USEFUL SUBJECT INDEX TERMS

Administration
Agents
Financial operations
Accounting
Funding
Payroll
Taxes
Legal aspects
Censorship
Contracts
Copyright
Liabilities
Regulations
Personnel
Labor relations
Planning/operation
Producing
Public relations
Advertising
Community relations
Marketing

Audience
Audience composition
Audience-performer relationship
Audience reactions/comments

Basic theatrical documents
Choreographies
Film treatments
Librettos
Miscellaneous texts
Playtexts
Promptbooks
Scores

Design/technology
Costuming
Equipment
Lighting
Make-up
Masks
Projections
Properties
Puppets
Scenery
Sound
Technicians/crews
Wigs
Special effects

Institutions
Institutions, associations
Institutions, producing
Institutions, research
Institutions, service
Institutions, social
Institutions, special
Institutions, training

Performance/production
Acting
Acrobatics
Aerialists
Aquatics
Animal acts
Choreography
Clowning
Dancing
Equestrian acts
Equilibrists
Instrumentalists
Juggling
Magic
Martial arts

Puppeteers
Singing
Staging
Ventriloquism

Performance spaces
Amphitheatres/arenas
Fairgrounds
Found spaces
Halls
Religious structures
Show boats
Theatres
Auditorium
Foyer
Orchestra pit
Stage,
Adjustable
Apron
Arena
Proscenium
Support areas

Plays/librettos/scripts
Adaptations
Characters/roles
Dramatic structure
Editions
Language
Plot/subject/theme

Reference materials
Bibliographies
Catalogues
Collected materials
Databanks
Descriptions of resources
Dictionaries
Directories
Discographies
Encyclopedias
Glossaries
Guides
Iconographies
Indexes
Lists
Videographies
Yearbooks

Relation to other fields
Anthropology
Economics
Education
Ethics
Literature
Figurative arts
Philosophy
Politics
Psychology
Religion
Sociology

Research/historiography
Methodology
Research tools

Theory/criticism
Aesthetics
Deconstruction
Dialectics
Phenomenology
Semiotics

Training
Apprenticeship
Teaching methods
Training aids

INTERNATIONAL BIBLIOGRAPHY OF THEATRE: 1986

International Bibliography of Theatre: 1986

Published by the Theatre Research Data Center, Brooklyn College, City University of New York, NY 11210 USA.

© Theatre Research Data Center, 1991: ISBN 0-945419-01-5. All rights reserved.

This publication was made possible in part by grants from the National Endowment for the Humanities and the American Society for Theatre Research, by gifts from individual members of the Society and by in-kind support and services provided by Brooklyn College of the City University of New York.

The paper used in this book complies with the Permanent Paper Standard issued by the National Information Standards Organization (Z39.48-1984).

THE THEATRE RESEARCH DATA CENTER

The Theatre Research Data Center at Brooklyn College houses, publishes and distributes the International Bibliography of Theatre. Inquiries about the bibliographies and the databank are welcome. Telephone (718) 780-5998; FAX (718) 951-7428; E-Mail RXWBC@CUNYVM on BITNET.

INTERNATIONAL BIBLIOGRAPHY OF THEATRE: 1986

Benito Ortolani, Editor

Associate Editors

Catherine Hilton

Margaret Loftus Ranald   Rosabel Wang

Louis A. Rachow, Consultant

Theatre Research Data Center

Irving M. Brown, Director

Rosabel Wang, Systems Analyst

Rose Bonczek, Helen Huff, Donna Mehle, Technical Assistants

The International Bibliography of Theatre project is sponsored by the American Society for Theatre Research and the International Association of Libraries and Museums of the Performing Arts in cooperation with the International Federation for Theatre Research.

Theatre Research Data Center
New York 1991

QUICK ACCESS GUIDE

GENERAL

The Classed Entries are equivalent to library shelf arrangements.

The Indexes are equivalent to a library card catalogue.

SEARCH METHODS

By subject:

Look in the alphabetically arranged Subject Index for the relevant term(s), topic(s) or names(s): e.g., Staging; *Macbeth*; Shakespeare, William; etc.

Check the number at the end of each relevant précis.

Using that number, search the Classed Entries section to find full information.

By country:

Look in the Geographical-Chronological Index for the country related to the *content* of interest.

Note: Countries are arranged in alphabetical order and then subdivided chronologically.

Find the number at the end of each relevant précis.

Using that number, search the Classed Entries section to find full information.

By periods:

Determine the country of interest.

Look in the Geographical-Chronological Index, paying special attention to the chronological subdivisions.

Find the number at the end of each relevant précis.

Using that number, search the Classed Entries section to find full information.

By authors of listed books or articles:

Look in the alphabetically arranged Document Authors Index for the relevant names.

Using the number at the end of each Author Index entry, search the Classed Entries section to find full information.

SUGGESTIONS

Search a variety of possible subject headings.

Search the **most specific subject heading** first, e.g., if interested in acting in Ibsen plays, begin with Ibsen, Henrik, rather than the more generic Acting or Plays/librettos/scripts.

When dealing with large clusters of references under a single subject heading, note that items are listed in **alphabetical order of content geography** (Afghanistan to Zimbabwe). Under each country items are ordered alphabetically by author, following the same numerical sequence as that of the Classed Entries.

TABLE OF CONTENTS

PREFACE

This fifth volume of the **International Bibliography of Theatre** is our latest effort to document significant written theatre materials worldwide. Expansion of international coverage and filling of gaps, 1982-1986, characterize this effort. Furthermore, nationals of Australia, Belgium, China, Finland, France, Japan, Korea, and Switzerland have begun to submit data entries from the major publications of their respective countries. Gap-filling has been accomplished primarily in the publications of Canada, China, the UK and the USA. With the advent of the IBT Consortium (four universities sharing the data collection and editing loads) we expect IBT:87 to include full coverage of Latin American and African materials. And some day soon we hope to hear from India, Greece and the countries of Southeast Asia.

Editorial refinements for IBT:86 emphasize tighter control of the proliferation of subject heads and the reduction in the Classed Entries of single listings of each one of the plays in collected reviews of plays.

A finding list for periodical titles has been added to facilitate relating titles to acronyms. The finding list is simply an alphabetical listing of periodicals by title, each accompanied by its assigned acronym. Further information about a particular title will be found in the Periodicals List.

ACKNOWLEDGMENTS

We are grateful to the many institutions and individuals who have helped us make this volume possible, some for funds, some for good counsel, some for practical assistance when it was sorely needed:

The members and the leaders of ASTR: President Kalman Burnim, Past President Joseph Donohue and the Executive Committee.

President Robert Hess, Provost Christoph Kimmich and the members of the Theatre Department of Brooklyn College, City University of New York;

President Oscar Pausch, Past-President Harald Zielske and the International Bibliography Commission of SIBMAS: Heinrich Huesmann, Chair, Deutsches Theatermuseum, Munich; Hedvig Belitska-Scholtz, National Széchényi Library, Budapest; Rainer Köppl, Univ. of Vienna; Paul Ulrich, Berlin Public Library; and G. Heldt, Univ. of Munich;

President Wolfgang Greisenegger and the University Commission of FIRT;

Hedwig Belitska-Scholtz, National Széchényi Library, Budapest;

Marvin Carlson, Graduate Center, City University of New York;

William Gargan, Library, Brooklyn College, City University of New York;

Arturo García Giménez, Institut del Teatre, Barcelona;

Cécile Giteau, Bibliothèque Nationale, Paris;

Lindsay Newman, Univ. of Lancaster Library, and the SIBMAS of Great Britain;

Betsey Jackson, SPIRES Consortium, Stanford University;

Benjamin S. Klein and Pat Reber, CUNY/University Computer Center;

Tamara Il. Lapteva, Lenin State Library of the USSR, Moscow;

Jane Rosenberg, Division of Research Programs, National Endowment for the Humanities;

Helen Salmon, Library, University of Guelph, Ontario;

Alessandro Tinterri, Museo Biblioteca dell'Attore di Genova;

Zbigniew Wilski, Polska Akademia Nauk, Warsaw

And we thank our field bibliographers whose contributions have made this work a reality:

Patrick Atkinson	Univ. of Missouri, Columbia, MO
Sri Ram V. Bakshi	State Univ. of New York, Brockport
Jerry Bangham	Alcorn State Univ., Lorman, MS
Thomas L. Berger	St. Lawrence Univ., Canton, NY
Helen Bickerstaff	University of Sussex Library, UK
Magnus Blomkvist	Stockholm Univ. Bibliotek
Magdolna Both	National Széchényi Library, Budapest
Jane N. Brittain	Leicester Polytechnic Library, UK
David F. Cheshire	Middlesex Polytechnic, Cat Hill Cockfosters
Oh-kon Cho	State Univ. of New York, Brockport
Nancy Copeland	University of Toronto, ON
Clifford O. Davidson	Western Michigan Univ., Kalamazoo, MI
Angela M. Douglas	Central School of Speech and Drama, London
Veronika Eger	National Széchényi Library, Budapest
Ron Engle	Univ. of North Dakota, Grand Forks, ND
Elaine Etkin	State Univ. of New York, Stony Brook
Dorothy Faulkner	Dartington College of Arts, Devon
Gabriele Fischborn	Theaterhochschule Hans Otto, Leipzig
Linda Fitzsimmons	Univ. of Bristol, UK
Marian J. Fordom	Royal Scottish Academy of Music and Drama, Glasgow
David P. Gates	Univ. of Western Ontario, London, ON
Donatella Giuliano	Civico Museo Biblioteca dell'Attore, Genoa
Carol Goodger-Hill	Univ. of Guelph, ON
Guillem-Jordi Graells	Museo de Arts de l'Espectacle, Barcelona
Temple Hauptfleisch	Univ. of Stellenbosch, Rep. of South Africa
Heidi J. Holder	Univ. of Massachusetts, Amherst
Frank S. Hook	Lehigh Univ., Bethlehem, PA
Clare Hope	Royal Academy of Dramatic Arts, London
Brigitte Howard	State Univ. of New York, Stony Brook
Dennis W. Johnston	Vancouver, BC
Robert Jordan	Univ. of New South Wales, Australia
Oxanna Kaufman	Univ. of Pittsburg, PA
Christine King	State Univ. of New York, Stony Brook
Gerhard Knewitz	Institut für Theaterwissenschaft, Vienna
Danuta Kusznika	Polska Akademia Nauk, Warsaw
Nicole Leclercq	Archives et Musée de la Littérature A.S.B.L.
Shimon Lev-Ari	Tel Aviv Univ., Ramat Aviv
Felicia Hardison Londré	Univ. of Missouri, Kansas City, MO
Min-Huei Lu	State Univ. of New York, Stony Brook
Tamotsu Matsuda	Nishogakusha Univ., Japan
Jack W. McCullough	Trenton State College, Trenton, NJ
Eleanor Milton	Westmoreland County Comm. Coll., Youngwood, PA
Barbara Mittman	Univ. of Illinois, Chicago, IL
Clair Myers	Elon College, Elon, NC
Bill Nelson	Carnegie-Mellon Univ., Pittsburgh
Lauren Nesbitt	Univ. of Guelph, ON
Andrea Nouryeh	New York, NY
Nicholas F. Radel	Furman Univ., Greenville, SC
Elizabeth Rae	Puslinch, ON
Margaret Loftus Ranald	Queens College, City Univ. of New York
Maarten A. Reilingh	McNeese State Univ., LA
Bari Rolfe	Oakland, CA
Jörg Ryser	Schweizerische Theatersammlung, Bern
Johannes Schütz	Institut für Theaterwissenschaft, Vienna
Marilyn S. Smith	Granby, Mass.

ACKNOWLEDGMENTS—Cont'd

Monika Specht	Freie Universität Berlin
Annick Tillier	Bibliothèque Nationale, Paris
Ronald W. Vince	McMaster Univ., Hamilton, ON
Hélène Volat-Shapiro	State Univ. of New York, Stony Brook
Carla Waal	Univ. of Missouri, Columbia, MO
Daniel Watermeier	Univ. of Toledo, OH
Margaret Watson	Newcastle-upon-Tyne Polytechnic, UK
David Whitton	Univ. of Lancaster, UK

and the many students in the Theatre History and Research & Bibliography courses at Brooklyn College, CUNY.

A GUIDE FOR USERS

SCOPE OF THE BIBLIOGRAPHY

Materials Included

The *International Bibliography of Theatre: 1986* lists theatre books, book articles, dissertations, journal articles and miscellaneous other theatre documents published during 1986. It also includes items from 1982, 1983, 1984 and 1985 received too late for inclusion in earlier volumes. Published works (with the exceptions noted below) are included without restrictions on the internal organization, format, or purpose of those works. Materials selected for the Bibliography deal with any aspect of theatre significant to research, without historical, cultural or geographical limitations. Entries are drawn from theatre histories, essays, studies, surveys, conference papers and proceedings, catalogues of theatrical holdings of any type, portfolios, handbooks and guides, dictionaries, bibliographies, thesauruses and other reference works, records and production documents.

Materials Excluded

Reprints of previously published works are usually excluded unless they are major documents which have been unavailable for some time. In general only references to newly published works are included, though significantly revised editions of previously published works are treated as new works. Purely literary scholarship is generally excluded, since it is already listed in established bibliographical instruments. An exception is made for material published in journals completely indexed by *IBT*. Studies in theatre literature, textual studies, and dissertations are represented only when they contain significant components that examine or have relevance to theatrical performance.

Playtexts are excluded unless they are published with extensive or especially noteworthy introductory material, or when the text is the first translation or adaptation of a classic from an especially rare language into a major language. Book reviews and reviews of performances are not included, except for those reviews of sufficient scope to constitute a review article, or clusters of reviews published under one title.

Language

There is no restriction on language in which theatre documents appear, but English is the primary vehicle for compiling and abstracting the materials. The Subject Index gives primary importance to titles in their original languages, transliterated into the Roman Alphabet where necessary. Original language titles also appear in Classed Entries that refer to plays in translation and in the précis of Subject Index items.

CLASSED ENTRIES

Content

The **Classed Entries** section contains one entry for each document analyzed and provides the user with complete information on all material indexed in this volume. It is the only place where publication citations may be found and where detailed abstracts are furnished. Users are advised to familiarize themselves with the elements and structure of the Taxonomy to simplify the process of locating items indexed in the **Classed Entries** section.

Organization

Entries follow the order provided in Columns I, II and III of the Taxonomy.

Column I classifies theatre into nine categories beginning with Theatre in General and thereafter listed alphabetically from "Dance" to "Puppetry." Column II divides most of the nine Column I categories into a number of subsidiary components. Column III headings relate any of the previously selected Column I and Column II catagories to specific elements of the theatre. A list of Useful Subject Index Terms is also given (see frontpapers). These terms are also sub-components of the Column III headings.

Examples:

Items classified under "Theatre in General" appear in the Classed Entries before those classified under "Dance" in Column I, etc.

Items classified under the Column II heading of "Musical theatre" appear before those classified under the Column II heading of "Opera," etc.

Items further classified under the Column III heading of "Administration" appear before those classified under "Design/technology," etc.

Every group of entries under any of the divisions of the **Classed Entries** is printed in alphabetical order according to its content geography: e.g., a cluster of items concerned with plays related to Spain, classified under "Drama" (Column I) and "Plays/librettos/scripts" (Column III) would be printed together after items concerned with plays related to South Africa and before those related to Sweden. Within these country clusters, each group of entries is arranged alphabetically by author.

Relation to Subject Index
When in doubt concerning the appropriate Taxonomy category for a **Classed Entry** search, the user should refer to the **Subject Index** for direction. The **Subject Index** provides several points of access for each entry in the **Classed Entries** section. In most cases it is advisable to use the **Subject Index** as the first and main way to locate the information contained in the **Classed Entries**.

TAXONOMY TERMS

The following descriptions have been established to clarify the terminology used in classifying entries according to the Taxonomy. They are used for clarification only, as a searching tool for users of the Bibliography. In cases where clarification has been deemed unnecessary (as in the cases of "Ballet," "*Kabuki*," "Film," etc.) no further description appears below. Throughout the Classed Entries, the term "General" distinguishes miscellaneous items that cannot be more specifically classified by the remaining terms in the Column II category. Sufficient subject headings enable users to locate items regardless of their taxonomical classification.

THEATRE IN GENERAL: Only for items which cannot be properly classified by categories "Dance" through "Puppetry," or for items related to more than one theatrical category.

DANCE: Only for items published in theatre journals completely indexed by *IBT*, or for dance items with relevance to theatre.

DANCE-DRAMA: Items related to dramatic genres where dance is the dominant artistic element. Used primarily for specific forms of non-Western theatre, e.g., *Kathakali, Nō*.

DRAMA: Items related to playtexts and performances where the spoken word is traditionally considered the dominant element. (i.e., all Western dramatic literature and all spoken drama everywhere). An article on acting as a discipline will also fall into this category, as well as books about directing, unless these endeavors are more closely related to musical theatre forms or other genres.

MEDIA: Only for media-related items published in theatre journals completely indexed by *IBT*, or for media items with relevance to theatre.

MIME: Items related to performances where mime is the dominant element. This category comprises all forms of mime from every epoch and/or country.

PANTOMINE: Both Roman pantomine and the performance form epitomized in modern times by Étienne Decroux and Marcel Marceau. English pantomine is indexed under "Mixed Entertainment."

MIXED ENTERTAINMENT: Items related either 1) to performances consisting of a variety of performance elements among which none is considered dominant, or 2) to performances where the element of spectacle and the function of broad audience appeal are dominant. Because of the great variety of terminology in different circumstances, times, and countries for similar types of spectacle, such items as café-concert, quadrille réaliste, one-man-shows, night club acts, pleasure gardens, tavern concerts, night cellars, saloons, Spezialitätentheater, storytelling, divertissement, rivistina, etc., are classified under "General," "Variety acts," or "Cabaret," etc., depending on time period, circumstances and/or country.

Variety acts: Items related to variety entertainment of mostly unconnected "numbers," including some forms of vaudeville, revue, petite revue, intimate revue, burlesque, etc.

PUPPETRY: Items related to all kinds of puppets, marionettes and mechanically operated figures.

N.B.: Notice that entries related to individuals are classified according to the Column III category describing the individual's primary field of activity: e.g., a manager under "Administration," a set designer under "Design/technology," an actor under "Performance/production," a playwright under "Plays/librettos/scripts," a teacher under "Training," etc.

CITATION FORMS

Basic bibliographical information

Each citation includes the standard bibliographical information: author(s), title, publisher, pages, and notes, preface, appendices, etc., when present. Journal titles are usually given in the form of an acronym, whose corresponding title may be found in the **List of Periodicals**. Pertinent publication information is also provided in this list.

Translation of original language

When the play title is not in English, a translation in parentheses follows the original title. Established English translations of play titles or names of institutions are used when they exist. Names of institutions, companies, buildings, etc., unless an English version is in common use, are as a rule left untranslated. Geographical names are given in standard English form as defined by *Webster's New Geographical Dictionary* (1984).

Time and place

An indication of the time and place to which a document pertains is included wherever appropriate and possible. The geographical information refers usually to a country, sometimes to a larger region such as Europe or English-speaking countries. The geographical designation is relative to the time of the content: Russia is used before 1917, USSR after; East and West Germany 1945-1990; Roman Empire until its official demise, Italy thereafter. When appropriate, precise dates related to the content of the item are given. Otherwise the decade or century is indicated.

Abstract

Unless the content of a document is made sufficiently clear by the title, the classed entry provides a brief abstract. Titles of plays not in English are given in English translation in the abstract, except for most operas and titles that are widely known in their original language. If the original title does not appear in the document title, it is provided in the abstract.

Spelling

English form is used for transliterated personal names. In the **Subject Index** each English spelling refers the users to the international or transliterated spelling under which all relevant entries are listed.

Varia

Affiliation with a movement and influence by or on individuals or groups is indicated only when the document itself suggests such information.

When a document belongs to more than one Column I category of the Taxonomy, the other applicable Column I categories are cross-referenced in the **Subject Index**.

Document treatment

"Document treatment" indicates the type of scholarly approach used in the writing of the document. The following terms are used in the present bibliography:

Bibliographical studies treat as their primary subject bibliographic material.

Biographical studies are articles on part of the subject's life.

Biographies are book-length or extensive treatments of entire lives.

Critical studies present an evaluation resulting from the application of criteria.

Empirical research identifies studies that incorporate as part of their design an experiment or series of experiments.

Historical studies designate accounts of individual events, groups, movements, institutions, etc., whose primary purpose is to provide a historical record or evaluation.

Histories-general cover the whole spectrum of theatre—or most of it—over a period of time and typically appear in one or several volumes.

Histories-specific cover a particular genre, field, or component of theatre over a period of time and usually are published as a book.

Histories-sources designate source materials that provide an internal evaluation or account of the treated subject: e.g. interviews with theatre professionals.

Histories-reconstruction attempt to reconstruct some aspect of the theatre.

Instructional materials include textbooks, manuals, guides or any other publication to be used in teaching.

Reviews of performances examine one or several performances in the format of review articles, or clusters of reviews published under one title.

Technical studies examine theatre from the point of view of the applied sciences or discuss particular theatrical techniques.
Textual studies examine the texts themselves for origins, accuracy, and publication data.

Example with diagram

Here follows an example (in this case a book article) of a **Classed Entries** item with explanation of its elements:

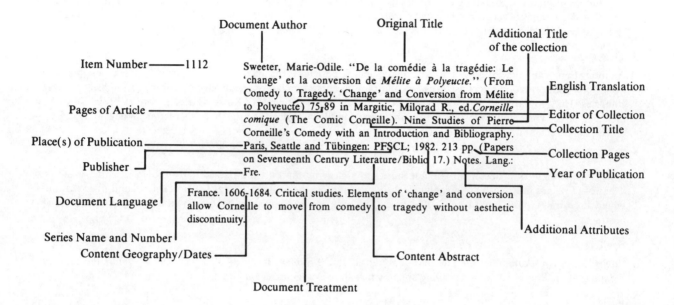

SUBJECT INDEX

Function

The **Subject Index** is a primary means of access to the major aspects of documents referenced by the **Classed Entries**.

Content

Each **Subject Index** item contains
- (a) subject headings, e.g., names of persons, names of institutions, forms and genres of theatre, elements of the theatre arts, titles of plays
- (b) column III category indicating primary focus of the entry
- (c) short abstracts describing the items of the **Classed Entries** related to the subject heading
- (d) content country, city, time and language of document
- (e) the number of the **Classed Entry** from which each Subject Index item was generated.

Standards

Names of persons, including titles of address, are listed alphabetically by last names according to the standard established in *Anglo-American Cataloguing Rules* (Library of Congress, 2nd edition, 1978).

All names and terms originating in non-Roman alphabets, including Russian, Greek, Chinese and Japanese have been transliterated and are listed by the transliterated forms.

Geographical names are spelled according to *Webster's New Geographical Dictionary* (1984).

"SEE" references direct users from common English spellings or titles to names or terms indexed in a less familiar manner.

Example:

Chekhov, Anton
SEE
Čechov, Anton Pavlovič

Individuals are listed in the Subject Index when:

- (a) they are the primary or secondary focus of the document;
- (b) the document addresses aspects of their lives and/or work in a primary or supporting manner;
- (c) they are the author of the document, but only when their life and/or work is also the document's primary focus;
- (d) their lives have influenced, or have been influenced by, the primary subject of the document or the writing of it, as evidenced by explicit statement in the document.

This Subject Index is particularly useful when a listed individual is the subject of numerous citations. In such cases a search should not be limited only to the main subject heading (e.g., Shakespeare). A more relevant one (e.g., *Hamlet*) could bring more specific results.

"SEE" references

Institutions, groups, and social or theatrical movements appear as subject headings, following the above criteria. Names of theatre companies, theatre buildings, etc. are given in their original languages or transliterated. "See" references are provided for the generally used or literally translated English terms;

Example: "Moscow Art Theatre" directs users to the company's original title:

Moscow Art Theatre
SEE
Moskovskij Chudožestvennyj Akedemičeskij Teat'r

No commonly used English term exists for "Comédie-Française," it therefore appears only under its title of origin. The same is true for *commedia dell'arte*, Burgtheater and other such terms.

Play titles appear in their original languages, with "SEE" references next to their English translations. Subject headings for plays in a third language may be provided if the translation in that language is of unusual importance.

Widely known opera titles are not translated.

Similar subject headings

Subject headings such as "Politics" and "Political theatre" are neither synonymous nor mutually exclusive. They aim to differentiate between a phenomenon and a theatrical genre. Likewise, such terms as "Feminism" refer to social and cultural movements and are not intended to be synonymous with "Women in theatre." The term "Ethnic theatre" is used to classify any type of theatrical literature or performance where the ethnicity of those concerned is of primary importance. Because of the number of items, and for reasons of accessibility, "Black theatre," "Native American theatre" and the theatre of certain other ethnic groups are given separate subject headings.

Groups/movements, periods, etc.

Generic subject headings such as "Victorian theatre," "Expressionism," etc., are only complementary to other more specific groupings and do not list all items in the bibliography related to that period or generic subject: e.g., the subject heading "Elizabethan theatre" does not list a duplicate of all items related to Shakespeare, which are to be found under "Shakespeare," but lists materials explicitly related to the actual physical conditions or style of presentation typical of the Elizabethan theatre. For a complete search according to periods, use the **Geographical-Chronological Index**, searching by country and by the years related to the period.

Subdivision of subject headings

Each subject heading is subdivided into Column III categories that identify the primary focus of the cited entry. These subcategories are intended to facilitate the user when searching under such broad terms as "Black theatre" or "*King Lear*." The subcategory helps to identify the relevant cluster of entries. Thus, for instance, when the user is interested only in Black theatre companies, the subheading "Institutions" groups all the relevant items together. Similarly, the subheading "Performance/production" groups together all the items dealing with production aspects of *King Lear*. It is, however, important to remember that these subheadings (i.e. Column III categories) are not subcategories of the subject heading itself, but of the main subject matter treated in the entry.

Printing order

Short abstracts under each subject heading are listed according to Column III categories. These Column categories are organized alphabetically. Short abstracts within each cluster, on the other hand, are arranged sequentially according to the item number they refer to in the Classed Entries. This enables the frequent user to recognize immediately the location and classification of the entry. If the user cannot find one specific subject heading, a related term may suffice, e.g., for Church dramas, see Religion. In some cases, a "SEE" reference is provided.

Example with diagram

Here follows an example of a **Subject Index** entry with explanation of its elements:

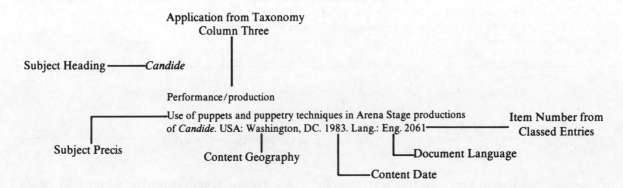

GEOGRAPHICAL-CHRONOLOGICAL INDEX

Organization

The **Geographical-Chronological Index** is arranged alphabetically by the country relevant to the subject or topic treated. The references under each country are then subdivided by date. References to articles with contents of the same date are then listed according to their category in the Taxonomy's Column III. The last item in each Geographical-Chronological Index listing is the number of the Classed Entry from which the listing was generated.

Example: For material on Drama in Italy between World Wars I and II, look under Italy, 1918-1939. In the example below, entries 2734, 2227 and 891 match this description.

Italy — cont'd

1907-1984.	**Theory/criticism.** Cruelty and sacredness in contemporary theatre poetics. Germany. France. Lang.: Ita.	2734
1914.	**Plays/librettos/scripts.** Comparative study of *Francesca da Rimini* by Riccardo Zandonai and *Tristan und Isolde* by Richard Wagner. Lang.: Eng.	3441
1920-1936.	**Plays/librettos/scripts.** Introductory analysis of twenty-one of Pirandello's plays Lang.: Eng.	2227
1923-1936.	**Institutions.** History of Teatro degli Indipendenti. Rome. Lang.; Ita.	891
1940-1984.	**Performance/production.** Italian tenor Giuseppe Giacomini speaks of his career and art. New York, NY. Lang.; Eng.	3324

Dates

Dates reflect the content period covered by the item, not the publication year. However, the publication year is used for theoretical writings and for assessments of old traditions, problems, etc. When precise dates cannot be established, the decade (e.g., 1970-1979) or the century (e.g., 1800-1899) is given.

Biographies and histories

In the case of biographies of people who are still alive, the year of birth of the subject and the year of publication of the biography are given. The same criterion is followed for histories of institutions such as theatres or companies which are still in existence. The founding date of such institutions and the date of publication of the entry are given - unless the entry explicitly covers only a specific period of the history of the institution.

Undatable content

No dates are given when the content is either theoretical or not meaningfully definable in time. Entries without date(s) print first.

DOCUMENT AUTHORS INDEX

The term "Document Author" means the author of the article or book cited in the **Classed Entries**. The author of the topic under discussion, e.g., Molière in an article about one of his plays, is *not* found in the **Document Authors Index**. (See Subject Index).

The **Document Authors Index** lists these authors alphabetically and in the Roman alphabet. The numbers given after each name direct the researcher to the full citations in the Classed Entries section.

N.B.: Users are urged to familiarize themselves with the Taxonomy and the indexes provided. The four-way access to research sources possible through consultation of the Classed Entries section, the Subject Index, the Geographical-Chronological Index and the Document Authors Index is intended to be sufficient to locate even the most highly specialized material.

CLASSED ENTRIES

THEATRE IN GENERAL

1   Hont, Ferenc, gen. ed.; Staud, Géza, ed.; Székely, György, ed. *A szinház világtörténete.* (World History of the Theatre.) Budapest: Gondolat; 1986. vol. 1: 491 pp., vol. 2: 865 pp. Pref. Index. Tables. Biblio. Illus.: Photo. B&W. Grd.Plan. 528: var. sizes. [2nd expanded edition.] Lang.: Hun.
Histories-general. ■Detailed history of the theatre from ancient times to present day based on most current research.

2   Ottai, Antonella, ed. *Teatro Oriente/Occidente.* (Theatre: East/West.) Rome: Bulzoni; 1986. viii, 565 pp. (Biblioteca Teatrale 47.) Lang.: Ita.
1986. Historical studies. ■Proceedings of conference on theatre held at the University of Rome. Related to Dance-Drama.

3   Zamponi, Linda. "Vom Schlacht–ins Kornhaus." (From Slaughterhouse to the Kornhaus.) *Buhne.* 1986 Feb.; 29(2): 38-39. Illus.: Photo. Print. B&W. Lang.: Ger.
Austria: Bregenz. 1818-1986. Historical studies. ■Theatre history of Vorarlberg, especially the history of Theater für Vorarlberg.

4   Hsu, Tao-Ching. *The Chinese Conception of the Theatre.* Seattle, WA: Univ. of Washington; 1986. 710 pp. Tables. Biblio. Illus.: Photo. Dwg. Lang.: Eng.
China. 600 B.C.-1985 A.D. Histories-general. ■History of Chinese classical theatre with comparisons to Ancient Greek and Elizabethan theatre and *commedia dell'arte.*

5   Stupnikov, I.V. *Anglijskij teatr: konec XVII načalo XVIII.* (English Theatre of the Late Seventeenth and Early Eighteenth Centuries.) Leningrad: Iskusstvo; 1986. 349 pp. Lang.: Rus.
England. 1660-1737. Histories-general.

6   "Vita a szinházi struktúráról. Az utópiáktól a szinház valóságaig. Vitazáró jegyzetek." (Discussion on Theatre Structure: From Utopias to the Reality of Theatre. Final Notes to the Discussion.) *Krit.* 1986; 14(5): 17-18. Lang.: Hun.
Hungary. Critical studies. ■Summary of articles in a series on Hungarian theatre structure.

7   Davoli, Susi, ed. *Civiltà teatrale e Settecento emiliano.* (Theatrical Civilization in Emilia in the Eighteenth Century.) Bologna: Il Mulino; 1986. 465 pp. (Proscenio 3.) Pref. Index. Notes. Tables. Biblio. Illus.: Photo. Plan. Dwg. Sketches. B&W. Lang.: Ita.
Italy: Emilia. 1700-1799. Historical studies. ■Presentations made at a 1985 conference in Reggio Emilia on theatre, opera, architecture and scene design.

8   Griševeva, L.D. *Formirovanie japonskoi nacional'noj kultury: konec XVI-načalo XX veka.* (Formation of Japanese National Culture From the Late Sixteenth to the Early Twentieth Century.) Moscow: Nauka; 1986. 285 pp. Lang.: Rus.
Japan. 1596-1941. Historical studies. ■Development of performing arts.

9   Chang, Han-Ki. *Hanguk yeongŭksa.* (History of the Korean Theatre.) Dongguk Univ: Lee, Chi-Kwan; 1986. 360 pp. Pref. Index. Tables. Biblio. Append. Illus.: Photo. B&W. 49: 15.5 cm. x 23 cm. Lang.: Kor.
Korea. 57 B.C.-1945 A.D. Histories-general. ■History of Korean theatre up to 1945.

10   Sławińska, Irena. "Z życia teatralnego szkoły. Wspomnienia z miłego miasta." (On the Theatrical Life of a School: Recollections from the Nice City.) *PaT.* 1986 Second & Third Qtr; 2-3: 431-440. Notes. Lang.: Pol.
Poland: Vilna. 1908-1986. Histories-sources. ■Description of various theatrical activities in Vilna when it was a Polish city, including performances at school, home theatres and festivals.

11   Pilipŭk, R. "...V predščepkinskij period." (In the Time Before Ščepkinskij.) *UTeatr.* 1986; 2: 26-29 . Lang.: Ukr.
Russia: Char'kov, Poltava. 1808-1816. Historical studies. ■History of theatre in Char'kov and Poltava.

12   Salvat, Ricard, ed. *El Teatre durant l'Edat Mitjana i el Renaixement.* (The Theatre during the Middle Ages and the Renaissance.) Barcelona: Publicacions i Edicions de la Universitat de Barcelona; 1986. xxviii, 322 pp. (El Pla de les Comèdies 2.) Notes. Pref. Index. Append. Illus.: Photo. Print. B&W. 16: var. sizes. Lang.: Cat, Spa, Ita.
Spain. Italy. 1000-1680. Historical studies. ■Proceedings of the First International Symposium titled *L'Edat Mitjana i el Renaixement en el Teatre.* Sitges, October, 1983.

13   Skoglund, Hans. "Trötta kan finna en inspirationskälla." (The Tired Can Find a Source of Inspiration.) *Teaterf.* 1986; 19(6): 13. Lang.: Swe.
Sweden: Stockholm. 1986. Histories-sources. ■Report from a conference on modern Swedish theatre: professionals discussed the stagnation of the theatre while ignoring the country's vital amateur theatres.

14   Čemortan, L.M.; Barboj, Ju. M., ed. *Stanovlenie moldavskogo sovetskogo teatra: Stanicy istorii.* (The Formation of Moldavian Soviet Theatre: Pages from a History.) Kišinev: Štiinca; 1986. 166 pp. Lang.: Rus.
USSR. 1917-1986. Historical studies. ■Formation and development of Moldavian Soviet theatre.

15   Mamedov, M. *Teatr, dramaturgija i sovremennost.* (Theatre, Dramaturgy and Contemporaneity.) Baku: Jšyg; 1986. 393 pp. Lang.: Rus.
USSR. 1980-1986. Critical studies. ■Research on the theatre and dramaturgy of Soviet Azerbajdžan.

Administration

16   "In Death As In Life: The Remains of Elvis Presley." *JAP&M.* 1986 May; 2(3): 21. Lang.: Eng.
1986. Historical studies. ■Promotion and marketing of the work of deceased artists, using Elvis Presley as an example.

THEATRE IN GENERAL: —Administration

17 Kuomantos, George; Stewart, Stephen. "Review of Conference on the Berne Convention Proceedings." *ColJL&A.* 1986 Fall; 11 (1): 225-249. [Closing Speech.] Lang.: Eng.
1886-1986. Histories-sources. ■Future trends in copyright, particularly in international protection, lessons from history and evolution of new copyright problems.

18 Lieberman, Susan B. "Getting Your Subscribers to Byte." *ThCr.* 1986 Feb.; 20(2): 28-29, 58-59. Lang.: Eng.
1986. Technical studies. ■Consumer marketing techniques to convert one-time ticket buyers into subscribers, a guide to the latest box office and subscription software.

19 Novotny, Oscar; Ács, Eva, transl. "A szinházi numka társadalmi-gaz dasági feltételei." (Socioeconomic Conditions of Theatre Work.) *Sz.* 1986 Dec.; 19(12): 18-24. Lang.: Hun.
1986. Critical studies. ■Critical analysis of theatrical working conditions, economic problems in social connection.

20 Sorokin, B., ed. *Ekonomika u organizacija teatra: Sbornik.* (The Economics and Organization of the Theatre: A Collection Vol. 7.) Leningrad: Iskusstvo; 1986. 215 pp. Lang.: Rus.
1980-1986. Critical studies. ■Current problems of theatrical organizations in the Soviet Union and elsewhere, including the training of personnel.

21 Ndiaye, Ndéné. "The Berne Convention and Developing Countries." *ColJL&A.* 1986 Fall; 11(1): 47-56. Lang.: Eng.
Africa. Asia. 1963-1986. Historical studies. ■Ability of developing countries to grant rules of protection of Berne Convention, development of 1967 Protocol to deal with developing countries.

22 Blaylock, Malcolm; Levy, Graham. "Subsidy, Community, and Excellence in Australian Theatre." *NTQ.* 1986 Feb.; 11(5): 75-79. Lang.: Eng.
Australia. 1985. Histories-sources. ■Malcolm Blaylock: director of a community-based company and member of a federal funding body, and some background on the present funding policy.

23 Brokensha, Peter; Tonks, Ann. *Culture and Community: Economics and Expectations of Arts in South Australia.* Wentworth Falls, NSW, Australia: Social Science P; 1986. 162 pp. Index. Biblio. Lang.: Eng.
Australia. 1986. Critical studies. ■Discusses the economic condition of arts in Australia and the difficulty of obtaining government subsidies. Includes a detailed description of arts and crafts organizations in South Australia.

24 Heckenberg, Pamela. "The Australian Playwright in the Commercial Theatre: 1914/1939." 99-110 in Univ. New England, ed. *Australian Drama 1920-1955.* Papers presented at a conference at the University of New England, Armidale, September 1-4, 1984. Armidale, N.S.W: Univ. of New England; 1986. 157 pp. Lang.: Eng.
Australia: Sydney. 1914-1939. Historical studies. ■Analyzes decline in the number of commercially produced Australian plays. Considers entrepreneurial policy, entertainment taxes, the advent of film and the trend toward suburban living, using Sydney as the test case.

25 Löbl, Hermi. "Ich bin ein Ermöglicher." (I Am a Person Who Makes Things Possible.) *Buhne.* 1986 June; 29(6): 12-15. Illus.: Photo. Print. Color. B&W. Lang.: Ger.
Austria: Vienna. 1928-1986. Biographical studies. ■Robert Jungbluth, how he became involved in theatre, why he did not become an actor and his management of the Österreichische Bundestheater.

26 Jaumain, Michel. "Le Secteur Théâtral de la Comunauté Française de Belgique: Activités, Audience et Flux Économiques (Essai de Description)." (The Theatrical Field in Belgium's French Community: Activity, Audience and Financial Tides.) 170-197 in Archives et Musée de la Littérature, ed. *Annuaire du spectacle de la Communauté française de Belgique 1983-1984.* Bruxelles: Archives et Musée de la Littérature; 1984. 216 pp. Illus.: Plan. Lang.: Fre.

Belgium. 1983-1984. Technical studies. ■Description of the theatre as a part of the economy producing 'products' as well as 'consumers' and a 'financial flow'.

27 Brunner, Astrid. "From *Othello* to *Endgame*, John Neville at the Neptune." *ArtsAtl.* 1983 Spr; 4(4): 22-23. Illus.: Photo. Print. B&W. 5: 10 cm. x 4 cm., 8 cm. x 6 cm. Lang.: Eng.
Canada: Halifax, NS. 1979-1983. Historical studies. ■John Neville's control of the Neptune Theatre has brought about economic stability, encouragement of young actors and experimental theatre.

28 Lapierre, Laurent. "Visions partagées... ou partage de préoccupations." (Shared Visions... or Sharing of Concerns.) *JCT.* 1985; 35: 93-110. Lang.: Fre.
Canada. 1985. Histories-sources. ■Colloquium of Artistic Directors of Institutional Companies, with discussion of the difficulties of being both a 'visionary' and an administrator.

29 Usin, Léa V. "Creon's City: A History of Ottawa's Town Theatre." *CDr.* 1986 Spr; 12(1): 8-17. Illus.: Photo. Print. B&W. 3: 5 in. x 7 in. Lang.: Eng.
Canada: Ottawa, ON. 1948-1970. Historical studies. ■History of the Town Theatre, which failed because of financial problems, conservative audiences and the National Arts Centre.

30 Shoukang, Guo. "The Berne Union and Developing Countries, with Particular Reference to the People's Republic of China." *ColJL&A.* 1986 Fall; 11(1): 121-127. Notes. Lang.: Eng.
China, People's Republic of. 1908-1986. Historical studies. ■Chinese copyright law, particular issues relating to China and international copyright.

31 Elliott, John R., Jr. "Plays at Christ Church in 1636: A New Document." *TN.* 1985; 39(I): 7-13. Notes. Biblio. Lang.: Eng.
England: Oxford. 1636. Historical studies. ■Analysis of expense account discovered in the Christ Church archives which details expenses incurred for a production in 1636, outlining items purchased, names of artisans and costs.

32 Milhous, Judith; Hume, Robert D. "The Drury Lane Actors' Petition of 1705." *TN.* 1985; 39(2): 62-67. Illus.: Photo. B&W. 1. Lang.: Eng.
England. 1705. Historical studies. ■Analysis of petition drawn up by actors of the successful Drury Lane Theatre to protest merging with the ailing Haymarket in 1705. Struggle between the company's managers over the years.

33 Mitchell, Louis D. "Command Performances During the Reign of George II." *Restor.* 1986 Sum; 2nd ser.1(1): 18-33. Notes. Tables. Lang.: Eng.
England: London. 1727-1760. Historical studies. ■Royal theatrical patronage during the reign of George II.

34 Pry, Kevin. "The Opera House Petition of 1799." *TN.* 1986; 40(3): 101-106. Notes. Lang.: Eng.
England: London. 1799. Historical studies. ■Performers petitioned Lord Chamberlain for redress of their grievances against their manager.

35 Sawyer, Paul. "Charles Fleetwood's Debts." *TN.* 1985; 39(1): 3-7. Biblio. Lang.: Eng.
England: London. 1734-1745. Historical studies. ■A look at how under the ownership and management of Charles Fleetwood, quality at the Drury Lane plummetted.

36 Freegard, Michael. "The Berne Convention, Compulsory Licensing and Collecting Societies." *ColJL&A.* 1986 Fall; 11(1): 137-155. Notes. Tables. Lang.: Eng.
Europe. 1908-1986. Historical studies. ■History of compulsory licensing in the Berne Convention, future developments of collective administration techniques as alternatives to compulsory licensing.

37 Ricketson, Sam. "The Birth of the Berne Union." *ColJL&A.* 1986 Fall; 11(1): 9-32. Biblio. Lang.: Eng.
Europe. 1709-1886. Historical studies. ■Background and events leading up to Berne Convention, development of European copyright laws and bilateral copyright agreements.

38 "L'organisation du public de Jean Vilar." (Jean Vilar's Organization of his Public.) *CTL.* 1986 June; 19(56-57):

THEATRE IN GENERAL: —Administration

9-18. [International colloquium on Jean Vilar, Venice, November 1985.] Lang.: Fre.
France: Paris. 1948-1968. Historical studies. ■Jean Vilar was able to build a working class audience for the Théâtre National Populaire by locating theatres in the suburbs, fostering an hospitable atmosphere for the audience and selling subscriptions through community groups.

39 Carlson, Marvin. "The French Censorship Enquiries of 1849 and 1891." *ET.* 1986 Nov.; 5(1): 5-14. Notes. Lang.: Eng.
France: Paris. 1791-1891. Historical studies. ■Analysis of censorship in post-Revolutionary France, focusing on testimony of witnesses before Parliamentary commissions.

40 Gobin, Alain. *Le Droit des auteurs, des artistes et des gens du spectacle: guide pratique.* (The Rights of Authors, Artists and Performers: A Practical Guide.) Paris: Entreprise Moderne d'Édition; 1986. 159 pp. Index. Append. Lang.: Fre.
France. 1957-1986. Histories-specific. ■Study of the problems of copyright with respect to theatrical productions. Includes text of some French laws and sample contracts.

41 Guibert, Noëlle; Houssaye, Arsène; Touchard, Pierre-Aimé; Vincent, Jean-Pierre. "Les Administrateurs." (The Administrators.) *CF.* 1986 Sep.; 16(151): 20-27. Illus.: Photo. B&W. Lang.: Fre.
France: Paris. 1680-1986. Histories-specific. ■Several short pieces on the history of the various administrators-in-chief of the Comédie-Française.

42 Hue, Jean-Pierre. *Le Théâtre et son droit.* (The Theatre and Its Law.) Paris: Librairie Théâtrale; 1986. 207 pp. Pref. Biblio. Append. Lang.: Fre.
France. 1945-1985. Histories-specific. ■Theatrical legislation in France. Covers public and private theatres, government involvement in subsidy, assistance and training. Includes texts of significant laws, sample contracts and a list of subsidized companies.

43 Plaisant, Robert. "The Protection of *Droit Moral* and *Droit de Suite.*" *ColJL&A.* 1986 Fall; 11(1): 157-164. Notes. Lang.: Eng.
France. 1971-1986. ■Background, viability and continuation of *droit de suite* and *droit moral* under Berne Convention.

44 Stewart, E.R. *The Decentralisation of French Theatre, 1940-1952: The Association Jeune France and the Centres Dramatiques.* Warwick: Univ. of Warwick; 1985. Notes. Biblio. [M.A. dissertation, *Index to Theses*, 37-0091.] Lang.: Eng.
France. 1940-1952. Historical studies. ■Traces the decentralization of French popular theatre by individuals and the state, and studies the work of Jeanne Laurent in the establishment of permanent provincial theatre companies.

45 Bőgel, József. "Vita a szinházi strukturáról. Szinházi struktúra '85-86. Vita, helyzet, jövő." (Discussion on Theatre Structure: Theatre Structure '85-86: Discussion—Position—Future.) *Krit.* 1986; 14(4): 20-23 . Print. 3: 7 cm. x 9 cm. Lang.: Hun.
Hungary. 1985-1986. Critical studies. ■Contribution to the discussion on the Hungarian theatre structure.

46 Boytha, György. "The Berne Convention and the Socialist Countries with Particular Reference to Hungary." *ColJL&A.* 1986 Fall; 11(1): 51-72. Notes. Lang.: Eng.
Hungary. 1917-1986. Historical studies. ■History of Berne Convention in socialist countries, including typical provisions and distinctive characteristics of socialist copyright law.

47 Czinner, Karolina; Margitics, Imre. "'SRS' Számitógépes szinházi helyfoglaló és jegyeladó rendszer." ('SRS'—Computer Based Ticket Selling and Reservation System for Theatres.) *SFo.* 1986; 13(1): 33-34. Lang.: Hun.
Hungary: Budapest. 1982-1985. Technical studies. ■Discussion of SCI-L, a Budapest computer firm that developed a computerized ticketing system for use in Western Europe.

48 Illés, Jenő. "Vita a szinházi struktúráról. A közös felelősségről." (Discussion on Theatre Structure: On the Common Responsibility.) *Krit.* 1986; 14(1): 16-17. Illus.: Dwg. 3. Lang.: Hun.

Hungary. 1985-1986. Critical studies. ■Study on the Hungarian theatre structure, program policy, different theatrical workshops, responsibility of the director, lack of quality in productions.

49 Mészáros, Tamás. "Vita a szinházi struktúráról. Struktúrára várva." (Discussion of Theatre Structure: Waiting for Structure.) *Krit.* 1986; 14(3): 18-19. Illus.: Dwg. 2: 6.5 cm. x 8 cm. Lang.: Hun.
Hungary. 1985-1986. Critical studies. ■Contribution to the discussion on theatre structure in Hungary.

50 Mihályi, Gábor. "Vita a szinházi struktúráról. Szép álom vagy gazdasági szükségszerüség." (Discussion on Theatre Structure: A Nice Dream, or Economic Necessity.) *Krit.* 1986; 14(5): 15-16. Illus.: Dwg. 3: 6.5 cm. x 8 cm., 7 cm. x 7.5 cm., 7 cm. x 9.5 cm. Lang.: Hun.
Hungary. 1985-1986. Critical studies. ■Contribution to the discussion on the Hungarian theatre structure.

51 Sivó, Emil. "Vita a szinházi struktúráról. Szinházi gondok—a másik oldalról." (Discussion on Theatre Structure: Troubles of the Theatre from the Other Side.) *Krit.* 1986; 14(2): 21. Illus.: Dwg. 1: 7 cm. x 7.5 cm. Lang.: Hun.
Hungary. 1985-1986. Critical studies. ■Economic problems of the theatre and critical notes on state subsidy.

52 Har'el, Vered. "Reaion Im Yehoshua Sobol Gedalya Besser-Menahalav Haomanutyim Shel Hateatron Hayroni Haifa." (An Interview with Jehoshua Sobol and Gedalya Besser, Directors of the Haifa Municipal Theatre.) *Bamah.* 1986; 21(103): 43-58. Illus.: Photo. Print. B&W. 6. Lang.: Heb.
Israel: Haifa. 1982-1986. Histories-sources. ■On the artistic management of the Haifa Municipal Theatre, the cooperation between Jehoshua Sobol, playwright manager, and Gedalya Besser, director manager, their artistic credo.

53 Cervetti, Valerio, ed. *Dietro il sipario. 1881-1898. Memorie e appunti del Segretario della Commissione Teatrale Giulio Ferrarini.* (Behind the Curtain, 1881-1898: Memoirs and Notes of the Secretary of the Theatrical Board, Giulio Ferrarini.) Parma: Grafiche STEP; 1986. xxi, 381 pp. (Archivo Storico Teatro Regio 1.) Pref. Index. Notes. Tables. Biblio. Illus.: Photo. Pntg. Dwg. Poster. B&W. Lang.: Ita.
Italy: Parma. 1881-1898. Histories-sources. ■The theatrical board as seen by its administrator, with period documentation and biographical dictionary. Related to Music-Drama: Opera.

54 Mangini, Nicola. "L'organizzazione teatrale a Venezia nel Settecento." (Theatrical Organization in Eighteenth-Century Venice.) *Ariel.* 1986 Jan-Apr.; 1(1): 59-74. Notes. Tables. B&W. 2: 16 cm. x 24 cm. Lang.: Ita.
Italy: Venice. 1700-1799. Historical studies. ■Privatization and management of theatrical activity.

55 "Daehammimguk Yeongukjae Lo-Nyeon, Eotteoke Gayahal Geoshimga?" (How Should the Korean Theatre Festival Be Run?)*KTR.* 1986 Dec.; 127(12): 21-27. Illus.: Photo. B&W. 1: 8.5 cm. x 25.7 cm. Lang.: Kor.
Korea. 1986. Critical studies. ■Problems of and solutions for the Korean Theatre Festival.

56 Lee, Gun-Sam; Jeong, Jin-Soo; Lee, Jung-Han. "Yeonguk Jeojakgwan Symposium." (Theatre-Copyright Symposium.) *KTR.* 1986 Sep.; 124(9): 16-31. Illus.: Photo. B&W. 1: 18.5 cm. x 26 cm. Lang.: Kor.
Korea. USA. 1986. Critical studies. ■Copyright agreement between Korea and the United States and the future of Korean theatre.

57 Shim, Woo-Seong. "Jeontong Yesul." (Traditional Art.) *KTR.* 1986 Jan.; 116(1): 32-33. Illus.: Photo. B&W. 2: 18.5 cm. x 26 cm. Lang.: Kor.
Korea: Seoul. 1985. Histories-sources. ■Record of the Korean Traditional Art Masters Festival.

58 Shim, Woo-Seong. "'86 Seoul Gukjae Minsok Chukjae." ('86 Seoul International Folklore Festival.) *KTR.* 1986 Oct.; 125 (10): 67. Illus.: Photo. B&W. 1: 18.5 cm. x 26 cm. Lang.: Kor.

CLASSED ENTRIES

THEATRE IN GENERAL: —Administration

Korea: Seoul. 1986. Critical studies. ■Review of the festival.

59   Åberg, Lars. "Malmö." *NT.* 1986; 33: 18-19. Lang.: Swe.
Sweden: Malmö. 1986. Historical studies. ■Changes in the structure of government funding will result in greater artistic achievement and lower ticket prices.

60   Dahlberg, Christer. "Den första tiden kändes allting själv-klart." (For the First Time Everything Was Obvious.) *Teaterf.* 1986; 19(1): 11-12. Illus.: Photo. Dwg. Lang.: Swe.
Sweden: Gävle. 1984-1986. ■Folkteatern i Gävleborgs Län has a special adviser for the amateur theatres in the country, to organize training for the amateurs.

61   Engblom, Sören. "Tecken för föreställningen." (Signs For the Performance.) *NT.* 1986; 35: 11-13. Illus.: Photo. Lang.: Swe.
Sweden. 1985-1986. Critical studies. ■Discrepancies between the visual performance and the poorly designed programs.

62   Hägglund, Kent. "Skånskan." (The Skånska Theatre.) *Entre.* 1986; 13(1): 14-28. Illus.: Photo. B&W. 24: var. sizes. Lang.: Swe.
Sweden: Landskrona, Malmö. 1963-1986. Historical studies. ■Skånska Teatern, a successful provincial theatre, works with amateur groups and schools. Despite budget problems and changes of personnel, the theatre is an integral part of the Landskrona community.

63   Sjöqvist, Hans-Åke. "Portättet: STTF:s ordförande Bernt Thorell." (The Portrait: The President of STTF, Bernt Thorell.) *ProScen.* 1986; 10(2): 24-27. Illus.: Photo. Lang.: Swe.
Sweden. 1966-1986. Histories-sources. ■Interview with Bernt Thorell about his background as an operating engineer of the first Swedish nuclear power station, his twenty years as head technician at Kungliga Dramatiska Teatern and his view of the Swedish Society for Theatre Technicians.

64   Fabiani, Mario. "WIPO Report." *ColJL&A.* 1986 Win; 11(2): 315-330. Lang.: Eng.
Switzerland. 1986. Historical studies. ■Report on drafts by World Intellectual Property Organization to serve as models for national laws concerning rights and obligations of employed authors.

65   Hoehne, Verena, ed.; Jauslin, Christian, ed. *Dramatiker-Förderung: Dokumentation zum Schweizer Dramatiker-Förderungsmodell.* (Encouraging Playwrights: Documentation on the Project to Encourage Swiss Playwrights.) Bonstetten: Theaterkultur; 1986. 240 pp. (Schweizer Theaterjahrbuch 48.) Pref. Biblio. Illus.: Photo. B&W. Lang.: Fre, Ger.
Switzerland. 1983-1986. Critical studies. ■Evaluation of a program designed to provide financial and artistic support for Swiss playwrights, including modifications relevant to legal issues.

66   Strasser, Hannes. "Theater und Gewerkschaft." (Theatre and Trade Unions.) 66-71 in Reich, Dietbert, ed.; Waltisbühl, Christine, ed. *Opernhaus Zürich–Jahrbuch 86/87.* Zürich: Orell Füssli Verlag; 1986. 168 pp. Illus.: Photo. B&W. Lang.: Ger.
Switzerland. 1986-1987. Historical studies. ■Contract problems in theatrical professions, concentrating on partnership rather than interdependent hierarchy.

67   Arnold-Baker, Charles. *The Five Thousand, or the Living Constitution.* London: Longcross; 1986. 207 pp. Biblio. Lang.: Eng.
UK. 1986. Historical studies. ■Discussion of a network of British government officials who manage virtually all the country's affairs.

68   Davis, Ivor. "A Century of Copyright: The United Kingdom and the Berne Convention." *ColJL&A.* 1986 Fall; 11(1): 33-46. Lang.: Eng.
UK. 1850-1986. Historical studies. ■Origin of UK copyright law, international copyright in UK prior to Berne Convention, application of Berne Convention, recent and future changes in UK law.

69   de Freitas, Denis. "The Berne Convention and the Market Economy Countries." *ColJL&A.* 1986 Fall; 11(1): 73-87. Notes. Lang.: Eng.

UK. USA. 1886-1986. Critical studies. ■Distinguishing features of market economy countries reflected in way copyright systems operate.

70   Herbert, Ian. "Cork Is Out." *Sin.* 1986; 20(2): 5. Lang.: Eng.
UK. 1986. Historical studies. ■Summary of the Cork report including discussion of the training of theatre technicians, generation of revenues and maximum use of theatre buildings. Also includes recommendations on how the results can be used.

71   Jennings, Antony. "Cables and Satellites." *ColJL&A.* 1986 Fall; 11(1): 129-136. Notes. Lang.: Eng.
UK. 1971-1986. Historical studies. ■Effect of copyright law on Direct Broadcast and Point-to-Point satellites and cable, conflict between copyright law, telecommunications law and media policy in era of electronic communications.

72   Langton, Robert Gore. "On the Road." *PlPl.* 1986 Nov.; 398: 14-15. B&W. 2. Lang.: Eng.
UK. 1986. Histories-sources. ■Interview with Ron Daniels and Caro Mackay, director and tour manager, respectively, of Royal Shakespeare Company, on the cultural importance of touring and its financial and administrative difficulties.

73   Llewelyn, David. "Computers, Software, & International Protection." *ColJL&A.* 1986 Fall; 11(1): 183-193. Notes. Lang.: Eng.
UK. USA. 1956-1986. Critical studies. ■Discusses debate over copyright protection for computer programs, including problems of infringement and definition of ownership.

74   Miller, Jonathan. "The Doctor's Diagnosis." *Drama.* 1986; 160(2): 5-6. Illus.: Photo. B&W. 1. Lang.: Eng.
UK. 1945-1986. Critical studies. ■Pros and cons of subsidy: institutional theatre becomes boring.

75   Phillips, Jeremy. "The Berne Convention and the Public Interest." *ColJL&A.* 1986 Fall; 11(1): 165-182. Notes. Lang.: Eng.
UK. 1886-1986. Historical studies. ■History of the concept of public interest and its relation to copyright law, including its use as a defense in copyright infringement cases.

76   Pilbrow, Richard. "The Way We Were." *Sin.* 1986; 20(1): 19-25. Illus.: Diagram. Photo. B&W. 7. Lang.: Eng.
UK. 1986. Historical studies. ■Formation and development of the Association of British Theatre Technicians (ABTT).

77   Smart, John. "RITA: No Trouble at T'Mill." *Sin.* 1986; 20(1): 35-37. Illus.: Photo. B&W. 2: var. sizes. Lang.: Eng.
UK. 1980-1986. Technical studies. ■Real-time Integrated Ticketing and Administration (RITA) designed by the Royal Shakespeare Company and British Telecom, is an adaptable system that can be used in large and small theatres and can handle box office, accounts, membership database, mailing, management information and word processing.

78   Werson, Gerard. "Centres of Excellence." *PI.* 1986 Jan.; 1(6): 20-21. Illus.: Photo. Print. B&W. 1. [Cont. in 1986 Feb, pp 12-14.] Lang.: Eng.
UK. 1978-1986. Historical studies. ■Britain's art centers and their cash problems.

79   Adams, John. "Reprography." *ColJL&A.* 1986 Fall; 11(1): 195-223. Notes. Append. Lang.: Eng.
UK-England. 1911-1986. Historical studies. ■Conflict between Berne Convention reproduction rights of authors and permission to reproduce, current UK legislation and suggestions for future schemes.

80   Bogsch, Arpad. "Conference Celebrating the Centenary of the Berne Convention: Opening of Conference." *ColJL&A.* 1986 Fall; 11(1): 3-7. Lang.: Eng.
UK-England: London. 1986. Histories-sources. ■Opening speech at 1986 London conference celebrating Berne Convention centenary discusses background and purpose of meeting.

81   Delamothe, Tony. "The Great Abolition Cock-up." *PI.* 1986 Apr.; 1(9): 10-11, 25. Illus.: Photo. Print. B&W. 1. Lang.: Eng.
UK-England: London. 1981-1986. Historical studies. ■Discusses the chaos ensuing from the dissolution of the Greater London Council, resulting in limited funds for over one hundred theatres and theatre companies.

THEATRE IN GENERAL: —Administration

82 Doyle, John; Allen, Paul. "UK Regions." *PI*. 1986 Mar.; 1(8): 32-33. Illus.: Photo. Print. B&W. 2. Lang.: Eng.
UK-England: Cheltenham. UK-Wales: Mold. 1986. Histories-sources. ■The artistic directors of Theatre Clwyd and Cheltenham's Everyman Theatre discuss their theatres' history and policy.

83 Delamothe, Tony. "Edinburgh's International Theatre Year." *PI*. 1986 Aug.; 2(1): 20-22. B&W. 3. Lang.: Eng.
UK-Scotland: Edinburgh. 1986. Histories-sources. ■Frank Dunlop, director of the Edinburgh Festival, discusses the World Theatre season he has planned.

84 Authors' League of America. "Final Report of the Ad-Hoc Working Group on U.S. Adherence to the Berne Convention." *ColJL&A*. 1986 Sum; 10(4): 513-736. Notes. Append. Lang.: Eng.
USA. 1985. Histories-sources. ■Report investigating whether US Copyright Act and other Federal and State Statutes and Common Law provide protection required by the 1971 Paris Act of the Berne Convention for works originating in countries not covered by the Berne Convention.

85 Anthoine, Robert. "Charitable Contributions After the 1986 Tax Act and Problems in Valuation of Appreciated Property." *ColJL&A*. 1986 Win; 11(2): 283-314. Notes. Lang.: Eng.
USA. 1986-1987. Technical studies. ■Selected case analysis details effect of 1986 tax law on charitable contributions, especially to arts. Includes discussion of deduction law, Internal Revenue Service regulations and guidelines for determining fair market value of gifts.

86 Bank, Rosemarie K. "A Reconsideration of the Death of Nineteenth-Century American Repertory Companies and the Rise of the Combinations." *ET*. 1986 Nov.; 5(1): 61-75. Notes. Lang.: Eng.
USA. 1850-1900. Historical studies. ■Analysis of the causes of rapid shift from resident stock to touring combination, with discussion of the use of sources.

87 Beach, Claudia Anne. *Henry Greenwall: Theatre Manager*. Austin, TX: Texas Tech Univ; 1986. 231 pp. Pref. Notes. Biblio. [Ph.D. dissertation, Univ. Microfilms order No. DA8627700.] Lang.: Eng.
USA: Galveston, TX. 1867-1890. Biographical studies. ■Investigates Henry Greenwall's contribution to the theatre as an independent manager in the South and his opposition to the theatrical syndicate.

88 Benisch, Barbara. "Individual Fundraising." *TT*. 1983 Nov/Dec.; 3(2): 9. Lang.: Eng.
USA. 1983. Instructional materials. ■Fundraising methods for maximizing individual donations, including benefits, direct mail.

89 Benisch, Barbara. "Foundation Fundraising: A Crash Course." *TT*. 1983 June; 2(7): 6-7. Lang.: Eng.
USA: New York, NY. 1983. Technical studies. ■Defines a variety of foundations, identifies likely prospects and describes application procedures. Includes list of Foundation Center publications.

90 Benisch, Barbara. "Corporate In-Kind Gifts." *TT*. 1984 Feb.; 3(4): 8-9. Lang.: Eng.
USA: New York, NY. 1984. Historical studies. ■Potential of in-kind giving between corporations and new theatre companies. Random sampling of nine companies and their policies.

91 Bishop, André. "Direct Mail Marketing for the Arts: Solution or Problem?" *TT*. 1982; 1(3): 5-8. Illus.: Photo. B&W. 6: var. sizes. Lang.: Eng.
USA: New York, NY. 1982. Critical studies. ■Keynote address of direct mail marketing seminar given by André Bishop, artistic director of Playwrights Horizons. State of the art techniques and the type of audience being developed through these campaigns.

92 Borchard, William M.; Hart, William D. "Solving Common Problems Arising from Use of Trademarks in the Arts." *ColJL&A*. 1986 Win; 10(2): 171-196. Notes. Lang.: Eng.
USA. 1985. Histories-sources. ■Common trademark protection problems in the arts.

93 Brennan, Scott. "Technology Takes Over: Computers in the Theatre." *TT*. 1986 Jan.; 5(2): 11-12. Illus.: Sketches. 1. Lang.: Eng.
USA: New York, NY. 1985. Historical studies. ■How computers are used by Alliance of Resident Theatres/New York's member organizations. Focus on management, planning, payroll, and ART/NY Cooperative Computer Project.

94 Busch, Kate. "The New Approved Production Contract." *TT*. 1985 June/July; 4(6): 7. Lang.: Eng.
USA: New York, NY. 1985. Historical studies. ■League of American Theatres and Producers and Dramatists Guild release details of the new Approved Production Contract which replaces the Minimum Basic Production Contract.

95 Chandler, Margaret K.; Hall, John C., Jr.; Brockway, Michael; Bronson, Michael; Berman, Noel B. "Future Issues in Collective Bargaining." *JAML*. 1986 Spr; 16(1): 61-90. Pref. Lang.: Eng.
USA. 1986. Histories-sources. ■Panel discussion on technological advances and their effects on the arts, institutional developments, career progression for the artist.

96 Cohen, Ruth. "For the Benefit of Your Theatre." *TT*. 1986 May; 5(4): 10-11. Lang.: Eng.
USA: New York, NY. 1986. Technical studies. ■Organization and planning of a benefit to be used as an effective fundraising tool for nonprofit theatres.

97 Conable, Anne E. "You *Can* Overcome Fear of Phoning." *TT*. 1984 Apr.; 3(6): 4-5. Illus.: Sketches. 1. Lang.: Eng.
USA: New York, NY. 1984. Historical studies. ■New techniques of telemarketing, focusing on Circle in the Square's new and effective sales methods.

98 DiMaggio, Paul. "Can Culture Survive the Marketplace?" *JAML*. 1983 Spr; 13(1): 61-87. Notes. Lang.: Eng.
USA. 1940-1983. Critical studies. ■What sort of culture will survive Reagan's Economic Recovery Act? Designing strategies of arts support to meet challenges of public and private patronage.

99 Faine, Hyman R. "Cooperative Bargaining in Nonprofit Arts Organizations." *JAML*. 1986 Spr; 16(1): 48-60. Pref. Notes. Lang.: Eng.
USA. 1986. Critical studies. ■Overview of the functions of management and administration and their relationship to unions in collective bargaining process.

100 Feldman, Franklin. "Commodities and Art: A Delicate Relationship." *ColJL&A*. 1986 Win; 10(2): 197-210. Notes. Illus.: Sketches. B&W. 16: 5 cm. x 4 cm. Lang.: Eng.
USA. 1986. Historical studies. ■Arts as a commodity to be bought, kept or sold.

101 Fichandler, Zelda. "On Risk and Money." *AmTh*. 1986 Nov.; 3(8): 26-27, 97-100. Illus.: Photo. 1: 3 in. x 5 in. Lang.: Eng.
USA: Washington, DC. 1986. Histories-sources. ■Producing Director of Arena Stage discusses artistic risk in relation to fiscal deficits.

102 Gelber, Jack. "Julian Beck, Businessman." *TDR*. 1986 Sum; 30(2): 6-29. Notes. Illus.: Photo. B&W. 16: 3 in. x 3 in. Lang.: Eng.
USA: New York, NY. 1947-1983. Historical studies. ■Business acumen of Julian Beck has allowed the Living Theatre to operate on a shoestring for forty years.

103 Gillespie, Fern. "Black Theater." *Crisis*. 1986 Jan.; 93(1): 35-39, 44-46. Illus.: Photo. Print. B&W. 6. Lang.: Eng.
USA: St. Louis, MO, New York, NY, Los Angeles, CA, Detroit, MI. 1985. Historical studies. ■Alternative funding for small theatres previously dependent on government subsidy.

104 Godfrey, Marian A. "The Calculus of Art & Money: Building a Board." *TT*. 1986 May; 5(4): 1-3. Illus.: Photo. Sketches. 3. Lang.: Eng.
USA: New York, NY. 1986. Critical studies. ■Creation and role of board of directors in nonprofit theatre. Profile of individual theatres and some board members.

105 Godfrey, Marian A. "Funding for Individual Productions." *TT*. 1985 Jan.; 4(3): 6-7. Illus.: Photo. B&W. 2: var. sizes. Lang.: Eng.

THEATRE IN GENERAL: —Administration

USA: New York, NY. 1985. Historical studies. ■Development of funding sources for special projects, individual productions and individual fellowships.

106 Goldbard, Arlene; Adams, Don. "The Right to Culture." *JAML*. 1983 Spr; 13(25-27). Lang.: Eng.
USA. 1983. Critical studies. ■Failure of democratic ideals to protect and promote culture.

107 Golden, Joseph. "Ten Terrific Ways to Become Obsolete." *Gap*. 1986; 6(5): 17-21. [Speed Up Your Organization's Decline.] Lang.: Eng.
USA. 1986. Critical studies. ■Satirical analysis of the strategies used in managing an arts organization that will insure failure.

108 Golodner, Jack. "Overview." *JAML*. 1986 Spr; 16(1): 8-15. Pref. Lang.: Eng.
USA. 1986. Histories-sources. ■Text of a speech on the effects of new technology. The expanding scope of the arts and the role of government in arts on the bargaining relationship in the performing arts.

109 Hale, Alice M. "Solid As A Rock." *ThCr*. 1986 Feb.; 20(2): 16-21, 43-45, 48-49. Illus.: Photo. 8: var. sizes. Lang.: Eng.
USA: Baltimore, MD. 1963-1986. Historical studies. ■Profile of Center Stage, focusing on the strong cooperation between the administration and production department.

110 Hale, Alice M. "The Acting Company." *ThCr*. 1986 Mar.; 20(3): 38, 42-43. Lang.: Eng.
USA: New York, NY. 1986. Historical studies. ■Fundraising strategy of The Acting Company.

111 Hale, Alice M. "Hugh Landwehr: Associate Artist." *ThCr*. 1986 Feb.; 20(2): 20-21, 51-52. Lang.: Eng.
USA: Baltimore, MD. 1977-1986. Historical studies. ■A profile of Center Stage's resident set designer who functions as part of a directorate that helps plan the theatre's season.

112 Hale, Alice M. "Karen Brooks Hopkins." *ThCr*. 1986 Mar.; 20(3): 40, 56-59. Lang.: Eng.
USA: New York, NY. Historical studies. ■Fundraising strategy of Karen Brooks Hopkins, development director for the Brooklyn Academy of Music.

113 Harris, William. "Marion Godfrey." *ThCr*. 1986 Mar.; 20(3): 39, 49-52. Lang.: Eng.
USA: New York, NY. 1986. Historical studies. ■Fundraising strategies of Marion Godfrey, development director for various theatres.

114 Harris, William. "Barbara Groves." *ThCr*. 1986 Mar.; 20(3): 40, 52. Lang.: Eng.
USA: New York, NY. 1986. Historical studies. ■Fundraising strategy of Barbara Groves, development director for Lincoln Center.

115 Harrow, Gustave. "Creativity and Control." *JAML*. 1986 Sum; 16(2): 47-76. Notes. Lang.: Eng.
USA. 1986. Critical studies. ■Discusses artists with respect to societal control.

116 Havlicèk, Franklin J.; Kelso, J. Clark. "The Rights of Composers and Lyricists: Before and After Bernstein." *JAML*. 1986 Sum; 16(2): 77-93. Notes. Lang.: Eng.
USA. 1986. Critical studies. ■Proposal of terms and agreements to protect composers' and lyricists' rights.

117 Hirsch, Foster. "Still Savvy After All These Years." *AmTh*. 1986 Mar.; 2(11): 12-15. Illus.: Photo. Print. B&W. 3: 5 in. x 5 in., 7 in. x 8 in. Lang.: Eng.
USA: New York, NY, Atlanta, GA. 1936-1986. Historical studies. ■Sandra Deer's *So Long on Lonely Street* occasions Cheryl Crawford's return to producing on Broadway, where she has been a figure for 50 years.

118 James, Luther. "Theatre." *Crisis*. 1986 Feb.; 93(2): 13, 60. Illus.: Photo. Print. B&W. 1: 4 in. x 5 in. Lang.: Eng.
USA. 1985. Historical studies. ■Developments in increasing arts funding to minority arts projects as called for by the Multicultural Advisory Coalition of the California Arts Council.

119 Jaros, Susan Steven. "Copyright." *PuJ*. 1986 Fall; 38(1): 23. Illus.: Design. B&W. 1: 2.5 in. x 2.5 in. Lang.: Eng.
USA. 1985. Technical studies. ■Reprint of general information and background on procedure and protection of work. Related to Puppetry.

120 Joyce, Michael. "Government: Patron of Last Resort." *JAML*. 1983 Spr; 13(1): 35-37. Lang.: Eng.
USA. 1854-1983. Critical studies. ■Cultural patronage: should the American government engage in it if cultural patronage is to keep alive the essential ideals, values, perspectives and dimensions of any assembly of citizens calling itself a group?.

121 Katz, Jonathan. "Decentralization and the Arts: Principles, Practice, and Policy." *JAML*. 1983 Spr; 13(1): 109-120. Notes. Biblio. Lang.: Eng.
USA. 1980-1983. Historical studies. ■Decentralization of government policies on the arts and the delegation of responsibility to organizations of more local or specific purview.

122 Kaufman, Gary. "Exposing the Suspicious Foundations of Society's Primacy in Copyright Law: Five Accidents." *ColJL&A*. 1986 Win; 10(2): 381-420. Notes. Lang.: Eng.
USA. 1557-1985. Historical studies. ■Five historical cases involving English and U.S. copyright law: conflict of interest between author's and society's interests regarding 'fair use,' factual works and private copying.

123 Keller, Anthony. "Private Initiative and the Public Good." *JAML*. 1983 Spr; 13(1): 100-108. Lang.: Eng.
USA. 1983. Histories-sources. ■Interview with Richard Carter on differences between government and corporate support of the arts.

124 Keller, Anthony. "The Artist and Public Policy: An Interview with Douglas Davis." *JAML*. 1983 Spr; 13(1): 129-137. Lang.: Eng.
USA. 1983. Histories-sources. ■Davis discusses the unique features of artist-state relationship in the U.S.: preservation of the old, desire for the new, variety of regional preferences.

125 Kohn, Rita. "In Regional Theater as in New York, Lady Luck Can Be Capricious." *DGQ*. 1986 Spr; 23(1): 15-17.
USA: New York, NY. 1986. Histories-sources. ■Playwright Rita Kohn discusses attempts to get her play *Necessities* produced in New York and regional theatre.

126 Kramer, Ian. "Fundraising from Individuals: Guidelines for Small Theatres." *TT*. 1986 Jan.; 5(2): 6-7. Illus.: Sketches. 6. Lang.: Eng.
USA: New York, NY. 1985. Technical studies. ■Guidelines for fundraising from individuals.

127 Kreig, Patricia A. "Copyright, Free Speech, and the Visual Arts." *JAML*. 1986 Win; 15(4): 59-80. Notes. Lang.: Eng.
USA. 1986. Critical studies. ■Examines inadequacy of first amendment in relation to arts and proposes more idealistic copyright laws that would guarantee artists' freedom of speech.

128 LaRue, Michèle. "Community Theatre." *ThCr*. 1986 Mar.; 20(3): 39, 45-59. Lang.: Eng.
USA. 1986. Historical studies. ■Fundraising strategies of various community theatres.

129 Leibowitz, Leonard; Eisenberg, Alan; Webster, Albert K.; Waldeck, Lewis; Schoenfeld, Gerald. "The Bargaining Table: Current Issues." *JAML*. 1986 Spr; 16(1): 15-45. Pref. Lang.: Eng.
USA. 1986. Histories-sources. ■General discussion on the problems of profit versus not-for-profit arts institutions. The need for Equity's protection, salaries, status.

130 Lerner, Ruby. "If a Play Falls Outside Manhattan Does it Make a Sound?" *TT*. 1984 Jan.; 3(3): 3,9. Illus.: Photo. B&W. 1: 3 in. x 4 in. Lang.: Eng.
USA: New York, NY. 1983. Historical studies. ■Executive director of Alternate ROOTS, an alliance of Southern artists and art groups, discusses advantages for regional groups to perform in New York.

131 Lesnick, Howard. "Artists, Workers, and the Law of Work: Keynote Address." *JAML*. 1986 Sum; 16(2): 39-46. Pref. Notes. Lang.: Eng.
USA: New York, NY. 1986. Histories-sources. ■Distinctions made between artists and other workers.

132 Levine, Mindy N. "How Does a Literary Manager Manage?" *TT*. 1983 Feb.; 2(4): 1-2, 11. Illus.: Photo. B&W. 2. Lang.: Eng.

THEATRE IN GENERAL: —Administration

USA: New York, NY. 1983. Histories-sources. ■Discussion with several literary managers on their roles and responsibilities in nonprofit theatre.

133 Levine, Mindy N. "An Interview with Zuri McKie, NY-SCA's New Theatre program Director." *TT*. 1983 Oct.; 3(1): 4-5. Illus.: Photo. B&W. 1: 3 in. x 4 in. Lang.: Eng.
USA: New York, NY. 1983. Histories-sources. ■Zuri McKie, New York State Council on the Arts Theatre Program Director, discusses her theatre background, perceptions of NYSCA and their funding policies, and the need to increase communication with individuals and smaller organizations.

134 Levine, Mindy N. "Is It Better to Give than to Receive?" *TT*. 1984 May/June; 3(7): 3-4, 8. Illus.: Photo. B&W. 2: var. sizes. Lang.: Eng.
USA: New York, NY. 1984. Histories-sources. ■Corporate grant officers and arts management heads discuss corporate giving and the difference for those who went from working in nonprofit theatre to corporate grants departments.

135 Levine, Mindy N. "Between the Play and the Production: The Art and Business of Play Agents." *TT*. 1985 Nov.; 5(1): 1, 4-5. Illus.: Photo. B&W. 2. Lang.: Eng.
USA: New York, NY. 1985. Critical studies. ■Role of a writer's agent in finding a script and getting it produced. Legal aspects, contracts and negotiations are discussed.

136 Lewis, William. "Decades of Exclusion." *JAML*. 1983 Spr; 13(1): 54-57. Lang.: Eng.
USA. 1983. Critical studies. ■How minority artists, arts institutions and organizations obtain and maintain access to priorities, issues and decisions that shape public policy as funds become more limited.

137 Lieberman, Susan B. "Children's Theatre Company." *ThCr*. 1986 Mar.; 20(3): 39, 43-45. Lang.: Eng.
USA: Minneapolis, MN. 1986. Historical studies. ■Fundraising strategy of the Children's Theatre Company.

138 Long, Robert. "The Costume Building Eyes Manhattan." *ThCr*. 1986 Aug/Sep.; 20(7): 31, 41-43. Lang.: Eng.
USA: New York, NY. 1986. Historical studies. ■Costume shop owners and designers collaborate to strike a real estate deal with the City of New York.

139 Louloudes, Virginia. "Beyond Danny Newman: New Trends in Brochure Design." *TT*. 1986 Nov.; 6(1): 7-8. Illus.: Handbill. B&W. 1. Lang.: Eng.
USA: New York, NY. 1986. Critical studies. ■Marketing directors seek innovative approaches to brochure design which break from the 'Danny Newman' style.

140 Louloudes, Virginia. "More Than Selling Tickets: The Job of the Marketing Director." *TT*. 1986 Mar.; 5(3): 7, 12. Illus.: Sketches. 3. Lang.: Eng.
USA: New York, NY. 1986. Historical studies. ■Role of the marketing director in nonprofit theatre, focusing on audience development and new marketing techniques for Manhattan Theatre Club, New Wave Festival and the Ark Theatre.

141 Lowrey, W. McNeil. "Tradition and Evolution in Public Arts Policy." *JAML*. 1983 Spr; 13(1): 17-23. Notes. Lang.: Eng.
USA. 1776-1983. Critical studies. ■Difficulty in formulation of public policy in the arts traced to the dual base of American society—public and private, official and voluntary.

142 Lowry, W. McNeil. "Purging the Citadel." *AmTh*. 1984 Oct.; 1(6): 22-23. Illus.: Photo. B&W. 1. Lang.: Eng.
USA. 1984. Histories-sources. ■The former vice president for humanities and the arts of the Ford Foundation discusses funding for the arts and the relationship between institutions and their boards.

143 Marable, Manning. "In Pursuit of Cultural Democracy." *JAML*. 1983 Spr; 13: 28-31. Notes. Lang.: Eng.
USA. 1857-1983. Critical studies. ■Relationship among aesthetics, cultural work and the state, and the tension created by melting-pot ideals and cultural suppression.

144 Martin, Scott M. "Museum Copyright Licensing Agreements and Visual Artists." *ColJL&A*. 1986 Win; 10(2): 421-452. Notes. Lang.: Eng.
USA. 1976-1985. Historical studies. ■Copyright licensing agreements between museums and artists whose works are reproduced for public sale, and a proposed model licensing agreement.

145 McCaslin, Nellie. "Where Yellow Brick Road and Madison Avenue Meet, or Packaging the Artist in Children's Theatre." *ChTR*. 1986 Spr; 35(1): 14-15. Notes. Illus.: Photo. B&W. 1: 3 in. x 7 in. Lang.: Eng.
USA: Cleveland, OH. 1985-1986. Historical studies. ■Use of business and promotional techniques to bring Aurand Harris, children's theatre performer, to Cleveland by getting community leaders to fund his residency.

146 McClimon, Timothy J. "Denial of the Preliminary Injunction in Copyright Infringement Cases: An Emerging Judicially Crafted Compulsory License." *ColJL&A*. 1986 Win; 10(2): 277-308. Notes. Lang.: Eng.
USA. 1976-1985. Historical studies. ■Examination of the authority of courts to grant or deny these injunctions.

147 McCulloch-Lovell, Ellen. "The Heritage of the Future." *JAML*. 1983 Spr; 13(1): 40-53. Notes. Lang.: Eng.
USA. 1904-1983. Critical studies. ■Argument for congruence between cultural history and arts policy, with discussion of 'new regionalism'.

148 Milch, Neal. "Protection for Utilitarian Works of Arts: The Design Patent/Copyright Conundrum." *ColJL&A*. 1986 Win; 10 (2): 211-244. Notes. Lang.: Eng.
USA. 1842-1985. Historical studies. ■Design patent problems within U.S. copyright law: historical origins, examples of problems and a proposal to replace design patents with comprehensive copyright protection.

149 Moore, Kate L. "Seeking Clarity at the National Endowment for the Arts." *JAML*. 1983 Spr; 13(1): 93-99. Append. Lang.: Eng.
USA. 1981-1983. Critical studies. ■Identifying the most pressing needs of the arts today and how the NEA can make the ever diminishing funds stretch further in support of the arts.

150 Moynihan, D.S. "Sarah Pearson." *ThCr*. 1986 Mar.; 20(3): 40, 59-63. Lang.: Eng.
USA: Cambridge, MA. 1986. Historical studies. ■Fundraising strategy of Sarah Pearson, development director for American Repertory Theatre.

151 Nelson, Richard. "Nonprofit Theatre in America: Where We Are." *TT*. 1983 Nov/Dec.; 3(2): 2-3. Lang.: Eng.
USA. 1983. Historical studies. ■Complacency and institutional stability have superseded artistic achievement and social responsibility in American nonprofit theatre. A slightly different version of this article appears in *PerAJ* 19 and 21.

152 Remer, Jane. "Arts Policy in Public Education." *JAML*. 1983 Spr; 13(1): 121-125. Lang.: Eng.
USA. 1960-1983. Critical studies. ■Lack of consensus on what is acceptable in the arts reflected in neglect of arts in the classroom.

153 Robinson, Alma. "Dispute Resolution for the Arts Community." *ColJL&A*. 1986 Win; 11(2): 333-345. Lang.: Eng.
USA: San Francisco, CA. 1980-1986. Historical studies. ■Development of model project offering dispute resolution services to artists by Bay Area Lawyers for the Arts, including case resolutions, fee structure, evaluation methods and training of arbitrators.

154 Rosenak, David; Hale, Alice M. "Sweet Charity." *ThCr*. 1986 Aug/Sep.; 20(7): 29, 93-95. Lang.: Eng.
USA. 1986. Technical studies. ■Theatres approach individual foundations in the face of shrinking federal arts funding.

155 Rosenak, David. "Brother, Can You Spare Ten Grand?" *ThCr*. 1986 Aug/Sep.; 20(7): 29, 95-105. Lang.: Eng.
USA. 1986. Technical studies. ■Guide to some of the largest private foundations and a profile of The Foundation Center.

156 Rowe, Katharine. "The New Cost of Theatre: Public Liability Insurance." *TT*. 1986 May; 5(4): 5-6. Lang.: Eng.
USA: New York, NY. 1986. Historical studies. ■Escalating insurance rates create economic hardship for Off Broadway theatres. Analysis of why rates are rising and projections for the future.

CLASSED ENTRIES

THEATRE IN GENERAL: —Administration

157 Sandison, Hamish. "The Berne Union and the Universal Copyright Convention: The American Experience." *ColJL&A.* 1986 Fall ; 11(1): 89-120. Notes. Lang.: Eng.
USA. 1776-1986. Historical studies. ■History of American copyright law and relationship to Berne Convention, including obstacles in U.S. adherence.

158 Sansone, Marleen. "Policy and Politics." *JAML.* 1983 Spr; 13(1): 88-92. Notes. Lang.: Eng.
USA. 1980-1983. Critical studies. ■Relationships between politicians and cultural leaders.

159 Schaffer, Robert; Levine, Mindy N., ed. *Showcase Primer: Producing Off-off Broadway.* New York, NY: ART/NY; 1981. 62 pp. Pref. Biblio. Lang.: Eng.
USA: New York, NY. Technical studies. ■All aspects of showcase production, including information on the Actors Equity Association showcase code, contracts, promotion and budgeting as well as lists of publication and organizations assisting independent producers.

160 Sheffer, Isaiah. "The Symphony Space Victory and its Implications for New York State Arts Organizations." *TT.* 1983 Oct. ; 3(1): 3, 9. Illus.: Photo. B&W. 1: 3 in. x 3.5 in. Lang.: Eng.
USA: New York, NY. 1979-1983. Historical studies. ■Court appeals by Symphony Space on New York City's interpretation of the tax laws created a ruling favorable to arts organizations paying municipal property taxes.

161 Somners, Michael. "Working With the General Contractor." *ThCr.* 1986 Dec.; 20(20): 20, 48-51. Illus.: Plan. Photo. 1: var. sizes. Lang.: Eng.
USA. 1986. Technical studies. ■Early consultation, concrete specifications and close supervision are advised when working with general contractors.

162 Steuer, Gary P. "The NYSCA Reorganization Explained." *TT.* 1984 Aug.; 3(8): 7, 10. Lang.: Eng.
USA: New York, NY. 1984. Historical studies. ■Primary organizational changes at New York State Council on the Arts discussed: creation of Multi-Year Support Program, general operating grant category, Individual Artists Program and elimination of separate fiscal and program staffs.

163 Steuer, Gary P. "Going...Going...Gone! The Auction as a Fundraising Tool." *TT.* 1986 Mar.; 5(3): 6-7. Illus.: Sketches. 1. Lang.: Eng.
USA: New York, NY. 1986. Technical studies. ■Effective use of an auction as a fundraising tool for small nonprofit theatres.

164 Steuer, Gary P. "Banking on the Arts." *TT.* 1985 Nov.; 5(1): 12-13. Lang.: Eng.
USA: New York, NY. 1985. Critical studies. ■Banking industry in New York as a strong source of corporate contributions. Includes grant-giving history and policies of some major banks.

165 Steuer, Gary P. "The Showcase Code in 1983." *TT.* 1982 Oct.; 2(1): 5, 8. Illus.: Photo. B&W. 1. Lang.: Eng.
USA: New York, NY. 1982. Historical studies. ■Revisions in the Showcase Code by Actors' Equity Association as a result of a dispute with playwrights wanting to retain greater control over future productions of their works.

166 Steuer, Gary P. "Deciphering the New Showcase and Nonprofit Theatre Codes." *TT.* 1983 Oct.; 3(1): 6-7. Illus.: Photo. B&W. 1: 3 in. x 3 in. Lang.: Eng.
USA. 1983. Historical studies. ■Changes in the Showcase and Nonprofit Theatre codes granted by Actors' Equity Association. New regulations affect compensation to actors in various tiers, conversion rights.

167 Steuer, Gary P. "Getting the Picture—First Stats on N.Y. Nonprofit Theatre." *TT.* 1983 Nov/Dec.; 3(2): 1, 11. Illus.: Graphs. B&W. 1: 6.5 in. x 4.5 in. Lang.: Eng.
USA: New York, NY. 1980-1983. Historical studies. ■Statistics of income and expenses of New York Off and Off-off Broadway nonprofit theatres for the 1980-81 and 1981-82 seasons. Results compared with those in a Theatre Communications Group study of nonprofit theatres nationally.

168 Steuer, Gary P.; Tarlow, Mindy. "Beyond DCA: Tapping the Board of Estimate and City Council." *TT.* 1984 Oct.; 4(1): 5-6. Notes. Lang.: Eng.
USA: New York, NY. 1984. Historical studies. ■The role of the New York City Board of Estimate in allocating large sums of money to arts groups. Includes breakdown of monetary distributions.

169 Steuer, Gary P. "Managing Directors." *TT.* 1985 Jan.; 4(3): 1-3. Illus.: Photo. B&W. 4: var. sizes. Lang.: Eng.
USA: New York, NY. 1984. Historical studies. ■Focus on several managing directors in nonprofit theatre, discussing skills and abilities necessary to meet demands of the job.

170 Steuer, Gary P. "Computers in the Theatre: Boon or Bane?" *TT.* 1982 Nov/Dec.; 2(2): 1-2, 4. Illus.: Photo. B&W. 2. Lang.: Eng.
USA: New York, NY. 1982. Technical studies. ■Benefits and uses of computers in non-profit theatre organizations.

171 Stewart, William; Fichandler, Zelda; White, David R.; Dean, Laura; Bikel, Theodore. "Professional Standards and Managerial Realities." *JAML.* 1986 Sum; 16(2): 8-36. Notes. Lang.: Eng.
USA. 1986. Histories-sources. ■Panel discussion on encouraging growth and change in artists and institutions.

172 Thompson, Tom. "Single Ticket Discounts." *TT.* 1984 Dec.; 4(2): 5-6. Illus.: Dwg. 1. Lang.: Eng.
USA: New York, NY. 1984. Historical studies. ■Pros and cons of single ticket discount policies, advertising them and combining with subscription, how they encourage audiences.

173 Van Den Haag, Ernest. "The Government Should Stay Away." *JAML.* 1983 Spr; 13(1): 32-34. Lang.: Eng.
USA. 1983. Critical studies. ■Argument against government subsidy of the arts as well as government censorship.

174 Weil, Stephen E. "Artists, Workers, and the Law of Work: Introductory Comments." *JAML.* 1986 Sum; 16(2): 37-38. Pref. Notes. Lang.: Eng.
USA. 1986. Histories-sources. ■Effects of classification (artist, layman, executive) on ways of envisioning work.

175 Weiss, Will Maitland. "Turn On, Tune In...To Radio Advertising." *TT.* 1986 June; 5(5): 8-9. Lang.: Eng.
USA: New York, NY. 1986. Critical studies. ■Advantages of radio advertising for live theatre. Several ad agency executives address the marketing strategies involved. Related to Media: Audio forms.

176 Weiss, Will Maitland. "Trick Question: When Is One Grant Better than Three?" *TT.* 1985 May; 4(5): 6-7. Lang.: Eng.
USA: New York, NY. 1985. Technical studies. ■Advantages and drawbacks of consortium fundraising. Joint grant requests have better chance of success.

177 Wetzsteon, Ross. "Joe Papp Gets Big Ideas." *AmTh.* 1986 Sep.; 3(6): 10-17. Illus.: Photo. 5: 3 in. x 4 in., 11 in. x 11 in. Lang.: Eng.
USA: New York, NY. 1959-1986. Histories-sources. ■Joe Papp discusses building new audiences on Broadway and in the barrios.

178 Whitfield, Vantile E. "Artistic Director As Nightmare." *OvA.* 1985 Win; 13(1): 13-14. Lang.: Eng.
USA. 1986. Critical studies. ■Satiric examination of what not to do if one is to become an effective artistic director.

179 Wiener, Sally Dixon. "Artistic Directors Review Problems and Aspirations of Regional Theatre." *DGQ.* 1986 Spr; 23(1): 10-14.
USA: New York, NY. 1986. Histories-sources. ■Panel discussion at a meeting of the League of Professional Theatre Women answering the question 'is theatre commerce or a resource to its community?'.

180 Ziff, Charles. "Taking Aims...Or How to Stop Worrying and Love Your Computer." *AmTh.* 1984 June; 1(3): 40-41. Illus.: Sketches. 1. Lang.: Eng.
USA: New York, NY. 1984. Critical studies. ■Detailed history and analysis of the capabilities of AIMS (Arts Income Management System), a computer software package to aid marketing and fundraising for arts organizations.

THEATRE IN GENERAL: —Administration

181 Zimmerman, Jory Bard. "Exclusivity of Personal Services: The Viability and Enforceability of Contracted Rights." *JAML*. 1986 Fall; 16(3): 61-84. Notes. Lang.: Eng.
USA. 1986. Technical studies. ■Procedures of writing and maintaining contracts.

182 Adžiev, M. "Ekonomika i tvorčestvo ešče kak sovmestimy." (Economics and Creative Work: Still Compatible.) *TeatZ*. 1986; 29(15): 12-13. Lang.: Rus.
USSR. 1980-1986. Histories-sources. ■Independent financing of experimental theatre.

183 Belkin, A. "Vremja trebuet." (Time Makes Demands.) *TeatZ*. 1986; 29(7): 9. Lang.: Rus.
USSR. 1986. Critical studies. ■Notes on how to rebuild theatre business and develop actor training following meeting of All-Union Theatre Society (Vsesojuznyj teatral'nyj obščestvo).

184 Drozdov, G. "O mečtah, kotorym pora sbyvat'sja." (Of Dreams Whose Time Has Come.) *TeatZ*. 1986; 29(8): 12-13. Lang.: Rus.
USSR. 1986. Critical studies. ■On the need for radical change in theatrical management and financing.

185 Efremov, A. "Nužno pobeždat' každyj den'." (Each Day One Must Overcome.) *TeatrM*. 1986; 9: 40-47. Lang.: Rus.
USSR: Moscow. 1980. Histories-sources. ■Interview with V.R. Beljakovič, manager of the collective Teat'r studija na Jugo-Zapade on the collective, its principles and methodology.

186 Efremov, O. "Slovo dolžno stat' postupkom." (The Word Must Become Deed.) *TeatrM*. 1986; 5: 34-36. Lang.: Rus.
USSR. 1980-1986. Critical studies. ■Need for change in the organization of theatrical management.

187 Ešalieva, E.S. *Problemy finansirovanija učreždenij kul'tury (na primere teatral' no-zreliščhnyh predrpijatij): Avtoref. dis. ... kand. ekonom. nauk.* (Problems of Financing Cultural Institutions—On the Example of Theatrical Performance Enterprises: Synopsis of a Dissertation by a Candidiate in Economics.) Moscow: Moskovskij finansovyj institut; 1986. 23 pp. Lang.: Rus.
USSR. 1986. Critical studies.

188 Kolbin, G. "Kadry kul'tury i kul'tura kadrov." (Cadres of Culture and the Culture of Cadres.) *TeatrM*. 1986; 2: 27-34. Lang.: Rus.
USSR. 1980-1986. Historical studies. ■On personnel problems in theatres.

189 Pidust, A.M. *Tvorčeskoe razvitije oblastnogo dramatičeskogo teatra v uslovijach kompleksnogo planirovanija ego dejatel'nosti: Avtoref. diss. ... kand. iskusstvovedenija.* (The Creative Development of the Regional Dramatic Theatre under the Conditions of the Group Planning of Its Activity: Synopsis of a Dissertation by a Candidate in Art Criticism.) Leningrad: Leningradskij gosudarstvennyj institut teatra, muzyki i kinematografii; 1986. 25 pp. Lang.: Rus.
USSR. 1980-1986. Critical studies.

190 Pivovarov, O. "Sobrat'sja vmeste vsem zavlitam." (Literary Directors Get Together.) *TeatZ*. 1986; 29(8): 19. Lang.: Rus.
USSR. 1986. Critical studies. ■Proposals for reorganizing theatrical business, including financing, producing and the formation of companies.

191 Plavskaja, E. "Obeščanija kotorye vypolnjajutsja." (Promises That are Being Fulfilled.) *TeatZ*. 1986; 29(24): 23 . Lang.: Rus.
USSR: Moscow. 1980-1986. Critical studies. ■Transition of amateur theatre groups to professional collectives: problems and perspectives.

192 Serdjuk, L. "Naši potomki—naše buduščej." (Our Descendents, Our Future.) *UTeatr*. 1986; 5: 3-4. Lang.: Ukr.
USSR. 1980-1986. Critical studies. ■Ukrainian actors and teachers on rebuilding theatre business.

193 Tarasenko, A. "Kto pervy?: polemičeskije razmyšlenija." (Who Is First? Polemical Reflections.) *UTeatr*. 1986; 2: 9-11. Lang.: Ukr.

USSR. 1980-1986. Critical studies. ■Problems of present-day reality in Ukrainian theatres.

194 Volček, G.; Vorob'ev, B.; Golubovskij, B. "Naš sovremennik—teatr." (Our Contemporary, the Theatre.) *TeatrM*. 1986; 4: 145-155. Lang.: Rus.
USSR. 1980-1986. Historical studies. ■Articles on the organizational problems of theatre.

195 Zajcev, E. "Obnovlenie teatra." (Renewal of the Theatre.) *TeatrM*. 1986; 12: 46-53. Lang.: Rus.
USSR. 1980-1986. Histories-sources. ■On the conditions of a composite experiment in the broadening of creative independence and the rebuilding of the economic principles of the work of theatres.

196 Žuhovicckij, L. "Zagadki teatral'nogo goroda." (Riddles of a Theatre Town.) *TeatrM*. 1986; 1: 72-80. Lang.: Rus.
USSR. 1980-1986. Historical studies. ■Problems of theatres in USSR-Russian SFSR.

Audience

197 Toyama, Shizuo. "An Experiment in Visual Acuity Affecting Audience Seating." *TD&T*. 1986 Sum; 22(2): 11-14. Tables. Illus.: Diagram. 8: var. sizes. Lang.: Eng.
1986. Empirical research. ■Results of a series of experiments to determine the maximum distance from the stage at which seats may be placed in an auditorium and still allow the perception of subtle features and expressions.

198 Roy, Claude. "Le Répertoire Classique: Modernité et Actualité." (The Classical Repertory: Modernity and Actuality.) *CTL*. 1986 June; 19(56-57): 38-46. [International colloquium on Vilar, Venice, November 1985.] Lang.: Fre.
France: Paris. 1951-1963. Historical studies. ■Jean Vilar, while expressing the desire to produce modern works, kept returning to the classics which he felt to have more revolutionary power than agit-prop theatre.

199 Weitz, Shoshana; Avigal, Shoshana. "Cultural and Ideological Variables in Audience Response: The Case of *The Trojan Women*, Tel-Aviv, 1982-1983." *ASSAPHc*. 1986; 3: 6-42. Notes. Tables. Illus.: Photo. B&W. 5: var. sizes. Lang.: Eng.
Israel: Tel-Aviv. 1982-1983. Historical studies. ■The influence of the circumstances of reception on audience perception observed at a production of *Troádes (The Trojan Women)* by Euripides by HaBimah Theatre.

200 Kim, Oh-Jung. "Kwangaek Chukmyeon Egeo Bön Hänguk Yeinkükui Panghyangseong Yeöngu." (Study of Present Korean Theatre through a Survey of Theatre-Goers.) 85-152 in Lee, Young-Tack, ed. *Dong-Guk Dramatic Art*. Seoul: Dong-Guk Univ; 1986. 231 pp. Lang.: Kor.
Korea: Seoul. 1975-1985. Empirical studies. ■Report on audience preferences for commercial theatre, including an analysis of audience statistics.

201 Busch, Kate. "Students in the Audience." *TT*. 1985 Jan.; 4(3): 1, 3-4. Illus.: Photo. B&W. 2: var. sizes. Lang.: Eng.
USA: New York, NY. 1984. Historical studies. ■Several New York theatres discuss their student outreach programs, encouraging and developing the theatre audience of the future.

202 Salazar, Laura Gardner. "Crusade Against Children in the Theatre, 1900-1910." *ChTR*. 1984 July; 33(3): 8-10. Notes. Lang.: Eng.
USA: New York, NY. 1900-1910. Critical studies. ■Examination of the rise in children's attendance at theatrical performances in New York at the beginning of the century, and the concerns of social workers that such attendance adversely affected children's education and moral development.

203 Weiss, Will Maitland. "Subscribers: The Folks We Love to Hate." *TT*. 1984 Dec.; 4(2): 1,7. Illus.: Sketches. 1. Lang.: Eng.
USA: New York, NY. 1984. Critical studies. ■Profile of subscribers to nonprofit theatre, the role subscribers play in advance planning, finances, and influence on direction of theatre season.

THEATRE IN GENERAL: —Audience

204 "Teatr i zritel' utračennyj dialog." (Theatre and Audience: A Lost Dialogue.) *TeatZ.* 1986; 29(23): 14-15, 18. Lang.: Rus.
USSR: Moscow. 1986. Critical studies. ■G. Damadjan, A. Rubinštejn, V. Židkov and others discuss the audience-performer relationship in experimental theatre.

205 Al'tšuller, A.Ja., ed. *Teatr i gorod: Sbornik statej.* (The Theatre and the City: Collected Articles.) Moscow: Vseros. teatr. o-vo; 1986. 156 pp. Lang.: Rus.
USSR. 1950-1985. Critical studies. ■Social role of urban theatres.

206 Belkin, A. "Zritel' real'nyj i zritel' mifičeskij." (The Real Audience and the Mythical Audience.) *TeatZ.* 1986; 29 (20): 12-13. Lang.: Rus.
USSR. 1980-1986. Historical studies. ■Discusses the absence of an audience for non-mainstream theatre.

207 Dmitrievskij, V. *Teatr pora neotložnyh rešenij: 'Psihologiceskij bar'er' i real 'nost' situacii.* (Theatre 86: A Time of Urgent Decisions: 'The Psychological Hurdle' and the Reality of the Situation.) *TeatrM.* 1986; 4: 56-65.
USSR: Kujbyšev. 1980-1986. Histories-sources. ■Conference on low attendance in city theatres.

208 Ivčenko, V. "Teat'r i zritel'." (Theatre and Audience.) *Mastactva Belarusi.* 1986; 2: 33-34. Lang.: Rus.
USSR: Minsk. 1983-1984. Empirical research. ■Results of a study of Minsk theatre audiences.

209 Kon, I. "Ravnopravnyj sobesednik teatra." (An Equitable Interlocutor of the Theatre.) *TeatrM.* 1986; 12: 123-128. Lang.: Rus.
USSR. 1980-1986. Critical studies. ■On the role of the theatre in the life of contemporary youth.

210 Kornijenko, N.N. *Teatr segodnja—teatr zavtra: socioestetičeskie zametki o drame, scene i zritele 70-80.* (The Theatre Today, The Theatre Tomorrow: Socio-Aesthetic Notes on Drama, the Stage and the Audiences of the Seventies and Eighties.) Kiev: Mistectvo; 1986. 221 pp. Lang.: Rus.
USSR. 1970-1980. Critical studies.

211 Lattik, V. "Mesto Žitel'stva—Moskva." (Place of Residence: Moscow.) *DruzNar.* 1986; 8: 199-216. Lang.: Rus.
USSR: Moscow. 1980-1986. Historical studies. ■Overview of Moscow theatrical life.

212 Ljaguščenko, A. "Na puti k novumu zritelju: Iz istorii sociologičeskich issledovanij teatralnoj zizni na Ukraine v 20-e gody." (Toward a New Audience: Sociological Studies of Ukrainian Theatrical Life in the 1920s.) *UTeatr.* 1986; 2: 30-32. Lang.: Ukr.
USSR. 1920. Historical studies. ■Sociological studies of Ukrainian theatrical life.

213 Soham, Hayim. "Kahal Veteatron—Teatron Vekahal." (Public and Theatre—Theatre and Public.) *Bamah.* 1986; 21(103): 5-11. Notes. Lang.: Heb.
USSR: Moscow. 1918-1925. Critical studies. ■The relationship between HaBimah theatre and its audience with respect to repertory.

214 Velechova, N. "Dobryj, zloj, chorošij." (Kind, Evil, Good.) *TeatrM.* 1986; 3: 102-111. Lang.: Rus.
USSR. 1980-1986. Critical studies. ■Aesthetic education through theatre.

Basic theatrical documents

215 Jennings, Coleman A., ed.; Berghammer, Gretta, ed. *Theatre for Youth: Twelve Plays with Mature Themes.* Austin, TX: Univ. of Texas; 1986. 512 pp. Biblio. Lang.: Eng.
■Collection of plays intended to be performed by children 12-15 for an adult audience.

216 Bajza, József. *Szózat a pesti Magyar Szinház ügyében.* (An Appeal in the Cause of the Hungarian Theatre of Pest.) Preface by Gábor Szigethy. Budapest: Magvető; 1986. 92 pp. (Gondolkodó magyarok.) Pref. Notes. Lang.: Hun.
Austro-Hungarian Empire: Pest. 1839. Histories-sources. ■The 1839 pamphlet by the author and critic József Bajza, manager of the National Theatre, concerning the situation of the Hungarian Theatre of Pest.

217 Brooker, Bertram. "*Within: A Drama of Mind in Revolt.*" *CDr.* 1985; 11(1): 269-279. Illus.: Handbill. Poster. 2. Lang.: Eng.
Canada: Toronto, ON. 1935. ■Playtext of Brooker's *Within*, first produced by The Play Workshop, directed by Herman Voaden.

218 Deverell, Rex. "*Beyond Batoche.*" *CDr.* 1985 Sum; 11(2): 376-427. Illus.: Photo. B&W. 2. Lang.: Eng.
Canada: Regina, SK. 1985. ■Text of Rex Deverell's play *Beyond Batoche,* first performed April 10, 1985, at the Globe Theatre, Regina.

219 Hirsch, John, dir.; Shakespeare, William. *As You Like It.* Norwood, MA: Beacon Films; 1986. Lang.: Eng.
Canada: Stratford, ON. 1983. ■Videotape of a live performance of Shakespeare's *As You Like It.* Includes a study guide for classroom use and an annotated edition of the play with an introduction by John Hirsch.

220 Milhous, Judith; Hume, Robert D. "Charles Killigrew's 'Abstract of Title to the Playhouse' British Library Add. Ms 20, 726, Fols. 1-14." *THSt.* 1986; 6: 57-71. Notes. Illus.: Photo. Print. B&W. 1: 6.5 in. x 4.5 in. Lang.: Eng.
England. 1661-1684. ■Transcription of manuscript giving ownership of shares in the King's Company by the Killigrew Family.

221 Delcampe, Armand. "Poétique et travail théâtral: *Memento.*" (*Memento:* Poetic and Theatrical Work.) *CTL.* 1986 June; 19(56-57): 19-27. [International colloquium on Vilar, Venice, November 1985.] Lang.: Fre.
France: Paris. 1951-1981. Biographical studies. ■Compares entries in Jean Vilar's diary, begun in 1952 and published in 1981 as *Memento,* with polemics against him.

222 France, Richard. "Virgil Thomson/Gertrude Stein: A Correspondence." *THSt.* 1986; 6: 72-86. Notes. Lang.: Eng.
France. USA. 1926-1946. ■Correspondence between Gertrude Stein and Virgil Thomson regarding their collaboration on *The Mother of Us All.*

223 Kilián, István, ed. "A Kézdivásárhelyi betlehemesről." (On the Nativity Play of Kézdivásárhely.) *Napj.* 1986; 25(12): 20-23. Lang.: Hun.
Hungary: Kézdivásárhely. 1700-1730. ■Text of a Nativity play from Kézdivásárhely with commentary.

224 Sciascia, Leonardo; Fusco, Mario, transl. "'Je pense ce que je sens...'." ('I Think What I Feel...'.) *ThE.* 1986 Apr.; 10: 5-6. Illus.: Photo. B&W. 1. Lang.: Fre.
Italy: Agrigento. 1927. Biographical studies. ■Studies a letter from Pirandello to Silvio D'Amico indicating Pirandello's distrust of Adriano Tilgher's ideological criticism.

225 Betancourt, Helia. "El protocolo de Julián Bravo (1599): primer contrato de una agrupación teatral en América." (Julian Bravo's Protocol (1599): First Theatrical Contract in America.) *LATR.* 1986 Spr; 19(2): 17-22. Notes. Lang.: Spa.
Peru: Lima. 1599-1620. Histories-sources. ■Text of a contract drawn by the notary public of Lima for the first known theatre company in America, headed by Francisco Pérez de Robles.

226 Roy, Donald, ed. *Plays by James Robinson Planché.* Cambridge: Cambridge UP; 1986. xi, 241 pp. Pref. Notes. Biblio. Append. Illus.: Photo. B&W. 5: var. sizes. Lang.: Eng.
UK-England. 1818-1872. ■Text of plays by James Robinson Planché with an introduction discussing his influence on the development of English pantomime and his anticipation of the operas of Gilbert and Sullivan. Related to Mime: Pantomime.

Design/technology

227 Behl, Dennis. "Architect of the Open Stage." *ThCr.* 1986 Aug/Sep.; 20(7): 16-23, 108-115. Illus.: Photo. Plan. Sketches. 15: var. sizes. Lang.: Eng.
1934-1986. Biographical studies. ■Profile of theatre designer Tanya Moiseiwitsch, her training, career and association with composer Benjamin Britten.

THEATRE IN GENERAL: —Design/technology

228 Brady, Paul J., ed.; Glerum, Jay O., ed. "Recommended Guidelines for Stage Rigging and Stage Machinery." *TD&T*. 1986 Sum ; 22(2): 8-9, 42-50. Lang.: Eng.
Technical studies. ■Stage rigging and stage machinery guidelines developed and recommended by the United States Institute for Theatre Technology for universal adoption within the theatre industry.

229 Corson, Richard. *Stage Makeup.* New York, NY: Meredith; 1986. 448 pp. Pref. Index. Append. Illus.: Photo. Dwg. Print. B&W. 163: var. sizes. [7th ed.] Lang.: Eng.
1986. Instructional materials. ■Comprehensive guide to basic techniques for creative design and application of make-up for the performing artist.

230 Gorier, Jacquie. *Theaterwerkstatt: Bühnenrequisiten selbstgemacht.* (Theatre Workshop: Stage Props Self-made.) Wiesbaden/Berlin: Bauverlag; 1986. 220 pp. Pref. Index. Illus.: Design. Plan. Dwg. Sketches. Lang.: Ger.
1986. Instructional materials. ■Part 1: reader is made familiar with basic techniques of stage prop production. Part 2: suggestions for stage props from various epochs of theatre (from antiquity to science fiction), and different genres.

231 Leiterman, Eugene. "Hanging Cardboards." *TechB*. 1981 Oct.: 1-2. Illus.: Diagram. 2. Lang.: Eng.
1986. Technical studies. ■Cardboards used as reference guides for handing, circuiting and focusing a light plot.

232 Seligman, Kevin. "Costume Pattern Drafts." *TD&T*. 1986 Spr; 22(1): 24-28. Tables. Illus.: Diagram. B&W. 3: 4 in. x 5 in. [Overcoats: The Inverness, the MacFarlane and the Dress Cape.] Lang.: Eng.
1986. Technical studies. ■How-to article on cutting and assembling overcoats from early 20th century patterns.

233 Seligman, Kevin. "Costume Pattern Drafts." *TD&T*. 1986 Fall; 22(3): 17-18. Illus.: Diagram. B&W. 4: var. sizes. Lang.: Eng.
1986. Technical studies. ■How-to article on cutting and assembling capes from patterns published in the early 20th century.

234 Sööt, Olaf. "Single Failure-Proof Design for Theatre Safety." *TD&T*. 1986 Sum; 22(2): 4-7, 32. Illus.: Diagram. B&W. Architec. Detail. 7: var. sizes. Lang.: Eng.
1986. Technical studies. ■Application of safety codes and examples of precautions that could help prevent damage or injury as a result of the failure of individual parts of various theatre machinery.

235 Unruh, Delbert. "Scenography, Ethics, and the American Tradition of Theatrical Design." *TD&T*. 1986 Spr; 22(1): 16-19, 62-64. Notes. Lang.: Eng.
1986. Historical studies. ■The confrontation of American realism with European scenography has created a moral as well as aesthetic crisis in American design.

236 Vanni Menichi, Carlo, ed. *Le maschere dell'uomo. Segni plastici da oriente ad occidente.* (The Masks of Man: Plastic Signs from East to West.) Pistoia: Tellini; 1986. 80 pp. Index. Notes. Tables. Biblio. Illus.: Photo. Pntg. Dwg. Color. B&W. Lang.: Ita.
Asia. Europe. Africa. Historical studies. ■Survey of the use of masks from tribal societies to *commedia dell'arte*.

237 Répászky, Ernő. "A bécsi Állami Szinházak Központi Mütermei." (Central Workshops for the Theatres of Vienna.) *SFo*. 1986; 13(4): 15-16. Illus.: Photo. B&W. 5: var. sizes. Lang.: Hun.
Austria: Vienna. 1963-1980. Technical studies.

238 Szinte, Gábor. "Látogatás Salzburgban." (A Visit in Salzburg.) *SFo*. 1986; 13(2): 8. Illus.: Photo. B&W. Lang.: Hun.
Austria: Salzburg. 1986. Histories-sources. ■Study tour of Hungarian students of stage and costume design in the Mozarteum.

239 Zoglauer, Franz. "Hans Schavernoch: Räume der Zukunft." (Hans Schavernoch: Future Spaces.) *Parnass*. 1986 Jul-Aug.; 6(4): 56-61. Illus.: Photo. Print. Color. B&W. Lang.: Ger.
Austria: Vienna. 1945-1986. Biographical studies. ■On scene designer Hans Schavernoch and his work.

240 Grossman, Harry; Westerlund, Hedvig. "A Portable Cruciform Theatre." *TD&T*. 1986 Fall; 22(3): 11-14, 53. Illus.: Photo. Dwg. Plan. 7: var. sizes. Lang.: Eng.
Belgium. 1986. Technical studies. ■Design of a performer-spectator space in which the audience is seated on four sides, yet no section sees exactly the same thing.

241 Garebian, Keith. "Vision and Vitality in Stage Design." *PAC*. 1983 Apr.; 20(1): 40-45. Illus.: Photo. B&W. 2. Lang.: Eng.
Canada. 1972-1983. Histories-sources. ■Careers of stage designers Murray Laufer, Michael Eagan and Susan Benson, including comments from the designers on matters of style, inspiration and technique.

242 Larrue, Jean-Marc. "Les créations scéniques de Louis-Honoré Fréchette: Juin 1880." (The Scenic Creations of Louis-Honoré Fréchette: June 1880.) *THC*. 1986 Fall; 7(2): 161-167. Lang.: Fre.
Canada: Montreal, PQ. 1880-1900. Historical studies. ■Detailed study of the production of two plays by L.H. Fréchette: *Pampineau* and *Le Retour de l'exil (Return from Exile)*. Focus on scenery and the use of spectacle.

243 Sisk, Douglass, F. "Multi-Site Consulting." *ThCr*. 1986 Aug/Sep.; 20(7): 28, 46-47. Illus.: Diagram. 1. Lang.: Eng.
Canada: Vancouver, BC. 1986. Technical studies. ■How theatre consultant S. Leonard Auerbach tracked the technical specifications and contract bidding for Expo '86's multi-site performance spaces.

244 Young, Richard. "Nicholas Cernovitch and the Dynamics of Light Design." *PAC*. 1983 Apr.; 20(1): 63-65. Illus.: Photo. B&W. 3. Lang.: Eng.
Canada: Montreal, PQ. 1970-1983. Critical studies. ■An overview of Cernovitch's career at Les Grands Ballets Canadiens (LGBC) as lighting designer, focusing on his technique and on his theories about lighting for dance as opposed to theatre.

245 Wang, Bangxiong. "Shijue, Xinli, Wutai Meishu." (Visual Sense, Psychology and Stage Design.) *XYishu*. 1982 May; 5(2): 86-90. Lang.: Chi.
China. 1308-1982. Critical studies. ■Ways of emphasizing visual imagery and metaphor in scenery and lighting.

246 Wang, Jingguo. "Lou Feng Tou Yue." (More Wind and Moon.) *XYishu*. 1982 Aug.; 5(3): 147-148. Lang.: Chi.
China. 700-1980. Critical studies. ■Argues that the principles of Chinese garden design should be applied to set design, i.e., let the audience's imagination complement the design.

247 Chen, Ming. "Ni Wu Qu Xin." (Making Objects Reflect the Soul.) *XYishu*. 1982 Aug.; 5(3): 136-139. Lang.: Chi.
China, People's Republic of. 1265-1981. Critical studies. ■Color, shape and structure as functions of symbolism in set design.

248 Wang, Mingguo. "Bujing Xingxiang Chien Tan." (On the Imagery of Scenery.) *XYishu*. 1982 Aug.; 5(3): 144-146. Lang.: Chi.
China, People's Republic of. 1960-1982. Critical studies. ■Need for a balance between realism and fantasy in set design.

249 Wei, Zhaoping. "Wutai Si Wei Kongjian." (Four Dimensions of Stage.) *XYishu*. 1982 Aug.; 5(3): 140-143. Lang.: Chi.
China, People's Republic of. 1900-1982. Critical studies. ■Ongoing transformation provided by lighting and scenery changes in theatrical productions contrasted with the static presentation of the plastic arts.

250 Yun, Duan. "Wutai Meishu de Yuyan he Xingshi Gan." (Language and Sense of Form in the Art of Stage Design.) *XYishu*. 1982 Nov.; 5(4): 102-108. Lang.: Chi.
China, People's Republic of. 1960-1982. Critical studies. ■Elements of set design and their emotional impact.

251 Zhu, Shichang. "Hua yu Hua—Shilun Xiju Huazhuang." (Make-up and Painting: On Make-up in Theatre.) *XYishu*. 1982 May; 5 (2): 79-85. Lang.: Chi.
China, People's Republic of. 1907-1980. Instructional materials. ■Similarities and differences between painting and make-up techniques to achieve realism and characterization.

252 Hu, Miaosheng. "Huodong yu Guang de Xiju: Guanyu Yuesefu Siwoboda de Wutai Sheji." (The Theatre of

CLASSED ENTRIES

THEATRE IN GENERAL: —Design/technology

Motion and Light: Josef Svoboda's Stage Design.) *XYishu.* 1982 Aug.; 5(3): 49-60. Illus.: Photo. 18: var. sizes. [Continued in *XYishu* 5:4 (1982 Nov), 115-124.] Lang.: Chi.
Czechoslovakia. 1887-1982. Historical studies. ■Survey of Svoboda's work, especially his original use of projection. Part II includes some of Svoboda's creations: disconnected multi-screen, light and mirrors, moving architecture, collage, psycho-plastic space.

253 Kovalenko, G.F. "Češskij teatral'nyi konstruktivizm." (Czech Theatrical Constructivism.) 133-153 in Rubanova, I.I., ed. *Aktual'nye voprosy iskusstva socialističeskich stran.* Moscow: Nauka; 1986. Lang.: Rus.
Czechoslovakia. 1960-1979. Critical studies. ■Constructivism in Czech stage design.

254 Pullar, Jenny. "Josef Svoboda Master Class." *Cue.* 1986 Jan/Feb.; 8(39): 15-16. Illus.: Photo. Print. B&W. 1: 8 cm. x 6 cm. Lang.: Eng.
Czechoslovakia. Canada: Banff, AB. 1985. Histories-sources. ■Description of a master class given by scene designer Josef Svoboda at the Banff School of Fine Arts, Canada.

255 Répászky, Ernő. "A Szlovák Nemzeti Szinház, Pozsony Központi Mütermei." (The Central Workshops of the Slovakian National Theatre in Pozsony.) *SFo.* 1986; 13(4): 8-9. Illus.: Photo. B&W. Grd.Plan. 5: var. sizes. Lang.: Hun.
Czechoslovakia: Bratislava. 1960-1986. Technical studies.

256 Cohen-Stratyner, Barbara Naomi, ed.; Ault, C. Thomas, transl. *Scenes and Machines from the 18th Century: The Stagecraft of Jacopo Fabris & Citoyen Boullet.* New York, NY: Theatre Library Assn; 1986. xviii, 146 pp. (Performing Arts Resources 11.) Notes. Illus.: Design. Plan. Dwg. Diagram. Print. B&W. Architec. Explod.Sect. Fr.Elev. Grd.Plan. 36: 3 in. X 5 in. Lang.: Eng.
Denmark: Copenhagen. France: Paris. 1760-1801. Historical studies. ■Works by and about designers Jacopo Fabris and Citoyen Boullet.

257 Fabris, Jacopo; Ault, C. Thomas, transl. "Instruction in Theatre, Architecture, & Mechanics." 2-51 in Cohen-Stratyner, Barbara Naomi, ed. *Scenes & Machines from the 18th Century: The Stagecraft of Jacopo Fabris & Citoyen Boullet.* New York, NY: Theatre Library Assn; 1986. xviii, 146 pp. (Performing Arts Resources 11.) Illus.: Design. Plan. Dwg. Print. B&W. Architec. Explod.Sect. Fr.Elev. Grd.Plan. 21: 2.5 in. X 5 in. Lang.: Eng.
Denmark: Copenhagen. Italy. 1760-1801. Histories-sources. ■Folio drawings illustrating how to paint perspective scenery and build theatrical machinery.

258 Astington, John H. "Descent Machinery in the Playhouses." *MRenD.* 1985; 2: 119-134. Notes. Illus.: Photo. Dwg. Print. B&W. R.Elev. 3: 8.5 in. x 11 in. Lang.: Eng.
England. 1576-1595. Histories-reconstruction. ■Beginnings of various ascending and descending machinery for special effects, including the appearance of rope and pulley expenditures in conjunction with the 'heavens' or stage roof.

259 Barlow, Graham. "Lighting at Hampton Court Theatre, 1718." *TN.* 1986; 40(2): 51-55. Notes. [Postscript to the author's article in *TN* 18:2 (1983), pp 51-63.] Lang.: Eng.
England: London, Hampton Court. 1718. Historical studies. ■Comparison of lighting in English theatres and the Comédie-Française.

260 "Les Peintres et le théâtre." (Painters and the Theatre.) *ThE.* 1986; 11: 5-96. Pref. Illus.: Pntg. Dwg. Sketches. Print. Color. B&W. 184: var. sizes. [Painting/Theatre Exhibit at Festival of Avignon, 1986.] Lang.: Fre.
Europe. 1890-1980. ■Anthology of writings of painters who designed for the theatre.

261 González, Josep Maria; Passans, Jaume; Delgado, Eduard, intro. *28 màscares. Caretes, carotes i antifaços.* (28 Masks.) Barcelona: Editorial Graó; 1986. 94 pp. (Instruments Guix 3.) Biblio. Index. Tables. Illus.: Design. 82: var. sizes. Lang.: Cat.
Europe. 1986. Instructional materials. ■Directions for making masks from various materials. Includes a brief history and introduction to the uses of masks. Intended for school use.

262 Ingemark, Peter. "Spektakel med rök och ljus inte bara på rockkonserter." (Shows of Smoke and Light, Not Only for Rock Concerts.) *ProScen.* 1986; 10(3-4): 48-50. Illus.: Dwg. Lang.: Swe.
Europe. North America. 1986. 1890-1920. Historical studies. ■How fire, smoke and lighting effects were created during the 19th century according to A. Hopkins, *The World of Magic.*

263 Tirelli, Umberto, ed.; Poma, Maria Cristina, ed.; Carrieri, Mario, photo. *Donazione Tirelli. La vita nel costume, il costume nella vita.* (Tirelli Donation: Life in Costume, Costume in Life.) Milan: Mondadori; 1986. 240 pp. Pref. Index. Notes. Tables. Biblio. Illus.: Photo. Color. Lang.: Ita.
Europe. 1700-1984. Histories-specific. ■Tirelli collection of period dress and theatrical, operatic and film costumes at the Galleria del Costume in Florence.

264 Boullet, Citoyen; Ault, C. Thomas, transl. "Essay on the Art of Constructing Theatres, Their Machines, and Their Operations." 52-146 in Cohen-Stratyner, Barbara Naomi, ed. *Scenes & Machines from the 18th Century: The Stagecraft of Jacopo Fabris & Citoyen Boullet.* New York, NY: Theatre Library Assn; 1986. xviii, 146 pp. (Performing Arts Resources 11.) Pref. Notes. Illus.: Design. Plan. Dwg. Print. B&W. Architec. Explod.Sect. Fr.Elev. Detail. Grd.Plan. 13: 3 in. x 5 in. Lang.: Eng.
France: Paris. 1760-1801. Histories-sources. ■Eighteenth-century designer discusses stage construction and the design, construction and operation of stage machinery, as well as lighting, storage, heating, and a description of how to mount an opera.

265 Canonge, Sarah; Guntheret, André. "Les métiers du Français: si l'amidon m'était compté." (Working at the Comédie-Française: If I Had to Pay for the Starch.) *CF.* 1986 Nov.; 16(153): 36-38. 4: var. sizes. Lang.: Fre.
France. 1961-1986. Histories-sources. ■Recollections of two employees of the Comédie-Française who iron the elaborate costumes of the French classical theatre.

266 Guibert, Noëlle; Razgonnikoff, Jacqueline. "Mode et haute couture, cour et jardin." (High Fashion and the Theatre.) *CF.* 1986 Sep.; 16(151): 42-51. Illus.: Photo. Dwg. B&W. [A series of four articles.] Lang.: Fre.
France: Paris. 1620-1930. Histories-specific. ■A history of the symbiotic relationship between Parisian high fashion and costuming on the Paris stage. Continued in *CF* 16:152 (1986 Oct.), 52-61, *CF* 16:153 (1986 Nov.), 46-53, *CF* 16:154 (1986 Dec.), 46-53.

267 Lagorio, Michele. "Sculpting the Silent Majority." *ThCr.* 1986 Mar.; 20(3): 65-67. Illus.: Photo. 8: var. sizes. Lang.: Eng.
France: Paris. 1986. Technical studies. ■Théâtre du Soleil director Ariane Mnouchkine and her design staff create a Cambodian mask for *Norodom Sihanouk.*

268 "A színháztechnika fejlesztéséért. Plenáris ülés Berlinben." (For the Development of Theatre Technology: The 5th Plenary Session, East Berlin, December 2-6, 1986.) *SFo.* 1986; 13(4): 3-4. Lang.: Hun.
Germany, East: Berlin, East. 1986. Histories-sources. ■Report of the session of the IVth Working Commission for the 'Development of Equipment and Products of Theatre Technology' of the Ministries of Culture of the Socialist Countries.

269 Kárpáti, Imre. "Eduard Fischer szinház-és jelmezplasztikái az NDK-ból." (Theatre and Costume Modelling Art of Eduard Fischer from GDR.) *SFo.* 1986; 13(1): 3-4. Illus.: Photo. B&W. Lang.: Hun.
Germany, East: Berlin, East. Hungary: Budapest. 1985. Histories-sources. ■Report on an exhibition of models by Eduard Fischer of the Berliner Ensemble.

270 Répászky, Ernő. "Szinházi mühelyek. Semper Opera, Drezda." (Theatre Workshops, Semper Opera, Dresden.) *SFo.* 1986; 13(4): 13-14. Illus.: Photo. Graphs. B&W. 3: var. sizes. Lang.: Hun.
Germany, East: Dresden. 1977-1981. Technical studies.

271 Véghelyi, József. "Paul Jähnichen 1935-1986." *SFo.* 1986; 13(4): 5. Illus.: Photo. B&W. 1. Lang.: Hun.

THEATRE IN GENERAL: —Design/technology

Germany, East: Berlin, East. 1935-1986. Biographical studies. ■Commemoration of the many-sided theatre expert Paul Jähnichen.

272 Véghelyi, József. "Tájékoztatás." (Information.) *SFo.* 1986; 13(4): 3-5. Lang.: Hun.

Germany, East: Berlin, East. 1986. Historical studies. ■About the activities of the IVth Working Commission for the 'Development of Equipment and Products of Theatre Technology' of the Ministries of Culture of the Socialist Countries.

273 "Showtech '86." *SFo.* 1986; 13(2): 8-12. Illus.: Graphs. Photo. B&W. 2. Lang.: Hun.

Germany, West: Berlin, West. 1986. Histories-sources. ■Short reports on the Showtech conference and exhibition by six Hungarian technicians.

274 Boskovsky, Corinna. "Pictures of Mystery." *ThCr.* 1986 Oct.; 20(8): 32-35, 90. Illus.: Photo. 6: var. sizes. Lang.: Eng.

Germany, West. 1944-1986. Biographical studies. ■Profile of set and lighting designer Erich Wonder.

275 Répászky, Ernő. "A müncheni Állami Operaház új mühelyháza." (The New Production Building of the State Opera House of Munich.) *SFo.* 1986; 13(4): 10-12. Illus.: Photo. B&W. Grd.Plan. 3: var. sizes. Lang.: Hun.

Germany, West: Munich. 1983. Technical studies. ■Details of the new production building at the State Opera House in Munich.

276 "8. Szinháztéchnikai Napok, Szeged, 1987. június 4-6., Szegedi Nemzeti Szinház." (VIIIth Convention for Theatre Technology: The National Theatre of Szeged, June 4-6, 1987.) *SFo.* 1986; 13(4): 2. Lang.: Hun.

Hungary: Szeged. 1986. Histories-sources. ■Advance program of the meeting organized by the Section for Theatre Technology of the Hungarian Optical, Acoustical and Cinematographical Society.

277 "Villamos berendezések." (Electrical Installations.) *SFo.* 1986; 13(3): 29-31. Illus.: Photo. B&W. Lang.: Hun.

Hungary: Szeged. 1983-1986. Technical studies. ■Details of new electrical system of rebuilt Szeged National Theatre, including sound and lighting specifications.

278 Bodrogi, János. "Gyártáselőkészités a Magyar Televizió Diszletés Jelmezgyártó Üzemében." (Production Engineering in the Scene and Costume Manufacturing Works of Television.) *SFo.* 1986; 13(4): 27-31. Lang.: Hun.

Hungary: Budapest. 1986. Technical studies. ■The differences in scene and costume design for television versus theatre. Related to Media: Video forms.

279 Bőgel, József. "Magyar szcenográfia a felszabadulás után II. Nyitottabb színházpolitika." (Hungarian Scenography after the Liberation: A More Open Theatre Policy.) *Sz.* 1986 Jan.; 19(1): 46-48. Lang.: Hun.

Hungary. 1957-1970. Historical studies. ■Reviews the changes and most important figures of Hungarian scenography and costume design.

280 Bőgel, József. "A magyar szcenográfia története a felszabadulás után III. A hetvenes évek." (History of Hungarian Scenography after Liberation, Part 3: The Seventies.) *Sz.* 1986 June; 19(6): 39-44. Lang.: Hun.

Hungary. 1965-1980. Historical studies. ■Historical overview of scene and costume design.

281 Bőgel, József. "A magyar szcenográfia története a felszabadulás után IV. A nyolcvanas évek elején." (History of Hungarian Scenography after Liberation, Part 4: The Early Eighties.) *Sz.* 1986 July; 19(7): 44-47. Lang.: Hun.

Hungary. 1980-1984. Historical studies. ■Post-liberation Hungarian design.

282 Császár, Miklós. "Elektroakusztikai, információs és video rendszer." (The Sound—Information—and Video-System.) *SFo.* 1986; 13(3): 36-39. Illus.: Photo. B&W. Lang.: Hun.

Hungary: Szeged. 1986. Technical studies. ■The sound and video systems at the reconstructed Szeged National Theatre.

283 Kárpáti, Imre. "Uj utakon a Tungsram Rt. Elektronikai Gyára." (The Electronics Factory of Tungsram Rt. on a New Path.) *SFo.* 1986; 13(1): 11-14. Illus.: Photo. Graphs. B&W. Lang.: Hun.

Hungary: Budapest. 1980-1986. Histories-sources. ■Interviews with engineers and officials involved with the Tungsram Rt. Electronics factory.

284 Kárpáti, Imre. "A szakmunkásképzés lehetősége Zalaegerszegen." (Possibilities of Training Skilled Workers in Zalaegerszeg.) *SFo.* 1986; 13(4): 32-33. Illus.: Photo. B&W. 3. Lang.: Hun.

Hungary: Zalaegerszeg. 1983-1986. Histories-sources. ■Interview with Sándor Bishof, scenographer of the Hevesi Sándor Theatre of Salaegerszeg.

285 Kiss, István. "Két rövid hir nyomában." (About Two Short News Items.) *SFo.* 1986; 13(2): 17-18. Lang.: Hun.

Hungary. 1977-1986. Histories-sources. ■Interview with Gyula Ember, president of ÉCSÁSZ on the widening of the activities of the technical theatre workshop and with president Gyula Asztalos on the foundation of a cooperative of technical theatre equipment.

286 Kiss, István. "Zenelectro Elektronikai Gazdasági Munkaközösség." (The Electronic Economic Working Party Zenelectro.) *SFo.* 1986; 13(1): 15-17. Illus.: Photo. B&W. Lang.: Hun.

Hungary. 1983-1986. Technical studies. ■The history of a small sound and lighting equipment company and their good products.

287 Kiss, István. "Utazó együttesek." (Travelling Ensembles.) *SFo.* 1986; 13(1): 31-32. Illus.: Photo. B&W. Lang.: Hun.

Hungary: Győr. 1979-1986. Histories-sources. ■First in a series on theatre organization. János Hani, leading technician of Győr Ballet, discusses his working methods and international work experience.

288 Korponai, Ferenc. "A szinpadtechnikai berendezések rekonstrukciója." (The Reconstruction of the Mechanical Equipment of the Stage.) *SFo.* 1986; 13(3): 11-16. Illus.: Photo. B&W. Lang.: Hun.

Hungary: Szeged. 1981-1986. Technical studies. ■The reconstruction of the mechanical equipment, especially the revolving stage, of the Szeged National Theatre.

289 Pálfi, Ferenc. "A nemzetközi együttmüködés lehetségei a szinháztechnikában." (Possibilities of International Cooperation in Theatre Techniques.) *SFo.* 1986; 13(2): 12-13. Lang.: Hun.

Hungary. Germany, West: Berlin, West. 1986. Histories-sources. ■A short version of the lecture delivered at Showtech '86.

290 Répászky, Ernő. "A Szinházak Központi Mütermei, Budapest Központi diszletmühely terve." (The Central Theatre Workshops: Budapest Central Scene Shop Project.) *SFo.* 1986; 13(4): 18-19. Illus.: Plan. Lang.: Hun.

Hungary: Budapest. 1953-1986. Technical studies. ■Description of the central scene shop as an example of the 'official' architectural style of the 1950s.

291 Répászky, Ernő. "Tanulmányterv a Csokonai utcai épület korszerüsitésére, KÖZTI, 1976." (Study for the Modernization of the Production Building in Csokonai Street, KÖZTI, 1976.) *SFo.* 1986; 13(4): 19-20. Lang.: Hun.

Hungary: Budapest. 1976. Technical studies. ■The planned renovation of the building was combined with the modernization of the establishment.

292 Répászky, Ernő. "Uj központi mütermek és raktárak terve, IPARTERV, 1980." (Project of New Central Workshops and Stores, IPARTERV, 1980.) *SFo.* 1986; 13(4): 20-21. Illus.: Plan. Explod.Sect. Grd.Plan. 3. Lang.: Hun.

Hungary: Budapest. 1980. Technical studies. ■Description of plans for new central theatre scene shop and storage areas.

293 Selmeczky, Ernő. "Épületgépészeti leirás." (Description of the Sanitary Installations.) *SFo.* 1986; 13(3): 32-33. Illus.: Photo. B&W. 1: 12 cm. x 10 cm. Lang.: Hun.

Hungary: Szeged. 1978-1986. Technical studies. ■Report on the new heating, plumbing and air-conditioning at reconstructed Szeged National Theatre.

294 Szabó-Jilek, Iván. "Kulisszatitkok." (Backstage Secrets.) *SFo.* 1986; 13(4): 1. Lang.: Hun.

Hungary. 1980-1986. Critical studies. ■The editorial refers to a series of problems concerning the creation of theatrical 'art of scenery'.

CLASSED ENTRIES

THEATRE IN GENERAL: —Design/technology

295   Szabó-Jilek, Iván. "A Csokonai utcai mühelyház újabb tanulmányterve, KOMPLETTERV G.M., 1984." (A New Project for the Renovation of the Production Building in Csokonai Street—KOMPLETTERV G.M., 1984.) *SFo.* 1986; 13(4): 22. Lang.: Hun.
Hungary: Budapest. 1984. Technical studies. ■Description of planned renovation for scene shop and production building.

296   Szabó-Jilek, Iván. "A Szinházak Központi Mütermeinek új telephelye, TÉVTERV, 1986." (The New Central Theatre Workshops—TÉVTERV, 1986.) *SFo.* 1986; 13(4): 23-26. Illus.: Plan. Grd.Plan. Lang.: Hun.
Hungary: Budapest. 1986. Technical studies. ■Sale of textile shops permitted rebuilding and renovation of scene shops.

297   "Theatrefile: Arnon Adar." *ASSAPHc.* 1986; 3: 186-190. Illus.: Photo. B&W. 9: var. sizes. Lang.: Eng.
Israel: Tel-Aviv. 1955-1971. Historical studies. ■Photographs of settings designed by Israeli designer Arnon Adar issued as a tribute to his work.

298   Belkin, Ahuva. "Leone de' Sommi's Pastoral Conception and the Design of the Shepherds' Costumes for the Mantuan Production of Guarini's *Il Pastor Fido.*" *ASSAPHc.* 1986; 3: 58-74. Notes. Illus.: Photo. B&W. 5: var. sizes. Lang.: Eng.
Italy: Mantua. 1500-1600. Historical studies. ■Literary and artistic tradition of shepherds' clothing influenced Francesco Valesio's costume designs of Giambattista Guarini's *Il Pastor Fido (The Faithful Shepherd).*

299   De Santi, Pier Marco. *Il totale artificiale. Guglielminetti.* (The Artificial Total: Guglielminetti.) Rome: Gremese; 1986. 223 pp. (Gremese Cultura.) Index. Notes. Tables. Biblio. Illus.: Photo. Dwg. Color. B&W. Lang.: Ita.
Italy. 1946-1986. Historical studies. ■Recounts 40-year career of Eugenio Guglielminetti, costume and stage designer for theatre and television. Related to Media: Video forms.

300   Isgrò, Giovanni. *Fortuny e il teatro.* (Fortuny and Theatre.) Palermo: Novecento; 1986. 198 pp. (Logos 5.) Pref. Index. Notes. Tables. Biblio. Illus.: Photo. Plan. Dwg. Sketches. B&W. Lang.: Ita.
Italy. 1871-1949. Historical studies. ■Importance of Mariano Fortuny, costumer, architect, set designer, and inventor of lighting techniques.

301   Monti, Raffaele, ed. *Il Maggio Musicale Fiorentino 1. Pittori e scultori.* (Florentine Musical May, Vol. 1: Painters and Sculptors.) Rome: De Luca; 1986. 251 pp. Pref. Index. Tables. Illus.: Photo. Pntg. Dwg. Color. B&W. Lang.: Ita.
Italy: Florence. 1933-1982. Histories-sources. ■Volume I of a series on the productions of the spring arts festival 'Maggio Musicale Fiorentino'. Includes critical and photographic documentation on the sculptors and painters involved in various productions.

302   Cho, Jong-gi. *Hängük Mudae Design ui Pyoenhwa äe Kwanhän Yëongü.* (History of Korean Stage Setting: from 1945 to Present.) Seoul: Kim Im-Ode; 1986. 281 pp. Illus.: Photo. Print. B&W. 21: 4 in. x 6 in., 2 in. x 3 in. Lang.: Kor.
Korea: Seoul. 1945-1986. Historical studies. ■Development of Korean scenography.

303   Shin, Seon-Hee; Song, Ae-Gyung; Kim, Dong-Jim; Lee, Ju-Gyung. "Hanguk Yeonguk-ui Hyeonjuso. IV: Mudae Yesulga." (The Present State of Korean Theatre. IV: The Set Designer.) *KTR.* 1986 June; 121(6): 12-39. Illus.: Photo. B&W. 1: 18.5 cm. x 26 cm. Lang.: Kor.
Korea. 1986. Histories-sources. ■Includes an interview with set designer Chang Jong-Seong.

304   Vajda, Ferenc. "Az OISTAT Végrehajtó Bizottságának ülése 1986. június 4-6, Amsterdam." (The Meeting of the Executive Committee of OISTAT, June 4-6, 1986, Amsterdam.) *SFo.* 1986; 13(3): 5-6. Lang.: Hun.
Netherlands: Amsterdam. 1986. Histories-sources. ■Account of meeting of OISTAT Executive Committee.

305   Cormack, Randy. "Theatre Technology in North America." *Sin.* 1986; 20(2): 26-27. Illus.: Photo. B&W. 1. Lang.: Eng.

North America. UK-England. 1980-1987. Historical studies. ■Overview of sound systems used in North American theatres, similarities with those used in British theatres.

306   Reid, Francis. "NOTT '86 Norvégia, Geilo 1986. május 25-28." (NOTT '86 Norway: Geilo, May 25-28, 1986.) *SFo.* 1986; 13(4): 6-7. Lang.: Hun.
Norway: Geilo. 1986. ■Hungarian translation of a report on the NOTT conference from *Cue* (May-June, 1986).

307   Koecher-Hensel, Agnieszka. "Premières Rencontres du théâtre de la vision et de la plastique colloque de la commission de l'histoire de la théorie et de la critique de l'OISTAT à Katowice." (The 1st Meetings of Theatre of the Visual Arts Symposium of the OISTAT Commission on History, Theory and Criticism at Katowice.) *TP.* 1986; 29(9-10): 13-17. Illus.: Photo. Print. B&W. 2: 14 cm. x 12 cm., 22 cm. x 14 cm. Lang.: Eng, Fre.
Poland. 1986. Historical studies. ■Overview of a conference on visual art in the theatre and the influence of scenography on production. Includes proceedings of OISTAT symposium.

308   Nagy, Károly. "Szinháztechnikai kiállitás. 1986. október 6-8, Varsó." (An Exposition of Theatre Technology, 6-8 October, 1986, Warsaw.) *SFo.* 1986; 13(3): 3-4. Illus.: Photo. B&W. Lang.: Hun.
Poland: Warsaw. Hungary: Budapest. 1986. Technical studies. ■Report on exhibition in Warsaw, especially on the S20 dimmer used by the lighting director of the Thália Theatre in Budapest.

309   Raszewski, Zbigniew. "Trzy spisy dekoracji Teatru Narodowego." (Three Lists of the Decor Equipment of Narodowy Theatre.) *PaT.* 1986 First Qtr; 1: 87-134. Notes. Illus.: Diagram. 1. Lang.: Pol.
Poland: Warsaw. 1779-1833. Histories-sources. ■Description of the decor equipment used in the Narodowy Theatre between 1779 and 1833. Original listing of items (in German) included with Polish translation.

310   Répászky, Ernő. "A Technikus Bizottság ülése (OISTAT): 1986. Október 6-8., Varsó." (Meeting of the Committee of Technicians (OISTAT) 6-8 October, 1986, Warsaw.) *SFo.* 1986; 13(3): 6. Lang.: Hun.
Poland: Warsaw. 1986. Histories-sources. ■Account of meeting of OISTAT technicians' committee.

311   Bravo i Pijoan, Isidre; Saura, Salvador, illus.; Torrente, Ramon, illus. *L'Escenografia Catalana.* (Catalan Stage Design.) Barcelona: Diputació de Barcelona; 1986. 352 pp. 747: var. sizes. Lang.: Cat.
Spain-Catalonia. 200 B.C.-1986 A.D. Histories-specific. ■History of Catalan scenography.

312   Engvén, Ingvar; Hultén, Henrietta; Uggelberg, Ameli; Lindström, Kristina; Pauser, Anders. "Nio scenografer." (Nine Set Designers.) *NT.* 1986; 35: 40-56. Illus.: Photo. Lang.: Swe.
Sweden. 1980-1986. Histories-sources. ■Swedish set designers discuss their working methods.

313   Eriksson, Lasse. "Reflektioner över modern teknik." (Some Reflections on Modern Techniques.) *ProScen.* 1986; 10(3-4): 34-37. Lang.: Swe.
Sweden. 1940-1986. Historical studies. ■A critical comparison of the manual dimmer rack and the sophisticated computer dimmer of today.

314   Janflod, Lars-Olof. "'Sankan' Carl-Eric Sandgren." *ProScen.* 1986; 10(1): 29-32. Illus.: Photo. Plan. Lang.: Swe.
Sweden: Gävle. 1952-1986. Biographical studies. ■A portrait of Carl-Eric Sandgren and his technical innovations in scene design.

315   Lind, Ingela. "Teatern som mental tidsmaskin." (The Theatre As a Mental Time Machine.) *NT.* 1986; 35: 6-10. Illus.: Photo. Lang.: Swe.
Sweden. 1980-1986. Critical studies. ■The absence of stylization in scene designs of the 1980s reflects a lack of courage.

316   Möller, Klas. "Ros och ris om teknikerutbildningen." (Praise and Blame for the Training of Technicians.) *ProScen.* 1986; 10(2): 40-42. Illus.: Photo. Lang.: Swe.

THEATRE IN GENERAL: —Design/technology

Sweden: Stockholm. 1985-1986. Critical studies. ■Opinions on the first year of training theatre technicians at Dramatiska Institutet. The cooperation of theory and practice.

317   Nylén, Leif. "Formbröd, kulturkitsch och förbränd klassicism i 80-talets scenografi." (Tin Loaf, Popular Culture and Burned-up Classicism in the Set Designs of the Eighties.) *NT*. 1986; 35: 4-6. Illus.: Photo. Lang.: Swe.
Sweden: Stockholm. 1980-1986. Critical studies. ■The craftsmen and the engineers have taken over from the artists on the set designs.

318   Sjöberg, Staffan. "Teaterteknikerutbildning har startat." (The Education of Theatre Technicians Has Started.) *ProScen*. 1986; 10(1): 26-27. Illus.: Photo. Lang.: Swe.
Sweden: Stockholm. 1985. Histories-sources. ■A presentation of the two-year basic training of theatre technicians at Dramatiska Institutet.

319   Wiktorsson, Stefan. "Ljussättaren och färgen." (The Lighting Designer and Color.) *ProScen*. 1986; 10(3-4): 4-10. Illus.: Photo. Lang.: Swe.
Sweden: Gävle. 1986. Critical studies. ■The function of colored light for our perception of a play's psychological message, as practiced in three productions at the Folkteatern i Gävleborgs Län.

320   Burrell, John. "Nearly 40 Years On." *Tabs*. 1986; 43(1): 8-9. Illus.: Photo. B&W. 8: var. sizes. Lang.: Eng.
UK. 1946-1986. Histories-sources. ■Amateur lighting technician describes his work in schools, colleges and churches over the last forty years.

321   Bentham, Frederick. "I Was There!" *Tabs*. 1986; 43(1): 20-22. Illus.: Dwg. Photo. B&W. 2. Lang.: Eng.
UK-England: London. 1935-1986. Histories-sources. ■Details the installation and use, in the Palladium Theatre and later in the New Festival Hall, of a 1935 Strand lighting console designed by the author.

322   Bentley, J.S. "Tips." *Tabs*. 1986; 43(1): 13. Lang.: Eng.
UK-England. Instructional materials. ■Lighting tips for amateur theatre groups working in church and community halls and schools.

323   Edwards, Philip. "Trade Show 86." *Sin*. 1986; 20(1): 16-17. Illus.: Photo. B&W. 5. Lang.: Eng.
UK-England: London. 1986. Technical studies. ■Overview of performance technology show at Riverside Studios highlighting particular displays.

324   Graham, Bill. "A Long Way from the Panatrope." *Sin*. 1986; 20(1): 13-14. Illus.: Photo. B&W. 2. Lang.: Eng.
UK-England. Technical studies. ■Technical guidelines introduced by ABTT for sound and communications systems in the theatre, intended for architects, managers and consulting engineers as a basis for new installations.

325   Greenwald, Michael L. "New Directions for the RSC." *TheatreS*. 1984-85/1985-86; 31/32: 5-14. Lang.: Eng.
UK-England: London. 1967-1986. Historical studies. ■Changes in the Royal Shakespeare Company under current directors Adrian Noble, John Caird and Bill Alexander, most notably in its emphasis on design-oriented theatre.

326   Horsley, R. "Half a Mile from Shakespeare." *Tabs*. 1986; 43(1): 7. Illus.: Diagram. Photo. B&W. 3. Lang.: Eng.
UK-England: Stratford. 1980-1986. Histories-sources. ■Lighting concerts, plays and pantomimes in a church hall with the second largest stage in Stratford-upon-Avon and minimal lighting facilities.

327   Simpson, Catherine. "How We Lit *Godspell*." *Tabs*. 1986; 43(1): 10-11. Illus.: Photo. B&W. 3. Lang.: Eng.
UK-England. 1980-1986. Histories-sources. ■Secondary school's unique staging of a production of *Godspell* including a lighting outline for each scene.

328   Szabó-Jilek, Iván. "Rosco—Londonban." (Rosco in London.) *SFo*. 1986; 13(4): 5-6. Illus.: Photo. B&W. 2: var. sizes. Lang.: Hun.
UK-England: London. 1986. ■Report on the first European subsidiary of Rosco Laboratories.

329   Szabó-Jilek, Iván. "Meghalt a király—éljen a király." (The King Is Dead—Long Live the King.) *SFo*. 1986; 13(1): 5. Illus.: Photo. B&W. Lang.: Hun.

UK-England. 1986. Technical studies. ■Brief report on Rank Strand Ltd. and its subsidiary lighting companies operating throughout the world.

330   Tempe, Ruth; Kaposi, Ágota, transl. "A szinházi müszakiak helyzete Angliában." (The Situation of Theatre Technicians in England.) *SFo*. 1986; 13(2): 33-36. Lang.: Hun.
UK-England. 1983-1985. Critical studies. ■Study published in the 1985 Jan. issue of the Employment Gazette of the ABTT News.

331   Wolfe, Debbie. "Design for Acting." *Drama*. 1986; 160(2): 13-15. Illus.: Photo. B&W. 7. Lang.: Eng.
UK-England. 1945-1986. Histories-sources. ■Interview with designer Ralph Koltai on achieving balance between designer and production.

332   Hanley, P.L. "Two to Bear My Soul Away: An Encounter with Gemini." *Tabs*. 1986; 43(1): 30-31. Lang.: Eng.
UK-Scotland: Edinburgh. 1980-1986. Technical studies. ■Describes the Gemini computerized lighting system that was used by the National Youth Music Theatre at the Edinburgh Festival.

333   "Visual Recall." *ThCr*. 1986 Mar.; 20(3): 22-27, 63-65. Illus.: Photo. 12: var. sizes.
USA. 1972-1986. Biographical studies. ■Career of lighting designer Beverly Emmons, spanning the avant-garde, dance, Broadway and resident theatres.

334   "Out, Damned Spot, Out I Say." *ThCr*. 1986 Oct.; 20(8): 28, 82-83. Lang.: Eng.
USA. 1986. Technical studies. ■A report on the leading brands of stage blood for washability.

335   "The Search for Perfect Sound of Intelligent Life." *ThCr*. 1986 Oct.; 20(8): 36-41. Illus.: Photo. 3: var. sizes. Lang.: Eng.
USA: New York, NY. 1986. Technical studies. ■Sound design for Lily Tomlin's *The Search for Signs of Intelligent Life in the Universe*.

336   "Directory 86/87." *ThCr*. 1986 June/July; 20(6). Lang.: Eng.
USA. 1986. Technical studies. ■Theatre Crafts' annual directory of theatre equipment and manufacturers.

337   "What the Manufacturers Say." *ThCR*. 1986 Oct.; 20(8): 29, 76, 79-80, 82. Lang.: Eng.
USA. 1986. Technical studies. ■Prices, quantities and manufacturers' official line on stage blood.

338   "There's Intelligent Life on Broadway." *LDim*. 1986 Mar-Apr.; 10(2): 80-83, 85-88, 90-92. Illus.: Photo. Print. Color. B&W. Schematic. 7: var. sizes. Lang.: Eng.
USA: New York, NY, Portland, OR, Boston, MA. 1985-1986. Histories-sources. ■Interview with lighting designer Neil-Peter Jampoks, on his work on Lily Tomlin's *The Search for Signs of Intelligent Life in the Universe*.

339   Aronson, Arnold. "The Adventures of Eugene Lee." *AmTh*. 1984 Dec.; 1(8): 4-9, 41. Notes. Illus.: Photo. Plan. B&W. 7: var. sizes. Lang.: Eng.
USA: Providence, RI. 1965-1984. Histories-sources. ■Eugene Lee, resident scene designer of Trinity Square Repertory, discusses his career, his techniques and his work for both theatre and film. Includes brief interview with artistic director Adrian Hall about his working relationship with Lee. Related to Media: Film.

340   Aronson, Arnold. "The Facts of Light." *AmTh*. 1986 Jan.; 2(10): 11-16. Illus.: Photo. Print. B&W. 7: 2 in. x 3 in., 5 in. x 7 in. Lang.: Eng.
USA. 1986. Histories-sources. ■Interview with Arden Fingerhut, Tharon Musser and Jennifer Tipton on lighting design in contemporary show business and performing arts.

341   Aronson, Arnold. "Design and the Next Wave." *TD&T*. 1986 Spr; 22(1): 6-15, 71. Illus.: Photo. Color. B&W. 9: var. sizes. Lang.: Eng.
USA. 1984-1986. Historical studies. ■A definite style of design has emerged out of the fusion of post-modern aesthetics and the performance spaces of the Brooklyn Academy of Music. Examination of various works by designers at BAM.

342   Aronson, Arnold, ed. "Theatre Architecture." *TD&T*. 1986 Spr; 22(1): 20-23, 45-61. Illus.: Plan. Photo. B&W. Architec.

Explod.Sect. Grd.Plan. 22: var. sizes. [Design 85.] Lang.: Eng.
USA. 1976-1987. Histories-sources. ■Reproductions of panels displayed at the United States Institute for Theatre Technology (USITT) conferences showing examples of contemporary theatre architecture: Series continued in TD&T 22:2 (1986 Sum), 20-30, 22:3 (1986, Fall), 29-33 and 22:4 (1986 Win), 12-15, 28-37, 40.

343 Bacon, Bruce W. "Flying Drops in Limited Fly Space." TechB. 1983 Apr.: 1-3. Notes. Illus.: Dwg. B&W. 1. [TB 1129.] Lang.: Eng.
USA. 1983. Technical studies. ■Construction of a droproller that operates like a window shade. Lists materials, procedure and operation.

344 Baker, Rob. "Creating the Circumstances." ThCr. 1986 Jan.; 20(1): 22-25, 58-62. Illus.: Photo. 8: var. sizes.
USA: New York, NY. 1975-1986. Histories-sources. ■Director Wilford Leach discusses his career as a director and erstwhile designer at La Mama and the Public Theatre.

345 Barrecu, Christopher H. "Photo-Murals for the Stage." TechB. 1982 Jan.: 1-3. Illus.: Diagram. 4. [TB 1113.] Lang.: Eng.
USA. 1982. Technical studies. ■Materials and methods for creating photo murals.

346 Bell, David C. "Notes on Designing and Building a Concussion Mortar." TechB. 1986 Oct.: 1-2. Illus.: Dwg. B&W. 2. [TB 1167.] Lang.: Eng.
USA. 1986. Technical studies. ■An economical method of constructing a concussion mortar for realistic explosions.

347 Bender, James. "Zero-Throw Casters." TechB. 1984 Apr.: 1-3. Illus.: Dwg. B&W. 4. [TB 1141.] Lang.: Eng.
USA. 1984. Technical studies. ■The use of zero-throw casters, as opposed to swivel casters, allows a platform to move in any direction on stage.

348 Bliese, Thomas G. "Nylon Rollers Modified." TechB. 1986 Apr.. Notes. Illus.: Dwg. B&W. 1. [TB 1137 Addendum.] Lang.: Eng.
USA. 1986. Technical studies. ■Modification in the nylon roller construction explained in TB 1137 by Ray Forton.

349 Braunstein, Sharon. "Artificial Canapes." TechB. 1981 Oct.: 1-2. [TB 1108.] Lang.: Eng.
USA. 1981. Technical studies. ■A method for creating artificial canapes for the stage.

350 Buck, William. "Lap-Joint Decks." TechB. 1983 Apr.: 1-2. Notes. Illus.: Plan. Dwg. 2. [TB 1128.] Lang.: Eng.
USA. 1983. Technical studies. ■Construction and assembly of a lap-joint deck as an alternative to traditional bolted decks.

351 Buck, William. "Underhung Hinges." TechB. 1983 Oct.: 1-2. Notes. Illus.: Dwg. B&W. 2. [TB 1134.] Lang.: Eng.
USA. 1983. Technical studies. ■Illustrates assembly procedure for a hinged trap door that can be completely concealed in the decking.

352 Cantor, Roy. "Theatre Technology in America." Sin. 1986; 20(1): 27-29. Illus.: Photo. Dwg. B&W. 4: var. sizes. Lang.: Eng.
USA. 1986. Technical studies. ■Outlines the United States Institute for Theatre Technology (USITT) trade exhibition. Notably different from British trade exhibitions because of the better balance of exhibitors representing rigging, lighting, sound, seating, Rostra fabrics, counterweight flying practices.

353 Carter, Paul. "Determining Tensions in Bridling Lines." TechB. 1983 Jan.: 1-2. Notes. Tables. Illus.: Graphs. Dwg. B&W. 3. [TB 1126.] Lang.: Eng.
USA. 1983. Technical studies. ■Techniques of bridling to stabilize a load and how to determine tension in various lines.

354 Catalano, Cosmo, Jr. "A Remote-Controlled Portable Water Source." TechB. 1982 Apr.: 1-2. Illus.: Diagram. [TB 1116.] Lang.: Eng.
USA. 1982. Technical studies. ■The materials and construction of a remote-controlled portable water source.

355 Chase, Rob. "Styrofoam Molding Cutter." TechB. 1983 Oct.: 1-3. Notes. Illus.: Dwg. B&W. 4. [TB 1131.] Lang.: Eng.
USA. 1983. Technical studies. ■Construction and use of a wood lathe attachment designed to produce styrofoam molding.

356 Cohen-Stratyner, Barbara Naomi. "Using Pre-Packaged Makeup Kits." ThCr. 1986 Jan.; 20(1): 36-38, 53-57. Illus.: Graphs.
USA. 1986. Technical studies. ■Expert users discuss how to make the 'major manufacturers' kits work for the user.

357 Crum, Jane Ann. "Three Generations of Lighting Design: An Interview with Peggy Clark Kelley, Jennifer Tipton, and Danianne Mizzy." ThM. 1985 Win; 17(1): 45-50. Illus.: Photo. B&W. 3. Lang.: Eng.
USA. 1946-1983. Histories-sources. ■Three lighting designers discuss changes in equipment, working with directors, differences in lighting, dance and drama and acceptance of women in the technical professions.

358 Cunningham, David. "Two Methods of Constructing Terrain Decks." TechB. 1986 Apr.: 1-3. Illus.: Dwg. B&W. 2. [TB 1164.] Lang.: Eng.
USA. 1986. Technical studies. ■Two ways of constructing contoured decking with lath and mesh or stud substructures.

359 Dace, Tish. "Fosse's Cross-Fade." ThCr. 1986 Aug/Sep.; 20(7): 24-25, 90-92. Lang.: Eng.
USA. 1986. Technical studies. ■Challenges faced by designers in creating cinematic style of Bob Fosse's Broadway production of Big Deal. Related to Media: Film.

360 Dace, Tish. "From the Ridiculous to the Sublime." ThCr. 1986 Mar.; 20(3): 34-37, 67-70. Illus.: Photo. 8: var. sizes.
USA: New York, NY. 1986. Biographical studies. ■Charles Ludlam's role as set designer, artistic director and lead actor of The Ridiculous Theatre Company.

361 Dennstaedt, Jeffrey V. "A Pantograph Molding Jig." TechB. 1986 Apr.: 1-3. Illus.: Dwg. B&W. 1. [TB 1165.] Lang.: Eng.
USA. 1986. Technical studies. ■A shop-built jig, the pantograph transfers angles with sets of interconnected pivoting arms.

362 Dolan, Jill. "Love Of Light." ThCr. 1986 Feb.; 20(2): 22-25, 52, 54-55. Lang.: Eng.
USA. 1986. Technical studies. ■Artist Leni Schwendinger discusses her lighting designs for theatre, dance, film, television and galleries, focusing on her design for original production of Lie of the Mind.

363 Dolan, Jill. "Curator of the Culture." ThCr. 1986 Apr.; 20(4): 20-25, 90-95. Illus.: Photo. 11: var. sizes.
USA: New Haven, CT. 1986. Technical studies. ■Yale Repertory Theatre's resident costume designer Dunya Ramicova discusses the aesthetics of design.

364 Duro, Dan. "Wired for Sound." ThCr. 1986 Mar.; 20(3): 32, 80.
USA. 1986. Technical studies. ■Sound designers at resident theatres discuss their use of the latest technology in stage reinforcement.

365 Eller, Claudia. "Fresh Ideas." ThCr. 1986 Nov.; 20(9): 24-26, 28-29, 52-54. Illus.: Photo.
USA: Los Angeles, CA. 1977-1986. Biographical studies. ■A profile of Cliff Faulkner, 12-time dramalogue recipient, and resident designer at South Coast Repertory.

366 Fain, Michael D. "Simple Smoke." TechB. 1982 Jan.: 1. [TB 1114.] Lang.: Eng.
USA. 1982. Technical studies. ■The use of ammonium chloride for smoke effects.

367 Forton, Ray. "Nylon Rollers." TechB. 1984 Jan.: 1-2. Notes. Illus.: Dwg. B&W. 2. [TB 1137.] Lang.: Eng.
USA. 1984. Technical studies. ■Construction of nylon rollers as an alternative to casters when there is a height limitation.

368 Fullerton, Randy. "Stage Blood." TechB. 1982 Jan.: 1-2. [TB 1112.] Lang.: Eng.
USA. 1982. Technical studies. ■Several methods of making blood for the stage.

THEATRE IN GENERAL: —Design/technology

369   Graham, Jaylene. "Acid-Cut Gobos." *TechB*. 1985 Jan.:
       1-3. Notes. [TB 1149.] Lang.: Eng.
USA. 1985. Technical studies. ■How to make acid-cut gobos.

370   Grammer, Charles. "Painting Photographic Scenery Using
       Friskets." *TechB*. 1984 Jan.: 1-2. Notes. [TB 1136.] Lang.:
       Eng.
USA. 1984. Technical studies. ■The 'frisket principle' is a process which
quickly duplicates the look of a high contrast black and white photo on
large scale.

371   Hacker, Philip E. "A Non-Skid Ground Cloth." *TechB*.
       1986 Apr.: 1-2. [TB 1166.] Lang.: Eng.
USA. 1986. Technical studies. ■Materials and methods for assembling a
non-skid ground cloth.

372   Hale, Alice M.; Long, Robert. "Cut From Different Cloth."
       ThCr. 1986 Aug/Sep.; 20(7): 30-41. Lang.: Eng.
USA: New York, NY. 1986. Technical studies. ■Profile of costume
shops discusses those that turn to work in film, television and other
industries. Includes a list of shops.

373   Hale, Alice M. "Stage Blood: What's Your Type." *ThCr*.
       1986 Oct.; 20(8): 26-27, 74, 76. Illus.: Photo. 3: var. sizes.
       Lang.: Eng.
USA. 1986. Technical studies. ■Aesthetic and practical application of
stage blood, including homemade recipes.

374   Hale, Alice M. "Grasping the Intangible." *ThCr*. 1986
       Nov.; 20(9): 18-23, 46-51. Illus.: Photo. 8: var. sizes.
USA. 1980-1986. Biographical studies. ■A profile of lighting designer
James Ingalls, whose work includes *Ajax* at the American National
Theatre, *Galileo* at the Goodman and *The Front Page* at Seattle
Repertory Theatre.

375   Hardison, Curtis. "Frosting Plexiglass Windows with Beer
       and Epsom Salts." *TechB*. 1986 Oct.: 1. [TB 1169.] Lang.:
       Eng.
USA. 1986. Technical studies. ■An economical and efficient way to frost
plexiglass.

376   Harvey, Donald A. "Homosote 'Brick' Facings for the
       Stage." *TechB*. 1984 Apr.: 1-2. Illus.: Dwg. B&W. 1. [TB
       1140.] Lang.: Eng.
USA. 1984. Technical studies. ■Homosote as an alternative to plywood
for use in making brick facings on stage.

377   Haye, Bethany. "The Manhattan Project." *ThCr*. 1986
       Apr.; 20(4): 73-76. Illus.: Photo. 4: var. sizes.
USA. 1986. Technical studies. ■How special effects designer Bran
Ferren employed on-camera lasers and nuclear salvage in *The Manhattan Project*.

378   Haye, Bethany. "A House Apart." *ThCr*. 1986 Jan.; 20(1):
       84-87. Illus.: Sketches.
USA. 1986. Technical studies. ■Art director Steven Graham and his
work on the film *The Money Pit*. Related to Media: Film.

379   Hood, John Robert. "Corrugated (Kraft) Cardboard as a
       Scene Material." *TechB*. 1973 Jan.: 1. [TB 1101.] Lang.:
       Eng.
USA. 1973. Technical studies. ■The use and texturing of corrugated
cardboard on stage.

380   Jaehnig, Chris P. "Remote-Control Live Fire." *TechB*. 1984
       Jan.: 1-2. Notes. Illus.: Dwg. 1. [TB 1138.] Lang.: Eng.
USA. 1984. Technical studies. ■Presents a safe and proven method of
controlling live fire onstage from a remote position.

381   Jerant, Frederick. "Sound Reduction Door at Bagley
       Wright Theatre." *TD&T*. 1986 Sum; 22(2): 16-17. Illus.:
       Photo. Dwg. B&W. Detail. 4: var. sizes. Lang.: Eng.
USA: Seattle, WA. 1986. Technical studies. ■Specifications of a door
constructed to reduce noise between the shop and the stage at the
Seattle Repertory Theatre.

382   Knox, Barbara. "Cruising Along with the WPA." *ThCr*.
       1986 Apr.; 20(4): 34-36, 67-79. Illus.: Photo. 8: var. sizes.
USA: New York, NY. 1977-1986. Biographical studies. ■The WPA
Theatre's resident designer, Edward Gianfrancesco.

383   LaCourt, Anne. "Scenic Uses For Double-Stick Foam
       Tape." *TechB*. 1985 Jan.: 1-2. [TB 1147.] Lang.: Eng.

USA. 1985. Technical studies. ■Double-stick foam tape provides a tight
seal between almost any two surfaces.

384   Lagerquist, Jon. "Sandwich Batten Clamps." *TechB*. 1984
       Jan.: 1-2. Notes. Illus.: Dwg. B&W. 2. [TB 1135.] Lang.:
       Eng.
USA. 1984. Technical studies. ■Installation and parts of a clamp
capable of attaching sandwich battens to a drop or scrim.

385   Lagerquist, Jon. "A Comparison of Rope Braking Devices."
       TechB. 1984 Oct.: 1-3. Notes. Tables. Illus.: Dwg. B&W. 5.
       [TB 1144.] Lang.: Eng.
USA. 1984. Technical studies. ■Five alternative braking devices for
lowering flown scenery.

386   Lagerquist, Jon. "High-Volume Low-Cost Modelling Clay."
       TechB. 1985 Apr.: 1. [TB 1151.] Lang.: Eng.
USA. 1985. Technical studies. ■How to make low-cost modeling clay in
large amounts.

387   LaRue, Michèle. "The World Theatre." *ThCr*. 1986 Dec.;
       20(10): 34-35, 70-73. Illus.: Photo. Diagram. 2: var. sizes.
       Lang.: Eng.
USA: St. Paul, MN. 1982-1986. Technical studies. ■The complete
overhaul of St. Paul's 1910 road house, owned by Minnesota Public
Radio, to create an up-to-date radio broadcasting facility and music
presentation hall. Related to Media: Audio forms.

388   Leventhal, Max. "Two Periscopes for Full-Scale Cartooning." *TechB*. 1985 Jan.: 1-3. Notes. Illus.: Dwg. B&W. 2.
       [TB 1150.] Lang.: Eng.
USA. 1985. Technical studies. ■The flying and cart periscopes allow
designers to project drawings ('cartoons') onto the floor instead of the
wall.

389   Levine, Mindy N. "William Ivey Long on Costume Design." *TT*. 1986 May; 5(4): 1, 4-5. Illus.: Photo. B&W. 4:
       var. sizes. Lang.: Eng.
USA: New York, NY. 1986. Technical studies. ■Costume designer
William Ivey Long discusses his work for Off Broadway theatres.
Methodology and economic hardships for nonprofit companies.

390   Levine, Mindy N. "Speaking About Design: Jim Clayburgh." *TT*. 1983 Mar/Apr.; 2(5): 5-7. Illus.: Photo. Pntg.
       Grd.Plan. 7: var. sizes. Lang.: Eng.
USA: New York, NY. 1972-1983. Histories-sources. ■Discussion with
set designer Jim Clayburgh on his career, technique and productions,
especially with the Wooster Group.

391   Lewis, Kenneth J. "A Low-Voltage Remote Controller for
       Special Effects." *TechB*. 1985 Apr.: 1-2. Illus.: Dwg. B&W.
       2. [TB 1153.] Lang.: Eng.
USA. 1985. Technical studies. ■Special effects that respond to on/off
signals can be operated by a magnetic reed-switch controller instead of
a sophisticated electronic system.

392   Limoncelli, Jerry. "A System to Facilitate Hanging Lights."
       TechB. 1983 Apr.: 1. Notes. Illus.: Dwg. B&W. 1. [TB 1130.]
       Lang.: Eng.
USA. 1983. Technical studies. ■System of index cards and sash cords to
facilitate hanging lights in repetitive situations.

393   Lindsay, George. "Compliance with Fire Safety." *TechB*.
       1976 May: 1. [TB 1106.] Lang.: Eng.
USA. 1976. Technical studies. ■General fire safety regulations and
fireproofing of many materials common to the theatre.

394   Loney, Glenn. "Tracking a Wardrobe." *ThCr*. 1986 Apr.;
       20(4): 32-37, 57-67.
USA: Ashland, OR. 1986. Histories-sources. ■Resident costume designer Jeannie Davidson discusses the organization of the shop at the
Oregon Shakespeare Festival and the use of computer lists to keep track
of costume stock.

395   Long, Robert; Opitz, Larry. "Giving Them The Business."
       ThCr. 1986 Mar.; 20(3): 33, 71-80.
USA: New York, NY. 1986. Technical studies. ■The changing face of
Broadway's union scene shops in their struggle to remain solvent.

396   Long, Robert. "Major Non-Union Scene Shops Serving
       New York." *ThCr*. 1986 Nov.; 20(9): 16, 81-87.

THEATRE IN GENERAL: —Design/technology

USA: New York, NY. 1986. Historical studies. ■Review of non-union scene shops.

397 Marean, John. "Allowable Loads on Lumber-Nail Joints." *TechB.* 1983 Oct.: 1-3. Notes. Tables. Illus.: Dwg. B&W. 2. [TB 1133.] Lang.: Eng.
USA. 1983. Technical studies. ■Number of nails needed in supporting a non-legged platform that rests on a wood carrying strip.

398 Markle, Patrick. "A Jig For Installing Roto-Locks in Platform Decks." *TechB.* 1984 Apr.: 1-3. Notes. Illus.: Dwg. 2. [TB 1139.] Lang.: Eng.
USA. 1984. Technical studies. ■Description and installation of a jig made to simplify the installation of roto-locks or coffin locks onto platform decks.

399 McClintock, Robert. "Basic Hydraulics." *TechB.* 1981 Oct.: 1-2. [TB 1107.] Lang.: Eng.
USA. 1981. Technical studies. ■The basic principles of hydraulics and formula applications for moving scenery.

400 Miller, James Hull. "Improved Soft-Covered Stock Masking Units." *TechB.* 1984 Oct.: 1-2. Notes. Illus.: Dwg. B&W. 2. [TB 1146.] Lang.: Eng.
USA. 1984. Technical studies. ■Masking screen uses a cloth version of a paper hinge to facilitate storage and shipping.

401 Monsey, Steven E. "A Touch-Tone Relay Controller for Special Effects." *TechB.* 1986 Apr.: 1-2. Illus.: Dwg. B&W. 1. [TB 1163.] Lang.: Eng.
USA. 1986. Technical studies. ■An electronic touch-tone relay controller for operating numerous special effects.

402 Neil, Jane Snyder. "Mask and Headgear of Native American Ritual/Theatre on the Northwest Coast." *TJ.* 1986 Dec.; 38(4): 453-462. Notes. Lang.: Eng.
USA. 1800-1900. Historical studies. ■A survey of the styles and uses of Native American headgear, including examination of the changing categories of performance such as ritual, dance and song.

403 Neville, Tom. "Spider-Cable Clamps." *TechB.* 1984 Oct.: 1-2. Illus.: Dwg. B&W. 2. [TB 1143.] Lang.: Eng.
USA. 1984. Technical studies. ■Spider-cable clamps as a solution for excess cable at a grid.

404 Ohl, Theodore G. "Theatrical Applications of Aniline Dye." *TechB.* 1976 Jan.: 1. [TB 1102.] Lang.: Eng.
USA. 1976. Technical studies. ■Preparation and application of aniline dye for stage use.

405 Ohl, Theodore G. "Snowballs for the Stage." *TechB.* 1976 Jan.: 1. [TB 1103.] Lang.: Eng.
USA. 1976. Technical studies. ■A method for creating snowballs out of Ivory soap.

406 Ohl, Theodore G. "General Specifications for Stairs and Ladders." *TechB.* 1976 Jan.: 1. [TB 1104.] Lang.: Eng.
USA. 1976. Technical studies. ■Safety considerations in constructing stairs and ladders.

407 Olinex, Arthur. "Sliding Electrical Contacts." *TechB.* 1985 Jan.: 1-2. Illus.: Dwg. B&W. 3. [TB 1148.] Lang.: Eng.
USA. 1985. Technical studies. ■Sliding electrical contacts provide an easy way to get power to electrically operated devices that are mounted on tracked pallets or wagons.

408 Opitz, Lary; Pollock, Steve; Sisk, Douglass F. "Lighting Control R&D: High End Products." *ThCr.* 1986 Apr.; 20(4): 26, 43.
USA. 1986. Technical studies. ■Latest research and development of major lighting manufacturers.

409 Opitz, Lary. "Sound Around." *ThCr.* 1986 Jan.; 20(1): 30, 39-45.
USA. 1986. Technical studies. ■Resident sound designers at regional theatres evaluate the condition of their equipment and reveal their wish-lists for new purchases.

410 Ossorguine, Serge. "Using a Piano to Create a Reverberation Effect." *TechB.* 1983 Apr.: 1-2. Notes. Illus.: Dwg. B&W. 1. [TB 1127.] Lang.: Eng.

USA. 1983. Technical studies. ■Technique for creating reverb by using a piano and the phenomenon of sympathetic vibrations induced by sound waves across piano strings.

411 Pollock, Steve. "Followspots: Who's Hot and Who's Hotter?" *ThCr.* 1986 Nov.; 20(9): 37-42.
USA. 1986. Technical studies. ■A comprehensive equipment buyer's guide presents the photometrics and throw ranges of followspots.

412 Pollock, Steve. "Remote Controlled Luminaires." *ThCr.* 1986 Oct.; 20(8): 30, 67-69.
USA. Technical studies. ■Review of the leading manufacturers of remote controlled luminaires and their equipment.

413 Pollock, Steve. "Pars for the Course." *ThCr.* 1986 Jan.; 20(1): 31, 48-51.
USA. 1986. Technical studies. ■Part 3 of a series on low voltage lighting: a guide to sealed beam lamps.

414 Pollock, Steve. "Sound in the 21st Century." *ThCr.* 1986 Feb.; 20(2): 34-36, 98-99. Illus.: Plan. 2: 7 in. x 9 in., 7 in. x 7 in. Lang.: Eng.
USA: New York, NY. 1986. Technical studies. ■Sound designer Abe Jacob discusses refurbishing older theatres to update them with modern acoustics.

415 Rusk, Douglas L. "Sawdust Street Bricks." *TechB.* 1981 Oct.: 1. [TB 1109.] Lang.: Eng.
USA. 1981. Technical studies. ■An easy method of creating durable street bricks.

416 Russell, Douglas A. "Adolphe Appia's Influence on the Work of Lee Simonson." *TD&T.* 1986 Fall; 22(3): 5-10, 51. Illus.: Photo. Dwg. B&W. 13: var. sizes. Lang.: Eng.
USA. 1900-1950. Historical studies. ■Adolphe Appia's influence on Lee Simonson as seen in examples from the Simonson collection at the Stanford University Library.

417 Sammler, Bronislaw. "A Platform System." *TechB.* 1984 Oct.: 1-3. Illus.: Dwg. Diagram. B&W. Detail. 2. [TB 1145.] Lang.: Eng.
USA. 1984. Technical studies. ■A quick and easily assembled platform system that is more efficient than the more traditional system.

418 Sammler, Bronislaw. "Stressed-Skin Platform Units." *TechB.* 1976 Jan.: 1. [TB 1105.] Lang.: Eng.
USA. 1976. Technical studies. ■Use of long-span platform stringers constructed in I-beam fashion.

419 Schwartz, Larry. "Computer-Assisted Lighting Design." *TechB.* 1983 Oct.: 1-3. Notes. [TB 1132.] Lang.: Eng.
USA. 1983. Technical studies. ■Computer program used to store lighting design data which assists designers in recording changes.

420 Shankman, Sarah, ed. "Lighting Design and Application." *L&DA.* 1986; 16(4): 64. Index. Illus.: Dwg. Photo. Print. Color. B&W. Architec. Grd.Plan. Chart. 55. Lang.: Eng.
USA. 1985. ■Magazine for lighting designers, interior designers, architects, consulting engineers and manufacturers covering all aspects of lighting.

421 Sisk, Douglass F. "Byte That Barking Dog." *ThCr.* 1986 Nov.; 20(9): 36, 64, 76-78, 80-81.
USA. 1986. Technical studies. ■A review of the capabilities of the two available computer-controlled sound systems.

422 Stach, David A. "Photocopy Transfers." *TechB.* 1984 Apr.: 1-2. [TB 1142.] Lang.: Eng.
USA. 1984. Technical studies. ■Process of reproducing photocopies of drawings or photographs onto any type of natural-fiber fabric.

423 Sullivan, Thomas. "A Laminated Plywood Turntable." *TechB.* 1986 Oct.: 1-3. Illus.: Diagram. B&W. 3. [TB 1168.] Lang.: Eng.
USA. 1986. Technical studies. ■Complete description of method and supplies for building a frameless laminated plywood turntable.

424 Waskow, Darryl S. "A Quick And Simple Rigging System." *TechB.* 1985 Apr.: 1-2. Illus.: Dwg. B&W. 2. [TB 1152.] Lang.: Eng.
USA. 1985. Technical studies. ■The use of webbing slings and carib-iners makes quick rigging connections possible.

THEATRE IN GENERAL: —Design/technology

425 Williams, Walter. "Decision Trees." *TechB.* 1982 Jan.: 1-3. Illus.: Diagram. 1. [TB 1111.] Lang.: Eng.
USA. 1982. Technical studies. ∎A formula used to make decisions under conditions of uncertainty.

426 Zanotti, Judy. "Metallic Painting Process." *TechB.* 1982 Apr.: 1. [TB 1115.] Lang.: Eng.
USA. 1982. Technical studies. ∎The method and materials needed for putting a metallic finish on stage props.

427 Zimmer, Elizabeth. "Women in Scene Design." *TT.* 1985 Jan.; 4(3): 12-13. Illus.: Photo. B&W. 3: var. sizes. Lang.: Eng.
USA: New York, NY. 1985. Technical studies. ∎Report and excerpts from panel held on women's roles in the field of design. Working conditions, sexism and pay discrimination.

428 Chidekel, R. "Vyjavljaja svoe prednaznačenie." (Revealing One's Intentions.) *TeatrM.* 1986; 5: 14, 147. Lang.: Rus.
USSR. 1980-1986. Technical studies. ∎Stage design for the small stage.

429 Gerasimova, E.M., comp. "Proizvedenija M.Gor'kogo v tvorčestve chudožnikov teatra i kino." (The Works of M. Gorkij in the Works of Theatre and Film Artists.) 166-198 in *Chudožestvennye materialy muzeja A.M. Gor'kogo/ ANSSR. In-t mirovoj literatury im A.M. Gor'kogo.* Moscow: Nauka; 1986. Lang.: Rus.
USSR. 1868-1986. Critical studies. ∎Scene design for works of Maksim Gorkij.

430 Glagoleva, V.S., comp.; Vinogradov, V.M., ed. *Material-'naja sreda spektaklja: Sbornik rekomenduemyh materialov.* (Material Environment of Performance: A Collection of Recommended Materials.) Moscow: Un-t Giproteatr; 1986. 120 pp. Lang.: Rus.
USSR. 1980-1986. Instructional materials. ∎Collected materials on stage equipment, costuming, etc..

431 Kočergin, E. "P'esa glazami chudožnika." (A Play Through the Eyes of an Artist.) *SovD.* 1986; 4: 232-235. Lang.: Rus.
USSR. 1986. Histories-sources. ∎Scene designer E. Kočergin discusses his work.

432 Krasil'nikova, O. "Muzyka—osnova Vdohnovenija." (Music, the Basis of Inspiration.) *TeatZ.* 1986; 29(1): 28-29. Illus.: Photo. B&W. Lang.: Rus.
USSR: Kiev. 1960-1986. Biographical studies. ∎Work of principal designer F. F. Nirod of the Teat'r Opery i Baleta im. T.G. Sevčenko.

433 Kulešova, V.N. *Sovetskie chudožniki teatra i kino 7: Sbornik statej.* (Soviet Artists of Theatre and Film, 7: A Collection of Articles.) M.: Sov. chudožnik; 1986. 329. Lang.: Rus.
USSR. 1980-1986. Critical studies. ∎Survey of the year's exhibits, with analysis of the work of three designers.

434 Kuznecov, A. "S ljud'mi i dlja ljudei." (With People and For People.) *Chudožnik.* 1986; 7: 51-55. Lang.: Rus.
USSR. 1980-1986. Critical studies. ∎Problems and goals of designers for theatre and film.

435 Levitin, G.J. "Tat'jana Georgijevna Bruni." Lang.: Rus.
USSR. 1923-1981. Biographical studies. ∎Career of stage designer Tat'jana Georgijevna Bruni.

436 Šepovalov, V.M. *Scenografija v chudožestvennoj celostnosti spektaklja: Avtoref. diss. ... kand. iskusstvovedenija.* (Stage Design in the Artistic Integrity of the Performance: Synopsis of a Dissertation by a Candidate in Art Criticism.) Leningrad: Leningradskij gosudarstvennyj institut teatra, muzyki i kinematografii; 1986. 24 pp. Lang.: Rus.
USSR. 1980-1986. Critical studies.

Institutions

437 Brand, Mona. "A Writer's Thirty Six Years in Radical Theatre: New Theatre's Formative Years 1932/1955 and Their Influence on Australian Drama." 1-8 in Univ. New England, ed. *Australian Drama 1920-1955.* Papers presented at a conference at the University of New England, Armidale, September 1-4, 1984. Armidale, N.S.W.: Univ. of New England; 1986. 157 pp. Lang.: Eng.
Australia: Sydney, Melbourne. 1932-1955. Historical studies. ∎An account of the left-wing New Theatre movement in Australia, dealing almost exclusively with the Sydney company. The article, by a playwright associated with the company, emphasizes New Theatre's commitment to Australian writers and its introduction to Australia of political street theatre and Brechtian theatre forms.

438 Herliner, Paul. "A New Direction for 'The New'?" *ADS.* 1986 Apr.; 8: 97-112. Notes. Illus.: Photo. 2: 10.5 x 16.5 cm., 10.5 x 14.5 cm. Lang.: Eng.
Australia: Sydney, N.S.W. 1932-1986. Historical studies. ∎Sydney's oldest alternative, radical-political theatre (New Theatre) established in 1932.

439 Hibberd, Jack. "Theatre: Pram and Crib." in Davidson, Jim, ed. *The Sydney/Melbourne Book.* Sydney: Allen & Unwin; 1986. 337 pp. Lang.: Eng.
Australia: Melbourne, Sydney. 1850-1986. Historical studies. ∎Melbourne playwright Jack Hibberd compares the theatrical cultures of Sydney and Melbourne, asserting the continued dominance of English models in the former and the more innovative and nationalist quality of the latter.

440 Böhm, Gotthard. "Mörbisch am Bodensee?" (Mörbisch at Lake Constance?)*Buhne.* 1986 Jan.; 29(1): 41-42. Illus.: Photo. Print. B&W. Lang.: Ger.
Austria: Bregenz. 1985-1986. Histories-sources. ∎Financial difficulties of the Bregenzer Festspiele and their influence on programming.

441 Böhm, Gotthard. "Das Ganze ist ein Abenteuer." (The Whole Thing Is an Adventure.) *Buhne.* 1986 Jan.; 29(1): 13-14. Lang.: Ger.
Austria: Vienna. 1986. Histories-sources. ∎Wiener Festwochen 1986, focusing on Wolfgang Amadeus Mozart and modern art: includes notes on Ursula Pasterk's concept for managing its productions.

442 Böhm, Gotthard. "Kein Platz für Euphorie." (No Place for Euphoria.) *Buhne.* 1986 Mar.; 29(3): 38. Illus.: Photo. Print. B&W. Lang.: Ger.
Austria: Bregenz. 1986-1987. Histories-sources. ∎Solving the financial problems of the Bregenzer Festspiele by increasing subsidies and taking suitable measures to get more spectators.

443 Böhm, Gotthard. "Abseits von Modetrends." (Aside from Modish Trends.) *Buhne.* 1986 May; 29(5): 39. Illus.: Photo. Print. B&W. Lang.: Ger.
Austria: Klagenfurt. 1985-1987. Histories-sources. ∎Notes on three productions at the Stadttheater Klagenfurt and program plans for the 1986/87 season.

444 Böhm, Gotthard. "Kunst und Logistik." (Art and Logistics.) *Buhne.* 1986 Aug.; 29(8): 36, 38. Illus.: Photo. Print. B&W. Lang.: Ger.
Austria: Salzburg. Germany, West. 1957-1986. Biographical studies. ∎Franz Willnauer, new secretary-general of the Salzburger Festspiele: his former work and his plans for working with the festival, particularly the Mozart-cycle in 1991.

445 Kutschera, Edda. "Bausteine setzen." (Laying Bricks.) *Buhne.* 1986 Feb.; 29(2): 39-40. Illus.: Photo. Print. B&W. Lang.: Ger.
Austria. 1986. Histories-sources. ∎Program planning for the festival, Carinthischer Sommer.

446 Kutschera, Edda. "Lebensbedürfnis decken." (To Satisfy Necessities of Life.) *Buhne.* 1986 Mar.; 29(3): 17. (Serie Publikumsorganisationen 8.) Illus.: Photo. Print. Color. Lang.: Ger.
Austria: Salzburg. 1947-1986. Histories-specific. ∎On the audience-society, Salzburger Kulturvereinigung: its history, function and activities.

447 Kutschera, Edda. "Sprachlos, aber ausdruckstart." (Speechless, but Strong in Expression.) *Buhne.* 1986 June; 29(6): 6-7. Illus.: Photo. Print. B&W. Lang.: Ger.
Austria: Vienna. 1986. Histories-sources. ∎The Microtheater Festival in the Wiener Festwochen, including a discussion of the term Microtheater and notes on the origin and history of this kind of theatre.

CLASSED ENTRIES

THEATRE IN GENERAL: —Institutions

448 Kutschera, Edda. "Lachen sollen d'Leut." (People Should Laugh.) *Buhne.* 1986 June; 29(6): 41-42. Illus.: Photo. Print. Color. B&W. Lang.: Ger.
Austria. 1980-1986. Histories-sources. ■Niederösterreichischer Theatersommer: concept for producing summer theatre at festivals in different places.

449 Kutschera, Edda. "Die Spannung bleibt erhalten." (Tension Is Preserved.) *Buhne.* 1986 Nov.; 29(11): 22-23. Lang.: Ger.
Austria: Vienna. 1986. Histories-sources. ■The collaboration of the Theater an der Wien, the Raimundtheater and Ronacher with the Verbund Wiener Theater brought about by financial problems and concepts for using these theatres.

450 Mayer, Gerhard. "Das ist nicht zu verachten." (That's Not To Be Sneezed at.) *Buhne.* 1986 Feb.; 29(2): 6-7. Illus.: Photo. Print. B&W. Lang.: Ger.
Austria: Vienna. 1985. Histories-sources. ■Activities of Teletheater-Gesellschaft, a society for managing summer performances of Austrian theatres or groups, including performances in the media and foreign touring.

451 Mayer, Gerhard. "In die Zielgerade." (To Home Straight.) *Buhne.* 1986 Dec.; 29(12): 10-11. Illus.: Photo. Print. B&W. Lang.: Ger.
Austria: Salzburg. 1986. Histories-sources. ■Postponement of the remodeling of the Kleines Festspielhaus, and the concept and program for the Salzburger Festspiele in 1987.

452 Mayer, Gerhard. "Der Weg ist vorgezeichnet." (The Way Is Indicated.) *Buhne.* 1986 Aug.; 29(8): 6-7. Illus.: Photo. Print. B&W. Lang.: Ger.
Austria: Salzburg. 1986. Histories-sources. ■Management and plans for the Salzburger Festspiele in 1987.

453 Mertl, Monika. "Damen-Wahl und Divas." (Ladies' Choice and Stars.) *Buhne.* 1986 May; 29(5): 7-8. Illus.: Photo. Print. B&W. Lang.: Ger.
Austria: Vienna. 1986. Histories-sources. ■Themes of productions at the Wiener Festwochen.

454 Mertl, Monika. "Bewusstsein erweitern." (Extending Consciousness.) *Buhne.* 1986 Dec.; 29(12): 30-31. Illus.: Photo. Print. B&W. Lang.: Ger.
Austria: Vienna. 1986. Histories-sources. ■On new productions and concepts of groups or persons producing theatre for children, especially on training children for productions.

455 Mertl, Monika. "Zehn Jahre *auf der Walz.*" (*On the Road* for Ten Years.) *Buhne.* 1986 Dec.; 29(12): 31-32. Illus.: Photo. Print. B&W. Lang.: Ger.
Austria. 1976-1986. Histories-sources. ■Tours of the Volksoper, Staatsoper and Burgtheater in Austria.

456 Mertl, Monika. "Im Keller und auf Wanderschaft." (In Cellars and on Tours.) *Buhne.* 1986 Feb.; 29(2): 18-19. (Serie Kindertheater 5.) Illus.: Photo. Print. B&W. Lang.: Ger.
Austria. 1985-1986. Critical studies. ■Working conditions of theatres and groups producing theatre for children, including notes on some of their projects for 1986.

457 Mertl, Monika. "Mehr sein als eine Ware." (To Be More than a Commodity.) *Buhne.* 1986 June; 29(6): 10-11. Illus.: Photo. Print. B&W. Lang.: Ger.
Austria: Vienna. 1986. Histories-sources. ■The Jura Soyfer Theater, its financial situation and plans for productions in the 1986/87 season.

458 Mertl, Monika. "Brainstorm." *Buhne.* 1986 July; 29(7): 102. Illus.: Photo. Print. B&W. Lang.: Ger.
Austria: Burgenland. 1983-1986. Histories-sources. ■Concept and functions of Schlossspiele Kobersdorf, notes on budget and productions in 1986.

459 Raitmayr, Babette. "Theater zum Marktplatz machen." (To Take Theatre to the Market Place.) *Buhne.* 1986 Sep.; 29(9): 41-42. Illus.: Photo. Print. B&W. Lang.: Ger.
Austria: Salzburg. 1986. Histories-sources. ■Lutz Hochstraate's ideas about managing the Salzburg Landestheater and biographical notes on him.

460 Schwabender, Franz. "Revolution ist nicht im Plan." (Revolution Is Not Planned.) *Buhne.* 1986 Dec.; 29(12): 36-37. Illus.: Photo. Print. B&W. Lang.: Ger.
Austria: Linz. 1986. Histories-sources. ■Manager Roman Zeilinger's plans for managing the Landestheater, with notes on its artistic program.

461 Alpár, Ágnes. *Az István Téri Szinház, 1872-1874.* (The Theatre of István Square, 1872-1874.) Budapest: Magyar Szinházi Intézet; 1986. 142 pp. (Szinháztörténeti füzetek 76.) Index. Biblio. Illus.: Photo. Poster. B&W. Lang.: Hun.
Austro-Hungarian Empire: Budapest. 1872-1874. Historical studies. ■Critical study and index of the theatre operating in a Budapest suburb under the management of Gyula Miklósy.

462 Kolta, Magdolna. *A Népszinház iratai.* (The Archives of the Popular Theatre.) Budapest: Magyar Szinházi Intézet; 1986. 359 pp. (Szinháztörténeti könyvtár 16.) Pref. Notes. Index. Lang.: Hun.
Austro-Hungarian Empire: Budapest. 1872-1918. Histories-sources. ■Collection of the surviving documents of the foundation and operation of the Népszinház Popular Theatre of Budapest (1875-1907) with the register of its documents in the Metropolitan Archives of Budapest.

463 Mayer, Gerhard. "... damit die Jugend zur Oper findet." (...So That Youth May Find the Way to Opera.) *Buhne.* 1986 Jan.; 29(1): 43-45. Illus.: Photo. Print. B&W. Color. Lang.: Ger.
Bulgaria: Stara Zagora. 1966-1985. Histories-sources. ■Festival for children and youth, including notes on productions in 1985.

464 Aaron, Susan. "Edmonton's Catalyst Theatre: A Voice for the Community." *PAC.* 1983 Apr.; 20(1): 66-68. Illus.: Photo. B&W. 3. Lang.: Eng.
Canada: Edmonton, AB. 1977-1983. Critical studies. ■An overview of the productions of Catalyst Theatre, examining the company's relation to the community and emphasis on social issues such as disabilities and drug abuse.

465 Anthony, Brian. "Applebaum-Hébert Report: The Many Stages of Cultural Stocktaking." *PAC.* 1983 Apr.; 20(1): 25-28. Illus.: Photo. B&W. 1. Lang.: Eng.
Canada. 1982-1983. Historical studies. ■A discussion of the significance of the 1982 Applebaum-Hébert Report on Federal Cultural Policy in Canada, arguing for consideration of and response to the report. Related to Dance.

466 Bains, Yashdip Singh. "Popular-Priced Stock Companies and Their Repertory in Montreal and Toronto in the 1890's." *CDr.* 1986 Fall; 12(2): 332-341. Notes. Append. 3: var. sizes. Lang.: Eng.
Canada: Montreal, PQ, Toronto, ON. 1890-1940. Historical studies. ■Compares the organization and financial success of two stock companies that catered to 1890s' audience expectations by avoiding shock or confrontation.

467 Beauchamp, Hélène. "Des jeunes en festival." (Of Youth in Festival.) *JCT.* 1984; 30(1): 38-42. Notes. Illus.: Photo. B&W. 3. Lang.: Fre.
Canada: Montreal, PQ. 1966-1984. Historical studies. ■An overview of the second Festival de Créations Jeunesse held in April 1984 in Montreal with background on the origin and structure of the festival.

468 Bertin, Raymond. "Le théâtre à l'école de la vie." (Theatre at the School of Life.) *JCT.* 1984; 30(1): 93-105. Notes. Illus.: Photo. B&W. 7. Lang.: Fre.
Canada. 1980-1984. Critical studies. ■An examination of the techniques and philosophy of two Quebecois children's theatre troupes, focusing on the differences between theatre for children and adolescents and theatre for adults.

469 Carrier, Denis. "Les Circonstances de la Fondation du Théâtre National Français de Montréal." (The Circumstances of the Founding of the Théâtre National Français de Montréal.) *THC.* 1986 Fall; 7(2): 168-175. Notes. Lang.: Fre.
Canada: Montreal, PQ. 1889-1901. Historical studies. ■Describes context of the founding of the Théâtre National Français de Montréal

CLASSED ENTRIES

THEATRE IN GENERAL: —Institutions

in 1900, with attention to the importance of structure and financial arrangements.

470 Dusting, Gillian. "A Positive Direction for Learning and Vancouver Playhouse." *PAC.* 1983 Apr.; 20(1): 59-62. Illus.: Photo. B&W. 3. Lang.: Eng.
Canada: Vancouver, BC. 1982-1983. Critical studies. ■A consideration of the beginning of Walter Learning's career as artistic director of Vancouver Playhouse, discussing the projected repertory and funding opportunities.

471 Fortin, Marcel. "Le Caveau d'Ottawa: Une Troupe Amateur en Quête de Légitimité (1932-1951)." (The Caveau d'Ottawa: An Amateur Troupe in Search of Legitimacy (1932-1951).) *THC.* 1986 Spr; 7(1): 33-49. Notes. Append. Illus.: Photo. B&W. 3: var. sizes. Lang.: Fre.
Canada: Ottawa, ON. 1932-1951. Historical studies. ■A study of the amateur troupe Le Caveau d'Ottawa and its relation to professional companies from France and Montreal.

472 Friedlander, Mira. "The Quality and Quantity of Canadian Theatre Awards." *PAC.* 1983 Apr.; 20(1): 52-53. Illus.: Photo. B&W. 2. Lang.: Eng.
Canada: Toronto, ON. 1983. Critical studies. ■A consideration of the increase in theatre awards in Canada, particularly Toronto, and their effect of diluting theatre honors. The author suggests consolidation of awards.

473 Gaboriau, Linda. "Un théâtre miroir pour la jeunesse: entretien avec Dennis Foon." (Theatre As a Mirror for Youth: An Interview with Dennis Foon.) *JCT.* 1984; 30(1): 107-119. Notes. Illus.: Photo. 6. Lang.: Fre.
Canada: Vancouver, BC. 1975-1984. Histories-sources. ■Director of the Green Thumb Theatre for young people discusses innovations in theme and staging, areas in which Foon sees Canada as leading the U.S..

474 Gascon, Annie; Cyr, René Richard. "À la recherche du théâtre pour adolescents: carnets de voyage du petit à petit." (In Search of Theatre for Youth: Notes on the Tour of Petit à Petit.) *JCT.* 1984; 30(1): 77-82. Lang.: Fre.
Canada: Montreal, PQ. France. 1981-1984. Historical studies. ■An account of Théâtre Petit à Petit's production of *Où est-ce qu'elle est ma gang (Where's My Gang?)* with background on the company's philosophy, techniques and tour of France.

475 Gilbert, Sky. "Rhubarb!: Inside the Rhubarb! Festival." *CTR.* 1986 Win; 13(49): 40-43. Illus.: Photo. Print. B&W. 3: 4 in. x 5 in., 1 in. x 5 in., 3 in. x 3 in. Lang.: Eng.
Canada: Toronto, ON. 1979-1986. Histories-sources. ■The founder of the annual Rhubarb festival reviews its original aesthetic stance and the ways in which that stance has changed over seven years.

476 Grulin, Adrien. "L'Enseignement du théâtre au Cegep: une pédagogie active et signifiante." (Teaching Theatre in Secondary Education: An Active and Meaningful Pedagogy.) *JCT.* 1984; 30(1): 21-37. Illus.: Photo. 6. Lang.: Fre.
Canada. 1984. Histories-sources. ■A group of academics in the field of theatre discusses the role of theatre programs and theatrical production in education.

477 Gruslin, Adrien; Vais, Michel. "La N.C.T.: éducation et théâtre: entretien avec Françoise Graton et Gilles Pelletier." (The N.C.T.: Education and Theatre: An Interview with Françoise Graton and Gilles Pelletier.) *JCT.* 1984; 30(1): 140-157. Illus.: Photo. B&W. 11. Lang.: Fre.
Canada: Montreal, PQ. 1964-1984. Histories-sources. ■Two of the founders of the Nouvelle Compagnie Théâtrale discuss issues of repertory, politics and theatre for children.

478 Hoffman, James. "Carroll Aikins and the Home Theatre." *THC.* 1986 Spr; 7(1): 50-70. Notes. Illus.: Photo. B&W. Grd.Plan. 8. Lang.: Eng.
Canada: Naramata, BC. 1920-1922. Historical studies. ■An overview of the Canadian Players and the ideas and practices of founder Carroll Aikins, with discussion of problems and successes at the Home Theatre.

479 Lavore, Pierre. "Festival de Théâtre des Amériques: 16e festival Québecois de jeune théâtre." (Festival of Theatre of the Americas: The 16th Quebec Festival of Children's Theatre.) *JCT.* 1986 1st Trimester; 38: 11-115. Notes. Illus.: Photo. Dwg. B&W. 69. Lang.: Fre.
Canada. 1985. Critical studies. ■A symposium on and overview of the festival and its international offerings, with analysis of individual productions and theoretical analysis of the festival.

480 Noonan, James. "The National Arts Centre: Fifteen Years at Play." *THC.* 1985 Spr; 6(1): 56-81. Notes. Append. Lang.: Eng.
Canada: Ottawa, ON. 1969-1985. Historical studies. ■Overview of productions and policies of the National Arts Centre, its status as a 'National theatre,' and its problems in repertory and funding.

481 Pavlovic, Diane. "Répertoire analytique de la N.C.T." (An Account of the Repertory of the N.C.T.)*JCT.* 1984; 30(1): 164-173. Notes. Tables. Illus.: Photo. B&W. 4. Lang.: Fre.
Canada: Montreal, PQ. 1964-1984. Historical studies. ■Analysis of the repertory of the Nouvelle Compagnie Théâtrale including a breakdown of genres, directors and audience attendance.

482 Pavlovic, Diane; Cardinal, Clothilde; Beauchamp, Hélène; Cusson, Chantal; Rousseau, Pierre; Barret, Gisèle. "Festival international de théâtre jeunes publics du Québec, 12e édition." (Quebec International Festival of Theatre for Young Audiences, 12th Edition.) *JCT.* 1986 2nd Trimester; 39: 9-48. Notes. Illus.: Photo. B&W. 19. Lang.: Fre.
Canada. Japan. 1985. Histories-sources. ■A report on the 1985 Quebec International Festival of Theatre for Young Audiences, giving an overview of the productions with special attention to children's theatre in Japan.

483 Perkyns, Richard. "Two Decades of Neptune Theatre." *THC.* 1985 Fall; 6(2): 148-186. Notes. Append. Illus.: Photo. B&W. 8. Lang.: Eng.
Canada: Halifax, NS. 1963-1983. Historical studies. ■An overview of the history of the Neptune Theatre and the styles of its five artistic directors.

484 Pilbrow, Richard; Mackintosh, Iain; Staples, David; Godden, Jerry. "Calgary Quartet." *Cue.* 1986 Mar/Apr.; 8(40): 6-12. Illus.: Photo. Dwg. Print. Color. 8: var. sizes. Lang.: Eng.
Canada: Calgary, AB. 1978-1985. Histories-sources. ■Description of the new downtown arts district by four of those involved.

485 Rittenhouse, Jonathan. "Festival Lennoxville: An All-Canadian Story." *CDr.* 1984 Spr; 10(1): 84-114. Illus.: Photo. Sketches. Diagram. B&W. 9: var. sizes. Lang.: Eng.
Canada: Lennoxville, PQ. 1972-1982. Historical studies. ■Overview of Festival Lennoxville, with particular attention to funding, administration and the place of anglophone drama in Quebec.

486 Usin, Léa V. "'A Local Habitation and a Name': Ottawa's Great Canadian Theatre Company." *THC.* 1986 Spr; 7(1): 71-90 . Notes. Illus.: Photo. B&W. 4. Lang.: Eng.
Canada: Ottawa, ON. 1975-1986. Historical studies. ■Analysis of the structure and political viewpoint of the Great Canadian Theatre Company, with an overview of its productions of Canadian plays.

487 Vaïs, Michel. "Le théâtre anglo-québécois à l'heure du renouveau." (The Anglo-Quebec Theatre at the Time of Reawakening.) *JCT.* 1986 1st Trimester; 38: 131-187. Notes. Illus.: Photo. Poster. B&W. 27. Lang.: Fre.
Canada. 1985. Histories-sources. ■Texts of interviews with theatrical professionals in Quebec, focusing on the practical and theoretical problems and interests in workshops and companies.

488 Tao, Hsiung. "Shanghai Ling Chieh Lien He Hui." (The United Association of Performing Artists of Shanghai.) *XYanj.* 1986 Apr.; 18: 270-272. Lang.: Chi.
China, People's Republic of: Shanghai. 1912-1931. Histories-specific. ■One of the first labor organizations to be constituted for the purpose of improving the welfare of performing artists.

489 Arnell, Helena. "Vi sjöng en sång." (We Did Sing a Song.) *Teaterf.* 1986; 19(5): 14. Lang.: Swe.
Denmark: Vordingborg. 1986. Historical studies. ■A report from the European drama camp for children, organized by Amatørteatersellskab.

490 Lewin, Jan. "København." (Copenhagen.) *Entre.* 1986; 13(2): 28-37. Illus.: Photo. B&W. 19: var. sizes. Lang.: Swe.

THEATRE IN GENERAL: —Institutions

Denmark: Copenhagen. 1976-1986. Critical studies. ■Worries about economy, repertory, artistic standards, marketing, and training dominate bleak theatre scene in Copenhagen. Some younger directors do good work at smaller theatres.

491 Burling, William J.; Hume, Robert D. "Theatrical Companies at the Little Haymarket, 1720-1737." *ET.* 1986 May; 4(2): 98-118. Notes. Illus.: Dwg. 1. Lang.: Eng.
England: London. 1720-1737. Historical studies. ■A listing of the groups and actors using the Little Haymarket Theatre from 1720 until the Licensing Act of 1737.

492 Poesio, Paolo Emilio, ed. "Passaporto per il palcoscenico." (Passport to the Stage.) *QT.* 1986 May; 8(32): 3-58. Lang.: Ita.
Europe. 1888-1985. Histories-sources. ■Collection of texts referring to drama schools.

493 "Outi Nyytäjä Principal of Finnish Theatre Academy." *NFT.* 1986; 38: 19. Lang.: Eng, Fre.
Finland: Helsinki. 1967-1986. Historical studies. ■Overview of the career of dramaturgist and teacher Outi Nyytäjä, announcement of his appointment as head of the Theatre Academy of Finland.

494 Vestheim, Katri. "Lilla teatern: Big Little Theatre." *NFT.* 1986(38): 14-17. Illus.: Photo. B&W. 5: var. sizes. Lang.: Eng, Fre.
Finland: Helsinki. 1940-1986. Historical studies. ■History of Swedish-language Lilla-teatern (Little Theatre) covering its evolution from intimate avant-garde productions to topical cabarets, classics and new European plays. Related to Mixed Entertainment: Cabaret.

495 Beauchamp, Hélène. "Point de départ: zéro...et quelques décimales: réflexions sur le théâtre pour adolescents en France." (Point of Departure: Zero...and Some Decimals: Reflections on the Theatre for Adolescents in France.) *JCT.* 1984; 30(1): 83-92. Notes. Illus.: Photo. B&W. 5. Lang.: Fre.
France. 1968-1984. Critical studies. ■Theatre for adolescents in France, particularly the attempts of theatre companies to connect with aspects of 'youth culture' such as rock music.

496 Carlson, Marvin. "August von Kotzebue's Surveys of the Parisian Stage." *THSt.* 1986; 6: 22-31. Notes. Lang.: Eng.
France: Paris. Germany. 1790-1804. Historical studies. ■Kotzebue's views of Parisian stage as reflected in his travel journals of 1790 and 1804.

497 Cohn, Ruby. "Ariane Mnouchkine: Twenty-One Years of Théâtre du Soleil." *ThM.* 1985 Win; 17(1): 78-84. Illus.: Photo... 2. Lang.: Eng.
France: Paris. 1959-1985. Critical studies. ■Overview of Mnouchkine's work with Théâtre du Soleil, focusing on her collaborative work with the company in playwriting, staging and film. Related to Media: Film.

498 Ullrich, Renate. *Schweriner Entdeckungen. Ein Theatre im Gespräch.* (Discoveries in Schwerin. A Theatre under Discussion.) Berlin: Dietz; 1986. 191 pp. B&W. 24. Lang.: Ger.
Germany, East: Schwerin. 1970-1986. Histories-specific. ■Development of the Mecklenburgisches Staatstheater Schwerin drama ensemble under the artistic lead of Christoph Schroth.

499 Arntzen, Knut Ove; Bramsjö, Henrik, transl. "Tiden sviktar." (The Time Is Yielding.) *NT.* 1986; 34: 8-10. Illus.: Photo. Lang.: Swe.
Germany, West: Berlin, West. 1981-1986. Historical studies. ■About Transformtheater, which combines the physical theatre of the East with the avant garde of the West, and their staging of Jürgen Lederach's *Japanische Spiele (Japanese Play)*.

500 Belitska-Scholtz, Hedvig. "Hol a közvélemény?" (Where is Public Opinion?)*SFo.* 1986; 13(2): 1. Lang.: Hun.
Hungary: Budapest. 1986. Histories-sources. ■Interview with director of theatrical history collection at Széchény, National Library as an exhibit of evidence of early theatrical history, as well as organizational problems, lack of public interest.

501 Kazimir, Károly. *Szinház a Városligetben és egyéb történetek.* (Theatre in the Town Park and Other Stories.) Budapest: Magvető; 1986. xvi, 349 pp. Illus.: Photo. B&W. Lang.: Hun.

Hungary: Budapest. 1958-1986. Histories-sources. ■Recollections of Károly Kazimir, stage director, theatre manager, founder and artistic director of the summer Arena Theatre (Körszinház).

502 Mészöly, Tibor. *Szinház a század küszöbén. Ditrói Mór és a Vigszinház stilusforradalma.* (Theatre at the Gates of Our Century: Mór Ditrói and the Stylistic Revolution in the Comedy Theatre.) Budapest: Múzsák; 1986. 72 pp. (Szkénetéka.) Illus.: Photo. Dwg. B&W. Lang.: Hun.
Hungary: Budapest. 1896-1916. Historical studies. ■The first two decades of the Comedy Theatre, under the management of Mór Ditrói.

503 Nagy, István Attila. "Szinháztörténet—interjúkból." (Theatre History—in Interviews.) *Alfold.* 1986; 37(8): 59-66. Lang.: Hun.
Hungary: Debrecen. 1974-1986. Histories-sources. ■Three interviews with József Bényei, Lászlo Gali and Gyula Kertész, former managing directors of Csokonai Theatre.

504 Reid, Francis. "The Museum Theatre in Madras." *Cue.* 1986 Mar/Apr.; 8(40): 4-5. Illus.: Photo. Print. Color. 4: 11 cm. x 7 cm. Lang.: Eng.
India: Madras. 1895-1985. Historical studies. ■Description of the Museum Theatre in Madras and its history.

505 Al-Hadethy, Waleed Hassan. *Educational Theatre in Iraq: Elementary and Secondary Levels, Late 19th Century to 1985.* Boulder, CO: Univ of Colorado; 1986. 399 pp. Pref. Notes. Biblio. [Ph.D. dissertation, University Microfilms order No. DA 8618919.] Lang.: Eng.
Iraq. 1885-1985. Historical studies. ■Survey of educational theatre in Iraq based on interviews, literature survey and classroom observation.

506 *Teatroinaria 1976. 1986.* (Theatre in the Air, 1976-1986.) Rome: Teatroinaria; 1986. 24 pp. Tables. Illus.: Photo. Dwg. Color. B&W. Lang.: Ita.
Italy. 1976-1986. Histories-sources. ■History of Compagnia Teatroinaria on its tenth anniversary, with lists of its activities and productions.

507 Hall, Robin. "Children's Theatre in Japan." *ATJ.* 1986 Spr; 3(1): 102-109. Notes. Illus.: Photo. Print. B&W. 4: 3 in. x 5 in. Lang.: Eng.
Japan. 1950-1984. Historical studies. ■Japan's Kaze-no-Ko theatre company, a professional travelling children's theatre combining mime, games, *origami*, magic and puppets with traditional practices and folk literature.

508 Cha, Beom-Seok; Kim, Seouk-Man. "Hanguk Yeonguk Hyeophoe-ui Hyeonshil-gwa Banghyang." (Reality and the Future Course of the Korean National Theatre Association.) *KTR.* 1986 Feb.; 117(2): 11-27. Illus.: Photo. B&W. 1: 18.5 cm. x 26 cm. Lang.: Kor.
Korea. 1985-1986. Critical studies. ■Controversial aspects of the Korean National Theatre Association and the theatre people's demands of the KNTA.

509 Yoo, Min-Young. "Tôwēal Gūkdän." (The Toweal Theatre.) 241-256 in Yoo, Min-Young, ed. *Illusion and Reality.* Seoul: Aum, In-Gue; 1986. 362 pp. Lang.: Kor.
Korea: Seoul. 1922-1924. Historical studies. ■Detailed information about Korea's first theatre production company founded by Kim Woo-Jin.

510 Harter, Patricia; Martin, Carol; Nanney, Nancy K.; Tsubaki, Andrew T. "Report of the American Theatre Association Panel: Asian Theatre Through Conferences and Festivals." *ATJ.* 1985 Fall; 2(2): 212-220. Notes. Lang.: Eng.
Philippines: Manila. Malaysia: Kuala Lumpur. Japan: Toga. India: Calcutta. 1981-1984. Histories-sources. ■Reports on four Asian theatre conferences and festivals: Styles and Functions of Theatre for Youth in Asia (Manila), Mustika Malaysia (Kuala Lumpur), International Theatre Festival (Toga), and International Seminar on Indian Dance Traditions (Calcutta).

511 Drewnowski, Tadeusz. "Poza kryzysem. Trzydzieści roczników 'Dialogu'." (Outside the Crisis: Thirty Years of *Dialog*.) *PaT.* 1986 Fourth Qtr; 4: 447-462. Illus.: Photo. Print. B&W. 8: var. sizes. Lang.: Pol.

CLASSED ENTRIES

THEATRE IN GENERAL: —Institutions

Poland: Warsaw. 1956-1986. Historical studies. ■Profile of theatrical journal *Dialog* including aesthetic criteria, major critics on editorial board, contributors and esteem of theatrical community.

512 Maciejewski, Jarosław. *Teatry poznańskie w latach panowania króla Stanisława Augusta.* (Theatres in Poznań during the Reign of Stanislas August.) Warsaw: Państwowe Wydawnictwo Naukowe; 1986. 287 pp. (Bibliotek Kroniki Miasta Poznania.) Index. Illus.: Photo. Plan. Pntg. B&W. 20: var. sizes. Lang.: Pol.

Poland: Poznań. 1782-1793. Historical studies. ■Foundation of Polish theatre in Poznań in 1783, its repertoire and political contexts.

513 Pyžova, O.V. *Fragmenty teatral'noj sud'by.* (Fragments of a Theatrical Destiny.) Moscow: Sov. Russia; 1986. 336 pp. Lang.: Rus.

Russia: Moscow. 1898-1986. Historical studies. ■Foundation and brief history of Moscow Art Theatre.

514 Blasco, Ricard. *El teatre al País Valencià durant la Guerra Civil (1936-1939).* (The Theatre in the Valencia Area during the Civil War (1936-1939).) Barcelona: Curial Edicions Catalanes; 1986. 302 pp., 240 pp. (Biblioteca de Cultura Catalana 62/63.) Index. Notes. Pref. Append. [2 vols.] Lang.: Cat.

Spain: Valencia. 1817-1982. Histories-specific. ■Covers the nineteenth and twentieth century with emphasis on the Civil War period. Includes organization of performances, programming, etc.

515 Cabal, Fermín. "El Teatro español entre dos fuegos." (Spanish Theatre Caught in the Cross-Fire.) *Estreno.* 1986 Fall; 12(2): 29-30. Lang.: Spa.

Spain. 1959-1985. Historical studies. ■Lack of growth in conservative, naturalistic, commercial Spanish theatre and the movement of audiences to smaller independent theatres.

516 Gómez Grande, Fernando, ed.; Máñez, Julio A., intro., notes. *Sessions Extraordinàries de Treball del Consell Assessor de Teatre. Octobre 1984.* (Extraordinary Sessions of the Theatre Advisory Board. October 1984.) Valencia: Direcció General de Cultura. Conselleria de Cultura, Educació i Ciència de la Generalitat Valenciana; 1986. 252 pp. (Textos Teòrics.) Notes. Index. Append. Lang.: Fre, Eng, Spa, Ita, Cat.

Spain: Valencia. 1959-1984. Histories-sources. ■Debates on public theatre in Europe and particularly in Spain, including a discussion of the planned Centre Dramàtic de la Generalitat Valenciana. Includes documentation.

517 Font i Guillé, Josep Maria; Berney, Joan; Cots, Joan; Villatoro, Vicenç; Llonch, Jordi; Corbella, Jordi; Perramon, Rosa M.; Clua, Francesc. *10 anys de Rialles a Terrassa.* (Ten Years of Rialles in Terrassa.) Barcelona: Omium Cultural; 1986. 46 pp. Tables. Illus.: Photo. Design. Handbill. Maps. Poster. Print. B&W. 30: var. sizes. Lang.: Cat.

Spain-Catalonia: Terrassa. 1972-1982. Histories-sources. ■Commemorative booklet on the tenth anniversary of the founding of Rialles, an organization dedicated to children's activities, especially with respect to performance.

518 Blomqvist, Kurt. "Teknikgruppen." (The Section for Technicians.) *ProScen.* 1986; 10(2): 14-17. Illus.: Photo. Lang.: Swe.

Sweden. 1976-1986. Historical studies. ■How the collaboration between technical directors and theatre technicians has developed in the last ten years, and plans for the future of the Swedish Society for Theatre Technicians (STFF).

519 Eriksson, Ann-Christine. "Mannen med det vita skägget." (The Man with the White Beard.) *Teaterf.* 1986; 19(1): 6-9. Illus.: Photo. Lang.: Swe.

Sweden: Fagersta. 1918-1986. Historical studies. ■Interview with Einar Bergvin founder of Fagersta Amatörteaterstudio Teaterforum, the organization for Swedish Amateurs and the magazine of the organization.

520 Hoogland, Rikard. "Det började 1953." (It Began in 1953.) *Teaterf.* 1986; 19(5): 3-6. Illus.: Photo. Lang.: Swe.

Sweden: Södertälje. 1953-1986. Historical studies. ■History of Södertälje Amateur Theatre, which works with children, adults and elderly amateurs.

521 Janflod, Lars-Olof. "En personlig återblick." (A Personal Retrospect.) *ProScen.* 1986; 10(2): 28-31. Illus.: Photo. Lang.: Swe.

Sweden. 1976-1986. Historical studies. ■Discusses the first ten years of the Swedish Society for Theatre Technicians, including technician training plans and safety issues.

522 Janflod, Lars-Olof. "Skottes Musikteater." *ProScen.* 1986; 10(3-4): 18-19. Illus.: Photo. Lang.: Swe.

Sweden: Gävle. 1976-1986. Historical studies. ■The independent group Skottes Musikteater, with 10 permanent posts, manage touring on a government grant of 1 million Swedish kroner a year.

523 Nilsson, Nils-Gunnar. "Arkitekturgruppen." (The Section for Architecture.) *ProScen.* 1986; 10(2): 8-10. Illus.: Photo. Lang.: Swe.

Sweden. 1976-1986. Historical studies. ■The theatrical architecture of the last ten years, and the importance of the Swedish Society for Theatre Technicians (STFF).

524 Samuelsson, Björn. "Jag ville absolut int vara pedagog." (I Didn't Want on Any Account to be a Pedagogue.) *Teaterf.* 1986; 19(4): 13-14. Illus.: Photo. Lang.: Swe.

Sweden: Stockholm. 1933-1986. Historical studies. ■Gamla Stans Teater has staged open-air performances every summer since 1980. Recently, they have staged *The Prince and the Pauper.*

525 Samuelsson, Björn. "Galeasen. En egen väg i oskuld." (Galeasen: A Way of Its Own in Innocence.) *NT.* 1986; 33: 35-38. Illus.: Photo. Lang.: Swe.

Sweden: Stockholm. 1986. Historical studies. ■Discussion of the production of *Baal* with twelve young actors without formal training.

526 Sander, Anki. "Att dansa i kyrkan och ge kollekten till Amnesty." (To Dance in the Church and Give the Collection to Amnesty.) *Teaterf.* 1986; 19(6): 8-10. Illus.: Photo. Lang.: Swe.

Sweden: Lund. 1960-1986. Historical studies. ■Lunds Stifts Kyrkospel (The Church Play of The Diocese of Lund) has under Birgitta Hellerstedt-Thorin developed liturgical drama and dance for amateurs to be practiced in the Swedish church.

527 Sander, Anki. "Rapport från Nordiskt Arbetar-och Lokalspelseminarium." (Report from the Seminar of the Nordic Local Plays of the Workers.) *Teaterf.* 1986; 19(2-3): 25. Lang.: Swe.

Sweden: Norrköping. 1970-1986. Histories-sources. ■Seminar by Nordiskt Amatörteaterråd, NAR (Council of Nordic Amateur Theatre) on the development of worker's theatre and local plays.

528 Sander, Anki. "Huvudsaken är att vi kan försörja oss på teater." (The Important Thing Is That We Can Support Ourselves By Theatre.) *Teaterf.* 1986; 19(2-3): 22-23. Illus.: Photo. Lang.: Swe.

Sweden: Norrköping. 1960-1986. Historical studies. ■Marieborg Folkhögskola has training programs, aimed at leaders of amateur groups, in acting and directing.

529 Sjögren, Frederik. "Återkommande favoritord." (Frequent Favorite Words.) *Teaterf.* 1986; 19(2-3): 18-19. Illus.: Photo. Lang.: Swe.

Sweden: Stockholm. 1977-1986. Historical studies. ■The festival at Skeppsholmen, the Folkkulturcentrum, has tried to get ordinary people to be creative and stage their own productions.

530 Grin, Claude; Aeby, Raymond. "9e Biennale de La Chaux-de-Fonds (7-25 mai 1986): Le théâtre amateur dans le monde." (9th Biennial of La Chaux-de-Fonds (May 7-25, 1986): Amateur Theatre All Over the World.) *TPR.* 1986 Sep.; 166: 1-14. Illus.: Photo. B&W. Lang.: Fre.

Switzerland: La Chaux-de-Fonds. Histories-sources. ■For the duration of a theatre festival, problems of amateur theatre productions (infrastructure/finance/acting) were discussed, and various specimens of amateur productions from all over the world were staged.

531 Weibel, Paul. "Die Vereinigten Theaterschaffenden der Schweiz (VTS): Das 'andere' Theater organisiert sich."

THEATRE IN GENERAL: —Institutions

(The Swiss Union of Theatre Makers (VTS): The 'Other' Theatre Gets Organized.) *ASTEJ.* 1986 Sep.(42): 37-41. Lang.: Fre, Ger.
Switzerland. 1983-1986. Historical studies. ■The financial and special status and conditions of alternative theatre (street theatre, variety shows, cabaret, children's theatre) have so far been badly neglected. VTS tries to give support to those working under these conditions and to open national financial resources.

532   Shank, Theodore. "The Welfare State Theater." 233-248 in McNamara, Brooks, ed.; Dolan, Jill, ed. *The Drama Review: Thirty Years of Commentary on the Avant-Garde.* Ann Arbor, MI: UMI Research P; 1986. xii, 371 pp. (Theatre and Dramatic Studies 35.) Print. B&W. 3: 5 in. x 8 in. Lang.: Eng.
UK. 1977. Historical studies. ■Function of Welfare State International detailing its efforts to provide controversial theatre that invites audience participation and reaction.

533   "UK Rep Guide." *PI.* 1986 Mar.; 1(8): 37-38. Lang.: Eng.
UK-England. 1986. Histories-sources. ■Survey of nine repertory theatres.

534   Marcus, Paul. "Present Imperfect—Future Indefinite." *PI.* 1986 Nov.; 2(4): 14-15. B&W. 1. Lang.: Eng.
UK-England: London. 1986. Historical studies. ■*Not the RSC Festival* at the Almeida Theatre included debates on theatre subsidy, training for directors, theatre composers, new writing, actors and designers.

535   Motton, Gregory; Bloom, Stanley, transl. "London fringeteater på väg att kvävas." (The Fringe Theatre of London On Its Way To Suffocation.) *NT.* 1986; 32: 33-34. Lang.: Swe.
UK-England: London. 1980-1986. Historical studies. ■Timorous and conservative administrators are slowly choking the fringe theatre of London.

536   Motton, Gregory; Bloom, Stanley, transl. "Lumière & Son tror på bildens bärkraft." (Lumière & Son Believes in the Supporting Capacity of the Picture.) *NT.* 1986; 32: 35-37. Illus.: Photo. Lang.: Swe.
UK-England: London. 1973-1986. Histories-sources. ■Interview with Hilary Westlake on financial and administrative aspects of Lumière & Son, compared to other fringe theatre groups.

537   Brennan, Mary. "Festival at Forty." *Drama.* 1986; 3(161): 24-25. Illus.: Photo. B&W. 3: var. sizes. Lang.: Eng.
UK-Scotland: Edinburgh. 1984-1986. Historical studies. ■Director Frank Dunlop extends the fortieth Edinburgh Festival with an International World Theatre Season.

538   Oliver, Cordelia. "The Edinburgh Traverse." *PI.* 1986 Sept; 2(2): 53-56. Lang.: Eng.
UK-Scotland: Edinburgh. 1986. Historical studies. ■Description of the Edinburgh Traverse Theatre and the arrival of new director Jerry Killick.

539   Oliver, Cordelia. "Edinburgh Festival Drama (1986)." *PI.* 1986 Oct.; 2(3): 33-37. B&W. 2. Lang.: Eng.
UK-Scotland: Edinburgh. 1986. Reviews of performances. ■Edinburgh Festival plays, including Ingmar Bergman's production of *John Gabriel Borkman* by Henrik Ibsen, *Crime and Punishment* from Cracow and *Yerma* performed by Nuria Espert's company.

540   "Stormy Weather." *AmTh.* 1984 June; 1(3): 28-30. Illus.: Photo. B&W. 4: var. sizes. Lang.: Eng.
USA: Washington, DC. 1984. Historical studies. ■Debate between NEA Chairman Frank Hodsoll and Rep. Sidney R. Yates in Congressional hearings regarding the NEA budget. Proposed budget is seen as detrimental to growth in the arts.

541   "City Help on Real Estate Problems." *TT.* 1984 Feb.; 3(4): 1-2, 5. Lang.: Eng.
USA: New York, NY. 1984. Histories-sources. ■Sara Garretson, director, office for not-for-profit sector, Office of Business Development, discusses how her office can assist theatres, strategies for confronting the real estate crisis afflicting theatres in New York.

542   "New York Theatre Workshop." *TT.* 1984; 3(4): 7, 10. Illus.: Photo. B&W. 1: 3 in. x 3.5 in. Lang.: Eng.

USA: New York, NY. 1980-1984. Historical studies. ■Profile of New York Theatre Workshop, dedicated to developing new works for the theatre, including commissioning new plays. Future plans discussed by artistic director Jean Passanante, along with a brief history of past productions.

543   "Merry Enterprises Theatre." *TT.* 1984 Feb.; 3(4): 10. Illus.: Photo. B&W. 1: 3 in. x 4 in. Lang.: Eng.
USA: New York, NY. 1975-1984. Historical studies. ■Profile of Merry Enterprises Theatre, dedicated to building a stable family of artists and managers, and to the comic tradition.

544   "In Search of Security: A Real Estate Update." *TT.* 1984 Oct.; 4(1): 1, 14-15. Lang.: Eng.
USA: New York, NY. 1984. Historical studies. ■Several New York nonprofit theatres secure new spaces. Details of the structures, financial arrangements and negotiations.

545   Adelman, Louis C. "We Need a Living Library on the Stage." *DGQ.* 1986 Win; 23(4): 30-31.
USA: New York, NY. 1986. Critical studies. ■A call for a government-subsidized repertory acting ensemble.

546   Auslander, Philip. "Staying Alive." *AmTh.* 1984 July/Aug.; 1(4): 10-14. Illus.: Photo. B&W. 4: var. sizes. Lang.: Eng.
USA. 1964. Historical studies. ■Avant-garde style and technique of Living Theatre, early productions, and how they have influenced theatre over the last 20 years.

547   Bagby, Beth. "El Teatro Campesino: Interviews with Luis Valdez." 127-139 in McNamara, Brooks, ed.; Dolan, Jill, ed. *The Drama Review: Thirty Years of Commentary on the Avant-Garde.* Ann Arbor, MI: UMI Research P; 1986. xii, 371 pp. (Theatre and Dramatic Studies 35.) Print. B&W. 1: 2 in. x 3 in. Lang.: Eng.
USA. Mexico. 1965-1986. Histories-sources. ■Luis Valdez describes the origins and evolution of El Teatro Campesino (California), its key individuals and union groups.

548   Barlow, Arthur. "Double Jeopardy." *AmTh.* 1986 Feb.; 2(11): 10-17. Illus.: Photo. Print. B&W. 7: 2 in. x 3 in., 9 in. x 12 in. Lang.: Eng.
USA: Providence, RI, Dallas, TX. 1966-1986. Histories-sources. ■Adrian Hall, artistic director and founder of Trinity Square Repertory, discusses added challenge of simultaneously running Dallas Theatre Center.

549   Bradley, Janet; Bradley, Reg. "Design for Growth: Tears of Joy Theatre 1986." *PuJ.* 1986 Spr; 37(3): 10-13. Illus.: Photo. Print. B&W. 3: var. sizes. Lang.: Eng.
USA: Vancouver, WA. 1974-1985. Histories-sources. ■Growth and organization of Tears of Joy Puppet Theatre, including management techniques that benefit the company and its personnel.

550   Brennan, Scott. "A Working Vacation in the Theatre." *TT.* 1985 June/July; 4(6): 8-9. Lang.: Eng.
USA. 1985. ■Theatre companies that spend summers outside of New York City to promote artistic growth and development.

551   Durham, Weldon B. "The Revival and Decline of the Stock Company Mode of Organization, 1886-1930." *ThSt.* 1986; 6: 165-188. Notes. Tables. Lang.: Eng.
USA. 1886-1930. Historical studies. ■Causes and effects of the revival and then decline of resident acting companies in the U.S. based on case studies of stock companies in San Francisco, Brooklyn, Philadelphia, Bronx, Boston and Kansas City.

552   Gin, Sue-Jeung. "The Circle in the Square, 1950-1960." 325-342 in Yoo, Min-Young, ed. *Illusion and Reality.* Seoul: Aum, In-Gue; 1986. 362 pp. Lang.: Kor.
USA: New York, NY. 1950-1960. Historical studies. ■Early origins of the Off Broadway movement.

553   Godfrey, Marian A. "Taking Stock of the NEA Ongoing Ensembles Grant." *TT.* 1986 July/Aug.; 5(6): 1-3. Illus.: Photo. B&W. 3. Lang.: Eng.
USA: New York, NY. 1986. Historical studies. ■Ensemble companies have developed and grown with the aid of the National Endowment's Ongoing Ensembles Program.

554   Godfrey, Marian A. "The Second Largest Cultural Agency in the United States." *TT.* 1984 Jan.; 3(3): 6-8. Lang.: Eng.

THEATRE IN GENERAL: —Institutions

USA: New York, NY. 1983. Historical studies. ■Structure and functions of the New York City Department of Cultural Affairs, focus on programs affecting nonprofit theatre.

555 Guthrie, Tyrone. "A Fruitful Union." *AmTh.* 1986 Nov.; 3(8): 24-25. Pref. Illus.: Photo. 2: 5 in. x 7 in. Lang.: Eng.
USA: Minneapolis, MN. 1963. Histories-sources. ■Tyrone Guthrie sums up the aspirations of the fledgling Guthrie Theatre and the regional theatre movement of which it became a symbol.

556 Holley, Robert. "Unfair Competition: Business vs. NonProfits." *AmTh.* 1984 May; 1(2): 24-25. Illus.: Sketches. 1. Lang.: Eng.
USA. 1984. Historical studies. ■Small Business Administration issues a report claiming unfair competition from nonprofit organizations. Report proposes IRS restrict current regulations for nonprofit status.

557 Holley, Robert. "The Arts in Congress: A Legislative Preview." *AmTh.* 1984 Apr.; 1(1): 26-27. Illus.: Sketches. 1. Lang.: Eng.
USA: Washington, DC. 1984. Historical studies. ■Effects of recent legislation on arts organizations and how election year politics will impact on funding for the NEA.

558 Honigberg, Nadine. "The Women's Project: An Interview with Julia Miles." *ThM.* 1985 Win; 17(1): 57-62. Illus.: Photo. B&W. 4. Lang.: Eng.
USA: New York, NY. 1978-1985. Histories-sources. ■Director of the Women's Project at the American Place Theatre discusses the history of the project and her views on feminism and theatre.

559 Houseman, John. "The Good Old Days." *AmTh.* 1986 Nov.; 3(8): 18-19, 95-96. Illus.: Photo. Print. B&W. 2: 2 in. x 3 in., 3 in. x 3 in. Lang.: Eng.
USA: New York, NY, Washington, DC. 1935-1940. Histories-sources. ■John Houseman details the history of the Federal Theatre.

560 LeGallienne, Eva. "On Repertory and Audiences." *AmTh.* 1986 Nov.; 3(8): 21-21. Pref. Illus.: Photo. Print. B&W. 2: 4 in. x 5 in., 6 in. x 7 in. Lang.: Eng.
USA: New York, NY. 1933-1953. Histories-sources. ■The struggle to create repertory companies at Civic Rep and American Repertory Theatres.

561 Levine, Mindy N. "International Theatre in New York." *TT.* 1985 Mar.; 4(4): 1, 6-7, 11. Illus.: Photo. B&W. 6. Lang.: Eng.
USA: New York, NY. 1986. Historical studies. ■Discussion of the few theatres—La Mama, Japan House, Repertorio Español—that promote international plays and companies.

562 Levine, Mindy N. "Writers Theatre." *TT.* 1983 Nov/Dec.; 3(2): 10. Lang.: Eng.
USA: New York, NY. 1975-1983. Historical studies. ■Profile of Writers Theatre, focusing on adaptations of poetry and literature for theatre. Organization gives information regarding prizes, funding, etc..

563 Levine, Mindy N. "Economy Tires Theater." *TT.* 1984 Jan.; 3(3): 10. Illus.: Photo. B&W. 1: 3 in. x 2 in. Lang.: Eng.
USA: New York, NY. 1978-1983. Historical studies. ■Profile of Economy Tires Theatre, producing arm of Dance Theatre Workshop. Success, future plans and commitment to produce independent artists.

564 Pianca, Marina. "A Dialogue Among the Americas on Brecht." *ComIBS.* 1984 Nov.; 14(1): 55-56.
USA: New York, NY. 1984. Historical studies. ■A report on the symposium at the Festival Latino discusses Bertolt Brecht and the Nuevo Teatro movement in Latin America.

565 Regan, F. Scott. "Theatre with Children." *ChTR.* 1985 Apr.; 34(2): 13-21. Append. Lang.: Eng.
USA. 1949-1985. Historical studies. ■Structure and goals of eight youth theatres that use child performers. Includes actor training.

566 Renick, Kyle. "Is Bigger Really Better: Thoughts on Institutionalization." *TT.* 1986 June; 5(5): 1-3. Illus.: Sketches. 6: var. sizes. Lang.: Eng.
USA: New York, NY. 1977-1986. Histories-sources. ■The pros and cons of the institutionalization of theatre companies, focusing on WPA Theatre and economic factors that influence growth of theatre.

567 Salazar, Laura Gardner. "Professional and University Youth Theatre Programs: Problems and Perceptions." *YTJ.* 1986 Fall; 1(2): 10-13. Illus.: Graphs. 2. Lang.: Eng.
USA. 1984-1986. Critical studies. ■A study of the administration of professional and university youth theatre programs, using responses from a survey of professionals in the field, focusing on problems in administration and production.

568 Smith, Abby. "New Forms for Old Dreams." *Drama.* 1986; 160(2): 23-25. Illus.: Photo. B&W. 5. Lang.: Eng.
USA: Washington, DC. 1984. Historical studies. ■Establishment of America's National Theatre and background of artistic director Peter Sellars.

569 Somners, Michael. "South Coast Rep." *ThCr.* 1986 Nov.; 20(9): 26-29, 54-58. Illus.: Photo.
USA: Los Angeles, CA. 1964-1986. Historical studies. ■A profile of this southern California theatre, which boasts new scripts, agreeable working conditions and careful planning.

570 Steuer, Gary P. "Theatre for the New City." *TT.* 1983 Oct.; 3(1): 10. Illus.: Photo. B&W. 2: 3 in. x 3 in. Lang.: Eng.
USA: New York, NY. 1970-1983. Histories-sources. ■Goals and accomplishments of Theatre for the New City, focusing on experimental works. Quotes George Bartenieff and Crystal Field, co-artistic directors.

571 Steuer, Gary P. "Co-Production: The Wave of the Future?" *TT.* 1985 May; 4(5): 1, 10-11. Illus.: Photo. B&W. 3. Lang.: Eng.
USA: New York, NY. 1985. Historical studies. ■Financial necessity, space limitations and scarcity of quality scripts force New York theatres to co-produce. Problems and advantages that arise from joint productions.

572 Ward, Douglas Turner. "For Whites Only?" *AmTh.* 1986 Nov.; 3(8): 30-31, 100-101. Pref. Print. B&W. 1: 4 in. x 4 in. Lang.: Eng.
USA: New York, NY. 1966. Histories-sources. ■Reprint of an article that resulted in the founding of the Negro Ensemble Company.

573 Zesch, Lindy. "A Plan, A Process...A Puzzlement." *AmTh.* 1984 Apr.; 1(1): 28-30. Illus.: Sketches. 1. Lang.: Eng.
USA: Washington, DC. 1984. Historical studies. ■A 5-year plan of operations delivered to Congress by the NEA creates controversy over artistic deficits and funding.

574 Zimmer, Elizabeth. "The Play is Not the Only Thing." *TT.* 1984 May/June; 3(7): 6-7. Illus.: Photo. B&W. 2: var. sizes. Lang.: Eng.
USA: New York, NY. 1984. Historical studies. ■Member organizations of Alliance of Resident Theatres/New York expand their play seasons to include programs in poetry, media and music. Related to Media.

575 Bulavincev, N. "Ostrov otkrytij: Muzej teatra v Penze." (An Island of Discoveries: The Theatre Museum in Penze.) *Volga.* 1986(2): 181-191. Lang.: Rus.
USSR: Penze. 1986. Critical studies.

576 Demin, V. "GITIS: An International University." *KZ.* 1986 Jul.; 30(7): 25-27. Lang.: Rus.
USSR: Moscow. 1980-1986. Historical studies. ■The State Institute of Theatrical Art.

577 Gorbačëv, I. "Tvorit' dlja naroda." (To Create for the People.) *KZ.* 1986 Feb.; 30(2): 31. Lang.: Rus.
USSR: Leningrad. 1980-1986. Critical studies. ■Actor and artistic director of the Puškin Theatre speaks about the goals of the theatre collective.

578 Krymova, N. "'My vse ucilis'..." (We All Studied...) *SovD.* 1986; 2: 236-249. Lang.: Rus.
USSR. Histories-sources. ■Scholar of theatre reminisces about her teachers: P.A. Markov, M.O. Knebel and others who worked at Moscow Art Theatre.

Performance spaces

579 Dahle, Terje Nils, ed. *Theaterbau im Ausland.* (Theatre Building Abroad.) Stuttgart: Informationszentrum Raum und Bau; 1985. 167 pp. (IRB Literaturauslese 873.) Pref. Index. Lang.: Ger.

THEATRE IN GENERAL: —Performance spaces

Historical studies. ■Constructed and planned examples of playhouses in Europe and overseas. History of theatre buildings, technique, planning and restoration. Indexes of subject matter, persons, institutions and places.

580 "Wharf Theatre." *Builder NSW.* 1986 Feb.; 15(4): 210-219. Illus.: Photo. Plan. Lang.: Eng.
Australia: Sydney, N.S.W. 1986. Technical studies. ■Extremely successful conversion of a wharf into the headquarters of the Sydney Theatre Company. Includes building specifications, general description, photographs and simple plans.

581 Irving, D.C. "Taking Australia's Oldest Theatre into the Twenty-first Century." *Cue.* 1986 Nov-Dec.; 8(44): 19-22. Illus.: Photo. Plan. Print. B&W. Color. 9: var. sizes. Lang.: Eng.
Australia: Hobart, Tasmania. 1834-1986. Histories-sources. ■Restoration of the Theatre Royal.

582 Böhm, Gotthard. "Sicherheit über alles." (Safety First.) *Buhne.* 1986 Aug.; 29(8): 35-36. Illus.: Photo. Print. B&W. Lang.: Ger.
Austria: Salzburg. 1986. Histories-sources. ■Remodeling the stage of the Kleines Festspielhaus.

583 Kräftner, Johann. "Das Kulissendepot des k.k. Hoftheaters: Spuren einstiger Bestimmung." (The Scene-Depot of K.K. Hoftheater: Marks of Former Determination.) *Parnass.* 1986 Sep-Oct.; 6(5): 42-53. Illus.: Photo. Plan. Dwg. B&W. Color. Lang.: Ger.
Austria: Vienna. 1872-1986. Historical studies. ■On Semper Depot, a scene shop built by Gottfried Semper and Carl Hasenauer for the K.K. Hoftheater.

584 Kutschera, Edda. "Aber glauben muss man d'ran!" (But One Must Believe in It!)*Buhne.* 1986 May; 29(5): 12-14. Illus.: Photo. Print. Color. Lang.: Ger.
Austria: Vienna. 1871-1986. Historical studies. ■Concept for the use of the Ronacher theatre after its renovation, including notes on the 1986 production of *Cagliostro in Wien (Cagliostro in Vienna)* by Johann Strauss. Related to Music-Drama: Operetta.

585 Persson, Lasse. "Lyudmila Zhivkova, kulturpalatset i Sofia." (Lyudmila Zhivkova, the Palace of Culture in Sofia.) *ProScen.* 1986; 10(1): 49-56. Illus.: Photo. Lang.: Swe.
Bulgaria: Sofia. 1983-1985. Technical studies. ■Description of the palace of culture, built in 1983, with its 9 public halls (600-3,880 cap.) and all its technical facilities under, on and above the stages.

586 Blagrave, Mark. "Saint John: The Bi-Capitol Project." *CTR.* 1986 Fall; 13(48): 111-116. Illus.: Photo. Plan. Print. B&W. Explod.Sect. 3:3 in. x 5 in., 5 in. x 4 in. Lang.: Eng.
Canada: St. John, NB. 1913-1986. Historical studies. ■In 1982 a local group was formed to purchase the former Imperial Theatre, once a handsome playhouse and cinema. By 1983, the group had raised enough money to complete the purchase, and to begin seeking funds for the theatre's renovation as a new civic performing arts center.

587 Milliken, Paul. "The Complex Restoration at Adelaide Court." *PAC.* 1983 Apr.; 20(1): 22-24. Illus.: Photo. B&W. 3. Lang.: En .
Canada: Toronto, ON. 1979-1983. Historical studies. ■An overview of the troubles faced by the Adelaide Court theatre complex, opened in 1979, with attention to financial arrangements and the facilities' use by various companies.

588 Smith, H.M. Scott. "Reclamation of the Imperial Theatre." *ArtsAtl.* 1985 Spr; 6(2): 30-31. Illus.: Photo. Print. B&W. 4: 4 cm. x 12 cm., 12 cm. x 8 cm., 12 cm. x 23 cm., 7 cm. x 5 cm. Lang.: Eng.
Canada: St. John, NB. 1913-1985. Historical studies. ■The Imperial Theatre in St. John, built in 1913, has been reacquired by the theatre community through public fundraising and preservation campaign. It will be restored as a centre for the dramatic arts.

589 Winn, Steven. "International Performance Spaces." *ThCr.* 1986 Aug/Sep.; 20(7): 26-28, 43-45. Illus.: Photo. Diagram. 3: var. sizes. Lang.: Eng.
Canada: Vancouver, BC. 1986. Technical studies. ■The planning of 18 different performance venues for Expo '86.

590 LaRue, Michèle. "F.J. Harquail Theatre." *ThCr.* 1986 Dec.; 20(20): 26, 28-29, 38-40. Illus.: Photo. Diagram. 1: size 3 in. x 4.5 in. Lang.: Eng.
Cayman Islands. UK-England. 1986. Technical studies. ■Grand Cayman's National Theatre, designed in England and assembled on the island.

591 Lee, Huai-Sun. "Fu Peng Tang Tang Shih Tsu Tang Ku Hsi Tai." (Ancient Theatre Stage of Tang's Temple at Fu Peng Tang.) *XYanj.* 1986 Apr.; 18: 220-227. Lang.: Chi.
China. 710-905. Historical studies. ■Use of temples as theatre spaces during the Tang dynasty.

592 Berry, Herbert. *The Boar's Head Playhouse.* Cranbury, NJ: Folger Books/Associated Univ. Presses; 1986. 238 pp. Index. Illus.: Photo. Lang.: Eng.
England: London. 1558-1603. Histories-reconstruction. ■Conjectural reconstruction of a theatre based on property deeds, lawsuits and production history, presenting a detailed picture of theatrical life.

593 Somerset, J.A.B. "Local Drama and Playing Places at Shrewsbury: New Findings from the Borough Records." *MRenD.* 1985; 2: 1-32. Pref. Notes. Illus.: Photo. Maps. Dwg. B&W. 14: 8.5 in. x 11 in. Lang.: Eng.
England: Shrewsbury. 1445-1575. Histories-reconstruction. ■A consideration of theatrical activities and fixed outdoor playing spaces in Shrewsbury using surviving fragmentary records such as maps, leases, and recorded lawsuits concerning quarry activities. Descriptive evidence examines a semi-circular outdoor fixed amphitheatre—one of the few known.

594 Hofer, Miklós. "Előkészületek agy századvégi szinházi leltárhoz." (Preparations for a Theatre Inventory to be Made at the End of the Century.) *SFo.* 1986; 13(1): 23-29. Illus.: Photo. B&W. Grd.Plan. Lang.: Hun.
Europe. North America. 1920-1985. Critical studies. ■An architect discusses theory of theatre construction.

595 Clément, Robert. *Les Théâtres de Nîmes au cours des siècles.* (Theatre of Nîmes Through the Centuries.) Nîmes: R. Clément; 1986. Pref. Illus.: Design. Plan. Photo. Sketches. 260: var. sizes. Lang.: Fre.
France: Nîmes. 1739-1985. Historical studies. ■History of the theatres of the city of Nîmes.

596 Lawrenson, T. E. *The French Stage and Playhouse in the XVIIth Century.* 2nd ed., revised. enlarged. New York: AMS P; 1986. xxix, 285 pp. (AMS Studies in the Seventeenth Century 1.) Pref. Notes. Biblio. Index. Illus.: Photo. Print. B&W. Architec. 118. Lang.: Eng, Fre.
France. Italy. 500 B.C.-1726 A.D. Histories-specific. ■Development of theatres, stages and how the Italianate proscenium arch theatre altered the social nature of French drama.

597 Mullin, Donald; Bell, J.M. "The Problem with Pollux." *TN.* 1986; 40(1): 9-22. Notes. Lang.: Eng.
Greece. Italy: Rome. 600-400 B.C. Critical studies. ■Renaissance and subsequent sources offer ambiguous translations of facts of Greek theatrical production.

598 "Pályaudvari hangversenyterem." (A Concert Hall in a Railway Station.) *SFo.* 1986; 13(2): 25-28. Illus.: Photo. B&W. Grd.Plan. 5. Lang.: Hun.
Hungary: Budapest. 1985-1986. Technical studies. ■Design competition for the construction of a concert hall in the former booking offices of the reconstructed Budapest West Railway Station.

599 Füredi, Ferenc. "A lebonyolitó tapasztalatai." (Experiences.) *SFo.* 1986; 13(3): 35-36. Illus.: Photo. B&W. Lang.: Hun.
Hungary: Szeged. 1978-1986. Technical studies. ■Renovation of the Szeged National Theatre.

600 Giday, Kálmán. "A szinház égése 1885. április 22-én." (The Burning of the Theatre on 22 April, 1885.) *SFo.* 1986; 13(3): 8. Lang.: Hun.
Hungary: Szeged. 1885. Historical studies. ■Burning of Szeged National Theatre.

601 Illés, Jenő. "Szinházfelújitások sorozatban." (Theatre Reconstructions in Series.) *SFo.* 1986; 13(4) : 2-3. Lang.: Hun.

THEATRE IN GENERAL: —Performance spaces

Hungary. 1980-1986. Historical studies. ■Survey of the program of renovation and reconstruction of theatres in Hungary.

602 Kádár, Ferenc. "Épületdiagnosztikai vizsgálat." (Solutions of Structural Design.) *SFo.* 1986; 13(3): 25-27. Lang.: Hun.

Hungary: Szeged. 1977-1986. Technical studies. ■How structural design problems were solved in the reconstruction of the Szeged National Theatre.

603 Maár, Márton. "A Szegedi Nemzeti Szinház. A szinház épitésének története." (The National Theatre of Szeged: The History of the Theatre Building.) *SFo.* 1986; 13(3): 7-8. Lang.: Hun.

Hungary: Szeged. 1800-1883. Historical studies. ■Chronicles various uses of the theatre building, its destruction by flood and its reconstruction.

604 Maár, Márton. "A szinház felújitásának előzményei." (Preliminaries of the Present-Day Reconstruction.) *SFo.* 1986; 13(3): 9-10. Lang.: Hun.

Hungary: Szeged. 1948-1980. Technical studies. ■Modernization details of the reconstruction of the Szeged National Theatre.

605 Maár, Márton. "A felújitás. Tervezés és épités." (The Reconstruction of the National Theatre of Szeged: Design and Construction.) *SFo.* 1986; 13(3): 17-21. Illus.: Photo. B&W. Explod.Sect. Grd.Plan. Lang.: Hun.

Hungary: Szeged. 1978-1986. Technical studies. ■Details of the reconstruction of the house at Szeged National Theatre.

606 Máté, Sándor. "Angyalföldi nézőtér." (Theatre in Angyalföld.) *SFo.* 1986; 13(1): 8-10. Illus.: Photo. B&W. Lang.: Hun.

Hungary: Budapest. 1986. Technical studies. ■The reconstruction of the auditorium of the József Attila Culture Centre in the municipal district of Angyaföld from a technical point of view.

607 Nagy, László. "Uj szinház született." (A New Theatre has Been Created.) *SFo.* 1986; 13(3): 1. Lang.: Hun.

Hungary: Szeged. 1978-1986. Histories-sources. ■A brief summary given by the theatre director of the last eight years of the reconstructed National Theatre of Szeged.

608 Szekeres, Mihály. "Belsőépitészet." (Interior Design.) *SFo.* 1986; 13(3): 33-34. Illus.: Photo. B&W. Lang.: Hun.

Hungary: Szeged. 1981-1986. Technical studies. ■Design of the Szeged National Theatre renovation.

609 Mukhopadhyay, Durgadas; Marsan, Valentine Aymone, transl. "Il teatro dell'antica India e le sue regole." (The Ancient Indian Stage and its Conventions.) 365-370 in Ottai, Antonella, ed. *Teatro Oriente/Occidente.* Rome: Bulzoni; 1986. viii, 565 pp. (Biblioteca Teatrale 47.) Lang.: Ita.

India. 200 B.C. Technical studies. ■Conventions governing the size and disposition of the stage in Ancient Indian theatre.

610 Vannuccini, Riccardo, ed. *Lo spazio scenico. Storia dell'arte teatrale attraverso i teatri di Roma e Lazio.* (Scenic Space: History of Theatrical Art in the Theatres of Rome and Lazio.) Rome: Bulzoni; 1986. 156 pp. Pref. Index. Tables. Biblio. Append. Illus.: Photo. Plan. Pntg. Dwg. Poster. B&W. Lang.: Ita.

Italy: Rome. 55 B.C.-1983 A.D. Historical studies. ■Brief descriptions and pictures of theatres from ancient Rome to the present.

611 Król-Kaczorowska, Barbara. "O teatrach Czesława Przybylskiego." (On Czesław Przybylski's Theatres.) *PaT.* 1986 Fourth Qtr; 4: 486-506. Notes. Illus.: Design. Photo. Print. B&W. Detail. Fr.Elev. 14: var. sizes. Lang.: Pol.

Poland: Warsaw, Vilna, Kalisz. 1880-1985. Historical studies. ■Description of theatre buildings designed by architect Czesław Przybylski.

612 "The Natal Playhouse." *Scenaria.* 1986 Apr.; 63: 3-31. Illus.: Photo. Plan. Color. B&W. 43: var. sizes. Lang.: Eng.

South Africa, Republic of: Durban. 1897-1986. Historical studies. ■A description of this last of the large state-funded theatre complexes, along with its history, its place in theatre history of Natal and a description of its opening and its facilities as a revamped new complex.

613 "Sand du Plessis Theatre, Bloemfontein." *Architect and Builder.* 1986 Oct.: 8-13. Illus.: Photo. B&W. Lang.: Afr.

South Africa, Republic of: Bloemfontein. 1986. Technical studies. ■A technical description of the facilities, specifications and aesthetic principles involved in this new theatre complex.

614 Eichbaum, Julius; Viljoen, Henning. "The New Secunda Theatre." *Scenaria.* 1986 Sep.; 68: 9-14. Illus.: Photo. B&W. 7: 4 in. x 5 in. Lang.: Eng.

South Africa, Republic of: Secunda. 1986. Historical studies. ■A brief description and history of this new city theatre, with reviews of its opening performances, during 1986.

615 Gleuck, Germaine. "The Port Elizabeth Opera House—Past and Present." *Scenaria.* 1986 Mar.; 62: 5-11, 16-18. Illus.: Photo. B&W. 15: 5 in. x 8 in. Lang.: Eng.

South Africa, Republic of: Port Elizabeth. 1892-1986. Historical studies. ■A brief overview of the history and uses of the Port Elizabeth Opera House, including a description of the theatre.

616 Massip, Jesús-Francesc. "Algunes notes sobre l'evolució de l'espai escènic medieval als Països Catalans." (Some Notes about the Evolution of the Medieval Stage Space in the Catalan Countries.) 1-12 in Salvat, Ricard, ed. *El Teatre durant l'Edat Mitjana i el Renaixement.* Barcelona: Publicacions i Edicions de la Universitat de Barcelona; 1986. xxviii, 322 pp. (El Pla de les Comèdies 2.) Notes. [Presented at First International Symposium on Medieval and Renaissance Theatre, Sitges, 1983.] Lang.: Cat.

Spain-Catalonia. Italy: Florence. 1388-1538. Historical studies. ■Analysis of spatial orientation in the performance of medieval Catalan religious dramas, including a comparison with the scene designs of Filippo Brunelleschi.

617 "Sommarturné med *Cyrano de Bergerac.*" (Summer Tour of *Cyrano de Bergerac.*) *ProScen.* 1986; 10(3-4): 12-16. Illus.: Photo. Lang.: Swe.

Sweden. 1986. Histories-sources. ■The tour around northern Sweden with Regionteatern i Västernorrland from the crew's point of view.

618 Jonson, Lotta. "Orionteatern." *ProScen.* 1986; 10(3-4): 42-47. Illus.: Photo. Lang.: Swe.

Sweden: Stockholm. 1983-1986. Historical studies. ■Orionteatern is a former mechanical factory, a hall with a length of 35 m. and a height of 12 m., which is used in many ways to realize a unique theatrical design for every production.

619 Pauser, Anders. "Norrland. Här byggs de nya teatrarna." (Norrland: Here Are the New Theatres Constructed.) *NT.* 1986; 35: 20-23. Illus.: Photo. B&W. Lang.: Swe.

Sweden. 1986-1987. Historical studies. ■Two new theatres have recently been built in Norrland: Norrbottenteatern at Luleå and Idunteatern for Norrlandsoperan at Umeå.

620 Thorell, Bernt. "En ny scen: Lejonkulan." (A New Stage: Lejonkulan.) *ProScen.* 1986; 10(2): 32-33. Illus.: Photo. Lang.: Swe.

Sweden: Stockholm. 1986. Technical studies. ■The architectural and technical points of Lejonkulan (The Lion's Den), the new small stage of Kungliga Dramatiska Teatern.

621 Westerlund, Erik. "Renovering Husumgården." (Renovating the Husumgården.) *ProScen.* 1986; 10(1): 46-48. Illus.: Photo. Lang.: Swe.

Sweden: Husum. 1928-1985. Technical studies. ■The assembly hall of Husumgården, built in the year 1928, and the renovation of 1985, which resulted in a bigger stage and better sight lines.

622 Nilsson, Nils-Gunnar. "Teaterbyggnader i Schweiz." (Theatres in Switzerland.) *ProScen.* 1986; 10(1): 36-40. Illus.: Photo. Plan. Lang.: Swe.

Switzerland. 1968-1985. Technical studies. ■Some notes about the theatres in Saint Gallen, Winterthur and Zug.

623 Anderson, Bob. "Alhambra Theatre Bradford." *Cue.* 1986 Sep/Oct.; 8(43): 16-17. Illus.: Photo. Plan. Print. B&W. 2: 14 x 7 cm. Lang.: Eng.

UK-England: Bradford. 1914-1986. Histories-sources. ■Description of the modernization of the Alhambra Theatre.

624 Anderson, Bob. "In the Round, In the Garden." *Sin.* 1986; 20(2): 19-23. Illus.: Photo. Plan. B&W. 4. Lang.: Eng.

THEATRE IN GENERAL: —Performance spaces

UK-England: Stoke-on-Trent. 1980-1986. Historical studies. ∎Technical design features of New Victoria Theatre.

625 Bentham, Frederick. "From War Back to Art Deco." *Sin.* 1986; 20(1): 30-33. Illus.: Photo. B&W. 4: var. sizes. Lang.: Eng.

UK-England: London. 1930-1986. Technical studies. ∎Outlines the restoration of the Whitehall Theatre to its original Art Deco style.

626 Foley, Mike. "A Pub Crawl Round the Troupe." *Sin.* 1986; 20(2): 31-37. Illus.: Photo. Handbill. B&W. 10. Lang.: Eng.

UK-England: London. 1980-1987. Historical studies. ∎Overview of pub-theatres: the Bush, the Gate, Kings Head and the Old Red Lion, highlighting the restricted space and facilities both on and backstage and the very high standard of production that is maintained.

627 Hutchinson, J.A. "The Ultimate Vanishing Trick!" *Tabs.* 1986; 43(1): 19. Illus.: Photo. B&W. 4. Lang.: Eng.

UK-England: London. 1875-1986. Technical studies. ∎Peculiar proportions of Alexander Palace Theatre led to its use as a stage for Victorian pantomime.

628 Mackintosh, Iain. "Courtyard Coincidences?" *Sin.* 1986; 20(1): 4-7. Illus.: Photo. Plan. B&W. Grd.Plan. 8. Lang.: Eng.

UK-England. 1986. Historical studies. ∎Analysis of trends in theatre design focusing on the influence of cultural stimuli on different designers leading to the formation of movements in theatre design.

629 Maitland, Sally. "Peter Cheeseman." *PI.* 1986 Aug.; 2(1): 37-38. B&W. 2. Lang.: Eng.

UK-England: Stoke-on-Trent. 1962-1986. Histories-sources. ∎Peter Cheeseman, artistic director of the New Victoria Theatre, describes the new theatre opening in Stoke-on-Trent and the old theatre, The Old Vic, he has been using since 1962.

630 Parker, J.R. "Restoration of an Opera House." *Cue.* 1986 Nov-Dec.; 8(44): 7-9. Illus.: Photo. Plan. Print. B&W. 3: 12 x 8 cm., 18 x 12 cm. Lang.: Eng.

UK-England: Wakefield. 1954-1986. Histories-sources. ∎Restoration of Wakefield Theatre Royal and Opera House.

631 Parker, Kate. "Women in Warwickshire." *PI.* 1986 Apr.; 1(9): 12-17. Illus.: Photo. Print. B&W. 8. Lang.: Eng.

UK-England: Stratford. 1986. Historical studies. ∎Describes the new Swan Theatre, previews the 1986 Royal Shakespeare Company season, and lists all the Shakespeare-related buildings in Stratford.

632 Thomsen, Christian W. "Der Schwan entfaltet neue Schwingen: Der Neubau der Royal Shakespeare Company in Stratford-on-Avon wurde eröffnet." (The Swan Unfolds New Wings: The New Building of the Royal Shakespeare Company at Stratford-on-Avon.) *Parnass.* 1986 Jul-Aug.; 6(4): 40-46. Illus.: Photo. Plan. Dwg. Print. Color. B&W. Lang.: Ger.

UK-England: Stratford. 1977-1986. Histories-sources. ∎The new building of Swan Theatre, reason for its erection, its history from the plans by John Napier after theatres of Elizabethan period to its opening, concepts for using it.

633 "Marquis Theatre." *ThCr.* 1986 Dec.; 20(20): 22, 56-61. Illus.: Plan. Photo. 2: var. sizes. Lang.: Eng.

USA: New York, NY. 1986. Technical studies. ∎Design challenges faced by architect Robert Morgan in construction of Broadway's newest theatre.

634 "Alabama Shakespeare Festival." *ThCr.* 1986 Dec.; 20(20): 30-33, 51-56. Illus.: Photo. Diagram. 3: var. sizes. Lang.: Eng.

USA: Montgomery, AL. 1982-1986. Historical studies. ∎History of the design and construction of Alabama Shakespeare Festival's two-theatre complex.

635 Auerbach, S. Leonard. "In Search of Excellence." *ThCr.* 1986 Dec.; 20(10): 17, 36-38. Lang.: Eng.

USA. 1986. Histories-sources. ∎Theatre consultant reflects upon the past, present and future of theatre architecture.

636 Elder, Eldon; Imhof, Marsha; Ryder, Sharon Lee; Sagarin, Judy, ed. *Will It Make a Theatre.* New York, NY: Drama Book Specialists; 1979. 2-206 pp, i-ix, intro.. Index. Tables. Biblio. Illus.: Design. Plan. Maps. Dwg. Diagram. B&W.

Architec. Explod.Sect. Fr.Elev. Detail. R.Elev. Grd.Plan. Chart. 78: var. sizes. Lang.: Eng.

USA: New York, NY. 1979. Technical studies. ∎A comprehensive guide to locating, designing and planning a performance space for non-traditional theatre, including methods of evaluation, plans and design suggestions, and regulations to bring space up to code.

637 Hale, Alice M. "Horton Plaza Lyceum Theatre." *ThCr.* 1986 Dec.; 20(20): 24, 44-48. Illus.: Photo. Diagram. 2: var. sizes. Lang.: Eng.

USA: San Diego, CA. 1986. Technical studies. ∎Architectural design of the Horton Plaza Lyceum Theatre, new home of the San Diego Repertory, a two-theatre structure built under a shopping center.

638 Levine, Mindy N.; Weisman, Sari E. *Space to Create: The Theatre Community in Crisis.* Real Estate and New York's Nonprofit Theatres. New York, NY: Alliance of Resident Theatres/New York; 1986. 1-61 pp. Pref. Append. Illus.: Graphs. B&W. 17: var. sizes. Lang.: Eng.

USA: New York, NY. 1986. Technical studies. ∎Results of a survey issued to 80 Off Broadway theatres focusing on the crisis of limited space and real estate costs.

639 Levine, Mindy N. "The Shape of Things to Come." *TT.* 1986 July/Aug.; 5(6): 8-10. Illus.: Photo. Plan. Sketches. Architec. Grd.Plan. 10: var. sizes. Lang.: Eng.

USA: New York, NY. 1986. Technical studies. ∎Theatre for the New City and the Vineyard Theatre design new theatre spaces. Includes plans, audience seating design.

640 Levine, Mindy N. "Alternative Spaces." *TT.* 1984 Dec.; 4(2): 1-2, 12. Illus.: Photo. B&W. 3: var. sizes. Lang.: Eng.

USA: New York, NY. 1984. Technical studies. ∎Alternative performance spaces for experimental theatre and dance works, generally founded and run by artists themselves.

641 Lindy, Sharon. "The 1986 Chicago Conclave." *MarqJTHS.* 1986; 18(3): 33-34. Illus.: Photo. B&W. 3: var. sizes. Lang.: Eng.

USA: Chicago, IL. 1986. Histories-sources. ∎A description of the Theatre Historical Society's 1986 Chicago Conclave which involved tours of theatres in Illinois, Iowa and Wisconsin. Related to Media: Film.

642 Persson, Lasse. "Studieresa i USA." (Study Touring in USA.) *ProScen.* 1986; 10(3-4): 24-32. Illus.: Photo. Lang.: Swe.

USA: Chicago, IL, New York, NY. 1986. Technical studies. ∎The technical facilities and labor relations at De Paul University, Body Politic Theatre and Civic Opera at Chicago, and Vivian Beaumont Theatre and Metropolitan Opera at New York, as seen from a Swedish point of view.

643 Pert, Hisan X. "Bidding the Building." *ThCr.* 1986 Dec.; 20(20): 27, 74-79. Lang.: Eng.

USA. 1986. Technical studies. ∎Bidding process for theatre building, the role of the theatre consultant and current equipment research and development.

644 Steuer, Gary P. "The New Off Broadway Theatres." *TT.* 1984 Apr.; 3(6): 6-8. Illus.: Photo. B&W. 8: var. sizes. Lang.: Eng.

USA: New York, NY. 1984. Historical studies. ∎Brief descriptions of newly constructed theatres, who developed spaces, how financed, architects and theatre consultants involved, and theatre's distinguishing features.

645 Wolff, Robert. "Controlling Costs." *ThCr.* 1986 Dec.; 20(20): 29, 40-44. Lang.: Eng.

USA. 1986. Technical studies. ∎Estimating and managing the cost of building a theatre.

646 Lazarev, D. "Eto naš dom." (This is Our Home.) *TeatrM.* 1986; 5: 78-84. Lang.: Rus.

USSR. 1980-1986. Critical studies. ∎Problems of designing and building theatrical buildings.

647 Ustinov, B.; Gusejnov, G. "Teatr v gorode." (Theatre in the City.) *DekorIsk.* 1986 Jul.; 29(7): 23. Lang.: Rus.

THEATRE IN GENERAL: —Performance spaces

USSR. Historical studies. ■Social role of theatre and theatrical space.

Performance/production

648 Cairns, Adrian. "Zen and the Art of Acting." *NTQ.* 1986 Feb.; 11(5): 26-28. Notes. Lang.: Eng.
Critical studies. ■Ways in which the tenets of Zen mesh with the principles common to most western styles of acting.

649 George, David E.R. "Letter to a Poor Actor." *NTQ.* 1986 Nov.; 11(8): 352-363. Notes. Illus.: Diagram. 4. Lang.: Eng.
Critical studies. ■Theatricality on and off-stage.

650 Jones, David Richard. *Great Directors at Work: Stanislavsky, Brecht, Kazan, Brook.* Berkeley & Los Angeles, CA: Univ. of California; 1986. 380 pp. Index. Lang.: Eng.
1898-1964. Critical studies. ■Study of the directorial process through examination of four important productions—Stanislavskij, Čechov's *Čajka (The Seagull)*: Brecht, *Mutter Courage und ihre Kinder (Mother Courage and Her Children)*: Kazan, Williams' *A Streetcar Named Desire*: Brook, Weiss's *Marat/Sade.*

651 Javier, Francisco. "Panorama du théâtre argentin récent, 1978-1983." (Panorama of Recent Argentine Theatre, 1978-1983.) *JCT.* 1985; 34(1): 59-80. Notes. Tables. Illus.: Photo. B&W. 15: var. sizes. Lang.: Fre.
Argentina: Buenos Aires. 1978-1983. Critical studies. ■Overview of recent Argentine Theatre emphasizing developments in playwriting and scenography.

652 Bayaly, Kassim. "La tragedia religiosa araba." (Arabian Religious Tragedy.) *QT.* 1986 May; 8(32): 111-115. Lang.: Ita.
Asia. Arabic countries. 680-1970. Historical studies. ■The history and practice of Arabic religious tragedy and its performance.

653 Savarese, Nicola. "Una categoria della cultura teatrale occidentale—l'improvvisazione—a confronto con alcune pratiche dell'attore orientale." (A Category of Western Theatrical Culture—Improvisation—Compared with Certain Practices of the Eastern Actor.) 171-182 in Ottai, Antonella, ed. *Teatro Oriente/Occidente.* Rome: Bulzoni; 1986. viii, 565 pp. (Biblioteca Teatrale 47.) Lang.: Ita.
Asia. Europe. 1900-1986. Critical studies. ■Improvisation as practiced by the Eastern and Western actor.

654 "Satire: Interview with Max Gillies." *Meanjin.* 1986; 45(2): 213-222. Lang.: Eng.
Australia. 1986. Histories-sources. ■Actor and political satirist discusses his work and that of Barry Humphries.

655 Britton, David. "The Making of an Aboriginal Theatre." *Fremantle Arts Review.* 1986 July; 1(7): 12-13. Lang.: Eng.
Australia. 1986. Historical studies. ■An account of the collaboration between Aboriginal playwright Jack Davis and European-Australian director Andrew Ross to produce Davis' plays in his home state, Western Australia, and for tours interstate and overseas.

656 Goldie, Terry. "Indigenous Stages: The Indigene in Canadian, New Zealand and Australian Drama." *ADS.* 1986 Oct.; 9: 5-20 . Notes. Illus.: Photo. B&W. 4: 10.5 cm. x 13.5 cm., 10.5 x 15.5 cm. Lang.: Eng.
Australia. New Zealand. Canada. 1830-1980. Critical studies. ■Image of the indigène in the cultures of Canada, Australia and New Zealand existing within a limited semiotic field.

657 Harmer, Wendy. "Standing Up for Myself." *Meanjin.* 1986; 45(2): 175-179. Lang.: Eng.
Australia: Melbourne. 1986. Histories-sources. ■Stand-up comic writes about the Melbourne cabaret scene, concepts of women's comedy, feminism and comedy, and the female comic's relationship with a male audience.

658 Böhm, Gotthard. "Ich geniesse das Singen so." (I Enjoy Singing So Much.) *Buhne.* 1986 May; 29(5): 25-26. Illus.: Photo. Print. Color. Lang.: Ger.
Austria: Vienna. Germany, West. 1914-1985. Biographical studies. ■Playwright and director George Tabori and his work, especially his staging of Ruggiero Leoncavallo's *Der Bajazzo* at the Wiener Kammeroper.

659 Löbl, Hermi. "Theater dürfen nicht verstaubt sein." (Theatres Must Not Be Stuffy.) *Buhne.* 1986 Sep.; 29(9): 13-15. Illus.: Photo. Print. Color. B&W. Lang.: Ger.
Austria: Vienna. Switzerland. Germany, West. Biographical studies. ■Manager and director Claus Helmut Drese: his career and how he got his present position as manager of the Vienna Staatsoper.

660 Quaghebeur, Marc. "Introduction to Belgian Theatre." *GAMBIT.* 1986; 11(42-43): 9-24. Lang.: Eng.
Belgium: Brussels, Liège. Historical studies. ■Effects of two separate language communities, French and Flemish, on Belgian theatre: lack of unity and autonomy, no real repertory theatres.

661 Quaghebeur, Marc. "Une institution théâtrale à la croisée des chemins." (A Theatrical Institution at the Crossroads.) *JCT.* 1985; 35: 111-125. Lang.: Fre.
Belgium. 1985. Historical studies. ■A study of recent French-language theatre in Belgium.

662 Dzjubinskaja, O. "V poiskah sobesednika." (In Search of an Interlocutor.) *TeatrM.* 1986; 7: 170-176. Lang.: Rus.
Bulgaria. 1980-1986. Reviews of performances. ■Notes on various performances.

663 Bains, Yashdip Singh; Jenckes, Norma. "Fanny Kemble and Charles Kemble: As Canadians Saw Them in 1833." *THC.* 1984 Fall; 5(2): 115-131. Notes. Illus.: Photo. B&W. 5. Lang.: Eng.
Canada. 1832-1834. Historical studies. ■A study of the Kembles' tour of Canada in 1833, focusing on public and critical reception, particularly in Montreal and Quebec City, with extensive use of contemporary newspaper reviews.

664 Blanchard, Sharon. "Esse W. Ljungh and the Winnipeg Little Theatre." *THC.* 1984 Fall; 5(2): 185-201. Notes. Illus.: Photo. B&W. 2. Lang.: Eng.
Canada: Winnipeg, MB. 1921-1937. Historical studies. ■Acting career at Winnipeg Little Theatre of Esse Ljungh, later a producer and director of radio drama. Related to Media: Audio forms.

665 Brunner, Astrid. "The Mermaid Theatre, Almost a Miller's Tale." *ArtsAtl.* 1985 Spr; 6(2): 38-40. Illus.: Photo. Print. B&W. 3: 8 cm. x 15 cm., 8 cm. x 8 cm., 12 cm. x 7 cm. Lang.: Eng.
Canada: Wolfville, NS. 1972-1985. Historical studies. ■Use of puppets, masks and people by director Graham Whitehead and designer Tom Miller at the Mermaid Theatre.

666 Eizenstadt, Michael. "Festival Expo BeVancouver." (Theatre Festival Expo 86 in Vancouver.) *Bamah.* 1986; 21(104): 110-113. Illus.: Photo. Print. B&W. 2: var. sizes. Lang.: Heb.
Canada: Vancouver, BC. 1986. Historical studies. ■Overview of performances at the Expo Festival.

667 Gaudet, Paul. "Lorenzo's 'Infidel': The Staging of Difference in *The Merchant of Venice*." *TJ.* 1986 Oct.; 38(3): 275-290. Notes. Illus.: Photo. B&W. 1. Lang.: Eng.
Canada: Stratford, ON. 1984. Histories-specific. ■Production analysis of Mark Lamos's 1984 production of *The Merchant of Venice*, focusing on the importance of the Lorenzo/Jessica relationship.

668 Gruslin, Adrien. "Le Théâtre politique au Québec: une espèce en voie de disparition." (Political Theatre in Quebec: A Species on the Way to Extinction.) *JCT.* 1985; 36: 32-39. Lang.: Fre.
Canada. 1985. Historical studies. ■Dangers of assimilation of French-Canadian theatre into Anglo-Canadian culture. Asserts importance of theatre to cultural politics.

669 Hébert, Lorraine. "Sauve qui peut le théâtre: itinéraire d'un théâtre populaire." (The Theatre in Danger: Itinerary of a Popular Theatre.) *JCT.* 1985; 36: 25-31. Lang.: Fre.
Canada. USA. 1985. Critical studies. ■Relations of Canadian to U.S. theatre, with emphasis on the choice between resistance and assimilation. Argues for a 'critical' theatre that will resist the standard modes of interpretation.

670 Joubert, Ingrid. "Quoi de neuf dans l'ouest Canadien-Français?" (What's New in the French-Canadian West?)*THC.* 1986 Fall; 7(2): 186-201. Notes. Illus.: Photo. B&W. 2. Lang.: Fre.

THEATRE IN GENERAL: —Performance/production

Canada. 1983-1986. Critical studies. ■Opposition to realism in *Aucun motif (No Motive)* by Rhéal Cenerini and *Les Partisans (The Partisans)* by Cercle Molière, with particular emphasis on the techniques used to subvert dramatic illusion.

671 Juleus, Nels. "Lady Dufferin's Amateur Theatricals." *CDr.* 1985 Spr; 11(1): 245-250. Notes. Lang.: Eng.
Canada: Ottawa, ON. India. 1873-1888. Historical studies. ■Examination of Lady Dufferin's amateur theatrical productions, mainly those staged at the Government House in Ottawa in the 1870s.

672 Leonard, Paul. "Rhubarb!: Towards a New Dramaturgy." *CTR.* 1986 Win; 13(49): 44-50. Illus.: Photo. Print. B&W. 5: var. sizes. Lang.: Eng.
Canada: Toronto, ON. 1986. Historical studies. ■Toronto's annual Rhubarb Festival provides an important antithesis to the usual workshop process for new plays and to the notion that the playwright is the 'aristocrat of the theatrical process'.

673 Wallace, Robert. "Issues in Performance: An Introduction." *CTR.* 1986 Sum; 13(47): 4. Illus.: Photo. Print. B&W. 1: 2 in. x 1 in. Lang.: Eng.
Canada. 1986. Critical studies. ■Introduction to a special issue dealing with performance.

674 Pearn, J.C. *Poetry as a Performing Art in the English-Speaking Caribbean.* Sheffield: Univ. of Sheffield; 1986. Notes. Biblio. [Ph.D. dissertation, *Index to Theses* 37-4378.] Lang.: Eng.
Caribbean. 1937-1985. Histories-specific. ■Studies the emergence of poetry as a performing art and its relationship to nationalist agitation.

675 Bravo-Elizondo, Pedro. "Ramón Griffero: Nuevos espacios, nuevo teatro." (Ramón Griffero: New Spaces, New Theatre.) *LATR.* 1986 Fall; 20(1): 95-101. Illus.: Photo. Print. B&W. 2: 3 in. x 4 in., 4.5 in. x 5.5 in. Lang.: Spa.
Chile: Santiago. 1953-1986. Histories-sources. ■Ramón Griffero, Chilean playwright, director, actor and filmmaker, reminisces about his work in theatre. Related to Media: Film.

676 Kalvodovà, Dana; Marsan, Valentine Aymone, transl. "Sistemi di adattamento alla scena occidentale di opera e messe in scena tradizionali della Cina orientale." (Methods for Adapting East Chinese Traditional Works and Stagings to the Western Stage.) 303-313 in Ottai, Antonella, ed. *Teatro Oriente/Occidente.* Rome: Bulzoni; 1986. viii, 565 pp. (Biblioteca Teatrale 47.) Lang.: Ita.
China. Europe. Critical studies. ■Methods of transposing staging techniques from eastern to western theatre.

677 Ottaviani, Gioia. "L'Oriente come specchio: le testimonianze dello spettacolo cinese e giapponese nelle relazioni di viaggio tra '500 e '600." (The East as Mirror: The Testimonies of Chinese and Japanese Performances in the Travel Relations between 1500 and 1600.) 477-485 in Ottai, Antonella, ed. *Teatro Oriente/Occidente.* Rome: Bulzoni; 1986. viii, 565 pp. (Biblioteca Teatrale 47.) Lang.: Ita.
China. Japan. 1500-1600. Critical studies. ■Account of documentation of performances in China and Japan as related by Western travelers.

678 Wu, Boying; Hu, Yue. "Wu Renzhi Daoyan Jifa Sanshi Tiao." (Thirty Directing Techniques of Wu Renzhi.) *XYishu.* 1982 Aug. ; 5(3): 1-4. Lang.: Chi.
China. 1930-1980. Instructional materials. ■Director's guide based upon reinforcement and reduction. Includes categories such as concentration, repetition, softening, etc.

679 Chin, Tsai. "Teaching and Directing in China: Chinese Theatre Revisited." *ATJ.* 1986 Spr; 3(1): 118-131. Notes. Illus.: Photo. Print. B&W. 3: 3 in. x 5 in, 5 in. x 7 in. Lang.: Eng.
China, People's Republic of: Beijing. 1981-1985. Histories-sources. ■Use of Western training to teach and direct a class for a production of *The Tempest* by William Shakespeare at the Central Academy of Drama.

680 Leal, Rine. "Una branca cubana del teatre català." (A Cuban Branch of the Catalan Theatre.) *SdO.* 1986 Dec.; 28(327) : 91-95. Notes. Tables. Illus.: Design. Photo. Print. B&W. 3: var. sizes. Lang.: Cat.

Cuba. Spain-Catalonia. 1838-1972. Historical studies. ■Brief history of the Robreño family, Catalan immigrants to Cuba, and their impact on Cuban theatre.

681 Mugersija, M. "Vzgljad na sovremennyj kubinskij teatr." (A Look at Contemporary Cuban Theatre.) *TeatrM.* 1986; 6: 167-173. Lang.: Rus.
Cuba. 1980-1986. Critical studies. ■Survey of articles on Cuban theatre.

682 Bérczes, László. "Pisektől Amerikáig. Beszámoló egy 'amatőr' fesztiválról." (From Pisek to America, Report on an 'Amateur' Festival.) *Sz.* 1986 Sep.; 19(9): 32-34. Illus.: Photo. B&W. 1: 7 cm. x 12 cm. Lang.: Hun.
Czechoslovakia: Pisek. 1986. Reviews of performances. ■Notes on the amateur festival of Pisek.

683 Dahlberg, Christer; Sander, Anki; Ytterborg, Jan. "Internationellt samarbete." (International Cooperation.) *Teaterf.* 1986; 19(6): 3-5. Illus.: Photo. Lang.: Swe.
Denmark: Copenhagen. 1986. Reviews of performances. ■Report from an international amateur theatre festival where music and dance were prominent. Related to Music-Drama.

684 Gabnai, Katalin. "Gyerekszínjátszók Dániában." (Child Actors in Denmark.) *Sz.* 1986 Nov.; 19(11): 25-27. Lang.: Hun.
Denmark: Vordingborg. 1986. Histories-sources. ■Report on the Third European Child Acting Workshop.

685 Moatty, Mohammed Abdel; Sirabella, Mariabruna, transl. "Il teatro egiziano contemporaneo tra la cultura araba e quella europea." (Contemporary Egyptian Theatre Between Arabic and European Cultures.) 377-386 in Ottai, Antonella, ed. *Teatro Oriente/Occidente.* Rome: Bulzoni; 1986. viii, 565 pp. (Biblioteca Teatrale 47.) Lang.: Ita.
Egypt. 1798-1986. Critical studies. ■European and Arabic influences on Egyptian theatre.

686 Colgan, Gerard. "Dublin." *PI.* 1986 Mar.; 1(8): 42,58. Lang.: Eng.
Eire: Dublin. 1985. Reviews of performances. ■Survey of the 1985 Dublin theatre season.

687 Barker, Kathleen. "Thirty Years of Struggle: Entertainment in Provincial Towns Between 1840 and 1870 (Part 1)." *TN.* 1985; 39(1): 25-31. Notes. Biblio. [Part 2 in *TN* 39:2 (1985), 68-75.] Lang.: Eng.
England. 1840-1870. Historical studies. ■Development of and influences on regional theatre and other entertainments.

688 Barker, Kathleen. "Thirty Years of Struggle: Entertainment in Provincial Towns Between 1840 and 1870." *TN.* 1985; 39(2): 68-75. Notes. Biblio. Illus.: Photo. Poster. Plan. [Continued in *TN* 39:3 (1985), 140-149.] Lang.: Eng.
England. 1840-1870. Historical studies. ■Development of and influences on theatre and other regional entertainments.

689 Berry, Herbert. "The Globe Bewitched and *El Hombre Fiel.*" *MRenD.* 1984; 1: 211-230. Notes. Lang.: Eng.
England. 1634. Historical studies. ■Context of Heywood and Brome's *The Late Lancaster Witches*, focusing on the authors' use of witch-trial documents. A significant account of the play is discussed and analyzed.

690 Bond, David. "Nell Gwyn's Birthdate." *TN.* 1986; 40(1): 3-9. Notes. Biblio. Lang.: Eng.
England: London. 1642-1671. Biographical studies. ■Re-establishes actress Nell Gwyn's birthdate as 1650, using evidence and comparisons from contemporary accounts to show *The Bibliographical Dictionary of Actors & Actresses* is unjustified in suggesting 1642.

691 Boswell, Jackson Campbell. "Seven Actors in Search of a Biographer." *MRenD.* 1985; 2: 51-62. Notes. Lang.: Eng.
England. 1526-1587. Biographical studies. ■Brief investigation of seven actors updates Edwin Nungezer's *Dictionary of Actors.*

692 Kendall, Alan. *David Garrick: A Biography.* New York, NY: St. Martin's; 1986. 224 pp. Biblio. Index. Illus.: Photo. Lang.: Eng.
England: London. 1717-1779. Biographies. ■Realistic portrayal of the actor who brought Shakespeare back to the stage.

THEATRE IN GENERAL: —Performance/production

693 Milhous, Judith. "The First Production of Rowe's *Jane Shore.*" *TJ.* 1986 Oct.; 38(3): 309-321. Notes. Lang.: Eng.
England: London. 1713-1714. Historical studies. ■A detailed study of the first production of *Jane Shore* by Nicholas Rowe using extensive financial records, with particular reference to costuming.

694 Ranger, Paul. "I Was Present at the Representation..." *TN.* 1985; 39(1): 18-25. Notes. Biblio. Illus.: Photo. Pntg. Sketches. B&W. 7: var. sizes. Lang.: Eng.
England. 1700-1985. Historical studies. ■Analysis of 18th-century acting styles to show a dynamism in technique, with watercolors of Sarah Siddons in performance.

695 Roach, Joseph R. "Garrick, the Ghost and the Machine." *TJ.* 1982 Dec.; 34(4): 431-440. Illus.: Sketches. Lang.: Eng.
England. 1734-1779. Critical studies. ■David Garrick's familiarity with mechanical physiology influenced his practical execution of performance and staging.

696 Styan, J.L. *Restoration Comedy in Performance.* Cambridge, MA: Cambridge UP; 1986. 271 pp. Index. Biblio. Illus.: Photo. Lang.: Eng.
England. 1660-1986. Critical studies. ■Study of Restoration comedy intended for use by actors and directors. Includes reviews of modern performances.

697 Taylor, John Russell. "The Wonderful World of Jonathan Miller." *PlPl.* 1986 Dec.; 399: 10-11. B&W. 2: 4 in. x 4 in. Lang.: Eng.
England: London. 1961-1986. Biographical studies. ■A review of Miller's career in theatre prompted by the autobiography *Subsequent Performances.* Argues that Miller's strength lies in instinct tempered by intellect.

698 Tydeman, William. *English Medieval Theatre, 1400-1500.* London/Boston: Routledge & Kegan Paul/Methuen; 1986. Notes. Illus.: Photo. Sketches. Lang.: Eng.
England. 1400-1500. Histories-specific. ■Theories of production and acting techniques based partly on modern productions of medieval plays. *Mankynde*, *The Castle of Perseverance* and *Fulgens and Lucres* are specifically examined.

699 Wasson, John. "Professional Actors in the Middle Ages and Early Renaissance." *MRenD.* 1984; 1: 1-11. Notes. Lang.: Eng.
England: London. 1200-1600. Historical studies. ■An examination of recently available evidence suggesting that professional actors appeared earlier than has been assumed by theatre historians.

700 "Russkij ljubitelskij teat'r v Tartu v XIX v." (Russian Amateur Theatre in Tartu in the Nineteenth Century.) *Sovetskije archivy.* 1986; 4: 73-74. Lang.: Rus.
Estonia: Tartu. 1882-1913. Historical studies. ■Survey of documents from the Central State Historical Archive of the Estonia SSR about theatrical activities of Russian amateurs.

701 *Bor'ba tendencij v sovremannom zapadnom iskusstve: Sbornik statej.* (The Struggle of Tendencies in Contemporary Western Art: A Collection of Articles.) Moscow: Nauka; 1986. 244. Lang.: Rus.
Europe. USA. 1960-1980. Critical studies. ■Analyses of the major trends in theatre, film and other art forms. Related to Media: Film.

702 Leonard, William Torbert. *Masquerade in Black.* Metuchen, NJ: Scarecrow; 1986. 431 pp. Index. Biblio. Lang.: Eng.
Europe. USA. 1560-1979. Historical studies. ■Study of white actors who performed in blackface, with emphasis on *Othello.*

703 Mehta, C.C.; Chini, Antonella, transl. "Il teatro orientale ed occidentale." (Eastern and Western Theatre.) 371-373 in Ottai, Antonella, ed. *Teatro Oriente/Occidente.* Rome: Bulzoni; 1986. viii, 565 pp. (Biblioteca Teatrale 47.) Lang.: Ita.
Europe. India. 1884-1986. Critical studies. ■History and influence of Indian theatre on Western drama.

704 Roach, Joseph R. *The Player's Passion: Studies in the Science of Acting.* Newark, DE: Univ. of Delaware P; 1986. 255 pp. Index. Notes. Biblio. Illus.: Photo. Lang.: Eng.
Europe. North America. 1700-1985. Histories-specific. ■Study of the history of acting theory.

705 Šachmatova, Je.V. *Idejno-estetičeskie iskanija europejskoj režissury na rubeže XIX-XX vekov i tradicii vostočnogo teatra: Avtoref. diss. ... kand. iskusstvovedenija.* (Ideo-Aesthetic Quests of European Directors at the Turn of the Century and the Traditions of Eastern Theatre.) Moscow: GITIS; 1986. 22 pp. Lang.: Rus.
Europe. Asia. 1890-1910. Critical studies.

706 Segerberg, Tom. "Behov av en nationell identitet." (The Need of a National Identity.) *Teaterf.* 1986; 19(2-3): 5-8. Illus.: Photo. Lang.: Swe.
Finland. 1920-1986. Historical studies. ■History of amateur theatre in Finland, where all professional companies have evolved from amateur groups. Includes discussion of workers' theatre, bourgeois theatre, and Swedish-language theatre.

707 Smeds, Barbro; Nyytäjä, Outi. "Finlandia. Liv av överblivet." (Finlandia: Life of Leftovers.) *NT.* 1986; 33 : 14-17. Illus.: Photo. Lang.: Swe.
Finland: Helsinki. 1986. Reviews of performances. ■Impressions of Ryhmäteatteri's aesthetics, based on their staging of *Finlandia.*

708 "Mysli posle festivalja." (Thoughts After the Festival.) *UTeatr.* 1986; 1: 29-31. Lang.: Ukr.
France: Lyons. 1985. Histories-sources. ■On international festival of children's theatre and youth theatre.

709 Blumenthal, Eileen. "The Unfinished History of Ariane Mnouchkine." *AmTh.* 1986 Apr.; 3(3): 4-11. Illus.: Photo. Print. B&W. 8: 2 in. x 3 in., 14 in. x 14 in. Lang.: Eng.
France: Paris. 1964-1986. Historical studies. ■Ariane Mnouchkine's Théâtre du Soleil's epic *Norodom Sihanouk*, blending Shakespeare with Asian theatre styles.

710 Boudet, Micheline. "Les raisons de l'emploi." (Reasons for Typecasting.) *CF.* 1986 Nov.; 16(153): 24. Lang.: Fre.
France. 1925-1986. Critical studies. ■Stresses physical suitability for a role.

711 Demur, Guy. "Le côté Marigny." (The Marigny Side.) *CRB.* 1986; 34(112): 10-17. Lang.: Fre.
France. 1943-1956. Biographical studies. ■Recollection of actor, director Jean-Louis Barrault's life and career.

712 Dort, Bernard. "L'oeuvre de Vilar: 'Une Utopie nécessaire'." (The Work of Vilar: 'A Necessary Utopia'.) *CTL.* 1986 June; 19(56-57): 28-37. Notes. [International Colloquium on Jean Vilar, Venice, November 1985.] Lang.: Fre.
France: Paris. 1912-1971. Histories-sources. ■Personal recollections and a critique of Jean Vilar and his work.

713 Dort, Bernard; Lepri, Laura, transl. "L'opera di Vilar: un'utopia necessaria." (The Work of Vilar: A Necessary Utopia.) *BiT.* 1986; 1: 3-13. Notes. Biblio. Lang.: Ita.
France. 1912-1971. Critical studies. ■The work of director Jean Vilar interpreted as an impossible attempt to meet the demands of actors, audience and text.

714 Dullin, Charles; Seragnoli, Daniele, ed.; Guccini, Gerardo, transl. *La ricerca degli dei. Pedagogia di attori e professione di teatro.* (The Quest for Gods: Actor Training and the Theatrical Profession.) Florence: Usher; 1986. 285 pp. (Oggi, del teatro 8.) Pref. Index. Notes. Biblio. Lang.: Ita.
France. 1885-1949. Histories-sources. ■Anthology of writings by and about Charles Dullin, with biographical notes and a critical essay by the editor.

715 Goodden, Angelica. *Action and Persuasion: Dramatic Performance in Eighteenth-Century France.* Oxford: Clarendon; 1986. 224 pp. Illus.: Photo. Print. B&W. 8. Lang.: Eng.
France: Paris. 1700-1799. Historical studies. ■History of the struggle to raise the professional status of acting to the level of other arts based on the rhetorical notion of *actio*, a theory of gesture, attitude and facial expression.

716 Héliot, Armelle. "Une femme superbe: Edwige Feuillère." (A Superb Woman: Edwige Feuillère.) *CF.* 1986 Nov.; 16(153): 15. Lang.: Fre.
France. 1931-1986. Histories-sources. ■Feuillère's recollections of her theatre debuts and role in Henry Becque's *La Parisienne.*

THEATRE IN GENERAL: —Performance/production

717 Jakubovskij, A. "Teatr nevozmoznosti." (Theatre of the Impossible.) *TeatrM*. 1986; 4: 173-186. Lang.: Rus.
France. 1980-1986. Critical studies. ■Problems of contemporary French theatre.

718 Lengyel, György. "A szinházi ember. Arcképvázlat Michel Saint-Denis-ről." (The Theatre Man: Portrait of Michel Saint-Denis.) *Sz*. 1986 Dec.; 19(12): 28-31. Lang.: Hun.
France. UK-England. 1920-1960. Biographical studies. ■Survey of the career of director Michel Saint-Denis.

719 McEwen, Barbara. "Au-delà del'exoticisme: Le Théâtre québécois devant la critique parisienne, 1955-1985." (Beyond Exoticism: Quebec Theatre as Seen by Parisian Criticism.) *THC*. 1986 Fall; 7(2): 134-148. Notes. Lang.: Fre.
France: Paris. Canada. 1955-1985. Histories-specific. ■A consideration of the reception of Quebec theatre productions by Parisian critics, focusing on the status of the productions as regional theatre of France.

720 Meyer-Plantureux, Chantal. "Quelque chose s'est passé mais quoi? Évolution de la photographie de théâtre de la fin du 19e s. à 1986." (Something Happened, But What? The Evolution of Theatre Photography from the End of the 19th Century to 1986.) 76-99 in Roegiers, Patrick, ed. *L'Ecart constant*. Brussels/Paris: Didascalies; 1986. 147 pp. Illus.: Photo. Print. B&W. 37: var. sizes. Lang.: Fre.
France. 1872-1986. Historical studies. ■The development of stage photography especially since the 1920s and its aesthetic evolution since 1945.

721 Muraškinceva, E.D. "Francuzskij srednevekovyj teat'r: aktery i roli." (French Theatre of the Middle Ages: Actors and Roles.) 58-67 in Piskunova, S.J., ed. *Literatura v kontekste kul'tury*. Moscow: Izd-vo Mosk un-ta; 1986. Lang.: Rus.
France. 900-1499. Historical studies. ■Actors and roles in medieval French theatre.

722 Seigner, Françoise. "Un paradoxe: la notion d'emploi." (The Paradox of Typecasting.) *CF*. 1986 Nov.; 16(153): 26. Lang.: Fre.
France. 1940-1986. Critical studies. ■Arguments against typecasting, including actors' difficulty of changing their type.

723 Sueur, Monique. *Le théâtre et les jours...* (Theatre and Days...)Paris: Flammarion; 1986. 259 pp. Lang.: Fre.
France: Paris. 1950-1986. Histories-sources. ■Interview with actor and director of Théâtre National de l'Odéon, Jean-Pierre Miquel.

724 Toja, Jacques. "Être le personnage." (To Be the Character.) *CF*. 1986; 16(153): 28. Lang.: Fre.
France. 1950-1986. Critical studies. ■Learning many roles and avoiding being typecast said to be enriching for both actor and audience. Situations of French and American actors compared.

725 Vouzelot, Jean-Michel. "Aimer le jeu, tout simplement." (Quite Simply to Love Acting.) *JCT*. 1986 2nd Trimester; 39: 113-121. Illus.: Photo. B&W. 4. Lang.: Fre.
France: Paris. 1985. Histories-sources. ■Interview with director and actor Daniel Mesguich on his teaching at the Paris Conservatory and his ideas of the function of 'truth' and 'falsity' in the craft of acting.

726 Zanger, Abby. "Acting as Counteracting in Molière's *The Impromptu of Versailles*." *TJ*. 1986 May; 38(2): 180-195. Notes. Lang.: Eng.
France. 1663. Critical studies. ■Analysis of the relation of actor to role as depicted in Molière's *L'Impromptu de Versailles*, and this relation's function as a model of signification.

727 Drese, Claus Helmut. *Theaterarbeit in drei deutschsprachigen Ländern*. (Theatrical Work in Three German-Speaking Countries.) Basel: Schweizerischer Bühnenverband; 1986. 24 pp. (Schriftenreihe.) Pref. Lang.: Ger.
Germany. Switzerland. Austria. 1945-1985. Historical studies. ■Speech to the general meeting of Schweizerischer Bühnenverband (Zürich) comparing theatrical work in three German speaking countries from a historical angle.

728 Williams, Simon. "The 'Great Guest' Arrives: Early German Hamlets." *TJ*. 1986 Oct.; 38(3): 291-308. Notes. Lang.: Eng.
Germany: Hamburg. 1770-1811. Historical studies. ■Production and textual analyses of German versions of Shakespeare's *Hamlet*, with consideration of differing acting styles.

729 Suvin, Darko. "Brechtian or Pseudo-Brechtian: Mythical Estrangement in the Berliner Ensemble Adaptation of *Coriolanus*." *ASSAPHc*. 1986; 3: 135-158. Notes. Biblio. Illus.: Photo. B&W. 5: var. sizes. Lang.: Eng.
Germany, East: Berlin, East. 1964. Historical studies. ■Description of a production of William Shakespeare's *Coriolanus* by the Berliner Ensemble (East Berlin).

730 Weimann, Robert; Schumacher, Ernst; Heinz, Wolfgang; Schroth, Christoph; Wekwerth, Manfred. *Wechselwirkungen der darstellenden Künste*. (Interplay of the Performing Arts.) Berlin: Akademie der Künste der DDR; 1986. 99 pp. (Arbeitshefte 39.) [International colloquy.] Lang.: Ger.
Germany, East. 1983. Critical studies. ■The actor's craft in theatre, film and television: interplay and differences in working methods.

731 Siedlicki, Krzysztof. "Warszawskie Spotkania Petera Steina." (Meeting with Peter Stein in Warsaw.) *TeatrW*. 1984 May; 39 (812): 25-30. 2: 10 cm. x 16 cm., 16 cm. x 8 cm. Lang.: Pol.
Germany, West: Berlin, West. Poland: Warsaw. 1984. Histories-sources. ■Interview with Peter Stein, director of Schaubühne am Helleschen Ufer.

732 Spiegel, Mechthild; Komar, Kathleen, transl. "Interview with Hilmar Thate." *ComIBS*. 1985 Apr.; 84(2): 57-60.
Germany, West. Germany, East. 1949-1984. Biographical studies. ■Actor Hilmar Thate reflects on his encounter with Bertolt Brecht and his theatre.

733 "Szinikritikusok dija 1985/86." (Theatre Critics' Prizes 1985/86.) *Sz*. 1986 Oct.; 19(10): 1-13. Lang.: Hun.
Hungary. 1985-1986. Critical studies. ■Hungarian critics vote at the end of every season for the best Hungarian play, performance, male and female actor, scenery and costume of the season.

734 Belitska-Scholtz, Hedvig. "Színháztörténeti emlékek. Iskolai, főúri és német szinjátszás Magyarországon." (The Early Remains of Theatrical History: Scholastic, Aristocratic and German Theatre in Hungary.) *SFo*. 1986; 13(2): 19-24. Illus.: Photo. B&W. Lang.: Hun.
Hungary. 1610-1850. Histories-sources. ■Review of the exhibition held in April 1986 in the Széchényi National Library prepared by the Theatre History Collection.

735 Nánay, István. "Kazincbarcikai számvetés." (Accounting and Survey in Kazincbarcika.) *Sz*. 1986 Sep.; 19 (9): 18-23. Illus.: Photo. B&W. 4: 9 cm. x 12 cm., 12 cm. x 12 cm. Lang.: Hun.
Hungary. 1986. Critical studies. ■Covers Eighth National Theatre Festival and the status of Hungarian amateur theatre.

736 Nánay, István. "Mozgásszínházi találkozó." (Calisthenic-Theatre Meeting.) *Sz*. 1986 May; 19 (5): 33-36. Illus.: Photo. B&W. 5: var. sizes. Lang.: Hun.
Hungary: Budapest. 1985. Histories-sources. ■Notes on the meeting of experimental theatre groups at Szkéné Theatre of the Budapest Technical University. Related to Dance.

737 Novák, Mária. "Csurgó régen és most. A diákszínjátszó fesztiválok húsz éve." (Csurgó in the Old Times and Now: Theatre Festivals for Students 20 Years Ago.) *Sz*. 1986 Sep.; 19(9): 24-27. Illus.: Photo. B&W. 2: 9 cm. x 12 cm. Lang.: Hun.
Hungary: Csurgó. 1967-1986. Critical studies. ■Review and notes on Festival Days for students.

738 Staud, Géza. "A magyar szinmüészet a harmincas években." (Hungarian Theatre in the 1930s.) 34-44 in Herbai, Ágnes, ed. *Müvészeti élet Magyarországon az 1930-as években (Art in Hungary in the 1930s)*. Budapest: TIT; 1985. 164 pp. Lang.: Hun.

THEATRE IN GENERAL: —Performance/production

Hungary. 1932-1938. Historical studies. ■Text of a speech delivered to the Society for the Propagation of Knowledge.

739 Verebes, István. "Vita a szinházi struktúráról. A sajátos bármilyen." (Discussion on Theatre Structure: The Peculiar Whatever.) *Krit.* 1986; 14(2): 20-21. Illus.: Dwg. 1: 14 cm. x 8 cm. Lang.: Hun.

Hungary. Critical studies. ■Contribution to the discussion from actors' viewpoint about the quality of the Hungarian theatre work focusing on staging.

740 Sander, Anki. "Det nordiska kulturarvet." (The Nordic Cultural Heritage.) *Teaterf.* 1986; 19(4): 8-10. Illus.: Photo. Lang.: Swe.

Iceland: Reykjavik. 1986. Critical studies. ■Report from the Third Nordic Festival for Amateur Theatre, now including Iceland and Greenland, with the slogan: 'The Nordic cultural heritage as inspiration for the theatre of today'.

741 Verdone, Mario. "*Persepolis* e *Orghast*." (Persepolis and Orghast.) 421-430 in Ottai, Antonella, ed. *Teatro Oriente/ Occidente.* Rome: Bulzoni; 1986. viii, 565 pp. (Biblioteca Teatrale 47.) Lang.: Ita.

Iran: Shiraz. 1971. Critical studies. ■Description of the Persepolis-Shiraz theatre festival of 1971, featuring *Persepolis* by Jannis Xenakis and *Orghast* by Peter Brook, text by Ted Hughes.

742 Rapp, Uri; Sirabella, Mariabruna, transl. "Il teatro israeliano fra Oriente e Occidente." (Israeli Theatre Between East and West.) 387-394 in Ottai, Antonella, ed. *Teatro Oriente/Occidente.* Rome: Bulzoni; 1986. viii, 565 pp. (Biblioteca Teatrale 47.) Lang.: Ita.

Israel. 1920-1986. Critical studies. ■Development of a nationalist theatre in Israel after an initial period of strong European, especially Russian, influence.

743 *L'isola dei pappagalli con Bonaventura prigioniero degli antropofagi.* (The Island of Parrots with Bonaventura Captured by Cannibals.) Casalecchio di Reno (Bologna): Grafis; 1986. 48 pp. Index. Biblio. Illus.: Dwg. Photo. Lang.: Ita.

Italy: Turin. 1986. Histories-sources. ■Program of *L'isola dei pappagalli* (*The Island of Parrots*) by Sergio Tofano on the occasion of repeat performances by the Teatro Stabile di Torino.

744 Brandon, James R. "Theatre East and West: An International Congress." *ATJ.* 1985 Fall; 2(2): 231-233. Lang.: Eng.

Italy: Rome. Asia. 1984. Histories-sources. ■Review of an international conference on the confrontation of Asian and Western theatre.

745 Cappelletti, Salvatore. *Luigi Riccoboni e la riforma del teatro. Dalle* commedie dell'arte *alla commedia borghese.* (Luigi Riccoboni and the Reformation of Theatre: From *Commedia dell'arte* to Bourgeois Comedy.) Ravenna: Longo; 1986. 155 pp. (L'interprete 45.) Pref. Index. Notes. Biblio. Lang.: Ita.

Italy. France. 1676-1753. Historical studies. ■Reconstructs the intellectual career of actor, author and theatre historian Luigi Riccoboni through his works.

746 Casini-Ropa, Eugenia, ed.; Calore, Marina, ed.; Guccini, Gerardo, ed.; Valenti, Cristina, ed. *Uomini di teatro nel settecento in Emilia e Romagna. Il teatro della cultura. Prospettive documentarie.* (Men of Theatre During the Eighteenth Century in Emilia and Romagna. The Theatre of Culture: Documentary Perspectives.) Modena: Mucchi; 1986. viii, 318 pp. Pref. Index. Tables. Illus.: Dwg. B&W. 61: var. sizes. Lang.: Ita.

Italy. 1700-1799. Histories-sources. ■Anthology of extracts pertaining to theatrical life of the period, including letters, articles, dedications, diaries, treatises and designs, with explanatory notes.

747 Damkjaer, Nils; Gustafson, Ann, transl. "Kulturen som hävstang." (Culture as a Lever.) *Teaterf.* 1986; 19(6): 6-7. Illus.: Photo. Lang.: Swe.

Italy: Amandola. 1980-1986. Historical studies. ■Members of Teatret La Luna have, with the local mayor, started an amateur festival for and by the people of Amandola.

748 Grotowski, Jerzy. "Teatro Oriente/Occidente." (Theatre East and West.) 7-19 in Ottai, Antonella, ed. *Teatro Oriente/Occidente.* Rome: Bulzoni; 1986. viii, 565 pp. (Biblioteca Teatrale 47.) Lang.: Ita.

Italy: Rome. 1986. Historical studies. ■Keynote speech given by Jerzy Grotowski at the conference *Teatro Oriente/Occidente.* General comparison of Eastern and Western theatre.

749 Jenkins, Ron. "Dario Fo, The Roar of the Clown." *TDR.* 1986 Spr; 30(1): 171-179. Illus.: Photo. Print. B&W. 7: 2 in. x 3 in., 8 in. x 10 in. Lang.: Eng.

Italy. 1960-1986. Critical studies. ■Dario Fo's fusion of subversive politics and poetic slapstick in his plays and one-man shows.

750 Livio, Gigi. "L'orientalismo fine secolo nel linguaggio della scena italiana: quattro rappresentazioni di *Salomè.*" (Fin-de-siècle Orientalism in the Language of the Italian Stage: Four Performances of *Salome.*) 495-525 in Ottai, Antonella, ed. *Teatro Oriente/Occidente.* Rome: Bulzoni; 1986. viii, 565 pp. (Biblioteca Teatrale 47.) Lang.: Ita.

Italy. 1904-1963. Critical studies. ■Compares the effect of late nineteenth-century Orientalism on four productions of Oscar Wilde's *Salome.*

751 Memola, Massimo Marino. "Tramonto del teatro moderno e nuova drammaturgia." (Decline of Modern Theatre and New Dramaturgy.) *QT.* 1986 May; 8(32): 96-110. Notes. Biblio. Lang.: Ita.

Italy. 1970-1985. Critical studies. ■Examination of Italian avant-garde theatre.

752 Monti, Raffaele, ed. *Il Maggio Musicale Fiorentino 2. I grandi spettacoli.* (Florentine Musical May, Vol. 2: The Great Performances.) Rome: De Luca; 1986. 268 pp. Pref. Index. Notes. Tables. Biblio. Illus.: Photo. Dwg. Color. B&W. Lang.: Ita.

Italy: Florence. 1933-1985. Histories-sources. ■Volume II of a series on the spring arts festival 'Maggio Musicale Fiorentino' discusses directors and stage designers. Includes ample critical and photographic documentation.

753 Palombi, Claudia. *Il gergo del teatro. L'attore italiano di tradizione.* (The Jargon of Theatre: The Italian Traditional Actor.) Rome: Bulzoni; 1986. 231 pp. (Biblioteca di cultura 304.) Pref. Index. Notes. Tables. Biblio. Gloss. Illus.: Photo. Dwg. B&W. 14: var. sizes. Lang.: Ita.

Italy. 1885-1940. Historical studies. ■Reconstruction of the life of Italian actors and acting companies with a vocabulary of their jargon.

754 Zeffirelli, Franco. *Zeffirelli: The Autobiography of Franco Zeffirelli.* New York, NY: Weidenfeld & Nicolson; 1986. 348 pp. Index. Illus.: Photo. Lang.: Eng.

Italy. UK-England. 1923-1986. Biographical studies. ■Theatre and film director recounts his work with notable actors and singers.

755 Adedeji, Joel; Chini, Antonella, transl. "La maschera come ombelico del teatro orientale e occidente." (The Mask as the Umbilicus of Theatre East and West.) 95-110 in Ottai, Antonella, ed. *Teatro Oriente/Occidente.* Rome: Bulzoni; 1986. viii, 565 pp. (Biblioteca Teatrale 47.) Lang.: Ita.

Japan. Africa. Europe. Historical studies. ■The mask as source of energy and central point of popular theatre.

756 Ortolani, Benito. "Il teatro occidentale alla ricerca dell'energia profonda 'rilassata e composita' dell'Oriente." (Western Theatrical Quest for the Deep 'Relaxed and Composite' Energy of the East.) 185-195 in Ottai, Antonella, ed. *Teatro Oriente/Occidente.* Rome: Bulzoni; 1986. viii, 565 pp. (Biblioteca Teatrale 47.) Lang.: Ita.

Japan. Historical studies. ■Energy of Oriental performances a source of interest to Occidental actors.

757 Osasa, Yoshio. *Nihon gendai engekishi taisho: Shōwa shokihen.* (History of Contemporary Japanese Theatre: The Early Shōwa Period.) Tokyo: Hakusuisha; 1986. 616 pp. Lang.: Jap.

Japan: Tokyo. 1950-1986. Histories-specific. ■History of contemporary Japanese theatre.

THEATRE IN GENERAL: —Performance/production

758 Ahn, Mim-soo; Yeo, Suk-ki; Lee, Tae-ju. *Yēun-Ki.* (Acting.) Seoul: Yeo, Suk-gi; 1988. 267 pp. Lang.: Kor.
Korea: Seoul. Technical studies. ■Theory, practice and body-training for the beginner.

759 Kim, Jae-Hung; Kim, Seok-Man; Song, Ae-Gyung; Yu, Yong-Hwan; Bang, Tae-Soo; Jeong, Jin-Soo; Kim, Yeong-Tae; Lee, Seong-Soo; Kim, Cheol-Li. "Hanguk yeongukin-ui Hyeonjuso. VI: Gogukjang.'' (The Present Korean Theatre. VI: The Small Theatre.) *KTR.* 1986 Aug.; 123(8): 4-45. Illus.: Photo. B&W. 1: 18.5 cm. x 26 cm. Lang.: Kor.
Korea. 1950-1986. Histories-specific. ■Yesterday and today of the 'small theatre': Korea's 'Off Broadway' movement.

760 Kim, Woo-Ok. "Hanguk Yeonguk-ui Hyeonjuso. II: Yeonchulga.'' (The Present State of Korean Theatre. II: The Director.) *KTR.* 1986 Apr.; 119(4): 12-51. Illus.: Photo. B&W. 1: 18.5 cm. x 26 cm. Lang.: Kor.
Korea. 1986. Histories-sources. ■Includes interviews with several well-known directors.

761 Lee, Gun-Sam; Jeong, Jin-soo; Kim, Soo-nam; Lee, Sung-Gyu; Kim, Woo-Ok. "Hanguk Yeonguk-ui Hyeonjuso. I: Baewoo.'' (The Present State of Korean Theatre. I: The Actor.) *KTR.* 1986 Mar.; 118(3): 9-36. Illus.: Photo. B&W. 1: 18.5 cm. x 26 cm. Lang.: Kor.
Korea. 1986. Histories-sources. ■Includes interviews with famous actors.

762 Seo, Yeon-Ho; Lee, Chang-gu; Kim, Dong-gyu; Lee, Han-seop; Kim, Sung-gyu; Kim, Mun-Hong; Kim, Si-Ra; Song, Ae-Gyung; Kim, Yang-Hui; Kim, Un-Jeong; Yu, Hyeon-Ok; Han, Seong-ju. "Hanguk Yeongukim-ui Hyeonjuso. V: Jibang Yeongukin.'' (The Present State of Korean Theatre. V: The Theatre People.) *KTR.* 1986 July; 122(7): 12-54. Illus.: Photo. B&W. 1: 18.5 cm. Lang.: Kor.
Korea. 1986. Critical studies. ■Activities of theatre people outside Seoul.

763 Baycroft, Bernardo. "Brecht in Latin America: The Ideology and Aesthetics of the New Theater.'' *ComIBS.* 1986 Apr.; 15(2): 43-47.
Latin America. Critical studies. ■The New Theatre movement of Latin America combines the methodologies of collective creation with the Brechtian epic to create an original Latin American theatre.

764 Ščedraui, Ja. *Problemy režissury na sovremennoj livanskoj scene: Avtoref. diss. ... kand. iskusstvovedenija.* (Problems of Directing on the Contemporary Lebanese Stage: Synopsis of a Dissertation by a Candidate in Art Criticism.) Moscow: GITIS; 1986. 24 pp. Lang.: Rus.
Lebanon. 1980-1986. Critical studies.

765 Metz, Katalin. "Változatok a donquijotizmusra. Holland Fesztivál '86.'' (Variations on Donquijotism: Holland Festival '86.) *Sz.* 1986 Nov.; 19(11): 39-42. Illus.: Photo. B&W. 4: var. sizes. Lang.: Hun.
Netherlands: Amsterdam. 1986. Reviews of performances. ■Overview of the productions presented at the festival.

766 O'Farrell, Lawrence. "*Shut Up* and *Gather Before the Bride*—Examples of Divergent Trends in Theatre for Young Audiences in the Netherlands.'' *YTJ.* 1986 Fall; 1(2): 22-24. Illus.: Photo. B&W. 1: 3 in. x 6 in. Lang.: Eng.
Netherlands: Amsterdam. 1986. Reviews of performances. ■Productions by Optater and Wederzijds.

767 White, Helen C. "Women in the Theatre in Aotearoa.'' *Hecate.* 1986; 12(1-2): 158-165. Lang.: Eng.
New Zealand. 1980-1986. Critical studies. ■Growing impact of women and the emergence of the woman's perspective in New Zealand theatre as a revolution in that theatre, in relation to a similar growth of Maori involvement in theatre.

768 Rose, Mark V. *The Actor and his Double: Mime and Movement for the Theatre of Cruelty.* Chicago, IL: Actor Training Research Institute; 1986. xiv, 66 pp. Pref. Notes. Biblio. Append. Illus.: Photo. B&W. 11: var. sizes. Lang.: Eng.
North America. 1938-1986. Instructional materials. ■Antonin Artaud's concepts of gesture and movement: techniques include breathing, movement styles, effect of costumes and objects, use of media and exaggeration related to emotion.

769 Bonifert, Mária. "*Ez nem Broadway.* Beszélgetés Mario Delgado Vásquezzel, a perui Cuoatrotablas együttes vezetőjével.'' (*This Is Not Broadway*: Interview with Mario Delgado Vásquez, Leader of the Peruvian Cuatrotablas Ensemble.) *Sz.* 1986 May; 19(5): 40-42. Illus.: Photo. B&W. 1: 9 cm. x 18 cm. Lang.: Hun.
Peru: Lima. 1971-1985. Histories-sources. ■Discusses the ensemble's theatrical goals, style, artistic and political position. Defines Cuatrotablas as an 'educational centre for theatre' with a primarily pedagogical function.

770 Fremsin, Joanna. "Sanningen sägs på scenskolans fik.'' (The Truth Is Told at the Café of the Theatre School.) *NT.* 1986; 32: 38-39. Illus.: Photo. Lang.: Swe.
Poland: Warsaw. 1986. Histories-sources. ■Impressions of Warsaw's theatres and the training of Polish actors.

771 Késmárky, Nóra. "Bepillantás Jerzy Grotowski szinházi laboratóriumába.'' (A Look into the Theatre Laboratory of Jerzy Grotowski.) *SzSz.* 1986; 10(19): 149-178. Notes. Lang.: Hun.
Poland. 1959-1984. Critical studies. ■Analysis and review of Jerzy Grotowski's theatrical experiments, his method and productions.

772 Korzeniewski, Bohdan. "Wspomnienie o Zelwerowiczu.'' (On Zelwerowicz, A Recollection.) *PaT.* 1986 First Qtr; 1: 3-12. Illus.: Photo. B&W. 6: var. sizes. Lang.: Pol.
Poland. 1920-1986. Histories-sources. ■Director Bohdan Korzeniewski recalls Aleksander Zelwerowicz (1877-1955), an outstanding Polish actor, director and professor.

773 Osiński, Zbigniew; Vallee, Lillian, transl.; Findlay, Robert, transl. *Grotowski and His Laboratory.* New York, NY: PAJ; 1986. 185 pp. Illus.: Photo. Lang.: Eng.
Poland. 1933-1976. Biographies. ■Study of director Jerzy Grotowski and his work.

774 Wanat, Andrzej; Wojtkiewicz, Witold, illus. "Apoteoza Rewolucji i *Consilium Facultatis.*'' (Revolutionary Apotheosis and *Consilium Facultatis.*) *TeatrW.* 1983 Apr.; 38(759): 29-31. Illus.: Dwg. Print. B&W. 2: 25 cm. x 15 cm., 11 cm. x 18 cm. Lang.: Pol.
Poland. 1878-1914. Historical studies. ■Book review of *Zycie Teatralne Polskiego Proletariatu 1878-1914 (A Theatre Society of Polish Proletariats 1878-1914)* by Józef Kołowski.

775 Wierciński, Edmund; Chojnacka, Anna, ed. "Pamiętnik z pierwszego objazdu Reduty.'' (Memoirs from the First Tour of Reduta Theatre.) *PaT.* 1986 First Qtr; 1: 45-70. Pref. Notes. Illus.: Photo. B&W. 10: var. sizes. Lang.: Pol.
Poland. 1924. Historical studies. ■Recollections of actor and director Edmund Wierciński (1899-1955) of Reduta Theatre tour, the Reduta acting style and psychological and aesthetic aspects of outdoor performance.

776 Nánay, István. "Impressziók a portugál színházról.'' (Impressions of the Portuguese Theatre.) *Sz.* 1986 Apr.; 19(4): 38-42. Illus.: Photo. B&W. 3: 9 cm. x 12 cm., 12 cm. x 16 cm. Lang.: Hun.
Portugal. 1985. Critical studies. ■General survey of Portuguese theatrical life, including discussion of both large and small theatres.

777 Beare, William; De Nonno, Mario, transl. *I romani a teatro.* (The Roman Stage.) Bari: Editori Laterza; 1986. xxvi, 294 pp. (Biblioteca Universale Laterza 169.) Pref. Index. Notes. Biblio. Lang.: Ita.
Roman Republic: Rome. 100 B.C. Histories-general. ■Translation of *The Roman Stage* by William Beare.

778 Berlogea, Ileana; Sirabella, Mariabruna, transl. "Drammi giapponesi sulle scene rumene.'' (Japanese Plays on the Romanian Stage.) 267-278 in Ottai, Antonella, ed. *Teatro Oriente/Occidente.* Rome: Bulzoni; 1986. viii, 565 pp. (Biblioteca Teatrale 47.) Lang.: Ita.
Romania. Japan. 1900-1986. Historical studies. ■Plays from Japan performed in Romania.

THEATRE IN GENERAL: —Performance/production

779 Zaslavskaja, A. "O teatre, mino i okolo." (On Theatre Far and Near.) *TeatrM.* 1986; 3: 147-152. Lang.: Rus.
Romania: Bucharest. 1980. Reviews of performances. ■On performances at Romanian theaters: Teatrul Mic, Teatrul C.I. Nottara and Teatrul Lucia Sturdza Bulandra.

780 "Čackij v Tiflise: Iz istoriii Tiflisskogog russkogo teatra XIX veka." (Čackij in Tbilisi: From a History of the Tbilisi Russian Theatre of the Nineteenth Century.) *LitGruzia.* 1986 Jul.; 29(7): 207-221. Lang.: Rus.
Russia. 1845-1900. Historical studies. ■History of productions of A.S. Griboedov's *Gore ot uma (Wit Works Woe).*

781 Abroskina, I.I., comp.; Ivanova, M.S., comp.; Krylova, N.A., comp. *Michajl Čechov: Lit.nasledie v 2 t. T.1: Vospominanija, Pis'ma. T.2: Ob iskusstve aktera.* (Michajl Čechov: Literary Legacy in Two Volumes. Vol. 1: Reminiscences, Letters. Vol. 2: On the Actor's Art.) Moscow: Iskusstvo; 1986. 462 pp., 560 pp. Lang.: Rus.
Russia. USA. 1891-1955. Histories-sources. ■Literary legacy of Michajl A. Čechov.

782 Danilova, L., comp.; Al'tšuller, A.Ja., ed. *Vasilij Vasil'jevič Merkur'jev. Vospominanija: Stat'i.* (Vasilij Vasil'jevič Merkur'jev: Reminiscences, Articles.) Leningrad: LGIT-MiK; 1986. 200 pp. Lang.: Rus.
Russia: Leningrad. 1904-1978. Historical studies. ■Collection devoted to leading actor of Leningrad Puškin Drama Theatre.

783 Kinkul'kina, N. "Perekrestki sudeb: Vercharn i Moskva." (The Crossroads of Destiny: Vorhaeren and Moscow.) *Moskva.* 1986 ; 2: 180-182. Lang.: Rus.
Russia. Belgium. 1912-1914. Historical studies. ■Belgian poet and playwright Émile Verhaeren's visit to Russia's artistic and free theatres, productions of his plays.

784 Poljakova, E.I. *Sadovskije.* (The Sadovskijes.) Moscow: Iskusstvo; 1986. 344 pp. (Ser. Zizn'v Iskusstve.) Lang.: Rus.
Russia: Moscow. 1800-1917. Biographies. ■The life and activities of a family of Russian actors in the Malyj Theatre, reknowned for roles from the native repertoire, above all in plays by A.N. Ostrovskij.

785 Smeljanskij, A.M.; Efremov, O.H., intro. *Michajl Bulgakov v Ch'udožestvennom Teatre.* (Michajl Bulgakov in the Art Theatre.) Moscow: Iskusstvo; 1986. 383 pp. Lang.: Rus.
Russia: Moscow. 1891-1940. Historical studies. ■Playwright's ties with Moscow Art Theatre, production history of his plays *Dni Turbinych (Days of the Turbins), Beg (The Escape)* and *Moj'jer (Molière).*

786 Starikova, L.M. *Problema faktologičeskogo izučenija žizni i tvorčestva F.G. Volkova i russkogo teatra ego vremeni.* (The Problem of a Factual Study of the Life and Work of F.G. Volkov and the Russian Theatre of His Time.) Moscow: VNII iskusstvoznanija; 1986. 25 pp. [Synopsis of a Dissertation.] Lang.: Rus.
Russia. 1729-1763. Biographical studies. ■Life and work of first great Russian actor.

787 "The Government White Paper on the Creative Arts." *Scenaria.* 1986 July; 65: 20. Lang.: Eng.
South Africa, Republic of. 1986. Critical studies. ■A critical appraisal of the report of the commision of inquiry into the creative arts and the government's reaction to the report.

788 Moropa, C.K. "Art of Drama in 'Intsomi' Narration." *South African Journal of African Languages.* 1986(2): 91-93. Biblio. Lang.: Eng.
South Africa, Republic of. 1800-1985. Critical studies. ■The way in which the storyteller (*intsomi*) in Xhosa traditional performance uses dramatic techniques.

789 Lecoq, Jacques; Tanaka, Min; Angiolillo, Mary; González Vilar, José Manuel; de Marinis, Marco. "Les formes dramàtiques no verbals. Internacionalització o decodificació." (Non-Verbal Dramatic Forms. Internationalization or Codification.) 87-186 in Coca, Jordi, ed.; Conesa, Laura, comp. *Congrés Internacional de Teatre a Catalunya 1985. Actes. Volum II. Seccions 1, 2 i 3.* Barcelona: Institut del Teatre; 1986. 340 pp. Notes. Biblio. Lang.: Eng, Fre, Spa.

Spain. 1985. Critical studies. ■Reports and discussions of Section II, International Congress on Theatre in Catalonia, focusing on nonverbal communication.

790 Mason, Susan. "The San Francisco Mime Troupe's *Spain/36.*" *ThM.* 1986 Fall/Win; 18(1): 94-97. Illus.: Photo. Print. B&W. 1: 5 in. x 7 in. Lang.: Eng.
Spain. USA: San Francisco, CA. 1936-1986. Reviews of performances. ■San Francisco Mime Troupe's 1986 show based on the Spanish Civil War.

791 García Giménez, Arturo, ed. *Resum de la temporada teatral a Barcelona 1985-1986.* (Summary of the Theatrical Season in Barcelona 1985-1986.) Barcelona: Institut del Teatre; 1986. 20 pp. Tables. Illus.: Photo. Print. B&W. 12: var. sizes. Lang.: Cat.
Spain-Catalonia: Barcelona. 1985-1986. Reviews of performances. ■Collection of newspaper articles on the theatre season, including information on 143 productions, both professional and semi-professional.

792 Romeu i Figueras, Josep. "El Teatre Assumpcionista de Tècnica medieval als Països Catalans." (Medieval Style Assumption Plays in Catalan Countries.) 207-213 in Salvat, Ricard, ed. *El Teatre durant l'Edat Mitjana i el Renaixement.* Barcelona: Publicacions i Edicions de la Universitat de Barcelona; 1986. xxviii, 322 pp. (El Pla de les Comèdies 2.) [Presented at First International Symposium on Medieval and Renaissance Theatre, Sitges, 1983.] Lang.: Cat.
Spain-Catalonia. 1000-1709. Historical studies. ■Christian tradition relating to the Assumption of the Virgin Mary reflected in three medieval plays on the subject in Catalan.

793 Siljunas, B. "Lir i drugie." (Lear and Others.) *TeatrM.* 1986; 5: 174-181. Lang.: Rus.
Spain-Catalonia: Barcelona. 1985. Histories-sources. ■Report on International Theatre Congress.

794 "Additionen, teaterfoton." (The Addition, Photographs of Performances.) *NT.* 1986; 35: 57-64, 67. Illus.: Photo. Lang.: Swe.
Sweden. 1985-1986. Historical studies. ■Seven photographers choose and comment on their photographs of theatrical performances.

795 Berlin, Ulla. "En vecka som manar till efterföljd." (A Week That Invites Imitation.) *Teaterf.* 1986; 19(2-3): 20-21. Illus.: Photo. Lang.: Swe.
Sweden: Trelleborg. 1986. Historical studies. ■During a week in April 400 pupils performed for all their school fellows at Trelleborg, under the slogan 'Without Pretensions'.

796 Bramsjö, Henrik, ed. "På spaning efter en tid." (On the Search For a Time.) *NT.* 1986; 34: 36-39. Illus.: Photo. Lang.: Swe.
Sweden. 1980-1986. Historical studies. ■Directors Maud Backéus, Stefan Johansson, Annika Silkeberg and Lena Stefenson and dramaturg Claes-Peter Hellwig look for what is typical of the 1980s.

797 Fagerström, Henrik. "350 aktörer i *Kung Ubu.*" (350 Actors in *Ubu roi.*) *Teaterf.* 1986; 19(1): 10. Illus.: Photo. Lang.: Swe.
Sweden: Kristianstad. 1986. Historical studies. ■How Kristianstad's Musikteater produced *Ubu roi,* which engaged 350 amateurs, schoolchildren and some professionals, with of music by Björn Larsson (which will be for sale as a record), all within a budget of 500,000 Swedish kroner.

798 Forser, Tomas; Florin, Magnus; Janzon, Leif; Samuelsson, Björn; Hägglund, Kent; Öhrn, K. Anders; Holmberg, Henric; Lysell, Roland; Ludawska, Janina; Weyler, Svante; Gredeby, Nils; Kindstrand, Gunilla; Enckell, Johanna; Harlén, Carl; Backéus, Maud; Sjögren, Frederik; Narti, Ana Maria; Johansson, Stefan; Smeds, Barbro. "Drabbad på teatern." (Affected by the Theatre.) *NT.* 1986; 33: 39-45. Lang.: Swe.
Sweden. 1986. Reviews of performances. ■19 critics, directors and dramaturgs tell which of the season's performances affected them most.

799 Hoogland, Rikard. "Det visade sig att vi hade gjort något nytt." (It Turned Out That We Had Created Something

CLASSED ENTRIES
CLASSED ENTRIES

THEATRE IN GENERAL: —Performance/production

New.) *Teaterf.* 1986; 19(2-3): 28-29. Illus.: Dwg. Lang.: Swe.
Sweden: Vänersborg. 1982-1986. Historical studies. ■Ändockgruppen has staged *De dövas historia (The Story of the Deaf)* with hearing and deaf amateurs, and developed a new language of theatre.

800 Ibom, Hans-Ola. "Allt behöver inte vara perfekt." (Everything Doesn't Have to Be Perfect.) *Teaterf.* 1986; 19(2-3): 17. Illus.: Photo. Lang.: Swe.
Sweden: Sandviken. 1986. Historical studies. ■Report from an amateur theatre festival at Västerbergs Folkhögskola.

801 Samuelsson, Björn. "Ett strävsamt gäng." (A Strenuous Gang.) *Teaterf.* 1986; 19(5): 12-13. Lang.: Swe.
Sweden: Stockholm. 1979-1986. Historical studies. ■The staging of Mats Ödeen's *Det enda raka (The Only Straight Thing)* by TURteaterns amatörteatergrupp, directed by Elisabeth Frick.

802 Sander, Anki. "Varför spelar man amatörteater?" (Why Do You Play Amateur Theatre?)*Teaterf.* 1986; 19(4): 11-12. Lang.: Swe.
Sweden: Malmö. 1985-1986. Historical studies. ■Interview with judge Bo Severin, who has never acted on stage, and now has begun at Studioteatern as an amateur.

803 Sanders, Anki. "Den funkar inte på bebisar." (It Won't Work on Babies.) *Teaterf.* 1986; 19(2-3): 14-16. Illus.: Photo. Lang.: Swe.
Sweden: Västerås. 1986. Historical studies. ■Report from the sixth annual festival of amateur theatre.

804 Appia, Adolphe; Bablet, Denis, intro. *Oeuvres Complètes.* (Complete Works.) Lausanne: L'Age d'Homme; 1986. 493 pp. Pref. Notes. Tables. Biblio. Illus.: Photo. B&W. [Vol. 2.] Lang.: Fre, Ger.
Switzerland. 1895-1905. Critical studies. ■Annotated edition of Appia's theoretical works and stage designs, with commentary.

805 Dukore, Bernard F. "Newer Peter Barnes, With Links to Past." *ET.* 1986 Nov.; 15(1): 47-59. Notes. Lang.: Eng.
UK-England. 1981-1986. Critical studies. ■Production analysis of four plays by Peter Barnes: *Not as Bad as They Seem, Somersaults, The Real Long John Silver,* and *It's Cold, Wanderer, It's Cold.*

806 Dymkowski, Christine. *Harley Granville Barker: A Preface to Modern Shakespeare.* Washington, DC/London: Folger Shakespeare Library/Associated Univ. Presses; 1986. 240 pp. Index. Biblio. Lang.: Eng.
UK-England. 1912-1940. Critical studies. ■Discussion of Granville-Barker's innovative Shakespeare stagings at the Savoy Theatre (1912-1914) and his influence on John Gielgud's *King Lear* (1940).

807 Granville-Barker, Harley; Salmon, Eric, ed. *Granville Barker and His Correspondents: A Selection of Letters by Him and to Him.* Detroit, MI: Wayne State UP; 1986. 602 pp. Notes. Index. Append. Illus.: Photo. Lang.: Eng.
UK-England. 1877-1946. Histories-sources. ■Includes letters to and from John Gielgud, George Bernard Shaw and T.E. Lawrence.

808 Hobson, Harold. "The Goodness of Guinness." *Drama.* 1986; 159: 5. Illus.: Photo. B&W. 1. Lang.: Eng.
UK-England. 1933-1984. Biographical studies. ■Appreciation of actor Alec Guinness, emphasizing the importance of religion in his life.

809 Jacob, W.L. "Amateur Theatricals at Sir Percy Shelley's Theatre, Boscombe Manor." *TN.* 1985; 39(1): 13-18. Biblio. Lang.: Eng.
UK-England: London. 1876. Historical studies. ■The development and production of Sir Percy Shelley's amateur production of *The Doom of St. Querec,* adapted by Herbert Gardner from the novel by Sir Francis Burnand and Arthur à Becket.

810 Kaplan, Joel H. "The False Dawn of 1883: London's Operatic and Dramatic Fare in an Unremarkable Year." *THSt.* 1986; 6: 1-21. Notes. Illus.: Photo. Sketches. Print. B&W. 6: var. sizes. Lang.: Eng.
UK-England: London. 1883. Historical studies. ■Dramatic and operatic performances in the London season of 1883. Season reflects progress and improvement in both domestic and political life in England and demands for a new operatic repertory and a national drama. Related to Music-Drama: Opera.

811 Langton, Robert Gore. "Gentleman's Relish." *PlPl.* 1986 Sep.; 396: 8-9. B&W. 3: var. sizes. Lang.: Eng.
UK-England: London. 1936-1986. Histories-sources. ■Interview with John Mills on his acting career.

812 Langton, Robert Gore. "Kick for Coriolanus." *PlPl.* 1986 Sep.; 396: 18-19. B&W. 2. Lang.: Eng.
UK-England: London. 1985-1986. Histories-sources. ■Director Deborah Warner of KICK on her production of Shakespeare's *Coriolanus* and limited public funding for the non-touring company.

813 Petrova, O.G. *Osobennosti formirovanija režissury v anglijskom teatre vtoroj poloviny XIX veka: Avtoref. dis. ... kand. iskusstvovedenija.* (The Particulars of the Training of Directors in the English Theatre of the Second Half of the Nineteenth Century: Synopsis of a Dissertation by a Candidate in Art Criticism.) Moscow: GITIS; 1986. 19 pp. Lang.: Rus.
UK-England. 1850-1900. Historical studies.

814 Rea, Kenneth; Fox, John. "Welfare State Goes to Africa." *Drama.* 1986; 160(2): 18-20. Illus.: Photo. B&W. 4. Lang.: Eng.
UK-England. Tanzania. 1970-1986. Historical studies. ■History of alternative theatre group, including recent work with Tanzanian performers. Related to Mixed Entertainment.

815 Reinelt, Janelle. "Beyond Brecht: Britain's New Feminist Drama." *TJ.* 1986 May; 38(2): 154-163. Notes. Lang.: Eng.
UK-England. 1956-1979. Critical studies. ■Analysis of use of Brechtian technique in contemporary feminist drama, particularly notions of past and present.

816 Rissik, Andrew. "Favouring Curry." *Drama.* 1986; 160(2): 7-8. Illus.: Photo. B&W. 4. Lang.: Eng.
UK-England. 1968-1986. Critical studies. ■Analysis of flamboyant acting style of Tim Curry.

817 Senter, Al. "Life and Death in Covent Garden." *PI.* 1986 Feb.; 1(7): 16-17. Illus.: Photo. Print. B&W. 2. Lang.: Eng.
UK-England: London. 1633-1986. Biographical studies. ■A survey of the actors' church, St. Paul's, Covent Garden, where there are memorials to many actors.

818 Timaševa, M.A. "Nezavisimyi teat'r D. Greina." (J.T. Grein's Independent Theatre.) 117-124 in *Tradicii i novaterstvo v zarubežnom teatre.* Leningrad: Leningr. in-t teatre, muzyki i kinematografii; Lang.: Rus.
UK-England: London. 1891. Historical studies. ■The Independent Theatre of Jacob Thomas Grein, established in imitation of André Antoine's Théâtre Libre.

819 Bjelkendahl, Göran. "I Edinburgh kan man mötas." (You Can Meet in Edinburgh.) *Teaterf.* 1986; 19(5): 8-11. Illus.: Photo. Lang.: Swe.
UK-Scotland: Edinburgh. 1986. Historical studies. ■A report from Edinburgh International Fringe Festival, including information on how to join the Festival, National Youth Music Theatre.

820 Alpert, Hollis. *Burton.* New York: Putnam; 1986. 268 pp. Lang.: Eng.
UK-Wales. 1925-1984. Biographies. ■A biography of Richard Burton, focusing on *Camelot,* his relationship with Elizabeth Taylor, the film *Who's Afraid of Virginia Woolf* and his drinking problem. Related to Media: Film.

821 "In Memoriam, Alan Schneider: 1917-1984." *AmTh.* 1984 July/Aug.; 1(4): 26-27, 41. Illus.: Photo. B&W. 2. Lang.: Eng.
USA: New York, NY. 1984. Histories-sources. ■Excerpts from memorial service held in honor of director Alan Schneider at Circle in the Square.

822 Aaron, Stephen. *Stage Fright: Its Role in Acting.* Chicago, IL: U of Chicago P; 1986. 172 pp. Lang.: Eng.
USA. 1986. Technical studies. ■The author, a clinical psychologist and director, analyzes the psychological elements that routinely produce stress in actors.

823 Bahr, Gisela; Wheeler, Ulrike, transl. "Interview with Walfriede Schmitt." *ComIBS.* 1986 Nov.; 16(1): 14-17.

THEATRE IN GENERAL: —Performance/production

USA. 1986. Histories-sources. ■Actress Walfriede Schmitt, artist-in-residence at Miami University, discusses her training, playing Brecht and her performance in the university's production of *The Good Person of Szechwan.*

824 Beck, Julian; Ruffini, Franco, ed. "Il Living Theatre." (The Living Theatre.) *QT.* 1986 Aug.; 9(33): 1-100. Pref. Index. Tables. Biblio. Illus.: Photo. B&W. 20: var. sizes. Lang.: Ita.
USA. Europe. 1960-1985. Histories-specific. ■Includes previously unpublished extracts from the writings of Julian Beck, an account of the Living Theatre's activity 1975-1985 and a bibliography of works in Italian.

825 Bruder, Melissa. *A Practical Handbook for the Actor.* New York, NY: Vintage Books; 1986. 94 pp. Biblio. Lang.: Eng.
USA. 1986. Instructional materials. ■Brief analysis of the acting process: physical action as the essential task of the actor.

826 Collier, Richard. *Make-Believe: The Magic World of International Theatre.* New York, NY: Dodd; 1986. 255 pp. Biblio. Lang.: Eng.
USA. England. 1800-1986. Histories-specific. ■A history of the British and American stage, including anecdotes about actors, directors, playwrights, producers and designers.

827 Cypkin, Diane. *Second Avenue: The Yiddish Broadway.* New York, NY: New York Univ; 1986. 584 pp. Pref. Notes. Biblio. [Ph.D. dissertation, Univ. Microfilms order No. DA8626859.] Lang.: Eng.
USA: New York, NY. 1900-1939. Historical studies. ■History of Yiddish theatre district, including history of the theatre, related businesses and puppet theatre, vaudeville and night club entertainment.

828 Daniel, Walter C. *'De Lawd': Richard B. Harrison and* The Green Pastures. Westport, CT: Greenwood; 1986. 180 pp. (Contributions in Afro-American and African Studies 99.) Index. Biblio. Lang.: Eng.
USA. 1930-1939. Biographical studies. ■Life of the actor whose career in professional theatre began at age 65 in Marc Connelly's all-black play *The Green Pastures.* Includes a detailed analysis of the play and its reflection of race relations.

829 Eder, Richard. "The World According to Brook." *AmTh.* 1984 May; 1(2): 4-9, 38. Illus.: Photo. B&W. 4: var. sizes. Lang.: Eng.
USA: New York, NY. 1948-1984. Historical studies. ■Development of director Peter Brook's technique, his collaboration with actors and audience, focusing on his most recent work *Tragedy of Carmen.*

830 Ellis, Roger. *An Audition Handbook for Student Actors.* Chicago, IL: Nelson-Hall; 1986. 234 pp. Index. Biblio. Lang.: Eng.
USA. 1986. Instructional materials. ■Selection of materials, preparation, rehearsal and auditioning techniques for dramatic and musical theatre. Includes numerous quotations from professional actors. Related to Music-Drama: Musical theatre.

831 Feinsod, Arthur Bennett. *The Origins of Minimalist Mise-en-scene in the U.S.* New York, NY: New York Univ; 1986. 419 pp. Pref. Notes. Biblio. [Ph.D. dissertation, Univ. Microfilms order No. DA8614502.] Lang.: Eng.
USA. 1912-1922. Historical studies. ■Study of the origins of the radically simplified stage.

832 Fichandler, Zelda. "The Essential Actor." *AmTh.* 1986 Mar.; 2(11): 16-17, 41. Illus.: Photo. Print. B&W. 2: 2 in. x 4 in. Lang.: Eng.
USA: Washington, DC. 1951-1986. Histories-sources. ■Founder and artistic director of Arena Stage discusses the place of the actor in contemporary theatre life.

833 Földes, Anna. "Nemzetek Szinháza, 1986. Baltimore-i tudósitás." (Theatre of Nations 1986: A Report from Baltimore.) *Sz.* 1986 Nov.; 19(11): 30-38. Illus.: Photo. B&W. 7: var. sizes. Lang.: Hun.
USA: Baltimore, MD. 1986. Critical studies. ■Survey of the program of Theatre of Nations Festival held in the USA for the first time.

834 Henderson, Mary C. *Theater in America.* New York, NY: Harry N. Abrams; 1986. 327 pp. Pref. Biblio. Index. Append. Illus.: Photo. Pntg. Dwg. Poster. Print. Color.

B&W. Grd.Plan. Blprnt. 373: var. sizes. [200 Years of Plays, Players, and Productions.] Lang.: Eng.
USA. 1750-1985. Histories-general. ■American theatre history, examining trends in playwriting, acting, audience reaction, technology and playhouse design. Includes an extensive bibliography.

835 Henry, Marilyn; Rogers, Lynne. *How to Be a Working Actor: An Insider's Guide to Finding Jobs in Theatre, Film, and Television.* New York, NY: M. Evans; 1986. 302 pp.. Biblio. Append. Illus.: Photo. Print. B&W. 8: var. sizes. Lang.: Eng.
USA. 1986. Instructional materials. ■Includes counseling on agents, unions, contracts, script analysis, audition technique and the varied demands of stage, television, film and soap opera acting. Related to Media.

836 Jenkins, Linda Walsh; Ogden-Malouf, Susan. "The (Female) Actor Prepares." *ThM.* 1985 Win; 17(1): 66-69. Illus.: Photo. B&W. 1. Lang.: Eng.
USA. 1985. Histories-sources. ■Interviews with female theatre professionals assessing the importance of gender roles to the actor's preparation. Includes feminist strategies in contemporary production.

837 Leiter, Samuel L. *Ten Seasons: New York Theatre in the Seventies.* New York, NY/Westport, CT/London: Greenwood P; 1986. xii, 245 pp. Pref. Notes. Index. Tables. [New York Theatre in the Seventies.] Lang.: Eng.
USA: New York, NY. 1970-1980. Histories-specific. ■Comprehensive survey of ten years of theatre in New York City, including Broadway, Off and Off-off Broadway plays, playwrights, musicals, revues, revivals, audience composition, actors, critics and theatre buildings.

838 Leverett, James. "You Have to Be There: Notes on Robert Wilson." *AmTh.* 1984 Nov.; 1(7): 26-27. Illus.: Photo. B&W. 1. Lang.: Eng.
USA. Germany, East. 1984. Histories-sources. ■The work of Robert Wilson, and speculation on the fate of his *CIVIL warS* after its cancellation in Los Angeles.

839 Levine, Mindy N. "Commercialism and Self-Censorship in the American Theatre." *TT.* 1982; 1(3): 3, 8. Lang.: Eng.
USA: New York, NY. 1982. Histories-sources. ■Interview with Ellen Rudolph of Alliance of Resident Theatres/New York discussing her observations of foreign artists on a cultural exchange tour of the US and the artists' observations of American production values, technical prowess and brief rehearsal schedules.

840 Levine, Mindy N. "Impressions of German Theatre Today: A Conversation with Harvey Seifter." *TT.* 1984 Apr.; 3(6): 3, 11. Illus.: Photo. B&W. 1. Lang.: Eng.
USA: New York, NY. Germany, West. 1984. Histories-sources. ■Interview with Harvey Seifter, development director of Theatre for the New City, discussing performance spaces, funding and artistic direction in contemporary Germany.

841 London, Todd. "Off Broadway on TV." *TT.* 1986 Nov.; 6(1): 3-5. Illus.: Photo. Print. B&W. 4: var. sizes. Lang.: Eng.
USA: New York, NY. 1980-1986. Critical studies. ■Off Broadway companies have not gained financially or artistically from adaptations and transference of plays from stage to television. Contracts, negotiations and aspects of production are discussed. Related to Media: Video forms.

842 Lundriyan, Paul J. *Ensemble: The Group Approach to Performing.* Carbondale, IL: Southern Illinois Univ; 1986. 309 pp. Pref. Notes. Biblio. [Ph.D. dissertation, Univ. Microfilms order No. DA8622996.] Lang.: Eng.
USA. Historical studies. ■Examines gradual changes in ensemble theatre practice from emphasis on aesthetic qualities to interrelational qualities.

843 Marowitz, Charles. *Prospero's Staff: Acting and Directing in the Contemporary Theatre.* Bloomington, IN: Indiana UP; 1986. 194 pp. Lang.: Eng.
USA. 1965-1985. Critical studies. ■Director's analysis of his role in avant-garde theatre. Includes interviews with Robert Lewis and Glenda Jackson.

CLASSED ENTRIES

844 Marowitz, Charles. "Discovering 'The Life of Our Times'." *AmTh.* 1986 Apr.; 3(1): 11-17, 48. Illus.: Photo. Print. B&W. 3: 6 in. x 16 in., 6 in. x 6 in., 3 in. x 4 in. Lang.: Eng.
USA: New York, NY. 1930-1986. Histories-sources. ▪Robert Lewis discusses the influence of 'the method' on contemporary acting technique.

845 Munk, Erika. "The Rite of Women." *PerAJ.* 1986; 10(2): 35-42. Illus.: Photo. Print. B&W. 5: var. sizes. Lang.: Eng.
USA. Denmark. 1985. Histories-sources. ▪Critique of International School of Theatre Anthropology (ISTA) conference on female roles as anti-feminist.

846 Myers, Norman J. "Josephine Clifton: 'Manufactured' Star." *THSt.* 1986; 6: 109-123. Notes. Illus.: Dwg. Print. B&W. 4: 6.5 in. x 4.5 in. Lang.: Eng.
USA. 1813-1847. Biographical studies. ▪An account and assessment of the career of Josephine Clifton.

847 Nightingale, Benedict. *Fifth Row Center: A Critic's Year On and Off Broadway.* New York, NY: Times Bks; 1986. 308 pp. Lang.: Eng.
USA: New York, NY. 1983-1984. Reviews of performances.

848 Pearson-Davis, Susan. "Working with Deaf and Hearing Actors in the Same Cast—Even If You Don't Know Sign Language." *YTJ.* 1986 Sum; 1(1): 15-19, 81. Biblio. Lang.: Eng.
USA. 1984-1986. Instructional materials. ▪Guidelines for working with deaf actors and sign interpreters.

849 Savran, David. *The Wooster Group, 1975-1985: Breaking the Rules.* Ann Arbor, MI: UMI Research P; 1986. 238 pp. (Theatre and dramatic studies 39.) Index. Notes. Biblio. Illus.: Photo. Dwg. Lang.: Eng.
USA: New York, NY. 1975-1985. Histories-specific. ▪Importance of the Wooster Group in recent experimental theatre.

850 Savran, David. "Terrorists of the Text." *AmTh.* 1986 Dec.; 3(9): 19-24, 45. Illus.: Photo. 5: 3 in. x 5 in., 8.5 in. x 11 in. Lang.: Eng.
USA: New York, NY. 1975-1986. Critical studies. ▪The Wooster Group mounts a retrospective of original works.

851 Shewey, Don. "A Boot in Two Camps." *AmTh.* 1986 Oct.; 3(7): 12-17. Print. B&W. 6: 2 in. x 3 in., 10 in. x 12 in. Lang.: Eng.
USA: San Francisco, CA, New York, NY, La Jolla, CA. 1976-1986. Histories-sources. ▪Robert Woodruff, an established practitioner of American realism, turns to greater theatricality in staging.

852 Spector, Susan. "Margaret Webster's *Othello*: The Principal Players Versus the Director." *THSt.* 1986; 6: 93-108. Notes. Illus.: Photo. Print. B&W. 3: 5.5 in. x 4.5 in. Lang.: Eng.
USA: New York, NY. 1942-1944. Historical studies. ▪History of the Margaret Webster-Paul Robeson production of *Othello*.

853 Sweet, Jeffrey. "From Second City to New York City." *TT.* 1984 Aug.; 3(8): 3-4. Notes. Illus.: Photo. B&W. 3: var. sizes. Lang.: Eng.
USA: New York, NY, Chicago, IL. 1984. Critical studies. ▪Current trend of productions moving from Chicago to New York, observations on Chicago theatre scene and its differences from New York.

854 Watermeier, Daniel, J. "Edwin Booth's Iago." *THSt.* 1986; 6: 32-55. Notes. Illus.: Pntg. Dwg. Photo. Print. B&W. 7: 6.5 in. x 4.5 in. Lang.: Eng.
USA. 1852-1890. Historical studies. ▪History and reconstruction of Edwin Booth's performance of Iago in Shakespeare's *Othello*.

855 White, David. "The International Marketplace." *TT.* 1984 Aug.; 3(8): 1-2, 11-12. Notes. Illus.: Photo. B&W. 1. Lang.: Eng.
USA: New York, NY. 1984. Critical studies. ▪Attraction of performing in Europe for American experimental artists. Financial and artistic opportunities examined. Includes list of international service organizations.

856 Wilk, John R.; Edmondson, Belinda, ed. *The Creation of an Ensemble: The First Years of The American Conservatory Theatre.* Carbondale/Edwardsville: Southern Illinois Univ; 1986. xiii, 214 pp. Pref. Notes. Biblio. Index. Append. Illus.: Photo. Print. B&W. 35: var. sizes. Lang.: Eng.
USA. Europe. 1950-1972. Historical studies. ▪History of the American Conservatory Theatre, including its philosophy, development, training methods and backing by Ford Foundation.

857 *Teat'r im. Kamala: očerk istorii.* (The Kamal Theatre: Sketch of a History.) Kazan': Tatarskoje knižnoje izdatelstvo; 1986. 327 pp. Lang.: Rus.
USSR: Kazan. 1906-1985. Histories-specific. ▪Description of the major activities of the Tatar State Academic Theatre, known as the Kamal Theatre.

858 "Naš sovremennik—teatr." (Our Contemporary, the Theatre.) *TeatrM.* 1986; 2: 71-79. Lang.: Rus.
USSR. 1980-1986. Histories-sources. ▪Summary of discussion at a round table on problems of contemporary theatre.

859 "Cem živ akter?" (What Makes an Actor Tick?) *TeatZ.* 1986; 29(9): 24-25. Lang.: Rus.
USSR. 1986. Histories-sources. ▪Interview with critic T. Zabozlaeva and actress G. Karelina on acting.

860 "V poiskah radosti." (In Search of Happiness.) *TeatZ.* 1986; 29(19): 2-5. Lang.: Rus.
USSR: Moscow. 1960-1986. Histories-sources. ▪Similarities and differences at the turning point in Soviet theatre of the 1960s and 1980s are examined at a round table discussion by E. Surkov, I. Krymova and others.

861 "V zerkale tvorčestva: Vl. Vysockij kak javlenije kultury." (In the Mirror of Creative Work: Vladimir Vysockij as a Cultural Phenomenon.) *VFil.* 1986; 7: 112-124. Lang.: Rus.
USSR. 1938-1980. Biographical studies. ▪Social significance of Vysockij's work as actor, poet and singer.

862 "Ot nadežd do real'nych sveršenij." (From Hopes to Real Achievements.) *UTeatr.* 1986; 3: 2-4. Lang.: Rus.
USSR. 1970-1986. Critical studies. ▪On developments in the theatres of the Ukraine.

863 Andreev, A.V. "Sovetsko-amerikanskie kul'turnye i naučnye svjazi." (Soviet-American Cultural and Scientific Ties.) *USA—Ekonomika, politika, ideologija.* 1986(10): 14-24. Lang.: Rus.
USSR. USA. 1960-1986. Historical studies. ▪Includes material on theatrical relations.

864 Anninskij, L. "Iskrjaščie kremni." (Sparking Flints.) *TeatrM.* 1986; 9: 30-39. Lang.: Rus.
USSR: Moscow. 1980-1986. Historical studies. ▪Working life of theatrical collective Teat'r-studija na Jugo-Zapade.

865 Banionis, D. "Samaja glavnaja rol'." (The Most Important Role.) *Kommunist.* 1986; 10: 91-96. Lang.: Rus.
USSR. 1980-1986. Critical studies. ▪Social role of the actor.

866 Bogdanov, I.A. *Plastičnost' aktera estrady i osnovnye sposoby ee formirovanija v vysšej škole: Avtoref. diss... kand. iskusstvovedenija.* (Plasticity of the Stage Actor—Basic Methods of University Training: Synopsis of a Dissertation by a Candidate in Art Criticism.) Leningrad: LGITMIK; 1986. 22 pp. Lang.: Rus.
USSR. Critical studies.

867 Carev, M. "Na poroge peremen." (On the Threshold of Change.) *TeatZ.* 1986; 29(2): 9-10. Lang.: Rus.
USSR. 1980-1986. Critical studies. ▪On the problems of professionalism and training of young actors.

868 Davydov, V.G. *Elementy teatral'noj vyrazitel'nosti. Opyt sistemnogo analiza: Avtoref. diss... kand. iskusstvovedenija.* (Elements of Theatrical Expression—An Attempt at Systematic Analysis: Synopsis of a Dissertation by a Candidate in Art Criticism.) Moscow: VNII Iskusstvosnanija; 1986. 26 pp. Lang.: Rus.
USSR. 1986. Critical studies.

869 Demidov, A. "Čto i kak nazyvat'." (What and How to Name.) *TeatZ.* 1986; 29(2): 18-20. Lang.: Rus.

CLASSED ENTRIES

THEATRE IN GENERAL: —Performance/production

USSR. 1980-1986. Critical studies. ■Problems of experimental theatre.

870 Dodin, L. "Začem režisseru 'kompanija'?" (What Does a Director Need a 'Company' For?)*TeatZ.* 1986; 29(18): 19-20 . Lang.: Rus.
USSR. 1986. Critical studies. ■Discussion of director's role in a theatrical company.

871 Efros, Anatolij. "Voprosy...voprosy." (Questions, Questions.) *VFil.* 1986; 10: 128-131. Lang.: Rus.
USSR. 1980-1986. Histories-sources. ■Director discusses realism and convention in contemporary theatre, audience and perception.

872 El'kis, G. Ya. *O plastičeskom trenaže aktera: Iz opyta pedagoga.* (On the Plastic Training of the Actor: From the Experience of the Teacher.) Kiev: Mistecvo; 1986. 115 pp. Lang.: Rus.
USSR. 1986. Histories-sources. ■On the physical training of actors.

873 Gasan-Gusejnov, M. "Pora zrelosti." (A Season for Maturity.) *TeatZ.* 1986; 29(2): 22-23. Lang.: Rus.
USSR. 1935-1985. Historical studies. ■Overview of Avarskij Musykal'no-Dramatičeskij Teat'r im. G. Cadasy on its jubilee.

874 Gladyševa, A. "Sceničeskoje slovo i professionalizm aktera." (The Stage Word and Professionalism of the Actor.) *UTeatr.* 1986; 2: 13-15. Lang.: Ukr.
USSR. 1986. Critical studies. ■Actor professionalism and the spoken word.

875 Golubovskij, B.G. *Plastika v iskusstve aktera.* (Plasticity of the Actor's Art.) Moscow: Iskusstvo; 1986. 189 pp. Lang.: Rus.
USSR. 1980-1986. Critical studies. ■Plastic aspects of the actor's appearance on stage.

876 Grinšpun, I.A. *O druz'jach moich i učiteljach.* (About My Friends and Teachers.) Kiev: Mistecvo; 1986. 167 pp. Lang.: Rus.
USSR. 1930-1986. Histories-sources. ■Soviet director's recollection of famous actors, directors and playwrights.

877 Gul'čenko, V. "Oni i my." (Them and Us.) *TeatrM.* 1986; 7: 57-73. Lang.: Rus.
USSR: Moscow. 1980-1986. Reviews of performances. ■Discusses performances of adolescents on the Moscow stage.

878 Gulčenko, V. "'Prošlogodnij cvet'." ('Last Year's Bloom'.) *TeatrM.* 1986; 2: 85-101. Lang.: Rus.
USSR: Moscow. 1985. Reviews of performances. ■Russian and Soviet classics produced during the 1985 season.

879 Gurbanidze, N. "Svet i teni Gruzinskogo teatra." (Light and Shadows of the Georgian Theatre.) *Kommunist Grusii.* 1986; 5 : 48-53. Lang.: Rus.
USSR. 1980-1986. Critical studies. ■Social role of Georgian theatre today.

880 Ivanova, V.V., ed. *Akter. Personaž. Rol'. Obraz: (Sbornik naučnych trudov).* (Actor, Character, Role, Image: A Collection of Scientific Articles.) Leningrad: LGITMIK; 1986. 168. Lang.: Rus.
USSR. 1960-1980. Historical studies. ■Development of a system of stage appearance, based on materials from productions.

881 Jaškin, V.K. *Teatral'nost i teatralizacija v iskusstve sovetskoj estrady: Avtoref. diss. ... kand. iskusstvovedenija.* (Theatricality and Dramatization in the Art of the Soviet Stage: Synopsis of a Dissertation by a Candidate in Art Criticism.) Moscow: VNII Iskusstvoznanija; 1986. 21 pp. Lang.: Rus.
USSR. 1980-1986. Critical studies.

882 Jermakova, N. "I snova ob uslovijach uspecha: polemičeskije zametki kritika." (Once More on the Conditions of Success: Polemical Notes of a Critic.) *UTeatr.* 1986; 4: 7-9. Lang.: Ukr.
USSR. 1980-1986. Critical studies. ■Discusses issues of acting and directing using Ukrainian productions as examples.

883 Jermolin, J.A. *Žanr melodramy v sovremennych zreliščnych iskusstvah: Avtoref. dis... kand. iskusstvovedenija.* (Genre of Melodrama in Contemporary Performing Arts: Synopsis of a Dissertation by a Candidate in Art Criticism.) Moscow: VNII Iskusstvosnanija; 1986. 22 pp. Lang.: Rus.
USSR. 1980-1986. Critical studies.

884 Kaufmann, S.S., ed.; Ščedrovickaja, M.V., ed.; Zachava, N.I., ed.; Tolčanov, I.M., intro. *Pervaja Turandot: kniga o žizni i tvorcestve narodnoj artistki SSSR C.L. Mansurovoi.* (The First Turandot: The Life and Work of Folk Artist C.L. Mansurova.) Moscow: VTO; 1986. 406 pp. Lang.: Rus.
USSR. 1920-1986. Biographical studies. ■Articles, reminiscences and documents relating to actress C.L. Mansurova and her relations with Je. B. Vachtangov and the Vachtangov Theatre.

885 Kiknadze, V. "Žizn' Sandro Achmeteli: K 100-letiju režissera." (The Life of Sandro Achmeteli: For the One Hundredth Anniversary of the Director's Birth.) *SovCh.* 1986; 1: 143-155. Lang.: Rus.
USSR. 1866-1937. Biographical studies. ■Life and career of director Aleksand'r Achmeteli.

886 Kiknadze, V. "Goreč." (The Mountaineer.) *TeatM.* 1986; 2: 39-44. Lang.: Rus.
USSR. 1866-1937. Biographical studies. ■Life and career of director Aleksand'r Achmeteli.

887 Kindelan, Nancy. "A Solution for Children's Theatre: Michael Chekhov's 'Psychology of Style'." *ChTR.* 1985 Apr.; 34(2): 7-12. Notes. Tables. Lang.: Eng.
USSR: Moscow. USA: Ridgefield, CT. 1938. Critical studies. ■Analysis of Michael Chekhov's theories of acting and staging and the significance of his ideas to children's theatre, particularly his emphasis on a visual language.

888 Kozakov, M. "Fragmenty." (Fragments.) *DruzNar.* 1986; 8: 226-233. Lang.: Rus.
USSR: Moscow. 1980-1986. Histories-sources. ■Actor discusses work on recitation programs for stage, radio and television and recording. Related to Media.

889 Kutateladze, A. "Teat'r dolžen izobražat' svoje vremja." (The Theatre Must Portray Its Own Age.) *TeatM.* 1986; 1 (1): 11-14. Lang.: Rus.
USSR. 1980-1986. Critical studies. ■Performances and goals of recent Georgian theatre.

890 Kuz'mina, S.M., ed. *Russkoe sceničeskoe proiznošenie.* (Russian Stage Pronunciation.) Moscow: Nauka; 1986. 236. Lang.: Rus.
USSR. 1980-1986. Technical studies. ■Essays on various theatrical issues in contemporary Russian stage pronunciation.

891 Lordkipanidze, G. "Edinstvenny put'." (The Sole Path.) *TeatM.* 1986; 1(1): 26-30. Lang.: Rus.
USSR. 1980-1986. Critical studies. ■Recent achievements of Georgian theatre.

892 Mareckajte, G. "Dver' raspachnutaja na maluju scenu." (A Door Thrown Open Onto the Small Stage.) *Kulturos baraj.* 1986 (7): 18-19. Lang.: Lit.
USSR. 1980-1986. Critical studies. ■Small stages of the dramatic theatres.

893 Mejnerte, S.Ja. *Paralingvističeskiie i kommunikativnye osobennosti sceničeskoj reč: Avtoref. dis. ... kand. filo. nauk.* (Paralinguistic and Communicative Features of Stage Speech: Synopsis of a Dissertation by a Candidate in Philology.) Moscow: Mosk. pedagogičeskij institut inostrannych jazykov; 1986. 22 pp. Lang.: Rus.
USSR. 1986. Critical studies.

894 Orenov, V. "Neskol'ko slov o jazyke teatra." (A Few Words on the Language of Theatre.) *TeatZ.* 1986; 29(18): 21-22. Lang.: Rus.
USSR. Critical studies. ■Aesthetic criteria in theatre and the role of the director.

895 Pimenov, V.F. *Narodnye artisty: Teatr. Portrety.* (Artists of the People: Theatrical Portraits.) Moscow: Iskusstvo; 1986. 171 pp. Lang.: Rus.
USSR. 1917-1980. Biographical studies. ■Sketches of leading Soviet actors and directors.

THEATRE IN GENERAL: —Performance/production

896 Sarkosjan, N.S. *Osnovnye tendencii razvitija armjanskoj režissury (50-70 gg.).* (Basic Tendencies in the Development of Armenian Directing, 1950s-1960s.) Moscow: GITIS; 1986. 18 pp. [Synopsis of a Dissertation.] Lang.: Rus.
USSR. 1950-1979. Historical studies. ■ Development of Armenian directing.

897 Šitova, V.V. *K.S. Stanislavskij.* Moscow: Iskusstvo; 1986. 166 pp. Lang.: Rus.
USSR. 1863-1938. Biographies. ■Biography of Konstantin S. Stanislavskij.

898 Skvorcov, L.I., ed.; Kuznecova, L.N., ed. *Kul'tura reči na scene i na ecrane.* (The Culture of Speech on Stage and Screen.) Moscow: Nauka; 1986. 188 pp. Lang.: Rus.
USSR. 1980-1986. Critical studies. ■Articles concerning issues in stage pronunciation and speech as it relates to dramatic performance. Related to Media: Film.

899 Sokolinskij, E. "Po uzkomu, šatkomu mostiku." (Along a Narrow, Shaky Little Bridge.) *TeatZ.* 1986; 29(13): 6-8. Lang.: Rus.
USSR: Moscow. 1980-1986. Critical studies. ■Problems of young people's theatre.

900 Solnceva, A.; Ufimceva, E. "Mužskoj razgovor." (A Man's Conversation.) *TeatZ.* 1986; 29(12): 9-11. Lang.: Rus.
USSR: Moscow. 1986. Histories-sources. ■Actors from Moscow theatres participate in a round table discussion on problems facing young actors, focusing on working conditions and professional growth.

901 Stanislavskij, K.S.; Prokof'ev, V.N., comp. *Iz zapishyh knižek: V 2 t.* (From Notebooks: In Two Volumes.) Moscow: Vseros. teatr. o-vo; 1986. 608 pp., 446 pp. [Vol. 1: 1888-1911, Vol. 2: 1912-1938.] Lang.: Rus.
USSR. 1888-1938. Histories-sources.

902 Starosel'skaja, N. "'Issleduem': filosofskie problemy kul'tury." ('We Investigate': Philosophical Problems of Culture.) *VFil.* 1986; II: 128-133. Lang.: Rus.
USSR: Moscow. 1980. Histories-sources. ■Interview with A. Džigorchanjan of the Majakovskij Theatre on the philosophical comprehension of the world in the works of Eduard Radzinskij.

903 Štejn, A. "Leonid Viv'en." *TeatrM.* 1986; 9: 122-131. Lang.: Rus.
USSR: Leningrad. 1887-1966. Biographical studies. ■Work of actor-director Leonid Viv'en.

904 Tabakov, Oleg; Ščerbakov, K. "Rubeži i nadeždy." (Boundaries and Hopes.) *DruzNar.* 1986; 5: 229-238. Lang.: Rus.
USSR: Moscow. 1950-1986. Histories-sources. ■Tabakov's work in the context of Soviet cultural and theatre life, in the Sovremennik theatre, Moscow Art Theatre and as a teacher.

905 Ul'janov, M.A. "Uroki pravdy." (The Lessons of Truth.) *Kommunist.* 1986; 5: 72-75. Lang.: Rus.
USSR: Moscow. 1986. Critical studies. ■Actor of Vachtangov Theatre discusses the tasks of Soviet theatre.

906 Uvarova, Je.D. *Arkadij Rajkin.* Moscow: Iskusstvo; 1986. 303 pp. Lang.: Rus.
USSR: Leningrad, Moscow. 1911-1987. Biographies. ■Life of the founder of the Leningrad Theatre of Miniatures.

907 Vajl', M. "Liki teatral'noj studii." (The Faces of a Studio Theatre.) *TeatrM.* 1986; 10: 97-108. Lang.: Rus.
USSR: Taškent. 1980-1986. Histories-sources. ■Discussion with one of the directors of Il'chom studio theatre.

908 Vysockij, Ju. "I ešše raz o chudožestvennom maksimalizme." (Once Again on Artistic Maximalism.) *UTeatr.* 1986; 6: 6-7. Lang.: Ukr.
USSR. 1980-1986. Critical studies. ■Professional standards of contemporary actors and directors.

909 Zacharov, Mark; Szeredás, Agnes, transl. "A főrendező monológja." (Director's Monologue.) *Sz.* 1986 Jan. ; 19(1): 35-38. Illus.: Photo. B&W. 2: 9 cm. x 12 cm., 8 cm. x 19 cm. Lang.: Hun.
USSR: Moscow. 1927-1985. Critical studies. ■Director of the Lenin Comsomol Theatre speaks about the history and repertory of the theatre, as well as the birth of Ribnikov's modern opera *Junona i Avos (Juno and Avos).*

910 Zacharov, Mark. "Koridor poiska: Zametki režissera." (Corridor of Searching: A Director's Notes.) *TeatrM.* 1986; 1: 143-151. Lang.: Rus.
USSR: Moscow. 1980-1986. Histories-sources. ■Artistic director of Komsomol Theatre discusses his profession.

911 Zacharov, Mark. "Režissura zigzagov imontaž ekstremal-'nyh situacij." (Directing Zigzags and Mounting Extremely Critical Situations.) *TeatrM.* 1986; 12: 145-154. Lang.: Rus.
USSR. 1980-1986. Critical studies. ■On the methodology of acting and directing.

912 Zacharov, Mark. "Kontakty na raznykh urovnjach." (Contacts at Various Levels.) *DruzNar.* 1986; 7: 211-222. Lang.: Rus.
USSR: Moscow. 1980-1986. Histories-sources. ■Principal director of the Komsomol Theatre speaks about his work in the theatre, film and television. Related to Media: Film.

913 Zacharov, S. "Pozarčera i včera: Iz zapisok starogo sverdlovčanina." (The Day Before Yesterday and Yesterday: From the Notes of an Elderly Sverdlovian.) *Ural.* 1986(3): 146-153. Lang.: Rus.
USSR: Sverdlovsk. 1932-1947. Histories-sources. ■Memoirs of Sverdlovsk's theatrical and concert fare.

914 Zarubina, T. "Sosed: K 85-letiju So dnja rozdenija N.P. Akimova." (Neighbor: For the Eightieth Anniversary of the Birth of N.P. Akimov.) *Neva.* 1986; 4: 169-175. Lang.: Rus.
USSR. 1901-1968. Histories-sources. ■Recollections of director, designer and teacher Nikolaj Pavlovič Akimov.

915 Duró, Győző. "Cheo. Egy igazi népszínház." (Cheo: A Real Popular Theatre.) *Sz.* 1986 Sep.; 19(9) : 35-40. Illus.: Photo. B&W. 4: 9 cm. x 12 cm. Lang.: Hun.
Vietnam: Thai Binh. Hungary. 1986. Historical studies. ■Production in Hungary of *Quan-em Thi Kinh (Thi Kinh, The Merciful Buddha Woman)* by Cheo Theatre Ensemble. Review of performances and notes on Vietnamese dramatic art.

916 Nánay, István. "Gyerekszinházi fesztivál Šibenikben." (Children's Theatre Festival in Šibenik.) *Sz.* 1986 Nov.; 19(11): 27-29. Illus.: Photo. B&W. 1: 12 cm. x 18 cm. Lang.: Hun.
Yugoslavia: Šibenik. 1986. Reviews of performances. ■Overview of festival activities and reviews of productions focusing on puppet performances. Related to Puppetry.

Plays/librettos/scripts

917 Durang, Christopher; Margulies, Donald; Sweet, Jeffrey; Wasserstein, Wendy. "Ethics and Responsibilities." *DGQ.* 1986 Sum; 23(2): 15-23.
1986. Histories-sources. ■Transcript of a discussion on ethics and playwriting among Christopher Durang, Donald Margulies, Jeffrey Sweet and Wendy Wasserstein.

918 Sweet, Jeffrey. "The Dramaturg: A Single Name for Many Functions, Including That of Playwright's Helper." *DGQ.* 1986 Win ; 23(4): 18-22.
Historical studies. ■Symposium addresses confusion over the role of the dramaturg.

919 Magnier, Bernard. "Dramaturgies africaines d'aujourd'hui: inventaire d'un imaginaire (dans les pays de l'Afrique noire d'expression française)." (Present-Day African Theatre: Inventory of the Imaginary Person in French Black Africa.) 225-239 in Coca, Jordi, ed.; Conesa, Laura, comp. *Congrés Internacional de Teatre a Catalunya 1985. Actes. Volum II. Seccions 1, 2 i 3.* Barcelona: Institut del Teatre; 1986. 340 pp. Lang.: Fre.
Africa. 1985. Critical studies. ■Analysis of various theatrical forms of francophone Africa, both traditional and colonial.

920 Brandon, James R. "Foreign Influence on the Theatres of Asia." 203-211 in Coca, Jordi, ed.; Conesa, Laura, comp.

THEATRE IN GENERAL: —Plays/librettos/scripts

Congrés Internacional de Teatre a Catalunya 1985. Actes. Volum II. Seccions 1, 2 i 3. Barcelona: Institut del Teatre; 1986. 340 pp. Notes. Lang.: Eng.
Asia. 500-1985. Historical studies. ■Analysis of influences on various theatrical genres, both from other Asian countries and from the West.

921 Ellis, Bob. "The Monologue." *Meanjin.* 1986; 45(2): 169-173. Lang.: Eng.
Australia. 1985. Critical studies. ■Speculations on the success of the dramatic monologue in Australian theatre cabaret, television, etc., by a scriptwriter, journalist, raconteur and playwright.

922 Humphries, Barry. "A Fugitive Art." *Meanjin.* 1986; 45(2): 270-295. Lang.: Eng.
Australia. UK-England. 1950-1986. Histories-sources. ■Interview with Barry Humphries, writer/performer of satiric monologues on Australian character types, on his major creations—Edna Everage, Sandy Stone, Les Paterson and Barry McKenzie—and their relationship to Australian society and their success in England.

923 Melrose, Susan. "Dramatic Holes, Theatre Discourse/s." *AJCS.* 1986; 4(1): 103-113. Lang.: Eng.
Australia: Perth, W.A. 1986. Critical studies. ■Semiotic analysis of a production by the Hole-in-the-Wall Theatre of Sophocles' *Antigone* as a 'transaction, a negotiation of meaning, between intricately constituted participants', particularly the director, the designer, the actors and the audience.

924 Tilley, Christine. "A Writer's Thirty-Six Years in Radical Theatre: Perspectives on Mona Brand's Isolation from Mainstream Australian Theatre." 9-16 in Univ. New England, ed. *Australian Drama 1920-1955.* Papers presented at a conference at the University of New England, Armidale, September 1-4, 1984. Armidale, N.S.W: Univ. of New England; 1986. 157 pp. Lang.: Eng.
Australia: Sydney, N.S.W. 1932-1968. Critical studies. ■Describes Brand's work with Sydney's New Theatre, the effect on her development of a fifteen-year ban on reviews of the company's productions in the conservative press, the tendency for critics to dismiss her as didactic, and the lack of recognition of her innovative techniques.

925 Zimmer, Wolfgang. "'Chanter pour ceux qui n'ont pas le droit de chanter'. Entretien avec René Philombe sur son oeuvre dramatique." ('To Sing for Those Who Aren't Allowed to Sing': Interview with René Philombe on His Dramatic Work.) *Pnpa.* 1986 May-June; 9(51): 59-77. Notes. Lang.: Fre.
Cameroon. 1930-1986. Histories-sources. ■Interview with playwright René Philombe on the educative function of theatre.

926 Godin, Jean-Cléo. "Sur le théâtre québécois inédit, 1900-1980." (On Unpublished Quebec Theatre, 1900-1980.) *JCT.* 1985; 34(1): 51-57. Notes. Illus.: Photo. B&W. 5. Lang.: Fre.
Canada. 1900-1980. Critical studies. ■Revisionist view of twentieth-century Québec theatre. Author finds that most productions were of popular genres such as melodrama and burlesque, argues that reliance on published plays distorts theatre history.

927 Grace, Sherrill E. "Another Part in the Brooker Quartetttttte (sic)." *CDr.* 1985 Spr; 11(1): 251-253. Biblio. Lang.: Eng.
Canada. 1928-1936. Critical studies. ■A brief introduction to the work of Bertram Brooker, emphasizing his connection with Herman Voaden and his place in modernist theatre. This piece introduces the text of two of Brooker's plays.

928 Herzberg, Rota Lister. "Beverley Simons and the Influence of Oriental Theatre." *CDr.* 1984 Sum; 10(2): 218-226. Notes. Lang.: Eng.
Canada: Vancouver, BC. 1962-1975. Critical studies. ■Influence of oriental theatre—specifically its structure and patterning—on the later plays of Beverley Simons.

929 Innes, Christopher. "The Many Faces of Rita Joe: The Anatomy of a Playwright's Development." *CDr.* 1984 Sum; 10(2): 145-166. Notes. Lang.: Eng.
Canada: Vancouver, BC. 1966-1982. Textual studies. ■An examination of the drafts of George Ryga's *Ecstasy of Rita Joe*, originally produced at the Vancouver Playhouse in 1966, focusing on the alterations in the title and character.

930 Johnson, Chris. "Amerindians and Aborigines in English, Canadian and Australian Drama." *CDr.* 1984 Sum; 10(2): 167-187. Notes. Lang.: Eng.
Canada. Australia. 1606-1975. Critical studies. ■Argues that the use of Amerindian and Aborigine characters by white playwrights indicates a development toward identification with non-white figures.

931 Johnson, Denis W. "George F. Walker: Liberal Idealism and the 'Power Plays'." *CDr.* 1984 Sum; 10(2): 195-206. Notes. Lang.: Eng.
Canada: Toronto, ON. 1970-1984. Critical studies. ■A study of Walker's progression from 'esoteric' to 'popular' playwright, focusing on three plays with the same central figure, journalist-detective 'Tyrone Power'.

932 Lapierre, Laurent. "Le dévoué, la pure, le naif et le méchant." (The Devoted Man, the Pure Woman, the Naive Man and the Wicked Man.) *JCT.* 1986 4th Trimester; 41: 117-125. Notes. Illus.: Photo. B&W. 3. Lang.: Eng.
Canada: Montreal, PQ. Europe. 1604-1986. Critical studies. ■An analysis of the role of envy in Shakespeare's *Othello* and Peter Shaffer's *Amadeus*, partly inspired by the 1986 Théâtre du Nouveau Monde production of *Othello*.

933 Lapointe, Gilles. "*Vie et mort du Roi Boiteaux* de Jean-Pierre Ronfard." (*Life and Death of King Boiteaux* by Jean-Pierre Ronfard.) *CDr.* 1983; 9(2): 220-225. Notes. Lang.: Fre.
Canada: Montreal, PQ. 1983. Critical studies. ■Ronfard's use of historical characters across time and space to achieve a 'wax museum' effect.

934 Messenger, Ann. "Imagination in the Cellar: Rex Deverell's *Boiler Room Suite*." *CDr.* 1984 Sum; 10(2): 188-194. Notes. Lang.: Eng.
Canada: Regina, SK. 1977. Critical studies. ■The use of symbolism of Deverell's *Boiler Room Suite*, and its significance to his development of an intellectual drama. Also considered are allusions to Neil Simon and Samuel Beckett.

935 Nunn, Robert C. "Sharon Pollock's Plays: A Review Article." *THC.* 1984 Spr; 5(1): 72-83. Notes. Lang.: Eng.
Canada. 1971-1983. Critical studies. ■Innovations in dramatic structure and use of social and political themes.

936 O'Neill, Patrick B. "Reflections in a Cracked Mirror: Canadian Drama and World War I." *CDr.* 1984 Sum; 10(2): 207-217. Notes. Lang.: Eng.
Canada. UK. 1901-1918. Critical studies. ■Discussion of plays written by Canadian soldiers, mainly for theatre concert parties. Attention is given to the plays' importance to the development of a Canadian national drama.

937 Pavlovic, Diane. "Par amour, un jeu: *Li jus de Robin et Marion*." (By Way of Love, the Play of Joy: *The Play of Robin and Marion*.) *JCT.* 1986, 4th Trimester; 41: 101-114. Illus.: Photo. B&W. 7. Lang.: Fre.
Canada: Montreal, PQ. 1986. Reviews of performances. ■Review essay on Adam de la Halle's *Play of Robin and Marion*, directed by Jean Asselin at the Espace libre, focusing on the popularity today of Medieval drama.

938 Bennett, Robert B. "The Royal Ruse: Malcontentedness in John Marston's *The Malcontent*." *MRenD.* 1984; 1: 71-84. Notes. Lang.: Eng.
England. 1590-1600. Critical studies. ■An essay providing a corrective view of the prevailing critical opinion of Marston as intellectually confused and uncontrolled. Marston is placed in the context of the satirists of the 1590s, and his play *The Malcontent* is seen as a carefully constructed satire.

939 Cohen, Robert. "Spoken Dialogue in Written Drama." *ET.* 1986 May; 4(2): 85-97. Notes. Lang.: Eng.
England. USA. 1600-1986. Critical studies. ■Comparison of natural and dramatic speech, using works by David Mamet, Caryl Churchill, Tennessee Williams, William Shakespeare as examples.

CLASSED ENTRIES

THEATRE IN GENERAL: —Plays/librettos/scripts

940 Colley, Scott. "Marston, Calvinism, and Satire." *MRenD*. 1984; 1: 85-96. Notes. Lang.: Eng.
England. 1595-1609. Critical studies. ■Relation between religious ideas and structure and theme in Marston's satirical plays with particular attention to the use of doubleness and artificiality in such plays as *The Malcontent*.

941 Hees, Edwin. "Unity of Vision in Ben Jonson's Tragedies and Masques." *Theoria*. 1986 Oct.; 67: 21-32. Notes. Lang.: Eng.
England. 1597-1637. Critical studies. ■A comparison of Jonson's historical tragedies and his masques, showing how the same dramatic techniques inform both genres.

942 Ide, Richard S. "Exploiting the Tradition: The Elizabethan Revenger as Chapman's 'Complete Man'." *MRenD*. 1984; 1: 159-172. Notes. Lang.: Eng.
England. 1603. Critical studies. ■Analysis of critical confusion regarding the title character of *The Revenge of Bussy D'Ambois* by George Chapman.

943 Orlin, Lena Cowen. "Man's House as His Castle in *Arden of Faversham*." *MRenD*. 1985; 2: 57-90. Pref. Notes. Lang.: Eng.
England. 1536-1592. Historical studies. ■Rise of English home and landowner influence on Elizabethan domestic tragedy as exemplified in *Arden of Faversham*.

944 Pavlova, T.V. "*Vera ili Nigilisty* 'Russkaja' drama Oskara Vajl'da." (*Vera, or The Nihilists*: The 'Russian' Drama of Oscar Wilde.) *Russkaja literatura*. 1986; 3: 171-181. Lang.: Rus.
England. Russia. USA: New York, NY. 1883. Historical studies. ■On the play, its Russian publication and the first production in New York.

945 Turner, Robert Y. "Heroic Passion in the Early Tragicomedies of Beaumont and Fletcher." *MRenD*. 1984; 1: 109-130. Notes. Lang.: Eng.
England. 1608-1611. Critical studies. ■A study of the use of plots with 'extreme passion' in the plays of Beaumont and Fletcher, arguing that such plots are 'heroic' in quality.

946 Nicastro, Guido, ed. *Istituzioni culturali e sceniche nell'età delle riforme*. (Cultural and Scenic Institutions in the Age of Reform.) Milan: Franco Angeli; 1986. 287 pp. (Il Settecento 7.) Pref. Notes. Biblio. Index. Lang.: Ita.
Europe. 1985. Critical studies. ■Conference in Catania on aspects of theatre and culture in the eighteenth century.

947 Baženova, L.Je. *Problema stilja v teatre Pera Kornelja (do 1636 goda): Avtoref. diss... kand. iskusstvovedenija*. (Problem of Style in the Theatre of Pierre Corneille to 1636: Synopsis of a Dissertation by a Candidate in Art Criticism.) Moscow: GITIS; 1986. 25 pp. Lang.: Rus.
France. 1606-1636. Critical studies.

948 Cholakian, Patricia Francis. "The Itinerary of Desire in Molière's *Le Tartuffe*." *TJ*. 1986 May; 38(2): 165-179. Notes. Illus.: Photo. B&W. 1. Lang.: Eng.
France. 1660-1669. Critical studies. ■A reconsideration of the role of the servant in *Tartuffe* in the light of psychoanalytic and post-structuralist theory.

949 Dunn, E. Catherine. "The Saint's Legend as Mimesis: Gallican Liturgy and Mediterranean Culture." *MRenD*. 1984; 1: 13-27. Notes. Lang.: Eng.
France. 500-900. Critical studies. ■An argument for the Gallican liturgy (the recitation of saints' lives in Gaul) as a form of drama, and as a starting point for medieval French drama, focusing on connections with Roman classical drama and on the use of dance with the liturgy.

950 Kápolnai Molnár, Ilona. "Metz, a színházi kommunikáció városa." (Metz, the Town of Theatrical Communication.) *Sz*. 1986 July; 19(7): 48. Lang.: Hun.
France: Metz. 1982-1986. Histories-sources. ■Metz theatre festival and competition of one-act plays.

951 Sandoval, Enrique. *The Metaphoric Style in Politically Censored Theatre*. Edmonton, AB: Concordia Univ; 1986. Pref. Notes. Biblio. [Ph.D. dissertation.] Lang.: Eng.
France. South Africa, Republic of. Chile. 1940-1986. Historical studies. ■Examines the use by playwrights Jean-Paul Sartre, Athol Fugard and Juan Radrigán of metaphoric style as a device to circumvent censorship.

952 Arzeni, Flavia. "Giochi esotici e rituali politici: motivi giapponesi in Klabund e Brecht." (Exotic Tricks and Political Rituals: Japanese Motifs in Klabund and Brecht.) 237-252 in Ottai, Antonella, ed. *Teatro Oriente/Occidente*. Rome: Bulzoni; 1986. viii, 565 pp. (Biblioteca Teatrale 47.) Lang.: Ita.
Germany. Japan. 1900-1950. Historical studies. ■*Nō* and *kabuki* influences on the plays of Bertolt Brecht and Klabund (Alfred Henschke).

953 Chiarini, Paolo, ed.; Gargano, Antonella, ed.; Vlad, Roman, ed. *Expressionismus. Una enciclopedia interdisciplinare*. (Expressionism. An Interdisciplinary Encyclopedia.) Rome: Bulzoni; 1986. xi, 608 pp. (Studi di filologia tedesca 11.) Index. Notes. Tables. Append. Illus.: Photo. Pntg. Dwg. B&W. 22: var. sizes. Lang.: Ger, Ita.
Germany. Austria. 1891-1933. Critical studies. ■Collection of essays on all facets of German expressionism, including sections on theatre and dance.

954 Kumbatovic, Filip Kalan; Marsan, Valentine Aymone, transl. "Addio giorni felici (Omaggio a Klabund)." (Adieu, Happy Days (An Homage to Klabund).) 487-493 in Ottai, Antonella, ed. *Teatro Oriente/Occidente*. Rome: Bulzoni; 1986. viii, 565 pp. (Biblioteca Teatrale 47.) Lang.: Ita.
Germany. 1890-1928. Biographical studies. ■Influence of Japanese drama on the works of Klabund (Alfred Henschke).

955 Pollock, Della. *Brecht and Expressionism: An Assessment of Rhetorical Continuity*. Evanston, IL: Northwestern Univ; 1986. 463 pp. Pref. Notes. Biblio. [Ph.D. dissertation, University Microfilms order No. DA 8621851.] Lang.: Eng.
Germany. 1919-1944. Historical studies. ■Reassessment of Bertolt Brecht's relationship with the Expressionist movement, including the use of 'negational' rhetoric.

956 Hill, Errol. "The Revolutionary Tradition in Black Drama." *TJ*. 1986 Dec.; 38(4): 408-426. Notes. Lang.: Eng.
Haiti. Jamaica. 1820-1970. Historical studies. ■Revolutionary heroes and themes of nineteenth and twentieth century black theatre that preceded the revolutionary theatre of the 1960s.

957 Ablonczy, László. "Vidám siratók." (The Merry Mourners.) *Tisz*. 1986; 40(3): 81-90. Lang.: Hun.
Hungary. Romania. 1965-1985. Histories-sources. ■Interview with András Sütő on his plays.

958 Antal, Gábor. "Benedek András: *Színházi műhelytitkok*." (András Benedek: *Theatre Workshop Secrets*.) *Sz*. 1986 Apr.; 19(4): 45-46. Lang.: Hun.
Hungary. 1952-1984. Critical studies. ■Review of András Benedek's book containing essays on outstanding Hungarian playwrights, adaptations of dramas, theoretical questions and portraits of excellent Hungarian artists.

959 Antonucci, Giovanni. *Storia del teatro italiano del Novecento*. (History of Italian Theatre in the Twentieth Century.) Rome: Edizioni Studium; 1986. 284 pp. (Nuova Universale Studium 49.) Pref. Index. Notes. Biblio. Lang.: Ita.
Italy. 1900-1985. Histories-specific. ■Overview of twentieth-century Italian theatre from D'Annunzio to the present.

960 Molodcova, M.M. "Pul'činella v tvorčestve E. de Filippo." (Pulchinella in the Works of Eduardo De Filippo.) 138-150 in *Tradicii i novaterstvo v zarubežnom teatre*. Leningrad: Leningr. in-t teatre, muzyki i kinematografii; Lang.: Rus.
Italy. 1900-1985. Critical studies. ■Pulchinella figures in the plays of Eduardo De Filippo.

961 Yun, Jo-Byeong; Yu, Min-Yeong; Lee, Gang-Baek; No, Gyeong-Shik. "Hanguk Yeonguk-ui Hyeonjuso. III: Gukjakga." (The Present State of Korean Theatre. III: The Playwright.) *KTR*. 1986 May; 120(5): 14-49. Illus.: Photo. B&W. 1: 18.5 cm. x 26 cm. Lang.: Kor.

THEATRE IN GENERAL: —Plays/librettos/scripts

Korea. 1986. Histories-sources. ■History of Korean modern drama, including interviews with leading playwrights.

962 Kaynar, Gad. "Patiah Letargum *Eiolf Hakatan.*" (Introduction to the Translation of *Little Eyolf.*) *Bamah.* 1986; 21 (105-106): 50-52. Notes. Lang.: Heb.

Norway. Israel. 1884-1985. Historical studies. ■Introductory note on the first translation of Henrik Ibsen's *Lille Eyolf (Little Eyolf)* into Hebrew.

963 Czinege-Károly, Anna. *Dramatikus játékok a csikmenasági lakodalomban.* (Dramatic Plays in the Wedding Festivities of Csikmenaság.) Szeged: JATE; 1984. 100-109 pp. (Néprajzi dolgozatok 44.) Lang.: Hun.

Romania: Armăseni. 1978. Historical studies. ■Discussion of the motifs in two plays performed at wedding festivities in Csikmenaság, on the basis of recordings from 1978.

964 Ivanova, V.V. "Slavjanskaja pora v poeticheskom jazyke i poezii Chlebnikova." (The Time of Slavs in the Poetic Language and Poetry of Chlebnikov.) *SovSlav.* 1986; 22(3): 62-71. Lang.: Rus.

Russia. 1885-1922. Critical studies. ■Studies Chlebnikov's language in the plays *Snežimocka* and *Devij bog (The Maiden God).*

965 Kafanova, O.B.; Alekseev, M.P., ed.; Danilevskij, R. Ju., ed. "N.M. Karamzin i zapadnoevropejskij teat'r." (N.M. Karamzin and Western European Theatre.) 62-89 in *Russkaja literatura i zarubežnoe iskusstvo.* Leningrad: Nauka; 1986. Lang.: Rus.

Russia. 1766-1826. ■Western European influences on playwright Nikolaj M. Karamzin.

966 Krovčenko, Je. "Na jasnyi svet." (Into a Bright World.) *Pod'jem (Voronež).* 1986; 6: 133-135. Lang.: Rus.

Russia. 1899-1951. Critical studies. ■Analysis of A. Platonov's comedy *Vysokoe naprjaženic (High Tension).*

967 Sitas, Ari. "Culture and Production: The Contradictions of Working Class Theatre in South Africa." *AfricaP.* 1986; 1 (1/2): 84-111. Notes. Lang.: Eng.

South Africa, Republic of. 1976-1986. Critical studies. ■A look at the role of the working class in the evolution of a theatre of resistance in South Africa.

968 "Dramatic Convention and Poetic Discourse: Dialogue, Monologue, and Aside in Luis de Góngora's *Las Firmezas de Isabela.*" *BCom.* 1985; 37(2): 225-248. Lang.: Eng.

Spain. 1561-1627. Critical studies. ■Study of Góngora's use of language and structure in *The Decisions of Isabela* as a deliberate response to the playwriting techniques of Lope de Vega.

969 Conlon, Raymond. "Female Psychosexuality in Tirso's *El vergonzoso en palacio.*" *BCom.* 1985; 37(1): 55-70. Lang.: Eng.

Spain. 1580-1648. Critical studies. ■Argues that female characters in *El vergonzoso en palacio (The Shy Man at Court)* represent aspects of female sexuality, moving from ignorance to fulfilment.

970 Smith, Dawn L. "Tirso's Use of Emblems as a Technique of Representation in *La mujer que manda en casa.*" *BCom.* 1985; 37(1): 71-82. Lang.: Eng.

Spain. 1580-1648. Critical studies. ■Relationship between emblematic pictorialism in Tirso de Molina's *The Woman Who Rules the Roost* and its moral function as a biblical story.

971 Stainton, Leslie. "The Tragic Landscapes of Federico García Lorca." *AmTh.* 1986 Dec.; 3(9): 12-17. Pref. Illus.: Photo. Print. B&W. 6: 3 in. x 5 in., 5 in. x 7 in. Lang.: Eng.

Spain: Granada, Madrid. USA: New York, NY. 1898-1936. Biographical studies. ■A short history of the life of Federico García Lorca, including what little is known of his death.

972 Huerta Viñas, Ferran. "Els drames de Nadal al Teatre Medieval Català i les tradicions llegendàries." (The Christmas Dramas in the Catalan Medieval Theatre and the Legendary Traditions.) 39-47 in Salvat, Ricard, ed. *El Teatre durant l'Edat Mitjana i el Renaixement.* Barcelona: Publicacions i Edicions de la Universitat de Barcelona; 1986. xxviii, 322 pp. (El Pla de les Comèdies 2.) Notes. [Presented at First International Symposium on Medieval and Renaissance Theatre, Sitges, 1983.] Lang.: Cat.

Spain-Catalonia. 1400-1599. Historical studies. ■Analysis of various medieval Catalan Nativity plays and their relationships with religious dogma and tradition.

973 Molas, Joaquim, ed.; Cassany, Enric; Fàbregas, Xavier; Jorba, Manuel; Tayadella, Antònia. *Història de la literatura catalana, Volum 7.* (History of Catalan Literature, Volume 7.) Barcelona: Editorial Ariel, S.A; 1986. xxiv, 714 pp. (Història de la literatura catalana 7.) Index. Notes. Pref. Illus.: Design. Pntg. Dwg. Photo. Maps. Print. Color. B&W. 371: var. sizes. Lang.: Cat.

Spain-Catalonia. France. 1800-1926. Histories-specific. ■History of Catalan literature, including chapters on playwrights Serafía Pitarra (Frederic Soler), Àngel Guimerà, Apel.les Mestres, Josep Pin i Soler and Narcís Oller.

974 Molas, Joaquim, ed.; Castellanos, Jordi; Fàbregas, Xavier; Gallén, Enric; Marfany, Joan-Lluís; Massot, Josep. *Història de la literatura catalana, Volum 8.* (History of Catalan Literature, Volume 8.) Barcelona: Editorial Ariel, S.A; 1986. xxiv, 637 pp. (Història de la literatura catalana 8.) Index. Notes. Illus.: Design. Pntg. Dwg. Photo. Plan. Poster. Print. B&W. 272: var. sizes. Lang.: Cat.

Spain-Catalonia. 1800-1974. Histories-specific. ■Includes chapters on Catalan theatre, Santiago Rusiñol, Víctor Català and other playwrights.

975 Ciesielski, Zenon. *Od Fredry do Różewicza. Dramat i teatr polski w Szwecji w latach 1835-1976.* (From Fredro to Różewicz: Polish Drama and Theatre in Sweden: 1835-1976.) Gdańsk: Wydawnictwo Morskie; 1986. 399 pp. Append. Illus.: Photo. B&W. 60: var. sizes. [English summary.] Lang.: Pol.

Sweden. Poland. 1835-1976. Historical studies. ■Enumeration and interpretation of Polish plays performed in Sweden, including visits by Polish actors and theatre groups. Also touches on opera, ballet and puppetry.

976 Huberman, Jeffrey H. *Late Victorian Farce.* Ann Arbor, MI: UMI Research P; 1986. (Theater and Dramatic Studies 40.) Illus.: Photo. Lang.: Eng.

UK-England. 1875-1900. Histories-specific. ■Development and subsequent decline of the three-act farce.

977 Obrazcova, A. "Terroristy ili patrioty?" (Terrorists or Patriots?)*TeatrM.* 1986; 2: 138-149. Lang.: Rus.

UK-Ireland. 1980-1986. Critical studies. ■Representation of political struggle in Northern Ireland in English theatre and film. Related to Media: Film.

978 Austin, Addell Patricia. *Pioneering Black Authorized Dramas: 1924-27.* East Lansing, MI: Michigan State Univ; 1986. 241 pp. Pref. Notes. Biblio. Append. [Ph.D. dissertation, University Microfilms order No. DA 8625006.] Lang.: Eng.

USA. 1924-1927. Historical studies. ■History of literary contests intended to encourage Black writers, with detailed discussion of the winners.

979 Cummings, Scott. "Seeing with Clarity: The Visions of Maria Irene Fornes." *ThM.* 1985 Win; 17(1): 51-56. Illus.: Photo. B&W. 3. Lang.: Eng.

USA. 1965-1985. Histories-sources. ■Interview with Fornes focusing on her playwriting technique, her views on language and its relation to character development.

980 Foreman, Richard; Alevras, Jorgos, transl. "14 uppmaningar till mig själv då jag faller för frestelsen att låta skrivandet efterbilda 'erfarenheten'." (14 Appeals to Myself When I'm Yielding to the Temptation to Let Writing Imitate 'Experience'.) *NT.* 1986; 34: 14-18. Lang.: Swe.

USA. Histories-sources. ■Advice on how to write about events before they have happened.

981 Levine, Mindy N. "A Conversation with Al Carmines." *TT.* 1985 Mar.; 4(4): 1-2, 4. Illus.: Photo. B&W. 2. Lang.: Eng.

USA: New York, NY. 1985. Histories-sources. ■Interview with playwright Al Carmines on his career and inspirations.

THEATRE IN GENERAL: —Plays/librettos/scripts

982 Rea, Charlotte. "Women's Theatre Groups." 197-208 in McNamara, Brooks, ed.; Dolan, Jill, ed. *The Drama Review: Thirty Years of Commentary on the Avant-Garde.* Ann Arbor, MI: UMI Research P; 1986. xii, 371 pp. (Theatre and Dramatic Studies 35.) Print. B&W. 1: 2 in. x 3 in. Lang.: Eng.
USA. 1971-1986. Critical studies. ■Plays and themes concerning the Women's Movement created from contrasting images of women in society.

983 Renick, Kyle. "On Rights...And Wrongs." *TT.* 1984 Mar.; 3(5): 4-5. Illus.: Photo. B&W. 2. Lang.: Eng.
USA: New York, NY. 1984. Historical studies. ■Process of obtaining legal rights to a property when adapting a play from another source. Copyright and contracts are discussed.

984 Reynolds, Richard C. *Stage Left: The Development of the American Social Drama in the Thirties.* Troy, NY: Whitston; 1986. 175 pp. Lang.: Eng.
USA. 1930-1939. Histories-specific. ■Treatment of social problems in the plays of the period, particularly those of Lillian Hellman and Clifford Odets.

985 Segal, Errol. *George Sklar: Playwright for a Socially Committed Theatre.* Ann Arbor, MI: Univ of Michigan; 1986. 322 pp. Pref. Notes. Biblio. [Ph.D. dissertation, University Microfilms order No. DA 8621373.] Lang.: Eng.
USA: New York, NY. 1920-1967. Critical studies. ■Career of Marxist playwright George Sklar, including discussion of his distorted presentation of social and political reality.

986 Sukari, Alamba. "Ossie Davis Speaks." *OvA.* 1986 Win; 14(1): 25-26. Illus.: Photo. Print. B&W. 1: 4 in. x 3 in. Lang.: Eng.
USA: Davis, CA. 1986. Histories-sources. ■Summary of speech given by playwright Ossie Davis at Third World Theatre Conference calling for self-sufficiency in funding and a return to folk idioms in creating Black theatre.

987 Szilassy, Zoltán. *American Theater of the 1960's.* Carbondale & Edwardsville, IL: Southern Illinois; 1986. 113 pp. Index. Notes. Lang.: Eng.
USA. 1960-1979. Histories-specific. ■Survey of the achievements and spirit of American theatre of the 1960s and a discussion of whether that spirit continued in the 1970s.

988 "Kogda istorija sovremenna: V glubinach folklornogo vremeni." (When History Is Contemporary: In the Depths of Folkloric Time.) *Minsk.* 1986; 7: 155-162. Lang.: Rus.
USSR. 1980-1986. Historical studies. ■History of dramaturgy in northern Byelorussia.

989 Klado, N. "Begom ili polzkom." (Running or Crawling.) *SovD.* 1986; 2: 229-235. Lang.: Rus.
USSR. 1986. Critical studies. ■Critical analysis of *Tri devuški v golubom (Three Girls in Blue)* by Ljudmila Petruševskaja.

990 Mamčur, M. "Dramaturgija i teat'r: v ožidanii peremen." (Dramaturgy and Theatre: In Expectation of Changes.) *UTeatr.* 1986; 1: 14-16. Lang.: Ukr.
USSR. 1980-1986. Critical studies. ■Predicted changes in Russian dramaturgy and theatre.

991 Ninov, A. "O dramaturgii i teatre Michajla Bulgakova: itogi i perspektivy izučenija." (On the Dramaturgy and Theatre of Michajl Bulgakov: Results and Perspectives of a Study.) *VLit.* 1986; 9: 84-111. Lang.: Rus.
USSR. 1925-1940. Critical studies. ■Dramaturgy of Michajl Afanasjević Bulgakov.

992 Promtova, I. "Slovo na scene." (The Word on the Stage.) *SovD.* 1986; 3: 260-267. Lang.: Rus.
USSR. 1986. Critical studies. ■On the necessity of preserving the actor's text in a play.

993 Reznik, G.M. "Beskorystnyj prestupnik v žizni i na scene." (The Unselfish Criminal in Life and on the Stage.) *Sov. gosudarstvo i pravo.* 1986; 9: 125-128. Lang.: Rus.
USSR. 1980-1986. Critical studies. ■Sociological problems in contemporary drama.

994 Stroeva, M. "Mera otkrovennosti: Opyt dramaturgii Ljudmily Petruševskoj." (A Measure of Frankness: The Experience of Ljudmila Petruševskaja's Dramaturgy.) *SovD.* 1986; 2: 218-228. Lang.: Rus.
USSR. 1986. Critical studies. ■Analyses of the plays of Ljudmila Petruševskaja.

Reference materials

995 Brauneck, Manfred, ed.; Schneilin, Gérard, ed. *Theaterlexicon: Begriffe und Epochen, Bühnen und Ensembles.* (Lexicon of the Theatre: Concepts and Epochs, Stages and Companies.) Reinbek bei Hamburg: Rowohlt Taschenbuch V; 1986. 1113 pp. (Rowohlts Enzyklopädie RE 417.) Lang.: Ger.
700 B.C.-1986 A.D. ■Comprehensive lexicon of the theatre with articles on a wide range of theatrical subjects.

996 Dahle, Terje Nils, ed. *Theater in Mehrzweckbauten.* (Theatre in Buildings Serving Multiple Purposes.) Stuttgart: Informationszentrum Raum und Bau; 1986. 92 pp. (IRB Literaturauslese 874.) Pref. Index. Lang.: Ger.
■List of technical details of multifunctional buildings and halls, town halls and congress centres with stages.

997 Dietrich, Margret, comp.; Krauss, Cornelia, comp.; Gregor, Joseph, gen. ed. *Der Schauspielführer: Das Schauspiel von 1980-1983.* (Drama Guide: Dramatic Publications, 1980-1983.) Vol. 13. Stuttgart: Hiersemann; 1986. ix, 235 pp. Pref. Index. Biblio. Lang.: Ger.
1980-1983. ■Summaries of the most important plays published and performed worldwide.

998 Fleshman, Bob, ed. *Theatrical Movement: A Bibliographical Anthology.* Metuchen, NJ/London: Scarecrow; 1986. xiv, 742 pp. Pref. Lang.: Eng.
■Physical aspects of theatre.

999 Kullman, Colby H., ed.; Young, William C., ed. *Theatre Companies of the World.* Westport, CT: Greenwood; 1986. 979 pp. [In two volumes.] Lang.: Eng.
■Covers theatre companies which have national reputation and historical importance, possess innovative technology or produce experimental drama.

1000 Fotheringham, Richard. "Copyright Sources for Australian Drama and Film." *Archives and Manuscripts.* 1986; 14(2): 144-153. Lang.: Eng.
Australia. 1870-1969. Bibliographical studies. ■Organization and significance of Australian archives of early filmmaking and unpublished plays.

1001 Kefala, Antigone. *Multiculturalism and the Arts.* Sydney: Australia Council; 1986. 69 pp. Lang.: Eng.
Australia. 1986. ■Introductory article on multiculturalism and the arts, formal statement of the Australia Council Multicultural Program and brief accounts of some Australian artists of non-English-speaking backgrounds, several of whom are active in theatre.

1002 Kirsop, Wallace. "A Theatrical Library in Nineteenth-Century Melbourne and its Dispersal: Solving a Problem." *LLJ.* 1986; 10(7pp 1-8). Lang.: Eng.
Australia: Melbourne. 1866. Bibliographical materials. ■Describes the contents of a theatrical library sold by auction in 1866, placing it in the context of bookbuying in late 19th century Melbourne and identifying the seller as James Smith, a leading journalist and writer of the time.

1003 Pausch, Oskar; Höller, Gertrud, comp. *Theaterkostüme aus zwei Jahrhunderten.* (Theatre Costumes of Two Centuries.) Exposition of the 'Österreichische Theatermuseum' in Schloss Grafenegg bei Krems/NÖ, 1986. Vienna: Österreichisches Theatermuseum: Theatersammlung d. Österr. Nationalbibliothek; 1986. 28 pp. (Biblos-Schriften 134.) Tables. Illus.: Photo. Color. 8: 15 cm. x 17 cm. Lang.: Ger.
Austria: Vienna. 1831-1960. Histories-sources. ■Photos of costumes of state and former court theatres, dressing of Viennese folk comedy and design realizations by modern costume designers. All costumes originated from famous Viennese actors.

CLASSED ENTRIES

THEATRE IN GENERAL: —Reference materials

1004   *Annuaire du Spectacle de la Communauté Française de Belgique 1981-1982.* (Yearbook of Performing Arts in Belgium's French Community 1981-1982.) Bruxelles: Archives et Musée de la Littérature; 1983. 119 pp. Pref. Index. Illus.: Photo. B&W. 109. Lang.: Fre.
Belgium. 1981-1982. Reviews of performances. ■Annals of theatre productions in Belgium's French community for the 1981-1982 season.

1005   *Annuaire du Spectacle de la Communauté Française de Belgique 1982-1983.* (Yearbook of Performing Arts in Belgium's French Community 1982-1983.) Bruxelles: Archives et Musée de la Littérature; 1984. 160 pp. Pref. Index. Illus.: Photo. B&W. 159. Lang.: Fre.
Belgium. 1982-1983. Reviews of performances. ■Annals of theatre production in Belgium's French community for the 1982-1983 season.

1006   *Annuaire de Spectacle de la Communauté Française de Belgique 1983-1984.* (Yearbook of Performing Arts in Belgium's French Community 1983-1984.) Bruxelles: Archives et Musée de la Littérature; 1984. 216 pp. Pref. Index. Illus.: Photo. B&W. 192. Lang.: Fre.
Belgium. 1983-1984. Reviews of performances. ■Annals of theatre productions in Belgium's French community for the 1983-1984 season.

1007   *Annuaire du Spectacle de la Communauté Française de Belqique 1984-1985.* (Yearbook of Performing Arts in Belgium's French Community 1984-1985.) Bruxelles: Archives et Musée de la Littérature; 1986. 240 pp. Pref. Illus.: Photo. B&W. 213. Lang.: Fre.
Belgium. 1984-1985. Reviews of performances. ■Annals of theatre productions in Belgium's French community for the 1984-1985 season.

1008   Brown, J. Frederick. "The Charlottetown Festival in Review: An Update." *CDr.* 1986 Spr; 12(1): 75-143. Illus.: Photo. Poster. Print. B&W. 25: 3 in. x 5 in., 5 in. x 7 in. [Update of *CDr* 9: 2(1983), 227-308.] Lang.: Eng.
Canada: Charlottetown, PE. 1972-1983. Historical studies. ■A calendar of 17 productions at the Charlottetown Festival including cast and production lists, plot digests, musical numbers, extracts of reviews and performance records.

1009   Conolly, Leonard W., ed. "Modern Canadian Drama: Some Critical Perspective." *CDr.* 1985 Spr; 11(1): 1-229. Lang.: Eng.
Canada. 1934-1983. Reviews of performances. ■Collection of reviews of productions of 31 major Canadian plays, from *Hill-Land* to *The Canadian Brothers.*

1010   Plant, Richard. "Hearts of the West." *BooksC.* 1983 Apr.; 12(4): 14-16. Lang.: Eng.
Canada. 1982. Historical studies. ■Survey of Canadian theatre publications uncovers leading contributions coming from the Prairies, as well as collections in both French and English.

1011   Han, Rixin, ed. "Xiong Foxi Zhuzuo Xinian." (Chronicle of Xiong Foxi's Works.) *XYishu.* 1982 May; 5(2): 17-30. Lang.: Chi.
China, People's Republic of. 1917-1963. ■Bibliography of all published articles, plays and books of Xiong Foxi, from 1917 to 1963.

1012   Ritchey, David. "An Index to the Theatrical Materials in Five Eighteenth-Century American Theatre Journals." *Restor.* 1986 Sum; 2nd ser.1(1): 34-52. Notes. Lang.: Eng.
Colonial America. 1758-1800. ■Cross-indexed by title, author, playwright, performer, subject heading.

1013   Hensel, Georg. *Spielplan: Schauspielführer von der Antike bis zur Gegenwart.* (Repertory: Play Guide from Antiquity to the Present.) Frankfurt-am-Main/Berlin: Propyläen-Ullstein; 1986. 1640 pp. Index. Biblio. Illus.: Design. Handbill. Photo. Dwg. Sketches. 383: var. sizes. [Two volumes: revised edition of 1966.] Lang.: Ger.
Europe. 600 B.C.-1986 A.D. Histories-general. ■Short description of dramas of Western theatre and introduction to theatre history with references to dramatists, production styles, stages, decoration and administrative questions.

1014   "Haosef shel Betzalel London Sahkan Teatron 'Hamatate' Ve 'Ohel'." (New in the Archives: The Collection of Betzalel London.) *Bamah.* 1986; 21(105-106): 134. Illus.: Photo. Print. B&W. 1: 7 cm. x 6 cm. Lang.: Heb.
Israel: Jerusalem. 1925-1971. ■Announcement of the deposition of the theatrical archives of Betzalel London at Hebrew University.

1015   "Hatzagot Bechora Bateatron Haisraeli 1/3/86-31/7/86." (Opening Nights of Israeli Theatres 1/3/86-31/7/86.) *Bamah.* 1986 ; 21(104): 122-123. Lang.: Heb.
Israel. 1986. ■List of the season's opening nights.

1016   "Hatzagot Bechora Bateatron Haisraeli 1/9/85-28/2/86." (Opening Nights of Israeli Theatres 9/1/85-2/28/86.) *Bamah.* 1986 ; 21(103): 83-85. Lang.: Heb.
Israel. 1985-1986. Historical studies. ■A list of opening nights of the 1985/86 theatrical season in Israel.

1017   "Hatzagot Bechora Bateatron Haisraeli 1/8/86-30/11/86." (Opening Nights of Israeli Theatres 8/1/86-11/30/86.) *Bamah.* 1986; 21(105-106): 150-157. Notes. Lang.: Heb.
Israel. 1986. ■A list of opening nights of the theatrical season in Israel.

1018   Gilula, Dvora; Di-Nur, Shlomo; Levin, Dov; Shadletzki, Ephraim. "Bikoret Sfarim." (Book Reviews.) *Bamah.* 1986; 21(103): 71-82. Biblio. Lang.: Heb.
Israel: Tel-Aviv. 1983-1985. ■Bibliography of book reviews.

1019   Zemach, Benjamin. "Emuna, Hazon—Ahava." (Faith, Vision and Love.) *Bamah.* 1986; 21(105-106): 130-133. Illus.: Photo. Print. B&W. 3: var. sizes. Lang.: Heb.
Israel: Jerusalem. 1986. Historical studies. ■Speech given by Benjamin Zemach on the deposition of Nachum Zemach's archive at Hebrew University.

1020   *Teatro festival Parma—Meeting europeo dell'attore.* (Parma Festival Theatre—Actors' European Meeting.) Parma: Teatro festival Parma; 1986. 143 pp. Tables. Illus.: Photo. Poster. B&W. Lang.: Ita.
Italy: Parma. 1986. Histories-sources. ■Program of European Actors' Meeting, including criticism, texts and performances.

1021   Amministrazione provinciale di Pavia. *Leggere lo spettacolo 1985.* (Reading Show-Business 1985.) Milan: Bibliografica; 1986. 362 pp. (Cataloghi di Biblioteche 5.) Index. Lang.: Ita.
Italy. 1985. ■Catalogue of books on film, theatre, music and dance published in Italy in 1985. Related to Media: Film.

1022   *Teatro italiano 85: Annuario dell'Istituto del Dramma Italiano e della Società Italiana Autori ed Editori (IDI-SIAE).* (Italian Theatre 1985: IDI-SIAE Yearbook.) Rome: SIAE-IDI; 1986. 364 pp. Pref. Index. Tables. Illus.: Photo. B&W. 66: var. sizes. Lang.: Ita.
Italy. 1984-1985. Histories-specific. ■Yearbook of information on the Italian theatre season.

1023   Società Italiana Autori ed Editori (SIAE). *Lo spettacolo in Italia. Annuario statistico Anno 1984.* (Show-business in Italy: Statistical Yearbook, 1984.) Rome: SIAE; 1986. xxi, 289 pp. Pref. Index. Tables. Illus.: Graphs. Maps. Diagram. Color. 23: var. sizes. Lang.: Ita.
Italy. 1984. Histories-specific. ■Statistics on film, television, theatre and sports.

1024   Botto, Ida Maria, ed. *Il teatro Carlo Felice di Genova: storia e progetti.* (Carlo Felice Theatre of Genoa: History and Projects.) Genoa: Sagep; 1986. 300 pp. Illus.: Photo. Plan. Pntg. Dwg. Poster. Color. B&W. Lang.: Ita.
Italy: Genoa. 1600-1985. Historical studies. ■Catalogue of a 1985 exhibit on the Carlo Felice Theatre, which was destroyed in World War II: history, stage designs, architecture, proposed reconstruction.

1025   Quadri, Franco, ed.; Bergero, Silvia, ed.; Ponte di Pino, Oliviero, ed. *Il Patalogo 9: annuario dello spettacolo: teatro.* (The Patalogo 9.) Milan: Ubulibri; 1986. 262 pp. [1986 Theatre Yearbook.] Lang.: Ita.
Italy. 1986. Histories-sources. ■Yearbook of Italian theatrical productions, including performers and criticism.

1026   Waseda Daigaku Engeki Hakubutsu-kan. *Engeki Nenpō 1986.* (Theatre Yearbook 1986.) Tokyo: Waseda Daigaku Shuppan-bu; 1986. 185 pp. Illus.: Photo. B&W. 60: var. sizes. Lang.: Jap.

THEATRE IN GENERAL: —Reference materials

Japan: Tokyo. 1986. Critical studies. ■Comprehensive yearbook of important performances in all areas of Japanese theatre.

1027 Shōyō Kyōkai. *Tsubouchi Shōyō Jiten.* (Companion to Tsubouchi Shōyō.) Tokyo: Heibonsha; 1986. 573 pp. Illus.: Photo. B&W. 30: var. sizes. Lang.: Jap.
Japan: Tokyo. 1859-1986. ■Comprehensive lexicon of items related to the life and work of Tsubouchi Shōyō.

1028 Watanabe, Moriaki; Kisaragi, Koharu. *Engi suru toshi.* (The Theatre Season.) Tokyo: Heibonsha; 1986. Lang.: Jap.
Japan: Tokyo. 1200-1500. ■Listing of theatrical productions.

1029 Korean National Theatre Association. "Hanguk Yeomgukin-ui Sahoe—Gyeomgjae—Yesul Hwaldong-ae Gwanhan Josa Yeomgu." (A Study of the Social, Economic, and Artistic Activity of the Korean Theatre People.) *KTR*. 1986 Nov.; 126(11): 12-36. Illus.: Photo. B&W. 1: 18.5 cm. x 25.7 cm. Lang.: Kor.
Korea. 1985-1986. Historical studies. ■Includes demographic characteristics and problems in Korean theatre.

1030 Gràcia, Josep, ed. *Teatres de Catalunya.* (Theatres of Catalonia.) Barcelona: Institut del Teatre/Generalitat de Catalunya/Caixa de Barcelona; 1986. 328 pp. Index. Illus.: Graphs. Plan. Photo. Print. B&W. Grd.Plan. Explod.Sect. 1147: var. sizes. [2 vols.] Lang.: Cat.
Spain-Catalonia. 1848-1986. Histories-sources. ■Guide to 570 Catalan theatres.

1031 Englund, Claes, ed.; Ånnerud, Annika, ed. *Teaterårsboken 86.* (Theatre Yearbook 86.) Jönköping: Entré/Riksteatern; 1986. 248 pp. Pref. Biblio. Index. Illus.: Photo. Print. B&W. 407. Lang.: Swe.
Sweden. 1985-1986. Histories-sources. ■Yearbook of theatre with the theatres in alphabetic order, including radio and television drama.

1032 Loor, Hillar. "STTF-medlemsblads artiklar genom åren." (The Articles of the Bulletin STTF Through the Years.) *ProScen.* 1986; 10(2): 51-60. Index. Illus.: Photo. Lang.: Swe.
Sweden. 1977-1986. ■A list of all articles that have appeared in *STTF-medlemsblad* 1977-1985 and *ProScen* 1986.

1033 Apothèloz, Anne-Lise, comp. *Szene Schweiz—Scène Suisse—Scena Svizzera: Eine Dokumentation des Theaterlebens in der Schweiz.* (Scene Switzerland: A Documentation of Theatrical Activity in Switzerland.) Bonstetten: Theaterkultur; 1986. xvi, 214 pp. (SSSS 14.) Index. Biblio. B&W. [Vol. 14.] Lang.: Ger, Fre, Ita.
Switzerland. 1986-1987. ■Listing of all theatrical productions, both dramatic and musical, and a detailed bibliography of Swiss theatrical activity.

1034 Howard, Diana. *Directory of Theatre Resources.* London: The Library Association & The Society for Theatre Research; 1986. 144 pp. Pref. Index. [2nd ed.] Lang.: Eng.
UK. 1985-1986. ■Lists 292 research collections and information sources, most of which are open to the public.

1035 *British Theatre Directory, 1986/87.* London: Richmond House; 1986. 600 pp. Illus.: Photo. B&W. 12: var. sizes. [15th ed.] Lang.: Eng.
UK-England. 1985-1986. ■Includes sections on venues, municipal entertainment facilities, production (managements, companies, orchestras, etc.), agents, publishers, booksellers, training and education, as well as suppliers and services.

1036 Senter, Al. "Down Memory Lane." *PI.* 1986 July; 1(12): 24-25. B&W. 1. Lang.: Eng.
UK-England: London. 1986. ■Wealth of theatre memorabilia in British museums is considered, from portraits of actors and playwrights in the art galleries, to autographed letters in the British Museum.

1037 *Theatre Member Directory.* New York, NY: ART/NY; 1986. 91 pp. Lang.: Eng.
USA: New York, NY. 1986. ■Directory of member organizations of ART/NY (Alliance of Resident Theatres/New York), an organization which provides services to increase managerial strength and which serves as an advocate for the theatre community.

1038 "Members' Services Directory." *DGQ.* 1986 Fall; 23(3).
USA. 1986. Historical studies. ■A directory of services available to Dramatists Guild members.

1039 "1986-87 Directory of Institutional Theaters Cross-Country and in New York City." *DGQ.* 1986 Spr; 23(1).
USA. 1986. Historical studies. ■List of institutional theatres.

1040 "1984-1985 Season Production Schedules." *TT.* 1984 Oct.; 4(1): 7-9. Lang.: Eng.
USA: New York, NY. 1984. Historical studies. ■Production schedules of member theatres of Alliance of Resident Theatres/New York. Includes plays, directors, dates.

1041 "Directory of Support: Play Contests, Agents, Producers On and Off Broadway." *DGQ.* 1986 Sum; 23(2).
USA. 1986. Historical studies. ■Directory of support sources for the playwright.

1042 *NYC Rehearsal Space List.* New York, NY: ART/NY; 1986. 38 pp. Lang.: Eng.
USA: New York, NY. ■Comprehensive list of rehearsal and performance spaces in NYC, including prices and details of physical layout of space.

1043 "Twenty-Five Years in the American Theatre." *AmTh.* 1986 Nov.; 3(8): 43-61. Pref. Illus.: Photo. Print. B&W. 58: 3 in. x 4 in., 5 in. x 7 in. Lang.: Eng.
USA. 1961-1986. Historical studies. ■A chronology of landmark events and memorable productions from the American not-for-profit theatre, with historic photographs.

1044 Frank, Susan; Levine, Mindy N. *In Print.* Englewood Cliffs, NJ: Prentice-Hall; 1984. ix-xii, 146 pp. Pref. Index. Append. Gloss. Illus.: Design. Photo. Dwg. Sketches. B&W. 20: var. sizes. Lang.: Eng.
USA. 1984. ■Concise guide to graphic arts and printing for small businesses and nonprofit organizations.

1045 Istel, John, ed. *Theatre Directory 1986-87.* New York, NY: Theatre Communications Group; 1986. 67 pp. Notes. Tables. Lang.: Eng.
USA. 1986. Histories-sources. ■Annual directory listing repertory schedules, contact and contract information of member theatres and organizations of Theatre Communications Group.

1046 McCaslin, Nellie. *Historical Guide to Children's Theatre in America.* Westport, CT: Greenwood; 1986. xvii, 348 pp. Pref. Index. Biblio. Append. Lang.: Eng.
USA. 1903-1985. ■Alphabetically arranged profiles of professional and amateur theatres for children with a comprehensive history of theatrical entertainment for children. Appendix includes chronology of events, personality roster and geographical directory.

1047 Parker, Kate. "When in Manhattan." *PI.* 1986 Mar.; 1(8): 18-19. Illus.: Photo. Print. B&W. 2. Lang.: Eng.
USA: New York, NY. 1986. Histories-sources. ■Three theatre shops — The Drama Bookshop, Theatre Books and One Shubert Alley — all in Manhattan, are described.

Relation to other fields

1048 Alasjärvi, Ulla; Miralles, Francesc, transl. *El joc dramàtic.* (The Dramatic Game.) Barcelona: Editorial Graó; 1986. 94 pp. (Col.lecció Guix 3.) Biblio. Notes. Pref. Illus.: Design. Photo. Print. Color. 28: var. sizes. Lang.: Cat.
1986. Instructional materials. ■Use of theatrical performance in teaching, including the elaboration of plots on a basic theme, use of masks for characterization.

1049 Antal, Gábor. "*Quo vadis, Thalia?* Sándor Iván szinibirálatai." (*Quo vadis, Thalia?* Iván Sándor's Reviews.) *Sz.* 1986 Dec.; 19(12): 47-48. Lang.: Hun.
1986. Critical studies. ■Review of Iván Sándor's essays on Hungarian and foreign playwrights, productions, actors and traditions.

1050 Csillag, Ilona. "A zsidó kultusz teátrális elemei a múltban és jelenben." (The Theatrical Elements of Jewish Religion in the Past and the Present.) *SzSz.* 1986; 10(19): 25-52. Biblio. Lang.: Hun.

THEATRE IN GENERAL: —Relation to other fields

1300 B.C.-1986 A.D. Historical studies. ■Study of the historical motives, theatrical elements and lack of creative power in Jewish religious ceremonies.

1051 Deldime, Roger. "Alternatives théâtrales et stratégies de l'animation." (Theatrical Alternatives and Strategies of Bringing to Life.) *JCT*. 1985; 35: 134-138. Lang.: Fre.
Critical studies. ■Suggestions for reviving political theatre and for reaching an apolitical audience.

1052 Deverell, Rita Shelton. "When the Performer is Black." *CTR*. 1986 Sum; 13(47): 56-62. Biblio. Illus.: Photo. Print. B&W. 2: 4 in. x 5 in. Lang.: Eng.
1986. Critical studies. ■Control of language and of decision-making involved in performances by Blacks.

1053 Epskamp, Kees Paul; Chini, Antonella, transl. "Alla ricerca dell'autenticità: i registi teatrali del nord-Atlantico ed il teatro tradizionale nel Terzo Mondo." (The Search for Authenticity: Directors of the North Atlantic States and Traditional Theatre in the Third World.) 111-130 in Ottai, Antonella, ed. *Teatro Oriente/Occidente*. Rome: Bulzoni; 1986. viii, 565 pp. (Biblioteca Teatrale 47.) Lang.: Ita.
1900-1986. Historical studies. ■Interaction of Western directors with third world traditional theatre: Antonin Artaud, Peter Brook, Eugenio Barba.

1054 Harrison, James. "The Myth of Free Trade." *Theatrum*. 1985-86 Fall-Win; 3: 23-24. Lang.: Eng.
1985-1986. Historical studies. ■Warns that economic partnership with the USA will harm the cultural character of Canada.

1055 Lorenz, Dagmar C.G.; Geiger, Gerlinda, transl. "Female Projections in Brecht's Love Poetry." *ComIBS*. 1986 Nov.; 16(1): 29-37.
1920-1928. Critical studies. ■The use of women and homosexuality in Brecht's sexual lyric poetry.

1056 Magli, Adriano. *Prospettive sociologiche e antropologiche nella storia dello spettacolo*. (Sociological and Anthropological Perspectives on the History of Performance.) Rome: Bulzoni; 1986. 221 pp. Index. Notes. Illus.: Photo. B&W. 4: var. sizes. Lang.: Ita.
Historical studies. ■Collection of articles on various anthropological aspects of theatre, including shamanism, in primitive theatre and the religious theatre of the Middle Ages.

1057 Morris, Desmond; Sosio, Libero, transl. *Il nostro corpo: anatomia, evoluzione, linguaggio*. (Our Body: Anatomy, Evolution, Language.) Milan: Mondadori; 1986. 256 pp. Index. Tables. Biblio. Illus.: Photo. Pntg. Dwg. Color. B&W. Lang.: Ita.
Instructional materials. ■Translation of *Bodywatching: A Field Guide to the Human Species* (1985).

1058 Sándor, Iván. *Quo vadis Thalia?* (Quo vadis Thalia?)Budapest: Kozmosz; 1986. 236 pp. Lang.: Hun.
1962-1986. Historical studies. ■Essays and reviews presented in the frame of a Greek travelogue, on Hungarian and foreign playwrights, productions, actors and traditions.

1059 Schafer, R. Murray. "The Theatre of Confluence II." *CTR*. 1986 Sum; 13(47): 5-19. Illus.: Photo. Print. B&W. 8: var. sizes. [Sequel to 'The Theatre of Confluence I,' published in *Open Letter* in 1979.] Lang.: Eng.
1986. Critical studies. ■The original sacred purposes of art have been profaned with the rise of civilization. New contexts must be sought, perhaps echoing the significance of surviving modern rituals, to allow for the true celebration of and participation in art. Related to Dance-Drama.

1060 Turner, Victor; Capriolo, Paola, transl. *Dal rito al teatro*. (From Ritual to Theatre.) Bologna: Il Mulino; 1986. 218 pp. (Intersezioni 27.) Pref. Index. Notes. Biblio. Lang.: Ita.
Historical studies. ■Translation of *From Ritual to Theatre: The Human Seriousness of Play* (New York, 1982).

1061 Faik, Ala Yahya. *Theatrical Elements in Religious Storytelling of Medieval Islamic Culture*. Ann Arbor, MI: Univ of Michigan; 1986. 154 pp. Pref. Notes. Biblio. [Ph.D. dissertation, University Microfilms order No. DA 8621278.] Lang.: Eng.
Asia. 700-1200. Historical studies. ■Analyzes the theatrical nature of religious storytelling in medieval Islam and its development into a ritualistic performance medium with theatrical conventions.

1062 Burgess, Roma; Gaudry, Pamela. *Time for Drama*. Philadelphia, PA: Open UP; 1986. xii, 270 pp. Pref. Index. Biblio. Append. Illus.: Diagram. [A Handbook for Secondary Teachers.] Lang.: Eng.
Australia. 1974-1985. Instructional materials. ■Teacher handbook includes comprehensive discussion of dramatic process, distinction between drama and theatre and the role of the teacher. Contains lesson plans for various age groups.

1063 Rickard, John. "Cultural History: The 'High' and the 'Popular'." *ACH*. 1986; 5: 32-43. Lang.: Eng.
Australia. 1860-1930. Critical studies. ■Analyzes Australian theatre with special reference to the nineteenth century, to indicate the problem of sustaining a distinction between high and popular culture and the way it obscures questions of cultural significance. Looks at the social role of opera, the programming and marketing strategies of actor-managers, and the status of actors.

1064 Löbl, Hermi. "Gemässigt in der Form, fest in der Sache." (Moderate in Form, Rigid in Substance.) *Buhne*. 1986 July; 29(7): 8-9. Illus.: Photo. Print. Color. Lang.: Ger.
Austria. 1986. Histories-sources. ■Minister Herbert Moritz and his cultural politics relating to theatres, specifically the roles played by Thomas Bernhard and Claus Peymann.

1065 Vay, Sarolta; Steinert, Agota, ed. *Régi magyar társasélet*. (Society Life in Hungary in the Past.) Budapest: Magvető; 1986. 608 pp. (Magyar hirmondó.) Notes. Lang.: Hun.
Austro-Hungarian Empire. 1740-1848. Histories-sources. ■Cultural-historical sketches of Countess Sarolta Vay published in 1900 including several of theatrical interest.

1066 Popovic, Pierre. "À Liège: le théâtre d'une mémoire en crise." (At Liège: The Theatre of a Memory in Crisis.) *JCT*. 1985; 35: 126-133. Lang.: Fre.
Belgium. 1985. Historical studies. ■Discussion of political theatre in Wallonia.

1067 Blagrave, Mark. "Temperance and the Theatre in the Nineteenth-Century Maritimes." *THC*. 1986 Spr; 7(1): 23-32. Notes. Illus.: Photo. B&W. 1. Lang.: Eng.
Canada. 1800-1900. Historical studies. ■Analysis of the use of theatricals by nineteenth-century temperance societies in the Maritime provinces. John Sparrow Thompson's *Cadets of Temperance* and the anonymous *Harvest Queen's Coronation* are discussed.

1068 Cusson, Chantal; Pace, Marc. "Au delà des modes: table ronde avec des praticiens." (Beyond Fashions: A Round Table With Professionals.) *JCT*. 1984; 30(1): 50-64. Notes. Illus.: Photo. B&W. 8. Lang.: Fre.
Canada: Quebec, PQ. 1984. Histories-sources. ■Discussion among theatre professionals on theatre for adolescents, focusing on repertory, theme and technique.

1069 Filewod, Alan. "The Interactive Documentary in Canada: Catalyst Theatre's *It's About Time*." *THC*. 1985 Fall; 6(2): 133-147. Notes. Illus.: Photo. B&W. 2. Lang.: Eng.
Canada: Edmonton, AB. 1982. Critical studies. ■Use of interactive theatre in this production compared to political theatre in Canada and to the techniques of Augusto Boal.

1070 Hoffman, James. "Towards an Early British Columbian Theatre: The Homatsa Ceremony as Drama." *CDr*. 1985 Spr; 11(1): 231-244. Notes. Illus.: Diagram. Lang.: Eng.
Canada. 1890-1900. Critical studies. ■Kwakiutl Homatsa (winter) ceremony as drama, with discussion of staging, 'script,' roles and community function.

1071 Knowles, Richard Paul. "*Homo Ludens*: Canadian Theatre, Canadian Football, Shakespeare and the NHL." *CDr*. 1984 Spr; 10 (1): 65-74. Notes. Lang.: Eng.

THEATRE IN GENERAL: —Relation to other fields

Canada. 1972-1983. Critical studies. ∎The relation of nationalism to theatre, connections between theatre and audience, and theatre and sports, focusing on the meaning of 'play'.

1072 Laplante, Benoît. "Le théâtre est-il une affaire?" (Is Theatre a Business?)*JCT*. 1986 1st Trimester; 38: 215-228. Notes. Illus.: Photo. B&W. 4. Lang.: Fre.

Canada: Quebec, PQ. 1985. Historical studies. ∎Report of a conference on theatre and economics, focusing on public and private funding and its effect on artistic independence.

1073 Mullaly, Edward. "The Saint John Theatre Riot of 1845." *THC*. 1985 Spr; 6(1): 44-55. Notes. Lang.: Eng.

Canada: St. John, NB. 1845. Historical studies. ∎Examination of the riot at the St. John Theatre provoked by Thomas Hill's political satire *The Provincial Association*.

1074 Smith, Mary Elizabeth. "*Measure by Measure* and Other Political Satires from New Brunswick." *THC*. 1984 Fall; 5(2): 172-184. Notes. Lang.: Eng.

Canada. 1798-1871. Historical studies. ∎A study of anonymous political satires published in New Brunswick newspapers, with particular attention to the use of Shakespearean allusions.

1075 Wagner, Anton. "'A Country of the Soul': Herman Voaden, Lowrie Warrener and the Writing of *Symphony*." *CDr*. 1983; 9(2) : 203-219. Notes. Lang.: Eng.

Canada. 1914-1933. Critical studies. ∎An examination of the collaboration of Voaden and Warrener on the 1930 mixed-media piece *Symphony* which is seen as testing Voaden's thesis of the development of a Canadian drama through heightened aesthetic awareness. Grp/movt: Expressionism. Related to Media: Mixed media.

1076 Jin, Shonliang. "Yishu Daode Sanlun." (On Art and Morality.) *XYishu*. 1982 Aug.; 5(3): 125-130. Lang.: Chi.

China. 1949-1982. Instructional materials. ∎In a socialist country, artists should have strong sense of collective principle, loyalty to socialist arts and vigilance against decadent Western culture.

1077 Chen, Bohong. "Pen Yuan Ju hsing Yishu Daode Jiaoyu Zuotanhui." (Roundtable Discussion on Teaching Ethics in Art.) *XYishu*. 1982 Aug.; 5(3): 130-135. Lang.: Chi.

China, People's Republic of. 1949-1982. Critical studies. ∎Arts education should emphasize the role of being a socialist artist, not merely an individual artist.

1078 Wei, Zhaofeng. "Cong *Maoguo Chungiu* dao *Shengguan Tu*." (From *The Cat Country Era* to *Pictures of Official Promotions*.) *XYishu*. 1982 May; 5(2): 95-99. Illus.: Dwg. 4. Lang.: Chi.

China, People's Republic of. 1942-1981. Biographical studies. ∎Anecdotes about caricaturist Liao Bingxiong and comedian Chen Baichen, based upon Liao's exhibit and Chou's farce, both satirizing the Nationalist Government of the 1940s.

1079 Booth, Michael R. "Art and the Classical Actor: Painting, Sculpture, and the English Stage." *AUMLA*. 1986; 66: 260-271. Lang.: Eng.

England. 1700-1900. Critical studies. ∎Impact of the visual arts on eighteenth and nineteenth century theatre, including the use of sculptures and paintings as models for tragic gesture, the *tableau vivant*, the stage set as a painting and the entire stage composition as a picture.

1080 Kropf, C.R. "William Popple: Dramatist, Critic, and Diplomat." *Restor*. 1986 Sum; 2nd ser.1(1): 1-17. Notes. Lang.: Eng.

England. 1737-1764. Biographical studies. ∎William Popple's career as author of comedies, contributor to *The Prompter* and politician.

1081 Leinwand, Theodore B. *The City Staged: Jacobean Comedy 1603-1613*. Madison, WI: Univ. of Wisconsin P; 1986. 233 pp. Index. Biblio. Lang.: Eng.

England: London. 1603-1613. Critical studies. ∎Social critique and influence of Jacobean drama.

1082 Moritz, William; Gulli, Caterina, transl. "La drammaturgia cromatica." (Chromatic Dramaturgy.) *TeatrC*. 1985-1986; 6 (11-12): 167-186. Notes. Biblio. Lang.: Ita.

Europe. USA. 1900-1985. Critical studies. ∎Study of attempts to create a 'visual' music using light instead of sound. Related to Media: Film.

1083 Verdone, Mario. "Coesistenza delle avanguardie." (Coexistence of the Avant-gardes.) *TeatrC*. 1986; 6(13): 77-81. Lang.: Ita.

Europe. 1900-1930. Critical studies. ∎Brief account of the results of an international colloquium on the ideals, contrasts and consequences of artistic, literary and theatrical avant-garde movements.

1084 Erenstein, Robert; Marcantoni, Marilena, transl. "Claude Gillot e il Théâtre Italien." (Claude Gillot and the 'Théâtre Italien'.) *BiT*. 1986; 2: 23-43. Notes. Tables. Biblio. Illus.: Pntg. Dwg. B&W. 4: 11 cm. x 18 cm. Lang.: Ita.

France. 1673-1722. Historical studies. ∎The work of painter and scene designer Claude Gillot.

1085 Sohlich, Wolfgang. "The Théâtre du Soleil's *Mephisto* and the Problematics of Political Theatre." *TJ*. 1986 May ; 38(2): 137-153. Notes. Lang.: Eng.

France: Paris. 1979. Historical studies. ∎A detailed analysis of the production of Klaus Mann's *Mephisto* by Théâtre du Soleil, focusing on the self-conscious critique of the relation between politics and theatre.

1086 Zenkin, S.N. "Teat'r i akterskaja igra v chudožestvennoj proze Teofilja Got'e." (Theatre and the Actor's Performance in the Artistic Prose of Théophile Gautier.) *VMGUf*. 1986; 21(3): 50-57. Lang.: Rus.

France. 1811-1872. Historical studies. ∎Théophile Gautier's ideas on theatre and performance.

1087 Davies, Ronald Austin. *Christian Dietrich Grabbe (1801-1836) and the Third Reich*. Stanford, CA: Stanford Univ; 1986. 294 pp. Pref. Notes. Biblio. [Ph.D. dissertation, University Microfilms order No. DA 8619735.] Lang.: Eng.

Germany. 1801-1946. Historical studies. ∎Studies the role of ideology in the success of writers through the case study of playwright Christian Dietrich Grabbe, made a literary hero of the Nazis.

1088 Habermann, Günther. "Die Stimme als Ausdrucksmittel beim Lachen und Weinen." (Voice as Means of Expressiveness While Laughing and Crying.) 69-86 in Spitzer, Leopold, ed. *Probleme der Sängerausbildung: Bericht über das 5. gesangspädagogische Symposion in Bad Ischl vom 18. bis 22. März 1985*. Vienna: Hochschule für Musik u. darst. Kunst in Wien, Abt. f. Sologesang u. musikdramat. Darstellung; 1986. 175 pp. Illus.: Photo. Dwg. B&W. 2: 12 cm. x 8 cm. Lang.: Ger.

Germany. USA. 1935-1983. Instructional materials. ∎Study describes the vocal and mimetic characteristics of different forms of laughing and crying for the purpose of performance. References to psychic conditions on the basis of empiric inquiries.

1089 Jesse, Horst; Vansant, Jacqueline. "The Young Bertolt Brecht and Religion." *ComIBS*. 1986 Apr.; 15(2): 17-27.

Germany. 1913-1918. Critical studies. ∎The young Brecht's fascination with religion and his use of the Bible to criticize the Church and society.

1090 Pflüger, Kurt; Herbst, Helmut. *Schreibers Kindergarten: Eine Monographie*. (Schreiber's Kindergarten: A Monograph.) Pinneberg: Renate Raecke; 1986. 212 pp. Pref. Index. Notes. Biblio. Illus.: Photo. B&W. Lang.: Ger.

Germany. 1878-1921. Histories-specific. ∎History of children's paper theatres, which were used to teach middle-class behavior and values.

1091 Wardetzky, Jutta. *Theaterpolitik im faschistischen Deutschland. Studien und Dokumente*. (Theatre Policy in Fascist Germany: Studies and Documents.) Berlin: Henschelverlag; 1983. 398 pp. Index. Notes. Append. Lang.: Ger.

Germany: Berlin. 1933-1944. Histories-specific. ∎Essence and methods of Fascist theatre policy, theatre as instrument of resistance for some theatre people.

1092 Althoff, Gabriele; Allkempen, Alo; Halverson, Rachel, transl.; Gilbert, Michael, transl. "A Commentary on Brecht's Love Poems." *ComIBS*. 1986 Nov.; 16(1): 29-37.

Germany, East. 1898-1956. Critical studies. ∎The underlying materialistic sobriety in Brecht's love poetry.

1093 Knopf, Jan; Pieper, Dietmar, transl. "Reflections on the New Poetry Edition." *ComIBS*. 1986 Apr.; 15(2): 3-10.

THEATRE IN GENERAL: —Relation to other fields

Germany, East. 1898-1956. Critical studies. ■Review of the 5-volume edition of Bertolt Brecht's poetry, focusing on the sequence of arrangement, including excerpts from the poetic commentary in the collection.

1094 Voris, Renate. "The Autobiographical 'Phallacy'." *ComIBS*. 1986 Nov.; 16(1): 52-58.

Germany, East. 1898-1956. Critical studies. ■Critique of two articles which examine Brecht's love poetry from a feminist perspective.

1095 Magli, Adriano. "Civiltà di vergogna e civiltà di colpa." (Civilization of Shame and Civilization of Guilt.) 59-72 in Ottai, Antonella, ed. *Teatro Oriente/Occidente*. Rome: Bulzoni; 1986. viii, 565 pp. (Biblioteca Teatrale 47.) [In Relation to Influences of Shamanistic Performance.] Lang.: Ita.

Greece. Asia. 500 B.C.-1986 A.D. Historical studies. ■Influences of shamanism on Eastern and Western theatre.

1096 Albee, Edward. "Governments Fear the Word." *DGQ*. 1986 Win; 23(4): 9-11.

Hungary: Budapest. 1986. Histories-sources. ■Albee's observations on government censorship and freedom of artistic expression at the Budapest Cultural Forum.

1097 Csik, István. "A kedvcsináló. Varga Győző és Színházi plakátjai." (The Man Who Makes a Good Mood: Győző Varga and his Theatre Posters.) *Sz.* 1986 June; 19(6): 45-47. Illus.: Photo. B&W. 1: 12 cm. x 17 cm. Lang.: Hun.

Hungary. 1986. Histories-sources. ■Interview with graphic artist Győző Varga on the occasion of an exhibit on his posters.

1098 Dömötör, Tekla. *Régi és mai magyar népszokások.* (Ancient and Contemporary Hungarian Folk Customs.) Budapest: Tankönyvkiadó; 1986. 163 pp. (Néprajz mindenkinek 3.) Illus.: Photo. Dwg. Color. B&W. 74: var. sizes. Lang.: Hun.

Hungary. 1986. Historical studies. ■Folklorist Tekla Dömötör incorporates customs of mimicry and dramatic characterization into her work.

1099 Lapu, Istvánné; Korkes, Zsuzsa, comp. *Viseletek és szokások Zsámbokon.* (Relics and Customs of Zsámbok.) Aszád: Petőfi Múzeum; 1986. 227 pp. (Múzeumi füzetek 33.) Illus.: Photo. Dwg. B&W. 57: var. sizes. Lang.: Hun.

Hungary: Zsámbok. 1930-1985. Histories-sources. ■The ethnographic remains of Zsámbok: the memoirs and the recitals of Istvánné Lapu, collector of intellectual traditions and material relics of her village for several decades.

1100 Szinetár, Miklós. "Vita a szinházi strukturáról. A szinház társadalmasitása." (Discussion on Theatre Structure: Socialization of the Theatre.) *Krit.* 1986; 14(3): 15-17. Illus.: Dwg. 4: var. sizes. Lang.: Hun.

Hungary. Critical studies. ■Contribution to the discussion on theatre structure analyzing the function of theatre in society.

1101 Varga, Imre, ed. *Ujabb párbeszédek a müvészetpolitikáról 1981-1984.* (Recent Dialogues on Arts Policies 1981-1984.) Budapest: Müvészeti Szakszervezetek Szöv; 1985. 194 pp. Index. Lang.: Hun.

Hungary. 1981-1984. Histories-sources. ■Minutes of debates organized by the Association of Artists' Unions, on socialist arts policy, including theatre.

1102 Bernova, A.A. "Religioznye obrjady kak odin iz istokov tradicionnogo teatra narodov Indonezii." (Religious Ritual as a Source of Traditional Theatre for the People of Indonesia.) 89-107 in Žukovskaja, N.L., ed. *Mify, Kulty, obrjady naradov zarubežnoj Azii/AN SSSR. In-t etnografii.* Moscow: Nauka; 1986. Lang.: Rus.

Indonesia. Historical studies. ■Uses of religious ritual in traditional theatre.

1103 Asor Rosa, Alberto, ed. *Letterature italiana. Teatro, musica, tradizione dei classici.* (Italian Literature: Theatre, Music, and the Classical Tradition.) Turin: Einaudi; 1986. 964 pp. (Letteratura italiana 6.) Index. Notes. Tables. Biblio. Illus.: Pntg. Dwg. Color. B&W. 37: var. sizes. Lang.: Ita.

Italy. 800-1985. Histories-specific. ■Essays investigating the interaction between literary language and the languages of theatre, music, spectacle in general.

1104 Barberi-Squarotti, Giorgio. "La sfida di Serafino Gubbio operatore." (The Challenge of Serafino Gubbio, Cameraman.) *Ariel.* 1986 Sep-Dec.; 1(3): 189-210. Lang.: Ita.

Italy. 1915-1925. Critical studies. ■Study of Luigi Pirandello's novel, *I quaderni di Serafino Gubbio operatore (The Notebooks of Serafino Gubbio, Cameraman).*

1105 Gennaro, Pietro, ed.; Teoldi, Massimo, ed. *Spettacolo come industria.* (Show Business as Industry.) Florence: Passigli; 1986. 213 pp. Index. Notes. Tables. Illus.: Diagram. B&W. Lang.: Ita.

Italy. 1970-1985. Technical studies. ■Show business in the process of adopting modern industrial methods. Includes reports of a seminar on the subject (Rome, 1982).

1106 Lattarulo, Leonardo. "Pirandello tra Croce e Gentile." (Pirandello between Croce and Gentile.) *Ariel.* 1986 Sep-Dec.; 1 (3): 59-68. Notes. Biblio. Lang.: Ita.

Italy. 1867-1936. Critical studies. ■Playwright Luigi Pirandello's relationship with the two major Italian philosophers of his time.

1107 Maier, Bruno. "Pirandello, Trieste e Svevo." (Pirandello, Trieste and Svevo.) *Ariel.* 1986 Sep-Dec.; 1(3): 27-39. Notes. Biblio. Lang.: Ita.

Italy: Trieste. 1925-1926. Historical studies. ■The meeting of playwright Luigi Pirandello and novelist Italo Svevo.

1108 Pirandello, Luigi; Guglielmino, Salvatore, intro. *L'umorismo.* (Humor.) Milan: Mondadori; 1986. 170 pp. (Oscar Saggi 106.) Pref. Index. Notes. Biblio. Lang.: Ita.

Italy. 1200-1906. Critical studies. ■New edition of Pirandello's 1908 essay on the dynamics of humor with examples from European literature.

1109 Varanini, Giorgio. "Per la protostoria della lauda drammatica." (The Protohistory of the 'Lauda Drammatica'.) *Ariel.* 1986 May-Aug.; 1(2): 55-68. Notes. Tables. Biblio. Illus.: Pntg. B&W. 4: var. sizes. Lang.: Ita.

Italy. 1200-1400. Historical studies. ■Literary origins of the 'lauda drammatica'.

1110 Zolla, Elémire. "La seduta sciamanica coreana come teatro primordiale." (The Korean Shamanistic Seance as Primordial Theatre.) 73-86 in Ottai, Antonella, ed. *Teatro Oriente/Occidente.* Rome: Bulzoni; 1986. viii, 565 pp. (Biblioteca Teatrale 47.) Lang.: Ita.

Korea. 1900-1986. Historical studies. ■Description of shamanistic rituals, trances and their connections to the origins of theatre.

1111 Assaf, Roger; Formosa, Feliu; Grilli, Giuseppe; Plaza, Sixto; Lapeña, Antonio Andrés. "La expressió verbal. Factor de comunicació, factor d'aillament." (Verbal Expression: Factor of Communication, Factor of Isolation.) 5-86 in Coca, Jordi, ed.; Conesa, Laura, comp. *Congrés Internacional de Teatre a Catalunya 1985. Actes. Volum II. Seccions 1, 2 i 3.* Barcelona: Institut del Teatre; 1986. 340 pp. Notes. Index. Lang.: Fre, Spa, Cat.

Lebanon. Spain-Catalonia. USA. 1985. Critical studies. ■Reports and discussions of Section I, International Congress on Theatre in Catalonia, focusing on restrictions on cultural communication.

1112 Pillai, Janet. "Children's Theatre in Malaysia." *ChTR.* 1985 Jan.; 34(1): 7-10. Notes. Lang.: Eng.

Malaysia. 1930-1985. Critical studies. ■The development of children's theatre in Malaysia focusing on the relation between traditional Malay forms and European elements that appeared in the colonial and post-colonial periods, including some discussion of political context.

1113 Ritch, Pamela. "Children's Drama in Mexico: An Interview with Socorro Merlin." *ChTR.* 1985 July; 34(3): 15-18. Notes. Lang.: Eng.

Mexico: Mexico City. 1947-1985. Histories-sources. ■Interview with Socorro Merlin, director of the Centro de Investigaciones Teatro Rodolfo Usigli, Instituto de Bellas Artes, Mexico City, discussing the administration, funding and philosophy of children's theatre in Mexico.

1114 Bolt, Alan. "Magic Theater—Political Theater." *ComIBS.* 1986 Apr.; 15(2): 48-51.

Nicaragua. 1985. Histories-sources. ■An excerpt from a talk at Yale University by Alan Bolt, director of the Nicaraguan National Theater

THEATRE IN GENERAL: —Relation to other fields

Workshop, who sees the process of theatre as a way of building democracy.

1115 Rue, Victoria. "Art and Politics in Central America." *TT.* 1983 Nov/Dec.; 3(2): 4. Illus.: Maps. B&W. 1: 3 in. x 6.5 in. Lang.: Eng.

Nicaragua. 1983. Historical studies. ■Author's visit to Nicaragua, the role of culture since the revolution.

1116 Dudzik, Wojciech. "Franciszka Siedleckiego 'Teatre duszy'." (Franciszek Siedlecki's 'Theatre of the Soul'.) *DialogW.* 1986; 4: 124-135. Notes. Lang.: Pol.

Poland. 1909-1934. Critical studies. ■Stage designer and theatre critic F. Siedlecki's writings, his relationship to Rudolph Steiner's anthroposophy and program for theatre in Poland.

1117 Findlay, Robert; Filipowicz, Halina. "Grotowski's Laboratory Theatre: Dissolution and Diaspora." *TDR.* 1986 Fall; 30(3): 200-225. Biblio. Illus.: Handbill. Photo. B&W. 12: 4 in. x 4 in. Lang.: Eng.

Poland: Wrocław. 1959-1985. Historical studies. ■Account of the Laboratory Theatre's dissolution due to evolving political and personal events and possible evolving directions for members of the company.

1118 Guszpit, Ireneusz. "Poglady na teatr w zapiskach Osterwy." (Theatrical Ideas in Osterwa's Writings.) *DialogW.* 1986; 4: 103-114. Notes. Lang.: Pol.

Poland. 1918-1947. Historical studies. ■Actor-director Juliusz Osterwa's ideas about theatre's place in society, its relationship to religion and anthropology, and the mystical dimensions of acting.

1119 Jawłowska, Aldona. "Idee kontrkultury a teatr studencki." (Alternative Culture and Student Theatre.) *DialogW.* 1986; 1: 125-136. Notes. Lang.: Pol.

Poland. 1960-1986. Historical studies. ■Alternative theatre and the political situation in Poland. Jerzy Grotowski and the Gardzienice Theatre.

1120 Kuligowska, Anna. "Powrót teatru polskiego (5-7 lipca 1905)." (Restitution of the Polish Theatre (July 5-7, 1905).) *PaT.* 1986 Second & Third Qtr; 2-3: 301-320. Notes. Illus.: Photo. Print. B&W. 1. Lang.: Pol.

Poland: Vilna. 1905. Historical studies. ■In 1864, after the Polish insurrection of 1863, Tsarist Russia, along with other repressive measures, closed the Polish theatre in Vilna. In 1905, after a period of turmoil and social unrest, the Polish theatre was restored. Opening night and the happy reaction of the audience are described.

1121 Kwaskowski, Stanisław. "Z pamiątnika aktora. Fragmenty." (From the Actor's Memoirs (Fragments).) *PaT.* 1986 First Qtr; 1: 23-44. Pref. Illus.: Photo. B&W. 7: var. sizes. Lang.: Pol.

Poland. 1918-1920. Histories-sources. ■Recollections of actor Stanisław Kwaskowski (1897-1986) about theatrical life under the political and economic conditions of independence.

1122 Osterwa, Juliusz; Guszpit, Ireneusz, ed. "Obrachunek." (An Account.) *DialogW.* 1986; 4: 115-123. Pref. Notes. Lang.: Pol.

Poland. 1940-1947. Histories-sources. ■Actor-director Juliusz Osterwa's understanding of historical processes and their influence on theatre: World War II as punishment for the human race.

1123 Rutkiewicz, Anna. "Plakat Teatralny?" (Theatre Poster?) *TeatrW.* 1984 July; 39(814): 37-39. Lang.: Pol.

Poland. 1984. Critical studies. ■Polish theatre posters.

1124 Novackij, V.; Uvarova, I. "I plyvet korabl'..." (And the Ship Sails...) *DekorIsk.* 1986 Jul.; 29(7): 24-28. Lang.: Rus.

Russia. Historical studies. ■Ancient Russian rituals linked with the 'ship of souls' theme in world culture.

1125 Hauptfleisch, Temple, ed.; Groenewald, H.C., ed.; Kohler, P., ed.; Marais, J.L., ed. *Research on South African Literature and Race Relations.* Pretoria: Human Sciences Research Council; 1986. 80 pp. (CENSAL/CESAT Publication 1.) Pref. Lang.: Afr.

South Africa, Republic of. Critical studies. ■The proceedings of a symposium on the way in which the arts and theatre and literature reflect and influence race relations in South Africa, with contributions by fifteen art historians and critics.

1126 Kotze, Astrid von. "Workers' Plays in South Africa." *ComIBS.* 1985 Nov.; 15(1): 3-16.

South Africa, Republic of. 1985. Critical studies. ■The development of worker plays adheres to socio-historical needs rather than aesthetic considerations or consumer demands.

1127 Hernando, Josep. "Los moralistas frente a los espectáculos de la Edad Media." (The Moralists and the Entertainments of the Middle Ages.) 21-37 in Salvat, Ricard, ed. *El Teatre durant l'Edat Mitjana i el Renaixement.* Barcelona: Publicacions i Edicions de la Universitat de Barcelona; 1986. xxviii, 322 pp. (El Pla de les Comèdies 2.) Notes. Append. [Presented at First International Symposium on Medieval and Renaissance Theatre, Sitges, 1983.] Lang.: Spa.

Spain. 1000-1316. Historical studies. ■Development of Church attitude toward performers.

1128 Scaffi, Saviana; Brandon, James R.; Copfermann, Émile; Boal, Augusto; Magnier, Bernard; Adler, Heidrun; Antei, Giorgio; Cao, Antonio F.; Pearson, Michael; Pérez-Stanfield, María Pilar; Polito, Juan Carlos D.; Purkey, Malcolm; Revuelta, Vicente; Margaritis, Alcibiade E. "Influència cultural i colonització. Enriquiment de les formes d'expressió pròpies i modificació de la trajectoria cultural." (Cultural Influence and Colonization. Enrichment of Indigenous Forms of Expression and Modification of Cultural Evolution.) 189-336 in Coca, Jordi, ed.; Conesa, Laura, comp. *Congrés Internacional de Teatre a Catalunya 1985. Actes. Volum II. Seccions 1, 2 i 3.* Barcelona: Institut del Teatre; 1986. 340 pp. Notes. Biblio. Lang.: Eng, Fre, Spa, Cat.

Spain. Latin America. 1185. Critical studies. ■Reports and discussions of Section III, International Congress of Theatre in Catalonia, focusing primarily on Latin American theatre.

1129 Cohen, Hilary U. "Vår Teater: A Swedish Model of Children's Theater for Participants with Disabilities." *ChTR.* 1985 Oct.; 34(4): 14-16. Notes. Lang.: Eng.

Sweden: Stockholm. 1975-1985. Historical studies. ■Participation of disabled children in the production of Stockholm's city-run Vår Teater (Our Theatre), including discussion of two productions, *Naturalem* and *The Clock,* and speculation on the application of similar productions in the U.S.

1130 Hermand, Jost; Poore, Carol, transl. "Brecht in *Die Ästhetik des Widerstands.*" *ComIBS.* 1984 Apr.; 12(2): 3-12.

Sweden: Stockholm. 1939-1940. Critical studies. ■A portrait of Brecht as the superfather according to Peter Weiss's narrator in the novel *Die Ästhetik des Widerstands.*

1131 Slayton, Ralph. "Do We Value Our Children Less?" *ChTR.* 1986 Spr; 35(1): 28. Lang.: Eng.

Sweden: Stockholm. USA. 1986. Histories-sources. ■Inadequacy of U.S. children's theatre as compared to Vår Teater of Stockholm. Asks if we value our children less and care less about what they have to say. Bemoans commercialization of children's theatre in USA.

1132 Lipgens, Anselm. "Theaterpädagogik die wandelnde Identitätskrise." (Acting Teachers-Teaching Actors: A Job Looks for Its Identity.) *TM.* 1986 Dec.; 1(1): 6-7. Illus.: Photo. B&W. Lang.: Ger.

Switzerland: Zurich. 1980-1986. Historical studies. ■Training course at School of Acting for teacher/actors, who would teach children to express themselves through drama—however, no employment opportunities yet exist for them.

1133 Raunicher, Herta. "Münzen prägen Schweizer Kultur." (Official Coins for Swiss Culture.) *MuT.* 1986 Oct.; 7(10): 32-33. Lang.: Ger.

Switzerland. 1982-1986. Histories-sources. ■Criticizes the present structure of government support for playwrights and official attitudes toward funding for the arts.

1134 Lihamba, A. *Politics and Theatre in Tanzania after the Arusha Declaration.* Leeds: Univ. of Leeds; 1985. Notes. Biblio. [Ph.D. dissertation, *Index to Theses,* 36-6920.] Lang.: Eng.

Tanzania. 1967-1984. Historical studies. ■Study of the historical background, the Arusha Declaration and the role of the theatre within

THEATRE IN GENERAL: —Relation to other fields

Ujamaa and for social development, with a discussion of the works of Ebrahim Hussein.

1135 Berghaus, Günter. "Theatre in Exile." *PlPl.* 1986 Sep.; 396: 14-17. B&W. 4. Lang.: Eng.
UK-England. Germany. 1937-1947. Historical studies. ▪Refugee artists from Nazi Germany and the flowering of German culture in Britain.

1136 Langton, Robert Gore. "Macbeth's Barclaymoan." *PlPl.* 1986 Dec.; 399: 14-15. Lang.: Eng.
UK-England: London. South Africa, Republic of. 1986. Histories-specific. ▪Argues that the Royal Shakespeare Company (RSC) was wrong to turn down Barclay sponsorship to show disapproval of apartheid.

1137 Mezei, Éva. "Színház a nevelésben." (Theatre-in-Education.) *Sz.* 1986 Nov.; 19(11): 22-25. Illus.: Photo. B&W. 1: 18 cm. x 13 cm. Lang.: Hun.
UK-England: London, Greenwich. 1986. Critical studies. ▪The possible application of different theatrical-dramatic techniques in education, in a wider sense in social connection.

1138 Protherough, Robert. "The Rhetoric of Sir Keith Joseph." *JAP&M.* 1986 May; 2(3): 4-8. Lang.: Eng.
UK-England. 1985. Critical studies. ▪Attitude and language of England's Secretary of State for Education, Sir Keith Joseph, as demonstrated in his public addresses.

1139 Sibley, Adrian. "Altered Images." *PlPl.* 1986 Oct.; 397: 9-11. B&W. 5. Lang.: Eng.
UK-England. 1979-1986. Critical studies. ▪Studies the work of disabled theatre groups which challenge basic assumptions and attitudes of audiences to performers.

1140 Barba, Eugenio. "Theatre Anthropology." 275-304 in McNamara, Brooks, ed.; Dolan, Jill, ed. *The Drama Review: Thirty Years of Commentary on the Avant-Garde.* Ann Arbor, MI: UMI Research P; 1986. xii, 371 pp. (Theatre and Dramatic Studies 35.) Illus.: Photo. Print. B&W. 15: var. sizes. Lang.: Eng.
USA. Japan. 1982. Empirical research. ▪Sociocultural and physiological study of human behavior in a performance situation focusing on an analysis of the actor's language. References are made to the Oriental theatre.

1141 Chamberlain, Oliver. "Pricing Management for the Performing Arts." *JAML.* 1986 Fall; 16(3): 49-59. Notes. Tables. Lang.: Eng.
USA. 1986. Critical studies. ▪Goals and strategies of pricing decisions includi̇ g price systemization.

1142 Collins, Patrick M. "Toward Dramatic Literacy: A Position Paper." *ChTR.* 1985 Oct.; 34(4): 3-6. Notes. Biblio. Lang.: Eng.
USA. 1944-1985. Critical studies. ▪Asserts the need for 'dramatic literacy' to be included in the concept of 'cultural literacy' in the schools. Ways to incorporate drama into the curriculum.

1143 Cooley, Edna Hammer. *Women in American Theatre 1850-1870: A Study in Professional Equity.* College Park, MD: Univ. of Maryland; 1986. 281 pp. Pref. Notes. Biblio. [Ph.D. dissertation, Univ. Microfilms order No. DA 8620759.] Lang.: Eng.
USA: New York, NY. 1850-1870. Historical studies. ▪Demonstrates that careers in theatre offered women professional equality with men in respect to salary and career opportunities.

1144 Demo, Mary Penasack. "The ERIC Connection." *ChTR.* 1984 Oct.; 33(4): 21-23. Notes. Lang.: Eng.
USA. 1980-1985. Critical studies. ▪A paper offering examples of the research and practice of role-playing from the ERIC database, arguing for innovation in role-playing and increased use of the data system.

1145 Dezseran, Catherine; Katz, Barbara Myerson. "Theatre-in-Education and Child Sexual Abuse: A Descriptive Study." *ChTR.* 1985 Oct.; 34(4): 7-13. Biblio. Lang.: Eng.
USA: St. Louis, MO. 1976-1984. Critical studies. ▪Development of Choices, an educational theatre program on child sexual abuse designed for a third-grade audience, with emphasis on the responses of test-group audiences, including students, teachers and parents.

1146 Dunn, Tom. "On Paying Playwrights." *TT.* 1984 Feb.; 3(4): 3. Illus.: Photo. B&W. 1: 3 in. x 3 in. Lang.: Eng.
USA: New York, NY. 1984. Historical studies. ▪Argument for increase of financial rewards for playwrights to prevent them from fleeing to other media.

1147 Fox, Deborah Jean. "The ERIC Connection." *YTJ.* 1986 Fall; 1(2): 19-20. Lang.: Eng.
USA. 1983-1985. Instructional materials. ▪A selection of documents from the ERIC computer system, discussing dramatic exercises in the classroom and their use as a pedagogical technique.

1148 Gilman, Richard. "Good Company." *AmTh.* 1984 June; 1(3): 12-13. Illus.: Photo. B&W. 2: var. sizes. Lang.: Eng.
USA: Los Angeles, CA. 1984. Critical studies. ▪The Twenty-third Olympiad Arts Festival is scheduled to coincide with the 1984 Olympics. A comparison and analysis of theatre and sports, citing Mejerchol'd and Brecht.

1149 Goldberg, Moses. "Aesthetic Development: A Position Paper." *ChTR.* 1985 Jan.; 34(1): 3-6. Tables. Lang.: Eng.
USA. 1985. Critical studies. ▪A discussion of the integration of theatre into children's education based on a three-part model of aesthetics: techniques, processes, and experience. The paper emphasizes the importance of the arts in general to a complete education in values.

1150 Goodwin, Dorothy A. "An Investigation of the Efficacy of Creative Drama as a Method for Teaching Social Skills to Mentally Retarded Youth and Adults." *ChTR.* 1985 Apr.; 34(2): 23-26. Biblio. Lang.: Eng.
USA. 1984. Critical studies. ▪Dramatic activities in teaching social interaction to handicapped children and adults, with suggestions for conducting programs.

1151 Gourgey, Annette F.; Bosseau, Jason. "The Impact of an Improvisational Dramatics Program on Student Attitudes and Achievement." *ChTR.* 1985 July; 34(3): 9-14. Tables. Biblio. Lang.: Eng.
USA: Newark, NJ. Critical studies. ▪A study of the effects of an improvisational drama program on 150 disadvantaged minority students, asserting that such a program improves both reading and social skills.

1152 Holley, Robert. "Advocacy Clampdown." *AmTh.* 1984 July/Aug.; 1(4): 28-29. Illus.: Sketches. 1. Lang.: Eng.
USA: Washington, DC. 1984. Historical studies. ▪Office of Management and Budget (OMB) issues new rules restricting lobbying activities by voluntary organizations that receive federal grants and contracts.

1153 Jenkins, Linda Walsh. "Children and Community: Bondings and Deep Stirrings." *ChTR.* 1984 July; 33(3): 3-7. Lang.: Eng.
USA. 1970-1984. Critical studies. ▪Analysis of the relation between children's theatre and community, specifically the usefulness of theatre for teaching children about such problems as dilemmas and paradoxes. Also discussed is the importance of funding.

1154 Levine, Mindy N. "The Art of Theatrical Letters: A Conversation with *Performing Arts Journal*'s Publishers." *TT.* 1984 Feb.; 3(4): 6-7. Illus.: Photo. B&W. 2: 3 in. x 4 in. Lang.: Eng.
USA: New York, NY. 1984. Historical studies. ▪Mission of *Performing Arts Journal* and PAJ publications to increase stature of drama as part of American literature by increased publication of playtexts and criticism.

1155 Levine, Mindy N. "Making (And Not Making) A Living in the Theatre." *TT.* 1983 July; 2(8): 1-2, 8-9. Illus.: Photo. B&W. 2. Lang.: Eng.
USA: New York, NY. 1983. Histories-sources. ▪Economic survival of the individual theatre artist discussed by several directors and designers. Salaries, alternate jobs and the curtailing of private and public support for the arts.

1156 Lima, Maria H. "The Tropical Brecht Comes to New York." *ComIBS.* 1984 Nov.; 14(1): 57-59.
USA: New York, NY. 1984. Historical studies. ▪The Nuevo Teatro movement, which focuses on colonialism and the resultant deformation of Latin America, and the status of Bertolt Brecht in the U.S.

THEATRE IN GENERAL: —Relation to other fields

1157 MacDonald, Judith B. "Understanding Communication Patterns Through Playmaking." *YTJ*. 1986 Fall; 1(2): 3-9. Biblio. Tables. Lang.: Eng.
USA: New York, NY. 1986. Critical studies. ■Effect of playmaking on a group of sixth and seventh-grade students hypothesizing that playmaking allows for a different type of discourse among students.

1158 McCaslin, Nellie. "Good Theatre for Today's Changing Child." *ChTR*. 1984 July; 33(3): 11-13. Notes. Lang.: Eng.
USA. 1903-1985. Critical studies. ■Overview of the changes in the forms and goals of the children's theatre movement in this century, particularly in the areas of genre, plots and characters, and the relation of performance to social or 'adult' issues.

1159 Michell, Monica. "Creative Drama: Bridging the Gap Between the Elementary School and the Art Museum." *ChTR*. 1985 July; 34(3): 5-7. Notes. Biblio. Lang.: Eng.
USA: Austin, TX. 1985. Critical studies. ■A proposal for integrating museum visits and study of the visual arts into the elementary school curriculum by using creative drama and story-making before, during and after museum trips.

1160 Mulcahy, Kevin V. "The Arts and Their Economic Impact: The Values of Utility." *JAML*. 1986 Fall; 16(3): 33-48. Notes. Lang.: Eng.
USA. 1986. Critical studies. ■The role of the arts in the urban economy.

1161 Rudolph, Ellen B. "Artist As Outsider: Some Thoughts and Feelings About Artists in the Schools." *TT*. 1984 Jan.; 3(3): 1-2, 8-9. Illus.: Photo. B&W. 2: 3 in. x 3.5 in., 6 in. x 2.5 in. Lang.: Eng.
USA: New York, NY. 1983. Historical studies. ■Distrust between artists and educators, conflicts between individual creativity and academic regimen, advantages to teachers and artists from increased contact.

1162 Salazar, Laura Gardner. "Reflections, Innovation and Concurrence: Style in Children's Theatre." *ChTR*. 1985 Apr.; 34(2): 3-6. Tables. Biblio. Lang.: Eng.
USA. UK. France. 1600-1980. Critical studies. ■Style of children's theatre in the context of Philippe Ariès' theories of the passage of cultural forms through adult and juvenile phases, with attention to pantomime, absurdist works and vaudeville.

1163 Schwartz, Dorothy T.; Bedard, Roger L. "Children's Theatre Association of America: Issues of the Past, Challenges of the Future." *ChTR*. 1984 Oct.; 33(4): 3-9. Notes. Lang.: Eng.
USA. 1940-1984. Critical studies. ■Methods and aims of the Children's Theatre Association from the 1940s to the present, considering such issues as connections with social issues, the international exchange of ideas and the use of professional and volunteer workers.

1164 Steuer, Gary P. "Economic Impact of Theatre in New York City." *TT*. 1984 Jan.; 3(3): 4-5. Lang.: Eng.
USA: New York, NY. 1983. Historical studies. ■Highlights of study: *The Arts as An Industry: Their Economic Importance to the New York-New Jersey Metropolitan Region* issued by the Port Authority of New York and the Cultural Assistance Center, Inc.

1165 Stewig, John W. "The Classroom Connection—Elementary School Principals and Creative Drama." *YTJ*. 1986 Fall; 1(2): 15-18 . Notes. Tables. Lang.: Eng.
USA. 1986. Critical studies. ■Study of how principals perceive the use of drama in the curriculum.

1166 Stewig, John W. "The Classroom Connection: Creative Drama Content In Current College Language Arts Textbooks." *ChTR*. 1986 Spr; 35(1): 20-21. Biblio. Tables. Lang.: Eng.
USA. 1986. Critical studies. ■Survey of 21 college Language Arts textbooks to determine how much attention is paid to drama and which drama topics are most commonly addressed.

1167 Turner, Victor. "Body, Brain and Culture." *PerAJ*. 1986; 10(2): 26-34. Notes. Lang.: Eng.
USA. 1986. Technical studies. ■Stimulation of both hemispheres of the brain by ritual and rhythm.

1168 Wills, J. Robert. "Who Are You? A Question for Children's Theatre." *ChTR*. 1985 July; 34(3): 3-4. Lang.: Eng.

USA. 1985. Critical studies. ■A position paper arguing for the establishment of graduate programs in children's theatre, citing the demands of specialization and the necessity of expanding and enhancing children's theatre.

1169 Wright, Carolyn. "ESIPA: A Case Study In Innovative Arts and Education." *ChTR*. 1984 Oct.; 33(4): 11-17. Notes. Lang.: Eng.
USA: Albany, NY. 1970-1984. Historical studies. ■Development of the Empire State Institute for the Performing Arts: its administrations, goals, facilities and funding.

1170 Zesch, Lindy. "Artists Fall Victim to McCarthy Era Law." *AmTh*. 1984 Dec.; 1(8): 26-29. Notes. Illus.: Photo. B&W. 3: var. sizes. Lang.: Eng.
USA: Washington, DC. 1984. Historical studies. ■International artists are denied entry visas to the United States as undesirables under the McCarthy era 'ideological exclusionary clauses' of the Immigration and Nationality Act. Includes remarks by Producer Bernard Gersten to the Conference on Free Trade in Ideas in Washington, D.C.

1171 "Koncepcija čeloveka v sovremennom teatral'nom processe." (The Conception of Man in the Contemporary Theatre Process.) *TeatrM*. 1986; 10: 120-139. Lang.: Rus.
USSR. 1980. Critical studies. ■First of a two-part series continued in *TeatrM* 11 (1986), 116-138.

1172 Čepalov, A. "Teat'r est' prostranstvo neevklidovo." (The Theatre is Non-Euclidean Space.) *TeatrM*. 1986; 11: 161-169 . Lang.: Rus.
USSR. 1980-1986. Historical studies. ■Relates theatrical art and progressive scientific thought.

1173 Čičkov, B. "Eto tema vybrala menja." (It is the Theme that Chose Me.) *TeatZ*. 1986; 29(1): 12-13. Lang.: Rus.
USSR. 1980-1986. Historical studies. ■Traditions of political theatre and drama.

1174 Garon, L. "Načnem s sebja." (Let's Start With Ourselves.) *SovD*. 1986; 3: 223-234. Lang.: Rus.
USSR. 1986. Histories-sources. ■Interview with Oleg Jéfremov, principal director at Moscow Art Theatre, on the aims of theatre with respect to social change.

1175 Kapeljus, J. "Čto zritel' vyberet? Zametki sociologa." (What Will the Audience Select? Notes of a Sociologist.) *TeatrM*. 1986; 12: 141-143. Lang.: Rus.
USSR. 1985. Histories-sources. ■Statistical index of theatre attendance in the regional and provincial centers of the USSR-Russian SFSR.

1176 Krymova, I. "Gorod ne molčit." (The City is Not Silent.) *TeatZ*. 1986; 29(5): 14-15. Lang.: Rus.
USSR. 1980. Critical studies. ■A sociologist's view of the audience-performer relationship.

1177 Lichačev, D. "Nravstvennost'—osnova kul'tury." (Morals: The Foundation of Culture.) *SovD*. 1986; 3: 211-222. Lang.: Rus.
USSR. 1980-1986. Critical studies. ■The role of theatre and television in the moral education of society. Related to Media: Video forms.

1178 Smelkov, Ju. "Sezon peremen." (A Season of Changes.) *Znamja*. 1986(9): 213-222. Lang.: Rus.
USSR. 1980. Critical studies. ■New tendencies in Soviet theatre.

1179 Stourac, Richard; McCreery, Kathleen. *Theatre As a Weapon: Workers' Theatre in the Soviet Union, Germany and Britain, 1917-1934*. London/New York, NY: Routledge & Kegan Paul/Methuen; 1986. 336 pp. Index. Biblio. Illus.: Photo. Lang.: Eng.
USSR. Germany. UK-England. 1917-1934. Histories-specific. ■Organization and aims of theatre for the proletariat.

1180 Švydkoj, M. "Zloba dnja i vdochnovenije poeta." (Daily Evil and the Poet's Inspiration.) *DruzNar*. 1986; 6: 220-228. Lang.: Rus.
USSR. 1980-1986. Critical studies. ■Reaction of theatre to changed social conditions.

1181 Švydkoj, M. "Kakoj teatr nuzen ljudjam? Razmyšlenja serediny 80-h gg." (What Kind of Theatre do the People

CLASSED ENTRIES

THEATRE IN GENERAL: —Relation to other fields

Need? Reflections of the Mid-1980s.) *TeatrM*. 1986; 2: 6-25. Lang.: Rus.
USSR. 1980-1986. Critical studies. ■Reflections on the role of theatre in society.

1182 Zagradskaja, S. "Obrjad včera i segodnja." (The Rite of Yesterday and Today.) *KZ*. 1986 June; 30(6): 14-16. Lang.: Rus.
USSR. Historical studies. ■Elements of ritual and ceremony in outdoor festivities.

1183 Turner, Edith. "Philip Kabwita, Ghost Doctor: The Ndembu in 1985." *TDR*. 1986 Win; 30(4): 12-35. Notes. Illus.: Handbill. Photo. Maps. B&W. 14: 4 in. x 4 in. Lang.: Eng.
Zambia. 1985. Historical studies. ■Healers of the Ndembu tribe of Zambia use theatrical rituals and props in order to effect a cure.

Research/historiography

1184 McDonald, Larry. "On Writing Alternative Theatre History: Hypernaturalism—Whose Theatre of the 70s?" *CDr*. 1984 Sum; 10 (2): 227-231. Lang.: Eng.
Canada. 1970-1980. Critical studies. ■Response to William Weiss's essay in *CDr* 9:2 (1983), which asserted the dominance of 'hyperrealist' style in the 70s. McDonald considers the theatrical movements ignored by Weiss, particularly in the Canadian theatre.

1185 Adler, Doris. "Dekker Observed: Review Article." *MRenD*. 1984; 1: 231-242. Notes. Lang.: Eng.
England: London. USA. 1600-1980. Critical studies. ■An overview of Cyrus Hoy's critical introductions to Fredson Bower's collected works of Thomas Dekker, assessing Hoy's presentation of historical facts, stage history and critical responses to Dekker's work.

1186 Owomoyela, Oyekan. "Creative Historiography and Critical Determinism in Nigerian Theater." *RAL*. 1986 Sum; 17(2): 234-251. Notes. Lang.: Eng.
Nigeria. 1826-1986. Historical studies. ■Examination of Joel Adedeji's thesis on *alàrìnjó*, a Yoruba theatrical art form, contrasting his account with his sources and focusing on whether such entertainments were done by professional performers.

1187 Edwards, Christopher; Herbert, Ian. "Computer Databases for the Performing Arts: Tandem and International Bibliography of Theatre." *TN*. 1985; 39(3): 149-152. Notes. Lang.: Eng.
UK-England. 1985. Historical studies. ■Development of two databases, TANDEM and IBT to aid in theatre research on an international level.

1188 Herbert, Ian. "Computer Databases for Theatre Studies." *NTQ*. 1986 May; 11(6): 175-180. Notes. Lang.: Eng.
UK-England: London. 1985. Historical studies. ■An account of a conference held in London, 13-14 September, 1985, of leading world specialists in theatre information, sharing their experience of computers in their work, and discussing their future use on a national and international scale.

Theory/criticism

1189 Bécsy, Tamás; Eszenyi, Sándor, transl. *Drama As a Genre and Its Kinds*. Budapest: Hungarian Centre of ITI; 1986. 87 pp. Biblio. Lang.: Eng.
Critical studies. ■Problematic issues of the aesthetic theories of theatre and drama.

1190 Carlson, Marvin. "Psychic Polyphony." *JDTC*. 1986 Fall; 1(1): 35-47. Notes. Lang.: Eng.
1600-1986. Critical studies. ■Unique power of live theatre to express different psychic lines of action giving the spectator a choice of focus.

1191 Fergusson, Francis; Földényi, F. László, transl. *A szinház nyomában. A dráma müvészete változó perspektívában*. (The Idea of a Theatre: The Art of Drama in Changing Perspective.) Budapest: Európa; 1986. 328 pp. (Modern könyvtár.) Lang.: Hun.
1949. Critical studies. ■Hungarian translation of *The Idea of a Theatre*, Princeton University Press.

1192 Józsa, Péter. *Az esztétikai élmény nyomában*. (In Quest of the Aesthetic Experience.) Budapest: Akadémiai K.; 1986. 278 pp. (Muszeion könyvtár 5.) Biblio. Lang.: Hun.
Critical studies. ■Essays on the sociology of art and semiotics, universal problems of aesthetic reception, film in particular and, by inference, theatre. Related to Media: Film.

1193 Kissel, Howard. "The Wise Counselor? The Critic's Role in Contemporary Theatre." *TheatreS*. 1984-85/1985-86; 31/32: 41-48. Lang.: Eng.
1986. Critical studies. ■Objectivity and high standards of the theatre critic are essential for effective evaluation.

1194 Kramer, Hilton; Dasgupta, Gautam; Rabkin, Gerald; Blau, Herbert. "Interface: Hilton Kramer." *PerAJ*. 1986; 10(1): 59-76. Lang.: Eng.
1986. Histories-sources. ■Transcript of a discussion of the nature and development of modernism and postmodernism as artistic movements.

1195 Müller, Péter P. "Színházelméleti kérdések a nyolcvanas években. Áttekintés." (Theoretical Questions for Theatre in the Eighties: Review.) *Sz*. 1986 Nov.; 19(11): 43-48. Biblio. Lang.: Hun.
1977-1986. Critical studies. ■Survey on the major trends of theatre theory in the 1980s.

1196 Ruffini, Franco. "Horizontal and Vertical Montage in the Theatre." *NTQ*. 1986 Feb.; 11(5): 29-37. Notes. Illus.: Diagram. B&W. 1. Lang.: Eng.
Critical studies. ■Actors and audiences 'select' from the full theatrical vocabulary and its many means of expression, to make live performance subject to creative self-assembly and juxtaposition ('montage') as in film.

1197 Székely, György. *A szinjáték világa. Egy müvészeti ág társadalom-történetének vázlata*. (The World of the Play: The Outlines of the Social History of Theatre.) Budapest: Gondolat; 1986. 483 pp. Biblio. Lang.: Hun.
Histories-general. ■A comprehensive history of the theatre in its social context, from its beginnings to the present, based on the theory of theatre types.

1198 Wang, Bangxiong. "Xitong, Xinhi Zidonghua, Wutai Meishu." (System, Psychological Motivation, Stage Design.) *Xyishu*. 1982 Nov.; 5(4): 109-114. Lang.: Chi.
1950-1980. Critical studies. ■Systematic analysis of the interrelations of the theatrical elements and audience reaction in a theatre space.

1199 Fiebach, Joachim. *Die Toten als die Macht der Lebenden. Zur Theorie and Geschichte von Theater in Afrika*. (The Dead as the Power of the Living. On Theory and History of Theatre in Africa.) Berlin: Henschelverlag; 1986. 447 pp. Pref. Index. Notes. Illus.: Photo. B&W. 35: 11 cm. x 7 cm. Lang.: Ger.
Africa. 1400-1985. Histories-specific. ■Pre-capitalistic (pre-colonial) African culture and 20th century African theatre.

1200 Lee, Du-Heyun; Brandon, James R. "Tongseŏ Yeonguk Pigyŏ Yeongu." (Comparative Study of Eastern and Western Theatre.) 6-82 in Yeo, Suk-Gi, ed. *A Collection of Essays*. Seoul: Korea UP; 1986. 295 pp. Lang.: Kor.
Asia. Europe. Histories-general. ■Comparative study of characteristics that distinguish the Oriental theatre from Western theatre.

1201 Copfermann, Émile; Boal, Augusto. "Le Théâtre de l'Opprimé, réponse à la colonisation Culturelle—Théâtre de l'Opprimé. L'arsenal théorique." (The Theatre of the Oppressed: A Response to Cultural Colonization—Theatre of the Oppressed: The Theoretical Arsenal.) 213-223 in Coca, Jordi, ed.; Conesa, Laura, comp. *Congrés Internacional de Teatre a Catalunya 1985. Actes. Volum II. Seccions 1, 2 i 3*. Barcelona: Institut del Teatre; 1986. 340 pp. Lang.: Eng.
Brazil. France. 1956-1978. Critical studies. ■Compares Boal's concept of the theatre of the oppressed with similar theories of Brecht and Fernández Retamar, describes Boal's evolution and ideas.

1202 Gu, Zhongyi; Sun, Huizhu, ed. "Gu Zhongyi Di Xiju Lilun." (Gu Zhongyi's Theories of Theatre.) *XYishu*. 1982 Aug.; 5(3): 5-16. Lang.: Chi.

THEATRE IN GENERAL: —Theory/criticism

China. 1920-1963. Critical studies. ■Western theory synthesized and adapted to Chinese drama by Gu Zhongyi. Includes listing of plays by Gu.

1203 Su, Kun. "Jinian *Zai Yan'an Wenyi Zuotanhui Shang de Jiang-hua* Fabiao Sishi Zhounian." (Commemorating the 40th Anniversary of the Publication of *Talks At Yan'an Forum of Literature and Art*.) *XYishu*. 1982 May; 5(2): 1-5. Lang.: Chi.

China, People's Republic of: Shanghai, Yan'an. 1942-1982. Critical studies. ■Round-table discussion about historical and current significance of Mao's talks from 40 years ago on the purpose of literature and art, and the role of the artist.

1204 Cruciani, Fabrizio, ed.; Falletti, Clelia, ed. *Civiltà teatrale nel XX secolo*. (Theatrical Civilization in the Twentieth Century.) Bologna: Il Mulino; 1986. 393 pp. (Problemi e prospettive. Musica e spettacolo.) Pref. Index. Notes. Biblio. Lang.: Ita.

Europe. 1880-1985. Critical studies. ■Anthology of excerpts from the writings of critics and theatre professionals on the theory of modern theatre. Includes works by Stanislavskij, György Lukács and Jerzy Grotowski.

1205 Korhonen, Kaisa; Stormbom, Nils-Börje, transl. "Varför dör inte teatern?" (Why Doesn't the Theatre Die?)*NT*. 1986; 32: 3-7. Lang.: Swe.

Finland: Tammerfors. 1986. Critical studies. ■University of Tammerfors' inaugural lecture investigating the nature of theatre.

1206 Har'el, Vered. "Siha Im Patris Pavis." (Interview with Patrice Pavis.) *Bamah*. 1986; 21(105-106): 122-123. Lang.: Heb.

France: Paris. 1923-1986. Histories-sources. ■Interview with semiologist Patrice Pavis about the theatre institute at the Sorbonne, his semiotic approach to theatre and modern French theatre.

1207 Huston, Hollis. "The Performance/Thought of Roland Barthes." *JDTC*. 1986 Fall; 1(1): 99-115. Notes. Lang.: Eng.

France. Critical studies. ■A dialogue performed by an imaginary performer and critic about the nature of Roland Barthes' work.

1208 Zverev, A. "Magičeskije mosty." (Magical Bridges.) *VLit*. 1986; 5: 241-249. Lang.: Rus.

France. 1846-1949. Critical studies. ■Influence of the theatrical culture of the East on Antonin Artaud.

1209 Leidner, Alan C. "The Dream of Identity: Lenz and the Problem of *Standpunkt*." *GQ*. 1986 Sum; 59(3): 387-400. Lang.: Eng.

Germany. 1774. Critical studies. ■Concept of *Standpunkt* in J.M.R. Lenz's poetics *Anmerkungen Ubers Theater (Notes on the Theatre)* and its application to the search for identity in the 'Sturm und Drang' period.

1210 Conradie, P.J. "Enkele moderne benaderings van die Griekse Tragedie." (A Few Modern Approaches to Greek Tragedy.) *Acta Classica*. 1986; 29(29): 3-17. Biblio. Lang.: Afr.

Greece. UK-England. Germany. Critical studies. ■A look at the way recent developments in literary and dramatic theory may influence critical approaches to Greek theatre studies.

1211 Hermann, István. *A hitvitától a drámáig*. (From Religious Controversy to Drama.) Budapest: Szépirodalmi K; 1986. 526 pp. Lang.: Hun.

Hungary. 1971-1983. Critical studies. ■Selected studies on the theory of the theatre and the drama, including television and film reviews.

1212 Tahy, Nóra. "A teátrális szokás. Eddigi szerepe a magyar színháztörténet megértésében és rendszeres vizsgálatának alapjai." (The Theatrical Habit: Its Role so Far in the Understanding of the Hungarian Theatre History and Basis of its Regular Study.) *SzSz*. 1986; 10(19): 53-83. Notes. [From a dissertation *Das theatralische Brauchtum des ungarischen Sprachbereichs* (Vienna, 1984).] Lang.: Hun.

Hungary. Critical studies. ■Study on restatement of the question of theatrical habit on the basis of its international literature and methodological application.

1213 Watanabe, Tomoya; Chini, Antonella, transl. "Alcuni aspetti dello sviluppo del teatro europeo e giapponese." (Aspects of the Development of European and Japanese Theatre.) 87-94 in Ottai, Antonella, ed. *Teatro Oriente/Occidente*. Rome: Bulzoni; 1986. viii, 565 pp. (Biblioteca Teatrale 47.) Lang.: Ita.

Japan. Europe. 500 B.C.-1986 A.D. Historical studies. ■Development and mutual influence of Japanese and European theatre. Origin of theatre in ritual and religion. Diet as a major factor in cultural background.

1214 Chang, Han-Gi. *Hängǔk Yěongǔksä*. (History of Korean Theatre.) Seoul: Lee, Gi-guan; 1986. 361 pp. Lang.: Kor.

Korea: Seoul. 200 B.C.-1986 A.D. Histories-general. ■Theory and history of Korean theatre.

1215 Kim, Ho-Sung. "Dôngyäng Yèongǔk." (Theatre of the Orient.) 376-341 in Sung, Gim-Kwang, ed. *Understanding Theatre*. Seoul: Sung, Gim-Kwang; 1986. 344 pp. Lang.: Kor.

Korea: Seoul. Japan: Tokyo. China: Beijing. 200-1986. Histories-general. ■Discussion of the primary genres: Korean mask play, *nō* and *kabuki* (Japan) and Beijing Opera (China).

1216 Shae, Yung-Ho. "Kim Woo-Jin ui Yěongǔk Pigyö." (Kim Woo-Jin's Theatre Criticism.) 257-278 in Yoo, Min-Young, ed. *Illusion and Reality*. Seoul: Aum, In-Gue; 1986. 362 pp. Lang.: Kor.

Korea: Seoul. 1920-1929. Critical studies. ■Major critic's views on Korean plays and theatre productions.

1217 Hausbrandt, Andrzej; Holoubek, Gustaw. *Teatr jest światem*. (Theatre is World.) Cracow: Wydawnictwo Literackie; 1986. 256 pp. Lang.: Pol.

Poland. Critical studies. ■Critic Andrzej Hausbrandt and actor Gustaw Holoubek discuss their views on the general problems of theatre: its origins, time and space, acting, audience, etc..

1218 Batalov, R.H. *Estetičeskie vozzrenija K.S. Stanislavskogo. Avtoref. diss... kand. filos. nauk*. (The Aesthetic Views of K.S. Stanislavskij: Synopsis of a Dissertation by a Candidate in Philosophy.) Moscow: MGU; 1986. 23 pp. Lang.: Rus.

Russia. 1863-1938. Critical studies.

1219 "Ingmar Bergman's *King Lear*. A Discussion with Eugenio Barba." *ATJ*. 1986 Fall; 3(2): 261-269. Illus.: Photo. Print. B&W. 2: 5.5 in. x 5 in., 4 in. x 5 in. Lang.: Eng.

Spain-Catalonia: Barcelona. 1985. Histories-sources. ■Eugenio Barba and an *ATJ* editor discuss the Ingmar Bergman production of *King Lear* in terms of Asian aesthetics and performance pictures, with comparisons to *Nō* and *Kabuki*.

1220 Grilli, Giuseppe. "Models de transformació del text teatral: la segona oportunitat." (Transformation Models of a Play: The Second Opportunity.) 35-51 in Coca, Jordi, ed.; Conesa, Laura, comp. *Congrés Internacional de Teatre a Catalunya 1985. Actes. Volum II. Seccions 1, 2 i 3*. Compiled by Laura Conesa. Barcelona: Institut del Teatre; 1986. 340 pp. Lang.: Cat.

Spain-Catalonia. 1400-1963. Critical studies. ■Historical difficulties in creating a paradigm for Catalan theatre, with examples from plays from different historical periods.

1221 Ay, Lufti. "Relazione e influenze del teatro occidentale nel campo delle arti dello spettacolo in Turchia." (Relations and Influences of Western Theatre in the Domain of the Performing Arts in Turkey.) 395-414 in Ottai, Antonella, ed. *Teatro Oriente/Occidente*. Rome: Bulzoni; 1986. viii, 565 pp. (Biblioteca Teatrale 47.) Lang.: Ita.

Turkey. 1524-1986. Critical studies. ■Study of western influences on theatrical development in Turkey.

1222 Özgü, Melâhat. "L'influenza dell'oriente e dell'occidente sul concetto turco di teatro." (The Influence of East and West on the Turkish Conception of the Theatre.) 415-420 in Ottai, Antonella, ed. *Teatro Oriente/Occidente*. Rome: Bulzoni; 1986. viii, 565 pp. (Biblioteca Teatrale 47.) Lang.: Ita.

CLASSED ENTRIES

THEATRE IN GENERAL: —Theory/criticism

Turkey. 1000-1986. Critical studies. ■Influences of Eastern and Western theatre on theatrical development in Turkey.

1223 "Getting Press." *TT.* 1983 July; 2(8): 6-8. Illus.: Photo. B&W. 7: var. sizes. Lang.: Eng.
USA: New York, NY. 1983. Histories-sources. ■Report on seminar on theatre criticism sponsored by Alliance of Resident Theatres/New York, with quotations from several critics and press agents on the role of the critic in theatre today.

1224 Breuer, Lee. "The Theatre and Its Trouble." *AmTh.* 1986 Nov.; 3(8): 38-39. Pref. Illus.: Photo. Print. B&W. 2: 2 in. x 3 in., 5 in. x 7 in. Lang.: Eng.
USA. Histories-sources. ■A tongue-in-cheek deconstructionist manifesto.

1225 Brustein, Robert; Nelson, Richard; Bishop, André; Maguire, Matthew; Renick, Kyle; Gurney, A.R., Jr. "Theatre vs. the Movies." *TT.* 1985 May; 4(5): 2-5. Illus.: Handbill. B&W. 1. Lang.: Eng.
USA: New York, NY. 1985. ■Six directors and playwrights challenge article in *Atlantic* in which David Denby asserted that theatre is a weak form of communication in comparison to film and television. Related to Media: Film.

1226 Cattaneo, Anne. "New York Theatre Critics: Partners or Adversaries?" *TT.* 1983 June; 2(7): 1-2, 8-10. Illus.: Photo. B&W. 5: var. sizes. Lang.: Eng.
USA: New York, NY. 1983. Histories-sources. ■Discussion with several artistic directors, reviewers and writers regarding the role of the critic in theatre today, their relationship to avant-garde theatre, the lack of qualified critics for the future.

1227 Dolan, Jill. "The Politics of Feminist Performance." *TT.* 1986 July/Aug.; 5(6): 11-12. Illus.: Dwg. 2. Lang.: Eng.
USA: New York, NY. 1982-1986. Historical studies. ■Lack of representation of women in theatre examined from plays of ancient Greece to today. Politicization occurs as women press for voice in the mainstream.

1228 Dziewulska, Małgorzata. "'Performing Arts Journal' i tło z wiewiórkami." ('Performing Arts Journal' and the Background with Squirrels.) *DialogW.* 1986; 12: 110-116. Lang.: Pol.
USA. 1976-1986. Critical studies. ■Critical profile of *Performing Arts Journal* and of recent theatrical trends.

1229 Gilman, Richard. "Eric Bentley...and Me." *AmTh.* 1986 Oct.; 3(7): 23-25. Illus.: Photo. Print. B&W. 2: 3 in. x 5 in., 5 in. x 6 in. Lang.: Eng.
USA. 1962-1986. Histories-sources. ■Describes the influence of Eric Bentley on his own work and on a generation of theatrical theorists.

1230 Huston, Hollis. "Dedthtre." *PerAJ.* 1986; 10(2): 17-25. Lang.: Eng.
USA. Critical studies. ■Is the theatre dead? How technological advances have altered the spiritual and aesthetic role of the actor in society.

1231 Kirby, Michael; Schechner, Richard. "An Interview with John Cage." 79-100 in McNamara, Brooks, ed.; Dolan, Jill, ed. *The Drama Review: Thirty Years of Commentary on the Avant-Garde.* Ann Arbor, MI: UMI Research P; 1986. xii, 371 pp. (Theatre and Dramatic Studies 35.) Lang.: Eng.
USA. 1965. Histories-sources. ■John Cage discusses his struggle to define art through his exploration of definitions for dance, music, painting, theatre and structure.

1232 Kirby, Michael. "TDR Statement." 193-196 in McNamara, Brooks, ed.; Dolan, Jill, ed. *The Drama Review: Thirty Years of Commentary on the Avant-Garde.* Ann Arbor, MI: UMI Research P; 1986. xii, 371 pp. (Theatre and Dramatic Studies 35.) Lang.: Eng.
USA. 1971-1986. Critical studies. ■Michael Kirby defends the liberal outlook of *The Drama Review* citing its documentation of trends and movements in theatre as well as significant performances.

1233 O'Quinn, Jim. "Experiencing the Other." *AmTh.* 1984 Sep.; 1(5): 14-18. Notes. Illus.: Photo. B&W. 8: var. sizes. Lang.: Eng.
USA: Amherst, MA. Histories-sources. ■Theatre Communications Group's 1984 National Conference titled 'An Examination of Process:

Exploring Creative Collaboration in the Theatre'. International collaborations also discussed. Includes excerpts from keynote speech given by John Hirsch, artistic director of the Stratford Festival.

1234 Schechner, Richard. "Schechner's Farewell." 175-176 in McNamara, Brooks, ed.; Dolan, Jill, ed. *The Drama Review: Thirty Years of Commentary on the Avant-Garde.* Ann Arbor, MI: UMI Research P; 1986. xii, 371 pp. (Theatre and Dramatic Studies 35.) Lang.: Eng.
USA. 1969-1986. Histories-sources. ■Richard Schechner bids farewell to *The Drama Review* and suggests areas of future theatrical investigation.

1235 Schneider, Alan. "Things to Come: Crystal-Gazing at the Near and Distant Future of a Durable Art." *AmTh.* 1984 Apr.; 1 (1): 14-17, 40. Illus.: Sketches. 2. Lang.: Eng.
USA. 1984. Histories-sources. ■Director Alan Schneider presents satirical predictions for the future of theatre along with serious questions as to who will guide the development of the art form.

1236 Tatlow, Antony. "Aimez-vous Brecht? A Polemic." *ComIBS.* 1985 Nov.; 15(1): 38-42.
USA. 1974. Critical studies. ■Critique of James Fenton's review of John Willett's *Brecht in Context* and Ronald Hayman's *Brecht: A Biography* as a hostile polemic on their subject.

1237 Bondarenko, V. "Den' zavtrašnij." (The Future.) *SovD.* 1986; 1: 255-262. Lang.: Rus.
USSR. 1986. Critical studies. ■'New Wave' drama and contemporary Soviet dramaturgy.

1238 Efros, Anatolij. "Kritika dolžna byt' vyše nas." (Criticism Must be Superior to Us.) *TeatZ.* 1986; 29(20): 19-20 . Lang.: Rus.
USSR. 1980-1986. Critical studies. ■The role of criticism in the creative theatrical process.

1239 Il'inskaja, O. "Govorjascee molčanie." (A Speaking Silence.) *SovD.* 1986; 4: 236-250. Lang.: Rus.
USSR. 1986. Critical studies. ■Correlation of word and image in dramaturgy.

1240 Jakubovskij, D. "Talant vsegda raduet." (Talent Always Gladdens.) *TeatZ.* 1986; 29(5): 12-13. Lang.: Rus.
USSR: Moscow. 1986. Critical studies. ■Round table on the problems of synthesis of the arts in the theatrical process with dancer L. Semenjaka, theatre critic and producer of the Malyj Teat'r, B. L'vov-Anoshin, and producer of Kamernyj Muzykal'nyj Teat'r, Ju. Borisov.

1241 Karp, P. "Professionalnye paradoksy." (Professional Paradoxes.) *Neva.* 1986; 6: 170-175. Lang.: Rus.
USSR. 1980-1986. Critical studies. ■Problems and tasks of contemporary theatre criticism.

1242 Klimova, L.P. *K.S. Stanislavskij v russkoj i sovetskoj kritike.* (K.S. Stanislavskij in Russian and Soviet Criticism.) Leningrad: Iskusstvo; 1986. 149 pp. Lang.: Rus.
USSR: Russia. 1888-1986. Critical studies. ■Stanislavskij in Russian and Soviet criticism.

1243 Kupcova, O.N. *Kritičeskie diskussii o putjach stanovlenija sovetskogo teatra (1917-1927 gg.).* (Critical Discussions about the Paths of Formation of the Soviet Theatre, 1917-1927.) Moscow: MGU; 1986. 22 pp. [Synopsis of a Dissertation.] Lang.: Rus.
USSR. 1917-1927. Historical studies. ■Overview of the development of theatre criticism in the press.

1244 Kuznecov, F. "Vnimanie k žizni." (Attention to Life.) *SovD.* 1986; 1: 234-245. Lang.: Rus.
USSR. Critical studies. ■The aims of literature, including drama.

1245 Ljubimov, B. "Ne bud' ja kritik..." (Let Me Not Be a Critic...)*TeatZ.* 1986; 29(14): 20-22. Lang.: Rus.
USSR. Critical studies. ■Ethical and moral position of criticism.

1246 Šagin, I. "Den' segodnjasnij." (The Present.) *SovD.* 1986; 1: 246-254. Lang.: Rus.
USSR. 1986. Critical studies. ■Problems, tendencies and basic features of Soviet dramaturgy.

1247 Ščerbakov, K. "O teatre, mino i okolo." (On Theatre Far and Near.) *TeatrM.* 1986; 3: 134-141. Lang.: Rus.

THEATRE IN GENERAL: —Theory/criticism

USSR. 1980. Critical studies. ■On theatre criticism.

1248 Seleznev, Ju. "Glasami naroda." (With the Eyes of the People.) *SovD.* 1986; 2: 266-277. Lang.: Rus.
USSR. 1986. Critical studies. ■National features of Russian literature and dramaturgy.

1249 Simukov, A. "Moe remeslo: zametki dramaturga." (My Craft: Notes of a Playwright.) *SovD.* 1986; 2: 205-217. Lang.: Rus.
USSR. 1986. Critical studies. ■Director of the Gorky Literary Institute discusses specific characteristics of the playwright's craft.

1250 Voršavskij, Ja. "Na perekrestkacn iskusstv." (At the Cross-roads of the Arts.) *Iskusstvo kino.* 1986; 6: 95-106. Lang.: Rus.
USSR. 1980-1986. Critical studies. ■The interpenetration of theatre, film, and 'tele-art', and the reflection of the artistic in works of art criticism in recent years.

Training

1251 Antal, Gábor. "A szinésznevelés breviáriuma." (Breviary of the Education of Artists.) *Sz.* 1986 Sep.; 19 (9): 47-48. Lang.: Hun.
Historical studies. ■Review of training materials in Hungary and elsewhere since antiquity.

1252 Barba, Eugenio. "Le Corps dilaté." (The Dilated Body.) *JCT.* 1985; 35: 40-58. Lang.: Fre.
Critical studies. ■Physical training of actors, emphasizing the concept of negation, which involves first doing the opposite of the intended action.

1253 Coblenzer, Horst; Muhar, Franz. *Atem und Stimme: Anleitung zum guten Sprechen.* (Breath and Voice: Guide to Good Speech.) Vienna: Österreichischer Bundesverlag; 1986. 119 pp. (Schriften zur Lehrerbildung und Lehrerfortbildung 13.) Index. Notes. Biblio. Illus.: Dwg. B&W. [First printing in 1976, 6th ed.] Lang.: Ger.
Austria. 1985. Instructional materials. ■The use of voice as a special function of breathing and its economy. Phonation adapted to breath rhythmics, wrong use of voice and acoustic impression. Physiological processes while speaking and singing. Numerous exercises for self-instruction.

1254 Gissenwehrer, Michael; Chini, Antonella, transl. "Il sistema di addestramento nel teatro cinese. Una possibile fonte di nuovi metodi di addestramento nell'Occidente?" (The Training System in the Chinese Theatre: A Potential Source of New Training Methods in the West?)345-361 in Ottai, Antonella, ed. *Teatro Oriente/Occidente.* Rome: Bulzoni; 1986. viii, 565 pp. (Biblioteca Teatrale 47.) Lang.: Ita.
China. Europe. Critical studies. ■Potential training techniques available in Chinese theatre for Western artists.

1255 Zhao, Mingyi. "Xu *Zhongguo Huaju Jiaoyu Shihua.*" (Preface to *Chinese Spoken Drama Training: A History.*) *XYishu.* 1982 May; 5(2): 91-94. Lang.: Chi.
China, People's Republic of. 1907-1982. Critical studies. ■Drama training programs should always support the political goals of the time.

1256 Kiernander, Adrian. "Actor Training at the Centre National d'Art et d'Essai." *ADS.* 1986 Oct.; 9: 53-61. Lang.: Eng.
France: Paris. 1984. Historical studies. ■Record and background study of director Luce Berthomme's actor training methods at the Centre National d'Art et d'Essai.

1257 Wolfe, Debbie. "Directing the Directors." *Drama.* 1986; 3(161): 13-14. Illus.: Photo. B&W. 2: var. sizes. Lang.: Eng.
UK-England. 1986. Critical studies. ■Insufficient courses and facilities are available for training directors.

1258 Curry, Richard Jerome. *A Practical Philosophy of Theatre Education for the Disabled.* New York, NY: New York Univ; 1986. 190 pp. Pref. Notes. Biblio. [Ph.D. dissertation, Univ. Microfilms order No. DA8614319.] Lang.: Eng.
USA. 1986. Critical studies. ■Study of the development of a practical philosophy for the training of disabled students in theatre arts.

1259 Ginsburg, Loren; Hale, Alice M. "Resources: A Guide to Internship Training Programs." *ThCr.* 1986 Jan.; 20(1): 18, 62-73 .
USA. 1986. ■A guide to internship training programs.

1260 London, Todd. "Lost in Manhattan: Directors in Search of Training." *TT.* 1986 Jan.; 5(2): 1-3. Illus.: Photo. B&W. 3. Lang.: Eng.
USA: New York, NY. 1985. Historical studies. ■Lack of opportunities, programs and training for beginning directors. Some options and existing programs are discussed.

1261 Mason, Susan. "An Interview with Kristin Linklater." *ThM.* 1985 Win; 17(1): 40-44. Illus.: Photo. B&W. 1. Lang.: Eng.
USA: New York, NY. UK-England: London. 1954-1985. Histories-sources. ■Director of training and acting company member at Shakespeare and Co. discusses her training and voice techniques.

1262 Romanov, P.V., ed. *Problemy i perspectivy teatral'nogo obrazovanija: sb. nauč. trudov.* (Problems and Perspectives of Theatrical Training: A Collection of Scholarly Works.) Leningrad: Leningr. in-t teatra muzyki i kinematografii; Lang.: Rus.
USSR. 1980-1986. Histories-sources. ■Collected articles on the theory and practice of actor training.

1263 Sazonova, V.A. *Idejno-esteticeskie principy teatralnoj pedagogiki Iu.A. Zavadskogo.* (Ideo-aesthetic Principles of the Theatrical Pedagogy of Ju.A. Zavadskij.) Moscow: GITIS; 1986. 16 pp. [Synopsis of a Dissertation.] Lang.: Rus.
USSR. 1894-1977. Historical studies. ■Pedagogical principles of director, actor and teacher Jurij Aleksandrovič Zavadskij.

1264 Sibirjakov, N. "Magičeskoe 'esli by...': Sistema Stanislavskogo i rumynskij teatr." (The Magical 'If Only...': The Stanislavskij System and Romanian Theatre.) *TeatrM.* 1986; 1: 171-179. Lang.: Rus.
USSR. Romania. 1980-1986. Historical studies. ■Influence of Stanislavskij on Romanian theatre.

DANCE

General

Basic theatrical documents

1265 Ohno, Kazuo. "Selections From the Prose of Kazuo Ohno." *TDR.* 1986 Sum; 30(2): 156-162. Illus.: Photo. B&W. 5: 3 in. x 3 in. Lang.: Eng.
Japan. Histories-sources. ■Butō choreographer Ohno Kazuo's thoughts on the inspiration for his dances.

1266 Ohno, Kazuo. "The Dead Sea Vienna Waltz and Ghost." *TDR.* 1986 Sum; 30(2): 170. Lang.: Eng.
Japan. 1986. ■Notes for butō dance about the bewilderment of the dead searching for love.

1267 Tanaka, Min. "Stand By Me!" *TDR.* 1986 Sum; 30(2): 152. Lang.: Eng.
Japan. 1985. Histories-sources. ■Poem by Tanaka Min that speaks of the reasons he dances.

1268 Tanaka, Min. "I Am an Avant-Garde Who Crawls the Earth." *TDR.* 1986 Sum; 30(2): 153-155. Lang.: Eng.
Japan. 1976-1985. Histories-sources. ■Homage to butō dancer Hijikata Tatsumi, as an influence on Tanaka Min.

Institutions

1269 Zamponi, Linda. "Alles tanzt." (Everybody Is Dancing.) *Buhne.* 1986 Feb.; 29(2): 12-16. Illus.: Photo. Print. Color. B&W. Lang.: Ger.
Austria: Vienna. 1986. Histories-sources. ■Tanz '86, an international dance-festival.

1270 Levkojeva, N. "Družba i Sotrudnichestvo." (Friendship and Collaboration.) *SovBal.* 1986; 2: 58. Lang.: Rus.
Canada: Montreal, PQ, Toronto, ON. 1985. Histories-sources. ■Notes on the dance committee meetings at the 21st congress of the International Theatre Institute.

DANCE: General—Performance/production

Performance/production

1271 Hood, Robley Munger. *Ballets Suédois: Modernism and the Painterly Stage.* Denver, CO: Univ of Denver; 1986. 208 pp. Pref. Notes. Biblio. [Ph.D. dissertation, Univ. Microfilms order No. DA8612843.] Lang.: Eng.
France: Paris. 1920-1925. Critical studies. ■Study of four works presented by the experimental ballet troupe, Ballets Suédois.

1272 Daly, Ann. "The Thrill of the Lynch Mob or the Rage of a Woman?" *TDR.* 1986 Sum; 30(2): 46-56. Lang.: Eng.
Germany, West. 1973-1985. Historical studies. ■Symposium of German and American critics concerning the influence of Pina Bausch on *Tanztheater*, particularly the violence in her work.

1273 Martin, Carol. "Mechthild Grossman: The Art of Anti-Heroes." *TDR.* 1986 Sum; 30(2): 98-106. Illus.: Photo. B&W. 2: 3 in. x 4 in. Lang.: Eng.
Germany, West. 1984-1985. Histories-sources. ■Interview with choreographer Mechthild Grossman: *Antigone* and her treatment of sex roles.

1274 Kővágó, Zsuzsa. "A *Magyar Csupajáték* története documentumok tükrében. Válogatás Bordy Bella hagyatékából." (The History of the *Hungarian All-Play* in the Light of Documents: Selection from The Bequest of Bella Bordy.) *SzSz.* 1986; 10(20): 25-42. Notes. Illus.: Photo. B&W. 3: var. sizes. Lang.: Hun.
Hungary: Budapest. 1938-1939. Historical studies. ■Study on the characteristically Hungarian artistic programme, *Magyar Csupajáték (Hungarian All-Play)*, which adapted and stylized elements of folksongs and dance to the stage.

1275 Milloss, Aurél; István, Mária, transl. "Közös munkám Chiricóval." (My Common Work with Chirico.) *SzSz.* 1986; 10(19): 144-148. [Originally published in *Bühne und bildende Kunst im XX. Jahrhundert*, Henning Rischbieter ed. Friedrich Verlag, 1968.] Lang.: Hun.
Hungary. Italy: Milan, Rome. 1942-1945. Histories-sources. ■Choreographer Aurél Milloss's collaboration with artist and scene designer Giorgio de Chirico on a production of *Amphion* by Paul Valéry at La Scala and on other projects.

1276 Pór, Anna. "Találkozások. (Tánc és szinház)." (Meetings: Dance and Theatre.) *SzSz.* 1986; 10 (20): 111-131. 5: var. sizes. Lang.: Hun.
Hungary. 1980-1986. Critical studies. ■Combination of movement, dance and acting in the development of theatrical art in the 1980s.

1277 Pór, Anna. "Változatok kolindára. A szarvassá változott fiak." (Variations on Colinda: *The Sons Who Turned into Stags.*) *Sz.* 1986 Oct.; 19(10): 35-36. Illus.: Photo. B&W. 1: 12 cm. x 15 cm. Lang.: Hun.
Hungary: Győr. 1985-1986. Critical studies. ■*A szarvassá változott fiak (The Sons Who Turned Into Stags)*, choreographed by Iván Markó and Ferenc Novák is a special meeting of modern ballet and traditional folk dance.

1278 Schechner, Richard. "Kazuo Ohno Doesn't Commute." *TDR.* 1986 Sum; 30(2): 163-169. Illus.: Photo. B&W. 4: 2 in. x 2 in. Lang.: Eng.
Japan. 1906-1985. Histories-sources. ■Interview with *butō* choreographer dancer Ohno Kazuo, the spiritual aspects of his work.

1279 Stein, Bonnie Sue. "*Butō*: 'Twenty Years Ago We Were Crazy, Dirty, and Mad'." *TDR.* 1986 Sum; 30(2): 107-125. Notes. Biblio. Illus.: Photo. B&W. 19: 3 in. x 3 in. Lang.: Eng.
Japan. 1960-1986. Historical studies. ■*Butō*, an avant-garde Japanese dance movement, seeks to erase the heavy imprint of Japan's strict society by offering unprecedented freedom of artistic expression.

1280 Stein, Bonnie Sue. "Min Tanaka: Farmer/Dancer or Dancer/Farmer." *TDR.* 1986 Sum; 30(2): 142-151. Illus.: Photo. B&W. 2: 3 in. x 3 in. Lang.: Eng.
Japan. 1950-1985. Histories-sources. ■Interview with *butō* dancer Tanaka Min on the influences of other *butō* dancers, especially Ohno and Hijikata.

1281 Tanaka, Min. "Tradition of the Body and of Avant-Garde Dance." 99-103 in Coca, Jordi, ed.; Conesa, Laura, comp. *Congrés Internacional de Teatre a Catalunya 1985. Actes.*

Volum II. Seccions 1, 2 i 3. Barcelona: Institut del Teatre; 1986. 340 pp. Lang.: Eng.
Japan: Tokyo. 1945-1985. Histories-sources. ■Brief autobiography of dancer, including reflections on improvisation.

1282 Gleuck, Germaine. "Dance Takes Centre Spotlight at Grahamstown Festival." *Scenaria.* 1986 July; 65: 9-15. Illus.: Photo. B&W. 12: 4 in. x 6 in. Lang.: Eng.
South Africa, Republic of: Grahamstown. 1986. Reviews of performances. ■A review of the range and themes of the dance and mime at the annual Festival of the Arts. Related to Mime.

1283 Barnes, Clive; Beaufort, John; Henry, William A., III; Kissel, Howard; Kroll, Jack; Rich, Frank; Watt, Douglas; Wilson, Edwin; Winer, Linda. "*Big Deal.*" *NYTCR.* 1986 Mar 17; 47(5): 327-333. Lang.: Eng.
USA: New York, NY. 1986. Reviews of performances. ■Collection of newspaper reviews of *Big Deal*, based on *Big Deal on Madonna Street*, written, staged and choreographed by Bob Fosse at the Broadway Theatre.

1284 Barnes, Clive; Beaufort, John; Kissel, Howard; Rich, Frank; Storey, Richard David; Watt, Douglas. "*Uptown...It's Hot.*" *NYTCR.* 1986 Jan 13; 47(2): 384-386. Lang.: Eng.
USA: New York, NY. 1986. Reviews of performances. ■Collection of newspaper reviews of *Uptown...It's Hot*, staged, choreographed and conceived by Maurice Hines at the Lunt-Fontanne Theatre.

1285 Kirby, Michael. "Post-Modern Dance: An Introduction." 225-228 in McNamara, Brooks, ed.; Dolan, Jill, ed. *The Drama Review: Thirty Years of Commentary on the Avant-Garde.* Ann Arbor, MI: UMI Research P; 1986. xii, 371 pp. (Theatre and Dramatic Studies 35.) Lang.: Eng.
USA. 1975-1986. Historical studies. ■Merce Cunningham, Alwin Nikolais, Meredith Monk and Yvonne Rainer on post-modern dance and their attempts to join what the spectator perceives to the intentions of the creator.

Reference materials

1286 Kerényi, Ferenc, ed. "Tánctörténeti documentumok Pest megye Levéltárában (1833-1840)." (Documents on the History of Dance in the County Archives of Pest, 1833-1840.) *SzSz.* 1986; 10(20): 133-190. Pref. Notes. Lang.: Hun.
Hungary: Pest. 1833-1840. Histories-specific. ■Source materials of the history of the Hungarian art of dance.

1287 Kuniyoshi, Kazuko. "*Butō* Chronology 1959-1984." *TDR.* 1986 Sum; 30(2): 127-141. Illus.: Photo. B&W. 1: 2 in. x 3 in. Lang.: Eng.
Japan. 1959-1984. ■Includes major works, choreographers and film and art events.

Relation to other fields

1288 Brodbeck, Christine. "Wir müssen ins Leben flüchten." (Flight into Life.) *KB.* 1986 Oct.; 10: 8-15. Illus.: Photo. B&W. Lang.: Ger.
Switzerland. Critical studies. ■Analyzes the absence of body awareness in modern art, especially dance, resulting in a disparity between social structure and bodily well-being. Sees dance performance as a means to body awareness.

Theory/criticism

1289 Birringer, Johannes. "Pina Bausch: Dancing Across Borders." *TDR.* 1986 Sum; 30(2): 85-97. Biblio. Illus.: Photo. B&W. 9: 3 in. x 3 in. Lang.: Eng.
Germany, West. 1977-1985. Historical studies. ■Pina Bausch seen as heir of epic theater of Bertolt Brecht.

1290 Manning, Susan Allene. "An American Perspective on Tanztheater." *TDR.* 1986 Sum; 30(2): 57-79. Biblio. Illus.: Photo. B&W. 26: 3 in. x 3 in. Lang.: Eng.
Germany, West. USA. 1933-1985. Historical studies. ■American critics of dance with a largely formalist aesthetic tend to dismiss the efforts of the German *Tanztheater* movement which relies more on a social and anti-formalist aesthetic.

DANCE: General—Theory/criticism

1291   Supree, Burt. "What the Critics Say about Tanztheater."
TDR. 1986 Sum; 30(2): 80-84. Lang.: Eng.
USA. Germany, West. 1984-1986. Reviews of performances. ■Collection of American dance critics' reviews of Pina Bausch's work.

Ballet

Administration

1292   Lušin, S. "Bogatstvo duchovnoj kul'tury." (The Wealth of Spiritual Culture.) *SovMuzyka*. 1986; 2: 30-32. Lang.: Rus.
USSR: Moscow. 1986. Histories-sources. ■The general director of the Bolšoj Theatre speaks about the problems and tasks standing before the theatre in the years 1986-1990: repertoire, financial problems. Related to Music-Drama: Opera.

1293   Vinogradov, O. "Tol'ko o problemah." (Only About Problems.) *SovBal*. 1986; 3: 5-9. Lang.: Rus.
USSR. 1980-1986. Histories-sources. ■The principal choreographer of the Kirov Theatre discusses the goals, creative and organizational problems of Soviet ballet theatre.

Institutions

1294   Kutschera, Edda. "Politik des Möglichen." (Politics of Possibilities.) *Buhne*. 1986 Feb.; 29(2): 10. (Serie Publikumsorganisationen 7.) Lang.: Ger.
Austria: Vienna. 1985-1986. Histories-specific. ■Origins, functions and activities of the audience-society, Gesellschaft der Freunde der Ballettschule der Österreichischen Bundestheater.

1295   Crabb, Michael. "Alexander Grant's Dismissal From the Complex National Ballet: An Artistic Director's Lot." *PAC*. 1983 Apr.; 20(1): 34-39. Illus.: Photo. B&W. 6. Lang.: Eng.
Canada: Toronto, ON. 1975-1982. Critical studies. ■An analysis of the controversial 1982 firing of Grant, considering his conflicts with dancers, choreographers and other administrators.

1296   Crabb, Michael. "New Directions for the National with Eric Bruhn." *PAC*. 1983 Aug.; 20(2): 24-28. Illus.: Photo. B&W. 2. Lang.: Eng.
Canada: Toronto, ON. 1967-1983. Critical studies. ■An analysis of the problems facing the National Ballet of Canada, and a discussion of the plans and background of newly named artistic director Eric Bruhn.

1297   "V tvorčeskoj obstanovke." (In Creative Conditions.) *SovBal*. 1986; 2: 58-59. Lang.: Rus.
China: Beijing. 1980-1986. Historical studies. ■The contemporary state of ballet theatre in China, including specific characteristics of the teaching of choreography.

1298   Chapman, J.V. *Dancers, Critics and Ballet Masters, Paris 1790-1848*. Lodon: CNAA, Laban Centre for Music and Dance; 1986. Notes. Biblio. [Ph.D. dissertation *Index to Theses* 37-4372.] Lang.: Eng.
France: Paris. 1790-1848. Historical studies. ■Development of dancing and the ballet aesthetic at the Paris Opéra.

1299   Heubi, Peter. "État de l'enseignement professionel de la danse en Suisse." (State of Professional Dance Education in Switzerland.) *NB*. 1986 Aug-Sep.; 10(28): 5-7. Lang.: Fre.
Switzerland. 1986. Historical studies. ■Private and public professional ballet education and the problems brought upon the institutions by different practices of subsidization in different cantons.

Performance spaces

1300   Stuart, Anders; Eriksson, Björn. "Balett i sporthallar." (Ballet in Sports Arenas.) *ProScen*. 1986; 10(1): 34-35. Illus.: Photo. Lang.: Swe.
Sweden. 1986. Technical studies. ■Description of construction of the stage for touring ballet company Cullbergbaletten.

Performance/production

1301   Gelencsér, Ágnes; Körtvélyes, Géza; Maácz, László. *Két évtized táncmüvészeti irásai a 'Magyar Nemzet'-ben: Válogatás*. (Selected Dance Reviews from the *Magyar* Daily Newspaper.) Budapest: Magyar Táncmüvészek Szövetséte; 1985. 187 pp. Lang.: Hun.

1964-1984. Reviews of performances.

1302   Thorpe, Edward. *Kenneth MacMillan: The Man and the Ballets*. London: Hamish Hamilton; 1986. 239 pp. Index. Illus.: Photo. Lang.: Eng.
Europe. USA. 1929-1986. Biographies. ■Career of choreographer, including lists of ballets, companies, designers, dancers, excerpts of reviews.

1303   Zorina, Vera. *Zorina*. New York, NY: Farrar, Straus & Giroux; 1986. 288 pp. Index. Illus.: Photo. Lang.: Eng.
Europe. 1917-1986. Biographies. ■Memoirs of Vera Zorina, star of stage and screen.

1304   Alfejevskaja, G. "Baletnaja muzyka Rameau." (Ballet Music of Rameau.) *SovBal*. 1986; 2: 45-47. Lang.: Rus.
France. 1683-1764. Historical studies. ■On productions of lyric comedies and opera ballets by Jean-Philippe Rameau. Related to Music-Drama: Opera.

1305   Fuchs, Livia. "*A csodálatos mandarin* a magyar szinpadokon (1956-1985)." (*The Miraculous Mandarin* on Hungarian Stages, 1956-1985.) *SzSz*. 1986; 10(20): 73-110. Notes. Illus.: Photo. B&W. 5: var. sizes. Lang.: Hun.
Hungary. 1956-1985. Historical studies. ■Stage history of Bela Bartók's dance drama with analyses of various adaptations.

1306   Major, Rita. "A *Giselle* a régi magyar szinpadon." (*Giselle* on the Hungarian Stage.) *SzSz*. 1986; 10(20): 7-23. Notes. Lang.: Hun.
Hungary: Pest. 1847-1880. Historical studies. ■Stage career of Adolphe Adam's ballet *Giselle* in the National Theatre of Pest.

1307   Pór, Anna. "'Merj szeretni, gyulölni'. Prokofjef-Seregi Rómeó és Júlia-balettje az Operaházban." ('Dare to Love and Hate': Opera House Premiere of *Romeo and Juliet* by Prokofiev and Seregi.) *Sz*. 1986 Apr.; 19(4): 29-32. Illus.: Photo. B&W. 3: 9 cm. x 12 cm., 12 cm. x 15 cm. Lang.: Hun.
Hungary: Budapest. 1985. Reviews of performances. ■Prokofjěv's ballet *Romeo and Juliet* choreographed by László Seregi.

1308   Pór, Anna. "Passiók Liszt zenéjére. *Requiem, Via crucis* és *Jézus, az ember fia*." (Passion Plays on Liszt's Music: *Requiem, Via crucis* and *Jesus the Son of Man*.) *Sz*. 1986 July; 19(7): 10-12. Illus.: Photo. B&W. 2: 12 cm. x 14 cm. Lang.: Hun.
Hungary: Zalaegerszeg, Budapest. 1986. Reviews of performances. ■József Ruszt's movement theatrical production on Franz Liszt's works *Requiem* and *Via Crucis*, and the Ballet Ensemble of Győr's production *Jesus, the Son of Man* in Budapest.

1309   Vanslov, V. "Na forume evropejskich stran." (In the Forum of European Countries.) *SovBal*. 1986; 2: 56-58. Lang.: Rus.
Hungary: Budapest. USSR. 1985. Histories-sources. ■Remarks on the cultural forum of European countries (Budapest, 1985) and the collaboration of the Soviet Union with foreign countries in the field of ballet.

1310   Verdone, Mario. "La drammaturgia ballettistica di Aurelio Milloss." (Ballet Dramaturgy of Aurél Milloss.) *TeatrC*. 1985-1986; 6(11-12): 105-108. Tables. Illus.: Photo. B&W. 8: var. sizes. Lang.: Ita.
Hungary. Italy. 1906-1985. Critical studies. ■Notes on the choreography of Aurél Milloss.

1311   Kotychov, B. "100 let so dnja rozdenija I.L. Rubinstein." (The Hundredth Anniversary of the Birth of I.L. Rubinstein.) *SovBal*. 1986; 3: 58. Lang.: Rus.
Russia. France. 1885-1960. Biographical studies. ■On the career of dancer and actress Ida Rubinstein, member of Diaghilew's 'Russian Seasons'.

1312   Viale, Maria Teresa. "Ritratto di Djagilev, impresario in Europa." (A Portrait of Diaghilew, Manager in Europe.) *BiT*. 1986; 3: 61-82. Notes. Biblio. Lang.: Ita.
Russia. France. 1872-1929. Biographical studies. ■European career of Serge de Diaghilew.

1313   Čabukiani, V. "Moj opyt—argument v diskussii." (My Experience: An Argument in a Debate.) *SovBal*. 1986; 5: 6-8. Lang.: Rus.

DANCE: Ballet—Performance/production

USSR. 1980-1986. Histories-sources. ■Dancer and choreographer V. Čabukiani discusses contemporary and classical ballet.

1314 Černova, N. "V prostranstve žizni." (In the Expanse of Life.) *TeatZ*. 1986; 29(1): 21. Illus.: Photo. B&W. Lang.: Rus.

USSR. Hungary: Budapest. 1985. Reviews of performances. ■Notes from International Choreographic Symposium 'Interbalet'.

1315 Davlekamova, S. "Parad virtuozov." (A Parade of Virtuosos.) *TeatrM*. 1986; 1: 129-142. Lang.: Rus.

USSR: Moscow. 1985. Histories-sources. ■Notes on the 5th International Competition of Ballet Dancers.

1316 Erofeeva-Litvinskaja, E. "Majja Pliseckaja: 'Vmet'voshiščat'sja—tože iskusstvo'." (Majja Pliseckaja: 'Knowing How to be Carried Away is Also an Art'.) *TeatZ*. 1986; 29(2): 12-13. Lang.: Rus.

USSR. 1985. Histories-sources. ■Interview with ballerina Majja Pliseckaja.

1317 Il'čeva, M.A. *Irina Kolpakova*. Leningrad: Iskusstvo; 1986. 204 pp. Lang.: Rus.

USSR: Leningrad. 1950-1985. Biographies. ■Creative development of leading ballerina of the Kirov Theatre.

1318 Kasatkina, N.D.; Vasil'jèv, V.Ju. "Sotvorčestvo." (Co-Authorship.) *MuZizn*. 1986; 14: 2-3. Lang.: Rus.

USSR: Moscow. 1980-1985. Histories-sources. ■Artistic directors of the Ballet Theatre of the Soviet Union speak about music and ballet, and the creative plans of the theatre.

1319 Lepešinskaja, O.; Džofri, P.; Leskova, T. "Vstreči na konkurse." (Meetings at a Competition.) *TeatrM*. 1986; 1: 171-179. Lang.: Rus.

USSR: Moscow. 1985. Reviews of performances. ■Reviews of 5th International Competition of Ballet Dancers.

1320 Lopuchov, R. "Rossijskie apostoly tanca." (Russian Apostles of Dance.) *SovBal*. 1986; 5: 48-52. Lang.: Rus.

USSR. Biographical studies. ■Discusses careers of Asaf Messerer, Vladimir Vasiljèv, Jurij Solovjèv and Boris Breguadze.

1321 Vanslov, V. "Mnogogrannyj talant." (Multifaceted Talent.) *TeatrM*. 1986; 8: 126-132. Lang.: Rus.

USSR. 1925-1986. Biographical studies. ■The life and career of Ju. T. Ždanov of the Bolshoi Ballet.

Plays/librettos/scripts

1322 "Shakespeare v smene baletnych epoch." (Shakespeare at the Changing of Ballet Epochs.) *SovBal*. 1986; 1: 30-33. [Cont. in 1986(2): 27-30.] Lang.: Rus.

USSR. Germany, West. 1980-1986. Historical studies. ■The production of ballets based on themes from the works of Shakespeare in the Soviet Union and the Federal Republic of Germany.

1323 Vanslov, V. "Položitel'nyj opyt preobladaet." (Positive Experience Prevails.) *SovBal*. 1986; 1: 19-22. Lang.: Rus.

USSR. 1980-1986. Critical studies. ■Realization of contemporary themes in Soviet ballet theatre.

Reference materials

1324 Koegler, Horst; Weissenböck, Jarmila, comp. *Christl Zimmerl und das Ballett der Wiener Staatsoper 1955-1975*. (Christl Zimmerl and the Ballet of the Viennese State Opera 1955-1975.) Vienna: Österreichischer Bundestheaterverband und Österr. Theatermuseum; 1986. 28 pp. Tables. Illus.: Photo. B&W. 9. Lang.: Ger.

Austria: Vienna. 1939-1976. Biographical studies. ■The late prima ballerina of the Vienna State Opera: her personal and artistic importance, photos of her roles and extracts of letters to her. Includes chronology of her roles.

1325 *Zsuzsi Roboz grafikus és festőművész balett-és szinházi grafikáinak kiállitása a Magyar Állami Operaház Erkel Szinházában: 1985. március 22-április 28*. (Drawings of Theatre and Ballet by Graphic Artist Zsuzsi Roboz: An Exhibit in the Erkel Theatre of the Hungarian National Opera House, 22 March-28 April 1985.) Pref. Notes. Dwg.

12: 15 cm. x 20.5 cm., 16 cm. x 20.5 cm., 20.5 cm. x 20.5 cm. Lang.: Hun.

Hungary: Budapest. 1985. Histories-sources. ■Catalogue of the exhibition held in the Erkel Theatre during the Budapest Spring Festival.

1326 Huguenin, Claire, ed. *Serge Lifar: Une vie pour la danse*. (Serge Lifar: Dancing a Life.) Lausanne: Musée historique de l'Ancien-Évêché; 1986. 166 pp. Pref. Index. Illus.: Photo. B&W. Color. Lang.: Fre.

Switzerland: Lausanne. 1986. Biographical studies. ■Exhibition catalogue showing life and work (text and pictures) of the famous Russian dancer Serge Lifar, who has been living near Lausanne since 1981.

Relation to other fields

1327 Šlaustas, N. "Gravjury rasskazyvajut." (Prints Narrate.) *SovBal*. 1986; 2: 42-43. Lang.: Rus.

France. 1700-1799. Historical studies. ■Eighteenth-century prints depict dancers Marie Sallé and Marie Anne de Cupis de Camargo.

1328 Platek, Ja. "Podslušat' u muzyki." (Listening In Through Music.) *MuZizn*. 1986(14): 15-17. Lang.: Rus.

USSR. 1889-1966. Critical studies. ■The world of choreography in the work of poet Anna Achmatova.

Ethnic dance

Performance/production

1329 Parry, Caroline Balderston. "The Maypole is up, now give me the cup..." *REEDN*. 1986; 11(1): 7-9. Lang.: Eng.

England. 1244-1985. Historical studies. ■Maypole dancing as an historical activity and as currently revived with emphasis upon the modern introduction of ribbons woven around the pole. Related to Mixed Entertainment.

1330 Buonaventura, Wendy; Nobile, Giovanna, transl. *Il serpente e la sfinge*. (The Snake and the Sphinx.) Como: Lyra; 1986. 221 pp. (I sensi dell'amore 7.) Pref. Index. Notes. Tables. Biblio. Illus.: Photo. Pntg. Dwg. B&W. Lang.: Ita.

Europe. Asia. Africa. Historical studies. ■Translation of *Belly-dancing* (London 1983).

1331 Maácz, László. *A magyar néptánc szinpadi pályafutása a XIX-XX. században*. (Hungarian Folk Dance on the Stage in the 19th and 20th Centuries.) Budapest: Népművelési Intézet; 1985. 30 pp. [3rd ed..] Lang.: Hun.

Hungary. 1773-1985. Historical studies. ■A brief historical survey of the adaptation of folk dance to the stage.

1332 Maácz, László. "Kisérlet egy müvészportrëra: Rábai Miklós (1921-1974)." (Attempt at a Portrait of an Artist: Miklós Rábai, 1921-1974.) *SzSz*. 1986; 10(20): 43-72. Illus.: Photo. B&W. 4: var. sizes. Lang.: Hun.

Hungary. 1921-1974. Biographical studies. ■Life and career of choreographer Miklós Rábai.

1333 De Dancan, Llyn. "The Blossom Falling: Movement and Allusion in a Malay Dance." *ATJ*. 1986 Spr; 3(1): 110-116. Notes. Illus.: Photo. Print. B&W. 1: 3 in. x 5 in. Lang.: Eng.

Malaysia. 1950-1984. Historical studies. ■Traditional rules and training in the lyric dance of Malay, and their influence on staging. Use of dances, many based on the *Rāmāyana*, for entertainment, communication, ritual and healing.

1334 Burden, Mathilda. "Tradisionele danse van die Afrikaner wat tot in die twintigste eeu bly voortbestaan het." (Traditional Dances of the Afrikaner Which Have Survived into the Twentieth Century.) *Tydskrif vir Volkskunde en Volkstaal*. 1986 Apr.; 42(1): 32-40. Illus.: Photo. Lang.: Afr.

South Africa, Republic of. 1700-1986. Historical studies. ■A description of some folk dances derived from European popular dance forms and their modern counterparts in Afrikaner culture.

1335 Snow, Stephen. "Intercultural Performance: The Balinese American Model." *ATJ*. 1986 Fall; 3(2): 204-232. Notes. Illus.: Photo. Print. B&W. 18: var. sizes. Lang.: Eng.

USA: New York, NY. Indonesia. 1952-1985. Historical studies. ■Influence of Asian, especially Balinese, theatre traditions on three American artists: dancer-choreographer Islene Pinder, actor-director John Emigh, and director/designer Julie Taymor.

DANCE: Ethnic dance—Performance/production

Research/historiography

1336   Cravath, Paul. "The Ritual Origins of the Classical Dance Drama of Cambodia." *ATJ*. 1986 Fall; 3(1): 179-203. Notes. Illus.: Photo. Print. B&W. 6: var. sizes. Lang.: Eng.
Cambodia. 4 B.C.-1986 A.D. Historical studies. ■Ritual elements and functions found in the Khmer dance of Cambodia concentrating on fertility and funeral rites, relationship between the dancers, spirit world and the kings, and the decline of this ancient form since the 1970s.

1337   Honore, Jasmine. *Towards a Transcription System for Xhosa Umtshotsho Dances*. Stellenbosch: Dept. of Physical Education, Univ. of Stellenbosch; 1986. Notes. Biblio. Illus.: Photo. Dwg. [Research report, part 3.] Lang.: Eng.
South Africa, Republic of. 1980-1985. Technical studies. ■A description of a system for transcribing ethnic dance forms in movement terms, illustrated through a description of Xhosa Umtshotsho dances.

1338   Katsenellenbogen, Edith. *Die dokumentasie en ontleding van sosio-etniese danse en musiek van bepaalde volksgroepe in Suider Afrika, in antropologiese verband*. (The Documentation and Analysis of Socio-Ethnic Dance and Music of Specific Cultural Groups in Southern Africa, in an Anthropological Context.) Stellenbosch: Dept. of Physical Education, Univ. of Stellenbosch; 1986. Notes. Biblio. Illus.: Photo. B&W. [Project leader's report.] Lang.: Afr.
South Africa, Republic of. 1980-1985. Technical studies. ■Summary of the results of a series of studies on ethnic dances in South Africa, including guidelines for a system for transcription and descriptions of various dances.

Modern dance

Administration

1339   Dieterle, Regina, ed. *Tanztheater—wie zeigen—was fördern?* (Dance Theatre: How to Show—What to Promote?)Boswil: Stiftung Künstlerhaus; 1986. 72 pp. Pref. Lang.: Fre, Ger.
Switzerland: Boswil. 1986. Histories-sources. ■Account of symposium on dance theatre at Künstlerhaus, focusing on questions of finance and subsidy.

Design/technology

1340   Bowen, Ken. "Lighting for the Real World of Dance: How to Survive in the Real World of High Expectations on a Tight Budget." *LDim*. 1986 Mar-Apr.; 10(2): 47-53. Illus.: Photo. Print. Color. 5: 5 in. x 7 in, 3 in. x 4 in. Lang.: Eng.
1985-1986. Technical studies. ■Discusses ways to stretch the lighting budget without compromising quality. Gives several examples of simple but effective lighting.

1341   Charles-Roux, Edmonde. *Yves Saint-Laurent et le théâtre*. (Yves Saint-Laurent and the Theatre.) Paris: Herscher; 1986. 130 pp. Pref. Index. Illus.: Design. Photo. Print. Color. B&W. 141: var. sizes. [Accompanies exhibit at the Musée des Arts décoratifs (Paris), June-Sept. 1986.] Lang.: Fre.
France. 1959-1984. Histories-sources. ■Yves Saint-Laurent's costume designs for theatre, the Ballet Roland Petit and music halls, with biographical information.

1342   Bush, Catherine. "Art Design for Dance." *ThCr*. 1986 Jan.; 20(1): 32-35, 51-53. Illus.: Photo. 4: var. sizes.
USA. 1986. Technical studies. ■Visual artists Keith Haring, Robert Longo and Gretchen Bender create an eclectic look for the dance repertory of choreographers Bill T. Jones and Arnie Zane.

Institutions

1343   Citron, Paula. "Formolo and Urban's New Steps in Dance." *PAC*. 1983 Apr.; 20(1): 30-33. Illus.: Photo. B&W. 4. Lang.: Eng.
Canada: Regina, SK, Edmonton, AB. 1980-1983. Histories-sources. ■An overview of the careers of Maria Formolo and Keith Urban, artistic directors of Formolo and Urban Dance Co., focusing on the difficulties of developing choreography and repertory for regional audiences.

1344   Citron, Paula. "A Step Back to Move Forward: Transition at Toronto Dance Theatre." *PAC*. 1983 Aug.; 20(2): 15-18. Illus.: Photo. B&W. 5. Lang.: Eng.
Canada: Toronto, ON. 1968-1982. Critical studies. ■A discussion of problems in repertory and funding at Toronto Dance Theatre, with some consideration of the group's commitment to the technique and principles of Martha Graham.

Performance/production

1345   *Compagnie l'Esquisse: Joëlle Bouvier-Régis Obadia*. (The Esquisse Company: Joëlle Bouvier and Régis Obadia.) Paris: L'Esquisse; 1986. 128 pp. (Angle d'ailes 1.) Append. Illus.: Photo. Print. B&W. 94: var. sizes. Lang.: Fre.
France: Paris. 1981-1985. Histories-sources. ■Black-and-white photos of dance productions by the company l'Esquisse, and an interview with Joëlle Bouvier and Régis Obadia.

1346   Yehouda Moraly, Jean-Bernard. "Danser la Bible." (Dancing the Bible.) *RHT*. 1986; 38(2): 199-212. Notes. [Text of speech to Ninth Intl. Congress of Jewish Studies, Jerusalem, August 1985.] Lang.: Fre.
France. 1934-1936. Historical studies. ■Author's recollections of collaboration with Paul Claudel in the production of theatrical material on Biblical subjects for dancer/choreographer Ida Rubinstein.

1347   *Pina Bausch*. Paris: Solin; 1986. 199 pp. (Danse.) Tables. Illus.: Photo. Print. B&W. 161: var. sizes. Lang.: Fre.
Germany. 1970-1985. Histories-sources. ■Interview with choreographer Pina Bausch on her life, career, training and work. Analysis of her choreographies, with photographs.

1348   Müller, Hedwig. *Mary Wigman: Leben und Werk der grossen Tänzerin*. (Mary Wigman: Life and Work of the Great Dancer.) Weinheim/Berlin: Quadriga; 1986. 324 pp. Pref. Index. Biblio. Illus.: Photo. Color. B&W. Lang.: Ger.
Germany. Switzerland. 1886-1973. Biographies. ■Biographical account of the importance of Mary Wigman as revolutionary of the modern dance movement.

1349   Wigman, Mary; Robinson, Jacqueline, transl. *Le Langage de la danse*. (The Language of Dance.) Paris: Papiers; 1986. Illus.: Photo. Sketches. B&W. 65: var. sizes. Lang.: Fre.
Germany. 1914-1961. Biographical studies. ■Choreographer Mary Wigman discusses her major works and her theory of dance. Original version published 1983.

1350   Goldberg, Marianne. "Trisha Brown, All of the Person's Person Arriving." *TDR*. 1986 Spr; 30(1): 149-170. Pref. Illus.: Photo. Print. B&W. 16: 2 in. x 3 in., 8 in. x 10. Lang.: Eng.
North America. 1983-1985. Histories-sources. ■Interview with choreographer Trisha Brown covers recent work in proscenium stages.

1351   "Roger George—65 Jahre." (Roger George: 65 Years.) *TanzG*. 1986 Oct.; 42(3): 22-24. Illus.: Photo. B&W. Lang.: Ger.
Switzerland. Germany, West. 1921-1986. Biographical studies. ■Homage to one of Switzerland's most celebrated representatives of expressionist modern dance: dancer, choreographer, now director of a school for children in northern Germany.

1352   Rainer, Yvonne. "Yvonne Rainer Interviews Ann Halprin." 101-121 in McNamara, Brooks, ed.; Dolan, Jill, ed. *The Drama Review: Thirty Years of Commentary on the Avant-Garde*. Ann Arbor, MI: UMI Research P; 1986. xii, 371 pp. (Theatre and Dramatic Studies 35.) Lang.: Eng.
USA. 1965. Histories-sources. ■Modern dancer Ann Halprin and how her work with artists in other media created an awareness of the changing reality of performance.

Relation to other fields

1353   Manning, Susan Allene; Benson, Melissa. "Interrupted Continuities: Modern Dance in Germany." *TDR*. 1986 Sum; 30(2): 30-45. Illus.: Photo. Pntg. Diagram. Poster. B&W. 21: 3 in. x 3 in. Lang.: Eng.
Germany. 1902-1985. Historical studies. ■Development of modern dance interrupted by the climate of the Third Reich: German artists fled

DANCE: Modern dance—Relation to other fields

to the United States. Current American artists are now influencing German artists in recreating dance theatre.

Training

1354   Aster, Regina. "Bewegte Strukturen: Tanz und Bewegung mit Betina Nisoli." (Moved Structures: Dance and Motion with Betina Nisoli.) *Parnass.* 1986 Nov-Dec.; 6(6): 20-21. Illus.: Photo. Print. B&W. Lang.: Ger.
Austria: Vienna. 1986. Histories-sources. ∎Report on a lesson with dancer and teacher Betina Nisoli and her ideas about her work.

Other entries with significant content related to Dance: 465, 736, 1656, 2987, 3277, 3361, 3665, 3684, 3870.

DANCE-DRAMA

General

Basic theatrical documents

1355   Panikkar, Kāvālam Nārāyana; Zachariya, Paul, transl.; Zarrilli, Philip, ed. "*Karimkutty.*" *ATJ.* 1985 Fall; 2(2): 172-211. Pref. Notes. Illus.: Photo. 5: 3 in. x 2.5 in. Lang.: Eng.
India. 1983. Textual studies. ∎Text of *Karimkutty* by K. N. Panikkar, a modern parable of the transition from traditional to post-traditional society.

1356   Lee, Meewon, transl.; Lee, Duhyun, transl. "The Mask-Dance Play of Kasan Village (*Kasan ogwangdae*)." *ATJ.* 1985 Fall; 2(2): 139-171. Pref. Biblio. Illus.: Photo. B&W. 5: 3 in. x 2.5 in. Lang.: Eng.
Korea: Kasan. 1975. Textual studies. ∎Translation of mask-dance play, *Kasan ogwangdae (The Five Buffoons of Kasan).*

Performance/production

1357   Ariyanto, Marianne. "*Gambuh*: The Source of Balinese Dance." *ATJ.* 1985 Fall; 2(2): 221-230. Notes. Index. B&W. 1: 3 in. x 2.5 in. Lang.: Eng.
Bali. 1100-1982. Histories-specific. ∎Traces the history of *gambuh*, the oldest form of classical Balinese dance-drama, from its origins in court entertainment to the present.

1358   Cravath, Paul. *Earth in Flower: An Historical and Descriptive Study of the Classical Dance of Cambodia.* Honolulu, HI: Univ of Hawaii; 1986. 684 pp. Pref. Notes. Biblio. [Ph.D. dissertation, Univ. Microfilms order No. DA8629034.] Lang.: Eng.
Cambodia. 1860-1985. Historical studies. ∎Complete history of classical Cambodian dance, including evidence of dance at Angkor, mythological basis of dance, training, ritual function, repertoire and role of dance under each ruler since 1860.

1359   Banu, Georges, int.; Schechner, Richard, ed. "Talking with the Playwright, the Musician, and the Designer." *TDR.* 1986 Spr; 30(1): 72-81. Illus.: Photo. Print. B&W. 3: 2 in. x 3 in., 5 in. x 7 in. Lang.: Eng.
France: Avignon. 1973-1985. Histories-sources. ∎Discussion with playwright, musician, and designer of Peter Brook's *Mahabharata.*

1360   Millon, Martini, int.; Schechner, Richard, ed. "Talking with Three Actors." *TDR.* 1986 Spr; 30(1): 15-53. Illus.: Photo. Print. B&W. 3: 5 in. x 7 in. Lang.: Eng.
France: Avignon. 1985. Histories-sources. ∎Interview with three actors of Peter Brook's company performing the *Mahabharata.*

1361   Schechner, Richard; La Bardonnie, Mathílde; Jouanneau, Joël; Banu, Georges. "*The Mahabharata*, Talking with Peter Brook." *TDR.* 1986 Spr; 30(1): 52-71. Pref. Illus.: Maps. Print. B&W. Grd.Plan. 6: 4 in. x 5 in., 3 in. x 5 in. Lang.: Eng.
France: Avignon. India. 1965-1986. Histories-sources. ∎Interviews with Peter Brook on development of *Mahabharata.*

1362   Richmond, Karen Farley; Richmond, Yasmin. "The Multiple Dimensions of Time and Space in Kūtyāṭṭam, the Sanskrit Theatre of Kerala." *ATJ.* 1985 Spr; 2(1): 50-60. Notes. Illus.: Photo. B&W. 1: 2 in. X 2 in. Lang.: Eng.
India. 1974-1980. Critical studies. ∎An examination of how the Indian concept of time and space and the Hindu world view are reflected in the setting, gestures and language of *Kūtyāṭṭam*, the Sanskrit theatre of Kerala.

1363   Foley, Kathy. "The Dancer and the Danced: Trance Dance and Theatrical Performance in West Java." *ATJ.* 1985 Spr; 2(1): 28-49. Notes. Illus.: Photo. Color. B&W. 8: var. sizes. Lang.: Eng.
Indonesia. 1977-1982. Historical studies. ∎Analysis of three significant trance forms found in West Java. Looks at the similarities between trancers and performers in conventional theatrical entertainments of West Java.

1364   Brandon, James R.; Marsan, Valentine Aymone, transl. "Un modello di spettacolo teatrale asiatico." (A Model of Asian Theatre Performance.) 149-164 in Ottai, Antonella, ed. *Teatro Oriente/Occidente.* Rome: Bulzoni; 1986. viii, 565 pp. (Biblioteca Teatrale 47.) Illus.: Diagram. 3. Lang.: Ita.
Japan. 1363-1986. Critical studies. ∎An outline formula of performance as derived from Asian theatre and its importance in the creation of change.

1365   Farrimond, William. "Proiezione del principio *Kata* nello sviluppo del repertorio espressivo dell'attore occidentale." (Projection of the *Kata* Principle in the Development of the Western Actor's Repertory of Expressions.) 165-170 in Ottai, Antonella, ed. *Teatro Oriente/Occidente.* Rome: Bulzoni; 1986. viii, 565 pp. (Biblioteca Teatrale 47.) Lang.: Ita.
Japan. Denmark. Australia. 1981-1986. Critical studies. ∎Influence of the Japanese *kata* on acting techniques of Western actors, based on observation of Odin Teatret (Holstebro) and Rune Theatre (Sydney).

1366   Hoff, Frank. "Killing the Self: How the Narrator Acts." *ATJ.* 1985 Spr; 2(1): 1-27. Notes. Illus.: Photo. B&W. 4: var. sizes. Lang.: Eng.
Japan. 1960-1983. Critical studies. ∎Examines Japanese storytelling tradition of *Katari*, especially the qualitative differences in sound that differentiate the dual roles of the narrator.

1367   Vsevolodskaja-Goluškevič, O. "Balety Aleksandra Sumarokova." (The Ballets of Aleksand'r Sumarokov.) *SovBal.* 1986; 4: 37-40. Lang.: Rus.
Russia. 1717-1777. Historical studies. ∎Dance-pantomime dramas based on the plots of plays by Aleksand'r Sumarokov.

1368   Baker, Rob. "The Visionary Art of Meredith Monk." *AmTh.* 1984 Oct.; 1(6): 4-9, 34. Notes. Illus.: Photo. B&W. 7: var. sizes. Lang.: Eng.
USA: New York, NY. 1964-1984. Histories-sources. ∎Choreographer Meredith Monk discusses her career, methodology, and collaboration with Ping Chong for their production of *The Games.*

1369   Green, William; Chini, Antonella, transl. "L'Occidente incontra l'Oriente: l'influenza sul teatro moderno americano della messinscena del *Sumurun* di Max Reinhardt nel 1912 a New York." (West Meets East: The Influence on Modern American Theatre of Max Reinhardt's 1912 New York Production of *Sumurun*.) 527-538 in Ottai, Antonella, ed. *Teatro Oriente/Occidente.* Rome: Bulzoni; 1986. viii, 565 pp. (Biblioteca Teatrale 47.) Lang.: Ita.
USA: New York, NY. 1912. Critical studies. ∎Influence of Max Reinhardt's 'drama with music and without words', based on episodes from the *Thousand and One Nights.*

1370   Leverett, James. "From the Repertoire: The (Im)Pure Theatre of Twyla Tharp." *AmTh.* 1984 Apr.; 1(1): 22-23. Illus.: Photo. B&W. 1. Lang.: Eng.
USA. 1984. Reviews of performances. ∎Criticizing the poor quality in theatre, Leverett presents choreographer Twyla Tharp's *Fait Accompli* as an exciting blend of dance and theatre.

DANCE-DRAMA: General—Performance/production

1371   Yohalem, John. "Bosch is Alive: In Martha Clarke's 'Garden'." *AmTh.* 1984 Nov.; 1(7): 16-18. Illus.: Photo. B&W. 3: var. sizes. Lang.: Eng.
USA: New York, NY. 1979-1984. Historical studies. ■Martha Clarke's *The Garden of Earthly Delights*, inspired by a painting of Hieronymous Bosch incorporates elements of theatre and dance.

1372   Drewel, Henry John. "Flaming Crowns, Cooling Waters: Masquerades of the Ijebu Yoruba." *AAinNYLH.* 1986 Nov.; 20(1): 32-41, 99. Notes. Illus.: Photo. Print. Color. B&W. 22: var. sizes. Lang.: Eng.
Western Africa. Historical studies. ■Costumes, satiric dances and processions of the Ijebu Yoruba masquerades, rituals of purification and renewal that mark the transition of seasons.

1373   Drewel, Margaret Thompson. "Art and Trance Among Yoruba Shango Devotees." *AAinNYLH.* 1986 Nov.; 20(1): 60-67, 98. Notes. Illus.: Photo. Print. Color. B&W. 18. Lang.: Eng.
Western Africa. Historical studies. ■Costumes, dance steps and music in initiation rites of Yoruba priesthood where initiate becomes medium, possession dances performed by the shaman.

1374   Kamlongera, Christopher F. "An Example of Syncretic Drama from Malawi: Malipenga." *RAL.* 1986 Sum; 17(2): 197-210. Notes. Lang.: Eng.
Zambia: Malawi. 1914-1985. Historical studies. ■Origins of *malipenga*, known also as *mganda* and *beni*, a form of dance-drama combining Western and African elements, and the celebrations at which these burlesques of military parades are performed.

Plays/librettos/scripts

1375   Kim, Han-Young. "Yängjubyealsändae ui Inmööl Bunsuck." (A Study of Characters in *Yängjubyulsändae*.) 23-51 in Kim, Han-Young, ed. *A Study of Yängjubyulsändae.* Seoul: Bae, Min-Chon; 1986. vi, 281 pp. Lang.: Kor.
Korea: Yängju. 1700-1900. Critical studies. ■Characteristic features of the roles in the mask-dance play *Yängjubyulsändae*.

Research/historiography

1376   Zarrilli, Philip. "The Aftermath, When Peter Brook Came to India." *TDR.* 1986 Spr; 30(1): 92-99. Illus.: Photo. Print. B&W. 2: 5 in. x 7 in. Lang.: Eng.
India: Kerala, Calcutta. 1980-1985. Histories-sources. ■Discussion among scholars and practitioners of Indian theatre on research methods and impact of Peter Brook's *Mahabharata*.

Theory/criticism

1377   Chang, Han-Ki. "Hängük-gwa Ilban-ui Minsôkgük Pigyo Yeongü." (Comparative Study of Folklore in Japan and Korea.) 5-28 in Lee, Young-Tack, ed. *Dong-Guk Dramatic Art.* Seoul: Dong-Guk Univ; 1986. 231 pp. Illus.: Photo. B&W. 8: 3 in. x 4 in., 4 in. x 8 in. Lang.: Kor.
Korea: Seoul. Japan. 1400-1600. Histories-specific. ■Influence of Korean traditional theatre on the Japanese traditional mask-dance play.

1378   Kim, Bäng-Ock. "Hängük Kämyoenguk ni Yôenguk Mihäk." (Aesthetics of the Korean Mask-Dance Drama.) 213-242 in Kim, Ook-gil, ed. *Mask-Dance Drama.* Seoul: Ewha Women's UP; 1986. 370 pp. Lang.: Kor.
Korea: Seoul. Japan: Tokyo. China: Beijing. 1400-1986. Critical studies. ■Comparative analysis of differences between the Korean mask-dance drama and other traditional mask-dance drama in Asia.

1379   Lim, Heä-Kyung. "Tai chum äe Nätamän Häehäk ui: Sanging Seüng." (Symbolic Formation of Humor in the Mask-Dance Drama.) 179-212 in Kim, Ook-gil, ed. *Mask-Dance Drama.* Seoul: Ewha Women's UP; 1986. 370 pp. Illus.: Photo. Neg. B&W. 4: 2 in. x 4 in., 2 in. x 6 in. Lang.: Kor.
Korea: Seoul. 700-1986. Histories-specific. ■Evolution of the Mask-Dance drama detailing the symbolic references of the genre.

Kabuki

Basic theatrical documents

1380   Kabuki Daichō Kenkyūkai. *Kabuki Dozichō Shūsei No. 9-12.* (Collection of Kabuki Texts, No. 9-12.) Tokyo: Benseisha; 1986. 639 pp. Illus.: Photo. Lang.: Jap.
Japan: Tokyo. 1600-1980. ■Collection of *kabuki* texts assembled by the Society for Kabuki.

Performance/production

1381   Bandō, Tamasaburō; Ōkura, Shunji; Watanabe, Tamotsu. *Kabuki—Onnagata.* (Kabuki—Female Impersonators.) Tokyo: Shinchōsha; 1986. Illus.: Photo. Lang.: Jap.
Japan: Tokyo. Histories-sources. ■Collection of pictures of famous *onnagata*.

1382   Brandon, James R. "Time and Tradition in Modern Japanese Theatre." *ATJ.* 1985 Spr; 2(1): 71-79. Notes. Illus.: Photo. B&W. 2: 3 in. x 5 in. Lang.: Eng.
Japan. 1983-1984. Reviews of performances. ■Examines the balance of old and new forms of Japanese theatre through a series of reviews. Related to Puppetry.

Nō

Basic theatrical documents

1383   Beichman, Janine. "*Drifting Fires*: An American Nō." *ATJ.* 1986 Fall; 3(2): 231-260. Notes. Append. Illus.: Photo. Print. B&W. 2: 5 in. x 7 in., 3 in. x 5 in. Lang.: Eng.
Japan: Ibaraki. 1984-1985. Histories-sources. ■Playtext of an English language drama *Drifting Fires* by Janine Beichman, with author's afterword on use of *Nō* elements.

1384   Kenny, Don. "The Snail: A *Kyōgen* Play as Performed by the Izumi School." *ATJ.* 1986 Spr; 3(1): 34-53. Biblio. Illus.: Photo. Print. B&W. 9: 3 in. x 5 in, 5 in. x 7 in. Lang.: Eng.
Japan. 1060-1982. Historical studies. ■Introduction to the Japanese comic theatre form of *kyōgen*, its birth as an art form, its costuming, staging and traditional training. Includes the text of Nomura Mansai's *The Snail*, photographs and stage directions from the Izumi School production.

1385   Sekine, Masaru. *Zeami and His Theories of Nō Drama.* Gerrards Cross: C. Smythe; 1985. 184 pp. Biblio. Index. Illus.: Photo. B&W. Lang.: Eng.
Japan. 1363-1443. Historical studies. ■Edition of the essays of Zeami arranged according to subject matter.

Design/technology

1386   Bethe, Monica. "*Nō* Costume as Interpretation." *MimeJ.* 1984: 148-155. Illus.: Photo. 6: var. sizes.
Japan. Critical studies. ■An actor's interpretive costume choice within the strictly prescribed costume tradition of *Nō* theatre.

1387   Blundall, John M. "The Noh Theatre of Japan." *Cue.* 1986 Sep/Oct.; 8(43): 4-6. Illus.: Photo. Print. Color. B&W. 7: 9 x 6 cm., 8 x 10 cm. Lang.: Eng.
Japan. 1363-1986. Technical studies. ■Description of how *Nō* masks are made.

1388   Ichinen, Kitazawa; Teele, Rebecca, transl. "The Expression of Ko-omote." *MimeJ.* 1984: 125-129. Lang.: Eng.
Japan. Critical studies. ■The aesthetic qualities of the Yuki *no* ko-omote mask.

1389   Iwao, Kongō. *Yūgen no hana, Nō shōzoku no meihin.* (Flowers of *Yūgen*: Famous Costumes of the *Nō*.) Tokyo: Kōrinsha Shuppan; 1986. 119 pp. Illus.: Photo. Lang.: Jap.
Japan. 1300-1986. Histories-sources. ■Collection of pictures of *nō* costumes.

1390   Kyōun, Iwasaki; Teele, Rebecca, transl. "*Kyōgen* Masks." *MimeJ.* 1984: 183-193. Illus.: Photo. 17: var. sizes.
Japan. Historical studies. ■Compares the development of *nō* and *kyōgen* masks, the use of the woman's mask in *kyōgen* and the concerns of the mask carver.

DANCE-DRAMA: *Nō*—Design/technology

1391   Manzō, Nomura; Kenny, Don, transl. "Mask Making."
MimeJ. 1984: 171-176. Illus.: Photo. 4: var. sizes.
Japan. 1984. 1984. Histories-sources. ■An analysis of mask carving,
back finishing and coloring based on traditional methods and the
author's experience.

1392   Nakamura, Yasuo; Teele, Rebecca. "*Nō* Masks: Their
History and Development." *MimeJ*. 1984: 114-124. Illus.:
Photo. 10: var. sizes. Lang.: Eng.
Japan. Technical studies. ■Characteristics of different *nō* masks and
modeling devices found in *ko-omote*.

1393   Nearman, Mark J. "Behind the Mask of *Nō*." *MimeJ*. 1984:
20-65. Illus.: Photo. 40: var. sizes. Lang.: Eng.
Japan. Critical studies. ■The meaning and significance of the *nō* mask
from the perspective of medieval artists connected to its tradition.

1394   Nishimura, Jeanne Chizuko. "A Life-Giving Art: Traditional Art of *Nō* Mask Carving." *MimeJ*. 1984: 140-147.
Illus.: Photo. 12: var. sizes. Lang.: Eng.
Japan. Technical studies. ■Carving techniques used in making the *ko-
omote* mask.

1395   Teele, Rebecca. "Interview with Udaka Michishige, Actor
of the Kongō School." *MimeJ*. 1984: 130-139. Illus.: Photo.
6: var. sizes. Lang.: Eng.
Japan. Histories-sources. ■Udaka Michishige discusses how his work as
a mask carver influences his awareness of the mask as a *nō* actor.

Performance/production

1396   "Recent Experiments in the Use of *Nō* and *Kyōgen* Traditions: *At the Hawk's Well*: An Experiment in Japan With *Nō*
Techniques in English." *MimeJ*. 1984: 215-232.
Japan: Kyoto, Tokyo. 1984. 1981-1982. Histories-sources. ■Directors,
dancers and music directors discuss the movement demands, concept,
use of mask and timing and delivery of lines in a *nō* production of *At the
Hawk's Well*.

1397   Alberry, Nobuko. *The House of Kanze: A Saga of Four-
teenth-Century Japan*. New York, NY: Simon & Schuster;
1985. 302 pp. Lang.: Eng.
Japan. 1357-1441. Histories-reconstruction. ■A novel reconstructing the
life of the founders of *nō*, Kanami and Zeami.

1398   Banu, Georges. *L'Acteur qui ne revient pas: journées de
travail au Japon*. (The Actor Who Doesn't Come Back:
Working Days in Japan.) Paris: Aubier; 1986. 121 pp. Illus.:
Photo. Print. B&W. 16: var. sizes. Lang.: Fre.
Japan. 1986. Empirical research. ■Collection of essays on Japanese
theatre written after a study trip to Japan.

1399   Bethe, Monica. "Okina: An Interview with Takabayashi
Kōji." *MimeJ*. 1984: 93-103. Illus.: Dwg. Photo. 4: var.
sizes. Lang.: Eng.
Japan. Histories-sources. ■Kita school actor Takabayashi Kōji discusses
the centrality of *Okina* to the *nō* actor's repertory.

1400   Horigami, Ken. *Nō, 'shura' to 'en' no sekai*. (Nō: The World
of 'Shura' and 'En'.) Tokyo: Nōgaku-shorin; 1986. 184 pp.
Illus.: Photo. Lang.: Jap.
Japan. 1350-1986. Histories-sources. ■Collection of pictures about *nō*
theatre.

1401   Immoos, Thomas; Sirabella, Mariabruna, transl. "La Teoria
mistica della recitazione in Zeami." (Zeami's Mystical
Theory of Acting.) 213-229 in Ottai, Antonella, ed. *Teatro
Oriente/Occidente*. Rome: Bulzoni; 1986. viii, 565 pp.
(Biblioteca Teatrale 47.) Illus.: TA. 1. Lang.: Ita.
Japan. 1363-1443. Historical studies. ■Zeami's theories regarding
performance techniques.

1402   Kanze, Hisao; Kenny, Don, transl. "Life With the *Nō*
Mask." *MimeJ*. 1984: 65-73. Illus.: Photo. 4: var. sizes.
Lang.: Eng.
Japan. Critical studies. ■*Nō* actor Kanze Hisao discusses the actor's
relationship with the *Nō* mask.

1403   Matsuda, Tamotsu. *Nō utai meisho kyūseki shiryō*. (Ninth
Century Sources of *Nō Utai* Masterpieces.) Tokyo: Kasama-
shoin; 1986. 54 pp. Lang.: Jap.

Japan. 800-899. Histories-sources. ■Ancient sources relating to *nō*
drama.

1404   Myerscongh, Marie. "East Meets West: On the Art of
Tadashi Suzuki." *AmTh*. 1986 Jan.; 2(10): 4-10. Illus.:
Photo. Print. B&W. 6: 3 in. x 4 in., 12 in. x 12 in., 5 in. x 7 in.
Lang.: Eng.
Japan: Toga. 1985. Historical studies. ■Western content, Japanese form,
enforced through rigorous training of Tadashi Suzuki's SCOT Suzuki
Company of Toga.

1405   Nakamura, Hachirō. "*Nō*, Chūgoku-mono no butai to
rekishi." (*Nō*: Performance and History of Chinese Subject
Plays.) *Umewaka*. 1986: 273-277. Lang.: Jap.
Japan. 1300-1400. Historical studies. ■Examination of *nō* plays with
Chinese subjects.

1406   Nomura, Mansaku; Kenny, Don, transl. "Some Thoughts
on *Kyōgen* Masks." *MimeJ*. 1984: 177-182. Illus.: Photo. 5:
var. sizes.
Japan. Histories-sources. ■*Kyōgen* actor discusses the differences
between *nō* and *kyōgen*, and their connection with mask work.

1407   Omote, Akira. "Kitashichidayū-Nagayoshi o meguru
shomondai." (Questions Regarding the Life Work of
Nagayoshi.) *Nōgaku-kenkyū*. 1986 Mar.; 11: 1-106. Lang.:
Jap.
Japan. Biographies. ■Career and life achievements of *nō* artist Kitashi-
chidayū Nagayoshi.

1408   Richie, Donald. "*Nō* Masks." *MimeJ*. 1984: 17-19. Lang.:
Eng.
Japan. Critical studies. ■The relationship between the *nō* actor and the
mask.

1409   Shigeyama, Sengorō; Teele, Rebecca, transl. "The *Kyōgen*
Actor and His Relationship With the Mask." *MimeJ*. 1984:
148-155. Illus.: Photo. 18: var. sizes.
Japan. 1984. Critical studies. ■Compares the *kyōgen* actor's goals to
those of other oriental traditions and describes different categories of
masks.

1410   Takano, Toshio. *Zeami, manazashi no chōkoku*. (Zeami:
The Sculpture of a Beautiful Image.) Tokyo: Kawade-
shobō-shinsha; 1986. 272 pp. Lang.: Jap.
Japan. 1364-1443. Biographical studies. ■Aesthetic evaluation of
Zeami's techniques and work.

1411   Teele, Rebecca. "Recollections and Thoughts on *Nō*."
MimeJ. 1984: 74-92. Illus.: Photo. Sketches. 11: var. sizes.
Lang.: Eng.
Japan. Histories-sources. ■Interview with Kongō Iwao, head of the
Kongō School of *Nō*, his training, experience and the use of masks.

1412   Teele, Rebecca. "*Nō* and *Kyōgen*: An Introduction."
MimeJ. 1984: 4-16.
Japan. Historical studies. ■General introduction to *nō* and *kyōgen*,
including a discussion of the masks, types of plays and the stage.

1413   Tsumura, Reijirō; Teele, Rebecca, transl. "Dojoji: Preparation for a Second Performance." *MimeJ*. 1984: 104-113.
Illus.: Photo. 8: var. sizes. Lang.: Eng.
Japan. 1983. Histories-sources. ■Kanze School actor Tsumura Reijirō
discusses his decision to perform the *nō* play *Dōjōji* a second time and
the subsequent physical preparation and rehearsal process.

1414   Yagi, Zengorō; Yagi, Seiya. *Mibu dainenbutsu kyōgen.
Tōdai 25-nenshi nenpyō*. (List of the Last 25 Years of Mibu
Dainenbutsu Kyōgen.) Kyoto: Mibu dainenbutsu kō; 1986.
135 pp. Lang.: Jap.
Japan: Kyoto. Historical studies. ■Special performances of *kyōgen*
presented at the Mibu Temple.

1415   Yokomichi, Mario. *Nōgeki no kenkyū*. (Studies on *Nō*
Plays.) Tokyo: Iwanami-shoten; 1986. 481 pp. Lang.: Jap.
Japan. Historical studies. ■Dramaturgy and performance of *nō* drama.

1416   Doi, Yuriko; Graham, Robert. "Recent Experiments in the
Use of *Nō* and *Kyōgen* Traditions: Masks in Fusion Theatre." *MimeJ*. 1984: 201-207. Illus.: Photo. 2: var. sizes.

DANCE-DRAMA: *Nō*—Performance/production

USA: San Francisco, CA. 1984. 1978-1984. Histories-sources. ▪Yuriko Doi discusses her directorial approach on *Antigone* as influenced by *nō* and *kyōgen*.

1417 Kenny, Don. "The Face and the Mask." *MimeJ.* 1984: 194-199. Illus.: Photo. 6: var. sizes.
USA. 1984. Histories-sources. ▪Author discusses his experiences performing the *kyōgen* play *Shimizu* in English and discovering the life of the mask.

Plays/librettos/scripts

1418 Taguchi, Kazuo. *Teikyō-nenkan, Ōkura-ryū ai-kyōgen-bon nishu.* (Two Types of Texts of *Ai-kyōgen* in the Ōkura School.) Tokyo: Wanya-shoten; 1986. 249 pp. Lang.: Jap.
Japan. 1600-1800. Historical studies. ▪A study of the *ai-kyōgen* texts in the Okura school.

Relation to other fields

1419 Fukuda, Yasukawa. *Ezra Pound kenkyū.* (A Study of Ezra Pound.) Tokyo: Yamaguchi-shoten; 1986. 297 pp. Lang.: Jap.
Japan. 1885-1972. Critical studies. ▪Work of Ezra Pound and his relationship to *nō*.

Theory/criticism

1420 Dōmoto, Masaki. *Zeami.* Tokyo: Geki-shobō; 1986. 804 pp. Lang.: Jap.
Japan. 1364-1443. Biographical studies. ▪Comprehensive look at the life and work of Zeami Motokiyo.

1421 Ortolani, Benito. "La spiritualità per il danzatore-attore negli scritti di Zeami e Zenchiku sul teatro Nō." (Spirituality for the Actor-Dancer in the Writings of Zeami and Zenchiku on *Nō* Theatre.) 195-211 in Ottai, Antonella, ed. *Teatro Oriente/Occidente.* Rome: Bulzoni; 1986. viii, 565 pp. (Biblioteca Teatrale 47.) Lang.: Ita.
Japan. 1363-1470. Critical studies. ▪Spiritual and practical training to reach sublime levels of performance in the *nō*.

1422 Satake, Akihiro. *Kogo zōdan.* (Discussion of Old Words.) Tokyo: Iwanami-shoten; 1986. 251 pp. Lang.: Jap.
Japan. 1300-1986. Critical studies. ▪Various aspects of *kyōgen*.

1423 Zeami, Motokiyo; De Poorter, Erika. *Zeami's Talks on Sarugaku.* Japonica Neerlandica. Amsterdam: J.C. Greben; 1986. 303 pp. (Monographs of the Netherlands Association for Japanese Studies 2.) Pref. Notes. Biblio. Gloss. Index. Tables. Append. Lang.: Eng.
Japan. 1430. Critical studies. ▪Translation of Zeami's *Sarugaku dangi*, with introduction and commentary.

Training

1424 Turner, Craig. "Recent Experiments in the Use of *Nō* and *Kyōgen* Traditions: *Nō* and *Kyōgen* Masks in Actor Training." *MimeJ.* 1984: 208-214.
USA. 1984. Histories-sources. ▪A specialist in movement training uses *nō* masks to teach actors communication through movement.

Other entries with significant content related to Dance-Drama: 2, 1059, 1750.

DRAMA

1425 Adler, Thomas P. "'Daddy Spoke to Me!': Gods Lost and Found in *Long Day's Journey Into Night* and *Through a Glass Darkly*." *CompD.* 1986; 20(4): 341-348. Notes. Lang.: Eng.
USA. Sweden. 1957-1961. Critical studies. ▪Intertextual analysis of Eugene O'Neill's play *Long Day's Journey Into Night* and Ingmar Bergman's film, *Through a Glass Darkly*. Related to Media: Film.

Administration

1426 Kutschera, Edda. "Es gibt viel Grund, um mich zu freu'n." (There Are Many Reasons for Me To Be Pleased.) *Buhne.* 1986 Mar.; 29(3): 11-12. Illus.: Photo. Print. Color. B&W. Lang.: Ger.
Austria: Vienna. 1930-1986. Biographical studies. ▪On manager Heinrich Kraus and his work.

1427 Löbl, Hermi. "Ich habe alles ausgestanden." (I Have Endured Everything.) *Buhne.* 1986 Apr.; 29(4): 12-14. Illus.: Photo. Print. Color. Lang.: Ger.
Austria: Vienna. Germany, West. 1925-1986. Biographical studies. ▪On manager, actor and director Boy Gobert and his plans for managing the Theater in der Josefstadt.

1428 Lossmann, Hans. "Ich werde wie der Teufel improvisieren müssen." (I Shall Have to Improvise Like the Devil.) *Buhne.* 1986 Mar.; 29(3): 4-5. Illus.: Photo. Print. B&W. Lang.: Ger.
Austria: Vienna. 1986. Histories-sources. ▪Changes in selling tickets at the Burgtheater and Akademietheater under new manager Claus Peymann, includes notes on the program of his first season.

1429 Eizenstadt, Michael. "Onat Teatron BeVancouver." (A Theatre Season in Vancouver, BC.) *Bamah.* 1986; 21(103): 65-70. Illus.: Photo. Print. B&W. 2. Lang.: Heb.
Canada: Vancouver, BC. 1986. Historical studies. ▪The theatrical activities of the Vancouver Playhouse, Arts Club House Theatre, Carousel Theatre and the Theatre Arts Department at the University of Vancouver.

1430 Garebian, Keith. "Risks: the 1985 Shaw Festival." *JCNREC.* 1986 Mar.; 20(4): 148-158. Illus.: Photo. Print. B&W. 2: 11 cm. x 7 cm., 11 cm. x 8 cm. Lang.: Eng.
Canada: Niagara-on-the-Lake, ON. 1985. Historical studies. ▪Under the leadership of Christopher Newton, this was a successful season of risks, complex plays and problems solved with technological resourcefulness.

1431 Tromly, F.B. "Authority on the Wane: Stratford's Thirty-Third Season." *JCNREC.* 1986 March; 20(4): 140-148. Lang.: Eng.
Canada: Stratford, ON. 1985. Historical studies. ▪John Hirsch's final season as artistic director of the Stratford Festival was marked by an air of caution, even defensiveness. Under his leadership the Festival has become a tourist theatre with a large deficit. His greatest achievement is seen in the development of the Young Company.

1432 Ingram, William. "The Playhouse as an Investment, 1607-1614: Thomas Woodford and Whitefriars." *MRenD.* 1985; 2: 209-229. Pref. Notes. Lang.: Eng.
England: London. 1607-1614. Historical studies. ▪An investigation of the history and management of the Whitefriars Playhouse, including its various leaseholders and shareholders.

1433 Ingram, William. "Robert Keysar, Playhouse Speculator." *SQ.* 1986 Win; 37(4): 476-485. Notes. Lang.: Eng.
England: London. 1608. Historical studies. ▪Involvement of Robert Keysar with Harry Evans and Blackfriars' Children's Company and what we can learn about Elizabethan-Jacobean theatre by examining lives and works of theatrical producers and financial speculators.

1434 Jason, Philip K. "The Afterpiece: Origins and Early Development." *Restor.* 1986 Sum; 2nd ser.1(1): 53-63. Notes. Tables. Lang.: Eng.
England: London. 1603-1747. Historical studies. ▪Afterpieces added to program as result of competition and practice of taking 'after-money'.

1435 Kujawińska-Courtney, Krystyna. "Wpływ współczesnej Szekspirowi cenzury na jego sztuki o historii Anglii." (Censorship's Influence on Shakespeare's History Plays.) *PaT.* 1986 Fourth Qtr; 4: 507-515. Notes. Lang.: Pol.
England. 1593-1603. Historical studies. ▪Effect of censorship on Shakespeare's *Richard III* and *Henry IV*.

1436 Giovanelli, Paola; Mancini, Andrea. "Ernesto Rossi a Ferdinando Martini." (Ernesto Rossi to Ferdinando Martini.) *BiT.* 1986; 2: 93-116. Notes. Biblio. Lang.: Ita.

DRAMA: —Administration

Italy. 1891. Histories-sources. ■Letter from actor Ernesto Rossi to author and theatre critic Ferdinando Martini on the organization of a mutual aid society for actors. Includes extensive explanatory notes.

1437 Viziano, Teresa. "Le disavventure di una attrice e del suo capocomico durante il Risorgimento." (The Mishaps of an Actress and Her Company Manager during the Risorgimento.) *TArch.* 1986 Sep.; 10: 113-148. Notes. Biblio. Illus.: Maps. B&W. 2: 13 cm. x 21 cm. Lang.: Ita.
Italy. 1847-1849. Historical studies. ■Lawsuit of actress Adelaide Ristori against her company manager for nonfulfillment of contract.

1438 Secomska, Henryka. "Wielki reprtuar a aktach Warszawskiego Komitetu Cenzury (1873-1907)." (Great Repertory in Reports of the Censorship Committee in Warsaw 1873-1907.) *PaT.* 1986 Fourth Qtr; 4: 581-600. Pref. Notes. Lang.: Rus, Pol.
Poland: Warsaw. Russia. 1873-1907. Histories-sources. ■Effect of Russian censorship on both texts and performances of plays by Shakespeare, Victor Hugo, Friedrich Schiller, Juliusz Słowacki and Aleksander Fredro in Polish theatres.

1439 Davis, Tracy C. "The Employment of Children in the Victorian Theatre." *NTQ.* 1986 May; 11(6): 116-135. Notes. Illus.: Photo. B&W. 9. Lang.: Eng.
UK. 1837-1901. Histories-specific. ■The exploitation and adulation inflicted on Victorian child-actors, gradually curbed by well-intentioned legislation.

1440 "Black Theater Stages a Comeback: Despite the Crippling Loss of Government Grants Small Regional Companies are Alive and Well." *Ebony.* 1986 Nov.; 42(1): 54, 56, 58, 61. Illus.: Photo. Print. Color. B&W. 8. Lang.: Eng.
USA. 1960-1984. Historical studies. ■Growing activity of Black regional theatre companies. Loss of government funding leading to dependency upon the community for financial support. Trends in using theater as a vehicle for educating the public and for social change. Focus on Kuumba Theater (Chicago).

1441 Levine, Mindy N. "From West Broadway to Broadway: The Life and Death of the Glines Theatre." *TT.* 1983 Jan.; 2(3): 6-7. Illus.: Photo. B&W. 2. Lang.: Eng.
USA: New York, NY. 1983. Historical studies. ■Restructuring of the Glines producing organization into the Glines Foundation to fund individuals and groups producing gay playwrights.

1442 Parker, Kate. "Is There Life Off Broadway." *PI.* 1986 Sept; 2(2): 30-31. Illus.: Photo. B&W. 2. Lang.: Eng.
USA: New York, NY. 1972-1986. Histories-sources. ■Lynne Meadow, artistic director of the Manhattan Theatre Club, describes her fourteen years there, and the theatre's move to City Center.

1443 Renick, Kyle. "How I Learned to Stop Worrying and Love the Shubert Organization." *TT.* 1983 Jan.; 2(3): 1-2, 8. Illus.: Photo. B&W. 2. Lang.: Eng.
USA: New York, NY. 1983. Histories-sources. ■Transfer of a play first produced by a nonprofit theatre to commercial theatre. WPA Theatre's experience with *Little Shop of Horrors, Gorey Stories* and *Nuts.*

Audience

1444 Knowles, Richard Paul. "The Mulgrave Road Co-op: Theatre and the Community in Guysborough County, N.S." *CDr.* 1986 Spr; 12(1): 18-32. Illus.: Photo. B&W. 6: 3 in. x 5 in., 5 in. x 7 in. Lang.: Eng.
Canada: Guysborough, NS. 1977-1985. Historical studies. ■The Mulgrave Road Co-op produces theatre based on the lives of local small-town Nova Scotians, contributing to their social and economic development.

1445 Kindermann, Heinz. *Das Theaterpublikum der Renaissance: Band 2.* (The Theatre Audience of the Renaissance: Volume 2.) Salzburg: Müller; 1986. 263 pp. Pref. Notes. Biblio. Illus.: Photo. Dwg. Sketches. B&W. 148: var. sizes. [Volume 1, published in 1984, concerned the audiences of Renaissance theatre in Italy.] Lang.: Ger.
Europe. 1480-1630. Histories-specific. ■Audience composition and reactions in the humanistic and school-theatre. Audience's role in political and religious theatre as witnesses and participants.

1446 Gourdon, Anne-Marie, ed. *Animation, théâtre et société.* (Cultural Policy, Theatre and Society.) Paris: CNRS; 1986. 228 pp. Index. Biblio. Illus.: Photo. Print. B&W. 57: var. sizes. Lang.: Fre.
France. Germany. UK-England. 1789-1986. Historical studies. ■Official policy regarding education and culture in France, Germany, Belgium and the United Kingdom: relations between the creation of dramatic texts and their theatrical representation examined through the experience of several directors.

1447 Hemmings, F.W.J. "La Claque: une institution contestée." (The Claque, a Contested Institution.) *RHT.* 1986; 38(3): 293-309. Lang.: Fre.
France. 1800. Historical studies. ■Examines claques as a theatrical institution.

1448 Adling, Wilfried; Dressler, Roland; Wiedemann, Dieter; Werner, Gabriele; Stanicki, Andreas. *Theater und Publikum.* (Theatre and Audience.) Berlin: Verband d. Theaterschaffenden d. DDR; 1984. 96 pp. (MT 182.) Lang.: Ger.
Germany, East: Leipzig, Schwerin, Helle. 1980-1983. Critical studies. ■Presentations at a colloquium dealing with aspects of the performer/audience relationship: sociological, receptional, perceptional, with special study on juvenile public.

1449 Rozik, Eli. "The Syntax of Theatrical Communication." *ASSAPHc.* 1986; 3: 43-57. Notes. Illus.: Diagram. Lang.: Eng.
Israel. 1986. Critical studies. ■Differentiation between aspects that identify the entity referred to (the subject) and those that describe the changing aspects (the predicate) in dramatic dialogue.

1450 Shoham, Chaim. "Programming the Spectator's Reaction in the Theatre." *ASSAPHc.* 1986; 3: 214-236. Notes. Lang.: Eng.
Israel. 1986. Critical studies. ■Use of primary material as an artistic dramatic strategy to organize audience reaction.

1451 Hannowa, Anna. "Młodzież o sztukach Różewicza." (Teenagers' Opinion about Różewicz's Plays.) *DialogW.* 1986; 11: 117-127. Lang.: Pol.
Poland. 1986. Histories-sources. ■Reactions of Polish teenagers to the plays (1920s) of poet and playwright Tadeusz Różewicz.

1452 Kaynar, Gad. "A Rhetorically Oriented Analysis of Strindberg's *The Dance of Death.*" *ASSAPHc.* 1986; 3: 109-134. Notes. Illus.: Diagram. Lang.: Eng.
Sweden. 1900. Critical studies. ■Rhetorical analysis of *Dödsdansen (The Dance of Death)* by August Strindberg suggests that he attempted to change his audience's conception of reality.

1453 Page, Malcolm. "Canadian Plays in Britain 1972-85." *CDr.* 1986 Spr; 12(1): 64-73. Append. 2: var. sizes. Lang.: Eng.
UK. Canada. 1949-1985. Reviews of performances. ■Surveys critical responses to Canadian plays produced by Canadian or British companies in Britain.

1454 Blau, Herbert. "Odd, Anonymous Needs: The Audience in a Dramatized Society." *PerAJ.* 1986; 10(1): 34-42. [Second of a two-part essay.] Lang.: Eng.
USA. 1985-1986. Critical studies. ■Analysis of the concepts of individual, audience and public as related to dramatic content, form and convention in postmodern theatre and society.

1455 Davy, Kate. "Constructing the Spectator: Reception, Context, and Address in Lesbian Performance." *PerAJ.* 1986; 10(2): 43-52. Illus.: Photo. Print. B&W. 3: var. sizes. Lang.: Eng.
USA: New York, NY. 1985. Critical studies. ■Semiotic analysis of the context and design of specific lesbian performances and their effect on audiences.

1456 Wilkerson, Margaret B. "*A Raisin in the Sun*: Anniversary of an American Classic." *TJ.* 1986 Dec.; 38(4): 441-452. Notes. Illus.: Photo. B&W. 2: var. sizes. Lang.: Eng.
USA. 1959-1986. Historical studies. ■Analysis of the continuing success of *A Raisin in the Sun* by Lorraine Hansberry, with special attention to historical context and audience response.

DRAMA: —Basic theatrical documents

Basic theatrical documents

1457 Chekhov, Anton. *Orchards.* New York, NY: Knopf; 1986. 288 pp. Lang.: Eng.
■A collection of seven Čechov stories and seven one-act plays based on them, commissioned for the 1985-86 season of the Acting Company.

1458 Long, William B. "'A Bed for Woodstock': A Warning for the Unwary." *MRenD.* 1985; 2: 91-118. Notes. Illus.: Photo. Neg. B&W. 6. Lang.: Eng.
1594-1633. Textual studies. ■Use of notes and promptbook of *Thomas England of Woodstock* to reconstruct performances and revivals.

1459 Roland, Betty. "*War on the Waterfront.*" *ADS.* 1986 Apr.; 8: 74-79. Lang.: Eng.
Australia. 1939. ■Text of Betty Roland's *War on the Waterfront* as published in the *Communist Review*, February 1939.

1460 Roland, Betty. "Prosperity Around the Corner." *ADS.* 1986 Apr.; 8: 69-74. Lang.: Eng.
Australia. 1938. ■Text of Act I, Scene 3 of Betty Roland's *Are You Ready Comrade?* as published in the *Communist Review*, April 1938.

1461 Decker, Jacques de. "Jeu d'intérieur." (Indoor Games.) *GAMBIT.* 1986; 11(42-43): 139-161. B&W. 1. Lang.: Eng.
Belgium. 1979. ■Complete playtext of *Jeu d'intérieur (Indoor Games)* by Jacques de Decker.

1462 Kalisky, René; Glasheen, Anne-Marie, transl. "Sur les ruines de Carthage." (On the Ruins of Carthage.) *GAMBIT.* 1986 ; 11(42-43): 105-138. Illus.: Photo. B&W. 2. Lang.: Eng.
Belgium. 1980. ■Complete playtext of *Sur les ruines de Carthage (On the Ruins of Carthage).*

1463 Sigrid, Jean; Glasheen, Anne-Marie, transl. "L'Ange couteau." (Angel Knife.) *GAMBIT.* 1986; 11(42-43): 75-104. Illus.: Photo. B&W. 2. Lang.: Eng.
Belgium. 1980. ■Complete playtext of Jean Sigrid's *L'ange couteau (Angel Knife).*

1464 Willems, Paul; Glasheen, Anne-Marie, transl. "Il pleut dans ma maison." (It's Raining in My House.) *GAMBIT.* 1986; 11 (42-43): 25-74. Illus.: Photo. B&W. 1. Lang.: Eng.
Belgium. 1963. ■Complete playtext of Paul Willems' *Il pleut dans ma maison (It's Raining in My House).*

1465 Beasley, David, intro. "Major John Richardson's *The Miser Outwitted* Discovered." *THC.* 1986 Spr; 7(1): 3-22. Notes. Illus.: Photo. B&W. 1. Lang.: Eng.
Canada. UK-Ireland: Dublin. 1838-1848. ■Text of a nineteenth-century farce attributed to Major John Richardson. Introduction includes discussion of possible production of play at Queen's Royal Theatre, Dublin, in 1848.

1466 Brooker, Bertram. "*The Dragon*: A Parable of Illusion and Disillusion." *CDr.* 1985; 11(1): 254-268. Illus.: Handbill. Poster. Lang.: Eng.
Canada: Toronto, ON. 1936. ■Playtext of Brooker's *The Dragon*, first produced by The Play Workshop, directed by Herman Voaden.

1467 Camirand, François; Lauvaux, Yves; Rioux, Monique; Noel, Michel O.; Van Burek, John, transl. "Umiak, the Collective Boat." *CTR.* 1986 Spr; 13(46): 79-94. Illus.: Photo. Print. B&W. 6: var. sizes. Lang.: Eng.
Canada: Toronto, ON. 1983. ■Text of *Umiak* by Théâtre de la Marmaille, a play for young audiences based on Inuit tradition.

1468 Cowan, Cindy. "*A Woman from the Sea.*" *CTR.* 1986 Fall; 13(48): 62-110. Pref. Illus.: Photo. Dwg. Print. B&W. 6: var. sizes. Lang.: Eng.
Canada. 1986. ■Two-act drama, first performed in 1986, about a woman coming to grips with her first pregnancy, with the help of a marine spirit.

1469 Godin, Jean Cléo, intro. "Alain Grandbois et le Théâtre." (Alain Grandbois and the Theatre.) *THC.* 1986 Fall ; 7(2): 149-159. Notes. Illus.: Dwg. B&W. 1. Lang.: Fre.
Canada. 1934-1975. ■Text of *J'ai Vingt Ans (I Am Twenty Years Old)*, by Alain Grandbois, published with a brief critical introduction.

1470 Parker, Gilbert; Ripley, John, ed. *Gilbert Parker and Herbert Beerbohm Tree Stage* The Seats of the Mighty.

Toronto: Simon and Pierre; 1986. 160 pp. Illus.: Dwg. Photo. Lang.: Eng.
Canada. 1897. Histories-sources. ■Text of Gilbert Parker's play, *The Seats of the Mighty*, about a Scottish major in Quebec, 1757-59, with stage directions, biographies of Parker and Herbert Beerbohm Tree, bibliography and introduction by the editor on the historical background of the production.

1471 Reay, Corey. *Caught in the Act.* Toronto: Simon and Pierre; 1986. 144 pp. [Forty Comic Characters for Readers and Performers.] Lang.: Eng.
Canada. ■A collection of satirical monologues by playwright Corey Reay.

1472 Smith, Mary Elizabeth. "Three Political Dramas from New Brunswick." *CDr.* 1986 Spr; 12(1): 144-228. Lang.: Eng.
Canada. 1833-1879. Critical studies. ■Reprints and comments on three political dramas published serially in New Brunswick newspapers.

1473 Whittaker, Herbert; Lister, Rota Herzberg, ed. "Whittaker's Montreal: A Theatrical Autobiography 1910-1949." *CDr.* 1986 Fall; 12(2): 233-331. Notes. Lang.: Eng.
Canada: Montreal, PQ. 1910-1949. Biographical studies. ■Whittaker's theatrical autobiography, covering his early years in Montreal as designer, director and critic.

1474 Hughes, Leo; Scouten, Arthur H. "Dryden with Variations: Three Prompt Books." *ThR.* 1986; 11(2): 91-105. Notes. Print. B&W. 6. Lang.: Eng.
England. 1700-1799. Textual studies. ■Promptbooks for *The Comic Lovers, Oedipus, King of Thebes* and *Don Sebastiani* by John Dryden, ascribed to Drury Lane Theatre, offer backstage view of the company at work.

1475 Milhous, Judith; Hume, Robert D. "A 1660s Promptbook of Shirley's *Loves Crueltie.*" *ThR.* 1986; 11(1): 1-13. Notes. Lang.: Eng.
England: London. 1660-1669. Textual studies. ■Prompt markings on a copy of James Shirley's *Loves Crueltie* performed by the King's Company.

1476 Kilpinen, Inkeri; Tullberg, Diana, transl. "Verily Verily." *MID.* 1985 Apr.; 18(2): 5-52. Lang.: Eng, Fin.
Finland. 1982-1983. ■Translation of *Totisesti totisesti* by Inkeri Kilpinen.

1477 "Journal d'Edouard Bourdet." (Journal of Edouard Bourdet.) *RHT.* 1986; 38(4): 326-353. Notes. Lang.: Fre.
France: Paris. 1936. Histories-sources. ■Journal of playwright from period just preceding his promotion to general administrator of the Comédie-Française includes his connections with literary world. Biographical notes by Marie-Odile Descolas, pp. 323-325.

1478 Cocteau, Jean; Graells, Guillem-Jordi, intro. *L'àguila de dos caps.* (The Eagle With Two Heads.) Barcelona: Institut del Teatre; 1986. 104 pp. (Biblioteca Teatral 43.) Biblio. Lang.: Cat.
France. 1946. ■Catalan translation of Cocteau's *L'aigle à deux têtes.*

1479 Gilbert, Huguette. "*Les Nopces ducales* et la querelle de *L'École des Femmes.*" (Ducal Nuptials and the Quarrel about *The School for Wives.*) *DSS.* 1986 Jan/Mar.; 38(1): 73-74. Notes. Lang.: Fre.
France. 1663. Histories-sources. ■Seventeenth century document clarifies a detail regarding performance site of three polemical 'impromptus' about Molière's *L'école des femmes (The School for Wives).*

1480 Howe, Alan. "Bruscambille, qui était-il?" (Who Was Bruscambille?)*DSS.* 1986 Oct/Dec.; 38(4): 390-396. Notes. Lang.: Fre.
France. 1600-1634. Histories-specific. ■Discovery of certain documents allows identification of Jean Gracieux as the actor who used the name Bruscambille for farce and Des Lauriers for comedy.

1481 Mongrédien, Georges, ed. *Comédies et pamphlets sur Molière.* (Comedies and Pamphlets about Molière.) Paris: Nizet; 1986. 308 pp. Pref. Notes. Lang.: Fre.
France. 1660-1670. Histories-sources. ■Critical edition of comedies and pamphlets about Molière.

1482 Dorst, Tankred; Casas, Joan, ed., intro. *Gran imprecació davant la muralla de la ciutat—Toller.* (Great Tirade before

DRAMA: —Basic theatrical documents

the City Wall and *Toller*.) Barcelona: Institut del Teatre; 1986. 140 pp. (Biblioteca Teatral 39.) Biblio. Lang.: Cat.
Germany. 1961. ■Catalan translations of *Grosse Schmährede an der Stadtmauer (Great Tirade before the City Wall)* and *Toller*.

1483 Shakespeare, William; Müller, Heiner, transl.; Scheib, Hans, illus. *Wie es euch gefällt. (As You Like It.)* Leipzig: Reclam; 1986. 91 pp. B&W. 32. Lang.: Ger.
Germany, East. 1986. ■New German translation of Shakespeare's *As You Like It* by Heiner Müller with interpretive illustrations.

1484 Déry, Tibor; Goldstein, Imre, transl. "The Giant Baby." *MID.* 1986 Oct.; 20(1): 5-48. Lang.: Eng, Hun.
Hungary. 1894-1977. ■Translation of *Az Óriáscsecsemő*.

1485 Pirandello, Luigi; Abellan, Joan, intro. *El jocs dels papers. (The Rules of the Game.)* Barcelona: Institut del Teatre; 1986. 84 pp. (Biblioteca Teatral 48.) Biblio. Lang.: Cat.
Italy. 1918. ■Catalan translation of *Il giuoco delle parti (The Rules of the Game)*.

1486 Rame, Franca; Fo, Dario; Hood, Stuart, transl. *"An Open Couple—Very Open."* ThM. 1985 Win; 17(1): 19-31. Illus.: Photo. B&W. 2. Lang.: Eng.
Italy: Trieste. 1983. ■Stuart Hood's translation of Rame and Fo's 1983 play *Coppia aperta*.

1487 Mishima, Yukio. *La senyora de Sade. (Madame de Sade.)* Sant Boi del Llobregat: Llibres del Mall; 1986. 104 pp. (Sèrie Oberta.) Notes. Lang.: Cat.
Japan. 1960-1970. ■Catalan translation of *Madame de Sade*.

1488 Vilalta, Maruxa; Nigro, Kirsten, transl. *"A Little Tale of Horror (and Unbridled Love)."* MID. 1986 Apr.; 19(2): 25-60 . Lang.: Eng.
Mexico. 1932. ■Translation of *Pequeña historia de horror*.

1489 Ibsen, Henrik. *"Eiolf Hakatan."* (*Little Eyolf.*) Bamah. 1986; 21(105-106): 51-100. Illus.: Photo. Print. B&W. 1: 7 cm. x 7 cm. Lang.: Heb.
Norway. Israel. 1884-1985. Textual studies. ■Text of *Eiolf Hakatan*, Hebrew translation of Henrik Ibsen's *Lille Eyolf (Little Eyolf)* by Gad Kaynar.

1490 Kantor, Tadeusz. "The Writings of Tadeusz Kantor 1956-1985." *TDR.* 1986 Fall; 30(3): 114-176. Lang.: Eng.
Poland. 1956-1985. ■Writings of director Tadeusz Kantor on the nature of theatre.

1491 Timoszewicz, Jerzy. "Z teki afiszów wileńskich." (From the Collection of Playbills from Vilna.) PaT. 1986 Second & Third Qtr; 2-3: 221-284. Notes. Illus.: Photo. Print. B&W. 53. Lang.: Pol.
Poland: Vilna. 1800-1863. Histories-sources. ■Photographs of 51 playbills from theatres in Vilna are published for the first time for Polish researchers. Access to original playbills is very difficult because they are in theatre archives in USSR.

1492 Čechov, Anton Pavlovič; Frayn, Michael; Garin, Imma, transl. *Mel salvatge. (Wild Honey.)* Barcelona: Centre Dramàtic de la Generalitat/Edhasa; 1986. 128 pp. (Els Textos des Centre Dramàtic 7.) Lang.: Cat.
Russia. 1878. ■Catalan translation of an untitled play by Čechov usually called *Platonov*, in a version by Michael Frayn.

1493 Aub, Max; Reed, Cary, transl. "The Remarkable Misanthrope." *MID.* 1986 Apr.; 19(2): 5-24. Lang.: Eng, Spa.
Spain. 1903-1972. ■Translation of *El desconfiado prodigioso*.

1494 Martínez Ballesteros, Antonio. *"Los Comediantes."* (*The Players.*) Estreno. 1986 Aut; 12(2): 36-61. Notes. Illus.: Photo. Print. B&W. 4. Lang.: Spa.
Spain. 1982. ■Playtext of *Los Comediantes (The Players)* by Antonio Martínez Ballesteros.

1495 Capmany, Maria Aurelía; Valdivieso, L. Teresa, transl. *"Tú y el hipócrita."* (*You and the Hypocrite.*) Estreno. 1986 Spr; 12(1): 11-32. Lang.: Spa.
Spain-Catalonia: Barcelona. 1959. ■Text of *Tu i l'hipócrita (You and the Hypocrite)*, by Maria Aurélia Capmany, translated into Castilian Spanish by L. Teresa Valdivieso as *Tú y el hipócrita*.

1496 Espriu, Salvador; Masoliver, Joan Ramón, transl.; Pinyol-Balasch, R., ed., intro. *Primera historia de Esther/Primera història d'Esther.* (First Story of Esther.) Barcelona: Marca Hispànica, S.A./Diputació de Barcelona; 1986. 198 pp. (Marca Hispànica.) Lang.: Spa, Cat.
Spain-Catalonia: Barcelona. 1913-1985. ■Bilingual edition of the play with biography of the author, textual and performance history of the play.

1497 Morell i Montaldi, Carme; Mas i Vives, Joan, intro. *La famosa comèdia de la gala està en son punt. Edició i estudi.* (The Famous Comedy of the Gala Done to a Turn: Edition and Study.) Barcelona: Curial Edicions Catalanes/Publicacions de l'Abadia de Montserrat; 1986. 178 pp. (Textos i Estudis de Cultura Catalana 14.) Notes. Pref. Index. Lang.: Cat.
Spain-Catalonia. 1625-1680. ■Text of an anonymous burlesque comedy, *La famosa comèdia de la gala està en son punt (The Famous Comedy of the Gala Done to a Turn)* with notes on the genre of burlesque comedy and an analysis of the play.

1498 Mundi i Pedret, Francesc, ed.; Anton i Clavé, Salvador, ed. *La 'Tragèdia de Sant Sebastià'. Una mostra de teatre popular a Riudoms.* (The Tragedy of Saint Sebastian: An Example of Popular Theatre in Riudoms.) Riudoms: Centre d'Estudis Riudomencs 'Arnau de Palomar'; 1986. 108 pp. (Quaderns de Divulgació Cultural 12.) Notes. Biblio. Illus.: Photo. Print. B&W. 2: 16 cm. x 11 cm. Lang.: Cat.
Spain-Catalonia: Riudoms. 1400-1880. Textual studies. ■Edition of popular tragedy with prologue by the editors discussing the cult of Saint Sebastian in Catalonia, other forms of popular theatre and formal and content analysis of the play.

1499 Palau i Fabre, Josep; Guillamón, Julià, intro. *Avui, Romeo i Julieta seguida de El porter i el penalty. (Today, Romeo and Juliet and The Goalkeeper and the Penalty.)* Barcelona: Institut del Teatre; 1986. 68 pp. (Biblioteca Teatral 54.) Notes. Biblio. Lang.: Cat.
Spain-Catalonia. 1917-1982. ■Texts of two plays by Josep Palau i Fabre.

1500 Pedrolo, Manuel de; Wellworth, George E., transl. "The Use of Matter." *MID.* 1986 Oct.; 20(1): 49-103. Lang.: Cat, Eng.
Spain-Catalonia. 1963. ■Translation of *L'ús de la matèria*.

1501 Sagarra, Josep Maria de; Permanyer, Lluís, intro. *Josep M. de Sagarra en els seus millors escrits.* (Josep M. de Sagarra in His Better Writings.) Barcelona: Editorial Miguel Arimany, S.A; 1986. 168 pp. (Els dies i els homes 13.) Illus.: Photo. Print. B&W. 1: 9 cm. x 14 cm. Lang.: Cat.
Spain-Catalonia. 1917-1964. ■Anthology of poetry, prose, plays and translations by Sagarra, with introductory material by various scholars.

1502 Shakespeare, William; Sagarra, Josep Maria de, transl.; Coca, Jordi, intro. *Obres Completes. Traduccions. Teatre de W. Shakespeare. Volum I.* (Complete Works, Translations, Plays of William Shakespeare, Volume I.) Barcelona: Editorial Selecta Catalònia; 1986. xxxi, 1065 pp. (Biblioteca Perenne 34.) Notes. Lang.: Cat.
Spain-Catalonia. UK-England. 1590-1986. ■Sagarra's translations with an introduction on Sagarro's knowledge of Shakespeare, comparisons with other translators, influence of Shakespeare on Sagarra's own plays and the language of Elizabethan theatre.

1503 Teixidor, Jordi; Broch, Alex, intro. *David, rei. (David, King.)* Barcelona: Institut del Teatre; 1986. 78 pp. (Biblioteca Teatral 49.) Lang.: Cat.
Spain-Catalonia. 1970-1985. ■Complete playtext.

1504 Dürrenmatt, Friedrich; Kerr, Charlotte. *Rollenspiele. (Role Games.)* Zürich: Diogen; 1986. 346 pp. Notes. Illus.: Dwg. Lang.: Ger.
Switzerland. ■Contains the third version of *Achterloo*, written after a fictional stage production discussed with the author's wife, Charlotte Kerr. Discussion published in this volume, plus sketches drawn with felt-pen by Dürrenmatt.

DRAMA: —Basic theatrical documents

1505 Kopf, Peter. *Schicksalzug-Kreuzweg.* (*Train of Fate* and *Crossroads.*) Bern: Mad Theater; 1986. 164 pp. Illus.: Photo. B&W. Lang.: Ger.
Switzerland: Bern. 1933-1985. ■Two plays dealing with refugees in Switzerland, Jewish in the 1940s and Tamil in the 1980s. Includes documentation on the refugees' politics not normally published.

1506 Osborne, John; Mallafré, Joaquim, intro. *Amb la ràbia al cos.* (*Look Back in Anger.*) Barcelona: Institut del Teatre; 1986. 112 pp. (Biblioteca Teatral 47.) Notes. Biblio. Lang.: Cat.
UK-England. 1956. ■Catalan translation of Osborne's play.

1507 Pinter, Harold; Mallafré, Joaquim, intro. *Qui a casa torna.* (*The Homecoming.*) Barcelona: Institut del Teatre; 1986. 104 pp. (Biblioteca Teatral 44.) Notes. Biblio. Lang.: Cat.
UK-England. 1965. ■Catalan translation of Pinter's play. Related to Media: Film.

1508 Sams, Eric, ed. *Shakespeare's Lost Play:* Edmund Ironside. New York: St. Martin's; 1986. 367 pp. Pref. Notes. Index. Lang.: Eng.
UK-England: London. 1580-1600. ■Attribution of early Elizabethan play *Edmund Ironside* to Shakespeare, based on cryptographic analysis. Includes the text of the play.

1509 Wesker, Arnold; Lorés, Maite, intro. *Sopa de pollastre amb ordi.* (*Chicken Soup with Barley.*) Barcelona: Institut del Teatre; 1986. 104 pp. (Biblioteca Teatral 53.) Biblio. Lang.: Cat.
UK-England. 1958. ■Catalan translation of Arnold Wesker's play.

1510 Benedetti, Mario; Beberfall, Freda, transl. "Pedro and the Captain." *MID.* 1985 Oct.; 19(1): 33-52. Lang.: Eng.
Uruguay. 1979. ■Translation of *Pedro y el capitán* by Benedetti, a Uruguayan playwright living in Spain.

1511 Miller, Arthur; Carandell, Josep Maria, intro. *Del pont estant.* (*A View From the Bridge.*) Barcelona: Institut del Teatre; 1986. 108 pp. (Biblioteca Teatral 46.) Biblio. Lang.: Cat.
USA. 1955. ■Catalan translation of Arthur Miller's play.

1512 Williams, Tennessee; Melendres, Jaume, intro. *Advertència per a embarcacions petites.* (*Small Craft Warnings.*) Barcelona: Institut del Teatre; 1986. 94 pp. (Biblioteca Teatral 41.) Notes. Lang.: Cat.
USA. 1972. ■Catalan translation of *Small Craft Warnings* by Tennessee Williams.

Design/technology

1513 Van Der Merwe, Pieter. "Sketches for Scenery by Clarkson Stanfield: New Finds, 1980-1984." *TN.* 1986; 40(1): 22-29. Notes. Illus.: Sketches. B&W. 7: var. sizes. Lang.: Eng.
England: London. 1793-1867. Histories-sources. ■Describes and reproduces recently discovered sketches by set designer Clarkson Stanfield.

1514 Isgrò, Giovanni. "Appia e Fortuny." (Appia and Fortuny.) *TeatrC.* 1985-1986; 6(11-12): 109-116. Notes. Biblio. Lang.: Ita.
France. 1903. Historical studies. ■Adolphe Appia's use of some innovative lighting techniques of Mariano Fortuny.

1515 Newman, L. M. "Gordon Craig in Germany." *GL&L.* 1986; 40(1): 11-33. Notes. Illus.: Photo. Print. B&W. 3. Lang.: Eng.
Germany. Austria. USA. 1904-1930. Historical studies. ■Travelling exhibitions of Edward Gordon Craig and his first book *The Art of the Theatre.*

1516 Rorrison, Hugh. "Designing for Reinhardt: The Work of Ernst Stern." *NTQ.* 1986 Aug.; 11(7): 217-232. Notes. Illus.: Dwg. B&W. 22. Lang.: Eng.
Germany: Berlin. UK-England: London. 1905. Biographical studies. ■Stern's contribution to Max Reinhardt's theatre in particular, and 20th-century scenography in general.

1517 Lista, Giovanni. "La ricerca dei pittori futuristi per la scena o la poetica del teatro come 'imago urbis'." (The Research of Futurist Painters for Stage or the Poetics of Theatre as 'Imago Urbis'.) *TeatrC.* 1985-1986; 6(11-12): 159-166. Illus.: Photo. Pntg. Dwg. B&W. 8: var. sizes. Lang.: Ita.
Italy. 1910-1928. Critical studies. ■Scene designs and theoretical texts of futurist painters working in the theatre.

1518 Bravo i Pijoan, Isidre; Graells, Guillem-Jordi. *Quadern introductori al Teatrí de l'escenografia d'Oleguer Junyent (any 1917) per a l'acte tercer, quadre primer de L'auca del senyor Esteve de Santiago Rusiñol.* (Introductory Booklet to Model of the Stage Design of Oleguer Junyent for *Mr. Esteve's 'Auca'* III.i, by Santiago Rusiñol (1917).) Barcelona: Institut del Teatre; 1986. 16 pp. (Col.lecció de facsímils del fons documental 3.) Illus.: Dwg. Poster. Plan. Design. Photo. Print. Color. B&W. Grd.Plan. Fr.Elev. 50: var. sizes. Lang.: Cat.
Spain-Catalonia: Barcelona. 1861-1984. Historical studies. ■Introduction provides information on the author, the play, Teatre Victòria, subsequent productions, the designer and the model. Includes staging instructions.

1519 Junyent i Sants, Oleguer; Bravo i Pijoan, Isidre, intro.; Graells, Guillem-Jordi, intro. *Teatrí de l'escenografia d'Oleguer Junyent (any 1917) per a l'acte tercer, quadre primer de L'auca del senyor Esteve* de Santiago Rusiñol. (Model of the Stage Design of Oleguer Junyent for *Mr. Esteve's 'Auca'* III.i, by Santiago Rusiñol (1917).) Barcelona: Institut del Teatre; 1986. 4 pp. (Biblioteca Teatral 54.) Illus.: Dwg. Print. Color. 4: 48 cm. x 69 cm. Lang.: Cat.
Spain-Catalonia: Barcelona. 1917. Histories-sources. ■Facsimile edition of the design for *L'auca del senyor Esteve (Mr. Esteve's 'Auca'),* or story told in drawings and rhymed texts.

1520 Liljequist, Ann-Margret. "Att skulptera rum." (To Sculpture a Room.) *NT.* 1986; 35: 14-17. Illus.: Photo. Lang.: Swe.
Sweden: Stockholm. 1927. Historical studies. ■The collaboration between Per Lindberg and Sandro Malmquist that resulted in a unique production of Calderón's *Life Is a Dream* at Kungliga Dramatiska Teatern.

1521 Graham, Bill. "Bradford's Wonderful Theatre." *Sin.* 1986; 20(2): 14-17. Illus.: Photo. Diagram. B&W. Grd.Plan. 3. Lang.: Eng.
UK-England: Bradford. 1980-1987. Historical studies. ■Overview of the renovation of the Alhambra Theatre including flaws uncovered in the counterweight, sound and light systems.

1522 Palmer, S.R. "4 Into 3 Will Go!" *Tabs.* 1986; 43(1): 14. Illus.: Plan. Photo. B&W. 3. Lang.: Eng.
UK-England. 1980-1986. Instructional materials. ■Amateur technician describes how three one-act plays can be lit with four lanterns.

1523 Parker, Kate. "The Costume Business (Part 1)." *PI.* 1986 June; 1(11): 14. B&W. 5. Lang.: Eng.
UK-England: London. 1950-1986. Historical studies. ■Overview of the costume department of the National Theatre, the staff, theatres it serves, and various productions it has worked on.

1524 Parker, Kate. "The Costume Business (Part 2)." *PI.* 1986 July; 1(12): 21-23. B&W. 2. Lang.: Eng.
UK-England: London. 1790-1986. Historical studies. ■Broad survey of costuming in England.

1525 Sporre, Dennis J. "Charles Kean's Antiquarianism: The Designs for *Richard III* 1857." *TID.* 1986; 8: 93-111. Notes. Illus.: Sketches. B&W. 11: 5 in. x 7 in. Lang.: Eng.
UK-England: London. 1857. Historical studies. ■An account of actor-director Charles Kean's production of Shakespeare's *Richard III,* which attempted to achieve historical accuracy in scenery and costumes. Includes reactions of contemporaries.

1526 Oliver, Cordelia. "Tom MacDonald, Painter and Stage Designer 1914-1985." *STN.* 1986 May-June; 9(50): 8-10. Illus.: Photo. B&W. 3. Lang.: Eng.
UK-Scotland: Glasgow. 1914-1985. Biographical studies. ■Discussion of the stage design work of Tom MacDonald.

1527 "Lighting Fugard's *The Blood Knot.*" *LDim.* 1986 Mar-Apr.; 10(2). Notes. Illus.: Photo. Print. Color. B&W. 8: var. sizes. Lang.: Eng.

DRAMA: —Design/technology

USA: New Haven, CT. 1985-1986. Histories-sources. ■Interview with lighting designer William Warfel on his career and lighting design for *The Blood Knot* by Athol Fugard.

1528 "Ming Cho Lee:An Interview." *LDim.* 1986 Mar-Apr.; 10(2): 39-44. Notes. Illus.: Design. Photo. Print. Color. 2: 5 in. x 7 in. Lang.: Eng.

USA: New Haven, CT. Histories-sources. ■Interview with scene designer Ming Cho Lee on his approach to lighting which he does not design himself.

1529 Halcomb, Richard. *New Stagecraft Principles Applied to Two Musical Comedy Costume Designs of Miles White.* Lubbock, TX: Texas Tech Univ; 1986. 182 pp. Pref. Notes. Biblio. [Ph.D. dissertation, Univ. Microfilms order No: DA8615354.] Lang.: Eng.

USA: New York, NY. 1944-1960. Historical studies. ■Analysis of costume designs by Miles White for two musicals, *Bloomer Girl* and *Bye Bye Birdie*.

1530 Levine, Mindy N. "Adrianne Lobel." *TT.* 1986 Nov.; 6(1): 6-7. Illus.: Photo. B&W. 5: var. sizes. Lang.: Eng.

USA: New York, NY. 1986. Histories-sources. ■Set designer Adrianne Lobel discusses her collaborations with playwright John Patrick Shanley, focusing on the set of several of his plays.

1531 Williams, Mike. "Tom Skelton's Dark Dreams." *LDim.* 1986 May/June; 10(3): 97-98, 100-102. Illus.: Design. Print. Color. 2: var. sizes. Lang.: Eng.

USA: New York, NY. 1985-1986. Histories-sources. ■Interview with lighting designer Tom Skelton about his work on the recent revival of *The Iceman Cometh* by Eugene O'Neill.

Institutions

1532 Böhm, Gotthard. "Das Theater ist kein Fahrplan." (Theatre Is Not a Schedule.) *Buhne.* 1986 July; 29(7): 5-7. Illus.: Photo. Print. B&W. Lang.: Ger.

Austria: Vienna. 1986. Histories-sources. ■Claus Peymann's concept for managing the Burgtheater and the Akademietheater, and his plans for the current season.

1533 Grancy, Christine de; Gilsing, Monika; Hove, Oliver von; Urbach, Reinhard, ed.; Benning, Achim, ed. *Burgtheater Wien 1776-1986, Ebenbild und Widerspruch: Zweihundert und zehn Jahre.* (Burgtheater Vienna 1776-1986, Image and Contradiction: Two Hundred and Ten Years.) Vienna: Schroll; 1986. 263 pp. Tables. Illus.: Photo. Dwg. B&W. 266. Lang.: Ger.

Austria: Vienna. 1776-1986. Histories-specific. ■Ten years of the Burgtheater under the auspices of Achim Benning. Detailed chronicle of productions and events with speeches, essays, letters and scene photos. Focus on productions of *Hamlet*. Includes repertory list.

1534 Kathrein, Karin; Türk, Annemarie, comp.; Wiesinger, Toni, comp. *Schauspielhaus Wien, 1978-1986.* (Schauspielhaus Vienna, 1978-1986.) Vienna: Löcker; 1986. 92 pp. Illus.: Photo. B&W. 104. Lang.: Ger.

Austria: Vienna. 1978-1986. Histories-sources. ■Photos show performance styles, scenery and costumes of various productions including Shakespeare, French existentialists, Handke and musicals.

1535 Kutschera, Edda. "Wir wollen ein Theater-Zuhause schaffen." (We Want to Create a Theatre Which Is a Home.) *Buhne.* 1986 Jan.; 29(1): 8. (Serie Publikumsorganisationen 6.) Illus.: Photo. Print. B&W. Lang.: Ger.

Austria: Vienna. 1985-1986. Histories-specific. ■The audience-society, Freunde des Theaters in der Josefstadt, its beginnings in 1985, function and activities.

1536 Kutschera, Edda. "Im Zeichen des Kreises." (In the Sign of the Circle.) *Buhne.* 1986 Dec.; 29(12): 7-8. Illus.: Photo. Print. B&W. Lang.: Ger.

Austria: Vienna. 1986-1987. Histories-sources. ■On the new group, Der Kreis, managed by George Tabori: its concept and program for the 1986/87 season.

1537 Mayer, Gerhard. "Freunden und Qualen." (Pleasures and Pains.) *Buhne.* 1986 Apr.; 29(4): 6. Illus.: Photo. Print. B&W. Lang.: Ger.

Austria: Vienna. 1976-1986. Histories-sources. ■The last ten years of Achim Benning's management of the Burgtheater.

1538 Mayer, Gerhard. "Theater mit Haltung." (Theatre with Attitudes.) *Buhne.* 1986 May; 29(5): 6-7. Illus.: Photo. Print. B&W. Lang.: Ger.

Austria: Vienna. 1986-1987. Histories-sources. ■Paul Blaha's plans for managing the current Volkstheater.

1539 Ackerman, Marianne. "A Crisis of Vision." *CTR.* 1986 Spr; 13(46): 21-27. Illus.: Photo. Print. B&W. 3: var. sizes. Lang.: Eng.

Canada: Montreal, PQ. 1980-1986. Critical studies. ■The malaise in English-language theatre in Montreal may yet be overcome by dynamic leadership.

1540 Allen, Deb; Mair, Elizabeth; Knowles, Richard Paul. "Prince Edward Island: The Charlottetown Alternatives." *CTR.* 1986 Fall; 13(48): 23-24. Illus.: Photo. Print. B&W. 1: 4 in. x 3 in. Lang.: Eng.

Canada: Charlottetown, PE. 1982-1986. Historical studies. ■The chief alternatives to the Charlottetown Festival are Theatre Bandwagon and Theatre After All, but at present their survival is precarious.

1541 Barker, Kevin. "Going through a Stage." *BooksC.* 1986 Apr.; 15(3): 11-12. Illus.: Dwg. Print. B&W. 1: 9 cm. x 11 cm. Lang.: Eng.

Canada: Vancouver, BC. 1975-1986. Historical studies. ■Green Thumb is a theatre company for young people which presents plays on social issues.

1542 Bosley, Vivien. "Edmonton: Alive, Well, and in French." *CTR.* 1986 Sum; 13(47): 140-143. Illus.: Photo. Print. B&W. 1: 3 in. x 5 in. Lang.: Eng.

Canada: Edmonton, AB. 1970-1986. Historical studies. ■A history of the Théâtre français d'Edmonton, as well as a brief description of a francophone children's theatre in Edmonton, La Boîte à Popicos.

1543 Brennan, Brian. "Finishing School: The Banff Playwrights Colony." *CTR.* 1986 Win; 13(49): 30-35. Illus.: Photo. Print. B&W. 3: 3 in. x 5 in.,4 in. x 5 in., 5 in. x 5 in. Lang.: Eng.

Canada: Banff, AB. 1974-1986. Historical studies. ■Since its founding in 1974, the emphasis of the Banff Playwrights Colony has changed from initiating new plays to providing final polish for plays-in-progress.

1544 Chiasson, Zénon; Viger, Roland, transl. "The Acadian Theatre." *CTR.* 1986 Spr; 13(46): 50-57. Notes. Illus.: Photo. Print. B&W. 4: var. sizes. Lang.: Eng.

Canada. 1969-1986. Historical studies. ■French-language theatre in Canada's Atlantic provinces began by expressing themes of exile and marginalization, like the Acadian tradition from which it springs.

1545 Cowan, Cindy. "Halifax: Towards an Atlantic Playwrights' Colony." *CTR.* 1986 Win; 13(49): 120-122. Lang.: Eng.

Canada: Halifax, NS. 1986. Histories-sources. ■Attempts by the Dramatists' Co-op of Nova Scotia to get funds from the Canadian Council to found an Atlantic Playwrights' Colony.

1546 Etheridge, David; Fitch, Sheree; Ruganda, John. "New Brunswick: Enterprise Theatre Inc." *CTR.* 1986 Fall; 13(48): 33-36. Tables. Illus.: Photo. Print. B&W. 1: 4 in. x 5 in. Lang.: Eng.

Canada. 1983-1986. Histories-sources. ■The principles and history of Enterprise Theatre are explained by the company's founding directors.

1547 Fancy, Alex. "Acadie: The Lights Around the Shore." *CTR.* 1986 Fall; 13(48): 37-42. Notes. Illus.: Photo. Print. B&W. 2: 3 in. x 5 in., 4 in. x 5 in. Lang.: Eng.

Canada. 1985-1986. Historical studies. ■While Acadian playwrights continue to be in short supply, Acadian directors maintain a great deal of French-language theatre in New Brunswick through a wide variety of performance and repertory strategies.

1548 Furlong, Gary T. "Equity Turns On Its Own." *Theatrum.* 1986 Win; 5: 15-17. Lang.: Eng.

Canada: Toronto, ON. 1983-1986. Historical studies. ■Purpose and function of Canada's professional performers' union, its support of smaller companies, its pay scales and the consequences of inflexibility.

1549 Gilbert, Sky. "A New Dramaturgy: Inside the Rhubarb Festival." *Theatrum.* 1986 Sum; 4: 5-8. Lang.: Eng.

DRAMA: —Institutions

Canada: Toronto, ON. 1986. Historical studies. ■The artistic director of the Rhubarb Festival discusses its experimental work within the context of its history and programming.

1550 Goldie, Terry. "Newfoundland: The Powers That Be." *CTR*. 1986 Fall; 13(48): 6-15. Illus.: Photo. Print. B&W. 7: var. sizes. Lang.: Eng.

Canada. 1976-1986. Historical studies. ■Alternative theatre in Newfoundland has been the envy of other regions in Canada, beginning with the Mummers' Troupe and Codco in the mid-1970s.

1551 Harrison, James. "In the Heart of the Heart of Stratford: An Interview with John Neville." *Theatrum*. 1985-86 Fall-Win; 3: 3-6. Pref. Lang.: Eng.

Canada: Stratford, ON. 1985. Histories-sources. ■John Neville discusses plans for the future scope and seasons of the Stratford Festival, emphasizing professional training to expand theatrical traditions.

1552 Klein, Jeanne. "Le Théâtre de la Marmaille: A Québécois Collective Founded on Research." *ChTR*. 1986 Spr ; 35(1): 3-8. Notes. Append. Illus.: Photo. B&W. 2: 9 in. x 7 in. Lang.: Eng.

Canada: Quebec, PQ. 1973-1986. Historical studies. ■Le Théâtre de la Marmaille, a professional Québécois children's theatre collective, and research oriented, child advocacy theatre group.

1553 Knaapen, Jacoba. "Looking Ahead." *Theatrum*. 1986 Sum; 4: 4. Lang.: Eng.

Canada: Toronto, ON. 1985. Histories-sources. ■The journal's managing editor comments on the first anniversary of publication, giving a summary of intent and purpose. Changes are outlined for production, scope and staff.

1554 Lapointe, Gilles. "*Canadian Theatre Review*: Une sobriété un peu terne." (*Canadian Theatre Review*: A Rather Dry Sobriety.) *CDr*. 1986 Fall; 12(2): 375-377. Notes. Lang.: Fre.

Canada. 1985. Critical studies. ■The author criticizes the journal *Canadian Theatre Review* for its conservative, non-confrontational approach to Canadian theatre history and promotion of contemporary Canadian theatre.

1555 Love, Myron. "Fleeing Things." *BooksC*. 1986 Apr.; 15(3): 3. Lang.: Eng.

Canada: Winnipeg, MB. 1980-1986. Historical studies. ■The Shared Stage company and its commitment to experimental theatre.

1556 Mair, Elizabeth. "Prince Edward Island: Theatre: Who's It For?" *CTR*. 1986 Fall; 13(48): 19-22. Illus.: Photo. Print. B&W. 3: 4 in. x 3 in., 3 in. x 5 in., 4 in. x 2 in. Lang.: Eng.

Canada. 1981-1986. Historical studies. ■The development of community-based theatre in Prince Edward Island is being led by the Island Community Theatre and by two summer companies, the King's Playhouse (Georgetown) and the Victoria Playhouse (Victoria-by-the-Sea).

1557 McKenna, Ed. "Nova Scotia: The Halifax Problem, Inside and Out." *CTR*. 1986 Fall; 13(48): 43-54. Illus.: Photo. Dwg. Print. B&W. 7: var. sizes. Lang.: Eng.

Canada: Halifax, NS. 1962-1986. Historical studies. ■The Neptune Theatre, one of Canada's first regional theatres, has been largely unsuccessful in creating indigenous or community-based drama. Since the early 1970s, however, a number of short-lived companies have provided alternatives.

1558 Metcalfe, Robin. "Playing to Win, the Dramatists' Co-op of Nova Scotia." *ArtsAtl*. 1986 Sum; 7(2): 38-39. Illus.: Photo. Print. B&W. 1: 12 cm. x 11 cm. Lang.: Eng.

Canada. 1976-1986. Historical studies. ■The Dramatists' Co-op and its aspirations to establish an Eastern playwrights' colony and produce a collection of plays for use in high schools.

1559 Munday, Jenny. "New Brunswick: The Comedy Asylum." *CTR*. 1986 Fall; 13(48): 26-31. Illus.: Photo. Print. B&W. 3: 3 in. x 3 in, 3 in. x 5 in. Lang.: Eng.

Canada: Fredericton, NB. 1982-1986. Historical studies. ■Origins and development of a dinner-theatre and touring company in Fredericton, called the Comedy Asylum, described by one of the company's founding members.

1560 Page, Malcolm. "British Columbia: White Rock Summer Theatre, 1976-85." *CTR*. 1986 Spr; 13(46): 100-105. Illus.: Photo. Print. B&W. 1: 4 in. x 5 in. Lang.: Eng.

Canada: White Rock, BC. 1976-1985. Historical studies. ■The first decade of White Rock Summer Theatre, a summer stock operation near Vancouver.

1561 Poteet, Susan. "A Matter of Voice." *CTR*. 1986 Spr; 13(46): 28-35. Illus.: Photo. Diagram. Print. B&W. Chart. 4: var. sizes. Lang.: Eng.

Canada: Montreal, PQ. 1976-1986. Critical studies. ■The current state of English-language new play development in Montreal gives little opportunity for local playwrights to be produced locally.

1562 Silk, Ilkay; Young, Vicki. "New Brunswick: TNB's Contact Theatre." *CTR*. 1986 Fall; 13(48): 31-33. Illus.: Photo. Print. B&W. 2: 3 in. x 5 in. Lang.: Eng.

Canada. 1985-1986. Historical studies. ■Theatre New Brunswick created its own alternative stage called Theatre Contact to broaden its programming.

1563 Tourangeau, Rémi; Duhaime, Julien. *125 Ans de Théâtre au Séminaire de Trois-Rivières*. (One Hundred and Twenty-Five Years of Theatre at the Trois-Rivières Seminary.) Trois-Rivières, PQ: Editions Cédoleq; 1985. Lang.: Fre.

Canada: Trois-Rivières, PQ. 1860-1985. Histories-specific. ■Gives a history of the theatrical activity at the College (now Seminary) of Trois-Rivières, in souvenir-album form.

1564 Wade, Bryan. "Down and Out in the Can Lit Ghetto." *CTR*. 1986 Spr; 13(46): 106-109. Illus.: Photo. Print. B&W. 1: 3 in. x 5 in. Lang.: Eng.

Canada. 1986. Critical studies. ■A playwright surveys Canadian university offerings in Canadian literature, drama and playwriting.

1565 Wallace, Robert. "Garrison Theatre: An Introduction." *CTR*. 1986 Spr; 13(46): 4-5. Illus.: Photo. Print. B&W. 1:2 in. x 1 in. Lang.: Eng.

Canada. 1986. Critical studies. ■Special issue on minority-language theatre in Canada, termed here 'Garrison theatre'.

1566 Wallace, Robert. "Tales of Two Cities." *CTR*. 1986 Spr; 13(46): 6-20. Illus.: Photo. Print. B&W. 8: var. sizes. Lang.: Eng.

Canada: Montreal, PQ, Toronto, ON. 1986. Histories-sources. ■Interviews with the artistic directors of Canada's two most important minority-language theatres, Maurice Podbrey (of Centaur Theatre, Montreal) and John Van Burek (of Théâtre du P'tit Bonheur, Toronto).

1567 Wright, Heather. "On n'est plus loin de Toronto." *CTR*. 1986 Spr; 13(46): 42-49. Notes. Tables. Append. Illus.: Photo. Diagram. Print. B&W. Chart. 5: var. sizes. Lang.: Eng.

Canada. 1968-1986. Historical studies. ■The development of French-language theatre in Ontario has greatly accelerated in the past decade.

1568 Gao, Mei. "Yiai Zaixing Yong Nanwang." (The Unforgettable Love He Passed On.) *XYishu*. 1982 May; 5(2): 14-16. Lang.: Chi.

China, People's Republic of: Chengdu. 1901-1981. Biographical studies. ■Former students of the Sichuan Province Theatre/Music School (1938-1941) remember their principal, Xiong Foxi.

1569 Gao, Qun. "Chinian Enshi—Xiong Foxi." (Remembering a Beloved Teacher—Xiong Foxi.) *XYishu*. 1982 May; 5(2): 11-13. Lang.: Chi.

China, People's Republic of: Jinan, Chengdu. 1901-1982. Histories-sources. ■The author recalls the days as a student actor under Xiong Foxi's supervision and care.

1570 Ma, Ming. "Zhang Boling yu Nankai Xin Jutuan." (Zhang Boling and Nankai's New Drama Company.) *XYishu*. 1982 Nov.; 5(4): 139-151. Lang.: Chi.

China, People's Republic of: Tianjin. 1907-1951. Historical studies. ■Account of Zhang's company, one of the earliest and longest lasting spoken drama companies.

1571 Su, Kun. "Huigu, Zongjie, Zhanwang." (Review, Summary, Forecast.) *XYishu*. 1982 Nov.; 5(4): 3-12. Lang.: Chi.

China, People's Republic of: Shanghai. 1945-1982. Historical studies. ■Influence of politics on the programs of the Shanghai Drama Institute.

CLASSED ENTRIES

DRAMA: —Institutions

1572 "Timo Tiusanen in Memoriam." *NFT*. 1986; 38: 18. Illus.: Photo. B&W. 1: 2 cm. x 2 cm. Lang.: Eng, Fre.
Finland: Helsinki. 1957-1985. Historical studies. ■Overview of the career of theatre manager, director, critic and scholar Timo Tiusanen.

1573 "Les Quarante ans de la compagnie." (Forty Years of the Company.) *CRB*. 1986; 112: 1-133. 5: var. sizes. Lang.: Fre.
France: Paris. 1946-1986. Reviews of performances. ■Special issue devoted to Jean-Louis Barrault and actress Madeleine Renaud and a retrospective of the activities of the Compagnie Renaud-Barrault.

1574 Goodwin, Michael. "Shakespeare and Le Théâtre Soleil." *Theatrum*. 1985-86 Fall-Win; 3: 15-18. Lang.: Eng.
France: Paris. 1963-1985. Historical studies. ■Development of Théâtre du Soleil as an ensemble, its artistic goals and influence of Shakespeare.

1575 Kiernander, Adrian. "The Théâtre du Soleil, Part One: a Brief History of the Company." *NTQ*. 1986 Aug.; 11(7): 195-203. Notes. Illus.: Photo. B&W. 9. Lang.: Eng.
France: Paris. 1964-1986. Histories-specific. ■A survey of the company's work and its distinctive qualities.

1576 Sueur, Monique. *Deux siècles au Conservatoire national d'art dramatique.* (Two Centuries at the Conservatoire National d'Art Dramatique.) Paris: C.N.S.A.D.; 1986. 236 pp. Pref. Append. Illus.: Photo. Plan. Dwg. Print. B&W. 157: var. sizes. Lang.: Fre.
France: Paris. 1786-1986. Historical studies. ■Evolution and current status of the teaching of acting in France. Details of current teaching methods, list of teachers since 1807 and list of students since 1947.

1577 Seydel, Renate, ed. *Verweile doch...Erinnerungen von Schauspielern des Deutschen Theaters Berlin.* (Stay Please...Remembrances by Actors of Deutsches Theater Berlin.) Berlin: Henschelverlag; 1984. 837 pp. Illus.: Photo. Print. B&W. 192: var. sizes. Lang.: Ger.
Germany: Berlin. 1884-1955. Biographical studies. ■Autobiographical documents by 50 prominent managing directors, stage directors and actors on their work in the Deutsches Theater.

1578 Tenschert, Joachim; Kleber, Pia; Blostein, David. "Theatrical Production at the Berliner Ensemble." *Theatrum*. 1986 Win; 5: 19-22, 33. Pref. Lang.: Eng.
Germany, East: Berlin, East. 1930-1986. Histories-sources. ■Director Joachim Tenschert describes the repertory work of the Berliner Ensemble group, their methods of training, production, acting and direction.

1579 Coveney, Michael. "Sophocles: Dress Informal." *PlPl*. 1986 Dec.; 399: 12-13. B&W. 3: var. sizes. Lang.: Eng.
Italy: Parma. 1982-1986. Critical studies. ■Collettivo di Parma, a company that explores its own culture through experimental productions of classics.

1580 Ferrone, Siro. "La Compagnia dei Comici 'Confidenti' al servizio di Don Giovanni dei Medici (1613-1621)." (The 'Confidenti' Company in the Service of Don Giovanni dei Medici (1613-1621).) 153-175 in Salvat, Ricard, ed. *El Teatre durant l'Edat Mitjana i el Renaixement.* Barcelona: Publicacions i Edicions de la Universitat de Barcelona; 1986. xxviii, 322 pp. (El Pla de les Comèdies 2.) Notes. [Presented at First International Symposium on Medieval and Renaissance Theatre, Sitges, 1983.] Lang.: Ita.
Italy: Venice. 1613-1621. Historical studies. ■Relations between a company and its patron, as revealed through contemporary correspondence.

1581 Osiński, Zbigniew. "Analyse du texte dramatique dans le théâtre 'Reduta' de Juliusz Osterwa et de Mieczysław Limanowski." (Analysis of Dramatic Text in the Reduta Theatre of Juliusz Osterwa and Mieczysław Limanowski.) 51-65 in Heistein, Józef, ed. *Le texte dramatique. La lecture et la scène.* Wrocław: Wydawnictwo Uniwersytetu Wrocławskiego; 1986. 248 pp. (Acta Universitatis Wratislaviensis 895, Romanica Wratislaviensia 26.) Lang.: Fre.
Poland: Warsaw. 1919-1939. Historical studies. ■The Reduta theatre approach to drama as the predecessor of Grotowski's Laboratory.

1582 Miralles, Alberto. "El nuevo teatro español ha muerto y mueran sus asesinos!" (The New Spanish Theatre is Dead: Death to Its Assassins!)*Estreno*. 1986 Fall; 12(2): 21-24. Lang.: Spa.
Spain. 1975-1985. Historical studies. ■Factors leading to the decline of Spanish theatre, including lack of recognition by the minister of culture, decreasing subsidies, declining production quality, critical and public indifference and lack of new plays.

1583 Candel, Francisco; Rodríguez Méndez, José María; Carmona i Rístol, Àngel; Munné-Jordà, Antoni, transl. "Dossier La Pipironda." *EECIT*. 1986 Dec.; 28: 9-48. Lang.: Cat.
Spain-Catalonia: Barcelona. 1958-1986. Histories-sources. ■Three essays on the evolution of the Catalan theatre company La Pipironda.

1584 Johansson, Ingrid. "Alla deltar i skapande." (Everybody Join in the Creation.) *Teaterf*. 1986; 19(1): 3-4. Illus.: Photo. Lang.: Swe.
Sweden: Handen. 1982-1986. Historical studies. ■Amateur production of *La Casa de Bernarda Alba (The House of Bernarda Alba)* by Kulturföreningen ROJ, directed by Margerete Kuhn.

1585 Samuelsson, Björn. "Lön blir det om det inte regnar." (Salaries Will Be Paid If It Doesn't Rain.) *Teaterf*. 1986 ; 19(4): 3-6. Illus.: Photo. Lang.: Swe.
Sweden: Södertälje. 1980-1986. Historical studies. ■Sommarteatern (Summer Theatre) is an open-air theatre with professionals cooperating with amateurs, who will now try to perform year-round.

1586 Abbotson, S.P. *Creating a Fiction: Theatre, Creativity and the Research Process.* Bath: Univ. of Bath; 1986. [Ph.D. dissertation, *Index to Theses*, 36-6913.] Lang.: Eng.
UK-England: London. 1981-1986. Empirical research. ■Study of the creative process of an alternative theatre group whose interpretation of the text and interaction with the audience are used as a metaphor for understanding the research process of interpreting data and writing a thesis.

1587 Lucre, Andrew. "David Porter." *PI*. 1986 Oct.; 2(3): 32-33. B&W. 1. Lang.: Eng.
UK-England: Leicester. 1986. Histories-sources. ■David Porter, the new artistic director of Leicester Haymarket Theatre, discusses his policy.

1588 Lustig, Vera. "Rising Tide." *WomanR*. 1986 Sep.; 2(11): 34-35. Illus.: Photo. B&W. 3. Lang.: Eng.
UK-England: London. 1986. Histories-specific. ■Place of women in Britain's National Theatre. Includes comment on Sarah Daniels' *Neaptide* by designer Alison Ghitty and performer Jessica Turner.

1589 Nevitt, Roy. "Community Spirit." *Drama*. 1986; 162(4): 11-14. Illus.: Photo. B&W. 3: var. sizes. Lang.: Eng.
UK-England: Milton Keynes. 1976-1986. Historical studies. ■Social and educational value of the community documentary plays created by the Living Archive Project.

1590 Parrish, Sue. "Enter Women, Centre Stage." *WomenR*. 1986 Oct.; 2(12): 9-11. Illus.: Photo. B&W. 6. Lang.: Eng.
UK-England: London. 1984-1986. Histories-specific. ■The context for the formation of the Women's Playhouse Trust in Britain, its progress and its aims.

1591 Reid, Francis. "The Royal Shakespeare Theatre Museum." *Cue*. 1986 Sep/Oct.; 8(43): 10-11. Illus.: Photo. Print. B&W. 4: 9 x 6 cm. Lang.: Eng.
UK-England: Stratford. 1932-1986. Histories-sources. ■Description of an exhibit on 'Stages and Staging' in the RSC Collection at the Shakespeare Memorial Theatre.

1592 Roberts, Peter. "Shakespeare Our Contemporary." *PI*. 1986 Oct.; 2(3): 20-21,57. B&W. 1. Lang.: Eng.
UK-England. 1986. Historical studies. ■Actor Michael Pennington and director Michael Bogdanov discuss the formation of the English Shakespeare Company and its tour of England and abroad performing *Henry IV Parts 1 and 2* and *Henry V*.

1593 Zong, Bai; Li, Ching-Te. "Ying Kuo Huangjia Shashibiya Jutuan Zongheng Tan." (Report on England's Royal Shakespeare Company.) *XYishu*. 1982 May; 5(2): 127-129. Lang.: Chi.
UK-England. 1960-1980. Historical studies. ■Survey of RSC's productions, particularly those of Peter Hall and Peter Brook.

DRAMA: —Institutions

1594 Melville, Bill. "Borderline." *STN*. 1985 Dec-Jan.; 9(48): 5-7. Illus.: Photo. B&W. 1. Lang.: Eng.
UK-Scotland. 1974-1985. Historical studies. ■History of Borderline Theatre Company and their projected move to new premises.

1595 Oliver, Cordelia. "The Long March Towards a Scottish National Theatre." *STN*. 1986 Spr; 9(49): 23-30. Lang.: Eng.
UK-Scotland. 1940-1986. Critical studies. ■Discussion of the attempts made to establish a Scottish National Theatre.

1596 Paterson, Tony. "Something of a Miracle: The Wilson Barrett Achievement." *STN*. 1986 Spr; 9(49): 3-7. Illus.: Photo. B&W. 3: var. sizes. Lang.: Eng.
UK-Scotland. 1930-1955. Historical studies. ■Description of the Wilson Barrett Theatre Company (UK-Scotland).

1597 Bloom, Arthur W. "The Jefferson Company, 1830-1845." *ThS*. 1986 May & Nov.; 27(1-2): 89-153. Notes. Lang.: Eng.
USA. 1830-1845. Historical studies. ■Careful examination of repertory, schedule, and personnel of the Jefferson Company confirms, corrects and expands Douglas McDermott's thesis concerning the development of theatre on the American frontier (*Theatre Survey*, 1978).

1598 Graham, Billy. "Alaska to Miami: Black Theatre on Tour." *BlackM*. 1986 Jan-Feb.: 2-3. Lang.: Eng.
USA: New York, NY. 1969-1982. Historical studies. ■History of two major Black touring companies, the National Black Touring Circuit out of the New Federal Theatre (New York, NY) and the Negro Ensemble Touring Company (NEC, New York, NY), focusing on choice of plays, mounting productions and cost factors.

1599 Kanellos, Nicolás. *Mexican American Theatre: Legacy & Reality*. Houston, TX: Arte Publico; 1986. 128 pp. Lang.: Eng.
USA. 1850-1985. Historical studies. ■Includes studies of the Los Angeles playwriting boom in the 1920s, an overview of the evolution of the Mexican American circus/tent show, folklore and popular culture in Chicano theatre and an evaluation of by Luis Valdez and other Chicano theatres. Related to Mixed Entertainment: Circus.

1600 Kirfel-Lenk, Thea. *Erwin Piscator im Exil in den USA. 1939-1951*. (Erwin Piscator: Exile in the USA.) Deutsches Theater im Exil. Berlin: Henschelverlag; 1984. 268 pp. Notes. Index. Illus.: Photo. Print. B&W. 68: var. sizes. Lang.: Ger.
USA: New York, NY. 1939-1951. Historical studies. ■Detailed description of Piscator's work at the Dramatic Workshop of the New School for Social Research.

1601 Loving-Sloane, Cecilia. "Theater." *Crisis*. 1986 Oct.; 93(8): 12-14. Illus.: Photo. Print. B&W. 3: 3 in. x 2 in., 4 in. x 3 in., 3 in. x 5 in. Lang.: Eng.
USA: New York, NY. 1980-1986. Historical studies. ■Discusses Vi Higginsen's *Mama I Want to Sing* and examines the history of the Mumbo-Jumbo Theatre Company.

1602 Loving-Sloane, Cecilia. "Eubie Blake Children's Theatre Company." *OvA*. 1986 Win; 14(1): 9, 31. Illus.: Photo. Print. B&W. 1: 4 in. x 7 in. Lang.: Eng.
USA: New York, NY. 1986. Historical studies. ■Curriculum and expectation of students in Eubie Blake's Children's Theatre Company, offshoot of musical theatre company AMAS Repertory (New York, NY). Related to Music-Drama: Musical theatre.

1603 Perry, Shauneille. "Reclaiming Our Theaters: Thoughts on Survival." *BlackM*. 1986 Sum: 4, 10. Illus.: Photo. Print. B&W. 2: 1.5 in. x 2 in. [Part 3.] Lang.: Eng.
USA: New York, NY. 1970-1986. Historical studies. ■History of Black Spectrum, a Black community-based theatre which has survived through community involvement, a dinner theatre, three distinct repertory companies and a film production company.

1604 Perry, Shauneille. "Reclaiming Our Theatres: Thoughts on Survival." *BlackM*. 1986 Feb-Mar.: 4, 10. Illus.: Photo. Print. B&W. 2: 2 in. x 3 in. [Part 2.] Lang.: Eng.
USA: New York, NY. 1970-1986. Historical studies. ■Brief histories of the H.A.D.L.E.Y. Players and the Cynthia Belgrave Theatre Workshop and their survival.

1605 Raymond, Gerard. "The New York Shakespeare Festival in the Schools." *OvA*. 1986 Win; 14(1): 15, 28. Illus.: Photo. Print. B&W. 2: 4 in. x 5 in. Lang.: Eng.
USA: New York, NY. 1986. Historical studies. ■Efforts of New York Shakespeare Festival to develop an audience for Shakespearean drama through its Playwriting-in-the-schools program, multi-racial company and its offering of plays for school audiences.

1606 Ryzuk, Mary S. *The Circle Repertory Company—The First 15 Years*. New York, NY: City Univ. of New York; 1986. 477 pp. Pref. Notes. Biblio. [Ph.D. dissertation, Univ. Microfilms order No. DA8611378.] Lang.: Eng.
USA: New York, NY. 1969-1984. Histories-specific. ■Evolution of the Circle Repertory Company founded by Marshall W. Mason, Rob Thirkield, Lanford Wilson and Tanya Berezin.

1607 Shewey, Don. "The Many Voices of Mabou Mines." *AmTh*. 1984 Apr.; 1(3): 4-11, 42. Illus.: Photo. B&W. 9: var. sizes. Lang.: Eng.
USA: New York, NY. 1984. Histories-sources. ■Interview with members of Mabou Mines, analysis of their work, collaboration process and individual techniques. Includes chronological list of their productions.

1608 Simpson, David. "Black Theater: Alive, Well, and Living in Philly." *BlackM*. 1985 Dec. 15-1986 Jan. 15: 2, 3, 10. Lang.: Eng.
USA: Philadelphia, PA. 1966-1985. Historical studies. ■Survey of Black theatre companies and their respective histories showing how each group serves the cultural life of its community.

1609 Thomas, Veona. "Michigan's McCree Theater: A Fifteen Year Odyssey." *BlackM*. 1986 Apr-May: 4. Illus.: Design. Print. B&W. 1: 2 in. x 4 in. Lang.: Eng.
USA: Flint, MI. 1971-1986. Historical studies. ■Brief history of the McCree Theatre (associated with the theatre department of C.S. Mott Community College) its acceptance of contributions from local artists and its efforts to address the needs of the community.

1610 Turner, Beth. "Marjorie Moon: Opportunity's Door-keeper." *BlackM*. 1986 Sep.: 2-3, 9. Illus.: Photo. Print. B&W. 1: 4 in. x 5 in. Lang.: Eng.
USA: New York, NY, Cleveland, OH. 1973-1986. Historical studies. ■Career of Marjorie Moon, artistic director of the Billie Holliday Theatre (New York, NY) and how the theatre has grown under her leadership.

1611 Wang, Yiqun. "Meiguo Xiaojuchang Yundong jiqi dui Meiguo Xiandai Xiju de Yingxiang." (The Little Theatre Movement in the United States and Its Impact on Modern American Plays.) *XYishu*. 1982 May; 5(2): 114-120. Lang.: Chi.
USA. 1887-1967. Historical studies. ■Includes its role in the development of American regional theatre.

Performance spaces

1612 Harrison, Wayne. "Designing for the Mailbox." *Sin*. 1986; 20(2): 24-25. Illus.: Photo. B&W. 3. Lang.: Eng.
Australia: Sydney, N.S.W. 1980-1986. Historical studies. ■Problematic dimensions of the Sydney Opera House's Drama Theatre and the solutions of designer Brian Thompson.

1613 Regan, Tom. "Nova Scotia: The Start of a Beautiful Relationship?" *CTR*. 1986 Fall; 13(48): 55-58. Illus.: Photo. Print. B&W. 2: 4 in. x 5 in, 2 in. x 3 in. Lang.: Eng.
Canada: Halifax, NS. 1986. Historical studies. ■The opening of the new Cunard Street Theatre, founded by the Nova Scotia Drama League to encourage more alternative theatre in Halifax by providing an accessible, affordable rental space.

1614 Vingoe, Mary. "Parrsboro: Environmental Marine Theatre." *CTR*. 1986 Fall; 13(48): 116-121. Illus.: Photo. Print. B&W. 3:3 in. x 5 in. Lang.: Eng.
Canada. 1982-1986. Historical studies. ■In 1982 a heritage society was formed to restore a derelict 1920s small coastal cruise ship, and in 1984 the Ship's Company Theatre began producing summer theatre on the ship.

DRAMA: —Performance spaces

1615 Astington, John H. "Staging at St. James' Palace in the Seventeenth Century." *ThR.* 1986; 11(3): 187-213. Notes. Illus.: Plan. Dwg. B&W. Grd.Plan. 2. Lang.: Eng.
England: London. 1600-1986. Histories-reconstruction. ■Reconstructing a theatrical organization at St. James Palace using architectural, textual and financial evidence.

1616 Burkhart, Robert E. "The Dimensions of Middle Temple Hall." *SQ.* 1986 Fall; 37(3): 370-371. Notes. Illus.: Plan. Architec. Grd.Plan. 1. Lang.: Eng.
England: London. 1602. Historical studies. ■Overview of the great hall in which *Twelfth Night* by William Shakespeare was performed, includes a revision of the screen measurements made by Richard Hosley in his book *The Origins of the Shakespearean Playhouse.*

1617 Easterbrook, Anthony. "Swan." *Sin.* 1986; 20(2): 7-10. Illus.: Photo. Plan. B&W. Architec. 6. Lang.: Eng.
UK-England: Stratford. Historical studies. ■Outlines the technical and architectural features of the Swan Theatre at Stratford-upon-Avon.

1618 Emmet, Alfred. "*She Stoops to Conquer.* New Victoria Theatre. Newcastle-under-Lyme." *Sin.* 1986; 20(2): 38. Biblio. Illus.: Photo. B&W. 1. Lang.: Eng.
UK-England: Newcastle-under-Lyme. 1980-1986. Critical studies. ■A technical review of *She Stoops to Conquer* by Oliver Goldsmith, performed at the New Victoria Theatre commending the full use of the theatre in the round.

1619 Reid, Francis. "A Swan for the Avon." *Cue.* 1986 May/June; 8(41): 4-7. Illus.: Photo. Dwg. Print. Color. B&W. 10: var. sizes. Lang.: Eng.
UK-England: Stratford. 1978-1985. Histories-sources. ■Description of the new Swan Theatre.

1620 Russell, Barry. "Launching the Swan." *Drama.* 1986; 3(161): 11-12. Illus.: Photo. B&W. 3: 8 cm. x 12 cm. Lang.: Eng.
UK-England: Stratford. 1986. Technical studies. ■Effect of the RSC's new Swan Theatre on actors and audiences.

1621 Eppes, William D. "Alabama Shakespeare Festival: The State Theatre, Montgomery." *MarqJTHS.* 1986; 18(3): 9-12. Illus.: Photo. Plan. B&W. Grd.Plan. 5: var. sizes. Lang.: Eng.
USA: Montgomery, AL. 1972-1986. Historical studies. ■A history of the Alabama Shakespeare Festival and a description of the new theatre built in 1985 in Montgomery.

1622 Harris, Stephen. "Marquee Picture Portfolio: The Theatres of Birmingham." *MarqJTHS.* 1986; 18(3): 16-22. Illus.: Photo. B&W. 13: var. sizes. Lang.: Eng.
USA: Birmingham, AL. 1890-1983. Historical studies. ■Photographs, with descriptive captions, of various legitimate, vaudeville and film theatres.

1623 Headley, Robert K. "THS—1986—Conclave Chicago-Midwest." *MarqJTHS.* 1986; 18(2): 1-40. Illus.: Photo. Plan. B&W. Grd.Plan. 82: var. sizes. Lang.: Eng.
USA: Chicago, IL, Milwaukee, WI. 1889-1986. Historical studies. ■Short descriptions and photographs of 36 legitimate and film theatres visited during the Theatre Historical Society's 1986 Chicago-Midwest Conclave.

1624 Marotta, Dario S. "The Bowery Theatre." *MarqJTHS.* 1986; 18(1): 24-27. Illus.: Photo. B&W. 4: var. sizes. Lang.: Eng.
USA: New York, NY. 1826-1929. Historical studies. ■Originally built in 1826, and due to fires, rebuilt in 1828, 1837, 1839 and 1845. The Thalia Theatre was built on the same site in 1879.

1625 Robinson, Jack. "New York's Most Elegant, The Century Theatre." *MarqJTHS.* 1986; 18(4): 9-15. Biblio. Illus.: Photo. B&W. 5: var. sizes. [Winner of Third Prize in the 1985 Jeffrey Weiss Contest.] Lang.: Eng.
USA: New York, NY. 1905-1930. Historical studies. ■In 1905, a group of social leaders decided to build a theatre worthy of their patronage. Despite its elegance, the New (later Century) Theatre was a financial failure.

1626 Segan, Leone. "New Faces on Old Spaces." *MarqJTHS.* 1986; 18(1): 1, 3-18, 32. Illus.: Photo. B&W. DR. 34: var. sizes. Lang.: Eng.
USA: New York, NY. 1861-1986. Historical studies. ■Descriptions of the 42 theatres featured in the touring exhibit 'New Faces on Old Spaces' sponsored by the New York State Assembly and AT&T.

Performance/production

1627 Davis, Tracy C. "Acting in Ibsen." *TN.* 1985; 39(3): 113-123. Lang.: Eng.
1885-1905. Historical studies. ■Realistic and sensationalistic acting styles in productions of plays by Ibsen.

1628 Dort, Bernard; Kruger, Loren. "The Site of Epic Representation." *ComIBS.* 1985 Apr.; 84(2): 3-19.
1985. Critical studies. ■Characteristics of the stage space in epic theatre, including openess, neutrality, mobility and lack of perspective.

1629 Finkel, Shimon. "Neshumale Lezichra Shel Elisabeth Bergner." (Elisabeth Bergner.) *Bamah.* 1986; 21(104): 114-118. Illus.: Photo. Print. B&W. 1: 16.5 cm. x 11.5 cm. Lang.: Heb.
1922-1986. Biographical studies. ■Obituary of actress Elisabeth Bergner.

1630 Gruber, William E. *Comic Theatres: Studies in Performance and Audience Response.* Athens, GA: Univ of Georgia P; 1986. ix, 198 pp. Biblio. Index. Notes. Lang.: Eng.
Critical studies. ■Argues that meaning in dramatic texts depends on performance and the relationship between performer and audience. Focuses on inherent tensions between actor and character, actor and audience, stage and world.

1631 Miller, Jonathan. *Subsequent Performances.* London/Boston: Faber & Faber; 1986. 288 pp. Index. Illus.: Photo. Color. Lang.: Eng.
1986. Critical studies. ■Director's theory of performance based on genre, consideration of how plays can have both historical continuity and relevance to contemporary life.

1632 Peters, Steven James. *Modern to Post Modern Acting and Directing: An Historical Perspective.* Lubbock, TX: Texas Tech. Univ.; 1986. 305 pp. Pref. Notes. Biblio. [Ph.D. dissertation, Univ. Microfilms order No. DA8615367.] Lang.: Eng.
1898-1986. Histories-specific. ■Study surveying the historical and stylistic influences on an expanding methodology for acting and directing through the equation of stages of self-development with production responsibilities.

1633 Stern, Gary. "A Nice Place to Live." *AmTh.* 1984 July/Aug.; 1(4): 15-19. Illus.: Photo. B&W. 11: var. sizes. Lang.: Eng.
1961-1984. Historical studies. ■Focus on five actors—Ed Hall, Joan Allen, Adale O'Brien, Clayton Corzatte and Barbara Dirickson— who have committed themselves to working solely in regional theatres.

1634 Wyatt, Eliza. "Include Character Conferences." *DGQ.* 1986 Win; 23(4): 25-28.
1986. Critical studies. ■Eliza Wyatt urges fellow playwrights to establish a routine of character conferences with actors during the rehearsal process.

1635 Zhu, Duanjun; Yang, Ying, ed.; Yao, Tiagheng, ed. "Zhu Duanjun Tan Yi Lu." (Zhu Duanjun's Lecture on the Arts.) *XYishu.* 1982 Nov.; 5(4): 29-36. Lang.: Chi.
1890-1978. Histories-sources. ■Director and teacher Zhu's last lecture on actor's characterization, basic physical training, Stanislavskij, and spoken drama's relation to Chinese opera.

1636 Loney, Glenn. "Talking to Carlos Gimenez, Creator of the Rajatabla in Caracas." *NTQ.* 1986 Aug.; 11(7): 243-249. Illus.: Photo. B&W. 4. Lang.: Eng.
Argentina. Venezuela: Caracas. 1969-1986. Histories-sources. ■Interview with Carlos Gimenez, Argentinine director currently working in exile in Venezuela.

1637 Borny, Geoffrey. "Williams and Kazan: the Creative Synthesis." *ADS.* 1986 Apr.; 8: 33-47. Notes. Lang.: Eng.

CLASSED ENTRIES

DRAMA: —Performance/production

Australia. Historical studies. ■Collaboration between Tennessee Williams and director Elia Kazan on productions of Williams' plays.

1638 Burvill, Tom. "Sidetrack: Discovering the Theatricality of Community." *NTQ.* 1986 Feb.; 11(5): 80-89. Illus.: Photo. B&W. 5. Lang.: Eng.

Australia: Sydney, N.S.W. 1980-1986. Historical studies. ■Sidetrack's recent work in the context of understanding of community theatre according to Brecht and Benjamin.

1639 Gallasch, Keith. "Promise and Participation: Youth Theatre in Australia." *NTQ.* 1986 Feb.; 11(5): 90-93. Illus.: Photo. B&W. 1. Lang.: Eng.

Australia. 1982-1986. Histories-specific. ■The developing youth theatre movement seen as part of reaction to the drama-in-education of the 70s. Some of its dilemmas and prospects.

1640 Kelly, Veronica. "Garnet Walch in Sydney." *ADS.* 1986 Oct.; 9: 92-109. Notes. Illus.: Photo. 3: 11 cm. x 14 cm., 11 cm. x 16 cm. Lang.: Eng.

Australia: Sydney, N.S.W. 1860-1890. Historical studies. ■Exploration of Australian playwright Garnet Walch's dramatic apprenticeship in the 1870s including an account of the personalities and kinds of theatrical organizations of the time.

1641 Love, Harold. "Chinese Theatre on the Victorian Goldfields, 1858-1870." *ADS.* 1985 Apr.; 3(2): 45-86. Illus.: Maps. Dwg. 5: var. sizes. Lang.: Eng.

Australia. 1858-1870. Historical studies. ■Account of Chinese theatre companies on the Victorian Goldfields with a description of theatrical practices.

1642 Böhm, Gotthard. "Theater ist Lebenskunst." (Theatre Is the Art of Life.) *Buhne.* 1986 June; 29(6): 25-56. Illus.: Photo. Print. Color. Lang.: Ger.

Austria: Vienna. Switzerland. Germany, East. 1922-1986. Biographical studies. ■Manager and director Benno Besson, and his concept for staging *Don Juan* by Molière at the Burgtheater.

1643 Havel, Václav. "Fern vom Theater." (Far from Theatre.) 48-50 in Urbach, Reinhard, ed.; Benning, Achim, ed. *Burgtheater Wien 1776-1986, Ebenbild und Widerspruch: Zweihundert und zehn Jahre (Burgtheater Vienna 1776-1986, Image and Contradiction: Two Hundred and Ten Years).* Lang.: Ger.

Austria: Vienna. Czechoslovakia. 1976-1986. Histories-sources. ■Playwright Václav Havel's career and experiences with censorship. Production of his plays at Burgtheater.

1644 Kutschera, Edda. "Theater—das muss ein Muss sein!" (Theatre—That Has To Be a Must!)*Buhne.* 1986 Nov.; 29(11): 27-28. Illus.: Photo. Print. B&W. Lang.: Ger.

Austria: Vienna. 1938-1986. Biographical studies. ■Actor Heinz Petters: his popularity, his career, his work at the Volkstheater and his role as Striese in *Der Raub der Sabinerinnen (The Rape of the Sabine Women)* by Franz and Paul Schönthan, with notes on the production of this play at the Volkstheater.

1645 Lederer, Herbert. *Bevor alles verweht...: Wiener Kellertheater 1945 bis 1960.* (Before Everything's Gone...: Viennese Cellar Theatres 1945-1960.) Vienna: Österreichischer Bundesverlag; 1986. 188 pp. Pref. Index. Notes. Tables. Illus.: Photo. B&W. 40. Lang.: Ger.

Austria: Vienna. 1945-1960. Histories-specific. ■Resumption of theatre productions after World War II: the founding of cellar theatres. Living conditions, aims and styles of actors. Includes a listing of repertory and actors.

1646 Löbl, Hermi. "Mit Geld nicht erpressbar." (Not Blackmailed by Money.) *Buhne.* 1986 Nov.; 29(11): 17-18. Illus.: Photo. Print. Color. Lang.: Ger.

Austria: Vienna. 1957-1986. Biographical studies. ■Actor and playwright Gabriel Barylli: his childhood, his training, his plays and reasons for acting and playwriting.

1647 Löbl, Hermi. "Ich hab gern masslose Produkte." (I Like Excessive Products.) *Buhne.* 1986 Dec.; 29(12): 15-17. Illus.: Photo. Print. Color. Lang.: Ger.

Austria: Vienna. 1946-1986. Biographical studies. ■On actor Franz Morak and his work at the Burgtheater.

1648 Löbl, Hermi. "Der Weg ist das Ziel." (The Way Is the Aim.) *Buhne.* 1986 Jan.; 29(1): 23-26. Illus.: Photo. Print. Color. B&W. Lang.: Ger.

Austria: Vienna. 1944-1986. Biographical studies. ■Actor Klaus Maria Brandauer and his role as Hamlet at the Burgtheater.

1649 Löbl, Hermi. "Jede Rolle hat tausend Möglichkeiten." (Every Role Offers a Thousand Possibilities.) *Buhne.* 1986 Oct.; 29(10): 14-15. Illus.: Photo. Print. B&W. Lang.: Ger.

Austria: Vienna. Germany, West. 1941-1986. Biographical studies. ■Actor Gert Voss, his way of acting, his cooperation with director Claus Peymann and his relationship to Vienna.

1650 Löbl, Hermi. "Seit Jahren diktiert der Spielplan." (For Years the Program Has Dictated.) *Buhne.* 1986 Apr.; 29(4): 24-26. Illus.: Photo. Print. Color. Lang.: Ger.

Austria. 1936-1986. Biographical studies. ■Actress Elisabeth Orth, her life and work, her training at the Reinhardt Seminar and some of her roles at the Burgtheater.

1651 Raitmayr, Babette. "Das Leben ist nicht zu bändigen." (Life Can't Be Subdued.) *Buhne.* 1986 Aug.; 29(8): 22-23. Illus.: Photo. Print. B&W. Lang.: Ger.

Austria: Salzburg. Germany, West: Munich. 1986. Histories-sources. ■Director Dieter Dorn and his ideas about staging Heinrich von Kleist's *Der zerbrochene Krug (The Broken Jug)* for the Munich Kammerspiele and the Salzburger Festspiele.

1652 Reichert, Franz. *Durch meine Brille: Theater in bewegter Zeit (1925-1950).* (Through My Glasses: Theatre in Rough Times (1925-1950).) Ein Österreich-Thema aus dem Bundesverlag. Vienna: Österreichischer Bundesverlag; 1986. 287 pp. Index. Illus.: Photo. B&W. 31. Lang.: Ger.

Austria: Vienna. Germany: Berlin. Czechoslovakia: Prague. 1925-1950. Biographies. ■Actor and stage manager Franz Reichert remembers his roles and productions in various German-speaking cities, his colleagues and experiences with the Nazi regime.

1653 Reitl, Josef. *Richard Eybner: Ich möcht so leben können wie ich leb. Erinnerungen ans Burgtheater und anderes.* (Richard Eybner: I'd Like to Be Able to Live As I Live: Reminiscences on the Burgtheater and Other Things.) Vienna/Munich: Amalthea; 1986. 325 pp. Tables. Append. Illus.: Handbill. Photo. Dwg. Sketches. B&W. 105: var. sizes. Lang.: Ger.

Austria: Vienna. 1896-1986. Biographies. ■Biography of actor Richard Eybner of the Burgtheater: his experiences during the Nazi occupation, colleagues and work in film and theatre. Includes list of stage roles. Related to Media: Film.

1654 Urbach, Reinhard. "Hamlet: Exkurs über die begehrteste Rolle." (Hamlet: Essay about this Most Desired Role.) 35-40 in Urbach, Reinhard, ed.; Benning, Achim, ed. *Burgtheater Wien 1776-1986, Ebenbild und Widerspruch: Zweihundert und zehn Jahre (Burgtheater Vienna 1776-1986, Image and Contradiction: Two Hundred and Ten Years).* Vienna: Schroll; 1986. 263 pp. Illus.: Photo. B&W. 10: 7 cm. x 9 cm. Lang.: Ger.

Austria: Vienna. 1803-1985. Historical studies. ■Portrayal of Hamlet at the Burgtheater, style and interpretation by various actors.

1655 Molnár Gál, Péter. *A Latabárok. Egy szinészdinasztia a magyar szinháztörténetben.* (The Latabars: An Actor Dynasty in Hungarian Theatre History.) Budapest: Múzsák; 1986. 564 pp. (Szkénetéka.) Illus.: Photo. B&W. 88: var. sizes. Lang.: Hun.

Austro-Hungarian Empire. 1811-1970. Biographies. ■The Latabár acting dynasty, its continuity and importance in Hungarian theatre history.

1656 Hunt, Nigel. "Beckett, Boal, and Other Things in Brazil." *Theatrum.* 1985-86 Fall-Win; 3: 19-22. Lang.: Eng.

Brazil: Rio de Janeiro. 1985-1986. Historical studies. ■Describes 50 productions performed during the Christmas season which were primarily Brazilian. Several plays performed in Portuguese. Related to Dance: Ethnic dance.

1657 "Raising the Standard." *Drama.* 1986; 4(162): 23-24. Illus.: Photo. B&W. 4: var. sizes. Lang.: Eng.

DRAMA: —Performance/production

Canada: Stratford, ON. 1974-1986. Critical studies. ■John Neville revitalizes the Stratford Festival with productions of Shakespeare's *The Winter's Tale*, *Pericles* and *Cymbeline*.

1658 Borlase, Tim. "Newfoundland: Giving Culture a Shape." *CTR*. 1986 Fall; 13(48): 16-18. Illus.: Photo. Print. B&W. 2: 2 in. x 4 in., 4 in. x 5 in. Lang.: Eng.

Canada. 1983-1986. Historical studies. ■Recent increase in locally produced documentary and sociological productions, particularly in small Inuit communities.

1659 Brask, Per. "Canadian Dramaturgy: Dramaturgia." *CTR*. 1986 Win; 13(49): 11-14. Illus.: Photo. Print. B&W. 2: 2 in. x 2 in., 4 in. x 5 in. Lang.: Eng.

Canada. 1986. Historical studies. ■In developing new plays, the dramaturg has to understand the world of the playwright in order to resolve conflicts between it and the motivations of the characters.

1660 Clark, Annette. "St. John's: The Pursuits of Cathy Jones." *CTR*. 1986 Sum; 13(47): 143-146. Illus.: Photo. Print. B&W. 1: 4 in. x 3 in. Lang.: Eng.

Canada: St. John's, NF. 1986. Critical studies. ■The origins and styles of Cathy Jones' one-woman shows, in particular *Wedding in Texas*.

1661 Desson, Jim; Filson, Bruce K. "Where is David Fennario Now?" *CTR*. 1986 Spr; 13(46): 36-41. Illus.: Photo. Print. B&W. 2: var. sizes. Lang.: Eng.

Canada: Montreal, PQ. 1980-1986. Biographical studies. ■The work of playwright David Fennario, since his award-winning *Balconville* (1979), has been concentrated on political commitment in a working-class community theatre.

1662 Downton, Dawn Rae. "Maxim Mazumdar in Nova Scotia." *ArtsAtl*. 1986 Sum; 7(2): 40-41. Illus.: Photo. Print. B&W. 1: 4 cm. x 13 cm. Lang.: Eng.

Canada: Wolfville, NS. 1985-1986. Biographical studies. ■Actor, teacher, director Maxim Mazumdar.

1663 Furlong, Gary T. "An Actor's Profile: Stephen Ouimette." *Theatrum*. 1986 Win; 5: 9-14. Pref. Illus.: Photo. Print. B&W. 1: 5 in. x 6 in. Lang.: Eng.

Canada. 1960-1986. Histories-sources. ■Interview with actor Stephen Ouimette recounting his reasons for choosing professional theatre, his background, his training and his future plans.

1664 Grace-Warrick, Christa. "Vancouver: Getting Physical." *CTR*. 1986 Sum; 13(47): 125-130. Illus.: Photo. Print. B&W. 4: var. sizes. Lang.: Eng.

Canada: Vancouver, BC. 1986. Critical studies. ■The increase in the use of movement scores in dramatic production, and improvised dialogue in mime production, reflects a greater concern for physical aspects of theatre in several Vancouver companies. Related to Mime.

1665 Hayes, Elliott. "Stasis: The Workshop Syndrome." *CTR*. 1986 Win; 13(49): 36-39. Illus.: Photo. Print. B&W. 2: 3 in. x 5 in. Lang.: Eng.

Canada: Stratford, ON. 1986. Histories-sources. ■The dramaturg of the Stratford Festival analyzes the causes and effects of 'workshopitis' in new plays in Canada, and the Festival's own role in developing new plays.

1666 Hughes, Alan. "Coppin and the Australians of Vancouver Island." *ADS*. 1986 Oct.; 9: 82-91. Notes. Illus.: Photo. 3: 11 cm. x 15 cm., 11 cm. x 13.5 cm. Lang.: Eng.

Canada: Victoria, BC. 1864. Biographical studies. ■Profile of Australian actor-entrepreneur George Seth Coppin's performances in Victoria while serving as Charles Kean's manager on an 1864 North American tour.

1667 Kareda, Urjo. "Canadian Dramaturgy: They Also Serve Who Only Stand and Wait for Rewrites." *CTR*. 1986 Win; 13(49): 6-11. Illus.: Photo. Print. B&W. 2: 2 in. x 2 in., 4 in. x 5 in. Lang.: Eng.

Canada: Toronto, ON. 1986. Histories-sources. ■The author describes his experience in two types of dramaturgy: with a classical company and with a company devoted to new plays.

1668 Knowles, Richard Paul. "Robin Phillips' *Richard III*: History and Human Will." *THC*. 1984 Spr; 5(1): 36-50. Notes. Append. Illus.: Photo. B&W. 4. Lang.: Eng.

Canada: Stratford, ON. 1977. Critical studies. ■Analysis of Shakespeare's *Richard III* as staged by Robin Phillips at the Stratford Festival.

1669 Knowles, Richard Paul. "New Brunswick: Life After TNB." *CTR*. 1986 Fall; 13(48): 25. Illus.: Photo. Print. B&W. 1: 2 in. x 4 in. Lang.: Eng.

Canada. 1986. Historical studies. ■Introduction to three articles about small theatre companies in New Brunswick.

1670 Knowles, Richard Paul. "Atlantic Alternatives: An Introduction." *CTR*. 1986 Fall; 13(48): 4-5. Illus.: Photo. Print. B&W. 1: 2 in. x 1 in. Lang.: Eng.

Canada. 1986. Historical studies. ■Introduction to a special issue on alternative theatre in Canada's Atlantic provinces.

1671 Lazarus, John. "A Playwright's Guide to Workshop Survival." *CTR*. 1986 Win; 13(49): 27-29. Illus.: Photo. Print. B&W. 1: 3 in. x 3 in. Lang.: Eng.

Canada. 1986. Histories-sources. ■A playwright's advice on how to derive the most benefit from workshopping a new play.

1672 Lépine, Stéphane. "'Les cauchemars du grand monde': de l'art de pointe à la singularité." ('Nightmares of High Society': From Standardized Art to Singularity.) *JCT*. 1984; 30(1): 120-133. Notes. Illus.: Photo. B&W. 6. Lang.: Fre.

Canada: Montreal, PQ. 1984. Critical studies. ■Readings of Gilbert Turp's play *Les cauchemars du grand monde (Nightmares of High Society)* by three directors: Turp, Claude Poissant and Jean-Luc Denis.

1673 McDonald, Peter. "The Towneley Cycle at Toronto." *MET*. 1986; 8(1): 51-60. Lang.: Eng.

Canada: Toronto, ON. 1985. Reviews of performances. ■Stresses value of the place-and-scaffold staging in Victoria College Quandrangle which created fluid and multiple acting areas.

1674 Neil, Boyd. "The Wright Stuff." *BooksC*. 1986 Apr.; 15(3): 7-10. Illus.: Photo. Print. B&W. 1: 9 cm. x 11 cm. Lang.: Eng.

Canada: Toronto, ON. 1965-1986. Biographical studies. ■Bill Glassco, founder of Toronto's Tarragon Theatre, is currently artistic director of CentreStage. He considers himself an actor's director and feels that regionalism is a strength in Canadian drama.

1675 Salter, Denis. "At Home and Abroad: The Acting Career of Julia Arthur (1869-1950)." *THC*. 1984 Spr; 5(1): 1-35. Notes. Illus.: Photo. B&W. 6. Lang.: Eng.

Canada. UK-England. USA. 1869-1950. Biographical studies. ■Career of Julia Arthur's work as manager, director and actor. Particular attention given to her performances as Lady Macbeth and St. Joan.

1676 Selman, Jan. "Workshopping Plays." *CTR*. 1986 Win; 13(49): 15-23. Illus.: Photo. Print. B&W. 6: var. sizes. Lang.: Eng.

Canada. 1986. Historical studies. ■An experienced workshop leader and director of new plays evaluates principles of effective play workshopping, including the value of workshop series and public readings.

1677 Sinclair, Carol. "My Brilliant Career as a Maritimes Actor." *CTR*. 1986 Fall; 13(48): 59-61. Illus.: Photo. Print. B&W. 1: 2 in. x 2 in. Lang.: Eng.

Canada. 1986. Histories-sources. ■An experienced professional actress weighs the advantages of making a career in small cities and towns rather than in New York, Los Angeles, or Toronto.

1678 Smith, Brian. "The Dream in High Park." *CTR*. 1986 Sum; 13(47): 29-37. Notes. Illus.: Photo. Print. B&W. 5: var. sizes. Lang.: Eng.

Canada: Toronto, ON. 1983-1986. Historical studies. ■The outdoor Shakespeare project 'The Dream in High Park', its origins, annual increase in technical sophistication, effects on actors and impact on audience.

1679 Tepperman, Shelley. "Two Brothers/Two Cultures—At Work With Felipe Santander." *Theatrum*. 1986 Win; 5: 27-30. Illus.: Photo. Print. B&W. 4: 1 in. x 3 in. Lang.: Eng.

Canada: Toronto, ON. Mexico. 1986. Historical studies. ■Account of the production process and public response to mounting a translated work by Mexican director Felipe Santander.

DRAMA: —Performance/production

1680 Thompson, Peggy. "Vancouver: Who Is Peter Eliot Weiss." *CTR.* 1986 Sum; 13(47): 131-139. Illus.: Photo. Print. B&W. 4: var. sizes. Lang.: Eng.
Canada: Vancouver, BC. 1986. Histories-sources. ■Interview with playwright Peter Eliot Weiss, with illustrative excerpts from his plays *Going Down for the Count, West End* and *Sex Tips for Modern Girls*, all of which contain strong elements of improvisation and kinesthetics.

1681 Wallace, Robert. "New Play Development: An Introduction." *CTR.* 1986 Win; 13(49): 4-5. Illus.: Photo. Print. B&W. 2: 2 in. x 2 in., 3 in. x 5 in. Lang.: Eng.
Canada. 1986. Historical studies. ■Introduction to a special issue on new play development.

1682 Wallace, Robert. "Edmonton: Fringe Binge." *CTR.* 1986 Win; 13(49): 117-120. Illus.: Photo. Print. B&W. 2: 2 in. x 2 in., 3 in. x 5 in. Lang.: Eng.
Canada: Edmonton, AB. 1986. Reviews of performances. ■The fifth annual Edmonton Fringe Festival was its most successful to date, although innovative theatre seems to be discouraged by the Festival's structure.

1683 Warren, Roger. "Shakespeare at Stratford, Ontario: The John Hirsch Years." *ShS.* 1986; 39: 179-190. Notes. Illus.: Photo. Print. B&W. 6:3 in. x 5 in., 5 in. x 8 in. Lang.: Eng.
Canada: Stratford, ON. 1981-1985. Reviews of performances. ■Reviews of productions at the Stratford Festival, under the artistic direction of John Hirsch.

1684 Weiss, Peter Eliot. "The Collective from a Playwright's Perspective." *CTR.* 1986 Win; 13(49): 58-66. Illus.: Photo. Print. B&W. 5: var. sizes. Lang.: Eng.
Canada: Vancouver, BC. 1984-1985. Histories-sources. ■The playwright/dramaturg of the collective creation *Sex Tips for Modern Girls* describes the origins of the project and his own role in shaping the material toward a finished production.

1685 Wylie, Betty Jane. "A Playwright's Guide to Workshop Survival." *CTR.* 1986 Win; 13(49): 24-26. Illus.: Photo. Print. B&W. 1: 3 in. x 4 in. Lang.: Eng.
Canada. 1986. Histories-sources. ■Advice on how to derive the most benefit from workshopping a new play.

1686 Bravo-Elizondo, Pedro. "Temporada teatral en Chile: 1985." (The 1985 Theatre Season in Chile.) *LATR.* 1986 Fall; 20(1): 85-90. Lang.: Spa.
Chile. 1984-1985. Historical studies. ■Humorous and political trends in Chilean theatre season.

1687 Lu, Xiaoyan. "Zai Xiangxiang de Shijie Li—He Jiaose de Duihua." (In an Imaginary World: A Dialogue with the Character.) *XYishu.* 1982 May; 5(2): 145-149. Lang.: Chi.
China. USA. 1939-1982. Histories-sources. ■Account of the author/ actress's effort to enter the soul of her character, Alexandra, by various associations in Lillian Hellman's *The Little Foxes.*

1688 Ma, Ye. "Zhangguo Xiqu Wutai Shikong de Yundong Texing." (Special Characteristics of the Space-Time Movement in Chinese Theatres.) *XYishu.* 1982 May; 5(2): 69-78. Lang.: Chi.
China. 1127-1980. Critical studies. ■Differences in portraying time and locale in Sung drama and in contemporary *spoken drama.*

1689 Wang, Xiaoping. "Zuigao Renwu, Guanchuan Dongtso Xijie." (Primary Objective, Plan of Action, Details.) *XYishu.* 1982 May ; 5(2): 31-37. Lang.: Chi.
China: Shanghai. 1900-1982. Instructional materials. ■Dynamics between objectives and action, with the examples of some plays the author directed.

1690 Zhang, Ying Xiang. "Ta Chongmanzhe Meili." (She Is Filled with Enchanting Attraction.) *XYishu.* 1982 May; 5(2): 38-46. Illus.: Photo. Lang.: Chi.
China: Shanghai. 1982. Critical studies. ■Directorial design for Dürrenmatt's *Die Physiker (The Physicists).*

1691 Zhu, Yu. "Biaoyan Yishu de Qinggan Shijie Tanwei." (Exploring the World of Emotion in Acting.) *XYishu.* 1982 May; 5(2): 136-140. Lang.: Chi.

China. 1850-1981. Critical studies. ■Empathy in acting is derived from both association and inner imitation: broad experience is crucial to the actor's world of emotion.

1692 Huang, Chünyao. "K'o Chung-p'ing yü shan kan ning pieh ch'ü min chung chü t'uan." (K'o Chung-p'ing and the People's Theater Groups in Shan, Kan and Ning.) *XYanj.* 1986 Dec.; 21: 113-128. Notes. Lang.: Chi.
China, People's Republic of. 1938-1940. Historical studies. ■Describes the development and influence of people's theatre groups in the provinces of Shansi, Kansu and Liaoning under the leadership of K'o Chung-p'ing.

1693 Wang, Jingdi. "Huaju Biaoyan Ruogan Wenti Dabian." (Answers to Some Issues in Acting.) *XYishu.* 1982 May; 5(2): 141-144. Lang.: Chi.
China, People's Republic of. 1978-1982. Critical studies. ■Purpose of acting is to fulfill a character's being, not merely to imitate the appearance or manner of the character.

1694 Díaz, Néstor Gustavo. "Reseña del VIII Festival Internacional de Teatro." (Review of the 8th International Theatre Festival.) *LATR.* 1986 Fall; 20(1): 109-111. Lang.: Spa.
Colombia: Manizales. 1985. Historical studies. ■The festival included 12 plays, 7 professional companies, 5 university groups and many 'fringe' productions.

1695 Bruna, Otakar; Balogh, Géza, transl. "A gondolat és a forma keresése." (The Quest for Idea and Form.) *Sz.* 1986 Dec.; 19(12): 32-37. Illus.: Photo. 4: var. sizes. Lang.: Hun.
Czechoslovakia: Prague, Brno. Poland: Warsaw. 1986. Reviews of performances. ■Overview of the season's productions, with emphasis on Czechoslovakian authors.

1696 Ciccotti, Eusebio. "Teatro futurista italiano a Praga." (Italian Futurist Theatre in Prague.) *TeatrC.* 1986; 6(13): 69-76. Notes. Biblio. Lang.: Ita.
Czechoslovakia: Prague. 1921. Historical studies. ■An evening of Italian futurist theatre.

1697 Day, Barbara. "Czech Theatre from the National Revival to the Present Day." *NTQ.* 1986 Aug.; 11(7): 250-274. Notes. Illus.: Photo. Dwg. Poster. 15. Lang.: Eng.
Czechoslovakia. 1781-1986. Histories-specific. ■Czechoslovakia's theatre has been distinguished less by the work of individual dramatists than through collective creation, 'small forms' such as cabaret, and through scenography and other aspects of technical innovation. These features are related to the political and social conditions and to repression and censorship.

1698 Nánay, István. "Prága kisszinházaiban." (In Studio Theatre of Prague.) *Sz.* 1986 Oct.; 19(10): 42-45. Illus.: Photo. B&W. 3: 12 cm. x 9 cm., 18.5 cm. x 11.5 cm. Lang.: Hun.
Czechoslovakia: Prague. 1986. Reviews of performances. ■Overview of the season's productions by studio theatres in Prague. Related to Mime: Pantomime.

1699 Adler, Doris. "The Unlacing of Cleopatra." *TJ.* 1982 Dec.; 34(4): 450-466. Illus.: Photo. Sketches. 2: var. sizes. Lang.: Eng.
England. 1813-1890. Critical studies. ■Portrayal of Shakespeare's Cleopatra by various actresses, focusing on the change in the character's mode of dress and physical configuration.

1700 Amberg, Anthony. "Moore's *Gamester* on the London stage, 1771-1871." *TN.* 1986; 40(2): 55-60. Notes. Lang.: Eng.
England: London. 1771-1871. Historical studies. ■Evidence of the continuing popularity of *The Gamester* compared to other tragedies.

1701 Elliott, John R., Jr.; Buttrey, John. "The Royal Plays at Christ Church in 1636: A New Document." *ThR.* 1985 Sum; 10(2): 93-106. Notes. Illus.: Photo. B&W. 3. Lang.: Eng.
England: Oxford. 1636. Historical studies. ■Analysis of the document detailing expenses for performances given at Christ Church (Oxford) for Charles I, suggesting involvement by Inigo Jones as stage director.

1702 Kaplan, Joel H. "'Have We No Chairs': Pinero's *Trelawny* and the Myth of Tom Robertson." *ET.* 1986 May; 4(2): 114-133. Notes. Illus.: Photo. Dwg. B&W. 2. Lang.: Eng.

DRAMA: —Performance/production

England: London. 1840-1848. Historical studies. ▪Comparison of the image of Tom Robertson as a stage reformer, as depicted in Arthur Wing Pinero's *Trelawny of the Wells*, with the facts of his career as a theatrical innovator.

1703 Kohler, Richard C. "Kyd's Ordered Spectacle: 'Behold... What 'tis to be subject to destiny'." *MRenD*. 1986; 3: 27-49. Notes. Lang.: Eng.

England: London. 1592. Historical studies. ▪An attempt to reconstruct the staging of Act I of the first production of Thomas Kyd's *The Spanish Tragedy*. Examines the play scene by scene to see how spectacle is arranged to clarify exposition using the theatre structure of the day.

1704 LaBranche, Linda. "Visual Patterns and Linking Analogues in *Troilus and Cressida*." *SQ*. 1986 Win; 37(4): 440-450. Notes. Lang.: Eng.

England: London. 1597-1600. Critical studies. ▪Visual patterns of staging and how they link diverse moments in a play by providing recurring figures, situations or conflicts that create a coherent dramatic experience.

1705 Metz, G. Harold. "Stage History of *Cardenio—Double Falshood*." *THSt*. 1986; 6: 87-92. Notes. Illus.: Dwg. Print. B&W. Lang.: Eng.

England: London. 1613-1847. Historical studies. ▪History of productions of *Cardenio* by William Shakespeare and John Fletcher.

1706 Milhous, Judith. "Elizabeth Bowtell and Elizabeth Davenport: Some Puzzles Solved." *TN*. 1985; 39(3): 124-134. Illus.: Photo. Sketches. Dwg. 4: var. sizes. Lang.: Eng.

England. 1664-1715. Historical studies. ▪The career of actress Elizabeth Bowtell, who first acted with the King's Company under the name Elizabeth Davenport.

1707 Mullaly, Edward. "Charles Freer, 1802-1857: The Life of a 'Support' Actor in America." *NCTR*. 1986; 14(1-2): 1-19. Illus.: Photo. Print. B&W. 1: 4 in. x 7 in. Lang.: Eng.

England: London. USA: New York, NY. 1808-1858. Biographical studies. ▪Frustrations and poverty of non-star actors who hoped to achieve success by leaving England for America, exemplified by the career of Charles Freer.

1708 Pederson, Steven I. "The Staging of *The Castle of Perseverance*: A Re-Analysis." *TN*. 1985; 39(2): 51-62. Biblio. Notes. Lang.: Eng.

England. 1343-1554. Historical studies. ▪Analysis and interpretation of the staging of *The Castle of Perseverance* based on oldest extant stage plan drawing. Compares play to elements of tournaments of Middle Ages.

1709 Pederson, Steven I. "The Staging of *The Castle of Perseverance*: Testing the List Theory." *TN*. 1985; 39(3): 104-113. Notes. Biblio. Lang.: Eng.

England. 1343-1554. Historical studies. ▪Text of *The Castle of Perseverance* examined for clues to audience placement, and the necessity of a moat. Physical plan suggested by script is discussed.

1710 Rodgers, Anton. "A Director's Hat." *PlPl*. 1986 Dec.; 399: 7-8. B&W. 1: 4 in. x 4 in. Lang.: Eng.

England: London. 1986. Histories-sources. ▪Interview with actor Michael Leech on his staging of Eugène Labiche's *Un chapeau de Paille d'Italie (An Italian Straw Hat)*.

1711 Scouten, Arthur H. "A Reconsideration of the King's Company Casts in John Downes' *Roscius Anglicanus*." *TN*. 1986; 40 (2): 74-85. Notes. Lang.: Eng.

England: London. 1660-1708. Historical studies. ▪Speculations on the accuracy of Restoration lists.

1712 Stokes, James D. "Robin Hood and the Churchwardens in Yeovil." *MRenD*. 1986; 3: 1-25. Notes. Append. Lang.: Eng.

England. 1475-1588. Historical studies. ▪Investigation of Robin Hood entertainments, including plays, performed in the Somerset parish of Yeovil based upon parish records.

1713 Thomson, Leslie. "'On Ye Walls': The Staging of *Hengist, King of Kent* V, ii." *MRenD*. 1986; 3: 165-176. Notes. Lang.: Eng.

England: London. 1619-1661. Historical studies. ▪Discussion of the staging of Thomas Middleton's *Hengist, King of Kent* using historical records and the text to support the use of an upper stage in the first production of this play.

1714 Wikander, Mathew H. "As Secret as Maidenhead: The Profession of the Boy-Actress in *Twelfth Night*." *CompD*. 1986; 20(4): 349-363. Notes. Lang.: Eng.

England. 1601. Critical studies. ▪Discusses the implications of 'boy-actresses' in the role of Viola. Argues that the character is poised between a 'woman's part' and 'man's estate' and embodies 'subversive tensions'.

1715 Woods, Leigh. "Garrick's *King Lear* and the English Malady." *ThS*. 1986 May & Nov.; 27(1-2): 17-35. Notes. Illus.: Dwg. 2: 9 cm. x 11 cm., 15 cm. x 11 cm. Lang.: Eng.

England. 1680-1779. Historical studies. ▪David Garrick's approach to adapting and playing *King Lear* reveals changing attitudes concerning the nature of madness.

1716 Kirillov, A.A. "*Hamlet* W. Shakespeare i problema novatorstra v sceničeskom iskusstre pervoj četverti XX veka (ot. G. Craiga do M. Čechova)." (Shakespeare's *Hamlet* and Innovative Stage Art in the Early Twentieth Century (From Gordon Craig to Michajl Čechov).) 125-137 in *Tradicii i novaterstvo v zarubežnom teatre*. Leningrad: Leningr. in-t teatre, muzyki i kinematografii; 1986. Lang.: Rus.

Europe. 1700-1950. Historical studies. ▪Innovative stagings of Shakespeare's *Hamlet*.

1717 Pavis, Patrice. "De l'importance du rhythme dans le travail de la mise en scène." (Importance of Rhythm in the Work of the Director.) 87-96 in Heistein, Józef, ed. *Le texte dramatique. La lecture et la scène*. Wrocław: Wydawnictwo Uniwersytetu Wrocławskiego; 1986. 248 pp. (Acta Universitatis Wratislaviensis 895, Romanica Wratislaviensia 26.) Lang.: Fre.

Europe. 1900-1984. Critical studies. ▪Functions of rhythm in the reading and performance of text introduced by the director and the actors.

1718 Regős, János. "Érzelmekre ható színház. Beszélgetés Eugenio Barbával, az Odin Teatret rendezőjével." (Theatre Affecting Sentiments: Interview with Eugenio Barba, Director of Odin Teatret.) *Sz*. 1986 May; 19 (5): 37-39. Illus.: Photo. B&W. 1: 11 cm. x 12 cm. Lang.: Hun.

Europe. 1985. Histories-sources. ▪The leader of the Odin Theatre of Denmark, Eugenio Barba, tells of his theatrical goals and working methods.

1719 "Jalmari Rinne in Memoriam." *NFT*. 1986; 38: 18. Illus.: Photo. B&W. 1: 2 in. x 2 in. Lang.: Eng, Fre.

Finland: Helsinki, Tampere, Turku. 1893-1985. Historical studies. ▪Career of Finnish actor Jalmari Rinne. Related to Media: Film.

1720 Edwards, Susanna. "Skådespelaren är mer än ett tänkande huvud." (The Actor is More Than a Thinking Head.) *NT*. 1986; 33: 10-13. Illus.: Photo. Lang.: Swe.

Finland. 1986. Histories-sources. ▪Interview with Juoko Turkka about his views of acting and his directorial method.

1721 "Le Cantique des cantiques, 'Sa main gauche sous ma tête'..." (*The Song of Songs*: 'Let His Left Hand Be Under My Head' ...) *CF*. 1986 Nov-Dec.; 153: 5-7. Illus.: Pntg. Color. 3. Lang.: Fre.

France: Paris. 1986. Histories-sources. ▪Evolution of a recent Comédie-Française production of *Le Cantique des cantiques (The Song of Songs)* directed by Jacques Destoop focusing on the gradual blending of music, dance and the spoken word.

1722 "Jouer Claudel aujourd'hui." (Playing Claudel Today.) *RHT*. 1986; 38(2): 181-188. Lang.: Fre.

France. Belgium. 1943-1985. Histories-sources. ▪Panel discussion of actors on performing in plays by Paul Claudel.

1723 "Mettre en scène Claudel aujourd'hui." (Staging Claudel Today.) *RHT*. 1986; 38(2): 140-156. Illus.: Photo. Print. B&W. 8: var. sizes. Lang.: Fre.

France. Belgium. 1985. Histories-sources. ▪Directors' panel discussion on how to stage the plays of Paul Claudel.

DRAMA: —Performance/production

1724 Auclaire Tamaroff, Elisabeth, ed.; Barthélémy, ed. *Jean-Marie Serreau découvreur de théâtres.* (Jean-Marie Serreau's Theatrical Discoveries.) Paris: L'Arbre verdoyant; 1986. 224 pp. Append. Illus.: Design. Photo. Print. B&W. 164: var. sizes. Lang.: Fre.
France. 1938-1973. Biographical studies. ■Collection of unpublished notes and interviews with Jean-Marie Serreau, as well as a study of his production concepts. Examines his importance as actor, director and producer in the discovery of such playwrights as Ionesco, Beckett, Genet, Aimé Césaire and Kateb Yacine.

1725 Berling, Philippe; Sinding, Terje; Varda, Rosalie; De Beaumarchais, Jean-Pierre; Guibert, Noëlle. *"Un Chapeau de paille d'Italie."* (An Italian Straw Hat.) CF. 1986 Apr.; 16(147/148): 6-41. Illus.: Photo. Sketches. B&W. Lang.: Fre.
France: Paris. 1850-1986. Histories-sources. ■A series of short pieces about the performance in 1986 and history of performance of *Un Chapeau de paille d'Italie (An Italian Straw Hat)* by Eugène Labiche

1726 Blin, Roger; Bellity Peskine, Lynda, ed. *Souvenirs et propos.* (Recollections and Remarks.) Paris: Gallimard; 1986. 342 pp. Pref. Index. Illus.: Photo. Print. B&W. 1: 13 cm. x 18 cm. Lang.: Fre.
France. 1930-1983. Biographies. ■Reminiscences of actor-director Roger Blin on his work with Antonin Artuad, Jacques Prévert, the theatrical company Le Groupe Octobre and Jean-Louis Barrault, as well as his principal stagings of the plays of Samuel Beckett and Jean Genet. Includes the cast list of plays he has directed.

1727 Bricage, Claude. "La Galérie photo." (The Photo Gallery.) CF. 1986 May; 16(149/150): 40-53. Illus.: Photo. B&W. Lang.: Fre.
France: Paris. 1986. Histories-sources. ■Photographs of the 1986 production of *Un Chapeau de paille d'Italie (An Italian Straw Hat)* by Eugène Labiche.

1728 Camus, Albert. "Madeleine Renaud." CRB. 1986; 34(112): 83-87. Lang.: Fre.
France. 1950. Biographical studies. ■Prints Camus' praise of actress Madeleine Renaud.

1729 Didym, Eric. "La Galérie photo." (The Photo Gallery.) CF. 1986 Apr.; 16(147/148): 42-51. Illus.: Photo. B&W. Lang.: Fre.
France: Paris. 1986. Histories-sources. ■Photographs of the 1986 production of Pierre Corneille's *Le Menteur (The Liar)* at the Comédie-Française.

1730 Dumur, Guy. "La cohorte des fantômes." (The Cohort of Ghosts.) ThE. 1986 Apr.; 10: 28-30. Illus.: Photo. B&W. 4: 4 in. x 5 in. Lang.: Fre.
France: Paris. 1951-1986. Critical studies. ■Luigi Pirandello's reinvention of theatrical illusion in *Sei personaggi in cerca d'autore (Six Characters in Search of an Author)* and its staging by Georges Pitoëff.

1731 Dumur, Guy; Benedetti, Tere, transl. "Vilar prima di Vilar." (Vilar Before Vilar.) BiT. 1986; 1: 35-47. Lang.: Ita.
France. Critical studies. ■An emotional account of Jean Vilar's early career by a young spectator.

1732 Enckell, Johanna. "Elektra. Som insekter krälar människorna." (Electra: As Insects the Men Are Swarming.) NT. 1986; 34: 4-7. Illus.: Photo. Lang.: Swe.
France: Paris. 1986. Historical studies. ■Sophocles' *Electra* staged by Antoine Vitez as a conflict of deceit.

1733 Fernandes, Marie-Pierre. *Travailler avec Duras: la Musica deuxième.* (Working with Duras: La Musica Deuxième.) Paris: Gallimard; 1986. 209 pp. Illus.: Photo. Print. B&W. 4: 12 cm. x 19 cm. Lang.: Fre.
France: Paris. 1985. Histories-reconstruction. ■Journal of the production of the text and show of *La Musica deuxième*, by Marguerite Duras, at the Théâtre du Rond-Point.

1734 Földes, Anna. "Sárkányok közt védtelen. Párizsi színházi levél." (Without Protection Among Dragons: Theatre Letter from Paris.) Sz. 1986 Aug.; 19(8): 38-43. Lang.: Hun.

France: Paris. 1986. Reviews of performances. ■Theatre experiences in Paris during one week: review of three performances.

1735 Françon, Alain; Bailly, Jean-Christophe; Marin, Louis. *"Le Menteur."* (The Liar.) CF. 1986 Feb.; 16(145/146): 6-33. Illus.: Photo. B&W. Lang.: Fre.
France: Paris. 1644-1985. Histories-sources. ■Several brief pieces having to do with performance of Pierre Corneille's *Le Menteur (The Liar)* at the Comédie-Française.

1736 Gisselbrecht, André. "Vilar e Brecht." (Vilar and Brecht.) BiT. 1986; 1: 22-34. Lang.: Ita.
France. 1951-1960. Critical studies. ■Jean Vilar's introduction into France of the work of Bertolt Brecht and his refusal to adopt the epic method.

1737 Graver, David. "The Théâtre du Soleil, Part Three: The Production of *Sihanouk.*" NTQ. 1986 Aug.; 11(7): 212-215. Illus.: Photo. B&W. 2. Lang.: Eng.
France: Paris. 1985. Historical studies. ■Cixous's script of *Norodom Sihanouk* as realized in production.

1738 Guibert, Noëlle. "Le Menteur mis en scène." (Staging The Liar.) CF. 1986 Feb.; 16(145/146): 34-41. Illus.: Photo. Lang.: Fre.
France: Paris. 1644-1985. Histories-specific. ■Staging of Pierre Corneille's *Le Menteur (The Liar)* at the Comédie-Française.

1739 Heed, Sven Åke. "Kärleken som handelsvara." (Love As Commodity.) NT. 1986; 32: 8-13. Illus.: Photo. Lang.: Swe.
France: Nanterre. Germany, West: Berlin, West. 1985. Historical studies. ■A presentation of two stagings of Marivaux's comedies *La Fausse suivante (Between Two Women)* by Patrice Chéreau, and *Le Triomphe de l'amour (The Triumph of Love)* by Luc Bondy.

1740 Laplace, Roselyne. "1778: une année de registres à la Comédie-Française." (1778: One Year of Registers at the Comédie-Française.) RHT. 1986; 38(4): 354-369. Lang.: Fre.
France: Paris. 1778. Histories-sources. ■View of the Comédie-Française through its records: repertory, activities, historical context.

1741 Latour, Geneviève, comp. *Petites scènes, grand théatre.* (Small Stage, Great Theatre.) Paris: Délégation à l'action artistique de la Ville de Paris; 1986. 303 pp. Pref. Index. Illus.: Photo. Dwg. Poster. Print. B&W. 82: var. sizes. [Accompanies exhibit at the Mairie of the 5th arrondissement of Paris, 1986.] Lang.: Fre.
France: Paris. 1944-1960. Histories-reconstruction. ■Information on theatrical productions, including cast lists, opening dates and reviews.

1742 Londré, Felicia Hardison. *"Coriolanus* and Stavisky: The Interpenetration of Art and Politics." ThR. 1986; 11(2): 119-32. Notes. Lang.: Eng, Fre.
France: Paris. 1934. Critical studies. ■Polemic surrounding Sacha Stavisky's production of *Coriolanus* by William Shakespeare at the Comédie-Française.

1743 Marko, Susanne. "Teatern är i maskopi med sin tid." (The Theatre Is in Collusion With Its Time.) Entre. 1986; 13(4): 30-31. Illus.: Photo. B&W. 1: 6 in. x 4 in. Lang.: Swe.
France: Paris. 1981-1986. Reviews of performances. ■Reflection of modern society in Antoine Vitez's production of Sophocles' *Electra* at Théâtre National Populaire.

1744 Miquel, Jean-Pierre. *Le Théâtre et les jours: réflexions sur une pratique.* (Theatre and Days: Reflections on a Practice.) Paris: Flammarion; 1986. 259 pp. Lang.: Fre.
France. 1955-1986. Biographical studies. ■Biography of Jean-Pierre Vincent, actor, director and head of the Conservatoire National d'Art Dramatique. Discusses his work and his view of contemporary theatre.

1745 Morteo, Gian Renzo. "Vilar e la scrittura." (Vilar and Writing.) BiT. 1986; 1: 14-21. Lang.: Ita.
France. 1871-1912. Critical studies. ■Analysis of theoretical writings of Jean Vilar.

1746 Pavis, Patrice. *Marivaux à l'épreuve de la scène.* (Marivaux on Stage.) Université de Paris III-Panthéon Sorbonne. Paris: Publications de la Sorbonne; 1986. 466 pp. (Langues et langages 12.) Notes. Biblio. Lang.: Fre.

CLASSED ENTRIES

DRAMA: —Performance/production

France. 1723-1981. Historical studies. ■Compares the initial productions (1723-1744) of four plays by Marivaux—*La Dispute (The Dispute), La Double Inconstance (The Double Infidelity), Le Jeu de l'Amour et du Hasard (Play of Love and Chance)* and *Les Fausses Confidences (False Confidences)*—and their contemporary presentations (1968-1981) with textual analysis.

1747   Regnault, François. *Le Spectateur.* (The Spectator.) Paris, Nanterre: Beba, Théâtre des Amandiers, Théâtre National de Chaillot; 1986. 173 pp. Illus.: Photo. Print. B&W. 28: var. sizes. Lang.: Fre.

France. 1970-1985. Critical studies. ■Collection of articles on aesthetics of theatre and critical essays on major productions.

1748   Sagne, Jean. "Théâtre et photographie au XIXe s.: de l'illusionisme à la pétrification." (Theatre and Photography in the 19th Century: From Illusionism to Petrification.) 9-19 in Roegiers, Patrick, ed. *L'Écart constant.* Bruxelles: Didascalies; 1986. 147 pp. Illus.: Photo. Print. B&W. 9: var. sizes. Lang.: Fre.

France. 1818-1899. Historical studies. ■Early use of stage photography by Jacques Daguerre and Cicéri, influence of stage sets on photographic aesthetics, popularity of actors' portraits.

1749   Schumacher, Claude. "Un ritorno alle fonti? *Riccardo II* al 'Théâtre du Soleil' (Dicembre 1981)." (A Return to the Source? *Richard II* at the 'Théâtre du Soleil', December 1981.) 261-266 in Ottai, Antonella, ed. *Teatro Oriente/Occidente.* Rome: Bulzoni; 1986. viii, 565 pp. (Biblioteca Teatrale 47.) Lang.: Ita.

France: Paris. 1981. Critical studies. ■Eastern influences on the production of *Richard II* by the Théâtre du Soleil.

1750   Shionoya, Kei. *Cyrano et les samurai: le théâtre japonais en France dans la Ière moitié du 20e s. et l'effet de retour.* (Cyrano and the Samurai: Japanese Theatre in France During the First Half of the Twentieth Century and the Feedback Effect.) Paris: Publications orientalistes de France; 1986. 142 pp. (Bibliothèque japonaise.) Pref. Index. Notes. Lang.: Fre.

France. Japan. 1900-1945. Historical studies. ■Influence of Japanese theatre on acting technique and theatrical aesthetics in France, and European influence on Japanese theatre. Related to Dance-Drama.

1751   Stricker, Jean-Marc. "Portrait, Dominique Constanza." *CF.* 1986 Nov-Dec.; 153: 16-21. B&W. 13: var. sizes. Lang.: Fre.

France: Paris. 1986. Histories-sources. ■Interview with Comédie-Française actress Dominique Constanza focusing on her influences and preferences in her work.

1752   Tarr, Carrie. "The Sun Queen." *WomenR.* 1986 Apr.; 2(6): 38-40. Illus.: Photo. B&W. 2. Lang.: Eng.

France. Cambodia. 1964-1986. Reviews of performances. ■The collaboration between Ariane Mnouchkine and Hélène Cixous in producing *Norodom Sihanouk.*

1753   Tonkin, Boyd; Colvin, Clare. "Maha Marathon." *Drama.* 1986; 159: 21-23. Illus.: Photo. B&W. 3. Lang.: Eng.

France: Avignon, Paris. 1985-1986. Reviews of performances. ■Peter Brook's nine-hour production of *The Mahabharata*, transferred from the Avignon Festival to the Théâtre des Bouffes du Nord (Paris), employs all crafts of theatre in recreating the atmosphere of Indian legend.

1754   Veinstein, Jacqueline, ed. "*La Mort de Judas* de Paul Claudel: Entretien avec Sophie Lucachevsky." (*The Death of Judas* by Paul Claudel: A Conversation with Sophie Lucachevsky.) *RHT.* 1986; 38(2): 178-180. Lang.: Fre.

France: Brangues. 1985. Histories-sources. ■Director discusses her adaptation of a prose work by Paul Claudel for production at the Château de Brangues, July 1985.

1755   Weber-Caflisch, Antoinette. "Claudel et les mises en scène impossibles." (Claudel and Impossible Staging.) *RHT.* 1986; 38(2): 157-175. Lang.: Fre.

France. 1910-1931. Critical studies. ■Difficulties in staging the plays of Paul Claudel.

1756   Cometa, Michele. *Il teatro di Pirandello in Germania.* (Pirandello's Theatre in Germany.) Palermo: Novecento; 1986. 393 pp. Pref. Index. Notes. Tables. Biblio. Append. Illus.: Photo. Pntg. Dwg. Poster. Color. B&W. Lang.: Ita.

Germany. Italy. 1924-1931. Histories-specific. ■German productions of plays by Luigi Pirandello and their reception.

1757   Jacobs, Margaret, ed.; Warren, John, ed. *Max Reinhardt: The Oxford Symposium.* Oxford: Oxford Polytechnic; 1986. xiii, 198 pp. Notes. Illus.: Photo. Print. B&W. Lang.: Eng, Ger.

Germany. Austria. 1890-1938. Historical studies. ■Max Reinhardt's work with his contemporaries, his varied performance spaces and productions of *A Midsummer Night's Dream* by William Shakespeare.

1758   Meech, Anthony. "Giving the Wrong Signs." *NTQ.* 1986 May; 11(6): 181-183. Notes. Lang.: Eng.

Germany. Critical studies. ■An exploration of Brecht's *Gestus.*

1759   Rössner, Michael. "La fortuna di Pirandello in Germania e le messinscene di Max Reinhardt." (The Fortune of Pirandello in Germany and the Stagings of Max Reinhardt.) *QT.* 1986 Nov.; 9(34): 40-53. Notes. Biblio. Lang.: Ita.

Germany. Italy. 1924-1934. Historical studies. ■Pirandello's image in Germany seen through Max Reinhardt's notes on directing *Sei personaggi in cerca d'autore (Six Characters in Search of an Author).*

1760   Williams, Simon. "Shakespeare and Weimar Classicism: A Study in Cross-Purposes." *ET.* 1986 Nov.; 5(1): 27-46. Notes. Lang.: Eng.

Germany: Weimar. 1771-1812. Historical studies. ■Analysis of Shakespeare's influence on German neoclassicism, with detailed analysis of two Weimar court productions: *Macbeth* and *Romeo and Juliet.*

1761   "Berliner Ensemble: A Pictorial Retrospective, 1949-84." *NTQ.* 1986 May; 11(6): 106-115. Illus.: Photo. B&W. 20. Lang.: Eng.

Germany, East: Berlin, East. 1949-1984. Histories-sources. ■The development of the Berliner Ensemble, shown in photographs, to commemorate the 40th anniversary celebrations of the founding of the company and of the GDR.

1762   Brecht-Schall, Barbara; Schall, Eckhardt. "Acting with the Berliner Ensemble: Elements of Brechtian Acting Discussed by an Acknowledged Master." *NTQ.* 1986 May; 11(6): 99-105. Illus.: Photo. B&W. 2. Lang.: Eng.

Germany, East: Berlin, East. UK-England: London. 1952-1986. Histories-sources. ■A discussion at the Riverside Studios, in which Schall explains the practical application of concepts relating to Brechtian acting, and his own approach to such major roles as the Brecht-Shakespeare *Coriolanus.*

1763   Funke, Michael, ed. *Dantons Tod von Georg Büchner.* (*Danton's Death* by Georg Büchner.) Berlin: Verband d. Theaterschaffenden d. DDR; 1983. 258 pp. (Theaterarbeit in der DDR 8.) Illus.: Photo. Print. B&W. 106: var. sizes. Lang.: Ger.

Germany, East: Berlin, East. 1984. Histories-reconstruction. ■Alexander Lang's famous production of *Danton's Death*, Deutsches Theater: preparatory and rehearsal process, interpretation of characters, aesthetics of acting, reviews.

1764   Heinz, Wolfgang. *Theater—Darsteller—Gesellschaft. Aus Reden, Aufsätzen, Gesprächen.* (Theatre—Performer—Society: From Speeches, Essays, Talks.) Berlin: Verband d. Theaterschaffenden d. DDR; 1985. 131 pp. (MT 187.) Lang.: Ger.

Germany, East: Berlin, East. 1980-1984. Histories-sources. ■On acting, problems of East German theatre, actor's personality.

1765   Küchenmeister, Wera; Küchenmeister, Claus; Buchmann, Ditte, ed. *Eine Begabung muss man entmutigen...* (A Talent Has to Be Discouraged...)Berlin (East): 1986. 176 pp. Illus.: Photo. B&W. 43. Lang.: Ger.

Germany, East: Berlin, East. 1950-1956. Biographical studies. ■Two scholars of Brecht remember their years with the Berliner Ensemble (dramaturgical work and staging). Includes materials about the productions *Die Mutter (The Mother)* (1950), *Urfaust* (1953), and *Hans Pfriem* (1954).

CLASSED ENTRIES

DRAMA: —Performance/production

1766 Hill, Holly. "Playing Joan." *AmTh.* 1986 Nov.; 3(7): 18-22. Print. B&W. 3: 8.5 in. x 11 in., 2.5 in. x 10 in. Lang.: Eng.
Germany, West: Berlin, West. UK-England: Malvern. USA: Washington, DC. Histories-sources. ■Interview with actresses Elisabeth Bergner and Jane Alexander on their portrayals of the title role in Shaw's *Saint Joan.*

1767 Kächele, Heinz. *Bertolt Brecht.* Leipzig: Bibliographisches Institut; 1984. 139 pp. Illus.: Photo. Print. B&W. 86: var. sizes. Lang.: Ger.
Germany, West: Augsburg. Germany, East: Berlin, East. USA. 1898-1956. Biographies. ■Concise survey of Brecht's life and work.

1768 Osterloff, Barbara; Waltz, Ruth, photo. "*Oresteja* Petera Steina." (*Oresteia* by Peter Stein.) *TeatrW.* 1984 Jan.; 39 (808): 7-10. Illus.: Photo. 2: 10 cm. x 5 cm, 22 cm. x 18 cm. Lang.: Pol.
Germany, West: Berlin, West. Poland: Warsaw. 1983. Reviews of performances. ■Production analysis of the *Oresteia* of Aeschylus, directed by Peter Stein and staged by Schaubühne am Lehniner Platz/ Berlin at Teatr Wielki (Warsaw).

1769 Haus, Heinz-Uwe; Lynch, Bonnie, transl. "Notes on *Baal*— The Greek Premiere." *ComIBS.* 1984 Apr.; 12(2): 66-67.
Greece: Athens. 1983. Histories-sources. ■Program notes for the Athens Ensemble production of *Baal* by Bertolt Brecht.

1770 "Vienna börtön. A *Szeget Szeggel* Veszprémben." (Vienna Prison: *Measure for Measure* in Veszprém.) *Sz.* 1986 Feb.; 19(2): 22-26. Illus.: Photo. B&W. 2: 9 cm. x 12 cm. Lang.: Hun.
Hungary: Veszprém. 1985. Reviews of performances. ■Shakespeare's *Measure for Measure* at Petőfi Theatre directed by István Paál.

1771 "Valami változik. Három színielőadás gyerekeknek." (Something Is Changing: Three Performances for Children.) *Sz.* 1986 Mar.; 19(3): 20-23. Illus.: Photo. B&W. 3: 9 cm. x 12 cm. Lang.: Hun.
Hungary: Pécs, Budapest. 1985. Reviews of performances. ■Performances of *Alice in Wonderland, The Two Gentlemen of Verona* and *Tobbsincs Királyfi (No More Crown Prince).*

1772 "Pusztító és teremtő közeg. Sam Shepard-bemutató a Radnóti Színpadon." (Destroying and Creating Medium: Sam Shepard Play on the Radnóti Stage.) *Sz.* 1986 Apr.; 19(4): 17-20. Illus.: Photo. B&W. 2: 9 cm. x 12 cm., 12 cm. x 12 cm. Lang.: Hun.
Hungary: Budapest. 1986. Reviews of performances. ■Discussion of Sam Shepard's *True West,* directed by István Verebes at the Radnóti Miklós Theatre, includes consideration of how audience reaction transforms a performance.

1773 "Élektra, haragszol még? A Stúdió K bemutatója." (Electra, Are You Still Angry? First Night at Studio K Ensemble.) *Sz.* 1986 May; 19(5): 16-20. Illus.: Photo. B&W. 1: 10 cm. x 12 cm. Lang.: Hun.
Hungary: Budapest. 1986. Critical studies. ■Discusses production of *Vázlatsor (Series of Sketches),* a montage of various dramatic adaptations of the story of Electra, by Stúdió K, an experimental theatre ensemble.

1774 "Magyar drámát a stúdiószínházakba! Beszélgetés Giricz Mátyással." (Hungarian Drama Into the Studio Theatres! Interview with Mátyás Giricz.) *Sz.* 1986 Sep.; 19(9): 30-32. Lang.: Hun.
Hungary. 1986. Histories-sources. ■Interview with director Mátyás Giricz on his opinion that the studio theatres ought to undertake performing new Hungarian plays.

1775 "Szilveszter: Mácsai Pál." (Sylvester: Pál Mácsai.) *Sz.* 1986 Oct.; 19(10): 37-39. Illus.: Photo. B&W. 3: 5.5 cm. x 12 cm., 5.5 cm. x 11 cm., 5.5 cm. x 8 cm. Lang.: Hun.
Hungary: Szentendre. 1986. Histories-sources. ■Interview with Pál Mácsai on his career and his role in Molière's *Les Fourberies de Scapin (Scapin's Tricks)* performed in Szentendre.

1776 "Portré öniróniával. Major Tamással beszélget Marton Frigyes." (A Portrait with Self-Irony: Frigyes Marton Talks with Tamás Major.) *Krit.* 1986; 14(5): 18-22. Illus.: Photo. B&W. 1: 7.9 cm. x 25.5 cm. Lang.: Hun.

Hungary. 1910-1986. Histories-sources. ■Interview with Tamás Major, the central figure of postwar theatre in Hungary, on his career as managing director, artistic director and leading actor of the National Theatre of Budapest.

1777 "Szabó Magda: *A macskák szerdája.* Bemutató a Csokonai Szinházban." (Magda Szabó: *Cat Wednesday.* A New Production in the Csokonai Theatre.) *Alfold.* 1986; 37(12): 112-115. Lang.: Hun.
Hungary: Debrecen. 1986. Reviews of performances. ■Magda Szabó's *A macskák szerdája (Cat Wednesday)* at Csokonai Theatre directed by László Gali.

1778 A., M. "Dosztojevszkij: *Ördögök.*" (Dostojévskij: *The Devils.*) *Krit.* 1986; 14(11): 35-36. Illus.: Photo. B&W. 1: 6.9 cm. x 9.5 cm. Lang.: Hun.
Hungary: Budapest. 1986. Reviews of performances. ■Guest director Tamás Ascher's staging of *The Devils,* a stage adaptation of Dostojévskij's novel *Besy (The Possessed),* based on adaptations by Camus (*Les possédés*) and Wajda.

1779 Ablonczy, László. "Hófúvásos időben." (When Blizzards Come.) *Tisz.* 1986; 40(3): 91-96. Lang.: Hun.
Hungary: Budapest. 1984-1985. Reviews of performances. ■András Sütő's *Advent a Hargitán (Advent in the Harghita Mountains)* at the National Theatre directed by Ferenc Sik.

1780 Abody, Béla. *Arcok, képek, önarcképek.* (Faces, Pictures, Self-Portraits.) Budapest: Szépirodalmi K; 1985. 337 pp. Lang.: Hun.
Hungary. 1970-1980. Histories-sources. ■Writer, critic and theatre director Béla Abody remembers some of his contemporaries, including actors and singers.

1781 Almási, Miklós. "Molnár Ferenc: *A farkas.*" (Ferenc Molnár: *The Wolf.*) *Krit.* 1986; 14(1): 34. Illus.: Photo. B&W. 1: 7 cm. x 3 cm. Lang.: Hun.
Hungary: Budapest. 1985. Reviews of performances. ■Remarks on Ferenc Molnár's *A farkas (The Wolf)* presented at Comedy Theatre directed by István Verebes.

1782 Almási, Miklós. "Dürrenmatt: *Az öreg hölgy látogatása.*" (Dürenmatt: *The Visit.*) *Krit.* 1986; 14(3): 41-42. Illus.: Photo. B&W. 1: 7 cm. x 6.5 cm. Lang.: Hun.
Hungary: Budapest. 1986. Reviews of performances. ■Review of a successful production of Friedrich Dürrenmatt's *Der Besuch der Alten Dame (The Visit)* at Comedy Theatre directed by Péter Gothár.

1783 Almási, Miklós. "Bulgakov: *Iván, a rettentő.*" (Bulgakov: *Ivan Vasiljevič.*) *Krit.* 1986; 14 (7): 39. Lang.: Hun.
Hungary: Budapest. 1986. Reviews of performances. ■*Ivan Vasiljevič* by Michajl Afanasjévič Bulgakov directed by László Marton at Vigszinház.

1784 Almási, Miklós. "Csehov: *Cseresznyéskert.*" (Čechov: *The Cherry Orchard.*) *Krit.* 1986; 14(9): 39. Lang.: Hun.
Hungary: Miskolc. 1986. Reviews of performances. ■Illusion and reality in the performance of *Višněvyj sad (The Cherry Orchard)* by Anton Pavlovič Čechov directed at the National Theatre of Miskolc by Imre Csiszár.

1785 Almási, Miklós. "Shakespeare: *Szeget szeggel.*" (Shakespeare: *Measure for Measure.*) *Krit.* 1986; 14(2): 35-36. Lang.: Hun.
Hungary: Budapest. 1985. Reviews of performances. ■Notes on the performance of Shakespeare's *Measure for Measure* at Madách Chamber Theatre directed by Tamás Szirtes.

1786 Almási, Miklós. "Szakonyi Károly: *Ki van a képen?.*" (Károly Szakonyi: *Who Is In the Picture?.*) *Krit.* 1986; 14(6): 44. Lang.: Hun.
Hungary: Budapest. 1986. Reviews of performances. ■Notes on the world premiere of *Ki van a képan? (Who Is in the Picture?)* by Károly Szakonyi at Madách Chamber Theatre directed by Tamás Szirtes.

1787 Antal, Gábor. *Dajka Margit.* (Margit Dajka.) Budapest: Múzsák; 1986. 95pp. Illus.: Photo. B&W. Lang.: Hun.
Hungary. 1907-1986. Biographical studies. ■Career, prominent roles and personality of actress Margit Dajka.

1788 Bécsy, Tamás. "Az önmanipuláció és a látszat. Dürrenmatt: *Az öreg hölgy látogatása* Győrött." (Self-Manipulation and Appearance: Dürrenmatt's *The Visit* in Győr.) *Sz.* 1986 Jan.

CLASSED ENTRIES

DRAMA: —Performance/production

; 19(1): 17-22. Illus.: Photo. B&W. 3: 9 cm. x 12 cm. Lang.: Hun.

Hungary: Győr. 1985. Reviews of performances. ■Friedrich Dürrenmatt's *Der Besuch der alten Dame (The Visit)* directed by György Emőd in Kisfaludy Theatre.

1789 Bécsy, Tamás. "A zsarnok és a megbocsátó." (The Tyrant and the Forgiver.) *Sz.* 1986 Feb.; 19(2): 17-22. Illus.: Photo. B&W. 3: 9 cm. x 12 cm., 12 cm. x 13 cm., 12 cm. x 17 cm. Lang.: Hun.

Hungary: Budapest. 1985. Reviews of performances. ■Shakespeare's *Measure for Measure* at Madách Studio Theatre directed by Tamás Szirtes.

1790 Bécsy, Tamás. "*Szent Bertalan nappala.*" (*Saint Bartholomew's Day.*) *Sz.* 1986 June; 19(6): 1-4. Illus.: Photo. B&W. 2: 9 cm. x 12 cm. Lang.: Hun.

Hungary: Budapest. 1986. Critical studies. ■Notes on Magda Szabó's play directed by György Lengyel at Madách Theatre.

1791 Bécsy, Tamás. "Trónbitorlás és következményei." (Usurpation and Its Consequences.) *Sz.* 1986 July; 19(7): 18-22. Illus.: Photo. B&W. 2: 12 cm. x 14 cm., 12 cm. x 16 cm. Lang.: Hun.

Hungary: Szeged. 1985. Critical studies. ■Shakespeare's *Henry IV* directed by János Sándor at the Szeged National Theatre.

1792 Bécsy, Tamás. "Euripidész: *A trójai nők.*" (Euripides: *The Trojan Women.*) *Krit.* 1986; 14(4): 29-30. Lang.: Hun.

Hungary: Budapest. 1986. Reviews of performances. ■Notes on the performance of *Les Troyennes (The Trojan Women)* by Jean-Paul Sartre after Euripides, adapted by Gyula Illyés for the Hungarian stage directed at the National Theatre by László Vámos.

1793 Bécsy, Tamás. "G.B. Shaw: *Megtört szivek háza.*" (G.B. Shaw: *Heartbreak House.*) *Krit.* 1986; 14(5): 31-32. Illus.: Dwg. 1: 7 cm. x 10 cm. Lang.: Hun.

Hungary: Budapest. 1985. Reviews of performances. ■Notes on the performance of *Heartbreak House* by George Bernard Shaw at Pest Theatre directed by István Horvai.

1794 Bérczes, László. "A pusztulás képei. Az *Ének Phaedráért.*" (Pictures of Decay: *Song for Phaedra* in Miskolc.) *Sz.* 1986 June; 19(6): 29-31. Illus.: Photo. B&W. 1: 9 cm. x 12 cm. Lang.: Hun.

Hungary: Miskolc. 1985. Reviews of performances. ■Per Olof Enquist's *Til Faedra (Song for Phaedra)* directed by Imre Csiszár at the Miskolc National Theatre.

1795 Bérczes, László. "Májusi eső. Az *esőcsináló* Békéscsabán." (May Rain: *The Rainmaker* in Békéscsaba.) *Sz.* 1986 July; 19(7): 26-29. Illus.: Photo. B&W. 3: 9 cm. x 12 cm. Lang.: Hun.

Hungary: Békéscsaba. 1986. Reviews of performances. ■Performance of *The Rainmaker* directed by Mátyás Giricz at Jókai Theatre.

1796 Berkes, Erzsébet. "Böbe—avagy az öncsalás vége. Molnár Piroska játékáról." (Böbe, or The End of Self-Deceit: On the Performance of Piroska Molnár.) *Sz.* 1986 July; 19(7): 37-39. Illus.: Photo. B&W. 3: 9 cm. x 12 cm. Lang.: Hun.

Hungary: Kaposvár. 1986. Critical studies. ■Notes on Piroska Molnár's performance in Mihály Kornis' *Kozma* at Csiky Gergely Theatre.

1797 Berkes, Erzsébet. "Sütő András: *Advent a Hargitán.*" (András Sütő: *Advent in the Harghita Mountains.*) *Krit.* 1986; 14(4): 27-28. Illus.: Photo. B&W. 1: 6.8 cm. x 6.9 cm. Lang.: Hun.

Hungary: Budapest. 1986. Reviews of performances. ■Analysis of Sütő's new poetic play about the tragedy of love, the sinking hope of old Hungarians in Transylvania and the Great Evil that is burying everything and everybody. The performance at the National Theatre was staged by Ferenc Sik.

1798 Bóna, László. "A természet mint kellék. (Motivumkereső szinházi táborozás) Kaméleon Szinházi Csoport - 1983. július, Kurd község." (Nature as a Requisite (Motive Searching Theatre Camping) Chameleon Theatre Group July 1983, Kurd.) *SzSz.* 1986; 10(19): 253-270. Append. Lang.: Hun.

Hungary: Kurd. 1982-1985. Histories-sources. ■Experimental theatrical training in natural surroundings for the explanation of human being's connection to the world.

1799 Bóna, László. "Amerikai-magyar közös emberáldozat (David Rabe: *Bot és gitár* cimü drámájának 1974-es pesti szinházi bemutatójáról)." (American-Hungarian Human Sacrifice: On the Premiere of David Rabe's *Sticks and Bones*, Pesti Theatre in 1974.) *SzSz.* 1986; 10(21): 75-110. Biblio. Lang.: Hun.

Hungary: Budapest. 1971-1975. Critical studies. ■Analysis of David Rabe's play *Sticks and Bones* and its performance at Pesti Theatre directed by Dezső Kapás.

1800 Budai, Katalin. "Milyenek hazánk fiai? Kolozsvári Papp László komédiája a Józsefvárosi Színházban." (How Are the Sons of Our Country? László Papp's Comedy at Józsefváros Theatre.) *Sz.* 1986 Feb. ; 19(2): 8-9. Illus.: Photo. B&W. 1: 8 cm. x 12 cm. Lang.: Hun.

Hungary: Budapest. 1985. Reviews of performances. ■First night of László Kolozsvári Papp's comedy *Hazánk fiai (Sons of Our Country)* at Józsefvárosi Theatre directed by József Petrik.

1801 Budai, Katalin. "Tegnapi újságok. Három vígjáték a Józsefvárosi Színházban." (Yesterday's News: Three Comedies at Józsefvárosi Theatre.) *Sz.* 1986 Mar.; 19(3): 27-30. Illus.: Photo. B&W. 3: 9 cm. x 12 cm., 12 cm. x 15 cm. Lang.: Hun.

Hungary: Budapest. 1985. Reviews of performances. ■Notes on performances of *Hongkongi paróka (Wig Made in Hong Kong)*, *Egérút (Narrow Escape)* and *Róza néni (Aunt Rosa)*.

1802 Cenner, Mihály. "Hivatás és küldetés. Várady Gyrgy emlékezete." (Vocation and Mission: The Memory of György Várady.) *Muhely.* 1986; 9(2): 56-59. Lang.: Hun.

Hungary. Romania. 1945-1980. Biographical studies. ■Overview of career of actor and director György Várady.

1803 Csáki, Judit. "Igy vagy úgy. A stúdiószínházakról." (In This Way Or In Another: On the Studio Theatres.) *Sz.* 1986 Sep.; 19(9): 7-14. Illus.: Photo. B&W. 8: var. sizes. Lang.: Hun.

Hungary. 1985-1986. Critical studies. ■Evaluation of the 1985/86 studio theatre productions on the occasion of the National Chamber Theatre Meeting and of the Chamber and Studio Theatre Meeting.

1804 Csáki, Judit. "Lanford Wilson: *Mint két tojás.*" (Lanford Wilson: *Talley's Folly.*) *Krit.* 1986; 14(12): 46. Lang.: Hun.

Hungary: Dunaújváros. 1986. Reviews of performances. ■Hungarian performance of Lanford Wilson's *Talley's Folly* presented at Dunaújváros Premiere Theatre directed by András Bálint.

1805 Csáki, Judit. "Freud—zöldben. *A farkas* a Vígszínházban." (Freud—in Green: *The Wolf* at Comedy Theatre.) *Sz.* 1986 Jan.; 19(1): 14-16. Illus.: Photo. B&W. 2: 8 cm. x 12 cm., 12 cm. x 12 cm. Lang.: Hun.

Hungary: Budapest. 1985. Reviews of performances. ■Ferenc Molnár's comedy, *The Wolf*, at Comedy Theatre directed by István Verebes.

1806 Csáki, Judit. "*Alkony.* Babel szinmüve a Tháliában." (*Sunset*: Babel's Play at Thália Theatre.) *Sz.* 1986 May; 19(5): 20-22. Illus.: Photo. B&W. 2: 9 cm. x 12 cm. Lang.: Hun.

Hungary: Budapest. 1985. Reviews of performances. ■Notes on Isaak Babel's drama *Zakat (Sunset)* performed at Thália Theatre directed by Károly Kazimir.

1807 Csáki, Judit. "Tanulságos siker. Az *Emil és a detektívek* az Arany János Színházban." (An Instructive Success: *Emil and the Detectives* at the Arany János Theatre.) *Sz.* 1986 July; 19(7): 31-33. Illus.: Photo. B&W. 2: 9 cm. x 12 cm. Lang.: Hun.

Hungary: Budapest. 1986. Reviews of performances. ■Erich Kästner's novel, *Emil und die Detektive (Emil and the Detectives)* adapted to the stage by Alíz Mosonyi and directed by István Keleti at Arany János Theatre.

1808 Csáki, Judit. "Megannyi megátkozott. Páskándi-ősbemutató Kőszegen." (So Many Damned: World Premiere of Páskándi's Play in Kőszeg.) *Sz.* 1986 Oct.; 19(10): 20-22.

CLASSED ENTRIES

DRAMA: —Performance/production

Illus.: Photo. B&W. 2: 12 cm. x 9 cm., 12 cm. x 13 cm. Lang.: Hun.
Hungary: Kőszeg. 1986. Reviews of performances. ■Géza Páskándi's historical play, *Átkozottak (The Damned)* at Castle Theatre directed by László Romhányi.

1809 Csáki, Judit. "Tennessee Williams: *Macska a forró bádogtetőn.*" (Tennessee Williams: *Cat on a Hot Tin Roof.*) *Krit.* 1986; 14(1): 34. Illus.: Photo. B&W. 1: 7 cm. x 9 cm. Lang.: Hun.
Hungary: Budapest. 1985. Reviews of performances. ■Tennessee Williams' drama at Castle Theatre directed by Miklós Szurdi.

1810 Csáki, Judit. "Bertolt Brecht: *A nevelő.*" (Bertolt Brecht: *The Tutor.*) *Krit.* 1986; 14(4): 30. Lang.: Hun.
Hungary: Kaposvár. 1985. Reviews of performances. ■Jakob Lenz's drama adapted by Bertolt Brecht at Csiky Gergely Theatre directed by Gábor Máté.

1811 Csáki, Judit. "Ivan Kušan: *Galócza.*" (Ivan Kušan: *Death Cap.*) *Krit.* 1986; 14(9): 41. Lang.: Hun.
Hungary: Budapest. 1986. Reviews of performances. ■Review of Ivan Kušan's musical comedy *Čaruga (Death Cap)*, directed by Miklós Benedek, Katona József Theatre, as *Galócza*, includes discussion of acting and dramatic art.

1812 Csáki, Judit. "Vészi Endre: *Don Quijote utolsó kalandja.*" (Endre Vészi: *Don Quixote's Last Adventure.*) *Krit.* 1986; 14(10): 35. Illus.: Photo. B&W. 1: 8.2 cm. x 8 cm. Lang.: Hun.
Hungary: Gyula. 1986. Reviews of performances. ■Endre Vészi's tragicomedy at the Gyula Summer Theatre directed by Imre Kerényi.

1813 Csáki, Judit. "Sarkadi Imre: *Oszlopos Simeon.*" (Imre Sarkadi: *The Man On the Pillar.*) *Krit.* 1986; 14(11): 36-37. Lang.: Hun.
Hungary: Miskolc. 1986. Reviews of performances. ■István Szőke's staging of Imre Sarkadi's *Oszlopos Simeon (The Man on the Pillar)*, which poses vital questions about the relationship of the individual and society.

1814 Cserje, Zsuzsa. "Fojtott indulatok." (Pressed Emotions.) *Sz.* 1986 Mar.; 19(3): 30-32. Illus.: Photo. B&W. 2: 12 cm. x 12 cm. Lang.: Hun.
Hungary: Budapest. 1985. Critical studies. ■Soljonij and Kuligin played by Géza Balkay and László Vajda in *Tri sestry (Three Sisters)*, directed by Tamás Ascher at the Katona József Theatre.

1815 Csernus, Mariann. *Eszterlánc.* (Roundelay.) Budapest: Magvető; 1986. 299 pp. (Rakéta regénytár.) Lang.: Hun.
Hungary. 1928-1950. Biographies. ■Memoir of Mariann Csernus, actress and poetry recitalist, emphasizing her relationship with an older woman which influenced her life and art.

1816 Csizner, Ildikó. "Feketén vagy fehéren. Csernus Mariann a Várszínházban." (Black Or White: Mariann Csernus in the Várszinház.) *Sz.* 1986 Jan.; 19(1): 44-46. Illus.: Photo. B&W. 2: 9 cm. x 12 cm., 12 cm. x 16 cm. Lang.: Hun.
Hungary: Budapest. 1985. Reviews of performances. ■Simone de Beauvoir's *La Femme rompue (The Broken Woman)* and the autobiography of Liv Ullmann *Forandringen (Changing)* staged and performed by Mariann Csernus.

1817 Csizner, Ildikó. "Vizsgák és buktatók. Két Mrozek-előadásról." (Examinations and Tippers. On Performances of Two Mrozek-Plays.) *Sz.* 1986 June; 19(6): 18-22. Illus.: Photo. B&W. 2: 9 cm. x 12 cm. Lang.: Hun.
Hungary: Budapest. 1986. Reviews of performances. ■Two plays by Sławomir Mrożek: *Rzeźnia (The Slaughterhouse)* at Józsefvárosi Theatre directed by Sándor Beke and *Dom na granicy (The Home on the Border)* at University Stage directed by Csaba Ivánka.

1818 Csizner, Ildikó. "In Memoriam 1963. A *Villa Negra* a Játékszínben." (In Memoriam 1963: *Villa Negra* at The Stage.) *Sz.* 1986 Aug.; 19(8): 24-27. Illus.: Photo. B&W. 3: 9 cm. x 12 cm., 12 cm. x 16 cm. Lang.: Hun.
Hungary: Budapest. 1986. Reviews of performances. ■Anikó and Katalin Vajda's *Villa Negra* at The Stage directed by Miklós Szurdi.

1819 Csizner, Ildikó. "A büvös kettős. A *Mikszáth különös házassága* Szegeden." (The Magic Duet: *Mikszáth and His Peculiar Marriage* in Szeged.*) *Sz.* 1986 Oct.; 19(10): 40-41. Illus.: Photo. B&W. 2: 9 cm. x 7 cm. Lang.: Hun.
Hungary: Szeged. 1986. Reviews of performances. ■*Mikszáth kölönös házassága (Mikszáth and His Peculiar Marriage)* by Gábor Görgey, with Lászlo Mensáros and Klári Tolnay as the Hungarian writer Kálmán Mikszáth and his wife. Directed by János Sándor at the Szegedi Szabadteri Játékok.

1820 Csizner, Ildikó. "A harmadfeledik úton. Vörösmarty-dráma Debrecenben." (The Third Half of the Way: Vörösmarty-Play in Debrecen.) *Sz.* 1986 May; 19(5): 9-11. Illus.: Photo. B&W. 2: 9 cm. x 12 cm. Lang.: Hun.
Hungary: Debrecen. 1986. Reviews of performances. ■Mihály Vörösmarty's play *Csongor és Tünde (Csongor and Tünde)* at Csokonai Theatre directed by László Gergely.

1821 Deák, Attila. "Gogol: *Háztüznéző.*" (Gogol: *The Marriage.*) *Krit.* 1986; 14(5): 32. Illus.: Dwg. 1: 7 cm. x 8.5 cm. Lang.: Hun.
Hungary: Békéscsaba. 1985. Reviews of performances. ■Gogol's comedy at Jókai Theatre in Békéscsaba directed by Anatolij Ivanov as a guest.

1822 Deák, Attila. "Páskándi Géza: *Átkozottak.*" (Géza Páskándi: *The Damned.*) *Krit.* 1986; 14(10): 37. Lang.: Hun.
Hungary: Kőszeg. 1986. Reviews of performances. ■World premiere of Géza Páskándi's historical chronicle about Erzsébet Báthory, a disreputable figure of Transylvanian history, presented at Kőszeg Castle Theatre directed by László Romhányi.

1823 Enyedi, Sándor. "A súgólyukból a szinpadra. Paulay Ede Győrben." (From the Prompter's Box to the Stage: Ede Paulay in Győr.) *Muhely.* 1986; 9(4): 68-70. Lang.: Hun.
Hungary: Győr. 1855. Historical studies. ■Study of the young Ede Paulay who was prompter, actor and secretary of Boldiszár Láng's touring company in the early period of Hungarian theatre history.

1824 Enyedi, Sándor. "Paulay Ede útban a Nemzeti Színház felé." (Ede Paulay and the National Theatre.) *Sz.* 1986 May; 19(5): 46-48. Lang.: Hun.
Hungary: Budapest. 1852-1864. Critical studies. ■Career of Ede Paulay, actor, director, stage manager and dramaturg.

1825 Erdei, János. "Az átgondolatlanság kaotikus hatása. A *Cyrano* a Madách Színházban." (The Chaotic Effect of Lack of Reflection: *Cyrano* at Madach Theatre.) *Sz.* 1986 Mar.; 19(3): 24-27. Illus.: Photo. B&W. 2: 9 cm. x 12 cm., 12 cm. x 17 cm. Lang.: Hun.
Hungary: Budapest. 1985. Reviews of performances. ■*Cyrano de Bergerac* by Edmond Rostand at Madách Theatre, directed by György Lengyel.

1826 Erdei, János. "A sivárság ünnepe. A *Bűnhődés* a Szkéné Színházban." (Feast of Bleakness: *Punishment* at Szkéné Theatre.) *Sz.* 1986 May; 19(5): 22-26. Illus.: Photo. B&W. 2: 9 cm. x 12 cm. Lang.: Hun.
Hungary: Budapest. Reviews of performances. ■*The Idiot* adapted to the stage by Andrzej Wajda and directed by Dezső Kapás at Szkéné Theatre with the title *Punishment*, performed by actors of Comedy Theatre.

1827 Erdei, János. "Itélni Isten helyett. A *Hamlet* Debrecenben." (Judge Instead of God: *Hamlet* in Debrecen.) *Sz.* 1986 Aug.; 19(8): 28-33. Illus.: Photo. B&W. 3: 12 cm. x 14 cm. Lang.: Hun.
Hungary: Debrecen. 1986. Reviews of performances. ■Shakespeare's tragedy directed by László Gali at Csokonai Theatre.

1828 Erdei, János. "Saint-Exupéry: *A kis herceg.*" (Saint-Exupéry: *The Little Prince.*) *Krit.* 1986; 14(5): 32. Illus.: Photo. B&W. 1: 8 cm. x 10 cm. Lang.: Hun.
Hungary: Budapest. 1985. Reviews of performances. ■Stage adaptation of Saint-Exupéry's *Le petit prince (The Little Prince)* by Anna Belia and Péter Valló at József Attila Theatre directed by Péter Valló.

1829 Esztergályos, Cecilia. *Adj békét, urami.* (Give Me Peace, O Lord!)Budapest: Sportpropaganda; 1986. 166 pp. Illus.: Photo. B&W. Lang.: Hun.

CLASSED ENTRIES

DRAMA: —Performance/production

Hungary. 1945-1986. Histories-sources. ■Autobiographical recollections of Cecilia Esztergályos, a ballet-dancer turned actress. Related to Media: Film.

1830 Ézsiás, Erzsébet. "Nyitány a Radnóti Miklós Szinpadon." (Overture on the Radnóti Miklós Theatre.) *Sz.* 1986 Feb.; 19(2): 15-17. Illus.: Photo. B&W. 2: 9 cm. x 12 cm., 12 cm. x 17 cm. Lang.: Hun.

Hungary: Budapest. 1985. Historical studies. ■Radnóti Miklós Theatre opened the 1985 autumn season with a new director, András Bálint, and with new artistic ideas.

1831 Ézsiás, Erzsébet. "Színészi jutalomjáték. Az *Edith és Marlene* a Pesti Színházban." (Benefit Performance: *Edith and Marlene* at Pesti Theatre.) *Sz.* 1986 Apr.; 19(4): 32-34. Illus.: Photo. B&W. 2: 12 cm. x 16 cm. Lang.: Hun.

Hungary: Budapest. 1986. Reviews of performances. ■Erzsébet Kútvölgyi and Judit Hernádi as Edith Piaf and Marlene Dietrich in Éva Pataki's play at Comedy Theatre.

1832 Földes, Anna. "A századik *Macskajáték.*" (The Hundredth *Catsplay.*) *Sz.* 1986 Jan.; 19(1): 9-13. Illus.: Photo. B&W. 3: 9 cm. x 12 cm., 12 cm. x 15 cm. Lang.: Hun.

Hungary: Budapest. 1985. Reviews of performances. ■*Macskajáték (Catsplay)* by István Örkény, one of Hungary's most performed plays, is presently in its hundredth production at the Magyar Játékszin, directed by Gábor Berényi.

1833 Földes, Anna. "*Deficit,* Szolnok, 1985." *Sz.* 1986 Feb.; 19(2): 10-14. Illus.: Photo. B&W. 3: 9 cm. x 12 cm., 12 cm. x 14 cm. Lang.: Hun.

Hungary: Szolnok, Budapest. 1970-1985. Critical studies. ■István Csurka's *Deficit* performed in 1979 at Pesti Theatre directed by István Horvai and in 1985 in the Studio Theatre of Szigligeti Theatre.

1834 Földes, Anna. "Megkésett tanúk. Déry Tibor drámájának szolnoki bemutatója alkalmából." (Late Witnesses: Premiere of Tibor Déry's Play in Szolnok.) *Sz.* 1986 Apr.; 19(4): 1-6. Illus.: Photo. B&W. 3: 9 cm. x 12 cm., 12 cm. x 12 cm. Lang.: Hun.

Hungary: Szolnok. 1945-1985. Historical studies. ■History of *A Tanúk (The Witnesses)* by Tibor Déry, written in 1945 but not produced until 1985 at the Szigligeti Theatre under the direction of Tibor Csizmadia.

1835 Földes, Anna. "Csoportkép vendéggel. Szakonyi-bemutató a Madách Kamarában." (Tableau With a Guest: Premiere of Szakonyi's Play at Madách Studio Theatre.) *Sz.* 1986 June; 19(6): 5-8. Illus.: Photo. B&W. 2: 9 cm. x 12 cm. Lang.: Hun.

Hungary: Budapest. 1986. Critical studies. ■Károly Szakonyi's play *Ki van a képen? (Who Is in the Picture?)* at Madách Studio Theatre directed by Tamás Szirtes.

1836 Futaky, Hajna. "Szinészportrék pécsi háttérrel. 4. Avar István." (Portraits of Actors With a Background in Pécs, 4: István Avar.) *Jelenkor.* 1986; 29(4): 333-340. Lang.: Hun.

Hungary. 1954-1985. Histories-sources. ■Interview with actor István Avar.

1837 Futaky, Hajna. "Szinészportrék pécsi háttérrel. 3. Spányik Éva." (Portraits of Actors With a Background in Pécs, 3: Éva Spányik.) *Jelenkor.* 1986; 29(2): 137-143. Lang.: Hun.

Hungary. 1957-1985. Histories-sources. ■Interview with actress Éva Spányik.

1838 Futaky, Hajna. "Szinészportrék pécsi háttérrel 5. Pásztor Erzsi." (Portraits of Actors With a Background in Pécs, 5: Erzsi Pásztor.) *Jelenkor.* 1986; 29(7/8): 679-686. Lang.: Hun.

Hungary. 1970-1980. Histories-sources. ■Interview with actor Erzsi Pásztor.

1839 Futaky, Hajna. "Szinészportrék pécsi háttérel. 6. Bálint András." (Portrait of Actors With a Background in Pécs, 6: András Bálint.) *Jelenkor.* 1986; 29(12): 1109-1115. Lang.: Hun.

Hungary. 1965-1986. Histories-sources. ■Interview with actor András Bálint.

1840 György, Péter. "A karrier, avagy az ára. Brecht: *A nevelő* Kaposvárott." (The Career Or Its Price. Brecht: *The Tutor*

at Kaposvár.) *Sz.* 1986 Jan.; 19(1): 22-24. Illus.: Photo. B&W. 3: 9 cm. x 12 cm., 12 cm. x 12 cm., 12 cm. x 17 cm. Lang.: Hun.

Hungary: Kaposvár. 1985. Reviews of performances. ■Notes on Bertolt Brecht's *Der Hofmeister (The Tutor)* at the Csiky Gergely Theatre, directed by Gábor Máté and starring Ander Lukács.

1841 Hegedüs, Sándor, ed. *IV. Országos Szinházi Találkozó 1985. május 27-június 9.* (Fourth National Theatre Meeting May 27-June 9, 1985.) Budapest: Magyar Szinházmüvészeti Szövetség; 1986. 454 pp. Lang.: Hun.

Hungary: Budapest. 1985. Histories-sources. ■The minutes of the meetings and discussions of the symposium of the Budapest and provincial theatres, organized by the Hungarian Theatre Association.

1842 Huszti, Péter. *Királyok az alagútban.* (Kings in the Tunnel.) Budapest: Szépirodalmi K; 1986. 239 pp. Illus.: Photo. B&W. Lang.: Hun.

Hungary. 1944-1986. Biographical studies. ■Career, roles and contemporaries of actor Péter Huszti, of the Madách Theatre.

1843 Illés, Jenő. "Sütő András: *Egy lócsiszár virágvasárnapja.*" (András Sütő: *Palm Sunday of a Horse Dealer.*) *Krit.* 1986; 14(7): 37. Illus.: Photo. B&W. 1: 6.8 cm. x 9.7 cm. Lang.: Hun.

Hungary: Budapest. 1986. Reviews of performances. ■Analysis of *Egy lócsiszár virágvasárnapja (The Palm Sunday of a Horse Dealer)* by András Sütő after Heinrich von Kleist and its performance at Madách Theatre directed by Ottó Ádám.

1844 Illisz, L. László. "Shakespeare: *Hamlet.*" *Krit.* 1986; 14(9): 41. Lang.: Hun.

Hungary: Debrecen. 1986. Reviews of performances. ■Character analysis of Hamlet as played by Károly Sziki at Csokonai Theatre, directed by László Gali.

1845 Illisz, L. László. "Görgey Gábor: *Huzatos ház.*" (Gábor Görgey: *Drafty House.*) *Krit.* 1986; 14(7): 37-38. Illus.: Photo. B&W. 1: 6.8 cm. x 7.9 cm. Lang.: Hun.

Hungary: Budapest. 1986. Reviews of performances. ■Gábor Görgey's cabaret-farce brings to life various occurrences from 1939 to the present in a villa in Budapest. World premiere at Vidám Színpad directed by Gyula Bodrogi.

1846 Illisz, L. László. "Pelle János: *Casanova.*" (János Pelle: *Casanova.*) *Krit.* 1986; 14(10): 36-37. Illus.: Photo. B&W. 1: 6.7 cm. x 10.4 cm. Lang.: Hun.

Hungary: Budapest. 1986. Reviews of performances. ■János Pelle's *Casanova,* based on Casanova's memoirs, directed by Károly Kazimir at Körszinház.

1847 István, Mária. "Koreográfus egy prózai szinházban. Milloss Aurél emlékezése a Nemzetiben töltött évekről." (A Choreographer in the Theatre: Recollections of Aurél Milloss on the Years Spent at the National Theatre.) *SzSz.* 1986; 10(19): 139-144. Lang.: Hun.

Hungary: Budapest. 1935-1938. Historical studies. ■Discussion of Aurél Milloss' choreographies for theatrical productions directed by Antal Németh.

1848 K., T. "Schwajda György: *Segitség.*" (György Schwajda: *Help.*) *Krit.* 1986; 14(9): 41. Lang.: Hun.

Hungary: Debrecen. 1986. Reviews of performances. ■György Schwajda's *Segitség (Help),* a longer version of his one-act play *Anthem,* directed at Csokonai Theatre by István Pinczés.

1849 K., T. "Móricz Zsigmond: *Légy jó mindhalálig.*" (Zsigmond Móricz: *Be Good Till Death.*) *Krit.* 1986; 14(11): 36. Illus.: Photo. B&W. 1: 6.9 cm. x 9.5 cm. Lang.: Hun.

Hungary: Budapest. 1986. Reviews of performances. ■Stage adaptation of novel by Zsigmond Móricz, *Légy jó minhalálig (Be Good Till Death)* is frequently revived. Review of performance staged by András Béhés, National Theatre.

1850 Kállai, Katalin. "Iszaak Babel: *Alkony.*" (Isaac Babel: *Sunset.*) *Krit.* 1986; 14(3): 43. Illus.: Photo. B&W. 1: 7 cm. x 7 cm. Lang.: Hun.

Hungary: Budapest. 1985. Reviews of performances. ■Notes on the performance of Isaak Babel's *Zakat (Sunset)* at Thália Theatre directed by Károly Kazimir.

CLASSED ENTRIES

DRAMA: —Performance/production

1851 Kállai, Katalin. "Samuel Beckett: *Az utolsó tekercs.*" (Samuel Beckett: *Krapp's Last Tape.*) *Krit.* 1986; 14 (4): 30-31. Lang.: Hun.
Hungary: Budapest. 1985. Reviews of performances. ■*Eh, Joe!* and *Krapp's Last Tape* by Samuel Beckett directed by András Matkócsik at Vigszinház.

1852 Kamody, Miklós. "Sóhivatalnokok, postamesterek: és egy szinész. A Paulay család nyomában Észak-Magyarországon." (Bureaucrats, Postmasters—and an Actor: Tracing the Paulay Family of Northern Hungary.) *Napj.* 1986; 25(12): 36-37. Lang.: Hun.
Hungary. 1731-1982. Historical studies. ■Contribution to the biography of the outstanding actor and director Ede Paulay, including additional material on the history of the Paulay family.

1853 Kéry, László. "Shakespeare: *A velencei Kalmár.*" (Shakespeare: *The Merchant of Venice.*) *Krit.* 1986; 14(6): 41. Illus.: Photo. B&W. 1: 6.6 cm. x 7.1 cm. Lang.: Hun.
Hungary: Budapest. 1986. Reviews of performances. ■Discussion of *The Merchant of Venice* by Shakespeare focusing on the character of Shylock, in connection with a performance at National Theatre directed by Ferenc Sik.

1854 Kiss, Eszter. "Két színházi este Győrben." (Two Theatre Evenings in Győr.) *Sz.* 1986 Apr.; 19(4): 6-11. Illus.: Photo. B&W. 4: 9 cm. x 12 cm., 12 cm. x 13 cm. Lang.: Hun.
Hungary: Győr. 1985. Reviews of performances. ■Primarily discusses *Ágyrajárók (Night Lodgers)* by Péter Szántó, directed in the Kisfaludy Studio Theatre by György Emőd.

1855 Kiss, Eszter. "A *Trójai nők* a Nemzetiben." (*The Trojan Women* at National Theatre.) *Sz.* 1986 May; 19(5): 14-16. Illus.: Photo. B&W. 1: 9 cm. x 12 cm. Lang.: Hun.
Hungary: Budapest. 1986. Reviews of performances. ■Euripides' drama adapted by Sartre at National Theatre directed by László Vámos.

1856 Kiss, Eszter. "Közhelytörténelem. Görgey Gábor színműve a Vidám Színpadon." (A Commonplace History: Gábor Görgey's Play at Gaiety Theatre.) *Sz.* 1986 June; 19(6): 11-12. Illus.: Photo. B&W. 1: 7 cm. x 12 cm. Lang.: Hun.
Hungary: Budapest. 1986. Reviews of performances. ■Gábor Görgey's *Huzatos ház (Drafty House)* directed by Gyula Bodrogi at Vidám Színpad.

1857 Kiss, Eszter. "Arthur Miller: *Az ügynök halála* és Tennessee Williams: *A vágy villamosa* cimü drámájának magyarországi bemutatóiról." (On Hungarian Premieres of Arthur Miller's *Death of a Salesman* and Tennessee Williams' *A Streetcar Named Desire.*) *SzSz.* 1986; 10(21): 21-42. Notes. Append. Lang.: Hun.
Hungary. 1959-1983. Critical studies. ■Survey of the various interpretations of Arthur Miller's *Death of a Salesman* and Tennessee Williams' *A Streetcar Named Desire* in Hungary.

1858 Kőháti, Zsolt. "Por száll. G.B. Shaw: *Megtört szívek háza.*" (Dust Is Floating: G.B. Shaw's *Heartbreak House.*) *Sz.* 1986 Mar.; 19(3): 16-17. Illus.: Photo. B&W. 2: 9 cm. x 12 cm. Lang.: Hun.
Hungary: Budapest. 1985. Reviews of performances. ■Shaw's comedy *Heartbreak House* at Pesti Theatre directed by István Horvai.

1859 Kőháti, Zsolt. "Leszakadt az ágy. Tömöry Péter: *Sip a tökre.*" (The Bed Broke Down. Péter Tömöry: *Play a Trump in Diamonds.*) *Sz.* 1986 Oct.; 19(10): 28. Lang.: Hun.
Hungary: Kisvárda. 1986. Reviews of performances. ■Péter Tömöry's musical comedy *Sip a tökre (Play a Trump in Diamonds)* at Castle Theatre directed by Imre Halasi.

1860 Koltai, Tamás. *Szinváltozások.* (Changes of Scenery.) Budapest: Szépirodalmi; 1986. 576 pp. Lang.: Hun.
Hungary. 1979-1983. Reviews of performances. ■Selected drama reviews of the productions of Hungarian and foreign plays.

1861 Koltai, Tamás. *Közjáték, Szinházi irások.* (Intermezzo: Theatrical Writings.) Budapest: Magvető; 1986. 431 pp. (Elvek és utak.) Lang.: Hun.
Hungary. 1976-1983. Critical studies. ■A collection of critical reviews of productions and performances at home and abroad.

1862 Koltai, Tamás. "Alex Koenigsmark: *Agyő, kedvesem.*" (Alex Koenigsmark: *Good-bye Darling.*) *Krit.* 1986; 14(4): 28-29. Illus.: Photo. B&W. 2: 8 cm. x 8 cm. Lang.: Hun.
Hungary: Kaposvár. 1985. Reviews of performances. ■Péter Gothár's staging is a conscious combination of Central-Eastern-European absurd play and traditional farce in the performance of Koenigsmark's play *Adié, milacku! (Good-bye, Darling!)* at Csiky Gergely Theatre.

1863 Koltai, Tamás. "Előszó egy Major-könyvhöz." (Preface to a Major Book.) *Sz.* 1986 Nov.; 19(11): 1-6. Illus.: Photo. B&W. 5: var. sizes. Lang.: Hun.
Hungary. 1930-1986. Biographical studies. ■Tamás Koltai's introduction to his book about Tamás Major, the central figure of postwar theatre in Hungary, managing director, artistic director and leading actor of Budapest National Theatre.

1864 Koltai, Tamás. "A Márkus-szerep." (The 'Márkus' Role.) *Krit.* 1986; 14(2): 22. Illus.: Photo. B&W. 2: 7 cm. x 9 cm. Lang.: Hun.
Hungary. 1986. Biographical studies. ■Commemoration of actor László Márkus, his artistic figure and his roles on the stage and in his life.

1865 Koltai, Tamás. "Mrożek: *Mészárszék.*" (Mrożek: *The Slaughterhouse.*) *Krit.* 1986; 14(3): 42. Lang.: Hun.
Hungary: Budapest. 1985. Reviews of performances. ■Notes on the Hungarian premiere of Sławomir Mrożek's play *Rzeźnia (The Slaughterhouse)* at Józsefvárosi Szinház directed by Sándor Beke.

1866 Koltai, Tamás. "Shakespeare: *Ahogy tetszik.*" (Shakespeare: *As You Like It.*) *Krit.* 1986; 14(5): 29. Lang.: Hun.
Hungary: Miskolc. 1986. Reviews of performances. ■Shakespeare's *As You Like It* at the National Theatre of Miskolc directed by István Szőke.

1867 Koltai, Tamás. "Teleki László: *Kegyenc.*" (László Teleki: *The Favorite.*) *Krit.* 1986; 14(9): 39-40. Lang.: Hun.
Hungary: Zalaegerszeg. 1986. Reviews of performances. ■Review of László Teleki's *A Kegyenc (The Favorite)* as directed by József Ruszt, Hevesi Sándor Theatre, discusses problems in the text.

1868 Koltai, Tamás. "Szenvedélyes szinház. Beszélgetés Major Tamással." (Passionate Theatre: Interview with Tamás Major.) *Krit.* 1986; 14(12): 19-23. Illus.: Photo. Plan. B&W. 5: var. sizes. Lang.: Hun.
Hungary. 1945-1986. Histories-sources. ■Excerpts from a forthcoming biography of Tamás Major, managing director, artistic director and leading actor of the National Theatre.

1869 Koltai, Tamás. "Mondjunk-e le önmagunkról? Gondolatritmus kaposvári előadásokban." (Shall We Give Up Our Own Selves? Rhythms of Ideas in Productions in Kaposvár.) *Jelenkor.* 1986; 29(5): 443-446. Lang.: Hun.
Hungary: Kaposvár. 1985-1986. Reviews of performances. ■Reviews of four performances at Csiky Gergely Theatre.

1870 Koltai, Tamás. "*Villa Negra.*" *Krit.* 1986; 14(7): 39. Lang.: Hun.
Hungary: Budapest. 1986. Reviews of performances. ■Review of adaptation for the stage by Anikó Vajda and Katalin Vajda of Imre Dobozy's screenplay *Villa Negra,* directed at Játékszin by Miklós Szurdi.

1871 Koltai, Tamás. "*Ruttkai.*" *Krit.* 1986; 14(11): 15-16. Illus.: Photo. B&W. 1: 6.8 cm. x 7 cm. Lang.: Hun.
Hungary. 1927-1986. Biographical studies. ■Commemoration of actress Éva Ruttkai's career. Related to Media: Film.

1872 Kovács, Dezső. "Hercegek ketrecben. A *Szeget szeggel* veszprémi bemutatójáról." (Caged Princes: On the Premiere of *Measure for Measure* in Veszprém.) *Sz.* 1986 Feb.; 19(2): 26-28. Illus.: Photo. B&W. 1: 9 cm. x 12 cm. Lang.: Hun.
Hungary: Veszprém. 1985. Reviews of performances. ■*Measure for Measure* at Petőfi Theatre in Veszprém directd by István Paál.

1873 Kovács, Dezső. "Színeváltozások. Az *Ahogy tetszik* Miskolcon." (Transfigurations: *As You Like It* in Miskolc.) *Sz.* 1986 Apr.; 19(4): 21-22. Illus.: Photo. B&W. 2: 9 cm. x 12 cm. Lang.: Hun.

DRAMA: —Performance/production

Hungary: Miskolc. 1986. Reviews of performances. ∎Shakespeare's *As You Like It* at Miskolc National Theatre directed by István Szőke.

1874 Kovács, Dezső. "A tragédia kezdete és vége. Kornis Mihály új drámája Kaposváron." (Beginning and the End of Tragedy: Mihály Kornis' New Play in Kaposvár.) *Sz.* 1986 July; 19(7): 3-6. Illus.: Photo. B&W. 3: 7 cm. x 12 cm., 9 cm. x 12 cm. Lang.: Hun.

Hungary: Kaposvár. 1986. Critical studies. ∎*Kozma*, by Mihály Kornis directed by János Ács at Csiky Gergely Theatre.

1875 Kovács, Dezső. "A képtelenség természetrajza. A *Császári futam* Gyulán." (Natural History of Nonsense: The *Imperial Round* in Gyula.) *Sz.* 1986 Oct.; 19(10): 19-20. Illus.: Photo. B&W. 1: 12 cm. x 9 cm. Lang.: Hun.

Hungary: Gyula. 1986. Reviews of performances. ∎Dramaturgical problems of Miklós Gyárfás' play presented at Gyulai Várszinház directed by Géza Tordy.

1876 Kovács, Dezső. "Történelmi 'magánügyek'. A *Bánk Bán* szolnoki bemutatójáról." (Historical Private Affairs. On the premiere of *Banus Bánk* in Szolnok.) *Sz.* 1986 Dec.; 19(12): 1-3. Illus.: Photo. B&W. 3: 12 cm. x 16 cm., 6 cm. x 10 cm. Lang.: Hun.

Hungary: Szolnok. 1986. Reviews of performances. ∎János Ács' production at Szigligeti Szinház abstains from the traditional compulsory pathos of the classical drama.

1877 Kovács, Dezső. "Vörösmarty Mihály: *Csongor és Tünde*." (Mihály Vörösmarty: *Csongor and Tünde*.) *Krit.* 1986; 14(6): 42. Illus.: Photo. B&W. 1: 8.4 cm. x 10.9 cm. Lang.: Hun.

Hungary: Eger. 1985. Reviews of performances. ∎A new interpretation of Mihály Vörösmarty's classic play *Csongor és Tünde (Csongor and Tünde)* directed at Gárdonyi Géza Szinház by János Szikora.

1878 Kovássy, Zoltán. "Szinházi esték Máramarosszigeten (Beszélgetések szép emlékekről)." (Theatre Evenings in Máramarossziget (Talks on Happy Memories).) *SzSz.* 1986; 10(21): 111-176. Pref. Notes. Append. Illus.: Photo. B&W. 9. Lang.: Hun.

Hungary: Máramarossziget. 1833-1938. Biographical studies. ∎Theatrical recollections focusing on the career of actress Kornélia Prielle.

1879 Major, Tamás; Koltai, Tamás, pref. *A Mester monológja.* (The Master's Monologue.) Budapest: ILK; 1986. 140 pp. Illus.: Photo. B&W. Lang.: Hun.

Hungary. 1910-1986. Biographical studies. ∎Actor, director and theatre manager Tamás Major remembers his career and his contemporaries.

1880 Mészáros, Tamás. "A stílus—a színész?" (Is the Style the Actor?) *Sz.* 1986 Feb.; 19(2): 1-7. Illus.: Photo. B&W. 6: var. sizes. Lang.: Hun.

Hungary. 1985. Critical studies. ∎Consideration of the place of the actor in a director's theatre and the possibility of genuiness in acting.

1881 Mészáros, Tamás. "Urának hű szolgája. Grillparzer-mű Nyiregyházán." (A Faithful Servant of His Lord: Grillparzer's Work in Nyiregyháza.) *Sz.* 1986 Apr.; 19(4): 14-17. Illus.: Photo. B&W. 3: 9 cm. x 12 cm. Lang.: Hun.

Hungary: Nyiregyháza. 1985. Reviews of performances. ∎Grillparzer's work under the title *A Faithful Servant of His Lord* in the Móricz Zsigmond Theatre at Nyiregyháza directed by László Salamon Suba.

1882 Mihályi, Gábor. "Neonaturalista inferno. Lars Norén *Az éjszaka a nappal anyja* című drámája Dunaújvárosban." (Neo-naturalistic Inferno: Lars Norén's *Night Is the Mother of the Day* at Dunaújváros.) *Sz.* 1986 Apr.; 19(4): 23-27. Illus.: Photo. B&W. 2: 9 cm. x 12 cm. Lang.: Hun.

Hungary: Dunaújváros. 1986. Critical studies. ∎Notes on the performance of Lars Norén's *Night is the Mother of the Day* at Dunaújváros Stage of the Miskolc National Theatre, directed by Imre Csiszár, compared with the world premiere in Sweden.

1883 Molnár Gál, Péter. "Shakespeare: *A vihar*." (Shakespeare: *The Tempest*.) *Krit.* 1986; 14(5): 30. Lang.: Hun.

Hungary: Kaposvár. 1986. Reviews of performances. ∎Discusses interpretations of Shakespeare's *The Tempest* in connection with a performance at Csiky Gergely Theatre staged by film director Gyula Gazdag.

1884 Molnár Gál, Péter. "*Bánk Bán, 1986.*" *Krit.* 1986; 14(12): 44-45. Lang.: Hun.

Hungary: Szolnok. 1986. Reviews of performances. ∎A strange present-day interpretation of József Katona's classic drama *Banus Bánk* at Szigligeti Theatre directed by János Ács.

1885 Molnár Gál, Péter. "Kornis Mihály: *Kozma*." (Mihály Kornis: *Kozma*.) *Krit.* 1986; 14(6): 44-45. Illus.: Photo. B&W. 1: 6.8 cm. x 11.4 cm. Lang.: Hun.

Hungary: Kaposvár. 1986. Reviews of performances. ∎Notes on world premiere of *Kozma* by Mihály Kornis at Csiky Gergely Theatre directed by János Ács.

1886 Molnár Gál, Péter. "Dajka Margit halálára." (On Margit Dajka's Death.) *Krit.* 1986; 14(7): 17. Lang.: Hun.

Hungary. 1986. Histories-sources. ∎Recollections of the author's interview with late actress Margit Dajka.

1887 Móricz, Zsigmond. *Shakespeare*. Preface by Gábor Szigethy. Budapest: Magvető; 1986. 80 pp. (Gondolkodó magyarok.) Pref. Notes. Lang.: Hun.

Hungary: Budapest. 1923. Reviews of performances. ∎Nine reviews of Shakespeare productions in the National Theatre, written since 1923 by Hungarian realist writer, Zsigmond Móricz. Grp/movt: Realism.

1888 Müller, Péter P. "Göcseji Hamlet. Ivo Brešan drámája Zalában." (Hamlet of Göcsej: Ivo Brešan's Drama in Zala.) *Sz.* 1986 May; 19(5): 29-32. Illus.: Photo. B&W. 3: 9 cm. x 12 cm., 12 cm. x 14 cm. Lang.: Hun.

Hungary: Zalaegerszeg. 1986. Reviews of performances. ∎Production of *Predstava 'Hamleta' u selu Mrduša Donja (Hamlet Performed at Lower Mrduša)* by Yugoslavian playwright Ivo Brešan, directed by Béla Merő at Hevesi Sándor Theatre as *Paraszt Hamlet (The Peasant Hamlet)*.

1889 Müller, Péter P. "Feloldozatlanul. *Az öreg hölgy látogatása* a Vígszínházban." (Unshriven: *The Visit* at Comedy Theatre.) *Sz.* 1986 Apr.; 19(4): 11-14. Illus.: Photo. B&W. 2: 9 cm. x 12 cm. Lang.: Hun.

Hungary: Budapest. 1986. Reviews of performances. ∎*Der Besuch der alten Dame (The Visit)* by Friedrich Dürrenmatt directed by Péter Gothár.

1890 Müller, Péter P. "Galócza, a gyilkos. Ivan Kušan komédiája a Katona József Színházban." (Charuga, the Killer. Ivan Kušan's Comedy at Katona József Theatre.) *Sz.* 1986 June; 19(6): 15-18. Illus.: Photo. B&W. 3: 9 cm. x 12 cm., 12 cm. x 13 cm. Lang.: Hun.

Hungary: Budapest. 1986. Reviews of performances. ∎Notes on *Čaruga (Death Cap)*, by Ivan Kušan, directed by Miklós Benedek, Katona József Theatre, under the title *Galócza*.

1891 Müller, Péter P. "Az ideologikus színház korlátai. Teleki László *Kegyence* Zalaegerszegen." (Limits of Ideological Theatre: László Teleki's *The Favorite* in Zalaegerszeg.) *Sz.* 1986 Aug.; 19(8): 19-21. Illus.: Photo. B&W. 2: 9 cm. x 12 cm. Lang.: Hun.

Hungary: Zalaegerszeg. 1986. Critical studies. ∎Notes on the performance of *A kegyenc (The Favorite)* directed by József Ruszt at Hevesi Sándor Theatre.

1892 Müller, Péter P. "Kórkép az egész vidék. A *Knock* Kaposvárott." (Pathology Is the Whole Point: *Knock* in Kaposvár.) *Sz.* 1986 Dec.; 19(12): 12-15. Illus.: Photo. B&W. 3: 12 cm. x 17 cm., 12 cm. x 8 cm. Lang.: Hun.

Hungary: Kaposvár. 1986. Reviews of performances. ∎Critical essay on Jules Romains' play presented at Csiky Gergely Theatre in Kaposvár directed by Gábor Máté.

1893 Müller, Péter P. "Pécsi szinházi esték." (Theatre Evenings at Pécs.) *Jelenkor.* 1986; 29(1): 56-59. Lang.: Hun.

Hungary: Pécs. 1985. Reviews of performances. ∎Čechov's *Diadia Vania (Uncle Vanya)* directed by Róbert Nógrádi and Shaw's *Candida* directed by Iván Vas-Zoltán at the Pécs National Theatre.

1894 Müller, Péter P. "Da Capo al (In)fine. Koenigsmark-bemutató Kaposvárott." (Da Capo al (In)finite: First Night of Koenigsmark's Play in Kaposvár.) *Sz.* 1986 Jan.; 19(1): 29-33. Illus.: Photo. B&W. 3: 9 cm. x 12 cm. Lang.: Hun.

CLASSED ENTRIES

DRAMA: —Performance/production

Hungary: Kaposvár. 1985. Critical studies. ▪Péter Gothár directs *Agyő, kedvesem*, a Hungarian translation of *Adié, milacku! (Goodbye, Darling!)* by Alex Koenigsmark, at Csiky Gergely Theatre.

1895 Müller, Péter P. "Ars critica. Koltai Tamás: Szinváltozások." (Ars Critica. Tamás Koltai: Changes of Scenery.) *Jelenkor.* 1986; 29(11): 1045-1047. Lang.: Hun.
Hungary. 1978-1983. Critical studies. ▪Review of collection of essays by drama critic Tamás Koltai.

1896 Müller, Péter P. "Szabó Magda: *Szent Bertalan nappala.*" (Magda Szabó: *St. Bartholomew's Day.*) *Krit.* 1986; 14(6): 43-44. Illus.: Photo. B&W. 1: 6.8 cm. x 17.3 cm. Lang.: Hun.
Hungary: Budapest. 1986. Reviews of performances. ▪Review of the world premiere of *Szent Bertalan nappala (Saint Bartholomew's Day)* by Magda Szabó at Madach Theatre directed by György Lengyel.

1897 Müller, Péter P. "Pécsi szinházi esték." (Theatre Evenings at Pécs.) *Jelenkor.* 1986; 29(7/8): 692-693. Lang.: Hun.
Hungary: Pécs. 1986. Reviews of performances. ▪Dezső Szomory's *Bella* at the Pécs National Theatre directed by István Jeney.

1898 Müller, Péter P. "Pécsi szinházi esték." (Theatre Evenings at Pécs.) *Jelenkor.* 1986; 29(6): 545-550. Lang.: Hun.
Hungary: Pécs. 1986. Reviews of performances. ▪Review of three productions at the Pécs National Theatre: *Hagyaték (Legacy)* by Gyula Hernádi, *We've Come Through* by Edward Bond and *El perro del hortelano (The Gardener's Dog)* by Lope de Vega.

1899 Multanowski, Andrzej. "Pasja Z Csiksomlyó." (*The Passion of Csiksomlyó.*) *TeatrW.* 1984 Jan.; 39(808): 5-6. Lang.: Pol.
Hungary: Budapest. Poland: Warsaw. 1983. Reviews of performances. ▪Production analysis of *Pasja Z Csiksolmyó (The Passion of Csiksolmyó)* directed by Imre Kerényi, with the National Theatre of Budapest at National Theatre (Teatr Narodowy) in Warsaw.

1900 Nádra, Valéria. "A kertész kutyája. Bemutató a Józsefvárosi Szinházban." (*The Gardener's Dog*: Premiere in Józsefváros Theatre.) *Sz.* 1986 Jan.; 19(1): 28-29. Illus.: Photo. B&W. 1: 12 cm. x 17 cm. Lang.: Hun.
Hungary: Budapest. 1985. Reviews of performances. ▪Production of Lope de Vega's *El Perro del hortelano (The Gardener's Dog)* by Mátyás Giricz.

1901 Nádra, Valéria. "Füst Milán: *Margit Kisasszony.*" (Milán Füst: *Miss Margit.*) *Krit.* 1986; 14 (6): 42-43. Lang.: Hun.
Hungary: Budapest. 1986. Reviews of performances. ▪Notes on Milán Füst's plays and on the performance of *Miss Margit* at The Stage directed by István Dégi.

1902 Nagy, Ibolya, ed. '...a Múlt idü nem délibáb': Válogatás Ratkó József: Segitsd a királyt! cimü drámájának kritikáiból. ('...the Past Is No Mirage': A Selection of the Critical Reviews of *Help the King* by József Ratkó.) Nyiregyháza: Móricz Megyei és Városi Könyvtár; 1986. 95 pp. Pref. Illus.: Photo. B&W. Lang.: Hun.
Hungary: Nyiregyháza. 1985. Reviews of performances. ▪Selected reviews of 1985 production of a play by József Ratkó about King Stephen, founder of the Hungarian State.

1903 Nánay, István. "Változatok a reménytelenségre. A *Három nővér* két előadása." (Versions of Hopelessness: Two Adaptations of *Three Sisters.*) *Sz.* 1986 Mar.; 19(3): 6-13. Illus.: Photo. B&W. 8: var. sizes. Lang.: Hun.
Hungary: Zalaegerszeg, Budapest. 1985. Reviews of performances. ▪Čechov's *Tri sestry (Three Sisters)* produced in two theatres at the same time: at Hevesi Sándor Theatre (Zalaegerszeg) directed by József Ruszt and at Katona József Theatre (Budapest) directed by Tamás Ascher.

1904 Nánay, István. "Gyerekeknek, játszanak." (Play to the Children.) *Sz.* 1986 Nov.; 19(11): 14-19. Illus.: Photo. B&W. 5: var. sizes. Lang.: Hun.
Hungary. 1985-1986. Reviews of performances. ▪Overview of the season's productions for children and critical evaluation of performances.

1905 Nánay, István. "Kell a romantika! *A kőszívü ember fiai* Zalaegerszegen." (We Need Romantics! *The Sons of the Stone-Hearted Man* in Zalaegerszeg.) *Sz.* 1986 June; 19(6): 34-37. Illus.: Photo. B&W. 2: 12 cm. x 14 cm. Lang.: Hun.
Hungary: Zalaegerszeg. 1986. Reviews of performances. ▪Mór Jókai's novel adapted to the stage by Mihály Földes and directed by János Ács at Hevesi Sándor Theatre.

1906 Nánay, István. "Amatőr szinházak tündöklése és bukása." (The Rise and Fall of Amateur Theatres.) *SzSz.* 1986; 10(19): 179-251. Notes. Lang.: Hun.
Hungary. 1960-1980. Historical studies. ▪Survey of various amateur theatrical groups and workshops with analyses of their productions.

1907 Nánay, István. "*A velencei kalmár.* Shakespeare-bemutató a Nemzeti Színházban." (*The Merchant of Venice*: Opening Night of Shakespeare's Play at National Theatre.) *Sz.* 1986 July; 19(7): 12-17. Illus.: Photo. B&W. 2: 9 cm. x 12 cm., 12 cm. x 17 cm. Lang.: Hun.
Hungary: Budapest. 1986. Critical studies. ▪Notes on the play and on the performance of *The Merchant of Venice* directed by Ferenc Sik.

1908 Nánay, István. "Félreértett *Forgatókönyv.* Örkény István drámája Békéscsabán." (Misunderstood *Film Script*: István Örkény's Play in Békéscsaba.) *Sz.* 1986 May; 19 (5): 12-14. Illus.: Photo. B&W. 1: 9 cm. x 12 cm. Lang.: Hun.
Hungary: Békéscsaba. 1986. Reviews of performances. ▪István Örkény's play, *Film Script*, at Jókai Theatre in Békéscsaba directed by Gábor Balogh.

1909 Novák, Mária. "Poszeidón átka. A *Trójai nők* Debrecenben." (Poseidon's Curse: *Trojan Women* in Debrecen.) *Sz.* 1986 Jan.; 19(1): 25-28. Illus.: Photo. B&W. 2: 9 cm. x 11 cm. Lang.: Hun.
Hungary: Debrecen. 1985. Reviews of performances. ▪The drama of Euripides and Jean-Paul Sartre directed by László Gergely at Csokonai Theatre in Debrecen.

1910 Novák, Mária. "Nevetés és leleplezés. Brecht *Koldusoperája* Debrecenben." (Laughter and Revelation: Brecht's *Three Penny Opera* in Debrecen.) *Sz.* 1986 June; 19(6): 37-39. Illus.: Photo. B&W. 1: 9 cm. x 12 cm. Lang.: Hun.
Hungary: Debrecen. 1986. Reviews of performances. ▪*Die dreigroschenoper (The Three Penny Opera)* directed by István Pinczés at Csokonai Theatre.

1911 Palotai, Erzsi. *Arcok fényben és homályban.* (Faces In Light and Shadow.) Budapest: Szépirodalmi K; 1986. 391 pp. Lang.: Hun.
Hungary. 1954-1985. Histories-sources. ▪Actress/poetry recitalist Erzsi Palotai recalls her life and career.

1912 Pályi, András. "A 'mérték utáni' Ionesco. Két egyfelvonásos Kaposvárott." (Ionesco 'Made to Measure': Two One-act Plays in Kaposvár.) *Sz.* 1986 June; 19(6): 31-34. Illus.: Photo. B&W. 2: 12 cm. x 15 cm., 12 cm. x 17 cm. Lang.: Hun.
Hungary: Kaposvár. 1986. Reviews of performances. ▪*La Cantatrice chauve (The Bald Soprano)* and *La Leçon (The Lesson)* by Eugène Ionesco directed by Tamás Ascher at Csiky Gergely Theatre.

1913 Pályi, András. "Szinházi előadások Budapesten." (Theatre Performances in Budapest.) *Jelenkor.* 1986; 29(4): 341-345. Lang.: Hun.
Hungary: Budapest. 1986. Reviews of performances. ▪Two plays by András Sütő: *Advent a Hargitán (Advent in the Harghita Mountains)*, directed by Ferenc Sik, National Theatre, and *Egy lócsiszár virágvasárnapja (The Palm Sunday of a Horse Dealer)*, directed by Ottó Adám, Madách Theatre.

1914 Pályi, András. "Szinházi előadások Budapesten." (Theatre Performances in Budapest.) *Jelenkor.* 1986; 29(6): 539-544. Lang.: Hun.
Hungary: Budapest. 1985. Reviews of performances. ▪Čechov's *Tri sestry (Three Sisters)* at Katona József Theatre directed by Tamás Ascher.

1915 Pályi, András. "'Csak egy ember'. Dajka Margitról." ('Just a Human Being'—About Margit Dajka.) *Sz.* 1986 Nov.; 19(11): 7-8. Illus.: Photo. 2: 12 cm. x 17 cm., 12 cm. x 8.5 cm. Lang.: Hun.

CLASSED ENTRIES

DRAMA: —Performance/production

Hungary. 1929-1986. Biographical studies. ■Recollections of Margit Dajka's unforgettable performances.

1916 Pályi, András. "Szinházi előadások Budapesten." (Theatre Performances in Budapest.) *Jelenkor*. 1986; 29(7/8): 687-691. Lang.: Hun.

Hungary: Budapest. 1985-1986. Reviews of performances. ■Reviews of *Margit kisasszony (Miss Margit), Az Ibolya (The Violet), Az Árny (The Ghost)* and *Róza néni (Aunt Rosa)*.

1917 Papp, Lajos. "A szinész érverése milyen?" (How Quick Is the Pulse of the Actor?)*Napj*. 1986; 25(10): 32-36. Lang.: Hun.

Hungary: Miskolc. 1986. Histories-sources. ■An interview with actor Imre Kulcsár, of the National Theatre of Miskolc, at the start of the season.

1918 Peterdi Nagy, László. "Libák és gúnárok. A *Ványa bácsi* a Pécsi Nemzeti Színházban." (Geese and Ganders: *Uncle Vanya* in the National Theatre in Pécs.) *Sz*. 1986 Mar.; 19(3): 13-15. Illus.: Photo. B&W. 2: 9 cm. x 12 cm., 12 cm. x 14 cm. Lang.: Hun.

Hungary: Pécs. 1985. Reviews of performances. ■Čechov's *Diadia Vania (Uncle Vanya)* in the Pécs National Theatre directed by Róbert Nógrádi. Some words about the birth of the play and its former performances.

1919 Radics, Viktória. "A megalkuvó szinház." (The Theatre of Compromise.) *Elet*. 1986; 23(1): 64-65. Lang.: Hun.

Hungary: Budapest. 1985. Reviews of performances. ■Miklós Mészöly's *Bunker* at Népszinház directed by Mátyás Giricz.

1920 Rátonyi, Róbert. *Szeretném ha nevetnének*. (I'd Love to Make You Laugh.) Budapest: Ifjúsági Lap-és Könyvkiadó; 1985. 317 pp. Lang.: Hun.

Hungary. 1944-1985. Critical studies. ■Selected short comic prose sketches of Róbert Rátony, actor, showman and writer.

1921 Reményi, József Tamás. "Csehov nagyoperettje. A *Cseresznyéskert* Miskolcon." (Čechov's Light Opera: *The Cherry Orchard* in Miskolc.) *Sz*. 1986 Aug.; 19(8): 33-35. Illus.: Photo. B&W. 1: 9 cm. x 12 cm. Lang.: Hun.

Hungary: Miskolc. 1986. Reviews of performances. ■Čechov's *The Cherry Orchard* directed by Imre Csiszár at Miskolc National Theatre.

1922 Reményi, József Tamás. "Megváltás nélkül. Dosztojevszkij-adaptációk Budapesten és Debrecenben." (Without Redemption: Dostojévskij Adaptations in Budapest and Debrecen.) *Sz*. 1986 Feb.; 19(2): 28-32. Illus.: Photo. B&W. 5: 9 cm. x 12 cm. Lang.: Hun.

Hungary: Budapest, Debrecen. 1985. Reviews of performances. ■Dostoyevsky's *Idiot* adapted to the stage by G.A. Tovstonogov at József Attila Theatre, director István Iglódi, and *Bratja Karamazov (The Brothers Karamazov)* at Csokonai Theatre in Debrecen directed by László Gali.

1923 Reményi, József Tamás. "'Boldogságba eltemetve'. A *Csongor és Tünde* Egerben." ('Buried in Happiness': *Csongor and Tünde* in Eger.) *Sz*. 1986 May; 19(5): 6-8. Illus.: Photo. B&W. 2: 9 cm. x 12 cm., 12 cm. x 16 cm. Lang.: Hun.

Hungary: Eger. 1985. Reviews of performances. ■Mihály Vörösmarty's *Csongor and Tünde* at Gárdonyi Géza Theatre directed by János Szikora.

1924 Róna, Katalin. "A színpad tragédiája. A *Hangok komédiája* a Thália Stúdióban." (Tragedy of the Stage: The *Comedy of Sounds* at Thália Studio Theatre.) *Sz*. 1986 Jan.; 19(1): 16-17. Illus.: Photo. B&W. 1: 11 cm. x 12 cm. Lang.: Hun.

Hungary: Budapest. 1985. Reviews of performances. ■Criticizes the adaptation for stage by Károly Kazimir of a radio play *Hangok komédiája (Comedy of Sounds)* by Miklós Gyárfás.

1925 Róna, Katalin. "Csak dünnyögünk. a *Színházkomédia* a debreceni Csokonai Színházban." (We Are Only Mumbling: *Theatre Comedy* at Csokonai Theatre in Debrecen.) *Sz*. 1986 Apr.; 19(4): 27-29. Illus.: Photo. B&W. 2: 11 cm. x 12 cm. Lang.: Hun.

Hungary: Debrecen. 1985. Reviews of performances. ■Bengt Ahlfors' comedy at Csokonai Theatre in Debrecen directed by András Márton.

1926 Siposhegyi, Péter. "Hol a kétfejü feje." (Where is the Head of the Two-Headed Beast?)*Elet*. 1986; 23(3): 244-248. Lang.: Hun.

Hungary. Reviews of performances. ■Study of *A Kétfejü fenerad (The Two-Headed Beast)* by Sándor Weöres in connection with its productions.

1927 Siposhegyi, Péter. "Az első gongtól a fődijig." (From the First Stroke of the Gong to the First Prize.) *Elet*. 1986; 23(1): 69-73. Lang.: Hun.

Hungary: Zalaegerszeg. 1983-1986. Critical studies. ■Evaluation of three seasons of Hevesi Sándor Theatre opened in 1983, with analyses of productions focusing on József Ruszt's stagings.

1928 Stuber, Andrea. "Szikora János útjai." (Ways of János Szikora.) *Sz*. 1986 Sep.; 19(9): 27-30. Lang.: Hun.

Hungary. 1982-1986. Histories-sources. ■Interview with János Szikora about his activities as a director.

1929 Stuber, Andrea. "A Körszinház tragédiája. *Casanova* a Városligetben." (Tragedy of Theatre in the Round: *Casanova* in the Town Park.) *Sz*. 1986 Oct.; 19(10): 15-18. Illus.: Photo. B&W. 3: 12 cm. x 16 cm., 8 cm. x 12 cm., 9 cm. x 12 cm. Lang.: Hun.

Hungary: Budapest. 1986. Reviews of performances. ■The play written by János Pelle based on Casanova's memoirs was performed at Körszinház directed by Károly Kazimir.

1930 Stuber, Andrea. "Dajka-hagyaték." (The Dajka Legacy.) *Sz*. 1986 Nov.; 19(11): 9-14. 5: var. sizes. Lang.: Hun.

Hungary. 1929-1986. Biographical studies. ■Memoir of actress Margit Dajka's outstanding personality, her career and most prominent roles.

1931 Stuber, Andrea. "Uborkafán. Az *Úrhatnám polgár* Nyiregy-házán." (On the Cucumber Tree: *The Bourgeois Gentleman* in Nyiregyháza.) *Sz*. 1986 Dec.; 19(12): 9-12. Illus.: Photo. B&W. 2: 12 cm. x 16 cm., 18 cm. x 12 cm. Lang.: Hun.

Hungary: Nyiregyháza. 1986. Reviews of performances. ■Critical review of Molière's comedy directed at Móricz Zsigmond Theatre by Péter Gellért.

1932 Stuber, Andrea. "Verebes István: *Kettős ünnep*." (István Verebes: *A Double Holiday*.) *Krit*. 1986; 14 (10): 38. 1: 7.7 cm. x 12.5 cm. Lang.: Hun.

Hungary: Budapest. 1986. Reviews of performances. ■Review of *Kettős ünnep (A Double Holiday)*, written and staged by István Verebes.

1933 Szanki, F. Csaba. "Tollvonások Törőcsik Mari arcképéhez." (Strokes of the Pen—Contributions to Mari Törőcsik's Portrait.) *Tisz*. 1986; 40(4): 103-108. Lang.: Hun.

Hungary. 1956-1986. Critical studies. ■Survey of the life and career of actress Mari Tórócsik on the occasion of her fiftieth birthday. Related to Media: Film.

1934 Szántó, Judit. "*Pán Péter* a gyermekszínház fogságában." (*Peter Pan* in the Captivity of Children's Theatre.) *Sz*. 1986 Mar.; 19(3): 17-20. Illus.: Photo. B&W. 2: 9 cm. x 12 cm. Lang.: Hun.

Hungary: Kaposvár. 1985. Reviews of performances. ■Barrie's *Peter Pan* at Csiky Gergely Theatre, directed by Géza Pártos.

1935 Szántó, Judit. "Elfoszlott csoda. *A kis herceg* a József Attila Színházban." (The Miracle that Faded Away: *The Little Prince* at József Attila Theatre.) *Sz*. 1986 July; 19(7): 29-31. Illus.: Photo. B&W. 1: 9 cm. x 12 cm. Lang.: Hun.

Hungary: Budapest. 1985. Reviews of performances. ■*Le petit prince (The Little Prince)* of Antoine de Saint-Exupéry adapted to the stage by Anna Belia and Péter Valló at József Attila Theatre directed by Péter Valló.

1936 Szántó, Judit. "Szomor-y és Kéj-i. A *Bella* Pécsett." (*Bella* in Pécs.) *Sz*. 1986 Aug.; 19(8) : 21-24. Illus.: Photo. B&W. 2: 9 cm. x 12 cm. Lang.: Hun.

Hungary: Pécs. 1986. Critical studies. ■Dezső Szomory's *Bella* at Pécs National Theatre directed by István Jeney.

1937 Szántó, Judit. "Enquist: *Ének Phaedráért*." (Enquist: *Song for Phaedra*.) *Krit*. 1986; 14(3): 42-43. Illus.: Photo. B&W. 1: 7 cm. x 9 cm. Lang.: Hun.

CLASSED ENTRIES

DRAMA: —Performance/production

Hungary: Miskolc. 1985. Reviews of performances. ■Review of the Hungarian premiere of Per Olof Enquist's *Til Faedra (Song for Phaedra)* at the National Theatre of Miskolc directed by Imre Csiszár.

1938 Szántó, Judit. "Shakespeare: *Szeget szeggel.*" (Shakespeare: *Measure for Measure.*) *Krit.* 1986; 14(4): 30. Lang.: Hun.

Hungary: Veszprém. 1985. Reviews of performances. ■Shakespeare's *Measure for Measure* at Petőfi Theatre of Veszprém directed by István Paál.

1939 Szántó, Judit. "Sam Shepard: *Valódi vadnyugat.*" (Sam Shepard: *True West.*) *Krit.* 1986; 14(5): 30-31. Lang.: Hun.

Hungary: Budapest. 1986. Reviews of performances. ■Review of Sam Shepard's play *True West* at Radnóti Miklós Theatre directed by István Verebes.

1940 Szántó, Judit. "Még nem vagyunk kinn a vízből. Bond drámája Pécsett." (Not Yet Saved: Bond's Drama in Pécs.) *Sz.* 1986 June; 19(6): 22-25. Illus.: Photo. B&W. 2: 9 cm. x 12 cm. Lang.: Hun.

Hungary: Pécs. 1986. Critical studies. ■Edward Bond's *Saved* directed by István Szőke at Pécs National Theatre.

1941 Szántó, Judit. "Ritkán jön jobb. Füst Milán *Margit Kisasszonya* a Játékszínben." (Rarely Follows Something Better: Milán Füst's *Miss Margit* at The Stage.) *Sz.* 1986 May; 19(5): 1-4. Illus.: Photo. B&W. 3: 9 cm. x 12 cm., 12 cm. x 13 cm. Lang.: Hun.

Hungary: Budapest. 1986. Reviews of performances. ■Review of *Margit kisasszony (Miss Margit)* directed by István Dégi.

1942 Szántó, Judit. "Fábián László: *Levéltetvek.*" (László Fábián: *Plant-Lice.*) *Krit.* 1986; 14(7): 38. Lang.: Hun.

Hungary: Miskolc. 1986. Reviews of performances. ■Notes on *Levéltetvek az akasztófán (Plant-Lice on the Gallows)* by László Fábián and its world premiere at Studio Stage of the National Theatre of Miskolc directed by István Szőke.

1943 Szántó, Judit. "Klasszikus születik. Háy Gyula két drámájának hazai bemutatójáról." (A Classic is Born: Premiere of Two Plays of Gyula Háy in Hungary.) *Sz.* 1986 Sep.; 19(9): 1-5. Illus.: Photo. B&W. 3: 9 cm. x 12 cm., 12 cm. x 16 cm. Lang.: Hun.

Hungary: Veszprém, Gyula. 1986. Reviews of performances. ■Ferenc Sik directs two plays of Gyula Háy: *A ló (The Horse)* at Petőfi Theatre, *Attila éjszakái (The Nights of Attila)* at Gyula Várszinház.

1944 Székely, György. "Paulay Ede, a Nemzeti Színház 'drámai igzagatója'." (Ede Paulay, 'Dramatic Manager' of the National Theatre.) *Sz.* 1986 Mar.; 19(3): 1-6. Illus.: Photo. 6: 6 cm. x 8 cm., 6 cm. x 10 cm., 9 cm. x 12 cm. Lang.: Hun.

Hungary: Budapest. 1878-1894. Historical studies. ■Career of Ede Paulay, actor, director, dramaturg, translator and author and his work with the Hungarian National Theatre.

1945 Szepesi, Dóra. "Státusváltás. Beszélgetés Katona Imrével." (From Amateurism to Professionalism: Interview with Imre Katona.) *Sz.* 1986 Mar.; 19(3): 33-34. Lang.: Hun.

Hungary: Budapest. 1961-1985. Histories-sources. ■Interview with actor, director and dramaturg Imre Katona on the theatrical activity of Gropius Társulat (The Gropius Ensemble), which grew out of Universitas Együttes (Universitas Ensemble).

1946 Szilassy, Zoltán. "A *Nem félünk a farkastól* magyarországi fogadtatásáról." (On the Reception of *Who's Afraid of Virginia Woolf?* in Hungary.) *SzSz.* 1986; 10(21): 59-74. Notes. Append. Lang.: Hun.

Hungary: 1963-1984. Critical studies. ■Production history of Edward Albee's *Who's Afraid of Virginia Woolf?* in Hungary.

1947 Szűcs, Katalin. "Komikus, nem groteszk. Alekszej Dudarëv drámája a Józsefvárosi Színházban." (Comical, Not Grotesque: Aleksej Dudarëv's Drama at Józsefvárosi Theatre.) *Sz.* 1986 Sep.; 19(9): 5-7. Illus.: Photo. B&W. Lang.: Hun.

Hungary: Budapest. 1986. Reviews of performances. ■Aleksej Dudarëv's *Večer (An Evening)* directed by Mátyas Giricz at Józsefvárosi Theatre.

1948 Szűcs, Katalin. "Rendezte m. v. Előadások Veszprémben és Békéscsabán." (Guest Director: Performances in Veszprém

and Békéscsaba.) *Sz.* 1986 Feb.; 19(2): 32-34. Illus.: Photo. B&W. 2: 7 cm. x 12 cm., 9 cm. x 12 cm. Lang.: Hun.

Hungary: Veszprém, Békéscsaba. 1985. Reviews of performances. ■Stage adaptation of Gončarov's *Obiknovenna'a istori'a (Weekday History)* adapted by Viktor Rozov in the Petőfi Theatre, directed by Oleg Tabakov and Gogol's *Ženitba (The Marriage)* in the Jókai Theatre directed by Anatolij Ivanov.

1949 Szűcs, Katalin. "A nem vállalás válalása. Hernádi Gyula *Hagyaték* című drámája Pécsett." (Undertaking the 'Non-Undertaking': Gyula Hernádi's *Legacy* in Pécs.) *Sz.* 1986 June; 19(6): 8-11. Illus.: Photo. B&W. 2: 9 cm. x 12 cm. Lang.: Hun.

Hungary: Pécs. 1986. Critical studies. ■Gyula Hernádi's *Hagyaték (Legacy)* directed by Menyhért Szegvári at Pécs National Theatre.

1950 Szűcs, Katalin. "'Rendet teremteni igyekvő tiszta szándék'. Gáll István drámája Nyiregyházán." ('Pure Intention to Make Order': István Gáll's Drama in Nyiregyháza.) *Sz.* 1986 June; 19(7): 1-3. 1: 9 cm. x 12 cm. Lang.: Hun.

Hungary: Nyiregyháza. 1986. Reviews of performances. ■*Nő a körúton (Woman on the Boulevard)* by István Gáll directed by Péter Léner at Móricz Zsigmond Theatre.

1951 Szűcs, Katalin. "Kényelmetlen eszmék. Vészi Endre drámája Gyulán." (Uncomfortable Ideas: Endre Vészi's Drama in Gyula.) *Sz.* 1986 Oct.; 19(10): 23-25. Illus.: Photo. B&W. 2: 12 cm. x 16 cm. Lang.: Hun.

Hungary: Gyula. 1986. Reviews of performances. ■Endre Vészi's *Don Quijote utolsó kalandja (Don Quixote's Last Adventure)* at Gyulai Várszinház directed by Imre Kerényi.

1952 Szűcs, Katalin. "(Pre)koncepció nélkül. Az *Oszlopos Simeon* Miskolcon." (Without (Pre)conceptions. *The Man on the Pillar* in Miskolc.) *Sz.* 1986 Dec.; 19(12): 7-9. Illus.: Photo. B&W. 2: 12 cm. x 17 cm. Lang.: Hun.

Hungary: Miskolc. 1986. Reviews of performances. ■Imre Sarkadi's *Oszlopos Simeon (The Man on the Pillar)* directed by István Szőke at Nemzeti Szinház.

1953 Szűcs, Katalin. "Rostand: *Cyrano de Bergerac.*" *Krit.* 1986; 14(2): 35. Illus.: Photo. B&W. 1: 7 cm. x 7.5 cm. Lang.: Hun.

Hungary: Budapest. 1985. Reviews of performances. ■Notes on Edmond Rostand's *Cyrano de Bergerac* and its performance at Madách Theatre directed by György Lengyel.

1954 Szűcs, Katalin. "Déry Tibor: *A tanúk.*" (Tibor Déry: *The Witnesses.*) *Krit.* 1986; 14(9): 40-41. Lang.: Hun.

Hungary: Szolnok. 1986. Reviews of performances. ■World premiere of *A tanúk (The Witnesses)* by the late Tibor Déry, directed at Szigligeti Theatre by Tibor Csizmadia.

1955 Szűcs, Katalin. "Csáth Géza: *Janika.*" (Géza Csáth: *Our Son.*) *Krit.* 1986; 14(12): 45-46. Lang.: Hun.

Hungary: Szolnok. 1986. Reviews of performances. ■Notes on an outstanding performance of Géza Csáth's tragicomedy *Janika (Our Son)* at the Pocket Theatre of Szigligeti Theatre directed by Tamás Fodor. Review focuses on György Kézdy's performance in the title role.

1956 Szűcs, Katalin. "A hallgatás balladája. Sütő András-színjáték a Nemzeti Színházban." (The Ballad of Silence: András Sütő's Play at the National Theatre.) *Sz.* 1986 May; 19(5): 4-6. Illus.: Photo. B&W. 2: 12 cm. x 16 cm. Lang.: Hun.

Hungary: Budapest. 1986. Reviews of performances. ■*Advent a Hargitán (Advent in the Harghita Mountains)*, by András Sütő, directed by Ferenc Sik.

1957 Szűcs, Katalin. "Molière: *Scapin furfangjai.*" (Molière: *Scapin's Tricks.*) *Krit.* 1986; 14(10): 36. Illus.: Photo. B&W. 1: 6.6 cm. x 9.8 cm. Lang.: Hun.

Hungary: Szentendre. 1986. Reviews of performances. ■A summer production of *Les Fourberies de Scapin (Scapin's Tricks)* by Molière at Szentendre Theatre directed by László Vámos.

1958 Takács, István. "A felülbírált Schnitzler." (The Criticized Schnitzler.) *Sz.* 1986 Aug.; 19(8): 35-38 . Illus.: Photo. B&W. 1: 12 cm. x 15 cm. Lang.: Hun.

DRAMA: —Performance/production

Hungary: Budapest, Zalaegerszeg. 1986. Critical studies. ■Two plays by Arthur Schnitzler directed by Imre Halasi: *Reigen (Round)* at Thália Studio and *Der grüne Kakadu (The Green Cockatoo)* in a musical version at Hevesi Sándor Theatre. Related to Music-Drama: Musical theatre.

1959 Takács, István. "Telitalálat és félreértés." (Direct Hit and Misunderstanding.) *Sz.* 1986 July; 19(7): 22-26. Illus.: Photo. B&W. 3: 9 cm. x 12 cm., 12 cm. x 13 cm. Lang.: Hun.

Hungary: Szeged. 1986. Reviews of performances. ■Performances of *Hair*, directed by János Sándor, and *Desire Under the Elms*, directed by Géza Bodolay at the National Theatre of Szeged. Related to Music-Drama: Musical theatre.

1960 Tarján, Tamás. "A sziget nem elég magas. *A vihar* Kaposváron." (The Island Is Not High Enough: *The Tempest* in Kaposvár.) *Sz.* 1986 May; 19(5): 26-28. Illus.: Photo. B&W. 1: 9 cm. x 12 cm. Lang.: Hun.

Hungary: Kaposvár. 1986. Critical studies. ■*The Tempest* by William Shakespeare at Csiky Gergely Theatre directed by Gyula Gazdag.

1961 Tarján, Tamás. "Sörfuccs. A *Levéltetvek az akasztfán* bemutatójáról." (Beer Fail: On the Premiere of *Plant-Lice on the Gallows*.) *Sz.* 1986 July; 19(7): 6-9. Illus.: Photo. B&W. 3: 9 cm. x 12 cm., 12 cm. x 12 cm. Lang.: Hun.

Hungary: Miskolc. 1986. Reviews of performances. ■László Fábián's play at the National Theatre of Miskolc directed by István Szőke.

1962 Tarján, Tamás. "Örkény István: *Macskajáték*." (István Örkény: *Catsplay*.) *Krit.* 1986; 14(1): 33. Lang.: Hun.

Hungary: Budapest. 1985. Reviews of performances. ■One of the best Hungarian plays of the recent past, *Macskajáték (Catsplay)* by István Örkény, at Magyar Játékszin directed by Gábor Berényi.

1963 Tarján, Tamás. "Sütő András szinjátéka a próbáktól a premierig." (András Sütő's Play from Rehearsals to the Premiere.) *Krit.* 1986; 14(4): 26-27. Illus.: Photo. B&W. 1: 7 cm. x 11 cm. Lang.: Hun.

Hungary: Budapest. 1985-1986. Histories-sources. ■Discussion of rehearsals of *Advent a Hargitán (Advent in the Harghita Mountains)* by András Sütő's directed at the National Theatre by Ferenc Sik and of a photography exhibit on the rehearsals.

1964 Tarján, Tamás. "Csehov: *Három nővér*." (Čechov: *Three Sisters*.) *Krit.* 1986; 14(2): 34-35. Lang.: Hun.

Hungary: Budapest, Zalaegerszeg. 1985. Reviews of performances. ■Comparison of two productions of Čechov's *Tri sestry (Three Sisters)* presented at Katona József Theatre in Budapest directed by Tamás Ascher and at Hevesi Sándor Theatre in Zalaegerszeg directed by József Ruszt.

1965 Tarján, Tamás. "Witkiewicz: *Az őrült és az apáca*." (Witkiewicz: *The Madman and the Nun*.) *Krit.* 1986; 14(10): 37. Lang.: Hun.

Hungary: Szeged. 1986. Reviews of performances. ■*Wariat i zakonnica (The Madman and the Nun)* by Stanisław Ignacy Witkiewicz, directed by János Sándor at Szeged National Theatre.

1966 Tarján, Tamás. "*A nevelő*. Brecht bemutató Kaposváron." (*The Tutor*. A Play of Brecht in Kaposvár.) *Somo.* 1986; 14(1): 99-101. Lang.: Hun.

Hungary: Kaposvár. 1985. Reviews of performances. ■Bertolt Brecht's play *Der Hofmeister (The Tutor)* at Csiky Gergely Theatre directed by Gábor Máté.

1967 Tóth, Dénes. "Avantgarde szinházi hagyományok." (Avant-garde Theatre Traditions.) *Alfold.* 1986; 37(9): 90-92. Lang.: Hun.

Hungary: Budapest. 1931. Critical studies. ■Synthesis of music, dance, song and speech in *Ayrus Leánya (Ayrus' Daughter)* by Ödön Palasovszky.

1968 Várszegi, Tibor. "Szophoklész: *Oidipusz*." (Sophocles: *Oedipus the King*.) *Krit.* 1986; 14(10): 38. Lang.: Hun.

Hungary: Szolnok. 1986. Reviews of performances. ■Analysis of Sophocles' tragedy presented at Szigligeti Chamber Theatre directed by Róbert Vörös.

1969 Vinkó, József. "A megszelidített Übü papa." (Father Ubu Domesticated.) *Sz.* 1985 May; 18: 26-29. Illus.: Photo. Print. B&W. Lang.: Hun.

Hungary: Budapest. 1984. Critical studies. ■Production analysis of *Ubu roi* by Alfred Jarry staged for the first time in Hungary by Gábor Zsámbéki at the József Katona Theatre.

1970 Zappe, László. "Nem írta át Dürrenmatt. *II. Richárd* a Várszinházban." (It Wasn't Rewritten by Dürrenmatt: *Richard II* at Castle Theatre.) *Sz.* 1986 June; 19(6): 13-14. Illus.: Photo. B&W. 2: 9 cm. x 11 cm. Lang.: Hun.

Hungary: Budapest. 1986. Reviews of performances. ■Shakespeare's *Richard II* at Castle Theatre directed by Imre Kerényi.

1971 Zappe, László. "Illyés Gyula: *Kegyenc*." (Gyula Illyés: *The Favorite*.) *Krit.* 1986; 14(1): 33-34. Illus.: Photo. B&W. 1: 14 cm. x 11 cm. Lang.: Hun.

Hungary: Miskolc. 1985. Reviews of performances. ■Notes on *A kegyenc (The Favorite)*, by Gyula Illyés, based on a play by László Teleki, at the National Theatre of Miskolc directed by János Sándor.

1972 Zappe, László. "Reginald Rose: *Tizenkét dühös ember*." (Reginald Rose: *Twelve Angry Men*.) *Krit.* 1986; 14(5): 29-30. Lang.: Hun.

Hungary: Budapest. 1985. Reviews of performances. ■Analysis of Reginald Rose's *Twelve Angry Men* and its performance at the National Theatre directed by András Béhés.

1973 Zappe, László. "Gáll István: *Nő a körúton*." (István Gáll: *Woman on the Boulevard*.) *Krit.* 1986; 14(7): 36-37. Lang.: Hun.

Hungary: Nyiregyháza. 1986. Reviews of performances. ■Dramaturgical problems of István Gáll's play and notes on the performance at Móricz Zsigmond Theatre directed by Péter Léner.

1974 Zsigmond, Gyula. "'Add vissza nekünk, Uram, a kiáltás jogát...!'." ('Give us Back, Our Lord, the Right to Cry...!'.) *Confes.* 1986; 10(3): 76-77. Lang.: Hun.

Hungary: Budapest. 1986. Reviews of performances. ■András Sütő's *Advent a Hargitán (Advent in the Harghita Mountains)* at the National Theatre directed by Ferenc Sik.

1975 Bharucha, Rustom. "*Request Concert* in Bombay." *ThM.* 1986 Fall/Win; 18(1): 42-51. Illus.: Photo. Print. B&W. 1: 5 in. x 7 in. Lang.: Eng.

India: Calcutta, Madras, Bombay. Historical studies. ■An adaptation of Franz Xaver Kroetz's *Request Concert (Wunschkonzert)*, a wordless monodrama, performed in three Indian cities with local casts.

1976 Free, Katharine B. "The *Bhavāī* of Gujarat: Religious Drama in Honour of the Mother Goddess of India." *ThR.* 1986; 11(1): 48-60. Notes. Lang.: Eng.

India. 1980-1986. Histories-reconstruction. ■Description of several *Bhavāī* performances.

1977 "Pras Meir Margalit Leomanut Hateatron, Tav-Shin-Memvav." (Meir Margalith Prize for 1986.) *Bamah.* 1986; 21(104): 119-121. Illus.: Photo. Print. B&W. 2: 8 cm. x 12 cm. Lang.: Heb.

Israel: Jerusalem. 1986. Historical studies. ■Announcement of 1986 Margalith Prize winners: director Gedalya Besser and scene designer Roni Toren.

1978 Blumert, Ruth. "Shtei Sichot." (Interviews with Dan Horowitz and Ya'akov Raz.) *Bamah.* 1986; 21(104): 86-94. Lang.: Heb.

Israel. 1978-1986. Histories-sources. ■Artistic cooperation between playwright Dan Horowitz and director Ya'akov Raz in four theatrical productions in various theatres.

1979 Finkel, Shimon. "Habamai Liubimov Ve *Hashkia* Be 'HaBima'." (Stage Director Liubimov and the *Sunset* at the HaBimah Theatre.) *Bamah.* 1986; 21(105-106): 113-115. Illus.: Photo. Print. B&W. 1: 8.5 cm. x 6.5 cm. [Excerpt from *In the Shadow of Conflicts*.] Lang.: Heb.

Israel: Tel-Aviv. 1984-1986. Historical studies. ■Work of director Jurij Petrovič Liubimov on *Zakat (Sunset)* by Isaak Emmanuilovič Babel presented at the HaBimah Theatre.

1980 Kofman, Sarit. "Prakim Mitoh Yoman-Hahazarot shel *Eyolf Hakatan* Bahan HaIerushalmi, Tav-Shin-Mem-Zain." (Chapters from the Rehearsal Diary of *Little Eyolf*

DRAMA: —Performance/production

at the Jerusalem Khan Theatre.) *Bamah.* 1986; 21(105-106): 101-107. Illus.: Photo. Print. B&W. 3: var. sizes. Lang.: Heb.

Israel: Jerusalem. 1986. Histories-sources. ∎Notes on the process of staging *Eiolf Hakatan*, a Hebrew translation of Henrik Ibsen's *Lille Eyolf (Little Eyolf)*, directed by Yossi Israeli at the Kahn theatre.

1981 Lanzini, Daniel. "*Hazaiot Kamot Bamizrah—Yomano shel Bamai.*" (*Fantasies Awakening in the East*—Diary of a Stage Director.) *Bamah.* 1986; 21(105-106): 116-121. Illus.: Photo. Print. B&W. 1: 11.5 cm. x 11.5 cm. Lang.: Heb.

Israel: Acre. 1986. Historical studies. ∎Daniel Lanzini's notes on writing and staging his play *Hazaiot Kamot Bamizrah (Fantasies Awakening in the East)* at the Acre Theatre Festival.

1982 Rokem, Freddie. "*Eiolf Hakatan* Beteatron Hahan—Reshamim Mitahalich Hahazarot." (*Little Eyolf* At the Kahn: Impressions from the Rehearsal Process.) *Bamah.* 1986; 21(105-106): 108-112. Lang.: Heb.

Israel: Jerusalem. 1986. Histories-sources. ∎Notes on the rehearsals of Henrik Ibsen's *Eiolf Hakatan (Lille Eyolf)* directed by Yossi Israeli, at the Kahn Theatre.

1983 Sneh, Shlomo. "Ahavat Hakahal Muvtahat—Reaion Im Hasachkanit Rachel Marcus." (An Interview with Rachel Marcus.) *Bamah.* 1986; 21(103): 59-64. Illus.: Photo. Print. B&W. 2. Lang.: Heb.

Israel: Tel-Aviv. 1935-1986. Histories-sources. ∎Rachel Marcus on theatre and on her life in Israeli theatre.

1984 Zvi, Aza. "Rafael Zvi—Bamai Meshorer." (Raphael Zvi—A Stage Director, Poet and Teacher.) *Bamah.* 1986; 21(105/106): 5-37 . Illus.: Photo. Dwg. Print. B&W. 10: var. sizes. Lang.: Heb.

Israel. 1898-1985. Biographical studies. ∎Obituary of director Raphael Zvi.

1985 Teatro Regionale Toscano; Teatro Comunale Metastasio di Prato. Ignorabimus *di Arno Holz.* (Ignorabimus by Arno Holz.) NP: 1986. 104 pp. Illus.: Photo. B&W. Lang.: Ita.

Italy: Prato. 1986. Critical studies. ∎Biographical and critical notes, interviews and photos of Luca Ronconi's production of *Ignorabimus* by Arno Holz.

1986 Aliprandini, Luisa de. "La representación en Roma de la Tinellaria de Torres Naharro." (The Performance in Rome of the *Tinellaria* by Torres Naharro.) 127-135 in Salvat, Ricard, ed. *El Teatre durant l'Edat Mitjana i el Renaixement.* Barcelona: Publicacions i Edicions de la Universitat de Barcelona; 1986. xxviii, 322 pp. (El Pla de les Comèdies 2.) Notes. [Presented at First International Symposium on Medieval and Renaissance Theatre, Sitges, 1983.] Lang.: Spa.

Italy: Rome, Venice. 1508-1537. Histories-sources. ∎Reconstructs Roman performance of Torres Naharro's *Comedia Tinellaria* and considers its possible influence on the work of Pietro Aretino.

1987 Alonge, Roberto. "La riscoperta di Pirandello sulle scene italiane del secondo dopoguerra." (The Rediscovery of Pirandello on Italian Stages After World War II.) *QT.* 1986 Nov.; 9(34): 102-118. Notes. Biblio. Lang.: Ita.

Italy. 1947-1985. Historical studies. ∎The scarcity of Pirandello productions in the post-war period and some recent productions.

1988 Anderlini, Serena. "Franca Rame: Her Life and Works." *ThM.* 1983 Win; 17(1): 32-39. Illus.: Photo. B&W. 5. Lang.: Eng.

Italy. 1929-1983. Biographical studies. ∎Rame's work in the theatre, her background in a theatrical family, her collaborations with Fo and her political feminist work.

1989 Benedetti, Tere. "Zaccaria Seriman, il teatro, Goldoni e alcune chiavi inglesi." (Zaccaria Seriman, Theatre, Goldoni and Some English Clues.) *BiT.* 1986; 4: 61-87. Notes. Biblio. Lang.: Ita.

Italy: Venice. 1708-1784. Historical studies. ∎Judgments of Venetian man of letters Zaccaria Seriman on the theatre of his day, including his disapproval of the vulgarity of the comedies of Carlo Goldoni.

1990 Dort, Bernard. "Une écriture de la représentation." (Performance Writing.) *ThE.* 1986 Apr.; 10: 18-21. Notes. Illus.: Photo. B&W. 1: 9 in. x 7 in. Lang.: Fre.

Italy. 1921-1986. Critical studies. ∎Luigi Pirandello's concern with staging and distance exemplified by *Sei personaggi in cerca d'autore (Six Characters in Search of an Author)* and *Enrico Quarto (Henry IV)*.

1991 Mele, Rino. "The Theater of Memè Perlini." 249-254 in McNamara, Brooks, ed.; Dolan, Jill, ed. *The Drama Review: Thirty Years of Commentary on the Avant-Garde.* Ann Arbor, MI: UMI Research P; 1986. xii, 371 pp. (Theatre and Dramatic Studies 35.) Lang.: Eng.

Italy. 1978. Critical studies. ∎Working environment of director Memè Perlini, the type of lighting, imagery, dialogue and space he uses to create his theatrical world.

1992 Menichi, Angela. "Virgilio Talli, fra tradizione e avanguardia, primo regista del teatro italiano." (Virgilio Talli, Between Tradition and Avant-Garde, First Director of Italian Theatre.) *TeatrC.* 1985-1986; 6(11-12): 117-134. Notes. Biblio. Lang.: Ita.

Italy. 1917-1920. Critical studies. ∎Chronicles intense collaboration of director Virgilio Talli and playwright Pier Maria Rosso di San Secondo in the first productions of *Marionette che passione! (Marionettes, What Passion!)* and *La bella addormentata (Sleeping Beauty)*.

1993 Menichi, Angela. "Il rapporto tra Luigi Pirandello e Virgilio Talli negli anni tra il 1917 e il 1921." (The Relationship of Luigi Pirandello and Virgilio Talli, 1917-1921.) *QT.* 1986 Nov.; 9(34): 7-22. Notes. Biblio. Lang.: Ita.

Italy. 1917-1921. Critical studies. ∎Pirandello's dealings with actor, manager and director Virgilio Talli.

1994 Mitchell, Tony. "Milan." *PI.* 1986 Sept; 2(2): 34-35. B&W. Lang.: Eng.

Italy: Milan. 1986. Historical studies. ∎Current productions in Milan especially Giorgio Strehler's *Elvira, o la passione teatrale* and Dario Fo's *Mistero Buffo*.

1995 Molinari, Cesare. "La (s)fortuna teatrale di Manzoni." (The Theatrical (Mis)fortune of Manzoni.) *BiT.* 1986; 1: 77-93. Lang.: Ita.

Italy. 1827-1882. Historical studies. ∎The unsuccessful production of the tragedies of Alessandro Manzoni and his rewriting of *I promessi sposi (The Betrothed)*.

1996 Pezzana Capranica del Grillo, Aldo. "Il matrimonio di Giuliano Capranica del Grillo e di Adelaide Ristori." (The Marriage of Giuliano Capranica del Grillo and Adelaide Ristori.) *TArch.* 1986 Sep.; 10: 109-112. Lang.: Ita.

Italy. 1848. Biographical studies. ∎Information on the marriage of actress Adelaide Ristori based on archival material.

1997 Picchi, Arnaldo. "Didascalie. Una descrizione de *L'uomo, la bestia, e la virtù.*" (Stage Directions. A Description of *Man, Animal and Virtue.*) *QT.* 1986 Nov.; 9(34): 65-76. Notes. Biblio. Lang.: Ita.

Italy. 1919. Critical studies. ∎Notes on the first production of Luigi Pirandello's *L'uomo, la bestia, e la virtù (Man, Animal and Virtue)*.

1998 Poesio, Paolo Emilio. "Intorno alla 'prima' de *I giganti della montagna.*" (On the First Performance of *The Giants of the Mountain.*) *QT.* 1986 Nov.; 9(34): 94-101. Notes. Biblio. Lang.: Ita.

Italy: Florence. 1937. Historical studies. ∎Notes on the posthumous premiere of Luigi Pirandello's *I giganti della montagna (The Giants of the Mountain)* at the spring arts festival 'Maggio Musicale Fiorentino'.

1999 Rasi, Luigi; Schino, Mirella, ed. *La Duse.* Rome: Bolzoni; 1986. 245 pp. (Biblioteca teatrale-Memorie di teatro 3.) Pref. Index. Notes. Append. Lang.: Ita.

Italy. 1858-1901. Biographical studies. ∎New edition of a critical-biographical study of actress Eleonora Duse (1901) by actor Luigi Rasi. Includes an essay by Mirella Schina, 'Duse vs. the Theatre of her Time'.

2000 Russo, Maria. "Una 'Lady' in Progress." (A 'Lady' in Progress.) *BiT.* 1986; 4: 107-133. Notes. Biblio. Lang.: Ita.

Italy. England. USA. 1822-1906. Historical studies. ∎Career of Adelaide Ristori, first Italian actress to perform in English for anglophone

DRAMA: —Performance/production

audiences, including reactions of the press and public to her role as Lady Macbeth (London, 1882).

2001 Schino, Mirella. "Ritorno al teatro. Lettere di Eleonora Duse ad Ermete Zacconi e a Silvio D'Amico." (Back to the Theatre: Letters of Eleonora Duse to Ermete Zacconi and Silvio D'Amico.) *TArch*. 1986 Sep.; 10: 149-254. Notes. Biblio. Lang.: Ita.
Italy. 1920-1923. Biographical studies. ■Reconstruction of the last professional activities of actress Eleonora Duse based on her letters to two major theatrical figures.

2002 Scrivano, Enzo, ed. *Teatro: teoria e prassi*. (Theatre: Theory and Practice.) Rome: La Nuova Italia Scientifica; 1986. 200 pp. Pref. Index. Notes. Biblio. Lang.: Spa.
Italy: Agrigento. 1900-1940. Critical studies. ■Presentations from a conference sponsored by the Pirandellian Studies Center, Agrigento (1985).

2003 Štětka, Boris. "Ljubimov e l'Italia." (Liubimov and Italy.) *BiT*. 1986; 3: 83-99. Lang.: Ita.
Italy. USSR. 1973-1986. Critical studies. ■Creative development of director Jurij Liubimov in Italy, including his work with Italian companies.

2004 Tinterri, Alessandro. "Pirandello regista del suo teatro: 1925-1928." (Pirandello, Director of His Plays: 1925-1928.) *QT*. 1986 Nov.; 9(34): 54-63. Notes. Biblio. Lang.: Ita.
Italy: Rome. 1925-1928. Critical studies. ■Luigi Pirandello's staging of his own works at the Teatro d'Arte.

2005 Dillon, John. "*Salesman no shi*: A Director Discovers the Japanese Essence in an American Classic." *AmTh*. 1984 Nov.; 1 (7): 12-15. Illus.: Photo. Handbill. B&W. 4: var. sizes. Lang.: Eng.
Japan. 1984. Histories-sources. ■Director John Dillon discusses his experiences staging and adapting Arthur Miller's *Death of a Salesman* in Japan.

2006 Nánay, István. "Örkény-dráma japánul. A *Tóték* bemutatója Tojamában." (An Örkény Drama in Japanese. First Night of *The Tót Family* in Toyama.) *Sz*. 1986 Jan.; 19(1): 39-42. Illus.: Photo. B&W. 3: 6 cm. x 12 cm., 9 cm. x 12 cm. Lang.: Hun.
Japan: Toyama. 1985. Reviews of performances. ■Production of István Örkény's *Tóték (The Tót Family)*, directed by István Pinezés and performed by Bungei-za.

2007 Suzuki, Tadashi; Rimer, J. Thomas, transl. *The Way of Acting: The Theatre Writings of Tadashi Suzuki*. New York, NY: Theatre Communications Group; 1986. 155 pp. Pref. Illus.: Photo. 26: var. sizes. Lang.: Eng.
Japan. 1980-1983. Critical studies. ■Essays on Suzuki's training method, the art of stage performance, the nature of individual and ensemble work as a basis for human communication and the importance of a permanent theatre.

2008 Nanney, Nancy K. "Observing Modern Korean Plays." *ATJ*. 1985 Spr; 2(1): 67-70. Notes. Lang.: Eng.
Korea: Seoul. 1983-1984. Reviews of performances. ■A series of reviews of plays given during the 1983-1984 season in Seoul, including *0.917, Agnes of God, Pumba, Dream of a Strong Man* and *All Kinds of Birds Are Flying In*, a *madang guk*, or yard play.

2009 Shim, Jungsoon. "Modernizing the Myth: A Summary Review of the 1986 National Theatre Festival." *KoJ*. 1986 Dec.; 26(12): 60-63. Illus.: Photo. B&W. 4. Lang.: Eng.
Korea. 1986. Reviews of performances. ■Reviews of the play productions at the 1986 National Theatre Festival.

2010 Shim, Jungsoon. "Reinterpreting History: A Summary Review of the 1985 National Theatre Festival." *KoJ*. 1986 Jan.; 26(1) : 57-59. Illus.: Photo. B&W. 3. Lang.: Eng.
Korea. 1985. Reviews of performances. ■Review of the play productions at the 1985 National Theatre Festival held in Korea.

2011 Assaf, Roger. "Mémoire collective et travail théâtral au Liban Sud." (Collective Memory and Theatrical Work in South Lebanon.) 9-18 in Coca, Jordi, ed.; Conesa, Laura, comp. *Congrés Internacional de Teatre a Catalunya 1985.*

Actes. Volum II. Seccions 1, 2 i 3. Barcelona: Institut del Teatre; 1986. 340 pp. Lang.: Fre.
Lebanon. 1918-1985. Critical studies. ■Description of the conditions of performance for several genres: *hikâyâ* (popular tale), *hakawâti* (narrative theatre) and *Da'ziya* (epic poetry).

2012 Chevalley, Sylvie. "Politique et théâtre: une visite impériale en Hollande en 1811." (Politics and Theatre: An Imperial Visit to The Netherlands in 1811.) *RHT*. 1986; 38(4): 370-394. Illus.: Design. Print. B&W. 22: var. sizes. Lang.: Fre.
Netherlands. 1811. Histories-reconstruction. ■Performances in Amsterdam by actors of the Comédie-Française during a visit by Napoleon. Includes notes by Dutch actor Johanes Jelgerhuis Rienkzoon.

2013 Baniewicz, Elzbieta; Pajchel, Renate, photo. "Jeszcze Jedno Zwyciestwo Pisarza." (One More Victory of the Writer.) *TeatrW*. 1984 Oct.; 39(817): 9-11. 1: 19 cm. x 11 cm. Lang.: Pol.
Poland: Warsaw. 1984. Reviews of performances. ■Production analysis of *Popiol i Diament (Ashes and Diamonds)* by Jerzy Andrzejewski directed by Andrej Marczewski at Teatr Rozmaitości.

2014 Boltuć, Irena. "Centenaire de la naissance de Leon Schiller (1887-1954): Anniversaires UNESCO de personnalités éminentes et d'événements historiques." (Leon Schiller, His Hundredth Birthday (1887-1954): UNESCO Anniversaries of Great Personalities and Historical Events.) *TP*. 1986; 29(11-12): 3-10. Illus.: Photo. Print. B&W. 6. Lang.: Eng, Fre.
Poland. 1887-1954. Biographical studies. ■Life and work of Leon Schiller from cabaret singer to Poland's most eminent stage director. Related to Mixed Entertainment: Cabaret.

2015 Braun, Kazimierz. "Le metteur en scène—lecteur du drame." (Director as Reader of Drama.) 109-124 in Heistein, Józef, ed. *Le texte dramatique. La lecture et la scène*. Wrocław: Wydawnictwo Uniwersytetu Wrocławskiego; 1986. 248 pp. (Acta Universitatis Wratislaviensis 895, Romanica Wratislaviensia 26.) Illus.: Graphs. Lang.: Eng.
Poland: Wrocław. 1976-1983. Critical studies. ■Director Kazimierz Braun presents his experiences in reading dramas and other texts designed for production: uses his adaptation of Camus' *La Peste (The Plague)*.

2016 Brumer, Wiktor; Udalska, Eleonora, ed. *Tradycja i styl w teatrze*. (Tradition and Style in Theatre.) Warsaw: Państwowe Wydawnictwo Naukowe; 1986. 530 pp. Pref. Index. Illus.: Photo. B&W. 27: var. sizes. Lang.: Pol.
Poland. 1765-1930. Histories-sources. ■Collection of articles of eminent critic and theatre historian Wiktor Brumer (1894-1941) including reviews of performances in Warsaw theatres, 1918-1939, as well as historical studies and theoretical articles.

2017 Byrski, Tadeusz; Byrska, Irena; Nowak, Maciej, ed. "Wspomnienia z lat trzydziestych." (Recollection of the Thirties.) *PaT*. 1986 Second & Third Qtr; 2-3: 408-421. Notes. Illus.: Photo. Print. B&W. 1: 12 cm. x 6 cm. Lang.: Pol.
Poland: Vilna. 1930-1939. Histories-sources. ■Actor-directors Irena and Tadeusz Byrski recall various aspects of theatrical life in Vilna: political background, public relations, artistic events, social life of the theatre ensemble.

2018 Chałupka, Jerzy. "Interesy Ludwika Adama Dmuszewskiego." (Adam Dmuszewski's Businesses.) *PaT*. 1986 Fourth Qtr; 4: 469-485. Notes. Lang.: Pol.
Poland. 1799-1883. Historical studies. ■Business dealings of actor Adam Dmuszewski.

2019 Csik, István. "Wroclaw '86." *Sz*. 1986 Oct.; 19(10): 46-48. 1: 12 cm. x 15.5 cm. Lang.: Hun.
Poland: Wrocław. 1986. Reviews of performances. ■Performances of the 15th festival of contemporary Polish drama.

2020 Drohocka, Halina; Romer, Helena Ochenkowska. "Wspomnienia o Wileńskim Teatrze Objasdowym." (Recollections of Wileński Teatr Objazdowy.) *PaT*. 1986 Second & Third Qtr; 2-3: 422-430. Append. Lang.: Pol.

DRAMA: —Performance/production

Poland: Vilna. 1935-1936. Histories-sources. ∎Description of everyday life on tour in Wileński Touring Theatre, including repertory, casting, and difficult performance conditions.

2021 Godlewska, Joanna. "*Cyd* Uniewazniony." (*Le Cid* Annotated.) *TeatrW.* 1985 Mar.; 40(827): 17-18. Lang.: Pol.

Poland: Warsaw. 1984. Reviews of performances. ∎Production analysis of *Le Cid (The Cid)* by Pierre Corneille, directed by Adam Hanuszkiewicz, staged by Teatr Ateneum.

2022 Godlewska, Joanna. "Leon Schiller et Gordon Craig: L'amitié des deux artistes du théâtre." (Leon Schiller and Gordon Craig: The Friendship of Two Theatre Artists.) *TP.* 1986; 11-12: 11-16. Illus.: Photo. Print. B&W. 4. Lang.: Eng, Fre.

Poland: Warsaw. France: Paris. 1900-1954. Historical studies. ∎Overview of correspondence between Leon Schiller and Edward Gordon Craig and their meetings in Paris and Warsaw.

2023 Harrison, Wilfred. "*Othello* in Poland: Notes from a Director's Diary." *NTQ.* 1986 May; 11(6): 154-174. Illus.: Photo. B&W. 4. Lang.: Eng.

Poland: Toruń. 1980. Histories-sources. ∎Rehearsals for the Wilama Horzycy Theatre production of *Othello*, in a translation by Bohdan Drozdowski.

2024 Howard, Tony. "A Piece of Our Life: The Theatre of the Eighth Day: The Techniques and Trials of the Innovative Polish Company." *NTQ.* 1986 Nov.; 11(8): 291-305. Illus.: Photo. B&W. 6. Lang.: Eng.

Poland: Poznań. 1963-1985. Histories-sources. ∎Interviews with Tadeusz Janiszewski, Adam Borowski, Leszek Sczaniecki, Lech Raczak and Marcin Keszycki, discussing Jerzy Grotowski, their working method, the function of poetry in physical theatre, their major productions and their survival strategies.

2025 Jacoby, Oren. "Wajda's Dostoevsky....Darkness Visible." *ThM.* 1986 Fall/Win; 18(1): 60-64. Illus.: Photo. Print. B&W. 1: 4 in. x 4 in. Lang.: Eng.

Poland: Cracow. USA. 1986. Histories-sources. ∎Interview with director and cast of Wajda's adaptation of *Crime and Punishment*, as staged at Pepsico Summerfare.

2026 Jędrychowski, Zbigniew. "Aktorowie wileńscy w podróży." (Actors from Vilna on Tour.) *PaT.* 1986 Second & Third Qtr; 2-3: 201-220. Notes. Illus.: Photo. Print. B&W. 12. Lang.: Pol.

Poland. 1789-1864. Historical studies. ∎Description of the repertory, casting and stagings of performances by touring companies from Vilna in the cities of Grodno, Petersburg and Druskienniki.

2027 Kallaanvaara, Michael. "Andrzej Wajda." *Entre.* 1986; 13(1): 3-7. Illus.: Photo. B&W. 5: var. sizes. Lang.: Swe.

Poland: Warsaw. 1926-1986. Histories-sources. ∎Andrzej Wajda, leading Polish film and stage director, stresses form and literature in theatre. Polish Romantic drama seems modern today. Polish audiences have limited access to Wajda productions of *Crime and Punishment* and *Antigone*.

2028 Klossowicz, Jan. "Tadeusz Kantor's Journey." *TDR.* 1986 Fall; 30(3): 98-113. Notes. Illus.: Photo. B&W. 17: 3 in. x 3 in. Lang.: Eng.

Poland. 1915-1985. Historical studies. ∎Career of experimental director Tadeusz Kantor: his interest in theatre as a spectacle or a mirror of his inner process.

2029 Kobialka, Michal. "Let the Artists Die? An Interview with Tadeusz Kantor." *TDR.* 1986 Fall; 30(3): 177-183. Illus.: Photo. B&W. 4: 3 in. x 3 in. Lang.: Eng.

Poland. 1967-1985. Histories-sources. ∎Director Tadeusz Kantor: his journey to the present stultification of the creative process.

2030 Komorowski, Jarosław. "Shakespeare w Wilnie (1786-1864)." (Shakespeare in Vilna (1786-1864).) *PaT.* 1986 Second & Third Qtr; 2-3: 181-200. Notes. Illus.: Photo. Print. B&W. 9. Lang.: Pol.

Poland: Vilna. 1786-1864. Historical studies. ∎Description of first translations and adaptations of Shakespeare's dramas on the Polish stage as well as information on staging.

2031 Konic, Paweł. "Nadzieja na Fredre." (A Hope on Friday.) *TeatrW.* 1985 Mar.; 40(822): 16-17. Lang.: Pol.

Poland: Warsaw. 1984. Reviews of performances. ∎Production analysis of *Śluby Panienskie (Maiden Vows)* by Aleksander Fredro, directed by Andrzej Łapicki, staged by Teatr Polski.

2032 Majcherek, Janusz. "Temat Na Inne Opowiadanie." (Theme in Another Story.) *TeatrW.* 1985 Jan.; 40(820): 10-12. Lang.: Pol.

Poland: Cracow. 1984. Reviews of performances. ∎Adaptation of Dostojévskij's *Crime and Punishment* directed by Andrzej Wajda, Teatr Stary.

2033 Majcherer, Janusz. "Rzeczy, Nie Słowa." (Things, Not Words.) *TeatrW.* 1984 Oct.; 39(817): 6-7. Lang.: Pol.

Poland: Warsaw. 1984. Reviews of performances. ∎Production analysis of *Affabulazione* by Pier Paolo Pasolini directed by Tadeusz Łomnicki at Centrum Sztuki Studio.

2034 Marczak-Oborski, Stanisław. *Obszary teatru.* (Regions of Theatre.) Wrocław: Zakład Narodowy im. Ossolińskich; 1986. 273 pp. (Studia i Materiały do Dziejów Teatru Polskiego 18.) Lang.: Pol.

Poland. 1918-1986. Critical studies. ∎Collection of articles of eminent critic and theatre historian Stanisław Marczak-Oborski (1921-1987) including his reflections on traditions and avant-garde in Polish theatre and its place in Europe.

2035 Marrodań, Ewa. "Opowiesz o Balladynie." (A Story About Balladyna.) *TeatrW.* 1985 Apr.; 40(823): 24. Lang.: Pol.

Poland: Toruń. 1984. Reviews of performances. ∎Production analysis of *Balladyna* by Juliusz Słowacki directed by Krystyna Meissner, staged by Teatr Horzycy.

2036 Nawrat, Elżbieta. "Teatr Miejski na Pohulance za dyrekcji Leopolda Pobóg-Kielanowskiego (1938-1940)." (Na Pohulance City Theatre under the Director Leopold Pobóg-Kielanowski (1938-1940).) *PaT.* 1986 Second & Third Qtr; 2-3: 320-358. Notes. Append. Illus.: Photo. Design. Print. B&W. 36. Lang.: Pol.

Poland: Vilna. 1938-1940. Historical studies. ∎Repertory and main artistic achievements of Na Pohulance Theatre, with a listing of repertory and casting.

2037 Nyczek, Tadeusz. "Akademia Ruchu: Poza smugą cienia." (Akademia Ruchu: Beyond the Shadow.) *DialogW.* 1986; 12: 117-123. Lang.: Pol.

Poland: Warsaw. 1973-1986. Critical studies. ∎Artistic profile and main achievements of the Polish experimental theatre from Akademia Ruchu.

2038 Osterloff, Barbara. "'...aby Heńka Z Karolem'." ('...In Order that Heńka and Karol'.) *TeatrW.* 1984 Feb.; 39(809): 21-22. Lang.: Pol.

Poland: Warsaw. 1983. Reviews of performances. ∎Production analysis of *Pornografia (Pornography)* by Witold Gombrowicz, directed by Andrzej Pawłowski at Teatr Ateneum.

2039 Osterloff, Barbara. "Miedzy Gottgerem a Gombrowiczem." (Between Gottger and Gombrowicz.) *TeatrW.* 1984 Mar.; 39(810): 7-9. Illus.: Photo. 1: 10 cm. x 20 cm. Lang.: Pol.

Poland: Poznań. 1984. Reviews of performances. ∎Production analysis of *Dom Otwarty (Open House)* by Michał Bałucki, directed by Janusz Nyczak at Teatr Nowy.

2040 Osterloff, Barbara. "Babicki i *Pulapka*." (Babicki and Trap.) *TeatrW.* 1985 Jan.; 40(820): 20-21. Lang.: Pol.

Poland: Gdansk. 1984. Reviews of performances. ∎Production analysis of *Pulapka (Trap)* by Tadeusz Różewicz, directed by Krzysztof Babicki at Teatr Wybrzeże.

2041 Osterloff, Barbara. "Elzbieta, Krówlowa Anglii." (*Elizabeth, The Queen of England.*) *TeatrW.* 1985 Feb.; 40(821): 21-22. Lang.: Pol.

Poland: Cracow. 1984. Reviews of performances. ∎Performance analysis of *Elisabeth von England (Elizabeth of England)* by Ferdinand Brückner, directed by Laco Adamik, staged by Teatr Telewizji.

2042 Pawlicki, Maciej. "Perwersja i Słodycz." (Perversion and Sweetness.) *TeatrW.* 1985 Mar.; 40(822): 21-22. Lang.: Pol.

DRAMA: —Performance/production

Poland: Bydgoszcz. 1984. Reviews of performances. ■Production analysis of *Iwona, Księzniczka Burgundia (Ivona, Princess of Burgundia)* by Witold Gombrowicz, directed by Krzysztof Rościszewski staged by Teatr Polski.

2043 Prussak, Maria. "Rosjanie w Warszawie." (Russians in Warsaw.) *PaT.* 1986 Fourth Qtr; 4: 601-632. Notes. Illus.: Photo. Print. B&W. 24: 8 cm. x 5 cm., 10 cm. x 7 cm. Lang.: Pol.

Poland. Russia. 1882-1913. Histories-sources. ■Information on visits in Poland of the Russian actors and theatre as well as their political and sociological aspects. Letters of the Russian actors about their visits in Poland are included.

2044 Siedlicki, Krzysztof; Okoński, Ryszard. "Po Grotowskim." (After Grotowski.) *TeatrW.* 1985 Jan.; 40(820): 3-7. Illus.: Photo. 2: 10 cm. x 15 cm. Lang.: Pol.

Poland: Wrocław. 1959-1984. Critical studies. ■Production and style analysis of staging by Teatr Laboratorium directed by Jerzy Grotowski.

2045 Siedlicki, Krzysztof. "O Nas Współczesnych?" (About Us, Contemporary?) *TeatrW.* 1985 Feb.; 40(821): 24-25. Lang.: Pol.

Poland: Warsaw. 1984. Reviews of performances. ■Production analysis of *Dačniki (Summer Folk)* by Maksim Gorkij, directed by Józef Skwark, staged by Teatr Mały.

2046 Sieradzka, Zofia; Plewinski, Wojciech, photo. "Kościół Boga Czy Czarta?" (God's or Evil's Church?) *TeatrW.* 1984 Jan.; 39(808): 14-15. Illus.: Photo. 1: 15 cm. x 11 cm. Lang.: Pol.

Poland: Cracow. 1983. Reviews of performances. ■Production analysis of *Irydion* by Zygmunt Krasiński, directed by Mikołaj Grabowski staged at Teatr im. Słowacki.

2047 Sieradzki, Jacek. "Krzysztof Babicki: Przed sadyszką?" (Krzysztof Babicki: Before a Short Breath?) *DialogW.* 1986; 12 : 124-130. Notes. Lang.: Pol.

Poland. 1982-1986. Critical studies. ■Director Krzysztof Babicki's main artistic achievements as well as analysis of his directorial style.

2048 Sinko, Grzegorz. "Konferencja W Jałcie." (Yalta Conference.) *TeatrW.* 1985 Feb.; 40(821): 15-17. Lang.: Pol.

Poland: Warsaw. 1984. Reviews of performances. ■Production analysis of *Jalta (Yalta)* by Ryszard Frelka, directed by Jerzy Krasowski, staged by Teatr Mały.

2049 Sokolowski, Jerzy. "10e Festival du Théâtre russe et soviétique à Katowice." (10th Festival of Russian and Soviet Drama in Katowice.) *TP.* 1986; 29(4-5): 18-24. Illus.: Photo. Print. B&W. 8. Lang.: Eng, Fre.

Poland: Katowice. USSR. 1985. Critical studies. ■Description of the festival, critical reviews of some productions, the majority of which were classics.

2050 Szydlowski, Roman. "Brecht in Poland." *ComIBS.* 1984 Apr.; 12(2): 61-65.

Poland. 1923-1984. Historical studies. ■A stage history of Brecht's work.

2051 Treugutt, Stefan; Rytka, Zygmunt, photo. "Ksztalt Jnacisk Czasu." (Structure and Time Pressure.) *TeatrW.* 1983 Aug.; 38(803): 18-19. Illus.: Photo. Print. B&W. 1: 20 cm. x 13 cm. Lang.: Pol.

Poland: Warsaw. 1983. Reviews of performances. ■Production analysis of *Hamlet* by William Shakespeare directed by Janusz Warmiński at Teatr Ateneum.

2052 Treugutt, Stefan. "Gombrowicz Nieseminaryjny." (Gombrowicz as Non-Intellectual.) *TeatrW.* 1984 Feb.; 39(809): 20-21. Lang.: Pol.

Poland: Warsaw. 1983. Reviews of performances. ■Production analysis of *Iwona, Ksieznizka Burgundia (Ivona, Princess of Burgundia)* by Witold Gombrowicz, directed by Zygmunt Hübner at Teatr Powszechny.

2053 Treugutt, Stefan. "Wzlot W Zniszczenie." (Flight in Destruction.) *TeatrW.* 1984 Apr.; 39(811): 9-11. Illus.: Photo. 1: 13 cm. x 11 cm. Lang.: Pol.

Poland: Warsaw. 1984. Reviews of performances. ■Production analysis of *Pulapka (Trap)* by Tadeusz Różewicz directed by Jerzy Grzegorzewski staged at Centrum Sztuki Studio.

2054 Vallef, Lillian; Findlay, Robert. *Grotowski and His Laboratory.* New York, NY: Performing Arts Journal; 1986. 185 pp. Append. Illus.: Photo. Sketches. Poster. 34: var. sizes. Lang.: Eng.

Poland. 1958-1986. Biographical studies. ■Chronological portrait of Jerzy Grotowski based on a collection of newspaper accounts, magazine articles and review journals discussing his theatrical experiments, training methodology and his thoughts on the purpose of theatre.

2055 Vinkó, József. "Dögöljenek meg a művészek! Beszélgetés Tadeusz Kantorral." (Let the Artists Strike Dead! Interview with Tadeusz Kantor.) *Sz.* 1986 Feb.; 19(2): 45-48. Illus.: Photo. B&W. 2: 9 cm. x 12 cm. Lang.: Hun.

Poland. 1942-1985. Histories-sources. ■Polish director Tadeusz Kantor speaks about his career, his working methods and his views on art and theatre in general.

2056 Wanat, Andrezej; Hawałej, Adam, photo. "Nowy Don Juan." (A New Don Juan.) *TeatrW.* 1984 Oct.; 39(817): 3-6. Illus.: Photo. 2: 22 cm. x 15 cm., 21 cm. x 16 cm. Lang.: Pol.

Poland: Wrocław. 1984. Reviews of performances. ■Production analysis of *Śmierć Komandura (The Death of the Commander)* by Tomasz Tubieński directed by Eugeniusz Korin at Teatr Polski.

2057 Wanat, Andrzej. "Nie Tylko O *Weselu*." (Not Only About *The Wedding*.) *TeatrW.* 1985 Apr.; 40(823): 12-16. Lang.: Pol.

Poland: Warsaw. 1984. Reviews of performances. ■Production analysis of *Wesele (The Wedding)* by Stanisław Wypiański, directed by Kazimierz Dejmek, staged by Teatr Polski.

2058 Wanat, Andrzej. "*Antygona* ze Starego Teatru." (*Antigone* from Stary Teatr.) *TeatrW.* 1984 June; 39(813): 17-19. 2: 16 cm. x 10 cm., 17 cm. x 11 cm. Lang.: Pol.

Poland: Cracow. 1984. Reviews of performances. ■Production analysis of *Antigone* by Sophocles directed by Andrzej Wajda staged at Stary Teatr.

2059 Wójcik, Lidia. "Koncept Narodowy Gaśnie." (National Concept Is on the Wane.) *TeatrW.* 1985 Feb.; 40(821): 12-14. Lang.: Pol.

Poland: Lublin. 1984. Reviews of performances. ■Production analysis of *Wesele (The Wedding)* by Stanisław Wyspiański directed by Ignacy Gogolewski and staged by Teatr Osterwy.

2060 Žegin, N. "Pol'skie vstreči." (Polish Encounters.) *TeatrM.* 1986; 6: 174-181. Lang.: Rus.

Poland: Katowice. USSR. 1986. Reviews of performances. ■On the Tenth Festival of Russian and Soviet Theatre in Poland.

2061 Zmudzka, Elzbieta; Suchecki, Marek, photo. "Kantor I Jego Niegdysiejsze Śniegi." (Kantor and His Snows of Yesteryear.) *TeatrW.* 1984 Oct.; 39(817): 8-9. Illus.: Photo. 1: 8 cm. x 19 cm. Lang.: Pol.

Poland: Cracow. 1984. Reviews of performances. ■Production analysis of *Gdzie sa Niegdysiejsze Śniegi (Where Are the Snows of Yesteryear)* by Tadeusz Kantor, directed by him and staged by Cricot 2.

2062 Zmudzka, Elzbieta; Pajchel, Elzbieta, photo. "O Gladajac Kartoteke." (Watching *Card Index.*) *TeatrW.* 1984 Aug.; 39(815): 9-11. Illus.: Photo. 1: 21 cm. x 15 cm. Lang.: Pol.

Poland: Warsaw. 1984. Reviews of performances. ■Production analysis of *Kartoteka (Card Index)* by Tadeusz Różewicz directed by Michał Ratyński at Teatr Powszechny.

2063 Kántor, Lajos. "A szinház élete. Kolozsvári jegyzetek." (Life of the Theatre: Notes from Kolozsvár (Cluj).) *Sz.* 1986 Dec.; 19(12): 37-42. Illus.: Photo. 2: var. sizes. Lang.: Hun.

Romania: Cluj. 1984-1985. Critical studies. ■Overview of the season's productions at Állami Magyar Szinház and notes on director György Harag, who died in 1985, including his influence on Hungarian-language theatre in Transylvania.

2064 Majlat, Maria. "Beszélgetés Harag Györggyel." (Interview with György Harag.) *Sz.* 1986 Jan.; 19(1): 42-44. Lang.: Hun.

DRAMA: —Performance/production

Romania: Tîrgu-Mures. 1925-1985. Histories-sources. ■Interview with director György Harag, an ethnic Hungarian of Transylvania, on his final production *Višněvyj sad (The Cherry Orchard)* by Čechov.

2065 Eaton, Katherine Bliss. *The Theater of Meyerhold and Brecht.* Westport, CT: Greenwood; 1986. 142 pp. (Contributions in Drama and Theatre Studies 19.) Pref. Index. Notes. Biblio. Illus.: Photo. Print. B&W. 8: 5 in. x 8 in. Lang.: Eng.

Russia: Moscow. Germany, East: Berlin, East. 1903-1957. Historical studies. ■Study of the techniques and influence of V. E. Mejerchol'd on the work of Bertolt Brecht.

2066 Kovács, Léna. "Ny. Ny. Jevreinov munkássága (1879-1953). Pályakép." (Life and Career of N. N. Jevreinov (1879-1953).) *SzSz.* 1986; 10(19): 85-103. Notes. Lang.: Hun.

Russia. USSR. 1879-1953. Biographical studies. ■Character, career and theories of the director and symbolist playwright Nikolaj Nikolajěvič Jevreinov. Grp/movt: Symbolism.

2067 Lakšin, V. "Lica i 'maski' *Gorjačego serdca.*" (The Faces and 'Masks' of *The Burning Heart.*) *TeatrM.* 1986; 7: 119-133. Lang.: Rus.

Russia. 1869. Historical studies. ■Performance history of *Gorjačego serdca (The Burning Heart)* by Aleksand'r Nikolajěvič Ostrovskij.

2068 Papernyj, Z. *Strelka uskusstva.* (Art's Arrow.) Moscow: Sovremennik; 1986. 254 pp. Lang.: Rus.

Russia. 1860-1986. Historical studies. ■Collection of articles on productions of the plays of Anton Pavlovič Čechov on the dramatic and ballet stage.

2069 Pavan Pagnini, Stefania. "Gogol e il teatro: Le prime del *Revizor.*" (Gogol and Theatre. The First Performances of *Revizor.*) *BiT.* 1986; 3: 7-38. Notes. Biblio. Lang.: Ita.

Russia. 1836. Critical studies. ■Nikolaj Gogol's collaboration in the first production of his play *Revizor (The Inspector General)* revealed particular sensitivity to staging.

2070 Stanislavskij, Konstantin Sergejěvič; Malcovati, Fausto, ed. *Le mie regie (1). Tre sorelle, Il giardino dei ciliegi.* (My Directions (1): *Three Sisters* and *The Cherry Orchard.*) Milan: Ubulibri; 1986. 354 pp. (I libri bianchi.) Pref. Index. Notes. Tables. Biblio. Illus.: Photo. Dwg. B&W. Lang.: Ita.

Russia. 1901-1904. Histories-sources. ■Translation of Čechov's text of *Višněvyj sad (The Cherry Orchard)* and *Tri sestry (Three Sisters)* with Stanislavskij's production notes and photos of the first production. First appeared in Moscow, 1983.

2071 Suchodolov, V. "V bol'šom *Fontannom dome.*" (In the Great *Fontannyj Dom.*) *Neva.* 1986; 5: 196-199. Lang.: Rus.

Russia. 1768-1803. Biographical studies. ■Serf actress P.I. Žemčugova.

2072 Riach, D.W. *A Reconstruction of the 1552 Performance at Cupar of Sir David Lindsay's Ane Satyre of the Thrie Estaitis.* Edinburgh: Univ. of Edinburgh; 1986. Notes. Biblio. Illus.: Maps. [M.Litt. dissertation, *Index to Theses,* 36-6921.] Lang.: Eng.

Scotland: Cupar. 1552-1554. Histories-reconstruction. ■Detailed account of the production, with analysis of the script and variant texts, and a discussion of French influence on Scottish culture.

2073 Schach, Leonard. "Bad Timing." *Drama.* 1986; 160(2): 31-32. Illus.: Photo. B&W. 1. Lang.: Eng.

South Africa, Republic of. UK-England: London. 1986. Critical studies. ■Director of Ronald Harwood's play about apartheid, *Tramway Road,* discusses reception in South Africa.

2074 Arias, Ricardo. "*La navaja,* de Eduardo Quiles: Poética de dramaturgo en espacio escénico." (*The Razor* by Eduardo Quiles: Poetic Text in Scenic Space.) *Estreno.* 1986 Spr; 12(1): 3-4. Lang.: Spa.

Spain. 1980. Historical studies. ■Production description of the symbolist drama *La navaja (The Razor)* by Eduardo Quiles focusing on the extreme contrasts in the sound and lighting effects and the use of sculpted puppets. Related to Puppetry.

2075 Elliott, John R., Jr. "The Rio Gordo Passion Play." *MET.* 1986; 8(1): 63-65. Lang.: Eng.

Spain. 1951-1986. Historical studies. ■Tasks and behavior of stage-hands in a production of this modern passion play.

2076 Martínez Ballesteros, Antonio. "*Los Comediantes*: un poco de historia." (*The Players*: A Bit of History.) *Estreno.* 1986 Aut; 12(2): 35. Illus.: Photo. Print. B&W. 1: 3 1/2 in. x 5 in. Lang.: Spa.

Spain: Toledo. USA: Cincinnati, OH. 1982-1985. Histories-sources. ■Playwright Antonio Martínez Ballesteros discusses the production history of his play *Los Comediantes (The Players)* which he directed and later brought on tour.

2077 Wallace, Robert. "Festival Follies." *CTR.* 1986 Win; 13(49): 111-116. Illus.: Photo. Print. B&W. 3: 4 in. x 5 in., 6 in. x 4 in., 6 in. x 5 in. Lang.: Eng.

Spain. Canada: Montreal, PQ, Toronto, ON. 1986. Critical studies. ■A review of the offerings of international theatre festivals in Spain and Canada.

2078 Zatlin, Phyllis. "Women Directors in Spain: Josefina Molina." *WPerf.* 1986; 3(1): 52-58. Notes. Illus.: Photo. Print. B&W. 2: 2 in. x 3 in. Lang.: Eng.

Spain. 1952-1985. Historical studies. ■Directing career of Josefina Molina, including description of production of *Cinco horas con Mario (Five Hours with Mario).*

2079 Zatlin, Phyllis. "Lope de Vega Winner at Teatro de la Comedia." *Estreno.* 1986 Spr; 12(1): 4-5. Lang.: Eng.

Spain: Madrid. USA: Miami, FL. 1983-1985. Historical studies. ■Production history of *Hay que deshacer la casa (Undoing the Housework)* a two-woman psychological drama by Sebastián Junyent.

2080 Heras, Guillermo; Munné-Jordà, Antoni, transl. "El personatge i el director d'escena en el treball amb els clàssics." (The Character and the Stage Manager Working With Classics.) *EECIT.* 1986 Dec.; 28: 89-106. Biblio. Lang.: Cat.

Spain-Catalonia. 1984. Critical studies. ■Describes conditions attending modern productions of classic plays, arguing the necessity to integrate new analytical methods, such as semiotics, in the recreation of classics.

2081 Lavellim, Jorg; Sadowska-Guillon, Irena; Amsellem, Gerard, photo. "Magia Teatru." (The Magic of Theatre.) *TeatrW.* 1983 Oct.; 38(805): 28-30. Illus.: Photo. Print. B&W. 3: 5 cm. x 4.5 cm., 8 cm. x 13 cm., 8 cm. x 5 cm. Lang.: Pol.

Spain-Catalonia: Barcelona. 1983. Histories-sources. ■Interview with director Jorge Lavelli about Shakespeare production with Estudio Faixat.

2082 Pérez de Olaguer, Gonzalo, ed. *Documents del Centre Dramàtic, 8.* (Documents of the Centre Dramàtic, 8.) Barcelona: Centre Dramàtic de la Generalitat de Catalunya; 1986. 12 pp. Index. Illus.: Design. Pntg. Photo. Print. B&W. 13: var. sizes. Lang.: Cat.

Spain-Catalonia: Barcelona. 1986. Reviews of performances. ■Collected articles on productions of *Savannah Bay* by Marguerite Duras and *Reigen (Round)* by Arthur Schnitzler by the Centre Dramàtic de la Generalitat de Catalunya.

2083 Pérez de Olaguer, Gonzalo, ed. *Documents del Centre Dramàtic, 9.* (Documents of the Centre Dramàtic, 9.) Barcelona: Centre Dramàtic de la Generalitat de Catalunya; 1986. 12 pp. Tables. Illus.: Poster. Photo. Print. B&W. 24: var. sizes. Lang.: Cat.

Spain-Catalonia: Barcelona. France. 1986. Reviews of performances. ■Articles on the 1986-87 theatre season.

2084 Pérez de Olaguer, Gonzalo, ed. *Documents del Centre Dramàtic, 7.* (Documents of the Centre Dramàtic, 7.) Barcelona: Centre Dramàtic de la Generalitat de Catalunya; 1986. 12 pp. Index. Tables. Illus.: Design. Photo. Print. B&W. 22: var. sizes. Lang.: Cat.

Spain-Catalonia: Barcelona. 1976-1986. Reviews of performances. ■Covers the commemoration of Xavier Regàs, the 1985-86 Centre Dramàtic season, a production of *Mutter Courage (Mother Courage)* by the Centro Dramático Nacional and the tenth anniversary of Teatre Lliure.

DRAMA: —Performance/production

2085 Bergman, Gunilla; Edwards, Susanna. "Gastkramande. Bortom skammen." (Hair-raising: Beyond Shame.) *NT.* 1986; 33: 4-9. Illus.: Photo. Lang.: Swe.
Sweden: Gothenburg. 1986. Histories-sources. ■Impressions from the rehearsal of Juoko Turkka's *Kött och kärlek (Flesh and Love)* where the actors are instructed not to 'act'.

2086 Bergström, Gunnel. "Teater samtalet: hur vi talar med varanda i teaterns värld i landet Sverige." (Theatre Conversation: How We Talk to Each Other in the World of Theatre in the Country of Sweden.) *Entre.* 1986; 13(4): 32-34. Illus.: Photo. B&W. 2: 3.5 in. x 8.25 in., 1.75 in. x 3.25 in. Lang.: Swe.
Sweden: Stockholm. 1986. Critical studies. ■A Stanislavskij symposium in Stockholm in May provided a rare opportunity to discuss not only Stanislavskij but also basic issues in acting and directing.

2087 Bladh, Curt. "Det är människan det gäller." (It Is a Matter of Human Beings.) *TArsb.* 1986; 5: 12-16. Illus.: Photo. Print. B&W. Lang.: Swe.
Sweden: Stockholm. 1985-1986. Reviews of performances. ■Productions in the region of Norrland and in Stockholm.

2088 Englund, Claes. "Formens attraktion — eller det passionerade berättandet." (The Attraction of Form — or Telling a Story Passionately.) *TArsb.* 1986; 5: 24-29. Illus.: Photo. Print. B&W. 5. Lang.: Swe.
Sweden: Stockholm, Gothenburg. 1985-1986. Reviews of performances. ■Regional theatre productions in Sweden.

2089 Englund, Claes; Hägglund, Kent; Marko, Susanne; Ring, Lars. "Sommarteater 86." (Summer Theatre 86.) *Entre.* 1986; 13 (4): 2-19. Illus.: Photo. B&W. 22: var. sizes. Lang.: Swe.
Sweden: Stockholm, Södertälje, Karlskrona. 1986. Critical studies. ■Survey of summer 1986 productions throughout Sweden. Great variety of offerings, mostly by amateurs, including several productions of *Fröken Julie (Miss Julie)*.

2090 Larsson, Lisbeth; Ånnerud, Annika, ed. "Fröken Julie och Jean x 3." (Miss Julie and Jean x 3.) *TArsb.* 1986; 5: 9-11. Illus.: Photo. Print. B&W. 3. Lang.: Swe.
Sweden: Stockholm. Denmark: Copenhagen. South Africa, Republic of. 1985-1986. Reviews of performances. ■Review of one television and two theatre productions of Strindberg's *Miss Julie (Fröken Julie)*.

2091 Marklund, Björn. "Vem är galen?" (Who Is Crazy?) *Teaterf.* 1986; 19(2-3): 26. Lang.: Swe.
Sweden: Hedemora. 1985-1986. Histories-sources. ■The staging of an amateur performance of *Leka med elden (Playing With Fire)*.

2092 Marko, Susanne. "Agneta Ekmanner." *Entre.* 1986; 13(2): 3-11. Illus.: Photo. B&W. 8: var. sizes. Lang.: Swe.
Sweden: Stockholm. 1950-1986. Histories-sources. ■Interview with actress Agneta Ekmanner of Stockholm Stadsteater on her approach to role study, collaboration with director Suzanne Osten and her roles in plays by Čechov and Strindberg.

2093 Perrelli, Franco. *August Strindberg. Sul dramma moderno e il teatro moderno.* (August Strindberg: On Modern Drama and Modern Theatre.) Florence: Leo S. Olschki Editore; 1986. 137 pp. (Teatro studi e testi 6.) Pref. Index. Notes. Biblio. Append. Lang.: Ita.
Sweden. 1887-1910. Critical studies. ■Study of playwright August Strindberg's writings on modern theatre, with selections from the works themselves.

2094 Sjögren, Frederik. "Teme Stanislavskij." (Theme Stanislavskij.) *Entré.* 1986; 13(3): 2-32. Illus.: Photo. B&W. 24: var. sizes. Lang.: Swe.
Sweden. 1890-1986. Histories-sources. ■Numerous Swedish and foreign artists trace the history of Stanislavskij's influence on their work as artists and Swedish theatre in general.

2095 Sjögren, Frederik. "Turandot." *Teaterf.* 1986; 19(2-3): 9-10. Illus.: Photo. Lang.: Swe.
Sweden: Stockholm. 1986. Historical studies. ■The cooperation between amateurs and professionals in Fria Proteatern's staging of Brecht's *Turandot*.

2096 Kachler, Karl Gotthilf. *Maskenspiele aus Basler Tradition.* (Tradition of Mask Plays in Basel.) Basel: Christoph Merian; 1986. 224 pp. Pref. Index. Notes. Append. Illus.: Photo. Color. B&W. Lang.: Ger.
Switzerland: Basel. 1936-1974. Histories-specific. ■Function and use of mask in Greek and Roman drama is explained and exemplified in a detailed and widely illustrated account of plays put on stage in the original Roman theatre of Augst near Basel.

2097 Yaron, Elyakim. "Space, Scenery and Action in Dürrenmatt's Plays." *ASSAPHc.* 1986; 3: 191-206. Notes. Lang.: Eng.
Switzerland. 1949-1986. Historical studies. ■Contribution of stage directions concerning stage design and directing to producing plays by Friedrich Dürrenmatt.

2098 Hatch, Jim; Billops, Camille. "Wu Jing-Jyi: Director and Producer." *AInf.* 1986; 4: 134-151. [April 10, 1983.] Lang.: Eng.
Taiwan. USA: Minneapolis, MN, New York, NY. 1939-1980. Histories-sources. ■Wu Jing-Jyi about his life as a young man in Taiwan, his start in theater in New York in 1967, his return to Taiwan to develop the Lan-Ling Experimental Theatre Workshop using a blend of ancient Chinese theatre techniques and Western experimental theatre training.

2099 "Reviews of Productions." *LTR.* 1986 Jan 29-Feb 11; 6(3): 133-139. Lang.: Eng.
UK. 1986. ■*Hamlet* by William Shakespeare, dir by Cicely Berry at the Cottesloe Theatre: rev by Hiley, Lee. *Hippolytus* by Euripides, transl. by Mark McGlynn, dir by Kathryn Mead at the Gate Theatre (Notting Hill, London): rev by Edwardes, Kouril. *Totally Foxed* by Justin Greene and Steve Cooke, dir by Greene at the Nuffield Theatre (Southampton): rev by Martin, Shorter, Young. *John Bull's Other Island* by George Bernard Shaw, dir by Bill Pryde and Stephen Rayne at the Arts Theatre (Cambridge, UK): rev by Coveney, Morley, Shorter. *Are You Sitting Comfortably* by Sue Townsend, dir by Naria Aitken at the Palace Theatre (Watford, UK): rev by Barber, Billington, Hoyle, King. *Friends and Lovers* by Carlo Goldoni, transl by Robert David Macdonald, for the Citizen's Theatre Company at the Citizen's Theatre (Glasgow): rev by Ratcliffe. *Medea* by Euripides, transl by Jeremy Brooks, dir by Toby Robertson at the Theatre Clwyd (Mold, Wales): rev by Billington, Hoyle, Ratcliffe, Shorter.

2100 "Reviews of Productions." *LTR.* 1986 Jan 15-28; 6(2): 82-85. Lang.: Eng.
UK: London. 1986. ■*The Scarlet Pimpernel* by Baroness Orczy, adapted by Beverley Cross, dir by Nicholas Hytner at Her Majesty's Theatre: rev by Chaillet. *Les Liaisons Dangereuses* by Christopher Hampton, dir by Howard Davies at The Pit: rev by Tinker. *The Little Clay Cart* adapted by Jatinder Verma from classic by Shudraka, dir by Verma at the Arts Theatre: rev by Bryce. *The Pajama Game*, a musical based on Richard Bissell's *7 1/2 Cents*, dir by Mike Ockrent at the Leicester Theatre: rev by Ratcliffe. *Gregory's Girl* by Bill Forsyth, dir by Ian Forrest at the Coliseum (Oldham): rev by Keatley. *Hotel Vietnam* by Phil Melling at the Taliesin Arts Centre, Swansea: rev by Adams. *The Spanish Bawd* by Fernando De Rojas, dir by Philip Prowse at the Citizens' Theatre (Glasgow): rev by Billington, Ratcliffe, Shorter. *The Enchanted Birds' Nest* by J.C. Grimmelhauser, transl by Julian Hilton for the Medieval Players Warwich Arts Centre at the Citizens' Theatre (Glasgow): rev by Ratcliffe.

2101 "Reviews of Productions." *LTR.* 1986 Jan 15-28; 6(2): 75-82. Lang.: Eng.
UK. 1986. ■*No Son of Mine* by Philippe Gaulier, dir by Gaulier at the ICA Theatre: rev by Cotton, de Jongh, Edwardes. *The Merry Wives of Windsor* by William Shakespeare, the Royal Shakespeare Company production, dir by Bill Alexander at the Barbican Theatre: rev by Barber, Billington, Coveney, Edwards, Harron, Hirschhorn, Hoyle, King, Morley, Nathan, Nightingale, Rose, St. George, Shulman, Tinker. *Ourselves Alone* by Anne Devlin, dir by Simon Curtis at the Royal Court Theatre: rev by Morley. *Hamlet* by William Shakespeare, dir by Cicely Berry at the Cottesloe Theatre: rev by Atkins, de Jongh, Rissik. *Beauty and the Beast*, Louise Page's adaptation by Jules Wright for the Women's Playhouse Trust at the Old Vic Theatre: rev by Chaillet. *Peter Pan*, a musical production of the play by James M. Barrie, dir by Roger Redfarn at the Aldwych Theatre: rev by Chaillet. *As You Like It* by

DRAMA: —Performance/production

William Shakespeare, dir by Nicholas Hytner at the Royal Exchange Theatre (Manchester): rev by Chaillet. *The Cherry Orchard* by Anton Čechov, dir by Mike Alfreds at the Cottesloe Theatre: rev by Chaillet.

2102 "Reviews of Productions." *LTR*. 1986 Feb 26-Mar 11; 6(5): 238-240. Lang.: Eng.

UK. 1986. ■*Bailegangaire* by Tom Murphy, dir by Garry Hynes at the Donmar Warehouse: rev by Pascal. *The Apple Cart* by George Bernard Shaw, dir by Val May at the Theatre Royal, Haymarket: rev by Pascal. *Rakshasa's Ring* by Visakhadatta, dir by Anton Phillips at the Arts Theatre: rev by Bryce. *No Son of Mine* by Philippe Gaulier, dir by Gaulier at the ICA Theatre: rev by Bryce. *Travelling Nowhere*, rev by Connor. *The Game of Love and Chance* by Marivaux, at the Nuffield Theatre (Southampton): rev by Lewis, Shorter. *Hedda Gabler* by Henrik Ibsen, dir by Annie Castledine at the Theatre Clwyd (Mold, Wales): rev by Hoyle, Thornber. *Peer Gynt* by Henrik Ibsen, dir by John Doyle at the Ralph Richardson Studio, Cheltenham: rev by Young.

2103 "Reviews of Productions." *LTR*. 1986 Mar 12-25; 6(6): 295-299. Lang.: Eng.

UK. 1986. ■*Shirley Valentine or St. Joan of the Fitted Units* by Willy Russell, dir by Glen Walford at the Everyman Theatre (Liverpool): rev by Coveney, Shorter, Thornber, Williams. *Carmen Jones* book and lyrics by Oscar Hammerstein II, dir by Steven Pimlott and Clare Venables at the Crucible Theatre (Sheffield): rev by Ratcliffe, Shorter, Thornber, Young. *The Mad Adventures of a Knight* by Richard Curtis and others, dir by John Retallack at the Coliseum Theatre (Oldham): rev by Flint. *Mr. Government* by Stuart Paterson, dir by Hugh Hodgart at the Royal Lyceum Theatre (Edinburgh): rev by Clifford, Hoyle, Royal. *The Cheeky Chappie* by Dave Simpson, dir by Howard Lloyd-Lewis at the Library Theatre (Manchester): rev by O'Neill. *Orphans* by Lyle Kessler, dir by Gary Sinise at the Hampstead Theatre: rev by Couling, Morley. Liza Minnelli with The Footlockers at the London Palladium: rev by Morley.

2104 Cousin, Geraldine. "The Touring of the Shrew." *NTQ*. 1986 Aug.; 11(7): 275-281. Illus.: Photo. B&W. 3. Lang.: Eng.

UK. 1985-1986. Historical studies. ■An examination of two touring productions of *The Taming of the Shrew* by the Medieval Players and the Royal Shakespeare Company and a discussion of the problems in staging the play's politics.

2105 Evans, Peter. "'To the oak, to the oak!' The Finale of *The Merry Wives of Windsor*." *TN*. 1986; 40(3): 106-114. Notes. Illus.: Photo. Print. B&W. 1: 6 in. x 4 in. Lang.: Eng.

UK. 1874-1985. Critical studies. ■A comparison of alternative solutions to problems of reconciling the final scene of Shakespeare's *The Merry Wives of Windsor* with a naturalistic framework, with 19th and 20th century examples.

2106 Guinness, Alec. *Blessings In Disguise*. New York, NY: Knopf; 1986. xiv, 238 pp. Notes. Index. Illus.: Photo. Sketches. Print. B&W. 16: var. sizes. Lang.: Eng.

UK. USA. 1914-1985. Biographies. ■Autobiography of actor Alec Guinness. Related to Media: Film.

2107 "Plays International December 1986 Bumper Theatre Annual Issue." *PI*. 1986 Dec.; 2(5). Lang.: Eng.

UK-England: London. 1986. Reviews of performances. ■Theatre season in London.

2108 "Fringe Life after the Death of the GLC." *PI*. 1986 Dec.; 2(5): 38-39. Illus.: Photo. B&W. 1. Lang.: Eng.

UK-England: London. 1986. Reviews of performances. ■Review of alternative theatre productions including *Joyriders* and *The Great White Hope* at the Tricycle Theatre, *Road* and *Ourselves Alone* at the Royal Court Theatre.

2109 "Reviews of Productions." *LTR*. 1986 Jan 1-14; 6(1): 5-20. Lang.: Eng.

UK-England: London. 1986. ■*The Story of the Eye and the Tooth* presented by the El Hakawati Theatre at the Almeida, dir by François Abu Salem: rev by Billington, Coveney, Hiley, King, Mackenzie, Nathan, Pascal, Ratcliffe. *Pulp*, Siren Theatre Company, dir by Noelle Janaczewski at Drill Hall: rev by Radin. *Othello* by William Shakespeare, dir by Terry Hands at the Barbican: rev by Barber, Couling, Coveney, de Jongh, Edwards, Gardner, Hiley, Hirschhorn,

King, Nightingale, Nathan, Shulman, Tinker. *Father's Lying Dead on the Ironing Board* written and directed by Agnes Bernelle at King's Head: rev by Connor, Ratcliffe. *Les Liaisons Dangereuses* by Christopher Hampton, dir by Howard Davies at The Pit: rev by Barber, Bardsley, Billington, Coveney, Edwards, Gardner, Hirschhorn, Hurren, Morley, Nathan, Nightingale, Say, Shulman. *Beryl and the Perils*, written and performed by Beryl and the Perils at the Watermans: rev by Rea. *The Little Clay Cart* adapted by Jatinder Verma from the 8th century classic by Shudraka, dir by Verma at the Arts: rev by Dickson, Eccles, Hall, Hiley, Murdin, Nathan, Rea, St. George.

2110 "Reviews of Productions." *LTR*. 1986 Jan 1-14; 6(1): 21-36. Lang.: Eng.

UK-England: London. 1986. ■*Hamlet* by William Shakespeare, dir by Cicely Berry at the Cottesloe: rev by Coveney. *Frikzhan* by Marius Brill, dir by Mike Afford at the Soho Poly: rev by Kaye, Mackenzie. *Elmer Gantry*, musical by Steve Brown adapted from the novel by Sinclair Lewis, dir by Giles Croft at the Gate: rev by Barber, Billington, Cotton, Coveney, Hiley, Mackenzie, Morley, Murdin, Nathan, Ratcliffe, Say. *Striking Silence* by Louise Hide, dir by Christa van Raalte at the Tabard: rev by Eccles, Radin. *Ourselves Alone* by Anne Devlin, dir by Simon Curtis at the Theatre Upstairs: rev by Nightingale. *American Buffalo* by David Mamet, dir by Robert Walker at the Old Red Lion: rev by Billington, Edwards, Hay, King, Renton, Say. *The Life and Adventures of Nicholas Nickleby* adapted by David Edgar from the novel by Charles Dickens, dir by Trevor Nunn and John Caird at the RSC: rev by Barber, Billington, Gardner, Hurren, Keatley, King, Morley, Ratcliffe.

2111 "Reviews of productions." *LTR*. 1986 Jan 1-14; 6(1): 36-41. Lang.: Eng.

UK-England. 1986. ■*As You Like It* by William Shakespeare at the Royal Exchange (Manchester), dir by Nicholas Hytner: rev by Barber, Coveney, O'Neill, Ratcliffe, Thornber. *The Importance of Being Earnest* by Oscar Wilde, dir by Richard Williams at the Oxford Playhouse: rev by Billington, Shorter. *Travesties* by Tom Stoppard, dir by Richard Williams at the Oxford Playhouse: rev by Ratcliffe, Young. *Cinderella*, a pantomime by Warner Brown, at the London Palladium: rev by Hiley. *Beauty and the Beast* adapted by Louise Page, a Women's Playhouse Trust production dir by Jules Wright at the Old Vic: rev by Hiley, Nightingale, Pascal. *Peter Pan*, a musical production of the play by James M. Barrie, dir by Roger Redfarn at the Aldwych: rev by Hiley, Morley. *Judy* by Terry Wales, dir by John David at the Greenwich: rev by Hay. *The Go-Go Boys*, written, dir and performed by Howard Lester and Andrew Alty at the Lyric Studio: rev by Connor.

2112 "Reviews of productions." *LTR*. 1986 Jan 1-14; 6(1): 41-43. Lang.: Eng.

UK-England: London. 1986. ■*The Cherry Orchard* by Anton Čechov, dir by Mike Alfreds at the Cottesloe: rev by Morley, O'Shaughnessy. *As You Like It* by William Shakespeare, dir by Adrian Noble at the Barbican Theatre: rev by O'Shaughnessy. *The Tell-Tale Heart* by Edgar Allan Poe, performed by Steven Berkoff at the Donmar Warehouse Theatre: rev by Morley, Nightingale. *Yonadab* by Peter Shaffer, dir by Peter Hall at the Olivier Theatre: rev by Morley. *Edmond* by David Mamet, dir by Richard Eyre at the Royal Court: rev by Morley. *Harry's Christmas* performed and written by Steven Berkoff at the Donmar Warehouse: rev by Morley, Nightingale. *Dracula, or Out For The Count* adapted by Charles McKeown from the novel by Bram Stoker, dir by Peter James at the Lyric Hammersmith: rev by Nightingale. *Melons* by Bernard Pomerance, dir by Alison Sutcliffe at The Pit: rev by Bardsley, Couling, Morley, St. George, Slater.

2113 "Reviews of Productions." *LTR*. 1986 Jan 29-Feb 11; 6(3): 93-110. Lang.: Eng.

UK-England: London. 1986. ■*Philistines* by Maksim Gorkij adapted by Dusty Hughes, dir by John Caird for the Royal Shakespeare Company at The Pit: rev by Couling, de Jongh, Gardner, Harron, Hiley, Hoyle, King, Mackenzie, Murdin, Nathan, Nightingale, Shorter, Slater. *Better Than A Leech* devised and directed by Brian Stirner at Soho Poly: rev by de Jongh, Mackenzie, Osborne-Clarke. *Pride and Prejudice*, David Pownell's adaptation of Jane Austen, dir by Bill Pryde at the Old Vic Theatre: rev by Barber, Billington, Chaillet, Coveney, Denselow, Hirschhorn, Hurren, Jacobs, Kaye, King, Morley, Ratcliffe, Rose, Shulman, Tinker. *Don Carlos* by Friedrich von Schiller, transl by R.D.

DRAMA: —Performance/production

Boylan, dir by Malcolm Edwards at the Bridge Lane: rev by Eccles, Lee. *Enough/Footfalls/Rockaby*, three pieces by Samuel Beckett, dir by Alan Schneider at the Riverside Studios: rev by Couling, Coveney, Gill, Hiley, King, Radin, Ratcliffe, Wolf. *Blithe Spirit* by Noël Coward, dir by Peter Farago at the Vaudeville Theatre: rev by Barber, Billington, Coveney, Dickson, Edwards, Hiley, Hirschhorn, Hurren, Jameson, King, Mackenzie, Morley, Nathan, Ratcliffe, Shulman, Tinker. *Alterations* by Michael Abbensetts, dir by Steve Addison at the Theatre Royal: rev. by Barber, Billington, Hay, Hoyle, McKenley, Nathan, Ratcliffe.

2114   "Reviews of Productions." *LTR*. 1986 Jan 29-Feb 11; 6(3): 111-126. Lang.: Eng.
UK-England. 1986. ■*A Quiet End* by Robin Swados, dir by Noel Greig at the Offstage Downstairs: rev by de Jongh, Gardner, Mackenzie, Morley. *Spinning a Yarn* by Noel Greig, dir by Nic Fine at Drill Hall: rev by Gordon, McFerran, Radin, Wolf. *The Trapping Antelope* by Rachel Silver and Anne Rigel, dir by Chris Salt at the Young Vic Studio: rev by Barber, Cotton, Mackenzie, Nathan, Radin. *Rakshasa's Ring* by Visakhadatta, dir by Anton Phillips at the Arts Theatre: rev by Billington, Hay, King, McKenley. *Three Storeys and A Dark Cellar*, the IOU Theatre Company at the Almeida Theatre: rev by Coveney. *Ravens* by Kate Martin, dir by D. Shemilt-Duly presented by Meta-Obscura Theatre Company at the Man In The Moon: rev by Horsford, Rose. *Women Beware Women* by Thomas Middleton, adapted and completed by Howard Backer, dir by William Gaskill at the Royal Court Theatre: rev by Barber, Barkley, Billington, Coveney, Edwards, Gardner, Grant, Hiley, Hurren, King, Morley, Nathan, Nightingale, Ratcliffe, Shulman, Tinker.

2115   "Reviews of Productions." *LTR*. 1986 Jan 29-Feb 11; 6(3): 126-133. Lang.: Eng.
UK-England. 1986. ■*Cloud 9* by Caryl Churchill, dir by Chris Fisher at the Latchmere Theatre: rev by Eccles, Fox. *A Month of Sundays* by Bob Larbey, dir by Justin Greene at the Duchess Theatre: rev by Barber, Barkley, Hurren, Nathan, Shulman, Tinker, Young. *An Independent Woman* devised by Natasha Morgan, dir by Dusty Hughes at the Watermans Theatre (Brentford): rev by Billington, Coveney, Gardner, Gordon, Kent, Mackenzie, Nathan. *Romeo and Juliet* by William Shakespeare, dir by David Thacker at the Young Vic: rev by Barber, Fox, Gordon, Grier, Tinker, Wolf. *Ladies in Waiting* by Ellen Fox, dir by Simon Usher at the Finborough Theatre Club: rev by Gawthrop, McFerran. *Mamma December* by Nigel D. Moffat, dir by Alby James at The Place: rev by Hay, McKenley. *Les Liaisons Dangereuses* by Christopher Hampton, dir by Howard Davies at The Pit: rev by Chaillet.

2116   "Reviews of Productions." *LTR*. 1986 Jan 15-28; 6(2): 53-58. Lang.: Eng.
UK-England: London. 1986. ■*A Day Down A Goldmine*, a collaboration between actor Bill Paterson, sculptor George Wyllie and musician Tony Gorman, dir by Kenny Ireland at the ICA Theatre: rev by Connor, McFerran, Radin, Shulman. *Chameleon* by Michael Ellis, dir by Alby James at the YAA Asantewa Arts Centre (London): rev by Hay, McKenley. *All You Deserve* by Debbie Horsfield, dir by Alby James at the YAA Asantewa Arts Centre: rev by Hay, McKenley. *The Promise* by Aleksej Arbuzov, dir by Nicholas Mahon at the Latchmere: rev by Alexander, Renton. *Flann O'Brien's Hard Life* by Kerry Crabbe, dir by Deborah Bestwick at the Tricycle Theatre: rev by Hiley, Kaye, Mackenzie, Shulman. *Charlie and the Chocolate Factory*, Jeremy Raison's adaptation of Roald Dahl's book, dir by Kim Grant at Sadler's Wells: rev by Jameson, McFerran. *Balls and Chains*, written, dir and performed by Howard Lester and Andrew Alty at the Lyric Studio: rev by Bryce, de Jongh, Gardner, Hiley, Hoyle, King, Rose, Shorter.

2117   "Reviews of Productions." *LTR*. 1986 Jan 15-28; 6(2): 59-74. Lang.: Eng.
UK-England: London. 1986. ■*Bouncers* by John Godber, dir by Godber at the Donmar Warehouse: rev by King, Lee, Morley, Rose. *Traitors* by Melanie Phillips, dir by Julia Pascale at Drill Hall: rev by Bryce, Eccles, Hoyle, Hurren, Nathan, Wolf. *The Jackpot* by Kevin Clarke, dir by Clarke at the Finborough Theatre Club: rev by Eccles, Horsford. *The Light Rough* by Brian Thompson, dir by Michael Attenborough at the Hampstead: rev by Billington, Denselow, Fox,

Hirschhorn, Hoyle, Hurren, King, Mackenzie, Morley, Nathan, Nightingale, Shorter, Shulman, Ratcliffe, Tinker. *A Journey to London* by John Vanbrush and James Saunders, dir by Sam Water at the Orange Tree: rev by Billington, Coveney, Edwards, Hay, King, Matheou. *The Oven Glove Murders* by Nick Darke, dir by Mike Bradwell at the Bush: rev by Barber, Billington, Coveney, Denselow, Edwards, Gardener, Hiley, Kent, Morley, Nathan, Ratcliffe, Shulman.

2118   "Reviews of Productions." *LTR*. 1986 Feb 12-25; 6(4): 149-163. Lang.: Eng.
UK-England: London. 1986. ■*Progress* by Doug Lucie, dir by David Hayman at the Lyric Hammersmith: rev by Barber, Barkley, Coveney, de Jongh, Fox, Gordon, Hiley, Hurren, King, McFerran, Morley, Nathan, Nightingale, Shulman, Tinker. *Not About Heroes* by Stephen MacDonald, dir by Michael Simpson at the Cottesloe Theatre: rev by Barber, Connor, Coveney, de Jongh, Hurren, King, Morley, Nathan, Nightingale, Rose, Shulman, Tinker. *One of Us* by Robin Chapman, dir by Alan Strachan at the Greenwich Theatre: rev by Barber, Coveney, de Jongh, Gardner, Gordon, Hiley, Jacobs, King, Hurren, Mackenzie, Morley, Murdin. *Joyriders* by Christina Reid, dir by Pip Broughton at the Tricycle Theatre: rev by Connor, Coveney, de Jongh, Denselow, Mackenzie, Nathan, Ratcliffe. *Satre Day/Night* by Adrian Mitchell, dir by Richard Williams at the Lyric Studio: rev by Edwardes, Hoyle, King, Morley, Scaife, Shorter, Shulman.

2119   "Reviews of Productions." *LTR*. 1986 Feb 12-25; 6(4): 163-176. Lang.: Eng.
UK-England: London. 1986. ■*A Taste of Orton*, two works by Joe Orton, dir by Paul Tomlinson at the King's Head Theatre: rev by Connor, de Jongh, Rose. *Bailegangaire* by Tom Murphy, dir by Garry Hynes at the Donmar Warehouse: rev by Barber, Coveney, de Jongh, Fox, Hurren, King, Mackenzie, Ratcliffe, St. George, Shulman. *The Apple Cart* by George Bernard Shaw, dir by Val May at the Theatre Royal, Haymarket (London): rev by Barber, Barkley, Coveney, de Jongh, Edwards, Gordon, Hiley, Hurren, Jameson, King, Mackenzie, Morley, Nathan, Shulman, Tinker. *Thee Thy Thou Thine* devised and performed by Rose English at the ICA Theatre: rev by Wolf. *The Power of Theatrical Madness*, conceived and dir by Jan Fabre at Royal Albert Hall: rev by de Jongh, Mackenzie, Wolf.

2120   "Reviews of Productions." *LTR*. 1986 Feb 12-25; 6(4): 177-190. Lang.: Eng.
UK-England. 1986. ■*Glengarry Glen Ross* by David Mamet, dir by Bill Bryden at the Mermaid Theatre: rev by Barber, de Jongh, Edwards, Gardner, Grant, Hiley, Hoyle, Hurren, King, Jacobs, Morley, Shulman, Tinker. *Brighton Beach Memoirs* by Neil Simon, dir by Michael Rudman at the Lyttelton Theatre: rev by Barber, Barkley, Billington, Coveney, Edwards, Gardner, Grant, Hiley, Hurren, Jameson, King, Morley, Nathan, Nightingale, St. George, Shulman, Tinker. *A Month of Sundays* by Bob Larbey, dir by Justin Greene at the Duchess Theatre: rev by Connor, Edwardes, Hiley, Jameson, Morley. *Riddley Walker* by Russell Hoben, dir by Brahan Murray at the Royal Exchange Theatre (Manchester): rev by Hoyle, Ratcliff. *Three Sisters (Tri sestry)* by Anton Čechov, dir by Paul Unwin at the Old Vic Theatre (Bristol): rev by Shorter. *Goat* by Louise Page, dir by Pip Broughton at the Croydon Warehouse: rev by Billington.

2121   "Reviews of Productions." *LTR*. 1986 Feb 26-Mar 11; 6(5): 197-208. Lang.: Eng.
UK-England: London. 1986. ■*The Black Jacobins* by C.L.R. James, dir by Yvonne Brewster at the Riverside Studios: rev by Bryce, Couling, Coveney, de Jongh, Edwardes, Fox, Gordon, Shorter. *The Pirate Princess*, a Jamaican pantomime by Barbara Gloudon, dir by Alby James and Paulette Randall at the Arts Theatre: rev by Hay, McKenley. *I Do Not Like Thee Doctor Fell* by Bernard Farrell, dir by Robert Shaw at the Old Red Lion Theatre: rev by Connor. *Across From the Garden of Allah* by Charles Wood, dir by Ron Daniels at the Comedy Theatre: rev by Barber, Billington, Couling, Coveney, Hiley, Hurren, Jameson, King, McFerran, Morley, Nathan, Nightingale, Ratcliffe, Shulman, Tinker, Wheen, Wolf. *My Song Is Free* by Joyce Diaz, dir by Susan Todd at Drill Hall Theatre: rev by Eccles, Lee. *The Saxon Shore* by David Rudkin, dir by Pierre Audi at the Almeida Theatre: rev by Barber, Billington, Couling, Coveney, Gordon, Hiley, Hurren, King, Nightingale, Pascal, Ratcliffe, Rissik, Shulman.

CLASSED ENTRIES

DRAMA: —Performance/production

2122 "Reviews of Productions." *LTR*. 1986 Feb 26-Mar 11; 6(5): 208-220. Lang.: Eng.
UK-England: London. 1986. ▪*Short Change* by Terry Heaton, dir by Tim Fywell at the Theatre Upstairs: rev by Billington, Coveney, Gardner, Gordon, Rose, Shorter. *Jeanne*, a musical by Shirlie Roden, dir by Bill Kenwright at Sadler's Wells Theatre: rev by Barber, Billington, Coveney, Gardener, Hiley, Hurren, King, McFerran, Nathan, Ratcliffe, St. George, Shulman, Tinker, Wheen. *Sauce For The Goose*, transl. by Peter Meyer of *Le Dindon* by Georges Feydeau, dir by Sam Walters at the Orange Tree Theatre: rev by Fox, Hoyle. *Medea* by Euripides, transl by David Wiles, dir by Marina Caldarone at the Gate Theatre (Notting Hill, London): rev by Edwardes, Hoyle, McGivering, Shorter. *When We Are Married* by J.B. Priestley, dir by Ronald Eyre at the Whitehall Theatre: rev by Coveney, de Jongh, Denselow, Gordon, Hiley, Hirschhorn, Hurren, Jameson, King, Nathan, Nightingale, Ratcliffe, Rose, Shannon, Shorter, Shulman, Tinker, Wolf.

2123 "Reviews of Productions." *LTR*. 1986 Feb 26-Mar 11; 6(5): 220-238. Lang.: Eng.
UK-England: London. 1986. ▪*Lend Me a Tenor* by Ken Ludwig, dir by David Gilmore at the Globe Theatre: rev by Barber, Billington, Coveney, Edwardes, Gordon, Hiley, Hirschhorn, Hurren, Jameson, King, Nathan, Ratcliffe, Shulman, Tinker, Wheen, Wolf. *Rowan Atkinson: the New Revue* by Dick Curtis and Ben Elton with Rowan Atkinson, dir by Robin Lefevre at the Shaftsbury Arts Centre: rev by Barber, Billington, Connor, Coveney, Edwardes, Gordon, Hiley, Hirschhorn, Jacobs, Jameson, King, Nightingale, Ratcliffe, Shannon, Shulman, Tinker, Wheen. Liza Minnelli with The Footlockers at the London Palladium: rev by Bamigboye, Billson, Brooks, Brown, Clayton, Grant, Harron, Hirschhorn, Hoyle, Murdin, Shorter. *Blood, Sweat and Tears* by John Godber, dir by Godber at the Tricycle Theatre: rev by Barber, Coveney, Gardner, Hiley, Rose, Say, Shulman. *Orphans* by Lyle Kessler, dir by Gary Sinise at the Hampstead Theatre: rev by Barber, Billington, Coveney, Edwardes, Edwards, Fox, Hiley, Hirschhorn, Hurren, King, Nathan, Ratcliffe, Shulman, Tinker.

2124 "Reviews of Productions." *LTR*. 1986 Mar 12-25; 6(6): 249-265. Lang.: Eng.
UK-England: London. 1986. ▪*Matthew, Mark, Luke and Charlie* by Robert Gillespie, dir by Gillespie at the Latchmere Theatre: rev by Billington, Dickson, Hoyle, McFerran, St. George. *Cafe Puccini* by Robin Ray based on the life and music of Giacomo Puccini, dir by Christopher Renshaw at Wyndham's Theatre: rev by Billington, Coveney, Denselow, Edwardes, Hurren, Jameson, King, Morley, Murdin, Nathan, Nightingale, Shannon, Shorter, Tinker, Wheen, Wolf. *I Do Like To Be* by Shane Connaughton, dir by Jeff Teace at the Soho Poly Theatre: rev by de Jongh, Hoyle, McKenley, Rose. *The Three Penny Opera* by Bertolt Brecht and Kurt Weill, dir by Peter Wood at the Olivier Theatre: rev by Billington, Connor, Couling, Coveney, Edwards, Hiley, Hirschhorn, Hurren, Jameson, King, Morley, Nathan, Nightingale, Ratcliffe, Rose, St. George, Shannon, Shulman, Stadlen, Tinker. *The Futurists* by Dusty Hughes, dir by Richard Eyre at the Cottesloe Theatre: rev by Barber, Billington, Couling, Coveney, Edwards, Gardner, Harron, Hiley, Hurren, King, Lawson, Nathan, Nightingale, Shannon, Shulman, Tinker.

2125 "Reviews of Productions." *LTR*. 1986 Mar 12-25; 6(6): 266-281. Lang.: Eng.
UK-England: London. 1986. ▪*Made in Bangkok* by Anthony Minghella, dir by Michael Blakemore at the Aldwych Theatre: rev by Barber, Billington, Coveney, Edwardes, Gardner, Harron, Hiley, Hirschhorn, Hurren, Jameson, King, Morley, Nathan, Sharman, Shulman, Tinker. *A Midsummer Night's Dream* by William Shakespeare, dir by Declan Donnellan at the Donmar Warehouse: rev by Connor, de Jongh, Harron, Hoyle, Rose, Shorter. *After Aida* by Julian Mitchell, dir by Howard Davies at the Old Vic Theatre: rev by Barber, Billington, Coveney, Gardner, Harron, Hiley, King, Hirschhorn, Hurren, Jameson, Morley, Nathan, Nightingale, Rose, St. George, Shannon, Shulman, Tinker, Wheen, Williamson. *Eleanor and Felix* by Dot Rubin, dir by Deborah Hearn at the Man In The Moon Theatre: rev by Matheou, Senter. *Far From the Madding Crowd*, adapted from the novel by Thomas Hardy, at the Man In The Moon Theatre: rev by Matheou.

2126 "Reviews of Productions." *LTR*. 1986 Mar 12-25; 6(6): 282-295. Lang.: Eng.

UK-England: London. 1986. ▪*Circus Senso*, a Rock and Roll circus presented by Alternative Arts, J.H. Productions and the Combination Ltd., dir by John Turner at the Little Big Top, Jubilee Gardens (London): rev by Burno, Hall, Khan. *China* by Mark Brennan, dir by Simon Stokes at the Bush Theatre: rev by de Jongh, Edwardes, Gardner, Hurren, Murdin, Nathan, Shorter, Thorncroft. *The Man of Mode* by George Etherege, dir by Declan Donnellan at the Donmar Warehouse: rev by de Jongh, Edwards, Hoyle, King, Shorter, Shulman. *Milva Sings Brecht* dir by Giorgio Strehler at the Almeida Theatre: rev by Brown, Clements. *Moon On A Rainbow Shawl* by Errol John, dir by Errol John at the Theatre Royal, Stratford East (London): rev by Coveney, Fox, Hay, Hiley. *The Normal Heart* by Larry Kramer, dir by David Hayman at the Royal Court Theatre: rev by Coveney, de Jongh, Gardner, Gill, Hiley, Hirschhorn, Hurren, Jameson, King, Nathan, Nightingale, Ratcliffe, Shannon, Shorter, Shulman, Usher, Wheen.

2127 Allen, David. "Exploring the Limitless Depths: Mike Alfreds Directs Chekhov." *NTQ*. 1986 Nov.; 11(8): 320-335. Notes. Illus.: Photo. B&W. 7. Lang.: Eng.
UK-England: London. USSR. 1975-1986. Historical studies. ▪Mike Alfreds' Čechov productions show a recognition of the distinctively 'Russian' qualities of the plays, and an ability to render these in terms of the choices available to British actors.

2128 Bardsley, Barney. "Othello Unchained." *Drama*. 1986; 159(1): 14-16. Illus.: Photo. B&W. 2. Lang.: Eng.
UK-England. 1986. Histories-sources. ▪Interview with actors Ben Kingsley and David Suchet on their roles as Othello and Iago in the Royal Shakespeare Company production of Shakespeare's *Othello*.

2129 Berry, Ralph. "Hamlet's Doubles." *SQ*. 1986 Sum; 37(2): 204-212. Notes. Lang.: Eng.
UK-England: London. 1900-1985. Critical studies. ▪Doubling of roles in *Hamlet* by William Shakespeare for purely conceptual reasons, special references to performances in which Ghost/Claudius, Ghost/Hamlet, Ghost/Player, King/Fortinbras are doubled.

2130 Billington, Michael. "Not a Grand National Year." *PI*. 1986 Dec.; 2(5): 28-31. B&W. 4. Lang.: Eng.
UK-England: London. 1986. Reviews of performances. ▪Survey of the season at the National Theatre: *The Cherry Orchard* directed by Mike Alfreds, *Yonadab* directed by Peter Shaffer. Also Arthur Schnitzler's *Dalliance*, Arthur Miller's *The American Clock* and Miguel Piñero's *The Magistrate*.

2131 Bogdanov, Michael. "Touring the Classics." *Drama*. 1986; 162: 15. Illus.: Photo. B&W. 1. Lang.: Eng.
UK-England. 1986. Historical studies. ▪Establishment of new touring company, the English Shakespeare Company.

2132 Bruce, Jane. "Tutin in her Fifties." *PI*. 1986 May; 1(10): 12-13. B&W. 1. Lang.: Eng.
UK-England: Chichester. 1986. Histories-sources. ▪Actress Dorothy Tutin, about to play Miss Madrigal in *The Chalk Garden*, discusses her career.

2133 Cincotti, Joseph A. "Theatre with Bite." *PI*. 1986 Jan.; 1(6): 18-19. Illus.: Photo. Print. B&W. 2. Lang.: Eng.
UK-England: London. 1986. Histories-sources. ▪Interviews with writers of three Christmas shows. Louise Page: *Beauty and the Beast*. Charles McKeown: *Dracula, or Out For The Count*. Malcolm Sircon: *The Mr. Men Musical*.

2134 Colvin, Clare. "As You Like It or Not." *Drama*. 1986; 160(2): 11-13. Illus.: Photo. B&W. 2. Lang.: Eng.
UK-England. 1985. Histories-sources. ▪Interview with actress Glenda Jackson on her approach to her craft.

2135 Coveney, Michael. "More Than a Year of Musicals." *PI*. 1986 Dec.; 2(5): 22-25. Illus.: Photo. B&W. 3. Lang.: Eng.
UK-England: London. 1986. Reviews of performances. ▪Michael Coveney surveys the London season.

2136 Cowhig, Ruth M. "Ira Aldridge in Manchester." *ThR*. 1986; 11(3): 239-246. Illus.: Photo. B&W. 4. Lang.: Eng.
UK-England: Manchester. 1827. Historical studies. ▪Impact and influence of the highly successful tour by black American actor Ira Aldridge.

2137 Curtis, Simon. "New Blood at the Court." *PI*. 1986 July; 1(12): 23,41. B&W. 2. Lang.: Eng.

DRAMA: —Performance/production

UK-England: London. 1986. Histories-sources. ▪Director Simon Curtis discusses his production of Jim Cartwright's *Road* at the Royal Court Theatre, and the training he has had as a director at the Royal Court.

2138   Delamothe, Tony. "Up and Running with the Ball." *PI.* 1986 Sept; 2(2): 50-52. B&W. 1. Lang.: Eng.

UK-England: Bristol. 1970-1986. Histories-sources. ▪Roger Rees, associate director at Bristol Old Vic, discusses his career, the season, Dario Fo and *Hindle Wakes.*

2139   Delamothe, Tony. "Hunting for Truffles." *PI.* 1986 Nov.; 2(4): 18-19. B&W. 1. Lang.: Eng.

UK-England: London. 1986. Histories-sources. ▪Simon Callow talks about his production of Jean Cocteau's *The Infernal Machine* at the Lyric Hammersmith.

2140   Dessen, Alan C. "Price Tags and Trade-Offs: Chivalry and the Shakespearean Hero in 1985." *SQ.* 1986 Spr; 37(1): 102-105. Notes. Lang.: Eng.

UK-England: London, Stratford. USA: Ashland, OR. 1985. Reviews of performances. ▪Reviews of three Shakespearean productions: *All's Well that Ends Well* by the Oregon Shakespearean Festival, *Troilus and Cressida* by the Royal Shakespeare Company and *Coriolanus* by the National Theatre.

2141   Edwards, Anne; Sarlós, Szuzsa, transl. *Vivien Leigh.* Budapest: Zenemükiadó; 1986. 301 pp. Illus.: Photo. B&W. Lang.: Hun.

UK-England. 1913-1967. Biographies. ▪Hungarian translation of *Vivien Leigh: A Biography,* London, 1977. Related to Media: Film.

2142   Forry, Steven Earl. "An Early Conflict Involving the Production of R.B. Peake's *Presumption, or The Fate of Frankenstein.*" *TN.* 1985; 39(3): 99-103. Notes. Biblio. Illus.: Handbill. Lang.: Eng.

UK-England: London. 1818-1840. Critical studies. ▪The controversy and public protests surrounding the productions of *Presumption, or The Fate of Frankenstein* by Richard Brinsley Peake, based on the novel by Mary Shelley. Play was seen as an amoral attack on Christian faith.

2143   Gardner, Lyn. "Three Power Houses." *PI.* 1986 Dec.; 2(5): 40-41. B&W. 2. Lang.: Eng.

UK-England: London. 1986. Historical studies. ▪Overview of performances transferred from The Royal Court, Greenwich and Lyric Hammersmith theatres including *The House of Bernarda Alba* and *The Normal Heart.*

2144   Gow, Gordon. "Debut of the New Theatre Company." *PI.* 1986 Aug.; 2(1): 14-15. B&W. 2. Lang.: Eng.

UK-England: London. 1986. Histories-sources. ▪Director John Dexter and impresario Eddie Kulukundis discuss the formation of the New Theatre company and its mission to present classic plays beginning with T.S. Eliot's *The Cocktail Party.*

2145   Gow, Gordon. "Going Straight." *PI.* 1986 Sept; 2(2): 16-17. B&W. 1. Lang.: Eng.

UK-England: London. Histories-sources. ▪Actress Julie McKenzie discusses her numerous musical performances and her role in *Woman in Mind* by Alan Ayckbourn.

2146   Gow, Gordon. "Of Frances and Lillian." *PI.* 1986 Nov.; 2(4): 16-17. B&W. 1. Lang.: Eng.

UK-England: London. USA. 1986. Histories-sources. ▪Actress Frances de la Tour discusses her work *Lillian* by William Luce, a one-woman show about the life and work of Lillian Hellman.

2147   Gow, Gordon. "Welcome Back." *PI.* 1986 Oct.; 2(3): 18-19. B&W. 2. Lang.: Eng.

UK-England: London. 1970-1986. Histories-sources. ▪Actresses Jane Lapotaire and Elizabeth Spriggs discuss their affiliation with the Royal Shakespeare Company and their work in *Misalliance* by George Bernard Shaw.

2148   Happé, Peter. "Aspects of Dramatic Technique in Thomas Garter's *Susanna.*" *MET.* 1986; 8(1): 61-63. Lang.: Eng.

UK-England: Lancaster. 1985. Reviews of performances. ▪The production by the Joculatores Lancastrienses shows new value in three underestimated aspects of this interlude.

2149   Harris, Laurilyn J. "Peter Brook's *King Lear.* Aesthetic Achievement or Far Side of the Moon?" *ThR.* 1986; 11(3): 223-229. Notes. Lang.: Eng.

UK-England. 1962-1970. Historical studies. ▪Comparison of stage production and film version of *King Lear* by William Shakespeare, both directed by Peter Brook. Related to Media: Film.

2150   Harrison, David. "The West Country." *PI.* 1986 Dec.; 2(5): 46-48. Lang.: Eng.

UK-England. 1986. Historical studies. ▪Survey of theatrical performances in the low country including the Bristol Old Vic, Cheltenham, Weston-super-Mare.

2151   Hawkins, Bobbie. "All Those Ladies: Notes on Bettina Jonic." *WomenR.* 1986 July; 2(9): 44. Illus.: Photo. B&W. 1. Lang.: Eng.

UK-England. 1970-1986. Biographical Studies. ▪Theatre work of Bettina Jonic.

2152   Herbert, Ian. "A Patchy Year in the City." *PI.* 1986 Dec.; 2(5): 35-37. Illus.: Photo. B&W. 3. Lang.: Eng.

UK-England: London. 1986. Reviews of performances. ▪Royal Shakespeare Company's performances at the Barbican Theatre including *As You Like It, Othello, Les Liaisons Dangereuses, The Danton Affair, The Merry Wives of Windsor, Mephisto, The Philistines, Misalliance, Melons, The Archbishop's Ceiling.*

2153   Hill, Holly. "Saint Joan's Voices: Actresses on Shaw's Maid." *ShawR.* 1986; 6: 127-155. Notes. Lang.: Eng.

UK-England: London. 1936-1983. Histories-sources. ▪Eileen Atkins, Judi Dench, Wendy Hiller and Barbara Jefford discuss playing Saint Joan.

2154   Hobson, Harold. "Scofield Observed." *Drama.* 1986; 162: 17. Illus.: Photo. B&W. 1. Lang.: Eng.

UK-England. 1945-1986. Critical studies. ▪An assessment of actor Paul Scofield.

2155   Kachur, Barbara Anne. *Herbert Beerbohm Tree, Shakespearean Actor/Manager, Vols I-IV.* Columbus, OH: Ohio State Univ.; 1986. 1070 pp. Pref. Notes. Biblio. [Ph.D. dissertation, Univ. Microfilms order No. DA8618790.] Lang.: Eng.

UK-England: London. 1887-1917. Histories-reconstruction. ▪Reconstruction of a number of Shakespeare plays staged and performed by Herbert Beerbohm Tree.

2156   Kendal, Geoffrey. "The Shakespeare Wallah." *Drama.* 1986; 160(2): 26-30. Illus.: Photo. B&W. 10. Lang.: Eng.

UK-England. 1930-1933. Historical studies. ▪Trials and tribulations of touring Edward Dunstan Shakespearean Company.

2157   Key, Philip. "Merseyside." *PI.* 1986 Dec.; 2(5). Lang.: Eng.

UK-England. 1986. Historical studies. ▪Survey of theatre season in Merseyside including Liverpool's Everyman and Playhouse Theatres.

2158   Leech, Michael. "National Ayckbourn." *Drama.* 1986; 162: 9-10. Illus.: Photo. B&W. 3. Lang.: Eng.

UK-England: London. 1986. Histories-sources. ▪Playwright Alan Ayckbourn moves to direct at the National Theatre.

2159   Leech, Michael. "Miller's Journey." *PlPl.* 1986 Sep.; 396: 11-13. B&W. 4. Lang.: Eng.

UK-England: London. 1941-1986. Histories-sources. ▪Interview with Jonathan Miller on his production of Eugene O'Neill's *Long Day's Journey Into Night* and the play's history and context.

2160   Lynn, Jonathan. "Laugh Along with Lynn." *PI.* 1986 Aug.; 2(1): 16-18. B&W. 3. Lang.: Eng.

UK-England: London. UK-England: Cambridge. 1986. Histories-sources. ▪Director Jonathan Lynn discusses his work on three comedies performed at the National Theatre.

2161   Lynne, Gillian. "Top Cat." *PlPl.* 1986 Oct.; 397: 6-7. B&W. 2. Lang.: Eng.

UK-England: London. USA. 1940-1986. Histories-sources. ▪Biographical notes by the choreographer/director of *Cats, Cabaret, Phantom of the Opera,* etc..

2162   Marowitz, Charles. "The In-House Critic." *PI.* 1986 Feb.; 1(7): 15-29. Lang.: Eng.

UK-England. USA. Critical studies. ▪Proposes that critics should be employed by theatres to evaluate productions from the first run-through, the first dress rehearsal, the first preview, etc., for the benefit of the members of the theatre company.

DRAMA: —Performance/production

2163 Mathers, Pete. "Edward Bond Directs *Summer* at the Cottesloe, 1982." *NTQ.* 1986 May; 11(6): 136-153. Notes. Illus.: Photo. B&W. 7. Lang.: Eng.

UK-England: London. 1982. Critical studies. ■An assessment of *Summer* in close relationship to its original production by Bond, examining every element through which audiences experienced the production, including the poster, program, design, performance and the 'gests' through which they interconnect.

2164 Merck, Mandy. "Hard At It." *WomenR.* 1986 Feb.; 2(4): 28-30. Illus.: Photo. B&W. 1. Lang.: Eng.

UK-England. 1984-1986. Histories-specific. ■Interview with Hard Corps, lesbian feminist theatre company.

2165 Mills, David. "The Comedy of Virtuous and Godly Susanna." *MET.* 1986; 8(1): 67-71. Illus.: Photo. B&W. 2. Lang.: Eng.

UK-England. 1986. Historical studies. ■Performed by the Joculatores Lancastrienses before the original free-standing screen in the timber-framed Gothic hall of Rufford Old Hall, Burscough.

2166 Mitchell, Nicola. "Stage of the New." *WomenR.* 1986 Jan.; 2(3): 8-9. Illus.: Photo. B&W. 1. Lang.: Eng.

UK-England. 1980-1986. Histories-sources. ■Interview with Pip Broughton, director of Paines Plough Theatre Company, dedicated to producing and developing new writing.

2167 Moore, Oscar. "Lou Stein at Watford." *PI.* 1986 July; 1(12): 36-37. B&W. 1. Lang.: Eng.

UK-England: Watford. 1982-1986. Histories-sources. ■Lou Stein talks about his policy at the Watford Palace Theatre and his experience on the fringe where he founded the Gate Theatre at Notting Hill and the Gate at the Latchmere.

2168 Morley, Sheridan. "Six of the Best." *PI.* 1986 Dec.; 2(5): 18-19. Illus.: Photo. B&W. 6. Lang.: Eng.

UK-England: London. 1986. Historical studies. ■Overview of the top six male acting performances of the season.

2169 Nathan, David. "Half a Dozen of the Other." *PI.* 1986 Dec.; 2(5): 20-21. Illus.: Photo. B&W. 6. Lang.: Eng.

UK-England: London. 1986. Historical studies. ■Overview of the top six female acting performances of the season.

2170 Olivier, Laurence. *On Acting.* New York, NY: Simon & Schuster; 1986. 397 pp. Pref. Index. Filmography. Illus.: Photo. Print. B&W. Lang.: Eng.

UK-England: London. USA: New York, NY. 1907-1986. Biographies. ■Laurence Olivier discusses his career, approach to acting and characterization developed for specific roles. Includes brief history of eighteenth and nineteenth century actors and their styles and a chronological listing of Olivier's performances: stage, screen, television.

2171 Paczuska, Anna. "Perilous." *WomenR.* 1986 June; 2(8): 34. Illus.: Dwg. B&W. 1. Lang.: Eng.

UK-England. 1986. Reviews of performances. ■The work of British feminist theatre group, Beryl and the Perils.

2172 Philips, Deborah. "Billie Whitelaw Talks to Deborah Philips." *WomenR.* 1986 Feb.; 2(4): 6-8. Illus.: Photo. B&W. 3. Lang.: Eng.

UK-England. 1956-1986. Histories-sources. ■Interview with actress Billie Whitelaw about her career and her interpretations of Samuel Beckett's plays.

2173 Quinn, Michael. "The Northeast." *PI.* 1986 Dec.; 2(5): 48-49. Lang.: Eng.

UK-England. 1986. Historical studies. ■Survey of performances in England's Northeast, including the Tyne Weare Company, Empire Theatre, and the Playhouse.

2174 Roberts, Peter. "The Year of the Swan." *PI.* 1986 Dec.; 2(5): 32-34. Illus.: Photo. B&W. 4. Lang.: Eng.

UK-England: Stratford. 1986. Reviews of performances. ■Success of the new Swan Theatre at Stratford and overview of its season and the Royal Shakespeare Company's season.

2175 Roberts, Peter. "*La Cage*'s Smooth Start." *PI.* 1986 May; 1(10): 10-11. Illus.: Photo. Print. B&W. 1. Lang.: Eng.

UK-England: London. USA: New York. 1983-1986. Histories-sources. ■Harvey Fierstein discusses *La Cage aux Folles* and *Torch Song Trilogy*

while in London to take over the leading role of Arnold in *Torch Song Trilogy.*

2176 Roberts, Peter. "Our Man From Ulster." *PI.* 1986 June; 1(11): 12,24. B&W. 1. Lang.: Eng.

UK-England: London. 1950-1986. Histories-sources. ■Actor Colin Blakely discusses his career focussing on his work in *A Chorus of Disapproval* by Alan Ayckbourn.

2177 Roberts, Peter. "Return of the National Theatre's First Ophelia." *PI.* 1986 Aug.; 2(1): 12-13. B&W. 1. Lang.: Eng.

UK-England: London. USA: New York, NY. 1948-1986. Histories-sources. ■Actress Rosemary Harris discusses her work in Brian Clark's *The Petition*, and her career in New York with Ellis Rabb and the Association of Performing Artists (APA) and in England at the Chichester Festival Theatre, and the National Theatre.

2178 Roberts, Peter. "Lorca Portrays the Fascists." *PI.* 1986 Aug.; 2(1): 14-15,27. B&W. 1. Lang.: Eng.

UK-England. Spain. Histories-sources. ■Nuria Espert talks about Federico García Lorca and her production of *The House of Bernarda Alba* at the Lyric Hammersmith with Glenda Jackson as Bernarda Alba.

2179 Roberts, Peter. "A Not So Welsh Macbeth." *PI.* 1986 Nov.; 2(4): 12-13,45. B&W. 2. Lang.: Eng.

UK-England: Stratford. 1970-1986. Histories-sources. ■Jonathan Pryce discusses playing the role of Macbeth at Stratford and his acting career to date.

2180 Roberts, Peter. "Hancock's Finest Hour." *PI.* 1986 Jan.; 1(6): 12-13. Illus.: Photo. PW. B&W. 1. Lang.: Eng.

UK-England: London. 1986. Histories-sources. ■Actress Sheila Hancock talks about her role as Madame Ranevskaya in *Višněvyj sad (The Cherry Orchard)* at the National Theatre.

2181 Russell, Barry. "Reflections on Jeremy Irons." *Drama.* 1986; 4(162): 5-7. Illus.: Photo. B&W. 5: var. sizes. Lang.: Eng.

UK-England. USA. 1970-1985. Critical studies. ■The different techniques of acting required for theatre, television and film are related to the growth of Irons' career.

2182 Shaw, William P. "Meager Lead and Joyous Consequences: RSC Triumphs Among Shakespeare's Minor Plays." *ThS.* 1986 May & Nov.; 27(1-2): 37-67. Notes. Illus.: Photo. Print. B&W. 3:11 cm. x 15 cm., 15 cm. x 10 cm. Lang.: Eng.

UK-England: Stratford. 1946-1977. Historical studies. ■Detailed discussion of four successful Royal Shakespeare Company productions of Shakespeare's minor plays reveals strong directorial approaches.

2183 Shrimpton, Nicholas. "Shakespeare Performances in London and Stratford-upon-Avon 1984-1985." *ShS.* 1986; 39: 191-206. Illus.: Photo. Print. B&W. 6:3 in. x 5 in., 5 in. x 8 in. Lang.: Eng.

UK-England: Stratford, London. 1984-1985. Reviews of performances. ■Reviews of several Shakespearean plays of the National Theatre, the Royal Shakespeare Company and the Orange Tree Theatre.

2184 Siemon, James R. "'Nay That's Not Next': *Othello*, V.ii. in Performance, 1760-1900." *SQ.* 1986 Spr; 37(1): 38-51. Notes. Lang.: Eng.

UK-England: London. USA. 1760-1900. Critical studies. ■Analysis of predominant mode of staging final scene of Shakespeare's *Othello* suggesting ways text can be changed to conform to tragic mold favoured by an audience, including stage business, placing of Desdemona's bed, Othello's use of sword, Desdemona's struggle.

2185 Trewin, J.C. "Silver Jubilee of Mixed Delights." *PI.* 1986 Dec.; 2(5): 42-43. B&W. 2. Lang.: Eng.

UK-England: Chichester. 1986. Historical studies. ■Survey of the Chichester Festival: *The Relapse, The Chalk Garden, Annie Get Your Gun, Jane Eyre* and *A Funny Thing Happened on the Way to the Forum.*

2186 Wheeler, David. "*Sweet Bird of Youth.* By Tennessee Williams. Theatre Royal, Haymarket, London, Summer, 1985." *SAD.* 1986; 1: 105-107. Lang.: Eng.

UK-England: London. 1985. Reviews of performances. ■Tennessee Williams' *Sweet Bird of Youth* starring Lauren Bacall and directed by Harold Pinter.

DRAMA: —Performance/production

2187   Williams, D. *Theatre of Innocence and of Experience: Peter Brook.* Canterbury: Univ. of Kent; 1983. Pref. Biblio. [M.A. dissertation, *Index to Theses*, 36-6920.] Lang.: Eng.
UK-England. France. 1964-1980. Critical studies. ∎Chronological study of Brook's work.

2188   Fleming, Maurice. "The Making of an M.D." *STN*. 1986 Spr; 9(49): 12-14. Illus.: Photo. B&W. 1. Lang.: Eng.
UK-Scotland: Perth. 1948-1986. Biographical studies. ∎Career of John Scrimger, musical director at Perth Theatre.

2189   Fleming, Maurice. "Controlling the Explosion!" *STN*. 1986 Fall; 9(52): 4-8. Illus.: Photo. B&W. 2. Lang.: Eng.
UK-Scotland. 1970-1986. Histories-sources. ∎Interview with Royston Maldoom, a choreographer involved with community dance in Scotland and now dance direction at Dundee Rep.

2190   Hart, Charles. "Morag Fullarton." *STN*. 1986 Fall; 9(52): 16-18. Illus.: Photo. B&W. 2. Lang.: Eng.
UK-Scotland. 1979-1986. Historical studies. ∎Interview with Morag Fullarton, Artistic Director of Borderline Theatre Company.

2191   Kennedy, Flloyd. "The Triple Life of Anne Downie." *STN*. 1986 May-June; 9(50): 20-22. Illus.: Photo. B&W. 1. Lang.: Eng.
UK-Scotland. 1970-1986. Biographical studies. ∎Description of the career of Anne Downie.

2192   Kennedy, Flloyd. "David Hayman." *STN*. 1986 Sum; 9(51): 6-10. Illus.: Photo. B&W. 1. Lang.: Eng.
UK-Scotland. 1986. Histories-sources. ∎Interview with David Hayman on his production of Joe Corrie's play *Robert Burns* with the Scottish Theatre Company, and on his views and plans.

2193   Melville, Bill. "Focus on Focus." *STN*. 1986 May-June; 9(50): 13-16. Illus.: Photo. B&W. 2. Lang.: Eng.
UK-Scotland. 1973-1986. Histories-sources. ∎Interview with Jules Cranfield which discusses her career and the work of Focus (a theatre group in Scotland).

2194   Oliver, Cordelia. "On the Year in Scotland." *PI*. 1986 Dec.; 2(5): 44-46. B&W. 1. Lang.: Eng.
UK-Scotland. 1986. Historical studies. ∎A survey of the year in Scottish theatre, including the Tron Theatre, Pitlochry Festival Byre Theatre and Theatre Alba.

2195   "Spring Production Schedules." *TT*. 1984 Mar.; 3(5): 7-10. Illus.: Photo. B&W. 11: var. sizes. Lang.: Eng.
USA: New York, NY. 1984. Histories-sources. ∎Spring production schedules for member companies of Alliance of Resident Theatres/New York.

2196   Aksyonov, Vassily. "From the Barracks to the Market: Vassily Aksyonov in Conversation with Yury Ljubimov." *PerAJ*. 1986; 10(2): 62-68. Illus.: Photo. B&W. 2. Lang.: Eng.
USA: Washington, DC. USSR: Moscow. 1986. Histories-sources. ∎Director Jurij Liubimov: his personal history, political views and his directorial techniques.

2197   Atlas, Caron; Hannan, Ted. "Theatre of Committment: The Latino Festival in New York." *TT*. 1984 May/June; 3(7): 1-2, 8. Notes. Illus.: Photo. B&W. 4: var. sizes. Lang.: Eng.
USA: New York, NY. 1984. Historical studies. ∎Profile of theatre companies featured in Festival Latino de Nueva York at the Public Theatre: the political and social conditions that influence their work.

2198   Barbera, Jack V. "*As Is*. By William Hoffman. Lyceum Theatre, New York City. 1 May 1985." *SAD*. 1986; 1: 109-112. Notes. Illus.: Photo. B&W. 1: 4.5 in. x 4.5 in. Lang.: Eng.
USA: New York, NY. 1985. Reviews of performances. ∎William Hoffman's *As Is*, a play about AIDS, opening May 1, 1985 after an initial run at Circle Repertory Theatre.

2199   Barker, Kathleen. "A Provincial Tragedian Abroad." *ThR*. 1986; 11(1): 31-48. Notes. Illus.: Maps. Print. B&W. 1. Lang.: Eng.
USA.. 1861-1867. Biographical studies. ∎World tour by English tragedian Charles Dillon.

2200   Barnes, Clive; Beaufort, John; Cohen, Ron; Gold, Sylviane; Kissel, Howard; Rich, Frank; Wallach, Allan; Watt, Douglas. "*Coastal Disturbances.*" *NYTCR*. 1986 Nov 24; 47(16): 127-131. Lang.: Eng.
USA: New York, NY. 1986. Reviews of performances. ∎Collection of newspaper reviews of *Coastal Disturbances*, a play by Tina Howe, staged by Carole Rothman at the Second Stage.

2201   Barnes, Clive; Beaufort, John; Gussow, Mel; Kissel, Howard; Wallach, Allan; Watt, Douglas. "*Grouch: A Life in Revue.*" *NYTCR*. 1986 Nov 24; 47(16): 143-146. Lang.: Eng.
USA: New York, NY. 1986. Reviews of performances. ∎Collection of newspaper reviews of *Grouch: A Life in Revue*, by Arthur Marx and Robert Fisher, staged by Arthur Marx at the Lucille Lortel Theatre.

2202   Barnes, Clive; Beaufort, John; Cohen, Ron; Gold, Sylviane; Henry, William A., III; Rich, Frank; Wallach, Allan; Watt, Douglas; Winer, Linda. "*The Common Pursuit.*" *NYTCR*. 1986 Nov 24; 47(16): 137-142. Lang.: Eng.
USA: New York, NY. 1986. Reviews of performances. ∎Collection of newspaper reviews of *The Common Pursuit*, a play by Simon Gray, staged by Simon Gray and Michael McGuire at the Promenade Theatre.

2203   Barnes, Clive; Beaufort, John; Cohen, Ron; Kissel, Howard; Kroll, Jack; Rich, Frank; Wallach, Allan; Watt, Douglas. "*The Colored Museum.*" *NYTCR*. 1986 Nov 24; 47(16): 131-136. Lang.: Eng.
USA: New York, NY. 1986. Reviews of performances. ∎Collection of newspaper reviews of The Colored Museum, a play by George C. Wolfe, staged by L. Kenneth Richardson at the Public Theatre.

2204   Barnes, Clive; Beaufort, John; Cohen, Ron; Gold, Sylviane; Kissel, Howard; Rich, Frank; Wallach, Allan; Watt, Douglas; Winer, Linda. "*Lily Dale.*" *NYTCR*. 1986 Nov 24; 47(16): 122-126. Lang.: Eng.
USA: New York, NY. 1986. Reviews of performances. ∎Collection of newspaper reviews of *Lily Dale*, a play by Horton Foote, staged by William Alderson at the Samuel Beckett Theatre.

2205   Barnes, Clive; Beaufort, John; Henry, William A., III; Kissel, Howard; Lida, David; Rich, Frank; Siegel, Joel; Wallach, Allan; Watt, Douglas; Wilson, Edwin; Winer, Linda. "*Wild Honey.*" *NYTCR*. 1986 Dec 22; 47(17): 104-111. Lang.: Eng.
USA: New York, NY. 1986. Reviews of performances. ∎Collection of newspaper reviews of *Wild Honey*, a play by Michael Frayn from an untitled play (usually called *Platonov*) by Anton Čechov, conceived and staged by Christopher Morahan at the Virginia Theatre.

2206   Barnes, Clive; Beaufort, John; Henry, William A., III; Kissel, Howard; Kroll, Jack; Rich, Frank; Siegel, Joel; Wallach, Allan; Watt, Douglas; Wilson, Edwin; Winer, Linda. "*Broadway Bound.*" *NYTCR*. 1986 Dec 22; 47(17): 112-120. Lang.: Eng.
USA: New York, NY. 1986. Reviews of performances. ∎Collection of newspaper reviews of *Broadway Bound*, by Neil Simon, staged by Gene Saks at the Broadhurst Theatre.

2207   Barnes, Clive; Beaufort, John; Kissel, Howard; Lida, David; Shepard, Richard; Siegel, Joel; Williams, Stephen. "*Jackie Mason's 'World According to Me'.*" *NYTCR*. 1986 Dec 31; 47(18): 99-102. Lang.: Eng.
USA: New York, NY. 1986. Reviews of performances. ∎Collection of newspaper reviews of *Jackie Mason's 'World According to Me'*, written and created by Mason at the Brooks Atkinson Theatre.

2208   Barnes, Clive; Gold, Sylviane; Gussow, Mel; Kissel, Howard; McGuigan, Catherine; Nelson, Don; Sterritt, David; Wallach, Allan. "*Terrors of Pleasure.*" *NYTCR*. 1986 Sep 22; 47(12): 216-220. Lang.: Eng.
USA: New York, NY. 1986. Reviews of performances. ∎Collection of newspaper reviews of *Terrors of Pleasure*, a monologue by Spalding Gray at the Mitzi E. Newhouse Theatre.

2209   Barnes, Clive; Gerard, Jeremy; Gold, Sylviane; Henry, William A., III; Kroll, Jack; Nelson, Don; Rich, Frank.

CLASSED ENTRIES

DRAMA: —Performance/production

"Vienna: Lusthaus." NYTCR. 1986 Sep 22; 47(12): 220-224. Lang.: Eng.
USA: New York, NY. 1986. Reviews of performances. ■Collection of newspaper reviews of *Vienna: Lusthaus*, conceived and staged by Martha Clarke at the St. Clement's Theatre (April 20) and Public Newman Theatre (June 4).

2210 Barnes, Clive; Berman, Janice; Clarke, Gerald; Kissel, Howard; Kisselgoff, Anna; Mazo, Joseph H.; Siegel, Joel; Story, Richard David. *"Flamenco Puro." NYTCR.* 1986 Oct 13; 47(13): 180-184. Lang.: Eng.
USA: New York, NY. 1986. Reviews of performances. ■Collection of newspaper reviews of *Flamenco Puro*, conceived, staged and designed by Claudio Segovia and Hector Orezzoli at the Mark Hellinger Theatre.

2211 Barnes, Clive; Cohen, Ron; Kissel, Howard; Rich, Frank; Watt, Douglas; Wallach, Allan; Wilson, Edwin; Winer, Linda. *"Rowan Atkinson at the Atkinson." NYTCR.* 1986 Oct 13; 47(13): 188-192. Lang.: Eng.
USA: New York, NY. 1986. Reviews of performances. ■Collection of newspaper reviews of *Rowan Atkinson at the Atkinson*, a play by Richard Curtis, Rowan Atkinson and Ben Elton, staged by Mike Ockrent at the Brooks Atkinson Theatre.

2212 Barnes, Clive; Beaufort, John; Cohen, Ron; Henry, William A., III; Kissel, Howard; Rich, Frank; Wallach, Allan; Watt, Douglas; Wilson, Edwin; Winer, Linda. *"You Never Can Tell." NYTCR.* 1986 Oct 13; 47(13): 192-198. Lang.: Eng.
USA: New York, NY. 1986. Reviews of performances. ■Collection of newspaper reviews of *You Never Can Tell*, by George Bernard Shaw, staged by Stephen Porter at the Circle in the Square.

2213 Barnes, Clive; Beaufort, John; Cohen, Ron; Kaufman, Bill; Kissel, Howard; Shepard, Richard; Watt, Douglas; Winer, Linda. *"A Little Like Magic." NYTCR.* 1986 Oct 27; 47(14): 171-174. Lang.: Eng.
USA: New York, NY. 1986. Reviews of performances. ■Collection of newspaper reviews of *A Little Like Magic*, conceived and staged by Diane Lynn Dupuy at the Lyceum Theatre.

2214 Barnes, Clive; Beaufort, John; Cohen, Ron; Henry, William A., III; Kissel, Howard; Rich, Frank; Siegel, Joel; Wallach, Allan; Watt, Douglas; Wilson, Edwin; Winer, Linda. *"The Front Page." NYTCR.* 1986 Nov 17; 47(15): 158-164. Lang.: Eng.
USA: New York, NY. 1986. Reviews of performances. ■Collection of newspaper reviews of *The Front Page*, a play by Ben Hecht and Charles MacArthur, staged by Jerry Zaks at the Vivian Beaumont Theatre.

2215 Barnes, Clive; Beaufort, John; Gold, Sylviane; Kissel, Howard; Nelson, Don; Rich, Frank; Wallach, Allan; Winer, Linda. *"Arsenic and Old Lace." NYTCR.* 1986 July 7; 47(9): 257-262. Lang.: Eng.
USA: New York, NY. 1986. Reviews of performances. ■Collection of newspaper reviews of *Arsenic and Old Lace*, a play by Joseph Kesselring, staged by Brian Murray at the 46th Street Theatre.

2216 Barnes, Clive; Beaufort, John; Cohen, Ron; Rich, Frank; Storey, Richard David; Wallach, Allan; Watt, Douglas. *"Master Class." NYTCR.* 1986 Sep 22; 47(12): 205-209. Lang.: Eng.
USA: New York, NY. 1986. Reviews of performances. ■Collection of newspaper reviews of *Master Class*, a play by David Pownell, staged by Frank Corsaro at the Roundabout Theatre.

2217 Barnes, Clive; Beaufort, John; Gussow, Mel; Kissel, Howard; Nelson, Don; Storey, Richard David; Wallach, Allan; Wilson, Edwin. *"Twelfth Night." NYTCR.* 1986 Sep 22; 47(12): 200-204. Lang.: Eng.
USA: New York, NY. 1986. Reviews of performances. ■Collection of newspaper reviews of *Twelfth Night* by Shakespeare, staged by Wilford Leach at the Delcorte Theatre.

2218 Barnes, Clive; Beaufort, John; Cohen, Ron; Holden, Stephen; Seligsohn, Leo; Watt, Douglas; Winer, Linda. *"Olympus On My Mind." NYTCR.* 1986 Sep 22; 47(12): 212-215. Lang.: Eng.

USA: New York, NY. 1986. Reviews of performances. ■Collection of newspaper reviews of *Olympus On My Mind* based on *Amphitryon*, by Heinrich von Kleist, staged by Barry Harmon at Actors Outlet Theatre.

2219 Barnes, Clive; Beaufort, John; Cohen, Ron; Henry, William A., III; Kroll, Jack; Rich, Frank; Siegel, Joel; Watt, Douglas; Wilson, Edwin; Winer, Linda. *"Long Day's Journey Into Night." NYTCR.* 1986 Apr 7; 47(6): 302-308. Lang.: Eng.
USA: New York, NY. 1986. Reviews of performances. ■Collection of newspaper reviews of *Long Day's Journey Into Night*, by Eugene O'Neill, staged by Jonathan Miller at the Broadhurst Theatre.

2220 Barnes, Clive; Cohen, Ron; Henry, William A., III; Kroll, Jack; Rich, Frank; Watt, Douglas; Wilson, Edwin. *"The House of Blue Leaves." NYTCR.* 1986 Apr 21; 47(7): 296-300. Lang.: Eng.
USA: New York, NY. 1986. Reviews of performances. ■Collection of newspaper reviews of *The House of Blue Leaves*, a play by John Guare, staged by Jerry Zaks at the Mitzi Newhouse Theatre (March 29), and the Vivian Beaumont Theatre (April 29).

2221 Barnes, Clive; Beaufort, John; Henry, William A., III; Kissel, Howard; Rich, Frank; Siegel, Joel; Watt, Douglas; Wilson, Edwin; Winer, Linda. *"The Boys in Autumn." NYTCR.* 1986 Apr 21; 47(7): 292-295. Lang.: Eng.
USA: New York, NY. 1986. Reviews of performances. ■Collection of newspaper reviews of *The Boys in Autumn*, a play by Bernard Sabath, staged by Theodore Mann at Circle in the Square.

2222 Barnes, Clive; Beaufort, John; Gold, Sylviane; Gussow, Mel; Kissel, Howard; Watt, Douglas. *"Orchards." NYTCR.* 1986 May 5; 47(8): 270-272. Lang.: Eng.
USA: New York, NY. 1986. Reviews of performances. ■Collection of newspaper reviews of *Orchards*, seven one-act plays based on Anton Čechov's plays by Robert Falls, staged by Falls at the Lucille Lortel Theatre.

2223 Barnes, Clive; Beaufort, John; Henry, William A., III; Rich, Frank; Sharp, Christopher; Watt, Douglas. *"Principia Scriptoriae." NYTCR.* 1986 May 5; 47(8): 273-276. Lang.: Eng.
USA: New York, NY. 1986. Reviews of performances. ■Collection of newspaper reviews of *Principia Scriptoriae*, a play by Richard Nelson, staged by Lynne Meadow at the City Center Theatre.

2224 Barnes, Clive; Beaufort, John; Gold, Sylviane; Henry, William A., III; Kissel, Howard; Rich, Frank; Watt, Douglas; Winer, Linda. *"The Perfect Party." NYTCR.* 1986 May 5; 47(8): 276-279. Lang.: Eng.
USA: New York, NY. 1986. Reviews of performances. ■Collection of newspaper reviews of *The Perfect Party*, a play by A. R. Gurney, Jr., staged by John Tillinger at Playwrights Horizons.

2225 Barnes, Clive; Gussow, Mel; Sharp, Christopher; Watt, Douglas. *"Williams and Walker." NYTCR.* 1986 May 5; 47(8): 280-282. Lang.: Eng.
USA: New York, NY. 1986. Reviews of performances. ■Collection of newspaper reviews of *Williams and Walker*, a play by Vincent D. Smith, staged by Shaunelle Percy at the Henry Street Settlement's New Federal Theatre.

2226 Barnes, Clive; Beaufort, John; Gussow, Mel; Henry, William A., III; Kissel, Howard; Watt, Douglas; Winer, Linda. *"Hamlet." NYTCR.* 1986 May 5; 47(8): 283-287. Lang.: Eng.
USA: New York, NY. 1986. Reviews of performances. ■Collection of newspaper reviews of *Hamlet*, by William Shakespeare, staged by Liviu Ciulei at the Public Newman Theatre.

2227 Barnes, Clive; Beaufort, John; Cohen, Ron; Gussow, Mel; Henry, William A., III; Watt, Douglas; Winer, Linda. *"The Circle." NYTCR.* 1986 May 5; 47(8): 287-290. Lang.: Eng.
USA: New York, NY. 1986. Reviews of performances. ■Collection of newspaper reviews of *The Circle*, by W. Somerset Maugham, staged by Stephen Porter, performed by the Mirror Repertory Company at St. Peter's Church.

2228 Barnes, Clive; Beaufort, John; Gussow, Mel; Henry, William A., III; Kissel, Howard; Kroll, Jack; Story, Richard

DRAMA: —Performance/production

David; Wallach, Allan; Watt, Douglas. *"Cuba and His Teddy Bear."* NYTCR. 1986 July 7; 47(9): 263-268. Lang.: Eng.

USA: New York, NY. 1986. Reviews of performances. ■Collection of newspaper reviews of *Cuba and His Teddy Bear*, a play by Reinaldo Povod, staged by Bill Hart at the Public's Susan Stein Theatre (May 18) and Longacre Theatre (July 16).

2229   Barnes, Clive; Beaufort, John; Henry, William A., III; Kissel, Howard; Rich, Frank; Watt, Douglas; Winer, Linda. *"Loot."* NYTCR. 1986 Feb 10; 47(3): 358-361. Lang.: Eng.

USA: New York, NY. 1986. Reviews of performances. ■Collection of newspaper reviews of *Loot*, by Joe Orton, staged by John Tillinger at the City Center Theatre.

2230   Barnes, Clive; Beaufort, John; Cohen, Ron; Gussow, Mel; Watt, Douglas; Wilson, Edwin. *"Execution of Justice."* NYTCR. 1986 Mar 3; 47(4): 348-352. Lang.: Eng.

USA: New York, NY. 1986. Reviews of performances. ■Collection of newspaper reviews of *Execution of Justice*, written and staged by Emily Mann at the Virginia Theatre.

2231   Barnes, Clive; Beaufort, John; Henry, William A., III; Kissel, Howard; Kroll, Jack; Rich, Frank; Siegel, Joel; Watt, Douglas; Wilson, Edwin; Winer, Linda. *"Precious Sons."* NYTCR. 1986 Mar 3; 47(4): 342-347. Lang.: Eng.

USA: New York, NY. 1986. Reviews of performances. ■Collection of newspaper reviews of *Precious Sons*, by George Furth, staged by Norman Rene at the Longacre Theatre.

2232   Barnes, Clive; Beaufort, John; Cohen, Ron; Gold, Sylviane; Henry, William A., III; Rich, Frank; Siegel, Joel; Watt, Douglas. *"So Long on Lonely Street."* NYTCR. 1986 Mar 17; 47(5): 334-337. Lang.: Eng.

USA: New York, NY. 1986. Reviews of performances. ■Collection of newspaper reviews of *So Long on Lonely Street*, by Sandra Deer, staged by Kent Stephens at the Jack Lawrence Theatre.

2233   Barnes, Clive; Beaufort, John; Henry, William A., III; Kissel, Howard; Rich, Frank; Siegel, Joel; Watt, Douglas; Winer, Linda. *"Social Security."* NYTCR. 1986 Mar 17; 47(5): 322-326. Lang.: Eng.

USA: New York, NY. 1986. Reviews of performances. ■Collection of newspaper reviews of *Social Security*, by Andrew Bergman, staged by Mike Nichols at the Ethel Barrymore Theatre.

2234   Barnes, Clive; Beaufort, John; Cohen, Ron; Henry, William A., III; Kroll, Jack; Rich, Frank; Watt, Douglas; Wilson, Edwin; Winer, Linda. *"The Petition."* NYTCR. 1986 Apr 7; 47(6): 315-320. Lang.: Eng.

USA: New York, NY. 1986. Reviews of performances. ■Collection of newspaper reviews of *The Petition*, by Brian Clark, staged by Peter Hall at the John Golden Theatre.

2235   Barnes, Clive; Beaufort, John; Kissel, Howard; Rich, Frank; Watt, Douglas; Wilson, Edwin; Winer, Linda. *"Corpse!."* NYTCR. 1986 Jan 1; 47(1): 397-400. Lang.: Eng.

USA: New York, NY. 1986. Reviews of performances. ■Collection of newspaper reviews of *Corpse!*, by Gerald Moon, staged by John Tillinger at the Helen Hayes Theatre.

2236   Barnes, Clive; Beaufort, John; Cohen, Ron; Rich, Frank; Siegel, Joel; Watt, Douglas; Winer, Linda. *"The Caretaker."* NYTCR. 1986 Jan 1; 47(1): 380-383. Lang.: Eng.

USA: New York, NY. 1986. Reviews of performances. ■Collection of newspaper reviews of *The Caretaker*, by Harold Pinter, staged by John Malkovich at the Circle in the Square.

2237   Barnes, Clive; Beaufort, John; Kissel, Howard; Rich, Frank; Stearns, David Patrick; Watt, Douglas. *"Jerome Kern Goes to Hollywood."* NYTCR. 1986 Jan 13; 47(2): 387-390. Lang.: Eng.

USA: New York, NY. 1986. Reviews of performances. ■Collection of newspaper reviews of *Jerome Kern Goes to Hollywood*, conceived and staged by David Kernan at the Ritz Theatre.

2238   Barnes, Clive; Beaufort, John; Cohen, Ron; Gussow, Mel; Watt, Douglas. *"Gertrude Stein and a Companion."* NYTCR. 1986 Feb 10; 47(3): 375-377. Lang.: Eng.

USA: New York, NY. 1986. Reviews of performances. ■Collection of newspaper reviews of *Gertrude Stein and a Companion*, by Win Wells, staged by Ira Cirker at the Lucille Lortel Theatre.

2239   Barnes, Clive; Rich, Frank. *"Caligula."* NYTCR. 1986 Feb 10; 47(3): 369-371. Lang.: Eng.

USA: New York, NY. 1986. Reviews of performances. ■Collection of newspaper reviews of *Caligula*, by Albert Camus, staged by Marshall W. Mason, Circle in the Square production at the Triplex (Theatre II).

2240   Barnes, Clive; Beaufort, John; Gold, Sylviane; Rich, Frank; Sharp, Christopher; Watt, Douglas; Winer, Linda. *"The Mound Builders."* NYTCR. 1986 Feb 10; 47(3): 371-375. Lang.: Eng.

USA: New York, NY. 1986. Reviews of performances. ■Collection of newspaper reviews of *The Mound Builders*, by Lanford Wilson, staged by Marshall W. Mason, Circle in the Square production at Triplex (Theatre II).

2241   Barnes, Clive; Beaufort, John; Henry, William A., III; Kissel, Howard; Rich, Frank; Watt, Douglas. *"Rum and Coke."* NYTCR. 1986 Feb 10; 47(3): 366-369. Lang.: Eng.

USA: New York, NY. 1986. Reviews of performances. ■Collection of newspaper reviews of *Rum and Coke*, by Keith Reddin, staged by Leo Waters at the Public Theatre.

2242   Barnes, Clive; Beaufort, John; Gold, Sylviane; Henry, William A., III; Rich, Frank; Sharp, Christopher; Watt, Douglas; Winer, Linda. *"Room Service."* NYTCR. 1986 Feb 10; 47(3): 361-365. Lang.: Eng.

USA: New York, NY. 1986. Reviews of performances. ■Collection of newspaper reviews of *Room Service*, by John Murray and Allan Boretz, staged by Alan Arkin at the Roundabout.

2243   Barnes, Noreen Claire. *Actress of all Work: A Survey of the Performance Career of Louisa Lane Drew.* Medford, MA: Tufts Univ; 1986. 159 pp. Pref. Notes. Biblio. [Ph.D. dissertation, Univ. Microfilms order No. DA8616313.] Lang.: Eng.

USA. 1820-1897. Biographical studies. ■Career of actress and theatrical manager Louisa Lane Drew.

2244   Beaufort, John; Iyer, Pico; Kissel, Howard; Kroll, Jack; Rich, Frank; Stasio, Marilyn; Wallach, Allan. *"Asinamali."* NYTCR. 1986 Nov 24; 47(16): 146-150. Lang.: Eng.

USA: New York, NY. 1986. Reviews of performances. ■Collection of newspaper reviews of *Asinamali*, a play written and staged by Mbongeni Ngema at the Mitzi E. Newhouse Theatre.

2245   Beaufort, John; Henry, William A., III; Kissel, Howard; Rich, Frank; Stasio, Marilyn; Watt, Douglas; Wilson, Edwin; Winer, Linda. *"Lillian."* NYTCR. 1986 Jan 1; 47(1): 391-396. Lang.: Eng.

USA: New York, NY. 1986. Reviews of performances. ■Collection of newspaper reviews of *Lillian*, by William Luce, staged by Robert Whitehead at the Ethel Barrymore Theatre.

2246   Benzow, Gregg. "Interview with Director Christoph Nel." ComIBS. 1984 Nov.; 14(1): 23-27.

USA: Seattle, WA. 1984. Histories-sources. ■Director Christoph Nel discusses staging *Im Dickicht der Städte (In the Jungle of the Cities)* at the Intiman Theatre.

2247   Bertin, Michael. "Washington." PI. 1986 Nov.; 2(4): 50-51. Illus.: Photo. B&W. 1. Lang.: Eng.

USA: Washington, DC. 1986. Reviews of performances. ■Survey of Peter Sellars productions at the Kennedy Center's National Theatre, including *The Count of Monte Cristo, The Seagull, Ajax, Idiot's Delight* and *Two Figures in Dense Violet Light*.

2248   Bly, Mark. "Dramaturgy at Large: An Interview with Arthur Ballet." ThM. 1986 Sum/Fall; 17(3): 29-32. Illus.: Photo. Print. B&W. 1: 3 in. x 4 in. Lang.: Eng.

USA. 1950-1986. Histories-sources. ■Dramaturg Arthur Ballet discusses the clarification vs. the simplification of a play's theme.

2249   Bly, Mark. "Dramaturgy at the Magic and the O'Neill: An Interview with Martin Esslin." ThM. 1986 Sum/Fall; 17(3): 19-24 . Illus.: Photo. Print. B&W. 3: 3 in. x 4 in. Lang.: Eng.

CLASSED ENTRIES

DRAMA: —Performance/production

USA: Waterford, CT, San Francisco, CA. 1936-1986. Histories-sources. ■Martin Esslin discusses dramaturg's need to balance roles of naive spectator and informed academic.

2250 Bly, Mark. "Dramaturgy at the Eureka: An Interview with Oskar Eustis." *ThM.* 1986 Sum/Fall; 17(3): 7-12. Illus.: Photo. Print. B&W. 4: 3 in. x 3 in. Lang.: Eng.
USA: San Francisco, CA. 1975-1986. Histories-sources. ■Oskar Eustis, dramaturg of Eureka Theatre, talks of confronting social and aesthetic problems of a community.

2251 Bly, Mark. "Dramaturgy at the Yale Rep: An Interview with Gitta Honegger." *ThM.* 1986 Sum/Fall; 17(3): 33-37. Illus.: Photo. Print. B&W. 3: 3 in. x 4 in. Lang.: Eng.
USA: New Haven, CT. 1960-1986. Histories-sources. ■Yale Repertory dramaturg Gitta Honegger discusses training student dramaturgs and the European tradition of dramaturgy.

2252 Bly, Mark. "Dramaturgy at the Brooklyn Academy of Music: An Interview with Richard Nelson." *ThM.* 1986 Sum/Fall; 17(3): 38-42. Illus.: Photo. Print. B&W. 3: 3 in. x 3 in. Lang.: Eng.
USA: New York, NY. 1979-1986. Histories-sources. ■Brooklyn Academy of Music dramaturg Richard Nelson discusses communication with a variety of directors.

2253 Bly, Mark. "Dramaturgy at the Mark Taper Forum: An Interview with Russell Vandenbroucke." *ThM.* 1986 Sum/Fall; 17(3): 13-18. Illus.: Photo. Print. B&W. 3: 3 in. x 3 in. Lang.: Eng.
USA: Los Angeles, CA. 1974-1985. Histories-sources. ■Mark Taper dramaturg Russell Vandenbroucke discusses the necessity of proper timing when giving notes to director or playwright.

2254 Bly, Mark. "Dramaturgy at Second Stage and the Phoenix: An Interview with Anne Cattaneo." *ThM.* 1986 Sum/Fall; 17(3): 25-28. Illus.: Photo. Print. B&W. 2: 3 in. x 4 in. Lang.: Eng.
USA: New York, NY. 1971-1986. Histories-sources. ■Dramaturg Anne Cattaneo discusses the definition of the 'spine' of a play and the process of collaboration with the playwright to focus and strengthen it.

2255 Boardman, True. "I Always Drive Fast Through Fresno." *PAA.* 1986: 68-77. Illus.: Photo. Print. B&W. 6: var. sizes. Lang.: Eng.
USA: Fresno, CA. 1927. Histories-sources. ■An autobiographical account of one actor's experiences with the Fresno Paramount Players. The actors' living conditions, the process by which they learned their lines, their relationships and the surprise ending of the company are detailed.

2256 Breslauer, Jan. "Ellis Island with Palms." *ThM.* 1986 Fall/Win; 18(1): 91-93. Lang.: Eng.
USA: Los Angeles, CA. Reviews of performances. ■A review of JoAnne Akalaitis' *Green Card*, the result of a two-year collaboration with the Mark Taper Forum.

2257 Brown, Jared. *The Fabulous Lunts: A Biography of Alfred Lunt and Lynn Fontanne.* New York, NY: Atheneum; 1986. 512 pp. Index. Biblio. Illus.: Photo. Lang.: Eng.
USA. 1922-1972. Biographies. ■A scholarly study on the careers of Alfred Lunt and Lynn Fontanne, the premier husband-wife acting team on the English-speaking stage, including information on the history of theatre ideas and practices during their career.

2258 Cattaneo, Anne. "Do New York Critics Hate L.A. Theatre?" *TT.* 1984 Apr.; 3(6). Illus.: Photo. Print. B&W. 4. Lang.: Eng.
USA: Los Angeles, CA, New York, NY. 1983-1984. Critical studies. ■Examining reasons for negative critical responses by New York critics to plays which began and were successful in Los Angeles.

2259 Colby, Donald. "Second Chances in New York." *PI.* 1986 Mar.; 1(8): 44-46. Illus.: Photo. Print. B&W. 2. Lang.: Eng.
USA: New York, NY. 1986. Histories-sources. ■The Second Stage theatre company revives plays that deserve a second showing, for example, Lanford Wilson's *Lemon Sky*.

2260 Dace, Tish. "The Singular Careers of Tandy & Cronyn." *AmTh.* 1984 Oct.; 1(6): 10-15. Illus.: Photo. Print. B&W. 6: var. sizes. Lang.: Eng.
USA. 1932-1984. Histories-sources. ■Jessica Tandy and Hume Cronyn discuss their lives, careers, and views on acting.

2261 Davis, Peter A. "William Winter and E.C. Stedman on Lawrence Barrett's *Harebell.*" *NCTR.* 1986; 14(1-2): 45-50. Notes. Illus.: Photo. Print. B&W. 1: 5 in. x 6 in. Lang.: Eng.
USA: New York, NY. 1871-1909. Histories-sources. ■A letter from William Winter and a poem by E.C. Stedman lamenting the lack of success and praising the talent of actor Lawrence Barrett.

2262 Davis, R.G. "Seven Anarchists I Have Known: American Approaches to Dario Fo." *NTQ.* 1986 Nov.; 11(8): 313-319. Illus.: Photo. B&W. 4. Lang.: Eng.
USA. Canada. Italy. 1970-1986. Histories-sources. ■The author looks at his own and six other productions of Fo's *Morte accidentale di un anarchico (Accidental Death of an Anarchist)* in North America and asserts that it is impossible to direct Fo's work successfully without an understanding of his politics.

2263 Davy, Kate. "Foreman's PAIN(T) and Vertical Mobility." 209-224 in McNamara, Brooks, ed.; Dolan, Jill, ed. *The Drama Review: Thirty Years of Commentary on the Avant-Garde.* Ann Arbor, MI: UMI Research P; 1986. xii, 371 pp. (Theatre and Dramatic Studies 35.) Print. B&W. 10: var. sizes. Lang.: Eng.
USA. 1974-1986. Critical studies. ■Analysis of aesthetics, styles, rehearsal techniques of Richard Foreman emphasizing the three elements in his work: content, space and performer.

2264 Drucker, Trudy. "The Return of O'Neill's Play of Old Sorrow." *EON.* 1986 Win; 10(3): 12-23. Lang.: Eng.
USA. 1956-1986. Reviews of performances. ■An examination of character and structure in Eugene O'Neill's *Long Day's Journey Into Night* in relation to Jonathan Miller's 1986 production.

2265 Freedland, Michael. *The Secret Life of Danny Kaye.* New York, NY: St. Martin's; 1986. 261 pp. Illus.: Photo. Print. B&W. 16: var. sizes. Lang.: Eng.
USA: New York, NY. 1912-1985. Biographies. ■Study concentrating on the unique acting style of Danny Kaye.

2266 Fuchs, Elinor, inter.; Marranca, Bonnie, ed. "*Alcestis.*" *PerAJ.* 1986; 10(1): 78-115. Illus.: Dwg. Photo. Print. B&W. 16. [The PAJ Casebook.] Lang.: Eng.
USA: Cambridge, MA. 1986. Histories-sources. ■Interviews with key persons, including director Robert Wilson, involved in a production of Euripides' *Alcestis* by American Repertory Theatre. Excerpts from texts.

2267 Gadon, Ann. "*Lux in Tenebris* in Chicago." *ComIBS.* 1985 Nov.; 15(1): 24-27.
USA: Chicago, IL. 1985. Histories-sources. ■Director discusses her intention in staging *Lux in Tenebris* as part of the the festival 'Brecht on Film'.

2268 Garvey, Sheila Hickey. "Rethinking O'Neill." *EON.* 1986 Win; 10(3): 13-20. Notes. Lang.: Eng.
USA: New York, NY, New London, CT. 1986. Histories-sources. ■Interview with actor Peter Gallagher who played Edmund in Eugene O'Neill's *Long Day's Journey Into Night*, directed by Jonathan Miller.

2269 Gonzalez, Gloria. "Foreign Language Theater." *DGQ.* 1986 Sum; 23(2).
USA: New York, NY. 1986. Historical studies. ■Spanish-language production of author's play *Café Con Leche (Coffee with Milk)* at the Teatro Repertorio Español.

2270 Gray, Spalding. "Commune." *AmTh.* 1986 Nov.; 3(8): 36-37, 101-103. Pref. Illus.: Photo. Print. B&W. 2: 3 in. x 4 in., 5 in. x 7 in. Lang.: Eng.
USA. France. Poland. 1970. Histories-sources. ■Spalding Gray's account of the development and production of *Commune*, with anecdotes about the cost and touring.

2271 Gussow, Mel; Henry, William A., III; Kissel, Howard; Kroll, Jack; Nelson, Don; Siegel, Joel; Stasio, Marilyn; Sterritt, David; Wallach, Allan; Wilson, Edwin. "The Life and Adventures of Nicholas Nickleby." *NYTCR.* 1986 Sep 8; 47(11): 226-232. Lang.: Eng.
USA: New York, NY. 1986. Reviews of performances. ■Collection of newspaper reviews of *The Life and Adventures of Nicholas Nickleby*,

DRAMA: —Performance/production

book by Charles Dickens, adapted by David Edgar, staged by Trevor Nunn at the Broadhurst Theatre.

2272 Heiss, Christine. "Gerhart Hauptmanns *Die Weber* auf deutschen Bühnen der USA im neunzehnten Jahrhundert." (Gerhart Hauptmann's *The Weavers* on the German Stages of the USA in the Nineteenth Century.) *GQ*. 1986 Sum; 59(3): 361-374. Lang.: Ger.

USA. Germany. 1892-1900. Historical studies. ■Productions of *Die Weber (The Weavers)* by Gerhart Hauptmann on German speaking stages of the USA as an example of the interest of the workers in its presumably revolutionary message.

2273 Jackson, Caroline. "*Fences*: The Odyssey of a Play." *BlackM*. 1986 Feb-Mar.: 4, 11. Illus.: Photo. Print. B&W. 1: 3 in. x 5 in. Lang.: Eng.

USA. 1982-1986. Historical studies. ■Brief history of the genesis of August Wilson's *Fences* and its progress from the O'Neill Theatre Center to Chicago's Goodman Theatre and finally to Broadway.

2274 Jenkins, Linda Walsh; Pettingill, Richard. "Dramaturgy at the Court and Wisdom Bridge." *ThM*. 1986 Sum/Fall; 17(3): 51-55. Illus.: Photo. Print. B&W. 2: 3 in. x 3 in. Lang.: Eng.

USA: Chicago, IL. 1984-1986. Histories-sources. ■Chicago dramaturgs acknowledge a common ground in educating their audience.

2275 Katz, Vera J. "Mike Malone: Weaver of History and Musical Magic." *BlackM*. 1986 Apr-May: 2-3. Illus.: Photo. Print. B&W. 1: 4 in. x 5 in. Lang.: Eng.

USA: Washington, DC, Cleveland, OH. 1968-1985. Historical studies. ■Career of director/choreographer Mike Malone and his affiliation with The Everyman Theatre Company (Washington, D.C.), Workshops for Careers in the Arts, the DC Black Repertory Company (Washington, DC), Karamu House Theatre (Cleveland, OH), Washington, D.C. chapter of Young Audiences and Howard University.

2276 Kings, W.D. "Nailed to a Circus of Blood: *Ajax* at the American National Theatre." *ThM*. 1986 Fall/Win; 18(1): 9-15. Illus.: Photo. Print. B&W. 1: 5 in. x 7 in. Lang.: Eng.

USA: Washington, DC. 1986. Reviews of performances. ■Review of Robert Auletta's 1986 Pentagon version of *Ajax* by Sophocles as produced at the American National Theatre.

2277 Kirby, Michael. "The New Theatre." 61-78 in McNamara, Brooks, ed.; Dolan, Jill, ed. *The Drama Review: Thirty Years of Commentary on the Avant-Garde*. Ann Arbor, MI: UMI Research P; 1986. xii, 371 pp. (Theatre and Dramatic Studies 35.) Lang.: Eng.

USA. 1965. Critical studies. ■Explorative structure and manner of performance in avant-garde theatre and its search for evaluation of the theatre as a whole.

2278 Knust, Herbert. "Interview with Director John Ahart." *ComIBS*. 1984 Nov.; 14(1): 28-37.

USA: Urbana, IL. 1984. Histories-sources. ■Director John Ahart discusses staging *Der Kaukasische Kreidekreis (The Caucasian Chalk Circle)* at the University of Illinois.

2279 Koltai, Tamás. "Beckett Beckettet rendez." (Beckett Stages Beckett.) *Sz*. 1986 Mar.; 19(3): 35. Lang.: Hun.

USA. 1985. Critical studies. ■Analyzes Samuel Beckett's direction of his own play *Krapp's Last Tape* with the San Quentin Drama Workshop.

2280 Larson, Catherine. "The 11th Golden Age Drama Festival." *LATR*. 1986 Fall; 20(1): 103-107. Illus.: Photo. Print. B&W. 1: 4.5 in. x 6.5 in. Lang.: Eng.

USA: El Paso, TX. 1986. Historical studies. ■Competition among productions of Spanish Golden Age plays by U.S., Spanish and Latin American companies. List of winners.

2281 Leipzig, Adam. "Arts Across the Finish Line." *AmTh*. 1984 June; 1(3): 14-17. Illus.: Photo. Print. B&W. 2. Lang.: Eng.

USA: Los Angeles, CA. 1984. Historical studies. ■The organization of the Twenty-third Olympiad Arts Festival, its staging and technical requirements. Includes list of participants, productions and show dates.

2282 Leming, Warren. "On Directing Brecht." *ComIBS*. 1985 Nov.; 15(1): 28-29.

USA: Chicago, IL. 1985. Histories-sources. ■Notes from a production of *Mahagonny* by the Remains Ensemble.

2283 Levine, Mindy N. "Sign of the Times." *TT*. 1986 June; 5(5): 6-7. Illus.: Photo. B&W. 3. Lang.: Eng.

USA: New York, NY. 1980-1986. Historical studies. ■Signing for the deaf for theatre and comedy shows. Focus on Hands On, an organization of deaf language interpreters.

2284 Levine, Mindy N. "Extending One's Range: Dancers, Artists and Film Directors in the Theatre." *TT*. 1982 Nov/Dec.; 2(2): 6-8. Illus.: Photo. B&W. 4: var. sizes. Lang.: Eng.

USA: New York, NY. 1982. Historical studies. ■Focus on several artists who made their reputations in the fields of dance, film and television now working in Off and Off-off Broadway theatres. Related to Media.

2285 Levine, Mindy N. "Taking to the Streets: Outdoor Performance in New York City." *TT*. 1982 Oct.; 2(1): 1-2, 8. Illus.: Photo. B&W. 2. Lang.: Eng.

USA: New York, NY. 1960-1982. Historical studies. ■Political origins of street theatre in the 1960s compared to conditions surrounding recent resurgence. Several companies and their productions, techniques and origins are examined.

2286 Levine, Mindy N. "Beyond the RSC: Alternative British Theatre Comes to New York." *TT*. 1983 May; 2(6): 1-2. Illus.: Photo. B&W. 2. Lang.: Eng.

USA: New York, NY. 1970-1983. Historical studies. ■Britain Salutes New York, a festival to commemorate the bicentennial, brings several avant-garde theatre companies from Britain to New York. Includes list of presenting companies.

2287 Levine, Mindy N. "Drama of the Inarticulate: Two Kroetz Plays Come to New York." *TT*. 1984 Feb.; 3(4): 1, 9. Illus.: Photo. B&W. 3: 3 in. x 4 in. Lang.: Eng.

USA: New York, NY. Germany, West. 1984. Historical studies. ■Life and technique of Franz Xaver Kroetz, past productions of his plays and focus on current New York productions of *Wer durchs Laub geht (Through the Leaves)* and *Mensch Meier*.

2288 Levine, Mindy N. "An Interview with Elizabeth Le-Compte." *TT*. 1984 Aug.; 3(8): 1, 13-14. Lang.: Eng.

USA: New York, NY. 1984. Histories-sources. ■Interview with Wooster Group's artistic director Elizabeth LeCompte. Discussion of group's production history, controversial works and contemporary American theatre.

2289 Lindenbaum, Sheila. "Census of Medieval Drama Productions." *RORD*. 1986; 29: 109-112. Lang.: Eng.

USA: Washington, DC. UK-England: Lancaster. France: Perpignan. 1986. Reviews of performances. ■Descriptions of productions of *Li Jus de Robin et Marion (The Play of Robin and Marion)*, *The Comedy of Virtuous and Godly Susanna* and *The Second Shepherds Play*.

2290 Lyon, James. "Interview with Peter Sellars." *ComIBS*. 1984 Apr.; 12(2): 35-53.

USA. 1983. Histories-sources. ■Director Peter Sellars talks about staging Bertolt Brecht's plays.

2291 Marowitz, Charles. "The Jackson Approach." *PI*. 1986 Jan.; 1(6): 14-17. Illus.: Photo. Print. B&W. 1. Lang.: Eng.

USA: New York, NY. 1986. Histories-sources. ■Glenda Jackson talks about her method of acting.

2292 McCree, Cree. "Long Night's Journey." *AmTh*. 1984 Dec.; 1(8): 18-20. Illus.: Photo. B&W. 1. Lang.: Eng.

USA. 1984. Historical studies. ■Murray Mednick's 7-play Coyote Cycle performed outdoors from dusk to dawn.

2293 Micheli, Linda McJ. "Margaret Webster's *Henry VIII*: The Survival of 'Scenic Shakespeare' in America." *ThR*. 1986; 11 (3): 213-222. Notes. Lang.: Eng.

USA: New York, NY. 1910-1949. Historical studies. ■Margaret Webster's scenic approach to Shakespeare compared with those of Herbert Beerbohm Tree and Tyrone Guthrie.

2294 Moore, David, Jr. "Dramaturgy at the Guthrie: An Interview with Mark Bly." *ThM*. 1986 Sum/Fall; 17(3): 43-50. Illus.: Photo. Print. B&W. 4: 3 in. x 3 in. Lang.: Eng.

USA: Minneapolis, MN. 1981-1986. Histories-sources. ■Guthrie Theatre dramaturg Mark Bly discusses the dramaturg's responsibility to question.

CLASSED ENTRIES

DRAMA: —Performance/production

2295 Oumano, Ellen. *Sam Shepard: The Life and Work of an American Dreamer.* New York, NY: St. Martin's; 1986. 192 pp. Biblio. Lang.: Eng.
USA. 1943-1986. Biographies. ■Analysis of Shepard's life and work as poet, actor, playwright, screenwriter and musician. Related to Media: Film.

2296 Overbeck, L.M., ed.; Fehsenfeld, Martha, ed. "The Beckett Circle." *BCl.* 1985 Spr; 6(2): 8. Lang.: Eng.
USA: Boston, MA. 1984. Historical studies. ■Conflict over artistic control and interpretation in the American Repertory Theatre's production of *Fin de partie (Endgame)* between Barney Rosset, president of Grove Press, representing Samuel Beckett and Robert Brustein, artistic director of ART.

2297 Payne, Deborah C. "*Streamers.* By David Rabe. Steppenwolf Theatre Company, Washington, D.C. 3 August 1985." *SAD.* 1986; 1: 107-109. Illus.: Photo. B&W. 1: 5.5 in. x 4 in. Lang.: Eng.
USA: Washington, DC. 1985. Reviews of performances. ■Review of the Steppenwolf Theatre Company's production of *Streamers* by David Rabe, at the J.F. Kennedy Center.

2298 Pinkston, C. Alex, Jr. "The Stage Première of *Dr. Jekyll and Mr. Hyde.*" *NCTR.* 1986; 14(1-2): 21-43. Notes. Illus.: Photo. Sketches. Print. B&W. 7. Lang.: Eng.
USA: New York, NY. USA: Boston, MA. 1886-1888. Histories-specific. ■A detailed description of the first theatrical production of *Dr. Jekyll and Mr. Hyde,* based on the book by Robert Louis Stevenson and starring Richard Mansfield. The show, which influenced later film versions, is described through reviews, specific scenes and script changes made from the original book.

2299 Renick, Kyle. "Lillian Hellman: 1905-1984." *TT.* 1984 Oct.; 4(1): 3-4. Illus.: Photo. Sketches. 2. Lang.: Eng.
USA: New York, NY. 1984. Histories-sources. ■Kyle Renick recounts personal experiences with playwright Lillian Hellman in directing her plays at the WPA theatre. Brief overview of her career, and quotes from her writings.

2300 Richman, David. "The *King Lear* Quarto in Rehearsal and Performance." *SQ.* 1986 Fall; 37(3): 374-382. Notes. [Critical Review.] Lang.: Eng.
USA: Rochester, NY. 1985. Historical studies. ■Attempt to produce Quarto version of *King Lear* at University of Rochester, staging issues that seem to have demanded revision by Shakespeare or associates in Folio version, argument for conflated text of Folio and Quarto versions.

2301 Rogers, Priscilla Sue Marquardt. *Greek Tragedy in the New York Theatre: A History and Interpretation.* Ann Arbor, MI: Univ of Michigan; 1986. 352 pp. Pref. Notes. Biblio. [Ph.D. dissertation, University Microfilms order No. DA8612611.] Lang.: Eng.
USA: New York, NY. 1854-1984. Historical studies. ■Examination of professional productions of Greek tragedy highlighting those with greatest impact on New York theatre.

2302 Roudané, Matthew C. "*Seduced.* By Sam Shepard. Seven Stages, Atlanta, Georgia. 30 May 1985." *SAD.* 1986; 1: 103-105. Illus.: Photo. B&W. 1: 5.5 in. x 8 in. Lang.: Eng.
USA: Atlanta, GA. 1985. Reviews of performances. ■Sam Shepard's play *Seduced* (1978), based on billionaire Howard Hughes, as produced at Seven Stages and directed by George Nickas.

2303 Schneider, Alan. "Who's Afraid?" *AmTh.* 1986 Feb.; 2(11): 4-9. Illus.: Photo. Print. B&W. 3: 3 in. x 5 in., 9 in. x 12 in., 5 in. x 5 in. Lang.: Eng.
USA: New York, NY. 1962. Histories-sources. ■Director Alan Schneider's account of the original Broadway production of Edward Albee's *Who's Afraid of Virginia Woolf?.*

2304 Serban, Andrei. "The Life in a Sound." 229-232 in McNamara, Brooks, ed.; Dolan, Jill, ed. *The Drama Review: Thirty Years of Commentary on the Avant-Garde.* Ann Arbor, MI: UMI Research P; 1986. xii, 371 pp. (Theatre and Dramatic Studies 35.) Lang.: Eng.
USA. 1976. Critical studies. ■Discusses the effect of audible vibrations on listeners, suggests an exercise to free the voice.

2305 Sheffer, Isaiah. "'Einstein' Equation: Reviving a Classic = Setting it Free." *TT.* 1984 Oct.; 4(1): 1-2. Lang.: Eng.
USA: New York, NY. 1976-1984. Historical studies. ■Revival of Philip Glass and Robert Wilson's *Einstein on the Beach* at Brooklyn Academy of Music and the opportunities it presents for the authors to improve the piece. Related to Music-Drama: Opera.

2306 Smith, Ronn. "Wilson Weaves Classical Magic." *ThCr.* 1986 Nov.; 20(9): 30-32, 88-92. Illus.: Photo. 4: var. sizes.
USA: Cambridge, MA. 1986. Historical studies. ■A look at Robert Wilson's production of Euripides' *Alcestis* at the American Repertory Theatre.

2307 Stevens, Martin. "The Nativity Cycle at Irvine." *RORD.* 1986; 29: 95-97. Lang.: Eng.
USA: Irvine, CA. 1986. Reviews of performances. ■Account of University of California at Irvine production of a nativity play with composite text drawn from York, N-town and Wakefield cycles.

2308 Turner, Beth. "Lloyd Richards: The Quiet Force in American Theatre." *BlackM.* 1986 Sum: 2-3, 9. Illus.: Photo. Print. B&W. 1: 4 in. x 5 in. Lang.: Eng.
USA: Detroit, MI, New York, NY, New Haven, CT. 1920-1980. Historical studies. ■Lloyd Richard's career as an actor, director, artistic director and academic dean, with particular focus on his pivotal role in shaping Lorraine Hansberry's *A Raisin in the Sun.*

2309 Urbani, Serene, ed.; Valenti, Cristina, ed. *Dedicato a Julian Beck.* (Dedicated to Julian Beck.) Pontedera: Centro per la sperimentazione e la ricerca teatrale di Pontedera; 1986. 43 pp. Index. Tables. Append. Filmography. Illus.: Dwg. B&W. 6: var. sizes. Lang.: Ita.
USA. Europe. 1925-1985. Histories-sources. ■Writings by and about Julian Beck, founder of Living Theatre.

2310 Versényi, Adam. "1985 Festival Latino." *LATR.* 1986 Spr; 9(2): 111-120. Illus.: Photo. Print. B&W. 4: 3 1/4 in. x 4 1/2 in. Lang.: Eng.
USA: New York, NY. 1985. Reviews of performances. ■A dozen productions that were seen in the annual festival of Latin American plays at the Public Theatre including some by companies in exile.

2311 Wainscott, Ronald H. "Harnessing O'Neill's Furies, Philip Moeller Directs *Dynamo.*" *EON.* 1986 Win; 10(3): 3-13. Notes. Lang.: Eng.
USA: New York, NY. 1929. Reviews of performances. ■Analysis of the reviews of the 1929 Broadway production of O'Neill's *Dynamo* concluding that director Philip Moeller and designer Lee Simonson gave an excellent mounting to a weak play.

2312 Walsh, Martin. "The Brecht Company." *ComIBS.* 1984 Nov.; 14(1): 51-54.
USA: Ann Arbor, MI. 1979-1984. Historical studies. ■A profile of The Brecht Company, the first theatre devoted to the works and methods of Brecht since the early 1970s.

2313 Weiss, Judith A. "Primer Festival de Nuevo Teatro en Washington: Trayectoria y análisis." (First Festival of New Theatre in Washington: Trajectory and Analysis.) *LATR.* 1986 Spr; 19(2): 105-109. Lang.: Spa.
USA: Washington, DC. 1984-1986. Historical studies. ■Nuevo Teatro is distinguished from traditional or commercial theatre by its emphasis on production *process.* The festival brought together various theatre groups and included a symposium on Nuevo Teatro.

2314 White, Patricia S. "*Everybody*: On Stage in New York." *RORD.* 1986; 29: 105-107. Lang.: Eng.
USA: New York, NY. 1986. Reviews of performances. ■Account of a modern production of the medieval play *Everyman.*

2315 Wilkins, Frederick C. "Family Reunion at the Bottom of the Sea." *EON.* 1985 Win; 9(3): 23-28. Illus.: Photo. Print. B&W. 8: 5 in. x 7 in., 2 in. x 3 in. Lang.: Eng.
USA: New York, NY. 1985. Reviews of performances. ■Review of Eugene O'Neill's *The Iceman Cometh* directed by José Quintero.

2316 Ardamatskij, V. "Razgovory s Ranevskoj." (Conversations with Ranevskaja.) *TeatrM.* 1986; 11: 182-191. Lang.: Rus.
USSR. 1896-1984. Histories-sources. ■Recollections of actress Faina Ranevskaja.

DRAMA: —Performance/production

2317 Čeček, N.P. *Zapadnaja klassika na ukrainskoj sovetskoj scene 20-h godov (problema tragedijnogo spektaklja).* (Western Classics in the Ukrainian Soviet Stage of the Twenties—The Problem of Tragic Performance.) Moscow: VNII iskusstvoznanija; 1986. 25 pp. [Synopsis of a Dissertation.] Lang.: Rus.
USSR. 1920-1930. Critical studies. ■Ukrainian performances of classical Western tragedies.

2318 Csizner, Ildikó. "Tablókép Moszkvából. Tabakov-tanítványok vendégjátéka." (Tableau from Moscow: Guest Play of the Tabakov Students.) *Sz.* 1986 July; 19(7): 33-36. Illus.: Photo. B&W. 3: 9 cm. x 12 cm., 12 cm. x 12 cm. Lang.: Hun.
USSR: Moscow. Hungary: Budapest. 1986. Critical studies. ■Four performances in Budapest by the students of Oleg Tabakov of GITIS, the Institute of Dramatic Art, Moscow.

2319 Demin, G.G. *Vampilovskie tradicii v social'no-bytovoj drame i ee vopeoscenie na stoličnoj 70- godov: Avtoref. diss... kand. iskusstvovedenija.* (The Vampilov Tradition in Social-Domestic Drama—Its Realization on the Metropolitan Stage of the Seventies: Synopsis of a Dissertation by a Candidate in Art Criticism.) Moscow: GITIS; 1986. 16 pp. Lang.: Rus.
USSR. 1970-1979. Historical studies.

2320 Douglas, James B. "Impressions of Russia." *Theatrum.* 1985-86 Fall-Win; 3: 13-14. Lang.: Eng.
USSR: Leningrad, Moscow. 1984. Historical studies. ■Dispels western myths about Soviet theatre, providing an overview of the variety, volume and quality of performance in a subsidized, state-run system and noting the growth of East-West exchange.

2321 Gladil'ščikov, Ju. "'Za' i 'protiv' sovesti." ('For' and 'Against' Conscience.) *SovD.* 1986; 4: 215-222. Lang.: Rus.
USSR: Moscow. 1985-1986. Reviews of performances. ■Moscow theatre season surveyed.

2322 Golubovskij, B.G. *Mesto raboty—teatr.* (Place of Work—The Theatre.) Moscow: VTO; 1986. 288 pp. Lang.: Rus.
USSR: Moscow. 1940-1980. Biographies. ■Autobiography of director of the Gogol Theatre.

2323 Gudkova, V. "Temnoe mesto: Polemičeskie razmyšlenija." (A Dark Place: Polemical Reflections.) *TeatrM.* 1986; 9: 97-110. Lang.: Rus.
USSR: Moscow. 1980-1986. Reviews of performances. ■On interpretations of the works of Michajl Afanasjěvič Bulgakov at several theatres.

2324 Jurskij, S. "Poslednjaja rol' Ranevskoj." (Ranevskaja's Last Role.) *TeatrM.* 1986; 11: 170-182. Lang.: Rus.
USSR: Moscow. 1896-1984. Historical studies. ■On the participation of actress Faina Ranevskaja in Ostrovskij's play *Pravda—chorošo, a sčast'e lučše (Truth is Good, But Happiness is Better)* at Teat'r im. Mossověta.

2325 Jurskij, S. "Ishožu iz opyta." (Proceed from Experience.) *SovD.* 1986; 3: 248-255. Lang.: Rus.
USSR. 1986. Histories-sources. ■Interview with actor-director S. Jurskij on the staging of both classical drama and the contemporary plays of the Leningrad school.

2326 Kadyrova, S.M. *Svoeobrazie uzbekskoi Komedii i principy ee sceničeskogo voploščenija (70-perzv. pol: 80-h godov).* (The Distinctive Qualities of Uzbek Comedy and the Principles of Its Stage Realization, Seventies to First Half of Eighties.) Taškent: In-t iskusstvoznanija; 1986. 21 pp. [Synopsis of a Dissertation.] Lang.: Rus.
USSR. 1970-1985. Critical studies. ■Staging of Uzbek comedy.

2327 Kapralov, G. "Edigej i arbatskije staruški: 'Anatomija' odnoj roli." (Edigej and the Arbat Elders: The 'Anatomy' of a Role.) *TeatrM.* 1986; 9: 65-74. Lang.: Rus.
USSR: Moscow. 1980-1986. Reviews of performances. ■Performance of actor M.A. Ul'janovas Edigej in *I dolše veka dlitsja den' (A Day Lasts Longer than a Century)* by Čingiz Ajtmatov, at Teat'r im. Je. Vachtangova.

2328 Kaskabasov, S.A. *Rodniki iskusstva: Folkloristskie etjudy.* (Wellsprings of Art Folklore Sketches.) Alma-Ata: Oner; 1986. 123 pp. Lang.: Rus.

USSR. Critical studies. ■Descriptions of the folk drama of Kazakhstan.

2329 Koltai, Tamás. "Hajózni kell. A Komszomol Színház vendégjátéka." (One Has to Sail: Guest Play of the Comsomol Theatre.) *Sz.* 1986 Jan.; 19(1): 33-35. Illus.: Photo. B&W. 2: 10 cm. x 12 cm., 12 cm. x 13 cm. Lang.: Hun.
USSR: Moscow. Hungary: Budapest. 1985. Reviews of performances. ■Aleksej Ribnikov's modern opera *Junona i Avos (Juno and Avos)* and V.V. Višnevskij's *Optimista tragédia (Optimistic Tragedy)* performed by visiting Moscow Theatre of Lenin Comsomol, directed by Mark Zacharov at Comedy Theatre.

2330 Kulešov, V.I. "Kak my igraem klassiku." (How We Perform the Classics.) 202-230 in Kulešov, V.I., ed. *V poiskach točnosti i istiny.* Lang.: Rus.
USSR: Moscow. 1980-1986. Critical studies. ■Realization of classic works on the Moscow stage.

2331 Ljubimov, B. "Duchovnaja reforma." (Spiritual Reform.) *SovD.* 1986; 4: 202-215. Lang.: Rus.
USSR: Moscow. 1985-1986. Reviews of performances. ■Survey of the season's theatrical offerings, with analysis of repertoire.

2332 Mirchajdarova, Z.M. *Muyzka v dramatičeckom teatre Uzbekistana.* (Music in the Dramatic Theatre of Uzbekistan.) Taškent: Izdetelstvo literatury i iskusstva im. G. Guljama; 1986. 102 pp. Lang.: Rus.
USSR. Critical studies.

2333 Orlov, V. "Teatral'nye memuary." (Theatre Memoirs.) *Sibirskije ogni.* 1986; 3: 140-150. [Cont. in vol. 4, pp. 130-145 and vol. 5, 141-154.] Lang.: Rus.
USSR: Leningrad, Novosidirsk. 1947-1971. Histories-sources. ■Recollections of children's theatre in two Soviet cities.

2334 Ovčinnikova, S. "Slovo beret teat'r." (The World Takes the Theatre.) *NovyjMir.* 1986; 9: 242-255. Lang.: Rus.
USSR: Moscow. 1980-1986. Critical studies. ■Discussion of contemporary plays being staged in Moscow.

2335 Savickaja, O. "Uvidet' i ponjat': Zritelnoje načalo v režissure." (To See and To Understand: The Visual Principles in Directing.) *Tvorčestvo.* 1986; 8: 17-19. Lang.: Rus.
USSR: Leningrad. 1980-1986. Critical studies. ■Correlation of scenery and direction exemplified by performances of *Dom (Home)* and F. Abramov's *Bratja i sёstry (Brothers and Sisters)*, directed by L. Dodin at Malyj Dramatičeskij Teat'r.

2336 Sieradzki, Jacek. "Gruzini: Inne Problemy, Inny Teatr." (Georgians: Different Problems, Different Theatre.) *TeatrW.* 1984 Jan.; 39(808): 10-12. Lang.: Pol.
USSR: Tbilisi. Poland: Warsaw. 1983. Reviews of performances. ■production analysis of Bertolt Brecht's *Der Kaukasische Kreidekreis (The Caucasian Chalk Circle)* and Shakespeare's *Richard III* directed by Robert Sturua and staged by Georgian Academic Theatre at Teatr Dramatyczny in Warsaw.

2337 Starosel'skaja, N. "I ochertan'ja Fausta vdali..." (And in the Distance, Outlines of Faust.) *Literaturno obozrenie.* 1986; 9: 81-85. Lang.: Rus.
USSR. 1980-1986. Critical studies. ■Some features of the interpretation of classics for television and theatre, based on the directorial works of M. Kozakov.

2338 Tachmazov, N.N. *Problemy stanovlenija režissury v azerbajdžanskom dramatičeskom teatre.* (Problems of the Formation of the Art of Directing the Azerbajžan Dramatic Theatre From Its Origins to 1920.) Taškent: In-t iskusstvoznanija; 1986. 23 pp. [Synopsis of a Dissertation.] Lang.: Rus.
USSR. 1920. Historical studies. ■Development of Azerbajžani directing.

2339 Vasilinina, I. "Teatr čitaet p'esu." (A Theatre Reads a Play.) *TeatrM.* 1986; 7: 79-87. Lang.: Rus.
USSR. Moscow. 1986. Critical studies. ■Discusses Mekke's production of *Vinotavye (The Guilty)* by Aleksej Nikolajěvič Arbuzov at Teat'r im. Mossověta.

2340 Bőgel, József. "Vietnami *Bánk Bán*." (*Bánus Bánk* in Vietnam.) *Sz.* 1986 Sep.; 19(9): 41-46. Illus.: Photo. B&W. 2: 12 cm. x 17 cm. Lang.: Hun.

DRAMA: —Performance/production

Vietnam: Hanoi. 1986. Reviews of performances. ■József Katona's *Bánk Bán* presented by the Hanoi Tuong Theatre directed by Doan Anh Thang.

2341 Bőgel, József. "BITEF '85, Egy színházi fesztivál 'filozófiája'." (BITEF '85: 'Philosophy' of a Theatre Festival.) *Sz.* 1986 Feb.; 19(2): 41-44. Illus.: Photo. B&W. 2: 12 cm. x 15 cm., 12 cm. x 18 cm. Lang.: Hun.

Yugoslavia: Belgrade. 1985. Reviews of performances. ■Notes on theatrical events of nineteenth annual international theatre festival.

2342 Gul'čenko, V. "Ispoved' stranstvujuščego čeloveka." (Confessions of a Wandering Man.) *TeatrM.* 1986; 12: 174-179. Lang.: Rus.

Yugoslavia. 1980. Reviews of performances. ■Survey of plays from 21st festival of Yugoslavian theatre.

2343 Pályi, András. "A BITEF és környéke. Belgrád, Ljubljana, Zenica." (BITEF and Its Environment: Belgrade, Ljubljana, Zenica.) *Sz.* 1986 Feb.; 19(2): 35-40. Illus.: Photo. B&W. 4: 8 cm. x 12 cm., 10 cm. x 12 cm., 12 cm. x 16 cm. Lang.: Hun.

Yugoslavia. 1985. Reviews of performances. ■Report on the performances at the International Theatre Festival and on the theatrical events accompanying the meeting.

2344 Szakolczay, Lajos. "Egy drámai életút drámája. Sinkó Ervin és színpadai utóélete." (Drama of a Dramatic Life Career: Ervin Sinkó's Life on Stage.) *Sz.* 1986 Aug.; 19(8): 43-48. Illus.: Photo. B&W. 3: 9 cm. x 12 cm., 11 cm. x 12 cm. Lang.: Hun.

Yugoslavia: Belgrade. 1986. Critical studies. ■Slobodan Šnajder's play about Ervin Sinkó, *Confiteor*, directed by Janez Pipan at the National Theatre of Belgrade.

2345 Takács, István. "Mi lesz veled, Dubrovnik?" (What Will Be with You, Dubrovnik?)*Sz.* 1986 Apr.; 19(4): 43-45. Lang.: Hun.

Yugoslavia: Dubrovnik. 1984-1985. Critical studies. ■Preview of 1985 Summer Festival and comparison with the program of the previous year.

Plays/librettos/scripts

2346 Bécsy, Tamás. "Csehov—nem-verbális jelekkel." (Čechov—With Non-Verbal Signals.) *Jelenkor.* 1986; 29(5): 447-450. Lang.: Hun.

Critical studies. ■Analysis of four plays by Čechov: *Čajka (The Seagull), Diadia Vania (Uncle Vanya), Tri sestry (Three Sisters)* and *Višněvyj sad (The Cherry Orchard).*

2347 Bécsy, Tamás. "A csehovi dráma." (The Drama of Čechov.) *Sz.* 1986 Mar.; 19(3): 36-46. Lang.: Hun.

Critical studies. ■Study of the dramatic nature of Čechov's plays.

2348 Goetz, Ruth. "What is Dramatizing, Exactly?" *DGQ.* 1986 Win; 23:is 4: 8, 11-13.

Critical studies. ■Playwright Ruth Goetz defines dramatization as an emphasis on character over narrative and the visualization of an idea.

2349 Grote, David. "Where Are the Borderlines of the 'Essential' Playscript?" *DGQ.* 1986 Win; 23(4): 14-17.

Critical studies. ■Definition of the essentials of a script which should not be altered by directors or performers.

2350 Laurel, Brenda Kay. *Toward the Design of a Computer-Based Interactive Fantasy System.* Columbus, OH: Ohio State Univ; 1986. 324 pp. Pref. Biblio. Notes. [Ph.D. dissertation, Univ. Microfilms order No. DA8612387.] Lang.: Eng.

Technical studies. ■Feasibility study detailing theoretical and practical considerations for a computer-based dramatic interaction system programmed for 'expert playwriting' based on Aristotelian dramatic theory.

2351 Lehota, János. "A *Bánk Bán* szereplőinek magatartászázlata." (Behavior Draft of the Characters of *Banus Bánk.*) *Sz.* 1986 Dec.; 19(12): 24-28. Lang.: Hun.

Critical studies. ■Analysis of the characters of József Katona's classic drama focusing on the motivations behind their actions in the plot.

2352 Lord, Mark. "The Good and the Faithful at the Place of the Skull: Notes for a Theory of Translation." *ThM.* 1986 Fall/Win; 18(3): 70-73. Lang.: Eng.

1950-1986. Critical studies. ■Problems in translating discussed in relation to Eric Bentley's theories and Samuel Beckett's work.

2353 Mouton, Marisa. "Gehoordeelname en die deurbreking van die teaterillusie." (Audience Participation and Breaking Through the Theatrical Illusion.) *Acta Academica.* 1986; 13: 51-66. Notes. Biblio. Lang.: Afr.

1985. Critical studies. ■Theoretical look at the way in which playwrights try to break through theatrical illusion by forcing audience participation.

2354 Olsson, Jan; Victor-Rood, Juliette. "Brecht, Schweyk and the Military Review Motif." *ComIBS.* 1986 Apr.; 15(2): 28-36.

Critical studies. ■Brecht's use of the epically structured motif of the military review in *Furcht und Elend des III Reiches (Fear and Misery of the Third Reich)* and *Schweyk im Zweiten Weltkrieg (Schweyk in the Second World War).*

2355 Schechter, Joel. "Translations, Adaptations, Variations: A Conversation with Eric Bentley." *ThM.* 1986 Fall/Win; 18(1): 4-8. Illus.: Photo. 3: 3 in. x 4 in., 3 in. x 5 in., 3 in. x 2 in. Lang.: Eng.

1986. Textual studies. ■Interview with Eric Bentley on playwriting, translating and adapting texts.

2356 Slaff, Jerry. "Avoid These Pitfalls of Computerized Scripts." *DGQ.* 1986 Fall; 23(3): 34-35.

Instructional materials. ■Advice to playwrights from a manuscript reader on how to create an attractive computer-generated script.

2357 Szpakowska, Małgorzata. "Farsa czyli coś do śmiechu." (Farce, i.e., Something Funny.) *DialogW.* 1986; 11: 128-133. Notes. Lang.: Pol.

Critical studies. ■Characteristics of farce, mainly of the nineteenth century, and the problem of humor.

2358 Winston, Mathew. "The Incoherent Self in Contemporary Comedy." *MD.* 1986 Sep.; 29(3): 388-402. Notes. Lang.: Eng.

1954-1986. Critical studies. ■The centerless, protean, hapless and unreliable protagonist of modern comedy.

2359 Jain, Jasbir. "The Unfolding of a Text: Soyinka's *Death and the King's Horseman.*" *RAL.* 1986 Sum; 17(2): 252-260. Notes. Lang.: Eng.

Africa. 1975. Critical studies. ■Ritualistic elements in the structure of Wole Soyinka's *Death and the King's Horseman*, style of language, use of repetition, and reliance upon pageantry and ceremony.

2360 Artesi, Catalina Julia. "Una nueva forma para la farsa: *Fidela* de Aurelio Ferretti." (A New Form for Farce: Aurelio Ferretti's *Fidela.*) *LATR.* 1986 Fall; 20(1): 49-56. Notes. Lang.: Spa.

Argentina. 1930-1960. Critical studies. ■Use of various experimental techniques including puppets and the grotesque to depict contemporary life with tragicomic overtones in *Fidela* by Aurelio Ferretti. Related to Puppetry.

2361 Espinosa Domínguez, Carlos. "'Para mi el teatro es un ascesis, una cura de adelgazamiento': Entrevista a Mario Vargas Llosa." ('For Me Theatre Is Ascetic, A Cure for Narrowness': Interview with Mario Vargas Llosa.) *LATR.* 1986 Fall; 20(1): 57-60. Lang.: Spa.

Argentina. 1952-1986. Histories-sources. ■Mario Vargas Llosa discusses his three plays, *La señorita de Tacna (The Lady from Tacna), Kathie y el hippótamo (Kathy and the Hippopotamus)* and *La Chunga (The Joke)*, differences between narrative and dramatic writing and his response to productions of his plays.

2362 Laughlin, Karen L. "The Language of Cruelty: Dialogue, Strategies and the Spectator in Gambaro's *El desatino (The Blunder)* and Pinter's *The Birthday Party.*" *LATR.* 1986 Fall; 20(1): 1-20. Lang.: Eng.

Argentina. 1950-1980. Critical studies. ■Use of violent language in *El desatino (The Blunder)* by Griselda Gambaro in light of the theories of Antonin Artaud and its similarities to the techniques of Harold Pinter.

CLASSED ENTRIES

DRAMA: —Plays/librettos/scripts

2363 Magnarelli, Sharon. "Art and the Audience in O'Donnell's *Vincent y los cuervos.*" *LATR.* 1986 Spr; 19(2): 45-55. Notes. Illus.: Photo. Print. B&W. 3: var. sizes. Lang.: Eng.
Argentina: Buenos Aires. 1984. Critical studies. ■Analysis of Pacho O'Donnell's play about Van Gogh *Vincent y los cuervos (Vincent and the Crows)* as produced by Teatro del Bosque.

2364 Marcos, Juan Manuel. "Puig, Plutarco, Goethe: La dramaticidad cronotópica de *El beso de la mujer araña.*" (Puig, Plutarch, Goethe: The Chronotopical Dramatic Structure of *The Kiss of the Spider Woman.*) *LATR.* 1986 Fall; 20(1): 5-9. Notes. Lang.: Spa.
Argentina. 1976-1986. Critical studies. ■Applies Mikhail Bakhtin's theories of the chronotopos in Goethe and Plutarch to Manuel Puig's play *El beso de la mujer araña (The Kiss of the Spider Woman)* showing how language and space interact to produce psychological changes in the characters.

2365 Pelletieri, Osvaldo. "Presencia del sainete en el teatro argentino de las últimas décadas." (Presence of the *Sainete* in Argentine Theatre of Recent Decades.) *LATR.* 1986 Fall; 20(1): 71-77. Notes. Lang.: Spa.
Argentina. 1800-1980. Historical studies. ■Development in the genre of the *sainete,* or comic afterpiece.

2366 Seibel, Beatriz. "Festival Nacional de Teatro: Córdoba '85." (National Theatre Festival: Córdoba 1985.) *LATR.* 1986 Fall; 20(1): 91-94. Notes. Lang.: Spa.
Argentina: Córdoba. 1985. Historical studies. ■Theatre companies from various provinces of Argentina were represented at the festival which included many new Latin American plays.

2367 "Alma de Groen: An Interview." *LiNQ.* 1986; 14(3): 6-14. Lang.: Eng.
Australia. Histories-sources. ■Interview with Alma de Groen, focusing chiefly on her plays *Vocations* and *Rivers of China* and her attitude toward feminism.

2368 "Dorothy Hewett." 184-209 in Baker, Candida, ed. *Yacker: Australian Writers Talk about Their Work.* Sydney: Pan; 1986. 315 pp. Lang.: Eng.
Australia: Sydney, N.S.W. 1986. Histories-sources. ■An interview largely devoted to the biography, thoughts and life-style of Dorothy Hewett, but with comments on her writing methods and on particular plays and their productions, notably *Pandora's Cross* and *The Fields of Heaven.*

2369 "David Williamson." 290-315 in Baker, Candida, ed. *Yacker: Australia Writers Talk About Their Work.* Sydney: Pan; 1986. 315. Lang.: Eng.
Australia. 1986. Histories-sources. ■Interview with Williamson on the process of directing his own play, *Sons of Cain,* and the concerns of the play. Includes comments on productions of *The Removalists,* and Williamson's working methods.

2370 Ackland, Michael. "Plot and Counter-Plot in Charles Harpur's *The Bushrangers.*" *ADS.* 1986 Apr.; 8: 49-61. Notes. Lang.: Eng.
Australia. 1835-1853. Critical studies. ■Examination, exploration and assessment of Australian poet Charles Harpur's unproduced play originally titled *The Tragedy of Donohoe* written in 1835.

2371 Akerholt, May-Brit. "Translations and the Australian Theatre." *ADS.* 1986 Apr.; 8: 5-16. Notes. Illus.: Photo. B&W. 3: 11 x 15 cm. [Conference paper.] Lang.: Eng.
Australia: Armidale, N.S.W. 1985. Critical studies. ■Discussion of attitudes toward translating and adapting 'non-Australian English' and foreign plays for the Australian stage.

2372 Blair, Ron. "Understanding the Past." *ADS.* 1986 Oct.; 9: 21-24. Notes. Illus.: Photo. B&W. 5: 10.5 cm. x 13.5 cm., 10.5 cm. x 15 cm., 9.5 cm. x 15.5 cm. Lang.: Eng.
Australia. 1960-1970. Histories-sources. ■Playwright-director Ron Blair on technical virtuosity and dramatic content in writing for the theatre.

2373 Carroll, Dennis. "Mateship and Individualism in Modern Australian Drama." *TJ.* 1982 Dec.; 34(4): 467-480. Illus.: Photo. 3: var. sizes. Lang.: Eng.
Australia. 1940-1980. Critical studies. ■The limits on individuality in the face of male solidarity and its affect on male-female relationships.

2374 Fitzpatrick, Peter. "After the Wave: Australian Theatre since 1975." *NTQ.* 1986 Feb.; 11(5): 54-67. Illus.: Photo. B&W. 4. Lang.: Eng.
Australia. 1975-1986. Histories-specific. ■Developments in Australian playwriting since 1975.

2375 Fitzpatrick, Peter. "Sewell's *Dreams* at the Adelaide Festival." *ADS.* 1986 Oct.; 9: 35-51. Notes. Illus.: Photo. 6: 11 cm. x 15 cm. Lang.: Eng.
Australia: Adelaide. Critical studies. ■Evaluation and exploration of playwright Stephen Sewell's political orientation in *Dreams in an Empty City.*

2376 Hillel, Angela. "Oriel Gray: A Forgotten Playwright." 17-27 in Univ. New England, ed. *Australian Drama 1920-1955.* Papers presented at a conference at the University of New England, Armidale, September 1-4, 1984. Armidale, N.S.W: Univ. of New England; 1986. 157 pp. Lang.: Eng.
Australia. 1942-1958. Critical studies. ■Describes the plays of Oriel Gray, from early political pieces, through domestic dramas with a social conscience, to satirical plays of ideas with an historical setting, arguing for the value of the domestic dramas.

2377 Hooton, Joy. "Lawler's Demythologizing of the Doll: Kid Stakes and Other Times." *Australian Literary Studies.* 1986 May; 4(3): 335-346. Lang.: Eng.
Australia. 1955-1977. Critical studies. ■Argues that Ray Lawler's *Summer of the Seventeenth Doll,* when approached through the later plays dealing with the same characters, loses many of its ambiguities and takes on a darker tone.

2378 Kavanagh, Paul; Kuch, Peter. "What Are the Shades of Grey? David Williamson Talks to Paul Kavanagh and Peter Kuch." *Southerly.* 1986 June; 46(2): 131-141. Lang.: Eng.
Australia. 1986. Histories-sources. ■Interview with playwright David Williamson on the social and personal issues that have inspired his more recent plays. Describes his working methods, point of view on characters and preoccupation with the tension between idealism and pragmatism.

2379 Kiernan, Brian. "Comic Satiric Realism: David Williamson's Plays since *The Department.*" *Southerly.* 1986 Mar.; 46(1): 3-18. Lang.: Eng.
Australia. 1976-1985. Critical studies. ■Analysis of David Williamson's plays: *A Handful of Friends, The Club, Travelling North, Celluloid Heroes, The Perfectionist* and *Sons of Cain.*

2380 McCallum, John. "'Something with a Cow in It': Louis Esson's Imported Nationalism." 39-52 in Univ. New England, ed. *Australian Drama 1920-1955.* Papers presented at a conference at the University of New England, September 1-4, 1984. Armidale, N.S.W: Univ. of New England; 1986. 157 pp. Lang.: Eng.
Australia. Eire. 1905-1943. Critical studies. ■Influences on playwright Louis Esson in his efforts to create an Australian national drama, arguing for the inappropriateness of the Abbey Theatre model to which he committed himself and describing his later tentative moves toward an epic-form.

2381 McCallum, John. "The *Doll* and the Legend." *ADS.* 1985 Apr.; 3(2): 32-44. Illus.: Photo. B&W. 8: 4 in. x 6 in. Lang.: Eng.
Australia. 1959-1983. Critical studies. ■Impact of Ray Lawler's *Summer of the Seventeenth Doll* on Australian theatre.

2382 Modjeska, Drusilla. "Betty Roland Talks to Drusilla Modjeska." *ADS.* 1986 Apr.; 8: 63-69. Notes. Lang.: Eng.
Australia: Sydney, N.S.W. 1928-1985. Histories-sources. ■Excerpt from a 1985 recorded discussion of playwright Betty Roland's life and stage work.

2383 Perkins, Elizabeth. "Aspects of the Heroic in Australian Verse Drama: Douglas Stewart, Tom Inglis Moore and Catherine Duncan." 53-70 in Univ. New England, ed. *Australian Drama 1920-1955.* Papers presented at a conference at the University of New England, Armidale, September 1-4, 1984. Armidale, N.S.W: Univ. of New England; 1986. 157 pp. Lang.: Eng.

DRAMA: —Plays/librettos/scripts

Australia. 1941-1943. Critical studies. ■Analyzes and contrasts the nihilistic vision of Stewart's *Fire on the Snow*, the ironic stoicism of Moore's *We're Going Through* and the thesis drama of Duncan's *Songs of the Morning.*

2384 Ryan, J.S. "Forgotten Poetic Sensibilities: The Plays of Charles Jury and Ray Mathew." 71-88 in Univ. New England, ed. *Australian Drama 1920-1955*. Papers presented at a conference at the University of New England, Armidale, September 1-4, 1984. Armidale, N.S.W: Univ. of New England; 1986. 157 pp. Lang.: Eng.
Australia. 1905-1967. Critical studies. ■Analysis of Jury's verse plays, chiefly on Greek and Arthurian subjects, but with modern reverberations, and the lyric realism of Mathew's evocations of country life, which could have made him a fruitful contributor to the emerging Australian drama of the 1950s and 1960s.

2385 Sirmai, Geoffrey. "An Interview with Alex Buzo." *Southerly*. 1986 Mar.; 46(1): 80-91. Lang.: Eng.
Australia. 1986. Histories-sources. ■Playwright Alex Buzo discusses the style of his work and its relationship to absurdism, audience response, adaptations for film and television and his change of direction after *Martello Towers.*

2386 Sykes, Arlene. "Interview: Ray Lawler Talks to Arlene Sykes." *ADS*. 1985 Apr.; 3(2): 21-31. Lang.: Eng.
Australia: Melbourne. 1984. Histories-sources. ■Interview with playwright Ray Lawler on his work with Melbourne Theatre Company and the play *Godsend.*

2387 Thomas, Sue. "Betty Roland's *The Touch of Silk* and *Granite Peak.*" *ADS*. 1986 Apr.; 8: 81-94. Notes. Lang.: Eng.
Australia. 1928-1981. Critical studies. ■Assessment and exploration of Betty Roland's plays, *The Touch of Silk* and *Granite Peak.*

2388 Throssell, Ric. "Paths Towards Purpose: The Political Plays of Katherine Susannah Prichard and Ric Throssell." 28-38 in Univ. New England, ed. *Australian Drama 1920-1955*. Papers presented at a conference at the University of New England, Armidale, September 1-4, 1984. Armidale, N.S.W: Univ. of New England; 1986. 157 pp. Lang.: Eng.
Australia. 1909-1966. Critical studies. ■Describes the largely unpublished left-wing political plays of Prichard, mainly agit-prop in style, and comments on Throssell's political work.

2389 Fuerst, Norbert. *Das Dramenwerk Max Zweigs.* (The Dramatic Opus of Max Zweig.) Klagenfurt: Johannes Heyn; 1986. 111 pp. Pref. Append. Lang.: Ger.
Austria: Vienna. Germany: Berlin. Israel: Tel Aviv. 1892-1986. Critical studies. ■Excerpts from the dramatist's letters give a view of his life and work: realization, reception and judgment of his plays.

2390 Greiner, Bernhard. "Die Rede des Unbewussten als Komödie: Hofmannsthals Lustspiel *Der Schwierige.*" (The Speech of the Unconcious as Comedy: Hofmannsthal's Comedy *The Difficult Man.*) *GQ*. 1986 Spr; 59(2): 228-251. Lang.: Ger.
Austria. 1921. Critical studies. ■Analysis of the use of language in *Der Schwierige (The Difficult Man)* by Hugo von Hofmannsthal focusing on its similarities with Freudian theories of the unconscious.

2391 Mertl, Monika. "Eingestürzte Brücke." (Collapsed Bridges.) *Buhne*. 1986 Apr.; 29(4): 17-18. Illus.: Photo. Print. Color. [Autoren in Österreich 1.] Lang.: Ger.
Austria. 1986. Critical studies. ■The bad relationship between contemporary Austrian playwrights and theatres in Austria.

2392 Mertl, Monika. "Voneinander lernen." (Learning from Each Other.) *Buhne*. 1986; 29(5): 10-11. Illus.: Photo. Print. B&W. Lang.: Ger.
Austria: Vienna. 1985-1986. Critical studies. ■Training for new playwrights in cooperation with theatres or groups where they mostly work as dramaturgists.

2393 Mertl, Monika. "Kein Platz für Experimente." (No Place for Experiment.) *Buhne*. 1986 July; 29(7): 97-98. Illus.: Photo. Print. B&W. [Autoren in Österreich 4.] Lang.: Ger.

Austria. 1980-1986. Critical studies. ■Programming theatres in order to draw large audiences and obtain subsidies vs. presenting works of new playwrights in cooperation with the playwrights-in-training program.

2394 Mertl, Monika. "Der bessere Auftrag." (The Better Mandate.) *Buhne*. 1986 Aug.; 29(8): 40-41. Illus.: Photo. Print. B&W. Lang.: Ger.
Austria: Vienna. 1938-1986. Histories-specific. ■Cooperation between playwright Heinz Rudolf Unger and the Vienna Volkstheater is supported by the mandate of the theatre.

2395 Mertl, Monika. "Der Trend, das unbekannte Wesen." (The Trend, the Unknown Being.) *Buhne*. 1986 June; 29(6): 16, 18. Illus.: Photo. Print. Color. B&W. [Autoren in Österreich 3.] Lang.: Ger.
Austria. 1976-1986. Critical studies. ■The difficulties of new playwrights in getting their plays performed or promoted by publishers.

2396 Naumenko, A.M. "Dramaturgija F.T. Čokora do vtoroj mirovoj voiny: problemy poetiki." (The Dramaturgy of Franz Csokor up to World War II: Problems of Poetics.) *FN*. 1986; 29(3): 74-78. Lang.: Rus.
Austria. 1920-1939. Historical studies. ■Life and work of playwright Franz Csokor.

2397 Schwarzinger, Heinz. "Sie wollen *Die letzten Tage der Menschheit* übersetzen? Bumstinazi!: Bemerkungen zum französischen Übersetzungsprojekt." (You Want to Translate *The Last Days of Mankind*? Nonsense!: Notes on the French Translation Project.) 8-12 in Lunzer, Heinz, ed. *Karl Kraus 1874-1936: Katalog einer Ausstellung des Bundesministeriums für Auswärtige Angelegenheiten (Karl Kraus 1874-1936: Exhibition Catalogue of the Foreign Office).* Vienna: Dokumentationsstelle für neuere österreichische Literatur; 1986. 83 pp. (Zirkular, Sondernummer 8.) Biblio. Notes. Lang.: Ger.
Austria: Vienna. France: Paris. 1918-1986. Critical studies. ■Difficulties of translating play into French: special names and terminology, distinction between social and geographical origins of the dramatis personae, orthographical onomatopoeia, and special lengthening.

2398 Widrich, Hans. "Er träumt die Menschheitsträume." (He Dreams the Dreams of Mankind.) *Buhne*. 1986 Jan.; 29(1): 9-12. Illus.: Photo. Print. Color. B&W. Lang.: Ger.
Austria: Salzburg. Greece. 1985-1986. Histories-sources. ■Interview with Peter Handke about his new play *Prometheus gefesselt*, a translation and adaptation of *Prometheus desmotes (Prometheus Bound)* by Aeschylus: the problems of translation, and the first production at the Salzburger Festspiele in 1986.

2399 Lorenz, Dagmar C.G. *Grillparzer—Dichter des sozialen Konflikts.* (Grillparzer—Poet of Social Conflicts.) Vienna, Cologne, Graz: Böhlau; 1986. 211 pp. (Literatur und Leben, Neue Folge 33.) Pref. Index. Notes. Tables. Biblio. Lang.: Ger.
Austro-Hungarian Empire: Vienna. 1791-1872. Critical studies. ■Analysis of social themes in Franz Grillparzer's dramas: his revolutionary view of women's rights, nationalism, racism, antisemitism, monarchic and bourgeois rulership and class distinctions. Women's roles are especially characterized. Includes discussion of private and political actions in his dramas.

2400 Glasheen, Anne-Marie. "Jacques de Decker." *GAMBIT*. 1986; 11(42-43): 165, 168. Lang.: Eng.
Belgium. 1945-1986. Biographical studies. ■Biography of playwright Jacques de Decker with a list of his plays.

2401 Glasheen, Anne-Marie. "René Kalisky." *GAMBIT*. 1986; 11(42-43): 164-165,167-168. Lang.: Eng.
Belgium. 1936-1981. Biographical studies. ■Biography of playwright René Kalisky including a list of his plays.

2402 Glasheen, Anne-Marie. "Jean Sigrid." *GAMBIT*. 1986; 11(42-43): 163-164,167-168. Lang.: Eng.
Belgium. 1920-1986. Biographical studies. ■Biography of playwright Jean Sigrid, including a list of his plays and awards.

2403 Glasheen, Anne-Marie. "Paul Willems." *GAMBIT*. 1986; 11(42-43): 162-163,167-168. B&W. 1. Lang.: Eng.

DRAMA: —Plays/librettos/scripts

Belgium. 1912-1986. Biographical studies. ■Biography of playwright Paul Willems, including a list of his writings and awards.

2404 Albuquerque, Severino João. "Conflicting Signs of Violence in Augusto Boal's *Torquemada*." *MD*. 1986 Sep.; 29(3): 452-459. Notes. [Expanded version of paper read in Luso-Brazilian Session of Kentucky Foreign Languages and Literature Conference, Lexington, KY April 26, 1985.] Lang.: Eng.
Brazil. 1971. Critical studies. ■Interplay of verbal and nonverbal signs in Augusto Boal's *Torquemada*.

2405 Albuquerque, Severino João. "Verbal Violence and the Pursuit of Power in *Apareceu a Margarida*." *LATR*. 1986 Spr; 19(2): 23-29. Notes. Lang.: Eng.
Brazil. 1808-1973. Historical studies. ■Analysis of the use of language as an instrument of tyranny in Roberto Athayde's *Miss Margarida's Way*.

2406 Bardijewska, Liliana. "Literatura bułgarska: Dyskurs o narodzie." (Bulgarian Literature: Discourse about the Nation.) *DialogW*. 1986; 7: 118-129. Notes. Lang.: Pol.
Bulgaria. 1945-1986. Historical studies. ■Main subjects of Bulgarian drama after World War II, typical dramaturgical techniques, leading playwrights.

2407 Anthony, Geraldine. "Coulter's *Riel*: A Reappraisal." *CDr*. 1985 Sum; 11(2): 321-328. Notes. Lang.: Eng.
Canada. 1950. Critical studies. ■An analysis of John Coulter's play *Riel*, arguing that the depiction of Louis Riel as heroic is based on a carefully constructed parallel with the Passion of Christ.

2408 Bessai, Diane. "A Literary Perspective on the Plays of W.O. Mitchell." *CDr*. 1984 Spr; 10(1): 75-82. Lang.: Eng.
Canada. 1975. Critical studies. ■Structure and characterization in radio and stage plays by W.O. Mitchell, with some consideration of the connection between his novels and plays. Related to Media: Audio forms.

2409 Brunner, Astrid. "Halifax: Walter Borden, Child of Time." *CTR*. 1986 Fall; 13(48): 126-128. Illus.: Photo. Print. B&W. 1:2 in. x 2 in. Lang.: Eng.
Canada: Halifax, NS. 1960-1986. Biographical studies. ■Career of actor and prose-poet Walter Borden is epitomized by his play *Tight Rope Time*, first performed in 1986.

2410 Collet, Paulette. "Fennario's *Balconville* and Tremblay's *En Pièces détachées*: A Universe of Backyards and Despair." *CDr*. 1984 Spr; 10(1): 35-43. Notes. Lang.: Eng.
Canada: Quebec, PQ. 1970-1980. Critical studies. ■Poverty, despair and class in two Quebecois plays with comment on characterization, theme and structure.

2411 Copeman, Peter. "Rick Salutin and the Popular Dramatic Tradition: Towards a Dialectical Theatre in Canada." *CDr*. 1984 Spr; 10(1): 25-34. Notes. Lang.: Eng.
Canada: Montreal, PQ, Toronto, ON. 1976-1981. Critical studies. ■The dialectic of literary and popular theatrical forms in the plays of Rick Salutin in the context of colonialism in Canada.

2412 Devine, Michael. "Piscator/Meyerhold: Slicing Life in Epic Portions." *Theatrum*. 1986 Sum; 4: 17-20. Pref. Illus.: Dwg. B&W. 1: 2 in. x 3 in. Lang.: Eng.
Canada. Russia: Moscow. Germany. 1900-1986. Historical studies. ■Comparison of early 20th century German and Russian precedents of theatrical innovation with recent Canadian theatre.

2413 Doucette, L.E. "Louis Riel sur scène: L'État de la dramaturgie québécoise en 1886." (Louis Riel on Stage: The State of Quebec Dramaturgy in 1886.) *THC*. 1985 Fall; 6(2): 123-132. Notes. Lang.: Fre.
Canada: Montreal, PQ. 1886. Historical studies. ■An examination of two unproduced historical dramas on the subject of the death of the French-Canadian patriot Louis Riel.

2414 Garay, Kathleen. "John Coulter's *Riel*: The Shaping of 'A Myth for Canada'." *CDr*. 1985 Fall; 11(2): 293-309. Notes. Illus.: Handbill. Photo. Poster. 5. Lang.: Eng.
Canada: Toronto, ON, Ottawa, ON. 1936-1980. Critical studies. ■Examination of the writing and production of John Coulter's *Riel*, including the play's difficult production history.

2415 Garay, Kathleen. "'Highest Hopes and Deepest Disappointments:' John Coulter's London Diaries, 1951-1957." *CDr*. 1984 Spr; 10(1): 1-24. Notes. Illus.: Poster. B&W. 1. Lang.: Eng.
Canada: Toronto, ON. UK-England: London. 1951-1957. Biographical studies. ■An overview of the later years in the career of playwright John Coulter based on diary entries. The emphasis is on practical problems in playwriting and production.

2416 Garebian, Keith. "The Dusk to Dawn Journey of *RA*: Dangerous Moments in the Theatrical Underworld." *PAC*. 1983 Aug.; 20(2): 22-23. Illus.: Photo. B&W. 2. Lang.: Eng.
Canada: Toronto, ON. 1983. Critical studies. ■An overview of the Comus Music Theatre's 11-hour religious drama *RA*, a mixed-media production based on the Egyptian Book of the Dead. Related to Media: Mixed media.

2417 Gay, Paul. "Paul-André Paiement (1950-1978) ou le Désespoir du Colonisé." (Paul-André Paiement (1950-1978), or the Despair of the Colonial.) *THC*. 1986 Fall; 7(2): 176-185. Notes. Illus.: Photo. B&W. 1. Lang.: Fre.
Canada. 1970-1978. Critical studies. ■An analysis of the life and plays of Paul-André Paiement focusing on his status as a 'colonial' in English-speaking Ontario and on his use of the forms of comedy.

2418 Grace, Sherrill E. "'The Living Soul of Man': Bertram Brooker and Expressionist Theatre." *THC*. 1985 Spr; 6(1): 3-22. Notes. Illus.: Sketches. 1. Lang.: Eng.
Canada: Toronto, ON. 1888-1949. Critical studies. ■Career of playwright Bertram Brooker, with particular attention to two plays produced in 1935 and 1936 *Within* and *The Dragon*. Brooker's expressionism is compared to that of Jèvreinov and Andrejèv.

2419 Harrison, James. "At Issue With *As Is* and *The Dolly*." *Theatrum*. 1986 Sum; 4: 13-16. Lang.: Eng.
Canada: Toronto, ON. 1985. Critical studies. ■Comparison of two plays which present topical social issues but which fail to resolve their dramatic conflicts. Plot summaries are given as well as the critical criteria by which the plays fail.

2420 Heide, Christopher. "Wolfville: Playwright-in-Residence, Horton District High." *CTR*. 1986 Fall; 13(48): 122-126. Illus.: Photo. Print. B&W. 1:3 in. x 2 in. Lang.: Eng.
Canada. 1984-1985. Histories-sources. ■Playwright Christopher Heide, at age 33, attended high school as a student for a year to do research for a play.

2421 Johnson, Chris. "Ned Kelly: Australia's Theatrical Louis Riel." *CDr*. 1985 Sum; 11(2): 310-320. Notes. Lang.: Eng.
Canada. Australia. 1900-1976. Critical studies. ■A comparison of Australia's Ned Kelly with Canada's Louis Riel as central figures in historical dramas, focusing on anti-authoritarian strains in popular theatre.

2422 Kaplan, Jon. "New York: Sam Shikaze, Private Eye." *CTR*. 1986 Spr; 13(46): 98-100. Illus.: Photo. Print. B&W. 1: 3 in. x 4 in. Lang.: Eng.
Canada: Toronto, ON. USA: New York, NY. USA: San Francisco, CA. 1970-1986. Biographical studies. ■Production history of *Yellow Fever* by R.A. Shiomi, featuring a Japanese-Canadian private eye, and Shiomi's subsequent plays and development as a playwright.

2423 Lacombe, Michèle. "Antonine Maillet: Breaking the Silence of Centuries." *CTR*. 1986 Spr; 13(46): 58-64. Notes. Illus.: Photo. Print. B&W. 4: var. sizes. Lang.: Eng.
Canada. 1971-1979. Critical studies. ■The plays of Antonine Maillet, especially *La Sagouine (The Slattern)*, led to a revival of Acadian theatre in the 1970s.

2424 Leonard, Paul. "Toronto: Bilingual Fables." *CTR*. 1986 Spr; 13(46): 95-97. Illus.: Photo. Print. B&W. 1: 2 in. x 4 in. Lang.: Eng.
Canada: Toronto, ON. 1984-1985. Critical studies. ■The creation, performance, and implications of *La Storia* and *La Storia II*, two plays performed in Italian and English by the Acting Company of Toronto.

2425 Leonard, Paul. "Unnecessary Literature: *Five from the Fringe*." *CDr*. 1986 Fall; 12(2): 378-381. Lang.: Eng.

DRAMA: —Plays/librettos/scripts

Canada: Edmonton, AB. 1986. Critical studies. ■Criticizes Nancy Bell, editor of *Five from the Fringe*, for denigrating the theatrical vitality of Edmonton's Fringe Festival by choosing to publish five inferior scripts.

2426 McCaffrey, Mark. "Latin American Theatre in Montreal." *LATR*. 1986 Spr; 19(2): 121-125. Lang.: Eng.

Canada: Montreal, PQ. 1985. Historical studies. ■Interview with actress Pilar Romero of Grupo Rajatabla about her performance in *Bolívar* by José Antonio Rial at the Festival de Théâtre des Amériques, and with director Roberto Blanco of Teatre Irrumpe on his production of *María Antonia* by Eugenio Hernandez Espinosa.

2427 Meadwell, Kenneth W. "*125 Ans de théâtre au Séminaire de Trois-Rivières.*" (*125 Years of Theatre at the Trois-Rivières Seminary.*) *CDr*. 1986 Spr; 12(1): 229-230. Lang.: Fre.

Canada: Trois-Rivières, PQ. 1985. Critical studies. ■Praises the book *125 Ans de Théâtre au Séminaire de Trois-Rivières* by Rémi Tourangeau and Julien Duhaime for its use of illustrations and anecdotes, but criticizes the book's lack of depth.

2428 Moss, Jane. "The Body as Spectacle: Women's Theatre in Quebec." *WPerf*. 1986; 3(1): 5-16. Notes. Lang.: Eng.

Canada: Quebec, PQ. 1969-1985. Historical studies. ■Discusses feminist theatre with themes concerning the female body.

2429 Nelson, Ian C.; Wittlin, Curt. "'What Has He Done?'–'Mé que cést qu'y'a don faite?'." (Observations on Garneau's *Macbeth* in Québecois.) *CDr*. 1986 Fall; 12(2): 351-359. Notes. Lang.: Eng.

Canada: Montreal, PQ. 1978. Textual studies. ■Criticizes Michel Garneau's Québecois *joual* translation of *Macbeth* for failing to convey the universal themes of the original Shakespeare text.

2430 O'Neill, Patrick B. "*Fitzallan.*" *CDr*. 1986 Fall; 12(2): 372-374. Notes. Lang.: Eng.

Canada: Halifax, NS. 1833. Historical studies. ■Argues that the melodrama *Fitzallan* was the first production in Canada of a play written by a native-born Canadian author (William Rufus Blake).

2431 Perkyns, Richard. "Pioneers: Two Contrasting Dramatic Treatments." *CDr*. 1984 Spr; 10(1): 56-64. Notes. Lang.: Eng.

Canada. 1934-1950. Critical studies. ■Representations of the immigrant in *Hill-Land* by Herman Voaden and *At My Heart's Core* by Robertson Davies.

2432 Reprecht, Alvina. "Les voix scéniques de René-Daniel Dubois: discours et post-modernité." (René-Daniel Dubois' Scenic Voices: Speech and Post-Modernism.) *CDr*. 1986 Fall; 12(2): 360-371. Notes. Lang.: Fre.

Canada. 1980. Critical studies. ■Examines *Ne blâmez jamais les Bédouins* (*Don't Blame It on the Bedouins*) by Dubois as a post-modernist play which upsets audience stereotypes by playing with language and borrowing images from Dadaism and surrealism.

2433 Rewa, Natalie. "A Reflection of French-Canadian Nationalism: *Le Drapeau de Carillon.*" *TID*. 1986; 8: 177-194. Notes. Lang.: Eng.

Canada: Montreal, PQ. 1759-1901. Critical studies. ■Theme of French-Canadian nationalism in Laurent-Olivier David's 1901 production of *Le Drapeau de Carillon* (*The Flag of Carillon*) based on the poem by Octave Crémazie.

2434 Rioux, Monique; Van Burek, John, transl. "Discovering the Inuit People." *CTR*. 1986 Spr; 13(46): 72-78. Notes. Illus.: Photo. Print. B&W. 4: var. sizes. Lang.: Eng.

Canada. 1982-1983. Histories-sources. ■After a tour of northern Quebec, Le Théâtre de la Marmaille created the play *Umiak* based on Inuit legends and traditions.

2435 Rubess, Banuta. "Vancouver: Hamlet, a New Canadian Play." *CTR*. 1986 Win; 13(49): 131-135. Illus.: Photo. Print. B&W. 2: 5 in. x 5 in., 5 in. x 4 in. Lang.: Eng.

Canada: Vancouver, BC. 1986. Critical studies. ■*The Haunted House Hamlet*, produced by Tamahnous Theatre, employed elements of environmental theatre, simultaneous scenes, text transposition and interpolation, gender changes and new text, with Shakespeare's text treated as a mythic source.

2436 Ruprecht, Alvina. *Michel Tremblay et le temps perdu d'Albertine.* (Michel Tremblay and the Lost Time of Albertine.) *CDr*. 1986 Spr; 12(1): 1-7.

Canada. 1984. Critical studies. ■Tremblay's use of multiple time periods occurring simultaneously in *Albertine, en cinq temps* is compared to Proust's recollections of another Albertine in *A la recherche du temps perdu*.

2437 Scholar, Michael. "*Beyond Batoche*: The Playwright in Mid-Career." *CDr*. 1985 Sum; 11(2): 329-339. Notes. Lang.: Eng.

Canada: Regina, SK. 1985. Critical studies. ■Analysis of Rex Deverell's application of his documentary style, anti-realist techniques to the subject of Louis Riel in order to point up tensions between history and myth.

2438 Skene, Reg. "The Actor as Playwright: Alan Williams." *CTR*. 1986 Win; 13(49): 51-57. Illus.: Photo. Print. B&W. 4: var. sizes. Lang.: Eng.

Canada: Toronto, ON, Winnipeg, MB. UK-England: Hull. 1976-1986. Histories-sources. ■Interview with Alan Williams, English-born actor and playwright, about his methodological development and recent plays.

2439 Usmiani, Renate. "Antonine Maillet: Recycling an Archetype." *CTR*. 1986 Spr; 13(46): 65-71. Notes. Illus.: Photo. Print. B&W. 3: var. sizes. Lang.: Eng.

Canada. 1968-1975. Critical studies. ■The characters drawn by Acadian playwright Antonine Maillet debunk the romantic Acadian myth of Henry Wadsworth Longfellow's *Evangeline*.

2440 Wilson, Ann. "*Willful Acts: Five Plays.*" *CDr*. 1986 Fall; 12(2): 381-382. Lang.: Eng.

Canada. Critical studies. ■Welcomes the publication of five plays by Margaret Hollingsworth, which explore female lives and issues.

2441 Thomas, Charles P. "Chilean Theatre in Exile: The Teatro del Angel in Costa Rica, 1974-1984." *LATR*. 1986 Spr; 19(2): 97-101. Notes. Lang.: Eng.

Chile. Costa Rica. 1955-1984. Historical studies. ■Chilean playwright Alejandro Sieveking and his wife, actress Bélgica Castro, founded the Teatro del Angel, a theatre company in exile during the period of political problems in Chile. A list of productions is appended.

2442 Villegas, Juan. "Los Marginados como personajes: teatro chileno de la década de los sesenta." (Characters from the Margins of Society: Chilean Theatre of the 1960s.) *LATR*. 1986 Spr; 19(2): 85-95. Lang.: Eng.

Chile. 1960-1971. Historical studies. ■Emerging political influence of marginal social groups exemplified in the plays of Jorge Díaz, Egon Wolff and Luis Alberto Heiremans.

2443 Kaplan, Randy Barbara. *The Pre-Leftist One-Act Dramas of Tian Han.* Columbus, OH: Ohio State Univ.; 1986. 490 pp. Pref. Notes. Biblio. [Ph.D. dissertation, Univ. Microfilms order No. DA8618792.] Lang.: Eng.

China. 1898-1968. Biographies. ■Historical study focusing on the life, work and major contributions to Chinese theatre by Tian Han, who used foreign playwriting form and style combined with Chinese themes and subject matter.

2444 Kung, I-chiang. "Hsi, Li Shih, Li Shih Chu—Tsung Chi Chu San Kuo Hsi Tan Li Shih Chu Chuang Tso." (Talking about Creating Historical Drama: *The Romance of the Three Kingdoms.*) *XYanj*. 1986 Apr.; 18: 147-162. Lang.: Chi.

China. 960-1983. Historical studies. ■History and its recreation as a subject for traditional Chinese drama.

2445 Me, Shu-i. "Yuan Chu Chia Tso Tan." (Discourse on Yuan Dynasty Playwrights.) *XYanj*. 1986 Apr.; 18: 254-267. Lang.: Chi.

China. 1256-1341. Biographical studies. ■Profiles of Wang Shih-Fu, Kuan Han-Ching and Chu Ling-Hsiu drawn from historical documents.

2446 Wang, Zhendong. "Ding Xilin Dumu Xiju Jiewei Yishu Tan." (The Endings of Ding Xilin's One-Act Comedies.) *XYishu*. 1982 Aug.; 5(3): 110-115. Lang.: Chi.

DRAMA: —Plays/librettos/scripts

China. 1923-1962. Critical studies. ■Surprising reversals in Ding's short comedies were foreshadowed and presented with ingenious handling of irony.

2447 Zhou, Duanmu; Sun, Zuping. "Lun Dumuju." (On One-Act Plays.) *XYishu*. 1982 Aug.; 5(3): 98-109. Lang.: Chi.
China. 1500-1980. Critical studies. ■Approaches to the subject: condensation, enlargement, collage. Characterizations: concentration on main roles and their primary characteristics. Structural patterns.

2448 Liu, Jingyuan. "Yi He Mengfu." (Remembering He Mengfu.) *XYishu*. 1982 May; 5(2): 100-103. Illus.: Photo. 2. Lang.: Chi.
China, People's Republic of. 1911-1945. Biographical studies. ■Career of the playwright, screenwriter and director emphasizing World War II era. Related to Media: Film.

2449 Ye, Zi. "Huiyi Xiong Foxi de Yishu Shenghuo." (Remembering Xiong Foxi's Life As An Artist.) *XYishu*. 1982 May; 5(2): 6-11. Lang.: Chi.
China, People's Republic of: Beijing, Shanghai. USA: New York, NY. 1901-1965. Biographical studies. ■Xiong Foxi's life as a playwright, theatre organizer and educator.

2450 Alvarez-Borland, Isabel; George, David. "*La noche de los asesinos*: Text, Staging and Audience." *LATR*. 1986 Fall; 20 (1): 37-48. Notes. Lang.: Eng.
Cuba. Brazil. 1973-1974. Critical studies. ■Ritual and archetypal communication in University of São Paulo production of *La noche de los asesinos (The Night of the Assassins)* by José Triana.

2451 Escarpanter, José A. "Veinticinco años de teatro cubano en exilio." (Twenty-five Years of Cuban Theatre in Exile.) *LATR*. 1986 Spr; 19(2): 57-66. Notes. Lang.: Spa.
Cuba. USA: New York, NY. 1959-1986. Historical studies. ■Cuban exile theatre is headquartered in New York. Most of those plays refer to the Cuban experience: life before 1959, the revolutionary experience or problems in exile.

2452 Muñoz, Elías Miguel. "Teatro cubano de transición (1958-1964): Piñera y Estorino." (Cuban Theatre in Transition (1958-1964): Piñera and Estorino.) *LATR*. 1986 Spr; 19(2): 39-44. Notes. Lang.: Eng.
Cuba. 1958-1964. Historical studies. ■Two plays on revolution are considered as representative of the period: *Aire frío (Cold Air)* by Virgilio Piñera and *La casa vieja (The Old House)* by Abelardo Estorino.

2453 Graff, Yveta Synek. "Facts of Life." *OpN*. 1986 Jan 4; 50(8): 16, 44. Illus.: Handbill. Photo. B&W. 5. Lang.: Eng.
Czechoslovakia: Brno. 1880-1900. Critical studies. ■Evaluation of the dramatic work of Gabriela Preissová, whose play *Její Pastorkyna (Her Stepdaughter)* was the source of *Jenufa* by Leoš Janáček.

2454 Larsson, Peter. "Kohout." *Entre*. 1986; 13(2): 24-27. Illus.: Photo. B&W. 5. Lang.: Swe.
Czechoslovakia: Prague. Austria: Vienna. 1928-1986. Histories-sources. ■Interview with Czechoslovakian playwright, director and actor Pavel Kohout, living in exile in Vienna. His works treat social and political themes.

2455 McGrory, Moy. "Sisters of Eve." *WomenR*. 1986 Jan.; 2(3): 36. Illus.: Photo. B&W. 1. Lang.: Eng.
Eire. 1984-1986. Histories-specific. ■Tricia Burden's *Sisters of Eve*, a Theatre-in-Education show based on the case of the Kerry Babies: background of the case and its presentation in the show.

2456 Schrank, Bernice. "Anatomizing an Insurrection: Sean O'Casey's *The Plough and the Stars*." *MD*. 1986 June; 29(2): 216-228. Notes. Lang.: Eng.
Eire. 1926-1986. Critical studies. ■*The Plough and the Stars* by Sean O'Casey as a pessimistic play that shows the characters doomed by their limited perceptions.

2457 Thomson, Leslie. "Opening the Eyes of the Audience: Visual and Verbal Imagery in *Juno and the Paycock*." *MD*. 1986 Dec.; 29(4): 556-566. Notes. Lang.: Eng.
Eire. 1924. Critical studies. ■Pessimism of Sean O'Casey's *Juno and the Paycock* revealed through verbal and visual imagery.

2458 Ardolino, Frank R. "*Corrida* of Blood in *The Spanish Tragedy*: Kyd's Use of Revenge as National Destiny." *MRenD*. 1984 ; 1: 37-49. Notes. Lang.: Eng.
England. 1500-1600. Critical studies. ■An analysis of Kyd's use of a parallel between bullfighting and the revenge masque he presents in *The Spanish Tragedy*, asserting the political irony of such an analogy.

2459 Barber, C.L.; Wheeler, Richard P. *The Whole Journey: Shakespeare's Power of Development*. Berkeley & Los Angeles, CA: Univ. of California P; 1986. xxvii, 354 pp. Index. Lang.: Eng.
England. 1564-1616. Critical studies. ■Influence of the middle class and popularization of domestic comedy on the plays and sonnets of William Shakespeare.

2460 Bergeron, David M. "Art Within *The Second Maiden's Tragedy*." *MRenD*. 1984; 1: 173-186. Notes. Lang.: Eng.
England: London. 1611. Critical studies. ■An examination of the two apparently unconnected plots of the anonymous 1611 play arguing that the connections are made by imagery and language—especially that of the theatre—rather than by traditional plot and theme.

2461 Bergeron, David M. "'Lend me your Dwarf': Romance in *Volpone*." *MRenD*. 1986; 3: 99-113. Notes. Lang.: Eng.
England. 1575-1600. Critical studies. ■Refutation of critical viewpoint that Ben Jonson was merely a realist, through analysis of his use of romance in *Volpone*.

2462 Bilderback, Walter. "*Ein Jux* Through the Terrain of Nestroy and Stoppard." *ThM*. 1986 Fall/Win; 18(1): 65-69. Illus.: Photo. Print. B&W. 1: 2 in. x 8 in. Lang.: Eng.
England. Austria: Vienna. 1927-1981. Critical studies. ■*Einen Jux will er sich machen* by Johann Nestroy as adapted by Tom Stoppard in *On the Razzle*.

2463 Bliss, Lee. "Three Plays in One: Shakespeare and *Philaster*." *MRenD*. 1985; 2: 153-170. Notes. Lang.: Eng.
England. 1609. Critical studies. ■Influence of Shakespeare's *Hamlet*, *Othello* and *Twelfth Night* on Beaumont and Fletcher's *Philaster*.

2464 Bovard, Richard W. "Mockery and Mangling in Shakespeare's *Henry V*." *TID*. 1986; 8: 67-77. Notes. Lang.: Eng.
England. 1598-1599. Critical studies. ■Analysis of the importance of ceremony in distinguishing kings from peasants in *Henry V*.

2465 Burns-Harper, Carolyn. *A Looker-On Here in Vienna: Measure for Measure as Paradigm of Contraries*. Boulder, CO: Univ of Colorado; 1986. 264 pp. Pref. Notes. Biblio. [Ph.D. dissertation, University Microfilms order No. DA 8618950.] Lang.: Eng.
England. 1604-1605. Critical studies. ■Hypothesizes that Shakespeare used the paradigm of contraries to reinforce the Elizabethan world view in *Measure for Measure* in which Vienna, representing a Catholic country with separation of church and state is diametrically opposed to England's temporal/spiritual monarchy.

2466 Butler, Guy. "Blessing and Cursing in *King Lear*." *Unisa English Studies*. 1986 May; 24(1): 7-11. Biblio. Lang.: Eng.
England. 1605-1606. Textual studies. ■A study of the way in which blessing and cursing are used by Shakespeare in *King Lear*.

2467 Calderwood, James L. "Creative Uncreation in *King Lear*." *SQ*. 1986 Spr; 37(1): 5-19. Notes. Lang.: Eng.
England: London. 1605-1606. Critical studies. ■Semiotic analysis of *King Lear* by William Shakespeare focusing on the effect of the transformation of his sources.

2468 Champion, Larry S. "'Disaster With My So Many Joys': Structure and Perspective in Massinger and Dekker's *The Virgin Martyr*." *MRenD*. 1984; 1: 199-209. Notes. Lang.: Eng.
England: London. 1620-1625. Critical studies. ■An examination of the relation of religious subject matter and popular dramatic form in Massinger and Dekker's *The Virgin Martyr* focusing on the authors' use of a wide variety of generic types, plots and structures.

2469 Cohen, Eileen Z. "Virtue Is Bold: The Bed-trick and Characterization in *All's Well that Ends Well* and *Measure for Measure*." *PQ*. 1986 Spr; 65(2): 171-186. Notes. Lang.: Eng.

DRAMA: —Plays/librettos/scripts

England. 1603. Critical studies. ■Analysis of *All's Well that Ends Well* and *Measure for Measure* by William Shakespeare focusing on the unconventional and complex heroines in each play.

2470 Colaco, Jill. "The Window Scene in *Romeo and Juliet* and Folk Songs of the Night Visit." *MP*. 1986 Spr; 83(2): 138-157. Notes. Lang.: Eng.
England: London. 1594-1597. Critical studies. ■Influence of Elizabethan folk songs and Child ballads of the Night Visit motif on Shakespeare's *Romeo and Juliet*.

2471 Cook, Carol. "Unbodied Figures of Desire." *TJ*. 1986 Mar.; 38(1): 34-52. Lang.: Eng.
England. 1602. Critical studies. ■Plot and theme study of homosexual and heterosexual desires in William Shakespeare's *Troilus and Cressida* via character comparisons of Helen and Cressida.

2472 Cramer, James Douglas. *Theophany in the English Corpus Christi Play (Volumes I and II)*. Ann Arbor, MI: Univ of Michigan; 1986. 579 pp. Pref. Notes. Biblio. Append. [Ph.D. dissertation, University Microfilms order No. DA 8621268.] Lang.: Eng.
England. 1350-1550. Critical studies. ■Analysis of theophany in English *Corpus Christi* plays.

2473 Daalder, Joost. "The Role of 'Senex' in Kyd's *The Spanish Tragedy*." *CompD*. 1986; 20(3): 247-260. Notes. Lang.: Eng.
England. 1587. Critical studies. ■An analysis of the character variously referred to as 'Old Man', 'Senex', and 'Bazulto'. Argues that 'Senex' underscores the Senecan cast of *The Spanish Tragedy*.

2474 Daley, A. Stuart. "To Moralize a Spectacle: *As You Like It*, Act 2, Scene 1." *PQ*. 1986 Spr; 65(2): 147-170. Notes. Lang.: Eng.
England. 1598. Critical studies. ■Allegorical representation of and commentary upon the corrupt society using the imagery of the hunt.

2475 Dammers, Richard H. "Female Characterization in English Platonic Drama: A Background for the Eighteenth Century Tragedies of Nicholas Rowe." *Restor*. 1986 Win; 2nd ser.1(2): 34-41. Notes. Lang.: Eng.
England. 1629-1720. Critical studies. ■The essential difference between men and caricatured women in platonic drama, as opposed to their common humanity and mutual dependence in Rowe's drama.

2476 Dollimore, Jonathan. "Subjectivity, Sexuality and Transgression: The Jacobean Connection." *RenD*. 1986; 17: 53-81. Notes. Biblio. Lang.: Eng.
England: London. 1600-1625. Critical studies. ■Post-structuralist insights on sexuality and transgression as depicted in transvestite roles in Jacobean plays.

2477 Drucker, Trudy. "Lillo's Liberated Women." *Restor*. 1986 Win; 2nd ser.1(2): 42-43. Notes. Lang.: Eng.
England. 1730-1759. Critical studies. ■The important female characters in the plays of George Lillo are independent and assertive, applying reason to their dilemmas, usually with success.

2478 Duane, Carol Leventen. "Marlowe's Mixed Messages: A Model for Shakespeare?" *MRenD*. 1986; 3: 51-67. Notes. Lang.: Eng.
England. 1580-1620. Critical studies. ■Analysis of the deliberate contradictions and ambiguities of Christopher Marlowe's plays and the possible influence of this approach on the plays of William Shakespeare.

2479 Durbach, Errol. "*Antony and Cleopatra* and *Rosmersholm*: 'Third Empire' Love Tragedies." *CompD*. 1986; 20(1): 1-16. Notes. Lang.: Eng.
England. Norway. 1607-1885. Critical studies. ■Comparative study of *Antony and Cleopatra* and *Rosmersholm* as erotic tragedies, the first a tragedy of erotic indulgence, the second a tragedy of sexual sublimation.

2480 Dutton, Richard. "*King Lear, The Triumphs of Reunited Britannia* and the 'Matter of Britain'." *L&H*. 1986 Fall; 12(2): 139-151. Notes. Lang.: Eng.
England. 1605-1606. Critical studies. ■Reexamines the historical context of *King Lear* by comparing it to Anthony Munday's Lord Mayor's Show *The Triumphs of Reunited Britannia*.

2481 Endel, Peggy. "Profane Icon: The Throne Scene of Shakespeare's *Richard III*." *CompD*. 1986; 20(2): 115-123. Notes. Illus.: Pntg. B&W. 2: 5 in. x 8 in. Lang.: Eng.
England. 1591-1592. Critical studies. ■Traces the iconography of the throne scene from a detail in Sir Thomas More's *Historia Richardi III (History of King Richard III)* and links it to the tradition linking the devil with anality.

2482 Feinberg, Anat. "The Representation of the Poor in Elizabethan and Stuart Drama." *L&H*. 1986 Fall; 12(2): 152-163. Notes. Lang.: Eng.
England. 1558-1642. Critical studies. ■The image of poverty presented in Elizabethan and Stuart plays and how that image corresponds to historical reality.

2483 Flachmann, Michael. "*Epicoene*: A Comic Hell for a Comic Sinner." *MRenD*. 1984; 1: 131-142. Notes. Lang.: Eng.
England: London. 1609-1668. Critical studies. ■Importance of sounds in Jonson's *Epicoene* and their ironic use as both punishment and remedy.

2484 Frye, Northrop; De Angelis, Maria Pia, transl.; Poggi, Valentina, transl. *Tempo che opprime, tempo che redime. Riflessioni sul teatro di Shakespeare.* (Oppressing Time, Redeeming Time: Reflections on Shakespeare's Theatre.) Bologna: Il Mulino; 1986. 201 pp. (Intersezioni 91.) Pref. Index. Lang.: Ita.
England. 1564-1616. Critical studies. ■Translation of *Fools of Time: Study in Shakespearean Tragedy* (Toronto 1967) and *The Myth of Deliverance: Reflections on Shakespeare's Problem Comedies* (Toronto 1983).

2485 Fuzier, Jean, ed.; Larique, François, ed. *All's Well that Ends Well: Nouvelles perspectives critiques.* (*All's Well that Ends Well*: New Critical Perspectives.) Montpellier: Publications de l'Université Paul Valéry; 1986. 144 pp. (Astrea 1.) Biblio. [Proceedings of a colloquium, Paris, November 1985.] Lang.: Eng, Fre.
England. 1603. Textual studies. ■Essays on aspects of *All's Well that Ends Well* by William Shakespeare, including the courtly tradition, dramaturgy, language, dramatic structure and anthropological study.

2486 Gagen, Jean. "The Design of the High Plot in Etherege's *The Comical Revenge*." *Restor*. 1986 Win; 2nd ser.1(2): 1-15. Notes. Lang.: Eng.
England. 1664. Critical studies. ■George Etherege's play *The Comical Revenge* is unified because high plot is an ironic parody of heroic ethos.

2487 Gourtney, Cathy. "One Very Extraordinary Woman." *WomenR*. 1986 July; 2(9): 30-31. Illus.: Photo. B&W. 1. Lang.: Eng.
England: Coventry. USA. 1960-1986. Histories-sources. ■Interview with playwright Kathleen Betsko, about her work.

2488 Goy-Blanquet, Dominique. *Le Roi mis à nu: l'histoire d'Henri VI, de Hall à Shakespeare.* (The Denuded King: The Story of Henry VI, from Hall to Shakespeare.) Paris: Didier; 1986. 420 pp. (Etudes anglaises 92.) Notes. Biblio. Illus.: Photo. Dwg. Print. B&W. 4: 15 cm. x 18 cm. Lang.: Fre.
England. 1542-1592. Historical studies. ■Elizabethan historical drama as exemplified by Shakespeare's *Henry VI* trilogy, which is compared with the version in Hall's *Chronicles*.

2489 Graham-White, Anthony. "Elizabethan Punctuation and the Actor: *Gammer Gurton's Needle* as a Case Study." *TJ*. 1982 Mar. ; 34(1): 96-106.
England. 1575-1920. Critical studies. ■Elizabethan punctuation in *Gammer Gurton's Needle* indicates style of performance, controls pace and reveals character.

2490 Grantley, Darryll. "*The Winter's Tale* and Early Religious Drama." *CompD*. 1986; 20(1): 17-37. Notes. Lang.: Eng.
England. 1611. Critical studies. ■Relates theme of redemption in *The Winter's Tale* by William Shakespeare to the forms and stage pictures of early Tudor drama.

2491 Hamer, Mary. "Shakespeare's Rosalind and Her Public Image." *ThR*. 1986; 11(2): 105-118. Notes. Illus.: Photo. Print. B&W. 4. Lang.: Eng.

CLASSED ENTRIES

DRAMA: —Plays/librettos/scripts

England. 1600-1986. Historical studies. ■Varying identity and appeal of the role of Rosalind in *As You Like It* by William Shakespeare.

2492 Hanna, Cliff. "'A Bit of Cackle': Australia's Beginnings in English Drama." *ADS*. 1985 Apr.; 3(2): 5-20. Illus.: Handbill. B&W. 3: 4 in. x 6 in. Lang.: Eng.

England: London. Australia. 1787-1791. Historical studies. ■Four dramatic spectacles relating to Botany Bay appeared on English stages, thus marking the beginning of Australian drama.

2493 Homan, Richard L. "Devotional Themes in the Violence and Humor of the *Play of the Sacrament*." *CompD*. 1986; 20(4): 327-340. Notes. Lang.: Eng.

England. 1400-1499. Critical studies. ■Thematic significance of the scenes of humor and violence, indicating a work of serious devotional art.

2494 Horner, Olga. "Susanna's Double Life." *MET*. 1986; 8(2): 76-102. Notes. Lang.: Eng.

England: London. 1563. Critical studies. ■Examines the legalistic character of *The Comedy of Virtuous and Godly Susanna* and its source.

2495 Hughes, Derek. "Cibber and Vanbrugh: Language, Place, and Social Order in *Love's Last Shift*." *CompD*. 1986; 20(4): 287-304. Notes. Lang.: Eng.

England. 1696. Critical studies. ■Compares assumption about the relationship between language and social position in *Love's Last Shift* by Colley Cibber and *The Relapse* by Sir John Vanbrugh.

2496 Hunter, G. K. "The Beginnings of Elizabethan Drama: Revolution and Continuity." *RenD*. 1986; 17: 19-52. Notes. Biblio. Lang.: Eng.

England: London. 1575-1600. Historical studies. ■Tension in Renaissance drama between Protestant individualism and traditional popular forms and values.

2497 Kessel, Marie L. "*The Broken Heart*: An Allegorical Reading." *MRenD*. 1986; 3: 217-230. Notes. Lang.: Eng.

England. 1633. Critical studies. ■Allegorical romantic conventions in John Ford's *The Broken Heart*.

2498 Kiefer, Frederick. "Heywood as Moralist in *A Woman Killed with Kindness*." *MRenD*. 1986; 3: 83-98. Notes. Lang.: Eng.

England. 1560. Critical studies. ■Analysis of the moral issues inherent in Thomas Heywood's *A Woman Killed with Kindness*, especially the roles of Anne, John and Wendoll.

2499 Kroll, Norma. "Cosmic Characters and Human Form: Dramatic Interaction and Conflict in the Chester Cycle *Fall of Lucifer*." *MRenD*. 1985; 2: 33-50. Pref. Notes. Lang.: Eng.

England. 1400-1550. Critical studies. ■The function of the dramatic dynamics between Lucifer, God and angels in Chester cycle play *Fall of Lucifer* in comparison with York, Towneley and N-town cycle plays.

2500 Latham, Jacqueline, E.M. "Machiavelli, Policy and *The Devil's Charter*." *MRenD*. 1984; 1: 97-108. Notes. Lang.: Eng.

England. 1584-1607. Critical studies. ■An argument for Barnaby Barnes' *The Devil's Charter* as an important dramatic treatment of Machiavelli's theories of political leadership and policy.

2501 Levin, Richard. "The Contemporary Perception of Marlowe's *Tamburlane*." *MRenD*. 1984; 1: 51-70. Notes. Lang.: Eng.

England. 1984. Critical studies. ■An overview of contemporary responses to the title character in Marlowe's *Tamburlane*, attempting to determine a positive or negative response and refuting the 'ironic' reading of the play that has been proposed by some critics.

2502 McCandless, David Foley. *The Winter's Tale*: Summary and Summit of Shakespeare's Canon. Stanford, CA: Stanford U; 1986. 275 pp. Pref. Notes. Biblio. [Ph.D. dissertation, Univ. Microfilms order No. DA8608189.] Lang.: Eng.

England: London. 1604. Critical studies. ■Analysis of William Shakespeare's *The Winter's Tale*, examining the artistic techniques used in previous plays and how they culminate in this work.

2503 Miedzyrzecka, Daniela; Kott, Jan. "The Bottom Translation." *ThM*. 1986 Fall/Win; 18(1): 74-87. Notes. Illus.: Photo. Print. B&W. 1: 3 in. x 4 in. Lang.: Eng.

England. 1595-1986. Critical studies. ■Light and dark interpretations of *A Midsummer Night's Dream* as illuminated by Bottom's transformation.

2504 Milhous, Judith; Hume, Robert D. "Manuscript Casts for Revivals of Three Plays by Shirley in the 1660's." *TN*. 1985; 39 (1): 32-36. Notes. Biblio. Lang.: Eng.

England. 1653-1669. Historical studies. ■Cast lists in James Shirley's *Six New Plays* suggest that plays were performed frequently in repertory and therefore more popular than previously thought.

2505 Millard, Barbara C. "'An Acceptable Violence': Sexual Contest in Jonson's *Epicoene*." *MRenD*. 1984; 1: 143-158. Notes. Lang.: Eng.

England: London. 1609-1909. Critical studies. ■Discussion of gender roles and audience perception of them in Jonson's *Epicoene*, arguing the crucial status of the boy-actor to the meaning of the play.

2506 Munakata, Kuniyoshi; Marsan, Valentine Aymone, transl. "L'adattamento dell' *Amleto* per il teatro Nō." (Adaptation of *Hamlet* for the Nō Theatre.) 253-260 in Ottai, Antonella, ed. *Teatro Oriente/Occidente*. Rome: Bulzoni; 1986. viii, 565 pp. (Biblioteca Teatrale 47.) Lang.: Ita.

England. Japan. 1600-1982. Critical studies. ■The author's experiences with adapting Shakespeare's *Hamlet* for the nō theatre throughout his career.

2507 Orkin, Martin. "Civility and the English Colonial Enterprise: Notes on Shakespeare's *Othello*." *Theoria*. 1986 Dec.; 68 : 1-14. Notes. Biblio. Lang.: Eng.

England. South Africa, Republic of. 1597-1637. Textual studies. ■A Marxist analysis of the way in which British colonial expansion is treated in *Othello*. Related to present day views of the colonial enterprise, also in South Africa today.

2508 Ostovich, Helen. "'Jeered by Confederacy': Group Aggression in Jonson's Comedies." *MRenD*. 1986; 3: 115-128. Notes. Lang.: Eng.

England. 1575-1600. Critical studies. ■Discussion of the use of group aggression in Ben Jonson's comedies to illustrate particular kinds of social behavior.

2509 Oz, Avraham. "The Egall Yoke of Love: Prophetic Unions in *The Merchant of Venice*." *ASSAPHc*. 1986; 3: 75-108. Notes. Lang.: Eng.

England. 1598. Critical studies. ■Suggests that the proposal and response to prophetic riddles offer a key to understanding William Shakespeare's *The Merchant of Venice*.

2510 Pedicord, Harry William. "Garrick Produces *King John*." *TJ*. 1982 Dec.; 34(4): 441-449. Lang.: Eng.

England: London. 1736-1796. Critical studies. ■Using a manuscript partbook and promptbook, the author demonstrates that Garrick's adaptation of *King John* was coherent and fast-paced.

2511 Rackin, Phyllis. "Temporality, Anachronism and Presence in Shakespeare's English Histories." *RenD*. 1986; 17: 101-123. Notes. Biblio. Lang.: Eng.

England: London. 1590-1601. Critical studies. ■Anachronisms in Shakespeare's plays create tension as events are seen as both past and present.

2512 Radel, Nicholas F. "'Then Thus I Turne My Language to You': The Transformation of Theatrical Language in *Philaster*." *MRenD*. 1986; 3: 129-147. Notes. Lang.: Eng.

England. 1609. Critical studies. ■Discussion of the use of language in Beaumont and Fletcher's *Philaster* to explore rhetorical conventions that fail to motivate reasonable behavior.

2513 Randall, Dale B.J. "Some New Perspectives on the Spanish Setting of *The Changeling* and Its Source." *MRenD*. 1986; 3: 189-215. Notes. Illus.: Dwg. Sketches. B&W. 6: var. sizes. Lang.: Eng.

England. 1607-1622. Critical studies. ■Spanish setting of *The Changeling* by Middleton and Rowley traced to writings of John Reynolds.

2514 Reese, Max Meredith; Monari, Stefania, transl. *Shakespeare. Il suo mondo e la sua opera*. (Shakespeare: His World and His Work.) Bologna: Il Mulino; 1986. 626 pp. (Saggi 298.) Pref. Index. Notes. Biblio. Append. Lang.: Ita.

CLASSED ENTRIES

DRAMA: —Plays/librettos/scripts

England. 1564-1616. Biographies. ■Translation of Reese's 1980 biography.

2515 Riggs, David. "Ben Jonson's Family." *RORD*. 1986; 29: 1-5. Lang.: Eng.

England: London. 1596-1604. Historical studies. ■Reflections of Ben Jonson's personal life in his poems and plays.

2516 Rivero, Albert S. "Fielding's Artistic Accommodations in *The Author's Farce* (1730)." *Restor*. 1986 Win; 2nd ser.1(2): 16-33. Notes. Lang.: Eng.

England. 1730. Critical studies. ■Henry Fielding's manipulations of comic conventions, popular theatrical forms and authorial presence to create a play that is both stageworthy and intelligent.

2517 Ronan, Clifford J. "Snakes in *Catiline*." *MRenD*. 1986; 3: 149-163. Notes. Lang.: Eng.

England. 1611. Critical studies. ■Discussion of the symbolism and use of herpetological imagery in Ben Jonson's *Catiline* and compares it to Roman snake symbolism.

2518 Scanlon, Thomas F. "Historia Quasi Fabula: The Catiline Theme in Sallust and Jonson." *TID*. 1986; 8: 17-29. Notes. Lang.: Eng.

England. Italy. 43 B.C.-1611 A.D. Critical studies. ■Compares Ben Jonson's *Catiline* with Sallust's account of the Catiline conspiracy (64-63 B.C.) in intent, structure and content.

2519 Schuler, Robert M. "Jonson's Alchemists, Epicures, and Puritans." *MRenD*. 1985; 2: 171-208. Pref. Notes. Lang.: Eng.

England. 1610. Critical studies. ■Theme of Puritanism in *The Alchemist* by Ben Jonson.

2520 Sharp, Ronald A. "Gift Exchange and the Economies of Spirit in *The Merchant of Venice*." *MP*. 1986 Feb.; 83(3): 250-265 . Notes. Lang.: Eng.

England: London. 1594-1597. Critical studies. ■Contrasts gift exchange and the exchange of commodities in Shakespeare's *The Merchant of Venice*.

2521 Shepherd, Simon. *Marlowe and the Politics of Elizabethan Theatre*. New York, NY: St. Martin's P.; 1986. xix, 231 pp. Pref. Index. Biblio. Lang.: Eng.

England: London. Critical studies. ■Analysis of political ideas expressed in Elizabethan drama, focusing on the work of Christopher Marlowe.

2522 Sherbo, Arthur. "The Original of Dr. Last in Samuel Foote's *The Devil Upon Two Sticks*." *Restor*. 1986 Win; 2nd ser.1 (2): 44. Lang.: Eng.

England. 1768-1774. Historical studies. ■Identification of Thomas Cockup as the source for Dr. Last.

2523 Soellner, Rolf. "Chapman's *Caesar and Pompey* and the Fortunes of Prince Henry." *MRenD*. 1985; 2: 135-152. Pref. Notes. Lang.: Eng.

England. 1605-1631. Critical studies. ■George Chapman's *Caesar and Pompey* as a disguised version of the story of Prince Henry.

2524 Soto-Morettini, Donna. "Disrupting the Spectacle: Brenton's *Magnificence*." *TJ*. 1986 Mar.; 38: 82-96. Lang.: Eng.

England. 1970-1980. Critical studies. ■Structural and thematic analysis of Howard Brenton's play *Magnificence* and the play's significance in disrupting capitalism in England.

2525 Sousa, Gerald U. de. "Boundaries of Genre in Ben Jonson's *Volpone* and *The Alchemist*." *ET*. 1986 May; 4(2): 134-146. Notes. Lang.: Eng.

England: London. 1606-1610. Critical studies. ■A study of the violation of genre divisions in Jonson's plays using the idea of deferral to explore problems of textuality and genre in the Renaissance.

2526 Spinrad, Phoebe S. "Ceremonies of Complement: The Symbolic Marriage in Ford's *The Broken Heart*." *PQ*. 1986 Win; 65(1): 23-37. Notes. Lang.: Eng.

England. 1629. Critical studies. ■Final scene of John Ford's *The Broken Heart* as marriage of sense and sensibility, Stoicism and Christianity, Elizabethan and Caroline tragedy.

2527 Taylor, Richard C. "The Originality of John Caryll's *Sir Salomon*." *CompD*. 1986; 20(3): 261-269. Notes. Lang.: Eng.

England. France. 1662-1669. Critical studies. ■An examination of Caryll's adaptation of Molière's *L'École des femmes (The School for Wives)*.

2528 Teague, Frances. "*Othello* and New Comedy." *CompD*. 1986; 20(1): 54-64. Notes. Lang.: Eng.

England. 1604. Critical studies. ■An exploration of the perceived comic structure of Shakespeare's *Othello*, which finds in Roman New Comedy analogous dramatic techniques designed to facilitate acceptance of the events of the plot.

2529 Tempera, Mariangela, ed. Romeo and Juliet *dal testo alla scena*. (*Romeo and Juliet* from Text to Stage.) Bologna: CLUEB; 1986. 330 pp. Pref. Index. Notes. Tables. Biblio. Illus.: Photo. Pntg. Dwg. B&W. 8: var. sizes. Lang.: Ita.

England. 1595-1597. Critical studies. ■Collection of essays on various aspects and interpretations of Shakespeare's *Romeo and Juliet*.

2530 Tempera, Mariangela, ed. King Lear *dal testo alla scena*. (*King Lear* from Text to Stage.) Bologna: CLUEB; 1986. 351 pp. Pref. Index. Notes. Tables. Biblio. Illus.: Photo. B&W. 8: 10.5 cm. x 16 cm. Lang.: Ita.

England. 1605. Critical studies. ■Collection of essays on Shakespeare's *King Lear* by various critics and directors.

2531 Tricomi, H. Albert. "*A New Way to Pay Old Debts* and the Country-House Poetic Tradition." *MRenD*. 1986; 3: 177-187. Notes. Lang.: Eng.

England. 1621. Critical studies. ■Analysis of *A New Way to Pay Old Debts*, comparing it to the great English 'country-house' poems, but adapted to the values of aristocratic culture.

2532 Tyler, Sharon. "Shakespeare's Stepchildren: or Clio, Sedition Unlimited." *TID*. 1986; 8: 79-91. Notes. Lang.: Eng.

England. 1590-1940. Historical studies. ■Discusses the accuracy of portrayals of historical figures in Shakespeare's history plays and later adaptations.

2533 Wallace, John M. "*Timon of Athens* and the Three Graces: Shakespeare's Senecan Study." *MP*. 1986 May; 83(4): 349-363. Notes. Lang.: Eng.

England: London. 1601-1608. Critical studies. ■Interprets Shakespeare's *Timon of Athens* as an exploration of ideas set forth by Seneca in *De beneficiis*.

2534 Weil, Judith. "George Peele's Singing School: *David and Bethsabe* and the Elizabethan History Play." *TID*. 1986; 8: 51-66. Notes. Lang.: Eng.

England. 1560-1650. Critical studies. ■George Peele's use of metaphor, dramatic structure and the treatment of historical characters in *David and Bethsabe* compared to the treatment of historical figures by other Elizabethan playwrights.

2535 Wikander, Mathew H. "The Spitted Infant: Scenic Emblems and Exclusionist Politics in Restoration Adaptations of Shakespeare." *SQ*. 1986 Fall; 37(3): 340-358. Notes. Lang.: Eng.

England: London. 1660-1690. Critical studies. ■Revision of dramaturgy and stagecraft in Restoration adaptations of plays by William Shakespeare to focus attention on the connection between play's political themes and current political issues.

2536 Wilson, Richard. "'A Mingled Yarn': Shakespeare and the Cloth Workers." *L&H*. 1986 Fall; 12(2): 164-180. Notes. Lang.: Eng.

England. 1590-1986. Critical studies. ■The political stance apparent in Shakespeare's crowd scenes and the paternalistic dread of popular solidarity evidenced in modern criticism of such scenes.

2537 Pankhurst, Richard. "Shakespeare in Ethiopia." *RAL*. 1986 Sum; 17(2): 169-196. Notes. Lang.: Eng.

Ethiopia: Addis Ababa. 1941-1984. Historical studies. ■Discussion of translations of plays by William Shakespeare into Amharic and Tegrenna, the most important languages in Ethiopia, and publication and performances of these translations.

2538 Bogumil, Sieghild. "Poésie et violence: Tankred Dorst, Heiner Müller, Jean Genet." (Poetry and Violence: Tankred Dorst, Heiner Müller, Jean Genet.) *RHT*. 1986; 38(1): 20-38. Notes. Lang.: Fre.

DRAMA: —Plays/librettos/scripts

Europe. Critical studies. ■Effect of history on poetic and violent language in *Grosse Schmährede an der Stadtmauer (Great Tirade before the City Wall)* and *Merlin, oder, Das wüste Land (Merlin, or The Waste Land)* by Tankred Dorst, *Verkommenes Ufer Medeamaterial Landschaft mit Argonauten (Deserted Shore Matter for Medea Landscape with Argonauts)* by Heiner Müller and *Les Paravents (The Screens)* by Jean Genet.

2539 Brink, André P. *Aspekte van die Nuwe Drama.* (Aspects of the New Drama.) Pretoria: Academica; 1986. 268 pp. Pref. Index. Biblio. [2d ed.] Lang.: Afr.
Europe. South Africa, Republic of. 1800-1985. Textual studies. ■Comparative study of plays, termed 'New Drama', from Georg Büchner to Samuel Beckett, with application to contemporary Afrikaans drama.

2540 Hornby, Richard. *Drama, Metadrama, and Perception.* Cranbury, NJ: Bucknell UP; 1986. 189 pp. Index. Lang.: Eng.
Europe. 429 B.C.-1978 A.D. Critical studies. ■Attacks realism in theatre, explores metadrama and the theme of perception.

2541 Redmond, James, ed. *Historical Drama.* London/New York: Cambridge UP; 1986. xiv, 251 pp. Pref. Notes. Index. Illus.: Photo. Print. B&W. 20: 5 in. x 7 in. [Annual issue of themes in drama.] Lang.: Eng.
Europe. North America. Indonesia. 375 B.C.-1983 A.D. Critical studies. ■Collection of articles dedicated to the treatment of history in drama.

2542 Rosenmeyer, Thomas G. "Stoick Seneca." *MD.* 1986 Mar.; 29(1): 92-109. Notes. Lang.: Eng.
Europe. 65-1986. Critical studies. ■Stoicism and modern elements in the plays of Lucius Annaeus Seneca and his imitators.

2543 Vandenbossche, Lieven; Ryan, Thomas E., transl. "Where We Can Talk the Way We Want to Talk: An Interview with Kollektief Internationale Nieuwe Scene." *ComIBS.* 1984 Apr.; 12(2): 54-60.
Europe. 1984. Histories-sources. ■Founders of the travelling theatre collective International New Stage discuss their tent adaptation of *Mutter Courage und ihre Kinder (Mother Courage and Her Children)* by Bertolt Brecht.

2544 "Le Cantique des cantiques, un texte-phare, Entretien avec Josy Eisenberg." (*The Song of Songs*, a Seminal Text: Interview with Josy Eisenberg.) *CF.* 1986 Nov-Dec.; 153: 8. Illus.: Pntg. Color. 1: 5 in. x 7 in. Lang.: Fre.
France: Paris. 1986. Histories-sources. ■Josy Eisenberg, translator of *Le Cantique des cantiques (The Song of Songs)* recently produced at the Comédie-Française, discusses the meaning and influence of the Biblical text.

2545 *Dramaturgies, langages dramatiques.* (Dramaturgies, Dramatic Languages.) Paris: Nizet; 1986. Notes. Biblio. Illus.: Photo. Print. B&W. 1: 11 cm. x 16 cm. [Mélanges pour Jacques Schérer.] Lang.: Fre.
France. 1500-1985. Critical studies. ■Collection of essays on theatrical form, genre and language as well as dramaturgy, production and audience reception.

2546 *Samuel Beckett.* Toulouse: Privat; 1986. 475 pp. (Revue d'esthétique.) Biblio. Illus.: Handbill. Photo. Pntg. Dwg. Dwg. Print. B&W. 119: var. sizes. Lang.: Fre.
France. UK. 1947-1985. Critical studies. ■Special issue of *Revue d'esthétique* devoted to the works of Samuel Beckett as writer and director for stage and television. Analyzes the genesis of his dramatic writing and his directing notebooks. Includes statements by actors who have worked with him.

2547 Abastado, Claude; Xiao, He, transl. "He Fa Kuo Huangdanpai Xijujia Youjin Youniesiku de Tanhua." (Interview with French Absurdist Playwright Eugène Ionesco.) *XYishu.* 1982 May; 5(2): 121-126. Lang.: Chi.
France. 1949-1970. Histories-sources. ■Ionesco explains his ideas about intervening theatre and pure theatre. *La soif et la faim (Hunger and Thirst)* and *Rhinocéros* are examples.

2548 Balmas, Enea. *Il mito di Don Giovanni nel seicento francese.* (The Myth of Don Juan in Seventeenth-Century France.) Rome: Lucarini; 1986. 161 pp. (Universale.) Pref. Index. Notes. Biblio. Lang.: Ita.

France. 1657-1682. Historical studies. ■Studies six versions of the Don Juan legend, both preceding and following that of Molière.

2549 Bishop, Tom. "Du langage au silence: trajet du discours beckettien." (From Language to Silence: Trajectory of Beckett's Discourse.) *CRB.* 1986; 34(113): 113-127. Lang.: Fre.
France. 1930-1980. Critical studies. ■Language and the permanent dialectic of truth and lie in the plays of Samuel Beckett.

2550 Blanchard, Marc Eli. "The Reverse View: Greece and Greek Myths in Modern French Theatre." *MD.* 1986 Mar.; 29(1): 41-48. Notes. Lang.: Eng.
France. 1935-1944. Critical studies. ■The superficial and reductive use of classical myth in modern French theatre.

2551 Bouvier, Michel. "Dom Juan et les moralistes." (Don Juan and the Moralists.) *DSS.* 1986 Apr/June; 38(2): 153-158. Notes. Lang.: Fre.
France. 1660-1986. Critical studies. ■Molière's character Dom Juan reinterpreted on the basis of writings by seventeenth-century moralists as a desperate man excluded from the paradise of love.

2552 Brewer, Daniel. "Stages of the Enlightened Sublime: Narrating Sublimation." *TJ.* 1986 Mar.; 38(1): 5-18. Notes. Lang.: Eng.
France. 1700-1800. Historical studies. ■Influence of the Enlightenment narrative on French dramatists, especially Voltaire.

2553 Bruneau, Marie-Florine. *Racine, le Jansénisme et la modernité.* (Racine, Jansenism and Modernity.) Paris: Corit; 1986. 142 pp. Notes. Biblio. Lang.: Fre.
France. 1664-1691. Critical studies. ■Modern thought in the works of Jean Racine, including reflections on power, absolutism, self-affirmation and the possibility of progress.

2554 Brunel, Pierre. "Electre ou la chute des Masques de Marguerite Yourcenar." (*Electra or The Fall of the Masks* by Marguerite Yourcenar.) 27-35 in Real, Elena, ed. *Actes du Colloque International. Valence (Espagne) 1984. Marguerite Yourcenar.* Valencia: Universitat de València; 1986. 194 pp. Notes. Lang.: Fre.
France. 1944-1954. Critical studies. ■Analysis of the play with comparisons to previous versions by Euripides, Sophocles, Aeschylus and Jean Giraudoux.

2555 Calderwood, James L. "Ways of Waiting in *Waiting for Godot.*" *MD.* 1986 Sep.; 29(3): 363-375. Notes. Lang.: Eng.
France. 1953. Critical studies. ■Various implications of 'waiting' in *Waiting for Godot (En attendant Godot)*: semiotic, temporal, theatrical, existential.

2556 Calendoli, Giovanni. "Paul Claudel e il teatro Nō." (Paul Claudel and the Nō Theatre.) 231-236 in Ottai, Antonella, ed. *Teatro Oriente/Occidente.* Rome: Bulzoni; 1986. viii, 565 pp. (Biblioteca Teatrale 47.) Lang.: Ita.
France. 1868-1955. Historical studies. ■Influence of Nō drama on the plays of Paul Claudel, particularly his Biblical works.

2557 Catanzaro, Mary F. "The Psychic Structure of the Couple in *Waiting for Godot.*" *JDTC.* 1986 Fall; 1(1): 87-98. Notes. Lang.: Eng.
France. UK-Ireland. 1931-1958. Critical studies. ■*Waiting for Godot* interpreted as an assessment of the quality of life of the couple, which Beckett finds arduous and inadequate.

2558 Cooper, Barbara T. "Breaking Up/Down/Apart: 'L'Eclatement' as a Unifying Principle in Musset's *Lorenzaccio.*" *PQ.* 1986 Win; 65(1): 103-112. Lang.: Eng.
France. 1834. Critical studies. ■Fragmentation as a source of the play's thematic unity and modernity.

2559 Declercq, Gilles. "Le Lieu commun dans les tragédies de Racine." (The Commonplace in the Tragedies of Racine.) *DSS.* 1986 Jan/Mar.; 38(1): 43-60. Notes. Lang.: Fre.
France. 1650-1986. Critical studies. ■The function of the commonplace in the rhetoric and poetry of the tragedies of Jean Racine.

2560 Dort, Bernard. *Théâtres: essais.* (Theatres: Essays.) Paris: Seuil; 1986. 296 pp. (Coll. Points 185. Littérature.) Pref. Lang.: Fre.

DRAMA: —Plays/librettos/scripts

France. Italy. Germany, West. 1700-1964. Critical studies. ■Great dramatic works considered in light of modern theatre and social responsibility.

2561 Dufournet, Jean; Rousse, Michel. *Sur La Farce de Maître Pierre Pathelin.* (On *The Farce of Master Pierre Pathelin.*) Paris: Champion; 1986. 139 pp. (Unichamp 13.) Notes. Biblio. Illus.: Sketches. Print. B&W. 8: 18 cm. x 21 cm. Lang.: Fre.

France. 1485-1970. Textual studies. ■Language, comedy, ambiguity and dramatic structure. Includes a chronology of editions and performances from 1706 to 1970, and analysis of the most recent productions.

2562 Gautam, Kripa K.; Sharma, Manjula. "Dialogue in *Waiting for Godot* and Grice's Concept of Implicature." *MD.* 1986 Dec.; 29(4): 580-586. Notes. Lang.: Eng.

France. 1953. Critical studies. ■Application of H.P. Grice's maxims of conversation to *Waiting for Godot* reveals that Estragon controls discourse and finally alters Vladimir's attitude.

2563 Gautier, Roger. "Le thème de l'amour dans le théâtre de Jean-Jacques Rousseau." (The Theme of Love in the Plays of Jean-Jacques Rousseau.) *RHT.* 1986; 38(3): 281-292. Notes. Lang.: Fre.

France. Switzerland. 1712-1778. Critical studies. ■Rousseau's observations of all kinds of love as seen in his plays and operas. Related to Music-Drama: Opera.

2564 Goyet, Thérèse. "Au moment que je parle...Requête pour une lecture du théâtre au temps présent." (At the Moment When I am Speaking: Proposition of Reading the Theatre in Present Tense.) 203-213 in Heistein, Józef, ed. *Le texte dramatique. La lecture et la scène.* Wrocław: Wydawnictwo Uniwersytetu Wrocławskiego; 1986. 248 pp. (Acta Universitatis Wratislaviensis 895, Romanica Wratislaviensia 26.) Lang.: Fre.

France. 1600-1700. Critical studies. ■Relationship between grammar and metaphysics: use of the present tense in some of the tragedies of Corneille and Racine.

2565 Graells, Guillem-Jordi. "Pròleg a *L'àguila de dos caps* de Jean Cocteau." (Prologue to *The Eagle with Two Heads* by Jean Cocteau.) 5-13 in Institut del Teatre, ed. *L'àguila de dos caps.* Barcelona: Institut del Teatre; 1986. 104 pp. (Biblioteca Teatral 43.) Lang.: Cat.

France. 1889-1963. Critical studies. ■Analysis of *L'aigle à deux têtes* (The Eagle With Two Heads) focusing on the conflict between the two main characters. Bibliography includes Cocteau's cinematic works. Related to Media: Film.

2566 Hays, Michael. "On Maeterlinck Reading Shakespeare." *MD.* 1986 Mar.; 29(1): 49-59. Notes. Lang.: Eng.

France. 1590-1911. Critical studies. ■Comparative analysis of the works of Maurice Maeterlinck and William Shakespeare.

2567 Henry, Patrick. "Paradox in *Le Misanthrope.*" *PQ.* 1986 Spr; 65: 187-195. Notes. Lang.: Eng.

France. 1666. Critical studies. ■Molière's dialectical method, which challenges audience assumptions.

2568 Howarth, W.D. "Bonaparte on Stage: The Napoleonic Legend in the Nineteenth Century French Drama." *TID.* 1986; 8: 139-161 . Notes. Illus.: Pntg. B&W. 1: 4 in. x 5 in. Lang.: Eng.

France. England. 1797-1958. Critical studies. ■Treatment of Napoleon Bonaparte by French and English dramatists.

2569 Kaufman, Daliah. "Naval Hatzadic O HamitHased. Haibud Haivri Hamaskili shel *Tartif* Le Molièr." (*Naval-Righteous or Self Righteous,* A Hebrew Adaptation of *Tartuffe* by Molière in the Enlightenment Period.) *Bamah.* 1986; 21(105-106): 38-49. Notes. Lang.: Heb.

France. 1874. Critical studies. ■Examination of the first Hebrew adaptation of Molière's *Tartuffe* by David Vexler.

2570 Kiernander, Adrian. "The Théâtre du Soleil, Part 2: The Road to Cambodia." *NTQ.* 1986 Aug.; 11(7): 203-212. Notes. Illus.: Photo. B&W. 2. Lang.: Eng.

France: Paris. 1985. Histories-specific. ■Théâtre du Soleil considers the relationships between theatre and life, the place of theatre in society and its ability to modify the order of things in some way in *Norodom Sihanouk.*

2571 Le Marinel, Jacques. "L'importance du rhythme dans la réécriture des *Esprits* de Larivey par Albert Camus." (The Importance of Rhythm in the Rewriting of Larivey's *The Spirits* by Albert Camus.) *RHT.* 1986; 38(4): 395-405. Notes. Lang.: Fre.

France. 1570-1953. Critical studies. ■Stylistic study of the adaptation by Albert Camus of *Les Esprits (The Spirits)* by Pierre de Larivey, produced by the Festival d'art dramatique, Angers, 1953.

2572 Levy, Shimon. "The Case of the Three I's." *ASSAPHc.* 1986; 3: 159-185. Notes. Lang.: Eng.

France. 1953-1986. Critical studies. ■Beckett's three I's: the 'I' of Beckett, the 'I' of the actor and the 'I' of the audience.

2573 Mallet, Francine. *Molière.* Paris: Grasset; 1986. 475 pp. Notes. Biblio. Lang.: Fre.

France. 1622-1673. Biographical studies. ■Biography examines Molière's personality through his plays and traces religious and philosophical influences on his work. Includes judgment of his work by his contemporaries.

2574 Manifold, Gay. "Solidarity and Ensemble: George Sand and a People's Theatre." *NTQ.* 1986 Aug.; 11(7): 233-236. Notes. Lang.: Eng.

France. 1830-1844. Historical studies. ■An examination of *Père va-tout-seul (Old Man Go-It-Alone)* within the context of Sand's life, career and framework of beliefs.

2575 Marie, Charles P. "L'onde où se mire le théâtre de la cruauté (Camus—Artaud—Bachelard)." (Reflections of the Theatre of Cruelty: Camus, Artaud, Bachelard.) *RHT.* 1986; 38(3): 246-280. Notes. Lang.: Fre.

France. Critical studies. ■Structuralist analysis of plays by Albert Camus and Antonin Artaud, and the works of Gaston Bachelard, based on the idea that poetry and philosophy are united by action on stage.

2576 Marie, Charles P. "Avant-garde et sincérité: Ionesco." (Avant-Garde and Sincerity: Ionesco.) *RHT.* 1986; 38(1): 39-66. Notes. Lang.: Fre.

France. 1950-1980. Critical studies. ■Essentialism and avant-garde in the plays of Eugène Ionesco.

2577 Miguet, Marie. "Tardieu: un mot pour un sexe." (Tardieu: Sexual Metaphors.) *RHT.* 1986; 38(3): 310-314. Notes. Lang.: Fre.

France. 1955. Critical studies. ■Unusual and delicate sexual metaphors in the plays of Jean Tardieu.

2578 Moleski, Joseph J.; Stroupe, John H. "Jean Anouilh and Eugene O'Neill: Repetition and Negativity." *CompD.* 1986; 20(4): 315-326. Notes. Lang.: Eng.

France. USA. 1922-1960. Critical studies. ■Plays of Jean Anouilh and Eugene O'Neill compared.

2579 Nissim, Liana. "Une lecture moderne du théâtre symboliste: *Axël* de Villiers de l'Isle-Adam." (Modern Reading As Symbolistic Theatre: *Axël* by Villiers de l'Isle-Adam.) 185-201 in Heistein, Józef, ed. *Le texte dramatique. La lecture et la scène.* Wrocław: Wydawnictwo Uniwersytetu Wrocławskiego; 1986. 248 pp. (Acta Universitatis Wratislaviensis 895, Romanica Wratislaviensia 26.) Lang.: Fre.

France. 1862-1894. Critical studies. ■Analysis of *Axël* using the method of 'actants', proving that Villiers de l'Isle-Adam was a forerunner of contemporary theatre.

2580 Pavlides, Merope. *Restructuring the Traditional: Myth in Selected Works of Cixous, Chedid, Wittig and Yourcenar.* Madison, WI: Univ. of Wisconsin; 1986. 285 pp. Pref. Notes. Biblio. [Ph.D. dissertation, Univ. Microfilms order No. DA8611427.] Lang.: Eng.

France. Critical studies. ■Examination of selected works of Hélène Cixous, Andrée Chedid, Monique Wittig and Marguerite Yourcenar, focusing on the relationship between theatre and mythology and women and mythology.

2581 Pizzari, Serafino. *Le Mythe de Don Juan et la comédie de Molière.* (The Myth of Don Juan and the Comedy of

CLASSED ENTRIES

DRAMA: —Plays/librettos/scripts

Molière.) Paris: Nizet; 1986. 180 pp. Pref. Notes. Biblio. Lang.: Eng.
France. 1630-1980. Critical studies. ■History of Don Juan legend in literature and film, with analysis of Molière's play.

2582 Prigent, Michel. *Le Héros et l'État dans la tragédie de Pierre Corneille.* (The Hero and the State in the Tragedy of Pierre Corneille.) Paris: P.U.F.; 1986. vii, 571 pp. (Ecrivains.) Pref. Biblio. Lang.: Fre.
France. 1636-1674. Critical studies. ■Study of the works of Corneille as political tragedies based on history. Traces the evolution of his conception of the State from *Le Cid* to *Suréna*.

2583 Ronzeaud, Pierre. *Racine: La Romaine, la Turque, La Juive (regards sur Bérénice, Bajazet, Athalie).* (Racine: The Roman, the Turk, the Jewess (Looks at *Bérénice, Bajazet, Athalie*).) Aix-en-Provence: Université de Provence; 1986. 115. Notes. Lang.: Fre.
France. 1670-1691. Textual studies. ■Jean Racine's poetics and dramaturgy as seen through his plays *Bérénice, Athalie* and *Bajazet*.

2584 Thévenin, Paule. "Antonin Artaud: lettre à une amie." (Antonin Artaud: Letter to a Friend.) *CCIEP.* 1986; 169: 3-37. Illus.: Photo. Print. B&W. 3: 11 cm. x 15 cm. Lang.: Fre.
France. 1946-1967. Histories-specific. ■Meeting with playwright Antonin Artaud and the publication of his complete works by Gallimard.

2585 Vila, Pep. "Introducció a *Jesús batejat per Sant Joan Baptista.*" (Introduction to *Jesus Christ Baptized by St. John the Baptist.*) *EECIT.* 1986 Dec.; 28: 163-182. Notes. Lang.: Cat.
France. 1753-1832. Historical studies. ■Introduction to a pastoral play from the classical period of Rousillon drama, when the theme of John the Baptist was quite popular.

2586 Vlasopolos, Anca. "The Perils of Authorship in *Le voyageur sans bagage.*" *MD.* 1986 Dec.; 29(4): 601-612. Notes. Lang.: Eng.
France. 1937. Critical studies. ■Rival claims on the amnesiac Gaston in the *Le voyageur sans bagage* by Jean Anouilh represent attempts by a patriarchal society to regain dominance.

2587 Weber-Caflisch, Antoinette. *Dramaturgie et poésie: essais sur le texte et l'écriture du* Soulier de Satin. (Dramaturgy and Poetry: Essays On the Text and the Writing of *Le Soulier de Satin.*) Paris: Les Belles Lettres; 1986. 397 pp. (Annales littéraires de l'Université de Besançon 335. Centre de Recherches Jacques Petit 46.) Pref. Notes. Biblio. [Vol. 2.] Lang.: Fre.
France. 1928. Textual studies. ■Poetic and dramatic language in *Le Soulier de Satin (The Satin Slipper)* by Paul Claudel. Different versions of the playtext and stage directions included.

2588 Yehouda Moraly, Jean-Bernard. "Les cinq vies de Jean Genet: Quelques éléments nouveaux pour une biographie de Jean Genet." (The Five Lives of Jean Genet: Some New Elements Toward a Biography of Jean Genet.) *RHT.* 1986; 38(3): 219-245. Notes. Lang.: Fre.
France. 1910-1985. Biographical studies. ■Includes Genet's relations with Jean Cocteau, personal life, films, plays and politics. Related to Media: Film.

2589 Buffinga, John O. "From 'Bocksgesang' to 'Ziegenlied': The Transformation of a Myth in Georg Kaiser's *Zweimal Amphitryon (Amphitryon x 2).*" *GerSR.* 1986 Oct.; 9(3): 475-495. Lang.: Eng.
Germany. 1943. Critical studies. ■An investigation of Georg Kaiser's treatment of the old myth of Amphitryon, focusing on the motif of the double in order to establish the position of the play within the context of Kaiser's work in general.

2590 Burgess, G.J.A. "Differing Treatments of History: Gryphius's *Carolus Stuardus* and Schiller's *Maria Stuart.*" *TID.* 1986; 8: 113-128. Notes. Illus.: Photo. B&W. 1: 5 in. x 7 in. Lang.: Eng.
Germany. England. 1651-1800. Critical studies. ■Comparative study of *Carolus Stuardus* by Andreas Gryphius and *Maria Stuart* by Friedrich

von Schiller, focusing on their contrasting treatment of parallel historical incidents.

2591 Casas, Joan. "Presentació de l'obra de Tankred Dorst." (Presentation of the Work of Tankred Dorst.) 5-14 in Institut del Teatre, ed. *Gran imprecació davant la muralla de la ciutat—Toller.* Barcelona: Institut del Teatre; 1986. 140 pp. (Biblioteca Teatral 39.) Lang.: Cat.
Germany. 1925-1982. Biographical studies. ■Situates *Grosse Schmährede an der Stadtmauer (Great Tirade before the City Wall)* and *Toller* within the works of Tankred Dorst.

2592 Černenkov, V.I. *Dramaturgija Karla Immermana (specifika tvorčeskogo metoda pisatelja): Avtoreferat diss... kand. filol. nauk.* (The Dramaturgy of Karl Immermann—The Specific Character of the Writer's Creative Method: Synopsis of a Dissertation by a Candidate in Philology.) Moscow: Mosk. ped. in-t; 1986. 16 pp. Lang.: Rus.
Germany. 1796-1840. Critical studies.

2593 Coles, Martin. "Heinrich von Kleist: The Quest for Grace and Purity." *THSt.* 1986; 6: 189-198. Notes. Lang.: Eng.
Germany. 1777-1811. Critical studies. ■The idea of grace and the relationship between intellect and passion in life and art.

2594 Damm, Sigrid. *Vögel, die verkünden Land. Das Leben des Jakob Michael Reinhold Lenz.* (Birds Announcing Land: The Life of the Playwright J.M.R. Lenz.) Berlin/Weimar: Aufbau; 1985. 403 pp. Lang.: Ger.
Germany. Russia: Moscow. 1751-1792. Biographies. ■Biography of playwright Jakob Lenz.

2595 Ehrlich, Lothar. *Christian Dietrich Grabbe.* Leipzig: Reclam; 1986. 291 pp. Index. Notes. Tables. Biblio. Illus.: Photo. Print. B&W. 113: var. sizes. Lang.: Ger.
Germany. 1801-1836. Biographies. ■Grabbe's work as a playwright, with analysis of eight plays.

2596 Kaeding, Peter. *August von Kotzebue.* Berlin: Union; 1985. 319 pp. Print. B&W. 17: var. sizes. Lang.: Ger.
Germany: Weimar. Russia: St. Petersburg. 1761-1819. Biographies. ■Life of the extremely productive minor playwright seen in close connection to theatre history.

2597 Kieser, Harro, ed. *Carl Zuckmayer: Materialien zu Leben und Werk.* (Carl Zuckmayer: Information Concerning His Life and Work.) Frankfurt am Main: Fischer Taschenbuch; 1986. 243 pp. Pref. Notes. Biblio. Lang.: Ger.
Germany. Switzerland. 1920-1977. Biographical studies. ■Collection of essays (plus two autobiographical sketches) on dramatist, novelist and poet Carl Zuckmayer.

2598 Knust, Herbert. "Fuchs, du hast die Gans gestohlen...: Zu einem Motiv bei Hauptmann, Brecht und Frisch." (Fox, You Have Stolen the Goose...: Towards a Motif in Hauptmann, Brecht and Frisch.) *GQ.* 1986 Win; 59(1): 34-51. Lang.: Ger.
Germany. Switzerland. 1700-1976. Critical studies. ■Fox lore and fox symbolism as a source of dramatic reference in Gerhart Hauptmann's *Die Weber (The Weavers)*, Bertolt Brecht's *Leben des Galilei (The Life of Galileo)* and Max Frisch's *Biedermann und die Brandstifter (The Firebugs)*.

2599 Landau, Edwin Maria. *Paul Claudel auf deutschsprachigen Bühnen.* (Paul Claudel on German-Speaking Stages.) Munich: Prestel; 1986. 392 pp. Pref. Index. Append. Illus.: Photo. B&W. Lang.: Ger.
Germany. Switzerland. Austria. 1913-1986. Critical studies. ■General discussion of Claudel's theatrical work. Chronological list of performances, details plus review excerpts referring to the specific performances. Biographical details and the playwright's aesthetic conceptions in the introduction.

2600 Leader, Elliot. "Who is Galileo?" *TID.* 1986; 8: 225-248. Notes. Lang.: Eng.
Germany. 1938-1955. Critical studies. ■Examines the distortion of historical fact in *Leben des Galilei (The Life of Galileo)* by Bertolt Brecht. Also discusses Brecht's collaboration with Charles Laughton in preparing an adaptation for production in the U.S..

DRAMA: —Plays/librettos/scripts

2601 Lozovič, T.K. *Svoeobrazie tragičeskogo v dramaturgii Genricha fon Kleista: Avtoref. diss... kand. filol. nauk.* (The Distinctive Qualities of the Tragic in the Dramaturgy of Heinrich von Kleist: Synopsis of a Dissertation by a Candidate in Philology.) Moscow: MGU; 1986. 22 pp. Lang.: Rus.
Germany. 1777-1811. Critical studies.

2602 Matinjan, K.R. *Žanr komedii v literature nemeckogo romantizma konca XVIII načala XIXv. (Tik, Brentano).* (The Genre of Comedy in the Literature of German Romaticism, Late Eighteenth to Early Nineteenth Centuries: Tieck, Brentano.) Moscow: MGU; 1986. 18 pp. [Synopsis of a Dissertation.] Lang.: Rus.
Germany. 1795-1850. Historical studies.

2603 Mueller, Martin. "Hofmannsthal's *Electra* and its Dramatic Models." *MD*. 1986 Mar.; 29(1): 71-91. Notes. Lang.: Eng.
Germany. 1909. Critical studies. ■Comparative analysis of *Elektra* by Hugo von Hofmannsthal and its sources.

2604 Musolf, Peter M. "Parallelism in Büchner's *Leonce and Lena*: A Tragicomedy of Tautology." *GQ*. 1986 Spr; 59(2): 216-227. Lang.: Eng.
Germany. 1836. Critical studies. ■Roman Jakobson's strategy of literary analysis and his idea of paralellism applied to *Leonce und Lena* by Georg Büchner.

2605 Newman, Jane O. "Textuality Versus Performativity in Neo-Latin Drama: Johannes Reuchlin's *Henno*." *TJ*. 1986 Oct.; 38 (3): 259-274. Notes. Lang.: Eng.
Germany: Heidelberg. 1497-1522. Historical studies. ■A discussion of conflict between text and performance, classicism and the vernacular acts, as it appears in Johannes Reuchlin's *Henno*.

2606 Okljanskij, Ju. M. "Ostorožnaja mudrost' Galileja: Istoričeskoe i avtobiografičeskoe v p'ese B. Brechta *Zizn' Galileja*." (The Prudent Wisdom of Galileo: History and Autobiography in Brecht's *Life of Galileo*.) 70-115 in Okljanskij, Ju. M., ed. *Biografija i tvorčestvo. Portrety: Vstreči. Rasskazy iteraturoveda.* Moscow: Sov. pisatel'; 1986. Lang.: Rus.
Germany. 1938. Critical studies. ■Analysis of *Leben des Galilei (The Life of Galileo)* by Bertolt Brecht.

2607 Parri, Mario Graziano. "Arno Holz: dramma della poesia." (Arno Holz: The Drama of Poetry.) *QT*. 1986 Aug.; 9(33): 101-108. Lang.: Ita.
Germany. 1863-1929. Critical studies. ■Reflections on the works of Arno Holz.

2608 Paul, Arno; Marsan, Valentine Aymone, transl. "Brecht e l'arte teatrale cinese." (Brecht and Chinese Theatrical Art.) 335-343 in Ottai, Antonella, ed. *Teatro Oriente/Occidente.* Rome: Bulzoni; 1986. viii, 565 pp. (Biblioteca Teatrale 47.) Lang.: Ita.
Germany: Berlin. China. 1900-1950. Critical studies. ■Influence of Chinese theatre on the work of Bertolt Brecht.

2609 Salumets, Thomas. "Mündige Dichter und verkrüppelte Helden: F. M. Klingers Trauerspiel *Die Zwillinge*." (Poets Come of Age and Crippled Heroes: F. M. Klinger's Tragedy *The Twins*.) *GQ*. 1986 Sum; 59(3): 401-413. Lang.: Ger.
Germany. 1775. Critical studies. ■Analysis of *Die Zwillinge (The Twins)* by Friedrich Maximilian Klinger focusing on the denial of an opportunity to translate promises of the Enlightenment into sociopolitical reality and thus the dilemma of the advocates of the *Sturm und Drang* movement.

2610 Weisinger, Kenneth D. "*Götz von Berlichingen*: History Writing Itself." *GerSR*. 1986 May; 9(2): 211-232. Lang.: Eng.
Germany. 1773. Critical studies. ■An analysis of Goethe's *Götz von Berlichingen* from the standpoint of creating historical fiction from historical fact, or history revealing itself in the process of being written.

2611 Werner, Hans-Georg, ed. *Bausteine zu einer Wirkungsgeschichte. Gotthold Ephraim Lessing.* (Building Blocks of a Reception History: Gotthold Ephraim Lessing.) Berlin/Weimar: Aufbau; 1984. 519 pp. Index. Notes. Lang.: Ger.
Germany. 1748-1984. Critical studies. ■Fifteen essays on Lessing criticism at different times and on individual aspects of his plays.

2612 *Dialogstrukturen in Brechts Stück Die Gewehre der Frau Carrar.* (Structures of the Dialogue in Brecht's Play *Señora Carrar's Rifles*.) Berlin: Brecht-Zentrum der DDR; 1986. 239 pp. (Brecht-Studien 17.) Notes. Tables. Biblio. Lang.: Ger.
Germany, East. Critical studies. ■Description of a method of analyzing dialogue for the reading of dramatic texts.

2613 Davis, R.G. "A Short Statement on Re-Visioning." *ComIBS*. 1985 Nov.; 15(1): 30-31.
Germany, East. 1985. Critical studies. ■Describes a way of revising Brecht's plays that insures a socially relevant production.

2614 Emigh, John. "Euripides and the A-Effect." *ComIBS*. 1985 Apr.; 84(2): 20-28.
Germany, East. Greece. 450 B.C.-1956 A.D. Critical studies. ■Application of Bertolt Brecht's dramatic principles to the plays of Euripides.

2615 Fischetti, Renate. "A Feminist Reading of Brecht's Pirate Jenny." *ComIBS*. 1985 Apr.; 84(2): 29-33.
Germany, East. Critical studies. ■Brecht's partriarchal view of women as seen in his characterization of Jenny in *The Three Penny Opera*.

2616 Kruger, Loren. "Theater Translation as Reception: The Example of Brecht's *Galileo*." *ComIBS*. 1985 Apr.; 84(2): 34-48.
Germany, East. 1938-1953. Critical studies. ■Evaluation of translated text of *Leben des Galilei (The Life of Galileo)*, using reader and spectator as participants.

2617 Lamb, Stephen. "Hero or Villain? Notes on the Reception of Ernst Toller in the GDR." *GQ*. 1986 Sum; 59(3): 375-386. Lang.: Eng.
Germany, East. 1945-1984. Historical studies. ■Reception of the plays of Ernst Toller in the German Democratic Republic and the premiere of his play *Hoppla, wir leben! (Upsy-Daisy, We Are Alive)*.

2618 Lug, Sieglinde. "The 'Good' Woman Demystified." *ComIBS*. 1984 Nov.; 14(1): 3-16.
Germany, East. 1984. Critical studies. ■Brecht's demystification of the feminine myth through the *Verfremdungseffekt*.

2619 Prophet, Becky B. *Aspects of Traditional Chinese Theatre in the Plays of Bertolt Brecht (Volumes I and II).* Ann Arbor, MI: Univ of Michigan; 1986. 502 pp. Pref. Biblio. Notes. [Ph.D. dissertation, Univ. Microfilms order No. DA8612603.] Lang.: Eng.
Germany, East: Berlin, East. China. 1935-1956. Critical studies. ■Detailed comparative study of Chinese influence on all aspects of Bertolt Brecht's theatrical work.

2620 Rouse, John. "Adapting the Adapter." *ComIBS*. 1984 Nov.; 14(1): 17-22.
Germany, East. 1984. Critical studies. ■A look at Bertolt Brecht as adapter suggests that his plays as well as his interpretational techniques should be re-examined according to the current historical perspective.

2621 Siegert, Wolf; Komar, Kathleen L., transl. "Brecht's Children of the Commune." *ComIBS*. 1984 Apr.; 12(2): 13-27.
Germany, East. 1948-1956. Critical studies. ■Examines Brecht's concept of *Naivität* in *Die Tage der Kommune (The Days of the Commune)*.

2622 Teraoka, Arlene Akiko. "*Der Auftrag* and *Die Massnahme*: Models of Revolution in Heiner Müller and Bertolt Brecht." *GQ*. 1986 Win; 59(1): 65-84. Lang.: Eng.
Germany, East. 1930-1985. Critical studies. ■Comparative analysis of Heiner Müller's *Der Auftrag (The Mission)* and its model, Bertolt Brecht's *Die Massnahme (The Measures Taken)*.

2623 Cummings, Scott T. "'Dreams Against the Cold': Characterization in Kroetz's *Help Wanted*." *MD*. 1986 Dec.; 29(4): 587-592. Notes. Lang.: Eng.
Germany, West. 1984-1986. Critical studies. ■Self-consciousness of apparently naturalistic characters in Franz Xaver Kroetz's *Furcht und Hoffnung der BRD (Help Wanted)*.

DRAMA: —Plays/librettos/scripts

2624 Hensel, Georg. "Lobrede auf Dürrenmatt." (Praise for Dürrenmatt.) *Mykenae.* 1986 Oct.; 37(8): 2-4. Lang.: Ger.
Germany, West: Darmstadt. Switzerland: Neuchâtel. 1942-1986. Histories-sources. ■Text of a speech given on the presentation of the Büchner Prize to playwright Friedrich Dürrenmatt. Compares Dürrenmatt's dramatic and narrative works with those of Georg Büchner and contrasts them with those of Bertolt Brecht.

2625 Kleber, Pia. "Stefan Schütz: Beyond Beckett & Brecht." *Theatrum.* 1986 Win; 5: 23-24. Lang.: Eng.
Germany, West. 1944-1986. Critical studies. ■Playwright Stefan Schütz in relation to his predecessors in the modern theatre, and his departure from the terminal to the utopian viewpoint in his most recent play *Sappa.*

2626 Mittenzwei, Werner. *Das Leben des Bertolt Brecht oder Der Umgang mit den Welträtseln.* (The Life of Bertolt Brecht or Dealing with the Enigmas of the World.) Berlin/Weimar: Aufbau; 1986. Vol. 1: 774 pp., vol. 2: 740 pp. Index. Notes. Append. Lang.: Ger.
Germany, West: Augsburg. Germany, East: Berlin, East. USA: Los Angeles, CA. 1898-1956. Biographies. ■Comprehensive representation of Brecht's life and work in correlation to his social, political and cultural conditions.

2627 Rouse, John. "Brecht and the West German Theatre: A Case Study." *ComIBS.* 1986 Apr.; 15(2): 37-42.
Germany, West. 1956-1986. Critical studies. ■Brecht's interpretational legacy is best understood in West Germany where this approach is used in reinterpreting classical texts.

2628 Schütz, Stefan. "From Drama to Prose." *Theatrum.* 1986 Win; 5: 25-26, 32. Illus.: Photo. Print. B&W. 1: 2 in. x 3 in. Lang.: Eng.
Germany, West. 1970-1986. Histories-sources. ■An interview with Stefan Schütz in which the playwright discusses the departure of his work from the 'terminal' tradition and the socio-political views which shape his work.

2629 Deforge, Bernard. *Eschyle, poète cosmique.* (Aeschylus, Cosmic Poet.) Paris: Belles lettres; 1986. 345 pp. (Collection d'études mythologiques.) Index. Notes. Biblio. Append. Lang.: Fre.
Greece. 472-458 B.C. Critical studies. ■Cosmic themes in the plays of Aeschylus.

2630 Gilula, Dvora. "Beriut Vetehila, Sof Shekulo Tov? Kria BeFiloctetes Shel Sophocles." (Health and Glory, a Happy End? Reading *Philoctetes* by Sophocles.) *Bamah.* 1986; 21(103): 26-37. Notes. Lang.: Heb.
Greece. 409 B.C. Critical studies. ■Interpretation of the *Deus Ex Machina* in the final scenes of Sophocles' *Philoctetes*, proving that the play is classical.

2631 Haus, Heinz-Uwe. "Notes on *Ui* in Greece." *ComIBS.* 1985 Nov.; 15(1): 32-34.
Greece. 1985. Histories-sources. ■Program notes from Haus's production of Brecht's *Arturo Ui* in which he discusses the timeliness, language demands and structure of the play.

2632 Mitterrand, François. "Le pacte des Eumenides." (The Eumenides' Pact.) *CRB.* 1986; 34(112): 77-82. Lang.: Fre.
Greece. 458 B.C. Critical studies. ■The *Oresteia* of Aeschylus interpreted as a message about democracy and human self-determination.

2633 Polesso, Paola. "Parados." *QT.* 1986 Feb.; 8(31): 77-84. Notes. Biblio. Lang.: Ita.
Greece. 450-425 B.C. Critical studies. ■Analyzes the formal and textual analogues between the chorus of comedy and that of drama in classical Greek theatre.

2634 Romilly, Jacqueline de. *La Modernité d'Euripide.* (The Modernity of Euripides.) Paris: P.U.F.; 1986. (Écrivains.) Notes. Lang.: Fre.
Greece: Athens. 438-408 B.C. Historical studies. ■Examines the traces of the political and moral crisis of 5th-century B.C. Athens in the work of Euripides, finding the forms of the playwright's modernity in pathetic effects, the debate of ideas and political actuality.

2635 Thiercy, Pascal. *Aristophane: fiction et dramaturgie.* (Aristophanes: Fiction and Dramaturgy.) Paris: Les Belles Lettres; 1986. 408 pp. Notes. Index. Biblio. Illus.: Photo. Sketches. Print. B&W. 16: var. sizes. Lang.: Fre.
Greece. 446-385 B.C. Critical studies. ■Aristophanes' conception of comedy as seen through performance conditions, characters and playwriting techniques.

2636 Vernant, Jean-Pierre; Vidal-Naquet, Pierre. *Mythe et tragédie en Grèce ancienne.* (Myth and Tragedy in Ancient Greece.) Paris: La Découverte; 1986. 298 pp. Pref. Notes. Biblio. Index. Illus.: Dwg. Print. B&W. 5: var. sizes. [vol. 2.] Lang.: Fre.
Greece. 499-401 B.C. Historical studies. ■Collection of studies on Greek tragedy of the 5th century B.C., including the masked god as a tragic subject in the works of Aeschylus, Sophocles and Euripides. (Volume 1 appeared 1972).

2637 Arnold, A. James. "D'Haiti à l'Afrique: *La Tragédie du roi Christophe* de Césaire." (From Haiti to Africa: *The Tragedy of King Christopher* by Césaire.) *RLC.* 1986 Apr-June; 2: 133-148. Lang.: Fre.
Haiti. Africa. Martinique. 1939. Critical studies. ■Analysis of *La Tragédie du roi Christophe (The Tragedy of King Christopher)* by Aimé Césaire and its rewritings in light of Caribbean and African politics, questing for a new type of hero.

2638 Clark, Vèvè. "Haiti's Brechtian Playwrights." *ComIBS.* 1984 Apr.; 12(2): 28-34.
Haiti. 1970-1979. Critical studies. ■Examines the anti-establishment aesthetic of Haiti's exiled playwright Frank Fouché and the group Kovidor as inspired by Brecht.

2639 Bakonyi, István. "Egy kevésbé ismert Vörösmarty-dráma." (A Little-Known Play of Vörösmarty.) *Somo.* 1986; 14(3): 12-16. Lang.: Hun.
Hungary. 1800-1855. Critical studies. ■Analysis of Mihály Vörösmarty's *A bújdosók (Refugees).*

2640 Bécsy, Tamás. "Lehet-e ma drámát írni? Kérdések új magyar drámák kapcsán." (Is it Possible to Write a Drama Today? Questions in Connection with New Hungarian Dramas.) *Sz.* 1986 Aug.; 19(8): 1-11. Illus.: Photo. B&W. 6: 9 cm. x 12 cm., 12 cm. x 14 cm. Lang.: Hun.
Hungary. Critical studies. ■On the basis of the Hungarian dramas presented in the 1985/86 season, a few ideas on the contemporary problems, 'crisis', possibilities of drama writing.

2641 Bécsy, Tamás. "A benső világ drámáiról. Radnóti Zsuzsa: *Cselekvés-nosztalgia.*" (On the Internal Dramas. Zsuzsa Radnóti: *Nostalgia for Action.*) *Jelenkor.* 1986; 29(4): 346-349. Lang.: Hun.
Hungary. 1967-1983. Critical studies. ■Review of a study by Zsuzsa Radnóti, dramaturg of Vigszinház (Budapest), on experimental plays and playwrights.

2642 Bóna, László. "A belső szinház útja. Radnóti Zsuzsa: *Cselekvés-nosztalgia.*" (The Way of the Theatre Inside. Zsuzsa Radnóti: *Nostalgia for Action.*) *Muhely.* 1986; 9(3): 72-75. Lang.: Hun.
Hungary. 1967-1983. Critical studies. ■Review of the dramaturgist Zsuzsa Radnóti's study of form-breaking plays and playwrights wishing to renew the form.

2643 Davidson, Clifford. "A bölcsesség és a bolondság ikonográfiája a *Lear király*ban." (Iconography of Wisdom and Foolery in the Play *King Lear.*) *SzSz.* 1986; 10(19): 5-24. Notes. Illus.: Graphs. 3: var. sizes. Lang.: Hun.
Hungary: Budapest. Critical studies. ■Text of a lecture to the Hungarian Theatre Institute by a professor from Western Michigan University, Kalamazoo, MI.

2644 Deák, Tamás. "Száz év Madách." (A Hundred Years of Madách.) *Elet.* 1986; 23(1): 52-63. Lang.: Hun.
Hungary. 1883-1983. Critical studies. ■Philosophy and morality of Imre Madách's classical dramatic poem *Az ember tragédiája (The Tragedy of a Man).*

2645 Ézsiás, Erzsébet. *Mai magyar dráma.* (The Hungarian Drama Today.) Budapest: Kossuth; 1986. 262 pp. (Esztétikai kiskönyvtár.) Lang.: Hun.

DRAMA: —Plays/librettos/scripts

Hungary. 1960-1985. Historical studies. ■Survey of the development of Hungarian drama.

2646 Ézsiás, Erzsébet. "Szakonyi Károly drámairói portréja." (Portrait of the Playwright Károly Szakonyi.) *Somo.* 1986; 14(1): 38-42. Lang.: Hun.
Hungary. 1963-1982. Critical studies. ■Comparison of plays and short stories by Károly Szakonyi.

2647 Grezsa, Ferenc. "Katona József és Németh László." (József Katona and László Németh.) *Forras.* 1986; 18(5): 12-17. Lang.: Hun.
Hungary. 1985. Critical studies. ■Analysis of László Németh's study of *Bánk Bán* by József Katona and a portrait of the playwright.

2648 Hubay, Miklós. "Naplójegyzetek." (Diary Notes.) *Krit.* 1986; 14(5): 13. Illus.: Photo. B&W. 2: 14 cm. x 9 cm., 7 cm. x 10 cm. Lang.: Hun.
Hungary. 1984-1985. Histories-sources. ■Recollections of playwright Miklós Hubay: notes on his plays, the performances and reception.

2649 Hubay, Miklós. "Naplójegyzetek." (Diary Notes.) *Krit.* 1986; 14(6): 15. Illus.: Dwg. 1: 6.5 cm. x 10 cm. Lang.: Hun.
Hungary. 1969-1984. Histories-sources. ■Excerpts from playwright Miklós Hubay's diary.

2650 Kiss, Irén. "Nyílt fórum Egerváron. Tanácskozás a fiatal drámáiról műveiről." (Open Forum in Egervár: Conference on Works of the Young Playwrights.) *Sz.* 1986 May; 19(5): 42-44. Lang.: Hun.
Hungary: Zalaegerszeg. 1985. Critical studies. ■Conference on the situation of young Hungarian playwrights, with group analysis of plays and production workshops.

2651 Kröplin, Wolfgang. *Theater braucht Meisterschaft. Dialog über die Groteske. Interviews mit István Örkény.* (Theatre Requires Mastery: A Dialogue on the Grotesque. Interviews with István Örkény.) Berlin: Verband der Theaterschaffenden; 1986. 108 pp. (MT 190.) Lang.: Ger.
Hungary. 1947-1979. Histories-sources. ■Interviews with playwright István Örkény on the aesthetics of the grotesque in his work.

2652 Müller, Péter P. "Megsokszorozódás és eggyé válás." (Multiplication and Merging.) *Elet.* 1986; 23(2): 184-188. Lang.: Hun.
Hungary. Critical studies. ■Analysis of István Örkény's grotesque play, *Pisti a vérzivatarban (Steve in the Bloodbath).*

2653 Nagy, András. "Egervár, december három, hégy, öt, hat." (Egervár, December 3-6.) *Sz.* 1986 May; 19(5): 44-46. Lang.: Hun.
Hungary: Zalaegerszeg. 1985. Critical studies. ■Notes on the Open Forum in Zalaegerszeg.

2654 Nagy, Imre. "Küzdelem a groteszkkel." (Struggling With the Grotesque.) *Jelenkor.* 1986; 29(12): 1116-1119. Lang.: Hun.
Hungary. 1976-1985. Critical studies. ■Study of Tibor Gyurkovics' eight plays.

2655 Nagy, Miklós. "Arany János a Bánk bánról." (János Arany on *Bánk Bán.*) *Elet.* 1986; 23 (3): 238-243. Lang.: Hun.
Hungary. Critical studies. ■Analysis of plot, structure and national character of *Bánk Bán* by József Katona.

2656 Nyerges, László. "A klasszikusokhoz való megváltozott viszonyról. Magyar-olasz színházi tanácskozás." (On Changed Relations with the Classics: Hungarian-Italian Conference on Theatre.) *Sz.* 1986 Apr.; 19(4): 35-38. Lang.: Hun.
Hungary. Italy. 1985. Critical studies. ■Summary of a conference on the problems of adapting, interpreting and staging classical works.

2657 Pomogáts, Béla. "Sajátosság és egyetemesseg." (Particular and Universal.) *Napj.* 1986; 25(12): 27-28 . Lang.: Hun.
Hungary. Romania. 1927-1984. Critical studies. ■Review of a study of playwright András Sütö written by András Görömbei.

2658 Radnóti, Zsuzsa. "Átváltozások." (*Metamorphoses.*) *Jelenkor.* 1986; 29(1): 49-55. Lang.: Hun.
Hungary. 1980. Critical studies. ■Study of four contemporary Hungarian plays published in the anthology *Metamorphoses.*

2659 Spiró, György; Kocsis, L. Mihály. "Van itt valaki. Spiró György *Az imposztorról.*" (Is Somebody Here. György Spiró on *The Impostor.*) *Krit.* 1986; 14(1): 18-19. Lang.: Hun.
Hungary. 1983. Histories-sources. ■Excerpt from a book by L. Mihály Kocsis reproduces notes of playwright György Spiró on his play *Az imposztor (The Impostor),* about Wojciech Bogusławski, 'father of the Polish theatre'.

2660 Szántó, Judit. "Egy életmű fele. Sárospataky István drámáiról." (Half-Way: On the Dramas of István Sárospataky.) *Sz.* 1986 Jan.; 19(1): 1-4. Illus.: Photo. B&W. 5: 6 cm. x 7 cm., 8 cm. x 12 cm., 12 cm. x 17 cm. Lang.: Hun.
Hungary. 1974-1985. Critical studies. ■Survey of István Sárospatsky's activity as a playwright and a brief comprehensive analysis of his eight plays.

2661 Vigh, Károly. "A Bajcsy-Zsilinszky-dráma problémái." (The Problems of Plays About Bajcsy-Zsilinszky.) *Forras.* 1986; 18(6): 8-15. Lang.: Hun.
Hungary. 1960-1980. Critical studies. ■Survey of various dramatizations of the life of Endre Bajcsy-Zsilinszky, a major Hungarian political figure from 1920 to 1945.

2662 Lal, Ananda. *Three Plays by Rabindranath Tagore: Translated, and with an Introduction.* Urbana, IL: Univ. of Illinois; 1986. 619 pp. Pref. Notes. Biblio. Append. MU. [Ph.D. dissertation, Univ. Microfilms order No. DA8623344.] Lang.: Eng.
India. 1861-1941. Critical studies. ■Translations of three plays by Rabindranath Tagore—*Tapatī, Rakta-karavī (Red Oleander)* and *Arūp Ratan (Formless Jewel)*—with discussion of Tagore's evolution as a dramatist, productions of the plays and negative reviews.

2663 Armstrong, Gordon. "Symbols, Signs, and Language: The Brothers Yeats and Samuel Beckett's Art of the Theater." *CompD.* 1986; 20(1): 38-53. Notes. Lang.: Eng.
Ireland. France. 1945-1970. Critical studies. ■Based on a comparison of communicative gestures, the conclusion is that Beckett was influenced more by the artist Jack Yeats than by the poet W.B. Yeats.

2664 Fletcher, Alan J. "'Farte Prycke in Cule': A Late-Elizabethan Analogue from Ireland." *MET.* 1986; 8(2): 134-139. Notes. Lang.: Eng.
Ireland. 1602. Historical studies. ■The cock-fight in *Fulgens and Lucres* may have been a traditional Christmas game, known in Ulster as 'Skewer the Goose'.

2665 Kearney, Eileen M. *Teresa Deevy (1894-1963): Ireland's Forgotten Second Lady of the Abbey Theatre.* Eugene, OR: Univ of Oregon; 1986. 219 pp. Pref. Notes. Biblio. [Ph.D. dissertation, Univ. Microfilms order No. DA8622506.] Lang.: Eng.
Ireland. 1894-1963. Biographies. ■Playwright Teresa Deevy's feminism, her six plays produced at the Abbey Theatre and their significance.

2666 Malick, Javed. "The Polarized Universe of *The Island of the Mighty*: The Dramaturgy of Arden and D'Arcy." *NTQ.* 1986 Feb.; 11(5): 38-53. Notes. Lang.: Eng.
Ireland. UK. 1950-1972. Critical studies. ■*The Island of the Mighty* forms an important part of the Arden canon, expressing in its fullest and most coherent form themes and attitudes discernible in the earliest plays.

2667 Orian, Dan. "Ibudim Vetargumim shel 'Tartif' Leivrit." (Adaptations and Translations of *Tartuffe* into Hebrew.) *Bamah.* 1986; 21(104): 61-85. Notes. Illus.: Photo. Print. B&W. 4: var. sizes. Lang.: Heb.
Israel. France. 1794-1985. Historical studies. ■Overview of adaptations and translations of *Tartuffe* by Molière into Hebrew.

2668 *Tutto Pirandello. Poesie-Saggi-Romanzi-Novelle-Teatro.* (All About Pirandello: Poems, Essays, Stories, Theatre.) Agrigento: Centro Nazionale di Studi Pirandelliani; 1986. 398 pp. Index. Notes. Biblio. Lang.: Ita.
Italy. 1867-1936. Critical studies. ■Collection of seventeen presentations made by various authors at Pirandello conferences sponsored by the Pirandellian Studies Center at Agrigento, 1970-1985.

CLASSED ENTRIES

DRAMA: —Plays/librettos/scripts

2669 *Testo e messa in scena in Pirandello.* (Text and Staging in Pirandello.) Rome: La Nuova Italia Scientifica; 1986. 208 pp. Index. Notes. Biblio. Lang.: Ita.
Italy: Agrigento. 1867-1936. Critical studies. ▪Nine studies presented at a 1986 conference on textual meaning and staging in Pirandello's theatre, sponsored by the Pirandellian Studies Center (Agrigento).

2670 Abellan, Joan. "Pròleg. Ombres vives, màscares nues." (Prologue. Live Shadows, Naked Masks.) 5-17 in Institut del Teatre, ed. *El joc dels papers.* Barcelona: Institut del Teatre; 1986. 84 pp. (Biblioteca Teatral 48.) Lang.: Cat.
Italy. 1867-1936. Critical studies. ▪Evaluation of Pirandello's effect on the theatre of his time and evaluation of *Il giuoco delle parti (The Rules of the Game).*

2671 Alberti, Carmelo, ed. *Pietro Chiari e il teatro Europeo del settecento.* (Pietro Chiari and Eighteenth-Century European Theatre.) Vicenza: Neri Pozza; 1986. 315 pp. (Nuova Biblioteca di Cultura 43.) Pref. Index. Notes. Biblio. Lang.: Ita.
Italy. 1712-1785. Critical studies. ▪Papers presented at a conference on 'A Rival of Carlo Goldoni: Abbot Chiari and Eighteenth-Century European Theatre' (Venice, 1985).

2672 Antonucci, Giovanni, ed. "Lettere inedite di Diego Fabbri." (Unpublished Letters of Diego Fabbri.) *Ariel.* 1986 May-Aug. ; 1(2): 121-134. Notes. Lang.: Ita.
Italy. 1960-1978. Histories-sources. ▪Letters from playwright Diego Fabbri to various Italian directors and actors.

2673 Barbina, Alfredo. "Trent'anni dalla morte di Corrado Alvaro." (Thirty Years After the Death of Corrado Alvaro.) *Ariel.* 1986 May-Aug.; 1(2): 35-54. Notes. Tables. Biblio. Illus.: Photo. B&W. 3: 16 cm. x 24 cm. Lang.: Ita.
Italy. 1895-1956. Histories-sources. ▪Summary of author and critic Corrado Alvaro's involvement in theatre, with unpublished notes and letters.

2674 Barbina, Alfredo. "1) Il romanzo di una vocazione letteraria: 2) Repertorio delle lettere edite." (1) The Romance of a Literary Vocation: 2) Inventory of Published Letters.) *Ariel.* 1986 Sep-Dec.; 1(3): 108-125. Notes. Biblio. Lang.: Ita.
Italy. 1867-1936. Biographical studies. ▪Part 1 traces important moments in playwright Luigi Pirandello's artistic development through his letters, Part 2 is a guide to Pirandello's published letters.

2675 Barbina, Alfredo, ed. "Lettere d'amore di Luigi ad Antonietta." (Love Letters from Luigi to Antonietta.) *Ariel.* 1986 Sep-Dec.; 1(3): 211-229. Notes. Tables. Biblio. Illus.: Photo. B&W. 6: 5 cm. x 7 cm. Lang.: Ita.
Italy. 1893-1894. Histories-sources. ▪Luigi Pirandello's letters to his fiancée.

2676 Barsotti, Anna. "'Questi fantasmi!' o dell'ambiguità dei vivi." (These Phantoms! or on the Ambiguity of the Living.) *Ariel.* 1986 Jan-Apr.; 1(1): 75-100. Notes. Tables. Biblio. Illus.: Photo. Dwg. B&W. 2: 10 cm. x 13 cm. Lang.: Ita.
Italy. 1946. Critical studies. ▪Realism and fantasy in *Questi fantasmi! (These Phantoms!)* by Eduardo De Filippo.

2677 Barsotti, Anna. "Un 'Abito nuovo' da Pirandello a Eduardo." (A 'New Suit' from Pirandello to Eduardo.) *Ariel.* 1986 Sep-Dec.; 1(3): 81-99. Notes. Biblio. Illus.: Photo. B&W. 1: 8 cm. x 10 cm. Lang.: Ita.
Italy. 1935-1937. Critical studies. ▪Notes on a draft of *L'abito nuovo (The New Suit)* by Eduardo De Filippo and Luigi Pirandello based on a short story by Pirandello.

2678 Barsotti, Anna. "*La grande magia* secondo Eduardo." (*The Great Magic* According to Eduardo.) *QT.* 1986 Feb.; 8(31): 137-157. Notes. Biblio. Lang.: Ita.
Italy. 1948. Critical studies. ▪Critical discussion of *La grande magia (The Great Magic)* by Eduardo De Filippo.

2679 Beniscelli, Alberto. *La finzione del fiabesco. Studi sul teatro di Carlo Gozzi.* (Fiction of the Fabulous: Studies on the Theatre of Carlo Gozzi.) Casale Monferrato: Marietti; 1986. 156 pp. (Collana di saggistica 19.) Pref. Index. Notes. Biblio. Lang.: Ita.
Italy. 1720-1806. Critical studies. ▪Analysis of the theatrical poetics of the fantastic works of playwright Carlo Gozzi.

2680 Bougnoux, Daniel. "Au passé inachevé." (Past Incomplete.) *ThE.* 1986 Apr.; 10: 39-42. Illus.: Photo. B&W. 3: 9 in. x 6 in. Lang.: Fre.
Italy. 1867-1936. Critical studies. ▪Actuality and modernity of the plays of Luigi Pirandello.

2681 Cavallini, Giorgio. *La dimensione civile e sociale del quotidiano nel teatro comico di Carlo Goldoni.* (The Civil and Social Dimension of Everyday Life in the Comic Theatre of Carlo Goldoni.) Rome: Bulzoni; 1986. 143 pp. (Biblioteca di Cultura 314.) Pref. Index. Notes. Biblio. Lang.: Ita.
Italy. 1743-1760. Critical studies. ▪Personal and social relationships in Goldoni's comedies.

2682 Corsinovi, Graziella. "Suggestioni dell'Espressionismo Tedesco nel Teatro di Pirandello." (Suggestions of German Expressionism in Pirandello's Theatre.) *QT.* 1986 Nov.; 9(34): 23-39. Notes. Biblio. Lang.: Ita.
Italy. Germany. 1917-1930. Critical studies. ▪Influence of German expressionism on the plays of Luigi Pirandello.

2683 Ferraro, Bruno. "*L'esaltazione della croce*: rapporto tra 'figura' e 'figurato'." (*The Exaltation of the Cross*: Relation between the 'Figure' and the 'Figured'.) *QT.* 1986 Nov.; 9(34): 123-134. Notes. Biblio. Lang.: Ita.
Italy. 1585-1589. Critical studies. ▪Discussion of *L'esaltazione della croce (The Exaltation of the Cross)* by Giovanni Maria Cecchi.

2684 Ferrone, Siro. "I ruoli teatrali secondo Pirandello. *Pensaci Giacomino!.*" (Theatrical Parts According to Pirandello. *Think of It Jamie!.*) *Ariel.* 1986 Sep-Dec.; 1(3): 100-107. Notes. Biblio. Lang.: Ita.
Italy. 1916-1917. Critical studies. ▪Angelo Musco's interpretation of *Pensaci Giacomino! (Think of it, Jamie!)* by Luigi Pirandello.

2685 Fiorato, Adelin Charles. "Les *Six personnages* de Pirandello et le mal du théâtre." (The *Six Characters* of Pirandello and the Problem of Theatre.) 125-133 in Heistein, Józef, ed. *Le texte dramatique. La lecture et la scène.* Wrocław: Wydawnictwo Uniwersytetu Wrocławskiego; 1986. 248 pp. (Acta Universitatis Wratislaviensis 895, Romanica Wratislaviensia 26.) Lang.: Fre.
Italy. 1911-1929. Critical studies. ▪Analysis of *Sei personaggi in cerca d'autore (Six Characters in Search of an Author)* in terms of the opposition between the text and its theatrical realization.

2686 Guccini, Gerardo. "Esploratori e 'indigeni' nei teatri del '700: un viaggio intorno al pubblico e alla sua cultura." (Explorers and 'Natives' in Eighteenth-Century Theatre: A Journey Around the Audience and its Culture.) *BiT.* 1986; 4: 107-133. Notes. Biblio. Lang.: Ita.
Italy. France. 1700-1800. Historical studies. ▪Theatrical renderings of the experiences of French travelers in Italy and vice-versa.

2687 Herry, Ginette; Benedetti, Tere, transl. "Goldoni, Tartuffe e Molière. La difficoltà di essere autore di commedie." (Goldoni, Tartuffe and Molière. The Difficulty of Being an Author of Comedy.) *BiT.* 1986; 2: 45-68. Lang.: Ita.
Italy. 1751-1755. Biographical studies. ▪Three autobiographical comedies of Carlo Goldoni—*Molière, Terenzio (Terence)* and *Il Tasso*—reflect the playwright's nervous and anxious personality.

2688 Jenkins, Ron. "Clowns, Politics and Miracles: The Epic Satire of Dario Fo." *AmTh.* 1986 June; 3(3): 10-16. Illus.: Photo. B&W. 5: var. sizes. Lang.: Eng.
Italy. 1986. Historical studies. ▪The link between comic and survival instincts.

2689 Joly, Jacques; Buonomini, Camilla, transl. "Il sistema dell'immaginario nel *Calderón* di Pasolini." (The System of Imagining in *Calderón* by Pasolini.) *QT.* 1986 May; 8(32): 88-95. Lang.: Ita.

DRAMA: —Plays/librettos/scripts

Italy. 1973. Critical studies. ■Notes on Pier Paolo Pasolini's *Calderón*.

2690 Kowsar, Mohammad. "Deleuze on Theatre: A Case Study of Carmelo Bene's *Richard III*." *TJ*. 1986 Mar.; 38(1): 19-33. Notes. Lang.: Eng.

Italy. France. Critical studies. ■Application of Gilles Deleuze's philosophical principles to Carmelo Bene's avant-garde production of *Riccardo III*, a version of Shakespeare's *Richard III*.

2691 Lattarulo, Leonardo. "Protesta e parodia nel teatro di Landolfi." (Protest and Parody in Landolfi's Theatre.) *Ariel*. 1986 May-Aug.; 1(2): 91-98. Notes. Biblio. Lang.: Ita.

Italy. 1908-1979. Critical studies. ■Antinaturalism in the plays of Tommaso Landolfi.

2692 Lazo, Alessandra. "*La Turca* di Giovan Battista Andreini. Un caso di editoria teatrale nel Seicento." (*The Turkish Woman* by Giovan Battista Andreini: A Theatrical Publishing Case in the Eighteenth-Century.) *QT*. 1986 May; 8(32): 61-72. Notes. Biblio. Lang.: Ita.

Italy. 1611. Historical studies. ■History of the difficulties involved in publishing Giovan Battista Andreini's first comedy, *La Turca (The Turkish Woman)*.

2693 Maier, Bruno. "Il teatro di Italo Svevo e la sua cronologia." (The Theatre of Italo Svevo and its Chronology.) *Ariel*. 1986 May-Aug.; 1(2): 83-90. Notes. Biblio. Lang.: Ita.

Italy. 1861-1928. Textual studies. ■Study of the dating of plays by novelist Italo Svevo.

2694 Mancini, Andrea. "Pirandello, Ferrieri, *Il Convegno*." (Pirandello, Ferrieri, *The Meeting*.) *Ariel*. 1986 Sep-Dec.; 1 (3): 139-152. 2: 14 cm. x 20.5 cm. Lang.: Ita.

Italy. 1921-1924. Biographical studies. ■Reconstruction of the relationship of Luigi Pirandello and Ezio Ferrieri, editor of the literary magazine *Il Convegno*, through their letters.

2695 Marchiori, Donatella. "Aspetti del teatro di Achille Campanile." (Aspects of the Theatre of Achille Campanile.) *BiT*. 1986; 4: 141-158. Notes. Biblio. Lang.: Ita.

Italy. 1920-1930. Critical studies. ■Theatrical work of comedian Achille Campanile and his involvement in the theatrical experimentation of various groups.

2696 Marsili, Renata, ed. "L'album da disegno di Lina e Luigi Pirandello." (The Sketchbook of Lina and Luigi Pirandello.) *Ariel*. 1986 Sep-Dec.; 1(3): 247-255. Illus.: Photo. Dwg. Color. B&W. 8: var. sizes. Lang.: Ita.

Italy. 1883-1899. Histories-sources. ■Childhood drawings by Luigi Pirandello and his sister Lina.

2697 Momo, Arnaldo. "La carriera di Arlecchino in due commedie goldoniane." (Harlequin's Progress in Two Comedies by Goldoni.) *BiT*. 1986; 2: 69-92. Lang.: Ita.

Italy. 1751-1752. Critical studies. ■Analysis of the character of Harlequin in two comedies by Carlo Goldoni: *I pettegolezzi delle donne (Ladies' Gossip)* and *Le donne gelose (Jealous Ladies)*.

2698 Oliva, Gianni. "Pirandello tra D'Annunzio e Antonelli." (Pirandello Between D'Annunzio and Antonelli.) *Ariel*. 1986 Sep-Dec.; 1(3): 40-51. Notes. Biblio. Lang.: Ita.

Italy. 1900-1936. Biographical studies. ■Luigi Pirandello's relationship with author Gabriele D'Annunzio and reviewer Luigi Antonelli.

2699 Petrocchi, Giorgio. "Il carteggio Pirandello-Malipiero." (The Correspondence of Pirandello and Malipiero.) *Ariel*. 1986 Sep-Dec.; 1(3): 126-138. Notes. Tables. Biblio. Illus.: Photo. B&W. 2: 16 cm. x 24 cm. Lang.: Ita.

Italy. 1832-1938. Histories-sources. ■Correspondence between Luigi Pirandello and composer Gian Francesco Malipiero on a draft of an opera, *La favola del figlio cambiato (The Fable of the Changeling)*, with explanatory notes. Related to Music-Drama: Opera.

2700 Petronion, Giuseppe, ed. *Il punto su: Goldoni*. (The Point on Goldoni.) Bari: Laterza; 1986. 211 pp. (Universale Laterza 684.) Pref. Index. Notes. Biblio. Lang.: Ita.

Italy. 1707-1793. Critical studies. ■The poetics of Carlo Goldoni's plays as shown through an anthology of writings by and about him.

2701 Pirandello, Andrea, ed. "Quella tristissima estate del Ventuno." (That Sad Summer of 1921.) *Ariel*. 1986 Sep-Dec.; 1(3): 230-246. Notes. Biblio. Lang.: Ita.

Italy: Rome. 1921. Histories-sources. ■Reconstruction of life in the Pirandello household on the basis of letters from the writer's son Stefano to his fiancée.

2702 Puppa, Paolo. "*La nuova colonia*, ovvero il mito dell'attrice infelice." (*The New Colony*, or the Myth of the Unhappy Actress.) *QT*. 1986 Nov.; 9(34): 77-93. Notes. Biblio. Lang.: Ita.

Italy. 1928. Critical studies. ■Critical notes on *La nuova colonia (The New Colony)* by Luigi Pirandello.

2703 Puppa, Paolo. "Il teatro di Svevo ovvero il soggetto tagliato." (Svevo's Theatre or the Cut Subject.) *BiT*. 1986; 1: 48-76. Notes. Biblio. Lang.: Ita.

Italy. 1903-1926. Critical studies. ■Difficulties in staging two theatrical works by Italo Svevo: *Un marito (A Husband)* and *La regenerazione (Regeneration)*.

2704 Puppa, Paolo. "Il Signor Bonaventura, ovvero il teatro rallentato." (Signor Bonaventura' or Slowed Theatre.) *BiT*. 1986; 4: 135-140. Lang.: Ita.

Italy. 1927-1953. Historical studies. ■Playwright Sergio Tofano and the hero of his comedies, Bonaventura.

2705 Puppa, Paolo. *La morte in scena: Rosso di San Secondo*. (Death on Stage: Rosso di San Secondo.) Naples: Guida; 1986. 191 pp. Index. Notes. Biblio. Lang.: Ita.

Italy. 1918-1919. Critical studies. ■Disorientation and death-wish in *Marionette che passione! (Marionettes, What Passion!)* and *Lo Spirito della Morte (The Spirit of Death)* by Pier Maria Rosso di San Secondo.

2706 Roda i Pérez, Frederic, ed. *Homenatge a Luigi Pirandello en el .L. aniversari de la sevamort*. (Homage to Luigi Pirandello on the Fiftieth Anniversary of his Death.) Barcelona: Institut del Teatre; 1986. 16 pp. (Fulls informatius.) Biblio. Tables. Illus.: Photo. Dwg. Print. B&W. 7: var. sizes. [Published material in relation to the Act of Homage celebrated in December 10, 1986, at Barcelona.] Lang.: Spa, Cat.

Italy. Spain-Catalonia. 1867-1985. Critical studies. ■Contributions by directors, actors, writers, professors, critics, translators and journalists on the significance of Pirandello's work and its influence in Catalonia.

2707 Russo, Maria. "L'immagine del gesto nei *I promessi sposi*." (The Image of the Gesture in *The Betrothed*.) *BiT*. 1986; 1: 94-112. Notes. Biblio. Lang.: Ita.

Italy. 1842. Critical studies. ■Gesture as a means of characterization in *I promessi sposi (The Betrothed)* by Alessandro Manzoni.

2708 Sallenave, Danièle. "Lire la préface." (Reading the Preface.) *ThE*. 1986 Apr.; 10: 35-39. Notes. Illus.: Photo. B&W. 1: 7 in. x 7 in. Lang.: Fre.

Italy. 1923-1986. Critical studies. ■Importance of Luigi Pirandello's preface to *Sei personaggi in cerca d'autore (Six Characters in Search of an Author)* in helping Sallenave's translation into French. Relation between translation and staging.

2709 Sawecka, Halina. "Proposition d'une relecture de *Henri IV* de Pirandello sous l'angle des rapports entre le théâtre et la folie." (A Proposal to Reread Pirandello's *Henry IV* from the Point of View of Relations between Theatre and Madness.) 135-144 in Heistein, Józef, ed. *Le texte dramatique. La lecture et la scène*. Wrocław: Wydawnictwo Uniwersytetu Wrocławskiego; 1986. 248 pp. (Acta Universitatis Wratislaviensis 895, Romanica Wratislaviensia 26.) Lang.: Fre.

Italy. 1922. Critical studies. ■Analysis of Pirandello's *Enrico Quarto (Henry IV)* emphasizing the relation between theatre and role-playing in real life.

2710 Scaffi, Saviana; Curell, Mireia, transl. "L'expressió teatral del punt de vista de les dones." (Theatrical Expression from a Woman's Viewpoint.) 191-202 in Coca, Jordi, ed.; Conesa, Laura, comp. *Congrés Internacional de Teatre a Catalunya 1985. Actes. Volum II. Seccions 1, 2 i 3*. Barcelona: Institut del Teatre; 1986. 340 pp. Lang.: Cat.

Italy. 1985. Critical studies. ■Causes of the absence of drama written for women until the twentieth century, description of present tendencies toward return to classics and themes of daily life.

DRAMA: —Plays/librettos/scripts

2711 Sciascia, Leonardo, ed. *Omaggio a Pirandello.* (Homage to Pirandello.) Milan: Bompiani; 1986. 101 pp. Pref. Index. Tables. Append. Illus.: Photo. Pntg. Dwg. Poster. B&W. Lang.: Ita.
Italy. 1867-1936. Critical studies. ▪Collection of writings on various aspects of the life and work of playwright Luigi Pirandello.

2712 Scrivano, Riccardo. "'La ragione degli altri' o l'invenzione del teatro." (*The Reason of the Others* or the Invention of Theatre.) *Ariel.* 1986 Sep-Dec.; 1(3): 69-80. Notes. Biblio. Append. Lang.: Ita.
Italy. 1899-1917. Critical studies. ▪Development of Pirandello's *La ragione degli altri (The Reason of the Others)* from novel to play.

2713 Tamburini, Elena. "Filippo Acciajoli: un 'avventuriere' e il teatro." (Filippo Acciajoli: An 'Adventurer' and the Theatre.) 449-476 in Ottai, Antonella, ed. *Teatro Oriente/Occidente.* Rome: Bulzoni; 1986. viii, 565 pp. (Biblioteca Teatrale 47.) Lang.: Ita.
Italy. 1637-1700. Biographical studies. ▪Influence of a trip to Asian countries on the theatrical work of Filippo Acciajoli. Includes chronology of his life and work.

2714 Tanant, Myriam. "Une, aucune et cent mille." (One, None and a Hundred Thousand.) *ThE.* 1986; 10(2): 45-47. Illus.: Photo. B&W. 3. Lang.: Fre.
Italy. 1867-1936. Critical studies. ▪Luigi Pirandello's interest in the problems of women evidenced in his plays and novels.

2715 Tesio, Giovanni. "Premesse sul teatro dialettale in Piemonte, dall'Unità alla Prima Guerra Mondiale." (Introductions to Dialectal Theatre in the Piemonte, from Unity to the First World War.) *Ariel.* 1986 May-Aug.; 1(2): 69-82. Notes. Biblio. Lang.: Ita.
Italy: Turin. 1857-1914. Historical studies. ▪The lively tradition of Piemontese dialect theatre.

2716 Tinterri, Alessandro. "*Alcesti di Samuele* di Alberto Savinio." (*Alcesti of Samuel* by Alberto Savinio.) *TArch.* 1986 May; 9: 3-28. Notes. Tables. Biblio. Illus.: Photo. B&W. 6: var. sizes. Lang.: Ita.
Italy. 1947-1950. Historical studies. ▪Vicissitudes of Alberto Savinio's play *Alcesti di Samuele (Alcesti of Samuel)* seen through the author's correspondence.

2717 Zappulla Muscarà, Sarah. "*A patenti* di Luigi Pirandello." (*The Licence* by Luigi Pirandello.) *TArch.* 1986 May; 9: 29-107. Notes. Biblio. Lang.: Ita.
Italy. 1916-1918. Historical studies. ▪Text and historical study of the one-act *A patenti (The License)*, a Sicilian dialect play by Luigi Pirandello, with notes on productions, 1918-1934.

2718 Uhrbach, Jan R. "A Note on Language and Naming in *Dream on Monkey Mountain*." *Callaloo.* 1986 Fall; 9(4): 578-582. Lang.: Eng.
Jamaica. 1967. Critical studies. ▪Symbolism in Derek Walcott's *Dream on Monkey Mountain* focusing on the naming of characters, imagery and the use of cross-cultural linguistic references.

2719 Abe, Itaru. *Gendai geki bungaku no kenkyū.* (Studies on Contemporary Dramatic Literature.) Tokyo: Otusha; 1986. 331 pp. Illus.: Photo. Lang.: Jap.
Japan: Tokyo. 1900-1986. Biographical studies. ▪Major contemporary playwrights Kara, Betsuyaku, Abe, Izawa, Mishima and Tanaka are analyzed in their lives and works.

2720 Guifreu, Patrick. "Sade—Bataille—Mishima: L'escàndol i la veritat." (Sade—Bataille—Mishima: The Scandal and the Truth.) 9-18 in Guifreu, Patrick, ed. *La senyora de Sade.* Sant Boi del Llobregat: Llibres del Mall; 1986. 104 pp. (Sèrie Oberta.) Notes. [Prologue to *Madame de Sade*, by Yukio Mishima.] Lang.: Cat.
Japan. 1960-1970. Critical studies. ▪Analysis of Sade's ideology as read by Mishima through the work of Georges Bataille and of the themes and psychological characterization of *Madame de Sade.*

2721 Poh Sim Plowright, Lin; Sirabella, Mariabruna, transl. "Le similitudini fra il *Nō* e Beckett: un caso di convergenza di stile." (Similarities between *Nō* and Beckett: A Case of Convergence of Style.) 279-300 in Ottai, Antonella, ed. *Teatro Oriente/Occidente.* Rome: Bulzoni; 1986. viii, 565 pp. (Biblioteca Teatrale 47.) Lang.: Ita.
Japan. France. 1954-1986. Histories-sources. ▪Comparison of *nō* drama and the plays of Samuel Beckett. Includes interview with *nō* actor Kanze Hisao.

2722 Di Puccio, Denise M. "Metatheatrical Histories in *Corona de luz*." *LATR.* 1986 Fall; 20(1): 29-36. Notes. Biblio. Lang.: Eng.
Mexico. 1960-1980. Critical studies. ▪Metaphysical interpretation of *Corona de luz (Crown of Light)* by Rodolfo Usigli viewing the play as a comment on the process of dramatizing an historical event.

2723 Larson, Catherine. "'No conoces el precio de las palabras': Language and Meaning in Usigli's *El gesticulador*." ('You Don't Know the Value of Words': Language and Meaning in Usigli's *The Gesticulator*.) *LATR.* 1986 Fall; 20(1): 21-28. Notes. Biblio. Lang.: Spa.
Mexico. 1970-1980. Critical studies. ▪Self-reflexivity of language and its use in exposing role-playing and corruption in *El gesticulador (The Gesticulator)* by Rodolfo Usigli.

2724 White, Helen. "Paths for a Flightless Bird: Roles for Women on the New Zealand Stage Since 1950." *ADS.* 1985 Apr.; 3(2): 105-143. Lang.: Eng.
New Zealand. 1950-1984. Historical studies. ▪Focusing on dramatic work inated for performance on the local stage and the participation of women directly in the creative process.

2725 Gibbs, James. "The Living Dramatist and Shakespeare: A Study of Shakespeare's Influence on Wole Soyinka." *ShS.* 1986; 39: 169-178. Notes. Lang.: Eng.
Nigeria. UK-England: Leeds. 1957-1981. Critical studies. ▪Shakespeare's influence on playwright Wole Soyinka.

2726 Leland, Charles. "The Irresistible Calling: The Idea of Vocation in Ibsen." *MD.* 1986 Mar.; 29(2): 169-184. Notes. Lang.: Eng.
Norway. 1849-1899. Critical studies. ▪Thematic analysis of the plays of Henrik Ibsen focusing on self-transcendence through grace as embodied in the female characters.

2727 Tufts, Carol Strongin. "Recasting *A Doll's House*: Narcissism As Character Motivation in Ibsen's Play." *CompD.* 1986; 20(2): 140-159. Notes. Lang.: Eng.
Norway. 1879. Critical studies. ▪Finds in *Et Dukkehjem (A Doll's House)* an isolating narcissism that ensures the play's continuing relevance.

2728 Van Laan, Thomas F. "Generic Complexity in Ibsen's *An Enemy of the People*." *CompD.* 1986; 20(2): 95-114. Notes. Lang.: Eng.
Norway. 1882. Critical studies. ▪An analysis of Henrik Ibsen's *En Folkefiende (An Enemy of the People)* that finds it a complex generic experiment combining elements from comedy, tragedy and the social problem play.

2729 Van Laan, Thomas F. "The Novelty of *The Wild Duck*: The Author's Absence." *JDTC.* 1986 Fall; 1(1): 17-33. Notes. Lang.: Eng.
Norway. 1882. Critical studies. ▪In *Vildanden (The Wild Duck)* Henrik Ibsen deliberately undercuts every device by which a dramatist can make his presence felt.

2730 Morris, Robert J. "The Theatre of Julio Ortega since His 'Peruvian Hell'." *LATR.* 1986 Spr; 19(2): 31-37. Notes. Lang.: Eng.
Peru. 1970-1984. Historical studies. ▪The 19 plays by Julio Ortega have influenced the development of Peruvian theatre. Since 1980, his plays have become more political.

2731 Rivera-Rodas, Oscar. "El código temporal en *La señorita de Tacna*." (The Temporal Code in *The Lady from Tacna*.) *LATR.* 1986 Spr; 19(2): 5-16. Notes. Tables. Biblio. Lang.: Spa.
Peru. Historical studies. ▪Five temporal levels are interwoven in *La señorita de Tacna (The Lady from Tacna)* by Mario Vargas Llosa.

2732 Gaspar, Karl. "Passion Play, Philippines, 1984." *NTQ.* 1986 Feb.; 11(5): 12-15. B&W. 1. Lang.: Eng.

CLASSED ENTRIES

DRAMA: —Plays/librettos/scripts

Philippines: Davao City. 1983-1985. Histories-specific. ▪Orthodox belief and revolutionary political thinking in the creation of a passion play in a prison camp with Christ portrayed as a labor organizer.

2733 "Witkiewicz et le théâtre: symposium international à Varsovie." (Witkiewicz and Theatre: International Symposium in Warsaw.) *TP.* 1986; 29(6-8): 6, 8. Lang.: Eng, Fre.
Poland. 1985. Histories-sources. ▪Description of international symposium discussing the work of Stanisław Ignacy Witkiewicz. Includes list of papers presented.

2734 Bardijewska, Sława. "Tomasz Łubieński i problem mitu." (Tomasz Łubieński and the Problem of Myth.) *DialogW.* 1986; 9: 130-139. Notes. Lang.: Pol.
Poland. 1986. Critical studies. ▪Łubieński's dramas and his attitude toward romanticism and national myths.

2735 Błoński, Jan. "Le censeur—lecteur." (Censor—Reader.) 67-73 in Heistein, Józef, ed. *Le texte dramatique. La lecture et la scène.* Wrocław: Wydawnictwo Uniwersytetu Wrocławskiego; 1986. 248 pp. (Acta Universitatis Wratislaviensis 895, Romanica Wratislaviensia 26.) Lang.: Fre.
Poland. 1958. Historical studies. ▪Mrożek's *Policja (The Police)* as read by the censor and the alleged reasons why it was not forbidden.

2736 Csik, István. "A jövő közönsége—a színház jövője." (The Future's Audience—the Future of the Theatre.) *Sz.* 1986 Sep.; 19(9): 46-47. Lang.: Hun.
Poland: Wrocław. 1986. Histories-sources. ▪Interview with Jan Prochyra, director of the Teatr Współczésny of Wroclaw about the drama competition announced for children.

2737 Gębala, Stanisław. "Śmierci piękne i brzydkie." (Beautiful and Ugly Deaths.) *DialogW.* 1986; 11: 105-110 . Notes. Lang.: Pol.
Poland. 1986. Critical studies. ▪Treatment of death in Tadeusz Różewicz's drama and S. Żeromski's novels.

2738 Gerould, Daniel. "Laocoön at the Frontier, or the Limits of Limits." *MD.* 1986 Mar.; 29(1): 23-40. Notes. Lang.: Eng.
Poland. USSR. 1961-1979. Critical studies. ▪Analysis of *The Laocoön Group (Grupa Laokoona)* by Tadeusz Różewicz and *The Heron (Tsaplia)* by Vasilij Aksönov focusing on the debasement and politicization of art by mass culture.

2739 Godlewska, Joanna. "Samotność w polskim dramacie." (Problem of Solitude in Polish Drama.) *DialogW.* 1986; 2: 123-129. Notes. Lang.: Pol.
Poland. 1986. Critical studies. ▪Analysis of contemporary Polish plays dealing in various ways with the problem of solitude.

2740 Grotowski, Jerzy. "*Doctor Faustus* in Poland." 51-60 in McNamara, Brooks, ed.; Dolan, Jill, ed. *The Drama Review: Thirty Years of Commentary on the Avant-Garde.* Ann Arbor, MI: UMI Research P; 1986. xii, 371 pp. (Theatre and Dramatic Studies 35.) Illus.: Photo. Print. B&W. 2: 4 in. x 6 in. Lang.: Eng.
Poland. 1964. Critical studies. ▪Jerzy Grotowski discusses *mise en scène,* theme, plot and textual interpretation of his adaptation of *Doctor Faustus.*

2741 Heistein, Józef. "Écrivains et dramaturges—lecteurs des *Noces* de Wyspiański." (Writers and Playwrights as Readers of Wyspiański's *The Wedding.*) 171-183 in Heistein, Józef, ed. *Le texte dramatique. La lecture et la scène.* Wrocław: Wydawnictwo Uniwersytetu Wrocławskiego; 1986. 248 pp. (Acta Universitatis Wratislaviensis 895, Romanica Wratislaviensia 26.) Lang.: Fre.
Poland. 1901-1984. Historical studies. ▪Analysis of subject material used by various Polish playwrights.

2742 Heistein, Józef, ed. *Le texte dramatique. La lecture et la scène.* (Dramatic Text: Reading and Staging.) Wrocław: Wydawnictwo Uniwersytetu Wrocławskiego; 1986. 248 pp. (Acta Universitatis Wratislaviensis 895, Romanica Wratislaviensia 26.) Lang.: Fre.
Poland. 1600-1984. Critical studies. ▪Papers presented at the 1984 symposium organized by Wrocław University and University Paris III in Karpacz, Poland. Related to Media: Film.

2743 Inglot, Mieczysław. "Les drames de Juliusz Słowacki dans l'enseignement scolaire après la deuxième guerre mondiale." (Juliusz Słowacki's Dramas in Education after World War II.) 145-158 in Heistein, Józef, ed. *Le texte dramatique. La lecture et la scène.* Wrocław: Wydawnictwo Uniwersytetu Wrocławskiego; 1986. 248 pp. (Acta Universitatis Wratislaviensis 895, Romanica Wratislaviensia 26.) Lang.: Fre.
Poland. 1945-1984. Historical studies. ▪Interpretations of Słowacki's dramas in Polish high schools as a reflection of the changing political situation.

2744 Jenkins, Ron. "Ringmaster in a Circus of Dreams." *AmTh.* 1986 Mar.; 2(11): 4-11. Illus.: Photo. Print. B&W. 7: 2 in. x 3 in., 11 in. x 19 in. Lang.: Eng.
Poland: Cracow. 1944-1986. Critical studies. ▪Polish director Tadeusz Kantor's recent work as influenced by his past and Poland's national political milieu.

2745 Kelera, Józef. "Lata czterdzieste: Współczesność, historia, mit." (Forties: Contemporary, History and Myth.) *DialogW.* 1986; 1: 110-118. Notes. Lang.: Pol.
Poland. 1945-1955. Historical studies. ▪Two main subjects of the Polish dramaturgy of the 1940s were World War II and daily life in the postwar period.

2746 Kelera, Józef. "Lata czterdzieste: Kruczkowski, Szaniawski, Gałczyński." (The Forties: Kruczkowski, Szaniaski, Gałczyński.) *DialogW.* 1986; 3: 106-113. Notes. Lang.: Pol.
Poland. 1940-1949. Critical studies. ▪Plays published by Leon Kruczkowski, Jerzy Szaniawski and Konstanty I. Gałczyński: problems and techniques.

2747 Klossowicz, Jan. "Quelques impressions du symposium 'Witkiewicz et le théâtre'." (Impressions of the Symposium 'Witkiewicz and Theatre'.) *TP.* 1986; 29(6-8): 10-12. Lang.: Eng, Fre.
Poland. 1985. Histories-sources. ▪Overview of symposium discussing the drama of Stanisław Ignacy Witkiewicz. Papers presented on a broad range of topics including the playwright's philosophy and reception of his works in Poland and other countries.

2748 Kobialka, Michal. "*After Hamlet*: Two Perspectives." *TJ.* 1986 May; 38(2): 196-205. Notes. Lang.: Eng.
Poland. UK-England. 1945. Historical studies. ▪Study of the importance of the figure of Fortinbras in Shakespearean adaptations in Poland and Western Europe, with analysis of his changing political meaning.

2749 Kopka, Krzysztof. "Dramaturgia Bogusława Schaeffera." (Bogusław Schaeffer's Dramaturgy.) *DialogW.* 1986; 12: 131-138. Notes. Lang.: Pol.
Poland. 1929-1986. Critical studies. ▪Philosophical aspects and structure of plays by Bogusław Schaeffer.

2750 Majchrowski, Zbigniew. "Paradoks o Różewiczu." (Różewicz's Paradox.) *DialogW.* 1986; 11: 111-116. Notes. Lang.: Pol.
Poland. 1920-1986. Critical studies. ▪Philosophical aspects of Tadeusz Różewicz's drama and his use of obscene language.

2751 Miklaszewski, Krzysztof. "*Qu'ils crèvent les artistes*: compte rendu du spectacle à travers un entretien avec Tadeusz Kantor." (*Let the Artists Die*: Tadeusz Kantor Speaks About the Production.) *TP.* 1986; 29(1-3): 3-8, 11-16. Illus.: Photo. Print. B&W. 6. Lang.: Eng, Fre.
Poland. 1985. Histories-sources. ▪Playwright Tadeusz Kantor comments on themes, particularly death and the tragic story of Wit Stwosz, in his play *Niech szezna artyszi (Let the Artists Die).*

2752 Müller, Péter P. "Egy mai kelet-európai drámamodell: az elveszett identitás drámája." (A Present Type of East-European Drama: The Drama of Loss of Identity.) *Valo.* 1986; 29(9): 81-91. Notes. Lang.: Hun.
Poland. Hungary. 1955-1980. Critical studies. ▪Study of plays of loss of identity characterized by a grotesque and satirical viewpoint, especially those of István Örkény's and Sławomir Mrożek.

2753 Nastulanka, Krystyna. "Centenaire de la naissance de Jerzy Szaniawski (1886-1970): Anniversaires UNESCO de personnalités éminentes et d'événements historiques." (Jerzy

CLASSED ENTRIES

DRAMA: —Plays/librettos/scripts

Szaniawski's Birth Centenary (1886-1970) Included in UNESCO's Anniversaries of Great Personalities and Historical Events.) *TP*. 1986; 29(9-10): 3-12. Illus.: Photo. Print. B&W. 8. Lang.: Eng, Fre.

Poland. 1886-1970. Critical studies. ■Overview of major productions of playwright Jerzy Szaniawski, analysis of their content and impact on the theatre.

2754 Puzyna, Konstanty. "Witkacy au théâtre polonais." (Witkacy in the Polish Theatre.) *TP*. 1986; 29(6-8): 13-18. Lang.: Eng, Fre.

Poland. 1921-1985. Critical studies. ■Production history of plays by Stanisław Ignacy Witkiewicz analyzing the relevance of his works and their message for the modern world.

2755 Spiró, György. *A közép-kelet-európai dráma. A felvilágosodástól Wyspianski szintéziséig*. (The Drama in Central Eastern Europe: From the Enlightenment to the Synthesis of Wyspianski.) Budapest: Magvető; 1986. 395 pp. (Elvek és utak.) Lang.: Hun.

Poland. Hungary. Czechoslovakia. 1800-1915. Histories-specific. ■A comparative study in literary and theatrical history, with particular reference to the drama in Poland.

2756 Sugiera, Małgorzata. "*La Non-divine Comédie* de Krasiński dans la lecture littéraire et théâtrale." (*The Undivine Comedy* of Krasiński in the Literary and Theatrical Reading.) 159-169 in Heistein, Józef, ed. *Le texte dramatique. La lecture et la scène*. Wrocław: Wydawnictwo Uniwersytetu Wrocławskiego; 1986. 248 pp. (Acta Universitatis Wratislaviensis 895, Romanica Wratislaviensia 26.) Lang.: Fre.

Poland. 1835-1984. Historical studies. ■Different interpretations of *Neboska komedia (Undivine Comedy)* by scholar, and by directors producing this work.

2757 Tomassucci, Giovanna. "Bestiarium Witkiewicz." (Witkiewicz's Bestiary.) *DialogW*. 1986; 8: 115-123. Notes. Lang.: Pol.

Poland. 1920-1935. Critical studies. ■Analysis of the characters in Witkiewicz's dramas: their animal-like characteristics and outlook as projected by the playwright.

2758 Trojanowska, Tamara. "Teatralne konsekwencje operetki w *Operetce*." (Theatrical Consequences of the Operetta in *Operetka*.) *DialogW*. 1986; 5-6: 168-174. Notes. Lang.: Pol.

Poland. 1986. Textual studies. ■Witold Gombrowicz's play, *Operetka (Operetta)*, is analyzed in terms of the musical form: similarities of dramatic structure in the play and true operetta are underlined.

2759 Zmudzka, Elzbieta; Hartwig, Edward, photo. "Kantor—Realność Najniższej." (Kantor—Reality of the Lowest Degree.) *TeatrW*. 1984 Jan.; 39(808): 31-34. Illus.: Photo. 6: var. sizes. Lang.: Pol.

Poland: Cracow. 1973-1983. Critical studies. ■Analysis of the theatrical ideas of Tadeusz Kantor.

2760 Ramos-Perea, Roberto. "Nueva dramaturgia puertorriqueña." (New Puerto Rican Dramaturgy.) *LATR*. 1986 Fall; 20(1): 61-70. Notes. Lang.: Spa.

Puerto Rico. 1960-1980. Historical studies. ■Development of recent Puerto Rican drama from photographic realism to the more recent socio-political plays.

2761 Elek, Tibor. "Az első magyarországi monodrámakötetről." (The First Volume of Monodrama in Hungary.) *Elet*. 1986; 23(1): 66-68. Lang.: Hun.

Romania. Hungary. 1976-1984. Critical studies. ■Discusses monodramas of playwright István Kocsis.

2762 Görömbei, András. *Sütő András*. (András Sütő.) Budapest: Akadémiai K; 1986. 313 pp. (Kortársaink.) Biblio. Lang.: Hun.

Romania. Hungary. 1950-1984. Biographies. ■Monograph on the Hungarian prose-writer and playwright András Sütő, a famous figure in Transylvanian literature after 1945.

2763 Szakolczay, Lajos. "A megmaradás esztétikája. Görömbei András: *Sütő András*." (The Aesthetics of Survival. András Görömbei: *András Sütő*.) *Alfold*. 1986; 37(12): 104-110. Lang.: Hun.

Romania. 1950-1984. Critical studies. ■Review of a study of playwright and novelist András Sütő.

2764 Frayn, Michael; Garin, Imma, transl. "Introducció a *Mel salvatge* d'Anton Txèkhov." (Introduction to *Wild Honey* by Anton Čechov.) 5-21 in Centre Dramàtic, ed. *Mel salvatge*. Barcelona: Centre Dramàtic de la Generalitat/ Edhasa; 1986. 128 pp. (Els Textos del Centre Dramàtic 7.) Lang.: Cat.

Russia. USSR. 1878-1960. Historical studies. ■History of the writing and diffusion of *Platonov* by Anton Čechov.

2765 Gitovič, N.I., comp. *A.P. Čechov v vospominanijach sovremennikov*. (A.P. Čechov in the Reminiscences of Contemporaries.) Moscow: Chudožestvennaja literatura; 1986. 735 pp. Lang.: Rus.

Russia. 1860-1904. Histories-sources. ■One of a series on recollections of prominent masters of the Moscow Art Theatre.

2766 Karpova, G.I. *Problema sootnošenija Liričeskogo i dramatičeskogo v dramaturgii Aleksandra Bloka*. (The Problem of the Correlation of the Lyric and the Dramatic in the Dramaturgy of Aleksand'r Blok.) Tomsk: Tom. in-t; 1986. 20 pp. [Synopsis of a Dissertation.] Lang.: Rus.

Russia. 1880-1921. Critical studies. ■Poetic and dramatic elements in the plays of Aleksand'r Blok.

2767 Man'kova, L.V. *A.F. Pisemskij—dramaturg*. (A.F. Pisemskij—Playwright.) Moscow: MGU; 1986. 25 pp. [Synopsis of a Dissertation.] Lang.: Rus.

Russia. 1821-1881. Biographies. ■Life and work of playwright Aleksej Feofilaktovič Pisemskij.

2768 Muratov, A.B. "Dramaturgija Turgeneva." (The Dramaturgy of Turgenjev.) 3-38 in *Turgenev I.S. Sceny i komedii. 1842-1852*. (B-ka rus. dzamatuzgii). Lang.: Rus.

Russia. 1842-1852. Critical studies.

2769 Ren, He. "Gaorji de Xiju Chuangzuo." (The Drama of Gorky.) *XYishu*. 1982 Aug.; 5(3): 116-124. Lang.: Chi.

Russia. 1868-1936. Critical studies. ■Analysis of the major plays of Maksim Gorkij.

2770 Vinnikova, G.E. "Teat'r Turgeneva." (The Theatre of Turgenjev.) 50-75 in Vinnikova, G.E., ed. *Turgenev i Rossija*. Moscow: Sov. Rossika; 1986. Lang.: Rus.

Russia. 1818-1883. Historical studies. ■Analysis of the plays of Ivan Turgenjev.

2771 Žuravleva, A.I. "Tragedijnoje v dramaturgii Ostrovskogo." (The Tragic in Ostrovskij's Dramaturgy.) *VMGUf*. 1986; 21 (3): 26-32. Lang.: Rus.

Russia. 1823-1886. Critical studies. ■Analysis of plays by Aleksand'r Nikolajěvič Ostrovskij.

2772 Žuravleva, A.I. *Žanrovaja sistema dramaturgii A.N. Ostrovskogo: Avtoref. diss... d-rz filol. nauk*. (The Genre System of A.N. Ostrovskij's Dramaturgy: Synopsis of a Dissertation by a Candidate in Philology.) Moscow: MGU; 1986. 32 pp. Lang.: Rus.

Russia. 1823-1886. Critical studies.

2773 Gray, Stephen. "A Chair Called Agamemnon: Athol Fugard's Use of Greek Dramatic Myths." *Standpunte*. 1986 Aug.; 39(4): 19-27. Notes. Lang.: Afr.

South Africa, Republic of. 1959-1986. Critical studies. ■A critical analysis of Fugard's plays, concentrating on his use of Greek myths in writing about contemporary issues in South Africa.

2774 Hesse, G.H. "Die individu en die gemeenskap in P.G. du Plessis se *Die Nag van Legio* en Friedrich Dürrenmatt se *Der Besuch der alten Dame*." (Individual and Society in P.G. du Plessis's *The Night of Legio* and Friedrich Dürrenmatt's *The Visit*.) *Tydskrif vir Letterkunde*. 1986 Aug.; 24: 56-62. Notes. Lang.: Afr.

South Africa, Republic of. Switzerland. 1955-1970. Critical studies. ■Use of a closed community in order to examine the individual's function in society.

2775 Ross, Laura. "A Question of Certainties." *AmTh*. 1984 Sep.; 1(5): 4-9. Illus.: Photo. B&W. 4: var. sizes. Lang.: Eng.

DRAMA: —Plays/librettos/scripts

South Africa, Republic of. USA: New Haven, CT. 1984. Histories-sources. ■Athol Fugard discusses his views on theatre and playwriting, his plays *The Road to Mecca* and *Master Harold...and the boys*, and his sources of creativity.

2776 Salomi, Louw. "Koor en illusie in *Don Juan onder die Boere*." (Chorus and Illusion in *Don Juan Among the 'Boere'*.) *Standpunte*. 1986 Feb.; 39(1): 35-38. Notes. Lang.: Afr.
South Africa, Republic of. 1970-1986. Critical studies. ■Bartho Smit's comedy is analyzed to show how the serious theme is highlighted through the innovative use of the chorus and illusion.

2777 Steadman, Ian. *Popular Culture and Performance in South Africa*. Durban: Contemporary Cultural Studies Unit; 1986. 76 pp. Pref. Notes. Biblio. Illus.: Photo. Dwg. B&W. Lang.: Eng.
South Africa, Republic of: Soweto. 1976-1986. Critical studies. ■A study of working class culture and its influence on the form and content of the theatre of resistance in South Africa.

2778 Vandenbroucke, Russel. *Truths the Hand Can Touch: The Theatre of Athol Fugard*. Johannesburg: Ad Donker; 1986. 306 pp. Notes. Biblio. Append. Lang.: Eng.
South Africa, Republic of. 1932-1983. Biographical studies. ■A comprehensive critical study of the life and works of Athol Fugard.

2779 Wertheim, Albert. "The Darkness of Bondage, The Freedom of Light: Athol Fugard's *The Road to Mecca*." *ET*. 1986 Nov.; 5 (1): 15-25. Notes. Lang.: Eng.
South Africa, Republic of. 1961-1984. Critical studies. ■Thematic study of character of the artist in opposition to convention in *The Road to Mecca* by Athol Fugard.

2780 "En clave tragicómica." (In a Tragi-Comic Key.) *Estreno*. 1986 Spr; 12(1): 4. [Reprinted from *El Paíso*, 5 Jan. 1985.] Lang.: Spa.
Spain. 1940-1985. Historical studies. ■Description of plays by Eduardo Quiles including *La navaja (The Razor)* a tragicomedy for two actors and puppets. Related to Puppetry.

2781 Ashworth, Peter P. "Silence and Self-Portraits: The Artist as Young Girl, Old Man, and Scapegoat in *El Espíritu de la colmena* and *El Sueño de la razón*." *Estreno*. 1986 Aut; 12(2): 66-71. Biblio. Lang.: Eng.
Spain. 1970-1973. Historical studies. ■Comparing self-reflexive aspects in *El Sueño de la razón (The Sleep of Reason)* by Antonio Buero Vallejo and a film by Victor Erice, *El Espíritu de la colmena (The Spirit of the Beehive)*. Related to Media: Film.

2782 Cascardi, Anthony J. "The Old and the New: The Spanish *Comedia* and the Resistance to Historical Change." *RenD*. 1986; 17: 1-18. Notes. Biblio. Lang.: Eng.
Spain. 1600-1700. Historical studies. ■Conservative and reactionary nature of the Spanish *Comedia* and the argument against Lope de Vega's claim of modernizing in *Arte Nuevo*.

2783 Cazorla, Hazel. "Antonio Gala Vanguardista arrepentido?" (Antonio Gala, a Repentant Avant-Gardist?)*Estreno*. 1986 Fall; 12(2): 25-28. Notes. Lang.: Spa.
Spain. 1963-1985. Historical studies. ■Decrease of surrealistic and avant-garde elements in the plays of Antonio Gala and his current preoccupation with realistic characters and the meaning of indvidual existence.

2784 Cocozzella, Peter. "Salvador Espriu's Idea of a Theatre: The *Sotjador* versus the Demiurge." *MD*. 1986 Sep.; 29(3): 472-489. Notes. [Revision of a paper read at Memphis State University Symposium on Twentieth-Century Spanish Theatre, Memphis TN, Nov. 13, 1982.] Lang.: Eng.
Spain. 1965. Critical studies. ■Centrality of Shalom of Sinera to Salvador Espriu's essentially tragic vision in *Ronda de Mort a Sinera (Death Round at Sinera)*.

2785 Díez Borque, José María. "Juan del Enzina: Una poética de la modernidad de lo rústico-pastoril." (Juan del Enzina: A Poetics of the Modernity of the Rustic-Pastoral Genre.) 107-126 in Salvat, Ricard, ed. *El Teatre durant l'Edat Mitjana i el Renaixement*. Barcelona: Publicacions i Edicions de la Universitat de Barcelona; 1986. xxviii, 322 pp. (El Pla de les Comèdies 2.) Notes. [Presented at First International Symposium on Medieval and Renaissance Theatre, Sitges, 1983.] Lang.: Spa.
Spain. 1469-1529. Critical studies. ■Juan del Enzina's defense of his use of rustic and pastoral styles in his work instead of courtly forms, analyzed as reflecting the poet's conceptual modernity.

2786 Dowling, John. "La *Bestia Fiera* de Federico García Lorca: El Autor Dramático y su Público." (Federico García Lorca's *Proud Beast*: The Playwright and His Audience.) *Estreno*. 1986 Fall; 12(2): 16-20. Notes. Biblio. Lang.: Spa.
Spain: Madrid. 1609-1950. Historical studies. ■Examples of playwrights whose work was poorly received by theatrical audiences in Madrid.

2787 Dupuccio, Denise. "Ambiguous Voices and Beauties in Calderón's *Eco y Narciso* and Their Tragic Consequences." *BCom*. 1985; 37(1): 129-154. Lang.: Eng.
Spain. 1600-1680. Critical studies. ■Use of prophecy in Calderón's *Echo and Narcissus* and its effect on dramatic action and characterization.

2788 El Saffar, Ruth. "Way Stations in the Errancy of the Word: A Study of Calderón's *La vida es sueño*." *RenD*. 1986; 17: 83-100. Notes. Biblio. Lang.: Eng.
Spain. 1635-1681. Critical studies. ■Thematic analysis of *La vida es sueño (Life Is a Dream)* by Pedro Calderón de la Barca.

2789 Hanrahan, Thomas. "Calderón's Man in Mexico: The Mexican Source of *El gran duque de Gandía*." *BCom*. 1985; 37(1): 115-128. Lang.: Eng.
Spain. Mexico. 1600-1680. Critical studies. ■Comparison of dramatic technique in Calderón's historical drama *The Grand Duke of Gandía* and its Mexican source *La Comedia de San Francisco de Borja (The Comedy of Saint Francis of Borja)* by Matías Bocanegra.

2790 Hernández, José A. "El teatro de la crueldad en *Tórtolas, Crepúsculo y ... Telón* de Francisco Nieva." (The Theatre of Cruelty in Francisco Nieva's *Turtledoves, Twilight and ...Curtain*.) *Estreno*. 1986 Fall; 12(2): 72-74. Biblio. Lang.: Spa.
Spain. 1953. Historical studies. ■Compares *Tórtolas, crepúscula y ...telón (Turtledoves, Twilight and ...Curtain)*, a non-realistic, metatheatrical play by Francisco Nieva, with Antonin Artaud's theory of the Theatre of Cruelty.

2791 Jones, Margaret E.W. "Psychological and Visual Planes in Buero Vallejo's *Diálogo secreto*." *Estreno*. 1986 Spr; 12 (1): 33-35. Notes. Lang.: Eng.
Spain: Madrid. 1984. Historical studies. ■Poor reception of *Diálogo secreto (Secret Dialogue)* by Antonio Buero Vallejo in Spain because of the challenging nature of his themes.

2792 Lamartina-Lens, Iride. "Myth of Penelope and Ulysses in *La Tejadora de Sueños (Dream Weaver)*, *¿Porqué corres Ulises (Why do you Run, Ulysses?)* and *Ulises no Vuelve (Ulysses Does Not Return)*." *Estreno*. 1986 Fall; 12(2): 31-34. Notes. Lang.: Eng.
Spain. 1952-1983. Historical studies. ■Thematic and stylistic comparison of three plays influenced by the *Odyssey*: *Tejadora de sueños (Dream Weaver)* by Antonio Buero Vallejo, *¿Porque corres Ulises? (Why do you Run, Ulysses?)* by Antonio Gala and *Ulises no vuelve (Ulysses Does Not Return)* by Carmen Resino.

2793 López Mozo, Jerónimo. "¿Dónde está el nuevo teatro español?" (Where Is the New Spanish Theatre?) *Estreno*. 1986 Spr; 12(1): 36-39, 35. Lang.: Spa.
Spain. 1972-1985. Historical studies. ■Examines the failure of a new Spanish drama to emerge after the death of Franco.

2794 MacKay, Angus; McKendrick, Geraldine. "The Crowd in Theater and the Crowd in History: *Fuente Ovejuna*." *RenD*. 1986; 17: 125-147. Notes. Biblio. Lang.: Eng.
Spain. 1476. Historical studies. ■Reconstructs from historical sources the rebellion depicted in *Fuente Ovejuna (The Sheep Well)* by Lope de Vega as ritual behavior.

2795 Moon, Harold K. "Alejandro Casona and the Christian Tradition." *Estreno*. 1986 Fall; 12(2): 9-11. Notes. Lang.: Eng.
Spain. 1940-1980. Historical studies. ■Discusses Christian outlook in plays by Alejandro Casona beginning with his first play *La Sirena*

DRAMA: —Plays/librettos/scripts

varada (The Beached Mermaid), and with special focus on *La Barca sin pescador (The Boat Without a Fisherman)*.

2796 Mullen, Edward J. "Simón Aguado's *Entremés de los negros: Text and Context.*" *CompD*. 1986; 20(3): 231-246. Notes. Lang.: Eng.
Spain. 1600-1699. Critical studies. ■Examines Simón Aguado's *Entremés de los negros (Play of the Blacks)* in terms of its depiction of Blacks and concludes that the play is primarily about slavery as an institution.

2797 Nicholas, Robert L. "Illusions and Hallucinations (Antonio Buero Vallejo): Three Recent Plays." *Estreno*. 1986 Fall; 12 (2): 63-65. Notes. Lang.: Eng.
Spain. 1974-1979. Critical studies. ■Intent of radical subjectivism in three plays by Antonio Buero Vallejo: *La Fundación (The Foundation)*, *La Detonación (The Detonation)* and *Jueces en la noche (Judges at Night)*.

2798 Nicholson, David. "Valle-Inclán's *The Dragon's Head*: Symbolist Fairy Tale and Satyr Play." *MD*. 1986 Sep.; 29(3): 460-471. Notes. Lang.: Eng.
Spain. 1909. Critical studies. ■Parody and satire co-exist successfully with magical atmosphere in *La cabeza del dragón (The Dragon's Head)* by Ramón del Valle-Inclán.

2799 Pennington, Eric. "La ceguera del crítico: Reexamining Buero's Premise in *Diálogo secreto.*" *Estreno*. 1986 Fall; 12(2): 2-3. Notes. Lang.: Eng.
Spain: Madrid. 1984. Critical studies. ■Refutes critical position that Antonio Buero Vallejo's *Diálogo secreto (Secret Dialogue)* is unbelievable.

2800 Rogers, Elizabeth S. "*La Jaula*: An Ortegan View of Mass-Man." *Estreno*. 1986 Fall; 12(2): 12-15. Notes. Lang.: Eng.
Spain. 1971-1984. Critical studies. ■Thematic analysis of *La Jaula (The Cage)* by José Fernando Dicenta focusing on the degradation of the indvidual by mass-man.

2801 Ruyer-Tognotti, Danièle de. *De la prison à l'exil: structures relationnelles et structures spatiales dans trois pièces d'Arrabal.* (From Prison to Exile: Relational Structures and Spatial Structures in Three Plays of Arrabal.) Paris: Nizet; 1986. 310 pp. Notes. Biblio. Lang.: Fre.
Spain. France. ■Political and aesthetic thought of playwright Fernando Arrabal seen through the dramatic writing and themes of three of his plays: ...*Et ils passèrent les menottes aux fleurs (And They Handcuffed the Flowers)*, *Sur le fil ou La Ballade du train fantôme (On the Wire, or The Ballad of the Phantom Train)*, and *La Tour de Babel (The Tower of Babel)*.

2802 Sastre, Alfonso. "En lugar de una ponencia (Para el simposio de *Estreno*)." (Instead of a Presentation for the *Estreno* Symposium.) *Estreno*. 1986 Spr; 12(1): 2-3. Lang.: Spa.
Spain. 1983-1986. Histories-sources. ■Playwright Alfonso Sastre discusses the content of three of his recent plays and the reasons his plays have not been produced in Spain since 1983.

2803 Schmidhuber de la Mora, Guillermo. "Buero y Usigli: Dos Teatros y un abiso." (Buero and Usigli: Two Theatres and an Abyss.) *Estreno*. 1986 Fall; 12(2): 6-8. Notes. Lang.: Spa.
Spain. Mexico. Historical studies. ■Reflections and influence of playwrights Rodolfo Usigli of Mexico and Antonio Buero Vallejo of Spain on theatre in their native countries.

2804 Silverman, Joseph H. "Perduración del paradigma antisemita medieval en el teatro de Lope de Vega." (Persistence of the Medieval Anti-Semitic Paradigm in Lope de Vega's Theatre.) 63-70 in Salvat, Ricard, ed. *El Teatre durant l'Edat Mitjana i el Renaixement*. Barcelona: Publicacions i Edicions de la Universitat de Barcelona; 1986. xxviii, 322 pp. (El Pla de les Comèdies 2.) Notes. [Presented at First International Symposium on Medieval and Renaissance Theatre, Sitges, 1983.] Lang.: Spa.
Spain. 1562-1635. Historical studies. ■Analysis of the social standing of Jews in modern and medieval Spain, focusing on the converted Jew in Lope de Vega's *San Diego de Alcalá (Saint James of Alcalá)*.

2805 Uribe, María de la Luz. "Las influencias de la Comedia del Arte en España." (The Influences of the *Commedia dell'arte* in Spain.) 13-20 in Salvat, Ricard, ed. *El Teatre durant l'Edat Mitjana i el Renaixement*. Barcelona: Publicacions i Edicions de la Universitat de Barcelona; 1986. xxviii, 322 pp. (El Pla de les Comèdies 2.) [Presented at First International Symposium on Medieval and Renaissance Theatre, Sitges, 1983.] Lang.: Spa.
Spain. Italy. 1330-1623. Historical studies. ■Analysis of the mutual influence of Italian *commedia dell'arte* troupes and some Spanish baroque authors, including Lope de Vega and Cervantes.

2806 Valdivieso, L. Teresa. "A propósito de la versión castellana de *Tu i l'hipócrita.*" (Concerning the Translation into Castilian Spanish of *You and the Hypocrite*.) *Estreno*. 1986 Spr; 12(1): 9-10. Illus.: Photo. Print. B&W. 1: 7 in. x 8 in. Lang.: Spa.
Spain. 1959-1976. Historical studies. ■Translator discusses her Spanish version (*Tú y el hipócrita*) of Maria Aurélia Capmany's Catalan play *Tu i l'hipócrita (You and the Hypocrite)*.

2807 Villegas, Juan. "*La Celestina* de Alfonso Sastre: Niveles de intertextualidad y lector potencial." (Alfonso Sastre's *The Nun*: Levels of Intertextuality and Potential Reader.) *Estreno*. 1986 Spr; 12(1): 40-41. Notes. Lang.: Spa.
Spain. 1978. Critical studies. ■Alfonso Sastre's theory of complex tragedy in his play *La Celestina (The Nun)*.

2808 Zatlin, Phyllis. "Staged Reading of Salom's *The Cock's Short Flight.*" *Estreno*. 1986 Spr; 12(1): 2-3. Lang.: Eng.
Spain. USA: New York, NY. 1980-1985. Historical studies. ■Description of a staged reading of *The Cock's Short Flight* by Jaime Salom, translated by Marion Peter Holt, at Columbia University.

2809 Broch, Alex. "*David, rei* dins de l'obra dramàtica de Jordi Teixidor." (*David, King* within the Dramatic Work of Jordi Teixidor.) 5-21 in Institut del Teatre, ed. *David, rei*. Barcelona: Institut del Teatre; 1986. 78 pp. (Biblioteca Teatral 49.) Notes. Lang.: Cat.
Spain-Catalonia. 1970-1985. Critical studies. ■Analysis of the six published plays of Jordi Teixidor.

2810 Coca, Jordi. "El teatre de Josep Maria de Sagarra." (The Theatre by Josep Maria de Sagarra.) 91-97 in Permanyer, Lluís, ed. *Josep M. de Sagarra en els seus millors escrits*. Barcelona: Editorial Miguel Arimany, S.A; 1986. 168 pp. (Els dies i els homes 13.) Lang.: Cat.
Spain-Catalonia. 1917-1955. Critical studies. ■Evaluation of Sagarra's work, with particular focus on his use of language. Related to Mixed Entertainment: Variety acts.

2811 Coca, Jordi. "Sagarra, traductor de Shakespeare." (Sagarra, Translator of Shakespeare.) 139-144 in Permanyer, Lluís, ed. *Josep M. de Sagarra en els seus millors escrits*. Barcelona: Editorial Miguel Arimany, S.A; 1986. 186 pp. (Els dies i els homes 13.) Lang.: Cat.
Spain-Catalonia: Barcelona. 1940-1964. Critical studies. ■Evaluation of Sagarra's translations of Shakespeare (*The Merchant of Venice, The Merry Wives of Windsor*), and comparison of his translations with those of other Catalan translators.

2812 Díez Borque, José María; Munné-Jordà, Antoni, transl. "Lucas Fernández: una retòrica afectiva per a la Passió." (Lucas Fernández: An Affective Rhetoric for the Passion.) *EECIT*. 1986 Dec.; 28: 109-131. Lang.: Cat.
Spain-Catalonia. 1510-1514. Critical studies. ■Analysis of dramatic language used by Lucas Fernández in his *Auto de Pasión (Passion Play)*.

2813 Formosa, Feliu. "La incorporació de textos teatrals a una tradició escènica d'àmbit restringit i amb grans ruptures històriques." (The Incorporation of Plays into a Stage Tradition of Limited Diffusion with Important Historical Changes.) 5-86 in Coca, Jordi, ed.; Conesa, Laura, comp. *Congrés Internacional de Teatre a Catalunya 1985. Actes. Volum II. Seccions 1, 2 i 3*. Barcelona: Institut del Teatre; 1986. 340 pp. Notes. Lang.: Fre.

DRAMA: —Plays/librettos/scripts

Spain-Catalonia. 1848-1984. Historical studies. ■Notes on the history of translation into Catalan of plays by Ibsen, Shaw, Shakespeare and others.

2814 Guillamón, Julià. "Josep Palau i Fabre: teoria i pràctica de la representació teatral." (Josep Palau i Fabre: Theory and Practice of the Theatrical Performance.) 5-21 in Institut del Teatre, ed. *Avui, Romeo i Julieta* seguit de *El porter i el penalty*. Barcelona: Institut del Teatre; 1986. 68 pp. (Biblioteca Teatral 54.) Lang.: Cat.

Spain-Catalonia. 1917-1982. Critical studies. ■Introduction to plays by Josep Palau i Fabre contrasts his dramatic production with his theoretical writings, particularly his reflections on the nature of tragedy.

2815 Medina, Jaume. "*La Santa Espina* i l'amor d'en Guimerà." (*The Holy Thorn* and Guimerà's Love.) *SdO*. 1986 Jan. ; 28(316): 39-42. Notes. Illus.: Photo. Print. B&W. 15: var. sizes. [Continued in 28(317):35-39.] Lang.: Cat.

Spain-Catalonia. 1897-1907. Historical studies. ■Analysis of *La Santa Espina (The Holy Thorn)* by Àngel Guimerà, relating the play to the author's biography, Catholic tradition and veneration of relics.

2816 Miracle, Josep. *Víctor Català*. Barcelona: Edicions de Nou Art Thor; 1986. 52 pp. (Gent Nostra 45.) Tables. Illus.: Photo. Design. Dwg. Print. B&W. 70: var. sizes. Lang.: Cat.

Spain-Catalonia. 1869-1966. Biographies. ■Life and work of Caterina Albert, who wrote under the name Víctor Català, relating her dramatic works to other art forms that she practiced.

2817 Miracle, Josep. "El llenguatge d'Àngel Guimerá." (The Language of Àngel Guimerá.) *EECIT*. 1986 Dec.; 28: 133-148. Lang.: Cat.

Spain-Catalonia. 1860-1967. Critical studies. ■Defense of the literary value of the language of playwright Àngel Guimerà and comparison to that of Jacint Verdaguer.

2818 Miracle, Josep. "Pompeu Fabra, traductor teatral." (Pompeu Fabra, Theatrical Translator.) *EECIT*. 1986 Dec.; 28: 149-162 . Lang.: Cat.

Spain-Catalonia. 1890-1905. Historical studies. ■Discusses Pompeu Fabre's translations into Catalan of plays by Henrik Ibsen, Maurice Maeterlinck and Edgar Allan Poe as well as his work with the group l'Avenç.

2819 Möller-Soler, Maria-Lourdes. "La Mujer de la pre- y postguerra civil Española en las obras teatrales de Carme Montoriol y de Maria Aurélia Capmany." (Women in the Pre- and Post-Spanish Civil War Dramatic Works of Carme Montoriol and Maria Aurélia Capmany.) *Estreno*. 1986 Spr; 12(1): 6-8. Notes. Lang.: Spa.

Spain-Catalonia. 1700-1960. Historical studies. ■Roles of women in middle-class Catalonian society as reflected in the plays of Carme Montoriol and Maria Aurélia Capmany.

2820 Roda, Frederic. "Un príncep desheredat." (A Disinherited Prince.) *SdO*. 1986 Sep.; 28(324): 39-41. Illus.: Photo. Print. B&W. 5: var. sizes. [Issue on Joan Oliver.] Lang.: Cat.

Spain-Catalonia. 1920-1986. Histories-sources. ■Memoir concerning the plays and translations of Joan Oliver and their influence on the author's professional career.

2821 Bellquist, John Eric. "Strindberg's *Father*: Symbolism, Nihilism, Myth." *MD*. 1986 Dec.; 29(4): 532-543. Notes. Lang.: Eng.

Sweden. 1887. Critical studies. ■Symbolist, mythopoeic presentation of problem of atheism in *Fadren (The Father)*.

2822 Bramsjö, Henrik. "Carl Otto Ewers." *NT*. 1986; 33: 32. Illus.: Photo. Lang.: Swe.

Sweden. 1986. Histories-sources. ■Interview with playwright Carl Otto Ewers about why it is more difficult to write for school children than for an ordinary audience.

2823 Bramsjö, Henrik. "'I bland gör de saker, jag aldrig kunnat ana'." ('Sometimes They Do Things I Never Would Have Imagined'.) *NT*. 1986; 32: 28. Illus.: Photo. Lang.: Swe.

Sweden. 1984-1986. Histories-sources. ■Interview with playwright Ingegerd Monthan about the merging of history and current events in her *Drottningmötet (The Meeting of the Queens)*.

2824 Bramsjö, Henrik. "Pojken i tornet—Calderon för barn." (The Boy in the Tower: Calderón For Children.) *NT*. 1986; 34: 26. Illus.: Photo. Lang.: Swe.

Sweden: Malmö. 1985-1986. Histories-sources. ■Interview with playwright Irena Kraus about *Lilla livet (The Little Life)*, her very personal variation for children of Calderón's *Life Is a Dream*.

2825 Hoogland, Rikard. "Innerst inne." (At Heart.) *Teaterf*. 1986; 19(2-3): 11-12. Illus.: Photo. Lang.: Swe.

Sweden: Karlskoga. 1981-1986. Historical studies. ■At a celebration of Karlskoga's fourth century, theatre workshop performed *Innerst inne (At Heart)*, dramatizing conflicting wishes for peace and a job at a gun factory.

2826 Marko, Susanne. "Staffan Göthe: Att utifrån livet dikta vidare." (Staffan Göthe: Starting With Life, To Create.) *Entre*. 1986; 13(4): 20-27. Illus.: Photo. B&W. 7: var. sizes. Lang.: Swe.

Sweden: Luleå. 1972-1986. Histories-sources. ■Interview with director, actor and playwright Staffan Göthe about his stage and radio plays and his attempts to create an Elizabethan theatre of heightened realism.

2827 Mitchell, Stephen A. "The Path from *Inferno* to the Chamber Plays: *Easter* and Swedenborg." *MD*. 1986 Mar.; 29(2): 157-168. Notes. Lang.: Eng.

Sweden. 1900. Critical studies. ■Biblical and Swedenborgian influences on the development of August Strindberg's chamber play *Påsk (Easter)*.

2828 Harms, Klaus B. "Ich bin ein Mensch ohne Bühne." (I Am a Man Without a Stage.) *DB*. 1986 Nov.; 57(11): 8-11. Illus.: Photo. B&W. Lang.: Ger.

Switzerland. 1986. Histories-sources. ■Interview with playwright Friedrich Dürrenmatt on his work, philosophy, and relationship to the contemporary stage.

2829 Pickar, Gertrud Bauer. "Hades Revisited: Max Frisch's *Triptychon*." *GQ*. 1986 Win; 59(1): 52-64. Lang.: Eng.

Switzerland. 1939-1983. Critical studies. ■Analysis of *Triptychon (Triptych)* by Max Frisch, Thornton Wilder's influence and Frisch's experimentation with the potential of the stage for manipulating spatial and temporal boundaries, and a comparison of the play with Frisch's earlier *Nun singen sie wieder (Now They Sing Again)*.

2830 "A Question of Confidence." *WomenR*. 1986 May; 2(7): 8-9. Illus.: Photo. B&W. 2. Lang.: Eng.

UK-England. 1985-1986. Histories-sources. ■Literary manager's view of the current state of women's playwriting in Britain, and strategies for getting more women's work performed.

2831 "The Abuse of Power." *PI*. 1986 May; 1(10): 27-33. B&W. 1. Lang.: Eng.

UK-England: London. 1986. Histories-sources. ■Marius Brill discusses the background to his prize winning play *Frikzhan* about the confrontation between a black Social Security official and a white ex-policeman on the dole.

2832 Barker, Frank Granville. "Old Letters and New Plays." *PI*. 1986 Jan.; 1(6): 52-56. Illus.: Photo. Print. B&W. Lang.: Eng.

UK-England: London. 1986. Histories-sources. ■Rosemary Wilton discusses her life and writing *Bouncing*.

2833 Bulman, James C. "Bond, Shakespeare, and the Absurd." *MD*. 1986 Mar.; 29(1): 60-70. Notes. Lang.: Eng.

UK-England. 1971-1973. Critical studies. ■Edward Bond's attacks on Shakespeare's absurdism and nihilism in *Bingo* and *Lear*.

2834 Bulman, James C. "*The Woman* and Greek Myth: Bond's Theatre of History." *MD*. 1986 Dec.; 29(4): 505-515. Notes. Lang.: Eng.

UK-England. 1978. Critical studies. ■Edward Bond's use of Homeric, Sophoclean, and Euripidean models in transforming myth into history.

2835 Burkman, Katherine H. "Harold Pinter's *Betrayal*: Life Before Death—and After." *TJ*. 1982 Dec.; 34(4): 505-518.

UK-England. 1978. Critical studies. ■The use of backward narrative in Pinter's *Betrayal* highlights the theme of renewal.

2836 Burkman, Katherine H. "'Family Voices' and the Voice of the Family in Pinter's Plays." 164-174 in Gale, Steven H., ed. *Harold Pinter:Critical Approaches*. London/Toronto:

CLASSED ENTRIES

DRAMA: **—Plays/librettos/scripts**

Associated University Presses; 1986. 232 pp. Notes. Lang.: Eng.

UK-England. 1957-1981. Critical studies. ■Theme of the family in *Family Voices* and other plays by Harold Pinter.

2837   Cardullo, Bert. "The Mystery of *Candida*." *ShawR.* 1986; 6: 91-100. Notes. Lang.: Eng.

UK-England: London. 1894. Critical studies. ■Thematic analysis of *Candida* by George Bernard Shaw focusing on the spiritual development of Marchbanks.

2838   Colvin, Clare. "Quest for Perfection." *Drama.* 1986; 159: 11-13. Illus.: Photo. B&W. 5. Lang.: Eng.

UK-England: London. 1958-1986. Histories-sources. ■Interview with playwright Peter Shaffer about his craft, with special reference to his play *Yonadab*.

2839   Colvin, Clare. "The Real Tom Stoppard." *Drama.* 1986; 161: 9-10. Illus.: Photo. B&W. 3. Lang.: Eng.

UK-England. 1986. Histories-sources. ■Interview with playwright Tom Stoppard on the creative process and techniques of adaptation.

2840   Dean, Joan F. "Joe Orton and the Redefinition of Farce." *TJ.* 1982 Dec.; 34(4): 481-492. Lang.: Eng.

UK-England. 1960-1969. Critical studies. ■Orton redefined farce as a genre by moving it beyond facile amusement to accommodate his insight into humanity's unbounded energies.

2841   Delamothe, Tony. "The Color Pink." *PI.* 1986 Oct.; 2(3): 12-17. B&W. 8. Lang.: Eng.

UK-England: London. 1970-1986. Historical studies. ■Overview of plays with homosexual themes. *Torch Song Trilogy, The Normal Heart, La Cage Aux Folles* and theatre groups such as Gay Sweatshop and Bloolips producing their own plays.

2842   Dereuck, J.A. "*Old Times* and Pinter's Dramatic Method." *English Studies in Africa.* 1986; 29(2): 121-130. Notes. Lang.: Eng.

UK-England. 1971. Critical studies. ■Using insights gained from recent narratological theory, this study discusses the way Pinter communicates a sense of menace to his audiences.

2843   Diamond, Elin. "Stoppard's *Dogg's Hamlet, Cahoot's Macbeth*: The Uses of Shakespeare." *MD.* 1986 Dec.; 29(4): 593-600. Notes. [Originally presented to Shakespeare Association of America.] Lang.: Eng.

UK-England. 1979-1986. Critical studies. ■Criticism of the institutionalization of Shakespeare in Tom Stoppard's *Dogg's Hamlet, Cahoot's Macbeth.*

2844   Dohmen, William F. "Time After Time: Pinter Plays with Disjunctive Chronologies." 187-201 in Gale, Steven H., ed. *Harold Pinter:Critical Approaches.* London/Toronto: Associated University Presses; 1986. 232 pp. Lang.: Eng.

UK-England. 1957-1979. Critical studies. ■Playwright Harold Pinter's use of disjunctive chronologies.

2845   Donesky, Finlay. "Oppression, Resistance, and the Writer's Testament: Howard Barker interviewed by Finlay Donesky." *NTQ.* 1986 Nov.; 11(8): 336-344. Illus.: Photo. B&W. 4. Lang.: Eng.

UK-England. 1981-1985. Histories-sources. ■The development of Howard Barker's writing since 1981, and his thinking about society and playwriting.

2846   Dukore, Bernard F. "'My, How We've Changed'." 25-29 in Gale, Steven H., ed. *Harold Pinter: Critical Approaches.* London/Toronto: Associated University Presses; 1986. 232 pp. Notes. Lang.: Eng.

UK-England. 1957-1982. Critical studies. ■Impact of Harold Pinter on contemporary understanding of theater.

2847   Forry, Steven Earl. "The Hideous Progenies of Richard Brinsley Peake: *Frankenstein* on the Stage, 1823-26." *ThR.* 1986; 11(1): 13-31. Notes. Illus.: Photo. Print. B&W. 4. Lang.: Eng.

UK-England. France. 1823-1826. Historical studies. ■Frankenstein myth in gothic melodramas, *Presumption, The Man and the Monster* and *Le Monstre et le magicien (The Monster and the Magician).*

2848   Foulkes, Richard. "'The Cure is Removal of Guilt': Faith, Fidelity and Fertility in the Plays of Peter Nichols." *MD.* 1986 June; 29(2): 207-215. Notes. Lang.: Eng.

UK-England. 1967-1984. Critical studies. ■Sterility and redemption in plays by Peter Nichols interpreted in the light of Jungian psychological theories of John Layard.

2849   Fuegi, John. "The Uncertainty Principle and Pinter's Modern Drama." 202-207 in Gale, Steven H., ed. *Harold Pinter:Critical Approaches.* London/Toronto: Associated University Presses; 1986. 232 pp. Notes. Lang.: Eng.

UK-England. 1932-1986. Critical studies. ■Relation of Harold Pinter's plays to modern developments in science and philosophy.

2850   Gabbard, Lucina Paquet. "The Pinter Surprise." 175-186 in Gale, Steven H., ed. *Harold Pinter:Critical Approaches.* London/Toronto: Associated University Presses; 1986. 232 pp. Notes. Lang.: Eng.

UK-England. 1960-1977. Critical studies. ■Playwright Harold Pinter's use of dramatic reversals and surprise.

2851   Gale, Steven H., ed. *Harold Pinter: Critical Approaches.* London/Toronto: Associated University Presses; 1986. 232 pp. Pref. Notes. Index. Tables. Lang.: Eng.

UK-England. 1957-1984. Biographical studies. ■Collection of articles with an introductory survey of the career and dramatic works by Harold Pinter.

2852   Garr, Helen. "French Mistresses." *WomenR.* 1986 Apr.; 2(6): 10-11. Illus.: Photo. B&W. 1. Lang.: Eng.

UK-England. France. Critical studies. ■Attitudes toward sexuality in plays using French sources: Pam Gems' *Camille*, Christopher Hampton's *Les Liaisons Dangereuses* and Lerner and Loewe's *Gigi.*

2853   Gawood, Mal. "Whistling in the Wilderness: Edward Bond's Most Recent Plays." *Red Letters.* 1986 May(19): 11-23. Lang.: Eng.

UK-England: London. 1986. Critical studies. ■Failure of *The War Plays* to communicate Bond's ideas.

2854   Gems, Pam. "The Danton Affair." *Drama.* 1986; 161: 5-9. Illus.: Photo. B&W. 4. Lang.: Eng.

UK-England. 1985-1986. Histories-sources. ■The author's journal of research and writing at the Royal Shakespeare Company.

2855   Giantvalley, Scott. "Toying with *The Dwarfs*: The Textual Problems with Pinter's Corrections." 72-81 in Gale, Steven H., ed. *Harold Pinter: Critical Approaches.* London/Toronto: Associated University Presses; 1986. 232 pp. Notes. Lang.: Eng.

UK-England. 1960-1976. Critical studies. ■Effect of rewrites on different versions of Harold Pinter's *The Dwarfs.*

2856   Gillen, Francis. "Harold Pinter's *The Birthday Party*: Menace Reconsidered." 38-46 in Gale, Steven H., ed. *Harold Pinter: Critical Approaches.* London/Toronto: Associated University Presses; 1986. 232 pp. Notes. Lang.: Eng.

UK-England. 1958. Critical studies. ■Thematic analysis of Harold Pinter's *The Birthday Party.*

2857   Goodall, Jane. "Musicality and Meaning in the Dialogue of *Saint's Day*." *MD.* 1986 Dec.; 29(4): 567-579. Notes. Lang.: Eng.

UK-England. 1951. Critical studies. ■Meaning is conveyed through musical structuring of language and other aural components rather than through disquisition.

2858   Gray, Simon. *An Unnatural Pursuit and Other Pieces.* New York, NY: St. Martin's; 1986. 256 pp. Index. Illus.: Photo. Lang.: Eng.

UK-England. 1983. Histories-sources. ■Playwright's journal of the creation of his play, *The Common Pursuit*, directed by Harold Pinter.

2859   Hampton, Christopher; Langton, Robert Gore. "An Old Liaison." *PlPl.* 1986 Oct.; 397: 12-13. B&W. 2. Lang.: Eng.

UK-England: London. 1971-1986. Histories-sources. ■Interview with playwright Christopher Hampton about his *Les Liaisons dangereuses*, adapted from the novel by Pierre Chloderlos de Laclos.

2860   Hinchliffe, Arnold P. "After 'No Man's Land': A Progress Report." 153-163 in Gale, Steven H., ed. *Harold Pinter:*

DRAMA: —Plays/librettos/scripts

Critical Approaches. London/Toronto: Associated University Presses; 1986. 232 pp. Notes. Lang.: Eng.
UK-England. 1975-1983. Critical studies. ■History of Harold Pinter's work and critical reception.

2861 Hudgins, Christopher C. "Intended Audience Response, *The Homecoming,* and the Ironic Mode of Identification." 102-117 in Gale, Steven H., ed. *Harold Pinter: Critical Approaches.* London/Toronto: Associated University Presses; 1986. 232 pp. Notes. Lang.: Eng.
UK-England. 1952-1965. Critical studies. ■Reader-response theory used to interpret Harold Pinter's *The Homecoming.*

2862 Kauffman, Stanley. "George Bernard Shaw: Twentieth Century Victorian." *PerAJ.* 1986; 10(2): 54-61. Lang.: Eng.
UK-England. 1856-1950. Critical studies. ■Examination of George Bernard Shaw's contemporary relevance using examples from Volume 3 of his letters.

2863 Lee, J. Scott. "Comic Unity in *Arms and the Man.*" *ShawR.* 1986; 6: 100-122. Notes. Lang.: Eng.
UK-England: London. 1894. Critical studies. ■Argues that Shaw's *Arms and the Man* is a coherent whole, emphasizing recurring comedic elements.

2864 Lorés, Maite. "Pròleg a *Sopa de pollastre amb ordi* d'Arnold Wesker." (Prologue to *Chicken Soup with Barley* by Arnold Wesker.) 5-19 in Institut del Teatre, ed. *Sopa de pollastre amb ordi.* Barcelona: Institut del Teatre; 1986. 104 pp. (Biblioteca Teatral 53.) Lang.: Cat.
UK-England: London. 1932-1986. Critical studies. ■Analysis of the play in the context of Wesker's semi-autobiographical trilogy: *Chicken Soup with Barley* (1958), *Roots* (1959) and *I'm Talking about Jerusalem* (1960).

2865 Mallafré, Joaquim. "Pròleg a *Qui a casa torna* d'Harold Pinter." (Prologue to *The Homecoming* by Harold Pinter.) 5-13 in Institut del Teatre, ed. *Qui a casa torna.* Barcelona: Institut del Teatre; 1986. 104 pp. (Biblioteca Teatral 44.) Lang.: Cat.
UK-England: London. 1930-1985. Critical studies. ■Analysis of *The Homecoming,* with Pinter bibliography. Related to Media: Film.

2866 Mallafré, Joaquim. "Pròleg a *Amb la ràbia al cos* de John Osborne." (Prologue to *Look Back in Anger* by John Osborne.) 5-19 in Institut del Teatre, ed. *Amb la ràbia al cos.* Barcelona: Institut del Teatre; 1986. 112 pp. (Biblioteca Teatral 47.) Lang.: Cat.
UK-England: London. 1929-1978. Historical studies. ■Analysis of post-war British theatre as the background of Osborne's play, with analysis of the character Jimmy Porter. Includes an Osborne bibliography.

2867 Pack, Alison. "Conflict Among the Artists." *Drama.* 1986; 160(2): 21-22. Illus.: Photo. B&W. 2. Lang.: Eng.
UK-England. 1980. Histories-sources. ■Interview with playwright Dusty Hughes about his play, *The Futurists.*

2868 Peacock, Keith D. "Chronicles of Wasted Time." *TID.* 1986; 8: 195-212. Notes. Illus.: Photo. Print. B&W. 1: 5 in. x 7 in. Lang.: Eng.
UK-England. 1945-1983. Critical studies. ■Study of the evocation of World War II in plays questioning the quality of post-war change.

2869 Powlick, Leonard. "What the Hell is *That* All About?: A Peek at Pinter's Dramaturgy." 30-37 in Gale, Steven H., ed. *Harold Pinter: Critical Approaches.* London/Toronto: Associated University Presses; 1986. 232 pp. Notes. Lang.: Eng.
UK-England. 1957-1986. Critical studies. ■Harold Pinter's use of psychological metaphors and dream images.

2870 Quigley, Austin E. "Design and Discovery in Pinter's *The Lover.*" 82-101 in Gale, Steven H., ed. *Harold Pinter: Critical Approaches.* London/Toronto: Associated University Presses; 1986. 232 pp. Notes. Lang.: Eng.
UK-England. 1963. Critical studies. ■Thematic analysis of Harold Pinter's *The Lover.*

2871 Reinelt, Janelle. "Elaborating Brecht—Churchill's Domestic Drama." *ComIBS.* 1985 Apr.; 84(2): 49-56.

UK-England. 1980. Critical studies. ■Caryl Churchill combines Brecht's alienation effect with traditional comic structure in *Cloud 9* to create a popular play.

2872 Sammells, Neil. "Earning Liberties: *Travesties* and *The Importance of Being Earnest.*" *MD.* 1986 Sep.; 29(3): 376-387. Notes. Lang.: Eng.
UK-England. 1895-1974. Critical studies. ■In its form, Tom Stoppard's *Travesties* embodies Oscar Wilde's aesthetic asserting freedom of art to separate itself from conventional alternatives of conformity and delinquency.

2873 Sawyer, Paul. "The Last Line of *Arms and the Man.*" *ShawR.* 1986; 6: 123-125. Lang.: Eng.
UK-England: London. 1894-1982. Textual studies. ■Textual history of the variations in the final line of *Arms and the Man.*

2874 Shafer, Yvonne. "Aristophanic and Chekhovian Structure in the Plays of Simon Gray." *TheatreS.* 1984-85/1985-86; 31/32: 33-40. Illus.: Photo. 2: var. sizes. Lang.: Eng.
UK-England. 1986. Critical studies. ■Aristophanic structure of Simon Gray's *Otherwise Engaged* whose central figure searches for order in a chaotic world, and the chekhovian atmosphere of *Quartermaine's Terms,* whose main character moves through a landscape of despair.

2875 Smith, Bridget. "*Elizabeth: Almost by Chance a Woman.*" *WomenR.* 1986 Dec.; 2(14-15): 44-45. Illus.: Photo. B&W. 1. Lang.: Eng.
UK-England: London. Italy. 1986. Histories-sources. ■Interview with Gillian Hanna about her translation of and performance in Dario Fo's *Elisabetta: Quasì per caso una donna (Elizabeth: Almost by Chance a Woman).*

2876 Spencer, Jenny. "Edward Bond's *Bingo*: History, Politics and Subjectivity." *TID.* 1986; 8: 213-222. Notes. Lang.: Eng.
UK-England. 1974. Critical studies. ■Uses ideas of Bertolt Brecht on the history play to justify liberties taken by Edward Bond in *Bingo,* a play about the last year in the life of Shakespeare.

2877 Swanson, Michael. "Mother/Daughter Relationships in Three Plays by Caryl Churchill." *TheatreS.* 1984-85/1985-86; 31/32: 49-66. Illus.: Photo. 3: var. sizes. Lang.: Eng.
UK-England. 1986. Critical studies. ■Caryl Churchill explores women's roles in society and potential changes through mother/daughter relationships in *Cloud 9, Fen* and *Top Girls.*

2878 Tetzeli von Rosador, Kurt. "Christian Historical Drama: The Exemplariness of *Murder in the Cathedral.*" *MD.* 1986 Dec.; 29(4): 516-531. Notes. Lang.: Eng.
UK-England. 1935. Critical studies. ■T.S. Eliot's play dramatizes the Christian theory of history.

2879 Werson, Gerard. "MacDonald's Heroes." *PI.* 1986 Mar.; 1(8): 16-17. Illus.: Photo. Print. B&W. 1. Lang.: Eng.
UK-England: London. 1917-1986. Histories-sources. ■Stephen MacDonald discusses his play *Not About Heroes,* about World War I poets Siegfried Sassoon and Wilfred Owen.

2880 Wertheim, Albert. "Tearing of Souls: Harold Pinter's *A Slight Ache* on Radio and Stage." 64-71 in Gale, Steven H., ed. *Harold Pinter: Critical Approaches.* London/Toronto: Associated University Presses; 1986. 232 pp. Notes. Lang.: Eng.
UK-England. 1959-1961. Critical studies. ■Comparison of the radio and staged versions of Harold Pinter's *A Slight Ache.*

2881 Wesker, Arnold. "The Nature of Theatre Dialogue." *NTQ.* 1986 Nov.; 11(8): 364-368. Lang.: Eng.
UK-England. 1950-1986. Critical studies. ■The constituent elements of stage dialogue in supposedly 'realistic' drama are examined as is the rigorous if not always conscious process of artistic selection and shaping. Illustrated with examples from his own work.

2882 Yandell, Claire. "Beauty and the Beast." *WomenR.* 1986 Jan.; 2(3): 30-31. Illus.: Photo. B&W. 1. Lang.: Eng.
UK-England. 1979-1986. Histories-sources. ■Interview with playwright Louise Page.

2883 Zelenak, Michael X. "The Politics of History: Howard Brenton's Adaptations." *ThM.* 1986 Fall/Win; 18(1): 53-55. Notes. Lang.: Eng.

CLASSED ENTRIES

DRAMA: —Plays/librettos/scripts

UK-England. 1973-1986. Critical studies. ■Adaptations by Howard Brenton represent his changing political analysis.

2884 Zimmermann, Heinz. "Wesker and Utopia in the Sixties." *MD*. 1986 June; 29(2): 185-206. Notes. Lang.: Eng.

UK-England. 1958-1970. Critical studies. ■Utopia as an essential, though unrealizable, ideal in early plays by Arnold Wesker.

2885 Oliver, Cordelia. "New Voice from Scotland." *PI*. 1986 Feb.; 1(7): 46-57. Illus.: Photo. Print. B&W. 1. Lang.: Eng.

UK-Scotland: Edinburgh. 1960-1986. Histories-sources. ■John Clifford talks about his life and how he came to write plays.

2886 Whitebrook, Peter. "Ena Lamont Stewart Trilogy." *STN*. 1985 Dec-Jan.; 9(48): 9-10. Illus.: Photo. B&W. 1. Lang.: Eng.

UK-Scotland. 1940-1985. Historical studies. ■Description of Ena Lamont Stewart trilogy *Will You Still Need Me* which has just completed a major Scottish tour.

2887 Blaylock, Curtis. "Una obra uruguayana en Madrid." (An Uruguayan Work in Madrid.) *LATR*. 1986 Spr; 19(2): 103-104. Lang.: Spa.

Uruguay. Spain: Madrid. 1985. Historical studies. ■Description of Pedro Corradi's *Retrato de señora con espejo—Vida y pasión de Margarita Xirgu (Portrait of a Lady with Mirror—The Life and Passion of Margarita Xirgu)*, a play written in homage to the late director Xirgu.

2888 "Diaper Drama?: Nine Responses." *TT*. 1984 Mar.; 3(5): 1-2, 13. Illus.: Photo. B&W. 5: var. sizes. Lang.: Eng.

USA. 1984. Histories-sources. ■Interviews with artists committed to new plays about their reactions to *New York Times* article that condemned current state of American playwriting, attacking narrowness of plot and thematic material.

2889 Afanas'eva, E.A. *Novellistika i dramaturgija Karson makkallers (k probleme vzaimosvjazi žanrov): Avtoref. diss... kand. filol. nauk.* (Short Stories and Dramaturgy of Carson McCullers—Toward the Problem of the Correlation of Genres: Synopsis of a Dissertation by a Candidate in Philology.) Leningrad: Leningr. ped. in-t; 1986. 16 pp. Lang.: Rus.

USA. 1917-1967. Critical studies.

2890 Alevras, Jorgos. "Richard Foreman: Kroppen liknar en själ." (Richard Foreman: The Body Is Like a Soul.) *NT*. 1986; 34: 11-13. Illus.: Photo. Lang.: Swe.

USA. 1960-1986. Historical studies. ■Since founding the Ontological-Hysteric Theater Company, Richard Foreman has investigated consciousness in mind and body.

2891 Auletta, Robert. "Notes on Writing *Ajax*." *ThM*. 1986 Fall/Win; 18(1): 16-17. Lang.: Eng.

USA: Washington, DC. 1986. Histories-sources. ■Playwright Robert Auletta discusses the process of adapting Sophocles' *Ajax* for the American National Theatre production set at the Pentagon.

2892 Austin, Gayle. "Entering a Cold Ocean: The Playwriting Process." *TT*. 1984 Mar.; 3(5): 3, 14. Illus.: Photo. B&W. 2. Lang.: Eng.

USA: New York, NY. 1984. Histories-sources. ■Interview with playwright Maria Irene Fornes discussing her plays and the playwriting process.

2893 Ben-Zvi, Linda. "Susan Glaspell and Eugene O'Neill: The Imagery of Gender." *EON*. 1986 Spr; 10(1): 22-27. Lang.: Eng.

USA: New York, NY, Provincetown, MA. 1916-1922. Critical studies. ■*The Verge* by Susan Glaspell as a seminal influence on Eugene O'Neill, with discussion of gender reversal between these playwrights.

2894 Bermel, Albert. "The Liberation of Eugene O'Neill." *AmTh*. 1984 July/Aug.; 1(4): 4-9. Notes. Illus.: Photo. B&W. 7: var. sizes. Lang.: Eng.

USA. Critical studies. ■Examination of the popularity and relevance of the plays of Eugene O'Neill 30 years after his death. Actors and directors who have performed his work are interviewed.

2895 Black, Stephen A. "Letting the Dead be Dead: A Reinterpretation of *A Moon for the Misbegotten*." *MD*. 1986 Dec.; 29(4): 544-555. Notes. Lang.: Eng.

USA. 1922-1947. Critical studies. ■Central action of *A Moon for the Misbegotten* by Eugene O'Neill is Josie's mourning for Jim, which reflects the playwright's mourning for his brother.

2896 Bower, Martha. "The Cycle Women and Carlotta Monterey O'Neill." *EON*. 1986 Sum/Fall; 10(2): 29-33. Notes. Biblio. Lang.: Eng.

USA. 1927-1953. Critical studies. ■O'Neill's wife as model for the women in the Cycle plays: gender role and reversal reflects her domination of the playwright.

2897 Brooks, Marshall. "Eugene O'Neill's Boston." *EON*. 1984 Sum/Fall; 8(2): 19-21. Illus.: Photo. Print. B&W. 5: 2 in. x 3 in. Lang.: Eng.

USA: Boston, MA. 1914-1953. Histories-sources. ■Discussion of locations inhabited and frequented by Eugene O'Neill.

2898 Byers-Pevitts, Beverley. "Imaging Women in Theatre: Departures from Dramatic Tradition." *TA*. 1986; 40: 1-6. Lang.: Eng.

USA. 1900-1985. Critical studies. ■Introduction to and overview of articles contained in Volume 40 of *Theatre Annual*.

2899 Callens, Johan. "Memories of the Sea in Sam Shepard's *Illinois*." *MD*. 1986 Sep.; 29(3): 403-415. Notes. Lang.: Eng.

USA. 1978. Critical studies. ■Water imagery and the positive role of women in attempt to revive American dream in Sam Shepard's *Buried Child*.

2900 Canaday, Nicholas. "Toward the Creation of a Collective Form: The Plays of Ed Bullins." *SAD*. 1986; 1: 33-47. Biblio. Notes. Lang.: Eng.

USA. 1968-1973. Critical studies. ■Summary and commentary on the plays of Ed Bullins from two volumes, *Five Plays by Ed Bullins* (1969) and *The Theme is Blackness* (1973).

2901 Carandell, Josep Maria. "Comentari a *Del pont estant*." (Commentary on *A View From the Bridge*.) 5-19 in Institut del Teatre, ed. *Del pont estant*. Barcelona: Institut del Teatre; 1986. 108 pp. (Biblioteca Teatral 46.) Lang.: Cat.

USA: New York, NY. UK-England: London. 1915-1985. Critical studies. ■Analysis of Arthur Miller's play as a tragedy in the Greek tradition as well as a problem play.

2902 Cooper, Pamela. "David Rabe's *Sticks and Bones*: The Adventures of Ozzie and Harriet." *MD*. 1986 Dec.; 29(4): 613-625. Notes. Lang.: Eng.

USA. 1971. Critical studies. ■Playwright David Rabe's treatment of cliche in *Sticks and Bones*.

2903 Davis, R.G. "Eric Bentley." *ComIBS*. 1986 Nov.; 16(1): 24-28.

USA. Critical studies. ■An attack on Eric Bentley as one of the major forces in the subversion and depoliticization of Brecht.

2904 Debusscher, Gilbert. "And the Sailor Turned into a Princess: New Light on the Genesis of *Sweet Bird of Youth*." *SAD*. 1986; 1: 25-31. Biblio. Notes. Lang.: Eng.

USA. 1958. Critical studies. ■About a short sketch by Tennessee Williams, untitled, undated, but related in overall concept and in details of setting, characterization and dialogue to the first act of *Sweet Bird of Youth*.

2905 Duffy, Susan; Duffy, Bernard K. "Theatrical Responses to Technology During the Depression: Three Federal Theatre Project Plays." *THSt*. 1986; 6: 142-164. Notes. Illus.: Photo. Print. B&W. 4: 6.5 in. x 4.5 in. Lang.: Eng.

USA. 1935-1939. Critical studies. ■Attitude towards technology as reflected in the Federal Theatre Project 'Living Newspaper' productions *Power*, *Medicine Show* and *Spirochete*.

2906 Elam, Harry J., Jr. "Ritual Theory and Political Theatre: *Quinta Temporada* and *Slave Ship*." *TJ*. 1986 Dec.; 38(4): 463-472. Notes. Lang.: Eng.

USA. 1965-1967. Critical studies. ■In the light of ritual theory, analyzes the function on their communities of *The Slave Ship* by LeRoi Jones (Amiri Baraka), produced by Spirit House Movers, and *Quinta Temporada (Fifth Season)* by Luis Valdez, performed by Teatro Campesino (California).

DRAMA: —Plays/librettos/scripts

2907 Fambrough, Preston. "The Tragic Cosmology of O'Neill's *Desire Under the Elms.*" *EON.* 1986 Sum/Fall; 10(2): 25-29. Notes. Biblio. Lang.: Eng.
USA. 1924. Critical studies. ▪Irreducible core of mystery at the center of human experience as prime element of classic and neoclassic tragedy, as well as O'Neill's tragedy.

2908 Fisher, James. "Eugene O'Neill and Edward Gordon Craig." *EON.* 1986 Spr; 10(1): 27-30. Lang.: Eng.
USA. UK-England. 1912-1928. Historical studies. ▪Influence of Craig on American theatre, and his grudging recognition of O'Neill's importance.

2909 Frank, Leah D. "Gay Theatre in the Mainstream." *TT.* 1985 June/July; 4(6): 1-2. Illus.: Photo. B&W. 2. Lang.: Eng.
USA. 1933-1985. Critical studies. ▪Progress in audience perception of gay characters in plays.

2910 Groppali, Enrico. "Henry James e il teatro." (Henry James and the Theatre.) *QT.* 1986 May; 8(32): 116-125. Lang.: Ita.
USA. 1843-1916. Critical studies. ▪Notes on theatrical works by Henry James.

2911 Grunes, Dennis. "God and Albee: *Tiny Alice.*" *SAD.* 1986; 1: 61-71. Biblio. Lang.: Eng.
USA. 1965. Critical studies. ▪God as image and symbol in Edward Albee's *Tiny Alice.*

2912 Hart, Steven. "The Theme of 'Race' in Inner-City Prison Theatre: The Family, Inc." *TJ.* 1986 Dec.; 38(4): 427-440. Notes. Illus.: Photo. B&W. 1. Lang.: Eng.
USA. 1970-1986. Historical studies. ▪An examination of the function of race on both the individual and community level as seen in the prison dramas of Miguel Piñero, Marvin Felix Camillo, Lonnie Elder III and Ed Bullins.

2913 Joseph, Artur. "'Theater, unter vier Augen, Gespräche mit Prominente': Nauseated by Language (From an Interview with Peter Handke)." 185-192 in McNamara, Brooks, ed.; Dolan, Jill, ed. *The Drama Review: Thirty Years of Commentary on the Avant-Garde.* Ann Arbor, MI: UMI Research P; 1986. xii, 371 pp. (Theatre and Dramatic Studies 35.) Lang.: Eng.
USA. Austria. 1970-1986. Histories-sources. ▪Distinguishes between the natural flow of words and present forms of linguistic alienation.

2914 Kazakov, S.E. *Tvorčestvo E. Albee 60-h godov i problemy.* (The Work of Edward Albee in the Sixties and Problems of the Dramaturgical Method.) Moscow: Mosk. obl. ped. in-t; 1986. 16 pp. [Synopsis of a Dissertation.] Lang.: Rus.
USA. 1960-1970. Critical studies. ▪Analysis of the plays of Edward Albee.

2915 Kilkelly, Ann Gavere. "Who's in the House?" *WPerf.* 1986; 3(1): 28-34. Biblio. Lang.: Eng.
USA. 1933-1983. Critical studies. ▪Wendy Kesselman's treatment of a sensational murder that took place in LeMans, France, in *My Sister in This House.*

2916 Kiralyfalvi, Bela. "The Catonsville 'Trilogy': History, Testimony and Art." *THSt.* 1986; 6: 133-141. Lang.: Eng.
USA: Catonsville, MD. 1968-1973. Critical studies. ▪Analysis of the relationships among the actual event, the consequent trial and the play entitled *The Trial of the Catonsville Nine.*

2917 Koldenhoven, James John. *A Structuralist Approach to the Realistic Drama of William Vaughn Moody.* Minneapolis, MN: Univ. of Minnesota P; 1986. 169 pp. Pref. Notes. Biblio. [Ph.D. dissertation, Univ. Microfilms order No. DA8608894.] Lang.: Eng.
USA. 1869-1910. Critical studies. ▪Analysis of the plays of William Vaughn Moody from a structuralist point of view.

2918 Kolin, Philip C. "Staging *Hurlyburly*: David Rabe's Parable for the 1980s." *TA.* 1986; 41: 63-78. Notes. Print. B&W. 2: 3.5 in. x 5.5 in. Lang.: Eng.
USA. 1984. Critical studies. ▪Demonstration of how language, costume, gesture, movement and stage symbol reveal character and idea in David Rabe's *Hurlyburly.*

2919 Krafchick, Marcelline. "*Hughie* and *The Zoo Story.*" *EON.* 1986 Spr; 10(1): 15-16. Lang.: Eng.
USA: New York, NY. 1941-1958. Critical studies. ▪Similarities in technique and idea of these two plays by Eugene O'Neill and Edward Albee.

2920 Lamont, Rosette C. "Rosalyn Drexler's Semiotics of Instability." *ThM.* 1985 Win; 17(1): 70-77. Illus.: Photo. B&W. 2. Lang.: Eng.
USA. 1964-1985. Critical studies. ▪An analysis of Drexler's plays, focusing on their use of language and their manipulation and burlesquing of established genres, plots and roles.

2921 Lamos, Mark. "An Afternoon with Arthur Miller." *AmTh.* 1986 May; 3(2): 18-22, 44. Illus.: Photo. Print. B&W. Lang.: Eng.
USA. 1985. Histories-sources. ▪Arthur Miller discusses several of his plays, particularly *Death of a Salesman* and *The Crucible.* Related to Media: Video forms.

2922 Lappin, Louis; Wasserstein, Wendy. "Chekov and the American Imagination." *ThM.* 1986 Fall/Win; 18(1): 97-99. Illus.: Photo. Print. B&W. 1: 5 in. x 7 in. Lang.: Eng.
USA: New York, NY. 1986. Reviews of performances. ▪Review of stage adaptations of seven Čechov short stories by seven prominent American playwrights.

2923 Laughlin, Karen L. "Criminality, Desire and Community: A Feminist Approach to Beth Henley's *Crimes of the Heart.*" *WPerf.* 1986; 3(1): 35-51. Notes. Biblio. Lang.: Eng.
USA. 1980-1986. Critical studies. ▪Beth Henley's play *Crimes of the Heart* as an example of female criminality in response to a patriarchal culture.

2924 Lion, John. "Rock'n Roll Jesus with a Cowboy Mouth." *AmTh.* 1984 Apr.; 1(1): 4-8. Illus.: Photo. B&W. 4: var. sizes. Lang.: Eng.
USA: San Francisco, CA, New York, NY. 1970-1984. Histories-sources. ▪Director of the Magic Theatre discusses his collaboration with Sam Shepard, focusing on the development of *Fool for Love*, critical response and analysis of Shepard's work.

2925 Lippman, Amy. "Rhythm & Truths: An Interview with Sam Shepard." *AmTh.* 1984 Apr.; 1(1): 9-13, 40-41. Illus.: Photo. B&W. 4: var. sizes. Lang.: Eng.
USA. 1984. Histories-sources. ▪Playwright Sam Shepard discusses his technique, influences on his work and the role of music in his plays.

2926 Long, Deborah Marie. *The Existential Quest: Family and Form in Selected American Plays.* Eugene, OR: Univ of Oregon; 1986. 258 pp. Pref. Notes. Biblio. [Ph.D. dissertation, Univ. Microfilms order No. DA8613360.] Lang.: Eng.
USA. 1949-1956. Critical studies. ▪Comparison of *Long Day's Journey Into Night* by Eugene O'Neill, *Death of a Salesman* by Arthur Miller and *Cat on a Hot Tin Roof* by Tennessee Williams.

2927 Manheim, Michael. "O'Neill's Early Debt to David Belasco." *THSt.* 1986; 6: 124-131. Lang.: Eng.
USA: New York, NY. 1908-1922. Critical studies. ▪Correspondences between melodramas written and produced by David Belasco—including Belasco's *Peter Grimm* (1911) and Eugene Walters' *The Easiest Way* (1908—and early plays of Eugene O'Neill: *The Web* (1914), *Where the Cross Is Made* (1919), *Anna Christie* (1922).

2928 Marranca, Bonnie; Rabkin, Gerald; Birringer, Johannes. "Controversial 1985-86 Theatre Season: A Politics of Reception." *PerAJ.* 1986; 10(1): 7-33. Illus.: Photo. Print. B&W. 8. [Transcript of discussion taped April 1986.] Lang.: Eng.
USA: New York, NY. 1985-1986. Critical studies. ▪Analysis of issues raised, especially religion, race, gender, liberal politics and use of technology in performance.

2929 Melendres, Jaume. "Una visita a la sala de màquines." (A Visit to the Engine Room.) 5-12 in Institut del Teatre, ed. *Advertència per a embarcacions petites.* Barcelona: Institut del Teatre; 1986. 94 pp. (Biblioteca Teatral 41.) [Prologue to *Small Craft Warnings* by Tennessee Williams.] Lang.: Cat.

DRAMA: —Plays/librettos/scripts

USA: New York, NY. Spain-Catalonia: Barcelona. 1972-1983. Critical studies. ▪Analysis of the play focusing on linguistic duality as the basis of its structure, with references to its productions in New York and Barcelona.

2930 Mikoś, Michael; Mulroy, David. "Reymont's *The Peasants*: A Probable Influence on *Desire Under the Elms*." *EON*. 1986 Spr; 10(1): 4-14. Notes. Biblio. Lang.: Eng.

USA. 1902-1924. Critical studies. ▪The tale-type of the lustful stepmother in Euripides, Eugene O'Neill and Polish novelist Władysław Reymont.

2931 Morley, Sheridan. "Dear Octopus (Part 1)." *PI*. 1986 Mar.; 1(8): 14-15. [Cont. in 1986 Apr, pp 18-19.] Lang.: Eng.

USA: New York, NY. 1927-1986. Histories-sources. ▪Neil Simon talks about his life and his trio of autobiographical plays *Brighton Beach Memoirs*, *Biloxi Blues* and *Broadway Bound*.

2932 Morrow, Lee Alan; Pike, Frank. *Creating Theatre: The Professional's Approach to New Plays*. New York, NY: Random House; 1986. 320 pp. Lang.: Eng.

USA. 1986. Histories-sources. ▪Interviews with a number of playwrights, actors, directors, producers, designers and critics about the writing and production of successful new plays.

2933 Murray, Brenda. "*Beyond the Horizon*'s Narrative Sentence: An American Intertext for O'Neill." *TA*. 1986; 41: 49-62. Notes. Illus.: Photo. Print. B&W. 4: 3.5 in. x 5.5 in. Lang.: Eng.

USA. 1879-1918. Critical studies. ▪Analysis of the narrative structure and theme of Eugene O'Neill's *Beyond the Horizon*, comparing it with plays by David Belasco and James A. Herne.

2934 Naumljuk, M.V. *Dramaturgija Elmera Rajsa i problemy stanovlenija amerikanskoj dramy: Avtoref. diss... kand. filol. nauk*. (The Dramaturgy of Elmer Rice and the Problem of the Formation of American Drama: Synopsis of a Dissertation by a Candidate in Philology.) Leningrad: Leningrad. ped. in-t; 1986. 16 pp. Lang.: Rus.

USA. 1892-1967. Critical studies.

2935 O'Neill, Michael C. "History as Dramatic Present: Arthur L. Kopit's *Indians*." *TJ*. 1982 Dec.; 34(4): 493-504.

USA. 1969. Critical studies. ▪Mosaic structure, overt theatricality and use of ritual enable Kopit's *Indians* to transcend Vietnam-era America to address timeless issues.

2936 Pauwels, Gerard W. *A Critical Analysis of the Plays of Lanford Wilson*. Bloomington, IN: Indiana Univ.; 1986. 213 pp. Pref. Notes. Biblio. [Ph.D. dissertation, Univ. Microfilms order No. DA8617762.] Lang.: Eng.

USA. 1963-1985. Critical studies. ▪Examination of structural patterns and thematic concerns of the plays of Lanford Wilson which constitute a coherent body of dramatic writing directed by a distinct philosophical and aesthetic perspective.

2937 Ramsey, Dale. "The One Act: An Enormously Challenging Form, At the Heart of What Theater Is." *DGQ*. 1986 Win; 23(4): 23-24.

USA. 1986. Histories-sources. ▪Practical advice, musings and career testimonials from playwrights Romulus Linney, William Hauptman, Israel Horovitz, Shirley Lano and Terrence McNally.

2938 Roudané, Matthew C. "An Interview with David Mamet." *SAD*. 1986; 1: 73-80. Pref. Illus.: Photo. B&W. 1: 5.5 in. x 5 in. Lang.: Eng.

USA. 1984. Histories-sources. ▪Mamet discusses the American Dream myth, his use of structure and language, today's audience, his role as a storyteller.

2939 Rouse, John. "Structuring Stories: Robert Wilson's *Alcestis*." *ThM*. 1986 Fall/Win; 18(1): 56-59. Illus.: Photo. Print. B&W. 1: 5 in. x 7 in. Lang.: Eng.

USA: Cambridge, MA. 1979-1986. Critical studies. ▪Robert Wilson's adaptation of Euripides' *Alcestis* at the American Repertory Theatre includes more emotional content and recognizable idea than his previous works.

2940 Savran, David. "Adaptation as Clairvoyance: The Wooster Group's *Saint Anthony*." *ThM*. 1986 Fall/Win; 18(1): 36-41. Illus.: Photo. Print. B&W. 1: 5 in. x 7 in. Lang.: Eng.

USA: New York, NY, Boston, MA, Washington, DC. 1983-1986. Historical studies. ▪Development of Wooster Group's *Saint Anthony* from Flaubert and Peter Sellars.

2941 Sheffer, Isaiah. "An Interview with Israel Horovitz." *TT*. 1986 Jan.; 5(2): 8-9. Illus.: Photo. B&W. 3. Lang.: Eng.

USA: New York, NY. 1985. Histories-sources. ▪Interview with playwright Israel Horovitz, discusses his life and career, sources for *Today I Am a Fountain Pen*, *A Rosen By Any Other Name* and *The Chopin Playoffs*.

2942 Sheingorn, Pamela; Tomasello, Andrew. "Indiana Presents St. Nicholas at Kalamazoo." *RORD*. 1986; 29: 99-103. Lang.: Eng.

USA: Kalamazoo, MI. 1986. Reviews of performances. ▪Account of presentation of four St. Nicholas plays from Fleury Playbook.

2943 Simard, Rodney. "American Gothic: Sam Shepard's Family Trilogy." *TA*. 1986; 41: 21-36. Notes. Illus.: Photo. Print. B&W. 1: 3.5 in. x 5.5 in. Lang.: Eng.

USA. 1972-1985. Critical studies. ▪Analysis of Sam Shepard's *Curse of the Starving Class*, *Buried Child* and *True West*, emphasizing the shift from presentation to dramatization of experience.

2944 Skloot, Robert. "Warpaths and Boulevards: Sam Shepard on the Road of American Non-Realism." *ASSAPHc*. 1986; 3: 207-213. Notes. Lang.: Eng.

USA. 1943-1986. Critical studies. ▪Interpretation of Sam Shepard's plays as a reaction to traditional American drama.

2945 Terkel, Studs. "Make New Sounds." *AmTh*. 1984 Nov.; 1(7): 4-11, 41. Notes. Append. Illus.: Photo. B&W. 14: var. sizes. Lang.: Eng.

USA. 1959. Histories-sources. ▪Interview with playwright Lorraine Hansberry discussing characters and themes of her play *A Raisin in the Sun*. Reprinted from 1959 radio interview for 25th anniversary of play. Appended: 10 Prominent writers and directors discuss the play's impact over the years.

2946 Turner, Beth. "The Multi-Talented Samm-Art Williams." *BlackM*. 1986 Feb-Mar.: 2-3, 9-10. Illus.: Photo. Print. B&W. 1: 2 in. x 4 in. Lang.: Eng.

USA: Burgaw, NC, New York, NY. 1940-1986. Biographical studies. ▪Playwright/performer Samm-Art Williams, his play *Home* and his television credits.

2947 Vlasopolos, Anca. "Authorizing History: Victimization in *A Streetcar Named Desire*." *TJ*. 1986 Oct.; 38(3): 322-338. Notes. Lang.: Eng.

USA. 1960-1980. Critical studies. ▪The conflict between authority and victimization in *A Streetcar Named Desire* by Tennessee Williams, with particular attention to the significance of the audience response to the character of Blanche.

2948 Watt, Stephen. "O'Neill and Otto Rank: Doubles, 'Death Instincts', and the Trauma of Birth." *CompD*. 1986; 20(3): 211-230. Notes. Lang.: Eng.

USA. 1888-1953. Critical studies. ▪Applies the theories of Otto Rank to the analysis of the death instinct in the drama of Eugene O'Neill.

2949 Wattenburg, Richard. "America Redeemed: The Shape of History in Robert E. Sherwood's *The Petrified Forest* and *Abe Lincoln in Illinois*." *TID*. 1986; 8: 163-175. Notes. Lang.: Eng.

USA. 1930-1950. ▪Evolution of Robert E. Sherwood's conception of history, from cyclical (*The Petrified Forest*) to linear (*Abe Lincoln in Illinois*).

2950 Wheeler, David Mark. *Perceptions of Money and Wealth on Gilded Age Stages: A Study of Four Long Run Productions in New York City*. Eugene, OR: Univ of Oregon; 1986. 333 pp. Pref. Notes. Biblio. [Ph.D. dissertation, Univ. Microfilms order No. DA8622541.] Lang.: Eng.

USA: New York, NY. 1870-1889. Historical studies. ▪Study of the philosophy of wealth in four plays of the gilded age: *Gilded Age, or Colonel Sellers*, *The Big Bonanza*, *The Mighty Dollar* and *The Henrietta*.

2951 Whiting, Charles G. "Inverted Chronology in Sam Shepard's *La Turista*." *MD*. 1986 Sep.; 29(3): 416-422. Notes. Lang.: Eng.

CLASSED ENTRIES

DRAMA: —Plays/librettos/scripts

USA. 1967. Critical studies. ■Implications that the events of Act II precede those of Act I.

2952　Zinman, Toby Silverman. "Shepard Suite." *AmTh.* 1984 Dec.; 1(8): 15-17. Illus.: Photo. B&W. 3: var. sizes. Lang.: Eng.

USA: New York, NY. 1984. Critical studies. ■Director George Ferencz and jazz musician Max Roach collaborate on music in Sam Shepard's *Suicide in B-flat, Angel City* and *Back Bog Beast Bait.* Related to Music-Drama.

2953　*Evoljucija žanra narodnoj dramy v Belorusskom teatre: Avtoref. diss... kand. iskusstvovedenija.* (Evolution of the Genre of Folk Drama in the Byelorussian Theatre: Synopsis of a Dissertation by a Candidate in Art Criticism.) Moscow: VNII iskusstvoznanija; 1986. 24 pp. Lang.: Rus.

USSR. Critical studies.

2954　"Istorik, Publicist, Chudožnik: Dramaturgija M. Šatrova." (Historian, Publicist, Artist: The Dramaturgy of M. Šatrov.) *Neva.* 1986; 1: 167-174. Lang.: Rus.

USSR. 1932-1986. Biographical studies.

2955　"Vscsojuznyj seminar dramaturgov v Picunde." (All-Union Seminar of Playwrights in Picunde.) *TeatZ.* 1986; 29(15): 20-21. Lang.: Rus.

USSR: Picunde. 1986. Histories-sources. ■Conversation with leaders of an annual seminar for playwrights.

2956　"Škola vysokoj idejnosti: vstrečaja VIIIs' ez sovetskih pisatelej." (The School of High-Principled Character: Welcoming the Eighth Congress of Soviet Writers.) *TeatrM.* 1986; 6: 85-95. Lang.: Rus.

USSR. 1986. Critical studies. ■Answers to questions from the editorial staff on contemporary dramaturgy.

2957　"Govorjat učastniki zasedanija." (The Participants of the Conference Speak.) *TeatrM.* 1986; 11: 44-72. Lang.: Rus.

USSR: Moscow. 1986. Histories-sources. ■Selections from the speeches of Soviet playwrights before the commission on drama of the 8th Congress of Soviet Writers.

2958　"O psichologii literaturnogo tvorčestva." (On the Psychology of Literary Creation.) *TeatrM.* 1986; 2: 121-130. Lang.: Rus.

USSR. Bulgaria. 1986. Histories-sources. ■Five playwrights—Aleksej Nikolajěvič Arbuzov, V. Arro, J. Radičkov, M. Roščin and Nina Seměnova—reply to a questionnaire.

2959　Anninskij, L. "Bilet v raj." (Ticket to Paradise.) *SovD.* 1986; 4: 222-231. Lang.: Rus.

USSR. 1986. Critical studies. ■Analysis of the plays of Aleksej Gel'man.

2960　Borovik, G. "Segodnja i zavtra dramaturgii." (The Today and Tomorrow of Drama.) *TeatrM.* 1986; 11: 30-43. Lang.: Rus.

USSR: Moscow. 1986. Histories-sources. ■A report on the meeting of the commission on drama of the 8th Congress of Soviet Writers.

2961　Bugrov, B.S. *Russkaja sovetskaja dramaturgija 50-70 godov: osnovyje tendencii razvitija: Avtoref. diss... d-ra filol. nauk.* (Russian Soviet Dramaturgy, 1950s-1970s—Basic Tendencies of Development: Synopsis of a Dissertation by a Candidate in Philology.) Moscow: MGU; 1986. 46 pp. Lang.: Rus.

USSR. 1950-1979. Critical studies.

2962　Chegaj, S.M. *Rol' fol'klora v formirovanii žanra dramy v uzbekskoj literature: Avtoref. diss... kand. filol. nauk.* (The Role of Folklore in the Formation of the Genre of Drama in Uzbek Literature: Synopsis of a Dissertation by a Candidate in Philology.) Taškent: Institut jazyka i literatury; 1986. 21 pp. Lang.: Rus.

USSR. Critical studies.

2963　Ljubimov, B. "Pamjat' i nadežda." (Memory and Hope.) *TeatZ.* 1986; 29(1): 10-11. Lang.: Rus.

USSR: Kiev. 1980-1986. Critical studies. ■Motifs of moral and social renewal in Soviet theatre, changes in economic and organizational structure of theatre administration.

2964　Mironova, V.M. *Teatr Vsevoloda Višnevskogo.* (The Theatre of Vsevolod Višnevskij.) Leningrad: Iskusstvo; 1986. 144 pp. Lang.: Rus.

USSR. 1920-1959. Critical studies. ■Ideological and aesthetic analysis of Višnevskjij's work, literary relationships, analysis of productions of his plays during his lifetime.

2965　Moskvina, F.; Šolochov, S.; Fadeev, V.V., comp. "Dissonans—O nekotorych problemach v sovremennoj dramaturgii." (Dissonance—On Some Problems in Contemporary Dramaturgy.) 258-278 in *Poiski i tradicii.* Leningrad: Lenizdati; 1986. Lang.: Rus.

USSR. 1980-1986. Critical studies. ■Analysis of contemporary Soviet dramaturgy using the examples of Semyan Zlotnikov and Ljudmila Petruševskaja.

2966　Reich, Bernhard; Haus, Heinz-Uwe; Broyles, Yolande Julia, transl. "Correspondence." *ComIBS.* 1985 Apr.; 84(2): 61-64.

USSR. 1971-1972. Histories-sources. ■Letters from scholar Bernhard Reich and director Heinz-Uwe Haus on Shakespeare's *Richard III.*

2967　Sindikova, L.S. *Problema konflikta i charaktera v sovetskoj dramaturgii 70-h-nacal 80-x godov (na materiale 'proizvodstvennoj' dramy).* (Problem of Conflict and Character in Soviet Dramaturgy of the Seventies and Eighties, Based on Material of 'Production' Drama. Synopsis of a Dissertation by a Candidate in Philology.) Moscow: Mosk. ped. in-t im. V.I. Lenina; 1986. 16 pp. Lang.: Rus.

USSR. 1970-1980. Critical studies. ■Conflict and characterization in recent Soviet dramaturgy.

2968　Stanislavskij, Konstantin Sergejěvič; Rolander, Vera, transl.; Rolander, Julius, transl. "Othello." *NT.* 1986; 34: 33-34. Illus.: Photo. Lang.: Swe.

USSR. 1929-1930. Histories-sources. ■An excerpt from Stanislavskij's working method for the role of Othello.

2969　Vasilinina, I. "Každyj sobiraet svoj buket." (Each Gathers his Own Bouquet.) *TeatrM.* 1986; 2: 62-70. Lang.: Rus.

USSR. 1980-1986. Critical studies. ■Discussion of the hero in modern drama.

2970　Vasilinina, I. "U každogo svoj Puškin." (To Each his Own Puškin.) *TeatrM.* 1986; 1: 152-159. Lang.: Rus.

USSR. 1980-1986. Critical studies. ■The elaboration of moral and ethical themes in contemporary drama.

2971　Višnevskaja, I. "Bez straha i upreka." (Without Fear of Reproach.) *TeatrM.* 1986; 2: 55-61. Lang.: Rus.

USSR. 1980-1986. Critical studies. ■The positive hero in contemporary drama.

2972　Azparren Giménez, Leonardo. "El teatro venezolano en una encrucijada." (Venezuelan Theatre at a Cross-Road.) *LATR.* 1986 Fall; 20(1): 79-84. Lang.: Spa.

Venezuela. 1958-1980. Historical studies. ■Traces development of political trends in Venezuelan drama.

2973　Bravo-Elizondo, Pedro. "*Regreso sin causa*: Jaime Miranda y sus razones." (*Return Without Cause*: Jaime Miranda and his Reasons.) *LATR.* 1986 Spr; 19(2): 79-84. Lang.: Eng.

Venezuela. Chile. USA. 1956-1985. Historical studies. ■Interview with Chilean playwright Jaime Miranda on his award-winning *Regreso sin causa (Return Without Cause)* and his exile in Venezuela.

2974　Persson, Mats. "Teater i Vietnam: Tradition och förnyelse." (Theatre in Vietnam: Tradition and Renewal.) *Entre.* 1986; 13(3): 33-41. Illus.: Photo. B&W. 10: var. sizes. Lang.: Swe.

Vietnam. 1940-1986. Historical studies. ■Study of development of modern Vietnamese drama from its origins in traditional dramatic, musical and oratorical forms.

Reference materials

2975　Berger, Karl Heinz, comp.; Böttcher, Gerda, comp.; Böttcher, Kurt, comp.; Hoffmann, Ludwig, comp.; Naumann, Manfred, comp.; Seeger, Gisela, comp. *Schauspielführer A-Z.* (Play Guide A to Z.) East Berlin: Henschelverlag Kunst und Gesellschaft; 1986. Vol. 1: 716 pp., vol. 2: 740 pp. Index. Lang.: Ger.

CLASSED ENTRIES

DRAMA: —Reference materials

■Short biographies and content descriptions of the world's most famous plays and their authors.

2976 Carpenter, Charles A., comp. "Modern Drama Studies: An Annual Bibliography." *MD.* 1986 June; 29(2): 241-353. Lang.: Eng.
1985. ■Comprehensive bibliography of scholarship, criticism and commentary on modern world drama.

2977 Maticka, Margaret. "The Campbell Howard Collection of Australian Plays in Manuscript." 115-124 in Univ. New England, ed. *Australian Drama 1920-1955.* Papers presented at a conference at the University of New England, Armidale, September 1-4, 1984. Armidale, N.S.W: Univ. of New England; 1986. 157 pp. Lang.: Eng.
Australia. 1920-1955. Histories-sources. ■A general description of a significant collection of transcripts and original manuscripts of unpublished Australian plays, focusing on the period 1920-1955, held at the University of New England and collected by Campbell Howard.

2978 Sykes, Arlene. "The Australian Drama Bibliography Project." 111-114 in Univ. New England, ed. *Australian Drama 1920-1955.* Papers presented at a conference at the University of New England, September 1-4, 1984. Armidale, N.S.W: Univ. of New England; 1986. 157 pp. Lang.: Eng.
Australia. 1788-1984. ■A description of the systems used, and the progress made, at the Department of English, University of Queensland, in a project to compile a bibliography of all the plays written in Australia or by Australians since European settlement.

2979 Grieshofer, Franz; Riss, Ulrike; Zwiauer, Herbert. *Papiertheatre: Eine Sonderausstellung aus Wiener Sammmlungen. II. Teil: Ferdinand Raimund und das Wiener Theatre seiner Zeit im Spiegel des Papiertheaters.* (Toy Theatre: A Special Exhibition of the Viennese Collections. Part 2: Ferdinand Raimund and the Viennese Theatre of His Time Reflected by Toy Theatre.) Vienna: Österreichisches Museum für Volkskunde; 1986. 35 pp. Tables. Illus.: Dwg. B&W. Lang.: Ger.
Austria: Vienna. 1790-1836. Historical studies. ■Development, history and essence of the Toy Theatre in Europe. Ferdinand Raimund's dramas as pattern for the Toy Theatre productions.

2980 Lunzer, Heinz, ed.; Scheichl, Sigurd Paul; Lensing, Leo A.; Schwarzinger, Heinz; Sonino, Claudia. *Karl Kraus 1874-1936: Katalog einer Ausstellung des Bundesministeriums für Auswärtige Angelegenheiten.* (Karl Kraus 1874-1936: Exhibition Catalogue of the Foreign Office.) Vienna: Dokumentationsstelle für neuere österreichische Literatur; 1986. 83 pp. (Zirkular, Sondernummer 8.) Notes. Biblio. Illus.: Handbill. Photo. Dwg. B&W. 15. Lang.: Ger.
Austria: Vienna. USA: New York, NY. France: Paris. 1874-1986. Biographical studies. ■Exhibition catalogue about the influence of Karl Kraus's polemic writing. Translation and reaction to him in other countries. Includes bibliographies of primary and secondary sources.

2981 Mantler, Anton; Patzer, Franz, ed. *Ferdinand Raimund und die Nachwelt.* (Ferdinand Raimund and Posterity.) Vienna: Wiener Stadt-und Landesbibliothek; 1986. 36 pp. Pref. Tables. Illus.: Photo. Dwg. Sketches. B&W. 32. Lang.: Ger.
Austria: Vienna. 1790-1986. Histories-sources. ■Exhibition of works of Ferdinand Raimund's dramas produced after his death. Explores autobiographical elements in his plays and style of acting.

2982 Rajec, Elizabeth Molnár. *Ferenc Molnár: Bibliography. Part 1: Primary Sources. Part 2: Secondary Sources.* Vienna, Cologne, Graz: Böhlau; 1986. Vol 1: xviii, 160 pp./vol. 2: xi, 420 pp. Pref. Index. Tables. Lang.: Eng.
Austria: Vienna. Hungary: Budapest. USA: New York, NY. 1878-1982. Bibliographical studies. ■Listing of published primary sources in English, German and Hungarian. Includes list of films based on his writings, important dates of premieres and revivals of his plays. Part II is selected bibliography of secondary sources (interpretations, reviews, criticisms, etc.).

2983 Zimmer, Wolfgang. *Répertoire du théâtre camerounais.* (Theatrical Repertory of Cameroon.) Paris: L'Harmattan; 1986. 119 pp. Index. Biblio. Lang.: Fre.
Cameroon. 1940-1985. Bibliographical studies. ■Works of Cameroonian playwrights listed by author. Includes 700 plays by 260 authors, bibliographical references, and index of titles.

2984 Nardocchio, Elaine F. "1958-1968: Ten Formative Years in Quebec's Theatre History." *CDr.* 1986 Spr; 12(1): 33-63. Tables. Illus.: Graphs. 8: var. sizes. Lang.: Eng.
Canada: Montreal, PQ. 1958-1968. Historical studies. ■A calendar of French-language plays produced at 10 Montreal theatres over 10 years, with audience attendance figures.

2985 O'Neill, Patrick B. "Checklist of Canadian Dramatic Materials to 1967, Part II, L-Z." *CDr.* 1983; 9(2): 369-506. Biblio. Lang.: Eng.
Canada. 1800-1967. ■A bibliography of Canadian drama, including unpublished manuscripts and typescripts as well as published plays.

2986 Smith, Susan Harris. "Twentieth-Century Plays Using Classical Mythic Themes: A Checklist." *MD.* 1986 Mar.; 29(1): 110-134. Lang.: Eng.
Europe. USA. 1898-1986. ■Modern plays using mythic themes, grouped according to subject.

2987 Desgraves, Louis. *Répertoire des programmes des pièces de théâtre jouées dans les collèges de France (1601-1700).* (Repertory of Programs of Theatrical Plays Given in French Colleges 1601-1700.) Genève: Droz; 1986. (EPHE. IVe section, Sciences historiques et philologiques 6. Histoire et civilisation du livre 17.) Index. Biblio. Lang.: Fre.
France. 1601-1700. Histories-sources. ■Listed by college within each city. Includes location of programs in libraries and an index of plays. Related to Dance: Ballet.

2988 Koch, Philip. "Nature et signification des *Sujets de plusieurs comédies italiennes.*" (Nature and Signification of the *Sujets de plusieurs comédies italiennes.*) *RHT.* 1986; 38(1): 67-87. Notes. Lang.: Fre.
France. Italy. 1670-1740. Histories-reconstruction. ■Present state of research on the manuscript, which contains 20 theatrical texts in French, mostly scenarios translated from the Italian.

2989 Rosenberg, James L. "Ödön von Horváth." *NTQ.* 1986 Nov.; 11(8): 376-384. Illus.: Photo. B&W. 2. [NTQ Checklist No. 2.] Lang.: Eng.
Germany. 1901-1938. ■A checklist of Ödön von Horváth's plays and their productions with a biographical and critical introduction, suggesting aspects of his undervalued importance.

2990 *Én a komédiát lejátsztam, Mulattattam, de nem mulattam.* (I Have Performed the Comedy—You Enjoyed It...But I Didn't.) Preface by Hilda Gotti. Budapest: Magyar Szinházi Intézet; 1986. 237 pp. Illus.: Photo. B&W. 223: var. sizes. Lang.: Hun.
Hungary: Budapest. 1850-1986. ■Illustrated guide to exhibits at the Bajor Gizi Actors' Museum of Budapest on the lives and careers of more than 200 actors, actresses, directors and stage designers.

2991 Kotvász, Márta; Somoskövi, Istvánné. *Mohácsi Jenő 1886-1944. Bibliográfia.* (Jenő Mohácsi 1886-1944: Bibliography.) Mohács: Mohácsi Jenő Városi; 1986. 32 pp. Index. Lang.: Hun.
Hungary. 1886-1944. ■Works of Jenő Mohácsi, writer and translator, who adapted to German the classic Hungarian plays *Az Ember Tragédiája (The Tragedy of a Man), Csongor and Tünde* and *Bánk Bán.*

2992 Feingold, Ben-Ami. "Mahazot Israeliym Sherau Or Bishnat Tav-Shin-Mem-Vav." (Israeli Plays Published in 1986.) *Bamah.* 1986; 21(104): 95-105. Lang.: Heb.
Israel. 1985-1986. ■Overview of seven newly published Israeli plays.

2993 Dugulin, Adriano, ed. *Moissi.* Trieste: Civici Musei di Storia ed arte; 1986. 109 pp. (Civico Museo teatrale C. Schmidl-Trieste.) Pref. Index. Biblio. Append. Filmography. Illus.: Photo. Poster. B&W. Lang.: Ita.

DRAMA: —Reference materials

Italy: Trieste. Austria. 1880-1935. Biographical studies. ■Catalogue of a 1986 exhibit in Trieste on the life and roles of Italo-Austrian actor Alessandro Moissi.

2994 Zappulla, Sarah Muscarà; Zappulla, Enzo. *Pirandello e il teatro siciliano.* (Pirandello and Sicilian Theatre.) Catania: Maimone; 1986. 869 pp. Index. Notes. Tables. Biblio. Illus.: Photo. Pntg. Dwg. Poster. B&W. Lang.: Eng, Fre, Ger, Ita.

Italy. 1902-1936. ■Catalogue of photographic documentation on Luigi Pirandello's writings in dialect and on Sicilian actors of his time.

2995 Kobialka, Michal. "Bibliography: Writings By and About Tadeusz Kantor." *TDR.* 1986 Fall; 30(3): 184-198. Lang.: Eng.

Poland. 1946-1986.

2996 Maresz, Barbara; Szydłowska, Mariola. "O lwowskich egzemplarzach teatralnych w Bibliotece Śląskiej." (Śląska Library Collection of Playtexts from Theatres of Lvov.) *PaT.* 1986 Fourth Qtr; 4: 516-580. Notes. Illus.: Design. Photo. Print. B&W. 14: var. sizes. Lang.: Pol.

Poland: Lvov, Katowice. 1800-1978. Histories-sources. ■In 1939, USSR took possession of Lvov. In 1945, archives of the Polish theatre in Lvov were repatriated and placed in Katowice. Description of theatre documents as well as listing of playtexts (1800-1848) and censored playtexts (1810-1918).

2997 Podol, Peter L.; Pérez-Pineda, Frederico. "El drama español del siglo XX: bibliografía selecta del año 1984." (Twentieth-century Spanish Drama: Select Bibliography for 1984.) *Estreno.* 1986 Fall; 12(2): 75-78. Lang.: Spa.

Spain. 1984. ■Bibliography of twentieth century Spanish drama.

2998 Arnold, Peter, comp.; Cathomas, Vreni, comp. *Stück für Stück.* (Play After Play.) Kinder- und Jugendtheater. Basel: Lenos; 1986. 174 pp. (Jahrbuch 1986/87.) Pref. Index. Illus.: Photo. B&W. Lang.: Ger.

Switzerland. ■Essays presenting workshop activities for children and young adults. Also contains one integral playtext, plus addresses and descriptions of various youth theatres in Switzerland.

2999 Fridštejn, Ju.G. *Sovremennaja anglijskaja dramaturgija 1981-1985. Bibliogr. ukaz.* (Contemporary English Dramaturgy, 1981-85: A Bibliography.) Moscow: VGBIL; 1986. 167 pp. Lang.: Rus.

UK. 1981-1985. Bibliographical studies. ■Bibliography of English drama.

3000 Howard, Tony. "Census of Renaissance Drama Productions (1986)." *RORD.* 1986; 29: 47-71. Lang.: Eng.

UK. USA. New Zealand. 1986. ■List of 37 productions of 23 Renaissance plays, with commentary.

3001 Barnes, Philip. *Companion to Post-War British Theatre.* Totowa, NJ/London: Barnes & Noble/Croom Helm; 1986. 288 pp. Lang.: Eng.

UK-England. 1945-1986. ■Alphabetically arranged comprehensive guide to contemporary playwrights, plays, directors, actors, theatre groups and training institutions.

3002 Herbert, Ian, ed. *London Theatre Index 1985.* London: London Theatre Record; 1986. 48 pp. Pref. Illus.: Photo. Print. B&W. 16. Lang.: Eng.

UK-England: London. 1985. ■Chronological list of 407 London productions mounted in 1985 with an index to actors, writers and production personnel.

3003 Wearing, J.P. "Additions and Corrections to Allardyce Nicoll's Handlist of Plays 1900-1930." *NCTR.* 1986; 14(1-2): 51-96 . Lang.: Eng.

UK-England: London. 1900-1930. ■Errors and omissions the author discovered in Nicoll's sourcebook during the course of his own theatrical research are listed by the page. The author found typographical errors, mistaken dates and some overlooked productions.

3004 "1984-85 Season Schedules." *AmTh.* 1984 Oct.; 1(6). Illus.: Sketches. 1. Lang.: Eng.

USA. 1984-1985. Historical studies. ■A comprehensive listing of productions, dates and directors for the 1984-85 season at TCG constituent theatres nationwide.

3005 "The 1985-1986 Season Theatre Members Production Schedules." *TT.* 1985 Nov.; 5(1): 7-9. Illus.: Photo. B&W. 8: var. sizes. Lang.: Eng.

USA: New York, NY. 1985-1986. Histories-sources. ■Production schedules for member theatres of Alliance of Resident Theatres/New York.

3006 "Production Schedules: February-June, 1983." *TT.* 1983 Feb.; 2(4): 5-8. Illus.: Photo. B&W. 10: var. sizes. Lang.: Eng.

USA: New York, NY. 1983. Histories-sources. ■Production schedules for member theatres of Alliance of Resident Theatres/New York.

3007 Bailey, A. Peter. "Take It From the Top." *OvA.* 1986 Win; 13(1): 10-14. Lang.: Eng.

USA: New York, NY. 1973-1984. Histories-sources. ■Lists the annual Audelco Awards for Outstanding Playwright since 1973 and highlights the current work of these playwrights.

3008 Davis, J. Madison; Coleman, John. "David Mamet: A Classified Bibliography." *SAD.* 1986; 1: 82-102. Pref. Lang.: Eng.

USA. 1973-1986. ■David Mamet: plays, non-fiction, interviews, criticism, reviews and biographical materials.

3009 Guernsey, Otis L.; Swope, Martha, photo.; Hirshfeld, Al, illus. *Curtain Times: The New York Theatre 1965-1985.* New York, NY: Applause; 1986. viii, 613 pp. Index. Illus.: Photo. Dwg. Print. B&W. 30: var. sizes. Lang.: Eng.

USA: New York, NY. 1965-1985. ■Chronological listing of 20 theatre seasons in New York City containing synopses, reviews, details of events backstage, offstage and in the theatrical community and a discussion of what impact these events had on performance.

3010 Morley, Sheridan. *The Great Stage Stars: Distinguished Theatrical Careers of the Past and Present.* New York, NY: Facts on File; 1986. x, 425 pp. Illus.: Photo. Print. B&W. 55: var. sizes. Lang.: Eng.

USA. UK. 1717-1986. ■Alphabetically arranged series of biographical entries.

3011 Zimmer, Elizabeth. "Hot Time!—Summer in (And Out of) The City." *TT.* 1984 Aug.; 3(8): 8-9. Lang.: Eng.

USA: New York, NY. 1984. Histories-sources. ■Summer performance schedules for several New York companies that perform in and out of the Metropolitan area in the summer months.

Relation to other fields

3012 Halizev, V.E. *Drama kak rod literatury—Poetika, genezis, funkcionirovanie.* (Drama as a Genre of Literature—Poetics, Genesis, Functioning.) Moscow: Izd-vo Mosk. universiteta; 1986. 259 pp. Lang.: Rus.

Critical studies. ■Drama as a genre of literature.

3013 Komlósi, Piroska, comp. *Pszichodráma.* (Psychodrama.) Budapest: Adadémiai K; 1986. 211 pp. (Pszichológiai műhely 5.) Pref. Lang.: Hun.

Critical studies. ■Discusses theory of psychodrama and its applications in analysis and education.

3014 Horowitz, Michael. *Karl Kraus: Bildbiographie.* (Karl Kraus: Illustrated Biography.) Ein Trend-Profil-Buch. Vienna: Orac; 1986. 172 pp. Biblio. Illus.: Photo. Dwg. B&W. 236: var. sizes. Lang.: Ger.

Austria: Vienna. 1874-1936. Biographies. ■Critic and playwright Karl Kraus as a product of the literature and culture of his time. His discovery of unknown artists, and characteristics of his friends.

3015 Horowitz, Michael, ed. *Karl Kraus und seine Nachwelt: Ein Buch des Gedenkens. Nicht mehr publizierte Erste Veröffentlichung des Karl Kraus-Archivs im Verlag Richard Lányi, Wien (März) 1938.* (Karl Kraus and His Posterity: A Book of Unpublished Remembrances. First Edition of Karl Kraus Archives published by Richard Lányi, Vienna (March) 1938.) Vienna/Munich: Brandstätter; 1986. xv, 96 pp. 3: 12 cm. x 8 cm., 14 cm. x 10 cm. [Facsimile of the proof sheet of 1938.] Lang.: Ger.

DRAMA: —Relation to other fields

Austria: Vienna. 1933-1937. Histories-sources. ■Facsimile-edition of a book, not published because of the Nazi occupation. Poems, letters and obituary notes written by Kraus's contemporaries.

3016   Ruiss, Gerhard, comp.; Vyoral, Johannes A., comp. *Das Wir-wollen-ja-aber-es-geht-nicht Theater.* (The We-Want-But-It-Does-Not-Work-Theatre.) Vienna: IG Autoren; 1986. 126 pp. (Autorensolidarität 9/10.) Pref. Biblio. Append. [Proceeding of the Autoren-Theater-Enquete 1985.] Lang.: Ger.
Austria: Vienna. 1971-1986. Histories-sources. ■Conference of dramatists, theatre artists and critics discussing the financial situation of living playwrights: possibilities of performance, relationship to dramaturgy, reception by critics. Appendix chronicles the closing of the Künstlerhaustheater.

3017   Weigel, Hans. *Karl Kraus oder Die Macht der Ohnmacht: Versuch eine Motivenberichts zur Erhellung eines vielfachen Lebenswerks.* (Karl Kraus or the Power of Powerlessness: Attempt of a Motif Report for Enlightening a Multiple Lifework.) Vienna, Munich: Brandstätter; 1986. 341 pp. Index. Notes. [2d ed on the occasion of Kraus's death.] Lang.: Ger.
Austria: Vienna. 1874-1936. Biographies. ■Karl Kraus's plays and writings as author and critic and his efforts for the rediscovery of Nestroy and Offenbach. Originally published in 1968.

3018   Devine, Michael. "Eight Men Speak (A Metafictional Recreation)." *Theatrum.* 1986 Win; 5: 31-32. Lang.: Eng.
Canada: Toronto, ON. 1931-1933. Historical studies. ■Through a fictionalized diary excerpt by a cast member, describes a revolutionary political play banned by police after its first production in Toronto in 1933. Describes workers theatre and audiences in Canada during the 1930s.

3019   Enright, Robert. "The Theatre of the Oppressed: To Dynamize the Audience." *CTR.* 1986 Sum; 13(47): 41-49. Illus.: Photo. Print. B&W. 3: var. sizes. [Transcript of CBC radio broadcast, May 1985.] Lang.: Eng.
Canada: Montreal, PQ. France. Brazil: São Paulo. 1952-1986. Histories-sources. ■Interview with Augusto Boal about his career, techniques and approaches to theatre.

3020   Harrison, James. "Brecht, Bitterness and a First Born." *Theatrum.* 1986 Win; 5: 3-4. Lang.: Eng.
Canada: Toronto, ON. 1985. Historical studies. ■Welcomes participants to the *Brecht: Thirty Years After* conference, and describes Brecht's role in modern theatre, especially political theatre.

3021   Innes, Christopher. "The Psychology of Politics: George Ryga's *Captives of the Faceless Drummer.*" *THC.* 1985 Spr; 6(1): 23-43. Notes. Lang.: Eng.
Canada: Vancouver, BC. 1968-1971. Critical studies. ■Controversy surrounding the 1971 production of George Ryga's play at the Vancouver Playhouse, with attention to the problems of funding and staging political drama.

3022   Spry, Lib. "The Theatre of the Oppressed: But Not in Canada?" *CTR.* 1986 Sum; 13(47): 50-55. Notes. Illus.: Photo. Diagram. Print. B&W. Chart. 2: 3 in. x 5 in. Lang.: Eng.
Canada: Toronto, ON. 1986. Critical studies. ■Workshops in 'Theatre for the Oppressed' have significance in a highly developed country like Canada, as well as in the Third World.

3023   Usmiani, Renate. "The Theatre of the Oppressed: To Rehearse the Revolution." *CTR.* 1986 Sum; 13(47): 38-40. Illus.: Photo. Print. B&W. 1: 3 in. x 5 in. Lang.: Eng.
Canada: Montreal, PQ. 1985. Reviews of performances. ■Description of workshops conducted by Augusto Boal at the Festival des Amériques, in particular Boal's techniques called newspaper theatre, image theatre, invisible theatre and forum theatre.

3024   Velechov, L.Ju. *Problemy razvitija kubinskogo teatra i obščestvennaja žizn' revoljucionnoj Cuby 1960-1980 godov: Avtoref. diss... kand. iskusstvovedenija.* (Problems in the Development of Cuban Theatre and the Social Life of Revolutionary Cuba, 1960s-1980s: Synopsis of a Dissertation by a Candidate in Art Criticism.) Moscow: LGITMIK; 1986. 24 pp. Lang.: Rus.
Cuba. 1960-1986. Historical studies.

3025   Griswold, Wendy. *Renaissance Revivals: City Comedy and Revenge Tragedy in the London Theatre, 1576-1980.* Chicago, IL: Univ. of Chicago P; 1986. 288 pp. Index. Biblio. Illus.: Photo. Lang.: Eng.
England: London. 1576-1980. Critical studies. ■Study by a sociologist of the initial popularity of two genres and their reflection of trends in the social history of English drama.

3026   Nichols, Ann Eljenholm. "Costume in the Moralities: The Evidence of East Anglican Art." *CompD.* 1986; 20(4): 305-314. Notes. Lang.: Eng.
England. 1463-1544. Historical studies. ■Thirty-three baptismal fonts bearing carved representations of the seven sacraments examined for evidence concerning costuming of morality plays.

3027   Krzemiński, Adam. "Toller: Sześć dni u władzy." (Toller: Six Days in Authority.) *DialogW.* 1986; 1: 81-89. Notes. Lang.: Pol.
Europe. 1893-1939. Biographical studies. ■Ernst Toller's influence on the political situation in Europe.

3028   Sieradzki, Jacek. "Skansen i świat." (Skansen and the World.) *DialogW.* 1986; 9: 91-96. Lang.: Pol.
Europe. 1820-1986. Critical studies. ■Dramaturgy of Polish émigrés: its political and sociological aspects.

3029   Aston, Elaine. "Feminism in the French Theatre: A Turn-of-the-Century Perspective." *NTQ.* 1986 Aug.; 11(7): 237-242. Notes. Lang.: Eng.
France. 1897-1901. Historical studies. ■Attitudes toward feminism in turn-of-the-century France, with reference to contemporary plays and journals, indicating a growing willingness to question prevailing assumptions and a belief in the power of theatre to effect social change.

3030   Couton, Georges. *Richelieu et le théâtre.* (Richelieu and the Theatre.) Lyon: Presses Universitaires de Lyon; 1986. 91 pp. Notes. Lang.: Fre.
France. 1634-1642. Historical studies. ■Theatrical policies of Cardinal Richelieu, statesman, patron of the arts and author, including rehabilitation of the theatre and the acting profession, government control and subsidy, and the development of critical and theoretical thought on theatre.

3031   Davril, Anselme. "Johann Drumbl and the Origin of the *Quem Quaeritis*: A Review Article." *CompD.* 1986; 20(1): 65-75. Notes. Lang.: Eng.
France. Italy. 900-999. Historical studies. ■A review of Johann Drumbl's *Quem Quaeritis: Teatro Sacro dell' Alto Mediaevo* (1981), in which Davril explores the question of why the *Quem Quaeritis* trope emerged as a new liturgical ceremony.

3032   Proskurnikova, T. "*Mahabharata*—zerkalo mira." (*Mahabharata*: Mirror of the World.) *TeatrM.* 1986; 7: 177-182. Lang.: Rus.
France: Paris. 1985. Critical studies. ■On Peter Brook's *Mahabharata*, produced by the International Center of Theatre Research.

3033   *Für Theater Schreiben: Über zeitgenössische deutschsprachige Theaterautorinnen.* (Writing for the Stage: Contemporary German-Speaking Female Playwrights.) Schreiben. Bremen: Zeichen und Spuren, Frauenliteraturverlag; 1986. 214 pp. (Frauen-Literatur-Forum IX 29/30.) Pref. Biblio. Illus.: Photo. Lang.: Ger.
Germany. Switzerland. Austria. 1900-1986. Critical studies. ■Feminist criticism of the works of women playwrights and list of plays by women.

3034   Stark, Gary D. "La Police berlinoise et la Freie Volksbühne: une étude de l'intégration socialiste." (The Berlin Police and the Freie Volksbühne: A Study of Socialist Integration.) *RHT.* 1986; 38(1): 7-18. Notes. Lang.: Fre.
Germany: Berlin. 1890-1912. Historical studies. ■Police attempts to limit the freedom of action of the Freie Volksbühne, with the result that the company gave up its radical program and socialist goals.

DRAMA: —Relation to other fields

3035 Castellani, Victor. "Clio vs Melpomene: or Why so Little Historical Drama from Classical Athens?" *TID*. 1986; 8: 1-16. Notes. Lang.: Eng.
Greece: Athens. 475-375 B.C. Historical studies. ∎Examines the literary, political and social conditions that discouraged serious theatrical treatment of historical themes.

3036 Kolta, Magdolna. "Howard Fast: *Harminc ezüstpénz* c. drámájának fogadtatása Magyarországon." (Reception of Howard Fast's Play, *Thirty Pieces of Silver* in Hungary.) *SzSz*. 1986; 10(21): 5-19. Lang.: Hun.
Hungary. 1951-1986. Historical studies. ∎Ideology of the cold war period in Eastern Europe in connection with the premiere of Howard Fast's *Thirty Pieces of Silver*.

3037 Teatro Stabile di Catania, ed. *Giovanni Verga e il teatro.* (Giovanni Verga and the Theatre.) Catania: Assessorato Regionale ai Beni Culturali e Pubblica Istruzione; 1986. 156 pp. Index. Notes. Biblio. Filmography. Lang.: Ita.
Italy. 1840-1922. Histories-specific. ∎Studies presented at a 1984 conference on novelist Giovanni Verga and his theatrical connections and influences.

3038 Alberti, Carmelo. "Della probità teatrale. Giambattista Roberti e il teatro del settecento. Annotazioni e documenti." (On Theatrical Probity: Giambattista Roberti and Eighteenth-Century Theatre. Notes and Documents.) *BiT*. 1986; 4: 159-187. Notes. Biblio. Lang.: Ita.
Italy. 1719-1786. Histories-sources. ∎A short poem in praise of playwright Carlo Goldoni and some notes and reflections on the theatre by Jesuit writer Giambattista Roberti.

3039 Barilli, Renato. *Pirandello. Una rivoluzione culturale.* (Pirandello: A Cultural Revolution.) Milan: Mursia; 1986. 335 pp. (Saggi 39.) Pref. Index. Notes. Biblio. Lang.: Ita.
Italy. 1867-1936. Critical studies. ∎Collection of the author's critical writings on Luigi Pirandello since 1964.

3040 Cro, Stelio. "Pirandello lettore di Don Quijote." (Pirandello, Reader of Don Quixote.) *TeatrC*. 1986; 6(13): 1-20. Notes. Biblio. Lang.: Ita.
Italy. Spain. 1615-1936. Critical studies. ∎Comparison of playwright Luigi Pirandello and novelist Miguel de Cervantes, finding each revolutionary yet moderate in his genre.

3041 Oldoni, Massimo. "Intersezioni da Terenzio nella letteratura drammatica del X secolo: Liutprando da Cremona." (Intersections with Terence in Dramatic Literature of the Tenth Century: Liutprando of Cremona.) *Ariel*. 1986 Jan-Apr.; 1(1): 41-58 . Tables. Biblio. Illus.: Photo. Dwg. B&W. 6: var. sizes. Lang.: Ita.
Italy: Cremona. 920-972. Historical studies. ∎Examines the influence of the plays of Terence on the historical works of Bishop Liutprando of Cremona.

3042 Pasquini, Emilio. "Agnizioni pirandelliane nella poesia di Montale." (Recognition of Pirandello in Montale's Poetry.) *Ariel*. 1986 Sep-Dec.; 1(3): 52-58. Notes. Biblio. Lang.: Ita.
Italy. 1896-1981. Critical studies. ∎The influence of playwright Luigi Pirandello on the poems of Eugenio Montale.

3043 Pullini, Giorgio. *Tra esistenza e coscienza. Narrative e teatro del '900.* (Between Existence and Conscience: Narrative and Theatre in the Twentieth Century.) Milan: Mursia; 1986. 479 pp. (Saggi 37.) Index. Notes. Biblio. Lang.: Ita.
Italy. 1890-1970. Critical studies. ∎Describes great moments in the lives of major literary and dramatic figures on the issue of the relationship between existence and conscience.

3044 Sonino, Claudia. "Zur Karl-Kraus-Rezeption in Italien." (About the Reception of Karl Kraus in Italy.) 25-33 in Lunzer, Heinz, ed. *Karl Kraus 1874-1936: Katalog einer Ausstellung des Bundesministeriums für Auswärtige Angelegenheiten (Karl Kraus 1874-1936: Exhibition Catalogue of the Foreign Office).* Vienna: Dokumentationsstelle für neuere österreichische Literatur; 1986. 83 pp. (Zirkular, Sondernummer 8.) Biblio. Notes. Lang.: Ger.
Italy. Austria: Vienna. 1911-1985. Historical studies. ∎Discovering the author's importance: translation, scientific and literary analysis of his works. Includes bibliography of primary and secondary sources in Italy.

3045 Stewart, Pamela D. *Retorica e mimica nel Decamerone e nella commedia del cinquecento.* (Rhetoric and Mimesis in *The Decameron* and in the Comedy of the Sixteenth Century.) Florence: Olschki; 1986. 296 pp. (Saggi di 'Lettere Italiane' 35.) Pref. Index. Notes. Biblio. Lang.: Ita.
Italy. 1350-1550. Critical studies. ∎Reciprocal influence of Italian comedy and Boccaccio's *Il Decamerone (The Decameron)*.

3046 Potter, Robert. "Abraham and Human Sacrifice: The Exfoliation of Medieval Drama in Aztec Mexico." *NTQ*. 1986 Nov.; 11(8) : 306-312. Notes. Illus.: Dwg. B&W. 1. Lang.: Eng.
Mexico. Spain. 1519-1559. Historical studies. ∎The 'dramatic' qualities of Aztec forms of worship. The Spaniards, in their attempts to convert the Aztecs to Christianity, employed their own forms of 'sacrificial drama' for the purpose, while also assimilating some elements from the supplanted cultural forms.

3047 Solomon, Alisa. "The Road From Nigeria." *AmTh*. 1984 Dec.; 1(8): 10-14. Illus.: Photo. B&W. 5: var. sizes. Lang.: Eng.
Nigeria. USA: New Haven, CT. 1967-1984. Histories-sources. ∎Playwright Wole Soyinka discusses the violent political climate in his native Nigeria and its impact on his views and plays.

3048 Cioffi, Kathleen; Ceynowa, Andrzej. "An Interview with Director Lech Raczak." *TDR*. 1986 Fall; 30(3): 81-90. Illus.: Photo. B&W. 9: 3 in. x 3 in. Lang.: Eng.
Poland: Poznań. 1968-1985. Histories-sources. ∎Director of Teatr Osmego Dnia (Theatre of the Eighth Day): improvisational techniques lead to the creation of original theatre pieces.

3049 Koenig, Jerzy. "To nie takie proste." (It Is Not So Simple.) *DialogW*. 1986; 10: 110-116. Lang.: Pol.
Poland. 1945-1986. Critical studies. ∎Contemporary drama, analyzed by hypothetical playwright, director, critic and Polish authorities.

3050 Micińska, Anna. "Samobójstwo Witkiewicza." (Witkiewicz's Suicide.) *DialogW*. 1986; 8: 91-99. Notes. Lang.: Pol.
Poland. 1931-1939. Biographical studies. ∎Stanisław Witkiewicz's suicide in the light of his letters and papers, with recollections of his friends and contemporaries.

3051 Sokolowski, Jerzy. "Przełom lat pięćdziesiątych: Fala debiutów." (Wave of Debuts at the Turn of the Fifties and Sixties.) *DialogW*. 1986; 10: 106-109. Lang.: Pol.
Poland. 1958-1962. Critical studies. ∎Political situation and new plays on the Polish stage.

3052 Stolzman, Małgorzata. "Teatralne wierszyki Władysława Syrokomli." (Władysław Syrokomla's Theatrical Short Poems.) *PaT*. 1986 Second & Third Qtr; 2-3: 285-300. Notes. Illus.: Photo. Print. B&W. 8. Lang.: Pol.
Poland: Vilna, Warsaw. 1844-1861. Historical studies. ∎Discusses the relations of poet Władysław Syrokomla with Polish theatrical world, his reviews of performances, his own plays and satirical poems and his relationships with actors.

3053 Zadorožnaja, S.V. *Ukrainskaja dramaturgija pervoj poloviny XIX veka i ee istoki (k voprosu o sootnošenii literatury i folklora): Avtoref. diss... kand. filol. nauk.* (Ukrainian Dramaturgy of the Early Nineteenth Century and its Sources—Toward the Question of the Correlation of Literature and Folklore: Synopsis of a Dissertation by a Candidate in Philology.) Kiev: Kiev. in-t; 1986. 24 pp. Lang.: Rus.
Russia. 1800-1850.

3054 Hornbrook, David. "Drama, Education, and the Politics of Change: Part 2." *NTQ*. 1986 Feb.; 11(5): 16-25. Notes. Lang.: Eng.
UK. Histories-sources. ∎Proposals for a positive approach to drama-in-education giving the subject a greater curricular authority.

3055 Morton, David; Nixon, Jon; Graham, Tony. "Drama, Education, and Social Change: The Debate Continues." *NTQ*. 1986 Aug.; 11(7): 283-288. Notes. Lang.: Eng.

CLASSED ENTRIES

DRAMA: —Relation to other fields

UK. ■Responses to David Hornbrook's articles in *NTQ* 4 and 5, by theatre-in-education workers on the history of drama in education, a critique of present practice and practitioners, and some proposals for the future place of the subject in the curriculum.

3056 Bate, Jonathan. "Shakespearean Allusion in English Caricature in the Age of Gillray." *JWCI.* 1986; 49: 196-210. Notes. Illus.: Dwg. 1: 3 in. x 5 in. Lang.: Eng.
UK-England. 1780-1820. Historical studies. ■Selected satirical caricatures illustrate Shakespearean allusion in theatrical and political satire.

3057 Bolton, Gavin; Dobson, Warwick. "Drama, Education, and Social Change: The Debate Continues, 2." *NTQ.* 1986 Nov.; 11(8): 369-375. Lang.: Eng.
UK-England. Critical studies. ■Theatre-in-education's present practices and practitioners, and the place of the subject in the curriculum.

3058 Haigh, Anthony Russell. *The Essential Unity of Arnold Wesker's Vision with Special Reference to his Non-Dramatic Texts.* East Lansing, MI: Michigan State Univ; 1986. 235 pp. Pref. Notes. Biblio. [Ph.D. dissertation, Univ. Microfilms order No. DA8613294.] Lang.: Eng.
UK-England. 1932-1986. ■Exploration of the non-theatrical writings of playwright Arnold Wesker.

3059 Kelly, Katherine E. "Tom Stoppard's *Artist Descending a Staircase*: Outdoing the 'Dada' Duchamp." *CompD.* 1986; 20(3): 191-200. Notes. Lang.: Eng.
UK-England. 1913-1972. Critical studies. ■An exploration of the relationship between Marcel Duchamp's *Nude Descending a Staircase* and Stoppard's radio mystery.

3060 Peacock, D. Keith. "Fact Versus History: Two Attempts to Change the Audience's Political Perspective." *TheatreS.* 1984-85/1985-86; 31/32: 15-32. Illus.: Photo. 4: var. sizes. Lang.: Eng.
UK-England. 1971-1978. Critical studies. ■The form of John McGrath's agit-prop plays and the social realism of David Hare's *Plenty* reflect each author's political attitudes.

3061 Woddis, Carole. "(The) Woman." *PlPl.* 1986 Nov.; 398: 7-8. B&W. 2. Lang.: Eng.
UK-England: London. 1936-1986. Historical studies. ■Interview with actress Maria Aitken on a revival of *The Women* by Clare Boothe Luce, touching on the women's issues involved.

3062 Cima, Gay Gibson. "Shifting Perspectives: Combining Shepard and Rauschenberg." *TJ.* 1986 Mar.; 38(1): 67-81. Illus.: Pntg. Photo. B&W. 2: 4 in. x 5 in. Lang.: Eng.
USA. 1960-1980. Critical studies. ■Comparison of Robert Rauschenberg's painting 'Canyon' and sculpture 'Monogram' and the dramatic structure of Sam Shepard's *Buried Child*, *Action* and *Angel City*.

3063 Gaffney, Floyd. "Black Drama and Revolutionary Consciousness: What a Difference a Difference Makes." *TA.* 1986; 41: 1-19. Notes. Illus.: Photo. Print. B&W. 3: 3 in. x 6 in. Lang.: Eng.
USA. 1960-1985. Historical studies. ■Definition of 'Black theatre' with emphasis on dramatic characteristics and textual aspects which are culturally or socially based.

3064 Gay, Elisabeth. *Gert Schattner's Drama Sessions for Short Term Inpatients.* New York, NY: New York Univ.; 1986. 243 pp. Pref. Notes. Biblio. [Ph.D. dissertation, Univ. Microfilms order No. DA8614324.] Lang.: Eng.
USA: New York, NY. Austria. 1968. Histories-specific. ■Study dealing with the work of Gertrud Schattner as a founder of drama therapy, especially her work at Bellevue Hospital (New York, NY). Also includes a history of drama therapy and a videotape of Schattner at work.

3065 Janney, Kay Print; Galbraith-Jones, Marian. "The Young Playwright's Festival: Another Perspective." *ChTR.* 1986 Spr; 35 (1): 10-12. Notes. Biblio. Lang.: Eng.
USA: Groton, CT. 1983-1986. Historical studies. ■Description of the Cutler Playwright's Festival held at the Cutler School in Groton and designed for junior high school students. Suggestions for implementation by teachers and observations about themes and subject matter of plays submitted to the festival since 1983.

3066 Kim, Yun-Cheol. *A Critical Examination of Individual, Familial, and Social Destructiveness in Pulitzer Prize Plays, 1969-1984.* Provo, UT: Brigham Young Univ; 1986. 174 pp. Pref. Biblio. Notes. [Ph.D. dissertation, Univ. Microfilms order No. DA8610395.] Lang.: Eng.
USA. Historical studies. ■Examination of Pulitzer Prize plays illuminating racism, the decay of the American family and the pressure of the American success ethic as destructive forces in American society.

3067 Lensing, Leo A. "Karl Kraus im englischen Sprachraum." (Karl Kraus in the English-Speaking World.) 13-24 in Lunzer, Heinz, ed. *Karl Kraus 1874-1936: Katalog einer Ausstellung des Bundesministeriums für Auswärtige Angelegenheiten (Karl Kraus 1874-1936: Exhibition Catalogue of the Foreign Office).* Vienna: Dokumentationsstelle für neuere österreichische Literatur; 1986. 83 pp. (Zirkular, Sondernummer 8.) Biblio. Lang.: Ger.
USA: New York, NY. Austria: Vienna. UK-Scotland: Glasgow. 1909-1985. Historical studies. ■Reception of the Viennese critic and playwright's work in the English speaking world. Translations, critical studies, first performances of his play in English. Bibliography of primary and secondary sources in English.

3068 Sukari, Alamba. "Theatre Directors Giving Our Children Hope." *OvA.* 1986 Win; 14(1): 5, 7, 26, 28. Illus.: Photo. Print. B&W. 3: 5 in. x 6 in., 3 in. x 5 in. Lang.: Eng.
USA: New York, NY, Omaha, NE, Washington, DC. 1986. Historical studies. ■Theatre companies that use improvisation and workshop, as well as productions, to educate children about Afro-American history and folklore.

3069 Zinman, Toby Silverman. "Sam Shepard and Super-Realism." *MD.* 1986 Sep.; 29(3): 423-430. Notes. Lang.: Eng.
USA. 1978-1983. Critical studies. ■Shepard's recent plays and super-realist painting.

Research/historiography

3070 Courtney, Richard. "Drama as a Generic Skill." *YTJ.* 1986 Sum; 1(1): 5-10. Notes. Biblio. Lang.: Eng.
Canada: Toronto, ON. 1985. Empirical research. ■Study of educational drama from the perspective of generic skills.

3071 Werstine, Paul. "Printing History and Provenance in Two Revels Plays: Review Article." *MRenD.* 1984; 1: 243-278. Lang.: Eng.
England: London. 1514-1980. Critical studies. ■An assessment of two recent Revels Plays editions, one of George Peele's *Old Wives Tale* and another of two anonymous Tudor plays, focusing on manuscript sources and textual problems.

3072 Sokoljanskij, A.Ju. *Problemy metogiki analiza i opisanija dramatičeskogo spektaklja v teatral'no-kritičeskoj recenzii (70-e-80-e gody).* (Problems of the Method and Analysis of Dramatic Performance in Theatrical Reviews of the 70s and 80s.) Moscow: GITIS; 1986. 22 pp. [Synopsis of a Dissertation.] Lang.: Rus.
USSR. 1970-1980. Critical studies. ■Analysis and description in reviews of performances.

Theory/criticism

3073 Bachmann, Ueli. *Theatertext im Bühnenraum.* (Playtext and Performance Space.) Zürich & Schwäbisch Hall: Orell Füssli; 1986. 176 pp. Pref. Notes. Biblio. Illus.: Diagram. Lang.: Ger.
Critical studies. ■Discussion of the process of transposing a text into a performance, including stage directions inherent in dialogue.

3074 Free, William J. "A Theory of Evaluating Drama and Theatre." *JDTC.* 1986 Fall; 1(1): 77-85. Notes. Biblio. Lang.: Eng.
Critical studies. ■A theory of drama based on Max Scheler's philosophy, that posits different kinds of judgment at different points in the theatrical experience.

3075 Horville, Robert. "Théâtre à lire et théâtre à voir." (Theatre for Reading and Theatre for Seeing.) 11-19 in Heistein, Józef, ed. *Le texte dramatique. La lecture et la scène.* Wrocław: Wydawnictwo Uniwersytetu Wrocławskiego;

DRAMA: —Theory/criticism

1986. 248 pp. (Acta Universitatis Wratislaviensis 895, Romanica Wratislaviensia 26.) Lang.: Fre.
Critical studies. ■Analysis of two aspects of dramatic composition: the text perceived and completed by the imagination of the reader, and the performance of the same text seen by the spectator.

3076 Kelera, Józef. "La lecture du drame." (Reading of Drama.) 21-28 in Heistein, Józef, ed. *Le texte dramatique. La lecture et la scène*. Wrocław: Wydawnictwo Uniwersytetu Wrocławskiego; 1986. 248 pp. (Acta Universitatis Wratislaviensis 895, Romanica Wratislaviensia 26.) Lang.: Fre.
Critical studies. ■Different ways dramatic text is read by the scholar, the critic, the dramaturg, the director and the actor.

3077 Leverett, James. "From the Repertoire: Adding to Beckett." *AmTh*. 1984 June; 1(3): 26-27. Illus.: Photo. B&W. 1. Lang.: Eng.
1984. Critical studies. ■The influence of Samuel Beckett's later works on contemporary writers and directors.

3078 Ratajczak, Dobrochna. "Lire—Voir—Savoir." (To Read—To See—To Know.) 41-49 in Heistein, Józef, ed. *Le texte dramatique. La lecture et la scène*. Wrocław: Wydawnictwo Uniwersytetu Wrocławskiego; 1986. 248 pp. (Acta Universitatis Wratislaviensis 895, Romanica Wratislaviensia 26.) Lang.: Fre.
Critical studies. ■Attempt to establish a more theatrical view of drama.

3079 Rozik, Eli. "Theatrical Irony." *ThR*. 1986; 11(2): 132-51. Notes. Lang.: Eng.
Critical studies. ■Identifies types of irony within a general theory of theatrical communication and the emotional pleasure associated with irony.

3080 Shaked, Gershon. "Hamachaze Kederech Lehidavrut Tarbutit." (The Play as Means to Cultural Dialogue.) *Bamah*. 1986; 21 (104): 5-25. Notes. Lang.: Heb.
Critical studies. ■Semiotic analysis of the way a director's interpretation affects audience's ability to absorb new ideas and cultures.

3081 Swiontek, Sławomir. "La situation théâtrale inscrite dans le texte dramatique." (Theatrical Situation Inscribed in the Dramatic Text.) 97-107 in Heistein, Józef, ed. *Le texte dramatique. La lecture et la scène*. Wrocław: Wydawnictwo Uniwersytetu Wrocławskiego; 1986. 248 pp. (Acta Universitatis Wratislaviensis 895, Romanica Wratislaviensia 26.) Lang.: Fre.
Critical studies. ■Theoretical explanation of how only with dialogue can one construct the story and how the linguistic material can be transformed in theatrical situations.

3082 Ubersfeld, Anne. "Pour la théorie des actes de langage au théâtre." (Theory of Speech Acts in the Theatre.) 75-86 in Heistein, Józef, ed. *Le texte dramatique. La lecture et la scène*. Wrocław: Wydawnictwo Uniwersytetu Wrocławskiego; 1986. 248 pp. (Acta Universitatis Wratislaviensis 895, Romanica Wratislaviensia 26.) Lang.: Fre.
Critical studies. ■Justification of existence of the speech acts in theatre and their special functions in it.

3083 Docker, John. "In Defence of Melodrama: Towards a Libertarian Aesthetic." *ADS*. 1986 Oct.; 9: 63-81. Notes. Lang.: Eng.
Australia. 1850-1986. Critical studies. ■Appraisal of melodrama as an aesthetic theatre form from 19th-century theatre to today's television serial including concepts of cultural theorists Mikhail Bakhtin and Peter Brook.

3084 Fotheringham, Richard. "Sports Lovers and Sports Haters: Attitudes to Sport in Some Australian Plays." 89-98 in Univ. New England, ed. *Australian Drama 1920-1955*. Papers presented at a conference at the University of New England, Armidale, September 1-4, 1984. Armidale, N.S.W: Univ. of New England; 1986. 157 pp. Lang.: Eng.
Australia. 1876-1965. Historical studies. ■Negative attitudes toward sports in plays of Marcus Clark, Louis Esson, Katherine Susannah Prichard, Betty Roland and George Landen Dann.

3085 Morley, Michael. "A Critical State: Theatre Reviewing in Australia." *NTQ*. 1986 Feb.; 11(5): 94-96. Notes. Lang.: Eng.
Australia. 1985. Critical studies. ■Low standard of much Australian theatre reviewing.

3086 Bryden, Ronald, ed.; Neil, Boyd, ed. *Whittaker's Theatre: A Critic Looks at Stages in Canada and Thereabouts: 1944-1975*. Toronto: Univ of Toronto; 1985. xxii, 190 pp. Lang.: Eng.
Canada. 1944-1975. Reviews of performances. ■Reprints and critiques of fifty of Herbert Whittaker's theatre reviews.

3087 Lister, Rota Herzberg. "Whittaker's Theatre: A Critic Looks at Stages in Canada and Thereabouts: 1944-1975." *CDr*. 1986 Spr; 12(1): 231-232. Lang.: Eng.
Canada: Toronto, ON. 1944-1985. Critical studies. ■The reviewer praises editors Ronald Bryden and Boyd Neil for their valuable addition to Canadian theatre resource books. Their introductions to fifty of critic Herbert Whittaker's reviews trace the course of Canada's developing theatre scene as Whittaker both reflected and shaped it.

3088 Wagner, Anton. "A National or International Dramatic Art: B.K. Sandwell and *Saturday Night* 1932-1951." *CDr*. 1986 Fall ; 12(2): 342-350. Notes. Lang.: Eng.
Canada. 1932-1951. Biographical studies. ■Assesses the importance of critic, journalist and editor B.K. Sandwell, who maintained high international standards of criticism while encouraging the growth of visual, literary and theatrical arts in Canada.

3089 Ding, Luonan. "Xiong Foxi Xiju Sixiang Jianlun." (On Xiong Foxi's Thoughts on Theatre.) *XYishu*. 1982 Nov.; 5(4): 13-26. Lang.: Chi.
China, People's Republic of. 1920-1965. Critical studies. ■Includes discussion of his concepts of theatre for people's lives, theatre for fun and theatre as art.

3090 Ye, Qianrong. "Kongjian de Kaifang." (Liberating Space.) *XYishu*. 1982 May; 5(2): 130-135. Lang.: Chi.
China, People's Republic of. 1960-1981. Critical studies. ■How to overcome the impact of film and TV by adopting the Western idea of small, experimental theatres.

3091 Avetisjan, V.A. "Svojeobrazije getevskoj recenzii tvorchestvo W. Shakespeare." (Originality of Goethe's Reviews of the Work of Shakespeare.) *FN*. 1986; 29(2): 35-41. Lang.: Rus.
England. Germany. 1749-1832. Historical studies.

3092 Davidson, Clifford. "Iconography and Some Problems of Terminology in the Study of the Drama and Theater of the Renaissance." *RORD*. 1986; 29: 7-14. Notes. Lang.: Eng.
England. 1300-1642. Critical studies. ■Attempts to define such terms as 'emblematic' and 'iconographic' for purposes of dramatic criticism.

3093 Desai, Rupin W. "'Spectacles Fashioned With Such Perspective Art': A Phenomenological Reading of Webster's *The White Devil*." *MRenD*. 1984; 1: 187-198. Notes. Lang.: Eng.
England: London. 1610-1612. Critical studies. ■A phenomenological study arguing for a morally neutral world-view in the play, and for the play's status as a unique type of tragedy.

3094 Styan, J.L. "Quince's Questions and the Mystery of the Play Experience." *JDTC*. 1986 Fall; 1(1): 3-16. Biblio. Lang.: Eng.
England. 1600-1921. Critical studies. ■Some pitfalls of a semiotic analysis of theatre as illustrated by *A Midsummer Night's Dream*.

3095 Brook, Peter; Fei, Chunfang, transl. "Jishi Xiju Lilun Xuanyi." (Theory of Immediate Theatre: Selected Translations.) *XYishu*. 1982 Nov.; 5(4): 81-90. Lang.: Chi.
EUROPE. 1929-1982. Critical studies. ■First Chinese translation of the chapter 'Immediate Theatre,' from *The Empty Space*, an overview of Peter Brook's theory of theatre.

3096 Mango, Achille. "Theatre and Mind." *BiT*. 1986; 4: 1-20. Lang.: Ita.
Europe. 1986. Critical studies. ■The primacy of thought over representation because of the inability to represent fully the text and its concepts.

DRAMA: —Theory/criticism

3097 Pidoux, Jean-Yves. *Acteurs et Personnages: L'interprétation dans les esthétiques théâtrales du XXe siècle.* (Actors and Their Personalities: Aspects of Interpretations in 20th-Century Theatrical Aesthetics.) Montreux: L'Aire; 1986. 372 pp. Pref. Notes. Biblio. Lang.: Fre.
Europe. North America. 1900-1985. Critical studies. ■An approach to the interrelationships of interpretation, creation and text based on the ideas of Theodor Adorno and the Frankfurt School. Discusses the work of Bertolt Brecht, Konstantin Stanislavskij, Lee Strasberg, Jerzy Grotowski and Julian Beck.

3098 Tessari, Roberto. "Miti orientali e occidentali sull'origine del teatro." (Eastern and Western Myths on the Origin of Theatre.) 23-58 in Ottai, Antonella, ed. *Teatro Oriente/ Occidente.* Rome: Bulzoni; 1986. viii, 565 pp. (Biblioteca Teatrale 47.) Lang.: Ita.
Europe. Asia. 1986. Historical studies. ■Origins of the theatre as illustrated by the myths of Uzume and Baubo.

3099 Artaud, Antonin; Li, Hong, transl.; Wu, Baohe, transl. "Canku Xiju Lilun Xuanyi." (Theory of the Theatre of Cruelty: Selected Translations.) *XYishu.* 1982 Nov.; 5(4): 71-80. Lang.: Chi.
France. 1896-1949. Critical studies. ■Brief overviews of Artaud's life, work and theory with selections from his *The Theatre and Its Double*, translated into Chinese for the first time.

3100 Couprie, Alain. "Corneille et le mythe pastoral." (Corneille and the Pastoral Myth.) *DSS.* 1986 Apr/June; 38(2): 159-166. Notes. Lang.: Fre.
France. 1636-1986. Critical studies. ■The influence of the pastoral myth (nostalgia for a lost paradise) on the political tragedies and heroic comedies of Pierre Corneille.

3101 Diderot, Denis; Casas, Joan, transl. *Diderot i el teatre.* (Diderot and the Theatre.) Barcelona: Institut del Teatre; 1986. 76 pp. (Materials Pedagògics 2nd series 2.) Biblio. Tables. Index. Lang.: Cat.
France. 1713-1834. Instructional materials. ■Selection of Diderot's theoretical writings on theatre with introduction and commentary by Joan Casas.

3102 Jeung, Bang-hee. "Kōjeēn Yēongǔk." (Neoclassical Theatre.) 159-168 in Sung, Gim-Kwang, ed. *Understanding Theatre.* Seoul: Sung, Gim-Kwang; 1986. 344 pp. Lang.: Kor.
France. 1600-1700. Critical studies. ■Molière, Racine and Corneille: their plays and contributions.

3103 Mortier, Daniel. *Celui qui dit oui, celui qui dit non ou la réception de Brecht en France, 1945-1956.* (The Yes Man and the No Man: The Reception of Brecht in France, 1945-1956.) Geneva/Paris: Slatkine: Champion; 1986. 314 pp. Index. Notes. Lang.: Fre.
France. 1945-1956. Historical studies. ■Early introduction of the works of Bertolt Brecht in France: editions, the role of the review *Théâtre populaire* and Brecht's influence on French playwrights.

3104 Pavis, Patrice; Kruger, Loren, transl. "The Classical Heritage of Modern Drama: The Case of Postmodern Theatre." *MD.* 1986 Mar.; 29(1): 1-22. Notes. Lang.: Eng.
France. 1986. Critical studies. ■Comparative analysis of classical, modern and postmodern theatre and their delineation through oppositions (classical/modern, heritage/memory) and setting.

3105 Brecht, Bertolt; Li, Jianming, transl. "Wutai Shang de Bianzhengfa Biji." (Notes about Dialectic on the Stage.) *XYishu.* 1982 May; 5(2): 104-113. Lang.: Chi.
Germany. 1898-1956. Critical studies. ■*Coriolanus* according to Bertolt Brecht's socio-political mission.

3106 Chen, Shixiong. "Heige Lun Xiju de Neizai Yinsu Yu Waizai Yinsu." (Hegel on a Play's Internal and External Factors.) *XYishu.* 1982 May; 5(2): 62-68. Lang.: Chi.
Germany. 1770-1982. Critical studies. ■In the light of Hegel's theory, examines how 20th-century dramatists externalize internal contradictions.

3107 Graver, David. "Gottfried Benn's Impossible Plays: Dramatic Anarchy and Solipsism." *TJ.* 1986 Mar.; 38(1): 53-66. Lang.: Eng.
Germany: Berlin. 1914-1934. Critical studies. ■Study of solipsism, expressionism and aesthetics via dialogue and plot in Gottfried Benn's anti-rational dramas *Ithaca, Karandasch* and *Étappe.*

3108 Nietzsche, Friedrich; Kertész, Imre, transl. *A tragédia születése avagy Görögség és pesszimizmus.* (The Birth of Tragedy, or Greeks and Pessimism.) Budapest: Európa; 1986. 225 pp. (Mérleg.) Notes. Lang.: Hun.
Germany. 1872. Critical studies. ■Hungarian translation of *Die Geburt der Tragödie.*

3109 Orduña, Javier. "L'evolució cap el classicisme als escrits dramatúrgics de Schiller." (The Evolution Toward Classicism in Schiller's Theatrical Writings.) 7-28, 65-70 in *Schiller, escrits dramatúrgics.* Barcelona: Institut del Teatre; 1986. 76 pp. (Materials Pedagògics 2nd series 1.) Biblio. Tables. [Prologue to *Schiller, Theatrical Writings.*] Lang.: Cat.
Germany. 1759-1805. Instructional materials. ■Analysis of the different periods of Schiller's writings, including the influences of Kant, classical culture and nationalism.

3110 Schiller, Friedrich von; Orduña, Javier, ed.; Vinardell, Teresa, transl. *Schiller, escrits dramatúrgics.* (Schiller, Theatrical Writings.) Barcelona: Institut del Teatre; 1986. 76 pp. (Materials Pedagògics 2nd series 1.) Biblio. Tables. Index. Lang.: Cat.
Germany. 1759-1805. Instructional materials. ■Selection of writings on theatre by Schiller, including extracts from his *Von Pathetischen und Erhabenen (On the Pathetic and the Sublime)* and from letters to Goethe.

3111 Xue, Mu. "Bulaixite Yanjiu Zhong di Ruogan Wenti." (Exploration of Some Issues in Brecht Studies.) *XYishu.* 1982 Aug.; 5 (3): 34-43. Lang.: Chi.
Germany. China. 1400-1982. Critical studies. ■Comparison of Brechtian theatre and Chinese traditional theatre.

3112 Schäfer, Helmut; Heinze, Mona, transl. "On the Necessary Non-Sense of Production Dramaturgy." *ThM.* 1986 Sum/Fall; 17(3): 57-58. Lang.: Eng.
Germany, West. 1979. Critical studies. ■Dramaturgy, as a rational enterprise, is limited in relationship to artistic proces.

3113 Cavander, Kenneth. "Imagining the Greeks." *AmTh.* 1984 Sep.; 1(5): 11-13, 42. Illus.: Photo. B&W. 3: var. sizes. Lang.: Eng.
Greece: Athens. 450 B.C. Historical studies. ■Social and political conflicts and daily concerns of Greek society are examined to determine sources for their plays. Language, characters and playwrights are discussed.

3114 Peterdi Nagy, László. "Mi lesz velünk, Anton Pavlovics? Almási Miklós új könyve." (What Will Become of Us, Anton Pavlovič? Miklós Almási's New Book.) *Sz.* 1986 June; 19(6): 48. Lang.: Hun.
Hungary. 1986. Critical studies. ■Discusses Miklós Almási's treatment of the structural, interpretational and performance problems of the four most frequently played works of Čechov.

3115 Poszler, György. "Az ontológiai esztétika nyomában. Bécsy Tamás irásairól." (In Quest of an Onthological Aesthetic: On the Writings of Tamás Bécsy.) *Jelenkor.* 1986; 29(7/8): 715-718. Lang.: Hun.
Hungary. 1986. Critical studies. ■A critique of Tamás Bécsy's theory of theatre and of his writings.

3116 Varjas, Endre. "Van-e, ami van?" (Do We Really Have What We Have?) *Sz.* 1986 Apr.; 19(4): 47-48. Lang.: Hun.
Hungary. 1986. Critical studies. ■Review of two books on theatre: one by Anna Földes on playwright István Örkény and one by Szuzsa Radnóti on the Hungarian avant-garde.

3117 Cini, Lucia. "Macchina scenica e utopia nelle *Fiabe* teatrali di Carlo Gozzi." (Stage Machinery and Utopia in the Theatrical *Fables* of Carlo Gozzi.) *QT.* 1986 Feb.; 8(31): 123-136. Notes. Biblio. Lang.: Ita.

DRAMA: —Theory/criticism

Italy: Venice. 1761-1765. Critical studies. ■Semiotic analysis of Carlo Gozzi's *Fiabe (Fables)*.

3118 Harrison, James. "'Everytime I Speak, I Say Something.' *La Storia*: A Table of Fables." *Theatrum*. 1985-86 Fall-Win; 3 : 9-11, 22. Lang.: Eng.
Italy. 1985. Critical studies. ■Considers *La Storia* as an expression of the language of images, where (in a metatheatrical style) the spoken word clarifies the visual image.

3119 Stäuble, Antonio. "La dialectique texte-spectacle dans le théâtre italien du XX siècle." (Text-Performance Dialectics in the Italian Theatre of the Twentieth Century.) 29-40 in Heistein, Józef, ed. *Le texte dramatique. La lecture et la scène*. Wrocław: Wydawnictwo Uniwersytetu Wrocławskiego; 1986. 248 pp. (Acta Universitatis Wratislaviensis 895, Romanica Wratislaviensia 26.) Lang.: Fre.
Italy. 1900-1984. Critical studies. ■Decreasing importance of the playwright in theatre: documentary theatre, adaptations of the classics, participation of the audience in the performance.

3120 Hyun, Kyung-Ae. "Ibsenui kūgi Hängūk Yēangūkae Michin Yeonghyang." (Henrik Ibsen's Dramatic Thought and His Influence on Korean Theatre.) 49-83 in Lee, Tae-Ju, ed. *A Study of Realism*. Seoul: Kim, Moon-Han; 1986. 268 pp. Lang.: Kor.
Korea: Seoul. Norway. 1884-1986. Critical studies. ■Ibsen's major plays and their production values in Korea.

3121 Jeung, Kyung-Hee. "Chilshipnyoendāe Hangūk Huigökmunhākui Hyangsänggwa Mùnjaejeom." (Problems of Korean Drama During the 1970s.) 121-173 in Yeo, Suk-Gi, ed. *A Collection of Essays*. Seoul: Korea UP; 1986. 295 pp. Lang.: Kor.
Korea: Seoul. 1970-1979. Critical studies. ■Including some solutions by playwright/director, Oh Tāe-Suck.

3122 Lee, Shung-il. *Chuk-jāe Hwä Mädōng Juk*. (Festival and Street Plays.) Seoul: Bang, Wu-Young; 1986. 311 pp. Lang.: Kor.
Korea: Seoul. 200 B.C.-1986 A.D. Histories-specific. ■Origins of street theatre in festivals. Work of playwright/director Lim Gin-Tack used as example.

3123 Elías, Eduardo F. "Carlos Fuentes and Movie Stars (Intertextuality in a Mexican Drama)." *LATR*. 1986 Spr; 19(2): 67-77. Notes. Lang.: Eng.
Mexico. 1982-1986. Critical studies. ■A semiotic reading of Carlos Fuentes' play *Orquídeas a la luz de la luna (Orchids in the Moonlight)*.

3124 Maduakor, Obiajuru. "Soyinka as Literary Critic." *RAL*. 1986 Spr; 17(1): 1-38. Notes. Illus.: Diagram. Dwg. Print. B&W. Schematic. 3: 3 in. x 5 in., 5 in. x 5 in., 4 in. x 4 in. Lang.: Eng.
Nigeria. 1960-1980. Historical studies. ■An analysis of Wole Soyinka's major critical essays, focusing on how the essays illuminate Soyinka's plays.

3125 Gerould, Daniel. "From Adam Mickiewicz's *Lectures on Slavic Literature* Given at the Collège de France." *TDR*. 1986 Fall; 30(3): 91-97. Lang.: Eng.
Poland. 1798-1855. Critical studies. ■Translation of excerpts from Mickiewicz's lectures with discussion of his belief that theatrical poetry must be a communion with the dead as well as with the living.

3126 Grotowski, Jerzy; Mao, Baiyu, transl. "*Zhipu Xiju* Yu *Lei Xiju* Lilun Xuanyi." (Selected Translations from *Poor Theatre* and *Paratheatrics*.) *XYishu*. 1982 Nov.; 5(4): 91-101. Lang.: Chi.
Poland. 1933-1982. Critical studies. ■Overview of Grotowski's work and thoughts on theatre, and translation of two articles, 'The Actor's Technique' and 'Statement of Principles' from *Towards a Poor Theatre*.

3127 Klossowicz, Jan. "Conférence polono-américaine de théoriciens." (Polish-American Conference of Theorists.) *TP*. 1986; 29(4-5): 26-29. Lang.: Eng, Fre.
Poland. USA. 1985. Historical studies. ■Overview of conference discussing theoretical and practical problems related to the term 'performance'.

3128 Zieliński, Jan. "Tymona Terleckiego sztuka eseju." (Tymon Terlecki's Essays.) *DialogW*. 1986; 9: 110-124. Notes. Lang.: Pol.
Poland. 1905-1986. Textual studies. ■Critic Tymon Terlecki's essays, his language and main theoretical concepts.

3129 Agiševa, N. "Andrej Belyj i teatr." (Andrej Belyj and the Theatre.) *SovD*. 1986; 3: 268-276. Lang.: Rus.
Russia. 1880-1934. Historical studies. ■Andrej Belyj's views on Symbolist and Realist theatre, dramaturgy.

3130 Egri, Péter. *Chekhov and O'Neill: The Use of the Short Story in Chekhov's and O'Neill's Plays*. Budapest: Akadémiai K; 1986. 182 pp. Biblio. Lang.: Eng.
Russia. USA. Critical studies. ■Aesthetic and dramatic analysis of the relationship between the plays and short stories of Eugene O'Neill and Anton Čechov.

3131 Rizzi, Daniela. "Il teatro simbolista russo tra scena e letteratura: Valerij Brjusov." (Russian Symbolist Theatre Between Stage and Literature: Valerij Brjusov.) *BiT*. 1986; 3: 39-59. Notes. Biblio. Lang.: Ita.
Russia. 1873-1924. Critical studies. ■Study of symbolist poet Valerij Brjusov's theatrical experimentation and his manifesto of theatrical symbolism, 'A Needless Truth'.

3132 Rodríguez, Alemán, Mario. "La ideología teatral de Lope de Vega." (Lope de Vega's Theatrical Ideology.) 215-234 in Salvat, Ricard, ed. *El Teatre durant l'Edat Mitjana i el Renaixement*. Barcelona: Publicacions i Edicions de la Universitat de Barcelona; 1986. xxviii, 322 pp. (El Pla de les Comèdies 2.) Notes. [Presented at First International Symposium on Medieval and Renaissance Theatre, Sitges, 1983.] Lang.: Spa.
Spain. 1609-1624. Historical studies. ■Lope de Vega's dramatic theories applied to comedy, with comparisons to his contemporaries and to the history of world theatre.

3133 Zeij, Hanneke; Ingen Schenau, Karin van, transl. "Per l'esegesi del contenuto drammatico." (For the Exegesis of Dramatic Content.) *BiT*. 1986; 2: 1-21. Notes. Biblio. Lang.: Ita.
Sweden. 1889-1986. Critical studies. ■Semiotic analysis of the active function of the audience in performance, using the example of *Fröken Julie (Miss Julie)* by August Strindberg.

3134 Merritt, Susan Hollis. "Pinter's 'Semantic Uncertainty' and Critically 'Inescapable' Certainties." *JDTC*. 1986 Fall; 1 (1): 49-76. Notes. Biblio. Lang.: Eng.
UK. 1957-1986. Critical studies. ■Changing directions in Pinter criticism in relation to the uncertainty inherent in Harold Pinter's works.

3135 Dietrich, Richard F. "Deconstruction as Devil's Advocacy: A Shavian Alternative." *MD*. 1986 Sep.; 29(3): 431-451. Notes. Lang.: Eng.
UK-England. 1900-1986. Critical studies. ■Compares the devil's advocacy of George Bernard Shaw's plays and criticism to deconstruction, proposes Shavian method as model of criticism.

3136 Kuhn, Patricia Lenchan. *Kenneth Tynan and the Renaissance of Post-War British Drama*. Detroit, MI: Wayne State Univ; 1986. 306 pp. Pref. Notes. Biblio. [Ph.D. dissertation, Univ. Microfilms order No. DA8615408.] Lang.: Eng.
UK-England. 1950-1960. Historical studies. ■Examination and assessment of the critical works of Kenneth Tynan.

3137 "Experimental Theatre: What's Next?" *TT*. 1985 June/July; 4(6): 1, 4-6. Illus.: Photo. B&W. 3. Lang.: Eng.
USA: New York, NY. 1985. Histories-sources. ■Excerpts from symposium on experimental theatre. 11 panelists discuss their personal directions and the direction of the genre.

3138 Centola, Steven R. "The Monomyth and Arthur Miller's *After the Fall*." *SAD*. 1986; 1: 49-60. Biblio. Notes. Lang.: Eng.
USA. 1964-1984. Critical studies. ■Similarities between dramatic structure of Arthur Miller's *After the Fall* and structural organization of the monomyth as presented in Joseph Campbell's *The Hero with a Thousand Faces*.

DRAMA: —Theory/criticism

3139 Corrigan, Robert; Schechner, Richard. "Corrigan on TDR and TDR on Corrigan." 43-50 in McNamara, Brooks, ed.; Dolan, Jill, ed. *The Drama Review: Thirty Years of Commentary on the Avant-Garde.* Ann Arbor, MI: UMI Research P; 1986. xii, 371 pp. (Theatre and Dramatic Studies 35.) Lang.: Eng.
USA. 1964-1986. Critical studies. ■Forums: Dispute regarding the content and aims of *The Drama Review,* between past conservative editor Robert Corrigan and the new editorial board.

3140 Corrigan, Robert. "TDR's First Ten Years." 123-125 in McNamara, Brooks, ed.; Dolan, Jill, ed. *The Drama Review: Thirty Years of Commentary on the Avant-Garde.* Ann Arbor, MI: UMI Research P; 1986. xii, 371 pp. (Theatre and Dramatic Studies 35.) Lang.: Eng.
USA. 1966. Critical studies. ■Details ten-year anniversary celebration of *The Drama Review* and reasons for its longevity, with special attention to the first issue containing an essay by Friedrich Dürrenmatt entitled *Problems of the Theatre.*

3141 Fly, Richard. "The Evolution of Shakespearean Metadrama: Abel, Burckhardt, and Calderwood." *CompD.* 1986; 20(2): 124-139 . Notes. Lang.: Eng.
USA. 1963-1983. Critical studies. ■Analyses of self-reflexive themes in Shakespeare in the writings of three major critics: Lionel Abel, Sigurd Burckhardt and James L. Calderwood.

3142 Hauger, George. "When Is a Play Not a Play?" 27-38 in McNamara, Brooks, ed.; Dolan, Jill, ed. *The Drama Review: Thirty Years of Commentary on the Avant-garde.* Ann Arbor, MI: UMI Research P; 1986. xii, 371 pp. (Theatre and Dramatic Studies 35.) Lang.: Eng.
USA. 1960-1986. Critical studies. ■Analysis of the essentials of art, especially in theatre.

3143 Kachel, A. Theodore. "Does Dickens Deliver More Than Money?" *AmTh.* 1984 Dec.; 1(8): 23, 41. Lang.: Eng.
USA. 1984. Critical studies. ■The popularity of Charles Dicken's *A Christmas Carol* in American theatres and its themes of greed and generosity.

3144 Mamet, David. *Writing in Restaurants.* New York, NY: Viking Penguin; 1986. xii, 160 pp. Pref. Lang.: Eng.
USA: New York, NY, Los Angeles, CA. 1986. Critical studies. ■Playwright's essays on several artistic media, including photography, film and radio, as well as some character sketches.

3145 McNamara, Brooks, ed.; Dolan, Jill, ed. *The Drama Review: Thirty Years of Commentary on the Avant-garde.* Ann Arbor, MI: UMI Research P; 1986. xii, 371 pp. (Theatre and Dramatic Studies 35.) Lang.: Eng.
USA. 1955-1986. Critical studies. ■Collection of essays on the avant-garde.

3146 Moss, Jane. "Frank Rich Speaks Out: The Craft of the Critic." *TT.* 1986 Mar.; 5(3): 1-3. Illus.: Photo. B&W. 1. Lang.: Eng.
USA: New York, NY. 1986. Histories-sources. ■Editorial transcript of theatre critic Frank Rich's remarks at the 92nd St. YMHA series 'Critics on Criticism: Theatre.' Discusses his life, career and influences on his work.

3147 Norman, Marsha. "Articles of Faith: A Conversation with Lillian Hellman." *AmTh.* 1984 May; 1(2): 10-15. Illus.: Photo. B&W. 4: var. sizes. Lang.: Eng.
USA: Martha's Vineyard, MA. 1983. Histories-sources. ■Playwright Marsha Norman (assisted by Robert Brustein) interviews playwright Lillian Hellman regarding her philosophy and personal life, focusing on her book *An Unfinished Woman.*

3148 Paolucci, Anne. "Albee and the Restructuring of the Modern Stage." *SAD.* 1986; 1: 3-23. Biblio. Lang.: Eng.
USA. 1964-1980. Critical studies. ■Edward Albee as a playwright of the Absurd, his development of a realistic setting to enhance the surreal and cryptic, with special regard to *A Delicate Balance.*

3149 Redina, O.N. *Literaturno-estetičeskie iskanija T.Uajldera 30-40 godov (dramaturgija, esseistika): Avtoref. diss... kand. filol nauk.* (Literary-Aesthetic Quests of .T. Wilder in the Thirties and Forties—Dramaturgy, Essays: Synopsis of a Dissertation by a Candidate in Philology.) Moscow: Mosk. obl. ped. in-t; 1986. 24 pp. Lang.: Rus.
USA. 1930-1949. Critical studies. ■Aesthetic considerations in the plays and essays of Thornton Wilder.

3150 Schechner, Richard; Hoffman, Theodore. "TDR: 1963-?" 39-42 in McNamara, Brooks, ed.; Dolan, Jill, ed. *The Drama Review: Thirty Years of Commentary on the Avant-Garde.* Ann Arbor, MI: UMI Research P; 1986. xii, 371 pp. (Theatre and Dramatic Studies 35.) Lang.: Eng.
USA. 1963-1986. Critical studies. ■Intents and purposes of *The Drama Review.*

3151 Schechner, Richard. "Six Axioms for Environmental Theatre." 151-171 in McNamara, Brooks, ed.; Dolan, Jill, ed. *The Drama Review: Thirty Years of Commentary on the Avant-Garde.* Ann Arbor, MI: UMI Research P; 1986. xii, 371 pp. (Theatre and Dramatic Studies 35.) Print. B&W. 2: var. sizes. Lang.: Eng.
USA. 1968-1986. Critical studies. ■Theatrical theory suggesting focus on its six rules renders socially desirable elements of performance superfluous.

3152 Schechner, Richard. "Intercultural Performance: An Introduction." 271-274 in McNamara, Brooks, ed.; Dolan, Jill, ed. *The Drama Review: Thirty Years of Commentary on the Avant-Garde.* Ann Arbor, MI: UMI Research P; 1986. xii, 371 pp. (Theatre and Dramatic Studies 35.) Lang.: Eng.
USA. 1982. Critical studies. ■Richard Schechner discusses the importance of translating and performing the work of all cultures.

3153 Surkov, E. "A kak s charakterom?" (And How Do You Deal With Character?)*TeatZ.* 1986; 29(17): 10-11. Lang.: Rus.
USSR. 1980-1986. Critical studies. ■Character as an aesthetic category in contemporary dramaturgy.

Training

3154 Zhang, Yingxiang. "Duomuju Pailian Zhong de Jiaoxue Neirong yu Jiaoxue Fa." (Content and Methods of Teaching in the Course of Rehearsing Full-Length Plays.) *XYishu.* 1982 Aug.; 5(3): 22-26. Lang.: Chi.
1980-1982. Instructional materials. ■How-to on getting it together.

3155 Hu, Dao. "Tan Dongwu Guancha—Moni Xunlian." (Essay on the Observation of Animals—Exercise in Imitation.) *XYishu.* 1982 Aug.; 5(3): 17-21. Lang.: Chi.
China, People's Republic of: Shanghai. 1949-1982. Instructional materials. ■Imitating animals as an approach to training in movement, imagination and characterizations.

3156 Zhang, Jichun. "Jinian Foxi Shi." (Remembering Teacher Foxi.) *XYishu.* 1982 Nov.; 5(4): 27-29. Lang.: Chi.
China, People's Republic of: Ch'eng-tu. 1928-1940. Histories-sources. ■Author recalls how Xiong Foxi taught and worked to promote the social status of actors.

3157 Linklater, Kristin. "Animating the Actor's Body." *AmTh.* 1986 July-Aug.; 3(4): 38-39. Illus.: Photo. B&W. 1: 2 1/4 in. x 3 in. Lang.: Eng.
Europe. North America. 1985. Technical studies. ■The broad range of possibilities in the physical aspects of actor training.

3158 Simon, Zsuzsa. *Menjetek, készüljetek...A szinész alkotó müvész.* (Go, Get Ready...The Actor Is a Creative Artist.) Budapest: Múzsák; 1986. 97 pp. Biblio. Lang.: Hun.
Hungary. 1945-1985. Histories-sources. ■The author's experiences as teacher at the actors' academy for four decades.

3159 De Filippo, Eduardo. *Lezioni di teatro all'Università di Roma 'La Sapienza'.* (Lessons of Theatre at 'La Sapienza' University of Rome.) Turin: Einaudi; 1986. xxv, 178 pp. (Gli Struzzi 304.) Pref. Index. Notes. Lang.: Ita.
Italy: Rome. 1981-1982. Histories-sources. ■Transcription of the author's course on the production of theatrical texts.

3160 Hobgood, Burnet M. "Stanislavski's Books: An Untold Story." *ThS.* 1986 May & Nov.; 27(1-2): 155-165. Notes. Lang.: Eng.

DRAMA: —Training

USA. USSR. 1928-1986. Historical studies. ■Examination of materials in the Elizabeth Reynolds Hapgood Archive and the files of Theatre Arts Books reveals new details concerning the translation and publication in the USA of Stanislavskij's works.

3161   Lichti, Esther Sundell. *Richard Schechner and the Performance Group: A Study of Acting Technique and Methodology.* Lubbock, TX: Texas Tech Univ; 1986. 211 pp. Pref. Notes. Biblio. [Ph.D. dissertation, Univ. Microfilms order No. DA8515348.] Lang.: Eng.

USA. 1960. Historical studies. ■History and analysis of the Performance Group centering particularly on the development of a methodology for actor training.

3162   Crohn Schmitt, Natalie. "Stanislavski, Creativity, and the Unconscious." *NTQ.* 1986 Nov.; 11(8): 345-351. Notes. Lang.: Eng.

USSR: Moscow. 1900-1986. Historical studies. ■Konstantin Sergejēvič Stanislavskij believed that his 'system' was simply the application of natural laws to acting technique. He was indebted to the psychological theories of Ribot. The decline of Stanislavskij's system reflects the growing belief that creativity is 'process'.

3163   Westerfield, Bo. "An Interview with Zinovy Korogodsky: The Soviet Union's Leading Theatrical Director and Pedagogue." *ChTR.* 1986 Spr; 35(1): 18-19. Lang.: Eng.

USSR: Moscow, Leningrad. 1970-1984. Histories-sources. ■Russian actor training, specialization for children's theatre performers which begins in the fourth year of training, and relevance of Stanislavskij's theories today.

MEDIA
General

Administration

3164   Kim, Judy A. "The Performers' Plight in Sound Recordings Unique to the U.S.: A Comparative Study of the Development of Performers' Rights in the United States, England, and France." *ColJL&A.* 1986 Win; 10(2): 453-510. Notes. Lang.: Eng.

USA. UK-England. France. 1976-1985. Historical studies. ■Performers' rights in Great Britain and France as examples of feasible alternatives to existing American copyright legislation.

3165   Mulcahy, Kevin V.; Widoff, Joseph. "The Administrative Foundations of American Public Broadcasting." *JAML.* 1986 Win; 15 (4): 31-57. Notes. Tables. Lang.: Eng.

USA. 1986. Critical studies. ■Overview of the origins, finances and administration of public broadcasting including statistics on support from government, community, and institutions.

Audience

3166   Hoffman, Abbie. "Media Freaking." 177-183 in McNamara, Brooks, ed.; Dolan, Jill, ed. *The Drama Review: Thirty Years of Commentary on the Avant-Garde.* Ann Arbor, MI: UMI Research P; 1986. xii, 371 pp. (Theatre and Dramatic Studies 35.) Print. B&W. 1: 4 in. x 6 in. Lang.: Eng.

USA. 1969-1986. Historical studies. ■Susceptibility of American audiences to media manipulation.

Performance/production

3167   Higham, Charles. *Lucy: The Life of Lucille Ball.* New York, NY: St. Martin's; 1986. 320 pp. Illus.: Photo. Lang.: Eng.

USA. 1911-1986. Biographies. ■Career of film and television actress Lucille Ball.

Plays/librettos/scripts

3168   Corner, John, ed. *Documentary and the Mass Media.* London: Edward Arnold; 1986. 178 pp. (Stratford-upon-Avon Studies, Second Series.) Pref. Biblio. Index. Illus.: Photo. B&W. 18. Lang.: Eng.

UK-England. 1928-1986. Historical studies. ■The documentary in radio, television, and film.

Relation to other fields

3169   Scheffler, Ingrid. *Albin Zollinger, Max Frisch und Friedrich Dürrenmatt als Publizisten und ihr Verhältnis zu den Medien.* (Zollinger, Frisch and Dürrenmatt as Political Commentators and their Relation to the Media.) Bern/ Frankfurt am Main: Peter Lang; 1986. 541 pp. (Beiträge zur Literatur und Lit. wissenschaft des 20. Jhts. 7.) Pref. Notes. Biblio. Lang.: Ger.

Critical studies. ■Approach to the non-fictional and non-dramatic work by Albin Zollinger, Max Frisch and Friedrich Dürrenmatt from a non-literary viewpoint: questions relating to contemporary literary situations, literary theory and politics.

3170   Wagner, Anton. "Herman Voaden's 'New Religion'." *THC.* 1985 Fall; 6(2): 187-201. Notes. Illus.: Photo. B&W. 5. Lang.: Eng.

Canada: Toronto, ON. 1929-1943. Critical studies. ■Philosophical content of Voaden's plays, usually noted for their production style. The importance of Voaden's 'new religion' to his ideas of 'symphonic expressionism'.

3171   Mango, Achille. "La tecnologia mentale." (Mental Technology.) 131-148 in Ottai, Antonella, ed. *Teatro Oriente/ Occidente.* Rome: Bulzoni; 1986. viii, 565 pp. (Biblioteca Teatrale 47.) Lang.: Ita.

Italy. 1980-1986. Critical studies. ■Contrasts between culture and mass media, using several avant-garde productions as examples.

Theory/criticism

3172   Davies, Anthony. "Shakespeare and the Media of Film, Radio, and Television: A Retrospect." *ShS.* 1986; 39: 1-11. Notes. Lang.: Eng.

UK-England. USA. Japan. 1899-1985. Critical studies. ■Reviews Shakespeare productions on film, radio and television and evaluates criticism of them.

Audio forms

Basic theatrical documents

3173   Findley, Timothy. "*The Journey:* A Montage for Radio." *CDr.* 1984 Spr; 10(1): 115-140. Lang.: Eng.

Canada. 1970. ■Text of radio play originally produced by James Anderson for the CBC series 'Ideas' on April 3, 1970.

3174   Hébert, Anne; Benson, Eugene; Benson, Renate, transl. "*Les invités au procès.*" (The Guests on Trial.) *CDr.* 1983; 9(1): 165-194. Lang.: Eng.

Canada. 1952. Histories-sources. ■Translation of Anne Hébert's radio play *Les Invités au procès (The Guests on Trial).*

3175   Ritter, Erika. "*Miranda.*" *CTR.* 1986 Sum; 13(47): 73-120. Pref. Illus.: Photo. Print. B&W. 3: var. sizes. Lang.: Eng.

Canada: Montreal, PQ. UK-Scotland: Edinburgh. South Africa, Republic of: Cape Town. 1809-1859. ■Radio play, first broadcast in 1985, about a woman doctor who masqueraded as a man throughout her entire career.

Design/technology

3176   Paul, David. "Biomusic and the Brain: An Interview with David Rosenboom." *PerAJ.* 1986; 10(2): 12-16. Illus.: Photo. B&W. 1: 2 in. x 3 in. Lang.: Eng.

USA. 1986. Critical studies. ■Techniques and aesthetics of using biofeedback to create electronic music.

Institutions

3177   Page, Malcolm. "From 'Stage' to 'Sunday Matinee': Canadian Radio Drama in English, 1981-1982." *CDr.* 1983; 9(1): 23-29. Notes. Lang.: Eng.

Canada. 1981-1982. Historical studies. ■Negative evaluation of recent Canadian Broadcasting Corporation drama.

Performance/production

3178   Evans, Stuart. "Shakespeare on Radio." *ShS.* 1986; 39: 113-121. Lang.: Eng.

MEDIA: Audio forms—Performance/production

UK-England. 1935-1980. Technical studies. ■Problems of producing Shakespeare on radio, including casting, soliloquies, sound effects, background noises, etc.

3179 Jewell, Derek. *Frank Sinatra: A Celebration.* New York: Little; 1986. 192 pp. Discography. Filmography. Lang.: Eng.

USA. 1900-1986. Biographies. ■Music critic Derek Jewell traces Sinatra's career along with his own in this picture book, including a well-annotated filmography and discography. Related to Media: Film.

3180 Kelley, Kitty. *His Way: The Unauthorized Biography of Frank Sinatra.* New York, NY: Bantam; 1986. xvi, 587 pp. Pref. Index. Notes. Biblio. Filmography. Illus.: Photo. Print. B&W. Lang.: Eng.

USA. 1915-1984. Biographies. ■Documented account of the life and career of Frank Sinatra. Includes bibliography, discography and filmography. Related to Media: Film.

Plays/librettos/scripts

3181 Blouin, Louise; Page, Raymond. "Le phénomène des adaptations à la Radio Québécoise (1939-1949)." (The Phenomenon of Adaptations on Quebec Radio (1939-1949).) *THC.* 1986 Fall; 7(2): 202-214. Notes. Illus.: Photo. B&W. 1. Lang.: Fre.

Canada. 1939-1949. Historical studies. ■A study of the many adaptations of foreign works broadcast over Quebec radio over a ten-year period, with analysis of the repertory and its function as an 'acculturating' force.

3182 Lane, Harry. "CBC Radio and Scandinavian Literature." *CDr.* 1984 Spr; 10(1): 44-55. Notes. Lang.: Eng.

Canada. Scandinavia. 1939-1982. Historical studies. ■Survey of the offerings of Scandinavian drama on Canadian radio, asserting the primary importance of the radio adaptations to Canada's experience of Ibsen, in particular, the productions of director Esse Ljungh are examined.

3183 Pavelich, Joan E. "*Nazaire et Barnabé*: Learning to Live in an Americanized World." *CDr.* 1983 Spr; 9(1): 16-22. Notes. Lang.: Eng.

Canada. 1939-1958. Critical studies. ■Analysis of the popular Quebec radio series *Nazaire et Barnabé* with particular attention to the series' play on urban and rural, Anglo and French, and Canadian and American differences.

3184 Posesorski, Sherie. "A Way with Words." *BooksC.* 1986 Apr.; 15(3): 3-4. Lang.: Eng.

Canada. 1968-1986. Critical studies. ■Linda Zwicker's radio plays: sharp dialogue, history and interpersonal relationships.

3185 Wyatt, Rachel. "Passion Plays." *BooksC.* 1986 Apr.; 15(3): 5-6. Lang.: Eng.

Canada. 1985-1986. Critical studies. ■CBC radio producer John Juliani asked 6 women playwrights to write hour-long dramas on themes they felt passionate about.

3186 Esslin, Martin. "Harold Pinter's Work for Radio." 47-63 in Gale, Steven H., ed. *Harold Pinter: Critical Approaches.* London/Toronto: Associated University Presses; 1986. 232 pp. Notes. Lang.: Eng.

UK-England. 1957-1981. Historical studies. ■Harold Pinter's work for radio and its influence on his stage plays.

Relation to other fields

3187 Fink, Howard. "*The Jinker*, A Radio Play from the 50's." *CDr.* 1983; 9(1): 3-15. Notes. Lang.: Eng.

Canada. 1950-1955. Critical studies. ■An analysis of the social function of radio drama as a vehicle for articulating cultural ambiguities using as an example Joseph Schull's *The Jinker.*

Research/historiography

3188 Toeman, R. *A Grammar of Radio Drama.* UK: Open Univ; 1986. 3 vols and 3 reel-to-reel tapes. Notes. Biblio. Append. [M. Phil. dissertation, *Index to Theses*, 36-6922.] Lang.: Eng.

UK-England. 1981-1986. Critical studies. ■Identification of characteristics distinguishing radio drama, with a critical methodology.

Film

3189 Barbina, Alfredo, ed. "Lettere di Emilio Cecchi a Luigi Pirandello." (Letters from Emilio Cecchi to Luigi Pirandello.) *Ariel.* 1986 Jan-Apr.; 1(1): 150-154. Notes. Biblio. Lang.: Ita.

Italy. 1932-1933. Histories-sources. ■Letters on cinema from a major literary critic.

Administration

3190 "Hollywood Extra." *ThCr.* 1986 Mar.; 20(3): 94-96. Illus.: Photo. 2: var. sizes. Lang.: Eng.

USA: Los Angeles, CA. 1986. Histories-sources. ■Directors of the film festival Filmex discuss their plans for the future.

3191 Fleming, David. "The Deal: Start With What You Know." *ThCr.* 1986 Feb.; 20(2): 94-96. Illus.: Photo. 3: var. sizes. Lang.: Eng.

USA. 1986. Historical studies. ■Ken Copel's challenges as a producer in his transition from undergraduate to independent filmmaker.

3192 Gioia, Joseph. "The Deal: Hard Cash Hopscotch." *ThCr.* 1986 Apr.; 20(4): 86-88. Lang.: Eng.

USA: New York, NY. 1984-1986. Historical studies. ■Attempts by producer Paul Smart and writer/director Alexandre Rockwell to raise money for the film *Cheat'n Heart.*

3193 Harris, William. "Wine Bottle and Rooftops." *ThCr.* 1986 Jan.; 20(1): 82-83.

USA: New York, NY. 1986. Histories-sources. ■Independent filmmaker Leon Ichaso discusses raising money to produce his films.

3194 Lazare, Lewis. "Perversity Adversity." *ThCr.* 1986 May; 20(5): 79-80. Lang.: Eng.

USA. Historical studies. ■Stuart Oken and Jason Brett's efforts to produce the film of David Mamet's *Sexual Perversity in Chicago.*

3195 Oman, Ralph. "Source Licensing: The Latest Skirmish in an Old Battle." *ColJL&A.* 1986 Win; 11(2): 251-281. Notes. Lang.: Eng.

USA. 1897-1987. Historical studies. ■Historical development of customs and practices of licensing performing rights in TV and motion picture music, analysis of source licensing bills and proposed legislation.

Audience

3196 Richardson, Dallas; Headley, Robert K. "Reminiscences of Movie-Going in Charlotte, NC." *MarqJTHS.* 1986; 18(3): 7. Illus.: Photo. B&W. 1: 2 in. x 3.5 in. Lang.: Eng.

USA: Charlotte, NC. 1919-1986. Histories-sources. ■An oral history of movie-going in Charlotte, NC.

Basic theatrical documents

3197 Bjelkendahl, Göran. "*Lux in Tenebris*: A Scenario." *ComIBS.* 1985 Nov.; 15(1): 17-23.

1985. Historical studies. ■A film scenario for *Lux in Tenebris* along with an author's note chronicling how he secured the rights to Brecht's play.

Design/technology

3198 "Playback Prerogative." *ThCr.* 1986 Mar.; 20(3): 97-98. Illus.: Photo. 2: var. sizes. Lang.: Eng.

Technical studies. ■Production and sound applications of the Nagra IV Stereo Time Code Portable Recorder.

3199 Pirani, Adam. "*Santa Claus—The Movie.*" *ThCr.* 1986 Jan.; 20(1): 75-78. Illus.: Photo. 5: var. sizes.

Greenland. 1986. Technical studies. ■Designers and special effects supervisor collaborate to make Santa's sleigh fly.

3200 Hirano, Kyoko. "The Director: Kurosawa." *ThCr.* 1986 Feb.; 20(2): 88-93. Illus.: Photo. 7: var. sizes. Lang.: Eng.

Japan. 1986. Technical studies. ■Film director Akira Kurosawa discusses designing his film *Ran.*

3201 Haye, Bethany. "Pirates." *ThCr.* 1986 Aug/Sep.; 20(7): 77-81. Illus.: Photo. 5: var. sizes. Lang.: Eng.

Tunisia. 1986. Technical studies. ■Pierre Guffroy's Oscar award-winning design of an $8 million ship that can sail for Roman Polanski's film *Pirates.*

MEDIA: Film—Design/technology

3202   Harris, William. "Low Suds Success." *ThCr.* 1986 Aug/
Sep.; 20(7): 85-86.
UK-England: London. 1986. Technical studies. ■The making of the film
My Beautiful Laundrette by Hanif Kureishi.

3203   Pirani, Adam. "Absolute Beginners." *ThCr.* 1986 Mar.;
20(3): 83-87. Illus.: Photo. 6: var. sizes. Lang.: Eng.
UK-England: London. 1986. Technical studies. ■Challenges faced by
the designers of the movie musical *Absolute Beginners*.

3204   "A Trip to the Other Side." *LDim.* 1986 May-June; 10(3):
18, 52-57. Illus.: Photo. Print. Color. 2: var. sizes. Lang.:
Eng.
USA: Los Angeles, CA. USA: New York, NY. 1985-1986. Histories-
sources. ■Interview with lighting designer Andrew Lazlo on his work on
Poltergeist II.

3205   Comer, Brooke Sheffield. "From Stage to Screen." *ThCr.*
1986 Jan.; 20(1): 79-81. Illus.: Photo. 2: var. sizes.
USA: New York, NY. 1986. Technical studies. ■Problems faced by
sound designer Chris Newman in filming *A Chorus Line*.

3206   Conway, Lyle. "Disney & Dorothy in Oz." *PuJ.* 1985 Fall;
37(1): 19-22.
USA. Historical studies. ■The making of the Disney movie, *Return to
Oz*, directed by Walter Murch, focusing on its special effects and
creature design. Related to Puppetry.

3207   Eller, Claudia. "Second That Emotion." *ThCr.* 1986 May;
20(5): 69-72. Illus.: Photo. 6: var. sizes. Lang.: Eng.
USA. Technical studies. ■Cinematographer Stephen Burum's work on
Hal Ashby's film *Eight Million Ways to Die*.

3208   Gentry, Rick. "From Beyond." *ThCr.* 1986 Dec.; 20(10):
63-66. Illus.: Photo. 4: var. sizes. Lang.: Eng.
USA. 1986. Technical studies. ■Four special effects teams join efforts on
the film *From Beyond*, by the director of *Re-Animator*, Stuart Gordon.

3209   Gowin, Steve. "Black and White in Color." *ThCr.* 1986
Aug/Sep.; 20(7): 85-86.
USA. 1986. Technical studies. ■Using half-inch Betacam decks with
Ikegami green channel only to make black and white video for a tape-
to-film transfer of Rob Nilsson's *Heat and Sunlight*.

3210   Haye, Bethany. "Structuring the Image." *ThCr.* 1986 Apr.;
20(4): 77-80. Illus.: Photo. 4: var. sizes.
USA. 1986. Technical studies. ■Cinematographer Billy Williams discusses soft light, projection standards and temperamental directors.

3211   Knox, Barbara. "*Sid and Nancy.*" *LDim.* 1986 Nov.; 10(6):
46-49. Illus.: Photo. Print. Color. 4: var. sizes. Lang.: Eng.
USA: New York, NY, Los Angeles, CA. UK-England: London. 1976-
1986. Histories-sources. ■Interview with cinematographer Roger
Deakins about lighting for his work in the film *Sid and Nancy*.

3212   Latshaw, George; Latshaw, Pat. "*Little Shop of Horrors.*"
PuJ. 1986 Win; 38(2): 7-10. Illus.: Photo. B&W. 4: 7 1/2 in.
x 11 in., 5 in. x 5 in., 3 1/2 in. x 5 in. Lang.: Eng.
USA. Technical studies. ■Description of process involved in creating
Audrey II, the man-eating plant in the film version of *Little Shop of
Horrors*.

3213   Lebow, Jean. "Find That Tree." *ThCr.* 1986 Jan.; 20(1):
88-90. Illus.: Photo. 3: var. sizes.
USA. 1986. Technical studies. ■The role of the location scout in film
production.

3214   Melkin, Michael R. "Cosmekinetics and the Cave Bear."
PuJ. 1986 Fall; 38(1): 19-22. Illus.: Photo. Print. B&W. 5:
var. sizes. Lang.: Eng.
USA. 1985-1986. Technical studies. ■Detailed design information,
techniques, and materials used in the construction of mechanical bears
in *Clan of the Cave Bear*.

3215   Schwartz, David. "Saxophones in Space." *ThCr.* 1986 May;
20(5): 76-78. Illus.: Photo. 2: var. sizes. Lang.: Eng.
USA. Technical studies. ■Editing and post production on Shirley
Clarke's jazz documentary film about saxophonist Ornette Coleman
Ornette: Made in America.

Institutions

3216   Preiser, Howard. "Meeting of the Minds." *ThCr.* 1986
May; 20(5): 73-75. Illus.: Photo. 3: var. sizes. Lang.: Eng.
France: Avignon. 1986. Technical studies. ■The French-American Film
Workshop, designed to showcase the work of independents and
encourage cultural exchange.

Performance spaces

3217   Ruwedel, Mark. "Marquee Picture Portfolio: The Theatres
of Montreal." *MarqJTHS.* 1986; 18(4): 18-23. Illus.: Photo.
B&W. 11: var. sizes. Lang.: Eng.
Canada: Montreal, PQ. 1909-1982. Historical studies. ■Photographs of
the exteriors of eleven Montreal theatres. Some were built as legitimate
theatres, but all were used as film theatres.

3218   Costigan, Daniel M. "The Rahway: A Survivor in the
Shadow of the Mighty." *MarqJTHS.* 1986; 18(4): 24-30.
Notes. Illus.: Photo. B&W. 9: var. sizes. Lang.: Eng.
USA: Rahway, NJ. 1926-1986. Historical studies. ■The Rahway
Theatre was completed in 1928. Despite many management changes,
the theatre survived and is now the Union County Arts Center.

3219   Eppes, William D. "The STRAND, Shreveport, Louisi-
ana." *MarqJTHS.* 1986; 18(3): 13-15. Illus.: Photo. B&W.
3: var. sizes. Lang.: Eng.
USA: Shreveport, LA. 1925-1986. Historical studies. ■The Strand
theatre was built in 1925 as a joint venture of the Saenger and Ehrlich
theatre chains. It was later bought by Paramount Publix and is now an
arts center.

3220   Lewallen, Jim; Gomery, Douglas. "Chronicling the Caroli-
nas' Theaters." *MarqJTHS.* 1986; 18(3): 3-6, 8. Notes.
Append. Illus.: Photo. B&W. 6: var. sizes. Lang.: Eng.
USA. 1920-1986. Historical studies. ■History of film theatres in North
and South Carolina, followed by an annotated checklist of theatres.
Follow-up article in *MargJTHS* 18:4 (1986), 31-32.

3221   Mosser, Dorothy B. "The Capitol Theatre, Pottsville, PA."
MarqJTHS. 1986; 18(4): 16-17. Illus.: Photo. B&W. 3: var.
sizes. Lang.: Eng.
USA: Pottsville, PA. 1927-1982. Historical studies. ■The Capitol
Theatre opened in 1927 and was demolished in 1982. It was a typical
small city movie theatre.

3222   Robinson, Jack. "The Eastman Theatre: The House that
Kodaks Built." *MarqJTHS.* 1986; 18(1): 19-21. Notes.
Illus.: Photo. B&W. 2: var. sizes. Lang.: Eng.
USA: Rochester, NY. 1922-1986. Historical studies. ■The history of this
'Palladian Classic' motion picture theatre and concert hall built by
George Eastman in 1922 and restored in 1972.

Performance/production

3223   Dachs, Robert. *Willi Forst: Eine Biographie.* (Willi Forst: A
Biography.) Vienna: Kremayr und Scheriau; 1986. 192 pp.
Tables. Biblio. Filmography. Illus.: Handbill. Photo. Plan.
B&W. Grd.Plan. 165: var. sizes. Lang.: Ger.
Austria: Vienna. Germany: Berlin. 1903-1980. Biographies. ■Life and
films of actor/director Willi Forst, post-war theatrical conditions,
personal anecdotes.

3224   Deák, Attila. *Ruttkai Éva.* (Éva Ruttkai.) Budapest:
Múzsák; 1986. 103 pp. (Filmbarátok kiskönyvtára.)
Filmography. Illus.: Photo. B&W. Lang.: Hun.
Hungary. 1934-1976. Biographies. ■Critical appreciation of the film
career of Éva Ruttkai, outstanding actress of the Hungarian stage.

3225   del Ministro, Maurizio. "La cultura cinematografica e
teatrale di Ejzenštejn tra Oriente ed Occidente." (Eisenste-
in's Cinematographic and Theatrical Culture between East
and West.) 315-334 in Ottai, Antonella, ed. *Teatro Oriente/
Occidente.* Rome: Bulzoni; 1986. viii, 565 pp. (Biblioteca
Teatrale 47.) Illus.: Diagram. 1. Lang.: Ita.
Russia. 1898-1948. Critical studies. ■Eastern and Western elements in
Sergej Eisenstein's work.

3226   Csengery, Judit. *Greta Garbo.* Budapest: Zenemükiadó;
1986. 207 pp. Biblio. Filmography. Illus.: Photo. B&W.
Lang.: Hun.

CLASSED ENTRIES

MEDIA: Film—Performance/production

Sweden. USA: Hollywood, CA. 1905-1985. Biographies. ■Life and career of film star Greta Garbo.

3227 Rothwell, Kenneth S. "Representing *King Lear* on Screen: From Metatheatre to Metacinema." *ShS*. 1986; 39: 75-90. Notes. Filmography. Illus.: Photo. Print. B&W. 7: var. sizes. Lang.: Eng.

UK. USA. 1916-1983. Critical studies. ■Traces self-referential, metacinematic qualities in *King Lear* from Edwin Thahouser (1916) to Peter Brook (1953 and 1970), Grigori Kozintsev (1971), Jonathan Miller (1982) and Michael Elliot/Laurence Olivier (1983).

3228 Schickel, Richard. *James Cagney: A Celebration.* Boston: Little, Brown; 1986. 192 pp. Filmography. Illus.: Photo. Lang.: Eng.

USA. 1904-1986. Biographies. ■Includes critical evaluation of Cagney's career and discussion of his image with respect to film archetypes.

3229 Watson, Thomas J.; Chapman, Bill. *Judy: Portrait of An American Legend.* New York, NY: McGraw-Hill; 1986. 122 pp. Illus.: Photo. Color. B&W. Lang.: Eng.

USA. 1922-1969. Biographies. ■Career of singer/actress Judy Garland, with hundreds of photographs.

3230 Plachov, A. "Dokumental'nyj portret v inter'ere: k problem 'teatralizacii' v kino." (An Interior Documentary Portrait: The Problem of 'Theatricalization' in the Cinema.) *TeatrM*. 1986; 4: 135-141. Lang.: Rus.

USSR. 1980-1986. Critical studies. ■On the 'theatricalization' of film.

Plays/librettos/scripts

3231 Ottai, Antonella. "*Insel der Dämonen, Insel der Glücklichen*: campi, eventi, scenari nei mari del Sud." (*Island of Demons, Island of the Happy*: Fields, Events, Landscapes in the South Seas.) 539-552 in Ottai, Antonella, ed. *Teatro Oriente/Occidente.* Rome: Bulzoni; 1986. viii, 565 pp. (Biblioteca Teatrale 47.) Lang.: Ita.

Europe. USA. Indonesia. 1930. Critical studies. ■Conception of the South Sea islands in works of F.W. Murnau, Antonin Artaud and Walter Spies.

3232 Adler, Thomas P. "Pinter/Proust/Pinter." 128-137 in Gale, Steven H., ed. *Harold Pinter:Critical Approaches.* London/Toronto: Associated University Presses; 1986. 232 pp. Notes. Lang.: Eng.

France. UK-England. 1913-1978. Critical studies. ■Comparison of Harold Pinter and Marcel Proust, focusing on Pinter's filmscript *The Proust Screenplay.*

3233 Gleber, Anke. "Das Fräulein von Tellheim: Die ideologische Funktion der Frau in der nationalsozialistischen Lessing-Adaption." (The Lady of Tellheim: The Ideological Function of Women in National Socialism's Adaptation of Lessing.) *GQ*. 1986 Fall; 59(4): 547-568. Lang.: Ger.

Germany. 1940. Critical studies. ■Hans Schweikart's *Das Fräulein von Tellheim (The Lady of Tellheim)*, a cinematic adaptation of Gotthold Ephraim Lessing's *Minna von Barnhelm*, as an example of the ideological functionalization of women created by Nazi manipulation of literary history.

3234 Verdone, Mario. "Beckett dal teatro al cinema." (Beckett: From Theatre to Cinema.) *TeatrC*. 1986; 6(13): 21-23. Lang.: Ita.

Ireland. France. 1958-1986. Critical studies. ■Notes on film treatments of plays by Samuel Beckett.

3235 Kezich, Tullio. "Il pipistrello uno e due." (The Bat One and Two.) *Ariel.* 1986 Sep-Dec.; 1(3): 155-159. Lang.: Ita.

Italy. 1925-1928. Critical studies. ■Analysis of two versions of Luigi Pirandello's screenplay *Il pipistrello (The Bat)*, which was never produced.

3236 Marchi, Bruno de. "*Umberto D.*, 1952, lectures comparées: sujet, scenario, texte filmique." (*Umberto D.*, 1952, Comparative Reading: Subject, Screenplay, Film Text.) 215-248 in Heistein, József, ed. *Le texte dramatique. La lecture et la scène.* Wrocław: Wydawnictwo Uniwersytetu Wrocławskiego; 1986. 248 pp. (Acta Universitatis Wratislaviensis 895, Romanica Wratislaviensia 26.) Lang.: Fre.

Italy. 1952. Critical studies. ■Comparison of the screenplay and Victoria De Sica's finished film seen as a text.

3237 Verdone, Mario. "Luigi e Stefano Pirandello soggettisti e sceneggiatori di cinema." (Luigi and Stefano Pirandello, Script Writers and Scenarists.) *TeatrC*. 1985-1986; 6(11-12): 189-198. Notes. Tables. Biblio. Illus.: Dwg. B&W. 8: var. sizes. Lang.: Ita.

Italy. 1925-1933. Historical studies. ■Examines Luigi Pirandello's work as a scriptwriter and his collaboration with his son.

3238 Brater, Enoch. "*The French Lieutenant's Woman*: Screenplay and Adaptation." 139-152 in Gale, Steven H., ed. *Harold Pinter:Critical Approaches.* London/Toronto: Associated University Presses; 1986. 232 pp. Notes. Lang.: Eng.

UK-England. 1969-1981. Critical studies. ■Thematic analysis of Harold Pinter's screenplay of John Fowles' novel, *The French Lieutenant's Woman.*

3239 Hapgood, Robert. "*Chimes at Midnight* from Stage to Screen: The Art of Adaptation." *ShS*. 1986; 39: 39-52. Notes. Illus.: Sketches. Print. B&W. 5: 3 in. x 5 in., 2 in. x 2 in. Lang.: Eng.

UK-England. 1938-1965. Critical studies. ■Compares film versions of *Chimes at Midnight* by Orson Welles with two preceding stage adaptations on the same subject, Shakespeare's character, Falstaff.

3240 Tucker, Stephen. "Cinematic Proust Manifested by Pinter." *TA*. 1986; 41: 37-47. Notes. Lang.: Eng.

UK-England. 1972. Critical studies. ■Analysis of Harold Pinter's technique in adapting *A la Recherche du Temps Perdu (Remembrance of Things Past)* by Marcel Proust as a screenplay.

3241 "Orson Welles's *Othello*: A Study of Time in Shakespeare's Tragedy." *ShS*. 1986; 39: 53-65. Notes. Lang.: Eng.

USA. 1952. Critical studies. ■Using images of time and rhythm sound effects, Welles's film version of Shakespeare's *Othello* dramatizes Iago's control over Othello's perception of time.

3242 Eller, Claudia. "True Stories." *ThCr*. 1986 Nov.; 20(9): 67-71. Illus.: Photo. 5: var. sizes.

USA. 1986. Historical studies. ■How David Byrne worked on his first feature film, *True Stories*, beginning with drawings, doodles and snapshots to build a script.

3243 Pearlman, E. "*Macbeth* on Film." *ShS*. 1986; 39: 67-74. Notes. Lang.: Eng.

USA. Japan. 1948-1971. Critical studies. ■Analysis of the ways in which film versions of William Shakespeare's *Macbeth* by Orson Welles, Akira Kurosawa and Roman Polanski confront the play's monarchy.

Reference materials

3244 Prossnitz, Gisela; Fuhrich, Edda. *Die Reinhardt-Schauspieler machen Filmgeschichte: Eine Ausstellung der Max Reinhardt Forschungstätte Salzburg. Schloss Arenberg 28. Juli bis 31. August 1986.* (Reinhardt's Actors Make Film History: An Exhibition of the Max Reinhardt Forschungsstätte in Salzburg. Schloss Arenburg.) Salzburg: Max-Reinhardt-Forschungs und Gedenkstätte; 1986. 8 pp. Illus.: Photo. B&W. 35. Lang.: Ger.

Germany: Berlin. Austria: Vienna. 1913-1945. Historical studies. ■Exhibition's content and aims, Max Reinhardt's film projects, influence on other film producers, and use of stage actors as film actors. Includes actors' photos from various films.

3245 Holderness, Graham; McCullough, Christopher. "Shakespeare on the Screen: A Selective Filmography." *ShS*. 1986; 39: 13-37 . Notes. Lang.: Eng.

UK-England. USA. 1899-1984.

Relation to other fields

3246 Bickford, Laura. "Because It's There." *ThCr*. 1986 Nov.; 20(9): 72-74. Illus.: Photo. 2: 3 in. x 4 in.

Tibet. 1986. Historical studies. ■How mountain climber/cinematographer David Breashears climbed Mt. Everest to prove on film that British climbers George Mallory and Andrew Irving actually made it to the top in 1924.

Theory/criticism

3247 Mueller, Roswitha. "Brecht and Communications." *ComIBS*. 1986 Nov.; 16(1): 18-23.
Historical studies. ■Brecht's experience with the film industry and his assertion that producing artists must be independent of financial pressures and be in constant collaboration with their audience.

Mixed media

Basic theatrical documents

3248 Skipitares, Theodora. "*The Age of Invention.*" *ThM*. 1985 Win; 17(1): 5-15. Illus.: Photo. B&W. 7: var. sizes. Lang.: Eng.
USA: New York, NY. 1985. ■Text of Skipitares' play, first produced at Theatre for the New City.

Design/technology

3249 Birringer, Johannes. "Overexposure: *Les Immatériaux.*" *PerAJ*. 1986; 10(2): 6-11. Illus.: Dwg. B&W. 1: 3 in. x 3 in. Lang.: Eng.
France: Paris. 1986. Critical studies. ■Report on *Les Immatériaux* at the Pompidou Center. Exhibit is a self-enclosed structure in which a spectator journeys through a conglomeration of sound, projections, spoken theatre text, mirrors, robots, and interactive computer components.

Performance/production

3250 McIntosh, Diana. "Communicating Through Music." *MimeJ*. 1986: 72-81. Illus.: Photo. B&W. 5. Lang.: Eng.
Canada: Winnipeg, MB. 1979-1986. Histories-sources. ■Diana McIntosh describes her music/lecture/mixed media presentations on the state of contemporary music.

3251 Harris, William. "An Interview with Theodora Skipitares." *ThM*. 1985 Win; 17(1): 16-18. Illus.: Photo. B&W. 1. Lang.: Eng.
USA. 1974-1985. Histories-sources. ■An interview with Theodora Skipitares, a mixed-media artist who works with puppets. She discusses the production of the trilogy *The Age of Invention* and her use of historical material.

Video forms

Basic theatrical documents

3252 Findley, Timothy. "*The Paper People.*" *CDr*. 1983; 9(1): 62-164. Lang.: Eng.
Canada. 1967. Histories-sources. ■Text of television drama *The Paper People*.

Design/technology

3253 Bentham, Frederick. "Television Lighting—The Live Years." *Sin*. 1986; 20(2): 11-13. Illus.: Photo. B&W. 3. Lang.: Eng.
UK-England. 1930-1960. Historical studies. ■Examines the importance of lighting control in early live TV productions.

3254 Harris, Richard. "Light Rig." *Tabs*. 1986; 43(1): 16-17. Illus.: Dwg. B&W. 10. Lang.: Eng.
UK-England. 1980-1986. Technical studies. ■Overview of a completely new suspension lighting system for the drama area of a small video studio.

3255 Laws, Jim. "Lighting up *Lost Empires.*" *Sin*. 1986; 20(2): 28-29. Illus.: Photo. B&W. 3. Lang.: Eng.
UK-England. 1986. Historical studies. ■Lighting requirements for television production of J.B. Priestley's *Lost Empires* described by designer.

3256 Harris, Richard. "Setting a Television Lighting Trend." *Tabs*. 1986; 43(1): 28-29. Illus.: Photo. Color. 4. Lang.: Eng.
UK-Scotland: Glasgow. 1980-1986. Technical studies. ■Examination of the latest Strand TV lighting console in Studio A at BBC Scotland.

3257 Carlson, Verne; Carlson, Sylvia. "A Lesson in Using the Fixture." *LDim*. 1986 Jan-Feb.; 10(1): 55-58, 60, 62, 64, 77-78, 80. Illus.: Photo. Print. B&W. 6: 4 in. x 5 in. Lang.: Eng.

USA. 1986. Technical studies. ■Excerpt from *Professional Lighting Handbook* discusses various video and film lighting techniques.

3258 Eller, Claudia. "Amazing Stories." *ThCr*. 1986 Oct.; 20(8): 85-86. Illus.: Photo. 2: var. sizes. Lang.: Eng.
USA. 1986. Technical studies. ■Rick Carter's production design for Stephen Spielberg's television series *Amazing Stories*.

3259 Gardlin, Martin. "Lighting Up *The Cosby Show.*" *LDim*. 1986 Nov.; 10(6): 24, 26-27. Illus.: Photo. Print. B&W. 1: 3 in. x 4 in. Lang.: Eng.
USA: New York, NY. 1986. Histories-sources. ■Overview of the new lighting technology in the NBC television studio used for *The Cosby Show*.

3260 Gowin, Steve. "Technique: Walking on Water." *ThCr*. 1986 Feb.; 20(2): 86-87. Illus.: Photo. 2: 3 in. x 4.5 in. Lang.: Eng.
USA. 1986. Technical studies. ■Discussion of ultimatte, a television matting technique used at Shelley Duvall's Platypus Productions.

3261 Koyama, Christine. "Folklore and Faeries." *ThCr*. 1986 Feb.; 20(2): 81-85. Illus.: Photo. Sketches. 3: var. sizes. Lang.: Eng.
USA. 1986. Technical studies. ■Production designer Michael Erler and art director Jane Osmann's design concepts for the television series *Tall Tales*.

3262 Malkin, Michael R. "Muppet Manipulations." *ThCr*. 1986 Aug/Sep.; 20(7): 82-84. Illus.: Photo. 3: var. sizes. Lang.: Eng.
USA. 1986. Technical studies. ■Faz Fazakas, director of electronics and mechanical design for the Muppets, develops puppet simulacra to be used as offscreen controllers when characters must make elaborate movements.

3263 Williams, Mike. "Tales from the Oscars." *LDim*. 1986 Jul-Aug.; 10(4): 24-25, 45-50. Illus.: Photo. Print. Color. 2: var. sizes. Lang.: Eng.
USA: Los Angeles, CA. 1983-1986. Histories-sources. ■Interview with lighting designer Bob Dickinson on his work on the 1986 Oscar award ceremony.

3264 Williams, Mike. "On the *Moonlighting* Set." *LDim*. 1986 Sep/Oct.; 10(5): 16,18,62-65. Illus.: Photo. Print. B&W. 2: var. sizes. Lang.: Eng.
USA: Los Angeles, CA. 1985-1986. Histories-sources. ■Interview with cameraman Gerald Perry Finnerman about lighting for the television show *Moonlighting* focusing on color filters and equipment, different types of lighting for actors, stylization of light and problems on location.

3265 Williams, Mike. "On the Road with Live Video." *LDim*. 1986 Sep/Oct.; 10(5): 80-82. Illus.: Photo. Print. Color. 1: 4 in. x 5 in. Lang.: Eng.
USA. 1982-1986. Histories-sources. ■Interview with lighting designer Kieran Healy on lighting techniques for lighting live concert videos.

3266 Abramjan, M. "Cudožnik i televizionnyj teat'r." (The Artist and Television Theatre.) 130-144 in *Televidenie včera, segodnja, zavtra: Sb. Vyp. 6*. Moscow: Iskusstvo; 1986. Lang.: Rus.
USSR. 1980-1986. Critical studies. ■The art of set design for television.

Institutions

3267 Miller, Mary Jane. "Canadian Television Drama 1952-1970: Canada's National Theatre." *THC*. 1984 Spr; 5(1): 51-71. Notes. Illus.: Photo. B&W. 3. Lang.: Eng.
Canada. 1952-1970. Historical studies. ■Function of television drama in Canada as a training ground for actors, playwrights and directors.

Performance/production

3268 Burnett, Carol. *One More Time*. New York: Random House; 1986. 320 pp. Lang.: Eng.
1960's-1986. Biographies. ■An autobiography focusing on the entertainer's childhood and ending with Burnett finding fame and fortune on the Garry Moore TV show.

3269 Malkin, Michael R. "Behind the Fraggle's Rock." *PuJ*. 1986 Spr; 37(3): 14-17. Illus.: Photo. B&W. 6: var. sizes. Lang.: Eng.

MEDIA: Video forms—Performance/production

Canada: Toronto, ON. 1984. Historical studies. ■Behind-the-scenes visit to the production meetings, conferences, location shoots, studios and workshops of *Fraggle Rock*. Related to Puppetry: Muppets.

3270 Párkány, László, ed. *Stúdió 81-84: Interjúk, vitairatok, portrék.* (Studio 1981-1984: Interviews, Pamphlets, Portraits.) Budapest: RTV-Minerva; 1986. 383 pp. Lang.: Hun.
Hungary. 1981-1984. Histories-sources. ■Selections from the weekly cultural show of Hungarian Television, including theatrical events and interviews with actors.

3271 Fridell, Squire. *Acting in Television Commercials For Fun and Profit.* New York: Harmony; 1986. vii, 211 pp. Pref. Append. Illus.: Photo. Sketches. B&W. 12: var. sizes. [Revised First Edition with New Information.] Lang.: Eng.
USA. 1977-1986. Technical studies. ■Focuses on all aspects of working in television commercials, including updates on photographs, preparation and waiting, auditions, call-back hints and the job.

3272 Gray, Herman. "Television and the New Black Man: Black Male Images in Prime-Time Situation Comedy." *MC&S.* 1986; 8(2): 223-242. Lang.: Eng.
USA. 1980. Critical studies. ■Representation of Black assimilation: television's idealization of racial harmony.

3273 Rose, Brian G. *Television and the Performing Arts.* Westport, CT: Greenwood P; 1986. xi, 270 pp. Pref. Notes. Index. [A Handbook and Reference Guide to American Cultural Programming.] Lang.: Eng.
USA. 1930-1985. Critical studies. ■Dance, music, opera and theatre on television: aesthetic, economic, marketing and historical considerations that go into producing and broadcasting performing arts for the wide audience.

3274 Rothaus, James R. *The Cosby Show.* Mankato, MN: Creative Education; 1986. 31 pp. Illus.: Photo. Print. B&W. 11: var. sizes. Lang.: Eng.
USA. 1986. Biographies. ■Profile of actor Bill Cosby, including 'The Cosby Show', his awards and his position on the products he endorses.

3275 Sander, Nancy; Wells, Linda. "Hickory Hideout." *PuJ.* 1986 Sum; 37(4): 21. Illus.: Photo. B&W. 1: 3 in. x 5 in. Lang.: Eng.
USA: Cleveland, OH. 1982-1986. Histories-sources. ■Discusses NBC pre-school television program *Hickory Hideout*, including the influence of the Joy Puppeteers who created the characters on the show. Related to Puppetry.

3276 Stockman, Todd. "Kermit the Person: Kermit Love." *PuJ.* 1986 Spr; 37(3): 5-9. Illus.: Photo. Print. B&W. 4: 9 1/2 in. x 7 in., 5 in. x 6 in. Lang.: Eng.
USA: New York, NY. 1935-1985. Biographical studies. ■Life and work of Kermit Love, creator of Big Bird for *Sesame Street* and other puppets used in commercials. Related to Puppetry: Muppets.

3277 Belova, Je. "Osvaivaja novyj žanr." (Mastering a New Genre.) *SovMuzyka.* 1986; 4: 69-74. Lang.: Rus.
USSR: Leningrad. 1980-1986. Historical studies. ■Ballet for television produced by A. Belinskij. Related to Dance: Ballet.

Plays/librettos/scripts

3278 Howe, Jan. "Interview: Peter Yeldham Talks to Jan Howe." *ADS.* 1985 Apr.; 3: 88-104. Illus.: Photo. B&W. 1: 4 in. x 6 in. Lang.: Eng.
Australia: Sydney, N.S.W. 1985. Histories-sources. ■Interview with Peter Yeldham on his adaptations of novels to the television mini-series format.

3279 Feldman, Seth. "The Electronic Fable: Aspects of the Docudrama in Canada." *CDr.* 1983; 9(1): 39-48. Notes. Lang.: Eng.
Canada. 1970-1983. Critical studies. ■Cultural models and types in docudrama, e.g. civilization/wilderness, students/teacher, etc..

3280 Miller, Mary Jane. "An Analysis of *The Paper People.*" *CDr.* 1985; 9(1): 49-59. Notes. Lang.: Eng.
Canada. 1967. Critical studies. ■Analysis of the critical debate over Timothy Findley's television drama *The Paper People*, examining its self-conscious view of art and its use of a documentary-within-a-play structure.

3281 Nelson, Joyce. "TV Formulas: Notes for a Zeitgeist of Prime Time." *CDr.* 1983; 9(1): 30-38. Notes. Lang.: Eng.
Canada. USA. 1965-1983. Critical studies. ■Analysis of the ideology of commercial television, specifically crime dramas and situation comedies, focusing on the disjunction between public and private worlds. Includes treatment of technical factors.

3282 Fehsenfeld, Martha. "'Everything Out but the Faces': Beckett's Reshaping of *What Where* for Television." *MD.* 1986 June ; 29(2): 229-240. Notes. Lang.: Eng.
France. 1983-1985. Critical studies. ■Comparison of the television version of *What Where* by Samuel Beckett with the stage version including accounts of the adaptation process by the participants.

3283 Taylor, Neil. "Two Types of Television Shakespeare." *ShS.* 1986; 39: 103-111. Notes. Lang.: Eng.
UK-England: London. 1978-1985. Critical studies. ■Compares Jane Howell's theatrical techniques with Elijah Moshinsky's cinematic methods in their productions for the BBC Shakespeare series.

3284 Willems, Michele. "Verbal-Visual, Verbal-Pictorial or Textual-Televisual? Reflections on the BBC Shakespeare Series." *ShS.* 1986; 39: 91-102. Notes. Lang.: Eng.
UK-England: London. 1978-1985. Critical studies. ■Retrospective on BBC Shakespeare series finds stylized productions more successful than those in a naturalistic or pictorial style.

3285 Asam, Richard Henry. *A Genre Analysis of Television Docudrama.* Athens, GA: Univ of Georgia; 1986. 176 pp. Pref. Notes. Biblio. [Ph.D. dissertation, Univ. Microfilms order No. DA8628862.] Lang.: Eng.
USA. 1965-1986. Historical studies. ■Defines docudramas as television melodramas about familiar, recent events restructured to provide the viewer with an emotionally satisfying experience.

Relation to other fields

3286 Gordon, Steve. "Theatre on TV: There is Life After CBS Cable." *TT.* 1983 June; 2(7): 12-13. Illus.: Photo. B&W. 1. Lang.: Eng.
USA. 1983. Historical studies. ■Use of non-commercial cable television stations to promote activities of non-profit theatre. Public and leased access, municipal cable and the future of cable are discussed. Includes list of community access resources and publications.

Training

3287 Petrilli, Sally. "Training Creative Drama Teachers with Television." *YTJ.* 1986 Sum; 1(1): 12-14. Illus.: Photo. B&W. 1: 4 in. x 6 in. Lang.: Eng.
USA: University Park, IL. 1986. Critical studies. ■Instructional television programming for the advancement of arts in education.

———

Other entries with significant content related to Media: 175, 278, 299, 339, 359, 378, 387, 497, 574, 641, 664, 675, 701, 820, 835, 841, 888, 898, 912, 977, 1021, 1075, 1082, 1177, 1192, 1225, 1425, 1507, 1653, 1719, 1829, 1871, 1933, 2106, 2141, 2149, 2284, 2295, 2408, 2416, 2448, 2565, 2588, 2742, 2781, 2865, 2921, 3179, 3180, 3321, 3327, 3350, 3441, 3756, 3758, 3828, 3953, 4014.

MIME

General

Institutions

3288 Mertl, Monika. "Ewiges Suchen." (Eternally Searching.) *Buhne.* 1986 Oct.; 29(10): 37. Illus.: Photo. Print. B&W. Lang.: Ger.
Austria: Vienna. 1986-1987. Histories-sources. ■Theater Brett's programming for the 1986/87 season, and ideas for solving their financial problems.

3289 Lecoq, Jacques. "A propos du théâtre et du mouvement." (On Theatre and Movement.) 91-98 in Coca, Jordi, ed.; Conesa, Laura, comp. *Congrés Internacional de Teatre a*

MIME: General—Institutions

Catalunya 1985. Actes. Volum II. Seccions 1, 2 i 3. Barcelona: Institut del Teatre; 1986. 340 pp. Lang.: Fre.
France: Paris. 1962-1985. Histories-sources. ■Gesture and image in theatrical representation: the author's experiences at the École de Mime et Théâtre with clowning, melodrama and *commedia dell'arte*.

Performance/production

3290 Gapihan, Jean-Pierre, photo. "Introduction to Gestural Theatre: A Photographic Essay." *MimeJ.* 1983: 59-159. Illus.: Photo. 169: var. sizes.
1986. Historical studies. ■A photographic essay of 42 soloists and groups performing mime or gestural theatre.

3291 Gélinas, Aline. "The Traces of Becoming: A Look at Montreal's Omnibus." *MimeJ.* 1986: 82-91. Illus.: Photo. B&W. 7. Lang.: Eng.
Canada: Montreal, PQ. 1970-1988. Historical studies. ■Founding and continuance of the Omnibus mime troupe, their major works and the philosophy of their artistic director, Jean Asselin.

3292 Leabhart, Thomas. "Cirque du Soleil." *MimeJ.* 1986: 1-7. Illus.: Photo. B&W. 7. Lang.: Eng.
Canada: Montreal, PQ. 1984-1986. Historical studies. ■Influences upon post-modern Cirque du Soleil including Jacques Copeau and Etienne Decroux. Excerpts from interviews with two company members about how they came to the company. Shows fusion of elements characteristic of post-modernistic performance.

3293 Leabhart, Thomas; Doyle, Sandra. "The Winnipeg International Mime Festival." *MimeJ.* 1986: 56-71. Illus.: Photo. B&W. 16. Lang.: Eng.
Canada: Winnipeg, MB. 1983-1986. Historical studies. ■The founding of the Winnipeg International Mime Festival in 1983 by Giuseppe Condello, the events that were part of the festival and the performers and troupes who attended. Similar information is given more briefly for the festivals in 1985 and 1986.

3294 Savannah, Walling; Hunter, Terry; Weiss, Peter Eliot; Boyko, Debbie; Partlett, Mark. "Special Delivery Moving Theatre." *MimeJ.* 1986: 8-55. Illus.: Photo. DK. B&W. 27. Lang.: Eng.
Canada: Vancouver, BC. 1976-1986. Historical studies. ■Special Delivery company members contribute sections about the artistic purpose, historical context, training and character development methods of the company. Special focus on the work *Samarambi: Pounding of the Heart.*

3295 Mandel, Dorothy. *Uncommon Eloquence. A Biography of Angna Enters.* Denver, CO: Arden; 1986. Pref. Notes. Biblio. Index. Illus.: Photo. B&W. 43: var. sizes. Lang.: Eng.
Europe. USA. 1907-1986. Biographies. ■Angna Enters, mime artist, painter, writer, musician and designer: her tours, books and art shows.

3296 Ånnerud, Annika. "Der är ju roligt." (Why, It's Fun.) *Teaterf.* 1986; 19(2-3): 3-4. Illus.: Photo. Lang.: Swe.
Sweden: Stockholm. 1984-1986. Historical studies. ■Mimensemblan has staged *Outsidern*, a dramatization of Hesse's *Steppenwolf* directed by Per Eric Asplund, together with unpaid amateurs, an experiment that turned out well.

3297 Bührer, Michel. *Mummenschanz.* New York, NY: Rizzoli; 1986. 128 pp. Lang.: Eng.
Switzerland: Zurich. USA. 1984. Historical studies. ■A profile of the three performers trained in classical mime known collectively as Mummenschanz, focusing on their biographies, the history of their collaboration and the creation of a new program for a US tour.

3298 Barnes, Clive; Beaufort, John; Gold, Sylviane; Kisselgoff, Anna; Mazo, Joseph H.; Nelson, Don; Storey, Richard David; Wallach, Allan. "Mummenschanz 'The New Show'." *NYTCR.* 1986 Sep 8; 47(11): 233-236. Lang.: Eng.
USA: New York, NY. 1986. Reviews of performances. ■Collection of newspaper reviews of *Mummenschanz 'The New Show'*, a mime trio with Andres Bossard, Floriana Frassetto and Bernie Schurch at the Joyce Theatre.

3299 Toomey, Susie Kelly. *Mime Ministry.* Colorado Springs, CO: Meriwether; 1986. 167 pp. Illus.: Dwg. Photo. B&W. 182: var. sizes. Lang.: Eng.

USA. 1986. Instructional materials. ■Guide for organizing, programming and training a troupe of Christian mimes: technique, interpretation, makeup, costume, six skits, list of resources.

Theory/criticism

3300 "Mimes, Clowns and the Twentieth Century." *MimeJ.* 1983: 9-58. Illus.: Photo. 41: var. sizes.
Historical studies. ■Mime theatre, its current position and projection of where it is headed.

3301 Vogels, Fritz. "Three Statements." *MimeJ.* 1983: 160-179.
Europe. 1975-1986. Critical studies. ■Fritz Vogels of Grifteater discusses the aesthetics of movement theatre.

Pantomime

Design/technology

3302 Bryant, Joy. "How I Lit Part of the Show." *Tabs.* 1986; 43(1): 12-13. Illus.: Photo. B&W. 2. Lang.: Eng.
UK-England: Brighton. 1980-1986. Histories-sources. ■Amateur lighting designer describes her first job.

3303 March, David. "Sing a Song of Sixpence." *Tabs.* 1986; 43(1): 11. Illus.: Diagram. Photo. B&W. 2. Lang.: Eng.
UK-England. 1980-1986. Histories-sources. ■Outlines the lighting of an amateur pantomime.

3304 Rump, Mike. "Ali-Din and the Dirty Dixie." *Tabs.* 1986; 43(1): 12-13. Illus.: Dwg. Photo. B&W. 2. Lang.: Eng.
UK-England: Brighton. 1980-1986. Histories-sources. ■Amateur technician outlines his experience of lighting a pantomime in a hall with a ceiling 8 feet high.

3305 "Mummenschanz in New York." *LDim.* 1986 Sep/Oct.; 10(5): 24,26. Illus.: Photo. Print. B&W. 2: var. sizes. Lang.: Eng.
USA: New York, NY. 1986. Histories-sources. ■Interview with Beverly Emmons, lighting designer for Mummenschanz's USA tour.

Performance/production

3306 Silber, Glenn, dir.; Vianello, Claudia, dir. *Troupers.* New York, NY: Icarus Films; 1986. Lang.: Eng.
USA: San Francisco, CA. 1960-1986. ■Videocassette of performances and interviews of the San Francisco Mime Troupe, demonstrating the troupe's continuing commitment to political and social issues.

3307 Tichonova, N. "Teatr klouna Polunina." (Polonin's Theatre of Clowns.) *KZ.* 1986 Apr.; 30(4): 25. Lang.: Rus.
USSR: Leningrad. 1980-1986. Historical studies. ■Licedej Studio, directed by Viačeslav Polunin.

Other entries with significant content related to Mime: 226, 1282, 1664, 1698, 3990.

MIXED ENTERTAINMENT
General

Administration

3308 Blumenthal, Eileen. "Vancouver's First Asia Pacific Festival." *ATJ.* 1986 Fall; 3(2): 270-274. Lang.: Eng.
Canada: Vancouver, BC. 1985. Historical studies. ■Account of benefits and problems encountered. Festival included representatives from all over Asia as well as the Northwest Kwakuitl Indians.

3309 MacLean, Sally-Beth. "King Games and Robin Hood: Play and Profit at Kingston upon Thames." *RORD.* 1986; 29: 85-94. Notes. Illus.: Maps. Lang.: Eng.
England: Kingston. 1504-1538. Historical studies. ■Survey of records relating to performances of Robin Hood and King Games: chart of receipts and expenses for the Kingston shows.

Design/technology

3310 Liu, Nientzu. "Nan ang hsi hsiang." (Nanyang's Theatrical Engraving.) *XYanj.* 1986 Dec.; 21: 193-204. Notes. Illus.:

MIXED ENTERTAINMENT: General—Design/technology

Photo. B&W. 10: 10 cm. x 3 cm., 10 cm. x 5.5 cm. Lang.: Chi.
China: Nanyang. 202 B.C.-220 A.D. Histories-sources. ▪Discussion of the characteristics, types and significance of costumes used through the Han dynasty, drawn from the engravings found at Nanyang.

3311 Zorzi, Elvira Garbero. "La festa cerimoniale del Rinascimento. L'ingresso trionfale e il banchetto d'onore." (The Ceremonial Feast of the Renaissance. The Triumphal Entry and the Banquet of Honor.) 49-62 in Salvat, Ricard, ed. *El Teatre durant l'Edat Mitjana i el Renaixement.* Barcelona: Publicacions i Edicions de la Universitat de Barcelona; 1986. xxviii, 322 pp. (El Pla de les Comèdies 2.) Notes. [Presented at First International Symposium on Medieval and Renaissance Theatre, Sitges, 1983.] Lang.: Ita.
Italy. 1400-1600. Historical studies. ▪Description of civic ceremonies in Renaissance Italy, with special attention to scenography and machinery.

3312 "Hands Across the Water." *LDim.* 1986 Jan-Feb.; 10(1): 28-34, 36-38, 40. Notes. Illus.: Dwg. Print. Color. B&W. 12: var. sizes. Lang.: Eng.
Japan: Tokyo. 1985. Technical studies. ▪Technical aspects relating to Toyota's showing of its new automobile designs. Descriptions of rigging, lighting design, scheduling problems of lighting the cars.

3313 Bravo i Pijoan, Isidre; Graells, Guillem-Jordi. *Quadern introductori al Teatrí de l'escenografia de Francesc Soler i Rovirosa (any 1878) per a l'acte tercer, quadre divuitè de La almoneda del diablo de Rafael M. Liern.* (Introductory Pamphlet to Model of the Stage Design of Francesc Soler i Rovirosa for The Devil's Auction III.xviii by Rafael M. Liern (1878).) Barcelona: Institut del Teatre; 1986. 16 pp. (Col.lecció de facsímils del fons documental 4.) Illus.: Pntg. Plan. Dwg. Photo. Print. Color. B&W. Grd.Plan. Fr.Elev. 52: var. sizes. Lang.: Cat.
Spain-Catalonia: Barcelona, Valencia, Madrid. 1832-1900. Historical studies. ▪Introduction to the facsimile edition of Soler's drawings gives information on comedies of magic, the designer, the author, the play and the design. Includes mounting instructions.

3314 Soler i Rovirosa, Francesc; Bravo i Pijoan, Isidre, intro.; Graells, Guillem-Jordi, intro. *Teatrí de l'escenografia de Francesc Soler i Rovirosa (any 1878) per a l'acte tercer, quadre divuitè de La almoneda del diablo de Rafael M. Liern.* (Model of the Stage Design of Francesc Soler i Rovirosa for The Devil's Auction III.xviii by Rafael M. Liern (1878).) Barcelona: Institut del Teatre; 1986. 4 pp. (Col.lecció de facsímils del fons documental 4.) Illus.: Dwg. Print. Color. 4: 48 cm. x 69 cm. Lang.: Cat.
Spain-Catalonia: Barcelona. 1878. Histories-sources. ▪Facsimile edition of Soler's stage design.

3315 "Baltimore's Amazement Park." *LDim.* 1986 Jan-Feb.; 10(1): 42-51, 74. Notes. Illus.: Diagram. Photo. Print. B&W. 10: var. sizes. Lang.: Eng.
USA: Baltimore, MD. 1971-1986. Technical studies. ▪Describes Baltimore's new theme park based on life and times of Phineas Flagg, the lighting of various exhibitions and shows, including film projections and types of equipment used.

3316 Cole, Holly. "Costume Design and the New Vaudevillians." *TD&T.* 1986 Win; 22(4): 4-11. Illus.: Photo. B&W. 10: var. sizes. Lang.: Eng.
USA: New York, NY. 1984. Historical studies. ▪Survey and analysis of costume trends and concepts of over 200 performers seen at the New York International Clown Festival.

3317 Cooper, Jerry. "The Light of Liberty." *LDim.* 1986 July/Aug.; 10(4): 21-23, 40-43. Illus.: Photo. Print. Color. B&W. 4: var. sizes. Lang.: Eng.
USA: New York, NY. 1986. Historical studies. ▪Howard Brandston's approach to lighting the Statue of Liberty.

3318 Sisk, Douglass, F. "The Liberty Weekend Fête." *LDim.* 1986 Sep/Oct.; 10(5): 72, 74. Illus.: Photo. Print. B&W. 1: 2 in. x 5 in. Lang.: Eng.
USA: New York, NY. 1986. Technical studies. ▪Details of the lighting arrangements for the four-day Statue of Liberty centennial celebration

discussing the many sites involved, types of equipment used, amounts of cable necessary and number of people involved.

3319 Williams, Mike. "Birthday Bash for an American Classic." *LDim.* 1986 Sep/Oct.; 10(5): 42-47, 60-61. Illus.: Diagram. Photo. Print. B&W. Color. 5: var. sizes. Lang.: Eng.
USA: Atlanta, GA. 1986. Histories-sources. ▪Interview with lighting designer John Ingram about his lighting for the Coca-Cola centennial, including types of equipment used and the problems of using smoke-air currents.

3320 Williams, Mike. "Rock 'n' Roll History." *LDim.* 1986 Nov.; 10(6): 50-52. Illus.: Photo. Print. Color. 2: var. sizes. Lang.: Eng.
USA. 1968-1986. Histories-sources. ▪Interview with manager Tony Smith and lighting designer Alan Owen of the rock band Genesis focusing on the lighting technology used on their latest tour.

Institutions

3321 Tauber, Reinhold. "Zukunftsorientierte Kunst mit Technik." (Future Oriented Art with Technology.) *Parnass.* 1986 May-June; 6(3): 50-56. Illus.: Photo. Print. Color. B&W. Lang.: Ger.
Austria: Linz. 1979-1986. Historical studies. ▪Development of Ars Electronica at Linz since its beginning in 1979, with notes on productions in 1986. Related to Media: Video forms.

3322 Davis, Jim. "The Royal Dramatic College Fetes." *TN.* 1986; 40(2): 61-70. Notes. Print. B&W. 1: 8 in. x 6 in. Lang.: Eng.
England: London. 1858-1877. Historical studies. ▪A popular charity fair and theatre festival established to raise funds for retired theatre professionals.

3323 Frenkiel, Yechiel. "Teatron Ufeyiut Omanutit Aheret Beghetto Lodz 1940-1944." (Theatre and Other Artistic Activities in Łódź Ghetto 1940-1944.) *Bamah.* 1986; 21(103): 12-42. Notes. Illus.: Photo. Print. B&W. 12. Lang.: Heb.
Poland: Łódź. 1940-1944. Historical studies. ▪Children's theatre, puppet theatre, cabaret and avant-garde theatre at public kitchens and cultural institutions. Continues in *Bamah* 21:104 (1986), 38-60.

3324 Widen, Larry. "Milwaukee's Dime Museum Era." *MarqJTHS.* 1986; 18(4): 3-8. Biblio. Notes. Illus.: Photo. Handbill. B&W. 4: var. sizes. [Winner of Second Prize in the 1986 Jeffrey Weiss Contest.] Lang.: Eng.
USA: Milwaukee, WI. 1882-1916. Historical studies. ▪The author of the article refers to the Dime Museum as 'a curious amalgam of vaudeville, freak show, and science'. Several Milwaukee Dime Museums are described.

Performance spaces

3325 Mamone, Sara. "Slittamenti progressivi della festa (da Firenze a Lione per le nozze di Maria di Medici con Enrico IV di Francia) Anno 1600." (Progression of the Wedding Feast of Maria dei Medici and Henri IV of France, Florence to Lyon, 1600.) 71-84 in Salvat, Ricard, ed. *El Teatre durant l'Edat Mitjana i el Renaixement.* Barcelona: Publicacions i Edicions de la Universitat de Barcelona; 1986. xxviii, 322 pp. (El Pla de les Comèdies 2.) Notes. [Presented at First International Symposium on Medieval and Renaissance Theatre, Sitges, 1983.] Lang.: Ita.
Italy: Florence. France: Lyon. 1568-1600. Historical studies. ▪Description of the various ceremonies and public celebrations in honor of the bride on her journey to the French court.

3326 Loor, Hillar. "Det räcker nu!" (Now, It's Enough!) *ProScen.* 1986; 10(1): 42-45. Illus.: Photo. Lang.: Swe.
Sweden: Stockholm. 1985. Technical studies. ▪The problems of raising and furnishing a tent for theatrical performances.

Performance/production

3327 Harris, Max. "Mo." *Meanjin.* 1986; 45(2): 250-253. Lang.: Eng.

MIXED ENTERTAINMENT: General—Performance/production

Australia. 1892-1954. Critical studies. ■Art and personality of vaude-ville artist Roy Rene, who created the comic persona 'Mo' and performed in variety theatres, films and on radio. Related to Media.

3328 Cashman, Cheryl. "Canada's Clowns." *CTR*. 1986 Sum; 13(47): 63-72. Illus.: Photo. Print. B&W. 9: var. sizes. Lang.: Eng.

Canada: Toronto, ON, Vancouver, BC. 1967-1986. Critical studies. ■The development of Canadian clown performers beginning with Richard Pochinko in the late 1960s, has resulted in a distinctive style of Canadian clowning.

3329 Forzley, Richard. "Vancouver: a Stage for the World." *PAC*. July 1986; 23(1): 9-13. Illus.: Photo. B&W. 5: var. sizes. Lang.: Eng.

Canada: Vancouver, BC. 1986. Reviews of performances. ■A preview of the main cultural events and performances at the Expo '86 World Festival.

3330 Grace-Warrick, Christa. "Vancouver: Doing It in the Road." *CTR*. 1986 Win; 13(49): 122-130. Illus.: Photo. Print. B&W. 4: 3 in. x 5 in., 4 in. x 5 in., 4 in. x 4 in. Lang.: Eng.

Canada: Vancouver, BC. 1986. Historical studies. ■Street theatre as a vital component in the success of Expo 86 in Vancouver.

3331 "*The Tournament of Tottenham*: An Alliterative Poem and an Exeter Performance." *REEDN*. 1986; 11(2): 1-3. Notes. Lang.: Eng.

England: Exeter. 1432. Historical studies. ■How a mock tournament of the type described in a 15th-century poem seems to have been performed in Exeter in 1432, and of the links between the name of the event and the name of the poem.

3332 Heaney, Michael. "Must Every Fiddler Play a Fiddle?" *REEDN*. 1986; 11(1): 10-11. Lang.: Eng.

England. 1589-1816. Historical studies. ■Cautions researchers that the word 'fiddler' is not exclusive to string/violin players. Texts are provided to show that pipe-and-tabor is included during certain eras, and possibly other instruments as well.

3333 Lefebre, Paul. "Du bouffon: Entretien avec Philippe Gaulier." (On the Clown: A Conversation with Philippe Gaulier.) *JCT*. 1986 4th Trimester; 41: 42-51. Illus.: Photo. B&W. 6. Lang.: Fre.

Europe. 1500-1986. Histories-sources. ■Interview with clown, teacher and writer Philippe Gaulier, which presents his views on the history of the jester figure, with references to such figures as Christ and Père Ubu.

3334 Széles, Klára. "Mágikus kör—mágia nélkül. Sándor György a Mikroszkópban." (Magic Circle without Magic: György Sándor on the Mikroszkóp Stage.) *Sz*. 1986 July; 19(7): 40-41. Illus.: Photo. B&W. 1: 9 cm. x 12 cm. Lang.: Hun.

Hungary: Budapest. 1985. Reviews of performances. ■Humorist György Sándor's one-man show *Magic Heap* at Mikroszkóp Stage.

3335 Emigh, John; Emigh, Ulrike. "Hajari Bhand of Rajasthan: A Joker in the Deck." *TDR*. 1986 Spr; 30(1): 101-130. Notes. Illus.: Photo. Print. B&W. 14: 3 in. x 4 in., 5 in. x 7 in. Lang.: Eng.

India: Rajasthan. 1940-1985. Historical studies. ■Life and work of Hajari Bhand as an example of a *bahurupiya* or wandering mimic.

3336 Ancillotto, Paola. "Un buffone a Venezia nella prima metà del Cinquecento." (A Buffoon in Venice During the First Half of the Sixteenth-Century.) *QT*. 1986 Feb.; 8(31): 85-122. Notes. Biblio. Lang.: Ita.

Italy: Venice. 1500-1540. Biographical studies. ■Career of comic author and clown Zuanpolo Leopardi.

3337 Di Palma, Guido. "Le *Vastasate*, lo spettacolo in Sicilia nell'ultimo ventennio del Settecento." (The *Vastasate*: Performance in Sicily 1780-1800.) *BiT*. 1986; 3: 101-131. Notes. Biblio. Lang.: Ita.

Italy. 1780-1800. Historical studies. ■Study of *vastasate*, a form of farcical popular entertainment and an early form of Sicilian dialect theatre.

3338 Paladini Volterra, Angela. "Lo spettacolo mendicante." (The Mendicant Performance.) *TeatrC*. 1986; 6(13): 25-62. Notes. Biblio. Lang.: Ita.

Italy. 1700-1800. Historical studies. ■Discussion of outdoor perform-ances before the circus, with documentation.

3339 Piccat, Marco. *Rappresentazioni popolari e feste in Ravello nella metà del XV secolo*. (Popular Performances and Feasts in Ravello in the Mid-Fifteenth Century.) Collana di testi e studi piemontesi. Turin: Centro Studi Piemontesi; 1986. 173 pp. (Nuova serie 4.) Pref. Index. Notes. Tables. Biblio. Illus.: Photo. Maps. B&W. 7: var. sizes. Lang.: Ita.

Italy: Ravello. 1400-1503. Historical studies. ■Reconstruction of reli-gious spectacles based on archival documentation.

3340 Slichenko, Nikolaj. "Il teatro tzigano." (Gypsy Theatre.) *TeatrC*. 1986; 6(13): 63-67. Lang.: Ita.

Italy. 1900-1986. Histories-sources. ■A gypsy discusses the theatrical traditions of his people.

3341 Adams, Monni. "Women and Masks Among the Western We of the Ivory Coast." *AAinNYLH*. 1986 Feb.; 19(2): 46-55, 90. Notes. Illus.: Photo. Print. Color. B&W. 17. Lang.: Eng.

Ivory Coast. Historical studies. ■Types of maskers and the organization of the masquerades performed at tribal festivals and funerals of the We peoples.

3342 Honda, Yasuji. *Watashi no Album*. (My Album.) Tokyo: Kinsei-sha; 1986. 371 pp. Illus.: Photo. B&W. 30: var. sizes. Lang.: Jap.

Japan: Tokyo. 1986. Histories-sources. ■Anthology of popular entertain-ments in the country. Includes *kagura, ennen, dengaku*.

3343 Misumi, Haruo. *Geinō no Tani Inadani*. (The Valley of Popular Entertainment: Inadani.) Iida: Shinyosha; 1986. 282 pp. Illus.: Photo. [First of 4 volumes.] Lang.: Jap.

Japan: Iida. 1986. Historical studies. ■The popular entertainment of *Inadani* in Nagano province.

3344 Burzyński, Tadeusz. "3e Festival international du théâtre de rue à Jelenia Góra." (3rd International Festival of Street Theatre in Jelenia Góra.) *TP*. 1986; 29(1-3): 28-39. Illus.: Photo. Print. B&W. 10. Lang.: Eng, Fre.

Poland: Jelenia Góra. 1985. Historical studies. ■Description of street theatre festival and evaluation of performances by groups from various countries.

3345 Konecnyi, A. "Raёk—narodnaja zabava." (The *Raёk*, a Folk Amusement.) *DekorIsk*. 1986 Jul.; 29(9): 13-15. Lang.: Rus.

Russia. 1800-1917. Historical studies. ■Development of the *raёk* or gallery as a folk entertainment.

3346 Soberanas, Amadeu J. "El drama Assumpcionista de Tar-ragona del segle XIV." (The Assumption Drama from Tarragona in the XIVth Century.) 93-97 in Salvat, Ricard, ed. *El Teatre durant l'Edat Mitjana i el Renaixement*. Barcelona: Publicacions i Edicions de la Universitat de Barcelona; 1986. xxviii, 322 pp. (El Pla de les Comèdies 2.) [Presented at First International Symposium on Medieval and Renaissance Theatre, Sitges, 1983.] Lang.: Cat.

Spain-Catalonia: Tarragona. 1350-1388. Historical studies. ■Compares the Tarragona Assumption play with similar pieces in the Catalan language.

3347 Baisez, Mathilde. "Le clown contemporain: vers une nou-velle approche de l'art clownesque." (The Contemporary Clown: Toward a New Approach to the Art of Clowning.) *JCT*. 1986 4th Trimester; 41: 29-41. Notes. Illus.: Photo. B&W. 6. Lang.: Fre.

UK. 1769-1985. Historical studies. ■Development of clowning from its origins in an earthly 'clod' figure to an increasingly refined parody of the social environment.

3348 Barnes, Clive; Bruckner, D. J. R.; Cohen, Ron; Hinckley, David; Kroll, Jack; Sterritt, David; Seligsohn, Leo. "Na-tional Lampoon's *Class of 86*." *NYTCR*. 1986 Sep 22; 47(12): 209-212. Lang.: Eng.

USA: New York, NY. 1986. Reviews of performances. ■Collection of newspaper reviews of National Lampoon's *Class of 86*, staged by Jerry Adler at the Village Gate Theatre.

MIXED ENTERTAINMENT: General—Performance/production

3349 Barnes, Clive; Beaufort, John; Gussow, Mel; Kissel, Howard; Wilson, Edwin. *"Juggling and Cheap Theatrics."* *NYTCR.* 1986 Mar 17; 47(5): 337-340. Lang.: Eng.
USA: New York, NY. 1986. Reviews of performances. ■Collection of newspaper reviews of *Juggling and Cheap Theatrics*, an entertainment with the Flying Karamazov Brothers, staged by George Mosher at the Vivian Beaumont Theatre.

3350 Crystal, Billy; Schaap, Dick. *Absolutely Mahvelous.* New York: Putnam; 1986. 128 pp. Illus.: Photo. Print. B&W. 38: var. sizes. Lang.: Eng.
USA. 1955. Biographies. ■The rise to comedy stardom of Billy Crystal. Related to Media.

3351 Lehmann, Barbara. "Speaking in Tongues." *PM.* 1986 May-June; 41: 10-15. Illus.: Photo. Print. B&W. 1. Lang.: Eng.
USA. 1986. Histories-sources. ■Interview with performance artist Laurie Anderson discussing her new film *Home of the Brave* and the image of herself that is conveyed.

3352 Rivers, Joan; Meryman, John. *Enter Talking.* New York, NY: Delacorte; 1986. 398 pp. Index. Illus.: Photo. Print. B&W. 24: var. sizes. Lang.: Eng.
USA: New York, NY. 1928-1965. Biographies. ■Comedienne Joan Rivers' account of her life and early career.

3353 Smith, Ronald Lande. *Cosby.* New York, NY: St. Martin's Press; 1986. 217 pp. Index. Illus.: Photo. Print. B&W. 37. Lang.: Eng.
USA. 1937-1986. Biographies. ■Life and accomplishments of popular entertainer Bill Cosby. Includes chronological listing of shows, awards and discography.

Plays/librettos/scripts

3354 Bullins, Ed. "A Short Statement on Street Theatre." 173-174 in McNamara, Brooks, ed.; Dolan, Jill, ed. *The Drama Review: Thirty Years of Commentary on the Avant-Garde.* Ann Arbor, MI: UMI Research P; 1986. xii, 371 pp. (Theatre and Dramatic Studies 35.) Print. B&W. 2: var. sizes. Lang.: Eng.
USA. 1968-1986. Histories-sources. ■Identifies dramatic elements unique to street theatre.

Reference materials

3355 Font i Font, Presentació. "Festes majors i cíviques, aplecs i fires." (Feast Days and Civic Festivities, Meetings and Fairs.) *Arrel.* 1986 Feb.; 13: 48-53. Notes. Illus.: Photo. Print. B&W. 8: var. sizes. Lang.: Cat.
Spain-Catalonia. 1947-1986. Histories-sources. ■Description of popular entertainments, both sacred and secular.

Relation to other fields

3356 Mills, David. "'Bishop Brian' and the Dramatic Entertainments of Cheshire." *REEDN.* 1986; 11(1): 1-7. Notes. Lang.: Eng.
England: Cheshire. 1560-1641. Historical studies. ■Puritan attitudes against entertainment as displayed in a biography of a Cheshire squire, and Puritan attempts to use local legislation to ban entertainments allowed by King James.

3357 Stephens, John Russell. "Thespis' Poorest Children: Penny Theatres and the Law in the 1830's." *TN.* 1986; 40(3): 123-130. Notes. Lang.: Eng.
England: London. 1820-1839. Historical studies. ■The growth of penny theatres or 'gaffs,' their bad reputation with public authorities and the failure to outlaw them.

3358 Vovelle, Michel; Ruffo Landucci, Patrizio, transl. *Le metamorfosi della festa. Provenza 1750-1820.* (Metamorphoses of Celebration: Provence 1750-1820.) Bologna: Il Mulino; 1986. xix, 354 pp. (Saggi 309.) Pref. Index. Notes. Tables. Biblio. Illus.: Pntg. Dwg. Diagram. B&W. 8: var. sizes. Lang.: Ita.
France. 1750-1820. Historical studies. ■Translation of *Les métamorphoses de la fête en Provence de 1750 à 1820* (Paris 1976).

3359 Dibia, I Wayan. "*Odalan* of Hindu Bali: A Religious Festival, a Social Occasion, and a Theatrical Event." *ATJ.* 1985 Spr; 2(1): 61-65. Lang.: Eng.
Indonesia. ■*Odalan* integrates the religious, communal and artistic lives of the Hindu population of Bali.

3360 Ushio, Michio. *Ushio Michio Chosakushū, 2.* (Collected Works of Ushio Michio, Vol. 2.) Tokyo: Meicho Shuppan; 1986. 506 pp. Lang.: Jap.
Japan: Tokyo. 1986. Historical studies. ■Research on songs and dances related to the agriculture of rice (*taue*).

3361 Urkizu, Patrizio. "Teatro popular vasco en la Edad Media y el Renacimiento: las Pastorales, los Charivaris y las Tragicomedias de Carnaval." (Popular Basque Theatre in the Middle Ages and the Renaissance: Pastorals, Charivaris and Carnival Tragicomedies.) 137-152 in Salvat, Ricard, ed. *El Teatre durant l'Edat Mitjana i el Renaixement.* Barcelona: Publicacions i Edicions de la Universitat de Barcelona; 1986. xxviii, 322 pp. (El Pla de les Comèdies 2.) Notes. [Presented at First International Symposium on Medieval and Renaissance Theatre, Sitges, 1983.] Lang.: Spa.
Spain. France. 674-1963. Historical studies. ■Description of Basque popular theatrical forms, with discussion of studies and literary references and their relation to European popular theatre. Related to Dance: Ethnic dance.

3362 Fàbregas, Xavier. "Breve noticia sobre el teatro en la corte de Germana de Foix y en las fiestas populares." (A Brief Report on Theatre at the Court of Germaine de Foix and in Popular Celebrations.) 99-104 in Salvat, Ricard, ed. *El Teatre durant l'Edat Mitjana i el Renaixement.* Barcelona: Publicacions i Edicions de la Universitat de Barcelona; 1986. xxviii, 322 pp. (El Pla de les Comèdies 2.) [Presented at First International Symposium on Medieval and Renaissance Theatre, Sitges, 1983.] Lang.: Spa.
Spain-Catalonia: Valencia. 1330-1970. Historical studies. ■Discusses Renaissance theatre at the Court of Germaine de Foix as well as paraliturgical and popular Catalan festivals from the Middle Ages to the present.

Cabaret

Performance/production

3363 Böhm, Gotthard. "Ein Mann des Hintersinns." (A Man of Ambiguity.) *Buhne.* 1986 Apr.; 29(4): 10. Illus.: Photo. Print. B&W. Lang.: Ger.
Austria. 1924-1986. Biographical studies. ■Notes on Otto Grünmandl and his satiric revues.

3364 Veigl, Hans. *Lachen im Keller: Von den Budapestern zum Wiener Werkel. Kabarett und Kleinkunst in Wien.* (Laughing in the Cellar: From the Budapester to the Wiener Werkel. Cabaret and Variety in Vienna.) Vienna: Löcker; 1986. 239 pp. PA. Notes. Biblio. Illus.: Handbill. Dwg. Sketches. B&W. 138: 12 cm. x 10 cm., 5 cm. x 7 cm. Lang.: Ger.
Austria: Vienna. 1890-1945. Histories-specific. ■Viennese cabaret recorded by newspaper articles, critics, handbills and biographical notes. Historical and political context of cabaret.

3365 Gábor, István. "Jó hagyományok méltó folytatása. A Mikroszkóp Szinpad egy évada." (Worthy Continuation of Good Traditions: One Season of the Mikroszkóp Stage.) *Sz.* 1986 Sep.; 19(9): 15-17. Illus.: Photo. B&W. 4: 6 cm. x 9 cm., 9 cm. x 12 cm. Lang.: Hun.
Hungary: Budapest. 1985-1986. Reviews of performances. ■Four performances of the 1985/86 season of the Mikroszkóp Stage, the home of the political cabaret.

3366 Bren, Frank. "Comedy Boom." *Drama.* 1986; 3(161): 15-17. Illus.: Photo. B&W. 3: var. sizes. Lang.: Eng.
UK-England. 1979-1986. Critical studies. ■Increasingly popular comedy cabaret is discussed in terms of artists, the contents of their acts and their venues.

3367 Steuer, Gary P. "Cabaret Theatre in New York." *TT.* 1983 Mar/Apr.; 2(5): 1-2, 8. Illus.: Photo. B&W. 3. Lang.: Eng.

MIXED ENTERTAINMENT: Cabaret—Performance/production

USA: New York, NY. 1983. Historical studies. ∎Analysis of political cabaret and cabaret revue, its history and the current form of the genre.

Plays/librettos/scripts

3368 Thompson, Tom. "Political Satire in Sydney." *Meanjin.* 1986; 45(2): 223-227. Lang.: Eng.
Australia: Sydney, N.S.W. 1983-1986. Histories-sources. ∎Development of the political cabaret entertainment *Balmain Boys Don't Cry*, and analysis of its success and comments on its sequel by one of the writers involved in the work.

Reference materials

3369 Budzinski, Klaus. *Hermes Handlexikon: Das Kabarett.* (Hermes Handbook of Cabaret.) Düsseldorf: ECON Taschenbuch; 1985. 287 pp. (Hermes Handlexikon.) Pref. Biblio. Illus.: Photo. B&W. Lang.: Ger.
Germany. Switzerland. Austria. 1900-1965. ∎Terminology and portraits of specific artists and groups. Alphabetically ordered, additional analyses of satires, reflection of and effect on political and social conditions.

Relation to other fields

3370 Hippen, Reinhard. *Satire gegen Hitler.* (Satire Against Hitler.) Zürich: Dendo; 1986. 179 pp. (Kabarettgeschichten 14.) Pref. Index. Illus.: Photo. B&W. Lang.: Ger.
Germany. Switzerland: Zurich. 1933-1945. Histories-specific. ∎Historical account of the major anti-Nazi satirists. Refers especially to Erika Mann, who emigrated temporarily to Zürich. Added are some of the seminal satirical texts.

3371 Pelzer, Jürgen. "Satire oder Unterhaltung? Wirkungskonzepte im deutschen Kabarett zwischen Bohemerevolte und antifaschistischer Opposition." (Satire or Entertainment? Concepts of Effectiveness in German Cabaret between Bohemian Revolt and Anti-Fascist Opposition.) *GerSR.* 1986 Feb.; 9(1): 45-65. Lang.: Ger.
Germany. 1896-1945. Critical studies. ∎Historical function of cabaret entertainment.

Theory/criticism

3372 Cahn, Roger. "Lachen, die beste Medizin." (Laughing: There's no Better Remedy.) *MuT.* 1986 Mar.; 7(3): 32-35. Illus.: Photo. B&W. Lang.: Ger.
Switzerland. 1985. Histories-sources. ∎Interview with comedian Emil Steinberger about humor and laughter: their preliminaries, conditions and limits.

Carnival

3373 A., K. "Petersburgskije guljanija." (Petersburg Outdoor Festivals.) *DekorIsk.* 1986; 29(9): 34-35. Lang.: Rus.
Russia: St. Petersburg. 1712-1914. Historical studies. ∎Report on exhibit at State Historical Museum, Leningrad, dedicated to pre- and post-Lenten public festivals.

Performance/production

3374 Messen-Jaschin, Youri; Bering, Florian; Cuneo, Anne; Sidler, Peter. *Die Welt der Schausteller—Le Monde des Forains.* (The World of Show People.) Lausanne: Trois Continents; 1986. 211 pp. Pref. Illus.: Photo. B&W. Color. Lang.: Fre, Ger.
1500-1985. Histories-specific. ∎Historical survey of the world of the fun fair: carousels, roller-coasters and freak-shows. Concentrates on the most famous show families and their attractions.

3375 Bloodgood, 'Doc' Fred Foster. "'Sold Out, Doctor!'—The Medicine Show Life." *TT.* 1983 Oct.; 3(1): 1-2, 9. Pref. Illus.: Photo. B&W. 3: 3 in. x 3 in. Lang.: Eng.
USA. 1983. Historical studies. ∎Excerpted from *The Vi-Ton-Ka Medicine Show Book*, a record of a recreation of a medicine show featuring 'Doc' Fred Foster Bloodgood, staged by American Place Theatre.

Relation to other fields

3376 Harris, Wilson. "Carnival Logic." *PM.* 1986 Sep-Oct.; 43: 22-23. Lang.: Eng.

Europe. 1986. Historical studies. ∎Analysis of the function of carnival and its cultural and political implications.

3377 Fincardi, Marco. "Guastalla. Feste di Mezza Quaresima. Un Carnevale tra Risorgimento e Belle-époque." (Guastella. Feasts of Mid-Lent. A Carnival between Risorgimento and Belle-époque.) *QT.* 1986 May; 8(32): 73-87. Notes. Biblio. Lang.: Ita.
Italy: Guastalla. 1857-1895. Historical studies. ∎Reflections of social and historical conditions in the carnival celebration of a small Emilian town.

Circus

Administration

3378 Thayer, Stuart. "The Lent and Rockwell Papers at Somers." *Band.* 1985 July-Aug.; 29(4): 29-31. Illus.: Handbill. Photo. Print. B&W. 4: 2 in. x 6 in. Lang.: Eng.
USA. 1836-1843. Historical studies. ∎Bookkeeping records of two circus managers reveal the economic aspects of operating circuses before the Civil War.

3379 Rusakov, A. "Prognozy na zavtra." (Prognosis for the Future.) *SovEC.* 1986 Feb.; 2: 1-3. Lang.: Rus.
USSR. 1986. Histories-sources. ∎V.S. Skotorenko, head of the artistic section of the Union of State Circuses, comments on the program for new productions of circus art.

Institutions

3380 Mertl, Monika. "Nicht nur rote Nasen." (Not Only Red Noses.) *Buhne.* 1986 May; 29(5): 36. Illus.: Photo. Print. Color. Lang.: Ger.
Austria: Vienna. 1983-1986. Histories-sources. ∎On the event of the Festival der Clowns in the Wiener Festwochen 1986, including notes on financial operations and history of this event.

Performance spaces

3381 Speaight, George. "Rickett's Amphitheatre." *Band.* 1986 Mar-Apr.; 30(2): 17. Illus.: Dwg. B&W. 2: 2 in. x 3 in. Lang.: Eng.
USA: Philadelphia, PA. 1795-1799. Historical studies. ∎A history of one of the earliest American circus buildings.

Performance/production

3382 Hudern, Christopher. "Clowning Around." *PuJ.* 1985 Spr; 36(3): 5-8. Illus.: Photo. 6: var. sizes.
Histories-sources. ∎Ringling Bros. & Barnum & Bailey Circus clown discusses becoming a clown, his training and work with puppets.

3383 Zoglauer, Franz. "Hellers chinesische Engel." (Heller's Chinese Angels.) *Parnass.* 1986 Jan-Feb.; 6(1): 54-59. Illus.: Photo. Print. Color. B&W. Lang.: Ger.
Europe. China, People's Republic of. 1984-1985. Reviews of performances. ∎On André Heller's project *Begnadete Körper (Blessed Bodies)*, a show of Chinese acrobats.

3384 Borovik, E. "Pobeda molodyh artistov." (Young Artists Carry the Day.) *SovEC.* 1986 May; 5: 4-5. Lang.: Rus.
France: Paris. 1986. Histories-sources. ∎Interview with V.A. Noskov, deputy director of the Union of State Circuses on Ninth International Conference on the circus of tomorrow (Paris).

3385 Bradbury, Joseph T. "John Robinson Circus 1925." *Band.* 1985 July-Aug.; 24(4): 4-19. Illus.: Photo. Handbill. Poster. B&W. 24: 2 in. x 8 in. Lang.: Eng.
USA. 1925. Historical studies. ∎Owned by the American Circus Corporation, one of three shows sent on the road, this one managed by Sam Dill. Article cites four stops, audience reaction and material from contemporary newspaper reviews.

3386 Bradbury, Joseph T. "John Robinson Circus 1926." *Band.* 1985 Nov-Dec.; 29(6): 17-30. Illus.: Handbill. Photo. Print. B&W. 20: var. sizes. Lang.: Eng.
USA. Canada. 1926. Historical studies. ∎Details of the American Circus Corporation's season, including an elephant stampede in British Columbia and a reduction in number of railroad cars.

MIXED ENTERTAINMENT: Circus—Performance/production

3387 Carver, Gordon M. "The Carl Hagenbeck and Great Wallace Circus, 1913." *Band.* 1985 July-Aug.; 24(4): 20-28. Illus.: Photo. Handbill. Poster. Print. B&W. 20: 2 in. x 8 in. Lang.: Eng.
USA. 1913. Historical studies. ■Company formed by merger of two circuses ultimately solely owned and managed by B. E. Wallace. Article traces movement of a financially successful season. Types of attractions listed.

3388 Carver, Gordon M. "Hagenbeck Wallace Circus Seasons of 1914." *Band.* 1985 Nov-Dec.; 29(6): 37-45. Illus.: Handbill. Photo. Print. B&W. 15: var. sizes. Lang.: Eng.
USA: St. Louis, MO, Youngstown, OH, Sturgis, MI. 1914. Historical studies. ■A detailed history of the 1914 season of the Hagenbeck Wallace Circus, including the collapse of a tent which killed several people for which the circus was sued.

3389 Chang, Reynolds. "The Impact of Domestic Animal Diseases Upon the Circus." *Band.* 1985 Nov-Dec.; 29(6): 59-62. Illus.: Handbill. Photo. Print. B&W. 6: 2 in. x 4 in. Lang.: Eng.
USA. France. 1890-1985. Historical studies. ■Quarantine and other problems due to animal diseases, such as hoof and mouth, glanders and anthrax, have directly affected circus operations over the years.

3390 Cummings, Scott T. "An Interview with Dolly Jacobs." *ThM.* 1985 Win; 17(1): 63-65. Illus.: Photo. B&W. 1. Lang.: Eng.
USA. 1970-1985. Histories-sources. ■Interview with Dolly Jacobs, an aerialist who works on 'roman rings,' discussing her training and the development of her routine.

3391 Dahlinger, Fred, Jr. "Circus Wagon History File: The Barnum & Bailey London and New York Tableaus." *Band.* 1986 Jan-Feb. ; 30(1): 26-28. Illus.: Handbill. Photo. Print. B&W. 7: var. sizes. Lang.: Eng.
USA: New York, NY. 1864-1920. Historical studies. ■The use of 'tableau wagons' covered with historical tableaux and rococo details in the Barnum and Bailey Circus.

3392 Lentz, John. "Glasier's Historic Circus Photographs." *Band.* 1985 Nov-Dec.; 29(6): 32-34. Notes. Illus.: Photo. Print. B&W. 14: var. sizes. Lang.: Eng.
USA. 1896-1920. Histories-sources. ■A collection of photographs which features details and scenes of circus life.

3393 Pfening, Fred D., Jr. "The Lion King: His Career and His Circuses, Part I." *Band.* 1985 Nov-Dec.; 29(6): 5-13. Illus.: Handbill. Photo. Print. B&W. 20: var. sizes. Lang.: Eng.
USA. 1903-1943. Biographical studies. ■Captain Terrell Jacobs, a wild animal trainer, worked with 40 to 52 lions at one time, the largest number by a single man. Noted for 'breaking' all his animals personally.

3394 Pfening, Fred D., Jr. "The Circus Year in Review (1985 season)." *Band.* 1986 Jan-Feb.; 30(1): 4-15. Illus.: Handbill. Photo. Print. B&W. 26: var. sizes. Lang.: Eng.
USA. Canada. 1985. Historical studies. ■A review of the 1985 season including increased costs in liability insurance, dishonest phone promoters and harassment by animal rights groups.

3395 Pfening, Fred D., Jr. "Scenes of the 1985 Season: Holton Rowes, Photographer." *Band.* 1986 Mar-Apr.; 30(2): 26-27. Notes. Illus.: Dwg. B&W. 9: var. sizes. Lang.: Eng.
USA: New York, NY. 1985. Historical studies. ■Photographs of the Carson & Barnes, the Toby Tyler and the Big Apple circuses.

3396 Polacsek, John T. "The Stowe Brothers Circus: A Real Family Tradition, Part 1." *Band.* 1985 Nov-Dec.; 29(6): 49-56. Illus.: Handbill. Photo. Print. B&W. 6: var. sizes. Lang.: Eng.
USA. 1850-1920. Historical studies. ■History of the circus, including performances, travel and audiences.

3397 Thayer, Stuart. "Herr Driesbach: Lord of the Brute Creation." *Band.* 1986 Jan-Feb.; 30(1): 29-31. Illus.: Handbill. Photo. Print. B&W. 4: var. sizes. Lang.: Eng.
USA. 1807-1878. Biographical studies. ■Career of one of the top performers in field show history, a lion tamer whose act involved a fight between lion or tiger and the trainer himself.

3398 Dmitriev, Ju. "Ser' eznyj razgovor." (An Earnest Conversation.) *SovEC.* 1986 Feb.; 2: 11-12. Lang.: Rus.
USSR. 1986. Critical studies. ■Problems of the contemporary circus.

3399 Durova, N. "Iz novoj knigi." (From a New Book.) *SovEC.* 1986 May; 5: 14-15. Lang.: Rus.
USSR: Moscow. 1986. Historical studies. ■Excerpt from book by manager of Durov Theatre of Wild Animals.

3400 Ganešin, K. "V čem sovremennost?" (What is the Present Made Of?) *SovEC.* 1986 Apr.; 4: 11-12. Lang.: Rus.
USSR. 1980-1986. Critical studies. ■Achievements and problems of the contemporary circus.

3401 Makarov, S.M. *Sovetskaja klounada.* (Soviet Clownery.) Moscow: Iskusstvo; 1986. 272 pp. Lang.: Rus.
USSR. 1980-1986. Instructional materials. ■Textbook on clowning for circus and vaudeville acts.

3402 Marčenko, T. "Neobyčnoe prostranstvo čelovečeskogo tvorčestva." (The Unusual Space of Human Creative Work.) *SovEc.* 1986 Feb.; 2: 6-8. Lang.: Rus.
USSR. 1980-1986. Critical studies. ■On masters of the Soviet circus.

3403 Slavskij, R. "Zametki i komičeskom trjuke." (Notes on Comic Stunts.) *SovEC.* 1986 Sep.; 9: 16-18. Lang.: Rus.
USSR. 1986. Historical studies. ■Notes on comic stunts.

Relation to other fields

3404 Vladimirov, V. *Cirk kak fenomen kul'tury: Avtoref. diss... kand. filol. nauk.* (The Circus as a Cultural Phenomenon: Synopsis of a Dissertation by a Candidate in Philosophy.) Moscow: MGU; 1986. 23 pp. Lang.: Rus.
1980-1986. Critical studies.

Theory/criticism

3405 Lévesque, Solange. "Quand cirque et théâtre se font signe...sous le chapiteau du soleil." (When Circus and Theatre Speak to One Another...Under the Big Top of the Sun.) *JCT.* 1986 First Trimester; 38: 190-207. Illus.: Photo. B&W. 8. Lang.: Fre.
1985. Critical studies. ■An examination of the links between theatre and the circus, with a phenomenological reading of the history and development of the circus.

3406 Vladimirov, V.; Beljakova, G. "Spory o cirke: voprosy teorie." (A Debate on the Circus: Questions of Theory.) *SovEC.* 1986 June; 6: 6-10. Lang.: Rus.
USSR. 1980-1986. Critical studies. ■Debate on characteristics of the circus as art form.

Commedia dell'arte

Design/technology

3407 Knight, Malcolm. "Masks and the Commedia Dell'Arte." *Anim.* 1986 Dec-Jan.; 9(2): 30-31. Biblio. Illus.: Photo. Print. B&W. 7: 5 in. x 4 in., 2 in. x 5 in., 2 in. x 3 in., 2 in. x 2 in. Lang.: Eng.
Italy. Europe. USA. 1500-1986. Historical studies. ■Origins and development of *commedia dell'arte* detailing the costume and attributes of the stock characters.

Institutions

3408 Gilmour, Dean. "Images from Far Away." *Theatrum.* 1985-86 Fall-Win; 3: 7-8. Illus.: Sketches. B&W. 2: 1 in. x 1 in., 2 in. x 3 in. Lang.: Eng.
Canada: Toronto, ON. 1970-1986. Critical studies. ■Discusses the differences between popular theatre and stylized realism and outlines the author's discoveries of traditional methods of expression for use in his own work and theatre.

Performance/production

3409 Camerlain, Lorraine. "Art de la comédie, comédie de l'art: entretien avec Carlo Boso." (Art of Comedy, Comedy of Art: Conversation with Carlo Boso.) *JCT.* 1985; 35: 59-92. Lang.: Fre.

MIXED ENTERTAINMENT: *Commedia dell'arte*—Performance/production

Europe. 1985. Histories-sources. ■Interview with expert on *commedia dell'arte*, including the idea of the carnavalesque and Jean Racine's links with the *commedia*.

3410   Taviani, Ferdinando. "Attori ed attrici della Commedia dell'Arte." (Actors and Actresses of the *Commedia dell'Arte*.) 177-205 in Salvat, Ricard, ed. *El Teatre durant l'Edat Mitjana i el Renaixement*. Barcelona: Publicacions i Edicions de la Universitat de Barcelona; 1986. xxviii, 322 pp. (El Pla de les Comèdies 2.) Notes. [Presented at First International Symposium on Medieval and Renaissance Theatre, Sitges, 1983.] Lang.: Ita.
France. 1575-1670. Historical studies. ■Interpretive technique of *commedia dell'arte* actors, including recitation, mime, dance, acrobatics and masks. Based on records of Italian companies performing in France.

3411   Checchi, Giovanna. *Silvio Fiorillo, in arte Capitan Mattamoros*. (Silvio Fiorillo, Stage-Name Capitan Mattamoros.) Capua: Capuanuova; 1986. 135 pp. (Quaderni di storia ed arte campana 9.) Index. Notes. Tables. Biblio. Illus.: Photo. Pntg. Dwg. B&W. 28: var. sizes. Lang.: Ita.
Italy. 1565-1634. Historical studies. ■Life and works of actor and playwright Silvio Fiorillo, father of Tiberio.

3412   Florescu, Ileana. "Harlequin, nom de comédien." (Harlequin, Stage Name.) *BiT*. 1986; 4: 21-59. Notes. Biblio. Lang.: Ita.
Italy. France. 1550-1600. Historical studies. ■Life and experiences of Italian actors in France, focusing on comic actor Tristano Martinelli, who probably created the role of Harlequin.

3413   Fulchignoni, Enrico. "Le influenze orientali sulla commedia dell'arte—Per una ipotesi di ricerca." (Oriental Influences on the *Commedia dell'arte*—Toward an Hypothesis of Research.) 433-447 in Ottai, Antonella, ed. *Teatro Oriente/Occidente*. Rome: Bulzoni; 1986. viii, 565 pp. (Biblioteca Teatrale 47.) Lang.: Ita.
Italy. 1550-1650. Historical studies. ■Influences from the Orient on the *commedia dell'arte*.

3414   Royce, Anya Peterson. "The Venetian Commedia: Actors and Masques in the Development of the *Commedia dell'arte*." *ThS*. 1986 May & Nov.; 27(1-2): 69-87. Notes. Biblio. Lang.: Eng.
Italy: Venice. 1400-1620. Historical studies. ■Examination of private and popular entertainments, early performance and textual conventions which anticipated the conventions of *maschere* and *lazzi* associated with *commedia dell'arte*.

3415   Rea, Kenneth. "Reconstructing the *Commedia dell'arte*." *Drama*. 1986; 159(1): 17-19. Illus.: Photo. B&W. 4. Lang.: Eng.
UK-England. Italy. 1947-1986. Histories-sources. ■Interview with Carlo Boso on his reconstructions of *commedia dell'arte* for modern audiences, focusing on physical technique.

Plays/librettos/scripts

3416   Molinari, Cesare. "La vita nova del buffone." (The Buffoon's New Life.) 85-92 in Salvat, Ricard, ed. *El Teatre durant l'Edat Mitjana i el Renaixement*. Barcelona: Publicacions i Edicions de la Universitat de Barcelona; 1986. xxviii, 322 pp. (El Pla de les Comèdies 2.) [Presented at First International Symposium on Medieval and Renaissance Theatre, Sitges, 1983.] Lang.: Ita.
Italy. 1576-1646. Historical studies. ■Analysis of text of *Cicalamento, o vero trattato di matrimonio tra Buffetto e Colombina comici (Chatter, or True Treatise of the Wedding of Buffetto and Columbine)* by Carlo Cantú, including discussion of the actor's identification with his mask.

Court entertainment

Administration

3417   Streitberger, W. R. "The Revels at Court from 1541 to 1559." *RORD*. 1986; 29: 25-45. Notes. Append. Lang.: Eng.

England: London. 1510-1559. Historical studies. ■Organization and operation of Office of Revels mainly under Thomas Cawarden: appendix listing references from Feuillerat, Loseley MS and other sources.

Institutions

3418   Streitberger, W. R. "William Cornish and the Players of the Chapel." *MET*. 1986; 8(1): 1-20. Notes. Lang.: Eng.
England: London. 1504-1524. Historical studies. ■Emergence of the Chapel Royal as a dominant force of early Tudor court entertainment was due to William Cornish.

Performance/production

3419   Butler, Martin. "A Provincial Masque of *Comus*, 1636." *RenD*. 1986; 17: 149-173. Notes. Biblio. Lang.: Eng.
England: Shipton. 1600-1650. Historical studies. ■Discussion of records relating to Clifford family's production of a masque including *Comus* and the implications for history of provincial theatrical activities.

3420   Streitberger, W.R. "Henry VIII's Entertainment for the Queen of Scots, 1516: A New Revels Account and Cornish's Play." *MRenD*. 1984; 1: 29-49. Notes. Lang.: Eng.
England: Greenwich. 1504-1516. Critical studies. ■Documentary evidence relating to the cost of costumes and players with references to a dramatic piece by William Cornish.

Pageants/parades

3421   Russell, Robert. "An English Influence on Russian Revolutionary Festivals." *TN*. 1986; 40(3): 115-123. Notes. Illus.: Photo. Print. B&W. 3: var. sizes. Lang.: Eng.
Russia. UK-England: London. 1907-1920. ■Influence of Hampstead Garden Suburb pageant on the Russian Proletkult movement.

Design/technology

3422   Osberg, Richard H. "The Goldsmiths' 'Chastell' of 1377." *ThS*. 1986 May & Nov.; 27(1-2): 1-15. Notes. Illus.: Dwg. 5: var. sizes. Lang.: Eng.
England: London. 1377-1392. Historical studies. ■Contemporary descriptions and records accounting for the costs of the goldsmiths' pageants indicate that the construction of the castle was similar to that of siege engines constructed for similar purposes.

Performance/production

3423   Tourangeau, Rémi; Fortin, Marcel. "Le Phénomène des pageants au Québec." (The Phenomenon of Pageants in Quebec.) *THC*. 1986 Fall; 7(2): 215-238. Notes. Illus.: Photo. B&W. 4: var. sizes. Lang.: Fre.
Canada. 1900-1960. Historical studies. ■A classification of pageants in Quebec, comparing their function and development with the pageants of the United States and Britain. Includes discussion of both social and technical factors.

3424   Muir, Lynette. "Liturgy and Drama at St-Omer in the Thirteenth through the Sixteenth Centuries." *EDAM*. 1986 Fall; 9(1): 7-12. Lang.: Eng.
France: Saint-Omer. 1200-1600. Historical studies. ■Description of a Rituale preserved in the church that documents processions and plays presented under the supervision of the clergy.

3425   Mitchell, Bonner. *The Majesty of the State: Triumphal Progresses of Foreign Sovereigns in Renaissance Italy (1494-1600)*. Florence: Olschki; 1986. viii, 238 pp. (Biblioteca dell'Archivum Romanicum I 203.) Pref. Index. Notes. Tables. Biblio. Illus.: Pntg. Dwg. B&W. 8: 9 cm. x 12 cm., 12 cm. x 18 cm. Lang.: Eng.
Italy. 1494-1600. Historical studies. ■Reconstruction of triumphal entry pageants for French and Spanish sovereigns in Italy.

3426   Lester, Geoffrey. "Holy Week Processions in Seville." *MET*. 1986; 8(2): 103-118. Notes. Illus.: Photo. Diagram. B&W. 5. Lang.: Eng.
Spain: Seville. 1986. Historical studies. ■History, organization, themes and performances of the Holy Week Processions reveal many areas of relevance to the English Mystery plays.

MIXED ENTERTAINMENT: Pageants/parades—Performance/production

3427 Portillo, Rafael; Gomez Lara, Manuel. "Vestiges of Dramatic Performances of the Passion in Andalusia's Holy Week Procession." *MET*. 1986; 8(2): 119-133. Notes. Tables. Illus.: Maps. 1. Lang.: Eng.
Spain. 1986. Histories-sources. ■Identifies 48 occurrences of costumed characters and dramatic or quasi-dramatic action in Holy Week processions. Arranged by province, with table of themes.

3428 Hinckley, Priscilla Baird. "The Dodo Masquerade of Burkina Faso." *AAinNYLH*. 1986 Feb.; 19(2): 74-77, 91. Notes. Illus.: Photo. Print. B&W. Color. 6. Lang.: Eng.
Upper Volta: Ouagadougou. Historical studies. ■Types of costumes, dances and songs performed by groups of boys for the Dodo masquerades during Ramadan.

Plays/librettos/scripts

3429 Bergeron, David M. "The Bible in English Renaissance Civic Pageants." *CompD*. 1986; 20(2): 160-170. Notes. Lang.: Eng.
England. 1519-1639. Historical studies. ■Focusing on Midsummer Shows, Royal Entries and Lord Mayor's Shows, the author argues that biblical references in the pageants served political purposes.

3430 Wright, Stephen K. *The Historie of King Edward the Fourth*: A Chronicle Play on the Coventry Pageant Wagons." *MRenD*. 1986; 3: 69-81. Notes. Lang.: Eng.
England: Coventry, London. 1560-1600. Historical studies. ■Analysis of a history play written specifically for a festival in Coventry and performed on a pageant wagon and its similarities to *Edward IV* by Thomas Heywood.

3431 Knight, Alan E. "Manuscript Painting and Play Production: Evidence from the Processional Plays of Lille." *EDAM*. 1986 Fall; 9(1): 1-5. Illus.: Pntg. B&W. 1: 2 in. x 3.5 in. Lang.: Eng.
France: Lille. 1450-1500. Textual studies. ■Relationship between playtexts and illustrations in the Lille plays manuscript, the only extant medieval French plays known to have been presented processionally on wagons.

Relation to other fields

3432 Farràs i Farràs, Jaume. *La Patum de Berga*. (The *Patum* of Berga.) Barcelona: Edicions de Nou Art Thor; 1986. 64 pp. (Terra Nostra 3.) Index. Notes. Biblio. Illus.: Photo. Print. Color. B&W. 102: var. sizes. Lang.: Cat.
Spain-Catalonia: Berga. 1264-1986. Critical studies. ■Origins and characteristics of the *Patum*, a popular festival commemorating Corpus Christi but with pre-Christian roots.

Performance art

Audience

3433 Babel, Tara. "What Do Sixth-Formers Think about Performance Art?" *PM*. 1986 May-June; 41: 33-35. Illus.: Photo. B&W. 1. Lang.: Eng.
UK-England: Newcastle. 1986. Histories-sources. ■Results of a questionnaire and question and answer session with audiences evaluating performance art productions.

Design/technology

3434 Williams, Mike. "Japan's Follow Spot Spectacular." *LDim*. 1986 Jul-Aug.; 10(4): 26-29, 52-54. Illus.: Photo. Print. Color. 3: var. sizes. Lang.: Eng.
Japan: Yokohama. 1985-1986. Histories-sources. ■Interview with Kazuo Inoue on his lighting design for a rock concert in Yokohama Stadium.

3435 "A City in Concert." *LDim*. 1986 Jul-Aug.; 10(4): 12, 60, 62. Illus.: Photo. Print. Color. 1: 3 in. x 7 in. Lang.: Eng.
USA: Houston, TX. 1986. Historical studies. ■Discusses lighting by Jacques Rouverollis of 150th anniversary spectacle. People stopped on freeway to watch spectacle.

3436 Winer, Steve. "Broadcast Zones." *ThCr*. 1986 Jan.; 20(1): 26-29, 46-48. Illus.: Photo. 7: var. sizes.

USA. 1986. Histories-sources. ■Performance artist Chris Hardman discusses wiring his audience for sound and guiding them through constructed environments by taped directives.

Performance spaces

3437 "View from the South." *PM*. 1986 July-Aug.; 42: 18-19. Illus.: Photo. Print. B&W. 1. Lang.: Eng.
Australia: Adelaide. 1974-1986. Histories-sources. ■Overview of the Experimental Art Foundation, the first 'alternative' art space to be started up in Australia.

3438 La Frenais, Rob. "The Spaces between the Myth." *PM*. 1986 July-Aug.; 42: 7-9. Illus.: Photo. Print. B&W. 2. Lang.: Eng.
Australia. 1986. Historical studies. ■Overview of performance spaces in several Australian cities.

Performance/production

3439 Helyer, Nigel. "Kill the Word!" *PM*. 1986 July-Aug.; 42: 12-14. Illus.: Photo. Print. B&W. 4. Lang.: Eng.
Australia. 1986. Historical studies. ■Overview of the Soundworks Festival that brought together performances and critical forums exploring language, sound, image and gesture.

3440 La Frenais, Rob. "No One Wants You." *PM*. 1986 July-Aug.; 42: 15-17. Illus.: Photo. Print. B&W. 1. Lang.: Eng.
Australia. 1986. Histories-sources. ■Interview with performance artist Mike Mullins discussing the development of his work and his performances at the Australia Day ceremony.

3441 La Frenais, Rob. "Jill Scott." *PM*. 1986 July-Aug.; 42: 25-26. Illus.: Photo. Print. B&W. 1. Lang.: Eng.
Australia. 1986. Histories-sources. ■Interview with performance artist Jill Scott discussing the influence of science fiction and mythology on her work. Related to Media.

3442 Miller, Sarah. "Putting on an Act—Performing Femininity." *PM*. 1986 July-Aug.; 42. Illus.: Photo. Print. B&W. 2. Lang.: Eng.
Australia: Sydney, N.S.W. 1986. Historical studies. ■Success of performances by women on women's issues.

3443 Lushington, Kate. "Montreal: La Soirée des Murmures." *CTR*. 1986 Sum; 13(47): 121-125. Illus.: Photo. Print. B&W. 2: var. sizes. Lang.: Eng.
Canada: Montreal, PQ. 1986. Reviews of performances. ■Description of the interaction between audience and performers in an evening of eroticism in performance, entitled *La Soirée des murmures (The Evening of Murmurs)*.

3444 Zylin, Svetlana. "Performance Art: An Interpretation." *Theatrum*. 1986 Win; 5: 5-8, 34-35. Append. Illus.: Photo. Poster. Print. B&W. 3: var. sizes. Lang.: Eng.
Canada: Toronto, ON. USA: New York, NY. 1980-1986. Histories-sources. ■History of performance art, difficulties in precisely defining it and interviews with six Toronto performance artists.

3445 Cerezo, Francesc A. "*Accions* i La Fura dels Baus." (*Actions* and La Fura dels Baus.) *EECIT*. 1986 Dec.; 28: 51-88. Tables. Illus.: Graphs. Photo. Plan. Print. B&W. Schematic. 8: var. sizes. Lang.: Cat.
Spain-Catalonia. 1979-1984. Critical studies. ■Analysis of the show *Accions (Actions)* by the group La Fura dels Baus, with a brief history of the group and its members.

3446 La Frenais, Rob. "In Deep." *PM*. 1986 Mar-Apr.; 40: 25-28. Print. B&W. 4. Lang.: Eng.
UK. 1965-1986. Histories-sources. ■Interview with a performance artist undergoing ten years of training as a deep-sea diver to experience living in an extreme environment.

3447 Selwood, Sara. "Artists in the Theatre." *PM*. 1986 Sep-Oct.; 43: 13-15. Lang.: Eng.
UK. 1900-1986. Historical studies. ■Description of 'Artists in the Theatre,' a touring exhibition focusing on the influence of visual artists on the development of performance art.

3448 Briers, David. "Furniturisation." *PM*. 1986 Sep-Oct.; 43: 19-21. Lang.: Eng.

MIXED ENTERTAINMENT: Performance art—Performance/production

UK-England. 1986. Historical studies. ■How furniture affects our performance in everyday life.

3449 Greenhaigh, Jill. "Magdalena." *PM.* 1986 July-Aug.; 42: 32-33. Illus.: Photo. Print. B&W. 7. Lang.: Eng.

UK-England. 1986. Histories-sources. ■Overview of an international festival of performance art by women.

3450 La Frenais, Rob. "Slow Slow Quick Quick." *PM.* 1986 Mar-Apr.; 40: 19-23. Illus.: Photo. Print. B&W. 4. Lang.: Eng.

UK-England. 1986. Histories-sources. ■Experiences of two performance artists acquiring ballroom dancing skills.

3451 La Frenais, Rob. "Notes from the Engine Room." *PM.* 1986 Mar-Apr.; 40: 29-30. Illus.: Photo. Print. B&W. 1. Lang.: Eng.

UK-England. 1986. Histories-sources. ■Interview with member of Bow Gamelan Ensemble discussing skills acquired as a result of trying to discover creative elements in machines.

3452 Marjoram, Bol. "Mona Hatoum: Not an Entertainer." *PM.* 1986 May-June; 41: 20-23. Illus.: Photo. Print. B&W. 3. Lang.: Eng.

UK-England. 1975-1986. Histories-sources. ■Interview with performance artist Mona Hatoum discussing her recent performances and whether her work is inspired by her experience as a Palestinian in Britain.

3453 Rogers, Steve. "Rose English." *PM.* 1986 July-Aug.; 42: 29-31. Illus.: Photo. Print. B&W. 7. Lang.: Eng.

UK-England. 1970-1986. Histories-sources. ■Interview with performance artist Rose English contrasting her works of the seventies with her recent show *Thee Thy Thou Thine*.

3454 Rogers, Steve. "Entranced by Butterflies." *PM.* 1986 Sep-Oct.; 43: 16-18. Illus.: Photo. Print. B&W. 5. Lang.: Eng.

UK-England. 1980-1986. Histories-sources. ■Profile of the work of Lumière & Son Circus (London).

3455 Walwin, Jeni. "Close to the Horns." *PM.* 1986 Sep-Oct.; 43: 8-12. Illus.: Photo. Print. B&W. 4. Lang.: Eng.

UK-England. 1986. Historical studies. ■Examination of the work of performance artist Rose Finn-Kelcey in light of her most recent work that centers on the aesthetics, ambiguities and traditions of the bullfight.

3456 La Frenais, Rob. "A Specialization on Memory." *PM.* 1986 Sep-Oct.; 43: 24-25. Illus.: Photo. Print. B&W. 2. Lang.: Eng.

UK-Scotland: Glasgow. 1986. Histories-sources. ■Description of a three-day live performance by performance artist Stuart Brisley.

3457 Burnham, Linda Frye. "*High Performance*, Performance Art, and Me." *TDR.* 1986 Spr; 30(1): 15-53. Illus.: Diagram. Photo. Print. B&W. 27: 2 in. x 3 in., 5 in. x 7 in. Lang.: Eng.

USA. 1972-1986. Historical studies. ■A survey of the performance art movement by the founder of the magazine *High Performance*.

3458 Bush, Catherine. "Club Performance: The Changing East Village Scene." *TT.* 1986 Jan.; 5(2): 1, 4-5. Illus.: Photo. B&W. 3. Lang.: Eng.

USA: New York, NY. 1975-1985. Historical studies. ■Shifting aesthetics and changing econonomic and legal conditions bring transition to the East Village performance scene.

3459 Schechner, Richard. "Uprooting the Garden: Thoughts around 'The Prometheus Project': The Overlapping of Art, Parody, and Experience." *NTQ.* 1986 Feb.; 11(5): 3-11. Notes. Lang.: Eng.

USA. Historical studies. ■Avant-gardes confronting the prospect of global genocide, an explanation of the parodic tone which increasingly characterizes performance work.

3460 Winn, Steven. "See Here Now." *ThCr.* 1986 Apr.; 20(4): 37-38, 40-43. Illus.: Photo. 5: var. sizes.

USA: Berkeley, CA. 1986. Historical studies. ■A profile of performance artist George Coates.

Theory/criticism

3461 Pavis, Patrice. "Notes Toward a Semiotic Analysis." 255-270 in McNamara, Brooks, ed.; Dolan, Jill, ed. *The Drama*

Review: Thirty Years of Commentary on the Avant-Garde. Ann Arbor, MI: UMI Research P; 1986. xii, 371 pp. (Theatre and Dramatic Studies 35.) Print. B&W. 10. Lang.: Eng.

Europe. 1979. Critical studies. ■Semiotic analysis of theatrical elements to find a middle ground between concrete description and abstract theory.

3462 Rapaport, Herman. "Can You Say Hello?: Laurie Anderson's *United States*." *TJ.* 1986 Oct.; 38(3): 339-354. Notes. Lang.: Eng.

USA. 1984. Critical studies. ■An analysis of the relation between performer and society, high and low culture in Laurie Anderson's performance piece *United States* using semiotic and post-modern theory.

Variety acts

Institutions

3463 Barker, Felix. "The Players Theatre." *PlPl.* 1986 Dec.; 399: 9. B&W. 1: 4 in. x 2 in. Lang.: Eng.

UK-England: London. 1936-1986. Historical studies. ■Celebrates the Golden Jubilee of a small theatre which has occupied several premises and been a seed bed for many variety acts.

3464 Minsky, Morton; Machlin, Milt. *Minsky's Burlesque.* New York, NY: Arbor House; 1986. 312 pp. Append. Illus.: Photo. Dwg. Poster. Print. B&W. 18: var. sizes. Lang.: Eng.

USA: New York, NY. 1910-1937. Histories-sources. ■First-hand account of the history of Minsky Burlesque: the theatres played, its entertainers and its eventual disbandment.

Performance spaces

3465 Robinson, Jack. "Brooklyn's Magnificent Ruin: The Bushwick Theatre." *MarqJTHS.* 1986; 18(1): 22-23. Illus.: Photo. B&W. 4: var. sizes. Lang.: Eng.

USA: New York, NY. 1911-1986. Historical studies. ■Originally designed by William McElfatrick and built by Percy Williams as a vaudeville house. Later used as a movie house and, in 1970, a church.

Performance/production

3466 Jay, Ricky. *Learned Pigs & Fireproof Women.* Secaucus, NJ: Villard; 1986. 224 pp. Illus.: Photo. Dwg. Color. B&W. Lang.: Eng.

1600-1986. Histories-specific. ■Magician's account of unusual entertainers, including talking animals, mind readers and freaks.

3467 Martin, Linda; Segrave, Kerry. *Women in Comedy.* Citadel; 1986. 466 pp. Biblio. Illus.: Photo. Lang.: Eng.

1900-1986. Historical studies. ■Consists of overview of the type of comedy in a given period followed by discussion of the careers of successful women comics of the time.

3468 Crass, Randall F. "Fela Anikulapo-Kuti, The Art of an Afrobeat Rebel." *TDR.* 1986 Spr; 30(1): 131-148. Illus.: Photo. Poster. Print. B&W. 15: 2 in. x 3 in., 5 in. x 7 in. Lang.: Eng.

Nigeria: Lagos. 1960-1985. Biographical studies. ■Nigerian popular musician, Fela Anikulapo-Kuti, a theatrical performer and political voice through his songs and lyrics and how he became imprisoned.

3469 Hobson, Harold. "The Comic Spirit." *Drama.* 1986; 160(2): 9. Illus.: Photo. B&W. 1. Lang.: Eng.

UK-England. 1900. Critical studies. ■Recollection of performances by music-hall comedian Billy Danvers.

3470 Jackson, Delilah. "When Harlem Was Hot." *AInf.* 1986; 4: 124-133. [Hy Curtis, Marion Egbert, Charles Cook, Tondaleyo, March 9, 1986.] Lang.: Eng.

USA: New York, NY, Savannah, GA. 1930-1950. Histories-sources. ■Four nightclub entertainers on their particular acts and the atmosphere of the late night clubs and theaters in Harlem.

3471 Narita, Cobi. "Dakota Stanton, Entertainer: February 9, 1986." *AInf.* 1986; 4: 115-123. Lang.: Eng.

USA: Pittsburgh, PA, New York, NY. 1950-1980. Histories-sources. ■Dakota Stanton discussing her career as a singer and dancer in

MIXED ENTERTAINMENT: Variety acts—Performance/production

nightclubs and reviews on tour as well as on her workshops for the Universal Jazz Coalition in New York.

Reference materials

3472 Smith, Ronald Lande. *The Stars of Stand-Up Comedy: A Biographical Encyclopedia.* New York, NY: Garland; 1986. 227 pp. (Reference Library of the Humanities Vol. 564.) Illus.: Photo. Lang.: Eng.
USA. 1900-1986. Biographical studies. ■Brief biographies of 101 stand-up comics and comedy teams, including analysis of style and material, quotation of typical bits.

———

Other entries with significant content related to Mixed Entertainment: 494, 814, 1329, 1599, 2014, 2810.

MUSIC-DRAMA

General

3473 Kernochan, John M. "Music Performing Rights Organizations in the United States of America: Special Characteristics, Restraints and Public Attitudes." *ColJL&A.* 1986 Win; 10(2): 333-380. Notes. Lang.: Eng.
USA. 1856-1986. Historical studies. ■Overview of the U.S. legal arrangements regarding music performing rights, emphasizing features of the U.S. system which differ from the legal requirements of other countries.

Administration

3474 Field, Anthony. "The Economics of the Orchestra." *JAP&M.* 1986 May; 2(3): 9-11. Lang.: Eng.
Histories-specific. ■The financial situation of orchestras worldwide with brief history of orchestral funding and discussion of the 1985 Swedish National European Music Year Conference.

3475 Kite, Ulla Renton. "The Twentieth Century Promotion of Early Music." *JAP&M.* 1986 May; 2(3): 17-20. Notes. Lang.: Eng.
Historical studies. ■The revival of 'early music' performed on authentic, restored instruments. The development, financial backing, and promotion of 'early music' to attract contemporary audiences.

3476 Pinkos, Cynthia; Bomser, Alan H. "The Musician's Personal Management Contract: Sample Contract and Comments." *ColJL&A.* 1986 Win; 10(2): 245-276. Notes. Biblio. Lang.: Eng.
USA. 1986. Histories-sources. ■Detailed examination of the standard Musician's Personal Management Contract.

Design/technology

3477 Mills-Cockell, John. "Incidental Music in Contemporary Theatre." *Theatrum.* 1986 Sum; 4: 9-11, 22-24. Illus.: Photo. Print. B&W. 1: 3 in. x 4 in. Lang.: Eng.
Canada: Toronto, ON. 1985. Instructional materials. ■The composer, using examples from his own work in the theatre, contrasts the differences in the use of music in film and theatre.

3478 Jackman, Sharon. "Watching and Listening: Lighting for Orchestras." *LDim.* 1986 Mar-Apr.; 10(2): 72-73, 75, 77-78. Illus.: Photo. Print. Color. 2: 5 in. x 7 in. Lang.: Eng.
USA: Washington, DC, Boston, MA, New York, NY. 1910-1986. Technical studies. ■The problems of lighting symphony orchestras, especially in older buildings, so that both audience and musicians are comfortable. Special problems in lighting for television.

Institutions

3479 Kutschera, Edda. "Strauss plus Mozart mal zwei." (Strauss Plus Mozart Times Two.) *Buhne.* 1986 July; 29(7): 16-17. Illus.: Photo. Print. Color. Lang.: Ger.
Austria: Vienna. 1986. Histories-sources. ■Wiener Sommer 1986: productions of the Volksoper at Staatsoper, and of the Wiener Kammeroper between seasons during summer, promoted by Teletheater-Gesellschaft especially for tourists.

3480 Mertl, Monika. "Besondere Kategorie." *Buhne.* 1986 July; 29(7): 17-19. Illus.: Photo. Print. B&W. Lang.: Ger.
Austria: Vienna. 1986. Histories-sources. ■Manager Franz Eugen Dostal's concept for the festival Spectaculum produced at the old quarter of the University of Vienna, and his plans for productions in 1986.

Performance spaces

3481 Klüver, Reymer, ed. *Die grossen Opern- und Konzerthäuser der Welt.* (Great Opera Houses and Concert Halls of the World.) Ostfildern: J. Fink, Kümmerly & Frey; 1986. 360 pp. Pref. Index. Illus.: Photo. Color. Lang.: Ger.
Historical studies. ■Accounts of eighty opera houses around the world by various authors.

Performance/production

3482 Kesting, Jürgen. *Die grossen Sänger.* (Great Singers.) Düsseldorf: Claassen; 1986. 2094 pp. Pref. Index. Biblio. Append. Gloss. Illus.: Photo. B&W. [3 vols.] Lang.: Ger.
1901-1985. Histories-specific. ■Historical account of singers and the art of singing: biographies, analyses of vocal qualities, schools of vocal art.

3483 Taylor, Dennis. "Constructing the TV Drama Audience: a Case-Study of Channel 2's *Sweet and Sour.*" *ADS.* 1986 Apr.; 8: 18-32. Notes. Illus.: Photo. B&W. 1: 11 x 14 cm. Lang.: Eng.
Australia: Sydney, N.S.W. 1980-1984. Critical studies. ■Case-study of the production, scheduling and shaping of the rock music drama *Sweet and Sour*, for Australian's television audience by the Australian Broadcasting Corporation.

3484 Zamponi, Linda. "Es gibt keinen Mittelweg." (There is No Middle Course.) *Buhne.* 1986 June; 29(6): 20-22. Illus.: Photo. Print. Color. Lang.: Ger.
Austria: Vienna. 1955-1986. Biographical studies. ■Singer Elisabeth Kales and her work, especially her performance of the main role in Leo Fall's operetta *Madame Pompadour* at the Volksoper.

3485 Schafer, R. Murray. "The Princess of the Stars." *CTR.* 1986 Sum; 13(47): 20-28. Illus.: Photo. Print. B&W. 4: var. sizes. Lang.: Eng.
Canada: Banff, AB. 1985. Histories-sources. ■Description of a performance of *The Princess and the Stars* by R. Murray Schafer, an environmental performance piece first performed at dawn on Two Jack Lake near Banff, AB.

3486 Lucre, Andrew. "In Paris, Strehler Rehearses *The Three Penny Opera.*" *PI.* 1986 Dec.; 2(5): 78. Lang.: Eng.
France: Paris. 1986. Historical studies. ■Overview of *Die Dreigroschenoper (The Three Penny Opera)* rehearsal directed by Giorgio Strehler.

3487 Csáki, Judit. "A Novák. Cseh Tamás új műsoráról." (The Novák: On Tamás Cseh's New Show.) *Sz.* 1986 Aug.; 19(8): 16-18. Illus.: Photo. B&W. 1: 6 cm. x 9 cm. Lang.: Hun.
Hungary: Budapest. 1986. Critical studies. ■Notes on Tamás Cseh's *Melyrepülés (Flying at Low Altitude)*, text by Dénes Csengey.

3488 Nánay, István. "Nosztalgia és leszámolás. Zenés darabok a hatvanas évekről." (Nostalgia and Showdown: Musical Plays About the Sixties.) *Sz.* 1986 Aug.; 19(8): 11-15. Illus.: Photo. B&W. 3: 9 cm. x 12 cm., 9 cm. x 19 cm. Lang.: Hun.
Hungary. 1985-1986. Critical studies. ■Notes on three musical plays: *Melyrepülés (Flying at Low Altitude)*, Táncdalfesztivál '66 (Dance Music Festival '66), and *Munkásoperett (Workers' Operetta)*.

3489 Takács, István. "'Mondd, te kit választanál?' Az *István, a király* a Nemzetiben." ('Say, Whom Would You Choose?' *King Stephen* at the National Theatre.) *Sz.* 1986 Jan.; 19(1): 5-9. Illus.: Photo. B&W. 4: 9 cm. x 12 cm. Lang.: Hun.
Hungary: Budapest. 1985. Reviews of performances. ■The rock-opera of Miklós Boldizsár, Levente Szörényi and János Bródy at the National Theatre directed by Imre Kerényi in comparison with previous open-air performances.

3490 Treugutt, Stefan; Myszkowski, F., photo. "Spotkanie Z Rotbaumem." (Meeting with Rotbaum.) *TeatrW.* 1984

MUSIC-DRAMA: General—Performance/production

July; 39(814): 20-22. Illus.: Photo. 3: 10 cm. x 7 cm. Lang.: Pol.

Poland: Warsaw. 1984. Reviews of performances. ■Production analysis of *Sen O Goldfadenie (Dream About Goldfaden)* directed by Jacub Rotbaum at Teatr Zydowski, songs and music by Abraham Goldfaden.

3491 King, Pamela M.; Salvador-Rabaza, Asunción. "La Festa d'Elx: The Festival of the Assumption of the Virgin, Elche (Alicante)." *MET*. 1986; 8(1): 21-50. Notes. Illus.: Photo. Diagram. B&W. 22. Lang.: Eng.

Spain: Elche. 1370-1985. Reviews of performances. ■The evolution of the *Festa d'Agost* from 1370 is discussed in relation to a contemporary performance.

3492 "New Music Theatre." *TT*. 1985 Nov.; 5(1): 1-2, 14. Lang.: Eng.

USA. 1985. Histories-sources. ■Interview with composer-musician Peter Gordon, discussing the process of composing for the theatre and the relationship of his work to other forms of music theatre.

3493 Petter, Robert. "Hildegard of Bingen's *Ordo Virtutum*." *MET*. 1986; 8(1): 66-67. Lang.: Eng.

USA: Stanford, CA. 1986. Reviews of performances. ■Musical cloister drama performed by Sequentia, a German-based early medieval group, in Stanford University's Memorial Church.

3494 *Musykal'no-dramatičeskij spectakl'na sovremennoj sovetskoj scene: Avtoref. dis. ... kand. iskusstvovedenija.* (The Musical-Dramatic Performance on the Contemporary Soviet Stage: Synopsis of a Dissertation by a Candidate in Art Criticism.) Moscow: GITIS; 1986. 25 pp. Lang.: Rus.

USSR. 1980-1986. Critical studies.

3495 Šiškov, A. "Chto slyshim my..." (What We Listen To.) *Molodoj kommunist*. 1986; 8: 53-59. Lang.: Rus.

USSR. 1986. Histories-sources. ■Interview with composer Aleksej Ribnikov on current musical drama: rock music, opera and rock opera.

Plays/librettos/scripts

3496 Altieri, Joanne. *The Theatre of Praise: The Panegyric Tradition in Seventeenth-Century English Drama*. Newark, DE: Univ. of Delaware; 1986. 240 pp. Biblio. Index. Lang.: Eng.

England. 1642-1699. Histories-specific. ■Development of Restoration musical theatre from its origins in the court masque, city pageant and history play, primarily by Jonson, Davenant and Dryden.

3497 Rodnajanzkaja, M.L. *Anglijskije tradicii v muzykal'no-drama-tičeskich proizvedenijah Persela: Avtoref. diss... kand. iskusstvovedenija.* (English Traditions in the Musical-Dramatic Works of Purcell: Synopsis of a Dissertation by a Candidate in Art Criticism.) Moscow: LGITMIK; 1986. 24 pp. Lang.: Rus.

England. 1659-1695. Critical studies.

3498 Potter, Robert. "The *Ordo Virtutum*: Ancestor of the English Moralities?" *CompD*. 1986; 20(3): 201-210. Notes. Lang.: Eng.

Germany: Bingen. 1151. Critical studies. ■An analysis of Hildegard of Bingen's *Ordo Virtutum* as a morality play. Concludes that the play is not a direct ancestor of the later vernacular moralities, but stands alone as a unique creation.

3499 Cho, Tong-il. "The General Nature of *P'ansori*." *KoJ*. 1986 Apr.; 26(4): 10-22. Lang.: Eng.

Korea. Historical studies. ■Description of *p'ansori*, a one-man singing drama performed with an accompanying drum.

Reference materials

3500 Rich, Maria F. "Opera USA—Perspective: The Stravinsky Legacy." *OQ*. 1985 Spr; 3(1): 80-98. Illus.: Photo. Pntg. Dwg. Sketches. Print. B&W. 10: 3 in. x 5 in., 8 in. x 5 in. Lang.: Eng.

Switzerland: Basel. USA: New York, NY. 1930-1985. ■The Stravinsky collection of writing, music and art was purchased by the Paul Sacher Foundation and brought to Switzerland, and a joint exhibit of music, art and manuscripts of Stravinsky was created by Sacher and Christian Geelhaar at Kunstmuseum (Basel).

Relation to other fields

3501 Gilbert, Michael. "The Musical Dimensions of Brecht's Work as a Poet." *ComIBS*. 1986 Apr.; 15(2): 11-16.

Critical studies. ■A look at Brecht's talents in the area of musical-poetic improvisation and his emphasis on musical setting as a fundamental element of his poetry's sociopolitical utility.

Training

3502 Vitkauskete, A.D.Ju. *Plastičeskoe vospitanie na sovremen-nom etape razvitija muzykal'nogo teatra: Avtoref. diss... kand. iskusstvovedenija.* (The Plastic Education of the Actor-Vocalist at the Contemporary Stage of Development of the Music Theatre: Synopsis of a Dissertation by a Candidate in Art Criticism.) Moscow: GITIS; 1986. 24 pp. Lang.: Rus.

USSR. 1980. Critical studies.

Chinese opera

3503 Chang, Shih-k'uei. "Chi ch'eng yü ko hsin kai nien te keng hsin." (Renewal of the Concepts of Tradition and Innovation.) *XYanj*. 1986 Dec.; 21: 106-112. Notes. Lang.: Chi.

China, People's Republic of. 1949-1980. Critical studies. ■Influence of Wagner on the music of contemporary Chinese opera.

Design/technology

3504 Zhou, Xibao. "Heguan Kao Lue." (Research on the Pheasant-Feather Helmet.) *XYishu*. 1982 Aug.; 5(3): 71-75. Illus.: Photo. 14: var. sizes. Lang.: Chi.

China. 300 B.C.-1980 A.D. Historical studies. ■Origin, use and significance of the two pheasant feathers on the warrior's helmet in Chinese traditional theatre.

Performance/production

3505 Chang, Chiu. "Tao Yuan Tang Chia Wan Hsi Tai, Hsi Hui Kao Cha." (Research on Tao Yuan Tang Chia Wan's Theatre Stages and Activities.) *XYanj*. 1986 Apr.; 18: 228-253. Lang.: Chi.

China. 1868-1935. Historical studies. ■Use of early performance records to infer theatre activities of a later period.

3506 Chou, Ch'uanchia. "Wei ch'ang sheng lun." (Discourse on Wei Ch'angsheng.) *XYanj*. 1986 Dec.; 21: 172-192. Notes. Lang.: Chi.

China. 1795-1850. Biographical studies. ■Life and influence of Wei Ch'angsheng, famous actor and playwright.

3507 Folch, Maria-Dolors. "L'òpera de Pequín. Un art subtilment codificat." (The Bejing Opera. A Subtly Codified Art.) *SdO*. 1986 Jul-Aug.; 28(322-323): 79-81. Notes. Illus.: Photo. Pntg. Print. B&W. 8: var. sizes. Lang.: Cat.

China: Beijing. 800-1986. Historical studies. ■Description of the antecedents of the Beijing Opera, its principal characteristics and its most recent developments.

3508 Gao, Tzu. "Gudian Xiqu de Daoyan Tiaoben (Xu)." (Classical Opera's Directorial Prompt-book (Continued).) *XYishu*. 1982 Aug.; 5(3): 44-48. Lang.: Chi.

China: Suzhou. 1574-1646. Critical studies. ■Pro and con of Feng Menglong's detailed guide to producing traditional Beijing opera.

3509 Gao, Yu. "Gudian Xiqu de Daoyan Jiaoben." (Classical Opera's Directorial Prompt-Books.) *XYishu*. 1982 May; 5(2): 47-61. Notes. Lang.: Chi.

China: Suzhou. 1574-1646. Critical studies. ■Staging during the Ming dynasty according to the annotated classical scripts of Feng Menglong used as promptbooks.

3510 Guo, Liang. "Zaoqi Nanxi Biaoyan Tanyuan." (Trace of Acting in Early Southern Opera.) *XYishu*. 1982 Nov.; 5(4): 37-49. Lang.: Chi.

China: Wenzhou. 1101-1250. Critical studies. ■Analysis of the script for *Top Scholar Zhang Xie* shows traces of the first mature theatrical acting in China.

3511 Hsu, Shuo-fang. "Tu Tang Hsien-Tsu (I Huang Hsien Hsi Shen Ching Yuan Shin Miao Chi)." (Discourse on an Essay

MUSIC-DRAMA: Chinese opera—Performance/production

by Tang Hsien-tsu.) *XYanj.* 1986 Apr.; 18: 211-219. Lang.: Chi.

China. 1598-1984. Critical studies. ■Comparison of traditional and modern performance styles using Tang's essay as a foundation.

3512 Hu, Xuegang; Xu, Shunping. "Shilun Nanxi yu Minjian Wen Xue." (Southern Sung Drama and Folk Arts.) *XYishu.* 1982 Aug.; 5 (3): 76-88. Lang.: Chi.

China: Wenzhou. 1127-1234. Historical studies. ■Southern opera (*Nanxi*), the first mature theatrical genre in China, derived from various folk arts such as puppet shows, shadow puppets, oral imitation, acrobatics, joke shows, dance and folk songs. Related to Puppetry.

3513 Jiang, Weiguo. "Qu Qi Jingsui, Wei Wo Suoyong." (Take Its Quintessence and Apply It to Ours.) *XYishu.* 1982 Nov.; 5(4): 61-70. Lang.: Chi.

China. 1100-1980. Critical studies. ■Spoken drama actors can learn natural communication with audience, symbolic style and high physical skills from the Sung dramas.

3514 Liu, Tungshen. "Ching chü ming ching hou hsi jui." (Famous Beijing Opera Actor: Hou Hsijui.) *XYanj.* 1986 Dec.; 21 (156-171). Notes. Lang.: Chi.

China. 1920-1983. Biographical studies. ■Career of Hou Hsijui.

3515 Liu, Zhiqun. "Zangxi di Fazhan jiqi Zai Zhongguo Xijushi Shang de Diwei." (Development of Tibetan Opera and Its Place in the History of Chinese Theatre.) *XYishu.* 1982 Aug.; 5(3): 89-97. Lang.: Chi.

China. Tibet. 1700-1981. Historical studies. ■Influence of Tibetan drama on theatre in the Western provinces.

3516 Lu, Qing; Zhao, Bi. "Kong Fu De Xi Qu Huo Dong." (Theatrical Activities of the Kong Family.) *XYanj.* 1986 Nov.; 20: 262-279. Lang.: Chi.

China: Beijing. 1912-1936. Historical studies. ■Participation in the activities of Chinese opera after the Ching dynasty by descendants of Confucius.

3517 Ma, Ye. "Lun Zhongguo Xiqu Xuni Biaoyan Chan Sheng de Yuanyin." (Origins of Symbolic Acting in Chinese Opera.) *XYishu.* 1982 Nov.; 5(4): 50-60. Lang.: Chi.

China. 1127-1278. Critical studies. ■Dance-turned-narrative and daily-movement-turned-dance lead to stylized acting.

3518 Wei, Shihch'eng. "Ch'ing tai ch'ien chia shih ch'i ching shih te ch'in ch'iang." (Music of the Ch'in Opera in Beijing during the Ch'ing Dynasty.) *XYanj.* 1986 Dec.; 21: 220-232. Notes. Illus.: Photo. B&W. Lang.: Chi.

China: Beijing. 1795-1850. Historical studies. ■Analysis of the Shensi style of chanting and its influence on singing styles in the provinces of Szechuan and Yunnan.

3519 Wen, Yüpo. "Wei ch'ang sheng pu shih ch'in ch'iang yen yüan." (Wei Ch'angsheng Is Not an Actor of Ch'in Opera.) *XYanj.* 1986 Dec.; 21: 241-250. Notes. Lang.: Chi.

China. 1700-1800. Historical studies. ■Analysis of cast and production lists reveals that Wei Ch'angsheng was a Szechuan opera actor.

3520 Zheng, Guang-Hua. "Gui Zhou Tu Jia Zhu Tan Tan Xi." (The Tan Tan Play in Gui Zhou.) *XYanj.* 1986 Nov.; 20: 252-261. Lang.: Chi.

China. 1349-1949. Historical studies. ■Origins, costumes, music and performance style of the traditional Tan Tan play in Gui Zhou province.

3521 Banu, Georges; Wiswell, Ella L., transl.; Gibson, June V., transl. "Mei Lanfang: A Case Against and a Model for the Occidental Stage." *ATJ.* 1986 Fall; 3(1): 153-178. Notes. Biblio. Illus.: Photo. Print. B&W. 3: 3 in. x 5 in. Lang.: Eng.

China, People's Republic of. USSR. Germany. 1900-1935. Historical studies. ■Influence of Beijing opera performer Mei Lanfang on European acting and staging traditions, theories of Konstantin Stanislavskij, Vsevolod Mejerchol'd, Sergej Eisenstein and Bertolt Brecht.

3522 Liao, Pen; Le, Guan-hua; Wu, Yu-hua; Zhang, Min; Liu, Yan-jun. "1985 Nien Quan Guo Xi Qu Guan Mo Yan Chu SHu Ping." (Review of the 1985 Season of the National Opera.) *XYanj.* 1986; 20: 1-70. Lang.: Chi.

China, People's Republic of: Beijing. 1985. Reviews of performances. ■Includes discussions of performance styles, staging, design, playwriting and use of music.

3523 Lu, Chyuanlih. "Liaunan Yingdiaw Shih te choan sheng yu fa jaan." (The Creation and Development of Yingdiaw Opera.) *XYanj.* 1986 Dec.; 21: 267-268. Lang.: Chi.

China, People's Republic of. 1959-1980. Historical studies. ■Summary of theatre activities.

3524 Xu, Shu-hua. "Shi Tan Zheng Mian Xi Ju Xing Xiang De Shu Zhao." (Essay on Creation of Positive Comedy in Chinese Opera.) *XYanj.* 1986 Nov.; 20: 161-170. Lang.: Chi.

China, People's Republic of: Beijing. 1964-1985. Technical studies. ■Techniques of comedians in modern Beijing opera.

Plays/librettos/scripts

3525 Chin, Naichün. "Lun tou erh yüan kai pieh chung te chi ke wen t'i." (Discourse on the Adaptations of *The Injustice of Miss Tou.*) *XYanj.* 1986 Dec.; 21: 84-95. Notes. Lang.: Chi.

China. 1360-1960. Critical studies. ■Discussion of the plots and themes.

3526 Chu, Naishu. "Shen ching san k'ao." (Shen Ching, from Three Views.) *XYanj.* 1986 Dec.; 21: 233-240. Lang.: Chi.

China. 1368-1644. Biographical studies. ■Life, activities and works of playwright Shen Ching.

3527 Fu, Hsueh-i. "*Chan Ta Fei Chuan Ta.*" (*Chan Ta* Is Not *Chuan Ta.*) *XYanj.* 1986 Apr.; 18: 194-210. Lang.: Chi.

China. 1200-1986. Critical studies. ■Differences between the Southern Sung dynasty's lyric song-drama and the traditional Chinese opera.

3528 Fu, Xiao-Hang. "Jin Pi Xi Xiang Zhu Kan Ben Ji Lue." (Review of Various Editions of *Xi Xiang Zhu* by Jin Sheng Tan.) *XYanj.* 1986 Nov.; 20: 222-237. Lang.: Chi.

China. 1669-1843. Historical studies. ■Publishing dates, locations and contents of 32 extant editions of this classical play.

3529 Hua, Chia. "Hsi Chu Te I Ching." (The Mood of Beijing Opera.) *XYanj.* 1986 Apr.; 18: 123-131. Lang.: Chi.

China: Beijing. 1030-1984. Critical studies. ■Analyzes use of poetic elements to create mood in Beijing opera.

3530 Liu, Tahai. "Shih Hsiao." (Interpretation of *Hsiao.*) *XYanj.* 1986 Dec.; 21: 265-266. Notes. B&W. Lang.: Chi.

China. 618-1580. Historical studies. ■Definition and characteristics of the role *Hsiao.*

3531 Luo, Di. "Jieyan *Tiqu* Lun *Huanhun.*" (Commenting on *The Peony Pavilion* through *Tiqu.*) *XYishu.* 1982 Nov.; 5(4): 125-129. Lang.: Chi.

China. 1600-1980. Critical studies. ■*Tiqu*, a scene from Wu Bing's play, is in fact Wu's critique of Tang Xianzu's masterpiece, *The Peony Pavilion.*

3532 Shih, Lei. "Fan Ts'ui t'ing chi ch'i tso p'in." (Fan Ts'ui-t'ing and His Plays.) *XYanj.* 1986 Dec.; 21: 129-142. Notes. Lang.: Chi.

China. 1900-1980. Critical studies. ■Characteristics and influence and historical meaning of Fan Ts'ui-t'ing's plays.

3533 Zhan, Mutao. "Lun Li Yu de Weiren, Juzuo he Xiju guan." (Li Yu's Personality, Plays and Theory of Theatre.) *XYishu.* 1982 Nov.; 5(4): 130-139. Lang.: Chi.

China. 1611-1930. Critical studies. ■Disagreeing with Shen Yao and Lin Kecheng, the author argues that Li Yu, the famous Qing dynasty playwright, was a talented philistine intellectual, his plays are technically ingenious and his theory of theatre is generally valuable.

3534 Zhang, Xin-jian. "Wang Ji-De Yu Xu Wei." (Wang Ji-De and Xu Wei.) *XYanj.* 1986 Nov.; 20: 209-221. Lang.: Chi.

China. 1620-1752. Historical studies. ■Stylistic differences in the works of the playwrights Wang Ji-De and Xu Wei.

3535 An, Kui. "Ge Xin De Ju Zhuo Jia Long Luan Tong Zhong Huo De Re You Shi—Lun Xu Jin De Xi Qu Chuang Zhuo." (Reformed Dramatists Learn From Tradition: Discussion of Xu Jin's Newly-Created Chinese Operas.) *XYanj.* 1986 Nov.; 20: 190-208. Lang.: Chi.

China, People's Republic of: Beijing. 1952-1985. Critical studies. ■Adapting traditional theatre to modern needs.

3536 He, Wei. "Ma Ke Yu Xi Qu Yin Yue—Ji Nian Ma Ke Tong Zhi." (Ma Ke and Chinese Opera Music—To Commemorate Ma Ke.) *XYanj.* 1986 Nov.; 20: 175-189. Lang.: Chi.

MUSIC-DRAMA: Chinese opera—Plays/librettos/scripts

China, People's Republic of: Beijing. 1951-1985. Critical studies. ■An account of Ma Ke's musical works, contribution and influence upon Chinese opera.

3537 Hsing, Jen. "Hsi Chu Chu Pen Te Chieh Kou Te Tien." (The Special Structure of Opera Librettos.) *XYanj.* 1986 Apr.; 18: 112-122. Lang.: Chi.
China, People's Republic of: Beijing. 1983. Critical studies. ■Use of poetical and lyrical elements to add beauty to a play.

3538 Ke, Zi-ming. "Tan Pu Xian Mu Lian Xi." (Discourse on *Mu Lian* by Pu Xian.) *XYanj.* 1986 Nov.; 20: 246-251. Lang.: Chi.
China, People's Republic of: Beijing. 1962-1985. Critical studies. ■History, characteristics and performance styles of the Chinese folk play *Mu Lian*.

3539 Lee, Kuot'ing. "Chien lun Chen jen Chien." (Brief Discourse on Chen Jenchien.) *XYanj.* 1986 Dec.; 21: 143-155. Notes. Lang.: Chi.
China, People's Republic of. 1913-1986. Biographical studies. ■Chen Jenchien's life and contributions, especially his innovations which combined the characteristics of Chinese opera and Western theatre.

3540 Lee, Ling. "Hsü hsi shih fei t'an." (Discussion on Sequels to Plays.) *XYanj.* 1986 Dec.; 21: 96-105. Lang.: Chi.
China, People's Republic of. 1949-1980. Historical studies. ■Types of sequels and their characteristics.

3541 Qian, Shiming. "Lun Cheng Shi." (Essay on the Formulas of Chinese Operas.) *XYanj.* 1986 Nov.; 20: 96-111. Lang.: Chi.
China, People's Republic of: Beijing. 1903-1985. Critical studies. ■Origins, characteristics and structure of the standard schemes.

3542 Wei, Minglun, transl.; Nan, Guo, transl.; Hu, Dongsheng, transl.; Dai, Ling, transl.; Wang, Xiuping, transl.; Wichmann, Elizabeth, transl. "Scholar from Bashan County: A Sichuan Opera." *ATJ.* 1986 Spr; 3(1): 54-101. Illus.: Photo. Print. B&W. 14: var. sizes. Lang.: Eng.
China, People's Republic of. 1876-1983. Histories-sources. ■Introduction to the opera of Sichuan province, especially its all-percussion orchestra. Includes translations of a new play, *Scholar from Bashan County: A Sichuan Opera.*

3543 Yen, Ch'angfa. "Ku tien ming chü te t'ui ch'en ch'u hsin." (Adapting Classical Plays.) *XYanj.* 1986 Dec.; 21: 61-83. Notes. Lang.: Chi.
China, People's Republic of. 1986. Histories-sources. ■Interview with four playwrights about the problems of adaptations. Example used is the classic, *Pi Pa Chi (The Story of the Guitar).*

Reference materials

3544 Shun, Mei. "Guo Wai Yan Jiu Zong Guo Xi Qu De Ying Yu Wen Xian Shuo Yin." (Index of Foreign Research in English about Chinese Opera.) *XYanj.* 1986 Nov.; 20: 290-300. Lang.: Chi.
China. 1817-1974. Bibliographical studies. ■Annotated list of 121 documents.

3545 Wen, Shi. "Xian Dai Xi Ju Yan Jiu De Luo Gu—Xi Qu Xian Dai Xi Yan Jiu Hui 1985 Nian Nian Hui." (To Evoke the Study on Modern Comedy—Analysis of Chinese Modern Drama Research Committee's 1985 Annual Dissertations.) *XYanj.* 1986 Nov.; 20: 171-174. Lang.: Chi.
China, People's Republic of: Beijing. 1985. Critical studies. ■Review of 1985 dissertations and research directed by the Chinese Opera's Modern Drama Research Committee.

Relation to other fields

3546 Liao, Pen. "Chung Chou Chu Tu Pei Sung Hsi Chu Wen Wo Lun Kao." (Analysis of Archaeological Discoveries of Theatrical Documents and Equipment of the Northern Sung Dynasty.) *XYanj.* 1986 Apr.; 18: 163-193. Illus.: Photo. B&W. 6. Lang.: Chi.

1032-1126. Histories-sources.

3547 "Hsi Chu Te Hsien Tai Hua Yu Jen Te Hsien Tai Hua." (Modernization of Opera and Dramatists.) *XYanj.* 1986 Apr.; 18: 97-111. Lang.: Chi.
China, People's Republic of: Beijing. 1985. Historical studies. ■Art of the Beijing opera should follow the times and serve the needs of the people.

3548 Chang, Chen. "I Fung Shu Hsin Lun Chen Hsing." (To Promote the Beijing Opera—From A Letter.) *XYanj.* 1986 Apr.; 18: 75-78. Lang.: Chi.
China, People's Republic of: Beijing. 1985. Historical studies. ■Function of the Beijing opera is to educate the people about the principles of the revolution and current government policy.

3549 Ching, Chih. "Lun I Shu Pu Mieh—Tu Pai Hua Chi Fang, Tui Chen Chu Hsing Fang Chen Te Tsai Jen Shih." (It Is Not to Extinguish Art—Reinterpreting the Policy of 'All Assemble the Thought and Revolutionize the Tradition'.) *XYanj.* 1986 Apr.; 18: 49-74. Lang.: Chi.
China, People's Republic of: Beijing. 1920-1985. Historical studies. ■Mao Zedong's policy concerning theatre's role in the revolution.

Research/historiography

3550 Fan, Chihhsin. "Tien kuei-pu chi lu kuei-pu pien." (Controversy About Whether Tien Kuei-pu Could Be Lu Kuei-pu.) *XYanj.* 1986 Dec.; 21: 256-264. Notes. Lang.: Chi.
China. 1500-1644. Historical studies. ■Examination of historical documents proves that Tien Kuei-pu is not Lu Kuei-pu.

3551 Hsu, Hung-Tu; Lee, Chao-Chin. "Lu Yao, Lui Yao, Liu Yao." (Lu Yao, Lui Yao and Liu Yao.) *XYanj.* 1986 Apr.; 18: 268-269. Lang.: Chi.
China. 1032-1420. Critical studies. ■Three seemingly different types of dance-dramas prove to be the same dramatic work.

3552 Lu, Lin. "Yüan ch'ü szu ta chia chih yi te chih yi." (Question on the Question of the Four Great Playwrights of the Yüan Dynasty.) *XYanj.* 1986 Dec.; 21: 251-255. Lang.: Chi.
China. 1271-1368. Historical studies. ■Analysis of historical documents confirms that Cheng Kuangtsu was one of the four.

3553 Meng, Fanshu. "Kuan yü sheng ch'iang chü chung shih te yen chin fang fa wen t'i." (Problems of Methodology in the Research of Characterization throughout the History of Singing.) *XYanj.* 1986 Dec.; 21: 205-219. Lang.: Chi.
China. 1600-1980. Historical studies. ■Includes discussion of traditional musical notation and contemporary interpretation.

3554 Wang, Ren-yuan. "Ching Chao Jing Ju Lu Hua He Deng Gong Chi Pu Yi Jie." (Introducing the Translation of Musical Notes of Four Old Plays.) *XYanj.* 1986 Nov.; 20: 280-289. Lang.: Chi.
China: Beijing. 1674-1985. Instructional materials. ■Traditional music notation of *Lu Hua He, Er Jin Gong, Dang Liang* and *Man Ban Er Huang* translated and transformed into modern notation.

3555 Guo, Bing-zhen. "Yue Ju Ji Ju Bian Ge De Li Shi Pou Shi." (Historical Analysis of the Rapid Evolution of Cantonese Opera.) *XYanj.* 1986 Nov.; 20: 129-151. Lang.: Chi.
China, People's Republic of: Kuang Tung. 1885-1985. Historical studies. ■Development of Cantonese opera and its influence.

3556 Shen, Yao. "Hsi Chu I Shu Te Te Shu Tsung Ho Li Cheng." (Beijing Opera—A Special Kind of Synthesis.) *XYanj.* 1986 Apr.; 18: 1-34. Lang.: Chi.
China, People's Republic of: Beijing. 1755-1984. Historical studies. ■Traces the origins and history.

3557 Wang, Lin. "Ping Hsi Tsai Tienchin Te Fa Chan." (The Development of *Ping Hsi* in Tienchin.) *XYanj.* 1986 Apr.; 18: 273-287. Lang.: Chi.
China, People's Republic of: Tienchin. 1885-1948. Historical studies. ■Also discusses the influence of folksongs and theatre of Tienchin.

Theory/criticism

3558 "Chung Kuo Ku Tien Hsi Chu Chung Te Yu Huan I Shih—Hsi Chu Mei Hsueh Tuan Hsiang Chih I." (Chinese

MUSIC-DRAMA: Chinese opera—Theory/criticism

Classical Opera's 'Anxiety about Fate'—One of the Aesthetic Principles of Chinese Opera.) *XYanj.* 1986 Apr.; 18: 35-48. Lang.: Chi.

China: Beijing. 5 B.C.-1985 A.D. Critical studies. ∎Concern of traditional Chinese philosophy, applied to Beijing Opera.

3559 Chen, Shao-hua. "Chiao Chieh Tzu Jan—Ma Tzu Yuan Chu Tso Jung Shih Ju Chu Chu Li." (Artful, Natural—Ma Tzu-Yuan's Combination of Poetry with Opera.) *XYanj.* 1986 Apr.; 18: 139-146. Lang.: Chi.

China: Beijing. 1279-1368. Critical studies. ∎Extols Ma's use of poetic elements.

3560 Ding, Daoxi. "Xiqu Wutai Secai Guan." (Theory of Stage Colors of Traditional Theatre.) *XYishu.* 1982 Aug.; 5(3): 61-70. Lang.: Chi.

China. 200 B.C.-1982 A.D. Critical studies. ∎Significance, meaning and use of red, white and black in traditional theatre.

3561 Hu, T'ien-Ch'eng. "Lun tuan an chieh te hsien tan shuo." (Discourse on Tuan Anchieh's Aesthetics.) *XYanj.* 1986 Dec.; 21 : 44-60. Notes. Lang.: Chi.

China. 800-1644. Critical studies. ∎Development of Tuan's aesthetic theories and their influence on playwrights and critics.

3562 Qian, Yingyu. "Xigu Yishu de Zai Renshi." (Reconsideration of Theatre Arts.) *XYishu.* 1982 Aug.; 5(3): 27-33. Lang.: Chi.

China. 200 B.C.-1982 A.D. Critical studies. ∎Defense of tradition, especially Beijing opera.

3563 Xiao, Shi-xiong. "Chuan Ju Ga Qiang De Chuan Tong Li Lun Yu Bang Qiang." (The Theory of Traditional Music of Chuan Opera.) *XYanj.* 1986 Nov.; 20: 238-245. Lang.: Chi.

China. 1866-1952. Critical studies. ∎Analysis of the form, sources and theory of Szechuan Opera singing style.

3564 Dai, Ping. "Yi Ge Du Te Di Xin Xi Fu Hao Xi Tong—Lun Xi Ou Cheng Shi." (A Unique Symbolic System—Discussion of the Format of Chinese Opera.) *XYanj.* 1986 Nov.; 20: 71-95. Lang.: Chi.

China, People's Republic of: Beijing. 1935-1985. Critical studies. ∎Symbolism and aesthetics in the performance styles of Chinese opera.

3565 Gao, Xing-jing. "Xi Qu Bu Yao Gai Ge Yu Yao Gai Ge." (To Reform Chinese Opera or Not.) *XYanj.* 1986 Dec.; 21: 6-10. Lang.: Chi.

China, People's Republic of: Beijing. 1935-1985. Critical studies. ∎Strengths and weaknesses in Beijing opera, and suggested areas for improvement.

3566 Hua, Jia. "Shi Lun Xi Qu De Te Zheng." (Essay on the Special Characteristics of Chinese Opera.) *XYanj.* 1986 Nov.; 20: 112-128. Lang.: Chi.

China, People's Republic of. 1955-1985. Critical studies. ∎Use of dance, rhythm, illusion, symbolism in a formalized structure to produce enjoyment.

3567 Lin, Zhao-hua. "Bing Fei Ta Shan Shi." (The Stone Tool Is Not Foreign.) *XYanj.* 1986 Dec.; 21: 1-5. Lang.: Chi.

China, People's Republic of: Beijing. 1935-1985. Critical studies. ∎Influence of Western dramatic theories on Beijing opera.

3568 Tao, Mu-ning. "Fei *Kan Chien Nu* Hsi Chu Shuo." (Appeal for the Comedy *Kan Chien Nu.*) *XYanj.* 1986 Apr.; 18: 132-138. Lang.: Chi.

China, People's Republic of: Beijing. 1970-1983. Critical studies. ∎Compares *Kan Chien Nu* with Molière's plays and argues that *Kan Chien Nu* is a tragicomedy, not a comedy.

3569 Wang, Ping-chang. "Tang Tai Fu Chien Hsi Chu Tso Chia Te Chui Chiu." (Research on Contemporary Fuchien Dramatists.) *XYanj.* 1986 Apr.; 18: 79-96. Lang.: Chi.

China, People's Republic of. 1981-1985. Critical studies. ∎Aesthetics and antecedents in the work of four dramatists from Fuchien province.

3570 Yu, Yi. "Chuan Ju Yi Shu Ji Ben Te Zheng Chu Tan." (Analysis of the Basic Characteristics of the Art of Szechuan Opera.) *XYanj.* 1986 Nov.; 20: 152-160. Lang.: Chi.

China, People's Republic of. 1963-1985. Critical studies. ∎Discussion of performance style and use of language, song and orchestra.

Musical theatre

Administration

3571 "Producing Musicals." *ThCr.* 1986 May; 20(5): 17, 38. Lang.: Eng.

USA. 1984-1986. Historical studies. ∎Renewed interest in musicals in regional theatre.

3572 Hale, Alice M. "What Artistic and Managing Directors Say: Papermill Playhouse." *ThCr.* 1986 May; 20(5): 23, 46-47. Lang.: Eng.

USA: Millburn, NJ. Technical studies. ∎Papermill Playhouse's executive producer Angelo Del Rossi discusses producing musicals.

3573 Hale, Alice M. "What Artistic and Managing Directors Say: Playhouse on the Square." *ThCr.* 1986 May; 20(5): 23, 47. Lang.: Eng.

USA: Memphis, TN. Technical studies. ∎Playhouse on the Square's executive director Jackie Nichols discusses producing musicals.

3574 LaRue, Michèle. "What Artistic and Managing Directors Say: Seattle Repertory Theatre." *ThCr.* 1986 May; 20(5): 22, 45. Lang.: Eng.

USA: Seattle, WA. Histories-sources. ∎Seattle Repertory's artistic director Dan Sullivan discusses producing musicals.

3575 LaRue, Michèle. "What Artistic and Managing Directors Say: Walnut Street Theatre." *ThCr.* 1986 may; 20(5): 22, 45-46 . Lang.: Eng.

USA: Philadelphia, PA. Technical studies. ∎Walnut Street Theatre's executive producer discusses producing musicals.

3576 LaRue, Michèle. "Revues: Alive and Well." *ThCr.* 1986 May; 20(5): 24, 62. Lang.: Eng.

USA. 1986. Historical studies. ∎Popularity of musical revues in regional theatre.

Audience

3577 Harris, Dale. "New Perceptions in Lyric Theatre." *OC.* 1986 Spr; 27(1): 18-21. Illus.: Photo. B&W. 6. Lang.: Eng.

North America. 1950-1986. Critical studies. ∎The first of a two-part article on the growth of opera and musical theatre after World War II. Related to Music-Drama: Opera.

Basic theatrical documents

3578 Astley, Ed; Astley, Susan; Seary, Kim; Sereda, John; Strang, Hilary; Willes, Christine; Weiss, Peter Eliot. "*Sex Tips for Modern Girls.*" *CTR.* 1986 Win; 13(49): 67-110. Pref. Illus.: Photo. Print. B&W. 4: var. sizes. Lang.: Eng.

Canada: Vancouver, BC. 1985. ∎Two-act musical comedy about the concerns of sex and love among single heterosexual career-oriented women.

3579 McGee, Timothy J. "The Musical Setting of *La Conversion d'un pêcheur de la Nouvelle-Écosse.*" *THC.* 1984 Fall; 5(2): 141-171. Notes. Lang.: Eng.

Canada. 1851-1887. ∎Musical setting by Jean-Baptiste Labelle for *La conversion d'un pêcheur de la Nouvelle-Écosse (The Conversion of a Nova Scotian Fisherman)*, an operetta by Elzéar Labelle. Brief critical introduction.

3580 Hart, Lorenz; Hart, Dorothy, ed.; Kimball, Robert, ed. *The Complete Lyrics of Lorenz Hart.* New York, NY: Knopf; 1986. 317 pp. Index. Illus.: Photo. Lang.: Eng.

USA. 1920-1943.

Design/technology

3581 Stigsdotter, Annika; Frisk, Jerry; Nielsen, Ulf; Löw, Kalle; Sevnolt, Elisabeth. "Malmöteknikerna presenterar 'La Cage aux Folles, the Broadway Musical'." (The Technicians of Malmö Present *La Cage aux Folles, the Broadway Musical.*) *ProScen.* 1986; 10(1): 7-24. Illus.: Photo. Lang.: Swe.

Sweden: Malmö. 1985. Technical studies. ∎The artists responsible for costumes, lighting, sound, props and wigs, of Malmö Stadsteater, write about how they transferred the Broadway version of *La Cage aux Folles* to a Swedish theatre on one-tenth of the original budget.

3582 Foley, Mike. "*Les Misérables* at the Palace." *Sin.* 1986; 20(1): 8-11. Illus.: Photo. B&W. 5. Lang.: Eng.

MUSIC-DRAMA: Musical theatre—Design/technology

UK-England: London. 1980-1987. Critical studies. ■Analysis of the technological aspects of *Les Misérables* and the overabundance of technical elements in the production.

3583 Haye, Bethany. "*Les Misérables.*" *ThCr.* 1986 Nov.; 20(9): 32-35, 58-59. Illus.: Photo. 4: var. sizes.
UK-England: London. 1986. Technical studies. ■Set designer John Napier's work on the pop opera *Les Misérables.*

3584 Loney, Glenn. "The Ship in the Bottle." *ThCr.* 1986 Feb.; 20(2): 33, 100-101. Illus.: Photo. 3: var. sizes. Lang.: Eng.
UK-England: London. 1986. Technical studies. ■Designer William Dudley's life-like replica of the ship Bounty for David Essex's *Mutiny!*, a musical adaptation of *Mutiny on the Bounty.*

3585 Rea, Kenneth. "In Defence of Hi-Tech." *Drama.* 1986; 3(161): 19-21. Illus.: Photo. B&W. 4: var. sizes. Lang.: Eng.
UK-England: London. 1980-1986. Histories-sources. ■Designer John Napier argues the case for technologically spectacular productions of musicals.

3586 Hale, Alice M. "*Guys and Dolls.*" *ThCr.* 1986 May; 20(5): 19, 38-40. Illus.: Photo. 5: var. sizes. Lang.: Eng.
USA. 1984-1986. Technical studies. ■Costume and lighting designers discuss challenges in designing regional productions of *Guys and Dolls.*

3587 Hale, Alice M. "*She Loves Me.*" *ThCr.* 1986 May; 20(5): 26, 47-48, 50. Illus.: Photo. 4: var. sizes. Lang.: Eng.
USA. 1984-1986. Technical studies. ■Costume and lighting designers discuss challenges in designing regional productions of *She Loves Me.*

3588 Hale, Alice M. "*Gypsy.*" *ThCr.* 1986 May; 20(5): 32, 54-56. Illus.: Photo. Diagram. 4: var. sizes.
USA. 1984-1986. Technical studies. ■Costume and lighting designers discuss challenges in designing regional productions of *Gypsy.*

3589 LaRue, Michèle. "*The Music Man.*" *ThCr.* 1986 May; 20(5): 20-21, 41-42. Illus.: Sketches. Photo. 3: var. sizes. Lang.: Eng.
USA. 1983-1986. Technical studies. ■Costume and lighting designers discuss challenges in designing regional productions of *The Music Man.*

3590 LaRue, Michèle. "*Once Upon a Mattress.*" *ThCr.* 1986 May; 20(5): 30-31, 52-53. Illus.: Photo. 4: var. sizes.
USA. 1984-1986. Technical studies. ■Costume and lighting designers discuss challenges in designing regional productions of *Once Upon a Mattress.*

3591 LaRue, Michèle. "*Ain't Misbehavin'.*" *ThCr.* 1986 May; 20(5): 25, 63-64. Illus.: Photo. 2: var. sizes. Lang.: Eng.
USA. 1984-1986. Technical studies. ■Costume and lighting designers discuss challenges in designing regional productions of *Ain't Misbehavin'.*

3592 LaRue, Michèle. "*TinTypes.*" *ThCr.* 1986 May; 20(5): 25, 64. Lang.: Eng.
USA. 1984-1986. Technical studies. ■Costume and lighting designers discuss challenges in designing regional productions of *Tintypes.*

3593 LaRue, Michèle. "*Side-by-Side by Sondheim.*" *ThCr.* 1986 May; 20(5): 24, 62. Lang.: Eng.
USA. 1984. Technical studies. ■Costume and lighting designers discuss challenges in designing regional productions of *Side-by-Side by Sondheim.*

3594 Lieberman, Susan. "*The Sound of Music.*" *ThCr.* 1986 May; 20(5): 22-23, 42-44. Illus.: Photo. 4: var. sizes. Lang.: Eng.
USA. 1983-1986. Technical studies. ■Costume and lighting designers discuss challenges in designing regional productions of *The Sound of Music.*

3595 Lieberman, Susan. "*Fiddler on the Roof.*" *ThCr.* 1986 May; 20(5): 28-29, 50-52. Illus.: Photo. 4: var. sizes. Lang.: Eng.
USA. 1984-1986. Technical studies. ■Costume and lighting designers discuss challenges in designing regional productions of *Fiddler on the Roof.*

3596 Moynihan, D.S. "*Oklahoma.*" *ThCr.* 1986 May; 20(5): 36-37, 64-67. Illus.: Photo. 5: var. sizes. Lang.: Eng.
USA. 1984-1986. Technical studies. ■Costume and lighting designers discuss challenges in designing regional productions of *Oklahoma.*

3597 Moynihan, D.S. "*Grease.*" *ThCr.* 1986 May; 20(5): 34-35, 57-61. Illus.: Photo. 3: var. sizes. Lang.: Eng.
USA. 1984-1986. Technical studies. ■Costume and lighting designers discuss challenges in designing regional productions of *Grease.*

Performance/production

3598 Grote, David. *Staging the Musical: Planning, Rehearsing, and Marketing the Amateur Production.* New York, NY: Prentice-Hall; 1986. 250 pp. Biblio. Lang.: Eng.
1986. Instructional materials. ■Detailed instructions on the mounting of a musical.

3599 Doucette, L.E. "Theatre and the Politics of Confederation: Elzéar Labelle's *La Conversion d'un pêcheur de la Nouvelle-Écosse.*" *THC.* 1984 Fall; 5(2): 132-140. Notes. Lang.: Eng.
Canada: Quebec, PQ. 1837-1867. Historical studies. ■Development of drama in Quebec up to the Confederation. Labelle's *La Conversion d'un pêcheur de la Nouvelle-Écosse*, a highly popular operetta, is seen as exemplifying a movement toward public performance.

3600 "Az ismétlés előnyei. A *Lakat alá a lányokat* a Diósgyőri Várszinpadon." (Advantages of Repetition: *Lock Up Your Daughters* At Castle Stage of Diósgyőr.) *Sz.* 1986 Oct.; 19(10): 33-34. Illus.: Photo. B&W. 1: 12 cm. x 8 cm. Lang.: Hun.
Hungary: Diósgyőr. 1986. Reviews of performances. ■Stage adaptation of Henry Fielding's *Rape upon Rape*, music by Laurie Johnson and songs by Lionel Bart directed at Castle Stage by Imre Halasi.

3601 Budai, Katalin. "A *My Fair Lady* fogadtatása Magyarországon." (Reception of *My Fair Lady* in Hungary.) *SzSz.* 1986; 10(21): 43-57. Lang.: Hun.
Hungary. 1966-1970. Critical studies. ■The premiere of *My Fair Lady* by Lerner and Loewe represented the first appearance of the traditional Broadway musical on the Hungarian stage.

3602 Csáki, Judit. "Megalkuvásokkal. A *Vértestvérek* Pécsett." (With Compromises: *Blood Brothers* at Pécs.) *Sz.* 1986 June; 19(6): 25-28. Illus.: Photo. B&W. 2: 12 cm. x 15 cm. Lang.: Hun.
Hungary: Pécs. 1986. Reviews of performances. ■Willy Russell's musical *Blood Brothers* at Pécs National Theatre directed by Iván Vas-Zoltán.

3603 Illisz, L. László. "Pataki Éva: *Edith és Marlene.*" (Éva Pataki: *Edith and Marlene.*) *Krit.* 1986; 14(5): 32. Lang.: Hun.
Hungary: Budapest. 1986. Reviews of performances. ■The most popular songs of Edith Piaf and Marlene Dietrich in Eva Pataki's musical play at Pest National Theatre directed by film director Márta Mészáros.

3604 Molnár Gál, Péter. "Webber-Rice: *Jézus Krisztus Szupersztár.*" (Webber-Rice: *Jesus Christ Superstar.*) *Krit.* 1986; 14(10): 35-36. Illus.: Photo. B&W. 2: 7.5 cm. x 5.5 cm., 7.5 cm. x 5 cm. Lang.: Hun.
Hungary: Szeged. 1986. Reviews of performances. ■Notes on the Hungarian premiere of *Jézus Krisztus Szupersztár (Jesus Christ Superstar)* by Andrew Lloyd Webber and Tim Rice presented by the Rock Theatre at Szeged Open-Air Festival directed by János Szikora.

3605 Takács, István. "Szupersztár—magyarul. Bemutató Szegeden és a Margitszigeten." (Superstar in Hungarian: Premiere in Szeged and on Margaret Island.) *Sz.* 1986 Oct.; 19(10): 29-33. Illus.: Photo. B&W. 3: 12 cm. x 9 cm. Lang.: Hun.
Hungary: Szeged, Budapest. 1986. Reviews of performances. ■Summer productions of *Jesus Christ Superstar* by Andrew Lloyd Webber and Tim Rice presented by the Rock Theatre on Margaret Island in Budapest and at Szeged Open-Air Festival directed by János Szikora.

3606 Hägglund, Kent. "På fjärran platser men mitt i 80-talet." (Far Away and Yet in the Middle of the Eighties.) *TArsb.* 1986; 5: 16-19. Illus.: Photo. Print. B&W. 3. Lang.: Swe.
Sweden. 1985-1986. Reviews of performances. ■Three Swedish musical theatre productions.

3607 Barajas, DeVina. "Singing Brecht." *ComIBS.* 1985 Nov.; 15(1): 35-37.

MUSIC-DRAMA: Musical theatre—Performance/production

Switzerland. Germany, West. USA. 1978-1985. Histories-sources. ■DeVina Barajas of the Brecht Chansonettes discusses why she sings Brecht's songs, as well as the demands and joys of performing this material.

3608 Brace, Jane. "A Rock Star Comes to Chichester." *PI*. 1986 Apr.; 1(9): 20-21. Illus.: Photo. Print. B&W. 1. Lang.: Eng.
UK-England: Chichester. 1986. Histories-sources. ■Suzi Quatro describes her life as a rock star and her Annie Oakley in *Annie Get Your Gun* at Chichester Festival Theatre.

3609 Caird, John. "Making a Musical." *Drama*. 1986; 159: 7-9. Illus.: Photo. B&W. 4. Lang.: Eng.
UK-England. 1980. Critical studies. ■Problems of adapting the novel *Les Misérables* to the stage: collaborative nature of a musical.

3610 Cushman, Robert. "The Year of the Phantom." *PI*. 1986 Dec.; 2(5): 26-27. Illus.: Photo. B&W. 1. Lang.: Eng.
UK-England: London. 1986. Reviews of performances. ■Reviews of musicals including *Phantom of the Opera, Wonderful Town, La Cage Aux Folles, Chess, Annie Get Your Gun*.

3611 Barnes, Clive; Beaufort, John; Cohen, Ron; Henry, William A., III; Kroll, Jack; Rich, Frank; Siegel, Joel; Watt, Douglas; Wilson, Edwin; Winer, Linda. "*Sweet Charity*." *NYTCR*. 1986 Apr 7; 47(6): 309-314. Lang.: Eng.
USA: New York, NY. 1986. Reviews of performances. ■Collection of newspaper reviews of *Sweet Charity* by Neil Simon, based on an original screenplay by Federico Fellini, *et al.*, staged and choreographed by Bob Fosse at the Minskoff Theatre.

3612 Barnes, Clive; Gussow, Mel; Kissel, Howard; Wallach, Allan; Winer, Linda. "*Honky Tonk Nights*." *NYTCR*. 1986 July 7; 47 (9): 254-257. Lang.: Eng.
USA: New York, NY. 1986. Reviews of performances. ■Collection of newspaper reviews of *Honky Tonk Nights*, book and lyrics by Ralph Allen and David Campbell, staged and choreographed by Ernest O. Flatt at the Biltmore Theatre.

3613 Barnes, Clive; Beaufort, John; Cohen, Ron; Henry, William A., III; Kissel, Howard; Rich, Frank; Siegel, Joel; Wallach, Allan; Watt, Douglas; Wilson, Edwin; Winer, Linda. "*Smile*." *NYTCR*. 1986 Nov 17; 47(15): 152-157. Lang.: Eng.
USA: New York, NY. 1986. Reviews of performances. ■Collection of newspaper reviews of *Smile*, music by Marvin Hamlisch, book and lyrics by Howard Ashman at the Lunt-Fontanne Theatre.

3614 Barnes, Clive; Kissel, Howard; Rich, Frank; Sharp, Christopher; Wallach, Allan; Wilson, Edwin; Winer, Linda. "*Raggedy Ann*." *NYTCR*. 1986 Oct 13; 47(13): 184-188. Lang.: Eng.
USA: New York, NY. 1986. Reviews of performances. ■Collection of newspaper reviews of *Raggedy Ann*, book by William Gibon, music and lyrics by Joe Raposo, staged and choreographed by Patricia Birch at the Nederlander Theatre.

3615 Barnes, Clive; Cohen, Ron; Kissel, Howard; Rich, Frank; Wallach, Allan; Winer, Linda. "*Into the Light*." *NYTCR*. 1986 Oct 27; 47(14): 175-178. Lang.: Eng.
USA: New York, NY. 1986. Reviews of performances. ■Collection of newspaper reviews of *Into the Light*, book by Jeff Tamborniro, music by Lee Holdridge, lyrics by John Forster, staged by Michael Maurer at the Neil Simon Theatre.

3616 Barnes, Clive; Beaufort, John; Cohen, Ron; Gussow, Mel; Kissel, Howard; Wallach, Allan; Watt, Douglas; Wilson, Edwin; Winer, Linda. "*Oh Coward!*." *NYTCR*. 1986 Oct 27; 47(14): 166-170. Lang.: Eng.
USA: New York, NY. 1986. Reviews of performances. ■Collection of newspaper reviews of *Oh Coward!*, lyrics and music by Noël Coward, devised and staged by Roderick Cook at the Helen Hayes Theatre.

3617 Barnes, Clive; Beaufort, John; Kissel, Howard; Kroll, Jack; Rich, Frank; Siegel, Joel; Wallach, Allan; Watt, Douglas; Wilson, Edwin; Winer, Linda. "*Rags*." *NYTCR*. 1986 Aug 11; 47(10): 238-243. Lang.: Eng.
USA: New York, NY. 1986. Reviews of performances. ■Collection of newspaper reviews of *Rags*, book by Joseph Stein, music by Charles Strouse, lyrics by Stephen Schwartz, staged by Gene Saks at the Mark Hellinger Theatre.

3618 Barnes, Clive; Beaufort, John; Henry, William A., III; Kissel, Howard; Rich, Frank; Siegel, Joel; Shapiro, Laura; Wallach, Allan; Watt, Douglas; Wilson, Edwin; Winer, Linda. "*Me and My Girl*." *NYTCR*. 1986 Aug 11; 47(10): 244-251. Lang.: Eng.
USA: New York, NY. 1986. Reviews of performances. ■Collection of newspaper reviews of *Me and My Girl*, book and lyrics by L. Arthur Rose and Douglas Furber, staged by Mike Ockrent at the Marquis Theatre.

3619 Barnes, Clive; Beaufort, John; Dibble, Peter David; Hoelterhoff, Manuela; Rockwell, John; Watt, Douglas; Winer, Linda. "*Brigadoon*." *NYTCR*. 1986 Mar 3; 47(4): 352-356. Lang.: Eng.
USA: New York, NY. 1986. Reviews of performances. ■Collection of newspaper reviews of *Brigadoon*, a musical with book and lyrics by Alan Jay Lerner, music by Frederick Loewe, staged by Gerald Freedman at the New York State Theatre.

3620 Challender, James Winston. *The Function of Choreographer in the Development of the Conceptual Musical: An Examination of the Work of Jerome Robbins, Bob Fosse, and Michael Bennett on Broadway between 1944 and 1981*. Tallahassee, FL: Florida State Univ; 1986. 427 pp. Pref. Notes. Biblio. [Ph.D. dissertation, Univ. Microfilms order No. DA8626788.] Lang.: Eng.
USA: New York, NY. 1944-1981. Historical studies. ■Choreography in musical theatre.

3621 Lerner, Alan Jay. *The Musical Theatre: A Celebration*. New York, NY: McGraw-Hill; 1986. 240 pp. Index. Biblio. Illus.: Photo. Color. Lang.: Eng.
USA: New York, NY. UK-England: London. 1900-1985. Histories-specific. ■Informal history of musical theatre with anecdotes of the author's career.

3622 Levine, Mindy N. "The New Musical Theatre: An Alternative to Broadway." *TT*. 1982; 1(3): 1-2. Illus.: Photo. B&W. 1. Lang.: Eng.
USA: New York, NY. 1982. Critical studies. ■Development of new musicals by Off and Off-off Broadway theatres is providing opportunity for exploration and experimentation with new forms and artists.

3623 Turner, Beth. "Uptown or Downtown, Maurice Hines is Hot!" *BlackM*. 1986 Feb-Mar.: 2-3. Illus.: Photo. Print. B&W. 1: 3 in. x 5 in. Lang.: Eng.
USA: New York, NY. 1949-1986. Historical studies. ■Tap dancing career of Maurice Hines and the creation of his new company Balletap, USA.

3624 Zadan, Craig. *Sondheim & Co*. New York, NY: Harper & Row; 1986. 408 pp. (2nd edition.) Discography. Append. Illus.: Photo. Lang.: Eng.
USA: New York, NY. 1930-1986. Biographical studies. ■Updated version of a 1974 study includes quotations from Stephen Sondheim's associates, detailed listings of productions.

3625 Chrennikov, T. "Glavnoje-tvorcheskij poisk." (The Principal Thing is Creative Endeavor.) *SovBal*. 1986; 4: 4-5. Lang.: Rus.
USSR. 1980-1986. Critical studies. ■Problems in the development of Soviet musical theatre.

Plays/librettos/scripts

3626 Comden, Betty; Green, Adolph; Guare, John. "Comden and Green and Guare." *DGQ*. 1986 Fall; 23(3): 15-28.
Histories-sources. ■Betty Comden and Adolph Green reflect on their careers in a session moderated by playwright John Guare.

3627 Callari, Francesco; Fusco, Mario, transl. "*Proprio like that*." *ThE*. 1986 Apr.: 10: 105-111. Illus.: Photo. B&W. 1. Lang.: Fre.
Italy: Rome. 1930-1953. Histories-sources. ■Discovery in the Amministrazione Eredi Pirandello of unpublished documentation of *Proprio like that*, a musical by Luigi Pirandello.

MUSIC-DRAMA: Musical theatre—Plays/librettos/scripts

3628 Barker, Frank Granville. "After Amadeus." *PI*. 1986 Mar.; 1(8): 12-13,58. Illus.: Photo. Print. B&W. 2. Lang.: Eng.
UK-England: London. Italy. 1986. Historical studies. ∎Discussions of plays on the lives of the composers Verdi and Puccini: Robin Ray's *Cafe Puccini* and Julian Mitchell's *After Aida*.

3629 Sherrin, Ned. "Alan Jay Lerner." *PlPl*. 1986 Sep.; 396: 20-21. B&W. 3. Lang.: Eng.
UK-England. USA: New York, NY. 1918-1986. Biographical studies. ∎Career of lyricist Alan Jay Lerner.

3630 "Alan Jay Lerner 1918-1986." *DGQ*. 1986 Fall; 23(3): 12-14.
USA: New York, NY. 1986. Histories-sources. ∎Remarks by former Dramatists Guild president Sidney Kingsley and composer Leonard Bernstein at a memorial service for Alan Jay Lerner.

3631 Guernsey, Otis L.; McNally, Terrence, intro. *Broadway Song & Story: Playwrights/Lyricists/Composers Discuss Their Hits*. New York, NY: Dodd, Mead; 1986. 480 pp. Index. Lang.: Eng.
USA: New York, NY. 1900-1985. Histories-sources. ∎Collection of articles, mainly transcripts of colloquia, from the *Dramatists Guild Quarterly*.

3632 Weill, Kurt. "The Alchemy of Music." *KWN*. 1986 Fall; 4(2): 7-8. Lang.: Eng.
USA: New York, NY. 1936. Histories-sources. ∎Reprint of an essay from *Stage* magazine by Kurt Weill in which he argues that music transforms the play into living theatre, using examples of Paul Green, Clifford Odets and Maxwell Anderson as evidence of the restoration of poetry to drama.

Reference materials

3633 Suskin, Steven. *Show Tunes, 1905-1985: The Songs, Shows, and Careers of Broadway's Major Composers*. New York, NY: Dodd, Mead; 1986. 728 pp. Index. Biblio. Lang.: Eng.
1905-1985. ∎Guide to the work of thirty principal composers of Broadway musicals, including notes on productions, lists of published songs and other numbers, plus detailed listings for other composers.

3634 Lucha-Burns, Carol. *Musical Notes: A Practical Guide to Staffing and Staging Standards of the American Musical Theatre*. Westport, CT: Greenwood P; 1986. xvii, 581 pp. Pref. Index. Biblio. Append. Gloss. Lang.: Eng.
USA. 1951-1985. ∎Detailed listing of major American musicals and their production requirements. Composer, lyricist, librettist, principal roles and vocal type, plot synopsis, instrumentation, rights and script availability, information on original productions, song chart, and chronology of long running musicals are included.

3635 Munsing Winkelbauer, Stefanie; Pistorius, Hedwig, transl.; Höller, Gertrud, transl.; Pausch, Oskar, pref. *Wake Up and Dream! Costume Designs for Broadway Musicals 1900-1925 from the Theatre Collection of the Austrian National Library*. (Kostümentwürfe zu Broadway-Musicals 1900-1925 in der Theatersammlung der Österreichischen Nationalbibliothek.) Vienna/Cologne/Graz: Böhlau; 1986. 96 pp. (Cortina 7/Biblos-Schriften 137.) Pref. Tables. Biblio. Illus.: Dwg. Color. B&W. 36: 9 cm. x 15 cm., 15 cm. x 12 cm. Lang.: Eng, Ger.
USA: New York, NY. 1900-1925. Historical studies. ∎Catalogue of costume designs, notes about costumes for Broadway musicals and the dominance of European fashion houses. Short biographies of costume designers whose work is displayed.

Opera

3636 O'Carroll, John. "Voss, the Opera: Romanticism Rewritten." *Hermes*. 1986; 2(1): 29-31. Lang.: Eng.
Australia. 1980-1986. Critical studies. ∎Analyzes the balance between innovation and tradition in *Voss*, composed by Richard Meale, libretto by David Malouf.

3637 Reiber, Joachim. "Carl Maria von Weber in Wien: Eine biographische Skizze zum 200. Geburtstag des Komponisten." (Carl Maria von Weber in Vienna: A Biographical Sketch on the Occasion of his 200th Birthday.) *Parnass*.
1986 Nov-Dec.; 6(6): 70-73. Illus.: Photo. Dwg. Print. B&W. Lang.: Ger.
Austria: Vienna. Germany. 1803-1826. Biographical studies. ∎Composer Carl Maria von Weber, his operas, his stay in Vienna and productions of his operas in Vienna during his lifetime.

3638 Dan'ko, L. "Majakovskij—Naš savremennik." (Majakovskij, Our Contemporary.) *SovMuzyka*. 1986; 2: 73-76. Lang.: Rus.
USSR. Critical studies. ∎On *Majakovskij načinajetsja (Majakovskij Begins)*, an opera by A. Petrov.

Administration

3639 Hughes, Howard. "Tourism and the Live Performance of Opera and Classical Music." *JAP&M*. 1986 May; 2(3): 12-15. Notes. Lang.: Eng.
Historical studies. ∎'Cultural tourism' and its importance to opera and classical music.

3640 Hume, Robert D. "Handel and Opera Management in London in the 1730s." *MLet*. 1986 Oct.; 67(4): 347-362. Lang.: Eng.
England: London. 1729-1739. Historical studies. ∎A re-evaluation of accepted accounts of George Frideric Handel's declining success and his relationship with John Rich, the manager of Covent Garden, based on recently discovered sources.

3641 Scott, Michael. "Raoul Gunsbourg and the Monte Carlo Opera." *OQ*. 1985/86 Win; 3(4): 70-78. Notes. Lang.: Eng.
Monaco: Monte Carlo. 1893-1951. Biographical studies. ∎Overview of the life and managerial accomplishments of Raoul Gunsbourg, director of the Monte Carlo Opera for 59 years.

3642 Calhoun, John. "Alternate Programs." *ThCr*. 1986 Oct.; 20(8): 24-25, 63-64, 66. Lang.: Eng.
USA. Historical studies. ∎Alternate programs produced by opera houses.

3643 Duffie, Bruce. "Conversation Piece: Edward Downes." *OJ*. 1986 Fall; 19(3): 34-40. Lang.: Eng.
USA: New York, NY. 1911-1986. Histories-sources. ∎Edward Downes talks about his life in the opera, in particular his association with the Metropolitan Opera.

3644 Mayer, Martin. "Taking Charge." *OpN*. 1986 Sep.; 51(3): 10-14. Illus.: Design. Dwg. Photo. Color. B&W. 5. Lang.: Eng.
USA: New York, NY. 1985-1986. Histories-sources. ∎Account of the first year of new management at the Metropolitan Opera with Bruce Crawford as general manager and James Levine as artistic director.

3645 Waleson, Heidi. "Look for the Union Label." *OpN*. 1986 Nov.; 51(5): 47-49, 71. Illus.: Photo. B&W. 1. Lang.: Eng.
USA. 1936-1986. Histories-sources. ∎History and achievements of the American Guild of Musical Artists during its fifty years of existence.

3646 Waleson, Heidi; Englander, Maury. "Facing Forward." *OpN*. 1986 Mar 29; 50(14): 34-37. Illus.: Photo. B&W. 17: var. sizes. Lang.: Eng.
USA: New York, NY. 1986. Histories-sources. ∎Account of an international symposium on the future of opera held in New York (Nov 1-2, 1986) by the Central Opera Service in celebration of the fiftieth anniversary of the Metropolitan Opera Guild.

Audience

3647 Deshoulière, Christophe. "Scénographie du succès: l'organisation 'rationnelle' de la claque á l'opéra vue par les écrivains du XIXe." (Scenography of Success: The 'Rational' Organization of the Claque at the Opera, Seen by 19th Century Writers.) *Textuel*. 1986; 18: 34-44. Lang.: Fre.
France. 1800-1899. Critical studies. ∎The claque as seen by Auguste Villiers de l'Isle-Adam, George Sand, Honoré de Balzac and Hector Berlioz.

3648 Burlina, Je. "Opernaja publika: predstavlenije i realnost'." (The Opera Audience: Conception and Reality.) *SovMuzyka*. 1986; 5: 69-74. Lang.: Rus.

CLASSED ENTRIES

MUSIC-DRAMA: Opera—Basic theatrical documents

USSR. 1986. Empirical research.

Basic theatrical documents

3649 Tusa, Michael C. "Richard Wagner and Weber's *Euryanthe.*" *NCM*. 1986 Spr; 9(3): 206-221. Illus.: Diagram. Lang.: Eng.
Germany: Dresden. 1824-1879. Critical studies. ■The influence of Weber's opera *Euryanthe* on Wagner, especially on *Tannhäuser* and *Lohengrin*, with musical examples and comparative diagrams of structure.

Design/technology

3650 Moring, Kirsikka. "Stage Designer Ralf Forsström." *NFT*. 1986; 38: 11-13. Illus.: Photo. B&W. 3. Lang.: Eng, Fre.
Finland: Helsinki. 1963-1986. Biographical studies. ■Career of designer Ralf Forsström discussing his influences and stylistic preferences.

3651 Ramsaur, Michael F. "Lighting the *Ring* and *Tannhäuser* at Bayreuth." *Cue*. 1986 Sep/Oct.; 8(43): 27-32. Illus.: Photo. Plan. Print. B&W. Color. 14: var. sizes. Lang.: Eng.
Germany, West: Bayreuth. 1981-1986. Technical studies. ■Lighting techniques for productions of *Der Ring des Nibelungen* and *Tannhäuser*.

3652 Johansson, Stefan. "Bortglömd?" (Forgotten?)*NT*. 1986; 35: 18-19. Illus.: Photo. Lang.: Swe.
Sweden: Stockholm. 1950-1986. Critical studies. ■Contrasts the boldness of scene designs for the Royal Opera from the 1950s and 1960s to the present.

3653 Dreier, Martin. "Adolphe Appia—der Genfer Bühnenreformator." (Adolphe Appia—Stage Reformer from Geneva.) 35-38 in Fabian, Imre, ed.: Persché, Gerhard, ed. *Oper 1986: Jahrbuch der Zeitschrift 'Opernwelt'*. Zürich: Orell Füssli Verlag; 1986. 128 pp. Illus.: Photo. B&W. Lang.: Ger.
Switzerland: Geneva. 1862-1928. Biographical studies. ■Essay concentrating on Appia's theory of Wagner's *Ring* and present-day evaluation.

3654 "Grand Designs at the Met." *LDim*. 1986 Mar-Apr.; 10(2): 55-58, 60-61, 63-66, 68, 70-71, 94. Illus.: Photo. Print. Color. B&W. 12: var. sizes. Lang.: Eng.
USA: New York, NY. 1883-1986. Histories-sources. ■Interview with lighting designer Gil Wechsler on his work at the Metropolitan Opera.

3655 Calhoun, John. "Employment Networks." *ThCr*. 1986 Oct.; 20(8): 23, 61-63. Lang.: Eng.
USA. 1986. Technical studies. ■Tips on how to look for work as a designer or technician in opera.

3656 Hale, Alice M. "Stage Managers: A Polymorphic Position." *ThCr*. 1986 Oct.; 20(8): 20, 42-44, 46-48.
USA. Technical studies. ■The role of the stage manager in regional opera houses.

3657 Heymont, George. "Hunting the Wild Things." *OpN*. 1986 Sep.; 51(3): 24-26, 70. Illus.: Photo. Color. 1. Lang.: Eng.
USA. 1930-1986. Histories-sources. ■Profile of and interview with illustrator Maurice Sendak, designer of numerous opera productions.

3658 LaRue, Michèle. "Wigs and Music: Facing the Music." *ThCr*. 1986 Oct.; 20(8): 23, 55-56, 58-61. Lang.: Eng.
USA. Technical studies. ■The wigmaker's role in regional opera houses.

3659 Moynihan, D.S. "Costume Supervisors: Dressing the Diva." *ThCr*. 1986 Oct.; 20(8): 22, 52-55. Lang.: Eng.
USA. Technical studies. ■The role of the costumer in regional opera houses.

3660 Sisk, Douglass F. "Technical Directors: The Long and Short of It." *ThCr*. 1986 Oct.; 20(8): 21, 48-50. Lang.: Eng.
USA. Technical studies. ■The role of the technical director in regional opera houses.

3661 Somners, Michael. "Nights and Days at the Opera." *ThCr*. 1986 Oct.; 20(8): 20, 41-42. Lang.: Eng.
USA. Technical studies. ■Roles, skills and special needs of the regional opera scene and its artisans.

3662 Winn, Steve. "Second Thoughts." *ThCr*. 1986 Feb.; 20(2): 26-27, 55-58. Illus.: Photo. 3: var. sizes. Lang.: Eng.
USA: San Francisco, CA. 1986. Technical studies. ■Set designer John Conklin reconsiders his choices for the San Francisco Opera's production of Wagner's *Ring*.

3663 Wong, Carey. "Save Money With Creative Set Recycling." *ThCr*. 1986 Oct.; 20(8): 25, 66. Illus.: Photo. 3: var. sizes. Lang.: Eng.
USA. Technical studies. ■The resident designer of the Portland Opera discusses advantages to recycling opera sets.

3664 Gedgaudas, E. "Dialog chudožnika s muzykoj." (Dialogue of a Scene Designer with Music.) *SovMuzyka*. 1986; 2: 138. Lang.: Rus.
USSR. Lithuania. 1986. Critical studies. ■Opera set designs by L. Trujkis.

Institutions

3665 Kutschera, Edda. "Laufen lernen." (Learning On-Going.) *Buhne*. 1986 Dec.; 29(12): 6-7. Illus.: Photo. Print. B&W. Lang.: Ger.
Austria: Vienna. 1986-1987. Histories-sources. ■New concept for using the Theater im Künstlerhaus for the Opernwerkstatt productions of the Staatsoper. Includes the program of the Opernwerkstatt for the 1986/87 season. Related to Dance: Ballet.

3666 Löbl, Hermi. "Und ich schaffe es doch." (I'll Get It Done Anyhow.) *Buhne*. 1986 Mar.; 29(3): 8-10. Illus.: Photo. Print. Color. B&W. Lang.: Ger.
Austria: Salzburg. 1964-1986. Historical studies. ■History of the Salzburger Osterfestspiele.

3667 Lossmann, Hans. "Evolution statt Revolution." (Evolution Instead of Revolution.) *Buhne*. 1986 July; 29(7): 15. Illus.: Photo. Print. B&W. Lang.: Ger.
Austria: Vienna. 1986-1987. Histories-sources. ■Manager Claus Helmut Drese's plans for the new season at the Staatsoper.

3668 Lossmann, Hans. "Ich bin weder Revolutionär noch Gralshüter." (I Am Neither a Revolutionist nor a Guardian of Tradition.) *Buhne*. 1986 Jan.; 29(1): 4-6. Illus.: Photo. Print. B&W. Lang.: Ger.
Austria: Vienna. 1986-1991. Histories-sources. ■Claus Helmut Drese's plans for managing the Staatsoper until the 1990/91 season, including notes on planned productions.

3669 Mayer, Gerhard. "Österliche Exerzitien." (Easter Exercises.) *Buhne*. 1986 May; 29(5): 37-38. Illus.: Photo. Print. Color. Lang.: Ger.
Austria: Salzburg. 1986. Histories-sources. ■Report on the Salzburger Osterfestspiele.

3670 Parschalk, Volkmar. "Zwischen Publikum, Autoren und Komponisten." (Between Audience, Writers and Composers.) *Parnass*. 1986 Jul-Aug.; 6(4): 71-74. Illus.: Photo. Print. B&W. Lang.: Ger.
Austria: Vienna. Germany, West. Switzerland. 1930-1986. Histories-sources. ■Interview with manager Claus Helmut Drese: his work and plans for managing the Vienna Staatsoper.

3671 Patterson, Tom. "The Stratford Story." *OC*. 1986 Win; 27(4): 16-18, 24. Illus.: Photo. B&W. 6: var. sizes. Lang.: Eng.
Canada: Stratford, ON. 1951-1985. Historical studies. ■An outline of the history of music performances, especially opera, at the Stratford Festival. Related to Music-Drama: Musical theatre.

3672 Bakal, Shirley. "From the Nation to Itself: Prague's Opera Centennial." *OQ*. 1985 Spr; 3(1): 30-40. Notes. Illus.: Photo. B&W. 7: 4 in. x 6 in., 5 in. x 7 in. Lang.: Eng.
Czechoslovakia: Prague. 1787-1985. Historical studies. ■An historical summary of opera and theatre in Czechoslovakia from the time of Mozart, focusing on the construction, development and structure of the Prague National Theatre (Národní Divadlo) within a social and political context.

3673 "Aux origines d'Aix en Provence." (The Origins of Aix-en-Provence.) *CorpsE*. 1986; 20: 21-36. Lang.: Fre.
France: Aix-en-Provence. 1960. Histories-sources. ■Unpublished extracts from the participation of George Auric, Henri Sauguet, Yves Florenne, Roland Manuel and Francis Poulenc in discussions that took place at the Aix-en-Provence festival, which was intended to effect a renaissance of opera in France and the funding of a modern French opera.

MUSIC-DRAMA: Opera—Institutions

3674 Kahane, Martine, comp. *L'Ouverture du Nouvel Opéra: 5 janvier 1875.* (The Inauguration of the New Opera: January 5, 1875.) Paris: Ed. de la Réunion des Musées nationaux; 1986. 54 pp. (Les dossiers du Musée d'Orsay.) Append. Illus.: Design. Pntg. Dwg. Poster. Photo. Print. B&W. Schematic. 53: var. sizes. [Accompanies exhibit at Musée d'Orsay, Paris, Dec. 1980-Mar. 1981.] Lang.: Fre.
France: Paris. 1875. Histories-reconstruction. ■Includes architecture of the building, the opening program, reaction of the press and art world.

3675 "House of Hanover." *OpN.* 1986 May; 50(16): 24-26. Illus.: Photo. B&W. 7. Lang.: Eng.
Germany, West: Hanover. 1689-1986. Histories-sources. ■History of the former Royal Opera House of Hanover and its plans for the future.

3676 Battaglia, Carl. "Venetian Renaissance." *OpN.* 1986 May; 50(16): 14-16, 18. Illus.: Photo. Color. B&W. 3. Lang.: Eng.
Italy: Venice. 1980-1986. Histories-specific. ■Teatro La Fenice has become the most innovative opera house in Italy under the direction of Italo Gomez.

3677 Sachs, Harvey. "Historic Anniversary at La Scala." *OC.* 1986 Fall; 27(3): 13-16. Illus.: Photo. Print. B&W. 5. Lang.: Eng.
Italy: Milan. 1898-1986. Historical studies. ■History of the Teatro alla Scala on the fortieth anniversary of its post-war restoration and reopening.

3678 Carroll, Charles Michael. "Santa Fe's Thirtieth Season." *OJ.* 1986 Fall; 19(3): 16-23. Illus.: Photo. Print. B&W. 2: 5 in. x 8 in. Lang.: Eng.
USA: Santa Fe, NM. 1957-1986. Historical studies. ■The survival and prosperity of the Santa Fe Opera Company for the past 30 years.

3679 Heymont, George. "All in the Family." *OpN.* 1986 June; 50(17): 14, 16, 18. Illus.: Photo. B&W. 2. Lang.: Eng.
USA: St. Louis, MO. 1976-1986. Histories-sources. ■Since the retirement of Richard Gaddes, founding director of the Opera Theatre of St. Louis, the company is being managed by Charles MacKay, Colin Graham and John Nelson.

3680 Schmidgall, Gary. "News from Philadelphia." *OpN.* 1986 Apr 12; 50(15): 36, 38-41. Illus.: Photo. B&W. 5. Lang.: Eng.
USA: Philadelphia, PA. 1976-1986. Histories-specific. ■The history and plans of the Pennsylvania Opera Theatre as it begins a new decade.

3681 Sloan, Irene; Sloan, Sherwin. "Work." *OQ.* 1986 Spr; 4(1): 1-14. Notes. Illus.: Photo. B&W. 10: 3 in. x 4 in., 4 in. x 5 in. Lang.: Eng.
USA: Santa Fe, NM. 1956-1986. Historical studies. ■An editorial reflecting on the first thirty years of the Santa Fe Opera, under the general direction of John Crosby, including a list of all productions.

Performance spaces

3682 Boutwell, Jane. "A Space for Liberty." *OpN.* 1986 May; 50(16): 32-33. Illus.: Photo. Color. 2. Lang.: Eng.
France: Paris. 1981-1986. Histories-sources. ■Description of the new home of the Paris Opéra, L'Opéra Bastille.

3683 Levine, Robert. "Unser Haus." *OpN.* 1986 Mar 29; 50(14): 14-16. Illus.: Photo. B&W. 4. Lang.: Eng.
Germany, West: Stuttgart. 1909-1976. Histories-specific. ■The renovation of the Württemberg State Theatre by the citizens of Stuttgart.

3684 Artal, Margarida; Rocha, Adelita. *El Gran Teatre del Liceo.* Barcelona: Institut d'Educació Municipal; 1986. 32 pp. (Sèrie Didàctiques 9.) Pref. Biblio. Tables. Illus.: Design. Photo. Plan. Poster. 7: var. sizes. Lang.: Cat.
Spain-Catalonia: Barcelona. 1845-1986. Historical studies. ■History of the Gran Teatre del Liceo. Intended for children. Related to Dance: Ballet.

Performance/production

3685 Korn, I.M.; Kopu, U.U. *Problemy teatral'nosti opery.* (Problems of the Theatricality of the Opera.) Vil'njus: Gos. konservatoriga; 1986. 22 pp. [Synopsis of a Dissertation.] Lang.: Rus.

Historical studies. ■Theatricality in opera.

3686 Simoneau, Leopold. "Style and Mozart." *OC.* 1986 Sum; 27(2): 14-18, 24. Illus.: Photo. Print. B&W. 7. Lang.: Eng.
Histories-sources. ■A definition of what constitutes proper Mozartian style in singing and dramatic presentation by one of the foremost Mozart singers of the 1940s and 1950s.

3687 Farkas, Andrew. "Enrico Caruso: Tenor, Baritone, Bass." *OQ.* 1986-87 Win; 4(4): 53-60. Notes. Illus.: Photo. B&W. 1: 4 in. x 5 in. Lang.: Eng.
Argentina: Buenos Aires. 1906-1917. Critical studies. ■Discussion of evidence that Caruso sang the baritone prologue to *I Pagliacci.*

3688 Heymont, George. "News from Sydney." *OpN.* 1986 May; 50(16): 28-30, 47. Illus.: Photo. B&W. 2. Lang.: Eng.
Australia: Sydney, N.S.W. 1973-1986. Histories-specific. ■History and current state of Australian Opera at the Sydney Opera House.

3689 Scovell, Jane. "La Stupenda-II." *OpN.* 1986 Dec 6; 51(6): 12-15. Illus.: Dwg. 2. Lang.: Eng.
Australia: Sydney, N.S.W. 1926-1986. Histories-sources. ■Appreciation of the career of Joan Sutherland.

3690 "Wien hat mich geprägt." (Vienna Has Moulded Me.) *Buhne.* 1986 Sep.; 29(9): 16-17. Illus.: Photo. Print. Color. Lang.: Ger.
Austria: Vienna. Italy. 1950-1986. Biographical studies. ■Claudio Abbado: his relationship to Austria and Vienna, his ideas about conducting at the Vienna Staatsoper and his future plans.

3691 "Fragen der Aufführungspraxis am Beispiel W.A. Mozarts." (Questions about Representation Practice Shown by the Example of W.A. Mozart.) 148-175 in Spitzer, Leopold, ed. *Probleme der Sängerausbildung: Bericht über das 5. gesangspädagogische Symposion in Bad Ischl vom 18. bis 22. März 1985.* Vienna: Hochschule für Musik u. darst. Kunst in Wien, Abt. f. Sologesang u. musikdramat. Darstellung; 1986. 175 pp. Notes. Lang.: Ger.
Austria: Vienna. 1700-1799. Instructional materials. ■Performance rules during Mozart's time as a guidance for interpreting his works. Relationship between word and music in Mozart's opus: correct declamation, appoggiatures and fioriture, musical rhetoric figures and dynamics.

3692 Dusek, Peter; Irrgeher, Heinz; Parschalk, Volkmar; Springer, Georg; Freunde der Wiener Staatsoper, ed. *Nicht nur Tenöre: Das Beste aus der Opernwerkstatt.* (Not Only Tenors: The Best of the Opera Workshop.) Vienna, Munich: Jugend und Volk; 1986. Vol 1: 280 pp./vol. 2: 207 pp. Pref. Illus.: Photo. Color. B&W. 69. [Preface in Volume 2 by Claus H. Drese.] Lang.: Ger.
Austria: Vienna. 1909-1986. Histories-sources. ■Interviews with opera singers, stage managers and ballet dancers of the Viennese State Opera about their experiences, careers and opinions about art.

3693 Jacobson, Robert. "I'm Still Here." *OpN.* 1986 Mar 15; 50(13): 10-14, 48-50. Illus.: Photo. Color. B&W. 4. Lang.: Eng.
Austria: Vienna. 1926-1986. Histories-sources. ■Profile of and interview with soprano Leonie Rysanek.

3694 Kutschera, Edda. "Goldene Hochzeit mit der Oper." (Golden Wedding Anniversary with Opera.) *Buhne.* 1986 Oct.; 29(10): 6-8. Illus.: Photo. Print. B&W. Lang.: Ger.
Austria: Vienna. Italy. Europe. 1916-1986. Histories-sources. ■Opera singer Giuseppe Taddei and his work, especially at the Staatsoper.

3695 Kutschera, Edda. "Die Formel muss stimmen." (The Formula Must Suit.) *Buhne.* 1986 Sep.; 29(9): 18-20. Illus.: Photo. Print. Color. B&W. Lang.: Ger.
Austria: Vienna. 1924-1986. Histories-sources. ■Opera singer Oskar Czerwenka: his motivation for singing, his hobby of painting and his opinions about present opera singers.

3696 Löbl, Hermi. "Oper muss erregen." (Opera Has to Provoke.) *Buhne.* 1986 Aug.; 29(8): 13-14. Illus.: Photo. Print. Color. Lang.: Ger.
Austria. Germany, East. 1935-1985. Histories-sources. ■Harry Kupfer and his work, especially his ideas for staging operas.

MUSIC-DRAMA: Opera—Performance/production

3697 Löbl, Hermi. "Vom Herrgott noch ein Zuckerl." (Still a Good Thing More From God.) *Buhne.* 1986 Nov.; 29(10): 10-13. Illus.: Photo. Print. B&W. Color. Lang.: Ger.
Austria: Vienna. USA: New York, NY. 1926-1986. Histories-sources. ▪Opera singer Leonie Rysanek, her work and life with her husband Ernst Ludwig Gausmann.

3698 Löbl, Hermi. "Leicht ist gar nichts." (Easy Is Nothing at All.) *Buhne.* 1986 July; 29(7): 29-31. Illus.: Photo. Print. Color. Lang.: Ger.
Austria: Salzburg. Italy. 1946-1949. Histories-sources. ▪Opera singer Ferruccio Furlanetto and his work with Herbert von Karajan at Salzburg and his future plans.

3699 Marker, Frederick J.; Marker, Lise-Lone. "Retheatricalizing Opera: A Conversation with Jean-Pierre Ponnelle." *OQ.* 1985 Sum; 3(2): 25-44. Illus.: Photo. B&W. 16: 4 in. x 5 in. Lang.: Eng.
Austria: Salzburg. 1984. Technical studies. ▪An interview with Jean-Pierre Ponnelle about his set designs, directing style and work with James Levine.

3700 Mayer, Gerhard. "Realität and Halluzination." (Reality and Hallucination.) *Buhne.* 1986 Aug.; 29(8): 8-11. Illus.: Photo. Print. B&W. Lang.: Ger.
Austria: Salzburg. Poland. 1933-1986. Biographical studies. ▪Composer Krzystof Penderecki and his work, his new opera *Die schwarze Maske (The Black Mask),* based on a play by Gerhart Hauptmann, and its first production at Salzburg.

3701 Roschitz, Karlheinz; Wenzel-Jelinek, Margret, photo. *Dirigenten: Claudio Abbado, Leonard Bernstein, Riccardo Chailly...* (Conductors: Claudio Abbado, Leonard Bernstein, Riccardo Chailly...)332. Lang.: Ger.
Austria: Vienna, Salzburg. Histories-sources. ▪Photos of famous conductors during their rehearsals in Austrian music institutions. Brief biographies and an introduction to the history of conducting.

3702 Sandow, Gregory. "The Road Not Taken." *OpN.* 1986 Feb 15; 50(11): 30-31. Illus.: Photo. B&W. 1. Lang.: Eng.
Austria: Vienna. 1780. Critical studies. ▪*Idomeneo* is the most daring opera written by Wolfgang Amadeus Mozart.

3703 Scherer, Barrymore Laurence. "Sounds of Love." *OpN.* 1986 Mar 29; 50(14): 18-19. Illus.: Photo. B&W. 1. Lang.: Eng.
Austria: Vienna. 1911-1986. Critical studies. ▪The love-music of *Der Rosenkavalier* by Richard Strauss.

3704 Traubner, Richard. "Champagne Celebration." *OpN.* 1986 Dec 20; 51(7): 11-14. Illus.: Design. Dwg. Photo. Color. B&W. 11. Lang.: Eng.
Austria: Vienna. 1874-1986. Histories-specific. ▪Performance history of *Die Fledermaus* by Richard Strauss.

3705 Kerényi, Mária. *Neményi Lili.* (Lili Neményi.) Budapest: Zenemükiadó; 1986. 284 pp. Illus.: Photo. B&W. Lang.: Hun.
Austro-Hungarian Empire. Hungary. 1908-1986. Histories-sources. ▪Life and career of actress-singer Lili Neményi based on documents and interviews.

3706 Forrester, Maureen. "Forrester: Bewitched, Bothered and Airborne." *OC.* 1986 Win; 27(4): 19-21, 26. Illus.: Photo. B&W. 4: var. sizes. Lang.: Eng.
Canada. 1970-1984. Biographical studies. ▪An excerpt from singer Maureen Forrester's autobiography telling of the shift from serious roles to character and comic parts after her appearance as the witch in *Hansel and Gretel* for the CBC.

3707 Leper, Muriel. "Revival of Canada's First Opera." *PAC.* 1986 Sep.; 23(3): 10-14. Illus.: Photo. B&W. 4: 5 cm. x 7 cm., 8.5 cm. x 7 cm. Lang.: Eng.
Canada: Toronto, ON, Montreal, PQ. 1986. Reviews of performances. ▪Discusses the revival by Comus Music Theatre of Toronto of Joseph Quesnel's *Colas and Colinette* first performed in Montreal in 1790.

3708 Mercer, Ruby. "Spotlight on Judith Forst." *OC.* 1986 Fall; 27(3): 11-12. Illus.: Photo. Print. B&W. 3: 6 cm. x 7 cm., 6 cm. x 8 cm. Lang.: Eng.
Canada. 1975-1986. Histories-sources. ▪An interview with mezzo-soprano Judith Forst, discussing her return to Canada, collaboration with Joan Sutherland and special roles.

3709 Mercer, Ruby. "Spotlight on John Fanning." *OC.* 1986 Sum; 27(2): 11-12. Illus.: Photo. Print. B&W. 2: 6 cm. x 6 cm. Lang.: Eng.
Canada: Toronto, ON. 1980-1986. Histories-sources. ▪A talk with John Fanning, Canadian baritone, about his training at the University of Toronto and the start of his career.

3710 Mercer, Ruby. "Spotlight on Joanne Kolomyjec." *OC.* 1986 Spr; 27(1): 12-13. Illus.: Photo. Print. B&W. 2: 6 cm. x 7 cm., 6 cm. x 10 cm. Lang.: Eng.
Canada: Toronto, ON. 1986. Histories-sources. ▪An interview with soprano Joanne Kolomyjec discussing her education at the University of Toronto and work with the Canadian Opera Company Ensemble.

3711 Mercer, Ruby. "Spotlight on Gino Quilico." *OC.* 1986 Win; 27(4): 13-15. Illus.: Photo. B&W. 4: var. sizes. Lang.: Eng.
Canada: Toronto, ON. 1984-1986. Histories-sources. ▪An interview with Canadian baritone Gino Quilico, son of Louis, on his training and the start of his international career.

3712 Mulgan, Felicity. "Winthrop." *PAC.* 1986 Sep.; 23(2): 6-8. Illus.: Photo. B&W. 3: 7 cm. x 14 cm., 12.5 cm. x 10 cm. Lang.: Eng.
Canada: Toronto, ON. 1949-1985. Historical studies. ▪Discusses *Winthrop*, a new opera about the founder of Boston, John Winthrop, with a profile of the composer, Istvan Anhalt.

3713 Sutcliffe, Tom. "Strongman." *OpN.* 1986 Mar 15; 50(12): 18-21, 42-44. Illus.: Photo. B&W. 2. Lang.: Eng.
Canada: Prince Albert, AB. 1926-1986. Histories-sources. ▪Profile of and interview with tenor Jon Vickers about his career and his leading role in *Samson* by George Frideric Handel.

3714 Symcox, Peter. "The Four Faces of Opera." *OQ.* 1985 Spr; 3(1): 1-18. Gloss. Illus.: Diagram. Dwg. Photo. B&W. 13: 3 in. x 5 in. Lang.: Eng.
Canada. 1960-1980. Critical studies. ▪A discussion of the differences between presenting opera on the stage and for the TV camera with examples from the author's CBC productions of *Madama Butterfly* and *Macbeth.* Includes a glossary of terms.

3715 Graff, Yveta Synek. "Under the Linden Tree." *OpN.* 1986 Mar 1; 50(12): 29-31. Illus.: Photo. Pntg. Color. B&W. 5: var. sizes. Lang.: Eng.
Czechoslovakia: Prague. USA: New York, NY. 1883-1986. Historical studies. ▪Account of the neglected opera *Libuše* by Jan Smetana on the occasion of its New York premiere.

3716 Kutschera, Edda. "Musik ist meine beste Therapie." (Music Is the Best Therapy for Me.) *Buhne.* 1986 Mar.; 29(3): 6-7. Illus.: Photo. Print. B&W. Lang.: Ger.
Czechoslovakia: Bratislava. Austria: Vienna. 1951-1986. Biographical studies. ▪Opera singer Peter Dvorsky: his life and work.

3717 Robinson, Harlow. "The Folk Connection." *OpN.* 1986 Jan 4; 50(8): 18,20-21. Illus.: Photo. B&W. 1. Lang.: Eng.
Czechoslovakia. 1800-1910. Critical studies. ▪The native roots of Czechoslovakian literature and music.

3718 Simon, John. "Body from the Soul." *OpN.* 1986 Jan 4; 50(8): 10-13. Illus.: Photo. B&W. 3. [The speech-melody of Janáček characters.] Lang.: Eng.
Czechoslovakia: Brno. 1894-1903. Critical studies. ▪Thematic, character and musical analysis of *Jenufa* by Leoš Janáček.

3719 Conrad, Peter. "Let There Be Light: Body and Soul." *OpN.* 1986 Mar 1; 50(12): 16-17, 40. Illus.: Pntg. Color. 1. Lang.: Eng.
England: London. 1741-1986. Critical studies. ▪The mixture of opera and oratory in *Samson* by George Frideric Handel.

3720 Rossi, N. "Handel's *Muzio Scevola.*" *OQ.* 1985 Fall; 3(3): 17-38. Notes. Biblio. Illus.: Pntg. Photo. Print. B&W. 9: 3 in. x 5 in., 8 in. x 5 in. Lang.: Eng.
England: London. 1718-1980. Histories-reconstruction. ▪The creation of the Royal Academy of Music and its commission to Handel to compare the third act of *Muzio Scevola* analyzes the composition and looks at its first modern production.

MUSIC-DRAMA: Opera—Performance/production

3721 Association Internationale Sémiologie du spectacle. *Approches de l'opéra: actes du colloque AISS.* (Approaches of the Opera: Proceedings of the IASP Seminar.) Paris: Didier; 1986. 333 pp. (Langages, discours et sociétés.) Pref. Notes. Illus.: Graphs. Photo. Print. B&W. 32: var. sizes. Lang.: Eng, Fre.
Europe. 1600-1985. Critical studies. ■Semiology of opera, including methodological problems, formal analysis, the study of performance and reception. Opera as an intercultural practice.

3722 Blanchard, Roger; Candé, Roland de. *Dieux et divas de l'opéra: des origines à la Malibran.* (Divinities and Divas of the Opera: From the Origins to Malibran.) Paris: Plon; 1986. 429 pp. Biblio. Append. Illus.: Pntg. Dwg. Print. B&W. 137: var. sizes. [vol. 1.] Lang.: Fre.
Europe. 1600-1820. Biographical studies. ■Biographical dictionary of opera singers up to the Romantic period.

3723 Robinson, Harlow. "Believer." *OpN.* 1986 Feb 1; 50(10): 30-32. Illus.: Photo. Color. 2. Lang.: Eng.
Finland. 1935-1986. Histories-sources. ■Profile of and interview with Finnish Bass Martti Talvela.

3724 Suur-Kujala, Anneli. "Opera Director Ilkka Kuusisto: Opera Has Found the General Public." *NFT.* 1986; 38: 6-7. Illus.: Photo. B&W. 4: var. sizes. Lang.: Eng, Fre.
Finland: Helsinki, Suomussalmi. 1967-1986. Histories-sources. ■Interview with composer and director of the Finnish National Opera Ilkka Kuusisto discussing the public's change in attitude toward opera and the popularity of festivals.

3725 Conrad, Peter. "Fatal Charms." *OpN.* 1986 Mar 15; 50(13): 32-34, 36. Illus.: Photo. B&W. 2. Lang.: Eng.
France. 1875-1986. Critical studies. ■Performance analysis of the title role of *Carmen.*

3726 Kauffman, Dorothy. "Les Wagnériens." *OpN.* 1986 Apr 12; 50(15): 16-18. Illus.: Dwg. Photo. B&W. 3. Lang.: Eng.
France: Paris. Germany, West: Bayreuth. 1860-1986. Critical studies. ■The influence of Richard Wagner on the work of the French Symbolists and their publication *La Revue Wagnérienne.*

3727 Loney, Glenn. "Paris Postscript." *OpN.* 1986 June 18; 50(9): 32-34. Illus.: Photo. . 1. Lang.: Eng.
France. 1960-1985. Histories-sources. ■Profile of Bernard Lefort, former Intendant of the Palais Garnier of Paris.

3728 Pendle, Karin. "A Night at the Opera: The Parisian Prima Donna, 1830-1850." *OQ.* 1986 Spr; 4(1): 77-89. Notes. Append. Lang.: Eng.
France: Paris. 1830-1850. Histories-reconstruction. ■A brief account of the debuts and careers of young Parisian prima donnas and other popular French female singers, along with a list of roles in repertoire.

3729 Scherer, Barrymore Laurence. "Decline and Fall." *OpN.* 1986 Dec 6; 51(6): 18-20, 22. Illus.: Photo. B&W. 14: var. sizes. Lang.: Eng.
France. 1950-1986. Critical studies. ■Currently French singing and opera are both in decline, the result of a failure to understand the required style. Includes discussion of the great French stylists.

3730 Festival international de Radio-France et de Montpellier, ed. *Divas, parcours d'un mythe.* (Divas, Travel Through a Myth.) Arles: Actes Sud; 1986. 139 pp. Pref. Biblio. Illus.: Pntg. Photo. Dwg. Print. B&W. 78: var. sizes. [Accompanies exhibit at Musée Fabre, Montpellier, July-Sept. 1986.] Lang.: Fre.
France. Italy. USA. 1830-1970. Biographical studies. ■Analysis of the diva as a sociocultural phenomenon.

3731 Zohar, Uriel. "*Hatragedia shel Carmen* Lefi Piter Brook." (*Carmen's Tragedy* According to Peter Brook.) *Bamah.* 1986; 21(105-106): 124-129. Notes. Lang.: Heb.
France: Paris. 1981-1983. Historical studies. ■Peter Brook's direction and adaptation of the opera *Carmen* by Georges Bizet.

3732 Ardoin, John. "Furtwängler and Opera: Part IV—*Der Ring des Nibelungen.*" *OQ.* 1985 Spr; 3(1): 44-51. Pref. Notes. Biblio. [Part 4 of 4 drawn from a book in progress on Furtwängler and his recording legacy.] Lang.: Eng.

Germany: Bayreuth. Italy: Milan, Rome. 1901-1954. Biographical studies. ■The conversion of the conductor Wilhelm Furtwängler from a dissenter of Wagner's work to the foremost Wagnerian conductor of post World War I.

3733 Ashbrook, William. "The First Singers of *Tristan und Isolde.*" *OQ.* 1985/86 Win; 3(4): 11-23. Notes. Lang.: Eng.
Germany: Munich. 1857-1869. Historical studies. ■Researches the first singers that were cast in the early development and subsequent productions of Wagner's *Tristan und Isolde.*

3734 Assoun, Paul-Laurent. "Opéra et mise en scène des voix du désir: genèse d'une vocation." (Opera and the Staging of the Voices of Desire: Genesis of a Vocation.) *CorpsE.* 1986; 20: 69-76. Lang.: Fre.
Germany. 1800-1909. Critical studies. ■Analysis of staging as language, linking opera with drama, based on texts of Richard Wagner and on Sigmund Freud's story of Little Hans (Herbert Graf).

3735 Felsenstein, Walter. *...nicht Stimmungen, sondern Absichten. Gespräche mit Walter Felsenstein.* (...Not Moods But Intentions: Talks with Walter Felsenstein.) Berlin: Verband d. Theaterschaffenden d. DDR; 1986. 84 pp. (MT 200.) Lang.: Ger.
Germany: Berlin. 1921-1971. Histories-sources. ■Interviews with the universal theatre man Walter Felsenstein on his biography, opera, film, staging, singing, singers' training, understanding of music theatre.

3736 Giannini, Vera. "Fritz Busch: A Son Remembers His Father." *OQ.* 1986 Sum; 4(2): 57-74. Notes. Illus.: Photo. B&W. 3: 4 in. x 4 in., 5 in. x 7 in., 5 in. x 8 in. Lang.: Eng.
Germany. USA. 1922-1949. Biographical studies. ■Nazi persecution of the conductor of the Dresden Opera Theatre and the events that led up to his exile, followed by details of his associations with Carl Ebert and his son Hans Busch.

3737 Kraus, Gottfried, ed. *Ein Mass, das heute fehlt: Wilhelm Furtwängler im Echo der Nachwelt.* (The Measure Missing Today: Wilhelm Furtwängler in Response to Posterity.) Salzburg: Otto Müller; 1986. 249 pp. Biblio. Append. Illus.: Photo. B&W. 7: 9 cm. x 12 cm. Lang.: Ger.
Germany: Berlin. Austria: Salzburg. 1886-1986. Biographical studies. ■Collection of statements by various authors about the life and career of conductor Wilhelm Furtwängler, including his importance in musical interpretation and tonal music.

3738 Adam, Theo. *Die 100. Rolle oder Ich mache einen neuen Adam.* (The 100th Part or I Create a New Adam.) Berlin: Henschelverlag; 1986. 292 pp. Append. Illus.: Photo. B&W. 45. Lang.: Ger.
Germany, East: Dresden, Berlin, East. 1970-1985. Biographical studies. ■Bass-baritone Harry Kupfer on his work and career as singer and director. Includes discussion on Friedrich Cerha's *Baal,* Beethoven's *Fidelio* and the work of Richard Strauss.

3739 Koltai, Tamás. "Az opera: konfrontáció. Beszélgetés Harry Kupferral." (Opera Means Confrontation: An Interview with Harry Kupfer.) *Muzsika.* 1986; 29(2): 18-24. Illus.: Photo. B&W. Lang.: Hun.
Germany, East: Berlin, East. 1981-1986. Histories-sources. ■Interview with director Harry Kupfer of Komische Oper.

3740 Viola, György. "Bayreuthi beszélgetések Wolfgang Wagnerrel." (Talks with Wolfgang Wagner in Bayreuth.) *Sz.* 1986 Dec.; 19(12): 42-47. Illus.: Photo. B&W. 3: var. sizes. Lang.: Hun.
Germany, West: Bayreuth. 1975-1985. Histories-sources. ■Interview with Wolfgang Wagner on his stagings at Bayreuth Festspiele of Richard Wagner's *Parsifal, Die Meistersinger von Nürnberg* and *Tannhäuser.*

3741 Ardoin, John. "Maria Callas: The Early Years." *OQ.* 1985 Sum; 3(2): 6-13. Notes. Lang.: Eng.
Greece: Athens. 1937-1945. Biographical studies. ■Overview of Polyvius Marchand's study of Maria Callas' life during the period she spent performing in Greece.

3742 Fodor, Géza. *Operai napló.* (Opera Diary.) Budapest: Magvető; 1986. 637 pp. (Elvek és utak.) Lang.: Hun.

MUSIC-DRAMA: Opera—Performance/production

Hungary. 1982-1985. Critical studies. ■Critical essays, studies and recording reviews of opera performances.

3743 Fodor, Géza. "A mitosz megkisértése II. A *Manon Lescaut* új betanulásban." (Attempting the Myth, II: A New Production of *Manon Lescaut*.) *Muzsika*. 1986; 29(1): 36-44. Illus.: Photo. B&W. Lang.: Hun.
Hungary: Budapest. 1985. Reviews of performances. ■Puccini's *Manon Lescaut* at the Hungarian State Opera House directed by András Mikó.

3744 Fodor, Géza. "Operai napló." (Opera Diary.) *Muzsika*. 1986; 29(2): 27-33. Illus.: Photo. B&W. 4. Lang.: Hun.
Hungary: Budapest. 1985-1986. Reviews of performances. ■Critical evaluation of newly interpreted works in the Hungarian State Opera House season.

3745 Fodor, Géza. "*Rózsalovag.*" (*Der Rosenkavalier.*) *Muzsika*. 1986; 29(3): 18-27. Illus.: Photo. B&W. Lang.: Hun.
Hungary: Budapest. 1985. Reviews of performances. ■Richard Strauss' comic opera *Der Rosenkavalier* at the Hungarian State Opera House directed by András Mikó.

3746 Fodor, Géza. "Az álarcosbál." (*Un ballo in maschere.*) *Muzsika*. 1986; 29(4): 25-33. Illus.: Photo. B&W. Lang.: Hun.
Hungary: Budapest. 1986. Reviews of performances. ■Verdi's *Un ballo in maschera* at the Hungarian State Opera House directed by András Fehér.

3747 Fodor, Géza. "Operai napló." (Opera Diary.) *Muzsika*. 1986; 29(5): 22-31. Illus.: Photo. B&W. 7. Lang.: Hun.
Hungary: Budapest. 1986. Reviews of performances. ■Verdi's *Simon Boccanegra* directed by András Mikó and Puccini's *La Bohème* with guest star Luciano Pavarotti directed by Kálmán Nádasdy presented in the Hungarian State Opera House and Erkel Theatre.

3748 Halász, Péter. "A *Carmen* Szegeden." (*Carmen* at Szeged.) *Muzsika*. 1986; 29(2): 34-36. Illus.: Photo. B&W. Lang.: Hun.
Hungary: Szeged. 1985. Reviews of performances. ■Bizet's *Carmen* at National Theatre of Szeged directed by Géza Oberfrank.

3749 Halász, Péter. "Rossini a Népszinházban." (Rossini at the Popular Theatre.) *Muzsika*. 1986; 29(5): 32-33 . Lang.: Hun.
Hungary: Budapest. 1986. Reviews of performances. ■Rossini's *L'occasione fa il ladro* at the Popular Theatre directed by László Kertész.

3750 Kerényi, Mária. "A győri *Trubadúr.*" (*Il Trovatore* in Győr.) *Muzsika*. 1986; 29(1): 45. Lang.: Hun.
Hungary: Győr. 1985. Reviews of performances. ■Verdi's *Il Trovatore* at Kisfaludy Theatre directed by József Bor.

3751 Kerényi, Mária. "A *Don Pasquale* Pécsett." (*Don Pasquale* at Pécs.) *Muzsika*. 1986; 29(3): 30-31. Illus.: Photo. B&W. Lang.: Hun.
Hungary: Pécs. 1985. Reviews of performances. ■Donizetti's comic opera *Don Pasquale* at the National Theatre of Pécs directed by Zoltán Horváth.

3752 Lise, Giorgio; Rescigno, Eduardo, ed.; Tallián, Tibor, transl. *A 18. századi opera Scarlattitól Mozartig.* (Eighteenth Century Opera from Scarlatti to Mozart.) Budapest: Zenemükiadó; 1986. 71 pp. (Európa zenéje.) Index. Biblio. Illus.: Photo. B&W. Color. Lang.: Hun.
Hungary: Budapest. 1700-1800. Histories-general. ■Hungarian translation of *L'Opera nel Settecento*, (Milan, 1983) in the series *Grande Storia della Musica*.

3753 Simándy, József. *Bánk bán elmondja...krónikás Dalos László.* (Bán Bánk Tells All...the Chronicler: László Dalos.) Budapest: Zenemükiadó; 1986. 303 pp. Illus.: Photo. B&W. [Second ed.] Lang.: Hun.
Hungary. 1916-1984. Histories-sources. ■József Simándy, the internationally known tenor, remembers his life and the events of his career.

3754 Szitha, Tünde. "A debreceni *Tosca.*" (*Tosca* in Debrecen.) *Muzsika*. 1986; 29(3): 32. Lang.: Hun.
Hungary: Debrecen. 1985. Reviews of performances. ■Puccini's *Tosca* at Csokonai Theatre directed by Gyula Kertész.

3755 Viola, György. *Operafejedelmek.* (Royalty of the Opera.) Budapest: Népszava; 1986. 208 pp. Illus.: Photo. B&W. Lang.: Hun.
Hungary. 1925-1979. Biographical studies. ■Lives and careers of three Hungarian opera stars: Mária Gyurkovics, Sándor Svéd and Mihály Székely.

3756 Connolly, Robert. "Raider of the Lost Archives." *OpN.* 1986 Aug.; 51(2): 16-18, 20. Illus.: Photo. B&W. 10. Lang.: Eng.
Italy: Castelnuovo del Porto. 1950-1986. Histories-sources. ■Maurizio Tiberi and his Tima Club records preserve the work of little-known singers of the past as well as famous artists who made few recordings. Related to Media: Audio forms.

3757 Habermann, Günther. "Kastratensänger im 18. Jahrhundert in ihrer äusseren Erscheinung und ihrem Verhalten—nach zeitgenössischen Bildern." (Castrati Singers in the 18th Century, How They Looked and Their Behavior—According to Contemporary Pictures.) 126-147 in Spitzer, Leopold, ed. *Probleme der Sängerausbildung: Bericht über das 5. gesangspädagogische Symposion in Bad Ischl vom 18. bis 22. März 1985.* Vienna: Hochschule für Musik u. darst. Kunst in Wien, Abt. f. Sologesang u. musikdramat. Darstellung; 1986. 175 pp. Illus.: Photo. Dwg. Color. B&W. 23. Lang.: Ger.
Italy: Rome, Venice. England: London. 1700-1799. Historical studies. ■Physical characteristics, social behavior and stage presence of the *castrati*.

3758 Lebrecht, Norman. "Esultate! A Film of *Otello.*" *OpN.* 1986 Oct.; 51(4): 38-40, 42-43. Illus.: Photo. Color. B&W. 13. Lang.: Eng.
Italy: Rome. 1985-1986. Histories-sources. ■The Franco Zeffirelli film of *Otello* by Giuseppe Verdi, an account of the production. Related to Media: Film.

3759 Löbl, Hermi. "Ein grosses G gewonnen." (Won a Capital G.) *Buhne.* 1986 Feb.; 29(2): 20-21. Print. Color. Lang.: Ger.
Italy. Austria. 1935-1986. Biographical studies. ■Opera-singer Mirella Freni, née Fregni, married to Nicolai Ghiaurov: her roles and her plans.

3760 Mayer, Martin; Bliokh, Vladimir; Hayward, Bill. "Tenor of the Times." *OpN.* 1986 Mar 29; 50(14): 10-13. Illus.: Photo. B&W. 10. Lang.: Eng.
Italy: Modena. 1935-1986. Histories-sources. ■Profile of and interview with Italian tenor Luciano Pavarotti.

3761 Peschel, Enid Rhodes. "Medicine and Music: The Castrati in Opera." *OQ.* 1986-87 Win; 4(4): 21-38. Notes. TZ. Illus.: Dwg. B&W. 2: var. sizes. Lang.: Eng.
Italy. 1599-1797. Historical studies. ■History and medical perspective of castration for the purpose of creating the adult male soprano.

3762 Pleasants, Henry. "Giuseppina Cobelli: A Personal Memoir." *OQ.* 1985/86 Win; 3(4): 38-47. Notes. Illus.: Photo. B&W. 4: var. sizes. Lang.: Eng.
Italy. 1898-1948. Histories-sources. ■An overview of the life and career of Italian opera singer Giuseppina Cobelli.

3763 Ronconi, Luca. *Inventare l'opera. L'Orfeo, Il viaggio a Reims, Aida: tre opere d'occasione alla Scala.* (Inventing Opera: *Orfeo, Il viaggio a Reims,* and *Aida* at La Scala.) Milan: Ubulibri; 1986. 191 pp. (I libri quadrati.) Pref. Index. Tables. Append. Illus.: Photo. Dwg. Poster. Color. B&W. Lang.: Ita.
Italy: Milan. 1985. Histories-sources. ■Ronconi's productions of three operas at the Teatro alla Scala.

3764 Rosenbaum. "Concerted Effort." *OpN.* 1986 Mar 15; 50(13): 20, 50-51. Illus.: Photo. B&W. 1. Lang.: Eng.
Italy. 1856-1881. Critical studies. ■The council scene in *Simon Boccanegra* is a successful musico-dramatic collaboration between Giuseppe Verdi and his librettist Arrigo Boito.

3765 Sandow, Gregory. "Toward Uncharted Shores." *OpN.* 1986 Jan 4; 50(8): 30, 32, 34. Illus.: Photo. B&W. 1. Lang.: Eng.

MUSIC-DRAMA: Opera—Performance/production

Italy. 1800-1900. Critical studies. ∎*L'Italiana in Algeri* by Gioacchino Rossini is successful in itself and also an important innovative influence on Italian music.

3766   Waleson, Heidi. "In Love with Life." *OpN*. 1986 May; 50(16): 10-12, 48. Illus.: Photo. Color. B&W. 3. Lang.: Eng.

Italy: Castiglione del Pepoli. 1943-1986. Histories-sources. ∎Profile of and interview with Italian baritone Leo Nucci.

3767   Zucker, Stefan. "Heroes on the Rise." *OpN*. 1986 Jan 4; 50(8): 35-37. Illus.: Photo. B&W. 1. Lang.: Eng.

Italy: Bergamo. 1788-1860. Historical studies. ∎The growth and development of the Italian tenor singing style.

3768   Fraser, Antonia. "My Heroine." *OpN*. 1986 Dec 20; 51(7): 20-23. Illus.: Photo. Color. 1. Lang.: Eng.

New Zealand: Gisborne. USA: New York, NY. 1944-1986. Histories-sources. ∎Profile of and interview with New Zealand soprano Kiri Te Kanawa.

3769   Rich, Maria F. "Cause for Concern." *OpN*. 1986 Nov.; 51(5): 32, 34, 36-41. Illus.: Photo. B&W. 3. Lang.: Eng.

North America. 1985-1986. Histories-sources. ∎Evaluation, with statistics, of the 1985-86 North American opera season.

3770   Latus, Jan. "Bel Canto W Warszawie." (Bel Canto in Warsaw.) *TeatrW*. 1985 Feb.; 40(821): 22-23. Lang.: Pol.

Poland: Warsaw. 1984. Reviews of performances. ∎Production analysis of *Lucia di Lammermoor* by Gaetano Donizetti, music directed by Andrzej Straszyński, staged by Teatr Wielki.

3771   Stearns, David Patrick. "Opera Addict." *OpN*. 1986 May; 50(16): 20-22. Illus.: Photo. B&W. 2. Lang.: Eng.

Romania. USA: New York, NY. 1950-1986. Histories-sources. ∎Profile of and interview with Romanian-born conductor Christian Berea.

3772   Čajkovskij, Pëtr Iljic. *Muzykal'no-kritičeskie stat'i.* (Articles on Musical Criticism.) Leningrad: Muzyka; 1986. 364 pp. Lang.: Rus.

Russia. 1850-1900. Reviews of performances. ∎The composer's articles and reviews on opera in Russia and Western Europe.

3773   Dmitrijevskaja, E.R.; Dmitrijevskij, V. *Šaljapin v Moskve.* (Šaljapin in Moscow.) Moscow: Moskovski rabočij; 1986. 238 pp. Lang.: Rus.

Russia: Moscow. 1873-1938. Biographies. ∎Life and career of singer Fëdor J. Šaljapin.

3774   Groševa, E.A., comp.; Gul'janc, E.I. *Mark Rejzen: Avtobiogr. zapisi. Ctat'i. Vospominanija.* (Mark Rejzen: Autobiographical Notes, Articles, Memoirs.) Moscow: Sov.kompozitor; 1986. 304 pp. Lang.: Rus.

Russia: Moscow. 1895-1986. Biographies. ∎Biographical materials on Bolšoj singer Mark Rejzen.

3775   Oldani, Robert William. "Mussorgsky's *Boris* On the Stage of the Maryinsky Theater: A Chronicle of the First Production." *OQ*. 1986 Sum; 4(2): 75-92. Notes. Illus.: Dwg. 6: 3 in. x 4 in. Lang.: Eng.

Russia: St. Petersburg. 1874. Critical studies. ∎Production analysis of the first full performance of Modest Mussorgskij's opera, *Boris Godunov*, at the Mariinskij Theatre.

3776   Poljanovski, G.A. *N.A. Obychova.* Moscow: Muzyka; 1986. 158 pp. Lang.: Rus.

Russia. 1886-1961. Biographies. ∎Biography of singer N.A. Obychova.

3777   Stearns, David Patrick. "Decline and Fall." *OpN*. 1986 Feb 1; 50(10): 18-21. Illus.: Photo. B&W. 1. Lang.: Eng.

Russia: St. Petersburg. 1850-1890. Biographical studies. ∎The alcoholism of Modest Pavlovič Mussorgskij prevented the completion of *Chovanščina*.

3778   Buchau, Stephanie von. "Like a Ray of Light." *OpN*. 1986 Sep.; 51(3): 16-18, 20. Illus.: Photo. Color. B&W. 3. Lang.: Eng.

Spain: Zaragoza. USA: San Francisco, CA. 1928-1986. Histories-sources. ∎Profile of and interview with Spanish soprano Pilar Lorengar.

3779   Stearns, David Patrick; Schüller, Beatriz. "The Other Side of Domingo." *OpN*. 1986 Dec 6; 51(6): 24, 26. Illus.: Photo. B&W. 1. Lang.: Eng.

Spain: Madrid. 1941-1986. Histories-sources. ∎Profile of and interview with Spanish tenor Plácido Domingo focusing on his work as an operatic conductor.

3780   Fierz, Gerold. "Mensch und Natur: *Der magische Kreis.*" (Man and Nature: *The Magic Circle.*) *Opw*. 1986 Sep.; 27(9): 38. Illus.: Photo. B&W. Lang.: Ger.

Switzerland: Chur. 1986. Reviews of performances. ∎The first opera written in Romansch, Switzerland's fourth language, is about the destruction of forests. Music by Gion Antoni Derungs, libretto by Lothar Deplazes.

3781   Barker, Frank Granville. "Monteverdi Our Contemporary." *PI*. 1986 Apr.; 1(9): 54-55. Illus.: Photo. Print. B&W. 1. Lang.: Eng.

UK-England: Kent. 1986. Histories-sources. ∎Director Jonathan Hale's approach to Claudio Monteverdi's opera *L'incoronazione di Poppea* at the Kent Opera.

3782   Barker, Frank Granville. "A Dream at its Garden." *PI*. 1986 June; 1(11): 36-37. B&W. 2. Lang.: Eng.

UK-England: London. 1986. Histories-sources. ∎Christopher Renshaw talks about his production of Benjamin Britten's opera *A Midsummer Night's Dream* at Covent Garden.

3783   Bedford, Steuart. "Composer and Conductor—Annals of a Collaboration." *OQ*. 1986 Fall; 4(3): 60-74. Illus.: Photo. Sketches. B&W. 5: var. sizes. Lang.: Eng.

UK-England: London. 1967-1976. Histories-sources. ∎The collaboration and relationship of conductor Steuart Bedford and Benjamin Britten.

3784   Crozier, Eric. "Sir Peter Pears—An Appreciation." *OQ*. 1986 Fall; 4(3): 1-3. Lang.: Eng.

UK-England: London. 1937-1986. Biographical studies. ∎Tribute to opera singer Peter Pears, with brief overview of his career and relationship with composer Benjamin Britten.

3785   Davis, Peter G. "Sir Peter Pears." *OpN*. 1986 Aug.; 51(2): 32, 34, 46-47. Illus.: Photo. B&W. 4. Lang.: Eng.

UK-England: Aldeburgh. 1910-1986. Histories-sources. ∎Appreciation and obituary of the late English tenor Sir Peter Pears.

3786   Forbes, Elizabeth; Crowthers, Malcolm. "Six Days to Make an Opera." *OpN*. 1986 Nov.; 51(5): 24-26, 28-30, 70. Illus.: Photo. B&W. 10. Lang.: Eng.

UK-England: London. 1986. Histories-sources. ∎The Metropolitan Opera Guild Teacher Workshop demonstrates its techniques for London teachers.

3787   Roberts, Peter. "*Fidelio* as Morality Play." *PI*. 1986 Aug.; 2(1): 48-50. B&W. 4. Lang.: Eng.

UK-England: London. 1986. Histories-sources. ∎Andrei Serban discusses his production of Beethoven's *Fidelio* for Covent Garden.

3788   Lipton, Gary J. "Prime Time." *OpN*. 1986 Mar 29; 50(14): 30-32. Illus.: Photo. B&W. 4. Lang.: Eng.

UK-Wales: Pontnewynydd. 1936-1986. Histories-sources. ∎Profile of and interview with Welsh soprano Gwyneth Jones.

3789   Roberts, Peter. "*Otello* with a Political Dimension." *PI*. 1986 Mar.; 1(8): 50-52. Illus.: Photo. Print. B&W. 1. Lang.: Eng.

UK-Wales: Cardiff. 1986. Histories-sources. ∎Peter Stein discusses his approach to *Otello* and Verdi for his production of *Otello* at the Welsh National Opera Company.

3790   "Vienna Staatsoper Telecast." *OpN*. 1986 Mar 29; 50(14): 24-25. Illus.: Photo. Color. [*Elektra*.] Lang.: Eng.

USA: New York, NY. 1986. Histories-sources. ∎Stills from telecast performances. Lists of principals, conductors and production staff included.

3791   "Washington Opera Telecast." *OpN*. 1986 Nov.; 51(5): 18. [*Goya*.] Lang.: Eng.

USA: Washington, DC. 1986. Histories-sources. ∎Stills from telecast performance. List of principals, conductor and production staff included.

3792   Ardoin, John. "Horn of Plenty." *OQ*. 1986 Spr; 4(1): 43-53. Lang.: Eng.

MUSIC-DRAMA: Opera—Performance/production

USA. 1906-1925. Reviews of performances. ∎Brief reviews of 10 vintage recordings of complete operas (from the acoustic era) that are still available on LP.

3793 Battaglia, Carl. "June in Bloom." *OpN*. 1986 Aug.; 51(2): 10-14. Illus.: Photo. Color. B&W. 4. Lang.: Eng.
USA: New York, NY. 1955-1986. Histories-sources. ∎Profile of and interview with American soprano June Anderson.

3794 Bergman, Beth. "Metropolitan Opera: Radio Broadcast Performances." *OpN*. 1986; 50. Discography. Illus.: Design. Diagram. Plan. Dwg. Photo. Print. Color. B&W. [*L'Italiana in Algeri* (Jan 4): pp 22-24, *Jenufa* (Jan 4): pp 26-28, *Tosca* (Jan 18): pp 24-26, *Roméo et Juliette* (Jan 18): pp 28-30, *Khovanshchina* (Feb 1): pp 22-24, *Porgy and Bess* (Feb 1): pp 26-28, *Idomeneo* (Feb 15): pp 19-22, *Francesca da Rimini* (Feb 15): pp 26-28, *Samson* (Mar 1): pp 22-24, *Falstaff* (Mar 1): pp 26-28, *Simon Boccanegra* (Mar 15): pp 24-26, *Carmen* (Mar 15): pp 28-30, *Aida* (Mar 29): pp 20-22, *Der Rosenkavalier* (Mar 29): pp 26-28, *Don Carlo* (Apr 12): pp 26-26, *Parsifal* (Apr 12): pp 30-32.] Lang.: Eng.
USA: New York, NY. 1986. Histories-sources. ∎Photographs, cast lists, synopses, and discographies of Metropolitan Opera radio broadcast performances.

3795 Bergman, Beth; Heffernan, James. "Metropolitan Opera Telecasts." *OpN*. 1986; 50. Discography. Illus.: Design. Dwg. Photo. Color. [*L'Italiana in Algeri* (Jan 4): pp 22-24, *Lohengrin* (Mar 15): pp 23-24, *Die Fledermaus* (Dec 20): pp 30-32.] Lang.: Eng.
USA: New York, NY. 1986. Histories-sources. ∎Stills from telecast performances. Lists of principals, conductors and production staff included.

3796 Bergman, Beth; Swope, Martha. "New York City Opera Telecast." *OpN*. 1986 Nov.; 50(5): 44-45. Illus.: Photo. Color. [*Candide*.] Lang.: Eng.
USA: New York, NY. 1986. Histories-sources. ∎Stills from telecast performance. List of principals, conductor and production staff included.

3797 Bergman, Beth. "Metropolitan Opera: Radio Broadcast Performances." *OpN*. 1986; 51. Discography. Illus.: Design. Diagram. Plan. Dwg. Photo. Color. B&W. [*Roméo et Juliette* (Dec 6): pp 32-34, *I Puritani* (Dec 6): pp 38-40, *Fidelio* (Dec 20): pp 24-26, *Die Fledermaus* (Dec 20): pp 30-32.] Lang.: Eng.
USA: New York, NY. 1986. Histories-sources. ∎Photographs, cast lists, synopses, and discographies of Metropolitan Opera radio broadcast performances.

3798 Blumenfeld, Harold. "*Three Oranges* in Cincinnati." *OJ*. 1986 Fall; 19(3): 24-26. Illus.: Photo. Print. B&W. 1: 5 in. x 8 in. Lang.: Eng.
USA: Cincinnati, OH. 1986. Reviews of performances. ∎Harold Blumenfeld reviews Prokofjèv's *Love for Three Oranges* at the Corbett Center of Performing Arts, with a new translation by Tom Stoppard.

3799 Blumenfeld, Harold. "Opera Theatre at St. Louis Starts Second Decade." *OJ*. 1986 Fall; 19(3): 27-33. Illus.: Photo. Print. B&W. 1: 5 in. x 8 in. Lang.: Eng.
USA: St. Louis, MO. 1975-1986. Reviews of performances. ∎Reviews of *Death in the Family, Viaggio a Reims, Abduction from the Seraglio* and *Tales of Hoffmann*.

3800 Buchau, Stephanie von. "An Agreeable Man." *OpN*. 1986 Oct.; 51(4): 44, 36, 48, 79. Illus.: Photo. Color. B&W. 3. Lang.: Eng.
USA: San Francisco, CA. 1921-1986. Histories-sources. ∎Profile of and interview with Sir John Pritchard, music director of the San Francisco Opera.

3801 Carroll, Charles Michael. "Seattle's New *Die Walküre*." *OJ*. 1985; 18(3): 28-34. Illus.: Photo. 1: 5 in. x 9 in. Lang.: Eng.
USA: Seattle, WA. 1985. Reviews of performances. ∎Review of *Die Walküre*, Seattle Opera directed by François Rochaix.

3802 Davis, Peter G. "Growing with Opera." *OpN*. 1986 Oct.; 51(4): 13-20, 22, 24-25, 27-28. Illus.: Plan. Dwg. Photo. Print. Color. B&W. 11: var. sizes. Lang.: Eng.
USA: New York, NY. 1936-1986. Histories-specific. ∎Fifty years of *Opera News*.

3803 Driggers, Sam. "*Clair de Lune* by Libby Larsen." *OJ*. 1985; 18(1): 38-40. Lang.: Eng.
USA: Little Rock, AR. 1985. Reviews of performances. ∎Reactions to music by Libby Larsen, libretto by Patricia Hampl. World premiere February 22, 1985.

3804 Duffie, Bruce. "Conversation Piece: Marilyn Zschau." *OJ*. 1986 Spr; 19(1): 34-40. Lang.: Eng.
USA: Chicago, IL. 1976-1986. Histories-sources. ∎Marilyn Zschau discusses her singing career and life with Bruce Duffie.

3805 Duffie, Bruce. "Conversation Piece: Nathaniel Merrill." *OJ*. 1986 Sum; 19(2): 33-40. Lang.: Eng.
USA: New York, NY. 1958-1986. Histories-sources. ∎Opera director Nathaniel Merrill discusses his concepts and productions of operas at New York's Metropolitan Opera and Opera Colorado with Bruce Duffie.

3806 Duffie, Bruce. "Conversation Piece: Teresa Berganza." *OJ*. 1985; 18(3): 35-40. Lang.: Eng.
USA: Chicago, IL. 1984. Histories-sources. ∎Interview with mezzo Teresa Berganza: contemporary audiences, favorite roles, recording vs. live performance and the demands of a singer's life.

3807 Duffie, Bruce. "Conversation Piece: Terry Cook." *OJ*. 1985; 18(4): 35-38. Notes. Lang.: Eng.
USA: Chicago, IL. 1985. Histories-sources. ∎Interview with Terry Cook, bass, talking about the audition process, the demands placed upon a young singer and the problems of a black male regarding casting.

3808 Farwell, Harold. "The Hills Are Alive." *OpN*. 1986 Jul.; 51(1): 28, 30-31. Illus.: Photo. B&W. 4. Lang.: Eng.
USA: Charlotte, NC. 1936-1986. Histories-specific. ∎History and achievements of the Brevard Music Center on the occasion of its fiftieth season.

3809 Freeman, John W. "A Search for Style." *OpN*. 1986 Nov.; 51(5): 20-21, 23. Illus.: Photo. Color. 1. Lang.: Eng.
USA: Chicago, IL. 1925-1986. Histories-sources. ∎Interview with Sir Charles Mackerras on the subject of authenticity in musical performance.

3810 Freis, Richard. "Southern Exposure." *OpN*. 1986 June; 50(17): 24, 26. Illus.: Handbill. Photo. B&W. 3. Lang.: Eng.
USA: Charleston, SC. 1986. Histories-sources. ∎The program of Spoleto U.S.A. includes *Lord Byron's Love Letter* by Raffaello de Banfield with libretto by Tennessee Williams. An account of the collaboration is given.

3811 Graff, Yveta Synek; Horton, Rick. "Tosca Talks." *OpN*. 1986 Jan 18; 50(9): 18-23. Illus.: Photo. Color. 15. Lang.: Eng.
USA. 1935-1986. Histories-sources. ∎Famous sopranos discuss their interpretations of Tosca.

3812 Green, London. "*Otello* on Records: A Tragic Vision." *OQ*. 1986 Sum; 4(2): 49-56. Notes. Discography. Lang.: Eng.
USA. 1902-1978. Critical studies. ∎An analysis of Verdi and Boito's translation of Shakespeare's *Othello* for their opera *Otello* and its reflection in various recordings.

3813 Harrison, John. "*Martin Audéich: A Christmas Miracle* by Robert Downard." *OJ*. 1986 Spr; 19(1): 29-30. Lang.: Eng.
USA: Denver, CO. 1985. Reviews of performances. ∎The first performance of Robert Downard's opera *Martin Audéich: A Christmas Miracle* is reviewed by John Harrison.

3814 Heymont, George. "News from Honolulu." *OpN*. 1986 Feb 15; 50(11): 34-35. Illus.: Photo. Color. 3. Lang.: Eng.
USA: Honolulu, HI. 1950-1985. Histories-specific. ∎The operations of the Hawaii Opera Theatre.

3815 Hunter, Mead. "Sellars and Mozart at Summerfare." *ThM*. 1986 Fall/Win; 18(1): 100-102. Illus.: Photo. Print. B&W. 1: 5 in. x 7 in. Lang.: Eng.

MUSIC-DRAMA: Opera—Performance/production

USA: Purchase, NY. 1986. Reviews of performances. ■Review of Peter Sellars' 1986 modern dress *Così fan tutte* by Mozart, set in a jukebox diner.

3816 Jacobson, Robert; Hayward, Bill. "Its Own Reward." *OpN*. 1986 Feb 15; 50(11): 10-14, 43-44. Illus.: Photo. Color. 2. Lang.: Eng.

USA. 1940-1986. Histories-sources. ■Profile of and interview with American soprano Benita Valente.

3817 Jacobson, Robert. "Lucky Lady." *OpN*. 1986 Apr 12; 50(15): 9-14, 50-52. Illus.: Photo. Color. B&W. 6: var. sizes. Lang.: Eng.

USA: San Diego, CA. 1950-1986. Histories-sources. ■Profile of and interview with American soprano Carol Vaness.

3818 Jacobson, Robert. "World on a String." *OpN*. 1986 Jul.; 51(1): 10-14, 41-43, 46. Illus.: Photo. Color. B&W. 5. Lang.: Eng.

USA: New York, NY. 1952-1986. Histories-sources. ■Profile of and interview with American tenor Jerry Hadley.

3819 Kaufman, Thomas G. "The Arditi Tour: The Midwest Gets Its First Real Taste of Italian Opera." *OQ*. 1986-87 Win; 4(4): 39-52. Notes. Append. Lang.: Eng.

USA. Canada: Montreal, PQ, Toronto, ON. 1853-1854. Historical studies. ■Luigi Arditi's U.S. and Canada tour with the New York Opera Company with works by Bellini, Donizetti, Mozart, Rossini and Verdi.

3820 Law, Joe K. "Linking the Past with the Present: A Conversation with Nancy Evans and Eric Crozier." *OQ*. 1985 Spr; 3(1): 72-79. Lang.: Eng.

USA: Columbia, MO. UK-England: London. 1940-1985. Histories-sources. ■Interview with singer Nancy Evans and writer Eric Crozier discussing their relationship with Benjamin Britten, the creation of *Beggar's Opera* and the founding of the English Opera Group.

3821 Leverett, James. "Updating Classics: A Revamped Verdi Fuels the Fray." *AmTh*. 1984 Sep.; 1(5): 26-27. Illus.: Photo. B&W. 1. Lang.: Eng.

USA. 1984. Critical studies. ■Controversy over director Jonathan Miller's updated interpretation of Verdi's *Rigoletto*.

3822 Marvin, Marajean. "Pasatieri Premiere in Columbus." *OJ*. 1986 Sum; 19(2): 23-27. Illus.: Photo. Print. B&W. 1: 5 in. x 8 in. Lang.: Eng.

USA: Columbus, OH. 1968-1986. Reviews of performances. ■Reviews world premiere of the opera *Three Sisters* by Thomas Pasatieri and Ken Ward Elmslie.

3823 McArthur, Edwin. "Dusolina Giannini." *OpN*. 1986 Dec 6; 51(6): 28, 30. Illus.: Photo. B&W. 3. Lang.: Eng.

USA: Philadelphia, PA. 1902-1986. Histories-sources. ■An appreciation and obituary of American soprano Dusolina Giannini.

3824 McDonald, Ellen. "Women in Benjamin Britten's Operas." *OQ*. 1986 Fall; 4(3): 83-101. Notes. Illus.: Photo. B&W. 5: 3 in. x 5 in., 5 in. x 7 in. Lang.: Eng.

USA. 1940-1979. Critical studies. ■Analysis, description and comparison of women's roles in the operas of Benjamin Britten.

3825 Mobley, Cole. "Parody Meets Passion." *OpN*. 1986 Jul.; 51(1): 20-23, 41. Illus.: Photo. Color. B&W. 9. Lang.: Eng.

USA: New York, NY. 1973-1986. Histories-sources. ■Profile of and interview with opera parodist Charles Ludlam of The Ridiculous Theatre Company.

3826 Novick, Julius. "Interlopers in the Opera House." *AmTh*. 1986 May; 3(2): 10-17. Illus.: Photo. Print. B&W. Lang.: Eng.

USA: New York, NY. 1970-1986. Historical studies. ■Revitalization of opera due to work of directors such as Harold Prince, Peter Sellars, Andrei Serban and Frank Corsaro.

3827 O'Connor, Patrick. "Tête à Tate." *OpN*. 1986 Dec 20; 51(7): 16-18. Illus.: Photo. Color. 2. Lang.: Eng.

USA: New York, NY. 1940-1946. Histories-sources. ■Profile of and interview with American conductor Jeffrey Tate, concerning his approach to *Die Fledermaus* by Richard Strauss at the Metropolitan Opera.

3828 Price, Walter. "Treasure of Sight and Sound." *OpN*. 1986 Sep.; 51(3): 42-43. Illus.: Photo. B&W. 2. Lang.: Eng.

USA: New York, NY. 1985-1986. Histories-sources. ■The videotaped opera showings at the Museum of Broadcasting. Related to Media: Audio forms.

3829 Rhein, John von. "In the Milieu." *OpN*. 1986 June; 15(17): 20-22. Illus.: Photo. B&W. 4. Lang.: Eng.

USA: Chicago, IL. 1984-1986. Histories-sources. ■Profile of and interview with American composer William Neill, composer-in-residence at the Lyric Opera of Chicago, whose work *The Guilt of William Sloan*, with libretto by Frank Galati, was performed in June 1986.

3830 Rubinstein, Leslie. "Dr. Miracle." *OpN*. 1986 June; 50(17): 30-31, 48. Illus.: Photo. B&W. 1. Lang.: Eng.

USA: New York, NY. 1938-1986. Histories-sources. ■Memoir of Dr. Eugen Grabscheid, throat specialist.

3831 Scherer, Barrymore Laurence. "Let There Be Light: Chained Heroics." *OpN*. 1986 Mar 1; 50(12): 10-14, 16. Illus.: Dwg. Photo. Color. B&W. 5. Lang.: Eng.

USA: New York, NY. 1986. Critical studies. ■*Samson*, by George Frideric Handel, usually considered an oratorio, is staged at the Metropolitan Opera.

3832 Schmidgall, Gary. "A Long Voyage." *OpN*. 1986 June; 50(17): 10-13. Illus.: Design. Photo. Color. B&W. 5. Lang.: Eng.

USA: Long Eddy, NJ. 1926-1986. Histories-sources. ■Profile of and interview with Lee Hoiby, American composer of *The Tempest* with libretto by Mark Schulgasser.

3833 Scovell, Jane. "George Cehanovsky." *OpN*. 1986 June; 50(17): 28-29. Illus.: Photo. B&W. 4. Lang.: Eng.

USA: New York, NY. 1892-1986. Histories-sources. ■Appreciation and obituary of the late baritone of the Metropolitan Opera, George Cehanovsky.

3834 Seligman, Gerald. "The Road to X." *OpN*. 1986 Sep.; 51(3): 28-30. Illus.: Photo. Color. B&W. 3. Lang.: Eng.

USA: New York, NY. Histories-sources. ■Profile of and interview with Anthony Davis, composer of the opera *X*, on the life and times of Malcolm X.

3835 Shaffer, Allen. "*Harriet, the Woman Called Moses* by Thea Musgrave." *OJ*. 1985; 18(1): 31-37. Lang.: Eng.

USA: Norfolk, VA. 1985. Reviews of performances. ■Sources for and development of the opera about Harriet Tubman commissioned primarily by the Virginia Opera Association. Reactions to the staging by director Gordon Davidson and the libretto, also by the composer. World premiere March 1, 1985.

3836 Sloan, Irene; Sloan, Sherwin. "Work." *OQ*. 1985/86 Win; 3(4): 1-10. Illus.: Photo. B&W. 7: var. sizes. Lang.: Eng.

USA: Los Angeles, CA. 1985. Critical studies. ■Peter Hemmings, executive director of the Music Center Opera Association, and Götz Friedrich, director of the Deutsche Oper Berlin, collaborated to provide Los Angeles with its first full season of opera.

3837 St. Clair, F.B. "Designs on the Ring." *OpN*. 1986 Jul.; 51(1): 16-19. Illus.: Dwg. Photo. Color. B&W. 4. Lang.: Eng.

USA: Seattle, WA. 1986. Histories-sources. ■The controversial scenic designs by Robert Israel and François Rochaix for the Seattle production of *Der Ring des Nibelungen* by Richard Wagner.

3838 Stearns, David Patrick. "The Man Behind the Artist." *OpN*. 1986 Nov.; 51(5): 14-18. Illus.: Pntg. Photo. Color. B&W. 9. Lang.: Eng.

USA: New York, NY. 1911-1986. Histories-sources. ■Profile of and interview with Gian Carlo Menotti with emphasis on his new opera *Goya*.

3839 Story, Rosalyn. "Black Divas." *Essence*. 1986 June; 17(2): 36. Illus.: Photo. Print. B&W. 5. Lang.: Eng.

USA: Enid, OK, New York, NY. 1961-1985. Historical studies. ■Outlines rising number of Black opera stars focusing on career of Leona Mitchell and the need for such organizations as the all Black opera company, Opera Ebony.

3840 Wakefield-Wright, JoElyn. "*Chinchilla*." *OJ*. 1986 Spr; 19(1): 31-33. Lang.: Eng.

MUSIC-DRAMA: Opera—Performance/production

USA: Binghamton, NY. 1986. Reviews of performances. ■Premiere performance of Myron Fink's opera *Chinchilla*.

3841 Williams, Jeannie. "A Singer's Roundtable: We Are the Music-Makers." *OQ*. 1986 Spr; 4(1): 61-76. Notes. Illus.: Photo. B&W. 1: 3 in. x 5 in. Lang.: Eng.

USA: Philadelphia, PA, New York, NY. 1985. Histories-sources. ■Collection of performance highlights and personal experiences of several great American opera singers at the inauguration of the AVA Hall of Fame.

3842 Winer, Deborah Grace. "Kid Sister." *OpN*. 1986 Feb 1; 50(10): 34-35, 46. Illus.: Photo. B&W. 1. Lang.: Eng.

USA: New York, NY. 1900-1986. Histories-sources. ■Profile of and interview with Frances Gershwin Godowsky, younger sister of George and Ira Gershwin who reminisces about her brothers.

3843 Zytowski, Carl. "*Lunatics and Lovers* by W. A. Mozart." *OJ*. 1985; 18(3): 25-27. Lang.: Eng.

USA: Santa Barbara, CA. 1985. Reviews of performances. ■*Lunatics and Lovers*, an English version of *La finta giardiniera*, directed and adapted by Richard Pearlman and staged at the Music Academy of the West, Santa Barbara, CA, August 19-22, 1985.

3844 "Za sceničeskuju pravdu." (For Stage Truth.) *SovMuzyka*. 1986; 7: 48-50. Lang.: Rus.

USSR. 1980-1986. Critical studies. ■Problems of directing, acting and vocal execution of roles in opera theatres in the USSR.

3845 Akulova, N.; Nest'eva, M.; Poljakova, N. "Vnimanie opernoj kul'ture." (The Attention of Opera Culture.) *SovMuzyka*. 1986 ; 10: 2-17. Lang.: Rus.

USSR. 1980-1986. Critical studies. ■Condition of operatic art in USSR repertoire, acting, staging.

3846 Archipova, I. "Aktivnoje edinstvo." (An Active Unity.) *Kommunist*. 1986; 6: 60-62. Lang.: Rus.

USSR. 1980-1986. Critical studies. ■Soloist of Bol'šoj theatre discusses tasks of Soviet operatic theatre.

3847 Gozenpud, A.A. *Ivan Jeršov: Zizn' i sceničeskaja dejatel'nost'*. (Ivan Jeršov: His Life and Stage Activity.) Leningrad: Sov. Kompozitor; 1986. 304 pp. Lang.: Rus.

USSR. 1867-1943. Biographies. ■Life and work of operatic tenor and teacher.

3848 Kožuchova, G. "Smertel 'nyj nomer licedejstva." (The Final Number on the Program.) *TeatrM*. 1986; 4: 102-112. Lang.: Rus.

USSR: Tbilisi. 1980-1986. Reviews of performances. ■Based on a conversation with Georgian producer Robert Sturua, composer G. Kančeli and conductor D. Kachidze on the staging of Kančeli's opera *Muzyka dlja živych (Music for the Living)* at the Z. Paliašvili theater of opera and ballet.

3849 Rorem, Ned. "Variations on Mussorgsky." *OpN*. 1986 Feb 1; 50(10): 10-14, 16-17, 44. Illus.: Photo. Pntg. Color. B&W. 3. Lang.: Eng.

USSR. 1839-1881. Critical studies. ■Analysis and appreciation of the work of Modest Pavlovič Mussorgskij by American composer Ned Rorem.

3850 Tret'jakova, Je.; Čepurov, A.; Potapova, N. "Čto delat? Perestraivat'sja!" (What Is To Be Done? Reform!) *SovMuzyka*. 1986; 12: 28-35. Lang.: Rus.

USSR: Leningrad. 1985-1986. Reviews of performances. ■Reviews of the opera season: problems of repertoire, the status of youth, organizational questions.

Plays/librettos/scripts

3851 Greene, Susan. "Wozzeck and Marie—Outcasts in Search of an Honest Morality." *OQ*. 1985 Fall; 3(3): 75-86. Notes. Biblio. MU. Lang.: Eng.

1821. Critical studies. ■The search for morality in *Wozzeck* by Alban Berg.

3852 Lee, M. Owen. "Pfitzner's *Palestrina*: A Musical Legend." *OQ*. 1986 Spr; 4(1): 54-60. Notes. Lang.: Eng.

1900-1982. Critical studies. ■An evaluation of the use of German and Christian myths in Hans Pfitzner's opera *Palestrina*, particularly in the theme, second act and characters, along with biographical information given on Hans Pfitzner and its relation to the character Palestrina.

3853 Peschel, Enid Rhodes; Peschel, Richard E. "Medicine, Music and Literature: The Figure of Dr. Miracle in Offenbach's *Les contes d'Hoffmann*." *OQ*. 1985 Sum; 3(2): 59-70. Pref. Notes. Lang.: Eng.

1700-1900. Critical studies. ■Analysis of the character 'Dr. Miracle' from Jacques Offenbach's *Les contes d'Hoffmann*, his roots in E.T.A. Hoffmann's *Councillor Krespel* and his relationship to eighteenth and nineteenth century medicine.

3854 Štejnpress, B.S. "Russkaja literatura v zasrubežnoj opere." (Russian Literature in Foreign Opera.) *SovMuzyka*. 1986; 6: 93-96. Lang.: Rus.

Historical studies. ■Plots of works of Russian literature by Korolenko, Gorkij, Saltykov-Ščedrin and others in operas by non-Russian composers. Continued in *SovMuzyka* 8 (1986), 93-96.

3855 Ardoin, John. "Apropos *Wozzeck*." *OQ*. 1985 Fall; 3(3): 68-74. Notes. Biblio. Lang.: Eng.

Austria: Vienna. 1821-1925. Critical studies. ■The origins and influences of Büchner's *Woyzeck* on Alban Berg's opera *Wozzeck*, examining segments of the score for structure.

3856 Brody, Elaine. "Operas in Search of Brahms." *OQ*. 1985/86 Win; 3(4): 24-37. Notes. Lang.: Eng.

Austria: Vienna. 1863-1985. Historical studies. ■An unfinished opera libretto by Turgenjev is discovered in Johannes Brahms's personal library. An investigation ensues to determine if there is any existing music composed for it.

3857 Green, London. "Lulu Wakens." *OQ*. 1985 Fall; 3(3): 112-122. Notes. Biblio. Illus.: Photo. B&W. 1: 4 in. x 6 in. Lang.: Eng.

Austria: Vienna. 1891-1979. Critical studies. ■Discusses the historical treatment of the character Lulu as being misunderstood as a personified myth of destructive instinct rather than an extraordinarily vivid character.

3858 Mertl, Monika. "Glauben und Wissen." (Believing and Knowing.) *Buhne*. 1986 July; 29(7): 98-99. Illus.: Photo. Print. B&W. Lang.: Ger.

Austria: Ossiach. 1986. Histories-sources. ■The idea for composing the church opera *Kain* by Karl Heinz Füssl, libretto by Herbert Lederer, based on the biblical story of Cain and Abel for the Carinthischer Sommer Festival.

3859 Perle, George. "An Introduction to *Lulu*." *OQ*. 1985 Fall; 3(3): 87-111. Pref. Notes. Biblio. MU. Lang.: Eng.

Austria: Vienna. 1907-1979. Critical studies. ■Discusses how specific events and people in Berg's life influenced *Lulu*.

3860 Rovira Belloso, Josep M. "La clemència a les darreres òperes de Mozart." (Clemency in Mozart's Last Operas.) *SdO*. 1986 Sep.; 28(324): 57-60. Illus.: Pntg. Dwg. Print. B&W. 8: var. sizes. Lang.: Cat.

Austria: Vienna. 1782-1791. Historical studies. ■Analysis of the theme of clemency as central to the ideology of *Così fan tutte*, *Le nozze di Figaro*, *Don Giovanni* and *Die Zauberflöte* by Wolfgang Amadeus Mozart.

3861 Kephart, Carolyn. "Thomas Durfey's *Cinthia and Endimion*: A Reconsideration." *TN*. 1985; 39(3): 134-139. Notes. Biblio. Lang.: Eng.

England. 1690-1701. Historical studies. ■Examination of the text and music of Thomas Durfey's opera *Cinthia and Endimion*.

3862 Potter, John; Potter, Susan. "Let There Be Light: Heavenly Blaze." *OpN*. 1986 Mar 1; 50(12): 13-14, 16. Illus.: Photo. B&W. 1. Lang.: Eng.

England: London. 1743. Critical studies. ■Comparison of the *Samson Agonistes* of John Milton and the *Samson* of George Frideric Handel.

3863 Ardoin, John. "Three Facsimiles." *OQ*. 1985/86 Win; 3(4): 38-47. Notes. Lang.: Eng.

Europe. 1814-1985. Textual studies. ■An examination of the operatic facsimiles for Mozart's *Die Zauberflöte*, Bellini's *Norma* and Verdi's *Falstaff*.

CLASSED ENTRIES

MUSIC-DRAMA: Opera—Plays/librettos/scripts

3864 Sagardía, Ángel. *Albèniz*. Barcelona: Edicions de Nou Art Thor; 1986. 52 pp. (Gent Nostra 46.) Tables. Illus.: Photo. Design. Dwg. Print. B&W. 54: var. sizes. Lang.: Cat.
Europe. 1860-1909. Biographies. ■Life and work of composer Isaac Albèniz, his relations with other composers, including a description of his operas and *zarzuelas* and their premieres.

3865 Niemi, Irmeli. "New Finnish Opera." *NFT*. 1986; 38: 2-5. Illus.: Photo. B&W. 6: var. sizes. Lang.: Eng, Fre.
Finland: Helsinki, Savonlinna. 1909-1986. Critical studies. ■Respected literary works dealing with national themes and folk life as source material for recent Finnish opera, including *The Horseman* by Aulis Sallinen and *Viimeiset kiusaukset (The Last Temptation)* by Joonas Kokkonen.

3866 Räsänen, Auli. "Sallinen Working on His Fourth Opera." *NFT*. 1986; 38: 8-10. Illus.: Photo. B&W. 3: 2 cm. x 3 cm., 8 cm. x 7.5 cm., 7.5 cm. x 6 cm. Lang.: Eng, Fre.
Finland: Helsinki. 1975-1986. Histories-sources. ■Interview with opera composer Aulis Sallinen discussing theme, form and his use of the national epic, the *Kalevala*, in his new opera being composed for the inauguration of the new Helsinki opera house.

3867 Alper, Clifford D. "A Meditation on *Thaïs*." *OJ*. 1985; 18(2): 2-7. Lang.: Eng.
France. 1894. Critical studies. ■How the use of the 'Meditation' theme in Massenet's opera *Thaïs* becomes a central element of the dramatic structure and enhances characterization.

3868 Bailbé, Jean-Michel. "*Lélio* ou l'opéra fragmenté." (*Lélio* or the Fragmented Opera.) *CorpsE*. 1986; 20: 101-112. Lang.: Fre.
France. Historical studies. ■Aesthetic concerns of composer Hector Berlioz during the writing of his opera *Lélio*.

3869 Edelman, Susanne Popper. "Rigoletto's Cryptic Aside: 'Marullo—Signore'." *OJ*. 1985; 18(2): 8-12. Lang.: Eng.
France. 1496-1851. Histories-sources. ■Origins of the characters Rigoletto and Marullo in Verdi's *Rigoletto* traced from their historical models through Victor Hugo's play *Le Roi s'amuse*, upon which Verdi based his libretto.

3870 Ollier, Jacqueline. "Carmen d'hier et d'aujourd'hui." (Carmen Yesterday and Today.) *CorpsE*. 1986; 20: 113-122. Lang.: Fre.
France. Spain. 1845-1983. Historical studies. ■Various adaptations of *Carmen* by Prosper Mérimée: the opera by Georges Bizet and contemporary treatments in musical theatre, ballet and film. Related to Dance: Ballet.

3871 Steptoe, Andrew. "Mozart, Mesmer, and *Così Fan Tutte*." *MLet*. 1986 July; 67(3): 248-255. Lang.: Eng.
France: Paris. Austria: Vienna. 1734-1789. Historical studies. ■A biographical sketch of the scandalous career of Franz Anton Mesmer and a discussion of why Mozart parodied him in the first act finale of *Così fan tutte*.

3872 Cook, Susan C. "*Der Zar lässt sich photographieren*: Weill and Comic Opera." 83-102 in Kowalke, Kim H., ed. *A New Orpheus*. New Haven, CT: Yale UP; 1986. xvi, 374 pp. Lang.: Eng.
Germany: Berlin. 1926-1929. Historical studies. ■Notes on the premiere of Kurt Weill's opera *Der Zar lässt sich photographieren* and an analysis of why the work was considered a landmark.

3873 Darcy, William. "The Pessimism of *The Ring*." *OQ*. 1986 Sum; 4(2): 24-48. Notes. Lang.: Eng.
Germany. 1852-1856. Critical studies. ■A dramatic and musical comparative analysis of Schopenhauerian pessimism in Richard Wagner's *Ring* and *Götterdämmerung*.

3874 Evans, John. "*Death in Venice*: The Apollonian/Dionysian Conflict." *OQ*. 1986 Fall; 4(3): 102-115. Notes. Lang.: Eng.
Germany. UK-England. 1911-1970. Biographical studies. ■The struggle with homosexuality as it relates to art, creativity and passion in Benjamin Britten's *Death in Venice* and its source, *Der Tod in Venedig* by Thomas Mann.

3875 Jarman, Douglas. "Weill and Berg: *Lulu* as Epic Opera." 147-156 in Kowalke, Kim H., ed. *A New Orpheus*. New Haven, CT: Yale UP; 1986. xvi, 374 pp. Lang.: Eng.
Germany. 1920-1932. Critical studies. ■Kurt Weill's choice of Alban Berg as a collaborator on *Lulu*, and his debates on the content of the opera with Arnold Schönberg.

3876 Kemp, Ian. "Music as Metaphor: Aspects of *Der Silbersee*." 131-146 in Kowalke, Kim H., ed. *A New Orpheus*. New Haven, CT: Yale UP; 1986. xvi, 374 pp. Lang.: Eng.
Germany: Leipzig. 1930-1933. Critical studies. ■Analysis of the ideas and emotions expressed through the musical phrasing of *Der Silbersee*, an opera by Kurt Weill and Georg Kaiser.

3877 Kowalke, Kim H., ed. *A New Orpheus*. New Haven, CT: Yale UP; 1986. xvi, 374 pp. Pref. Index. Append. Illus.: Photo. 15: var. sizes. Lang.: Eng.
Germany: Berlin, Leipzig. 1900-1950. Critical studies. ■Essays on Kurt Weill's life and art, focusing on musical analysis of his operatic works.

3878 Martin, George. "Verdi's Imitation of Shakespeare: *La forza del destino*." *OQ*. 1985 Spr; 3(1): 19-29. Notes. Lang.: Eng.
Germany. Italy. Austria. 1750-1850. Critical studies. ■Detailed discussion of Shakespeare's influence on Verdi with particular emphasis on *La forza del destino*, *Otello* and *Falstaff*.

3879 Ringer, Alexander L. "*Kleinkunst* and *Kuchenlied* in the Socio-Musical World of Kurt Weill." 37-50 in Kowalke, Kim H., ed. *A New Orpheus*. New Haven, CT: Yale UP; 1986. xvi, 374 pp. Lang.: Eng.
Germany: Berlin. 1756-1950. Critical studies. ■Compares Kurt Weill's career to that of Mozart, discusses Mahler's influence on Weill.

3880 Williams, Simon. "Wagner's *Das Liebesverbot*—From Shakespeare to the Well-Made Play." *OQ*. 1985/86 Win; 3(4): 56-69. Notes. MU. Lang.: Eng.
Germany. 1834. Critical studies. ■Wagner's composition of *Das Liebesverbot*, an operatic adaptation of Shakespeare's *Measure for Measure*, was an arduous process as he attempted to follow the doctrine and confines of the 'well-made' play.

3881 Detels, Claire. "*Simon Boccanegra*: The Making of the 1881 Revision." *OJ*. 1986 Spr; 19(1): 16-28. Notes. Lang.: Eng.
Italy: Milan. 1857-1881. Historical studies. ■Why Verdi changed his mind and revised the 1857 version of *Simon Boccanegra* in 1881.

3882 Detels, Claire. "*Simon Boccanegra*: Notes on the 1857 Version." *OJ*. 1985; 18(4): 12-20. Notes. Lang.: Eng.
Italy: Venice. 1856-1881. Historical studies. ■The creation of the 1857 version of *Simon Boccanegra* by Verdi with libretto by Piave (rewritten by another librettist and Verdi in 1881) based on the play by García Gutiérrez.

3883 Donin-Janz, Beatrice. "Il libretto d'opera contemporaneo al 'Teatro delle novità' di Bergamo dal 1950 al 1973: aspetti tematici e linguistici. Cronologia." (Contemporary Librettos at 'Theatre of Novelties' in Bergamo from 1950 to 1973: Thematic and Linguistic Aspects. Chronology.) *TeatrC*. 1985-1986; 6(11-12): 135-158. Notes. Biblio. Lang.: Ita.
Italy: Bergamo. 1950-1973. Critical studies. ■Study of the librettos of operas premiered at the Teatro delle Novità festival.

3884 Donin-Janz, Beatrice. "*La panchina* di Italo Calvino: dal racconto al libretto." (*The Bench* by Italo Calvino: from Short Story to Libretto.) *TeatrC*. 1985-1986; 6(11-12): 339-347. Notes. Biblio. Lang.: Ita.
Italy. 1956. Critical studies. ■Italo Calvino's first libretto is based on one of his Marcovaldo stories.

3885 Hunter, Mary. "The Fusion and Juxtaposition of Genres in Opera Buffa 1770-1800: Anelli and Piccinni's *Griselda*." *MLet*. 1986 Oct.; 67(4): 363-375. Lang.: Eng.
Italy: Venice. Austria: Vienna. 1770-1800. Historical studies. ■A discussion of the popularity of the tale of Patient Griselda as a subject for *opera seria*, and an analysis of the conventions as they appear in the version by Angelo Anelli and Niccolo Piccinni.

3886 Kestner, Joseph. "Deathless Love." *OpN*. 1986 Jan 18; 50(9): 10-15. Illus.: Pntg. Color. 5. Lang.: Eng.
Italy. 1476-1900. Historical studies. ■The Romeo and Juliet theme as interpreted in the musical and visual arts.

MUSIC-DRAMA: Opera—Plays/librettos/scripts

3887 Lee, Owen. "Tragic Lives." *OpN.* 1986 Apr 12; 50(15): 20, 22, 25, 52. Illus.: Photo. B&W. 2. Lang.: Eng.
Italy. 1867-1883. Histories-specific. ■Changes from the Friedrich von Schiller source in *Don Carlo* by Giuseppe Verdi.

3888 Modi, Sorab. "A Doge in His Day." *OpN.* 1986 Mar 15; 50(13): 38-39. Illus.: Photo. B&W. 3. Lang.: Eng.
Italy: Genoa. 900-1857. Biographical studies. ■The historical Simon Boccanegra.

3889 Pistone, Danièle. *L'Opéra italien au XIXe s. : de Rossini à Puccini.* (Italian Opera in the Nineteenth Century: from Rossini to Puccini.) Paris: Champion; 1986. 206 pp. (Musique-Musicologie.) Biblio. Append. Illus.: Photo. Dwg. Sketches. Print. B&W. 29: var. sizes. Lang.: Fre.
Italy. 1810-1920. Critical studies. ■A thematic and aesthetic study of librettos, musical forms, voices, staging, opera houses, singers and audiences. Includes a dictionary of singers and conductors.

3890 Weaver, William; Davidson, Erika. "Poetic Vista." *OpN.* 1986 Feb 15; 50(11): 16-19. Illus.: Photo. Color. B&W. 7. Lang.: Eng.
Italy: Rimini. 1986. Histories-specific. ■The city of Rimini and its importance to *Francesca da Rimini* by Francesco Zandonai, its librettist Gabriele D'Annunzio, and the actress Eleonora Duse.

3891 Ewell, Barbara C. "*The Queen of Spades* and the Process of Artistic Transformation." *OJ.* 1985; 18(1): 19-26. Notes. Lang.: Eng.
Russia. 1833-1890. Critical studies. ■Summary of Puškin's story and Čajkovskij's libretto showing how the austerity of the story was expanded and elaborated to provide the conflict and color necessary for opera.

3892 Neef, Sigrid. *Handbuch der russischen und sowjetischen Oper.* (Handbook of Russian and Soviet Opera.) Berlin: Henschelverlag; 1985. 760 pp. Index. Lang.: Ger.
Russia. 1700-1985. Histories-specific. ■Surveys of the different national opera developments in part 1, very detailed articles on 64 composers and 152 operas in part 2.

3893 Ringger, Rolf Urs. "Jovialität und Dissonanzen: Eine Begegnung mit dem Komponisten Wolfgang Rihm." (Joviality and Dissonances: Meeting Wolfgang Rihm, Composer.) *NZZ.* 1986 Nov.; 272(22/23): 69. Illus.: Photo. B&W. Lang.: Ger.
Switzerland. 1974-1986. Histories-sources. ■Composer Wolfgang Rihm talks about his career, his best-known opera *Jakob Lenz* and his activities as composition teacher. Added is his speech on 'Musical Theatre from the Composer's Viewpoint' (1986).

3894 Alexander, Peter F. "The Process of the Composition of the Libretto of Britten's *Gloriana.*" *MLet.* 1986 Apr.; 67(2): 147-158. Lang.: Eng.
UK-England: London. 1952-1953. Historical studies. ■Development of the libretto for Benjamin Britten's opera *Gloriana* based on correspondence between Britten and librettist William Plomer.

3895 Crozier, Eric. "The Writing of *Billy Budd.*" *OQ.* 1986 Fall; 4(3): 11-27. Notes. Illus.: Photo. B&W. 2: var. sizes. Lang.: Eng.
UK-England: London. 1949-1964. Historical studies. ■The collaboration of E.M. Forster, Eric Crozier and Benjamin Britten in writing the opera *Billy Budd.*

3896 Elliott, Graham. "The Operas of Benjamin Britten." *OQ.* 1986 Fall; 4(3): 28-44. Notes. Illus.: Photo. B&W. 5: var. sizes. Lang.: Eng.
UK-England: London. 1946-1976. Historical studies. ■A chronology and analysis of the compositions of Benjamin Britten.

3897 Mitchell, Donald. "The Serious Comedy of *Albert Herring.*" *OQ.* 1986 Fall; 4(3): 45-59. Notes. Illus.: Photo. B&W. 7: var. sizes. Lang.: Eng.
UK-England: London. 1947. Critical studies. ■An in-depth analysis of Benjamin Britten's opera *Albert Herring* and an exploration of the 'seriousness' of its comedy.

3898 Stimpson, Mansel. "Drama and Meaning in *The Turn of the Screw.*" *OQ.* 1986 Fall; 4(3): 75-82. Notes. Illus.: Photo. B&W. 1. Lang.: Eng.

UK-England. 1954. Critical studies. ■Analysis and interpretation of the characters and their motivations in Britten's opera *The Turn of the Screw.*

3899 Sutcliffe, James Helme. "A Life for Music—Benjamin Britten: A Biographical Sketch." *OQ.* 1986 Fall; 4(3): 5-10. Notes. Lang.: Eng.
UK-England: London. 1913-1976. Biographical studies. ■The life, career and compositions of Benjamin Britten.

3900 Ardoin, John. "Tippett in America." *OQ.* 1986-87 Win; 4(4): 1-20. Notes. Illus.: Photo. B&W. 6: var. sizes. Lang.: Eng.
USA: Dallas, TX. 1965-1985. Histories-sources. ■The author's correspondence and personal contact with Sir Michael Tippett during his 20 years of work in American opera.

3901 Beeson, Jack. "The Autobiography of Lizzie Borden." *OQ.* 1986 Spr; 4(1): 15-42. Notes. Illus.: Diagram. Photo. B&W. 3: 4 in. x 5 in., 2 in. x 3 in. Lang.: Eng.
USA. 1954-1965. Critical studies. ■The author's creation and development of the opera *Lizzie Borden.*

3902 Brownlow, Art. "Menotti and the Critics." *OJ.* 1986 Spr; 19(1): 2-15. Notes. Lang.: Eng.
USA: New York, NY. UK-Scotland: Edinburgh. Italy: Cadegliano. 1938-1988. Critical studies. ■Gian Carlo Menotti's reactions to harsh criticism dealing with his opera scores—librettos and direction are discussed.

3903 Frayne, John P. "Mozart Revised—The Auden/Kallman Version of *The Magic Flute.*" *OQ.* 1985 Spr; 3(1): 52-71. Notes. Biblio. Lang.: Eng.
USA. 1951-1956. Critical studies. ■W.H. Auden and Chester Kallman's English translation of *The Magic Flute* is analyzed and compared to other versions through their interpretation of theme, character, structure and language.

3904 Sloan, Irene; Sloan, Sherwin, ed. "Work." *OQ.* 1985 Sum; 3(2): 1-5. Illus.: Photo. B&W. 2: 4 in. x 8 in. Lang.: Eng.
USA: Georgetown. 1985. Critical studies. ■A review of Southwestern University's Brown Symposium VII entitled 'Benjamin Britten and the Ceremony of Innocence'.

3905 Kröplin, Eckart. *Frühe sowjetische Oper. Schostakowitsch. Prokofiew.* (Early Soviet Opera: Šostakovič, Prokofjév.) Berlin: Henschelverlag; 1985. 722 pp. Notes. Index. Biblio. Append. Lang.: Ger.
USSR: Moscow. 1917-1941. Histories-specific. ■History and aesthetics of Soviet opera after the October Revolution, with analyses of operas by Šostakovič and Prokofjév.

3906 Paklin, N.A., ed. "Neizvestnye pis'ma M. Gor'kogo." (Unknown Letters of Maksim Gorkij.) *NovyjMir.* 1986; 1: 183-192. Lang.: Rus.
USSR. 1922-1930. Histories-sources. ■Correspondence of Maksim Gorkij and singer Fëdor Šaljapin.

Reference materials

3907 Gozenpud, A.A. *Kratkij opernyj slovar'.* (A Concise Opera Dictionary.) Kiev: Muzyčna Ukraina; 1986. 247 pp. Lang.: Rus.
Critical studies.

3908 Štejnpress, B.S. *Opernye prem'ery XX veka. 1941-1960 Slovar.* (Opera Premieres of the Twentieth Century: 1941-1960. A Dictionary.) Moscow: Sov. kompozitor; 1986. 341 pp. Lang.: Rus.
1941-1960. Critical studies. ■Covers opera premieres worldwide.

3909 "Great Performance Telecasts." *OpN.* 1986; 51. Illus.: Photo. B&W. [*Hänsel und Gretel.*] Lang.: Eng.
Austria: Vienna. 1986. Histories-sources. ■Stills from telecast performances. Lists of principals, conductors and production staff included.

3910 Fayer, Vienna, photo. *Wiener Opernkalander 1987.* (Calendar of the Opera in Vienna 1987.) Photo. Color. B&W. 14: 33 cm. x 40 cm. Lang.: Ger.
Austria: Vienna. 1985-1986. Histories-sources. ■Photos of all premieres at the Staatsoper during the 1985/86 season indicate scenery and performance style.

MUSIC-DRAMA: Opera—Reference materials

3911 Milnes, Rodney, ed. *Opera Index 1986*. London: Opera; 1986. 81 pp. Lang.: Eng.
Europe. UK-England. USA. 1986. ■Volume 37 offers a general subject index, with separate listings of contributors, operas and artists.

3912 Czeglédi, Imre. *Gyula, Erkel Ferenc Emlékház*. (Ferenc Erkel Museum, Gyula.) Budapest: Tájak, Korok, Múzeumok; 1986. 16 pp. (Tájak, korok, múzeumok kiskönyvtára.) Illus.: Photo. B&W. 11. Lang.: Hun.
Hungary: Gyula. 1810-1893. Histories-specific. ■Guide to the exhibition installed in the house where composer Ferenc Erkel, father of the Hungarian opera, was born.

3913 Schmidgall, Gary, comp.; Drueding, Alice. "The *Opera News* 1986-87 Opera Forecast." *OpN*. 1986 Sep.; 51(3): np. Illus.: Dwg. Color. Lang.: Eng.
North America. 1986. Histories-sources. ■Calendar of opera performances scheduled for the 1986-87 season throughout North America.

Relation to other fields

3914 Rich, Maria F. "Alban Berg and the Vienna of His Time." *OQ*. 1985 Fall; 3(3): 39-67. Notes. Biblio. Illus.: Pntg. Dwg. Photo. Print. B&W. 12: 5 in. x 8 in. Lang.: Eng.
Austria: Vienna. 1894-1935. Critical studies. ■In depth reporting of the political and artistic movements in Vienna in the early part of the century and how Berg was influenced by the times.

3915 Apter, Ronnie. "The Psychological Subtlety of Smetana and Züngel's *The Widows*." *OJ*. 1986 Sum; 19(2): 3-22. Notes. Gloss. Lang.: Eng.
Czechoslovakia-Bohemia. 1877-1878. Technical studies. ■Discusses psychological and sociological studies of main characters of *The Widows* by Bedřich Smetana and Emanuel Züngel.

3916 Hatch, Christopher. "The 'Cockney' Writers and Mozart's Operas." *OQ*. 1985 Sum; 3(2): 45-58. Notes. Lang.: Eng.
England: London. 1760-1840. Critical studies. ■The influence of Mozart's operas on the 'Cockney' school of writers and John Keats's poetry.

3917 Cazeaux, Isabelle. "The Gautier Family and the French Operatic Scene." *OJ*. 1985; 18(1): 3-10. Notes. Lang.: Eng.
France. 1811-1917. Histories-sources. ■Selection of writings about opera by Théophile Gautier from his reviews and novels. His daughter Judith Gautier's relationship with Richard Wagner and her championship of German music.

3918 Chapman, Alan. "Crossing the Cusp: The Schoenberg Connection." 103-130 in Kowalke, Kim H., ed. *A New Orpheus*. New Haven, CT: Yale UP; 1986. xvi, 374 pp. Lang.: Eng.
Germany. 1909-1940. Biographical studies. ■Analysis of the relationship between Kurt Weill and Arnold Schönberg, giving specific examples of how they influenced each other's music.

3919 Hailey, Christopher. "Creating a Public, Addressing a Market: Kurt Weill and Universal Edition." 21-36 in Kowalke, Kim H., ed. *A New Orpheus*. New Haven, CT: Yale UP; 1986. xvi, 374 pp. Lang.: Eng.
Germany: Berlin. 1924-1931. Historical studies. ■A look at the relationship between Kurt Weill and his publishers and the circumstances under which he was first published.

3920 Hinton, Stephen. "Weill: *Neue Sachlichkeit*, Surrealism, and *Gebrauchsmusik*." 61-82 in Kowalke, Kim H., ed. *A New Orpheus*. New Haven, CT: Yale UP; 1986. xvi, 374 pp. Lang.: Eng.
Germany: Berlin. 1923-1930. Critical studies. ■Involvement and influence of Kurt Weill in the German expressionist movement.

3921 Rockwell, John. "Kurt Weill's Operatic Reform and Its Context." 51-60 in Kowalke, Kim H., ed. *A New Orpheus*. New Haven, CT: Yale UP; 1986. xvi, 374 pp. Lang.: Eng.
Germany: Berlin. 1920-1959. Critical studies. ■Operatic reforms brought about by the introduction of socialism and the operas and essays of Kurt Weill.

3922 Pieczulis, Irena. "Wokł *Diabla wloskiego*." (Around *Italian Devil*.) *DialogW*. 1986; 7: 86-95. Notes. Lang.: Pol.

Poland. 1772-1821. Historical studies. ■Polish and Italian actors' competition on the stage of the Narodowy Teatr in Warsaw is the background for Stanisław Kostka Potocki's comic opera *Diabel wloski (Italian Devil)*.

3923 Reel, Jerome V., Jr. "Agatha and the Opera." *OJ*. 1985; 18(2): 30-36. Lang.: Eng.
UK-England. 1985. Critical studies. ■Compilation of references to operas in the works of Agatha Christie.

3924 Dorr, Donald. "Chosen Image: The Afro-American Vision in the Operas of William Grant Still." *OQ*. 1986 Sum. Notes. Illus.: Photo. B&W. 9: var. sizes. Lang.: Eng.
USA. 1895-1978. Critical studies. ■A critical analysis of William Grant Still as a composer and the effects of racism on his work *Minette Fontaine*.

3925 Wolf, Muriel Hebert. "Opera As a Forum for the Insanity Defense." *OQ*. 1985 Sum; 3(2): 14-24. Notes. Lang.: Eng.
USA. 1980-1985. Critical studies. ■Comparison between the courtroom insanity defense and opera with the audience as jury, examining characters and motivations in *Otello, Boris Gudonov, Wozzeck* and *Peter Grimes*.

Research/historiography

3926 Larsen, Jens P. "Oratorio Versus Opera." *OQ*. 1985 Fall; 3(3): 10-16. Notes. Lang.: Eng.
England: London. 1740-1900. Technical studies. ■Comparison and contrast of oratorio and opera styles as developed by Handel and a consideration of further developments introduced after his death.

3927 Kowalke, Kim H. "Looking Back: Toward a New Orpheus." 1-20 in Kowalke, Kim H., ed. *A New Orpheus*. New Haven, CT: Yale UP; 1986. xvi, 374 pp. Lang.: Eng.
Germany: Berlin. 1925-1926. Biographical studies. ■Kurt Weill's lifestyle: how the lack of research has diminished the acknowledged importance of his work.

3928 Simon, Stephen. "Handel: An Eighteenth Century Messiah for Italian Opera." *OQ*. 1985 Fall; 3(3): 1-9. Notes. Lang.: Eng.
Italy. England: London. Germany. 1685-1985. Historical studies. ■Highlights in the life of George Frideric Handel and his role in the advancement of the popularity of eighteenth-century Italian opera.

Theory/criticism

3929 Daverio, John J. "'Total Work of Art' or 'Nameless Deeds of Music': Some Thoughts on German Romantic Opera." *OQ*. 1986-87 Win; 4(4): 61-74. Notes. Lang.: Eng.
Germany. 1797-1953. Critical studies. ■The concept of *Gesamtkunstwerk* in which nineteenth-century German composers believed in the glorification of music alone.

3930 Maher, Terence J. "*Melos* and *Arete* in Richard Wagner's Art and Theory." *OJ*. 1985; 18(2): 13-29. Notes. Lang.: Eng.
Germany. 1813-1883. Critical studies. ■How concepts derived from Greek theatre influenced Richard Wagner at an early age, and how these concepts can be used to create a unified framework to evaluate the various stages in Wagner's development of music-drama.

3931 Kim, Woo-Tack. *Chänggük Yeongü*. (A Study of *Chänggük*.) Seoul: Kim, Woo-Tack; 1986. 216 pp. Lang.: Kor.
Korea: Seoul. 1800-1950. Histories-specific. ■Analysis of the traditional *Chäng-gük* play and stage designs, including a model for a proper stage.

3932 Rudneva, A.N. *Opernaja kritika na Ukraine. Problemy i tendencii (1917-1932 gg.)*. (Opera Criticism in the Ukraine—Problems and Tendencies, 1917-1932.) Leningrad: Leningr. konservatorija; 1986. 15 pp. [Synopsis of a Dissertation.] Lang.: Rus.
USSR. 1917-1932. Historical studies. ■Development of Ukrainian opera criticism.

Training

3933 Frank, Friedrich; Donner, Franz. "Wissenschaftliche Auswertung des stimmtechnisch-künstlerischen Deckvorganges." (Scientific Analysis of the Technical-Artistic

MUSIC-DRAMA: Opera—Training

Covering of Voice.) 19-27 in Spitzer, Leopold, ed. *Probleme der Sängerausbildung: Bericht über das 5. gesangspädagogische Symposion in Bad Ischl vom 18. bis 22. März 1985.* Vienna: Hochschule für Musik u. darst. Kunst in Wien, Abt. f. Sologesang u. musikdramat. Darstellung; 1986. 175 pp. Biblio. Illus.: Diagram. B&W. 8: 9 cm. x 12 cm. Lang.: Ger.

Austria. 1980-1984. Empirical research. ■Attempt at an objective consideration of technical and artistic covering of the voice. Sonographic analysis of covered and uncovered voices.

3934 Prosser-Bitterlich, Sigrid. "Individuelle Gesangspädagogik, Hindernisse und Entwicklungen." (Individual Vocal Pedagogy, Handicaps and Developments.) 103-116 in Spitzer, Leopold, ed. *Probleme der Sängerausbildung: Bericht über das 5. gesangspädagogische Symposion in Bad Ischl vom 18. bis 22. März 1985.* Vienna: Hochschule für Musik u. darst. Kunst in Wien, Abt. f; 1986. 175 pp. Lang.: Ger.

Austria: Vienna. 1980-1984. Instructional materials. ■Psychological problems during voice training. Behavioral patterns and student/teacher relationships.

3935 Spitzer, Leopold. "Psychologische Aspekte in der Gesangspädogogik." (Psychological Aspects of Vocal Pedagogy.) 87-102 in Spitzer, Leopold, ed. *Probleme der Sängerausbildung: Bericht über das 5. gesangspädagogische Symposion in Bad Ischl vom 18. bis 22. März 1985.* Vienna: Hochschule für Musik u. darst. Kunst in Wien, Abt. f. Sologesang u. musikdramat. Darstellung; 1986. 175 pp. Lang.: Ger.

Austria. USA. 1750-1984. Instructional materials. ■Short history of voice training, physiological and psychological methods. Difficulties of music students shown by examples from the practice.

3936 Spitzer, Leopold, ed.; Frank, Friedrich; Kittel, Gerhard; Habermann, Günther; Krones, Hartmut. *Probleme der Sängerausbildung: Bericht über das 5. gesangspädagogische Symposion in Bad Ischl vom 18. bis 22. März 1985.* (Problems of Singer Training: Documentation on the 5th Vocal Educational Symposium in Bad Ischl, 18-22 March 1985.) Vienna: Hochschule für Musik u. darst. Kunst in Wien, Abt. f. Sologesang u. musikdramat. Darstellung; 1986. 175 pp. Notes. Biblio. Illus.: Photo. Dwg. Diagram. Color. B&W. 46. Lang.: Ger.

Austria: Vienna. Italy: Rome. England: London. 1700-1984. Instructional materials. ■Collected papers of a conference about voice training. Rhetorical-phonetic, physiologic-medical, psychological and didactic aspects. Includes a paper about *castrati*.

3937 Frank, Friedrich. "Zum synchronverhalten von Kehle und Zwerchfell." (About Synchronous Work of Larynx and Diaphragm.) 7-18 in Spitzer, Leopold, ed. *Probleme der Sängerausbildung: Bericht über das 5. gesangspädagogische Symposium in Bad Ischl vom 18. bis 22. März 1985.* Vienna: Hochschule für Musik u. darst. Kunst in Wien, Abt. f. Sologesang u. musikdramat. Darstellung; 1986. 175 pp. Biblio. Lang.: Ger.

Europe. North America. 1929-1984. Instructional materials. ■Physiological description of reactions while breathing correctly and singing. Synchronization of larynx and diaphragm. Includes references in existing literature.

3938 Kittel, Gerhard. "Offenes und gedecktes Singen in der objektiven Stimmanalyse." (Open and Covered Singing in Objective Voice Analysis.) 30-48 in Spitzer, Leopold, ed. *Probleme der Sängerausbildung: Bericht über das 5. gesangspädagogische Symposion in Bad Ischl vom 18. bis 22. März 1985.* Vienna: Hochschule für Musik u. darst. Kunst in Wien, Abt. f. Sologesang u. musikdramat. Darstellung; 1986. 175 pp. Biblio. Illus.: Diagram. B&W. 13. Lang.: Ger.

Europe. 1980-1984. Empirical research. ■Essay about medical treatment of singers, including scientific analysis of covered singing.

3939 Mal'ter, N. "Opernyi pevec—kakim emu byt." (The Opera Singer: What Is He To Be?)*SovMuzyka*. 1986; 12: 35-37. Lang.: Rus.

USSR. 1986. Critical studies. ■Seminar on the problems of training actors for musical theatre in educational institutions, organized by the Soviet national committee of the International Theatre Institute, led by B. Pokrovskij.

Operetta

Performance/production

3940 Bános, Tibor. *Aki szelet vet...Fejezetek Fedák Sári életéből.* (We Reap As We Sow...Chapters from the Life of Sári Fedák.) Budapest: Magvető; 1986. 458 pp. Illus.: Photo. B&W. Lang.: Hun.

Austro-Hungarian Empire. 1879-1955. Biographies. ■Profile of Sári Fedák, actress, dancer, prima donna of operettas.

3941 Curtis, A. Ross. "Historical Celebrities and the Vaudeville Imagination." *TID*. 1986; 8: 129-137. Notes. Lang.: Eng.

France: Paris. 1808. Historical studies. ■Account of *Poisson Chez Colbert* as performed at Théâtre du Vaudeville with a discussion of the popularity of vaudeville in Paris.

3942 Müller, Péter P. "Operett és komédia. A *Mágnás Miska* Pécsett." (Operetta and Comedy: *Miska the Magnate* in Pécs.) *Sz.* 1986 Oct.; 19(10): 25-27. Illus.: Photo. B&W. 2: 12 cm. x 8 cm. Lang.: Hun.

Hungary: Pécs. 1986. Reviews of performances. ■Albert Szirmai's operetta at Pécs Summer Theatre, directed by László Bagossy, adds living and effective comedy to the anachronistic genre.

Plays/librettos/scripts

3943 Bujdosó, Dezső; Ráth, Zsolt; Regős, János; Szemere, Anna; Vörös, Gizella B. *Állami Áruház. Egy téma több arca.* (State Stores: Several Facets of One Subject.) Budapest: Müvelődéskutató Intézet; 1986. 227 pp. Illus.: Photo. B&W. Lang.: Hun.

Hungary. 1952-1977. Historical studies. ■Reconstruction of the three versions and productions of the 1952 operetta *State Stores* with study of their different 'ideological messages'.

3944 Smith, Joseph. "The Firebrand of Florence: A Musical Inventory." *KWN*. 1986 Spr; 4(1): 10-12. Illus.: Photo. Print. B&W. 1: 2 in. x 3 in. Lang.: Eng.

USA: New York, NY. Italy: Florence. 1945. Critical studies. ■Analysis of the operetta *Firebrand* by Kurt Weill and Ira Gershwin based upon the Edwin Justus Mayer play, *The Firebrand*, which concerned Benvenuto Cellini. Suggests script's/score's deficiencies might be advantages in a revival.

———

Other entries with significant content related to Music-Drama: 53, 584, 683, 810, 830, 1292, 1304, 1602, 1958, 1959, 2305, 2563, 2699, 2952, 3577, 3671, 4008.

PUPPETRY

General

Basic theatrical documents

3945 Volly, István. "Bábos betlehemesek a Balatonnál." (Nativity Puppet Plays at Lake Balaton.) *Somo.* 1986; 14 (6): 73-77. Lang.: Hun.

Hungary: Balatonberényi. 1970-1980. ■Text of a Nativity play performed in 1981 compared with other readings.

Design/technology

3946 Blanco, Tony. "A.K.A. Octopus Puppeteers." *PuJ.* 1985 Sum; 36(4): 13-16.

Technical studies. ■Logistics of a clown gag with puppetry that uses a third arm jacket.

3947 Herrick, Ron. "Marionette Construction—Installment II." *PuJ.* 1985 Fall; 37(1): 17-18. Illus.: Dwg.

Technical studies. ■Instructions in creating a modeled puppet head.

3948 Magon, Jero. "Let's Create a Character." *PuJ.* 1985 Fall; 37(1): 14-16. Illus.: Photo. 2.

PUPPETRY: General—Design/technology

Technical studies. ■Creating physical attributes for puppets which efficiently convey a sense of character.

3949   Polus, Betty. "The Dinosaur Show." *PuJ*. 1985 Win; 37(2): 9-11. Illus.: Photo. Dwg. 3: var. sizes.

Histories-sources. ■Puppeteer Betty Polus discusses the development of her dinosaur puppet show.

3950   Coad, Luman. "Mechanical Characters." *PuJ*. 1985 Win; 37(2): 13-14. Illus.: Photo. 2: var. sizes.

Canada. Historical studies. ■Working with robots for the program of the British Columbia Mobile Pavilion promoting Expo '86.

3951   Cotarella, Lia. *Realizzare burattini, marionette e maschere.* (Making Puppets, Marionettes and Masks.) Milan: Gammalibri-Kaos; 1986. 107 pp. (Manuali del sole.) Index. Tables. Append. Illus.: Photo. Dwg. Color. B&W. Lang.: Ita.

Italy. 1986. Instructional materials. ■Handbook of mask and puppet construction.

3952   Pikiel, Irena; Waszkiel, Marek, ed. "W szopkowym zwierciadle. Ze wspomnień o wileńskich szopkach adademickich (1921-1933)." (Satire's Mirror Image: Recollections of University Satirical Performances, 1921-1933.) *PaT*. 1986 Second & Third Qtr; 2-3: 383-407. Notes. Append. Illus.: Photo. Print. B&W. 10: var. sizes. Lang.: Pol.

Poland: Vilna. 1921-1933. Histories-sources. ■Recollections of puppet theatre stage designer Irena Pikiel, with original playtexts and photos of puppets.

3953   Callahan, Pegg. "Music for the Puppet Theatre." *PuJ*. 1986 Win; 38(2): 17-19. Illus.: Photo. B&W. 2: 5 in. x 6 in., 5 1/2 in. x 7 1/2 in. Lang.: Eng.

USA. Technical studies. ■Choosing music and sound effects for puppet theatre. Related to Media: Audio forms.

3954   Nelson, Michael W. "A Trip to the Hardware Store." *PuJ*. 1986 Win; 38(2): 14-16. Illus.: Photo. B&W. 4: 3 1/2 in. x 5 in. Lang.: Eng.

USA. 1986. Technical studies. ■General information on basic puppet design and construction techniques and tools.

3955   Schubert, Lettie Connell. "And You Thought Tomie DePaola Only Illustrated Children's Books!" *PuJ*. 1986 Sum; 37(4): 18-20. Illus.: Photo. B&W. 3: var. sizes. Lang.: Eng.

USA: New London, NH. 1970-1985. Biographical studies. ■Profile of illustrator Tomie DePaola and his work in puppetry.

Institutions

3956   Selmeczi, Elek. *Világhódító bábok.* (World-Conquering Puppets.) Budapest: Corvina; 1986. 212 pp. Append. Illus.: Photo. Color. B&W. 256: var. sizes. Lang.: Hun.

Hungary. 1773-1985. Histories-general. ■Chronicle of the Hungarian State Puppet Theatre (1949-1985) and survey on the history of puppetry from the beginning.

3957   Tömöry, Márta. "Huszonöt éves a Bóbita." (Bóbita Is Twenty-five Years Old.) *Sz*. 1986 Dec.; 19(12): 16-18. Illus.: Photo. B&W. 2: 12 cm. x 8 cm. 12 cm. x 18 cm. Lang.: Hun.

Hungary: Pécs. 1961-1986. Historical studies. ■The chronicle of Bóbita Puppet Theatre in connection with an exposition showing the history of the theatre.

3958   Porter, Lynne. "Pantijn Muziekpoppentheater." *Anim*. 1986; 10(2): 26. Illus.: Photo. Print. B&W. 2: 3 in. x 3 in. Lang.: Eng.

Netherlands: Amsterdam. 1980-1987. Historical studies. ■History of Pantijn Muziekpoppentheater.

3959   Roccoberton, Bart P., Jr. "Documentation: Now—Forever." *PuJ*. 1986 Sum; 37(4): 14-15. Illus.: Photo. Print. B&W. 6: var. sizes. Lang.: Eng.

USA: Waterford, CT. 1986. Historical studies. ■Exhibition, restoration and preservation of puppetry artifacts at the Institute of Professional Puppetry Arts as a resource for a new generation of puppeteers. Stresses usefulness of audio and video documentation.

3960   Secci, Sergio; Buscarino, Maurizio, photo. *Il teatro dei sogni materializzato. Storia e mito del Bread and Puppet Theatre.* (The Theatre of Materialized Dreams: History and Myth of Bread and Puppet Theatre.) Florence: Usher; 1986. 108 pp. Pref. Index. Tables. Biblio. Illus.: Photo. Dwg. Poster. B&W. 38: var. sizes. Lang.: Ita.

USA: New York, NY. 1961-1978. Historical studies. ■Analysis of the poetics and technique of Bread and Puppet Theatre, with bio-bibliography of playwright Peter Schumann.

Performance/production

3961   Currell, David. *The Complete Book of Puppet Theatre.* Totowa, NJ: Barnes & Noble; 1986. 342 pp. Illus.: Photo. [Revised and expanded edition.] Lang.: Eng.

Instructional materials. ■Resource book on construction and performance in puppetry.

3962   Holquist, David. "Stealing the Show." *PuJ*. 1985 Sum; 36(4): 24-25.

Critical studies. ■Advice for puppeteers in regards to stealing the creative ideas of others.

3963   Davidson, Clifford. "Medieval Puppet Theater at Witney, Oxfordshire and Pentecost Ceremony at St. Paul's, London." *EDAM*. 1986 Fall; 9(1): 15-16. Lang.: Eng.

England: London, Witney. 1540-1560. Histories-sources. ■Use of puppets reported by William Lambarde in annual Resurrection play, Witney, Oxfordshire, and in Pentecost ceremony, St. Paul's Cathedral, London.

3964   "Kukly služat miru." (Puppets Serve the World.) *Teatr*. Minsk. 1986; 1: 29-32. Lang.: Rus.

France. Histories-sources. ■Report on international puppet festival.

3965   Tömöry, Márta. "Bábos fórum Provence-ban." (Puppet Forum in Provence.) *Sz*. 1986 Nov.; 19(11): 20-22 . Illus.: Photo. B&W. 2: 12 cm. x 8 cm. Lang.: Hun.

France: Gareoult. 1986. Reviews of performances. ■Survey of productions presented at the first regional puppet forum at the French UNIMA Centre.

3966   Ebert, Fa Chu. "Aric Bass—Bubanai Hadshan." (Eric Bass—Innovative Puppeteer.) *Bamah*. 1986; 21(104): 106-109. Illus.: Photo. Print. B&W. 3: var. sizes. Lang.: Heb.

Israel: Jerusalem. 1984-1986. Biographical studies. ■Brief biography of puppeteer Eric Bass and his work at the Hakaron Puppet Theatre.

3967   Bendini, Fiorenza, ed. "Fingere figure." (Feigning Figures.) *QT*. 1986 Feb.; 8(31): 3-72. Pref. Index. Notes. Biblio. Lang.: Ita.

Italy. 1984. Critical studies. ■Papers presented at the 'Days of Study and Performances in Puppetry' conference held in Certaldo, November 6-11, 1984.

3968   Wojtczak, Bohdan; Hulej, Bolesław, photo. "Tropami Swiatków." (Tracing Holies.) *TeatrW*. 1984 Feb.; 39(809): 24-26. 1: 9 cm. x 13 cm. Lang.: Pol.

Poland: Szczecin. 1983. Reviews of performances. ■Production analysis of *Rzecz Ojedrzeju Wowrze (A Subject About Jedrzej Wowrze)* based on Polish folk legend, directed by Jan Wolkowski at Teatr Lalek Pleciuga.

3969   Friedman, Gary. "Puppets Against Apartheid: From a Series of Letters, Papers & Press Cuttings." *Anim*. 1986 Feb-Mar.; 9 (3): 48-49. Illus.: Photo. Print. B&W. 2: 3 in. x 4 in. Lang.: Eng.

South Africa, Republic of. 1805-1986. Historical studies. ■History of puppet theatre including recent developments in political satire and agit-prop.

3970   Martin, Sally. "Horse and Bamboo: A Company of the Byways." *Anim*. 1986 Aug-Sep.; 9(6): 103-104. Illus.: Photo. Print. B&W. 5: 3 in. x 2 in. Lang.: Eng.

UK-England: Rossendale. 1978-1986. Historical studies. ■Overview of Horse and Bamboo Theatre, a professional company specializing in community puppet theatre, including a horse-drawn summer tour and work with mentally handicapped people.

3971   "Interview: Lettie Connell Schubert." *PuJ*. 1985 Spr; 36(3): 8-10. Illus.: Photo. Dwg. 1.

USA. 1947-1985. Histories-sources. ■Puppeteer Lettie Connell discusses her career.

CLASSED ENTRIES

PUPPETRY: General—Performance/production

3972 Boylan, Eleanor. "Presenting the Poppinjays!" *PuJ*. 1986 Sum; 37(4): 9-13. Illus.: Photo. B&W. 8: var. sizes. Lang.: Eng.
USA: Cleveland, OH. 1968-1986. Histories-sources. ■Interview with puppeteers Roger Dennis and Bob Vesely and a profile of their partnership.

3973 Brown, Helen; Seitz, Jane. "With the Bread and Puppet Theatre: An Interview with Peter Schumann." 141-150 in McNamara, Brooks, ed.; Dolan, Jill, ed. *The Drama Review: Thirty Years of Commentary on the Avant-Garde*. Ann Arbor, MI: UMI Research P; 1986. xii, 371 pp. (Theatre and Dramatic Studies 35.) Print. B&W. 1: 3 in. x 6 in. Lang.: Eng.
USA: New York, NY. 1968-1986. Histories-sources. ■Peter Schumann discusses his work with the Bread and Puppet Theatre and explains the relationship of street theatre, radical theatre, art, time and money to the company.

3974 Burn, Jean Reyes. "Some Strings Attached." *PuJ*. 1985 Fall; 37(1): 11-13. Illus.: Photo. 4: var. sizes.
USA. 1986. Historical studies. ■Puppets in Performance, part of the 50th anniversary celebration of the WPA Federal Theatre Project, featuring puppeteers Bil Baird, Molka Reich, Ralph Chessé and Burr Tillstrom.

3975 Hider, Mitch. "Sparky's Puppets Quite a Feat." *PuJ*. 1986 Win; 38(2): 5-6, 29. Illus.: Photo. Dwg. B&W. 2: 3 1/2 in. x 5 1/2 in., 2 in. x 6 in. Lang.: Eng.
USA. 1986. Histories-sources. ■Interview with Judy 'Sparky' Roberts about her various puppets and characters, focusing on the puppets that she wears on her feet from a head-stand position.

3976 Jones, Kenneth Lee. "Interview: Blanche Hardig." *PuJ*. 1985 Sum; 36(4): 21-23. Illus.: Photo. 2: var. sizes.
USA. 1932-1985. Histories-sources. ■A profile of puppeteer Blanche Hardig.

3977 Levine, Mindy N. "Julie Taymor at the Ark Theatre." *TT*. 1984 Apr.; 3(6): 10-11. Illus.: Photo. B&W. 1. Lang.: Eng.
USA: New York, NY. 1984. Historical studies. ■Puppeteer Julie Taymor adapts Thomas Mann's novella *Die vertauschten Köpfe (The Transposed Heads)* for performance at the Ark Theatre. Primary use of shadow puppets.

3978 Martin, Sharon Stockard. "Show Stopper Gary Jones." *Essence*. 1986 Nov.; 17(7): 35. Illus.: Photo. Print. B&W. 1: 8 in. x 11 in. Lang.: Eng.
USA: Chicago, IL, Los Angeles, CA. 1970-1986. Historical studies. ■Career of Gary Jones, puppeteer, with emphasis on his Black Street, USA Puppet Theatre.

3979 Mattson, Jean M. "Puppets As Bridges." *PuJ*. 1986 Fall; 38(1): 24-25. Illus.: Photo. B&W. 3: 3 in. x 5 in., 3 in. x 4 in. Lang.: Eng.
USA: Seattle, WA. Japan. 1984. Historical studies. ■Planning, preparation and experiences of puppeteers Jean Mattson and Joan King on Japanese tour with their show *The Return of the Bounce*.

3980 Moore, Milton C. "Interview: Ellen Proctor." *PuJ*. 1986 Spr; 37(3): 20-22. Illus.: Photo. Dwg. B&W. Lang.: Eng.
USA: Chicago/Springfield, IL, St. Louis, MO. 1923-1985. Histories-sources. ■Puppeteer Ellen Proctor discusses her career and that of her late husband Romain Proctor, including their influence on puppetry as an art form.

3981 Murray, Steve. "Tokyo Marie." *PuJ*. 1986 Fall; 38(1): 11-12. Illus.: Photo. B&W. 3: var. sizes. Lang.: Eng.
USA: Los Angeles, CA. Japan: Tokyo. 1979-1986. Critical studies. ■Discusses *Marie Antoinette Tonight!* by puppeteer Bruce D. Schwartz.

3982 Sainer, Arthur. "Taymor's Odyssey: The Unusual Education of a Puppet-Master." *AmTh*. 1984 Dec.; 1(8): 30-32. Notes. Illus.: Photo. Sketches. B&W. 3: var. sizes. Lang.: Eng.
USA. 1970-1984. Histories-sources. ■Puppeteer Julie Taymor's training, productions and views on her craft.

3983 Schwartz, Bruce D. "Marie Antoinette Tonight!" *PuJ*. 1986 Fall; 38(1): 13-14. Illus.: Photo. Poster. B&W. 3: 2 1/2 in. x 3 1/2 in., 5 in. x 7 in. Lang.: Eng.

USA: Atlanta, GA. 1986. Histories-sources. ■Puppeteer Bruce D. Schwartz discusses the production and historical background of his play *Marie Antoinette Tonight!*.

3984 Snyder, Barry. "Creatures of Whimsy." *PuJ*. 1985 Sum; 36(4): 17-20. Illus.: Photo. 6: var. sizes.
USA. 1934-1985. Historical studies. ■Profile of puppeteer Basil Milovsaroff on the occasion of an exhibition of his work at the Robert Hall Fleming Museum.

3985 "Iz tihoi lagun–v okeanskij prostor." (From a Peaceful Lagoon into an Oceanic Expanse.) *TeatZ*. 1986; 29(1): 18-20. Lang.: Rus.
USSR: Moscow, Leningrad. 1986. Critical studies. ■Round table on puppet theatre with B. Goldovskij, head of the literary section, Moscow regional puppet theatre, G. Turoev, director of Leningrad puppet theatre Skazka, and P. Štejn, director of puppet theatre.

3986 "Bezumnoe čaepitie po povodu kukol'noj dramy." (A Mad Tea Party in Puppetry.) *TeatZ*. 1986; 29(3): 14-15. Lang.: Rus.
USSR: Moscow. 1986. Histories-sources. ■Interview with B. Goldovskij, head of the literary section, Moscow regional puppet theatre, and writer J. Uspenskij on the problems of contemporary puppet dramaturgy.

3987 Uvarova, I. "Dorogi kotorye my vybiraem." (The Roads We Choose.) *TeatZ*. 1986; 29(11): 18-19. Lang.: Rus.
USSR-Russian SFSR. 1986. Reviews of performances. ■Reviews of the 5th annual festival of puppet theatre.

Reference materials

3988 *I burattini di Ferrari*. (The Puppets of the Ferrari Family.) Ravenna: Centro Teatro di Figura; 1986. 35 pp. (Arrivano dal mare 1.) Pref. Index. Tables. Biblio. Illus.: Photo. Pntg. Dwg. B&W. Lang.: Ita.
Italy. 1877-1986. Histories-specific. ■Catalogue of a 1986 exhibition on the Ferrari family and their puppets.

3989 Ganim, Carole. "Vent Haven Museum." *PuJ*. 1985 Win; 37(2): 15-19. Illus.: Photo. 8: var. sizes.
USA: Fort Mitchell, KY. 1985. Historical studies. ■A profile of a museum of ventriloquism lore.

Relation to other fields

3990 Jurkowski, Henry K. "Puppets and the Power of the State." *Anim*. 1986 Oct-Nov.; 10(1): 3-5. Illus.: Photo. Print. B&W. 3: 5 in. x 3 in., 3 in. x 2 in., 4 in. x 3 in. Lang.: Eng.
Europe. 600 B.C.-1986 A.D. Histories-general. ■Overview of political impact of puppet theatre. Related to Mime.

3991 Szacsvay, Éva. *Bábos betlehemes játékok Kelet-Közép-Európában*. (Nativity Plays for Puppets in Eastern Central Europe.) Budapest: ELTE; 1985. 43-58 pp. (Folklór, folklorisztika és etnológia 121.) Illus.: Photo. B&W. 5. Lang.: Hun.
Europe. 1600-1985. Historical studies. ■A comparative study of the traditions of the nativity puppet play in Eastern Europe.

3992 Foley, Kathy. "At the Graves of the Ancestors: Chronicle Plays in the *Wayang Cepak* Puppet Theatre of Cirebon, Indonesia." *TID*. 1986; 8: 31-49. Notes. Illus.: Photo. Print. B&W. 7: 5 in. x 7 in. Lang.: Eng.
Indonesia. 1045-1986. Historical studies. ■Discussion of *Gusti Sinuhan*, an example of the *Wayang cepak*, puppet plays traditionally performed at the graves of ancestors, and its role in the transmission of Hindu beliefs.

3993 Bone, Geraldine; Lynch, Elizabeth. "Why Use Puppets for Community Development Projects?" *Anim*. 1986 Aug-Sep.; 9(6): 96-98. Illus.: Photo. Print. B&W. 5: 2 in. x 3 in. Lang.: Eng.
UK-England: London. 1986. Historical studies. ■Reflections on a 3-day workshop on using puppet theatre for social action and communication.

3994 Schumann, Peter. "Puppetry and Politics." *AmTh*. 1986 Nov.; 3(8): 32-33. Pref. Illus.: Photo. Print. B&W. 2: 3 in. x 3 in., 5 in. x 8 in. Lang.: Eng.
USA. 1970-1986. Historical studies. ■Relation of puppetry and the arts in general to politics.

PUPPETRY: General—Relation to other fields

Bunraku

Basic theatrical documents

3995 Kinseibungaku Sōsakuin Hensan Iinkai. *Kinseibungaku Sōsakuin Chikamatsu Monzaemon.* (Writings of Chikamatsu Monzaemon, 6 vols.) Tokyo: Kyōikusha; 1986. Vol 1: 746 pp. (Literature of the Early Modern Period.) Lang.: Jap.
Japan: Tokyo. 1653-1724.

3996 Chikamatsu, Hanji; Miyoshi, Shōraku; Takemoto, Saburōbei; Jones, Stanleigh H., Jr., transl. *"Moritsuna's Camp:* An Eighteenth-Century Play from Japan's Puppet Theatre." *ATJ.* 1985 Fall; 2(2): 99-138. Notes. Biblio. Illus.: Photo. Dwg. Print. Color. B&W. 12: var. sizes. Lang.: Eng.
Japan. 1760-1770. ■A translation of an 18th-century *Bunraku* play based on the campaign mounted against Osaka Castle by Tokugawa Ieyasu, in which Ieyasu destroyed the heir to the unification efforts of Hideyoshi and established his own dynasty.

Design/technology

3997 Saito, Seijirō. *Kashira: Ningyō jōruri no kubi.* (Puppet-heads of Bunraku.) Tokyo: Iwasaki Bijutsu Shuppansha; 1986. 181 pp. Illus.: Photo. Lang.: Jap.
Japan: Tokyo. Histories-sources. ■Collection of pictures of *bunraku* puppet heads.

Performance/production

3998 Boyd, Julianne *The Bunraku Puppet Theatre from 1945-1964: Changes in Administration and Organization.* New York, NY: City Univ. of New York; 1986. 155 pp. Pref. Notes. Biblio. [Ph.D. dissertation, Univ. Microfilms order No. DA8614659.] Lang.: Eng.
Japan. 1945-1964. Historical studies. ■Detailed account chronicling the events leading up to the separation of *Bunraku* into two rival groups, the Chinamikai and the Mitsuwakai.

3999 Farrell, John; Farrell, Carol. "Creating *Anerca.*" *PuJ.* 1986 Sum; 37(4): 5-8. Illus.: Photo. Print. B&W. 4: var. sizes. Lang.: Eng.
USA: Freeport, ME. 1985. Historical studies. ■Development of *Anerca*, a puppet play by Figures of Speech Theater based on Inuit culture, reflecting the collision of cultures throughout the world.

Plays/librettos/scripts

4000 Gerstle, C. Andrew. *Circles of Fantasy: Convention in the Plays of Chikamatsu.* Cambridge, MA/London: Council on East Asian Studies/Harvard UP; 1986. xii, 248 pp. (Harvard East Asian Monographs 116.) Pref. Notes. Biblio. Gloss. Index. Append. Illus.: Photo. B&W. 21. Lang.: Eng.
Japan. 1653-1725. Critical studies. ■Analysis of the musical structure of *jōruri* drama by Chikamatsu Monzaemon.

Marionettes

4001 Blackwood, Pady. "The Cottage Marionette Theatre." *PuJ.* 1985 Win; 37(2): 5-8. Illus.: Photo. 7: var. sizes.
USA: New York, NY. 1939-1985. Historical studies. ■A history of the Marionette Theatre, created in 1939 as a touring theatre for the parks.

Basic theatrical documents

4002 Dinesen, Isak; Hannah, Donald, transl. *"The Revenge of Truth*: A Marionette Comedy." *PerAJ.* 1986; 10(2): 107-126. Notes. Lang.: Eng.
Denmark. 1914. ■Text of *The Revenge of Truth* with notes by Bonnie Marranca.

Design/technology

4003 Herrick, Ron. "Marionette Construction." *PuJ.* 1985 Sum; 36(4): 9-12. Illus.: Photo. 4: var. sizes. [Part 2.]
USA. 1985-1986. Technical studies. ■Creating the proportions and constructing a pattern plan for marionettes. Part 3, on making a plaster of paris cast for a puppet head, in *PuJ* 37:2 (1985 Win), 20-21. Part 4,

on marionette construction tools and techniques, in *PuJ* 37:3 (1986 Spr), 18-19. Part 5, instructions, *PuJ* 37:4 (1986 Sum), 16-17.

4004 Preddy, Jane. "Norman Bel Geddes and Bluebeard." *PuJ.* 1986 Win; 38(2): 11-13. Notes. Illus.: Dwg. B&W. 4: var. sizes. Lang.: Eng.
USA. 1928. ■The influence and contribution of Norman Bel Geddes in design and creation of puppets for *Bluebeard* and a mobile marionette theatre for the Yale Puppeteers.

Institutions

4005 Francis, Penny. "Moving Stage Marionettes and the Puppet Barge: An Adventure." *Anim.* 1986 Feb-Mar.; 9(3): 51-52. Illus.: Photo. Print. B&W. 4: 4 in. x 5 in., 3 in. x 3 in. Lang.: Eng.
UK-England: London. 1976-1986. Historical studies. ■Experiences of a couple who converted a coal barge into a touring puppet theatre.

Performance/production

4006 Speaight, George. "A North of England Marionette Theatre in the 1860's." *TN.* 1986; 40(3): 130-133. Notes. Lang.: Eng.
England: Sunderland. 1860-1869. Historical studies. ■Examines the list of plays performed and concludes that, with a few exceptions, the repertoire lagged 50 years behind live theatre.

4007 Speaight, George. "The Little Angel Theatre—25 Years." *Anim.* 1986 Oct-Nov.; 10(1): 19-20. Illus.: Photo. Print. B&W. 4: 4 in. x 3 in., 3 in. x 3 in., 3 in. x 2 in. Lang.: Eng.
UK-England: London. 1961-1986. Historical studies. ■History of The Little Angel Theatre (Islington, UK), including their work with the physically and mentally handicapped, and teacher-training.

4008 Ballard, Frank. "Design." *PuJ.* 1986 Fall; 38(1): 17-18. Illus.: Sketches. 1: 3 1/2 in. x 4 1/2 in. [Part I.] Lang.: Eng.
USA. 1986. Technical studies. ■Concept and design for puppet production of Mozart's *Die Zauberflöte (The Magic Flute)* at the University of Connecticut. Related to Music-Drama: Opera.

Plays/librettos/scripts

4009 Amico, Nino. "Allied Against the Devil: A Study of a Sacred Play of the *Opera dei Pupi.*" *Anim.* 1986 Dec-Jan.; 10(2): 23, 35. Lang.: Eng.
Italy: Sicily, Naples. 1651-1986. Critical studies. ■Cultural and popular elements in a traditional nativity performance.

Relation to other fields

4010 Marranca, Bonnie. "Triptych: Isak Dinesen in Three Parts." *PerAJ.* 1986; 10(2): 91-106. Lang.: Eng.
Denmark. Kenya. 1885-1985. Biographical studies. ■Introduction to text of Dinesen's Marionette play *The Revenge of Truth* focuses on her theatrical lifestyle and interest in storytelling.

4011 *Colloque international Marionnettes et thérapie.* (International Symposium: Marionettes and Therapy.) Paris: Association Marionnettes et Thérapie; 1986. 126 pp. (Marionnettes et thérapie 18.) [Proceedings, 7th World Marionette Theatre Festival, 1985.] Lang.: Fre.
France. Belgium. 1980-1986. Empirical research. ■Reports on experiments in the use of marionettes in psychiatry and psychotherapy.

4012 Kleist, Heinrich von; Cusatelli, Giorgio, ed.; Pocar, Ervino, transl. *Sul teatro di marionette. Aneddoti. Saggi.* (On Marionette Theatre: Anecdotes and Essays.) Parma: Guanda; 1986. 145 pp. (Biblioteca della fenice.) Pref. Index. Notes. Biblio. Lang.: Ita.
Germany. 1810-1811. Critical studies. ■Essays and descriptions of marionette theatre.

Rod puppets

Performance/production

4013 Nimen, T.R. "Age of Invention." *PuJ.* 1985 Fall; 37(1): 5-8. Illus.: Photo. 4: var. sizes.
USA: New York, NY. 1986. Historical studies. ■Theodora Skipitares' puppet trilogy *Age of Invention* celebrates famous inventors Ben Franklin, Thomas Edison and Michael Conner.

PUPPETRY: Rod puppets—Performance/production

Shadow puppets

Design/technology

4014 Johnson, Jonibeth. "The Boy and the Magic." *PuJ.* 1985 Spr; 36(3): 17-19. Illus.: Dwg.
USA. Technical studies. ∎Creating overhead shadow sequence for puppet production involving full-color shadow figures and cross-fading of projections. Related to Media: Video forms.

Institutions

4015 Webb, Tim; Webb, Amanda. "(The) Puppet Theatre in China Today." *Anim.* 1986; 9(1): 9. Illus.: Photo. Print. B&W. 4: 2 in. x 2 in., 2 in. x 3 in. Lang.: Eng.
China: Beijing, Shanghai. 1986. Histories-sources. ∎Current state of the official puppet theatre, and the hope that political change may encourage the development of small companies.

Performance/production

4016 Allison, Drew; Devet, Donald. "Adapting George Orwell's *Animal Farm*." *PuJ.* 1985 Sum; 36(4): 5-8.

Historical studies. ∎Use of shadow puppets in an adaptation of *Animal Farm*.

4017 Reed, C.L. "Bima-Suarga: A Balinese Shadow Play as Performed by Ida Ragne Ngurah." *ATJ.* 1986 Spr; 3(1): 1-33. Illus.: Photo. Print. B&W. 7: 3 in. x 5 in. Lang.: Eng.
Bali. 1976-1985. Historical studies. ∎The use of shadow puppetry in the Balinese theatre as a way of passing on myth, ritual and culture. Includes playtext of *Bima Suarga*, a shadow play drawn from the *Mahābhārata* and usually performed on the eve of a cremation.

4018 Coudrin, Gildas-Louis; Sunander, Asep, illus.; Sumawijaya, Emdin, illus. *Wayang Golek, tradition vivante.* (Wayang Golek, a Living Tradition.) La Gaubretière (85130): C.E.P.M.A.; 1986. 155 pp. Append. Illus.: Design. Maps. B&W. 30: var. sizes. Lang.: Fre.
Indonesia. 1983-1986. Empirical research. ∎Notes from an Indonesian research trip to study *Wayang* puppetry. Describes puppetry techniques and characters from the cycles of the *Mahābhārata* and the *Rāmāyana*.

Other entries with significant content related to Puppetry: 119, 916, 1382, 2074, 2360, 2780, 3206, 3269, 3275, 3276, 3512. [QW]

SUBJECT INDEX

A la recherche du temps perdu (Remembrance of Things Past)
Plays/librettos/scripts
Compares Michel Tremblay's *Albertine en cing temps (Albertine in Five Times)* to Marcel Proust's *A la recherche du temps perdu (Remembrance of Things Past)*. Canada. 1984.   2436

Analysis of Harold Pinter's technique in adapting *A la Recherche du Temps Perdu (Remembrance of Things Past)* by Marcel Proust as a screenplay. UK-England. 1972. Lang.: Eng.   3240

A patenti (License, The)
Plays/librettos/scripts
Text and information on Luigi Pirandello's *A patenti (The License)*. Italy. 1916-1918. Lang.: Ita.   2717

Abbado, Claudio
Performance/production
Conductor Claudio Abbado and his work at the Staatsoper. Austria: Vienna. Italy. 1950-1986. Lang.: Ger.   3690

Abbensetts, Michael
Performance/production
Collection of newspaper reviews by London theatre critics. UK-England: London. 1986. Lang.: Eng.   2113

Abbey Theatre (Dublin)
Plays/librettos/scripts
Louis Esson's attempts to create an Australian national drama based on the Irish model. Australia. Eire. 1905-1943. Lang.: Eng.   2380

Biography of playwright Teresa Deevy. Ireland. 1894-1963. Lang.: Eng.   2665

Abbott, Bud
Institutions
History of the Minsky Burlesque. USA: New York, NY. 1910-1937. Lang.: Eng.   3464

Abduction from the Seraglio, The
SEE
Entführung aus dem Serail, Die.

Abe Lincoln in Illinois
Plays/librettos/scripts
Robert E. Sherwood's conception of history in *The Petrified Forest* and *Abe Lincoln in Illinois*. USA. 1930-1950. Lang.: Eng.   2949

Abe, Kōbō
Plays/librettos/scripts
Lives and works of major contemporary playwrights in Japan. Japan: Tokyo. 1900-1986. Lang.: Jap.   2719

Abel, Lionel
Plays/librettos/scripts
Corona de luz (Crown of Light) by Rodolfo Usigli as a self-reflexive comment on the process of dramatizing an historical event. Mexico. 1960-1980. Lang.: Eng.   2722

Theory/criticism
Self-reflexivity in Shakespeare as seen by Lionel Abel, Sigurd Burckhardt and James L. Calderwood. USA. 1963-1983. Lang.: Eng.   3141

Abito nuovo, L' (New Suit, The)
Plays/librettos/scripts
Study of a draft of *L'abito nuovo (The New Suit)* by Eduardo De Filippo and Luigi Pirandello. Italy. 1935-1937. Lang.: Ita.   2677

Abody, Béla
Performance/production
Memoir of writer, critic, theatre director Béla Abody. Hungary. 1970-1980. Lang.: Hun.   1780

About Last Night
Administration
Efforts to produce the film *Sexual Perversity in Chicago*. USA. Lang.: Eng.   3194

Abramov, F.
Performance/production
Correlation of scenery and direction. USSR: Leningrad. 1980-1986. Lang.: Rus.   2335

Absolute Beginners
Design/technology
Design challenges of the film *Absolute Beginners*. UK-England: London. 1986. Lang.: Eng.   3203

Absurdism
Plays/librettos/scripts
Interview with playwright Alex Buzo. Australia. 1986. Lang.: Eng.   2385

Relation of 'New Drama'—from Büchner to Beckett—to Afrikaans drama. Europe. South Africa, Republic of. 1800-1985. Lang.: Afr.   2539

Relation to other fields
Style in children's theatre in light of theories of Philippe Ariès. USA. UK. France. 1600-1980. Lang.: Eng.   1162

Theory/criticism
Edward Albee's development of realistic setting for absurdist drama. USA. 1964-1980. Lang.: Eng.   3148

ABTT
SEE
Association of British Theatre Technicians.

Abu Salem, François
Performance/production
Collection of newspaper reviews by London theatre critics. UK-England: London. 1986. Lang.: Eng.   2109

Academic Drama Theatre of A.S. Pushkin
SEE
Akademičeskij Teat'r Dramy im. A. S. Puškina.

Acciajoli, Filippo
Plays/librettos/scripts
Influence of Asian theatre on work of Filippo Acciajoli. Italy. 1637-1700. Lang.: Ita.   2713

Accidental Death of an Anarchist
SEE
Morte accidentale di un anarchico.

Accions (Actions)
Performance/production
Detailed description of the performance titled *Accions (Actions)* by La Fura dels Baus. Spain-Catalonia. 1979-1984. Lang.: Cat.   3445

Accounting
Administration
An expense account in Christ Church details production expenses. England: Oxford. 1636. Lang.: Eng.   31
Satirical view of arts management. USA. 1986. Lang.: Eng.   107

Accounting — cont'd

Survey of records relating to performances of Robin Hood and King Games. England: Kingston. 1504-1538. Lang.: Eng. 3309

Bookkeeping records of two pre-Civil War circuses. USA. 1836-1843. Lang.: Eng. 3378

Performance/production

Study of first production of *Jane Shore* by Nicholas Rowe at Drury Lane Theatre. England: London. 1713-1714. Lang.: Eng. 693

Relation to other fields

New regulations governing lobbying activities of nonprofit organizations. USA: Washington, DC. 1984. Lang.: Eng. 1152

Achintre, Auguste

Performance/production

Elzéar Labelle's operetta *La Conversion d'un pêcheur de la Nouvelle-Écosse (The Conversion of a Nova Scotian Fisherman)* as an example of the move toward public performance. Canada: Quebec, PQ. 1837-1867. Lang.: Eng. 3599

Achmatova, Anna Andrejevna

Relation to other fields

The world of choreography in the work of poet Anna Achmatova. USSR. 1889-1966. Lang.: Rus. 1328

Achmeteli, Aleksand'r

Performance/production

Life and career of director Aleksand'r Achmeteli. USSR. 1866-1937. Lang.: Rus. 885

Life and career of director Aleksand'r Achmeteli. USSR. 1866-1937. Lang.: Rus. 886

Achterloo

Basic theatrical documents

Third version of Friedrich Dürrenmatt's *Achterloo* with documentary materials on the rewriting process. Switzerland. Lang.: Ger. 1504

Achurch, Janet

Performance/production

Acting style in plays by Henrik Ibsen. 1885-1905. Lang.: Eng. 1627

Acker, Kathy

Plays/librettos/scripts

Discussion of issues raised in plays of 1985-86 season. USA: New York, NY. 1985-1986. Lang.: Eng. 2928

Ackermann, Erika

Performance/production

A photographic essay of 42 soloists and groups performing mime or gestural theatre. 1986. 3290

Acme Harpoon Company (Montreal, PQ)

Institutions

Interviews with theatre professionals in Quebec. Canada. 1985. Lang.: Fre. 487

Acosta, Ivan

Plays/librettos/scripts

The history of Cuban exile theatre. Cuba. USA: New York, NY. 1959-1986. Lang.: Spa. 2451

Acoustics

Design/technology

Creating reverberation effects with a piano. USA. 1983. Lang.: Eng. 410

Acre Theatre Festival

Performance/production

Daniel Lanzini's notes on writing and staging his play *Hazaiot Kamot Bamizrah (Fantasies Awakening in the East)* at the Acre Theatre Festival. Israel: Acre. 1986. Lang.: Heb. 1981

Acrobatics

Performance/production

Influences upon the post-modern mime troupe, Cirque du Soleil. Canada: Montreal, PQ. 1984-1986. Lang.: Eng. 3292

On André Heller's project *Begnadete Körper (Blessed Bodies)*. Europe. China, People's Republic of. 1984-1985. Lang.: Ger. 3383

Across From the Garden of Allah

Performance/production

Collection of newspaper reviews by London theatre critics. UK-England: London. 1986. Lang.: Eng. 2121

Ács, János

Performance/production

János Ács directs *Kozma* by Mihály Kornis. Hungary: Kaposvár. 1986. Lang.: Hun. 1874

Review of József Katona's *Bánk Bán* directed by János Ács at Szigligeti Színház. Hungary: Szolnok. 1986. Lang.: Hun. 1876

Bánk Bán by József Katona at Szigligeti Theatre directed by János Ács. Hungary: Szolnok. 1986. Lang.: Hun. 1884

Kozma by Mihály Kornis directed by János Ács, Csiky Gergely Szinház. Hungary: Kaposvár. 1986. Lang.: Hun. 1885

János Ács directs *A kőszívű ember fiai (The Sons of the Stone-Hearted Man)* by Mór Jókai. Hungary: Zalaegerszeg. 1986. Lang.: Hun. 1905

Reviews of three musicals about the 1960s. Hungary. 1985-1986. Lang.: Hun. 3488

Acting

Administration

John Neville's administration of the Neptune Theatre. Canada: Halifax, NS. 1979-1983. Lang.: Eng. 27

Ukrainian actors and teachers on rebuilding theatre business. USSR. 1980-1986. Lang.: Ukr. 192

Letter from actor Ernesto Rossi concerning actors' labor movement. Italy. 1891. Lang.: Ita. 1436

Lawsuit of actress Adelaide Ristori against her company manager for nonfulfillment of contract. Italy. 1847-1849. Lang.: Ita. 1437

Legislation for the protection of Victorian child-actors. UK. 1837-1901. Lang.: Eng. 1439

Basic theatrical documents

Edition of Zeami's essays on *nō* theatre, organized by subject. Japan. 1363-1443. Lang.: Eng. 1385

Gilbert Parker's *The Seats of the Mighty* as staged by Herbert Beerbohm Tree. Canada. 1897. Lang.: Eng. 1470

A collection of satirical monologues by playwright Corey Reay. Canada. Lang.: Eng. 1471

Photographs of playbills from Soviet archives. Poland: Vilna. 1800-1863. Lang.: Pol. 1491

Design/technology

Nō actors make interpretive costume choices. Japan. 1386

Nō actor talks about his work as a mask carver. Japan. Lang.: Eng. 1395

Institutions

List of actors and companies using Little Haymarket Theatre. England: London. 1720-1737. Lang.: Eng. 491

History of theatre in Valencia area focusing on Civil War period. Spain: Valencia. 1817-1982. Lang.: Cat. 514

Development of several companies funded by the NEA's Ongoing Ensembles Program. USA: New York, NY. 1986. Lang.: Eng. 553

Training and use of child performers. USA. 1949-1985. Lang.: Eng. 565

Photos of productions at the Schauspielhaus under the leadership of Hans Gratzer. Austria: Vienna. 1978-1986. Lang.: Ger. 1534

Former students remember Xiong Foxi. China, People's Republic of: Chengdu. 1901-1981. Lang.: Chi. 1568

Recollections of a student actor under Xiong Foxi's direction. China, People's Republic of: Jinan, Chengdu. 1901-1982. Lang.: Chi. 1569

History of Zhang Boling's spoken drama company. China, People's Republic of: Tianjin. 1907-1951. Lang.: Chi. 1570

History of the Théâtre du Soleil. France: Paris. 1963-1985. Lang.: Eng. 1574

History of the teaching of acting at the Conservatoire national d'art dramatique. France: Paris. 1786-1986. Lang.: Fre. 1576

Autobiographical documents by personnel of the Deutsches Theater. Germany: Berlin. 1884-1955. Lang.: Ger. 1577

Actor Michael Pennington and director Michael Bogdanov discuss the formation of the English Shakespeare Company. UK-England. 1986. Lang.: Eng. 1592

Director of school of mime and theatre on gesture and image in theatrical representation. France: Paris. 1962-1985. Lang.: Fre. 3289

Discussion of techniques and theories of Bread and Puppet Theatre. USA: New York, NY. 1961-1978. Lang.: Ita. 3960

Performance spaces

Impact of Swan Theatre on actors, audiences. UK-England: Stratford. 1986. Lang.: Eng. 1620

Performance/production

Zen and Western acting styles. Lang.: Eng. 648

Theatricality on and off-stage. Lang.: Eng. 649

Improvisation in East and West. Asia. Europe. 1900-1986. Lang.: Ita. 653

Interview with political satirist Max Gillies. Australia. 1986. Lang.: Eng. 654

Discussion of women's comedy by one of its practitioners. Australia: Melbourne. 1986. Lang.: Eng. 657

Notes on Bulgarian theatre. Bulgaria. 1980-1986. Lang.: Rus. 662

Acting — cont'd

Acting — cont'd

History of Yiddish theatre district. USA: New York, NY. 1900-1939. Lang.: Eng. 827

Biography of actor Richard B. Harrison, who played God in *The Green Pastures*. USA. 1930-1939. Lang.: Eng. 828

Overview of the career and work of director Peter Brook. USA: New York, NY. 1948-1984. Lang.: Eng. 829

Guide to auditioning for dramatic and musical productions. USA. 1986. Lang.: Eng. 830

The artistic director of the Arena Stage discusses the place of the actor in contemporary theatre. USA: Washington, DC. 1951-1986. Lang.: Eng. 832

History of theatre in America. USA. 1750-1985. Lang.: Eng. 834

Guide to finding acting jobs in theatre, film and television. USA. 1986. Lang.: Eng. 835

Gender roles in the work of female theatre professionals. USA. 1985. Lang.: Eng. 836

Changes in ensemble theatre practice. USA. Lang.: Eng. 842

Director Charles Marowitz on the role of the director. USA. 1965-1985. Lang.: Eng. 843

Interview with producer, director, actor Robert Lewis. USA: New York, NY. 1930-1986. Lang.: Eng. 844

Feminist criticism of theatre anthropology conference on women's roles. USA. Denmark. 1985. Lang.: Eng. 845

Career of actress Josephine Clifton. USA. 1813-1847. Lang.: Eng. 846

Collection of reviews by Benedict Nightingale on New York theatre. USA: New York, NY. 1983-1984. Lang.: Eng. 847

Guidelines for working with deaf actors and sign interpreters. USA. 1984-1986. Lang.: Eng. 848

History of the Wooster Group. USA: New York, NY. 1975-1985. Lang.: Eng. 849

Wooster Group retrospective of original works. USA: New York, NY. 1975-1986. Lang.: Eng. 850

Director Robert Woodruff's shift from naturalism to greater theatricality. USA: San Francisco, CA, New York, NY, La Jolla, CA. 1976-1986. Lang.: Eng. 851

History of the Margaret Webster-Paul Robeson production of *Othello*. USA: New York, NY. 1942-1944. Lang.: Eng. 852

Edwin Booth's portrayal of Iago in Shakespeare's *Othello*. USA. 1852-1890. Lang.: Eng. 854

History of the American Conservatory Theatre. USA. Europe. 1950-1972. Lang.: Eng. 856

Interview about the acting profession with T. Zabozlaeva and G. Karelina. USSR. 1986. Lang.: Rus. 859

Soviet actor, poet and singer Vladimir Vysockij. USSR. 1938-1980. Lang.: Rus. 861

Essay on actor's place in society. USSR. 1980-1986. Lang.: Rus. 865

Actor training methods. USSR. Lang.: Rus. 866

Professionalism and training of actors. USSR. 1980-1986. Lang.: Rus. 867

Elements of theatrical expression. USSR. 1986. Lang.: Rus. 868

On the physical training of actors. USSR. 1986. Lang.: Rus. 872

Actor professionalism and the spoken word. USSR. 1986. Lang.: Ukr. 874

Plastic aspects of the actor's appearance on stage. USSR. 1980-1986. Lang.: Rus. 875

Director I.A. Grinšpun recalls famous actors, directors and playwrights. USSR. 1930-1986. Lang.: Rus. 876

Performances of adolescents. USSR: Moscow. 1980-1986. Lang.: Rus. 877

Development of a system of stage appearance for actors. USSR. 1960-1980. Lang.: Rus. 880

Theatricality and dramatization on the Soviet stage. USSR. 1980-1986. Lang.: Rus. 881

Acting and directing using Ukrainian productions as examples. USSR. 1980-1986. Lang.: Ukr. 882

Biographical materials on actress C.L. Mansurova. USSR. 1920-1986. Lang.: Rus. 884

Michael Chekhov's theories of acting and directing. USSR: Moscow. USA: Ridgefield, CT. 1938. Lang.: Eng. 887

Actor discusses work in recitation programs. USSR: Moscow. 1980-1986. Lang.: Rus. 888

Issues in contemporary Russian stage productions. USSR. 1980-1986. Lang.: Rus. 890

Paralinguistic and communicative aspects of stage speech. USSR. 1986. Lang.: Rus. 893

Sketches of leading Soviet actors and directors. USSR. 1917-1980. Lang.: Rus. 895

Issues in speech pronunciation in performance. USSR. 1980-1986. Lang.: Rus. 898

Problems of young people's theatre. USSR: Moscow. 1980-1986. Lang.: Rus. 899

Actors' round table on the problems facing young actors. USSR: Moscow. 1986. Lang.: Rus. 900

The career of actor-director Leonid Viv'en, focusing on his work at Teat'r Dramy im. A.S. Puškina. USSR: Leningrad. 1887-1966. Lang.: Rus. 903

Career of actor-director Oleg Tabakov. USSR: Moscow. 1950-1986. Lang.: Rus. 904

Actor M. Ul'janov on tasks of Soviet theatre. USSR: Moscow. 1986. Lang.: Rus. 905

Biography of Arkadij Rajkin, founder of Theatre of Miniatures. USSR: Leningrad, Moscow. 1911-1987. Lang.: Rus. 906

Professional standards of contemporary actors and directors. USSR. 1980-1986. Lang.: Ukr. 908

Director Mark Zacharov discusses his methods. USSR. 1980-1986. Lang.: Rus. 911

Recollections of director, designer and teacher Nikolaj Pavlovič Akimov. USSR. 1901-1968. Lang.: Rus. 914

Review and discussion of Vietnamese performance in Hungary. Vietnam: Thai Binh. Hungary. 1986. Lang.: Hun. 915

Motion, dance and acting in the development of theatrical art. Hungary. 1980-1986. Lang.: Hun. 1276

On the career of dancer and actress Ida Rubinstein, member of Diaghilew's 'Russian Seasons'. Russia. France. 1885-1960. Lang.: Rus. 1311

History of classical dance-drama *gambuh*. Bali. 1100-1982. Lang.: Eng. 1357

Interview with Peter Brook's designer, musician, and costumer for *Mahabharata*. France: Avignon. 1973-1985. Lang.: Eng. 1359

Interviews with actors in Peter Brook's *Mahabharata*. France: Avignon. 1985. Lang.: Eng. 1360

Influence of *kata* principle on Western acting technique. Japan. Denmark. Australia. 1981-1986. Lang.: Ita. 1365

Narrator in *Katari* story-telling tradition. Japan. 1960-1983. Lang.: Eng. 1366

A production of *At the Hawk's Well* using *nō* techniques. Japan: Kyoto, Tokyo. 1984. 1981-1982. 1396

Essays on Japanese theatre. Japan. 1986. Lang.: Fre. 1398

Nō actor discusses the centrality of *Okina* to his repertory. Japan. Lang.: Eng. 1399

Collection of pictures about *nō* theatre. Japan. 1350-1986. Lang.: Jap. 1400

Zeami's theories of performance technique. Japan. 1363-1443. Lang.: Ita. 1401

Nō actor Kanze Hisao and the actor's relationship with the mask. Japan. Lang.: Eng. 1402

Suzuki's SCOT fuses diverse world cultures in ensemble theatre company. Japan: Toga. 1985. Lang.: Eng. 1404

Kyōgen actor on the difference between *nō* and *kyōgen*. Japan. 1406

The relationship between the *nō* actor and the mask. Japan. Lang.: Eng. 1408

The *kyōgen* actor's goals, relationship to mask work and training. Japan. 1984. 1409

Aesthetic evaluation of Zeami's techniques and work. Japan. 1364-1443. Lang.: Jap. 1410

Interview with *nō* actor Kongō Iwao. Japan. Lang.: Eng. 1411

Nō actor's preparation and rehearsal for the play, *Dōjōji*. Japan. 1983. Lang.: Eng. 1413

Dramaturgy and performance of *nō* drama. Japan. Lang.: Jap. 1415

Performing the *kyōgen* play *Shimizu* in English. USA. 1984. 1417

Acting — cont'd

Acting style in plays by Henrik Ibsen. 1885-1905. Lang.: Eng. 1627

Obituary of actress Elisabeth Bergner. 1922-1986. Lang.: Heb. 1629

Meaning in dramatic texts as a function of performance. Lang.: Eng. 1630

Historical development of acting and directing techniques. 1898-1986. Lang.: Eng. 1632

Five actors who work solely in regional theatre. 1961-1984. Lang.: Eng. 1633

Call for playwrights to hold character conferences with actors in rehearsal. 1986. 1634

Last lecture of director Zhu Duanjun. 1890-1978. Lang.: Chi. 1635

Dilemmas and prospects of youth theatre movement. Australia. 1982-1986. Lang.: Eng. 1639

On actor Heinz Petters and the production of *Der Raub der Sabinerinnen* at the Volkstheater. Austria: Vienna. 1938-1986. Lang.: Ger. 1644

Viennese cellar theatres as alternative theatre spaces. Austria: Vienna. 1945-1960. Lang.: Ger. 1645

On actor and playwright Gabriel Barylli. Austria: Vienna. 1957-1986. Lang.: Ger. 1646

Actor Franz Morak and his work at the Burgtheater. Austria: Vienna. 1946-1986. Lang.: Ger. 1647

Klaus Maria Brandauer as Hamlet. Austria: Vienna. 1944-1986. Lang.: Ger. 1648

On actor Gert Voss and his work. Austria: Vienna. Germany, West. 1941-1986. Lang.: Ger. 1649

Actress Elisabeth Orth, her life and work. Austria. 1936-1986. Lang.: Ger. 1650

Biography of actor and stage manager Franz Reichert. Austria: Vienna. Germany: Berlin. Czechoslovakia: Prague. 1925-1950. Lang.: Ger. 1652

Biography of Burgtheater actor Richard Eybner. Austria: Vienna. 1896-1986. Lang.: Ger. 1653

Playing Hamlet at the Burgtheater. Austria: Vienna. 1803-1985. Lang.: Ger. 1654

The Latabár acting dynasty, its continuity and importance in Hungarian theatre history. Austro-Hungarian Empire. 1811-1970. Lang.: Hun. 1655

Playwright and performer Cathy Jones. Canada: St. John's, NF. 1986. Lang.: Eng. 1660

Biographical study of actor/teacher/director Maxim Mazumdar. Canada: Wolfville, NS. 1985-1986. Lang.: Eng. 1662

Interview with actor Stephen Ouimette. Canada. 1960-1986. Lang.: Eng. 1663

Increased use of physical aspects of theatre in Vancouver. Canada: Vancouver, BC. 1986. Lang.: Eng. 1664

Profile of actor-entrepeneur George Coppin. Canada: Victoria, BC. 1864. Lang.: Eng. 1666

Career of actress, manager and director Julia Arthur. Canada. UK-England. USA. 1869-1950. Lang.: Eng. 1675

Actress compares advantages of small-town and metropolitan careers. Canada. 1986. Lang.: Eng. 1677

Description of an outdoor Shakespeare theatre project. Canada: Toronto, ON. 1983-1986. Lang.: Eng. 1678

Actress Lu Xiaoyan's experiences in preparing to play a role in *The Little Foxes*. China. USA. 1939-1982. Lang.: Chi. 1687

Objectives and action in staging of director Wang Xiaoping. China: Shanghai. 1900-1982. Lang.: Chi. 1689

Directorial design for Dürrenmatt's *Die Physiker (The Physicists)*. China: Shanghai. 1982. Lang.: Chi. 1690

Exploring the world of emotion in acting. China. 1850-1981. Lang.: Chi. 1691

On the goal of acting. China, People's Republic of. 1978-1982. Lang.: Chi. 1693

The portrayal of Cleopatra by various actresses. England. 1813-1890. Lang.: Eng. 1699

Career of actress Elizabeth Bowtell, who first acted under her maiden name of Davenport. England. 1664-1715. Lang.: Eng. 1706

Unsuccessful career of actor Charles Freer. England: London. USA: New York, NY. 1808-1858. Lang.: Eng. 1707

Restoration era cast lists of the King's Company. England: London. 1660-1708. Lang.: Eng. 1711

Significance of 'boy-actresses' in role of Viola in Shakespeare's *Twelfth Night*. England. 1601. Lang.: Eng. 1714

Changing attitudes toward madness reflected in David Garrick's adaptation of Shakespeare's *King Lear*. England. 1680-1779. Lang.: Eng. 1715

Innovative stagings of Shakespeare's *Hamlet*. Europe. 1700-1950. Lang.: Rus. 1716

Career of actor Jalmari Rinne. Finland: Helsinki, Tampere, Turku. 1893-1985. Lang.: Eng, Fre. 1719

Interview with Juoko Turkka on acting and directing. Finland. 1986. Lang.: Swe. 1720

Actors discuss performing in plays by Paul Claudel. France. Belgium. 1943-1985. Lang.: Fre. 1722

Notes, interviews and evolution of actor/director Jean-Marie Serreau. France. 1938-1973. Lang.: Fre. 1724

Pieces related to performance at Comédie-Française of *Un Chapeau de Paille d'Italie (An Italian Straw Hat)* by Eugène Labiche. France: Paris. 1850-1986. Lang.: Fre. 1725

Reminiscences of actor-director Roger Blin. France. 1930-1983. Lang.: Fre. 1726

Albert Camus' appreciation of actress Madeleine Renaud. France. 1950. Lang.: Fre. 1728

An emotional account of Jean Vilar's early career by a young spectator. France. Lang.: Ita. 1731

Pieces related to performance at the Comédie-Française of *Le Menteur (The Liar)* by Pierre Corneille. France: Paris. 1644-1985. Lang.: Fre. 1735

Actor, director and teacher Jean-Pierre Vincent. France. 1955-1986. Lang.: Fre. 1744

Relationship between theatre and early photography. France. 1818-1899. Lang.: Fre. 1748

Reciprocal influences of French and Japanese theatre. France. Japan. 1900-1945. Lang.: Fre. 1750

Interview with Comédie-Française actress Dominique Constanza. France: Paris. 1986. Lang.: Fre. 1751

An exploration of Brecht's *Gestus*. Germany. Lang.: Eng. 1758

Application of Brechtian concepts by Eckhardt Schall. Germany, East: Berlin, East. UK-England: London. 1952-1986. Lang.: Eng. 1762

Description of Georg Büchner's *Dantons Tod (Danton's Death)* staged by Alexander Lang at Deutsches Theater. Germany, East: Berlin, East. 1984. Lang.: Ger. 1763

Essays on acting by Wolfgang Heinz. Germany, East: Berlin, East. 1980-1984. Lang.: Ger. 1764

Interview with Elisabeth Bergner and Jane Alexander on their portrayals of Joan of Arc. Germany, West: Berlin, West. UK-England: Malvern. USA: Washington, DC. Lang.: Ger. 1766

István Verebes directs *Valódi Vadnyugat (True West)* by Sam Shepard. Hungary: Budapest. 1986. Lang.: Hun. 1772

Interview with actor Pál Mácsai on his role in *Scapin furfangjai (Scapin's Tricks)* by Molière. Hungary: Szentendre. 1986. Lang.: Hun. 1775

Interview with actor, director and manager Tamás Major. Hungary. 1910-1986. Lang.: Hun. 1776

Memoir of writer, critic, theatre director Béla Abody. Hungary. 1970-1980. Lang.: Hun. 1780

Career of actress Margit Dajka. Hungary. 1907-1986. Lang.: Hun. 1787

Szent Bertalan nappala (Saint Bartholomew's Day) by Magda Szabó directed by György Lengyel. Hungary: Budapest. 1986. Lang.: Hun. 1790

Piroska Molnár's performance in *Kozma* by Mihály Kornis. Hungary: Kaposvár. 1986. Lang.: Hun. 1796

Experimental training method used by Kaméleon Szinház Csoport. Hungary: Kurd. 1982-1985. Lang.: Hun. 1798

Career of actor/director György Várady. Hungary. Romania. 1945-1980. Lang.: Hun. 1802

Review of Ivan Kušan's musical comedy *Čaruga (Death Cap)*, directed by Miklós Benedek, Katona József Theatre, as *Galócza*, includes discussion of acting and dramatic art. Hungary: Budapest. 1986. Lang.: Hun. 1811

Čechov's *Három nővér (Three Sisters)* directed by Tamás Ascher. Hungary: Budapest. 1985. Lang.: Hun. 1814

Acting — cont'd

Memoir of actress and poetry recitalist Mariann Csernus. Hungary. 1928-1950. Lang.: Hun. 1815

Mariann Csernus' stage adaptations and performance in works of Simone de Beauvoir and Liv Ullmann. Hungary: Budapest. 1985. Lang.: Hun. 1816

Review of Gábor Görgey's *Mikszáth különös házassága (Mikszáth and His Peculiar Marriage)* directed by János Sándor. Hungary: Szeged. 1986. Lang.: Hun. 1819

Study of Hungarian actor Ede Paulay. Hungary: Győr. 1855. Lang.: Hun. 1823

Career of theatrical professional Ede Paulay. Hungary: Budapest. 1852-1864. Lang.: Hun. 1824

Autobiographical recollections of Cecilia Esztergályos, ballet-dancer turned actress. Hungary. 1945-1986. Lang.: Hun. 1829

Edith és Marlene (Edith and Marlene) by Éva Pataki at Comedy Theatre. Hungary: Budapest. 1986. Lang.: Hun. 1831

Interview with actor István Avar. Hungary. 1954-1985. Lang.: Hun. 1836

Interview with actress Éva Spányik. Hungary. 1957-1985. Lang.: Hun. 1837

Interview with actor Erzsi Pásztor. Hungary. 1970-1980. Lang.: Hun. 1838

Interview with actor András Bálint. Hungary. 1965-1986. Lang.: Hun. 1839

Production of *A nevelő (The Tutor)* by Bertolt Brecht. Hungary: Kaposvár. 1985. Lang.: Hun. 1840

Recollections of actor Péter Huszti. Hungary. 1944-1986. Lang.: Hun. 1842

Review of Shakespeare's *Hamlet* directed by László Gali at Csokonai Theatre, with attention to Károly Sziki's performance as Hamlet. Hungary: Debrecen. 1986. Lang.: Hun. 1844

Historical data on actor Ede Paulay and his family. Hungary. 1731-1982. Lang.: Hun. 1852

Reprinted preface to biography of Tamás Major. Hungary. 1930-1986. Lang.: Hun. 1863

Commemoration of actor László Márkus. Hungary. 1986. Lang.: Hun. 1864

Interview with Tamás Major, director and actor. Hungary. 1945-1986. Lang.: Hun. 1868

Career of actress Éva Ruttkai. Hungary. 1927-1986. Lang.: Hun. 1871

Theatrical recollections focusing on the career of actress Kornélia Prielle. Hungary: Máramarossziget. 1833-1938. Lang.: Hun. 1878

Recollections of actor, director and theatre manager Tamás Major. Hungary. 1910-1986. Lang.: Hun. 1879

Consideration of actor's place in a director's theatre. Hungary. 1985. Lang.: Hun. 1880

Recollections of actress Margit Dajka. Hungary. 1986. Lang.: Hun. 1886

Survey of various Hungarian amateur theatres and workshops. Hungary. 1960-1980. Lang.: Hun. 1906

Actress/poetry recitalist Erzsi Palotai recalls her life and career. Hungary. 1954-1985. Lang.: Hun. 1911

Tribute to late actress Margit Dajka. Hungary. 1929-1986. Lang.: Hun. 1915

Interview with actor Imre Kulcsár. Hungary: Miskolc. 1986. Lang.: Hun. 1917

Selected short comic prose sketches of Róbert Rátony, actor, showman and writer. Hungary. 1944-1985. Lang.: Hun. 1920

János Pelle's *Casanova* directed by Károly Kazimir at Körszinház. Hungary: Budapest. 1986. Lang.: Hun. 1929

Recollections of actress Margit Dajka. Hungary. 1929-1986. Lang.: Hun. 1930

The life and career of actress Mari Törőcsik. Hungary. 1956-1986. Lang.: Hun. 1933

Interview with actor, director and dramaturg Imre Katona of the Gropius Társulat. Hungary: Budapest. 1961-1985. Lang.: Hun. 1945

Janika (Our Son) by Géza Csáth, directed by Tamás Fodor and starring György Kézdy. Hungary: Szolnok. 1986. Lang.: Hun. 1955

Macskajáték (Catsplay) by István Örkény, directed by Gábor Berényi, at Magyar Játékszin. Hungary: Budapest. 1985. Lang.: Hun. 1962

Rehearsals of András Sütő's *Advent a Hargitán (Advent in the Harghita Mountains)* at the National Theatre directed by Ferenc Sik. Hungary: Budapest. 1985-1986. Lang.: Hun. 1963

Comparison of two Hungarian productions of *Háram nővér (Three Sisters)* by Anton Pavlovič Čechov. Hungary: Budapest, Zalaegerszeg. 1985. Lang.: Hun. 1964

Description of several *Bhavāi* performances. India. 1980-1986. Lang.: Eng. 1976

Notes on the rehearsals of Henrik Ibsen's *Lille Eyolf (Little Eyolf)* directed by Yossi Israeli, at the Kahn Theatre. Israel: Jerusalem. 1986. Lang.: Heb. 1982

Interview with actress Rachel Marcus. Israel: Tel-Aviv. 1935-1986. Lang.: Heb. 1983

Obituary of director Raphael Zvi. Israel. 1898-1985. Lang.: Heb. 1984

Life and work of actress-playwright Franca Rame. Italy. 1929-1983. Lang.: Eng. 1988

Information on the marriage of actress Adelaide Ristori. Italy. 1848. Lang.: Ita. 1996

Biographical study of actress Eleonora Duse. Italy. 1858-1901. Lang.: Ita. 1999

English-language performances of Italian actress Adelaide Ristori. Italy. England. USA. 1822-1906. Lang.: Ita. 2000

Letters of actress Eleanora Duse. Italy. 1920-1923. Lang.: Ita. 2001

Director John Dillon on his Japanese production of *Death of a Salesman* by Arthur Miller. Japan. 1984. Lang.: Eng. 2005

Essays by Suzuki Tadashi encompassing his approach to theatre, training, and performance. Japan. 1980-1983. Lang.: Eng. 2007

Performance conditions of specific theatrical genres. Lebanon. 1918-1985. Lang.: Fre. 2011

Performance of Comédie-Française actors in Amsterdam. Netherlands. 1811. Lang.: Fre. 2012

Collection of articles by critic and theatre historian Wiktor Brumer. Poland. 1765-1930. Lang.: Pol. 2016

Recollections of actor-directors Irena and Tadeusz Byrski. Poland: Vilna. 1930-1939. Lang.: Pol. 2017

Business dealings of actor Adam Dmuszewski. Poland. 1799-1883. Lang.: Pol. 2018

Othello, translated by Bohdan Drozdowski and directed by Wilfred Harrison at the Wilama Horzycy Theatre. Poland: Toruń. 1980. Lang.: Eng. 2023

Interviews with Polish theatre professionals. Poland: Poznań. 1963-1985. Lang.: Eng. 2024

Interview with director and cast of Wajda's *Crime and Punishment*. Poland: Cracow. USA. 1986. Lang.: Eng. 2025

Visits to Poland by Russian theatre troupes. Poland. Russia. 1882-1913. Lang.: Pol. 2043

Plays of Čechov interpreted in theatre and ballet. Russia. 1860-1986. Lang.: Rus. 2068

Serf actress P.I. Žemčugova. Russia. 1768-1803. Lang.: Rus. 2071

Role of the director working with classics today. Spain-Catalonia. 1984. Lang.: Cat. 2080

Rehearsals of *Kött och kärlek (Flesh and Love)* by Juoko Turkka. Sweden: Gothenburg. 1986. Lang.: Swe. 2085

Discussion of basic theatrical issues during Stanislavskij symposium. Sweden: Stockholm. 1986. Lang.: Swe. 2086

The staging of an amateur performance of *Leka med elden (Playing With Fire)*. Sweden: Hedemora. 1985-1986. Lang.: Swe. 2091

Interview with actress Agneta Ekmanner. Sweden: Stockholm. 1950-1986. Lang.: Swe. 2092

Discussion of Stanislavskij's influence by a number of artists. Sweden. 1890-1986. Lang.: Swe. 2094

Political difficulties in staging two touring productions of Shakespeare's *The Taming of the Shrew*. UK. 1985-1986. Lang.: Eng. 2104

Autobiography of actor Alec Guinness. UK. USA. 1914-1985. Lang.: Eng. 2106

Director Mike Alfreds' interpretation of the plays of Čechov. UK-England: London. USSR. 1975-1986. Lang.: Eng. 2127

Actors Ben Kingsley and David Suchet discuss their roles in Shakespeare's *Othello*. UK-England. 1986. Lang.: Eng. 2128

Acting — cont'd

Interview with actress Dorothy Tutin. UK-England: Chichester. 1986. Lang.: Eng. 2132

Interview with actress Glenda Jackson. UK-England. 1985. Lang.: Eng. 2134

Impact and influence of the tour by black American actor Ira Aldridge. UK-England: Manchester. 1827. Lang.: Eng. 2136

Roger Rees, associate director at Bristol Old Vic discusses his career and the season. UK-England: Bristol. 1970-1986. Lang.: Eng. 2138

Hungarian translation of *Vivien Leigh: A Biography*. UK-England. 1913-1967. Lang.: Hun. 2141

Actress Julie McKenzie discusses her role in *Woman in Mind* by Alan Ayckbourn. UK-England: London. Lang.: Eng. 2145

Actress Frances de la Tour discusses her work in *Lillian* by William Luce. UK-England: London. USA. 1986. Lang.: Eng. 2146

Actresses Jane Lapotaire and Elizabeth Spriggs discuss their careers in the Royal Shakespeare Company. UK-England: London. 1970-1986. Lang.: Eng. 2147

Theatre work of Bettina Jonic. UK-England. 1970-1986. Lang.: Eng. 2151

Eileen Atkins, Judi Dench, Wendy Hiller and Barbara Jefford discuss playing Saint Joan in Shaw's play. UK-England: London. 1936-1983. Lang.: Eng. 2153

An assessment of actor Paul Scofield. UK-England. 1945-1986. Lang.: Eng. 2154

Reconstruction of a number of Shakespeare plays staged and performed by Herbert Beerbohm Tree. UK-England: London. 1887-1917. Lang.: Eng. 2155

Comparative analysis of productions of *Summer* by Edward Bond. UK-England: London. 1982. Lang.: Eng. 2163

Interview with Lesbian feminist theatre company Hard Corps. UK-England. 1984-1986. Lang.: Eng. 2164

Overview of the top six male acting performances of the season. UK-England: London. 1986. Lang.: Eng. 2168

Overview of the top six female acting performances of the season. UK-England: London. 1986. Lang.: Eng. 2169

Actor Laurence Olivier's memoirs. UK-England: London. USA: New York, NY. 1907-1986. Lang.: Eng. 2170

Feminist theatre group Beryl and the Perils. UK-England. 1986. Lang.: Eng. 2171

Career of actress Billie Whitelaw, interpreter of Samuel Beckett's plays. UK-England. 1956-1986. Lang.: Eng. 2172

Interview with actor/playwright Harvey Fierstein. UK-England: London. USA: New York. 1983-1986. Lang.: Eng. 2175

Actor Colin Blakely discusses his career. UK-England: London. 1950-1986. Lang.: Eng. 2176

Actress Rosemary Harris discusses her work in *The Petition*. UK-England: London. USA: New York, NY. 1948-1986. Lang.: Eng. 2177

Jonathan Pryce in the role of Macbeth. UK-England: Stratford. 1970-1986. Lang.: Eng. 2179

Actress Sheila Hancock discusses role of Madame Ranevskaya in Čechov's *Višněvyj sad (The Cherry Orchard)*. UK-England: London. 1986. Lang.: Eng. 2180

Career of actor Jeremy Irons in theatre, television and film. UK-England. USA. 1970-1985. Lang.: Eng. 2181

Analysis of predominant mode of staging final scene of *Othello* by William Shakespeare. UK-England: London. USA. 1760-1900. Lang.: Eng. 2184

World tour by English tragedian Charles Dillon. USA.. 1861-1867. Lang.: Eng. 2199

Career of actress and theatrical manager Louisa Lane Drew. USA. 1820-1897. Lang.: Eng. 2243

An historical account of one actor's experiences with the Fresno Paramount Players. USA: Fresno, CA. 1927. Lang.: Eng. 2255

A scholarly study of the careers of Alfred Lunt and Lynn Fontanne. USA. 1922-1972. Lang.: Eng. 2257

Interview with actors Jessica Tandy and Hume Cronyn. USA. 1932-1984. Lang.: Eng. 2260

Career of actor Lawrence Barrett. USA: New York, NY. 1871-1909. Lang.: Eng. 2261

Review of Eugene O'Neill's *Long Day's Journey Into Night* directed by Jonathan Miller. USA. 1956-1986. Lang.: Eng. 2264

Biography of actor Danny Kaye. USA: New York, NY. 1912-1985. Lang.: Eng. 2265

Interview with Peter Gallagher on his portrayal of Edmund in *Long Day's Journey Into Night*. USA: New York, NY, New London, CT. 1986. Lang.: Eng. 2268

Spalding Gray's memories of the development and tour of Richard Schechner's *Commune*. USA. France. Poland. 1970. Lang.: Eng. 2270

Beckett's direction of *Krapp's Last Tape* at San Quentin Drama Workshop. USA. 1985. Lang.: Hun. 2279

The organization of the Olympiad Arts Festival. USA: Los Angeles, CA. 1984. Lang.: Eng. 2281

Interview with actress Glenda Jackson. USA: New York, NY. 1986. Lang.: Eng. 2291

Biography of playwright and actor Sam Shepard. USA. 1943-1986. Lang.: Eng. 2295

Description of first stage adaptation of Robert Louis Stevenson's *Dr. Jekyll and Mr. Hyde*. USA: New York, NY. USA: Boston, MA. 1886-1888. Lang.: Eng. 2298

Andrei Serban discusses the vibration of a sound and its effect on the listener. USA. 1976. Lang.: Eng. 2304

Lloyd Richard's career as an actor, director, artistic director and academic dean. USA: Detroit, MI, New York, NY, New Haven, CT. 1920-1980. Lang.: Eng. 2308

Writings by and about Julian Beck, founder of Living Theatre. USA. Europe. 1925-1985. Lang.: Ita. 2309

Recollections of actress Faina Ranevskaja. USSR. 1896-1984. Lang.: Rus. 2316

Ukrainian performances of classical Western tragedies. USSR. 1920-1930. Lang.: Rus. 2317

Four performances in Budapest by the students of Oleg Tabakov of GITIS, the Institute of Dramatic Art, Moscow. USSR: Moscow. Hungary: Budapest. 1986. Lang.: Hun. 2318

Overview of Soviet theatre. USSR: Leningrad, Moscow. 1984. Lang.: Eng. 2320

Faina Ranevskaja's role in *Pravda—chorošo, a sčast'e lučše (Truth is Good, But Happiness is Better)* by A.N. Ostrovskij. USSR: Moscow. 1896-1984. Lang.: Rus. 2324

Interview with actor-director S. Jurskij. USSR. 1986. Lang.: Rus. 2325

Actor M.A. Ul'janov in *I dol'še veka dlitsja den' (A Day Lasts Longer than a Century)* at Teat'r im. Je. Vachtangova. USSR: Moscow. 1980-1986. Lang.: Rus. 2327

Recollections of children's theatre in two Soviet cities. USSR: Leningrad, Novosidirsk. 1947-1971. Lang.: Rus. 2333

Theatrical events of nineteenth annual international theatre festival. Yugoslavia. 1985. Lang.: Hun. 2343

Career of film and television actress Lucille Ball. USA. 1911-1986. Lang.: Eng. 3167

Biography of singer Frank Sinatra. USA. 1915-1984. Lang.: Eng. 3180

Life and films of actor and director Willi Forst. Austria: Vienna. Germany: Berlin. 1903-1980. Lang.: Ger. 3223

Biography of actress Éva Ruttkai. Hungary. 1934-1976. Lang.: Hun. 3224

Life and career of film star Greta Garbo. Sweden. USA: Hollywood, CA. 1905-1985. Lang.: Hun. 3226

Biography of actor James Cagney. USA. 1904-1986. Lang.: Eng. 3228

Biography of singer/actress Judy Garland. USA. 1922-1969. Lang.: Eng. 3229

An autobiography focusing on Carol Burnett's early years. 1960-1986. Lang.: Eng. 3268

Selected interviews and reports from Hungarian television's weekly cultural show. Hungary. 1981-1984. Lang.: Hun. 3270

Handbook for acting in television commercials. USA. 1977-1986. Lang.: Eng. 3271

Profile of actor Bill Cosby. USA. 1986. Lang.: Eng. 3274

Biography of mime Angna Enters. Europe. USA. 1907-1986. Lang.: Eng. 3295

A profile of the three performers known collectively as Mummenschanz. Switzerland: Zurich. USA. 1984. Lang.: Eng. 3297

Acting — cont'd

Videotaped performances and interviews of San Francisco Mime Troupe. USA: San Francisco, CA. 1960-1986. Lang.: Eng.   3306

Career of vaudeville comedian Roy Rene, creator of 'Mo'. Australia. 1892-1954. Lang.: Eng.   3327

Distinctive style of Canadian clowns. Canada: Toronto, ON, Vancouver, BC. 1967-1986. Lang.: Eng.   3328

Review of *Mágiarakás (Magic Heap)* by humorist György Sándor. Hungary: Budapest. 1985. Lang.: Hun.   3334

Life and work of an Indian street performer. India: Rajasthan. 1940-1985. Lang.: Eng.   3335

Career of comic author and clown Zuanpolo Leopardi. Italy: Venice. 1500-1540. Lang.: Ita.   3336

Development of the *raëk* or gallery as a folk entertainment. Russia. 1800-1917. Lang.: Rus.   3345

Autobiography of comedian Billy Crystal. USA. 1955. Lang.: Eng.   3350

Comedienne Joan Rivers' account of her life and career. USA: New York, NY. 1928-1965. Lang.: Eng.   3352

Career of popular entertainer Bill Cosby. USA. 1937-1986. Lang.: Eng.   3353

Season review of Mikroszkóp Stage. Hungary: Budapest. 1985-1986. Lang.: Hun.   3365

Discussion of increasingly popular comedy cabaret. UK-England. 1979-1986. Lang.: Eng.   3366

Interpretive technique of *commedia dell'arte* actors. France. 1575-1670. Lang.: Ita.   3410

Life and works of actor and playwright Silvio Fiorillo. Italy. 1565-1634. Lang.: Ita.   3411

Comic actor Tristano Martinelli, probable creator of the character Harlequin. Italy. France. 1550-1600. Lang.: Ita.   3412

Precursors of *commedia dell'arte*. Italy: Venice. 1400-1620. Lang.: Eng.   3414

Interview with Carlo Boso on *commedia dell'arte* reconstruction. UK-England. Italy. 1947-1986. Lang.: Eng.   3415

Detailed description of the performance titled *Accions (Actions)* by La Fura dels Baus. Spain-Catalonia. 1979-1984. Lang.: Cat.   3445

Performance art and its current characteristic tone. USA. Lang.: Eng.   3459

History of unusual entertainers. 1600-1986. Lang.: Eng.   3466

Careers of fifty successful female comics. 1900-1986. Lang.: Eng.   3467

Recollection of performances by music-hall comedian Billy Danvers. UK-England. 1900. Lang.: Eng.   3469

Life and influence of Wei Ch'angsheng, actor and playwright. China. 1795-1850. Lang.: Chi.   3506

History of the Beijing Opera. China: Beijing. 800-1986. Lang.: Cat.   3507

Acting during the Southern Sung dynasty. China: Wenzhou. 1101-1250. Lang.: Chi.   3510

Modern and traditional performance styles compared. China. 1598-1984. Lang.: Chi.   3511

Origins of Southern Sung drama (*Nanxi*). China: Wenzhou. 1127-1234. Lang.: Chi.   3512

What spoken drama actors can learn from Sung drama. China. 1100-1980. Lang.: Chi.   3513

Career of Beijing opera actor, Hou Hsijui. China. 1920-1983. Lang.: Chi.   3514

Origins of the stylized acting in Southern drama (Nanxi). China. 1127-1278. Lang.: Chi.   3517

Wei Ch'angsheng: actor of Szechuan opera, not Shensi opera. China. 1700-1800. Lang.: Chi.   3519

Influence of Beijing opera performer Mei Lanfang on European acting and staging traditions. China, People's Republic of. USSR. Germany. 1900-1935. Lang.: Eng.   3521

Review of the 1985 season of the Chinese National Opera. China, People's Republic of: Beijing. 1985. Lang.: Chi.   3522

Techniques of comedians in modern Beijing opera. China, People's Republic of: Beijing. 1964-1985. Lang.: Chi.   3524

Detailed instructions on the mounting of a musical. 1986. Lang.: Eng.   3598

Interview with actress and rock star Suzi Quatro. UK-England: Chichester. 1986. Lang.: Eng.   3608

Choreography in musical theatre. USA: New York, NY. 1944-1981. Lang.: Eng.   3620

Artistic and technological differences in presenting opera for stage and television. Canada. 1960-1980. Lang.: Eng.   3714

Mussorgskij's opera *Boris Godunov* at the Mariinskij Theatre. Russia: St. Petersburg. 1874. Lang.: Eng.   3775

Profile of and interview with opera parodist Charles Ludlam of The Ridiculous Theatre Company. USA: New York, NY. 1973-1986. Lang.: Eng.   3825

Problems in the performance and production of opera in Soviet theatres. USSR. 1980-1986. Lang.: Rus.   3844

Condition of operatic art in USSR: repertoire, acting, staging. USSR. 1980-1986. Lang.: Rus.   3845

Review of opera season and discussion of problems. USSR: Leningrad. 1985-1986. Lang.: Rus.   3850

Profile of actress Sári Fedák. Austro-Hungarian Empire. 1879-1955. Lang.: Hun.   3940

Jan Wolkowski directs an adaptation of a folk legend about Jedrzej Wowrze. Poland: Szczecin. 1983. Lang.: Pol.   3968

Plays/librettos/scripts

Popularity of dramatic monologue on stage and television. Australia. 1985. Lang.: Eng.   921

On the necessity of preserving the actor's text in a play. USSR. 1986. Lang.: Rus.   992

Punctuation in *Gammer Gurton's Needle* indicates style of performance. England. 1575-1920.   2489

Role of Rosalind in Shakespeare's *As You Like It*. England. 1600-1986. Lang.: Eng.   2491

Cast lists in James Shirley's *Six New Playes* suggest popularity of plays. England. 1653-1669. Lang.: Eng.   2504

Gender roles in *Epicoene* by Ben Jonson. England: London. 1609-1909. Lang.: Eng.   2505

Popularity and relevance of Eugene O'Neill. USA. Lang.: Eng.   2894

Introduction to and overview of articles contained in Volume 40 of *Theatre Annual*. USA. 1900-1985. Lang.: Eng.   2898

Interview with theatre professionals on successful writing and production. USA. 1986. Lang.: Eng.   2932

Stanislavskij's method for the role of Othello. USSR. 1929-1930. Lang.: Swe.   2968

Analysis of *commedia dell'arte* text of Carlo Cantú's *Cicalamento*. Italy. 1576-1646. Lang.: Ita.   3416

Description of *p'ansori*, a traditional Korean entertainment. Korea. Lang.: Eng.   3499

Definition and characteristics of *Hsiao* role. China. 618-1580. Lang.: Chi.   3530

The town of Rimini and its attachment to *Francesca da Rimini*. Italy: Rimini. 1986. Lang.: Eng.   3890

Reference materials

Physical aspects of theatre. Lang.: Eng.   998

Western theatre from ancient times to the present. Europe. 600 B.C.-1986 A.D. Lang.: Ger.   1013

Program of European Actors' Meeting, including criticism, texts and performances. Italy: Parma. 1986. Lang.: Ita.   1020

Chronology of events and productions of non-profit theatre. USA. 1961-1986. Lang.: Eng.   1043

Interpretation of Ferdinand Raimund's dramas after his death. Austria: Vienna. 1790-1986. Lang.: Ger.   2981

Illustrated guide to Actor's Museum. Hungary: Budapest. 1850-1986. Lang.: Hun.   2990

Exhibit on life and work of actor Alessandro Moissi. Italy: Trieste. Austria. 1880-1935. Lang.: Ita.   2993

Catalogue of documentation on Pirandello's writings in dialect. Italy. 1902-1936. Lang.: Eng, Fre, Ger, Ita.   2994

Guide to postwar British theatre. UK-England. 1945-1986. Lang.: Eng.   3001

Theatrical careers of famous actors. USA. UK. 1717-1986. Lang.: Eng.   3010

Influence of stage director Max Reinhardt on film production. Germany: Berlin. Austria: Vienna. 1913-1945. Lang.: Ger.   3244

Biographical encyclopedia of stand-up comics and comedy teams. USA. 1900-1986. Lang.: Eng.   3472

Acting — cont'd

Relation to other fields

Review of Iván Sándor's essays on Hungarian theatre. 1986. Lang.: Hun. 1049

Translation of *Bodywatching* by Desmond Morris. Lang.: Ita. 1057

Essays and reviews on Hungarian and foreign playwrights, productions, actors and traditions. 1962-1986. Lang.: Hun. 1058

Difficulties of distinction between 'high' and 'popular' culture. Australia. 1860-1930. Lang.: Eng. 1063

Impact of painting and sculpture on theatre. England. 1700-1900. Lang.: Eng. 1079

Théophile Gautier's ideas on theatre and performance. France. 1811-1872. Lang.: Rus. 1086

Typical characteristics of laughing and crying. Germany. USA. 1935-1983. Lang.: Ger. 1088

Reports and discussions of restricted cultural communication. Lebanon. Spain-Catalonia. USA. 1985. Lang.: Fre, Spa, Cat. 1111

Actor-director Juliusz Osterwa's ideas about theatre's role in society. Poland. 1918-1947. Lang.: Pol. 1118

Actor Stanisław Kwaskowski talks about the first years of independent Poland. Poland. 1918-1920. Lang.: Pol. 1121

Development of Church attitude toward performers. Spain. 1000-1316. Lang.: Spa. 1127

Anthropological approach to performance and language. USA. Japan. 1982. Lang.: Eng. 1140

Poet, dramatist, critic and satirist Władysław Syrokomla. Poland: Vilna, Warsaw. 1844-1861. Lang.: Pol. 3052

The reception of critic and playwright Karl Kraus in the English speaking world. USA: New York, NY. Austria: Vienna. UK-Scotland: Glasgow. 1909-1985. Lang.: Ger. 3067

Psychological and sociological study of *The Widows* by Smetana and Züngel. Czechoslovakia-Bohemia. 1877-1878. Lang.: Eng. 3915

Theory/criticism

Lecture on the nature of theatre. Finland: Tammerfors. 1986. Lang.: Swe. 1205

Andrzej Hausbrandt (critic) and Gustaw Holoubek (actor) discuss their views on general problems of theatre. Poland. Lang.: Pol. 1217

Technology and the spiritual/aesthetic role of the actor. USA. Lang.: Eng. 1230

Life and work of Zeami Motokiyo. Japan. 1364-1443. Lang.: Jap. 1420

Spiritual dimension of *nō* actor training. Japan. 1363-1470. Lang.: Ita. 1421

Selection from Peter Brook's *The Empty Space*. EUROPE. 1929-1982. Lang.: Chi. 3095

Comparison of Brechtian theatre and Chinese traditional theatre. Germany. China. 1400-1982. Lang.: Chi. 3111

Selections from Jerzy Grotowski's *Towards a Poor Theatre*. Poland. 1933-1982. Lang.: Chi. 3126

Interview on the nature of humor with comedian Emil Steinberger. Switzerland. 1985. Lang.: Ger. 3372

Symbolism and aesthetics in the performance styles of Chinese opera. China, People's Republic of: Beijing. 1935-1985. Lang.: Chi. 3564

Influence of Western dramatic theories on Beijing opera. China, People's Republic of: Beijing. 1935-1985. Lang.: Chi. 3567

Characteristics of Chinese opera in Szechuan province. China, People's Republic of. 1963-1985. Lang.: Chi. 3570

Training

Concept of negation in actor training. Lang.: Fre. 1252

Potential use of Chinese actor-training methods in the West. China. Europe. Lang.: Ita. 1254

Overview of spoken drama training programs. China, People's Republic of. 1907-1982. Lang.: Chi. 1255

Interview with actress and acting trainer Kristin Linklater. USA: New York, NY. UK-England: London. 1954-1985. Lang.: Eng. 1261

Collected articles on the theory and practice of actor training. USSR. 1980-1986. Lang.: Rus. 1262

USSR. 1894-1977. Lang.: Rus. 1263

Use of *nō* masks in actor training. USA. 1984. 1424

Guide for teachers on getting a full-length play together. 1980-1982. Lang.: Chi. 3154

Actor-training approach based on imitation of animals. China, People's Republic of: Shanghai. 1949-1982. Lang.: Chi. 3155

Xiong Foxi, playwright and teacher. China, People's Republic of: Ch'eng-tu. 1928-1940. Lang.: Chi. 3156

Experiences of acting teacher Zsuzsa Simon. Hungary. 1945-1985. Lang.: Hun. 3158

Discussion of archival material relating to translation and U.S. publication of books by Stanislavskij. USA. USSR. 1928-1986. Lang.: Eng. 3160

Collected papers from a conference on voice training. Austria: Vienna. Italy: Rome. England: London. 1700-1984. Lang.: Ger. 3936

Seminar on training of opera and musical theatre performers. USSR. 1986. Lang.: Rus. 3939

Acting Company (New York, NY)
Administration
The Acting Company's fundraising strategy. USA: New York, NY. 1986. Lang.: Eng. 110

Basic theatrical documents
A collection of seven Čechov stories. Lang.: Eng. 1457

Plays/librettos/scripts
Review of adaptations for the stage of short stories by Čechov. USA: New York, NY. 1986. Lang.: Eng. 2922

Acting Company (Toronto, ON)
Plays/librettos/scripts
La Storia and *La Storia II* performed in Italian and English by the Acting Company. Canada: Toronto, ON. 1984-1985. Lang.: Eng. 2424

Action
Relation to other fields
Comparison of works of playwright Sam Shepard and artist Robert Rauschenberg. USA. 1960-1980. Lang.: Eng. 3062

Actor behavior
SEE
Behavior/psychology, actor.

Actor psychology
SEE
Behavior/psychology, actor.

Actor training
SEE
Training, actor.

Actors
SEE
Acting.

Actors Collective
Plays/librettos/scripts
Biographical sketch of playwright/performer Samm-Art Williams. USA: Burgaw, NC, New York, NY. 1940-1986. Lang.: Eng. 2946

Actors Outlet Theatre (New York, NY)
Performance/production
Reviews of *Olympus On My Mind* based on *Amphitryon*, by Heinrich von Kleist, staged by Barry Harmon. USA: New York, NY. 1986. Lang.: Eng. 2218

Actors Studio (New York, NY)
Performance/production
Interview with producer, director, actor Robert Lewis. USA: New York, NY. 1930-1986. Lang.: Eng. 844

Plays/librettos/scripts
Interview with playwright Maria Irene Fornes. USA. 1965-1985. Lang.: Eng. 979

Theory/criticism
Aesthetic theory of interpretation. Europe. North America. 1900-1985. Lang.: Fre. 3097

Training
Effect of changing ideas about psychology and creativity on the Stanislavskij system. USSR: Moscow. 1900-1986. Lang.: Eng. 3162

Actors' Equity Association (Canada)
Institutions
Role of the Canadian Actors' Equity Association. Canada: Toronto, ON. 1983-1986. Lang.: Eng. 1548

Actors' Equity Association (USA)
Administration
Economics and labor relations in performing arts. USA. 1986. Lang.: Eng. 129

Revisions in the Showcase Code by Actors' Equity Association. USA: New York, NY. 1982. Lang.: Eng. 165

Changes in the Showcase and Nonprofit Theatre codes. USA. 1983. Lang.: Eng. 166

Adam de la Halle

Performance/production

Descriptions of productions of *Li Jus de Robin et Marion (The Play of Robin and Marion), The Comedy of Virtuous and Godly Susanna* and *The Second Shepherds Play*. USA: Washington, DC. UK-England: Lancaster. France: Perpignan. 1986. Lang.: Eng.　　2289

Plays/librettos/scripts

Review essay on *Li jus de Robin et Marion (The Play of Robin and Marion)* directed by Jean Asselin. Canada: Montreal, PQ. 1986. Lang.: Fre.　　937

Adam le Bossu

SEE

Adam de la Halle.

Adam, Adolphe

Performance/production

Stage history of *Giselle* by Adolphe Adam at Pest National Theatre. Hungary: Pest. 1847-1880. Lang.: Hun.　　1306

Adám, Ottó

Performance/production

Ottó Adám directs *Egy lócsiszár virágvasárnapja (The Palm Sunday of a Horse Dealer)* by András Sütő after Kleist. Hungary: Budapest. 1986. Lang.: Hun.　　1843

Review of two performances of András Sütő's plays. Hungary: Budapest. 1986. Lang.: Hun.　　1913

Adamik, Laco

Performance/production

Laco Adamik directs Ferdinand Brückner's *Elisabeth von England* under the title *Elzbieta, Królowa Anglii*. Poland: Cracow. 1984. Lang.: Pol.　　2041

Adamov, Arthur

Plays/librettos/scripts

Great dramatic works considered in light of modern theatre and social reponsibility. France. Italy. Germany, West. 1700-1964. Lang.: Fre.　　2560

Adani, Laura

Performance/production

Orientalism in four productions of Wilde's *Salome*. Italy. 1904-1963. Lang.: Ita.　　750

Adaptations

Basic theatrical documents

Text of Čechov's *Platonov* in a version by Michael Frayn. Russia. 1878. Lang.: Cat.　　1492

Design/technology

William Dudley's life-like replica of the Bounty for David Essex's *Mutiny!*. UK-England: London. 1986. Lang.: Eng.　　3584

Institutions

Profile of Writers Theatre, an organization focusing on adaptations of poetry and literature for theatre. USA: New York, NY. 1975-1983. Lang.: Eng.　　562

Performance/production

Influence of Indian theatre on Western drama. Europe. India. 1884-1986. Lang.: Ita.　　703

Examination of German versions of Shakespeare's *Hamlet*. Germany: Hamburg. 1770-1811. Lang.: Eng.　　728

Development and production of Sir Percy Shelley's amateur production of *The Doom of St. Querec*. UK-England: London. 1876. Lang.: Eng.　　809

Overview of the career and work of director Peter Brook. USA: New York, NY. 1948-1984. Lang.: Eng.　　829

Process and results of adaptating plays from Off Broadway to TV. USA: New York, NY. 1980-1986. Lang.: Eng.　　841

Hungarian folksongs and dance adapted to the stage in *Magyar Csupajáték (Hungarian All-Play)*. Hungary: Budapest. 1938-1939. Lang.: Hun.　　1274

Production history of Bela Bartók's ballet *A csodálatos mandarin (The Miraculous Mandarin)* on Hungarian stages. Hungary. 1956-1985. Lang.: Hun.　　1305

Interview with Peter Brook's designer, musician, and costumer for *Mahabharata*. France: Avignon. 1973-1985. Lang.: Eng.　　1359

Changing attitudes toward madness reflected in David Garrick's adaptation of Shakespeare's *King Lear*. England. 1680-1779. Lang.: Eng.　　1715

Stage adaptation of *La Mort de Judas (The Death of Judas)* by Paul Claudel. France: Brangues. 1985. Lang.: Fre.　　1754

Production analysis of a montage of sketches about Electra by Stúdió K. Hungary: Budapest. 1986. Lang.: Hun.　　1773

Review of *A trójai nők (The Trojan Women)* adapted from Euripides and Sartre by Gyula Illyés, directed by László Vámos. Hungary: Budapest. 1986. Lang.: Hun.　　1792

Stage adaptation of Erich Kästner's novel *Emil und die Detektive (Emil and the Detectives)* directed by István Keleti. Hungary: Budapest. 1986. Lang.: Hun.　　1807

Der Hofmeister (The Tutor), Jakob Lenz's drama adapted by Bertolt Brecht, directed by Gábor Máté. Hungary: Kaposvár. 1985. Lang.: Hun.　　1810

Mariann Csernus' stage adaptations and performance in works of Simone de Beauvoir and Liv Ullmann. Hungary: Budapest. 1985. Lang.: Hun.　　1816

Review of *Bűnhődés (Punishment)*, a stage adaptation of *The Idiot* by Dostojěvskij. Hungary: Budapest. Lang.: Hun.　　1826

A kis herceg (The Little Prince) by Antoine de Saint-Exupéry adapted and staged by Anna Belia and Péter Valló. Hungary: Budapest. 1985. Lang.: Hun.　　1828

Review of *Trójai Nők (The Trojan Women)* by Jean-Paul Sartre, produced at Nemzeti Szinház. Hungary: Budapest. 1986. Lang.: Hun.　　1855

Ivo Brešan's *Paraszt Hamlet (The Peasant Hamlet)* directed by Béla Merő. Hungary: Zalaegerszeg. 1986. Lang.: Hun.　　1888

János Ács directs *A kőszívű ember fiai (The Sons of the Stone-Hearted Man)* by Mór Jókai. Hungary: Zalaegerszeg. 1986. Lang.: Hun.　　1905

Stage adaptations of Dostojěvskij novels *A Félkesgyelmű (The Idiot)* and *A Karamazov testvérek (The Brothers Karamazov)*. Hungary: Budapest, Debrecen. 1985. Lang.: Hun.　　1922

Criticizes stage adaptation of *Hangok komédiája (Comedy of Sounds)* by Miklós Gyárfás. Hungary: Budapest. 1985. Lang.: Hun.　　1924

A kis herceg (The Little Prince) by Saint-Exupéry adapted and staged by Anna Belia and Péter Valló. Hungary: Budapest. 1985. Lang.: Hun.　　1935

Stage adaptations of prose works by Gogol and Gončarov. Hungary: Veszprém, Békéscsaba. 1985. Lang.: Hun.　　1948

A kegyenc (The Favorite) by Gyula Illyés, directed by János Sándor, National Theatre of Miskolc. Hungary: Miskolc. 1985. Lang.: Hun.　　1971

Director John Dillon on his Japanese production of *Death of a Salesman* by Arthur Miller. Japan. 1984. Lang.: Eng.　　2005

Director Kazimierz Braun on his adaptation of *La Peste (The Plague)* by Albert Camus. Poland: Wrocław. 1976-1983. Lang.: Eng.　　2015

Description of first translations and adaptations of Shakespeare's dramas on the Polish stage. Poland: Vilna. 1786-1864. Lang.: Pol.　　2030

Adaptation of Dostojěvskij's *Prestuplenijě i nakazanijě (Crime and Punishment)* directed by Andrzej Wajda at Teatr Stary under the title *Zdrodnia i Kara*. Poland: Cracow. 1984. Lang.: Pol.　　2032

Interviews with playwrights Louise Page, Charles McKeown and Malcolm Sircon. UK-England: London. 1986. Lang.: Eng.　　2133

Controversy surrounding *Presumption, or The Fate of Frankenstein* by Richard Brinsley Peake. UK-England: London. 1818-1840. Lang.: Eng.　　2142

Description of first stage adaptation of Robert Louis Stevenson's *Dr. Jekyll and Mr. Hyde*. USA: New York, NY. USA: Boston, MA. 1886-1888. Lang.: Eng.　　2298

Attempt to produce Quarto version of *King Lear* at University of Rochester. USA: Rochester, NY. 1985. Lang.: Eng.　　2300

Account of University of California at Irvine production of a nativity play with composite text drawn from York, N-town and Wakefield cycles. USA: Irvine, CA. 1986. Lang.: Eng.　　2307

On the 'theatricalization' of film. USSR. 1980-1986. Lang.: Rus.　　3230

Lakat alá lányokat (Lock Up Your Daughters), a stage adaptation of Henry Fielding's *Rape Upon Rape*, directed by Imre Halasi. Hungary: Diósgyőr. 1986. Lang.: Hun.　　3600

Adapting and staging of *Les Misérables* by Victor Hugo. UK-England. 1980. Lang.: Eng.　　3609

Peter Brook's direction and adaptation of the opera *Carmen* by Georges Bizet. France: Paris. 1981-1983. Lang.: Heb.　　3731

Significance of the translation in recordings of Verdi's *Otello*. USA. 1902-1978. Lang.: Eng.　　3812

Adaptations — cont'd

Review of the world premiere of the opera *Three Sisters*. USA: Columbus, OH. 1968-1986. Lang.: Eng.   3822

Puppeteer Julie Taymor adapts *Die vertauschten Köpfe (The Transposed Heads)* by Thomas Mann for performance at the Ark Theatre. USA: New York, NY. 1984. Lang.: Eng.   3977

Use of shadow puppets in an adaptation of *Animal Farm*.   4016

Plays/librettos/scripts

Reviews of books on Hungarian theatre. Hungary. 1952-1984. Lang.: Hun.   958

Introductory note on the first translation of *Lille Eyolf (Little Eyolf)* into Hebrew. Norway. Israel. 1884-1985. Lang.: Heb.   962

Obtaining legal rights to a property when adapting a play. USA: New York, NY. 1984. Lang.: Eng.   983

Ballets based on works of William Shakespeare. USSR. Germany, West. 1980-1986. Lang.: Rus.   1322

The essentials of a script which should not be altered.   2349

Theory of translation, using ideas of Eric Bentley and plays of Samuel Beckett. 1950-1986. Lang.: Eng.   2352

Eric Bentley on playwriting, translating and adapting. 1986. Lang.: Eng.   2355

Translations, adaptations and the Australian theatre. Australia: Armidale, N.S.W. 1985. Lang.: Eng.   2371

Interview with playwright Alex Buzo. Australia. 1986. Lang.: Eng.   2385

Interview with Peter Handke about his play *Prometheus gefesselt*. Austria: Salzburg. Greece. 1985-1986. Lang.: Ger.   2398

Discusses Michel Garneau's *joual* translation of *Macbeth*. Canada: Montreal, PQ. 1978. Lang.: Eng.   2429

Environmental theatre version of *Hamlet*. Canada: Vancouver, BC. 1986. Lang.: Eng.   2435

Tom Stoppard's *On the Razzle*, an adaptation of *Einen Jux will er sich machen* by Johann Nestroy. England. Austria: Vienna. 1927-1981. Lang.: Eng.   2462

Semiotic analysis of Shakespeare's *King Lear*. England: London. 1605-1606. Lang.: Eng.   2467

Adapting *Hamlet* for the *nō* theatre. England. Japan. 1600-1982. Lang.: Ita.   2506

An appraisal of David Garrick's adaptation of Shakespeare's *King John*. England: London. 1736-1796. Lang.: Eng.   2510

George Chapman's *Caesar and Pompey* as a disguised version of the story of Prince Henry. England. 1605-1631. Lang.: Eng.   2523

Comparison of John Caryll's *Sir Salomon* with its source, *L'École des femmes (The School for Wives)* by Molière. England. France. 1662-1669. Lang.: Eng.   2527

Accuracy of portrayal of historical figures in Shakespeare and his adaptors. England. 1590-1940. Lang.: Eng.   2532

Revision of dramaturgy and stagecraft in Restoration adaptations of Shakespeare. England: London. 1660-1690. Lang.: Eng.   2535

Interview with founders of Internationale Nieuwe Scene. Europe. 1984.   2543

Interview with Josy Eisenberg, translator of *Le Cantique des cantiques (The Song of Songs)* for the Comédie-Française. France: Paris. 1986. Lang.: Fre.   2544

Superficial and reductive use of classical myth in modern French theatre. France. 1935-1944. Lang.: Eng.   2550

Examination of the first Hebrew adaptation of Molière's *Tartuffe* by David Vexler. France. 1874. Lang.: Heb.   2569

Adaptation by Albert Camus of *Les Esprits (The Spirits)* by Pierre de Larivey. France. 1570-1953. Lang.: Fre.   2571

The role of the double in Georg Kaiser's *Zweimal Amphitryon (Amphitryon x 2)* and other works. Germany. 1943. Lang.: Eng.   2589

Revising Brecht's plays to insure socially relevant productions. Germany, East. 1985.   2613

Criteria for evaluating translations, using the example of Brecht's *Galileo*. Germany, East. 1938-1953.   2616

Work of Bertolt Brecht should be re-examined according to the current historical perspective. Germany, East. 1984.   2620

Conference on the problems of adapting, interpreting and staging the classics. Hungary. Italy. 1985. Lang.: Hun.   2656

Overview of Hebrew adaptations and translations of *Tartuffe* by Molière. Israel. France. 1794-1985. Lang.: Heb.   2667

Development of Pirandello's *La ragione degli altri (The Reason of the Others)* from novel to play. Italy. 1899-1917. Lang.: Ita.   2712

Jerzy Grotowski and his adaptation of *Doctor Faustus*. Poland. 1964. Lang.: Eng.   2740

History of the writing and diffusion of Čechov's *Platonov (Wild Honey)*. Russia. USSR. 1878-1960. Lang.: Cat.   2764

Translations of Shakespeare by Josep Maria de Sagarra. Spain-Catalonia: Barcelona. 1940-1964. Lang.: Cat.   2811

Short history of Catalan translations of plays. Spain-Catalonia. 1848-1984. Lang.: Fre.   2813

Plays translated into Catalan by Pompeu Fabra. Spain-Catalonia. 1890-1905. Lang.: Cat.   2818

Interview with Irena Kraus about her play *Lilla livet (The Little Life)*, based on *La vida es sueño (Life Is a Dream)* by Calderón. Sweden: Malmö. 1985-1986. Lang.: Swe.   2824

Playwright Edward Bond's use of Greek models in *The Woman*. UK-England. 1978. Lang.: Eng.   2834

Interview with playwright Tom Stoppard. UK-England. 1986. Lang.: Eng.   2839

Interview with Christopher Hampton on his adaptation of *Les Liaisons dangereuses*. UK-England: London. 1971-1986. Lang.: Eng.   2859

Political views of Howard Brenton as evidenced in his adaptations. UK-England. 1973-1986. Lang.: Eng.   2883

Playwright Robert Auletta on his adaptation of Sophocles' *Ajax*. USA: Washington, DC. 1986. Lang.: Eng.   2891

Eric Bentley as one of the major forces in the subversion of Brecht. USA.   2903

Review of adaptations for the stage of short stories by Čechov. USA: New York, NY. 1986. Lang.: Eng.   2922

Robert Wilson's adaptation of Euripides' *Alcestis*. USA: Cambridge, MA. 1979-1986. Lang.: Eng.   2939

Contributing sources to Wooster Group's *Saint Anthony*. USA: New York, NY, Boston, MA, Washington, DC. 1983-1986. Lang.: Eng.   2940

Radio adaptations of foreign works, their effect on culture. Canada. 1939-1949. Lang.: Fre.   3181

Scandinavian drama on Canadian radio. Canada. Scandinavia. 1939-1982. Lang.: Eng.   3182

Comparison of Harold Pinter and Marcel Proust, focusing on Pinter's filmscript *The Proust Screenplay*. France. UK-England. 1913-1978. Lang.: Eng.   3232

Nazi ideology and Hans Schweikart's film adaptation of Lessing's *Minna von Barnhelm*. Germany. 1940. Lang.: Ger.   3233

Harold Pinter's screenplay for *The French Lieutenant's Woman* by John Fowles. UK-England. 1969-1981. Lang.: Eng.   3238

Orson Welles' adaptation of Shakespeare's Falstaff scenes, *Chimes at Midnight*. UK-England. 1938-1965. Lang.: Eng.   3239

Analysis of Harold Pinter's technique in adapting *A la Recherche du Temps Perdu (Remembrance of Things Past)* by Marcel Proust as a screenplay. UK-England. 1972. Lang.: Eng.   3240

Film versions of Shakespeare's *Macbeth* by Orson Welles, Akira Kurosawa and Roman Polanski. USA. Japan. 1948-1971. Lang.: Eng.   3243

Interview with scriptwriter Peter Yeldham. Australia: Sydney, N.S.W. 1985. Lang.: Eng.   3278

Comparison of the stage and television versions of *What Where* by Samuel Beckett. 1983-1985. Lang.: Eng.   3282

Productions of Jane Howell and Elijah Moshinsky for the BBC Shakespeare series. UK-England: London. 1978-1985. Lang.: Eng.   3283

Review articles on the BBC Shakespeare series. UK-England: London. 1978-1985. Lang.: Eng.   3284

Plots and themes in adaptations of *Tou Erh Yüan (The Injustice of Miss Tou)*. China. 1360-1960. Lang.: Chi.   3525

Problems of adapting classic plays. China, People's Republic of. 1986. Lang.: Chi.   3543

Analysis and origins of the character 'Dr. Miracle' in Offenbach's *Les contes d'Hoffmann*. 1700-1900. Lang.: Eng.   3853

Origins of the characters Rigoletto and Marullo in Verdi's *Rigoletto*. France. 1496-1851. Lang.: Eng.   3869

Adaptations of *Carmen* by Prosper Mérimée. France. Spain. 1845-1983. Lang.: Fre.   3870

Adaptations — cont'd

Shakespeare's influence on Verdi's operas. Germany. Italy. Austria. 1750-1850. Lang.: Eng.   3878

Wagner's *Das Liebesverbot*, an operatic adaptation of *Measure for Measure*. Germany. 1834. Lang.: Eng.   3880

Why Verdi revised the 1857 version of *Simon Boccanegra*. Italy: Milan. 1857-1881. Lang.: Eng.   3881

Creation of the 1857 version of *Simon Boccanegra* by Verdi, libretto by Piave. Italy: Venice. 1856-1881. Lang.: Eng.   3882

Changes from the Friedrich von Schiller source in *Don Carlo* by Giuseppe Verdi. Italy. 1867-1883. Lang.: Eng.   3887

Puškin's *Queen of Spades* adapted for opera by Čajkovskij. Russia. 1833-1890. Lang.: Eng.   3891

Collaboration of authors and composers of *Billy Budd*. UK-England: London. 1949-1964. Lang.: Eng.   3895

A chronology and analysis of the compositions of Benjamin Britten. UK-England: London. 1946-1976. Lang.: Eng.   3896

Auden and Kallman's English translation of *Die Zauberflöte (The Magic Flute)*. USA. 1951-1956. Lang.: Eng.   3903

Reconstruction of the three versions and productions of the operetta *Állami Áruház (State Stores)*. Hungary. 1952-1977. Lang.: Hun. 3943

Reference materials
Adaptation of Ferdinand Raimund's dramas for children's theatre. Austria: Vienna. 1790-1836. Lang.: Ger.   2979

Theory/criticism
Decreasing importance of the playwright in Italian theatre. Italy. 1900-1984. Lang.: Fre.   3119

Adar, Arnon
Design/technology
Photographs of settings designed by set designer Arnon Adar. Israel: Tel-Aviv. 1955-1971. Lang.: Eng.   297

Addison, Steve
Performance/production
Collection of newspaper reviews by London theatre critics. UK-England: London. 1986. Lang.: Eng.   2113

Adedeji, Joel
Research/historiography
Examination of Joel Adedeji's thesis on *alárìnjó*, a Yoruba theatrical art form. Nigeria. 1826-1986. Lang.: Eng.   1186

Adelaide Court (Toronto, ON)
Performance spaces
Troubles faced by Adelaide Court theatre complex. Canada: Toronto, ON. 1979-1983. Lang.: En .   587

Adié, milacku! (Good-bye, Darling!)
Performance/production
Review of Alex Koenigsmark's *Adié, milacku! (Good-bye, Darling!)* directed by Péter Gothár at Csiky Gergely Theatre under the title *Agyő, kedvesem*. Hungary: Kaposvár. 1985. Lang.: Hun.   1862

Adié, milacku! (Goodbye, Darling!)
Performance/production
Péter Gothár directs *Agyő, kedvesem (Goodbye, Darling!)* by Alex Koenigsmark, at Csiky Gergely Theatre. Hungary: Kaposvár. 1985. Lang.: Hun.   1894

Adler, Jerry
Performance/production
Reviews of National Lampoon's *Class of 86*, staged by Jerry Adler. USA: New York, NY. 1986. Lang.: Eng.   3348

Administration
SEE ALSO
Classed Entries.
Administration
Problems of present-day reality in Ukrainian theatres. USSR. 1980-1986. Lang.: Ukr.   193
Audience
Profile and role of subscribers in nonprofit theatre. USA: New York, NY. 1984. Lang.: Eng.   203

Effect of official educational and cultural policies on theatre. France. Germany. UK-England. 1789-1986. Lang.: Fre.   1446
Basic theatrical documents
Transcription of manuscript assigning shares in the King's Company. England. 1661-1684. Lang.: Eng.   220
Design/technology
Fire safety regulations and fireproofing. USA. 1976. Lang.: Eng. 393
Institutions
Financial difficulties of the Bregenzer Festspiele. Austria: Bregenz. 1985-1986. Lang.: Ger.   440

Wiener Festwochen 1986: Mozart and Modern Art. Austria: Vienna. 1986. Lang.: Ger.   441

Solving the financial problems of the Bregenzer Festspiele. Austria: Bregenz. 1986-1987. Lang.: Ger.   442

Concept for programs at the Stadttheater. Austria: Klagenfurt. 1985-1987. Lang.: Ger.   443

Program for the festival Carinthischer Sommer. Austria. 1986. Lang.: Ger.   445

Niederösterreichischer Theatersommer: producing summer theatre at festivals in different places. Austria. 1980-1986. Lang.: Ger.   448

Union of three theaters in Vienna to the Verbund Wiener Theatre. Austria: Vienna. 1986. Lang.: Ger.   449

Activities and functions of the Teletheater-Gesellschaft. Austria: Vienna. 1985. Lang.: Ger.   450

The Jura Soyfer Theater and its plans for the 1986/87 season. Austria: Vienna. 1986. Lang.: Ger.   457

Concept and functions of Schlossspiele Kobersdorf. Austria: Burgenland. 1983-1986. Lang.: Ger.   458

Roman Zeilinger's plans for managing the Landestheater. Austria: Linz. 1986. Lang.: Ger.   460

Significance of Applebaum-Hébert report on Canadian cultural policy. Canada. 1982-1983. Lang.: Eng.   465

Career of Walter Learning, artistic director, Vancouver Playhouse. Canada: Vancouver, BC. 1982-1983. Lang.: Eng.   470

Overview of Festival Lennoxville and the role of anglophone drama in Quebec. Canada: Lennoxville, PQ. 1972-1982. Lang.: Eng.   485

Structure and political viewpoint of Great Canadian Theatre Company. Canada: Ottawa, ON. 1975-1986. Lang.: Eng.   486

History of drama ensemble Mecklenburgisches Staatstheater Schwerin. Germany, East: Schwerin. 1970-1986. Lang.: Ger.   498

History of Korea's first theatre production company. Korea: Seoul. 1922-1924. Lang.: Kor.   509

Administrators seen as destroying the fringe theatre. UK-England: London. 1980-1986. Lang.: Swe.   535

Interview with Hilary Westlake of Lumière & Son. UK-England: London. 1973-1986. Lang.: Swe.   536

Interview with Adrian Hall, artistic director of both Trinity Square Repertory Theatre and Dallas Theatre Center. USA: Providence, RI, Dallas, TX. 1966-1986. Lang.: Eng.   548

Management techniques for growth at Tears of Joy Puppet Theatre. USA: Vancouver, WA. 1974-1985. Lang.: Eng.   549

Artistic director of WPA Theatre Kyle Renick discusses institutionalization of theatre companies. USA: New York, NY. 1977-1986. Lang.: Eng.   566

Notes on the dance committee meetings at the 21st congress of the International Theatre Institute. Canada: Montreal, PQ, Toronto, ON. 1985. Lang.: Rus.   1270

Account of the firing of Alexander Grant, artistic director of National Ballet of Canada. Canada: Toronto, ON. 1975-1982. Lang.: Eng.   1295

Goals of Eric Bruhn, new artistic director of National Ballet of Canada. Canada: Toronto, ON. 1967-1983. Lang.: Eng.   1296

Claus Peymann's concept for managing the Akademietheater and the Burgtheater. Austria: Vienna. 1986. Lang.: Ger.   1532

Achim Benning's management of the Burgtheater. Austria: Vienna. 1976-1986. Lang.: Ger.   1537

Paul Blaha's management of the Volkstheater. Austria: Vienna. 1986-1987. Lang.: Ger.   1538

Analysis of documentation on Jefferson theatre company. USA. 1830-1845. Lang.: Eng.   1597

History of two major Black touring companies. USA: New York, NY. 1969-1982. Lang.: Eng.   1598

The Festival of Clowns in the Wiener Festwochen. Austria: Vienna. 1983-1986. Lang.: Ger.   3380

Spectaculum 1986 and the concept for this festival. Austria: Vienna. 1986. Lang.: Ger.   3480

Claus Helmut Drese's plans for the new season at the Staatsoper. Austria: Vienna. 1986-1987. Lang.: Ger.   3667

Claus Helmut Drese's plans as manager of the Staatsoper. Austria: Vienna. 1986-1991. Lang.: Ger.   3668

Claus Helmut Drese and his plans for managing the Vienna Staatsoper. Austria: Vienna. Germany, West. Switzerland. 1930-1986. Lang.: Ger.   3670

SUBJECT INDEX

Administration — cont'd

The survival and prosperity of the Santa Fe Opera Company. USA: Santa Fe, NM. 1957-1986. Lang.: Eng.   3678

New administrative personnel at the Opera Theatre of St. Louis. USA: St. Louis, MO. 1976-1986. Lang.: Eng.   3679

The first thirty years of the Santa Fe Opera. USA: Santa Fe, NM. 1956-1986. Lang.: Eng.   3681

Performance spaces

Troubles faced by Adelaide Court theatre complex. Canada: Toronto, ON. 1979-1983. Lang.: En .   587

Results of an Off Broadway survey on the crisis of limited space and real estate costs. USA: New York, NY. 1986. Lang.: Eng.   638

Estimating and managing the cost of building a theatre. USA. 1986. Lang.: Eng.   645

History of the Century Theatre. USA: New York, NY. 1905-1930. Lang.: Eng.   1625

Performance/production

On manager and director Claus Helmut Drese. Austria: Vienna. Switzerland. Germany, West. Lang.: Ger.   659

Development of regional theatre and other entertainments. England. 1840-1870. Lang.: Eng.   687

History of theatre in America. USA. 1750-1985. Lang.: Eng.   834

Interview with Ellen Rudolph on recent cultural exchange tour of foreign artists in the US. USA: New York, NY. 1982. Lang.: Eng.
839

Problems of contemporary theatre. USSR. 1980-1986. Lang.: Rus.
858

Problems of young people's theatre. USSR: Moscow. 1980-1986. Lang.: Rus.   899

Komsomol Theatre director Mark Zacharov on his profession. USSR: Moscow. 1980-1986. Lang.: Rus.   910

Career of director Bill Glassco. Canada: Toronto, ON. 1965-1986. Lang.: Eng.   1674

Analysis of the document detailing expenses for performances given at Christ Church (Oxford) for Charles I, suggesting involvement by Inigo Jones as stage director. England: Oxford. 1636. Lang.: Eng.
1701

Analysis of Robin Hood entertainments in the parish of Yeovil. England. 1475-1588. Lang.: Eng.   1712

Career of actress and theatrical manager Louisa Lane Drew. USA. 1820-1897. Lang.: Eng.   2243

Advantages and limitations of television medium in producing, recording and broadcasting performing arts. USA. 1930-1985. Lang.: Eng.   3273

Details of the 1926 American Circus Corporation season. USA. Canada. 1926. Lang.: Eng.   3386

A general review of the 1985 circus season. USA. Canada. 1985. Lang.: Eng.   3394

Problems of the contemporary circus. USSR. 1986. Lang.: Rus. 3398

Excerpt from book by manager of Durov Theatre of Wild Animals. USSR: Moscow. 1986. Lang.: Rus.   3399

Achievements and problems of the contemporary circus. USSR. 1980-1986. Lang.: Rus.   3400

Problems in the development of Soviet musical theatre. USSR. 1980-1986. Lang.: Rus.   3625

Plays/librettos/scripts

Cooperation between theatres in Austria and playwrights-in-training. Austria. 1980-1986. Lang.: Ger.   2393

Career of Xiong Foxi. China, People's Republic of: Beijing, Shanghai. USA: New York, NY. 1901-1965. Lang.: Chi.   2449

Interview with theatre professionals on successful writing and production. USA. 1986. Lang.: Eng.   2932

Motif of renewal in Soviet theatre and reorganization of theatre administration. USSR: Kiev. 1980-1986. Lang.: Rus.   2963

Reference materials

Directory of member organizations of ART/NY. USA: New York, NY. 1986. Lang.: Eng.   1037

Listing of repertory schedules, contact and contract information. USA. 1986. Lang.: Eng.   1045

Relation to other fields

Modern business methods in show business. Italy. 1970-1985. Lang.: Ita.   1105

Cardinal Richelieu's theatrical policies. France. 1634-1642. Lang.: Fre.   3030

Theory/criticism

Forums: Dispute regarding content and aims of *The Drama Review.* USA. 1964-1986. Lang.: Eng.   3139

Adolphson, Per B.

Performance/production

Stage photographs with comment by photographers. Sweden. 1985-1986. Lang.: Swe.   794

Advent a Hargitán (Advent in the Harghita Mountains)

Performance/production

Ferenc Sik directs András Sütő's *Advent a Hargitán (Advent in the Harghita Mountains)* at the National Theatre. Hungary: Budapest. 1984-1985. Lang.: Hun.   1779

Review of *Advent a Hargitán (Advent in the Harghita Mountains)* by András Sütő, directed by Ferenc Sik. Hungary: Budapest. 1986. Lang.: Hun.   1797

Review of two performances of András Sütő's plays. Hungary: Budapest. 1986. Lang.: Hun.   1913

Advent a Hargitán (Advent in the Harghita Mountains) by András Sütő, directed at National Theatre by Ferenc Sik. Hungary: Budapest. 1986. Lang.: Hun.   1956

Rehearsals of András Sütő's *Advent a Hargitán (Advent in the Harghita Mountains)* at the National Theatre directed by Ferenc Sik. Hungary: Budapest. 1985-1986. Lang.: Hun.   1963

András Sütő's *Advent a Hargitán (Advent in the Harghita Mountains)* directed by Ferenc Sik. Hungary: Budapest. 1986. Lang.: Hun.   1974

Advertising

Administration

Marketing directors seek innovative approaches to brochure design. USA: New York, NY. 1986. Lang.: Eng.   139

Guide to producing Off-off Broadway showcases. USA: New York, NY. Lang.: Eng.   159

Advantages of radio advertising for live theatre. USA: New York, NY. 1986. Lang.: Eng.   175

Institutions

Brief histories of the H.A.D.L.E.Y. Players and the Cynthia Belgrave Theatre Workshop. USA: New York, NY. 1970-1986. Lang.: Eng.
1604

Reference materials

Guide to producing printed material. USA. 1984. Lang.: Eng.   1044

AEA

SEE

Actor's Equity Association.

Aerialists

Performance/production

Interview with aerialist Dolly Jacobs. USA. 1970-1985. Lang.: Eng.
3390

Aeschylus

Performance/production

Peter Stein directs Aeschylus' *Oresteia* in Warsaw. Germany, West: Berlin, West. Poland: Warsaw. 1983. Lang.: Pol.   1768

Plays/librettos/scripts

Interview with Peter Handke about his play *Prometheus gefesselt.* Austria: Salzburg. Greece. 1985-1986. Lang.: Ger.   2398

Marguerite Yourcenar's treatment of Electra story compared to other versions. France. 1944-1954. Lang.: Fre.   2554

Cosmic themes in the works of Aeschylus. Greece. 472-458 B.C. Lang.: Fre.   2629

Topicality of Aeschylus' *Oresteia.* Greece. 458 B.C. Lang.: Fre. 2632

Masked god as tragic subject in works of Aeschylus, Sophocles and Euripides. Greece. 499-401 B.C. Lang.: Fre.   2636

Relation to other fields

Factors that discouraged historical drama in the classical period. Greece: Athens. 475-375 B.C. Lang.: Eng.   3035

Aesthetics

Development of performing arts related to formation of Japanese national culture. Japan. 1596-1941. Lang.: Rus.   8

Administration

Aesthetics and culture—relationship with the state. USA. 1857-1983. Lang.: Eng.   143

Audience

Socio-aesthetic notes on contemporary theatre and audiences. USSR. 1970-1980. Lang.: Rus.   210

Aesthetic education through theatre. USSR. 1980-1986. Lang.: Rus.
214

Aesthetics — cont'd

Basic theatrical documents

Poem by Tanaka Min about his reasons for dancing. Japan. 1985. Lang.: Eng. 1267

Homage to *butō* dancer Hijikata Tatsumi by Tanaka Min. Japan. 1976-1985. Lang.: Eng. 1268

Writings by Tadeusz Kantor on the nature of theatre. Poland. 1956-1985. Lang.: Eng. 1490

Design/technology

Visual imagery and metaphor in scenery and lighting. China. 1308-1982. Lang.: Chi. 245

Use of audience imagination to complement a set design. China. 700-1980. Lang.: Chi. 246

Realism and fantasy in set design. China, People's Republic of. 1960-1982. Lang.: Chi. 248

Elements of set design and their emotional impact. China, People's Republic of. 1960-1982. Lang.: Chi. 250

Role of stage design in production as an artistic whole. USSR. 1980-1986. Lang.: Rus. 436

Performance spaces

Ancient Indian theatre and its conventions. India. 200 B.C. Lang.: Ita. 609

Performance/production

Adaptation of Eastern theatre for the Western stage. China. Europe. Lang.: Ita. 676

On Western impressions of Eastern performances. China. Japan. 1500-1600. Lang.: Ita. 677

European and Arabic influences on Egyptian theatre. Egypt. 1798-1986. Lang.: Ita. 685

Influence of Oriental theatre on European directors. Europe. Asia. 1890-1910. Lang.: Rus. 705

Review of *Finlandia*, produced by Ryhmäteatteri. Finland: Helsinki. 1986. Lang.: Swe. 707

Development of stage photography. France. 1872-1986. Lang.: Fre. 720

Western actors and the energy of Oriental performance. Japan. Lang.: Ita. 756

Aesthetic criteria in theatre and the role of the director. USSR. Lang.: Rus. 894

Interview with choreographer Ohno Kazuo. Japan. 1906-1985. Lang.: Eng. 1278

Description of *butō*, avant-garde dance movement of Japan. Japan. 1960-1986. Lang.: Eng. 1279

Dance in the Malaysian culture. Malaysia. 1950-1984. Lang.: Eng. 1333

Analysis of Twyla Tharp's *Fait Accompli*. USA. 1984. Lang.: Eng. 1370

Differences in portraying time and locale in Sung drama and in contemporary *spoken drama*. China. 1127-1980. Lang.: Chi. 1688

Critical essays on major productions and aesthetics. France. 1970-1985. Lang.: Fre. 1747

Reciprocal influences of French and Japanese theatre. France. Japan. 1900-1945. Lang.: Fre. 1750

Description of Georg Büchner's *Dantons Tod (Danton's Death)* staged by Alexander Lang at Deutsches Theater. Germany, East: Berlin, East. 1984. Lang.: Ger. 1763

Essays by Suzuki Tadashi encompassing his approach to theatre, training, and performance. Japan. 1980-1983. Lang.: Eng. 2007

Interview with director Tadeusz Kantor. Poland. 1967-1985. Lang.: Eng. 2029

Overview of the career of Jerzy Grotowski, his theatrical experiments, training methodology and thoughts on the purpose of theatre. Poland. 1958-1986. Lang.: Eng. 2054

Dramaturg Oskar Eustis on confronting social and aesthetic problems. USA: San Francisco, CA. 1975-1986. Lang.: Eng. 2250

Explorative structure and manner of performance in avant-garde theatre. USA. 1965. Lang.: Eng. 2277

Eastern and Western elements in Sergej Eisenstein's work. Russia. 1898-1948. Lang.: Ita. 3225

Oriental influences on *commedia dell'arte*. Italy. 1550-1650. Lang.: Ita. 3413

Origins of the stylized acting in Southern drama (Nanxi). China. 1127-1278. Lang.: Chi. 3517

Theatricality in opera. Lang.: Rus. 3685

Physical, social and theatrical aspects of *castrati*. Italy: Rome, Venice. England: London. 1700-1799. Lang.: Ger. 3757

Plays/librettos/scripts

Influence of oriental theatre on playwright Beverley Simons. Canada: Vancouver, BC. 1962-1975. Lang.: Eng. 928

Theory of translation, using ideas of Eric Bentley and plays of Samuel Beckett. 1950-1986. Lang.: Eng. 2352

Details on performances of plays by Paul Claudel in German-speaking countries. Germany. Switzerland. Austria. 1913-1986. Lang.: Ger. 2599

Influence of Chinese theatre on Bertolt Brecht. Germany: Berlin. China. 1900-1950. Lang.: Ita. 2608

The grotesque in the plays of István Örkény. Hungary. 1947-1979. Lang.: Ger. 2651

Nō and Beckett compared. Japan. France. 1954-1986. Lang.: Ita. 2721

Absence of the author in Henrik Ibsen's *Vildanden (The Wild Duck)*. Norway. 1882. Lang.: Eng. 2729

Politics and aesthetics in three plays of Fernando Arrabal. Spain. France. Lang.: Fre. 2801

Critical debate over Timothy Findley's *The Paper People*. Canada. 1967. Lang.: Eng. 3280

Structure of Beijing opera. China, People's Republic of: Beijing. 1983. Lang.: Chi. 3537

Aesthetic considerations in *Lélio* by Hector Berlioz. France. Lang.: Fre. 3868

Study of all aspects of Italian opera. Italy. 1810-1920. Lang.: Fre. 3889

History and aesthetics of Soviet opera. USSR: Moscow. 1917-1941. Lang.: Ger. 3905

Relation to other fields

Argument that theatre should return to art's roots in ritual and ceremony. 1986. Lang.: Eng. 1059

Dissolution of Jerzy Grotowski's Laboratory Theatre. Poland: Wrocław. 1959-1985. Lang.: Eng. 1117

Ethical value of theatre in education. USA. 1985. Lang.: Eng. 1149

Relates theatrical art and progressive scientific thought. USSR. 1980-1986. Lang.: Rus. 1172

Contrasts between culture and mass media. Italy. 1980-1986. Lang.: Ita. 3171

Kurt Weill and German expressionism. Germany: Berlin. 1923-1930. Lang.: Eng. 3920

Research/historiography

Indian theatre professionals criticize Peter Brook's *Mahabharata*. India: Kerala, Calcutta. 1980-1985. Lang.: Eng. 1376

Theory/criticism

Issues in theatrical aesthetics. Lang.: Eng. 1189

Hungarian translation of *The Idea of a Theatre* by Francis Fergusson. 1949. Lang.: Hun. 1191

Essays on the sociology of art and semiotics. Lang.: Hun. 1192

Theatre critic discusses objectivity and standards. 1986. Lang.: Eng. 1193

Critics discuss modernist and postmodernist movements. 1986. Lang.: Eng. 1194

History of theatre in its social context. Lang.: Hun. 1197

Analysis of audience reaction to theatre spaces. 1950-1980. Lang.: Chi. 1198

Characteristics of Eastern and Western theatre. Asia. Europe. Lang.: Kor. 1200

Influence of Western theory on Chinese drama of Gu Zhongyi. China. 1920-1963. Lang.: Chi. 1202

Purpose of literature and art, and the role of the artist. China, People's Republic of: Shanghai, Yan'an. 1942-1982. Lang.: Chi. 1203

An imagined dialogue on the work of Roland Barthes. France. Lang.: Eng. 1207

Concept of *Standpunkt* in J.M.R. Lenz's poetics and the search for identity in the 'Sturm und Drang' period. Germany. 1774. Lang.: Eng. 1209

Influences on the development of European and Japanese theatre. Japan. Europe. 500 B.C.-1986 A.D. Lang.: Ita. 1213

Theory and history of Korean theatre. Korea: Seoul. 200 B.C.-1986 A.D. Lang.: Kor. 1214

Aesthetics — cont'd

Development and characteristics of Oriental theatre. Korea: Seoul. Japan: Tokyo. China: Beijing. 200-1986. Lang.: Kor.   1215

Andrzej Hausbrandt (critic) and Gustaw Holoubek (actor) discuss their views on general problems of theatre. Poland. Lang.: Pol. 1217

Stanislavskij's aesthetic criteria. Russia. 1863-1938. Lang.: Rus.   1218

Ingmar Bergman production of *King Lear* and Asian influences. Spain-Catalonia: Barcelona. 1985. Lang.: Eng.   1219

Western influences on theatrical development in Turkey. Turkey. 1524-1986. Lang.: Ita.   1221

Eastern and Western influences on Turkish theatre. Turkey. 1000-1986. Lang.: Ita.   1222

Report of seminar on theatre criticism. USA: New York, NY. 1983. Lang.: Eng.   1223

Theatre professionals challenge assertions that theatre is a weaker form of communication than film. USA: New York, NY. 1985. Lang.: Eng.   1225

Interviews on the role of the critic in New York theatre. USA: New York, NY. 1983. Lang.: Eng.   1226

Lack of representation of women in theatre. USA: New York, NY. 1982-1986. Lang.: Eng.   1227

Critical profile of *Performing Arts Journal* and of recent theatrical trends. USA. 1976-1986. Lang.: Pol.   1228

Influence of drama critic Eric Bentley. USA. 1962-1986. Lang.: Eng.   1229

Technology and the spiritual/aesthetic role of the actor. USA. Lang.: Eng.   1230

John Cage discusses his struggle to define art. USA. 1965. Lang.: Eng.   1231

Michael Kirby defends the liberal outlook of *The Drama Review*. USA. 1971-1986. Lang.: Eng.   1232

Richard Schechner bids farewell to *The Drama Review* and suggests areas of future theatrical investigation. USA. 1969-1986. Lang.: Eng.   1234

Satirical essay on the future of the theatre. USA. 1984. Lang.: Eng.   1235

Critique of James Fenton's review of two books on Bertolt Brecht. USA. 1974.   1236

The role of criticism in the creative theatrical process. USSR. 1980-1986. Lang.: Rus.   1238

Synthesis of the arts in the theatrical process. USSR: Moscow. 1986. Lang.: Rus.   1240

Problems and tasks of contemporary theatre criticism. USSR. 1980-1986. Lang.: Rus.   1241

Stanislavskij in Russian and Soviet criticism. USSR: Russia. 1888-1986. Lang.: Rus.   1242

Overview of the development of theatre criticism in the press. USSR. 1917-1927. Lang.: Rus.   1243

Ethical and moral position of criticism. USSR. Lang.: Rus.   1245

Reflections on theatre criticism. USSR. 1980. Lang.: Rus.   1247

Playwright A. Simukov discusses his craft. USSR. 1986. Lang.: Rus.   1249

Mutual influences of theatre, film, and television. USSR. 1980-1986. Lang.: Rus.   1250

Pina Bausch seen as heir of epic theater of Bertolt Brecht. Germany, West. 1977-1985. Lang.: Eng.   1289

American criticisms of German *Tanztheater*. Germany, West. USA. 1933-1985. Lang.: Eng.   1290

American dance critics' reviews of Pina Bausch's work. USA. Germany, West. 1984-1986. Lang.: Eng.   1291

Influence of Korean mask-dance theatre in Japan. Korea: Seoul. Japan. 1400-1600. Lang.: Kor.   1377

Styles of mask-dance drama in Asia. Korea: Seoul. Japan: Tokyo. China: Beijing. 1400-1986. Lang.: Kor.   1378

Evolution and symbolism of the Mask-Dance drama. Korea: Seoul. 700-1986. Lang.: Kor.   1379

Life and work of Zeami Motokiyo. Japan. 1364-1443. Lang.: Jap.   1420

Various aspects of *kyōgen*. Japan. 1300-1986. Lang.: Jap.   1422

Theory of drama based on Max Scheler's philosophy. Lang.: Eng.   3074

The influence of Samuel Beckett's later works on contemporary writers and directors. 1984. Lang.: Eng.   3077

Identifies types of theatrical irony. Lang.: Eng.   3079

Melodrama as an aesthetic theatre form. Australia. 1850-1986. Lang.: Eng.   3083

Attitudes toward sports in serious Australian drama. Australia. 1876-1965. Lang.: Eng.   3084

Low standard of much Australian theatre reviewing. Australia. 1985. Lang.: Eng.   3085

Book review of *Whittaker's Theatre: A Critic Looks at Stages in Canada and Thereabouts: 1944-1975*, ed. Ronald Bryden and Boyd Neil. Canada: Toronto, ON. 1944-1985. Lang.: Eng.   3087

Discusses the impact of critic B.K. Sandwell. Canada. 1932-1951. Lang.: Eng.   3088

Playwright Xiong Foxi's concept of theatre. China, People's Republic of. 1920-1965. Lang.: Chi.   3089

Experimental theatres to offset the impact of film and theatre. China, People's Republic of. 1960-1981. Lang.: Chi.   3090

Analysis of Goethe's criticism of Shakespeare. England. Germany. 1749-1832. Lang.: Rus.   3091

Attempts to define such terms as 'emblematic' and 'iconographic' with respect to Renaissance theatre. England. 1300-1642. Lang.: Eng.   3092

Selection from Peter Brook's *The Empty Space*. EUROPE. 1929-1982. Lang.: Chi.   3095

Aesthetic theory of interpretation. Europe. North America. 1900-1985. Lang.: Fre.   3097

Selections from Antonin Artaud's *The Theatre and Its Double*. France. 1896-1949. Lang.: Chi.   3099

Selection and analysis of Diderot's theoretical writings about theatre. France. 1713-1834. Lang.: Cat.   3101

Corneille, Racine and Molière as neoclassisists. France. 1600-1700. Lang.: Kor.   3102

Introduction of the work and influence of Bertolt Brecht. France. 1945-1956. Lang.: Fre.   3103

Hegel's theory of theatre and its application by 20th-century dramatists. Germany. 1770-1982. Lang.: Chi.   3106

Solipsism, expressionism and aesthetics in the anti-rational dramas of Gottfried Benn. Germany: Berlin. 1914-1934. Lang.: Eng.   3107

Hungarian translation of Nietzsche's *Birth of Tragedy*. Germany. 1872. Lang.: Hun.   3108

Analysis of Friedrich Schiller's dramatic and theoretical works. Germany. 1759-1805. Lang.: Cat.   3109

Selection of Schiller's writings about drama. Germany. 1759-1805. Lang.: Cat.   3110

Comparison of Brechtian theatre and Chinese traditional theatre. Germany. China. 1400-1982. Lang.: Chi.   3111

Limited usefulness of dramaturgy in staging. Germany, West. 1979. Lang.: Eng.   3112

Review of *Mi lesz velünk Anton Pavlovics? (What Will Become of Us, Anton Pavlovič?)* by Miklós Almási. Hungary. 1986. Lang.: Hun.   3114

Tamás Bécsy's theory of the theatre. Hungary. 1986. Lang.: Hun.   3115

Reviews of books on Hungarian theatre. Hungary. 1986. Lang.: Hun.   3116

Influence of Henrik Ibsen on Korean theatre. Korea: Seoul. Norway. 1884-1986. Lang.: Kor.   3120

Problems in Korean drama. Korea: Seoul. 1970-1979. Lang.: Kor.   3121

Theory and origin of traditional street plays. Korea: Seoul. 200 B.C.-1986 A.D. Lang.: Kor.   3122

Analysis of Wole Soyinka's major critical essays. Nigeria. 1960-1980. Lang.: Eng.   3124

Adam Mickiewicz's theory of theatrical poetry. Poland. 1798-1855. Lang.: Eng.   3125

Selections from Jerzy Grotowski's *Towards a Poor Theatre*. Poland. 1933-1982. Lang.: Chi.   3126

Analysis of critic Tymon Terlecki's theoretical concepts. Poland. 1905-1986. Lang.: Pol.   3128

Relation of short story and drama in the plays of Anton Pavlovič Čechov and Eugene O'Neill. Russia. USA. Lang.: Eng.   3130

Lope de Vega's theories of comedy. Spain. 1609-1624. Lang.: Spa.   3132

Aesthetics — cont'd

Overview of Pinter criticism with emphasis on the works' inherent uncertainty. UK. 1957-1986. Lang.: Eng. 3134

Assessment of critic Kenneth Tynan's works. UK-England. 1950-1960. Lang.: Eng. 3136

Eleven theatre professionals discuss their personal direction and the direction of experimental theatre. USA: New York, NY. 1985. Lang.: Eng. 3137

Forums: Dispute regarding content and aims of *The Drama Review*. USA. 1964-1986. Lang.: Eng. 3139

Details ten-year anniversary celebration of *The Drama Review* and reasons for its longevity. USA. 1966. Lang.: Eng. 3140

The popularity of Charles Dicken's *A Christmas Carol* in American theatres. USA. 1984. Lang.: Eng. 3143

Essays on artistic media by playwright David Mamet. USA: New York, NY, Los Angeles, CA. 1986. Lang.: Eng. 3144

Collection of essays on the avant-garde. USA. 1955-1986. Lang.: Eng. 3145

Theatre critic Frank Rich discusses his life and work. USA: New York, NY. 1986. Lang.: Eng. 3146

Interview with playwright Lillian Hellman. USA: Martha's Vineyard, MA. 1983. Lang.: Eng. 3147

Aesthetic considerations in the plays and essays of Thornton Wilder. USA. 1930-1949. Lang.: Rus. 3149

Intents and purposes of *The Drama Review*. USA. 1963-1986. Lang.: Eng. 3150

Richard Schechner discusses the importance of translating and performing the work of all cultures. USA. 1982. Lang.: Eng. 3152

Character as an aesthetic category in contemporary dramaturgy. USSR. 1980-1986. Lang.: Rus. 3153

Shakespeare in media. UK-England. USA. Japan. 1899-1985. Lang.: Eng. 3172

The aesthetics of movement theatre. Europe. 1975-1986. 3301

Debate on characteristics of the circus as art form. USSR. 1980-1986. Lang.: Rus. 3406

Use of anxiety about fate in Beijing opera. China: Beijing. 5 B.C.-1985 A.D. Lang.: Chi. 3558

Ma Tzuyuan's use of poetic elements in Chinese opera. China: Beijing. 1279-1368. Lang.: Chi. 3559

Use of red, white and black colors in Chinese traditional theatre. China. 200 B.C.-1982 A.D. Lang.: Chi. 3560

Influence of Tuan Anchieh's aesthetics. China. 800-1644. Lang.: Chi. 3561

Defense of Chinese traditional theatre. China. 200 B.C.-1982 A.D. Lang.: Chi. 3562

Analyzes the singing style of Szechuan opera. China. 1866-1952. Lang.: Chi. 3563

Symbolism and aesthetics in the performance styles of Chinese opera. China, People's Republic of: Beijing. 1935-1985. Lang.: Chi. 3564

Strengths and weaknesses of Beijing opera. China, People's Republic of: Beijing. 1935-1985. Lang.: Chi. 3565

Dramatic structure in Beijing opera. China, People's Republic of. 1955-1985. Lang.: Chi. 3566

Influence of Western dramatic theories on Beijing opera. China, People's Republic of: Beijing. 1935-1985. Lang.: Chi. 3567

Analyzes works of four dramatists from Fuchien province. China, People's Republic of. 1981-1985. Lang.: Chi. 3569

Characteristics of Chinese opera in Szechuan province. China, People's Republic of. 1963-1985. Lang.: Chi. 3570

The concept of *Gesamtkunstwerk*. Germany. 1797-1953. Lang.: Eng. 3929

Affabulazione
Performance/production
Tadeusz Łomnicki directs Pasolini's *Affabulazione* at Centrum Sztuki Studio. Poland: Warsaw. 1984. Lang.: Pol. 2033

Afford, Mike
Performance/production
Collection of newspaper reviews by London theatre critics. UK-England: London. 1986. Lang.: Eng. 2110

Affré, Augustarello
Performance/production
Reviews of 10 vintage recordings of complete operas on LP. USA. 1906-1925. Lang.: Eng. 3792

Africapolis
Plays/librettos/scripts
Interview with playwright René Philombe on the educative function of theatre. Cameroon. 1930-1986. Lang.: Fre. 925

After Aida
Performance/production
Collection of newspaper reviews by London theatre critics. UK-England: London. 1986. Lang.: Eng. 2125

Plays/librettos/scripts
Discussion of plays about Verdi and Puccini by Julian Mitchell and Robin Ray. UK-England: London. Italy. 1986. Lang.: Eng. 3628

After the Fall
Theory/criticism
Arthur Miller's *After the Fall* seen an monomyth. USA. 1964-1984. Lang.: Eng. 3138

Age d'Or, L' (Golden Age, The)
Institutions
Overview of Ariane Mnouchkine's work with Théâtre du Soleil. France: Paris. 1959-1985. Lang.: Eng. 497

Age of Invention, The
Basic theatrical documents
Text of *The Age of Invention* by Theodora Skipitares. USA: New York, NY. 1985. Lang.: Eng. 3248

Performance/production
Interview with the mixed-media artist and puppeteer Theodora Skipitares. USA. 1974-1985. Lang.: Eng. 3251

Theodora Skipitares' puppet trilogy *Age of Invention*. USA: New York, NY. 1985. 4013

Agents
Administration
Function of playwright's agent in negotiation and production of a script. USA: New York, NY. 1985. Lang.: Eng. 135

Reference materials
Guide to theatrical services and productions. UK-England. 1985-1986. Lang.: Eng. 1035

Agnes of God
Performance/production
Reviews of plays performed in the 1983-84 Seoul theatre season. Korea: Seoul. 1983-1984. Lang.: Eng. 2008

Agrupació Dramàtica de Barcelona
Basic theatrical documents
Text of *Primera història d'Esther (First Story of Esther)* by Salvador Espriu, with introduction on the author and the play. Spain-Catalonia: Barcelona. 1913-1985. Lang.: Spa, Cat. 1496

Anthology and study of writings of Josep Maria de Sagarra. Spain-Catalonia. 1917-1964. Lang.: Cat. 1501

Plays/librettos/scripts
Translations of Shakespeare by Josep Maria de Sagarra. Spain-Catalonia: Barcelona. 1940-1964. Lang.: Cat. 2811

Memoir concerning playwright Joan Oliver. Spain-Catalonia. 1920-1986. Lang.: Cat. 2820

Relation to other fields
Reports and discussions of restricted cultural communication. Lebanon. Spain-Catalonia. USA. 1985. Lang.: Fre, Spa, Cat. 1111

Theory/criticism
Historical difficulties in creating a paradigm for Catalan theatre. Spain-Catalonia. 1400-1963. Lang.: Cat. 1220

Aguado, Simón
Plays/librettos/scripts
The institution of slavery as presented in *Entremés de los negros (Play of the Blacks)*. Spain. 1600-1699. Lang.: Eng. 2796

Agyó, kedvesem
SEE
Adié, milacku!.

Ágyrajárók (Night Lodgers)
Performance/production
Ágyrajárók (Night Lodgers) by Péter Szántó, directed by György Emőd at Kisfaludy Studio Theatre. Hungary: Győr. 1985. Lang.: Hun. 1854

Ahart, John
Performance/production
Director John Ahart discusses staging *The Caucasian Chalk Circle*. USA: Urbana, IL. 1984. 2278

Ahlfors, Bengt
Performance/production
Production of Bengt Ahlfors' *Színházkomédia (Theatre Comedy)* directed by András Márton. Hungary: Debrecen. 1985. Lang.: Hun. 1925

Ahlin, Maj-Britt
Institutions
The history of the Södertälje Teateramatörer. Sweden: Södertälje.
1953-1986. Lang.: Swe. 520

Ahn, Min-Soo
Performance/production
Directing and the current state of Korean theatre. Korea. 1986.
Lang.: Kor. 760

Aida
Performance/production
Productions of operas at La Scala by Luca Ronconi. Italy: Milan.
1985. Lang.: Ita. 3763
Photographs, cast list, synopsis, and discography of Metropolitan
Opera radio broadcast performances. USA: New York, NY. 1986.
Lang.: Eng. 3794

Aigle à deux têtes, L' (Eagle With Two Heads, The)
Basic theatrical documents
Catalan translation of *L'aigle à deux têtes (The Eagle With Two
Heads)* by Jean Cocteau. France. 1946. Lang.: Cat. 1478
Plays/librettos/scripts
Analysis of *L'Aigle à deux têtes (The Eagle With Two Heads)* by
Jean Cocteau. France. 1889-1963. Lang.: Cat. 2565

Aikins, Carroll
Institutions
Carroll Aikins, founder of Canadian Players. Canada: Naramata, BC.
1920-1922. Lang.: Eng. 478

Ain't Misbehavin'
Design/technology
Designers discuss regional productions of *Ain't Misbehavin'*. USA.
1984-1986. Lang.: Eng. 3591

Airdome Theatre (Fresno, CA)
Performance/production
An historical account of one actor's experiences with the Fresno
Paramount Players. USA: Fresno, CA. 1927. Lang.: Eng. 2255

Aire frío (Cold Air)
Plays/librettos/scripts
Cuban theatre in transition exemplified in the plays of Virgilio
Piñera and Abelardo Estorino. Cuba. 1958-1964. Lang.: Eng. 2452

Aischylos
SEE
Aeschylus.

Aitken, Maria
Relation to other fields
Interview with actress Maria Aitken on a revival of *The Women* by
Clare Boothe Luce. UK-England: London. 1936-1986. Lang.: Eng.
3061

Aitken, Naria
Performance/production
Collection of newspaper reviews by London theatre critics. UK.
1986. Lang.: Eng. 2099

Aix-en-Provence Festival (Aix-en-Provence)
Institutions
Discussions of opera at the festival of Aix-en-Provence. France: Aix-
en-Provence. 1960. Lang.: Fre. 3673

Ajax
Performance/production
Survey of productions at the Kennedy Center's National Theatre.
USA: Washington, DC. 1986. Lang.: Eng. 2247
Robert Auletta's updated version of Sophocles' *Ajax*. USA:
Washington, DC. 1986. Lang.: Eng. 2276
Plays/librettos/scripts
Playwright Robert Auletta on his adaptation of Sophocles' *Ajax*.
USA: Washington, DC. 1986. Lang.: Eng. 2891

Ajtmatov, Čingiz
Performance/production
Actor M.A. Ul'janov in *I dol'še veka dlitsja den' (A Day Lasts
Longer than a Century)* at Teat'r im. Je. Vachtangova. USSR:
Moscow. 1980-1986. Lang.: Rus. 2327

Akademia Ruchu (Warsaw)
Performance/production
Artistic profile and main achievements of Akademia Ruchu. Poland:
Warsaw. 1973-1986. Lang.: Pol. 2037

Akademičeskij Teat'r Dramy im. A.S. Puškina (Leningrad)
Institutions
Actor and artistic director of the Puškin Theatre on the theatre
collective. USSR: Leningrad. 1980-1986. Lang.: Rus. 577
Performance/production
Biographical articles on actor V.V. Merkur'jev. Russia: Leningrad.
1904-1978. Lang.: Rus. 782

The career of actor-director Leonid Viv'en, focusing on his work at
Teat'r Dramy im. A.S. Puškina. USSR: Leningrad. 1887-1966. Lang.:
Rus. 903

**Akademičeskij Teat'r Opery i Baleta im. S.M. Kirova
(Leningrad)**
Administration
Principal choreographer of Kirov Theatre on problems of Soviet
ballet theatre. USSR. 1980-1986. Lang.: Rus. 1293
Performance/production
Creative development of ballerina Irina Kolpakova. USSR:
Leningrad. 1950-1985. Lang.: Rus. 1317
Mussorgskij's opera *Boris Godunov* at the Mariinskij Theatre. Russia:
St. Petersburg. 1874. Lang.: Eng. 3775

Akademietheater (Vienna)
Administration
Selling tickets at the Burgtheater and Akademietheater. Austria:
Vienna. 1986. Lang.: Ger. 1428
Institutions
Claus Peymann's concept for managing the Akademietheater and the
Burgtheater. Austria: Vienna. 1986. Lang.: Ger. 1532

Akalaitis, JoAnne
Institutions
Interview with members of Mabou Mines. USA: New York, NY.
1984. Lang.: Eng. 1607
Performance/production
Review of *Green Card* by JoAnne Akalaitis. USA: Los Angeles, CA.
Lang.: Eng. 2256
Life and technique of Franz Xaver Kroetz. USA: New York, NY.
Germany, West. 1984. Lang.: Eng. 2287

Akimov, Nikolaj Pavlovič
Performance/production
Recollections of director, designer and teacher Nikolaj Pavlovič
Akimov. USSR. 1901-1968. Lang.: Rus. 914

Aksënov, Vasilij
Plays/librettos/scripts
Analysis of *Grupa Laokoona (The Laocoön Group)* by Tadeusz
Różewicz and *Tsaplia (The Heron)* by Vasilij Aksënov. Poland.
USSR. 1961-1979. Lang.: Eng. 2738

Al G. Barnes Circus (USA)
Performance/production
Career of lion tamer Captain Terrell Jacobs. USA. 1903-1943. Lang.:
Eng. 3393

Alabama Shakespeare Festival (Montgomery, AL)
Performance spaces
Design and construction of Alabama Shakespeare Festival's theatres.
USA: Montgomery, AL. 1982-1986. Lang.: Eng. 634
History of the Alabama Shakespeare Festival and new theatre. USA:
Montgomery, AL. 1972-1986. Lang.: Eng. 1621

Alabama Theatre (Birmingham, AL)
Performance spaces
History and photographs of various theatres. USA: Birmingham, AL.
1890-1983. Lang.: Eng. 1622

Alarcón, Juan Ruiz de
Plays/librettos/scripts
Examples of playwrights whose work was poorly received by
theatrical audiences in Madrid. Spain: Madrid. 1609-1950. Lang.:
Spa. 2786

Alárìnjó
Research/historiography
Examination of Joel Adedeji's thesis on *alárìnjó*, a Yoruba theatrical
art form. Nigeria. 1826-1986. Lang.: Eng. 1186

Alarma i Tastas, Salvador
Design/technology
Introduction to facsimile of Oleguer Junyent's set design for *L'Auca
del senyor Esteve (Mr. Esteve's 'Auca')* by Santiago Rusiñol. Spain-
Catalonia: Barcelona. 1861-1984. Lang.: Cat. 1518

Alaska Repertory Theatre (Anchorage, AL)
Design/technology
Designers discuss regional productions of *Ain't Misbehavin'*. USA.
1984-1986. Lang.: Eng. 3591

Alba, Pep
Institutions
History of theatre in Valencia area focusing on Civil War period.
Spain: Valencia. 1817-1982. Lang.: Cat. 514

Albanese, Licia
Performance/production
Famous sopranos discuss their interpretations of Tosca. USA. 1935-
1986. Lang.: Eng. 3811

Albee, Edward
Performance/production
Hungarian performance of Edward Albee's play *Nem félünk a farkastól (Who's Afraid of Virginia Woolf?)*. Hungary. 1963-1984. Lang.: Hun. 1946
Director of original production discusses Edward Albee's *Who's Afraid of Virginia Woolf?*. USA: New York, NY. 1962. Lang.: Eng. 2303
Plays/librettos/scripts
Survey of the achievements of American theatre of the 1960s. USA. 1960-1979. Lang.: Eng. 987
God as image and symbol in Edward Albee's *Tiny Alice*. USA. 1965. Lang.: Eng. 2911
Analysis of the plays of Edward Albee. USA. 1960-1970. Lang.: Rus. 2914
Similarities of *Hughie* by Eugene O'Neill and *The Zoo Story* by Edward Albee. USA: New York, NY. 1941-1958. Lang.: Eng. 2919
Relation to other fields
Edward Albee on government censorship and freedom of artistic expression. Hungary: Budapest. 1986. 1096
Theory/criticism
Edward Albee's development of realistic setting for absurdist drama. USA. 1964-1980. Lang.: Eng. 3148

Albert Herring
Performance/production
Interview with singer Nancy Evans and writer Eric Crozier discussing their association with Benjamin Britten. USA: Columbia, MO. UK-England: London. 1940-1985. Lang.: Eng. 3820
Plays/librettos/scripts
Analysis of Benjamin Britten's opera *Albert Herring*. UK-England: London. 1947. Lang.: Eng. 3897

Albert, Caterina
SEE
Català, Víctor.

Alberti, Rafael
Institutions
Factors leading to the decline of Spanish theatre. Spain. 1975-1985. Lang.: Spa. 1582

Albertine en cinq temps (Albertine in Five Times)
Plays/librettos/scripts
Compares Michel Tremblay's *Albertine en cinq temps (Albertine in Five Times)* to Marcel Proust's *A la recherche du temps perdu (Remembrance of Things Past)*. Canada. 1984. 2436

Alcesti di Samuele (Alcesti of Samuel)
Plays/librettos/scripts
Correspondence of Alberto Savinio, author of *Alcesti di Samuele (Alcesti of Samuel)*. Italy. 1947-1950. Lang.: Ita. 2716

Alchemist, The
Plays/librettos/scripts
Use of group aggression in Ben Jonson's comedies. England. 1575-1600. Lang.: Eng. 2508
Theme of Puritanism in *The Alchemist* by Ben Jonson. England. 1610. Lang.: Eng. 2519
Violation of genre divisions in the plays of Ben Jonson. England: London. 1606-1610. Lang.: Eng. 2525
Reference materials
List of 37 productions of 23 Renaissance plays, with commentary. UK. USA. New Zealand. 1986. Lang.: Eng. 3000

Alderson, William
Performance/production
Reviews of *Lily Dale*, by Horton Foote, staged by William Alderson. USA: New York, NY. 1986. Lang.: Eng. 2204

Aldridge, Ira
Performance/production
Impact and influence of the tour by black American actor Ira Aldridge. UK-England: Manchester. 1827. Lang.: Eng. 2136

Aldwych Theatre (London)
Performance/production
Collection of newspaper reviews by London theatre critics. UK. 1986. Lang.: Eng. 2101
Collection of newspaper reviews by London theatre critics. UK-England. 1986. Lang.: Eng. 2111
Collection of newspaper reviews by London theatre critics. UK-England: London. 1986. Lang.: Eng. 2125

Aleandro, Norma
Plays/librettos/scripts
Interview with author and playwright Mario Vargas Llosa. Argentina. 1952-1986. Lang.: Spa. 2361

Aleksandrinskij Theatre
SEE
Akademičeskij Teat'r Dramy im. A. S. Puškina.

Alekseev, Konstantin Sergeevič
SEE
Stanislavskij, Konstantin Sergejevič.

Alexander Palace Theatre (London)
Performance spaces
Alexander Palace Theatre as pantomime stage. UK-England: London. 1875-1986. Lang.: Eng. 627

Alexander, Bill
Design/technology
Changes in the Royal Shakespeare Company under its current directors. UK-England: London. 1967-1986. Lang.: Eng. 325
Performance/production
Collection of newspaper reviews by London theatre critics. UK. 1986. Lang.: Eng. 2101

Alexander, Jon
Performance/production
Opera greats reflect on performance highlights. USA: Philadelphia, PA, New York, NY. 1985. Lang.: Eng. 3841

Alexander, Roberta
Performance/production
Black opera stars and companies. USA: Enid, OK, New York, NY. 1961-1985. Lang.: Eng. 3839

Alexander, Susana
Performance/production
Annual festival of Latin American plays at the Public Theatre. USA: New York, NY. 1985. Lang.: Eng. 2310

Alfieri, Vittorio
Plays/librettos/scripts
Conference on eighteenth-century theatre and culture. Europe. 1985. Lang.: Ita. 946

Alfreds, Mike
Performance/production
Collection of newspaper reviews by London theatre critics. UK. 1986. Lang.: Eng. 2101
Collection of newspaper reviews by London theatre critics. UK-England: London. 1986. Lang.: Eng. 2112
Director Mike Alfreds' interpretation of the plays of Čechov. UK-England: London. USSR. 1975-1986. Lang.: Eng. 2127
Survey of the season at the National Theatre. UK-England: London. 1986. Lang.: Eng. 2130

Alhambra Theatre (Bradford, UK)
Design/technology
Renovation of the Alhambra Theatre. UK-England: Bradford. 1980-1987. Lang.: Eng. 1521
Performance spaces
Modernization of the Alhambra Theatre. UK-England: Bradford. 1914-1986. Lang.: Eng. 623

Alice in Wonderland
Performance/production
Performances of *Alice Csodaországban (Alice in Wonderland)*, *A Két Veronai nemes (The Two Gentlemen of Verona)* and *Tobbsincs királyfi (No More Crown Prince)*. Hungary: Pécs, Budapest. 1985. Lang.: Hun. 1771

Alin, Margareta
Administration
Role of Skånska Teatron in the community. Sweden: Landskrona, Malmö. 1963-1986. Lang.: Swe. 62

Aliwiyaya, Dalang
Relation to other fields
Analyses of *Wayang cepak* play, *Gusti Sinuhan*, and its role in the Hindu religion. Indonesia. 1045-1986. Lang.: Eng. 3992

Alkestis
Performance/production
Robert Wilson's production of *Alcestis* at the American Repertory Theatre. USA: Cambridge, MA. 1986. 2306
Plays/librettos/scripts
Robert Wilson's adaptation of Euripides' *Alcestis*. USA: Cambridge, MA. 1979-1986. Lang.: Eng. 2939

All Fools
Reference materials
List of 37 productions of 23 Renaissance plays, with commentary. UK. USA. New Zealand. 1986. Lang.: Eng. 3000

Amateur theatre — cont'd

De dövas historia (The Story of the Deaf) staged by Ändockgruppen using both hearing and deaf amateurs. Sweden: Vänersborg. 1982-1986. Lang.: Swe.   799

Report from an amateur theatre festival at Västerbergs Folkhögskola. Sweden: Sandviken. 1986. Lang.: Swe.   800

Mats Ödeen's *Det ende raka (The Only Straight Thing)* performed by TURteaterns amatörteatergrupp. Sweden: Stockholm. 1979-1986. Lang.: Swe.   801

Interview with judge and amateur actor Bo Severin. Sweden: Malmö. 1985-1986. Lang.: Swe.   802

Sixth annual amateur theatre festivals. Sweden: Västerås. 1986. Lang.: Swe.   803

Development and production of Sir Percy Shelley's amateur production of *The Doom of St. Querec.* UK-England: London. 1876. Lang.: Eng.   809

People's theatre groups in the provinces of Shansi, Kansu and Liaoning. China, People's Republic of. 1938-1940. Lang.: Chi.   1692

Experimental training method used by Kaméleon Szinház Csoport. Hungary: Kurd. 1982-1985. Lang.: Hun.   1798

Survey of various Hungarian amateur theatres and workshops. Hungary. 1960-1980. Lang.: Hun.   1906

Interview with actor, director and dramaturg Imre Katona of the Gropius Társulat. Hungary: Budapest. 1961-1985. Lang.: Hun.   1945

Survey of summer theatre offerings. Sweden: Stockholm, Södertälje, Karlskrona. 1986. Lang.: Swe.   2089

The staging of an amateur performance of *Leka med elden (Playing With Fire).* Sweden: Hedemora. 1985-1986. Lang.: Swe.   2091

The cooperation between amateurs and professionals in Fria Proteatern's staging of Brecht's *Turandot.* Sweden: Stockholm. 1986. Lang.: Swe.   2095

Outsidern (The Outsider), a production by Mimensemblan, based on Hermann Hesse's *Steppenwolf.* Sweden: Stockholm. 1984-1986. Lang.: Swe.   3296

Plays/librettos/scripts
Innerst inne (At Heart) dramatizes political and economic dilemma. Sweden: Karlskoga. 1981-1986. Lang.: Swe.   2825

Reference materials
Alphabetically arranged profiles and history of professional and amateur theatres for children. USA. 1903-1985. Lang.: Eng.   1046

Amateur Theatre Festival (Sweden)
SEE
Amatörteaterns Riksförbund.

Amatörteaterns Riksförbund (Västerås)
Institutions
Interview with Einar Bergvin, founder of amateur theatre groups and publication. Sweden: Fagersta. 1918-1986. Lang.: Swe.   519

Performance/production
Sixth annual amateur theatre festivals. Sweden: Västerås. 1986. Lang.: Swe.   803

Amatørteatersellskab (Vordingborg)
Institutions
A report from the European drama camp for children. Denmark: Vordingborg. 1986. Lang.: Swe.   489

Amatörteaterstudio (Fagersta)
Institutions
Interview with Einar Bergvin, founder of amateur theatre groups and publication. Sweden: Fagersta. 1918-1986. Lang.: Swe.   519

Amazing Stories
Design/technology
Production design for Stephen Spielberg's series *Amazing Stories.* USA. 1986. Lang.: Eng.   3258

American Ballet Theatre (New York, NY)
Performance/production
Career of choreographer Kenneth MacMillan. Europe. USA. 1929-1986. Lang.: Eng.   1302

American Buffalo
Performance/production
Collection of newspaper reviews by London theatre critics. UK-England: London. 1986. Lang.: Eng.   2110

American Circus Corporation
Performance/production
History of John Robinson Circus. USA. 1925. Lang.: Eng.   3385

Details of the 1926 American Circus Corporation season. USA. Canada. 1926. Lang.: Eng.   3386

American Clock, The
Performance/production
Survey of the season at the National Theatre. UK-England: London. 1986. Lang.: Eng.   2130

American Conservatory Theatre (San Francisco, CA)
Performance/production
History of the American Conservatory Theatre. USA. Europe. 1950-1972. Lang.: Eng.   856

American Guild of Musical Artists (New York, NY)
Administration
History and achievements of the American Guild of Musical Artists during its fifty years of existence. USA. 1936-1986. Lang.: Eng. 3645

American National Theatre (Washington, DC)
Design/technology
A profile of lighting designer James Ingalls. USA. 1980-1986.   374

Institutions
Discussion of America's National Theatre and Peter Sellars, artistic director. USA: Washington, DC. 1984. Lang.: Eng.   568

Performance/production
Survey of productions at the Kennedy Center's National Theatre. USA: Washington, DC. 1986. Lang.: Eng.   2247

Robert Auletta's updated version of Sophocles' *Ajax.* USA: Washington, DC. 1986. Lang.: Eng.   2276

Plays/librettos/scripts
Playwright Robert Auletta on his adaptation of Sophocles'*Ajax.* USA: Washington, DC. 1986. Lang.: Eng.   2891

American Place Theatre (New York, NY)
Institutions
Interview with Julia Miles, director of the Women's Project, American Place Theatre. USA: New York, NY. 1978-1985. Lang.: Eng.   558

Performance/production
Recreation of a medicine show featuring 'Doc' Bloodgood, staged by American Place Theatre. USA. 1983. Lang.: Eng.   3375

American Playhouse (Public Broadcasting System)
Performance/production
Process and results of adapting plays from Off Broadway to TV. USA: New York, NY. 1980-1986. Lang.: Eng.   841

American Repertory Theatre (Cambridge, MA)
Administration
Fundraising strategy of American Repertory Theatre's development director. USA: Cambridge, MA. 1986. Lang.: Eng.   150

Design/technology
A profile of lighting designer James Ingalls. USA. 1980-1986.   374

Institutions
Eva LeGallienne on Civic Repertory and American Repertory Theatres. USA: New York, NY. 1933-1953. Lang.: Eng.   560

Performance/production
Interview with individuals involved in production of *Alcestis* by Euripides. USA: Cambridge, MA. 1986. Lang.: Eng.   2266

Conflict over artistic control in American Repertory Theatre's production of *Endgame* by Samuel Beckett. USA: Boston, MA. 1984. Lang.: Eng.   2296

Robert Wilson's production of *Alcestis* at the American Repertory Theatre. USA: Cambridge, MA. 1986.   2306

Plays/librettos/scripts
Robert Wilson's adaptation of Euripides' *Alcestis.* USA: Cambridge, MA. 1979-1986. Lang.: Eng.   2939

Amiel
Performance/production
A photographic essay of 42 soloists and groups performing mime or gestural theatre. 1986.   3290

Amour en pagaille, L' (Love in a Muddle)
Plays/librettos/scripts
Interview with playwright René Philombe on the educative function of theatre. Cameroon. 1930-1986. Lang.: Fre.   925

Amphion
Performance/production
Collaboration of choreographer Aurél Milloss and scene designer Giorgio de Chirico. Hungary. Italy: Milan, Rome. 1942-1945. Lang.: Hun.   1275

Amphitheatres/arenas
Performance spaces
Outdoor performance spaces surveyed through fragmentary records. England: Shrewsbury. 1445-1575. Lang.: Eng.   593

Ambiguous translations of ancient Greek theatrical documentation. Greece. Italy: Rome. 600-400 B.C. Lang.: Eng.   597

Amphitheatres/arenas — cont'd

A history of one of the earliest American circus buildings. USA: Philadelphia, PA. 1795-1799. Lang.: Eng. 3381

Reference materials

Guide to Catalan theatres. Spain-Catalonia. 1848-1986. Lang.: Cat. 1030

Amphitryon

Performance/production

Reviews of *Olympus On My Mind* based on *Amphitryon*, by Heinrich von Kleist, staged by Barry Harmon. USA: New York, NY. 1986. Lang.: Eng. 2218

Amusement parks

Design/technology

Lighting techniques and equipment used at theme park. USA: Baltimore, MD. 1971-1986. Lang.: Eng. 3315

Ancient Greek theatre

History of classical Chinese theatre. China. 600 B.C.-1985 A.D. Lang.: Eng. 4

SEE ALSO

Geographical-Chronological Index under Greece 600 BC-100 AD.

Audience

HaBimah Theatre production of *Troádes (The Trojan Women)* by Euripides. Israel: Tel-Aviv. 1982-1983. Lang.: Eng. 199

Performance spaces

Ambiguous translations of ancient Greek theatrical documentation. Greece. Italy: Rome. 600-400 B.C. Lang.: Eng. 597

Performance/production

Masked Greek and Roman plays presented in original Roman theatre. Switzerland: Basel. 1936-1974. Lang.: Ger. 2096

Plays/librettos/scripts

Cosmic themes in the works of Aeschylus. Greece. 472-458 B.C. Lang.: Fre. 2629

Interpretation of final scenes of Sophocles' *Philoctetes*. Greece. 409 B.C. Lang.: Heb. 2630

Chorus in ancient Greek comedy and drama. Greece. 450-425 B.C. Lang.: Ita. 2633

Moral and political crises reflected in the plays of Euripides. Greece: Athens. 438-408 B.C. Lang.: Fre. 2634

Aristophanes and his conception of comedy. Greece. 446-385 B.C. Lang.: Fre. 2635

Masked god as tragic subject in works of Aeschylus, Sophocles and Euripides. Greece. 499-401 B.C. Lang.: Fre. 2636

Relation to other fields

Influences of shamanism on Eastern and Western theatre. Greece. Asia. 500 B.C.-1986 A.D. Lang.: Ita. 1095

Theory/criticism

Influence of literary theory on Greek theatre studies. Greece. UK-England. Germany. Lang.: Afr. 1210

Social and political conditions of Greek society as sources for dramatic material. Greece: Athens. 450 B.C. Lang.: Eng. 3113

Influence of Greek theatre on Richard Wagner's music-drama. Germany. 1813-1883. Lang.: Eng. 3930

And a Day Lasts Longer than a Century

SEE

I dolše vèka dlitsia dèn.

And People All Around

Plays/librettos/scripts

Career of Marxist playwright George Sklar. USA: New York, NY. 1920-1967. Lang.: Eng. 985

And They Handcuffed the Flowers

SEE

Et ils passèrent les menottes aux fleurs.

Anderson, Bob

Performance spaces

Technical review of *She Stoops to Conquer* by Oliver Goldsmith performed at the New Victoria Theatre. UK-England: Newcastle-under-Lyme. 1980-1986. Lang.: Eng. 1618

Anderson, June

Performance/production

Profile of and interview with American soprano June Anderson. USA: New York, NY. 1955-1986. Lang.: Eng. 3793

Anderson, Laurie

Performance/production

Interview with individuals involved in production of *Alcestis* by Euripides. USA: Cambridge, MA. 1986. Lang.: Eng. 2266

Interview with performance artist Laurie Anderson. USA. 1986. Lang.: Eng. 3351

Theory/criticism

Semiotic analysis of Laurie Anderson's *United States*. USA. 1984. Lang.: Eng. 3462

Anderson, Maxwell

Plays/librettos/scripts

The power of music to transform the play into living theatre, examples from the work of Paul Green, Clifford Odets, and Maxwell Anderson. USA: New York, NY. 1936. Lang.: Eng. 3632

Ändockgruppen (Vänersborg)

Performance/production

De dövas historia (The Story of the Deaf) staged by Ändockgruppen using both hearing and deaf amateurs. Sweden: Vänersborg. 1982-1986. Lang.: Swe. 799

Andreini, Giovan Battista

Plays/librettos/scripts

Giovan Battista Andreini's problems in publishing *La Turca (The Turkish Woman)*. Italy. 1611. Lang.: Ita. 2692

Andrejèv, Leonid

Plays/librettos/scripts

Career of expressionist playwright Bertram Brooker. Canada: Toronto, ON. 1888-1949. Lang.: Eng. 2418

Andrews, George H.

Performance/production

Survey of productions at the Kennedy Center's National Theatre. USA: Washington, DC. 1986. Lang.: Eng. 2247

Androcles and the Lion

Theory/criticism

Shaw's use of devil's advocacy in his plays compared to deconstructionism. UK-England. 1900-1986. Lang.: Eng. 3135

Andrzejewski, Jerzy

Performance/production

Andrzej Marczewski directs Andrzejewski's *Popioł i Diament (Ashes and Diamonds)*, Teatr Rozmaitości. Poland: Warsaw. 1984. Lang.: Pol. 2013

Anelli, Angelo

Plays/librettos/scripts

Use of the tale of Patient Griselda in *Griselda* by Angelo Anelli and Niccolo Piccinni. Italy: Venice. Austria: Vienna. 1770-1800. Lang.: Eng. 3885

Anerca

Performance/production

Development of *Anerca* by Figures of Speech Theater. USA: Freeport, ME. 1985. Lang.: Eng. 3999

Ange couteau, L' (Angel Knife)

Basic theatrical documents

Playtext of Jean Sigrid's *L'ange couteau (Angel Knife)* in English translation. Belgium. 1980. Lang.: Eng. 1463

Angel City

Plays/librettos/scripts

Director George Ferencz and jazz musician Max Roach collaborate on music in trio of Sam Shepard plays. USA: New York, NY. 1984. Lang.: Eng. 2952

Relation to other fields

Comparison of works of playwright Sam Shepard and artist Robert Rauschenberg. USA. 1960-1980. Lang.: Eng. 3062

Angel Knife

SEE

Ange couteau, L'.

Anglin, Margaret

Performance/production

Greek tragedy on the New York stage. USA: New York, NY. 1854-1984. Lang.: Eng. 2301

Angry Tenants and the Subterranean Sun

SEE

Unquilinos de la ira y el sol subterráneo, Los.

Angura

Plays/librettos/scripts

Lives and works of major contemporary playwrights in Japan. Japan: Tokyo. 1900-1986. Lang.: Jap. 2719

Angyalföldi Nézőtér (Budapest)

Performance spaces

Reconstruction of the auditorium of the József Attila Culture Centre. Hungary: Budapest. 1986. Lang.: Hun. 606

Anhalt, Istvan

Performance/production

Discusses the opera *Winthrop*, by composer Istvan Anhalt. Canada: Toronto, ON. 1949-1985. Lang.: Eng. 3712

Anikulapo-Kuti, Fela
Performance/production
Imprisoned Nigerian pop musician Fela Anikulapo-Kuti. Nigeria: Lagos. 1960-1985. Lang.: Eng. 3468
Animal acts
Performance/production
Details of the 1926 American Circus Corporation season. USA. Canada. 1926. Lang.: Eng. 3386

Detailed history of the 1914 Hagenbeck Wallace Circus season. USA: St. Louis, MO, Youngstown, OH, Sturgis, MI. 1914. Lang.: Eng. 3388

The effect of disease on circus animals. USA. France. 1890-1985. Lang.: Eng. 3389

Photographs of circus life taken by Frederick Glasier. USA. 1896-1920. Lang.: Eng. 3392

Career of lion tamer Captain Terrell Jacobs. USA. 1903-1943. Lang.: Eng. 3393

Photographs of three circuses by Holton Rowes. USA: New York, NY. 1985. Lang.: Eng. 3395

The career of Jacob Driesbach, a famous circus animal trainer in the circus. USA. 1807-1878. Lang.: Eng. 3397

Excerpt from book by manager of Durov Theatre of Wild Animals. USSR: Moscow. 1986. Lang.: Rus. 3399
Animal Farm
Performance/production
Use of shadow puppets in an adaptation of Animal Farm. 4016
Anna Christie
Plays/librettos/scripts
David Belasco's influence on Eugene O'Neill. USA: New York, NY. 1908-1922. Lang.: Eng. 2927
Annie Get Your Gun
Performance/production
Survey of the Chichester Festival. UK-England: Chichester. 1986. Lang.: Eng. 2185

Interview with actress and rock star Suzi Quatro. UK-England: Chichester. 1986. Lang.: Eng. 3608

Reviews of musicals. UK-England: London. 1986. Lang.: Eng. 3610
Anouilh, Jean
Plays/librettos/scripts
Superficial and reductive use of classical myth in modern French theatre. France. 1935-1944. Lang.: Eng. 2550

Repetition and negativism in plays of Jean Anouilh and Eugene O'Neill. France. USA. 1922-1960. Lang.: Eng. 2578

Patriarchy in Le Voyageur sans bagage (Traveler Without Luggage) by Jean Anouilh. France. 1937. Lang.: Eng. 2586
ANTA
SEE
American National Theatre and Academy.
Anthropology
Design/technology
Survey of the use of masks in theatre. Asia. Europe. Africa. Lang.: Ita. 236

Native American masks and headgear in various types of performances. USA. 1800-1900. Lang.: Eng. 402
Institutions
French-language theatre and the Acadian tradition. Canada. 1969-1986. Lang.: Eng. 1544
Performance/production
Reconstruction of the life of Italian actors and acting companies with a vocabulary of their jargon. Italy. 1885-1940. Lang.: Ita. 753

Feminist criticism of theatre anthropology conference on women's roles. USA. Denmark. 1985. Lang.: Eng. 845

Dance in the Malaysian culture. Malaysia. 1950-1984. Lang.: Eng. 1333

Costumes, satiric dances and processions of the Ijebu Yoruba masquerades. Western Africa. Lang.: Eng. 1372

Costumes, dance steps, and music in initiation rites of Yoruba priesthood. Western Africa. Lang.: Eng. 1373

Origins of malipenga, a form of dance-drama combining Western and African elements. Zambia: Malawi. 1914-1985. Lang.: Eng. 1374

Spalding Gray's memories of the development and tour of Richard Schechner's Commune. USA. France. Poland. 1970. Lang.: Eng. 2270

Maskers and masquerades of We tribal rituals. Ivory Coast. Lang.: Eng. 3341

Types of costumes, dances, and songs of Dodo masquerades during Ramadan. Upper Volta: Ouagadougou. Lang.: Eng. 3428

Imprisoned Nigerian pop musician Fela Anikulapo-Kuti. Nigeria: Lagos. 1960-1985. Lang.: Eng. 3468

Shadow puppetry as a way of passing on Balinese culture. Bali. 1976-1985. Lang.: Eng. 4017
Plays/librettos/scripts
The plays of Antonine Maillet and the revival of Acadian theatre. Canada. 1971-1979. Lang.: Eng. 2423

Umiak by Théâtre de la Marmaille of Toronto, based on Inuit tradition. Canada. 1982-1983. Lang.: Eng. 2434

Essays on Shakespeare's All's Well that Ends Well. England. 1603. Lang.: Eng, Fre. 2485

Analysis of La Tragédie du roi Christophe (The Tragedy of King Christopher) by Aimé Césaire. Haiti. Africa. Martinique. 1939. Lang.: Fre. 2637

Theatrical renderings of the experiences of French travelers in Italy and vice-versa. Italy. France. 1700-1800. Lang.: Ita. 2686

Ritual function of The Slave Ship by LeRoi Jones (Amiri Baraka) and Quinta Temporada (Fifth Season) by Luis Valdez. USA. 1965-1967. Lang.: Eng. 2906

Conceptions of the South Sea islands in works of Murnau, Artaud and Spies. Europe. USA. Indonesia. 1930. Lang.: Ita. 3231
Reference materials
Description of popular entertainments, both sacred and secular. Spain-Catalonia. 1947-1986. Lang.: Cat. 3355
Relation to other fields
Western directors and third-world theatre. 1900-1986. Lang.: Ita. 1053

Articles on anthropology of theatre. Lang.: Ita. 1056

Translation of Bodywatching by Desmond Morris. Lang.: Ita. 1057

Argument that theatre should return to art's roots in ritual and ceremony. 1986. Lang.: Eng. 1059

Translation of From Ritual to Theatre by Victor Turner. Lang.: Ita. 1060

Difficulties of distinction between 'high' and 'popular' culture. Australia. 1860-1930. Lang.: Eng. 1063

Kwakiutl Homatsa ceremony as drama. Canada. 1890-1900. Lang.: Eng. 1070

Influences of shamanism on Eastern and Western theatre. Greece. Asia. 500 B.C.-1986 A.D. Lang.: Ita. 1095

Enthnography of a Hungarian village. Hungary: Zsámbok. 1930-1985. Lang.: Hun. 1099

Origins of theatre in shamanistic ritual. Korea. 1900-1986. Lang.: Ita. 1110

Views of designer and critic Franciszek Siedlecki. Poland. 1909-1934. Lang.: Pol. 1116

Actor-director Juliusz Osterwa's ideas about theatre's role in society. Poland. 1918-1947. Lang.: Pol. 1118

Actor-director Juliusz Osterwa's views of historical processes. Poland. 1940-1947. Lang.: Pol. 1122

Anthropological approach to performance and language. USA. Japan. 1982. Lang.: Eng. 1140

Ritual, rhythmic activity: their effects upon brain systems. USA. 1986. Lang.: Eng. 1167

Theatrical nature of shamanistic rituals. Zambia. 1985. Lang.: Eng. 1183

Translation of Les métamorphoses de la fête en Provence de 1750 à 1820 (Paris 1976) by Michel Vovelle. France. 1750-1820. Lang.: Ita. 3358

Study of agriculture-related songs and dances. Japan: Tokyo. 1986. Lang.: Jap. 3360

Popular theatrical forms in the Basque country. Spain. France. 674-1963. Lang.: Spa. 3361

Reflections of social and historical conditions in the carnival celebration of a small Emilian town. Italy: Guastalla. 1857-1895. Lang.: Ita. 3377

Christian and pre-Christian elements of Corpus Christi celebration. Spain-Catalonia: Berga. 1264-1986. Lang.: Cat. 3432

Analysis of Northern Sung theatrical artifacts. 1032-1126. Lang.: Chi. 3546

Anthropology — cont'd

Research/historiography
Examination of Joel Adedeji's thesis on *alárìnjó*, a Yoruba theatrical art form. Nigeria. 1826-1986. Lang.: Eng. 1186

Ritual origins of the classical dance drama of Cambodia. Cambodia. 4 B.C.-1986 A.D. Lang.: Eng. 1336

Results of studies of ethnic dance with transcription system. South Africa, Republic of. 1980-1985. Lang.: Afr. 1338

Theory/criticism
Influences on the development of European and Japanese theatre. Japan. Europe. 500 B.C.-1986 A.D. Lang.: Ita. 1213

Eastern and western myths explaining the origin of theatre. Europe. Asia. 1986. Lang.: Ita. 3098

Antigone
Performance/production
Interview with choreographer Mechthild Grossman. Germany, West. 1984-1985. Lang.: Eng. 1273

Nō and *kyōgen* influences on interpretation of *Antigone*. USA: San Francisco, CA. 1984. 1978-1984. 1416

Djrector Andrzej Wajda's work, accessibility to Polish audiences. Poland: Warsaw. 1926-1986. Lang.: Swe. 2027

Andrzej Wajda directs Sophocles' *Antigone*, Stary Teatr. Poland: Cracow. 1984. Lang.: Pol. 2058

Plays/librettos/scripts
Semiotic analysis of a production of *Antigone* by Sophocles. Australia: Perth, W.A. 1986. Lang.: Eng. 923

Superficial and reductive use of classical myth in modern French theatre. France. 1935-1944. Lang.: Eng. 2550

Repetition and negativism in plays of Jean Anouilh and Eugene O'Neill. France. USA. 1922-1960. Lang.: Eng. 2578

Antoine, André
Performance/production
The Independent Theatre of Jacob Thomas Grein, established in imitation of André Antoine's Théâtre Libre. UK-England: London. 1891. Lang.: Rus. 818

Antoine, Mireille
Performance/production
Directors discuss staging of plays by Paul Claudel. France. Belgium. 1985. Lang.: Fre. 1723

Antonelli, Luigi
Plays/librettos/scripts
Luigi Pirandello's relationship with author Gabriele D'Annunzio and reviewer Luigi Antonelli. Italy. 1900-1936. Lang.: Ita. 2698

Antonio's Revenge
Reference materials
List of 37 productions of 23 Renaissance plays, with commentary. UK. USA. New Zealand. 1986. Lang.: Eng. 3000

Antony and Cleopatra
Performance/production
The portrayal of Cleopatra by various actresses. England. 1813-1890. Lang.: Eng. 1699

Reconstruction of a number of Shakespeare plays staged and performed by Herbert Beerbohm Tree. UK-England: London. 1887-1917. Lang.: Eng. 2155

Plays/librettos/scripts
Comparison of Shakespeare's *Antony and Cleopatra* and Ibsen's *Rosmersholm*. England. Norway. 1607-1885. Lang.: Eng. 2479

Antony, Béraud
Plays/librettos/scripts
Treatment of the Frankenstein myth in three gothic melodramas. UK-England. France. 1823-1826. Lang.: Eng. 2847

Antúnz, Marcel.lí
Performance/production
Detailed description of the performance titled *Accions (Actions)* by La Fura dels Baus. Spain-Catalonia. 1979-1984. Lang.: Cat. 3445

Apareceua Margarida (Miss Margarida's Way)
Plays/librettos/scripts
Language as an instrument of tyranny in Athayde's *Apareceua Margarida (Miss Margarida's Way)*. Brazil. 1808-1973. Lang.: Eng. 2405

Apfelbaum, Der (Vienna)
Institutions
On new activities of groups or persons producing theatre for children. Austria: Vienna. 1986. Lang.: Ger. 454

Appia, Adolphe
Design/technology
Adolphe Appia's influence on Lee Simonson. USA. 1900-1950. Lang.: Eng. 416

Adolphe Appia's use of some innovative lighting techniques of Mariano Fortuny. France. 1903. Lang.: Ita. 1514

Adolphe Appia's theory of Wagner's *Ring* and present-day evaluation. Switzerland: Geneva. 1862-1928. Lang.: Ger. 3653

Interview with lighting designer Gil Wechsler of the Metropolitan Opera. USA: New York, NY. 1883-1986. Lang.: Eng. 3654

Performance/production
Volume 2 of complete works of Adolphe Appia. Switzerland. 1895-1905. Lang.: Fre, Ger. 804

Technical innovation, scenography and cabaret in relation to political and social conditions. Czechoslovakia. 1781-1986. Lang.: Eng. 1697

Apple Cart, The
Performance/production
Collection of newspaper reviews by London theatre critics. UK. 1986. Lang.: Eng. 2102

Collection of newspaper reviews by London theatre critics. UK-England: London. 1986. Lang.: Eng. 2119

Apple in the Eye, The
Plays/librettos/scripts
Review of five published plays by Margaret Hollingsworth. Canada. Lang.: Eng. 2440

Applebaum, Louis
Institutions
Significance of Applebaum-Hébert report on Canadian cultural policy. Canada. 1982-1983. Lang.: Eng. 465

History of music performances, mainly opera, at the Stratford Festival. Canada: Stratford, ON. 1951-1985. Lang.: Eng. 3671

Apprenticeship
Training
A guide to internship training programs. USA. 1986. 1259

Arany János Szinház (Budapest)
Performance/production
Performances of *Alice Csodaországban (Alice in Wonderland)*, *A Két Veronai nemes (The Two Gentlemen of Verona)* and *Tobbsincs királyfi (No More Crown Prince)*. Hungary: Pécs, Budapest. 1985. Lang.: Hun. 1771

Stage adaptation of Erich Kästner's novel *Emil und die Detektive (Emil and the Detectives)* directed by István Keleti. Hungary: Budapest. 1986. Lang.: Hun. 1807

Arany, János
Plays/librettos/scripts
Plot, structure and national character of *Bánk Bán* by József Katona. Hungary. Lang.: Hun. 2655

Arbuzov, Aleksej Nikolajevič
Performance/production
Collection of newspaper reviews by London theatre critics. UK-England: London. 1986. Lang.: Eng. 2116

Vinotavye (The Guilty) at Teat'r im. Mossovèta. USSR: Moscow. 1986. Lang.: Rus. 2339

Plays/librettos/scripts
Replies to questionnaire by five Soviet playwrights. USSR. Bulgaria. 1986. Lang.: Rus. 2958

Archbishop's Ceiling, The
Performance/production
Royal Shakespeare Company performances at the Barbican Theatre. UK-England: London. 1986. Lang.: Eng. 2152

Archer, William
Performance/production
Letters to and from Harley Granville-Barker. UK-England. 1877-1946. Lang.: Eng. 807

Changes in English life reflected in 1883 theatre season. UK-England: London. 1883. Lang.: Eng. 810

Archipova, I.
Performance/production
Singer I. Archipova on tasks of Soviet opera. USSR. 1980-1986. Lang.: Rus. 3846

Architecture
Conference on aspects of theatre and opera in Emilia. Italy: Emilia. 1700-1799. Lang.: Ita. 7

Administration
Advice on working with general contractors in theatre. USA. 1986. Lang.: Eng. 161

Design/technology
Description of portable cruciform theatre. Belgium. 1986. Lang.: Eng. 240

Theatre consultant S. Leonard Auerbach's technical specifications for Expo '86. Canada: Vancouver, BC. 1986. Lang.: Eng. 243

SUBJECT INDEX

Architecture — cont'd

Works by and about designers Jacopo Fabris and Citoyen Boullet. Denmark: Copenhagen. France: Paris. 1760-1801. Lang.: Eng.   256

Translation of eighteenth-century treatise on stage machinery and construction. France: Paris. 1760-1801. Lang.: Eng.   264

Commemoration of theatre expert Paul Jähnichen. Germany, East: Berlin, East. 1935-1986. Lang.: Hun.   271

Theatre workshops of the Budapest Central Scene Shop Project. Hungary: Budapest. 1953-1986. Lang.: Hun.   290

The renovation and modernization of the theatre production building. Hungary: Budapest. 1976. Lang.: Hun.   291

Description of plans for new central theatre scene shops and storage areas. Hungary: Budapest. 1980. Lang.: Hun.   292

Description of planned renovation for scene shop and production building. Hungary: Budapest. 1984. Lang.: Hun.   295

Career of designer Mariano Fortuny. Italy. 1871-1949. Lang.: Ita.   300

Contemporary theatre architecture. USA. 1976-1987. Lang.: Eng.   342

Sound reduction door added to shop at Seattle Repertory Theatre. USA: Seattle, WA. 1986. Lang.: Eng.   381

Overhaul of The World Theatre as a radio broadcasting facility. USA: St. Paul, MN. 1982-1986. Lang.: Eng.   387

Institutions

Role of the Swedish Society for Theatre Technicians in recent theatre architecture. Sweden. 1976-1986. Lang.: Swe.   523

Illustrated discussion of the opening of the Théâtre National de l'Opéra. France: Paris. 1875. Lang.: Fre.   3674

Performance spaces

Description of Lyudmila Zhivkova, the palace of culture. Bulgaria: Sofia. 1983-1985. Lang.: Swe.   585

Planning of 18 performance venues for Expo 86. Canada: Vancouver, BC. 1986. Lang.: Eng.   589

Design and construction of Grand Cayman's National Theatre. Cayman Islands. UK-England. 1986. Lang.: Eng.   590

An architect discusses theory of theatre construction. Europe. North America. 1920-1985. Lang.: Hun.   594

History of the theatres of Nîmes. France: Nîmes. 1739-1985. Lang.: Fre.   595

Development of theatres, stages and the Italianate proscenium arch theatre. France. Italy. 500 B.C.-1726 A.D. Lang.: Eng, Fre.   596

Design of concert hall in part of a major railway station. Hungary: Budapest. 1985-1986. Lang.: Hun.   598

Renovation of the Szeged National Theatre. Hungary: Szeged. 1978-1986. Lang.: Hun.   599

Structural design problems and their solutions at the Szeged National Theatre in Hungary. Hungary: Szeged. 1977-1986. Lang.: Hun.   602

Reconstruction of the Szeged National Theatre. Hungary: Szeged. 1948-1980. Lang.: Hun.   604

Design and construction of rebuilt Szeged National Theatre. Hungary: Szeged. 1978-1986. Lang.: Hun.   605

Design of the Szeged National Theatre renovation. Hungary: Szeged. 1981-1986. Lang.: Hun.   608

Description of theatre buildings designed by architect Czesław Przybylski. Poland: Warsaw, Vilna, Kalisz. 1880-1985. Lang.: Pol.   611

Two newly constructed theatres in northern Sweden. Sweden. 1986-1987. Lang.: Swe.   619

Technical description of new small stage of Kungliga Dramatiska Teatern. Sweden: Stockholm. 1986. Lang.: Swe.   620

Technical design features of New Victoria Theatre. UK-England: Stoke-on-Trent. 1980-1986. Lang.: Eng.   624

Analysis of trends in theatre design. UK-England. 1986. Lang.: Eng.   628

Architect Robert Morgan's design for Broadway's Marquis Theatre. USA: New York, NY. 1986. Lang.: Eng.   633

Design and construction of Alabama Shakespeare Festival's theatres. USA: Montgomery, AL. 1982-1986. Lang.: Eng.   634

Reflections on theatre architecture by consultant S. Leonard Auerbach. USA. 1986. Lang.: Eng.   635

Architectural design of San Diego Repertory's new theatre. USA: San Diego, CA. 1986. Lang.: Eng.   637

Architectural design for new performance spaces for Theatre for the New City and the Vineyard Theatre. USA: New York, NY. 1986. Lang.: Eng.   639

Role of theatre consultant in bidding. USA. 1986. Lang.: Eng.   643

Descriptions of newly constructed Off Broadway theatres. USA: New York, NY. 1984. Lang.: Eng.   644

Estimating and managing the cost of building a theatre. USA. 1986. Lang.: Eng.   645

Problems of designing and building theatrical buildings. USSR. 1980-1986. Lang.: Rus.   646

Social role of theatre and theatrical space. USSR. Lang.: Rus.   647

Problematic dimensions of the Sydney Opera House's Drama Theatre. Australia: Sydney, N.S.W. 1980-1986. Lang.: Eng.   1612

Reconstructing a theatrical organization at Saint James Palace (London). England: London. 1600-1986. Lang.: Eng.   1615

Overview of the hall in which Shakespeare's *Twelfth Night* was performed. England: London. 1602. Lang.: Eng.   1616

Outlines the technical and architectural features of the Swan Theatre at Stratford-upon-Avon. UK-England: Stratford. Lang.: Eng.   1617

Historical Midwestern theatres. USA: Chicago, IL, Milwaukee, WI. 1889-1986. Lang.: Eng.   1623

New façades on 42 New York theatres. USA: New York, NY. 1861-1986. Lang.: Eng.   1626

History of the Eastman Theatre. USA: Rochester, NY. 1922-1986. Lang.: Eng.   3222

A history of one of the earliest American circus buildings. USA: Philadelphia, PA. 1795-1799. Lang.: Eng.   3381

History of the Bushwick Theatre. USA: New York, NY. 1911-1986. Lang.: Eng.   3465

Reference materials

Catalogue of an exhibit on the Carlo Felice Theatre, destroyed in World War II, and its proposed reconstruction. Italy: Genoa. 1600-1985. Lang.: Ita.   1024

Guide to Catalan theatres. Spain-Catalonia. 1848-1986. Lang.: Cat.   1030

Archives/libraries
Institutions

Puppetry documentation at Institute of Professional Puppetry Arts. USA: Waterford, CT. 1986. Lang.: Eng.   3959

Reference materials

Description of Australian archives relating to theatre and film. Australia. 1870-1969. Lang.: Eng.   1000

Description of the theatrical library of writer James Smith. Australia: Melbourne. 1866. Lang.: Eng.   1002

Betzalel London's archive deposited at Hebrew University. Israel: Jerusalem. 1925-1971. Lang.: Heb.   1014

Speech given by Benjamin Zemach on the deposition of Nachum Zemach's archive at Hebrew University. Israel: Jerusalem. 1986. Lang.: Heb.   1019

Wealth of theatre memorabilia in British museums. UK-England: London. 1986. Lang.: Eng.   1036

Description of a collection of unpublished Australian plays. Australia. 1920-1955. Lang.: Eng.   2977

Training

Discussion of archival material relating to translation and U.S. publication of books by Stanislavskij. USA. USSR. 1928-1986. Lang.: Eng.   3160

Arden of Faversham
Plays/librettos/scripts

Rise of English landowners reflected in *Arden of Faversham*. England. 1536-1592. Lang.: Eng.   943

Liberated female characters in the plays of George Lillo. England. 1730-1759. Lang.: Eng.   2477

Arden, John
Plays/librettos/scripts

The place of *The Island of the Mighty* in the John Arden canon. Ireland. UK. 1950-1972. Lang.: Eng.   2666

Arditi, Luigi
Performance/production

Details of Luigi Arditi's U.S. and Canada tour with the New York Opera Company. USA. Canada: Montreal, PQ, Toronto, ON. 1853-1854. Lang.: Eng.   3819

Ardoin, John
    Plays/librettos/scripts
    Correspondence and personal contact with Sir Michael Tippett. USA:
    Dallas, TX. 1965-1985. Lang.: Eng.   3900

Are You Ready Comrade?
    Basic theatrical documents
    Act I, Scene 3 of *Are You Ready Comrade?* by Betty Roland.
    Australia. 1938. Lang.: Eng.   1460

Are You Sitting Comfortably
    Performance/production
    Collection of newspaper reviews by London theatre critics. UK.
    1986. Lang.: Eng.   2099

Arena Stage (Washington, DC)
    Administration
    Zelda Fichandler discusses artistic risk and funding. USA:
    Washington, DC. 1986. Lang.: Eng.   101

    Design/technology
    Sound designers at regional theatres evaluate new equipment. USA.
    1986.   409

    Performance/production
    Interview with Elisabeth Bergner and Jane Alexander on their
    portrayals of Joan of Arc. Germany, West: Berlin, West. UK-
    England: Malvern. USA: Washington, DC. Lang.: Eng.   1766

Aretino, Pietro
    Performance/production
    Reconstruction of *Comedia Tinellaria* by Torres Naharro. Italy:
    Rome, Venice. 1508-1537. Lang.: Spa.   1986

Argenta Manhattan Workshop (New York, NY)
    Performance/production
    Profile of theatre companies featured in Festival Latino de Nueva
    York. USA: New York, NY. 1984. Lang.: Eng.   2197

Ariès, Philippe
    Relation to other fields
    Style in children's theatre in light of theories of Philippe Ariès.
    USA. UK. France. 1600-1980. Lang.: Eng.   1162

Aristophanes
    Plays/librettos/scripts
    Chorus in ancient Greek comedy and drama. Greece. 450-425 B.C.
    Lang.: Ita.   2633

    Aristophanes and his conception of comedy. Greece. 446-385 B.C.
    Lang.: Fre.   2635

    Influence of Aristophanes and Čechov on playwright Simon Gray.
    UK-England. 1986. Lang.: Eng.   2874

Aristoteles
    Performance/production
    Physical nature of acting. USA. 1986. Lang.: Eng.   825

    Plays/librettos/scripts
    Applying Brecht's dramatic principles to the plays of Euripides.
    Germany, East. Greece. 450 B.C.-1956 A.D.   2614

    Theory/criticism
    Influence of Western theory on Chinese drama of Gu Zhongyi.
    China. 1920-1963. Lang.: Chi.   1202

Aristotle
    SEE
    Aristoteles.

Ark Theatre (New York, NY)
    Administration
    Creation and role of board of directors in nonprofit theatre. USA:
    New York, NY. 1986. Lang.: Eng.   104

    Role of the marketing director in nonprofit theatre. USA: New
    York, NY. 1986. Lang.: Eng.   140

    Performance/production
    Puppeteer Julie Taymor adapts *Die vertauschten Köpfe (The
    Transposed Heads)* by Thomas Mann for performance at the Ark
    Theatre. USA: New York, NY. 1984. Lang.: Eng.   3977

Arkansas Opera Theatre (Little Rock, AR)
    Performance/production
    Review of Libby Larsen's opera *Clair de Lune*. USA: Little Rock,
    AR. 1985. Lang.: Eng.   3803

Arkin, Alan
    Performance/production
    Reviews of *Room Service*, by John Murray and Allan Boretz, staged
    by Alan Arkin. USA: New York, NY. 1986. Lang.: Eng.   2242

Arms and the Man
    Plays/librettos/scripts
    Argument for coherence of *Arms and the Man* by George Bernard
    Shaw. UK-England: London. 1894. Lang.: Eng.   2863

    Textual history of the final line of *Arms and the Man* by George
    Bernard Shaw. UK-England: London. 1894-1982. Lang.: Eng.   2873

Armstrong, Pat
    Institutions
    The first decade of White Rock Summer Theatre in British
    Columbia. Canada: White Rock, BC. 1976-1985. Lang.: Eng.   1560

Arnau, Josep Maria
    Plays/librettos/scripts
    History of Catalan literature, including playwrights. Spain-Catalonia.
    France. 1800-1926. Lang.: Cat.   973

Arnott, Peter D.
    Performance spaces
    Ambiguous translations of ancient Greek theatrical documentation.
    Greece. Italy: Rome. 600-400 B.C. Lang.: Eng.   597

Árny, Az (Ghost, The)
    Performance/production
    Reviews of *Margit kisasszony (Miss Margit)*, *Az Ibolya (The Violet)*,
    Az Árny (The Ghost) and *Róza néni (Aunt Rosa)*. Hungary:
    Budapest. 1985-1986. Lang.: Hun.   1916

Aronson, Boris
    Design/technology
    Designers discuss regional productions of *Fiddler on the Roof*. USA.
    1984-1986. Lang.: Eng.   3595

Arrabal, Fernando
    Plays/librettos/scripts
    Politics and aesthetics in three plays of Fernando Arrabal. Spain.
    France. Lang.: Fre.   2801

Arro, V.
    Plays/librettos/scripts
    Replies to questionnaire by five Soviet playwrights. USSR. Bulgaria.
    1986. Lang.: Rus.   2958

Ars Electronica (Linz)
    Institutions
    Productions in 1986 of Ars Electronica. Austria: Linz. 1979-1986.
    Lang.: Ger.   3321

Arsenic and Old Lace
    Performance/production
    Reviews of *Arsenic and Old Lace*, by Joseph Kesselring, staged by
    Brian Murray. USA: New York, NY. 1986. Lang.: Eng.   2215

Art of War, The
    Plays/librettos/scripts
    Development of playwright George F. Walker. Canada: Toronto,
    ON. 1970-1984. Lang.: Eng.   931

Art Theatre (Budapest)
    SEE
    Müvész Szinház.

Art Theatre (Moscow)
    SEE
    Moskovskij Chudožestvénnyj Akademičeskij Teat'r.

Artaud, Antonin
    Performance/production
    Antonin Artaud's conception of gesture and movement. North
    America. 1938-1986. Lang.: Eng.   768

    Reminiscences of actor-director Roger Blin. France. 1930-1983.
    Lang.: Fre.   1726

    Plays/librettos/scripts
    Use of violent language in the plays of Griselda Gambaro.
    Argentina. 1950-1980. Lang.: Eng.   2362

    Structuralist analysis of works of Albert Camus, Antonin Artaud and
    Gaston Bachelard. France. Lang.: Fre.   2575

    Personal memoir of playwright Antonin Artaud. France. 1946-1967.
    Lang.: Fre.   2584

    Artaud's concept of theatre of cruelty in Francisco Nieva's *Tórtolas,
    crepúscula y ...telón (Turtledoves, Twilight and ...Curtain)*. Spain.
    1953. Lang.: Spa.   2790

    Conceptions of the South Sea islands in works of Murnau, Artaud
    and Spies. Europe. USA. Indonesia. 1930. Lang.: Ita.   3231

    Relation to other fields
    Western directors and third-world theatre. 1900-1986. Lang.: Ita.
        1053

    Theory/criticism
    Eastern influences on the work of Antonin Artaud. France. 1846-
    1949. Lang.: Rus.   1208

    Selections from Antonin Artaud's *The Theatre and Its Double*.
    France. 1896-1949. Lang.: Chi.   3099

    Selections from Jerzy Grotowski's *Towards a Poor Theatre*. Poland.
    1933-1982. Lang.: Chi.   3126

Artaud, Antonin — cont'd

Analysis of the essentials of art, especially in theatre. USA. 1960-1986. Lang.: Eng. 3142

Arte Nuevo
Plays/librettos/scripts
Conservative and reactionary nature of the Spanish *Comedia*. Spain. 1600-1700. Lang.: Eng. 2782

Arthur, Julia
Performance/production
Career of actress, manager and director Julia Arthur. Canada. UK-England. USA. 1869-1950. Lang.: Eng. 1675

Artist Descending a Staircase
Relation to other fields
Influence of Marcel Duchamp's work on Tom Stoppard's radio play, *Artist Descending a Staircase*. UK-England. 1913-1972. Lang.: Eng. 3059

Artists Call (New York, NY)
Relation to other fields
The role of culture in Nicaragua since the revolution. Nicaragua. 1983. Lang.: Eng. 1115

Arts Club House Theatre (Vancouver, BC)
Administration
Theatrical activity on various Vancouver stages. Canada: Vancouver, BC. 1986. Lang.: Heb. 1429

Arts Council (Canada)
SEE
Canada Council.

Arts Income Management System (AIMS)
Administration
Computer software package designed for arts administration. USA: New York, NY. 1984. Lang.: Eng. 180

Arts Theatre (Cambridge, UK)
Performance/production
Collection of newspaper reviews by London theatre critics. UK. 1986. Lang.: Eng. 2099
Collection of newspaper reviews by London theatre critics. UK. 1986. Lang.: Eng. 2102
Collection of newspaper reviews by London theatre critics. UK-England. 1986. Lang.: Eng. 2114
Collection of newspaper reviews by London theatre critics. UK-England: London. 1986. Lang.: Eng. 2121

Arts Theatre (London)
Performance/production
Collection of newspaper reviews by London theatre critics. UK: London. 1986. Lang.: Eng. 2100
Collection of newspaper reviews by London theatre critics. UK-England: London. 1986. Lang.: Eng. 2109

ArtsConnection (New York, NY)
Relation to other fields
Problems of artists working in schools. USA: New York, NY. 1983. Lang.: Eng. 1161

Arŭp Ratan (Formless Jewel)
Plays/librettos/scripts
Translations of three plays by Rabindranath Tagore, with critical commentary. India. 1861-1941. Lang.: Eng. 2662

Arús, Jordi
Performance/production
Detailed description of the performance titled *Accions (Actions)* by La Fura dels Baus. Spain-Catalonia. 1979-1984. Lang.: Cat. 3445

As Is
Performance/production
Review of *As Is*, a play about AIDS by William Hoffman. USA: New York, NY. 1985. Lang.: Eng. 2198

Plays/librettos/scripts
Analysis of *As Is* by William Hoffman and *The Dolly* by Robert Locke. Canada: Toronto, ON. 1985. Lang.: Eng. 2419
Progress in audience perception of gay characters in plays. USA. 1933-1985. Lang.: Eng. 2909

As You Like It
Basic theatrical documents
Videotape of Shakespeare's *As You Like It* with study guide and edition of the play. Canada: Stratford, ON. 1983. Lang.: Eng. 219
New German translation of Shakespeare's *As You Like It*. Germany, East. 1986. Lang.: Ger. 1483

Institutions
Efforts of New York Shakespeare Festival to develop an audience for Shakespearean drama. USA: New York, NY. 1986. Lang.: Eng. 1605

Performance/production
John Hirsch's artistic career at the Stratford Festival Theatre. Canada: Stratford, ON. 1981-1985. Lang.: Eng. 1683
Ahogy tetszik (As You Like It) by William Shakespeare directed by István Szőke. Hungary: Miskolc. 1986. Lang.: Hun. 1866
István Szőke, directs *Ahogy tetszik (As You Like It)* by Shakespeare. Hungary: Miskolc. 1986. Lang.: Hun. 1873
Collection of newspaper reviews by London theatre critics. UK. 1986. Lang.: Eng. 2101
Collection of newspaper reviews by London theatre critics. UK-England. 1986. Lang.: Eng. 2111
Collection of newspaper reviews by London theatre critics. UK-England: London. 1986. Lang.: Eng. 2112
Royal Shakespeare Company performances at the Barbican Theatre. UK-England: London. 1986. Lang.: Eng. 2152
Shakespearean productions by the National Theatre, Royal Shakespeare Company and Orange Tree Theatre. UK-England: Stratford, London. 1984-1985. Lang.: Eng. 2183

Plays/librettos/scripts
Analysis, *As You Like It* II:i by William Shakespeare. England. 1598. Lang.: Eng. 2474
Possible influence of Christopher Marlowe's plays upon those of William Shakespeare. England. 1580-1620. Lang.: Eng. 2478
Role of Rosalind in Shakespeare's *As You Like It*. England. 1600-1986. Lang.: Eng. 2491
Study of realism vs metadrama. Europe. 429 B.C.-1978 A.D. Lang.: Eng. 2540

Ascend as the Sun
Relation to other fields
Philosophical context of the plays of Herman Voaden. Canada: Toronto, ON. 1929-1943. Lang.: Eng. 3170

Ascher, Tamás
Performance/production
Tamás Ascher directs *Ördögök (The Devils)*, an adaptation of *Besy (The Possessed)* by Dostojévskij. Hungary: Budapest. 1986. Lang.: Hun. 1778
Čechov's *Három nővér (Three Sisters)* directed by Tamás Ascher. Hungary: Budapest. 1985. Lang.: Hun. 1814
Two productions of Čechov's *Három Nővér (Three Sisters)*. Hungary: Zalaegerszeg, Budapest. 1985. Lang.: Hun. 1903
Tamás Ascher directs *A kopasz éneksnő (The Bald Soprano)* and *Különóra (The Lesson)* by Eugène Ionesco. Hungary: Kaposvár. 1986. Lang.: Hun. 1912
Tamás Ascher directs Čechov's *Tri sestry (Three Sisters)* at Katona József Theatre under the title *Három nővér*. Hungary: Budapest. 1985. Lang.: Hun. 1914
Comparison of two Hungarian productions of *Háram nővér (Three Sisters)* by Anton Pavlovič Čechov. Hungary: Budapest, Zalaegerszeg. 1985. Lang.: Hun. 1964

Ashby, Hal
Design/technology
Cinematographer Stephen Burum's work on *Eight Million Ways to Die*. USA. Lang.: Eng. 3207

Ashman, Howard
Performance/production
Reviews of *Smile*, music by Marvin Hamlisch, book by Howard Ashman. USA: New York, NY. 1986. Lang.: Eng. 3613

Asia Pacific Festival
Administration
Account of the first Asia Pacific Festival. Canada: Vancouver, BC. 1985. Lang.: Eng. 3308

Asian American Theatre Company (San Francisco, CA)
Plays/librettos/scripts
Work of playwright R.A. Shiomi, including production history of *Yellow Fever*. Canada: Toronto, ON. USA: New York, NY. USA: San Francisco, CA. 1970-1986. Lang.: Eng. 2422

Asian-American Repertory Theatre (New York, NY)
Performance/production
Director, producer Wu Jing-Jyi discusses his life and career in theatre. Taiwan. USA: Minneapolis, MN, New York, NY. 1939-1980. Lang.: Eng. 2098

Asinamali
Performance/production
Reviews of *Asinamali*, written and staged by Mbongeni Ngema. USA: New York, NY. 1986. Lang.: Eng. 2244

Aslan, Raoul
Performance/production
Playing Hamlet at the Burgtheater. Austria: Vienna. 1803-1985.
Lang.: Ger. 1654

Asplund, Per Eric
Performance/production
Outsidern (The Outsider), a production by Mimensemblan, based on
Hermann Hesse's *Steppenwolf*. Sweden: Stockholm. 1984-1986. Lang.:
Swe. 3296

Asselin, Jean
Performance/production
History of the Omnibus mime troupe. Canada: Montreal, PQ. 1970-
1988. Lang.: Eng. 3291

Plays/librettos/scripts
Review essay on *Li jus de Robin et Marion (The Play of Robin and
Marion)* directed by Jean Asselin. Canada: Montreal, PQ. 1986.
Lang.: Fre. 937

Association Jeune France
Administration
Development of regional theatre companies. France. 1940-1952.
Lang.: Eng. 44

Association of Artists' Unions
Relation to other fields
Minutes of debates organized by the Association of Artists' Unions,
on socialist arts policy, including theatre. Hungary. 1981-1984. Lang.:
Hun. 1101

Association of British Theatre Technicians (ABTT)
Administration
Summary of the Cork report with recommendations on how the
results can be used. UK. 1986. Lang.: Eng. 70

Formation and development of the Association of British Theatre
Technicians (ABTT). UK. 1986. Lang.: Eng. 76

Design/technology
Overview of performance technology show at Riverside Studios. UK-
England: London. 1986. Lang.: Eng. 323

ABTT technical guidelines for sound and communications systems in
the theatre. UK-England. Lang.: Eng. 324

Translation of article on theatre technicians in England from ABTT
News. UK-England. 1983-1985. Lang.: Hun. 330

Association of Performing Artists (APA, New York, NY)
Performance/production
Actress Rosemary Harris discusses her work in *The Petition*. UK-
England: London. USA: New York, NY. 1948-1986. Lang.: Eng.
2177

Association of Producing Artists
Institutions
Interviews with theatre professionals in Quebec. Canada. 1985.
Lang.: Fre. 487

Association Théâtrale des Etudiants de Paris (Paris)
Institutions
Work and distinctive qualities of the Théâtre du Soleil. France:
Paris. 1964-1986. Lang.: Eng. 1575

Associations
SEE
Institutions, associations.

Assumption plays
Performance/production
Medieval style Assumption plays. Spain-Catalonia. 1000-1709. Lang.:
Cat. 792

Comparison of Catalan Assumption plays. Spain-Catalonia:
Tarragona. 1350-1388. Lang.: Cat. 3346

Astley's Amphitheatre (London)
Performance/production
Development of clowning to include parody. UK. 1769-1985. Lang.:
Fre. 3347

Åström, Elisabeth
Design/technology
Swedish set designers discuss their working methods. Sweden. 1980-
1986. Lang.: Swe. 312

Asztalos, Gyula
Design/technology
Interviews with technicians Gyula Ember and Gyula Asztalos about
theatre technology. Hungary. 1977-1986. Lang.: Hun. 285

At My Heart's Core
Plays/librettos/scripts
The immigrant in plays by Herman Voaden and Robertson Davies.
Canada. 1934-1950. Lang.: Eng. 2431

At the Hawk's Well
Performance/production
A production of *At the Hawk's Well* using *nō* techniques. Japan:
Kyoto, Tokyo. 1984. 1981-1982. 1396

Atelier, Théâtre de l' (Paris)
SEE
Théâtre de l'Atelier.

Athalie
Plays/librettos/scripts
Study of *Bérénice, Athalie* and *Bajazet* by Jean Racine. France.
1670-1691. Lang.: Fre. 2583

Athayde, Roberto
Plays/librettos/scripts
Language as an instrument of tyranny in Athayde's *Apareceua
Margarida (Miss Margarida's Way)*. Brazil. 1808-1973. Lang.: Eng.
2405

Athens Ensemble
Performance/production
Program notes for the Athens Ensemble production of *Baal* by
Bertolt Brecht. Greece: Athens. 1983. 1769

Atherton, John Joseph
Plays/librettos/scripts
Analysis of plays by Canadian soldiers in World War I. Canada.
UK. 1901-1918. Lang.: Eng. 936

**ATINT (Associación de Trabajadores e Investigadores del Nuevo
Teatro)**
Institutions
A report on the symposium at the Festival Latino discusses Brecht
and the Nuevo Teatro movement. USA: New York, NY. 1984. 564

Atkins, Eileen
Performance/production
Eileen Atkins, Judi Dench, Wendy Hiller and Barbara Jefford
discuss playing Saint Joan in Shaw's play. UK-England: London.
1936-1983. Lang.: Eng. 2153

Atkinson, Rowan
Performance/production
Collection of newspaper reviews by London theatre critics. UK-
England: London. 1986. Lang.: Eng. 2123

Reviews of *Rowan Atkinson at the Atkinson*, by Richard Curtis,
Rowan Atkinson and Ben Elton, staged by Mike Ockrent. USA:
New York, NY. 1986. Lang.: Eng. 2211

Átkozottak (Damned, The)
Performance/production
Review of Géza Páskándi's *Átkozottak (The Damned)* directed by
László Romhányi. Hungary: Kőszeg. 1986. Lang.: Hun. 1808

Geza Páskándi's *Átkozottak (The Damned)* directed by László
Romhányi at Kőszegi Várszinház. Hungary: Kőszeg. 1986. Lang.:
Hun. 1822

Atlanta Child Murders, The
Plays/librettos/scripts
Analysis of television docudramas as ⟨a melodrama genre. USA.
1965-1986. Lang.: Eng. 3285

Atlas Slippers, The
SEE
Atlaczpapucs, Az.

ATR
SEE
Amatörteaterns Riksförbund.

Attenborough, Michael
Performance/production
Collection of newspaper reviews by London theatre critics. UK-
England: London. 1986. Lang.: Eng. 2117

Attias, Maurice
Performance/production
Directors discuss staging of plays by Paul Claudel. France. Belgium.
1985. Lang.: Fre. 1723

Attica
Plays/librettos/scripts
Analysis of television docudramas as a melodrama genre. USA.
1965-1986. Lang.: Eng. 3285

Attila éjszakái (Nights of Attila, The)
Performance/production
Ferenc Sik directs two plays by Gyula Háy. Hungary: Veszprém,
Gyula. 1986. Lang.: Hun. 1943

Attila Theatre
SEE
József Attila Szinház.

Aub, Max
Basic theatrical documents
English translation of *El desconfiado prodigioso (The Remarkable Misanthrope)* by Max Aub. Spain. 1903-1972. Lang.: Eng, Spa. 1493
Auca del senyor Esteve, L' (Mr. Esteve's 'Auca')
Design/technology
Introduction to facsimile of Oleguer Junyent's set design for *L'Auca del senyor Esteve (Mr. Esteve's 'Auca')* by Santiago Rusiñol. Spain-Catalonia: Barcelona. 1861-1984. Lang.: Cat. 1518
Facsimile edition of scene design drawings by Oleguer Junyent for *L'auca del senyor Esteve (Mr. Esteve's 'Auca')* by Santiago Rusiñol. Spain-Catalonia: Barcelona. 1917. Lang.: Cat. 1519
Auca del Senyor Esteve, L' (Mr. Esteve's 'Auca')
Plays/librettos/scripts
History of Catalan literature, including playwrights and theatre. Spain-Catalonia. 1800-1974. Lang.: Cat. 974
Aucun motif (No Motive)
Performance/production
Opposition to realism in plays from Francophone Manitoba. Canada. 1983-1986. Lang.: Fre. 670
Audelco Awards
SEE
Awards, Audelco.
Auden, W.H.
Plays/librettos/scripts
Auden and Kallman's English translation of *Die Zauberflöte (The Magic Flute)*. USA. 1951-1956. Lang.: Eng. 3903
Audi, Pierre
Performance/production
Collection of newspaper reviews by London theatre critics. UK-England: London. 1986. Lang.: Eng. 2121
Audience
SEE ALSO
Classed Entries.
Administration
Theatre as a generator of products, consumers, and financial flow. Belgium. 1983-1984. Lang.: Fre. 26
Institutions
Eva LeGallienne on Civic Repertory and American Repertory Theatres. USA: New York, NY. 1933-1953. Lang.: Eng. 560
Development of Prague National Theatre. Czechoslovakia: Prague. 1787-1985. Lang.: Eng. 3672
Performance spaces
Architectural design for new performance spaces for Theatre for the New City and the Vineyard Theatre. USA: New York, NY. 1986. Lang.: Eng. 639
Performance/production
Development of regional theatre and other entertainments. England. 1840-1870. Lang.: Eng. 687
Development of and influences on theatre and other regional entertainments. England. 1840-1870. Lang.: Eng. 688
Comprehensive survey of ten years of theatre in New York City. USA: New York, NY. 1970-1980. Lang.: Eng. 837
Director Anatolij Efros on theatrical conventions, audience and perception. USSR. 1980-1986. Lang.: Rus. 871
The Castle of Perseverance examined for clues to audience placement and physical plan of original production. England. 1343-1554. Lang.: Eng. 1709
Reciprocal influences of French and Japanese theatre. France. Japan. 1900-1945. Lang.: Fre. 1750
Djrector Andrzei Wajda's work, accessibility to Polish audiences. Poland: Warsaw. 1926-1986. Lang.: Swe. 2027
Chicago dramaturgs acknowledge a common ground in educating their audience. USA: Chicago, IL. 1984-1986. Lang.: Eng. 2274
Detailed history of the 1914 Hagenbeck Wallace Circus season. USA: St. Louis, MO, Youngstown, OH, Sturgis, MI. 1914. Lang.: Eng. 3388
Detailed history of the Stowe Brothers (family) Circus. USA. 1850-1920. Lang.: Eng. 3396
Case-study of *Sweet and Sour* by the Australian Broadcasting Corporation. Australia: Sydney, N.S.W. 1980-1984. Lang.: Eng. 3483
Plays/librettos/scripts
Cooperation between theatres in Austria and playwrights-in-training. Austria. 1980-1986. Lang.: Ger. 2393
Study of all aspects of Italian opera. Italy. 1810-1920. Lang.: Fre. 3889

Relation to other fields
Concept of play in theatre and sport. Canada. 1972-1983. Lang.: Eng. 1071
Theory/criticism
History of theatre in Africa. Africa. 1400-1985. Lang.: Ger. 1199
Andrzej Hausbrandt (critic) and Gustaw Holoubek (actor) discuss their views on general problems of theatre. Poland. Lang.: Pol. 1217
Audience behavior
SEE
Behavior/psychology, audience.
Audience composition
Administration
Causes of decline in number of commercially produced plays. Australia: Sydney. 1914-1939. Lang.: Eng. 24
Jean Vilar's development of a working class audience for the Théâtre National Populaire. France: Paris. 1948-1968. Lang.: Fre. 38
Keynote address of direct mail marketing seminar by Andre Bishop. USA: New York, NY. 1982. Lang.: Eng. 91
Satirical view of arts management. USA. 1986. Lang.: Eng. 107
Pros and cons of single ticket discount policies. USA: New York, NY. 1984. Lang.: Eng. 172
Interview with Joe Papp. USA: New York, NY. 1959-1986. Lang.: Eng. 177
Edward Downes on his life in the opera. USA: New York, NY. 1911-1986. Lang.: Eng. 3643
Audience
Several New York theatres discuss their student outreach programs. USA: New York, NY. 1984. Lang.: Eng. 201
Moral objections to children's attendance of theatres. USA: New York, NY. 1900-1910. Lang.: Eng. 202
Profile and role of subscribers in nonprofit theatre. USA: New York, NY. 1984. Lang.: Eng. 203
Absence of an audience for non-mainstream theatre. USSR. 1980-1986. Lang.: Rus. 206
Conference on low theatrical attendance. USSR: Kujbyšev. 1980-1986. 207
Results of a study of Minsk theatre audiences. USSR: Minsk. 1983-1984. Lang.: Rus. 208
Overview of Moscow theatrical life. USSR: Moscow. 1980-1986. Lang.: Rus. 211
Sociological studies of Ukrainian theatrical life. USSR. 1920. Lang.: Ukr. 212
Audience of the humanistic, religious and school-theatre of the European Renaissance. Europe. 1480-1630. Lang.: Ger. 1445
Claques as a theatrical institution. France. 1800. Lang.: Fre. 1447
Postmodern concepts of individual, audience, public. USA. 1985-1986. Lang.: Eng. 1454
Oral history of film audience. USA: Charlotte, NC. 1919-1986. Lang.: Eng. 3196
The growth of musical theatre and opera since World War II. North America. 1950-1986. Lang.: Eng. 3577
Claques as viewed by French writers. France. 1800-1899. Lang.: Fre. 3647
Study of the reality and misconception about opera audiences. USSR. 1986. Lang.: Rus. 3648
Institutions
Repertory of the Nouvelle Compagnie Théâtrale. Canada: Montreal, PQ. 1964-1984. Lang.: Fre. 481
Performance/production
Changes in East Village performance scene. USA: New York, NY. 1975-1985. Lang.: Eng. 3458
Interview with composer and director of the Finnish National opera Ilkka Kuusisto. Finland: Helsinki, Suomussalmi. 1967-1986. Lang.: Eng, Fre. 3724
Plays/librettos/scripts
Interview with director of Teatr Współczésny about children's drama competition. Poland: Wrocław. 1986. Lang.: Hun. 2736
Relation to other fields
Statistical index of theatre attendance in the regional and provincial centers of the USSR-Russian SFSR. USSR. 1985. Lang.: Rus. 1175
Circumstances surrounding a banned Workers' Experimental Theatre play. Canada: Toronto, ON. 1931-1933. Lang.: Eng. 3018
Audience psychology
SEE
Behavior/psychology, audience.

Auletta, Robert — cont'd

Plays/librettos/scripts
Playwright Robert Auletta on his adaptation of Sophocles'*Ajax*. USA: Washington, DC. 1986. Lang.: Eng.　　2891

Aunt Máli
SEE
Máli néni.

Aureng-Zebe
Plays/librettos/scripts
Female characterization in Nicholas Rowe's plays. England. 1629-1720. Lang.: Eng.　　2475

Aurics, Georges
Institutions
Discussions of opera at the festival of Aix-en-Provence. France: Aix-en-Provence. 1960. Lang.: Fre.　　3673

Austen, Jane
Performance/production
Collection of newspaper reviews by London theatre critics. UK-England: London. 1986. Lang.: Eng.　　2113

Austin, Gayle
Plays/librettos/scripts
Interview with playwright Maria Irene Fornes. USA: New York, NY. 1984. Lang.: Eng.　　2892

Australian Broadcasting Corporation
Performance/production
Case-study of *Sweet and Sour* by the Australian Broadcasting Corporation. Australia: Sydney, N.S.W. 1980-1984. Lang.: Eng.　　3483

Australian Performing Group (Melbourne)
Plays/librettos/scripts
Developments in Australian playwriting since 1975. Australia. 1975-1986. Lang.: Eng.　　2374

Austrian Federal Theatres
SEE
Österreichische Bundestheater.

Author's Farce, The
Plays/librettos/scripts
Analysis of Henry Fielding's play *The Author's Farce*. England. 1730. Lang.: Eng.　　2516

Auto de Pasión (Passion Play)
Plays/librettos/scripts
Linguistic study of *Auto de Pasión (Passion Play)* by Lucas Fernández. Spain-Catalonia. 1510-1514. Lang.: Cat.　　2812

Avant-garde theatre
SEE ALSO
Shōgekijō undō.
Alternative theatre.
Experimental theatre.

Institutions
History of Swedish language Lilla-teatern (Little Theatre). Finland: Helsinki. 1940-1986. Lang.: Eng, Fre.　　494
Production history and techniques of the Living Theatre. USA. 1964. Lang.: Eng.　　546
Early history of Circle in the Square. USA: New York, NY. 1950-1960. Lang.: Kor.　　552
Goals and accomplishments of Theatre for the New City. USA: New York, NY. 1970-1983. Lang.: Eng.　　570
History of the Shared Stage theatre company. Canada: Winnipeg, MB. 1980-1986. Lang.: Eng.　　1555
Interview with members of Mabou Mines. USA: New York, NY. 1984. Lang.: Eng.　　1607
Cultural activities in the Lodz ghetto. Poland: Łódź. 1940-1944. Lang.: Heb.　　3323

Performance/production
Examination of Italian avant-garde theatre. Italy. 1970-1985. Lang.: Ita.　　751
Director Charles Marowitz on the role of the director. USA. 1965-1985. Lang.: Eng.　　843
Synthesis of music, dance, song and speech in *Ayrus Leánya (Ayrus' Daughter)* by Ödön Palasovszky. Hungary: Budapest. 1931. Lang.: Hun.　　1967
Collection of articles by critic and theatre historian Stanisław Marczak-Oborski. Poland. 1918-1986. Lang.: Pol.　　2034
Aesthetics, styles, rehearsal techniques of director Richard Foreman. USA. 1974-1986. Lang.: Eng.　　2263
Explorative structure and manner of performance in avant-garde theatre. USA. 1965. Lang.: Eng.　　2277
Resurgence of street theatre productions and companies. USA: New York, NY. 1960-1982. Lang.: Eng.　　2285
Avant-garde theatre companies from Britain perform in New York festival. USA: New York, NY. 1970-1983. Lang.: Eng.　　2286
Writings by and about Julian Beck, founder of Living Theatre. USA. Europe. 1925-1985. Lang.: Ita.　　2309
Videotaped performances and interviews of San Francisco Mime Troupe. USA: San Francisco, CA. 1960-1986. Lang.: Eng.　　3306
Peter Schumann and his work with the Bread and Puppet Theatre. USA: New York, NY. 1968-1986. Lang.: Eng.　　3973

Plays/librettos/scripts
Survey of the achievements of American theatre of the 1960s. USA. 1960-1979. Lang.: Eng.　　987
Interview with founders of Internationale Nieuwe Scene. Europe. 1984.　　2543
Essentialism and avant-garde in the plays of Eugène Ionesco. France. 1950-1980. Lang.: Fre.　　2576
Deconstructionist analysis of *Riccardo III* by Carmelo Bene. Italy. France. Lang.: Eng.　　2690
Experimental theatrical productions of Achille Campanile. Italy. 1920-1930. Lang.: Ita.　　2695
Current thematic trends in the plays of Antonio Gala. Spain. 1963-1985. Lang.: Spa.　　2783
Analysis of the plays of Rosalyn Drexler. USA. 1964-1985. Lang.: Eng.　　2920

Relation to other fields
Artistic, literary and theatrical avant-garde movements. Europe. 1900-1930. Lang.: Ita.　　1083
Alternative theatre and the political situation. Poland. 1960-1986. Lang.: Pol.　　1119
Political influence of Ernst Toller's plays. Europe. 1893-1939. Lang.: Pol.　　3027
Contrasts between culture and mass media. Italy. 1980-1986. Lang.: Ita.　　3171

Theory/criticism
Interviews on the role of the critic in New York theatre. USA: New York, NY. 1983. Lang.: Eng.　　1226
Reviews of books on Hungarian theatre. Hungary. 1986. Lang.: Hun.　　3116
Collection of essays on the avant-garde. USA. 1955-1986. Lang.: Eng.　　3145

Avante Theatre Company (Philadelphia, PA)
Institutions
History of Black theater companies. USA: Philadelphia, PA. 1966-1985. Lang.: Eng.　　1608

Avar, István
Performance/production
Interview with actor István Avar. Hungary. 1954-1985. Lang.: Hun.　　1836

Avarskij Musykal'no-Dramatičeskij Teat'r im. G. Cadasy (Dagestan)
Performance/production
Jubilee of Avarskij Musykal'no-Dramatičeskij Teat'r im. G. Cadasy. USSR. 1935-1985. Lang.: Rus.　　873

Avenç, L' (Barcelona)
Plays/librettos/scripts
Plays translated into Catalan by Pompeu Fabra. Spain-Catalonia. 1890-1905. Lang.: Cat.　　2818

Avui, Romeo i Julieta (Today, Romeo and Juliet)
Basic theatrical documents
Texts of *Avui, Romeo i Julieta (Today, Romeo and Juliet)* and *El porter i el penalty (The Goalkeeper and the Penalty)* by Josep Palau i Fabre. Spain-Catalonia. 1917-1982. Lang.: Cat.　　1499

Plays/librettos/scripts
Analysis of Josep Palau's plays and theoretical writings. Spain-Catalonia. 1917-1982. Lang.: Cat.　　2814

Awards, Academy of Motion Picture Arts and Sciences
Design/technology
Lighting designer Bob Dickinson talks about lighting the 1986 Oscars ceremony. USA: Los Angeles, CA. 1983-1986. Lang.: Eng.　　3263

Awards, Audelco
Reference materials
Current work of Audelco award-winning playwrights. USA: New York, NY. 1973-1984. Lang.: Eng.　　3007

Bakhtin, Mikhail
Plays/librettos/scripts
Bertolt Brecht and the Expressionists. Germany. 1919-1944. Lang.: Eng. 955
Chronotopic analysis of *El beso de la mujer araña (The Kiss of the Spider Woman)* by Manuel Puigi. Argentina. 1976-1986. Lang.: Spa. 2364
Theory/criticism
Melodrama as an aesthetic theatre form. Australia. 1850-1986. Lang.: Eng. 3083

Bakker, Klaass
Institutions
History of Pantijn Muziekpoppentheater. Netherlands: Amsterdam. 1980-1987. Lang.: Eng. 3958

Balanchine, George
Performance/production
Memoirs of Vera Zorina, star of stage and screen. Europe. 1917-1986. Lang.: Eng. 1303

Balatri, Filippo
Performance/production
History of *castrati* in opera. Italy. 1599-1797. Lang.: Eng. 3761

Balconville
Performance/production
Playwright David Fennario's commitment to working-class community theatre. Canada: Montreal, PQ. 1980-1986. Lang.: Eng. 1661
Plays/librettos/scripts
Poverty in plays by Michel Tremblay and David Fennario. Canada: Quebec, PQ. 1970-1980. Lang.: Eng. 2410

Bald Prima Donna, The
SEE
Cantatrice chauve, La.

Bald Soprano, The
SEE
Cantatrice chauve, La.

Balet im S. M. Kirova
SEE
Akademičėskij Teat'r Opery i Baleta im S.M. Kirova.

Bálint, András
Performance/production
Lanford Wilson's play, *Talley's Folly (Mint két tojás)* directed by András Bálint. Hungary: Dunaújváros. 1986. Lang.: Hun. 1804
New director of Radnóti Miklós Theatre, András Bálint. Hungary: Budapest. 1985. Lang.: Hun. 1830
Interview with actor András Bálint. Hungary: 1965-1986. Lang.: Hun. 1839

Balkay, Géza
Performance/production
Čechov's *Három nővér (Three Sisters)* directed by Tamás Ascher. Hungary: Budapest. 1985. Lang.: Hun. 1814

Ball robat (Stolen Dance)
Plays/librettos/scripts
Memoir concerning playwright Joan Oliver. Spain-Catalonia. 1920-1986. Lang.: Cat. 2820

Ball, Lucille
Performance/production
Career of film and television actress Lucille Ball. USA. 1911-1986. Lang.: Eng. 3167

Balladyna
Performance/production
Krystyna Meissner directs Juliusz Słowacki's *Balladyna*, Teatr Horzycy. Poland: Toruń. 1984. Lang.: Pol. 2035

Ballard, Frank
Performance/production
Puppet production of Mozart's opera *Die Zauberflöte*. USA. 1986. Lang.: Eng. 4008

Ballet
SEE ALSO
Classed Entries under DANCE–Ballet: 1292-1328.
Design/technology
Career of lighting designer Nicholas Cernovitch. Canada: Montreal, PQ. 1970-1983. Lang.: Eng. 244
Costumes by Yves Saint-Laurent. France. 1959-1984. Lang.: Fre. 1341
Institutions
New concept for using the Theater im Künstlerhaus for the Opernwerkstatt productions. Austria: Vienna. 1986-1987. Lang.: Ger. 3665

Performance spaces
Children's history of the Gran Teatre del Liceo opera house. Spain-Catalonia: Barcelona. 1845-1986. Lang.: Cat. 3684
Performance/production
Analysis of choreography of *A szarvassá változott fiak (The Sons Who Turned Into Stags)*. Hungary: Győr. 1985-1986. Lang.: Hun. 1277
Dance and mime performances at annual Festival of the Arts. South Africa, Republic of: Grahamstown. 1986. Lang.: Eng. 1282
Autobiographical recollections of Cecilia Esztergályos, ballet-dancer turned actress. Hungary. 1945-1986. Lang.: Hun. 1829
Ballet for television produced by A. Belinskij. USSR: Leningrad. 1980-1986. Lang.: Rus. 3277
Interviews with various artists of the Viennese State Opera. Austria: Vienna. 1909-1986. Lang.: Ger. 3692
Plays/librettos/scripts
Adaptations of *Carmen* by Prosper Mérimée. France. Spain. 1845-1983. Lang.: Fre. 3870
Reference materials
Yearbook of major performances in all areas of Japanese theatre. Japan: Tokyo. 1986. Lang.: Jap. 1026
List and location of school playtexts and programs. France. 1601-1700. Lang.: Fre. 2987

Ballet training
SEE
Training, ballet.

Ballet, Arthur
Performance/production
Interview with dramaturg Arthur Ballet. USA. 1950-1986. Lang.: Eng. 2248
Plays/librettos/scripts
Report on a symposium addressing the role of the dramaturg. 918

Balletap, USA (New York, NY)
Performance/production
Tap dancing career of Maurice Hines and the creation of his new company Balletap, USA. USA: New York, NY. 1949-1986. Lang.: Eng. 3623

Ballets Russes (Monte Carlo)
Design/technology
Painters as designers for the theatrical productions. Europe. 1890-1980. Lang.: Fre. 260

Ballets Suédois (Paris)
Performance/production
Study of four works by Ballets Suédois. France: Paris. 1920-1925. Lang.: Eng. 1271

Ballettschule der Österreichischen Bundestheater (Vienna)
Institutions
Activities of the audience-society, Gesellschaft der Freunde der Ballettschule der Österreichischen Bundestheater. Austria: Vienna. 1985-1986. Lang.: Ger. 1294

Ballo in maschera, Un
Performance/production
András Fehér directs Verdi's *Un ballo in maschera* at the Hungarian State Opera House. Hungary: Budapest. 1986. Lang.: Hun. 3746

Balls and Chains
Performance/production
Collection of newspaper reviews by London theatre critics. UK-England: London. 1986. Lang.: Eng. 2116

Balmain Boys Don't Cry
Plays/librettos/scripts
Analysis of *Balmain Boys Don't Cry*, a political satire. Australia: Sydney, N.S.W. 1983-1986. Lang.: Eng. 3368

Balogh, Gábor
Performance/production
Forgatókönyv (Film Script) by István Örkény directed by Gábor Balogh. Hungary: Békéscsaba. 1986. Lang.: Hun. 1908

Baltsa, Agnes
Performance/production
Performance analysis of the title role of *Carmen*. France. 1875-1986. Lang.: Eng. 3725
Reference materials
Photos of the new opera productions at the Staatsoper. Austria: Vienna. 1985-1986. Lang.: Ger. 3910

Bałucki, Michał
Performance/production
Janusz Nyczak directs Michał Pałucki's *Dom Otwarty (Open House)* at Teatr Nowy. Poland: Poznań. 1984. Lang.: Pol. 2039

Balzac, Honoré de
Audience
Claques as viewed by French writers. France. 1800-1899. Lang.: Fre.
3647

BAM
SEE
Brooklyn Academy of Music.

Bán Bánk
SEE
Bánk Bán.

Bandler, Vivica
Institutions
History of Swedish language Lilla-teatern (Little Theatre). Finland: Helsinki. 1940-1986. Lang.: Eng, Fre.
494

Bandō, Tamasaburō
Performance/production
Collection of pictures of famous *onnagata*. Japan: Tokyo. Lang.: Jap.
1381

Banff Centre (Banff, AB)
Institutions
Shift in emphasis at Banff Centre. Canada: Banff, AB. 1974-1986. Lang.: Eng.
1543

Banfield, Rafaello de
Performance/production
Collaboration of Italian composer Rafaello de Banfield and American playwright Tennessee Williams on the opera *Lord Byron's Love Letter*. USA: Charleston, SC. 1986. Lang.: Eng.
3810

Bánk Bán
Performance/production
Review of József Katona's *Bánk Bán* directed by János Ács at Szigligeti Szinház. Hungary: Szolnok. 1986. Lang.: Hun.
1876

Bánk Bán by József Katona at Szigligeti Theatre directed by János Ács. Hungary: Szolnok. 1986. Lang.: Hun.
1884

József Katona's *Bánk Bán* presented by the Hanoi Tuong Theatre directed by Doan Anh Thang. Vietnam: Hanoi. 1986. Lang.: Hun.
2340

Plays/librettos/scripts
Analysis of the characters of *Bánk Bán* by József Katona. Lang.: Hun.
2351

Analysis of László Németh's study of *Bánk Bán* by József Katona and a portrait of the playwright. Hungary. 1985. Lang.: Hun.
2647

Plot, structure and national character of *Bánk Bán* by József Katona. Hungary. Lang.: Hun.
2655

Reference materials
Bibliography of Hungarian writer and translator Jenő Mohácsi. Hungary. 1886-1944. Lang.: Hun.
2991

Bánus Bánk
SEE
Bánk Bán.

Barajas, DeVina
Performance/production
DeVina Barajas discusses performing the songs of Brecht. Switzerland. Germany, West. USA. 1978-1985.
3607

Baraka, Imamu Amiri
Plays/librettos/scripts
Ritual function of *The Slave Ship* by LeRoi Jones (Amiri Baraka) and *Quinta Temporada (Fifth Season)* by Luis Valdez. USA. 1965-1967. Lang.: Eng.
2906

Relation to other fields
Sociocultural elements of Black theatre. USA. 1960-1985. Lang.: Eng.
3063

Baranowski, Henryk
Institutions
Production of Jürgen Lederach's *Japanische Spiele (Japanese Play)* by Transformtheater. Germany, West: Berlin, West. 1981-1986. Lang.: Swe.
499

Barba, Eugenio
Performance/production
Feminist criticism of theatre anthropology conference on women's roles. USA. Denmark. 1985. Lang.: Eng.
845

Influence of *kata* principle on Western acting technique. Japan. Denmark. Australia. 1981-1986. Lang.: Ita.
1365

Interview with Eugenio Barba, director of Odin Teatret. Europe. 1985. Lang.: Hun.
1718

Relation to other fields
Western directors and third-world theatre. 1900-1986. Lang.: Ita.
1053

Anthropological approach to performance and language. USA. Japan. 1982. Lang.: Eng.
1140

Theory/criticism
Creative self-assembly and juxtaposition in live performance and film. Lang.: Eng.
1196

Ingmar Bergman production of *King Lear* and Asian influences. Spain-Catalonia: Barcelona. 1985. Lang.: Eng.
1219

Training
Concept of negation in actor training. Lang.: Fre.
1252

Barber of Seville, The (opera)
SEE
Barbiere di Siviglia, Il.

Barberini, Urbano
Performance/production
The Franco Zeffirelli film of *Otello* by Giuseppe Verdi, an account of the production. Italy: Rome. 1985-1986. Lang.: Eng.
3758

Barbican Theatre (London)
SEE ALSO
Royal Shakespeare Company.
Performance/production
Collection of newspaper reviews by London theatre critics. UK. 1986. Lang.: Eng.
2101

Collection of newspaper reviews by London theatre critics. UK-England: London. 1986. Lang.: Eng.
2109

Collection of newspaper reviews by London theatre critics. UK-England: London. 1986. Lang.: Eng.
2112

Royal Shakespeare Company performances at the Barbican Theatre. UK-England: London. 1986. Lang.: Eng.
2152

Barbiere di Siviglia, Il
Performance/production
Reviews of 10 vintage recordings of complete operas on LP. USA. 1906-1925. Lang.: Eng.
3792

Barca d'Amílcar, La (Amilcar's Boat)
Plays/librettos/scripts
Memoir concerning playwright Joan Oliver. Spain-Catalonia. 1920-1986. Lang.: Cat.
2820

Barca sin pescador, La (Boat Without a Fisherman, The)
Plays/librettos/scripts
Discusses Christian outlook in plays by Alejandro Casona. Spain. 1940-1980. Lang.: Eng.
2795

Barchino, Josep
Institutions
History of theatre in Valencia area focusing on Civil War period. Spain: Valencia. 1817-1982. Lang.: Cat.
514

Barker, Howard
Plays/librettos/scripts
Interview with playwright Howard Barker. UK-England. 1981-1985. Lang.: Eng.
2845

Barna, Joseph
Design/technology
Computer program which stores lighting design data. USA. 1983. Lang.: Eng.
419

Barnes, Barnaby
Plays/librettos/scripts
Machiavellian ideas in *The Devil's Charter* by Barnaby Barnes. England. 1584-1607. Lang.: Eng.
2500

Barnes, Peter
Performance/production
Production analysis of four plays by Peter Barnes. UK-England. 1981-1986. Lang.: Eng.
805

Barnes, Will R.
Reference materials
Catalogue of an exhibition of costume designs for Broadway musicals. USA: New York, NY. 1900-1925. Lang.: Eng, Ger.
3635

Barnett, Henrietta
Influence of Hampstead Garden Suburb pageant on the Russian Proletkult movement. Russia. UK-England: London. 1907-1920. Lang.: Eng.
3421

Barnevelt Tragedy, The
SEE
Tragedy of Sir John van Olden Barnevelt, The.

Barney, Natalie
Performance/production
Interview with Lesbian feminist theatre company Hard Corps. UK-England. 1984-1986. Lang.: Eng.
2164

Barnum and Bailey Circus (Sarasota, FL)
SEE ALSO
Ringling Brothers and Barnum & Bailey Circus.

Barnum and Bailey Circus (Sarasota, FL) — cont'd

Performance/production
The history of 'tableau wagons' in the Barnum and Bailey circus.
USA: New York, NY. 1864-1920. Lang.: Eng.   3391

Baroque theatre
SEE ALSO
Geographical-Chronological Index under: Europe and other European
countries, 1594-1702.
Basic theatrical documents
Edition of *La famosa comèdia de la gala està en son punt (The
Famous Comedy of the Gala Done to a Turn)*, with analysis. Spain-
Catalonia. 1625-1680. Lang.: Cat.   1497
Plays/librettos/scripts
Mutual influences between *commedia dell'arte* and Spanish literature.
Spain. Italy. 1330-1623. Lang.: Spa.   2805

Barr, Richard
Performance/production
Director of original production discusses Edward Albee's *Who's
Afraid of Virginia Woolf?*. USA: New York, NY. 1962. Lang.: Eng.
2303

Barrault, Jean-Louis
Institutions
Retrospective of activities of Compagnie Renaud-Barrault. France:
Paris. 1946-1986. Lang.: Fre.   1573
Performance/production
Recollection of Jean-Louis Barrault's career as actor and director.
France. 1943-1956. Lang.: Fre.   711
Reminiscences of actor-director Roger Blin. France. 1930-1983.
Lang.: Fre.   1726

Barrett, Lawrence
Performance/production
Career of actor Lawrence Barrett. USA: New York, NY. 1871-1909.
Lang.: Eng.   2261

Barrett, Wilson
Institutions
Description of the Wilson Barrett Theatre Company. UK-Scotland.
1930-1955. Lang.: Eng.   1596
Performance/production
Changes in English life reflected in 1883 theatre season. UK-
England: London. 1883. Lang.: Eng.   810

Barrie, James M.
Performance/production
Performances of *Pán Peter (Peter Pan)* by J. M. Barrie, directed by
Géza Pártos. Hungary: Kaposvár. 1985. Lang.: Hun.   1934
Collection of newspaper reviews by London theatre critics. UK.
1986. Lang.: Eng.   2101
Collection of newspaper reviews by London theatre critics. UK-
England. 1986. Lang.: Eng.   2111

Barry, Dr. James
Basic theatrical documents
Text of radio play about a woman doctor who masqueraded as a
man. Canada: Montreal, PQ. UK-Scotland: Edinburgh. South Africa,
Republic of: Cape Town. 1809-1859. Lang.: Eng.   3175

Bart, Lionel
Performance/production
Lakat alá lányokat (Lock Up Your Daughters), a stage adaptation of
Henry Fielding's *Rape Upon Rape*, directed by Imre Halasi.
Hungary: Diósgyőr. 1986. Lang.: Hun.   3600

Bartenieff, George
Institutions
Goals and accomplishments of Theatre for the New City. USA: New
York, NY. 1970-1983. Lang.: Eng.   570
Performance/production
Resurgence of street theatre productions and companies. USA: New
York, NY. 1960-1982. Lang.: Eng.   2285

Bartered Bride, The
SEE
Prodana Nevesla.

Barth, John
Plays/librettos/scripts
The incoherent protagonist of modern comedy. 1954-1986. Lang.:
Eng.   2358

Barthes, Roland
Performance/production
Community theatre as interpreted by the Sidetrack Theatre
Company. Australia: Sydney, N.S.W. 1980-1986. Lang.: Eng.   1638
Theory/criticism
An imagined dialogue on the work of Roland Barthes. France.
Lang.: Eng.   1207

Pitfalls of a semiotic analysis of theatre. England. 1600-1921. Lang.:
Eng.   3094

Bartholomew Fair
Plays/librettos/scripts
Ben Jonson's use of romance in *Volpone*. England. 1575-1600. Lang.:
Eng.   2461
Use of group aggression in Ben Jonson's comedies. England. 1575-
1600. Lang.: Eng.   2508
Reference materials
List of 37 productions of 23 Renaissance plays, with commentary.
UK. USA. New Zealand. 1986. Lang.: Eng.   3000

Bartók, Bela
Performance/production
Production history of Bela Bartók's ballet *A csodálatos mandarin
(The Miraculous Mandarin)* on Hungarian stages. Hungary. 1956-
1985. Lang.: Hun.   1305

Barton, John
Design/technology
Changes in the Royal Shakespeare Company under its current
directors. UK-England: London. 1967-1986. Lang.: Eng.   325
Performance/production
Detailed discussion of four successful Royal Shakespeare Company
productions of Shakespeare's minor plays. UK-England: Stratford.
1946-1977. Lang.: Eng.   2182

Barylli, Gabriel
Performance/production
On actor and playwright Gabriel Barylli. Austria: Vienna. 1957-1986.
Lang.: Ger.   1646

Basement Workshop (New York, NY)
Performance/production
Director, producer Wu Jing-Jyi discusses his life and career in
theatre. Taiwan. USA: Minneapolis, MN, New York, NY. 1939-
1980. Lang.: Eng.   2098

Basic theatrical documents
SEE ALSO
Classed Entries.
Design/technology
Irena Pikiel, Polish puppet theatre stage-designer, describes her years
in satirical performances. Poland: Vilna. 1921-1933. Lang.: Pol. 3952
Performance/production
Stills from telecast performances of *Elektra*. List of principals,
conductor and production staff included. USA: New York, NY.
1986. Lang.: Eng.   3790
Stills from telecast performance of *Goya*. List of principals, conductor
and production staff included. USA: Washington, DC. 1986. Lang.:
Eng.   3791
Photographs, cast list, synopsis, and discography of Metropolitan
Opera radio broadcast performances. USA: New York, NY. 1986.
Lang.: Eng.   3794
Stills from telecast performances. List of principals, conductor and
production staff included. USA: New York, NY. 1986. Lang.: Eng.
3795
Stills from telecast performance of *Candide* by New York City
Opera. USA: New York, NY. 1986. Lang.: Eng.   3796
Photographs, cast list, synopsis, and discography of Metropolitan
Opera radio broadcast performances. USA: New York, NY. 1986.
Lang.: Eng.   3797
Plays/librettos/scripts
Text and information on Luigi Pirandello's *A patenti (The License)*.
Italy. 1916-1918. Lang.: Ita.   2717
Reference materials
Stills from telecast performances of *Hänsel und Gretel*. List of
principals, conductor and production staff included. Austria: Vienna.
1986. Lang.: Eng.   3909

Bass, Eric
Performance/production
Puppeteer Eric Bass of Hakaron Puppet Theatre. Israel: Jerusalem.
1984-1986. Lang.: Heb.   3966

Bassermann, Albert
Performance/production
Application of Brechtian concepts by Eckhardt Schall. Germany,
East: Berlin, East. UK-England: London. 1952-1986. Lang.: Eng.
1762

Bataille, Georges
Plays/librettos/scripts
Themes and characterization in *Madame de Sade* by Mishima Yukio.
Japan. 1960-1970. Lang.: Cat.   2720

Beckett, Samuel — cont'd

Conflict over artistic control in American Repertory Theatre's production of *Endgame* by Samuel Beckett. USA: Boston, MA. 1984. Lang.: Eng. 2296

Plays/librettos/scripts
Symbolism and allusion in *Boiler Room Suite* by Rex Deverell. Canada: Regina, SK. 1977. Lang.: Eng. 934

Theory of translation, using ideas of Eric Bentley and plays of Samuel Beckett. 1950-1986. Lang.: Eng. 2352

The incoherent protagonist of modern comedy. 1954-1986. Lang.: Eng. 2358

Beckett as writer and director. France. UK. 1947-1985. Lang.: Fre. 2546

Language and the permanent dialectic of truth and lie in the plays of Samuel Beckett. France. 1930-1980. Lang.: Fre. 2549

Various implications of 'waiting' in Samuel Beckett's *Waiting for Godot*. France. 1953. Lang.: Eng. 2555

Waiting for Godot as an assessment of the quality of life of the couple. France. UK-Ireland. 1931-1958. Lang.: Eng. 2557

Rhetorical analysis of Samuel Beckett's *Waiting for Godot*. France. 1953. Lang.: Eng. 2562

Multiple role of 'I' in plays of Sanuel Beckett. France. 1953-1986. Lang.: Eng. 2572

Work of playwright Stefan Schütz. Germany, West. 1944-1986. Lang.: Eng. 2625

Interview with playwright Stefan Schütz. Germany, West. 1970-1986. Lang.: Eng. 2628

Influence of artist Jack Yeats on playwright Samuel Beckett. Ireland. France. 1945-1970. Lang.: Eng. 2663

Nō and Beckett compared. Japan. France. 1954-1986. Lang.: Ita. 2721

Notes on film treatments of plays by Samuel Beckett. Ireland. France. 1958-1986. Lang.: Ita. 3234

Comparison of the stage and television versions of *What Where* by Samuel Beckett. France. 1983-1985. Lang.: Eng. 3282

Theory/criticism
The influence of Samuel Beckett's later works on contemporary writers and directors. 1984. Lang.: Eng. 3077

Assessment of critic Kenneth Tynan's works. UK-England. 1950-1960. Lang.: Eng. 3136

Phenomenological view of the history of the circus, its links with theatre. 1985. Lang.: Fre. 3405

Beckman, Anders
Administration
Role of Skånska Teatron in the community. Sweden: Landskrona, Malmö. 1963-1986. Lang.: Swe. 62

Becque, Henry
Performance/production
Recollections of actress Edwige Feuillère. France. 1931-1986. Lang.: Fre. 716

Bécsy, Tamás
Theory/criticism
Tamás Bécsy's theory of the theatre. Hungary. 1986. Lang.: Hun. 3115

Bedford, Brian
Performance/production
Robin Phillips' staging of Shakespeare's *Richard III*. Canada: Stratford, ON. 1977. Lang.: Eng. 1668

Bedford, Steuart
Performance/production
The relationship of Steuart Bedford and Benjamin Britten. UK-England: London. 1967-1976. Lang.: Eng. 3783

Beeson, Jack
Plays/librettos/scripts
Jack Beeson's opera *Lizzie Borden*. USA. 1954-1965. Lang.: Eng. 3901

Beethoven, Ludwig von
Performance/production
Collection of statements about the life and career of conductor Wilhelm Furtwängler. Germany: Berlin. Austria: Salzburg. 1886-1986. Lang.: Ger. 3737

Harry Kupfer: his work and career as singer and director. Germany, East: Dresden, Berlin, East. 1970-1985. Lang.: Ger. 3738

Andrei Serban discusses his production of Beethoven's *Fidelio*. UK-England: London. 1986. Lang.: Eng. 3787

Beg (Escape, The)
Performance/production
Michajl Bulgakov's ties with Moscow Art Theatre. Russia: Moscow. 1891-1940. Lang.: Rus. 785

Beggar's Opera
Performance/production
Interview with singer Nancy Evans and writer Eric Crozier discussing their association with Benjamin Britten. USA: Columbia, MO. UK-England: London. 1940-1985. Lang.: Eng. 3820

Begnadete Körper (Blessed Bodies)
Performance/production
On André Heller's project *Begnadete Körper (Blessed Bodies)*. Europe. China, People's Republic of. 1984-1985. Lang.: Ger. 3383

Behan, Brendan
Theory/criticism
Assessment of critic Kenneth Tynan's works. UK-England. 1950-1960. Lang.: Eng. 3136

Behavior/psychology, actor
Performance/production
Career and religious convictions of actor Alec Guinness. UK-England. 1933-1984. Lang.: Eng. 808

Rehearsals of *Kött och kärlek (Flesh and Love)* by Juoko Turkka. Sweden: Gothenburg. 1986. Lang.: Swe. 2085

Béhés, András
Performance/production
András Béhés directs *Légy jó mindhalálig (Be Good Till Death)* by Zsigmond Móricz at Nemzeti Szinház. Hungary: Budapest. 1986. Lang.: Hun. 1849

Tizenkét dühös ember (Twelve Angry Men) by Reginald Rose directed by András Béhés. Hungary: Budapest. 1985. Lang.: Hun. 1972

Behn, Aphra
Institutions
Progress and aims of Women's Playhouse Trust. UK-England: London. 1984-1986. Lang.: Eng. 1590

Beichman, Janine
Basic theatrical documents
Playtext of *Drifting Fires* by Janine Beichman, with author's afterword on use of *Nō* elements. Japan: Ibaraki. 1984-1985. Lang.: Eng. 1383

Beijing opera
SEE ALSO
Chinese opera.

Design/technology
Pheasant feathers in warrior's helmets in Chinese theatre. China. 300 B.C.-1980 A.D. Lang.: Chi. 3504

Performance/production
Life and influence of Wei Ch'angsheng, actor and playwright. China. 1795-1850. Lang.: Chi. 3506

History of the Beijing Opera. China: Beijing. 800-1986. Lang.: Cat. 3507

Guide for producing traditional Beijing opera. China: Suzhou. 1574-1646. Lang.: Chi. 3508

Career of Beijing opera actor, Hou Hsijui. China. 1920-1983. Lang.: Chi. 3514

Descendants of Confucius and Chinese opera after the Ching dynasty. China: Beijing. 1912-1936. Lang.: Chi. 3516

Influence of Beijing opera performer Mei Lanfang on European acting and staging traditions. China, People's Republic of. USSR. Germany. 1900-1935. Lang.: Eng. 3521

Techniques of comedians in modern Beijing opera. China, People's Republic of: Beijing. 1964-1985. Lang.: Chi. 3524

Plays/librettos/scripts
Use of poetic elements to create mood in Beijing opera. China: Beijing. 1030-1984. Lang.: Chi. 3529

Comparison of the works of Wang Ji-De and Xu Wei. China. 1620-1752. Lang.: Chi. 3534

Ma Ke's contribution and influence on Beijing opera. China, People's Republic of: Beijing. 1951-1985. Lang.: Chi. 3536

Structure of Beijing opera. China, People's Republic of: Beijing. 1983. Lang.: Chi. 3537

Introduction to the folk play, *Mu Lian*. China, People's Republic of: Beijing. 1962-1985. Lang.: Chi. 3538

Origins, characteristics and structures of Beijing operas. China, People's Republic of: Beijing. 1903-1985. Lang.: Chi. 3541

Beijing opera — cont'd

Relation to other fields

Role of Beijing opera today. China, People's Republic of: Beijing. 1985. Lang.: Chi. 3547

Political goals for Beijing opera. China, People's Republic of: Beijing. 1985. Lang.: Chi. 3548

Research/historiography

Transformation of traditional music notation into modern notation for four Chinese operas. China: Beijing. 1674-1985. Lang.: Chi. 3554

Origins and evolution of today's Beijing opera. China, People's Republic of: Beijing. 1755-1984. Lang.: Chi. 3556

Theory/criticism

Use of anxiety about fate in Beijing opera. China: Beijing. 5 B.C.-1985 A.D. Lang.: Chi. 3558

Defense of Chinese traditional theatre. China. 200 B.C.-1982 A.D. Lang.: Chi. 3562

Strengths and weaknesses of Beijing opera. China, People's Republic of: Beijing. 1935-1985. Lang.: Chi. 3565

Dramatic structure in Beijing opera. China, People's Republic of. 1955-1985. Lang.: Chi. 3566

Influence of Western dramatic theories on Beijing opera. China, People's Republic of: Beijing. 1935-1985. Lang.: Chi. 3567

Beijing Shadow Play Art Theatre (Beijing)

Institutions

Report on state puppet theatre. China: Beijing, Shanghai. 1986. Lang.: Eng. 4015

Beke, Sándor

Performance/production

Notes on performances of *Hongkongi paróka (Wig Made in Hong Kong)*, *Egérút (Narrow Escape)* and *Róza néni (Aunt Rosa)*. Hungary: Budapest. 1985. Lang.: Hun. 1801

Performances of Sławomir Mrożek's *Mészárszék (The Slaughterhouse)* and *Ház a határon (The Home on the Border)*. Hungary: Budapest. 1986. Lang.: Hun. 1817

Rzeźnia (The Slaughterhouse) by Sławomir Mrożek, directed by Sándor Beke at Józsefvárosi Szinház under the title *Mészárszék*. Hungary: Budapest. 1985. Lang.: Hun. 1865

Bel Geddes, Norman

Design/technology

Design and creation of puppets for the Yale Puppeteers' *Bluebeard*. USA. 1928. Lang.: Eng. 4004

Belasco, David

Plays/librettos/scripts

David Belasco's influence on Eugene O'Neill. USA: New York, NY. 1908-1922. Lang.: Eng. 2927

Theme and narrative structure in plays of Eugene O'Neill, David Belasco, and James A. Herne. USA. 1879-1918. Lang.: Eng. 2933

Belasco, Frederick

Institutions

Revival and decline of resident acting companies seen through case studies. USA. 1886-1930. Lang.: Eng. 551

Belgrave, Cynthia

Institutions

Brief histories of the H.A.D.L.E.Y. Players and the Cynthia Belgrave Theatre Workshop. USA: New York, NY. 1970-1986. Lang.: Eng. 1604

Belia, Anna

Performance/production

A kis herceg (The Little Prince) by Antoine de Saint-Exupéry adapted and staged by Anna Belia and Péter Valló. Hungary: Budapest. 1985. Lang.: Hun. 1828

A kis herceg (The Little Prince) by Saint-Exupéry adapted and staged by Anna Belia and Péter Valló. Hungary: Budapest. 1985. Lang.: Hun. 1935

Belinskij, A.

Performance/production

Ballet for television produced by A. Belinskij. USSR: Leningrad. 1980-1986. Lang.: Rus. 3277

Belitska-Scholtz, Hedvig

Institutions

Director of a theatrical history collection discusses organizational problems and lack of public interest. Hungary: Budapest. 1986. Lang.: Hun. 500

Beljakovič, V.R.

Administration

Interview with V.R. Beljakovič, manager of Teat'r-studija na Jugo-Zapade. USSR: Moscow. 1980. Lang.: Rus. 185

Bell, Nancy

Plays/librettos/scripts

Criticizes the plays in the collection *Five From the Fringe*. Canada: Edmonton, AB. 1986. Lang.: Eng. 2425

Bella

Performance/production

Dezső Szomory's *Bella* at the Pécs National Theatre directed by István Jeney. Hungary: Pécs. 1986. Lang.: Hun. 1897

Dezső Szomory's *Bella* at Pécs National Theatre directed by István Jeney. Hungary: Pécs. 1986. Lang.: Hun. 1936

Bella addormentata, La (Sleeping Beauty)

Performance/production

Collaboration of director Virgilio Talli and playwright Pier Maria Rosso di San Secondo. Italy. 1917-1920. Lang.: Ita. 1992

Bellini, Vincenzo

Performance/production

Photographs, cast list, synopsis, and discography of Metropolitan Opera radio broadcast performances. USA: New York, NY. 1986. Lang.: Eng. 3797

Plays/librettos/scripts

Operatic facsimiles by Mozart, Bellini and Verdi. Europe. 1814-1985. Lang.: Eng. 3863

The Romeo and Juliet theme as interpreted in the musical and visual arts. Italy. 1476-1900. Lang.: Eng. 3886

Belt and Braces (US)

Performance/production

Productions of Dario Fo's *Morte accidentale di un anarchico (Accidental Death of an Anarchist)* in the light of Fo's political ideas. USA. Canada. Italy. 1970-1986. Lang.: Eng. 2262

Beltran, Enric

Institutions

History of theatre in Valencia area focusing on Civil War period. Spain: Valencia. 1817-1982. Lang.: Cat. 514

Belyj, Andrej (Bugaev, Boris Nikolajevič)

Theory/criticism

Andrej Belyj's views on Symbolist and Realist theatre, dramaturgy. Russia. 1880-1934. Lang.: Rus. 3129

Bender, Gretchen

Design/technology

Keith Haring, Robert Longo and Gretchen Bender design for choreographers Bill T. Jones and Arnie Zane. USA. 1986. 1342

Bene, Carmelo

Performance/production

Orientalism in four productions of Wilde's *Salome*. Italy. 1904-1963. Lang.: Ita. 750

Examination of Italian avant-garde theatre. Italy. 1970-1985. Lang.: Ita. 751

Plays/librettos/scripts

Deconstructionist analysis of *Riccardo III* by Carmelo Bene. Italy. France. Lang.: Eng. 2690

Benedek, András

Plays/librettos/scripts

Reviews of books on Hungarian theatre. Hungary. 1952-1984. Lang.: Hun. 958

Benedek, Elek

Performance/production

Performances of *Alice Csodaországban (Alice in Wonderland)*, *A Két Veronai nemes (The Two Gentlemen of Verona)* and *Tobbsincs királyfi (No More Crown Prince)*. Hungary: Pécs, Budapest. 1985. Lang.: Hun. 1771

Benedek, Miklós

Performance/production

Review of Ivan Kušan's musical comedy *Čaruga (Death Cap)*, directed by Miklós Benedek, Katona József Theatre, as *Galócza*, includes discussion of acting and dramatic art. Hungary: Budapest. 1986. Lang.: Hun. 1811

Notes on *Čaruga (Death Cap)*, by Ivan Kušan, directed by Miklós Benedek, Katona József Theatre, under the title *Galócza*. Hungary: Budapest. 1986. Lang.: Hun. 1890

Benedetti, Mario

Basic theatrical documents

English translation of Mario Benedetti's *Pedro y el capitán (Pedro and the Captain)*. Uruguay. 1979. Lang.: Eng. 1510

Benjamin, Walter

Performance/production

Community theatre as interpreted by the Sidetrack Theatre Company. Australia: Sydney, N.S.W. 1980-1986. Lang.: Eng. 1638

SUBJECT INDEX

Benmussa, Simone
Performance/production
Collaboration of Hélène Cixous and Ariane Mnouchkine. France.
Cambodia. 1964-1986. Lang.: Eng.								1752

Benn, Gottfried
Theory/criticism
Solipsism, expressionism and aesthetics in the anti-rational dramas of
Gottfried Benn. Germany: Berlin. 1914-1934. Lang.: Eng.			3107

Bennett, Michael
Performance/production
Choreography in musical theatre. USA: New York, NY. 1944-1981.
Lang.: Eng.										3620

Bennett, R.B.
Relation to other fields
Circumstances surrounding a banned Workers' Experimental Theatre
play. Canada: Toronto, ON. 1931-1933. Lang.: Eng.				3018

Benning, Achim
Institutions
Ten years of the Burgtheater under the auspices of Achim Benning.
Austria: Vienna. 1776-1986. Lang.: Ger.						1533
Achim Benning's management of the Burgtheater. Austria: Vienna.
1976-1986. Lang.: Ger.								1537

Benson, Martin
Design/technology
A profile of Cliff Faulkner, resident designer at South Coast
Repertory. USA: Los Angeles, CA. 1977-1986.					365
Institutions
A profile of South Coast Repertory. USA: Los Angeles, CA. 1964-
1986.											569

Benson, Susan
Design/technology
Careers of stage designers, Murray Laufer, Michael Eagan and
Susan Benson. Canada. 1972-1983. Lang.: Eng.					241

Bentley, Eric
Plays/librettos/scripts
Theory of translation, using ideas of Eric Bentley and plays of
Samuel Beckett. 1950-1986. Lang.: Eng.						2352
Eric Bentley on playwriting, translating and adapting. 1986. Lang.:
Eng.											2355
Eric Bentley as one of the major forces in the subversion of Brecht.
USA.											2903
Theory/criticism
Influence of drama critic Eric Bentley. USA. 1962-1986. Lang.: Eng.
											1229

Bényei, József
Institutions
Interviews with former managing directors of Csokonai Theatre.
Hungary: Debrecen. 1974-1986. Lang.: Hun.					503

Beolco, Angelo
Performance/production
Precursors of *commedia dell'arte*. Italy: Venice. 1400-1620. Lang.:
Eng.											3414

Berea, Christian
Performance/production
Profile of and interview with Romanian-born conductor Christian
Berea. Romania. USA: New York, NY. 1950-1986. Lang.: Eng. 3771

Bérénice
Plays/librettos/scripts
Study of *Bérénice*, *Athalie* and *Bajazet* by Jean Racine. France.
1670-1691. Lang.: Fre.								2583

Berényi, Gábor
Performance/production
Gábor Berényi's production of *Macskajáték (Catsplay)* by István
Örkény at the Magyar Játékszin. Hungary: Budapest. 1985. Lang.:
Hun.											1832
Macskajáték (Catsplay) by István Örkény, directed by Gábor
Berényi, at Magyar Játékszin. Hungary: Budapest. 1985. Lang.: Hun.
											1962

Berezin, Tanya
Institutions
History of Circle Repertory Company. USA: New York, NY. 1969-
1984. Lang.: Eng.									1606

Berg, Alban
Performance/production
Opera director Nathaniel Merrill on his productions. USA: New
York, NY. 1958-1986. Lang.: Eng.						3805

Plays/librettos/scripts
The search for morality in *Wozzeck* by Alban Berg. 1821. Lang.:
Eng.											3851
Origins and influences of *Woyzeck* on Berg's opera *Wozzeck*.
Austria: Vienna. 1821-1925. Lang.: Eng.						3855
Title character in Alban Berg's *Lulu*. Austria: Vienna. 1891-1979.
Lang.: Eng.										3857
Influences on Alban Berg's *Lulu*. Austria: Vienna. 1907-1979. Lang.:
Eng.											3859
Collaboration of Kurt Weill, Alban Berg and Arnold Schönberg on
Lulu. Germany. 1920-1932. Lang.: Eng.						3875
Relation to other fields
Influence of political and artistic movements on composer Alban
Berg. Austria: Vienna. 1894-1935. Lang.: Eng.					3914
Comparison between insanity defense and opera productions with
audience as jury. USA. 1980-1985. Lang.: Eng.					3925
Theory/criticism
The concept of *Gesamtkunstwerk*. Germany. 1797-1953. Lang.: Eng.
											3929

Berg, Armin
Performance/production
History of the Viennese cabaret. Austria: Vienna. 1890-1945. Lang.:
Ger.											3364

Berganza, Teresa
Performance/production
Interview with mezzo Teresa Berganza. USA: Chicago, IL. 1984.
Lang.: Eng.										3806

Bergman, Andrew
Performance/production
Reviews of *Social Security*, by Andrew Bergman, staged by Mike
Nichols. USA: New York, NY. 1986. Lang.: Eng.				2233

Bergman, Ingmar
Intertextual analysis of Eugene O'Neill's play *Long Day's Journey
Into Night* and Ingmar Bergman's film, *Through a Glass Darkly*.
USA. Sweden. 1957-1961. Lang.: Eng.						1425
Performance/production
Reviews of regional productions. Sweden: Stockholm. 1985-1986.
Lang.: Swe.										2087
Reviews of three productions of *Fröken Julie (Miss Julie)* by August
Strindberg. Sweden: Stockholm. Denmark: Copenhagen. South Africa,
Republic of. 1985-1986. Lang.: Swe.						2090
Theory/criticism
Ingmar Bergman production of *King Lear* and Asian influences.
Spain-Catalonia: Barcelona. 1985. Lang.: Eng.					1219

Bergner, Elisabeth
Performance/production
Obituary of actress Elisabeth Bergner. 1922-1986. Lang.: Heb.	1629
Interview with Elisabeth Bergner and Jane Alexander on their
portrayals of Joan of Arc. Germany, West: Berlin, West. UK-
England: Malvern. USA: Washington, DC. Lang.: Eng.			1766

Bergvin, Einar
Institutions
Interview with Einar Bergvin, founder of amateur theatre groups and
publication. Sweden: Fagersta. 1918-1986. Lang.: Swe.				519

Bering Liisberg, Henrik
Institutions
Overview of current theatre scene. Denmark: Copenhagen. 1976-
1986. Lang.: Swe.									490

Berkeley Repertory Theatre (Berkeley, CA)
Design/technology
Sound desigers at regional theatres evaluate new equipment. USA.
1986.											409

Berkoff, Steven
Performance/production
Collection of newspaper reviews by London theatre critics. UK-
England: London. 1986. Lang.: Eng.						2112
New York critics respond negatively to plays successful in Los
Angeles. USA: Los Angeles, CA, New York, NY. 1983-1984. Lang.:
Eng.											2258

Berlin, Irving
Performance/production
Reviews of musicals. UK-England: London. 1986. Lang.: Eng.	3610

Berliner Ensemble (East Berlin)
Design/technology
Shows of models by Eduard Fischer of Berliner Ensemble. Germany,
East: Berlin, East. Hungary: Budapest. 1985. Lang.: Hun.			269

Berliner Ensemble (East Berlin) — cont'd

Institutions
Work of the Berliner Ensemble group. Germany, East: Berlin, East. 1930-1986. Lang.: Eng. 1578

Performance/production
Production of Shakespeare's *Coriolanus* by the Berliner Ensemble. Germany, East: Berlin, East. 1964. Lang.: Eng. 729

Photographic record of forty years of the Berliner Ensemble. Germany, East: Berlin, East. 1949-1984. Lang.: Eng. 1761

Application of Brechtian concepts by Eckhardt Schall. Germany, East: Berlin, East. UK-England: London. 1952-1986. Lang.: Eng. 1762

Brecht and the Berliner Ensemble. Germany, East: Berlin, East. 1950-1956. Lang.: Ger. 1765

Biography of Bertolt Brecht. Germany, West: Augsburg. Germany, East: Berlin, East. USA. 1898-1956. Lang.: Ger. 1767

Berlioz, Hector

Audience
Claques as viewed by French writers. France. 1800-1899. Lang.: Fre. 3647

Plays/librettos/scripts
Aesthetic considerations in *Lélio* by Hector Berlioz. France. Lang.: Fre. 3868

Berls, Jack

Plays/librettos/scripts
Unpublished documentation of *Proprio like that*, a musical by Luigi Pirandello. Italy: Rome. 1930-1953. Lang.: Fre. 3627

Berne Convention

Administration
Prediction of future copyright trends. 1886-1986. Lang.: Eng. 17

Berne Convention Protocol in developing countries. Africa. Asia. 1963-1986. Lang.: Eng. 21

Berne Convention in People's Republic of China. China, People's Republic of. 1908-1986. Lang.: Eng. 30

Berne Convention and compulsory licensing. Europe. 1908-1986. Lang.: Eng. 36

History of Berne Convention and copyright laws. Europe. 1709-1886. Lang.: Eng. 37

Protection of rights existing before Berne Convention. France. 1971-1986. Lang.: Eng. 43

Berne Convention and copyright in socialist countries. Hungary. 1917-1986. Lang.: Eng. 46

Copyright before and after Berne Convention. UK. 1850-1986. Lang.: Eng. 68

Berne Convention and copyright in market economy. UK. USA. 1886-1986. Lang.: Eng. 69

Berne Convention and public interest. UK. 1886-1986. Lang.: Eng. 75

Conflicts between reproduction permission and authors' rights. UK-England. 1911-1986. Lang.: Eng. 79

Discussion of Berne Convention (1886) establishing copyright agreement. UK-England: London. 1986. Lang.: Eng. 80

U.S. Copyright and the Berne Convention. USA. 1985. Lang.: Eng. 84

Berne Convention and U.S. copyright law. USA. 1776-1986. Lang.: Eng. 157

Bernelle, Agnes

Performance/production
Collection of newspaper reviews by London theatre critics. UK-England: London. 1986. Lang.: Eng. 2109

Bernhard, Thomas

Performance/production
On actor Gert Voss and his work. Austria: Vienna. Germany, West. 1941-1986. Lang.: Ger. 1649

Relation to other fields
Herbert Moritz and his views about cultural politics. Austria. 1986. Lang.: Ger. 1064

Bernhardt, Sarah

Performance/production
The portrayal of Cleopatra by various actresses. England. 1813-1890. Lang.: Eng. 1699

Bernstein, Leonard

Performance/production
Reviews of musicals. UK-England: London. 1986. Lang.: Eng. 3610

Stills from telecast performance of *Candide* by New York City Opera. USA: New York, NY. 1986. Lang.: Eng. 3796

Plays/librettos/scripts
Remarks on Alan Jay Lerner at his memorial service. USA: New York, NY. 1986. 3630

Berrigan, Daniel

Plays/librettos/scripts
Compares Daniel Berrigan's play *The Trial of the Catonsville Nine* with the trial itself and the action that occasioned it. USA: Catonsville, MD. 1968-1973. Lang.: Eng. 2916

Berry, Cicely

Performance/production
Collection of newspaper reviews by London theatre critics. UK. 1986. Lang.: Eng. 2099

Collection of newspaper reviews by London theatre critics. UK. 1986. Lang.: Eng. 2101

Collection of newspaper reviews by London theatre critics. UK-England: London. 1986. Lang.: Eng. 2110

Berthomme, Luce

Training
Actor training methods of Luce Berthomme. France: Paris. 1984. Lang.: Eng. 1256

Beryl and the Perils (UK)

Performance/production
Collection of newspaper reviews by London theatre critics. UK-England: London. 1986. Lang.: Eng. 2109

Feminist theatre group Beryl and the Perils. UK-England. 1986. Lang.: Eng. 2171

Beso de la mujer araña, El (Kiss of the Spider Woman, The)

Plays/librettos/scripts
Chronotopic analysis of *El beso de la mujer araña (The Kiss of the Spider Woman)* by Manuel Puigi. Argentina. 1976-1986. Lang.: Spa. 2364

Besser, Gedalya

Administration
Interview with directors of Teatron HaIroni. Israel: Haifa. 1982-1986. Lang.: Heb. 52

Performance/production
Announcement of Margalith Prize winners. Israel: Jerusalem. 1986. Lang.: Heb. 1977

Besson, Benno

Institutions
History of Swedish language Lilla-teatern (Little Theatre). Finland: Helsinki. 1940-1986. Lang.: Eng, Fre. 494

Performance/production
Benno Besson and his staging of *Don Juan* at the Burgtheater. Austria: Vienna. Switzerland. Germany, East. 1922-1986. Lang.: Ger. 1642

Hungarian reviewer discusses Paris performances. France: Paris. 1986. Lang.: Hun. 1734

Bestwick, Deborah

Performance/production
Collection of newspaper reviews by London theatre critics. UK-England: London. 1986. Lang.: Eng. 2116

Besuch der alten Dame, Der (Visit, The)

Performance/production
Öreg hölgy látogatása (The Visit) by Friedrich Dürrenmatt, directed by Péter Gothár at Vigszinház. Hungary: Budapest. 1986. Lang.: Hun. 1782

Production by György Emőd of Friedrich Dürrenmatt's *A Öreg hölgy látogatása (The Visit)*. Hungary: Győr. 1985. Lang.: Hun. 1788

Péter Gothár's production of *A Öreg hölgy látogatósa (The Visit)* by Friedrich Dürrenmatt. Hungary: Budapest. 1986. Lang.: Hun. 1889

Plays/librettos/scripts
Individual and society in *Die Nag van Legio (The Night of Legio)* by P.G. du Plessis and *Der Besuch der alten Dame (The Visit)* by Friedrich Dürrenmatt. South Africa, Republic of. Switzerland. 1955-1970. Lang.: Afr. 2774

Besy (Possessed, The)

Performance/production
Tamás Ascher directs *Ördögök (The Devils)*, an adaptation of *Besy (The Possessed)* by Dostojévskij. Hungary: Budapest. 1986. Lang.: Hun. 1778

Betrayal

Plays/librettos/scripts
Study of realism vs metadrama. Europe. 429 B.C.-1978 A.D. Lang.: Eng. 2540

Theme of renewal in Harold Pinter's *Betrayal*. UK-England. 1978. 2835

Billington, Ken — cont'd

Interview with lighting designer Gil Wechsler of the Metropolitan Opera. USA: New York, NY. 1883-1986. Lang.: Eng. 3654

Billington, Michael
Plays/librettos/scripts
Modern criticism of Shakespeare's crowd scenes. England. 1590-1986. Lang.: Eng. 2536

Billy Budd
Plays/librettos/scripts
Collaboration of authors and composers of *Billy Budd*. UK-England: London. 1949-1964. Lang.: Eng. 3895
A chronology and analysis of the compositions of Benjamin Britten. UK-England: London. 1946-1976. Lang.: Eng. 3896

Biloxi Blues
Plays/librettos/scripts
Interview with playwright Neil Simon. USA: New York, NY. 1927-1986. Lang.: Eng. 2931

Biltmore Theatre (New York, NY)
Performance/production
Reviews of *Honky Tonk Nights*, book and lyrics by Ralph Allen and David Campbell, staged and choreographed by Ernest O. Flatt. USA: New York, NY. 1986. Lang.: Eng. 3612

Bima Suarga
Performance/production
Shadow puppetry as a way of passing on Balinese culture. Bali. 1976-1985. Lang.: Eng. 4017

Bing, Rudolph
Administration
Edward Downes on his life in the opera. USA: New York, NY. 1911-1986. Lang.: Eng. 3643

Bingo
Plays/librettos/scripts
Beckettian elements in Shakespeare as seen by playwright Edward Bond. UK-England. 1971-1973. Lang.: Eng. 2833
Brecht's ideas about the history play as justification for Edward Bond's *Bingo*. UK-England. 1974. Lang.: Eng. 2876

Biographical studies
Performance/production
Tom Robertson as a theatrical innovator and as a character in Arthur Wing Pinero's *Trelawny of the Wells*. England: London. 1840-1848. Lang.: Eng. 1702

Birch, Patricia
Performance/production
Reviews of *Raggedy Ann*, book by William Gibon, music and lyrics by Joe Raposo, staged and choreographed by Patricia Birch. USA: New York, NY. 1986. Lang.: Eng. 3614

Birkmeyer, Michael
Institutions
Activities of the audience-society, Gesellschaft der Freunde der Ballettschule der Österreichischen Bundestheater. Austria: Vienna. 1985-1986. Lang.: Ger. 1294

Birth of Tragedy, The
SEE
Geburt der Tragödie, Die.

Birthday Party, The
Plays/librettos/scripts
Analysis of *The Birthday Party* by Harold Pinter. UK-England. 1958. Lang.: Eng. 2856

Bishof, Sándor
Design/technology
Interview with scene designer Sándor Bishof. Hungary: Zalaegerszeg. 1983-1986. Lang.: Hun. 284

Bishop, André
Administration
Literary managers discuss their roles and responsibilities in nonprofit theatre. USA: New York, NY. 1983. Lang.: Eng. 132

Plays/librettos/scripts
Artists react to *New York Times* condemnation of current playwriting. USA. 1984. Lang.: Eng. 2888

Theory/criticism
Theatre professionals challenge assertions that theatre is a weaker form of communication than film. USA: New York, NY. 1985. Lang.: Eng. 1225

Bisitratus
Relation to other fields
Factors that discouraged historical drama in the classical period. Greece: Athens. 475-375 B.C. Lang.: Eng. 3035

Bissell, Richard
Performance/production
Collection of newspaper reviews by London theatre critics. UK: London. 1986. Lang.: Eng. 2100

BITEF (Belgrade)
Performance/production
Notes on theatrical events of nineteenth annual international theatre festival. Yugoslavia: Belgrade. 1985. Lang.: Hun. 2341
Theatrical events of nineteenth annual international theatre festival. Yugoslavia. 1985. Lang.: Hun. 2343

Bizet, Georges
Performance/production
Production of *L'Histoire terrible mais inachevé de Norodom Sihanouk, roi du Cambodge (The Terrible but Unfinished History of Norodom Sihanouk, King of Cambodia)* by Hélène Cixous. France: Paris. 1985. Lang.: Eng. 1737
Peter Brook's direction and adaptation of the opera *Carmen* by Georges Bizet. France: Paris. 1981-1983. Lang.: Heb. 3731
Géza Oberfrank directs Bizet's *Carmen* at Szegedi Nemzeti Szinház. Hungary: Szeged. 1985. Lang.: Hun. 3748
Reviews of 10 vintage recordings of complete operas on LP. USA. 1906-1925. Lang.: Eng. 3792
Photographs, cast list, synopsis, and discography of Metropolitan Opera radio broadcast performances. USA: New York, NY. 1986. Lang.: Eng. 3794

Plays/librettos/scripts
Adaptations of *Carmen* by Prosper Mérimée. France. Spain. 1845-1983. Lang.: Fre. 3870

Bizot, Phillippe
Performance/production
A photographic essay of 42 soloists and groups performing mime or gestural theatre. 1986. Lang.: Eng. 3290

Bjørnager, Kjeld
Performance/production
Discussion of Stanislavskij's influence by a number of artists. Sweden. 1890-1986. Lang.: Swe. 2094

Black Bonspiel of Wullie MacCrimmon
Institutions
Career of Walter Learning, artistic director, Vancouver Playhouse. Canada: Vancouver, BC. 1982-1983. Lang.: Eng. 470

Black Jacobins, The
Performance/production
Collection of newspaper reviews by London theatre critics. UK-England: London. 1986. Lang.: Eng. 2121

Black Love
Institutions
History of Black Spectrum. USA: New York, NY. 1970-1986. Lang.: Eng. 1603

Black Nativity
Performance/production
Career of director/choreographer Mike Malone. USA: Washington, DC, Cleveland, OH. 1968-1985. Lang.: Eng. 2275

Black Picture Show
Reference materials
Current work of Audelco award-winning playwrights. USA: New York, NY. 1973-1984. Lang.: Eng. 3007

Black Rock Theatre (Montreal, PQ)
Performance/production
Playwright David Fennario's commitment to working-class community theatre. Canada: Montreal, PQ. 1980-1986. Lang.: Eng. 1661

Black Spectrum (New York, NY)
Relation to other fields
Black history and folklore taught in theatre workshops and productions. USA: New York, NY, Omaha, NE, Washington, DC. 1986. Lang.: Eng. 3068

Black Spectrum (Queens, NY)
Institutions
History of Black Spectrum. USA: New York, NY. 1970-1986. Lang.: Eng. 1603

Black Street, USA Puppet Theatre
Performance/production
Gary Jones, and the Black Street, USA Puppet Theatre. USA: Chicago, IL, Los Angeles, CA. 1970-1986. Lang.: Eng. 3978

Black theatre

Administration
Alternative funding for small theatres previously dependent on government subsidy. USA: St. Louis, MO, New York, NY, Los Angeles, CA, Detroit, MI. 1985. Lang.: Eng.   103

Developments in funding minority arts projects. USA. 1985. Lang.: Eng.   118

Growing activity and changing role of Black regional theatre companies. USA. 1960-1984. Lang.: Eng.   1440

Audience
Reception of Lorraine Hansberry's *A Raisin in the Sun*. USA. 1959-1986. Lang.: Eng.   1456

Institutions
Reprint of an article by Douglas Turner Ward that resulted in the founding of the Negro Ensemble Company. USA: New York, NY. 1966. Lang.: Eng.   572

History of two major Black touring companies. USA: New York, NY. 1969-1982. Lang.: Eng.   1598

Vi Higginsen's *Mama I Want to Sing* and history of the Mumbo-Jumbo Theatre Company. USA: New York, NY. 1980-1986. Lang.: Eng.   1601

Curriculum and expectation of students in Eubie Blake's Children's Theatre Company. USA: New York, NY. 1986. Lang.: Eng.   1602

History of Black Spectrum. USA: New York, NY. 1970-1986. Lang.: Eng.   1603

Brief histories of the H.A.D.L.E.Y. Players and the Cynthia Belgrave Theatre Workshop. USA: New York, NY. 1970-1986. Lang.: Eng.   1604

History of Black theater companies. USA: Philadelphia, PA. 1966-1985. Lang.: Eng.   1608

Brief history of the McCree Theatre. USA: Flint, MI. 1971-1986. Lang.: Eng.   1609

Career of Marjorie Moon, artistic director of Billie Holliday Theatre. USA: New York, NY, Cleveland, OH. 1973-1986. Lang.: Eng.   1610

Performance/production
Biography of actor Richard B. Harrison, who played God in *The Green Pastures*. USA. 1930-1939. Lang.: Eng.   828

Impact and influence of the tour by black American actor Ira Aldridge. UK-England: Manchester. 1827. Lang.: Eng.   2136

Brief history of August Wilson's *Fences*. USA. 1982-1986. Lang.: Eng.   2273

Career of director/choreographer Mike Malone. USA: Washington, DC, Cleveland, OH. 1968-1985. Lang.: Eng.   2275

Lloyd Richard's career as an actor, director, artistic director and academic dean. USA: Detroit, MI, New York, NY, New Haven, CT. 1920-1980. Lang.: Eng.   2308

Career of popular entertainer Bill Cosby. USA. 1937-1986. Lang.: Eng.   3353

Four nightclub entertainers on their particular acts and the atmosphere of the late night clubs and theaters in Harlem. USA: New York, NY, Savannah, GA. 1930-1950. Lang.: Eng.   3470

Dakota Stanton discusses her career as a singer and dancer in nightclubs and reviews. USA: Pittsburgh, PA, New York, NY. 1950-1980. Lang.: Eng.   3471

Tap dancing career of Maurice Hines and the creation of his new company Balletap, USA. USA: New York, NY. 1949-1986. Lang.: Eng.   3623

Black opera stars and companies. USA: Enid, OK, New York, NY. 1961-1985. Lang.: Eng.   3839

Plays/librettos/scripts
Precursors of revolutionary black theatre. Haiti. Jamaica. 1820-1970. Lang.: Eng.   956

Role of working class in development of theatre resistance. South Africa, Republic of. 1976-1986. Lang.: Eng.   967

Award-winning plays by Black writers. USA. 1924-1927. Lang.: Eng.   978

Summary of speech given by playwright Ossie Davis at Third World Theatre Conference. USA: Davis, CA. 1986. Lang.: Eng.   986

Analysis of *La Tragédie du roi Christophe (The Tragedy of King Christopher)* by Aimé Césaire. Haiti. Africa. Martinique. 1939. Lang.: Fre.   2637

Symbolism in Derek Walcott's *Dream on Monkey Mountain*. Jamaica. 1967. Lang.: Eng.   2718

Influence of working class on form and content of theatre of resistance. South Africa, Republic of: Soweto. 1976-1986. Lang.: Eng.   2777

Summary and discussion of the plays of Ed Bullins. USA. 1968-1973. Lang.: Eng.   2900

Ritual function of *The Slave Ship* by LeRoi Jones (Amiri Baraka) and *Quinta Temporada (Fifth Season)* by Luis Valdez. USA. 1965-1967. Lang.: Eng.   2906

Race in prison dramas of Piñero, Camillo, Elder and Bullins. USA. 1970-1986. Lang.: Eng.   2912

Interview with playwright Lorraine Hansberry. USA. 1959. Lang.: Eng.   2945

Biographical sketch of playwright/performer Samm-Art Williams. USA: Burgaw, NC, New York, NY. 1940-1986. Lang.: Eng.   2946

Identifies dramatic elements unique to street theatre. USA. 1968-1986. Lang.: Eng.   3354

Reference materials
Current work of Audelco award-winning playwrights. USA: New York, NY. 1973-1984. Lang.: Eng.   3007

Relation to other fields
Political issues for Black performers. 1986. Lang.: Eng.   1052

Reflections and influence of arts and race relations. South Africa, Republic of. Lang.: Afr.   1125

Sociocultural elements of Black theatre. USA. 1960-1985. Lang.: Eng.   3063

Black history and folklore taught in theatre workshops and productions. USA: New York, NY, Omaha, NE, Washington, DC. 1986. Lang.: Eng.   3068

Critical analysis of composer William Grant Still. USA. 1895-1978. Lang.: Eng.   3924

Black Theatre Workshop (Montreal, PQ)

Institutions
Interviews with theatre professionals in Quebec. Canada. 1985. Lang.: Fre.   487

Blackfriars' Children's Company (London)

Administration
Involvement of Robert Keysar with Harry Evans and Blackfriars' Children's Company. England: London. 1608. Lang.: Eng.   1433

Blaha, Paul

Institutions
Paul Blaha's management of the Volkstheater. Austria: Vienna. 1986-1987. Lang.: Ger.   1538

Blair, Ron

Plays/librettos/scripts
Ron Blair: considerations in writing for the theatre. Australia. 1960-1970. Lang.: Eng.   2372

Blake, Eubie

Institutions
Curriculum and expectation of students in Eubie Blake's Children's Theatre Company. USA: New York, NY. 1986. Lang.: Eng.   1602

Blake, William Rufus

Plays/librettos/scripts
William Rufus Blake's *Fitzallan* as the first play written and produced in Canada. Canada: Halifax, NS. 1833. Lang.: Eng.   2430

Blakely, Colin

Performance/production
Actor Colin Blakely discusses his career. UK-England: London. 1950-1986. Lang.: Eng.   2176

Blakemore, Michael

Performance/production
Collection of newspaper reviews by London theatre critics. UK-England: London. 1986. Lang.: Eng.   2125

Blanco, Roberto

Plays/librettos/scripts
Interviews with actress Pilar Romero and director Roberto Blanco at the Festival de Théâtre des Amériques. Canada: Montreal, PQ. 1985. Lang.: Eng.   2426

Blane, Sue

Design/technology
Design challenges of the film *Absolute Beginners*. UK-England: London. 1986. Lang.: Eng.   3203

Blin, Roger

Performance/production
Reminiscences of actor-director Roger Blin. France. 1930-1983. Lang.: Fre.   1726

Blithe Spirit
Performance/production
Collection of newspaper reviews by London theatre critics. UK-England: London. 1986. Lang.: Eng.   2113

Bloch, Ernst
Relation to other fields
Kurt Weill and German expressionism. Germany: Berlin. 1923-1930. Lang.: Eng.   3920

Blok, Aleksand'r Aleksandrovič
Plays/librettos/scripts
Poetic and dramatic elements in the plays of Aleksand'r Blok. Russia. 1880-1921. Lang.: Rus.   2766

Blood Brothers
Performance/production
Ivan Vas-Zoltán directs *Vértestvérek (Blood Brothers)* by Willy Russell. Hungary: Pécs. 1986. Lang.: Hun.   3602

Blood Knot, The
Design/technology
Interview with lighting designer William Warfel. USA: New Haven, CT. 1985-1986. Lang.: Eng.   1527

Blood Relations
Plays/librettos/scripts
Analysis of the plays of Sharon Pollock. Canada. 1971-1983. Lang.: Eng.   935

Blood, Sweat and Tears
Performance/production
Collection of newspaper reviews by London theatre critics. UK-England: London. 1986. Lang.: Eng.   2123

Bloodgood, Fred Foster
Performance/production
Recreation of a medicine show featuring 'Doc' Bloodgood, staged by American Place Theatre. USA. 1983. Lang.: Eng.   3375

Bloolips (UK)
Plays/librettos/scripts
Overview of plays with homosexual themes. UK-England: London. 1970-1986. Lang.: Eng.   2841

Bloomer Girl
Design/technology
Costume designs for musical comedy by Miles White. USA: New York, NY. 1944-1960. Lang.: Eng.   1529

Blues for a Gospel Queen
Institutions
Career of Marjorie Moon, artistic director of Billie Holliday Theatre. USA: New York, NY, Cleveland, OH. 1973-1986. Lang.: Eng.   1610

Bly, Mark
Performance/production
Mark Bly on the dramaturg's responsibility to question. USA: Minneapolis, MN. 1981-1986. Lang.: Eng.   2294

Boal, Augusto
Performance/production
Survey of productions in 1985/86. Brazil: Rio de Janeiro. 1985-1986. Lang.: Eng.   1656

Plays/librettos/scripts
Interplay of signs of violence in Augusto Boal's *Torquemada*. Brazil. 1971. Lang.: Eng.   2404

Relation to other fields
Interactive theatre in *It's About Time* by Catalyst Theatre. Canada: Edmonton, AB. 1982. Lang.: Eng.   1069
Interview with Augusto Boal. Canada: Montreal, PQ. France. Brazil: São Paulo. 1952-1986. Lang.: Eng.   3019
Workshops in Canada on 'Theatre for the Oppressed'. Canada: Toronto, ON. 1986. Lang.: Eng.   3022
Theatre workshops led by Augusto Boal. Canada: Montreal, PQ. 1985. Lang.: Eng.   3023
Current style of theatre-in-education. UK-England. Lang.: Eng.   3057

Theory/criticism
Augusto Boal's concept of theatre of the oppressed. Brazil. France. 1956-1978. Lang.: Eng.   1201

Boar's Head Playhouse (London)
Performance spaces
Conjectural reconstruction of the Boar's Head Playhouse. England: London. 1558-1603. Lang.: Eng.   592

Bóbita Bábszinház (Pécs)
Institutions
History of Bóbita Puppet Theatre. Hungary: Pécs. 1961-1986. Lang.: Hun.   3957

Bocanegra, Matías
Plays/librettos/scripts
Calderón's *El gran duque de Gandía (The Grand Duke of Gandía)* and its Mexican source. Spain. Mexico. 1600-1680. Lang.: Eng. 2789

Boccaccio, Giovanni
Relation to other fields
Reciprocal influence of Italian comedy and Boccaccio's *The Decameron*. Italy. 1350-1550. Lang.: Ita.   3045

Bodolay, Géza
Performance/production
Performances of *Hair*, directed by János Sándor, and *Desire Under the Elms*, directed by Géza Bodolay at the National Theatre of Szeged. Hungary: Szeged. 1986. Lang.: Hun.   1959

Bodrogi, Gyula
Performance/production
Gábor Görgey's *Huzatos ház (Drafty House)* directed by Gyula Bodrogi, Vidám Színpad. Hungary: Budapest. 1986. Lang.: Hun.
1845
Gábor Görgey's *Huzatos ház (Drafty House)* directed by Gyula Bodrogi at Vidám Színpad. Hungary: Budapest. 1986. Lang.: Hun.
1856

Body Politic Theatre (Chicago, IL)
Performance spaces
Technical facilities and labor practices at several U.S. theatres as seen by a Swedish visitor. USA: Chicago, IL, New York, NY. 1986. Lang.: Swe.   642

Bogart, Anne
Theory/criticism
Eleven theatre professionals discuss their personal direction and the direction of experimental theatre. USA: New York, NY. 1985. Lang.: Eng.   3137

Bogdanov, Michael
Institutions
Actor Michael Pennington and director Michael Bogdanov discuss the formation of the English Shakespeare Company. UK-England. 1986. Lang.: Eng.   1592

Bogusławski, Wojciech
Institutions
Foundation of Polish theatre in Poznań in 1783, its repertoire and political contexts. Poland: Poznań. 1782-1793. Lang.: Pol.   512
Plays/librettos/scripts
Notes on György Spiró's play about actor, director, manager and playwright Wojciech Bogusławski. Hungary. 1983. Lang.: Hun. 2659

Bohème, La
Performance/production
Verdi's *Simon Boccanegra* and Puccini's *La Bohème* at the Hungarian State Opera House and Erkel Theatre. Hungary: Budapest. 1986. Lang.: Hun.   3747

Böhm, Stefan
Performance/production
The cooperation between amateurs and professionals in Fria Proteatern's staging of Brecht's *Turandot*. Sweden: Stockholm. 1986. Lang.: Swe.   2095

Boiler Room Suite
Plays/librettos/scripts
Symbolism and allusion in *Boiler Room Suite* by Rex Deverell. Canada: Regina, SK. 1977. Lang.: Eng.   934

Boîte à Popicos, La (Edmonton, AB)
Institutions
A history of two French language theatres. Canada: Edmonton, AB. 1970-1986. Lang.: Eng.   1542

Boito, Arrigo
Performance/production
The successful collaboration of Arrigo Boito and Giuseppe Verdi in *Simon Boccanegra*. Italy. 1856-1881. Lang.: Eng.   3764
Photographs, cast list, synopsis, and discography of Metropolitan Opera radio broadcast performances. USA: New York, NY. 1986. Lang.: Eng.   3794
Plays/librettos/scripts
Why Verdi revised the 1857 version of *Simon Boccanegra*. Italy: Milan. 1857-1881. Lang.: Eng.   3881

Bol'šoj Teat'r Opery i Baleta Sojuza SSR (Moscow)
Performance/production
Singer I. Archipova on tasks of Soviet opera. USSR. 1980-1986. Lang.: Rus.   3846

Boldizsár, Miklós
Performance/production
Review of rock opera *István a király (King Stephen)* at the National Theatre. Hungary: Budapest. 1985. Lang.: Hun.   3489

Bolívar
Plays/librettos/scripts
Interviews with actress Pilar Romero and director Roberto Blanco at the Festival de Théâtre des Amériques. Canada: Montreal, PQ. 1985. Lang.: Eng.   2426

Bolshoi (Moscow)
SEE
Bolšoj Teat'r Opery i Baleta Sojuza SSR.

Bolshoi Ballet
SEE
Bolšoj Teat'r Opery i Baleta Sojuza SSR.

Bolshoi Opera
SEE
Bolšoj Teat'r Opery i Baleta Sojuza SSR.

Bolšoj Teat'r Opery i Baleta Sojuza SSR (Moscow)
Administration
General director of Bolšoj Ballet on problems of the future. USSR: Moscow. 1986. Lang.: Rus.   1292

Performance/production
Career of dancer Ju.T. Ždanov. USSR. 1925-1986. Lang.: Rus.   1321

Bolt, Alan
Relation to other fields
Director Alan Bolt of the Nicaraguan National Theater Workshop discusses the process of theatre. Nicaragua. 1985.   1114

Bolt, Carol
Plays/librettos/scripts
Amerindian and aborigine characters in the works of white playwrights. Canada. Australia. 1606-1975. Lang.: Eng.   930

Bolt, Robert
Plays/librettos/scripts
Accuracy of portrayal of historical figures in Shakespeare and his adaptors. England. 1590-1940. Lang.: Eng.   2532

Bolton, Gavin
Relation to other fields
Curricular authority for drama-in-education program. UK. Lang.: Eng.   3054

Discussion of theatre-in-education. UK. Lang.: Eng.   3055

Bonaparte, Napoleon
Plays/librettos/scripts
Treatment of Napoleon Bonaparte by French and English dramatists. France. England. 1797-1958. Lang.: Eng.   2568

Bond Street Theatre Coalition (New York, NY)
Institutions
Theatre companies that spend summers outside of New York City to promote artistic growth and development. USA. 1985. Lang.: Eng.
550

Performance/production
Resurgence of street theatre productions and companies. USA: New York, NY. 1960-1982. Lang.: Eng.   2285

Reference materials
Summer performance schedules for several New York companies. USA: New York, NY. 1984. Lang.: Eng.   3011

Bond, Christopher
Plays/librettos/scripts
Interview with Gillian Hanna about *Elisabetta: Quasì per caso una donna (Elizabeth: Almost by Chance a Woman)*. UK-England: London. Italy. 1986. Lang.: Eng.   2875

Bond, Edward
Performance/production
Productions of plays by Edward Bond, Gyula Hernádi and Lope de Vega at the Pécs National Theatre. Hungary: Pécs. 1986. Lang.: Hun.   1898

Kinn vagyunk a vízből (Saved) by Edward Bond directed by István Szőke. Hungary: Pécs. 1986. Lang.: Hun.   1940

Comparative analysis of productions of *Summer* by Edward Bond. UK-England: London. 1982. Lang.: Eng.   2163

Plays/librettos/scripts
Beckettian elements in Shakespeare as seen by playwright Edward Bond. UK-England. 1971-1973. Lang.: Eng.   2833

Playwright Edward Bond's use of Greek models in *The Woman*. UK-England. 1978. Lang.: Eng.   2834

Evaluation of *The War Plays* by Edward Bond. UK-England: London. 1986. Lang.: Eng.   2853

Brecht's ideas about the history play as justification for Edward Bond's *Bingo*. UK-England. 1974. Lang.: Eng.   2876

Bondy, Luc
Performance/production
Analysis of two productions of plays by Marivaux. France: Nanterre. Germany, West: Berlin, West. 1985. Lang.: Swe.   1739

Bonner, Marita
Plays/librettos/scripts
Precursors of revolutionary black theatre. Haiti. Jamaica. 1820-1970. Lang.: Eng.   956

Bononcini, Giovanni
Performance/production
Productions of Handel's *Muzio Scevola* and analysis of score and characters. England: London. 1718-1980. Lang.: Eng.   3720

Booker, Margaret
Administration
Panel discussion on theatre as commerce or resource to its community. USA: New York, NY. 1986.   179

Booth, Edwin
Performance/production
Edwin Booth's portrayal of Iago in Shakespeare's *Othello*. USA. 1852-1890. Lang.: Eng.   854

Booth, John N.
Reference materials
Catalogue of an exhibition of costume designs for Broadway musicals. USA: New York, NY. 1900-1925. Lang.: Eng, Ger.   3635

Booth, Junius Brutus
Performance/production
Career of actress and theatrical manager Louisa Lane Drew. USA. 1820-1897. Lang.: Eng.   2243

Bor, József
Performance/production
József Bor directs Verdi's opera *Il Trovatore* at Kisfaludy Theatre. Hungary: Győr. 1985. Lang.: Hun.   3750

Borden, Walter
Plays/librettos/scripts
Actor and prose-poet Walter Borden's play *Tight Rope Time*. Canada: Halifax, NS. 1960-1986. Lang.: Eng.   2409

Borderline Theatre Company (UK-Scotland)
Institutions
History of Borderline Theatre Company. UK-Scotland. 1974-1985. Lang.: Eng.   1594

Performance/production
Interview with Borderline Theatre Company artistic director Morag Fullarton. UK-Scotland. 1979-1986. Lang.: Eng.   2190

Borelli, Lyda
Performance/production
Orientalism in four productions of Wilde's *Salome*. Italy. 1904-1963. Lang.: Ita.   750

Boretz, Allan
Performance/production
Reviews of *Room Service*, by John Murray and Allan Boretz, staged by Alan Arkin. USA: New York, NY. 1986. Lang.: Eng.   2242

Boris Godunov
Performance/production
Mussorgskij's opera *Boris Godunov* at the Mariinskij Theatre. Russia: St. Petersburg. 1874. Lang.: Eng.   3775

Analysis and appreciation of the work of Modest Pavlovič Mussorgskij. USSR. 1839-1881. Lang.: Eng.   3849

Relation to other fields
Comparison between insanity defense and opera productions with audience as jury. USA. 1980-1985. Lang.: Eng.   3925

Borisov, Ju.
Theory/criticism
Synthesis of the arts in the theatrical process. USSR: Moscow. 1986. Lang.: Rus.   1240

Borowski, Adam
Performance/production
Interviews with Polish theatre professionals. Poland: Poznań. 1963-1985. Lang.: Eng.   2024

Bosch, Hieronymus
Performance/production
Martha Clarke's production of *The Garden of Earthly Delights*. USA: New York, NY. 1979-1984. Lang.: Eng.   1371

Plays/librettos/scripts
Iconography of throne scene in Shakespeare's *Richard III*. England. 1591-1592. Lang.: Eng.   2481

Boso, Carlo
Performance/production
Interview with Carlo Boso, expert on *commedia dell'arte*. Europe. 1985. Lang.: Fre.   3409

Boso, Carlo — cont'd

Interview with Carlo Boso on *commedia dell'arte* reconstruction. UK-England. Italy. 1947-1986. Lang.: Eng. 3415

Bouffes du Nord (Paris)
Performance/production
Peter Brook's *The Mahabharata* at the Théâtre aux Bouffes du Nord. France: Avignon, Paris. 1985-1986. Lang.: Eng. 1753

Bouffons de Bullion (Montreal)
Performance/production
Interview with clown, writer and teacher Philippe Gaulier. Europe. 1500-1986. Lang.: Fre. 3333

Boulez, Pierre
Performance/production
Recollection of Jean-Louis Barrault's career as actor and director. France. 1943-1956. Lang.: Fre. 711

Boullet, Citoyen
Design/technology
Works by and about designers Jacopo Fabris and Citoyen Boullet. Denmark: Copenhagen. France: Paris. 1760-1801. Lang.: Eng. 256

Folio drawings by Jacopo Fabris illustrating how to paint perspective scenery and build theatrical machinery. Denmark: Copenhagen. Italy. 1760-1801. Lang.: Eng. 257

Translation of eighteenth-century treatise on stage machinery and construction. France: Paris. 1760-1801. Lang.: Eng. 264

Boulton, Claudia
Performance/production
Feminist theatre group Beryl and the Perils. UK-England. 1986. Lang.: Eng. 2171

Bouncers
Performance/production
Collection of newspaper reviews by London theatre critics. UK-England: London. 1986. Lang.: Eng. 2117

Bouncing
Plays/librettos/scripts
Interview with playwright Rosemary Wilton, author of *Bouncing*. UK-England: London. 1986. Lang.: Eng. 2832

Bourdet, Edouard
Basic theatrical documents
Journal of playwright and general administrator of Comédie-Française. France: Paris. 1936. Lang.: Fre. 1477

Bourdet, Gildas
Performance/production
Directors discuss staging of plays by Paul Claudel. France. Belgium. 1985. Lang.: Fre. 1723

Bourgeois gentilhomme, Le (Bourgeois Gentleman, The)
Performance/production
Péter Gellért's production of *Urhatnám polgár (The Bourgeois Gentleman)* at Móricz Zsigmond Szinház. Hungary: Nyiregyháza. 1986. Lang.: Hun. 1931

Bouvier, Joëlle
Performance/production
Photos and interviews of dance company l'Esquisse. France: Paris. 1981-1985. Lang.: Fre. 1345

Bow Gamelan Ensemble (England)
Performance/production
Interview with performance artists Bow Gamelan Ensemble. UK-England. 1986. Lang.: Eng. 3451

Bower, Fredson
Research/historiography
Review of introductions to the plays of Thomas Dekker by Cyrus Hoy. England: London. USA. 1600-1980. Lang.: Eng. 1185

Bowery Theatre (New York, NY)
Performance spaces
The varied history of the Bowery Theatres. USA: New York, NY. 1826-1929. Lang.: Eng. 1624

Bowlaner, Marie-Julie
Performance/production
Careers of young Parisian prima donnas. France: Paris. 1830-1850. Lang.: Eng. 3728

Bowtell, Elizabeth
Performance/production
Career of actress Elizabeth Bowtell, who first acted under her maiden name of Davenport. England. 1664-1715. Lang.: Eng. 1706

Boy and the Magic, The
Design/technology
Creating overhead shadow sequence for puppet production. USA. 4014

Boyce, G.E.
Performance/production
History of Great Wallace Circus. USA. 1913. Lang.: Eng. 3387

Boyko, Debbi
Performance/production
Development of works by the Special Delivery Moving Theatre. Canada: Vancouver, BC. 1976-1986. Lang.: Eng. 3294

Boyle, Wickham
Theory/criticism
Eleven theatre professionals discuss their personal direction and the direction of experimental theatre. USA: New York, NY. 1985. Lang.: Eng. 3137

Boys in Autumn, The
Performance/production
Reviews of *The Boys in Autumn* by Bernard Sabath, staged by Theodore Mann. USA: New York, NY. 1986. Lang.: Eng. 2221

Bozó, László
Performance/production
Criticizes stage adaptation of *Hangok komédiája (Comedy of Sounds)* by Miklós Gyárfás. Hungary: Budapest. 1985. Lang.: Hun. 1924

Bradwell, Mike
Performance/production
Collection of newspaper reviews by London theatre critics. UK-England: London. 1986. Lang.: Eng. 2117

Brahms, Johannes
Plays/librettos/scripts
Investigates whether Brahms wrote music for an opera. Austria: Vienna. 1863-1985. Lang.: Eng. 3856

Brand
Plays/librettos/scripts
Self-transcendence through grace embodied in Henrik Ibsen's female characters. Norway. 1849-1899. Lang.: Eng. 2726

Brand, Mona
Institutions
Account of New Theatre movement by a participant. Australia: Sydney, Melbourne. 1932-1955. Lang.: Eng. 437

Plays/librettos/scripts
Playwright Mona Brand's work with New Theatre movement. Australia: Sydney, N.S.W. 1932-1968. Lang.: Eng. 924

Brandauer, Klaus Maria
Performance/production
Klaus Maria Brandauer as Hamlet. Austria: Vienna. 1944-1986. Lang.: Ger. 1648

Playing Hamlet at the Burgtheater. Austria: Vienna. 1803-1985. Lang.: Ger. 1654

Brandston, Howard
Design/technology
Howard Brandston's approach to lighting the Statue of Liberty. USA: New York, NY. 1986. Lang.: Eng. 3317

Brass Birds Don't Sing
Plays/librettos/scripts
Biographical sketch of playwright/performer Samm-Art Williams. USA: Burgaw, NC, New York, NY. 1940-1986. Lang.: Eng. 2946

Bratja i sëstry (Brothers and Sisters)
Performance/production
Correlation of scenery and direction. USSR: Leningrad. 1980-1986. Lang.: Rus. 2335

Bratja Karamazov (Brothers Karamazov, The)
Performance/production
Stage adaptations of Dostojèvskij novels *A Fëlkesgyelmü (The Idiot)* and *A Karamazov testvérek (The Brothers Karamazov)*. Hungary: Budapest, Debrecen. 1985. Lang.: Hun. 1922

Braun, Edward
Plays/librettos/scripts
Compares contemporary Canadian theatre with German and Russian theatre of the early 20th century. Canada. Russia: Moscow. Germany. 1900-1986. Lang.: Eng. 2412

Braun, Kazimierz
Performance/production
Director Kazimierz Braun on his adaptation of *La Peste (The Plague)* by Albert Camus. Poland: Wrocław. 1976-1983. Lang.: Eng. 2015

Braut von Messina, Die (Bride of Messina, The)
Theory/criticism
Analysis of Friedrich Schiller's dramatic and theoretical works. Germany. 1759-1805. Lang.: Cat. 3109

Bravo, Julian
Basic theatrical documents
Contract of first known theatre company in America. Peru: Lima. 1599-1620. Lang.: Spa. 225

Bray, Errol
Performance/production
Dilemmas and prospects of youth theatre movement. Australia. 1982-1986. Lang.: Eng. 1639

Bread and Dreams Festival (Winnipeg, MB)
Relation to other fields
Political issues for Black performers. 1986. Lang.: Eng. 1052

Bread and Puppet Theatre (New York, NY)
Institutions
Discussion of techniques and theories of Bread and Puppet Theatre. USA: New York, NY. 1961-1978. Lang.: Ita. 3960

Performance/production
Peter Schumann and his work with the Bread and Puppet Theatre. USA: New York, NY. 1968-1986. Lang.: Eng. 3973

Relation to other fields
Politics, performing arts and puppetry. USA. 1970-1986. Lang.: Eng. 3994

Breashears, David
Relation to other fields
Cinematographer David Breashears climbs Mt. Everest. Tibet. 1986. 3246

Brecht Chansonettes
Performance/production
DeVina Barajas discusses performing the songs of Brecht. Switzerland. Germany, West. USA. 1978-1985. 3607

Brecht Company, The (Ann Arbor, MI)
Performance/production
A profile of The Brecht Company. USA: Ann Arbor, MI. 1979-1984. 2312

Brecht-Schall, Barbara
Performance/production
Application of Brechtian concepts by Eckhardt Schall. Germany, East: Berlin, East. UK-England: London. 1952-1986. Lang.: Eng. 1762

Brecht, Bertolt
Basic theatrical documents
A film scenario for Bertolt Brecht's *Lux in Tenebris*. 1985. 3197

Institutions
Account of New Theatre movement by a participant. Australia: Sydney, Melbourne. 1932-1955. Lang.: Eng. 437
Production of Brecht's *Baal* by a troupe of untrained young actors. Sweden: Stockholm. 1986. Lang.: Swe. 525
A report on the symposium at the Festival Latino discusses Brecht and the Nuevo Teatro movement. USA: New York, NY. 1984. 564
Work of the Berliner Ensemble group. Germany, East: Berlin, East. 1930-1986. Lang.: Eng. 1578

Performance/production
Zen and Western acting styles. Lang.: Eng. 648
Directorial process as seen through major productions of Stanislavskij, Brecht, Kazan and Brook. 1898-1964. Lang.: Eng. 650
Production of Shakespeare's *Coriolanus* by the Berliner Ensemble. Germany, East: Berlin, East. 1964. Lang.: Eng. 729
Actor Hilmar Thate on Brecht. Germany, West. Germany, East. 1949-1984. 732
The New Theatre movement combines methodologies of collective creation with the Brechtian epic. Latin America. 763
Brechtian technique in the contemporary feminist drama of Caryl Churchill, Claire Luckham and others. UK-England. 1956-1979. Lang.: Eng. 815
Actress Walfriede Schmitt discusses performing Brecht. USA. 1986. 823
Characteristics of the stage space in Brecht's epic theatre. 1985. 1628
Historical development of acting and directing techniques. 1898-1986. Lang.: Eng. 1632
Community theatre as interpreted by the Sidetrack Theatre Company. Australia: Sydney, N.S.W. 1980-1986. Lang.: Eng. 1638
Jean Vilar's staging of plays by Bertolt Brecht. France. 1951-1960. Lang.: Ita. 1736
An exploration of Brecht's *Gestus*. Germany. Lang.: Eng. 1758
Photographic record of forty years of the Berliner Ensemble. Germany, East: Berlin, East. 1949-1984. Lang.: Eng. 1761

Application of Brechtian concepts by Eckhardt Schall. Germany, East: Berlin, East. UK-England: London. 1952-1986. Lang.: Eng. 1762
Brecht and the Berliner Ensemble. Germany, East: Berlin, East. 1950-1956. Lang.: Ger. 1765
Biography of Bertolt Brecht. Germany, West: Augsburg. Germany, East: Berlin, East. USA. 1898-1956. Lang.: Ger. 1767
Program notes for the Athens Ensemble production of *Baal* by Bertolt Brecht. Greece: Athens. 1983. 1769
Der Hofmeister (The Tutor), Jakob Lenz's drama adapted by Bertolt Brecht, directed by Gábor Máté. Hungary: Kaposvár. 1985. Lang.: Hun. 1810
Production of *A nevelő (The Tutor)* by Bertolt Brecht. Hungary: Kaposvár. 1985. Lang.: Hun. 1840
Die dreigroschenoper (The Three Penny Opera) directed by István Pinczés at Csokonai Theatre. Hungary: Debrecen. 1986. Lang.: Hun. 1910
Gábor Máté directs Brecht's *Der Hofmeister (The Tutor)* at Csiky Gergely Theatre under the title *A nevelő*. Hungary: Kaposvár. 1985. Lang.: Hun. 1966
A stage history of the work of Bertolt Brecht. Poland. 1923-1984. 2050
Mejerchol'd's influence on Bertolt Brecht. Russia: Moscow. Germany, East: Berlin, East. 1903-1957. Lang.: Eng. 2065
Articles about the productions of the Centre Dramàtic. Spain-Catalonia: Barcelona. 1976-1986. Lang.: Cat. 2084
The cooperation between amateurs and professionals in Fria Proteatern's staging of Brecht's *Turandot*. Sweden: Stockholm. 1986. Lang.: Swe. 2095
Collection of newspaper reviews by London theatre critics. UK-England: London. 1986. Lang.: Eng. 2124
Interview with director Jurij Liubimov. USA: Washington, DC. USSR: Moscow. 1986. Lang.: Eng. 2196
Director Christoph Nel discusses staging Brecht's *Im Dickicht der Städte (In the Jungle of the Cities)*. USA: Seattle, WA. 1984. 2246
Productions of Dario Fo's *Morte accidentale di un anarchico (Accidental Death of an Anarchist)* in the light of Fo's political ideas. USA. Canada. Italy. 1970-1986. Lang.: Eng. 2262
Director Ann Gadon on staging Brecht's *Lux in Tenebris*. USA: Chicago, IL. 1985. 2267
Director John Ahart discusses staging *The Caucasian Chalk Circle*. USA: Urbana, IL. 1984. 2278
Notes from a production of *Mahagonny* by the Remains Ensemble. USA: Chicago, IL. 1985. 2282
Director Peter Sellars talks about staging Brecht's plays. USA. 1983. 2290
A profile of The Brecht Company. USA: Ann Arbor, MI. 1979-1984. 2312
Robert Sturua of Georgian Academic Theatre directs Brecht and Shakespeare in Warsaw. USSR: Tbilisi. Poland: Warsaw. 1983. Lang.: Pol. 2336
Performance art and its current characteristic tone. USA. Lang.: Eng. 3459
Rehearsal of *Die Dreigroschenoper (The Three Penny Opera)* directed by Giorgio Strehler. France: Paris. 1986. Lang.: Eng. 3486
What spoken drama actors can learn from Sung drama. China. 1100-1980. Lang.: Chi. 3513
Influence of Beijing opera performer Mei Lanfang on European acting and staging traditions. China, People's Republic of. USSR. Germany. 1900-1935. Lang.: Eng. 3521
DeVina Barajas discusses performing the songs of Brecht. Switzerland. Germany, West. USA. 1978-1985. 3607

Plays/librettos/scripts
Japanese influences on works of Brecht and Klabund. Germany. Japan. 1900-1950. Lang.: Ita. 952
Bertolt Brecht and the Expressionists. Germany. 1919-1944. Lang.: Eng. 955
Brecht's use of the epically structured motif of the military review. 2354
Eric Bentley on playwriting, translating and adapting. 1986. Lang.: Eng. 2355
Interview with founders of Internationale Nieuwe Scene. Europe. 1984. 2543

Brecht, Bertolt — cont'd

Great dramatic works considered in light of modern theatre and social reponsibility. France. Italy. Germany, West. 1700-1964. Lang.: Fre.   2560

Fox symbolism in plays of Bertolt Brecht, Max Frisch and Gerhart Hauptmann. Germany. Switzerland. 1700-1976. Lang.: Ger.   2598

Distortion of historical fact in Brecht's *Leben des Galilei (The Life of Galileo)*. Germany. 1938-1955. Lang.: Eng.   2600

Analysis of *Leben des Galilei (The Life of Galileo)* by Bertolt Brecht. Germany. 1938. Lang.: Rus.   2606

Influence of Chinese theatre on Bertolt Brecht. Germany: Berlin. China. 1900-1950. Lang.: Ita.   2608

Dialogue analysis of *Die Gewehre der Frau Carrar (Señora Carrar's Rifles)* by Bertolt Brecht. Germany, East. Lang.: Ger.   2612

Revising Brecht's plays to insure socially relevant productions. Germany, East. 1985.   2613

Applying Brecht's dramatic principles to the plays of Euripides. Germany, East. Greece. 450 B.C.-1956 A.D.   2614

Brecht's patriarchal view of women as seen in the character of Jenny in *Die Dreigroschenoper (The Three Penny Opera)*. Germany, East.   2615

Criteria for evaluating translations, using the example of Brecht's *Galileo*. Germany, East. 1938-1953.   2616

Demystification of the feminine myth in Brecht's plays. Germany, East. 1984.   2618

Chinese influences on Bertolt Brecht. Germany, East: Berlin, East. China. 1935-1956. Lang.: Eng.   2619

Work of Bertolt Brecht should be re-examined according to the current historical perspective. Germany, East. 1984.   2620

Brecht's concept of *Naivität* in *Die Tage der Kommune (The Days of the Commune)*. Germany, East. 1948-1956.   2621

Comparison of Heiner Müller's *Der Auftrag (The Mission)* and Bertolt Brecht's *Die Massnahme (The Measures Taken)*. Germany, East. 1930-1985. Lang.: Eng.   2622

A *laudatio* in honor of playwright Friedrich Dürrenmatt, recipient of the 1986 Büchner Prize. Germany, West: Darmstadt. Switzerland: Neuchâtel. 1942-1986. Lang.: Ger.   2624

Work of playwright Stefan Schütz. Germany, West. 1944-1986. Lang.: Eng.   2625

Brecht's life and work. Germany, West: Augsburg. Germany, East: Berlin, East. USA: Los Angeles, CA. 1898-1956. Lang.: Ger.   2626

Brecht's interpretational legacy is best understood on West German stages. Germany, West. 1956-1986.   2627

Interview with playwright Stefan Schütz. Germany, West. 1970-1986. Lang.: Eng.   2628

Program notes from Heinz-Uwe Haus's production of *Arturo Ui*. Greece. 1985.   2631

The influence of Brecht on Haiti's exiled playwright Frank Fouché and the group Kovidor. Haiti. 1970-1979.   2638

Caryl Churchill combines Brecht's alienation effect with traditional comic structure in *Cloud 9*. UK-England. 1980.   2871

Brecht's ideas about the history play as justification for Edward Bond's *Bingo*. UK-England. 1974. Lang.: Eng.   2876

Political views of Howard Brenton as evidenced in his adaptations. UK-England. 1973-1986. Lang.: Eng.   2883

Eric Bentley as one of the major forces in the subversion of Brecht. USA.   2903

Correspondence between Bernhard Reich and Heinz-Uwe Haus. USSR. 1971-1972.   2966

Relation to other fields

The use of women and homosexuality in Brecht's sexual lyric poetry. 1920-1928.   1055

The young Brecht's use of the Bible to criticize the Church and society. Germany. 1913-1918.   1089

Analysis of Bertolt Brecht's love poetry. Germany, East. 1898-1956.   1092

A review of the 5-volume edition of Bertolt Brecht's poetry. Germany, East. 1898-1956.   1093

Critique of two articles which examine Brecht's love poetry from a feminist perspective. Germany, East. 1898-1956.   1094

A portrait of Brecht in Peter Weiss's *Die Ästhetik des Widerstands*. Sweden: Stockholm. 1939-1940.   1130

Comparison of Olympiad Arts Festival and the 1984 Olympic Games. USA: Los Angeles, CA. 1984. Lang.: Eng.   1148

A discussion of the Nuevo Teatro movement and the status of Brecht in the U.S. USA: New York, NY. 1984.   1156

Bertolt Brecht's contributions to modern theatre. Canada: Toronto, ON. 1985. Lang.: Eng.   3020

Brecht's talents in the area of musical-poetic improvisation.   3501

Theory/criticism

Influence of drama critic Eric Bentley. USA. 1962-1986. Lang.: Eng.   1229

Critique of James Fenton's review of two books on Bertolt Brecht. USA. 1974.   1236

Pina Bausch seen as heir of epic theater of Bertolt Brecht. Germany, West. 1977-1985. Lang.: Eng.   1289

Aesthetic theory of interpretation. Europe. North America. 1900-1985. Lang.: Fre.   3097

Introduction of the work and influence of Bertolt Brecht. France. 1945-1956. Lang.: Fre.   3103

Coriolanus from Bertolt Brecht's viewpoint. Germany. 1898-1956. Lang.: Chi.   3105

Comparison of Brechtian theatre and Chinese traditional theatre. Germany. China. 1400-1982. Lang.: Chi.   3111

Brecht's assertion that the producing artist must be independent of financial pressures.   3247

Influence of Western dramatic theories on Beijing opera. China, People's Republic of: Beijing. 1935-1985. Lang.: Chi.   3567

Bregenzer Festspiele (Bregenz)

Institutions

Financial difficulties of the Bregenzer Festspiele. Austria: Bregenz. 1985-1986. Lang.: Ger.   440

Solving the financial problems of the Bregenzer Festspiele. Austria: Bregenz. 1986-1987. Lang.: Ger.   442

Breguadze, Boris

Performance/production

Careers of four Russian 'apostles of dance'. USSR. Lang.: Rus. 1320

Brekte, Andris

Performance/production

Discussion of Stanislavskij's influence by a number of artists. Sweden. 1890-1986. Lang.: Swe.   2094

Brennan, Mark

Performance/production

Collection of newspaper reviews by London theatre critics. UK-England: London. 1986. Lang.: Eng.   2126

Brentano, Clemens

Plays/librettos/scripts

Comedies of Tieck and Brentano representing German Romanticism. Germany. 1795-1850. Lang.: Rus.   2602

Brenton, Howard

Plays/librettos/scripts

Analysis of *Magnificence* by Howard Brenton. England. 1970-1980. Lang.: Eng.   2524

Interview with playwright Howard Barker. UK-England. 1981-1985. Lang.: Eng.   2845

World War II as a theme in post-war British drama. UK-England. 1945-1983. Lang.: Eng.   2868

Political views of Howard Brenton as evidenced in his adaptations. UK-England. 1973-1986. Lang.: Eng.   2883

Brešan, Ivo

Performance/production

Ivo Brešan's *Paraszt Hamlet (The Peasant Hamlet)* directed by Béla Merő. Hungary: Zalaegerszeg. 1986. Lang.: Hun.   1888

Brett, Jason

Administration

Efforts to produce the film *Sexual Perversity in Chicago*. USA. Lang.: Eng.   3194

Brettschneider, Nika

Institutions

Program of Theater Brett for the 1986/87 season. Austria: Vienna. 1986-1987. Lang.: Ger.   3288

Breuer, Lee

Institutions

Interview with members of Mabou Mines. USA: New York, NY. 1984. Lang.: Eng.   1607

Performance/production

Historical development of acting and directing techniques. 1898-1986. Lang.: Eng.   1632

Brevard Music Center (Charlotte, NC)
Performance/production
History and achievements of the Brevard Music Center on the occasion of its fiftieth season. USA: Charlotte, NC. 1936-1986. Lang.: Eng. 3808

Brewster, Yvonne
Performance/production
Collection of newspaper reviews by London theatre critics. UK-England: London. 1986. Lang.: Eng. 2121

Brickman, Marshall
Design/technology
Bran Ferren's special effects for *The Manhattan Project*. USA. 1986. 377

Bricolo, Amédée
Performance/production
A photographic essay of 42 soloists and groups performing mime or gestural theatre. 1986. 3290

Bridge Lane Battersea Theatre (London)
Performance/production
Collection of newspaper reviews by London theatre critics. UK-England: London. 1986. Lang.: Eng. 2113

Brief History of Horror: and Wild Love
SEE
Pequeña historia de horror: y de amor desenfrenado.

Brigadoon
Performance/production
Reviews of *Brigadoon*, by Alan Jay Lerner, Frederick Loewe, staged by Gerald Freedman. USA: New York, NY. 1986. Lang.: Eng. 3619

Bright, John
Design/technology
Overview of the costume department of the National Theatre. UK-England: London. 1950-1986. Lang.: Eng. 1523

Brighton Beach Memoirs
Performance/production
Collection of newspaper reviews by London theatre critics. UK-England. 1986. Lang.: Eng. 2120

Plays/librettos/scripts
Interview with playwright Neil Simon. USA: New York, NY. 1927-1986. Lang.: Eng. 2931

Brill, Marius
Performance/production
Collection of newspaper reviews by London theatre critics. UK-England: London. 1986. Lang.: Eng. 2110

Plays/librettos/scripts
Playwright Marius Brill discusses his prize winning play *Frikzhan*. UK-England: London. 1986. Lang.: Eng. 2831

Brill, Steve
Design/technology
New lighting technology for *The Cosby Show*. USA: New York, NY. 1986. Lang.: Eng. 3259

Brink, André
Theory/criticism
Semiotic analysis of *La Storia*. Italy. 1985. Lang.: Eng. 3118

Brisley, Stuart
Performance/production
Description of a three-day live performance by performance artist Stuart Brisley. UK-Scotland: Glasgow. 1986. Lang.: Eng. 3456

Bristol Old Vic Theatre
Performance/production
Collection of newspaper reviews by London theatre critics. UK-England. 1986. Lang.: Eng. 2120
Roger Rees, associate director at Bristol Old Vic discusses his career and the season. UK-England: Bristol. 1970-1986. Lang.: Eng. 2138
Survey of theatrical performances in the low country. UK-England. 1986. Lang.: Eng. 2150

Bristolteatern (Copenhagen)
Institutions
Overview of current theatre scene. Denmark: Copenhagen. 1976-1986. Lang.: Swe. 490

British Broadcasting Corporation (BBC, London)
Design/technology
Examination of the latest Strand TV lighting console in Studio A at BBC Scotland. UK-Scotland: Glasgow. 1980-1986. Lang.: Eng. 3256

Plays/librettos/scripts
Interview with playwright Howard Barker. UK-England. 1981-1985. Lang.: Eng. 2845

Productions of Jane Howell and Elijah Moshinsky for the BBC Shakespeare series. UK-England: London. 1978-1985. Lang.: Eng. 3283
Review articles on the BBC Shakespeare series. UK-England: London. 1978-1985. Lang.: Eng. 3284

Britten, Benjamin
Design/technology
Profile of theatre designer Tanya Moiseiwitsch. 1934-1986. Lang.: Eng. 227

Performance/production
Christopher Renshaw talks about his production of Benjamin Britten's opera *A Midsummer Night's Dream* at Covent Garden. UK-England: London. 1986. Lang.: Eng. 3782
The relationship of Steuart Bedford and Benjamin Britten. UK-England: London. 1967-1976. Lang.: Eng. 3783
Life and career of singer Peter Pears. UK-England: London. 1937-1986. Lang.: Eng. 3784
Appreciation and obituary of the late English tenor Sir Peter Pears. UK-England: Aldeburgh. 1910-1986. Lang.: Eng. 3785
Interview with singer Nancy Evans and writer Eric Crozier discussing their association with Benjamin Britten. USA: Columbia, MO. UK-England: London. 1940-1985. Lang.: Eng. 3820
Women's roles in the operas of Benjamin Britten. USA. 1940-1979. Lang.: Eng. 3824

Plays/librettos/scripts
Treatment of homosexuality in *Death in Venice*. Germany. UK-England. 1911-1970. Lang.: Eng. 3874
Development of the libretto for Benjamin Britten's opera *Gloriana*. UK-England: London. 1952-1953. Lang.: Eng. 3894
Collaboration of authors and composers of *Billy Budd*. UK-England: London. 1949-1964. Lang.: Eng. 3895
A chronology and analysis of the compositions of Benjamin Britten. UK-England: London. 1946-1976. Lang.: Eng. 3896
Analysis of Benjamin Britten's opera *Albert Herring*. UK-England: London. 1947. Lang.: Eng. 3897
Character analysis in Britten's opera *The Turn of the Screw*. UK-England. 1954. Lang.: Eng. 3898
The life, career and compositions of Benjamin Britten. UK-England: London. 1913-1976. Lang.: Eng. 3899
A review of Southwestern University's Brown Symposium VII, 'Benjamin Britten and the Ceremony of Innocence'. USA: Georgetown. 1985. Lang.: Eng. 3904

Relation to other fields
Comparison between insanity defense and opera productions with audience as jury. USA. 1980-1985. Lang.: Eng. 3925

Brjusov, Valerij
Theory/criticism
Symbolist poet Valerij Brjusov's ideas on theatre. Russia. 1873-1924. Lang.: Ita. 3131

Broadhurst Theatre (New York, NY)
Performance/production
Reviews of *Broadway Bound*, by Neil Simon, staged by Gene Saks. USA: New York, NY. 1986. Lang.: Eng. 2206
Reviews of *Long Day's Journey Into Night* by Eugene O'Neill, staged by Jonathan Miller. USA: New York, NY. 1986. Lang.: Eng. 2219
Reviews of *The Life and Adventures of Nicholas Nickleby*, book by Charles Dickens, adapted by David Edgar, staged by Trevor Nunn. USA: New York, NY. 1986. Lang.: Eng. 2271

Broadway Bound
Performance/production
Reviews of *Broadway Bound*, by Neil Simon, staged by Gene Saks. USA: New York, NY. 1986. Lang.: Eng. 2206

Plays/librettos/scripts
Interview with playwright Neil Simon. USA: New York, NY. 1927-1986. Lang.: Eng. 2931

Broadway theatre
Design/technology
Challenges faced by designers of Bob Fosse's *Big Deal*. USA. 1986. Lang.: Eng. 359
Broadway's union scene shops struggle to remain solvent. USA: New York, NY. 1986. Lang.: Eng. 395

Performance spaces
Architect Robert Morgan's design for Broadway's Marquis Theatre. USA: New York, NY. 1986. Lang.: Eng. 633

Broadway theatre — cont'd

Performance/production

Comprehensive survey of ten years of theatre in New York City. USA: New York, NY. 1970-1980. Lang.: Eng. 837

Collection of reviews by Benedict Nightingale on New York theatre. USA: New York, NY. 1983-1984. Lang.: Eng. 847

Reviews of *Big Deal*, written, staged and choreographed by Bob Fosse. USA: New York, NY. 1986. Lang.: Eng. 1283

Reviews of *Uptown...It's Hot*, staged, choreographed and conceived by Maurice Hines. USA: New York, NY. 1986. Lang.: Eng. 1284

Reviews of *Broadway Bound*, by Neil Simon, staged by Gene Saks. USA: New York, NY. 1986. Lang.: Eng. 2206

Reviews of *Jackie Mason's 'World According to Me'*, written and created by Mason. USA: New York, NY. 1986. Lang.: Eng. 2207

Reviews of *Flamenco Puro*, conceived, staged and designed by Claudio Segovia and Hector Orezzoli. USA: New York, NY. 1986. Lang.: Eng. 2210

Reviews of *Rowan Atkinson at the Atkinson*, by Richard Curtis, Rowan Atkinson and Ben Elton, staged by Mike Ockrent. USA: New York, NY. 1986. Lang.: Eng. 2211

Reviews of *You Never Can Tell*, by George Bernard Shaw, staged by Stephen Porter. USA: New York, NY. 1986. Lang.: Eng. 2212

Reviews of *A Little Like Magic*, conceived and staged by Diane Lynn Dupuy. USA: New York, NY. 1986. Lang.: Eng. 2213

Reviews of *The Front Page*, by Ben Hecht and Charles MacArthur, staged by Jerry Zaks. USA: New York, NY. 1986. Lang.: Eng. 2214

Reviews of *Arsenic and Old Lace*, by Joseph Kesselring, staged by Brian Murray. USA: New York, NY. 1986. Lang.: Eng. 2215

Reviews of *Long Day's Journey Into Night* by Eugene O'Neill, staged by Jonathan Miller. USA: New York, NY. 1986. Lang.: Eng. 2219

Reviews of *The House of Blue Leaves* by John Guare, staged by Jerry Zaks. USA: New York, NY. 1986. Lang.: Eng. 2220

Reviews of *The Boys in Autumn* by Bernard Sabath, staged by Theodore Mann. USA: New York, NY. 1986. Lang.: Eng. 2221

Reviews of *Principia Scriptoriae* by Richard Nelson, staged by Lynne Meadow. USA: New York, NY. 1986. Lang.: Eng. 2223

Reviews of *Cuba and His Teddy Bear* by Reinaldo Povod, staged by Bill Hart. USA: New York, NY. 1986. Lang.: Eng. 2228

Reviews of *Execution of Justice*, written and staged by Emily Mann. USA: New York, NY. 1986. Lang.: Eng. 2230

Reviews of *Precious Sons* by George Furth, staged by Norman Rene. USA: New York, NY. 1986. Lang.: Eng. 2231

Reviews of *So Long on Lonely Street*, by Sandra Deer, staged by Kent Stephens. USA: New York, NY. 1986. Lang.: Eng. 2232

Reviews of *Social Security*, by Andrew Bergman, staged by Mike Nichols. USA: New York, NY. 1986. Lang.: Eng. 2233

Reviews of *The Petition*, by Brian Clark, staged by Peter Hall. USA: New York, NY. 1986. Lang.: Eng. 2234

Reviews of *Corpse!* by Gerald Moon, staged by John Tillinger. USA: New York, NY. 1986. Lang.: Eng. 2235

Reviews of *The Caretaker* by Harold Pinter, staged by John Malkovich. USA: New York, NY. 1986. Lang.: Eng. 2236

Reviews of *Jerome Kern Goes to Hollywood*, conceived and staged by David Kernan. USA: New York, NY. 1986. Lang.: Eng. 2237

Reviews of *Caligula* by Albert Camus, staged by Marshall W. Mason. USA: New York, NY. 1986. Lang.: Eng. 2239

Reviews of *Lillian* by William Luce, staged by Robert Whitehead. USA: New York, NY. 1986. Lang.: Eng. 2245

Reviews of *The Life and Adventures of Nicholas Nickleby*, book by Charles Dickens, adapted by David Edgar, staged by Trevor Nunn. USA: New York, NY. 1986. Lang.: Eng. 2271

Brief history of August Wilson's *Fences*. USA. 1982-1986. Lang.: Eng. 2273

Director of original production discusses Edward Albee's *Who's Afraid of Virginia Woolf?*. USA: New York, NY. 1962. Lang.: Eng. 2303

Reviews of *Juggling and Cheap Theatrics* with the Flying Karamazov Brothers, staged by George Mosher. USA: New York, NY. 1986. Lang.: Eng. 3349

Reviews of *Sweet Charity* by Neil Simon, staged and choreographed by Bob Fosse. USA: New York, NY. 1986. Lang.: Eng. 3611

Reviews of *Honky Tonk Nights*, book and lyrics by Ralph Allen and David Campbell, staged and choreographed by Ernest O. Flatt. USA: New York, NY. 1986. Lang.: Eng. 3612

Reviews of *Smile*, music by Marvin Hamlisch, book by Howard Ashman. USA: New York, NY. 1986. Lang.: Eng. 3613

Reviews of *Raggedy Ann*, book by William Gibon, music and lyrics by Joe Raposo, staged and choreographed by Patricia Birch. USA: New York, NY. 1986. Lang.: Eng. 3614

Reviews of *Into the Light*, book by Jeff Tamborniro, music by Lee Holdridge, lyrics by John Forster, staged by Michael Maurer. USA: New York, NY. 1986. Lang.: Eng. 3615

Reviews of *Oh Coward!*, lyrics and music by Noël Coward, devised and staged by Roderick Cook. USA: New York, NY. 1986. Lang.: Eng. 3616

Reviews of *Rags*, book by Joseph Stein, music by Charles Strouse, lyrics by Stephen Schwartz, staged by Gene Saks. USA: New York, NY. 1986. Lang.: Eng. 3617

Career of Broadway composer Stephen Sondheim. USA: New York, NY. 1930-1986. Lang.: Eng. 3624

Plays/librettos/scripts

Successful Broadway playwrights, lyricists, and composers discuss their hits. USA: New York, NY. 1900-1985. Lang.: Eng. 3631

Reference materials

Guide to the work of principal composers of Broadway musicals. 1905-1985. Lang.: Eng. 3633

Catalogue of an exhibition of costume designs for Broadway musicals. USA: New York, NY. 1900-1925. Lang.: Eng, Ger. 3635

Broadway Theatre (New York, NY)

Performance/production

Reviews of *Big Deal*, written, staged and choreographed by Bob Fosse. USA: New York, NY. 1986. Lang.: Eng. 1283

Brockbank, Philip

Plays/librettos/scripts

Modern criticism of Shakespeare's crowd scenes. England. 1590-1986. Lang.: Eng. 2536

Brockmann, Johann

Performance/production

Examination of German versions of Shakespeare's *Hamlet*. Germany: Hamburg. 1770-1811. Lang.: Eng. 728

Brod, Max

Plays/librettos/scripts

Reflections on Max Zweig's dramas. Austria: Vienna. Germany: Berlin. Israel: Tel Aviv. 1892-1986. Lang.: Ger. 2389

Bródy, János

Performance/production

Review of rock opera *István a király (King Stephen)* at the National Theatre. Hungary: Budapest. 1985. Lang.: Hun. 3489

Broken Heart, The

Plays/librettos/scripts

Allegorical romantic conventions in John Ford's *The Broken Heart*. England. 1633. Lang.: Eng. 2497

Analysis of the final scene of *The Broken Heart* by John Ford. England. 1629. Lang.: Eng. 2526

Brome, Richard

Performance/production

Historical context of *The Late Lancaster Witches* by Thomas Heywood and Richard Brome. England. 1634. Lang.: Eng. 689

Plays/librettos/scripts

Image of poverty in Elizabethan and Stuart plays. England. 1558-1642. Lang.: Eng. 2482

Brook, Peter

Institutions

Survey of Royal Shakespeare Company productions. UK-England. 1960-1980. Lang.: Chi. 1593

Performance/production

Zen and Western acting styles. Lang.: Eng. 648

Directorial process as seen through major productions of Stanislavskij, Brecht, Kazan and Brook. 1898-1964. Lang.: Eng. 650

Discussion of *Persepolis* and *Orghast* at Persepolis-Shiraz festival. Iran: Shiraz. 1971. Lang.: Ita. 741

Overview of the career and work of director Peter Brook. USA: New York, NY. 1948-1984. Lang.: Eng. 829

Director Charles Marowitz on the role of the director. USA. 1965-1985. Lang.: Eng. 843

Interview with Peter Brook's designer, musician, and costumer for *Mahabharata*. France: Avignon. 1973-1985. Lang.: Eng. 1359

Brook, Peter — cont'd

Interviews with actors in Peter Brook's *Mahabharata*. France: Avignon. 1985. Lang.: Eng.   1360

Peter Brook discusses development of *The Mahabharata*. France: Avignon. India. 1965-1986. Lang.: Eng.   1361

Peter Brook's *The Mahabharata* at the Théâtre aux Bouffes du Nord. France: Avignon, Paris. 1985-1986. Lang.: Eng.   1753

Comparison of stage production and film version of Shakespeare's *King Lear*, both directed by Peter Brook. UK-England. 1962-1970. Lang.: Eng.   2149

Theatre work of Bettina Jonic. UK-England. 1970-1986. Lang.: Eng.   2151

Detailed discussion of four successful Royal Shakespeare Company productions of Shakespeare's minor plays. UK-England: Stratford. 1946-1977. Lang.: Eng.   2182

Chronological study of the work of director Peter Brook. UK-England. France. 1964-1980. Lang.: Eng.   2187

Self-referential elements in several film versions of Shakespeare's *King Lear*. UK. USA. 1916-1983. Lang.: Eng.   3227

Performance analysis of the title role of *Carmen*. France. 1875-1986. Lang.: Eng.   3725

Peter Brook's direction and adaptation of the opera *Carmen* by Georges Bizet. France: Paris. 1981-1983. Lang.: Heb.   3731

Relation to other fields

Western directors and third-world theatre. 1900-1986. Lang.: Ita.   1053

On Peter Brook's *Mahabharata*, produced by the International Center of Theatre Research. France: Paris. 1985. Lang.: Rus.   3032

Research/historiography

Indian theatre professionals criticize Peter Brook's *Mahabharata*. India: Kerala, Calcutta. 1980-1985. Lang.: Eng.   1376

Theory/criticism

Melodrama as an aesthetic theatre form. Australia. 1850-1986. Lang.: Eng.   3083

Selection from Peter Brook's *The Empty Space*. EUROPE. 1929-1982. Lang.: Chi.   3095

Brooker, Bertram

Basic theatrical documents

Text of *Within* by Bertram Brooker. Canada: Toronto, ON. 1935. Lang.: Eng.   217

Text of *The Dragon* by Bertram Brooker. Canada: Toronto, ON. 1936. Lang.: Eng.   1466

Plays/librettos/scripts

Introduction to the plays of Bertram Brooker. Canada. 1928-1936. Lang.: Eng.   927

Career of expressionist playwright Bertram Brooker. Canada: Toronto, ON. 1888-1949. Lang.: Eng.   2418

Brookes, Joanna

Performance/production

Political difficulties in staging two touring productions of Shakespeare's *The Taming of the Shrew*. UK. 1985-1986. Lang.: Eng.   2104

Brooklyn Academy of Music (BAM, New York, NY)

Administration

Brooklyn Academy of Music development director's fundraising strategy. USA: New York, NY. Lang.: Eng.   112

Role of the marketing director in nonprofit theatre. USA: New York, NY. 1986. Lang.: Eng.   140

Design/technology

Development of scenic design at the Brooklyn Academy of Music. USA. 1984-1986. Lang.: Eng.   341

Performance/production

Interview with choreographer Meredith Monk. USA: New York, NY. 1964-1984. Lang.: Eng.   1368

Dramaturg Richard Nelson on communicating with different kinds of directors. USA: New York, NY. 1979-1986. Lang.: Eng.   2252

Revival of Philip Glass and Robert Wilson's *Einstein on the Beach* and opportunities to improve the piece. USA: New York, NY. 1976-1984. Lang.: Eng.   2305

Brooks Atkinson Theatre (New York, NY)

Performance/production

Reviews of *Jackie Mason's 'World According to Me'*, written and created by Mason. USA: New York, NY. 1986. Lang.: Eng.   2207

Reviews of *Rowan Atkinson at the Atkinson*, by Richard Curtis, Rowan Atkinson and Ben Elton, staged by Mike Ockrent. USA: New York, NY. 1986. Lang.: Eng.   2211

Brooks, Jeremy

Performance/production

Collection of newspaper reviews by London theatre critics. UK. 1986. Lang.: Eng.   2099

Brothers and Sisters

SEE

Bratja i sëstry.

Brothers Karamazov, Flying

SEE

Flying Karamazov Brothers.

Brothers Karamazov, The

SEE

Bratja Karamazov.

Broughton, Pip

Performance/production

Collection of newspaper reviews by London theatre critics. UK-England: London. 1986. Lang.: Eng.   2118

Collection of newspaper reviews by London theatre critics. UK-England. 1986. Lang.: Eng.   2120

Interview with Pip Broughton of Paines Plough Theatre Company. UK-England. 1980-1986. Lang.: Eng.   2166

Brown, Arvin

Administration

Panel discussion on theatre as commerce or resource to its community. USA: New York, NY. 1986.   179

Plays/librettos/scripts

Popularity and relevance of Eugene O'Neill. USA. Lang.: Eng.   2894

Brown, Bruce

A history of the Marionette Theatre. USA: New York, NY. 1939-1985.   4001

Brown, Joe E.

Performance/production

An historical account of one actor's experiences with the Fresno Paramount Players. USA: Fresno, CA. 1927. Lang.: Eng.   2255

Brown, Steve

Performance/production

Collection of newspaper reviews by London theatre critics. UK-England: London. 1986. Lang.: Eng.   2110

Brown, Trisha

Performance/production

Interview with choreographer Trisha Brown. North America. 1983-1985. Lang.: Eng.   1350

Brown, Warner

Performance/production

Collection of newspaper reviews by London theatre critics. UK-England. 1986. Lang.: Eng.   2111

Brown, William Henry

Plays/librettos/scripts

Precursors of revolutionary black theatre. Haiti. Jamaica. 1820-1970. Lang.: Eng.   956

Browne, Maurice

Performance/production

Origins of radically simplified stage in modern productions. USA. 1912-1922. Lang.: Eng.   831

Greek tragedy on the New York stage. USA: New York, NY. 1854-1984. Lang.: Eng.   2301

Brückner, Ferdinand

Performance/production

Laco Adamik directs Ferdinand Brückner's *Elisabeth von England* under the title *Elzbieta, Królowa Anglii*. Poland: Cracow. 1984. Lang.: Pol.   2041

Bruhn, Eric

Institutions

Goals of Eric Bruhn, new artistic director of National Ballet of Canada. Canada: Toronto, ON. 1967-1983. Lang.: Eng.   1296

Brumer, Wiktor

Performance/production

Collection of articles by critic and theatre historian Wiktor Brumer. Poland. 1765-1930. Lang.: Pol.   2016

Brunelleschi, Filippo

Performance spaces

Spatial orientation in medieval Catalan religious productions. Spain-Catalonia. Italy: Florence. 1388-1538. Lang.: Cat.   616

Bruni, Tat'jana Georgijevna

Design/technology

Career of stage designer Tat'jana Georgijevna Bruni. USSR. 1923-1981. Lang.: Rus.   435

Brunner, Gerhard
Institutions
Tanz '86 festival. Austria: Vienna. 1986. Lang.: Ger.   1269
Bruscambille
SEE
Gracieux, Jean.
Brustein, Robert
Performance/production
Conflict over artistic control in American Repertory Theatre's
production of *Endgame* by Samuel Beckett. USA: Boston, MA. 1984.
Lang.: Eng.   2296

Theory/criticism
Theatre professionals challenge assertions that theatre is a weaker
form of communication than film. USA: New York, NY. 1985.
Lang.: Eng.   1225
Interview with playwright Lillian Hellman. USA: Martha's Vineyard,
MA. 1983. Lang.: Eng.   3147
Bryceland, Yvonne
Performance/production
Comparative analysis of productions of *Summer* by Edward Bond.
UK-England: London. 1982. Lang.: Eng.   2163
Bryden, Bill
Performance/production
Collection of newspaper reviews by London theatre critics. UK-
England. 1986. Lang.: Eng.   2120
Bryden, Ronald
Theory/criticism
Book review of *Whittaker's Theatre: A Critic Looks at Stages in
Canada and Thereabouts: 1944-1975*, ed. Ronald Bryden and Boyd
Neil. Canada: Toronto, ON. 1944-1985. Lang.: Eng.   3087
Büchner, Georg
Performance/production
Description of Georg Büchner's *Dantons Tod (Danton's Death)*
staged by Alexander Lang at Deutsches Theater. Germany, East:
Berlin, East. 1984. Lang.: Ger.   1763

Plays/librettos/scripts
Study of realism vs metadrama. Europe. 429 B.C.-1978 A.D. Lang.:
Eng.   2540
Structuralist analysis of Georg Büchner's *Leonce und Lena*. Germany.
1836. Lang.: Eng.   2604
A *laudatio* in honor of playwright Friedrich Dürrenmatt, recipient of
the 1986 Büchner Prize. Germany, West: Darmstadt. Switzerland:
Neuchâtel. 1942-1986. Lang.: Ger.   2624
Origins and influences of *Woyzeck* on Berg's opera *Wozzeck*.
Austria: Vienna. 1821-1925. Lang.: Eng.   3855
Buck, Tim
Relation to other fields
Circumstances surrounding a banned Workers' Experimental Theatre
play. Canada: Toronto, ON. 1931-1933. Lang.: Eng.   3018
Buckley, Richard
Institutions
The survival and prosperity of the Santa Fe Opera Company. USA:
Santa Fe, NM. 1957-1986. Lang.: Eng.   3678
Budapest Art Theatre
SEE
Müvész Szinház (Budapest).
Budapest Opera
SEE
Magyar Állami Operaház.
Buddies in Bad Times Theatre (Toronto, ON)
Institutions
History of the Rhubarb Festival. Canada: Toronto, ON. 1986. Lang.:
Eng.   1549
Buero Vallejo, Antonio
Plays/librettos/scripts
Self-reflexivity in Antonio Buero Vallejo's play *El Sueño de la razón
(The Sleep of Reason)* and Victor Erice's film *El Espíritu de la
colmena (The Spirit of the Beehive)*. Spain. 1970-1973. Lang.: Eng.
     2781
Poor reception of *Diálogo secreto (Secret Dialogue)* by Antonio
Buero Vallejo in Spain. Spain: Madrid. 1984. Lang.: Eng.   2791
Thematic and stylistic comparison of three plays influenced by the
Odyssey. Spain. 1952-1983. Lang.: Eng.   2792
Radical subjectivism in three plays by Antonio Buero Vallejo: *La
Fundación (The Foundation)*, *La Detonación (The Detonation)* and
Jueces en la noche (Judges at Night). Spain. 1974-1979. Lang.: Eng.
     2797

Refutes critical position that Antonio Buero Vallejo's *Diálogo secreto
(Secret Dialogue)* is unbelievable. Spain: Madrid. 1984. Lang.: Eng.
     2799
Reflections and influence of playwrights Rodolfo Usigli of Mexico
and Antonio Buero Vallejo of Spain on theatre in their native
countries. Spain. Mexico. Lang.: Spa.   2803
Bújdosók, A (Refugees)
Plays/librettos/scripts
Analysis of Mihály Vörösmarty's *A bújdosók (Refugees)*. Hungary.
1800-1855. Lang.: Hun.   2639
Bulgakov, Michajl Afanasjěvič
Performance/production
Michajl Bulgakov's ties with Moscow Art Theatre. Russia: Moscow.
1891-1940. Lang.: Rus.   785
Ivan Vasiljěvič by Michajl Afanasjěvič Bulgakov directed by László
Marton at Vigszinház under the title *Iván, a rettentő*. Hungary:
Budapest. 1986. Lang.: Hun.   1783
Various interpretations of plays by Michajl Afanasjěvič Bulgakov.
USSR: Moscow. 1980-1986. Lang.: Rus.   2323
Plays/librettos/scripts
Dramaturgy of Michajl Afanasjěvič Bulgakov. USSR. 1925-1940.
Lang.: Rus.   991
Bull, Peter
Performance/production
Autobiography of actor Alec Guinness. UK. USA. 1914-1985. Lang.:
Eng.   2106
Bullins, Ed
Plays/librettos/scripts
Summary and discussion of the plays of Ed Bullins. USA. 1968-
1973. Lang.: Eng.   2900
Race in prison dramas of Piñero, Camillo, Elder and Bullins. USA.
1970-1986. Lang.: Eng.   2912
Identifies dramatic elements unique to street theatre. USA. 1968-
1986. Lang.: Eng.   3354
Bumbry, Grace
Performance/production
Famous sopranos discuss their interpretations of Tosca. USA. 1935-
1986. Lang.: Eng.   3811
Bungei-za (Japan)
Performance/production
Bungei-za performs *Tóték (The Tót Family)* by István Örkény.
Japan: Toyama. 1985. Lang.: Hun.   2006
Bünhődés (Punishment)
Performance/production
Review of *Bünhődés (Punishment)*, a stage adaptation of *The Idiot*
by Dostojěvskij. Hungary: Budapest. Lang.: Hun.   1826
Bunker
Performance/production
Miklós Mészöly's *Bunker* at Népszinház directed by Mátyás Giricz.
Hungary: Budapest. 1985. Lang.: Hun.   1919
Bunn, Alfred
Performance/production
Controversy surrounding *Presumption, or The Fate of Frankenstein*
by Richard Brinsley Peake. UK-England: London. 1818-1840. Lang.:
Eng.   2142
Bunraku
Performance/production
Old and new forms in Japanese theatre. Japan. 1983-1984. Lang.:
Eng.   1382
Puppeteer Bruce D. Scwartz discusses his play *Marie Antoinette
Tonight!*. USA: Atlanta, GA. 1986. Lang.: Eng.   3983
Reference materials
Yearbook of major performances in all areas of Japanese theatre.
Japan: Tokyo. 1986. Lang.: Jap.   1026
Burckhardt, Sigurd
Theory/criticism
Self-reflexivity in Shakespeare as seen by Lionel Abel, Sigurd
Burckhardt and James L. Calderwood. USA. 1963-1983. Lang.: Eng.
     3141
Burden, Tricia
Plays/librettos/scripts
Historical background of *Sisters of Eve* by Tricia Burden. Eire.
1984-1986. Lang.: Eng.   2455
Burger, Isabel
Relation to other fields
Description of the Cutler Playwright's Festival designed for junior
high school students. USA: Groton, CT. 1983-1986. Lang.: Eng.
     3065

SUBJECT INDEX

Caird, John
Design/technology
Changes in the Royal Shakespeare Company under its current directors. UK-England: London. 1967-1986. Lang.: Eng. 325
Set designer John Napier's work on *Les Misérables*. UK-England: London. 1986. 3583

Performance/production
Collection of newspaper reviews by London theatre critics. UK-England: London. 1986. Lang.: Eng. 2110
Collection of newspaper reviews by London theatre critics. UK-England: London. 1986. Lang.: Eng. 2113

Čajka (Seagull, The)
Performance/production
Directorial process as seen through major productions of Stanislavskij, Brecht, Kazan and Brook. 1898-1964. Lang.: Eng. 650
Survey of productions at the Kennedy Center's National Theatre. USA: Washington, DC. 1986. Lang.: Eng. 2247

Plays/librettos/scripts
Analysis of Čechov's plays. Lang.: Hun. 2346
Study of the dramatic nature of Čechov's plays. Lang.: Hun. 2347

Čajkovskij, Pëtr Iljič
Performance/production
Collected articles and reviews by composer Pëtr Iljič Čajkovskij. Russia. 1850-1900. Lang.: Rus. 3772

Plays/librettos/scripts
Puškin's *Queen of Spades* adapted for opera by Čajkovskij. Russia. 1833-1890. Lang.: Eng. 3891

Caldarone, Marina
Performance/production
Collection of newspaper reviews by London theatre critics. UK-England: London. 1986. Lang.: Eng. 2122

Calder, Angus
Plays/librettos/scripts
World War II as a theme in post-war British drama. UK-England. 1945-1983. Lang.: Eng. 2868

Calderón
Plays/librettos/scripts
Notes on Pier Paolo Pasolini's *Calderón*. Italy. 1973. Lang.: Ita. 2689

Calderón de la Barca, Pedro
Design/technology
Unusual production of *Life Is a Dream* by Kungliga Dramatiska Teatern. Sweden: Stockholm. 1927. Lang.: Swe. 1520

Plays/librettos/scripts
Notes on Pier Paolo Pasolini's *Calderón*. Italy. 1973. Lang.: Ita. 2689
Prophecy in Calderón's *Eco y Narciso (Echo and Narcissus)*. Spain. 1600-1680. Lang.: Eng. 2787
Thematic analysis of *La vida es sueño (Life Is a Dream)* by Pedro Calderón de la Barca. Spain. 1635-1681. Lang.: Eng. 2788
Calderón's *El gran duque de Gandía (The Grand Duke of Gandía)* and its Mexican source. Spain. Mexico. 1600-1680. Lang.: Eng. 2789
Interview with Irena Kraus about her play *Lilla livet (The Little Life)*, based on *La vida es sueño (Life Is a Dream)* by Calderón. Sweden: Malmö. 1985-1986. Lang.: Swe. 2824

Calderwood, James L.
Theory/criticism
Self-reflexivity in Shakespeare as seen by Lionel Abel, Sigurd Burckhardt and James L. Calderwood. USA. 1963-1983. Lang.: Eng. 3141

Caldwell, Zoe
Performance/production
Greek tragedy on the New York stage. USA: New York, NY. 1854-1984. Lang.: Eng. 2301

Calgary Centre for the Performing Arts (Calgary, AB)
Institutions
Description of new arts district. Canada: Calgary, AB. 1978-1985. Lang.: Eng. 484

California Suite
Plays/librettos/scripts
Symbolism and allusion in *Boiler Room Suite* by Rex Deverell. Canada: Regina, SK. 1977. Lang.: Eng. 934

Caligula
Performance/production
Reviews of *Caligula* by Albert Camus, staged by Marshall W. Mason. USA: New York, NY. 1986. Lang.: Eng. 2239

Calip, Rufus
Institutions
History of Black theater companies. USA: Philadelphia, PA. 1966-1985. Lang.: Eng. 1608

Callahan, Pegg
Design/technology
Choosing music and sound effects for puppet theatre. USA. Lang.: Eng. 3953

Callas, Maria
Performance/production
Overview of Maria Callas' early career. Greece: Athens. 1937-1945. Lang.: Eng. 3741

Calling
SEE
Besuchszeit.

Callow, Simon
Performance/production
Director Simon Callow talks about his production of Jean Cocteau's *The Infernal Machine*. UK-England: London. 1986. Lang.: Eng. 2139

Calmo, Andrea
Performance/production
Precursors of *commedia dell'arte*. Italy: Venice. 1400-1620. Lang.: Eng. 3414

Calms of Capricorn, The
Plays/librettos/scripts
Gender role-reversal in the Cycle plays of Eugene O'Neill. USA. 1927-1953. Lang.: Eng. 2896

Calvert Award
SEE
Awards, Calvert.

Calvino, Italo
Plays/librettos/scripts
Italo Calvino's first libretto is based on one of his Marcovaldo stories. Italy. 1956. Lang.: Ita. 3884

Camaleó, El (Barcelona)
Institutions
Three personal views of the evolution of the Catalan company La Pipironda. Spain-Catalonia: Barcelona. 1958-1986. Lang.: Cat. 1583

Camargo, Marie Anne de Cupis de
Relation to other fields
Eighteenth-century prints depict dancers Marie Sallé and Marie Anne de Cupis de Camargo. France. 1700-1799. Lang.: Rus. 1327

Cambria, Adele
Plays/librettos/scripts
Women's issues in Italian theatre. Italy. 1985. Lang.: Cat. 2710

Cambridge Theatre (London)
Performance/production
Director Jonathan Lynn discusses his works performed at the National Theatre. UK-England: London. UK-England: Cambridge. 1986. Lang.: Eng. 2160

Camelot
Performance/production
Biography of Richard Burton. UK-Wales. 1925-1984. Lang.: Eng. 820

Cameron, Bruce
Design/technology
Sound design for Lily Tomlin's *The Search for Signs of Intelligent Life in the Universe*. USA: New York, NY. 1986. Lang.: Eng. 335

Camille
Plays/librettos/scripts
Attitudes toward sexuality in plays from French sources. UK-England. France. Lang.: Eng. 2852

Camillo, Marvin Felix
Plays/librettos/scripts
Race in prison dramas of Piñero, Camillo, Elder and Bullins. USA. 1970-1986. Lang.: Eng. 2912

Camino Negro (Black Road)
Performance/production
Overview of recent Argentine theatre. Argentina: Buenos Aires. 1978-1983. Lang.: Fre. 651

Campanile, Achille
Plays/librettos/scripts
Experimental theatrical productions of Achille Campanile. Italy. 1920-1930. Lang.: Ita. 2695

250   International Bibliography of Theatre: 1986

Campbell, David
Performance/production
Reviews of *Honky Tonk Nights*, book and lyrics by Ralph Allen and David Campbell, staged and choreographed by Ernest O. Flatt. USA: New York, NY. 1986. Lang.: Eng. 3612

Campbell, Norman
Performance/production
Opera singer Maureen Forrester tells of her switch from serious roles to character and comic roles. Canada. 1970-1984. Lang.: Eng. 3706

Camus, Albert
Performance/production
Albert Camus' appreciation of actress Madeleine Renaud. France. 1950. Lang.: Fre. 1728

Tamás Ascher directs *Ördögök (The Devils)*, an adaptation of *Besy (The Possessed)* by Dostojêvskij. Hungary: Budapest. 1986. Lang.: Hun. 1778

Director Kazimierz Braun on his adaptation of *La Peste (The Plague)* by Albert Camus. Poland: Wrocław. 1976-1983. Lang.: Eng. 2015

Reviews of *Caligula* by Albert Camus, staged by Marshall W. Mason. USA: New York, NY. 1986. Lang.: Eng. 2239

Plays/librettos/scripts
Adaptation by Albert Camus of *Les Esprits (The Spirits)* by Pierre de Larivey. France. 1570-1953. Lang.: Fre. 2571
Structuralist analysis of works of Albert Camus, Antonin Artaud and Gaston Bachelard. France. Lang.: Fre. 2575

Canada Council
Institutions
The development of French-language theatre in Ontario. Canada. 1968-1986. Lang.: Eng. 1567

Canadian Broadcasting Association for the Study of Canadian Radio and Television (ACTH)
Institutions
Television drama as a virtual national theatre in Canada. Canada. 1952-1970. Lang.: Eng. 3267

Canadian Broadcasting Corporation (CBC)
Basic theatrical documents
Text of *The Journey* by Timothy Findley. Canada. 1970. Lang.: Eng. 3173

Text of *The Paper People* by Timothy Findley. Canada. 1967. Lang.: Eng. 3252

Institutions
Significance of Applebaum-Hébert report on Canadian cultural policy. Canada. 1982-1983. Lang.: Eng. 465

Performance/production
Opera singer Maureen Forrester tells of her switch from serious roles to character and comic roles. Canada. 1970-1984. Lang.: Eng. 3706
Artistic and technological differences in presenting opera for stage and television. Canada. 1960-1980. Lang.: Eng. 3714

Plays/librettos/scripts
Structure and characterization in the plays of W.O. Mitchell. Canada. 1975. Lang.: Eng. 2408
Radio adaptations of foreign works, their effect on culture. Canada. 1939-1949. Lang.: Fre. 3181
Plays by women on the CBC radio network. Canada. 1985-1986. Lang.: Eng. 3185
Cultural models and types in docudrama. Canada. 1970-1983. Lang.: Eng. 3279
Critical debate over Timothy Findley's *The Paper People*. Canada. 1967. Lang.: Eng. 3280

Relation to other fields
Social function of radio drama. Canada. 1950-1955. Lang.: Eng. 3187

Canadian Brothers, The
Reference materials
Collected reviews of 31 major Canadian plays. Canada. 1934-1983. Lang.: Eng. 1009

Canadian Opera Company (Toronto, ON)
Performance/production
Interview with soprano Joanne Kolomyjec. Canada: Toronto, ON. 1986. Lang.: Eng. 3710

Canadian Players (Toronto, ON)
Institutions
Carroll Aikins, founder of Canadian Players. Canada: Naramata, BC. 1920-1922. Lang.: Eng. 478

Canadian Theatre Review
Institutions
Criticism of *Canadian Theatre Review*. Canada. 1985. Lang.: Fre. 1554

Canadiens, Les (Canadians, The)
Plays/librettos/scripts
Literary and popular theatrical forms in the plays of Rick Salutin. Canada: Montreal, PQ, Toronto, ON. 1976-1981. Lang.: Eng. 2411

Relation to other fields
Concept of play in theatre and sport. Canada. 1972-1983. Lang.: Eng. 1071

Canberra Youth Theatre (Australia)
Performance/production
Dilemmas and prospects of youth theatre movement. Australia. 1982-1986. Lang.: Eng. 1639

Candelaria, La (Bogotá)
SEE
Teatro La Candelaria.

Candida
Performance/production
Performances of George Bernard Shaw's *Candida* and Čechov's *Diadia Vania (Uncle Vanya)*, under the title *Ványa bácsi*, at Pécs National Theatre. Hungary: Pécs. 1985. Lang.: Hun. 1893

Plays/librettos/scripts
Thematic analysis of *Candida* by George Bernard Shaw focusing on the spiritual development of Marchbanks. UK-England: London. 1894. Lang.: Eng. 2837

Candide
Performance/production
Stills from telecast performance of *Candide* by New York City Opera. USA: New York, NY. 1986. Lang.: Eng. 3796

Cannon, Doreen
Performance/production
Discussion of Stanislavskij's influence by a number of artists. Sweden. 1890-1986. Lang.: Swe. 2094

Cantatrice chauve, La (Bald Soprano, The)
Performance/production
Tamás Ascher directs *A kopasz éneksnő (The Bald Soprano)* and *Különóra (The Lesson)* by Eugène Ionesco. Hungary: Kaposvár. 1986. Lang.: Hun. 1912

Cantique des cantiques, Le (Song of Songs, The)
Performance/production
Evolution of *Le Cantique des cantiques (The Song of Songs)* directed by Jacques Destoop at Comédie-Française. France: Paris. 1986. Lang.: Fre. 1721

Plays/librettos/scripts
Interview with Josy Eisenberg, translator of *Le Cantique des cantiques (The Song of Songs)* for the Comédie-Française. France: Paris. 1986. Lang.: Fre. 2544

Cantonese opera
Research/historiography
Development of Cantonese opera and its influence. China, People's Republic of: Kuang Tung. 1885-1985. Lang.: Chi. 3555

Cantú, Carlo
Plays/librettos/scripts
Analysis of *commedia dell'arte* text of Carlo Cantú's *Cicalamento*. Italy. 1576-1646. Lang.: Ita. 3416

Čapek, Josef
Performance/production
Technical innovation, scenography and cabaret in relation to political and social conditions. Czechoslovakia. 1781-1986. Lang.: Eng. 1697

Capitol Theatre (Pottsville, PA)
Performance spaces
History of the Capitol Theatre. USA: Pottsville, PA. 1927-1982. Lang.: Eng. 3221

Capmany, Maria Aurélia
Basic theatrical documents
Text of *Tu i l'hipócrita (You and the Hypocrite)*, by Maria Aurélia Capmany, translated into Castilian Spanish by L. Teresa Valdivieso as *Tú y el hipócrita*. Spain-Catalonia: Barcelona. 1959. Lang.: Spa. 1495

Plays/librettos/scripts
Translator discusses her Spanish version of Maria Aurelia Capmany's Catalan play, *Tu i l'hipócrita (You and the Hypocrite)*. Spain. 1959-1976. Lang.: Spa. 2806
Roles of women in middle-class Catalonian society as reflected in the plays of Carme Montoriol and Maria Aurélia Capmany. Spain-Catalonia. 1700-1960. Lang.: Spa. 2819

Capobianco, Tito
Performance/production
Photographs, cast list, synopsis, and discography of Metropolitan Opera radio broadcast performances. USA: New York, NY. 1986. Lang.: Eng. 3794

Captives of the Faceless Drummer
Relation to other fields
Controversy about *Captives of the Faceless Drummer* by George Ryga. Canada: Vancouver, BC. 1968-1971. Lang.: Eng. 3021

Capuleti e i Montecchi, I
Plays/librettos/scripts
The Romeo and Juliet theme as interpreted in the musical and visual arts. Italy. 1476-1900. Lang.: Eng. 3886

Card Index, The
SEE
Kartoteka.

Cardenio
Performance/production
History of productions of *Cardenio* by William Shakespeare and John Fletcher. England: London. 1613-1847. Lang.: Eng. 1705

Cardon, Lola
Performance/production
Production history of *Hay que deshacer la casa (Undoing the Housework)*, winner of Lope de Vega prize. Spain: Madrid. USA: Miami, FL. 1983-1985. Lang.: Eng. 2079

Caretaker, The
Performance/production
Reviews of *The Caretaker* by Harold Pinter, staged by John Malkovich. USA: New York, NY. 1986. Lang.: Eng. 2236

Carinthischer Sommer Festival (Austria)
Institutions
Program for the festival Carinthischer Sommer. Austria. 1986. Lang.: Ger. 445

Plays/librettos/scripts
The church opera *Kain* written and composed for the Carinthiscer Sommer Festival. Austria: Ossiach. 1986. Lang.: Ger. 3858

Carlell, Lodowicke
Plays/librettos/scripts
Female characterization in Nicholas Rowe's plays. England. 1629-1720. Lang.: Eng. 2475

Carleton University (Ottawa, ON)
Institutions
Structure and political viewpoint of Great Canadian Theatre Company. Canada: Ottawa, ON. 1975-1986. Lang.: Eng. 486

Carmen
Performance/production
Performance analysis of the title role of *Carmen*. France. 1875-1986. Lang.: Eng. 3725

Peter Brook's direction and adaptation of the opera *Carmen* by Georges Bizet. France: Paris. 1981-1983. Lang.: Heb. 3731

Géza Oberfrank directs Bizet's *Carmen* at Szegedi Nemzeti Szinház. Hungary: Szeged. 1985. Lang.: Hun. 3748

Reviews of 10 vintage recordings of complete operas on LP. USA. 1906-1925. Lang.: Eng. 3792

Photographs, cast list, synopsis, and discography of Metropolitan Opera radio broadcast performances. USA: New York, NY. 1986. Lang.: Eng. 3794

Plays/librettos/scripts
Adaptations of *Carmen* by Prosper Mérimée. France. Spain. 1845-1983. Lang.: Fre. 3870

Carmen Jones
Performance/production
Collection of newspaper reviews by London theatre critics. UK. 1986. Lang.: Eng. 2103

Carmines, Al
Plays/librettos/scripts
Interview with playwright Al Carmines. USA: New York, NY. 1985. Lang.: Eng. 981

Carmona i Ristol, Àngel
Institutions
Three personal views of the evolution of the Catalan company La Pipironda. Spain-Catalonia: Barcelona. 1958-1986. Lang.: Cat. 1583

Carnevali, Ida
Performance/production
Distinctive style of Canadian clowns. Canada: Toronto, ON, Vancouver, BC. 1967-1986. Lang.: Eng. 3328

Carnival
SEE ALSO
Classed Entries under MIXED ENTERTAINMENT—Carnival: 3373-3377.
Performance/production
Street theatre at Expo 86. Canada: Vancouver, BC. 1986. Lang.: Eng. 3330

Maskers and masquerades of We tribal rituals. Ivory Coast. Lang.: Eng. 3341

Interview with Carlo Boso, expert on *commedia dell'arte*. Europe. 1985. Lang.: Fre. 3409

Reference materials
Description of popular entertainments, both sacred and secular. Spain-Catalonia. 1947-1986. Lang.: Cat. 3355

Theory/criticism
History of theatre in Africa. Africa. 1400-1985. Lang.: Ger. 1199

Carolus Stuardus
Plays/librettos/scripts
Contrasting treatment of history in *Carolus Stuardus* by Andreas Gryphius and *Maria Stuart* by Friedrich von Schiller. Germany. England. 1651-1800. Lang.: Eng. 2590

Carousel Theatre (Vancouver, BC)
Administration
Theatrical activity on various Vancouver stages. Canada: Vancouver, BC. 1986. Lang.: Heb. 1429

Carreras, José
Reference materials
Photos of the new opera productions at the Staatsoper. Austria: Vienna. 1985-1986. Lang.: Ger. 3910

Carrière, Jean-Claude
Performance/production
Interview with Peter Brook's designer, musician, and costumer for *Mahabharata*. France: Avignon. 1973-1985. Lang.: Eng. 1359

Interviews with actors in Peter Brook's *Mahabharata*. France: Avignon. 1985. Lang.: Eng. 1360

Peter Brook discusses development of *The Mahabharata*. France: Avignon. India. 1965-1986. Lang.: Eng. 1361

Carroll, Lewis
Performance/production
Performances of *Alice Csodaországban (Alice in Wonderland)*, *A Két Veronai nemes (The Two Gentlemen of Verona)* and *Tobbsincs királyfi (No More Crown Prince)*. Hungary: Pécs, Budapest. 1985. Lang.: Hun. 1771

Carson & Barnes Circus (New York, NY)
Performance/production
Photographs of three circuses by Holton Rowes. USA: New York, NY. 1985. Lang.: Eng. 3395

Carter, Richard
Administration
Differences between government and corporate support of the arts. USA. 1983. Lang.: Eng. 123

Carter, Rick
Design/technology
Production design for Stephen Spielberg's series *Amazing Stories*. USA. 1986. Lang.: Eng. 3258

Cartwright, Jim
Performance/production
Review of alternative theatre productions. UK-England: London. 1986. Lang.: Eng. 2108

Director Simon Curtis discusses his production of *Road*. UK-England: London. 1986. Lang.: Eng. 2137

Cartwright, William
Plays/librettos/scripts
Female characterization in Nicholas Rowe's plays. England. 1629-1720. Lang.: Eng. 2475

Čaruga (Death Cap)
Performance/production
Review of Ivan Kušan's musical comedy *Čaruga (Death Cap)*, directed by Miklós Benedek, Katona József Theatre, as *Galócza*, includes discussion of acting and dramatic art. Hungary: Budapest. 1986. Lang.: Hun. 1811

Notes on *Čaruga (Death Cap)*, by Ivan Kušan, directed by Miklós Benedek, Katona József Theatre, under the title *Galócza*. Hungary: Budapest. 1986. Lang.: Hun. 1890

Caruso, Enrico
Performance/production
Evidence that Enrico Caruso sang the baritone prologue to *I Pagliacci*. Argentina: Buenos Aires. 1906-1917. Lang.: Eng. 3687

SUBJECT INDEX

Caryll, John
Plays/librettos/scripts
Comparison of John Caryll's *Sir Salomon* with its source, *L'École des femmes (The School for Wives)* by Molière. England. France. 1662-1669. Lang.: Eng. 2527

Casa de Bernarda Alba, La (House of Bernarda Alba, The)
Institutions
Amateur production of García Lorca's *La Casa de Bernarda Alba (The House of Bernarda Alba).* Sweden: Handen. 1982-1986. Lang.: Swe. 1584

Performance/production
Overview of performances transferred from The Royal Court, Greenwich, and Lyric Hammersmith theatres. UK-England: London. 1986. Lang.: Eng. 2143
Nuria Espert talks about Federico García Lorca and her production of *The House of Bernarda Alba.* UK-England: London. Spain. Lang.: Eng. 2178

Plays/librettos/scripts
Biographical study of playwright Federico García Lorca. Spain: Granada, Madrid. USA: New York, NY. 1898-1936. Lang.: Eng. 971
Examples of playwrights whose work was poorly received by theatrical audiences in Madrid. Spain: Madrid. 1609-1950. Lang.: Spa. 2786

Casa Manana Musicals (Fort Worth, TX)
Design/technology
Designers discuss regional productions of *Oklahoma.* USA. 1984-1986. Lang.: Eng. 3596

Casa vieja, La (Old House, The)
Plays/librettos/scripts
Cuban theatre in transition exemplified in the plays of Virgilio Piñera and Abelardo Estorino. Cuba. 1958-1964. Lang.: Eng. 2452

Casanova
Performance/production
János Pelle's *Casanova* directed by Károly Kazimir at the Körszinház. Hungary: Budapest. 1986. Lang.: Hun. 1846
János Pelle's *Casanova* directed by Károly Kazimir at Körszinház. Hungary: Budapest. 1986. Lang.: Hun. 1929

Casei, Nedda
Administration
History and achievements of the American Guild of Musical Artists during its fifty years of existence. USA. 1936-1986. Lang.: Eng. 3645

Casiotheater (Zug)
Performance spaces
Notes on theatres in Saint Gallen, Winterthur and Zug. Switzerland. 1968-1985. Lang.: Swe. 622

Casona, Alejandro
Plays/librettos/scripts
Discusses Christian outlook in plays by Alejandro Casona. Spain. 1940-1980. Lang.: Eng. 2795

Casting
Performance/production
Arguments for typecasting. France. 1925-1986. Lang.: Fre. 710

Castle of Perseverance, The
Performance/production
Theories of medieval production and acting techniques. England. 1400-1500. Lang.: Eng. 698
Analysis and interpretation of the staging of *The Castle of Perseverance* based on original stage plan drawing. England. 1343-1554. Lang.: Eng. 1708
The Castle of Perseverance examined for clues to audience placement and physical plan of original production. England. 1343-1554. Lang.: Eng. 1709

Castle Theatre (Budapest)
SEE
Várszinház.

Castle Theatre (Kisvárda)
SEE
Kisvárdai Várszinház.

Castle Theatre (Kőszeg)
SEE
Kőszegi Várszinház.

Castledine, Annie
Performance/production
Collection of newspaper reviews by London theatre critics. UK. 1986. Lang.: Eng. 2102

Castrati
Performance/production
Physical, social and theatrical aspects of *castrati.* Italy: Rome, Venice. England: London. 1700-1799. Lang.: Ger. 3757

Training
Collected papers from a conference on voice training. Austria: Vienna. Italy: Rome. England: London. 1700-1984. Lang.: Ger. 3936

Castri, Massimo
Performance/production
Productions of plays by Luigi Pirandello after World War II. Italy. 1947-1985. Lang.: Ita. 1987

Castro, Bélgica
Plays/librettos/scripts
Chilean theatre in exile, Teatro del Angel. Chile. Costa Rica. 1955-1984. Lang.: Eng. 2441

Cat on a Hot Tin Roof
Performance/production
Macska a forró bádogtetőn (Cat on a Hot Tin Roof) by Tennessee Williams, directed by Miklós Szurdi at Városzinház. Hungary: Budapest. 1985. Lang.: Hun. 1809

Plays/librettos/scripts
Comparison of plays by Tennessee Williams, Arthur Miller and Eugene O'Neill. USA. 1949-1956. Lang.: Eng. 2926

Catalá, Victor (Albert, Caterina)
Plays/librettos/scripts
Roles of women in middle-class Catalonian society as reflected in the plays of Carme Montoriol and Maria Aurélia Capmany. Spain-Catalonia. 1700-1960. Lang.: Spa. 2819

Catalá, Víctor (Albert, Caterina)
Plays/librettos/scripts
History of Catalan literature, including playwrights and theatre. Spain-Catalonia. 1800-1974. Lang.: Cat. 974
Life and work of Caterina Albert, known as Víctor Catalá. Spain-Catalonia. 1869-1966. Lang.: Cat. 2816

Catalogues
Reference materials
Costumes of famous Viennese actors. Austria: Vienna. 1831-1960. Lang.: Ger. 1003
Program of European Actors' Meeting, including criticism, texts and performances. Italy: Parma. 1986. Lang.: Ita. 1020
Books on theatre, film, music and dance published in Italy in 1985. Italy. 1985. Lang.: Ita. 1021
Catalogue of an exhibit on the Carlo Felice Theatre, destroyed in World War II, and its proposed reconstruction. Italy: Genoa. 1600-1985. Lang.: Ita. 1024
Christl Zimmerl's career as prima ballerina at the Vienna State Opera. Austria: Vienna. 1939-1976. Lang.: Ger. 1324
Catalogue from an exhibit of theatrical and ballet art by Zsuzsi Roboz. Hungary: Budapest. 1985. Lang.: Hun. 1325
Catalogue of exhibition on dancer Serge Lifar. Switzerland: Lausanne. 1986. Lang.: Fre. 1326
Adaptation of Ferdinand Raimund's dramas for children's theatre. Austria: Vienna. 1790-1836. Lang.: Ger. 2979
Exhibition catalogue about context of the work and influence of Karl Kraus. Austria: Vienna. USA: New York, NY. France: Paris. 1874-1986. Lang.: Ger. 2980
Interpretation of Ferdinand Raimund's dramas after his death. Austria: Vienna. 1790-1836. Lang.: Ger. 2981
Exhibit on life and work of actor Alessandro Moissi. Italy: Trieste. Austria. 1880-1935. Lang.: Ita. 2993
Catalogue of documentation on Pirandello's writings in dialect. Italy. 1902-1936. Lang.: Eng, Fre, Ger, Ita. 2994
Influence of stage director Max Reinhardt on film production. Germany: Berlin. Austria: Vienna. 1913-1945. Lang.: Ger. 3244
Catalogue of an exhibition of costume designs for Broadway musicals. USA: New York, NY. 1900-1925. Lang.: Eng, Ger. 3635
Catalogue of a 1986 exhibition on the Ferrari family and their puppets. Italy. 1877-1986. Lang.: Ita. 3988

Catalyst Theatre (Edmonton, AB)
Institutions
Overview of the productions and goals of Catalyst Theatre. Canada: Edmonton, AB. 1977-1983. Lang.: Eng. 464

Relation to other fields
Interactive theatre in *It's About Time* by Catalyst Theatre. Canada: Edmonton, AB. 1982. Lang.: Eng. 1069

Catch Chang Hui-tsan Alive
SEE
Chu yen ch'u tong ho hsi.
Catilina (Catiline)
Plays/librettos/scripts
Self-transcendence through grace embodied in Henrik Ibsen's female
characters. Norway. 1849-1899. Lang.: Eng.   2726
Catiline
Plays/librettos/scripts
Herpetological imagery in Jonson's *Catiline*. England. 1611. Lang.:
Eng.   2517
Comparison of Ben Jonson's *Catiline* with its Latin prose source by
Sallust. England. Italy. 43 B.C.-1611 A.D. Lang.: Eng.   2518
Cattaneo, Anne
Performance/production
Interview with dramaturg Anne Cattaneo. USA: New York, NY.
1971-1986. Lang.: Eng.   2254
Plays/librettos/scripts
Review of adaptations for the stage of short stories by Čechov.
USA: New York, NY. 1986. Lang.: Eng.   2922
Caucasian Chalk Circle, The
SEE
Kaukasische Kreidekreis, Der.
Cauchemars du grand monde, Les (Nightmares of High Society)
Performance/production
Three directors' versions of *Les cauchemars du grand monde*
(Nightmares of High Society) by Gilbert Turp. Canada: Montreal,
PQ. 1984. Lang.: Fre.   1672
Cave of Salamanca, The
SEE
Cueva de Salamanca, La.
Caveau d'Ottawa, Le
Institutions
Amateur theatre troupe Le Caveau d'Ottawa. Canada: Ottawa, ON.
1932-1951. Lang.: Fre.   471
Caverna, La (Cavern, The)
Plays/librettos/scripts
Analysis of Josep Palau's plays and theoretical writings. Spain-
Catalonia. 1917-1982. Lang.: Cat.   2814
Cavero, Iñigo
Institutions
Factors leading to the decline of Spanish theatre. Spain. 1975-1985.
Lang.: Spa.   1582
Cawarden, Thomas
Administration
Organization and operation of Office of Revels mainly under
Thomas Cawarden. England: London. 1510-1559. Lang.: Eng.   3417
Cayman National Theatre Company (Cayman Islands)
Performance spaces
Design and construction of Grand Cayman's National Theatre.
Cayman Islands. UK-England. 1986. Lang.: Eng.   590
Cazeneuve, Paul
Institutions
Founding of Théâtre National Français de Montréal. Canada:
Montreal, PQ. 1889-1901. Lang.: Fre.   469
CBC
SEE
Canadian Broadcasting Corporation.
CBS
SEE
Columbia Broadcasting System.
CCA
SEE
Canadian Conference of the Arts.
Cecchi, Emilio
Letters from literary critic Emilio Cecchi to Luigi Pirandello. Italy.
1932-1933. Lang.: Ita.   3189
Cecchi, Giovanni Maria
Plays/librettos/scripts
Discussion of *L'esaltazione della croce (The Exaltation of the Cross)*
by Giovanni Maria Cecchi. Italy. 1585-1589. Lang.: Ita.   2683
Cechini, Piermaria
Institutions
Relations between the 'Confidenti' company and their patron Don
Giovanni dei Medici. Italy: Venice. 1613-1621. Lang.: Ita.   1580
Čechov, Anton Pavlovič
Basic theatrical documents
A collection of seven Čechov stories. Lang.: Eng.   1457

Text of Čechov's *Platonov* in a version by Michael Frayn. Russia.
1878. Lang.: Cat.   1492
Performance/production
Directorial process as seen through major productions of
Stanislavskij, Brecht, Kazan and Brook. 1898-1964. Lang.: Eng. 650
Čechov's *Višnëvyj sad (The Cherry Orchard)* directed at the National
Theatre of Miskolc by Imre Csiszár as *Cseresznyéshert*. Hungary:
Miskolc. 1986. Lang.: Hun.   1784
Čechov's *Három nővér (Three Sisters)* directed by Tamás Ascher.
Hungary: Budapest. 1985. Lang.: Hun.   1814
Performances of George Bernard Shaw's *Candida* and Čechov's
Diadia Vania (Uncle Vanya), under the title *Ványa bácsi*, at Pécs
National Theatre. Hungary: Pécs. 1985. Lang.: Hun.   1893
Two productions of Čechov's *Három Nővér (Three Sisters)*. Hungary:
Zalaegerszeg, Budapest. 1985. Lang.: Hun.   1903
Tamás Ascher directs Čechov's *Tri sestry (Three Sisters)* at Katona
József Theatre under the title *Három nővér*. Hungary: Budapest.
1985. Lang.: Hun.   1914
Production of *Ványa bácsi (Uncle Vanya)* by Čechov. Hungary: Pécs.
1985. Lang.: Hun.   1918
Čechov's *Višnëvyj sad (The Cherry Orchard)* directed by Imre
Csiszár under the title *Cseresznyéskert*. Hungary: Miskolc. 1986.
Lang.: Hun.   1921
Comparison of two Hungarian productions of *Háram nővér (Three
Sisters)* by Anton Pavlovič Čechov. Hungary: Budapest, Zalaegerszeg.
1985. Lang.: Hun.   1964
Interview with director György Harag. Romania: Tîrgu-Mures. 1925-
1985. Lang.: Hun.   2064
Plays of Čechov interpreted in theatre and ballet. Russia. 1860-1986.
Lang.: Rus.   2068
Documentation on Stanislavskij's productions of Čechov plays.
Russia. 1901-1904. Lang.: Ita.   2070
Interview with actress Agneta Ekmanner. Sweden: Stockholm. 1950-
1986. Lang.: Swe.   2092
Collection of newspaper reviews by London theatre critics. UK.
1986. Lang.: Eng.   2101
Collection of newspaper reviews by London theatre critics. UK-
England: London. 1986. Lang.: Eng.   2112
Collection of newspaper reviews by London theatre critics. UK-
England. 1986. Lang.: Eng.   2120
Director Mike Alfreds' interpretation of the plays of Čechov. UK-
England: London. USSR. 1975-1986. Lang.: Eng.   2127
Survey of the season at the National Theatre. UK-England: London.
1986. Lang.: Eng.   2130
Actress Sheila Hancock discusses role of Madame Ranevskaya in
Čechov's *Višnëvyj sad (The Cherry Orchard)*. UK-England: London.
1986. Lang.: Eng.   2180
Reviews of *Wild Honey*, by Michael Frayn after Čechov, conceived
and staged by Christopher Morahan. USA: New York, NY. 1986.
Lang.: Eng.   2205
Reviews of *Orchards* written and staged by Robert Falls after
Čechov. USA: New York, NY. 1986. Lang.: Eng.   2222
Survey of productions at the Kennedy Center's National Theatre.
USA: Washington, DC. 1986. Lang.: Eng.   2247
Review of the world premiere of the opera *Three Sisters*. USA:
Columbus, OH. 1968-1986. Lang.: Eng.   3822
Plays/librettos/scripts
Analysis of Čechov's plays. Lang.: Hun.   2346
Study of the dramatic nature of Čechov's plays. Lang.: Hun.   2347
History of the writing and diffusion of Čechov's *Platonov (Wild
Honey)*. Russia. USSR. 1878-1960. Lang.: Cat.   2764
Recollections of Anton Pavlovič Čechov by some of his
contemporaries. Russia. 1860-1904. Lang.: Rus.   2765
Influence of Aristophanes and Čechov on playwright Simon Gray.
UK-England. 1986. Lang.: Eng.   2874
Review of adaptations for the stage of short stories by Čechov.
USA: New York, NY. 1986. Lang.: Eng.   2922
Theory/criticism
Review of *Mi lesz velünk Anton Pavlovics? (What Will Become of
Us, Anton Pavlovič?)* by Miklós Almási. Hungary. 1986. Lang.: Hun.
3114
Relation of short story and drama in the plays of Anton Pavlovič
Čechov and Eugene O'Neill. Russia. USA. Lang.: Eng.   3130

Čechov, Michajl A.
Performance/production

Zen and Western acting styles. Lang.: Eng. 648

Literary legacy of Michajl A. Čechov. Russia. USA. 1891-1955. Lang.: Rus. 781

Michael Chekhov's theories of acting and directing. USSR: Moscow. USA: Ridgefield, CT. 1938. Lang.: Eng. 887

Innovative stagings of Shakespeare's *Hamlet*. Europe. 1700-1950. Lang.: Rus. 1716

CEDITADE (Paris)
Theory/criticism

Augusto Boal's concept of theatre of the oppressed. Brazil. France. 1956-1978. Lang.: Eng. 1201

Cehanovsky, George
Performance/production

Appreciation and obituary of the late baritone of the Metropolitan Opera, George Cehanovsky. USA: New York, NY. 1892-1986. Lang.: Eng. 3833

Celestina, La (Nun, The)
Plays/librettos/scripts

Alfonso Sastre's theory of complex tragedy in *La Celestina (The Nun)*. Spain. 1978. Lang.: Spa. 2807

Celluloid Heroes
Plays/librettos/scripts

Analysis of plays by David Williamson. Australia. 1976-1985. Lang.: Eng. 2379

Cenerini, Rhéal
Performance/production

Opposition to realism in plays from Francophone Manitoba. Canada. 1983-1986. Lang.: Fre. 670

Censorship
Administration

Censorship in post-Revolutionary France. France: Paris. 1791-1891. Lang.: Eng. 39

Relationships between politicians and cultural leaders. USA. 1980-1983. Lang.: Eng. 158

Argument against government involvement in the arts. USA. 1983. Lang.: Eng. 173

Problems of theatres in USSR-Russian SFSR. USSR. 1980-1986. Lang.: Rus. 196

Effect of censorship on Shakespeare's *Richard III* and *Henry IV*. England. 1593-1603. Lang.: Pol. 1435

Russian censorship of classic repertory in Polish theatres. Poland: Warsaw. Russia. 1873-1907. Lang.: Rus, Pol. 1438

Institutions

History of theatre in Valencia area focusing on Civil War period. Spain: Valencia. 1817-1982. Lang.: Cat. 514

Performance/production

Letters to and from Harley Granville-Barker. UK-England. 1877-1946. Lang.: Eng. 807

Interview with Ellen Rudolph on recent cultural exchange tour of foreign artists in the US. USA: New York, NY. 1982. Lang.: Eng. 839

Problems of contemporary theatre. USSR. 1980-1986. Lang.: Rus. 858

Comparison of Soviet theatre of the 1960s and 1980s. USSR: Moscow. 1960-1986. Lang.: Rus. 860

Problems of experimental theatre. USSR. 1980-1986. Lang.: Rus. 869

Playwright Václav Havel's experience with the Burgtheater. Austria: Vienna. Czechoslovakia. 1976-1986. Lang.: Ger. 1643

Technical innovation, scenography and cabaret in relation to political and social conditions. Czechoslovakia. 1781-1986. Lang.: Eng. 1697

Plays/librettos/scripts

Metaphoric style in the political drama of Jean-Paul Sartre, Athol Fugard and Juan Radrigán. France. South Africa, Republic of. Chile. 1940-1986. Lang.: Eng. 951

Social themes in the dramas of Franz Grillparzer. Austro-Hungarian Empire: Vienna. 1791-1872. Lang.: Ger. 2399

Interview with playwright, director and actor Pavel Kohout. Czechoslovakia: Prague. Austria: Vienna. 1928-1986. Lang.: Swe. 2454

Mrożek's *Policja (The Police)* as read by the censor. Poland. 1958. Lang.: Fre. 2735

Reference materials

Theatre documents and listing of playtexts in the Polish theatre in Lvov. Poland: Lvov, Katowice. 1800-1978. Lang.: Pol. 2996

Relation to other fields

Edward Albee on government censorship and freedom of artistic expression. Hungary: Budapest. 1986. 1096

Reopening of Polish theatre after over forty years of repression. Poland: Vilna. 1905. Lang.: Pol. 1120

Reflections and influence of arts and race relations. South Africa, Republic of. Lang.: Afr. 1125

Cardinal Richelieu's theatrical policies. France. 1634-1642. Lang.: Fre. 3030

Response of Freie Volksbühne to police pressure. Germany: Berlin. 1890-1912. Lang.: Fre. 3034

Examples of Puritan attempts to ban legal entertainments. England: Cheshire. 1560-1641. Lang.: Eng. 3356

Theory/criticism

Purpose of literature and art, and the role of the artist. China, People's Republic of: Shanghai, Yan'an. 1942-1982. Lang.: Chi. 1203

Census, The
SEE

Censo, El.

Centaur Theatre (Montreal, PQ)
Institutions

Interviews with theatre professionals in Quebec. Canada. 1985. Lang.: Fre. 487

New leadership in Montreal's English-speaking theatres. Canada: Montreal, PQ. 1980-1986. Lang.: Eng. 1539

Limited opportunities for English-language playwrights in Montreal. Canada: Montreal, PQ. 1976-1986. Lang.: Eng. 1561

Minority-language theatres in Canada. Canada: Montreal, PQ, Toronto, ON. 1986. Lang.: Eng. 1566

Center for Theatre Research (Paris)
Performance/production

Overview of the career and work of director Peter Brook. USA: New York, NY. 1948-1984. Lang.: Eng. 829

Center of Theatre Research (Paris)
Relation to other fields

On Peter Brook's *Mahabharata*, produced by the International Center of Theatre Research. France: Paris. 1985. Lang.: Rus. 3032

Center Stage (Baltimore, MD)
Administration

A profile of Center Stage. USA: Baltimore, MD. 1963-1986. Lang.: Eng. 109

Center Stage's resident set designer Hugh Landwehr. USA: Baltimore, MD. 1977-1986. Lang.: Eng. 111

Design/technology

Designers discuss regional productions of *She Loves Me*. USA. 1984-1986. Lang.: Eng. 3587

Central Academy of Drama (Beijing)
Performance/production

Training of Chinese students for a production of *The Tempest* by William Shakespeare. China, People's Republic of: Beijing. 1981-1985. Lang.: Eng. 679

Central Opera Service (New York, NY)
Administration

Account of an international symposium on the future of opera. USA: New York, NY. 1986. Lang.: Eng. 3646

Central Puppet Theatre (Moscow)
SEE

Gosudarstvénnyj Centralnyj Teat'r Kukol.

Centralnyj Teat'r Kukol (Moscow)
SEE

Gosudarstvénnyj Centralnyj Teat'r Kukol.

Centre d'Estudis Pirandellians (Barcelona)
Plays/librettos/scripts

Influence of Luigi Pirandello's work in Catalonia. Italy. Spain-Catalonia. 1867-1985. Lang.: Spa, Cat. 2706

Centre Dramàtic de la Generalitat de Catalunya (Barcelona)
Performance/production

Savannah Bay and *Reigen (Round)* produced by Centre Dramàtic. Spain-Catalonia: Barcelona. 1986. Lang.: Cat. 2082

Articles on the 1986-87 theatre season. Spain-Catalonia: Barcelona. France. 1986. Lang.: Cat. 2083

Articles about the productions of the Centre Dramàtic. Spain-Catalonia: Barcelona. 1976-1986. Lang.: Cat. 2084

Centre Georges Pompidou (Paris)
Design/technology
Les Immatériaux, multimedia exhibit by Jean-François Lyotard.
France: Paris. 1986. Lang.: Eng.   3249

Centre National d'Art et d'Essai (Paris)
Training
Actor training methods of Luce Berthomme. France: Paris. 1984.
Lang.: Eng.   1256

Centre Saidye Bronfman (Montreal, PQ)
Institutions
Interviews with theatre professionals in Quebec. Canada. 1985.
Lang.: Fre.   487

CentreStage (Toronto, ON)
Performance/production
Career of director Bill Glassco. Canada: Toronto, ON. 1965-1986.
Lang.: Eng.   1674

Centrum Sztuki Studio (Warsaw)
Performance/production
Tadeusz Łomnicki directs Pasolini's Affabulazione at Centrum Sztuki
Studio. Poland: Warsaw. 1984. Lang.: Pol.   2033

Jerzy Grzegorzewski directs Różewicz's Pułapka (Trap) at Centrum
Sztuki Studio. Poland: Warsaw. 1984. Lang.: Pol.   2053

Century Theatre (New York, NY)
Performance spaces
History of the Century Theatre. USA: New York, NY. 1905-1930.
Lang.: Eng.   1625

Cercle Molière (St. Banyace, MB)
Performance/production
Opposition to realism in plays from Francophone Manitoba. Canada.
1983-1986. Lang.: Fre.   670

Ceremonies in Dark Old Men
Plays/librettos/scripts
Race in prison dramas of Piñero, Camillo, Elder and Bullins. USA.
1970-1986. Lang.: Eng.   2912

Cereza, Xavier
Performance/production
Detailed description of the performance titled Accions (Actions) by
La Fura dels Baus. Spain-Catalonia. 1979-1984. Lang.: Cat.   3445

Cerha, Friedrich
Performance/production
Harry Kupfer: his work and career as singer and director. Germany,
East: Dresden, Berlin, East. 1970-1985. Lang.: Ger.   3738

Cernovitch, Nicholas
Design/technology
Career of lighting designer Nicholas Cernovitch. Canada: Montreal,
PQ. 1970-1983. Lang.: Eng.   244

Černyševskij Opera Theatre
SEE
Teat'r Opery i Baleta im. N. Černyševskovo (Saratov).

Certain Dark Joy, A
Performance/production
Career of director/choreographer Mike Malone. USA: Washington,
DC, Cleveland, OH. 1968-1985. Lang.: Eng.   2275

Cervantes Saavedra, Miguel de
Plays/librettos/scripts
Mutual influences between commedia dell'arte and Spanish literature.
Spain. Italy. 1330-1623. Lang.: Spa.   2805

Relation to other fields
Comparison of playwright Luigi Pirandello and novelist Miguel de
Cervantes. Italy. Spain. 1615-1936. Lang.: Ita.   3040

Césaire, Aimé
Performance/production
Notes, interviews and evolution of actor/director Jean-Marie Serreau.
France. 1938-1973. Lang.: Fre.   1724

Plays/librettos/scripts
Precursors of revolutionary black theatre. Haiti. Jamaica. 1820-1970.
Lang.: Eng.   956

Analysis of La Tragédie du roi Christophe (The Tragedy of King
Christopher) by Aimé Césaire. Haiti. Africa. Martinique. 1939. Lang.:
Fre.   2637

CFDC
SEE
Canadian Film Development Corporation.

CGALI
SEE
Centralnyj Gosudarstvênnyj Archiv Literatury i Iskusstva.

Chaikin, Joseph
Institutions
Production history and techniques of the Living Theatre. USA. 1964.
Lang.: Eng.   546

Chalbaud, Román
Plays/librettos/scripts
Traces development of political trends in Venezuelan drama.
Venezuela. 1958-1980. Lang.: Spa.   2972

Chalk Garden, The
Performance/production
Interview with actress Dorothy Tutin. UK-England: Chichester. 1986.
Lang.: Eng.   2132

Survey of the Chichester Festival. UK-England: Chichester. 1986.
Lang.: Eng.   2185

Chalmers Award
SEE
Awards, Chalmers.

Chamber Theatre (Moscow)
SEE
Kamernyj Teat'r.

Chamber Theatre (Munich)
SEE
Kammerspiele.

Chamber Theatre (Pest)
SEE
Kamaraszinház.

Chamber Theatre (Sopot)
SEE
Teatr Wybrzeżne.

Chamber Theatre (Tel Aviv)
SEE
Kameri.

Chameleon
Performance/production
Collection of newspaper reviews by London theatre critics. UK-
England: London. 1986. Lang.: Eng.   2116

Chan HaJerušalmi (Jerusalem)
Performance/production
Notes on the process of staging Eiolf Hakatan, a Hebrew translation
of Henrik Ibsen's Lille Eyolf (Little Eyolf), directed by Yossi Israeli
at the Kahn theatre. Israel: Jerusalem. 1986. Lang.: Heb.   1980

Notes on the rehearsals of Henrik Ibsen's Lille Eyolf (Little Eyolf)
directed by Yossi Israeli, at the Kahn Theatre. Israel: Jerusalem.
1986. Lang.: Heb.   1982

Chanal, Henri
Performance/production
Effect of dual-language society on Belgian theatre. Belgium: Brussels,
Liège. Lang.: Eng.   660

Chäng-gük
Theory/criticism
Theories about the stage for the traditional chäng-gük play. Korea:
Seoul. 1800-1950. Lang.: Kor.   3931

Chang, Heng
Design/technology
Profile of costuming during the Han dynasty. China: Nanyang. 202
B.C.-220 A.D. Lang.: Chi.   3310

Chang, Jong-Seon
Design/technology
Set design and the current state of Korean theatre. Korea. 1986.
Lang.: Kor.   303

Chang, Keng
Influence of Wagner on the music of contemporary Chinese opera.
China, People's Republic of. 1949-1980. Lang.: Chi.   3503

Plays/librettos/scripts
Characteristics and influences of Fan Ts'ui-T'ing's plays. China.
1900-1980. Lang.: Chi.   3532

Changeling, The
Plays/librettos/scripts
Origin of Spanish setting in Middleton and Rowley's The
Changeling. England. 1607-1622. Lang.: Eng.   2513

Reference materials
List of 37 productions of 23 Renaissance plays, with commentary.
UK. USA. New Zealand. 1986. Lang.: Eng.   3000

Chapeau de Paille d'Italie, Un (Italian Straw Hat, An)
Performance/production
Interview with actor-turned-director Michael Leech. England: London.
1986. Lang.: Eng.   1710

Chapeau de Paille d'Italie, Un (Italian Straw Hat, An) — cont'd

Production photos of *Un Chapeau de Paille d'Italie (An Italian Straw Hat)* by Eugène Labiche. France: Paris. 1986. Lang.: Fre.
1727

Chapel Royal (London)
Institutions
Importance of Chapel Royal in early Tudor court entertainment. England: London. 1504-1524. Lang.: Eng. 3418

Chapman, George
Plays/librettos/scripts
Critical confusion regarding *The Revenge of Bussy d'Ambois* by George Chapman. England. 1603. Lang.: Eng. 942

George Chapman's *Caesar and Pompey* as a disguised version of the story of Prince Henry. England. 1605-1631. Lang.: Eng. 2523

Stoicism and modern elements in Senecan drama. Europe. 65-1986. Lang.: Eng. 2542

Relation to other fields
Social critique and influence of Jacobean drama. England: London. 1603-1613. Lang.: Eng. 1081

Chapman, Gerald
Relation to other fields
Description of the Cutler Playwright's Festival designed for junior high school students. USA: Groton, CT. 1983-1986. Lang.: Eng.
3065

Chapman, Robin
Performance/production
Collection of newspaper reviews by London theatre critics. UK-England: London. 1986. Lang.: Eng. 2118

Characters/roles
Audience
History of the Mulgrave Road Co-op theatre. Canada: Guysborough, NS. 1977-1985. Lang.: Eng. 1444

Basic theatrical documents
Playtext of *Drifting Fires* by Janine Beichman, with author's afterword on use of *Nō* elements. Japan: Ibaraki. 1984-1985. Lang.: Eng. 1383

Design/technology
Origins and development of *commedia dell'arte* detailing the costume and attributes of the stock characters. Italy. Europe. USA. 1500-1986. Lang.: Eng. 3407

Performance/production
Production analysis of *The Merchant of Venice* directed by Mark Lamos. Canada: Stratford, ON. 1984. Lang.: Eng. 667

Influence of Indian theatre on Western drama. Europe. India. 1884-1986. Lang.: Ita. 703

Actors and roles in medieval French theatre. France. 900-1499. Lang.: Rus. 721

Careers of Sadovskije acting family. Russia: Moscow. 1800-1917. Lang.: Rus. 784

The artistic director of the Arena Stage discusses the place of the actor in contemporary theatre. USA: Washington, DC. 1951-1986. Lang.: Eng. 832

Edwin Booth's portrayal of Iago in Shakespeare's *Othello*. USA. 1852-1890. Lang.: Eng. 854

On actor Heinz Petters and the production of *Der Raub der Sabinerinnen* at the Volkstheater. Austria: Vienna. 1938-1986. Lang.: Ger. 1644

Klaus Maria Brandauer as Hamlet. Austria: Vienna. 1944-1986. Lang.: Ger. 1648

Playing Hamlet at the Burgtheater. Austria: Vienna. 1803-1985. Lang.: Ger. 1654

Career of actress, manager and director Julia Arthur. Canada. UK-England. USA. 1869-1950. Lang.: Eng. 1675

The portrayal of Cleopatra by various actresses. England. 1813-1890. Lang.: Eng. 1699

Tom Robertson as a theatrical innovator and as a character in Arthur Wing Pinero's *Trelawny of the Wells*. England: London. 1840-1848. Lang.: Eng. 1702

Analysis and interpretation of the staging of *The Castle of Perseverance* based on original stage plan drawing. England. 1343-1554. Lang.: Eng. 1708

Significance of 'boy-actresses' in role of Viola in Shakespeare's *Twelfth Night*. England. 1601. Lang.: Eng. 1714

Actors discuss performing in plays by Paul Claudel. France. Belgium. 1943-1985. Lang.: Fre. 1722

Description of Georg Büchner's *Dantons Tod (Danton's Death)* staged by Alexander Lang at Deutsches Theater. Germany, East: Berlin, East. 1984. Lang.: Ger. 1763

Interview with Elisabeth Bergner and Jane Alexander on their portrayals of Joan of Arc. Germany, West: Berlin, West. UK-England: Malvern. USA: Washington, DC. Lang.: Eng. 1766

Interview with actor Pál Mácsai on his role in *Scapin furfangjai (Scapin's Tricks)* by Molière. Hungary: Szentendre. 1986. Lang.: Hun. 1775

Career of actress Margit Dajka. Hungary. 1907-1986. Lang.: Hun. 1787

Piroska Molnár's performance in *Kozma* by Mihály Kornis. Hungary: Kaposvár. 1986. Lang.: Hun. 1796

Čechov's *Három nővér (Three Sisters)* directed by Tamás Ascher. Hungary: Budapest. 1985. Lang.: Hun. 1814

Review of Gábor Görgey's *Mikszáth különös házassága (Mikszáth and His Peculiar Marriage)* directed by János Sándor. Hungary: Szeged. 1986. Lang.: Hun. 1819

Edith és Marlene (Edith and Marlene) by Éva Pataki at Comedy Theatre. Hungary: Budapest. 1986. Lang.: Hun. 1831

Interview with actor István Avar. Hungary. 1954-1985. Lang.: Hun. 1836

Interview with actress Éva Spányik. Hungary. 1957-1985. Lang.: Hun. 1837

Interview with actor Erzsi Pásztor. Hungary. 1970-1980. Lang.: Hun. 1838

Interview with actor András Bálint. Hungary. 1965-1986. Lang.: Hun. 1839

Review of Shakespeare's *Hamlet* directed by László Gali at Csokonai Theatre, with attention to Károly Sziki's performance as Hamlet. Hungary: Debrecen. 1986. Lang.: Hun. 1844

Ferenc Sik directs *A velencei Kalmár (The Merchant of Venice)* by William Shakespeare. Hungary: Budapest. 1986. Lang.: Hun. 1853

Commemoration of actor László Márkus. Hungary. 1986. Lang.: Hun. 1864

Recollections of actor, director and theatre manager Tamás Major. Hungary. 1910-1986. Lang.: Hun. 1879

Recollections of actress Margit Dajka. Hungary. 1929-1986. Lang.: Hun. 1930

The life and career of actress Mari Törőcsik. Hungary. 1956-1986. Lang.: Hun. 1933

English-language performances of Italian actress Adelaide Ristori. Italy. England. USA. 1822-1906. Lang.: Ita. 2000

Director John Dillon on his Japanese production of *Death of a Salesman* by Arthur Miller. Japan. 1984. Lang.: Eng. 2005

Interview with actress Agneta Ekmanner. Sweden: Stockholm. 1950-1986. Lang.: Swe. 2092

Autobiography of actor Alec Guinness. UK. USA. 1914-1985. Lang.: Eng. 2106

Actors Ben Kingsley and David Suchet discuss their roles in Shakespeare's *Othello*. UK-England. 1986. Lang.: Eng. 2128

Doubling of roles in Shakespeare's *Hamlet*. UK-England: London. 1900-1985. Lang.: Eng. 2129

Eileen Atkins, Judi Dench, Wendy Hiller and Barbara Jefford discuss playing Saint Joan in Shaw's play. UK-England: London. 1936-1983. Lang.: Eng. 2153

Actor Colin Blakely discusses his career. UK-England: London. 1950-1986. Lang.: Eng. 2176

Analysis of predominant mode of staging final scene of *Othello* by William Shakespeare. UK-England: London. USA. 1760-1900. Lang.: Eng. 2184

Review of Eugene O'Neill's *Long Day's Journey Into Night* directed by Jonathan Miller. USA. 1956-1986. Lang.: Eng. 2264

Interview with Peter Gallagher on his portrayal of Edmund in *Long Day's Journey Into Night*. USA: New York, NY, New London, CT. 1986. Lang.: Eng. 2268

Director of original production discusses Edward Albee's *Who's Afraid of Virginia Woolf?*. USA: New York, NY. 1962. Lang.: Eng. 2303

Recollections of actress Faina Ranevskaja. USSR. 1896-1984. Lang.: Rus. 2316

Characters/roles — cont'd

Faina Ranevskaja's role in *Pravda—chorošo, a sčast'e lučše (Truth is Good, But Happiness is Better)* by A.N. Ostrovskij. USSR: Moscow. 1896-1984. Lang.: Rus. 2324

Comic actor Tristano Martinelli, probable creator of the character Harlequin. Italy. France. 1550-1600. Lang.: Ita. 3412

Ch'in opera and its influences. China: Beijing. 1795-1850. Lang.: Chi. 3518

Techniques of comedians in modern Beijing opera. China, People's Republic of: Beijing. 1964-1985. Lang.: Chi. 3524

Éva Pataki's *Edith és Marlene (Edith and Marlene)* directed by Márta Mészáros, Pest National Theatre. Hungary: Budapest. 1986. Lang.: Hun. 3603

Opera singer Maureen Forrester tells of her switch from serious roles to character and comic roles. Canada. 1970-1984. Lang.: Eng. 3706

Interview with mezzo-sporano Judith Forst. Canada. 1975-1986. Lang.: Eng. 3708

Profile of and interview with tenor Jon Vickers about his career and his leading role in *Samson* by George Frideric Handel. Canada: Prince Albert, AB. 1926-1986. Lang.: Eng. 3713

Productions of Handel's *Muzio Scevola* and analysis of score and characters. England: London. 1718-1980. Lang.: Eng. 3720

Performance analysis of the title role of *Carmen*. France. 1875-1986. Lang.: Eng. 3725

Opera-singer Mirella Freni: her roles and plans. Italy. Austria. 1935-1986. Lang.: Ger. 3759

Controversy over Jonathan Miller's production of *Rigoletto*. USA. 1984. Lang.: Eng. 3821

Women's roles in the operas of Benjamin Britten. USA. 1940-1979. Lang.: Eng. 3824

Description of characters and techniques of *Wayang* puppetry. Indonesia. 1983-1986. Lang.: Fre. 4018

Plays/librettos/scripts

Interview with satirist Barry Humphries. Australia. UK-England. 1950-1986. Lang.: Eng. 922

Semiotic analysis of a production of *Antigone* by Sophocles. Australia: Perth, W.A. 1986. Lang.: Eng. 923

Development of the title character of *The Ecstasy of Rita Joe* by George Ryga, seen in successive drafts. Canada: Vancouver, BC. 1966-1982. Lang.: Eng. 929

Development of playwright George F. Walker. Canada: Toronto, ON. 1970-1984. Lang.: Eng. 931

Envy in Shakespeare's *Othello* and Peter Shaffer's *Amadeus*. Canada: Montreal, PQ. Europe. 1604-1986. Lang.: Eng. 932

Defense of *The Malcontent* by John Marston as a well-constructed satire. England. 1590-1600. Lang.: Eng. 938

Critical confusion regarding *The Revenge of Bussy d'Ambois* by George Chapman. England. 1603. Lang.: Eng. 942

Psychoanalytic and post-structuralist analysis of Molière's *Tartuffe*. France. 1660-1669. Lang.: Eng. 948

Pulchinella figures in the plays of Eduardo De Filippo. Italy. 1900-1985. Lang.: Rus. 960

Interview with playwright Maria Irene Fornes. USA. 1965-1985. Lang.: Eng. 979

Discussion of plays and themes concerning the Women's Movement. USA. 1971-1986. Lang.: Eng. 982

Sociological problems in contemporary drama. USSR. 1980-1986. Lang.: Rus. 993

Role analysis of the mask-dance play, *Yängjubyulsändae* and the theories of Choe Sang-Su. Korea: Yängju. 1700-1900. Lang.: Kor. 1375

Dramatization as an emphasis on character over narrative. 2348

Analysis of the characters of *Bánk Bán* by József Katona. Lang.: Hun. 2351

The incoherent protagonist of modern comedy. 1954-1986. Lang.: Eng. 2358

Chronotopic analysis of *El beso de la mujer araña (The Kiss of the Spider Woman)* by Manuel Puigi. Argentina. 1976-1986. Lang.: Spa. 2364

Analysis of Ray Lawler's *Summer of the Seventeenth Doll* in the context of his later plays. Australia. 1955-1977. Lang.: Eng. 2377

Interview with playwright David Williamson. Australia. 1986. Lang.: Eng. 2378

Analysis of plays by David Williamson. Australia. 1976-1985. Lang.: Eng. 2379

Study of heroism in verse dramas by Douglas Stewart, Tom Inglis Moore and Catherine Duncan. Australia. 1941-1943. Lang.: Eng. 2383

Difficulties in French translation of Karl Kraus's *Die Letzten Tage der Menschheit (The Last Days of Mankind)*. Austria: Vienna. France: Paris. 1918-1986. Lang.: Ger. 2397

Social themes in the dramas of Franz Grillparzer. Austro-Hungarian Empire: Vienna. 1791-1872. Lang.: Ger. 2399

Poverty in plays by Michel Tremblay and David Fennario. Canada: Quebec, PQ. 1970-1980. Lang.: Eng. 2410

Study of two unproduced historical dramas about French-Canadian patriot Louis Riel. Canada: Montreal, PQ. 1886. Lang.: Fre. 2413

Writing and production of *Riel* by John Coulter. Canada: Toronto, ON, Ottawa, ON. 1936-1980. Lang.: Eng. 2414

Comparison of plays about Ned Kelly of Australia and Louis Riel of Canada. Canada. Australia. 1900-1976. Lang.: Eng. 2421

The immigrant in plays by Herman Voaden and Robertson Davies. Canada. 1934-1950. Lang.: Eng. 2431

Compares Michel Tremblay's *Albertine en cing temps (Albertine in Five Times)* to Marcel Proust's *A la recherche du temps perdu (Remembrance of Things Past)*. Canada. 1984. 2436

Marginal characters in plays of Jorge Díaz, Egon Wolff and Luis Alberto Heiremans. Chile. 1960-1971. Lang.: Eng. 2442

Use of history in Chinese traditional drama. China. 960-1983. Lang.: Chi. 2444

Analysis of one-act play structures. China. 1500-1980. Lang.: Chi. 2447

Limited perception in *The Plough and the Stars* by Sean O'Casey. Eire. 1926-1986. Lang.: Eng. 2456

Ceremony distinguishes kings from peasants in Shakespeare's *Henry V*. England. 1598-1599. Lang.: Eng. 2464

Shakespeare's complex, unconventional heroines in *All's Well that Ends Well* and *Measure for Measure*. England. 1603. Lang.: Eng. 2469

Connection between character Senex in Thomas Kyd's *The Spanish Tragedy* and Senecan drama. England. 1587. Lang.: Eng. 2473

Female characterization in Nicholas Rowe's plays. England. 1629-1720. Lang.: Eng. 2475

Liberated female characters in the plays of George Lillo. England. 1730-1759. Lang.: Eng. 2477

Punctuation in *Gammer Gurton's Needle* indicates style of performance. England. 1575-1920. 2489

Role of Rosalind in Shakespeare's *As You Like It*. England. 1600-1986. Lang.: Eng. 2491

Moral issues in *A Woman Killed with Kindness* by Thomas Heywood. England. 1560. Lang.: Eng. 2498

Contemporary responses to *Tamburlane the Great* by Christopher Marlowe. England. 1984. Lang.: Eng. 2501

Interpretations of Shakespeare's *A Midsummer Night's Dream* based on Bottom's transformation. England. 1595-1986. Lang.: Eng. 2503

Cast lists in James Shirley's *Six New Playes* suggest popularity of plays. England. 1653-1669. Lang.: Eng. 2504

Gender roles in *Epicoene* by Ben Jonson. England: London. 1609-1909. Lang.: Eng. 2505

Analysis of Henry Fielding's play *The Author's Farce*. England. 1730. Lang.: Eng. 2516

Character source for Dr. Last in Samuel Foote's play *The Devil Upon Two Sticks*. England. 1768-1774. Lang.: Eng. 2522

George Chapman's *Caesar and Pompey* as a disguised version of the story of Prince Henry. England. 1605-1631. Lang.: Eng. 2523

Analysis of the final scene of *The Broken Heart* by John Ford. England. 1629. Lang.: Eng. 2526

Accuracy of portrayal of historical figures in Shakespeare and his adaptors. England. 1590-1940. Lang.: Eng. 2532

Study of six French versions of the Don Juan legend. France. 1657-1682. Lang.: Ita. 2548

Molière's character Dom Juan reinterpreted. France. 1660-1986. Lang.: Fre. 2551

Theme of fragmentation in *Lorenzaccio* by Alfred de Musset. France. 1834. Lang.: Eng. 2558

Characters/roles — cont'd

Rhetorical analysis of Samuel Beckett's *Waiting for Godot*. France. 1953. Lang.: Eng.   2562

Dialectical method in the plays of Molière. France. 1666. Lang.: Eng.   2567

Treatment of Napoleon Bonaparte by French and English dramatists. France. England. 1797-1958. Lang.: Eng.   2568

The role of the double in Georg Kaiser's *Zweimal Amphitryon (Amphitryon x 2)* and other works. Germany. 1943. Lang.: Eng.   2589

Brecht's patriarchal view of women as seen in the character of Jenny in *Die Dreigroschenoper (The Three Penny Opera)*. Germany, East.   2615

Characterization in *Furcht und Hoffnung der BRD (Help Wanted)* by Franz Xaver Kroetz. Germany, West. 1984-1986. Lang.: Eng.   2623

Notes on György Spiró's play about actor, director, manager and playwright Wojciech Bogusławski. Hungary. 1983. Lang.: Hun.   2659

Dramatizations of the life of politician Endre Bajcsy-Zsilinszky. Hungary. 1960-1980. Lang.: Hun.   2661

Biography of playwright Teresa Deevy. Ireland. 1894-1963. Lang.: Eng.   2665

Angelo Musco's interpretation of *Pensaci Giacomino! (Think of it, Jamie!)* by Luigi Pirandello. Italy. 1916-1917. Lang.: Ita.   2684

Analysis of Harlequin in comedies by Carlo Goldoni. Italy. 1751-1752. Lang.: Ita.   2697

Playwright Sergio Tofano and the hero of his comedies, Bonaventura. Italy. 1927-1953. Lang.: Ita.   2704

Gestural characterization in *I promessi sposi (The Betrothed)* by Manzoni. Italy. 1842. Lang.: Ita.   2707

Women's issues in Italian theatre. Italy. 1985. Lang.: Cat.   2710

Influence of Asian theatre on work of Filippo Acciajoli. Italy. 1637-1700. Lang.: Ita.   2713

Use of language in *El Gesticulador (The Gesticulator)* by Rodolfo Usigli. Mexico. 1970-1980. Lang.: Spa.   2723

Self-transcendence through grace embodied in Henrik Ibsen's female characters. Norway. 1849-1899. Lang.: Eng.   2726

Narcissism in *Et Dukkehjem (A Doll's House)* by Henrik Ibsen. Norway. 1879. Lang.: Eng.   2727

Interpretation of Fortinbras in post-war productions of *Hamlet*. Poland. UK-England. 1945. Lang.: Eng.   2748

Tadeusz Kantor comments on his play *Niech szezna artyszi (Let the Artists Die)*. Poland. 1985. Lang.: Eng, Fre.   2751

Analysis of animal-like characters in Witkiewicz's dramas. Poland. 1920-1935. Lang.: Pol.   2757

Analysis of the major plays of Maksim Gorkij. Russia. 1868-1936. Lang.: Chi.   2769

The role of the artist in *The Road to Mecca* by Athol Fugard. South Africa, Republic of. 1961-1984. Lang.: Eng.   2779

Current thematic trends in the plays of Antonio Gala. Spain. 1963-1985. Lang.: Spa.   2783

Lope de Vega's characterization of the converted Jew. Spain. 1562-1635. Lang.: Spa.   2804

Mutual influences between *commedia dell'arte* and Spanish literature. Spain. Italy. 1330-1623. Lang.: Spa.   2805

Analysis of the six published dramatic works by Jordi Teixidor. Spain-Catalonia. 1970-1985. Lang.: Cat.   2809

Playwright Marius Brill discusses his prize winning play *Frikzhan*. UK-England: London. 1986. Lang.: Eng.   2831

Thematic analysis of *Candida* by George Bernard Shaw focusing on the spiritual development of Marchbanks. UK-England: London. 1894. Lang.: Eng.   2837

Treatment of the Frankenstein myth in three gothic melodramas. UK-England. France. 1823-1826. Lang.: Eng.   2847

Analysis of Arnold Wesker's *Chicken Soup with Barley*. UK-England: London. 1932-1986. Lang.: Cat.   2864

Analysis of John Osborne's *Look Back in Anger*. UK-England: London. 1929-1978. Lang.: Cat.   2866

Analysis of Pedro Corradi's *Retrato de señora con espejo—Vida y pasión de Margarita Xirgu (Portrait of a Lady with Mirror—The Life and Passion of Margarita Xirgu)*. Uruguay. Spain: Madrid. 1985. Lang.: Spa.   2887

Mourning in Eugene O'Neill's *A Moon for the Misbegotten*. USA. 1922-1947. Lang.: Eng.   2895

Gender role-reversal in the Cycle plays of Eugene O'Neill. USA. 1927-1953. Lang.: Eng.   2896

Imagery and the role of women in Sam Shepard's *Buried Child*. USA. 1978. Lang.: Eng.   2899

Progress in audience perception of gay characters in plays. USA. 1933-1985. Lang.: Eng.   2909

Analysis of *Hurlyburly* by David Rabe. USA. 1984. Lang.: Eng.   2918

Similarities of *Hughie* by Eugene O'Neill and *The Zoo Story* by Edward Albee. USA: New York, NY. 1941-1958. Lang.: Eng.   2919

Authority and victimization in *A Streetcar Named Desire* by Tennessee Williams. USA. 1960-1980. Lang.: Eng.   2947

Trends in Russian Soviet dramaturgy. USSR. 1950-1979. Lang.: Rus.   2961

Conflict and characterization in recent Soviet dramaturgy. USSR. 1970-1980. Lang.: Rus.   2967

Stanislavskij's method for the role of Othello. USSR. 1929-1930. Lang.: Swe.   2968

Discussion of the hero in modern drama. USSR. 1980-1986. Lang.: Rus.   2969

The positive hero in contemporary drama. USSR. 1980-1986. Lang.: Rus.   2971

Cultural models and types in docudrama. Canada. 1970-1983. Lang.: Eng.   3279

Ideology of commercial television. Canada. USA. 1965-1983. Lang.: Eng.   3281

Analysis of *commedia dell'arte* text of Carlo Cantú's *Cicalamento*. Italy. 1576-1646. Lang.: Ita.   3416

Plots and themes in adaptations of *Tou Erh Yüan (The Injustice of Miss Tou)*. China. 1360-1960. Lang.: Chi.   3525

Definition and characteristics of *Hsiao* role. China. 618-1580. Lang.: Chi.   3530

Characteristics and influences of Fan Ts'ui-T'ing's plays. China. 1900-1980. Lang.: Chi.   3532

Comparison of the works of Wang Ji-De and Xu Wei. China. 1620-1752. Lang.: Chi.   3534

Analysis of playwright Xu Jin's work. China, People's Republic of: Beijing. 1952-1985. Lang.: Chi.   3535

Structure of Beijing opera. China, People's Republic of: Beijing. 1983. Lang.: Chi.   3537

Introduction to the folk play, *Mu Lian*. China, People's Republic of: Beijing. 1962-1985. Lang.: Chi.   3538

Innovations of playwright Chen Jenchien. China, People's Republic of. 1913-1986. Lang.: Chi.   3539

Play sequels and their characteristics. China, People's Republic of. 1949-1980. Lang.: Chi.   3540

Origins, characteristics and structures of Beijing operas. China, People's Republic of: Beijing. 1903-1985. Lang.: Chi.   3541

Introduction to Sichuan opera, including translation of a new play. China, People's Republic of. 1876-1983. Lang.: Eng.   3542

The search for morality in *Wozzeck* by Alban Berg. 1821. Lang.: Eng.   3851

German and Christian myths in Hans Pfitzner's opera *Palestrina*. 1900-1982. Lang.: Eng.   3852

Analysis and origins of the character 'Dr. Miracle' in Offenbach's *Les contes d'Hoffmann*. 1700-1900. Lang.: Eng.   3853

Title character in Alban Berg's *Lulu*. Austria: Vienna. 1891-1979. Lang.: Eng.   3857

Influences on Alban Berg's *Lulu*. Austria: Vienna. 1907-1979. Lang.: Eng.   3859

Appearance of Franz Anton Mesmer as a character in Mozart's *Così fan tutte*. France: Paris. Austria: Vienna. 1734-1789. Lang.: Eng.   3871

Schopenhauerian pessimism in Wagner's *Ring* and *Götterdämmerung*. Germany. 1852-1856. Lang.: Eng.   3873

Use of the tale of Patient Griselda in *Griselda* by Angelo Anelli and Niccolo Piccinni. Italy: Venice. Austria: Vienna. 1770-1800. Lang.: Eng.   3885

Changes from the Friedrich von Schiller source in *Don Carlo* by Giuseppe Verdi. Italy. 1867-1883. Lang.: Eng.   3887

The historical Simon Boccanegra. Italy: Genoa. 900-1857. Lang.: Eng.   3888

Characters/roles — cont'd

A chronology and analysis of the compositions of Benjamin Britten. UK-England: London. 1946-1976. Lang.: Eng. 3896

Analysis of Benjamin Britten's opera *Albert Herring*. UK-England: London. 1947. Lang.: Eng. 3897

Character analysis in Britten's opera *The Turn of the Screw*. UK-England. 1954. Lang.: Eng. 3898

Jack Beeson's opera *Lizzie Borden*. USA. 1954-1965. Lang.: Eng. 3901

Reference materials
Review of 1985 dissertations. China, People's Republic of: Beijing. 1985. Lang.: Chi. 3545

Relation to other fields
Controversy about *Captives of the Faceless Drummer* by George Ryga. Canada: Vancouver, BC. 1968-1971. Lang.: Eng. 3021

Role of Beijing opera today. China, People's Republic of: Beijing. 1985. Lang.: Chi. 3547

Mao's policy on theatre in revolution. China, People's Republic of: Beijing. 1920-1985. Lang.: Chi. 3549

Research/historiography
Problems of research methodology applied to traditional singing styles. China. 1600-1980. Lang.: Chi. 3553

Development of Cantonese opera and its influence. China, People's Republic of: Kuang Tung. 1885-1985. Lang.: Chi. 3555

Rise of the *Ping Hsi* form in Tienchin. China, People's Republic of: Tienchin. 1885-1948. Lang.: Chi. 3557

Theory/criticism
Playwright A. Simukov discusses his craft. USSR. 1986. Lang.: Rus. 1249

Playwright Xiong Foxi's concept of theatre. China, People's Republic of. 1920-1965. Lang.: Chi. 3089

Character as an aesthetic category in contemporary dramaturgy. USSR. 1980-1986. Lang.: Rus. 3153

Influence of Tuan Anchieh's aesthetics. China. 800-1644. Lang.: Chi. 3561

Analyzes works of four dramatists from Fuchien province. China, People's Republic of. 1981-1985. Lang.: Chi. 3569

Characteristics of Chinese opera in Szechuan province. China, People's Republic of. 1963-1985. Lang.: Chi. 3570

Charley's Aunt
Plays/librettos/scripts
Development and subsequent decline of the three-act farce. UK-England. 1875-1900. Lang.: Eng. 976

Charlie and the Chocolate Factory
Performance/production
Collection of newspaper reviews by London theatre critics. UK-England: London. 1986. Lang.: Eng. 2116

Charlottetown Festival (Charlottetown, PE)
Institutions
Fragile alternatives to Charlottetown Festival. Canada: Charlottetown, PE. 1982-1986. Lang.: Eng. 1540

Reference materials
Overview of Charlottetown Festival productions. Canada: Charlottetown, PE. 1972-1983. Lang.: Eng. 1008

Cheat'n Heart
Administration
Fundraising for the film *Cheat'n Heart*. USA: New York, NY. 1984-1986. Lang.: Eng. 3192

Checheno-Ingush Drama Theatre
SEE
Čečeno-Ingušskij Dramatičeskij Teat'r im. Ch. Nuradilova.

Chedid, Andrée
Plays/librettos/scripts
Mythology in the works of Hélène Cixous, Andrée Chedid, Monique Wittig and Marguerite Yourcenar. France. Lang.: Eng. 2580

Cheeky Chappie, The
Performance/production
Collection of newspaper reviews by London theatre critics. UK. 1986. Lang.: Eng. 2103

Cheeseman, Peter
Performance spaces
Technical design features of New Victoria Theatre. UK-England: Stoke-on-Trent. 1980-1986. Lang.: Eng. 624

Peter Cheeseman, artistic director of the New Victoria Theatre, compares the new theatre with the Old Vic. UK-England: Stoke-on-Trent. 1962-1986. Lang.: Eng. 629

Technical review of *She Stoops to Conquer* by Oliver Goldsmith performed at the New Victoria Theatre. UK-England: Newcastle-under-Lyme. 1980-1986. Lang.: Eng. 1618

Chekhov Theatre Players (Ridgefield, CT)
Performance/production
Michael Chekhov's theories of acting and directing. USSR: Moscow. USA: Ridgefield, CT. 1938. Lang.: Eng. 887

Chekhov, Anton
SEE
Čechov, Anton Pavlovič.

Chekhov, Michael
SEE
Čechov, Michajl A..

Cheltenham Theatre (UK)
Performance/production
Survey of theatrical performances in the low country. UK-England. 1986. Lang.: Eng. 2150

Chen, Baichen
Relation to other fields
Anecdotes about caricaturist Liao Bingxiong and comedian Chen Baichen. China, People's Republic of. 1942-1981. Lang.: Chi. 1078

Chen, Ching
Relation to other fields
Mao's policy on theatre in revolution. China, People's Republic of: Beijing. 1920-1985. Lang.: Chi. 3549

Chen, Jenchien
Plays/librettos/scripts
Innovations of playwright Chen Jenchien. China, People's Republic of. 1913-1986. Lang.: Chi. 3539

Chen, Kuo
Plays/librettos/scripts
Differences between *Chan Ta* and *Chuan Ta* drama. China. 1200-1986. Lang.: Chi. 3527

Chen, Shaobai
Research/historiography
Development of Cantonese opera and its influence. China, People's Republic of: Kuang Tung. 1885-1985. Lang.: Chi. 3555

Chen, Tachang
Relation to other fields
Analysis of Northern Sung theatrical artifacts. 1032-1126. Lang.: Chi. 3546

Chen, Tesun
Performance spaces
Theatre activities during the Tang dynasty. China. 710-905. Lang.: Chi. 591

Cheng, Haijen
Performance spaces
Theatre activities during the Tang dynasty. China. 710-905. Lang.: Chi. 591

Cheng, Kuangtsu
Research/historiography
Great playwrights of the Yüan dynasty. China. 1271-1368. Lang.: Chi. 3552

Cheng, Ting Yu
Research/historiography
Great playwrights of the Yüan dynasty. China. 1271-1368. Lang.: Chi. 3552

Cheng, Yangqui
Theory/criticism
Characteristics of Chinese opera in Szechuan province. China, People's Republic of. 1963-1985. Lang.: Chi. 3570

Cheng, Yu
Relation to other fields
Role of Beijing opera today. China, People's Republic of: Beijing. 1985. Lang.: Chi. 3547

Cheo Theatre Ensemble (Thai Binh)
Performance/production
Review and discussion of Vietnamese performance in Hungary. Vietnam: Thai Binh. Hungary. 1986. Lang.: Hun. 915

Chéreau, Patrice
Performance/production
Analysis of two productions of plays by Marivaux. France: Nanterre. Germany, West: Berlin, West. 1985. Lang.: Swe. 1739

Plays/librettos/scripts
Great dramatic works considered in light of modern theatre and social reponsibility. France. Italy. Germany, West. 1700-1964. Lang.: Fre. 2560

Children's theatre — cont'd

Problems of young people's theatre. USSR: Moscow. 1980-1986.
Lang.: Rus.   899

Review of children's theatre festival. Yugoslavia: Šibenik. 1986.
Lang.: Hun.   916

Dilemmas and prospects of youth theatre movement. Australia. 1982-
1986. Lang.: Eng.   1639

Performances of *Alice Csodaországban (Alice in Wonderland)*, *A Két
Veronai nemes (The Two Gentlemen of Verona)* and *Tobbsincs
királyfi (No More Crown Prince)*. Hungary: Pécs, Budapest. 1985.
Lang.: Hun.   1771

Stage adaptation of Erich Kästner's novel *Emil und die Detektive
(Emil and the Detectives)* directed by István Keleti. Hungary:
Budapest. 1986. Lang.: Hun.   1807

Overview of children's theatre offerings. Hungary. 1985-1986. Lang.:
Hun.   1904

Recollections of children's theatre in two Soviet cities. USSR:
Leningrad, Novosidirsk. 1947-1971. Lang.: Rus.   2333

Plays/librettos/scripts

Umiak by Théâtre de la Marmaille of Toronto, based on Inuit
tradition. Canada. 1982-1983. Lang.: Eng.   2434

Playwright Sergio Tofano and the hero of his comedies,
Bonaventura. Italy. 1927-1953. Lang.: Ita.   2704

Interview with director of Teatr Współczésny about children's drama
competition. Poland: Wrocław. 1986. Lang.: Hun.   2736

Interview with playwright Carl Otto Ewers on writing for children.
Sweden. 1986. Lang.: Swe.   2822

Interview with Irena Kraus about her play *Lilla livet (The Little
Life)*, based on *La vida es sueño (Life Is a Dream)* by Calderón.
Sweden: Malmö. 1985-1986. Lang.: Swe.   2824

Reference materials

Alphabetically arranged profiles and history of professional and
amateur theatres for children. USA. 1903-1985. Lang.: Eng.   1046

Adaptation of Ferdinand Raimund's dramas for children's theatre.
Austria: Vienna. 1790-1836. Lang.: Ger.   2979

Text of a play with essays on workshop activities for children and
young adults. Switzerland. Lang.: Ger.   2998

Relation to other fields

Theatrical performance as a pedagogical tool. 1986. Lang.: Cat. 1048

Theatre professionals' round-table on issues in theatre for
adolescents. Canada: Quebec, PQ. 1984. Lang.: Fre.   1068

Children's paper theatres as educational tools. Germany. 1878-1921.
Lang.: Ger.   1090

Traditional Malay and European elements in children's theatre.
Malaysia. 1930-1985. Lang.: Eng.   1112

Participation of disabled children in Vår Teater. Sweden: Stockholm.
1975-1985. Lang.: Eng.   1129

Implications of commercialized American theatre for children.
Sweden: Stockholm. USA. 1986. Lang.: Eng.   1131

Argument for 'dramatic literacy' as part of 'cultural literacy'. USA.
1944-1985. Lang.: Eng.   1142

Examples of role-playing drawn from the ERIC database. USA.
1980-1985. Lang.: Eng.   1144

Development of educational theatre program dealing with child
sexual abuse. USA: St. Louis, MO. 1976-1984. Lang.: Eng.   1145

Documents from ERIC computer system detailing classroom exercises
in drama. USA. 1983-1985. Lang.: Eng.   1147

Ethical value of theatre in education. USA. 1985. Lang.: Eng. 1149

Drama as a tool for teaching social skills to the handicapped. USA.
1984. Lang.: Eng.   1150

Evaluation and social effects of improvisational drama program.
USA: Newark, NJ. Lang.: Eng.   1151

Children's theatre and the community. USA. 1970-1984. Lang.: Eng.
                                                             1153

Effect of playmaking on sixth and seventh grade pupils. USA: New
York, NY. 1986. Lang.: Eng.   1157

Development of forms and goals in the children's theatre movement.
USA. 1903-1985. Lang.: Eng.   1158

Proposal for using creative drama with museum visits and a study
of the visual arts. USA: Austin, TX. 1985. Lang.: Eng.   1159

Style in children's theatre in light of theories of Philippe Ariès.
USA. UK. France. 1600-1980. Lang.: Eng.   1162

Methods and goals of Children's Theatre Association of America.
USA. 1940-1984. Lang.: Eng.   1163

Study of how principals perceive the use of drama in the
curriculum. USA. 1986. Lang.: Eng.   1165

Creative drama content in college language arts textbooks. USA.
1986. Lang.: Eng.   1166

Argument for the establishment of graduate programs in children's
theatre. USA. 1985. Lang.: Eng.   1168

Development of arts-in-education program. USA: Albany, NY. 1970-
1984. Lang.: Eng.   1169

Description of the Cutler Playwright's Festival designed for junior
high school students. USA: Groton, CT. 1983-1986. Lang.: Eng.
                                                             3065

Research/historiography

Study of educational drama from the perspective of generic skills.
Canada: Toronto, ON. 1985. Lang.: Eng.   3070

Training

Interview with director and teacher Zinovy Korogodskij. USSR:
Moscow, Leningrad. 1970-1984. Lang.: Eng.   3163

Instructional television programming for the advancement of arts in
education. USA: University Park, IL. 1986. Lang.: Eng.   3287

Children's Theatre (Linz)
SEE
Theater des Kindes.

Children's Theatre (Moscow)
SEE
Oblastnoj Teat'r Junovo Zritelia.
Gosudarstvénnyj Centralnyj Detskij Teat'r.

Children's Theatre (USSR)
SEE
Teat'r Junych Zritélej.
Teat'r Junovo Zritélia.
Detskij Teat'r.

Children's Theatre Association of America (CTAA)
Relation to other fields
Argument for 'dramatic literacy' as part of 'cultural literacy'. USA.
1944-1985. Lang.: Eng.   1142

Methods and goals of Children's Theatre Association of America.
USA. 1940-1984. Lang.: Eng.   1163

Children's Theatre Company (Minneapolis, MN)
Administration
The Children's Theatre Company's fundraising strategy. USA:
Minneapolis, MN. 1986. Lang.: Eng.   137

Chimes at Midnight
Plays/librettos/scripts
Orson Welles' adaptation of Shakespeare's Falstaff scenes, *Chimes at
Midnight*. UK-England. 1938-1965. Lang.: Eng.   3239

Chin, Frank
Performance/production
Director, producer Wu Jing-Jyi discusses his life and career in
theatre. Taiwan. USA: Minneapolis, MN, New York, NY. 1939-
1980. Lang.: Eng.   2098

China
Performance/production
Collection of newspaper reviews by London theatre critics. UK-
England: London. 1986. Lang.: Eng.   2126

China Puppet Company (Beijing)
Institutions
Report on state puppet theatre. China: Beijing, Shanghai. 1986.
Lang.: Eng.   4015

Chinamikai
Performance/production
History of schism in *Bunraku* puppetry. Japan. 1945-1964. Lang.:
Eng.   3998

Chinchilla
Performance/production
Review of premiere performance of Myron Fink's opera *Chinchilla*.
USA: Binghamton, NY. 1986. Lang.: Eng.   3840

Chinese opera
SEE ALSO
Classed Entries under MUSIC-DRAMA—Chinese opera: 3503-3570.

Chinese opera
Performance/production
Last lecture of director Zhu Duanjun. 1890-1978. Lang.: Chi. 1635

Plays/librettos/scripts
Use of history in Chinese traditional drama. China. 960-1983. Lang.:
Chi.   2444

Profiles of Yuan dynasty playwrights. China. 1256-1341. Lang.: Chi.
                                                             2445

Chinese opera — cont'd

Theory/criticism
Development and characteristics of Oriental theatre. Korea: Seoul. Japan: Tokyo. China: Beijing. 200-1986. Lang.: Kor. 1215

Chiou, I
Theory/criticism
Analyzes works of four dramatists from Fuchien province. China, People's Republic of. 1981-1985. Lang.: Chi. 3569

Chlebnikov, Velimir
Plays/librettos/scripts
Poetic language in plays of Velimir Chlebnikov. Russia. 1885-1922. Lang.: Rus. 964

Chobot, Manfred
Plays/librettos/scripts
Training for new playwrights in Austria. Austria: Vienna. 1985-1986. Lang.: Ger. 2392

Chocrón, Isaac
Plays/librettos/scripts
Traces development of political trends in Venezuelan drama. Venezuela. 1958-1980. Lang.: Spa. 2972

Choe, Nam-Suen
Theory/criticism
Theory and history of Korean theatre. Korea: Seoul. 200 B.C.-1986 A.D. Lang.: Kor. 1214

Choe, Sang-Su
Plays/librettos/scripts
Role analysis of the mask-dance play, *Yängjubyulsändae* and the theories of Choe Sang-Su. Korea: Yängju. 1700-1900. Lang.: Kor. 1375

Theory/criticism
Theory and history of Korean theatre. Korea: Seoul. 200 B.C.-1986 A.D. Lang.: Kor. 1214
Theories about the stage for the traditional *chäng-gük* play. Korea: Seoul. 1800-1950. Lang.: Kor. 3931

Choi, Hap Pen
Performance/production
Chinese theatre companies on the Goldfields of Victoria. Australia. 1858-1870. Lang.: Eng. 1641

Choice, The
SEE
Vybor.

Choices (St. Louis, MO)
Relation to other fields
Development of educational theatre program dealing with child sexual abuse. USA: St. Louis, MO. 1976-1984. Lang.: Eng. 1145

Chong, Low
Performance/production
Chinese theatre companies on the Goldfields of Victoria. Australia. 1858-1870. Lang.: Eng. 1641

Chong, Ping
Performance/production
Interview with choreographer Meredith Monk. USA: New York, NY. 1964-1984. Lang.: Eng. 1368

Chopel, Farid
Performance/production
A photographic essay of 42 soloists and groups performing mime or gestural theatre. 1986. 3290

Chopin Playoffs, The
Plays/librettos/scripts
Interview with playwright Israel Horovitz. USA: New York, NY. 1985. Lang.: Eng. 2941

Choreographers
SEE
Choreography.

Choreographies
Basic theatrical documents
Notes for a *butō* dance. Japan. 1986. Lang.: Eng. 1266

Choreography
Administration
Principal choreographer of Kirov Theatre on problems of Soviet ballet theatre. USSR. 1980-1986. Lang.: Rus. 1293

Basic theatrical documents
Notes on the sources of inspiration for Ohno Kazuo dances. Japan. Lang.: Eng. 1265
Poem by Tanaka Min about his reasons for dancing. Japan. 1985. Lang.: Eng. 1267
Homage to *butō* dancer Hijikata Tatsumi by Tanaka Min. Japan. 1976-1985. Lang.: Eng. 1268

Design/technology
Strategies of lighting dance performances on a limited budget. 1985-1986. Lang.: Eng. 1340
Keith Haring, Robert Longo and Gretchen Bender design for choreographers Bill T. Jones and Arnie Zane. USA. 1986. 1342

Institutions
Current state of ballet theatre, including choreographic training. China: Beijing. 1980-1986. Lang.: Rus. 1297
Careers of choreographers Maria Formolo and Keith Urban. Canada: Regina, SK, Edmonton, AB. 1980-1983. Lang.: Eng. 1343

Performance/production
Study of four works by Ballets Suédois. France: Paris. 1920-1925. Lang.: Eng. 1271
Symposium on the violence in Pina Bausch's *Tanztheater*. Germany, West. 1973-1985. Lang.: Eng. 1272
Interview with choreographer Mechthild Grossman. Germany, West. 1984-1985. Lang.: Eng. 1273
Hungarian folksongs and dance adapted to the stage in *Magyar Csupajáték (Hungarian All-Play)*. Hungary: Budapest. 1938-1939. Lang.: Hun. 1274
Collaboration of choreographer Aurél Milloss and scene designer Giorgio de Chirico. Hungary. Italy: Milan, Rome. 1942-1945. Lang.: Hun. 1275
Analysis of choreography of *A szarvassá változott fiak (The Sons Who Turned Into Stags)*. Hungary: Győr. 1985-1986. Lang.: Hun. 1277
Interview with choreographer Ohno Kazuo. Japan. 1906-1985. Lang.: Eng. 1278
Description of *butō*, avant-garde dance movement of Japan. Japan. 1960-1986. Lang.: Eng. 1279
Butō dancer Tanaka Min speaks of early influences of Ohno and Hojikata. Japan. 1950-1985. Lang.: Eng. 1280
Reviews of *Big Deal*, written, staged and choreographed by Bob Fosse. USA: New York, NY. 1986. Lang.: Eng. 1283
Reviews of *Uptown...It's Hot*, staged, choreographed and conceived by Maurice Hines. USA: New York, NY. 1986. Lang.: Eng. 1284
Merce Cunningham, Alwin Nikolais, Meredith Monk and Yvonne Rainer on post-modern dance. USA. 1975-1986. Lang.: Eng. 1285
Career of choreographer Kenneth MacMillan. Europe. USA. 1929-1986. Lang.: Eng. 1302
Memoirs of Vera Zorina, star of stage and screen. Europe. 1917-1986. Lang.: Eng. 1303
Production history of Bela Bartók's ballet *A csodálatos mandarin (The Miraculous Mandarin)* on Hungarian stages. Hungary. 1956-1985. Lang.: Hun. 1305
Prokofjév's ballet *Romeo and Juliet* choreographed by László Seregi. Hungary: Budapest. 1985. Lang.: Hun. 1307
Notes on the choreography of Aurél Milloss. Hungary. Italy. 1906-1985. Lang.: Ita. 1310
Dancer and choreographer discusses contemporary and classical ballet. USSR. 1980-1986. Lang.: Rus. 1313
Notes from International Choreographic Symposium 'Interbalet'. USSR. Hungary: Budapest. 1985. Lang.: Rus. 1314
Careers of four Russian 'apostles of dance'. USSR. Lang.: Rus. 1320
Life and career of choreographer Miklós Rábai. Hungary. 1921-1974. Lang.: Hun. 1332
Dance in the Malaysian culture. Malaysia. 1950-1984. Lang.: Eng. 1333
Influence of Asian theatre traditions on American artists. USA: New York, NY. Indonesia. 1952-1985. Lang.: Eng. 1335
Paul Claudel's Biblical scripts for Ida Rubinstein. France. 1934-1936. Lang.: Eng. 1346
Illustrated interview with choreographer Pina Bausch. Germany. 1970-1985. Lang.: Fre. 1347
Choreographer Mary Wigman's theory of dance. Germany. 1914-1961. Lang.: Fre. 1349
Interview with choreographer Trisha Brown. North America. 1983-1985. Lang.: Eng. 1350
Homage to dancer and choreographer Roger George. Switzerland. Germany, West. 1921-1986. Lang.: Ger. 1351
History of classical Cambodian dance. Cambodia. 1860-1985. Lang.: Eng. 1358

Choreography — cont'd

Interview with choreographer Meredith Monk. USA: New York, NY. 1964-1984. Lang.: Eng.   1368

Analysis of Twyla Tharp's *Fait Accompli*. USA. 1984. Lang.: Eng.   1370

Martha Clarke's production of *The Garden of Earthly Delights*. USA: New York, NY. 1979-1984. Lang.: Eng.   1371

Collection of pictures of famous *onnagata*. Japan: Tokyo. Lang.: Jap.   1381

Directorial design for Dürrenmatt's *Die Physiker (The Physicists)*. China: Shanghai. 1982. Lang.: Chi.   1690

Choreography by Aurél Milloss for dramatic productions directed by Antal Németh at the National Theatre in Budapest. Hungary: Budapest. 1935-1938. Lang.: Hun.   1847

Biographical notes on choreographer and director Gillian Lynne. UK-England: London. USA. 1940-1986. Lang.: Eng.   2161

Interview with choreographer Royston Maldoom. UK-Scotland. 1970-1986. Lang.: Eng.   2189

Development of works by the Special Delivery Moving Theatre. Canada: Vancouver, BC. 1976-1986. Lang.: Eng.   3294

Dakota Stanton discusses her career as a singer and dancer in nightclubs and reviews. USA: Pittsburgh, PA, New York, NY. 1950-1980. Lang.: Eng.   3471

Reviews of *Sweet Charity* by Neil Simon, staged and choreographed by Bob Fosse. USA: New York, NY. 1986. Lang.: Eng.   3611

Reviews of *Honky Tonk Nights*, book and lyrics by Ralph Allen and David Campbell, staged and choreographed by Ernest O. Flatt. USA: New York, NY. 1986. Lang.: Eng.   3612

Reviews of *Raggedy Ann*, book by William Gibon, music and lyrics by Joe Raposo, staged and choreographed by Patricia Birch. USA: New York, NY. 1986. Lang.: Eng.   3614

Choreography in musical theatre. USA: New York, NY. 1944-1981. Lang.: Eng.   3620

Plays/librettos/scripts
Ballets based on works of William Shakespeare. USSR. Germany, West. 1980-1986. Lang.: Rus.   1322

Reference materials
Chronology of major *butō* works and choreographers. Japan. 1959-1984. Lang.: Eng.   1287

Christl Zimmerl's career as prima ballerina at the Vienna State Opera. Austria: Vienna. 1939-1976. Lang.: Ger.   1324

Relation to other fields
The world of choreography in the work of poet Anna Achmatova. USSR. 1889-1966. Lang.: Rus.   1328

The impact of the Third Reich on modern dance. Germany. 1902-1985. Lang.: Eng.   1353

Research/historiography
System for describing ethnic dance based on Xhosa dances. South Africa, Republic of. 1980-1985. Lang.: Eng.   1337

Results of studies of ethnic dance with transcription system. South Africa, Republic of. 1980-1985. Lang.: Afr.   1338

Theory/criticism
Pina Bausch seen as heir of epic theater of Bertolt Brecht. Germany, West. 1977-1985. Lang.: Eng.   1289

American criticisms of German *Tanztheater*. Germany, West. USA. 1933-1985. Lang.: Eng.   1290

American dance critics' reviews of Pina Bausch's work. USA. Germany, West. 1984-1986. Lang.: Eng.   1291

Chorus Line, A
Design/technology
Problems faced by sound designer Chris Newman in filming *A Chorus Line*. USA: New York, NY. 1986.   3205

Chorus of Disapproval, A
Performance/production
Actor Colin Blakely discusses his career. UK-England: London. 1950-1986. Lang.: Eng.   2176

Chou, Enlai
Performance/production
Development of opera in Liaoning province. China, People's Republic of. 1959-1980. Lang.: Chi.   3523

Chou, Yip'ai
Performance/production
Wei Ch'angsheng: actor of Szechuan opera, not Shensi opera. China. 1700-1800. Lang.: Chi.   3519

Chovanščina
Performance/production
The alcoholism of Modest Pavlovič Mussorgskij prevented the completion of *Chovanščina*. Russia: St. Petersburg. 1850-1890. Lang.: Eng.   3777

Photographs, cast list, synopsis, and discography of Metropolitan Opera radio broadcast performances. USA: New York, NY. 1986. Lang.: Eng.   3794

Analysis and appreciation of the work of Modest Pavlovič Mussorgskij. USSR. 1839-1881. Lang.: Eng.   3849

Chovanščina
Performance/production
Profile of and interview with Finnish bass Martti Talvela. Finland. 1935-1986. Lang.: Eng.   3723

Christ Church (Oxford)
Performance/production
Analysis of the document detailing expenses for performances given at Christ Church (Oxford) for Charles I, suggesting involvement by Inigo Jones as stage director. England: Oxford. 1636. Lang.: Eng.   1701

Christian Brothers, The
Plays/librettos/scripts
Ron Blair: considerations in writing for the theatre. Australia. 1960-1970. Lang.: Eng.   2372

Christian Hero, The
Plays/librettos/scripts
Liberated female characters in the plays of George Lillo. England. 1730-1759. Lang.: Eng.   2477

Christiani Wallace Brothers Combined
SEE
Wallace Brothers Circus.

Christie, Agatha
Relation to other fields
References to operas in the novels of Agatha Christie. UK-England. 1985. Lang.: Eng.   3923

Christmas Carol, A
Theory/criticism
The popularity of Charles Dicken's *A Christmas Carol* in American theatres. USA. 1984. Lang.: Eng.   3143

Christopher, Graham
Performance/production
Political difficulties in staging two touring productions of Shakespeare's *The Taming of the Shrew*. UK. 1985-1986. Lang.: Eng.   2104

Christopher, Tony
Design/technology
Lighting techniques and equipment used at theme park. USA: Baltimore, MD. 1971-1986. Lang.: Eng.   3315

Chronicles
Plays/librettos/scripts
Shakespeare's *Henry VI* and Hall's *Chronicles*. England. 1542-1592. Lang.: Fre.   2488

Chu, Linghsin
Plays/librettos/scripts
Profiles of Yuan dynasty playwrights. China. 1256-1341. Lang.: Chi.   2445

Chu, Pohsia
Research/historiography
Rise of the *Ping Hsi* form in Tienchin. China, People's Republic of: Tienchin. 1885-1948. Lang.: Chi.   3557

Chudožestvennyj Teat'r (Moscow)
SEE
Moskovskij Chudožestvennyj Akademičeskij Teat'r.

Chunga, La (Joke, The)
Plays/librettos/scripts
Interview with author and playwright Mario Vargas Llosa. Argentina. 1952-1986. Lang.: Spa.   2361

Churchill, Caryl
Institutions
Place of women in Britain's National Theatre. UK-England: London. 1986. Lang.: Eng.   1588

Performance/production
Brechtian technique in the contemporary feminist drama of Caryl Churchill, Claire Luckham and others. UK-England. 1956-1979. Lang.: Eng.   815

Collection of newspaper reviews by London theatre critics. UK-England. 1986. Lang.: Eng.   2115

Churchill, Caryl — cont'd

Dramaturg Oskar Eustis on confronting social and aesthetic problems. USA: San Francisco, CA. 1975-1986. Lang.: Eng. 2250

Avant-garde theatre companies from Britain perform in New York festival. USA: New York, NY. 1970-1983. Lang.: Eng. 2286

Plays/librettos/scripts

Comparison of natural and dramatic speech. England. USA. 1600-1986. Lang.: Eng. 939

Interview with playwright Kathleen Betsko. England: Coventry. USA. 1960-1986. Lang.: Eng. 2487

Current state of women's playwriting. UK-England. 1985-1986. Lang.: Eng. 2830

Caryl Churchill combines Brecht's alienation effect with traditional comic structure in *Cloud 9*. UK-England. 1980. 2871

Role of women in society in Caryl Churchill's plays. UK-England. 1986. Lang.: Eng. 2877

Cibber, Colley

Performance/production

Study of first production of *Jane Shore* by Nicholas Rowe at Drury Lane Theatre. England: London. 1713-1714. Lang.: Eng. 693

Plays/librettos/scripts

Language and society in Colley Cibber's *Love's Last Shift* and Sir John Vanbrugh's *The Relapse*. England. 1696. Lang.: Eng. 2495

Accuracy of portrayal of historical figures in Shakespeare and his adaptors. England. 1590-1940. Lang.: Eng. 2532

Cicalamento (Chatter)

Plays/librettos/scripts

Analysis of *commedia dell'arte* text of Carlo Cantú's *Cicalamento*. Italy. 1576-1646. Lang.: Ita. 3416

Cid, Le

Performance/production

Adam Hanuszkiewicz directs Corneille's *Le Cid* at Teatr Ateneum. Poland: Warsaw. 1984. Lang.: Pol. 2021

Cieslak, Ryszard

Relation to other fields

Dissolution of Jerzy Grotowski's Laboratory Theatre. Poland: Wrocław. 1959-1985. Lang.: Eng. 1117

Cigna, Gina

Performance/production

Famous sopranos discuss their interpretations of Tosca. USA. 1935-1986. Lang.: Eng. 3811

Cinco horas con Mario (Five Hours with Mario)

Performance/production

Directing career of Josefina Molina. Spain. 1952-1985. Lang.: Eng. 2078

Cinderella

Performance/production

Collection of newspaper reviews by London theatre critics. UK-England. 1986. Lang.: Eng. 2111

Cinderella by Kalmár

SEE

Hamupipőke.

Cine Mexico (Chicago, IL)

SEE

Congress Theatre.

Cinematography

Design/technology

Cinematographer Stephen Burum's work on *Eight Million Ways to Die*. USA. Lang.: Eng. 3207

Interview with cinematographer Billy Williams. USA. 1986. 3210

Relation to other fields

Cinematographer David Breashears climbs Mt. Everest. Tibet. 1986. 3246

Činoherní klub (Prague)

Performance/production

Overview of productions by the city's studio theatres. Czechoslovakia: Prague. 1986. Lang.: Hun. 1698

Cinthia and Endimion

Plays/librettos/scripts

Examination of the text and music of Thomas Durfey's opera *Cinthia and Endimion*. England. 1690-1701. Lang.: Eng. 3861

Cinthio

SEE

Giraldi Cinthio, Giovanbattista.

Cinti-Damoreau, Laure

Performance/production

Careers of young Parisian prima donnas. France: Paris. 1830-1850. Lang.: Eng. 3728

Cinzio

SEE

Giraldi Cinthio, Giovanbattista.

Circle in the Square (New York, NY)

Administration

New techniques of telemarketing instituted at Circle in the Square. USA: New York, NY. 1984. Lang.: Eng. 97

Institutions

Early history of Circle in the Square. USA: New York, NY. 1950-1960. Lang.: Kor. 552

Performance/production

Excerpts from memorial service for director Alan Schneider. USA: New York, NY. 1984. Lang.: Eng. 821

Reviews of *You Never Can Tell*, by George Bernard Shaw, staged by Stephen Porter. USA: New York, NY. 1986. Lang.: Eng. 2212

Reviews of *The Boys in Autumn* by Bernard Sabath, staged by Theodore Mann. USA: New York, NY. 1986. Lang.: Eng. 2221

Reviews of *The Caretaker* by Harold Pinter, staged by John Malkovich. USA: New York, NY. 1986. Lang.: Eng. 2236

Reviews of *Caligula* by Albert Camus, staged by Marshall W. Mason. USA: New York, NY. 1986. Lang.: Eng. 2239

Reviews of *The Mound Builders* by Lanford Wilson, staged by Marshall W. Mason. USA: New York, NY. 1986. Lang.: Eng. 2240

Circle Repertory (New York, NY)

Institutions

Development of several companies funded by the NEA's Ongoing Ensembles Program. USA: New York, NY. 1986. Lang.: Eng. 553

History of Circle Repertory Company. USA: New York, NY. 1969-1984. Lang.: Eng. 1606

Performance/production

Review of *As Is*, a play about AIDS by William Hoffman. USA: New York, NY. 1985. Lang.: Eng. 2198

Circle Theatre (Budapest)

SEE

Körszinház.

Circle, The

Performance/production

Reviews of *The Circle* by W. Somerset Maugham, staged by Stephen Porter, performed by the Mirror Repertory Company. USA: New York, NY. 1986. Lang.: Eng. 2227

Circus

SEE ALSO

Classed Entries under MIXED ENTERTAINMENT—Circus: 3378-3406.

Institutions

Collection of essays on the evolution of Chicano theatre. USA. 1850-1985. Lang.: Eng. 1599

Director of school of mime and theatre on gesture and image in theatrical representation. France: Paris. 1962-1985. Lang.: Fre. 3289

Performance/production

Development of regional theatre and other entertainments. England. 1840-1870. Lang.: Eng. 687

Development of and influences on theatre and other regional entertainments. England. 1840-1870. Lang.: Eng. 688

Reviews of *Juggling and Cheap Theatrics* with the Flying Karamazov Brothers, staged by George Mosher. USA: New York, NY. 1986. Lang.: Eng. 3349

Circus Senso

Performance/production

Collection of newspaper reviews by London theatre critics. UK-England: London. 1986. Lang.: Eng. 2126

Cirker, Ira

Performance/production

Reviews of *Gertrude Stein and a Companion*, by Win Wells, staged by Ira Cirker. USA: New York, NY. 1986. Lang.: Eng. 2238

Cirque Alfred

Performance/production

A photographic essay of 42 soloists and groups performing mime or gestural theatre. 1986. 3290

Cirque du Soleil (Montreal, PQ)

Performance/production

Influences upon the post-modern mime troupe, Cirque du Soleil. Canada: Montreal, PQ. 1984-1986. Lang.: Eng. 3292

Citizens' Theatre (Glasgow)

Performance/production

Collection of newspaper reviews by London theatre critics. UK. 1986. Lang.: Eng. 2099

Citizens' Theatre (Glasgow) — cont'd

Collection of newspaper reviews by London theatre critics. UK: London. 1986. Lang.: Eng.   2100

Relation to other fields
The reception of critic and playwright Karl Kraus in the English speaking world. USA: New York, NY. Austria: Vienna. UK-Scotland: Glasgow. 1909-1985. Lang.: Ger.   3067

City Center Theatre (New York, NY)
Administration
Lynne Meadow, artistic director of the Manhattan Theatre Club, describes her fourteen years on the job. USA: New York, NY. 1972-1986. Lang.: Eng.   1442

Performance/production
Reviews of *Principia Scriptoriae* by Richard Nelson, staged by Lynne Meadow. USA: New York, NY. 1986. Lang.: Eng.   2223
Reviews of *Loot*, by Joe Orton, staged by John Tillinger. USA: New York, NY. 1986. Lang.: Eng.   2229

City Theatre (Helsinki)
SEE
Helsingin Kaupunginteatteri.

Ciulei, Liviu
Performance/production
Reviews of Shakespeare's *Hamlet* staged by Liviu Ciulei. USA: New York, NY. 1986. Lang.: Eng.   2226
Dramaturg Richard Nelson on communicating with different kinds of directors. USA: New York, NY. 1979-1986. Lang.: Eng.   2252
Mark Bly on the dramaturg's responsibility to question. USA: Minneapolis, MN. 1981-1986. Lang.: Eng.   2294

Civic Opera (Chicago, IL)
Performance spaces
Technical facilities and labor practices at several U.S. theatres as seen by a Swedish visitor. USA: Chicago, IL, New York, NY. 1986. Lang.: Swe.   642

Civic Repertory Theatre (New York, NY)
Institutions
Eva LeGallienne on Civic Repertory and American Repertory Theatres. USA: New York, NY. 1933-1953. Lang.: Eng.   560

CIVIL warS
Performance/production
The development and production of Robert Wilson's *CIVIL warS*. USA. Germany, East. 1984. Lang.: Eng.   838

Cixous, Hélène
Design/technology
Théâtre du Soleil set for *Norodom Sihanouk*. France: Paris. 1986.   267

Performance/production
Shakespearean form, Asian content in *Norodom Sihanouk* by Ariane Mnouchkine's Théâtre du Soleil. France: Paris. 1964-1986. Lang.: Eng.   709
Production of *L'Histoire terrible mais inachevé de Norodom Sihanouk, roi du Cambodge (The Terrible but Unfinished History of Norodom Sihanouk, King of Cambodia)* by Hélène Cixous. France: Paris. 1985. Lang.: Eng.   1737
Collaboration of Hélène Cixous and Ariane Mnouchkine. France. Cambodia. 1964-1986. Lang.: Eng.   1752

Plays/librettos/scripts
Analysis of *L'Histoire terrible mais inachevé de Norodom Sihanouk, roi du Cambodge (The Terrible but Unfinished History of Norodom Sihanouk, King of Cambodia)* by Hélène Cixous. France: Paris. 1985. Lang.: Eng.   2570
Mythology in the works of Hélène Cixous, Andrée Chedid, Monique Wittig and Marguerite Yourcenar. France. Lang.: Eng.   2580

Clair de Lune
Performance/production
Review of Libby Larsen's opera *Clair de Lune*. USA: Little Rock, AR. 1985. Lang.: Eng.   3803

Clan of the Cave Bear
Design/technology
Mechanical bears in film, *Clan of the Cave Bear*. USA. 1985-1986. Lang.: Eng.   3214

Clarey, Cynthia
Performance/production
Black opera stars and companies. USA: Enid, OK, New York, NY. 1961-1985. Lang.: Eng.   3839

Clark Kelley, Peggy
Design/technology
Interview with three female lighting designers. USA. 1946-1983. Lang.: Eng.   357

Clark, Bradford
Design/technology
Designers discuss regional productions of *Grease*. USA. 1984-1986. Lang.: Eng.   3597

Clark, Brian
Performance/production
Actress Rosemary Harris discusses her work in *The Petition*. UK-England: London. USA: New York, NY. 1948-1986. Lang.: Eng.   2177
Reviews of *The Petition*, by Brian Clark, staged by Peter Hall. USA: New York, NY. 1986. Lang.: Eng.   2234

Clark, J. P.
Theory/criticism
Analysis of Wole Soyinka's major critical essays. Nigeria. 1960-1980. Lang.: Eng.   3124

Clarke, Kevin
Performance/production
Collection of newspaper reviews by London theatre critics. UK-England: London. 1986. Lang.: Eng.   2117

Clarke, Marcus
Theory/criticism
Attitudes toward sports in serious Australian drama. Australia. 1876-1965. Lang.: Eng.   3084

Clarke, Martha
Performance/production
Martha Clarke's production of *The Garden of Earthly Delights*. USA: New York, NY. 1979-1984. Lang.: Eng.   1371
Reviews of *Vienna: Lusthaus*, conceived and staged by Martha Clarke. USA: New York, NY. 1986. Lang.: Eng.   2209
Artists who began in dance, film or television move to Off Broadway theatre. USA: New York, NY. 1982. Lang.: Eng.   2284

Clarke, Shirley
Design/technology
Editing and post production on the documentary film *Ornette: Made in America*. USA. Lang.: Eng.   3215

Class of 86
Performance/production
Reviews of National Lampoon's *Class of 86*, staged by Jerry Adler. USA: New York, NY. 1986. Lang.: Eng.   3348

Claudel, Paul
Performance/production
Paul Claudel's Biblical scripts for Ida Rubinstein. France. 1934-1936. Lang.: Fre.   1346
Actors discuss performing in plays by Paul Claudel. France. Belgium. 1943-1985. Lang.: Fre.   1722
Directors discuss staging of plays by Paul Claudel. France. Belgium. 1985. Lang.: Fre.   1723
Stage adaptation of *La Mort de Judas (The Death of Judas)* by Paul Claudel. France: Brangues. 1985. Lang.: Fre.   1754
Difficulties in staging the plays of Paul Claudel. France. 1910-1931. Lang.: Fre.   1755

Plays/librettos/scripts
Influence of *Nō* on Paul Claudel. France. 1868-1955. Lang.: Ita.   2556
Poetic and dramatic language in version of *Le Soulier de Satin (The Satin Slipper)* by Paul Claudel. France. 1928. Lang.: Fre.   2587
Details on performances of plays by Paul Claudel in German-speaking countries. Germany. Switzerland. Austria. 1913-1986. Lang.: Ger.   2599

Clavé Santmartí, Antoni
Design/technology
History of Catalan scenography. Spain-Catalonia. 200 B.C.-1986 A.D. Lang.: Cat.   311

Clavé, Florenci
Institutions
Three personal views of the evolution of the Catalan company La Pipironda. Spain-Catalonia: Barcelona. 1958-1986. Lang.: Cat.   1583

Clay, Carl
Institutions
History of Black Spectrum. USA: New York, NY. 1970-1986. Lang.: Eng.   1603

Clayburgh, Jim
Design/technology
Interview with set designer Jim Clayburgh. USA: New York, NY. 1972-1983. Lang.: Eng.   390

Cleage, Pearl
Reference materials
Current work of Audelco award-winning playwrights. USA: New York, NY. 1973-1984. Lang.: Eng.   3007

CLETA
SEE
Centro Libre de Experimentación Teatral y Artistica.

Cleveland Playhouse (Cleveland, OH)
Administration
Community funding of residency for children's theatre performer, Aurand Harris. USA: Cleveland, OH. 1985-1986. Lang.: Eng.   145

Clifford, John
Plays/librettos/scripts
Interview with playwright John Clifford. UK-Scotland: Edinburgh. 1960-1986. Lang.: Eng.   2885

Clifton, Josephine
Performance/production
Career of actress Josephine Clifton. USA. 1813-1847. Lang.: Eng.   846

Cloud 9
Performance/production
Collection of newspaper reviews by London theatre critics. UK-England. 1986. Lang.: Eng.   2115

Plays/librettos/scripts
Caryl Churchill combines Brecht's alienation effect with traditional comic structure in Cloud 9. UK-England. 1980.   2871
Role of women in society in Caryl Churchill's plays. UK-England. 1986. Lang.: Eng.   2877

Clown Kompanie, La
Performance/production
A photographic essay of 42 soloists and groups performing mime or gestural theatre. 1986.   3290

Clowning
Design/technology
Costumes at New York International Clown Festival. USA: New York, NY. 1984. Lang.: Eng.   3316
Logistics of a clown gag with puppetry that uses a third arm jacket.   3946

Performance/production
Dario Fo's fusion of slapstick and politics. Italy. 1960-1986. Lang.: Eng.   749
Distinctive style of Canadian clowns. Canada: Toronto, ON, Vancouver, BC. 1967-1986. Lang.: Eng.   3328
Interview with clown, writer and teacher Philippe Gaulier. Europe. 1500-1986. Lang.: Fre.   3333
Life and work of an Indian street performer. India: Rajasthan. 1940-1985. Lang.: Eng.   3335
Career of comic author and clown Zuanpolo Leopardi. Italy: Venice. 1500-1540. Lang.: Ita.   3336
Development of clowning to include parody. UK. 1769-1985. Lang.: Fre.   3347
Circus clown discusses his training and work with puppets.   3382
Textbook on clowning for circus and vaudeville acts. USSR. 1980-1986. Lang.: Rus.   3401
Notes on comic stunts. USSR. 1986. Lang.: Rus.   3403

Club, The
Plays/librettos/scripts
Analysis of plays by David Williamson. Australia. 1976-1985. Lang.: Eng.   2379

Cluchey, Rick
Performance/production
Beckett's direction of Krapp's Last Tape at San Quentin Drama Workshop. USA. 1985. Lang.: Hun.   2279

Clurman, Harold
Administration
Cheryl Crawford's producing career discussed in light of her latest Broadway show. USA: New York, NY, Atlanta, GA. 1936-1986. Lang.: Eng.   117

Performance/production
Interview with producer, director, actor Robert Lewis. USA: New York, NY. 1930-1986. Lang.: Eng.   844

Coastal Disturbances
Performance/production
Reviews of Coastal Disturbances, by Tina Howe, staged by Carole Rothman. USA: New York, NY. 1986. Lang.: Eng.   2200

Coates, George
Performance/production
A profile of performance artist George Coates. USA: Berkeley, CA. 1986.   3460

Cobelli, Giuseppina
Performance/production
Life and career of singer Giuseppina Cobelli. Italy. 1898-1948. Lang.: Eng.   3762

Cochran, Felix
Institutions
Career of Marjorie Moon, artistic director of Billie Holliday Theatre. USA: New York, NY, Cleveland, OH. 1973-1986. Lang.: Eng.   1610

Cock's Short Flight, The
Plays/librettos/scripts
Description of a staged reading of The Cock's Short Flight by Jaime Salom. Spain. USA: New York, NY. 1980-1985. Lang.: Eng.   2808

Cocktail Party, The
Performance/production
Director John Dexter and impresario Eddie Kulukundis discuss the formation of the New Theatre Company. UK-England: London. 1986. Lang.: Eng.   2144

Cocteau, Jean
Basic theatrical documents
Catalan translation of L'aigle à deux têtes (The Eagle With Two Heads) by Jean Cocteau. France. 1946. Lang.: Cat.   1478

Performance/production
Director Simon Callow talks about his production of Jean Cocteau's The Infernal Machine. UK-England: London. 1986. Lang.: Eng.   2139

Plays/librettos/scripts
Analysis of L'Aigle à deux têtes (The Eagle With Two Heads) by Jean Cocteau. France. 1889-1963. Lang.: Cat.   2565
Biographical information on Jean Genet. France. 1910-1985. Lang.: Fre.   2588

Cocu imaginaire, Le
SEE
Sganarelle ou Le Cocu imaginaire.

Codco (St. John's, NF)
Institutions
Successful alternative theatre groups in Newfoundland. Canada. 1976-1986. Lang.: Eng.   1550

Coedès, George
Research/historiography
Ritual origins of the classical dance drama of Cambodia. Cambodia. 4 B.C.-1986 A.D. Lang.: Eng.   1336

Coffee House, The
SEE
Bottega del caffè, La.

Cohen, Bruce
Theory/criticism
Report of seminar on theatre criticism. USA: New York, NY. 1983. Lang.: Eng.   1223

Cohen, Nathan
Plays/librettos/scripts
Literary and popular theatrical forms in the plays of Rick Salutin. Canada: Montreal, PQ, Toronto, ON. 1976-1981. Lang.: Eng.   2411

Cohen, Robert
Performance/production
Discussion of basic theatrical issues during Stanislavskij symposium. Sweden: Stockholm. 1986. Lang.: Swe.   2086

Colas and Colinette
Performance/production
Review of Toronto performances of Colas and Colinette. Canada: Toronto, ON, Montreal, PQ. 1986. Lang.: Eng.   3707

Colette, Sidonie-Gabrielle
Plays/librettos/scripts
Attitudes toward sexuality in plays from French sources. UK-England. France. Lang.: Eng.   2852

Coliseum (Oldham)
Performance/production
Collection of newspaper reviews by London theatre critics. UK: London. 1986. Lang.: Eng.   2100
Collection of newspaper reviews by London theatre critics. UK. 1986. Lang.: Eng.   2103

Collected materials
Design/technology
Illustrated description of Umberto Tirelli costume collection. Europe. 1700-1984. Lang.: Ita.   263

Collected materials — cont'd

Institutions
Surviving documents relating to the Népszinház. Austro-Hungarian Empire: Budapest. 1872-1918. Lang.: Hun.   462

Reference materials
Description of Australian archives relating to theatre and film. Australia. 1870-1969. Lang.: Eng.   1000

Description of the theatrical library of writer James Smith. Australia: Melbourne. 1866. Lang.: Eng.   1002

Collected reviews of 31 major Canadian plays. Canada. 1934-1983. Lang.: Eng.   1009

Wealth of theatre memorabilia in British museums. UK-England: London. 1986. Lang.: Eng.   1036

Chronology of events and productions of non-profit theatre. USA. 1961-1986. Lang.: Eng.   1043

Source materials on the history of Hungarian dance. Hungary: Pest. 1833-1840. Lang.: Hun.   1286

The purchase and eventual exhibition of a collection of Stravinsky's work. Switzerland: Basel. USA: New York, NY. 1930-1985. Lang.: Eng.   3500

A profile of a museum of ventriloquism lore. USA: Fort Mitchell, KY. 1985.   3989

Collective creations

Basic theatrical documents
Text of *Sex Tips for Modern Girls* by Peter Eliot Weiss. Canada: Vancouver, BC. 1985. Lang.: Eng.   3578

Institutions
Overview of Ariane Mnouchkine's work with Théâtre du Soleil. France: Paris. 1959-1985. Lang.: Eng.   497

Production history and techniques of the Living Theatre. USA. 1964. Lang.: Eng.   546

History of the Théâtre du Soleil. France: Paris. 1963-1985. Lang.: Eng.   1574

Work and distinctive qualities of the Théâtre du Soleil. France: Paris. 1964-1986. Lang.: Eng.   1575

Performance/production
The New Theatre movement combines methodologies of collective creation with the Brechtian epic. Latin America.   763

Interview with playwright Peter Eliot Weiss. Canada: Vancouver, BC. 1986. Lang.: Eng.   1680

Playwright/dramaturg Peter Eliot Weiss discusses *Sex Tips for Modern Girls*. Canada: Vancouver, BC. 1984-1985. Lang.: Eng.   1684

Production of *L'Histoire terrible mais inachevé de Norodom Sihanouk, roi du Cambodge (The Terrible but Unfinished History of Norodom Sihanouk, King of Cambodia)* by Hélène Cixous. France: Paris. 1985. Lang.: Eng.   1737

Collectives

Institutions
Role of the Canadian Actors' Equity Association. Canada: Toronto, ON. 1983-1986. Lang.: Eng.   1548

College of Theatre Arts (Warsaw)
SEE
Panstova Akademia Sztuk Teatralnych.

College theatre
SEE
University theatre.

Collettivo di Parma (Parma)

Institutions
Experimental productions of classical works by Collettivo di Parma. Italy: Parma. 1982-1986. Lang.: Eng.   1579

Collettivo Isabella Morra (Rome)

Plays/librettos/scripts
Women's issues in Italian theatre. Italy. 1985. Lang.: Cat.   2710

Collins, Pat

Design/technology
Designers discuss regional productions of *Ain't Misbehavin'*. USA. 1984-1986. Lang.: Eng.   3591

Collins, Patrick

Relation to other fields
Description of the Cutler Playwright's Festival designed for junior high school students. USA: Groton, CT. 1983-1986. Lang.: Eng.   3065

Cologne Opera
SEE
Grosses Hause (Cologne).

Colombiaioni, Les

Performance/production
A photographic essay of 42 soloists and groups performing mime or gestural theatre. 1986.   3290

Color of Chambalén, The
SEE
Color de Chambalén, El.

Colored Balls
SEE
Bolles de colors.

Colored Museum, The

Performance/production
Reviews of *The Colored Museum*, by George C. Wolfe, staged by L. Kenneth Richardson. USA: New York, NY. 1986. Lang.: Eng.   2203

Comden, Betty

Performance/production
Reviews of musicals. UK-England: London. 1986. Lang.: Eng.   3610

Plays/librettos/scripts
Betty Comden and Adolph Green on their careers.   3626

Come and Go
SEE
Va et vient.

Comedia

Plays/librettos/scripts
Conservative and reactionary nature of the Spanish *Comedia*. Spain. 1600-1700. Lang.: Eng.   2782

Comedia de San Francisco de Borja, La (Comedy of Saint Francis of Borja, The)

Plays/librettos/scripts
Calderón's *El gran duque de Gandía (The Grand Duke of Gandía)* and its Mexican source. Spain. Mexico. 1600-1680. Lang.: Eng.   2789

Comedia Tinellaria

Performance/production
Reconstruction of *Comedia Tinellaria* by Torres Naharro. Italy: Rome, Venice. 1508-1537. Lang.: Spa.   1986

Comediantes, Los (Players, The)

Basic theatrical documents
Playtext of *Los Comediantes (The Players)* by Antonio Martínez Ballesteros. Spain. 1982. Lang.: Spa.   1494

Performance/production
Playwright Antonio Martínez Ballesteros discusses the production history of his play *Los Comediantes (The Players)*. Spain: Toledo. USA: Cincinnati, OH. 1982-1985. Lang.: Spa.   2076

Comédie-Française (Paris)

Administration
History of Comédie-Française administration. France: Paris. 1680-1986. Lang.: Fre.   41

Basic theatrical documents
Journal of playwright and general administrator of Comédie-Française. France: Paris. 1936. Lang.: Fre.   1477

Design/technology
Comparison of lighting in English theatres and Comédie-Française. England: London, Hampton Court. 1718. Lang.: Eng.   259

Recollections of workers who maintain costumes at the Comédie-Française. France. 1961-1986. Lang.: Fre.   265

Performance/production
Evolution of *Le Cantique des cantiques (The Song of Songs)* directed by Jacques Destoop at Comédie-Française. France: Paris. 1986. Lang.: Fre.   1721

Pieces related to performance at Comédie-Française of *Un Chapeau de Paille d'Italie (An Italian Straw Hat)* by Eugène Labiche. France: Paris. 1850-1986. Lang.: Fre.   1725

Production photos of *Un Chapeau de Paille d'Italie (An Italian Straw Hat)* by Eugène Labiche. France: Paris. 1986. Lang.: Fre.   1727

Production photographs of Pierre Corneille's *Le Menteur (The Liar)* at the Comédie-Française. France: Paris. 1986. Lang.: Fre.   1729

Pieces related to performance at the Comédie-Française of *Le Menteur (The Liar)* by Pierre Corneille. France: Paris. 1644-1985. Lang.: Fre.   1735

History of staging of *Le Menteur (The Liar)* by Pierre Corneille. France: Paris. 1644-1985. Lang.: Fre.   1738

Comédie-Française seen through its records for one year. France: Paris. 1778. Lang.: Fre.   1740

Polemic surrounding Sacha Stavisky's production of Shakespeare's *Coriolanus* at the Comédie-Française. France: Paris. 1934. Lang.: Eng, Fre.   1742

Comédie-Française (Paris) — cont'd

Interview with Comédie-Française actress Dominique Constanza. France: Paris. 1986. Lang.: Fre.　　1751

Performance of Comédie-Française actors in Amsterdam. Netherlands. 1811. Lang.: Fre.　　2012

Plays/librettos/scripts
Interview with Josy Eisenberg, translator of *Le Cantique des cantiques (The Song of Songs)* for the Comédie-Française. France: Paris. 1986. Lang.: Fre.　　2544

Comédie-Italienne (Paris)
Relation to other fields
The work of painter and scene designer Claude Gillot. France. 1673-1722. Lang.: Ita.　　1084

Comedy
Basic theatrical documents
Details of polemical impromptus about Molière's *L'école des Femmes (The School for Wives)*. France. 1663. Lang.: Fre.　　1479

Text of comedies and pamphlets about Molière. France. 1660-1670. Lang.: Fre.　　1481

New German translation of Shakespeare's *As You Like It*. Germany, East. 1986. Lang.: Ger.　　1483

English translation of *Pequeña historia de horror (Little Tale of Horror)*. Mexico. 1932. Lang.: Eng.　　1488

Edition of *La famosa comèdia de la gala està en son punt (The Famous Comedy of the Gala Done to a Turn)*, with analysis. Spain-Catalonia. 1625-1680. Lang.: Cat.　　1497

Performance/production
Discussion of women's comedy by one of its practitioners. Australia: Melbourne. 1986. Lang.: Eng.　　657

Performance-oriented study of Restoration comedy. England. 1660-1986. Lang.: Eng.　　696

Meaning in dramatic texts as a function of performance. Lang.: Eng.　　1630

Interview with actor-turned-director Michael Leech. England: London. 1986. Lang.: Eng.　　1710

Analysis of two productions of plays by Marivaux. France: Nanterre. Germany, West: Berlin, West. 1985. Lang.: Swe.　　1739

Premiere of László Kolozsvári Papp's *Hazánk fiai (Sons of Our Country)*. Hungary: Budapest. 1985. Lang.: Hun.　　1800

Notes on performances of *Hongkongi paróka (Wig Made in Hong Kong)*, *Egérút (Narrow Escape)* and *Róza néni (Aunt Rosa)*. Hungary: Budapest. 1985. Lang.: Hun.　　1801

István Verebes' production of *A farkas (The Wolf)* by Ferenc Molnár at the Vigszinház. Hungary: Budapest. 1985. Lang.: Hun.　　1805

G.B. Shaw's *Megtörtszívek háza (Heartbreak House)* directed by István Horvai. Hungary: Budapest. 1985. Lang.: Hun.　　1858

Notes on *Čaruga (Death Cap)*, by Ivan Kušan, directed by Miklós Benedek, Katona József Theatre, under the title *Galócza*. Hungary: Budapest. 1986. Lang.: Hun.　　1890

Selected short comic prose sketches of Róbert Rátony, actor, showman and writer. Hungary. 1944-1985. Lang.: Hun.　　1920

Production of Bengt Ahlfors' *Szinházkomédia (Theatre Comedy)* directed by András Márton. Hungary: Debrecen. 1985. Lang.: Hun.　　1925

Reconstruction of *Comedia Tinellaria* by Torres Naharro. Italy: Rome, Venice. 1508-1537. Lang.: Spa.　　1986

Feminist theatre group Beryl and the Perils. UK-England. 1986. Lang.: Eng.　　2171

Staging of Uzbek comedy. USSR. 1970-1985. Lang.: Rus.　　2326

Representation of Blacks in television programs. USA. 1980. Lang.: Eng.　　3272

Career of vaudeville comedian Roy Rene, creator of 'Mo'. Australia. 1892-1954. Lang.: Eng.　　3327

Review of *Mágiarakás (Magic Heap)* by humorist György Sándor. Hungary: Budapest. 1985. Lang.: Hun.　　3334

Autobiography of comedian Billy Crystal. USA. 1955. Lang.: Eng.　　3350

Notes on comic stunts. USSR. 1986. Lang.: Rus.　　3403

Comic actor Tristano Martinelli, probable creator of the character Harlequin. Italy. France. 1550-1600. Lang.: Ita.　　3412

Oriental influences on *commedia dell'arte*. Italy. 1550-1650. Lang.: Ita.　　3413

Careers of fifty successful female comics. 1900-1986. Lang.: Eng.　　3467

Techniques of comedians in modern Beijing opera. China, People's Republic of: Beijing. 1964-1985. Lang.: Chi.　　3524

Mágnás Miska (Miska the Magnate) by Albert Szirmai directed by László Bagossy. Hungary: Pécs. 1986. Lang.: Hun.　　3942

Plays/librettos/scripts
Luis de Góngora's plays as a response to Lope de Vega. Spain. 1561-1627. Lang.: Eng.　　968

Female sexuality in Tirso de Molina's *El vergonzoso en palacio (The Shy Man at Court)*. Spain. 1580-1648. Lang.: Eng.　　969

Emblematic pictorialism in *La mujer que manda en casa (The Woman Who Rules the Roost)* by Tirso de Molina. Spain. 1580-1648. Lang.: Eng.　　970

Characteristics of farce and the problem of humor. Lang.: Pol.　　2357

The incoherent protagonist of modern comedy. 1954-1986. Lang.: Eng.　　2358

Analysis of plays by David Williamson. Australia. 1976-1985. Lang.: Eng.　　2379

Influence of Western and Chinese traditional theatre upon works of Ding Xilin. China. 1923-1962. Lang.: Chi.　　2446

Shakespeare's complex, unconventional heroines in *All's Well that Ends Well* and *Measure for Measure*. England. 1603. Lang.: Eng.　　2469

Legalistic aspect of *Commody of the Moste Vertuous and Godlye Susana* by Thomas Garter. England: London. 1563. Lang.: Eng.　　2494

Language and society in Colley Cibber's *Love's Last Shift* and Sir John Vanbrugh's *The Relapse*. England. 1696. Lang.: Eng.　　2495

Character source for Dr. Last in Samuel Foote's play *The Devil Upon Two Sticks*. England. 1768-1774. Lang.: Eng.　　2522

Comparison of John Caryll's *Sir Salomon* with its source, *L'École des femmes (The School for Wives)* by Molière. England. France. 1662-1669. Lang.: Eng.　　2527

Comparison of Shakespeare's *Othello* with New Comedy of Rome. England. 1604. Lang.: Eng.　　2528

Dialectical method in the plays of Molière. France. 1666. Lang.: Eng.　　2567

Biography of Molière as seen through his plays. France. 1622-1673. Lang.: Fre.　　2573

Don Juan legend in literature and film. France. 1630-1980. Lang.: Eng.　　2581

Comedies of Tieck and Brentano representing German Romanticism. Germany. 1795-1850. Lang.: Rus.　　2602

Chorus in ancient Greek comedy and drama. Greece. 450-425 B.C. Lang.: Ita.　　2633

Aristophanes and his conception of comedy. Greece. 446-385 B.C. Lang.: Fre.　　2635

Personal and social relationships in Goldoni's comedies. Italy. 1743-1760. Lang.: Ita.　　2681

Playwright Carlo Goldoni's personality seen through autobiographical comedies. Italy. 1751-1755. Lang.: Ita.　　2687

The link between comic and survival instincts. Italy. 1986. Lang.: Eng.　　2688

Experimental theatrical productions of Achille Campanile. Italy. 1920-1930. Lang.: Ita.　　2695

Use of chorus in Bartho Smit's *Don Juan onder die Boere (Don Juan Among the 'Boere')*. South Africa, Republic of. 1970-1986. Lang.: Afr.　　2776

Argument for coherence of *Arms and the Man* by George Bernard Shaw. UK-England: London. 1894. Lang.: Eng.　　2863

Reference materials
List and location of school playtexts and programs. France. 1601-1700. Lang.: Fre.　　2987

Biographical encyclopedia of stand-up comics and comedy teams. USA. 1900-1986. Lang.: Eng.　　3472

Relation to other fields
Playwright Luigi Pirandello on the dynamics of humor. Italy. 1200-1906. Lang.: Ita.　　1108

Sociological analysis of city comedy and revenge tragedy. England: London. 1576-1980. Lang.: Eng.　　3025

Reciprocal influence of Italian comedy and Boccaccio's *The Decameron*. Italy. 1350-1550. Lang.: Ita.　　3045

Compagnie Madeleine Renaud#Jean-Louis Barrault (Paris) — cont'd

Performance/production
Collaboration of Hélène Cixous and Ariane Mnouchkine. France.
Cambodia. 1964-1986. Lang.: Eng.   1752

Compagnie Renaud-Barrault
SEE
Compagnie Madeleine Renaud—Jean-Louis Barrault.

Companies
SEE
Institutions, producing.

Competitions
Performance spaces
Design of concert hall in part of a major railway station. Hungary:
Budapest. 1985-1986. Lang.: Hun.   598

Performance/production
Notes on the 5th International Competition of Ballet Dancers.
USSR: Moscow. 1985. Lang.: Rus.   1315

Reviews of 5th International Competition of Ballet Dancers. USSR:
Moscow. 1985. Lang.: Rus.   1319

Account of competition in producing Spanish Golden Age plays.
USA: El Paso, TX. 1986. Lang.: Eng.   2280

Plays/librettos/scripts
Theatre festival and playwriting competition. France: Metz. 1982-
1986. Lang.: Hun.   950

Composers
SEE
Music.

Composition
SEE
Plays/librettos/scripts.

Compromise of 1867
SEE
Kiegyezés.

Computers
Administration
Marketing techniques for increasing subscriptions. 1986. Lang.: Eng.
                                                                  18

Computerized ticketing system developed in Budapest for use in
Western Europe. Hungary: Budapest. 1982-1985. Lang.: Hun.   47

Problems of copyright protection for computer programs. UK. USA.
1956-1986. Lang.: Eng.   73

Description of computerized ticketing and administration system. UK.
1980-1986. Lang.: Eng.   77

Conflicts between reproduction permission and authors' rights. UK-
England. 1911-1986. Lang.: Eng.   79

Use of computers by Alliance of Resident Theatres/New York's
member organizations. USA: New York, NY. 1985. Lang.: Eng.   93

Benefits and uses of computers in non-profit theatre organizations.
USA: New York, NY. 1982. Lang.: Eng.   170

Computer software package designed for arts administration. USA:
New York, NY. 1984. Lang.: Eng.   180

Design/technology
Comparison of manual and computerized dimmer systems. Sweden.
1940-1986. Lang.: Swe.   313

Use of the Gemini computerized lighting system used at the
Edinburgh Festival. UK-Scotland: Edinburgh. 1980-1986. Lang.: Eng.
                                                                  332

Computer program which stores lighting design data. USA. 1983.
Lang.: Eng.   419

Capabilities of available computer-controlled sound systems. USA.
1986.   421

Plays/librettos/scripts
Proposed computerized playwrighting system. Lang.: Eng.   2350
Advice on how to create an attractive computer-generated script.
                                                                  2356

Relation to other fields
Examples of role-playing drawn from the ERIC database. USA.
1980-1985. Lang.: Eng.   1144

Documents from ERIC computer system detailing classroom exercises
in drama. USA. 1983-1985. Lang.: Eng.   1147

Research/historiography
Computer databases for theatre studies. UK-England: London. 1985.
Lang.: Eng.   1188

Comsomol Theatre
SEE
Teat'r im. Leninskovo Komsomola.

Comune, La (Milan)
Performance/production
Productions of Dario Fo's *Morte accidentale di un anarchico
(Accidental Death of an Anarchist)* in the light of Fo's political
ideas. USA. Canada. Italy. 1970-1986. Lang.: Eng.   2262

Comus
Performance/production
Importance of records of a provincial masque. England: Shipton.
1600-1650. Lang.: Eng.   3419

Comus Music Theatre (Toronto, ON)
Performance/production
Review of Toronto performances of *Colas and Colinette*. Canada:
Toronto, ON, Montreal, PQ. 1986. Lang.: Eng.   3707

Plays/librettos/scripts
Analysis of *RA* by R. Murray Schafer, performed by Comus Music
Theatre. Canada: Toronto, ON. 1983. Lang.: Eng.   2416

Conant, Homer
Reference materials
Catalogue of an exhibition of costume designs for Broadway
musicals. USA: New York, NY. 1900-1925. Lang.: Eng, Ger.   3635

Conboy, Cornelius
Theory/criticism
Eleven theatre professionals discuss their personal direction and the
direction of experimental theatre. USA: New York, NY. 1985.
Lang.: Eng.   3137

Concentration in Theater
Relation to other fields
Black history and folklore taught in theatre workshops and
productions. USA: New York, NY, Omaha, NE, Washington, DC.
1986. Lang.: Eng.   3068

Condemned of Altona, The
SEE
Séquestrés d'Altona, Les.

Condemned Village
SEE
Pueblo rechazado.

Conducting
Performance/production
Profile of and interview with Romanian-born conductor Christian
Berea. Romania. USA: New York, NY. 1950-1986. Lang.: Eng. 3771

Interview with tenor and conductor Plácido Domingo. Spain: Madrid.
1941-1986. Lang.: Eng.   3779

Conductors
SEE
Music.

Confédération, La
Performance/production
Elzéar Labelle's operetta *La Conversion d'un pêcheur de la Nouvelle-
Écosse (The Conversion of a Nova Scotian Fisherman)* as an
example of the move toward public performance. Canada: Quebec,
PQ. 1837-1867. Lang.: Eng.   3599

Conference of the Birds
SEE
Aves.

Conferences
International conference on Eastern and Western theatre. 1986.
Lang.: Ita.   2

Conference on aspects of theatre and opera in Emilia. Italy: Emilia.
1700-1799. Lang.: Ita.   7

Proceedings of a symposium on theatre during the Middle Ages and
the Renaissance. Spain. Italy. 1000-1680. Lang.: Cat, Spa, Ita.   12

Report from conference on Swedish theatre. Sweden: Stockholm.
1986. Lang.: Swe.   13

Administration
Prediction of future copyright trends. 1886-1986. Lang.: Eng.   17

Berne Convention in People's Republic of China. China, People's
Republic of. 1908-1986. Lang.: Eng.   30

Berne Convention and compulsory licensing. Europe. 1908-1986.
Lang.: Eng.   36

History of Berne Convention and copyright laws. Europe. 1709-1886.
Lang.: Eng.   37

Protection of rights existing before Berne Convention. France. 1971-
1986. Lang.: Eng.   43

Berne Convention and copyright in socialist countries. Hungary.
1917-1986. Lang.: Eng.   46

Copyright before and after Berne Convention. UK. 1850-1986.
Lang.: Eng.   68

Conferences — cont'd

Berne Convention and copyright in market economy. UK. USA. 1886-1986. Lang.: Eng.   69

Effect of copyright on new broadcast technologies. UK. 1971-1986. Lang.: Eng.   71

Berne Convention and public interest. UK. 1886-1986. Lang.: Eng.   75

Discussion of Berne Convention (1886) establishing copyright agreement. UK-England: London. 1986. Lang.: Eng.   80

U.S. Copyright and the Berne Convention. USA. 1985. Lang.: Eng.   84

Berne Convention and U.S. copyright law. USA. 1776-1986. Lang.: Eng.   157

Panel discussion on theatre as commerce or resource to its community. USA: New York, NY. 1986.   179

Notes on theatre business following meeting of All-Union Theatre Society. USSR. 1986. Lang.: Rus.   183

Audience

Conference on low theatrical attendance. USSR: Kujbyšev. 1980-1986.   207

Various aspects of audience/performer relationship. Germany, East: Leipzig, Schwerin, Helle. 1980-1983. Lang.: Ger.   1448

Design/technology

Report on development of theatrical equipment in Socialist countries. Germany, East: Berlin, East. 1986. Lang.: Hun.   268

Activities of committee on development of theatre technology. Germany, East: Berlin, East. 1986. Lang.: Hun.   272

Reports on Showtech conference. Germany, West: Berlin, West. 1986. Lang.: Hun.   273

Advance program of the meeting of Theatre Technology Section of the Hungarian Optical, Acoustical and Cinematographical Society. Hungary: Szeged. 1986. Lang.: Hun.   276

Text of a lecture on international technical cooperation in theatre. Hungary. Germany, West: Berlin, West. 1986. Lang.: Hun.   289

Overview of conference on visual art in theatre. Poland. 1986. Lang.: Eng, Fre.   307

Institutions

Reports on theatre conferences and festivals in Asia. Philippines: Manila. Malaysia: Kuala Lumpur. Japan: Toga. India: Calcutta. 1981-1984. Lang.: Eng.   510

Seminar on local plays and worker's theatre. Sweden: Norrköping. 1970-1986. Lang.: Swe.   527

A report on the symposium at the Festival Latino discusses Brecht and the Nuevo Teatro movement. USA: New York, NY. 1984.   564

Notes on the dance committee meetings at the 21st congress of the International Theatre Institute. Canada: Montreal, PQ, Toronto, ON. 1985. Lang.: Rus.   1270

Performance/production

Comparative history of German-language theatre. Germany. Switzerland. Austria. 1945-1985. Lang.: Ger.   727

Meeting of experimental theatre groups at Szkéné Theatre. Hungary: Budapest. 1985. Lang.: Hun.   736

Discussion of international congress 'Theatre East and West'. Italy: Rome. Asia. 1984. Lang.: Eng.   744

Comparison of Eastern and Western theatre. Italy: Rome. 1986. Lang.: Ita.   748

Reports and discussions on nonverbal communication in theatre. Spain. 1985. Lang.: Eng, Fre, Spa.   789

Report on International Theatre Congress. Spain-Catalonia: Barcelona. 1985. Lang.: Rus.   793

Feminist criticism of theatre anthropology conference on women's roles. USA. Denmark. 1985. Lang.: Eng.   845

Actors' round table on the problems facing young actors. USSR: Moscow. 1986. Lang.: Rus.   900

Collaboration between USSR and other countries in ballet. Hungary: Budapest. USSR. 1985. Lang.: Rus.   1309

Notes from International Choreographic Symposium 'Interbalet'. USSR. Hungary: Budapest. 1985. Lang.: Rus.   1314

Account of nation-wide theatre conference. Hungary: Budapest. 1985. Lang.: Hun.   1841

Conference and theatrical theory and practice sponsored by Pirandellian Studies Center. Italy: Agrigento. 1900-1940. Lang.: Spa.   2002

Discussion of basic theatrical issues during Stanislavskij symposium. Sweden: Stockholm. 1986. Lang.: Swe.   2086

Festival of Latin American 'New Theatre'. USA: Washington, DC. 1984-1986. Lang.: Spa.   2313

Interview with V.A. Noskov of Union of State Circuses on international circus conference. France: Paris. 1986. Lang.: Rus.   3384

Review of the 1985 season of the Chinese National Opera. China, People's Republic of: Beijing. 1985. Lang.: Chi.   3522

Productions presented at the first regional puppet forum. France: Gareoult. 1986. Lang.: Hun.   3965

Plays/librettos/scripts

Report on a symposium addressing the role of the dramaturg.   918

Conference on eighteenth-century theatre and culture. Europe. 1985. Lang.: Ita.   946

Summary of speech given by playwright Ossie Davis at Third World Theatre Conference. USA: Davis, CA. 1986. Lang.: Eng.   986

Young playwright's conference. Hungary: Zalaegerszeg. 1985. Lang.: Hun.   2650

Notes on the Open Forum in Zalaegerszeg. Hungary: Zalaegerszeg. 1985. Lang.: Hun.   2653

Conference on the problems of adapting, interpreting and staging the classics. Hungary. Italy. 1985. Lang.: Hun.   2656

Collection of articles on playwright Luigi Pirandello. Italy. 1867-1936. Lang.: Ita.   2668

Studies on staging and meaning in plays of Luigi Pirandello. Italy: Agrigento. 1867-1936. Lang.: Ita.   2669

Presentations at a conference on playwright Pietro Chiari. Italy. 1712-1785. Lang.: Ita.   2671

Description of international symposium discussing the work of Stanisław Ignacy Witkiewicz. Poland. 1985. Lang.: Eng, Fre.   2733

Collection of essays on dramatic text and performance. Poland. 1600-1984. Lang.: Fre.   2742

Overview of symposium on playwright Stanisław Ignacy Witkiewicz. Poland. 1985. Lang.: Eng, Fre.   2747

Interview with leaders of playwrights' seminar. USSR: Picunde. 1986. Lang.: Rus.   2955

Problems of contemporary dramaturgy. USSR. 1986. Lang.: Rus.   2956

Excerpts from speeches by playwrights, 8th Congress of Soviet Writers. USSR: Moscow. 1986. Lang.: Rus.   2957

Report of drama commission, 8th Congress of Soviet Writers. USSR: Moscow. 1986. Lang.: Rus.   2960

Reference materials

Program of European Actors' Meeting, including criticism, texts and performances. Italy: Parma. 1986. Lang.: Ita.   1020

Relation to other fields

Report of conference on theatre and economics. Canada: Quebec, PQ. 1985. Lang.: Fre.   1072

Reports and discussions of restricted cultural communication. Lebanon. Spain-Catalonia. USA. 1985. Lang.: Fre, Spa, Cat.   1111

Reports and discussions on theatre and colonialism. Spain. Latin America. 1185. Lang.: Eng, Fre, Spa, Cat.   1128

Situation of playwrights in Austria. Austria: Vienna. 1971-1986. Lang.: Ger.   3016

Bertolt Brecht's contributions to modern theatre. Canada: Toronto, ON. 1985. Lang.: Eng.   3020

Conference on novelist Giovanni Verga and the theatre. Italy. 1840-1922. Lang.: Ita.   3037

Reflections on a 3-day workshop on using puppet theatre for social action and communication. UK-England: London. 1986. Lang.: Eng.   3993

Research/historiography

Computer databases for theatre studies. UK-England: London. 1985. Lang.: Eng.   1188

Theory/criticism

National Conference of Theatre Communications Group (TCG). USA: Amherst, MA. Lang.: Eng.   1233

Synthesis of the arts in the theatrical process. USSR: Moscow. 1986. Lang.: Rus.   1240

Conferences on theory of performance. Poland. USA. 1985. Lang.: Eng, Fre.   3127

Eleven theatre professionals discuss their personal direction and the direction of experimental theatre. USA: New York, NY. 1985. Lang.: Eng.   3137

Conferences — cont'd

Training
Collected papers from a conference on voice training. Austria: Vienna. Italy: Rome. England: London. 1700-1984. Lang.: Ger. 3936

Confession of a Wood
SEE
Spowiedź w driewnie.

Confiteor
Performance/production
Janez Pipan directs *Confiteor* by Slobodan Šnajder at National Theatre of Belgrade. Yugoslavia: Belgrade. 1986. Lang.: Hun. 2344

Conklin, John
Design/technology
Set designer John Conklin and the San Francisco Opera production of Wagner's *Ring*. USA: San Francisco, CA. 1986. Lang.: Eng. 3662

Performance/production
Interview with individuals involved in production of *Alcestis* by Euripides. USA: Cambridge, MA. 1986. Lang.: Eng. 2266
Robert Wilson's production of *Alcestis* at the American Repertory Theatre. USA: Cambridge, MA. 1986. 2306

Connaughton, Shane
Performance/production
Collection of newspaper reviews by London theatre critics. UK-England: London. 1986. Lang.: Eng. 2124

Connell, Lettie
Performance/production
Puppeteer Lettie Connell discusses her career. USA. 1947-1985. 3971

Connelly, Marc
Performance/production
Biography of actor Richard B. Harrison, who played God in *The Green Pastures*. USA. 1930-1939. Lang.: Eng. 828

Connie's Inn
Performance/production
Four nightclub entertainers on their particular acts and the atmosphere of the late night clubs and theaters in Harlem. USA: New York, NY, Savannah, GA. 1930-1950. Lang.: Eng. 3470

Conservatoire National de Paris
Performance/production
Interview with actor, director and teacher Daniel Mesguich. France: Paris. 1985. Lang.: Fre. 725

Conservatoire National Supérieur d'Art Dramatique (Paris)
Institutions
History of the teaching of acting at the Conservatoire national d'art dramatique. France: Paris. 1786-1986. Lang.: Fre. 1576

Performance/production
Actor, director and teacher Jean-Pierre Vincent. France. 1955-1986. Lang.: Fre. 1744

Constanza, Dominique
Performance/production
Interview with Comédie-Française actress Dominique Constanza. France: Paris. 1986. Lang.: Fre. 1751

Construction, mask
Design/technology
The development of *nō* and *kyōgen* masks and the concerns of the mask carver. Japan. 1390
Carving, back finishing and coloring of *nō* masks. Japan. 1984. 1984. 1391
Characteristics of different *nō* masks. Japan. Lang.: Eng. 1392
The meaning and significance of the *nō* mask. Japan. Lang.: Eng. 1393
Carving techniques used in making the *ko-omote* mask. Japan. Lang.: Eng. 1394
Nō actor talks about his work as a mask carver. Japan. Lang.: Eng. 1395
Handbook of mask and puppet construction. Italy. 1986. Lang.: Ita. 3951

Performance/production
The training and career of puppeteer Julie Taymor. USA. 1970-1984. Lang.: Eng. 3982

Construction, properties
Design/technology
Techniques of stage prop construction. 1986. Lang.: Ger. 230

Construction, puppet
Design/technology
Director of electronics and mechanical design for the Muppets, Faz Fazakas. USA. 1986. 3262
Instructions in creating a modeled puppet head. 3947

Handbook of mask and puppet construction. Italy. 1986. Lang.: Ita. 3951
Creating the proportions and constructing a pattern plan for marionettes. USA. 1985-1986. 4003
Performance/production
The training and career of puppeteer Julie Taymor. USA. 1970-1984. Lang.: Eng. 3982

Construction, theatre
Design/technology
Translation of eighteenth-century treatise on stage machinery and construction. France: Paris. 1760-1801. Lang.: Eng. 264
Construction of castle for goldsmith's guild pageant. England: London. 1377-1392. Lang.: Eng. 3422
Institutions
Several nonprofit theatres secure new spaces. USA: New York, NY. 1984. Lang.: Eng. 544
Performance spaces
Design and construction of Grand Cayman's National Theatre. Cayman Islands. UK-England. 1986. Lang.: Eng. 590
An architect discusses theory of theatre construction. Europe. North America. 1920-1985. Lang.: Hun. 594
Design and construction of Alabama Shakespeare Festival's theatres. USA: Montgomery, AL. 1982-1986. Lang.: Eng. 634
Architectural design for new performance spaces for Theatre for the New City and the Vineyard Theatre. USA: New York, NY. 1986. Lang.: Eng. 639
Role of theatre consultant in bidding. USA. 1986. Lang.: Eng. 643
Descriptions of newly constructed Off Broadway theatres. USA: New York, NY. 1984. Lang.: Eng. 644
Estimating and managing the cost of building a theatre. USA. 1986. Lang.: Eng. 645
Problems of designing and building theatrical buildings. USSR. 1980-1986. Lang.: Rus. 646

Constructivism
Design/technology
Constructivism in Czech stage design. Czechoslovakia. 1960-1979. Lang.: Rus. 253

Contes d'Hoffmann, Les
Performance/production
Reviews of *Death in the Family, Viaggio a Reims, Abduction from the Seraglio* and *Tales of Hoffmann*. USA: St. Louis, MO. 1975-1986. Lang.: Eng. 3799
Plays/librettos/scripts
Analysis and origins of the character 'Dr. Miracle' in Offenbach's *Les contes d'Hoffmann.* 1700-1900. Lang.: Eng. 3853

Contracts
Administration
Laws governing contracts and copyright. France. 1957-1986. Lang.: Fre. 40
Theatrical legislation. France. 1945-1985. Lang.: Fre. 42
Contractual problems in theatrical professions. Switzerland. 1986-1987. Lang.: Ger. 66
Details of the new Approved Production Contract. USA: New York, NY. 1985. Lang.: Eng. 94
Proposed copyright terms for composers and lyricists. USA. 1986. Lang.: Eng. 116
Function of playwright's agent in negotiation and production of a script. USA: New York, NY. 1985. Lang.: Eng. 135
Model dispute resolution project for artists. USA: San Francisco, CA. 1980-1986. Lang.: Eng. 153
Guide to producing Off-off Broadway showcases. USA: New York, NY. Lang.: Eng. 159
Revisions in the Showcase Code by Actors' Equity Association. USA: New York, NY. 1982. Lang.: Eng. 165
Procedures of writing and maintaining contracts. USA. 1986. Lang.: Eng. 181
History and management of Whitefriars Playhouse. England: London. 1607-1614. Lang.: Eng. 1432
Lawsuit of actress Adelaide Ristori against her company manager for nonfulfillment of contract. Italy. 1847-1849. Lang.: Ita. 1437
Transfer of plays from nonprofit to commercial theatre as experienced by WPA Theatre's artistic director Kyle Renick. USA: New York, NY. 1983. Lang.: Eng. 1443
The standard Musician's Personal Management Contract. USA. 1986. Lang.: Eng. 3476

Coriolanus
Performance/production
Production of Shakespeare's *Coriolanus* by the Berliner Ensemble. Germany, East: Berlin, East. 1964. Lang.: Eng. 729

Director Deborah Warner of KICK on her production of Shakespeare's *Coriolanus* and limited public funding for the non-touring company. UK-England: London. 1985-1986. Lang.: Eng. 812

Polemic surrounding Sacha Stavisky's production of Shakespeare's *Coriolanus* at the Comédie-Française. France: Paris. 1934. Lang.: Eng, Fre. 1742

Application of Brechtian concepts by Eckhardt Schall. Germany, East: Berlin, East. UK-England: London. 1952-1986. Lang.: Eng. 1762

Reviews of three Shakespearean productions. UK-England: London, Stratford. USA: Ashland, OR. 1985. Lang.: Eng. 2140

Shakespearean productions by the National Theatre, Royal Shakespeare Company and Orange Tree Theatre. UK-England: Stratford, London. 1984-1985. Lang.: Eng. 2183

Plays/librettos/scripts
Productions of Jane Howell and Elijah Moshinsky for the BBC Shakespeare series. UK-England: London. 1978-1985. Lang.: Eng. 3283

Theory/criticism
Coriolanus from Bertolt Brecht's viewpoint. Germany. 1898-1956. Lang.: Chi. 3105

Cork
Plays/librettos/scripts
Biographical sketch of playwright/performer Samm-Art Williams. USA: Burgaw, NC, New York, NY. 1940-1986. Lang.: Eng. 2946

Cork, Kenneth
Administration
Summary of the Cork report with recommendations on how the results can be used. UK. 1986. Lang.: Eng. 70

Corneille, Pierre
Performance/production
Production photographs of Pierre Corneille's *Le Menteur (The Liar)* at the Comédie-Française. France: Paris. 1986. Lang.: Fre. 1729

Pieces related to performance at the Comédie-Française of *Le Menteur (The Liar)* by Pierre Corneille. France: Paris. 1644-1985. Lang.: Fre. 1735

History of staging of *Le Menteur (The Liar)* by Pierre Corneille. France: Paris. 1644-1985. Lang.: Fre. 1738

Adam Hanuszkiewicz directs Corneille's *Le Cid* at Teatr Ateneum. Poland: Warsaw. 1984. Lang.: Pol. 2021

Plays/librettos/scripts
Style in the plays of Pierre Corneille. France. 1606-1636. Lang.: Rus. 947

Use of the present tense in some tragedies of Corneille and Racine. France. 1600-1700. Lang.: Fre. 2564

Evolution of concept of the State in the tragedies of Pierre Corneille. France. 1636-1674. Lang.: Fre. 2582

Theory/criticism
Influence of pastoral myth on works of Pierre Corneille. France. 1636-1986. Lang.: Fre. 3100

Corneille, Racine and Molière as neoclassisists. France. 1600-1700. Lang.: Kor. 3102

Cornish, William
Institutions
Importance of Chapel Royal in early Tudor court entertainment. England: London. 1504-1524. Lang.: Eng. 3418

Performance/production
Documenting evidence about a court entertainment of Henry VIII. England: Greenwich. 1504-1516. Lang.: Eng. 3420

Corona de luz (Crown of Light)
Plays/librettos/scripts
Corona de luz (Crown of Light) by Rodolfo Usigli as a self-reflexive comment on the process of dramatizing an historical event. Mexico. 1960-1980. Lang.: Eng. 2722

Corona of Light
SEE
Corona de luz.

Coronation of Poppea, The
SEE
Incoronazione di Poppea, L'.

Corpse!
Performance/production
Reviews of *Corpse!* by Gerald Moon, staged by John Tillinger. USA: New York, NY. 1986. Lang.: Eng. 2235

Corpus Christi
Performance/production
Account of University of California at Irvine production of a nativity play with composite text drawn from York, N-town and Wakefield cycles. USA: Irvine, CA. 1986. Lang.: Eng. 2307

Plays/librettos/scripts
Analysis of theophany in English *Corpus Christi* plays. England. 1350-1550. Lang.: Eng. 2472

Corradi, Pedro
Plays/librettos/scripts
Analysis of Pedro Corradi's *Retrato de señora con espejo—Vida y pasión de Margarita Xirgu (Portrait of a Lady with Mirror—The Life and Passion of Margarita Xirgu).* Uruguay. Spain: Madrid. 1985. Lang.: Spa. 2887

Corrales, José
Plays/librettos/scripts
The history of Cuban exile theatre. Cuba. USA: New York, NY. 1959-1986. Lang.: Spa. 2451

Corrie, Joe
Performance/production
Interview with director David Hayman of the Scottish Theatre Company. UK-Scotland. 1986. Lang.: Eng. 2192

Corrigan, Robert
Theory/criticism
Forums: Dispute regarding content and aims of *The Drama Review.* USA. 1964-1986. Lang.: Eng. 3139

Corsario do Rei, O (King's Corsair, The)
Performance/production
Survey of productions in 1985/86. Brazil: Rio de Janeiro. 1985-1986. Lang.: Eng. 1656

Corsaro, Frank
Performance/production
Reviews of *Master Class*, by David Pownell, staged by Frank Corsaro. USA: New York, NY. 1986. Lang.: Eng. 2216

Directors revitalizing opera. USA: New York, NY. 1970-1986. Lang.: Eng. 3826

Cortes, Hernán
Relation to other fields
Assimilation of dramatic elements of Aztec worship in Christianization process. Mexico. Spain. 1519-1559. Lang.: Eng. 3046

Corzatte, Clayton
Performance/production
Five actors who work solely in regional theatre. 1961-1984. Lang.: Eng. 1633

Cosby Show, The
Design/technology
New lighting technology for *The Cosby Show.* USA: New York, NY. 1986. Lang.: Eng. 3259

Cosby, Bill
Performance/production
Profile of actor Bill Cosby. USA. 1986. Lang.: Eng. 3274

Career of popular entertainer Bill Cosby. USA. 1937-1986. Lang.: Eng. 3353

Cosby, John
Institutions
The survival and prosperity of the Santa Fe Opera Company. USA: Santa Fe, NM. 1957-1986. Lang.: Eng. 3678

Così fan tutte
Performance/production
Peter Sellars' production of Mozart's *Così fan tutte.* USA: Purchase, NY. 1986. Lang.: Eng. 3815

Plays/librettos/scripts
The theme of clemency in the final operas of Mozart. Austria: Vienna. 1782-1791. Lang.: Cat. 3860

Appearance of Franz Anton Mesmer as a character in Mozart's *Così fan tutte.* France: Paris. Austria: Vienna. 1734-1789. Lang.: Eng. 3871

Cossa, Roberto
Performance/production
Overview of recent Argentine theatre. Argentina: Buenos Aires. 1978-1983. Lang.: Fre. 651

Plays/librettos/scripts
Development in the genre of the *sainete*, or comic afterpiece. Argentina. 1800-1980. Lang.: Spa. 2365

SUBJECT INDEX

Costumes
SEE
Costuming.

Costuming

Administration
Costume shop owners and designers make a real estate deal with the City of New York. USA: New York, NY. 1986. Lang.: Eng. 138

Basic theatrical documents
Kyōgen: history, training, and promotion. Japan. 1060-1982. Lang.: Eng. 1384

Design/technology
Profile of theatre designer Tanya Moiseiwitsch. 1934-1986. Lang.: Eng. 227

Assembling overcoats from early 20th century patterns. 1986. Lang.: Eng. 232

Assembling capes from early 20th century patterns. 1986. Lang.: Eng. 233

Hungarian students tour stage and costume designs at the Mozarteum. Austria: Salzburg. 1986. Lang.: Hun. 238

Careers of stage designers, Murray Laufer, Michael Eagan and Susan Benson. Canada. 1972-1983. Lang.: Eng. 241

Central workshops of the Slovak National Theatre. Czechoslovakia: Bratislava. 1960-1986. Lang.: Hun. 255

Painters as designers for the theatrical productions. Europe. 1890-1980. Lang.: Fre. 260

Illustrated description of Umberto Tirelli costume collection. Europe. 1700-1984. Lang.: Ita. 263

Recollections of workers who maintain costumes at the Comédie-Française. France. 1961-1986. Lang.: Fre. 265

Relationship between high fashion and costume design. France: Paris. 1620-1930. Lang.: Fre. 266

The differences in scene and costume design for television versus theatre. Hungary: Budapest. 1986. Lang.: Hun. 278

Development of modern Hungarian set and costume design. Hungary. 1957-1970. Lang.: Hun. 279

Historical overview of scene and costume design. Hungary. 1965-1980. Lang.: Hun. 280

Post-liberation Hungarian design. Hungary. 1980-1984. Lang.: Hun. 281

Costume design in a 16th century production in Milan of Guarini's *Il Pastor Fido*. Italy: Mantua. 1500-1600. Lang.: Eng. 298

Career of costume and stage designer Eugenio Guglielminetti. Italy. 1946-1986. Lang.: Ita. 299

Career of designer Mariano Fortuny. Italy. 1871-1949. Lang.: Ita. 300

Documentation on design work for arts festival, 'Maggio Musicale Fiorentino'. Italy: Florence. 1933-1982. Lang.: Ita. 301

History of Catalan scenography. Spain-Catalonia. 200 B.C.-1986 A.D. Lang.: Cat. 311

Costume designer Dunya Ramicova discusses the aesthetics of design. USA: New Haven, CT. 1986. 363

Profile of costume shops. USA: New York, NY. 1986. Lang.: Eng. 372

Costume designer William Ivey Long discusses his work for Off Broadway theatres. USA: New York, NY. 1986. Lang.: Eng. 389

Interview with costume designer Jeannie Davidson. USA: Ashland, OR. 1986. 394

Reproduction of the pattern of any photcopy to fabric. USA. 1984. Lang.: Eng. 422

Guide to materials necessary for theatrical performances. USSR. 1980-1986. Lang.: Rus. 430

Costumes by Yves Saint-Laurent. France. 1959-1984. Lang.: Fre. 1341

Nō actors make interpretive costume choices. Japan. 1386

Collection of pictures of *nō* costumes. Japan. 1300-1986. Lang.: Jap. 1389

Overview of the costume department of the National Theatre. UK-England: London. 1950-1986. Lang.: Eng. 1523

Broad survey of costuming in England. UK-England: London. 1790-1986. Lang.: Eng. 1524

Charles Kean's period production of Shakespeare's *Richard III*. UK-England: London. 1857. Lang.: Eng. 1525

Costume designs for musical comedy by Miles White. USA: New York, NY. 1944-1960. Lang.: Eng. 1529

Design challenges of the film *Absolute Beginners*. UK-England: London. 1986. Lang.: Eng. 3203

Profile of costuming during the Han dynasty. China: Nanyang. 202 B.C.-220 A.D. Lang.: Chi. 3310

Costumes at New York International Clown Festival. USA: New York, NY. 1984. Lang.: Eng. 3316

Pheasant feathers in warrior's helmets in Chinese theatre. China. 300 B.C.-1980 A.D. Lang.: Chi. 3504

Technical details of producing *La Cage aux Folles* on a small budget. Sweden: Malmö. 1985. Lang.: Swe. 3581

Designers discuss regional productions of *Guys and Dolls*. USA. 1984-1986. Lang.: Eng. 3586

Designers discuss regional productions of *She Loves Me*. USA. 1984-1986. Lang.: Eng. 3587

Designers discuss regional productions of *Gypsy*. USA. 1984-1986. 3588

Designers discuss regional productions of *The Music Man*. USA. 1983-1986. Lang.: Eng. 3589

Designers discuss regional productions of *Once Upon a Mattress*. USA. 1984-1986. 3590

Designers discuss regional productions of *Ain't Misbehavin'*. USA. 1984-1986. Lang.: Eng. 3591

Designers discuss regional productions of *Tintypes*. USA. 1984-1986. Lang.: Eng. 3592

Designers discuss regional productions of *Side-by-Side by Sondheim*. USA. 1984. Lang.: Eng. 3593

Designers discuss regional productions of *The Sound of Music*. USA. 1983-1986. Lang.: Eng. 3594

Designers discuss regional productions of *Fiddler on the Roof*. USA. 1984-1986. Lang.: Eng. 3595

Designers discuss regional productions of *Oklahoma*. USA. 1984-1986. Lang.: Eng. 3596

Designers discuss regional productions of *Grease*. USA. 1984-1986. Lang.: Eng. 3597

The role of the costumer in regional opera houses. USA. Lang.: Eng. 3659

The regional opera scene and its artisans. USA. Lang.: Eng. 3661

Institutions
Photos of productions at the Schauspielhaus under the leadership of Hans Gratzer. Austria: Vienna. 1978-1986. Lang.: Ger. 1534

Performance/production
On Western impressions of Eastern performances. China. Japan. 1500-1600. Lang.: Ita. 677

Study of first production of *Jane Shore* by Nicholas Rowe at Drury Lane Theatre. England: London. 1713-1714. Lang.: Eng. 693

Hungarian critics' awards for best actors, play, costume, scenery, etc. of the season. Hungary. 1985-1986. Lang.: Hun. 733

Role of the mask in popular theatre. Japan. Africa. Europe. Lang.: Ita. 755

History of contemporary Japanese theatre. Japan: Tokyo. 1950-1986. Lang.: Jap. 757

Costumes, satiric dances and processions of the Ijebu Yoruba masquerades. Western Africa. Lang.: Eng. 1372

Costumes, dance steps, and music in initiation rites of Yoruba priesthood. Western Africa. Lang.: Eng. 1373

The portrayal of Cleopatra by various actresses. England. 1813-1890. Lang.: Eng. 1699

Life and work of an Indian street performer. India: Rajasthan. 1940-1985. Lang.: Eng. 3335

Documenting evidence about a court entertainment of Henry VIII. England: Greenwich. 1504-1516. Lang.: Eng. 3420

Types of costumes, dances, and songs of Dodo masquerades during Ramadan. Upper Volta: Ouagadougou. Lang.: Eng. 3428

Four nightclub entertainers on their particular acts and the atmosphere of the late night clubs and theaters in Harlem. USA: New York, NY, Savannah, GA. 1930-1950. Lang.: Eng. 3470

Techniques of comedians in modern Beijing opera. China, People's Republic of: Beijing. 1964-1985. Lang.: Chi. 3524

Physical, social and theatrical aspects of *castrati*. Italy: Rome, Venice. England: London. 1700-1799. Lang.: Ger. 3757

Costuming — cont'd

Mussorgskij's opera *Boris Godunov* at the Mariinskij Theatre. Russia: St. Petersburg. 1874. Lang.: Eng.   3775

Plays/librettos/scripts
Compares pageant-wagon play about Edward IV with version by Thomas Heywood. England: Coventry, London. 1560-1600. Lang.: Eng.   3430

Reference materials
Costumes of famous Viennese actors. Austria: Vienna. 1831-1960. Lang.: Ger.   1003

Catalogue of an exhibition of costume designs for Broadway musicals. USA: New York, NY. 1900-1925. Lang.: Eng, Ger.   3635

Relation to other fields
Costuming evidence on carved baptismal fonts. England. 1463-1544. Lang.: Eng.   3026

Theory/criticism
Use of red, white and black colors in Chinese traditional theatre. China. 200 B.C.-1982 A.D. Lang.: Chi.   3560

Strengths and weaknesses of Beijing opera. China, People's Republic of: Beijing. 1935-1985. Lang.: Chi.   3565

Cottesloe Theatre (London)
SEE ALSO
National Theatre (London).

Performance/production
Collection of newspaper reviews by London theatre critics. UK. 1986. Lang.: Eng.   2099

Collection of newspaper reviews by London theatre critics. UK. 1986. Lang.: Eng.   2101

Collection of newspaper reviews by London theatre critics. UK-England: London. 1986. Lang.: Eng.   2110

Collection of newspaper reviews by London theatre critics. UK-England: London. 1986. Lang.: Eng.   2112

Collection of newspaper reviews by London theatre critics. UK-England: London. 1986. Lang.: Eng.   2118

Collection of newspaper reviews by London theatre critics. UK-England: London. 1986. Lang.: Eng.   2124

Comparative analysis of productions of *Summer* by Edward Bond. UK-England: London. 1982. Lang.: Eng.   2163

Cotton Club (New York, NY)
Performance/production
Four nightclub entertainers on their particular acts and the atmosphere of the late night clubs and theaters in Harlem. USA: New York, NY, Savannah, GA. 1930-1950. Lang.: Eng.   3470

Cotulí, Josepa Rosich
Plays/librettos/scripts
Roles of women in middle-class Catalonian society as reflected in the plays of Carme Montoriol and Maria Aurélia Capmany. Spain-Catalonia. 1700-1960. Lang.: Spa.   2819

Coulter, John
Plays/librettos/scripts
Analysis of religious symbolism in *Riel* by John Coulter. Canada. 1950. Lang.: Eng.   2407

Writing and production of *Riel* by John Coulter. Canada: Toronto, ON, Ottawa, ON. 1936-1980. Lang.: Eng.   2414

Overview of playwright John Coulter's later career. Canada: Toronto, ON. UK-England: London. 1951-1957. Lang.: Eng.   2415

Count of Monte Cristo, The
Performance/production
Survey of productions at the Kennedy Center's National Theatre. USA: Washington, DC. 1986. Lang.: Eng.   2247

County Museum (Umeå)
SEE
Länsmuseet.

Court entertainment
SEE ALSO
Classed Entries under MIXED ENTERTAINMENTS—Court entertainment: 3417-3420.

Performance/production
History of classical dance-drama *gambuh*. Bali. 1100-1982. Lang.: Eng.   1357

Court Theater (Chicago, IL)
Performance/production
Chicago dramaturgs acknowledge a common ground in educating their audience. USA: Chicago, IL. 1984-1986. Lang.: Eng.   2274

Court Theatre (London)
SEE
Royal Court Theatre.

Covent Garden
SEE
Royal Opera House, Covent Garden.

Covent Garden Theatre (London)
Administration
Royal theatrical patronage during the reign of George II. England: London. 1727-1760. Lang.: Eng.   33

Coventry, John
Design/technology
A lighting designer discusses the unique problems of lighting symphony orchestras. USA: Washington, DC, Boston, MA, New York, NY. 1910-1986. Lang.: Eng.   3478

Covivencia
Performance/production
Overview of recent Argentine theatre. Argentina: Buenos Aires. 1978-1983. Lang.: Fre.   651

Cowan, Cindy
Basic theatrical documents
Playtext of *A Woman from the Sea* by Cindy Cowan. Canada. 1986. Lang.: Eng.   1468

Coward, Noël
Performance/production
Collection of newspaper reviews by London theatre critics. UK-England: London. 1986. Lang.: Eng.   2113

Reviews of *Oh Coward!*, lyrics and music by Noël Coward, devised and staged by Roderick Cook. USA: New York, NY. 1986. Lang.: Eng.   3616

Cox, Alex
Design/technology
Cinematographer Roger Deakins discusses lighting for his work in the film *Sid and Nancy*. USA: New York, NY, Los Angeles, CA. UK-England: London. 1976-1986. Lang.: Eng.   3211

Coyote Cycle
Performance/production
Murray Mednick's 7-play Coyote Cycle performed outdoors from dusk to dawn. USA. 1984. Lang.: Eng.   2292

Crabbe, Kerry
Performance/production
Collection of newspaper reviews by London theatre critics. UK-England: London. 1986. Lang.: Eng.   2116

Craft, Robert
Reference materials
The purchase and eventual exhibition of a collection of Stravinsky's work. Switzerland: Basel. USA: New York, NY. 1930-1985. Lang.: Eng.   3500

Crage, Basil
Reference materials
Catalogue of an exhibition of costume designs for Broadway musicals. USA: New York, NY. 1900-1925. Lang.: Eng, Ger.   3635

Craig, Edward Gordon
Design/technology
Symbolism in set design. China, People's Republic of. 1265-1981. Lang.: Chi.   247

Travelling exhibitions of Edward Gordon Craig and his first book *The Art of the Theatre*. Germany. Austria. USA. 1904-1930. Lang.: Eng.   1515

Interview with lighting designer Gil Wechsler of the Metropolitan Opera. USA: New York, NY. 1883-1986. Lang.: Eng.   3654

Performance/production
Innovative Shakespeare stagings of Harley Granville-Barker. UK-England. 1912-1940. Lang.: Eng.   806

Origins of radically simplified stage in modern productions. USA. 1912-1922. Lang.: Eng.   831

Innovative stagings of Shakespeare's *Hamlet*. Europe. 1700-1950. Lang.: Rus.   1716

Max Reinhardt's work with his contemporaries. Germany. Austria. 1890-1938. Lang.: Eng, Ger.   1757

Overview of correspondence between Leon Schiller and Edward Gordon Craig. Poland: Warsaw. France: Paris. 1900-1954. Lang.: Eng, Fre.   2022

Plays/librettos/scripts
Influence of Gordon Craig on American theatre and his recognition of Eugene O'Neill's importance. USA. UK-England. 1912-1928. Lang.: Eng.   2908

Cranes Are Flying, The
SEE
Večno živyjě.

Cranfield, Jules
Performance/production
Interview with Jules Cranfield on Focus Theatre Group. UK-Scotland. 1973-1986. Lang.: Eng. 2193

Crawford, Bruce
Administration
Account of the first year of new management at the Metropolitan Opera. USA: New York, NY. 1985-1986. Lang.: Eng. 3644

Crawford, Cheryl
Administration
Cheryl Crawford's producing career discussed in light of her latest Broadway show. USA: New York, NY, Atlanta, GA. 1936-1986. Lang.: Eng. 117

Creative drama
SEE ALSO
Children's theatre.

Relation to other fields
Theatrical performance as a pedagogical tool. 1986. Lang.: Cat. 1048
Proposal for using creative drama with museum visits and a study of the visual arts. USA: Austin, TX. 1985. Lang.: Eng. 1159
Study of how principals perceive the use of drama in the curriculum. USA. 1986. Lang.: Eng. 1165

Research/historiography
Study of educational drama from the perspective of generic skills. Canada: Toronto, ON. 1985. Lang.: Eng. 3070

Training
Instructional television programming for the advancement of arts in education. USA: University Park, IL. 1986. Lang.: Eng. 3287

Crémazie, Octave
Plays/librettos/scripts
French-Canadian nationalism in *Le Drapeau de Carillon (The Flag of Carillon)*. Canada: Montreal, PQ. 1759-1901. Lang.: Eng. 2433

Crespin, Régine
Performance/production
Performance analysis of the title role of *Carmen*. France. 1875-1986. Lang.: Eng. 3725
Famous sopranos discuss their interpretations of Tosca. USA. 1935-1986. Lang.: Eng. 3811

Cribley, Roseann
Performance/production
The operations of the Hawaii Opera Theatre. USA: Honolulu, HI. 1950-1985. Lang.: Eng. 3814

Cricot 2 (Cracow)
Performance/production
Tadeusz Kantor directs his *Gdzie sa Niegdysiejsze Śniegi (Where Are the Snows of Yesteryear)*, Cricot 2. Poland: Cracow. 1984. Lang.: Pol. 2061

Plays/librettos/scripts
Influence of politics and personal history on Tadeusz Kantor and his Cricot 2 theatre company. Poland: Cracow. 1944-1986. Lang.: Eng. 2744

Crime and Punishment
SEE
Prestuplenijė i nakazanijė.

Institutions
Reviews of Edinburgh Festival plays. UK-Scotland: Edinburgh. 1986. Lang.: Eng. 539

Crimes of the Heart
Plays/librettos/scripts
Beth Henley's play *Crimes of the Heart* as an example of female criminality in response to a patriarchal culture. USA. 1980-1986. Lang.: Eng. 2923

Crimi, Gaetano
Plays/librettos/scripts
Cultural and popular elements in a traditional nativity puppet performance. Italy: Sicily, Naples. 1651-1986. Lang.: Eng. 4009

Critic, The
Performance/production
Lady Dufferin's amateur theatricals. Canada: Ottawa, ON. India. 1873-1888. Lang.: Eng. 671

Criticism
SEE
Theory/criticism.

Croatian National Theatre (Drama and Opera)
SEE
Hravatsko Narodno Kazalište.

Croce, Benedetto
Relation to other fields
Luigi Pirandello's relationship with philosophers Benedetto Croce and Giovanni Gentile. Italy. 1867-1936. Lang.: Ita. 1106

Croft, Giles
Performance/production
Collection of newspaper reviews by London theatre critics. UK-England: London. 1986. Lang.: Eng. 2110

Cronyn, Hume
Performance/production
Interview with actors Jessica Tandy and Hume Cronyn. USA. 1932-1984. Lang.: Eng. 2260

Crosby, John O.
Institutions
The first thirty years of the Santa Fe Opera. USA: Santa Fe, NM. 1956-1986. Lang.: Eng. 3681

Cross, Beverley
Performance/production
Collection of newspaper reviews by London theatre critics. UK: London. 1986. Lang.: Eng. 2100

Crossover Dreams
Administration
Interview with independent filmmaker Leon Ichaso. USA: New York, NY. 1986. 3193

Crown of Light
SEE
Corona de luz.

Crowne, John
Plays/librettos/scripts
Revision of dramaturgy and stagecraft in Restoration adaptations of Shakespeare. England: London. 1660-1690. Lang.: Eng. 2535

Croydon Warehouse (London)
Performance/production
Collection of newspaper reviews by London theatre critics. UK-England. 1986. Lang.: Eng. 2120

Crozier, Eric
Performance/production
Interview with singer Nancy Evans and writer Eric Crozier discussing their association with Benjamin Britten. USA: Columbia, MO. UK-England: London. 1940-1985. Lang.: Eng. 3820

Plays/librettos/scripts
Collaboration of authors and composers of *Billy Budd*. UK-England: London. 1949-1964. Lang.: Eng. 3895
A review of Southwestern University's Brown Symposium VII, 'Benjamin Britten and the Ceremony of Innocence'. USA: Georgetown. 1985. Lang.: Eng. 3904

Crucible Theatre (Sheffield)
Performance/production
Collection of newspaper reviews by London theatre critics. UK. 1986. Lang.: Eng. 2103

Crucible, The
Plays/librettos/scripts
Interview with playwright Arthur Miller. USA. 1985. Lang.: Eng. 2921

Crystal, Billy
Performance/production
Autobiography of comedian Billy Crystal. USA. 1955. Lang.: Eng. 3350

Császári futam (Imperial Round)
Performance/production
Géza Tordy directs *Császári futam (Imperial Round)* by Miklós Gyárfás at Gyulai Várszinház. Hungary: Gyula. 1986. Lang.: Hun. 1875

Csáth, Géza
Performance/production
Janika (Our Son) by Géza Csáth, directed by Tamás Fodor and starring György Kézdy. Hungary: Szolnok. 1986. Lang.: Hun. 1955

Cseh, Tamás
Performance/production
Melyrepülés (Flying at Low Altitude) by Tamás Cseh and Dénes Csengey. Hungary: Budapest. 1986. Lang.: Hun. 3487
Reviews of three musicals about the 1960s. Hungary. 1985-1986. Lang.: Hun. 3488

Csengey, Dénes
Performance/production
Melyrepülés (Flying at Low Altitude) by Tamás Cseh and Dénes Csengey. Hungary: Budapest. 1986. Lang.: Hun. 3487

D'Annunzio, Gabriele
Plays/librettos/scripts
Luigi Pirandello's relationship with author Gabriele D'Annunzio and reviewer Luigi Antonelli. Italy. 1900-1936. Lang.: Ita. 2698

The town of Rimini and its attachment to *Francesca da Rimini*. Italy: Rimini. 1986. Lang.: Eng. 3890

D'Arcy, Margaretta
Plays/librettos/scripts
The place of *The Island of the Mighty* in the John Arden canon. Ireland. UK. 1950-1972. Lang.: Eng. 2666

D'Auban, John
Administration
Legislation for the protection of Victorian child-actors. UK. 1837-1901. Lang.: Eng. 1439

Da'ziya
Performance/production
Performance conditions of specific theatrical genres. Lebanon. 1918-1985. Lang.: Fre. 2011

Relation to other fields
Reports and discussions of restricted cultural communication. Lebanon. Spain-Catalonia. USA. 1985. Lang.: Fre, Spa, Cat. 1111

Dačniki (Summer Folk)
Performance/production
Józef Skwark directs Gorkij's *Dačniki (Summer Folk)* under the title *Letnicy*. Poland: Warsaw. 1984. Lang.: Pol. 2045

Dadaism
Plays/librettos/scripts
Examines *Ne blâmez jamais les Bédouins (Don't Blame It on the Bedouins)* as a post-modernist play. Canada. 1980. Lang.: Fre. 2432

Relation to other fields
Artistic, literary and theatrical avant-garde movements. Europe. 1900-1930. Lang.: Ita. 1083

Influence of Marcel Duchamp's work on Tom Stoppard's radio play, *Artist Descending a Staircase*. UK-England. 1913-1972. Lang.: Eng. 3059

Daguerre, Jacques
Performance/production
Relationship between theatre and early photography. France. 1818-1899. Lang.: Fre. 1748

Dahl, Roald
Performance/production
Collection of newspaper reviews by London theatre critics. UK-England: London. 1986. Lang.: Eng. 2116

Dainty Shapes and Hairy Apes
SEE
Nabodnisie i koczkodany.

Dajka, Margit
Performance/production
Career of actress Margit Dajka. Hungary. 1907-1986. Lang.: Hun. 1787

Recollections of actress Margit Dajka. Hungary. 1986. Lang.: Hun. 1886

Tribute to late actress Margit Dajka. Hungary. 1929-1986. Lang.: Hun. 1915

Recollections of actress Margit Dajka. Hungary. 1929-1986. Lang.: Hun. 1930

Daley, Frank
Administration
History of the Town Theatre. Canada: Ottawa, ON. 1948-1970. Lang.: Eng. 29

Dallas Theatre Center (Dallas, TX)
Institutions
Interview with Adrian Hall, artistic director of both Trinity Square Repertory Theatre and Dallas Theatre Center. USA: Providence, RI, Dallas, TX. 1966-1986. Lang.: Eng. 548

Dallas, L.B.
Institutions
Interview with members of Mabou Mines. USA: New York, NY. 1984. Lang.: Eng. 1607

Dalliance
Performance/production
Survey of the season at the National Theatre. UK-England: London. 1986. Lang.: Eng. 2130

Dalton, Charles
Performance/production
Acting style in plays by Henrik Ibsen. 1885-1905. Lang.: Eng. 1627

Daly, Augustin
Plays/librettos/scripts
Philosophy of wealth in gilded age plays. USA: New York, NY. 1870-1889. Lang.: Eng. 2950

Damadjan, G.
Audience
Audience-performer relationship in experimental theatre. USSR: Moscow. 1986. Lang.: Rus. 204

Dance
SEE ALSO
Classed Entries under DANCE: 1265-1354.

Choreography.

Design/technology
Career of lighting designer Nicholas Cernovitch. Canada: Montreal, PQ. 1970-1983. Lang.: Eng. 244

Institutions
Significance of Applebaum-Hébert report on Canadian cultural policy. Canada. 1982-1983. Lang.: Eng. 465

New concept for using the Theater im Künstlerhaus for the Opernwerkstatt productions. Austria: Vienna. 1986-1987. Lang.: Ger. 3665

Performance spaces
Children's history of the Gran Teatre del Liceo opera house. Spain-Catalonia: Barcelona. 1845-1986. Lang.: Cat. 3684

Performance/production
Meeting of experimental theatre groups at Szkéné Theatre. Hungary: Budapest. 1985. Lang.: Hun. 736

History of contemporary Japanese theatre. Japan: Tokyo. 1950-1986. Lang.: Jap. 757

Costumes, satiric dances and processions of the Ijebu Yoruba masquerades. Western Africa. Lang.: Eng. 1372

Costumes, dance steps, and music in initiation rites of Yoruba priesthood. Western Africa. Lang.: Eng. 1373

Survey of productions in 1985/86. Brazil: Rio de Janeiro. 1985-1986. Lang.: Eng. 1656

Directorial design for Dürrenmatt's *Die Physiker (The Physicists)*. China: Shanghai. 1982. Lang.: Chi. 1690

Artists who began in dance, film or television move to Off Broadway theatre. USA: New York, NY. 1982. Lang.: Eng. 2284

Advantages and limitations of television medium in producing, recording and broadcasting performing arts. USA. 1930-1985. Lang.: Eng. 3273

Ballet for television produced by A. Belinskij. USSR: Leningrad. 1980-1986. Lang.: Rus. 3277

Development of works by the Special Delivery Moving Theatre. Canada: Vancouver, BC. 1976-1986. Lang.: Eng. 3294

Interpretive technique of *commedia dell'arte* actors. France. 1575-1670. Lang.: Ita. 3410

Types of costumes, dances, and songs of Dodo masquerades during Ramadan. Upper Volta: Ouagadougou. Lang.: Eng. 3428

Experiences of two performance artists acquiring ballroom dancing skills. UK-England. 1986. Lang.: Eng. 3450

Performance art and its current characteristic tone. USA. Lang.: Eng. 3459

Origins of Southern Sung drama (*Nanxi*). China: Wenzhou. 1127-1234. Lang.: Chi. 3512

Origins of the stylized acting in Southern drama (Nanxi). China. 1127-1278. Lang.: Chi. 3517

Three Swedish musical theatre productions. Sweden. 1985-1986. Lang.: Swe. 3606

Choreography in musical theatre. USA: New York, NY. 1944-1981. Lang.: Eng. 3620

Interviews with various artists of the Viennese State Opera. Austria: Vienna. 1909-1986. Lang.: Ger. 3692

Plays/librettos/scripts
Argument that the Gallican liturgy was a form of drama. France. 500-900. Lang.: Eng. 949

Essays on all facets of Expressionism including theatre and dance. Germany. Austria. 1891-1933. Lang.: Ger, Ita. 953

Conceptions of the South Sea islands in works of Murnau, Artaud and Spies. Europe. USA. Indonesia. 1930. Lang.: Ita. 3231

Adaptations of *Carmen* by Prosper Mérimée. France. Spain. 1845-1983. Lang.: Fre. 3870

Dance — cont'd

Reference materials
Theatre productions in the French community of Belgium. Belgium. 1981-1982. Lang.: Fre. 1004

Theatre productions in the French community of Belgium. Belgium. 1982-1983. Lang.: Fre. 1005

Theatre productions in the French community of Belgium. Belgium. 1983-1984. Lang.: Fre. 1006

Theatre productions in the French community of Belgium. Belgium. 1984-1985. Lang.: Fre. 1007

List and location of school playtexts and programs. France. 1601-1700. Lang.: Fre. 2987

Relation to other fields
Study of agriculture-related songs and dances. Japan: Tokyo. 1986. Lang.: Jap. 3360

Popular theatrical forms in the Basque country. Spain. France. 674-1963. Lang.: Spa. 3361

Dance ethnography
Research/historiography
System for describing ethnic dance based on Xhosa dances. South Africa, Republic of. 1980-1985. Lang.: Eng. 1337

Dance of Death, The
SEE
Dödsdansen.

Dödsdansen.

Dance Theatre Workshop (New York, NY)
Institutions
Profile of Economy Tires Theatre, producing arm of Dance Theatre Workshop. USA: New York, NY. 1978-1983. Lang.: Eng. 563

Dance-Drama
International conference on Eastern and Western theatre. 1986. Lang.: Ita. 2

SEE ALSO
Classed Entries under DANCE-DRAMA: 1335-1424.

Performance/production
Reciprocal influences of French and Japanese theatre. France. Japan. 1900-1945. Lang.: Fre. 1750

Plays/librettos/scripts
Influences on Asian theatrical genres. Asia. 500-1985. Lang.: Eng. 920

Reference materials
Theatre productions in the French community of Belgium. Belgium. 1981-1982. Lang.: Fre. 1004

Theatre productions in the French community of Belgium. Belgium. 1982-1983. Lang.: Fre. 1005

Theatre productions in the French community of Belgium. Belgium. 1983-1984. Lang.: Fre. 1006

Theatre productions in the French community of Belgium. Belgium. 1984-1985. Lang.: Fre. 1007

Relation to other fields
Argument that theatre should return to art's roots in ritual and ceremony. 1986. Lang.: Eng. 1059

Research/historiography
Analysis of three ancient types of dance-drama. China. 1032-1420. Lang.: Chi. 3551

Dancers
SEE
Dance.

Dancing
Institutions
Reports on theatre conferences and festivals in Asia. Philippines: Manila. Malaysia: Kuala Lumpur. Japan: Toga. India: Calcutta. 1981-1984. Lang.: Eng. 510

Liturgical drama and dance performed by amateur theatre group. Sweden: Lund. 1960-1986. Lang.: Swe. 526

Notes on the dance committee meetings at the 21st congress of the International Theatre Institute. Canada: Montreal, PQ, Toronto, ON. 1985. Lang.: Rus. 1270

Performance/production
Report from an international amateur theatre festival where music and dance were prominent. Denmark: Copenhagen. 1986. Lang.: Swe. 683

Motion, dance and acting in the development of theatrical art. Hungary. 1980-1986. Lang.: Hun. 1276

Brief autobiography of dancer Tanaka Min. Japan: Tokyo. 1945-1985. Lang.: Eng. 1281

Dance and mime performances at annual Festival of the Arts. South Africa, Republic of: Grahamstown. 1986. Lang.: Eng. 1282

Merce Cunningham, Alwin Nikolais, Meredith Monk and Yvonne Rainer on post-modern dance. USA. 1975-1986. Lang.: Eng. 1285

Dance reviews from the *Magyar* daily paper. 1964-1984. Lang.: Hun. 1301

Stage history of *Giselle* by Adolphe Adam at Pest National Theatre. Hungary: Pest. 1847-1880. Lang.: Hun. 1306

Prokofjév's ballet *Romeo and Juliet* choreographed by László Seregi. Hungary: Budapest. 1985. Lang.: Hun. 1307

Productions based on sacred music of Franz Liszt. Hungary: Zalaegerszeg, Budapest. 1986. Lang.: Hun. 1308

On the career of dancer and actress Ida Rubinstein, member of Diaghilew's 'Russian Seasons'. Russia. France. 1885-1960. Lang.: Rus. 1311

Dancer and choreographer discusses contemporary and classical ballet. USSR. 1980-1986. Lang.: Rus. 1313

Notes on the 5th International Competition of Ballet Dancers. USSR: Moscow. 1985. Lang.: Rus. 1315

Interview with ballerina Majja Pliseckaja. USSR. 1985. Lang.: Rus. 1316

Creative development of ballerina Irina Kolpakova. USSR: Leningrad. 1950-1985. Lang.: Rus. 1317

Artistic directors of Soviet Ballet Theatre on plans for the future. USSR: Moscow. 1980-1985. Lang.: Rus. 1318

Reviews of 5th International Competition of Ballet Dancers. USSR: Moscow. 1985. Lang.: Rus. 1319

Careers of four Russian 'apostles of dance'. USSR. Lang.: Rus. 1320

Career of dancer Ju.T. Ždanov. USSR. 1925-1986. Lang.: Rus. 1321

Translation of *Belly-dancing* by Wendy Buonaventura. Europe. Asia. Africa. Lang.: Ita. 1330

Adaptation of folk dance to the stage. Hungary. 1773-1985. Lang.: Hun. 1331

European-derived folk dances in contemporary Afrikaner culture. South Africa, Republic of. 1700-1986. Lang.: Afr. 1334

Biography of modern dancer Mary Wigman. Germany. Switzerland. 1886-1973. Lang.: Ger. 1348

History of classical dance-drama *gambuh*. Bali. 1100-1982. Lang.: Eng. 1357

History of classical Cambodian dance. Cambodia. 1860-1985. Lang.: Eng. 1358

Trance dance compared to role of dance in conventional theatre. Indonesia. 1977-1982. Lang.: Eng. 1363

Dance-pantomime dramas based on the plots of plays by Aleksand'r Sumarokov. Russia. 1717-1777. Lang.: Rus. 1367

Interview with choreographer Royston Maldoom. UK-Scotland. 1970-1986. Lang.: Eng. 2189

Experiences of two performance artists acquiring ballroom dancing skills. UK-England. 1986. Lang.: Eng. 3450

Imprisoned Nigerian pop musician Fela Anikulapo-Kuti. Nigeria: Lagos. 1960-1985. Lang.: Eng. 3468

Four nightclub entertainers on their particular acts and the atmosphere of the late night clubs and theaters in Harlem. USA: New York, NY, Savannah, GA. 1930-1950. Lang.: Eng. 3470

Dakota Stanton discusses her career as a singer and dancer in nightclubs and reviews. USA: Pittsburgh, PA, New York, NY. 1950-1980. Lang.: Eng. 3471

Reviews of three musicals about the 1960s. Hungary. 1985-1986. Lang.: Hun. 3488

Tap dancing career of Maurice Hines and the creation of his new company Balletap, USA. USA: New York, NY. 1949-1986. Lang.: Eng. 3623

Profile of actress Sári Fedák. Austro-Hungarian Empire. 1879-1955. Lang.: Hun. 3940

Research/historiography
System for describing ethnic dance based on Xhosa dances. South Africa, Republic of. 1980-1985. Lang.: Eng. 1337

Results of studies of ethnic dance with transcription system. South Africa, Republic of. 1980-1985. Lang.: Afr. 1338

Dang Liang
Research/historiography
Transformation of traditional music notation into modern notation for four Chinese operas. China: Beijing. 1674-1985. Lang.: Chi. 3554

Daniels, Ron
Administration
Interview with director and tour manager of Royal Shakespeare Company about touring. UK. 1986. Lang.: Eng.　72

Performance/production
Collection of newspaper reviews by London theatre critics. UK-England: London. 1986. Lang.: Eng.　2121

Daniels, Sarah
Institutions
Place of women in Britain's National Theatre. UK-England: London. 1986. Lang.: Eng.　1588

Progress and aims of Women's Playhouse Trust. UK-England: London. 1984-1986. Lang.: Eng.　1590

Dann, George Landen
Theory/criticism
Attitudes toward sports in serious Australian drama. Australia. 1876-1965. Lang.: Eng.　3084

Danny and the Deep Blue Sea
Performance/production
Interview with actor Stephen Ouimette. Canada. 1960-1986. Lang.: Eng.　1663

Danton Affair, The
Performance/production
Royal Shakespeare Company performances at the Barbican Theatre. UK-England: London. 1986. Lang.: Eng.　2152

Dantons Tod (Danton's Death)
Performance/production
Description of Georg Büchner's *Dantons Tod (Danton's Death)* staged by Alexander Lang at Deutsches Theater. Germany, East: Berlin, East. 1984. Lang.: Ger.　1763

Danube, The
Plays/librettos/scripts
Interview with playwright Maria Irene Fornes. USA: New York, NY. 1984. Lang.: Eng.　2892

Danvers, Billy
Performance/production
Recollection of performances by music-hall comedian Billy Danvers. UK-England. 1900. Lang.: Eng.　3469

Daoust, Julien
Institutions
Founding of Théâtre National Français de Montréal. Canada: Montreal, PQ. 1889-1901. Lang.: Fre.　469

Darke, Nick
Performance/production
Collection of newspaper reviews by London theatre critics. UK-England: London. 1986. Lang.: Eng.　2117

Dasgupta, Gautam
Relation to other fields
Performing Arts Journal attempts to increase stature of drama as literature. USA: New York, NY. 1984. Lang.: Eng.　1154

Dasté, Catherine
Institutions
Work and distinctive qualities of the Théâtre du Soleil. France: Paris. 1964-1986. Lang.: Eng.　1575

Databanks
Reference materials
Lists 292 research collections and information sources, most of which are open to the public. UK. 1985-1986. Lang.: Eng.　1034

Comprehensive list of rehearsal and performance spaces. USA: New York, NY. Lang.: Eng.　1042

Databases
Relation to other fields
Examples of role-playing drawn from the ERIC database. USA. 1980-1985. Lang.: Eng.　1144

Daudet, Léon
Performance/production
Influence of Richard Wagner on the work of the French Symbolists. France: Paris. Germany, West: Bayreuth. 1860-1986. Lang.: Eng.　3726

Daughter of Monsieur Occitania, The
SEE
Fille de Monsieur Occitania, La.

Davenant, William
Basic theatrical documents
Transcription of manuscript assigning shares in the King's Company. England. 1661-1684. Lang.: Eng.　220

Plays/librettos/scripts
Female characterization in Nicholas Rowe's plays. England. 1629-1720. Lang.: Eng.　2475

Image of poverty in Elizabethan and Stuart plays. England. 1558-1642. Lang.: Eng.　2482

Development of Restoration musical theatre. England. 1642-1699. Lang.: Eng.　3496

Davenport, Fanny
Performance/production
The portrayal of Cleopatra by various actresses. England. 1813-1890. Lang.: Eng.　1699

David and Bethsabe
Plays/librettos/scripts
Treatment of historical figures in plays by William Shakespeare, Christopher Marlowe and George Peele. England. 1560-1650. Lang.: Eng.　2534

David, Giacomo
Performance/production
The growth and development of the Italian tenor singing style. Italy: Bergamo. 1788-1860. Lang.: Eng.　3767

David, Guivanni
Performance/production
The growth and development of the Italian tenor singing style. Italy: Bergamo. 1788-1860. Lang.: Eng.　3767

David, John
Performance/production
Collection of newspaper reviews by London theatre critics. UK-England. 1986. Lang.: Eng.　2111

David, Laurent-Olivier
Plays/librettos/scripts
French-Canadian nationalism in *Le Drapeau de Carillon (The Flag of Carillon)*. Canada: Montreal, PQ. 1759-1901. Lang.: Eng.　2433

David, rei (David, King)
Basic theatrical documents
Text of *David, rei (David, King)* by Jordi Teixidor. Spain-Catalonia. 1970-1985. Lang.: Cat.　1503

Plays/librettos/scripts
Analysis of the six published dramatic works by Jordi Teixidor. Spain-Catalonia. 1970-1985. Lang.: Cat.　2809

Davidson, Clifford
Plays/librettos/scripts
Text of a lecture on Shakespeare's *King Lear* by Clifford Davidson. Hungary: Budapest. Lang.: Hun.　2643

Davidson, Gordon
Performance/production
Interview with dramaturg Russell Vandenbroucke. USA: Los Angeles, CA. 1974-1985. Lang.: Eng.　2253

Review of *Harriet, the Woman Called Moses*, an opera by Thea Musgrave, staged by Gordon Davidson. USA: Norfolk, VA. 1985. Lang.: Eng.　3835

Davidson, Jeannie
Design/technology
Interview with costume designer Jeannie Davidson. USA: Ashland, OR. 1986.　394

Davies, Howard
Performance/production
An exploration of Brecht's *Gestus*. Germany. Lang.: Eng.　1758

Collection of newspaper reviews by London theatre critics. UK: London. 1986. Lang.: Eng.　2100

Collection of newspaper reviews by London theatre critics. UK-England: London. 1986. Lang.: Eng.　2109

Collection of newspaper reviews by London theatre critics. UK-England. 1986. Lang.: Eng.　2115

Collection of newspaper reviews by London theatre critics. UK-England: London. 1986. Lang.: Eng.　2125

Shakespearean productions by the National Theatre, Royal Shakespeare Company and Orange Tree Theatre. UK-England: Stratford, London. 1984-1985. Lang.: Eng.　2183

Davies, Robertson
Plays/librettos/scripts
The immigrant in plays by Herman Voaden and Robertson Davies. Canada. 1934-1950. Lang.: Eng.　2431

Davis, Anthony
Performance/production
Profile of and interview with Anthony Davis, composer of the opera *X*, on the life and times of Malcolm X. USA: New York, NY. Lang.: Eng.　3834

Decker, Jacques de
Basic theatrical documents
Playtext of Jacques de Decker's *Jeu d'intérieur (Indoor Games)* in English translation. Belgium. 1979. Lang.: Eng.   1461

Plays/librettos/scripts
Biography and bibliography of playwright Jacques de Decker. Belgium. 1945-1986. Lang.: Eng.   2400

Deconstruction
Plays/librettos/scripts
Psychoanalytic and post-structuralist analysis of Molière's *Tartuffe*. France. 1660-1669. Lang.: Eng.   948

Examines *Ne blâmez jamais les Bédouins (Don't Blame It on the Bedouins)* as a post-modernist play. Canada. 1980. Lang.: Fre.   2432

Deconstructionist analysis of *Riccardo III* by Carmelo Bene. Italy. France. Lang.: Eng.   2690

Theory/criticism
Critics discuss modernist and postmodernist movements. 1986. Lang.: Eng.   1194

An imagined dialogue on the work of Roland Barthes. France. Lang.: Eng.   1207

Influence of literary theory on Greek theatre studies. Greece. UK-England. Germany. Lang.: Afr.   1210

A tongue-in-cheek deconstructionist manifesto. USA. Lang.: Eng.   1224

Classical, modern and postmodern theatre and their delineation through opposites. France. 1986. Lang.: Eng.   3104

Shaw's use of devil's advocacy in his plays compared to deconstructionism. UK-England. 1900-1986. Lang.: Eng.   3135

Analysis of the essentials of art, especially in theatre. USA. 1960-1986. Lang.: Eng.   3142

Six rules which render socially desirable elements of performance superfluous. USA. 1968-1986. Lang.: Eng.   3151

Decroux, Etienne
Performance/production
Influences upon the post-modern mime troupe, Cirque du Soleil. Canada: Montreal, PQ. 1984-1986. Lang.: Eng.   3292

Theory/criticism
Present and future of mime theatre.   3300

Decrouzol, Gérard
Performance/production
A photographic essay of 42 soloists and groups performing mime or gestural theatre. 1986.   3290

Deer, Sandra
Administration
Cheryl Crawford's producing career discussed in light of her latest Broadway show. USA: New York, NY, Atlanta, GA. 1936-1986. Lang.: Eng.   117

Performance/production
Reviews of *So Long on Lonely Street*, by Sandra Deer, staged by Kent Stephens. USA: New York, NY. 1986. Lang.: Eng.   2232

Deetz, Stanley
Plays/librettos/scripts
Bertolt Brecht and the Expressionists. Germany. 1919-1944. Lang.: Eng.   955

Deevy, Teresa
Plays/librettos/scripts
Biography of playwright Teresa Deevy. Ireland. 1894-1963. Lang.: Eng.   2665

Deficit
Performance/production
Productions of *Deficit* by István Csurka. Hungary: Szolnok, Budapest. 1970-1985. Lang.: Hun.   1833

Dégi, István
Performance/production
Milán Füst's *Margit kisasszony (Miss Margit)* directed by István Dégi at Játékszin. Hungary: Budapest. 1986. Lang.: Hun.   1901

Reviews of *Margit kisasszony (Miss Margit)*, *Az Ibolya (The Violet)*, *Az Árny (The Ghost)* and *Róza néni (Aunt Rosa)*. Hungary: Budapest. 1985-1986. Lang.: Hun.   1916

Review of *Margit kisasszony (Miss Margit)* directed by István Dégi. Hungary: Budapest. 1986. Lang.: Hun.   1941

Dejmek, Kazimierz
Performance/production
Kazimierz Dejmek directs Wyspiański's *Wesele (The Wedding)*, Teatr Polski. Poland: Warsaw. 1984. Lang.: Pol.   2057

Dekker, Thomas
Plays/librettos/scripts
Religion and popular entertainment in *The Virgin Martyr* by Philip Massinger and Thomas Dekker. England: London. 1620-1625. Lang.: Eng.   2468

Post-structuralist insights on sexuality and transgression in transvestite roles in Jacobean plays. England: London. 1600-1625. Lang.: Eng.   2476

Research/historiography
Review of introductions to the plays of Thomas Dekker by Cyrus Hoy. England: London. USA. 1600-1980. Lang.: Eng.   1185

Del Monaco, Mario
Performance/production
Significance of the translation in recordings of Verdi's *Otello*. USA. 1902-1978. Lang.: Eng.   3812

Del Rossi, Angelo
Administration
Papermill Playhouse's executive producer discusses producing musicals. USA: Millburn, NJ. Lang.: Eng.   3572

Del Valle-Inclán, Ramón
SEE
Valle-Inclán, Ramón del.

Delacorte Theatre (New York, NY)
Performance/production
Reviews of Shakespeare's *Twelfth Night*, staged by Wilford Leach. USA: New York, NY. 1986. Lang.: Eng.   2217

Delaney, Shelagh
Theory/criticism
Assessment of critic Kenneth Tynan's works. UK-England. 1950-1960. Lang.: Eng.   3136

Delcampe, Armond
Performance/production
Directors discuss staging of plays by Paul Claudel. France. Belgium. 1985. Lang.: Fre.   1723

Deleuze, Gilles
Plays/librettos/scripts
Deconstructionist analysis of *Riccardo III* by Carmelo Bene. Italy. France. Lang.: Eng.   2690

Delgado Vásquez, Mario
Performance/production
Interview with Mario Delgado Vásquez, director of Cuatrotablas. Peru: Lima. 1971-1985. Lang.: Hun.   769

Delgado, Judith
Relation to other fields
Evaluation and social effects of improvisational drama program. USA: Newark, NJ. Lang.: Eng.   1151

Delicate Balance, A
Theory/criticism
Edward Albee's development of realistic setting for absurdist drama. USA. 1964-1980. Lang.: Eng.   3148

DeMille, Agnes
Design/technology
Interview with three female lighting designers. USA. 1946-1983. Lang.: Eng.   357

Dempster, Curt
Plays/librettos/scripts
Artists react to *New York Times* condemnation of current playwriting. USA. 1984. Lang.: Eng.   2888

Denby, David
Theory/criticism
Theatre professionals challenge assertions that theatre is a weaker form of communication than film. USA: New York, NY. 1985. Lang.: Eng.   1225

Dench, Judi
Performance/production
An exploration of Brecht's *Gestus*. Germany. Lang.: Eng.   1758

Eileen Atkins, Judi Dench, Wendy Hiller and Barbara Jefford discuss playing Saint Joan in Shaw's play. UK-England: London. 1936-1983. Lang.: Eng.   2153

Dengaku
Performance/production
Anthology of Japanese popular entertainments. Japan: Tokyo. 1986. Lang.: Jap.   3342

Denis, Jean-Luc
Performance/production
Three directors' versions of *Les cauchemars du grand monde (Nightmares of High Society)* by Gilbert Turp. Canada: Montreal, PQ. 1984. Lang.: Fre.   1672

Design/technology — cont'd

Description of an outdoor Shakespeare theatre project. Canada: Toronto, ON. 1983-1986. Lang.: Eng.   1678

Technical innovation, scenography and cabaret in relation to political and social conditions. Czechoslovakia. 1781-1986. Lang.: Eng.   1697

Analysis and interpretation of the staging of *The Castle of Perseverance* based on original stage plan drawing. England. 1343-1554. Lang.: Eng.   1708

Relationship between theatre and early photography. France. 1818-1899. Lang.: Fre.   1748

Contribution of stage directions concerning stage design and directing to producing plays by Friedrich Dürrenmatt. Switzerland. 1949-1986. Lang.: Eng.   2097

The organization of the Olympiad Arts Festival. USA: Los Angeles, CA. 1984. Lang.: Eng.   2281

Analysis of reviews of 1929 *Dynamo* by Eugene O'Neill suggest strong production of a weak play. USA: New York, NY. 1929. Lang.: Eng.   2311

Detailed history of the 1914 Hagenbeck Wallace Circus season. USA: St. Louis, MO, Youngstown, OH, Sturgis, MI. 1914. Lang.: Eng.   3388

Classification and description of Quebec pageants. Canada. 1900-1960. Lang.: Fre.   3423

Review of the 1985 season of the Chinese National Opera. China, People's Republic of: Beijing. 1985. Lang.: Chi.   3522

Artistic and technological differences in presenting opera for stage and television. Canada. 1960-1980. Lang.: Eng.   3714

New designs for the Seattle Opera production of *Der Ring des Nibelungen* by Richard Wagner. USA: Seattle, WA. 1986. Lang.: Eng.   3837

Resource book on construction and performance in puppetry. Lang.: Eng.   3961

Plays/librettos/scripts
Interview with theatre professionals on successful writing and production. USA. 1986. Lang.: Eng.   2932

Ideology of commercial television. Canada. USA. 1965-1983. Lang.: Eng.   3281

Reference materials
A list of all articles that have appeared in *STTF-medlemsblad* 1977-1985 and *ProScen* 1986. Sweden. 1977-1986. Lang.: Swe.   1032

Illustrated guide to Actor's Museum. Hungary: Budapest. 1850-1986. Lang.: Hun.   2990

Review of 1985 dissertations. China, People's Republic of: Beijing. 1985. Lang.: Chi.   3545

Relation to other fields
The work of painter and scene designer Claude Gillot. France. 1673-1722. Lang.: Ita.   1084

Views of designer and critic Franciszek Siedlecki. Poland. 1909-1934. Lang.: Pol.   1116

Theory/criticism
Analysis of audience reaction to theatre spaces. 1950-1980. Lang.: Chi.   1198

Western influences on theatrical development in Turkey. Turkey. 1524-1986. Lang.: Ita.   1221

Eastern and Western influences on Turkish theatre. Turkey. 1000-1986. Lang.: Ita.   1222

Desire Under the Elms
Performance/production
Performances of *Hair*, directed by János Sándor, and *Desire Under the Elms*, directed by Géza Bodolay at the National Theatre of Szeged. Hungary: Szeged. 1986. Lang.: Hun.   1959

Plays/librettos/scripts
Concept of tragic character in Eugene O'Neill's *Desire Under the Elms*. USA. 1924. Lang.: Eng.   2907

The Peasants by Władysław Reymont as possible source for O'Neill's version of the lustful stepmother play. USA. 1902-1924. Lang.: Eng.   2930

Destinn, Emmy
Performance/production
Reviews of 10 vintage recordings of complete operas on LP. USA. 1906-1925. Lang.: Eng.   3792

Destoop, Jacques
Performance/production
Evolution of *Le Cantique des cantiques (The Song of Songs)* directed by Jacques Destoop at Comédie-Française. France: Paris. 1986. Lang.: Fre.   1721

Detonación, La (Detonation, The)
Plays/librettos/scripts
Radical subjectivism in three plays by Antonio Buero Vallejo: *La Fundación (The Foundation)*, *La Detonación (The Detonation)* and *Jueces en la noche (Judges at Night)*. Spain. 1974-1979. Lang.: Eng.   2797

Detroit Repertory Company (Detroit, MI)
Administration
Alternative funding for small theatres previously dependent on government subsidy. USA: St. Louis, MO, New York, NY, Los Angeles, CA, Detroit, MI. 1985. Lang.: Eng.   103

Deutsche Oper Ballet (West Berlin)
Performance/production
Career of choreographer Kenneth MacMillan. Europe. USA. 1929-1986. Lang.: Eng.   1302

Deutsche Oper Berlin (West Berlin)
Performance/production
Collaboration of Peter Hemmings and Götz Friedrich in Los Angeles' opera season. USA: Los Angeles, CA. 1985. Lang.: Eng.   3836

Deutsches Theater (East Berlin)
Institutions
Autobiographical documents by personnel of the Deutsches Theater. Germany: Berlin. 1884-1955. Lang.: Ger.   1577

Performance/production
Description of Georg Büchner's *Dantons Tod (Danton's Death)* staged by Alexander Lang at Deutsches Theater. Germany, East: Berlin, East. 1984. Lang.: Ger.   1763

Development
Audience
Several New York theatres discuss their student outreach programs. USA: New York, NY. 1984. Lang.: Eng.   201

Deverell, Rex
Basic theatrical documents
Text of *Beyond Batoche* by Rex Deverell. Canada: Regina, SK. 1985. Lang.: Eng.   218

Plays/librettos/scripts
Symbolism and allusion in *Boiler Room Suite* by Rex Deverell. Canada: Regina, SK. 1977. Lang.: Eng.   934

Rex Deverell's approach to history in plays about Louis Riel. Canada: Regina, SK. 1985. Lang.: Eng.   2437

Devij bog (Maiden God, The)
Plays/librettos/scripts
Poetic language in plays of Velimir Chlebnikov. Russia. 1885-1922. Lang.: Rus.   964

Devil Upon Two Sticks, The
Plays/librettos/scripts
Character source for Dr. Last in Samuel Foote's play *The Devil Upon Two Sticks*. England. 1768-1774. Lang.: Eng.   2522

Devil's Charter, The
Plays/librettos/scripts
Machiavellian ideas in *The Devil's Charter* by Barnaby Barnes. England. 1584-1607. Lang.: Eng.   2500

Devine, George
Performance/production
Career of actress Billie Whitelaw, interpreter of Samuel Beckett's plays. UK-England. 1956-1986. Lang.: Eng.   2172

Devlin, Anne
Institutions
Place of women in Britain's National Theatre. UK-England: London. 1986. Lang.: Eng.   1588

Performance/production
Collection of newspaper reviews by London theatre critics. UK. 1986. Lang.: Eng.   2101

Review of alternative theatre productions. UK-England: London. 1986. Lang.: Eng.   2108

Collection of newspaper reviews by London theatre critics. UK-England: London. 1986. Lang.: Eng.   2110

Plays/librettos/scripts
Current state of women's playwriting. UK-England. 1985-1986. Lang.: Eng.   2830

Devrient, Emil
Performance/production
Playing Hamlet at the Burgtheater. Austria: Vienna. 1803-1985. Lang.: Ger.   1654

Devries, Rosa
Performance/production
Details of Luigi Arditi's U.S. and Canada tour with the New York Opera Company. USA. Canada: Montreal, PQ, Toronto, ON. 1853-1854. Lang.: Eng. 3819

Dexter, John
Performance/production
Director John Dexter and impresario Eddie Kulukundis discuss the formation of the New Theatre Company. UK-England: London. 1986. Lang.: Eng. 2144

Diabel włoski (Italian Devil)
Relation to other fields
Commentary on *Diabel włoski (Italian Devil)* by Stanisław Potocki. Poland. 1772-1821. Lang.: Pol. 3922

Diadia Vania (Uncle Vanya)
Performance/production
Performances of George Bernard Shaw's *Candida* and Čechov's *Diadia Vania (Uncle Vanya)*, under the title *Ványa bácsi*, at Pécs National Theatre. Hungary: Pécs. 1985. Lang.: Hun. 1893
Production of *Ványa bácsi (Uncle Vanya)* by Čechov. Hungary: Pécs. 1985. Lang.: Hun. 1918
Plays/librettos/scripts
Analysis of Čechov's plays. Lang.: Hun. 2346
Study of the dramatic nature of Čechov's plays. Lang.: Hun. 2347

Diaghilev, Sergei
SEE
Diaghilew, Serge de.

Diaghilew, Serge de
Performance/production
On the career of dancer and actress Ida Rubinstein, member of Diaghilew's 'Russian Seasons'. Russia. France. 1885-1960. Lang.: Rus. 1311
European career of Serge de Diaghilew. Russia. France. 1872-1929. Lang.: Ita. 1312

Dialectics
Plays/librettos/scripts
Waiting for Godot as an assessment of the quality of life of the couple. France. UK-Ireland. 1931-1958. Lang.: Eng. 2557
Theory/criticism
Reflections on theatre criticism. USSR. 1980. Lang.: Rus. 1247
Analysis of dramatic composition: the text perceived and the text performed. Lang.: Fre. 3075
Dramatic text as read by actor, director, dramaturg, critic and scholar. Lang.: Fre. 3076
Attempt to establish a more theatrical view of drama. Lang.: Fre. 3078
Coriolanus from Bertolt Brecht's viewpoint. Germany. 1898-1956. Lang.: Chi. 3105
Decreasing importance of the playwright in Italian theatre. Italy. 1900-1984. Lang.: Fre. 3119

Diálogo secreto (Secret Dialogue)
Plays/librettos/scripts
Poor reception of *Diálogo secreto (Secret Dialogue)* by Antonio Buero Vallejo in Spain. Spain: Madrid. 1984. Lang.: Eng. 2791
Refutes critical position that Antonio Buero Vallejo's *Diálogo secreto (Secret Dialogue)* is unbelievable. Spain: Madrid. 1984. Lang.: Eng. 2799

Díaz, Jorge
Plays/librettos/scripts
Marginal characters in plays of Jorge Díaz, Egon Wolff and Luis Alberto Heiremans. Chile. 1960-1971. Lang.: Eng. 2442

Diaz, Joyce
Performance/production
Collection of newspaper reviews by London theatre critics. UK-England: London. 1986. Lang.: Eng. 2121

Díaz, Justino
Performance/production
The Franco Zeffirelli film of *Otello* by Giuseppe Verdi, an account of the production. Italy: Rome. 1985-1986. Lang.: Eng. 3758

Dicenta, José Fernando
Plays/librettos/scripts
Thematic analysis of *La Jaula (The Cage)* by José Fernando Dicenta. Spain. 1971-1984. Lang.: Eng. 2800

Dickens, Charles
Performance/production
Collection of newspaper reviews by London theatre critics. UK-England: London. 1986. Lang.: Eng. 2110

Reviews of *The Life and Adventures of Nicholas Nickleby*, book by Charles Dickens, adapted by David Edgar, staged by Trevor Nunn. USA: New York, NY. 1986. Lang.: Eng. 2271
Theory/criticism
The popularity of Charles Dicken's *A Christmas Carol* in American theatres. USA. 1984. Lang.: Eng. 3143

Dickinson, Bob
Design/technology
Lighting designer Bob Dickinson talks about lighting the 1986 Oscars ceremony. USA: Los Angeles, CA. 1983-1986. Lang.: Eng. 3263

Dictionaries
Administration
Notes and memoirs of secretary of theatrical board. Italy: Parma. 1881-1898. Lang.: Ita. 53
Performance/production
Reconstruction of the life of Italian actors and acting companies with a vocabulary of their jargon. Italy. 1885-1940. Lang.: Ita. 753
Plays/librettos/scripts
Study of all aspects of Italian opera. Italy. 1810-1920. Lang.: Fre. 3889
Reference materials
Lexicon of world theatre. 700 B.C.-1986 A.D. Lang.: Ger. 995
Dictionary of the life and work of Tsubouchi Shōyō. Japan: Tokyo. 1859-1986. Lang.: Jap. 1027
Dictionary of opera. Lang.: Rus. 3907
Dictionary of opera premieres. 1941-1960. Lang.: Rus. 3908

Diderot, Denis
Performance/production
Theatricality on and off-stage. Lang.: Eng. 649
Analysis of actor/character relationship in *L'impromptu de Versailles (The Impromptu of Versailles)* by Molière. France. 1663. Lang.: Eng. 726
Theory/criticism
Selection and analysis of Diderot's theoretical writings about theatre. France. 1713-1834. Lang.: Cat. 3101

Dietrich, Marlene
Performance/production
Edith és Marlene (Edith and Marlene) by Éva Pataki at Comedy Theatre. Hungary: Budapest. 1986. Lang.: Hun. 1831
Life and films of actor and director Willi Forst. Austria: Vienna. Germany: Berlin. 1903-1980. Lang.: Ger. 3223
Éva Pataki's *Edith és Marlene (Edith and Marlene)* directed by Márta Mészáros, Pest National Theatre. Hungary: Budapest. 1986. Lang.: Hun. 3603

Dill, Sam B.
Performance/production
History of John Robinson Circus. USA. 1925. Lang.: Eng. 3385

Dillon, Charles
Performance/production
World tour by English tragedian Charles Dillon. USA.. 1861-1867. Lang.: Eng. 2199

Dillon, H.R.
Plays/librettos/scripts
Analysis of plays by Canadian soldiers in World War I. Canada. UK. 1901-1918. Lang.: Eng. 936

Dillon, John
Performance/production
Director John Dillon on his Japanese production of *Death of a Salesman* by Arthur Miller. Japan. 1984. Lang.: Eng. 2005

Dillon, Melinda
Performance/production
Director of original production discusses Edward Albee's *Who's Afraid of Virginia Woolf?*. USA: New York, NY. 1962. Lang.: Eng. 2303

Dime Museum
Institutions
History of the Dime Museums. USA: Milwaukee, WI. 1882-1916. Lang.: Eng. 3324

Dimitri
Performance/production
A photographic essay of 42 soloists and groups performing mime or gestural theatre. 1986. 3290

Dindon, Le (Sauce for the Goose)
Performance/production
Collection of newspaper reviews by London theatre critics. UK-England: London. 1986. Lang.: Eng. 2122

Dinesen, Isak
Basic theatrical documents
Annotated text of *The Revenge of Truth* by Isak Dinesen. Denmark. 1914. Lang.: Eng. 4002

Relation to other fields
Introduction to *The Revenge of Truth* by Isak Dinesen. Denmark. Kenya. 1885-1985. Lang.: Eng. 4010

Ding, Xilin
Plays/librettos/scripts
Influence of Western and Chinese traditional theatre upon works of Ding Xilin. China. 1923-1962. Lang.: Chi. 2446

Dining Table with Romeo and Freesia, The
SEE
Romeo to Freesia no aru shokutaku.

Dinner Party Theatre (Queens, NY)
Institutions
History of Black Spectrum. USA: New York, NY. 1970-1986. Lang.: Eng. 1603

Dinner theatres
Institutions
Founding member discusses dinner-theatre Comedy Asylum. Canada: Fredericton, NB. 1982-1986. Lang.: Eng. 1559

Diósgyőri Várszinpad (Diósgyőr)
Performance/production
Lakat alá lányokat (Lock Up Your Daughters), a stage adaptation of Henry Fielding's *Rape Upon Rape*, directed by Imre Halasi. Hungary: Diósgyőr. 1986. Lang.: Hun. 3600

Directing
SEE
Staging.

Director training
SEE
Training, director.

Directories
Reference materials
Accounts of non-English-speaking artists. Australia. 1986. Lang.: Eng. 1001

Lists 292 research collections and information sources, most of which are open to the public. UK. 1985-1986. Lang.: Eng. 1034

Guide to theatrical services and productions. UK-England. 1985-1986. Lang.: Eng. 1035

Directory of member organizations of ART/NY. USA: New York, NY. 1986. Lang.: Eng. 1037

A directory of services available to Dramatists Guild members. USA. 1986. 1038

List of institutional theatres. USA. 1986. 1039

Directory of support sources for the playwright. USA. 1986. 1041

Comprehensive list of rehearsal and performance spaces. USA: New York, NY. Lang.: Eng. 1042

Listing of repertory schedules, contact and contract information. USA. 1986. Lang.: Eng. 1045

Directors
SEE
Staging.

Dirickson, Barbara
Performance/production
Five actors who work solely in regional theatre. 1961-1984. Lang.: Eng. 1633

Discipline, A
Plays/librettos/scripts
Biography of playwright Teresa Deevy. Ireland. 1894-1963. Lang.: Eng. 2665

Discographies
Performance/production
Biography of singer Frank Sinatra. USA. 1915-1984. Lang.: Eng. 3180

Stills from telecast performance of *Goya*. List of principals, conductor and production staff included. USA: Washington, DC. 1986. Lang.: Eng. 3791

Photographs, cast list, synopsis, and discography of Metropolitan Opera radio broadcast performances. USA: New York, NY. 1986. Lang.: Eng. 3794

Stills from telecast performances. List of principals, conductor and production staff included. USA: New York, NY. 1986. Lang.: Eng. 3795

Stills from telecast performance of *Candide* by New York City Opera. USA: New York, NY. 1986. Lang.: Eng. 3796

Photographs, cast list, synopsis, and discography of Metropolitan Opera radio broadcast performances. USA: New York, NY. 1986. Lang.: Eng. 3797

Reference materials
Stills from telecast performances of *Hänsel und Gretel*. List of principals, conductor and production staff included. Austria: Vienna. 1986. Lang.: Eng. 3909

Dispara, Flanaghan! (Shoot, Flanaghan!)
Plays/librettos/scripts
Analysis of the six published dramatic works by Jordi Teixidor. Spain-Catalonia. 1970-1985. Lang.: Cat. 2809

Dispute, La (Dispute, The)
Performance/production
Staging of plays by Marivaux compared to textual analysis. France. 1723-1981. Lang.: Fre. 1746

Ditrói, Mór
Institutions
History of Vigszinház (Comedy Theatre). Hungary: Budapest. 1896-1916. Lang.: Hun. 502

Diving
Plays/librettos/scripts
Review of five published plays by Margaret Hollingsworth. Canada. Lang.: Eng. 2440

Dmuszewski, Adam
Performance/production
Business dealings of actor Adam Dmuszewski. Poland. 1799-1883. Lang.: Pol. 2018

Dni Turbinych (Days of the Turbins)
Performance/production
Michajl Bulgakov's ties with Moscow Art Theatre. Russia: Moscow. 1891-1940. Lang.: Rus. 785

Dobozy, Imre
Performance/production
Adaptation for the stage by Anikó Vagda and Katalin Vajda of Imre Dobozy's screenplay *Villa Negra*, directed at Játékszin by Miklós Szurdi. Hungary: Budapest. 1986. Lang.: Hun. 1870

Docherty, Peter
Design/technology
Designers discuss regional productions of *Side-by-Side by Sondheim*. USA. 1984. Lang.: Eng. 3593

Doctor Faustus
Plays/librettos/scripts
Jerzy Grotowski and his adaptation of *Doctor Faustus*. Poland. 1964. Lang.: Eng. 2740

Reference materials
List of 37 productions of 23 Renaissance plays, with commentary. UK. USA. New Zealand. 1986. Lang.: Eng. 3000

Dodin, L.
Performance/production
Correlation of scenery and direction. USSR: Leningrad. 1980-1986. Lang.: Rus. 2335

Dödsdansen (Dance of Death, The)
Audience
Analysis of *Dödsdansen (The Dance of Death)*. Sweden. 1900. Lang.: Eng. 1452

Doepp, John
Design/technology
Designers discuss regional productions of *Ain't Misbehavin'*. USA. 1984-1986. Lang.: Eng. 3591

Dog in the Manger, The
SEE
Perro del hortelano, El.

Dogg's Hamlet, Cahoot's Macbeth
Plays/librettos/scripts
Links between Shakespeare's *Macbeth* and Tom Stoppard's *Dogg's Hamlet, Cahoot's Macbeth*. UK-England. 1979-1986. Lang.: Eng. 2843

Dōjōji
Performance/production
Nō actor's preparation and rehearsal for the play, *Dōjōji*. Japan. 1983. Lang.: Eng. 1413

Dol'še veka dlitsja den', I (Day Lasts Longer than a Century, A)
Performance/production
Actor M.A. Ul'janov in *I dol'še veka dlitsja den' (A Day Lasts Longer than a Century)* at Teat'r im. Je. Vachtangova. USSR: Moscow. 1980-1986. Lang.: Rus. 2327

Dramatic structure — cont'd

Reconstruction of staging of Act I, *The Spanish Tragedy* by Thomas Kyd. England: London. 1592. Lang.: Eng. 1703

Visual patterns of staging in Shakespeare's *Troilus and Cressida*. England: London. 1597-1600. Lang.: Eng. 1704

Interview with dramaturg Arthur Ballet. USA. 1950-1986. Lang.: Eng. 2248

Martin Esslin discusses dramaturg's need to balance roles of naive spectator and informed academic. USA: Waterford, CT, San Francisco, CA. 1936-1986. Lang.: Eng. 2249

Dramaturg Oskar Eustis on confronting social and aesthetic problems. USA: San Francisco, CA. 1975-1986. Lang.: Eng. 2250

Gitta Honegger on training dramaturgs and the European tradition of dramaturgy. USA: New Haven, CT. 1960-1986. Lang.: Eng. 2251

Dramaturg Richard Nelson on communicating with different kinds of directors. USA: New York, NY. 1979-1986. Lang.: Eng. 2252

Interview with dramaturg Russell Vandenbroucke. USA: Los Angeles, CA. 1974-1985. Lang.: Eng. 2253

Interview with dramaturg Anne Cattaneo. USA: New York, NY. 1971-1986. Lang.: Eng. 2254

Review of Eugene O'Neill's *Long Day's Journey Into Night* directed by Jonathan Miller. USA. 1956-1986. Lang.: Eng. 2264

Chicago dramaturgs acknowledge a common ground in educating their audience. USA: Chicago, IL. 1984-1986. Lang.: Eng. 2274

Explorative structure and manner of performance in avant-garde theatre. USA. 1965. Lang.: Eng. 2277

Mark Bly on the dramaturg's responsibility to question. USA: Minneapolis, MN. 1981-1986. Lang.: Eng. 2294

Plays/librettos/scripts

Influences on Asian theatrical genres. Asia. 500-1985. Lang.: Eng. 920

Popularity of dramatic monologue on stage and television. Australia. 1985. Lang.: Eng. 921

Development of the title character of *The Ecstasy of Rita Joe* by George Ryga, seen in successive drafts. Canada: Vancouver, BC. 1966-1982. Lang.: Eng. 929

Symbolism and allusion in *Boiler Room Suite* by Rex Deverell. Canada: Regina, SK. 1977. Lang.: Eng. 934

Analysis of the plays of Sharon Pollock. Canada. 1971-1983. Lang.: Eng. 935

Religious ideas in the satirical plays of John Marston. England. 1595-1609. Lang.: Eng. 940

Similar dramatic techniques in Ben Jonson's masques and tragedies. England. 1597-1637. Lang.: Eng. 941

Critical confusion regarding *The Revenge of Bussy d'Ambois* by George Chapman. England. 1603. Lang.: Eng. 942

Argument that the Gallican liturgy was a form of drama. France. 500-900. Lang.: Eng. 949

Luis de Góngora's plays as a response to Lope de Vega. Spain. 1561-1627. Lang.: Eng. 968

Development and subsequent decline of the three-act farce. UK-England. 1875-1900. Lang.: Eng. 976

Critical analysis of *Tri devuški v golubom (Three Girls in Blue)* by Ljudmila Petruševskaja. USSR. 1986. Lang.: Rus. 989

Analyses of the plays of Ljudmila Petruševskaja. USSR. 1986. Lang.: Rus. 994

Study of the dramatic nature of Čechov's plays. Lang.: Hun. 2347

Dramatization as an emphasis on character over narrative. 2348

Theoretical discussion of audience participation techniques to break through theatrical illusion. 1985. Lang.: Afr. 2353

Ritualistic elements in the structure of Wole Soyinka's *Death and the King's Horseman*. Africa. 1975. Lang.: Eng. 2359

Interview with author and playwright Mario Vargas Llosa. Argentina. 1952-1986. Lang.: Spa. 2361

Chronotopic analysis of *El beso de la mujer araña (The Kiss of the Spider Woman)* by Manuel Puigi. Argentina. 1976-1986. Lang.: Spa. 2364

Analysis of *Dreams in an Empty City* by Stephen Sewell. Australia: Adelaide. Lang.: Eng. 2375

Analysis of plays by David Williamson. Australia. 1976-1985. Lang.: Eng. 2379

Analysis of *The Touch of Silk* and *Granite Peak* by Betty Roland. Australia. 1928-1981. Lang.: Eng. 2387

Interplay of signs of violence in Augusto Boal's *Torquemada*. Brazil. 1971. Lang.: Eng. 2404

Structure and characterization in the plays of W.O. Mitchell. Canada. 1975. Lang.: Eng. 2408

Literary and popular theatrical forms in the plays of Rick Salutin. Canada: Montreal, PQ, Toronto, ON. 1976-1981. Lang.: Eng. 2411

Analysis of *As Is* by William Hoffman and *The Dolly* by Robert Locke. Canada: Toronto, ON. 1985. Lang.: Eng. 2419

Examines *Ne blâmez jamais les Bédouins (Don't Blame It on the Bedouins)* as a post-modernist play. Canada. 1980. Lang.: Fre. 2432

Compares Michel Tremblay's *Albertine en cing temps (Albertine in Five Times)* to Marcel Proust's *A la recherche du temps perdu (Remembrance of Things Past)*. Canada. 1984. 2436

Rex Deverell's approach to history in plays about Louis Riel. Canada: Regina, SK. 1985. Lang.: Eng. 2437

Influence of Western and Chinese traditional theatre upon works of Ding Xilin. China. 1923-1962. Lang.: Chi. 2446

Analysis of one-act play structures. China. 1500-1980. Lang.: Chi. 2447

Religion and popular entertainment in *The Virgin Martyr* by Philip Massinger and Thomas Dekker. England: London. 1620-1625. Lang.: Eng. 2468

Shakespeare's complex, unconventional heroines in *All's Well that Ends Well* and *Measure for Measure*. England. 1603. Lang.: Eng. 2469

Analysis of theophany in English *Corpus Christi* plays. England. 1350-1550. Lang.: Eng. 2472

Analysis, *As You Like It* II:i by William Shakespeare. England. 1598. Lang.: Eng. 2474

Possible influence of Christopher Marlowe's plays upon those of William Shakespeare. England. 1580-1620. Lang.: Eng. 2478

Essays on Shakespeare's *All's Well that Ends Well*. England. 1603. Lang.: Eng, Fre. 2485

Analysis of George Etherege's play, *The Comical Revenge*. England. 1664. Lang.: Eng. 2486

Allegorical romantic conventions in John Ford's *The Broken Heart*. England. 1633. Lang.: Eng. 2497

Analysis of *The Winter's Tale* by Shakespeare. England: London. 1604. Lang.: Eng. 2502

Origin of Spanish setting in Middleton and Rowley's *The Changeling*. England. 1607-1622. Lang.: Eng. 2513

Analysis of Henry Fielding's play *The Author's Farce*. England. 1730. Lang.: Eng. 2516

Violation of genre divisions in the plays of Ben Jonson. England: London. 1606-1610. Lang.: Eng. 2525

Comparison of Shakespeare's *Othello* with New Comedy of Rome. England. 1604. Lang.: Eng. 2528

Aristocratic culture and 'country-house' poetic theme in Massinger's *A New Way to Pay Old Debts*. England. 1621. Lang.: Eng. 2531

Treatment of historical figures in plays by William Shakespeare, Christopher Marlowe and George Peele. England. 1560-1650. Lang.: Eng. 2534

Revision of dramaturgy and stagecraft in Restoration adaptations of Shakespeare. England: London. 1660-1690. Lang.: Eng. 2535

Essays on dramatic form, genre and language. France. 1500-1985. Lang.: Fre. 2545

Beckett as writer and director. France. UK. 1947-1985. Lang.: Fre. 2546

Various implications of 'waiting' in Samuel Beckett's *Waiting for Godot*. France. 1953. Lang.: Eng. 2555

Theme of fragmentation in *Lorenzaccio* by Alfred de Musset. France. 1834. Lang.: Eng. 2558

Textual study of *La Farce de Maître Pierre Pathelin (The Farce of Master Pierre Pathelin)*. France. 1485-1970. Lang.: Fre. 2561

Analysis of *L'Aigle à deux têtes (The Eagle With Two Heads)* by Jean Cocteau. France. 1889-1963. Lang.: Cat. 2565

Comparative analysis of the works of Maurice Maeterlinck and William Shakespeare. France. 1590-1911. Lang.: Eng. 2566

Dialectical method in the plays of Molière. France. 1666. Lang.: Eng. 2567

Forerunner of contemporary theatre: *Axël* by Villiers de l'Isle-Adam. France. 1862-1894. Lang.: Fre. 2579

Dramatic structure — cont'd

Study of *Bérénice*, *Athalie* and *Bajazet* by Jean Racine. France. 1670-1691. Lang.: Fre.   2583

Biography of playwright Christian Dietrich Grabbe. Germany. 1801-1836. Lang.: Ger.   2595

Comedies of Tieck and Brentano representing German Romanticism. Germany. 1795-1850. Lang.: Rus.   2602

Comparative analysis of *Elektra* by Hugo von Hofmannsthal and its sources. Germany. 1909. Lang.: Eng.   2603

Applying Brecht's dramatic principles to the plays of Euripides. Germany, East. Greece. 450 B.C.-1956 A.D.   2614

Work of playwright Stefan Schütz. Germany, West. 1944-1986. Lang.: Eng.   2625

Interpretation of final scenes of Sophocles' *Philoctetes*. Greece. 409 B.C. Lang.: Heb.   2630

Program notes from Heinz-Uwe Haus's production of *Arturo Ui*. Greece. 1985.   2631

Aristophanes and his conception of comedy. Greece. 446-385 B.C. Lang.: Fre.   2635

Masked god as tragic subject in works of Aeschylus, Sophocles and Euripides. Greece. 499-401 B.C. Lang.: Fre.   2636

Analysis of Mihály Vörösmarty's *A bújdosók (Refugees)*. Hungary. 1800-1855. Lang.: Hun.   2639

Plot, structure and national character of *Bánk Bán* by József Katona. Hungary. Lang.: Hun.   2655

Influence of artist Jack Yeats on playwright Samuel Beckett. Ireland. France. 1945-1970. Lang.: Eng.   2663

Tension between text and realization in Pirandello's *Sei personaggi in cerca d'autore (Six Characters in Search of an Author)*. Italy. 1911-1929. Lang.: Fre.   2685

Influence of Luigi Pirandello's work in Catalonia. Italy. Spain-Catalonia. 1867-1985. Lang.: Spa, Cat.   2706

Role-playing and madness in Pirandello's *Enrico Quarto (Henry IV)*. Italy. 1922. Lang.: Fre.   2709

Analysis of *En Folkefiende (An Enemy of the People)* by Henrik Ibsen. Norway. 1882. Lang.: Eng.   2728

Absence of the author in Henrik Ibsen's *Vildanden (The Wild Duck)*. Norway. 1882. Lang.: Eng.   2729

Levels of time in *La señorita de Tacna (The Lady from Tacna)* by Mario Vargas Llosa. Peru. Lang.: Spa.   2731

Prison camp passion play with Christ as a labor organizer. Philippines: Davao City. 1983-1985. Lang.: Eng.   2732

Analysis of *Grupa Laokoona (The Laocoön Group)* by Tadeusz Różewicz and *Tsaplia (The Heron)* by Vasilij Aksënov. Poland. USSR. 1961-1979. Lang.: Eng.   2738

Analysis of plays of Kruczkowski, Szaniawski and Gałczyński. Poland. 1940-1949. Lang.: Pol.   2746

Philosophical aspects and structure of plays by Bogusław Schaeffer. Poland. 1929-1986. Lang.: Pol.   2749

Analysis of the play *Operetka (Operetta)* by Witold Gombrowicz. Poland. 1986. Lang.: Pol.   2758

Analysis of the major plays of Maksim Gorkij. Russia. 1868-1936. Lang.: Chi.   2769

System of genres in the work of A.N. Ostrovskij. Russia. 1823-1886. Lang.: Rus.   2772

Use of chorus in Bartho Smit's *Don Juan onder die Boere (Don Juan Among the 'Boere')*. South Africa, Republic of. 1970-1986. Lang.: Afr.   2776

Parody and satire in Ramón del Valle-Inclán's *La Cabeza del dragón (The Dragon's Head)*. Spain. 1909. Lang.: Eng.   2798

Analysis of the six published dramatic works by Jordi Teixidor. Spain-Catalonia. 1970-1985. Lang.: Cat.   2809

Analysis of Josep Palau's plays and theoretical writings. Spain-Catalonia. 1917-1982. Lang.: Cat.   2814

The presentation of atheism in August Strindberg's *The Father*. Sweden. 1887. Lang.: Eng.   2821

Biblical and Swedenborgian influences on the development of August Strindberg's chamber play *Påsk (Easter)*. Sweden. 1900. Lang.: Eng.   2827

Narratological analysis of Harold Pinter's *Old Times*. UK-England. 1971. Lang.: Eng.   2842

Interview with playwright Howard Barker. UK-England. 1981-1985. Lang.: Eng.   2845

Playwright Harold Pinter's use of dramatic reversals and surprise. UK-England. 1960-1977. Lang.: Eng.   2850

Playwright Simon Gray's journal about the production of his play *The Common Pursuit*. UK-England. 1983. Lang.: Eng.   2858

Argument for coherence of *Arms and the Man* by George Bernard Shaw. UK-England: London. 1894. Lang.: Eng.   2863

Analysis of the plot, characters and structure of *The Homecoming* by Harold Pinter. UK-England: London. 1930-1985. Lang.: Cat.   2865

Caryl Churchill combines Brecht's alienation effect with traditional comic structure in *Cloud 9*. UK-England. 1980.   2871

A comparison between Oscar Wilde's *The Importance of Being Earnest* and Tom Stoppard's *Travesties*. UK-England. 1895-1974. Lang.: Eng.   2872

Influence of Aristophanes and Čechov on playwright Simon Gray. UK-England. 1986. Lang.: Eng.   2874

T. S. Eliot's *Murder in the Cathedral* dramatizes Christian theory of history. UK-England. 1935. Lang.: Eng.   2878

Popularity and relevance of Eugene O'Neill. USA. Lang.: Eng.   2894

Analysis of the plays of Edward Albee. USA. 1960-1970. Lang.: Rus.   2914

Analysis of the plays of William Vaughn Moody. USA. 1869-1910. Lang.: Eng.   2917

Comparison of plays by Tennessee Williams, Arthur Miller and Eugene O'Neill. USA. 1949-1956. Lang.: Eng.   2926

Analysis of *Small Craft Warnings*, and report of audience reactions. USA: New York, NY. Spain-Catalonia: Barcelona. 1972-1983. Lang.: Cat.   2929

Theme and narrative structure in plays of Eugene O'Neill, David Belasco, and James A. Herne. USA. 1879-1918. Lang.: Eng.   2933

Mosaic structure of Arthur Kopit's *Indians*. USA. 1969.   2935

Themes and structures of the plays of Lanford Wilson. USA. 1963-1985. Lang.: Eng.   2936

A group of playwrights discuss the one-act play as a form. USA. 1986.   2937

Interview with playwright Israel Horovitz. USA: New York, NY. 1985. Lang.: Eng.   2941

Argument of reversed chronology in Acts I and II of *La Turista* by Sam Shepard. USA. 1967. Lang.: Eng.   2951

Analysis of the plays of Aleksej Gel'man. USSR. 1986. Lang.: Rus.   2959

Conflict and characterization in recent Soviet dramaturgy. USSR. 1970-1980. Lang.: Rus.   2967

Discussion of the hero in modern drama. USSR. 1980-1986. Lang.: Rus.   2969

A review of radio plays written by Linda Zwicker. Canada. 1968-1986. Lang.: Eng.   3184

Critical debate over Timothy Findley's *The Paper People*. Canada. 1967. Lang.: Eng.   3280

Identifies dramatic elements unique to street theatre. USA. 1968-1986. Lang.: Eng.   3354

Differences between *Chan Ta* and *Chuan Ta* drama. China. 1200-1986. Lang.: Chi.   3527

Use of poetic elements to create mood in Beijing opera. China: Beijing. 1030-1984. Lang.: Chi.   3529

Structure of Beijing opera. China, People's Republic of: Beijing. 1983. Lang.: Chi.   3537

Introduction to the folk play, *Mu Lian*. China, People's Republic of: Beijing. 1962-1985. Lang.: Chi.   3538

Play sequels and their characteristics. China, People's Republic of. 1949-1980. Lang.: Chi.   3540

Introduction to Sichuan opera, including translation of a new play. China, People's Republic of. 1876-1983. Lang.: Eng.   3542

Successful Broadway playwrights, lyricists, and composers discuss their hits. USA: New York, NY. 1900-1985. Lang.: Eng.   3631

The power of music to transform the play into living theatre, examples from the work of Paul Green, Clifford Odets, and Maxwell Anderson. USA: New York, NY. 1936. Lang.: Eng.   3632

Origins and influences of *Woyzeck* on Berg's opera *Wozzeck*. Austria: Vienna. 1821-1925. Lang.: Eng.   3855

Interview with opera composer Aulis Sallinen on his current work. Finland: Helsinki. 1975-1986. Lang.: Eng, Fre.   3866

Dramatic structure — cont'd

'Meditation' theme as a dramatic element in Massenet's *Thaïs*.
France. 1894. Lang.: Eng. 3867

Shakespeare's influence on Verdi's operas. Germany. Italy. Austria.
1750-1850. Lang.: Eng. 3878

Study of all aspects of Italian opera. Italy. 1810-1920. Lang.: Fre.
3889

Analysis of the operetta *Firebrand* by Kurt Weill and Ira Gershwin.
USA: New York, NY. Italy: Florence. 1945. Lang.: Eng. 3944

Relation to other fields
Reports and discussions of restricted cultural communication.
Lebanon. Spain-Catalonia. USA. 1985. Lang.: Fre, Spa, Cat. 1111

Theory/criticism
Playwright A. Simukov discusses his craft. USSR. 1986. Lang.: Rus.
1249

Analysis of dramatic composition: the text perceived and the text
performed. Lang.: Fre. 3075

Identifies types of theatrical irony. Lang.: Eng. 3079

Limited usefulness of dramaturgy in staging. Germany, West. 1979.
Lang.: Eng. 3112

Review of *Mi lesz velünk Anton Pavlovics? (What Will Become of
Us, Anton Pavlovič?)* by Miklós Almási. Hungary. 1986. Lang.: Hun.
3114

Dramatic structure in Beijing opera. China, People's Republic of.
1955-1985. Lang.: Chi. 3566

Comparison of Chinese play, *Kan Chien Nu*, with plays of Molière.
China, People's Republic of: Beijing. 1970-1983. Lang.: Chi. 3568

Dramatičeskij Teat'r im N. Gogolia (Moscow)
Performance/production
Autobiography of B.G. Golubovskij, director of the Gogol Theatre.
USSR: Moscow. 1940-1980. Lang.: Rus. 2322

Dramatiska Institutet (Stockholm)
Design/technology
Theory and practice in the training of theatre technicians at
Dramatiska Institutet. Sweden: Stockholm. 1985-1986. Lang.: Swe.
316

Training course for theatre technicians at Dramatiska Institutet.
Sweden: Stockholm. 1985. Lang.: Swe. 318

Dramatists Guild (New York, NY)
Administration
Details of the new Approved Production Contract. USA: New York,
NY. 1985. Lang.: Eng. 94

Dramatists' Co-op (Nova Scotia)
Institutions
Failure of Dramatists' Co-op of Nova Scotia to obtain funding for a
playwrights' colony. Canada: Halifax, NS. 1986. Lang.: Eng. 1545

History of the Dramatists' Co-op of Nova Scotia. Canada. 1976-
1986. Lang.: Eng. 1558

Dramaturgy
Research on the theatre and dramaturgy of Soviet Azerbajdžan.
USSR. 1980-1986. Lang.: Rus. 15

Audience
Socio-aesthetic notes on contemporary theatre and audiences. USSR.
1970-1980. Lang.: Rus. 210

Institutions
Ten years of the Burgtheater under the auspices of Achim Benning.
Austria: Vienna. 1776-1986. Lang.: Ger. 1533

Performance/production
Rhubarb Festival is alternative to playwriting and workshopping
conventions. Canada: Toronto, ON. 1986. Lang.: Eng. 672

Analyses of the major trends in theatre, film and other art forms.
Europe. USA. 1960-1980. Lang.: Rus. 701

Problems of contemporary French theatre. France. 1980-1986. Lang.:
Rus. 717

Examination of Italian avant-garde theatre. Italy. 1970-1985. Lang.:
Ita. 751

Gender roles in the work of female theatre professionals. USA.
1985. Lang.: Eng. 836

Dramaturgy and performance of *nō* drama. Japan. Lang.: Jap. 1415

Collaboration between playwright and dramaturg. Canada. 1986.
Lang.: Eng. 1659

Stratford Festival dramaturg discusses workshop trend. Canada:
Stratford, ON. 1986. Lang.: Eng. 1665

Dramaturg's experience with classical and new productions. Canada:
Toronto, ON. 1986. Lang.: Eng. 1667

Playwright John Lazarus on workshopping new play. Canada. 1986.
Lang.: Eng. 1671

Process and value of play workshops. Canada. 1986. Lang.: Eng.
1676

Playwright/dramaturg Peter Eliot Weiss discusses *Sex Tips for
Modern Girls*. Canada: Vancouver, BC. 1984-1985. Lang.: Eng. 1684

Playwright Betty Jane Wylie's advice on workshopping new plays.
Canada. 1986. Lang.: Eng. 1685

Career of theatrical professional Ede Paulay. Hungary: Budapest.
1852-1864. Lang.: Hun. 1824

Theatrical career of Ede Paulay. Hungary: Budapest. 1878-1894.
Lang.: Hun. 1944

Interview with actor, director and dramaturg Imre Katona of the
Gropius Társulat. Hungary: Budapest. 1961-1985. Lang.: Hun. 1945

Proposal to include theatre critics in pre-production evaluation of
plays. UK-England. USA. Lang.: Eng. 2162

Interview with dramaturg Arthur Ballet. USA. 1950-1986. Lang.:
Eng. 2248

Martin Esslin discusses dramaturg's need to balance roles of naive
spectator and informed academic. USA: Waterford, CT, San
Francisco, CA. 1936-1986. Lang.: Eng. 2249

Dramaturg Oskar Eustis on confronting social and aesthetic
problems. USA: San Francisco, CA. 1975-1986. Lang.: Eng. 2250

Gitta Honegger on training dramaturgs and the European tradition
of dramaturgy. USA: New Haven, CT. 1960-1986. Lang.: Eng. 2251

Dramaturg Richard Nelson on communicating with different kinds of
directors. USA: New York, NY. 1979-1986. Lang.: Eng. 2252

Interview with dramaturg Russell Vandenbroucke. USA: Los Angeles,
CA. 1974-1985. Lang.: Eng. 2253

Interview with dramaturg Anne Cattaneo. USA: New York, NY.
1971-1986. Lang.: Eng. 2254

Chicago dramaturgs acknowledge a common ground in educating
their audience. USA: Chicago, IL. 1984-1986. Lang.: Eng. 2274

Mark Bly on the dramaturg's responsibility to question. USA:
Minneapolis, MN. 1981-1986. Lang.: Eng. 2294

Discussion of contemporary plays being staged in Moscow. USSR:
Moscow. 1980-1986. Lang.: Rus. 2334

Interview on puppet theatre playwriting with B. Goldovskij and J.
Uspenskij. USSR: Moscow. 1986. Lang.: Rus. 3986

Plays/librettos/scripts
Report on a symposium addressing the role of the dramaturg. 918

History of dramaturgy in northern Byelorussia. USSR. 1980-1986.
Lang.: Rus. 988

Predicted changes in Russian dramaturgy and theatre. USSR. 1980-
1986. Lang.: Ukr. 990

Dramaturgy of Michajl Afanasjěvič Bulgakov. USSR. 1925-1940.
Lang.: Rus. 991

On the necessity of preserving the actor's text in a play. USSR.
1986. Lang.: Rus. 992

Life and work of playwright Franz Csokor. Austria. 1920-1939.
Lang.: Rus. 2396

Bulgarian drama after World War II. Bulgaria. 1945-1986. Lang.:
Pol. 2406

Interview with actor-playwright Alan Williams. Canada: Toronto,
ON, Winnipeg, MB. UK-England: Hull. 1976-1986. Lang.: Eng. 2438

Essays on Shakespeare's *All's Well that Ends Well*. England. 1603.
Lang.: Eng, Fre. 2485

Essays on dramatic form, genre and language. France. 1500-1985.
Lang.: Fre. 2545

Problems of modern dramatury exemplified in current Hungarian
theatre. Hungary. Lang.: Hun. 2640

Review of study of experimental plays and playwrights. Hungary.
1967-1983. Lang.: Hun. 2641

Review of a book on modern dramaturgy by playwright Zsuzsa
Radnóti. Hungary. 1967-1983. Lang.: Hun. 2642

World War II and post-war life as major subjects of Polish
dramaturgy. Poland. 1945-1955. Lang.: Pol. 2745

Philosophical aspects and structure of plays by Bogusław Schaeffer.
Poland. 1929-1986. Lang.: Pol. 2749

Development of recent Puerto Rican drama. Puerto Rico. 1960-1980.
Lang.: Spa. 2760

Dramaturgy of Turgenjev. Russia. 1842-1852. Lang.: Rus. 2768

Drumbl, Johann
Relation to other fields
Review article on Johann Drumbl's *Quem Quaeritis: Teatro Sacro dell'Alto Mediaevo*. France. Italy. 900-999. Lang.: Eng. 3031

Drury Lane Theatre (London)
Administration
Analysis of petition drawn up by actors of the Drury Lane Theatre. England. 1705. Lang.: Eng. 32

The Drury Lane Theatre under the management of Charles Fleetwood. England: London. 1734-1745. Lang.: Eng. 35

Basic theatrical documents
Promptbooks for three Dryden plays. England. 1700-1799. Lang.: Eng. 1474

Performance/production
Study of first production of *Jane Shore* by Nicholas Rowe at Drury Lane Theatre. England: London. 1713-1714. Lang.: Eng. 693

Dryden, John
Basic theatrical documents
Promptbooks for three Dryden plays. England. 1700-1799. Lang.: Eng. 1474

Plays/librettos/scripts
Female characterization in Nicholas Rowe's plays. England. 1629-1720. Lang.: Eng. 2475

Development of Restoration musical theatre. England. 1642-1699. Lang.: Eng. 3496

Du Maurier World Stage Festival (Toronto, ON)
Performance/production
Review of international theatre festivals. Spain. Canada: Montreal, PQ, Toronto, ON. 1986. Lang.: Eng. 2077

du Plessis, P.G.
Plays/librettos/scripts
Individual and society in *Die Nag van Legio (The Night of Legio)* by P.G. du Plessis and *Der Besuch der alten Dame (The Visit)* by Friedrich Dürrenmatt. South Africa, Republic of. Switzerland. 1955-1970. Lang.: Afr. 2774

Dubois, René-Daniel
Plays/librettos/scripts
Examines *Ne blâmez jamais les Bédouins (Don't Blame It on the Bedouins)* as a post-modernist play. Canada. 1980. Lang.: Fre. 2432

Dubois, Vashti
Institutions
Vi Higginsen's *Mama I Want to Sing* and history of the Mumbo-Jumbo Theatre Company. USA: New York, NY. 1980-1986. Lang.: Eng. 1601

Ducal Nuptials
SEE
Nopces ducales, Les.

Duchamp, Marcel
Relation to other fields
Influence of Marcel Duchamp's work on Tom Stoppard's radio play, *Artist Descending a Staircase*. UK-England. 1913-1972. Lang.: Eng. 3059

Duchess of Malfi, The
Reference materials
List of 37 productions of 23 Renaissance plays, with commentary. UK. USA. New Zealand. 1986. Lang.: Eng. 3000

Duchess Theatre (London)
Performance/production
Collection of newspaper reviews by London theatre critics. UK-England. 1986. Lang.: Eng. 2115

Collection of newspaper reviews by London theatre critics. UK-England. 1986. Lang.: Eng. 2120

Dudarëv, Aleksej
Performance/production
Aleksej Dudarëv's *Večer (An Evening)* directed by Mátyas Giricz at Józsefvárosi Theatre. Hungary: Budapest. 1986. Lang.: Hun. 1947

Dudley, William
Design/technology
William Dudley's life-like replica of the Bounty for David Essex's *Mutiny!*. UK-England: London. 1986. Lang.: Eng. 3584

Dufford, Stan
Design/technology
The wigmaker's role in regional opera houses. USA. Lang.: Eng. 3658

Duhaime, Julien
Plays/librettos/scripts
Book review of *125 Ans de Theatre au Seminaire de Trois-Rivières*. Canada: Trois-Rivières, PQ. 1985. Lang.: Fre. 2427

Dujardin, Édouard
Performance/production
Influence of Richard Wagner on the work of the French Symbolists. France: Paris. Germany, West: Bayreuth. 1860-1986. Lang.: Eng. 3726

Dukkehjem, Et (Doll's House, A)
Plays/librettos/scripts
Narcissism in *Et Dukkehjem (A Doll's House)* by Henrik Ibsen. Norway. 1879. Lang.: Eng. 2727

Theory/criticism
Influence of Henrik Ibsen on Korean theatre. Korea: Seoul. Norway. 1884-1986. Lang.: Kor. 3120

Dullin, Charles
Performance/production
Essays by and about Charles Dullin. France. 1885-1949. Lang.: Ita. 714

Dumas, Alexandre (fils)
Plays/librettos/scripts
Attitudes toward sexuality in plays from French sources. UK-England. France. Lang.: Eng. 2852

Dumas, Alexandre (père)
Plays/librettos/scripts
Treatment of Napoleon Bonaparte by French and English dramatists. France. England. 1797-1958. Lang.: Eng. 2568

Dumb Waiter, The
Theory/criticism
Overview of Pinter criticism with emphasis on the works' inherent uncertainty. UK. 1957-1986. Lang.: Eng. 3134

Dumont, Richard
Institutions
Interviews with theatre professionals in Quebec. Canada. 1985. Lang.: Fre. 487

Dunaújvárosi Bemutatószínpad (Dunaújváros)
Performance/production
Imre Csiszár directs *Az éjszaka a nappal anyja (Night is the Mother of the Day)* by Lars Norén. Hungary: Dunaújváros. 1986. Lang.: Hun. 1882

Dunaújvárosi Bemutatószinpad (Dunaújváros)
Performance/production
Lanford Wilson's play, *Talley's Folly (Mint két tojás)* directed by András Bálint. Hungary: Dunaújváros. 1986. Lang.: Hun. 1804

Dunbar, Andrea
Institutions
Place of women in Britain's National Theatre. UK-England: London. 1986. Lang.: Eng. 1588

Duncan, Catherine
Plays/librettos/scripts
Study of heroism in verse dramas by Douglas Stewart, Tom Inglis Moore and Catherine Duncan. Australia. 1941-1943. Lang.: Eng. 2383

Dundee Repertory Theatre (UK)
Performance/production
Interview with choreographer Royston Maldoom. UK-Scotland. 1970-1986. Lang.: Eng. 2189

Dunlop, Frank
Administration
Frank Dunlop, director of the Edinburgh Festival, discusses the World Theatre season he has planned. UK-Scotland: Edinburgh. 1986. Lang.: Eng. 83

Institutions
Edinburgh Festival extended by an international season. UK-Scotland: Edinburgh. 1984-1986. Lang.: Eng. 537

Dunn, Tom
Plays/librettos/scripts
Artists react to *New York Times* condemnation of current playwriting. USA. 1984. Lang.: Eng. 2888

Relation to other fields
Argument for increase of financial rewards for playwrights. USA: New York, NY. 1984. Lang.: Eng. 1146

Dunstan, Edward
Performance/production
History of the Edward Dunstan Shakespearean Company, a touring company. UK-England. 1930-1933. Lang.: Eng. 2156

Dupuy, Diane Lynn
Performance/production
Reviews of *A Little Like Magic*, conceived and staged by Diane Lynn Dupuy. USA: New York, NY. 1986. Lang.: Eng. 2213

École des femmes, L' (School for Wives, The) – cont'd

Plays/librettos/scripts

Comparison of John Caryll's *Sir Salomon* with its source, *L'École des femmes (The School for Wives)* by Molière. England. France. 1662-1669. Lang.: Eng.   2527

École Nationale de Théâtre, L' (Montreal, PQ)

Institutions

Interviews with theatre professionals in Quebec. Canada. 1985. Lang.: Fre.   487

Economics

Administration

Promotion and marketing the work of deceased artists. 1986. Lang.: Eng.   16

Analysis of theatrical working conditions. 1986. Lang.: Hun.   19

Berne Convention Protocol in developing countries. Africa. Asia. 1963-1986. Lang.: Eng.   21

Economic conditions of the arts in Australia. Australia. 1986. Lang.: Eng.   23

Theatre as a generator of products, consumers, and financial flow. Belgium. 1983-1984. Lang.: Fre.   26

Berne Convention and copyright in socialist countries. Hungary. 1917-1986. Lang.: Eng.   46

Contribution to the discussion on the Hungarian theatre structure. Hungary. 1985-1986. Lang.: Hun.   50

Economic problems of Hungarian theatre. Hungary. 1985-1986. Lang.: Hun.   51

Berne Convention and copyright in market economy. UK. USA. 1886-1986. Lang.: Eng.   69

Financial problems in British art centers. UK. 1978-1986. Lang.: Eng.   78

Strategies for funding under Reagan's Economic Recovery Act. USA. 1940-1983. Lang.: Eng.   98

Art as a commodity. USA. 1986. Lang.: Eng.   100

Economics and labor relations in performing arts. USA. 1986. Lang.: Eng.   129

Experiments with broadening creative independence and reestablishing economic basis of theatre operations. USSR. 1980-1986. Lang.: Rus.   195

The economics and promotion of the 'early music' revival. Lang.: Eng.   3475

'Cultural tourism' and its importance to opera and classical music. Lang.: Eng.   3639

Audience

History of the Mulgrave Road Co-op theatre. Canada: Guysborough, NS. 1977-1985. Lang.: Eng.   1444

Institutions

Overview of current theatre scene. Denmark: Copenhagen. 1976-1986. Lang.: Swe.   490

Problems and advantages of co-production. USA: New York, NY. 1985. Lang.: Eng.   571

Performance/production

Changes in East Village performance scene. USA: New York, NY. 1975-1985. Lang.: Eng.   3458

Plays/librettos/scripts

Analysis of *Magnificence* by Howard Brenton. England. 1970-1980. Lang.: Eng.   2524

Philosophy of wealth in gilded age plays. USA: New York, NY. 1870-1889. Lang.: Eng.   2950

Reference materials

Profile and problems of Korean theatre people. Korea. 1985-1986. Lang.: Kor.   1029

Relation to other fields

Negative cultural effects of free trade between the U.S. and Canada. 1985-1986. Lang.: Eng.   1054

Report of conference on theatre and economics. Canada: Quebec, PQ. 1985. Lang.: Fre.   1072

Modern business methods in show business. Italy. 1970-1985. Lang.: Ita.   1105

Actor Stanisław Kwaskowski talks about the first years of independent Poland. Poland. 1918-1920. Lang.: Pol.   1121

Essay arguing against the Royal Shakespeare Company's decision not to perform in South Africa. UK-England: London. South Africa, Republic of. 1986. Lang.: Eng.   1136

Goals and strategies of pricing decisions. USA. 1986. Lang.: Eng.   1141

Professional equality in theatrical careers for men and women. USA: New York, NY. 1850-1870. Lang.: Eng.   1143

Argument for increase of financial rewards for playwrights. USA: New York, NY. 1984. Lang.: Eng.   1146

Economic survival of the individual theatre artist. USA: New York, NY. 1983. Lang.: Eng.   1155

The role of the arts in the urban economy. USA. 1986. Lang.: Eng.   1160

Study on ecnomic impact of arts 'industry'. USA: New York, NY. 1983. Lang.: Eng.   1164

Economy Tires Theatre (New York, NY)

Institutions

Profile of Economy Tires Theatre, producing arm of Dance Theatre Workshop. USA: New York, NY. 1978-1983. Lang.: Eng.   563

Ecstasy of Rita Joe, The

Plays/librettos/scripts

Development of the title character of *The Ecstasy of Rita Joe* by George Ryga, seen in successive drafts. Canada: Vancouver, BC. 1966-1982. Lang.: Eng.   929

Amerindian and aborigine characters in the works of white playwrights. Canada. Australia. 1606-1975. Lang.: Eng.   930

Edel, Alfredo

Reference materials

Catalogue of an exhibition of costume designs for Broadway musicals. USA: New York, NY. 1900-1925. Lang.: Eng, Ger.   3635

Edgar, David

Performance/production

Collection of newspaper reviews by London theatre critics. UK-England: London. 1986. Lang.: Eng.   2110

Reviews of *The Life and Adventures of Nicholas Nickleby*, book by Charles Dickens, adapted by David Edgar, staged by Trevor Nunn. USA: New York, NY. 1986. Lang.: Eng.   2271

Edinburgh Festival

Administration

Frank Dunlop, director of the Edinburgh Festival, discusses the World Theatre season he has planned. UK-Scotland: Edinburgh. 1986. Lang.: Eng.   83

Design/technology

Use of the Gemini computerized lighting system used at the Edinburgh Festival. UK-Scotland: Edinburgh. 1980-1986. Lang.: Eng.   332

Institutions

Edinburgh Festival extended by an international season. UK-Scotland: Edinburgh. 1984-1986. Lang.: Eng.   537

Reviews of Edinburgh Festival plays. UK-Scotland: Edinburgh. 1986. Lang.: Eng.   539

Performance/production

Report from the international Fringe Festival. UK-Scotland: Edinburgh. 1986. Lang.: Swe.   819

Edith és Marlene (Edith and Marlene)

Performance/production

Edith és Marlene (Edith and Marlene) by Éva Pataki at Comedy Theatre. Hungary: Budapest. 1986. Lang.: Hun.   1831

Éva Pataki's *Edith és Marlene (Edith and Marlene)* directed by Márta Mészáros, Pest National Theatre. Hungary: Budapest. 1986. Lang.: Hun.   3603

Editions

Basic theatrical documents

Text of Čechov's *Platonov* in a version by Michael Frayn. Russia. 1878. Lang.: Cat.   1492

Text of *Primera història d'Esther (First Story of Esther)* by Salvador Espriu, with introduction on the author and the play. Spain-Catalonia: Barcelona. 1913-1985. Lang.: Spa, Cat.   1496

Edition of *La famosa comèdia de la gala està en son punt (The Famous Comedy of the Gala Done to a Turn)*, with analysis. Spain-Catalonia. 1625-1680. Lang.: Cat.   1497

Josep Maria de Sagarra's translations of Shakespeare with scholarly introduction. Spain-Catalonia. UK-England. 1590-1986. Lang.: Cat.   1502

Performance/production

Attempt to produce Quarto version of *King Lear* at University of Rochester. USA: Rochester, NY. 1985. Lang.: Eng.   2300

Plays/librettos/scripts

Personal memoir of playwright Antonin Artaud. France. 1946-1967. Lang.: Fre.   2584

Editions — cont'd

Introduction to *Jesús batejat per Sant Joan Baptista (Jesus Christ Baptized by St. John the Baptist)*. France. 1753-1832. Lang.: Cat.
2585

Differences among 32 extant editions of *Xi Xiang Zhu*. China. 1669-1843. Lang.: Chi.
3528

Edlund, Richard
  Design/technology
  Lighting designer Andrew Lazlo talks about his work on the film *Poltergeist II*. USA: Los Angeles, CA. USA: New York, NY. 1985-1986. Lang.: Eng.
3204

Edmond
  Performance/production
  Collection of newspaper reviews by London theatre critics. UK-England: London. 1986. Lang.: Eng.
2112

Edmonds, Randolph
  Plays/librettos/scripts
  Precursors of revolutionary black theatre. Haiti. Jamaica. 1820-1970. Lang.: Eng.
956

Edmonton Fringe Festival (Canada)
  Performance/production
  Review of Edmonton Fringe Festival. Canada: Edmonton, AB. 1986. Lang.: Eng.
1682
  Plays/librettos/scripts
  Criticizes the plays in the collection *Five From the Fringe*. Canada: Edmonton, AB. 1986. Lang.: Eng.
2425

Edmund Ironside
  Basic theatrical documents
  Text of *Edmund Ironside*, attributed to Shakespeare. UK-England: London. 1580-1600. Lang.: Eng.
1508
  Reference materials
  List of 37 productions of 23 Renaissance plays, with commentary. UK. USA. New Zealand. 1986. Lang.: Eng.
3000

Education
  Description of various theatrical activities. Poland: Vilna. 1908-1986. Lang.: Pol.
10
  Administration
  Lack of consensus on art linked to poor arts education. USA. 1960-1983. Lang.: Eng.
152
  Audience
  Moral objections to children's attendance of theatres. USA: New York, NY. 1900-1910. Lang.: Eng.
202
  On the role of the theatre in the life of contemporary youth. USSR. 1980-1986. Lang.: Rus.
209
  Aesthetic education through theatre. USSR. 1980-1986. Lang.: Rus.
214
  Effect of official educational and cultural policies on theatre. France. Germany. UK-England. 1789-1986. Lang.: Fre.
1446
  Design/technology
  Hungarian students tour stage and costume designs at the Mozarteum. Austria: Salzburg. 1986. Lang.: Hun.
238
  Institutions
  Interview with Dennis Foon, director of Green Thumb Theatre for Young People. Canada: Vancouver, BC. 1975-1984. Lang.: Fre. 473
  Academics in theatre discuss the role of theatre in education. Canada. 1984. Lang.: Fre.
476
  Educational theatre in Iraq. Iraq. 1885-1985. Lang.: Eng.
505
  History of the Dramatists' Co-op of Nova Scotia. Canada. 1976-1986. Lang.: Eng.
1558
  A playwright surveys Canadian university offerings in Canadian literature, drama and playwriting. Canada. 1986. Lang.: Eng.
1564
  History of the Shanghai Drama Institute. China, People's Republic of: Shanghai. 1945-1982. Lang.: Chi.
1571
  Efforts of New York Shakespeare Festival to develop an audience for Shakespearean drama. USA: New York, NY. 1986. Lang.: Eng.
1605
  Performance/production
  Report on the Third European Child Acting Workshop. Denmark: Vordingborg. 1986. Lang.: Hun.
684
  Interview with Mario Delgado Vásquez, director of Cuatrotablas. Peru: Lima. 1971-1985. Lang.: Hun.
769
  Dilemmas and prospects of youth theatre movement. Australia. 1982-1986. Lang.: Eng.
1639
  Profile of actor Bill Cosby. USA. 1986. Lang.: Eng.
3274
  Plays/librettos/scripts
  Interview with playwright René Philombe on the educative function of theatre. Cameroon. 1930-1986. Lang.: Fre.
925

School use of Juliusz Słowacki's dramas in Polish high schools as a reflection of the political situation. Poland. 1945-1984. Lang.: Fre.
2743

  Relation to other fields
  Theatrical performance as a pedagogical tool. 1986. Lang.: Cat. 1048
  Drama handbook for secondary school teachers. Australia. 1974-1985. Lang.: Eng.
1062
  Theatre professionals' round-table on issues in theatre for adolescents. Canada: Quebec, PQ. 1984. Lang.: Fre.
1068
  Importance of teaching proper values to theatre students. China, People's Republic of. 1949-1982. Lang.: Chi.
1077
  Children's paper theatres as educational tools. Germany. 1878-1921. Lang.: Ger.
1090
  Traditional Malay and European elements in children's theatre. Malaysia. 1930-1985. Lang.: Eng.
1112
  Interview with Socorro Merlin, director of the Institute of Fine Arts. Mexico: Mexico City. 1947-1985. Lang.: Eng.
1113
  Participation of disabled children in Vår Teater. Sweden: Stockholm. 1975-1985. Lang.: Eng.
1129
  Implications of commercialized American theatre for children. Sweden: Stockholm. USA. 1986. Lang.: Eng.
1131
  Training course for teacher/actors. Switzerland: Zurich. 1980-1986. Lang.: Ger.
1132
  Proposals on theatre in education. UK-England: London, Greenwich. 1986. Lang.: Hun.
1137
  Influence of Sir Keith Joseph upon the education system. UK-England. 1985. Lang.: Eng.
1138
  Argument for 'dramatic literacy' as part of 'cultural literacy'. USA. 1944-1985. Lang.: Eng.
1142
  Examples of role-playing drawn from the ERIC database. USA. 1980-1985. Lang.: Eng.
1144
  Development of educational theatre program dealing with child sexual abuse. USA: St. Louis, MO. 1976-1984. Lang.: Eng. 1145
  Documents from ERIC computer system detailing classroom exercises in drama. USA. 1983-1985. Lang.: Eng.
1147
  Ethical value of theatre in education. USA. 1985. Lang.: Eng. 1149
  Drama as a tool for teaching social skills to the handicapped. USA. 1984. Lang.: Eng.
1150
  Evaluation and social effects of improvisational drama program. USA: Newark, NJ. Lang.: Eng.
1151
  Children's theatre and the community. USA. 1970-1984. Lang.: Eng.
1153
  Effect of playmaking on sixth and seventh grade pupils. USA: New York, NY. 1986. Lang.: Eng.
1157
  Development of forms and goals in the children's theatre movement. USA. 1903-1985. Lang.: Eng.
1158
  Proposal for using creative drama with museum visits and a study of the visual arts. USA: Austin, TX. 1985. Lang.: Eng.
1159
  Problems of artists working in schools. USA: New York, NY. 1983. Lang.: Eng.
1161
  Style in children's theatre in light of theories of Philippe Ariès. USA. UK. France. 1600-1980. Lang.: Eng.
1162
  Methods and goals of Children's Theatre Association of America. USA. 1940-1984. Lang.: Eng.
1163
  Study of how principals perceive the use of drama in the curriculum. USA. 1986. Lang.: Eng.
1165
  Creative drama content in college language arts textbooks. USA. 1986. Lang.: Eng.
1166
  Argument for the establishment of graduate programs in children's theatre. USA. 1985. Lang.: Eng.
1168
  Development of arts-in-education program. USA: Albany, NY. 1970-1984. Lang.: Eng.
1169
  The role of theatre and television in the moral education of society. USSR. 1980-1986. Lang.: Rus.
1177
  Curricular authority for drama-in-education program. UK. Lang.: Eng.
3054
  Discussion of theatre-in-education. UK. Lang.: Eng. 3055
  Current style of theatre-in-education. UK-England. Lang.: Eng. 3057
  Description of the Cutler Playwright's Festival designed for junior high school students. USA: Groton, CT. 1983-1986. Lang.: Eng.
3065

Education — cont'd

Black history and folklore taught in theatre workshops and productions. USA: New York, NY, Omaha, NE, Washington, DC. 1986. Lang.: Eng. 3068

Political goals for Beijing opera. China, People's Republic of: Beijing. 1985. Lang.: Chi. 3548

Research/historiography
Study of educational drama from the perspective of generic skills. Canada: Toronto, ON. 1985. Lang.: Eng. 3070

Theory/criticism
Purpose of literature and art, and the role of the artist. China, People's Republic of: Shanghai, Yan'an. 1942-1982. Lang.: Chi. 1203

Training
Instructional television programming for the advancement of arts in education. USA: University Park, IL. 1986. Lang.: Eng. 3287

Educational Resources Information Center (ERIC, Annandale, VA)

Relation to other fields
Examples of role-playing drawn from the ERIC database. USA. 1980-1985. Lang.: Eng. 1144

Documents from ERIC computer system detailing classroom exercises in drama. USA. 1983-1985. Lang.: Eng. 1147

Edvall, Allan

Performance/production
Reviews of regional productions. Sweden: Stockholm. 1985-1986. Lang.: Swe. 2087

Discussion of Stanislavskij's influence by a number of artists. Sweden. 1890-1986. Lang.: Swe. 2094

Edward Dunstan Shakespearean Company (Liverpool)

Performance/production
History of the Edward Dunstan Shakespearean Company, a touring company. UK-England. 1930-1933. Lang.: Eng. 2156

Edward II

Plays/librettos/scripts
Possible influence of Christopher Marlowe's plays upon those of William Shakespeare. England. 1580-1620. Lang.: Eng. 2478

Reference materials
List of 37 productions of 23 Renaissance plays, with commentary. UK. USA. New Zealand. 1986. Lang.: Eng. 3000

Edward IV

Plays/librettos/scripts
Compares pageant-wagon play about Edward IV with version by Thomas Heywood. England: Coventry, London. 1560-1600. Lang.: Eng. 3430

Edwards, Ben

Performance/production
Greek tragedy on the New York stage. USA: New York, NY. 1854-1984. Lang.: Eng. 2301

Edwards, Malcolm

Performance/production
Collection of newspaper reviews by London theatre critics. UK-England: London. 1986. Lang.: Eng. 2113

Efremov, Oleg

SEE
Jefremov, Oleg.

Efros, Anatolij

Performance/production
Director Anatolij Efros on theatrical conventions, audience and perception. USSR. 1980-1986. Lang.: Rus. 871

Discussion of basic theatrical issues during Stanislavskij symposium. Sweden: Stockholm. 1986. Lang.: Swe. 2086

Egbert, Marion

Performance/production
Four nightclub entertainers on their particular acts and the atmosphere of the late night clubs and theaters in Harlem. USA: New York, NY, Savannah, GA. 1930-1950. Lang.: Eng. 3470

Egérút (Narrow Escape)

Performance/production
Notes on performances of *Hongkongi paróka (Wig Made in Hong Kong)*, *Egérút (Narrow Escape)* and *Róza néni (Aunt Rosa)*. Hungary: Budapest. 1985. Lang.: Hun. 1801

Egg, Augustus

Plays/librettos/scripts
Attitudes toward sexuality in plays from French sources. UK-England. France. Lang.: Eng. 2852

Egy lócsiszár virágvasárnapja (Palm Sunday of a Horse Dealer, The)

Performance/production
Ottó Adám directs *Egy lócsiszár virágvasárnapja (The Palm Sunday of a Horse Dealer)* by András Sütő after Kleist. Hungary: Budapest. 1986. Lang.: Hun. 1843

Review of two performances of András Sütő's plays. Hungary: Budapest. 1986. Lang.: Hun. 1913

Egyetemi Színpad (Budapest)

Performance/production
Performances of Sławomir Mrożek's *Mészárszék (The Slaughterhouse)* and *Ház a határon (The Home on the Border)*. Hungary: Budapest. 1986. Lang.: Hun. 1817

Eh, Joe!

Performance/production
András Matkócsik directs *Mondd, Joe! (Eh, Joe!)* and *Az utlosó tekercs (Krapp's Last Tape)* by Samuel Beckett. Hungary: Budapest. 1985. Lang.: Hun. 1851

Eichler, Lawrence

Design/technology
Charles Ludlam's role as set designer, artistic director and lead actor of The Ridiculous Theatre Company. USA: New York, NY. 1986. 360

Eight Men Speak

Relation to other fields
Circumstances surrounding a banned Workers' Experimental Theatre play. Canada: Toronto, ON. 1931-1933. Lang.: Eng. 3018

Eight Million Ways to Die

Design/technology
Cinematographer Stephen Burum's work on *Eight Million Ways to Die*. USA. Lang.: Eng. 3207

Eight Shining Palaces

SEE
Pa Chin Kung.

Einen Jux willer sich machen

SEE
Jux willer sich machen, Einen.

Einstein on the Beach

Performance/production
The development and production of Robert Wilson's *CIVIL warS*. USA. Germany, East. 1984. Lang.: Eng. 838

Revival of Philip Glass and Robert Wilson's *Einstein on the Beach* and opportunities to improve the piece. USA: New York, NY. 1976-1984. Lang.: Eng. 2305

Eisenberg, Josy

Plays/librettos/scripts
Interview with Josy Eisenberg, translator of *Le Cantique des cantiques (The Song of Songs)* for the Comédie-Française. France: Paris. 1986. Lang.: Fre. 2544

Eisenstein, Sergej Michajlovič

Performance/production
Eastern and Western elements in Sergej Eisenstein's work. Russia. 1898-1948. Lang.: Ita. 3225

Influence of Beijing opera performer Mei Lanfang on European acting and staging traditions. China, People's Republic of. USSR. Germany. 1900-1935. Lang.: Eng. 3521

Theory/criticism
Creative self-assembly and juxtaposition in live performance and film. Lang.: Eng. 1196

Ekmanner, Agneta

Performance/production
Interview with actress Agneta Ekmanner. Sweden: Stockholm. 1950-1986. Lang.: Swe. 2092

El Hakawati Theatre (Jerusalem)

Performance/production
Collection of newspaper reviews by London theatre critics. UK-England: London. 1986. Lang.: Eng. 2109

Elckerlijc

SEE
Everyman.

Elder, Lonnie III

Plays/librettos/scripts
Race in prison dramas of Piñero, Camillo, Elder and Bullins. USA. 1970-1986. Lang.: Eng. 2912

Eleanor and Felix

Performance/production
Collection of newspaper reviews by London theatre critics. UK-England: London. 1986. Lang.: Eng. 2125

Electra
Performance/production
Sophocles' *Electra* staged by Antoine Vitez as a conflict of deceit. France: Paris. 1986. Lang.: Swe.   1732

Reflection of modern society in Antoine Vitez's production of Sophocles' *Electra* at Théâtre National Populaire. France: Paris. 1981-1986. Lang.: Swe.   1743

Electra by Hofmannsthal
SEE
Elektra.

Elektra
Performance/production
Stills from telecast performances of *Elektra*. List of principals, conductor and production staff included. USA: New York, NY. 1986. Lang.: Eng.   3790

Plays/librettos/scripts
Comparative analysis of *Elektra* by Hugo von Hofmannsthal and its sources. Germany. 1909. Lang.: Eng.   2603

Eliot, Thomas Stearns
Performance/production
Director John Dexter and impresario Eddie Kulukundis discuss the formation of the New Theatre Company. UK-England: London. 1986. Lang.: Eng.   2144

Plays/librettos/scripts
T. S. Eliot's *Murder in the Cathedral* dramatizes Christian theory of history. UK-England. 1935. Lang.: Eng.   2878

Theory/criticism
Assessment of critic Kenneth Tynan's works. UK-England. 1950-1960. Lang.: Eng.   3136

Elisabeth von England (Elizabeth of England)
Performance/production
Laco Adamik directs Ferdinand Brückner's *Elisabeth von England* under the title *Elzbieta, Królowa Anglii*. Poland: Cracow. 1984. Lang.: Pol.   2041

Elisabetta: Quasì per case una donna (Elizabeth: Almost by Chance a Woman)
Plays/librettos/scripts
Interview with Gillian Hanna about *Elisabetta: Quasì per caso una donna (Elizabeth: Almost by Chance a Woman)*. UK-England: London. Italy. 1986. Lang.: Eng.   2875

Elizabethan theatre
History of classical Chinese theatre. China. 600 B.C.-1985 A.D. Lang.: Eng.   4

SEE ALSO
Geographical-Chronological Index under England 1558-1603.

Basic theatrical documents
Josep Maria de Sagarra's translations of Shakespeare with scholarly introduction. Spain-Catalonia. UK-England. 1590-1986. Lang.: Cat.   1502

Performance spaces
Conjectural reconstruction of the Boar's Head Playhouse. England: London. 1558-1603. Lang.: Eng.   592

Overview of the hall in which Shakespeare's *Twelfth Night* was performed. England: London. 1602. Lang.: Eng.   1616

Plays/librettos/scripts
Similar dramatic techniques in Ben Jonson's masques and tragedies. England. 1597-1637. Lang.: Eng.   941

Rise of English landowners reflected in *Arden of Faversham*. England. 1536-1592. Lang.: Eng.   943

Image of poverty in Elizabethan and Stuart plays. England. 1558-1642. Lang.: Eng.   2482

Marxist analysis of colonialism in Shakespeare's *Othello*. England. South Africa, Republic of. 1597-1637. Lang.: Eng.   2507

Political ideas expressed in Elizabethan drama, particularly the work of Christopher Marlowe. England: London. Lang.: Eng.   2521

Ellerbeck, Christine
Performance/production
Feminist theatre group Beryl and the Perils. UK-England. 1986. Lang.: Eng.   2171

Elliot, Michael
Performance/production
Self-referential elements in several film versions of Shakespeare's *King Lear*. UK. USA. 1916-1983. Lang.: Eng.   3227

Ellis, Michael
Performance/production
Collection of newspaper reviews by London theatre critics. UK-England: London. 1986. Lang.: Eng.   2116

Elmer Gantry
Performance/production
Collection of newspaper reviews by London theatre critics. UK-England: London. 1986. Lang.: Eng.   2110

Elmerick
Plays/librettos/scripts
Liberated female characters in the plays of George Lillo. England. 1730-1759. Lang.: Eng.   2477

Elmslie, Kennar D.
Plays/librettos/scripts
Jack Beeson's opera *Lizzie Borden*. USA. 1954-1965. Lang.: Eng.   3901

Elmslie, Kenward
Performance/production
Review of the world premiere of the opera *Three Sisters*. USA: Columbus, OH. 1968-1986. Lang.: Eng.   3822

Elton, Ben
Performance/production
Collection of newspaper reviews by London theatre critics. UK-England: London. 1986. Lang.: Eng.   2123

Reviews of *Rowan Atkinson at the Atkinson*, by Richard Curtis, Rowan Atkinson and Ben Elton, staged by Mike Ockrent. USA: New York, NY. 1986. Lang.: Eng.   2211

Elvira, o la passione teatrale (Elvira or the Theatrical Passion)
Performance/production
Overview of productions in Italy. Italy: Milan. 1986. Lang.: Eng.   1994

Elysian Theatre (St. John's, NF)
Institutions
Successful alternative theatre groups in Newfoundland. Canada. 1976-1986. Lang.: Eng.   1550

Ember tragédiája, Az (Tragedy of a Man, The)
Plays/librettos/scripts
Philosophy and morality of Imre Madách's classical dramatic poem *Az ember tragédiája (The Tragedy of a Man)*. Hungary. 1883-1983. Lang.: Hun.   2644

Reference materials
Bibliography of Hungarian writer and translator Jenő Mohácsi. Hungary. 1886-1944. Lang.: Hun.   2991

Ember, Gyula
Design/technology
Interviews with technicians Gyula Ember and Gyula Asztalos about theatre technology. Hungary. 1977-1986. Lang.: Hun.   285

Emery, Winifred
Administration
Legislation for the protection of Victorian child-actors. UK. 1837-1901. Lang.: Eng.   1439

Emigh, John
Performance/production
Influence of Asian theatre traditions on American artists. USA: New York, NY. Indonesia. 1952-1985. Lang.: Eng.   1335

Emil und die Detektive (Emil and the Detectives)
Performance/production
Stage adaptation of Erich Kästner's novel *Emil und die Detektive (Emil and the Detectives)* directed by István Keleti. Hungary: Budapest. 1986. Lang.: Hun.   1807

Emmes, David
Design/technology
A profile of Cliff Faulkner, resident designer at South Coast Repertory. USA: Los Angeles, CA. 1977-1986.   365

Institutions
A profile of South Coast Repertory. USA: Los Angeles, CA. 1964-1986.   569

Emmons, Beverly
Design/technology
Career of lighting designer Beverly Emmons. USA. 1972-1986.   333

Interview with Beverly Emmons, lighting designer for Mummenschanz's USA tour. USA: New York, NY. 1986. Lang.: Eng.   3305

Emmy Gifford Children's Theatre (Omaha, NE)
Institutions
Training and use of child performers. USA. 1949-1985. Lang.: Eng.   565

Emőd, György
Performance/production
Production by György Emőd of Friedrich Dürrenmatt's *A Öreg hölgy látogatása (The Visit)*. Hungary: Győr. 1985. Lang.: Hun.   1788

Emőd, György — cont'd

Ágyrajárók (Night Lodgers) by Péter Szántó, directed by György Emőd at Kisfaludy Studio Theatre. Hungary: Győr. 1985. Lang.: Hun. 1854

Emperor of Haiti
Plays/librettos/scripts
Precursors of revolutionary black theatre. Haiti. Jamaica. 1820-1970. Lang.: Eng. 956

Empire State Institute for the Performing Arts (ESIPA, Albany, NY)
Relation to other fields
Development of arts-in-education program. USA: Albany, NY. 1970-1984. Lang.: Eng. 1169

Empire Theatre (Sunderland, UK)
Performance/production
Survey of performances in England's Northeast. UK-England. 1986. Lang.: Eng. 2173

Employment
Design/technology
How to look for work as a designer or technician in opera. USA. 1986. Lang.: Eng. 3655

En attendant Godot (Waiting for Godot)
Plays/librettos/scripts
Language and the permanent dialectic of truth and lie in the plays of Samuel Beckett. France. 1930-1980. Lang.: Fre. 2549
Various implications of 'waiting' in Samuel Beckett's *Waiting for Godot*. France. 1953. Lang.: Eng. 2555
Waiting for Godot as an assessment of the quality of life of the couple. France. UK-Ireland. 1931-1958. Lang.: Eng. 2557
Rhetorical analysis of Samuel Beckett's *Waiting for Godot*. France. 1953. Lang.: Eng. 2562

En Pièces détachées (In Separate Pieces)
Plays/librettos/scripts
Poverty in plays by Michel Tremblay and David Fennario. Canada: Quebec, PQ. 1970-1980. Lang.: Eng. 2410

Enchanted Birds' Nest, The
Performance/production
Collection of newspaper reviews by London theatre critics. UK: London. 1986. Lang.: Eng. 2100

Encore Theatre (Montreal, PQ)
Institutions
New leadership in Montreal's English-speaking theatres. Canada: Montreal, PQ. 1980-1986. Lang.: Eng. 1539

Encyclopedias
Reference materials
Lexicon of world theatre. 700 B.C.-1986 A.D. Lang.: Ger. 995
Western theatre from ancient times to the present. Europe. 600 B.C.-1986 A.D. Lang.: Ger. 1013
Encyclopedia of cabaret in German. Germany. Switzerland. Austria. 1900-1965. Lang.: Ger. 3369
Biographical encyclopedia of stand-up comics and comedy teams. USA. 1900-1986. Lang.: Eng. 3472

Enda raka, Det (Only Straight Thing, The)
Performance/production
Mats Ödeen's *Det ende raka (The Only Straight Thing)* performed by TURteaterns amatörteatergrupp. Sweden: Stockholm. 1979-1986. Lang.: Swe. 801

Endgame
SEE
Fin de partie.

Engel, Erich
Performance/production
Photographic record of forty years of the Berliner Ensemble. Germany, East: Berlin, East. 1949-1984. Lang.: Eng. 1761

Engle, Claude
Design/technology
A lighting designer discusses the unique problems of lighting symphony orchestras. USA: Washington, DC, Boston, MA, New York, NY. 1910-1986. Lang.: Eng. 3478

English National Opera (London)
Performance/production
Profile of and interview with Romanian-born conductor Christian Berea. Romania. USA: New York, NY. 1950-1986. Lang.: Eng. 3771

English Opera Group
Performance/production
Interview with singer Nancy Evans and writer Eric Crozier discussing their association with Benjamin Britten. USA: Columbia, MO. UK-England: London. 1940-1985. Lang.: Eng. 3820

English Shakespeare Company (UK)
Institutions
Actor Michael Pennington and director Michael Bogdanov discuss the formation of the English Shakespeare Company. UK-England. 1986. Lang.: Eng. 1592
Performance/production
Establishment of the English Shakespeare Company. UK-England. 1986. Lang.: Eng. 2131

English Stage Company
SEE ALSO
Royal Court Theatre (London).

English, Rose
Performance/production
Collection of newspaper reviews by London theatre critics. UK-England: London. 1986. Lang.: Eng. 2119
Interview with performance artist Rose English. UK-England. 1970-1986. Lang.: Eng. 3453

Englund, Monica
Performance/production
Stage photographs with comment by photographers. Sweden. 1985-1986. Lang.: Swe. 794

Enlightenment
Plays/librettos/scripts
Enlightenment narrative and French dramatists. France. 1700-1800. Lang.: Eng. 2552
Theory/criticism
Analysis of Friedrich Schiller's dramatic and theoretical works. Germany. 1759-1805. Lang.: Cat. 3109

Ennen
Performance/production
Anthology of Japanese popular entertainments. Japan: Tokyo. 1986. Lang.: Jap. 3342

Ennosuke, Ichikawa
Performance/production
A photographic essay of 42 soloists and groups performing mime or gestural theatre. 1986. 3290

Enquist, Per Olof
Performance/production
Én99k Phaedráért (Song for Phaedra) by Per Olof Enquist directed by Imre Csiszár. Hungary: Miskolc. 1985. Lang.: Hun. 1794
Én99k Phaedráért (Song for Phaedra) by Per Olof Enquist, directed by Imre Csiszár at the National Theatre of Miskolc. Hungary: Miskolc. 1985. Lang.: Hun. 1937
Reviews of three productions of *Fröken Julie (Miss Julie)* by August Strindberg. Sweden: Stockholm. Denmark: Copenhagen. South Africa, Republic of. 1985-1986. Lang.: Swe. 2090

Enrico Quarto (Henry IV)
Performance/production
Luigi Pirandello's concerns with staging in *Sei personaggi in cerca d'autore (Six Characters in Search of an Author)* and *Enrico Quarto (Henry IV)*. Italy. 1921-1986. Lang.: Fre. 1990
Plays/librettos/scripts
Role-playing and madness in Pirandello's *Enrico Quarto (Henry IV)*. Italy. 1922. Lang.: Fre. 2709

Ensaio No. 02—O Pintor (Essay No. 2: The Painter)
Performance/production
Survey of productions in 1985/86. Brazil: Rio de Janeiro. 1985-1986. Lang.: Eng. 1656

Ensemble Studio Theatre (New York, NY)
Administration
Development director Marion Godfrey's fundraising strategies. USA: New York, NY. 1986. Lang.: Eng. 113
Reference materials
Summer performance schedules for several New York companies. USA: New York, NY. 1984. Lang.: Eng. 3011

Ensemble Theater (Austria)
Plays/librettos/scripts
Training for new playwrights in Austria. Austria: Vienna. 1985-1986. Lang.: Ger. 2392

Enterprise Theatre (Fredericton, NB)
Institutions
Founding directors explain history and principles of Enterprise Theatre. Canada. 1983-1986. Lang.: Eng. 1546

Enters, Angna
Performance/production
Biography of mime Angna Enters. Europe. USA. 1907-1986. Lang.: Eng. 3295

Equipment — cont'd

Review of the leading manufacturers of remote controlled luminaires. USA.   412

A guide to sealed beam lamps. USA. 1986.   413

Constructing durable street bricks. USA. 1981. Lang.: Eng.   415

Platform system that is more efficient and secure than those commonly used. USA. 1984. Lang.: Eng.   417

I-beam stringers used for stressed-skin platforms. USA. 1976. Lang.: Eng.   418

Computer program which stores lighting design data. USA. 1983. Lang.: Eng.   419

Capabilities of available computer-controlled sound systems. USA. 1986.   421

Construction of stage turntables. USA. 1986. Lang.: Eng.   423

Webbing slings and caribiners for quick rigging connections. USA. 1985. Lang.: Eng.   424

Guide to materials necessary for theatrical performances. USSR. 1980-1986. Lang.: Rus.   430

Renovation of the Alhambra Theatre. UK-England: Bradford. 1980-1987. Lang.: Eng.   1521

An introduction to the Nagra IV Stereo Time Code Portable Recorder. Lang.: Eng.   3198

Video and film lighting techniques. USA. 1986. Lang.: Eng.   3257

Interview with cameraman Gerald Perry Finnerman about lighting *Moonlighting*. USA: Los Angeles, CA. 1985-1986. Lang.: Eng.   3264

Interview with lighting designer Kieran Healy discussing techniques for lighting live concert videos. USA. 1982-1986. Lang.: Eng.   3265

Description of scenery, machinery and performance of Renaissance Italian feast. Italy. 1400-1600. Lang.: Ita.   3311

Technical aspects relating to Toyota's showing of its new automobile designs. Japan: Tokyo. 1985. Lang.: Eng.   3312

Lighting techniques and equipment used at theme park. USA: Baltimore, MD. 1971-1986. Lang.: Eng.   3315

Details of the lighting arrangements for the four-day Statue of Liberty centennial celebration. USA: New York, NY. 1986. Lang.: Eng.   3318

Lighting designer John Ingram discusses his lighting for the Coca-Cola centennial. USA: Atlanta, GA. 1986. Lang.: Eng.   3319

Analysis of the technological aspects of *Les Misérables*. UK-England: London. 1980-1987. Lang.: Eng.   3582

Performance spaces

Reconstruction of the Szeged National Theatre. Hungary: Szeged. 1948-1980. Lang.: Hun.   604

Guide to locating and designing performance spaces for non-traditional theatre. USA: New York, NY. 1979. Lang.: Eng.   636

Performance/production

Detailed history of the 1914 Hagenbeck Wallace Circus season. USA: St. Louis, MO, Youngstown, OH, Sturgis, MI. 1914. Lang.: Eng.   3388

The history of 'tableau wagons' in the Barnum and Bailey circus. USA: New York, NY. 1864-1920. Lang.: Eng.   3391

Equity
SEE
Actors' Equity.

Er Jin Gong
Research/historiography
Transformation of traditional music notation into modern notation for four Chinese operas. China: Beijing. 1674-1985. Lang.: Chi.   3554

Eran and Eclectic Theatre (Ontario)
Plays/librettos/scripts
Analysis of *As Is* by William Hoffman and *The Dolly* by Robert Locke. Canada: Toronto, ON. 1985. Lang.: Eng.   2419

Erdei, János
Performance/production
István Verebes directs *Valódi Vadnyugat (True West)* by Sam Shepard. Hungary: Budapest. 1986. Lang.: Hun.   1772

ERIC
SEE
Educational Resources Information Center.

Erice, Victor
Plays/librettos/scripts
Self-reflexivity in Antonio Buero Vallejo's play *El Sueño de la razón (The Sleep of Reason)* and Victor Erice's film *El Espíritu de la colmena (The Spirit of the Beehive)*. Spain. 1970-1973. Lang.: Eng.   2781

Erkel Szinház (Budapest)
Performance/production
Verdi's *Simon Boccanegra* and Puccini's *La Bohème* at the Hungarian State Opera House and Erkel Theatre. Hungary: Budapest. 1986. Lang.: Hun.   3747

Reference materials
Catalogue from an exhibit of theatrical and ballet art by Zsuzsi Roboz. Hungary: Budapest. 1985. Lang.: Hun.   1325

Erkel, Ferenc
Reference materials
Guide to Ferenc Erkel opera museum. Hungary: Gyula. 1810-1893. Lang.: Hun.   3912

Erler, Michael
Design/technology
Design concepts for television series *Tall Tales*. USA. 1986. Lang.: Eng.   3261

Ernst, Christina
Design/technology
Strategies of lighting dance performances on a limited budget. 1985-1986. Lang.: Eng.   1340

Esaltazione della croce, L' (Exaltation of the Cross, The)
Plays/librettos/scripts
Discussion of *L'esaltazione della croce (The Exaltation of the Cross)* by Giovanni Maria Cecchi. Italy. 1585-1589. Lang.: Ita.   2683

ESC
SEE
English Stage Company.

Escape, The
SEE
Běg.

Escola d'Art Dramàtic Adrià Gual (Barcelona)
Basic theatrical documents
Anthology and study of writings of Josep Maria de Sagarra. Spain-Catalonia. 1917-1964. Lang.: Cat.   1501

Plays/librettos/scripts
Translations of Shakespeare by Josep Maria de Sagarra. Spain-Catalonia: Barcelona. 1940-1964. Lang.: Cat.   2811

ESIPA
SEE
Empire State Institute for the Performing Arts.

Espace Libre (Montreal, PQ)
Plays/librettos/scripts
Review essay on *Li jus de Robin et Marion (The Play of Robin and Marion)* directed by Jean Asselin. Canada: Montreal, PQ. 1986. Lang.: Fre.   937

Espert, Nuria
Institutions
Reviews of Edinburgh Festival plays. UK-Scotland: Edinburgh. 1986. Lang.: Eng.   539

Performance/production
Nuria Espert talks about Federico García Lorca and her production of *The House of Bernarda Alba*. UK-England: London. Spain. Lang.: Eng.   2178

Espíritu de la colmena, El (Spirit of the Beehive, The)
Plays/librettos/scripts
Self-reflexivity in Antonio Buero Vallejo's play *El Sueño de la razón (The Sleep of Reason)* and Victor Erice's film *El Espíritu de la colmena (The Spirit of the Beehive)*. Spain. 1970-1973. Lang.: Eng.   2781

Esprits, Les (Spirits, The)
Plays/librettos/scripts
Adaptation by Albert Camus of *Les Esprits (The Spirits)* by Pierre de Larivey. France. 1570-1953. Lang.: Fre.   2571

Espriu, Salvador
Basic theatrical documents
Text of *Primera història d'Esther (First Story of Esther)* by Salvador Espriu, with introduction on the author and the play. Spain-Catalonia: Barcelona. 1913-1985. Lang.: Spa, Cat.   1496

Plays/librettos/scripts
Salvador Espriu's tragic vision in *Ronda de Mort a Sinera (Death Round at Sinera)*. Spain. 1965. Lang.: Eng.   2784

Relation to other fields
Reports and discussions of restricted cultural communication. Lebanon. Spain-Catalonia. USA. 1985. Lang.: Fre, Spa, Cat.   1111

Theory/criticism
Historical difficulties in creating a paradigm for Catalan theatre. Spain-Catalonia. 1400-1963. Lang.: Cat.   1220

Ethnic theatre — cont'd

Performance/production

History and performance practice of Arabic religious tragedy. Asia. Arabic countries. 680-1970. Lang.: Ita.   652

Collaboration of playwright Jack Davis and director Andrew Ross. Australia. 1986. Lang.: Eng.   655

Dangers of assimilation of French-Canadian theatre into Anglophone culture. Canada. 1985. Lang.: Fre.   668

Development of women's and Maori theatre. New Zealand. 1980-1986. Lang.: Eng.   767

Adaptation of folk dance to the stage. Hungary. 1773-1985. Lang.: Hun.   1331

Theatrical productions on local topics in small Inuit communities. Canada. 1983-1986. Lang.: Eng.   1658

Descriptions of the folk drama of Kazakhstan. USSR. Lang.: Rus.   2328

Early form of Sicilian dialect theatre. Italy. 1780-1800. Lang.: Ita.   3337

A gypsy discusses the theatrical traditions of his people. Italy. 1900-1986. Lang.: Ita.   3340

Plays/librettos/scripts

Work of playwright R.A. Shiomi, including production history of *Yellow Fever*. Canada: Toronto, ON. USA: New York, NY. USA: San Francisco, CA. 1970-1986. Lang.: Eng.   2422

The plays of Antonine Maillet and the revival of Acadian theatre. Canada. 1971-1979. Lang.: Eng.   2423

La Storia and *La Storia II* performed in Italian and English by the Acting Company. Canada: Toronto, ON. 1984-1985. Lang.: Eng.   2424

Umiak by Théâtre de la Marmaille of Toronto, based on Inuit tradition. Canada. 1982-1983. Lang.: Eng.   2434

Acadian characters of playwright Antonine Maillet contrasted with Longfellow's romantic myth. Canada. 1968-1975. Lang.: Eng.   2439

Piemontese dialect theatre. Italy: Turin. 1857-1914. Lang.: Ita.   2715

Text and information on Luigi Pirandello's *A patenti (The License)*. Italy. 1916-1918. Lang.: Ita.   2717

Ritual function of *The Slave Ship* by LeRoi Jones (Amiri Baraka) and *Quinta Temporada (Fifth Season)* by Luis Valdez. USA. 1965-1967. Lang.: Eng.   2906

Evolution of Byelorussian folk drama. USSR. Lang.: Rus.   2953

Folklore in Uzbek drama. USSR. Lang.: Rus.   2962

Reference materials

Accounts of non-English-speaking artists. Australia. 1986. Lang.: Eng.   1001

Relation to other fields

Kwakiutl Homatsa ceremony as drama. Canada. 1890-1900. Lang.: Eng.   1070

Etienne, Claude

Performance/production

Effect of dual-language society on Belgian theatre. Belgium: Brussels, Liège. Lang.: Eng.   660

Etxegarat, Jean

Relation to other fields

Popular theatrical forms in the Basque country. Spain. France. 674-1963. Lang.: Spa.   3361

Eubie Blake's Children's Theatre Company (New York, NY)

Institutions

Curriculum and expectation of students in Eubie Blake's Children's Theatre Company. USA: New York, NY. 1986. Lang.: Eng.   1602

Eugene Festival of Musical Theatre (Eugene, OR)

Design/technology

Designers discuss regional productions of *Fiddler on the Roof*. USA. 1984-1986. Lang.: Eng.   3595

Eugene Onegin

Performance/production

Analysis and appreciation of the work of Modest Pavlovič Mussorgskij. USSR. 1839-1881. Lang.: Eng.   3849

Eureka Theatre (San Francisco, CA)

Performance/production

Dramaturg Oskar Eustis on confronting social and aesthetic problems. USA: San Francisco, CA. 1975-1986. Lang.: Eng.   2250

Productions of Dario Fo's *Morte accidentale di un anarchico (Accidental Death of an Anarchist)* in the light of Fo's political ideas. USA. Canada. Italy. 1970-1986. Lang.: Eng.   2262

Euripides

Audience

HaBimah Theatre production of *Troádes (The Trojan Women)* by Euripides. Israel: Tel-Aviv. 1982-1983. Lang.: Eng.   199

Performance/production

Review of *A trójai nők (The Trojan Women)* adapted from Euripides and Sartre by Gyula Illyés, directed by László Vámos. Hungary: Budapest. 1986. Lang.: Hun.   1792

Review of *Trójai Nők (The Trojan Women)* by Jean-Paul Sartre, produced at Nemzeti Szinház. Hungary: Budapest. 1986. Lang.: Hun.   1855

Troádes (The Trojan Women) directed by László Gergely at Csokonai Theatre. Hungary: Debrecen. 1985. Lang.: Hun.   1909

Collection of newspaper reviews by London theatre critics. UK. 1986. Lang.: Eng.   2099

Collection of newspaper reviews by London theatre critics. UK-England: London. 1986. Lang.: Eng.   2122

Robert Wilson's production of *Alcestis* at the American Repertory Theatre. USA: Cambridge, MA. 1986.   2306

Plays/librettos/scripts

Marguerite Yourcenar's treatment of Electra story compared to other versions. France. 1944-1954. Lang.: Fre.   2554

Applying Brecht's dramatic principles to the plays of Euripides. Germany, East. Greece. 450 B.C.-1956 A.D.   2614

Moral and political crises reflected in the plays of Euripides. Greece: Athens. 438-408 B.C. Lang.: Fre.   2634

Masked god as tragic subject in works of Aeschylus, Sophocles and Euripides. Greece. 499-401 B.C. Lang.: Fre.   2636

The Peasants by Władysław Reymont as possible source for O'Neill's version of the lustful stepmother play. USA. 1902-1924. Lang.: Eng.   2930

Robert Wilson's adaptation of Euripides' *Alcestis*. USA: Cambridge, MA. 1979-1986. Lang.: Eng.   2939

Relation to other fields

Factors that discouraged historical drama in the classical period. Greece: Athens. 475-375 B.C. Lang.: Eng.   3035

Euryanthe

Basic theatrical documents

The influence of *Euryanthe* by Carl Maria von Weber on Richard Wagner. Germany: Dresden. 1824-1879. Lang.: Eng.   3649

Eurydice

Plays/librettos/scripts

Repetition and negativism in plays of Jean Anouilh and Eugene O'Neill. France. USA. 1922-1960. Lang.: Eng.   2578

Eustis, Oskar

Performance/production

Dramaturg Oskar Eustis on confronting social and aesthetic problems. USA: San Francisco, CA. 1975-1986. Lang.: Eng.   2250

Evans, Harry

Administration

Involvement of Robert Keysar with Harry Evans and Blackfriars' Children's Company. England: London. 1608. Lang.: Eng.   1433

Evans, John

Plays/librettos/scripts

A review of Southwestern University's Brown Symposium VII, 'Benjamin Britten and the Ceremony of Innocence'. USA: Georgetown. 1985. Lang.: Eng.   3904

Evans, Nancy

Performance/production

Interview with singer Nancy Evans and writer Eric Crozier discussing their association with Benjamin Britten. USA: Columbia, MO. UK-England: London. 1940-1985. Lang.: Eng.   3820

Plays/librettos/scripts

A review of Southwestern University's Brown Symposium VII, 'Benjamin Britten and the Ceremony of Innocence'. USA: Georgetown. 1985. Lang.: Eng.   3904

Eve of the Trial

Plays/librettos/scripts

Biographical sketch of playwright/performer Samm-Art Williams. USA: Burgaw, NC, New York, NY. 1940-1986. Lang.: Eng.   2946

Evening, An

SEE

Večer.

Ever Loving

Plays/librettos/scripts

Review of five published plays by Margaret Hollingsworth. Canada. Lang.: Eng.   2440

Everding, August
Performance/production
Stills from telecast performances. List of principals, conductor and production staff included. USA: New York, NY. 1986. Lang.: Eng.
3795

Every Man in His Humour
Plays/librettos/scripts
Ben Jonson's use of romance in *Volpone*. England. 1575-1600. Lang.: Eng.
2461
Use of group aggression in Ben Jonson's comedies. England. 1575-1600. Lang.: Eng.
2508
Reference materials
List of 37 productions of 23 Renaissance plays, with commentary. UK. USA. New Zealand. 1986. Lang.: Eng.
3000

Everyman
Performance/production
Account of a modern production of *Everyman*. USA: New York, NY. 1986. Lang.: Eng.
2314

Everyman Theatre (Cheltenham)
Administration
Artistic directors of Everyman Theatre and Theatre Clwyd discuss their theatres. UK-England: Cheltenham. UK-Wales: Mold. 1986. Lang.: Eng.
82

Everyman Theatre (Liverpool)
Performance/production
Collection of newspaper reviews by London theatre critics. UK. 1986. Lang.: Eng.
2103
Survey of theatre season in Merseyside. UK-England. 1986. Lang.: Eng.
2157

Everyman Theatre Company (Washington, DC)
Performance/production
Career of director/choreographer Mike Malone. USA: Washington, DC, Cleveland, OH. 1968-1985. Lang.: Eng.
2275

Evreinov, Nikolaj Nikolajevič
SEE
Jevrejnov, Nikolaj Nikolajevič.

Ewers, Carl Otto
Plays/librettos/scripts
Interview with playwright Carl Otto Ewers on writing for children. Sweden. 1986. Lang.: Swe.
2822

Ewing, Maria
Performance/production
Performance analysis of the title role of *Carmen*. France. 1875-1986. Lang.: Eng.
3725

Execution of Justice
Performance/production
Reviews of *Execution of Justice*, written and staged by Emily Mann. USA: New York, NY. 1986. Lang.: Eng.
2230
Mark Bly on the dramaturg's responsibility to question. USA: Minneapolis, MN. 1981-1986. Lang.: Eng.
2294

Exhibitions
Design/technology
Reports on Showtech conference. Germany, West: Berlin, West. 1986. Lang.: Hun.
273
Report on exhibition in Warsaw, especially on the S20 dimmer used by the lighting director of the Thália Theatre in Budapest. Poland: Warsaw. Hungary: Budapest. 1986. Lang.: Hun.
308
Overview of performance technology show at Riverside Studios. UK-England: London. 1986. Lang.: Eng.
323
Les Immatériaux, multimedia exhibit by Jean-François Lyotard. France: Paris. 1986. Lang.: Eng.
3249
Performance/production
Review of the Theatre History Collection exhibition in the Széchényi National Library. Hungary. 1610-1850. Lang.: Hun.
734
Touring exhibition 'Artists in the Theatre': influence of visual artists in the development of performance art. UK. 1900-1986. Lang.: Eng.
3447
A profile of puppeteer Basil Milovsaroff. USA. 1934-1985.
3984
Reference materials
Catalogue of an exhibit on the Carlo Felice Theatre, destroyed in World War II, and its proposed reconstruction. Italy: Genoa. 1600-1985. Lang.: Ita.
1024
Exhibition catalogue about context of the work and influence of Karl Kraus. Austria: Vienna. USA: New York, NY. France: Paris. 1874-1986. Lang.: Ger.
2980
Interpretation of Ferdinand Raimund's dramas after his death. Austria: Vienna. 1790-1986. Lang.: Ger.
2981

Exhibit on life and work of actor Alessandro Moissi. Italy: Trieste. Austria. 1880-1935. Lang.: Ita.
2993
Influence of stage director Max Reinhardt on film production. Germany: Berlin. Austria: Vienna. 1913-1945. Lang.: Ger.
3244
The purchase and eventual exhibition of a collection of Stravinsky's work. Switzerland: Basel. USA: New York, NY. 1930-1985. Lang.: Eng.
3500
Catalogue of an exhibition of costume designs for Broadway musicals. USA: New York, NY. 1900-1925. Lang.: Eng, Ger.
3635
Catalogue of a 1986 exhibition on the Ferrari family and their puppets. Italy. 1877-1986. Lang.: Ita.
3988

Existentialism
Plays/librettos/scripts
Relation of 'New Drama'—from Büchner to Beckett—to Afrikaans drama. Europe. South Africa, Republic of. 1800-1985. Lang.: Afr.
2539
Various implications of 'waiting' in Samuel Beckett's *Waiting for Godot*. France. 1953. Lang.: Eng.
2555

Experimental Art Foundation (Adelaide)
Performance spaces
History of the Experimental Art Foundation as an alternative space. Australia: Adelaide. 1974-1986. Lang.: Eng.
3437

Experimental theatre
SEE ALSO
Avant-garde theatre.
Alternative theatre.
Administration
John Neville's administration of the Neptune Theatre. Canada: Halifax, NS. 1979-1983. Lang.: Eng.
27
Independent financing of experimental theatre. USSR. 1980-1986. Lang.: Rus.
182
Audience
Audience-performer relationship in experimental theatre. USSR: Moscow. 1986. Lang.: Rus.
204
Absence of an audience for non-mainstream theatre. USSR. 1980-1986. Lang.: Rus.
206
Basic theatrical documents
Writings by Tadeusz Kantor on the nature of theatre. Poland. 1956-1985. Lang.: Eng.
1490
Design/technology
Interview with set designer Jim Clayburgh. USA: New York, NY. 1972-1983. Lang.: Eng.
390
Institutions
Production of Jürgen Lederach's *Japanische Spiele (Japanese Play)* by Transformtheater. Germany, West: Berlin, West. 1981-1986. Lang.: Swe.
499
On concept of the new group, Der Kreis. Austria: Vienna. 1986-1987. Lang.: Ger.
1536
History of the Shared Stage theatre company. Canada: Winnipeg, MB. 1980-1986. Lang.: Eng.
1555
Theories on incorporating traditional theatrical forms into popular theatre. Canada: Toronto, ON. 1970-1986. Lang.: Eng.
3408
Performance/production
Directorial process as seen through major productions of Stanislavskij, Brecht, Kazan and Brook. 1898-1964. Lang.: Eng.
650
Meeting of experimental theatre groups at Szkéné Theatre. Hungary: Budapest. 1985. Lang.: Hun.
736
Analysis of career and methods of director Jerzy Grotowski. Poland. 1959-1984. Lang.: Hun.
771
Director Deborah Warner of KICK on her production of Shakespeare's *Coriolanus* and limited public funding for the non-touring company. UK-England: London. 1985-1986. Lang.: Eng.
812
The development and production of Robert Wilson's *CIVIL warS*. USA. Germany, East. 1984. Lang.: Eng.
838
History of the Wooster Group. USA: New York, NY. 1975-1985. Lang.: Eng.
849
American experimental theatre artists performing in Europe: advantages and problems encountered. USA: New York, NY. 1984. Lang.: Eng.
855
Problems of experimental theatre. USSR. 1980-1986. Lang.: Rus. 869
Interview with director Carlos Gimenez. Argentina. Venezuela: Caracas. 1969-1986. Lang.: Eng.
1636
Notes, interviews and evolution of actor/director Jean-Marie Serreau. France. 1938-1973. Lang.: Fre.
1724

Experimental theatre — cont'd

Collaboration of Hélène Cixous and Ariane Mnouchkine. France.
Cambodia. 1964-1986. Lang.: Eng.   1752

Production analysis of a montage of sketches about Electra by
Stúdió K. Hungary: Budapest. 1986. Lang.: Hun.   1773

Experimental training method used by Kaméleon Szinház Csoport.
Hungary: Kurd. 1982-1985. Lang.: Hun.   1798

Performances of the 15th festival of contemporary Polish drama.
Poland: Wrocław. 1986. Lang.: Hun.   2019

Interviews with Polish theatre professionals. Poland: Poznań. 1963-
1985. Lang.: Eng.   2024

Career and philosophy of director Tadeusz Kantor. Poland. 1915-
1985. Lang.: Eng.   2028

Interview with director Tadeusz Kantor. Poland. 1967-1985. Lang.:
Eng.   2029

Artistic profile and main achievements of Akademia Ruchu. Poland:
Warsaw. 1973-1986. Lang.: Pol.   2037

Director, producer Wu Jing-Jyi discusses his life and career in
theatre. Taiwan. USA: Minneapolis, MN, New York, NY. 1939-
1980. Lang.: Eng.   2098

Interview with Wooster Group's artistic director Elizabeth LeCompte.
USA: New York, NY. 1984. Lang.: Eng.   2288

Conflict over artistic control in American Repertory Theatre's
production of Endgame by Samuel Beckett. USA: Boston, MA. 1984.
Lang.: Eng.   2296

Revival of Philip Glass and Robert Wilson's Einstein on the Beach
and opportunities to improve the piece. USA: New York, NY. 1976-
1984. Lang.: Eng.   2305

Description of street theatre festival. Poland: Jelenia Góra. 1985.
Lang.: Eng, Fre.   3344

Interview with composer-musician Peter Gordon. USA. 1985. Lang.:
Eng.   3492

Plays/librettos/scripts

Interview with playwright Al Carmines. USA: New York, NY. 1985.
Lang.: Eng.   981

Experimental farce techniques in Fidela by Aurelio Ferretti.
Argentina. 1930-1960. Lang.: Spa.   2360

Discusses feminist theatre with themes concerning the female body.
Canada: Quebec, PQ. 1969-1985. Lang.: Eng.   2428

Beckett as writer and director. France. UK. 1947-1985. Lang.: Fre.
                                                                    2546

Review of study of experimental plays and playwrights. Hungary.
1967-1983. Lang.: Hun.   2641

Experimental theatrical productions of Achille Campanile. Italy.
1920-1930. Lang.: Ita.   2695

Reasons for the lack of new Spanish drama and the few recent
significant realistic and experimental plays. Spain. 1972-1985. Lang.:
Spa.   2793

Discussion of issues raised in plays of 1985-86 season. USA: New
York, NY. 1985-1986. Lang.: Eng.   2928

Reference materials

Writings by and about director Tadeusz Kantor. Poland. 1946-1986.
Lang.: Eng.   2995

Relation to other fields

Interview with director Lech Raczak of Theatre of the Eighth Day.
Poland: Poznań. 1968-1985. Lang.: Eng.   3048

Theory/criticism

'New Wave' drama and contemporary Soviet dramaturgy. USSR.
1986. Lang.: Rus.   1237

Eleven theatre professionals discuss their personal direction and the
direction of experimental theatre. USA: New York, NY. 1985.
Lang.: Eng.   3137

Expo '86 (Vancouver, BC)

Design/technology

Theatre consultant S. Leonard Auerbach's technical specifications for
Expo '86. Canada: Vancouver, BC. 1986. Lang.: Eng.   243

Working with robots to promote Expo '86. Canada.   3950

Performance spaces

Planning of 18 performance venues for Expo 86. Canada:
Vancouver, BC. 1986. Lang.: Eng.   589

Performance/production

Previews cultural events and theatre at Expo '86. Canada:
Vancouver, BC. 1986. Lang.: Eng.   3329

Expressionism

Performance/production

Illustrated interview with choreographer Pina Bausch. Germany.
1970-1985. Lang.: Fre.   1347

Plays/librettos/scripts

Essays on all facets of Expressionism including theatre and dance.
Germany. Austria. 1891-1933. Lang.: Ger, Ita.   953

Bertolt Brecht and the Expressionists. Germany. 1919-1944. Lang.:
Eng.   955

Career of expressionist playwright Bertram Brooker. Canada:
Toronto, ON. 1888-1949. Lang.: Eng.   2418

The immigrant in plays by Herman Voaden and Robertson Davies.
Canada. 1934-1950. Lang.: Eng.   2431

Relation of 'New Drama'—from Büchner to Beckett—to Afrikaans
drama. Europe. South Africa, Republic of. 1800-1985. Lang.: Afr.
                                                                    2539

Influence of German expressionism on the plays of Luigi Pirandello.
Italy. Germany. 1917-1930. Lang.: Ita.   2682

Imagery of gender compared in works by Susan Glaspell and
Eugene O'Neill. USA: New York, NY, Provincetown, MA. 1916-
1922. Lang.: Eng.   2893

Origins and influences of Woyzeck on Berg's opera Wozzeck.
Austria: Vienna. 1821-1925. Lang.: Eng.   3855

Relation to other fields

Analysis of Symphony by Herman Voaden and Lowrie Warrener.
Canada. 1914-1933. Lang.: Eng.   1075

Philosophical context of the plays of Herman Voaden. Canada:
Toronto, ON. 1929-1943. Lang.: Eng.   3170

Kurt Weill and German expressionism. Germany: Berlin. 1923-1930.
Lang.: Eng.   3920

Theory/criticism

Solipsism, expressionism and aesthetics in the anti-rational dramas of
Gottfried Benn. Germany: Berlin. 1914-1934. Lang.: Eng.   3107

Eybner, Richard

Performance/production

Biography of Burgtheater actor Richard Eybner. Austria: Vienna.
1896-1986. Lang.: Ger.   1653

Eyes

Performance/production

Career of director/choreographer Mike Malone. USA: Washington,
DC, Cleveland, OH. 1968-1985. Lang.: Eng.   2275

Eyes of an American

Plays/librettos/scripts

Biographical sketch of playwright/performer Samm-Art Williams.
USA: Burgaw, NC, New York, NY. 1940-1986. Lang.: Eng.   2946

Eyre, Richard

Performance/production

Collection of newspaper reviews by London theatre critics. UK-
England: London. 1986. Lang.: Eng.   2112

Collection of newspaper reviews by London theatre critics. UK-
England: London. 1986. Lang.: Eng.   2124

Eyre, Ronald

Performance/production

Collection of newspaper reviews by London theatre critics. UK-
England: London. 1986. Lang.: Eng.   2122

Fabbri, Diego

Plays/librettos/scripts

Letters of playwright Diego Fabbri. Italy. 1960-1978. Lang.: Ita.
                                                                    2672

Fábián, László

Performance/production

László Fábián's Levéltetvek az akasztófán (Plant-Lice on the
Gallows) directed by István Szőke. Hungary: Miskolc. 1986. Lang.:
Hun.   1942

Isván Szőke directs Letvéltetvek az akasztófán (Plant-Lice on the
Gallows) by László Fábián. Hungary: Miskolc. 1986. Lang.: Hun.
                                                                    1961

Fabra, Pompeu

Plays/librettos/scripts

Short history of Catalan translations of plays. Spain-Catalonia. 1848-
1984. Lang.: Fre.   2813

Relation to other fields

Reports and discussions of restricted cultural communication.
Lebanon. Spain-Catalonia. USA. 1985. Lang.: Fre, Spa, Cat.   1111

Fabre, Jan
Performance/production
Collection of newspaper reviews by London theatre critics. UK-England: London. 1986. Lang.: Eng.   2119

Fabris, Jacopo
Design/technology
Works by and about designers Jacopo Fabris and Citoyen Boullet. Denmark: Copenhagen. France: Paris. 1760-1801. Lang.: Eng.   256

Folio drawings by Jacopo Fabris illustrating how to paint perspective scenery and build theatrical machinery. Denmark: Copenhagen. Italy. 1760-1801. Lang.: Eng.   257

Facio, Angel
Plays/librettos/scripts
Reasons for the lack of new Spanish drama and the few recent significant realistic and experimental plays. Spain. 1972-1985. Lang.: Spa.   2793

Factory Theatre Lab (FTL, Toronto, ON)
Performance spaces
Troubles faced by Adelaide Court theatre complex. Canada: Toronto, ON. 1979-1983. Lang.: En .   587

Faculty
SEE
Training, teacher.

Teaching methods.

Fadren (Father, The)
Plays/librettos/scripts
Study of realism vs metadrama. Europe. 429 B.C.-1978 A.D. Lang.: Eng.   2540

The presentation of atheism in August Strindberg's *The Father*. Sweden. 1887. Lang.: Eng.   2821

Fair Maid of the West
Reference materials
List of 37 productions of 23 Renaissance plays, with commentary. UK. USA. New Zealand. 1986. Lang.: Eng.   3000

Fait Accompli
Performance/production
Analysis of Twyla Tharp's *Fait Accompli*. USA. 1984. Lang.: Eng.   1370

Faithful Shepherdess, The
Plays/librettos/scripts
Passion in early plays of Beaumont and Fletcher. England. 1608-1611. Lang.: Eng.   945

Female characterization in Nicholas Rowe's plays. England. 1629-1720. Lang.: Eng.   2475

Falcon, Cornélie
Performance/production
Careers of young Parisian prima donnas. France: Paris. 1830-1850. Lang.: Eng.   3728

Fall, Leo
Performance/production
Elisabeth Kales and her performance in the main role of Leo Fall's operetta *Madame Pompadour*. Austria: Vienna. 1955-1986. Lang.: Ger.   3484

Falls, Robert
Performance/production
Reviews of *Orchards* written and staged by Robert Falls after Čechov. USA: New York, NY. 1986. Lang.: Eng.   2222

False Confidences
SEE
Fausses confidences, Les.

Falso Movimento (Milan)
Relation to other fields
Contrasts between culture and mass media. Italy. 1980-1986. Lang.: Ita.   3171

Falstaff
Performance/production
Photographs, cast list, synopsis, and discography of Metropolitan Opera radio broadcast performances. USA: New York, NY. 1986. Lang.: Eng.   3794

Plays/librettos/scripts
Operatic facsimiles by Mozart, Bellini and Verdi. Europe. 1814-1985. Lang.: Eng.   3863

Shakespeare's influence on Verdi's operas. Germany. Italy. Austria. 1750-1850. Lang.: Eng.   3878

Falstaff (Gothenburg)
Performance/production
Report from an international amateur theatre festival where music and dance were prominent. Denmark: Copenhagen. 1986. Lang.: Swe.   683

Familia/Family (New York, NY)
Performance/production
Profile of theatre companies featured in Festival Latino de Nueva York. USA: New York, NY. 1984. Lang.: Eng.   2197

Family Voices
Plays/librettos/scripts
Theme of family in plays of Harold Pinter. UK-England. 1957-1981. Lang.: Eng.   2836

Family, Inc.
Plays/librettos/scripts
Race in prison dramas of Piñero, Camillo, Elder and Bullins. USA. 1970-1986. Lang.: Eng.   2912

Famosa comèdia de la gala està en son punt, La (Famous Comedy of the Gala Done to a Turn, The)
Basic theatrical documents
Edition of *La famosa comèdia de la gala està en son punt (The Famous Comedy of the Gala Done to a Turn)*, with analysis. Spain-Catalonia. 1625-1680. Lang.: Cat.   1497

Fan, Chengming
Plays/librettos/scripts
Problems of adapting classic plays. China, People's Republic of. 1986. Lang.: Chi.   3543

Fan, Ts'ui-t'ing
Plays/librettos/scripts
Characteristics and influences of Fan Ts'ui-T'ing's plays. China. 1900-1980. Lang.: Chi.   3532

Fang, Tushu
Performance/production
Use of early performance records to infer theatre activities of a later period. China. 1868-1935. Lang.: Chi.   3505

Fanning, John
Performance/production
Interview with baritone John Fanning. Canada: Toronto, ON. 1980-1986. Lang.: Eng.   3709

Far From the Madding Crowd
Performance/production
Collection of newspaper reviews by London theatre critics. UK-England: London. 1986. Lang.: Eng.   2125

Farago, Peter
Performance/production
Collection of newspaper reviews by London theatre critics. UK-England: London. 1986. Lang.: Eng.   2113

Farce
Basic theatrical documents
Text of *The Miser Outwitted*, attributed to Major John Richardson, with introduction. Canada. UK-Ireland: Dublin. 1838-1848. Lang.: Eng.   1465

English translation of *El desconfiado prodigioso (The Remarkable Misanthrope)* by Max Aub. Spain. 1903-1972. Lang.: Eng, Spa. 1493

English translation of *L'ús de la matèria (The Use of Matter)* by Manuel de Pedrolo. Spain-Catalonia. 1963. Lang.: Cat, Eng.   1500
Performance/production
Review of Alex Koenigsmark's *Adié, milacku! (Good-bye, Darling!)* directed by Péter Gothár at Csiky Gergely Theatre under the title *Agyő, kedvesem*. Hungary: Kaposvár. 1985. Lang.: Hun.   1862

Productions of Dario Fo's *Morte accidentale di un anarchico (Accidental Death of an Anarchist)* in the light of Fo's political ideas. USA. Canada. Italy. 1970-1986. Lang.: Eng.   2262

Early form of Sicilian dialect theatre. Italy. 1780-1800. Lang.: Ita.   3337

Plays/librettos/scripts
Development and subsequent decline of the three-act farce. UK-England. 1875-1900. Lang.: Eng.   976

Characteristics of farce and the problem of humor. Lang.: Pol. 2357

Experimental farce techniques in *Fidela* by Aurelio Ferretti. Argentina. 1930-1960. Lang.: Spa.   2360

Textual study of *La Farce de Maître Pierre Pathelin (The Farce of Master Pierre Pathelin)*. France. 1485-1970. Lang.: Fre.   2561

Joe Orton's redefinition of farce as a genre. UK-England. 1960-1969. Lang.: Eng.   2840
Relation to other fields
Anecdotes about caricaturist Liao Bingxiong and comedian Chen Baichen. China, People's Republic of. 1942-1981. Lang.: Chi.   1078

Farce de Maître Pierre Pathelin, La (Farce of Master Pierre Pathelin, The)
Plays/librettos/scripts
Textual study of *La Farce de Maître Pierre Pathelin (The Farce of Master Pierre Pathelin)*. France. 1485-1970. Lang.: Fre. 2561

Farce of Master Pierre Pathelin, The
SEE
Farce de Maître Pierre Pathelin, La.

Farinelli
Performance/production
History of *castrati* in opera. Italy. 1599-1797. Lang.: Eng. 3761

Farkas, A (Wolf, The)
Performance/production
A farkas (The Wolf) by Ferenc Molnár, directed by István Verebes at Vigszinház. Hungary: Budapest. 1985. Lang.: Hun. 1781

István Verebes' production of *A farkas (The Wolf)* by Ferenc Molnár at the Vigszinház. Hungary: Budapest. 1985. Lang.: Hun. 1805

Farkas, Karl
Performance/production
History of the Viennese cabaret. Austria: Vienna. 1890-1945. Lang.: Ger. 3364

Farré, Ged Marlon Jean-Paul
Performance/production
A photographic essay of 42 soloists and groups performing mime or gestural theatre. 1986. 3290

Farrell, Bernard
Performance/production
Collection of newspaper reviews by London theatre critics. UK-England: London. 1986. Lang.: Eng. 2121

Farrell, Carol
Performance/production
Development of *Anerca* by Figures of Speech Theater. USA: Freeport, ME. 1985. Lang.: Eng. 3999

Farrell, John
Performance/production
Development of *Anerca* by Figures of Speech Theater. USA: Freeport, ME. 1985. Lang.: Eng. 3999

Fascism
Relation to other fields
Critique of the relation between politics and theatre in Klaus Mann's *Mephisto* performed by Théâtre du Soleil. France: Paris. 1979. Lang.: Eng. 1085

Fassbinder, Rainer Werner
Plays/librettos/scripts
Discussion of issues raised in plays of 1985-86 season. USA: New York, NY. 1985-1986. Lang.: Eng. 2928

Fast, Howard
Relation to other fields
The premiere of Howard Fast's play under the title *Harminc ezüstpénz (Thirty Pieces of Silver)* in Hungary. Hungary. 1951-1986. Lang.: Hun. 3036

Fatal Curiosity, The
Plays/librettos/scripts
Liberated female characters in the plays of George Lillo. England. 1730-1759. Lang.: Eng. 2477

Father's Lying Dead on the Ironing Board
Performance/production
Collection of newspaper reviews by London theatre critics. UK-England: London. 1986. Lang.: Eng. 2109

Faucit, Harriet
Performance/production
The portrayal of Cleopatra by various actresses. England. 1813-1890. Lang.: Eng. 1699

Faulkner, Cliff
Design/technology
A profile of Cliff Faulkner, resident designer at South Coast Repertory. USA: Los Angeles, CA. 1977-1986. 365

Fausse suivante, La (Between Two Women)
Performance/production
Analysis of two productions of plays by Marivaux. France: Nanterre. Germany, West: Berlin, West. 1985. Lang.: Swe. 1739

Fausses confidences, Les (False Confidences, The)
Performance/production
Staging of plays by Marivaux compared to textual analysis. France. 1723-1981. Lang.: Fre. 1746

Faust
Performance/production
Interpretation of classics for theatre and television. USSR. 1980-1986. Lang.: Rus. 2337

Reviews of 10 vintage recordings of complete operas on LP. USA. 1906-1925. Lang.: Eng. 3792

Faustino
Performance/production
A photographic essay of 42 soloists and groups performing mime or gestural theatre. 1986. 3290

Favola del figlio cambiato, La (Fable of the Changeling, The)
Plays/librettos/scripts
Correspondence between Luigi Pirandello and composer Gian Francesco Malipiero. Italy. 1832-1938. Lang.: Ita. 2699

Favorite, La
Performance/production
Reviews of 10 vintage recordings of complete operas on LP. USA. 1906-1925. Lang.: Eng. 3792

Fazakas, Faz
Design/technology
Director of electronics and mechanical design for the Muppets, Faz Fazakas. USA. 1986. 3262

Performance/production
Behind-the-scenes look at *Fraggle Rock*. Canada: Toronto, ON. 1984. Lang.: Eng. 3269

Fears of Fragmentation
Plays/librettos/scripts
Utopia in early plays by Arnold Wesker. UK-England. 1958-1970. Lang.: Eng. 2884

Fedák, Sári
Performance/production
Profile of actress Sári Fedák. Austro-Hungarian Empire. 1879-1955. Lang.: Hun. 3940

Federal Theatre (New York)
Plays/librettos/scripts
Career of Marxist playwright George Sklar. USA: New York, NY. 1920-1967. Lang.: Eng. 985

Federal Theatre Project (Washington, DC)
Institutions
John Houseman discusses Federal Theatre Project. USA: New York, NY, Washington, DC. 1935-1940. Lang.: Eng. 559

Plays/librettos/scripts
Attitudes toward technology reflected in some Living Newspaper productions of the Federal Theatre Project. USA. 1935-1939. Lang.: Eng. 2905

Feeling You're Behind
Plays/librettos/scripts
Jungian analysis of the plays of Peter Nichols. UK-England. 1967-1984. Lang.: Eng. 2848

Fefu and Her Friends
Plays/librettos/scripts
Interview with playwright Maria Irene Fornes. USA. 1965-1985. Lang.: Eng. 979

Fehér, András
Performance/production
András Fehér directs Verdi's *Un ballo in maschera* at the Hungarian State Opera House. Hungary: Budapest. 1986. Lang.: Hun. 3746

Fehle, Armin
Institutions
Activities and history of the audience-society, Freunde des Theaters in der Josefstadt. Austria: Vienna. 1985-1986. Lang.: Ger. 1535

Fehling, Jürgen
Relation to other fields
Study of Fascist theatrical policies. Germany: Berlin. 1933-1944. Lang.: Ger. 1091

Feingold, Michael
Performance/production
New York critics respond negatively to plays successful in Los Angeles. USA: Los Angeles, CA, New York, NY. 1983-1984. Lang.: Eng. 2258

Theory/criticism
Interviews on the role of the critic in New York theatre. USA: New York, NY. 1983. Lang.: Eng. 1226

Feld, Kenneth
Performance/production
A general review of the 1985 circus season. USA. Canada. 1985. Lang.: Eng. 3394

Felix, Bruno
History of the Theater für Vorarlberg. Austria: Bregenz. 1818-1986. Lang.: Ger. 3

Fellini, Federico
Performance/production
Reviews of *Sweet Charity* by Neil Simon, staged and choreographed by Bob Fosse. USA: New York, NY. 1986. Lang.: Eng. 3611

Fellner, Ferdinánd
Performance spaces
The history of the theatre building used by Szegedi Nemzeti Színház. Hungary: Szeged. 1800-1883. Lang.: Hun. 603

Felsenreitschule (Salzburg)
Performance/production
Interview with Jean-Pierre Ponnelle discussing his directing technique and set designs. Austria: Salzburg. 1984. Lang.: Eng. 3699

Felsenstein, Walter
Performance/production
Collection of interviews with Walter Felsenstein. Germany: Berlin. 1921-1971. Lang.: Ger. 3735

Feminism
Audience
Context and design of some lesbian performances. USA: New York, NY. 1985. Lang.: Eng. 1455
Basic theatrical documents
Text of radio play about a woman doctor who masqueraded as a man. Canada: Montreal, PQ. UK-Scotland: Edinburgh. South Africa, Republic of: Cape Town. 1809-1859. Lang.: Eng. 3175
Institutions
Interview with Julia Miles, director of the Women's Project, American Place Theatre. USA: New York, NY. 1978-1985. Lang.: Eng. 558
Place of women in Britain's National Theatre. UK-England: London. 1986. Lang.: Eng. 1588
Progress and aims of Women's Playhouse Trust. UK-England: London. 1984-1986. Lang.: Eng. 1590
Performance/production
Discussion of women's comedy by one of its practitioners. Australia: Melbourne. 1986. Lang.: Eng. 657
Development of women's and Maori theatre. New Zealand. 1980-1986. Lang.: Eng. 767
Brechtian technique in the contemporary feminist drama of Caryl Churchill, Claire Luckham and others. UK-England. 1956-1979. Lang.: Eng. 815
Gender roles in the work of female theatre professionals. USA. 1985. Lang.: Eng. 836
Feminist criticism of theatre anthropology conference on women's roles. USA. Denmark. 1985. Lang.: Eng. 845
Mariann Csernus' stage adaptations and performance in works of Simone de Beauvoir and Liv Ullmann. Hungary: Budapest. 1985. Lang.: Hun. 1816
Life and work of actress-playwright Franca Rame. Italy. 1929-1983. Lang.: Eng. 1988
Political difficulties in staging two touring productions of Shakespeare's *The Taming of the Shrew*. UK. 1985-1986. Lang.: Eng. 2104
Interview with Lesbian feminist theatre company Hard Corps. UK-England. 1984-1986. Lang.: Eng. 2164
Feminist theatre group Beryl and the Perils. UK-England. 1986. Lang.: Eng. 2171
Performances by women on women's issues. Australia: Sydney, N.S.W. 1986. Lang.: Eng. 3442
Careers of fifty successful female comics. 1900-1986. Lang.: Eng. 3467
Women's roles in the operas of Benjamin Britten. USA. 1940-1979. Lang.: Eng. 3824
Plays/librettos/scripts
Discussion of plays and themes concerning the Women's Movement. USA. 1971-1986. Lang.: Eng. 982
Interview with playwright Alma de Groen. Australia. Lang.: Eng. 2367
Betty Roland's life and stage work. Australia: Sydney, N.S.W. 1928-1985. Lang.: Eng. 2382
Discusses feminist theatre with themes concerning the female body. Canada: Quebec, PQ. 1969-1985. Lang.: Eng. 2428
Review of five published plays by Margaret Hollingsworth. Canada. Lang.: Eng. 2440

Historical background of *Sisters of Eve* by Tricia Burden. Eire. 1984-1986. Lang.: Eng. 2455
Interview with playwright Kathleen Betsko. England: Coventry. USA. 1960-1986. Lang.: Eng. 2487
Political aspects of George Sand's *Père va-tout-seul (Old Man Go-It-Alone)*. France. 1830-1844. Lang.: Eng. 2574
Brecht's patriarchal view of women as seen in the character of Jenny in *Die Dreigroschenoper (The Three Penny Opera)*. Germany, East. 2615
Biography of playwright Teresa Deevy. Ireland. 1894-1963. Lang.: Eng. 2665
Pirandello's interest in the problems of women evidenced in his plays and novels. Italy. 1867-1936. Lang.: Fre. 2714
Current state of women's playwriting. UK-England. 1985-1986. Lang.: Eng. 2830
Role of women in society in Caryl Churchill's plays. UK-England. 1986. Lang.: Eng. 2877
Introduction to and overview of articles contained in Volume 40 of *Theatre Annual*. USA. 1900-1985. Lang.: Eng. 2898
Beth Henley's play *Crimes of the Heart* as an example of female criminality in response to a patriarchal culture. USA. 1980-1986. Lang.: Eng. 2923
Plays by women on the CBC radio network. Canada. 1985-1986. Lang.: Eng. 3185
Relation to other fields
Theatre as a force of social change in turn-of-the-century France. France. 1897-1901. Lang.: Eng. 3029
Feminist criticism of plays written by women. Germany. Switzerland. Austria. 1900-1986. Lang.: Ger. 3033
Theory/criticism
Lack of representation of women in theatre. USA: New York, NY. 1982-1986. Lang.: Eng. 1227

Femme rompue, La (Broken Woman, The)
Performance/production
Mariann Csernus' stage adaptations and performance in works of Simone de Beauvoir and Liv Ullmann. Hungary: Budapest. 1985. Lang.: Hun. 1816

Fen
Plays/librettos/scripts
Role of women in society in Caryl Churchill's plays. UK-England. 1986. Lang.: Eng. 2877

Fences
Performance/production
Brief history of August Wilson's *Fences*. USA. 1982-1986. Lang.: Eng. 2273

Feng, Menglong
Performance/production
Guide for producing traditional Beijing opera. China: Suzhou. 1574-1646. Lang.: Chi. 3508
Staging during the Ming dynasty. China: Suzhou. 1574-1646. Lang.: Chi. 3509

Feng, Xia
Reference materials
Review of 1985 dissertations. China, People's Republic of: Beijing. 1985. Lang.: Chi. 3545

Fennario, David
Institutions
Minority-language theatres in Canada. Canada: Montreal, PQ, Toronto, ON. 1986. Lang.: Eng. 1566
Performance/production
Playwright David Fennario's commitment to working-class community theatre. Canada: Montreal, PQ. 1980-1986. Lang.: Eng. 1661
Plays/librettos/scripts
Poverty in plays by Michel Tremblay and David Fennario. Canada: Quebec, PQ. 1970-1980. Lang.: Eng. 2410

Fenoglio, Edmo
Plays/librettos/scripts
Letters of playwright Diego Fabbri. Italy. 1960-1978. Lang.: Ita. 2672

Fenton, James
Theory/criticism
Critique of James Fenton's review of two books on Bertolt Brecht. USA. 1974. 1236

Festivals — cont'd

Report on International Festival of Theatre for Young Audiences. Canada. Japan. 1985. Lang.: Fre. 482

Overview of Festival Lennoxville and the role of anglophone drama in Quebec. Canada: Lennoxville, PQ. 1972-1982. Lang.: Eng. 485

Reports on theatre conferences and festivals in Asia. Philippines: Manila. Malaysia: Kuala Lumpur. Japan: Toga. India: Calcutta. 1981-1984. Lang.: Eng. 510

Amateur theatre festival described. Switzerland: La Chaux-de-Fonds. Lang.: Fre. 530

Overview of the *Not the RSC Festival* at the Almeida Theatre. UK-England: London. 1986. Lang.: Eng. 534

Edinburgh Festival extended by an international season. UK-Scotland: Edinburgh. 1984-1986. Lang.: Eng. 537

Reviews of Edinburgh Festival plays. UK-Scotland: Edinburgh. 1986. Lang.: Eng. 539

Tanz '86 festival. Austria: Vienna. 1986. Lang.: Ger. 1269

Fragile alternatives to Charlottetown Festival. Canada: Charlottetown, PE. 1982-1986. Lang.: Eng. 1540

History of the Rhubarb Festival. Canada: Toronto, ON. 1986. Lang.: Eng. 1549

The French-American Film Workshop, designed to showcase the work of independents and encourage cultural exchange. France: Avignon. 1986. Lang.: Eng. 3216

Royal Dramatic College's charity for retired theatre professionals. England: London. 1858-1877. Lang.: Eng. 3322

The Festival of Clowns in the Wiener Festwochen. Austria: Vienna. 1983-1986. Lang.: Ger. 3380

Wiener Sommer 1986 promoted by Teletheater-Gesellschaft. Austria: Vienna. 1986. Lang.: Ger. 3479

Spectaculum 1986 and the concept for this festival. Austria: Vienna. 1986. Lang.: Ger. 3480

History of the Salzburger Osterfestspiele. Austria: Salzburg. 1964-1986. Lang.: Ger. 3666

Report on the Salzburger Osterfestspiele. Austria: Salzburg. 1986. Lang.: Ger. 3669

History of music performances, mainly opera, at the Stratford Festival. Canada: Stratford, ON. 1951-1985. Lang.: Eng. 3671

Discussions of opera at the festival of Aix-en-Provence. France: Aix-en-Provence. 1960. Lang.: Fre. 3673

Performance/production

Overview of performances at the Expo Festival. Canada: Vancouver, BC. 1986. Lang.: Heb. 666

Rhubarb Festival is alternative to playwriting and workshopping conventions. Canada: Toronto, ON. 1986. Lang.: Eng. 672

Notes on the amateur theatre festival of Pisek. Czechoslovakia: Pisek. 1986. Lang.: Hun. 682

On international festival of children's theatre and youth theatre. France: Lyons. 1985. Lang.: Ukr. 708

Reviews and discussion of amateur theatre. Hungary. 1986. Lang.: Hun. 735

Meeting of experimental theatre groups at Szkéné Theatre. Hungary: Budapest. 1985. Lang.: Hun. 736

Nordic Festival of Amateur Theatre now includes Iceland and Greenland. Iceland: Reykjavik. 1986. Lang.: Swe. 740

Discussion of *Persepolis* and *Orghast* at Persepolis-Shiraz festival. Iran: Shiraz. 1971. Lang.: Ita. 741

Amateur theatre festival initiated by Teatret La Luna (Århus). Italy: Amandola. 1980-1986. Lang.: Swe. 747

Documentation on staging of plays for 'Maggio Musicale Fiorentino'. Italy: Florence. 1933-1985. Lang.: Ita. 752

Overview of performances, 'Holland '86'. Netherlands: Amsterdam. 1986. Lang.: Hun. 765

Collected reviews of theatre season. Spain-Catalonia: Barcelona. 1985-1986. Lang.: Cat. 791

Report from an amateur theatre festival at Västerbergs Folkhögskola. Sweden: Sandviken. 1986. Lang.: Swe. 800

Sixth annual amateur theatre festivals. Sweden: Västerås. 1986. Lang.: Swe. 803

Report from the international Fringe Festival. UK-Scotland: Edinburgh. 1986. Lang.: Swe. 819

Theatre of Nations Festival reviewed. USA: Baltimore, MD. 1986. Lang.: Hun. 833

Review of children's theatre festival. Yugoslavia: Šibenik. 1986. Lang.: Hun. 916

Dance and mime performances at annual Festival of the Arts. South Africa, Republic of: Grahamstown. 1986. Lang.: Eng. 1282

Director Dieter Dorn and his idea for staging *Der zerbrochene Krug (The Broken Jug)*. Austria: Salzburg. Germany, West: Munich. 1986. Lang.: Ger. 1651

John Neville's productions of *The Winter's Tale*, *Pericles*, and *Cymbeline*. Canada: Stratford, ON. 1974-1986. Lang.: Eng. 1657

Interview with actor Stephen Ouimette. Canada. 1960-1986. Lang.: Eng. 1663

Review of Edmonton Fringe Festival. Canada: Edmonton, AB. 1986. Lang.: Eng. 1682

Account of eighth International Theatre Festival. Colombia: Manizales. 1985. Lang.: Spa. 1694

Evaluation of the season's studio theatre productions. Hungary. 1985-1986. Lang.: Hun. 1803

Daniel Lanzini's notes on writing and staging his play *Hazaiot Kamot Bamizrah (Fantasies Awakening in the East)* at the Acre Theatre Festival. Israel: Acre. 1986. Lang.: Heb. 1981

Premiere of Luigi Pirandello's *I giganti della montagna (The Giants of the Mountain)*. Italy: Florence. 1937. Lang.: Ita. 1998

Reviews of the play productions at the National Theatre Festival. Korea. 1986. Lang.: Eng. 2009

Review of the play productions at the National Theatre Festival. Korea. 1985. Lang.: Eng. 2010

Performances of the 15th festival of contemporary Polish drama. Poland: Wrocław. 1986. Lang.: Hun. 2019

Description of the festival of Russian and Soviet drama with reviews of performances. Poland: Katowice. USSR. 1985. Lang.: Eng, Fre. 2049

On the Tenth Festival of Russian and Soviet Theatre in Poland. Poland: Katowice. USSR. 1986. Lang.: Rus. 2060

Review of international theatre festivals. Spain. Canada: Montreal, PQ, Toronto, ON. 1986. Lang.: Eng. 2077

Profile of theatre companies featured in Festival Latino de Nueva York. USA: New York, NY. 1984. Lang.: Eng. 2197

Director Ann Gadon on staging Brecht's *Lux in Tenebris*. USA: Chicago, IL. 1985. 2267

The organization of the Olympiad Arts Festival. USA: Los Angeles, CA. 1984. Lang.: Eng. 2281

Avant-garde theatre companies from Britain perform in New York festival. USA: New York, NY. 1970-1983. Lang.: Eng. 2286

Annual festival of Latin American plays at the Public Theatre. USA: New York, NY. 1985. Lang.: Eng. 2310

Festival of Latin American 'New Theatre'. USA: Washington, DC. 1984-1986. Lang.: Spa. 2313

Notes on theatrical events of nineteenth annual international theatre festival. Yugoslavia: Belgrade. 1985. Lang.: Hun. 2341

Survey of plays from 21st festival of Yugoslavian theatre. Yugoslavia. 1980. Lang.: Rus. 2342

Theatrical events of nineteenth annual international theatre festival. Yugoslavia. 1985. Lang.: Hun. 2343

Preview of Dubrovnik Summer Theatre Festival, 1985. Yugoslavia: Dubrovnik. 1984-1985. Lang.: Hun. 2345

History of the International Mime Festival. Canada: Winnipeg, MB. 1983-1986. Lang.: Eng. 3293

Previews cultural events and theatre at Expo '86. Canada: Vancouver, BC. 1986. Lang.: Eng. 3329

Maskers and masquerades of We tribal rituals. Ivory Coast. Lang.: Eng. 3341

Description of street theatre festival. Poland: Jelenia Góra. 1985. Lang.: Eng, Fre. 3344

Comparison of Holy Week Processions of Seville with English Mystery plays. Spain: Seville. 1986. Lang.: Eng. 3426

Overview of the Soundworks Festival. Australia. 1986. Lang.: Eng. 3439

Overview of an international festival of performance art by women. UK-England. 1986. Lang.: Eng. 3449

Reviews of three musicals about the 1960s. Hungary. 1985-1986. Lang.: Hun. 3488

Festivals — cont'd

Contemporary performance of the traditional *Festa d'Elx*. Spain: Elche. 1370-1985. Lang.: Eng. 3491

Interview with composer and director of the Finnish National opera Ilkka Kuusisto. Finland: Helsinki, Suomussalmi. 1967-1986. Lang.: Eng, Fre. 3724

Interview with Wolfgang Wagner on his staging of 3 Wagnerian operas at the Bayreuth Festspiele. Germany, West: Bayreuth. 1975-1985. Lang.: Hun. 3740

Report on international puppet festival. France. Lang.: Rus. 3964

Puppets in Performance, part of the 50th anniversary celebration of the WPA Federal Theatre Project. USA. 1986. 3974

Festival of puppet theatre. USSR-Russian SFSR. 1986. Lang.: Rus. 3987

Plays/librettos/scripts

Theatre festival and playwriting competition. France: Metz. 1982-1986. Lang.: Hun. 950

Description of national theatre festival. Argentina: Córdoba. 1985. Lang.: Spa. 2366

Interview with Peter Handke about his play *Prometheus gefesselt*. Austria: Salzburg. Greece. 1985-1986. Lang.: Ger. 2398

Criticizes the plays in the collection *Five From the Fringe*. Canada: Edmonton, AB. 1986. Lang.: Eng. 2425

Interviews with actress Pilar Romero and director Roberto Blanco at the Festival de Théâtre des Amériques. Canada: Montreal, PQ. 1985. Lang.: Eng. 2426

Compares pageant-wagon play about Edward IV with version by Thomas Heywood. England: Coventry, London. 1560-1600. Lang.: Eng. 3430

The church opera *Kain* written and composed for the Carinthiscer Sommer Festival. Austria: Ossiach. 1986. Lang.: Ger. 3858

Study of the librettos of operas premiered at the Teatro delle Novità festival. Italy: Bergamo. 1950-1973. Lang.: Ita. 3883

Reference materials

Overview of Charlottetown Festival productions. Canada: Charlottetown, PE. 1972-1983. Lang.: Eng. 1008

Yearbook of theatre, including radio and television drama. Sweden. 1985-1986. Lang.: Swe. 1031

Relation to other fields

Comparison of Olympiad Arts Festival and the 1984 Olympic Games. USA: Los Angeles, CA. 1984. Lang.: Eng. 1148

Description of the Cutler Playwright's Festival designed for junior high school students. USA: Groton, CT. 1983-1986. Lang.: Eng. 3065

Religious, communal and artistic functions of Hindu *odalan* festival. Indonesia. Lang.: Eng. 3359

Renaissance theatre at Valencia court, Catalan festivals. Spain-Catalonia: Valencia. 1330-1970. Lang.: Spa. 3362

Theory/criticism

Theory and origin of traditional street plays. Korea: Seoul. 200 B.C.-1986 A.D. Lang.: Kor. 3122

Feuillère, Edwige

Performance/production

Recollections of actress Edwige Feuillère. France. 1931-1986. Lang.: Fre. 716

Feydeau, Georges

Performance/production

Collection of newspaper reviews by London theatre critics. UK-England: London. 1986. Lang.: Eng. 2122

Fiabe (Fables)

Theory/criticism

Semiotic analysis of Carlo Gozzi's *Fiabe (Fables)*. Italy: Venice. 1761-1765. Lang.: Ita. 3117

Fichandler, Zelda

Administration

Zelda Fichandler discusses artistic risk and funding. USA: Washington, DC. 1986. Lang.: Eng. 101

Performance/production

Excerpts from memorial service for director Alan Schneider. USA: New York, NY. 1984. Lang.: Eng. 821

The artistic director of the Arena Stage discusses the place of the actor in contemporary theatre. USA: Washington, DC. 1951-1986. Lang.: Eng. 832

Fiddler on the Roof

Design/technology

Designers discuss regional productions of *Fiddler on the Roof*. USA. 1984-1986. Lang.: Eng. 3595

Fidela

Plays/librettos/scripts

Experimental farce techniques in *Fidela* by Aurelio Ferretti. Argentina. 1930-1960. Lang.: Spa. 2360

Fidelio

Performance/production

Harry Kupfer: his work and career as singer and director. Germany, East: Dresden, Berlin, East. 1970-1985. Lang.: Ger. 3738

Andrei Serban discusses his production of Beethoven's *Fidelio*. UK-England: London. 1986. Lang.: Eng. 3787

Field, Ada

Reference materials

Catalogue of an exhibition of costume designs for Broadway musicals. USA: New York, NY. 1900-1925. Lang.: Eng, Ger. 3635

Field, Crystal

Institutions

Goals and accomplishments of Theatre for the New City. USA: New York, NY. 1970-1983. Lang.: Eng. 570

Field, Roy

Design/technology

Designer and special effects supervisor make sleigh fly in *Santa Claus—The Movie*. Greenland. 1986. 3199

Fielding, Henry

Performance/production

Lakat alá lányokat (Lock Up Your Daughters), a stage adaptation of Henry Fielding's *Rape Upon Rape*, directed by Imre Halasi. Hungary: Diósgyőr. 1986. Lang.: Hun. 3600

Plays/librettos/scripts

Analysis of Henry Fielding's play *The Author's Farce*. England. 1730. Lang.: Eng. 2516

Fields of Heaven, The

Plays/librettos/scripts

Interview with playwright Dorothy Hewett. Australia: Sydney, N.S.W. 1986. Lang.: Eng. 2368

Fierstein, Harvey

Performance/production

Interview with actor/playwright Harvey Fierstein. UK-England: London. USA: New York. 1983-1986. Lang.: Eng. 2175

Plays/librettos/scripts

Overview of plays with homosexual themes. UK-England: London. 1970-1986. Lang.: Eng. 2841

Progress in audience perception of gay characters in plays. USA. 1933-1985. Lang.: Eng. 2909

Fifth Season

SEE

Quinta Temporada.

Figurative arts

Design/technology

Shows of models by Eduard Fischer of Berliner Ensemble. Germany, East: Berlin, East. Hungary: Budapest. 1985. Lang.: Hun. 269

Documentation on design work for arts festival, 'Maggio Musicale Fiorentino'. Italy: Florence. 1933-1982. Lang.: Ita. 301

Scene designs and theoretical texts of futurist painters working in the theatre. Italy. 1910-1928. Lang.: Ita. 1517

Description of scenery, machinery and performance of Renaissance Italian feast. Italy. 1400-1600. Lang.: Ita. 3311

Performance/production

Touring exhibition 'Artists in the Theatre': influence of visual artists in the development of performance art. UK. 1900-1986. Lang.: Eng. 3447

Relation to other fields

Impact of painting and sculpture on theatre. England. 1700-1900. Lang.: Eng. 1079

Study of attempts to create a 'visual' music using light instead of sound. Europe. USA. 1900-1985. Lang.: Ita. 1082

Artistic, literary and theatrical avant-garde movements. Europe. 1900-1930. Lang.: Ita. 1083

The work of painter and scene designer Claude Gillot. France. 1673-1722. Lang.: Ita. 1084

Interview with designer of theatrical posters Győző Varga. Hungary. 1986. Lang.: Hun. 1097

Polish theatre posters. Poland. 1984. Lang.: Pol. 1123

Proposal for using creative drama with museum visits and a study of the visual arts. USA: Austin, TX. 1985. Lang.: Eng. 1159

Eighteenth-century prints depict dancers Marie Sallé and Marie Anne de Cupis de Camargo. France. 1700-1799. Lang.: Rus. 1327

Figurative arts — cont'd

Costuming evidence on carved baptismal fonts. England. 1463-1544. Lang.: Eng. 3026

Influence of Marcel Duchamp's work on Tom Stoppard's radio play, *Artist Descending a Staircase*. UK-England. 1913-1972. Lang.: Eng. 3059

Comparison of works of playwright Sam Shepard and artist Robert Rauschenberg. USA. 1960-1980. Lang.: Eng. 3062

Playwright Sam Shepard's recent plays and super-realist painting. USA. 1978-1983. Lang.: Eng. 3069

Figures of Speech Theater (Freeport, ME)
Performance/production
Development of *Anerca* by Figures of Speech Theater. USA: Freeport, ME. 1985. Lang.: Eng. 3999

Filla del mar, La (Daughter of the Sea, The)
Theory/criticism
Historical difficulties in creating a paradigm for Catalan theatre. Spain-Catalonia. 1400-1963. Lang.: Cat. 1220

Film
Intertextual analysis of Eugene O'Neill's play *Long Day's Journey Into Night* and Ingmar Bergman's film, *Through a Glass Darkly*. USA. Sweden. 1957-1961. Lang.: Eng. 1425

SEE ALSO
Classed Entries under MEDIA—Film: 3189-3247.

Audience
Oral history of film audience. USA: Charlotte, NC. 1919-1986. Lang.: Eng. 3196

Basic theatrical documents
Catalan translation of *The Homecoming* by Harold Pinter. UK-England. 1965. Lang.: Cat. 1507

Design/technology
Career of scenic designer Eugene Lee. USA: Providence, RI. 1965-1984. Lang.: Eng. 339

Challenges faced by designers of Bob Fosse's *Big Deal*. USA. 1986. Lang.: Eng. 359

Art director Steven Graham's work on the film *The Money Pit*. USA. 1986. 378

Problems and goals of designers for theatre and film. USSR. 1980-1986. Lang.: Rus. 434

Institutions
Overview of Ariane Mnouchkine's work with Théâtre du Soleil. France: Paris. 1959-1985. Lang.: Eng. 497

Performance spaces
Tour of theatres in Illinois, Iowa and Wisconsin. USA: Chicago, IL. 1986. Lang.: Eng. 641

A history of the film theatres in the Carolinas. USA. 1920-1986. Lang.: Eng. 3220

Performance/production
Interview with actor, director, playwright and filmmaker Ramón Griffero. Chile: Santiago. 1953-1986. Lang.: Spa. 675

Analyses of the major trends in theatre, film and other art forms. Europe. USA. 1960-1980. Lang.: Rus. 701

Acting for theatre, film and television. Germany, East. 1983. Lang.: Ger. 730

Biography of Richard Burton. UK-Wales. 1925-1984. Lang.: Eng. 820

Issues in speech pronunciation in performance. USSR. 1980-1986. Lang.: Rus. 898

Director Mark Zacharov of the Komsomol Theatre discusses his work. USSR: Moscow. 1980-1986. Lang.: Rus. 912

Biography of Burgtheater actor Richard Eybner. Austria: Vienna. 1896-1986. Lang.: Ger. 1653

Career of actor Jalmari Rinne. Finland: Helsinki, Tampere, Turku. 1893-1985. Lang.: Eng, Fre. 1719

Autobiographical recollections of Cecilia Esztergályos, ballet-dancer turned actress. Hungary. 1945-1986. Lang.: Hun. 1829

Career of actress Éva Ruttkai. Hungary. 1927-1986. Lang.: Hun. 1871

The life and career of actress Mari Törőcsik. Hungary. 1956-1986. Lang.: Hun. 1933

Director Andrzej Wajda's work, accessibility to Polish audiences. Poland: Warsaw. 1926-1986. Lang.: Swe. 2027

Autobiography of actor Alec Guinness. UK. USA. 1914-1985. Lang.: Eng. 2106

Hungarian translation of *Vivien Leigh: A Biography*. UK-England. 1913-1967. Lang.: Hun. 2141

Comparison of stage production and film version of Shakespeare's *King Lear*, both directed by Peter Brook. UK-England. 1962-1970. Lang.: Eng. 2149

Career of actor Jeremy Irons in theatre, television and film. UK-England. USA. 1970-1985. Lang.: Eng. 2181

Artists who began in dance, film or television move to Off Broadway theatre. USA: New York, NY. 1982. Lang.: Eng. 2284

Biography of playwright and actor Sam Shepard. USA. 1943-1986. Lang.: Eng. 2295

Music critic Derek Jewell traces Frank Sinatra's career along with his own. USA. 1900-1986. Lang.: Eng. 3179

Biography of singer Frank Sinatra. USA. 1915-1984. Lang.: Eng. 3180

Influence of Beijing opera performer Mei Lanfang on European acting and staging traditions. China, People's Republic of. USSR. Germany. 1900-1935. Lang.: Eng. 3521

Collection of interviews with Walter Felsenstein. Germany: Berlin. 1921-1971. Lang.: Ger. 3735

The Franco Zeffirelli film of *Otello* by Giuseppe Verdi, an account of the production. Italy: Rome. 1985-1986. Lang.: Eng. 3758

Plays/librettos/scripts
English theatrical representation of political struggle in Northern Ireland. UK-Ireland. 1980-1986. Lang.: Rus. 977

Career of He Mengfu, playwright and director. China, People's Republic of. 1911-1945. Lang.: Chi. 2448

Analysis of *L'Aigle à deux têtes (The Eagle With Two Heads)* by Jean Cocteau. France. 1889-1963. Lang.: Cat. 2565

Don Juan legend in literature and film. France. 1630-1980. Lang.: Eng. 2581

Biographical information on Jean Genet. France. 1910-1985. Lang.: Fre. 2588

Collection of essays on dramatic text and performance. Poland. 1600-1984. Lang.: Fre. 2742

Self-reflexivity in Antonio Buero Vallejo's play *El Sueño de la razón (The Sleep of Reason)* and Victor Erice's film *El Espíritu de la colmena (The Spirit of the Beehive)*. Spain. 1970-1973. Lang.: Eng. 2781

Analysis of the plot, characters and structure of *The Homecoming* by Harold Pinter. UK-England: London. 1930-1985. Lang.: Cat. 2865

History and practice of the documentary in radio, television, and film. UK-England. 1928-1986. Lang.: Eng. 3168

Adaptations of *Carmen* by Prosper Mérimée. France. Spain. 1845-1983. Lang.: Fre. 3870

Reference materials
Description of Australian archives relating to theatre and film. Australia. 1870-1969. Lang.: Eng. 1000

Books on theatre, film, music and dance published in Italy in 1985. Italy. 1985. Lang.: Ita. 1021

Relation to other fields
Study of attempts to create a 'visual' music using light instead of sound. Europe. USA. 1900-1985. Lang.: Ita. 1082

Theory/criticism
Essays on the sociology of art and semiotics. Lang.: Hun. 1192

Creative self-assembly and juxtaposition in live performance and film. Lang.: Eng. 1196

Theoretical writings and reviews on the performing arts. Hungary. 1971-1983. Lang.: Hun. 1211

Theatre professionals challenge assertions that theatre is a weaker form of communication than film. USA: New York, NY. 1985. Lang.: Eng. 1225

Experimental theatres to offset the impact of film and theatre. China, People's Republic of. 1960-1981. Lang.: Chi. 3090

Shakespeare in media. UK-England. USA. Japan. 1899-1985. Lang.: Eng. 3172

Filmex Festival (Los Angeles, CA)
Administration
Directors of the film festival Filmex discuss their plans for the future. USA: Los Angeles, CA. 1986. Lang.: Eng. 3190

Filmographies
Reference materials
Shakespeare on film. UK-England. USA. 1899-1984. Lang.: Eng. 3245

Financial operations — cont'd

Satiric examination of what not to do if one is to become an effective artistic director. USA. 1986. Lang.: Eng. 178

Computer software package designed for arts administration. USA: New York, NY. 1984. Lang.: Eng. 180

Independent financing of experimental theatre. USSR. 1980-1986. Lang.: Rus. 182

On the need for radical change in theatrical management and financing. USSR. 1986. Lang.: Rus. 184

Problems of funding cultural institutions, including theatres. USSR. 1986. Lang.: Rus. 187

Proposals for the reorganization of theatrical business. USSR. 1986. Lang.: Rus. 190

Experiments with broadening creative independence and reestablishing economic basis of theatre operations. USSR. 1980-1986. Lang.: Rus. 195

General director of Bol'šoj Ballet on problems of the future. USSR: Moscow. 1986. Lang.: Rus. 1292

Discussion of dance theatre subsidy. Switzerland: Boswil. 1986. Lang.: Fre, Ger. 1339

Selling tickets at the Burgtheater and Akademietheater. Austria: Vienna. 1986. Lang.: Ger. 1428

John Hirsch's final season as artistic director of the Stratford Festival. Canada: Stratford, ON. 1985. Lang.: Eng. 1431

Involvement of Robert Keysar with Harry Evans and Blackfriars' Children's Company. England: London. 1608. Lang.: Eng. 1433

Development of the afterpiece. England: London. 1603-1747. Lang.: Eng. 1434

Growing activity and changing role of Black regional theatre companies. USA. 1960-1984. Lang.: Eng. 1440

Overview of public broadcasting management. USA. 1986. Lang.: Eng. 3165

Fundraising for the film *Cheat'n Heart*. USA: New York, NY. 1984-1986. Lang.: Eng. 3192

Interview with independent filmmaker Leon Ichaso. USA: New York, NY. 1986. 3193

Survey of records relating to performances of Robin Hood and King Games. England: Kingston. 1504-1538. Lang.: Eng. 3309

Bookkeeping records of two pre-Civil War circuses. USA. 1836-1843. Lang.: Eng. 3378

Problems of orchestral funding. Lang.: Eng. 3474

Design/technology

Theatre consultant S. Leonard Auerbach's technical specifications for Expo '86. Canada: Vancouver, BC. 1986. Lang.: Eng. 243

Sale of textile shops permitted rebuilding and renovation of scene shops. Hungary: Budapest. 1986. Lang.: Hun. 296

Strategies of lighting dance performances on a limited budget. 1985-1986. Lang.: Eng. 1340

Institutions

Solving the financial problems of the Bregenzer Festspiele. Austria: Bregenz. 1986-1987. Lang.: Ger. 442

Compares two Canadian stock companies. Canada: Montreal, PQ, Toronto, ON. 1890-1940. Lang.: Eng. 466

Founding of Théâtre National Français de Montréal. Canada: Montreal, PQ. 1889-1901. Lang.: Fre. 469

History of the Neptune Theatre and its artistic directors. Canada: Halifax, NS. 1963-1983. Lang.: Eng. 483

How Skottes Musiktéater operates on a small government budget. Sweden: Gävle. 1976-1986. Lang.: Swe. 522

Interview with Hilary Westlake of Lumière & Son. UK-England: London. 1973-1986. Lang.: Swe. 536

Several nonprofit theatres secure new spaces. USA: New York, NY. 1984. Lang.: Eng. 544

Report issued by Small Business Administration claims unfair competition form nonprofit organizations. USA. 1984. Lang.: Eng. 556

Survey of problems of administration and production in youth theatre programs. USA. 1984-1986. Lang.: Eng. 567

Problems and advantages of co-production. USA: New York, NY. 1985. Lang.: Eng. 571

Controversy over proposed NEA plan. USA: Washington, DC. 1984. Lang.: Eng. 573

Career of Marjorie Moon, artistic director of Billie Holliday Theatre. USA: New York, NY, Cleveland, OH. 1973-1986. Lang.: Eng. 1610

The Festival of Clowns in the Wiener Festwochen. Austria: Vienna. 1983-1986. Lang.: Ger. 3380

Development of Prague National Theatre. Czechoslovakia: Prague. 1787-1985. Lang.: Eng. 3672

Performance spaces

Troubles faced by Adelaide Court theatre complex. Canada: Toronto, ON. 1979-1983. Lang.: En . 587

Results of an Off Broadway survey on the crisis of limited space and real estate costs. USA: New York, NY. 1986. Lang.: Eng. 638

Reconstructing a theatrical organization at Saint James Palace (London). England: London. 1600-1986. Lang.: Eng. 1615

Performance/production

Study of first production of *Jane Shore* by Nicholas Rowe at Drury Lane Theatre. England: London. 1713-1714. Lang.: Eng. 693

Amateur production of Alfred Jarry's *Kung Ubu (Ubu roi)* by Kristianstad Musikteater. Sweden: Kristianstad. 1986. Lang.: Swe. 797

Process and results of adapting plays from Off Broadway to TV. USA: New York, NY. 1980-1986. Lang.: Eng. 841

Business dealings of actor Adam Dmuszewski. Poland. 1799-1883. Lang.: Pol. 2018

Advantages and limitations of television medium in producing, recording and broadcasting performing arts. USA. 1930-1985. Lang.: Eng. 3273

Details of the 1926 American Circus Corporation season. USA. Canada. 1926. Lang.: Eng. 3386

History of Great Wallace Circus. USA. 1913. Lang.: Eng. 3387

A general review of the 1985 circus season. USA. Canada. 1985. Lang.: Eng. 3394

Problems of the contemporary circus. USSR. 1986. Lang.: Rus. 3398

Achievements and problems of the contemporary circus. USSR. 1980-1986. Lang.: Rus. 3400

Documenting evidence about a court entertainment of Henry VIII. England: Greenwich. 1504-1516. Lang.: Eng. 3420

Detailed instructions on the mounting of a musical. 1986. Lang.: Eng. 3598

Peter Schumann and his work with the Bread and Puppet Theatre. USA: New York, NY. 1968-1986. Lang.: Eng. 3973

Plays/librettos/scripts

Motif of renewal in Soviet theatre and reorganization of theatre administration. USSR: Kiev. 1980-1986. Lang.: Rus. 2963

Reference materials

Alphabetically arranged profiles and history of professional and amateur theatres for children. USA. 1903-1985. Lang.: Eng. 1046

Relation to other fields

New regulations governing lobbying activities of nonprofit organizations. USA: Washington, DC. 1984. Lang.: Eng. 1152

The role of the arts in the urban economy. USA. 1986. Lang.: Eng. 1160

Cardinal Richelieu's theatrical policies. France. 1634-1642. Lang.: Fre. 3030

Finborough Theatre Club (London)

Performance/production

Collection of newspaper reviews by London theatre critics. UK-England. 1986. Lang.: Eng. 2115

Collection of newspaper reviews by London theatre critics. UK-England: London. 1986. Lang.: Eng. 2117

Findley, Timothy

Basic theatrical documents

Text of *The Journey* by Timothy Findley. Canada. 1970. Lang.: Eng. 3173

Text of *The Paper People* by Timothy Findley. Canada. 1967. Lang.: Eng. 3252

Plays/librettos/scripts

Critical debate over Timothy Findley's *The Paper People*. Canada. 1967. Lang.: Eng. 3280

Fine, Nic

Performance/production

Collection of newspaper reviews by London theatre critics. UK-England. 1986. Lang.: Eng. 2114

Fingerhut, Arden

Design/technology

Interview with lighting designers Arden Fingerhut, Tharon Musser and Jennifer Tipton. USA. 1986. Lang.: Eng. 340

Fink, Myron
Performance/production
Review of premiere performance of Myron Fink's opera *Chinchilla*.
USA: Binghamton, NY. 1986. Lang.: Eng.   3840

Finlandia
Performance/production
Review of *Finlandia*, produced by Ryhmäteatteri. Finland: Helsinki.
1986. Lang.: Swe.   707

Finn-Kelcey, Rose
Performance/production
Work of performance artist Rose Finn-Kelcey. UK-England. 1986.
Lang.: Eng.   3455

Finnerman, Gerald Perry
Design/technology
Interview with cameraman Gerald Perry Finnerman about lighting
Moonlighting. USA: Los Angeles, CA. 1985-1986. Lang.: Eng.   3264

Finnish National Opera
SEE
Suomen Kansallisooppera.

Finnish National Theatre
SEE
Suomen Kansallisteatteri.

Finta Giardiniera, La
Performance/production
Review of *Lunatics and Lovers*, an adaptation of Mozart's *La finta
giardiniera*. USA: Santa Barbara, CA. 1985. Lang.: Eng.   3843

Fiorillo, Silvio
Performance/production
Life and works of actor and playwright Silvio Fiorillo. Italy. 1565-
1634. Lang.: Ita.   3411

Fire on the Snow
Plays/librettos/scripts
Study of heroism in verse dramas by Douglas Stewart, Tom Inglis
Moore and Catherine Duncan. Australia. 1941-1943. Lang.: Eng.
                                                           2383

Firebrand
Plays/librettos/scripts
Analysis of the operetta *Firebrand* by Kurt Weill and Ira Gershwin.
USA: New York, NY. Italy: Florence. 1945. Lang.: Eng.   3944

Firebugs, The
SEE
Biedermann und die Brandstifter.

Fireraiser, The
SEE
Biedermann und die Brandstifter.

Firmezas de Isabela, Las (Decisions of Isabela, The)
Plays/librettos/scripts
Luis de Góngora's plays as a response to Lope de Vega. Spain.
1561-1627. Lang.: Eng.   968

Fischer, Eduard
Design/technology
Shows of models by Eduard Fischer of Berliner Ensemble. Germany,
East: Berlin, East. Hungary: Budapest. 1985. Lang.: Hun.   269

Fish, Simon
Performance/production
Brief investigation of the lives of seven actors. England. 1526-1587.
Lang.: Eng.   691

Fisher, Chris
Performance/production
Collection of newspaper reviews by London theatre critics. UK-
England. 1986. Lang.: Eng.   2115

Fisher, Jules
Design/technology
Challenges faced by designers of Bob Fosse's *Big Deal*. USA. 1986.
Lang.: Eng.   359

Fisher, Robert
Performance/production
Reviews of *Grouch: A Life in Revue*, by Arthur Marx and Robert
Fisher, staged by Arthur Marx. USA: New York, NY. 1986. Lang.:
Eng.   2201

Fitch, Sheree
Institutions
Founding directors explain history and principles of Enterprise
Theatre. Canada. 1983-1986. Lang.: Eng.   1546

Fitzallan
Plays/librettos/scripts
William Rufus Blake's *Fitzallan* as the first play written and
produced in Canada. Canada: Halifax, NS. 1833. Lang.: Eng. 2430

Five Buffoons of Kasan, The
SEE
Kasan ogwangdae.

Flagg, Phineas
Design/technology
Lighting techniques and equipment used at theme park. USA:
Baltimore, MD. 1971-1986. Lang.: Eng.   3315

Flamenco Puro
Performance/production
Reviews of *Flamenco Puro*, conceived, staged and designed by
Claudio Segovia and Hector Orezzoli. USA: New York, NY. 1986.
Lang.: Eng.   2210

Flanagan, Hallie
Institutions
John Houseman discusses Federal Theatre Project. USA: New York,
NY, Washington, DC. 1935-1940. Lang.: Eng.   559

Plays/librettos/scripts
Attitudes toward technology reflected in some Living Newspaper
productions of the Federal Theatre Project. USA. 1935-1939. Lang.:
Eng.   2905

Flann O'Brien's Hard Life
Performance/production
Collection of newspaper reviews by London theatre critics. UK-
England: London. 1986. Lang.: Eng.   2116

Flannery, Daniel
Design/technology
Lighting techniques and equipment used at theme park. USA:
Baltimore, MD. 1971-1986. Lang.: Eng.   3315

Flatt, Ernest O.
Performance/production
Reviews of *Honky Tonk Nights*, book and lyrics by Ralph Allen and
David Campbell, staged and choreographed by Ernest O. Flatt.
USA: New York, NY. 1986. Lang.: Eng.   3612

Flaubert, Gustave
Plays/librettos/scripts
Contributing sources to Wooster Group's *Saint Anthony*. USA: New
York, NY, Boston, MA, Washington, DC. 1983-1986. Lang.: Eng.
                                                           2940

Fledermaus, Die
Performance/production
Performance history of *Die Fledermaus* by Richard Strauss. Austria:
Vienna. 1874-1986. Lang.: Eng.   3704

Reviews of 10 vintage recordings of complete operas on LP. USA.
1906-1925. Lang.: Eng.   3792

Stills from telecast performances. List of principals, conductor and
production staff included. USA: New York, NY. 1986. Lang.: Eng.
                                                           3795

Photographs, cast list, synopsis, and discography of Metropolitan
Opera radio broadcast performances. USA: New York, NY. 1986.
Lang.: Eng.   3797

Profile of and interview with American conductor Jeffrey Tate,
concerning his approach to *Die Fledermaus* by Richard Strauss.
USA: New York, NY. 1940-1946. Lang.: Eng.   3827

Fleetwood, Charles
Administration
The Drury Lane Theatre under the management of Charles
Fleetwood. England: London. 1734-1745. Lang.: Eng.   35

Fleming, Jill
Performance/production
Interview with Lesbian feminist theatre company Hard Corps. UK-
England. 1984-1986. Lang.: Eng.   2164

Fletcher, John
Performance/production
History of productions of *Cardenio* by William Shakespeare and
John Fletcher. England: London. 1613-1847. Lang.: Eng.   1705

Plays/librettos/scripts
Passion in early plays of Beaumont and Fletcher. England. 1608-
1611. Lang.: Eng.   945

Shakespeare's influence on Beaumont and Fletcher's *Philaster*.
England. 1609. Lang.: Eng.   2463

Female characterization in Nicholas Rowe's plays. England. 1629-
1720. Lang.: Eng.   2475

Image of poverty in Elizabethan and Stuart plays. England. 1558-
1642. Lang.: Eng.   2482

Use of language in Beaumont and Fletcher's *Philaster*. England.
1609. Lang.: Eng.   2512

Fleury Playbook
Plays/librettos/scripts
Account of presentation of four St. Nicholas plays from Fleury
Playbook. USA: Kalamazoo, MI. 1986. Lang.: Eng.   2942

Flint Youth Theatre (Flint, MI)
Institutions
Training and use of child performers. USA. 1949-1985. Lang.: Eng.
565

Florenne, Yves
Institutions
Discussions of opera at the festival of Aix-en-Provence. France: Aix-
en-Provence. 1960. Lang.: Fre.   3673

Florida Southern College (Lakeland, FL)
Design/technology
Designers discuss regional productions of *Grease*. USA. 1984-1986.
Lang.: Eng.   3597

Flying Karamazov Brothers
Performance/production
Reviews of *Juggling and Cheap Theatrics* with the Flying
Karamazov Brothers, staged by George Mosher. USA: New York,
NY. 1986. Lang.: Eng.   3349

Fo, Dario
Basic theatrical documents
English translation of *Coppia aperta, quasì spalancata (An Open
Couple–Very Open)* by Dario Fo and Franca Rame. Italy: Trieste.
1983. Lang.: Eng.   1486

Performance/production
Dario Fo's fusion of slapstick and politics. Italy. 1960-1986. Lang.:
Eng.   749

Life and work of actress-playwright Franca Rame. Italy. 1929-1983.
Lang.: Eng.   1988

Overview of productions in Italy. Italy: Milan. 1986. Lang.: Eng.
1994

Roger Rees, associate director at Bristol Old Vic discusses his career
and the season. UK-England: Bristol. 1970-1986. Lang.: Eng.   2138

Productions of Dario Fo's *Morte accidentale di un anarchico
(Accidental Death of an Anarchist)* in the light of Fo's political
ideas. USA. Canada. Italy. 1970-1986. Lang.: Eng.   2262

Plays/librettos/scripts
The link between comic and survival instincts. Italy. 1986. Lang.:
Eng.   2688

Interview with Gillian Hanna about *Elisabetta: Quasì per caso una
donna (Elizabeth: Almost by Chance a Woman)*. UK-England:
London. Italy. 1986. Lang.: Eng.   2875

Relation to other fields
Writers Gabriel García Márquez, Carlos Fuentes and Dario Fo
denied entry visas to the US on ideological grounds. USA:
Washington, DC. 1984. Lang.: Eng.   1170

Theory/criticism
Phenomenological view of the history of the circus, its links with
theatre. 1985. Lang.: Fre.   3405

Focus Theatre Group (UK-Scotland)
Performance/production
Interview with Jules Cranfield on Focus Theatre Group. UK-
Scotland. 1973-1986. Lang.: Eng.   2193

Fodor, Tamás
Performance/production
Production analysis of a montage of sketches about Electra by
Stúdió K. Hungary: Budapest. 1986. Lang.: Hun.   1773

Janika (Our Son) by Géza Csáth, directed by Tamás Fodor and
starring György Kézdy. Hungary: Szolnok. 1986. Lang.: Hun.   1955

Földes, Mihály
Performance/production
János Ács directs *A kőszívű ember fiai (The Sons of the Stone-
Hearted Man)* by Mór Jókai. Hungary: Zalaegerszeg. 1986. Lang.:
Hun.   1905

Folkefiende, En (Enemy of the People, An)
Plays/librettos/scripts
Analysis of *En Folkefiende (An Enemy of the People)* by Henrik
Ibsen. Norway. 1882. Lang.: Eng.   2728

Folketeatret (Copenhagen)
Institutions
Overview of current theatre scene. Denmark: Copenhagen. 1976-
1986. Lang.: Swe.   490

Folkkulturcentrum Festival (Stockholm)
Institutions
Activities of the Folkkulturcentrum Festival. Sweden: Stockholm.
1977-1986. Lang.: Swe.   529

Folklore
Basic theatrical documents
Edited text of a traditional Nativity play. Hungary: Kézdivásárhely.
1700-1730. Lang.: Hun.   223

Relation to other fields
Folklorist Tekla Dömötör includes traditional material in her popular
work. Hungary. 1986. Lang.: Hun.   1098

Enthnography of a Hungarian village. Hungary: Zsámbok. 1930-
1985. Lang.: Hun.   1099

Translation of *Les métamorphoses de la fête en Provence de 1750 à
1820* (Paris 1976) by Michel Vovelle. France. 1750-1820. Lang.: Ita.
3358

Nativity puppet plays in Eastern Europe. Europe. 1600-1985. Lang.:
Hun.   3991

Folkteatern i Gävleborg (Gävleborg)
Administration
Training of amateurs coordinated by Folkteatern in Gävleborgs Län.
Sweden: Gävle. 1984-1986. Lang.: Swe.   60

Design/technology
Designing with colored light to enhance the psychological impact of
productions. Sweden: Gävle. 1986. Lang.: Swe.   319

Folkwangschule
Relation to other fields
Refugee artists from Nazi Germany in Britain. UK-England.
Germany. 1937-1947. Lang.: Eng.   1135

Fontanne, Lynn
Performance/production
A scholarly study of the careers of Alfred Lunt and Lynn Fontanne.
USA. 1922-1972. Lang.: Eng.   2257

Fool for Love
Plays/librettos/scripts
Director John Lion on his work with playwright Sam Shepard. USA:
San Francisco, CA, New York, NY. 1970-1984. Lang.: Eng.   2924

Relation to other fields
Playwright Sam Shepard's recent plays and super-realist painting.
USA. 1978-1983. Lang.: Eng.   3069

Foon, Dennis
Institutions
Interview with Dennis Foon, director of Green Thumb Theatre for
Young People. Canada: Vancouver, BC. 1975-1984. Lang.: Fre.   473

History of the Green Thumb Theatre. Canada: Vancouver, BC.
1975-1986. Lang.: Eng.   1541

Foote, Horton
Performance/production
Reviews of *Lily Dale*, by Horton Foote, staged by William
Alderson. USA: New York, NY. 1986. Lang.: Eng.   2204

Foote, Samuel
Plays/librettos/scripts
Character source for Dr. Last in Samuel Foote's play *The Devil
Upon Two Sticks*. England. 1768-1774. Lang.: Eng.   2522

Footlockers, The
Performance/production
Collection of newspaper reviews by London theatre critics. UK.
1986. Lang.: Eng.   2103

Collection of newspaper reviews by London theatre critics. UK-
England: London. 1986. Lang.: Eng.   2123

For Colored Girls Who Have Considered Suicide
Reference materials
Current work of Audelco award-winning playwrights. USA: New
York, NY. 1973-1984. Lang.: Eng.   3007

Ford Foundation
Administration
W. McNeil Lowry of the Ford Foundation discusses funding for arts
institutions. USA. 1984. Lang.: Eng.   142

Computer software package designed for arts administration. USA:
New York, NY. 1984. Lang.: Eng.   180

Ford, John
Plays/librettos/scripts
Allegorical romantic conventions in John Ford's *The Broken Heart*.
England. 1633. Lang.: Eng.   2497

Analysis of the final scene of *The Broken Heart* by John Ford.
England. 1629. Lang.: Eng.   2526

Foreman, Richard
Performance/production
Historical development of acting and directing techniques. 1898-1986.
Lang.: Eng.   1632

Foreman, Richard — cont'd

Aesthetics, styles, rehearsal techniques of director Richard Foreman. USA. 1974-1986. Lang.: Eng. 2263

Performance art and its current characteristic tone. USA. Lang.: Eng. 3459

Plays/librettos/scripts
Richard Foreman's ideas about playwriting. USA. Lang.: Swe. 980

Richard Foreman, founder of Ontological-Hysteric Theater Company. USA. 1960-1986. Lang.: Swe. 2890

Discussion of issues raised in plays of 1985-86 season. USA: New York, NY. 1985-1986. Lang.: Eng. 2928

Theory/criticism
Eleven theatre professionals discuss their personal direction and the direction of experimental theatre. USA: New York, NY. 1985. Lang.: Eng. 3137

Forepaugh, John A.
Institutions
Revival and decline of resident acting companies seen through case studies. USA. 1886-1930. Lang.: Eng. 551

Forgatókönyv (Film Script)
Performance/production
Forgatókönyv (Film Script) by István Örkény directed by Gábor Balogh. Hungary: Békéscsaba. 1986. Lang.: Hun. 1908

Formolo and Urban Dance Company (Edmonton, AB)
Institutions
Careers of choreographers Maria Formolo and Keith Urban. Canada: Regina, SK, Edmonton, AB. 1980-1983. Lang.: Eng. 1343

Formolo, Maria
Institutions
Careers of choreographers Maria Formolo and Keith Urban. Canada: Regina, SK, Edmonton, AB. 1980-1983. Lang.: Eng. 1343

Fornes, Maria Irene
Plays/librettos/scripts
Interview with playwright Maria Irene Fornes. USA. 1965-1985. Lang.: Eng. 979

Interview with playwright Maria Irene Fornes. USA: New York, NY. 1984. Lang.: Eng. 2892

Review of adaptations for the stage of short stories by Čechov. USA: New York, NY. 1986. Lang.: Eng. 2922

Forrest, Edwin
Performance/production
Career of actress Josephine Clifton. USA. 1813-1847. Lang.: Eng. 846

Career of actress and theatrical manager Louisa Lane Drew. USA. 1820-1897. Lang.: Eng. 2243

Forrest, Ian
Performance/production
Collection of newspaper reviews by London theatre critics. UK: London. 1986. Lang.: Eng. 2100

Forrester, Maureen
Performance/production
Opera singer Maureen Forrester tells of her switch from serious roles to character and comic roles. Canada. 1970-1984. Lang.: Eng. 3706

Forsström, Ralf
Design/technology
Career of designer Ralf Forsström discussing his influences and stylistic preferences. Finland: Helsinki. 1963-1986. Lang.: Eng, Fre. 3650

Forst, Judith
Performance/production
Interview with mezzo-sporano Judith Forst. Canada. 1975-1986. Lang.: Eng. 3708

Forst, Willi
Performance/production
Life and films of actor and director Willi Forst. Austria: Vienna. Germany: Berlin. 1903-1980. Lang.: Ger. 3223

Forster, E.M.
Plays/librettos/scripts
Collaboration of authors and composers of Billy Budd. UK-England: London. 1949-1964. Lang.: Eng. 3895

Forster, John
Performance/production
Reviews of Into the Light, book by Jeff Tamborniro, music by Lee Holdridge, lyrics by John Forster, staged by Michael Maurer. USA: New York, NY. 1986. Lang.: Eng. 3615

Forsyth, Bill
Performance/production
Collection of newspaper reviews by London theatre critics. UK: London. 1986. Lang.: Eng. 2100

Forsythe, William
Performance/production
Performance art and its current characteristic tone. USA. Lang.: Eng. 3459

Fort Wayne Youth Theatre (Ft. Wayne, IN)
Institutions
Training and use of child performers. USA. 1949-1985. Lang.: Eng. 565

Forton, Raymond
Design/technology
Modification in the nylon roller construction explained in TB 1137 by Ray Forton. USA. 1986. Lang.: Eng. 348

Fortuny, Mariano
Design/technology
Career of designer Mariano Fortuny. Italy. 1871-1949. Lang.: Ita. 300

Adolphe Appia's use of some innovative lighting techniques of Mariano Fortuny. France. 1903. Lang.: Ita. 1514

Forty-seventh Street Theatre (New York, NY)
Performance spaces
Descriptions of newly constructed Off Broadway theatres. USA: New York, NY. 1984. Lang.: Eng. 644

Forza del destino, La
Plays/librettos/scripts
Shakespeare's influence on Verdi's operas. Germany. Italy. Austria. 1750-1850. Lang.: Eng. 3878

Fosse, Bob
Design/technology
Challenges faced by designers of Bob Fosse's Big Deal. USA. 1986. Lang.: Eng. 359

Performance/production
Reviews of Big Deal, written, staged and choreographed by Bob Fosse. USA: New York, NY. 1986. Lang.: Eng. 1283

Reviews of Sweet Charity by Neil Simon, staged and choreographed by Bob Fosse. USA: New York, NY. 1986. Lang.: Eng. 3611

Choreography in musical theatre. USA: New York, NY. 1944-1981. Lang.: Eng. 3620

Foucault, Michel
Plays/librettos/scripts
Deconstructionist analysis of Riccardo III by Carmelo Bene. Italy. France. Lang.: Eng. 2690

Interview with playwright Howard Barker. UK-England. 1981-1985. Lang.: Eng. 2845

Fouché, Frank
Plays/librettos/scripts
The influence of Brecht on Haiti's exiled playwright Frank Fouché and the group Kovidor. Haiti. 1970-1979. 2638

Found spaces
Description of various theatrical activities. Poland: Vilna. 1908-1986. Lang.: Pol. 10

Design/technology
Amateur technician outlines his experience of lighting a pantomime in a hall with a ceiling 8 feet high. UK-England: Brighton. 1980-1986. Lang.: Eng. 3304

Institutions
Cultural activities in the Lodz ghetto. Poland: Łodż. 1940-1944. Lang.: Heb. 3323

Experiences of a couple who converted a coal barge into a touring puppet theatre. UK-England: London. 1976-1986. Lang.: Eng. 4005

Performance spaces
Design of concert hall in part of a major railway station. Hungary: Budapest. 1985-1986. Lang.: Hun. 598

Description of Orionteatern, a former factory. Sweden: Stockholm. 1983-1986. Lang.: Swe. 618

Touring stage of ballet company Cullbergbaletten. Sweden. 1986. Lang.: Swe. 1300

Ceremonies celebrating the marriage of Maria dei Medici to Henri IV. Italy: Florence. France: Lyon. 1568-1600. Lang.: Ita. 3325

History of the Experimental Art Foundation as an alternative space. Australia: Adelaide. 1974-1986. Lang.: Eng. 3437

Overview of performance spaces in several Australian cities. Australia. 1986. Lang.: Eng. 3438

Performance/production
Viennese cellar theatres as alternative theatre spaces. Austria: Vienna. 1945-1960. Lang.: Ger. 1645

Details of Wileński Touring Theatre. Poland: Vilna. 1935-1936. Lang.: Pol. 2020

Found spaces — cont'd

Horse and Bamboo Theatre, specializing in community puppet theatre. UK-England: Rossendale. 1978-1986. Lang.: Eng.   3970

Foundation Center (New York, NY)
Administration
Types of foundations and procedures of application. USA: New York, NY. 1983. Lang.: Eng.   89

A guide to some of the largest private foundations. USA. 1986. Lang.: Eng.   155

Fourberies de Scapin, Les (Scapin's Tricks)
Performance/production
Interview with actor Pál Mácsai on his role in *Scapin furfangjai (Scapin's Tricks)* by Molière. Hungary: Szentendre. 1986. Lang.: Hun.   1775

Scapin furfangjai (Scapin's Tricks) by Molière, directed by László Vámos at Szentendrei Teátrum. Hungary: Szentendre. 1986. Lang.: Hun.   1957

Fowles, John
Plays/librettos/scripts
Harold Pinter's screenplay for *The French Lieutenant's Woman* by John Fowles. UK-England. 1969-1981. Lang.: Eng.   3238

Fox, Ellen
Performance/production
Collection of newspaper reviews by London theatre critics. UK-England. 1986. Lang.: Eng.   2115

Fraggle Rock
Performance/production
Behind-the-scenes look at *Fraggle Rock*. Canada: Toronto, ON. 1984. Lang.: Eng.   3269

Francesca da Rimini
Performance/production
Photographs, cast list, synopsis, and discography of Metropolitan Opera radio broadcast performances. USA: New York, NY. 1986. Lang.: Eng.   3794

Plays/librettos/scripts
The town of Rimini and its attachment to *Francesca da Rimini*. Italy: Rimini. 1986. Lang.: Eng.   3890

François, Guy-Claude
Performance/production
Production of *L'Histoire terrible mais inachevé de Norodom Sihanouk, roi du Cambodge (The Terrible but Unfinished History of Norodom Sihanouk, King of Cambodia)* by Hélène Cixous. France: Paris. 1985. Lang.: Eng.   1737

Frank Silvera Writers' Workshop (New York, NY)
Administration
Alternative funding for small theatres previously dependent on government subsidy. USA: St. Louis, MO, New York, NY, Los Angeles, CA, Detroit, MI. 1985. Lang.: Eng.   103

Frank, Mel
Performance/production
Biography of actor Danny Kaye. USA: New York, NY. 1912-1985. Lang.: Eng.   2265

Frankenstein
Plays/librettos/scripts
Treatment of the Frankenstein myth in three gothic melodramas. UK-England. France. 1823-1826. Lang.: Eng.   2847

Franklin Furnace (New York, NY)
Performance spaces
Alternative performance spaces for experimental theatre and dance works. USA: New York, NY. 1984. Lang.: Eng.   640

Fraser, Malcolm
Performance/production
Review of Prokofiév's *Love for Three Oranges*. USA: Cincinnati, OH. 1986. Lang.: Eng.   3798

Fraser, Winifred
Performance/production
Acting style in plays by Henrik Ibsen. 1885-1905. Lang.: Eng.   1627

Fraticelli, Rina
Institutions
Interviews with theatre professionals in Quebec. Canada. 1985. Lang.: Fre.   487

Limited opportunities for English-language playwrights in Montreal. Canada: Montreal, PQ. 1976-1986. Lang.: Eng.   1561

Fräulein von Tellheim, Das (Lady of Tellheim, The)
Plays/librettos/scripts
Nazi ideology and Hans Schweikart's film adaptation of Lessing's *Minna von Barnhelm*. Germany. 1940. Lang.: Ger.   3233

Frayn, Michael
Basic theatrical documents
Text of Čechov's *Platonov* in a version by Michael Frayn. Russia. 1878. Lang.: Cat.   1492

Performance/production
Reviews of *Wild Honey*, by Michael Frayn after Čechov, conceived and staged by Christopher Morahan. USA: New York, NY. 1986. Lang.: Eng.   2205

Frears, Stephen
Design/technology
The making of the film *My Beautiful Laundrette*. UK-England: London. 1986.   3202

Fréchette, Louis-Honoré
Design/technology
Design considerations in productions of two plays by Louis-Honoré Fréchette. Canada: Montreal, PQ. 1880-1900. Lang.: Fre.   242

Fredro, Aleksander
Administration
Russian censorship of classic repertory in Polish theatres. Poland: Warsaw. Russia. 1873-1907. Lang.: Rus, Pol.   1438

Performance/production
Andrzej Łapicki directs Aleksander Fredro's *Śluby Panienskie (Maiden Vows)*, Teatr Polski. Poland: Warsaw. 1984. Lang.: Pol.   2031

Plays/librettos/scripts
Polish drama performed in Sweden. Sweden. Poland. 1835-1976. Lang.: Pol.   975

Free German League of Culture (FDKB)
Relation to other fields
Refugee artists from Nazi Germany in Britain. UK-England. Germany. 1937-1947. Lang.: Eng.   1135

Freedman, Gerald
Performance/production
Reviews of *Brigadoon*, by Alan Jay Lerner, Frederick Loewe, staged by Gerald Freedman. USA: New York, NY. 1986. Lang.: Eng.   3619

Freedom Theatre of Philadelphia (Philadelphia, PA)
Institutions
History of Black theater companies. USA: Philadelphia, PA. 1966-1985. Lang.: Eng.   1608

Freeman, Ersky
Relation to other fields
Black history and folklore taught in theatre workshops and productions. USA: New York, NY, Omaha, NE, Washington, DC. 1986. Lang.: Eng.   3068

Freer, Charles
Performance/production
Unsuccessful career of actor Charles Freer. England: London. USA: New York, NY. 1808-1858. Lang.: Eng.   1707

Freie Volksbühne (East Berlin)
SEE
Volksbühne.

Freihart, Alex
History of the Theater für Vorarlberg. Austria: Bregenz. 1818-1986. Lang.: Ger.   3

Frelich, Phyllis
Performance/production
Guidelines for working with deaf actors and sign interpreters. USA. 1984-1986. Lang.: Eng.   848

Frelka, Ryszard
Performance/production
Jerzy Krasowski of Teatr Mały directs Ryszard Frelka's *Jalta (Yalta)*. Poland: Warsaw. 1984. Lang.: Pol.   2048

French Classicism
SEE
Neoclassicism.

French Lieutenant's Woman, The
Plays/librettos/scripts
Harold Pinter's screenplay for *The French Lieutenant's Woman* by John Fowles. UK-England. 1969-1981. Lang.: Eng.   3238

French-American Film Workshop (Avignon)
Institutions
The French-American Film Workshop, designed to showcase the work of independents and encourage cultural exchange. France: Avignon. 1986. Lang.: Eng.   3216

Freni, Mirella
Performance/production
Opera-singer Mirella Freni: her roles and plans. Italy. Austria. 1935-1986. Lang.: Ger.   3759

Freni, Mirella — cont'd

Reference materials
Photos of the new opera productions at the Staatsoper. Austria: Vienna. 1985-1986. Lang.: Ger. 3910

Fresno Paramount Players (Fresno, CA)
Performance/production
An historical account of one actor's experiences with the Fresno Paramount Players. USA: Fresno, CA. 1927. Lang.: Eng. 2255

Freud, Sigmund
Performance/production
Psychoanalytic study of staging as language. Germany. 1800-1909. Lang.: Fre. 3734

Plays/librettos/scripts
Psychoanalytic and post-structuralist analysis of Molière's *Tartuffe*. France. 1660-1669. Lang.: Eng. 948

Language in *Der Schwierige (The Difficult Man)* by Hugo von Hofmannsthal. Austria. 1921. Lang.: Ger. 2390

Relation to other fields
Curricular authority for drama-in-education program. UK. Lang.: Eng. 3054

Training
Effect of changing ideas about psychology and creativity on the Stanislavskij system. USSR: Moscow. 1900-1986. Lang.: Eng. 3162

Freunde des Theaters in der Josefstadt (Vienna)
Institutions
Activities and history of the audience-society, Freunde des Theaters in der Josefstadt. Austria: Vienna. 1985-1986. Lang.: Ger. 1535

Freytag, Gustav
Theory/criticism
Influence of Western theory on Chinese drama of Gu Zhongyi. China. 1920-1963. Lang.: Chi. 1202

Fria Proteatern (Stockholm)
Performance/production
The cooperation between amateurs and professionals in Fria Proteatern's staging of Brecht's *Turandot*. Sweden: Stockholm. 1986. Lang.: Swe. 2095

Frick, Elisabeth
Performance/production
Mats Ödeen's *Det ende raka (The Only Straight Thing)* performed by TURteaterns amatörteatergrupp. Sweden: Stockholm. 1979-1986. Lang.: Swe. 801

Friedell, Egon
Performance/production
History of the Viennese cabaret. Austria: Vienna. 1890-1945. Lang.: Ger. 3364

Friedrich, Götz
Performance/production
Collaboration of Peter Hemmings and Götz Friedrich in Los Angeles' opera season. USA: Los Angeles, CA. 1985. Lang.: Eng. 3836

Friends, The
Plays/librettos/scripts
Utopia in early plays by Arnold Wesker. UK-England. 1958-1970. Lang.: Eng. 2884

Frikzhan
Performance/production
Collection of newspaper reviews by London theatre critics. UK-England: London. 1986. Lang.: Eng. 2110

Plays/librettos/scripts
Playwright Marius Brill discusses his prize winning play *Frikzhan*. UK-England: London. 1986. Lang.: Eng. 2831

Frisch, Max
Plays/librettos/scripts
Fox symbolism in plays of Bertolt Brecht, Max Frisch and Gerhart Hauptmann. Germany. 1700-1976. Lang.: Ger. 2598

Analysis of plays by Max Frisch, and influences of Thornton Wilder. Switzerland. 1939-1983. Lang.: Eng. 2829

Relation to other fields
Nonfictional writings of Albin Zollinger, Max Frisch and Friedrich Dürrenmatt. Lang.: Ger. 3169

Fröken Julie (Miss Julie)
Performance/production
Survey of summer theatre offerings. Sweden: Stockholm, Södertälje, Karlskrona. 1986. Lang.: Swe. 2089

Reviews of three productions of *Fröken Julie (Miss Julie)* by August Strindberg. Sweden: Stockholm. Denmark: Copenhagen. South Africa, Republic of. 1985-1986. Lang.: Swe. 2090

Plays/librettos/scripts
Scandinavian drama on Canadian radio. Canada. Scandinavia. 1939-1982. Lang.: Eng. 3182

Theory/criticism
Semiotic analysis of audience involvement in *Fröken Julie (Miss Julie)* by August Strindberg. Sweden. 1889-1986. Lang.: Ita. 3133

From Beyond
Design/technology
Special effects in the film *From Beyond*. USA. 1986. Lang.: Eng. 3208

Front Page, The
Performance/production
Reviews of *The Front Page*, by Ben Hecht and Charles MacArthur, staged by Jerry Zaks. USA: New York, NY. 1986. Lang.: Eng. 2214

Front Room Boys, The
Plays/librettos/scripts
Individualism and male-female relationships as themes in Australian drama. Australia. 1940-1980. Lang.: Eng. 2373

Interview with playwright Alex Buzo. Australia. 1986. Lang.: Eng. 2385

Fry, Christopher
Theory/criticism
Assessment of critic Kenneth Tynan's works. UK-England. 1950-1960. Lang.: Eng. 3136

Frye, Northrop
Institutions
Introduction to the minority-language and 'Garrison theatre'. Canada. 1986. Lang.: Eng. 1565

FTL
SEE
Factory Theatre Lab.

Fu, Tu
Relation to other fields
Political goals for Beijing opera. China, People's Republic of: Beijing. 1985. Lang.: Chi. 3548

Fu, Xihua
Plays/librettos/scripts
Differences among 32 extant editions of *Xi Xiang Zhu*. China. 1669-1843. Lang.: Chi. 3528

Research/historiography
Transformation of traditional music notation into modern notation for four Chinese operas. China: Beijing. 1674-1985. Lang.: Chi. 3554

Fuente Ovejuna (Sheep Well, The)
Plays/librettos/scripts
Reconstructs from historical sources the rebellion depicted in *Fuente Ovejuna (The Sheep Well)* by Lope de Vega as ritual behavior. Spain. 1476. Lang.: Eng. 2794

Fuentes, Carlos
Relation to other fields
Writers Gabriel García Márquez, Carlos Fuentes and Dario Fo denied entry visas to the US on ideological grounds. USA: Washington, DC. 1984. Lang.: Eng. 1170

Theory/criticism
A semiotic reading of Carlos Fuentes' play *Orquídeas a la luz de la luna (Orchids in the Moonlight)*. Mexico. 1982-1986. Lang.: Eng. 3123

Fugard, Athol
Design/technology
Interview with lighting designer William Warfel. USA: New Haven, CT. 1985-1986. Lang.: Eng. 1527

Plays/librettos/scripts
Metaphoric style in the political drama of Jean-Paul Sartre, Athol Fugard and Juan Radrigán. France. South Africa, Republic of. Chile. 1940-1986. Lang.: Eng. 951

Use of Greek mythological themes in Athol Fugard's plays. South Africa, Republic of. 1959-1986. Lang.: Afr. 2773

Interview with playwright Athol Fugard. South Africa, Republic of. USA: New Haven, CT. 1984. Lang.: Eng. 2775

A comprehensive critical study of the life and works of Athol Fugard. South Africa, Republic of. 1932-1983. Lang.: Eng. 2778

The role of the artist in *The Road to Mecca* by Athol Fugard. South Africa, Republic of. 1961-1984. Lang.: Eng. 2779

Theory/criticism
History of theatre in Africa. Africa. 1400-1985. Lang.: Ger. 1199

Fulgens and Lucres
Performance/production
Theories of medieval production and acting techniques. England. 1400-1500. Lang.: Eng. 698

Plays/librettos/scripts
Possible source of cock fight in Henry Medwall's *Fulgens and Lucres*. Ireland. 1602. Lang.: Eng. 2664

Funding — cont'd

Funding, government

Fundraising

Funny House of a Negro

Funny Thing Happened on the Way to the Forum, A

SUBJECT INDEX

Fura dels Baus, La (Barcelona & Moià)
Performance/production
Detailed description of the performance titled *Accions (Actions)* by
La Fura dels Baus. Spain-Catalonia. 1979-1984. Lang.: Cat.   3445

Furber, Douglas
Performance/production
Review of *Me and My Girl*, book and lyrics by L. Arthur Rose and
Douglas Furber, staged by Mike Ockrent. USA: New York, NY.
1986. Lang.: Eng.   3618

Furcht und Elend des III Reiches (Fear and Misery of the Third Reich)
Plays/librettos/scripts
Brecht's use of the epically structured motif of the military review.
2354

Furcht und Hoffnung der BRD (Help Wanted)
Plays/librettos/scripts
Characterization in *Furcht und Hoffnung der BRD (Help Wanted)* by
Franz Xaver Kroetz. Germany, West. 1984-1986. Lang.: Eng.   2623

Furlanetto, Ferruccio
Performance/production
Opera singer Ferruccio Furlanetto and his career. Austria: Salzburg.
Italy. 1946-1949. Lang.: Ger.   3698

Furlong, Gary
Relation to other fields
Bertolt Brecht's contributions to modern theatre. Canada: Toronto,
ON. 1985. Lang.: Eng.   3020

Furth, George
Performance/production
Reviews of *Precious Sons* by George Furth, staged by Norman
Rene. USA: New York, NY. 1986. Lang.: Eng.   2231

Furtwängler, Wilhelm
Performance/production
Wilhelm Furtwängler's development as a Wagnerian conductor.
Germany: Bayreuth. Italy: Milan, Rome. 1901-1954. Lang.: Eng.
3732

Collection of statements about the life and career of conductor
Wilhelm Furtwängler. Germany: Berlin. Austria: Salzburg. 1886-1986.
Lang.: Ger.   3737

Füssl, Karl Heinz
Plays/librettos/scripts
The church opera *Kain* written and composed for the Carinthiscer
Sommer Festival. Austria: Ossiach. 1986. Lang.: Ger.   3858

Füst, Milán
Performance/production
Milán Füst's *Margit kisasszony (Miss Margit)* directed by István
Dégi at Játékszin. Hungary: Budapest. 1986. Lang.: Hun.   1901

Reviews of *Margit kisasszony (Miss Margit)*, *Az Ibolya (The Violet)*,
Az Árny (The Ghost) and *Róza néni (Aunt Rosa)*. Hungary:
Budapest. 1985-1986. Lang.: Hun.   1916

Review of *Margit kisasszony (Miss Margit)* directed by István Dégi.
Hungary: Budapest. 1986. Lang.: Hun.   1941

Futurism
Design/technology
Painters as designers for the theatrical productions. Europe. 1890-
1980. Lang.: Fre.   260

Scene designs and theoretical texts of futurist painters working in the
theatre. Italy. 1910-1928. Lang.: Ita.   1517

Performance/production
An evening of Italian futurist theatre. Czechoslovakia: Prague. 1921.
Lang.: Ita.   1696

Relation to other fields
Artistic, literary and theatrical avant-garde movements. Europe. 1900-
1930. Lang.: Ita.   1083

Theory/criticism
Decreasing importance of the playwright in Italian theatre. Italy.
1900-1984. Lang.: Fre.   3119

Futurists, The
Performance/production
Collection of newspaper reviews by London theatre critics. UK-
England: London. 1986. Lang.: Eng.   2124

Plays/librettos/scripts
Interview with playwright Dusty Hughes about his play, *The
Futurists*. UK-England. 1980. Lang.: Eng.   2867

Futzenhorst, Manuel
Performance/production
Adaptation of Kroetz's *Wunschkonzert (Request Concert)*. India:
Calcutta, Madras, Bombay. Lang.: Eng.   1975

Fywell, Tim
Performance/production
Collection of newspaper reviews by London theatre critics. UK-
England: London. 1986. Lang.: Eng.   2122

Gabe
Plays/librettos/scripts
Amerindian and aborigine characters in the works of white
playwrights. Canada. Australia. 1606-1975. Lang.: Eng.   930

Gable, Clark
Performance/production
An historical account of one actor's experiences with the Fresno
Paramount Players. USA: Fresno, CA. 1927. Lang.: Eng.   2255

Gaddes, Richard
Institutions
New administrative personnel at the Opera Theatre of St. Louis.
USA: St. Louis, MO. 1976-1986. Lang.: Eng.   3679

Gaia Scienza, La (Italy)
Relation to other fields
Contrasts between culture and mass media. Italy. 1980-1986. Lang.:
Ita.   3171

Gaiety Theatre (Budapest)
SEE
Vigszinház.

Gala, Antonio
Plays/librettos/scripts
Current thematic trends in the plays of Antonio Gala. Spain. 1963-
1985. Lang.: Spa.   2783

Thematic and stylistic comparison of three plays influenced by the
Odyssey. Spain. 1952-1983. Lang.: Eng.   2792

Alfonso Sastre's theory of complex tragedy in *La Celestina (The
Nun)*. Spain. 1978. Lang.: Spa.   2807

Galati, Frank
Performance/production
Profile of and interview with William Neill, composer-in-residence at
the Lyric Opera of Chicago. USA: Chicago, IL. 1984-1986. Lang.:
Eng.   3829

Galbraith-Jones, Marian
Relation to other fields
Description of the Cutler Playwright's Festival designed for junior
high school students. USA: Groton, CT. 1983-1986. Lang.: Eng.
3065

Gałczyński, Konstanty Ildefons
Plays/librettos/scripts
Analysis of plays of Kruczkowski, Szaniawski and Gałczyński.
Poland. 1940-1949. Lang.: Pol.   2746

Galeasen (Stockholm)
Institutions
Production of Brecht's *Baal* by a troupe of untrained young actors.
Sweden: Stockholm. 1986. Lang.: Swe.   525

Gali, László
Institutions
Interviews with former managing directors of Csokonai Theatre.
Hungary: Debrecen. 1974-1986. Lang.: Hun.   503

Performance/production
Magda Szabó's *A macskák szerdája (Cat Wednesday)* at Csokonai
Theatre directed by László Gali. Hungary: Debrecen. 1986. Lang.:
Hun.   1777

László Gali directs Shakespeare's *Hamlet*. Hungary: Debrecen. 1986.
Lang.: Hun.   1827

Review of Shakespeare's *Hamlet* directed by László Gali at
Csokonai Theatre, with attention to Károly Sziki's performance as
Hamlet. Hungary: Debrecen. 1986. Lang.: Hun.   1844

Stage adaptations of Dostojèvskij novels *A Fèlkesgyelmü (The Idiot)*
and *A Karamazov testvérek (The Brothers Karamazov)*. Hungary:
Budapest, Debrecen. 1985. Lang.: Hun.   1922

Galilei
SEE
Leben des Galilei.

Galileo Galilei
SEE
Leben des Galilei.

Gáll, István
Performance/production
Nő a körúton (Woman on the Boulevard) by István Gáll directed by
Péter Léner at Móricz Zsigmond Theatre. Hungary: Nyiregyháza.
1986. Lang.: Hun.   1950

Gáll, István — cont'd

István Gáll's *Nő a körúton (Woman on the Boulevard)* directed by Péter Léner at Móricz Zsigmond Szinház. Hungary: Nyiregyháza. 1986. Lang.: Hun.
1973

Gallagher, Peter
Performance/production
Interview with Peter Gallagher on his portrayal of Edmund in *Long Day's Journey Into Night*. USA: New York, NY, New London, CT. 1986. Lang.: Eng.
2268

Galleria del Costume (Florence)
Design/technology
Illustrated description of Umberto Tirelli costume collection. Europe. 1700-1984. Lang.: Ita.
263

Galsworthy, John
Performance/production
Esse Ljungh's acting career with Winnipeg Little Theatre. Canada: Winnipeg, MB. 1921-1937. Lang.: Eng.
664

Galthrop, Gatti
Performance/production
Interview with Lesbian feminist theatre company Hard Corps. UK-England. 1984-1986. Lang.: Eng.
2164

Galvin, Robert
Design/technology
New lighting technology for *The Cosby Show*. USA: New York, NY. 1986. Lang.: Eng.
3259

Gambaro, Griselda
Plays/librettos/scripts
Use of violent language in the plays of Griselda Gambaro. Argentina. 1950-1980. Lang.: Eng.
2362

Gambuh
Performance/production
History of classical dance-drama *gambuh*. Bali. 1100-1982. Lang.: Eng.
1357

Games, The
Performance/production
Interview with choreographer Meredith Monk. USA: New York, NY. 1964-1984. Lang.: Eng.
1368

Gamester, The
Performance/production
History of Edward Moore's *The Gamester* on London stages. England: London. 1771-1871. Lang.: Eng.
1700

Gamla Stans Teater (Stockholm)
Institutions
Recent outdoor productions of Gamla Stans Teater. Sweden: Stockholm. 1933-1986. Lang.: Swe.
524

Gammer Gurton's Needle
Plays/librettos/scripts
Punctuation in *Gammer Gurton's Needle* indicates style of performance. England. 1575-1920.
2489

Gan, Zhengwen
Performance/production
Techniques of comedians in modern Beijing opera. China, People's Republic of: Beijing. 1964-1985. Lang.: Chi.
3524

Ganz, Bruno
Plays/librettos/scripts
Brecht's interpretational legacy is best understood on West German stages. Germany, West. 1956-1986.
2627

Gao, Shen
Reference materials
Review of 1985 dissertations. China, People's Republic of: Beijing. 1985. Lang.: Chi.
3545

Garbo, Greta
Performance/production
Life and career of film star Greta Garbo. Sweden. USA: Hollywood, CA. 1905-1985. Lang.: Hun.
3226

García Gutierrez, Antonio
Plays/librettos/scripts
Examples of playwrights whose work was poorly received by theatrical audiences in Madrid. Spain: Madrid. 1609-1950. Lang.: Spa.
2786

Creation of the 1857 version of *Simon Boccanegra* by Verdi, libretto by Piave. Italy: Venice. 1856-1881. Lang.: Eng.
3882

García Lorca, Federico
Institutions
Amateur production of García Lorca's *La Casa de Bernarda Alba (The House of Bernarda Alba)*. Sweden: Handen. 1982-1986. Lang.: Swe.
1584

Performance/production
Overview of performances transferred from The Royal Court, Greenwich, and Lyric Hammersmith theatres. UK-England: London. 1986. Lang.: Eng.
2143

Nuria Espert talks about Federico García Lorca and her production of *The House of Bernarda Alba*. UK-England: London. Spain. Lang.: Eng.
2178

Plays/librettos/scripts
Biographical study of playwright Federico García Lorca. Spain: Granada, Madrid. USA: New York, NY. 1898-1936. Lang.: Eng.
971

Examples of playwrights whose work was poorly received by theatrical audiences in Madrid. Spain: Madrid. 1609-1950. Lang.: Spa.
2786

Interview with Gillian Hanna about *Elisabetta: Quasì per caso una donna (Elizabeth: Almost by Chance a Woman)*. UK-England: London. Italy. 1986. Lang.: Eng.
2875

García Márquez, Gabriel
Performance/production
Interview with director Carlos Gimenez. Argentina. Venezuela: Caracas. 1969-1986. Lang.: Eng.
1636

Annual festival of Latin American plays at the Public Theatre. USA: New York, NY. 1985. Lang.: Eng.
2310

Relation to other fields
Writers Gabriel García Márquez, Carlos Fuentes and Dario Fo denied entry visas to the US on ideological grounds. USA: Washington, DC. 1984. Lang.: Eng.
1170

Garden of Earthly Delights, The
Performance/production
Martha Clarke's production of *The Garden of Earthly Delights*. USA: New York, NY. 1979-1984. Lang.: Eng.
1371

Gardner, David
Plays/librettos/scripts
Critical debate over Timothy Findley's *The Paper People*. Canada. 1967. Lang.: Eng.
3280

Gardner, Herbert
Performance/production
Development and production of Sir Percy Shelley's amateur production of *The Doom of St. Querec*. UK-England: London. 1876. Lang.: Eng.
809

Gardner, Jake
Performance/production
Reviews of *Death in the Family*, *Viaggio a Reims*, *Abduction from the Seraglio* and *Tales of Hoffmann*. USA: St. Louis, MO. 1975-1986. Lang.: Eng.
3799

Gárdonyi Géza Szinház (Eger)
Performance/production
Csongor és Tünde (Csongor and Tünde) by Mihály Vörösmarty, directed by János Szikora at Gárdonyi Géza Szinház. Hungary: Eger. 1985. Lang.: Hun.
1877

Mihály Vörösmarty's *Csongor and Tünde* at Gárdonyi Géza Theatre directed by János Szikora. Hungary: Eger. 1985. Lang.: Hun.
1923

Gardzienice Theatre
Relation to other fields
Alternative theatre and the political situation. Poland. 1960-1986. Lang.: Pol.
1119

Garland, Judy
Performance/production
Biography of singer/actress Judy Garland. USA. 1922-1969. Lang.: Eng.
3229

Garneau, Michel
Plays/librettos/scripts
Discusses Michel Garneau's *joual* translation of *Macbeth*. Canada: Montreal, PQ. 1978. Lang.: Eng.
2429

Garnier, Charles
Institutions
Illustrated discussion of the opening of the Théâtre National de l'Opéra. France: Paris. 1875. Lang.: Fre.
3674

Garrick, David
Performance/production
Biography of actor David Garrick. England: London. 1717-1779. Lang.: Eng.
692

Influence of mechanical physiology on David Garrick. England. 1734-1779. Lang.: Eng.
695

Changing attitudes toward madness reflected in David Garrick's adaptation of Shakespeare's *King Lear*. England. 1680-1779. Lang.: Eng.
1715

Garrick, David — cont'd

Plays/librettos/scripts
An appraisal of David Garrick's adaptation of Shakespeare's *King John*. England: London. 1736-1796. Lang.: Eng.   2510

Garrigues, Malvina
Performance/production
The first singers to perform *Tristan und Isolde*. Germany: Munich. 1857-1869. Lang.: Eng.   3733

Garter, Thomas
Performance/production
Performance by Joculatores Lancastrienses of Thomas Garter's interlude, *Commody of the Moste Vertuous and Godlye Susanna*. UK-England: Lancaster. 1985. Lang.: Eng.   2148

Thomas Garter's *Commody of the Moste Vertuous and Godlye Susana* performed before orignial screen in timberframed gothic hall. UK-England. 1986. Lang.: Eng.   2165

Plays/librettos/scripts
Legalistic aspect of *Commody of the Moste Vertuous and Godlye Susana* by Thomas Garter. England: London. 1563. Lang.: Eng.   2494

Gas, Mario
Performance/production
Savannah Bay and *Reigen (Round)* produced by Centre Dramàtic. Spain-Catalonia: Barcelona. 1986. Lang.: Cat.   2082

Gaskill, William
Performance/production
Collection of newspaper reviews by London theatre critics. UK-England. 1986. Lang.: Eng.   2114

Gate at the Latchmere (London)
Performance/production
Director Lou Stein discusses his policy at the Watford Palace Theatre. UK-England: Watford. 1982-1986. Lang.: Eng.   2167

Gate Theatre (Notting Hill, London)
Performance spaces
Overview of pub theatres. UK-England: London. 1980-1987. Lang.: Eng.   626
Performance/production
Collection of newspaper reviews by London theatre critics. UK. 1986. Lang.: Eng.   2099

Collection of newspaper reviews by London theatre critics. UK-England: London. 1986. Lang.: Eng.   2110

Collection of newspaper reviews by London theatre critics. UK-England: London. 1986. Lang.: Eng.   2122

Director Lou Stein discusses his policy at the Watford Palace Theatre. UK-England: Watford. 1982-1986. Lang.: Eng.   2167

Gatell, Pep
Performance/production
Detailed description of the performance titled *Accions (Actions)* by La Fura dels Baus. Spain-Catalonia. 1979-1984. Lang.: Cat.   3445

Gaulier, Philippe
Performance/production
Collection of newspaper reviews by London theatre critics. UK. 1986. Lang.: Eng.   2101

Collection of newspaper reviews by London theatre critics. UK. 1986. Lang.: Eng.   2102

Interview with clown, writer and teacher Philippe Gaulier. Europe. 1500-1986. Lang.: Fre.   3333

Gautier, Judith
Relation to other fields
Théophile Gautier's views about opera. France. 1811-1917. Lang.: Eng.   3917

Gautier, Théophile
Relation to other fields
Théophile Gautier's ideas on theatre and performance. France. 1811-1872. Lang.: Rus.   1086

Théophile Gautier's views about opera. France. 1811-1917. Lang.: Eng.   3917

Gauvreau, Georges
Institutions
Founding of Théâtre National Français de Montréal. Canada: Montreal, PQ. 1889-1901. Lang.: Fre.   469

Gay Sweatshop (UK)
Plays/librettos/scripts
Overview of plays with homosexual themes. UK-England: London. 1970-1986. Lang.: Eng.   2841

Gay theatre
Administration
Restructuring of the Glines producing organization of the Glines Foundation. USA: New York, NY. 1983. Lang.: Eng.   1441

Performance/production
Interview with actor/playwright Harvey Fierstein. UK-England: London. USA: New York. 1983-1986. Lang.: Eng.   2175

Plays/librettos/scripts
Progress in audience perception of gay characters in plays. USA. 1933-1985. Lang.: Eng.   2909

Gazdag, Gyula
Performance/production
Gyula Gazdag directs *A vihar (The Tempest)* by William Shakespeare, Csiky Gergely Theatre. Hungary: Kaposvár. 1986. Lang.: Hun.   1883

Review of Gyula Gazdag's production of *A Vihar (The Tempest)* by Shakespeare, Csiky Gergely Theatre. Hungary: Kaposvár. 1986. Lang.: Hun.   1960

Gdzie sa Niegdysiejsze Śniegi (Where Are the Snows of Yesteryear)
Performance/production
Tadeusz Kantor directs his *Gdzie sa Niegdysiejsze Śniegi (Where Are the Snows of Yesteryear)*, Cricot 2. Poland: Cracow. 1984. Lang.: Pol.   2061

Geburt der Tragödie, Die (Birth of Tragedy, The)
Theory/criticism
Hungarian translation of Nietzsche's *Birth of Tragedy*. Germany. 1872. Lang.: Hun.   3108

Gee, Lee
Performance/production
Chinese theatre companies on the Goldfields of Victoria. Australia. 1858-1870. Lang.: Eng.   1641

Gee, Shirley
Plays/librettos/scripts
Current state of women's playwriting. UK-England. 1985-1986. Lang.: Eng.   2830

Geelhaar, Christian
Reference materials
The purchase and eventual exhibition of a collection of Stravinsky's work. Switzerland: Basel. USA: New York, NY. 1930-1985. Lang.: Eng.   3500

Gegerfelt, Calle von
Design/technology
Swedish set designers discuss their working methods. Sweden. 1980-1986. Lang.: Swe.   312

Geki, Mugon
Performance/production
A photographic essay of 42 soloists and groups performing mime or gestural theatre. 1986.   3290

Gel'man, Aleksej
Plays/librettos/scripts
Analysis of the plays of Aleksej Gel'man. USSR. 1986. Lang.: Rus.   2959

Gellért, Péter
Performance/production
Péter Gellért's production of *Urhatnám polgár (The Bourgeois Gentleman)* at Móricz Zsigmond Szinház. Hungary: Nyiregyháza. 1986. Lang.: Hun.   1931

Gems, Pam
Plays/librettos/scripts
Attitudes toward sexuality in plays from French sources. UK-England. France. Lang.: Eng.   2852

Diary of a playwright at Royal Shakespeare Company. UK-England. 1985-1986. Lang.: Eng.   2854

Genesis
Design/technology
Interview with manager Tony Smith and lighting designer Alan Owen of the rock band Genesis focusing on the lighting technology used on their latest tour. USA. 1968-1986. Lang.: Eng.   3320

Genet, Jean
Performance/production
Notes, interviews and evolution of actor/director Jean-Marie Serreau. France. 1938-1973. Lang.: Fre.   1724

Reminiscences of actor-director Roger Blin. France. 1930-1983. Lang.: Fre.   1726

Plays/librettos/scripts
History, poetry and violence in plays by Tankred Dorst, Heiner Müller and Jean Genet. Europe. Lang.: Fre.   2538

Great dramatic works considered in light of modern theatre and social reponsibility. France. Italy. Germany, West. 1700-1964. Lang.: Fre.   2560

Genet, Jean — cont'd

    Biographical information on Jean Genet. France. 1910-1985. Lang.:
    Fre.   2588

Gengangere (Ghosts)
    Plays/librettos/scripts
    Short history of Catalan translations of plays. Spain-Catalonia. 1848-
    1984. Lang.: Fre.   2813
    Plays translated into Catalan by Pompeu Fabra. Spain-Catalonia.
    1890-1905. Lang.: Cat.   2818
    Relation to other fields
    Reports and discussions of restricted cultural communication.
    Lebanon. Spain-Catalonia. USA. 1985. Lang.: Fre, Spa, Cat.   1111

Genres
    Basic theatrical documents
    Edition of *La famosa comèdia de la gala està en son punt (The
    Famous Comedy of the Gala Done to a Turn)*, with analysis. Spain-
    Catalonia. 1625-1680. Lang.: Cat.   1497
    Performance/production
    Comparison of Eastern and Western theatre. Italy: Rome. 1986.
    Lang.: Ita.   748
    Director Jonathan Miller's theory of performance based on genre.
    1986. Lang.: Eng.   1631
    Performance conditions of specific theatrical genres. Lebanon. 1918-
    1985. Lang.: Fre.   2011
    Origins of Southern Sung drama (*Nanxi*). China: Wenzhou. 1127-
    1234. Lang.: Chi.   3512
    Influence of Tibetan drama on Chinese theatre. China. Tibet. 1700-
    1981. Lang.: Chi.   3515
    Mágnás Miska (Miska the Magnate) by Albert Szirmai directed by
    László Bagossy. Hungary: Pécs. 1986. Lang.: Hun.   3942
    Plays/librettos/scripts
    Development in the genre of the *sainete*, or comic afterpiece.
    Argentina. 1800-1980. Lang.: Spa.   2365
    Violation of genre divisions in the plays of Ben Jonson. England:
    London. 1606-1610. Lang.: Eng.   2525
    Essays on dramatic form, genre and language. France. 1500-1985.
    Lang.: Fre.   2545
    Comedies of Tieck and Brentano representing German Romanticism.
    Germany. 1795-1850. Lang.: Rus.   2602
    System of genres in the work of A.N. Ostrovskij. Russia. 1823-1886.
    Lang.: Rus.   2772
    Juan del Enzina's defence of pastoral vs. courtly genre. Spain. 1469-
    1529. Lang.: Spa.   2785
    Joe Orton's redefinition of farce as a genre. UK-England. 1960-1969.
    Lang.: Eng.   2840
    Correlation between short stories and plays by Carson McCullers.
    USA. 1917-1967. Lang.: Rus.   2889
    Evolution of Byelorussian folk drama. USSR. Lang.: Rus.   2953
    Relation to other fields
    Reports and discussions of restricted cultural communication.
    Lebanon. Spain-Catalonia. USA. 1985. Lang.: Fre, Spa, Cat.   1111
    Drama as a genre of literature. Lang.: Rus.   3012
    Popular theatrical forms in the Basque country. Spain. France. 674-
    1963. Lang.: Spa.   3361
    Renaissance theatre at Valencia court, Catalan festivals. Spain-
    Catalonia: Valencia. 1330-1970. Lang.: Spa.   3362
    Theory/criticism
    Eleven theatre professionals discuss their personal direction and the
    direction of experimental theatre. USA: New York, NY. 1985.
    Lang.: Eng.   3137
    Present and future of mime theatre.   3300

Gentile, Giovanni
    Relation to other fields
    Luigi Pirandello's relationship with philosophers Benedetto Croce and
    Giovanni Gentile. Italy. 1867-1936. Lang.: Ita.   1106

George, David
    Plays/librettos/scripts
    Ritual and archetypal communication in *La noche de los asesinos
    (The Night of the Assassins)* by José Triana. Cuba. Brazil. 1973-
    1974. Lang.: Eng.   2450

George, Roger
    Performance/production
    Homage to dancer and choreographer Roger George. Switzerland.
    Germany, West. 1921-1986. Lang.: Ger.   1351

Georgian Academic Theatre (Tbilisi)
    SEE
    Gruzinskij Akademičeskij Teat'r im. Kote Mordžanišvili.

Performance/production
    Robert Sturua of Georgian Academic Theatre directs Brecht and
    Shakespeare in Warsaw. USSR: Tbilisi. Poland: Warsaw. 1983.
    Lang.: Pol.   2336

Gergely, László
    Performance/production
    Mihály Vörösmarty's *Csongor és Tünde (Csongor and Tünde)*
    directed by László Gergely. Hungary: Debrecen. 1986. Lang.: Hun.
    1820
    Troádes (The Trojan Women) directed by László Gergely at
    Csokonai Theatre. Hungary: Debrecen. 1985. Lang.: Hun.   1909

Gerou, Wayne
    Design/technology
    The wigmaker's role in regional opera houses. USA. Lang.: Eng.
    3658

Gershwin, George
    Performance/production
    Photographs, cast list, synopsis, and discography of Metropolitan
    Opera radio broadcast performances. USA: New York, NY. 1986.
    Lang.: Eng.   3794
    Profile of and interview with Frances Gershwin Godowsky, younger
    sister of George and Ira Gershwin. USA: New York, NY. 1900-
    1986. Lang.: Eng.   3842

Gershwin, Ira
    Performance/production
    Photographs, cast list, synopsis, and discography of Metropolitan
    Opera radio broadcast performances. USA: New York, NY. 1986.
    Lang.: Eng.   3794
    Profile of and interview with Frances Gershwin Godowsky, younger
    sister of George and Ira Gershwin. USA: New York, NY. 1900-
    1986. Lang.: Eng.   3842
    Plays/librettos/scripts
    Analysis of the operetta *Firebrand* by Kurt Weill and Ira Gershwin.
    USA: New York, NY. Italy: Florence. 1945. Lang.: Eng.   3944

Gersten, Bernard
    Relation to other fields
    Writers Gabriel García Márquez, Carlos Fuentes and Dario Fo
    denied entry visas to the US on ideological grounds. USA:
    Washington, DC. 1984. Lang.: Eng.   1170

Gertrude Stein and a Companion
    Performance/production
    Reviews of *Gertrude Stein and a Companion*, by Win Wells, staged
    by Ira Cirker. USA: New York, NY. 1986. Lang.: Eng.   2238

Geschonnek, Erwin
    Performance/production
    Photographic record of forty years of the Berliner Ensemble.
    Germany, East: Berlin, East. 1949-1984. Lang.: Eng.   1761

**Gesellschaft der Freunde der Ballettschule der Österreichischen
Bundestheater (Vienna)**
    Institutions
    Activities of the audience-society, Gesellschaft der Freunde der
    Ballettschule der Österreichischen Bundestheater. Austria: Vienna.
    1985-1986. Lang.: Ger.   1294

Gesticulador, El (Gesticulator, The)
    Plays/librettos/scripts
    Use of language in *El Gesticulador (The Gesticulator)* by Rodolfo
    Usigli. Mexico. 1970-1980. Lang.: Spa.   2723

Gesture
    Plays/librettos/scripts
    Gestural characterization in *I promessi sposi (The Betrothed)* by
    Manzoni. Italy. 1842. Lang.: Ita.   2707

Gewehre der Frau Carrar, Die (Señora Carrar's Rifles)
    Plays/librettos/scripts
    Dialogue analysis of *Die Gewehre der Frau Carrar (Señora Carrar's
    Rifles)* by Bertolt Brecht. Germany, East. Lang.: Ger.   2612

Ghelderode, Michel de
    Performance/production
    Effect of dual-language society on Belgian theatre. Belgium: Brussels,
    Liège. Lang.: Eng.   660

Gherson, Gad
    Plays/librettos/scripts
    Unpublished documentation of *Proprio like that*, a musical by Luigi
    Pirandello. Italy: Rome. 1930-1953. Lang.: Fre.   3627

Ghiaurov, Nicolai
    Performance/production
    Opera-singer Mirella Freni: her roles and plans. Italy. Austria. 1935-
    1986. Lang.: Ger.   3759

Ghitty, Alison
Institutions
Place of women in Britain's National Theatre. UK-England: London. 1986. Lang.: Eng. 1588

Ghosts
SEE
Gengangere.

Gi, Guk-Seo
Performance/production
Directing and the current state of Korean theatre. Korea. 1986. Lang.: Kor. 760

Gianfrancesco, Edward
Design/technology
The WPA Theatre's resident designer, Edward Gianfrancesco. USA: New York, NY. 1977-1986. 382

Giannini, Dusolina
Performance/production
Obituary of soprano Dusolina Giannini. USA: Philadelphia, PA. 1902-1986. Lang.: Eng. 3823

Gibon, William
Performance/production
Reviews of *Raggedy Ann*, book by William Gibon, music and lyrics by Joe Raposo, staged and choreographed by Patricia Birch. USA: New York, NY. 1986. Lang.: Eng. 3614

Gibson, Brian
Design/technology
Lighting designer Andrew Lazlo talks about his work on the film *Poltergeist II.* USA: Los Angeles, CA. USA: New York, NY. 1985-1986. Lang.: Eng. 3204

Gielgud, John
Performance/production
Innovative Shakespeare stagings of Harley Granville-Barker. UK-England. 1912-1940. Lang.: Eng. 806
Letters to and from Harley Granville-Barker. UK-England. 1877-1946. Lang.: Eng. 807
Actor Laurence Olivier's memoirs. UK-England: London. USA: New York, NY. 1907-1986. Lang.: Eng. 2170

Giffard, Henry
Administration
Royal theatrical patronage during the reign of George II. England: London. 1727-1760. Lang.: Eng. 33

Gigaku
Plays/librettos/scripts
Influences on Asian theatrical genres. Asia. 500-1985. Lang.: Eng. 920

Giganti della montagna, I (Giants of the Mountain, The)
Performance/production
Premiere of Luigi Pirandello's *I giganti della montagna (The Giants of the Mountain).* Italy: Florence. 1937. Lang.: Ita. 1998

Gigi
Plays/librettos/scripts
Attitudes toward sexuality in plays from French sources. UK-England. France. Lang.: Eng. 2852

Gilbert, Sky
Institutions
Founder Sky Gilbert discusses aesthetic goals of Rhubarb Festival. Canada: Toronto, ON. 1979-1986. Lang.: Eng. 475
History of the Rhubarb Festival. Canada: Toronto, ON. 1986. Lang.: Eng. 1549
Performance/production
Rhubarb Festival is alternative to playwriting and workshopping conventions. Canada: Toronto, ON. 1986. Lang.: Eng. 672

Gilbert, William Schwenck
Basic theatrical documents
Text of plays by James Robinson Planché, with introduction on his influence. UK-England. 1818-1872. Lang.: Eng. 226

Gilded Age or Colonel Sellers
Plays/librettos/scripts
Philosophy of wealth in gilded age plays. USA: New York, NY. 1870-1889. Lang.: Eng. 2950

Gilfert, Charles
Performance spaces
The varied history of the Bowery Theatres. USA: New York, NY. 1826-1929. Lang.: Eng. 1624

Gillespie, Robert
Performance/production
Collection of newspaper reviews by London theatre critics. UK-England: London. 1986. Lang.: Eng. 2124

Gillies, Max
Performance/production
Interview with political satirist Max Gillies. Australia. 1986. Lang.: Eng. 654

Gillot, Claude
Relation to other fields
The work of painter and scene designer Claude Gillot. France. 1673-1722. Lang.: Ita. 1084

Gillray, James
Relation to other fields
Shakespearean allusion in English caricature. UK-England. 1780-1820. Lang.: Eng. 3056

Gilmore, David
Performance/production
Collection of newspaper reviews by London theatre critics. UK-England: London. 1986. Lang.: Eng. 2123

Gilmour, Dean
Institutions
Theories on incorporating traditional theatrical forms into popular theatre. Canada: Toronto, ON. 1970-1986. Lang.: Eng. 3408
Performance/production
Distinctive style of Canadian clowns. Canada: Toronto, ON, Vancouver, BC. 1967-1986. Lang.: Eng. 3328

Gimenez, Carlos
Performance/production
Interview with director Carlos Gimenez. Argentina. Venezuela: Caracas. 1969-1986. Lang.: Eng. 1636

Gioacchino, Rossini
Performance/production
Photographs, cast list, synopsis, and discography of Metropolitan Opera radio broadcast performances. USA: New York, NY. 1986. Lang.: Eng. 3794

Gioconda, La
Reference materials
Photos of the new opera productions at the Staatsoper. Austria: Vienna. 1985-1986. Lang.: Ger. 3910

Girardi, Alexander
Reference materials
Costumes of famous Viennese actors. Austria: Vienna. 1831-1960. Lang.: Ger. 1003
Interpretation of Ferdinand Raimund's dramas after his death. Austria: Vienna. 1790-1986. Lang.: Ger. 2981
Relation to other fields
Life and work of playwright and critic Karl Kraus. Austria: Vienna. 1874-1936. Lang.: Ger. 3017

Giraudoux, Jean
Plays/librettos/scripts
Superficial and reductive use of classical myth in modern French theatre. France. 1935-1944. Lang.: Eng. 2550
Marguerite Yourcenar's treatment of Electra story compared to other versions. France. 1944-1954. Lang.: Fre. 2554

Giricz, Mátyás
Performance/production
Interview with director Mátyás Giricz. Hungary. 1986. Lang.: Hun. 1774
Az esőcsináló (The Rainmaker) by N. Richard Nash, directed by Mátyás Giricz. Hungary: Békéscsaba. 1986. Lang.: Hun. 1795
Mátyás Giricz directs *A kertész kutyája (The Gardener's Dog)* by Lope de Vega. Hungary: Budapest. 1985. Lang.: Hun. 1900
Miklós Mészöly's *Bunker* at Népszinház directed by Mátyás Giricz. Hungary: Budapest. 1985. Lang.: Hun. 1919
Aleksej Dudarëv's *Večer (An Evening)* directed by Mátyas Giricz at Józsefvárosi Theatre. Hungary: Budapest. 1986. Lang.: Hun. 1947

Giselle
Performance/production
Stage history of *Giselle* by Adolphe Adam at Pest National Theatre. Hungary: Pest. 1847-1880. Lang.: Hun. 1306

GITIS
SEE
Gosudarstvènnyj Institut Teatralnovo Iskusstva.

Giuoco delle parti, Il (Rules of the Game, The)
Basic theatrical documents
Catalan translation of *Il giuoco delle parti (The Rules of the Game)* by Luigi Pirandello. Italy. 1918. Lang.: Cat. 1485
Plays/librettos/scripts
Evaluation of *Il giuoco delle parti (The Rules of the Game)* in the context of Pirandello's oeuvre. Italy. 1867-1936. Lang.: Cat. 2670

Government subsidies
SEE
Funding, government.

Goya
Performance/production
Stills from telecast performance of *Goya*. List of principals, conductor and production staff included. USA: Washington, DC. 1986. Lang.: Eng. 3791

Profile of and interview with Gian Carlo Menotti with emphasis on his new opera *Goya*. USA: New York, NY. 1911-1986. Lang.: Eng. 3838

Gozzi, Carlo
Plays/librettos/scripts
Poetics of the fantastic in works of Carlo Gozzi. Italy. 1720-1806. Lang.: Ita. 2679

Theory/criticism
Semiotic analysis of Carlo Gozzi's *Fiabe (Fables)*. Italy: Venice. 1761-1765. Lang.: Ita. 3117

Grabbe, Christian Dietrich
Plays/librettos/scripts
Biography of playwright Christian Dietrich Grabbe. Germany. 1801-1836. Lang.: Ger. 2595

Relation to other fields
Nazi ideology and the revival of plays by Christian Dietrich Grabbe. Germany. 1801-1946. Lang.: Eng. 1087

Grabowski, Mikołaj
Performance/production
Mikołaj Grabowski directs *Irydion* by Zygmunt Krasiński. Poland: Cracow. 1983. Lang.: Pol. 2046

Grabscheid, Eugen
Performance/production
Memoir of Dr. Eugen Grabscheid, throat specialist. USA: New York, NY. 1938-1986. Lang.: Eng. 3830

Gracieux, Jean
Basic theatrical documents
Identity of actor Bruscambille, or Des Louriers. France. 1600-1634. Lang.: Fre. 1480

Graeae Theatre Group (London)
Relation to other fields
The work of disabled theatre companies in England. UK-England. 1979-1986. Lang.: Eng. 1139

Graham, Colin
Institutions
New administrative personnel at the Opera Theatre of St. Louis. USA: St. Louis, MO. 1976-1986. Lang.: Eng. 3679

Performance/production
Reviews of *Death in the Family*, *Viaggio a Reims*, *Abduction from the Seraglio* and *Tales of Hoffmann*. USA: St. Louis, MO. 1975-1986. Lang.: Eng. 3799

Graham, Martha
Institutions
Problems of Toronto Dance Theatre. Canada: Toronto, ON. 1968-1982. Lang.: Eng. 1344

Graham, Steven
Design/technology
Art director Steven Graham's work on the film *The Money Pit*. USA. 1986. 378

Gran duque de Gandía, El (Grand Duke of Gandía, The)
Plays/librettos/scripts
Calderón's *El gran duque de Gandía (The Grand Duke of Gandía)* and its Mexican source. Spain. Mexico. 1600-1680. Lang.: Eng. 2789

Gran Teatre del Liceo (Barcelona)
Performance spaces
Children's history of the Gran Teatre del Liceo opera house. Spain-Catalonia: Barcelona. 1845-1986. Lang.: Cat. 3684

Grand Opera House (New Orleans, LA)
Administration
Career of independent theatrical manager Henry Greenwall. USA: Galveston, TX. 1867-1890. Lang.: Eng. 87

Grandbois, Alain
Basic theatrical documents
Text of *J'ai Vingt Ans (I Am Twenty Years Old)* by Alain Grandbois. Canada. 1934-1975. Lang.: Fre. 1469

Grande magia, La (Great Magic, The)
Plays/librettos/scripts
Critical discussion of *La grande magia (The Great Magic)* by Eduardo De Filippo. Italy. 1948. Lang.: Ita. 2678

Grands Ballets Canadiens, Les (LGBC, Montreal, PQ)
Design/technology
Career of lighting designer Nicholas Cernovitch. Canada: Montreal, PQ. 1970-1983. Lang.: Eng. 244

Granite Peak
Plays/librettos/scripts
Analysis of *The Touch of Silk* and *Granite Peak* by Betty Roland. Australia. 1928-1981. Lang.: Eng. 2387

Grant, Alexander
Institutions
Account of the firing of Alexander Grant, artistic director of National Ballet of Canada. Canada: Toronto, ON. 1975-1982. Lang.: Eng. 1295

Grant, Kim
Performance/production
Collection of newspaper reviews by London theatre critics. UK-England: London. 1986. Lang.: Eng. 2116

Granville-Barker, Harley
Performance/production
Innovative Shakespeare stagings of Harley Granville-Barker. UK-England. 1912-1940. Lang.: Eng. 806

Letters to and from Harley Granville-Barker. UK-England. 1877-1946. Lang.: Eng. 807

Greek tragedy on the New York stage. USA: New York, NY. 1854-1984. Lang.: Eng. 2301

Graton, Françoise
Institutions
Interview with Françoise Graton and Gilles Pelletier of Nouvelle Compagnie Théâtrale. Canada: Montreal, PQ. 1964-1984. Lang.: Fre. 477

Gratzer, Hans
Institutions
Photos of productions at the Schauspielhaus under the leadership of Hans Gratzer. Austria: Vienna. 1978-1986. Lang.: Ger. 1534

Performance spaces
Plans for using the Ronacher theatre after its renovation. Austria: Vienna. 1871-1986. Lang.: Ger. 584

Gray, Oriel
Plays/librettos/scripts
Analysis of the plays of Oriel Gray. Australia. 1942-1958. Lang.: Eng. 2376

Gray, Simon
Performance/production
Reviews of *The Common Pursuit*, by Simon Gray, staged by Simon Gray and Michael McGuire. USA: New York, NY. 1986. Lang.: Eng. 2202

Plays/librettos/scripts
Playwright Simon Gray's journal about the production of his play *The Common Pursuit*. UK-England. 1983. Lang.: Eng. 2858

Influence of Aristophanes and Čechov on playwright Simon Gray. UK-England. 1986. Lang.: Eng. 2874

Gray, Spalding
Performance/production
Wooster Group retrospective of original works. USA: New York, NY. 1975-1986. Lang.: Eng. 850

Historical development of acting and directing techniques. 1898-1986. Lang.: Eng. 1632

Reviews of *Terrors of Pleasure*, a monologue by Spalding Gray. USA: New York, NY. 1986. Lang.: Eng. 2208

Plays/librettos/scripts
Review of adaptations for the stage of short stories by Čechov. USA: New York, NY. 1986. Lang.: Eng. 2922

Grazer Schauspielhaus (Graz)
Plays/librettos/scripts
Training for new playwrights in Austria. Austria: Vienna. 1985-1986. Lang.: Ger. 2392

Grease
Design/technology
Designers discuss regional productions of *Grease*. USA. 1984-1986. Lang.: Eng. 3597

Great Canadian Theatre Company (Ottawa, ON)
Institutions
Structure and political viewpoint of Great Canadian Theatre Company. Canada: Ottawa, ON. 1975-1986. Lang.: Eng. 486

Great Theatre of the World, The
SEE
Gran Teatro del Mundo, El.

SUBJECT INDEX

Great Wallace Circus
SEE
Wallace Brothers Circus.

Great White Hope, The
Performance/production
Review of alternative theatre productions. UK-England: London. 1986. Lang.: Eng. 2108

Career of director/choreographer Mike Malone. USA: Washington, DC, Cleveland, OH. 1968-1985. Lang.: Eng. 2275

Greater London Council (London)
Plays/librettos/scripts
Interview with playwright Howard Barker. UK-England. 1981-1985. Lang.: Eng. 2845

Greater Miami Opera (Miami, FL)
Design/technology
The wigmaker's role in regional opera houses. USA. Lang.: Eng. 3658

Greek Amphitheatre (Syracuse)
SEE
Teatro Greco.

Green Bird, The
SEE
Augellino belverde, L'.

Green Card
Performance/production
Review of *Green Card* by JoAnne Akalaitis. USA: Los Angeles, CA. Lang.: Eng. 2256

Green Cockatoo, The
SEE
Grüne Kakadu, Der.

Green Lawn Rest Home
Plays/librettos/scripts
Influence of oriental theatre on playwright Beverley Simons. Canada: Vancouver, BC. 1962-1975. Lang.: Eng. 928

Green Pastures, The
Performance/production
Biography of actor Richard B. Harrison, who played God in *The Green Pastures.* USA. 1930-1939. Lang.: Eng. 828

Green Thumb Theatre (Vancouver, BC)
Institutions
Interview with Dennis Foon, director of Green Thumb Theatre for Young People. Canada: Vancouver, BC. 1975-1984. Lang.: Fre. 473
History of the Green Thumb Theatre. Canada: Vancouver, BC. 1975-1986. Lang.: Eng. 1541

Green, Adolph
Performance/production
Reviews of musicals. UK-England: London. 1986. Lang.: Eng. 3610

Plays/librettos/scripts
Betty Comden and Adolph Green on their careers. 3626

Green, Jane
Theory/criticism
Report of seminar on theatre criticism. USA: New York, NY. 1983. Lang.: Eng. 1223

Green, Paul
Plays/librettos/scripts
The power of music to transform the play into living theatre, examples from the work of Paul Green, Clifford Odets, and Maxwell Anderson. USA: New York, NY. 1936. Lang.: Eng. 3632

Greene, Graham
Theory/criticism
Assessment of critic Kenneth Tynan's works. UK-England. 1950-1960. Lang.: Eng. 3136

Greene, Justin
Performance/production
Collection of newspaper reviews by London theatre critics. UK. 1986. Lang.: Eng. 2099
Collection of newspaper reviews by London theatre critics. UK-England. 1986. Lang.: Eng. 2115
Collection of newspaper reviews by London theatre critics. UK-England. 1986. Lang.: Eng. 2120

Greene, Robert
Plays/librettos/scripts
Image of poverty in Elizabethan and Stuart plays. England. 1558-1642. Lang.: Eng. 2482
Tradition and individualism in Renaissance drama. England: London. 1575-1600. Lang.: Eng. 2496

Greenfield, Bill
Design/technology
A lighting designer discusses the unique problems of lighting symphony orchestras. USA: Washington, DC, Boston, MA, New York, NY. 1910-1986. Lang.: Eng. 3478

Greenwall, Henry
Administration
Career of independent theatrical manager Henry Greenwall. USA: Galveston, TX. 1867-1890. Lang.: Eng. 87

Greenwich Theatre (London)
Performance/production
Collection of newspaper reviews by London theatre critics. UK-England. 1986. Lang.: Eng. 2111
Collection of newspaper reviews by London theatre critics. UK-England: London. 1986. Lang.: Eng. 2118
Overview of performances transferred from The Royal Court, Greenwich, and Lyric Hammersmith theatres. UK-England: London. 1986. Lang.: Eng. 2143

Greenwich Young Peoples Theatre
Relation to other fields
Proposals on theatre in education. UK-England: London, Greenwich. 1986. Lang.: Hun. 1137

Gregory, Isabella Augusta, Lady
Plays/librettos/scripts
Biography of playwright Teresa Deevy. Ireland. 1894-1963. Lang.: Eng. 2665

Gregory, Lady
SEE
Gregory, Isabella Augusta.

Gregory's Girl
Performance/production
Collection of newspaper reviews by London theatre critics. UK: London. 1986. Lang.: Eng. 2100

Greig, Noel
Performance/production
Collection of newspaper reviews by London theatre critics. UK-England. 1986. Lang.: Eng. 2114

Grein, Jacob Thomas
Performance/production
The Independent Theatre of Jacob Thomas Grein, established in imitation of André Antoine's Théâtre Libre. UK-England: London. 1891. Lang.: Rus. 818

Griboedov, A.S.
Performance/production
History of productions of A.S. Griboedov's *Gore ot uma (Wit Works Woe).* Russia. 1845-1900. Lang.: Rus. 780

Grice, H.P.
Plays/librettos/scripts
Rhetorical analysis of Samuel Beckett's *Waiting for Godot.* France. 1953. Lang.: Eng. 2562

Griffero, Ramón
Performance/production
Interview with actor, director, playwright and filmmaker Ramón Griffero. Chile: Santiago. 1953-1986. Lang.: Spa. 675

Griffin, Benjamin Pitt
Performance/production
Profile of actor-entrepeneur George Coppin. Canada: Victoria, BC. 1864. Lang.: Eng. 1666

Grifteater
Theory/criticism
The aesthetics of movement theatre. Europe. 1975-1986. 3301

Grillparzer, Franz
Performance/production
László Salamon Suba's production of *Urának hű szolgája (A Faithful Servant of His Lord)* by Franz Grillparzer. Hungary: Nyíregyháza. 1985. Lang.: Hun. 1881

Plays/librettos/scripts
Reflections on Max Zweig's dramas. Austria: Vienna. Germany: Berlin. Israel: Tel Aviv. 1892-1986. Lang.: Ger. 2389
Social themes in the dramas of Franz Grillparzer. Austro-Hungarian Empire: Vienna. 1791-1872. Lang.: Ger. 2399

Grimmelhauser, J.C.
Performance/production
Collection of newspaper reviews by London theatre critics. UK: London. 1986. Lang.: Eng. 2100

Grinšpun, I.A.
Performance/production
Director I.A. Grinšpun recalls famous actors, directors and
playwrights. USSR. 1930-1986. Lang.: Rus.   876

Griselda
Plays/librettos/scripts
Use of the tale of Patient Griselda in *Griselda* by Angelo Anelli and
Niccolo Piccinni. Italy: Venice. Austria: Vienna. 1770-1800. Lang.:
Eng.   3885

Griswold, Mary
Design/technology
Designers discuss regional productions of *Side-by-Side by Sondheim*.
USA. 1984. Lang.: Eng.   3593

Grizzard, George
Performance/production
Director of original production discusses Edward Albee's *Who's
Afraid of Virginia Woolf?*. USA: New York, NY. 1962. Lang.: Eng.
2303

Grön, Maria
Institutions
Training for amateur theatre leaders at Marieborg Folkhögskola.
Sweden: Norrköping. 1960-1986. Lang.: Swe.   528

Gropius Társulat (Budapest)
Performance/production
Performances of *Alice Csodaországban (Alice in Wonderland)*, *A Két
Veronai nemes (The Two Gentlemen of Verona)* and *Tobbsincs
királyfi (No More Crown Prince)*. Hungary: Pécs, Budapest. 1985.
Lang.: Hun.   1771
Interview with actor, director and dramaturg Imre Katona of the
Gropius Társulat. Hungary: Budapest. 1961-1985. Lang.: Hun.   1945

Grosse Schmährede an der Stadtmauer (Great Tirade before the City Wall)
Basic theatrical documents
Catalan translations of plays by Tankred Dorst, with critical
introduction. Germany. 1961. Lang.: Cat.   1482
Plays/librettos/scripts
History, poetry and violence in plays by Tankred Dorst, Heiner
Müller and Jean Genet. Europe. Lang.: Fre.   2538
Introduction to plays by Tankred Dorst. Germany. 1925-1982. Lang.:
Cat.   2591

Grosses Haus, Der (Stuttgart)
Performance spaces
The renovation of the Württemberg State Theatre by the citizens of
Stuttgart. Germany, West: Stuttgart. 1909-1976. Lang.: Eng.   3683

Grossman, Mechthild
Performance/production
Interview with choreographer Mechthild Grossman. Germany, West.
1984-1985. Lang.: Eng.   1273
Theory/criticism
American criticisms of German *Tanztheater*. Germany, West. USA.
1933-1985. Lang.: Eng.   1290

Grosz, George
Design/technology
Contribution of designer Ernst Stern to modern scenography.
Germany: Berlin. UK-England: London. 1905. Lang.: Eng.   1516

Grotowski, Jerzy
Institutions
The Reduta theatre as the predecessor of Grotowski's Laboratory.
Poland: Warsaw. 1919-1939. Lang.: Fre.   1581
Performance/production
Zen and Western acting styles. Lang.: Eng.   648
Theatricality on and off-stage. Lang.: Eng.   649
Comparison of Eastern and Western theatre. Italy: Rome. 1986.
Lang.: Ita.   748
Analysis of career and methods of director Jerzy Grotowski. Poland.
1959-1984. Lang.: Hun.   771
Career of director Jerzy Grotowski. Poland. 1933-1976. Lang.: Eng.
773
Historical development of acting and directing techniques. 1898-1986.
Lang.: Eng.   1632
Interviews with Polish theatre professionals. Poland: Poznań. 1963-
1985. Lang.: Eng.   2024
Analysis of the directorial style of Jerzy Grotowski. Poland:
Wrocław. 1959-1984. Lang.: Pol.   2044
Overview of the career of Jerzy Grotowski, his theatrical
experiments, training methodology and thoughts on the purpose of
theatre. Poland. 1958-1986. Lang.: Eng.   2054

Performance art and its current characteristic tone. USA. Lang.: Eng.
3459
Plays/librettos/scripts
Jerzy Grotowski and his adaptation of *Doctor Faustus*. Poland. 1964.
Lang.: Eng.   2740
Relation to other fields
Dissolution of Jerzy Grotowski's Laboratory Theatre. Poland:
Wrocław. 1959-1985. Lang.: Eng.   1117
Alternative theatre and the political situation. Poland. 1960-1986.
Lang.: Pol.   1119
Theory/criticism
Creative self-assembly and juxtaposition in live performance and
film. Lang.: Eng.   1196
Excerpts from writings of critics and theatre professionals on theory
of theatre. Europe. 1880-1985. Lang.: Ita.   1204
Experimental theatres to offset the impact of film and theatre.
China, People's Republic of. 1960-1981. Lang.: Chi.   3090
Aesthetic theory of interpretation. Europe. North America. 1900-1985.
Lang.: Fre.   3097
Selections from Jerzy Grotowski's *Towards a Poor Theatre*. Poland.
1933-1982. Lang.: Chi.   3126

Grouch: A Life in Revue
Performance/production
Reviews of *Grouch: A Life in Revue*, by Arthur Marx and Robert
Fisher, staged by Arthur Marx. USA: New York, NY. 1986. Lang.:
Eng.   2201

Group Theatre (New York, NY)
Administration
Cheryl Crawford's producing career discussed in light of her latest
Broadway show. USA: New York, NY, Atlanta, GA. 1936-1986.
Lang.: Eng.   117
Performance/production
Interview with producer, director, actor Robert Lewis. USA: New
York, NY. 1930-1986. Lang.: Eng.   844

Group 20 (New York, NY)
Performance/production
Actress Rosemary Harris discusses her work in *The Petition*. UK-
England: London. USA: New York, NY. 1948-1986. Lang.: Eng.
2177

Groupe Octobre (France)
Performance/production
Reminiscences of actor-director Roger Blin. France. 1930-1983.
Lang.: Fre.   1726

Grove, Barry
Administration
Skills required by managing directors. USA: New York, NY. 1984.
Lang.: Eng.   169

Groves, Barbara
Administration
Lincoln Center development director's fundraising strategy. USA:
New York, NY. 1986. Lang.: Eng.   114

Gruberova, Edita
Reference materials
Photos of the new opera productions at the Staatsoper. Austria:
Vienna. 1985-1986. Lang.: Ger.   3910

Grünbaum, Fritz
Performance/production
History of the Viennese cabaret. Austria: Vienna. 1890-1945. Lang.:
Ger.   3364

Gründgens, Gustaf
Performance/production
Playing Hamlet at the Burgtheater. Austria: Vienna. 1803-1985.
Lang.: Ger.   1654
Relation to other fields
Study of Fascist theatrical policies. Germany: Berlin. 1933-1944.
Lang.: Ger.   1091

Grüne Kakadu, Der (Green Cockatoo, The)
Performance/production
Reviews of two plays by Arthur Schnitzler directed by Imre Halasi.
Hungary: Budapest, Zalaegerszeg. 1986. Lang.: Hun.   1958

Grünmandl, Otto
Performance/production
Otto Grünmandl and his satiric revues. Austria. 1924-1986. Lang.:
Ger.   3363

Grupa Laokoona (Laocoön Group, The)
Plays/librettos/scripts
Analysis of *Grupa Laokoona (The Laocoön Group)* by Tadeusz Różewicz and *Tsaplia (The Heron)* by Vasilij Aksёnov. Poland. USSR. 1961-1979. Lang.: Eng.　2738

Grupo de Artistas Latinoamericanos (Washington, D.C.)
Relation to other fields
Reports and discussions of restricted cultural communication. Lebanon. Spain-Catalonia. USA. 1985. Lang.: Fre, Spa, Cat.　1111

Gruzinskij Akademičeskij Teat'r im. Kote Mordžanišvili
Performance/production
Robert Sturua of Georgian Academic Theatre directs Brecht and Shakespeare in Warsaw. USSR: Tbilisi. Poland: Warsaw. 1983. Lang.: Pol.　2336

Gryphius, Andreas
Plays/librettos/scripts
Contrasting treatment of history in *Carolus Stuardus* by Andreas Gryphius and *Maria Stuart* by Friedrich von Schiller. Germany. England. 1651-1800. Lang.: Eng.　2590

Grzegorzewski, Jerzy
Performance/production
Jerzy Grzegorzewski directs Różewicz's *Pulapka (Trap)* at Centrum Sztuki Studio. Poland: Warsaw. 1984. Lang.: Pol.　2053

Gu, Zhongyi
Theory/criticism
Influence of Western theory on Chinese drama of Gu Zhongyi. China. 1920-1963. Lang.: Chi.　1202

Gual, Adrià
Design/technology
History of Catalan scenography. Spain-Catalonia. 200 B.C.-1986 A.D. Lang.: Cat.　311
Plays/librettos/scripts
History of Catalan literature, including playwrights and theatre. Spain-Catalonia. 1800-1974. Lang.: Cat.　974

Guare, John
Performance/production
Reviews of *The House of Blue Leaves* by John Guare, staged by Jerry Zaks. USA: New York, NY. 1986. Lang.: Eng.　2220
Plays/librettos/scripts
Review of adaptations for the stage of short stories by Čechov. USA: New York, NY. 1986. Lang.: Eng.　2922
Betty Comden and Adolph Green on their careers.　3626
Theory/criticism
National Conference of Theatre Communications Group (TCG). USA: Amherst, MA. Lang.: Eng.　1233

Guarini, Giambattista
Design/technology
Costume design in a 16th century production in Milan of Guarini's *Il Pastor Fido*. Italy: Mantua. 1500-1600. Lang.: Eng.　298

Guarrera, Frank
Performance/production
Opera greats reflect on performance highlights. USA: Philadelphia, PA, New York, NY. 1985. Lang.: Eng.　3841

Guattari, Félix
Plays/librettos/scripts
Deconstructionist analysis of *Riccardo III* by Carmelo Bene. Italy. France. Lang.: Eng.　2690

Gubaku
Plays/librettos/scripts
Influences on Asian theatrical genres. Asia. 500-1985. Lang.: Eng.　920

Guerre de Troie n'aura pas lieu, La (Tiger at the Gates)
Plays/librettos/scripts
Superficial and reductive use of classical myth in modern French theatre. France. 1935-1944. Lang.: Eng.　2550

Guffroy, Pierre
Design/technology
Pierre Guffroy's design of a functional ship for Polanski's *Pirates*. Tunisia. 1986. Lang.: Eng.　3201

Guglielminetti, Eugenio
Design/technology
Career of costume and stage designer Eugenio Guglielminetti. Italy. 1946-1986. Lang.: Ita.　299

Guides
Administration
Guidelines for fundraising from individuals. USA: New York, NY. 1985. Lang.: Eng.　126
A guide to some of the largest private foundations. USA. 1986. Lang.: Eng.　155

Guide to producing Off-off Broadway showcases. USA: New York, NY. Lang.: Eng.　159
Basic theatrical documents
Videotape of Shakespeare's *As You Like It* with study guide and edition of the play. Canada: Stratford, ON. 1983. Lang.: Eng.　219
Design/technology
ABTT technical guidelines for sound and communications systems in the theatre. UK-England. Lang.: Eng.　324
Theatre Craft's annual directory of theatre equipment and manufacturers. USA. 1986. Lang.: Eng.　336
Using the 'major manufacturers' make-up kits. USA. 1986.　356
A guide to sealed beam lamps. USA. 1986.　413
Guide to materials necessary for theatrical performances. USSR. 1980-1986. Lang.: Rus.　430
Instructions in creating a modeled puppet head.　3947
Creating physical attributes for puppets which effectively communicate their character.　3948
Creating the proportions and constructing a pattern plan for marionettes. USA. 1985-1986.　4003
Performance/production
Guide to finding acting jobs in theatre, film and television. USA. 1986. Lang.: Eng.　835
Spring production schedules for member companies of Alliance of Resident Theatres/New York. USA: New York, NY. 1984. Lang.: Eng.　2195
Plays/librettos/scripts
Analysis and guide to Pirandello's published letters. Italy. 1867-1936. Lang.: Ita.　2674
Reference materials
Guide to plays of the world. 1980-1983. Lang.: Ger.　997
Guide to theatre companies around the world. Lang.: Eng.　999
Survey of Canadian theatre publications. Canada. 1982. Lang.: Eng.　1010
Listing of theatrical productions. Japan: Tokyo. 1200-1500. Lang.: Jap.　1028
Guide to Catalan theatres. Spain-Catalonia. 1848-1986. Lang.: Cat.　1030
Guide to theatrical services and productions. UK-England. 1985-1986. Lang.: Eng.　1035
A directory of services available to Dramatists Guild members. USA. 1986.　1038
Production schedules of member theatres of Alliance of Resident Theatres/New York. USA: New York, NY. 1984. Lang.: Eng.　1040
Directory of support sources for the playwright. USA. 1986.　1041
Guide to producing printed material. USA. 1984. Lang.: Eng.　1044
Alphabetically arranged profiles and history of professional and amateur theatres for children. USA. 1903-1985. Lang.: Eng.　1046
Guide to well-known plays and their authors. Lang.: Ger.　2975
Illustrated guide to Actor's Museum. Hungary: Budapest. 1850-1986. Lang.: Hun.　2990
Guide to postwar British theatre. UK-England. 1945-1986. Lang.: Eng.　3001
Production schedules for member theatres of Alliance of Resident Theatres/New York. USA: New York, NY. 1985-1986. Lang.: Eng.　3005
Production schedules for member theatres of Alliance of Resident Theatres, New York. USA: New York, NY. 1983. Lang.: Eng.　3006
Theatrical careers of famous actors. USA. UK. 1717-1986. Lang.: Eng.　3010
Summer performance schedules for several New York companies. USA: New York, NY. 1984. Lang.: Eng.　3011
Description of popular entertainments, both sacred and secular. Spain-Catalonia. 1947-1986. Lang.: Cat.　3355
Guide to the work of principal composers of Broadway musicals. 1905-1985. Lang.: Eng.　3633
Detailed listing of major American musicals and their production requirements. USA. 1951-1985. Lang.: Eng.　3634
Guide to Ferenc Erkel opera museum. Hungary: Gyula. 1810-1893. Lang.: Hun.　3912
Relation to other fields
Essays and reviews on Hungarian and foreign playwrights, productions, actors and traditions. 1962-1986. Lang.: Hun.　1058

Guides — cont'd

Training
A guide to internship training programs. USA. 1986.   1259

Guilt of William Sloan, The
Performance/production
Profile of and interview with William Neill, composer-in-residence at the Lyric Opera of Chicago. USA: Chicago, IL. 1984-1986. Lang.: Eng.   3829

Guilty, The
SEE
Vinovatyje.

Guimerà, Àngel
Basic theatrical documents
Anthology and study of writings of Josep Maria de Sagarra. Spain-Catalonia. 1917-1964. Lang.: Cat.   1501

Plays/librettos/scripts
History of Catalan literature, including playwrights. Spain-Catalonia. France. 1800-1926. Lang.: Cat.   973

Evaluation of the literary and dramatic work of Josep Maria de Sagarra. Spain-Catalonia. 1917-1955. Lang.: Cat.   2810

Analysis of *La Santa Espina (The Holy Thorn)* by Àngel Guimerà. Spain-Catalonia. 1897-1907. Lang.: Cat.   2815

A defense of Àngel Guimerà's language. Spain-Catalonia. 1860-1967. Lang.: Cat.   2817

Relation to other fields
Reports and discussions of restricted cultural communication. Lebanon. Spain-Catalonia. USA. 1985. Lang.: Fre, Spa, Cat.   1111

Theory/criticism
Historical difficulties in creating a paradigm for Catalan theatre. Spain-Catalonia. 1400-1963. Lang.: Cat.   1220

Guinness, Alec
Performance/production
Career and religious convictions of actor Alec Guinness. UK-England. 1933-1984. Lang.: Eng.   808

Autobiography of actor Alec Guinness. UK. USA. 1914-1985. Lang.: Eng.   2106

Gunn, Bill
Reference materials
Current work of Audelco award-winning playwrights. USA: New York, NY. 1973-1984. Lang.: Eng.   3007

Gunsbourg, Raoul
Administration
Raoul Gunsbourg, director of Monte Carlo Opera for 59 years. Monaco: Monte Carlo. 1893-1951. Lang.: Eng.   3641

Günther, Ricard
Institutions
Production of Brecht's *Baal* by a troupe of untrained young actors. Sweden: Stockholm. 1986. Lang.: Swe.   525

Gurney, A. R., Jr.
Performance/production
Reviews of *The Perfect Party* by A. R. Gurney, Jr., staged by John Tillinger. USA: New York, NY. 1986. Lang.: Eng.   2224

Gurney, A.R., Jr.
Theory/criticism
Theatre professionals challenge assertions that theatre is a weaker form of communication than film. USA: New York, NY. 1985. Lang.: Eng.   1225

Gusti Sinuhan
Relation to other fields
Analyses of *Wayang cepak* play, *Gusti Sinuhan*, and its role in the Hindu religion. Indonesia. 1045-1986. Lang.: Eng.   3992

Gute Mensch von Sezuan, Der (Good Person of Szechwan, The)
Performance/production
Actress Walfriede Schmitt discusses performing Brecht. USA. 1986.   823

Plays/librettos/scripts
Demystification of the feminine myth in Brecht's plays. Germany, East. 1984.   2618

Guthrie Theatre (Minneapolis, MN)
Design/technology
Sound designers at regional theatres evaluate new equipment. USA. 1986.   409

Designers discuss regional productions of *Guys and Dolls*. USA. 1984-1986. Lang.: Eng.   3586

Institutions
Tyrone Guthrie on Guthrie Theatre and regional theatre movement. USA: Minneapolis, MN. 1963. Lang.: Eng.   555

Performance/production
Dramaturg Richard Nelson on communicating with different kinds of directors. USA: New York, NY. 1979-1986. Lang.: Eng.   2252

Mark Bly on the dramaturg's responsibility to question. USA: Minneapolis, MN. 1981-1986. Lang.: Eng.   2294

Guthrie, Tyrone
Design/technology
Profile of theatre designer Tanya Moiseiwitsch. 1934-1986. Lang.: Eng.   227

Institutions
Tyrone Guthrie on Guthrie Theatre and regional theatre movement. USA: Minneapolis, MN. 1963. Lang.: Eng.   555

Performance/production
Actor Laurence Olivier's memoirs. UK-England: London. USA: New York, NY. 1907-1986. Lang.: Eng.   2170

Margaret Webster's scenic approach to Shakespeare compared with those of Herbert Beerbohm Tree and Tyrone Guthrie. USA: New York, NY. 1910-1949. Lang.: Eng.   2293

Greek tragedy on the New York stage. USA: New York, NY. 1854-1984. Lang.: Eng.   2301

Gutmacher, Benito
Performance/production
A photographic essay of 42 soloists and groups performing mime or gestural theatre. 1986.   3290

Guys and Dolls
Design/technology
Designers discuss regional productions of *Guys and Dolls*. USA. 1984-1986. Lang.: Eng.   3586

Performance/production
Tap dancing career of Maurice Hines and the creation of his new company Balletap, USA. USA: New York, NY. 1949-1986. Lang.: Eng.   3623

Gwyn, Nell
Performance/production
New determination of birthdate of actress Nell Gwyn. England: London. 1642-1671. Lang.: Eng.   690

Plays/librettos/scripts
Cast lists in James Shirley's *Six New Playes* suggest popularity of plays. England. 1653-1669. Lang.: Eng.   2504

Gyárfás, Miklós
Performance/production
Notes on performances of *Hongkongi paróka (Wig Made in Hong Kong)*, *Egérút (Narrow Escape)* and *Róza néni (Aunt Rosa)*. Hungary: Budapest. 1985. Lang.: Hun.   1801

Géza Tordy directs *Császári futam (Imperial Round)* by Miklós Gyárfás at Gyulai Várszinház. Hungary: Gyula. 1986. Lang.: Hun.   1875

Criticizes stage adaptation of *Hangok komédiája (Comedy of Sounds)* by Miklós Gyárfás. Hungary: Budapest. 1985. Lang.: Hun.   1924

Gye, Ernest
Performance/production
Changes in English life reflected in 1883 theatre season. UK-England: London. 1883. Lang.: Eng.   810

Gyóri Balett (Gyór)
Design/technology
Technician János Hani of Gyóri Balett discusses his work. Hungary: Gyór. 1979-1986. Lang.: Hun.   287

Performance/production
Analysis of choreography of *A szarvassá változott fiak (The Sons Who Turned Into Stags)*. Hungary: Gyór. 1985-1986. Lang.: Hun.   1277

Productions based on sacred music of Franz Liszt. Hungary: Zalaegerszeg, Budapest. 1986. Lang.: Hun.   1308

Gypsy
Design/technology
Designers discuss regional productions of *Gypsy*. USA. 1984-1986.   3588

Gyulai Várszinház (Gyula)
Performance/production
Géza Tordy directs *Császári futam (Imperial Round)* by Miklós Gyárfás at Gyulai Várszinház. Hungary: Gyula. 1986. Lang.: Hun.   1875

Ferenc Sik directs two plays by Gyula Háy. Hungary: Veszprém, Gyula. 1986. Lang.: Hun.   1943

Endre Vészi's *Don Quijote utolsó kalandja (Don Quixote's Last Adventure)* directed by Imre Kerényi. Hungary: Gyula. 1986. Lang.: Hun.   1951

Gyurkovics, Mária
Performance/production
Careers of three Hungarian opera stars. Hungary. 1925-1979. Lang.:
Hun. 3755

Gyurkovics, Tibor
Plays/librettos/scripts
Study of Tibor Gyurkovics' eight plays. Hungary. 1976-1985. Lang.:
Hun. 2654

H.A.D.L.E.Y. Players (New York, NY)
Institutions
Brief histories of the H.A.D.L.E.Y. Players and the Cynthia Belgrave
Theatre Workshop. USA: New York, NY. 1970-1986. Lang.: Eng.
1604

HaBimah (Moscow)
Audience
Relationship between HaBimah theatre and its audience. USSR:
Moscow. 1918-1925. Lang.: Heb. 213

HaBimah (Tel Aviv)
Audience
HaBimah Theatre production of *Troádes (The Trojan Women)* by
Euripides. Israel: Tel-Aviv. 1982-1983. Lang.: Eng. 199

Performance/production
Jurij Petrivič Liubimov directs Isaak Babel's *Hashhia (Sunset)*. Israel:
Tel-Aviv. 1984-1986. Lang.: Heb. 1979

HaBimah (Tel-Aviv)
Reference materials
Speech given by Benjamin Zemach on the deposition of Nachum
Zemach's archive at Hebrew University. Israel: Jerusalem. 1986.
Lang.: Heb. 1019

Hacker, Linda
Design/technology
Designers discuss regional productions of *Guys and Dolls*. USA.
1984-1986. Lang.: Eng. 3586

Designers discuss regional productions of *The Music Man*. USA.
1983-1986. Lang.: Eng. 3589

Designers discuss regional productions of *Once Upon a Mattress*.
USA. 1984-1986. 3590

Hadley, Jerry
Performance/production
Profile of and interview with American tenor Jerry Hadley. USA:
New York, NY. 1952-1986. Lang.: Eng. 3818

Haeussermann, Ernst
Administration
Manager Heinrich Kraus and his work. Austria: Vienna. 1930-1986.
Lang.: Ger. 1426

Hagen, Uta
Performance/production
History of the Margaret Webster-Paul Robeson production of
Othello. USA: New York, NY. 1942-1944. Lang.: Eng. 852

Director of original production discusses Edward Albee's *Who's
Afraid of Virginia Woolf?*. USA: New York, NY. 1962. Lang.: Eng.
2303

Hagenbeck Wallace Circus
Performance/production
Detailed history of the 1914 Hagenbeck Wallace Circus season.
USA: St. Louis, MO, Youngstown, OH, Sturgis, MI. 1914. Lang.:
Eng. 3388

Hagyaték (Legacy)
Performance/production
Productions of plays by Edward Bond, Gyula Hernádi and Lope de
Vega at the Pécs National Theatre. Hungary: Pécs. 1986. Lang.:
Hun. 1898

Hagyaték (Legacy) by Gyula Hernádi, directed by Menyhért
Szegvári. Hungary: Pécs. 1986. Lang.: Hun. 1949

Haidlen, Barbara
History of the Theater für Vorarlberg. Austria: Bregenz. 1818-1986.
Lang.: Ger. 3

Haifa Municipal Theatre
SEE
Teatron HaIroni Haifa.

Haimes, Todd
Administration
Skills required by managing directors. USA: New York, NY. 1984.
Lang.: Eng. 169

Hair
Performance/production
Performances of *Hair*, directed by János Sándor, and *Desire Under
the Elms*, directed by Géza Bodolay at the National Theatre of
Szeged. Hungary: Szeged. 1986. Lang.: Hun. 1959

Hair of the Dog
Plays/librettos/scripts
Gender role-reversal in the Cycle plays of Eugene O'Neill. USA.
1927-1953. Lang.: Eng. 2896

Hairy Ape, The
Plays/librettos/scripts
Repetition and negativism in plays of Jean Anouilh and Eugene
O'Neill. France. USA. 1922-1960. Lang.: Eng. 2578

Imagery of gender compared in works by Susan Glaspell and
Eugene O'Neill. USA: New York, NY, Provincetown, MA. 1916-
1922. Lang.: Eng. 2893

Hakaron Puppet Theatre (Jerusalem)
Performance/production
Puppeteer Eric Bass of Hakaron Puppet Theatre. Israel: Jerusalem.
1984-1986. Lang.: Heb. 3966

Hakawâti
Performance/production
Performance conditions of specific theatrical genres. Lebanon. 1918-
1985. Lang.: Fre. 2011

Relation to other fields
Reports and discussions of restricted cultural communication.
Lebanon. Spain-Catalonia. USA. 1985. Lang.: Fre, Spa, Cat. 1111

Halasi, Imre
Performance/production
Sip a tökre (Play a Trump in Diamonds) by Péter Tömöry, directed
by Imre Halasi. Hungary: Kisvárda. 1986. Lang.: Hun. 1859

Reviews of two plays by Arthur Schnitzler directed by Imre Halasi.
Hungary: Budapest, Zalaegerszeg. 1986. Lang.: Hun. 1958

Lakat alá lányokat (Lock Up Your Daughters), a stage adaptation of
Henry Fielding's *Rape Upon Rape*, directed by Imre Halasi.
Hungary: Diósgyőr. 1986. Lang.: Hun. 3600

Hale, Jonathan
Performance/production
Claudio Monteverdi's *L'incoronazione di Poppea (The Coronation of
Poppea)* directed by Jonathan Hale at the Kent Opera. UK-England:
Kent. 1986. Lang.: Eng. 3781

Hall, Adrian
Design/technology
Career of scenic designer Eugene Lee. USA: Providence, RI. 1965-
1984. Lang.: Eng. 339

Institutions
Interview with Adrian Hall, artistic director of both Trinity Square
Repertory Theatre and Dallas Theatre Center. USA: Providence, RI,
Dallas, TX. 1966-1986. Lang.: Eng. 548

Hall, Ed
Performance/production
Five actors who work solely in regional theatre. 1961-1984. Lang.:
Eng. 1633

Hall, Peter
Institutions
Survey of Royal Shakespeare Company productions. UK-England.
1960-1980. Lang.: Chi. 1593

Performance/production
Collection of newspaper reviews by London theatre critics. UK-
England: London. 1986. Lang.: Eng. 2112

Detailed discussion of four successful Royal Shakespeare Company
productions of Shakespeare's minor plays. UK-England: Stratford.
1946-1977. Lang.: Eng. 2182

Shakespearean productions by the National Theatre, Royal
Shakespeare Company and Orange Tree Theatre. UK-England:
Stratford, London. 1984-1985. Lang.: Eng. 2183

Reviews of *The Petition*, by Brian Clark, staged by Peter Hall.
USA: New York, NY. 1986. Lang.: Eng. 2234

Performance analysis of the title role of *Carmen*. France. 1875-1986.
Lang.: Eng. 3725

Photographs, cast list, synopsis, and discography of Metropolitan
Opera radio broadcast performances. USA: New York, NY. 1986.
Lang.: Eng. 3794

Plays/librettos/scripts
Modern criticism of Shakespeare's crowd scenes. England. 1590-1986.
Lang.: Eng. 2536

Hall, Radclyffe
Performance/production
Interview with Lesbian feminist theatre company Hard Corps. UK-England. 1984-1986. Lang.: Eng. 2164

Haller, Bernard
Performance/production
A photographic essay of 42 soloists and groups performing mime or gestural theatre. 1986. 3290

Halls
Design/technology
Lighting tips for amateur theatre groups working in church and community halls and schools. UK-England. Lang.: Eng. 322
Lighting concerts, plays and pantomimes in a church hall with minimum lighting facilities. UK-England: Stratford. 1980-1986. Lang.: Eng. 326
Amateur technician outlines his experience of lighting a pantomime in a hall with a ceiling 8 feet high. UK-England: Brighton. 1980-1986. Lang.: Eng. 3304
A lighting designer discusses the unique problems of lighting symphony orchestras. USA: Washington, DC, Boston, MA, New York, NY. 1910-1986. Lang.: Eng. 3478
Performance spaces
Design of concert hall in part of a major railway station. Hungary: Budapest. 1985-1986. Lang.: Hun. 598
Overview of the hall in which Shakespeare's *Twelfth Night* was performed. England: London. 1602. Lang.: Eng. 1616
Performance/production
Development of and influences on theatre and other regional entertainments. England. 1840-1870. Lang.: Eng. 688
Thomas Garter's *Commody of the Moste Vertuous and Godlye Susana* performed before orignial screen in timberframed gothic hall. UK-England. 1986. Lang.: Eng. 2165
Reference materials
Index of multifunctional halls used for theatrical performances. Lang.: Ger. 996

Halprin, Ann
Performance/production
Modern dancer Ann Halprin and her work with artists in other media. USA. 1965. Lang.: Eng. 1352

Hamblin, Thomas Sowerby
Performance spaces
The varied history of the Bowery Theatres. USA: New York, NY. 1826-1929. Lang.: Eng. 1624
Performance/production
Career of actress Josephine Clifton. USA. 1813-1847. Lang.: Eng. 846

Hamilton, Edith
Performance spaces
Ambiguous translations of ancient Greek theatrical documentation. Greece. Italy: Rome. 600-400 B.C. Lang.: Eng. 597

Hamlet
Institutions
Ten years of the Burgtheater under the auspices of Achim Benning. Austria: Vienna. 1776-1986. Lang.: Ger. 1533
Performance/production
Examination of German versions of Shakespeare's *Hamlet*. Germany: Hamburg. 1770-1811. Lang.: Eng. 728
Director Charles Marowitz on the role of the director. USA. 1965-1985. Lang.: Eng. 843
Klaus Maria Brandauer as Hamlet. Austria: Vienna. 1944-1986. Lang.: Ger. 1648
Playing Hamlet at the Burgtheater. Austria: Vienna. 1803-1985. Lang.: Ger. 1654
Innovative stagings of Shakespeare's *Hamlet*. Europe. 1700-1950. Lang.: Rus. 1716
Analysis of Shakespeare's influence on Weimar, German neoclassicism. Germany: Weimar. 1771-1812. Lang.: Eng. 1760
László Gali directs Shakespeare's *Hamlet*. Hungary: Debrecen. 1986. Lang.: Hun. 1827
Review of Shakespeare's *Hamlet* directed by László Gali at Csokonai Theatre, with attention to Károly Sziki's performance as Hamlet. Hungary: Debrecen. 1986. Lang.: Hun. 1844
Shakespeare's *Hamlet* directed by Janusz Warmiński. Poland: Warsaw. 1983. Lang.: Pol. 2051
Collection of newspaper reviews by London theatre critics. UK. 1986. Lang.: Eng. 2099

Collection of newspaper reviews by London theatre critics. UK. 1986. Lang.: Eng. 2101
Collection of newspaper reviews by London theatre critics. UK-England: London. 1986. Lang.: Eng. 2110
Doubling of roles in Shakespeare's *Hamlet*. UK-England: London. 1900-1985. Lang.: Eng. 2129
Reconstruction of a number of Shakespeare plays staged and performed by Herbert Beerbohm Tree. UK-England: London. 1887-1917. Lang.: Eng. 2155
Shakespearean productions by the National Theatre, Royal Shakespeare Company and Orange Tree Theatre. UK-England: Stratford, London. 1984-1985. Lang.: Eng. 2183
Reviews of Shakespeare's *Hamlet* staged by Liviu Ciulei. USA: New York, NY. 1986. Lang.: Eng. 2226
Plays/librettos/scripts
Environmental theatre version of *Hamlet*. Canada: Vancouver, BC. 1986. Lang.: Eng. 2435
Shakespeare's influence on Beaumont and Fletcher's *Philaster*. England. 1609. Lang.: Eng. 2463
Adapting *Hamlet* for the *nō* theatre. England. Japan. 1600-1982. Lang.: Ita. 2506
Translations of plays by William Shakespeare into Amharic and Tegrenna. Ethiopia: Addis Ababa. 1941-1984. Lang.: Eng. 2537
Interpretation of Fortinbras in post-war productions of *Hamlet*. Poland. UK-England. 1945. Lang.: Eng. 2748

Hamlisch, Marvin
Performance/production
Reviews of *Smile*, music by Marvin Hamlisch, book by Howard Ashman. USA: New York, NY. 1986. Lang.: Eng. 3613

Hammerstein, Oscar, II
Performance/production
Collection of newspaper reviews by London theatre critics. UK. 1986. Lang.: Eng. 2103

Hampl, Patricia
Performance/production
Review of Libby Larsen's opera *Clair de Lune*. USA: Little Rock, AR. 1985. Lang.: Eng. 3803

Hampstead Theatre (London)
Performance/production
Collection of newspaper reviews by London theatre critics. UK. 1986. Lang.: Eng. 2103
Collection of newspaper reviews by London theatre critics. UK-England: London. 1986. Lang.: Eng. 2117
Collection of newspaper reviews by London theatre critics. UK-England: London. 1986. Lang.: Eng. 2123

Hampton Court Theatre (UK)
Design/technology
Comparison of lighting in English theatres and Comédie-Française. England: London, Hampton Court. 1718. Lang.: Eng. 259

Hampton, Christopher
Performance/production
Collection of newspaper reviews by London theatre critics. UK: London. 1986. Lang.: Eng. 2100
Collection of newspaper reviews by London theatre critics. UK-England: London. 1986. Lang.: Eng. 2109
Collection of newspaper reviews by London theatre critics. UK-England: London. 1986. Lang.: Eng. 2115
Royal Shakespeare Company performances at the Barbican Theatre. UK-England: London. 1986. Lang.: Eng. 2152
Plays/librettos/scripts
Attitudes toward sexuality in plays from French sources. UK-England. France. Lang.: Eng. 2852
Interview with Christopher Hampton on his adaptation of *Les Liaisons dangereuses*. UK-England: London. 1971-1986. Lang.: Eng. 2859

Han, Sang-Cheol
Performance/production
Directing and the current state of Korean theatre. Korea. 1986. Lang.: Kor. 760

Han, Tian
Plays/librettos/scripts
Life and work of playwright Tian Han. China. 1898-1968. Lang.: Eng. 2443

Han, Yoo-Sung
Theory/criticism
Styles of mask-dance drama in Asia. Korea: Seoul. Japan: Tokyo.
China: Beijing. 1400-1986. Lang.: Kor.   1378
Evolution and symbolism of the Mask-Dance drama. Korea: Seoul.
700-1986. Lang.: Kor.   1379

Hancock, Sheila
Performance/production
Actress Sheila Hancock discusses role of Madame Ranevskaya in
Čechov's *Višněvyj sad (The Cherry Orchard)*. UK-England: London.
1986. Lang.: Eng.   2180

Handel, George Frideric
Administration
Reconsideration of George Frideric Handel's declining success.
England: London. 1729-1739. Lang.: Eng.   3640

Performance/production
Profile of and interview with tenor Jon Vickers about his career and
his leading role in *Samson* by George Frideric Handel. Canada:
Prince Albert, AB. 1926-1986. Lang.: Eng.   3713
The mixture of opera and oratory in *Samson* by George Frideric
Handel. England: London. 1741-1986. Lang.: Eng.   3719
Productions of Handel's *Muzio Scevola* and analysis of score and
characters. England: London. 1718-1980. Lang.: Eng.   3720
Photographs, cast list, synopsis, and discography of Metropolitan
Opera radio broadcast performances. USA: New York, NY. 1986.
Lang.: Eng.   3794
Opera director Nathaniel Merrill on his productions. USA: New
York, NY. 1958-1986. Lang.: Eng.   3805
Samson, by George Frideric Handel is staged at the Metropolitan
Opera. USA: New York, NY. 1986. Lang.: Eng.   3831

Plays/librettos/scripts
Comparison of the *Samson Agonistes* of John Milton and the
Samson of George Frideric Handel. England: London. 1743. Lang.:
Eng.   3862

Research/historiography
Comparison of oratorio and opera styles as developed by Handel.
England: London. 1740-1900. Lang.: Eng.   3926
The life of Handel and his influence in making Italian opera
popular in England. Italy. England: London. Germany. 1685-1985.
Lang.: Eng.   3928

Handful of Friends, A
Plays/librettos/scripts
Analysis of plays by David Williamson. Australia. 1976-1985. Lang.:
Eng.   2379

Handke, Peter
Plays/librettos/scripts
Interview with Peter Handke about his play *Prometheus gefesselt*.
Austria: Salzburg. Greece. 1985-1986. Lang.: Ger.   2398
Distinguishes between the natural flow of words and present forms
of linguistic alienation. USA. Austria. 1970-1986. Lang.: Eng. 2913

Hands On (New York, NY)
Performance/production
Hands On, a company which interprets plays and variety
performances for the deaf. USA: New York, NY. 1980-1986. Lang.:
Eng.   2283

Hands, Terry
Design/technology
Changes in the Royal Shakespeare Company under its current
directors. UK-England: London. 1967-1986. Lang.: Eng.   325

Performance/production
Collection of newspaper reviews by London theatre critics. UK-
England: London. 1986. Lang.: Eng.   2109
Detailed discussion of four successful Royal Shakespeare Company
productions of Shakespeare's minor plays. UK-England: Stratford.
1946-1977. Lang.: Eng.   2182
Shakespearean productions by the National Theatre, Royal
Shakespeare Company and Orange Tree Theatre. UK-England:
Stratford, London. 1984-1985. Lang.: Eng.   2183

**Handspring Puppet Theatre Company (Republic of South
Africa)**
Performance/production
History of puppet theatre including recent developments in political
satire and agit-prop. South Africa, Republic of. 1805-1986. Lang.:
Eng.   3969

Hangok komédiája (Comedy of Sounds)
Performance/production
Criticizes stage adaptation of *Hangok komédiája (Comedy of Sounds)*
by Miklós Gyárfás. Hungary: Budapest. 1985. Lang.: Hun.   1924

Hani, János
Design/technology
Technician János Hani of Győri Balett discusses his work. Hungary:
Győr. 1979-1986. Lang.: Hun.   287

Hanka, Erika
Reference materials
Christl Zimmerl's career as prima ballerina at the Vienna State
Opera. Austria: Vienna. 1939-1976. Lang.: Ger.   1324

Hankerson, Barry
Administration
Growing activity and changing role of Black regional theatre
companies. USA. 1960-1984. Lang.: Eng.   1440

Hanna, Gillian
Plays/librettos/scripts
Interview with Gillian Hanna about *Elisabetta: Quasi per caso una
donna (Elizabeth: Almost by Chance a Woman)*. UK-England:
London. Italy. 1986. Lang.: Eng.   2875

Hannah, Don
Performance/production
Dramaturg's experience with classical and new productions. Canada:
Toronto, ON. 1986. Lang.: Eng.   1667

Hanoi Tuong Theatre (Hanoi)
Performance/production
József Katona's *Bánk Bán* presented by the Hanoi Tuong Theatre
directed by Doan Anh Thang. Vietnam: Hanoi. 1986. Lang.: Hun.
                                                           2340

Hans Pfriem
Performance/production
Brecht and the Berliner Ensemble. Germany, East: Berlin, East.
1950-1956. Lang.: Ger.   1765

Hansberry, Lorraine
Audience
Reception of Lorraine Hansberry's *A Raisin in the Sun*. USA. 1959-
1986. Lang.: Eng.   1456

Performance/production
Lloyd Richard's career as an actor, director, artistic director and
academic dean. USA: Detroit, MI, New York, NY, New Haven, CT.
1920-1980. Lang.: Eng.   2308

Plays/librettos/scripts
Interview with playwright Lorraine Hansberry. USA. 1959. Lang.:
Eng.   2945

Hänsel und Gretel
Reference materials
Stills from telecast performances of *Hänsel und Gretel*. List of
principals, conductor and production staff included. Austria: Vienna.
1986. Lang.: Eng.   3909

Hanuszkiewicz, Adam
Performance/production
Adam Hanuszkiewicz directs Corneille's *Le Cid* at Teatr Ateneum.
Poland: Warsaw. 1984. Lang.: Pol.   2021

Hapgood, Elizabeth Reynolds
Training
Discussion of archival material relating to translation and U.S.
publication of books by Stanislavskij. USA. USSR. 1928-1986. Lang.:
Eng.   3160

Happenings
Performance/production
Survey of the performance art movement. USA. 1972-1986. Lang.:
Eng.   3457

Harag, György
Performance/production
Notes on production of the Állami Magyar Szinház and its late
director György Harag. Romania: Cluj. 1984-1985. Lang.: Hun. 2063
Interview with director György Harag. Romania: Tîrgu-Mures. 1925-
1985. Lang.: Hun.   2064

Harbage, Alfred
Plays/librettos/scripts
Modern criticism of Shakespeare's crowd scenes. England. 1590-1986.
Lang.: Eng.   2536

Hard Corps (UK)
Performance/production
Interview with Lesbian feminist theatre company Hard Corps. UK-
England. 1984-1986. Lang.: Eng.   2164

Hardig, Blanche
Performance/production
Profile of puppeteer Blanche Hardig. USA. 1932-1985.   3976

Hardman, Chris
Design/technology
Interview with performance artist Chris Hardman. USA. 1986.   3436

Hardy, Thomas
Performance/production
Collection of newspaper reviews by London theatre critics. UK-England: London. 1986. Lang.: Eng.   2125

Hare, David
Plays/librettos/scripts
Interview with playwright Howard Barker. UK-England. 1981-1985. Lang.: Eng.   2845
World War II as a theme in post-war British drama. UK-England. 1945-1983. Lang.: Eng.   2868

Relation to other fields
Reflections of political attitudes in plays by John McGrath and David Hare. UK-England. 1971-1978. Lang.: Eng.   3060

Harebell
Performance/production
Career of actor Lawrence Barrett. USA: New York, NY. 1871-1909. Lang.: Eng.   2261

Haring, Keith
Design/technology
Keith Haring, Robert Longo and Gretchen Bender design for choreographers Bill T. Jones and Arnie Zane. USA. 1986.   1342

Harlequin
Performance/production
Comic actor Tristano Martinelli, probable creator of the character Harlequin. Italy. France. 1550-1600. Lang.: Ita.   3412

Plays/librettos/scripts
Analysis of Harlequin in comedies by Carlo Goldoni. Italy. 1751-1752. Lang.: Ita.   2697

Harmer, Wendy
Performance/production
Discussion of women's comedy by one of its practitioners. Australia: Melbourne. 1986. Lang.: Eng.   657

Harmon, Barry
Performance/production
Reviews of *Olympus On My Mind* based on *Amphitryon*, by Heinrich von Kleist, staged by Barry Harmon. USA: New York, NY. 1986. Lang.: Eng.   2218

Harpur, Charles
Plays/librettos/scripts
Analysis of *The Bushrangers* by Charles Harpur. Australia. 1835-1853. Lang.: Eng.   2370

Harriet, the Woman Called Moses
Performance/production
Review of *Harriet, the Woman Called Moses*, an opera by Thea Musgrave, staged by Gordon Davidson. USA: Norfolk, VA. 1985. Lang.: Eng.   3835

Harris, Aurand
Administration
Community funding of residency for children's theatre performer, Aurand Harris. USA: Cleveland, OH. 1985-1986. Lang.: Eng.   145

Harris, Rosemary
Performance/production
Actress Rosemary Harris discusses her work in *The Petition*. UK-England: London. USA: New York, NY. 1948-1986. Lang.: Eng.   2177

Harrison, Richard B.
Performance/production
Biography of actor Richard B. Harrison, who played God in *The Green Pastures*. USA. 1930-1939. Lang.: Eng.   828

Harrison, Sharon
Performance/production
Review of premiere performance of Myron Fink's opera *Chinchilla*. USA: Binghamton, NY. 1986. Lang.: Eng.   3840

Harrison, Wilfred
Performance/production
Othello, translated by Bohdan Drozdowski and directed by Wilfred Harrison at the Wilama Horzycy Theatre. Poland: Toruń. 1980. Lang.: Eng.   2023

Harrison, William
Plays/librettos/scripts
Image of poverty in Elizabethan and Stuart plays. England. 1558-1642. Lang.: Eng.   2482

Harry's Christmas
Performance/production
Collection of newspaper reviews by London theatre critics. UK-England: London. 1986. Lang.: Eng.   2112

Hart, Bill
Performance/production
Reviews of *Cuba and His Teddy Bear* by Reinaldo Povod, staged by Bill Hart. USA: New York, NY. 1986. Lang.: Eng.   2228

Hart, Lorenz
Basic theatrical documents
Text of Lorenz Hart lyrics. USA. 1920-1943. Lang.: Eng.   3580

Hartelius, Claes
Institutions
Sommarteatern, using both amateur and professional actors, will attempt a year-round season. Sweden: Södertälje. 1980-1986. Lang.: Swe.   1585

Harvest Queen's Coronation
Relation to other fields
Theatricals used by temperance societies. Canada. 1800-1900. Lang.: Eng.   1067

Harwood, Ronald
Performance/production
Director discusses *Tramway Road* by Ronald Harwood. South Africa, Republic of. UK-England: London. 1986. Lang.: Eng.   2073

Hašek, Jaroslav
Plays/librettos/scripts
Brecht's use of the epically structured motif of the military review.   2354

Hasenauer, Carl
Performance spaces
Semper Depot and its history. Austria: Vienna. 1872-1986. Lang.: Ger.   583

Hashhia
SEE
Zakat.

Hashioka, Kazumichi
Design/technology
Carving techniques used in making the *ko-omote* mask. Japan. Lang.: Eng.   1394

Hassan, Noordin
Relation to other fields
Traditional Malay and European elements in children's theatre. Malaysia. 1930-1985. Lang.: Eng.   1112

Hatoum, Mona
Performance/production
Interview with performance artist Mona Hatoum. UK-England. 1975-1986. Lang.: Eng.   3452

Haunted House Hamlet, The
Plays/librettos/scripts
Environmental theatre version of *Hamlet*. Canada: Vancouver, BC. 1986. Lang.: Eng.   2435

Hauptman, William
Plays/librettos/scripts
A group of playwrights discuss the one-act play as a form. USA. 1986.   2937

Hauptmann, Gerhart
Performance/production
Max Reinhardt's work with his contemporaries. Germany. Austria. 1890-1938. Lang.: Eng, Ger.   1757
American productions of Hauptmann's *Die Weber (The Weavers)*. USA. Germany. 1892-1900. Lang.: Ger.   2272
Composer Krzystof Penderecki and his new opera *Die schwarze Maske (The Black Mask)*, based upon a play by Gerhart Hauptmann. Austria: Salzburg. Poland. 1933-1986. Lang.: Ger.   3700

Plays/librettos/scripts
Fox symbolism in plays of Bertolt Brecht, Max Frisch and Gerhart Hauptmann. Germany. Switzerland. 1700-1976. Lang.: Ger.   2598

Haus, Heinz-Uwe
Plays/librettos/scripts
Program notes from Heinz-Uwe Haus's production of *Arturo Ui*. Greece. 1985.   2631
Correspondence between Bernhard Reich and Heinz-Uwe Haus. USSR. 1971-1972.   2966

Hausbrandt, Andrzej
Theory/criticism
Andrzej Hausbrandt (critic) and Gustaw Holoubek (actor) discuss their views on general problems of theatre. Poland. Lang.: Pol.   1217

Heathcote, Dorothy
Institutions
Educational theatre in Iraq. Iraq. 1885-1985. Lang.: Eng. 505
Relation to other fields
Curricular authority for drama-in-education program. UK. Lang.: Eng. 3054
Discussion of theatre-in-education. UK. Lang.: Eng. 3055
Current style of theatre-in-education. UK-England. Lang.: Eng. 3057
Heaton, Terry
Performance/production
Collection of newspaper reviews by London theatre critics. UK-England: London. 1986. Lang.: Eng. 2122
Hébert, Anne
Basic theatrical documents
English translation of *Les invités au procès (The Guests on Trial)* by Anne Hébert. Canada. 1952. Lang.: Eng. 3174
Hébert, Jacques
Institutions
Significance of Applebaum-Hébert report on Canadian cultural policy. Canada. 1982-1983. Lang.: Eng. 465
Hebrew University Theatre Museum (Jerusalem)
Reference materials
Betzalel London's archive deposited at Hebrew University. Israel: Jerusalem. 1925-1971. Lang.: Heb. 1014
Hecht, Ben
Performance/production
Reviews of *The Front Page*, by Ben Hecht and Charles MacArthur, staged by Jerry Zaks. USA: New York, NY. 1986. Lang.: Eng. 2214
Hecht, Stuart
Performance/production
Chicago dramaturgs acknowledge a common ground in educating their audience. USA: Chicago, IL. 1984-1986. Lang.: Eng. 2274
Heckroth, Hein
Relation to other fields
Refugee artists from Nazi Germany in Britain. UK-England. Germany. 1937-1947. Lang.: Eng. 1135
Hedda Gabler
Performance/production
Collection of newspaper reviews by London theatre critics. UK. 1986. Lang.: Eng. 2102
Heeley, Desmond
Performance/production
John Hirsch's artistic career at the Stratford Festival Theatre. Canada: Stratford, ON. 1981-1985. Lang.: Eng. 1683
Hegel, Georg Wilhelm Friedrich
Theory/criticism
Hegel's theory of theatre and its application by 20th-century dramatists. Germany. 1770-1982. Lang.: Chi. 3106
Heide, Christopher
Institutions
History of the Dramatists' Co-op of Nova Scotia. Canada. 1976-1986. Lang.: Eng. 1558
Plays/librettos/scripts
Playwright Christopher Heide's research on high school students. Canada. 1984-1985. Lang.: Eng. 2420
Heinz, Wolfgang
Performance/production
Essays on acting by Wolfgang Heinz. Germany, East: Berlin, East. 1980-1984. Lang.: Ger. 1764
Heiremans, Luis Alberto
Plays/librettos/scripts
Marginal characters in plays of Jorge Díaz, Egon Wolff and Luis Alberto Heiremans. Chile. 1960-1971. Lang.: Eng. 2442
Helen Corning Warden Theatre (Philadelphia, PA)
Performance/production
Opera greats reflect on performance highlights. USA: Philadelphia, PA, New York, NY. 1985. Lang.: Eng. 3841
Helen Hayes Theatre (New York, NY)
Performance/production
Reviews of *Corpse!* by Gerald Moon, staged by John Tillinger. USA: New York, NY. 1986. Lang.: Eng. 2235
Reviews of *Oh Coward!*, lyrics and music by Noël Coward, devised and staged by Roderick Cook. USA: New York, NY. 1986. Lang.: Eng. 3616
Heller, André
Performance/production
On André Heller's project *Begnadete Körper (Blessed Bodies)*. Europe. China, People's Republic of. 1984-1985. Lang.: Ger. 3383

Hellerstedt-Thorin, Birgitta
Institutions
Liturgical drama and dance performed by amateur theatre group. Sweden: Lund. 1960-1986. Lang.: Swe. 526
Hellman, Lillian
Performance/production
Actress Lu Xiaoyan's experiences in preparing to play a role in *The Little Foxes*. China. USA. 1939-1982. Lang.: Chi. 1687
Actress Frances de la Tour discusses her work in *Lillian* by William Luce. UK-England: London. USA. 1986. Lang.: Eng. 2146
Director Kyle Renick's personal experiences with playwright Lillian Hellman. USA: New York, NY. 1984. Lang.: Eng. 2299
Plays/librettos/scripts
Treatment of social problems in the plays of Lillian Hellman and Clifford Odets. USA. 1930-1939. Lang.: Eng. 984
Theory/criticism
Interview with playwright Lillian Hellman. USA: Martha's Vineyard, MA. 1983. Lang.: Eng. 3147
Hellwig, Claes-Peter
Performance/production
Emblems of the 1980s in Swedish theatre. Sweden. 1980-1986. Lang.: Swe. 796
Helm, Hans
Reference materials
Photos of the new opera productions at the Staatsoper. Austria: Vienna. 1985-1986. Lang.: Ger. 3910
Helmer, Hermann
Performance spaces
The history of the theatre building used by Szegedi Nemzeti Színház. Hungary: Szeged. 1800-1883. Lang.: Hun. 603
Help the King!
SEE
Segitsd a királyst!.
Help Wanted
SEE
Furcht und Hoffnung der BRD.
Helsingin Kaupunginteatteri (Helsinki)
Design/technology
Career of designer Ralf Forsström discussing his influences and stylistic preferences. Finland: Helsinki. 1963-1986. Lang.: Eng, Fre. 3650
Institutions
Obituary of theatre manager, director, critic and scholar Timo Tiusanen. Finland: Helsinki. 1957-1985. Lang.: Eng, Fre. 1572
Helsinki City Theatre
SEE
Helsingin Kaupunginteatteri.
Helter Skelter
Plays/librettos/scripts
Analysis of television docudramas as a melodrama genre. USA. 1965-1986. Lang.: Eng. 3285
Hemingway, Ernest
Performance/production
Autobiography of actor Alec Guinness. UK. USA. 1914-1985. Lang.: Eng. 2106
Hemmings, Peter
Performance/production
Collaboration of Peter Hemmings and Götz Friedrich in Los Angeles' opera season. USA: Los Angeles, CA. 1985. Lang.: Eng. 3836
Hemphill, A. Marcus
Reference materials
Current work of Audelco award-winning playwrights. USA: New York, NY. 1973-1984. Lang.: Eng. 3007
Hemsky, Gil
Design/technology
Interview with lighting designer Gil Wechsler of the Metropolitan Opera. USA: New York, NY. 1883-1986. Lang.: Eng. 3654
Henderson, Jan
Performance/production
Distinctive style of Canadian clowns. Canada: Toronto, ON, Vancouver, BC. 1967-1986. Lang.: Eng. 3328
Hendry, Tom
Institutions
Shift in emphasis at Banff Centre. Canada: Banff, AB. 1974-1986. Lang.: Eng. 1543

Hengist, King of Kent
Performance/production
Original staging of Thomas Middleton's *Hengist, King of Kent.*
England: London. 1619-1661. Lang.: Eng.   1713

Henley, Beth
Plays/librettos/scripts
Beth Henley's play *Crimes of the Heart* as an example of female
criminality in response to a patriarchal culture. USA. 1980-1986.
Lang.: Eng.   2923

Henno
Plays/librettos/scripts
Critical problems in *Henno* by Johannes Reuchlin. Germany:
Heidelberg. 1497-1522. Lang.: Eng.   2605

Henrietta, The
Plays/librettos/scripts
Philosophy of wealth in gilded age plays. USA: New York, NY.
1870-1889. Lang.: Eng.   2950

Henry IV
Administration
Effect of censorship on Shakespeare's *Richard III* and *Henry IV.*
England. 1593-1603. Lang.: Pol.   1435

Institutions
Actor Michael Pennington and director Michael Bogdanov discuss
the formation of the English Shakespeare Company. UK-England.
1986. Lang.: Eng.   1592

Performance/production
Shakespearean form, Asian content in *Norodom Sihanouk* by Ariane
Mnouchkine's Théâtre du Soleil. France: Paris. 1964-1986. Lang.:
Eng.   709
IV. Henrik (Henry IV) by Shakespeare, directed by János Sándor.
Hungary: Szeged. 1985. Lang.: Hun.   1791
Reconstruction of a number of Shakespeare plays staged and
performed by Herbert Beerbohm Tree. UK-England: London. 1887-
1917. Lang.: Eng.   2155

Henry IV by Pirandello
SEE
Enrico Quarto.

Henry V
Institutions
Actor Michael Pennington and director Michael Bogdanov discuss
the formation of the English Shakespeare Company. UK-England.
1986. Lang.: Eng.   1592

Plays/librettos/scripts
Ceremony distinguishes kings from peasants in Shakespeare's *Henry
V.* England. 1598-1599. Lang.: Eng.   2464
Possible influence of Christopher Marlowe's plays upon those of
William Shakespeare. England. 1580-1620. Lang.: Eng.   2478

Henry VI
Performance/production
Detailed discussion of four successful Royal Shakespeare Company
productions of Shakespeare's minor plays. UK-England: Stratford.
1946-1977. Lang.: Eng.   2182

Plays/librettos/scripts
Shakespeare's *Henry VI* and Hall's *Chronicles.* England. 1542-1592.
Lang.: Fre.   2488
Productions of Jane Howell and Elijah Moshinsky for the BBC
Shakespeare series. UK-England: London. 1978-1985. Lang.: Eng.
                                                           3283

Henry VIII
Performance/production
Reconstruction of a number of Shakespeare plays staged and
performed by Herbert Beerbohm Tree. UK-England: London. 1887-
1917. Lang.: Eng.   2155
Margaret Webster's scenic approach to Shakespeare compared with
those of Herbert Beerbohm Tree and Tyrone Guthrie. USA: New
York, NY. 1910-1949. Lang.: Eng.   2293

Henschke, Alfred
SEE
Klabund (Henschke, Alfred).

Henson, Jim
Performance/production
Behind-the-scenes look at *Fraggle Rock.* Canada: Toronto, ON. 1984.
Lang.: Eng.   3269
Work of Kermit Love, creator of Big Bird for *Sesame Street.* USA:
New York, NY. 1935-1985. Lang.: Eng.   3276

Her Majesty's Theatre (London)
Performance/production
Collection of newspaper reviews by London theatre critics. UK:
London. 1986. Lang.: Eng.   2100
Reconstruction of a number of Shakespeare plays staged and
performed by Herbert Beerbohm Tree. UK-England: London. 1887-
1917. Lang.: Eng.   2155

Herbert, Jocelyn
Performance/production
Career of actress Billie Whitelaw, interpreter of Samuel Beckett's
plays. UK-England. 1956-1986. Lang.: Eng.   2172

Herbert, Marie-Francine
Institutions
History of the Théâtre de la Marmaille. Canada: Quebec, PQ. 1973-
1986. Lang.: Eng.   1552

Herbst, Janne
Performance/production
De dövas historia (The Story of the Deaf) staged by Ändockgruppen
using both hearing and deaf amateurs. Sweden: Vänersborg. 1982-
1986. Lang.: Swe.   799

Herder, Johann Gottfried
Theory/criticism
Analysis of Friedrich Schiller's dramatic and theoretical works.
Germany. 1759-1805. Lang.: Cat.   3109

Hernádi, Gyula
Performance/production
Productions of plays by Edward Bond, Gyula Hernádi and Lope de
Vega at the Pécs National Theatre. Hungary: Pécs. 1986. Lang.:
Hun.   1898
Hagyaték (Legacy) by Gyula Hernádi, directed by Menyhért
Szegvári. Hungary: Pécs. 1986. Lang.: Hun.   1949

Hernádi, Judit
Performance/production
Edith és Marlene (Edith and Marlene) by Éva Pataki at Comedy
Theatre. Hungary: Budapest. 1986. Lang.: Hun.   1831

Hernandez Espinosa, Eugenio
Plays/librettos/scripts
Interviews with actress Pilar Romero and director Roberto Blanco at
the Festival de Théâtre des Amériques. Canada: Montreal, PQ. 1985.
Lang.: Eng.   2426

Hernández, Francesc
Institutions
History of theatre in Valencia area focusing on Civil War period.
Spain: Valencia. 1817-1982. Lang.: Cat.   514

Herne, James A.
Plays/librettos/scripts
Theme and narrative structure in plays of Eugene O'Neill, David
Belasco, and James A. Herne. USA. 1879-1918. Lang.: Eng.   2933

Hesse, Hermann
Performance/production
Outsidern (The Outsider), a production by Mimensemblan, based on
Hermann Hesse's *Steppenwolf.* Sweden: Stockholm. 1984-1986. Lang.:
Swe.   3296

Heufeld, Franz
Performance/production
Examination of German versions of Shakespeare's *Hamlet.* Germany:
Hamburg. 1770-1811. Lang.: Eng.   728

Hevesi Sándor Szinház (Zalaegerszeg)
Design/technology
Interview with scene designer Sándor Bishof. Hungary: Zalaegerszeg.
1983-1986. Lang.: Hun.   284

Performance/production
Review of László Teleki's *A Kegyenc (The Favorite)* as directed by
József Ruszt, Hevesi Sándor Theatre. Hungary: Zalaegerszeg. 1986.
Lang.: Hun.   1867
Ivo Brešan's *Paraszt Hamlet (The Peasant Hamlet)* directed by Béla
Merő. Hungary: Zalaegerszeg. 1986. Lang.: Hun.   1888
Review of László Teleki's *A Kegyenc (The Favorite)* directed by
József Ruszt. Hungary: Zalaegerszeg. 1986. Lang.: Hun.   1891
Two productions of Čechov's *Három Nővér (Three Sisters).* Hungary:
Zalaegerszeg, Budapest. 1985. Lang.: Hun.   1903
János Ács directs *A kőszívű ember fiai (The Sons of the Stone-
Hearted Man)* by Mór Jókai. Hungary: Zalaegerszeg. 1986. Lang.:
Hun.   1905
Evaluation of József Ruszt's direction at Hevesi Sándor Theatre.
Hungary: Zalaegerszeg. 1983-1986. Lang.: Hun.   1927

Hevesi Sándor Szinház (Zalaegerszeg) — cont'd

Reviews of two plays by Arthur Schnitzler directed by Imre Halasi.
Hungary: Budapest, Zalaegerszeg. 1986. Lang.: Hun.   1958

Comparison of two Hungarian productions of *Háram nővér (Three
Sisters)* by Anton Pavlovič Čechov. Hungary: Budapest, Zalaegerszeg.
1985. Lang.: Hun.   1964

Hewett, Dorothy
Plays/librettos/scripts
Interview with playwright Dorothy Hewett. Australia: Sydney, N.S.W.
1986. Lang.: Eng.   2368

Developments in Australian playwriting since 1975. Australia. 1975-
1986. Lang.: Eng.   2374

Hewit, Andrew
Performance/production
Brief investigation of the lives of seven actors. England. 1526-1587.
Lang.: Eng.   691

Heyward, DuBose
Performance/production
Photographs, cast list, synopsis, and discography of Metropolitan
Opera radio broadcast performances. USA: New York, NY. 1986.
Lang.: Eng.   3794

Heywood, Thomas
Performance/production
Historical context of *The Late Lancaster Witches* by Thomas
Heywood and Richard Brome. England. 1634. Lang.: Eng.   689

Plays/librettos/scripts
Moral issues in *A Woman Killed with Kindness* by Thomas
Heywood. England. 1560. Lang.: Eng.   2498

Compares pageant-wagon play about Edward IV with version by
Thomas Heywood. England: Coventry, London. 1560-1600. Lang.:
Eng.   3430

Hibberd, Jack
Administration
Malcolm Blaylock on theatre and government funding policy.
Australia. 1985. Lang.: Eng.   22

Institutions
Playwright Jack Hibberd's analysis of nationalist and English-derived
theatrical cultures. Australia: Melbourne, Sydney. 1850-1986. Lang.:
Eng.   439

Performance/production
Community theatre as interpreted by the Sidetrack Theatre
Company. Australia: Sydney, N.S.W. 1980-1986. Lang.: Eng.   1638

Plays/librettos/scripts
Developments in Australian playwriting since 1975. Australia. 1975-
1986. Lang.: Eng.   2374

Hibbert, Alun
Institutions
Limited opportunities for English-language playwrights in Montreal.
Canada: Montreal, PQ. 1976-1986. Lang.: Eng.   1561

Hickory Hideout
Performance/production
Influence of the Joy Puppeteers on the television program *Hickory
Hideout.* USA: Cleveland, OH. 1982-1986. Lang.: Eng.   3275

Hide, Louise
Performance/production
Collection of newspaper reviews by London theatre critics. UK-
England: London. 1986. Lang.: Eng.   2110

Higginsen, Vi
Administration
Growing activity and changing role of Black regional theatre
companies. USA. 1960-1984. Lang.: Eng.   1440

Institutions
Vi Higginsen's *Mama I Want to Sing* and history of the Mumbo-
Jumbo Theatre Company. USA: New York, NY. 1980-1986. Lang.:
Eng.   1601

Highland Summer Theatre (Highland, IL)
Design/technology
Designers discuss regional productions of *Once Upon a Mattress.*
USA. 1984-1986.   3590

Hijikata, Tatsumi
Basic theatrical documents
Homage to *butō* dancer Hijikata Tatsumi by Tanaka Min. Japan.
1976-1985. Lang.: Eng.   1268

Performance/production
Description of *butō*, avant-garde dance movement of Japan. Japan.
1960-1986. Lang.: Eng.   1279

Butō dancer Tanaka Min speaks of early influences of Ohno and
Hojikata. Japan. 1950-1985. Lang.: Eng.   1280

Hikâyâ
Performance/production
Performance conditions of specific theatrical genres. Lebanon. 1918-
1985. Lang.: Fre.   2011

Relation to other fields
Reports and discussions of restricted cultural communication.
Lebanon. Spain-Catalonia. USA. 1985. Lang.: Fre, Spa, Cat.   1111

Hilar, Karel Hugo
Performance/production
Technical innovation, scenography and cabaret in relation to political
and social conditions. Czechoslovakia. 1781-1986. Lang.: Eng.   1697

Hildegard, Saint
Performance/production
Performance by Sequentia of *Ordo Virtutum* by Hildegard of Bingen.
USA: Stanford, CA. 1986. Lang.: Eng.   3493

Plays/librettos/scripts
Analysis of Hildegard of Bingen's *Ordo Virtutum* as a morality play.
Germany: Bingen. 1151. Lang.: Eng.   3498

Hill-Land
Plays/librettos/scripts
The immigrant in plays by Herman Voaden and Robertson Davies.
Canada. 1934-1950. Lang.: Eng.   2431

Reference materials
Collected reviews of 31 major Canadian plays. Canada. 1934-1983.
Lang.: Eng.   1009

Relation to other fields
Philosophical context of the plays of Herman Voaden. Canada:
Toronto, ON. 1929-1943. Lang.: Eng.   3170

Hill, Aaron
Performance/production
Influence of mechanical physiology on David Garrick. England.
1734-1779. Lang.: Eng.   695

Relation to other fields
William Popple's career in literature and politics. England. 1737-
1764. Lang.: Eng.   1080

Hill, Abram
Reference materials
Current work of Audelco award-winning playwrights. USA: New
York, NY. 1973-1984. Lang.: Eng.   3007

Hill, Arthur
Performance/production
Director of original production discusses Edward Albee's *Who's
Afraid of Virginia Woolf?.* USA: New York, NY. 1962. Lang.: Eng.
                                                                     2303

Hill, Thomas
Relation to other fields
Theatre riot provoked by Thomas Hill's *The Provincial Association.*
Canada: St. John, NB. 1845. Lang.: Eng.   1073

Hiller, Wendy
Performance/production
Eileen Atkins, Judi Dench, Wendy Hiller and Barbara Jefford
discuss playing Saint Joan in Shaw's play. UK-England: London.
1936-1983. Lang.: Eng.   2153

Hilpert, Heinz
Performance/production
Biography of actor and stage manager Franz Reichert. Austria:
Vienna. Germany: Berlin. Czechoslovakia: Prague. 1925-1950. Lang.:
Ger.   1652

Relation to other fields
Study of Fascist theatrical policies. Germany: Berlin. 1933-1944.
Lang.: Ger.   1091

Hilton, Julian
Performance/production
Collection of newspaper reviews by London theatre critics. UK:
London. 1986. Lang.: Eng.   2100

Hindle Wakes
Performance/production
Roger Rees, associate director at Bristol Old Vic discusses his career
and the season. UK-England: Bristol. 1970-1986. Lang.: Eng.   2138

Hines, Maurice
Performance/production
Reviews of *Uptown...It's Hot*, staged, choreographed and conceived
by Maurice Hines. USA: New York, NY. 1986. Lang.: Eng.   1284

Tap dancing career of Maurice Hines and the creation of his new
company Balletap, USA. USA: New York, NY. 1949-1986. Lang.:
Eng.   3623

Holder, Laurence
Reference materials
Current work of Audelco award-winning playwrights. USA: New York, NY. 1973-1984. Lang.: Eng. 3007

Holdridge, Lee
Performance/production
Reviews of *Into the Light*, book by Jeff Tamborniro, music by Lee Holdridge, lyrics by John Forster, staged by Michael Maurer. USA: New York, NY. 1986. Lang.: Eng. 3615

Hole-in-the Wall Theatre (Perth)
Plays/librettos/scripts
Semiotic analysis of a production of *Antigone* by Sophocles. Australia: Perth, W.A. 1986. Lang.: Eng. 923

Hollingsworth, Margaret
Plays/librettos/scripts
Review of five published plays by Margaret Hollingsworth. Canada. Lang.: Eng. 2440

Holmberg, Kalle
Plays/librettos/scripts
Analysis of thematic trends in recent Finnish Opera. Finland: Helsinki, Savonlinna. 1909-1986. Lang.: Eng, Fre. 3865
Interview with opera composer Aulis Sallinen on his current work. Finland: Helsinki. 1975-1986. Lang.: Eng, Fre. 3866

Holograms
Design/technology
Les Immatériaux, multimedia exhibit by Jean-François Lyotard. France: Paris. 1986. Lang.: Eng. 3249

Holoubek, Gustaw
Theory/criticism
Andrzej Hausbrandt (critic) and Gustaw Holoubek (actor) discuss their views on general problems of theatre. Poland. Lang.: Pol. 1217

Holz, Arno
Performance/production
Documentation on Arno Holz's *Ignorabimus* directed by Luca Ronconi. Italy: Prato. 1986. Lang.: Ita. 1985
Plays/librettos/scripts
Reflections on the works of Arno Holz. Germany. 1863-1929. Lang.: Ita. 2607

Home
Plays/librettos/scripts
Biographical sketch of playwright/performer Samm-Art Williams. USA: Burgaw, NC, New York, NY. 1940-1986. Lang.: Eng. 2946
Reference materials
Current work of Audelco award-winning playwrights. USA: New York, NY. 1973-1984. Lang.: Eng. 3007

Home of the Brave
Performance/production
Interview with performance artist Laurie Anderson. USA. 1986. Lang.: Eng. 3351

Home Theatre (Naramata, BC)
Institutions
Carroll Aikins, founder of Canadian Players. Canada: Naramata, BC. 1920-1922. Lang.: Eng. 478

Homecoming, The
Basic theatrical documents
Catalan translation of *The Homecoming* by Harold Pinter. UK-England. 1965. Lang.: Cat. 1507
Plays/librettos/scripts
Reader-response interpretation of *The Homecoming* by Harold Pinter. UK-England. 1952-1965. Lang.: Eng. 2861
Analysis of the plot, characters and structure of *The Homecoming* by Harold Pinter. UK-England: London. 1930-1985. Lang.: Cat. 2865

Honegger, Gitta
Performance/production
Gitta Honegger on training dramaturgs and the European tradition of dramaturgy. USA: New Haven, CT. 1960-1986. Lang.: Eng. 2251

Hong, Hae-Seong
Performance/production
Directing and the current state of Korean theatre. Korea. 1986. Lang.: Kor. 760

Hongkongi paróka (Wig Made in Hong Kong)
Performance/production
Notes on performances of *Hongkongi paróka (Wig Made in Hong Kong)*, *Egérút (Narrow Escape)* and *Róza néni (Aunt Rosa)*. Hungary: Budapest. 1985. Lang.: Hun. 1801

Honky Tonk Nights
Performance/production
Reviews of *Honky Tonk Nights*, book and lyrics by Ralph Allen and David Campbell, staged and choreographed by Ernest O. Flatt. USA: New York, NY. 1986. Lang.: Eng. 3612

Hopkins, A.
Design/technology
Nineteenth-century special effects. Europe. North America. 1986. 1890-1920. Lang.: Swe. 262

Hopkins, Arthur
Performance/production
Origins of radically simplified stage in modern productions. USA. 1912-1922. Lang.: Eng. 831

Hopkins, Didi
Performance/production
Feminist theatre group Beryl and the Perils. UK-England. 1986. Lang.: Eng. 2171

Hopkins, Karen Brooks
Administration
Brooklyn Academy of Music development director's fundraising strategy. USA: New York, NY. Lang.: Eng. 112

Hoppla, wir leben! (Upsy-Daisy, We Are Alive)
Plays/librettos/scripts
Premiere of Ernst Toller's play *Hoppla, wir leben! (Upsy Daisy, We Are Alive)*. Germany, East. 1945-1984. Lang.: Eng. 2617

Hornbrook, David
Relation to other fields
Discussion of theatre-in-education. UK. Lang.: Eng. 3055

Horne, Marilyn
Performance/production
Performance analysis of the title role of *Carmen*. France. 1875-1986. Lang.: Eng. 3725

Horovitz, Israel
Plays/librettos/scripts
A group of playwrights discuss the one-act play as a form. USA. 1986. 2937
Interview with playwright Israel Horovitz. USA: New York, NY. 1985. Lang.: Eng. 2941

Horowitz, Dan
Performance/production
Artistic cooperation between playwright Dan Horowitz and director Ya'akov Raz. Israel. 1978-1986. Lang.: Heb. 1978

Horse and Bamboo Theatre (Rossendale, UK)
Performance/production
Horse and Bamboo Theatre, specializing in community puppet theatre. UK-England: Rossendale. 1978-1986. Lang.: Eng. 3970

Horseman, The
Plays/librettos/scripts
Analysis of thematic trends in recent Finnish Opera. Finland: Helsinki, Savonlinna. 1909-1986. Lang.: Eng, Fre. 3865

Horsfield, Debbie
Institutions
Place of women in Britain's National Theatre. UK-England: London. 1986. Lang.: Eng. 1588
Performance/production
Collection of newspaper reviews by London theatre critics. UK-England: London. 1986. Lang.: Eng. 2116

Hortense Couldn't Care Less
SEE
Hortense a dit: 'Je m'en fous!'.

Horton Plaza Lyceum Theatre (San Diego, CA)
Performance spaces
Architectural design of San Diego Repertory's new theatre. USA: San Diego, CA. 1986. Lang.: Eng. 637

Horvai, István
Performance/production
István Horvai directs *Megtört szivek háza (Heartbreak House)* by George Bernard Shaw at Pest National Theatre. Hungary: Budapest. 1985. Lang.: Hun. 1793
Productions of *Deficit* by István Csurka. Hungary: Szolnok, Budapest. 1970-1985. Lang.: Hun. 1833
G.B. Shaw's *Megtörtszívek háza (Heartbreak House)* directed by István Horvai. Hungary: Budapest. 1985. Lang.: Hun. 1858

Horvat, Christa
Institutions
On new activities of groups or persons producing theatre for children. Austria: Vienna. 1986. Lang.: Ger. 454

SUBJECT INDEX

Hugo, Victor — cont'd

Performance/production
Adapting and staging of *Les Misérables* by Victor Hugo. UK-England. 1980. Lang.: Eng. 3609

Plays/librettos/scripts
Treatment of Napoleon Bonaparte by French and English dramatists. France. England. 1797-1958. Lang.: Eng. 2568

Origins of the characters Rigoletto and Marullo in Verdi's *Rigoletto*. France. 1496-1851. Lang.: Eng. 3869

Huidobro, Montes
Plays/librettos/scripts
The history of Cuban exile theatre. Cuba. USA: New York, NY. 1959-1986. Lang.: Spa. 2451

Hull Truck Theatre (Hull, England)
Plays/librettos/scripts
Interview with actor-playwright Alan Williams. Canada: Toronto, ON, Winnipeg, MB. UK-England: Hull. 1976-1986. Lang.: Eng. 2438

Humanism
Audience
Audience of the humanistic, religious and school-theatre of the European Renaissance. Europe. 1480-1630. Lang.: Ger. 1445

Humphries, Barry
Performance/production
Interview with political satirist Max Gillies. Australia. 1986. Lang.: Eng. 654

Plays/librettos/scripts
Interview with satirist Barry Humphries. Australia. UK-England. 1950-1986. Lang.: Eng. 922

Hunan opera
Plays/librettos/scripts
Characteristics and influences of Fan Ts'ui-T'ing's plays. China. 1900-1980. Lang.: Chi. 3532

Hunchback of Notre Dame, The
SEE
Notre Dame de Paris.

Hundson, Fred
Administration
Alternative funding for small theatres previously dependent on government subsidy. USA: St. Louis, MO, New York, NY, Los Angeles, CA, Detroit, MI. 1985. Lang.: Eng. 103

Hungarian National Theatre
SEE
Nemzeti Színház.

Hungarian State Opera
SEE
Magyar Állami Operaház.

Hungarian State Puppet Theatre
SEE
Állami Bábszínház.

Hungarian State Theatre (Kolozsvár)
SEE
Állami Magyar Szinház (Cluj).

Hungarian Theatre Association
Performance/production
Account of nation-wide theatre conference. Hungary: Budapest. 1985. Lang.: Hun. 1841

Hungarian Theatre Institute
SEE
Magyar Szinházi Intézet.

Hungarian Theatre of Kolozsvár
SEE
Allami Magyar Szinház (Cluj).

Hunger and Thirst
SEE
Soif et la faim, La.

Hunt, Leigh
Relation to other fields
Influence of Mozart's operas on the 'Cockney' school of writers. England: London. 1760-1840. Lang.: Eng. 3916

Hunter, Terry
Performance/production
Development of works by the Special Delivery Moving Theatre. Canada: Vancouver, BC. 1976-1986. Lang.: Eng. 3294

Hurlyburly
Plays/librettos/scripts
Analysis of *Hurlyburly* by David Rabe. USA. 1984. Lang.: Eng. 2918

Husband, A
SEE
Marito, Un.

Hussein, Ebrahim
Relation to other fields
Role of theatre after the Arusha Declaration. Tanzania. 1967-1984. Lang.: Eng. 1134

Husumgården (Husum)
Performance spaces
Details of renovation of Husumgården auditorium. Sweden: Husum. 1928-1985. Lang.: Swe. 621

Huszti, Péter
Performance/production
Recollections of actor Péter Huszti. Hungary. 1944-1986. Lang.: Hun. 1842

Huzatos ház (Drafty House)
Performance/production
Gábor Görgey's *Huzatos ház (Drafty House)* directed by Gyula Bodrogi, Vidám Színpad. Hungary: Budapest. 1986. Lang.: Hun. 1845

Gábor Görgey's *Huzatos ház (Drafty House)* directed by Gyula Bodrogi at Vidám Színpad. Hungary: Budapest. 1986. Lang.: Hun. 1856

Hycke Scorner
Research/historiography
Review of recent editions of Revels plays, including George Peele's *The Old Wives Tale.* England: London. 1514-1980. Lang.: Eng. 3071

Hynes, Garry
Performance/production
Collection of newspaper reviews by London theatre critics. UK. 1986. Lang.: Eng. 2102

Collection of newspaper reviews by London theatre critics. UK-England: London. 1986. Lang.: Eng. 2119

Hytner, Nicholas
Performance/production
Collection of newspaper reviews by London theatre critics. UK: London. 1986. Lang.: Eng. 2100

Collection of newspaper reviews by London theatre critics. UK. 1986. Lang.: Eng. 2101

Collection of newspaper reviews by London theatre critics. UK-England. 1986. Lang.: Eng. 2111

I Do Like To Be
Performance/production
Collection of newspaper reviews by London theatre critics. UK-England: London. 1986. Lang.: Eng. 2124

I Do Not Like Thee Doctor Fell
Performance/production
Collection of newspaper reviews by London theatre critics. UK-England: London. 1986. Lang.: Eng. 2121

I'm Talking about Jerusalem
Plays/librettos/scripts
Analysis of Arnold Wesker's *Chicken Soup with Barley.* UK-England: London. 1932-1986. Lang.: Cat. 2864

Utopia in early plays by Arnold Wesker. UK-England. 1958-1970. Lang.: Eng. 2884

Ibolya, Az (Violet, The)
Performance/production
Reviews of *Margit kisasszony (Miss Margit)*, *Az Ibolya (The Violet)*, *Az Árny (The Ghost)* and *Róza néni (Aunt Rosa)*. Hungary: Budapest. 1985-1986. Lang.: Hun. 1916

Ibsen, Henrik
Basic theatrical documents
Text of *Eiolf Hakatan*, Gad Kaynar's Hebrew translation of *Lille Eyolf (Little Eyolf)* by Henrik Ibsen. Norway. Israel. 1884-1985. Lang.: Heb. 1489

Institutions
Reviews of Edinburgh Festival plays. UK-Scotland: Edinburgh. 1986. Lang.: Eng. 539

Performance/production
Esse Ljungh's acting career with Winnipeg Little Theatre. Canada: Winnipeg, MB. 1921-1937. Lang.: Eng. 664

Acting style in plays by Henrik Ibsen. 1885-1905. Lang.: Eng. 1627

Notes on the process of staging *Eiolf Hakatan*, a Hebrew translation of Henrik Ibsen's *Lille Eyolf (Little Eyolf)*, directed by Yossi Israeli at the Kahn theatre. Israel: Jerusalem. 1986. Lang.: Heb. 1980

Im Dickicht der Städte (In the Jungle of the Cities)
Performance/production
Director Christoph Nel discusses staging Brecht's *Im Dickicht der Städte (In the Jungle of the Cities)*. USA: Seattle, WA. 1984.　2246

Image in the Clay
Plays/librettos/scripts
Amerindian and aborigine characters in the works of white playwrights. Canada. Australia. 1606-1975. Lang.: Eng.　930

Immatériaux, Les
Design/technology
Les Immatériaux, multimedia exhibit by Jean-François Lyotard. France: Paris. 1986. Lang.: Eng.　3249

Immermann, Karl
Plays/librettos/scripts
Playwright Karl Immermann's creative method. Germany. 1796-1840. Lang.: Rus.　2592

Imperial Theatre (St. John, NB)
Performance spaces
Renovation of Imperial Theatre as performing arts center. Canada: St. John, NB. 1913-1986. Lang.: Eng.　586
Planning and fundraising for the restoration of the Imperial Theatre. Canada: St. John, NB. 1913-1985. Lang.: Eng.　588

Importance of Being Earnest, The
Performance/production
Collection of newspaper reviews by London theatre critics. UK-England. 1986. Lang.: Eng.　2111

Plays/librettos/scripts
A comparison between Oscar Wilde's *The Importance of Being Earnest* and Tom Stoppard's *Travesties*. UK-England. 1895-1974. Lang.: Eng.　2872

Imposztor, Az (Impostor, The)
Plays/librettos/scripts
Notes on György Spiró's play about actor, director, manager and playwright Wojciech Bogusławski. Hungary. 1983. Lang.: Hun.　2659

Imprisonment of Obatala, The
Theory/criticism
Analysis of Wole Soyinka's major critical essays. Nigeria. 1960-1980. Lang.: Eng.　3124

Impromptu de Versailles, L' (Impromptu of Versailles, The)
Performance/production
Analysis of actor/character relationship in *L'impromptu de Versailles (The Impromptu of Versailles)* by Molière. France. 1663. Lang.: Eng.　726

Improvisation
Institutions
Production history and techniques of the Living Theatre. USA. 1964. Lang.: Eng.　546

Performance/production
Improvisation in East and West. Asia. Europe. 1900-1986. Lang.: Ita.　653
Interview with playwright Peter Eliot Weiss. Canada: Vancouver, BC. 1986. Lang.: Eng.　1680
Interviews with Polish theatre professionals. Poland: Poznań. 1963-1985. Lang.: Eng.　2024

Relation to other fields
Theatrical performance as a pedagogical tool. 1986. Lang.: Cat. 1048
Evaluation and social effects of improvisational drama program. USA: Newark, NJ. Lang.: Eng.　1151
Theatre workshops led by Augusto Boal. Canada: Montreal, PQ. 1985. Lang.: Eng.　3023
Brecht's talents in the area of musical-poetic improvisation.　3501

In the Jungle of the Cities
SEE
Im Dickicht der Städte.

Inacent Black and the Five Brothers
Institutions
Career of Marjorie Moon, artistic director of Billie Holliday Theatre. USA: New York, NY, Cleveland, OH. 1973-1986. Lang.: Eng. 1610

Reference materials
Current work of Audelco award-winning playwrights. USA: New York, NY. 1973-1984. Lang.: Eng.　3007

Inadani
Performance/production
The popular entertainment of *Inadani* in Nagano province. Japan: Iida. 1986. Lang.: Jap.　3343

Incoronazione di Poppea, L' (Coronation of Poppea, The)
Performance/production
Claudio Monteverdi's *L'incoronazione di Poppea (The Coronation of Poppea)* directed by Jonathan Hale at the Kent Opera. UK-England: Kent. 1986. Lang.: Eng.　3781

Independent Theatre (London)
Performance/production
The Independent Theatre of Jacob Thomas Grein, established in imitation of André Antoine's Théâtre Libre. UK-England: London. 1891. Lang.: Rus.　818

Independent Woman, An
Performance/production
Collection of newspaper reviews by London theatre critics. UK-England. 1986. Lang.: Eng.　2115

Indexes
Reference materials
Index of multifunctional halls used for theatrical performances. Lang.: Ger.　996
Theatrical materials in five early American magazines. Colonial America. 1758-1800. Lang.: Eng.　1012
A list of all articles that have appeared in *STTF-medlemsblad* 1977-1985 and *ProScen* 1986. Sweden. 1977-1986. Lang.: Swe.　1032
List and location of school playtexts and programs. France. 1601-1700. Lang.: Fre.　2987
Chronological list of 407 London productions mounted in 1985 with an index to actors, writers and production personnel. UK-England: London. 1985. Lang.: Eng.　3002
Annotated list of English-language research on Chinese opera. China. 1817-1974. Lang.: Chi.　3544
Index of operas, artists, contributors, etc. Europe. UK-England. USA. 1986. Lang.: Eng.　3911

Relation to other fields
Statistical index of theatre attendance in the regional and provincial centers of the USSR-Russian SFSR. USSR. 1985. Lang.: Rus. 1175

Indian
Plays/librettos/scripts
Amerindian and aborigine characters in the works of white playwrights. Canada. Australia. 1606-1975. Lang.: Eng.　930

Indiana Repertory (Indianapolis, IN)
Design/technology
Sound desigers at regional theatres evaluate new equipment. USA. 1986.　409

Indians
Plays/librettos/scripts
Mosaic structure of Arthur Kopit's *Indians*. USA. 1969.　2935

Indigenous theatre
Audience
History of the Mulgrave Road Co-op theatre. Canada: Guysborough, NS. 1977-1985. Lang.: Eng.　1444

Performance/production
Image of the *indigène*. Australia. New Zealand. Canada. 1830-1980. Lang.: Eng.　656
Amateur theatre festival initiated by Teatret La Luna (Århus). Italy: Amandola. 1980-1986. Lang.: Swe.　747
A gypsy discusses the theatrical traditions of his people. Italy. 1900-1986. Lang.: Ita.　3340

Plays/librettos/scripts
The history of Cuban exile theatre. Cuba. USA: New York, NY. 1959-1986. Lang.: Spa.　2451

Indoor Games
SEE
Jeu d'intérieur.

Infernal Machine, The
SEE
Machine Infernale, La.

Ingalls, James
Design/technology
A profile of lighting designer James Ingalls. USA. 1980-1986.　374

Ingram, John
Design/technology
Lighting designer John Ingram discusses his lighting for the Coca-Cola centennial. USA: Atlanta, GA. 1986. Lang.: Eng.　3319

Inner City Cultural Center (Los Angeles, CA)
Administration
Alternative funding for small theatres previously dependent on government subsidy. USA: St. Louis, MO, New York, NY, Los Angeles, CA, Detroit, MI. 1985. Lang.: Eng.　103

Institutions, producing — cont'd

Basic theatrical documents

Pamphlet of 1839 concerning the Hungarian Theatre of Pest. Austro-Hungarian Empire: Pest. 1839. Lang.: Hun. 216

Promptbooks for three Dryden plays. England. 1700-1799. Lang.: Eng. 1474

Design/technology

Details of new electrical system of rebuilt Szeged National Theatre. Hungary: Szeged. 1983-1986. Lang.: Hun. 277

Report on new heating, plumbing and air-conditioning at reconstructed Szeged National Theatre. Hungary: Szeged. 1978-1986. Lang.: Hun. 293

Changes in the Royal Shakespeare Company under its current directors. UK-England: London. 1967-1986. Lang.: Eng. 325

Institutions

Account of New Theatre movement by a participant. Australia: Sydney, Melbourne. 1932-1955. Lang.: Eng. 437

Historical perspective of the New Theatre. Australia: Sydney, N.S.W. 1932-1986. Lang.: Eng. 438

Playwright Jack Hibberd's analysis of nationalist and English-derived theatrical cultures. Australia: Melbourne, Sydney. 1850-1986. Lang.: Eng. 439

Financial difficulties of the Bregenzer Festspiele. Austria: Bregenz. 1985-1986. Lang.: Ger. 440

Wiener Festwochen 1986: Mozart and Modern Art. Austria: Vienna. 1986. Lang.: Ger. 441

Solving the financial problems of the Bregenzer Festspiele. Austria: Bregenz. 1986-1987. Lang.: Ger. 442

Concept for programs at the Stadttheater. Austria: Klagenfurt. 1985-1987. Lang.: Ger. 443

The new secretary-general of the Salzburger Festspiele, Franz Willnauer. Austria: Salzburg. Germany, West. 1957-1986. Lang.: Ger. 444

Program for the festival Carinthischer Sommer. Austria. 1986. Lang.: Ger. 445

Report on the Microtheater Festival in the Wiener Festwochen. Austria: Vienna. 1986. Lang.: Ger. 447

Niederösterreichischer Theatersommer: producing summer theatre at festivals in different places. Austria. 1980-1986. Lang.: Ger. 448

Union of three theaters in Vienna to the Verbund Wiener Theatre. Austria: Vienna. 1986. Lang.: Ger. 449

Concept and program for the Salzburger Festspiele in 1987. Austria: Salzburg. 1986. Lang.: Ger. 451

Management and plans for the Salzburger Festspiele. Austria: Salzburg. 1986. Lang.: Ger. 452

Themes of productions at the Wiener Festwochen. Austria: Vienna. 1986. Lang.: Ger. 453

On new activities of groups or persons producing theatre for children. Austria: Vienna. 1986. Lang.: Ger. 454

Tours of the Österreichische Bundestheater in Austria. Austria. 1976-1986. Lang.: Ger. 455

Working conditions of theatres and groups producing for children. Austria. 1985-1986. Lang.: Ger. 456

The Jura Soyfer Theater and its plans for the 1986/87 season. Austria: Vienna. 1986. Lang.: Ger. 457

Concept and functions of Schlossspiele Kobersdorf. Austria: Burgenland. 1983-1986. Lang.: Ger. 458

Lutz Hochstraate's ideas about managing the Salzburg Landestheater. Austria: Salzburg. 1986. Lang.: Ger. 459

Roman Zeilinger's plans for managing the Landestheater. Austria: Linz. 1986. Lang.: Ger. 460

Critical study and index of the Theatre of István Square. Austro-Hungarian Empire: Budapest. 1872-1874. Lang.: Hun. 461

Surviving documents relating to the Népszinház. Austro-Hungarian Empire: Budapest. 1872-1918. Lang.: Hun. 462

Festival for children and youth. Bulgaria: Stara Zagora. 1966-1985. Lang.: Ger. 463

Overview of the productions and goals of Catalyst Theatre. Canada: Edmonton, AB. 1977-1983. Lang.: Eng. 464

Significance of Applebaum-Hébert report on Canadian cultural policy. Canada. 1982-1983. Lang.: Eng. 465

Compares two Canadian stock companies. Canada: Montreal, PQ, Toronto, ON. 1890-1940. Lang.: Eng. 466

Overview of Festival de Créations Jeunesse. Canada: Montreal, PQ. 1966-1984. Lang.: Fre. 467

Techniques and philosophy of children's theatre compared to theatre for adults. Canada. 1980-1984. Lang.: Fre. 468

Founding of Théâtre National Français de Montréal. Canada: Montreal, PQ. 1889-1901. Lang.: Fre. 469

Career of Walter Learning, artistic director, Vancouver Playhouse. Canada: Vancouver, BC. 1982-1983. Lang.: Eng. 470

Amateur theatre troupe Le Caveau d'Ottawa. Canada: Ottawa, ON. 1932-1951. Lang.: Fre. 471

Interview with Dennis Foon, director of Green Thumb Theatre for Young People. Canada: Vancouver, BC. 1975-1984. Lang.: Fre. 473

Théâtre Petit à Petit and their production of *Où est-ce qu'elle est ma gang (Where's My Gang?)* by Louis-Dominique Lavigne. Canada: Montreal, PQ. France. 1981-1984. Lang.: Fre. 474

Founder Sky Gilbert discusses aesthetic goals of Rhubarb Festival. Canada: Toronto, ON. 1979-1986. Lang.: Eng. 475

Interview with Françoise Graton and Gilles Pelletier of Nouvelle Compagnie Théâtrale. Canada: Montreal, PQ. 1964-1984. Lang.: Fre. 477

Carroll Aikins, founder of Canadian Players. Canada: Naramata, BC. 1920-1922. Lang.: Eng. 478

Overview of the 16th Quebec Children's Theatre Festival. Canada. 1985. Lang.: Fre. 479

Productions and policies of National Art Centre. Canada: Ottawa, ON. 1969-1985. Lang.: Eng. 480

Repertory of the Nouvelle Compagnie Théâtrale. Canada: Montreal, PQ. 1964-1984. Lang.: Fre. 481

Report on International Festival of Theatre for Young Audiences. Canada. Japan. 1985. Lang.: Fre. 482

History of the Neptune Theatre and its artistic directors. Canada: Halifax, NS. 1963-1983. Lang.: Eng. 483

Description of new arts district. Canada: Calgary, AB. 1978-1985. Lang.: Eng. 484

Overview of Festival Lennoxville and the role of anglophone drama in Quebec. Canada: Lennoxville, PQ. 1972-1982. Lang.: Eng. 485

Structure and political viewpoint of Great Canadian Theatre Company. Canada: Ottawa, ON. 1975-1986. Lang.: Eng. 486

Interviews with theatre professionals in Quebec. Canada. 1985. Lang.: Fre. 487

Overview of current theatre scene. Denmark: Copenhagen. 1976-1986. Lang.: Swe. 490

List of actors and companies using Little Haymarket Theatre. England: London. 1720-1737. Lang.: Eng. 491

History of Swedish language Lilla-teatern (Little Theatre). Finland: Helsinki. 1940-1986. Lang.: Eng, Fre. 494

Assessment of theatre for adolescents. France. 1968-1984. Lang.: Fre. 495

Views of Parisian theatre from the journals of August von Kotzebue. France: Paris. Germany. 1790-1804. Lang.: Eng. 496

Overview of Ariane Mnouchkine's work with Théâtre du Soleil. France: Paris. 1959-1985. Lang.: Eng. 497

History of drama ensemble Mecklenburgisches Staatstheater Schwerin. Germany, East: Schwerin. 1970-1986. Lang.: Ger. 498

Production of Jürgen Lederach's *Japanische Spiele (Japanese Play)* by Transformtheater. Germany, West: Berlin, West. 1981-1986. Lang.: Swe. 499

Recollections of director Károly Kazimir, of Körszinház. Hungary: Budapest. 1958-1986. Lang.: Hun. 501

History of Vigszinház (Comedy Theatre). Hungary: Budapest. 1896-1916. Lang.: Hun. 502

Interviews with former managing directors of Csokonai Theatre. Hungary: Debrecen. 1974-1986. Lang.: Hun. 503

History of Museum Theatre. India: Madras. 1895-1985. Lang.: Eng. 504

History of Compagnia Teatroinaria. Italy. 1976-1986. Lang.: Ita. 506

The Kaze-no-Ko: professional travelling children's theatre of Japan. Japan. 1950-1984. Lang.: Eng. 507

History of Korea's first theatre production company. Korea: Seoul. 1922-1924. Lang.: Kor. 509

Institutions, producing — cont'd

Reports on theatre conferences and festivals in Asia. Philippines: Manila. Malaysia: Kuala Lumpur. Japan: Toga. India: Calcutta. 1981-1984. Lang.: Eng.　　510

Foundation of Polish theatre in Poznań in 1783, its repertoire and political contexts. Poland: Poznań. 1782-1793. Lang.: Pol.　　512

Foundation and brief history of Moscow Art Theatre. Russia: Moscow. 1898-1986. Lang.: Rus.　　513

History of theatre in Valencia area focusing on Civil War period. Spain: Valencia. 1817-1982. Lang.: Cat.　　514

Trend toward independent Spanish theatres. Spain. 1959-1985. Lang.: Spa.　　515

Discussion of public theatre in Europe, especially Spain. Spain: Valencia. 1959-1984. Lang.: Fre, Eng, Spa, Ita, Cat.　　516

The history of the Södertälje Teateramatörer. Sweden: Södertälje. 1953-1986. Lang.: Swe.　　520

How Skottes Musiktéater operates on a small government budget. Sweden: Gävle. 1976-1986. Lang.: Swe.　　522

Recent outdoor productions of Gamla Stans Teater. Sweden: Stockholm. 1933-1986. Lang.: Swe.　　524

Production of Brecht's *Baal* by a troupe of untrained young actors. Sweden: Stockholm. 1986. Lang.: Swe.　　525

Liturgical drama and dance performed by amateur theatre group. Sweden: Lund. 1960-1986. Lang.: Swe.　　526

Activities of the Folkkulturcentrum Festival. Sweden: Stockholm. 1977-1986. Lang.: Swe.　　529

Amateur theatre festival described. Switzerland: La Chaux-de-Fonds. Lang.: Fre.　　530

Function of the Welfare State Theater. UK. 1977. Lang.: Eng.　　532

Survey of nine repertory theatres. UK-England. 1986. Lang.: Eng.　　533

Overview of the *Not the RSC Festival* at the Almeida Theatre. UK-England: London. 1986. Lang.: Eng.　　534

Administrators seen as destroying the fringe theatre. UK-England: London. 1980-1986. Lang.: Swe.　　535

Interview with Hilary Westlake of Lumière & Son. UK-England: London. 1973-1986. Lang.: Swe.　　536

Edinburgh Festival extended by an international season. UK-Scotland: Edinburgh. 1984-1986. Lang.: Eng.　　537

Traverse Theatre and the new director Jerry Killick. UK-Scotland: Edinburgh. 1986. Lang.: Eng.　　538

Reviews of Edinburgh Festival plays. UK-Scotland: Edinburgh. 1986. Lang.: Eng.　　539

Profile of New York Theatre Workshop. USA: New York, NY. 1980-1984. Lang.: Eng.　　542

Profile of Merry Enterprises Theatre. USA: New York, NY. 1975-1984. Lang.: Eng.　　543

Several nonprofit theatres secure new spaces. USA: New York, NY. 1984. Lang.: Eng.　　544

A call for a government-subsidized repertory acting ensemble. USA: New York, NY. 1986.　　545

Production history and techniques of the Living Theatre. USA. 1964. Lang.: Eng.　　546

Origins and evolution of Teatro Campesino. USA. Mexico. 1965-1986. Lang.: Eng.　　547

Interview with Adrian Hall, artistic director of both Trinity Square Repertory Theatre and Dallas Theatre Center. USA: Providence, RI, Dallas, TX. 1966-1986. Lang.: Eng.　　548

Management techniques for growth at Tears of Joy Puppet Theatre. USA: Vancouver, WA. 1974-1985. Lang.: Eng.　　549

Theatre companies that spend summers outside of New York City to promote artistic growth and development. USA. 1985. Lang.: Eng.　　550

Revival and decline of resident acting companies seen through case studies. USA. 1886-1930. Lang.: Eng.　　551

Early history of Circle in the Square. USA: New York, NY. 1950-1960. Lang.: Kor.　　552

Development of several companies funded by the NEA's Ongoing Ensembles Program. USA: New York, NY. 1986. Lang.: Eng.　　553

Tyrone Guthrie on Guthrie Theatre and regional theatre movement. USA: Minneapolis, MN. 1963. Lang.: Eng.　　555

Interview with Julia Miles, director of the Women's Project, American Place Theatre. USA: New York, NY. 1978-1985. Lang.: Eng.　　558

John Houseman discusses Federal Theatre Project. USA: New York, NY, Washington, DC. 1935-1940. Lang.: Eng.　　559

Eva LeGallienne on Civic Repertory and American Repertory Theatres. USA: New York, NY. 1933-1953. Lang.: Eng.　　560

The few New York theatres that promote international plays and companies. USA: New York, NY. 1986. Lang.: Eng.　　561

Profile of Writers Theatre, an organization focusing on adaptations of poetry and literature for theatre. USA: New York, NY. 1975-1983. Lang.: Eng.　　562

Profile of Economy Tires Theatre, producing arm of Dance Theatre Workshop. USA: New York, NY. 1978-1983. Lang.: Eng.　　563

Training and use of child performers. USA. 1949-1985. Lang.: Eng.　　565

Artistic director of WPA Theatre Kyle Renick discusses institutionalization of theatre companies. USA: New York, NY. 1977-1986. Lang.: Eng.　　566

Survey of problems of administration and production in youth theatre programs. USA. 1984-1986. Lang.: Eng.　　567

Discussion of America's National Theatre and Peter Sellars, artistic director. USA: Washington, DC. 1984. Lang.: Eng.　　568

A profile of South Coast Repertory. USA: Los Angeles, CA. 1964-1986.　　569

Goals and accomplishments of Theatre for the New City. USA: New York, NY. 1970-1983. Lang.: Eng.　　570

Problems and advantages of co-production. USA: New York, NY. 1985. Lang.: Eng.　　571

Reprint of an article by Douglas Turner Ward that resulted in the founding of the Negro Ensemble Company. USA: New York, NY. 1966. Lang.: Eng.　　572

Member organizations of Alliance of Resident Theatres/New York include programs in poetry, media and music. USA: New York, NY. 1984. Lang.: Eng.　　574

Actor and artistic director of the Puškin Theatre on the theatre collective. USSR: Leningrad. 1980-1986. Lang.: Rus.　　577

Tanz '86 festival. Austria: Vienna. 1986. Lang.: Ger.　　1269

Account of the firing of Alexander Grant, artistic director of National Ballet of Canada. Canada: Toronto, ON. 1975-1982. Lang.: Eng.　　1295

Goals of Eric Bruhn, new artistic director of National Ballet of Canada. Canada: Toronto, ON. 1967-1983. Lang.: Eng.　　1296

Development of ballet at Opéra de Paris. France: Paris. 1790-1848. Lang.: Eng.　　1298

Careers of choreographers Maria Formolo and Keith Urban. Canada: Regina, SK, Edmonton, AB. 1980-1983. Lang.: Eng.　　1343

Problems of Toronto Dance Theatre. Canada: Toronto, ON. 1968-1982. Lang.: Eng.　　1344

Claus Peymann's concept for managing the Akademietheater and the Burgtheater. Austria: Vienna. 1986. Lang.: Ger.　　1532

Ten years of the Burgtheater under the auspices of Achim Benning. Austria: Vienna. 1776-1986. Lang.: Ger.　　1533

Photos of productions at the Schauspielhaus under the leadership of Hans Gratzer. Austria: Vienna. 1978-1986. Lang.: Ger.　　1534

On concept of the new group, Der Kreis. Austria: Vienna. 1986-1987. Lang.: Ger.　　1536

Achim Benning's management of the Burgtheater. Austria: Vienna. 1976-1986. Lang.: Ger.　　1537

Paul Blaha's management of the Volkstheater. Austria: Vienna. 1986-1987. Lang.: Ger.　　1538

New leadership in Montreal's English-speaking theatres. Canada: Montreal, PQ. 1980-1986. Lang.: Eng.　　1539

Fragile alternatives to Charlottetown Festival. Canada: Charlottetown, PE. 1982-1986. Lang.: Eng.　　1540

History of the Green Thumb Theatre. Canada: Vancouver, BC. 1975-1986. Lang.: Eng.　　1541

A history of two French language theatres. Canada: Edmonton, AB. 1970-1986. Lang.: Eng.　　1542

French-language theatre and the Acadian tradition. Canada. 1969-1986. Lang.: Eng.　　1544

Institutions, producing — cont'd

Institutions, producing — cont'd

Claus Helmut Drese and his plans for managing the Vienna Staatsoper. Austria: Vienna. Germany, West. Switzerland. 1930-1986. Lang.: Ger. 3670

History of music performances, mainly opera, at the Stratford Festival. Canada: Stratford, ON. 1951-1985. Lang.: Eng. 3671

Development of Prague National Theatre. Czechoslovakia: Prague. 1787-1985. Lang.: Eng. 3672

Discussions of opera at the festival of Aix-en-Provence. France: Aix-en-Provence. 1960. Lang.: Fre. 3673

Illustrated discussion of the opening of the Théâtre National de l'Opéra. France: Paris. 1875. Lang.: Fre. 3674

History of the former Royal Opera House of Hanover and its plans for the future. Germany, West: Hanover. 1689-1986. Lang.: Eng. 3675

Innovation at Teatro La Fenice under the directorship of Italo Gomez. Italy: Venice. 1980-1986. Lang.: Eng. 3676

History of the Teatro alla Scala. Italy: Milan. 1898-1986. Lang.: Eng. 3677

The survival and prosperity of the Santa Fe Opera Company. USA: Santa Fe, NM. 1957-1986. Lang.: Eng. 3678

New administrative personnel at the Opera Theatre of St. Louis. USA: St. Louis, MO. 1976-1986. Lang.: Eng. 3679

The history and plans of the Pennsylvania Opera Theatre. USA: Philadelphia, PA. 1976-1986. Lang.: Eng. 3680

The first thirty years of the Santa Fe Opera. USA: Santa Fe, NM. 1956-1986. Lang.: Eng. 3681

History of puppetry and the Hungarian State Puppet Theatre. Hungary. 1773-1985. Lang.: Hun. 3956

History of Bóbita Puppet Theatre. Hungary: Pécs. 1961-1986. Lang.: Hun. 3957

History of Pantijn Muziekpoppentheater. Netherlands: Amsterdam. 1980-1987. Lang.: Eng. 3958

Discussion of techniques and theories of Bread and Puppet Theatre. USA: New York, NY. 1961-1978. Lang.: Ita. 3960

Experiences of a couple who converted a coal barge into a touring puppet theatre. UK-England: London. 1976-1986. Lang.: Eng. 4005

Report on state puppet theatre. China: Beijing, Shanghai. 1986. Lang.: Eng. 4015

Performance spaces

History of various theatre buildings and the companies that perform in them. Lang.: Ger. 579

Troubles faced by Adelaide Court theatre complex. Canada: Toronto, ON. 1979-1983. Lang.: En . 587

Renovation of the Szeged National Theatre. Hungary: Szeged. 1978-1986. Lang.: Hun. 599

The burning of the Szeged National Theatre. Hungary: Szeged. 1885. Lang.: Hun. 600

Structural design problems and their solutions at the Szeged National Theatre in Hungary. Hungary: Szeged. 1977-1986. Lang.: Hun. 602

The history of the theatre building used by Szegedi Nemzeti Színhaz. Hungary: Szeged. 1800-1883. Lang.: Hun. 603

Reconstruction of the Szeged National Theatre. Hungary: Szeged. 1948-1980. Lang.: Hun. 604

Design and construction of rebuilt Szeged National Theatre. Hungary: Szeged. 1978-1986. Lang.: Hun. 605

Director of Szegedi Nemzeti Színhaz on reconstructed theatre. Hungary: Szeged. 1978-1986. Lang.: Hun. 607

Design of the Szeged National Theatre renovation. Hungary: Szeged. 1981-1986. Lang.: Hun. 608

Description of Orionteatern, a former factory. Sweden: Stockholm. 1983-1986. Lang.: Swe. 618

Notes on theatres in Saint Gallen, Winterthur and Zug. Switzerland. 1968-1985. Lang.: Swe. 622

Overview of pub theatres. UK-England: London. 1980-1987. Lang.: Eng. 626

Reconstructing a theatrical organization at Saint James Palace (London). England: London. 1600-1986. Lang.: Eng. 1615

Children's history of the Gran Teatre del Liceo opera house. Spain-Catalonia: Barcelona. 1845-1986. Lang.: Cat. 3684

Performance/production

On manager and director Claus Helmut Drese. Austria: Vienna. Switzerland. Germany, West. Lang.: Ger. 659

Recent French-language theatre. Belgium. 1985. Lang.: Fre. 661

Staging techniques employed at the Mermaid Theatre. Canada: Wolfville, NS. 1972-1985. Lang.: Eng. 665

Canadian theatre and its relations with U.S. theatre. Canada. USA. 1985. Lang.: Fre. 669

Amateur theatre festival initiated by Teatret La Luna (Århus). Italy: Amandola. 1980-1986. Lang.: Swe. 747

Theatre activities outside of Seoul. Korea. 1986. Lang.: Kor. 762

Interview with Mario Delgado Vásquez, director of Cuatrotablas. Peru: Lima. 1971-1985. Lang.: Hun. 769

Actor-director Edmund Wierciński on Reduta Theatre. Poland. 1924. Lang.: Pol. 775

Survey of Portuguese theatrical life, including discussion of both large and small theatres. Portugal. 1985. Lang.: Hun. 776

Collected reviews of theatre season. Spain-Catalonia: Barcelona. 1985-1986. Lang.: Cat. 791

Report from the international Fringe Festival. UK-Scotland: Edinburgh. 1986. Lang.: Swe. 819

Theatre of Nations Festival reviewed. USA: Baltimore, MD. 1986. Lang.: Hun. 833

Wooster Group retrospective of original works. USA: New York, NY. 1975-1986. Lang.: Eng. 850

Working life of theatrical collective Teat'r-studija na Jugo-Zapade. USSR: Moscow. 1980-1986. Lang.: Rus. 864

Jubilee of Avarskij Musykal'no-Dramatičeskij Teat'r im. G. Cadasy. USSR. 1935-1985. Lang.: Rus. 873

Biography of Arkadij Rajkin, founder of Theatre of Miniatures. USSR: Leningrad, Moscow. 1911-1987. Lang.: Rus. 906

Director of Lenin Comsomol Theatre discusses theatre's history and repertory, Ribnikov's *Juno és Avosz (Juno and Avos)*. USSR: Moscow. 1927-1985. Lang.: Hun. 909

Komsomol Theatre director Mark Zacharov on his profession. USSR: Moscow. 1980-1986. Lang.: Rus. 910

Career of dancer Ju.T. Ždanov. USSR. 1925-1986. Lang.: Rus. 1321

Five actors who work solely in regional theatre. 1961-1984. Lang.: Eng. 1633

Introduction to series of articles on small theatre companies. Canada. 1986. Lang.: Eng. 1669

Career of director Bill Glassco. Canada: Toronto, ON. 1965-1986. Lang.: Eng. 1674

Description of an outdoor Shakespeare theatre project. Canada: Toronto, ON. 1983-1986. Lang.: Eng. 1678

Interview with Eugenio Barba, director of Odin Teatret. Europe. 1985. Lang.: Hun. 1718

Comédie-Française seen through its records for one year. France: Paris. 1778. Lang.: Fre. 1740

Actor, director and teacher Jean-Pierre Vincent. France. 1955-1986. Lang.: Fre. 1744

New director of Radnóti Miklós Theatre, András Bálint. Hungary: Budapest. 1985. Lang.: Hun. 1830

Reprinted preface to biography of Tamás Major. Hungary. 1930-1986. Lang.: Hun. 1863

Interview with Tamás Major, director and actor. Hungary. 1945-1986. Lang.: Hun. 1868

Theatrical career of Ede Paulay. Hungary: Budapest. 1878-1894. Lang.: Hun. 1944

Interview with actor, director and dramaturg Imre Katona of the Gropius Társulat. Hungary: Budapest. 1961-1985. Lang.: Hun. 1945

Daniel Lanzini's notes on writing and staging his play *Hazaiot Kamot Bamizrah (Fantasies Awakening in the East)* at the Acre Theatre Festival. Israel: Acre. 1986. Lang.: Heb. 1981

Details of Wileński Touring Theatre. Poland: Vilna. 1935-1936. Lang.: Pol. 2020

Repertory and artistic achievements of the Na Pohulance Theatre. Poland: Vilna. 1938-1940. Lang.: Pol. 2036

Artistic profile and main achievements of Akademia Ruchu. Poland: Warsaw. 1973-1986. Lang.: Pol. 2037

Overview of the season at the new Swan Theatre. UK-England: Stratford. 1986. Lang.: Eng. 2174

Interview with Borderline Theatre Company artistic director Morag Fullarton. UK-Scotland. 1979-1986. Lang.: Eng. 2190

Institutions, producing — cont'd

Interview with director David Hayman of the Scottish Theatre Company. UK-Scotland. 1986. Lang.: Eng. 2192

Interview with Jules Cranfield on Focus Theatre Group. UK-Scotland. 1973-1986. Lang.: Eng. 2193

An historical account of one actor's experiences with the Fresno Paramount Players. USA: Fresno, CA. 1927. Lang.: Eng. 2255

New York critics respond negatively to plays successful in Los Angeles. USA: Los Angeles, CA, New York, NY. 1983-1984. Lang.: Eng. 2258

Brief history of August Wilson's *Fences*. USA. 1982-1986. Lang.: Eng. 2273

The organization of the Olympiad Arts Festival. USA: Los Angeles, CA. 1984. Lang.: Eng. 2281

Conflict over artistic control in American Repertory Theatre's production of *Endgame* by Samuel Beckett. USA: Boston, MA. 1984. Lang.: Eng. 2296

A profile of The Brecht Company. USA: Ann Arbor, MI. 1979-1984. 2312

Details of the 1926 American Circus Corporation season. USA. Canada. 1926. Lang.: Eng. 3386

Case-study of *Sweet and Sour* by the Australian Broadcasting Corporation. Australia: Sydney, N.S.W. 1980-1984. Lang.: Eng. 3483

History of the Beijing Opera. China: Beijing. 800-1986. Lang.: Cat. 3507

Interview with director Harry Kupfer of Komische Oper. Germany, East: Berlin, East. 1981-1986. Lang.: Hun. 3739

Interview with Sir John Pritchard, music director of the San Francisco Opera. USA: San Francisco, CA. 1921-1986. Lang.: Eng. 3800

The operations of the Hawaii Opera Theatre. USA: Honolulu, HI. 1950-1985. Lang.: Eng. 3814

Black opera stars and companies. USA: Enid, OK, New York, NY. 1961-1985. Lang.: Eng. 3839

Gary Jones, and the Black Street, USA Puppet Theatre. USA: Chicago, IL, Los Angeles, CA. 1970-1986. Lang.: Eng. 3978

History of The Little Angel Marionette Theatre. UK-England: London. 1961-1986. Lang.: Eng. 4007

Plays/librettos/scripts

Polish drama performed in Sweden. Sweden. Poland. 1835-1976. Lang.: Pol. 975

Description of national theatre festival. Argentina: Córdoba. 1985. Lang.: Spa. 2366

Cooperation between playwright Heinz Rudolf Unger and the Volkstheater. Austria: Vienna. 1938-1986. Lang.: Ger. 2394

Criticizes the plays in the collection *Five From the Fringe*. Canada: Edmonton, AB. 1986. Lang.: Eng. 2425

Interview with founders of Internationale Nieuwe Scene. Europe. 1984. 2543

Interview with director of Teatr Współczésny about children's drama competition. Poland: Wrocław. 1986. Lang.: Hun. 2736

Reference materials

Guide to theatre companies around the world. Lang.: Eng. 999

Overview of Charlottetown Festival productions. Canada: Charlottetown, PE. 1972-1983. Lang.: Eng. 1008

A list of opening nights of the theatrical season in Israel. Israel. 1986. Lang.: Heb. 1017

Guide to theatrical services and productions. UK-England. 1985-1986. Lang.: Eng. 1035

Directory of member organizations of ART/NY. USA: New York, NY. 1986. Lang.: Eng. 1037

List of institutional theatres. USA. 1986. 1039

Listing of repertory schedules, contact and contract information. USA. 1986. Lang.: Eng. 1045

Alphabetically arranged profiles and history of professional and amateur theatres for children. USA. 1903-1985. Lang.: Eng. 1046

Guide to postwar British theatre. UK-England. 1945-1986. Lang.: Eng. 3001

Production schedules for member theatres of Alliance of Resident Theatres/New York. USA: New York, NY. 1985-1986. Lang.: Eng. 3005

Summer performance schedules for several New York companies. USA: New York, NY. 1984. Lang.: Eng. 3011

Relation to other fields

Political theatre in Wallonia. Belgium. 1985. Lang.: Fre. 1066

Interactive theatre in *It's About Time* by Catalyst Theatre. Canada: Edmonton, AB. 1982. Lang.: Eng. 1069

Reports and discussions of restricted cultural communication. Lebanon. Spain-Catalonia. USA. 1985. Lang.: Fre, Spa, Cat. 1111

Participation of disabled children in Vår Teater. Sweden: Stockholm. 1975-1985. Lang.: Eng. 1129

On Peter Brook's *Mahabharata*, produced by the International Center of Theatre Research. France: Paris. 1985. Lang.: Rus. 3032

Black history and folklore taught in theatre workshops and productions. USA: New York, NY, Omaha, NE, Washington, DC. 1986. Lang.: Eng. 3068

Theory/criticism

Experimental theatres to offset the impact of film and theatre. China, People's Republic of. 1960-1981. Lang.: Chi. 3090

Institutions, research

Administration

An expense account in Christ Church details production expenses. England: Oxford. 1636. Lang.: Eng. 31

Copyright licensing agreement between museums and artists. USA. 1976-1985. Lang.: Eng. 144

Basic theatrical documents

Photographs of playbills from Soviet archives. Poland: Vilna. 1800-1863. Lang.: Pol. 1491

Institutions

Director of a theatrical history collection discusses organizational problems and lack of public interest. Hungary: Budapest. 1986. Lang.: Hun. 500

Scope and purpose of *Theatrum*. Canada: Toronto, ON. 1985. Lang.: Eng. 1553

Criticism of *Canadian Theatre Review*. Canada. 1985. Lang.: Fre. 1554

Exhibit on stages and staging by Royal Shakespeare Company. UK-England: Stratford. 1932-1986. Lang.: Eng. 1591

Performance/production

Review of the Theatre History Collection exhibition in the Széchényi National Library. Hungary. 1610-1850. Lang.: Hun. 734

Reference materials

Speech given by Benjamin Zemach on the deposition of Nachum Zemach's archive at Hebrew University. Israel: Jerusalem. 1986. Lang.: Heb. 1019

Theatre documents and listing of playtexts in the Polish theatre in Lvov. Poland: Lvov, Katowice. 1800-1978. Lang.: Pol. 2996

Institutions, service

U.S. laws on music performing rights. USA. 1856-1986. Lang.: Eng. 3473

Administration

Primary organizational changes at New York State Council on the Arts. USA: New York, NY. 1984. Lang.: Eng. 162

Design/technology

The renovation and modernization of the theatre production building. Hungary: Budapest. 1976. Lang.: Hun. 291

Institutions

On the audience-society, Salzburger Kulturvereinigung. Austria: Salzburg. 1947-1986. Lang.: Ger. 446

Activities of Rialles, including children's theatre and puppetry. Spain-Catalonia: Terrassa. 1972-1982. Lang.: Cat. 517

Interview with Sara Garretson, Office of Business Development. USA: New York, NY. 1984. Lang.: Eng. 541

Programs of the New York City Department of Cultural Affairs affecting nonprofit theatre. USA: New York, NY. 1983. Lang.: Eng. 554

Activities of the audience-society, Gesellschaft der Freunde der Ballettschule der Österreichischen Bundestheater. Austria: Vienna. 1985-1986. Lang.: Ger. 1294

Activities and history of the audience-society, Freunde des Theaters in der Josefstadt. Austria: Vienna. 1985-1986. Lang.: Ger. 1535

Role of the Canadian Actors' Equity Association. Canada: Toronto, ON. 1983-1986. Lang.: Eng. 1548

The French-American Film Workshop, designed to showcase the work of independents and encourage cultural exchange. France: Avignon. 1986. Lang.: Eng. 3216

Royal Dramatic College's charity for retired theatre professionals. England: London. 1858-1877. Lang.: Eng. 3322

Institutions, social
Performance/production
Analysis of Robin Hood entertainments in the parish of Yeovil.
England. 1475-1588. Lang.: Eng.   1712
Institutions, special
Institutions
Activities and functions of the Teletheater-Gesellschaft. Austria:
Vienna. 1985. Lang.: Ger.   450

Argument that Canadian theatre awards are too numerous. Canada:
Toronto, ON. 1983. Lang.: Eng.   472

Thirty years of the Polish theatrical monthly *Dialog*. Poland:
Warsaw. 1956-1986. Lang.: Pol.   511

Congressional debate over proposed NEA budget. USA: Washington,
DC. 1984. Lang.: Eng.   540

Impact of election year politics on NEA funding. USA: Washington,
DC. 1984. Lang.: Eng.   557

Controversy over proposed NEA plan. USA: Washington, DC. 1984.
Lang.: Eng.   573

Description of a theatre museum. USSR: Penze. 1986. Lang.: Rus.
                                                                      575

Shift in emphasis at Banff Centre. Canada: Banff, AB. 1974-1986.
Lang.: Eng.   1543

Failure of Dramatists' Co-op of Nova Scotia to obtain funding for a
playwrights' colony. Canada: Halifax, NS. 1986. Lang.: Eng.   1545

A history of theatre at the Séminaire de Trois-Rivières. Canada:
Trois-Rivières, PQ. 1860-1985. Lang.: Fre.   1563

Progress and aims of Women's Playhouse Trust. UK-England:
London. 1984-1986. Lang.: Eng.   1590

History of the Dime Museums. USA: Milwaukee, WI. 1882-1916.
Lang.: Eng.   3324
Institutions, training
Design/technology
Theory and practice in the training of theatre technicians at
Dramatiska Institutet. Sweden: Stockholm. 1985-1986. Lang.: Swe.
                                                                      316

Training course for theatre technicians at Dramatiska Institutet.
Sweden: Stockholm. 1985. Lang.: Swe.   318

Institutions
Significance of Applebaum-Hébert report on Canadian cultural
policy. Canada. 1982-1983. Lang.: Eng.   465

Academics in theatre discuss the role of theatre in education.
Canada. 1984. Lang.: Fre.   476

A report from the European drama camp for children. Denmark:
Vordingborg. 1986. Lang.: Swe.   489

Collection of texts referring to drama schools. Europe. 1888-1985.
Lang.: Ita.   492

Career of dramaturgist and teacher Outi Nyytäjä. Finland: Helsinki.
1967-1986. Lang.: Eng, Fre.   493

Educational theatre in Iraq. Iraq. 1885-1985. Lang.: Eng.   505

Training for amateur theatre leaders at Marieborg Folkhögskola.
Sweden: Norrköping. 1960-1986. Lang.: Swe.   528

Training and use of child performers. USA. 1949-1985. Lang.: Eng.
                                                                      565

The State Institute of Theatrical Art. USSR: Moscow. 1980-1986.
Lang.: Rus.   576

Reminiscences of study at Moscow Art Theatre. USSR. Lang.: Rus.
                                                                      578

Current state of ballet theatre, including choreographic training.
China: Beijing. 1980-1986. Lang.: Rus.   1297

The effect of subsidization on private and public professional ballet
schools in Switzerland. Switzerland. 1986. Lang.: Fre.   1299

Careers of choreographers Maria Formolo and Keith Urban.
Canada: Regina, SK, Edmonton, AB. 1980-1983. Lang.: Eng.   1343

Problems of Toronto Dance Theatre. Canada: Toronto, ON. 1968-
1982. Lang.: Eng.   1344

A playwright surveys Canadian university offerings in Canadian
literature, drama and playwriting. Canada. 1986. Lang.: Eng.   1564

Former students remember Xiong Foxi. China, People's Republic of:
Chengdu. 1901-1981. Lang.: Chi.   1568

Recollections of a student actor under Xiong Foxi's direction. China,
People's Republic of: Jinan, Chengdu. 1901-1982. Lang.: Chi.   1569

History of the Shanghai Drama Institute. China, People's Republic
of: Shanghai. 1945-1982. Lang.: Chi.   1571

Obituary of theatre manager, director, critic and scholar Timo
Tiusanen. Finland: Helsinki. 1957-1985. Lang.: Eng, Fre.   1572

History of the teaching of acting at the Conservatoire national d'art
dramatique. France: Paris. 1786-1986. Lang.: Fre.   1576

Erwin Piscator's work at the Dramatic Workshop of the New School
for Social Research. USA: New York, NY. 1939-1951. Lang.: Ger.
                                                              1600

Curriculum and expectation of students in Eubie Blake's Children's
Theatre Company. USA: New York, NY. 1986. Lang.: Eng.   1602

Efforts of New York Shakespeare Festival to develop an audience
for Shakespearean drama. USA: New York, NY. 1986. Lang.: Eng.
                                                              1605

Director of school of mime and theatre on gesture and image in
theatrical representation. France: Paris. 1962-1985. Lang.: Fre.   3289

Theories on incorporating traditional theatrical forms into popular
theatre. Canada: Toronto, ON. 1970-1986. Lang.: Eng.   3408

Puppetry documentation at Institute of Professional Puppetry Arts.
USA: Waterford, CT. 1986. Lang.: Eng.   3959
Performance/production
Training of Chinese students for a production of *The Tempest* by
William Shakespeare. China, People's Republic of: Beijing. 1981-
1985. Lang.: Eng.   679

Creative work of Il'chom studio theatre. USSR: Taškent. 1980-1986.
Lang.: Rus.   907

Actor, director and teacher Jean-Pierre Vincent. France. 1955-1986.
Lang.: Fre.   1744

Career of director/choreographer Mike Malone. USA: Washington,
DC, Cleveland, OH. 1968-1985. Lang.: Eng.   2275

Four performances in Budapest by the students of Oleg Tabakov of
GITIS, the Institute of Dramatic Art, Moscow. USSR: Moscow.
Hungary: Budapest. 1986. Lang.: Hun.   2318
Plays/librettos/scripts
Career of Xiong Foxi. China, People's Republic of: Beijing,
Shanghai. USA: New York, NY. 1901-1965. Lang.: Chi.   2449
Reference materials
Bibliography of Xiong Foxi's writings. China, People's Republic of.
1917-1963. Lang.: Chi.   1011

Guide to postwar British theatre. UK-England. 1945-1986. Lang.:
Eng.   3001
Relation to other fields
Development of arts-in-education program. USA: Albany, NY. 1970-
1984. Lang.: Eng.   1169
Theory/criticism
Interview with semiologist Patrice Pavis about the theatre institute at
the Sorbonne, his semiotic approach to theatre and modern French
theatre. France: Paris. 1923-1986. Lang.: Heb.   1206
Training
Overview of spoken drama training programs. China, People's
Republic of. 1907-1982. Lang.: Chi.   1255

Actor training methods of Luce Berthomme. France: Paris. 1984.
Lang.: Eng.   1256

Seminar on training of opera and musical theatre performers. USSR.
1986. Lang.: Rus.   3939
Instructional materials
Design/technology
Directions for making various masks, with historical information.
Europe. 1986. Lang.: Cat.   261

Guide to materials necessary for theatrical performances. USSR.
1980-1986. Lang.: Rus.   430

Handbook of mask and puppet construction. Italy. 1986. Lang.: Ita.
                                                              3951
Performance/production
Guide to auditioning for dramatic and musical productions. USA.
1986. Lang.: Eng.   830

Guide to finding acting jobs in theatre, film and television. USA.
1986. Lang.: Eng.   835

Guidelines for working with deaf actors and sign interpreters. USA.
1984-1986. Lang.: Eng.   848

Textbook on clowning for circus and vaudeville acts. USSR. 1980-
1986. Lang.: Rus.   3401

Guide for producing traditional Beijing opera. China: Suzhou. 1574-
1646. Lang.: Chi.   3508

Detailed instructions on the mounting of a musical. 1986. Lang.:
Eng.   3598

Instructional materials — cont'd

Resource book on construction and performance in puppetry. Lang.: Eng. 3961

Plays/librettos/scripts
Advice on how to create an attractive computer-generated script. 2356

Reference materials
Guide to producing printed material. USA. 1984. Lang.: Eng. 1044

Relation to other fields
Theatrical performance as a pedagogical tool. 1986. Lang.: Cat. 1048

Training
Guide for teachers on getting a full-length play together. 1980-1982. Lang.: Chi. 3154

Instrumentalists
Performance/production
Interview with Peter Brook's designer, musician, and costumer for *Mahabharata*. France: Avignon. 1973-1985. Lang.: Eng. 1359

Use of the term 'fiddler' in early works. England. 1589-1816. Lang.: Eng. 3332

Reviews of 10 vintage recordings of complete operas on LP. USA. 1906-1925. Lang.: Eng. 3792

INTAR (New York, NY)
Institutions
Member organizations of Alliance of Resident Theatres/New York include programs in poetry, media and music. USA: New York, NY. 1984. Lang.: Eng. 574

Interart Theatre (New York, NY)
Performance/production
Life and technique of Franz Xaver Kroetz. USA: New York, NY. Germany, West. 1984. Lang.: Eng. 2287

Interludes
Reference materials
List and location of school playtexts and programs. France. 1601-1700. Lang.: Fre. 2987

International Bibliography of Theatre (IBT, New York, NY)
Research/historiography
Development of two databases, TANDEM and IBT to aid in international theatre research. UK-England. 1985. Lang.: Eng. 1187

International Center of Theatre Research
SEE
Center for Theatre Research.

International Festival of Theatre (London)
SEE
London International Festival of Theatre.

International Folklore Festival (Seoul)
Administration
Account of the International Folklore Festival. Korea: Seoul. 1986. Lang.: Kor. 58

International Mime Festival (Winnipeg)
Performance/production
History of the International Mime Festival. Canada: Winnipeg, MB. 1983-1986. Lang.: Eng. 3293

International Organization of Scenographers, Theatre Technicians, and Architects
SEE
Organisation Internationale des Scénographes, Techniciens et Architectes de Theéâtre.

International School of Theatre Anthropology (ISTA)
SEE ALSO
Odin Teatret (Hosltebro).

International Seminar on Indian Dance Traditions (Calcutta)
Institutions
Reports on theatre conferences and festivals in Asia. Philippines: Manila. Malaysia: Kuala Lumpur. Japan: Toga. India: Calcutta. 1981-1984. Lang.: Eng. 510

International Theatre Festival (Toga)
Institutions
Reports on theatre conferences and festivals in Asia. Philippines: Manila. Malaysia: Kuala Lumpur. Japan: Toga. India: Calcutta. 1981-1984. Lang.: Eng. 510

International Theatre Institute (ITI)
Institutions
Notes on the dance committee meetings at the 21st congress of the International Theatre Institute. Canada: Montreal, PQ, Toronto, ON. 1985. Lang.: Rus. 1270

Training
Seminar on training of opera and musical theatre performers. USSR. 1986. Lang.: Rus. 3939

Intiman Theatre (Seattle, WA)
Design/technology
Sound desigers at regional theatres evaluate new equipment. USA. 1986. 409

Performance/production
Director Christoph Nel discusses staging Brecht's *Im Dickicht der Städte (In the Jungle of the Cities)*. USA: Seattle, WA. 1984. 2246

Into the Light
Performance/production
Reviews of *Into the Light*, book by Jeff Tamborniro, music by Lee Holdridge, lyrics by John Forster, staged by Michael Maurer. USA: New York, NY. 1986. Lang.: Eng. 3615

Invités au procès, Les (Guests on Trial, The)
Basic theatrical documents
English translation of *Les invités au procès (The Guests on Trial)* by Anne Hébert. Canada. 1952. Lang.: Eng. 3174

Ionesco, Eugène
Performance/production
Notes, interviews and evolution of actor/director Jean-Marie Serreau. France. 1938-1973. Lang.: Fre. 1724

Tamás Ascher directs *A kopasz éneksnö (The Bald Soprano)* and *Különóra (The Lesson)* by Eugène Ionesco. Hungary: Kaposvár. 1986. Lang.: Hun. 1912

Plays/librettos/scripts
The incoherent protagonist of modern comedy. 1954-1986. Lang.: Eng. 2358

Intervening and pure theatre acoording to Eugène Ionesco. France. 1949-1970. Lang.: Chi. 2547

Essentialism and avant-garde in the plays of Eugène Ionesco. France. 1950-1980. Lang.: Fre. 2576

Theory/criticism
Assessment of critic Kenneth Tynan's works. UK-England. 1950-1960. Lang.: Eng. 3136

IOU Theatre Company
Performance/production
Collection of newspaper reviews by London theatre critics. UK-England. 1986. Lang.: Eng. 2114

Iphigenie auf Tauris (Iphigenia in Taurus)
Plays/librettos/scripts
Comparative analysis of *Elektra* by Hugo von Hofmannsthal and its sources. Germany. 1909. Lang.: Eng. 2603

Ireland, David
Plays/librettos/scripts
Amerindian and aborigine characters in the works of white playwrights. Canada. Australia. 1606-1975. Lang.: Eng. 930

Ireland, Kenny
Performance/production
Collection of newspaper reviews by London theatre critics. UK-England: London. 1986. Lang.: Eng. 2116

Irish National Theatre Society (Dublin)
SEE
Abbey Theatre.

Irons, Jeremy
Performance/production
Career of actor Jeremy Irons in theatre, television and film. UK-England. USA. 1970-1985. Lang.: Eng. 2181

Irving, Henry
Performance/production
Changes in English life reflected in 1883 theatre season. UK-England: London. 1883. Lang.: Eng. 810

Career of actress, manager and director Julia Arthur. Canada. UK-England. USA. 1869-1950. Lang.: Eng. 1675

Irydion
Performance/production
Mikołaj Grabowski directs *Irydion* by Zygmunt Krasiński. Poland: Cracow. 1983. Lang.: Pol. 2046

Iser, Wolfgang
Plays/librettos/scripts
Bertolt Brecht and the Expressionists. Germany. 1919-1944. Lang.: Eng. 955

Island Community Theatre (Prince Edward Island)
Institutions
Development of community-based theatre on Prince Edward Island. Canada. 1981-1986. Lang.: Eng. 1556

Island of the Mighty, The
Plays/librettos/scripts
The place of *The Island of the Mighty* in the John Arden canon. Ireland. UK. 1950-1972. Lang.: Eng. 2666

Jefford, Barbara
Performance/production
Eileen Atkins, Judi Dench, Wendy Hiller and Barbara Jefford
discuss playing Saint Joan in Shaw's play. UK-England: London.
1936-1983. Lang.: Eng.   2153

Jéfremov, Oleg
Relation to other fields
Interview with director Oleg Jéfremov of Moscow Art Theatre on
social goals of theatre. USSR. 1986. Lang.: Rus.   1174

Její Pastorkyna (Her Stepdaughter)
Performance/production
Thematic, character and musical analysis of *Jenufa* by Leoš Janáček.
Czechoslovakia: Brno. 1894-1903. Lang.: Eng.   3718

Plays/librettos/scripts
Evaluation of the dramatic work of Gabriela Preissová, author of
the source play for *Jenufa* by Leoš Janáček. Czechoslovakia: Brno.
1880-1900. Lang.: Eng.   2453

Jelgerhuis Rienkzoon, Johanes
Performance/production
Performance of Comédie-Française actors in Amsterdam.
Netherlands. 1811. Lang.: Fre.   2012

Jellicoe, Ann
Plays/librettos/scripts
Current state of women's playwriting. UK-England. 1985-1986.
Lang.: Eng.   2830

Jeney, István
Performance/production
Performances of *Alice Csodaországban (Alice in Wonderland)*, *A Két
Veronai nemes (The Two Gentlemen of Verona)* and *Tobbsincs
királyfi (No More Crown Prince)*. Hungary: Pécs, Budapest. 1985.
Lang.: Hun.   1771

Dezső Szomory's *Bella* at the Pécs National Theatre directed by
István Jeney. Hungary: Pécs. 1986. Lang.: Hun.   1897

Dezső Szomory's *Bella* at Pécs National Theatre directed by István
Jeney. Hungary: Pécs. 1986. Lang.: Hun.   1936

Jenkins, Darwin
Institutions
History of Black theater companies. USA: Philadelphia, PA. 1966-
1985. Lang.: Eng.   1608

Jenkins, Linda Walsh
Performance/production
Chicago dramaturgs acknowledge a common ground in educating
their audience. USA: Chicago, IL. 1984-1986. Lang.: Eng.   2274

Jenufa
Performance/production
The native roots of Czechoslovakian literature and music.
Czechoslovakia. 1800-1910. Lang.: Eng.   3717

Thematic, character and musical analysis of *Jenufa* by Leoš Janáček.
Czechoslovakia: Brno. 1894-1903. Lang.: Eng.   3718

Photographs, cast list, synopsis, and discography of Metropolitan
Opera radio broadcast performances. USA: New York, NY. 1986.
Lang.: Eng.   3794

Plays/librettos/scripts
Evaluation of the dramatic work of Gabriela Preissová, author of
the source play for *Jenufa* by Leoš Janáček. Czechoslovakia: Brno.
1880-1900. Lang.: Eng.   2453

Jerome Kern Goes to Hollywood
Performance/production
Reviews of *Jerome Kern Goes to Hollywood*, conceived and staged
by David Kernan. USA: New York, NY. 1986. Lang.: Eng.   2237

Jeršov, Ivan
Performance/production
Biography of singer Ivan Jeršov. USSR. 1867-1943. Lang.: Rus. 3847

Jesuit theatre
Audience
Audience of the humanistic, religious and school-theatre of the
European Renaissance. Europe. 1480-1630. Lang.: Ger.   1445

**Jesús batejat per Sant Joan Baptista (Jesus Christ Baptized by
St. John the Baptist)**
Plays/librettos/scripts
Introduction to *Jesús batejat per Sant Joan Baptista (Jesus Christ
Baptized by St. John the Baptist)*. France. 1753-1832. Lang.: Cat.
                                                              2585

Jesus Christ Superstar
Performance/production
Jézus Krisztus Szupersztar (Jesus Christ Superstar) by Andrew Lloyd
Webber and Tim Rice directed by János Szikora (Rock Szinház).
Hungary: Szeged. 1986. Lang.: Hun.   3604

Summer productions of *Jézus Krisztus Szupersztár*. Hungary: Szeged,
Budapest. 1986. Lang.: Hun.   3605

Jesus, the Son of Man
Performance/production
Productions based on sacred music of Franz Liszt. Hungary:
Zalaegerszeg, Budapest. 1986. Lang.: Hun.   1308

Jeu d'intérieur (Indoor Games)
Basic theatrical documents
Playtext of Jacques de Decker's *Jeu d'intérieur (Indoor Games)* in
English translation. Belgium. 1979. Lang.: Eng.   1461

Jeu de l'amour et du hasard, Le (Play of Love and Chance)
Performance/production
Staging of plays by Marivaux compared to textual analysis. France.
1723-1981. Lang.: Fre.   1746

Jeu de l'amour et du hasard, Le (Play of Love and Chance, The)
Performance/production
Collection of newspaper reviews by London theatre critics. UK.
1986. Lang.: Eng.   2102

Jèvreinov, Nikolaj Nikolajèvič
Performance/production
Career of director and playwright, Nikolaj Nikolajèvič Jèvreinov.
Russia. USSR. 1879-1953. Lang.: Hun.   2066

Plays/librettos/scripts
Career of expressionist playwright Bertram Brooker. Canada:
Toronto, ON. 1888-1949. Lang.: Eng.   2418

Jew of Malta, The
Plays/librettos/scripts
Possible influence of Christopher Marlowe's plays upon those of
William Shakespeare. England. 1580-1620. Lang.: Eng.   2478

Reference materials
List of 37 productions of 23 Renaissance plays, with commentary.
UK. USA. New Zealand. 1986. Lang.: Eng.   3000

Jewell, Derek
Performance/production
Music critic Derek Jewell traces Frank Sinatra's career along with
his own. USA. 1900-1986. Lang.: Eng.   3179

Jewish Institute Players (Glasgow)
Design/technology
Life of stage designer Tom MacDonald. UK-Scotland: Glasgow.
1914-1985. Lang.: Eng.   1526

Jewish theatre
SEE
Yiddish theatre.

Jiao, Juyin
Theory/criticism
Symbolism and aesthetics in the performance styles of Chinese
opera. China, People's Republic of: Beijing. 1935-1985. Lang.: Chi.
                                                              3564

Jigsaw Theatre-in-education Company (Australia)
Performance/production
Dilemmas and prospects of youth theatre movement. Australia. 1982-
1986. Lang.: Eng.   1639

Jin, Shengtan
Plays/librettos/scripts
Differences among 32 extant editions of *Xi Xiang Zhu*. China. 1669-
1843. Lang.: Chi.   3528

Jinker, The
Relation to other fields
Social function of radio drama. Canada. 1950-1955. Lang.: Eng.
                                                              3187

Joculatores Lancastrienses (UK)
Performance/production
Performance by Joculatores Lancastrienses of Thomas Garter's
interlude, *Commody of the Moste Vertuous and Godlye Susanna*. UK-
England: Lancaster. 1985. Lang.: Eng.   2148

Thomas Garter's *Commody of the Moste Vertuous and Godlye
Susanna* performed before orignial screen in timberframed gothic hall.
UK-England. 1986. Lang.: Eng.   2165

Joe Beef
Performance/production
Playwright David Fennario's commitment to working-class
community theatre. Canada: Montreal, PQ. 1980-1986. Lang.: Eng.
                                                              1661

Jofjell, Staffan
Performance/production
Stage photographs with comment by photographers. Sweden. 1985-
1986. Lang.: Swe.   794

Johan the Husband
Performance/production
New evidence on the appearance of professional actors. England:
London. 1200-1600. Lang.: Eng.   699

Johanson, Robert
Design/technology
Designers discuss regional productions of *Side-by-Side by Sondheim*.
USA. 1984. Lang.: Eng.   3593

Johansson, Stefan
Performance/production
Emblems of the 1980s in Swedish theatre. Sweden. 1980-1986.
Lang.: Swe.   796

John Bull's Other Island
Performance/production
Collection of newspaper reviews by London theatre critics. UK.
1986. Lang.: Eng.   2099

John Gabriel Borkman
Institutions
Reviews of Edinburgh Festival plays. UK-Scotland: Edinburgh. 1986.
Lang.: Eng.   539

Plays/librettos/scripts
Self-transcendence through grace embodied in Henrik Ibsen's female
characters. Norway. 1849-1899. Lang.: Eng.   2726

John Golden Theatre (New York, NY)
Performance/production
Reviews of *The Petition*, by Brian Clark, staged by Peter Hall.
USA: New York, NY. 1986. Lang.: Eng.   2234

John Houseman Acting Company (New York, NY)
Plays/librettos/scripts
Biographical sketch of playwright/performer Samm-Art Williams.
USA: Burgaw, NC, New York, NY. 1940-1986. Lang.: Eng.   2946

John, Errol
Performance/production
Collection of newspaper reviews by London theatre critics. UK-
England: London. 1986. Lang.: Eng.   2126

Johnson, Andrew
Institutions
Interviews with theatre professionals in Quebec. Canada. 1985.
Lang.: Fre.   487

Johnson, Laurie
Performance/production
Lakat alá lányokat (Lock Up Your Daughters), a stage adaptation of
Henry Fielding's *Rape Upon Rape*, directed by Imre Halasi.
Hungary: Diósgyőr. 1986. Lang.: Hun.   3600

Johnson, Raymond
Performance/production
Origins of radically simplified stage in modern productions. USA.
1912-1922. Lang.: Eng.   831

Johnstone, Keith
Performance/production
Discussion of Stanislavskij's influence by a number of artists.
Sweden. 1890-1986. Lang.: Swe.   2094

Joint Stock Theatre Group (London)
Plays/librettos/scripts
Interview with playwright Howard Barker. UK-England. 1981-1985.
Lang.: Eng.   2845

Jókai Szinház (Békéscsaba)
Performance/production
Az esőcsináló (The Rainmaker) by N. Richard Nash, directed by
Mátyás Giricz. Hungary: Békéscsaba. 1986. Lang.: Hun.   1795

Anatoly Ivanov directs Gogol's *Ženitba (The Marriage)* at Jókai
Szinház under the title *Háztüznéző*. Hungary: Békéscsaba. 1985.
Lang.: Hun.   1821

Stage adaptations of prose works by Gogol and Gončarov. Hungary:
Veszprém, Békéscsaba. 1985. Lang.: Hun.   1948

Jókai, Mór
Performance/production
János Ács directs *A kőszívű ember fiai (The Sons of the Stone-
Hearted Man)* by Mór Jókai. Hungary: Zalaegerszeg. 1986. Lang.:
Hun.   1905

Jolivet, Tyrone
Performance/production
Black opera stars and companies. USA: Enid, OK, New York, NY.
1961-1985. Lang.: Eng.   3839

Joly, Christine
Performance/production
A photographic essay of 42 soloists and groups performing mime or
gestural theatre. 1986.   3290

Jomandi (Atlanta, GA)
Administration
Growing activity and changing role of Black regional theatre
companies. USA. 1960-1984. Lang.: Eng.   1440

Jones, Bill T.
Design/technology
Keith Haring, Robert Longo and Gretchen Bender design for
choreographers Bill T. Jones and Arnie Zane. USA. 1986.   1342

Jones, Cathy
Performance/production
Playwright and performer Cathy Jones. Canada: St. John's, NF.
1986. Lang.: Eng.   1660

Jones, David
Performance/production
Dramaturg Richard Nelson on communicating with different kinds of
directors. USA: New York, NY. 1979-1986. Lang.: Eng.   2252

Jones, Gary
Performance/production
Gary Jones, and the Black Street, USA Puppet Theatre. USA:
Chicago, IL, Los Angeles, CA. 1970-1986. Lang.: Eng.   3978

Jones, Gwyneth
Performance/production
Profile of and interview with Welsh soprano Gwyneth Jones. UK-
Wales: Pontnewynydd. 1936-1986. Lang.: Eng.   3788

Jones, Inigo
Performance/production
Analysis of the document detailing expenses for performances given
at Christ Church (Oxford) for Charles I, suggesting involvement by
Inigo Jones as stage director. England: Oxford. 1636. Lang.: Eng.
                                                                    1701

Jones, LeRoi
SEE
Baraka, Imamu Amiri.

Jones, Mrs. W.G.
Relation to other fields
Professional equality in theatrical careers for men and women. USA:
New York, NY. 1850-1870. Lang.: Eng.   1143

Jones, Robert Edmond
Performance/production
Origins of radically simplified stage in modern productions. USA.
1912-1922. Lang.: Eng.   831

Jones, Tom
Administration
Growing activity and changing role of Black regional theatre
companies. USA. 1960-1984. Lang.: Eng.   1440

Jonic, Bettina
Performance/production
Theatre work of Bettina Jonic. UK-England. 1970-1986. Lang.: Eng.
                                                                    2151

Jonson, Ben
Plays/librettos/scripts
Similar dramatic techniques in Ben Jonson's masques and tragedies.
England. 1597-1637. Lang.: Eng.   941

Ben Jonson's use of romance in *Volpone*. England. 1575-1600. Lang.:
Eng.   2461

Post-structuralist insights on sexuality and transgression in transvestite
roles in Jacobean plays. England: London. 1600-1625. Lang.: Eng.
                                                                    2476

Image of poverty in Elizabethan and Stuart plays. England. 1558-
1642. Lang.: Eng.   2482

Sounds in Ben Jonson's *Epicoene*. England: London. 1609-1668.
Lang.: Eng.   2483

Gender roles in *Epicoene* by Ben Jonson. England: London. 1609-
1909. Lang.: Eng.   2505

Use of group aggression in Ben Jonson's comedies. England. 1575-
1600. Lang.: Eng.   2508

Reflections of Ben Jonson's personal life in his poems and plays.
England: London. 1596-1604. Lang.: Eng.   2515

Herpetological imagery in Jonson's *Catiline*. England. 1611. Lang.:
Eng.   2517

Comparison of Ben Jonson's *Catiline* with its Latin prose source by
Sallust. England. Italy. 43 B.C.-1611 A.D. Lang.: Eng.   2518

Theme of Puritanism in *The Alchemist* by Ben Jonson. England.
1610. Lang.: Eng.   2519

Violation of genre divisions in the plays of Ben Jonson. England:
London. 1606-1610. Lang.: Eng.   2525

Jonson, Ben — cont'd

Development of Restoration musical theatre. England. 1642-1699.
Lang.: Eng. 3496

Jonson, Raymond
Performance/production
Greek tragedy on the New York stage. USA: New York, NY. 1854-1984. Lang.: Eng. 2301

Joos Leeder School of Dance
Relation to other fields
Refugee artists from Nazi Germany in Britain. UK-England. Germany. 1937-1947. Lang.: Eng. 1135

Joos, Kurt
Relation to other fields
Refugee artists from Nazi Germany in Britain. UK-England. Germany. 1937-1947. Lang.: Eng. 1135

Jorn, Karl
Performance/production
Reviews of 10 vintage recordings of complete operas on LP. USA. 1906-1925. Lang.: Eng. 3792

Jōruri
Design/technology
Collection of pictures of *bunraku* puppet heads. Japan: Tokyo. Lang.: Jap. 3997
Plays/librettos/scripts
Musical structure of dramas of Chikamatsu. Japan. 1653-1725. Lang.: Eng. 4000

Joseph, Sir Keith
Relation to other fields
Influence of Sir Keith Joseph upon the education system. UK-England. 1985. Lang.: Eng. 1138

Journey to London, A
Performance/production
Collection of newspaper reviews by London theatre critics. UK-England: London. 1986. Lang.: Eng. 2117

Journey, The
Basic theatrical documents
Text of *The Journey* by Timothy Findley. Canada. 1970. Lang.: Eng. 3173

Joy Puppeteers (Cleveland, OH)
Performance/production
Influence of the Joy Puppeteers on the television program *Hickory Hideout*. USA: Cleveland, OH. 1982-1986. Lang.: Eng. 3275

Joyce Theatre (New York, NY)
Performance spaces
Descriptions of newly constructed Off Broadway theatres. USA: New York, NY. 1984. Lang.: Eng. 644
Performance/production
Reviews of *Mummenschanz 'The New Show'*. USA: New York, NY. 1986. Lang.: Eng. 3298

Joyriders
Performance/production
Review of alternative theatre productions. UK-England: London. 1986. Lang.: Eng. 2108

Collection of newspaper reviews by London theatre critics. UK-England: London. 1986. Lang.: Eng. 2118

József Attila Szinház (Budapest)
Performance/production
A kis herceg (The Little Prince) by Antoine de Saint-Exupéry adapted and staged by Anna Belia and Péter Valló. Hungary: Budapest. 1985. Lang.: Hun. 1828

Stage adaptations of Dostojévskij novels *A Félkesgyelmű (The Idiot)* and *A Karamazov testvérek (The Brothers Karamazov)*. Hungary: Budapest, Debrecen. 1985. Lang.: Hun. 1922

A kis herceg (The Little Prince) by Saint-Exupéry adapted and staged by Anna Belia and Péter Valló. Hungary: Budapest. 1985. Lang.: Hun. 1935

József Katona Theatre
SEE
Katona József Szinház.

Józsefvárosi Szinház (Budapest)
Performance/production
Premiere of László Kolozsvári Papp's *Hazánk fiai (Sons of Our Country)*. Hungary: Budapest. 1985. Lang.: Hun. 1800

Notes on performances of *Hongkongi paróka (Wig Made in Hong Kong)*, *Egérút (Narrow Escape)* and *Róza néni (Aunt Rosa)*. Hungary: Budapest. 1985. Lang.: Hun. 1801

Performances of Sławomir Mrożek's *Mészárszék (The Slaughterhouse)* and *Ház a határon (The Home on the Border)*. Hungary: Budapest. 1986. Lang.: Hun. 1817

Rzeźnia (The Slaughterhouse) by Sławomir Mrożek, directed by Sándor Beke at Józsefvárosi Szinház under the title *Mészárszék*. Hungary: Budapest. 1985. Lang.: Hun. 1865

Mátyás Giricz directs *A kertész kutyája (The Gardener's Dog)* by Lope de Vega. Hungary: Budapest. 1985. Lang.: Hun. 1900

Reviews of *Margit kisasszony (Miss Margit)*, *Az Ibolya (The Violet)*, *Az Árny (The Ghost)* and *Róza néni (Aunt Rosa)*. Hungary: Budapest. 1985-1986. Lang.: Hun. 1916

Aleksej Dudarëv's *Večer (An Evening)* directed by Mátyas Giricz at Józsefvárosi Theatre. Hungary: Budapest. 1986. Lang.: Hun. 1947

Judy
Performance/production
Collection of newspaper reviews by London theatre critics. UK-England. 1986. Lang.: Eng. 2111

Jueces en la noche (Judges at Night)
Plays/librettos/scripts
Radical subjectivism in three plays by Antonio Buero Vallejo: *La Fundación (The Foundation)*, *La Detonación (The Detonation)* and *Jueces en la noche (Judges at Night)*. Spain. 1974-1979. Lang.: Eng. 2797

Juggling and Cheap Theatrics
Performance/production
Reviews of *Juggling and Cheap Theatrics* with the Flying Karamazov Brothers, staged by George Mosher. USA: New York, NY. 1986. Lang.: Eng. 3349

Juha
Performance/production
Interview with composer and director of the Finnish National opera Ilkka Kuusisto. Finland: Helsinki, Suomussalmi. 1967-1986. Lang.: Eng, Fre. 3724
Plays/librettos/scripts
Analysis of thematic trends in recent Finnish Opera. Finland: Helsinki, Savonlinna. 1909-1986. Lang.: Eng, Fre. 3865

Juhl, Jerry
Performance/production
Behind-the-scenes look at *Fraggle Rock*. Canada: Toronto, ON. 1984. Lang.: Eng. 3269

Juliani, John
Plays/librettos/scripts
Plays by women on the CBC radio network. Canada. 1985-1986. Lang.: Eng. 3185

Julius Caesar
Performance/production
Reconstruction of a number of Shakespeare plays staged and performed by Herbert Beerbohm Tree. UK-England: London. 1887-1917. Lang.: Eng. 2155
Plays/librettos/scripts
Translations of plays by William Shakespeare into Amharic and Tegrenna. Ethiopia: Addis Ababa. 1941-1984. Lang.: Eng. 2537

Junction Theatre (Australia)
Administration
Malcolm Blaylock on theatre and government funding policy. Australia. 1985. Lang.: Eng. 22

Jungbluth, Robert
Administration
Robert Jungbluth and his management of the Österreichische Bundestheater. Austria: Vienna. 1928-1986. Lang.: Ger. 25

Jungla sentimental, La (Sentimental Jungle, The)
Plays/librettos/scripts
Analysis of the six published dramatic works by Jordi Teixidor. Spain-Catalonia. 1970-1985. Lang.: Cat. 2809

Juno and the Paycock
Plays/librettos/scripts
Pessimism of Sean O'Casey's *Juno and the Paycock*. Eire. 1924. Lang.: Eng. 2457

Junona i Avos (Juno and Avos)
Performance/production
Director of Lenin Comsomol Theatre discusses theatre's history and repertory, Ribnikov's *Juno és Avosz (Juno and Avos)*. USSR: Moscow. 1927-1985. Lang.: Eng. 909

Plays by Ribnikov and Višnevskij performed by Moscow Theatre of Lenin Comsomal. USSR: Moscow. Hungary: Budapest. 1985. Lang.: Hun. 2329

Junyent i Sants, Oleguer
Design/technology
History of Catalan scenography. Spain-Catalonia. 200 B.C.-1986 A.D. Lang.: Cat. 311

Junyent i Sants, Oleguer — cont'd

Introduction to facsimile of Oleguer Junyent's set design for *L'Auca del senyor Esteve (Mr. Esteve's 'Auca')* by Santiago Rusiñol. Spain-Catalonia: Barcelona. 1861-1984. Lang.: Cat. 1518

Facsimile edition of scene design drawings by Oleguer Junyent for *L'auca del senyor Esteve (Mr. Esteve's 'Auca')* by Santiago Rusiñol. Spain-Catalonia: Barcelona. 1917. Lang.: Cat. 1519

Junyent, Sebastián
Performance/production
Production history of *Hay que deshacer la casa (Undoing the Housework)*, winner of Lope de Vega prize. Spain: Madrid. USA: Miami, FL. 1983-1985. Lang.: Eng. 2079

Jura Soyfer Theater (Vienna)
Institutions
The Jura Soyfer Theater and its plans for the 1986/87 season. Austria: Vienna. 1986. Lang.: Ger. 457

Jurskij, S.
Performance/production
Interview with actor-director S. Jurskij. USSR. 1986. Lang.: Rus. 2325

Jury, Charles
Plays/librettos/scripts
Analysis of plays by Charles Jury and Ray Mathew. Australia. 1905-1967. Lang.: Eng. 2384

Jus de Robin et Marion, Li (Play of Robin and Marion, The)
Performance/production
Descriptions of productions of *Li Jus de Robin et Marion (The Play of Robin and Marion)*, *The Comedy of Virtuous and Godly Susanna* and *The Second Shepherds Play*. USA: Washington, DC. UK-England: Lancaster. France: Perpignan. 1986. Lang.: Eng. 2289

Plays/librettos/scripts
Review essay on *Li jus de Robin et Marion (The Play of Robin and Marion)* directed by Jean Asselin. Canada: Montreal, PQ. 1986. Lang.: Fre. 937

Justification for the Bloodshed
SEE
Opravdanijė krovi.

K.K. Hoftheater (Vienna)
Performance spaces
Semper Depot and its history. Austria: Vienna. 1872-1986. Lang.: Ger. 583

K'o, Chung-p'ing
Performance/production
People's theatre groups in the provinces of Shansi, Kansu and Liaoning. China, People's Republic of. 1938-1940. Lang.: Chi. 1692

Kabale une Liebe (Love and Intrigue)
Theory/criticism
Analysis of Friedrich Schiller's dramatic and theoretical works. Germany. 1759-1805. Lang.: Cat. 3109

Kabuki
SEE ALSO
Classed Entries under DANCE-DRAMA—*Kabuki*: 1380-1382.

Basic theatrical documents
Text of *bunraku* play in English translation. Japan. 1760-1770. Lang.: Eng. 3996

Performance/production
Role of the mask in popular theatre. Japan. Africa. Europe. Lang.: Ita. 755

An outline formula of performance as derived from Asian theatre. Japan. 1363-1986. Lang.: Ita. 1364

Influence of *kata* principle on Western acting technique. Japan. Denmark. Australia. 1981-1986. Lang.: Ita. 1365

Essays on Japanese theatre. Japan. 1986. Lang.: Fre. 1398

Suzuki's SCOT fuses diverse world cultures in ensemble theatre company. Japan: Toga. 1985. Lang.: Eng. 1404

Reciprocal influences of French and Japanese theatre. France. Japan. 1900-1945. Lang.: Fre. 1750

Plays/librettos/scripts
Influences on Asian theatrical genres. Asia. 500-1985. Lang.: Eng. 920

Japanese influences on works of Brecht and Klabund. Germany. Japan. 1900-1950. Lang.: Ita. 952

Musical structure of dramas of Chikamatsu. Japan. 1653-1725. Lang.: Eng. 4000

Reference materials
Yearbook of major performances in all areas of Japanese theatre. Japan: Tokyo. 1986. Lang.: Jap. 1026

Dictionary of the life and work of Tsubouchi Shōyō. Japan: Tokyo. 1859-1986. Lang.: Jap. 1027

Theory/criticism
Development and characteristics of Oriental theatre. Korea: Seoul. Japan: Tokyo. China: Beijing. 200-1986. Lang.: Kor. 1215

Kabuki Daichō Kenkyūkai (Society for Kabuki, Tokyo)
Basic theatrical documents
Collection of *kabuki* texts. Japan: Tokyo. 1600-1980. Lang.: Jap. 1380

Kabwita, Philip
Relation to other fields
Theatrical nature of shamanistic rituals. Zambia. 1985. Lang.: Eng. 1183

Kachidze, D.
Performance/production
The staging of G. Kančeli's opera *Muzyka dlja živych (Music for the Living)* at the Z. Paliašvili theater. USSR: Tbilisi. 1980-1986. Lang.: Rus. 3848

Kadmon, Stella
Performance/production
History of the Viennese cabaret. Austria: Vienna. 1890-1945. Lang.: Ger. 3364

Kagura
Performance/production
Anthology of Japanese popular entertainments. Japan: Tokyo. 1986. Lang.: Jap. 3342

The popular entertainment of *Inadani* in Nagano province. Japan: Iida. 1986. Lang.: Jap. 3343

Kain
Plays/librettos/scripts
The church opera *Kain* written and composed for the Carinthiscer Sommer Festival. Austria: Ossiach. 1986. Lang.: Ger. 3858

Kainz, Josef
Performance/production
Playing Hamlet at the Burgtheater. Austria: Vienna. 1803-1985. Lang.: Ger. 1654

Kaiser, Georg
Plays/librettos/scripts
The role of the double in Georg Kaiser's *Zweimal Amphitryon (Amphitryon x 2)* and other works. Germany. 1943. Lang.: Eng. 2589

Analysis of *Der Silbersee* by Kurt Weill and Georg Kaiser. Germany: Leipzig. 1930-1933. Lang.: Eng. 3876

Kaiser, Herwig
Plays/librettos/scripts
Training for new playwrights in Austria. Austria: Vienna. 1985-1986. Lang.: Ger. 2392

Kalamazoo Civic Players (Kalamazoo, MI)
Administration
Fundraising strategies of various community theatres. USA. 1986. Lang.: Eng. 128

Kales, Elisabeth
Performance/production
Elisabeth Kales and her performance in the main role of Leo Fall's operetta *Madame Pompadour*. Austria: Vienna. 1955-1986. Lang.: Ger. 3484

Kalevala
Plays/librettos/scripts
Interview with opera composer Aulis Sallinen on his current work. Finland: Helsinki. 1975-1986. Lang.: Eng, Fre. 3866

Kalisky, René
Basic theatrical documents
Playtext of René Kalisky's *Sur les ruines de Carthage (On the Ruins of Carthage)* in English translation. Belgium. 1980. Lang.: Eng. 1462

Plays/librettos/scripts
Biography and bibliography of playwright René Kalisky. Belgium. 1936-1981. Lang.: Eng. 2401

Kallman, Chester
Plays/librettos/scripts
Auden and Kallman's English translation of *Die Zauberflöte (The Magic Flute)*. USA. 1951-1956. Lang.: Eng. 3903

Kalmar, Anni
Relation to other fields
Life and work of playwright and critic Karl Kraus. Austria: Vienna. 1874-1936. Lang.: Ger. 3017

Kamal Theatre
SEE
Tatarskij Gosudarstvėnnyj Akademičeskij Teat'r im. Kamala.

Kaméleon Szinházi Csoport (Kurd)
Performance/production
Experimental training method used by Kaméleon Szinház Csoport.
Hungary: Kurd. 1982-1985. Lang.: Hun. 1798

Kamernyj Muzykal'nyj Teat'r (Moscow)
Theory/criticism
Synthesis of the arts in the theatrical process. USSR: Moscow. 1986.
Lang.: Rus. 1240

Kamm, Tom
Performance/production
Interview with individuals involved in production of *Alcestis* by
Euripides. USA: Cambridge, MA. 1986. Lang.: Eng. 2266
Robert Wilson's production of *Alcestis* at the American Repertory
Theatre. USA: Cambridge, MA. 1986. 2306

Kammerspiele (Munich)
Performance/production
Director Dieter Dorn and his idea for staging *Der zerbrochene Krug
(The Broken Jug)*. Austria: Salzburg. Germany, West: Munich. 1986.
Lang.: Ger. 1651

Kan Chien Nu
Theory/criticism
Comparison of Chinese play, *Kan Chien Nu*, with plays of Molière.
China, People's Republic of: Beijing. 1970-1983. Lang.: Chi. 3568

Kanami
Performance/production
Novel about founders of *nō* theatre. Japan. 1357-1441. Lang.: Eng.
1397

Kančeli, G.
Performance/production
The staging of G. Kančeli's opera *Muzyka dlja živych (Music for the
Living)* at the Z. Paliašvili theater. USSR: Tbilisi. 1980-1986. Lang.:
Rus. 3848

Kantor, Tadeusz
Basic theatrical documents
Writings by Tadeusz Kantor on the nature of theatre. Poland. 1956-
1985. Lang.: Eng. 1490

Performance/production
Career and philosophy of director Tadeusz Kantor. Poland. 1915-
1985. Lang.: Eng. 2028
Interview with director Tadeusz Kantor. Poland. 1967-1985. Lang.:
Eng. 2029
Interview with director Tadeusz Kantor. Poland. 1942-1985. Lang.:
Hun. 2055
Tadeusz Kantor directs his *Gdzie sa Niegdysiejsze Śniegi (Where Are
the Snows of Yesteryear)*, Cricot 2. Poland: Cracow. 1984. Lang.:
Pol. 2061

Plays/librettos/scripts
Influence of politics and personal history on Tadeusz Kantor and his
Cricot 2 theatre company. Poland: Cracow. 1944-1986. Lang.: Eng.
2744
Tadeusz Kantor comments on his play *Niech szezna artyszi (Let the
Artists Die)*. Poland. 1985. Lang.: Eng, Fre. 2751
Analysis of the theatrical ideas of Tadeusz Kantor. Poland: Cracow.
1973-1983. Lang.: Pol. 2759

Reference materials
Writings by and about director Tadeusz Kantor. Poland. 1946-1986.
Lang.: Eng. 2995

Kanze
Performance/production
Novel about founders of *nō* theatre. Japan. 1357-1441. Lang.: Eng.
1397

Kanze, Hisao
Plays/librettos/scripts
Nō and Beckett compared. Japan. France. 1954-1986. Lang.: Ita.
2721

Kao, Tsecheng
Plays/librettos/scripts
Problems of adapting classic plays. China, People's Republic of.
1986. Lang.: Chi. 3543

Kapás, Dezső
Performance/production
David Rabe's play *Sticks and Bones* presented at the Pesti Theatre
in Hungary. Hungary: Budapest. 1971-1975. Lang.: Hun. 1799
Review of *Bünhődés (Punishment)*, a stage adaptation of *The Idiot*
by Dostojěvskij. Hungary: Budapest. Lang.: Hun. 1826

Kara, Jūrō
Plays/librettos/scripts
Lives and works of major contemporary playwrights in Japan.
Japan: Tokyo. 1900-1986. Lang.: Jap. 2719

Karajan, Herbert von
Institutions
History of the Salzburger Osterfestspiele. Austria: Salzburg. 1964-
1986. Lang.: Ger. 3666
Report on the Salzburger Osterfestspiele. Austria: Salzburg. 1986.
Lang.: Ger. 3669

Performance/production
Opera singer Ferruccio Furlanetto and his career. Austria: Salzburg.
Italy. 1946-1949. Lang.: Ger. 3698

Karamazov Brothers
SEE
Bratja Karamazov.

Karamazov Brothers, Flying
SEE
Flying Karamazov Brothers.

Karamu House Theatre (Cleveland, OH)
Institutions
Career of Marjorie Moon, artistic director of Billie Holliday Theatre.
USA: New York, NY, Cleveland, OH. 1973-1986. Lang.: Eng. 1610

Performance/production
Career of director/choreographer Mike Malone. USA: Washington,
DC, Cleveland, OH. 1968-1985. Lang.: Eng. 2275

Karamzin, Nikolaj M.
Plays/librettos/scripts
Western European influences on playwright Nikolaj M. Karamzin.
Russia. 1766-1826. Lang.: Rus. 965

Karandasch
Theory/criticism
Solipsism, expressionism and aesthetics in the anti-rational dramas of
Gottfried Benn. Germany: Berlin. 1914-1934. Lang.: Eng. 3107

Karelina, G.
Performance/production
Interview about the acting profession with T. Zabozlaeva and G.
Karelina. USSR. 1986. Lang.: Rus. 859

Karimkutty
Basic theatrical documents
Text of *Karimkutty* by K. N. Panikkar in English translation. India.
1983. Lang.: Eng. 1355

Kartoteka (Card Index)
Performance/production
Michał Ratyński directs Różewicz's *Kartoteka (Card Index)*, Teatr
Powszechny. Poland: Warsaw. 1984. Lang.: Pol. 2062

Kasan ogwangdae (Five Buffoons of Kasan, The)
Basic theatrical documents
Text of *Kasan ogwangdae (The Five Buffoons of Kasan)* in English
translation. Korea: Kasan. 1975. Lang.: Eng. 1356

Kasatkina, N.D.
Performance/production
Artistic directors of Soviet Ballet Theatre on plans for the future.
USSR: Moscow. 1980-1985. Lang.: Rus. 1318

Kassius, Katinka
Institutions
Recent outdoor productions of Gamla Stans Teater. Sweden:
Stockholm. 1933-1986. Lang.: Swe. 524

Kästner, Erich
Performance/production
Stage adaptation of Erich Kästner's novel *Emil und die Detektive
(Emil and the Detectives)* directed by István Keleti. Hungary:
Budapest. 1986. Lang.: Hun. 1807

Kata
Performance/production
Influence of *kata* principle on Western acting technique. Japan.
Denmark. Australia. 1981-1986. Lang.: Ita. 1365

Katari
Performance/production
Narrator in *Katari* story-telling tradition. Japan. 1960-1983. Lang.:
Eng. 1366

Katerina Ismailova
Plays/librettos/scripts
History and aesthetics of Soviet opera. USSR: Moscow. 1917-1941.
Lang.: Ger. 3905

Kathakali
Performance/production
Interview with Peter Brook's designer, musician, and costumer for
Mahabharata. France: Avignon. 1973-1985. Lang.: Eng. 1359

Kathakali — cont'd

Interviews with actors in Peter Brook's *Mahabharata*. France: Avignon. 1985. Lang.: Eng.   1360

Peter Brook discusses development of *The Mahabharata*. France: Avignon. India. 1965-1986. Lang.: Eng.   1361

Kathie y el hippótamo (Kathy and the Hippopotamus)

Plays/librettos/scripts

Interview with author and playwright Mario Vargas Llosa. Argentina. 1952-1986. Lang.: Spa.   2361

Katie Roche

Plays/librettos/scripts

Biography of playwright Teresa Deevy. Ireland. 1894-1963. Lang.: Eng.   2665

Katona József Szinház (Budapest)

Performance/production

Review of Ivan Kušan's musical comedy *Čaruga (Death Cap)*, directed by Miklós Benedek, Katona József Theatre, as *Galócza*, includes discussion of acting and dramatic art. Hungary: Budapest. 1986. Lang.: Hun.   1811

Čechov's *Három nővér (Three Sisters)* directed by Tamás Ascher. Hungary: Budapest. 1985. Lang.: Hun.   1814

Notes on *Čaruga (Death Cap)*, by Ivan Kušan, directed by Miklós Benedek, Katona József Theatre, under the title *Galócza*. Hungary: Budapest. 1986. Lang.: Hun.   1890

Two productions of Čechov's *Három Nővér (Three Sisters)*. Hungary: Zalaegerszeg, Budapest. 1985. Lang.: Hun.   1903

Tamás Ascher directs Čechov's *Tri sestry (Three Sisters)* at Katona József Theatre under the title *Három nővér*. Hungary: Budapest. 1985. Lang.: Hun.   1914

Comparison of two Hungarian productions of *Háram nővér (Three Sisters)* by Anton Pavlovič Čechov. Hungary: Budapest, Zalaegerszeg. 1985. Lang.: Hun.   1964

Production analysis of *Ubu roi* by Alfred Jarry staged for the first time in Hungary by Gábor Zsámbéki at the József Katona Theatre. Hungary: Budapest. 1984. Lang.: Hun.   1969

Melyrepülés (Flying at Low Altitude) by Tamás Cseh and Dénes Csengey. Hungary: Budapest. 1986. Lang.: Hun.   3487

Reviews of three musicals about the 1960s. Hungary. 1985-1986. Lang.: Hun.   3488

Katona, Imre

Performance/production

Performances of *Alice Csodaországban (Alice in Wonderland)*, *A Két Veronai nemes (The Two Gentlemen of Verona)* and *Tobbsincs királyfi (No More Crown Prince)*. Hungary: Pécs, Budapest. 1985. Lang.: Hun.   1771

Interview with actor, director and dramaturg Imre Katona of the Gropius Társulat. Hungary: Budapest. 1961-1985. Lang.: Hun.   1945

Katona, József

Performance/production

Review of József Katona's *Bánk Bán* directed by János Ács at Szigligeti Szinház. Hungary: Szolnok. 1986. Lang.: Hun.   1876

Bánk Bán by József Katona at Szigligeti Theatre directed by János Ács. Hungary: Szolnok. 1986. Lang.: Hun.   1884

József Katona's *Bánk Bán* presented by the Hanoi Tuong Theatre directed by Doan Anh Thang. Vietnam: Hanoi. 1986. Lang.: Hun.   2340

Plays/librettos/scripts

Analysis of the characters of *Bánk Bán* by József Katona. Lang.: Hun.   2351

Analysis of László Németh's study of *Bánk Bán* by József Katona and a portrait of the playwright. Hungary. 1985. Lang.: Hun.   2647

Plot, structure and national character of *Bánk Bán* by József Katona. Hungary. Lang.: Hun.   2655

Kaukasische Kreidekreis, Der (Caucasian Chalk Circle, The)

Institutions

Work of the Berliner Ensemble group. Germany, East: Berlin, East. 1930-1986. Lang.: Eng.   1578

Performance/production

Director John Ahart discusses staging *The Caucasian Chalk Circle*. USA: Urbana, IL. 1984.   2278

Robert Sturua of Georgian Academic Theatre directs Brecht and Shakespeare in Warsaw. USSR: Tbilisi. Poland: Warsaw. 1983. Lang.: Pol.   2336

Plays/librettos/scripts

Bertolt Brecht and the Expressionists. Germany. 1919-1944. Lang.: Eng.   955

Demystification of the feminine myth in Brecht's plays. Germany, East. 1984.   2618

Kaupunginteatteri (Helsinki)

SEE

Helsingin Kaupunginteatteri.

Kavin, Ludvik

Institutions

Program of Theater Brett for the 1986/87 season. Austria: Vienna. 1986-1987. Lang.: Ger.   3288

Kaye, Danny

Performance/production

Biography of actor Danny Kaye. USA: New York, NY. 1912-1985. Lang.: Eng.   2265

Kaynar, Gad

Basic theatrical documents

Text of *Eiolf Hakatan*, Gad Kaynar's Hebrew translation of *Lille Eyolf (Little Eyolf)* by Henrik Ibsen. Norway. Israel. 1884-1985. Lang.: Heb.   1489

Kaza no Ko (Tokyo)

Institutions

Report on International Festival of Theatre for Young Audiences. Canada. Japan. 1985. Lang.: Fre.   482

Kazan, Elia

Performance/production

Directorial process as seen through major productions of Stanislavskij, Brecht, Kazan and Brook. 1898-1964. Lang.: Eng.   650

Collaboration of Tennessee Williams and Elia Kazan. Australia. Lang.: Eng.   1637

Plays/librettos/scripts

Analysis of *A View From the Bridge* by Arthur Miller. USA: New York, NY. UK-England: London. 1915-1985. Lang.: Cat.   2901

Kaze-no-Ko Theatre Company (Japan)

Institutions

The Kaze-no-Ko: professional travelling children's theatre of Japan. Japan. 1950-1984. Lang.: Eng.   507

Kazimir, Károly

Institutions

Recollections of director Károly Kazimir, of Körszinház. Hungary: Budapest. 1958-1986. Lang.: Hun.   501

Performance/production

Review of *Alkony (Sunset)* by Isaak Babel, directed by Károly Kazimir at Thália Szinház. Hungary: Budapest. 1985. Lang.: Hun.   1806

János Pelle's *Casanova* directed by Károly Kazimir at the Körszinház. Hungary: Budapest. 1986. Lang.: Hun.   1846

Alkony (Sunset) by Isaak Babel, directed by Károly Kazimir at Thália Szinház. Hungary: Budapest. 1985. Lang.: Hun.   1850

Criticizes stage adaptation of *Hangok komédiája (Comedy of Sounds)* by Miklós Gyárfás. Hungary: Budapest. 1985. Lang.: Hun.   1924

János Pelle's *Casanova* directed by Károly Kazimir at Körszinház. Hungary: Budapest. 1986. Lang.: Hun.   1929

Kean, Charles

Design/technology

Charles Kean's period production of Shakespeare's *Richard III*. UK-England: London. 1857. Lang.: Eng.   1525

Performance/production

Profile of actor-entrepeneur George Coppin. Canada: Victoria, BC. 1864. Lang.: Eng.   1666

Keats, John

Relation to other fields

Influence of Mozart's operas on the 'Cockney' school of writers. England: London. 1760-1840. Lang.: Eng.   3916

Keene, Laura

Relation to other fields

Professional equality in theatrical careers for men and women. USA: New York, NY. 1850-1870. Lang.: Eng.   1143

Kegyenc, A (Favorite, The)

Performance/production

Review of László Teleki's *A Kegyenc (The Favorite)* as directed by József Ruszt, Hevesi Sándor Theatre. Hungary: Zalaegerszeg. 1986. Lang.: Hun.   1867

Review of László Teleki's *A Kegyenc (The Favorite)* directed by József Ruszt. Hungary: Zalaegerszeg. 1986. Lang.: Hun.   1891

A kegyenc (The Favorite) by Gyula Illyés, directed by János Sándor, National Theatre of Miskolc. Hungary: Miskolc. 1985. Lang.: Hun.   1971

Killigrew, Thomas — cont'd

Plays/librettos/scripts
Female characterization in Nicholas Rowe's plays. England. 1629-1720. Lang.: Eng.   2475

Kilpinen, Inkeri
Basic theatrical documents
Text of Inkeri Kilpinen's *Totisesti totisesti (Verily Verily)* in English translation. Finland. 1982-1983. Lang.: Eng, Fin.   1476

Kim, Cheol-Li
Performance/production
Directing and the current state of Korean theatre. Korea. 1986. Lang.: Kor.   760

Kim, Woo-Jin
Institutions
History of Korea's first theatre production company. Korea: Seoul. 1922-1924. Lang.: Kor.   509

Theory/criticism
Theatre criticism of Kim Woo-Jin. Korea: Seoul. 1920-1929. Lang.: Kor.   1216

King and No King
Plays/librettos/scripts
Passion in early plays of Beaumont and Fletcher. England. 1608-1611. Lang.: Eng.   945

King Goes Forth to France, The
SEE
Kuningas lähtee Ranskaan.

King John
Performance/production
Reconstruction of a number of Shakespeare plays staged and performed by Herbert Beerbohm Tree. UK-England: London. 1887-1917. Lang.: Eng.   2155

Plays/librettos/scripts
An appraisal of David Garrick's adaptation of Shakespeare's *King John*. England: London. 1736-1796. Lang.: Eng.   2510

King Lear
Institutions
Erwin Piscator's work at the Dramatic Workshop of the New School for Social Research. USA: New York, NY. 1939-1951. Lang.: Ger.   1600

Performance/production
Innovative Shakespeare stagings of Harley Granville-Barker. UK-England. 1912-1940. Lang.: Eng.   806
Changing attitudes toward madness reflected in David Garrick's adaptation of Shakespeare's *King Lear*. England. 1680-1779. Lang.: Eng.   1715
Comparison of stage production and film version of Shakespeare's *King Lear*, both directed by Peter Brook. UK-England. 1962-1970. Lang.: Eng.   2149
Actor Laurence Olivier's memoirs. UK-England: London. USA: New York, NY. 1907-1986. Lang.: Eng.   2170
Attempt to produce Quarto version of *King Lear* at University of Rochester. USA: Rochester, NY. 1985. Lang.: Eng.   2300
Self-referential elements in several film versions of Shakespeare's *King Lear*. UK. USA. 1916-1983. Lang.: Eng.   3227

Plays/librettos/scripts
Blessing and cursing in Shakespeare's *King Lear*. England. 1605-1606. Lang.: Eng.   2466
Semiotic analysis of Shakespeare's *King Lear*. England: London. 1605-1606. Lang.: Eng.   2467
Similarities between *King Lear* by Shakespeare and *The Trimphs of Reunited Britannia* by Munday. England. 1605-1606. Lang.: Eng.   2480
Critics and directors on Shakespeare's *King Lear*. England. 1605. Lang.: Ita.   2530
Text of a lecture on Shakespeare's *King Lear* by Clifford Davidson. Hungary: Budapest. Lang.: Hun.   2643

Theory/criticism
Ingmar Bergman production of *King Lear* and Asian influences. Spain-Catalonia: Barcelona. 1985. Lang.: Eng.   1219

King of Spain's Daughter, The
Plays/librettos/scripts
Biography of playwright Teresa Deevy. Ireland. 1894-1963. Lang.: Eng.   2665

King Shotaway
Plays/librettos/scripts
Precursors of revolutionary black theatre. Haiti. Jamaica. 1820-1970. Lang.: Eng.   956

King Stephen
SEE
István, a király.

King, Charmion
Basic theatrical documents
A collection of satirical monologues by playwright Corey Reay. Canada. Lang.: Eng.   1471

King, Joan
Performance/production
Tour of puppet show *The Return of the Bounce* by Jean Mattson and Joan King. USA: Seattle, WA. Japan. 1984. Lang.: Eng.   3979

King, Woodie, Jr.
Administration
Alternative funding for small theatres previously dependent on government subsidy. USA: St. Louis, MO, New York, NY, Los Angeles, CA, Detroit, MI. 1985. Lang.: Eng.   103
Institutions
History of two major Black touring companies. USA: New York, NY. 1969-1982. Lang.: Eng.   1598
Plays/librettos/scripts
Interview with playwright Lorraine Hansberry. USA. 1959. Lang.: Eng.   2945

King's Company (London)
Administration
Account of grievance petition by Opera House performers. England: London. 1799. Lang.: Eng.   34
Basic theatrical documents
Transcription of manuscript assigning shares in the King's Company. England. 1661-1684. Lang.: Eng.   220
Prompt markings on a copy of James Shirley's *Loves Crueltie* performed by the King's Company. England: London. 1660-1669. Lang.: Eng.   1475
Performance/production
Career of actress Elizabeth Bowtell, who first acted under her maiden name of Davenport. England. 1664-1715. Lang.: Eng.   1706
Restoration era cast lists of the King's Company. England: London. 1660-1708. Lang.: Eng.   1711
Plays/librettos/scripts
Cast lists in James Shirley's *Six New Playes* suggest popularity of plays. England. 1653-1669. Lang.: Eng.   2504

King's Head Theatre (London)
Performance spaces
Overview of pub theatres. UK-England: London. 1980-1987. Lang.: Eng.   626
Performance/production
Collection of newspaper reviews by London theatre critics. UK-England: London. 1986. Lang.: Eng.   2109
Collection of newspaper reviews by London theatre critics. UK-England: London. 1986. Lang.: Eng.   2119

King's Playhouse (Georgetown, PE)
Institutions
Development of community-based theatre on Prince Edward Island. Canada. 1981-1986. Lang.: Eng.   1556

King's Theatre (London)
Administration
Royal theatrical patronage during the reign of George II. England: London. 1727-1760. Lang.: Eng.   33

Kingsley, Ben
Performance/production
Actors Ben Kingsley and David Suchet discuss their roles in Shakespeare's *Othello*. UK-England. 1986. Lang.: Eng.   2128

Kingsley, Sidney
Plays/librettos/scripts
Remarks on Alan Jay Lerner at his memorial service. USA: New York, NY. 1986.   3630

Kirby, Michael
Theory/criticism
Michael Kirby defends the liberal outlook of *The Drama Review*. USA. 1971-1986. Lang.: Eng.   1232

Kirov Ballet
SEE
Akademičeskij Teat'r Opery i Baleta im. S. M. Kirova.

Kirov Opera
SEE
Akademičeskij Teat'r Opery i Baleta im. S. M. Kirova.

Kirov Theatre (Leningrad)
SEE
Akademičeskij Teat'r Opery i Baleta im. S. M. Kirova.

Kirsten, Dorothy
Performance/production
Famous sopranos discuss their interpretations of Tosca. USA. 1935-1986. Lang.: Eng.   3811

Kisfaludy Szinház (Győr)
Performance/production
Production by György Emöd of Friedrich Dürrenmatt's *A Öreg hölgy látogatása (The Visit)*. Hungary: Győr. 1985. Lang.: Hun. 1788
József Bor directs Verdi's opera *Il Trovatore* at Kisfaludy Theatre. Hungary: Győr. 1985. Lang.: Hun.   3750

Kisfaludy Szinház Kamaraszínháza (Győr)
Performance/production
Ágyrajárók (Night Lodgers) by Péter Szántó, directed by György Emöd at Kisfaludy Studio Theatre. Hungary: Győr. 1985. Lang.: Hun.   1854

Kisvárdai Várszinház (Kisvárda)
Performance/production
Sip a tökre (Play a Trump in Diamonds) by Péter Tömöry, directed by Imre Halasi. Hungary: Kisvárda. 1986. Lang.: Hun.   1859

Kitashichidayū, Nagayoshi
Performance/production
Career of *nō* artist Kitashichidayū Nagayoshi. Japan. Lang.: Jap.   1407

Kitchen, The
Plays/librettos/scripts
Utopia in early plays by Arnold Wesker. UK-England. 1958-1970. Lang.: Eng.   2884

Kitchen, The (New York, NY)
Performance spaces
Alternative performance spaces for experimental theatre and dance works. USA: New York, NY. 1984. Lang.: Eng.   640

Kite, The
Plays/librettos/scripts
Structure and characterization in the plays of W.O. Mitchell. Canada. 1975. Lang.: Eng.   2408

Kiviette (Kiviat, Y.S.)
Reference materials
Catalogue of an exhibition of costume designs for Broadway musicals. USA: New York, NY. 1900-1925. Lang.: Eng, Ger.   3635

Kiyotsune
Design/technology
Nō actors make interpretive costume choices. Japan.   1386

Klabund (Henschke, Alfred)
Plays/librettos/scripts
Japanese influences on works of Brecht and Klabund. Germany. Japan. 1900-1950. Lang.: Ita.   952
Influence of Japanese drama on the works of Klabund. Germany. 1890-1928. Lang.: Ita.   954

Kleines Festspielhaus (Salzburg)
Institutions
Concept and program for the Salzburger Festspiele in 1987. Austria: Salzburg. 1986. Lang.: Ger.   451

Performance spaces
Remodeling the stage at the Kleines Festspielhaus. Austria: Salzburg. 1986. Lang.: Ger.   582

Kleist, Heinrich von
Performance/production
Director Dieter Dorn and his idea for staging *Der zerbrochene Krug (The Broken Jug)*. Austria: Salzburg. Germany, West: Munich. 1986. Lang.: Ger.   1651
Ottó Ádám directs *Egy lócsiszár virágvasárnapja (The Palm Sunday of a Horse Dealer)* by András Sütő after Kleist. Hungary: Budapest. 1986. Lang.: Hun.   1843
Reviews of *Olympus On My Mind* based on *Amphitryon*, by Heinrich von Kleist, staged by Barry Harmon. USA: New York, NY. 1986. Lang.: Eng.   2218

Plays/librettos/scripts
Social themes in the dramas of Franz Grillparzer. Austro-Hungarian Empire: Vienna. 1791-1872. Lang.: Ger.   2399
The idea of grace in the life and work of Heinrich von Kleist. Germany. 1777-1811. Lang.: Eng.   2593
The tragic in plays of Heinrich von Kleist. Germany. 1777-1811. Lang.: Rus.   2601

Relation to other fields
Translation of works on puppetry by Heinrich von Kleist. Germany. 1810-1811. Lang.: Ita.   4012

Klimt, Gustav
Relation to other fields
Influence of political and artistic movements on composer Alban Berg. Austria: Vienna. 1894-1935. Lang.: Eng.   3914

Klingenberg, Fritz
History of the Theater für Vorarlberg. Austria: Bregenz. 1818-1986. Lang.: Ger.   3

Klinger, Friedrich Maximilian
Plays/librettos/scripts
Analysis of *Die Zwillinge (The Twins)* by Friedrich Maximilian Klinger and the dilemma of the *Sturm und Drang* movement. Germany. 1775. Lang.: Ger.   2609

Klotz, Florence
Design/technology
Designers discuss regional productions of *Side-by-Side by Sondheim*. USA. 1984. Lang.: Eng.   3593

Knebel, Maria Osipovna
Institutions
Reminiscences of study at Moscow Art Theatre. USSR. Lang.: Rus.   578

Knight of the Burning Pestle, The
Plays/librettos/scripts
Use of language in Beaumont and Fletcher's *Philaster*. England. 1609. Lang.: Eng.   2512

Knight, G. Wilson
Plays/librettos/scripts
Modern criticism of Shakespeare's crowd scenes. England. 1590-1986. Lang.: Eng.   2536

Knock ou triomphe de la médecine (Doctor Knock, or the Triumph of Medicine)
Performance/production
Knock by Jules Romains directed by Gábor Máté at Csiky Gergely Theatre. Hungary: Kaposvár. 1986. Lang.: Hun.   1892

Ko-omote
Design/technology
The aesthetic qualities of the Yuki *no ko-omote* mask. Japan. Lang.: Eng.   1388
Characteristics of different *nō* masks. Japan. Lang.: Eng.   1392
Carving techniques used in making the *ko-omote* mask. Japan. Lang.: Eng.   1394

Kočergin, E.
Design/technology
Scene designer E. Kočergin discusses his work. USSR. 1986. Lang.: Rus.   431

Kocsis, István
Plays/librettos/scripts
Monodramas of playwright István Kocsis. Romania. Hungary. 1976-1984. Lang.: Hun.   2761

Koenig, Rachel
Plays/librettos/scripts
Interview with playwright Kathleen Betsko. England: Coventry. USA. 1960-1986. Lang.: Eng.   2487

Koenigsmark, Alex
Performance/production
Review of Alex Koenigsmark's *Adié, milacku! (Good-bye, Darling!)* directed by Péter Gothár at Csiky Gergely Theatre under the title *Agyő, kedvesem*. Hungary: Kaposvár. 1985. Lang.: Hun.   1862
Péter Gothár directs *Agyő, kedvesem (Goodbye, Darling!)* by Alex Koenigsmark, at Csiky Gergely Theatre. Hungary: Kaposvár. 1985. Lang.: Hun.   1894

Kohout, Pavel
Plays/librettos/scripts
Interview with playwright, director and actor Pavel Kohout. Czechoslovakia: Prague. Austria: Vienna. 1928-1986. Lang.: Swe. 2454

Kokkonen, Joonas
Performance/production
Interview with composer and director of the Finnish National opera Ilkka Kuusisto. Finland: Helsinki, Suomussalmi. 1967-1986. Lang.: Eng, Fre.   3724

Plays/librettos/scripts
Analysis of thematic trends in recent Finnish Opera. Finland: Helsinki, Savonlinna. 1909-1986. Lang.: Eng, Fre.   3865

Kokoschka, Oskar
Reference materials
Costumes of famous Viennese actors. Austria: Vienna. 1831-1960. Lang.: Ger.   1003

Kott, Jan
Performance/production
Feminist criticism of theatre anthropology conference on women's roles. USA. Denmark. 1985. Lang.: Eng. 845

Kotzebue, August von
Institutions
Views of Parisian theatre from the journals of August von Kotzebue. France: Paris. Germany. 1790-1804. Lang.: Eng. 496

Plays/librettos/scripts
Biography of playwright August von Kotzebue. Germany: Weimar. Russia: St. Petersburg. 1761-1819. Lang.: Ger. 2596

Kovacs, Ernie
Performance/production
Autobiography of actor Alec Guinness. UK. USA. 1914-1985. Lang.: Eng. 2106

Kövary, Andreas
Plays/librettos/scripts
Training for new playwrights in Austria. Austria: Vienna. 1985-1986. Lang.: Ger. 2392

Kovidor
Plays/librettos/scripts
The influence of Brecht on Haiti's exiled playwright Frank Fouché and the group Kovidor. Haiti. 1970-1979. 2638

Kozakov, M.
Performance/production
Actor discusses work in recitation programs. USSR: Moscow. 1980-1986. Lang.: Rus. 888

Interpretation of classics for theatre and television. USSR. 1980-1986. Lang.: Rus. 2337

Kozintsev, Grigori
Performance/production
Self-referential elements in several film versions of Shakespeare's *King Lear*. UK. USA. 1916-1983. Lang.: Eng. 3227

Kozlik, Al
Institutions
The first decade of White Rock Summer Theatre in British Columbia. Canada: White Rock, BC. 1976-1985. Lang.: Eng. 1560

Kozma
Performance/production
Piroska Molnár's performance in *Kozma* by Mihály Kornis. Hungary: Kaposvár. 1986. Lang.: Hun. 1796

János Ács directs *Kozma* by Mihály Kornis. Hungary: Kaposvár. 1986. Lang.: Hun. 1874

Kozma by Mihály Kornis directed by János Ács, Csiky Gergely Szinház. Hungary: Kaposvár. 1986. Lang.: Hun. 1885

Kramer, Kenneth
Plays/librettos/scripts
Rex Deverell's approach to history in plays about Louis Riel. Canada: Regina, SK. 1985. Lang.: Eng. 2437

Kramer, Larry
Performance/production
Collection of newspaper reviews by London theatre critics. UK-England: London. 1986. Lang.: Eng. 2126

Overview of performances transferred from The Royal Court, Greenwich, and Lyric Hammersmith theatres. UK-England: London. 1986. Lang.: Eng. 2143

Plays/librettos/scripts
Overview of plays with homosexual themes. UK-England: London. 1970-1986. Lang.: Eng. 2841

Progress in audience perception of gay characters in plays. USA. 1933-1985. Lang.: Eng. 2909

Krapp's Last Tape
Performance/production
András Matkócsik directs *Mondd, Joe!* (*Eh, Joe!*) and *Az utlosó tekercs* (*Krapp's Last Tape*) by Samuel Beckett. Hungary: Budapest. 1985. Lang.: Hun. 1851

Beckett's direction of *Krapp's Last Tape* at San Quentin Drama Workshop. USA. 1985. Lang.: Hun. 2279

Krasiński, Zygmunt
Performance/production
Mikołaj Grabowski directs *Irydion* by Zygmunt Krasiński. Poland: Cracow. 1983. Lang.: Pol. 2046

Plays/librettos/scripts
Different interpretations of Zygmunt Krasiński's *Ne-boska komedia* (*Undivine Comedy*). Poland. 1835-1984. Lang.: Fre. 2756

Krasowski, Jerzy
Performance/production
Jerzy Krasowski of Teatr Mały directs Ryszard Frelka's *Jalta* (*Yalta*). Poland: Warsaw. 1984. Lang.: Pol. 2048

Krauliz, Alf
Institutions
The Festival of Clowns in the Wiener Festwochen. Austria: Vienna. 1983-1986. Lang.: Ger. 3380

Kraus, Heinrich
Administration
Manager Heinrich Kraus and his work. Austria: Vienna. 1930-1986. Lang.: Ger. 1426

Kraus, Irena
Plays/librettos/scripts
Interview with Irena Kraus about her play *Lilla livet* (*The Little Life*), based on *La vida es sueño* (*Life Is a Dream*) by Calderón. Sweden: Malmö. 1985-1986. Lang.: Swe. 2824

Kraus, Karl
Performance/production
History of the Viennese cabaret. Austria: Vienna. 1890-1945. Lang.: Ger. 3364

Plays/librettos/scripts
Difficulties in French translation of Karl Kraus's *Die Letzten Tage der Menschheit* (*The Last Days of Mankind*). Austria: Vienna. France: Paris. 1918-1986. Lang.: Ger. 2397

Reference materials
Exhibition catalogue about context of the work and influence of Karl Kraus. Austria: Vienna. USA: New York, NY. France: Paris. 1874-1986. Lang.: Ger. 2980

Relation to other fields
Karl Kraus, a reflection of Viennese culture and literature history. Austria: Vienna. 1874-1936. Lang.: Ger. 3014

Collection of obituary notes for the critic and dramatist Karl Kraus. Austria: Vienna. 1933-1937. Lang.: Ger. 3015

Life and work of playwright and critic Karl Kraus. Austria: Vienna. 1874-1936. Lang.: Ger. 3017

Study on the reception of critic and playwright Karl Kraus in Italy. Italy. Austria: Vienna. 1911-1985. Lang.: Ger. 3044

The reception of critic and playwright Karl Kraus in the English speaking world. USA: New York, NY. Austria: Vienna. UK-Scotland: Glasgow. 1909-1985. Lang.: Ger. 3067

Influence of political and artistic movements on composer Alban Berg. Austria: Vienna. 1894-1935. Lang.: Eng. 3914

Kreis, Der (Vienna)
Institutions
On concept of the new group, Der Kreis. Austria: Vienna. 1986-1987. Lang.: Ger. 1536

Kreuzweg (Crossroads)
Basic theatrical documents
Text of two plays about refugees in Switzerland. Switzerland: Bern. 1933-1985. Lang.: Ger. 1505

Kroetz, Franz Xaver
Performance/production
Adaptation of Kroetz's *Wunschkonzert* (*Request Concert*). India: Calcutta, Madras, Bombay. Lang.: Eng. 1975

Life and technique of Franz Xaver Kroetz. USA: New York, NY. Germany, West. 1984. Lang.: Eng. 2287

Plays/librettos/scripts
Characterization in *Furcht und Hoffnung der BRD* (*Help Wanted*) by Franz Xaver Kroetz. Germany, West. 1984-1986. Lang.: Eng. 2623

Kronik, John
Plays/librettos/scripts
Use of language in *El Gesticulador* (*The Gesticulator*) by Rodolfo Usigli. Mexico. 1970-1980. Lang.: Spa. 2723

Kruczkowski, Leon
Plays/librettos/scripts
Analysis of plays of Kruczkowski, Szaniawski and Gałczyński. Poland. 1940-1949. Lang.: Pol. 2746

Krull, Annie
Performance/production
Reviews of 10 vintage recordings of complete operas on LP. USA. 1906-1925. Lang.: Eng. 3792

Kruse, Max
Design/technology
Contribution of designer Ernst Stern to modern scenography. Germany: Berlin. UK-England: London. 1905. Lang.: Eng. 1516

Kuumba Theater (Chicago, IL)
Administration
Growing activity and changing role of Black regional theatre companies. USA. 1960-1984. Lang.: Eng. 1440

Kuusisto, Ilkaa
Performance/production
Interview with composer and director of the Finnish National opera Ilkka Kuusisto. Finland: Helsinki, Suomussalmi. 1967-1986. Lang.: Eng, Fre. 3724

Kvapil, Jaroslav
Performance/production
Technical innovation, scenography and cabaret in relation to political and social conditions. Czechoslovakia. 1781-1986. Lang.: Eng. 1697

Kwaskowski, Stanisław
Relation to other fields
Actor Stanisław Kwaskowski talks about the first years of independent Poland. Poland. 1918-1920. Lang.: Pol. 1121

Kwong, Leong Chan
Performance/production
Chinese theatre companies on the Goldfields of Victoria. Australia. 1858-1870. Lang.: Eng. 1641

Kyd, Thomas
Performance/production
Reconstruction of staging of Act I, *The Spanish Tragedy* by Thomas Kyd. England: London. 1592. Lang.: Eng. 1703

Plays/librettos/scripts
Bullfighting and revenge in *The Spanish Tragedy* by Thomas Kyd. England. 1500-1600. Lang.: Eng. 2458

Connection between character Senex in Thomas Kyd's *The Spanish Tragedy* and Senecan drama. England. 1587. Lang.: Eng. 2473

Tradition and individualism in Renaissance drama. England: London. 1575-1600. Lang.: Eng. 2496

Kyōgen
Basic theatrical documents
Kyōgen: history, training, and promotion. Japan. 1060-1982. Lang.: Eng. 1384

Design/technology
The development of *nō* and *kyōgen* masks and the concerns of the mask carver. Japan. 1390

Performance/production
A production of *At the Hawk's Well* using *nō* techniques. Japan: Kyoto, Tokyo. 1984. 1981-1982. 1396

Novel about founders of *nō* theatre. Japan. 1357-1441. Lang.: Eng. 1397

Kyōgen actor on the difference between *nō* and *kyōgen*. Japan. 1406

The *kyōgen* actor's goals, relationship to mask work and training. Japan. 1984. 1409

Introduction to *nō* and *kyōgen*. Japan. 1412

Special performances of *kyōgen* presented at the Mibu Temple. Japan: Kyoto. Lang.: Jap. 1414

Nō and *kyōgen* influences on interpretation of *Antigone*. USA: San Francisco, CA. 1984. 1978-1984. 1416

Performing the *kyōgen* play *Shimizu* in English. USA. 1984. 1417

Interview with individuals involved in production of *Alcestis* by Euripides. USA: Cambridge, MA. 1986. Lang.: Eng. 2266

Plays/librettos/scripts
A study of the *ai-kyōgen* texts in the Okura school. Japan. 1600-1800. Lang.: Jap. 1418

Reference materials
Yearbook of major performances in all areas of Japanese theatre. Japan: Tokyo. 1986. Lang.: Jap. 1026

Dictionary of the life and work of Tsubouchi Shōyō. Japan: Tokyo. 1859-1986. Lang.: Jap. 1027

Theory/criticism
Various aspects of *kyōgen*. Japan. 1300-1986. Lang.: Jap. 1422

L.O.V.E.
Relation to other fields
Black history and folklore taught in theatre workshops and productions. USA: New York, NY, Omaha, NE, Washington, DC. 1986. Lang.: Eng. 3068

L.S.D.
Performance/production
Wooster Group retrospective of original works. USA: New York, NY. 1975-1986. Lang.: Eng. 850

L'vov-Anochin, B.
Theory/criticism
Synthesis of the arts in the theatrical process. USSR: Moscow. 1986. Lang.: Rus. 1240

La Fenice (Venice)
SEE
Teatro La Fenice.

La Mama (New York, NY)
Institutions
The few New York theatres that promote international plays and companies. USA: New York, NY. 1986. Lang.: Eng. 561

La Scala
SEE
Teatro alla Scala.

Laban, Rudolf
Relation to other fields
Refugee artists from Nazi Germany in Britain. UK-England. Germany. 1937-1947. Lang.: Eng. 1135

Labelle, Elzéar
Basic theatrical documents
Musical setting for operetta *La conversion d'un pêcheur de la Nouvelle-Écosse (The Conversion of a Nova Scotian Fisherman)*. Canada. 1851-1887. Lang.: Eng. 3579

Performance/production
Elzéar Labelle's operetta *La Conversion d'un pêcheur de la Nouvelle-Écosse (The Conversion of a Nova Scotian Fisherman)* as an example of the move toward public performance. Canada: Quebec, PQ. 1837-1867. Lang.: Eng. 3599

Labelle, Jean-Baptiste
Basic theatrical documents
Musical setting for operetta *La conversion d'un pêcheur de la Nouvelle-Écosse (The Conversion of a Nova Scotian Fisherman)*. Canada. 1851-1887. Lang.: Eng. 3579

Labiche, Eugène
Performance/production
Interview with actor-turned-director Michael Leech. England: London. 1986. Lang.: Eng. 1710

Pieces related to performance at Comédie-Française of *Un Chapeau de Paille d'Italie (An Italian Straw Hat)* by Eugène Labiche. France: Paris. 1850-1986. Lang.: Fre. 1725

Production photos of *Un Chapeau de Paille d'Italie (An Italian Straw Hat)* by Eugène Labiche. France: Paris. 1986. Lang.: Fre. 1727

Labor relations
Administration
Analysis of theatrical working conditions. 1986. Lang.: Hun. 19

Analysis of petition drawn up by actors of the Drury Lane Theatre. England. 1705. Lang.: Eng. 32

Account of grievance petition by Opera House performers. England: London. 1799. Lang.: Eng. 34

Contractual problems in theatrical professions. Switzerland. 1986-1987. Lang.: Ger. 66

Formation and development of the Association of British Theatre Technicians (ABTT). UK. 1986. Lang.: Eng. 76

Panel discussion on collective bargaining issues. USA. 1986. Lang.: Eng. 95

Management and unions in collective bargaining. USA. 1986. Lang.: Eng. 99

New factors in arts and their impact on labor relations. USA. 1986. Lang.: Eng. 108

Economics and labor relations in performing arts. USA. 1986. Lang.: Eng. 129

Distinctions made between artists and other workers. USA: New York, NY. 1986. Lang.: Eng. 131

Work relationships: artist, layman and executive. USA. 1986. Lang.: Eng. 174

Personnel problems in theatres. USSR. 1980-1986. Lang.: Rus. 188

Articles on the organizational problems of theatre. USSR. 1980-1986. Lang.: Rus. 194

Letter from actor Ernesto Rossi concerning actors' labor movement. Italy. 1891. Lang.: Ita. 1436

Legislation for the protection of Victorian child-actors. UK. 1837-1901. Lang.: Eng. 1439

History and achievements of the American Guild of Musical Artists during its fifty years of existence. USA. 1936-1986. Lang.: Eng. 3645

Language — cont'd

Performance/production

Reconstruction of the life of Italian actors and acting companies with a vocabulary of their jargon. Italy. 1885-1940. Lang.: Ita. 753

Actor professionalism and the spoken word. USSR. 1986. Lang.: Ukr. 874

Issues in contemporary Russian stage productions. USSR. 1980-1986. Lang.: Rus. 890

Paralinguistic and communicative aspects of stage speech. USSR. 1986. Lang.: Rus. 893

Issues in speech pronunciation in performance. USSR. 1980-1986. Lang.: Rus. 898

Narrator in *Katari* story-telling tradition. Japan. 1960-1983. Lang.: Eng. 1366

Working environment of director Memè Perlini. Italy. 1978. Lang.: Eng. 1991

Producing *Café Con Leche (Coffee with Milk)* in Spanish. USA: New York, NY. 1986. 2269

Early form of Sicilian dialect theatre. Italy. 1780-1800. Lang.: Ita. 3337

Psychoanalytic study of staging as language. Germany. 1800-1909. Lang.: Fre. 3734

Plays/librettos/scripts

Comparison of natural and dramatic speech. England. USA. 1600-1986. Lang.: Eng. 939

Style in the plays of Pierre Corneille. France. 1606-1636. Lang.: Rus. 947

Poetic language in plays of Velimir Chlebnikov. Russia. 1885-1922. Lang.: Rus. 964

Luis de Góngora's plays as a response to Lope de Vega. Spain. 1561-1627. Lang.: Eng. 968

Interview with playwright Maria Irene Fornes. USA. 1965-1985. Lang.: Eng. 979

Summary of speech given by playwright Ossie Davis at Third World Theatre Conference. USA: Davis, CA. 1986. Lang.: Eng. 986

On the necessity of preserving the actor's text in a play. USSR. 1986. Lang.: Rus. 992

Ritualistic elements in the structure of Wole Soyinka's *Death and the King's Horseman*. Africa. 1975. Lang.: Eng. 2359

Use of violent language in the plays of Griselda Gambaro. Argentina. 1950-1980. Lang.: Eng. 2362

Language in *Der Schwierige (The Difficult Man)* by Hugo von Hofmannsthal. Austria. 1921. Lang.: Ger. 2390

Difficulties in French translation of Karl Kraus's *Die Letzten Tage der Menschheit (The Last Days of Mankind)*. Austria: Vienna. France: Paris. 1918-1986. Lang.: Ger. 2397

Language as an instrument of tyranny in Athayde's *Apareceua Margarida (Miss Margarida's Way)*. Brazil. 1808-1973. Lang.: Eng. 2405

Life and work of Francophone playwright Paul-André Paiement. Canada. 1970-1978. Lang.: Fre. 2417

La Storia and *La Storia II* performed in Italian and English by the Acting Company. Canada: Toronto, ON. 1984-1985. Lang.: Eng. 2424

Examines *Ne blâmez jamais les Bédouins (Don't Blame It on the Bedouins)* as a post-modernist play. Canada. 1980. Lang.: Fre. 2432

Pessimism of Sean O'Casey's *Juno and the Paycock*. Eire. 1924. Lang.: Eng. 2457

Language in *The Second Maiden's Tragedy*. England: London. 1611. Lang.: Eng. 2460

Blessing and cursing in Shakespeare's *King Lear*. England. 1605-1606. Lang.: Eng. 2466

Sounds in Ben Jonson's *Epicoene*. England: London. 1609-1668. Lang.: Eng. 2483

Essays on Shakespeare's *All's Well that Ends Well*. England. 1603. Lang.: Eng, Fre. 2485

Punctuation in *Gammer Gurton's Needle* indicates style of performance. England. 1575-1920. 2489

Language and society in Colley Cibber's *Love's Last Shift* and Sir John Vanbrugh's *The Relapse*. England. 1696. Lang.: Eng. 2495

Use of language in Beaumont and Fletcher's *Philaster*. England. 1609. Lang.: Eng. 2512

History, poetry and violence in plays by Tankred Dorst, Heiner Müller and Jean Genet. Europe. Lang.: Fre. 2538

Stoicism and modern elements in Senecan drama. Europe. 65-1986. Lang.: Eng. 2542

Essays on dramatic form, genre and language. France. 1500-1985. Lang.: Fre. 2545

Language and the permanent dialectic of truth and lie in the plays of Samuel Beckett. France. 1930-1980. Lang.: Fre. 2549

Commonplace as rhetorical device in plays of Jean Racine. France. 1650-1986. Lang.: Fre. 2559

Textual study of *La Farce de Maître Pierre Pathelin (The Farce of Master Pierre Pathelin)*. France. 1485-1970. Lang.: Fre. 2561

Rhetorical analysis of Samuel Beckett's *Waiting for Godot*. France. 1953. Lang.: Eng. 2562

Use of the present tense in some tragedies of Corneille and Racine. France. 1600-1700. Lang.: Fre. 2564

Adaptation by Albert Camus of *Les Esprits (The Spirits)* by Pierre de Larivey. France. 1570-1953. Lang.: Fre. 2571

Multiple role of 'I' in plays of Samuel Beckett. France. 1953-1986. Lang.: Eng. 2572

Sexual metaphors in plays of Jean Tardieu. France. 1955. Lang.: Fre. 2577

Study of *Bérénice*, *Athalie* and *Bajazet* by Jean Racine. France. 1670-1691. Lang.: Fre. 2583

Poetic and dramatic language in version of *Le Soulier de Satin (The Satin Slipper)* by Paul Claudel. France. 1928. Lang.: Fre. 2587

Structuralist analysis of Georg Büchner's *Leonce und Lena*. Germany. 1836. Lang.: Eng. 2604

Dialogue analysis of *Die Gewehre der Frau Carrar (Señora Carrar's Rifles)* by Bertolt Brecht. Germany, East. Lang.: Ger. 2612

Chorus in ancient Greek comedy and drama. Greece. 450-425 B.C. Lang.: Ita. 2633

Influence of artist Jack Yeats on playwright Samuel Beckett. Ireland. France. 1945-1970. Lang.: Eng. 2663

Piemontese dialect theatre. Italy: Turin. 1857-1914. Lang.: Ita. 2715

Text and information on Luigi Pirandello's *A patenti (The License)*. Italy. 1916-1918. Lang.: Ita. 2717

Symbolism in Derek Walcott's *Dream on Monkey Mountain*. Jamaica. 1967. Lang.: Eng. 2718

Corona de luz (Crown of Light) by Rodolfo Usigli as a self-reflexive comment on the process of dramatizing an historical event. Mexico. 1960-1980. Lang.: Eng. 2722

Use of language in *El Gesticulador (The Gesticulator)* by Rodolfo Usigli. Mexico. 1970-1980. Lang.: Spa. 2723

Philosophy and obscenity in the plays of Tadeusz Różewicz. Poland. 1920-1986. Lang.: Pol. 2750

Poetic and dramatic elements in the plays of Aleksand'r Blok. Russia. 1880-1921. Lang.: Rus. 2766

Evaluation of the literary and dramatic work of Josep Maria de Sagarra. Spain-Catalonia. 1917-1955. Lang.: Cat. 2810

Linguistic study of *Auto de Pasión (Passion Play)* by Lucas Fernández. Spain-Catalonia. 1510-1514. Lang.: Cat. 2812

A defense of Àngel Guimerà's language. Spain-Catalonia. 1860-1967. Lang.: Cat. 2817

Musical use of language conveys meaning in John Whiting's *Saint's Day*. UK-England. 1951. Lang.: Eng. 2857

Textual history of the final line of *Arms and the Man* by George Bernard Shaw. UK-England: London. 1894-1982. Lang.: Eng. 2873

Interview with Gillian Hanna about *Elisabetta: Quasi per caso una donna (Elizabeth: Almost by Chance a Woman)*. UK-England: London. Italy. 1986. Lang.: Eng. 2875

Playwright Arnold Wesker discusses the writing of dialogue. UK-England. 1950-1986. Lang.: Eng. 2881

Influence of Gordon Craig on American theatre and his recognition of Eugene O'Neill's importance. USA. UK-England. 1912-1928. Lang.: Eng. 2908

Distinguishes between the natural flow of words and present forms of linguistic alienation. USA. Austria. 1970-1986. Lang.: Eng. 2913

Analysis of the plays of Rosalyn Drexler. USA. 1964-1985. Lang.: Eng. 2920

Problems of adapting classic plays. China, People's Republic of. 1986. Lang.: Chi. 3543

Aesthetic considerations in *Lélio* by Hector Berlioz. France. Lang.: Fre. 3868

SUBJECT INDEX

Language — cont'd

Study of the librettos of operas premiered at the Teatro delle Novità festival. Italy: Bergamo. 1950-1973. Lang.: Ita. 3883

Reference materials

Exhibition catalogue about context of the work and influence of Karl Kraus. Austria: Vienna. USA: New York, NY. France: Paris. 1874-1986. Lang.: Ger. 2980

Catalogue of documentation on Pirandello's writings in dialect. Italy. 1902-1936. Lang.: Eng, Fre, Ger, Ita. 2994

Relation to other fields

Anthropological approach to performance and language. USA. Japan. 1982. Lang.: Eng. 1140

Theory/criticism

Correlation of word and image in dramaturgy. USSR. 1986. Lang.: Rus. 1239

Semiotic analysis of *La Storia*. Italy. 1985. Lang.: Eng. 3118

Lanner, Katti

Administration

Legislation for the protection of Victorian child-actors. UK. 1837-1901. Lang.: Eng. 1439

Lano, Shirley

Plays/librettos/scripts

A group of playwrights discuss the one-act play as a form. USA. 1986. 2937

Lanzini, Daniel

Performance/production

Daniel Lanzini's notes on writing and staging his play *Hazaiot Kamot Bamizrah (Fantasies Awakening in the East)* at the Acre Theatre Festival. Israel: Acre. 1986. Lang.: Heb. 1981

Lao, Se

Performance/production

Techniques of comedians in modern Beijing opera. China, People's Republic of: Beijing. 1964-1985. Lang.: Chi. 3524

LaPeyrette, Ketty

Performance/production

Reviews of 10 vintage recordings of complete operas on LP. USA. 1906-1925. Lang.: Eng. 3792

Łapicki, Andrzej

Performance/production

Andrzej Łapicki directs Aleksander Fredro's *Śluby Panienskie (Maiden Vows)*, Teatr Polski. Poland: Warsaw. 1984. Lang.: Pol. 2031

Lapine, James

Performance/production

Artists who began in dance, film or television move to Off Broadway theatre. USA: New York, NY. 1982. Lang.: Eng. 2284

Lapotaire, Jane

Performance/production

Actresses Jane Lapotaire and Elizabeth Spriggs discuss their careers in the Royal Shakespeare Company. UK-England: London. 1970-1986. Lang.: Eng. 2147

Theatre work of Bettina Jonic. UK-England. 1970-1986. Lang.: Eng. 2151

Larbey, Bob

Performance/production

Collection of newspaper reviews by London theatre critics. UK-England. 1986. Lang.: Eng. 2115

Collection of newspaper reviews by London theatre critics. UK-England. 1986. Lang.: Eng. 2120

Larivey, Pierre de

Plays/librettos/scripts

Adaptation by Albert Camus of *Les Esprits (The Spirits)* by Pierre de Larivey. France. 1570-1953. Lang.: Fre. 2571

Larkin, Peter

Design/technology

Challenges faced by designers of Bob Fosse's *Big Deal*. USA. 1986. Lang.: Eng. 359

Larson, Libby

Performance/production

Review of Libby Larsen's opera *Clair de Lune*. USA: Little Rock, AR. 1985. Lang.: Eng. 3803

Larsson, Björn

Performance/production

Amateur production of Alfred Jarry's *Kung Ubu (Ubu roi)* by Kristianstad Musikteater. Sweden: Kristianstad. 1986. Lang.: Swe. 797

Larsson, Gunilla

Administration

Role of Skånska Teatron in the community. Sweden: Landskrona, Malmö. 1963-1986. Lang.: Swe. 62

Last Street Play, The

Reference materials

Current work of Audelco award-winning playwrights. USA: New York, NY. 1973-1984. Lang.: Eng. 3007

Latabár family

Performance/production

The Latabár acting dynasty, its continuity and importance in Hungarian theatre history. Austro-Hungarian Empire. 1811-1970. Lang.: Hun. 1655

Latchmere Theatre (London)

SEE

Battersea Latchmere Theatre.

Late Lancaster Witches, The

Performance/production

Historical context of *The Late Lancaster Witches* by Thomas Heywood and Richard Brome. England. 1634. Lang.: Eng. 689

Laube, Heinrich

Plays/librettos/scripts

Social themes in the dramas of Franz Grillparzer. Austro-Hungarian Empire: Vienna. 1791-1872. Lang.: Ger. 2399

Laufer, Murray

Design/technology

Careers of stage designers, Murray Laufer, Michael Eagan and Susan Benson. Canada. 1972-1983. Lang.: Eng. 241

Laughton, Charles

Plays/librettos/scripts

Distortion of historical fact in Brecht's *Leben des Galilei (The Life of Galileo)*. Germany. 1938-1955. Lang.: Eng. 2600

Laundra, Linda

Institutions

Profile of Writers Theatre, an organization focusing on adaptations of poetry and literature for theatre. USA: New York, NY. 1975-1983. Lang.: Eng. 562

Laurence, Dan H.

Plays/librettos/scripts

Reference of George Bernard Shaw to contemporary society. UK-England. 1856-1950. Lang.: Eng. 2862

Laurent, Jeanne

Administration

Development of regional theatre companies. France. 1940-1952. Lang.: Eng. 44

Lavelli, Jorge

Performance/production

Interview with director Jorge Lavelli of Estudio Faixat. Spain-Catalonia: Barcelona. 1983. Lang.: Pol. 2081

Lavigne, Louis-Dominique

Institutions

Théâtre Petit à Petit and their production of *Où est-ce qu'elle est ma gang (Where's My Gang?)* by Louis-Dominique Lavigne. Canada: Montreal, PQ. France. 1981-1984. Lang.: Fre. 474

Lawler, Ray

Plays/librettos/scripts

Individualism and male-female relationships as themes in Australian drama. Australia. 1940-1980. Lang.: Eng. 2373

Analysis of Ray Lawler's *Summer of the Seventeenth Doll* in the context of his later plays. Australia. 1955-1977. Lang.: Eng. 2377

Impact of Ray Lawler's *Summer of the Seventeenth Doll* on Australian theatre. Australia. 1959-1983. Lang.: Eng. 2381

Interview with playwright Ray Lawler. Australia: Melbourne. 1984. Lang.: Eng. 2386

Lawrence, T.E.

Performance/production

Letters to and from Harley Granville-Barker. UK-England. 1877-1946. Lang.: Eng. 807

Laxenburger Kultursommer (Austria)

Institutions

Niederösterreichischer Theatersommer: producing summer theatre at festivals in different places. Austria. 1980-1986. Lang.: Ger. 448

Layard, John

Plays/librettos/scripts

Jungian analysis of the plays of Peter Nichols. UK-England. 1967-1984. Lang.: Eng. 2848

Lazarus, John
Performance/production
Playwright John Lazarus on workshopping new play. Canada. 1986.
Lang.: Eng.   1671

Lazlo, Andrew
Design/technology
Lighting designer Andrew Lazlo talks about his work on the film
Poltergeist II. USA: Los Angeles, CA. USA: New York, NY. 1985-
1986. Lang.: Eng.   3204

Lazzi
Performance/production
Precursors of *commedia dell'arte*. Italy: Venice. 1400-1620. Lang.:
Eng.   3414

Le Noire, Rosetta
Administration
Alternative funding for small theatres previously dependent on
government subsidy. USA: St. Louis, MO, New York, NY, Los
Angeles, CA, Detroit, MI. 1985. Lang.: Eng.   103
Institutions
Curriculum and expectation of students in Eubie Blake's Children's
Theatre Company. USA: New York, NY. 1986. Lang.: Eng.   1602

Le Roux, Jeanne
Institutions
History of the Théâtre de la Marmaille. Canada: Quebec, PQ. 1973-
1986. Lang.: Eng.   1552

Le Vern Jones, Herman
Institutions
History of two major Black touring companies. USA: New York,
NY. 1969-1982. Lang.: Eng.   1598

Leach, Wilford
Design/technology
Interview with director and former designer Wilford Leach. USA:
New York, NY. 1975-1986.   344
Performance/production
Reviews of Shakespeare's *Twelfth Night*, staged by Wilford Leach.
USA: New York, NY. 1986. Lang.: Eng.   2217

League of American Theatres and Producers
Administration
Details of the new Approved Production Contract. USA: New York,
NY. 1985. Lang.: Eng.   94

League of Professional Theatre Women (New York, NY)
Administration
Panel discussion on theatre as commerce or resource to its
community. USA: New York, NY. 1986.   179

Lear
Plays/librettos/scripts
Beckettian elements in Shakespeare as seen by playwright Edward
Bond. UK-England. 1971-1973. Lang.: Eng.   2833

Learning, Walter
Institutions
Career of Walter Learning, artistic director, Vancouver Playhouse.
Canada: Vancouver, BC. 1982-1983. Lang.: Eng.   470

Leavis, F.R.
Plays/librettos/scripts
Modern criticism of Shakespeare's crowd scenes. England. 1590-1986.
Lang.: Eng.   2536

Lebedev, Platon (aka Kerzhentsev)
Influence of Hampstead Garden Suburb pageant on the Russian
Proletkult movement. Russia. UK-England: London. 1907-1920.
Lang.: Eng.   3421

Leben des Galilei (Life of Galilei, The)
Plays/librettos/scripts
Fox symbolism in plays of Bertolt Brecht, Max Frisch and Gerhart
Hauptmann. Germany. Switzerland. 1700-1976. Lang.: Ger.   2598
Distortion of historical fact in Brecht's *Leben des Galilei (The Life
of Galileo)*. Germany. 1938-1955. Lang.: Eng.   2600
Analysis of *Leben des Galilei (The Life of Galileo)* by Bertolt
Brecht. Germany. 1938. Lang.: Rus.   2606
Criteria for evaluating translations, using the example of Brecht's
Galileo. Germany, East. 1938-1953.   2616

LeCompte, Elizabeth
Performance/production
History of the Wooster Group. USA: New York, NY. 1975-1985.
Lang.: Eng.   849
Wooster Group retrospective of original works. USA: New York,
NY. 1975-1986. Lang.: Eng.   850
Interview with Wooster Group's artistic director Elizabeth LeCompte.
USA: New York, NY. 1984. Lang.: Eng.   2288

Lecomte, Louis Henri
Plays/librettos/scripts
Treatment of Napoleon Bonaparte by French and English dramatists.
France. England. 1797-1958. Lang.: Eng.   2568

Leçon, La (Lesson, The)
Performance/production
Tamás Ascher directs *A kopasz éneksnő (The Bald Soprano)* and
Különóra (The Lesson) by Eugène Ionesco. Hungary: Kaposvár.
1986. Lang.: Hun.   1912

Lecoq, Jacques
Institutions
Director of school of mime and theatre on gesture and image in
theatrical representation. France: Paris. 1962-1985. Lang.: Fre.   3289
Theories on incorporating traditional theatrical forms into popular
theatre. Canada: Toronto, ON. 1970-1986. Lang.: Eng.   3408

Lederach, Jürgen
Institutions
Production of Jürgen Lederach's *Japanische Spiele (Japanese Play)*
by Transformtheater. Germany, West: Berlin, West. 1981-1986.
Lang.: Swe.   499

Lederer, Herbert
Performance/production
Viennese cellar theatres as alternative theatre spaces. Austria: Vienna.
1945-1960. Lang.: Ger.   1645
Plays/librettos/scripts
The church opera *Kain* written and composed for the Carinthiscer
Sommer Festival. Austria: Ossiach. 1986. Lang.: Ger.   3858

Lee Brothers Circus
Performance/production
Career of lion tamer Captain Terrell Jacobs. USA. 1903-1943. Lang.:
Eng.   3393

Lee, Chunyu
Research/historiography
Analysis of three ancient types of dance-drama. China. 1032-1420.
Lang.: Chi.   3551

Lee, Eugene
Design/technology
Career of scenic designer Eugene Lee. USA: Providence, RI. 1965-
1984. Lang.: Eng.   339

Lee, Hae-gu
Theory/criticism
Theory and history of Korean theatre. Korea: Seoul. 200 B.C.-1986
A.D. Lang.: Kor.   1214
Evolution and symbolism of the Mask-Dance drama. Korea: Seoul.
700-1986. Lang.: Kor.   1379

Lee, Kingshun
Research/historiography
Rise of the *Ping Hsi* form in Tienchin. China, People's Republic of:
Tienchin. 1885-1948. Lang.: Chi.   3557

Lee, Kueichun
Institutions
Beginnings of performing arts labor organizations. China, People's
Republic of: Shanghai. 1912-1931. Lang.: Chi.   488

Lee, Ming Cho
Design/technology
Interview with scene designer Ming Cho Lee. USA: New Haven,
CT. Lang.: Eng.   1528
Performance/production
Stills from telecast performances. List of principals, conductor and
production staff included. USA: New York, NY. 1986. Lang.: Eng.
3795
Relation to other fields
Economic survival of the individual theatre artist. USA: New York,
NY. 1983. Lang.: Eng.   1155

Lee, Pai
Relation to other fields
Political goals for Beijing opera. China, People's Republic of:
Beijing. 1985. Lang.: Chi.   3548

Lee, Tseho
Theory/criticism
Use of anxiety about fate in Beijing opera. China: Beijing. 5 B.C.-
1985 A.D. Lang.: Chi.   3558

Lee, Yu
Theory/criticism
Use of anxiety about fate in Beijing opera. China: Beijing. 5 B.C.-
1985 A.D. Lang.: Chi.   3558

SUBJECT INDEX

Leech, Michael
Performance/production
Interview with actor-turned-director Michael Leech. England: London.
1986. Lang.: Eng.   1710

Leela Means to Play
Plays/librettos/scripts
Influence of oriental theatre on playwright Beverley Simons. Canada:
Vancouver, BC. 1962-1975. Lang.: Eng.   928

Lefevre, Robin
Performance/production
Collection of newspaper reviews by London theatre critics. UK-
England: London. 1986. Lang.: Eng.   2123

Lefort, Bernard
Performance/production
Profile of Bernard Lefort, former Intendant of the Palais Garnier of
Paris. France: Paris. 1960-1985. Lang.: Eng.   3727

Legal aspects
U.S. laws on music performing rights. USA. 1856-1986. Lang.: Eng.
                                                                          3473

Administration
Prediction of future copyright trends. 1886-1986. Lang.: Eng.   17

Berne Convention Protocol in developing countries. Africa. Asia.
1963-1986. Lang.: Eng.   21

Causes of decline in number of commercially produced plays.
Australia: Sydney. 1914-1939. Lang.: Eng.   24

Berne Convention in People's Republic of China. China, People's
Republic of. 1908-1986. Lang.: Eng.   30

The Drury Lane Theatre under the management of Charles
Fleetwood. England: London. 1734-1745. Lang.: Eng.   35

Berne Convention and compulsory licensing. Europe. 1908-1986.
Lang.: Eng.   36

History of Berne Convention and copyright laws. Europe. 1709-1886.
Lang.: Eng.   37

Laws governing contracts and copyright. France. 1957-1986. Lang.:
Fre.   40

Theatrical legislation. France. 1945-1985. Lang.: Fre.   42

Protection of rights existing before Berne Convention. France. 1971-
1986. Lang.: Eng.   43

Berne Convention and copyright in socialist countries. Hungary.
1917-1986. Lang.: Eng.   46

Copyright protection in Korea. Korea. USA. 1986. Lang.: Kor.   56

Draft copyright laws of World Intellectual Property Organization.
Switzerland. 1986. Lang.: Eng.   64

Evaluation of a program of financial support for Swiss playwrights.
Switzerland. 1983-1986. Lang.: Fre, Ger.   65

Identification of important British officials responsible for most
government policies. UK. 1986. Lang.: Eng.   67

Copyright before and after Berne Convention. UK. 1850-1986.
Lang.: Eng.   68

Berne Convention and copyright in market economy. UK. USA.
1886-1986. Lang.: Eng.   69

Effect of copyright on new broadcast technologies. UK. 1971-1986.
Lang.: Eng.   71

Problems of copyright protection for computer programs. UK. USA.
1956-1986. Lang.: Eng.   73

Berne Convention and public interest. UK. 1886-1986. Lang.: Eng.
                                                                          75

Conflicts between reproduction permission and authors' rights. UK-
England. 1911-1986. Lang.: Eng.   79

Discussion of Berne Convention (1886) establishing copyright
agreement. UK-England: London. 1986. Lang.: Eng.   80

U.S. Copyright and the Berne Convention. USA. 1985. Lang.: Eng.
                                                                          84

Use of sources in analyzing shift from resident to touring companies.
USA. 1850-1900. Lang.: Eng.   86

Career of independent theatrical manager Henry Greenwall. USA:
Galveston, TX. 1867-1890. Lang.: Eng.   87

Trademark protection in the arts. USA. 1985. Lang.: Eng.   92

Details of the new Approved Production Contract. USA: New York,
NY. 1985. Lang.: Eng.   94

Management and unions in collective bargaining. USA. 1986. Lang.:
Eng.   99

Proposed copyright terms for composers and lyricists. USA. 1986.
Lang.: Eng.   116

General information on copyright. USA. 1985. Lang.: Eng.   119

Copyright, fair use, factual works, and private copying. USA. 1557-
1985. Lang.: Eng.   122

Uniquely American aspects of artist-state relationship. USA. 1983.
Lang.: Eng.   124

Proposed copyright laws to protect artists' free speech. USA. 1986.
Lang.: Eng.   127

Economics and labor relations in performing arts. USA. 1986. Lang.:
Eng.   129

Copyright licensing agreement between museums and artists. USA.
1976-1985. Lang.: Eng.   144

Injunctions in copyright infringement cases. USA. 1976-1985. Lang.:
Eng.   146

Design patent problems within U.S. copyright law. USA. 1842-1985.
Lang.: Eng.   148

Model dispute resolution project for artists. USA: San Francisco, CA.
1980-1986. Lang.: Eng.   153

Analysis of escalating insurance rates for Off Broadway theatres.
USA: New York, NY. 1986. Lang.: Eng.   156

Berne Convention and U.S. copyright law. USA. 1776-1986. Lang.:
Eng.   157

Guide to producing Off-off Broadway showcases. USA: New York,
NY. Lang.: Eng.   159

Revisions in the Showcase Code by Actors' Equity Association. USA:
New York, NY. 1982. Lang.: Eng.   165

Changes in the Showcase and Nonprofit Theatre codes. USA. 1983.
Lang.: Eng.   166

Argument against government involvement in the arts. USA. 1983.
Lang.: Eng.   173

Procedures of writing and maintaining contracts. USA. 1986. Lang.:
Eng.   181

Proposals for the reorganization of theatrical business. USSR. 1986.
Lang.: Rus.   190

History and management of Whitefriars Playhouse. England: London.
1607-1614. Lang.: Eng.   1432

Effect of censorship on Shakespeare's *Richard III* and *Henry IV.*
England. 1593-1603. Lang.: Pol.   1435

Lawsuit of actress Adelaide Ristori against her company manager for
nonfulfillment of contract. Italy. 1847-1849. Lang.: Ita.   1437

Russian censorship of classic repertory in Polish theatres. Poland:
Warsaw. Russia. 1873-1907. Lang.: Rus, Pol.   1438

Legislation for the protection of Victorian child-actors. UK. 1837-
1901. Lang.: Eng.   1439

Restructuring of the Glines producing organization of the Glines
Foundation. USA: New York, NY. 1983. Lang.: Eng.   1441

Transfer of plays from nonprofit to commercial theatre as
experienced by WPA Theatre's artistic director Kyle Renick. USA:
New York, NY. 1983. Lang.: Eng.   1443

Performers' rights in the United States, England and France. USA.
UK-England. France. 1976-1985. Lang.: Eng.   3164

History of source licensing for television and film scores. USA. 1897-
1987. Lang.: Eng.   3195

The standard Musician's Personal Management Contract. USA. 1986.
Lang.: Eng.   3476

Basic theatrical documents
Transcription of manuscript assigning shares in the King's Company.
England. 1661-1684. Lang.: Eng.   220

Institutions
Discussion of public theatre in Europe, especially Spain. Spain:
Valencia. 1959-1984. Lang.: Fre, Eng, Spa, Ita, Cat.   516

Performance spaces
Guide to locating and designing performance spaces for non-
traditional theatre. USA: New York, NY. 1979. Lang.: Eng.   636

Performance/production
Career of actress Elizabeth Bowtell, who first acted under her
maiden name of Davenport. England. 1664-1715. Lang.: Eng.   1706

Detailed history of the 1914 Hagenbeck Wallace Circus season.
USA: St. Louis, MO, Youngstown, OH, Sturgis, MI. 1914. Lang.:
Eng.   3388

The effect of disease on circus animals. USA. France. 1890-1985.
Lang.: Eng.   3389

Legal aspects — cont'd

A general review of the 1985 circus season. USA. Canada. 1985.
Lang.: Eng.   3394

Problems of the contemporary circus. USSR. 1986. Lang.: Rus.   3398

Achievements and problems of the contemporary circus. USSR.
1980-1986. Lang.: Rus.   3400

Changes in East Village performance scene. USA: New York, NY.
1975-1985. Lang.: Eng.   3458

Reference materials
Guide to producing printed material. USA. 1984. Lang.: Eng.   1044

Relation to other fields
Writers Gabriel García Márquez, Carlos Fuentes and Dario Fo
denied entry visas to the US on ideological grounds. USA:
Washington, DC. 1984. Lang.: Eng.   1170

Non-commercial cable television promotes activities of non-profit
theatre. USA. 1983. Lang.: Eng.   3286

LeGallienne, Eva
Institutions
Eva LeGallienne on Civic Repertory and American Repertory
Theatres. USA: New York, NY. 1933-1953. Lang.: Eng.   560

Légaré, Ovila
Plays/librettos/scripts
Analysis of French-language radio series *Nazaire et Barnabé*.
Canada. 1939-1958. Lang.: Eng.   3183

Léger, Viola
Plays/librettos/scripts
The plays of Antonine Maillet and the revival of Acadian theatre.
Canada. 1971-1979. Lang.: Eng.   2423

Acadian characters of playwright Antonine Maillet contrasted with
Longfellow's romantic myth. Canada. 1968-1975. Lang.: Eng.   2439

Légy jó mindhalálig (Be Good Till Death)
Performance/production
András Béhés directs *Légy jó mindhalálig (Be Good Till Death)* by
Zsigmond Móricz at Nemzeti Szinház. Hungary: Budapest. 1986.
Lang.: Hun.   1849

Lehmann, Hans-Peter
Institutions
History of the former Royal Opera House of Hanover and its plans
for the future. Germany, West: Hanover. 1689-1986. Lang.: Eng.
    3675

Leicester Theatre (Haymarket)
Performance/production
Collection of newspaper reviews by London theatre critics. UK:
London. 1986. Lang.: Eng.   2100

Leigh, Vivien
Performance/production
Hungarian translation of *Vivien Leigh: A Biography*. UK-England.
1913-1967. Lang.: Hun.   2141

Actor Laurence Olivier's memoirs. UK-England: London. USA: New
York, NY. 1907-1986. Lang.: Eng.   2170

Leka med elden (Playing With Fire)
Performance/production
The staging of an amateur performance of *Leka med elden (Playing
With Fire)*. Sweden: Hedemora. 1985-1986. Lang.: Swe.   2091

Lélio
Plays/librettos/scripts
Aesthetic considerations in *Lélio* by Hector Berlioz. France. Lang.:
Fre.   3868

Lemaire, Charles
Reference materials
Catalogue of an exhibition of costume designs for Broadway
musicals. USA: New York, NY. 1900-1925. Lang.: Eng, Ger.   3635

Lemmon, Jack
Performance/production
Review of Eugene O'Neill's *Long Day's Journey Into Night* directed
by Jonathan Miller. USA. 1956-1986. Lang.: Eng.   2264

Interview with Peter Gallagher on his portrayal of Edmund in *Long
Day's Journey Into Night*. USA: New York, NY, New London, CT.
1986. Lang.: Eng.   2268

Lemon Sky
Performance/production
Revivals by Second Stage. USA: New York, NY. 1986. Lang.: Eng.
    2259

Lend Me a Tenor
Performance/production
Collection of newspaper reviews by London theatre critics. UK-
England: London. 1986. Lang.: Eng.   2123

Léner, Péter
Performance/production
Nő a körúton (Woman on the Boulevard) by István Gáll directed by
Péter Léner at Móricz Zsigmond Theatre. Hungary: Nyiregyháza.
1986. Lang.: Hun.   1950

István Gáll's *Nő a körúton (Woman on the Boulevard)* directed by
Péter Léner at Móricz Zsigmond Szinház. Hungary: Nyiregyháza.
1986. Lang.: Hun.   1973

Lengyel, György
Performance/production
Szent Bertalan nappala (Saint Bartholomew's Day) by Magda Szabó
directed by György Lengyel. Hungary: Budapest. 1986. Lang.: Hun.
    1790

Rostand's *Cyrano de Bergerac* directed by György Lengyel. Hungary:
Budapest. 1985. Lang.: Hun.   1825

Magda Szabó's *Szent Bertalan nappala (Saint Bartholomew's Day)*
directed by György Lengyel at Madách Szinház. Hungary: Budapest.
1986. Lang.: Hun.   1896

Cyrano de Bergerac by Edmond Rostand, directed by György
Lengyel at Madách Szinház. Hungary: Budapest. 1985. Lang.: Hun.
    1953

Lengyel, Menyhért
Performance/production
Notes on performances of *Hongkongi paróka (Wig Made in Hong
Kong)*, *Egérút (Narrow Escape)* and *Róza néni (Aunt Rosa)*.
Hungary: Budapest. 1985. Lang.: Hun.   1801

Reviews of *Margit kisasszony (Miss Margit)*, *Az Ibolya (The Violet)*,
Az Árny (The Ghost) and *Róza néni (Aunt Rosa)*. Hungary:
Budapest. 1985-1986. Lang.: Hun.   1916

Lennon, Johan
Design/technology
Interview with manager Tony Smith and lighting designer Alan
Owen of the rock band Genesis focusing on the lighting technology
used on their latest tour. USA. 1968-1986. Lang.: Eng.   3320

Lenoir, Pierre
Institutions
Interviews with theatre professionals in Quebec. Canada. 1985.
Lang.: Fre.   487

Lenox Arts Center (Lenox, MA)
Institutions
Theatre companies that spend summers outside of New York City to
promote artistic growth and development. USA. 1985. Lang.: Eng.
    550

Lent, Lewis B.
Administration
Bookkeeping records of two pre-Civil War circuses. USA. 1836-1843.
Lang.: Eng.   3378

Lenz, Jakob Michael Reinhold
Performance/production
Der Hofmeister (The Tutor), Jakob Lenz's drama adapted by Bertolt
Brecht, directed by Gábor Máté. Hungary: Kaposvár. 1985. Lang.:
Hun.   1810

Plays/librettos/scripts
Biography of playwright Jakob Lenz. Germany. Russia: Moscow.
1751-1792. Lang.: Ger.   2594

Interview with composer Wolfgang Rihm. Switzerland. 1974-1986.
Lang.: Ger.   3893

Theory/criticism
Concept of *Standpunkt* in J.M.R. Lenz's poetics and the search for
identity in the 'Sturm und Drang' period. Germany. 1774. Lang.:
Eng.   1209

Leonard, Robert
Performance/production
Profile and interview with American soprano June Anderson.
USA: New York, NY. 1955-1986. Lang.: Eng.   3793

Leoncavallo, Ruggiero
Performance/production
Playwright and director George Tabori and his work. Austria:
Vienna. Germany, West. 1914-1985. Lang.: Ger.   658

Reviews of 10 vintage recordings of complete operas on LP. USA.
1906-1925. Lang.: Eng.   3792

Leonce und Lena
Plays/librettos/scripts
Structuralist analysis of Georg Büchner's *Leonce und Lena*. Germany.
1836. Lang.: Eng.   2604

Leopardi, Zuanpolo
Performance/production
Career of comic author and clown Zuanpolo Leopardi. Italy: Venice. 1500-1540. Lang.: Ita. 3336

Léotard, Philippe
Institutions
Work and distinctive qualities of the Théâtre du Soleil. France: Paris. 1964-1986. Lang.: Eng. 1575

Lerner, Alan Jay
Performance/production
Hungarian performance of *My Fair Lady*. Hungary. 1966-1970. Lang.: Hun. 3601

Reviews of *Brigadoon*, by Alan Jay Lerner, Frederick Loewe, staged by Gerald Freedman. USA: New York, NY. 1986. Lang.: Eng. 3619

Informal history of musical theatre. USA: New York, NY. UK-England: London. 1900-1985. Lang.: Eng. 3621

Plays/librettos/scripts
Attitudes toward sexuality in plays from French sources. UK-England. France. Lang.: Eng. 2852

Career of lyricist Alan Jay Lerner. UK-England. USA: New York, NY. 1918-1986. Lang.: Eng. 3629

Remarks on Alan Jay Lerner at his memorial service. USA: New York, NY. 1986. 3630

Lerner, Anders
Institutions
Sommarteatern, using both amateur and professional actors, will attempt a year-round season. Sweden: Södertälje. 1980-1986. Lang.: Swe. 1585

Lerner, Ruby
Administration
Advantages to regional theatre groups of New York performances. USA: New York, NY. 1983. Lang.: Eng. 130

Lesbian theatre
Audience
Context and design of some lesbian performances. USA: New York, NY. 1985. Lang.: Eng. 1455

Performance/production
Interview with Lesbian feminist theatre company Hard Corps. UK-England. 1984-1986. Lang.: Eng. 2164

Lessing, Gotthold Ephraim
Plays/librettos/scripts
Essays on Lessing and Lessing criticism. Germany. 1748-1984. Lang.: Ger. 2611

Nazi ideology and Hans Schweikart's film adaptation of Lessing's *Minna von Barnhelm*. Germany. 1940. Lang.: Ger. 3233

Theory/criticism
Analysis of Friedrich Schiller's dramatic and theoretical works. Germany. 1759-1805. Lang.: Cat. 3109

Lester, Howard
Performance/production
Collection of newspaper reviews by London theatre critics. UK-England. 1986. Lang.: Eng. 2111

Collection of newspaper reviews by London theatre critics. UK-England: London. 1986. Lang.: Eng. 2116

Let the Artists Die
SEE
Niech szezna artyszi.

Letzten Tage der Menschheit, Die (Last Days of Mankind, The)
Plays/librettos/scripts
Difficulties in French translation of Karl Kraus's *Die Letzten Tage der Menschheit (The Last Days of Mankind)*. Austria: Vienna. France: Paris. 1918-1986. Lang.: Ger. 2397

Reference materials
Exhibition catalogue about context of the work and influence of Karl Kraus. Austria: Vienna. USA: New York, NY. France: Paris. 1874-1986. Lang.: Ger. 2980

Relation to other fields
Karl Kraus, a reflection of Viennese culture and literature history. Austria: Vienna. 1874-1936. Lang.: Ger. 3014

Life and work of playwright and critic Karl Kraus. Austria: Vienna. 1874-1936. Lang.: Ger. 3017

Study on the reception of critic and playwright Karl Kraus in Italy. Italy. Austria: Vienna. 1911-1985. Lang.: Ger. 3044

The reception of critic and playwright Karl Kraus in the English speaking world. USA: New York, NY. Austria: Vienna. UK-Scotland: Glasgow. 1909-1985. Lang.: Ger. 3067

Levéltetvek az akasztófán (Plant-Lice on the Gallows)
Performance/production
László Fábián's *Levéltetvek az akasztófán (Plant-Lice on the Gallows)* directed by István Szőke. Hungary: Miskolc. 1986. Lang.: Hun. 1942

Isván Szőke directs *Letvéltetvek az akasztófán (Plant-Lice on the Gallows)* by László Fábián. Hungary: Miskolc. 1986. Lang.: Hun. 1961

Levinas, Emmanuel
Theory/criticism
Semiotic analysis of *La Storia*. Italy. 1985. Lang.: Eng. 3118

Levine, James
Administration
Edward Downes on his life in the opera. USA: New York, NY. 1911-1986. Lang.: Eng. 3643

Account of the first year of new management at the Metropolitan Opera. USA: New York, NY. 1985-1986. Lang.: Eng. 3644

Performance/production
Interview with Jean-Pierre Ponnelle discussing his directing technique and set designs. Austria: Salzburg. 1984. Lang.: Eng. 3699

Levy, Deborah
Plays/librettos/scripts
Interview with Gillian Hanna about *Elisabetta: Quasì per caso una donna (Elizabeth: Almost by Chance a Woman)*. UK-England: London. Italy. 1986. Lang.: Eng. 2875

Levy, Jonathan
Relation to other fields
Description of the Cutler Playwright's Festival designed for junior high school students. USA: Groton, CT. 1983-1986. Lang.: Eng. 3065

Levy, Tondaleyo
Performance/production
Four nightclub entertainers on their particular acts and the atmosphere of the late night clubs and theaters in Harlem. USA: New York, NY, Savannah, GA. 1930-1950. Lang.: Eng. 3470

Lewis, Robert
Performance/production
Director Charles Marowitz on the role of the director. USA. 1965-1985. Lang.: Eng. 843

Interview with producer, director, actor Robert Lewis. USA: New York, NY. 1930-1986. Lang.: Eng. 844

Training
Effect of changing ideas about psychology and creativity on the Stanislavskij system. USSR: Moscow. 1900-1986. Lang.: Eng. 3162

LGBC
SEE
Grands Ballets Canadiens, Les.

Li, Guoren
Performance/production
Techniques of comedians in modern Beijing opera. China, People's Republic of: Beijing. 1964-1985. Lang.: Chi. 3524

Li, Yingjie
Reference materials
Review of 1985 dissertations. China, People's Republic of: Beijing. 1985. Lang.: Chi. 3545

Li, Yu
Plays/librettos/scripts
Analysis of the work of playwright Li Yu. China. 1611-1930. Lang.: Chi. 3533

Liabilities
Administration
Analysis of escalating insurance rates for Off Broadway theatres. USA: New York, NY. 1986. Lang.: Eng. 156

Procedures of writing and maintaining contracts. USA. 1986. Lang.: Eng. 181

History and management of Whitefriars Playhouse. England: London. 1607-1614. Lang.: Eng. 1432

Performance/production
Detailed history of the 1914 Hagenbeck Wallace Circus season. USA: St. Louis, MO, Youngstown, OH, Sturgis, MI. 1914. Lang.: Eng. 3388

The effect of disease on circus animals. USA. France. 1890-1985. Lang.: Eng. 3389

A general review of the 1985 circus season. USA. Canada. 1985. Lang.: Eng. 3394

SUBJECT INDEX

Lighting — cont'd

Lists — cont'd

Career of popular entertainer Bill Cosby. USA. 1937-1986. Lang.: Eng. 3353

History of Great Wallace Circus. USA. 1913. Lang.: Eng. 3387

Details of Luigi Arditi's U.S. and Canada tour with the New York Opera Company. USA. Canada: Montreal, PQ, Toronto, ON. 1853-1854. Lang.: Eng. 3819

Plays/librettos/scripts

Cast lists in James Shirley's *Six New Playes* suggest popularity of plays. England. 1653-1669. Lang.: Eng. 2504

Details on performances of plays by Paul Claudel in German-speaking countries. Germany. Switzerland. Austria. 1913-1986. Lang.: Ger. 2599

Description of international symposium discussing the work of Stanisław Ignacy Witkiewicz. Poland. 1985. Lang.: Eng, Fre. 2733

Reference materials

Overview of Charlottetown Festival productions. Canada: Charlottetown, PE. 1972-1983. Lang.: Eng. 1008

List of the season's opening nights. Israel. 1986. Lang.: Heb. 1015

A list of opening nights of the theatrical season in Israel. Israel. 1985-1986. Lang.: Heb. 1016

A list of opening nights of the theatrical season in Israel. Israel. 1986. Lang.: Heb. 1017

Listing of theatrical productions. Japan: Tokyo. 1200-1500. Lang.: Jap. 1028

A list of all articles that have appeared in *STTF-medlemsblad* 1977-1985 and *ProScen* 1986. Sweden. 1977-1986. Lang.: Swe. 1032

List of institutional theatres. USA. 1986. 1039

Comprehensive list of rehearsal and performance spaces. USA: New York, NY. Lang.: Eng. 1042

Christl Zimmerl's career as prima ballerina at the Vienna State Opera. Austria: Vienna. 1939-1976. Lang.: Ger. 1324

Overview of French-language productions. Canada: Montreal, PQ. 1958-1968. Lang.: Eng. 2984

List and location of school playtexts and programs. France. 1601-1700. Lang.: Fre. 2987

Checklist of plays by Ödön von Horváth and their productions. Germany. 1901-1938. Lang.: Eng. 2989

Theatre documents and listing of playtexts in the Polish theatre in Lvov. Poland: Lvov, Katowice. 1800-1978. Lang.: Pol. 2996

List of 37 productions of 23 Renaissance plays, with commentary. UK. USA. New Zealand. 1986. Lang.: Eng. 3000

Chronological list of 407 London productions mounted in 1985 with an index to actors, writers and production personnel. UK-England: London. 1985. Lang.: Eng. 3002

Update of Allardyce Nicoll's handlist of plays. UK-England: London. 1900-1930. Lang.: Eng. 3003

Productions, dates and directors at TCG constituent theatres. USA. 1984-1985. Lang.: Eng. 3004

Production schedules for member theatres of Alliance of Resident Theatres/New York. USA: New York, NY. 1985-1986. Lang.: Eng. 3005

Current work of Audelco award-winning playwrights. USA: New York, NY. 1973-1984. Lang.: Eng. 3007

Chronological listing of 20 theatre seasons. USA: New York, NY. 1965-1985. Lang.: Eng. 3009

Index of operas, artists, contributors, etc. Europe. UK-England. USA. 1986. Lang.: Eng. 3911

Calendar of opera performances scheduled for the 1986-87 season throughout North America. North America. 1986. Lang.: Eng. 3913

Liszt, Franz

Performance/production

Productions based on sacred music of Franz Liszt. Hungary: Zalaegerszeg, Budapest. 1986. Lang.: Hun. 1308

Literary management

Administration

Literary managers discuss their roles and responsibilities in nonprofit theatre. USA: New York, NY. 1983. Lang.: Eng. 132

Literature

Institutions

Member organizations of Alliance of Resident Theatres/New York include programs in poetry, media and music. USA: New York, NY. 1984. Lang.: Eng. 574

Performance/production

Poetry as performing art and political tool. Caribbean. 1937-1985. Lang.: Eng. 674

Stage adaptation of Erich Kästner's novel *Emil und die Detektive (Emil and the Detectives)* directed by István Keleti. Hungary: Budapest. 1986. Lang.: Hun. 1807

A kis herceg (The Little Prince) by Antoine de Saint-Exupéry adapted and staged by Anna Belia and Péter Valló. Hungary: Budapest. 1985. Lang.: Hun. 1828

János Ács directs *A kőszívű ember fiai (The Sons of the Stone-Hearted Man)* by Mór Jókai. Hungary: Zalaegerszeg. 1986. Lang.: Hun. 1905

A kis herceg (The Little Prince) by Saint-Exupéry adapted and staged by Anna Belia and Péter Valló. Hungary: Budapest. 1985. Lang.: Hun. 1935

Lakat alá lányokat (Lock Up Your Daughters), a stage adaptation of Henry Fielding's *Rape Upon Rape*, directed by Imre Halasi. Hungary: Diósgyőr. 1986. Lang.: Hun. 3600

Use of shadow puppets in an adaptation of *Animal Farm.* 4016

Plays/librettos/scripts

Social themes in the dramas of Franz Grillparzer. Austro-Hungarian Empire: Vienna. 1791-1872. Lang.: Ger. 2399

Political ideas expressed in Elizabethan drama, particularly the work of Christopher Marlowe. England: London. Lang.: Eng. 2521

Correlation between short stories and plays by Carson McCullers. USA. 1917-1967. Lang.: Rus. 2889

Plots of works of Russian literature by Korolenko, Gorkij, Saltykov-Ščedrin and others in operas by non-Russian composers. Lang.: Rus. 3854

Italo Calvino's first libretto is based on one of his Marcovaldo stories. Italy. 1956. Lang.: Ita. 3884

Collaboration of authors and composers of *Billy Budd.* UK-England: London. 1949-1964. Lang.: Eng. 3895

Reference materials

Exhibition catalogue about context of the work and influence of Karl Kraus. Austria: Vienna. USA: New York, NY. France: Paris. 1874-1986. Lang.: Ger. 2980

Relation to other fields

Review of Iván Sándor's essays on Hungarian theatre. 1986. Lang.: Hun. 1049

The use of women and homosexuality in Brecht's sexual lyric poetry. 1920-1928. 1055

Essays and reviews on Hungarian and foreign playwrights, productions, actors and traditions. 1962-1986. Lang.: Hun. 1058

Selected cultural-historical sketches of Countess Sarolta Vay published in 1900 including several of theatrical interest. Austro-Hungarian Empire. 1740-1848. Lang.: Hun. 1065

William Popple's career in literature and politics. England. 1737-1764. Lang.: Eng. 1080

Artistic, literary and theatrical avant-garde movements. Europe. 1900-1930. Lang.: Ita. 1083

Théophile Gautier's ideas on theatre and performance. France. 1811-1872. Lang.: Rus. 1086

Analysis of Bertolt Brecht's love poetry. Germany, East. 1898-1956. 1092

A review of the 5-volume edition of Bertolt Brecht's poetry. Germany, East. 1898-1956. 1093

Critique of two articles which examine Brecht's love poetry from a feminist perspective. Germany, East. 1898-1956. 1094

Essays on literary and theatrical languages. Italy. 800-1985. Lang.: Ita. 1103

Study of Luigi Pirandello's novel, *I quaderni di Serafino Gubbio operatore (The Notebooks of Serafino Gubbio, Cameraman)*. Italy. 1915-1925. Lang.: Ita. 1104

The meeting of playwright Luigi Pirandello and novelist Italo Svevo. Italy: Trieste. 1925-1926. Lang.: Ita. 1107

Playwright Luigi Pirandello on the dynamics of humor. Italy. 1200-1906. Lang.: Ita. 1108

Literary origins of the 'lauda drammatica'. Italy. 1200-1400. Lang.: Ita. 1109

A portrait of Brecht in Peter Weiss's *Die Ästhetik des Widerstands.* Sweden: Stockholm. 1939-1940. 1130

Performing Arts Journal attempts to increase stature of drama as literature. USA: New York, NY. 1984. Lang.: Eng. 1154

Literature — cont'd

The world of choreography in the work of poet Anna Achmatova. USSR. 1889-1966. Lang.: Rus. 1328

Work of Ezra Pound and his relationship to *nō*. Japan. 1885-1972. Lang.: Jap. 1419

Drama as a genre of literature. Lang.: Rus. 3012

Karl Kraus, a reflection of Viennese culture and literature history. Austria: Vienna. 1874-1936. Lang.: Ger. 3014

Collection of obituary notes for the critic and dramatist Karl Kraus. Austria: Vienna. 1933-1937. Lang.: Ger. 3015

Situation of playwrights in Austria. Austria: Vienna. 1971-1986. Lang.: Ger. 3016

Life and work of playwright and critic Karl Kraus. Austria: Vienna. 1874-1936. Lang.: Ger. 3017

On Peter Brook's *Mahabharata*, produced by the International Center of Theatre Research. France: Paris. 1985. Lang.: Rus. 3032

Factors that discouraged historical drama in the classical period. Greece: Athens. 475-375 B.C. Lang.: Eng. 3035

Conference on novelist Giovanni Verga and the theatre. Italy. 1840-1922. Lang.: Ita. 3037

Reaction of a Jesuit priest to the theatre of Carlo Goldoni. Italy. 1719-1786. Lang.: Ita. 3038

Critical articles on playwright Luigi Pirandello. Italy. 1867-1936. Lang.: Ita. 3039

Comparison of playwright Luigi Pirandello and novelist Miguel de Cervantes. Italy. Spain. 1615-1936. Lang.: Ita. 3040

Influence of the plays of Terence on writings of Bishop Liutprando of Cremona. Italy: Cremona. 920-972. Lang.: Ita. 3041

Pirandello's influence on poet Eugenio Montale. Italy. 1896-1981. Lang.: Ita. 3042

Existence and conscience as seen by major writers. Italy. 1890-1970. Lang.: Ita. 3043

Study on the reception of critic and playwright Karl Kraus in Italy. Italy. Austria: Vienna. 1911-1985. Lang.: Ger. 3044

Reciprocal influence of Italian comedy and Boccaccio's *The Decameron*. Italy. 1350-1550. Lang.: Ita. 3045

Poet, dramatist, critic and satirist Władysław Syrokomla. Poland: Vilna, Warsaw. 1844-1861. Lang.: Pol. 3052

Sources of Ukrainian dramaturgy. Russia. 1800-1850. Lang.: Rus. 3053

Non-dramatic writings of playwright Arnold Wesker. UK-England. 1932-1986. Lang.: Eng. 3058

The reception of critic and playwright Karl Kraus in the English speaking world. USA: New York, NY. Austria: Vienna. UK-Scotland: Glasgow. 1909-1985. Lang.: Ger. 3067

Nonfictional writings of Albin Zollinger, Max Frisch and Friedrich Dürrenmatt. Lang.: Ger. 3169

Influence of Mozart's operas on the 'Cockney' school of writers. England: London. 1760-1840. Lang.: Eng. 3916

Théophile Gautier's views about opera. France. 1811-1917. Lang.: Eng. 3917

References to operas in the novels of Agatha Christie. UK-England. 1985. Lang.: Eng. 3923

Introduction to *The Revenge of Truth* by Isak Dinesen. Denmark. Kenya. 1885-1985. Lang.: Eng. 4010

Translation of works on puppetry by Heinrich von Kleist. Germany. 1810-1811. Lang.: Ita. 4012

Theory/criticism

Role of theatrical habit in Hungarian theatre history. Hungary. Lang.: Hun. 1212

The aims of literature, including drama. USSR. Lang.: Rus. 1244

National features of Russian literature and dramaturgy. USSR. 1986. Lang.: Rus. 1248

Litt, Jacob

Institutions

History of the Dime Museums. USA: Milwaukee, WI. 1882-1916. Lang.: Eng. 3324

Little Angel Marionette Theatre (Islington, UK)

Performance/production

History of The Little Angel Marionette Theatre. UK-England: London. 1961-1986. Lang.: Eng. 4007

Little Big Top, Jubilee Gardens (London)

Performance/production

Collection of newspaper reviews by London theatre critics. UK-England: London. 1986. Lang.: Eng. 2126

Little Eyolf

SEE

Lille Eyolf.

Little Foxes, The

Performance/production

Actress Lu Xiaoyan's experiences in preparing to play a role in *The Little Foxes*. China. USA. 1939-1982. Lang.: Chi. 1687

Little Haymarket Theatre (London)

Institutions

List of actors and companies using Little Haymarket Theatre. England: London. 1720-1737. Lang.: Eng. 491

Little Like Magic, A

Performance/production

Reviews of *A Little Like Magic*, conceived and staged by Diane Lynn Dupuy. USA: New York, NY. 1986. Lang.: Eng. 2213

Little Shop of Horrors

Administration

Transfer of plays from nonprofit to commercial theatre as experienced by WPA Theatre's artistic director Kyle Renick. USA: New York, NY. 1983. Lang.: Eng. 1443

Design/technology

Special effects in the film version of *Little Shop of Horrors*. USA. Lang.: Eng. 3212

Little Theatre (Leningrad)

SEE

Malyj Dramatičeskij Teat'r.

Little Theatre (Moscow)

SEE

Malyj Teat'r.

Little Theatre movement

Institutions

Influence of the Little Theatre movement on regional theatre. USA. 1887-1967. Lang.: Chi. 1611

Littlewood, Joan

Performance/production

Career of actress Billie Whitelaw, interpreter of Samuel Beckett's plays. UK-England. 1956-1986. Lang.: Eng. 2172

Littman, Max

Performance spaces

The renovation of the Württemberg State Theatre by the citizens of Stuttgart. Germany, West: Stuttgart. 1909-1976. Lang.: Eng. 3683

Littrell, Tom

Design/technology

Interview with manager Tony Smith and lighting designer Alan Owen of the rock band Genesis focusing on the lighting technology used on their latest tour. USA. 1968-1986. Lang.: Eng. 3320

Liturgical drama

Institutions

Liturgical drama and dance performed by amateur theatre group. Sweden: Lund. 1960-1986. Lang.: Swe. 526

Performance/production

Documents of religious processions and plays. France: Saint-Omer. 1200-1600. Lang.: Eng. 3424

Use of puppets in liturgical plays and ceremonies. England: London, Witney. 1540-1560. Lang.: Eng. 3963

Plays/librettos/scripts

Argument that the Gallican liturgy was a form of drama. France. 500-900. Lang.: Eng. 949

Analysis of Catalan Nativity plays. Spain-Catalonia. 1400-1599. Lang.: Cat. 972

Account of presentation of four St. Nicholas plays from Fleury Playbook. USA: Kalamazoo, MI. 1986. Lang.: Eng. 2942

Study of playtexts and illustrations in Lille plays manuscript. France: Lille. 1450-1500. Lang.: Eng. 3431

Liubimov, Jurij Petrovič

Performance/production

Jurij Petrivič Liubimov directs Isaak Babel's *Hashhia (Sunset)*. Israel: Tel-Aviv. 1984-1986. Lang.: Heb. 1979

Creative development of director Jurij Liubimov in Italy. Italy. USSR. 1973-1986. Lang.: Ita. 2003

Interview with director Jurij Liubimov. USA: Washington, DC. USSR: Moscow. 1986. Lang.: Eng. 2196

Liutprando, Bishop of Cremona
Relation to other fields
Influence of the plays of Terence on writings of Bishop Liutprando of Cremona. Italy: Cremona. 920-972. Lang.: Ita.   3041

Living Archive Project (Milton Keynes, UK)
Institutions
Community documentary plays of Living Archive Project. UK-England: Milton Keynes. 1976-1986. Lang.: Eng.   1589

Living Newspaper
Plays/librettos/scripts
Attitudes toward technology reflected in some Living Newspaper productions of the Federal Theatre Project. USA. 1935-1939. Lang.: Eng.   2905

Living Theatre (New York, NY)
Administration
Julian Beck's management of the Living Theatre. USA: New York, NY. 1947-1983. Lang.: Eng.   102

Institutions
Production history and techniques of the Living Theatre. USA. 1964. Lang.: Eng.   546

Performance/production
Extracts from unpublished writings by Julian Beck. USA. Europe. 1960-1985. Lang.: Ita.   824

Collection of reviews by Benedict Nightingale on New York theatre. USA: New York, NY. 1983-1984. Lang.: Eng.   847

Writings by and about Julian Beck, founder of Living Theatre. USA. Europe. 1925-1985. Lang.: Ita.   2309

Theory/criticism
Aesthetic theory of interpretation. Europe. North America. 1900-1985. Lang.: Fre.   3097

Livingstone, Ken
Plays/librettos/scripts
Interview with playwright Howard Barker. UK-England. 1981-1985. Lang.: Eng.   2845

Lizzie Borden
Plays/librettos/scripts
Jack Beeson's opera *Lizzie Borden*. USA. 1954-1965. Lang.: Eng.   3901

Ljungh, Esse W.
Performance/production
Esse Ljungh's acting career with Winnipeg Little Theatre. Canada: Winnipeg, MB. 1921-1937. Lang.: Eng.   664

Plays/librettos/scripts
Scandinavian drama on Canadian radio. Canada. Scandinavia. 1939-1982. Lang.: Eng.   3182

Lloyd Webber, Andrew
Performance/production
Jézus Krisztus Szupersztar (Jesus Christ Superstar) by Andrew Lloyd Webber and Tim Rice directed by János Szikora (Rock Szinház). Hungary: Szeged. 1986. Lang.: Hun.   3604

Summer productions of *Jézus Krisztus Szupersztár*. Hungary: Szeged, Budapest. 1986. Lang.: Hun.   3605

Reviews of musicals. UK-England: London. 1986. Lang.: Eng.   3610

Lloyd-Lewis, Howard
Performance/production
Collection of newspaper reviews by London theatre critics. UK. 1986. Lang.: Eng.   2103

Ló, A (Horse, The)
Performance/production
Ferenc Sik directs two plays by Gyula Háy. Hungary: Veszprém, Gyula. 1986. Lang.: Hun.   1943

Lobel, Adrianne
Design/technology
Panel held on women's roles in the field of design. USA: New York, NY. 1985. Lang.: Eng.   427

Interview with set designer Adrianne Lobel. USA: New York, NY. 1986. Lang.: Eng.   1530

Lochner, David
Design/technology
Designers discuss regional productions of *Ain't Misbehavin'*. USA. 1984-1986. Lang.: Eng.   3591

Lock Up Your Daughters (Lakat alá a lányokat)
Performance/production
Lakat alá lányokat (Lock Up Your Daughters), a stage adaptation of Henry Fielding's *Rape Upon Rape*, directed by Imre Halasi. Hungary: Diósgyőr. 1986. Lang.: Hun.   3600

Locke, Robert
Plays/librettos/scripts
Analysis of *As Is* by William Hoffman and *The Dolly* by Robert Locke. Canada: Toronto, ON. 1985. Lang.: Eng.   2419

Lodge, Thomas
Plays/librettos/scripts
Image of poverty in Elizabethan and Stuart plays. England. 1558-1642. Lang.: Eng.   2482

Loewe, Frederick
Performance/production
Hungarian performance of *My Fair Lady*. Hungary. 1966-1970. Lang.: Hun.   3601

Reviews of *Brigadoon*, by Alan Jay Lerner, Frederick Loewe, staged by Gerald Freedman. USA: New York, NY. 1986. Lang.: Eng.   3619

Plays/librettos/scripts
Attitudes toward sexuality in plays from French sources. UK-England. France. Lang.: Eng.   2852

Logan, Olive
Administration
Legislation for the protection of Victorian child-actors. UK. 1837-1901. Lang.: Eng.   1439

Lohengrin
Basic theatrical documents
The influence of *Euryanthe* by Carl Maria von Weber on Richard Wagner. Germany: Dresden. 1824-1879. Lang.: Eng.   3649

Performance/production
Stills from telecast performances. List of principals, conductor and production staff included. USA: New York, NY. 1986. Lang.: Eng.   3795

Łomnicki, Tadeusz
Performance/production
Tadeusz Łomnicki directs Pasolini's *Affabulazione* at Centrum Sztuki Studio. Poland: Warsaw. 1984. Lang.: Pol.   2033

London Merchant, The
Plays/librettos/scripts
Liberated female characters in the plays of George Lillo. England. 1730-1759. Lang.: Eng.   2477

London Palladium
Performance/production
Collection of newspaper reviews by London theatre critics. UK. 1986. Lang.: Eng.   2103

Collection of newspaper reviews by London theatre critics. UK-England. 1986. Lang.: Eng.   2111

Collection of newspaper reviews by London theatre critics. UK-England: London. 1986. Lang.: Eng.   2123

London, Betzalel
Reference materials
Betzalel London's archive deposited at Hebrew University. Israel: Jerusalem. 1925-1971. Lang.: Heb.   1014

Long Day's Journey Into Night
Intertextual analysis of Eugene O'Neill's play *Long Day's Journey Into Night* and Ingmar Bergman's film, *Through a Glass Darkly*. USA. Sweden. 1957-1961. Lang.: Eng.   1425

Performance/production
Jonathan Miller's production of Eugene O'Neill's *Long Day's Journey Into Night*. UK-England: London. 1941-1986. Lang.: Eng.   2159

Reviews of *Long Day's Journey Into Night* by Eugene O'Neill, staged by Jonathan Miller. USA: New York, NY. 1986. Lang.: Eng.   2219

Review of Eugene O'Neill's *Long Day's Journey Into Night* directed by Jonathan Miller. USA. 1956-1986. Lang.: Eng.   2264

Interview with Peter Gallagher on his portrayal of Edmund in *Long Day's Journey Into Night*. USA: New York, NY, New London, CT. 1986. Lang.: Eng.   2268

Plays/librettos/scripts
Popularity and relevance of Eugene O'Neill. USA. Lang.: Eng.   2894

Comparison of plays by Tennessee Williams, Arthur Miller and Eugene O'Neill. USA. 1949-1956. Lang.: Eng.   2926

Long, Robert
Design/technology
Keith Haring, Robert Longo and Gretchen Bender design for choreographers Bill T. Jones and Arnie Zane. USA. 1986.   1342

Long, William Ivey
Design/technology
Costume designer William Ivey Long discusses his work for Off Broadway theatres. USA: New York, NY. 1986. Lang.: Eng.   389

Longacre Theatre (New York, NY)
Performance/production
Reviews of *Cuba and His Teddy Bear* by Reinaldo Povod, staged by Bill Hart. USA: New York, NY. 1986. Lang.: Eng. 2228

Reviews of *Precious Sons* by George Furth, staged by Norman Rene. USA: New York, NY. 1986. Lang.: Eng. 2231

Look Back in Anger
Basic theatrical documents
Catalan translation of *Look Back in Anger* by John Osborne. UK-England. 1956. Lang.: Cat. 1506

Plays/librettos/scripts
Analysis of John Osborne's *Look Back in Anger*. UK-England: London. 1929-1978. Lang.: Cat. 2866

Looking for a Bride
SEE
Ženitba.

Loot
Performance/production
Reviews of *Loot*, by Joe Orton, staged by John Tillinger. USA: New York, NY. 1986. Lang.: Eng. 2229

Lope de Vega
SEE
Vega Carpio, Lope Félix de.

Lorca, Federico García
SEE
García Lorca, Federico.

Lord Byron's Love Letter
Performance/production
Collaboration of Italian composer Rafaello de Banfield and American playwright Tennessee Williams on the opera *Lord Byron's Love Letter*. USA: Charleston, SC. 1986. Lang.: Eng. 3810

Lorengar, Pilar
Performance/production
Profile of and interview with Spanish soprano Pilar Lorengar. Spain: Zaragoza. USA: San Francisco, CA. 1928-1986. Lang.: Eng. 3778

Lorenz, Dagmar C.G.
Relation to other fields
Critique of two articles which examine Brecht's love poetry from a feminist perspective. Germany, East. 1898-1956. 1094

Lorenzaccio
Plays/librettos/scripts
Theme of fragmentation in *Lorenzaccio* by Alfred de Musset. France. 1834. Lang.: Eng. 2558

Losey, Joseph
Plays/librettos/scripts
Analysis of Harold Pinter's technique in adapting *A la Recherche du Temps Perdu (Remembrance of Things Past)* by Marcel Proust as a screenplay. UK-England. 1972. Lang.: Eng. 3240

Losing Venice
Plays/librettos/scripts
Interview with playwright John Clifford. UK-Scotland: Edinburgh. 1960-1986. Lang.: Eng. 2885

Lost Empires
Design/technology
Lighting requirements for television production of *Lost Empires*. UK-England. 1986. Lang.: Eng. 3255

Lotman, Yuri
Plays/librettos/scripts
Development in the genre of the *sainete*, or comic afterpiece. Argentina. 1800-1980. Lang.: Spa. 2365

Love for Three Oranges
Performance/production
Review of Prokofiév's *Love for Three Oranges*. USA: Cincinnati, OH. 1986. Lang.: Eng. 3798

Love of Life Orchestra
Performance/production
Interview with composer-musician Peter Gordon. USA. 1985. Lang.: Eng. 3492

Love, Kermit
Performance/production
Work of Kermit Love, creator of Big Bird for *Sesame Street*. USA: New York, NY. 1935-1985. Lang.: Eng. 3276

Love's Labour's Lost
Performance/production
John Hirsch's artistic career at the Stratford Festival Theatre. Canada: Stratford, ON. 1981-1985. Lang.: Eng. 1683

Detailed discussion of four successful Royal Shakespeare Company productions of Shakespeare's minor plays. UK-England: Stratford. 1946-1977. Lang.: Eng. 2182

Plays/librettos/scripts
Productions of Jane Howell and Elijah Moshinsky for the BBC Shakespeare series. UK-England: London. 1978-1985. Lang.: Eng. 3283

Love's Last Shift
Plays/librettos/scripts
Language and society in Colley Cibber's *Love's Last Shift* and Sir John Vanbrugh's *The Relapse*. England. 1696. Lang.: Eng. 2495

Love's Sacrifice
Reference materials
List of 37 productions of 23 Renaissance plays, with commentary. UK. USA. New Zealand. 1986. Lang.: Eng. 3000

Lover, The
Plays/librettos/scripts
Thematic analysis of Harold Pinter's *The Lover*. UK-England. 1963. Lang.: Eng. 2870

Loves Crueltie
Basic theatrical documents
Prompt markings on a copy of James Shirley's *Loves Crueltie* performed by the King's Company. England: London. 1660-1669. Lang.: Eng. 1475

Lowry, W. McNeil
Administration
W. McNeil Lowry of the Ford Foundation discusses funding for arts institutions. USA. 1984. Lang.: Eng. 142

Lu Hua He
Research/historiography
Transformation of traditional music notation into modern notation for four Chinese operas. China: Beijing. 1674-1985. Lang.: Chi. 3554

Lu, Kuei-pu
Research/historiography
Controversy over identities of Tien Kuei-pu and Lu Kuei-pu. China. 1500-1644. Lang.: Chi. 3550

Lu, Xiaoyan
Performance/production
Actress Lu Xiaoyan's experiences in preparing to play a role in *The Little Foxes*. China. USA. 1939-1982. Lang.: Chi. 1687

Łubieński, Tomasz
Plays/librettos/scripts
Analysis of Tomasz Łubieński's plays. Poland. 1986. Lang.: Pol. 2734

Lucachevsky, Sophie
Performance/production
Hungarian reviewer discusses Paris performances. France: Paris. 1986. Lang.: Hun. 1734

Stage adaptation of *La Mort de Judas (The Death of Judas)* by Paul Claudel. France: Brangues. 1985. Lang.: Fre. 1754

Luce, Clare Boothe
Plays/librettos/scripts
Interview with Gillian Hanna about *Elisabetta: Quasi per caso una donna (Elizabeth: Almost by Chance a Woman)*. UK-England: London. Italy. 1986. Lang.: Eng. 2875

Relation to other fields
Interview with actress Maria Aitken on a revival of *The Women* by Clare Boothe Luce. UK-England: London. 1936-1986. Lang.: Eng. 3061

Luce, William
Performance/production
Actress Frances de la Tour discusses her work in *Lillian* by William Luce. UK-England: London. USA. 1986. Lang.: Eng. 2146

Reviews of *Lillian* by William Luce, staged by Robert Whitehead. USA: New York, NY. 1986. Lang.: Eng. 2245

Lucet, Jean-Paul
Performance/production
Directors discuss staging of plays by Paul Claudel. France. Belgium. 1985. Lang.: Fre. 1723

Lucia di Lammermoor
Performance/production
Andrzej Straszyński directs Donizetti's *Lucia di Lammermoor*, Teatr Wielki. Poland: Warsaw. 1984. Lang.: Pol. 3770

Lucie, Doug
Performance/production
Collection of newspaper reviews by London theatre critics. UK-England: London. 1986. Lang.: Eng. 2118

Lucille Lortel Theatre (New York, NY)
Performance/production
Reviews of *Grouch: A Life in Revue*, by Arthur Marx and Robert Fisher, staged by Arthur Marx. USA: New York, NY. 1986. Lang.: Eng. 2201

Reviews of *Orchards* written and staged by Robert Falls after Čechov. USA: New York, NY. 1986. Lang.: Eng. 2222

Reviews of *Gertrude Stein and a Companion*, by Win Wells, staged by Ira Cirker. USA: New York, NY. 1986. Lang.: Eng. 2238

Luckham, Claire
Institutions
Progress and aims of Women's Playhouse Trust. UK-England: London. 1984-1986. Lang.: Eng. 1590

Performance/production
Brechtian technique in the contemporary feminist drama of Caryl Churchill, Claire Luckham and others. UK-England. 1956-1979. Lang.: Eng. 815

Interview with Pip Broughton of Paines Plough Theatre Company. UK-England. 1980-1986. Lang.: Eng. 2166

Lucrècia
Theory/criticism
Historical difficulties in creating a paradigm for Catalan theatre. Spain-Catalonia. 1400-1963. Lang.: Cat. 1220

Ludlam, Charles
Design/technology
Charles Ludlam's role as set designer, artistic director and lead actor of The Ridiculous Theatre Company. USA: New York, NY. 1986. 360

Performance/production
Profile of and interview with opera parodist Charles Ludlam of The Ridiculous Theatre Company. USA: New York, NY. 1973-1986. Lang.: Eng. 3825

Ludwig, Ken
Performance/production
Collection of newspaper reviews by London theatre critics. UK-England: London. 1986. Lang.: Eng. 2123

Lukács, Andor
Performance/production
Production of *A nevelő (The Tutor)* by Bertolt Brecht. Hungary: Kaposvár. 1985. Lang.: Hun. 1840

Lukács, György
Theory/criticism
Excerpts from writings of critics and theatre professionals on theory of theatre. Europe. 1880-1985. Lang.: Ita. 1204

Lulu
Plays/librettos/scripts
Title character in Alban Berg's *Lulu*. Austria: Vienna. 1891-1979. Lang.: Eng. 3857

Influences on Alban Berg's *Lulu*. Austria: Vienna. 1907-1979. Lang.: Eng. 3859

Collaboration of Kurt Weill, Alban Berg and Arnold Schönberg on *Lulu*. Germany. 1920-1932. Lang.: Eng. 3875

Relation to other fields
Influence of political and artistic movements on composer Alban Berg. Austria: Vienna. 1894-1935. Lang.: Eng. 3914

Lumière & Son Circus (London)
Institutions
Interview with Hilary Westlake of Lumière & Son. UK-England: London. 1973-1986. Lang.: Swe. 536

Performance/production
Profile of the work of Lumière & Son Circus (London). UK-England. 1980-1986. Lang.: Eng. 3454

Lunatics and Lovers
SEE
Finta giardiniera, La.

Lundberg, Jan
Design/technology
Swedish set designers discuss their working methods. Sweden. 1980-1986. Lang.: Swe. 312

Lunds Stifts Kyrkospel (Lund)
Institutions
Liturgical drama and dance performed by amateur theatre group. Sweden: Lund. 1960-1986. Lang.: Swe. 526

Lunt-Fontanne Theatre (New York, NY)
Performance/production
Reviews of *Uptown...It's Hot*, staged, choreographed and conceived by Maurice Hines. USA: New York, NY. 1986. Lang.: Eng. 1284

Reviews of *Smile*, music by Marvin Hamlisch, book by Howard Ashman. USA: New York, NY. 1986. Lang.: Eng. 3613

Lunt, Alfred
Performance/production
A scholarly study of the careers of Alfred Lunt and Lynn Fontanne. USA. 1922-1972. Lang.: Eng. 2257

Lux in Tenebris
Basic theatrical documents
A film scenario for Bertolt Brecht's *Lux in Tenebris*. 1985. 3197

Performance/production
Director Ann Gadon on staging Brecht's *Lux in Tenebris*. USA: Chicago, IL. 1985. 2267

Lyceum Company (London)
Performance/production
Career of actress, manager and director Julia Arthur. Canada. UK-England. USA. 1869-1950. Lang.: Eng. 1675

Lyceum Theatre (Edinburgh)
SEE
Royal Lyceum Theatre.

Lyceum Theatre (New York, NY)
Performance/production
Reviews of *A Little Like Magic*, conceived and staged by Diane Lynn Dupuy. USA: New York, NY. 1986. Lang.: Eng. 2213

Lynn, Jonathan
Performance/production
Director Jonathan Lynn discusses his works performed at the National Theatre. UK-England: London. UK-England: Cambridge. 1986. Lang.: Eng. 2160

Lynne, Gillian
Performance/production
Biographical notes on choreographer and director Gillian Lynne. UK-England: London. USA. 1940-1986. Lang.: Eng. 2161

Lyotard, Jean-François
Design/technology
Les Immatériaux, multimedia exhibit by Jean-François Lyotard. France: Paris. 1986. Lang.: Eng. 3249

Lyric Hammersmith (London)
Performance/production
Collection of newspaper reviews by London theatre critics. UK-England: London. 1986. Lang.: Eng. 2112

Collection of newspaper reviews by London theatre critics. UK-England: London. 1986. Lang.: Eng. 2118

Director Simon Callow talks about his production of Jean Cocteau's *The Infernal Machine*. UK-England: London. 1986. Lang.: Eng. 2139

Overview of performances transferred from The Royal Court, Greenwich, and Lyric Hammersmith theatres. UK-England: London. 1986. Lang.: Eng. 2143

Nuria Espert talks about Federico García Lorca and her production of *The House of Bernarda Alba*. UK-England: London. Spain. Lang.: Eng. 2178

Lyric Opera of Chicago
Performance/production
Profile of and interview with William Neill, composer-in-residence at the Lyric Opera of Chicago. USA: Chicago, IL. 1984-1986. Lang.: Eng. 3829

Lyric Studio (London)
Performance/production
Collection of newspaper reviews by London theatre critics. UK-England. 1986. Lang.: Eng. 2111

Collection of newspaper reviews by London theatre critics. UK-England: London. 1986. Lang.: Eng. 2116

Collection of newspaper reviews by London theatre critics. UK-England: London. 1986. Lang.: Eng. 2118

Lyrics
Basic theatrical documents
Text of Lorenz Hart lyrics. USA. 1920-1943. Lang.: Eng. 3580

Lyttelton Theatre (London)
SEE ALSO
National Theatre (London).

Performance/production
Collection of newspaper reviews by London theatre critics. UK-England. 1986. Lang.: Eng. 2120

Lyudmila Zhivkova (Sofia)
Performance spaces
Description of Lyudmila Zhivkova, the palace of culture. Bulgaria: Sofia. 1983-1985. Lang.: Swe. 585

M. le Trouhadec Possessed by Debauchery
SEE
Monsieur le Trouhadec saisi par la débauche.

Ma Rainey's Black Bottom
Performance/production
Lloyd Richard's career as an actor, director, artistic director and academic dean. USA: Detroit, MI, New York, NY, New Haven, CT. 1920-1980. Lang.: Eng. 2308

Ma, Chihyüan
Research/historiography
Great playwrights of the Yüan dynasty. China. 1271-1368. Lang.: Chi. 3552

Ma, Ke
Plays/librettos/scripts
Ma Ke's contribution and influence on Beijing opera. China, People's Republic of: Beijing. 1951-1985. Lang.: Chi. 3536

Mabou Mines (New York, NY)
Administration
Development director Marion Godfrey's fundraising strategies. USA: New York, NY. 1986. Lang.: Eng. 113

Institutions
Interview with members of Mabou Mines. USA: New York, NY. 1984. Lang.: Eng. 1607

Performance/production
Life and technique of Franz Xaver Kroetz. USA: New York, NY. Germany, West. 1984. Lang.: Eng. 2287

Performance art and its current characteristic tone. USA. Lang.: Eng. 3459

MacArthur, Charles
Performance/production
Reviews of *The Front Page*, by Ben Hecht and Charles MacArthur, staged by Jerry Zaks. USA: New York, NY. 1986. Lang.: Eng. 2214

Macbeth
Performance/production
Career of actress, manager and director Julia Arthur. Canada. UK-England. USA. 1869-1950. Lang.: Eng. 1675

Analysis of Shakespeare's influence on Weimar, German neoclassicism. Germany: Weimar. 1771-1812. Lang.: Eng. 1760

English-language performances of Italian actress Adelaide Ristori. Italy. England. USA. 1822-1906. Lang.: Ita. 2000

Reconstruction of a number of Shakespeare plays staged and performed by Herbert Beerbohm Tree. UK-England: London. 1887-1917. Lang.: Eng. 2155

Jonathan Pryce in the role of Macbeth. UK-England: Stratford. 1970-1986. Lang.: Eng. 2179

Artistic and technological differences in presenting opera for stage and television. Canada. 1960-1980. Lang.: Eng. 3714

Plays/librettos/scripts
Discusses Michel Garneau's *joual* translation of *Macbeth*. Canada: Montreal, PQ. 1978. Lang.: Eng. 2429

Translations of plays by William Shakespeare into Amharic and Tegrenna. Ethiopia: Addis Ababa. 1941-1984. Lang.: Eng. 2537

Film versions of Shakespeare's *Macbeth* by Orson Welles, Akira Kurosawa and Roman Polanski. USA. Japan. 1948-1971. Lang.: Eng. 3243

MacDermot, Galt
Performance/production
Performances of *Hair*, directed by János Sándor, and *Desire Under the Elms*, directed by Géza Bodolay at the National Theatre of Szeged. Hungary: Szeged. 1986. Lang.: Hun. 1959

MacDonald, Glenn
Institutions
The first decade of White Rock Summer Theatre in British Columbia. Canada: White Rock, BC. 1976-1985. Lang.: Eng. 1560

MacDonald, Stephen
Performance/production
Collection of newspaper reviews by London theatre critics. UK-England: London. 1986. Lang.: Eng. 2118

Plays/librettos/scripts
Interview with playwright Stephen MacDonald. UK-England: London. 1917-1986. Lang.: Eng. 2879

MacDonald, Tom
Design/technology
Life of stage designer Tom MacDonald. UK-Scotland: Glasgow. 1914-1985. Lang.: Eng. 1526

Maceba Affairs (Houston, TX)
Administration
Growing activity and changing role of Black regional theatre companies. USA. 1960-1984. Lang.: Eng. 1440

MacGeachy, Cora
Reference materials
Catalogue of an exhibition of costume designs for Broadway musicals. USA: New York, NY. 1900-1925. Lang.: Eng, Ger. 3635

Machiavelli, Niccoló
Plays/librettos/scripts
Machiavellian ideas in *The Devil's Charter* by Barnaby Barnes. England. 1584-1607. Lang.: Eng. 2500

Machine Infernale, La
Performance/production
Director Simon Callow talks about his production of Jean Cocteau's *The Infernal Machine*. UK-England: London. 1986. Lang.: Eng. 2139

Machines
SEE
Equipment.

Mackay, Caro
Administration
Interview with director and tour manager of Royal Shakespeare Company about touring. UK. 1986. Lang.: Eng. 72

MacKay, Charles
Institutions
New administrative personnel at the Opera Theatre of St. Louis. USA: St. Louis, MO. 1976-1986. Lang.: Eng. 3679

Mackerras, Charles
Performance/production
Interview with Sir Charles Mackerras on the subject of authenticity in musical performance. USA: Chicago, IL. 1925-1986. Lang.: Eng. 3809

Mackintosh, Cameron
Design/technology
Set designer John Napier's work on *Les Misérables*. UK-England: London. 1986. 3583

Macklin, Charles
Administration
The Drury Lane Theatre under the management of Charles Fleetwood. England: London. 1734-1745. Lang.: Eng. 35

Macloma
Performance/production
A photographic essay of 42 soloists and groups performing mime or gestural theatre. 1986. 3290

MacMillan, Kenneth
Performance/production
Career of choreographer Kenneth MacMillan. Europe. USA. 1929-1986. Lang.: Eng. 1302

Macready, William Charles
Design/technology
Charles Kean's period production of Shakespeare's *Richard III*. UK-England: London. 1857. Lang.: Eng. 1525

Performance/production
Career of actress and theatrical manager Louisa Lane Drew. USA. 1820-1897. Lang.: Eng. 2243

Mácsai, Pál
Performance/production
Interview with actor Pál Mácsai on his role in *Scapin furfangjai (Scapin's Tricks)* by Molière. Hungary: Szentendre. 1986. Lang.: Hun. 1775

Macskajáték (Catsplay)
Performance/production
Gábor Berényi's production of *Macskajáték (Catsplay)* by István Örkény at the Magyar Játékszin. Hungary: Budapest. 1985. Lang.: Hun. 1832

Macskajáték (Catsplay) by István Örkény, directed by Gábor Berényi, at Magyar Játékszin. Hungary: Budapest. 1985. Lang.: Hun. 1962

Macskák szerdája, A (Cat Wednesday)
Performance/production
Magda Szabó's *A macskák szerdája (Cat Wednesday)* at Csokonai Theatre directed by László Gali. Hungary: Debrecen. 1986. Lang.: Hun. 1777

Macurdy, John
Performance/production
Opera greats reflect on performance highlights. USA: Philadelphia, PA, New York, NY. 1985. Lang.: Eng. 3841

Magyar Játékszin (Budapest)
Performance/production
Villa Negra by Anikó and Katalin Vajda directed by Miklós Szurdi. Hungary: Budapest. 1986. Lang.: Hun. 1818

Gábor Berényi's production of *Macskajáték (Catsplay)* by István Örkény at the Magyar Játékszin. Hungary: Budapest. 1985. Lang.: Hun. 1832

Adaptation for the stage by Anikó Vagda and Katalin Vajda of Imre Dobozy's screenplay *Villa Negra*, directed at Játékszin by Miklós Szurdi. Hungary: Budapest. 1986. Lang.: Hun. 1870

Milán Füst's *Margit kisasszony (Miss Margit)* directed by István Dégi at Játékszin. Hungary: Budapest. 1986. Lang.: Hun. 1901

Reviews of *Margit kisasszony (Miss Margit)*, *Az Ibolya (The Violet)*, *Az Árny (The Ghost)* and *Róza néni (Aunt Rosa)*. Hungary: Budapest. 1985-1986. Lang.: Hun. 1916

Review of *Margit kisasszony (Miss Margit)* directed by István Dégi. Hungary: Budapest. 1986. Lang.: Hun. 1941

Macskajáték (Catsplay) by István Örkény, directed by Gábor Berényi, at Magyar Játékszin. Hungary: Budapest. 1985. Lang.: Hun. 1962

Magyar Szinházi Intézet
Plays/librettos/scripts
Text of a lecture on Shakespeare's *King Lear* by Clifford Davidson. Hungary: Budapest. Lang.: Hun. 2643

Mahābhārata
Performance/production
Shadow puppetry as a way of passing on Balinese culture. Bali. 1976-1985. Lang.: Eng. 4017

Description of characters and techniques of *Wayang* puppetry. Indonesia. 1983-1986. Lang.: Fre. 4018

Mahabharata, The
Performance/production
Interview with Peter Brook's designer, musician, and costumer for *Mahabharata*. France: Avignon. 1973-1985. Lang.: Eng. 1359

Interviews with actors in Peter Brook's *Mahabharata*. France: Avignon. 1985. Lang.: Eng. 1360

Peter Brook discusses development of *The Mahabharata*. France: Avignon. India. 1965-1986. Lang.: Eng. 1361

Peter Brook's *The Mahabharata* at the Théâtre aux Bouffes du Nord. France: Avignon, Paris. 1985-1986. Lang.: Eng. 1753

Relation to other fields
On Peter Brook's *Mahabharata*, produced by the International Center of Theatre Research. France: Paris. 1985. Lang.: Rus. 3032

Research/historiography
Indian theatre professionals criticize Peter Brook's *Mahabharata*. India: Kerala, Calcutta. 1980-1985. Lang.: Eng. 1376

Mahagonny
SEE
Aufstieg und Fall der Stadt Mahagonny.

Mahalia's Song
Performance/production
Career of director/choreographer Mike Malone. USA: Washington, DC, Cleveland, OH. 1968-1985. Lang.: Eng. 2275

Mahler, Gustav
Plays/librettos/scripts
Mahler's influence on Kurt Weill's career. Germany: Berlin. 1756-1950. Lang.: Eng. 3879

Relation to other fields
Influence of political and artistic movements on composer Alban Berg. Austria: Vienna. 1894-1935. Lang.: Eng. 3914

Mahon, Nicholas
Performance/production
Collection of newspaper reviews by London theatre critics. UK-England: London. 1986. Lang.: Eng. 2116

Maid's Tragedy, The
Reference materials
List of 37 productions of 23 Renaissance plays, with commentary. UK. USA. New Zealand. 1986. Lang.: Eng. 3000

Maillet, Antonine
Institutions
French-language theatre and the Acadian tradition. Canada. 1969-1986. Lang.: Eng. 1544

Plays/librettos/scripts
The plays of Antonine Maillet and the revival of Acadian theatre. Canada. 1971-1979. Lang.: Eng. 2423

Acadian characters of playwright Antonine Maillet contrasted with Longfellow's romantic myth. Canada. 1968-1975. Lang.: Eng. 2439

Majakovskij načinajetsja (Majakovskij Begins)
On *Majakovskij načinajetskja (Majakovskij Begins)*, an opera by A. Petrov. USSR. Lang.: Rus. 3638

Majakovskij Theatre (Moscow)
SEE
Teat'r im. V. Majakovskovo.

Majakovskij, Vladimir Vladimirovič
On *Majakovskij načinajetskja (Majakovskij Begins)*, an opera by A. Petrov. USSR. Lang.: Rus. 3638

Major, Leon
Institutions
History of the Neptune Theatre and its artistic directors. Canada: Halifax, NS. 1963-1983. Lang.: Eng. 483

Major, Tamás
Performance/production
Interview with actor, director and manager Tamás Major. Hungary. 1910-1986. Lang.: Hun. 1776

Reprinted preface to biography of Tamás Major. Hungary. 1930-1986. Lang.: Hun. 1863

Interview with Tamás Major, director and actor. Hungary. 1945-1986. Lang.: Hun. 1868

Recollections of actor, director and theatre manager Tamás Major. Hungary. 1910-1986. Lang.: Hun. 1879

Makart, Hans
Reference materials
Costumes of famous Viennese actors. Austria: Vienna. 1831-1960. Lang.: Ger. 1003

Make-up
Design/technology
Basic techniques of make-up for the performing artist. 1986. Lang.: Eng. 229

Theatre make-up compared to painting. China, People's Republic of. 1907-1980. Lang.: Chi. 251

Report on the leading brands of stage blood. USA. 1986. Lang.: Eng. 334

Prices, quantities and manufacturers' official line on stage blood. USA. 1986. Lang.: Eng. 337

Using the 'major manufacturers' make-up kits. USA. 1986. 356

Application of stage blood. USA. 1986. Lang.: Eng. 373

Guide to materials necessary for theatrical performances. USSR. 1980-1986. Lang.: Rus. 430

Special effects in the film *From Beyond*. USA. 1986. Lang.: Eng. 3208

Performance/production
Life and work of an Indian street performer. India: Rajasthan. 1940-1985. Lang.: Eng. 3335

Techniques of comedians in modern Beijing opera. China, People's Republic of: Beijing. 1964-1985. Lang.: Chi. 3524

Theory/criticism
Strengths and weaknesses of Beijing opera. China, People's Republic of: Beijing. 1935-1985. Lang.: Chi. 3565

Malakova, Petra
Performance/production
The Franco Zeffirelli film of *Otello* by Giuseppe Verdi, an account of the production. Italy: Rome. 1985-1986. Lang.: Eng. 3758

Malamud, Hector
Performance/production
A photographic essay of 42 soloists and groups performing mime or gestural theatre. 1986. 3290

Malayālam
Basic theatrical documents
Text of *Karimkutty* by K. N. Panikkar in English translation. India. 1983. Lang.: Eng. 1355

Malcolm X
Performance/production
Profile of and interview with Anthony Davis, composer of the opera *X*, on the life and times of Malcolm X. USA: New York, NY. Lang.: Eng. 3834

Malcontent, The
Plays/librettos/scripts
Defense of *The Malcontent* by John Marston as a well-constructed satire. England. 1590-1600. Lang.: Eng. 938

Religious ideas in the satirical plays of John Marston. England. 1595-1609. Lang.: Eng. 940

Maldoom, Royston
Performance/production
Interview with choreographer Royston Maldoom. UK-Scotland. 1970-1986. Lang.: Eng.   2189

Maleczech, Ruth
Institutions
Interview with members of Mabou Mines. USA: New York, NY. 1984. Lang.: Eng.   1607

Malina, Judith
Administration
Julian Beck's management of the Living Theatre. USA: New York, NY. 1947-1983. Lang.: Eng.   102
Institutions
Production history and techniques of the Living Theatre. USA. 1964. Lang.: Eng.   546

Malipenga
Performance/production
Origins of *malipenga*, a form of dance-drama combining Western and African elements. Zambia: Malawi. 1914-1985. Lang.: Eng. 1374

Malipiero, Gian Francesco
Plays/librettos/scripts
Correspondence between Luigi Pirandello and composer Gian Francesco Malipiero. Italy. 1832-1938. Lang.: Ita.   2699

Malkovich, John
Performance/production
Reviews of *The Caretaker* by Harold Pinter, staged by John Malkovich. USA: New York, NY. 1986. Lang.: Eng.   2236

Mallarmé, Stéphane
Performance/production
Influence of Richard Wagner on the work of the French Symbolists. France: Paris. Germany, West: Bayreuth. 1860-1986. Lang.: Eng.   3726

Malmberg, Agneta
Performance/production
De dövas historia (The Story of the Deaf) staged by Ändockgruppen using both hearing and deaf amateurs. Sweden: Vänersborg. 1982-1986. Lang.: Swe.   799

Malmquist, Sandro
Design/technology
Unusual production of *Life Is a Dream* by Kungliga Dramatiska Teatern. Sweden: Stockholm. 1927. Lang.: Swe.   1520

Malone, Mike
Performance/production
Career of director/choreographer Mike Malone. USA: Washington, DC, Cleveland, OH. 1968-1985. Lang.: Eng.   2275

Malouf, David
Traditional innovation in *Voss* by Richard Meale and David Malouf. Australia. 1980-1986. Lang.: Eng.   3636

Maltz, Albert
Plays/librettos/scripts
Career of Marxist playwright George Sklar. USA: New York, NY. 1920-1967. Lang.: Eng.   985

Malyj Dramatičeskij Teat'r (Leningrad)
Performance/production
Correlation of scenery and direction. USSR: Leningrad. 1980-1986. Lang.: Rus.   2335

Malyj Teat'r (Leningrad)
SEE
Malyj Teat'r Opery i Baleta.
Malyj Dramatičeskij Teat'r.

Malyj Teat'r (Moscow)
Performance/production
Careers of Sadovskije acting family. Russia: Moscow. 1800-1917. Lang.: Rus.   784
Theory/criticism
Synthesis of the arts in the theatrical process. USSR: Moscow. 1986. Lang.: Rus.   1240

Mama I Want to Sing
Institutions
Vi Higginsen's *Mama I Want to Sing* and history of the Mumbo-Jumbo Theatre Company. USA: New York, NY. 1980-1986. Lang.: Eng.   1601

Mamet, David
Administration
Efforts to produce the film *Sexual Perversity in Chicago*. USA. Lang.: Eng.   3194
Performance/production
Collection of newspaper reviews by London theatre critics. UK-England: London. 1986. Lang.: Eng.   2110

Collection of newspaper reviews by London theatre critics. UK-England: London. 1986. Lang.: Eng.   2112
Collection of newspaper reviews by London theatre critics. UK-England. 1986. Lang.: Eng.   2120
Plays/librettos/scripts
Comparison of natural and dramatic speech. England. USA. 1600-1986. Lang.: Eng.   939
Review of adaptations for the stage of short stories by Čechov. USA: New York, NY. 1986. Lang.: Eng.   2922
Interview with playwright David Mamet. USA. 1984. Lang.: Eng.   2938

Reference materials
David Mamet bibliography. USA. 1973-1986. Lang.: Eng.   3008
Theory/criticism
Essays on artistic media by playwright David Mamet. USA: New York, NY, Los Angeles, CA. 1986. Lang.: Eng.   3144

Mamma December
Performance/production
Collection of newspaper reviews by London theatre critics. UK-England. 1986. Lang.: Eng.   2115

Mamouney, Don
Performance/production
Community theatre as interpreted by the Sidetrack Theatre Company. Australia: Sydney, N.S.W. 1980-1986. Lang.: Eng.   1638

Man and Superman
Theory/criticism
Shaw's use of devil's advocacy in his plays compared to deconstructionism. UK-England. 1900-1986. Lang.: Eng.   3135

Man and the Monster, The
Plays/librettos/scripts
Treatment of the Frankenstein myth in three gothic melodramas. UK-England. France. 1823-1826. Lang.: Eng.   2847

Man Ban Er Huang
Research/historiography
Transformation of traditional music notation into modern notation for four Chinese operas. China: Beijing. 1674-1985. Lang.: Chi. 3554

Man In The Moon Theatre (London)
Performance/production
Collection of newspaper reviews by London theatre critics. UK-England. 1986. Lang.: Eng.   2114
Collection of newspaper reviews by London theatre critics. UK-England: London. 1986. Lang.: Eng.   2125

Man of Mode, The
Performance/production
Collection of newspaper reviews by London theatre critics. UK-England: London. 1986. Lang.: Eng.   2126

Man, Animal and Virtue
SEE
Uomo, la bestia e la virtù, L'.

Management
SEE ALSO
Administration.
Administration
Contribution to the discussion on the Hungarian theatre structure. Hungary. 1985-1986. Lang.: Hun.   45
Contribution to the discussion on theatre structure in Hungary. Hungary. 1985-1986. Lang.: Hun.   49
Managing the Korean Theatre Festival. Korea. 1986. Lang.: Kor. 55
Use of computers by Alliance of Resident Theatres/New York's member organizations. USA: New York, NY. 1985. Lang.: Eng.   93
Panel discussion on collective bargaining issues. USA. 1986. Lang.: Eng.   95
Skills required by managing directors. USA: New York, NY. 1984. Lang.: Eng.   169
Panel discussion on encouraging growth and change in artists and institutions. USA. 1986. Lang.: Eng.   171
On the need for radical change in theatrical management and financing. USSR. 1986. Lang.: Rus.   184
Interview with V.R. Beljakovič, manager of Teat'r-studija na Jugo-Zapade. USSR: Moscow. 1980. Lang.: Rus.   185
Need for change in the organization of theatrical management. USSR. 1980-1986. Lang.: Rus.   186
Ukrainian actors and teachers on rebuilding theatre business. USSR. 1980-1986. Lang.: Ukr.   192
History and management of Whitefriars Playhouse. England: London. 1607-1614. Lang.: Eng.   1432

Manhattan Project, The
Design/technology
Bran Ferren's special effects for *The Manhattan Project*. USA. 1986.
377

Manhattan Theatre Club (New York, NY)
Administration
Creation and role of board of directors in nonprofit theatre. USA:
New York, NY. 1986. Lang.: Eng. 104
Role of the marketing director in nonprofit theatre. USA: New
York, NY. 1986. Lang.: Eng. 140
Lynne Meadow, artistic director of the Manhattan Theatre Club,
describes her fourteen years on the job. USA: New York, NY.
1972-1986. Lang.: Eng. 1442

Design/technology
Costume designer William Ivey Long discusses his work for Off
Broadway theatres. USA: New York, NY. 1986. Lang.: Eng. 389
Designers discuss regional productions of *Ain't Misbehavin'*. USA.
1984-1986. Lang.: Eng. 3591

Institutions
Several nonprofit theatres secure new spaces. USA: New York, NY.
1984. Lang.: Eng. 544

Mankato State College (Mankato, MN)
Design/technology
Designers discuss regional productions of *Grease*. USA. 1984-1986.
Lang.: Eng. 3597

Mankynde
Performance/production
Theories of medieval production and acting techniques. England.
1400-1500. Lang.: Eng. 698

Mann, Emily
Performance/production
Reviews of *Execution of Justice*, written and staged by Emily Mann.
USA: New York, NY. 1986. Lang.: Eng. 2230
Mark Bly on the dramaturg's responsibility to question. USA:
Minneapolis, MN. 1981-1986. Lang.: Eng. 2294

Mann, Erika
Relation to other fields
History of anti-Nazi satire. Germany. Switzerland: Zurich. 1933-1945.
Lang.: Ger. 3370

Mann, Klaus
Performance/production
Royal Shakespeare Company performances at the Barbican Theatre.
UK-England: London. 1986. Lang.: Eng. 2152

Relation to other fields
Critique of the relation between politics and theatre in Klaus
Mann's *Mephisto* performed by Théâtre du Soleil. France: Paris.
1979. Lang.: Eng. 1085
History of anti-Nazi satire. Germany. Switzerland: Zurich. 1933-1945.
Lang.: Ger. 3370

Mann, Paul
Performance/production
Lloyd Richard's career as an actor, director, artistic director and
academic dean. USA: Detroit, MI, New York, NY, New Haven, CT.
1920-1980. Lang.: Eng. 2308

Mann, Theodore
Performance/production
Reviews of *The Boys in Autumn* by Bernard Sabath, staged by
Theodore Mann. USA: New York, NY. 1986. Lang.: Eng. 2221

Mann, Thomas
Performance/production
Puppeteer Julie Taymor adapts *Die vertauschten Köpfe (The
Transposed Heads)* by Thomas Mann for performance at the Ark
Theatre. USA: New York, NY. 1984. Lang.: Eng. 3977

Plays/librettos/scripts
Treatment of homosexuality in *Death in Venice*. Germany. UK-
England. 1911-1970. Lang.: Eng. 3874

Manning, Barbara
Performance/production
Dilemmas and prospects of youth theatre movement. Australia. 1982-
1986. Lang.: Eng. 1639

Manon Lescaut
Performance/production
Puccini's opera *Manon Lescaut* at the Hungarian State Opera House.
Hungary: Budapest. 1985. Lang.: Hun. 3743

Reference materials
Photos of the new opera productions at the Staatsoper. Austria:
Vienna. 1985-1986. Lang.: Ger. 3910

Mansfield, Richard
Performance/production
Description of first stage adaptation of Robert Louis Stevenson's *Dr.
Jekyll and Mr. Hyde*. USA: New York, NY. USA: Boston, MA.
1886-1888. Lang.: Eng. 2298

Mansouri, Lofti
Performance/production
Opera singer Maureen Forrester tells of her switch from serious roles
to character and comic roles. Canada. 1970-1984. Lang.: Eng. 3706

Mansurova, C.L.
Performance/production
Biographical materials on actress C.L. Mansurova. USSR. 1920-1986.
Lang.: Rus. 884

Manuel, Roland
Institutions
Discussions of opera at the festival of Aix-en-Provence. France: Aix-
en-Provence. 1960. Lang.: Fre. 3673

Manzoni, Alessandro
Performance/production
Unsuccessful productions of works by Alessandro Manzoni. Italy.
1827-1882. Lang.: Ita. 1995

Plays/librettos/scripts
Gestural characterization in *I promessi sposi (The Betrothed)* by
Manzoni. Italy. 1842. Lang.: Ita. 2707

Mao, Zedong
Relation to other fields
Political goals for Beijing opera. China, People's Republic of:
Beijing. 1985. Lang.: Chi. 3548
Mao's policy on theatre in revolution. China, People's Republic of:
Beijing. 1920-1985. Lang.: Chi. 3549

Theory/criticism
Purpose of literature and art, and the role of the artist. China,
People's Republic of: Shanghai, Yan'an. 1942-1982. Lang.: Chi.
1203

Mar i cel (Sea and Sky)
Plays/librettos/scripts
A defense of Àngel Guimerà's language. Spain-Catalonia. 1860-1967.
Lang.: Cat. 2817

Marat/Sade
Performance/production
Directorial process as seen through major productions of
Stanislavskij, Brecht, Kazan and Brook. 1898-1964. Lang.: Eng. 650

Marceau, Marcel
Performance/production
A photographic essay of 42 soloists and groups performing mime or
gestural theatre. 1986. 3290

Theory/criticism
Present and future of mime theatre. 3300

Marchand, Polyvius
Performance/production
Overview of Maria Callas' early career. Greece: Athens. 1937-1945.
Lang.: Eng. 3741

Marcus, Rachel
Performance/production
Interview with actress Rachel Marcus. Israel: Tel-Aviv. 1935-1986.
Lang.: Heb. 1983

Marczak-Oborski, Stanisław
Performance/production
Collection of articles by critic and theatre historian Stanisław
Marczak-Oborski. Poland. 1918-1986. Lang.: Pol. 2034

Marczewski, Andrzej
Performance/production
Andrzej Marczewski directs Andrzejewski's *Popiol i Diament (Ashes
and Diamonds)*, Teatr Rozmaitości. Poland: Warsaw. 1984. Lang.:
Pol. 2013

Margit kisasszony (Miss Margit)
Performance/production
Milán Füst's *Margit kisasszony (Miss Margit)* directed by István
Dégi at Játékszin. Hungary: Budapest. 1986. Lang.: Hun. 1901
Reviews of *Margit kisasszony (Miss Margit)*, *Az Ibolya (The Violet)*,
Az Árny (The Ghost) and *Róza néni (Aunt Rosa)*. Hungary:
Budapest. 1985-1986. Lang.: Hun. 1916
Review of *Margit kisasszony (Miss Margit)* directed by István Dégi.
Hungary: Budapest. 1986. Lang.: Hun. 1941

Margitszigeti Szabadtéri Szinpad (Budapest)
Performance/production
Summer productions of *Jézus Krisztus Szupersztár*. Hungary: Szeged,
Budapest. 1986. Lang.: Hun. 3605

Marlowe, Christopher
Plays/librettos/scripts
Post-structuralist insights on sexuality and transgression in transvestite roles in Jacobean plays. England: London. 1600-1625. Lang.: Eng.
2476

Possible influence of Christopher Marlowe's plays upon those of William Shakespeare. England. 1580-1620. Lang.: Eng. 2478

Tradition and individualism in Renaissance drama. England: London. 1575-1600. Lang.: Eng. 2496

Contemporary responses to *Tamburlane the Great* by Christopher Marlowe. England. 1984. Lang.: Eng. 2501

Political ideas expressed in Elizabethan drama, particularly the work of Christopher Marlowe. England: London. Lang.: Eng. 2521

Treatment of historical figures in plays by William Shakespeare, Christopher Marlowe and George Peele. England. 1560-1650. Lang.: Eng. 2534

Jerzy Grotowski and his adaptation of *Doctor Faustus*. Poland. 1964. Lang.: Eng. 2740

Marquis Theatre (New York, NY)
Performance spaces
Architect Robert Morgan's design for Broadway's Marquis Theatre. USA: New York, NY. 1986. Lang.: Eng. 633

Performance/production
Review of *Me and My Girl*, book and lyrics by L. Arthur Rose and Douglas Furber, staged by Mike Ockrent. USA: New York, NY. 1986. Lang.: Eng. 3618

Marranca, Bonnie
Basic theatrical documents
Annotated text of *The Revenge of Truth* by Isak Dinesen. Denmark. 1914. Lang.: Eng. 4002

Performance/production
Interviews with performance artists. Canada: Toronto, ON. USA: New York, NY. 1980-1986. Lang.: Eng. 3444

Relation to other fields
Performing Arts Journal attempts to increase stature of drama as literature. USA: New York, NY. 1984. Lang.: Eng. 1154

Introduction to *The Revenge of Truth* by Isak Dinesen. Denmark. Kenya. 1885-1985. Lang.: Eng. 4010

Marriage of Figaro, The (Opera)
SEE
Nozze di Figaro, Le.

Marriot, B. Rodney
Plays/librettos/scripts
Artists react to *New York Times* condemnation of current playwriting. USA. 1984. Lang.: Eng. 2888

Mars, Tanya
Performance/production
Interviews with performance artists. Canada: Toronto, ON. USA: New York, NY. 1980-1986. Lang.: Eng. 3444

Marshall, Norman
Institutions
Profile of Merry Enterprises Theatre. USA: New York, NY. 1975-1984. Lang.: Eng. 543

Marston, John
Plays/librettos/scripts
Defense of *The Malcontent* by John Marston as a well-constructed satire. England. 1590-1600. Lang.: Eng. 938

Religious ideas in the satirical plays of John Marston. England. 1595-1609. Lang.: Eng. 940

Martello Towers
Plays/librettos/scripts
Interview with playwright Alex Buzo. Australia. 1986. Lang.: Eng. 2385

Mártha, István
Performance/production
Reviews of three musicals about the 1960s. Hungary. 1985-1986. Lang.: Hun. 3488

Martial arts
Performance/production
Evidence for performance of a mock tournament of the type described in a 15th-century poem. England: Exeter. 1432. Lang.: Eng. 3331

Martin Audéich: A Christmas Miracle
Performance/production
Review of Robert Downard's opera *Martin Audéich: A Christmas Miracle*. USA: Denver, CO. 1985. Lang.: Eng. 3813

Martin, Kate
Performance/production
Collection of newspaper reviews by London theatre critics. UK-England. 1986. Lang.: Eng. 2114

Martín, Manuel
Plays/librettos/scripts
The history of Cuban exile theatre. Cuba. USA: New York, NY. 1959-1986. Lang.: Spa. 2451

Martinelli, Giovanni
Performance/production
Significance of the translation in recordings of Verdi's *Otello*. USA. 1902-1978. Lang.: Eng. 3812

Martinelli, Tristano
Performance/production
Interpretive technique of *commedia dell'arte* actors. France. 1575-1670. Lang.: Ita. 3410

Comic actor Tristano Martinelli, probable creator of the character Harlequin. Italy. France. 1550-1600. Lang.: Ita. 3412

Martínez Ballesteros, Antonio
Basic theatrical documents
Playtext of *Los Comediantes (The Players)* by Antonio Martínez Ballesteros. Spain. 1982. Lang.: Spa. 1494

Performance/production
Playwright Antonio Martínez Ballesteros discusses the production history of his play *Los Comediantes (The Players)*. Spain: Toledo. USA: Cincinnati, OH. 1982-1985. Lang.: Spa. 2076

Martini, Ferdinando
Administration
Letter from actor Ernesto Rossi concerning actors' labor movement. Italy. 1891. Lang.: Ita. 1436

Márton, András
Performance/production
Production of Bengt Ahlfors' *Szinházkomédia (Theatre Comedy)* directed by András Márton. Hungary: Debrecen. 1985. Lang.: Hun. 1925

Marton, László
Performance/production
Ivan Vasiljèvič by Michajl Afanasjèvič Bulgakov directed by László Marton at Vigszinház under the title *Iván, a rettentő*. Hungary: Budapest. 1986. Lang.: Hun. 1783

Marx, Arthur
Performance/production
Reviews of *Grouch: A Life in Revue*, by Arthur Marx and Robert Fisher, staged by Arthur Marx. USA: New York, NY. 1986. Lang.: Eng. 2201

Marxism
Plays/librettos/scripts
Career of Marxist playwright George Sklar. USA: New York, NY. 1920-1967. Lang.: Eng. 985

Marxist analysis of colonialism in Shakespeare's *Othello*. England. South Africa, Republic of. 1597-1637. Lang.: Eng. 2507

Relation to other fields
Critique of the relation between politics and theatre in Klaus Mann's *Mephisto* performed by Théâtre du Soleil. France: Paris. 1979. Lang.: Eng. 1085

Maschere
Performance/production
Precursors of *commedia dell'arte*. Italy: Venice. 1400-1620. Lang.: Eng. 3414

Mask plays
Plays/librettos/scripts
Role analysis of the mask-dance play, *Yängjubyulsändae* and the theories of Choe Sang-Su. Korea: Yängju. 1700-1900. Lang.: Kor. 1375

Theory/criticism
Development and characteristics of Oriental theatre. Korea: Seoul. Japan: Tokyo. China: Beijing. 200-1986. Lang.: Kor. 1215

Influence of Korean mask-dance theatre in Japan. Korea: Seoul. Japan. 1400-1600. Lang.: Kor. 1377

Styles of mask-dance drama in Asia. Korea: Seoul. Japan: Tokyo. China: Beijing. 1400-1986. Lang.: Kor. 1378

Evolution and symbolism of the Mask-Dance drama. Korea: Seoul. 700-1986. Lang.: Kor. 1379

Masks
Design/technology
Survey of the use of masks in theatre. Asia. Europe. Africa. Lang.: Ita. 236

Máté, Gábor
Performance/production
Der Hofmeister (The Tutor), Jakob Lenz's drama adapted by Bertolt Brecht, directed by Gábor Máté. Hungary: Kaposvár. 1985. Lang.: Hun. 1810

Production of *A nevelő (The Tutor)* by Bertolt Brecht. Hungary: Kaposvár. 1985. Lang.: Hun. 1840

Knock by Jules Romains directed by Gábor Máté at Csiky Gergely Theatre. Hungary: Kaposvár. 1986. Lang.: Hun. 1892

Gábor Máté directs Brecht's *Der Hofmeister (The Tutor)* at Csiky Gergely Theatre under the title *A nevelő*. Hungary: Kaposvár. 1985. Lang.: Hun. 1966

Mathew, Ray
Plays/librettos/scripts
Analysis of plays by Charles Jury and Ray Mathew. Australia. 1905-1967. Lang.: Eng. 2384

Comparison of plays about Ned Kelly of Australia and Louis Riel of Canada. Canada. Australia. 1900-1976. Lang.: Eng. 2421

Mathews, W.H.
Reference materials
Catalogue of an exhibition of costume designs for Broadway musicals. USA: New York, NY. 1900-1925. Lang.: Eng, Ger. 3635

Matkócsik, András
Performance/production
András Matkócsik directs *Mondd, Joe! (Eh, Joe!)* and *Az utolsó tekercs (Krapp's Last Tape)* by Samuel Beckett. Hungary: Budapest. 1985. Lang.: Hun. 1851

Matkowsky, Adalbert
Performance/production
Application of Brechtian concepts by Eckhardt Schall. Germany, East: Berlin, East. UK-England: London. 1952-1986. Lang.: Eng. 1762

Matthew, Mark, Luke and Charlie
Performance/production
Collection of newspaper reviews by London theatre critics. UK-England: London. 1986. Lang.: Eng. 2124

Mattson, Jean
Performance/production
Tour of puppet show *The Return of the Bounce* by Jean Mattson and Joan King. USA: Seattle, WA. Japan. 1984. Lang.: Eng. 3979

Mattsson, Anders
Performance/production
Stage photographs with comment by photographers. Sweden. 1985-1986. Lang.: Swe. 794

Maugham, W. Somerset
Performance/production
Reviews of *The Circle* by W. Somerset Maugham, staged by Stephen Porter, performed by the Mirror Repertory Company. USA: New York, NY. 1986. Lang.: Eng. 2227

Maurer, Michael
Performance/production
Reviews of *Into the Light*, book by Jeff Tamborniro, music by Lee Holdridge, lyrics by John Forster, staged by Michael Maurer. USA: New York, NY. 1986. Lang.: Eng. 3615

Mauri, Vicent
Institutions
History of theatre in Valencia area focusing on Civil War period. Spain: Valencia. 1817-1982. Lang.: Cat. 514

May Blossom
Plays/librettos/scripts
Theme and narrative structure in plays of Eugene O'Neill, David Belasco, and James A. Herne. USA. 1879-1918. Lang.: Eng. 2933

May, Val
Performance/production
Collection of newspaper reviews by London theatre critics. UK. 1986. Lang.: Eng. 2102

Collection of newspaper reviews by London theatre critics. UK-England: London. 1986. Lang.: Eng. 2119

Mayakovsky Theatre (Moscow)
SEE
Teat'r im V. Majakovskovo.

Mayakovsky, Vladimir Vladimirovich
SEE
Majakovskij, Vladimir Vladimirovič.

Mayer, Edwin Justus
Plays/librettos/scripts
Analysis of the operetta *Firebrand* by Kurt Weill and Ira Gershwin. USA: New York, NY. Italy: Florence. 1945. Lang.: Eng. 3944

Mayer, Heinrich
Institutions
Activities and functions of the Teletheater-Gesellschaft. Austria: Vienna. 1985. Lang.: Ger. 450

Mayer, William
Performance/production
Reviews of *Death in the Family, Viaggio a Reims, Abduction from the Seraglio* and *Tales of Hoffmann*. USA: St. Louis, MO. 1975-1986. Lang.: Eng. 3799

Mayo, Janet
Design/technology
Overview of the costume department of the National Theatre. UK-England: London. 1950-1986. Lang.: Eng. 1523

Maypole dancing
Performance/production
History of Maypole dancing. England. 1244-1985. Lang.: Eng. 1329

Mazumdar, Maxim
Performance/production
Biographical study of actor/teacher/director Maxim Mazumdar. Canada: Wolfville, NS. 1985-1986. Lang.: Eng. 1662

McAnuff, Des
Performance/production
Director Robert Woodruff's shift from naturalism to greater theatricality. USA: San Francisco, CA, New York, NY, La Jolla, CA. 1976-1986. Lang.: Eng. 851

McArthur, Edwin
Performance/production
Obituary of soprano Dusolina Giannini. USA: Philadelphia, PA. 1902-1986. Lang.: Eng. 3823

McCaslin, Nellie
Administration
Community funding of residency for children's theatre performer, Aurand Harris. USA: Cleveland, OH. 1985-1986. Lang.: Eng. 145

McCormach, Suzanne
Administration
Directors of the film festival Filmex discuss their plans for the future. USA: Los Angeles, CA. 1986. Lang.: Eng. 3190

McCracken, Jack
Performance/production
The effect of disease on circus animals. USA. France. 1890-1985. Lang.: Eng. 3389

McCracken, James
Performance/production
Significance of the translation in recordings of Verdi's *Otello*. USA. 1902-1978. Lang.: Eng. 3812

McCray, Ivey
Reference materials
Current work of Audelco award-winning playwrights. USA: New York, NY. 1973-1984. Lang.: Eng. 3007

McCree Theatre (Flint, MI)
Institutions
Brief history of the McCree Theatre. USA: Flint, MI. 1971-1986. Lang.: Eng. 1609

McCullers, Carson
Plays/librettos/scripts
Correlation between short stories and plays by Carson McCullers. USA. 1917-1967. Lang.: Rus. 2889

McElfatrick, William
Performance spaces
History of the Bushwick Theatre. USA: New York, NY. 1911-1986. Lang.: Eng. 3465

McEwan, Ian
Plays/librettos/scripts
World War II as a theme in post-war British drama. UK-England. 1945-1983. Lang.: Eng. 2868

McGafferty, Nell
Plays/librettos/scripts
Historical background of *Sisters of Eve* by Tricia Burden. Eire. 1984-1986. Lang.: Eng. 2455

McGeary, W.C.
Plays/librettos/scripts
Analysis of plays by Canadian soldiers in World War I. Canada. UK. 1901-1918. Lang.: Eng. 936

McGlynn, Mark
Performance/production
Collection of newspaper reviews by London theatre critics. UK. 1986. Lang.: Eng. 2099

McGrath, John
Plays/librettos/scripts
Interview with playwright Howard Barker. UK-England. 1981-1985. Lang.: Eng. 2845

Interview with playwright Louise Page. UK-England. 1979-1986. Lang.: Eng. 2882

Relation to other fields
Reflections of political attitudes in plays by John McGrath and David Hare. UK-England. 1971-1978. Lang.: Eng. 3060

McGuinn-Cazale Theatre (New York, NY)
Performance spaces
Descriptions of newly constructed Off Broadway theatres. USA: New York, NY. 1984. Lang.: Eng. 644

McGuire, Michael
Performance/production
Reviews of *The Common Pursuit*, by Simon Gray, staged by Simon Gray and Michael McGuire. USA: New York, NY. 1986. Lang.: Eng. 2202

McIntosh, Diana
Performance/production
Diana McIntosh on her performance pieces involving contemporary music. Canada: Winnipeg, MB. 1979-1986. Lang.: Eng. 3250

McKenzie, Julie
Performance/production
Actress Julie McKenzie discusses her role in *Woman in Mind* by Alan Ayckbourn. UK-England: London. Lang.: Eng. 2145

McKeown, Charles
Performance/production
Collection of newspaper reviews by London theatre critics. UK-England: London. 1986. Lang.: Eng. 2112

Interviews with playwrights Louise Page, Charles McKeown and Malcolm Sircon. UK-England: London. 1986. Lang.: Eng. 2133

McKie, Zuri
Administration
Interview with NYSCA Theatre Program Director Zuri McKie. USA: New York, NY. 1983. Lang.: Eng. 133

McKim, Meade and White
Performance spaces
History of the Eastman Theatre. USA: Rochester, NY. 1922-1986. Lang.: Eng. 3222

McNair, Sarah
Performance/production
Interview with Lesbian feminist theatre company Hard Corps. UK-England. 1984-1986. Lang.: Eng. 2164

McNally, Terrence
Plays/librettos/scripts
A group of playwrights discuss the one-act play as a form. USA. 1986. 2937

Me and My Girl
Performance/production
Review of *Me and My Girl*, book and lyrics by L. Arthur Rose and Douglas Furber, staged by Mike Ockrent. USA: New York, NY. 1986. Lang.: Eng. 3618

Mead, Kathryn
Performance/production
Collection of newspaper reviews by London theatre critics. UK. 1986. Lang.: Eng. 2099

Meadow, Lynne
Administration
Lynne Meadow, artistic director of the Manhattan Theatre Club, describes her fourteen years on the job. USA: New York, NY. 1972-1986. Lang.: Eng. 1442

Performance/production
Reviews of *Principia Scriptoriae* by Richard Nelson, staged by Lynne Meadow. USA: New York, NY. 1986. Lang.: Eng. 2223

Meale, Richard
Traditional innovation in *Voss* by Richard Meale and David Malouf. Australia. 1980-1986. Lang.: Eng. 3636

Measure by Measure
Basic theatrical documents
Texts of three political dramas, with discussion. Canada. 1833-1879. Lang.: Eng. 1472

Relation to other fields
Shakespearean allusions in political satire. Canada. 1798-1871. Lang.: Eng. 1074

Measure for Measure
Performance/production
István Paál directs Shakespeare's *Szeget szeggel (Measure for Measure)*. Hungary: Veszprém. 1985. Lang.: Hun. 1770

Szeget szeggel (Measure for Measure) by William Shakespeare directed by Tamás Szirtes at Madách Kamaraszinház. Hungary: Budapest. 1985. Lang.: Hun. 1785

Tamás Szirtes directs *Szeget szeggel (Measure for Measure)* by Shakespeare. Hungary: Budapest. 1985. Lang.: Hun. 1789

Production of Shakespeare's *Szeget szeggel (Measure for Measure)* directed by István Paál. Hungary: Veszprém. 1985. Lang.: Hun. 1872

István Paál directs *Szeget szeggel (Measure for Measure)* by Shakespeare at Petőfi Szinház. Hungary: Veszprém. 1985. Lang.: Hun. 1938

Plays/librettos/scripts
Contrast between Shakespeare's England and the Vienna of *Measure for Measure*. England. 1604-1605. Lang.: Eng. 2465

Shakespeare's complex, unconventional heroines in *All's Well that Ends Well* and *Measure for Measure*. England. 1603. Lang.: Eng. 2469

Possible influence of Christopher Marlowe's plays upon those of William Shakespeare. England. 1580-1620. Lang.: Eng. 2478

Wagner's *Das Liebesverbot*, an operatic adaptation of *Measure for Measure*. Germany. 1834. Lang.: Eng. 3880

Mecklenburgisches Staatstheater (Schwerin)
Institutions
History of drama ensemble Mecklenburgisches Staatstheater Schwerin. Germany, East: Schwerin. 1970-1986. Lang.: Ger. 498

Meczner, János
Performance/production
Notes on performances of *Hongkongi paróka (Wig Made in Hong Kong)*, *Egérút (Narrow Escape)* and *Róza néni (Aunt Rosa)*. Hungary: Budapest. 1985. Lang.: Hun. 1801

Meddings, Derek
Design/technology
Designer and special effects supervisor make sleigh fly in *Santa Claus—The Movie*. Greenland. 1986. 3199

Medea
Performance/production
Collection of newspaper reviews by London theatre critics. UK. 1986. Lang.: Eng. 2099

Collection of newspaper reviews by London theatre critics. UK-England: London. 1986. Lang.: Eng. 2122

Media
Intertextual analysis of Eugene O'Neill's play *Long Day's Journey Into Night* and Ingmar Bergman's film, *Through a Glass Darkly*. USA. Sweden. 1957-1961. Lang.: Eng. 1425

SEE ALSO
Classed Entries under MEDIA: 3164-3287.

Administration
Effect of copyright on new broadcast technologies. UK. 1971-1986. Lang.: Eng. 71

Advantages of radio advertising for live theatre. USA: New York, NY. 1986. Lang.: Eng. 175

Basic theatrical documents
Catalan translation of *The Homecoming* by Harold Pinter. UK-England. 1965. Lang.: Cat. 1507

Design/technology
The differences in scene and costume design for television versus theatre. Hungary: Budapest. 1986. Lang.: Hun. 278

Career of costume and stage designer Eugenio Guglielminetti. Italy. 1946-1986. Lang.: Ita. 299

Career of scenic designer Eugene Lee. USA: Providence, RI. 1965-1984. Lang.: Eng. 339

Challenges faced by designers of Bob Fosse's *Big Deal*. USA. 1986. Lang.: Eng. 359

Art director Steven Graham's work on the film *The Money Pit*. USA. 1986. 378

Overhaul of The World Theatre as a radio broadcasting facility. USA: St. Paul, MN. 1982-1986. Lang.: Eng. 387

Choosing music and sound effects for puppet theatre. USA. Lang.: Eng. 3953

Creating overhead shadow sequence for puppet production. USA. 4014

Institutions
Overview of Ariane Mnouchkine's work with Théâtre du Soleil. France: Paris. 1959-1985. Lang.: Eng. 497

Member organizations of Alliance of Resident Theatres/New York include programs in poetry, media and music. USA: New York, NY. 1984. Lang.: Eng. 574

Media — cont'd

Productions in 1986 of Ars Electronica. Austria: Linz. 1979-1986.
Lang.: Ger.   3321

Performance spaces
Tour of theatres in Illinois, Iowa and Wisconsin. USA: Chicago, IL.
1986. Lang.: Eng.   641

Performance/production
Esse Ljungh's acting career with Winnipeg Little Theatre. Canada:
Winnipeg, MB. 1921-1937. Lang.: Eng.   664

Interview with actor, director, playwright and filmmaker Ramón
Griffero. Chile: Santiago. 1953-1986. Lang.: Spa.   675

Analyses of the major trends in theatre, film and other art forms.
Europe. USA. 1960-1980. Lang.: Rus.   701

Biography of Richard Burton. UK-Wales. 1925-1984. Lang.: Eng.
                                                                820

Guide to finding acting jobs in theatre, film and television. USA.
1986. Lang.: Eng.   835

Process and results of adaptating plays from Off Broadway to TV.
USA: New York, NY. 1980-1986. Lang.: Eng.   841

Actor discusses work in recitation programs. USSR: Moscow. 1980-
1986. Lang.: Rus.   888

Issues in speech pronunciation in performance. USSR. 1980-1986.
Lang.: Rus.   898

Director Mark Zacharov of the Komsomol Theatre discusses his
work. USSR: Moscow. 1980-1986. Lang.: Rus.   912

Biography of Burgtheater actor Richard Eybner. Austria: Vienna.
1896-1986. Lang.: Ger.   1653

Career of actor Jalmari Rinne. Finland: Helsinki, Tampere, Turku.
1893-1985. Lang.: Eng, Fre.   1719

Autobiographical recollections of Cecilia Esztergályos, ballet-dancer
turned actress. Hungary. 1945-1986. Lang.: Hun.   1829

Career of actress Éva Ruttkai. Hungary. 1927-1986. Lang.: Hun.
                                                                1871

The life and career of actress Mari Törőcsik. Hungary. 1956-1986.
Lang.: Hun.   1933

Autobiography of actor Alec Guinness. UK. USA. 1914-1985. Lang.:
Eng.   2106

Hungarian translation of *Vivien Leigh: A Biography*. UK-England.
1913-1967. Lang.: Hun.   2141

Comparison of stage production and film version of Shakespeare's
King Lear, both directed by Peter Brook. UK-England. 1962-1970.
Lang.: Eng.   2149

Career of actor Jeremy Irons in theatre, television and film. UK-
England. USA. 1970-1985. Lang.: Eng.   2181

Artists who began in dance, film or television move to Off
Broadway theatre. USA: New York, NY. 1982. Lang.: Eng.   2284

Biography of playwright and actor Sam Shepard. USA. 1943-1986.
Lang.: Eng.   2295

Music critic Derek Jewell traces Frank Sinatra's career along with
his own. USA. 1900-1986. Lang.: Eng.   3179

Biography of singer Frank Sinatra. USA. 1915-1984. Lang.: Eng.
                                                                3180

Career of vaudeville comedian Roy Rene, creator of 'Mo'. Australia.
1892-1954. Lang.: Eng.   3327

Autobiography of comedian Billy Crystal. USA. 1955. Lang.: Eng.
                                                                3350

Comedienne Joan Rivers' account of her life and career. USA: New
York, NY. 1928-1965. Lang.: Eng.   3352

Career of popular entertainer Bill Cosby. USA. 1937-1986. Lang.:
Eng.   3353

Interview with performance artist Jill Scott. Australia. 1986. Lang.:
Eng.   3441

Maurizio Tiberi and his Tima Club records of operatic rarities. Italy:
Castelnuovo del Porto. 1950-1986. Lang.: Eng.   3756

The Franco Zeffirelli film of *Otello* by Giuseppe Verdi, an account
of the production. Italy: Rome. 1985-1986. Lang.: Eng.   3758

The videotaped opera showings at the Museum of Broadcasting.
USA: New York, NY. 1985-1986. Lang.: Eng.   3828

Plays/librettos/scripts
Popularity of dramatic monologue on stage and television. Australia.
1985. Lang.: Eng.   921

English theatrical representation of political struggle in Northern
Ireland. UK-Ireland. 1980-1986. Lang.: Rus.   977

Structure and characterization in the plays of W.O. Mitchell. Canada.
1975. Lang.: Eng.   2408

Analysis of *RA* by R. Murray Schafer, performed by Comus Music
Theatre. Canada: Toronto, ON. 1983. Lang.: Eng.   2416

Career of He Mengfu, playwright and director. China, People's
Republic of. 1911-1945. Lang.: Chi.   2448

Analysis of *L'Aigle à deux têtes* (*The Eagle With Two Heads*) by
Jean Cocteau. France. 1889-1963. Lang.: Cat.   2565

Biographical information on Jean Genet. France. 1910-1985. Lang.:
Fre.   2588

Collection of essays on dramatic text and performance. Poland.
1600-1984. Lang.: Fre.   2742

Self-reflexivity in Antonio Buero Vallejo's play *El Sueño de la razón*
(*The Sleep of Reason*) and Victor Erice's film *El Espíritu de la
colmena* (*The Spirit of the Beehive*). Spain. 1970-1973. Lang.: Eng.
                                                                2781

Analysis of the plot, characters and structure of *The Homecoming* by
Harold Pinter. UK-England: London. 1930-1985. Lang.: Cat.   2865

Interview with playwright Arthur Miller. USA. 1985. Lang.: Eng.
                                                                2921

Reference materials
Theatre productions in the French community of Belgium. Belgium.
1981-1982. Lang.: Fre.   1004

Theatre productions in the French community of Belgium. Belgium.
1982-1983. Lang.: Fre.   1005

Theatre productions in the French community of Belgium. Belgium.
1983-1984. Lang.: Fre.   1006

Theatre productions in the French community of Belgium. Belgium.
1984-1985. Lang.: Fre.   1007

Books on theatre, film, music and dance published in Italy in 1985.
Italy. 1985. Lang.: Ita.   1021

Relation to other fields
Analysis of *Symphony* by Herman Voaden and Lowrie Warrener.
Canada. 1914-1933. Lang.: Eng.   1075

Study of attempts to create a 'visual' music using light instead of
sound. Europe. USA. 1900-1985. Lang.: Ita.   1082

The role of theatre and television in the moral education of society.
USSR. 1980-1986. Lang.: Rus.   1177

Theory/criticism
Essays on the sociology of art and semiotics. Lang.: Hun.   1192

Theatre professionals challenge assertions that theatre is a weaker
form of communication than film. USA: New York, NY. 1985.
Lang.: Eng.   1225

Experimental theatres to offset the impact of film and theatre.
China, People's Republic of. 1960-1981. Lang.: Chi.   3090

Medicine show
Performance/production
Recreation of a medicine show featuring 'Doc' Bloodgood, staged by
American Place Theatre. USA. 1983. Lang.: Eng.   3375

Medieval Players (Perth)
Performance/production
Political difficulties in staging two touring productions of
Shakespeare's *The Taming of the Shrew*. UK. 1985-1986. Lang.:
Eng.   2104

Medieval theatre
Administration
Survey of records relating to performances of Robin Hood and King
Games. England: Kingston. 1504-1538. Lang.: Eng.   3309

Basic theatrical documents
Edition and introduction to Catalan religious tragedy of Saint
Sebastian. Spain-Catalonia: Riudoms. 1400-1880. Lang.: Cat.   1498

Design/technology
Construction of castle for goldsmith's guild pageant. England:
London. 1377-1392. Lang.: Eng.   3422

Performance spaces
Outdoor performance spaces surveyed through fragmentary records.
England: Shrewsbury. 1445-1575. Lang.: Eng.   593

Spatial orientation in medieval Catalan religious productions. Spain-
Catalonia. Italy: Florence. 1388-1538. Lang.: Cat.   616

Performance/production
Theories of medieval production and acting techniques. England.
1400-1500. Lang.: Eng.   698

Actors and roles in medieval French theatre. France. 900-1499.
Lang.: Rus.   721

Medieval style Assumption plays. Spain-Catalonia. 1000-1709. Lang.:
Cat.   792

Medieval theatre — cont'd

Performance of *Towneley Cycle* in Victoria College Quadrangle. Canada: Toronto, ON. 1985. Lang.: Eng. 1673

Reconstruction of staging of Act I, *The Spanish Tragedy* by Thomas Kyd. England: London. 1592. Lang.: Eng. 1703

Analysis and interpretation of the staging of *The Castle of Perseverance* based on original stage plan drawing. England. 1343-1554. Lang.: Eng. 1708

Analysis of Robin Hood entertainments in the parish of Yeovil. England. 1475-1588. Lang.: Eng. 1712

Original staging of Thomas Middleton's *Hengist, King of Kent.* England: London. 1619-1661. Lang.: Eng. 1713

Performance by Joculatores Lancastrienses of Thomas Garter's interlude, *Commody of the Moste Vertuous and Godlye Susanna.* UK-England: Lancaster. 1985. Lang.: Eng. 2148

Thomas Garter's *Commody of the Moste Vertuous and Godlye Susana* performed before orignial screen in timberframed gothic hall. UK-England. 1986. Lang.: Eng. 2165

Descriptions of productions of *Li Jus de Robin et Marion (The Play of Robin and Marion), The Comedy of Virtuous and Godly Susanna* and *The Second Shepherds Play.* USA: Washington, DC. UK-England: Lancaster. France: Perpignan. 1986. Lang.: Eng. 2289

Account of University of California at Irvine production of a nativity play with composite text drawn from York, N-town and Wakefield cycles. USA: Irvine, CA. 1986. Lang.: Eng. 2307

Account of a modern production of *Everyman.* USA: New York, NY. 1986. Lang.: Eng. 2314

Reconstruction of religious dramatic spectacles. Italy: Ravello. 1400-1503. Lang.: Ita. 3339

Comparison of Catalan Assumption plays. Spain-Catalonia: Tarragona. 1350-1388. Lang.: Cat. 3346

Documents of religious processions and plays. France: Saint-Omer. 1200-1600. Lang.: Eng. 3424

Contemporary performance of the traditional *Festa d'Elx.* Spain: Elche. 1370-1985. Lang.: Eng. 3491

Performance by Sequentia of *Ordo Virtutum* by Hildegard of Bingen. USA: Stanford, CA. 1986. Lang.: Eng. 3493

Use of puppets in liturgical plays and ceremonies. England: London, Witney. 1540-1560. Lang.: Eng. 3963

Plays/librettos/scripts

Review essay on *Li jus de Robin et Marion (The Play of Robin and Marion)* directed by Jean Asselin. Canada: Montreal, PQ. 1986. Lang.: Fre. 937

Analysis of Catalan Nativity plays. Spain-Catalonia. 1400-1599. Lang.: Cat. 972

Ben Jonson's use of romance in *Volpone.* England. 1575-1600. Lang.: Eng. 2461

Analysis of theophany in English *Corpus Christi* plays. England. 1350-1550. Lang.: Eng. 2472

Possible influence of Christopher Marlowe's plays upon those of William Shakespeare. England. 1580-1620. Lang.: Eng. 2478

Function of humor and violence in the *Play of the Sacrament* (Croxton). England. 1400-1499. Lang.: Eng. 2493

Legalistic aspect of *Commody of the Moste Vertuous and Godlye Susana* by Thomas Garter. England: London. 1563. Lang.: Eng. 2494

Moral issues in *A Woman Killed with Kindness* by Thomas Heywood. England. 1560. Lang.: Eng. 2498

Dramatic dynamics of Chester cycle play, *The Fall of Lucifer.* England. 1400-1550. Lang.: Eng. 2499

Use of group aggression in Ben Jonson's comedies. England. 1575-1600. Lang.: Eng. 2508

Use of language in Beaumont and Fletcher's *Philaster.* England. 1609. Lang.: Eng. 2512

Herpetological imagery in Jonson's *Catiline.* England. 1611. Lang.: Eng. 2517

Critical problems in *Henno* by Johannes Reuchlin. Germany: Heidelberg. 1497-1522. Lang.: Eng. 2605

Possible source of cock fight in Henry Medwall's *Fulgens and Lucres.* Ireland. 1602. Lang.: Eng. 2664

Discussion of *L'esaltazione della croce (The Exaltation of the Cross)* by Giovanni Maria Cecchi. Italy. 1585-1589. Lang.: Ita. 2683

Linguistic study of *Auto de Pasión (Passion Play)* by Lucas Fernández. Spain-Catalonia. 1510-1514. Lang.: Cat. 2812

Compares pageant-wagon play about Edward IV with version by Thomas Heywood. England: Coventry, London. 1560-1600. Lang.: Eng. 3430

Study of playtexts and illustrations in Lille plays manuscript. France: Lille. 1450-1500. Lang.: Eng. 3431

Analysis of Hildegard of Bingen's *Ordo Virtutum* as a morality play. Germany: Bingen. 1151. Lang.: Eng. 3498

Relation to other fields

Articles on anthropology of theatre. Lang.: Ita. 1056

Literary origins of the 'lauda drammatica'. Italy. 1200-1400. Lang.: Ita. 1109

Costuming evidence on carved baptismal fonts. England. 1463-1544. Lang.: Eng. 3026

Assimilation of dramatic elements of Aztec worship in Christianization process. Mexico. Spain. 1519-1559. Lang.: Eng. 3046

Renaissance theatre at Valencia court, Catalan festivals. Spain-Catalonia: Valencia. 1330-1970. Lang.: Spa. 3362

Christian and pre-Christian elements of Corpus Christi celebration. Spain-Catalonia: Berga. 1264-1986. Lang.: Cat. 3432

Mednick, Murray
Performance/production
Murray Mednick's 7-play Coyote Cycle performed outdoors from dusk to dawn. USA. 1984. Lang.: Eng. 2292

Medusa
Plays/librettos/scripts
Work of playwright Stefan Schütz. Germany, West. 1944-1986. Lang.: Eng. 2625

Interview with playwright Stefan Schütz. Germany, West. 1970-1986. Lang.: Eng. 2628

Medwall, Henry
Plays/librettos/scripts
Possible source of cock fight in Henry Medwall's *Fulgens and Lucres.* Ireland. 1602. Lang.: Eng. 2664

Mehrten, Greg
Institutions
Interview with members of Mabou Mines. USA: New York, NY. 1984. Lang.: Eng. 1607

Mei, Lanfang
Performance/production
History of the Beijing Opera. China: Beijing. 800-1986. Lang.: Cat. 3507

What spoken drama actors can learn from Sung drama. China. 1100-1980. Lang.: Chi. 3513

Career of Beijing opera actor, Hou Hsijui. China. 1920-1983. Lang.: Chi. 3514

Influence of Beijing opera performer Mei Lanfang on European acting and staging traditions. China, People's Republic of. USSR. Germany. 1900-1935. Lang.: Eng. 3521

Theory/criticism
Symbolism and aesthetics in the performance styles of Chinese opera. China, People's Republic of: Beijing. 1935-1985. Lang.: Chi. 3564

Characteristics of Chinese opera in Szechuan province. China, People's Republic of. 1963-1985. Lang.: Chi. 3570

Meilleur, Daniel
Institutions
History of the Théâtre de la Marmaille. Canada: Quebec, PQ. 1973-1986. Lang.: Eng. 1552

Meinikov, Ivan
Performance/production
Mussorgskij's opera *Boris Godunov* at the Mariinskij Theatre. Russia: St. Petersburg. 1874. Lang.: Eng. 3775

Meissner, Krystyna
Performance/production
Krystyna Meissner directs Juliusz Słowacki's *Balladyna*, Teatr Horzycy. Poland: Toruń. 1984. Lang.: Pol. 2035

Meister, Otto
Institutions
History of the Dime Museums. USA: Milwaukee, WI. 1882-1916. Lang.: Eng. 3324

Meistersinger von Nürnberg, Die
Performance/production
Interview with Wolfgang Wagner on his staging of 3 Wagnerian operas at the Bayreuth Festspiele. Germany, West: Bayreuth. 1975-1985. Lang.: Hun. 3740

Mejerchol'd, Vsevolod Emiljèvič
Performance/production
Zen and Western acting styles. Lang.: Eng. 648

Mejerchol'd's influence on Bertolt Brecht. Russia: Moscow. Germany, East: Berlin, East. 1903-1957. Lang.: Eng. 2065

What spoken drama actors can learn from Sung drama. China. 1100-1980. Lang.: Chi. 3513

Influence of Beijing opera performer Mei Lanfang on European acting and staging traditions. China, People's Republic of. USSR. Germany. 1900-1935. Lang.: Eng. 3521
Plays/librettos/scripts
Compares contemporary Canadian theatre with German and Russian theatre of the early 20th century. Canada. Russia: Moscow. Germany. 1900-1986. Lang.: Eng. 2412
Relation to other fields
Comparison of Olympiad Arts Festival and the 1984 Olympic Games. USA: Los Angeles, CA. 1984. Lang.: Eng. 1148

Melbourne Theatre Company (Melbourne)
Administration
Malcolm Blaylock on theatre and government funding policy. Australia. 1985. Lang.: Eng. 22
Plays/librettos/scripts
Developments in Australian playwriting since 1975. Australia. 1975-1986. Lang.: Eng. 2374

Interview with playwright Ray Lawler. Australia: Melbourne. 1984. Lang.: Eng. 2386

Melià, Felip
Institutions
History of theatre in Valencia area focusing on Civil War period. Spain: Valencia. 1817-1982. Lang.: Cat. 514

Melling, Phil
Performance/production
Collection of newspaper reviews by London theatre critics. UK: London. 1986. Lang.: Eng. 2100

Mellot, Martha
Performance/production
Acting style in plays by Henrik Ibsen. 1885-1905. Lang.: Eng. 1627

Melodrama
Performance/production
Melodrama in the performing arts. USSR. 1980-1986. Lang.: Rus. 883
Plays/librettos/scripts
William Rufus Blake's *Fitzallan* as the first play written and produced in Canada. Canada: Halifax, NS. 1833. Lang.: Eng. 2430

Treatment of the Frankenstein myth in three gothic melodramas. UK-England. France. 1823-1826. Lang.: Eng. 2847

Analysis of television docudramas as a melodrama genre. USA. 1965-1986. Lang.: Eng. 3285
Relation to other fields
Difficulties of distinction between 'high' and 'popular' culture. Australia. 1860-1930. Lang.: Eng. 1063
Theory/criticism
Melodrama as an aesthetic theatre form. Australia. 1850-1986. Lang.: Eng. 3083

Melons
Performance/production
Collection of newspaper reviews by London theatre critics. UK-England: London. 1986. Lang.: Eng. 2112

Royal Shakespeare Company performances at the Barbican Theatre. UK-England: London. 1986. Lang.: Eng. 2152

Melville, Herman
Plays/librettos/scripts
Collaboration of authors and composers of *Billy Budd*. UK-England: London. 1949-1964. Lang.: Eng. 3895

Melyrepülés (Flying at Low Altitude)
Performance/production
Melyrepülés (Flying at Low Altitude) by Tamás Cseh and Dénes Csengey. Hungary: Budapest. 1986. Lang.: Hun. 3487

Reviews of three musicals about the 1960s. Hungary. 1985-1986. Lang.: Hun. 3488

Menotti, Gian Carlo
Performance/production
Stills from telecast performance of *Goya*. List of principals, conductor and production staff included. USA: Washington, DC. 1986. Lang.: Eng. 3791

Profile of and interview with Gian Carlo Menotti with emphasis on his new opera *Goya*. USA: New York, NY. 1911-1986. Lang.: Eng. 3838

Plays/librettos/scripts
Gian Carlo Menotti's reactions to harsh criticism of his operas. USA: New York, NY. UK-Scotland: Edinburgh. Italy: Cadegliano. 1938-1988. Lang.: Eng. 3902

Mensáros, László
Performance/production
Review of Gábor Görgey's *Mikszáth különös házassága (Mikszáth and His Peculiar Marriage)* directed by János Sándor. Hungary: Szeged. 1986. Lang.: Hun. 1819

Mensch Meier
Performance/production
Life and technique of Franz Xaver Kroetz. USA: New York, NY. Germany, West. 1984. Lang.: Eng. 2287

Menteur, Le (Liar, The)
Performance/production
History of staging of *Le Menteur (The Liar)* by Pierre Corneille. France: Paris. 1644-1985. Lang.: Fre. 1738

Menteur, Le (Liar, The)
Performance/production
Production photographs of Pierre Corneille's *Le Menteur (The Liar)* at the Comédie-Française. France: Paris. 1986. Lang.: Fre. 1729

Pieces related to performance at the Comédie-Française of *Le Menteur (The Liar)* by Pierre Corneille. France: Paris. 1644-1985. Lang.: Fre. 1735

Mephisto
Performance/production
Royal Shakespeare Company performances at the Barbican Theatre. UK-England: London. 1986. Lang.: Eng. 2152
Relation to other fields
Critique of the relation between politics and theatre in Klaus Mann's *Mephisto* performed by Théâtre du Soleil. France: Paris. 1979. Lang.: Eng. 1085

Merchant of Venice, The
Performance/production
Production analysis of *The Merchant of Venice* directed by Mark Lamos. Canada: Stratford, ON. 1984. Lang.: Eng. 667

John Hirsch's artistic career at the Stratford Festival Theatre. Canada: Stratford, ON. 1981-1985. Lang.: Eng. 1683

Ferenc Sik directs *A velencei Kalmár (The Merchant of Venice)* by William Shakespeare. Hungary: Budapest. 1986. Lang.: Hun. 1853

Ferenc Sik directs Shakespeare's *A velencei kalmár (The Merchant of Venice)*. Hungary: Budapest. 1986. Lang.: Hun. 1907
Plays/librettos/scripts
Possible influence of Christopher Marlowe's plays upon those of William Shakespeare. England. 1580-1620. Lang.: Eng. 2478

Prophetic riddles in Shakespeare's *The Merchant of Venice*. England. 1598. Lang.: Eng. 2509

Gift exchange and mercantilism in *The Merchant of Venice* by Shakespeare. England: London. 1594-1597. Lang.: Eng. 2520

Translations of Shakespeare by Josep Maria de Sagarra. Spain-Catalonia: Barcelona. 1940-1964. Lang.: Cat. 2811

Mercille, France
Institutions
History of the Théâtre de la Marmaille. Canada: Quebec, PQ. 1973-1986. Lang.: Eng. 1552

Merikanto, Aarre
Plays/librettos/scripts
Analysis of thematic trends in recent Finnish Opera. Finland: Helsinki, Savonlinna. 1909-1986. Lang.: Eng, Fre. 3865

Mérimée, Prosper
Plays/librettos/scripts
Adaptations of *Carmen* by Prosper Mérimée. France. Spain. 1845-1983. Lang.: Fre. 3870

Merkling, Frank
Performance/production
History of *Opera News* in its fiftieth year. USA: New York, NY. 1936-1986. Lang.: Eng. 3802

Merkur'jev, Vasilij Vasil'jevič
Performance/production
Biographical articles on actor V.V. Merkur'jev. Russia: Leningrad. 1904-1978. Lang.: Rus. 782

Merle, Jean-Toussaint
Plays/librettos/scripts
Treatment of the Frankenstein myth in three gothic melodramas. UK-England. France. 1823-1826. Lang.: Eng. 2847

Merlin, oder, Das wüste Lande (Merlin, or The Waste Land)
Plays/librettos/scripts
History, poetry and violence in plays by Tankred Dorst, Heiner
Müller and Jean Genet. Europe. Lang.: Fre.   2538

Merlin, Socorro
Relation to other fields
Interview with Socorro Merlin, director of the Institute of Fine Arts.
Mexico: Mexico City. 1947-1985. Lang.: Eng.   1113

Merlo, Ismael
Plays/librettos/scripts
Poor reception of *Diálogo secreto (Secret Dialogue)* by Antonio
Buero Vallejo in Spain. Spain: Madrid. 1984. Lang.: Eng. 2791

Mermaid Theatre (London)
Performance/production
Collection of newspaper reviews by London theatre critics. UK-
England. 1986. Lang.: Eng.   2120

Mermaid Theatre (Wolfville, NS)
Performance/production
Staging techniques employed at the Mermaid Theatre. Canada:
Wolfville, NS. 1972-1985. Lang.: Eng.   665

Merő, Béla
Performance/production
Ivo Brešan's *Paraszt Hamlet (The Peasant Hamlet)* directed by Béla
Merő. Hungary: Zalaegerszeg. 1986. Lang.: Hun.   1888

Merrill, Helen
Administration
Function of playwright's agent in negotiation and production of a
script. USA: New York, NY. 1985. Lang.: Eng.   135

Merrill, Nathaniel
Performance/production
Opera director Nathaniel Merrill on his productions. USA: New
York, NY. 1958-1986. Lang.: Eng.   3805
Review of Robert Downard's opera *Martin Audéich: A Christmas
Miracle.* USA: Denver, CO. 1985. Lang.: Eng.   3813

Merry Enterprises Theatre (New York, NY)
Institutions
Profile of Merry Enterprises Theatre. USA: New York, NY. 1975-
1984. Lang.: Eng.   543

Merry Wives of Windsor, The
Performance/production
John Hirsch's artistic career at the Stratford Festival Theatre.
Canada: Stratford, ON. 1981-1985. Lang.: Eng.   1683
Collection of newspaper reviews by London theatre critics. UK.
1986. Lang.: Eng.   2101
Solutions to staging the final scene of Shakespeare's *The Merry
Wives of Windsor.* UK. 1874-1985. Lang.: Eng.   2105
Royal Shakespeare Company performances at the Barbican Theatre.
UK-England: London. 1986. Lang.: Eng.   2152
Reconstruction of a number of Shakespeare plays staged and
performed by Herbert Beerbohm Tree. UK-England: London. 1887-
1917. Lang.: Eng.   2155
Shakespearean productions by the National Theatre, Royal
Shakespeare Company and Orange Tree Theatre. UK-England:
Stratford, London. 1984-1985. Lang.: Eng.   2183
Plays/librettos/scripts
Translations of Shakespeare by Josep Maria de Sagarra. Spain-
Catalonia: Barcelona. 1940-1964. Lang.: Cat.   2811

Merry-Go-Round
Plays/librettos/scripts
Career of Marxist playwright George Sklar. USA: New York, NY.
1920-1967. Lang.: Eng.   985

Mesguich, Daniel
Performance/production
Interview with actor, director and teacher Daniel Mesguich. France:
Paris. 1985. Lang.: Fre.   725

Mesmer, Franz Anton
Plays/librettos/scripts
Appearance of Franz Anton Mesmer as a character in Mozart's *Così
fan tutte.* France: Paris. Austria: Vienna. 1734-1789. Lang.: Eng.
                                                         3871

Messerer, Asaf
Performance/production
Careers of four Russian 'apostles of dance'. USSR. Lang.: Rus. 1320

Messina, Cedric
Plays/librettos/scripts
Review articles on the BBC Shakespeare series. UK-England:
London. 1978-1985. Lang.: Eng.   3284

Mestre, Jeaninne
Performance/production
Savannah Bay and *Reigen (Round)* produced by Centre Dramàtic.
Spain-Catalonia: Barcelona. 1986. Lang.: Cat.   2082

Mestres, Apel.les
Plays/librettos/scripts
History of Catalan literature, including playwrights. Spain-Catalonia.
France. 1800-1926. Lang.: Cat.   973

Mészáros, Márta
Performance/production
Éva Pataki's *Edith és Marlene (Edith and Marlene)* directed by
Márta Mészáros, Pest National Theatre. Hungary: Budapest. 1986.
Lang.: Hun.   3603

Mészöly, Miklós
Performance/production
Miklós Mészöly's *Bunker* at Népszinház directed by Mátyás Giricz.
Hungary: Budapest. 1985. Lang.: Hun.   1919

Meta-Obscura Theatre Company
Performance/production
Collection of newspaper reviews by London theatre critics. UK-
England. 1986. Lang.: Eng.   2114

Metamorphoses
Plays/librettos/scripts
Study of contemporary Hungarian plays. Hungary. 1980. Lang.: Hun.
                                                         2658

**Métamorphoses de la fête en Provence de 1750 à 1820, Les
(Metamorphoses of Celebration: Provence 1750-1820)**
Relation to other fields
Translation of *Les métamorphoses de la fête en Provence de 1750 à
1820* (Paris 1976) by Michel Vovelle. France. 1750-1820. Lang.: Ita.
                                                         3358

Metatheatre
Plays/librettos/scripts
Study of realism vs metadrama. Europe. 429 B.C.-1978 A.D. Lang.:
Eng.   2540
Corona de luz (Crown of Light) by Rodolfo Usigli as a self-reflexive
comment on the process of dramatizing an historical event. Mexico.
1960-1980. Lang.: Eng.   2722
Theory/criticism
Pitfalls of a semiotic analysis of theatre. England. 1600-1921. Lang.:
Eng.   3094
Semiotic analysis of *La Storia.* Italy. 1985. Lang.: Eng.   3118
Self-reflexivity in Shakespeare as seen by Lionel Abel, Sigurd
Burckhardt and James L. Calderwood. USA. 1963-1983. Lang.: Eng.
                                                         3141

Methodology
Administration
Use of sources in analyzing shift from resident to touring companies.
USA. 1850-1900. Lang.: Eng.   86
Institutions
Comparison of the creative process in theatre and in research. UK-
England: London. 1981-1986. Lang.: Eng.   1586
Performance/production
Director Mark Zacharov discusses his methods. USSR. 1980-1986.
Lang.: Rus.   911
Plays/librettos/scripts
Revisionist view of twentieth-century Québec theatre based on
published works. Canada. 1900-1980. Lang.: Fre.   926
Relation to other fields
Interview with Augusto Boal. Canada: Montreal, PQ. France. Brazil:
São Paulo. 1952-1986. Lang.: Eng.   3019
Research/historiography
Challenge to assertion that hyper-realism dominated theatre of the
1970s. Canada. 1970-1980. Lang.: Eng.   1184
Review of introductions to the plays of Thomas Dekker by Cyrus
Hoy. England: London. USA. 1600-1980. Lang.: Eng.   1185
Examination of Joel Adedeji's thesis on *alárinjó,* a Yoruba theatrical
art form. Nigeria. 1826-1986. Lang.: Eng.   1186
System for describing ethnic dance based on Xhosa dances. South
Africa, Republic of. 1980-1985. Lang.: Eng.   1337
Results of studies of ethnic dance with transcription system. South
Africa, Republic of. 1980-1985. Lang.: Afr.   1338
Indian theatre professionals criticize Peter Brook's *Mahabharata.*
India: Kerala, Calcutta. 1980-1985. Lang.: Eng.   1376
Study of educational drama from the perspective of generic skills.
Canada: Toronto, ON. 1985. Lang.: Eng.   3070

Methodology — cont'd

Review of recent editions of Revels plays, including George Peele's *The Old Wives Tale*. England: London. 1514-1980. Lang.: Eng. 3071

Analysis and description in reviews of performances. USSR. 1970-1980. Lang.: Rus. 3072

Characteristics of radio drama. UK-England. 1981-1986. Lang.: Eng. 3188

Problems of research methodology applied to traditional singing styles. China. 1600-1980. Lang.: Chi. 3553

Comparison of oratorio and opera styles as developed by Handel. England: London. 1740-1900. Lang.: Eng. 3926

The life of Handel and his influence in making Italian opera popular in England. Italy. England: London. Germany. 1685-1985. Lang.: Eng. 3928

Theory/criticism
Role of theatrical habit in Hungarian theatre history. Hungary. Lang.: Hun. 1212

Metropolitan Opera (New York, NY)

Administration
Edward Downes on his life in the opera. USA: New York, NY. 1911-1986. Lang.: Eng. 3643

Account of the first year of new management at the Metropolitan Opera. USA: New York, NY. 1985-1986. Lang.: Eng. 3644

Design/technology
Interview with lighting designer Gil Wechsler of the Metropolitan Opera. USA: New York, NY. 1883-1986. Lang.: Eng. 3654

Performance spaces
Technical facilities and labor practices at several U.S. theatres as seen by a Swedish visitor. USA: Chicago, IL, New York, NY. 1986. Lang.: Swe. 642

Performance/production
Opera singer Leonie Rysanek and her career. Austria: Vienna. USA: New York, NY. 1926-1986. Lang.: Ger. 3697

Stills from telecast performance of *Goya*. List of principals, conductor and production staff included. USA: Washington, DC. 1986. Lang.: Eng. 3791

Photographs, cast list, synopsis, and discography of Metropolitan Opera radio broadcast performances. USA: New York, NY. 1986. Lang.: Eng. 3794

Stills from telecast performances. List of principals, conductor and production staff included. USA: New York, NY. 1986. Lang.: Eng. 3795

Photographs, cast list, synopsis, and discography of Metropolitan Opera radio broadcast performances. USA: New York, NY. 1986. Lang.: Eng. 3797

Opera director Nathaniel Merrill on his productions. USA: New York, NY. 1958-1986. Lang.: Eng. 3805

Profile of and interview with American conductor Jeffrey Tate, concerning his approach to *Die Fledermaus* by Richard Strauss. USA: New York, NY. 1940-1946. Lang.: Eng. 3827

Samson, by George Frideric Handel is staged at the Metropolitan Opera. USA: New York, NY. 1986. Lang.: Eng. 3831

Appreciation and obituary of the late baritone of the Metropolitan Opera, George Cehanovsky. USA: New York, NY. 1892-1986. Lang.: Eng. 3833

Black opera stars and companies. USA: Enid, OK, New York, NY. 1961-1985. Lang.: Eng. 3839

Metropolitan Opera Guild (New York, NY)

Administration
Account of an international symposium on the future of opera. USA: New York, NY. 1986. Lang.: Eng. 3646

Performance/production
The Metropolitan Opera Guild Teacher Workshop demonstrates its techniques for London teachers. UK-England: London. 1986. Lang.: Eng. 3786

Metz Theatre Festival

Plays/librettos/scripts
Theatre festival and playwriting competition. France: Metz. 1982-1986. Lang.: Hun. 950

Meyer, Peter

Performance/production
Collection of newspaper reviews by London theatre critics. UK-England: London. 1986. Lang.: Eng. 2122

Meyerhold, Vsevolod

SEE
Mejerchol'd, Vsevolod Emil'evič.

Meyerson, Bess

Institutions
Programs of the New York City Department of Cultural Affairs affecting nonprofit theatre. USA: New York, NY. 1983. Lang.: Eng. 554

Mi, Tienchen

Performance spaces
Theatre activities during the Tang dynasty. China. 710-905. Lang.: Chi. 591

Mickiewicz, Adam

Theory/criticism
Adam Mickiewicz's theory of theatrical poetry. Poland. 1798-1855. Lang.: Eng. 3125

Microscope Stage

SEE
Mikroszkóp Szinpad.

Microtheater

Institutions
Report on the Microtheater Festival in the Wiener Festwochen. Austria: Vienna. 1986. Lang.: Ger. 447

Middleton, Grenville

Institutions
Experiences of a couple who converted a coal barge into a touring puppet theatre. UK-England: London. 1976-1986. Lang.: Eng. 4005

Middleton, Juliet

Institutions
Experiences of a couple who converted a coal barge into a touring puppet theatre. UK-England: London. 1976-1986. Lang.: Eng. 4005

Middleton, Thomas

Performance/production
Original staging of Thomas Middleton's *Hengist, King of Kent*. England: London. 1619-1661. Lang.: Eng. 1713

Collection of newspaper reviews by London theatre critics. UK-England. 1986. Lang.: Eng. 2114

Plays/librettos/scripts
Origin of Spanish setting in Middleton and Rowley's *The Changeling*. England. 1607-1622. Lang.: Eng. 2513

Relation to other fields
Social critique and influence of Jacobean drama. England: London. 1603-1613. Lang.: Eng. 1081

Midsummer Night's Dream, A

Performance/production
Innovative Shakespeare stagings of Harley Granville-Barker. UK-England. 1912-1940. Lang.: Eng. 806

Director Charles Marowitz on the role of the director. USA. 1965-1985. Lang.: Eng. 843

John Hirsch's artistic career at the Stratford Festival Theatre. Canada: Stratford, ON. 1981-1985. Lang.: Eng. 1683

Max Reinhardt's work with his contemporaries. Germany. Austria. 1890-1938. Lang.: Eng, Ger. 1757

Collection of newspaper reviews by London theatre critics. UK-England: London. 1986. Lang.: Eng. 2125

Christopher Renshaw talks about his production of Benjamin Britten's opera *A Midsummer Night's Dream* at Covent Garden. UK-England: London. 1986. Lang.: Eng. 3782

Plays/librettos/scripts
Interpretations of Shakespeare's *A Midsummer Night's Dream* based on Bottom's transformation. England. 1595-1986. Lang.: Eng. 2503

Productions of Jane Howell and Elijah Moshinsky for the BBC Shakespeare series. UK-England: London. 1978-1985. Lang.: Eng. 3283

Theory/criticism
Pitfalls of a semiotic analysis of theatre. England. 1600-1921. Lang.: Eng. 3094

Migenes-Johnson, Julia

Performance/production
Performance analysis of the title role of *Carmen*. France. 1875-1986. Lang.: Eng. 3725

Mighty Dollar, The

Plays/librettos/scripts
Philosophy of wealth in gilded age plays. USA: New York, NY. 1870-1889. Lang.: Eng. 2950

Mika'el, Josef-Habta

Plays/librettos/scripts
Translations of plays by William Shakespeare into Amharic and Tegrenna. Ethiopia: Addis Ababa. 1941-1984. Lang.: Eng. 2537

Designers discuss regional productions of *Side-by-Side by Sondheim*. USA. 1984. Lang.: Eng. 3593

Mime
SEE ALSO
Classed Entries under MIME: 3288-3307.
Pantomime.

Basic theatrical documents
Text of plays by James Robinson Planché, with introduction on his influence. UK-England. 1818-1872. Lang.: Eng. 226

Design/technology
Costumes at New York International Clown Festival. USA: New York, NY. 1984. Lang.: Eng. 3316

Institutions
Theories on incorporating traditional theatrical forms into popular theatre. Canada: Toronto, ON. 1970-1986. Lang.: Eng. 3408

Performance/production
Antonin Artaud's conception of gesture and movement. North America. 1938-1986. Lang.: Eng. 768

Dance and mime performances at annual Festival of the Arts. South Africa, Republic of: Grahamstown. 1986. Lang.: Eng. 1282

Increased use of physical aspects of theatre in Vancouver. Canada: Vancouver, BC. 1986. Lang.: Eng. 1664

Overview of productions by the city's studio theatres. Czechoslovakia: Prague. 1986. Lang.: Hun. 1698

Interpretive technique of *commedia dell'arte* actors. France. 1575-1670. Lang.: Ita. 3410

Relation to other fields
Overview of political impact of puppet theatre. Europe. 600 B.C.-1986 A.D. Lang.: Eng. 3990

Theory/criticism
The aesthetics of movement theatre. Europe. 1975-1986. 3301

Mimensemblan (Stockholm)
Performance/production
Outsidern (The Outsider), a production by Mimensemblan, based on Hermann Hesse's *Steppenwolf*. Sweden: Stockholm. 1984-1986. Lang.: Swe. 3296

Minetta Lane Theatre (New York, NY)
Performance spaces
Descriptions of newly constructed Off Broadway theatres. USA: New York, NY. 1984. Lang.: Eng. 644

Minette Fontaine
Relation to other fields
Critical analysis of composer William Grant Still. USA. 1895-1978. Lang.: Eng. 3924

Minetti, Bernhard
Performance/production
Biography of actor and stage manager Franz Reichert. Austria: Vienna. Germany: Berlin. Czechoslovakia: Prague. 1925-1950. Lang.: Ger. 1652

Minghella, Anthony
Performance/production
Collection of newspaper reviews by London theatre critics. UK-England: London. 1986. Lang.: Eng. 2125

Miniature Theatre (Moscow)
SEE
Teat'r Miniatiur.

Minks, Wilfried
Plays/librettos/scripts
Brecht's interpretational legacy is best understood on West German stages. Germany, West. 1956-1986. 2627

Minna von Barnhelm
Plays/librettos/scripts
Nazi ideology and Hans Schweikart's film adaptation of Lessing's *Minna von Barnhelm*. Germany. 1940. Lang.: Ger. 3233

Minnelli, Liza
Performance/production
Collection of newspaper reviews by London theatre critics. UK. 1986. Lang.: Eng. 2103

Collection of newspaper reviews by London theatre critics. UK-England: London. 1986. Lang.: Eng. 2123

Minnesota Opera Theatre (Minneapolis, MN)
Administration
Alternate programs produced by opera houses. USA. Lang.: Eng. 3642

Design/technology
The regional opera scene and its artisans. USA. Lang.: Eng. 3661

Minnesota Public Radio
Design/technology
Overhaul of The World Theatre as a radio broadcasting facility. USA: St. Paul, MN. 1982-1986. Lang.: Eng. 387

Minskoff Theatre (New York, NY)
Performance/production
Reviews of *Sweet Charity* by Neil Simon, staged and choreographed by Bob Fosse. USA: New York, NY. 1986. Lang.: Eng. 3611

Minsky, Morton
Institutions
History of the Minsky Burlesque. USA: New York, NY. 1910-1937. Lang.: Eng. 3464

Minzoku-geinō
Performance/production
The popular entertainment of *Inadani* in Nagano province. Japan: Iida. 1986. Lang.: Jap. 3343

Miquel, Jean-Pierre
Performance/production
Interview with actor, director Jean-Pierre Miquel. France: Paris. 1950-1986. Lang.: Fre. 723

Miraculous Mandarin
SEE
Csodálatos mandarin.

Miranda
Basic theatrical documents
Text of radio play about a woman doctor who masqueraded as a man. Canada: Montreal, PQ. UK-Scotland: Edinburgh. South Africa, Republic of: Cape Town. 1809-1859. Lang.: Eng. 3175

Miranda, Jaime
Performance/production
Humorous and political trends in Chilean theatre season. Chile. 1984-1985. Lang.: Spa. 1686

Plays/librettos/scripts
Interview with Chilean playwright Jaime Miranda. Venezuela. Chile. USA. 1956-1985. Lang.: Eng. 2973

Mirkin, Larry
Performance/production
Behind-the-scenes look at *Fraggle Rock*. Canada: Toronto, ON. 1984. Lang.: Eng. 3269

Miró, Toni
Performance/production
Savannah Bay and *Reigen (Round)* produced by Centre Dramàtic. Spain-Catalonia: Barcelona. 1986. Lang.: Cat. 2082

Mirror Repertory Company (New York, NY)
Performance/production
Reviews of *The Circle* by W. Somerset Maugham, staged by Stephen Porter, performed by the Mirror Repertory Company. USA: New York, NY. 1986. Lang.: Eng. 2227

Misalliance
Performance/production
Actresses Jane Lapotaire and Elizabeth Spriggs discuss their careers in the Royal Shakespeare Company. UK-England: London. 1970-1986. Lang.: Eng. 2147

Royal Shakespeare Company performances at the Barbican Theatre. UK-England: London. 1986. Lang.: Eng. 2152

Misanthrope, Le (Misanthrope, The)
Plays/librettos/scripts
Dialectical method in the plays of Molière. France. 1666. Lang.: Eng. 2567

Miscellaneous texts
Basic theatrical documents
Pamphlet of 1839 concerning the Hungarian Theatre of Pest. Austro-Hungarian Empire: Pest. 1839. Lang.: Hun. 216

Transcription of manuscript assigning shares in the King's Company. England. 1661-1684. Lang.: Eng. 220

Jean Vilar's diary compared to polemics against him. France: Paris. 1951-1981. Lang.: Fre. 221

Correspondence between Gertrude Stein and Virgil Thomson regarding their collaboration on *The Mother of Us All*. France. USA. 1926-1946. Lang.: Eng. 222

Letter from Luigi Pirandello to Silvio D'Amico. Italy: Agrigento. 1927. Lang.: Fre. 224

Contract of first known theatre company in America. Peru: Lima. 1599-1620. Lang.: Spa. 225

Notes on the sources of inspiration for Ohno Kazuo dances. Japan. Lang.: Eng. 1265

Miscellaneous texts — cont'd

Poem by Tanaka Min about his reasons for dancing. Japan. 1985. Lang.: Eng. 1267

Homage to *butō* dancer Hijikata Tatsumi by Tanaka Min. Japan. 1976-1985. Lang.: Eng. 1268

Edition of Zeami's essays on *nō* theatre, organized by subject. Japan. 1363-1443. Lang.: Eng. 1385

Autobiographical essays by drama critic Herbert Whittaker. Canada: Montreal, PQ. 1910-1949. Lang.: Eng. 1473

Journal of playwright and general administrator of Comédie-Française. France: Paris. 1936. Lang.: Fre. 1477

Details of polemical impromptus about Molière's *L'école des Femmes (The School for Wives)*. France. 1663. Lang.: Fre. 1479

Identity of actor Bruscambille, or Des Louriers. France. 1600-1634. Lang.: Fre. 1480

Writings by Tadeusz Kantor on the nature of theatre. Poland. 1956-1985. Lang.: Eng. 1490

Photographs of playbills from Soviet archives. Poland: Vilna. 1800-1863. Lang.: Pol. 1491

Miser Outwitted, The
Basic theatrical documents
Text of *The Miser Outwitted*, attributed to Major John Richardson, with introduction. Canada. UK-Ireland: Dublin. 1838-1848. Lang.: Eng. 1465

Misérables, Les
Design/technology
Analysis of the technological aspects of *Les Misérables*. UK-England: London. 1980-1987. Lang.: Eng. 3582

Set designer John Napier's work on *Les Misérables*. UK-England: London. 1986. 3583

Performance/production
Adapting and staging of *Les Misérables* by Victor Hugo. UK-England. 1980. Lang.: Eng. 3609

Mishima, Yukio
Basic theatrical documents
Catalan translation of *Madame de Sade* by Mishima Yukio. Japan. 1960-1970. Lang.: Cat. 1487

Plays/librettos/scripts
Lives and works of major contemporary playwrights in Japan. Japan: Tokyo. 1900-1986. Lang.: Jap. 2719

Themes and characterization in *Madame de Sade* by Mishima Yukio. Japan. 1960-1970. Lang.: Cat. 2720

Miskolci Nemzeti Szinház (Miskolc)
Performance/production
Čechov's *Višněvyj sad (The Cherry Orchard)* directed at the National Theatre of Miskolc by Imre Csiszár as *Cseresznyéshert*. Hungary: Miskolc. 1986. Lang.: Hun. 1784

Ének Phaedráért (Song for Phaedra) by Per Olof Enquist directed by Imre Csiszár. Hungary: Miskolc. 1985. Lang.: Hun. 1794

István Szőke directs *Oszlopos Simeon (The Man on the Pillar)* by Imre Sarkadi at Miskolc National Theatre. Hungary: Miskolc. 1986. Lang.: Hun. 1813

Ahogy tetszik (As You Like It) by William Shakespeare directed by István Szőke. Hungary: Miskolc. 1986. Lang.: Hun. 1866

István Szőke, directs *Ahogy tetszik (As You Like It)* by Shakespeare. Hungary: Miskolc. 1986. Lang.: Hun. 1873

Interview with actor Imre Kulcsár. Hungary: Miskolc. 1986. Lang.: Hun. 1917

Čechov's *Višněvyj sad (The Cherry Orchard)* directed by Imre Csiszár under the title *Cseresznyéskert*. Hungary: Miskolc. 1986. Lang.: Hun. 1921

Ének Phaedráért (Song for Phaedra) by Per Olof Enquist, directed by Imre Csiszár at the National Theatre of Miskolc. Hungary: Miskolc. 1985. Lang.: Hun. 1937

László Fábián's *Levéltetvek az akasztófán (Plant-Lice on the Gallows)* directed by István Szőke. Hungary: Miskolc. 1986. Lang.: Hun. 1942

Imre Sarkadi's *Oszlopos Simeon (The Man on the Pillar)* directed by István Szőke at Nemzeti Szinház. Hungary: Miskolc. 1986. Lang.: Hun. 1952

Isván Szőke directs *Letvéltetvek az akasztófán (Plant-Lice on the Gallows)* by László Fábián. Hungary: Miskolc. 1986. Lang.: Hun. 1961

A kegyenc (The Favorite) by Gyula Illyés, directed by János Sándor, National Theatre of Miskolc. Hungary: Miskolc. 1985. Lang.: Hun. 1971

Miss Julie
SEE
Fröken Julie.

Missiles of October
Plays/librettos/scripts
Analysis of television docudramas as a melodrama genre. USA. 1965-1986. Lang.: Eng. 3285

Mission, The
SEE
Auftrag, Der.

Mistero Buffo
Performance/production
Overview of productions in Italy. Italy: Milan. 1986. Lang.: Eng. 1994

Mistress of the Inn
SEE
Locandiera, La.

Mitchell, Adrian
Performance/production
Collection of newspaper reviews by London theatre critics. UK-England: London. 1986. Lang.: Eng. 2118

Mitchell, Julian
Performance/production
Collection of newspaper reviews by London theatre critics. UK-England: London. 1986. Lang.: Eng. 2125

Plays/librettos/scripts
Discussion of plays about Verdi and Puccini by Julian Mitchell and Robin Ray. UK-England: London. Italy. 1986. Lang.: Eng. 3628

Mitchell, Leona
Performance/production
Black opera stars and companies. USA: Enid, OK, New York, NY. 1961-1985. Lang.: Eng. 3839

Mitchell, Maggie
Relation to other fields
Professional equality in theatrical careers for men and women. USA: New York, NY. 1850-1870. Lang.: Eng. 1143

Mitchell, W.O.
Institutions
Career of Walter Learning, artistic director, Vancouver Playhouse. Canada: Vancouver, BC. 1982-1983. Lang.: Eng. 470

Plays/librettos/scripts
Structure and characterization in the plays of W.O. Mitchell. Canada. 1975. Lang.: Eng. 2408

Mitsuwakai
Performance/production
History of schism in *Bunraku* puppetry. Japan. 1945-1964. Lang.: Eng. 3998

Mitterwurzer, Friedrich
Performance/production
Playing Hamlet at the Burgtheater. Austria: Vienna. 1803-1985. Lang.: Ger. 1654

Mitzi Newhouse Theatre (New York, NY)
Performance/production
Reviews of *Terrors of Pleasure*, a monologue by Spalding Gray. USA: New York, NY. 1986. Lang.: Eng. 2208

Reviews of *The House of Blue Leaves* by John Guare, staged by Jerry Zaks. USA: New York, NY. 1986. Lang.: Eng. 2220

Reviews of *Asinamali*, written and staged by Mbongeni Ngema. USA: New York, NY. 1986. Lang.: Eng. 2244

Mixed Entertainment
SEE ALSO
Classed Entries under MIXED ENTERTAINMENT: 3308-3472.

Institutions
History of Swedish language Lilla-teatern (Little Theatre). Finland: Helsinki. 1940-1986. Lang.: Eng, Fre. 494

Collection of essays on the evolution of Chicano theatre. USA. 1850-1985. Lang.: Eng. 1599

Performance/production
English alternative theatre group Welfare State International works with Tanzanian performers. UK-England. Tanzania. 1970-1986. Lang.: Eng. 814

History of Maypole dancing. England. 1244-1985. Lang.: Eng. 1329

Selected short comic prose sketches of Róbert Rátony, actor, showman and writer. Hungary. 1944-1985. Lang.: Hun. 1920

Life and work of cabaret singer and stage director Leon Schiller. Poland. 1887-1954. Lang.: Eng, Fre. 2014

Molina, Josefina
Performance/production
Directing career of Josefina Molina. Spain. 1952-1985. Lang.: Eng.
2078

Molina, Tirso de
Plays/librettos/scripts
Female sexuality in Tirso de Molina's *El vergonzoso en palacio (The Shy Man at Court)*. Spain. 1580-1648. Lang.: Eng.   969
Emblematic pictorialism in *La mujer que manda en casa (The Woman Who Rules the Roost)* by Tirso de Molina. Spain. 1580-1648. Lang.: Eng.   970

Molnár, Ferenc
Performance/production
A farkas (The Wolf) by Ferenc Molnár, directed by István Verebes at Vigszinház. Hungary: Budapest. 1985. Lang.: Hun.   1781
István Verebes' production of *A farkas (The Wolf)* by Ferenc Molnár at the Vigszinház. Hungary: Budapest. 1985. Lang.: Hun.
1805
Reviews of *Margit kisasszony (Miss Margit)*, *Az Ibolya (The Violet)*, *Az Árny (The Ghost)* and *Róza néni (Aunt Rosa)*. Hungary: Budapest. 1985-1986. Lang.: Hun.   1916

Reference materials
Bibliography on and about the playwright-author Ferenc Molnár. Austria: Vienna. Hungary: Budapest. USA: New York, NY. 1878-1982. Lang.: Eng.   2982

Molnár, Piroska
Performance/production
Piroska Molnár's performance in *Kozma* by Mihály Kornis. Hungary: Kaposvár. 1986. Lang.: Hun.   1796

Money Pit, The
Design/technology
Art director Steven Graham's work on the film *The Money Pit*. USA. 1986.   378

Monk, Meredith
Performance/production
Merce Cunningham, Alwin Nikolais, Meredith Monk and Yvonne Rainer on post-modern dance. USA. 1975-1986. Lang.: Eng.   1285
Interview with choreographer Meredith Monk. USA: New York, NY. 1964-1984. Lang.: Eng.   1368

Monodrama
Performance/production
Interview with political satirist Max Gillies. Australia. 1986. Lang.: Eng.   654

Plays/librettos/scripts
Popularity of dramatic monologue on stage and television. Australia. 1985. Lang.: Eng.   921
Interview with satirist Barry Humphries. Australia. UK-England. 1950-1986. Lang.: Eng.   922
Monodramas of playwright István Kocsis. Romania. Hungary. 1976-1984. Lang.: Hun.   2761

Monserdà, Dolors
Plays/librettos/scripts
Roles of women in middle-class Catalonian society as reflected in the plays of Carme Montoriol and Maria Aurélia Capmany. Spain-Catalonia. 1700-1960. Lang.: Spa.   2819

Monstre et le magicien, Le (Monster and the Magician, The)
Plays/librettos/scripts
Treatment of the Frankenstein myth in three gothic melodramas. UK-England. France. 1823-1826. Lang.: Eng.   2847

Monstrous Regiment (London)
Plays/librettos/scripts
Interview with Gillian Hanna about *Elisabetta: Quasi per caso una donna (Elizabeth: Almost by Chance a Woman)*. UK-England: London. Italy. 1986. Lang.: Eng.   2875

Montagu, Walter
Plays/librettos/scripts
Female characterization in Nicholas Rowe's plays. England. 1629-1720. Lang.: Eng.   2475

Montale, Eugenio
Relation to other fields
Pirandello's influence on poet Eugenio Montale. Italy. 1896-1981. Lang.: Ita.   3042

Monte Carlo Opera
Administration
Raoul Gunsbourg, director of Monte Carlo Opera for 59 years. Monaco: Monte Carlo. 1893-1951. Lang.: Eng.   3641

Monteverdi, Claudio
Performance/production
Productions of operas at La Scala by Luca Ronconi. Italy: Milan. 1985. Lang.: Ita.   3763
Claudio Monteverdi's *L'incoronazione di Poppea (The Coronation of Poppea)* directed by Jonathan Hale at the Kent Opera. UK-England: Kent. 1986. Lang.: Eng.   3781

Montgomery, Kenneth
Institutions
The survival and prosperity of the Santa Fe Opera Company. USA: Santa Fe, NM. 1957-1986. Lang.: Eng.   3678

Month of Sundays, A
Performance/production
Collection of newspaper reviews by London theatre critics. UK-England. 1986. Lang.: Eng.   2115
Collection of newspaper reviews by London theatre critics. UK-England. 1986. Lang.: Eng.   2120

Monthan, Ingegard
Plays/librettos/scripts
Interview with Ingegerd Monthan, author of *Drottningmötet (The Meeting of the Queens)*. Sweden. 1984-1986. Lang.: Swe.   2823

Monthly Magazine and American Review
Reference materials
Theatrical materials in five early American magazines. Colonial America. 1758-1800. Lang.: Eng.   1012

Montoriol, Carme
Plays/librettos/scripts
Roles of women in middle-class Catalonian society as reflected in the plays of Carme Montoriol and Maria Aurélia Capmany. Spain-Catalonia. 1700-1960. Lang.: Spa.   2819

Montreal Repertory Theatre (Montreal, PQ)
Basic theatrical documents
Autobiographical essays by drama critic Herbert Whittaker. Canada: Montreal, PQ. 1910-1949. Lang.: Eng.   1473

Montreal Theatre Lab (Montreal, PQ)
Institutions
Interviews with theatre professionals in Quebec. Canada. 1985. Lang.: Fre.   487

Moody, William Vaughn
Plays/librettos/scripts
Analysis of the plays of William Vaughn Moody. USA. 1869-1910. Lang.: Eng.   2917

Moon for the Misbegotten, A
Plays/librettos/scripts
Mourning in Eugene O'Neill's *A Moon for the Misbegotten*. USA. 1922-1947. Lang.: Eng.   2895

Moon On A Rainbow Shawl
Performance/production
Collection of newspaper reviews by London theatre critics. UK-England: London. 1986. Lang.: Eng.   2126

Moon, Gerald
Performance/production
Reviews of *Corpse!* by Gerald Moon, staged by John Tillinger. USA: New York, NY. 1986. Lang.: Eng.   2235

Moon, Marjorie
Institutions
Career of Marjorie Moon, artistic director of Billie Holliday Theatre. USA: New York, NY, Cleveland, OH. 1973-1986. Lang.: Eng.   1610

Moonlighting
Design/technology
Interview with cameraman Gerald Perry Finnerman about lighting *Moonlighting*. USA: Los Angeles, CA. 1985-1986. Lang.: Eng.   3264

Moore, Edward
Performance/production
History of Edward Moore's *The Gamester* on London stages. England: London. 1771-1871. Lang.: Eng.   1700

Moore, Garry
Performance/production
An autobiography focusing on Carol Burnett's early years. 1960-1986. Lang.: Eng.   3268

Moore, Tom Inglis
Plays/librettos/scripts
Study of heroism in verse dramas by Douglas Stewart, Tom Inglis Moore and Catherine Duncan. Australia. 1941-1943. Lang.: Eng.
2383

Morahan, Christopher
Performance/production
Reviews of *Wild Honey*, by Michael Frayn after Čechov, conceived and staged by Christopher Morahan. USA: New York, NY. 1986. Lang.: Eng. 2205

Morak, Franz
Performance/production
Actor Franz Morak and his work at the Burgtheater. Austria: Vienna. 1946-1986. Lang.: Ger. 1647

Morales, Joan
Design/technology
History of Catalan scenography. Spain-Catalonia. 200 B.C.-1986 A.D. Lang.: Cat. 311

Morality plays
Plays/librettos/scripts
Analysis of Hildegard of Bingen's *Ordo Virtutum* as a morality play. Germany: Bingen. 1151. Lang.: Eng. 3498

Relation to other fields
Costuming evidence on carved baptismal fonts. England. 1463-1544. Lang.: Eng. 3026

Mordžanišvili Theatre (Tbilisi)
SEE
Gruzinskij Akademičeskij Teat'r im. Kote Mordžanišvili.

More Stately Mansions
Plays/librettos/scripts
Gender role-reversal in the Cycle plays of Eugene O'Neill. USA. 1927-1953. Lang.: Eng. 2896

More, Sir Thomas
Plays/librettos/scripts
Iconography of throne scene in Shakespeare's *Richard III*. England. 1591-1592. Lang.: Eng. 2481

Moreland, Donald
Performance/production
Review of premiere performance of Myron Fink's opera *Chinchilla*. USA: Binghamton, NY. 1986. Lang.: Eng. 3840

Morera, Enric
Plays/librettos/scripts
Analysis of *La Santa Espina (The Holy Thorn)* by Àngel Guimerà. Spain-Catalonia. 1897-1907. Lang.: Cat. 2815

Morgan, Fidelis
Institutions
Progress and aims of Women's Playhouse Trust. UK-England: London. 1984-1986. Lang.: Eng. 1590

Morgan, Natasha
Performance/production
Collection of newspaper reviews by London theatre critics. UK-England. 1986. Lang.: Eng. 2115

Morgan, Robert
Performance spaces
Architect Robert Morgan's design for Broadway's Marquis Theatre. USA: New York, NY. 1986. Lang.: Eng. 633

Morgenstern, Christian
Performance/production
Max Reinhardt's work with his contemporaries. Germany. Austria. 1890-1938. Lang.: Eng, Ger. 1757

Móricz Zsigmond Szinház (Nyiregyháza)
Performance/production
László Salamon Suba's production of *Urának hű szolgája (A Faithful Servant of His Lord)* by Franz Grillparzer. Hungary: Nyiregyháza. 1985. Lang.: Hun. 1881

Selected reviews of *Segitsd a király! (Help the King!)* by József Ratkó. Hungary: Nyiregyháza. 1985. Lang.: Hun. 1902

Péter Gellért's production of *Urhatnám polgár (The Bourgeois Gentleman)* at Móricz Zsigmond Szinház. Hungary: Nyiregyháza. 1986. Lang.: Hun. 1931

Nő a körúton (Woman on the Boulevard) by István Gáll directed by Péter Léner at Móricz Zsigmond Theatre. Hungary: Nyiregyháza. 1986. Lang.: Hun. 1950

István Gáll's *Nő a körúton (Woman on the Boulevard)* directed by Péter Léner at Móricz Zsigmond Szinház. Hungary: Nyiregyháza. 1986. Lang.: Hun. 1973

Móricz, Zsigmond
Performance/production
András Béhés directs *Légy jó mindhalálig (Be Good Till Death)* by Zsigmond Móricz at Nemzeti Szinház. Hungary: Budapest. 1986. Lang.: Hun. 1849

Reviews of Shakespeare productions written by Hungarian realist writer, Zsigmond Móricz. Hungary: Budapest. 1923. Lang.: Hun. 1887

Moritz, Herbert
Relation to other fields
Herbert Moritz and his views about cultural politics. Austria. 1986. Lang.: Ger. 1064

Moritz, Nils
Design/technology
Swedish set designers discuss their working methods. Sweden. 1980-1986. Lang.: Swe. 312

Mort de Judas, La (Death of Judas, The)
Performance/production
Stage adaptation of *La Mort de Judas (The Death of Judas)* by Paul Claudel. France: Brangues. 1985. Lang.: Fre. 1754

Morte accidentale di un anarchico (Accidental Death of an Anarchist)
Performance/production
Productions of Dario Fo's *Morte accidentale di un anarchico (Accidental Death of an Anarchist)* in the light of Fo's political ideas. USA. Canada. Italy. 1970-1986. Lang.: Eng. 2262

Morte, Andreu
Performance/production
Detailed description of the performance titled *Accions (Actions)* by La Fura dels Baus. Spain-Catalonia. 1979-1984. Lang.: Cat. 3445

Morton, Mark W.
Design/technology
Designers discuss regional productions of *She Loves Me*. USA. 1984-1986. Lang.: Eng. 3587

Designers discuss regional productions of *The Music Man*. USA. 1983-1986. Lang.: Eng. 3589

Mosakowski, Susan
Theory/criticism
Eleven theatre professionals discuss their personal direction and the direction of experimental theatre. USA: New York, NY. 1985. Lang.: Eng. 3137

Moscoso, Roberto
Institutions
Work and distinctive qualities of the Théâtre du Soleil. France: Paris. 1964-1986. Lang.: Eng. 1575

Moscow Art Theatre
SEE
Moskovskij Chudožestvennyj Akedemičeskij Teat'r.

Moscow Puppet Theatre
SEE
Gosudarstvėnnyj Centralnyj Teat'r Kukol.

Moscow Theatre Institute, GITIS
SEE
Gosudarstvėnnyj Institut Teatralnovo Iskusstva.

Moser, Albert
Institutions
Concept and program for the Salzburger Festspiele in 1987. Austria: Salzburg. 1986. Lang.: Ger. 451

Management and plans for the Salzburger Festspiele. Austria: Salzburg. 1986. Lang.: Ger. 452

Moser, Hans
Performance/production
Life and films of actor and director Willi Forst. Austria: Vienna. Germany: Berlin. 1903-1980. Lang.: Ger. 3223

Mosher, George
Performance/production
Reviews of *Juggling and Cheap Theatrics* with the Flying Karamazov Brothers, staged by George Mosher. USA: New York, NY. 1986. Lang.: Eng. 3349

Moshinsky, Elijah
Plays/librettos/scripts
Productions of Jane Howell and Elijah Moshinsky for the BBC Shakespeare series. UK-England: London. 1978-1985. Lang.: Eng. 3283

Review articles on the BBC Shakespeare series. UK-England: London. 1978-1985. Lang.: Eng. 3284

Moskovskij Chudožestvėnnyj Akademičeskij Teat'r (Moscow Art Theatre)
Institutions
Foundation and brief history of Moscow Art Theatre. Russia: Moscow. 1898-1986. Lang.: Rus. 513

Reminiscences of study at Moscow Art Theatre. USSR. Lang.: Rus. 578

Moskovskij Chudožestvènnyj Akademičeskij Teat'r (Moscow Art Theatre) — cont'd

Performance/production
Michajl Bulgakov's ties with Moscow Art Theatre. Russia: Moscow. 1891-1940. Lang.: Rus. 785

Career of actor-director Oleg Tabakov. USSR: Moscow. 1950-1986. Lang.: Rus. 904

Plays/librettos/scripts
Compares contemporary Canadian theatre with German and Russian theatre of the early 20th century. Canada. Russia: Moscow. Germany. 1900-1986. Lang.: Eng. 2412

Relation to other fields
Interview with director Oleg Jèfremov of Moscow Art Theatre on social goals of theatre. USSR. 1986. Lang.: Rus. 1174

Training
Effect of changing ideas about psychology and creativity on the Stanislavskij system. USSR: Moscow. 1900-1986. Lang.: Eng. 3162

Mosonyi, Alíz
Performance/production
Stage adaptation of Erich Kästner's novel *Emil und die Detektive (Emil and the Detectives)* directed by István Keleti. Hungary: Budapest. 1986. Lang.: Hun. 1807

Moss, Jane
Theory/criticism
Theatre critic Frank Rich discusses his life and work. USA: New York, NY. 1986. Lang.: Eng. 3146

Mossovèt Theatre
SEE
Teat'r im. Mossovèta.

Mot pour un autre, Un (One Word for Another)
Plays/librettos/scripts
Sexual metaphors in plays of Jean Tardieu. France. 1955. Lang.: Fre. 2577

Mother Courage
SEE
Mutter Courage und ihre Kinder.

Mother of Us All, The
Basic theatrical documents
Correspondence between Gertrude Stein and Virgil Thomson regarding their collaboration on *The Mother of Us All.* France. USA. 1926-1946. Lang.: Eng. 222

Mots de ritual per a Electra (Ritual Words for Electra)
Plays/librettos/scripts
Analysis of Josep Palau's plays and theoretical writings. Spain-Catalonia. 1917-1982. Lang.: Cat. 2814

Mouches, Les (Flies, The)
Plays/librettos/scripts
Superficial and reductive use of classical myth in modern French theatre. France. 1935-1944. Lang.: Eng. 2550

Mound Builders, The
Performance/production
Reviews of *The Mound Builders* by Lanford Wilson, staged by Marshall W. Mason. USA: New York, NY. 1986. Lang.: Eng. 2240

Moussorgsky, Modeste
SEE
Mussorgskij, Modest Pavlovič.

Movingstage Marionettes (London)
Institutions
Experiences of a couple who converted a coal barge into a touring puppet theatre. UK-England: London. 1976-1986. Lang.: Eng. 4005

Moy bedny Marat (Promise, The)
Performance/production
Collection of newspaper reviews by London theatre critics. UK-England: London. 1986. Lang.: Eng. 2116

Moyle, Thomas
Performance/production
Brief investigation of the lives of seven actors. England. 1526-1587. Lang.: Eng. 691

Mozart, Wolfgang Amadeus
Design/technology
Profile of and interview with illustrator Maurice Sendak, designer of numerous opera productions. USA. 1930-1986. Lang.: Eng. 3657

Institutions
Wiener Festwochen 1986: Mozart and Modern Art. Austria: Vienna. 1986. Lang.: Ger. 441

Performance/production
Leopold Simoneau on Mozartian style. Lang.: Eng. 3686

Performance rules of Mozart's time as guidance for singers. Austria: Vienna. 1700-1799. Lang.: Ger. 3691

The innovative quality of *Idomeneo.* Austria: Vienna. 1780. Lang.: Eng. 3702

Collection of statements about the life and career of conductor Wilhelm Furtwängler. Germany: Berlin. Austria: Salzburg. 1886-1986. Lang.: Ger. 3737

Photographs, cast list, synopsis, and discography of Metropolitan Opera radio broadcast performances. USA: New York, NY. 1986. Lang.: Eng. 3794

Reviews of *Death in the Family, Viaggio a Reims, Abduction from the Seraglio* and *Tales of Hoffmann.* USA: St. Louis, MO. 1975-1986. Lang.: Eng. 3799

Opera director Nathaniel Merrill on his productions. USA: New York, NY. 1958-1986. Lang.: Eng. 3805

Peter Sellars' production of Mozart's *Così fan tutte.* USA: Purchase, NY. 1986. Lang.: Eng. 3815

Review of *Lunatics and Lovers*, an adaptation of Mozart's *La finta giardiniera.* USA: Santa Barbara, CA. 1985. Lang.: Eng. 3843

Puppet production of Mozart's opera *Die Zauberflöte.* USA. 1986. Lang.: Eng. 4008

Plays/librettos/scripts
The power of music to transform the play into living theatre, examples from the work of Paul Green, Clifford Odets, and Maxwell Anderson. USA: New York, NY. 1936. Lang.: Eng. 3632

The theme of clemency in the final operas of Mozart. Austria: Vienna. 1782-1791. Lang.: Cat. 3860

Operatic facsimiles by Mozart, Bellini and Verdi. Europe. 1814-1985. Lang.: Eng. 3863

Appearance of Franz Anton Mesmer as a character in Mozart's *Così fan tutte.* France: Paris. Austria: Vienna. 1734-1789. Lang.: Eng. 3871

Mahler's influence on Kurt Weill's career. Germany: Berlin. 1756-1950. Lang.: Eng. 3879

Auden and Kallman's English translation of *Die Zauberflöte (The Magic Flute).* USA. 1951-1956. Lang.: Eng. 3903

Relation to other fields
Influence of Mozart's operas on the 'Cockney' school of writers. England: London. 1760-1840. Lang.: Eng. 3916

Training
Collected papers from a conference on voice training. Austria: Vienna. Italy: Rome. England: London. 1700-1984. Lang.: Ger. 3936

Mozarteum (Salzburg)
Design/technology
Hungarian students tour stage and costume designs at the Mozarteum. Austria: Salzburg. 1986. Lang.: Hun. 238

Mr. Government
Performance/production
Collection of newspaper reviews by London theatre critics. UK. 1986. Lang.: Eng. 2103

Mr. Men Musical, The
Performance/production
Interviews with playwrights Louise Page, Charles McKeown and Malcolm Sircon. UK-England: London. 1986. Lang.: Eng. 2133

Mrcchakatika (Little Clay Cart)
Performance/production
Collection of newspaper reviews by London theatre critics. UK-England: London. 1986. Lang.: Eng. 2109

Mrcchakatika (Little Clay Cart, The)
Performance/production
Collection of newspaper reviews by London theatre critics. UK: London. 1986. Lang.: Eng. 2100

Mrožek, Sławomir
Performance/production
Performances of Sławomir Mrožek's *Mészárszék (The Slaughterhouse)* and *Ház a határon (The Home on the Border).* Hungary: Budapest. 1986. Lang.: Hun. 1817

Rzeźnia (The Slaughterhouse) by Sławomir Mrožek, directed by Sándor Beke at Józsefvárosi Szinház under the title *Mészárszék.* Hungary: Budapest. 1985. Lang.: Hun. 1865

Plays/librettos/scripts
Polish drama performed in Sweden. Sweden. Poland. 1835-1976. Lang.: Pol. 975

Mrožek's *Policja (The Police)* as read by the censor. Poland. 1958. Lang.: Fre. 2735

Material derived from Stanisław Wyspiański's *Wesele (The Wedding)* by various Polish playwrights. Poland. 1901-1984. Lang.: Fre. 2741

Mrożek, Sławomir — cont'd

Loss of identity in plays by István Örkény's and Sławomir Mrożek. Poland. Hungary. 1955-1980. Lang.: Hun. 2752

Mu Lian
Plays/librettos/scripts
Introduction to the folk play, *Mu Lian*. China, People's Republic of: Beijing. 1962-1985. Lang.: Chi. 3538

Much Ado About Nothing
Performance/production
Reconstruction of a number of Shakespeare plays staged and performed by Herbert Beerbohm Tree. UK-England: London. 1887-1917. Lang.: Eng. 2155

Mud
Plays/librettos/scripts
Interview with playwright Maria Irene Fornes. USA: New York, NY. 1984. Lang.: Eng. 2892

Mujer que manda en casa, La (Woman Who Rules the Roost, The)
Plays/librettos/scripts
Emblematic pictorialism in *La mujer que manda en casa (The Woman Who Rules the Roost)* by Tirso de Molina. Spain. 1580-1648. Lang.: Eng. 970

Mulgrave Road Co-op (Guysborough, NS)
Audience
History of the Mulgrave Road Co-op theatre. Canada: Guysborough, NS. 1977-1985. Lang.: Eng. 1444

Müller, Heiner
Basic theatrical documents
New German translation of Shakespeare's *As You Like It*. Germany, East. 1986. Lang.: Ger. 1483

Performance/production
The development and production of Robert Wilson's *CIVIL warS*. USA. Germany, East. 1984. Lang.: Eng. 838

Plays/librettos/scripts
History, poetry and violence in plays by Tankred Dorst, Heiner Müller and Jean Genet. Europe. Lang.: Fre. 2538
Comparison of Heiner Müller's *Der Auftrag (The Mission)* and Bertolt Brecht's *Die Massnahme (The Measures Taken)*. Germany, East. 1930-1985. Lang.: Eng. 2622
Robert Wilson's adaptation of Euripides' *Alcestis*. USA: Cambridge, MA. 1979-1986. Lang.: Eng. 2939

Müller, Jürgen
Performance/production
Detailed description of the performance titled *Accions (Actions)* by La Fura dels Baus. Spain-Catalonia. 1979-1984. Lang.: Cat. 3445

Mullins, Mike
Performance/production
Interview with performance artist Mike Mullins. Australia. 1986. Lang.: Eng. 3440

Mumbo-Jumbo Theatre Company (New York, NY)
Institutions
Vi Higginsen's *Mama I Want to Sing* and history of the Mumbo-Jumbo Theatre Company. USA: New York, NY. 1980-1986. Lang.: Eng. 1601

Mummenschanz (Zurich)
Design/technology
Interview with Beverly Emmons, lighting designer for Mummenschanz's USA tour. USA: New York, NY. 1986. Lang.: Eng. 3305

Performance/production
A photographic essay of 42 soloists and groups performing mime or gestural theatre. 1986. 3290
A profile of the three performers known collectively as Mummenschanz. Switzerland: Zurich. USA. 1984. Lang.: Eng. 3297
Reviews of Mummenschanz 'The New Show'. USA: New York, NY. 1986. Lang.: Eng. 3298

Mummers' Troupe (St. John's, NF)
Institutions
Successful alternative theatre groups in Newfoundland. Canada. 1976-1986. Lang.: Eng. 1550

Münch, Edvard
Design/technology
Contribution of designer Ernst Stern to modern scenography. Germany: Berlin. UK-England: London. 1905. Lang.: Eng. 1516

Munch, Edvard
Plays/librettos/scripts
Work of playwright Stefan Schütz. Germany, West. 1944-1986. Lang.: Eng. 2625

Münchener Festspiele
SEE
Bayerische Staatsoper im Nationaltheater.

Munday, Anthony
Plays/librettos/scripts
Similarities between *King Lear* by Shakespeare and *The Trimphs of Reunited Britannia* by Munday. England. 1605-1606. Lang.: Eng. 2480

Munich Opera
SEE
Bayerische Staatsoper im Nationaltheater.

Municipal Theatre (Haifa)
SEE
Teatron haIroni Haifa.

Municipal Theatre (Helsinki)
SEE
Helsingin Kaupunginteatteri.

Munk, Erika
Theory/criticism
Report of seminar on theatre criticism. USA: New York, NY. 1983. Lang.: Eng. 1223

Munkásoperett (Workers' Operetta)
Performance/production
Reviews of three musicals about the 1960s. Hungary. 1985-1986. Lang.: Hun. 3488

Munro, Rona
Performance/production
Interview with Pip Broughton of Paines Plough Theatre Company. UK-England. 1980-1986. Lang.: Eng. 2166

Muppets
Design/technology
Director of electronics and mechanical design for the Muppets, Faz Fazakas. USA. 1986. 3262

Performance/production
Behind-the-scenes look at *Fraggle Rock*. Canada: Toronto, ON. 1984. Lang.: Eng. 3269
Work of Kermit Love, creator of Big Bird for *Sesame Street*. USA: New York, NY. 1935-1985. Lang.: Eng. 3276

Murch, Walter
Design/technology
Making of the movie *Return to Oz*, focusing on its special effects and creature design. USA. 3206

Murder in the Cathedral
Plays/librettos/scripts
T. S. Eliot's *Murder in the Cathedral* dramatizes Christian theory of history. UK-England. 1935. Lang.: Eng. 2878

Murnau, Friederich Wilhelm
Plays/librettos/scripts
Conceptions of the South Sea islands in works of Murnau, Artaud and Spies. Europe. USA. Indonesia. 1930. Lang.: Ita. 3231

Murobushi, Ko
Performance/production
A photographic essay of 42 soloists and groups performing mime or gestural theatre. 1986. 3290

Murphy, Tom
Performance/production
Collection of newspaper reviews by London theatre critics. UK. 1986. Lang.: Eng. 2102
Collection of newspaper reviews by London theatre critics. UK-England: London. 1986. Lang.: Eng. 2119

Murray, Brahan
Performance/production
Collection of newspaper reviews by London theatre critics. UK-England. 1986. Lang.: Eng. 2120

Murray, Brian
Performance/production
Reviews of *Arsenic and Old Lace*, by Joseph Kesselring, staged by Brian Murray. USA: New York, NY. 1986. Lang.: Eng. 2215

Murray, Gilbert
Performance/production
Letters to and from Harley Granville-Barker. UK-England. 1877-1946. Lang.: Eng. 807

Murray, John
Performance/production
Reviews of *Room Service*, by John Murray and Allan Boretz, staged by Alan Arkin. USA: New York, NY. 1986. Lang.: Eng. 2242

Murrell, John
Institutions
Shift in emphasis at Banff Centre. Canada: Banff, AB. 1974-1986. Lang.: Eng. 1543

Musco, Angelo
Plays/librettos/scripts
Angelo Musco's interpretation of *Pensaci Giacomino! (Think of it, Jamie!)* by Luigi Pirandello. Italy. 1916-1917. Lang.: Ita. 2684
Text and information on Luigi Pirandello's *A patenti (The License)*. Italy. 1916-1918. Lang.: Ita. 2717

Museum of Broadcasting (New York, NY)
Performance/production
The videotaped opera showings at the Museum of Broadcasting. USA: New York, NY. 1985-1986. Lang.: Eng. 3828

Museum Theatre (Madras, India)
Institutions
History of Museum Theatre. India: Madras. 1895-1985. Lang.: Eng. 504

Musgrave, Thea
Performance/production
Review of *Harriet, the Woman Called Moses*, an opera by Thea Musgrave, staged by Gordon Davidson. USA: Norfolk, VA. 1985. Lang.: Eng. 3835

Mushovin, Jeff
Performance/production
Robert Wilson's production of *Alcestis* at the American Repertory Theatre. USA: Cambridge, MA. 1986. 2306

Music
Influence of Wagner on the music of contemporary Chinese opera. China, People's Republic of. 1949-1980. Lang.: Chi. 3503

Administration
Proposed copyright terms for composers and lyricists. USA. 1986. Lang.: Eng. 116

Design/technology
Techniques and aesthetics of using biofeedback to create electronic music. USA. 1986. Lang.: Eng. 3176
Use of music in film and theatre. Canada: Toronto, ON. 1985. Lang.: Eng. 3477

Institutions
Discussions of opera at the festival of Aix-en-Provence. France: Aix-en-Provence. 1960. Lang.: Fre. 3673

Performance/production
History of contemporary Japanese theatre. Japan: Tokyo. 1950-1986. Lang.: Jap. 757
Interview with Peter Brook's designer, musician, and costumer for *Mahabharata*. France: Avignon. 1973-1985. Lang.: Eng. 1359
Martha Clarke's production of *The Garden of Earthly Delights*. USA: New York, NY. 1979-1984. Lang.: Eng. 1371
Use of music in Uzbekistan dramatic presentations. USSR. Lang.: Rus. 2332
Diana McIntosh on her performance pieces involving contemporary music. Canada: Winnipeg, MB. 1979-1986. Lang.: Eng. 3250
Use of the term 'fiddler' in early works. England. 1589-1816. Lang.: Eng. 3332
Interview with composer-musician Peter Gordon. USA. 1985. Lang.: Eng. 3492
Contemporary musical-dramatic performance. USSR. 1980-1986. Lang.: Rus. 3494
Ch'in opera and its influences. China: Beijing. 1795-1850. Lang.: Chi. 3518
Review of the 1985 season of the Chinese National Opera. China, People's Republic of: Beijing. 1985. Lang.: Chi. 3522
Reviews of *Honky Tonk Nights*, book and lyrics by Ralph Allen and David Campbell, staged and choreographed by Ernest O. Flatt. USA: New York, NY. 1986. Lang.: Eng. 3612
Reviews of *Raggedy Ann*, book by William Gibon, music and lyrics by Joe Raposo, staged and choreographed by Patricia Birch. USA: New York, NY. 1986. Lang.: Eng. 3614
Reviews of *Into the Light*, book by Jeff Tamborniro, music by Lee Holdridge, lyrics by John Forster, staged by Michael Maurer. USA: New York, NY. 1986. Lang.: Eng. 3615
Reviews of *Oh Coward!*, lyrics and music by Noël Coward, devised and staged by Roderick Cook. USA: New York, NY. 1986. Lang.: Eng. 3616

Reviews of *Rags*, book by Joseph Stein, music by Charles Strouse, lyrics by Stephen Schwartz, staged by Gene Saks. USA: New York, NY. 1986. Lang.: Eng. 3617
Reviews of *Brigadoon*, by Alan Jay Lerner, Frederick Loewe, staged by Gerald Freedman. USA: New York, NY. 1986. Lang.: Eng. 3619
Career of Broadway composer Stephen Sondheim. USA: New York, NY. 1930-1986. Lang.: Eng. 3624
Interviews with various artists of the Viennese State Opera. Austria: Vienna. 1909-1986. Lang.: Ger. 3692
Photos of famous conductors during their rehearsals. Austria: Vienna, Salzburg. Lang.: Ger. 3701
The native roots of Czechoslovakian literature and music. Czechoslovakia. 1800-1910. Lang.: Eng. 3717
Thematic, character and musical analysis of *Jenufa* by Leoš Janáček. Czechoslovakia: Brno. 1894-1903. Lang.: Eng. 3718
Influence of Richard Wagner on the work of the French Symbolists. France: Paris. Germany, West: Bayreuth. 1860-1986. Lang.: Eng. 3726
The successful collaboration of Arrigo Boito and Giuseppe Verdi in *Simon Boccanegra*. Italy. 1856-1881. Lang.: Eng. 3764
The innovative influence on Italian music of *L'Italiana in Algeri*. Italy. 1800-1900. Lang.: Eng. 3765
Profile of and interview with Romanian-born conductor Christian Berea. Romania. USA: New York, NY. 1950-1986. Lang.: Eng. 3771
The relationship of Steuart Bedford and Benjamin Britten. UK-England: London. 1967-1976. Lang.: Eng. 3783
Reviews of 10 vintage recordings of complete operas on LP. USA. 1906-1925. Lang.: Eng. 3792
Interview with Sir John Pritchard, music director of the San Francisco Opera. USA: San Francisco, CA. 1921-1986. Lang.: Eng. 3800
Interview with Sir Charles Mackerras on the subject of authenticity in musical performance. USA: Chicago, IL. 1925-1986. Lang.: Eng. 3809
Profile of and interview with American conductor Jeffrey Tate, concerning his approach to *Die Fledermaus* by Richard Strauss. USA: New York, NY. 1940-1946. Lang.: Eng. 3827
Profile of and interview with William Neill, composer-in-residence at the Lyric Opera of Chicago. USA: Chicago, IL. 1984-1986. Lang.: Eng. 3829
Profile of and interview with Lee Hoiby, American composer of *The Tempest* with libretto by Mark Schulgasser. USA: Long Eddy, NJ. 1926-1986. Lang.: Eng. 3832
Profile of and interview with Anthony Davis, composer of the opera *X*, on the life and times of Malcolm X. USA: New York, NY. Lang.: Eng. 3834
Profile of and interview with Gian Carlo Menotti with emphasis on his new opera *Goya*. USA: New York, NY. 1911-1986. Lang.: Eng. 3838
Profile of and interview with Frances Gershwin Godowsky, younger sister of George and Ira Gershwin. USA: New York, NY. 1900-1986. Lang.: Eng. 3842
Analysis and appreciation of the work of Modest Pavlovič Mussorgskij. USSR. 1839-1881. Lang.: Eng. 3849

Plays/librettos/scripts
Interview with playwright Al Carmines. USA: New York, NY. 1985. Lang.: Eng. 981
Interview with playwright Sam Shepard. USA. 1984. Lang.: Eng. 2925
Director George Ferencz and jazz musician Max Roach collaborate on music in trio of Sam Shepard plays. USA: New York, NY. 1984. Lang.: Eng. 2952
Conceptions of the South Sea islands in works of Murnau, Artaud and Spies. Europe. USA. Indonesia. 1930. Lang.: Ita. 3231
Ma Ke's contribution and influence on Beijing opera. China, People's Republic of: Beijing. 1951-1985. Lang.: Chi. 3536
Origins, characteristics and structures of Beijing operas. China, People's Republic of: Beijing. 1903-1985. Lang.: Chi. 3541
Successful Broadway playwrights, lyricists, and composers discuss their hits. USA: New York, NY. 1900-1985. Lang.: Eng. 3631
Examination of the text and music of Thomas Durfey's opera *Cinthia and Endimion*. England. 1690-1701. Lang.: Eng. 3861

Music — cont'd

Premiere of Kurt Weill's landmark opera *Der Zar lässt sich photographieren*. Germany: Berlin. 1926-1929. Lang.: Eng.　　3872

Collaboration of Kurt Weill, Alban Berg and Arnold Schönberg on *Lulu*. Germany. 1920-1932. Lang.: Eng.　　3875

Analysis of *Der Silbersee* by Kurt Weill and Georg Kaiser. Germany: Leipzig. 1930-1933. Lang.: Eng.　　3876

Essays on Kurt Weill's art and life. Germany: Berlin, Leipzig. 1900-1950. Lang.: Eng.　　3877

Mahler's influence on Kurt Weill's career. Germany: Berlin. 1756-1950. Lang.: Eng.　　3879

Collaboration of authors and composers of *Billy Budd*. UK-England: London. 1949-1964. Lang.: Eng.　　3895

The life, career and compositions of Benjamin Britten. UK-England: London. 1913-1976. Lang.: Eng.　　3899

Correspondence and personal contact with Sir Michael Tippett. USA: Dallas, TX. 1965-1985. Lang.: Eng.　　3900

Musical structure of dramas of Chikamatsu. Japan. 1653-1725. Lang.: Eng.　　4000

Reference materials

Guide to the work of principal composers of Broadway musicals. 1905-1985. Lang.: Eng.　　3633

Relation to other fields

Brecht's talents in the area of musical-poetic improvisation.　　3501

Mutual influence of Kurt Weill and Arnold Schönberg. Germany. 1909-1940. Lang.: Eng.　　3918

Kurt Weill's relationship with his publisher. Germany: Berlin. 1924-1931. Lang.: Eng.　　3919

Kurt Weill and German expressionism. Germany: Berlin. 1923-1930. Lang.: Eng.　　3920

Socialism and Kurt Weill's operatic reforms. Germany: Berlin. 1920-1959. Lang.: Eng.　　3921

Critical analysis of composer William Grant Still. USA. 1895-1978. Lang.: Eng.　　3924

Research/historiography

Transformation of traditional music notation into modern notation for four Chinese operas. China: Beijing. 1674-1985. Lang.: Chi.　3554

Inadequacy of research on the life of Kurt Weill. Germany: Berlin. 1925-1926. Lang.: Eng.　　3927

Theory/criticism

Strengths and weaknesses of Beijing opera. China, People's Republic of: Beijing. 1935-1985. Lang.: Chi.　　3565

The concept of *Gesamtkunstwerk*. Germany. 1797-1953. Lang.: Eng.　　3929

Music Academy of the West (Santa Barbara, CA)

Performance/production

Review of *Lunatics and Lovers*, an adaptation of Mozart's *La finta giardiniera*. USA: Santa Barbara, CA. 1985. Lang.: Eng.　　3843

Music Center Opera Association (Los Angeles, CA)

Performance/production

Collaboration of Peter Hemmings and Götz Friedrich in Los Angeles' opera season. USA: Los Angeles, CA. 1985. Lang.: Eng.　　3836

Music for the Living

SEE

Muzyka dlia živych.

Music hall

SEE ALSO

Classed Entries under MIXED ENTERTAINMENT—Variety acts: 3463-3472.

Music Man, The

Design/technology

Designers discuss regional productions of *The Music Man*. USA. 1983-1986. Lang.: Eng.　　3589

Music Theatre Group/Lenox Arts Center

Reference materials

Summer performance schedules for several New York companies. USA: New York, NY. 1984. Lang.: Eng.　　3011

Music-Drama

SEE ALSO

Classed Entries under MUSIC-DRAMA: 3473-3944.

Administration

Notes and memoirs of secretary of theatrical board. Italy: Parma. 1881-1898. Lang.: Ita.　　53

General director of Bolšoj Ballet on problems of the future. USSR: Moscow. 1986. Lang.: Rus.　　1292

Audience

The growth of musical theatre and opera since World War II. North America. 1950-1986. Lang.: Eng.　　3577

Institutions

Curriculum and expectation of students in Eubie Blake's Children's Theatre Company. USA: New York, NY. 1986. Lang.: Eng.　　1602

History of music performances, mainly opera, at the Stratford Festival. Canada: Stratford, ON. 1951-1985. Lang.: Eng.　　3671

Performance spaces

Plans for using the Ronacher theatre after its renovation. Austria: Vienna. 1871-1986. Lang.: Ger.　　584

Performance/production

Report from an international amateur theatre festival where music and dance were prominent. Denmark: Copenhagen. 1986. Lang.: Swe.　　683

Changes in English life reflected in 1883 theatre season. UK-England: London. 1883. Lang.: Eng.　　810

Guide to auditioning for dramatic and musical productions. USA. 1986. Lang.: Eng.　　830

On productions of lyric comedies and opera ballets by Jean-Philippe Rameau. France. 1683-1764. Lang.: Rus.　　1304

Reviews of two plays by Arthur Schnitzler directed by Imre Halasi. Hungary: Budapest, Zalaegerszeg. 1986. Lang.: Hun.　　1958

Performances of *Hair*, directed by János Sándor, and *Desire Under the Elms*, directed by Géza Bodolay at the National Theatre of Szeged. Hungary: Szeged. 1986. Lang.: Hun.　　1959

Revival of Philip Glass and Robert Wilson's *Einstein on the Beach* and opportunities to improve the piece. USA: New York, NY. 1976-1984. Lang.: Eng.　　2305

Puppet production of Mozart's opera *Die Zauberflöte*. USA. 1986. Lang.: Eng.　　4008

Plays/librettos/scripts

Love in the plays and operas of Jean-Jacques Rousseau. France. Switzerland. 1712-1778. Lang.: Fre.　　2563

Correspondence between Luigi Pirandello and composer Gian Francesco Malipiero. Italy. 1832-1938. Lang.: Ita.　　2699

Director George Ferencz and jazz musician Max Roach collaborate on music in trio of Sam Shepard plays. USA: New York, NY. 1984. Lang.: Eng.　　2952

Musica deuxième, La

Performance/production

Production journal of *La Musica deuxième* by Marguerite Duras. France: Paris. 1985. Lang.: Fre.　　1733

Musica II, La

SEE

Musica deuxième, La.

Musical theatre

SEE ALSO

Classed Entries under MUSIC-DRAMA—Musical theatre: 3571-3635.

Institutions

Curriculum and expectation of students in Eubie Blake's Children's Theatre Company. USA: New York, NY. 1986. Lang.: Eng.　　1602

History of music performances, mainly opera, at the Stratford Festival. Canada: Stratford, ON. 1951-1985. Lang.: Eng.　　3671

Performance/production

Guide to auditioning for dramatic and musical productions. USA. 1986. Lang.: Eng.　　830

Playwright/dramaturg Peter Eliot Weiss discusses *Sex Tips for Modern Girls*. Canada: Vancouver, BC. 1984-1985. Lang.: Eng.　1684

Memoir of writer, critic, theatre director Béla Abody. Hungary. 1970-1980. Lang.: Hun.　　1780

Review of Ivan Kušan's musical comedy *Čaruga (Death Cap)*, directed by Miklós Benedek, Katona József Theatre, as *Galócza*, includes discussion of acting and dramatic art. Hungary: Budapest. 1986. Lang.: Hun.　　1811

Sip a tökre (Play a Trump in Diamonds) by Péter Tömöry, directed by Imre Halasi. Hungary: Kisvárda. 1986. Lang.: Hun.　　1859

Die dreigroschenoper (The Three Penny Opera) directed by István Pinczés at Csokonai Theatre. Hungary: Debrecen. 1986. Lang.: Hun.　　1910

Reviews of two plays by Arthur Schnitzler directed by Imre Halasi. Hungary: Budapest, Zalaegerszeg. 1986. Lang.: Hun.　　1958

Performances of *Hair*, directed by János Sándor, and *Desire Under the Elms*, directed by Géza Bodolay at the National Theatre of Szeged. Hungary: Szeged. 1986. Lang.: Hun.　　1959

Musical theatre — cont'd

Career of John Scrimger, music director at Perth Theatre. UK-Scotland: Perth. 1948-1986. Lang.: Eng.   2188

Analysis of political cabaret and cabaret revue. USA: New York, NY. 1983. Lang.: Eng.   3367

Reviews of three musicals about the 1960s. Hungary. 1985-1986. Lang.: Hun.   3488

Mágnás Miska (Miska the Magnate) by Albert Szirmai directed by László Bagossy. Hungary: Pécs. 1986. Lang.: Hun.   3942

Plays/librettos/scripts
Interview with composer Wolfgang Rihm. Switzerland. 1974-1986. Lang.: Ger.   3893

Relation to other fields
Brecht's talents in the area of musical-poetic improvisation.   3501

Musicians
SEE
Music.

Musikteater (Kristianstad)
Performance/production
Amateur production of Alfred Jarry's *Kung Ubu (Ubu roi)* by Kristianstad Musikteater. Sweden: Kristianstad. 1986. Lang.: Swe.
                    797

Musser, Tharon
Design/technology
Interview with lighting designers Arden Fingerhut, Tharon Musser and Jennifer Tipton. USA. 1986. Lang.: Eng.   340

Musset, Alfred de
Plays/librettos/scripts
Theme of fragmentation in *Lorenzaccio* by Alfred de Musset. France. 1834. Lang.: Eng.   2558

Mussorgskij, Modest Pavlovič
Performance/production
Profile of and interview with Finnish bass Martti Talvela. Finland. 1935-1986. Lang.: Eng.   3723

Mussorgskij's opera *Boris Godunov* at the Mariinskij Theatre. Russia: St. Petersburg. 1874. Lang.: Eng.   3775

The alcoholism of Modest Pavlovič Mussorgskij prevented the completion of *Chovanščina*. Russia: St. Petersburg. 1850-1890. Lang.: Eng.   3777

Photographs, cast list, synopsis, and discography of Metropolitan Opera radio broadcast performances. USA: New York, NY. 1986. Lang.: Eng.   3794

Analysis and appreciation of the work of Modest Pavlovič Mussorgskij. USSR. 1839-1881. Lang.: Eng.   3849

Relation to other fields
Comparison between insanity defense and opera productions with audience as jury. USA. 1980-1985. Lang.: Eng.   3925

Mustika Malaysia (Kuala Lumpur)
Institutions
Reports on theatre conferences and festivals in Asia. Philippines: Manila. Malaysia: Kuala Lumpur. Japan: Toga. India: Calcutta. 1981-1984. Lang.: Eng.   510

Mutiny!
Design/technology
William Dudley's life-like replica of the Bounty for David Essex's *Mutiny!*. UK-England: London. 1986. Lang.: Eng.   3584

Mutter Courage und ihre Kinder (Mother Courage and Her Children)
Performance/production
Directorial process as seen through major productions of Stanislavskij, Brecht, Kazan and Brook. 1898-1964. Lang.: Eng.   650

Articles about the productions of the Centre Dramàtic. Spain-Catalonia: Barcelona. 1976-1986. Lang.: Cat.   2084

Plays/librettos/scripts
Interview with founders of Internationale Nieuwe Scene. Europe. 1984.   2543

Demystification of the feminine myth in Brecht's plays. Germany, East. 1984.   2618

Mutter, Die (Mother, The)
Performance/production
Brecht and the Berliner Ensemble. Germany, East: Berlin, East. 1950-1956. Lang.: Ger.   1765

Müvész Szinház (Budapest)
Performance/production
Hungarian folksongs and dance adapted to the stage in *Magyar Csupajáték (Hungarian All-Play)*. Hungary: Budapest. 1938-1939. Lang.: Hun.   1274

Muzio Scevola
Performance/production
Productions of Handel's *Muzio Scevola* and analysis of score and characters. England: London. 1718-1980. Lang.: Eng.   3720

Muzyka dlja živych (Music for the Living)
Performance/production
The staging of G. Kančeli's opera *Muzyka dlja živych (Music for the Living)* at the Z. Paliašvili theater. USSR: Tbilisi. 1980-1986. Lang.: Rus.   3848

My Beautiful Laundrette
Design/technology
The making of the film *My Beautiful Laundrette*. UK-England: London. 1986.   3202

My Fair Lady
Performance/production
Hungarian performance of *My Fair Lady*. Hungary. 1966-1970. Lang.: Hun.   3601

My Sister in This House
Plays/librettos/scripts
Wendy Kesselman's treatment of a murder in *My Sister in This House*. USA. 1933-1983. Lang.: Eng.   2915

My Song Is Free
Performance/production
Collection of newspaper reviews by London theatre critics. UK-England: London. 1986. Lang.: Eng.   2121

Mystery of Edwin Drood, The
Design/technology
Interview with director and former designer Wilford Leach. USA: New York, NY. 1975-1986.   344

Mystery plays
SEE ALSO
Passion plays.

Performance/production
Comparison of Holy Week Processions of Seville with English Mystery plays. Spain: Seville. 1986. Lang.: Eng.   3426

Mythology
Performance/production
Production analysis of a montage of sketches about Electra by Stúdió K. Hungary: Budapest. 1986. Lang.: Hun.   1773

Murray Mednick's 7-play Coyote Cycle performed outdoors from dusk to dawn. USA. 1984. Lang.: Eng.   2292

Plays/librettos/scripts
Analysis of Tomasz Łubieński's plays. Poland. 1986. Lang.: Pol.
                    2734

Use of Greek mythological themes in Athol Fugard's plays. South Africa, Republic of. 1959-1986. Lang.: Afr.   2773

Playwright Edward Bond's use of Greek models in *The Woman*. UK-England. 1978. Lang.: Eng.   2834

Treatment of the Frankenstein myth in three gothic melodramas. UK-England. France. 1823-1826. Lang.: Eng.   2847

German and Christian myths in Hans Pfitzner's opera *Palestrina*. 1900-1982. Lang.: Eng.   3852

Reference materials
Modern plays using mythic themes, grouped according to subject. Europe. USA. 1898-1986. Lang.: Eng.   2986

Relation to other fields
Ritual, rhythmic activity: their effects upon brain systems. USA. 1986. Lang.: Eng.   1167

Theory/criticism
Eastern and western myths explaining the origin of theatre. Europe. Asia. 1986. Lang.: Ita.   3098

Social and political conditions of Greek society as sources for dramatic material. Greece: Athens. 450 B.C. Lang.: Eng.   3113

Arthur Miller's *After the Fall* seen an monomyth. USA. 1964-1984. Lang.: Eng.   3138

N-town Plays
Performance/production
Account of University of California at Irvine production of a nativity play with composite text drawn from York, N-town and Wakefield cycles. USA: Irvine, CA. 1986. Lang.: Eng.   2307

Plays/librettos/scripts
Dramatic dynamics of Chester cycle play, *The Fall of Lucifer*. England. 1400-1550. Lang.: Eng.   2499

Na Pohulance Theatre (Vilna)
Performance/production
Repertory and artistic achievements of the Na Pohulance Theatre. Poland: Vilna. 1938-1940. Lang.: Pol.   2036

National Theatre (London) — cont'd

Survey of the season at the National Theatre. UK-England: London. 1986. Lang.: Eng. 2130

Reviews of three Shakespearean productions. UK-England: London, Stratford. USA: Ashland, OR. 1985. Lang.: Eng. 2140

Playwright Alan Ayckbourn's directing stint at the National Theatre. UK-England: London. 1986. Lang.: Eng. 2158

Director Jonathan Lynn discusses his works performed at the National Theatre. UK-England: London. UK-England: Cambridge. 1986. Lang.: Eng. 2160

Actor Colin Blakely discusses his career. UK-England: London. 1950-1986. Lang.: Eng. 2176

Actress Rosemary Harris discusses her work in *The Petition*. UK-England: London. USA: New York, NY. 1948-1986. Lang.: Eng. 2177

Actress Sheila Hancock discusses role of Madame Ranevskaya in Čechov's *Višněvyj sad (The Cherry Orchard)*. UK-England: London. 1986. Lang.: Eng. 2180

Shakespearean productions by the National Theatre, Royal Shakespeare Company and Orange Tree Theatre. UK-England: Stratford, London. 1984-1985. Lang.: Eng. 2183

Plays/librettos/scripts
Interview with playwright Howard Barker. UK-England. 1981-1985. Lang.: Eng. 2845

Relation to other fields
Current style of theatre-in-education. UK-England. Lang.: Eng. 3057

National Theatre (Miskolc)
SEE
Miskolci Nemzeti Szinház.

National Theatre (Munich)
SEE
Bayerische Staatsoper im Nationaltheater.

National Theatre (New York, NY)
SEE
American National Theatre and Academy.

National Theatre (Pest)
SEE
Pécsi Nemzeti Szinház.

National Theatre (Prague)
SEE
Národní Divadlo.

National Theatre (Szeged)
SEE
Szegedi Nemzeti Szinház.

National Theatre (Tel Aviv)
SEE
HaBima (Tel Aviv).

National Theatre Festival (Korea)
Performance/production
Reviews of the play productions at the National Theatre Festival. Korea. 1986. Lang.: Eng. 2009

Review of the play productions at the National Theatre Festival. Korea. 1985. Lang.: Eng. 2010

National Theatre Workshop of the Handicapped
Training
Training of disabled students in theatre arts. USA. 1986. Lang.: Eng. 1258

National Training School for Dancing (UK)
Administration
Legislation for the protection of Victorian child-actors. UK. 1837-1901. Lang.: Eng. 1439

National Youth Music Theatre (UK)
Design/technology
Use of the Gemini computerized lighting system used at the Edinburgh Festival. UK-Scotland: Edinburgh. 1980-1986. Lang.: Eng. 332

Performance/production
Report from the international Fringe Festival. UK-Scotland: Edinburgh. 1986. Lang.: Swe. 819

Nativity plays
Relation to other fields
Folklorist Tekla Dömötör includes traditional material in her popular work. Hungary. 1986. Lang.: Hun. 1098

Naturalism
Plays/librettos/scripts
Essays on Lessing and Lessing criticism. Germany. 1748-1984. Lang.: Ger. 2611

Concept of tragic character in Eugene O'Neill's *Desire Under the Elms*. USA. 1924. Lang.: Eng. 2907

Nātya-sāstra
Performance/production
An outline formula of performance as derived from Asian theatre. Japan. 1363-1986. Lang.: Ita. 1364

Navaja, La (Razor, The)
Performance/production
Production description of the symbolist drama *La navaja (The Razor)* by Eduardo Quiles. Spain. 1980. Lang.: Spa. 2074

Plays/librettos/scripts
Description of plays by Eduardo Quiles including *La navaja (The Razor)* a tragicomedy for two actors and puppets. Spain. 1940-1985. Lang.: Spa. 2780

Nazaire et Barnabé
Plays/librettos/scripts
Analysis of French-language radio series *Nazaire et Barnabé*. Canada. 1939-1958. Lang.: Eng. 3183

NCT
SEE
Nouvelle Companie Thâtrale.

Ne blâmez jamais les Bédouins (Don't Blame It on the Bedouins)
Plays/librettos/scripts
Examines *Ne blâmez jamais les Bédouins (Don't Blame It on the Bedouins)* as a post-modernist play. Canada. 1980. Lang.: Fre. 2432

Ne-boska komedia (Undivine Comedy)
Plays/librettos/scripts
Different interpretations of Zygmunt Krasiński's *Ne-boska komedia (Undivine Comedy)*. Poland. 1835-1984. Lang.: Fre. 2756

NEA
SEE
National Endowment for the Arts.

Neaptide
Institutions
Place of women in Britain's National Theatre. UK-England: London. 1986. Lang.: Eng. 1588

NEC
SEE
Negro Ensemble Company.

Necessities
Administration
Rita Kohn's attempts to get her play *Necessities* produced. USA: New York, NY. 1986. 125

Ned Kelly
Plays/librettos/scripts
Individualism and male-female relationships as themes in Australian drama. Australia. 1940-1980. Lang.: Eng. 2373

Comparison of plays about Ned Kelly of Australia and Louis Riel of Canada. Canada. Australia. 1900-1976. Lang.: Eng. 2421

Nederlander Theatre (New York, NY)
Performance/production
Reviews of *Raggedy Ann*, book by William Gibon, music and lyrics by Joe Raposo, staged and choreographed by Patricia Birch. USA: New York, NY. 1986. Lang.: Eng. 3614

Negro Ensemble Company (NEC, New York, NY)
Administration
Alternative funding for small theatres previously dependent on government subsidy. USA: St. Louis, MO, New York, NY, Los Angeles, CA, Detroit, MI. 1985. Lang.: Eng. 103

Growing activity and changing role of Black regional theatre companies. USA. 1960-1984. Lang.: Eng. 1440

Institutions
Reprint of an article by Douglas Turner Ward that resulted in the founding of the Negro Ensemble Company. USA: New York, NY. 1966. Lang.: Eng. 572

History of two major Black touring companies. USA: New York, NY. 1969-1982. Lang.: Eng. 1598

Plays/librettos/scripts
Biographical sketch of playwright/performer Samm-Art Williams. USA: Burgaw, NC, New York, NY. 1940-1986. Lang.: Eng. 2946

Neil Simon Theatre (New York, NY)
Performance/production
Reviews of *Into the Light*, book by Jeff Tamborniro, music by Lee Holdridge, lyrics by John Forster, staged by Michael Maurer. USA: New York, NY. 1986. Lang.: Eng. 3615

Neil, Bill
Design/technology
Lighting designer Andrew Lazlo talks about his work on the film *Poltergeist II*. USA: Los Angeles, CA. USA: New York, NY. 1985-1986. Lang.: Eng.   3204

Neil, Boyd
Theory/criticism
Book review of *Whittaker's Theatre: A Critic Looks at Stages in Canada and Thereabouts: 1944-1975*, ed. Ronald Bryden and Boyd Neil. Canada: Toronto, ON. 1944-1985. Lang.: Eng.   3087

Neill, William
Performance/production
Profile of and interview with William Neill, composer-in-residence at the Lyric Opera of Chicago. USA: Chicago, IL. 1984-1986. Lang.: Eng.   3829

Nel, Christoph
Performance/production
Director Christoph Nel discusses staging Brecht's *Im Dickicht der Städte (In the Jungle of the Cities)*. USA: Seattle, WA. 1984.   2246

Nelson, Don
Theory/criticism
Report of seminar on theatre criticism. USA: New York, NY. 1983. Lang.: Eng.   1223

Nelson, John
Institutions
New administrative personnel at the Opera Theatre of St. Louis. USA: St. Louis, MO. 1976-1986. Lang.: Eng.   3679

Nelson, Michael W.
Design/technology
Techniques and tools in puppet design and construction. USA. 1986. Lang.: Eng.   3954

Nelson, Richard
Performance/production
Reviews of *Principia Scriptoriae* by Richard Nelson, staged by Lynne Meadow. USA: New York, NY. 1986. Lang.: Eng.   2223
Dramaturg Richard Nelson on communicating with different kinds of directors. USA: New York, NY. 1979-1986. Lang.: Eng.   2252

Theory/criticism
Theatre professionals challenge assertions that theatre is a weaker form of communication than film. USA: New York, NY. 1985. Lang.: Eng.   1225

Neményi, Lili
Performance/production
Life and career of actress-singer Lili Neményi. Austro-Hungarian Empire. Hungary. 1908-1986. Lang.: Hun.   3705

Németh, Antal
Performance/production
Choreography by Aurél Milloss for dramatic productions directed by Antal Németh at the National Theatre in Budapest. Hungary: Budapest. 1935-1938. Lang.: Hun.   1847

Németh, László
Plays/librettos/scripts
Analysis of László Németh's study of *Bánk Bán* by József Katona and a portrait of the playwright. Hungary. 1985. Lang.: Hun.   2647

Nemzeti Szinház (Budapest)
Performance/production
Interview with actor, director and manager Tamás Major. Hungary. 1910-1986. Lang.: Hun.   1776
Ferenc Sik directs András Sütő's *Advent a Hargitán (Advent in the Harghita Mountains)* at the National Theatre. Hungary: Budapest. 1984-1985. Lang.: Hun.   1779
Review of *A trójai nők (The Trojan Women)* adapted from Euripides and Sartre by Gyula Illyés, directed by László Vámos. Hungary: Budapest. 1986. Lang.: Hun.   1792
Review of *Advent a Hargitán (Advent in the Harghita Mountains)* by András Sütő, directed by Ferenc Sik. Hungary: Budapest. 1986. Lang.: Hun.   1797
Career of theatrical professional Ede Paulay. Hungary: Budapest. 1852-1864. Lang.: Hun.   1824
Choreography by Aurél Milloss for dramatic productions directed by Antal Németh at the National Theatre in Budapest. Hungary: Budapest. 1935-1938. Lang.: Hun.   1847
András Béhés directs *Légy jó mindhalálig (Be Good Till Death)* by Zsigmond Móricz at Nemzeti Szinház. Hungary: Budapest. 1986. Lang.: Hun.   1849
Ferenc Sik directs *A velencei Kalmár (The Merchant of Venice)* by William Shakespeare. Hungary: Budapest. 1986. Lang.: Hun.   1853

Review of *Trójai Nők (The Trojan Women)* by Jean-Paul Sartre, produced at Nemzeti Szinház. Hungary: Budapest. 1986. Lang.: Hun.   1855
Reprinted preface to biography of Tamás Major. Hungary. 1930-1986. Lang.: Hun.   1863
Interview with Tamás Major, director and actor. Hungary. 1945-1986. Lang.: Hun.   1868
Reviews of Shakespeare productions written by Hungarian realist writer, Zsigmond Móricz. Hungary: Budapest. 1923. Lang.: Hun.   1887
Review of Biblical passion play by National Theatre of Budapest. Hungary: Budapest. Poland: Warsaw. 1983. Lang.: Pol.   1899
Ferenc Sik directs Shakespeare's *A velencei kalmár (The Merchant of Venice)*. Hungary: Budapest. 1986. Lang.: Hun.   1907
Review of two performances of András Sütő's plays. Hungary: Budapest. 1986. Lang.: Hun.   1913
Theatrical career of Ede Paulay. Hungary: Budapest. 1878-1894. Lang.: Hun.   1944
Advent a Hargitán (Advent in the Harghita Mountains) by András Sütő, directed at National Theatre by Ferenc Sik. Hungary: Budapest. 1986. Lang.: Hun.   1956
Rehearsals of András Sütő's *Advent a Hargitán (Advent in the Harghita Mountains)* at the National Theatre directed by Ferenc Sik. Hungary: Budapest. 1985-1986. Lang.: Hun.   1963
Tizenkét dühös ember (Twelve Angry Men) by Reginald Rose directed by András Béhés. Hungary: Budapest. 1985. Lang.: Hun.   1972
András Sütő's *Advent a Hargitán (Advent in the Harghita Mountains)* directed by Ferenc Sik. Hungary: Budapest. 1986. Lang.: Hun.   1974
Review of rock opera *István a király (King Stephen)* at the National Theatre. Hungary: Budapest. 1985. Lang.: Hun.   3489

Nemzeti Szinház (Miskolc)
SEE
Miskolci Nemzeti Szinház.

Nemzeti Szinház (Pécs)
SEE
Pécsi Nemzeti Szinház.

Nemzeti Szinház (Szeged)
SEE
Szegedi Nemzeti Szinház.

Neoclassicism
SEE ALSO
Geographical-Chronological Index under Europe 1540-1660, France 1629-1660, Italy 1540-1576.
Performance/production
Analysis of Shakespeare's influence on Weimar, German neoclassicism. Germany: Weimar. 1771-1812. Lang.: Eng.   1760
Plays/librettos/scripts
Treatment of Napoleon Bonaparte by French and English dramatists. France. England. 1797-1958. Lang.: Eng.   2568
Theory/criticism
Corneille, Racine and Molière as neoclassisists. France. 1600-1700. Lang.: Kor.   3102

Népszinház (Budapest)
Institutions
Surviving documents relating to the Népszinház. Austro-Hungarian Empire: Budapest. 1872-1918. Lang.: Hun.   462
Performance/production
Miklós Mészöly's *Bunker* at Népszinház directed by Mátyás Giricz. Hungary: Budapest. 1985. Lang.: Hun.   1919
László Kertész directs Rossini's *L'occasione fa il ladro* at Népszinház. Hungary: Budapest. 1986. Lang.: Hun.   3749

Neptune Theatre (Halifax, NS)
Administration
John Neville's administration of the Neptune Theatre. Canada: Halifax, NS. 1979-1983. Lang.: Eng.   27
Institutions
History of the Neptune Theatre and its artistic directors. Canada: Halifax, NS. 1963-1983. Lang.: Eng.   483
Several short-lived alternative theatre companies to the Neptune Theatre. Canada: Halifax, NS. 1962-1986. Lang.: Eng.   1557

Nessim, Louise
Performance/production
Stage photographs with comment by photographers. Sweden. 1985-1986. Lang.: Swe.   794

Nest of the Woodgrouse
SEE
Teterëvo gnezdo.

Nestroy-Festspiele au Burg Liechtenstein (Austria)
Institutions
Niederösterreichischer Theatersommer: producing summer theatre at festivals in different places. Austria. 1980-1986. Lang.: Ger.   448

Nestroy, Franz
Relation to other fields
Life and work of playwright and critic Karl Kraus. Austria: Vienna. 1874-1936. Lang.: Ger.   3017

Nestroy, Johann
Plays/librettos/scripts
Tom Stoppard's *On the Razzle*, an adaptation of *Einen Jux will er sich machen* by Johann Nestroy. England. Austria: Vienna. 1927-1981. Lang.: Eng.   2462

Reference materials
Costumes of famous Viennese actors. Austria: Vienna. 1831-1960. Lang.: Ger.   1003

Relation to other fields
Karl Kraus, a reflection of Viennese culture and literature history. Austria: Vienna. 1874-1936. Lang.: Ger.   3014
Life and work of playwright and critic Karl Kraus. Austria: Vienna. 1874-1936. Lang.: Ger.   3017

Network
SEE
Netzwerk.

Neumann, Fred
Institutions
Interview with members of Mabou Mines. USA: New York, NY. 1984. Lang.: Eng.   1607

Neville, John
Administration
John Neville's administration of the Neptune Theatre. Canada: Halifax, NS. 1979-1983. Lang.: Eng.   27

Institutions
History of the Neptune Theatre and its artistic directors. Canada: Halifax, NS. 1963-1983. Lang.: Eng.   483
Artistic director John Neville discusses future plans for the Stratford Festival. Canada: Stratford, ON. 1985. Lang.: Eng.   1551

Performance/production
John Neville's productions of *The Winter's Tale*, *Pericles*, and *Cymbeline*. Canada: Stratford, ON. 1974-1986. Lang.: Eng.   1657

New Colony, The
SEE
Nuova colonia, La.

New England Magazine
Reference materials
Theatrical materials in five early American magazines. Colonial America. 1758-1800. Lang.: Eng.   1012

New Federal Theatre (New York, NY)
Administration
Alternative funding for small theatres previously dependent on government subsidy. USA: St. Louis, MO, New York, NY, Los Angeles, CA, Detroit, MI. 1985. Lang.: Eng.   103

Institutions
History of two major Black touring companies. USA: New York, NY. 1969-1982. Lang.: Eng.   1598

Performance/production
Reviews of *Williams and Walker* by Vincent D. Smith, staged by Shaunelle Percy. USA: New York, NY. 1986. Lang.: Eng.   2225

Plays/librettos/scripts
Biographical sketch of playwright/performer Samm-Art Williams. USA: Burgaw, NC, New York, NY. 1940-1986. Lang.: Eng.   2946

New Festival Theatre (London)
Design/technology
Details the installation and use of a 1935 Strand lighting console. UK-England: London. 1935-1986. Lang.: Eng.   321

New Play Centre, The (Vancouver, BC)
Performance/production
Increased use of physical aspects of theatre in Vancouver. Canada: Vancouver, BC. 1986. Lang.: Eng.   1664

New School for Social Research (New York, NY)
Institutions
Erwin Piscator's work at the Dramatic Workshop of the New School for Social Research. USA: New York, NY. 1939-1951. Lang.: Ger.   1600

New Theatre (London)
Performance/production
Director John Dexter and impresario Eddie Kulukundis discuss the formation of the New Theatre Company. UK-England: London. 1986. Lang.: Eng.   2144

New Theatre (New York, NY)
Performance spaces
History of the Century Theatre. USA: New York, NY. 1905-1930. Lang.: Eng.   1625

New Theatre (Sydney)
Institutions
Account of New Theatre movement by a participant. Australia: Sydney, Melbourne. 1932-1955. Lang.: Eng.   437
Historical perspective of the New Theatre. Australia: Sydney, N.S.W. 1932-1986. Lang.: Eng.   438

Plays/librettos/scripts
Playwright Mona Brand's work with New Theatre movement. Australia: Sydney, N.S.W. 1932-1968. Lang.: Eng.   924
Analysis of the plays of Oriel Gray. Australia. 1942-1958. Lang.: Eng.   2376

New Theatre (Toronto, ON)
Performance spaces
Troubles faced by Adelaide Court theatre complex. Canada: Toronto, ON. 1979-1983. Lang.: En .   587

New Victoria Theatre (Newcastle-under-Lyme)
Performance spaces
Technical review of *She Stoops to Conquer* by Oliver Goldsmith performed at the New Victoria Theatre. UK-England: Newcastle-under-Lyme. 1980-1986. Lang.: Eng.   1618

New Victoria Theatre (Stoke-on-Trent)
Performance spaces
Technical design features of New Victoria Theatre. UK-England: Stoke-on-Trent. 1980-1986. Lang.: Eng.   624
Peter Cheeseman, artistic director of the New Victoria Theatre, compares the new theatre with the Old Vic. UK-England: Stoke-on-Trent. 1962-1986. Lang.: Eng.   629

New Way to Pay Old Debts, A
Plays/librettos/scripts
Aristocratic culture and 'country-house' poetic theme in Massinger's *A New Way to Pay Old Debts*. England. 1621. Lang.: Eng.   2531

New York City Department of Cultural Affairs (New York, NY)
Institutions
Programs of the New York City Department of Cultural Affairs affecting nonprofit theatre. USA: New York, NY. 1983. Lang.: Eng.   554

New York City Opera
Performance/production
Stills from telecast performance of *Candide* by New York City Opera. USA: New York, NY. 1986. Lang.: Eng.   3796
Profile of and interview with American tenor Jerry Hadley. USA: New York, NY. 1952-1986. Lang.: Eng.   3818
Profile of and interview with Anthony Davis, composer of the opera *X*, on the life and times of Malcolm X. USA: New York, NY. Lang.: Eng.   3834

New York International Clown Festival (New York)
Design/technology
Costumes at New York International Clown Festival. USA: New York, NY. 1984. Lang.: Eng.   3316

New York Magazine or Literary Repository
Reference materials
Theatrical materials in five early American magazines. Colonial America. 1758-1800. Lang.: Eng.   1012

New York Opera Company
Performance/production
Details of Luigi Arditi's U.S. and Canada tour with the New York Opera Company. USA. Canada: Montreal, PQ, Toronto, ON. 1853-1854. Lang.: Eng.   3819

New York Shakespeare Festival
SEE
Public Theater (New York, NY).

New York State Council on the Arts (NYSCA)
Administration
Interview with NYSCA Theatre Program Director Zuri McKie. USA: New York, NY. 1983. Lang.: Eng.   133
Primary organizational changes at New York State Council on the Arts. USA: New York, NY. 1984. Lang.: Eng.   162

New York State Theatre (New York, NY)
Performance/production
Reviews of *Brigadoon*, by Alan Jay Lerner, Frederick Loewe, staged by Gerald Freedman. USA: New York, NY. 1986. Lang.: Eng. 3619

New York Street Theatre Caravan
Performance/production
Resurgence of street theatre productions and companies. USA: New York, NY. 1960-1982. Lang.: Eng. 2285

New York Theatre Workshop (New York, NY)
Administration
Creation and role of board of directors in nonprofit theatre. USA: New York, NY. 1986. Lang.: Eng. 104

Institutions
Profile of New York Theatre Workshop. USA: New York, NY. 1980-1984. Lang.: Eng. 542

Problems and advantages of co-production. USA: New York, NY. 1985. Lang.: Eng. 571

Training
Lack of opportunities, programs and training for beginning directors. USA: New York, NY. 1985. Lang.: Eng. 1260

Newman, Chris
Design/technology
Problems faced by sound designer Chris Newman in filming *A Chorus Line*. USA: New York, NY. 1986. 3205

Newman, Danny
Administration
Marketing directors seek innovative approaches to brochure design. USA: New York, NY. 1986. Lang.: Eng. 139

Newton, Christopher
Administration
Resourcefulness of the Shaw Festival season. Canada: Niagara-on-the-Lake, ON. 1985. Lang.: Eng. 1430

Next Wave Festival (New York, NY)
Performance/production
Interview with choreographer Meredith Monk. USA: New York, NY. 1964-1984. Lang.: Eng. 1368

Ngema, Mbongeni
Performance/production
Reviews of *Asinamali*, written and staged by Mbongeni Ngema. USA: New York, NY. 1986. Lang.: Eng. 2244

Ngurah, Ida Bagus (a.k.a. Dalang Buduk)
Performance/production
Shadow puppetry as a way of passing on Balinese culture. Bali. 1976-1985. Lang.: Eng. 4017

Nha hat Kich (Hanoi)
Plays/librettos/scripts
Vietnamese drama focusing on its origins from traditional forms. Vietnam. 1940-1986. Lang.: Swe. 2974

Nichols, Jackie
Administration
Playhouse on the Square's executive producer discusses producing musicals. USA: Memphis, TN. Lang.: Eng. 3573

Nichols, Mike
Performance/production
Reviews of *Social Security*, by Andrew Bergman, staged by Mike Nichols. USA: New York, NY. 1986. Lang.: Eng. 2233

Nichols, Peter
Plays/librettos/scripts
Jungian analysis of the plays of Peter Nichols. UK-England. 1967-1984. Lang.: Eng. 2848

Nickas, George
Performance/production
Seduced by Sam Shepard, directed by George Nickas at Seven Stages. USA: Atlanta, GA. 1985. Lang.: Eng. 2302

Nicoll, Allardyce
Reference materials
Update of Allardyce Nicoll's handlist of plays. UK-England: London. 1900-1930. Lang.: Eng. 3003

Niech sczezna artyszi (Let the Artists Die)
Performance/production
Career and philosophy of director Tadeusz Kantor. Poland. 1915-1985. Lang.: Eng. 2028

Interview with director Tadeusz Kantor. Poland. 1967-1985. Lang.: Eng. 2029

Plays/librettos/scripts
Influence of politics and personal history on Tadeusz Kantor and his Cricot 2 theatre company. Poland: Cracow. 1944-1986. Lang.: Eng. 2744

Niech szezna artyszi (Let the Artists Die)
Plays/librettos/scripts
Tadeusz Kantor comments on his play *Niech szezna artyszi (Let the Artists Die)*. Poland. 1985. Lang.: Eng, Fre. 2751

Niederösterreichischer Theatersommer (Austria)
Institutions
Niederösterreichischer Theatersommer: producing summer theatre at festivals in different places. Austria. 1980-1986. Lang.: Ger. 448

Niese, Hansi
Performance/production
Biography of actor and stage manager Franz Reichert. Austria: Vienna. Germany: Berlin. Czechoslovakia: Prague. 1925-1950. Lang.: Ger. 1652

Nietzsche, Friedrich Wilhelm
Theory/criticism
Hungarian translation of Nietzsche's *Birth of Tragedy*. Germany. 1872. Lang.: Hun. 3108

Analysis of Wole Soyinka's major critical essays. Nigeria. 1960-1980. Lang.: Eng. 3124

Nieva, Francisco
Plays/librettos/scripts
Artaud's concept of theatre of cruelty in Francisco Nieva's *Tórtolas, crepúscula y ...telón (Turtledoves, Twilight and ...Curtain)*. Spain. 1953. Lang.: Spa. 2790

Night is the Mother of the Day
Performance/production
Imre Csiszár directs *Az éjszaka a nappal anyja (Night is the Mother of the Day)* by Lars Norén. Hungary: Dunaújváros. 1986. Lang.: Hun. 1882

Night of Legio, The
SEE
Nag van Legio, Die.

Night of the Assassins, The
SEE
Noche de los asesinos, La.

Nightclubs
Performance/production
Changes in East Village performance scene. USA: New York, NY. 1975-1985. Lang.: Eng. 3458

Four nightclub entertainers on their particular acts and the atmosphere of the late night clubs and theaters in Harlem. USA: New York, NY, Savannah, GA. 1930-1950. Lang.: Eng. 3470

Nightingale, Benedict
Performance/production
Collection of reviews by Benedict Nightingale on New York theatre. USA: New York, NY. 1983-1984. Lang.: Eng. 847

Nightwood Theatre (Toronto, ON)
Institutions
History of the Rhubarb Festival. Canada: Toronto, ON. 1986. Lang.: Eng. 1549

Nikolais, Alwin
Performance/production
Merce Cunningham, Alwin Nikolais, Meredith Monk and Yvonne Rainer on post-modern dance. USA. 1975-1986. Lang.: Eng. 1285

Nilsson, Birgit
Performance/production
Profile of and interview with soprano Leonie Rysanek. Austria: Vienna. 1926-1986. Lang.: Eng. 3693

Famous sopranos discuss their interpretations of Tosca. USA. 1935-1986. Lang.: Eng. 3811

Nilsson, Rob
Design/technology
Technique for transferring film to black and white videotape. USA. 1986. 3209

Nimrod Theatre Company (New South Wales)
Plays/librettos/scripts
Developments in Australian playwriting since 1975. Australia. 1975-1986. Lang.: Eng. 2374

Nirod, F.F.
Design/technology
Work of F.F. Nirod, principal designer of the Teat'r Opery i Baleta im. T.G. Sevčenko. USSR: Kiev. 1960-1986. Lang.: Rus. 432

Nisoli, Betina
Training
Modern dance lesson with Betina Nisoli. Austria: Vienna. 1986. Lang.: Ger. 1354

Nixon, Jon
Relation to other fields
Discussion of theatre-in-education. UK. Lang.: Eng. 3055

Nō
SEE ALSO
Classed Entries under DANCE-DRAMA—*Nō*: 1383-1424.
Basic theatrical documents
Playtext of *Drifting Fires* by Janine Beichman, with author's afterword on use of *Nō* elements. Japan: Ibaraki. 1984-1985. Lang.: Eng. 1383
Design/technology
Description of how *Nō* masks are made. Japan. 1363-1986. Lang.: Eng. 1387
Performance/production
Role of the mask in popular theatre. Japan. Africa. Europe. Lang.: Ita. 755
Western actors and the energy of Oriental performance. Japan. Lang.: Ita. 756
Influence of *kata* principle on Western acting technique. Japan. Denmark. Australia. 1981-1986. Lang.: Ita. 1365
Reciprocal influences of French and Japanese theatre. France. Japan. 1900-1945. Lang.: Fre. 1750
Plays/librettos/scripts
Japanese influences on works of Brecht and Klabund. Germany. Japan. 1900-1950. Lang.: Ita. 952
Adapting *Hamlet* for the *nō* theatre. England. Japan. 1600-1982. Lang.: Ita. 2506
Influence of *Nō* on Paul Claudel. France. 1868-1955. Lang.: Ita. 2556
Nō and Beckett compared. Japan. France. 1954-1986. Lang.: Ita. 2721
Reference materials
Yearbook of major performances in all areas of Japanese theatre. Japan: Tokyo. 1986. Lang.: Jap. 1026
Dictionary of the life and work of Tsubouchi Shōyō. Japan: Tokyo. 1859-1986. Lang.: Jap. 1027
Theory/criticism
Development and characteristics of Oriental theatre. Korea: Seoul. Japan: Tokyo. China: Beijing. 200-1986. Lang.: Kor. 1215
Various aspects of *kyōgen*. Japan. 1300-1986. Lang.: Jap. 1422
Training
Use of *nō* masks in actor training. USA. 1984. 1424

Nō a körúton (Woman on the Boulevard)
Performance/production
Nō a körúton (Woman on the Boulevard) by István Gáll directed by Péter Léner at Móricz Zsigmond Theatre. Hungary: Nyiregyháza. 1986. Lang.: Hun. 1950
István Gáll's *Nō a körúton (Woman on the Boulevard)* directed by Péter Léner at Móricz Zsigmond Szinház. Hungary: Nyiregyháza. 1986. Lang.: Hun. 1973

No Girls Allowed
Administration
Ken Copel's transition to independent filmmaker. USA. 1986. Lang.: Eng. 3191

No Place to Be Somebody
Institutions
Career of Marjorie Moon, artistic director of Billie Holliday Theatre. USA: New York, NY, Cleveland, OH. 1973-1986. Lang.: Eng. 1610

No Son of Mine
Performance/production
Collection of newspaper reviews by London theatre critics. UK. 1986. Lang.: Eng. 2101
Collection of newspaper reviews by London theatre critics. UK. 1986. Lang.: Eng. 2102

Noble, Adrian
Design/technology
Changes in the Royal Shakespeare Company under its current directors. UK-England: London. 1967-1986. Lang.: Eng. 325
Performance/production
Collection of newspaper reviews by London theatre critics. UK-England: London. 1986. Lang.: Eng. 2112
Jonathan Pryce in the role of Macbeth. UK-England: Stratford. 1970-1986. Lang.: Eng. 2179
Shakespearean productions by the National Theatre, Royal Shakespeare Company and Orange Tree Theatre. UK-England: Stratford, London. 1984-1985. Lang.: Eng. 2183

Noche de los asesinos, La (Night of the Assassins, The)
Plays/librettos/scripts
Ritual and archetypal communication in *La noche de los asesinos (The Night of the Assassins)* by José Triana. Cuba. Brazil. 1973-1974. Lang.: Eng. 2450

Nógrádi, Róbert
Performance/production
Performances of George Bernard Shaw's *Candida* and Čechov's *Diadia Vania (Uncle Vanya)*, under the title *Ványa bácsi*, at Pécs National Theatre. Hungary: Pécs. 1985. Lang.: Hun. 1893
Production of *Ványa bácsi (Uncle Vanya)* by Čechov. Hungary: Pécs. 1985. Lang.: Hun. 1918

Nolan, J.E.
Administration
Legislation for the protection of Victorian child-actors. UK. 1837-1901. Lang.: Eng. 1439

Nomura, Mansai
Basic theatrical documents
Kyōgen: history, training, and promotion. Japan. 1060-1982. Lang.: Eng. 1384

Nopces ducales, Les (Ducal Nuptials)
Basic theatrical documents
Details of polemical impromptus about Molière's *L'école des Femmes (The School for Wives)*. France. 1663. Lang.: Fre. 1479

Nordin, Mats
Institutions
Sommarteatern, using both amateur and professional actors, will attempt a year-round season. Sweden: Södertälje. 1980-1986. Lang.: Swe. 1585

Nordisk Teaterlaboratorium (Holstebro)
SEE ALSO
Odin Teatret.

Nordiskt Amatörteaterråd (Norrköping)
Institutions
Seminar on local plays and worker's theatre. Sweden: Norrköping. 1970-1986. Lang.: Swe. 527

Nordiskt Amatörteaterråd (Stockholm)
Performance/production
Nordic Festival of Amateur Theatre now includes Iceland and Greenland. Iceland: Reykjavik. 1986. Lang.: Swe. 740

Nordlöv, Svenne
Performance/production
Stage photographs with comment by photographers. Sweden. 1985-1986. Lang.: Swe. 794

Norén, Lars
Performance/production
Imre Csiszár directs *Az éjszaka a nappal anyja (Night is the Mother of the Day)* by Lars Norén. Hungary: Dunaújváros. 1986. Lang.: Hun. 1882

Norgård, Dag
Administration
Role of Skånska Teatron in the community. Sweden: Landskrona, Malmö. 1963-1986. Lang.: Swe. 62

Norma
Plays/librettos/scripts
Operatic facsimiles by Mozart, Bellini and Verdi. Europe. 1814-1985. Lang.: Eng. 3863

Normal Heart, The
Performance/production
Collection of newspaper reviews by London theatre critics. UK-England: London. 1986. Lang.: Eng. 2126
Overview of performances transferred from The Royal Court, Greenwich, and Lyric Hammersmith theatres. UK-England: London. 1986. Lang.: Eng. 2143
Plays/librettos/scripts
Overview of plays with homosexual themes. UK-England: London. 1970-1986. Lang.: Eng. 2841

Norman, Marsha
Theory/criticism
Interview with playwright Lillian Hellman. USA: Martha's Vineyard, MA. 1983. Lang.: Eng. 3147

Norodom Sihanouk
SEE
Histoire terrible mais inachevé de Norodom Sihanouk, roi du Cambodge, L'.

Nuts
Administration
Transfer of plays from nonprofit to commercial theatre as experienced by WPA Theatre's artistic director Kyle Renick. USA: New York, NY. 1983. Lang.: Eng.   1443

Nyczak, Janusz
Performance/production
Janusz Nyczak directs Michał Pałucki's *Dom Otwarty (Open House)* at Teatr Nowy. Poland: Poznań. 1984. Lang.: Pol.   2039

Nyytäjä, Outi
Institutions
Career of dramaturgist and teacher Outi Nyytäjä. Finland: Helsinki. 1967-1986. Lang.: Eng, Fre.   493

O'Brien, Adale
Performance/production
Five actors who work solely in regional theatre. 1961-1984. Lang.: Eng.   1633

O'Casey, Sean
Plays/librettos/scripts
Limited perception in *The Plough and the Stars* by Sean O'Casey. Eire. 1926-1986. Lang.: Eng.   2456

Pessimism of Sean O'Casey's *Juno and the Paycock*. Eire. 1924. Lang.: Eng.   2457

Biography of playwright Teresa Deevy. Ireland. 1894-1963. Lang.: Eng.   2665

Theory/criticism
Assessment of critic Kenneth Tynan's works. UK-England. 1950-1960. Lang.: Eng.   3136

O'Donnell, Pacho
Plays/librettos/scripts
Pacho O'Donnell's play *Vincent y los cuervos (Vincent and the Crows)*. Argentina: Buenos Aires. 1984. Lang.: Eng.   2363

O'Neill Theatre Center (Waterford, CT)
Performance/production
Interview with dramaturg Arthur Ballet. USA. 1950-1986. Lang.: Eng.   2248

Martin Esslin discusses dramaturg's need to balance roles of naive spectator and informed academic. USA: Waterford, CT, San Francisco, CA. 1936-1986. Lang.: Eng.   2249

Brief history of August Wilson's *Fences*. USA. 1982-1986. Lang.: Eng.   2273

O'Neill, Carlotta Monterey
Plays/librettos/scripts
Popularity and relevance of Eugene O'Neill. USA. Lang.: Eng.   2894

Gender role-reversal in the Cycle plays of Eugene O'Neill. USA. 1927-1953. Lang.: Eng.   2896

Discussion of locations inhabited and frequented by Eugene O'Neill. USA: Boston, MA. 1914-1953. Lang.: Eng.   2897

O'Neill, Eugene
Intertextual analysis of Eugene O'Neill's play *Long Day's Journey Into Night* and Ingmar Bergman's film, *Through a Glass Darkly*. USA. Sweden. 1957-1961. Lang.: Eng.   1425

Design/technology
Lighting designer Tom Skelton discussing his work on the recent revival of *The Iceman Cometh*. USA: New York, NY. 1985-1986. Lang.: Eng.   1531

Institutions
Influence of the Little Theatre movement on regional theatre. USA. 1887-1967. Lang.: Chi.   1611

Performance/production
Performances of *Hair*, directed by János Sándor, and *Desire Under the Elms*, directed by Géza Bodolay at the National Theatre of Szeged. Hungary: Szeged. 1986. Lang.: Hun.   1959

Jonathan Miller's production of Eugene O'Neill's *Long Day's Journey Into Night*. UK-England: London. 1941-1986. Lang.: Eng.   2159

Reviews of *Long Day's Journey Into Night* by Eugene O'Neill, staged by Jonathan Miller. USA: New York, NY. 1986. Lang.: Eng.   2219

Review of Eugene O'Neill's *Long Day's Journey Into Night* directed by Jonathan Miller. USA. 1956-1986. Lang.: Eng.   2264

Interview with Peter Gallagher on his portrayal of Edmund in *Long Day's Journey Into Night*. USA: New York, NY, New London, CT. 1986. Lang.: Eng.   2268

Analysis of reviews of 1929 *Dynamo* by Eugene O'Neill suggest strong production of a weak play. USA: New York, NY. 1929. Lang.: Eng.   2311

The Iceman Cometh by Eugene O'Neill, directed by José Quintero. USA: New York, NY. 1985. Lang.: Eng.   2315

Plays/librettos/scripts
Repetition and negativism in plays of Jean Anouilh and Eugene O'Neill. France. USA. 1922-1960. Lang.: Eng.   2578

Imagery of gender compared in works by Susan Glaspell and Eugene O'Neill. USA: New York, NY, Provincetown, MA. 1916-1922. Lang.: Eng.   2893

Popularity and relevance of Eugene O'Neill. USA. Lang.: Eng.   2894

Mourning in Eugene O'Neill's *A Moon for the Misbegotten*. USA. 1922-1947. Lang.: Eng.   2895

Gender role-reversal in the Cycle plays of Eugene O'Neill. USA. 1927-1953. Lang.: Eng.   2896

Discussion of locations inhabited and frequented by Eugene O'Neill. USA: Boston, MA. 1914-1953. Lang.: Eng.   2897

Concept of tragic character in Eugene O'Neill's *Desire Under the Elms*. USA. 1924. Lang.: Eng.   2907

Influence of Gordon Craig on American theatre and his recognition of Eugene O'Neill's importance. USA. UK-England. 1912-1928. Lang.: Eng.   2908

Similarities of *Hughie* by Eugene O'Neill and *The Zoo Story* by Edward Albee. USA: New York, NY. 1941-1958. Lang.: Eng.   2919

Comparison of plays by Tennessee Williams, Arthur Miller and Eugene O'Neill. USA. 1949-1956. Lang.: Eng.   2926

David Belasco's influence on Eugene O'Neill. USA: New York, NY. 1908-1922. Lang.: Eng.   2927

The Peasants by Władysław Reymont as possible source for O'Neill's version of the lustful stepmother play. USA. 1902-1924. Lang.: Eng.   2930

Theme and narrative structure in plays of Eugene O'Neill, David Belasco, and James A. Herne. USA. 1879-1918. Lang.: Eng.   2933

Theories of Otto Rank applied to plays of Eugene O'Neill. USA. 1888-1953. Lang.: Eng.   2948

Theory/criticism
Relation of short story and drama in the plays of Anton Pavlovič Čechov and Eugene O'Neill. Russia. USA. Lang.: Eng.   3130

O'Reilly, Terry
Institutions
Interview with members of Mabou Mines. USA: New York, NY. 1984. Lang.: Eng.   1607

Oakley, Barry
Plays/librettos/scripts
Developments in Australian playwriting since 1975. Australia. 1975-1986. Lang.: Eng.   2374

Oba Koso
Theory/criticism
Analysis of Wole Soyinka's major critical essays. Nigeria. 1960-1980. Lang.: Eng.   3124

Obadia, Régis
Performance/production
Photos and interviews of dance company l'Esquisse. France: Paris. 1981-1985. Lang.: Fre.   1345

Oberfrank, Géza
Performance/production
Géza Oberfrank directs Bizet's *Carmen* at Szegedi Nemzeti Szinház. Hungary: Szeged. 1985. Lang.: Hun.   3748

Obiknovenna'a istori'a (Weekday History)
Performance/production
Stage adaptations of prose works by Gogol and Gončarov. Hungary: Veszprém, Békéscsaba. 1985. Lang.: Hun.   1948

Oblomov
Plays/librettos/scripts
Overview of playwright John Coulter's later career. Canada: Toronto, ON. UK-England: London. 1951-1957. Lang.: Eng.   2415

Obratsova, Elena
Performance/production
Performance analysis of the title role of *Carmen*. France. 1875-1986. Lang.: Eng.   3725

Obraztsov Puppet Theatre
SEE
Gosudarstvènnyj Centralnyj Teat'r Kukol.

Obychova, N.A.
Performance/production
Biography of singer N.A. Obychova. Russia. 1886-1961. Lang.: Rus.   3776

SUBJECT INDEX

Off Broadway theatre — cont'd

Production schedules for member theatres of Alliance of Resident Theatres, New York. USA: New York, NY. 1983. Lang.: Eng. 3006

Summer performance schedules for several New York companies. USA: New York, NY. 1984. Lang.: Eng. 3011

Off-off Broadway theatre
Administration
Guide to producing Off-off Broadway showcases. USA: New York, NY. Lang.: Eng. 159

Statistics of income and expenses of New York Off and Off-off Broadway nonprofit theatres. USA: New York, NY. 1980-1983. Lang.: Eng. 167

Institutions
Goals and accomplishments of Theatre for the New City. USA: New York, NY. 1970-1983. Lang.: Eng. 570

Performance/production
Comprehensive survey of ten years of theatre in New York City. USA: New York, NY. 1970-1980. Lang.: Eng. 837

Artists who began in dance, film or television move to Off Broadway theatre. USA: New York, NY. 1982. Lang.: Eng. 2284

Development of new musicals by Off and Off-off Broadway theatres. USA: New York, NY. 1982. Lang.: Eng. 3622

Offenbach, Jacques
Performance/production
Reviews of *Death in the Family, Viaggio a Reims, Abduction from the Seraglio* and *Tales of Hoffmann*. USA: St. Louis, MO. 1975-1986. Lang.: Eng. 3799

Plays/librettos/scripts
Analysis and origins of the character 'Dr. Miracle' in Offenbach's *Les contes d'Hoffmann*. 1700-1900. Lang.: Eng. 3853

Relation to other fields
Life and work of playwright and critic Karl Kraus. Austria: Vienna. 1874-1936. Lang.: Ger. 3017

Offstage Downstairs Theatre (London)
Performance/production
Collection of newspaper reviews by London theatre critics. UK-England. 1986. Lang.: Eng. 2114

Oh Coward!
Performance/production
Reviews of *Oh Coward!*, lyrics and music by Noël Coward, devised and staged by Roderick Cook. USA: New York, NY. 1986. Lang.: Eng. 3616

Oh, Tae-Suck
Theory/criticism
Problems in Korean drama. Korea: Seoul. 1970-1979. Lang.: Kor. 3121

Ohno, Kazuo
Basic theatrical documents
Notes on the sources of inspiration for Ohno Kazuo dances. Japan. Lang.: Eng. 1265

Notes for a *butō* dance. Japan. 1986. Lang.: Eng. 1266

Performance/production
Interview with choreographer Ohno Kazuo. Japan. 1906-1985. Lang.: Eng. 1278

Description of *butō*, avant-garde dance movement of Japan. Japan. 1960-1986. Lang.: Eng. 1279

Butō dancer Tanaka Min speaks of early influences of Ohno and Hojikata. Japan. 1950-1985. Lang.: Eng. 1280

Oidípous Týrannos
Plays/librettos/scripts
Study of realism vs metadrama. Europe. 429 B.C.-1978 A.D. Lang.: Eng. 2540

Oidípous Týrannos
Performance/production
Hungary: Szolnok. 1986. Lang.: Hun. 1968

OISTAT
SEE
Organisation Internationale des Scénographes, Techniciens et Architectes de Théâtre.

Oken, Stuart
Administration
Efforts to produce the film *Sexual Perversity in Chicago*. USA. Lang.: Eng. 3194

Okina
Design/technology
The meaning and significance of the *nō* mask. Japan. Lang.: Eng. 1393

Performance/production
Nō actor discusses the centrality of *Okina* to his repertory. Japan. Lang.: Eng. 1399

Oklahoma
Design/technology
Designers discuss regional productions of *Oklahoma*. USA. 1984-1986. Lang.: Eng. 3596

Ōkura, Shunji
Performance/production
Collection of pictures of famous *onnagata*. Japan: Tokyo. Lang.: Jap. 1381

Okura, Toraakira
Plays/librettos/scripts
A study of the *ai-kyōgen* texts in the Okura school. Japan. 1600-1800. Lang.: Jap. 1418

Old Man Go-It-Alone
SEE
Père va-tout-seul.

Old Red Lion Theatre (London)
Performance spaces
Overview of pub theatres. UK-England: London. 1980-1987. Lang.: Eng. 626

Performance/production
Collection of newspaper reviews by London theatre critics. UK-England: London. 1986. Lang.: Eng. 2110

Collection of newspaper reviews by London theatre critics. UK-England: London. 1986. Lang.: Eng. 2121

Old Times
Plays/librettos/scripts
Narratological analysis of Harold Pinter's *Old Times*. UK-England. 1971. Lang.: Eng. 2842

Old Vic Theatre (Bristol)
SEE
Bristol Old Vic Theatre.

Old Vic Theatre (London)
Performance spaces
Peter Cheeseman, artistic director of the New Victoria Theatre, compares the new theatre with the Old Vic. UK-England: Stoke-on-Trent. 1962-1986. Lang.: Eng. 629

Performance/production
Collection of newspaper reviews by London theatre critics. UK. 1986. Lang.: Eng. 2101

Collection of newspaper reviews by London theatre critics. UK-England. 1986. Lang.: Eng. 2111

Collection of newspaper reviews by London theatre critics. UK-England: London. 1986. Lang.: Eng. 2113

Collection of newspaper reviews by London theatre critics. UK-England: London. 1986. Lang.: Eng. 2125

Old Wives Tale, The
Research/historiography
Review of recent editions of Revels plays, including George Peele's *The Old Wives Tale*. England: London. 1514-1980. Lang.: Eng. 3071

Oldman, Gary
Design/technology
Cinematographer Roger Deakins discusses lighting for his work in the film *Sid and Nancy*. USA: New York, NY, Los Angeles, CA. UK-England: London. 1976-1986. Lang.: Eng. 3211

Oliver, Edith
Plays/librettos/scripts
Report on a symposium addressing the role of the dramaturg. 918

Oliver, Joan
Plays/librettos/scripts
Short history of Catalan translations of plays. Spain-Catalonia. 1848-1984. Lang.: Fre. 2813

Memoir concerning playwright Joan Oliver. Spain-Catalonia. 1920-1986. Lang.: Cat. 2820

Relation to other fields
Reports and discussions of restricted cultural communication. Lebanon. Spain-Catalonia. USA. 1985. Lang.: Fre, Spa, Cat. 1111

Olivero, Magda
Performance/production
Famous sopranos discuss their interpretations of Tosca. USA. 1935-1986. Lang.: Eng. 3811

Olivier Theatre (London)
SEE ALSO
National Theatre (London).

Opera — cont'd

Revival of Philip Glass and Robert Wilson's *Einstein on the Beach* and opportunities to improve the piece. USA: New York, NY. 1976-1984. Lang.: Eng.   2305

Plays by Ribnikov and Višnevskij performed by Moscow Theatre of Lenin Comsomal. USSR: Moscow. Hungary: Budapest. 1985. Lang.: Hun.   2329

Advantages and limitations of television medium in producing, recording and broadcasting performing arts. USA. 1930-1985. Lang.: Eng.   3273

Puppet production of Mozart's opera *Die Zauberflöte*. USA. 1986. Lang.: Eng.   4008

Plays/librettos/scripts

Love in the plays and operas of Jean-Jacques Rousseau. France. Switzerland. 1712-1778. Lang.: Fre.   2563

Comparative analysis of *Elektra* by Hugo von Hofmannsthal and its sources. Germany. 1909. Lang.: Eng.   2603

Correspondence between Luigi Pirandello and composer Gian Francesco Malipiero. Italy. 1832-1938. Lang.: Ita.   2699

Development of Restoration musical theatre. England. 1642-1699. Lang.: Eng.   3496

Reference materials

Yearbook of major performances in all areas of Japanese theatre. Japan: Tokyo. 1986. Lang.: Jap.   1026

Dictionary of the life and work of Tsubouchi Shōyō. Japan: Tokyo. 1859-1986. Lang.: Jap.   1027

Relation to other fields

Difficulties of distinction between 'high' and 'popular' culture. Australia. 1860-1930. Lang.: Eng.   1063

Opera (Dresden)

SEE

Dresdner Hoftheater.

Opéra Bastille, L' (Paris)

Performance spaces

Description of the new home of the Paris Opéra, L'Opéra Bastille. France: Paris. 1981-1986. Lang.: Eng.   3682

Opera Colorado

Performance/production

Opera director Nathaniel Merrill on his productions. USA: New York, NY. 1958-1986. Lang.: Eng.   3805

Opéra de Paris

Institutions

Development of ballet at Opéra de Paris. France: Paris. 1790-1848. Lang.: Eng.   1298

Performance spaces

Description of the new home of the Paris Opéra, L'Opéra Bastille. France: Paris. 1981-1986. Lang.: Eng.   3682

Opera Ebony (New York, NY)

Performance/production

Black opera stars and companies. USA: Enid, OK, New York, NY. 1961-1985. Lang.: Eng.   3839

Opera Memphis (Memphis, TN)

Design/technology

Portland Opera's resident designer discusses set recycling. USA. Lang.: Eng.   3663

Opera News

Performance/production

History of *Opera News* in its fiftieth year. USA: New York, NY. 1936-1986. Lang.: Eng.   3802

Opera Orchestra of New York

Performance/production

Account of the neglected opera *Libuše* by Jan Smetana on the occasion of its New York premiere. Czechoslovakia: Prague. USA: New York, NY. 1883-1986. Lang.: Eng.   3715

Opera Theatre (USSR)

SEE

Teat'r Opery i Baleta.

Opera Theatre of St. Louis (St. Louis, MO)

Institutions

New administrative personnel at the Opera Theatre of St. Louis. USA: St. Louis, MO. 1976-1986. Lang.: Eng.   3679

Operetka (Operetta)

Plays/librettos/scripts

Analysis of the play *Operetka (Operetta)* by Witold Gombrowicz. Poland. 1986. Lang.: Pol.   2758

Operetta

SEE ALSO

Classed Entries under MUSIC-DRAMA—Operetta: 3940-3944.

Performance spaces

Plans for using the Ronacher theatre after its renovation. Austria: Vienna. 1871-1986. Lang.: Ger.   584

Performance/production

Biography of Burgtheater actor Richard Eybner. Austria: Vienna. 1896-1986. Lang.: Ger.   1653

Elisabeth Kales and her performance in the main role of Leo Fall's operetta *Madame Pompadour*. Austria: Vienna. 1955-1986. Lang.: Ger.   3484

Reviews of three musicals about the 1960s. Hungary. 1985-1986. Lang.: Hun.   3488

Elzéar Labelle's operetta *La Conversion d'un pêcheur de la Nouvelle-Écosse (The Conversion of a Nova Scotian Fisherman)* as an example of the move toward public performance. Canada: Quebec, PQ. 1837-1867. Lang.: Eng.   3599

Plays/librettos/scripts

Analysis of the play *Operetka (Operetta)* by Witold Gombrowicz. Poland. 1986. Lang.: Pol.   2758

Operettenspiele Amstetten (Austria)

Institutions

Niederösterreichischer Theatersommer: producing summer theatre at festivals in different places. Austria. 1980-1986. Lang.: Ger.   448

Opernwerkstatt

Institutions

New concept for using the Theater im Künstlerhaus for the Opernwerkstatt productions. Austria: Vienna. 1986-1987. Lang.: Ger.   3665

Optater (Amsterdam)

Performance/production

Youth theatre productions by Optater and Wederzijds. Netherlands: Amsterdam. 1986. Lang.: Eng.   766

Optimista tragédia (Optimistic Tragedy)

Performance/production

Plays by Ribnikov and Višnevskij performed by Moscow Theatre of Lenin Comsomal. USSR: Moscow. Hungary: Budapest. 1985. Lang.: Hun.   2329

Orange County Performing Arts Center (Los Angeles, CA)

Performance spaces

Reflections on theatre architecture by consultant S. Leonard Auerbach. USA. 1986. Lang.: Eng.   635

Orange Tree Theatre (London)

Performance/production

Collection of newspaper reviews by London theatre critics. UK-England: London. 1986. Lang.: Eng.   2117

Collection of newspaper reviews by London theatre critics. UK-England: London. 1986. Lang.: Eng.   2122

Shakespearean productions by the National Theatre, Royal Shakespeare Company and Orange Tree Theatre. UK-England: Stratford, London. 1984-1985. Lang.: Eng.   2183

Orchards

Performance/production

Reviews of *Orchards* written and staged by Robert Falls after Čechov. USA: New York, NY. 1986. Lang.: Eng.   2222

Orchids in the Moonlight

SEE

Orquideas a la luz de la luna.

Orczy, Baroness

Performance/production

Collection of newspaper reviews by London theatre critics. UK: London. 1986. Lang.: Eng.   2100

Ordeal of Patty Hearst, The

Plays/librettos/scripts

Analysis of television docudramas as a melodrama genre. USA. 1965-1986. Lang.: Eng.   3285

Ordo Virtutum

Performance/production

Performance by Sequentia of *Ordo Virtutum* by Hildegard of Bingen. USA: Stanford, CA. 1986. Lang.: Eng.   3493

Plays/librettos/scripts

Analysis of Hildegard of Bingen's *Ordo Virtutum* as a morality play. Germany: Bingen. 1151. Lang.: Eng.   3498

Ördögök (Devils, The)

Performance/production

Tamás Ascher directs *Ördögök (The Devils)*, an adaptation of *Besy (The Possessed)* by Dostojèvskij. Hungary: Budapest. 1986. Lang.: Hun.   1778

Österreichische Bundestheater (Vienna) — cont'd

Activities of the audience-society, Gesellschaft der Freunde der Ballettschule der Österreichischen Bundestheater. Austria: Vienna. 1985-1986. Lang.: Ger.   1294

Relation to other fields
Herbert Moritz and his views about cultural politics. Austria. 1986. Lang.: Ger.   1064

Osterwa, Juliusz
Institutions
The Reduta theatre as the predecessor of Grotowski's Laboratory. Poland: Warsaw. 1919-1939. Lang.: Fre.   1581

Relation to other fields
Actor-director Juliusz Osterwa's ideas about theatre's role in society. Poland. 1918-1947. Lang.: Pol.   1118

Actor-director Juliusz Osterwa's views of historical processes. Poland. 1940-1947. Lang.: Pol.   1122

Ostrovskij, Aleksand'r Nikolajèvič
Performance/production
Careers of Sadovskije acting family. Russia: Moscow. 1800-1917. Lang.: Rus.   784

Performance history of *Gorjačego serdca (The Burning Heart)* by Aleksand'r Nikolajèvič Ostrovskij. Russia. 1869. Lang.: Rus.   2067

Faina Ranevskaja's role in *Pravda—chorošo, a sčast'e lučše (Truth is Good, But Happiness is Better)* by A.N. Ostrovskij. USSR: Moscow. 1896-1984. Lang.: Rus.   2324

Plays/librettos/scripts
The tragedy in the plays of Aleksand'r Nikolajèvič Ostrovskij. Russia. 1823-1886. Lang.: Rus.   2771

System of genres in the work of A.N. Ostrovskij. Russia. 1823-1886. Lang.: Rus.   2772

Oszlopos Simeon (Man on the Pillar, The)
Performance/production
István Szőke directs *Oszlopos Simeon (The Man on the Pillar)* by Imre Sarkadi at Miskolc National Theatre. Hungary: Miskolc. 1986. Lang.: Hun.   1813

Imre Sarkadi's *Oszlopos Simeon (The Man on the Pillar)* directed by István Szőke at Nemzeti Szinház. Hungary: Miskolc. 1986. Lang.: Hun.   1952

Otello
Performance/production
The Franco Zeffirelli film of *Otello* by Giuseppe Verdi, an account of the production. Italy: Rome. 1985-1986. Lang.: Eng.   3758

Interview with Peter Stein about his production of Verdi's *Otello*. UK-Wales: Cardiff. 1986. Lang.: Eng.   3789

Significance of the translation in recordings of Verdi's *Otello*. USA. 1902-1978. Lang.: Eng.   3812

Plays/librettos/scripts
Shakespeare's influence on Verdi's operas. Germany. Italy. Austria. 1750-1850. Lang.: Eng.   3878

Relation to other fields
Comparison between insanity defense and opera productions with audience as jury. USA. 1980-1985. Lang.: Eng.   3925

Othello
Performance/production
Study of white actors who performed in blackface, with emphasis on *Othello*. Europe. USA. 1560-1979. Lang.: Eng.   702

History of the Margaret Webster-Paul Robeson production of *Othello*. USA: New York, NY. 1942-1944. Lang.: Eng.   852

Edwin Booth's portrayal of Iago in Shakespeare's *Othello*. USA. 1852-1890. Lang.: Eng.   854

Othello, translated by Bohdan Drozdowski and directed by Wilfred Harrison at the Wilama Horzycy Theatre. Poland: Toruń. 1980. Lang.: Eng.   2023

Collection of newspaper reviews by London theatre critics. UK-England: London. 1986. Lang.: Eng.   2109

Actors Ben Kingsley and David Suchet discuss their roles in Shakespeare's *Othello*. UK-England. 1986. Lang.: Eng.   2128

Royal Shakespeare Company performances at the Barbican Theatre. UK-England: London. 1986. Lang.: Eng.   2152

Reconstruction of a number of Shakespeare plays staged and performed by Herbert Beerbohm Tree. UK-England: London. 1887-1917. Lang.: Eng.   2155

Actor Laurence Olivier's memoirs. UK-England: London. USA: New York, NY. 1907-1986. Lang.: Eng.   2170

Shakespearean productions by the National Theatre, Royal Shakespeare Company and Orange Tree Theatre. UK-England: Stratford, London. 1984-1985. Lang.: Eng.   2183

Analysis of predominant mode of staging final scene of *Othello* by William Shakespeare. UK-England: London. USA. 1760-1900. Lang.: Eng.   2184

Significance of the translation in recordings of Verdi's *Otello*. USA. 1902-1978. Lang.: Eng.   3812

Plays/librettos/scripts
Envy in Shakespeare's *Othello* and Peter Shaffer's *Amadeus*. Canada: Montreal, PQ. Europe. 1604-1986. Lang.: Eng.   932

Shakespeare's influence on Beaumont and Fletcher's *Philaster*. England. 1609. Lang.: Eng.   2463

Marxist analysis of colonialism in Shakespeare's *Othello*. England. South Africa, Republic of. 1597-1637. Lang.: Eng.   2507

Comparison of Shakespeare's *Othello* with New Comedy of Rome. England. 1604. Lang.: Eng.   2528

Translations of plays by William Shakespeare into Amharic and Tegrenna. Ethiopia: Addis Ababa. 1941-1984. Lang.: Eng.   2537

Stanislavskij's method for the role of Othello. USSR. 1929-1930. Lang.: Swe.   2968

Sound effects and images of time in Orson Welles' film version of Shakespeare's *Othelllo*. USA. 1952. Lang.: Eng.   3241

Othello (opera)
SEE
Otello.

Other Place, The (Stratford, UK)
SEE ALSO
Royal Shakespeare Company (RSC, Stratford & London).

Other Times
Plays/librettos/scripts
Analysis of Ray Lawler's *Summer of the Seventeenth Doll* in the context of his later plays. Australia. 1955-1977. Lang.: Eng.   2377

Otherwise Engaged
Plays/librettos/scripts
Influence of Aristophanes and Čechov on playwright Simon Gray. UK-England. 1986. Lang.: Eng.   2874

Ott, Sharon
Design/technology
A profile of Cliff Faulkner, resident designer at South Coast Repertory. USA: Los Angeles, CA. 1977-1986.   365

Otto, Hans
Performance/production
Essays on acting by Wolfgang Heinz. Germany, East: Berlin, East. 1980-1984. Lang.: Ger.   1764

Otway, Thomas
Performance/production
Reception of the Kembles' Canadian tour. Canada. 1832-1834. Lang.: Eng.   663

Plays/librettos/scripts
Revision of dramaturgy and stagecraft in Restoration adaptations of Shakespeare. England: London. 1660-1690. Lang.: Eng.   2535

Où est-ce qu'elle est ma gang (Where's My Gang?)
Institutions
Théâtre Petit à Petit and their production of *Où est-ce qu'elle est ma gang (Where's My Gang?)* by Louis-Dominique Lavigne. Canada: Montreal, PQ. France. 1981-1984. Lang.: Fre.   474

Ouimette, Stephen
Performance/production
Interview with actor Stephen Ouimette. Canada. 1960-1986. Lang.: Eng.   1663

Ourselves Alone
Performance/production
Collection of newspaper reviews by London theatre critics. UK. 1986. Lang.: Eng.   2101

Review of alternative theatre productions. UK-England: London. 1986. Lang.: Eng.   2108

Collection of newspaper reviews by London theatre critics. UK-England: London. 1986. Lang.: Eng.   2110

Outsidern (The Outsider)
Performance/production
Outsidern (The Outsider), a production by Mimensemblan, based on Hermann Hesse's *Steppenwolf*. Sweden: Stockholm. 1984-1986. Lang.: Swe.   3296

Ouzanian, Richard
Institutions
Overview of Festival Lennoxville and the role of anglophone drama in Quebec. Canada: Lennoxville, PQ. 1972-1982. Lang.: Eng.   485

SUBJECT INDEX

Oven Glove Murders, The
Performance/production
Collection of newspaper reviews by London theatre critics. UK-England: London. 1986. Lang.: Eng. 2117

Owen, Alan
Design/technology
Interview with manager Tony Smith and lighting designer Alan Owen of the rock band Genesis focusing on the lighting technology used on their latest tour. USA. 1968-1986. Lang.: Eng. 3320

Owen, Wilfred
Plays/librettos/scripts
Interview with playwright Stephen MacDonald. UK-England: London. 1917-1986. Lang.: Eng. 2879

OxCart, The
Performance/production
Lloyd Richard's career as an actor, director, artistic director and academic dean. USA: Detroit, MI, New York, NY, New Haven, CT. 1920-1980. Lang.: Eng. 2308

Oxford Playhouse (Oxford, UK)
Performance/production
Collection of newspaper reviews by London theatre critics. UK-England. 1986. Lang.: Eng. 2111

Oz, Frank
Design/technology
Special effects in the film version of *Little Shop of Horrors*. USA. Lang.: Eng. 3212

P.B.I., or Mademoiselle of Bully Greway, The
Plays/librettos/scripts
Analysis of plays by Canadian soldiers in World War I. Canada. UK. 1901-1918. Lang.: Eng. 936

P'ansori
Plays/librettos/scripts
Description of *p'ansori*, a traditional Korean entertainment. Korea. Lang.: Eng. 3499

Paál, István
Performance/production
István Paál directs Shakespeare's *Szeget szeggel (Measure for Measure)*. Hungary: Veszprém. 1985. Lang.: Hun. 1770
Production of Shakespeare's *Szeget szeggel (Measure for Measure)* directed by István Paál. Hungary: Veszprém. 1985. Lang.: Hun. 1872
István Paál directs *Szeget szeggel (Measure for Measure)* by Shakespeare at Petőfi Szinház. Hungary: Veszprém. 1985. Lang.: Hun. 1938

Packer, Tina
Training
Interview with actress and acting trainer Kristin Linklater. USA: New York, NY. UK-England: London. 1954-1985. Lang.: Eng. 1261

Padrisa, Carles
Performance/production
Detailed description of the performance titled *Accions (Actions)* by La Fura dels Baus. Spain-Catalonia. 1979-1984. Lang.: Cat. 3445

Page, Louise
Performance/production
Collection of newspaper reviews by London theatre critics. UK. 1986. Lang.: Eng. 2101
Collection of newspaper reviews by London theatre critics. UK-England. 1986. Lang.: Eng. 2111
Collection of newspaper reviews by London theatre critics. UK-England. 1986. Lang.: Eng. 2120
Interviews with playwrights Louise Page, Charles McKeown and Malcolm Sircon. UK-England: London. 1986. Lang.: Eng. 2133
Interview with Pip Broughton of Paines Plough Theatre Company. UK-England. 1980-1986. Lang.: Eng. 2166
Plays/librettos/scripts
Interview with playwright Louise Page. UK-England. 1979-1986. Lang.: Eng. 2882

Pageants/parades
SEE ALSO
Processional theatre.
Classed Entries under MIXED ENTERTAINMENT—Pageants/parades: 3421-3432.
Performance/production
Origins of *malipenga*, a form of dance-drama combining Western and African elements. Zambia: Malawi. 1914-1985. Lang.: Eng. 1374
Analysis and interpretation of the staging of *The Castle of Perseverance* based on original stage plan drawing. England. 1343-1554. Lang.: Eng. 1708

The history of 'tableau wagons' in the Barnum and Bailey circus. USA: New York, NY. 1864-1920. Lang.: Eng. 3391
Plays/librettos/scripts
Similarities between *King Lear* by Shakespeare and *The Trimphs of Reunited Britannia* by Munday. England. 1605-1606. Lang.: Eng. 2480

Pagliacci, I
Performance/production
Evidence that Enrico Caruso sang the baritone prologue to *I Pagliacci*. Argentina: Buenos Aires. 1906-1917. Lang.: Eng. 3687
Reviews of 10 vintage recordings of complete operas on LP. USA. 1906-1925. Lang.: Eng. 3792

Pai, Chui
Theory/criticism
Ma Tzuyuan's use of poetic elements in Chinese opera. China: Beijing. 1279-1368. Lang.: Chi. 3559

Pai, P'u
Research/historiography
Great playwrights of the Yüan dynasty. China. 1271-1368. Lang.: Chi. 3552

PAIN(T)
Performance/production
Aesthetics, styles, rehearsal techniques of director Richard Foreman. USA. 1974-1986. Lang.: Eng. 2263

Paines Plough Theatre Company (London)
Performance/production
Interview with Pip Broughton of Paines Plough Theatre Company. UK-England. 1980-1986. Lang.: Eng. 2166
Plays/librettos/scripts
Current state of women's playwriting. UK-England. 1985-1986. Lang.: Eng. 2830

Painting
Design/technology
Theatre make-up compared to painting. China, People's Republic of. 1907-1980. Lang.: Chi. 251
'Frisket principle' duplicates black and white photo on large scale. USA. 1984. Lang.: Eng. 370
Plays/librettos/scripts
Study of playtexts and illustrations in Lille plays manuscript. France: Lille. 1450-1500. Lang.: Eng. 3431

Paisley, Brian
Performance/production
Review of Edmonton Fringe Festival. Canada: Edmonton, AB. 1986. Lang.: Eng. 1682

Pajama Game, The
Performance/production
Collection of newspaper reviews by London theatre critics. UK: London. 1986. Lang.: Eng. 2100

Palace Theatre (Watford, UK)
Performance/production
Collection of newspaper reviews by London theatre critics. UK. 1986. Lang.: Eng. 2099
Director Lou Stein discusses his policy at the Watford Palace Theatre. UK-England: Watford. 1982-1986. Lang.: Eng. 2167

Palais Garnier (Paris)
Performance/production
Profile of Bernard Lefort, former Intendant of the Palais Garnier of Paris. France: Paris. 1960-1985. Lang.: Eng. 3727

Palasovszky, Ödön
Performance/production
Synthesis of music, dance, song and speech in *Ayrus Leánya (Ayrus' Daughter)* by Ödön Palasovszky. Hungary: Budapest. 1931. Lang.: Hun. 1967

Palau i Fabre, Josep
Basic theatrical documents
Texts of *Avui, Romeo i Julieta (Today, Romeo and Juliet)* and *El porter i el penalty (The Goalkeeper and the Penalty)* by Josep Palau i Fabre. Spain-Catalonia. 1917-1982. Lang.: Cat. 1499
Plays/librettos/scripts
Analysis of Josep Palau's plays and theoretical writings. Spain-Catalonia. 1917-1982. Lang.: Cat. 2814

Palestrina
Plays/librettos/scripts
German and Christian myths in Hans Pfitzner's opera *Palestrina*. 1900-1982. Lang.: Eng. 3852

Paliashvili Opera Theatre (Tbilisi)
SEE
Teat'r Opery i Baleta im. Z. Paliašvili.

International Bibliography of Theatre: 1986   431

Palladium Theatre (London)
Design/technology
Details the installation and use of a 1935 Strand lighting console.
UK-England: London. 1935-1986. Lang.: Eng.   321

Palotai, Erzsi
Performance/production
Actress/poetry recitalist Erzsi Palotai recalls her life and career.
Hungary. 1954-1985. Lang.: Hun.   1911

Pampineau
Design/technology
Design considerations in productions of two plays by Louis-Honoré
Fréchette. Canada: Montreal, PQ. 1880-1900. Lang.: Fre.   242

Pan Asian Repertory Theatre (New York, NY)
Plays/librettos/scripts
Work of playwright R.A. Shiomi, including production history of
Yellow Fever. Canada: Toronto, ON. USA: New York, NY. USA:
San Francisco, CA. 1970-1986. Lang.: Eng.   2422

Panchina, La (Bench, The)
Plays/librettos/scripts
Italo Calvino's first libretto is based on one of his Marcovaldo
stories. Italy. 1956. Lang.: Ita.   3884

Pandora's Cross
Plays/librettos/scripts
Interview with playwright Dorothy Hewett. Australia: Sydney, N.S.W.
1986. Lang.: Eng.   2368

Panikkar, Kāvālam Nārāyana
Basic theatrical documents
Text of *Karimkutty* by K. N. Panikkar in English translation. India.
1983. Lang.: Eng.   1355

Pantages Theatre (Birmingham, AL)
Performance spaces
History and photographs of various theatres. USA: Birmingham, AL.
1890-1983. Lang.: Eng.   1622

Pantijn Muziekpoppentheater (Amsterdam)
Institutions
History of Pantijn Muziekpoppentheater. Netherlands: Amsterdam.
1980-1987. Lang.: Eng.   3958

Pantomime
SEE ALSO
Mime.
Classed Entries under MIME—Pantomime: 3302-3307.

Basic theatrical documents
Text of plays by James Robinson Planché, with introduction on his
influence. UK-England. 1818-1872. Lang.: Eng.   226

Institutions
Director of school of mime and theatre on gesture and image in
theatrical representation. France: Paris. 1962-1985. Lang.: Fre.   3289

Performance spaces
Alexander Palace Theatre as pantomime stage. UK-England:
London. 1875-1986. Lang.: Eng.   627

Performance/production
Dance-pantomime dramas based on the plots of plays by Aleksand'r
Sumarokov. Russia. 1717-1777. Lang.: Rus.   1367
Overview of productions by the city's studio theatres. Czechoslovakia:
Prague. 1986. Lang.: Hun.   1698

Relation to other fields
Style in children's theatre in light of theories of Philippe Ariès.
USA. UK. France. 1600-1980. Lang.: Eng.   1162

Pao, Yuehchiao
Institutions
Beginnings of performing arts labor organizations. China, People's
Republic of: Shanghai. 1912-1931. Lang.: Chi.   488

Paoli, Antonio
Performance/production
Reviews of 10 vintage recordings of complete operas on LP. USA.
1906-1925. Lang.: Eng.   3792

Papas, Irene
Performance/production
Greek tragedy on the New York stage. USA: New York, NY. 1854-
1984. Lang.: Eng.   2301

Paper People, The
Basic theatrical documents
Text of *The Paper People* by Timothy Findley. Canada. 1967. Lang.:
Eng.   3252

Plays/librettos/scripts
Critical debate over Timothy Findley's *The Paper People*. Canada.
1967. Lang.: Eng.   3280

Papermill Playhouse (Millburn, NJ)
Administration
Papermill Playhouse's executive producer discusses producing
musicals. USA: Millburn, NJ. Lang.: Eng.   3572

Design/technology
Designers discuss regional productions of *Side-by-Side by Sondheim*.
USA. 1984. Lang.: Eng.   3593
Designers discuss regional productions of *The Sound of Music*. USA.
1983-1986. Lang.: Eng.   3594

Papp, Gail Merrifield
Plays/librettos/scripts
Artists react to *New York Times* condemnation of current
playwriting. USA. 1984. Lang.: Eng.   2888

Papp, Joseph
Administration
Interview with Joe Papp. USA: New York, NY. 1959-1986. Lang.:
Eng.   177

Theory/criticism
Interviews on the role of the critic in New York theatre. USA: New
York, NY. 1983. Lang.: Eng.   1226

Paquin, Elzéar
Plays/librettos/scripts
Study of two unproduced historical dramas about French-Canadian
patriot Louis Riel. Canada: Montreal, PQ. 1886. Lang.: Fre.   2413

Parade
Plays/librettos/scripts
Career of Marxist playwright George Sklar. USA: New York, NY.
1920-1967. Lang.: Eng.   985

Parades
SEE
Pageants/parades.

Paradise Lost by Sarkadi
SEE
Elveszett paradicsom.

Paradoxe sur le comédien (Paradox of Acting, The)
Theory/criticism
Selection and analysis of Diderot's theoretical writings about theatre.
France. 1713-1834. Lang.: Cat.   3101

Parage, E.
Plays/librettos/scripts
Study of two unproduced historical dramas about French-Canadian
patriot Louis Riel. Canada: Montreal, PQ. 1886. Lang.: Fre.   2413

Paravents, Les (Screens, The)
Plays/librettos/scripts
History, poetry and violence in plays by Tankred Dorst, Heiner
Müller and Jean Genet. Europe. Lang.: Fre.   2538

Paris Opera
SEE
Opéra de Paris.

Parisienne, La (Woman of Paris, The)
Performance/production
Recollections of actress Edwige Feuillère. France. 1931-1986. Lang.:
Fre.   716

Parisio, Madeline
Design/technology
Analysis of the technological aspects of *Les Misérables*. UK-England:
London. 1980-1987. Lang.: Eng.   3582

Park Theatre (London)
SEE
Battersea Park Theatre.

Parker, Gilbert
Administration
Function of playwright's agent in negotiation and production of a
script. USA: New York, NY. 1985. Lang.: Eng.   135

Basic theatrical documents
Gilbert Parker's *The Seats of the Mighty* as staged by Herbert
Beerbohm Tree. Canada. 1897. Lang.: Eng.   1470

Parsifal
Performance/production
Interview with Wolfgang Wagner on his staging of 3 Wagnerian
operas at the Bayreuth Festspiele. Germany, West: Bayreuth. 1975-
1985. Lang.: Hun.   3740
Photographs, cast list, synopsis, and discography of Metropolitan
Opera radio broadcast performances. USA: New York, NY. 1986.
Lang.: Eng.   3794

Parsons, Estelle
Institutions
Efforts of New York Shakespeare Festival to develop an audience for Shakespearean drama. USA: New York, NY. 1986. Lang.: Eng.
1605

Partisans, Les (Partisans, The)
Performance/production
Opposition to realism in plays from Francophone Manitoba. Canada. 1983-1986. Lang.: Fre.
670

Partlett, Mark
Performance/production
Development of works by the Special Delivery Moving Theatre. Canada: Vancouver, BC. 1976-1986. Lang.: Eng.
3294

Partner
SEE
Companero.

Pártos, Géza
Performance/production
Performances of *Pán Peter (Peter Pan)* by J. M. Barrie, directed by Géza Pártos. Hungary: Kaposvár. 1985. Lang.: Hun.
1934

Partridge-Nedds, Laura
Relation to other fields
Black history and folklore taught in theatre workshops and productions. USA: New York, NY, Omaha, NE, Washington, DC. 1986. Lang.: Eng.
3068

Pasatieri, Thomas
Performance/production
Marilyn Zschau discusses her singing career and life. USA: Chicago, IL. 1976-1986. Lang.: Eng.
3804
Review of the world premiere of the opera *Three Sisters*. USA: Columbus, OH. 1968-1986. Lang.: Eng.
3822

Pascal, Julia
Performance/production
Collection of newspaper reviews by London theatre critics. UK-England: London. 1986. Lang.: Eng.
2117

Påsk (Easter)
Plays/librettos/scripts
Biblical and Swedenborgian influences on the development of August Strindberg's chamber play *Påsk (Easter)*. Sweden. 1900. Lang.: Eng.
2827

Páskándi, Géza
Performance/production
Review of Géza Páskándi's *Átkozottak (The Damned)* directed by László Romhányi. Hungary: Kőszeg. 1986. Lang.: Hun.
1808
Geza Páskándi's *Átkozottak (The Damned)* directed by László Romhányi at Kőszegi Várszinház. Hungary: Kőszeg. 1986. Lang.: Hun.
1822

Pasolini, Pier Paolo
Performance/production
Tadeusz Łomnicki directs Pasolini's *Affabulazione* at Centrum Sztuki Studio. Poland: Warsaw. 1984. Lang.: Pol.
2033

Plays/librettos/scripts
Notes on Pier Paolo Pasolini's *Calderón*. Italy. 1973. Lang.: Ita.
2689

Passanante, Jean
Institutions
Profile of New York Theatre Workshop. USA: New York, NY. 1980-1984. Lang.: Eng.
542
Problems and advantages of co-production. USA: New York, NY. 1985. Lang.: Eng.
571

Passe Muraille Theatre (Toronto, ON)
Plays/librettos/scripts
Literary and popular theatrical forms in the plays of Rick Salutin. Canada: Montreal, PQ, Toronto, ON. 1976-1981. Lang.: Eng.
2411

Passion According to Antígona Pérez
SEE
Pasión según Antígona Pérez, La.

Passion Play
Plays/librettos/scripts
Jungian analysis of the plays of Peter Nichols. UK-England. 1967-1984. Lang.: Eng.
2848

Passion plays
SEE ALSO
Mystery plays.

Performance/production
Use of stagehands in production of modern passion play. Spain. 1951-1986. Lang.: Eng.
2075

Past is Past, The
Reference materials
Current work of Audelco award-winning playwrights. USA: New York, NY. 1973-1984. Lang.: Eng.
3007

Pasterk, Ursula
Institutions
Wiener Festwochen 1986: Mozart and Modern Art. Austria: Vienna. 1986. Lang.: Ger.
441

Pastor Fido, Il (Faithful Shepherd, The)
Design/technology
Costume design in a 16th century production in Milan of Guarini's *Il Pastor Fido*. Italy: Mantua. 1500-1600. Lang.: Eng.
298

Pásztor, Erzsi
Performance/production
Interview with actor Erzsi Pásztor. Hungary. 1970-1980. Lang.: Hun.
1838

Pataki, Éva
Performance/production
Edith és Marlene (Edith and Marlene) by Éva Pataki at Comedy Theatre. Hungary: Budapest. 1986. Lang.: Hun.
1831
Éva Pataki's *Edith és Marlene (Edith and Marlene)* directed by Márta Mészáros, Pest National Theatre. Hungary: Budapest. 1986. Lang.: Hun.
3603

Paterson, Bill
Performance/production
Collection of newspaper reviews by London theatre critics. UK-England: London. 1986. Lang.: Eng.
2116

Paterson, Stuart
Performance/production
Collection of newspaper reviews by London theatre critics. UK. 1986. Lang.: Eng.
2103

Path of Promise, The
SEE
Weg der Verheissung, Der.

Pathelin
SEE
Farce de Maître Pierre Pathelin, La.

Patronage
Administration
Royal theatrical patronage during the reign of George II. England: London. 1727-1760. Lang.: Eng.
33

Patterson, Andrew
Performance/production
Interviews with performance artists. Canada: Toronto, ON. USA: New York, NY. 1980-1986. Lang.: Eng.
3444

Paukwa (Dar Es-Salaam)
Performance/production
Report from an international amateur theatre festival where music and dance were prominent. Denmark: Copenhagen. 1986. Lang.: Swe.
683

Paul Robeson
Performance/production
Lloyd Richard's career as an actor, director, artistic director and academic dean. USA: Detroit, MI, New York, NY, New Haven, CT. 1920-1980. Lang.: Eng.
2308

Paulay, Ede
Performance/production
Study of Hungarian actor Ede Paulay. Hungary: Győr. 1855. Lang.: Hun.
1823
Career of theatrical professional Ede Paulay. Hungary: Budapest. 1852-1864. Lang.: Hun.
1824
Historical data on actor Ede Paulay and his family. Hungary. 1731-1982. Lang.: Hun.
1852
Theatrical career of Ede Paulay. Hungary: Budapest. 1878-1894. Lang.: Hun.
1944

Paulini, Béla
Performance/production
Hungarian folksongs and dance adapted to the stage in *Magyar Csupajáték (Hungarian All-Play)*. Hungary: Budapest. 1938-1939. Lang.: Hun.
1274

Pavarotti, Luciano
Performance/production
Verdi's *Simon Boccanegra* and Puccini's *La Bohème* at the Hungarian State Opera House and Erkel Theatre. Hungary: Budapest. 1986. Lang.: Hun.
3747
Profile of and interview with Italian tenor Luciano Pavarotti. Italy: Modena. 1935-1986. Lang.: Eng.
3760

Pavarotti, Luciano — cont'd

Reference materials
Photos of the new opera productions at the Staatsoper. Austria: Vienna. 1985-1986. Lang.: Ger. 3910

Pavis, Patrice
Theory/criticism
Interview with semiologist Patrice Pavis about the theatre institute at the Sorbonne, his semiotic approach to theatre and modern French theatre. France: Paris. 1923-1986. Lang.: Heb. 1206

Classical, modern and postmodern theatre and their delineation through opposites. France. 1986. Lang.: Eng. 3104

Semiotic analysis of theatrical elements. Europe. 1979. Lang.: Eng. 3461

Pavolini, Corrado
Performance/production
Orientalism in four productions of Wilde's *Salome*. Italy. 1904-1963. Lang.: Ita. 750

Pawłowski, Andrzej
Performance/production
Andrzej Pawłowski directs Gombrowicz's *Pornografia (Pornography)*. Poland: Warsaw. 1983. Lang.: Pol. 2038

Payroll
Administration
Use of computers by Alliance of Resident Theatres/New York's member organizations. USA: New York, NY. 1985. Lang.: Eng. 93

Peace on Earth
Plays/librettos/scripts
Career of Marxist playwright George Sklar. USA: New York, NY. 1920-1967. Lang.: Eng. 985

Peacock, Trevor
Performance/production
An exploration of Brecht's *Gestus*. Germany. Lang.: Eng. 1758

Peake, Richard Brinsley
Performance/production
Controversy surrounding *Presumption, or The Fate of Frankenstein* by Richard Brinsley Peake. UK-England: London. 1818-1840. Lang.: Eng. 2142
Plays/librettos/scripts
Treatment of the Frankenstein myth in three gothic melodramas. UK-England. France. 1823-1826. Lang.: Eng. 2847

Pearlman, Richard
Performance/production
Review of *Lunatics and Lovers*, an adaptation of Mozart's *La finta giardiniera*. USA: Santa Barbara, CA. 1985. Lang.: Eng. 3843

Pears, Peter
Performance/production
Life and career of singer Peter Pears. UK-England: London. 1937-1986. Lang.: Eng. 3784

Appreciation and obituary of the late English tenor Sir Peter Pears. UK-England: Aldeburgh. 1910-1986. Lang.: Eng. 3785

Pearson, Sarah
Administration
Fundraising strategy of American Repertory Theatre's development director. USA: Cambridge, MA. 1986. Lang.: Eng. 150

Peasant, The
Plays/librettos/scripts
The Peasants by Władysław Reymont as possible source for O'Neill's version of the lustful stepmother play. USA. 1902-1924. Lang.: Eng. 2930

Peaslee, Richard
Performance/production
Martha Clarke's production of *The Garden of Earthly Delights*. USA: New York, NY. 1979-1984. Lang.: Eng. 1371

Pécsi Nemzeti Szinház (Pécs)
Performance/production
Performances of *Alice Csodaországban (Alice in Wonderland)*, *A Két Veronai nemes (The Two Gentlemen of Verona)* and *Tobbsincs királyfi (No More Crown Prince)*. Hungary: Pécs, Budapest. 1985. Lang.: Hun. 1771

Performances of George Bernard Shaw's *Candida* and Čechov's *Diadia Vania (Uncle Vanya)*, under the title *Ványa bácsi*, at Pécs National Theatre. Hungary: Pécs. 1985. Lang.: Hun. 1893

Dezső Szomory's *Bella* at the Pécs National Theatre directed by István Jeney. Hungary: Pécs. 1986. Lang.: Hun. 1897

Productions of plays by Edward Bond, Gyula Hernádi and Lope de Vega at the Pécs National Theatre. Hungary: Pécs. 1986. Lang.: Hun. 1898

Production of *Ványa bácsi (Uncle Vanya)* by Čechov. Hungary: Pécs. 1985. Lang.: Hun. 1918

Dezső Szomory's *Bella* at Pécs National Theatre directed by István Jeney. Hungary: Pécs. 1986. Lang.: Hun. 1936

Kinn vagyunk a vízből (Saved) by Edward Bond directed by István Szőke. Hungary: Pécs. 1986. Lang.: Hun. 1940

Ivan Vas-Zoltán directs *Vértestvérek (Blood Brothers)* by Willy Russell. Hungary: Pécs. 1986. Lang.: Hun. 3602

Zoltán Horváth directs Donizetti's *Don Pasquale* at the Pécsi Nemzeti Szinház. Hungary: Pécs. 1985. Lang.: Hun. 3751

Pécsi Nemzeti Szinház (Pest)
Performance/production
Hagyaték (Legacy) by Gyula Hernádi, directed by Menyhért Szegvári. Hungary: Pécs. 1986. Lang.: Hun. 1949

Pécsi Nyári Szinház (Pécs)
Performance/production
Mágnás Miska (Miska the Magnate) by Albert Szirmai directed by László Bagossy. Hungary: Pécs. 1986. Lang.: Hun. 3942

Pedro y el capitán (Pedro and the Captain)
Basic theatrical documents
English translation of Mario Benedetti's *Pedro y el capitán (Pedro and the Captain)*. Uruguay. 1979. Lang.: Eng. 1510

Pedrolo, Manuel de
Basic theatrical documents
English translation of *L'ús de la matèria (The Use of Matter)* by Manuel de Pedrolo. Spain-Catalonia. 1963. Lang.: Cat, Eng. 1500

Peele, George
Plays/librettos/scripts
Image of poverty in Elizabethan and Stuart plays. England. 1558-1642. Lang.: Eng. 2482

Treatment of historical figures in plays by William Shakespeare, Christopher Marlowe and George Peele. England. 1560-1650. Lang.: Eng. 2534
Research/historiography
Review of recent editions of Revels plays, including George Peele's *The Old Wives Tale*. England: London. 1514-1980. Lang.: Eng. 3071

Peer Gynt
Performance/production
Esse Ljungh's acting career with Winnipeg Little Theatre. Canada: Winnipeg, MB. 1921-1937. Lang.: Eng. 664

Collection of newspaper reviews by London theatre critics. UK. 1986. Lang.: Eng. 2102
Plays/librettos/scripts
Self-transcendence through grace embodied in Henrik Ibsen's female characters. Norway. 1849-1899. Lang.: Eng. 2726

Pelican Player Neighborhood Theatre (Toronto, ON)
Relation to other fields
Political issues for Black performers. 1986. Lang.: Eng. 1052

Pelle, János
Performance/production
János Pelle's *Casanova* directed by Károly Kazimir at the Körszinház. Hungary: Budapest. 1986. Lang.: Hun. 1846

János Pelle's *Casanova* directed by Károly Kazimir at Körszinház. Hungary: Budapest. 1986. Lang.: Hun. 1929

Pelletier, Gilles
Institutions
Interview with Françoise Graton and Gilles Pelletier of Nouvelle Compagnie Théâtrale. Canada: Montreal, PQ. 1964-1984. Lang.: Fre. 477

Peltz, Mary Ellis
Performance/production
History of *Opera News* in its fiftieth year. USA: New York, NY. 1936-1986. Lang.: Eng. 3802

Penderecki, Krzysztof
Performance/production
Composer Krzysztof Penderecki and his new opera *Die schwarze Maske (The Black Mask)*, based upon a play by Gerhart Hauptmann. Austria: Salzburg. Poland. 1933-1986. Lang.: Ger. 3700

Peng, Huating
Theory/criticism
Analyzes the singing style of Szechuan opera. China. 1866-1952. Lang.: Chi. 3563

Penka, Rudolf
Performance/production
Discussion of Stanislavskij's influence by a number of artists. Sweden. 1890-1986. Lang.: Swe. 2094

Pennington, Michael
Institutions
Actor Michael Pennington and director Michael Bogdanov discuss the formation of the English Shakespeare Company. UK-England. 1986. Lang.: Eng.   1592

Performance/production
Establishment of the English Shakespeare Company. UK-England. 1986. Lang.: Eng.   2131

Pennsylvania Opera Theatre (Philadelphia, PA)
Institutions
The history and plans of the Pennsylvania Opera Theatre. USA: Philadelphia, PA. 1976-1986. Lang.: Eng.   3680

Penny theatres
Relation to other fields
History of English penny theatres. England: London. 1820-1839. Lang.: Eng.   3357

Pensaci Giacomino! (Think of it, Jamie!)
Plays/librettos/scripts
Angelo Musco's interpretation of *Pensaci Giacomino! (Think of it, Jamie!)* by Luigi Pirandello. Italy. 1916-1917. Lang.: Ita.   2684

Peony Pavilion, The
Plays/librettos/scripts
Playwright Wu Bing mocks *The Peony Pavilion* by Tang Xianzu. China. 1600-1980. Lang.: Chi.   3531

People's Theatre (Budapest)
SEE
Népszinház.

People's War, The
Plays/librettos/scripts
World War II as a theme in post-war British drama. UK-England. 1945-1983. Lang.: Eng.   2868

Pequeña historia de horror (Little Tale of Horror)
Basic theatrical documents
English translation of *Pequeña historia de horror (Little Tale of Horror)*. Mexico. 1932. Lang.: Eng.   1488

Pera, Marília
Performance/production
Annual festival of Latin American plays at the Public Theatre. USA: New York, NY. 1985. Lang.: Eng.   2310

Perchtoldsdorfer Sommerspiele (Austria)
Institutions
Niederösterreichischer Theatersommer: producing summer theatre at festivals in different places. Austria. 1980-1986. Lang.: Ger.   448

Percy, Shaunelle
Performance/production
Reviews of *Williams and Walker* by Vincent D. Smith, staged by Shaunelle Percy. USA: New York, NY. 1986. Lang.: Eng.   2225

Père va-tout-seul (Old Man Go-It-Alone)
Plays/librettos/scripts
Political aspects of George Sand's *Père va-tout-seul (Old Man Go-It-Alone)*. France. 1830-1844. Lang.: Eng.   2574

Pereiras, Manuel
Plays/librettos/scripts
The history of Cuban exile theatre. Cuba. USA: New York, NY. 1959-1986. Lang.: Spa.   2451

Pérez de Robles, Francisco
Basic theatrical documents
Contract of first known theatre company in America. Peru: Lima. 1599-1620. Lang.: Spa.   225

Perez y Gonzalez, Felipe
Plays/librettos/scripts
Examples of playwrights whose work was poorly received by theatrical audiences in Madrid. Spain: Madrid. 1609-1950. Lang.: Spa.   2786

Perfect Party, The
Performance/production
Reviews of *The Perfect Party* by A. R. Gurney, Jr., staged by John Tillinger. USA: New York, NY. 1986. Lang.: Eng.   2224

Perfectionist, The
Plays/librettos/scripts
Interview with playwright David Williamson. Australia. 1986. Lang.: Eng.   2378
Analysis of plays by David Williamson. Australia. 1976-1985. Lang.: Eng.   2379

Performance art
SEE ALSO
Classed Entries under MIXED ENTERTAINMENTS—Performance art: 3433-3462.

Design/technology
Overview of conference on visual art in theatre. Poland. 1986. Lang.: Eng, Fre.   307
Institutions
Founder Sky Gilbert discusses aesthetic goals of Rhubarb Festival. Canada: Toronto, ON. 1979-1986. Lang.: Eng.   475
Performance/production
Rhubarb Festival is alternative to playwriting and workshopping conventions. Canada: Toronto, ON. 1986. Lang.: Eng.   672
Interview with choreographer Meredith Monk. USA: New York, NY. 1964-1984. Lang.: Eng.   1368
Review of international theatre festivals. Spain. Canada: Montreal, PQ, Toronto, ON. 1986. Lang.: Eng.   2077
Plays/librettos/scripts
Contributing sources to Wooster Group's *Saint Anthony*. USA: New York, NY, Boston, MA, Washington, DC. 1983-1986. Lang.: Eng.   2940

Performance Group (New York, NY)
Training
History of the Performance Group. USA. 1960. Lang.: Eng.   3161
Performance management
Performance/production
History of the American Conservatory Theatre. USA. Europe. 1950-1972. Lang.: Eng.   856

Performance Space 22 (New York, NY)
Performance spaces
Alternative performance spaces for experimental theatre and dance works. USA: New York, NY. 1984. Lang.: Eng.   640

Performance spaces
SEE ALSO
Classed Entries.
Administration
Guide to producing Off-off Broadway showcases. USA: New York, NY. Lang.: Eng.   159
Audience
Auditorium seating for maximum visibility of stage. 1986. Lang.: Eng.   197
Design/technology
Description of portable cruciform theatre. Belgium. 1986. Lang.: Eng.   240
Theatre consultant S. Leonard Auerbach's technical specifications for Expo '86. Canada: Vancouver, BC. 1986. Lang.: Eng.   243
Reconstruction of mechanical equipment at the Szeged National Theatre. Hungary: Szeged. 1981-1986. Lang.: Hun.   288
Lighting tips for amateur theatre groups working in church and community halls and schools. UK-England. Lang.: Eng.   322
Lighting concerts, plays and pantomimes in a church hall with minimum lighting facilities. UK-England: Stratford. 1980-1986. Lang.: Eng.   326
Adolphe Appia's influence on Lee Simonson. USA. 1900-1950. Lang.: Eng.   416
Amateur technician outlines his experience of lighting a pantomime in a hall with a ceiling 8 feet high. UK-England: Brighton. 1980-1986. Lang.: Eng.   3304
Institutions
Cultural activities in the Lodz ghetto. Poland: Łódź. 1940-1944. Lang.: Heb.   3323
Development of Prague National Theatre. Czechoslovakia: Prague. 1787-1985. Lang.: Eng.   3672
Illustrated discussion of the opening of the Théâtre National de l'Opéra. France: Paris. 1875. Lang.: Fre.   3674
History of the Teatro alla Scala. Italy: Milan. 1898-1986. Lang.: Eng.   3677
Performance spaces
Alexander Palace Theatre as pantomime stage. UK-England: London. 1875-1986. Lang.: Eng.   627
Touring stage of ballet company Cullbergbaletten. Sweden. 1986. Lang.: Swe.   1300
Summer theatre on a restored cruise ship. Canada. 1982-1986. Lang.: Eng.   1614
Performance/production
New evidence on the appearance of professional actors. England: London. 1200-1600. Lang.: Eng.   699
History of theatre in America. USA. 1750-1985. Lang.: Eng.   834
Interview with development director Harvey Seifter on German theatre. USA: New York, NY. Germany, West. 1984. Lang.: Eng.   840

Performance/production — cont'd

Essays and reviews on Hungarian and foreign playwrights, productions, actors and traditions. 1962-1986. Lang.: Hun. 1058

Théophile Gautier's ideas on theatre and performance. France. 1811-1872. Lang.: Rus. 1086

Absence of body awareness in modern art and dance. Switzerland. Lang.: Ger. 1288

Response of Freie Volksbühne to police pressure. Germany: Berlin. 1890-1912. Lang.: Fre. 3034

The reception of critic and playwright Karl Kraus in the English speaking world. USA: New York, NY. Austria: Vienna. UK-Scotland: Glasgow. 1909-1985. Lang.: Ger. 3067

Analysis of Northern Sung theatrical artifacts. 1032-1126. Lang.: Chi. 3546

Role of Beijing opera today. China, People's Republic of: Beijing. 1985. Lang.: Chi. 3547

Mao's policy on theatre in revolution. China, People's Republic of: Beijing. 1920-1985. Lang.: Chi. 3549

Research/historiography

Controversy over identities of Tien Kuei-pu and Lu Kuei-pu. China. 1500-1644. Lang.: Chi. 3550

Great playwrights of the Yüan dynasty. China. 1271-1368. Lang.: Chi. 3552

Theory/criticism

Theoretical writings and reviews on the performing arts. Hungary. 1971-1983. Lang.: Hun. 1211

Western influences on theatrical development in Turkey. Turkey. 1524-1986. Lang.: Ita. 1221

Eastern and Western influences on Turkish theatre. Turkey. 1000-1986. Lang.: Ita. 1222

Michael Kirby defends the liberal outlook of The Drama Review. USA. 1971-1986. Lang.: Eng. 1232

Discusses the impact of critic B.K. Sandwell. Canada. 1932-1951. Lang.: Eng. 3088

Review of Mi lesz velünk Anton Pavlovics? (What Will Become of Us, Anton Pavlovič?) by Miklós Almási. Hungary. 1986. Lang.: Hun. 3114

Collection of essays on the avant-garde. USA. 1955-1986. Lang.: Eng. 3145

Shakespeare in media. UK-England. USA. Japan. 1899-1985. Lang.: Eng. 3172

Debate on characteristics of the circus as art form. USSR. 1980-1986. Lang.: Rus. 3406

Strengths and weaknesses of Beijing opera. China, People's Republic of: Beijing. 1935-1985. Lang.: Chi. 3565

Performing Arts Center of the Borough of Manhattan Community College (New York, NY)

Performance spaces

Descriptions of newly constructed Off Broadway theatres. USA: New York, NY. 1984. Lang.: Eng. 644

Performing Arts Journal

Theory/criticism

Critical profile of Performing Arts Journal and of recent theatrical trends. USA. 1976-1986. Lang.: Pol. 1228

Performing Garage, The (New York, NY)

Performance/production

Wooster Group retrospective of original works. USA: New York, NY. 1975-1986. Lang.: Eng. 850

Performing Group (New York, NY)

Performance/production

Performance art and its current characteristic tone. USA. Lang.: Eng. 3459

Performing institutions

SEE

Institutions, producing.

Pericles

Performance/production

John Neville's productions of The Winter's Tale, Pericles, and Cymbeline. Canada: Stratford, ON. 1974-1986. Lang.: Eng. 1657

Periferia (Periphery)

Performance/production

Overview of recent Argentine theatre. Argentina: Buenos Aires. 1978-1983. Lang.: Fre. 651

Peris Celda, Josep

Institutions

History of theatre in Valencia area focusing on Civil War period. Spain: Valencia. 1817-1982. Lang.: Cat. 514

Perlini, Memè

Performance/production

Working environment of director Memè Perlini. Italy. 1978. Lang.: Eng. 1991

Perro del hortelano, El (Gardener's Dog, The)

Performance/production

Productions of plays by Edward Bond, Gyula Hernádi and Lope de Vega at the Pécs National Theatre. Hungary: Pécs. 1986. Lang.: Hun. 1898

Mátyás Giricz directs A kertész kutyája (The Gardener's Dog) by Lope de Vega. Hungary: Budapest. 1985. Lang.: Hun. 1900

Perry, David

Design/technology

Design challenges of the film Absolute Beginners. UK-England: London. 1986. Lang.: Eng. 3203

Persepolis

Performance/production

Discussion of Persepolis and Orghast at Persepolis-Shiraz festival. Iran: Shiraz. 1971. Lang.: Ita. 741

Personnel

Summary of articles on Hungarian theatre structure. Hungary. Lang.: Hun. 6

Administration

Analysis of theatrical working conditions. 1986. Lang.: Hun. 19

Current problems in theatrical organizations. 1980-1986. Lang.: Rus. 20

Analysis of petition drawn up by actors of the Drury Lane Theatre. England. 1705. Lang.: Eng. 32

Account of grievance petition by Opera House performers. England: London. 1799. Lang.: Eng. 34

Economic problems of Hungarian theatre. Hungary. 1985-1986. Lang.: Hun. 51

Interview with Bernt Thorell, president of Svensk Teaterteknisk Förening. Sweden. 1966-1986. Lang.: Swe. 63

Contractual problems in theatrical professions. Switzerland. 1986-1987. Lang.: Ger. 66

Formation and development of the Association of British Theatre Technicians (ABTT). UK. 1986. Lang.: Eng. 76

Benefit as fundraising tool for nonprofit theatres. USA: New York, NY. 1986. Lang.: Eng. 96

Management and unions in collective bargaining. USA. 1986. Lang.: Eng. 99

Creation and role of board of directors in nonprofit theatre. USA: New York, NY. 1986. Lang.: Eng. 104

New factors in arts and their impact on labor relations. USA. 1986. Lang.: Eng. 108

Discusses artists with respect to societal control. USA. 1986. Lang.: Eng. 115

Distinctions made between artists and other workers. USA: New York, NY. 1986. Lang.: Eng. 131

Literary managers discuss their roles and responsibilities in nonprofit theatre. USA: New York, NY. 1983. Lang.: Eng. 132

Corporate grant officers and arts management heads discuss corporate giving. USA: New York, NY. 1984. Lang.: Eng. 134

Guide to producing Off-off Broadway showcases. USA: New York, NY. Lang.: Eng. 159

Primary organizational changes at New York State Council on the Arts. USA: New York, NY. 1984. Lang.: Eng. 162

Work relationships: artist, layman and executive. USA. 1986. Lang.: Eng. 174

Satiric examination of what not to do if one is to become an effective artistic director. USA. 1986. Lang.: Eng. 178

Personnel problems in theatres. USSR. 1980-1986. Lang.: Rus. 188

Proposals for the reorganization of theatrical business. USSR. 1986. Lang.: Rus. 190

Articles on the organizational problems of theatre. USSR. 1980-1986. Lang.: Rus. 194

Letter from actor Ernesto Rossi concerning actors' labor movement. Italy. 1891. Lang.: Ita. 1436

Organization and operation of Office of Revels mainly under Thomas Cawarden. England: London. 1510-1559. Lang.: Eng. 3417

History and achievements of the American Guild of Musical Artists during its fifty years of existence. USA. 1936-1986. Lang.: Eng. 3645

Personnel — cont'd

Design/technology
Details of the lighting arrangements for the four-day Statue of Liberty centennial celebration. USA: New York, NY. 1986. Lang.: Eng.   3318

How to look for work as a designer or technician in opera. USA. 1986. Lang.: Eng.   3655

Institutions
Origins and evolution of Teatro Campesino. USA. Mexico. 1965-1986. Lang.: Eng.   547

Role of the Canadian Actors' Equity Association. Canada: Toronto, ON. 1983-1986. Lang.: Eng.   1548

Performance/production
Actors' round table on the problems facing young actors. USSR: Moscow. 1986. Lang.: Rus.   900

The organization of the Olympiad Arts Festival. USA: Los Angeles, CA. 1984. Lang.: Eng.   2281

Reference materials
Directory of member organizations of ART/NY. USA: New York, NY. 1986. Lang.: Eng.   1037

Relation to other fields
Methods and goals of Children's Theatre Association of America. USA. 1940-1984. Lang.: Eng.   1163

Perth Theatre Company (UK-Scotland)
Performance/production
Career of John Scrimger, music director at Perth Theatre. UK-Scotland: Perth. 1948-1986. Lang.: Eng.   2188

Perucci, Andrea (pseud. Ruggeri Ugone, Casimiro)
Plays/librettos/scripts
Cultural and popular elements in a traditional nativity puppet performance. Italy: Sicily, Naples. 1651-1986. Lang.: Eng.   4009

Peschel, Richard E.
Performance/production
History of *castrati* in opera. Italy. 1599-1797. Lang.: Eng.   3761

Peškov, Aleksey Maksimovič
SEE
Gorkij, Maksim.

Pessoal do Victor, Nucleo
Performance/production
Annual festival of Latin American plays at the Public Theatre. USA: New York, NY. 1985. Lang.: Eng.   2310

Pest National Theatre
SEE
Pesti Nemzeti Szinház.

Performance/production
István Horvai directs *Megtört szivek háza (Heartbreak House)* by George Bernard Shaw at Pest National Theatre. Hungary: Budapest. 1985. Lang.: Hun.   1793

Productions of *Deficit* by István Csurka. Hungary: Szolnok, Budapest. 1970-1985. Lang.: Hun.   1833

Peste, La (Plague, The)
Performance/production
Director Kazimierz Braun on his adaptation of *La Peste (The Plague)* by Albert Camus. Poland: Wrocław. 1976-1983. Lang.: Eng.   2015

Pesti Magyar Szinház
Basic theatrical documents
Pamphlet of 1839 concerning the Hungarian Theatre of Pest. Austro-Hungarian Empire: Pest. 1839. Lang.: Hun.   216

Pesti Nemzeti Szinház (Budapest)
Performance/production
Stage history of *Giselle* by Adolphe Adam at Pest National Theatre. Hungary: Pest. 1847-1880. Lang.: Hun.   1306

Performances of *Alice Csodaországban (Alice in Wonderland)*, *A Két Veronai nemes (The Two Gentlemen of Verona)* and *Tobbsincs királyfi (No More Crown Prince)*. Hungary: Pécs, Budapest. 1985. Lang.: Hun.   1771

Éva Pataki's *Edith és Marlene (Edith and Marlene)* directed by Márta Mészáros, Pest National Theatre. Hungary: Budapest. 1986. Lang.: Hun.   3603

Pesti Szinház (Budapest)
Performance/production
David Rabe's play *Sticks and Bones* presented at the Pesti Theatre in Hungary. Hungary: Budapest. 1971-1975. Lang.: Hun.   1799

G.B. Shaw's *Megtörtszívek háza (Heartbreak House)* directed by István Horvai. Hungary: Budapest. 1985. Lang.: Hun.   1858

Peter Grimes
Relation to other fields
Comparison between insanity defense and opera productions with audience as jury. USA. 1980-1985. Lang.: Eng.   3925

Peter Grimm
Plays/librettos/scripts
David Belasco's influence on Eugene O'Neill. USA: New York, NY. 1908-1922. Lang.: Eng.   2927

Peter Pan
Performance/production
Performances of *Pán Peter (Peter Pan)* by J. M. Barrie, directed by Géza Pártos. Hungary: Kaposvár. 1985. Lang.: Hun.   1934

Collection of newspaper reviews by London theatre critics. UK. 1986. Lang.: Eng.   2101

Collection of newspaper reviews by London theatre critics. UK-England. 1986. Lang.: Eng.   2111

Peters, Paul
Plays/librettos/scripts
Career of Marxist playwright George Sklar. USA: New York, NY. 1920-1967. Lang.: Eng.   985

Petit Prince, Le (Little Prince, The)
Performance/production
A kis herceg (The Little Prince) by Antoine de Saint-Exupéry adapted and staged by Anna Belia and Péter Valló. Hungary: Budapest. 1985. Lang.: Hun.   1828

A kis herceg (The Little Prince) by Saint-Exupéry adapted and staged by Anna Belia and Péter Valló. Hungary: Budapest. 1985. Lang.: Hun.   1935

Petit, Roland
Design/technology
Costumes by Yves Saint-Laurent. France. 1959-1984. Lang.: Fre.   1341

Petition, The
Performance/production
Actress Rosemary Harris discusses her work in *The Petition*. UK-England: London. USA: New York, NY. 1948-1986. Lang.: Eng.   2177

Reviews of *The Petition*, by Brian Clark, staged by Peter Hall. USA: New York, NY. 1986. Lang.: Eng.   2234

Petőfi Szinház (Veszprém)
Performance/production
István Paál directs Shakespeare's *Szeget szeggel (Measure for Measure)*. Hungary: Veszprém. 1985. Lang.: Hun.   1770

Production of Shakespeare's *Szeget szeggel (Measure for Measure)* directed by István Paál. Hungary: Veszprém. 1985. Lang.: Hun. 1872

István Paál directs *Szeget szeggel (Measure for Measure)* by Shakespeare at Petőfi Szinház. Hungary: Veszprém. 1985. Lang.: Hun.   1938

Ferenc Sik directs two plays by Gyula Háy. Hungary: Veszprém, Gyula. 1986. Lang.: Hun.   1943

Stage adaptations of prose works by Gogol and Gončarov. Hungary: Veszprém, Békéscsaba. 1985. Lang.: Hun.   1948

Petrified Forest, The
Plays/librettos/scripts
Robert E. Sherwood's conception of history in *The Petrified Forest* and *Abe Lincoln in Illinois*. USA. 1930-1950. Lang.: Eng.   2949

Petrik, József
Performance/production
Premiere of László Kolozsvári Papp's *Hazánk fiai (Sons of Our Country)*. Hungary: Budapest. 1985. Lang.: Hun.   1800

Petrov, A.
On *Majakovskij načinajetskja (Majakovskij Begins)*, an opera by A. Petrov. USSR. Lang.: Rus.   3638

Petruševskaja, Ljudmila
Plays/librettos/scripts
Critical analysis of *Tri devuški v golubom (Three Girls in Blue)* by Ljudmila Petruševskaja. USSR. 1986. Lang.: Rus.   989

Analyses of the plays of Ljudmila Petruševskaja. USSR. 1986. Lang.: Rus.   994

Playwrights Semyan Zlotnikov and Ljudmila Petruševskaja as representative of contemporary dramaturgy. USSR. 1980-1986. Lang.: Rus.   2965

Pettegolezzi delle donne, I (Ladies' Gossip)
Plays/librettos/scripts
Analysis of Harlequin in comedies by Carlo Goldoni. Italy. 1751-1752. Lang.: Ita.   2697

Petters, Heinz
Performance/production
On actor Heinz Petters and the production of *Der Raub der Sabinerinnen* at the Volkstheater. Austria: Vienna. 1938-1986. Lang.: Ger.   1644

Pettingill, Richard
Performance/production
Chicago dramaturgs acknowledge a common ground in educating their audience. USA: Chicago, IL. 1984-1986. Lang.: Eng.   2274

Peymann, Claus
Administration
Selling tickets at the Burgtheater and Akademietheater. Austria: Vienna. 1986. Lang.: Ger.   1428
Institutions
Claus Peymann's concept for managing the Akademietheater and the Burgtheater. Austria: Vienna. 1986. Lang.: Ger.   1532
Performance/production
On actor Gert Voss and his work. Austria: Vienna. Germany, West. 1941-1986. Lang.: Ger.   1649
Relation to other fields
Herbert Moritz and his views about cultural politics. Austria. 1986. Lang.: Ger.   1064

Pfitzner, Hans
Plays/librettos/scripts
German and Christian myths in Hans Pfitzner's opera *Palestrina*. 1900-1982. Lang.: Eng.   3852

Phaedra
Plays/librettos/scripts
Stoicism and modern elements in Senecan drama. Europe. 65-1986. Lang.: Eng.   2542

Phantom of the Opera
Performance/production
Reviews of musicals. UK-England: London. 1986. Lang.: Eng.   3610

Phenomenology
Theory/criticism
Live theatre gives the spectator a choice of focus. 1600-1986. Lang.: Eng.   1190
Theory of drama based on Max Scheler's philosophy. Lang.: Eng.   3074
Phenomenological study of *The White Devil* by John Webster. England: London. 1610-1612. Lang.: Eng.   3093
Edward Albee's development of realistic setting for absurdist drama. USA. 1964-1980. Lang.: Eng.   3148
Phenomenological view of the history of the circus, its links with theatre. 1985. Lang.: Fre.   3405

Philadelphia Monthly Magazine
Reference materials
Theatrical materials in five early American magazines. Colonial America. 1758-1800. Lang.: Eng.   1012

Philaster
Plays/librettos/scripts
Passion in early plays of Beaumont and Fletcher. England. 1608-1611. Lang.: Eng.   945
Shakespeare's influence on Beaumont and Fletcher's *Philaster*. England. 1609. Lang.: Eng.   2463
Use of language in Beaumont and Fletcher's *Philaster*. England. 1609. Lang.: Eng.   2512

Philistines
SEE
Varvary.

Phillips, Anton
Performance/production
Collection of newspaper reviews by London theatre critics. UK. 1986. Lang.: Eng.   2102
Collection of newspaper reviews by London theatre critics. UK-England. 1986. Lang.: Eng.   2114

Phillips, Melanie
Performance/production
Collection of newspaper reviews by London theatre critics. UK-England: London. 1986. Lang.: Eng.   2117

Phillips, Paulette
Performance/production
Interviews with performance artists. Canada: Toronto, ON. USA: New York, NY. 1980-1986. Lang.: Eng.   3444

Phillips, Robin
Performance/production
Dramaturg's experience with classical and new productions. Canada: Toronto, ON. 1986. Lang.: Eng.   1667

Robin Phillips' staging of Shakespeare's *Richard III*. Canada: Stratford, ON. 1977. Lang.: Eng.   1668
Relation to other fields
Concept of play in theatre and sport. Canada. 1972-1983. Lang.: Eng.   1071

Philoctetes
Plays/librettos/scripts
Interpretation of final scenes of Sophocles' *Philoctetes*. Greece. 409 B.C. Lang.: Heb.   2630

Philombe, René
Plays/librettos/scripts
Interview with playwright René Philombe on the educative function of theatre. Cameroon. 1930-1986. Lang.: Fre.   925

Philosophy
Institutions
Comparison of the creative process in theatre and in research. UK-England: London. 1981-1986. Lang.: Eng.   1586
Performance/production
Zen and Western acting styles. Lang.: Eng.   648
Critical essays on major productions and aesthetics. France. 1970-1985. Lang.: Fre.   1747
Plays/librettos/scripts
Moral issues in *A Woman Killed with Kindness* by Thomas Heywood. England. 1560. Lang.: Eng.   2498
Stoicism and modern elements in Senecan drama. Europe. 65-1986. Lang.: Eng.   2542
Enlightenment narrative and French dramatists. France. 1700-1800. Lang.: Eng.   2552
Modern thought in works of Jean Racine. France. 1664-1691. Lang.: Fre.   2553
Various implications of 'waiting' in Samuel Beckett's *Waiting for Godot*. France. 1953. Lang.: Eng.   2555
Waiting for Godot as an assessment of the quality of life of the couple. France. UK-Ireland. 1931-1958. Lang.: Eng.   2557
Biography of Molière as seen through his plays. France. 1622-1673. Lang.: Fre.   2573
Essentialism and avant-garde in the plays of Eugène Ionesco. France. 1950-1980. Lang.: Fre.   2576
The idea of grace in the life and work of Heinrich von Kleist. Germany. 1777-1811. Lang.: Eng.   2593
Cosmic themes in the works of Aeschylus. Greece. 472-458 B.C. Lang.: Fre.   2629
Moral and political crises reflected in the plays of Euripides. Greece: Athens. 438-408 B.C. Lang.: Fre.   2634
Philosophy and obscenity in the plays of Tadeusz Różewicz. Poland. 1920-1986. Lang.: Pol.   2750
Interview with playwright Friedrich Dürrenmatt. Switzerland. 1986. Lang.: Ger.   2828
Relation of Harold Pinter's plays to modern developments in science and philosophy. UK-England. 1932-1986. Lang.: Eng.   2849
Relation to other fields
Analysis of *Symphony* by Herman Voaden and Lowrie Warrener. Canada. 1914-1933. Lang.: Eng.   1075
Contribution to the discussion on theatre structure analyzing the function of theatre in society. Hungary. Lang.: Hun.   1100
Luigi Pirandello's relationship with philosophers Benedetto Croce and Giovanni Gentile. Italy. 1867-1936. Lang.: Ita.   1106
Conceptions of humankind as seen in contemporary theatre. USSR. 1980. Lang.: Rus.   1171
Existence and conscience as seen by major writers. Italy. 1890-1970. Lang.: Ita.   3043
Philosophical context of the plays of Herman Voaden. Canada: Toronto, ON. 1929-1943. Lang.: Eng.   3170
Theory/criticism
An imagined dialogue on the work of Roland Barthes. France. Lang.: Eng.   1207
Theory of drama based on Max Scheler's philosophy. Lang.: Eng.   3074
Selection of Schiller's writings about drama. Germany. 1759-1805. Lang.: Cat.   3110
Overview of Pinter criticism with emphasis on the works' inherent uncertainty. UK. 1957-1986. Lang.: Eng.   3134
Use of anxiety about fate in Beijing opera. China: Beijing. 5 B.C.-1985 A.D. Lang.: Chi.   3558

Phoenix Little Theatre Guild (Phoenix, AZ)
Administration
Fundraising strategies of various community theatres. USA. 1986.
Lang.: Eng.   128
Phoenix Theatre (New York, NY)
Performance/production
Interview with dramaturg Anne Cattaneo. USA: New York, NY.
1971-1986. Lang.: Eng.   2254
Phoenix Theatre (Toronto, ON)
Performance spaces
Troubles faced by Adelaide Court theatre complex. Canada: Toronto,
ON. 1979-1983. Lang.: En .   587
Phonetics
Training
Results of sonographic analysis of covered and uncovered singing.
Austria. 1980-1984. Lang.: Ger.   3933
Psychological aspects of voice training. Austria. USA. 1750-1984.
Lang.: Ger.   3935
Collected papers from a conference on voice training. Austria:
Vienna. Italy: Rome. England: London. 1700-1984. Lang.: Ger. 3936
Physiological regulation for correct breathing and singing. Europe.
North America. 1929-1984. Lang.: Ger.   3937
Photography
Design/technology
'Frisket principle' duplicates black and white photo on large scale.
USA. 1984. Lang.: Eng.   370
Reproduction of the pattern of any photcopy to fabric. USA. 1984.
Lang.: Eng.   422
Cinematographer Roger Deakins discusses lighting for his work in
the film *Sid and Nancy*. USA: New York, NY, Los Angeles, CA.
UK-England: London. 1976-1986. Lang.: Eng.   3211
Interview with cameraman Gerald Perry Finnerman about lighting
Moonlighting. USA: Los Angeles, CA. 1985-1986. Lang.: Eng.   3264
Performance/production
Development of stage photography. France. 1872-1986. Lang.: Fre.
                                                                      720
Stage photographs with comment by photographers. Sweden. 1985-
1986. Lang.: Swe.   794
Relationship between theatre and early photography. France. 1818-
1899. Lang.: Fre.   1748
Photographic record of forty years of the Berliner Ensemble.
Germany, East: Berlin, East. 1949-1984. Lang.: Eng.   1761
Rehearsals of András Sütő's *Advent a Hargitán (Advent in the
Harghita Mountains)* at the National Theatre directed by Ferenc Sik.
Hungary: Budapest. 1985-1986. Lang.: Hun.   1963
Photographs of circus life taken by Frederick Glasier. USA. 1896-
1920. Lang.: Eng.   3392
Photographs of three circuses by Holton Rowes. USA: New York,
NY. 1985. Lang.: Eng.   3395
Reference materials
Catalogue of documentation on Pirandello's writings in dialect. Italy.
1902-1936. Lang.: Eng, Fre, Ger, Ita.   2994
Physicists, The
SEE
    Physiker, Die.
Physiker, Die (Physicists, The)
Performance/production
Directorial design for Dürrenmatt's *Die Physiker (The Physicists)*.
China: Shanghai. 1982. Lang.: Chi.   1690
Physiology
Training
Results of sonographic analysis of covered and uncovered singing.
Austria. 1980-1984. Lang.: Ger.   3933
Collected papers from a conference on voice training. Austria:
Vienna. Italy: Rome. England: London. 1700-1984. Lang.: Ger. 3936
Pi Pa Chi (Story of the Guitar, The)
Plays/librettos/scripts
Problems of adapting classic plays. China, People's Republic of.
1986. Lang.: Chi.   3543
Piaf, Edith
Performance/production
Edith és Marlene (Edith and Marlene) by Éva Pataki at Comedy
Theatre. Hungary: Budapest. 1986. Lang.: Hun.   1831
Éva Pataki's *Edith és Marlene (Edith and Marlene)* directed by
Márta Mészáros, Pest National Theatre. Hungary: Budapest. 1986.
Lang.: Hun.   3603

Piave, Francesco Maria
Plays/librettos/scripts
Creation of the 1857 version of *Simon Boccanegra* by Verdi, libretto
by Piave. Italy: Venice. 1856-1881. Lang.: Eng.   3882
Piccadilly Theatre (London)
Design/technology
William Dudley's life-like replica of the Bounty for David Essex's
Mutiny!. UK-England: London. 1986. Lang.: Eng.   3584
Piccinni, Niccolo
Plays/librettos/scripts
Use of the tale of Patient Griselda in *Griselda* by Angelo Anelli and
Niccolo Piccinni. Italy: Venice. Austria: Vienna. 1770-1800. Lang.:
Eng.   3885
Pickwick Players (Midland, TX)
Institutions
Training and use of child performers. USA. 1949-1985. Lang.: Eng.
                                                                      565
Pielmeier, John
Performance/production
Reviews of plays performed in the 1983-84 Seoul theatre season.
Korea: Seoul. 1983-1984. Lang.: Eng.   2008
Plays/librettos/scripts
Report on a symposium addressing the role of the dramaturg.   918
Pien, Ka
Theory/criticism
Analyzes works of four dramatists from Fuchien province. China,
People's Republic of. 1981-1985. Lang.: Chi.   3569
Piggery, The (Montreal, PQ)
Institutions
Interviews with theatre professionals in Quebec. Canada. 1985.
Lang.: Fre.   487
Pikiel, Irena
Design/technology
Irena Pikiel, Polish puppet theatre stage-designer, describes her years
in satirical performances. Poland: Vilna. 1921-1933. Lang.: Pol. 3952
Piller, Heinar
Institutions
History of the Neptune Theatre and its artistic directors. Canada:
Halifax, NS. 1963-1983. Lang.: Eng.   483
Pimlott, Steven
Performance/production
Collection of newspaper reviews by London theatre critics. UK.
1986. Lang.: Eng.   2103
Pin i Soler, Josep
Plays/librettos/scripts
History of Catalan literature, including playwrights. Spain-Catalonia.
France. 1800-1926. Lang.: Cat.   973
Pinczés, István
Performance/production
Segítség (Help) by György Schwajda, directed by István Pinczés,
Csokonai Szinház. Hungary: Debrecen. 1986. Lang.: Hun.   1848
Die dreigroschenoper (The Three Penny Opera) directed by István
Pinczés at Csokonai Theatre. Hungary: Debrecen. 1986. Lang.: Hun.
                                                                      1910
Bungei-za performs *Tóték (The Tót Family)* by István Örkény.
Japan: Toyama. 1985. Lang.: Hun.   2006
Pinder, Islene
Performance/production
Influence of Asian theatre traditions on American artists. USA: New
York, NY. Indonesia. 1952-1985. Lang.: Eng.   1335
Piñera, Virgilio
Plays/librettos/scripts
Cuban theatre in transition exemplified in the plays of Virgilio
Piñera and Abelardo Estorino. Cuba. 1958-1964. Lang.: Eng.   2452
Pinero, Arthur Wing
Performance/production
Tom Robertson as a theatrical innovator and as a character in
Arthur Wing Pinero's *Trelawny of the Wells*. England: London.
1840-1848. Lang.: Eng.   1702
Plays/librettos/scripts
Development and subsequent decline of the three-act farce. UK-
England. 1875-1900. Lang.: Eng.   976
Piñero, Miguel
Performance/production
Survey of the season at the National Theatre. UK-England: London.
1986. Lang.: Eng.   2130
Plays/librettos/scripts
Race in prison dramas of Piñero, Camillo, Elder and Bullins. USA.
1970-1986. Lang.: Eng.   2912

Ping Hsi
Research/historiography
Rise of the *Ping Hsi* form in Tienchin. China, People's Republic of: Tienchin. 1885-1948. Lang.: Chi. 3557

Pinpoints Traveling Theatre Group (Washington, DC)
Relation to other fields
Black history and folklore taught in theatre workshops and productions. USA: New York, NY, Omaha, NE, Washington, DC. 1986. Lang.: Eng. 3068

Pinter, Harold
Basic theatrical documents
Catalan translation of *The Homecoming* by Harold Pinter. UK-England. 1965. Lang.: Cat. 1507

Institutions
Survey of Royal Shakespeare Company productions. UK-England. 1960-1980. Lang.: Chi. 1593

Performance/production
Review of Tennessee Williams' *Sweet Bird of Youth* starring Lauren Bacall, directed by Harold Pinter. UK-England: London. 1985. Lang.: Eng. 2186

Reviews of *The Caretaker* by Harold Pinter, staged by John Malkovich. USA: New York, NY. 1986. Lang.: Eng. 2236

Plays/librettos/scripts
Use of violent language in the plays of Griselda Gambaro. Argentina. 1950-1980. Lang.: Eng. 2362

Study of realism vs metadrama. Europe. 429 B.C.-1978 A.D. Lang.: Eng. 2540

Theme of renewal in Harold Pinter's *Betrayal*. UK-England. 1978. 2835

Theme of family in plays of Harold Pinter. UK-England. 1957-1981. Lang.: Eng. 2836

Narratological analysis of Harold Pinter's *Old Times*. UK-England. 1971. Lang.: Eng. 2842

Playwright Harold Pinter's use of disjunctive chronologies. UK-England. 1957-1979. Lang.: Eng. 2844

Interview with playwright Howard Barker. UK-England. 1981-1985. Lang.: Eng. 2845

Influence of playwright Harold Pinter. UK-England. 1957-1982. Lang.: Eng. 2846

Relation of Harold Pinter's plays to modern developments in science and philosophy. UK-England. 1932-1986. Lang.: Eng. 2849

Playwright Harold Pinter's use of dramatic reversals and surprise. UK-England. 1960-1977. Lang.: Eng. 2850

Articles on work of playwright Harold Pinter. UK-England. 1957-1984. Lang.: Eng. 2851

Different versions of *The Dwarfs* by Harold Pinter. UK-England. 1960-1976. Lang.: Eng. 2855

Analysis of *The Birthday Party* by Harold Pinter. UK-England. 1958. Lang.: Eng. 2856

Playwright Simon Gray's journal about the production of his play *The Common Pursuit*. UK-England. 1983. Lang.: Eng. 2858

History of Harold Pinter's work and critical reception. UK-England. 1975-1983. Lang.: Eng. 2860

Reader-response interpretation of *The Homecoming* by Harold Pinter. UK-England. 1952-1965. Lang.: Eng. 2861

Analysis of the plot, characters and structure of *The Homecoming* by Harold Pinter. UK-England: London. 1930-1985. Lang.: Cat. 2865

Metaphor and image in plays of Harold Pinter. UK-England. 1957-1986. Lang.: Eng. 2869

Thematic analysis of Harold Pinter's *The Lover*. UK-England. 1963. Lang.: Eng. 2870

Comparison of the radio and staged versions of Harold Pinter's *A Slight Ache*. UK-England. 1959-1961. Lang.: Eng. 2880

Influence of Harold Pinter's radio work on his stage plays. UK-England. 1957-1981. Lang.: Eng. 3186

Comparison of Harold Pinter and Marcel Proust, focusing on Pinter's filmscript *The Proust Screenplay*. France. UK-England. 1913-1978. Lang.: Eng. 3232

Harold Pinter's screenplay for *The French Lieutenant's Woman* by John Fowles. UK-England. 1969-1981. Lang.: Eng. 3238

Analysis of Harold Pinter's technique in adapting *A la Recherche du Temps Perdu (Remembrance of Things Past)* by Marcel Proust as a screenplay. UK-England. 1972. Lang.: Eng. 3240

Theory/criticism
Overview of Pinter criticism with emphasis on the works' inherent uncertainty. UK. 1957-1986. Lang.: Eng. 3134

Assessment of critic Kenneth Tynan's works. UK-England. 1950-1960. Lang.: Eng. 3136

Pipan, Janez
Performance/production
Janez Pipan directs *Confiteor* by Slobodan Šnajder at National Theatre of Belgrade. Yugoslavia: Belgrade. 1986. Lang.: Hun. 2344

Pipironda, La (Barcelona)
Institutions
Three personal views of the evolution of the Catalan company La Pipironda. Spain-Catalonia: Barcelona. 1958-1986. Lang.: Cat. 1583

Pipistrello, Il (Bat, The)
Plays/librettos/scripts
Analysis of two versions of a screenplay by Luigi Pirandello. Italy. 1925-1928. Lang.: Ita. 3235

Pique Dame (Queen of Spades)
Plays/librettos/scripts
Puškin's *Queen of Spades* adapted for opera by Čajkovskij. Russia. 1833-1890. Lang.: Eng. 3891

Pirandello, Luigi
Letters from literary critic Emilio Cecchi to Luigi Pirandello. Italy. 1932-1933. Lang.: Ita. 3189

Basic theatrical documents
Letter from Luigi Pirandello to Silvio D'Amico. Italy: Agrigento. 1927. Lang.: Fre. 224

Catalan translation of *Il giuoco delle parti (The Rules of the Game)* by Luigi Pirandello. Italy. 1918. Lang.: Cat. 1485

Performance/production
Theatrical illusion in *Sei personaggi in cerca d'autore (Six Characters in Search of an Author)* by Luigi Pirandello. France: Paris. 1951-1986. Lang.: Fre. 1730

Reception of Pirandello's plays in Germany. Germany. Italy. 1924-1931. Lang.: Ita. 1756

Max Reinhardt's notes on his production of *Sei personaggi in cerca d'autore (Six Characters in Search of an Author)* by Luigi Pirandello. Germany. Italy. 1924-1934. Lang.: Ita. 1759

Productions of plays by Luigi Pirandello after World War II. Italy. 1947-1985. Lang.: Ita. 1987

Luigi Pirandello's concerns with staging in *Sei personaggi in cerca d'autore (Six Characters in Search of an Author)* and *Enrico Quarto (Henry IV)*. Italy. 1921-1986. Lang.: Fre. 1990

Pirandello's dealings with actor, manager and director Virgilio Talli. Italy. 1917-1921. Lang.: Ita. 1993

Notes on the first production of Luigi Pirandello's *L'uomo, la bestia, e la virtù (Man, Animal and Virtue)*. Italy. 1919. Lang.: Ita. 1997

Premiere of Luigi Pirandello's *I giganti della montagna (The Giants of the Mountain)*. Italy: Florence. 1937. Lang.: Ita. 1998

Conference and theatrical theory and practice sponsored by Pirandellian Studies Center. Italy: Agrigento. 1900-1940. Lang.: Spa. 2002

Luigi Pirandello's staging of his own works at the Teatro d'Arte. Italy: Rome. 1925-1928. Lang.: Ita. 2004

Plays/librettos/scripts
Great dramatic works considered in light of modern theatre and social reponsibility. France. Italy. Germany, West. 1700-1964. Lang.: Fre. 2560

Collection of articles on playwright Luigi Pirandello. Italy. 1867-1936. Lang.: Ita. 2668

Studies on staging and meaning in plays of Luigi Pirandello. Italy: Agrigento. 1867-1936. Lang.: Ita. 2669

Evaluation of *Il giuoco delle parti (The Rules of the Game)* in the context of Pirandello's oeuvre. Italy. 1867-1936. Lang.: Cat. 2670

Analysis and guide to Pirandello's published letters. Italy. 1867-1936. Lang.: Ita. 2674

Luigi Pirandello's letters to his fiancée. Italy. 1893-1894. Lang.: Ita. 2675

Study of a draft of *L'abito nuovo (The New Suit)* by Eduardo De Filippo and Luigi Pirandello. Italy. 1935-1937. Lang.: Ita. 2677

Actuality and modernity of the plays of Luigi Pirandello. Italy. 1867-1936. Lang.: Fre. 2680

Influence of German expressionism on the plays of Luigi Pirandello. Italy. Germany. 1917-1930. Lang.: Ita. 2682

Pirandello, Luigi — cont'd

Angelo Musco's interpretation of *Pensaci Giacomino! (Think of it, Jamie!)* by Luigi Pirandello. Italy. 1916-1917. Lang.: Ita. 2684

Tension between text and realization in Pirandello's *Sei personaggi in cerca d'autore (Six Characters in Search of an Author)*. Italy. 1911-1929. Lang.: Fre. 2685

Letters of Luigi Pirandello and editor Ezio Ferrieri. Italy. 1921-1924. Lang.: Ita. 2694

Childhood drawings by Luigi Pirandello and his sister Lina. Italy. 1883-1899. Lang.: Ita. 2696

Luigi Pirandello's relationship with author Gabriele D'Annunzio and reviewer Luigi Antonelli. Italy. 1900-1936. Lang.: Ita. 2698

Correspondence between Luigi Pirandello and composer Gian Francesco Malipiero. Italy. 1832-1938. Lang.: Ita. 2699

Letters of Luigi Pirandello's son Stefano. Italy: Rome. 1921. Lang.: Ita. 2701

Critical notes on *La nuova colonia (The New Colony)* by Luigi Pirandello. Italy. 1928. Lang.: Ita. 2702

Influence of Luigi Pirandello's work in Catalonia. Italy. Spain-Catalonia. 1867-1985. Lang.: Spa, Cat. 2706

Study of Pirandello's preface to *Sei personaggi in cerca d'autore (Six Characters in Search of an Author)*. Italy. 1923-1986. Lang.: Fre. 2708

Role-playing and madness in Pirandello's *Enrico Quarto (Henry IV)*. Italy. 1922. Lang.: Fre. 2709

Writings on life and work of Luigi Pirandello. Italy. 1867-1936. Lang.: Ita. 2711

Development of Pirandello's *La ragione degli altri (The Reason of the Others)* from novel to play. Italy. 1899-1917. Lang.: Ita. 2712

Pirandello's interest in the problems of women evidenced in his plays and novels. Italy. 1867-1936. Lang.: Fre. 2714

Text and information on Luigi Pirandello's *A patenti (The License)*. Italy. 1916-1918. Lang.: Ita. 2717

Analysis of two versions of a screenplay by Luigi Pirandello. Italy. 1925-1928. Lang.: Ita. 3235

Luigi Pirandello's work as scriptwriter in collaboration with his son. Italy. 1925-1933. Lang.: Ita. 3237

Unpublished documentation of *Proprio like that*, a musical by Luigi Pirandello. Italy: Rome. 1930-1953. Lang.: Fre. 3627

Reference materials

Catalogue of documentation on Pirandello's writings in dialect. Italy. 1902-1936. Lang.: Eng, Fre, Ger, Ita. 2994

Relation to other fields

Study of Luigi Pirandello's novel, *I quaderni di Serafino Gubbio operatore (The Notebooks of Serafino Gubbio, Cameraman)*. Italy. 1915-1925. Lang.: Ita. 1104

Luigi Pirandello's relationship with philosophers Benedetto Croce and Giovanni Gentile. Italy. 1867-1936. Lang.: Ita. 1106

The meeting of playwright Luigi Pirandello and novelist Italo Svevo. Italy: Trieste. 1925-1926. Lang.: Ita. 1107

Playwright Luigi Pirandello on the dynamics of humor. Italy. 1200-1906. Lang.: Ita. 1108

Critical articles on playwright Luigi Pirandello. Italy. 1867-1936. Lang.: Ita. 3039

Comparison of playwright Luigi Pirandello and novelist Miguel de Cervantes. Italy. Spain. 1615-1936. Lang.: Ita. 3040

Pirandello's influence on poet Eugenio Montale. Italy. 1896-1981. Lang.: Ita. 3042

Existence and conscience as seen by major writers. Italy. 1890-1970. Lang.: Ita. 3043

Theory/criticism

Pitfalls of a semiotic analysis of theatre. England. 1600-1921. Lang.: Eng. 3094

Decreasing importance of the playwright in Italian theatre. Italy. 1900-1984. Lang.: Fre. 3119

Pirandello, Stefano

Plays/librettos/scripts

Letters of Luigi Pirandello's son Stefano. Italy: Rome. 1921. Lang.: Ita. 2701

Luigi Pirandello's work as scriptwriter in collaboration with his son. Italy. 1925-1933. Lang.: Ita. 3237

Pirate Princess, The

Performance/production

Collection of newspaper reviews by London theatre critics. UK-England: London. 1986. Lang.: Eng. 2121

Pirates

Design/technology

Pierre Guffroy's design of a functional ship for Polanski's *Pirates*. Tunisia. 1986. Lang.: Eng. 3201

Pirates, The

Plays/librettos/scripts

Dramatic spectacles relating to Botany Bay. England: London. Australia. 1787-1791. Lang.: Eng. 2492

Piscator, Erwin

Institutions

Erwin Piscator's work at the Dramatic Workshop of the New School for Social Research. USA: New York, NY. 1939-1951. Lang.: Ger. 1600

Plays/librettos/scripts

Brecht's use of the epically structured motif of the military review. 2354

Compares contemporary Canadian theatre with German and Russian theatre of the early 20th century. Canada. Russia: Moscow. Germany. 1900-1986. Lang.: Eng. 2412

Relation to other fields

Study of Fascist theatrical policies. Germany: Berlin. 1933-1944. Lang.: Ger. 1091

Refugee artists from Nazi Germany in Britain. UK-England. Germany. 1937-1947. Lang.: Eng. 1135

Pisemskij, Aleksej Feofilaktovič

Plays/librettos/scripts

Life and work of playwright Aleksej Feofilaktovič Pisemskij. Russia. 1821-1881. Lang.: Rus. 2767

Pisti a vérzivatarban (Steve in the Bloodbath)

Plays/librettos/scripts

Analysis of István Örkény's play, *Pisti a vérzivatarban (Steve in the Bloodbath)*. Hungary. Lang.: Hun. 2652

Pit, The (London)

SEE ALSO

Royal Shakespeare Company.

Performance/production

Collection of newspaper reviews by London theatre critics. UK: London. 1986. Lang.: Eng. 2100

Collection of newspaper reviews by London theatre critics. UK-England: London. 1986. Lang.: Eng. 2109

Collection of newspaper reviews by London theatre critics. UK-England: London. 1986. Lang.: Eng. 2112

Collection of newspaper reviews by London theatre critics. UK-England: London. 1986. Lang.: Eng. 2113

Collection of newspaper reviews by London theatre critics. UK-England. 1986. Lang.: Eng. 2115

Pitarra, Serafía (Soler, Frederic)

Plays/librettos/scripts

History of Catalan literature, including playwrights. Spain-Catalonia. France. 1800-1926. Lang.: Cat. 973

Pitlochry Festival (Scotland)

Performance/production

Survey of the year in Scottish theatre. UK-Scotland. 1986. Lang.: Eng. 2194

Pitoëff, Georges

Performance/production

Theatrical illusion in *Sei personaggi in cerca d'autore (Six Characters in Search of an Author)* by Luigi Pirandello. France: Paris. 1951-1986. Lang.: Fre. 1730

Pittsburgh Civic Light Opera (Pittsburgh, PA)

Design/technology

Designers discuss regional productions of *Guys and Dolls*. USA. 1984-1986. Lang.: Eng. 3586

Designers discuss regional productions of *Once Upon a Mattress*. USA. 1984-1986. 3590

Pittsburgh Opera (Pittsburgh, PA)

Design/technology

The regional opera scene and its artisans. USA. Lang.: Eng. 3661

Place, The (London)

SEE ALSO

Royal Shakespeare Company.

Performance/production

Collection of newspaper reviews by London theatre critics. UK-England. 1986. Lang.: Eng. 2115

Planché, James Robinson

Basic theatrical documents

Text of plays by James Robinson Planché, with introduction on his influence. UK-England. 1818-1872. Lang.: Eng. 226

SUBJECT INDEX

Platonov — cont'd

Plays/librettos/scripts
History of the writing and diffusion of Čechov's *Platonov (Wild Honey)*. Russia. USSR. 1878-1960. Lang.: Cat. 2764

Platonov, A.
Plays/librettos/scripts
Analysis of A. Platonov's comedy *Vysokoe naprjaženic (High Tension)*. Russia. 1899-1951. Lang.: Rus. 966

Platonova, Yulia
Performance/production
Mussorgskij's opera *Boris Godunov* at the Mariinskij Theatre. Russia: St. Petersburg. 1874. Lang.: Eng. 3775

Platt, Livingston
Performance/production
Origins of radically simplified stage in modern productions. USA. 1912-1922. Lang.: Eng. 831

Platypus Productions
Design/technology
Discussion of ultimatte, a television matting technique. USA. 1986. Lang.: Eng. 3260

Plautus, Titus Maccius
Plays/librettos/scripts
Critical problems in *Henno* by Johannes Reuchlin. Germany: Heidelberg. 1497-1522. Lang.: Eng. 2605

Play of Giants, A
Relation to other fields
Interview with playwright Wole Soyinka. Nigeria. USA: New Haven, CT. 1967-1984. Lang.: Eng. 3047

Play of Love and Chance, The
SEE
Jeu de l'amour et du hasard, Le.

Play of Saint Anthony from Viana
SEE
Comèdia de Sant Antoni de Viana.

Play of the Sacrament (Croxton)
Plays/librettos/scripts
Function of humor and violence in the *Play of the Sacrament* (Croxton). England. 1400-1499. Lang.: Eng. 2493

Play Workshop, The (Toronto, ON)
Basic theatrical documents
Text of *Within* by Bertram Brooker. Canada: Toronto, ON. 1935. Lang.: Eng. 217
Text of *The Dragon* by Bertram Brooker. Canada: Toronto, ON. 1936. Lang.: Eng. 1466

Players Theatre (London)
Institutions
History of variety act playhouse, the Players Theatre. UK-England: London. 1936-1986. Lang.: Eng. 3463

Playhouse on the Square (Memphis, TN)
Administration
Playhouse on the Square's executive producer discusses producing musicals. USA: Memphis, TN. Lang.: Eng. 3573

Design/technology
Designers discuss regional productions of *The Sound of Music*. USA. 1983-1986. Lang.: Eng. 3594

Playhouse Theatre (Liverpool, UK)
Performance/production
Survey of theatre season in Merseyside. UK-England. 1986. Lang.: Eng. 2157

Playhouse Theatre (Newcastle, UK)
Performance/production
Survey of performances in England's Northeast. UK-England. 1986. Lang.: Eng. 2173

Playhouse 91 (New York, NY)
Performance spaces
Descriptions of newly constructed Off Broadway theatres. USA: New York, NY. 1984. Lang.: Eng. 644

Plays/librettos/scripts
SEE ALSO
Classed Entries.
Playwriting.

Administration
Development of the afterpiece. England: London. 1603-1747. Lang.: Eng. 1434

Audience
History of the Mulgrave Road Co-op theatre. Canada: Guysborough, NS. 1977-1985. Lang.: Eng. 1444

Basic theatrical documents
Text of *Edmund Ironside*, attributed to Shakespeare. UK-England: London. 1580-1600. Lang.: Eng. 1508

Institutions
History of the Rhubarb Festival. Canada: Toronto, ON. 1986. Lang.: Eng. 1549

Performance/production
Image of the indigène. Australia. New Zealand. Canada. 1830-1980. Lang.: Eng. 656
Recent French-language theatre. Belgium. 1985. Lang.: Fre. 661
Problems of contemporary French theatre. France. 1980-1986. Lang.: Rus. 717
Plays from Japan performed in Romania. Romania. Japan. 1900-1986. Lang.: Ita. 778
Wooster Group retrospective of original works. USA: New York, NY. 1975-1986. Lang.: Eng. 850
Apprenticeship of playwright Garnet Walch. Australia: Sydney, N.S.W. 1860-1890. Lang.: Eng. 1640
Playwright Václav Havel's experience with the Burgtheater. Austria: Vienna. Czechoslovakia. 1976-1986. Lang.: Ger. 1643
Theatre Plus production of Santander's *Two Brothers*. Canada: Toronto, ON. Mexico. 1986. Lang.: Eng. 1679
Interview with playwright Peter Eliot Weiss. Canada: Vancouver, BC. 1986. Lang.: Eng. 1680
Differences in portraying time and locale in Sung drama and in contemporary *spoken drama*. China. 1127-1980. Lang.: Chi. 1688
Original staging of Thomas Middleton's *Hengist, King of Kent*. England: London. 1619-1661. Lang.: Eng. 1713
Notes, interviews and evolution of actor/director Jean-Marie Serreau. France. 1938-1973. Lang.: Fre. 1724
Critical essays on major productions and aesthetics. France. 1970-1985. Lang.: Fre. 1747
Difficulties in staging the plays of Paul Claudel. France. 1910-1931. Lang.: Fre. 1755
Memoir of writer, critic, theatre director Béla Abody. Hungary. 1970-1980. Lang.: Hun. 1780
Unsuccessful productions of works by Alessandro Manzoni. Italy. 1827-1882. Lang.: Ita. 1995
Notes on the first production of Luigi Pirandello's *L'uomo, la bestia, e la virtù (Man, Animal and Virtue)*. Italy. 1919. Lang.: Ita. 1997
Reviews of three productions of *Fröken Julie (Miss Julie)* by August Strindberg. Sweden: Stockholm. Denmark: Copenhagen. South Africa, Republic of. 1985-1986. Lang.: Swe. 2090
Autobiography of actor Alec Guinness. UK. USA. 1914-1985. Lang.: Eng. 2106
Eileen Atkins, Judi Dench, Wendy Hiller and Barbara Jefford discuss playing Saint Joan in Shaw's play. UK-England: London. 1936-1983. Lang.: Eng. 2153
Aesthetics, styles, rehearsal techniques of director Richard Foreman. USA. 1974-1986. Lang.: Eng. 2263
Producing *Café Con Leche (Coffee with Milk)* in Spanish. USA: New York, NY. 1986. 2269
Explorative structure and manner of performance in avant-garde theatre. USA. 1965. Lang.: Eng. 2277
Conflict over artistic control in American Repertory Theatre's production of *Endgame* by Samuel Beckett. USA: Boston, MA. 1984. Lang.: Eng. 2296
Various interpretations of plays by Michajl Afanasjèvič Bulgakov. USSR: Moscow. 1980-1986. Lang.: Rus. 2323
Reviews of National Lampoon's *Class of 86*, staged by Jerry Adler. USA: New York, NY. 1986. Lang.: Eng. 3348
Case-study of *Sweet and Sour* by the Australian Broadcasting Corporation. Australia: Sydney, N.S.W. 1980-1984. Lang.: Eng. 3483
Life and influence of Wei Ch'angsheng, actor and playwright. China. 1795-1850. Lang.: Chi. 3506
Acting during the Southern Sung dynasty. China: Wenzhou. 1101-1250. Lang.: Chi. 3510
Review of the 1985 season of the Chinese National Opera. China, People's Republic of: Beijing. 1985. Lang.: Chi. 3522
Problems in the development of Soviet musical theatre. USSR. 1980-1986. Lang.: Rus. 3625
The successful collaboration of Arrigo Boito and Giuseppe Verdi in *Simon Boccanegra*. Italy. 1856-1881. Lang.: Eng. 3764

Plays/librettos/scripts — cont'd

Interview on puppet theatre playwriting with B. Goldovskij and J. Uspenskij. USSR: Moscow. 1986. Lang.: Rus.　　3986

Reference materials

Description of Australian archives relating to theatre and film. Australia. 1870-1969. Lang.: Eng.　　1000

Bibliography of Xiong Foxi's writings. China, People's Republic of. 1917-1963. Lang.: Chi.　　1011

Western theatre from ancient times to the present. Europe. 600 B.C.-1986 A.D. Lang.: Ger.　　1013

Chronology of events and productions of non-profit theatre. USA. 1961-1986. Lang.: Eng.　　1043

Description of a collection of unpublished Australian plays. Australia. 1920-1955. Lang.: Eng.　　2977

Exhibition catalogue about context of the work and influence of Karl Kraus. Austria: Vienna. USA: New York, NY. France: Paris. 1874-1986. Lang.: Ger.　　2980

Bibliography on and about the playwright-author Ferenc Molnár. Austria: Vienna. Hungary: Budapest. USA: New York, NY. 1878-1982. Lang.: Eng.　　2982

Bibliography of plays by Cameroonians. Cameroon. 1940-1985. Lang.: Fre.　　2983

Current state of research on the manuscript *Sujets de plusieurs comédies italiennes (Subjects of Some Italian Comedies)*. France. Italy. 1670-1740. Lang.: Fre.　　2988

Checklist of plays by Ödön von Horváth and their productions. Germany. 1901-1938. Lang.: Eng.　　2989

Overview of seven newly published Israeli plays. Israel. 1985-1986. Lang.: Heb.　　2992

Guide to postwar British theatre. UK-England. 1945-1986. Lang.: Eng.　　3001

Chronological listing of 20 theatre seasons. USA: New York, NY. 1965-1985. Lang.: Eng.　　3009

Review of 1985 dissertations. China, People's Republic of: Beijing. 1985. Lang.: Chi.　　3545

Relation to other fields

Reports and discussions of restricted cultural communication. Lebanon. Spain-Catalonia. USA. 1985. Lang.: Fre, Spa, Cat.　　1111

Collection of obituary notes for the critic and dramatist Karl Kraus. Austria: Vienna. 1933-1937. Lang.: Ger.　　3015

Situation of playwrights in Austria. Austria: Vienna. 1971-1986. Lang.: Ger.　　3016

Bertolt Brecht's contributions to modern theatre. Canada: Toronto, ON. 1985. Lang.: Eng.　　3020

Study on the reception of critic and playwright Karl Kraus in Italy. Italy. Austria: Vienna. 1911-1985. Lang.: Ger.　　3044

Destructiveness in dramatic literature. USA. Lang.: Eng.　　3066

The reception of critic and playwright Karl Kraus in the English speaking world. USA: New York, NY. Austria: Vienna. UK-Scotland: Glasgow. 1909-1985. Lang.: Ger.　　3067

Analysis of Northern Sung theatrical artifacts. 1032-1126. Lang.: Chi.　　3546

Role of Beijing opera today. China, People's Republic of: Beijing. 1985. Lang.: Chi.　　3547

Research/historiography

Controversy over identities of Tien Kuei-pu and Lu Kuei-pu. China. 1500-1644. Lang.: Chi.　　3550

Analysis of three ancient types of dance-drama. China. 1032-1420. Lang.: Chi.　　3551

Great playwrights of the Yüan dynasty. China. 1271-1368. Lang.: Chi.　　3552

Theory/criticism

Dramatic text as read by actor, director, dramaturg, critic and scholar. Lang.: Fre.　　3076

Attempt to establish a more theatrical view of drama. Lang.: Fre.　　3078

Transformation of linguistic material into theatrical situations. Lang.: Fre.　　3081

Book review of *Whittaker's Theatre: A Critic Looks at Stages in Canada and Thereabouts: 1944-1975*, ed. Ronald Bryden and Boyd Neil. Canada: Toronto, ON. 1944-1985. Lang.: Eng.　　3087

Discusses the impact of critic B.K. Sandwell. Canada. 1932-1951. Lang.: Eng.　　3088

Playwright Xiong Foxi's concept of theatre. China, People's Republic of. 1920-1965. Lang.: Chi.　　3089

Introduction of the work and influence of Bertolt Brecht. France. 1945-1956. Lang.: Fre.　　3103

Review of *Mi lesz velünk Anton Pavlovics? (What Will Become of Us, Anton Pavlovič?)* by Miklós Almási. Hungary. 1986. Lang.: Hun.　　3114

Collection of essays on the avant-garde. USA. 1955-1986. Lang.: Eng.　　3145

Influence of Western dramatic theories on Beijing opera. China, People's Republic of: Beijing. 1935-1985. Lang.: Chi.　　3567

Comparison of Chinese play, *Kan Chien Nu*, with plays of Molière. China, People's Republic of: Beijing. 1970-1983. Lang.: Chi.　　3568

Playtexts

Basic theatrical documents

Collection of plays for adolescents. Lang.: Eng.　　215

Text of *Within* by Bertram Brooker. Canada: Toronto, ON. 1935. Lang.: Eng.　　217

Text of *Beyond Batoche* by Rex Deverell. Canada: Regina, SK. 1985. Lang.: Eng.　　218

Edited text of a traditional Nativity play. Hungary: Kézdivásárhely. 1700-1730. Lang.: Hun.　　223

Text of plays by James Robinson Planché, with introduction on his influence. UK-England. 1818-1872. Lang.: Eng.　　226

Text of *Karimkutty* by K. N. Panikkar in English translation. India. 1983. Lang.: Eng.　　1355

Text of *Kasan ogwangdae (The Five Buffoons of Kasan)* in English translation. Korea: Kasan. 1975. Lang.: Eng.　　1356

Collection of *kabuki* texts. Japan: Tokyo. 1600-1980. Lang.: Jap.　　1380

Playtext of *Drifting Fires* by Janine Beichman, with author's afterword on use of *Nō* elements. Japan: Ibaraki. 1984-1985. Lang.: Eng.　　1383

Kyōgen: history, training, and promotion. Japan. 1060-1982. Lang.: Eng.　　1384

A collection of seven Čechov stories. Lang.: Eng.　　1457

Text of *War on the Waterfront* by Betty Roland. Australia. 1939. Lang.: Eng.　　1459

Act I, Scene 3 of *Are You Ready Comrade?* by Betty Roland. Australia. 1938. Lang.: Eng.　　1460

Playtext of Jacques de Decker's *Jeu d'intérieur (Indoor Games)* in English translation. Belgium. 1979. Lang.: Eng.　　1461

Playtext of René Kalisky's *Sur les ruines de Carthage (On the Ruins of Carthage)* in English translation. Belgium. 1980. Lang.: Eng. 1462

Playtext of Jean Sigrid's *L'ange couteau (Angel Knife)* in English translation. Belgium. 1980. Lang.: Eng.　　1463

Playtext of Paul Willems' play *Il pleut dans ma maison (It's Raining in My House)* in English translation. Belgium. 1963. Lang.: Eng.　　1464

Text of *The Miser Outwitted*, attributed to Major John Richardson, with introduction. Canada. UK-Ireland: Dublin. 1838-1848. Lang.: Eng.　　1465

Text of *The Dragon* by Bertram Brooker. Canada: Toronto, ON. 1936. Lang.: Eng.　　1466

Text of *Umiak* by Théâtre de la Marmaille. Canada: Toronto, ON. 1983. Lang.: Eng.　　1467

Playtext of *A Woman from the Sea* by Cindy Cowan. Canada. 1986. Lang.: Eng.　　1468

Text of *J'ai Vingt Ans (I Am Twenty Years Old)* by Alain Grandbois. Canada. 1934-1975. Lang.: Fre.　　1469

Gilbert Parker's *The Seats of the Mighty* as staged by Herbert Beerbohm Tree. Canada. 1897. Lang.: Eng.　　1470

A collection of satirical monologues by playwright Corey Reay. Canada. Lang.: Eng.　　1471

Texts of three political dramas, with discussion. Canada. 1833-1879. Lang.: Eng.　　1472

Text of Inkeri Kilpinen's *Totisesti totisesti (Verily Verily)* in English translation. Finland. 1982-1983. Lang.: Eng, Fin.　　1476

Catalan translation of *L'aigle à deux têtes (The Eagle With Two Heads)* by Jean Cocteau. France. 1946. Lang.: Cat.　　1478

Text of comedies and pamphlets about Molière. France. 1660-1670. Lang.: Fre.　　1481

Catalan translations of plays by Tankred Dorst, with critical introduction. Germany. 1961. Lang.: Cat.　　1482

Playtexts — cont'd

New German translation of Shakespeare's *As You Like It*. Germany, East. 1986. Lang.: Ger.   1483

English translation of *Az óriáscsecsemö (The Giant Baby)* by Tibor Déry. Hungary. 1894-1977. Lang.: Eng, Hun.   1484

Catalan translation of *Il giuoco delle parti (The Rules of the Game)* by Luigi Pirandello. Italy. 1918. Lang.: Cat.   1485

English translation of *Coppia aperta, quasì spalancata (An Open Couple—Very Open)* by Dario Fo and Franca Rame. Italy: Trieste. 1983. Lang.: Eng.   1486

Catalan translation of *Madame de Sade* by Mishima Yukio. Japan. 1960-1970. Lang.: Cat.   1487

English translation of *Pequeña historia de horror (Little Tale of Horror)*. Mexico. 1932. Lang.: Eng.   1488

Text of *Eiolf Hakatan*, Gad Kaynar's Hebrew translation of *Lille Eyolf (Little Eyolf)* by Henrik Ibsen. Norway. Israel. 1884-1985. Lang.: Heb.   1489

Text of Čechov's *Platonov* in a version by Michael Frayn. Russia. 1878. Lang.: Cat.   1492

English translation of *El desconfiado prodigioso (The Remarkable Misanthrope)* by Max Aub. Spain. 1903-1972. Lang.: Eng, Spa. 1493

Playtext of *Los Comediantes (The Players)* by Antonio Martínez Ballesteros. Spain. 1982. Lang.: Spa.   1494

Text of *Tu i l'hipócrita (You and the Hypocrite)*, by Maria Aurélia Capmany, translated into Castilian Spanish by L. Teresa Valdivieso as *Tú y el hipócrita*. Spain-Catalonia: Barcelona. 1959. Lang.: Spa.   1495

Text of *Primera història d'Esther (First Story of Esther)* by Salvador Espriu, with introduction on the author and the play. Spain-Catalonia: Barcelona. 1913-1985. Lang.: Spa, Cat.   1496

Edition of *La famosa comèdia de la gala està en son punt (The Famous Comedy of the Gala Done to a Turn)*, with analysis. Spain-Catalonia. 1625-1680. Lang.: Cat.   1497

Texts of *Avui, Romeo i Julieta (Today, Romeo and Juliet)* and *El porter i el penalty (The Goalkeeper and the Penalty)* by Josep Palau i Fabre. Spain-Catalonia. 1917-1982. Lang.: Cat.   1499

English translation of *L'ús de la matèria (The Use of Matter)* by Manuel de Pedrolo. Spain-Catalonia. 1963. Lang.: Cat, Eng.   1500

Anthology and study of writings of Josep Maria de Sagarra. Spain-Catalonia. 1917-1964. Lang.: Cat.   1501

Josep Maria de Sagarra's translations of Shakespeare with scholarly introduction. Spain-Catalonia. UK-England. 1590-1986. Lang.: Cat.   1502

Text of *David, rei (David, King)* by Jordi Teixidor. Spain-Catalonia. 1970-1985. Lang.: Cat.   1503

Third version of Friedrich Dürrenmatt's *Achterloo* with documentary materials on the rewriting process. Switzerland. Lang.: Ger.   1504

Text of two plays about refugees in Switzerland. Switzerland: Bern. 1933-1985. Lang.: Ger.   1505

Catalan translation of *Look Back in Anger* by John Osborne. UK-England. 1956. Lang.: Cat.   1506

Catalan translation of *The Homecoming* by Harold Pinter. UK-England. 1965. Lang.: Cat.   1507

Text of *Edmund Ironside*, attributed to Shakespeare. UK-England: London. 1580-1600. Lang.: Eng.   1508

Catalan translation of *Chicken Soup with Barley* by Arnold Wesker. UK-England. 1958. Lang.: Cat.   1509

English translation of Mario Benedetti's *Pedro y el capitán (Pedro and the Captain)*. Uruguay. 1979. Lang.: Eng.   1510

Catalan translation of *A View From the Bridge* by Arthur Miller. USA. 1955. Lang.: Cat.   1511

Catalan translation of *Small Craft Warnings* by Tennessee Williams. USA. 1972. Lang.: Cat.   1512

Text of *The Journey* by Timothy Findley. Canada. 1970. Lang.: Eng.   3173

English translation of *Les invités au procès (The Guests on Trial)* by Anne Hébert. Canada. 1952. Lang.: Eng.   3174

Text of radio play about a woman doctor who masqueraded as a man. Canada: Montreal, PQ. UK-Scotland: Edinburgh. South Africa, Republic of: Cape Town. 1809-1859. Lang.: Eng.   3175

Text of *The Age of Invention* by Theodora Skipitares. USA: New York, NY. 1985. Lang.: Eng.   3248

Text of *The Paper People* by Timothy Findley. Canada. 1967. Lang.: Eng.   3252

Text of *Sex Tips for Modern Girls* by Peter Eliot Weiss. Canada: Vancouver, BC. 1985. Lang.: Eng.   3578

Text of a Nativity puppet play. Hungary: Balatonberényi. 1970-1980. Lang.: Hun.   3945

Works of playwright Chikamatsu Monzaemon. Japan: Tokyo. 1653-1724. Lang.: Jap.   3995

Text of *bunraku* play in English translation. Japan. 1760-1770. Lang.: Eng.   3996

Annotated text of *The Revenge of Truth* by Isak Dinesen. Denmark. 1914. Lang.: Eng.   4002

Performance/production

Shadow puppetry as a way of passing on Balinese culture. Bali. 1976-1985. Lang.: Eng.   4017

Plays/librettos/scripts

Translations of three plays by Rabindranath Tagore, with critical commentary. India. 1861-1941. Lang.: Eng.   2662

Playwrights

SEE

Playwriting.

Plays/librettos/scripts.

Playwrights Horizons (New York, NY)

Administration

Keynote addréss of direct mail marketing seminar by Andre Bishop. USA: New York, NY. 1982. Lang.: Eng.   91

Creation and role of board of directors in nonprofit theatre. USA: New York, NY. 1986. Lang.: Eng.   104

Performance/production

Reviews of *The Perfect Party* by A. R. Gurney, Jr., staged by John Tillinger. USA: New York, NY. 1986. Lang.: Eng.   2224

Playwrights Union of Canada (Toronto, ON)

Institutions

A playwright surveys Canadian university offerings in Canadian literature, drama and playwriting. Canada. 1986. Lang.: Eng.   1564

Playwrights Workshop (Montreal, PQ)

Institutions

Limited opportunities for English-language playwrights in Montreal. Canada: Montreal, PQ. 1976-1986. Lang.: Eng.   1561

Playwrights' Workshop (Montreal, PQ)

Institutions

Interviews with theatre professionals in Quebec. Canada. 1985. Lang.: Fre.   487

Playwriting

SEE ALSO

Plays/librettos/scripts.

Administration

Evaluation of a program of financial support for Swiss playwrights. Switzerland. 1983-1986. Lang.: Fre, Ger.   65

Function of playwright's agent in negotiation and production of a script. USA: New York, NY. 1985. Lang.: Eng.   135

Revisions in the Showcase Code by Actors' Equity Association. USA: New York, NY. 1982. Lang.: Eng.   165

Basic theatrical documents

Third version of Friedrich Dürrenmatt's *Achterloo* with documentary materials on the rewriting process. Switzerland. Lang.: Ger.   1504

Institutions

Shift in emphasis at Banff Centre. Canada: Banff, AB. 1974-1986. Lang.: Eng.   1543

Failure of Dramatists' Co-op of Nova Scotia to obtain funding for a playwrights' colony. Canada: Halifax, NS. 1986. Lang.: Eng.   1545

History of the Dramatists' Co-op of Nova Scotia. Canada. 1976-1986. Lang.: Eng.   1558

A playwright surveys Canadian university offerings in Canadian literature, drama and playwriting. Canada. 1986. Lang.: Eng.   1564

Performance/production

Collaboration of playwright Jack Davis and director Andrew Ross. Australia. 1986. Lang.: Eng.   655

Rhubarb Festival is alternative to playwriting and workshopping conventions. Canada: Toronto, ON. 1986. Lang.: Eng.   672

Interview with actor, director, playwright and filmmaker Ramón Griffero. Chile: Santiago. 1953-1986. Lang.: Spa.   675

Gender roles in the work of female theatre professionals. USA. 1985. Lang.: Eng.   836

Director I.A. Grinšpun recalls famous actors, directors and playwrights. USSR. 1930-1986. Lang.: Rus.   876

Paul Claudel's Biblical scripts for Ida Rubinstein. France. 1934-1936. Lang.: Fre.   1346

Playwriting — cont'd

Interview with playwright Athol Fugard. South Africa, Republic of. USA: New Haven, CT. 1984. Lang.: Eng. 2775

Interview with playwright Carl Otto Ewers on writing for children. Sweden. 1986. Lang.: Swe. 2822

Interview with Ingegerd Monthan, author of *Drottningmötet (The Meeting of the Queens)*. Sweden. 1984-1986. Lang.: Swe. 2823

Interview with Irena Kraus about her play *Lilla livet (The Little Life)*, based on *La vida es sueño (Life Is a Dream)* by Calderón. Sweden: Malmö. 1985-1986. Lang.: Swe. 2824

Interview with actor, director, playwright Staffan Göthe. Sweden: Luleå. 1972-1986. Lang.: Swe. 2826

Current state of women's playwriting. UK-England. 1985-1986. Lang.: Eng. 2830

Interview with playwright Peter Shaffer. UK-England: London. 1958-1986. Lang.: Eng. 2838

Interview with playwright Tom Stoppard. UK-England. 1986. Lang.: Eng. 2839

Playwright Harold Pinter's use of disjunctive chronologies. UK-England. 1957-1979. Lang.: Eng. 2844

Interview with playwright Howard Barker. UK-England. 1981-1985. Lang.: Eng. 2845

Playwright Harold Pinter's use of dramatic reversals and surprise. UK-England. 1960-1977. Lang.: Eng. 2850

Articles on work of playwright Harold Pinter. UK-England. 1957-1984. Lang.: Eng. 2851

Attitudes toward sexuality in plays from French sources. UK-England. France. Lang.: Eng. 2852

Playwright Simon Gray's journal about the production of his play *The Common Pursuit*. UK-England. 1983. Lang.: Eng. 2858

Metaphor and image in plays of Harold Pinter. UK-England. 1957-1986. Lang.: Eng. 2869

Playwright Arnold Wesker discusses the writing of dialogue. UK-England. 1950-1986. Lang.: Eng. 2881

Interview with playwright Louise Page. UK-England. 1979-1986. Lang.: Eng. 2882

Artists react to *New York Times* condemnation of current playwriting. USA. 1984. Lang.: Eng. 2888

Interview with playwright Maria Irene Fornes. USA: New York, NY. 1984. Lang.: Eng. 2892

Playwright David Rabe's treatment of cliche in *Sticks and Bones*. USA. 1971. Lang.: Eng. 2902

Distinguishes between the natural flow of words and present forms of linguistic alienation. USA. Austria. 1970-1986. Lang.: Eng. 2913

Director John Lion on his work with playwright Sam Shepard. USA: San Francisco, CA, New York, NY. 1970-1984. Lang.: Eng. 2924

Interview with playwright Sam Shepard. USA. 1984. Lang.: Eng. 2925

Interview with theatre professionals on successful writing and production. USA. 1986. Lang.: Eng. 2932

A group of playwrights discuss the one-act play as a form. USA. 1986. 2937

Interview with playwright David Mamet. USA. 1984. Lang.: Eng. 2938

Interview with playwright Israel Horovitz. USA: New York, NY. 1985. Lang.: Eng. 2941

Development of playwright Sam Shepard's style. USA. 1972-1985. Lang.: Eng. 2943

Interview with leaders of playwrights' seminar. USSR: Picunde. 1986. Lang.: Rus. 2955

Problems of contemporary dramaturgy. USSR. 1986. Lang.: Rus. 2956

Excerpts from speeches by playwrights, 8th Congress of Soviet Writers. USSR: Moscow. 1986. Lang.: Rus. 2957

Replies to questionnaire by five Soviet playwrights. USSR. Bulgaria. 1986. Lang.: Rus. 2958

Report of drama commission, 8th Congress of Soviet Writers. USSR: Moscow. 1986. Lang.: Rus. 2960

Interview with Chilean playwright Jaime Miranda. Venezuela. Chile. USA. 1956-1985. Lang.: Eng. 2973

Luigi Pirandello's work as scriptwriter in collaboration with his son. Italy. 1925-1933. Lang.: Ita. 3237

Successful Broadway playwrights, lyricists, and composers discuss their hits. USA: New York, NY. 1900-1985. Lang.: Eng. 3631

Examination of the text and music of Thomas Durfey's opera *Cinthia and Endimion*. England. 1690-1701. Lang.: Eng. 3861

Reference materials

Directory of support sources for the playwright. USA. 1986. 1041

Bibliography on and about the playwright-author Ferenc Molnár. Austria: Vienna. Hungary: Budapest. USA: New York, NY. 1878-1982. Lang.: Eng. 2982

Relation to other fields

Argument for increase of financial rewards for playwrights. USA: New York, NY. 1984. Lang.: Eng. 1146

Suicide of playwright Stanisław Witkiewicz. Poland. 1931-1939. Lang.: Pol. 3050

Description of the Cutler Playwright's Festival designed for junior high school students. USA: Groton, CT. 1983-1986. Lang.: Eng. 3065

Theory/criticism

'New Wave' drama and contemporary Soviet dramaturgy. USSR. 1986. Lang.: Rus. 1237

Problems, tendencies and basic features of Soviet dramaturgy. USSR. 1986. Lang.: Rus. 1246

Playwright A. Simukov discusses his craft. USSR. 1986. Lang.: Rus. 1249

Social and political conditions of Greek society as sources for dramatic material. Greece: Athens. 450 B.C. Lang.: Eng. 3113

Character as an aesthetic category in contemporary dramaturgy. USSR. 1980-1986. Lang.: Rus. 3153

Training

Transcription of a course on how theatrical texts are written. Italy: Rome. 1981-1982. Lang.: Ita. 3159

Plenty

Relation to other fields

Reflections of political attitudes in plays by John McGrath and David Hare. UK-England. 1971-1978. Lang.: Eng. 3060

Pliseckaja, Majja

Performance/production

Interview with ballerina Majja Pliseckaja. USSR. 1985. Lang.: Rus. 1316

Plomer, William

Plays/librettos/scripts

Development of the libretto for Benjamin Britten's opera *Gloriana*. UK-England: London. 1952-1953. Lang.: Eng. 3894

Plot/subject/theme

Intertextual analysis of Eugene O'Neill's play *Long Day's Journey Into Night* and Ingmar Bergman's film, *Through a Glass Darkly*. USA. Sweden. 1957-1961. Lang.: Eng. 1425

Basic theatrical documents

Playtext of *Drifting Fires* by Janine Beichman, with author's afterword on use of *Nō* elements. Japan: Ibaraki. 1984-1985. Lang.: Eng. 1383

Texts of three political dramas, with discussion. Canada. 1833-1879. Lang.: Eng. 1472

Institutions

Factors leading to the decline of Spanish theatre. Spain. 1975-1985. Lang.: Spa. 1582

Performance/production

Problems of contemporary French theatre. France. 1980-1986. Lang.: Rus. 717

Dance-pantomime dramas based on the plots of plays by Aleksand'r Sumarokov. Russia. 1717-1777. Lang.: Rus. 1367

Performances of *nō* plays dealing with Chinese subject matter. Japan. 1300-1400. Lang.: Jap. 1405

Tom Robertson as a theatrical innovator and as a character in Arthur Wing Pinero's *Trelawny of the Wells*. England: London. 1840-1848. Lang.: Eng. 1702

Significance of 'boy-actresses' in role of Viola in Shakespeare's *Twelfth Night*. England. 1601. Lang.: Eng. 1714

Working environment of director Memè Perlini. Italy. 1978. Lang.: Eng. 1991

Playwright Antonio Martínez Ballesteros discusses the production history of his play *Los Comediantes (The Players)*. Spain: Toledo. USA: Cincinnati, OH. 1982-1985. Lang.: Spa. 2076

Aesthetics, styles, rehearsal techniques of director Richard Foreman. USA. 1974-1986. Lang.: Eng. 2263

Plot/subject/theme — cont'd

Compares contemporary Canadian theatre with German and Russian theatre of the early 20th century. Canada. Russia: Moscow. Germany. 1900-1986. Lang.: Eng. 2412

Analysis of *RA* by R. Murray Schafer, performed by Comus Music Theatre. Canada: Toronto, ON. 1983. Lang.: Eng. 2416

Career of expressionist playwright Bertram Brooker. Canada: Toronto, ON. 1888-1949. Lang.: Eng. 2418

Analysis of *As Is* by William Hoffman and *The Dolly* by Robert Locke. Canada: Toronto, ON. 1985. Lang.: Eng. 2419

Work of playwright R.A. Shiomi, including production history of *Yellow Fever*. Canada: Toronto, ON. USA: New York, NY. USA: San Francisco, CA. 1970-1986. Lang.: Eng. 2422

The plays of Antonine Maillet and the revival of Acadian theatre. Canada. 1971-1979. Lang.: Eng. 2423

Criticizes the plays in the collection *Five From the Fringe*. Canada: Edmonton, AB. 1986. Lang.: Eng. 2425

Interviews with actress Pilar Romero and director Roberto Blanco at the Festival de Théâtre des Amériques. Canada: Montreal, PQ. 1985. Lang.: Eng. 2426

Book review of *125 Ans de Theatre au Seminaire de Trois-Rivières*. Canada: Trois-Rivières, PQ. 1985. Lang.: Fre. 2427

Discusses feminist theatre with themes concerning the female body. Canada: Quebec, PQ. 1969-1985. Lang.: Eng. 2428

Discusses Michel Garneau's *joual* translation of *Macbeth*. Canada: Montreal, PQ. 1978. Lang.: Eng. 2429

William Rufus Blake's *Fitzallan* as the first play written and produced in Canada. Canada: Halifax, NS. 1833. Lang.: Eng. 2430

The immigrant in plays by Herman Voaden and Robertson Davies. Canada. 1934-1950. Lang.: Eng. 2431

Examines *Ne blâmez jamais les Bédouins (Don't Blame It on the Bedouins)* as a post-modernist play. Canada. 1980. Lang.: Fre. 2432

French-Canadian nationalism in *Le Drapeau de Carillon (The Flag of Carillon)*. Canada: Montreal, PQ. 1759-1901. Lang.: Eng. 2433

Compares Michel Tremblay's *Albertine en cing temps (Albertine in Five Times)* to Marcel Proust's *A la recherche du temps perdu (Remembrance of Things Past)*. Canada. 1984. 2436

Acadian characters of playwright Antonine Maillet contrasted with Longfellow's romantic myth. Canada. 1968-1975. Lang.: Eng. 2439

Review of five published plays by Margaret Hollingsworth. Canada. Lang.: Eng. 2440

Chilean theatre in exile, Teatro del Angel. Chile. Costa Rica. 1955-1984. Lang.: Eng. 2441

Marginal characters in plays of Jorge Díaz, Egon Wolff and Luis Alberto Heiremans. Chile. 1960-1971. Lang.: Eng. 2442

Life and work of playwright Tian Han. China. 1898-1968. Lang.: Eng. 2443

Use of history in Chinese traditional drama. China. 960-1983. Lang.: Chi. 2444

Ritual and archetypal communication in *La noche de los asesinos (The Night of the Assassins)* by José Triana. Cuba. Brazil. 1973-1974. Lang.: Eng. 2450

The history of Cuban exile theatre. Cuba. USA: New York, NY. 1959-1986. Lang.: Spa. 2451

Cuban theatre in transition exemplified in the plays of Virgilio Piñera and Abelardo Estorino. Cuba. 1958-1964. Lang.: Eng. 2452

Interview with playwright, director and actor Pavel Kohout. Czechoslovakia: Prague. Austria: Vienna. 1928-1986. Lang.: Swe. 2454

Historical background of *Sisters of Eve* by Tricia Burden. Eire. 1984-1986. Lang.: Eng. 2455

Limited perception in *The Plough and the Stars* by Sean O'Casey. Eire. 1926-1986. Lang.: Eng. 2456

Pessimism of Sean O'Casey's *Juno and the Paycock*. Eire. 1924. Lang.: Eng. 2457

Bullfighting and revenge in *The Spanish Tragedy* by Thomas Kyd. England. 1500-1600. Lang.: Eng. 2458

Influence of middle class and of domestic comedy on the works of William Shakespeare. England. 1564-1616. Lang.: Eng. 2459

Language in *The Second Maiden's Tragedy*. England: London. 1611. Lang.: Eng. 2460

Ben Jonson's use of romance in *Volpone*. England. 1575-1600. Lang.: Eng. 2461

Shakespeare's influence on Beaumont and Fletcher's *Philaster*. England. 1609. Lang.: Eng. 2463

Contrast between Shakespeare's England and the Vienna of *Measure for Measure*. England. 1604-1605. Lang.: Eng. 2465

Religion and popular entertainment in *The Virgin Martyr* by Philip Massinger and Thomas Dekker. England: London. 1620-1625. Lang.: Eng. 2468

Influence of Night Visit folk notif on Shakespeare's *Romeo and Juliet*. England: London. 1594-1597. Lang.: Eng. 2470

Heterosexual and homosexual desires in Shakespeare's *Troilus and Cressida*. England. 1602. Lang.: Eng. 2471

Female characterization in Nicholas Rowe's plays. England. 1629-1720. Lang.: Eng. 2475

Post-structuralist insights on sexuality and transgression in transvestite roles in Jacobean plays. England: London. 1600-1625. Lang.: Eng. 2476

Liberated female characters in the plays of George Lillo. England. 1730-1759. Lang.: Eng. 2477

Comparison of Shakespeare's *Antony and Cleopatra* and Ibsen's *Rosmersholm*. England. Norway. 1607-1885. Lang.: Eng. 2479

Similarities between *King Lear* by Shakespeare and *The Trimphs of Reunited Britannia* by Munday. England. 1605-1606. Lang.: Eng. 2480

Iconography of throne scene in Shakespeare's *Richard III*. England. 1591-1592. Lang.: Eng. 2481

Image of poverty in Elizabethan and Stuart plays. England. 1558-1642. Lang.: Eng. 2482

Sounds in Ben Jonson's *Epicoene*. England: London. 1609-1668. Lang.: Eng. 2483

Translation of two works by Northrop Frye on Shakespeare. England. 1564-1616. Lang.: Ita. 2484

Interview with playwright Kathleen Betsko. England: Coventry. USA. 1960-1986. Lang.: Eng. 2487

Shakespeare's *Henry VI* and Hall's *Chronicles*. England. 1542-1592. Lang.: Eng. 2488

Theme of redemption in Shakespeare's *The Winter's Tale*. England. 1611. Lang.: Eng. 2490

Dramatic spectacles relating to Botany Bay. England: London. Australia. 1787-1791. Lang.: Eng. 2492

Function of humor and violence in the *Play of the Sacrament (Croxton)*. England. 1400-1499. Lang.: Eng. 2493

Legalistic aspect of *Commody of the Moste Vertuous and Godlye Susana* by Thomas Garter. England: London. 1563. Lang.: Eng. 2494

Tradition and individualism in Renaissance drama. England: London. 1575-1600. Lang.: Eng. 2496

Moral issues in *A Woman Killed with Kindness* by Thomas Heywood. England. 1560. Lang.: Eng. 2498

Dramatic dynamics of Chester cycle play, *The Fall of Lucifer*. England. 1400-1550. Lang.: Eng. 2499

Machiavellian ideas in *The Devil's Charter* by Barnaby Barnes. England. 1584-1607. Lang.: Eng. 2500

Analysis of *The Winter's Tale* by Shakespeare. England: London. 1604. Lang.: Eng. 2502

Interpretations of Shakespeare's *A Midsummer Night's Dream* based on Bottom's transformation. England. 1595-1986. Lang.: Eng. 2503

Gender roles in *Epicoene* by Ben Jonson. England: London. 1609-1909. Lang.: Eng. 2505

Marxist analysis of colonialism in Shakespeare's *Othello*. England. South Africa, Republic of. 1597-1637. Lang.: Eng. 2507

Use of group aggression in Ben Jonson's comedies. England. 1575-1600. Lang.: Eng. 2508

Prophetic riddles in Shakespeare's *The Merchant of Venice*. England. 1598. Lang.: Eng. 2509

Use of anachronism in William Shakespeare's history plays. England: London. 1590-1601. Lang.: Eng. 2511

Reflections of Ben Jonson's personal life in his poems and plays. England: London. 1596-1604. Lang.: Eng. 2515

Herpetological imagery in Jonson's *Catiline*. England. 1611. Lang.: Eng. 2517

Comparison of Ben Jonson's *Catiline* with its Latin prose source by Sallust. England. Italy. 43 B.C.-1611 A.D. Lang.: Eng. 2518

Plot/subject/theme — cont'd

Theme of Puritanism in *The Alchemist* by Ben Jonson. England. 1610. Lang.: Eng. 2519

Gift exchange and mercantilism in *The Merchant of Venice* by Shakespeare. England: London. 1594-1597. Lang.: Eng. 2520

Political ideas expressed in Elizabethan drama, particularly the work of Christopher Marlowe. England: London. Lang.: Eng. 2521

Analysis of *Magnificence* by Howard Brenton. England. 1970-1980. Lang.: Eng. 2524

Analysis of the final scene of *The Broken Heart* by John Ford. England. 1629. Lang.: Eng. 2526

Senecan ideas in Shakespeare's *Timon of Athens*. England: London. 1601-1608. Lang.: Eng. 2533

Revision of dramaturgy and stagecraft in Restoration adaptations of Shakespeare. England: London. 1660-1690. Lang.: Eng. 2535

Modern criticism of Shakespeare's crowd scenes. England. 1590-1986. Lang.: Eng. 2536

Relation of 'New Drama'—from Büchner to Beckett—to Afrikaans drama. Europe. South Africa, Republic of. 1800-1985. Lang.: Afr. 2539

Treatment of history in drama. Europe. North America. Indonesia. 375 B.C.-1983 A.D. Lang.: Eng. 2541

Stoicism and modern elements in Senecan drama. Europe. 65-1986. Lang.: Eng. 2542

Superficial and reductive use of classical myth in modern French theatre. France. 1935-1944. Lang.: Eng. 2550

Modern thought in works of Jean Racine. France. 1664-1691. Lang.: Fre. 2553

Marguerite Yourcenar's treatment of Electra story compared to other versions. France. 1944-1954. Lang.: Fre. 2554

Various implications of 'waiting' in Samuel Beckett's *Waiting for Godot*. France. 1953. Lang.: Eng. 2555

Waiting for Godot as an assessment of the quality of life of the couple. France. UK-Ireland. 1931-1958. Lang.: Eng. 2557

Theme of fragmentation in *Lorenzaccio* by Alfred de Musset. France. 1834. Lang.: Eng. 2558

Great dramatic works considered in light of modern theatre and social reponsibility. France. Italy. Germany, West. 1700-1964. Lang.: Fre. 2560

Love in the plays and operas of Jean-Jacques Rousseau. France. Switzerland. 1712-1778. Lang.: Fre. 2563

Comparative analysis of the works of Maurice Maeterlinck and William Shakespeare. France. 1590-1911. Lang.: Eng. 2566

Dialectical method in the plays of Molière. France. 1666. Lang.: Eng. 2567

Analysis of *L'Histoire terrible mais inachevé de Norodom Sihanouk, roi du Cambodge (The Terrible but Unfinished History of Norodom Sihanouk, King of Cambodia)* by Hélène Cixous. France: Paris. 1985. Lang.: Eng. 2570

Biography of Molière as seen through his plays. France. 1622-1673. Lang.: Fre. 2573

Political aspects of George Sand's *Père va-tout-seul (Old Man Go-It-Alone)*. France. 1830-1844. Lang.: Eng. 2574

Structuralist analysis of works of Albert Camus, Antonin Artaud and Gaston Bachelard. France. Lang.: Fre. 2575

Essentialism and avant-garde in the plays of Eugène Ionesco. France. 1950-1980. Lang.: Fre. 2576

Repetition and negativism in plays of Jean Anouilh and Eugene O'Neill. France. USA. 1922-1960. Lang.: Eng. 2578

Mythology in the works of Hélène Cixous, Andrée Chedid, Monique Wittig and Marguerite Yourcenar. France. Lang.: Eng. 2580

Don Juan legend in literature and film. France. 1630-1980. Lang.: Eng. 2581

Evolution of concept of the State in the tragedies of Pierre Corneille. France. 1636-1674. Lang.: Fre. 2582

Introduction to *Jesús batejat per Sant Joan Baptista (Jesus Christ Baptized by St. John the Baptist)*. France. 1753-1832. Lang.: Cat. 2585

Patriarchy in *Le Voyageur sans bagage (Traveler Without Luggage)* by Jean Anouilh. France. 1937. Lang.: Eng. 2586

The role of the double in Georg Kaiser's *Zweimal Amphitryon (Amphitryon x 2)* and other works. Germany. 1943. Lang.: Eng. 2589

Contrasting treatment of history in *Carolus Stuardus* by Andreas Gryphius and *Maria Stuart* by Friedrich von Schiller. Germany. England. 1651-1800. Lang.: Eng. 2590

Introduction to plays by Tankred Dorst. Germany. 1925-1982. Lang.: Cat. 2591

The idea of grace in the life and work of Heinrich von Kleist. Germany. 1777-1811. Lang.: Eng. 2593

Fox symbolism in plays of Bertolt Brecht, Max Frisch and Gerhart Hauptmann. Germany. Switzerland. 1700-1976. Lang.: Ger. 2598

Distortion of historical fact in Brecht's *Leben des Galilei (The Life of Galileo)*. Germany. 1938-1955. Lang.: Eng. 2600

The tragic in plays of Heinrich von Kleist. Germany. 1777-1811. Lang.: Rus. 2601

Comparative analysis of *Elektra* by Hugo von Hofmannsthal and its sources. Germany. 1909. Lang.: Eng. 2603

Critical problems in *Henno* by Johannes Reuchlin. Germany: Heidelberg. 1497-1522. Lang.: Eng. 2605

Analysis of *Leben des Galilei (The Life of Galileo)* by Bertolt Brecht. Germany. 1938. Lang.: Rus. 2606

Analysis of *Die Zwillinge (The Twins)* by Friedrich Maximilian Klinger and the dilemma of the *Sturm und Drang* movement. Germany. 1775. Lang.: Ger. 2609

History in Goethe's *Götz von Berlichingen*. Germany. 1773. Lang.: Eng. 2610

Essays on Lessing and Lessing criticism. Germany. 1748-1984. Lang.: Ger. 2611

Brecht's patriarchal view of women as seen in the character of Jenny in *Die Dreigroschenoper (The Three Penny Opera)*. Germany, East. 2615

Premiere of Ernst Toller's play *Hoppla, wir leben! (Upsy Daisy, We Are Alive)*. Germany, East. 1945-1984. Lang.: Eng. 2617

Demystification of the feminine myth in Brecht's plays. Germany, East. 1984. 2618

Chinese influences on Bertolt Brecht. Germany, East: Berlin, East. China. 1935-1956. Lang.: Eng. 2619

Brecht's concept of *Naivität* in *Die Tage der Kommune (The Days of the Commune)*. Germany, East. 1948-1956. 2621

Comparison of Heiner Müller's *Der Auftrag (The Mission)* and Bertolt Brecht's *Die Massnahme (The Measures Taken)*. Germany, East. 1930-1985. Lang.: Eng. 2622

Work of playwright Stefan Schütz. Germany, West. 1944-1986. Lang.: Eng. 2625

Brecht's interpretational legacy is best understood on West German stages. Germany, West. 1956-1986. 2627

Interview with playwright Stefan Schütz. Germany, West. 1970-1986. Lang.: Eng. 2628

Cosmic themes in the works of Aeschylus. Greece. 472-458 B.C. Lang.: Fre. 2629

Program notes from Heinz-Uwe Haus's production of *Arturo Ui*. Greece. 1985. 2631

Topicality of Aeschylus' *Oresteia*. Greece. 458 B.C. Lang.: Fre. 2632

Moral and political crises reflected in the plays of Euripides. Greece: Athens. 438-408 B.C. Lang.: Fre. 2634

Analysis of *La Tragédie du roi Christophe (The Tragedy of King Christopher)* by Aimé Césaire. Haiti. Africa. Martinique. 1939. Lang.: Fre. 2637

The influence of Brecht on Haiti's exiled playwright Frank Fouché and the group Kovidor. Haiti. 1970-1979. 2638

Problems of modern dramatury exemplified in current Hungarian theatre. Hungary. Lang.: Hun. 2640

Review of study of experimental plays and playwrights. Hungary. 1967-1983. Lang.: Hun. 2641

Review of a book on modern dramaturgy by playwright Zsuzsa Radnóti. Hungary. 1967-1983. Lang.: Hun. 2642

Text of a lecture on Shakespeare's *King Lear* by Clifford Davidson. Hungary: Budapest. Lang.: Hun. 2643

Philosophy and morality of Imre Madách's classical dramatic poem *Az ember tragédiája (The Tragedy of a Man)*. Hungary. 1883-1983. Lang.: Hun. 2644

Comparison of plays and short stories by Károly Szakonyi. Hungary. 1963-1982. Lang.: Hun. 2646

Plot/subject/theme — cont'd

Notes from the journal of playwright Miklós Hubay. Hungary. 1984-1985. Lang.: Hun. 2648

Young playwright's conference. Hungary: Zalaegerszeg. 1985. Lang.: Hun. 2650

The grotesque in the plays of István Örkény. Hungary. 1947-1979. Lang.: Ger. 2651

Analysis of István Örkény's play, *Pisti a vérzivatarban (Steve in the Bloodbath)*. Hungary. Lang.: Hun. 2652

Notes on the Open Forum in Zalaegerszeg. Hungary: Zalaegerszeg. 1985. Lang.: Hun. 2653

Study of Tibor Gyurkovics' eight plays. Hungary. 1976-1985. Lang.: Hun. 2654

Study of contemporary Hungarian plays. Hungary. 1980. Lang.: Hun. 2658

Notes on György Spiró's play about actor, director, manager and playwright Wojciech Bogusławski. Hungary. 1983. Lang.: Hun. 2659

Works of playwright István Sárospataky. Hungary. 1974-1985. Lang.: Hun. 2660

Dramatizations of the life of politician Endre Bajcsy-Zsilinszky. Hungary. 1960-1980. Lang.: Hun. 2661

Translations of three plays by Rabindranath Tagore, with critical commentary. India. 1861-1941. Lang.: Eng. 2662

Possible source of cock fight in Henry Medwall's *Fulgens and Lucres*. Ireland. 1602. Lang.: Eng. 2664

Biography of playwright Teresa Deevy. Ireland. 1894-1963. Lang.: Eng. 2665

The place of *The Island of the Mighty* in the John Arden canon. Ireland. UK. 1950-1972. Lang.: Eng. 2666

Evaluation of *Il giuoco delle parti (The Rules of the Game)* in the context of Pirandello's oeuvre. Italy. 1867-1936. Lang.: Cat. 2670

Realism and fantasy in *Questi fantasmi! (These Phantoms!)* by Eduardo De Filippo. Italy. 1946. Lang.: Ita. 2676

Poetics of the fantastic in works of Carlo Gozzi. Italy. 1720-1806. Lang.: Ita. 2679

Actuality and modernity of the plays of Luigi Pirandello. Italy. 1867-1936. Lang.: Fre. 2680

Personal and social relationships in Goldoni's comedies. Italy. 1743-1760. Lang.: Ita. 2681

Theatrical renderings of the experiences of French travelers in Italy and vice-versa. Italy. France. 1700-1800. Lang.: Ita. 2686

Deconstructionist analysis of *Riccardo III* by Carmelo Bene. Italy. France. Lang.: Eng. 2690

Antinaturalism in the plays of Tommaso Landolfi. Italy. 1908-1979. Lang.: Ita. 2691

Theme of death-wish in plays of Pier Maria Rosso di San Secondo. Italy. 1918-1919. Lang.: Ita. 2705

Study of Pirandello's preface to *Sei personaggi in cerca d'autore (Six Characters in Search of an Author)*. Italy. 1923-1986. Lang.: Fre. 2708

Pirandello's interest in the problems of women evidenced in his plays and novels. Italy. 1867-1936. Lang.: Fre. 2714

Symbolism in Derek Walcott's *Dream on Monkey Mountain*. Jamaica. 1967. Lang.: Eng. 2718

Lives and works of major contemporary playwrights in Japan. Japan: Tokyo. 1900-1986. Lang.: Jap. 2719

Themes and characterization in *Madame de Sade* by Mishima Yukio. Japan. 1960-1970. Lang.: Cat. 2720

Use of language in *El Gesticulador (The Gesticulator)* by Rodolfo Usigli. Mexico. 1970-1980. Lang.: Spa. 2723

Shakespeare's influence on playwright Wole Soyinka. Nigeria. UK-England: Leeds. 1957-1981. Lang.: Eng. 2725

Self-transcendence through grace embodied in Henrik Ibsen's female characters. Norway. 1849-1899. Lang.: Eng. 2726

Influence and development of the plays of Julio Ortega. Peru. 1970-1984. Lang.: Eng. 2730

Levels of time in *La señorita de Tacna (The Lady from Tacna)* by Mario Vargas Llosa. Peru. Lang.: Spa. 2731

Description of international symposium discussing the work of Stanisław Ignacy Witkiewicz. Poland. 1985. Lang.: Eng, Fre. 2733

Analysis of Tomasz Łubieński's plays. Poland. 1986. Lang.: Pol. 2734

Mrożek's *Policja (The Police)* as read by the censor. Poland. 1958. Lang.: Fre. 2735

Interview with director of Teatr Współczésny about children's drama competition. Poland: Wrocław. 1986. Lang.: Hun. 2736

Death in the plays of Tadeusz Różewicz. Poland. 1986. Lang.: Pol. 2737

Analysis of *Grupa Laokoona (The Laocoön Group)* by Tadeusz Różewicz and *Tsaplia (The Heron)* by Vasilij Aksënov. Poland. USSR. 1961-1979. Lang.: Eng. 2738

Analysis of contemporary Polish plays dealing with solitude. Poland. 1986. Lang.: Pol. 2739

Jerzy Grotowski and his adaptation of *Doctor Faustus*. Poland. 1964. Lang.: Eng. 2740

Material derived from Stanisław Wyspiański's *Wesele (The Wedding)* by various Polish playwrights. Poland. 1901-1984. Lang.: Fre. 2741

School use of Juliusz Słowacki's dramas in Polish high schools as a reflection of the political situation. Poland. 1945-1984. Lang.: Fre. 2743

Influence of politics and personal history on Tadeusz Kantor and his Cricot 2 theatre company. Poland: Cracow. 1944-1986. Lang.: Eng. 2744

World War II and post-war life as major subjects of Polish dramaturgy. Poland. 1945-1955. Lang.: Pol. 2745

Overview of symposium on playwright Stanisław Ignacy Witkiewicz. Poland. 1985. Lang.: Eng, Fre. 2747

Philosophical aspects and structure of plays by Bogusław Schaeffer. Poland. 1929-1986. Lang.: Pol. 2749

Tadeusz Kantor comments on his play *Niech szezna artyszi (Let the Artists Die)*. Poland. 1985. Lang.: Eng, Fre. 2751

Loss of identity in plays by István Örkény's and Sławomir Mrożek. Poland. Hungary. 1955-1980. Lang.: Hun. 2752

Overview of major productions of playwright Jerzy Szaniawski. Poland. 1886-1970. Lang.: Eng, Fre. 2753

Production history of plays by Stanisław Ignacy Witkiewicz. Poland. 1921-1985. Lang.: Eng, Fre. 2754

Literary and theatrical history of Eastern Europe. Poland. Hungary. Czechoslovakia. 1800-1915. Lang.: Hun. 2755

Different interpretations of Zygmunt Krasiński's *Ne-boska komedia (Undivine Comedy)*. Poland. 1835-1984. Lang.: Fre. 2756

Analysis of animal-like characters in Witkiewicz's dramas. Poland. 1920-1935. Lang.: Pol. 2757

Analysis of the theatrical ideas of Tadeusz Kantor. Poland: Cracow. 1973-1983. Lang.: Pol. 2759

Development of recent Puerto Rican drama. Puerto Rico. 1960-1980. Lang.: Spa. 2760

Monodramas of playwright István Kocsis. Romania. Hungary. 1976-1984. Lang.: Hun. 2761

Study of author and playwright András Sütő. Romania. Hungary. 1950-1984. Lang.: Hun. 2762

Review of a study of playwright and novelist András Sütő. Romania. 1950-1984. Lang.: Hun. 2763

Dramaturgy of Turgenjev. Russia. 1842-1852. Lang.: Rus. 2768

Analysis of the major plays of Maksim Gorkij. Russia. 1868-1936. Lang.: Chi. 2769

Analysis of the plays of Ivan Turgenjev. Russia. 1818-1883. Lang.: Rus. 2770

The tragedy in the plays of Aleksand'r Nikolajèvič Ostrovskij. Russia. 1823-1886. Lang.: Rus. 2771

Use of Greek mythological themes in Athol Fugard's plays. South Africa, Republic of. 1959-1986. Lang.: Afr. 2773

Individual and society in *Die Nag van Legio (The Night of Legio)* by P.G. du Plessis and *Der Besuch der alten Dame (The Visit)* by Friedrich Dürrenmatt. South Africa, Republic of. Switzerland. 1955-1970. Lang.: Afr. 2774

Interview with playwright Athol Fugard. South Africa, Republic of. USA: New Haven, CT. 1984. Lang.: Eng. 2775

Influence of working class on form and content of theatre of resistance. South Africa, Republic of: Soweto. 1976-1986. Lang.: Eng. 2777

A comprehensive critical study of the life and works of Athol Fugard. South Africa, Republic of. 1932-1983. Lang.: Eng. 2778

Plot/subject/theme — cont'd

The role of the artist in *The Road to Mecca* by Athol Fugard. South Africa, Republic of. 1961-1984. Lang.: Eng. 2779

Description of plays by Eduardo Quiles including *La navaja (The Razor)* a tragicomedy for two actors and puppets. Spain. 1940-1985. Lang.: Spa. 2780

Self-reflexivity in Antonio Buero Vallejo's play *El Sueño de la razón (The Sleep of Reason)* and Victor Erice's film *El Espíritu de la colmena (The Spirit of the Beehive)*. Spain. 1970-1973. Lang.: Eng. 2781

Conservative and reactionary nature of the Spanish *Comedia*. Spain. 1600-1700. Lang.: Eng. 2782

Current thematic trends in the plays of Antonio Gala. Spain. 1963-1985. Lang.: Spa. 2783

Salvador Espriu's tragic vision in *Ronda de Mort a Sinera (Death Round at Sinera)*. Spain. 1965. Lang.: Eng. 2784

Juan del Enzina's defence of pastoral vs. courtly genre. Spain. 1469-1529. Lang.: Spa. 2785

Examples of playwrights whose work was poorly received by theatrical audiences in Madrid. Spain: Madrid. 1609-1950. Lang.: Spa. 2786

Prophecy in Calderón's *Eco y Narciso (Echo and Narcissus)*. Spain. 1600-1680. Lang.: Eng. 2787

Thematic analysis of *La vida es sueño (Life Is a Dream)* by Pedro Calderón de la Barca. Spain. 1635-1681. Lang.: Eng. 2788

Calderón's *El gran duque de Gandía (The Grand Duke of Gandía)* and its Mexican source. Spain. Mexico. 1600-1680. Lang.: Eng. 2789

Artaud's concept of theatre of cruelty in Francisco Nieva's *Tórtolas, crepúscula y ...telón (Turtledoves, Twilight and ...Curtain)*. Spain. 1953. Lang.: Spa. 2790

Poor reception of *Diálogo secreto (Secret Dialogue)* by Antonio Buero Vallejo in Spain. Spain: Madrid. 1984. Lang.: Eng. 2791

Thematic and stylistic comparison of three plays influenced by the *Odyssey*. Spain. 1952-1983. Lang.: Eng. 2792

Reasons for the lack of new Spanish drama and the few recent significant realistic and experimental plays. Spain. 1972-1985. Lang.: Spa. 2793

Reconstructs from historical sources the rebellion depicted in *Fuente Ovejuna (The Sheep Well)* by Lope de Vega as ritual behavior. Spain. 1476. Lang.: Eng. 2794

Discusses Christian outlook in plays by Alejandro Casona. Spain. 1940-1980. Lang.: Eng. 2795

The institution of slavery as presented in *Entremés de los negros (Play of the Blacks)*. Spain. 1600-1699. Lang.: Eng. 2796

Radical subjectivism in three plays by Antonio Buero Vallejo: *La Fundación (The Foundation)*, *La Detonación (The Detonation)* and *Jueces en la noche (Judges at Night)*. Spain. 1974-1979. Lang.: Eng. 2797

Refutes critical position that Antonio Buero Vallejo's *Diálogo secreto (Secret Dialogue)* is unbelievable. Spain: Madrid. 1984. Lang.: Eng. 2799

Thematic analysis of *La Jaula (The Cage)* by José Fernando Dicenta. Spain. 1971-1984. Lang.: Eng. 2800

Politics and aesthetics in three plays of Fernando Arrabal. Spain. France. Lang.: Fre. 2801

Playwright Alfonso Sastre discusses three of his recent plays. Spain. 1983-1986. Lang.: Spa. 2802

Reflections and influence of playwrights Rodolfo Usigli of Mexico and Antonio Buero Vallejo of Spain on theatre in their native countries. Spain. Mexico. Lang.: Spa. 2803

Mutual influences between *commedia dell'arte* and Spanish literature. Spain. Italy. 1330-1623. Lang.: Eng. 2805

Translator discusses her Spanish version of Maria Aurelia Capmany's Catalan play, *Tu i l'hipócrita (You and the Hypocrite)*. Spain. 1959-1976. Lang.: Spa. 2806

Alfonso Sastre's theory of complex tragedy in *La Celestina (The Nun)*. Spain. 1978. Lang.: Spa. 2807

Description of a staged reading of *The Cock's Short Flight* by Jaime Salom. Spain. USA: New York, NY. 1980-1985. Lang.: Eng. 2808

Analysis of *La Santa Espina (The Holy Thorn)* by Àngel Guimerà. Spain-Catalonia. 1897-1907. Lang.: Cat. 2815

Life and work of Caterina Albert, known as Víctor Català. Spain-Catalonia. 1869-1966. Lang.: Cat. 2816

Roles of women in middle-class Catalonian society as reflected in the plays of Carme Montoriol and Maria Aurélia Capmany. Spain-Catalonia. 1700-1960. Lang.: Spa. 2819

Memoir concerning playwright Joan Oliver. Spain-Catalonia. 1920-1986. Lang.: Cat. 2820

The presentation of atheism in August Strindberg's *The Father*. Sweden. 1887. Lang.: Eng. 2821

Interview with playwright Carl Otto Ewers on writing for children. Sweden. 1986. Lang.: Swe. 2822

Interview with Ingegerd Monthan, author of *Drottningmötet (The Meeting of the Queens)*. Sweden. 1984-1986. Lang.: Swe. 2823

Innerst inne (At Heart) dramatizes political and economic dilemma. Sweden: Karlskoga. 1981-1986. Lang.: Swe. 2825

Interview with actor, director, playwright Staffan Göthe. Sweden: Luleå. 1972-1986. Lang.: Swe. 2826

Biblical and Swedenborgian influences on the development of August Strindberg's chamber play *Påsk (Easter)*. Sweden. 1900. Lang.: Eng. 2827

Analysis of plays by Max Frisch, and influences of Thornton Wilder. Switzerland. 1939-1983. Lang.: Eng. 2829

Current state of women's playwriting. UK-England. 1985-1986. Lang.: Eng. 2830

Playwright Marius Brill discusses his prize winning play *Frikzhan*. UK-England: London. 1986. Lang.: Eng. 2831

Interview with playwright Rosemary Wilton, author of *Bouncing*. UK-England: London. 1986. Lang.: Eng. 2832

Beckettian elements in Shakespeare as seen by playwright Edward Bond. UK-England. 1971-1973. Lang.: Eng. 2833

Theme of renewal in Harold Pinter's *Betrayal*. UK-England. 1978. 2835

Theme of family in plays of Harold Pinter. UK-England. 1957-1981. Lang.: Eng. 2836

Thematic analysis of *Candida* by George Bernard Shaw focusing on the spiritual development of Marchbanks. UK-England: London. 1894. Lang.: Eng. 2837

Interview with playwright Tom Stoppard. UK-England. 1986. Lang.: Eng. 2839

Overview of plays with homosexual themes. UK-England: London. 1970-1986. Lang.: Eng. 2841

Links between Shakespeare's *Macbeth* and Tom Stoppard's *Dogg's Hamlet, Cahoot's Macbeth*. UK-England. 1979-1986. Lang.: Eng. 2843

Playwright Harold Pinter's use of disjunctive chronologies. UK-England. 1957-1979. Lang.: Eng. 2844

Influence of playwright Harold Pinter. UK-England. 1957-1982. Lang.: Eng. 2846

Treatment of the Frankenstein myth in three gothic melodramas. UK-England. France. 1823-1826. Lang.: Eng. 2847

Jungian analysis of the plays of Peter Nichols. UK-England. 1967-1984. Lang.: Eng. 2848

Relation of Harold Pinter's plays to modern developments in science and philosophy. UK-England. 1932-1986. Lang.: Eng. 2849

Playwright Harold Pinter's use of dramatic reversals and surprise. UK-England. 1960-1977. Lang.: Eng. 2850

Articles on work of playwright Harold Pinter. UK-England. 1957-1984. Lang.: Eng. 2851

Attitudes toward sexuality in plays from French sources. UK-England. France. Lang.: Eng. 2852

Evaluation of *The War Plays* by Edward Bond. UK-England: London. 1986. Lang.: Eng. 2853

Different versions of *The Dwarfs* by Harold Pinter. UK-England. 1960-1976. Lang.: Eng. 2855

Analysis of *The Birthday Party* by Harold Pinter. UK-England. 1958. Lang.: Eng. 2856

Musical use of language conveys meaning in John Whiting's *Saint's Day*. UK-England. 1951. Lang.: Eng. 2857

History of Harold Pinter's work and critical reception. UK-England. 1975-1983. Lang.: Eng. 2860

Reader-response interpretation of *The Homecoming* by Harold Pinter. UK-England. 1952-1965. Lang.: Eng. 2861

Reference of George Bernard Shaw to contemporary society. UK-England. 1856-1950. Lang.: Eng. 2862

Plot/subject/theme — cont'd

Analysis of Arnold Wesker's *Chicken Soup with Barley*. UK-England: London. 1932-1986. Lang.: Cat.   2864

Analysis of the plot, characters and structure of *The Homecoming* by Harold Pinter. UK-England: London. 1930-1985. Lang.: Cat.   2865

Interview with playwright Dusty Hughes about his play, *The Futurists*. UK-England. 1980. Lang.: Eng.   2867

World War II as a theme in post-war British drama. UK-England. 1945-1983. Lang.: Eng.   2868

Metaphor and image in plays of Harold Pinter. UK-England. 1957-1986. Lang.: Eng.   2869

Thematic analysis of Harold Pinter's *The Lover*. UK-England. 1963. Lang.: Eng.   2870

A comparison between Oscar Wilde's *The Importance of Being Earnest* and Tom Stoppard's *Travesties*. UK-England. 1895-1974. Lang.: Eng.   2872

Brecht's ideas about the history play as justification for Edward Bond's *Bingo*. UK-England. 1974. Lang.: Eng.   2876

Role of women in society in Caryl Churchill's plays. UK-England. 1986. Lang.: Eng.   2877

Interview with playwright Stephen MacDonald. UK-England: London. 1917-1986. Lang.: Eng.   2879

Comparison of the radio and staged versions of Harold Pinter's *A Slight Ache*. UK-England. 1959-1961. Lang.: Eng.   2880

Interview with playwright Louise Page. UK-England. 1979-1986. Lang.: Eng.   2882

Utopia in early plays by Arnold Wesker. UK-England. 1958-1970. Lang.: Eng.   2884

Interview with playwright John Clifford. UK-Scotland: Edinburgh. 1960-1986. Lang.: Eng.   2885

A description of Ena Lamont Stewart's trilogy *Will you Still Need Me*. UK-Scotland. 1940-1985. Lang.: Eng.   2886

Analysis of Pedro Corradi's *Retrato de señora con espejo—Vida y pasión de Margarita Xirgu (Portrait of a Lady with Mirror—The Life and Passion of Margarita Xirgu)*. Uruguay. Spain: Madrid. 1985. Lang.: Spa.   2887

Artists react to *New York Times* condemnation of current playwriting. USA. 1984. Lang.: Eng.   2888

Correlation between short stories and plays by Carson McCullers. USA. 1917-1967. Lang.: Rus.   2889

Richard Foreman, founder of Ontological-Hysteric Theater Company. USA. 1960-1986. Lang.: Swe.   2890

Interview with playwright Maria Irene Fornes. USA: New York, NY. 1984. Lang.: Eng.   2892

Imagery of gender compared in works by Susan Glaspell and Eugene O'Neill. USA: New York, NY, Provincetown, MA. 1916-1922. Lang.: Eng.   2893

Popularity and relevance of Eugene O'Neill. USA. Lang.: Eng.   2894

Mourning in Eugene O'Neill's *A Moon for the Misbegotten*. USA. 1922-1947. Lang.: Eng.   2895

Gender role-reversal in the Cycle plays of Eugene O'Neill. USA. 1927-1953. Lang.: Eng.   2896

Introduction to and overview of articles contained in Volume 40 of *Theatre Annual*. USA. 1900-1985. Lang.: Eng.   2898

Imagery and the role of women in Sam Shepard's *Buried Child*. USA. 1978. Lang.: Eng.   2899

Summary and discussion of the plays of Ed Bullins. USA. 1968-1973. Lang.: Eng.   2900

Analysis of *A View From the Bridge* by Arthur Miller. USA: New York, NY. UK-England: London. 1915-1985. Lang.: Cat.   2901

Playwright David Rabe's treatment of cliche in *Sticks and Bones*. USA. 1971. Lang.: Eng.   2902

Genesis of *Sweet Bird of Youth* by Tennessee Williams. USA. 1958. Lang.: Eng.   2904

Attitudes toward technology reflected in some Living Newspaper productions of the Federal Theatre Project. USA. 1935-1939. Lang.: Eng.   2905

Ritual function of *The Slave Ship* by LeRoi Jones (Amiri Baraka) and *Quinta Temporada (Fifth Season)* by Luis Valdez. USA. 1965-1967. Lang.: Eng.   2906

Concept of tragic character in Eugene O'Neill's *Desire Under the Elms*. USA. 1924. Lang.: Eng.   2907

God as image and symbol in Edward Albee's *Tiny Alice*. USA. 1965. Lang.: Eng.   2911

Race in prison dramas of Piñero, Camillo, Elder and Bullins. USA. 1970-1986. Lang.: Eng.   2912

Wendy Kesselman's treatment of a murder in *My Sister in This House*. USA. 1933-1983. Lang.: Eng.   2915

Compares Daniel Berrigan's play *The Trial of the Catonsville Nine* with the trial itself and the action that occasioned it. USA: Catonsville, MD. 1968-1973. Lang.: Eng.   2916

Analysis of *Hurlyburly* by David Rabe. USA. 1984. Lang.: Eng.   2918

Similarities of *Hughie* by Eugene O'Neill and *The Zoo Story* by Edward Albee. USA: New York, NY. 1941-1958. Lang.: Eng.   2919

Interview with playwright Arthur Miller. USA. 1985. Lang.: Eng.   2921

Beth Henley's play *Crimes of the Heart* as an example of female criminality in response to a patriarchal culture. USA. 1980-1986. Lang.: Eng.   2923

Director John Lion on his work with playwright Sam Shepard. USA: San Francisco, CA, New York, NY. 1970-1984. Lang.: Eng.   2924

Interview with playwright Sam Shepard. USA. 1984. Lang.: Eng.   2925

David Belasco's influence on Eugene O'Neill. USA: New York, NY. 1908-1922. Lang.: Eng.   2927

Discussion of issues raised in plays of 1985-86 season. USA: New York, NY. 1985-1986. Lang.: Eng.   2928

The Peasants by Władysław Reymont as possible source for O'Neill's version of the lustful stepmother play. USA. 1902-1924. Lang.: Eng.   2930

Interview with playwright Neil Simon. USA: New York, NY. 1927-1986. Lang.: Eng.   2931

Theme and narrative structure in plays of Eugene O'Neill, David Belasco, and James A. Herne. USA. 1879-1918. Lang.: Eng.   2933

Themes and structures of the plays of Lanford Wilson. USA. 1963-1985. Lang.: Eng.   2936

Interview with playwright David Mamet. USA. 1984. Lang.: Eng.   2938

Interview with playwright Israel Horovitz. USA: New York, NY. 1985. Lang.: Eng.   2941

Account of presentation of four St. Nicholas plays from Fleury Playbook. USA: Kalamazoo, MI. 1986. Lang.: Eng.   2942

Development of playwright Sam Shepard's style. USA. 1972-1985. Lang.: Eng.   2943

Sam Shepard's plays as a response to traditional American drama. USA. 1943-1986. Lang.: Eng.   2944

Interview with playwright Lorraine Hansberry. USA. 1959. Lang.: Eng.   2945

Biographical sketch of playwright/performer Samm-Art Williams. USA: Burgaw, NC, New York, NY. 1940-1986. Lang.: Eng.   2946

Theories of Otto Rank applied to plays of Eugene O'Neill. USA. 1888-1953. Lang.: Eng.   2948

Robert E. Sherwood's conception of history in *The Petrified Forest* and *Abe Lincoln in Illinois*. USA. 1930-1950. Lang.: Eng.   2949

Interview with leaders of playwrights' seminar. USSR: Picunde. 1986. Lang.: Rus.   2955

Problems of contemporary dramaturgy. USSR. 1986. Lang.: Rus.   2956

Analysis of the plays of Aleksej Gel'man. USSR. 1986. Lang.: Rus.   2959

Trends in Russian Soviet dramaturgy. USSR. 1950-1979. Lang.: Rus.   2961

Folklore in Uzbek drama. USSR. Lang.: Rus.   2962

Motif of renewal in Soviet theatre and reorganization of theatre administration. USSR: Kiev. 1980-1986. Lang.: Rus.   2963

Playwrights Semyan Zlotnikov and Ljudmila Petruševskaja as representative of contemporary dramaturgy. USSR. 1980-1986. Lang.: Rus.   2965

Conflict and characterization in recent Soviet dramaturgy. USSR. 1970-1980. Lang.: Rus.   2967

Discussion of the hero in modern drama. USSR. 1980-1986. Lang.: Rus.   2969

Plot/subject/theme — cont'd

Moral and ethical themes in contemporary drama. USSR. 1980-1986. Lang.: Rus. 2970

The positive hero in contemporary drama. USSR. 1980-1986. Lang.: Rus. 2971

Traces development of political trends in Venezuelan drama. Venezuela. 1958-1980. Lang.: Spa. 2972

Interview with Chilean playwright Jaime Miranda. Venezuela. Chile. USA. 1956-1985. Lang.: Eng. 2973

Vietnamese drama focusing on its origins from traditional forms. Vietnam. 1940-1986. Lang.: Swe. 2974

Analysis of French-language radio series *Nazaire et Barnabé*. Canada. 1939-1958. Lang.: Eng. 3183

A review of radio plays written by Linda Zwicker. Canada. 1968-1986. Lang.: Eng. 3184

Plays by women on the CBC radio network. Canada. 1985-1986. Lang.: Eng. 3185

Influence of Harold Pinter's radio work on his stage plays. UK-England. 1957-1981. Lang.: Eng. 3186

Conceptions of the South Sea islands in works of Murnau, Artaud and Spies. Europe. USA. Indonesia. 1930. Lang.: Ita. 3231

Comparison of Harold Pinter and Marcel Proust, focusing on Pinter's filmscript *The Proust Screenplay*. France. UK-England. 1913-1978. Lang.: Eng. 3232

Nazi ideology and Hans Schweikart's film adaptation of Lessing's *Minna von Barnhelm*. Germany. 1940. Lang.: Ger. 3233

Analysis of two versions of a screenplay by Luigi Pirandello. Italy. 1925-1928. Lang.: Ita. 3235

Comparison of screenplay and film of *Umberto D.*, directed by Vittorio De Sica. Italy. 1952. Lang.: Fre. 3236

Harold Pinter's screenplay for *The French Lieutenant's Woman* by John Fowles. UK-England. 1969-1981. Lang.: Eng. 3238

Sound effects and images of time in Orson Welles' film version of Shakespeare's *Othelllo*. USA. 1952. Lang.: Eng. 3241

Cultural models and types in docudrama. Canada. 1970-1983. Lang.: Eng. 3279

Ideology of commercial television. Canada. USA. 1965-1983. Lang.: Eng. 3281

Analysis of television docudramas as a melodrama genre. USA. 1965-1986. Lang.: Eng. 3285

Identifies dramatic elements unique to street theatre. USA. 1968-1986. Lang.: Eng. 3354

Political use of biblical references in pageantry. England. 1519-1639. Lang.: Eng. 3429

Compares pageant-wagon play about Edward IV with version by Thomas Heywood. England: Coventry, London. 1560-1600. Lang.: Eng. 3430

Development of Restoration musical theatre. England. 1642-1699. Lang.: Eng. 3496

English traditions in works of Henry Purcell. England. 1659-1695. Lang.: Rus. 3497

Analysis of Hildegard of Bingen's *Ordo Virtutum* as a morality play. Germany: Bingen. 1151. Lang.: Eng. 3498

Description of *p'ansori*, a traditional Korean entertainment. Korea. Lang.: Eng. 3499

Plots and themes in adaptations of *Tou Erh Yüan (The Injustice of Miss Tou)*. China. 1360-1960. Lang.: Chi. 3525

Life and works of playwright Shen Ching. China. 1368-1644. Lang.: Chi. 3526

Playwright Wu Bing mocks *The Peony Pavilion* by Tang Xianzu. China. 1600-1980. Lang.: Chi. 3531

Characteristics and influences of Fan Ts'ui-T'ing's plays. China. 1900-1980. Lang.: Chi. 3532

Analysis of the work of playwright Li Yu. China. 1611-1930. Lang.: Chi. 3533

Comparison of the works of Wang Ji-De and Xu Wei. China. 1620-1752. Lang.: Chi. 3534

Analysis of playwright Xu Jin's work. China, People's Republic of: Beijing. 1952-1985. Lang.: Chi. 3535

Structure of Beijing opera. China, People's Republic of: Beijing. 1983. Lang.: Chi. 3537

Introduction to the folk play, *Mu Lian*. China, People's Republic of: Beijing. 1962-1985. Lang.: Chi. 3538

Innovations of playwright Chen Jenchien. China, People's Republic of. 1913-1986. Lang.: Chi. 3539

Play sequels and their characteristics. China, People's Republic of. 1949-1980. Lang.: Chi. 3540

Origins, characteristics and structures of Beijing operas. China, People's Republic of: Beijing. 1903-1985. Lang.: Chi. 3541

Introduction to Sichuan opera, including translation of a new play. China, People's Republic of. 1876-1983. Lang.: Eng. 3542

Unpublished documentation of *Proprio like that*, a musical by Luigi Pirandello. Italy: Rome. 1930-1953. Lang.: Fre. 3627

Discussion of plays about Verdi and Puccini by Julian Mitchell and Robin Ray. UK-England: London. Italy. 1986. Lang.: Eng. 3628

German and Christian myths in Hans Pfitzner's opera *Palestrina*. 1900-1982. Lang.: Eng. 3852

Plots of works of Russian literature by Korolenko, Gorkij, Saltykov-Ščedrin and others in operas by non-Russian composers. Lang.: Rus. 3854

Investigates whether Brahms wrote music for an opera. Austria: Vienna. 1863-1985. Lang.: Eng. 3856

The church opera *Kain* written and composed for the Carinthiscer Sommer Festival. Austria: Ossiach. 1986. Lang.: Ger. 3858

The theme of clemency in the final operas of Mozart. Austria: Vienna. 1782-1791. Lang.: Cat. 3860

Examination of the text and music of Thomas Durfey's opera *Cinthia and Endimion*. England. 1690-1701. Lang.: Eng. 3861

Comparison of the *Samson Agonistes* of John Milton and the *Samson* of George Frideric Handel. England: London. 1743. Lang.: Eng. 3862

Biography of composer Isaac Albèniz. Europe. 1860-1909. Lang.: Cat. 3864

Analysis of thematic trends in recent Finnish Opera. Finland: Helsinki, Savonlinna. 1909-1986. Lang.: Eng, Fre. 3865

Interview with opera composer Aulis Sallinen on his current work. Finland: Helsinki. 1975-1986. Lang.: Eng, Fre. 3866

Schopenhauerian pessimism in Wagner's *Ring* and *Götterdämmerung*. Germany. 1852-1856. Lang.: Eng. 3873

Treatment of homosexuality in *Death in Venice*. Germany. UK-England. 1911-1970. Lang.: Eng. 3874

Study of the librettos of operas premiered at the Teatro delle Novità festival. Italy: Bergamo. 1950-1973. Lang.: Ita. 3883

Use of the tale of Patient Griselda in *Griselda* by Angelo Anelli and Niccolo Piccinni. Italy: Venice. Austria: Vienna. 1770-1800. Lang.: Eng. 3885

The Romeo and Juliet theme as interpreted in the musical and visual arts. Italy. 1476-1900. Lang.: Eng. 3886

The town of Rimini and its attachment to *Francesca da Rimini*. Italy: Rimini. 1986. Lang.: Eng. 3890

History of Russian opera, with detailed articles on individual works and composers. Russia. 1700-1985. Lang.: Ger. 3892

Development of the libretto for Benjamin Britten's opera *Gloriana*. UK-England: London. 1952-1953. Lang.: Eng. 3894

Collaboration of authors and composers of *Billy Budd*. UK-England: London. 1949-1964. Lang.: Eng. 3895

Analysis of Benjamin Britten's opera *Albert Herring*. UK-England: London. 1947. Lang.: Eng. 3897

Jack Beeson's opera *Lizzie Borden*. USA. 1954-1965. Lang.: Eng. 3901

Gian Carlo Menotti's reactions to harsh criticism of his operas. USA: New York, NY. UK-Scotland: Edinburgh. Italy: Cadegliano. 1938-1988. Lang.: Eng. 3902

A review of Southwestern University's Brown Symposium VII, 'Benjamin Britten and the Ceremony of Innocence'. USA: Georgetown. 1985. Lang.: Eng. 3904

Cultural and popular elements in a traditional nativity puppet performance. Italy: Sicily, Naples. 1651-1986. Lang.: Eng. 4009

Reference materials
Interpretation of Ferdinand Raimund's dramas after his death. Austria: Vienna. 1790-1986. Lang.: Ger. 2981

Relation to other fields
Circumstances surrounding a banned Workers' Experimental Theatre play. Canada: Toronto, ON. 1931-1933. Lang.: Eng. 3018

Role of Beijing opera today. China, People's Republic of: Beijing. 1985. Lang.: Chi. 3547

Plot/subject/theme — cont'd

Mao's policy on theatre in revolution. China, People's Republic of: Beijing. 1920-1985. Lang.: Chi. 3549

Research/historiography
Development of Cantonese opera and its influence. China, People's Republic of: Kuang Tung. 1885-1985. Lang.: Chi. 3555

Theory/criticism
Playwright A. Simukov discusses his craft. USSR. 1986. Lang.: Rus. 1249

Identifies types of theatrical irony. Lang.: Eng. 3079

Transformation of linguistic material into theatrical situations. Lang.: Fre. 3081

Book review of *Whittaker's Theatre: A Critic Looks at Stages in Canada and Thereabouts: 1944-1975*, ed. Ronald Bryden and Boyd Neil. Canada: Toronto, ON. 1944-1985. Lang.: Eng. 3087

Playwright Xiong Foxi's concept of theatre. China, People's Republic of. 1920-1965. Lang.: Chi. 3089

Review of *Mi lesz velünk Anton Pavlovics? (What Will Become of Us, Anton Pavlovič?)* by Miklós Almási. Hungary. 1986. Lang.: Hun. 3114

Overview of Pinter criticism with emphasis on the works' inherent uncertainty. UK. 1957-1986. Lang.: Eng. 3134

Collection of essays on the avant-garde. USA. 1955-1986. Lang.: Eng. 3145

Influence of Tuan Anchieh's aesthetics. China. 800-1644. Lang.: Chi. 3561

Comparison of Chinese play, *Kan Chien Nu*, with plays of Molière. China, People's Republic of: Beijing. 1970-1983. Lang.: Chi. 3568

Analyzes works of four dramatists from Fuchien province. China, People's Republic of. 1981-1985. Lang.: Chi. 3569

Characteristics of Chinese opera in Szechuan province. China, People's Republic of. 1963-1985. Lang.: Chi. 3570

Plough and the Stars, The
Plays/librettos/scripts
Limited perception in *The Plough and the Stars* by Sean O'Casey. Eire. 1926-1986. Lang.: Eng. 2456

Plowright, Joan
Performance/production
Actor Laurence Olivier's memoirs. UK-England: London. USA: New York, NY. 1907-1986. Lang.: Eng. 2170

Po Hamlecie (After Hamlet)
Plays/librettos/scripts
Interpretation of Fortinbras in post-war productions of *Hamlet*. Poland. UK-England. 1945. Lang.: Eng. 2748

Pochinko, Richard
Performance/production
Distinctive style of Canadian clowns. Canada: Toronto, ON, Vancouver, BC. 1967-1986. Lang.: Eng. 3328

Podbrey, Maurice
Institutions
Minority-language theatres in Canada. Canada: Montreal, PQ, Toronto, ON. 1986. Lang.: Eng. 1566

Poe, Edgar Allan
Performance/production
Collection of newspaper reviews by London theatre critics. UK-England: London. 1986. Lang.: Eng. 2112

Plays/librettos/scripts
Plays translated into Catalan by Pompeu Fabra. Spain-Catalonia. 1890-1905. Lang.: Cat. 2818

Poel, William
Performance/production
Innovative Shakespeare stagings of Harley Granville-Barker. UK-England. 1912-1940. Lang.: Eng. 806

Poetry
Relation to other fields
The use of women and homosexuality in Brecht's sexual lyric poetry. 1920-1928. 1055

Poet, dramatist, critic and satirist Władysław Syrokomla. Poland: Vilna, Warsaw. 1844-1861. Lang.: Pol. 3052

Influence of Mozart's operas on the 'Cockney' school of writers. England: London. 1760-1840. Lang.: Eng. 3916

Pogany, Willy
Reference materials
Catalogue of an exhibition of costume designs for Broadway musicals. USA: New York, NY. 1900-1925. Lang.: Eng, Ger. 3635

Poissant, Claude
Performance/production
Three directors' versions of *Les cauchemars du grand monde (Nightmares of High Society)* by Gilbert Turp. Canada: Montreal, PQ. 1984. Lang.: Fre. 1672

Poisson Chez Colbert
Performance/production
Account of *Poisson Chez Colbert* as performed at Théâtre du Vaudeville with a discussion of the popularity of vaudeville in Paris. France: Paris. 1808. Lang.: Eng. 3941

Poitier, Sidney
Performance/production
Lloyd Richard's career as an actor, director, artistic director and academic dean. USA: Detroit, MI, New York, NY, New Haven, CT. 1920-1980. Lang.: Eng. 2308

Pokrovskij, B.
Training
Seminar on training of opera and musical theatre performers. USSR. 1986. Lang.: Rus. 3939

Polanski, Roman
Design/technology
Pierre Guffroy's design of a functional ship for Polanski's *Pirates*. Tunisia. 1986. Lang.: Eng. 3201

Plays/librettos/scripts
Film versions of Shakespeare's *Macbeth* by Orson Welles, Akira Kurosawa and Roman Polanski. USA. Japan. 1948-1971. Lang.: Eng. 3243

Poletti, John
Design/technology
Designers discuss regional productions of *Side-by-Side by Sondheim*. USA. 1984. Lang.: Eng. 3593

Polgar, Alfred
Performance/production
History of the Viennese cabaret. Austria: Vienna. 1890-1945. Lang.: Ger. 3364

Policja (The Police)
Plays/librettos/scripts
Mrożek's *Policja (The Police)* as read by the censor. Poland. 1958. Lang.: Fre. 2735

Political theatre
Audience
Jean Vilar's view of the revolutionary power of the classics. France: Paris. 1951-1963. Lang.: Fre. 198

Basic theatrical documents
Text of *War on the Waterfront* by Betty Roland. Australia. 1939. Lang.: Eng. 1459

Act I, Scene 3 of *Are You Ready Comrade?* by Betty Roland. Australia. 1938. Lang.: Eng. 1460

Text of two plays about refugees in Switzerland. Switzerland: Bern. 1933-1985. Lang.: Ger. 1505

Institutions
Account of New Theatre movement by a participant. Australia: Sydney, Melbourne. 1932-1955. Lang.: Eng. 437

Historical perspective of the New Theatre. Australia: Sydney, N.S.W. 1932-1986. Lang.: Eng. 438

The Jura Soyfer Theater and its plans for the 1986/87 season. Austria: Vienna. 1986. Lang.: Ger. 457

Foundation of Polish theatre in Poznań in 1783, its repertoire and political contexts. Poland: Poznań. 1782-1793. Lang.: Pol. 512

Progress and aims of Women's Playhouse Trust. UK-England: London. 1984-1986. Lang.: Eng. 1590

Discussion of techniques and theories of Bread and Puppet Theatre. USA: New York, NY. 1961-1978. Lang.: Ita. 3960

Performance/production
Interview with political satirist Max Gillies. Australia. 1986. Lang.: Eng. 654

Dangers of assimilation of French-Canadian theatre into Anglophone culture. Canada. 1985. Lang.: Fre. 668

Interview with Mario Delgado Vásquez, director of Cuatrotablas. Peru: Lima. 1971-1985. Lang.: Hun. 769

Interview with Ellen Rudolph on recent cultural exchange tour of foreign artists in the US. USA: New York, NY. 1982. Lang.: Eng. 839

Interview with director Carlos Gimenez. Argentina. Venezuela: Caracas. 1969-1986. Lang.: Eng. 1636

Community theatre as interpreted by the Sidetrack Theatre Company. Australia: Sydney, N.S.W. 1980-1986. Lang.: Eng. 1638

Political theatre — cont'd

Playwright Václav Havel's experience with the Burgtheater. Austria: Vienna. Czechoslovakia. 1976-1986. Lang.: Ger. 1643

Playwright David Fennario's commitment to working-class community theatre. Canada: Montreal, PQ. 1980-1986. Lang.: Eng. 1661

Production of *L'Histoire terrible mais inachevé de Norodom Sihanouk, roi du Cambodge (The Terrible but Unfinished History of Norodom Sihanouk, King of Cambodia)* by Hélène Cixous. France: Paris. 1985. Lang.: Eng. 1737

An exploration of Brecht's *Gestus*. Germany. Lang.: Eng. 1758

Photographic record of forty years of the Berliner Ensemble. Germany, East: Berlin, East. 1949-1984. Lang.: Eng. 1761

Application of Brechtian concepts by Eckhardt Schall. Germany, East: Berlin, East. UK-England: London. 1952-1986. Lang.: Eng. 1762

Performances of *Hair*, directed by János Sándor, and *Desire Under the Elms*, directed by Géza Bodolay at the National Theatre of Szeged. Hungary: Szeged. 1986. Lang.: Hun. 1959

Interview with director Jurij Liubimov. USA: Washington, DC. USSR: Moscow. 1986. Lang.: Eng. 2196

Productions of Dario Fo's *Morte accidentale di un anarchico (Accidental Death of an Anarchist)* in the light of Fo's political ideas. USA. Canada. Italy. 1970-1986. Lang.: Eng. 2262

Resurgence of street theatre productions and companies. USA: New York, NY. 1960-1982. Lang.: Eng. 2285

Interview with Wooster Group's artistic director Elizabeth LeCompte. USA: New York, NY. 1984. Lang.: Eng. 2288

Videotaped performances and interviews of San Francisco Mime Troupe. USA: San Francisco, CA. 1960-1986. Lang.: Eng. 3306

Analysis of political cabaret and cabaret revue. USA: New York, NY. 1983. Lang.: Eng. 3367

History of puppet theatre including recent developments in political satire and agit-prop. South Africa, Republic of. 1805-1986. Lang.: Eng. 3969

Peter Schumann and his work with the Bread and Puppet Theatre. USA: New York, NY. 1968-1986. Lang.: Eng. 3973

Plays/librettos/scripts

Playwright Mona Brand's work with New Theatre movement. Australia: Sydney, N.S.W. 1932-1968. Lang.: Eng. 924

Role of working class in development of theatre resistance. South Africa, Republic of. 1976-1986. Lang.: Eng. 967

Analysis of the plays of Oriel Gray. Australia. 1942-1958. Lang.: Eng. 2376

Betty Roland's life and stage work. Australia: Sydney, N.S.W. 1928-1985. Lang.: Eng. 2382

Political plays of Katharine Susannah Prichard and Ric Throssell. Australia. 1909-1966. Lang.: Eng. 2388

Review of five published plays by Margaret Hollingsworth. Canada. Lang.: Eng. 2440

The history of Cuban exile theatre. Cuba. USA: New York, NY. 1959-1986. Lang.: Spa. 2451

Analysis of *L'Histoire terrible mais inachevé de Norodom Sihanouk, roi du Cambodge (The Terrible but Unfinished History of Norodom Sihanouk, King of Cambodia)* by Hélène Cixous. France: Paris. 1985. Lang.: Eng. 2570

Political aspects of George Sand's *Père va-tout-seul (Old Man Go-It-Alone)*. France. 1830-1844. Lang.: Eng. 2574

The place of *The Island of the Mighty* in the John Arden canon. Ireland. UK. 1950-1972. Lang.: Eng. 2666

Influence and development of the plays of Julio Ortega. Peru. 1970-1984. Lang.: Eng. 2730

Prison camp passion play with Christ as a labor organizer. Philippines: Davao City. 1983-1985. Lang.: Eng. 2732

Development of recent Puerto Rican drama. Puerto Rico. 1960-1980. Lang.: Spa. 2760

Influence of working class on form and content of theatre of resistance. South Africa, Republic of: Soweto. 1976-1986. Lang.: Eng. 2777

Interview with playwright Howard Barker. UK-England. 1981-1985. Lang.: Eng. 2845

Evaluation of *The War Plays* by Edward Bond. UK-England: London. 1986. Lang.: Eng. 2853

Interview with Gillian Hanna about *Elisabetta: Quasì per caso una donna (Elizabeth: Almost by Chance a Woman)*. UK-England: London. Italy. 1986. Lang.: Eng. 2875

Attitudes toward technology reflected in some Living Newspaper productions of the Federal Theatre Project. USA. 1935-1939. Lang.: Eng. 2905

Discussion of issues raised in plays of 1985-86 season. USA: New York, NY. 1985-1986. Lang.: Eng. 2928

Analysis of *Balmain Boys Don't Cry*, a political satire. Australia: Sydney, N.S.W. 1983-1986. Lang.: Eng. 3368

Relation to other fields

Suggestions for reviving political theatre. Lang.: Fre. 1051

Political theatre in Wallonia. Belgium. 1985. Lang.: Fre. 1066

Reflections and influence of arts and race relations. South Africa, Republic of. Lang.: Afr. 1125

Traditions of political theatre and drama. USSR. 1980-1986. Lang.: Rus. 1173

Interview with Augusto Boal. Canada: Montreal, PQ. France. Brazil: São Paulo. 1952-1986. Lang.: Eng. 3019

Workshops in Canada on 'Theatre for the Oppressed'. Canada: Toronto, ON. 1986. Lang.: Eng. 3022

Theatre workshops led by Augusto Boal. Canada: Montreal, PQ. 1985. Lang.: Eng. 3023

Theatre as a force of social change in turn-of-the-century France. France. 1897-1901. Lang.: Eng. 3029

Interview with director Lech Raczak of Theatre of the Eighth Day. Poland: Poznań. 1968-1985. Lang.: Eng. 3048

Reflections of political attitudes in plays by John McGrath and David Hare. UK-England. 1971-1978. Lang.: Eng. 3060

Overview of political impact of puppet theatre. Europe. 600 B.C.-1986 A.D. Lang.: Eng. 3990

Theory/criticism

Critics discuss modernist and postmodernist movements. 1986. Lang.: Eng. 1194

Lack of representation of women in theatre. USA: New York, NY. 1982-1986. Lang.: Eng. 1227

National Conference of Theatre Communications Group (TCG). USA: Amherst, MA. Lang.: Eng. 1233

Politics

Administration

Censorship in post-Revolutionary France. France: Paris. 1791-1891. Lang.: Eng. 39

Strategies for funding under Reagan's Economic Recovery Act. USA. 1940-1983. Lang.: Eng. 98

Failure of democracy to protect culture. USA. 1983. Lang.: Eng. 106

New factors in arts and their impact on labor relations. USA. 1986. Lang.: Eng. 108

Questions about the role of government cultural patronage. USA. 1854-1983. Lang.: Eng. 120

Decentralization of government policy on the arts. USA. 1980-1983. Lang.: Eng. 121

Differences between government and corporate support of the arts. USA. 1983. Lang.: Eng. 123

Uniquely American aspects of artist-state relationship. USA. 1983. Lang.: Eng. 124

How minorities are getting access to public arts funding. USA. 1983. Lang.: Eng. 136

American cultural bases of arts policy problems. USA. 1776-1983. Lang.: Eng. 141

Aesthetics and culture—relationship with the state. USA. 1857-1983. Lang.: Eng. 143

'Sense of place' in developing arts policy. USA. 1904-1983. Lang.: Eng. 147

Lack of consensus on art linked to poor arts education. USA. 1960-1983. Lang.: Eng. 152

Relationships between politicians and cultural leaders. USA. 1980-1983. Lang.: Eng. 158

Argument against government involvement in the arts. USA. 1983. Lang.: Eng. 173

Effect of censorship on Shakespeare's *Richard III* and *Henry IV*. England. 1593-1603. Lang.: Pol. 1435

Russian censorship of classic repertory in Polish theatres. Poland: Warsaw. Russia. 1873-1907. Lang.: Rus, Pol. 1438

Politics — cont'd

Audience

History of the Mulgrave Road Co-op theatre. Canada: Guysborough, NS. 1977-1985. Lang.: Eng. 1444

Effect of official educational and cultural policies on theatre. France. Germany. UK-England. 1789-1986. Lang.: Fre. 1446

Susceptibility of American audiences to media manipulation by the bureaucratic establishment. USA. 1969-1986. Lang.: Eng. 3166

Basic theatrical documents

Letter from Luigi Pirandello to Silvio D'Amico. Italy: Agrigento. 1927. Lang.: Fre. 224

Text of *J'ai Vingt Ans (I Am Twenty Years Old)* by Alain Grandbois. Canada. 1934-1975. Lang.: Fre. 1469

Texts of three political dramas, with discussion. Canada. 1833-1879. Lang.: Eng. 1472

Text of two plays about refugees in Switzerland. Switzerland: Bern. 1933-1985. Lang.: Ger. 1505

Institutions

Playwright Jack Hibberd's analysis of nationalist and English-derived theatrical cultures. Australia: Melbourne, Sydney. 1850-1986. Lang.: Eng. 439

Overview of the 16th Quebec Children's Theatre Festival. Canada. 1985. Lang.: Fre. 479

Overview of Festival Lennoxville and the role of anglophone drama in Quebec. Canada: Lennoxville, PQ. 1972-1982. Lang.: Eng. 485

Structure and political viewpoint of Great Canadian Theatre Company. Canada: Ottawa, ON. 1975-1986. Lang.: Eng. 486

History of theatre in Valencia area focusing on Civil War period. Spain: Valencia. 1817-1982. Lang.: Cat. 514

Congressional debate over proposed NEA budget. USA: Washington, DC. 1984. Lang.: Eng. 540

Origins and evolution of Teatro Campesino. USA. Mexico. 1965-1986. Lang.: Eng. 547

Impact of election year politics on NEA funding. USA: Washington, DC. 1984. Lang.: Eng. 557

History of the Green Thumb Theatre. Canada: Vancouver, BC. 1975-1986. Lang.: Eng. 1541

Criticism of *Canadian Theatre Review*. Canada. 1985. Lang.: Fre. 1554

History of the Shanghai Drama Institute. China, People's Republic of: Shanghai. 1945-1982. Lang.: Chi. 1571

Relations between the 'Confidenti' company and their patron Don Giovanni dei Medici. Italy: Venice. 1613-1621. Lang.: Ita. 1580

Development of Prague National Theatre. Czechoslovakia: Prague. 1787-1985. Lang.: Eng. 3672

Performance/production

Dangers of assimilation of French-Canadian theatre into Anglophone culture. Canada. 1985. Lang.: Fre. 668

Canadian theatre and its relations with U.S. theatre. Canada. USA. 1985. Lang.: Fre. 669

Poetry as performing art and political tool. Caribbean. 1937-1985. Lang.: Eng. 674

Dario Fo's fusion of slapstick and politics. Italy. 1960-1986. Lang.: Eng. 749

Reaction to government white paper on creative arts. South Africa, Republic of. 1986. Lang.: Eng. 787

Changes in English life reflected in 1883 theatre season. UK-England: London. 1883. Lang.: Eng. 810

Brechtian technique in the contemporary feminist drama of Caryl Churchill, Claire Luckham and others. UK-England. 1956-1979. Lang.: Eng. 815

Biography of actor Richard B. Harrison, who played God in *The Green Pastures*. USA. 1930-1939. Lang.: Eng. 828

Gender roles in the work of female theatre professionals. USA. 1985. Lang.: Eng. 836

Comparison of Soviet theatre of the 1960s and 1980s. USSR: Moscow. 1960-1986. Lang.: Rus. 860

USA-USSR cultural ties, including theatre. USSR. USA. 1960-1986. Lang.: Rus. 863

Essay on actor's place in society. USSR. 1980-1986. Lang.: Rus. 865

Actor M. Ul'janov on tasks of Soviet theatre. USSR: Moscow. 1986. Lang.: Rus. 905

Biography of actor and stage manager Franz Reichert. Austria: Vienna. Germany: Berlin. Czechoslovakia: Prague. 1925-1950. Lang.: Ger. 1652

Humorous and political trends in Chilean theatre season. Chile. 1984-1985. Lang.: Spa. 1686

Technical innovation, scenography and cabaret in relation to political and social conditions. Czechoslovakia. 1781-1986. Lang.: Eng. 1697

Polemic surrounding Sacha Stavisky's production of Shakespeare's *Coriolanus* at the Comédie-Française. France: Paris. 1934. Lang.: Eng, Fre. 1742

Life and work of actress-playwright Franca Rame. Italy. 1929-1983. Lang.: Eng. 1988

Performance conditions of specific theatrical genres. Lebanon. 1918-1985. Lang.: Fre. 2011

Performance of Comédie-Française actors in Amsterdam. Netherlands. 1811. Lang.: Fre. 2012

Recollections of actor-directors Irena and Tadeusz Byrski. Poland: Vilna. 1930-1939. Lang.: Pol. 2017

Director Andrzej Wajda's work, accessibility to Polish audiences. Poland: Warsaw. 1926-1986. Lang.: Swe. 2027

Visits to Poland by Russian theatre troupes. Poland. Russia. 1882-1913. Lang.: Pol. 2043

Political difficulties in staging two touring productions of Shakespeare's *The Taming of the Shrew*. UK. 1985-1986. Lang.: Eng. 2104

Dramaturg Oskar Eustis on confronting social and aesthetic problems. USA: San Francisco, CA. 1975-1986. Lang.: Eng. 2250

American productions of Hauptmann's *Die Weber (The Weavers)*. USA. Germany. 1892-1900. Lang.: Ger. 2272

Resurgence of street theatre productions and companies. USA: New York, NY. 1960-1982. Lang.: Eng. 2285

Interview with the mixed-media artist and puppeteer Theodora Skipitares. USA. 1974-1985. Lang.: Eng. 3251

History of the Viennese cabaret. Austria: Vienna. 1890-1945. Lang.: Ger. 3364

Season review of Mikroszkóp Stage. Hungary: Budapest. 1985-1986. Lang.: Hun. 3365

A general review of the 1985 circus season. USA. Canada. 1985. Lang.: Eng. 3394

Classification and description of Quebec pageants. Canada. 1900-1960. Lang.: Fre. 3423

Interview with performance artist Mona Hatoum. UK-England. 1975-1986. Lang.: Eng. 3452

Imprisoned Nigerian pop musician Fela Anikulapo-Kuti. Nigeria: Lagos. 1960-1985. Lang.: Eng. 3468

Elzéar Labelle's operetta *La Conversion d'un pêcheur de la Nouvelle-Écosse (The Conversion of a Nova Scotian Fisherman)* as an example of the move toward public performance. Canada: Quebec, PQ. 1837-1867. Lang.: Eng. 3599

Nazi persecution of conductor Fritz Busch. Germany. USA. 1922-1949. Lang.: Eng. 3736

Singer I. Archipova on tasks of Soviet opera. USSR. 1980-1986. Lang.: Rus. 3846

History of puppet theatre including recent developments in political satire and agit-prop. South Africa, Republic of. 1805-1986. Lang.: Eng. 3969

Plays/librettos/scripts

Analysis of various theatrical forms of francophone Africa. Africa. 1985. Lang.: Fre. 919

Analysis of the plays of Sharon Pollock. Canada. 1971-1983. Lang.: Eng. 935

Metaphoric style in the political drama of Jean-Paul Sartre, Athol Fugard and Juan Radrigán. France. South Africa, Republic of. Chile. 1940-1986. Lang.: Eng. 951

Precursors of revolutionary black theatre. Haiti. Jamaica. 1820-1970. Lang.: Eng. 956

English theatrical representation of political struggle in Northern Ireland. UK-Ireland. 1980-1986. Lang.: Rus. 977

Treatment of social problems in the plays of Lillian Hellman and Clifford Odets. USA. 1930-1939. Lang.: Eng. 984

Career of Marxist playwright George Sklar. USA: New York, NY. 1920-1967. Lang.: Eng. 985

Politics — cont'd

Analysis of *Dreams in an Empty City* by Stephen Sewell. Australia: Adelaide. Lang.: Eng. 2375

Analysis of religious symbolism in *Riel* by John Coulter. Canada. 1950. Lang.: Eng. 2407

Poverty in plays by Michel Tremblay and David Fennario. Canada: Quebec, PQ. 1970-1980. Lang.: Eng. 2410

Literary and popular theatrical forms in the plays of Rick Salutin. Canada: Montreal, PQ, Toronto, ON. 1976-1981. Lang.: Eng. 2411

Compares contemporary Canadian theatre with German and Russian theatre of the early 20th century. Canada. Russia: Moscow. Germany. 1900-1986. Lang.: Eng. 2412

Study of two unproduced historical dramas about French-Canadian patriot Louis Riel. Canada: Montreal, PQ. 1886. Lang.: Fre. 2413

Analysis of *As Is* by William Hoffman and *The Dolly* by Robert Locke. Canada: Toronto, ON. 1985. Lang.: Eng. 2419

Comparison of plays about Ned Kelly of Australia and Louis Riel of Canada. Canada. Australia. 1900-1976. Lang.: Eng. 2421

French-Canadian nationalism in *Le Drapeau de Carillon (The Flag of Carillon)*. Canada: Montreal, PQ. 1759-1901. Lang.: Eng. 2433

Marginal characters in plays of Jorge Díaz, Egon Wolff and Luis Alberto Heiremans. Chile. 1960-1971. Lang.: Eng. 2442

Cuban theatre in transition exemplified in the plays of Virgilio Piñera and Abelardo Estorino. Cuba. 1958-1964. Lang.: Eng. 2452

Interview with playwright, director and actor Pavel Kohout. Czechoslovakia: Prague. Austria: Vienna. 1928-1986. Lang.: Swe. 2454

Bullfighting and revenge in *The Spanish Tragedy* by Thomas Kyd. England. 1500-1600. Lang.: Eng. 2458

Contrast between Shakespeare's England and the Vienna of *Measure for Measure*. England. 1604-1605. Lang.: Eng. 2465

Shakespeare's *Henry VI* and Hall's *Chronicles*. England. 1542-1592. Lang.: Fre. 2488

Machiavellian ideas in *The Devil's Charter* by Barnaby Barnes. England. 1584-1607. Lang.: Eng. 2500

Marxist analysis of colonialism in Shakespeare's *Othello*. England. South Africa, Republic of. 1597-1637. Lang.: Eng. 2507

Origin of Spanish setting in Middleton and Rowley's *The Changeling*. England. 1607-1622. Lang.: Eng. 2513

Political ideas expressed in Elizabethan drama, particularly the work of Christopher Marlowe. England: London. Lang.: Eng. 2521

Analysis of *Magnificence* by Howard Brenton. England. 1970-1980. Lang.: Eng. 2524

Modern criticism of Shakespeare's crowd scenes. England. 1590-1986. Lang.: Eng. 2536

Treatment of history in drama. Europe. North America. Indonesia. 375 B.C.-1983 A.D. Lang.: Eng. 2541

Enlightenment narrative and French dramatists. France. 1700-1800. Lang.: Eng. 2552

Modern thought in works of Jean Racine. France. 1664-1691. Lang.: Fre. 2553

Evolution of concept of the State in the tragedies of Pierre Corneille. France. 1636-1674. Lang.: Fre. 2582

Biographical information on Jean Genet. France. 1910-1985. Lang.: Fre. 2588

Revising Brecht's plays to insure socially relevant productions. Germany, East. 1985. 2613

Brecht's life and work. Germany, West: Augsburg. Germany, East: Berlin, East. USA: Los Angeles, CA. 1898-1956. Lang.: Ger. 2626

Interview with playwright Stefan Schütz. Germany, West. 1970-1986. Lang.: Eng. 2628

Topicality of Aeschylus' *Oresteia*. Greece. 458 B.C. Lang.: Fre. 2632

Moral and political crises reflected in the plays of Euripides. Greece: Athens. 438-408 B.C. Lang.: Fre. 2634

Analysis of *La Tragédie du roi Christophe (The Tragedy of King Christopher)* by Aimé Césaire. Haiti. Africa. Martinique. 1939. Lang.: Fre. 2637

Dramatizations of the life of politician Endre Bajcsy-Zsilinszky. Hungary. 1960-1980. Lang.: Hun. 2661

Mrożek's *Policja (The Police)* as read by the censor. Poland. 1958. Lang.: Fre. 2735

School use of Juliusz Słowacki's dramas in Polish high schools as a reflection of the political situation. Poland. 1945-1984. Lang.: Eng. 2743

Influence of politics and personal history on Tadeusz Kantor and his Cricot 2 theatre company. Poland: Cracow. 1944-1986. Lang.: Eng. 2744

Interpretation of Fortinbras in post-war productions of *Hamlet*. Poland. UK-England. 1945. Lang.: Eng. 2748

The role of the artist in *The Road to Mecca* by Athol Fugard. South Africa, Republic of. 1961-1984. Lang.: Eng. 2779

Politics and aesthetics in three plays of Fernando Arrabal. Spain. France. Lang.: Fre. 2801

Playwright Alfonso Sastre discusses three of his recent plays. Spain. 1983-1986. Lang.: Spa. 2802

Lope de Vega's characterization of the converted Jew. Spain. 1562-1635. Lang.: Spa. 2804

Innerst inne (At Heart) dramatizes political and economic dilemma. Sweden: Karlskoga. 1981-1986. Lang.: Swe. 2825

Beckettian elements in Shakespeare as seen by playwright Edward Bond. UK-England. 1971-1973. Lang.: Eng. 2833

Links between Shakespeare's *Macbeth* and Tom Stoppard's *Dogg's Hamlet, Cahoot's Macbeth*. UK-England. 1979-1986. Lang.: Eng. 2843

World War II as a theme in post-war British drama. UK-England. 1945-1983. Lang.: Eng. 2868

Political views of Howard Brenton as evidenced in his adaptations. UK-England. 1973-1986. Lang.: Eng. 2883

Utopia in early plays by Arnold Wesker. UK-England. 1958-1970. Lang.: Eng. 2884

Race in prison dramas of Piñero, Camillo, Elder and Bullins. USA. 1970-1986. Lang.: Eng. 2912

Analysis of the plays of Vsevolod Vitaljēvič Višnevskij. USSR. 1920-1959. Lang.: Rus. 2964

Traces development of political trends in Venezuelan drama. Venezuela. 1958-1980. Lang.: Spa. 2972

Interview with Chilean playwright Jaime Miranda. Venezuela. Chile. USA. 1956-1985. Lang.: Eng. 2973

Analysis of French-language radio series *Nazaire et Barnabé*. Canada. 1939-1958. Lang.: Eng. 3183

Nazi ideology and Hans Schweikart's film adaptation of Lessing's *Minna von Barnhelm*. Germany. 1940. Lang.: Ger. 3233

Ideology of commercial television. Canada. USA. 1965-1983. Lang.: Eng. 3281

Political use of biblical references in pageantry. England. 1519-1639. Lang.: Eng. 3429

Schopenhauerian pessimism in Wagner's *Ring* and *Götterdämmerung*. Germany. 1852-1856. Lang.: Eng. 3873

Reconstruction of the three versions and productions of the operetta *Állami Áruház (State Stores)*. Hungary. 1952-1977. Lang.: Hun. 3943

Reference materials

Accounts of non-English-speaking artists. Australia. 1986. Lang.: Eng. 1001

Overview of French-language productions. Canada: Montreal, PQ. 1958-1968. Lang.: Eng. 2984

Theatre documents and listing of playtexts in the Polish theatre in Lvov. Poland: Lvov, Katowice. 1800-1978. Lang.: Pol. 2996

Encyclopedia of cabaret in German. Germany. Switzerland. Austria. 1900-1965. Lang.: Ger. 3369

Relation to other fields

Suggestions for reviving political theatre. Lang.: Fre. 1051

Political issues for Black performers. 1986. Lang.: Eng. 1052

Negative cultural effects of free trade between the U.S. and Canada. 1985-1986. Lang.: Eng. 1054

Theatrical conventions in religious story-telling. Asia. 700-1200. Lang.: Eng. 1061

Herbert Moritz and his views about cultural politics. Austria. 1986. Lang.: Ger. 1064

Political theatre in Wallonia. Belgium. 1985. Lang.: Fre. 1066

Theatricals used by temperance societies. Canada. 1800-1900. Lang.: Eng. 1067

Interactive theatre in *It's About Time* by Catalyst Theatre. Canada: Edmonton, AB. 1982. Lang.: Eng. 1069

Politics — cont'd

Theatre riot provoked by Thomas Hill's *The Provincial Association.* Canada: St. John, NB. 1845. Lang.: Eng. 1073

Shakespearean allusions in political satire. Canada. 1798-1871. Lang.: Eng. 1074

Analysis of *Symphony* by Herman Voaden and Lowrie Warrener. Canada. 1914-1933. Lang.: Eng. 1075

Recommended ethical values for artists in a socialist country. China. 1949-1982. Lang.: Chi. 1076

Importance of teaching proper values to theatre students. China, People's Republic of. 1949-1982. Lang.: Chi. 1077

Anecdotes about caricaturist Liao Bingxiong and comedian Chen Baichen. China, People's Republic of. 1942-1981. Lang.: Chi. 1078

William Popple's career in literature and politics. England. 1737-1764. Lang.: Eng. 1080

Critique of the relation between politics and theatre in Klaus Mann's *Mephisto* performed by Théâtre du Soleil. France: Paris. 1979. Lang.: Eng. 1085

Nazi ideology and the revival of plays by Christian Dietrich Grabbe. Germany. 1801-1946. Lang.: Eng. 1087

Study of Fascist theatrical policies. Germany: Berlin. 1933-1944. Lang.: Ger. 1091

Edward Albee on government censorship and freedom of artistic expression. Hungary: Budapest. 1986. 1096

Minutes of debates organized by the Association of Artists' Unions, on socialist arts policy, including theatre. Hungary. 1981-1984. Lang.: Hun. 1101

Reports and discussions of restricted cultural communication. Lebanon. Spain-Catalonia. USA. 1985. Lang.: Fre, Spa, Cat. 1111

Traditional Malay and European elements in children's theatre. Malaysia. 1930-1985. Lang.: Eng. 1112

Director Alan Bolt of the Nicaraguan National Theater Workshop discusses the process of creation. Nicaragua. 1985. 1114

The role of culture in Nicaragua since the revolution. Nicaragua. 1983. Lang.: Eng. 1115

Dissolution of Jerzy Grotowski's Laboratory Theatre. Poland: Wrocław. 1959-1985. Lang.: Eng. 1117

Alternative theatre and the political situation. Poland. 1960-1986. Lang.: Pol. 1119

Reopening of Polish theatre after over forty years of repression. Poland: Vilna. 1905. Lang.: Pol. 1120

Actor Stanisław Kwaskowski talks about the first years of independent Poland. Poland. 1918-1920. Lang.: Pol. 1121

Socio-historical basis of worker plays. South Africa, Republic of. 1985. 1126

Reports and discussions on theatre and colonialism. Spain. Latin America. 1185. Lang.: Eng, Fre, Spa, Cat. 1128

Critique of government support and funding for the arts. Switzerland. 1982-1986. Lang.: Ger. 1133

Role of theatre after the Arusha Declaration. Tanzania. 1967-1984. Lang.: Eng. 1134

Refugee artists from Nazi Germany in Britain. UK-England. Germany. 1937-1947. Lang.: Eng. 1135

Essay arguing against the Royal Shakespeare Company's decision not to perform in South Africa. UK-England: London. South Africa, Republic of. 1986. Lang.: Eng. 1136

Professional equality in theatrical careers for men and women. USA: New York, NY. 1850-1870. Lang.: Eng. 1143

New regulations governing lobbying activities of nonprofit organizations. USA: Washington, DC. 1984. Lang.: Eng. 1152

A discussion of the Nuevo Teatro movement and the status of Brecht in the U.S. USA: New York, NY. 1984. 1156

Writers Gabriel García Márquez, Carlos Fuentes and Dario Fo denied entry visas to the US on ideological grounds. USA: Washington, DC. 1984. Lang.: Eng. 1170

Traditions of political theatre and drama. USSR. 1980-1986. Lang.: Rus. 1173

Interview with director Oleg Jefremov of Moscow Art Theatre on social goals of theatre. USSR. 1986. Lang.: Rus. 1174

The role of theatre and television in the moral education of society. USSR. 1980-1986. Lang.: Rus. 1177

New tendencies in Soviet theatre. USSR. 1980. Lang.: Rus. 1178

History of workers' theatre. USSR. Germany. UK-England. 1917-1934. Lang.: Eng. 1179

The impact of the Third Reich on modern dance. Germany. 1902-1985. Lang.: Eng. 1353

Circumstances surrounding a banned Workers' Experimental Theatre play. Canada: Toronto, ON. 1931-1933. Lang.: Eng. 3018

Interview with Augusto Boal. Canada: Montreal, PQ. France. Brazil: São Paulo. 1952-1986. Lang.: Eng. 3019

Bertolt Brecht's contributions to modern theatre. Canada: Toronto, ON. 1985. Lang.: Eng. 3020

Controversy about *Captives of the Faceless Drummer* by George Ryga. Canada: Vancouver, BC. 1968-1971. Lang.: Eng. 3021

Workshops in Canada on 'Theatre for the Oppressed'. Canada: Toronto, ON. 1986. Lang.: Eng. 3022

Theatre workshops led by Augusto Boal. Canada: Montreal, PQ. 1985. Lang.: Eng. 3023

Theatre and society in post-revolutionary Cuba. Cuba. 1960-1986. Lang.: Rus. 3024

Sociological analysis of city comedy and revenge tragedy. England: London. 1576-1980. Lang.: Eng. 3025

Political influence of Ernst Toller's plays. Europe. 1893-1939. Lang.: Pol. 3027

Political and sociological aspects of the dramaturgy of Polish émigrés. Europe. 1820-1986. Lang.: Pol. 3028

Theatre as a force for social change in turn-of-the-century France. France. 1897-1901. Lang.: Eng. 3029

Cardinal Richelieu's theatrical policies. France. 1634-1642. Lang.: Fre. 3030

Feminist criticism of plays written by women. Germany. Switzerland. Austria. 1900-1986. Lang.: Ger. 3033

Response of Freie Volksbühne to police pressure. Germany: Berlin. 1890-1912. Lang.: Fre. 3034

The premiere of Howard Fast's play under the title *Harminc ezüstpénz (Thirty Pieces of Silver)* in Hungary. Hungary. 1951-1986. Lang.: Hun. 3036

Interview with playwright Wole Soyinka. Nigeria. USA: New Haven, CT. 1967-1984. Lang.: Eng. 3047

Interview with director Lech Raczak of Theatre of the Eighth Day. Poland: Poznań. 1968-1985. Lang.: Eng. 3048

Analysis of contemporary drama from various viewpoints. Poland. 1945-1986. Lang.: Pol. 3049

Political situation and new plays on the Polish stage. Poland. 1958-1962. Lang.: Pol. 3051

Shakespearean allusion in English caricature. UK-England. 1780-1820. Lang.: Eng. 3056

Reflections of political attitudes in plays by John McGrath and David Hare. UK-England. 1971-1978. Lang.: Eng. 3060

Nonfictional writings of Albin Zollinger, Max Frisch and Friedrich Dürrenmatt. Lang.: Ger. 3169

Social function of radio drama. Canada. 1950-1955. Lang.: Eng. 3187

Examples of Puritan attempts to ban legal entertainments. England: Cheshire. 1560-1641. Lang.: Eng. 3356

Renaissance theatre at Valencia court, Catalan festivals. Spain-Catalonia: Valencia. 1330-1970. Lang.: Spa. 3362

History of anti-Nazi satire. Germany. Switzerland: Zurich. 1933-1945. Lang.: Ger. 3370

Historical function of cabaret entertainment. Germany. 1896-1945. Lang.: Ger. 3371

Function of carnival in society. Europe. 1986. Lang.: Eng. 3376

Christian and pre-Christian elements of Corpus Christi celebration. Spain-Catalonia: Berga. 1264-1986. Lang.: Cat. 3432

Role of Beijing opera today. China, People's Republic of: Beijing. 1985. Lang.: Chi. 3547

Political goals for Beijing opera. China, People's Republic of: Beijing. 1985. Lang.: Chi. 3548

Mao's policy on theatre in revolution. China, People's Republic of: Beijing. 1920-1985. Lang.: Chi. 3549

Influence of political and artistic movements on composer Alban Berg. Austria: Vienna. 1894-1935. Lang.: Eng. 3914

Socialism and Kurt Weill's operatic reforms. Germany: Berlin. 1920-1959. Lang.: Eng. 3921

Politics — cont'd

Overview of political impact of puppet theatre. Europe. 600 B.C.-1986 A.D. Lang.: Eng. 3990

Reflections on a 3-day workshop on using puppet theatre for social action and communication. UK-England: London. 1986. Lang.: Eng. 3993

Politics, performing arts and puppetry. USA. 1970-1986. Lang.: Eng. 3994

Theory/criticism
Augusto Boal's concept of theatre of the oppressed. Brazil. France. 1956-1978. Lang.: Eng. 1201

Purpose of literature and art, and the role of the artist. China, People's Republic of: Shanghai, Yan'an. 1942-1982. Lang.: Chi. 1203

Michael Kirby defends the liberal outlook of *The Drama Review*. USA. 1971-1986. Lang.: Eng. 1232

Richard Schechner bids farewell to *The Drama Review* and suggests areas of future theatrical investigation. USA. 1969-1986. Lang.: Eng. 1234

Overview of the development of theatre criticism in the press. USSR. 1917-1927. Lang.: Rus. 1243

Pina Bausch seen as heir of epic theater of Bertolt Brecht. Germany, West. 1977-1985. Lang.: Eng. 1289

American criticisms of German *Tanztheater*. Germany, West. USA. 1933-1985. Lang.: Eng. 1290

Attitudes toward sports in serious Australian drama. Australia. 1876-1965. Lang.: Eng. 3084

Selection of Schiller's writings about drama. Germany. 1759-1805. Lang.: Cat. 3110

Social and political conditions of Greek society as sources for dramatic material. Greece: Athens. 450 B.C. Lang.: Eng. 3113

Eleven theatre professionals discuss their personal direction and the direction of experimental theatre. USA: New York, NY. 1985. Lang.: Eng. 3137

Training
Overview of spoken drama training programs. China, People's Republic of. 1907-1982. Lang.: Chi. 1255

Polívka, Boleslav
Performance/production
Overview of productions by the city's studio theatres. Czechoslovakia: Prague. 1986. Lang.: Hun. 1698

A photographic essay of 42 soloists and groups performing mime or gestural theatre. 1986. 3290

Pollock, Sharon
Institutions
Shift in emphasis at Banff Centre. Canada: Banff, AB. 1974-1986. Lang.: Eng. 1543

Plays/librettos/scripts
Amerindian and aborigine characters in the works of white playwrights. Canada. Australia. 1606-1975. Lang.: Eng. 930

Analysis of the plays of Sharon Pollock. Canada. 1971-1983. Lang.: Eng. 935

Pollux, Julius
Performance spaces
Ambiguous translations of ancient Greek theatrical documentation. Greece. Italy: Rome. 600-400 B.C. Lang.: Eng. 597

Poltergeist II
Design/technology
Lighting designer Andrew Lazlo talks about his work on the film *Poltergeist II*. USA: Los Angeles, CA. USA: New York, NY. 1985-1986. Lang.: Eng. 3204

Polunin, Viačeslav
Performance/production
Licedej Studio, directed by Viačeslav Polunin. USSR: Leningrad. 1980-1986. Lang.: Rus. 3307

Polus, Betty
Design/technology
Puppeteer Betty Polus discusses the development of her dinosaur puppet show. 3949

Pomerance, Bernard
Performance/production
Collection of newspaper reviews by London theatre critics. UK-England: London. 1986. Lang.: Eng. 2112

Royal Shakespeare Company performances at the Barbican Theatre. UK-England: London. 1986. Lang.: Eng. 2152

Ponnelle, Jean-Pierre
Performance/production
Interview with Jean-Pierre Ponnelle discussing his directing technique and set designs. Austria: Salzburg. 1984. Lang.: Eng. 3699

Photographs, cast list, synopsis, and discography of Metropolitan Opera radio broadcast performances. USA: New York, NY. 1986. Lang.: Eng. 3794

Stills from telecast performances. List of principals, conductor and production staff included. USA: New York, NY. 1986. Lang.: Eng. 3795

Pop Music Festival '66
SEE
Táncdalfesztivál '66.

Popiol i Diament (Ashes and Diamonds)
Performance/production
Andrzej Marczewski directs Andrzejewski's *Popiol i Diament (Ashes and Diamonds)*, Teatr Rozmaitości. Poland: Warsaw. 1984. Lang.: Pol. 2013

Popple, William
Relation to other fields
William Popple's career in literature and politics. England. 1737-1764. Lang.: Eng. 1080

Popular entertainment
SEE ALSO
Classed Entries under MIXED ENTERTAINMENT: 3308-3472.

Poquelin, Jean-Baptiste
SEE
Molière.

Porgy and Bess
Performance/production
Photographs, cast list, synopsis, and discography of Metropolitan Opera radio broadcast performances. USA: New York, NY. 1986. Lang.: Eng. 3794

Profile of and interview with Frances Gershwin Godowsky, younger sister of George and Ira Gershwin. USA: New York, NY. 1900-1986. Lang.: Eng. 3842

Pornografia (Pornography)
Performance/production
Andrzej Pawłowski directs Gombrowicz's *Pornografia (Pornography)*. Poland: Warsaw. 1983. Lang.: Pol. 2038

¿Porque corres Ulises? (Why do you Run, Ulysses?)
Plays/librettos/scripts
Thematic and stylistic comparison of three plays influenced by the *Odyssey*. Spain. 1952-1983. Lang.: Eng. 2792

Port Elizabeth Opera House (Port Elizabeth)
Performance spaces
History of the Port Elizabeth Opera House. South Africa, Republic of: Port Elizabeth. 1892-1986. Lang.: Eng. 615

Porter i el penalty, El (Goalkeeper and the Penalty, The)
Basic theatrical documents
Texts of *Avui, Romeo i Julieta (Today, Romeo and Juliet)* and *El porter i el penalty (The Goalkeeper and the Penalty)* by Josep Palau i Fabre. Spain-Catalonia. 1917-1982. Lang.: Cat. 1499

Plays/librettos/scripts
Analysis of Josep Palau's plays and theoretical writings. Spain-Catalonia. 1917-1982. Lang.: Cat. 2814

Porter, David
Institutions
David Porter, the new artistic director of Leicester Haymarket Theatre, discusses his policy. UK-England: Leicester. 1986. Lang.: Eng. 1587

Porter, Stephen
Performance/production
Reviews of *You Never Can Tell*, by George Bernard Shaw, staged by Stephen Porter. USA: New York, NY. 1986. Lang.: Eng. 2212

Reviews of *The Circle* by W. Somerset Maugham, staged by Stephen Porter, performed by the Mirror Repertory Company. USA: New York, NY. 1986. Lang.: Eng. 2227

Portland Opera (Portland, OR)
Design/technology
Portland Opera's resident designer discusses set recycling. USA. Lang.: Eng. 3663

Posters
Relation to other fields
Interview with designer of theatrical posters Győző Varga. Hungary. 1986. Lang.: Hun. 1097

Postmodernism

Performance/production

Merce Cunningham, Alwin Nikolais, Meredith Monk and Yvonne Rainer on post-modern dance. USA. 1975-1986. Lang.: Eng. 1285

Influences upon the post-modern mime troupe, Cirque du Soleil. Canada: Montreal, PQ. 1984-1986. Lang.: Eng. 3292

Theory/criticism

Critics discuss modernist and postmodernist movements. 1986. Lang.: Eng. 1194

Classical, modern and postmodern theatre and their delineation through opposites. France. 1986. Lang.: Eng. 3104

Potocki, Stanisław Kostka

Relation to other fields

Commentary on *Diabel włoski (Italian Devil)* by Stanisław Potocki. Poland. 1772-1821. Lang.: Pol. 3922

Potter, Cora Urquardt

Performance/production

The portrayal of Cleopatra by various actresses. England. 1813-1890. Lang.: Eng. 1699

Pou i Pagès, Josep

Plays/librettos/scripts

History of Catalan literature, including playwrights and theatre. Spain-Catalonia. 1800-1974. Lang.: Cat. 974

Poulenc, Francis

Institutions

Discussions of opera at the festival of Aix-en-Provence. France: Aix-en-Provence. 1960. Lang.: Fre. 3673

Pound, Ezra

Relation to other fields

Work of Ezra Pound and his relationship to *nō*. Japan. 1885-1972. Lang.: Jap. 1419

Povod, Reinaldo

Performance/production

Reviews of *Cuba and His Teddy Bear* by Reinaldo Povod, staged by Bill Hart. USA: New York, NY. 1986. Lang.: Eng. 2228

Power of Theatrical Madness, The

Performance/production

Collection of newspaper reviews by London theatre critics. UK-England: London. 1986. Lang.: Eng. 2119

Pownall, Leon

Institutions

The first decade of White Rock Summer Theatre in British Columbia. Canada: White Rock, BC. 1976-1985. Lang.: Eng. 1560

Pownell, David

Performance/production

Collection of newspaper reviews by London theatre critics. UK-England: London. 1986. Lang.: Eng. 2113

Reviews of *Master Class*, by David Pownell, staged by Frank Corsaro. USA: New York, NY. 1986. Lang.: Eng. 2216

Pöysti, Lasse

Institutions

History of Swedish language Lilla-teatern (Little Theatre). Finland: Helsinki. 1940-1986. Lang.: Eng, Fre. 494

Practical Arts and Theatre with the Handicapped (PATH)

Relation to other fields

The work of disabled theatre companies in England. UK-England. 1979-1986. Lang.: Eng. 1139

Pradivadlo (Prague)

Performance/production

Overview of productions by the city's studio theatres. Czechoslovakia: Prague. 1986. Lang.: Hun. 1698

Prairie Home Companion, A

Design/technology

Overhaul of The World Theatre as a radio broadcasting facility. USA: St. Paul, MN. 1982-1986. Lang.: Eng. 387

Prampolini, Enrico

Design/technology

Scene designs and theoretical texts of futurist painters working in the theatre. Italy. 1910-1928. Lang.: Ita. 1517

Pravda—chorošo, a ščast'e lučše (Truth is Good, But Happiness is Better)

Performance/production

Faina Ranevskaja's role in *Pravda—chorošo, a ščast'e lučše (Truth is Good, But Happiness is Better)* by A.N. Ostrovskij. USSR: Moscow. 1896-1984. Lang.: Rus. 2324

Precious Sons

Performance/production

Reviews of *Precious Sons* by George Furth, staged by Norman Rene. USA: New York, NY. 1986. Lang.: Eng. 2231

Predstava 'Hamleta' u selu Mrduša Donja (Hamlet Performed at Lower Mrduša)

Performance/production

Ivo Brešan's *Paraszt Hamlet (The Peasant Hamlet)* directed by Béla Merő. Hungary: Zalaegerszeg. 1986. Lang.: Hun. 1888

Pregones (Puerto Rico)

Performance/production

Profile of theatre companies featured in Festival Latino de Nueva York. USA: New York, NY. 1984. Lang.: Eng. 2197

Preissová, Gabriela

Performance/production

Thematic, character and musical analysis of *Jenufa* by Leoš Janáček. Czechoslovakia: Brno. 1894-1903. Lang.: Eng. 3718

Plays/librettos/scripts

Evaluation of the dramatic work of Gabriela Preissová, author of the source play for *Jenufa* by Leoš Janáček. Czechoslovakia: Brno. 1880-1900. Lang.: Eng. 2453

Preparing

Plays/librettos/scripts

Influence of oriental theatre on playwright Beverley Simons. Canada: Vancouver, BC. 1962-1975. Lang.: Eng. 928

Preservation, theatre

Performance spaces

Planning and fundraising for the restoration of the Imperial Theatre. Canada: St. John, NB. 1913-1985. Lang.: Eng. 588

Historical Midwestern theatres. USA: Chicago, IL, Milwaukee, WI. 1889-1986. Lang.: Eng. 1623

New façades on 42 New York theatres. USA: New York, NY. 1861-1986. Lang.: Eng. 1626

History of the Strand theatre. USA: Shreveport, LA. 1925-1986. Lang.: Eng. 3219

Presley, Elvis

Administration

Promotion and marketing the work of deceased artists. 1986. Lang.: Eng. 16

Press

Institutions

Thirty years of the Polish theatrical monthly *Dialog*. Poland: Warsaw. 1956-1986. Lang.: Pol. 511

Criticism of *Canadian Theatre Review*. Canada. 1985. Lang.: Fre. 1554

Performance/production

New York critics respond negatively to plays successful in Los Angeles. USA: Los Angeles, CA, New York, NY. 1983-1984. Lang.: Eng. 2258

Plays/librettos/scripts

Artists react to *New York Times* condemnation of current playwriting. USA. 1984. Lang.: Eng. 2888

Theory/criticism

Theatre critic discusses objectivity and standards. 1986. Lang.: Eng. 1193

Report of seminar on theatre criticism. USA: New York, NY. 1983. Lang.: Eng. 1223

Interviews on the role of the critic in New York theatre. USA: New York, NY. 1983. Lang.: Eng. 1226

Overview of the development of theatre criticism in the press. USSR. 1917-1927. Lang.: Rus. 1243

Discusses the impact of critic B.K. Sandwell. Canada. 1932-1951. Lang.: Eng. 3088

Theatre critic Frank Rich discusses his life and work. USA: New York, NY. 1986. Lang.: Eng. 3146

Preston, Henry W.

Relation to other fields

Theatre riot provoked by Thomas Hill's *The Provincial Association*. Canada: St. John, NB. 1845. Lang.: Eng. 1073

Preston, John

Plays/librettos/scripts

Image of poverty in Elizabethan and Stuart plays. England. 1558-1642. Lang.: Eng. 2482

Prestuplenijė i nakazanijė (Crime and Punishment)

Performance/production

Interview with director and cast of Wajda's *Crime and Punishment*. Poland: Cracow. USA. 1986. Lang.: Eng. 2025

Prestuplenijė i nakazanijė (Crime and Punishment) — cont'd

Djrector Andrzei Wajda's work, accessibility to Polish audiences. Poland: Warsaw. 1926-1986. Lang.: Swe. 2027

Adaptation of Dostojėvskij's *Prestuplenijė i nakazanijė (Crime and Punishment)* directed by Andrzej Wajda at Teatr Stary under the title *Zdrodnia i Kara*. Poland: Cracow. 1984. Lang.: Pol. 2032

Presumption, or The Fate of Frankenstein
Performance/production
Controversy surrounding *Presumption, or The Fate of Frankenstein* by Richard Brinsley Peake. UK-England: London. 1818-1840. Lang.: Eng. 2142
Plays/librettos/scripts
Treatment of the Frankenstein myth in three gothic melodramas. UK-England. France. 1823-1826. Lang.: Eng. 2847

Prévert, Jacques
Performance/production
Reminiscences of actor-director Roger Blin. France. 1930-1983. Lang.: Fre. 1726

Prichard, Katharine Susannah
Plays/librettos/scripts
Political plays of Katharine Susannah Prichard and Ric Throssell. Australia. 1909-1966. Lang.: Eng. 2388
Theory/criticism
Attitudes toward sports in serious Australian drama. Australia. 1876-1965. Lang.: Eng. 3084

Prida, Dolores
Plays/librettos/scripts
The history of Cuban exile theatre. Cuba. USA: New York, NY. 1959-1986. Lang.: Spa. 2451

Pride and Prejudice
Performance/production
Collection of newspaper reviews by London theatre critics. UK-England: London. 1986. Lang.: Eng. 2113

Prielle, Kornélia
Performance/production
Theatrical recollections focusing on the career of actress Kornélia Prielle. Hungary: Máramarossziget. 1833-1938. Lang.: Hun. 1878

Priestley, J.B.
Design/technology
Lighting requirements for television production of *Lost Empires*. UK-England. 1986. Lang.: Eng. 3255
Performance/production
Collection of newspaper reviews by London theatre critics. UK-England: London. 1986. Lang.: Eng. 2122

Primer història d'Esther (First Story of Esther)
Theory/criticism
Historical difficulties in creating a paradigm for Catalan theatre. Spain-Catalonia. 1400-1963. Lang.: Cat. 1220

Primera història d'Esther (First Story of Esther)
Basic theatrical documents
Text of *Primera història d'Esther (First Story of Esther)* by Salvador Espriu, with introduction on the author and the play. Spain-Catalonia: Barcelona. 1913-1985. Lang.: Spa, Cat. 1496
Relation to other fields
Reports and discussions of restricted cultural communication. Lebanon. Spain-Catalonia. USA. 1985. Lang.: Fre, Spa, Cat. 1111

Prince and the Pauper, The
Institutions
Recent outdoor productions of Gamla Stans Teater. Sweden: Stockholm. 1933-1986. Lang.: Swe. 524

Prince, Harold
Performance/production
Directors revitalizing opera. USA: New York, NY. 1970-1986. Lang.: Eng. 3826

Princess and the Stars, The
Performance/production
Description of *The Princess and the Stars* by R. Murray Schafer. Canada: Banff, AB. 1985. Lang.: Eng. 3485

Princess Theatre (Toronto, ON)
Institutions
Compares two Canadian stock companies. Canada: Montreal, PQ, Toronto, ON. 1890-1940. Lang.: Eng. 466

Princesse, The
Plays/librettos/scripts
Female characterization in Nicholas Rowe's plays. England. 1629-1720. Lang.: Eng. 2475

Principia Scriptoriae
Performance/production
Reviews of *Principia Scriptoriae* by Richard Nelson, staged by Lynne Meadow. USA: New York, NY. 1986. Lang.: Eng. 2223

Prionti, Gary
Design/technology
Designers discuss regional productions of *The Sound of Music*. USA. 1983-1986. Lang.: Eng. 3594

Prison theatre
Performance/production
Beckett's direction of *Krapp's Last Tape* at San Quentin Drama Workshop. USA. 1985. Lang.: Hun. 2279
Plays/librettos/scripts
Race in prison dramas of Piñero, Camillo, Elder and Bullins. USA. 1970-1986. Lang.: Eng. 2912

Prisoners, The
Plays/librettos/scripts
Female characterization in Nicholas Rowe's plays. England. 1629-1720. Lang.: Eng. 2475

Pritchard, John
Performance/production
Interview with Sir John Pritchard, music director of the San Francisco Opera. USA: San Francisco, CA. 1921-1986. Lang.: Eng. 3800

Processional theatre
SEE ALSO
Classed Entries under MIXED ENTERTAINMENT—Pageants/parades: 3421-3432.

Pageants/parades.
Performance/production
Comparison of Holy Week Processions of Seville with English Mystery plays. Spain: Seville. 1986. Lang.: Eng. 3426

Instances of dramatic action and costume in Holy Week processions. Spain. 1986. Lang.: Eng. 3427

Prochyra, Jan
Plays/librettos/scripts
Interview with director of Teatr Współczésny about children's drama competition. Poland: Wrocław. 1986. Lang.: Hun. 2736

Proctor, Ellen
Performance/production
Interview with puppeteer Ellen Proctor. USA: Chicago/Springfield, IL, St. Louis, MO. 1923-1985. Lang.: Eng. 3980

Producing
Administration
Problems in the structural organization of Hungarian theatre. Hungary. 1985-1986. Lang.: Hun. 48

Panel discussion on collective bargaining issues. USA. 1986. Lang.: Eng. 95

Julian Beck's management of the Living Theatre. USA: New York, NY. 1947-1983. Lang.: Eng. 102

Satirical view of arts management. USA. 1986. Lang.: Eng. 107

Cheryl Crawford's producing career discussed in light of her latest Broadway show. USA: New York, NY, Atlanta, GA. 1936-1986. Lang.: Eng. 117

Rita Kohn's attempts to get her play *Necessities* produced. USA: New York, NY. 1986. 125

Function of playwright's agent in negotiation and production of a script. USA: New York, NY. 1985. Lang.: Eng. 135

Guide to producing Off-off Broadway showcases. USA: New York, NY. Lang.: Eng. 159

Interview with Joe Papp. USA: New York, NY. 1959-1986. Lang.: Eng. 177

Satiric examination of what not to do if one is to become an effective artistic director. USA. 1986. Lang.: Eng. 178

Interview with V.R. Beljakovič, manager of Teat'r-studija na Jugo-Zapade. USSR: Moscow. 1980. Lang.: Rus. 185

Proposals for the reorganization of theatrical business. USSR. 1986. Lang.: Rus. 190

Interview with independent filmmaker Leon Ichaso. USA: New York, NY. 1986. 3193

Efforts to produce the film *Sexual Perversity in Chicago*. USA. Lang.: Eng. 3194

Renewed interest in musicals in regional theatre. USA. 1984-1986. Lang.: Eng. 3571

Alternate programs produced by opera houses. USA. Lang.: Eng. 3642

Institutions
Interview with Adrian Hall, artistic director of both Trinity Square Repertory Theatre and Dallas Theatre Center. USA: Providence, RI, Dallas, TX. 1966-1986. Lang.: Eng. 548

Producing — cont'd

John Houseman discusses Federal Theatre Project. USA: New York, NY, Washington, DC. 1935-1940. Lang.: Eng. 559

Performance/production

History of the British and American stage. USA. England. 1800-1986. Lang.: Eng. 826

Career of actress, manager and director Julia Arthur. Canada. UK-England. USA. 1869-1950. Lang.: Eng. 1675

Collection of articles by critic and theatre historian Wiktor Brumer. Poland. 1765-1930. Lang.: Pol. 2016

Producing *Café Con Leche (Coffee with Milk)* in Spanish. USA: New York, NY. 1986. 2269

Description of first stage adaptation of Robert Louis Stevenson's *Dr. Jekyll and Mr. Hyde.* USA: New York, NY. USA: Boston, MA. 1886-1888. Lang.: Eng. 2298

Importance of records of a provincial masque. England: Shipton. 1600-1650. Lang.: Eng. 3419

Relation to other fields

Goals and strategies of pricing decisions. USA. 1986. Lang.: Eng. 1141

Theory/criticism

Brecht's assertion that the producing artist must be independent of financial pressures. 3247

Producing institutions
SEE
Institutions, producing.

Production histories
SEE
Staging.
Performance/production.

Productions (Toronto, ON)
Plays/librettos/scripts
Analysis of *As Is* by William Hoffman and *The Dolly* by Robert Locke. Canada: Toronto, ON. 1985. Lang.: Eng. 2419

Productions elite (Montreal, PQ)
Institutions
Interviews with theatre professionals in Quebec. Canada. 1985. Lang.: Fre. 487

Professional Lighting Handbook
Design/technology
Video and film lighting techniques. USA. 1986. Lang.: Eng. 3257

Programs
SEE ALSO
Collected materials.

Reference materials
List and location of school playtexts and programs. France. 1601-1700. Lang.: Fre. 2987

Progress
Performance/production
Collection of newspaper reviews by London theatre critics. UK-England: London. 1986. Lang.: Eng. 2118

Projections
Design/technology
Survey of Joseph Svoboda's lighting and design work. Czechoslovakia. 1887-1982. Lang.: Chi. 252

Les Immatériaux, multimedia exhibit by Jean-François Lyotard. France: Paris. 1986. Lang.: Eng. 3249

Prokofiev, Sergei
SEE
Prokofjev, Sergej Sergejèvič.

Prokofjev, Sergej Sergejèvič
Performance/production
Prokofjèv's ballet *Romeo and Juliet* choreographed by László Seregi. Hungary: Budapest. 1985. Lang.: Hun. 1307

Review of Prokofjèv's *Love for Three Oranges.* USA: Cincinnati, OH. 1986. Lang.: Eng. 3798

Plays/librettos/scripts
History and aesthetics of Soviet opera. USSR: Moscow. 1917-1941. Lang.: Ger. 3905

Proletkult
Influence of Hampstead Garden Suburb pageant on the Russian Proletkult movement. Russia. UK-England: London. 1907-1920. Lang.: Eng. 3421

Prolti, Aldo
Performance/production
Significance of the translation in recordings of Verdi's *Otello.* USA. 1902-1978. Lang.: Eng. 3812

Promenade Theatre (New York, NY)
Performance spaces
Descriptions of newly constructed Off Broadway theatres. USA: New York, NY. 1984. Lang.: Eng. 644

Performance/production
Reviews of *The Common Pursuit,* by Simon Gray, staged by Simon Gray and Michael McGuire. USA: New York, NY. 1986. Lang.: Eng. 2202

Promessi sposi, I (Betrothed, The)
Performance/production
Unsuccessful productions of works by Alessandro Manzoni. Italy. 1827-1882. Lang.: Ita. 1995

Plays/librettos/scripts
Gestural characterization in *I promessi sposi (The Betrothed)* by Manzoni. Italy. 1842. Lang.: Ita. 2707

Prometheus desmotes (Prometheus Bound)
Plays/librettos/scripts
Interview with Peter Handke about his play *Prometheus gefesselt.* Austria: Salzburg. Greece. 1985-1986. Lang.: Ger. 2398

Prometheus gefesselt (Prometheus Bound)
Plays/librettos/scripts
Interview with Peter Handke about his play *Prometheus gefesselt.* Austria: Salzburg. Greece. 1985-1986. Lang.: Ger. 2398

Promptbooks
Basic theatrical documents
Examination of promptbooks and notes for *Thomas England of Woodstock.* 1594-1633. Lang.: Eng. 1458

Promptbooks for three Dryden plays. England. 1700-1799. Lang.: Eng. 1474

Prompt markings on a copy of James Shirley's *Loves Crueltie* performed by the King's Company. England: London. 1660-1669. Lang.: Eng. 1475

Performance/production
Directorial process as seen through major productions of Stanislavskij, Brecht, Kazan and Brook. 1898-1964. Lang.: Eng. 650

Guide for producing traditional Beijing opera. China: Suzhou. 1574-1646. Lang.: Chi. 3508

Prompter, The
Relation to other fields
William Popple's career in literature and politics. England. 1737-1764. Lang.: Eng. 1080

Properties
Design/technology
Techniques of stage prop construction. 1986. Lang.: Ger. 230

Careers of stage designers, Murray Laufer, Michael Eagan and Susan Benson. Canada. 1972-1983. Lang.: Eng. 241

Central workshops of the Slovak National Theatre. Czechoslovakia: Bratislava. 1960-1986. Lang.: Hun. 255

Shows of models by Eduard Fischer of Berliner Ensemble. Germany, East: Berlin, East. Hungary: Budapest. 1985. Lang.: Hun. 269

Report on the leading brands of stage blood. USA. 1986. Lang.: Eng. 334

Prices, quantities and manufacturers' official line on stage blood. USA. 1986. Lang.: Eng. 337

Artificial canapes for the stage. USA. 1981. Lang.: Eng. 349

Making stage blood. USA. 1982. Lang.: Eng. 368

Application of stage blood. USA. 1986. Lang.: Eng. 373

Putting a metallic finish on props. USA. 1982. Lang.: Eng. 426

Guide to materials necessary for theatrical performances. USSR. 1980-1986. Lang.: Rus. 430

Technical details of producing *La Cage aux Folles* on a small budget. Sweden: Malmö. 1985. Lang.: Swe. 3581

Performance/production
New evidence on the appearance of professional actors. England: London. 1200-1600. Lang.: Eng. 699

How furniture affects our performance in everyday life. UK-England. 1986. Lang.: Eng. 3448

Plays/librettos/scripts
Compares pageant-wagon play about Edward IV with version by Thomas Heywood. England: Coventry, London. 1560-1600. Lang.: Eng. 3430

Proprio like that
Plays/librettos/scripts
Unpublished documentation of *Proprio like that,* a musical by Luigi Pirandello. Italy: Rome. 1930-1953. Lang.: Fre. 3627

Pumba
Performance/production
Reviews of plays performed in the 1983-84 Seoul theatre season. Korea: Seoul. 1983-1984. Lang.: Eng. 2008

Punaunen viiva (Red Line, The)
Performance/production
Interview with composer and director of the Finnish National opera Ilkka Kuusisto. Finland: Helsinki, Suomussalmi. 1967-1986. Lang.: Eng, Fre. 3724
Plays/librettos/scripts
Analysis of thematic trends in recent Finnish Opera. Finland: Helsinki, Savonlinna. 1909-1986. Lang.: Eng, Fre. 3865

Interview with opera composer Aulis Sallinen on his current work. Finland: Helsinki. 1975-1986. Lang.: Eng, Fre. 3866

Puppet Barge (London)
Institutions
Experiences of a couple who converted a coal barge into a touring puppet theatre. UK-England: London. 1976-1986. Lang.: Eng. 4005

Puppet Theatre (Budapest)
SEE
Állami Bábszínház.

Puppeteers
Institutions
Experiences of a couple who converted a coal barge into a touring puppet theatre. UK-England: London. 1976-1986. Lang.: Eng. 4005
Performance/production
Interview with the mixed-media artist and puppeteer Theodora Skipitares. USA. 1974-1985. Lang.: Eng. 3251

Behind-the-scenes look at Fraggle Rock. Canada: Toronto, ON. 1984. Lang.: Eng. 3269

Influence of the Joy Puppeteers on the television program Hickory Hideout. USA: Cleveland, OH. 1982-1986. Lang.: Eng. 3275

Work of Kermit Love, creator of Big Bird for Sesame Street. USA: New York, NY. 1935-1985. Lang.: Eng. 3276

Resource book on construction and performance in puppetry. Lang.: Eng. 3961

Advice for puppeteers in regards to stealing ideas. 3962

Use of puppets in liturgical plays and ceremonies. England: London, Witney. 1540-1560. Lang.: Eng. 3963

Report on international puppet festival. France. Lang.: Rus. 3964

Productions presented at the first regional puppet forum. France: Gareoult. 1986. Lang.: Hun. 3965

Puppeteer Eric Bass of Hakaron Puppet Theatre. Israel: Jerusalem. 1984-1986. Lang.: Heb. 3966

History of puppet theatre including recent developments in political satire and agit-prop. South Africa, Republic of. 1805-1986. Lang.: Eng. 3969

Horse and Bamboo Theatre, specializing in community puppet theatre. UK-England: Rossendale. 1978-1986. Lang.: Eng. 3970

Puppeteer Lettie Connell discusses her career. USA. 1947-1985. 3971

Interview with puppeteers Roger Dennis and Bob Vesely. USA: Cleveland, OH. 1968-1986. Lang.: Eng. 3972

Interview with puppeteer Judy 'Sparky' Roberts. USA. 1986. Lang.: Eng. 3975

Profile of puppeteer Blanche Hardig. USA. 1932-1985. 3976

Puppeteer Julie Taymor adapts Die vertauschten Köpfe (The Transposed Heads) by Thomas Mann for performance at the Ark Theatre. USA: New York, NY. 1984. Lang.: Eng. 3977

Gary Jones, and the Black Street, USA Puppet Theatre. USA: Chicago, IL, Los Angeles, CA. 1970-1986. Lang.: Eng. 3978

Tour of puppet show The Return of the Bounce by Jean Mattson and Joan King. USA: Seattle, WA. Japan. 1984. Lang.: Eng. 3979

Interview with puppeteer Ellen Proctor. USA: Chicago/Springfield, IL, St. Louis, MO. 1923-1985. Lang.: Eng. 3980

Discusses Marie Antoinette Tonight! by puppeteer Bruce D. Schwartz. USA: Los Angeles, CA. Japan: Tokyo. 1979-1986. Lang.: Eng. 3981

The training and career of puppeteer Julie Taymor. USA. 1970-1984. Lang.: Eng. 3982

Puppeteer Bruce D. Scwartz discusses his play Marie Antoinette Tonight!. USA: Atlanta, GA. 1986. Lang.: Eng. 3983

A profile of puppeteer Basil Milovsaroff. USA. 1934-1985. 3984

Round-table on puppet theatre. USSR: Moscow, Leningrad. 1986. Lang.: Rus. 3985

Interview on puppet theatre playwriting with B. Goldovskij and J. Uspenskij. USSR: Moscow. 1986. Lang.: Rus. 3986

Festival of puppet theatre. USSR-Russian SFSR. 1986. Lang.: Rus. 3987

History of The Little Angel Marionette Theatre. UK-England: London. 1961-1986. Lang.: Eng. 4007

Theodora Skipitares' puppet trilogy Age of Invention. USA: New York, NY. 1985. 4013

Use of shadow puppets in an adaptation of Animal Farm. 4016

Description of characters and techniques of Wayang puppetry. Indonesia. 1983-1986. Lang.: Fre. 4018
Plays/librettos/scripts
Polish drama performed in Sweden. Sweden. Poland. 1835-1976. Lang.: Pol. 975
Reference materials
Catalogue of a 1986 exhibition on the Ferrari family and their puppets. Italy. 1877-1986. Lang.: Ita. 3988

A profile of a museum of ventriloquism lore. USA: Fort Mitchell, KY. 1985. 3989
Relation to other fields
Development of educational theatre program dealing with child sexual abuse. USA: St. Louis, MO. 1976-1984. Lang.: Eng. 1145

Reflections on a 3-day workshop on using puppet theatre for social action and communication. UK-England: London. 1986. Lang.: Eng. 3993

Puppetry
SEE ALSO
Classed Entries under PUPPETRY: 3945-4018.
Administration
General information on copyright. USA. 1985. Lang.: Eng. 119
Design/technology
Making of the movie Return to Oz, focusing on its special effects and creature design. USA. 3206

Instructions in creating a modeled puppet head. 3947
Institutions
Report on the Microtheater Festival in the Wiener Festwochen. Austria: Vienna. 1986. Lang.: Ger. 447

Activities of Rialles, including children's theatre and puppetry. Spain-Catalonia: Terrassa. 1972-1982. Lang.: Cat. 517

Cultural activities in the Lodz ghetto. Poland: Łodż. 1940-1944. Lang.: Heb. 3323
Performance/production
History of Yiddish theatre district. USA: New York, NY. 1900-1939. Lang.: Eng. 827

Review of children's theatre festival. Yugoslavia: Šibenik. 1986. Lang.: Hun. 916

Influence of Asian theatre traditions on American artists. USA: New York, NY. Indonesia. 1952-1985. Lang.: Eng. 1335

Old and new forms in Japanese theatre. Japan. 1983-1984. Lang.: Eng. 1382

Production description of the symbolist drama La navaja (The Razor) by Eduardo Quiles. Spain. 1980. Lang.: Spa. 2074

Behind-the-scenes look at Fraggle Rock. Canada: Toronto, ON. 1984. Lang.: Eng. 3269

Influence of the Joy Puppeteers on the television program Hickory Hideout. USA: Cleveland, OH. 1982-1986. Lang.: Eng. 3275

Work of Kermit Love, creator of Big Bird for Sesame Street. USA: New York, NY. 1935-1985. Lang.: Eng. 3276

Origins of Southern Sung drama (Nanxi). China: Wenzhou. 1127-1234. Lang.: Chi. 3512

Report on international puppet festival. France. Lang.: Rus. 3964

Puppets in Performance, part of the 50th anniversary celebration of the WPA Federal Theatre Project. USA. 1986. 3974

Puppet production of Mozart's opera Die Zauberflöte. USA. 1986. Lang.: Eng. 4008

Theodora Skipitares' puppet trilogy Age of Invention. USA: New York, NY. 1985. 4013
Plays/librettos/scripts
Analysis of various theatrical forms of francophone Africa. Africa. 1985. Lang.: Fre. 919

Experimental farce techniques in Fidela by Aurelio Ferretti. Argentina. 1930-1960. Lang.: Spa. 2360

Description of plays by Eduardo Quiles including La navaja (The Razor) a tragicomedy for two actors and puppets. Spain. 1940-1985. Lang.: Spa. 2780

Puppetry Guild of Northeast Ohio
Performance/production
Interview with puppeteers Roger Dennis and Bob Vesely. USA:
Cleveland, OH. 1968-1986. Lang.: Eng. 3972
Puppets
Design/technology
Making of the movie *Return to Oz*, focusing on its special effects
and creature design. USA. 3206
Special effects in the film version of *Little Shop of Horrors*. USA.
Lang.: Eng. 3212
Mechanical bears in film, *Clan of the Cave Bear*. USA. 1985-1986.
Lang.: Eng. 3214
Director of electronics and mechanical design for the Muppets, Faz
Fazakas. USA. 1986. 3262
Logistics of a clown gag with puppetry that uses a third arm jacket.
3946
Instructions in creating a modeled puppet head. 3947
Creating physical attributes for puppets which effectively
communicate their character. 3948
Techniques and tools in puppet design and construction. USA. 1986.
Lang.: Eng. 3954
Tomie DePaola's work in puppetry. USA: New London, NH. 1970-
1985. Lang.: Eng. 3955
Collection of pictures of *bunraku* puppet heads. Japan: Tokyo.
Lang.: Jap. 3997
Creating the proportions and constructing a pattern plan for
marionettes. USA. 1985-1986. 4003
Design and creation of puppets for the Yale Puppeteers' *Bluebeard*.
USA. 1928. Lang.: Eng. 4004
Creating overhead shadow sequence for puppet production. USA.
4014

Performance/production
Staging techniques employed at the Mermaid Theatre. Canada:
Wolfville, NS. 1972-1985. Lang.: Eng. 665
Production description of the symbolist drama *La navaja (The
Razor)* by Eduardo Quiles. Spain. 1980. Lang.: Spa. 2074
Interview with the mixed-media artist and puppeteer Theodora
Skipitares. USA. 1974-1985. Lang.: Eng. 3251
Circus clown discusses his training and work with puppets. 3382
Peter Schumann and his work with the Bread and Puppet Theatre.
USA: New York, NY. 1968-1986. Lang.: Eng. 3973
Marionette theatre history in Northern England. England:
Sunderland. 1860-1869. Lang.: Eng. 4006
Shadow puppetry as a way of passing on Balinese culture. Bali.
1976-1985. Lang.: Eng. 4017

Plays/librettos/scripts
Influence of Asian theatre on work of Filippo Acciajoli. Italy. 1637-
1700. Lang.: Ita. 2713
Description of plays by Eduardo Quiles including *La navaja (The
Razor)* a tragicomedy for two actors and puppets. Spain. 1940-1985.
Lang.: Spa. 2780
Purcell, Henry
Plays/librettos/scripts
English traditions in works of Henry Purcell. England. 1659-1695.
Lang.: Rus. 3497
Puritani, I
Performance/production
Photographs, cast list, synopsis, and discography of Metropolitan
Opera radio broadcast performances. USA: New York, NY. 1986.
Lang.: Eng. 3797
Purple Flower, The
Plays/librettos/scripts
Precursors of revolutionary black theatre. Haiti. Jamaica. 1820-1970.
Lang.: Eng. 956
Pushkin Theatre (Leningrad)
SEE
Akademičeskij Teat'r Dramy im. A. Puškina.
Puškin, Aleksand'r Sergejevič
Plays/librettos/scripts
Puškin's *Queen of Spades* adapted for opera by Čajkovskij. Russia.
1833-1890. Lang.: Eng. 3891
Puzyna, Konstanty
Institutions
Thirty years of the Polish theatrical monthly *Dialog*. Poland:
Warsaw. 1956-1986. Lang.: Pol. 511

Pygmalion
Plays/librettos/scripts
Short history of Catalan translations of plays. Spain-Catalonia. 1848-
1984. Lang.: Fre. 2813
Relation to other fields
Reports and discussions of restricted cultural communication.
Lebanon. Spain-Catalonia. USA. 1985. Lang.: Fre, Spa, Cat. 1111
Pynchon, Thomas
Plays/librettos/scripts
The incoherent protagonist of modern comedy. 1954-1986. Lang.:
Eng. 2358
Pyramide Op De Punt
Theory/criticism
The aesthetics of movement theatre. Europe. 1975-1986. 3301
Pyrotechnics
Design/technology
Safe method of controlling live fire onstage from remote position.
USA. 1984. Lang.: Eng. 380
Qu'ils crèvent les artists
SEE
Niech szezna artyszi.
*Quaderni di Serafino Gubbio operatore, I (Notebooks of Serafino
Gubbio, Cameraman, The)*
Relation to other fields
Study of Luigi Pirandello's novel, *I quaderni di Serafino Gubbio
operatore (The Notebooks of Serafino Gubbio, Cameraman)*. Italy.
1915-1925. Lang.: Ita. 1104
Quadrennial (Prague)
SEE
Prague Quadrennial.
Quan-em Thi Kinh (Thi Kinh, The Merciful Buddha Woman)
Performance/production
Review and discussion of Vietnamese performance in Hungary.
Vietnam: Thai Binh. Hungary. 1986. Lang.: Hun. 915
Quartermaine's Terms
Plays/librettos/scripts
Influence of Aristophanes and Čechov on playwright Simon Gray.
UK-England. 1986. Lang.: Eng. 2874
Quatro, Suzi
Performance/production
Interview with actress and rock star Suzi Quatro. UK-England:
Chichester. 1986. Lang.: Eng. 3608
Quebec Drama Festival (Quebec, PQ)
Institutions
Limited opportunities for English-language playwrights in Montreal.
Canada: Montreal, PQ. 1976-1986. Lang.: Eng. 1561
Queen of Spades
SEE
Pique Dame.
Queen's Royal Theatre (Dublin)
Basic theatrical documents
Text of *The Miser Outwitted*, attributed to Major John Richardson,
with introduction. Canada. UK-Ireland: Dublin. 1838-1848. Lang.:
Eng. 1465
Queler, Eve
Performance/production
Account of the neglected opera *Libuše* by Jan Smetana on the
occasion of its New York premiere. Czechoslovakia: Prague. USA:
New York, NY. 1883-1986. Lang.: Eng. 3715
Quellet, René
Performance/production
A photographic essay of 42 soloists and groups performing mime or
gestural theatre. 1986. 3290
Quem Quaeritis
Relation to other fields
Review article on Johann Drumbl's *Quem Quaeritis: Teatro Sacro
dell'Alto Mediaevo*. France. Italy. 900-999. Lang.: Eng. 3031
Quesnel, Joseph
Performance/production
Review of Toronto performances of *Colas and Colinette*. Canada:
Toronto, ON, Montreal, PQ. 1986. Lang.: Eng. 3707
Questi fantasmi! (These Phantoms!)
Plays/librettos/scripts
Realism and fantasy in *Questi fantasmi! (These Phantoms!)* by
Eduardo De Filippo. Italy. 1946. Lang.: Ita. 2676
Quiet End, A
Performance/production
Collection of newspaper reviews by London theatre critics. UK-
England. 1986. Lang.: Eng. 2114

Quiet Place, A
Reference materials
Photos of the new opera productions at the Staatsoper. Austria: Vienna. 1985-1986. Lang.: Ger.   3910

Quiles, Eduardo
Performance/production
Production description of the symbolist drama *La navaja (The Razor)* by Eduardo Quiles. Spain. 1980. Lang.: Spa.   2074

Plays/librettos/scripts
Description of plays by Eduardo Quiles including *La navaja (The Razor)* a tragicomedy for two actors and puppets. Spain. 1940-1985. Lang.: Spa.   2780

Quilico, Gino
Performance/production
Interview with baritone Gino Quilico. Canada: Toronto, ON. 1984-1986. Lang.: Eng.   3711

Quilico, Louis
Performance/production
Interview with baritone Gino Quilico. Canada: Toronto, ON. 1984-1986. Lang.: Eng.   3711

Quinta Temporada (Fifth Season)
Plays/librettos/scripts
Ritual function of *The Slave Ship* by LeRoi Jones (Amiri Baraka) and *Quinta Temporada (Fifth Season)* by Luis Valdez. USA. 1965-1967. Lang.: Eng.   2906

Quintero, José
Design/technology
Lighting designer Tom Skelton discussing his work on the recent revival of *The Iceman Cometh*. USA: New York, NY. 1985-1986. Lang.: Eng.   1531

Performance/production
The Iceman Cometh by Eugene O'Neill, directed by José Quintero. USA: New York, NY. 1985. Lang.: Eng.   2315

Plays/librettos/scripts
Popularity and relevance of Eugene O'Neill. USA. Lang.: Eng.   2894

Quintessence of Ibsenism, The
Theory/criticism
Shaw's use of devil's advocacy in his plays compared to deconstructionism. UK-England. 1900-1986. Lang.: Eng.   3135

Quinto, José María
Plays/librettos/scripts
Examples of playwrights whose work was poorly received by theatrical audiences in Madrid. Spain: Madrid. 1609-1950. Lang.: Spa.   2786

Quinton, Everett
Design/technology
Charles Ludlam's role as set designer, artistic director and lead actor of The Ridiculous Theatre Company. USA: New York, NY. 1986.   360

Quinzaine internationale du théâtre (Montreal, PQ)
Performance/production
Review of international theatre festivals. Spain. Canada: Montreal, PQ, Toronto, ON. 1986. Lang.: Eng.   2077

Quivar, Florence
Performance/production
Black opera stars and companies. USA: Enid, OK, New York, NY. 1961-1985. Lang.: Eng.   3839

RA
Plays/librettos/scripts
Analysis of *RA* by R. Murray Schafer, performed by Comus Music Theatre. Canada: Toronto, ON. 1983. Lang.: Eng.   2416

Raalte, Christa van
Performance/production
Collection of newspaper reviews by London theatre critics. UK-England: London. 1986. Lang.: Eng.   2110

Rábai, Miklós
Performance/production
Life and career of choreographer Miklós Rábai. Hungary. 1921-1974. Lang.: Hun.   1332

Rabb, Ellis
Performance/production
Actress Rosemary Harris discusses her work in *The Petition*. UK-England: London. USA: New York, NY. 1948-1986. Lang.: Eng.   2177

Rabe, David
Performance/production
David Rabe's play *Sticks and Bones* presented at the Pesti Theatre in Hungary. Hungary: Budapest. 1971-1975. Lang.: Hun.   1799

Review of the Steppenwolf Theatre Company's production of *Streamers* by David Rabe. USA: Washington, DC. 1985. Lang.: Eng.   2297

Plays/librettos/scripts
Playwright David Rabe's treatment of cliche in *Sticks and Bones*. USA. 1971. Lang.: Eng.   2902

Analysis of *Hurlyburly* by David Rabe. USA. 1984. Lang.: Eng.   2918

Racine, Jean
Performance/production
Interview with Carlo Boso, expert on *commedia dell'arte*. Europe. 1985. Lang.: Fre.   3409

Plays/librettos/scripts
Stoicism and modern elements in Senecan drama. Europe. 65-1986. Lang.: Eng.   2542

Modern thought in works of Jean Racine. France. 1664-1691. Lang.: Fre.   2553

Commonplace as rhetorical device in plays of Jean Racine. France. 1650-1986. Lang.: Fre.   2559

Use of the present tense in some tragedies of Corneille and Racine. France. 1600-1700. Lang.: Fre.   2564

Study of *Bérénice*, *Athalie* and *Bajazet* by Jean Racine. France. 1670-1691. Lang.: Fre.   2583

Theory/criticism
Corneille, Racine and Molière as neoclassisists. France. 1600-1700. Lang.: Kor.   3102

Raczak, Lech
Performance/production
Interviews with Polish theatre professionals. Poland: Poznań. 1963-1985. Lang.: Eng.   2024

Relation to other fields
Interview with director Lech Raczak of Theatre of the Eighth Day. Poland: Poznań. 1968-1985. Lang.: Eng.   3048

RADA
SEE
Royal Academy of Dramatic Arts.

Radičkov, J.
Plays/librettos/scripts
Replies to questionnaire by five Soviet playwrights. USSR. Bulgaria. 1986. Lang.: Rus.   2958

Radio
SEE
Audio forms.

Radio drama
Basic theatrical documents
English translation of *Les invités au procès (The Guests on Trial)* by Anne Hébert. Canada. 1952. Lang.: Eng.   3174

Text of radio play about a woman doctor who masqueraded as a man. Canada: Montreal, PQ. UK-Scotland: Edinburgh. South Africa, Republic of: Cape Town. 1809-1859. Lang.: Eng.   3175

Institutions
Negative evaluation of recent Canadian Broadcasting Corporation drama. Canada. 1981-1982. Lang.: Eng.   3177

Performance/production
Esse Ljungh's acting career with Winnipeg Little Theatre. Canada: Winnipeg, MB. 1921-1937. Lang.: Eng.   664

Actor discusses work in recitation programs. USSR: Moscow. 1980-1986. Lang.: Rus.   888

Problems of producing Shakespeare on radio. UK-England. 1935-1980. Lang.: Eng.   3178

Plays/librettos/scripts
Interview with actor, director, playwright Staffan Göthe. Sweden: Luleå. 1972-1986. Lang.: Swe.   2826

Comparison of the radio and staged versions of Harold Pinter's *A Slight Ache*. UK-England. 1959-1961. Lang.: Eng.   2880

Radio adaptations of foreign works, their effect on culture. Canada. 1939-1949. Lang.: Fre.   3181

Scandinavian drama on Canadian radio. Canada. Scandinavia. 1939-1982. Lang.: Eng.   3182

A review of radio plays written by Linda Zwicker. Canada. 1968-1986. Lang.: Eng.   3184

Plays by women on the CBC radio network. Canada. 1985-1986. Lang.: Eng.   3185

Influence of Harold Pinter's radio work on his stage plays. UK-England. 1957-1981. Lang.: Eng.   3186

SUBJECT INDEX

Rame, Franca
Basic theatrical documents
English translation of *Coppia aperta, quasi spalancata (An Open Couple—Very Open)* by Dario Fo and Franca Rame. Italy: Trieste. 1983. Lang.: Eng.   1486

Performance/production
Life and work of actress-playwright Franca Rame. Italy. 1929-1983. Lang.: Eng.   1988

Productions of Dario Fo's *Morte accidentale di un anarchico (Accidental Death of an Anarchist)* in the light of Fo's political ideas. USA. Canada. Italy. 1970-1986. Lang.: Eng.   2262

Rameau, Jean-Philippe
Performance/production
On productions of lyric comedies and opera ballets by Jean-Philippe Rameau. France. 1683-1764. Lang.: Rus.   1304

Ramicova, Dunya
Design/technology
Costume designer Dunya Ramicova discusses the aesthetics of design. USA: New Haven, CT. 1986.   363

Ramis, Joan
Relation to other fields
Reports and discussions of restricted cultural communication. Lebanon. Spain-Catalonia. USA. 1985. Lang.: Fre, Spa, Cat.   1111

Theory/criticism
Historical difficulties in creating a paradigm for Catalan theatre. Spain-Catalonia. 1400-1963. Lang.: Cat.   1220

Ramsey
Performance/production
Brief investigation of the lives of seven actors. England. 1526-1587. Lang.: Eng.   691

Ran
Design/technology
Film director Akira Kurosawa discusses designing *Ran.* Japan. 1986. Lang.: Eng.   3200

Ranama, Norman
Performance/production
Biography of actor Danny Kaye. USA: New York, NY. 1912-1985. Lang.: Eng.   2265

Randall, Paulette
Performance/production
Collection of newspaper reviews by London theatre critics. UK-England: London. 1986. Lang.: Eng.   2121

Randazzo, Peter
Institutions
Problems of Toronto Dance Theatre. Canada: Toronto, ON. 1968-1982. Lang.: Eng.   1344

Ranevskaja, Faina
Performance/production
Recollections of actress Faina Ranevskaja. USSR. 1896-1984. Lang.: Rus.   2316

Faina Ranevskaja's role in *Pravda—chorošo, a sčast'e lučše (Truth is Good, But Happiness is Better)* by A.N. Ostrovskij. USSR: Moscow. 1896-1984. Lang.: Rus.   2324

Rank Strand Ltd. Lighting
Design/technology
Details the installation and use of a 1935 Strand lighting console. UK-England: London. 1935-1986. Lang.: Eng.   321

Information on Rank Strand Ltd. Lighting and its subsidiaries. UK-England. 1986. Lang.: Hun.   329

Rank, Otto
Plays/librettos/scripts
Theories of Otto Rank applied to plays of Eugene O'Neill. USA. 1888-1953. Lang.: Eng.   2948

Rape of Lucretia, The
Plays/librettos/scripts
A chronology and analysis of the compositions of Benjamin Britten. UK-England: London. 1946-1976. Lang.: Eng.   3896

Raphael, Tim
Institutions
Vi Higginsen's *Mama I Want to Sing* and history of the Mumbo-Jumbo Theatre Company. USA: New York, NY. 1980-1986. Lang.: Eng.   1601

Raposo, Joe
Performance/production
Reviews of *Raggedy Ann*, book by William Gibon, music and lyrics by Joe Raposo, staged and choreographed by Patricia Birch. USA: New York, NY. 1986. Lang.: Eng.   3614

Rasi, Luigi
Performance/production
Biographical study of actress Eleonora Duse. Italy. 1858-1901. Lang.: Ita.   1999

Ratkó, József
Performance/production
Selected reviews of *Segitsd a király! (Help the King!)* by József Ratkó. Hungary: Nyiregyháza. 1985. Lang.: Hun.   1902

Rátony, Róbert
Performance/production
Selected short comic prose sketches of Róbert Rátony, actor, showman and writer. Hungary. 1944-1985. Lang.: Hun.   1920

Rattigan, Terrence
Theory/criticism
Assessment of critic Kenneth Tynan's works. UK-England. 1950-1960. Lang.: Eng.   3136

Ratyński, Michał
Performance/production
Michał Ratyński directs Różewicz's *Kartoteka (Card Index)*, Teatr Powszechny. Poland: Warsaw. 1984. Lang.: Pol.   2062

Raub der Sabinerinnen, Der (Rape of the Sabine Women, The)
Performance/production
On actor Heinz Petters and the production of *Der Raub der Sabinerinnen* at the Volkstheater. Austria: Vienna. 1938-1986. Lang.: Ger.   1644

Raüber, Die (Bandits, The)
Theory/criticism
Analysis of Friedrich Schiller's dramatic and theoretical works. Germany. 1759-1805. Lang.: Cat.   3109

Rauschenberg, Robert
Relation to other fields
Comparison of works of playwright Sam Shepard and artist Robert Rauschenberg. USA. 1960-1980. Lang.: Eng.   3062

Rautavaara, Eionojuhani
Plays/librettos/scripts
Analysis of thematic trends in recent Finnish Opera. Finland: Helsinki, Savonlinna. 1909-1986. Lang.: Eng, Fre.   3865

Ravens
Performance/production
Collection of newspaper reviews by London theatre critics. UK-England. 1986. Lang.: Eng.   2114

Ravenscroft, Edward
Plays/librettos/scripts
Revision of dramaturgy and stagecraft in Restoration adaptations of Shakespeare. England: London. 1660-1690. Lang.: Eng.   2535

Ray, Robin
Performance/production
Collection of newspaper reviews by London theatre critics. UK-England: London. 1986. Lang.: Eng.   2124

Plays/librettos/scripts
Discussion of plays about Verdi and Puccini by Julian Mitchell and Robin Ray. UK-England: London. Italy. 1986. Lang.: Eng.   3628

Raymond, Bill
Institutions
Interview with members of Mabou Mines. USA: New York, NY. 1984. Lang.: Eng.   1607

Raymond, James
Performance/production
The career of Jacob Driesbach, a famous circus animal trainer in the circus. USA. 1807-1878. Lang.: Eng.   3397

Rayne, Stephen
Performance/production
Collection of newspaper reviews by London theatre critics. UK. 1986. Lang.: Eng.   2099

Raz, Ya'akov
Performance/production
Artistic cooperation between playwright Dan Horowitz and director Ya'akov Raz. Israel. 1978-1986. Lang.: Heb.   1978

Reading Theatre-in-Education Company (England)
Plays/librettos/scripts
Historical background of *Sisters of Eve* by Tricia Burden. Eire. 1984-1986. Lang.: Eng.   2455

Real Long John Silver, The
Performance/production
Production analysis of four plays by Peter Barnes. UK-England. 1981-1986. Lang.: Eng.   805

Realism

Performance/production

Director Robert Woodruff's shift from naturalism to greater theatricality. USA: San Francisco, CA, New York, NY, La Jolla, CA. 1976-1986. Lang.: Eng.   851

Reviews of Shakespeare productions written by Hungarian realist writer, Zsigmond Móricz. Hungary: Budapest. 1923. Lang.: Hun.   1887

Plays/librettos/scripts

Realism and fantasy in *Questi fantasmi! (These Phantoms!)* by Eduardo De Filippo. Italy. 1946. Lang.: Ita.   2676

Theory/criticism

Andrej Belyj's views on Symbolist and Realist theatre, dramaturgy. Russia. 1880-1934. Lang.: Rus.   3129

Reaney, James

Reference materials

Collected reviews of 31 major Canadian plays. Canada. 1934-1983. Lang.: Eng.   1009

Reapers

Plays/librettos/scripts

Biography of playwright Teresa Deevy. Ireland. 1894-1963. Lang.: Eng.   2665

Reardon, Michael

Performance spaces

Description of the new Swan Theatre and Shakespeare-related buildings. UK-England: Stratford. 1986. Lang.: Eng.   631

Outlines the technical and architectural features of the Swan Theatre at Stratford-upon-Avon. UK-England: Stratford. Lang.: Eng.   1617

Reay, Corey

Basic theatrical documents

A collection of satirical monologues by playwright Corey Reay. Canada. Lang.: Eng.   1471

Rebels, The by Ignác Nagy

SEE

Pártütők, A.

Rebombori 2 (Disturbance 2)

Plays/librettos/scripts

Analysis of the six published dramatic works by Jordi Teixidor. Spain-Catalonia. 1970-1985. Lang.: Cat.   2809

Reception theory

Theory/criticism

Essays on the sociology of art and semiotics. Lang.: Hun.   1192

Influence of literary theory on Greek theatre studies. Greece. UK-England. Germany. Lang.: Afr.   1210

Six rules which render socially desirable elements of performance superfluous. USA. 1968-1986. Lang.: Eng.   3151

Reconstruction, performance

Basic theatrical documents

Examination of promptbooks and notes for *Thomas England of Woodstock*. 1594-1633. Lang.: Eng.   1458

Gilbert Parker's *The Seats of the Mighty* as staged by Herbert Beerbohm Tree. Canada. 1897. Lang.: Eng.   1470

Performance spaces

Outdoor performance spaces surveyed through fragmentary records. England: Shrewsbury. 1445-1575. Lang.: Eng.   593

Performance/production

Theories of medieval production and acting techniques. England. 1400-1500. Lang.: Eng.   698

Performances of *nō* plays dealing with Chinese subject matter. Japan. 1300-1400. Lang.: Jap.   1405

Reconstruction of staging of Act I, *The Spanish Tragedy* by Thomas Kyd. England: London. 1592. Lang.: Eng.   1703

Original staging of Thomas Middleton's *Hengist, King of Kent*. England: London. 1619-1661. Lang.: Eng.   1713

Letters of actress Eleanora Duse. Italy. 1920-1923. Lang.: Ita.   2001

Reconstruction of a number of Shakespeare plays staged and performed by Herbert Beerbohm Tree. UK-England: London. 1887-1917. Lang.: Eng.   2155

Interview with Carlo Boso on *commedia dell'arte* reconstruction. UK-England. Italy. 1947-1986. Lang.: Eng.   3415

Reconstruction of triumphal entry pageants. Italy. 1494-1600. Lang.: Eng.   3425

Plays/librettos/scripts

Reconstruction of the three versions and productions of the operetta *Állami Áruház (State Stores)*. Hungary. 1952-1977. Lang.: Hun. 3943

Theory/criticism

Attempt to establish a more theatrical view of drama. Lang.: Fre.   3078

Reconstruction, theatre

Design/technology

Details of new electrical system of rebuilt Szeged National Theatre. Hungary: Szeged. 1983-1986. Lang.: Hun.   277

The sound and video systems at the Szeged National Theatre. Hungary: Szeged. 1986. Lang.: Hun.   282

Reconstruction of mechanical equipment at the Szeged National Theatre. Hungary: Szeged. 1981-1986. Lang.: Hun.   288

Report on new heating, plumbing and air-conditioning at reconstructed Szeged National Theatre. Hungary: Szeged. 1978-1986. Lang.: Hun.   293

Overhaul of The World Theatre as a radio broadcasting facility. USA: St. Paul, MN. 1982-1986. Lang.: Eng.   387

Performance spaces

Survey of renovations and reconstructions of theatres in Hungary. Hungary. 1980-1986. Lang.: Hun.   601

Structural design problems and their solutions at the Szeged National Theatre in Hungary. Hungary: Szeged. 1977-1986. Lang.: Hun.   602

The history of the theatre building used by Szegedi Nemzeti Színház. Hungary: Szeged. 1800-1883. Lang.: Hun.   603

Reconstruction of the Szeged National Theatre. Hungary: Szeged. 1948-1980. Lang.: Hun.   604

Design and construction of rebuilt Szeged National Theatre. Hungary: Szeged. 1978-1986. Lang.: Hun.   605

Reconstruction of the auditorium of the József Attila Culture Centre. Hungary: Budapest. 1986. Lang.: Hun.   606

Director of Szegedi Nemzeti Színház on reconstructed theatre. Hungary: Szeged. 1978-1986. Lang.: Hun.   607

Design of the Szeged National Theatre renovation. Hungary: Szeged. 1981-1986. Lang.: Hun.   608

Reconstructing a theatrical organization at Saint James Palace (London). England: London. 1600-1986. Lang.: Eng.   1615

Reference materials

Catalogue of an exhibit on the Carlo Felice Theatre, destroyed in World War II, and its proposed reconstruction. Italy: Genoa. 1600-1985. Lang.: Ita.   1024

Red Ladder Theatre (UK)

Performance/production

Brechtian technique in the contemporary feminist drama of Caryl Churchill, Claire Luckham and others. UK-England. 1956-1979. Lang.: Eng.   815

Reddin, Keith

Performance/production

Reviews of *Rum and Coke*, by Keith Reddin, staged by Leo Waters. USA: New York, NY. 1986. Lang.: Eng.   2241

Redfarn, Roger

Performance/production

Collection of newspaper reviews by London theatre critics. UK. 1986. Lang.: Eng.   2101

Collection of newspaper reviews by London theatre critics. UK-England. 1986. Lang.: Eng.   2111

Redgrave, Colin

Performance/production

Actress Frances de la Tour discusses her work in *Lillian* by William Luce. UK-England: London. USA. 1986. Lang.: Eng.   2146

Redgrave, Corin

Institutions

Overview of the *Not the RSC Festival* at the Almeida Theatre. UK-England: London. 1986. Lang.: Eng.   534

Redgrave, Vanessa

Institutions

Overview of the *Not the RSC Festival* at the Almeida Theatre. UK-England: London. 1986. Lang.: Eng.   534

Reduta Theatre (Poland)

Performance/production

Actor-director Edmund Wierciński on Reduta Theatre. Poland. 1924. Lang.: Pol.   775

Rees, Roger

Performance/production

Roger Rees, associate director at Bristol Old Vic discusses his career and the season. UK-England: Bristol. 1970-1986. Lang.: Eng.   2138

Regional theatre — cont'd

A profile of South Coast Repertory. USA: Los Angeles, CA. 1964-1986. 569

Careers of choreographers Maria Formolo and Keith Urban. Canada: Regina, SK, Edmonton, AB. 1980-1983. Lang.: Eng. 1343

Artistic director John Neville discusses future plans for the Stratford Festival. Canada: Stratford, ON. 1985. Lang.: Eng. 1551

Several short-lived alternative theatre companies to the Neptune Theatre. Canada: Halifax, NS. 1962-1986. Lang.: Eng. 1557

History of the Théâtre du Soleil. France: Paris. 1963-1985. Lang.: Eng. 1574

Influence of the Little Theatre movement on regional theatre. USA. 1887-1967. Lang.: Chi. 1611

Performance/production

Development of regional theatre and other entertainments. England. 1840-1870. Lang.: Eng. 687

Development of and influences on theatre and other regional entertainments. England. 1840-1870. Lang.: Eng. 688

Parisian criticism of Quebec theatre as French regional theatre. France: Paris. Canada. 1955-1985. Lang.: Fre. 719

Description of the major activities of the Tatar State Academic Theatre, known as the Kamal Theatre. USSR: Kazan. 1906-1985. Lang.: Rus. 857

Performances and goals of recent Georgian theatre. USSR. 1980-1986. Lang.: Rus. 889

Recent achievements of Georgian theatre. USSR. 1980-1986. Lang.: Rus. 891

Development of Armenian directing. USSR. 1950-1979. Lang.: Rus. 896

Five actors who work solely in regional theatre. 1961-1984. Lang.: Eng. 1633

Survey of productions in 1985/86. Brazil: Rio de Janeiro. 1985-1986. Lang.: Eng. 1656

Career of director Bill Glassco. Canada: Toronto, ON. 1965-1986. Lang.: Eng. 1674

Actress compares advantages of small-town and metropolitan careers. Canada. 1986. Lang.: Eng. 1677

Reviews of regional productions. Sweden: Stockholm. 1985-1986. Lang.: Swe. 2087

Ukrainian performances of classical Western tragedies. USSR. 1920-1930. Lang.: Rus. 2317

Use of music in Uzbekistan dramatic presentations. USSR. Lang.: Rus. 2332

Development of Azerbajžani directing. USSR. 1920. Lang.: Rus. 2338

Plays/librettos/scripts

Description of national theatre festival. Argentina: Córdoba. 1985. Lang.: Spa. 2366

Reference materials

Overview of Charlottetown Festival productions. Canada: Charlottetown, PE. 1972-1983. Lang.: Eng. 1008

List of institutional theatres. USA. 1986. 1039

Overview of French-language productions. Canada: Montreal, PQ. 1958-1968. Lang.: Eng. 2984

Relation to other fields

Statistical index of theatre attendance in the regional and provincial centers of the USSR-Russian SFSR. USSR. 1985. Lang.: Rus. 1175

Regionteatern i Västernorrland (Sweden)

Performance spaces

Touring production of *Cyrano de Bergerac* seen from crew's point of view. Sweden. 1986. Lang.: Swe. 617

Regreso sin causa (Return Without Cause)

Plays/librettos/scripts

Interview with Chilean playwright Jaime Miranda. Venezuela. Chile. USA. 1956-1985. Lang.: Eng. 2973

Regulations

U.S. laws on music performing rights. USA. 1856-1986. Lang.: Eng. 3473

Administration

Draft copyright laws of World Intellectual Property Organization. Switzerland. 1986. Lang.: Eng. 64

Details of the new Approved Production Contract. USA: New York, NY. 1985. Lang.: Eng. 94

Guide to producing Off-off Broadway showcases. USA: New York, NY. Lang.: Eng. 159

Primary organizational changes at New York State Council on the Arts. USA: New York, NY. 1984. Lang.: Eng. 162

Revisions in the Showcase Code by Actors' Equity Association. USA: New York, NY. 1982. Lang.: Eng. 165

Changes in the Showcase and Nonprofit Theatre codes. USA. 1983. Lang.: Eng. 166

Legislation for the protection of Victorian child-actors. UK. 1837-1901. Lang.: Eng. 1439

History of source licensing for television and film scores. USA. 1897-1987. Lang.: Eng. 3195

Institutions

List of actors and companies using Little Haymarket Theatre. England: London. 1720-1737. Lang.: Eng. 491

Plays/librettos/scripts

Obtaining legal rights to a property when adapting a play. USA: New York, NY. 1984. Lang.: Eng. 983

Reference materials

Guide to producing printed material. USA. 1984. Lang.: Eng. 1044

Relation to other fields

New regulations governing lobbying activities of nonprofit organizations. USA: Washington, DC. 1984. Lang.: Eng. 1152

Reich, Bernhard

Plays/librettos/scripts

Correspondence between Bernhard Reich and Heinz-Uwe Haus. USSR. 1971-1972. 2966

Reich, Molka

Performance/production

Puppets in Performance, part of the 50th anniversary celebration of the WPA Federal Theatre Project. USA. 1986. 3974

Reichert, Franz

Performance/production

Biography of actor and stage manager Franz Reichert. Austria: Vienna. Germany: Berlin. Czechoslovakia: Prague. 1925-1950. Lang.: Ger. 1652

Reid, Christina

Performance/production

Collection of newspaper reviews by London theatre critics. UK-England: London. 1986. Lang.: Eng. 2118

Reigen (Round)

Performance/production

Reviews of two plays by Arthur Schnitzler directed by Imre Halasi. Hungary: Budapest, Zalaegerszeg. 1986. Lang.: Hun. 1958

Savannah Bay and *Reigen (Round)* produced by Centre Dramàtic. Spain-Catalonia: Barcelona. 1986. Lang.: Cat. 2082

Reignolds, Kate

Relation to other fields

Professional equality in theatrical careers for men and women. USA: New York, NY. 1850-1870. Lang.: Eng. 1143

Reiling, Gil

Design/technology

Howard Brandston's approach to lighting the Statue of Liberty. USA: New York, NY. 1986. Lang.: Eng. 3317

Reinach, Edwige

Performance/production

Orientalism in four productions of Wilde's *Salome*. Italy. 1904-1963. Lang.: Ita. 750

Reinhardt, Max

Design/technology

Contribution of designer Ernst Stern to modern scenography. Germany: Berlin. UK-England: London. 1905. Lang.: Eng. 1516

Institutions

Autobiographical documents by personnel of the Deutsches Theater. Germany: Berlin. 1884-1955. Lang.: Ger. 1577

Performance/production

Origins of radically simplified stage in modern productions. USA. 1912-1922. Lang.: Eng. 831

Max Reinhardt's music-drama *Sumurun*. USA: New York, NY. 1912. Lang.: Ita. 1369

Max Reinhardt's work with his contemporaries. Germany. Austria. 1890-1938. Lang.: Eng, Ger. 1757

Max Reinhardt's notes on his production of *Sei personaggi in cerca d'autore (Six Characters in Search of an Author)* by Luigi Pirandello. Germany. Italy. 1924-1934. Lang.: Ita. 1759

Interview with Elisabeth Bergner and Jane Alexander on their portrayals of Joan of Arc. Germany, West: Berlin, West. UK-England: Malvern. USA: Washington, DC. Lang.: Eng. 1766

Reinhardt, Max — cont'd

Greek tragedy on the New York stage. USA: New York, NY. 1854-1984. Lang.: Eng. 2301

Reference materials

Influence of stage director Max Reinhardt on film production. Germany: Berlin. Austria: Vienna. 1913-1945. Lang.: Ger. 3244

Rejzen, Mark O.

Performance/production

Biographical materials on Bolšoj singer Mark Rejzen. Russia: Moscow. 1895-1986. Lang.: Rus. 3774

Relapse, The

Performance/production

Survey of the Chichester Festival. UK-England: Chichester. 1986. Lang.: Eng. 2185

Plays/librettos/scripts

Language and society in Colley Cibber's *Love's Last Shift* and Sir John Vanbrugh's *The Relapse*. England. 1696. Lang.: Eng. 2495

Religion

Audience

Moral objections to children's attendance of theatres. USA: New York, NY. 1900-1910. Lang.: Eng. 202

Audience of the humanistic, religious and school-theatre of the European Renaissance. Europe. 1480-1630. Lang.: Ger. 1445

Basic theatrical documents

Edited text of a traditional Nativity play. Hungary: Kézdivásárhely. 1700-1730. Lang.: Hun. 223

Edition and introduction to Catalan religious tragedy of Saint Sebastian. Spain-Catalonia: Riudoms. 1400-1880. Lang.: Cat. 1498

Text of a Nativity puppet play. Hungary: Balatonberényi. 1970-1980. Lang.: Hun. 3945

Institutions

A history of theatre at the Séminaire de Trois-Rivières. Canada: Trois-Rivières, PQ. 1860-1985. Lang.: Fre. 1563

Performance spaces

Spatial orientation in medieval Catalan religious productions. Spain-Catalonia. Italy: Florence. 1388-1538. Lang.: Cat. 616

Performance/production

History and performance practice of Arabic religious tragedy. Asia. Arabic countries. 680-1970. Lang.: Ita. 652

Occidental nature of Israeli theatre. Israel. 1920-1986. Lang.: Ita. 742

Medieval style Assumption plays. Spain-Catalonia. 1000-1709. Lang.: Cat. 792

Evolution of *Le Cantique des cantiques (The Song of Songs)* directed by Jacques Destoop at Comédie-Française. France: Paris. 1986. Lang.: Fre. 1721

Review of Biblical passion play by National Theatre of Budapest. Hungary: Budapest. Poland: Warsaw. 1983. Lang.: Pol. 1899

Description of several *Bhavāī* performances. India. 1980-1986. Lang.: Eng. 1976

Controversy surrounding *Presumption, or The Fate of Frankenstein* by Richard Brinsley Peake. UK-England: London. 1818-1840. Lang.: Eng. 2142

Guide to organizing Christian mime troupe. USA. 1986. Lang.: Eng. 3299

Reconstruction of religious dramatic spectacles. Italy: Ravello. 1400-1503. Lang.: Ita. 3339

Classification and description of Quebec pageants. Canada. 1900-1960. Lang.: Fre. 3423

Documents of religious processions and plays. France: Saint-Omer. 1200-1600. Lang.: Eng. 3424

Comparison of Holy Week Processions of Seville with English Mystery plays. Spain: Seville. 1986. Lang.: Eng. 3426

Instances of dramatic action and costume in Holy Week processions. Spain. 1986. Lang.: Eng. 3427

Types of costumes, dances, and songs of Dodo masquerades during Ramadan. Upper Volta: Ouagadougou. Lang.: Eng. 3428

Shadow puppetry as a way of passing on Balinese culture. Bali. 1976-1985. Lang.: Eng. 4017

Plays/librettos/scripts

Religious ideas in the satirical plays of John Marston. England. 1595-1609. Lang.: Eng. 940

Argument that the Gallican liturgy was a form of drama. France. 500-900. Lang.: Eng. 949

Emblematic pictorialism in *La mujer que manda en casa (The Woman Who Rules the Roost)* by Tirso de Molina. Spain. 1580-1648. Lang.: Eng. 970

Analysis of Catalan Nativity plays. Spain-Catalonia. 1400-1599. Lang.: Cat. 972

Analysis of religious symbolism in *Riel* by John Coulter. Canada. 1950. Lang.: Eng. 2407

Analysis of *RA* by R. Murray Schafer, performed by Comus Music Theatre. Canada: Toronto, ON. 1983. Lang.: Eng. 2416

Book review of *125 Ans de Theatre au Seminaire de Trois-Rivières*. Canada: Trois-Rivières, PQ. 1985. Lang.: Fre. 2427

Religion and popular entertainment in *The Virgin Martyr* by Philip Massinger and Thomas Dekker. England: London. 1620-1625. Lang.: Eng. 2468

Analysis of theophany in English *Corpus Christi* plays. England. 1350-1550. Lang.: Eng. 2472

Function of humor and violence in the *Play of the Sacrament* (Croxton). England. 1400-1499. Lang.: Eng. 2493

Moral issues in *A Woman Killed with Kindness* by Thomas Heywood. England. 1560. Lang.: Eng. 2498

Theme of Puritanism in *The Alchemist* by Ben Jonson. England. 1610. Lang.: Eng. 2519

Interview with Josy Eisenberg, translator of *Le Cantique des cantiques (The Song of Songs)* for the Comédie-Française. France: Paris. 1986. Lang.: Fre. 2544

Modern thought in works of Jean Racine. France. 1664-1691. Lang.: Fre. 2553

Biography of Molière as seen through his plays. France. 1622-1673. Lang.: Fre. 2573

Introduction to *Jesús batejat per Sant Joan Baptista (Jesus Christ Baptized by St. John the Baptist)*. France. 1753-1832. Lang.: Cat. 2585

The idea of grace in the life and work of Heinrich von Kleist. Germany. 1777-1811. Lang.: Eng. 2593

Discussion of *L'esaltazione della croce (The Exaltation of the Cross)* by Giovanni Maria Cecchi. Italy. 1585-1589. Lang.: Ita. 2683

Prison camp passion play with Christ as a labor organizer. Philippines: Davao City. 1983-1985. Lang.: Eng. 2732

Lope de Vega's characterization of the converted Jew. Spain. 1562-1635. Lang.: Spa. 2804

The presentation of atheism in August Strindberg's *The Father*. Sweden. 1887. Lang.: Eng. 2821

Biblical and Swedenborgian influences on the development of August Strindberg's chamber play *Påsk (Easter)*. Sweden. 1900. Lang.: Eng. 2827

Jungian analysis of the plays of Peter Nichols. UK-England. 1967-1984. Lang.: Eng. 2848

God as image and symbol in Edward Albee's *Tiny Alice*. USA. 1965. Lang.: Eng. 2911

Political use of biblical references in pageantry. England. 1519-1639. Lang.: Eng. 3429

Study of playtexts and illustrations in Lille plays manuscript. France: Lille. 1450-1500. Lang.: Eng. 3431

Analysis of Hildegard of Bingen's *Ordo Virtutum* as a morality play. Germany: Bingen. 1151. Lang.: Eng. 3498

Relation to other fields

Lack of theatricality in Jewish religious ceremonies. 1300 B.C.-1986 A.D. Lang.: Hun. 1050

Theatrical conventions in religious story-telling. Asia. 700-1200. Lang.: Eng. 1061

Theatricals used by temperance societies. Canada. 1800-1900. Lang.: Eng. 1067

The young Brecht's use of the Bible to criticize the Church and society. Germany. 1913-1918. 1089

Influences of shamanism on Eastern and Western theatre. Greece. Asia. 500 B.C.-1986 A.D. Lang.: Ita. 1095

Uses of religious ritual in traditional theatre. Indonesia. Lang.: Rus. 1102

Literary origins of the 'lauda drammatica'. Italy. 1200-1400. Lang.: Ita. 1109

Origins of theatre in shamanistic ritual. Korea. 1900-1986. Lang.: Ita. 1110

Actor-director Juliusz Osterwa's views of historical processes. Poland. 1940-1947. Lang.: Pol. 1122

Ancient Russian rituals linked with the 'ship of souls' theme in world culture. Russia. Lang.: Rus. 1124

Religion — cont'd

Development of Church attitude toward performers. Spain. 1000-
1316. Lang.: Spa.   1127

Elements of ritual and ceremony in outdoor festivities. USSR. Lang.:
Rus.   1182

Sociological analysis of city comedy and revenge tragedy. England:
London. 1576-1980. Lang.: Eng.   3025

Costuming evidence on carved baptismal fonts. England. 1463-1544.
Lang.: Eng.   3026

Review article on Johann Drumbl's *Quem Quaeritis: Teatro Sacro
dell'Alto Mediaevo*. France. Italy. 900-999. Lang.: Eng.   3031

Assimilation of dramatic elements of Aztec worship in
Christianization process. Mexico. Spain. 1519-1559. Lang.: Eng.   3046

Examples of Puritan attempts to ban legal entertainments. England:
Cheshire. 1560-1641. Lang.: Eng.   3356

Translation of *Les métamorphoses de la fête en Provence de 1750 à
1820* (Paris 1976) by Michel Vovelle. France. 1750-1820. Lang.: Ita.
     3358

Religious, communal and artistic functions of Hindu *odalan* festival.
Indonesia. Lang.: Eng.   3359

Christian and pre-Christian elements of Corpus Christi celebration.
Spain-Catalonia: Berga. 1264-1986. Lang.: Cat.   3432

Nativity puppet plays in Eastern Europe. Europe. 1600-1985. Lang.:
Hun.   3991

Analyses of *Wayang cepak* play, *Gusti Sinuhan*, and its role in the
Hindu religion. Indonesia. 1045-1986. Lang.: Eng.   3992

Research/historiography
Ritual origins of the classical dance drama of Cambodia. Cambodia.
4 B.C.-1986 A.D. Lang.: Eng.   1336

Theory/criticism
Influences on the development of European and Japanese theatre.
Japan. Europe. 500 B.C.-1986 A.D. Lang.: Ita.   1213

Religious ritual
SEE
Ritual-ceremony, religious.

Religious structures
Performance spaces
Spatial orientation in medieval Catalan religious productions. Spain-
Catalonia. Italy: Florence. 1388-1538. Lang.: Cat.   616

Religious theatre
Performance/production
Performance of *Towneley Cycle* in Victoria College Quadrangle.
Canada: Toronto, ON. 1985. Lang.: Eng.   1673

Use of stagehands in production of modern passion play. Spain.
1951-1986. Lang.: Eng.   2075

Contemporary performance of the traditional *Festa d'Elx*. Spain:
Elche. 1370-1985. Lang.: Eng.   3491

Performance by Sequentia of *Ordo Virtutum* by Hildegard of Bingen.
USA: Stanford, CA. 1986. Lang.: Eng.   3493

Plays/librettos/scripts
Linguistic study of *Auto de Pasión (Passion Play)* by Lucas
Fernández. Spain-Catalonia. 1510-1514. Lang.: Cat.   2812

Remains Ensemble (Chicago, IL)
Performance/production
Notes from a production of *Mahagonny* by the Remains Ensemble.
USA: Chicago, IL. 1985.   2282

Removalists, The
Plays/librettos/scripts
Interview with playwright David Williamson. Australia. 1986. Lang.:
Eng.   2369

Interview with playwright David Williamson. Australia. 1986. Lang.:
Eng.   2378

Renaissance theatre
Proceedings of a symposium on theatre during the Middle Ages and
the Renaissance. Spain. Italy. 1000-1680. Lang.: Cat, Spa, Ita.   12

SEE ALSO
Geographical-Chronological Index under Europe 1400-1600, France
1400-1600, Italy 1400-1600, Spain 1400-1600.

Administration
Organization and operation of Office of Revels mainly under
Thomas Cawarden. England: London. 1510-1559. Lang.: Eng.   3417

Audience
Audience of the humanistic, religious and school-theatre of the
European Renaissance. Europe. 1480-1630. Lang.: Ger.   1445

Design/technology
Description of scenery, machinery and performance of Renaissance
Italian feast. Italy. 1400-1600. Lang.: Ita.   3311

Performance spaces
Ambiguous translations of ancient Greek theatrical documentation.
Greece. Italy: Rome. 600-400 B.C. Lang.: Eng.   597

Plays/librettos/scripts
Tradition and individualism in Renaissance drama. England: London.
1575-1600. Lang.: Eng.   2496

Juan del Enzina's defence of pastoral vs. courtly genre. Spain. 1469-
1529. Lang.: Spa.   2785

Reference materials
List of 37 productions of 23 Renaissance plays, with commentary.
UK. USA. New Zealand. 1986. Lang.: Eng.   3000

Relation to other fields
Sociological analysis of city comedy and revenge tragedy. England:
London. 1576-1980. Lang.: Eng.   3025

Renaissance theatre at Valencia court, Catalan festivals. Spain-
Catalonia: Valencia. 1330-1970. Lang.: Spa.   3362

Theory/criticism
Attempts to define such terms as 'emblematic' and 'iconographic'
with respect to Renaissance theatre. England. 1300-1642. Lang.: Eng.
     3092

Renaixença (Catalonia)
Plays/librettos/scripts
A defense of Àngel Guimerà's language. Spain-Catalonia. 1860-1967.
Lang.: Cat.   2817

Plays translated into Catalan by Pompeu Fabra. Spain-Catalonia.
1890-1905. Lang.: Cat.   2818

Renart i Arús, Frances
Plays/librettos/scripts
History of Catalan literature, including playwrights and theatre.
Spain-Catalonia. 1800-1974. Lang.: Cat.   974

Renaud, Madeleine
Institutions
Retrospective of activities of Compagnie Renaud-Barrault. France:
Paris. 1946-1986. Lang.: Fre.   1573

Performance/production
Recollection of Jean-Louis Barrault's career as actor and director.
France. 1943-1956. Lang.: Fre.   711

Albert Camus' appreciation of actress Madeleine Renaud. France.
1950. Lang.: Fre.   1728

Rene, Norman
Performance/production
Reviews of *Precious Sons* by George Furth, staged by Norman
Rene. USA: New York, NY. 1986. Lang.: Eng.   2231

Rene, Roy
Performance/production
Career of vaudeville comedian Roy Rene, creator of 'Mo'. Australia.
1892-1954. Lang.: Eng.   3327

Renée, Madelyn
Performance/production
Verdi's *Simon Boccanegra* and Puccini's *La Bohème* at the
Hungarian State Opera House and Erkel Theatre. Hungary:
Budapest. 1986. Lang.: Hun.   3747

Renick, Kyle
Administration
Transfer of plays from nonprofit to commercial theatre as
experienced by WPA Theatre's artistic director Kyle Renick. USA:
New York, NY. 1983. Lang.: Eng.   1443

Institutions
Artistic director of WPA Theatre Kyle Renick discusses
institutionalization of theatre companies. USA: New York, NY.
1977-1986. Lang.: Eng.   566

Performance/production
Director Kyle Renick's personal experiences with playwright Lillian
Hellman. USA: New York, NY. 1984. Lang.: Eng.   2299

Plays/librettos/scripts
Artists react to *New York Times* condemnation of current
playwriting. USA. 1984. Lang.: Eng.   2888

Theory/criticism
Theatre professionals challenge assertions that theatre is a weaker
form of communication than film. USA: New York, NY. 1985.
Lang.: Eng.   1225

Renovation, theatre
Design/technology
Details of new electrical system of rebuilt Szeged National Theatre.
Hungary: Szeged. 1983-1986. Lang.: Hun.   277

The sound and video systems at the Szeged National Theatre.
Hungary: Szeged. 1986. Lang.: Hun.   282

Research/historiography — cont'd

Audience

Effect of official educational and cultural policies on theatre. France. Germany. UK-England. 1789-1986. Lang.: Fre.　　1446

Institutions

Comparison of the creative process in theatre and in research. UK-England: London. 1981-1986. Lang.: Eng.　　1586

Performance/production

Historical context of *The Late Lancaster Witches* by Thomas Heywood and Richard Brome. England. 1634. Lang.: Eng.　　689

New evidence on the appearance of professional actors. England: London. 1200-1600. Lang.: Eng.　　699

The Castle of Perseverance examined for clues to audience placement and physical plan of original production. England. 1343-1554. Lang.: Eng.　　1709

Documenting evidence about a court entertainment of Henry VIII. England: Greenwich. 1504-1516. Lang.: Eng.　　3420

History of *castrati* in opera. Italy. 1599-1797. Lang.: Eng.　　3761

Plays/librettos/scripts

Argument that the Gallican liturgy was a form of drama. France. 500-900. Lang.: Eng.　　949

Discussion of locations inhabited and frequented by Eugene O'Neill. USA: Boston, MA. 1914-1953. Lang.: Eng.　　2897

The Peasants by Władysław Reymont as possible source for O'Neill's version of the lustful stepmother play. USA. 1902-1924. Lang.: Eng.　　2930

Investigates whether Brahms wrote music for an opera. Austria: Vienna. 1863-1985. Lang.: Eng.　　3856

Reference materials

Update of Allardyce Nicoll's handlist of plays. UK-England: London. 1900-1930. Lang.: Eng.　　3003

Resino, Carmen

Plays/librettos/scripts

Thematic and stylistic comparison of three plays influenced by the *Odyssey*. Spain. 1952-1983. Lang.: Eng.　　2792

Resnik, Regina

Performance/production

Opera greats reflect on performance highlights. USA: Philadelphia, PA, New York, NY. 1985. Lang.: Eng.　　3841

Restoration theatre

History of English theatre. England. 1660-1737. Lang.: Rus.　　5

SEE ALSO

Geographical-Chronological Index under England 1660-1685.

Basic theatrical documents

Transcription of manuscript assigning shares in the King's Company. England. 1661-1684. Lang.: Eng.　　220

Performance/production

New determination of birthdate of actress Nell Gwyn. England: London. 1642-1671. Lang.: Eng.　　690

Performance-oriented study of Restoration comedy. England. 1660-1986. Lang.: Eng.　　696

Restoration era cast lists of the King's Company. England: London. 1660-1708. Lang.: Eng.　　1711

Plays/librettos/scripts

Revision of dramaturgy and stagecraft in Restoration adaptations of Shakespeare. England: London. 1660-1690. Lang.: Eng.　　2535

Development of Restoration musical theatre. England. 1642-1699. Lang.: Eng.　　3496

Restoration, theatre

Institutions

History of the Teatro alla Scala. Italy: Milan. 1898-1986. Lang.: Eng.　　3677

Performance spaces

History of various theatre buildings and the companies that perform in them. Lang.: Ger.　　579

Restoration of the Theatre Royal. Australia: Hobart, Tasmania. 1834-1986. Lang.: Eng.　　581

Planning and fundraising for the restoration of the Imperial Theatre. Canada: St. John, NB. 1913-1985. Lang.: Eng.　　588

Modernization of the Alhambra Theatre. UK-England: Bradford. 1914-1986. Lang.: Eng.　　623

Restoration of the Whitehall Theatre. UK-England: London. 1930-1986. Lang.: Eng.　　625

Restoration of Wakefield Theatre Royal and Opera House. UK-England: Wakefield. 1954-1986. Lang.: Eng.　　630

Outlines the technical and architectural features of the Swan Theatre at Stratford-upon-Avon. UK-England: Stratford. Lang.: Eng.　　1617

History of the Eastman Theatre. USA: Rochester, NY. 1922-1986. Lang.: Eng.　　3222

Retallack, John

Performance/production

Collection of newspaper reviews by London theatre critics. UK. 1986. Lang.: Eng.　　2103

Retaule del flautista, El (Flautist's Reredos, The)

Plays/librettos/scripts

Analysis of the six published dramatic works by Jordi Teixidor. Spain-Catalonia. 1970-1985. Lang.: Cat.　　2809

Retorberg, Elisabeth

Performance/production

Significance of the translation in recordings of Verdi's *Otello*. USA. 1902-1978. Lang.: Eng.　　3812

Retour de l'exil, Le (Return from Exile)

Design/technology

Design considerations in productions of two plays by Louis-Honoré Fréchette. Canada: Montreal, PQ. 1880-1900. Lang.: Fre.　　242

Retrato de señora con espejo—Vida y pasión de Margarita Xirgu (Portrait of a Lady with Mirror—The Life and Passion of Margarita Xirgu)

Plays/librettos/scripts

Analysis of Pedro Corradi's *Retrato de señora con espejo—Vida y pasión de Margarita Xirgu (Portrait of a Lady with Mirror—The Life and Passion of Margarita Xirgu)*. Uruguay. Spain: Madrid. 1985. Lang.: Spa.　　2887

Rettig, Claes von

Institutions

Activities of the Folkkulturcentrum Festival. Sweden: Stockholm. 1977-1986. Lang.: Swe.　　529

Return of the Bounce, The

Performance/production

Tour of puppet show *The Return of the Bounce* by Jean Mattson and Joan King. USA: Seattle, WA. Japan. 1984. Lang.: Eng.　　3979

Return to Oz

Design/technology

Making of the movie *Return to Oz*, focusing on its special effects and creature design. USA.　　3206

Reuchlin, Johannes

Plays/librettos/scripts

Critical problems in *Henno* by Johannes Reuchlin. Germany: Heidelberg. 1497-1522. Lang.: Eng.　　2605

Revels (London)

Administration

Organization and operation of Office of Revels mainly under Thomas Cawarden. England: London. 1510-1559. Lang.: Eng.　　3417

Research/historiography

Review of recent editions of Revels plays, including George Peele's *The Old Wives Tale*. England: London. 1514-1980. Lang.: Eng.　　3071

Revenge of Bussy D'Ambois, The

Plays/librettos/scripts

Critical confusion regarding *The Revenge of Bussy d'Ambois* by George Chapman. England. 1603. Lang.: Eng.　　942

Revenge of Truth, The

Basic theatrical documents

Annotated text of *The Revenge of Truth* by Isak Dinesen. Denmark. 1914. Lang.: Eng.　　4002

Relation to other fields

Introduction to *The Revenge of Truth* by Isak Dinesen. Denmark. Kenya. 1885-1985. Lang.: Eng.　　4010

Revenger's Tragedy, The

Reference materials

List of 37 productions of 23 Renaissance plays, with commentary. UK. USA. New Zealand. 1986. Lang.: Eng.　　3000

Revizor (Inspector General, The)

Performance/production

Collaboration of Nikolaj Gogol in first production of *Revizor (The Inspector General)*. Russia. 1836. Lang.: Ita.　　2069

Revolution Theatre

SEE

Teat'r im. V. Majakovskovo.

Reymont, Władysław

Plays/librettos/scripts

The Peasants by Władysław Reymont as possible source for O'Neill's version of the lustful stepmother play. USA. 1902-1924. Lang.: Eng.　　2930

Richards, Lloyd — cont'd

Interview with dramaturg Arthur Ballet. USA. 1950-1986. Lang.: Eng. 2248

Martin Esslin discusses dramaturg's need to balance roles of naive spectator and informed academic. USA: Waterford, CT, San Francisco, CA. 1936-1986. Lang.: Eng. 2249

Gitta Honegger on training dramaturgs and the European tradition of dramaturgy. USA: New Haven, CT. 1960-1986. Lang.: Eng. 2251

Lloyd Richard's career as an actor, director, artistic director and academic dean. USA: Detroit, MI, New York, NY, New Haven, CT. 1920-1980. Lang.: Eng. 2308

Plays/librettos/scripts
Interview with playwright Lorraine Hansberry. USA. 1959. Lang.: Eng. 2945

Richardson, John
Basic theatrical documents
Text of *The Miser Outwitted*, attributed to Major John Richardson, with introduction. Canada. UK-Ireland: Dublin. 1838-1848. Lang.: Eng. 1465

Richardson, L. Kenneth
Performance/production
Reviews of *The Colored Museum*, by George C. Wolfe, staged by L. Kenneth Richardson. USA: New York, NY. 1986. Lang.: Eng. 2203

Richardson, Ralph
Performance/production
Actor Laurence Olivier's memoirs. UK-England: London. USA: New York, NY. 1907-1986. Lang.: Eng. 2170

Richelieu, Armand Jean du Plessis, Cardinal de
Relation to other fields
Cardinal Richelieu's theatrical policies. France. 1634-1642. Lang.: Fre. 3030

Rickett's Amphitheatre (Philadelphia, PA)
Performance spaces
A history of one of the earliest American circus buildings. USA: Philadelphia, PA. 1795-1799. Lang.: Eng. 3381

Ricordi, Giulio
Plays/librettos/scripts
Why Verdi revised the 1857 version of *Simon Boccanegra*. Italy: Milan. 1857-1881. Lang.: Eng. 3881

Riddley Walker
Performance/production
Collection of newspaper reviews by London theatre critics. UK-England. 1986. Lang.: Eng. 2120

Ridiculous Theatre Company, The (New York, NY)
Performance/production
Profile of and interview with opera parodist Charles Ludlam of The Ridiculous Theatre Company. USA: New York, NY. 1973-1986. Lang.: Eng. 3825

Ridiculous Theatre Company, The (TRTC, New York, NY)
Design/technology
Charles Ludlam's role as set designer, artistic director and lead actor of The Ridiculous Theatre Company. USA: New York, NY. 1986. 360

Plays/librettos/scripts
Discussion of issues raised in plays of 1985-86 season. USA: New York, NY. 1985-1986. Lang.: Eng. 2928

Riel
Plays/librettos/scripts
Analysis of religious symbolism in *Riel* by John Coulter. Canada. 1950. Lang.: Eng. 2407

Study of two unproduced historical dramas about French-Canadian patriot Louis Riel. Canada: Montreal, PQ. 1886. Lang.: Fre. 2413

Writing and production of *Riel* by John Coulter. Canada: Toronto, ON, Ottawa, ON. 1936-1980. Lang.: Eng. 2414

Riel, Louis
Basic theatrical documents
Text of *Beyond Batoche* by Rex Deverell. Canada: Regina, SK. 1985. Lang.: Eng. 218

Plays/librettos/scripts
Analysis of religious symbolism in *Riel* by John Coulter. Canada. 1950. Lang.: Eng. 2407

Study of two unproduced historical dramas about French-Canadian patriot Louis Riel. Canada: Montreal, PQ. 1886. Lang.: Fre. 2413

Writing and production of *Riel* by John Coulter. Canada: Toronto, ON, Ottawa, ON. 1936-1980. Lang.: Eng. 2414

Comparison of plays about Ned Kelly of Australia and Louis Riel of Canada. Canada. Australia. 1900-1976. Lang.: Eng. 2421

Rex Deverell's approach to history in plays about Louis Riel. Canada: Regina, SK. 1985. Lang.: Eng. 2437

Riga Russian Drama Theatre
SEE
Teat'r Russkoj Dramy.

Rigel, Anne
Performance/production
Collection of newspaper reviews by London theatre critics. UK-England. 1986. Lang.: Eng. 2114

Rigging
Design/technology
Stage machinery guidelines. Lang.: Eng. 228

Webbing slings and caribiners for quick rigging connections. USA. 1985. Lang.: Eng. 424

Righteousness
Plays/librettos/scripts
Rex Deverell's approach to history in plays about Louis Riel. Canada: Regina, SK. 1985. Lang.: Eng. 2437

Rigoletto
Performance/production
Reviews of 10 vintage recordings of complete operas on LP. USA. 1906-1925. Lang.: Eng. 3792

Controversy over Jonathan Miller's production of *Rigoletto*. USA. 1984. Lang.: Eng. 3821

Plays/librettos/scripts
Origins of the characters Rigoletto and Marullo in Verdi's *Rigoletto*. France. 1496-1851. Lang.: Eng. 3869

Rihm, Wolfgang
Plays/librettos/scripts
Interview with composer Wolfgang Rihm. Switzerland. 1974-1986. Lang.: Ger. 3893

Ring des Nibelungen, Der
Design/technology
Lighting techniques for Wagnerian operas. Germany, West: Bayreuth. 1981-1986. Lang.: Eng. 3651

Adolphe Appia's theory of Wagner's *Ring* and present-day evaluation. Switzerland: Geneva. 1862-1928. Lang.: Ger. 3653

Set designer John Conklin and the San Francisco Opera production of Wagner's *Ring*. USA: San Francisco, CA. 1986. Lang.: Eng. 3662

Performance/production
Wilhelm Furtwängler's development as a Wagnerian conductor. Germany: Bayreuth. Italy: Milan, Rome. 1901-1954. Lang.: Eng. 3732

New designs for the Seattle Opera production of *Der Ring des Nibelungen* by Richard Wagner. USA: Seattle, WA. 1986. Lang.: Eng. 3837

Plays/librettos/scripts
Schopenhauerian pessimism in Wagner's *Ring* and *Götterdämmerung*. Germany. 1852-1856. Lang.: Eng. 3873

Ringling Brothers and Barnum & Bailey Circus (Sarasota, FL)
SEE ALSO
Barnum and Bailey Circus.

Performance/production
Circus clown discusses his training and work with puppets. 3382

Interview with aerialist Dolly Jacobs. USA. 1970-1985. Lang.: Eng. 3390

Ringling Museum of Art (Sarasota, FL)
Performance/production
Photographs of circus life taken by Frederick Glasier. USA. 1896-1920. Lang.: Eng. 3392

Rinne, Jalmari
Performance/production
Career of actor Jalmari Rinne. Finland: Helsinki, Tampere, Turku. 1893-1985. Lang.: Eng, Fre. 1719

Riou & Pouchain
Performance/production
A photographic essay of 42 soloists and groups performing mime or gestural theatre. 1986. 3290

Rioux, Monique
Institutions
History of the Théâtre de la Marmaille. Canada: Quebec, PQ. 1973-1986. Lang.: Eng. 1552

Rise and Fall of the City of Mahagonny
SEE
Aufstieg und Fall der Stadt Mahagonny.

Rising Tide (St. John's, NF)
Institutions
Successful alternative theatre groups in Newfoundland. Canada.
1976-1986. Lang.: Eng.   1550

Risorgimento
SEE ALSO
Geographical-Chronological Index under Italy 1815-1876.

Ristori, Adelaide
Administration
Lawsuit of actress Adelaide Ristori against her company manager for
nonfulfillment of contract. Italy. 1847-1849. Lang.: Ita.   1437

Performance/production
Information on the marriage of actress Adelaide Ristori. Italy. 1848.
Lang.: Ita.   1996

English-language performances of Italian actress Adelaide Ristori.
Italy. England. USA. 1822-1906. Lang.: Ita.   2000

Rites
SEE
Ritual-ceremony.

Ritual-ceremony
International conference on Eastern and Western theatre. 1986.
Lang.: Ita.   2

Basic theatrical documents
Text of *Kasan ogwangdae (The Five Buffoons of Kasan)* in English
translation. Korea: Kasan. 1975. Lang.: Eng.   1356

Design/technology
Native American masks and headgear in various types of
performances. USA. 1800-1900. Lang.: Eng.   402

Description of scenery, machinery and performance of Renaissance
Italian feast. Italy. 1400-1600. Lang.: Ita.   3311

Performance spaces
Ceremonies celebrating the marriage of Maria dei Medici to Henri
IV. Italy: Florence. France: Lyon. 1568-1600. Lang.: Ita.   3325

Performance/production
History of classical Cambodian dance. Cambodia. 1860-1985. Lang.:
Eng.   1358

Hindu world view reflected in Sanskrit theatre. India. 1974-1980.
Lang.: Eng.   1362

Trance dance compared to role of dance in conventional theatre.
Indonesia. 1977-1982. Lang.: Eng.   1363

Origins of *malipenga*, a form of dance-drama combining Western
and African elements. Zambia: Malawi. 1914-1985. Lang.: Eng. 1374

Description of several *Bhavāī* performances. India. 1980-1986. Lang.:
Eng.   1976

Maskers and masquerades of We tribal rituals. Ivory Coast. Lang.:
Eng.   3341

Comparison of Catalan Assumption plays. Spain-Catalonia:
Tarragona. 1350-1388. Lang.: Cat.   3346

Documents of religious processions and plays. France: Saint-Omer.
1200-1600. Lang.: Eng.   3424

Comparison of Holy Week Processions of Seville with English
Mystery plays. Spain: Seville. 1986. Lang.: Eng.   3426

Types of costumes, dances, and songs of Dodo masquerades during
Ramadan. Upper Volta: Ouagadougou. Lang.: Eng.   3428

Use of puppets in liturgical plays and ceremonies. England: London,
Witney. 1540-1560. Lang.: Eng.   3963

Plays/librettos/scripts
Dramatic elements in wedding celebrations. Romania: Armăseni.
1978. Lang.: Hun.   963

Ritualistic elements in the structure of Wole Soyinka's *Death and
the King's Horseman*. Africa. 1975. Lang.: Eng.   2359

Ritual and archetypal communication in *La noche de los asesinos
(The Night of the Assassins)* by José Triana. Cuba. Brazil. 1973-
1974. Lang.: Eng.   2450

Ceremony distinguishes kings from peasants in Shakespeare's *Henry
V*. England. 1598-1599. Lang.: Eng.   2464

Reconstructs from historical sources the rebellion depicted in *Fuente
Ovejuna (The Sheep Well)* by Lope de Vega as ritual behavior.
Spain. 1476. Lang.: Eng.   2794

Linguistic study of *Auto de Pasión (Passion Play)* by Lucas
Fernández. Spain-Catalonia. 1510-1514. Lang.: Cat.   2812

Ritual function of *The Slave Ship* by LeRoi Jones (Amiri Baraka)
and *Quinta Temporada (Fifth Season)* by Luis Valdez. USA. 1965-
1967. Lang.: Eng.   2906

Relation to other fields
Lack of theatricality in Jewish religious ceremonies. 1300 B.C.-1986
A.D. Lang.: Hun.   1050

Articles on anthropology of theatre. Lang.: Ita.   1056

Argument that theatre should return to art's roots in ritual and
ceremony. 1986. Lang.: Eng.   1059

Translation of *From Ritual to Theatre* by Victor Turner. Lang.: Ita.
                                                           1060

Theatrical conventions in religious story-telling. Asia. 700-1200.
Lang.: Eng.   1061

Kwakiutl Homatsa ceremony as drama. Canada. 1890-1900. Lang.:
Eng.   1070

Influences of shamanism on Eastern and Western theatre. Greece.
Asia. 500 B.C.-1986 A.D. Lang.: Ita.   1095

Uses of religious ritual in traditional theatre. Indonesia. Lang.: Rus.
                                                           1102

Origins of theatre in shamanistic ritual. Korea. 1900-1986. Lang.: Ita.
                                                           1110

Ancient Russian rituals linked with the 'ship of souls' theme in
world culture. Russia. Lang.: Rus.   1124

Ritual, rhythmic activity: their effects upon brain systems. USA.
1986. Lang.: Eng.   1167

Elements of ritual and ceremony in outdoor festivities. USSR. Lang.:
Rus.   1182

Theatrical nature of shamanistic rituals. Zambia. 1985. Lang.: Eng.
                                                           1183

Assimilation of dramatic elements of Aztec worship in
Christianization process. Mexico. Spain. 1519-1559. Lang.: Eng. 3046

Religious, communal and artistic functions of Hindu *odalan* festival.
Indonesia. Lang.: Eng.   3359

Renaissance theatre at Valencia court, Catalan festivals. Spain-
Catalonia: Valencia. 1330-1970. Lang.: Spa.   3362

Theory/criticism
History of theatre in Africa. Africa. 1400-1985. Lang.: Ger. 1199

Ritz Theatre (New York, NY)
Design/technology
Designers discuss regional productions of *Side-by-Side by Sondheim*.
USA. 1984. Lang.: Eng.   3593

Performance/production
Reviews of *Jerome Kern Goes to Hollywood*, conceived and staged
by David Kernan. USA: New York, NY. 1986. Lang.: Eng.   2237

Rivelles, Amparo
Performance/production
Production history of *Hay que deshacer la casa (Undoing the
Housework)*, winner of Lope de Vega prize. Spain: Madrid. USA:
Miami, FL. 1983-1985. Lang.: Eng.   2079

River Niger, The
Reference materials
Current work of Audelco award-winning playwrights. USA: New
York, NY. 1973-1984. Lang.: Eng.   3007

Rivers of China
Plays/librettos/scripts
Interview with playwright Alma de Groen. Australia. Lang.: Eng.
                                                           2367

Rivers, Joan
Performance/production
Comedienne Joan Rivers' account of her life and career. USA: New
York, NY. 1928-1965. Lang.: Eng.   3352

Riverside Studios (London)
Design/technology
Overview of performance technology show at Riverside Studios. UK-
England: London. 1986. Lang.: Eng.   323

Performance/production
Application of Brechtian concepts by Eckhardt Schall. Germany,
East: Berlin, East. UK-England: London. 1952-1986. Lang.: Eng.
                                                           1762

Collection of newspaper reviews by London theatre critics. UK-
England: London. 1986. Lang.: Eng.   2113

Collection of newspaper reviews by London theatre critics. UK-
England: London. 1986. Lang.: Eng.   2121

Roach, Max
Plays/librettos/scripts
Director George Ferencz and jazz musician Max Roach collaborate
on music in trio of Sam Shepard plays. USA: New York, NY. 1984.
Lang.: Eng.   2952

Road
SEE
Lu.
Performance/production
Review of alternative theatre productions. UK-England: London.
1986. Lang.: Eng.   2108

Director Simon Curtis discusses his production of *Road*. UK-
England: London. 1986. Lang.: Eng.   2137

Road to Immortality, The
Performance/production
Wooster Group retrospective of original works. USA: New York,
NY. 1975-1986. Lang.: Eng.   850

Road to Mecca, The
Plays/librettos/scripts
Interview with playwright Athol Fugard. South Africa, Republic of.
USA: New Haven, CT. 1984. Lang.: Eng.   2775

The role of the artist in *The Road to Mecca* by Athol Fugard.
South Africa, Republic of. 1961-1984. Lang.: Eng.   2779

Road, The
Relation to other fields
Interview with playwright Wole Soyinka. Nigeria. USA: New Haven,
CT. 1967-1984. Lang.: Eng.   3047

Theory/criticism
Analysis of Wole Soyinka's major critical essays. Nigeria. 1960-1980.
Lang.: Eng.   3124

Robards, Jason
Design/technology
Lighting designer Tom Skelton discussing his work on the recent
revival of *The Iceman Cometh*. USA: New York, NY. 1985-1986.
Lang.: Eng.   1531

Robbins, Jerome
Performance/production
Choreography in musical theatre. USA: New York, NY. 1944-1981.
Lang.: Eng.   3620

Robert Burns
Performance/production
Interview with director David Hayman of the Scottish Theatre
Company. UK-Scotland. 1986. Lang.: Eng.   2192

Robert, Emmerich
Performance/production
Playing Hamlet at the Burgtheater. Austria: Vienna. 1803-1985.
Lang.: Ger.   1654

Roberti, Giambattista
Relation to other fields
Reaction of a Jesuit priest to the theatre of Carlo Goldoni. Italy.
1719-1786. Lang.: Ita.   3038

Roberts, Judy
Performance/production
Interview with puppeteer Judy 'Sparky' Roberts. USA. 1986. Lang.:
Eng.   3975

Robertson, Toby
Administration
Artistic directors of Everyman Theatre and Theatre Clwyd discuss
their theatres. UK-England: Cheltenham. UK-Wales: Mold. 1986.
Lang.: Eng.   82

Performance/production
Collection of newspaper reviews by London theatre critics. UK.
1986. Lang.: Eng.   2099

Robertson, Tom
Performance/production
Tom Robertson as a theatrical innovator and as a character in
Arthur Wing Pinero's *Trelawny of the Wells*. England: London.
1840-1848. Lang.: Eng.   1702

Robeson, Paul
Performance/production
History of the Margaret Webster-Paul Robeson production of
Othello. USA: New York, NY. 1942-1944. Lang.: Eng.   852

Robin Hood plays
Administration
Survey of records relating to performances of Robin Hood and King
Games. England: Kingston. 1504-1538. Lang.: Eng.   3309

Performance/production
Analysis of Robin Hood entertainments in the parish of Yeovil.
England. 1475-1588. Lang.: Eng.   1712

Robins, Elizabeth
Performance/production
Acting style in plays by Henrik Ibsen. 1885-1905. Lang.: Eng.   1627

Robinson, Clarence
Performance/production
Four nightclub entertainers on their particular acts and the
atmosphere of the late night clubs and theaters in Harlem. USA:
New York, NY, Savannah, GA. 1930-1950. Lang.: Eng.   3470

Robman, Steven
Plays/librettos/scripts
Report on a symposium addressing the role of the dramaturg.   918

Robots
Design/technology
Working with robots to promote Expo '86. Canada.   3950

Roboz, Zsuzsi
Reference materials
Catalogue from an exhibit of theatrical and ballet art by Zsuzsi
Roboz. Hungary: Budapest. 1985. Lang.: Hun.   1325

Robreño family
Performance/production
Short history of the activities of the family Robreño. Cuba. Spain-
Catalonia. 1838-1972. Lang.: Cat.   680

Robreño, Josep
Plays/librettos/scripts
History of Catalan literature, including playwrights and theatre.
Spain-Catalonia. 1800-1974. Lang.: Cat.   974

Rochaix, François
Performance/production
Review of Wagner's *Die Walküre* staged by François Rochaix. USA:
Seattle, WA. 1985. Lang.: Eng.   3801

New designs for the Seattle Opera production of *Der Ring des
Nibelungen* by Richard Wagner. USA: Seattle, WA. 1986. Lang.:
Eng.   3837

Roche, David
Performance/production
Rhubarb Festival is alternative to playwriting and workshopping
conventions. Canada: Toronto, ON. 1986. Lang.: Eng.   672

Interviews with performance artists. Canada: Toronto, ON. USA:
New York, NY. 1980-1986. Lang.: Eng.   3444

Rock music
Design/technology
Interview with lighting designer Kieran Healy discussing techniques
for lighting live concert videos. USA. 1982-1986. Lang.: Eng.   3265

Interview with manager Tony Smith and lighting designer Alan
Owen of the rock band Genesis focusing on the lighting technology
used on their latest tour. USA. 1968-1986. Lang.: Eng.   3320

Lighting designer Kazuo Inoue discusses his lighting for a rock
concert. Japan: Yokohama. 1985-1986. Lang.: Eng.   3434

Performance/production
Case-study of *Sweet and Sour* by the Australian Broadcasting
Corporation. Australia: Sydney, N.S.W. 1980-1984. Lang.: Eng.   3483

Review of rock opera *István a király (King Stephen)* at the National
Theatre. Hungary: Budapest. 1985. Lang.: Hun.   3489

Rock opera
Performance/production
Review of rock opera *István a király (King Stephen)* at the National
Theatre. Hungary: Budapest. 1985. Lang.: Hun.   3489

Interview with composer Aleksej Ribnikov. USSR. 1986. Lang.: Rus.
                                                                     3495

Rock Szinház (Budapest)
Performance/production
Jézus Krisztus Szupersztar (Jesus Christ Superstar) by Andrew Lloyd
Webber and Tim Rice directed by János Szikora (Rock Szinház).
Hungary: Szeged. 1986. Lang.: Hun.   3604

Summer productions of *Jézus Krisztus Szupersztár*. Hungary: Szeged,
Budapest. 1986. Lang.: Hun.   3605

Rockaby
Performance/production
Collection of newspaper reviews by London theatre critics. UK-
England: London. 1986. Lang.: Eng.   2113
Theory/criticism
The influence of Samuel Beckett's later works on contemporary
writers and directors. 1984. Lang.: Eng.   3077

Rocktältet
Performance spaces
Technical problems of using tents for performances. Sweden:
Stockholm. 1985. Lang.: Swe.   3326

Rockwell, Alexandre
Administration
Fundraising for the film *Cheat'n Heart*. USA: New York, NY. 1984-
1986. Lang.: Eng.   3192

Rockwell, Henry
Administration
Bookkeeping records of two pre-Civil War circuses. USA. 1836-1843.
Lang.: Eng. 3378

Roden, Shirlie
Performance/production
Collection of newspaper reviews by London theatre critics. UK-England: London. 1986. Lang.: Eng. 2122

Rodgers, Richard
Basic theatrical documents
Text of Lorenz Hart lyrics. USA. 1920-1943. Lang.: Eng. 3580

Rodríguez Méndez, José María
Institutions
Three personal views of the evolution of the Catalan company La Pipironda. Spain-Catalonia: Barcelona. 1958-1986. Lang.: Cat. 1583

Roi s'amuse, Le
Plays/librettos/scripts
Origins of the characters Rigoletto and Marullo in Verdi's *Rigoletto*. France. 1496-1851. Lang.: Eng. 3869

Roland, Betty
Basic theatrical documents
Text of *War on the Waterfront* by Betty Roland. Australia. 1939. Lang.: Eng. 1459
Act I, Scene 3 of *Are You Ready Comrade?* by Betty Roland. Australia. 1938. Lang.: Eng. 1460
Plays/librettos/scripts
Betty Roland's life and stage work. Australia: Sydney, N.S.W. 1928-1985. Lang.: Eng. 2382
Analysis of *The Touch of Silk* and *Granite Peak* by Betty Roland. Australia. 1928-1981. Lang.: Eng. 2387
Theory/criticism
Attitudes toward sports in serious Australian drama. Australia. 1876-1965. Lang.: Eng. 3084

Roles
SEE
Characters/roles.

Rolli, Bernard
Performance/production
A photographic essay of 42 soloists and groups performing mime or gestural theatre. 1986. 3290

Rolli, Paolo
Performance/production
Productions of Handel's *Muzio Scevola* and analysis of score and characters. England: London. 1718-1980. Lang.: Eng. 3720

Romains, Jules
Performance/production
Knock by Jules Romains directed by Gábor Máté at Csiky Gergely Theatre. Hungary: Kaposvár. 1986. Lang.: Hun. 1892

Roman Actor
Reference materials
List of 37 productions of 23 Renaissance plays, with commentary. UK. USA. New Zealand. 1986. Lang.: Eng. 3000

Roman theatre
SEE ALSO
Geographical-Chronological Index under Roman Republic 509-27 BC, Roman Empire 27 BC-476 AD.
Performance/production
Translation of *The Roman Stage* by William Beare. Roman Republic: Rome. 100 B.C. Lang.: Ita. 777
Masked Greek and Roman plays presented in original Roman theatre. Switzerland: Basel. 1936-1974. Lang.: Ger. 2096
Plays/librettos/scripts
Comparison of Shakespeare's *Othello* with New Comedy of Rome. England. 1604. Lang.: Eng. 2528

Romanticism
SEE ALSO
Geographical-Chronological Index under Europe 1800-1850, France 1810-1857, Germany 1798-1830, Italy 1815-1876, UK 1801-1850.
Institutions
Views of Parisian theatre from the journals of August von Kotzebue. France: Paris. Germany. 1790-1804. Lang.: Eng. 496
Plays/librettos/scripts
Treatment of Napoleon Bonaparte by French and English dramatists. France. England. 1797-1958. Lang.: Eng. 2568
The idea of grace in the life and work of Heinrich von Kleist. Germany. 1777-1811. Lang.: Eng. 2593
Comedies of Tieck and Brentano representing German Romanticism. Germany. 1795-1850. Lang.: Rus. 2602

Theory/criticism
Analysis of Friedrich Schiller's dramatic and theoretical works. Germany. 1759-1805. Lang.: Cat. 3109

Romeo and Juliet
Institutions
Efforts of New York Shakespeare Festival to develop an audience for Shakespearean drama. USA: New York, NY. 1986. Lang.: Eng. 1605

Performance/production
Reception of the Kembles' Canadian tour. Canada. 1832-1834. Lang.: Eng. 663
Analysis of Shakespeare's influence on Weimar, German neoclassicism. Germany: Weimar. 1771-1812. Lang.: Eng. 1760
Collection of newspaper reviews by London theatre critics. UK-England. 1986. Lang.: Eng. 2115

Plays/librettos/scripts
Influence of Night Visit folk notif on Shakespeare's *Romeo and Juliet*. England: London. 1594-1597. Lang.: Eng. 2470
Essays on Shakespeare's *Romeo and Juliet*. England. 1595-1597. Lang.: Ita. 2529
Translations of plays by William Shakespeare into Amharic and Tegrenna. Ethiopia: Addis Ababa. 1941-1984. Lang.: Eng. 2537
The Romeo and Juliet theme as interpreted in the musical and visual arts. Italy. 1476-1900. Lang.: Eng. 3886

Romeo and Juliet (ballet)
Performance/production
Prokofjèv's ballet *Romeo and Juliet* choreographed by László Seregi. Hungary: Budapest. 1985. Lang.: Hun. 1307

Roméo et Juliette
Performance/production
Reviews of 10 vintage recordings of complete operas on LP. USA. 1906-1925. Lang.: Eng. 3792
Photographs, cast list, synopsis, and discography of Metropolitan Opera radio broadcast performances. USA: New York, NY. 1986. Lang.: Eng. 3794
Photographs, cast list, synopsis, and discography of Metropolitan Opera radio broadcast performances. USA: New York, NY. 1986. Lang.: Eng. 3797

Plays/librettos/scripts
The Romeo and Juliet theme as interpreted in the musical and visual arts. Italy. 1476-1900. Lang.: Eng. 3886

Romeril, John
Administration
Malcolm Blaylock on theatre and government funding policy. Australia. 1985. Lang.: Eng. 22
Plays/librettos/scripts
Developments in Australian playwriting since 1975. Australia. 1975-1986. Lang.: Eng. 2374

Romero, Mariela
Plays/librettos/scripts
Traces development of political trends in Venezuelan drama. Venezuela. 1958-1980. Lang.: Spa. 2972

Romero, Pilar
Plays/librettos/scripts
Interviews with actress Pilar Romero and director Roberto Blanco at the Festival de Théâtre des Amériques. Canada: Montreal, PQ. 1985. Lang.: Eng. 2426

Romhányi, László
Performance/production
Review of Géza Páskándi's *Átkozottak (The Damned)* directed by László Romhányi. Hungary: Kőszeg. 1986. Lang.: Hun. 1808
Geza Páskándi's *Átkozottak (The Damned)* directed by László Romhányi at Kőszegi Várszinház. Hungary: Kőszeg. 1986. Lang.: Hun. 1822

Rona, Nadia
Institutions
Interviews with theatre professionals in Quebec. Canada. 1985. Lang.: Fre. 487

Ronacher (Vienna)
Institutions
Union of three theaters in Vienna to the Verbund Wiener Theatre. Austria: Vienna. 1986. Lang.: Ger. 449
Performance spaces
Plans for using the Ronacher theatre after its renovation. Austria: Vienna. 1871-1986. Lang.: Ger. 584

Rostand, Edmond — cont'd

Cyrano de Bergerac by Edmond Rostand, directed by György Lengyel at Madách Színház. Hungary: Budapest. 1985. Lang.: Hun.
1953

Rostrup, Kaspar
Institutions
Overview of current theatre scene. Denmark: Copenhagen. 1976-1986. Lang.: Swe.
490

Rotbaum, Jacub
Performance/production
Abraham Goldfaden's *Sen O Goldfadenie (Dream About Goldfaden)* directed by Jacob Rotbaum, Teatr Zydowski. Poland: Warsaw. 1984. Lang.: Pol.
3490

Rothman, Carole
Performance/production
Reviews of *Coastal Disturbances*, by Tina Howe, staged by Carole Rothman. USA: New York, NY. 1986. Lang.: Eng.
2200

Revivals by Second Stage. USA: New York, NY. 1986. Lang.: Eng.
2259

Relation to other fields
Economic survival of the individual theatre artist. USA: New York, NY. 1983. Lang.: Eng.
1155

Roundabout Theatre (New York, NY)
Performance/production
Reviews of *Master Class*, by David Pownell, staged by Frank Corsaro. USA: New York, NY. 1986. Lang.: Eng.
2216

Reviews of *Room Service*, by John Murray and Allan Boretz, staged by Alan Arkin. USA: New York, NY. 1986. Lang.: Eng.
2242

Rousseau, Jean-Jacques
Plays/librettos/scripts
Love in the plays and operas of Jean-Jacques Rousseau. France. Switzerland. 1712-1778. Lang.: Fre.
2563

Theory/criticism
Selection and analysis of Diderot's theoretical writings about theatre. France. 1713-1834. Lang.: Cat.
3101

Hegel's theory of theatre and its application by 20th-century dramatists. Germany. 1770-1982. Lang.: Chi.
3106

Routes 1 & 9
Performance/production
Wooster Group retrospective of original works. USA: New York, NY. 1975-1986. Lang.: Eng.
850

Interview with Wooster Group's artistic director Elizabeth LeCompte. USA: New York, NY. 1984. Lang.: Eng.
2288

Routon, Yvonne
Reference materials
Catalogue of an exhibition of costume designs for Broadway musicals. USA: New York, NY. 1900-1925. Lang.: Eng, Ger.
3635

Rouverollis, Jacques
Design/technology
Lighting design for 150th anniversary spectacle. USA: Houston, TX. 1986. Lang.: Eng.
3435

Rowe, Nicholas
Performance/production
Study of first production of *Jane Shore* by Nicholas Rowe at Drury Lane Theatre. England: London. 1713-1714. Lang.: Eng.
693

Plays/librettos/scripts
Female characterization in Nicholas Rowe's plays. England. 1629-1720. Lang.: Eng.
2475

Rowes, Holton
Performance/production
Photographs of three circuses by Holton Rowes. USA: New York, NY. 1985. Lang.: Eng.
3395

Rowley, William
Plays/librettos/scripts
Origin of Spanish setting in Middleton and Rowley's *The Changeling*. England. 1607-1622. Lang.: Eng.
2513

Royal Academy of Music (London)
Performance/production
Productions of Handel's *Muzio Scevola* and analysis of score and characters. England: London. 1718-1980. Lang.: Eng.
3720

Royal Albert Hall (London)
Performance/production
Collection of newspaper reviews by London theatre critics. UK-England: London. 1986. Lang.: Eng.
2119

Royal Ballet (Cambodia)
Performance/production
History of classical Cambodian dance. Cambodia. 1860-1985. Lang.: Eng.
1358

Royal Ballet (London)
Performance/production
Career of choreographer Kenneth MacMillan. Europe. USA. 1929-1986. Lang.: Eng.
1302

Royal Court Theatre (London)
SEE ALSO
English Stage Company.

Institutions
Place of women in Britain's National Theatre. UK-England: London. 1986. Lang.: Eng.
1588

Progress and aims of Women's Playhouse Trust. UK-England: London. 1984-1986. Lang.: Eng.
1590

Performance/production
Collection of newspaper reviews by London theatre critics. UK. 1986. Lang.: Eng.
2101

Review of alternative theatre productions. UK-England: London. 1986. Lang.: Eng.
2108

Collection of newspaper reviews by London theatre critics. UK-England: London. 1986. Lang.: Eng.
2112

Collection of newspaper reviews by London theatre critics. UK-England. 1986. Lang.: Eng.
2114

Collection of newspaper reviews by London theatre critics. UK-England: London. 1986. Lang.: Eng.
2126

Director Simon Curtis discusses his production of *Road*. UK-England: London. 1986. Lang.: Eng.
2137

Overview of performances transferred from The Royal Court, Greenwich, and Lyric Hammersmith theatres. UK-England: London. 1986. Lang.: Eng.
2143

Career of actress Billie Whitelaw, interpreter of Samuel Beckett's plays. UK-England. 1956-1986. Lang.: Eng.
2172

Plays/librettos/scripts
Current state of women's playwriting. UK-England. 1985-1986. Lang.: Eng.
2830

Royal Dramatic College (London)
Institutions
Royal Dramatic College's charity for retired theatre professionals. England: London. 1858-1877. Lang.: Eng.
3322

Royal Dramatic Theatre of Stockholm
SEE
Kungliga Dramatiska Teatern.

Royal Exchange Theatre (Manchester)
Performance/production
Collection of newspaper reviews by London theatre critics. UK. 1986. Lang.: Eng.
2101

Collection of newspaper reviews by London theatre critics. UK-England. 1986. Lang.: Eng.
2111

Collection of newspaper reviews by London theatre critics. UK-England. 1986. Lang.: Eng.
2120

Royal Lyceum Theatre (Edinburgh)
Performance/production
Collection of newspaper reviews by London theatre critics. UK. 1986. Lang.: Eng.
2103

Royal Opera House (Hanover)
Institutions
History of the former Royal Opera House of Hanover and its plans for the future. Germany, West: Hanover. 1689-1986. Lang.: Eng.
3675

Royal Opera House (Stockholm)
SEE
Kungliga Operahus.

Royal Opera House, Covent Garden (London)
Administration
Reconsideration of George Frideric Handel's declining success. England: London. 1729-1739. Lang.: Eng.
3640

Performance/production
Christopher Renshaw talks about his production of Benjamin Britten's opera *A Midsummer Night's Dream* at Covent Garden. UK-England: London. 1986. Lang.: Eng.
3782

Andrei Serban discusses his production of Beethoven's *Fidelio*. UK-England: London. 1986. Lang.: Eng.
3787

Royal Puppet Company (Cape Town)
Performance/production
History of puppet theatre including recent developments in political satire and agit-prop. South Africa, Republic of. 1805-1986. Lang.: Eng.
3969

Royal Shakespeare Company (RSC, Stratford & London)

Administration
Interview with director and tour manager of Royal Shakespeare Company about touring. UK. 1986. Lang.: Eng. 72

Description of computerized ticketing and administration system. UK. 1980-1986. Lang.: Eng. 77

Design/technology
Changes in the Royal Shakespeare Company under its current directors. UK-England: London. 1967-1986. Lang.: Eng. 325

Broad survey of costuming in England. UK-England: London. 1790-1986. Lang.: Eng. 1524

Institutions
Overview of the *Not the RSC Festival* at the Almeida Theatre. UK-England: London. 1986. Lang.: Eng. 534

Place of women in Britain's National Theatre. UK-England: London. 1986. Lang.: Eng. 1588

Exhibit on stages and staging by Royal Shakespeare Company. UK-England: Stratford. 1932-1986. Lang.: Eng. 1591

Survey of Royal Shakespeare Company productions. UK-England. 1960-1980. Lang.: Chi. 1593

Performance spaces
Description of the new Swan Theatre and Shakespeare-related buildings. UK-England: Stratford. 1986. Lang.: Eng. 631

History of the new Swan Theatre. UK-England: Stratford. 1977-1986. Lang.: Ger. 632

Outlines the technical and architectural features of the Swan Theatre at Stratford-upon-Avon. UK-England: Stratford. Lang.: Eng. 1617

Impact of Swan Theatre on actors, audiences. UK-England: Stratford. 1986. Lang.: Eng. 1620

Performance/production
An exploration of Brecht's *Gestus*. Germany. Lang.: Eng. 1758

Collection of newspaper reviews by London theatre critics. UK. 1986. Lang.: Eng. 2101

Political difficulties in staging two touring productions of Shakespeare's *The Taming of the Shrew*. UK. 1985-1986. Lang.: Eng. 2104

Collection of newspaper reviews by London theatre critics. UK-England: London. 1986. Lang.: Eng. 2110

Collection of newspaper reviews by London theatre critics. UK-England: London. 1986. Lang.: Eng. 2113

Director Mike Alfreds' interpretation of the plays of Čechov. UK-England: London. USSR. 1975-1986. Lang.: Eng. 2127

Actors Ben Kingsley and David Suchet discuss their roles in Shakespeare's *Othello*. UK-England. 1986. Lang.: Eng. 2128

Reviews of three Shakespearean productions. UK-England: London, Stratford. USA: Ashland, OR. 1985. Lang.: Eng. 2140

Actresses Jane Lapotaire and Elizabeth Spriggs discuss their careers in the Royal Shakespeare Company. UK-England: London. 1970-1986. Lang.: Eng. 2147

Royal Shakespeare Company performances at the Barbican Theatre. UK-England: London. 1986. Lang.: Eng. 2152

Overview of the season at the new Swan Theatre. UK-England: Stratford. 1986. Lang.: Eng. 2174

Jonathan Pryce in the role of Macbeth. UK-England: Stratford. 1970-1986. Lang.: Eng. 2179

Detailed discussion of four successful Royal Shakespeare Company productions of Shakespeare's minor plays. UK-England: Stratford. 1946-1977. Lang.: Eng. 2182

Shakespearean productions by the National Theatre, Royal Shakespeare Company and Orange Tree Theatre. UK-England: Stratford, London. 1984-1985. Lang.: Eng. 2183

Adapting and staging of *Les Misérables* by Victor Hugo. UK-England. 1980. Lang.: Eng. 3609

Plays/librettos/scripts
The place of *The Island of the Mighty* in the John Arden canon. Ireland. UK. 1950-1972. Lang.: Eng. 2666

Interview with playwright Howard Barker. UK-England. 1981-1985. Lang.: Eng. 2845

Attitudes toward sexuality in plays from French sources. UK-England. France. Lang.: Eng. 2852

Evaluation of *The War Plays* by Edward Bond. UK-England: London. 1986. Lang.: Eng. 2853

Diary of a playwright at Royal Shakespeare Company. UK-England. 1985-1986. Lang.: Eng. 2854

Relation to other fields
Essay arguing against the Royal Shakespeare Company's decision not to perform in South Africa. UK-England: London. South Africa, Republic of. 1986. Lang.: Eng. 1136

Current style of theatre-in-education. UK-England. Lang.: Eng. 3057

Royal Slave, The
Plays/librettos/scripts
Female characterization in Nicholas Rowe's plays. England. 1629-1720. Lang.: Eng. 2475

Royalties
Relation to other fields
Situation of playwrights in Austria. Austria: Vienna. 1971-1986. Lang.: Ger. 3016

Róza néni (Aunt Rosa)
Performance/production
Notes on performances of *Hongkongi paróka (Wig Made in Hong Kong)*, *Egérút (Narrow Escape)* and *Róza néni (Aunt Rosa)*. Hungary: Budapest. 1985. Lang.: Hun. 1801

Reviews of *Margit kisasszony (Miss Margit)*, *Az Ibolya (The Violet)*, *Az Árny (The Ghost)* and *Róza néni (Aunt Rosa)*. Hungary: Budapest. 1985-1986. Lang.: Hun. 1916

Różewicz, Tadeusz
Audience
Reactions of Polish teenagers to the plays (1920s) of poet and playwright Tadeusz Różewicz. Poland. 1986. Lang.: Pol. 1451

Performance/production
Krzysztof Babicki directs Różewicz's *Pulapka (Trap)*. Poland: Gdansk. 1984. Lang.: Pol. 2040

Jerzy Grzegorzewski directs Różewicz's *Pulapka (Trap)* at Centrum Sztuki Studio. Poland: Warsaw. 1984. Lang.: Pol. 2053

Michał Ratyński directs Różewicz's *Kartoteka (Card Index)*, Teatr Powszechny. Poland: Warsaw. 1984. Lang.: Pol. 2062

Plays/librettos/scripts
Polish drama performed in Sweden. Sweden. Poland. 1835-1976. Lang.: Pol. 975

Death in the plays of Tadeusz Różewicz. Poland. 1986. Lang.: Pol. 2737

Analysis of *Grupa Laokoona (The Laocoön Group)* by Tadeusz Różewicz and *Tsaplia (The Heron)* by Vasilij Aksënov. Poland. USSR. 1961-1979. Lang.: Eng. 2738

Philosophy and obscenity in the plays of Tadeusz Różewicz. Poland. 1920-1986. Lang.: Pol. 2750

Rozov, Viktor
Performance/production
Stage adaptations of prose works by Gogol and Gončarov. Hungary: Veszprém, Békéscsaba. 1985. Lang.: Hun. 1948

Rubin, Dot
Performance/production
Collection of newspaper reviews by London theatre critics. UK-England: London. 1986. Lang.: Eng. 2125

Rubin, Leon
Performance/production
John Hirsch's artistic career at the Stratford Festival Theatre. Canada: Stratford, ON. 1981-1985. Lang.: Eng. 1683

Rubini, Giovanni Battista
Performance/production
The growth and development of the Italian tenor singing style. Italy: Bergamo. 1788-1860. Lang.: Eng. 3767

Rubins, Harry
Institutions
Interviews with theatre professionals in Quebec. Canada. 1985. Lang.: Fre. 487

Rubinstein, Ida
Performance/production
On the career of dancer and actress Ida Rubinstein, member of Diaghilew's 'Russian Seasons'. Russia. France. 1885-1960. Lang.: Rus. 1311

Paul Claudel's Biblical scripts for Ida Rubinstein. France. 1934-1936. Lang.: Fre. 1346

Rubinštejn, A.
Audience
Audience-performer relationship in experimental theatre. USSR: Moscow. 1986. Lang.: Rus. 204

Rudd, Paul
Performance/production
Interview with individuals involved in production of *Alcestis* by Euripides. USA: Cambridge, MA. 1986. Lang.: Eng. 2266

Rudet, Jacqueline
Institutions
Place of women in Britain's National Theatre. UK-England: London. 1986. Lang.: Eng.   1588

Performance/production
Interview with Pip Broughton of Paines Plough Theatre Company. UK-England. 1980-1986. Lang.: Eng.   2166

Rudkin, David
Performance/production
Collection of newspaper reviews by London theatre critics. UK-England: London. 1986. Lang.: Eng.   2121

Rudman, Michael
Performance/production
Collection of newspaper reviews by London theatre critics. UK-England. 1986. Lang.: Eng.   2120

Rudolfsson, Lars
Performance/production
Regional theatre productions in Sweden. Sweden: Stockholm, Gothenburg. 1985-1986. Lang.: Swe.   2088

Rudolph, Ellen B.
Relation to other fields
Problems of artists working in schools. USA: New York, NY. 1983. Lang.: Eng.   1161

Rueda, Lope de
Plays/librettos/scripts
Mutual influences between *commedia dell'arte* and Spanish literature. Spain. Italy. 1330-1623. Lang.: Spa.   2805

Ruffo, Titta
Performance/production
Evidence that Enrico Caruso sang the baritone prologue to *I Pagliacci*. Argentina: Buenos Aires. 1906-1917. Lang.: Eng.   3687

Rufus
Performance/production
A photographic essay of 42 soloists and groups performing mime or gestural theatre. 1986.   3290

Ruganda, John
Institutions
Founding directors explain history and principles of Enterprise Theatre. Canada. 1983-1986. Lang.: Eng.   1546

Ruggeri, Ruggero
Performance/production
Orientalism in four productions of Wilde's *Salome*. Italy. 1904-1963. Lang.: Ita.   750

Artistic and technological differences in presenting opera for stage and television. Canada. 1960-1980. Lang.: Eng.   3714

Ruiz Ramón, Francisco
Plays/librettos/scripts
Reasons for the lack of new Spanish drama and the few recent significant realistic and experimental plays. Spain. 1972-1985. Lang.: Spa.   2793

Ruiz, Vicente
Performance/production
Humorous and political trends in Chilean theatre season. Chile. 1984-1985. Lang.: Spa.   1686

Rules of the Game, The
SEE
Giuoco delle parti, Il.

Rum and Coke
Performance/production
Reviews of *Rum and Coke*, by Keith Reddin, staged by Leo Waters. USA: New York, NY. 1986. Lang.: Eng.   2241

Run'ers
Reference materials
Current work of Audelco award-winning playwrights. USA: New York, NY. 1973-1984. Lang.: Eng.   3007

Rune Theatre (Sydney)
Performance/production
Influence of *kata* principle on Western acting technique. Japan. Denmark. Australia. 1981-1986. Lang.: Ita.   1365

Rusiñol i Prats, Santiago
Design/technology
Introduction to facsimile of Oleguer Junyent's set design for *L'Auca del senyor Esteve (Mr. Esteve's 'Auca')* by Santiago Rusiñol. Spain-Catalonia: Barcelona. 1861-1984. Lang.: Cat.   1518

Facsimile edition of scene design drawings by Oleguer Junyent for *L'auca del senyor Esteve (Mr. Esteve's 'Auca')* by Santiago Rusiñol. Spain-Catalonia: Barcelona. 1917. Lang.: Cat.   1519

Rusiñol, Santiago
Plays/librettos/scripts
History of Catalan literature, including playwrights and theatre. Spain-Catalonia. 1800-1974. Lang.: Cat.   974

Russell, Willy
Performance/production
Collection of newspaper reviews by London theatre critics. UK. 1986. Lang.: Eng.   2103

Ivan Vas-Zoltán directs *Vértestvérek (Blood Brothers)* by Willy Russell. Hungary: Pécs. 1986. Lang.: Hun.   3602

Russia
Design/technology
Interview with performance artist Chris Hardman. USA. 1986.   3436

Ruszt, József
Performance/production
Productions based on sacred music of Franz Liszt. Hungary: Zalaegerszeg, Budapest. 1986. Lang.: Hun.   1308

Review of László Teleki's *A Kegyenc (The Favorite)* as directed by József Ruszt, Hevesi Sándor Theatre. Hungary: Zalaegerszeg. 1986. Lang.: Hun.   1867

Review of László Teleki's *A Kegyenc (The Favorite)* directed by József Ruszt. Hungary: Zalaegerszeg. 1986. Lang.: Hun.   1891

Two productions of Čechov's *Három Nővér (Three Sisters)*. Hungary: Zalaegerszeg, Budapest. 1985. Lang.: Hun.   1903

Evaluation of József Ruszt's direction at Hevesi Sándor Theatre. Hungary: Zalaegerszeg. 1983-1986. Lang.: Hun.   1927

Comparison of two Hungarian productions of *Háram nővér (Three Sisters)* by Anton Pavlovič Čechov. Hungary: Budapest, Zalaegerszeg. 1985. Lang.: Hun.   1964

Ruts, Jan
Theory/criticism
The aesthetics of movement theatre. Europe. 1975-1986.   3301

Ruttkai, Éva
Performance/production
Career of actress Éva Ruttkai. Hungary. 1927-1986. Lang.: Hun.
                                                                1871

Biography of actress Éva Ruttkai. Hungary. 1934-1976. Lang.: Hun.
                                                                3224

Ruzante
SEE
Beolco, Angelo.

Ryan, Oscar
Relation to other fields
Circumstances surrounding a banned Workers' Experimental Theatre play. Canada: Toronto, ON. 1931-1933. Lang.: Eng.   3018

Rydl, Kurt
Reference materials
Photos of the new opera productions at the Staatsoper. Austria: Vienna. 1985-1986. Lang.: Ger.   3910

Ryga, George
Plays/librettos/scripts
Development of the title character of *The Ecstasy of Rita Joe* by George Ryga, seen in successive drafts. Canada: Vancouver, BC. 1966-1982. Lang.: Eng.   929

Amerindian and aborigine characters in the works of white playwrights. Canada. Australia. 1606-1975. Lang.: Eng.   930

Relation to other fields
Controversy about *Captives of the Faceless Drummer* by George Ryga. Canada: Vancouver, BC. 1968-1971. Lang.: Eng.   3021

Ryhmäteatteri (Helsinki)
Performance/production
Review of *Finlandia*, produced by Ryhmäteatteri. Finland: Helsinki. 1986. Lang.: Swe.   707

Rysanek, Leonie
Performance/production
Profile of and interview with soprano Leonie Rysanek. Austria: Vienna. 1926-1986. Lang.: Eng.   3693

Opera singer Leonie Rysanek and her career. Austria: Vienna. USA: New York, NY. 1926-1986. Lang.: Ger.   3697

Famous sopranos discuss their interpretations of Tosca. USA. 1935-1986. Lang.: Eng.   3811

Rzecz Ojedrzeju Wowrze (A Subject About Jedrzej Wowrze)
Performance/production
Jan Wolkowski directs an adaptation of a folk legend about Jedrzej Wowrze. Poland: Szczecin. 1983. Lang.: Pol.   3968

SUBJECT INDEX

Rzeźnia (Slaughterhouse, The)
Performance/production
Performances of Sławomir Mrożek's *Mészárszék (The Slaughterhouse)* and *Ház a határon (The Home on the Border)*. Hungary: Budapest. 1986. Lang.: Hun.　　1817

Rzeźnia (The Slaughterhouse) by Sławomir Mrożek, directed by Sándor Beke at Józsefvárosi Szinház under the title *Mészárszék*. Hungary: Budapest. 1985. Lang.: Hun.　　1865

Sabath, Bernard
Performance/production
Reviews of *The Boys in Autumn* by Bernard Sabath, staged by Theodore Mann. USA: New York, NY. 1986. Lang.: Eng.　　2221

Sabourin, Marcel
Institutions
History of the Théâtre de la Marmaille. Canada: Quebec, PQ. 1973-1986. Lang.: Eng.　　1552

Sacher, Paul
Reference materials
The purchase and eventual exhibition of a collection of Stravinsky's work. Switzerland: Basel. USA: New York, NY. 1930-1985. Lang.: Eng.　　3500

Sackler, Howard
Performance/production
Review of alternative theatre productions. UK-England: London. 1986. Lang.: Eng.　　2108

Sadista Sisters (UK)
Performance/production
Interview with Lesbian feminist theatre company Hard Corps. UK-England. 1984-1986. Lang.: Eng.　　2164

Sadler's Wells Theatre (London)
Performance/production
Collection of newspaper reviews by London theatre critics. UK-England: London. 1986. Lang.: Eng.　　2116

Collection of newspaper reviews by London theatre critics. UK-England: London. 1986. Lang.: Eng.　　2122

Sadovskije family
Performance/production
Careers of Sadovskije acting family. Russia: Moscow. 1800-1917. Lang.: Rus.　　784

Safety
SEE
Health/safety.

Sagarra, Josep Maria de
Basic theatrical documents
Anthology and study of writings of Josep Maria de Sagarra. Spain-Catalonia. 1917-1964. Lang.: Cat.　　1501

Josep Maria de Sagarra's translations of Shakespeare with scholarly introduction. Spain-Catalonia. UK-England. 1590-1986. Lang.: Cat.　　1502

Plays/librettos/scripts
Evaluation of the literary and dramatic work of Josep Maria de Sagarra. Spain-Catalonia. 1917-1955. Lang.: Cat.　　2810

Translations of Shakespeare by Josep Maria de Sagarra. Spain-Catalonia: Barcelona. 1940-1964. Lang.: Cat.　　2811

Short history of Catalan translations of plays. Spain-Catalonia. 1848-1984. Lang.: Fre.　　2813

Sägayé, Gäbrä Mädhen
Plays/librettos/scripts
Translations of plays by William Shakespeare into Amharic and Tegrenna. Ethiopia: Addis Ababa. 1941-1984. Lang.: Eng.　　2537

Sagesse ou le parabole du festin, La (Wisdom, or The Parable of the Feast)
Plays/librettos/scripts
Influence of *Nō* on Paul Claudel. France. 1868-1955. Lang.: Ita.　　2556

Sagouine, La (Slattern, The)
Plays/librettos/scripts
The plays of Antonine Maillet and the revival of Acadian theatre. Canada. 1971-1979. Lang.: Eng.　　2423

Saidye Bronfman Theatre (Montreal, PQ)
Institutions
New leadership in Montreal's English-speaking theatres. Canada: Montreal, PQ. 1980-1986. Lang.: Eng.　　1539

Sainete
Plays/librettos/scripts
Development in the genre of the *sainete*, or comic afterpiece. Argentina. 1800-1980. Lang.: Spa.　　2365

Saint Anthony
Performance/production
Wooster Group retrospective of original works. USA: New York, NY. 1975-1986. Lang.: Eng.　　850

Plays/librettos/scripts
Contributing sources to Wooster Group's *Saint Anthony*. USA: New York, NY, Boston, MA, Washington, DC. 1983-1986. Lang.: Eng.　　2940

Saint Clements Theatre (New York, NY)
Performance/production
Reviews of *Vienna: Lusthaus*, conceived and staged by Martha Clarke. USA: New York, NY. 1986. Lang.: Eng.　　2209

Saint James Palace (London)
Performance spaces
Reconstructing a theatrical organization at Saint James Palace (London). England: London. 1600-1986. Lang.: Eng.　　1615

Saint Joan
Performance/production
Career of actress, manager and director Julia Arthur. Canada. UK-England. USA. 1869-1950. Lang.: Eng.　　1675

Interview with Elisabeth Bergner and Jane Alexander on their portrayals of Joan of Arc. Germany, West: Berlin, West. UK-England: Malvern. USA: Washington, DC. Lang.: Eng.　　1766

Eileen Atkins, Judi Dench, Wendy Hiller and Barbara Jefford discuss playing Saint Joan in Shaw's play. UK-England: London. 1936-1983. Lang.: Eng.　　2153

Saint John Theatre (St. John, NB)
Relation to other fields
Theatre riot provoked by Thomas Hill's *The Provincial Association*. Canada: St. John, NB. 1845. Lang.: Eng.　　1073

Saint-Denis, Michel
Performance/production
Zen and Western acting styles. Lang.: Eng.　　648

Survey of the career of director Michel Saint-Denis. France. UK-England. 1920-1960. Lang.: Hun.　　718

Saint-Exupéry, Antoine de
Performance/production
A kis herceg (The Little Prince) by Antoine de Saint-Exupéry adapted and staged by Anna Belia and Péter Valló. Hungary: Budapest. 1985. Lang.: Hun.　　1828

A kis herceg (The Little Prince) by Saint-Exupéry adapted and staged by Anna Belia and Péter Valló. Hungary: Budapest. 1985. Lang.: Hun.　　1935

Saint-Laurent, Yves
Design/technology
Costumes by Yves Saint-Laurent. France. 1959-1984. Lang.: Fre.　　1341

Saint's Day
Plays/librettos/scripts
Musical use of language conveys meaning in John Whiting's *Saint's Day*. UK-England. 1951. Lang.: Eng.　　2857

Saks, Gene
Performance/production
Reviews of *Broadway Bound*, by Neil Simon, staged by Gene Saks. USA: New York, NY. 1986. Lang.: Eng.　　2206

Reviews of *Rags*, book by Joseph Stein, music by Charles Strouse, lyrics by Stephen Schwartz, staged by Gene Saks. USA: New York, NY. 1986. Lang.: Eng.　　3617

Salamon Suba, László
Performance/production
László Salamon Suba's production of *Urának hű szolgája (A Faithful Servant of His Lord)* by Franz Grillparzer. Hungary: Nyiregyháza. 1985. Lang.: Hun.　　1881

Saleem, Adèle
Performance/production
Interview with Lesbian feminist theatre company Hard Corps. UK-England. 1984-1986. Lang.: Eng.　　2164

Šaljapin, Fëdor
Performance/production
Life and career of singer Fëdor J. Šaljapin. Russia: Moscow. 1873-1938. Lang.: Rus.　　3773

Plays/librettos/scripts
Correspondence of Maksim Gorkij and singer Fëdor Šaljapin. USSR. 1922-1930. Lang.: Rus.　　3906

Sallé, Marie
Relation to other fields
Eighteenth-century prints depict dancers Marie Sallé and Marie Anne de Cupis de Camargo. France. 1700-1799. Lang.: Rus.　　1327

SUBJECT INDEX

San Quentin Drama Workshop (San Quentin, CA)
Performance/production
Beckett's direction of *Krapp's Last Tape* at San Quentin Drama
Workshop. USA. 1985. Lang.: Hun. 2279
Sand Du Plessis Theatre (Bloemfontein)
Performance spaces
Description of new Sand du Plessis theatre complex. South Africa,
Republic of: Bloemfontein. 1986. Lang.: Afr. 613
Sand, George
Audience
Claques as viewed by French writers. France. 1800-1899. Lang.: Fre.
3647

Plays/librettos/scripts
Political aspects of George Sand's *Père va-tout-seul (Old Man Go-It-
Alone)*. France. 1830-1844. Lang.: Eng. 2574
Sander, Nancy
Performance/production
Influence of the Joy Puppeteers on the television program *Hickory
Hideout*. USA: Cleveland, OH. 1982-1986. Lang.: Eng. 3275
Sandgren, Carl-Eric
Design/technology
Innovator and scene designer Carl-Eric Sandgren. Sweden: Gävle.
1952-1986. Lang.: Swe. 314
Sandor, Anna
Plays/librettos/scripts
Cultural models and types in docudrama. Canada. 1970-1983. Lang.:
Eng. 3279
Sándor, György
Performance/production
Review of *Mágiarakás (Magic Heap)* by humorist György Sándor.
Hungary: Budapest. 1985. Lang.: Hun. 3334
Sándor, Iván
Relation to other fields
Review of Iván Sándor's essays on Hungarian theatre. 1986. Lang.:
Hun. 1049
Sándor, János
Performance/production
IV. Henrik (Henry IV) by Shakespeare, directed by János Sándor.
Hungary: Szeged. 1985. Lang.: Hun. 1791
Review of Gábor Görgey's *Mikszáth különös házassága (Mikszáth
and His Peculiar Marriage)* directed by János Sándor. Hungary:
Szeged. 1986. Lang.: Hun. 1819
Performances of *Hair*, directed by János Sándor, and *Desire Under
the Elms*, directed by Géza Bodolay at the National Theatre of
Szeged. Hungary: Szeged. 1986. Lang.: Hun. 1959
Wariat i zakonnica (The Madman and the Nun) by Stanisław Ignacy
Witkiewicz, directed by János Sándor at Szeged National Theatre
under the title *Az őrült és az apáca*. Hungary: Szeged. 1986. Lang.:
Hun. 1965
A kegyenc (The Favorite) by Gyula Illyés, directed by János Sándor,
National Theatre of Miskolc. Hungary: Miskolc. 1985. Lang.: Hun.
1971

Sandwell, Bernard K.
Theory/criticism
Discusses the impact of critic B.K. Sandwell. Canada. 1932-1951.
Lang.: Eng. 3088
Sanguinetti, Florentine
Performance/production
Evidence that Enrico Caruso sang the baritone prologue to *I
Pagliacci*. Argentina: Buenos Aires. 1906-1917. Lang.: Eng. 3687
Sankai Juku
Performance/production
Description of *butō*, avant-garde dance movement of Japan. Japan.
1960-1986. Lang.: Eng. 1279
Sankofa
Performance/production
Career of director/choreographer Mike Malone. USA: Washington,
DC, Cleveland, OH. 1968-1985. Lang.: Eng. 2275
Santa Claus—The Movie
Design/technology
Designer and special effects supervisor make sleigh fly in *Santa
Claus—The Movie*. Greenland. 1986. 3199
Santa Espina, La (Holy Thorn, The)
Plays/librettos/scripts
Analysis of *La Santa Espina (The Holy Thorn)* by Àngel Guimerà.
Spain-Catalonia. 1897-1907. Lang.: Cat. 2815

Santa Fe Opera (Santa Fe, NM)
Institutions
The first thirty years of the Santa Fe Opera. USA: Santa Fe, NM.
1956-1986. Lang.: Eng. 3681
Santa Fe Opera (Sante Fe, NM)
Administration
Alternate programs produced by opera houses. USA. Lang.: Eng.
3642

Design/technology
The wigmaker's role in regional opera houses. USA. Lang.: Eng.
3658

The role of the costumer in regional opera houses. USA. Lang.:
Eng. 3659

Institutions
The survival and prosperity of the Santa Fe Opera Company. USA:
Santa Fe, NM. 1957-1986. Lang.: Eng. 3678
Performance/production
Profile of and interview with opera parodist Charles Ludlam of The
Ridiculous Theatre Company. USA: New York, NY. 1973-1986.
Lang.: Eng. 3825
Santana, Rodolfo
Plays/librettos/scripts
Traces development of political trends in Venezuelan drama.
Venezuela. 1958-1980. Lang.: Spa. 2972
Santander, Felipe
Performance/production
Theatre Plus production of Santander's *Two Brothers*. Canada:
Toronto, ON. Mexico. 1986. Lang.: Eng. 1679
Sappa
Plays/librettos/scripts
Work of playwright Stefan Schütz. Germany, West. 1944-1986.
Lang.: Eng. 2625
Interview with playwright Stefan Schütz. Germany, West. 1970-1986.
Lang.: Eng. 2628
Sardou, Victorien
Administration
Censorship in post-Revolutionary France. France: Paris. 1791-1891.
Lang.: Eng. 39
Sarkadi, Imre
Performance/production
István Szőke directs *Oszlopos Simeon (The Man on the Pillar)* by
Imre Sarkadi at Miskolc National Theatre. Hungary: Miskolc. 1986.
Lang.: Hun. 1813
Imre Sarkadi's *Oszlopos Simeon (The Man on the Pillar)* directed by
István Szőke at Nemzeti Szinház. Hungary: Miskolc. 1986. Lang.:
Hun. 1952
Sarkola, Asko
Institutions
History of Swedish language Lilla-teatern (Little Theatre). Finland:
Helsinki. 1940-1986. Lang.: Eng, Fre. 494
Sárospataky, István
Plays/librettos/scripts
Works of playwright István Sárospataky. Hungary. 1974-1985. Lang.:
Hun. 2660
Sarsanedas, Jordi
Relation to other fields
Reports and discussions of restricted cultural communication.
Lebanon. Spain-Catalonia. USA. 1985. Lang.: Fre, Spa, Cat. 1111

Theory/criticism
Historical difficulties in creating a paradigm for Catalan theatre.
Spain-Catalonia. 1400-1963. Lang.: Cat. 1220
Sartori, Amleto
Design/technology
Origins and development of *commedia dell'arte* detailing the costume
and attributes of the stock characters. Italy. Europe. USA. 1500-
1986. Lang.: Eng. 3407
Sartre, Jean-Paul
Performance/production
Review of *A trójai nők (The Trojan Women)* adapted from
Euripides and Sartre by Gyula Illyés, directed by László Vámos.
Hungary: Budapest. 1986. Lang.: Hun. 1792
Review of *Trójai Nők (The Trojan Women)* by Jean-Paul Sartre,
produced at Nemzeti Szinház. Hungary: Budapest. 1986. Lang.: Hun.
1855

Troádes (The Trojan Women) directed by László Gergely at
Csokonai Theatre. Hungary: Debrecen. 1985. Lang.: Hun. 1909

Sartre, Jean-Paul — cont'd

Plays/librettos/scripts
Metaphoric style in the political drama of Jean-Paul Sartre, Athol Fugard and Juan Radrigán. France. South Africa, Republic of. Chile. 1940-1986. Lang.: Eng. 951

Superficial and reductive use of classical myth in modern French theatre. France. 1935-1944. Lang.: Eng. 2550

Sarugaku
Theory/criticism
Translation and discussion of Zeami's *Sarugaku dangi*. Japan. 1430. Lang.: Eng. 1423

Sassoon, Siegfried
Plays/librettos/scripts
Interview with playwright Stephen MacDonald. UK-England: London. 1917-1986. Lang.: Eng. 2879

Sastre, Alfonso
Plays/librettos/scripts
Playwright Alfonso Sastre discusses three of his recent plays. Spain. 1983-1986. Lang.: Spa. 2802

Alfonso Sastre's theory of complex tragedy in *La Celestina (The Nun)*. Spain. 1978. Lang.: Spa. 2807

Satin Slipper, The
SEE
Soulier de satin, Le.

Satire
Basic theatrical documents
A collection of satirical monologues by playwright Corey Reay. Canada. Lang.: Eng. 1471

Design/technology
Irena Pikiel, Polish puppet theatre stage-designer, describes her years in satirical performances. Poland: Vilna. 1921-1933. Lang.: Pol. 3952

Performance/production
Development of clowning to include parody. UK. 1769-1985. Lang.: Fre. 3347

Otto Grünmandl and his satiric revues. Austria. 1924-1986. Lang.: Ger. 3363

History of the Viennese cabaret. Austria: Vienna. 1890-1945. Lang.: Ger. 3364

Plays/librettos/scripts
Interview with satirist Barry Humphries. Australia. UK-England. 1950-1986. Lang.: Eng. 922

Defense of *The Malcontent* by John Marston as a well-constructed satire. England. 1590-1600. Lang.: Eng. 938

Religious ideas in the satirical plays of John Marston. England. 1595-1609. Lang.: Eng. 940

Analysis of plays by David Williamson. Australia. 1976-1985. Lang.: Eng. 2379

The link between comic and survival instincts. Italy. 1986. Lang.: Eng. 2688

Reference materials
Encyclopedia of cabaret in German. Germany. Switzerland. Austria. 1900-1965. Lang.: Ger. 3369

Relation to other fields
Shakespearean allusions in political satire. Canada. 1798-1871. Lang.: Eng. 1074

History of anti-Nazi satire. Germany. Switzerland: Zurich. 1933-1945. Lang.: Ger. 3370

Historical function of cabaret entertainment. Germany. 1896-1945. Lang.: Ger. 3371

Theory/criticism
Satirical essay on the future of the theatre. USA. 1984. Lang.: Eng. 1235

Satre Day/Night
Performance/production
Collection of newspaper reviews by London theatre critics. UK-England: London. 1986. Lang.: Eng. 2118

Šatrov, Michajl
Plays/librettos/scripts
Playwright Michajl Šatrov. USSR. 1932-1986. Lang.: Rus. 2954

Saturday Company (Australia)
Performance/production
Dilemmas and prospects of youth theatre movement. Australia. 1982-1986. Lang.: Eng. 1639

Satyre of the Thrie Estaitis, Ane
Performance/production
Account of a production of *Ane Satyre of the Thrie Estaitis* by David Lindsay. Scotland: Cupar. 1552-1554. Lang.: Eng. 2072

Sauce for the Goose: sp *Dindon, Le*
SEE

Sauguet, Henri
Institutions
Discussions of opera at the festival of Aix-en-Provence. France: Aix-en-Provence. 1960. Lang.: Fre. 3673

Saunders, James
Performance/production
Collection of newspaper reviews by London theatre critics. UK-England: London. 1986. Lang.: Eng. 2117

Savage in Limbo
Design/technology
Interview with set designer Adrianne Lobel. USA: New York, NY. 1986. Lang.: Eng. 1530

Savannah Bay
Performance/production
Savannah Bay and *Reigen (Round)* produced by Centre Dramàtic. Spain-Catalonia: Barcelona. 1986. Lang.: Cat. 2082

Savannah Club (Savannah, GA)
Performance/production
Four nightclub entertainers on their particular acts and the atmosphere of the late night clubs and theaters in Harlem. USA: New York, NY, Savannah, GA. 1930-1950. Lang.: Eng. 3470

Save Grand Central
Performance/production
Interview with dramaturg Anne Cattaneo. USA: New York, NY. 1971-1986. Lang.: Eng. 2254

Saved
Performance/production
Kinn vagyunk a vízböl (Saved) by Edward Bond directed by István Szőke. Hungary: Pécs. 1986. Lang.: Hun. 1940

Savinio, Alberto
Plays/librettos/scripts
Correspondence of Alberto Savinio, author of *Alcesti di Samuele (Alcesti of Samuel)*. Italy. 1947-1950. Lang.: Ita. 2716

Savonlinna Opera Festival
Design/technology
Career of designer Ralf Forsström discussing his influences and stylistic preferences. Finland: Helsinki. 1963-1986. Lang.: Eng, Fre. 3650

Performance/production
Interview with composer and director of the Finnish National opera Ilkka Kuusisto. Finland: Helsinki, Suomussalmi. 1967-1986. Lang.: Eng, Fre. 3724

Plays/librettos/scripts
Analysis of thematic trends in recent Finnish Opera. Finland: Helsinki, Savonlinna. 1909-1986. Lang.: Eng, Fre. 3865

Interview with opera composer Aulis Sallinen on his current work. Finland: Helsinki. 1975-1986. Lang.: Eng, Fre. 3866

Savoy Theatre (London)
Performance/production
Innovative Shakespeare stagings of Harley Granville-Barker. UK-England. 1912-1940. Lang.: Eng. 806

Saxon Shore, The
Performance/production
Collection of newspaper reviews by London theatre critics. UK-England: London. 1986. Lang.: Eng. 2121

Sbragia, Giancarlo
Plays/librettos/scripts
Letters of playwright Diego Fabbri. Italy. 1960-1978. Lang.: Ita. 2672

Scabia, Giuliano
Theory/criticism
Decreasing importance of the playwright in Italian theatre. Italy. 1900-1984. Lang.: Fre. 3119

Scala, Flaminio
Institutions
Relations between the 'Confidenti' company and their patron Don Giovanni dei Medici. Italy: Venice. 1613-1621. Lang.: Ita. 1580

Scarf, The
Performance/production
Profile of and interview with Lee Hoiby, American composer of *The Tempest* with libretto by Mark Schulgasser. USA: Long Eddy, NJ. 1926-1986. Lang.: Eng. 3832

Scarlet Pimpernel, The
Performance/production
Collection of newspaper reviews by London theatre critics. UK: London. 1986. Lang.: Eng. 2100

Scenery — cont'd

Institutions

Performance spaces

Scenery — cont'd

Technical design features of New Victoria Theatre. UK-England: Stoke-on-Trent. 1980-1986. Lang.: Eng.   624

Problematic dimensions of the Sydney Opera House's Drama Theatre. Australia: Sydney, N.S.W. 1980-1986. Lang.: Eng.   1612

Ceremonies celebrating the marriage of Maria dei Medici to Henri IV. Italy: Florence. France: Lyon. 1568-1600. Lang.: Ita.   3325

Performance/production

Short history of the activities of the family Robreño. Cuba. Spain-Catalonia. 1838-1972. Lang.: Cat.   680

Hungarian critics' awards for best actors, play, costume, scenery, etc. of the season. Hungary. 1985-1986. Lang.: Hun.   733

Documentation on staging of plays for 'Maggio Musicale Fiorentino'. Italy: Florence. 1933-1985. Lang.: Ita.   752

Volume 2 of complete works of Adolphe Appia. Switzerland. 1895-1905. Lang.: Fre, Ger.   804

History of the British and American stage. USA. England. 1800-1986. Lang.: Eng.   826

Origins of radically simplified stage in modern productions. USA. 1912-1922. Lang.: Eng.   831

Recollections of director, designer and teacher Nikolaj Pavlovič Akimov. USSR. 1901-1968. Lang.: Rus.   914

Collaboration of choreographer Aurél Milloss and scene designer Giorgio de Chirico. Hungary. Italy: Milan, Rome. 1942-1945. Lang.: Hun.   1275

Interview with Peter Brook's designer, musician, and costumer for *Mahabharata*. France: Avignon. 1973-1985. Lang.: Eng.   1359

The Castle of Perseverance examined for clues to audience placement and physical plan of original production. England. 1343-1554. Lang.: Eng.   1709

Overview of correspondence between Leon Schiller and Edward Gordon Craig. Poland: Warsaw. France: Paris. 1900-1954. Lang.: Eng, Fre.   2022

Contribution of stage directions concerning stage design and directing to producing plays by Friedrich Dürrenmatt. Switzerland. 1949-1986. Lang.: Eng.   2097

Analysis of reviews of 1929 *Dynamo* by Eugene O'Neill suggest strong production of a weak play. USA: New York, NY. 1929. Lang.: Eng.   2311

Detailed instructions on the mounting of a musical. 1986. Lang.: Eng.   3598

Interview with Jean-Pierre Ponnelle discussing his directing technique and set designs. Austria: Salzburg. 1984. Lang.: Eng.   3699

Mussorgskij's opera *Boris Godunov* at the Mariinskij Theatre. Russia: St. Petersburg. 1874. Lang.: Eng.   3775

Plays/librettos/scripts

Compares pageant-wagon play about Edward IV with version by Thomas Heywood. England: Coventry, London. 1560-1600. Lang.: Eng.   3430

Reference materials

Illustrated guide to Actor's Museum. Hungary: Budapest. 1850-1986. Lang.: Hun.   2990

Relation to other fields

Impact of painting and sculpture on theatre. England. 1700-1900. Lang.: Eng.   1079

The work of painter and scene designer Claude Gillot. France. 1673-1722. Lang.: Ita.   1084

Theory/criticism

Semiotic analysis of Carlo Gozzi's *Fiabe (Fables)*. Italy: Venice. 1761-1765. Lang.: Ita.   3117

Use of red, white and black colors in Chinese traditional theatre. China. 200 B.C.-1982 A.D. Lang.: Chi.   3560

Theories about the stage for the traditional *chäng-gük* play. Korea: Seoul. 1800-1950. Lang.: Kor.   3931

Sceny iz maskarada (Scenes from a Masquerade)

Performance/production

Interpretation of classics for theatre and television. USSR. 1980-1986. Lang.: Rus.   2337

Schach, Leonard

Performance/production

Director discusses *Tramway Road* by Ronald Harwood. South Africa, Republic of. UK-England: London. 1986. Lang.: Eng.   2073

Schaeffer, Bogusław

Plays/librettos/scripts

Philosophical aspects and structure of plays by Bogusław Schaeffer. Poland. 1929-1986. Lang.: Pol.   2749

Schafer, R. Murray

Performance/production

Description of *The Princess and the Stars* by R. Murray Schafer. Canada: Banff, AB. 1985. Lang.: Eng.   3485

Plays/librettos/scripts

Analysis of *RA* by R. Murray Schafer, performed by Comus Music Theatre. Canada: Toronto, ON. 1983. Lang.: Eng.   2416

Schall, Eckhardt

Performance/production

Application of Brechtian concepts by Eckhardt Schall. Germany, East: Berlin, East. UK-England: London. 1952-1986. Lang.: Eng.   1762

Schattner, Gertrud

Relation to other fields

Gertrud Schattner, a founder of drama therapy, and her work at Bellevue Hospital. USA: New York, NY. Austria. 1968. Lang.: Eng.   3064

Schaubühne am Helleschen Ufer (West Berlin)

Performance/production

Interview with Peter Stein, director of Schaubühne am Helleschen Ufer. Germany, West: Berlin, West. Poland: Warsaw. 1984. Lang.: Pol.   731

Schaubühne Am Lehniner Platz (West Berlin)

Performance/production

Peter Stein directs Aeschylus' *Oresteia* in Warsaw. Germany, West: Berlin, West. Poland: Warsaw. 1983. Lang.: Pol.   1768

Schauspielhaus (Vienna)

Institutions

Photos of productions at the Schauspielhaus under the leadership of Hans Gratzer. Austria: Vienna. 1978-1986. Lang.: Ger.   1534

On concept of the new group, Der Kreis. Austria: Vienna. 1986-1987. Lang.: Ger.   1536

Plays/librettos/scripts

Training for new playwrights in Austria. Austria: Vienna. 1985-1986. Lang.: Ger.   2392

Schavernoch, Hans

Design/technology

On scene designer Hans Schavernoch and his work. Austria: Vienna. 1945-1986. Lang.: Ger.   239

Schechner, Richard

Performance/production

Historical development of acting and directing techniques. 1898-1986. Lang.: Eng.   1632

Spalding Gray's memories of the development and tour of Richard Schechner's *Commune*. USA. France. Poland. 1970. Lang.: Eng.   2270

Plays/librettos/scripts

Jerzy Grotowski and his adaptation of *Doctor Faustus*. Poland. 1964. Lang.: Eng.   2740

Theory/criticism

John Cage discusses his struggle to define art. USA. 1965. Lang.: Eng.   1231

Richard Schechner bids farewell to *The Drama Review* and suggests areas of future theatrical investigation. USA. 1969-1986. Lang.: Eng.   1234

Forums: Dispute regarding content and aims of *The Drama Review*. USA. 1964-1986. Lang.: Eng.   3139

Intents and purposes of *The Drama Review*. USA. 1963-1986. Lang.: Eng.   3150

Six rules which render socially desirable elements of performance superfluous. USA. 1968-1986. Lang.: Eng.   3151

Richard Schechner discusses the importance of translating and performing the work of all cultures. USA. 1982. Lang.: Eng.   3152

Training

History of the Performance Group. USA. 1960. Lang.: Eng.   3161

Schechter, Joel

Plays/librettos/scripts

Report on a symposium addressing the role of the dramaturg.   918

Scheiderman, Perry

Institutions

Interviews with theatre professionals in Quebec. Canada. 1985. Lang.: Fre.   487

Scheler, Max

Theory/criticism

Theory of drama based on Max Scheler's philosophy. Lang.: Eng.   3074

Seattle Repertory Theatre (Seattle, WA) — cont'd

Designers discuss regional productions of *The Sound of Music*. USA.
1983-1986. Lang.: Eng.   3594

Second Maiden's Tragedy, The
Plays/librettos/scripts
Language in *The Second Maiden's Tragedy*. England: London. 1611.
Lang.: Eng.   2460

Second Shepherds Play
SEE
Secundum Pastorum.

Second Stage (New York, NY)
Performance/production
Reviews of *Coastal Disturbances*, by Tina Howe, staged by Carole
Rothman. USA: New York, NY. 1986. Lang.: Eng.   2200
Interview with dramaturg Anne Cattaneo. USA: New York, NY.
1971-1986. Lang.: Eng.   2254
Revivals by Second Stage. USA: New York, NY. 1986. Lang.: Eng.
2259

Secret Dialogues
SEE
Diálogos secretos.

Secunda Theatre (Secunda)
Performance spaces
Brief history of Secunda Theatre. South Africa, Republic of:
Secunda. 1986. Lang.: Eng.   614

Secundum Pastorum
Performance/production
Descriptions of productions of *Li Jus de Robin et Marion (The Play
of Robin and Marion)*, *The Comedy of Virtuous and Godly Susanna*
and *The Second Shepherds Play*. USA: Washington, DC. UK-
England: Lancaster. France: Perpignan. 1986. Lang.: Eng.   2289

Seduced
Performance/production
Seduced by Sam Shepard, directed by George Nickas at Seven
Stages. USA: Atlanta, GA. 1985. Lang.: Eng.   2302

Segitsd a király! (Help the King!)
Performance/production
Selected reviews of *Segitsd a király! (Help the King!)* by József
Ratkó. Hungary: Nyiregyháza. 1985. Lang.: Hun.   1902

Segitség (Help)
Performance/production
Segitség (Help) by György Schwajda, directed by István Pinczés,
Csokonai Szinház. Hungary: Debrecen. 1986. Lang.: Hun.   1848

Segovia, Claudio
Performance/production
Reviews of *Flamenco Puro*, conceived, staged and designed by
Claudio Segovia and Hector Orezzoli. USA: New York, NY. 1986.
Lang.: Eng.   2210

*Sei personaggi in cerca d'autore (Six Characters in Search of an
Author)*
Performance/production
Theatrical illusion in *Sei personaggi in cerca d'autore (Six
Characters in Search of an Author)* by Luigi Pirandello. France:
Paris. 1951-1986. Lang.: Fre.   1730
Max Reinhardt's notes on his production of *Sei personaggi in cerca
d'autore (Six Characters in Search of an Author)* by Luigi
Pirandello. Germany. Italy. 1924-1934. Lang.: Ita.   1759
Luigi Pirandello's concerns with staging in *Sei personaggi in cerca
d'autore (Six Characters in Search of an Author)* and *Enrico Quarto
(Henry IV)*. Italy. 1921-1986. Lang.: Fre.   1990

Plays/librettos/scripts
Tension between text and realization in Pirandello's *Sei personaggi
in cerca d'autore (Six Characters in Search of an Author)*. Italy.
1911-1929. Lang.: Fre.   2685
Study of Pirandello's preface to *Sei personaggi in cerca d'autore
(Six Characters in Search of an Author)*. Italy. 1923-1986. Lang.:
Fre.   2708

Seifter, Harvey
Performance/production
Interview with development director Harvey Seifter on German
theatre. USA: New York, NY. Germany, West. 1984. Lang.: Eng.
840

Sekiya, Yukio
Institutions
The Kaze-no-Ko: professional travelling children's theatre of Japan.
Japan. 1950-1984. Lang.: Eng.   507

Sellars, Peter
Design/technology
A profile of lighting designer James Ingalls. USA. 1980-1986.   374

Institutions
Discussion of America's National Theatre and Peter Sellars, artistic
director. USA: Washington, DC. 1984. Lang.: Eng.   568
Performance/production
Survey of productions at the Kennedy Center's National Theatre.
USA: Washington, DC. 1986. Lang.: Eng.   2247
Robert Auletta's updated version of Sophocles' *Ajax*. USA:
Washington, DC. 1986. Lang.: Eng.   2276
Director Peter Sellars talks about staging Brecht's plays. USA. 1983.
2290
The Iceman Cometh by Eugene O'Neill, directed by José Quintero.
USA: New York, NY. 1985. Lang.: Eng.   2315
Peter Sellars' production of Mozart's *Così fan tutte*. USA: Purchase,
NY. 1986. Lang.: Eng.   3815
Directors revitalizing opera. USA: New York, NY. 1970-1986. Lang.:
Eng.   3826
Plays/librettos/scripts
Playwright Robert Auletta on his adaptation of Sophocles'*Ajax*.
USA: Washington, DC. 1986. Lang.: Eng.   2891
Contributing sources to Wooster Group's *Saint Anthony*. USA: New
York, NY, Boston, MA, Washington, DC. 1983-1986. Lang.: Eng.
2940

Sells-Floto Circus
Performance/production
Career of lion tamer Captain Terrell Jacobs. USA. 1903-1943. Lang.:
Eng.   3393
Selody, Kim
Performance/production
Increased use of physical aspects of theatre in Vancouver. Canada:
Vancouver, BC. 1986. Lang.: Eng.   1664
Semën Kotko
Plays/librettos/scripts
History and aesthetics of Soviet opera. USSR: Moscow. 1917-1941.
Lang.: Ger.   3905
Semenjaka, L.
Theory/criticism
Synthesis of the arts in the theatrical process. USSR: Moscow. 1986.
Lang.: Rus.   1240
Semënova, Nina
Plays/librettos/scripts
Replies to questionnaire by five Soviet playwrights. USSR. Bulgaria.
1986. Lang.: Rus.   2958
Séminaire de Trois-Rivières (Trois-Rivières, PQ)
Institutions
A history of theatre at the Séminaire de Trois-Rivières. Canada:
Trois-Rivières, PQ. 1860-1985. Lang.: Fre.   1563
Plays/librettos/scripts
Book review of *125 Ans de Theatre au Seminaire de Trois-Rivières*.
Canada: Trois-Rivières, PQ. 1985. Lang.: Fre.   2427
Semiotics
Audience
The semiotics of dramatic dialogue. Israel. 1986. Lang.: Eng.   1449
Postmodern concepts of individual, audience, public. USA. 1985-
1986. Lang.: Eng.   1454
Context and design of some lesbian performances. USA: New York,
NY. 1985. Lang.: Eng.   1455
Performance/production
Image of the indigène. Australia. New Zealand. Canada. 1830-1980.
Lang.: Eng.   656
Merce Cunningham, Alwin Nikolais, Meredith Monk and Yvonne
Rainer on post-modern dance. USA. 1975-1986. Lang.: Eng.   1285
The functions of rhythm in reading and performance. Europe. 1900-
1984. Lang.: Fre.   1717
Role of the director working with classics today. Spain-Catalonia.
1984. Lang.: Cat.   2080
Aesthetics, styles, rehearsal techniques of director Richard Foreman.
USA. 1974-1986. Lang.: Eng.   2263
Semiology of opera. Europe. 1600-1985. Lang.: Eng, Fre.   3721
Plays/librettos/scripts
Semiotic analysis of a production of *Antigone* by Sophocles.
Australia: Perth, W.A. 1986. Lang.: Eng.   923
Semiotic analysis of Shakespeare's *King Lear*. England: London.
1605-1606. Lang.: Eng.   2467
Study of realism vs metadrama. Europe. 429 B.C.-1978 A.D. Lang.:
Eng.   2540

Semiotics — cont'd

Rhetorical analysis of Samuel Beckett's *Waiting for Godot*. France. 1953. Lang.: Eng.   2562

Forerunner of contemporary theatre: *Axël* by Villiers de l'Isle-Adam. France. 1862-1894. Lang.: Fre.   2579

Relation to other fields

Reports and discussions of restricted cultural communication. Lebanon. Spain-Catalonia. USA. 1985. Lang.: Fre, Spa, Cat.   1111

Theory/criticism

Live theatre gives the spectator a choice of focus. 1600-1986. Lang.: Eng.   1190

Essays on the sociology of art and semiotics. Lang.: Hun.   1192

Survey on the major trends of theatre theory in the 1980s. 1977-1986. Lang.: Hun.   1195

Creative self-assembly and juxtaposition in live performance and film. Lang.: Eng.   1196

Interview with semiologist Patrice Pavis about the theatre institute at the Sorbonne, his semiotic approach to theatre and modern French theatre. France: Paris. 1923-1986. Lang.: Heb.   1206

An imagined dialogue on the work of Roland Barthes. France. Lang.: Eng.   1207

Influence of literary theory on Greek theatre studies. Greece. UK-England. Germany. Lang.: Afr.   1210

Historical difficulties in creating a paradigm for Catalan theatre. Spain-Catalonia. 1400-1963. Lang.: Cat.   1220

Correlation of word and image in dramaturgy. USSR. 1986. Lang.: Rus.   1239

Transposition of text into performance. Lang.: Ger.   3073

Theory of drama based on Max Scheler's philosophy. Lang.: Eng.   3074

Semiotic analysis of audience-director relationship. Lang.: Heb. 3080

Pitfalls of a semiotic analysis of theatre. England. 1600-1921. Lang.: Eng.   3094

Semiotic analysis of Carlo Gozzi's *Fiabe (Fables)*. Italy: Venice. 1761-1765. Lang.: Ita.   3117

Semiotic analysis of *La Storia*. Italy. 1985. Lang.: Eng.   3118

A semiotic reading of Carlos Fuentes' play *Orquídeas a la luz de la luna (Orchids in the Moonlight)*. Mexico. 1982-1986. Lang.: Eng.   3123

Conferences on theory of performance. Poland. USA. 1985. Lang.: Eng, Fre.   3127

Semiotic analysis of audience involvement in *Fröken Julie (Miss Julie)* by August Strindberg. Sweden. 1889-1986. Lang.: Ita.   3133

Collection of essays on the avant-garde. USA. 1955-1986. Lang.: Eng.   3145

Semiotic analysis of theatrical elements. Europe. 1979. Lang.: Eng.   3461

Semiotic analysis of Laurie Anderson's *United States*. USA. 1984. Lang.: Eng.   3462

Semper Court Theatre
SEE
Dresdner Hoftheater.

Semper Opera
SEE
Dresdner Hoftheater.

Semper, Gottfried
Performance spaces
Semper Depot and its history. Austria: Vienna. 1872-1986. Lang.: Ger.   583

Sempronio
SEE
Artis, Avelli.

Sen O Goldfadenie (Dream About Goldfaden)
Performance/production
Abraham Goldfaden's *Sen O Goldfadenie (Dream About Goldfaden)* directed by Jacob Rotbaum, Teatr Zydowski. Poland: Warsaw. 1984. Lang.: Pol.   3490

Sendak, Maurice
Design/technology
Profile of and interview with illustrator Maurice Sendak, designer of numerous opera productions. USA. 1930-1986. Lang.: Eng.   3657

Sendin Galiana, Alfred
Institutions
History of theatre in Valencia area focusing on Civil War period. Spain: Valencia. 1817-1982. Lang.: Cat.   514

Seneca, Lucius Annaeus
Plays/librettos/scripts
Connection between character Senex in Thomas Kyd's *The Spanish Tragedy* and Senecan drama. England. 1587. Lang.: Eng.   2473

Senecan ideas in Shakespeare's *Timon of Athens*. England: London. 1601-1608. Lang.: Eng.   2533

Stoicism and modern elements in Senecan drama. Europe. 65-1986. Lang.: Eng.   2542

Señora Carrar's Rifles
SEE
Gewehre der Frau Carrar, Die.

Señorita de Tacna, La (Lady from Tacna, The)
Plays/librettos/scripts
Interview with author and playwright Mario Vargas Llosa. Argentina. 1952-1986. Lang.: Spa.   2361

Levels of time in *La señorita de Tacna (The Lady from Tacna)* by Mario Vargas Llosa. Peru. Lang.: Spa.   2731

Sequentia (West Germany)
Performance/production
Performance by Sequentia of *Ordo Virtutum* by Hildegard of Bingen. USA: Stanford, CA. 1986. Lang.: Eng.   3493

Serafí Pitarra
SEE
Soler, Frederic.

Serban, Andrei
Performance/production
Greek tragedy on the New York stage. USA: New York, NY. 1854-1984. Lang.: Eng.   2301

Andrei Serban discusses the vibration of a sound and its effect on the listener. USA. 1976. Lang.: Eng.   2304

Andrei Serban discusses his production of Beethoven's *Fidelio*. UK-England: London. 1986. Lang.: Eng.   3787

Directors revitalizing opera. USA: New York, NY. 1970-1986. Lang.: Eng.   3826

Seregi, László
Performance/production
Prokofjev's ballet *Romeo and Juliet* choreographed by László Seregi. Hungary: Budapest. 1985. Lang.: Hun.   1307

Seriman, Zaccaria
Performance/production
Writings of Zaccaria Seriman on the theatre of his time. Italy: Venice. 1708-1784. Lang.: Ita.   1989

Serreau, Jean-Marie
Performance/production
Notes, interviews and evolution of actor/director Jean-Marie Serreau. France. 1938-1973. Lang.: Fre.   1724

Service institutions
SEE
Institutions, service.

Sesame Street
Performance/production
Work of Kermit Love, creator of Big Bird for *Sesame Street*. USA: New York, NY. 1935-1985. Lang.: Eng.   3276

Set design
SEE
Scenery.

Seven and a Half Cents
Performance/production
Collection of newspaper reviews by London theatre critics. UK: London. 1986. Lang.: Eng.   2100

Seven Stages (Atlanta, GA)
Performance/production
Seduced by Sam Shepard, directed by George Nickas at Seven Stages. USA: Atlanta, GA. 1985. Lang.: Eng.   2302

Severin, Bo
Performance/production
Interview with judge and amateur actor Bo Severin. Sweden: Malmö. 1985-1986. Lang.: Swe.   802

Sewell, Stephen
Plays/librettos/scripts
Developments in Australian playwriting since 1975. Australia. 1975-1986. Lang.: Eng.   2374

Analysis of *Dreams in an Empty City* by Stephen Sewell. Australia: Adelaide. Lang.: Eng.   2375

Shakespeare, William — cont'd

István Paál directs Shakespeare's *Szeget szeggel (Measure for Measure)*. Hungary: Veszprém. 1985. Lang.: Hun. 1770

Performances of *Alice Csodaországban (Alice in Wonderland)*, *A Két Veronai nemes (The Two Gentlemen of Verona)* and *Tobbsincs királyfi (No More Crown Prince)*. Hungary: Pécs, Budapest. 1985. Lang.: Hun. 1771

Szeget szeggel (Measure for Measure) by William Shakespeare directed by Tamás Szirtes at Madách Kamaraszinház. Hungary: Budapest. 1985. Lang.: Hun. 1785

Tamás Szirtes directs *Szeget szeggel (Measure for Measure)* by Shakespeare. Hungary: Budapest. 1985. Lang.: Hun. 1789

IV. Henrik (Henry IV) by Shakespeare, directed by János Sándor. Hungary: Szeged. 1985. Lang.: Hun. 1791

László Gali directs Shakespeare's *Hamlet*. Hungary: Debrecen. 1986. Lang.: Hun. 1827

Review of Shakespeare's *Hamlet* directed by László Gali at Csokonai Theatre, with attention to Károly Sziki's performance as Hamlet. Hungary: Debrecen. 1986. Lang.: Hun. 1844

Ferenc Sik directs *A velencei Kalmár (The Merchant of Venice)* by William Shakespeare. Hungary: Budapest. 1986. Lang.: Hun. 1853

Ahogy tetszik (As You Like It) by William Shakespeare directed by István Szőke. Hungary: Miskolc. 1986. Lang.: Hun. 1866

Production of Shakespeare's *Szeget szeggel (Measure for Measure)* directed by István Paál. Hungary: Veszprém. 1985. Lang.: Hun. 1872

István Szőke, directs *Ahogy tetszik (As You Like It)* by Shakespeare. Hungary: Miskolc. 1986. Lang.: Hun. 1873

Gyula Gazdag directs *A vihar (The Tempest)* by William Shakespeare, Csiky Gergely Theatre. Hungary: Kaposvár. 1986. Lang.: Hun. 1883

Reviews of Shakespeare productions written by Hungarian realist writer, Zsigmond Móricz. Hungary: Budapest. 1923. Lang.: Hun. 1887

Ferenc Sik directs Shakespeare's *A velencei kalmár (The Merchant of Venice)*. Hungary: Budapest. 1986. Lang.: Hun. 1907

István Paál directs *Szeget szeggel (Measure for Measure)* by Shakespeare at Petőfi Szinház. Hungary: Veszprém. 1985. Lang.: Hun. 1938

Review of Gyula Gazdag's production of *A Vihar (The Tempest)* by Shakespeare, Csiky Gergely Theatre. Hungary: Kaposvár. 1986. Lang.: Hun. 1960

Performance of Shakespeare's *Richard II* at Várszinház, directed by Imre Kerényi. Hungary: Budapest. 1986. Lang.: Hun. 1970

Othello, translated by Bohdan Drozdowski and directed by Wilfred Harrison at the Wilama Horzycy Theatre. Poland: Toruń. 1980. Lang.: Hun. 2023

Description of first translations and adaptations of Shakespeare's dramas on the Polish stage. Poland: Vilna. 1786-1864. Lang.: Pol. 2030

Shakespeare's *Hamlet* directed by Janusz Warmiński. Poland: Warsaw. 1983. Lang.: Pol. 2051

Interview with director Jorge Lavelli of Estudio Faixat. Spain-Catalonia: Barcelona. 1983. Lang.: Pol. 2081

Collection of newspaper reviews by London theatre critics. UK. 1986. Lang.: Eng. 2099

Collection of newspaper reviews by London theatre critics. UK. 1986. Lang.: Eng. 2101

Political difficulties in staging two touring productions of Shakespeare's *The Taming of the Shrew*. UK. 1985-1986. Lang.: Eng. 2104

Solutions to staging the final scene of Shakespeare's *The Merry Wives of Windsor*. UK. 1874-1985. Lang.: Eng. 2105

Collection of newspaper reviews by London theatre critics. UK-England: London. 1986. Lang.: Eng. 2109

Collection of newspaper reviews by London theatre critics. UK-England: London. 1986. Lang.: Eng. 2110

Collection of newspaper reviews by London theatre critics. UK-England. 1986. Lang.: Eng. 2111

Collection of newspaper reviews by London theatre critics. UK-England: London. 1986. Lang.: Eng. 2112

Collection of newspaper reviews by London theatre critics. UK-England. 1986. Lang.: Eng. 2115

Collection of newspaper reviews by London theatre critics. UK-England: London. 1986. Lang.: Eng. 2125

Actors Ben Kingsley and David Suchet discuss their roles in Shakespeare's *Othello*. UK-England. 1986. Lang.: Eng. 2128

Doubling of roles in Shakespeare's *Hamlet*. UK-England: London. 1900-1985. Lang.: Eng. 2129

Reviews of three Shakespearean productions. UK-England: London, Stratford. USA: Ashland, OR. 1985. Lang.: Eng. 2140

Comparison of stage production and film version of Shakespeare's *King Lear*, both directed by Peter Brook. UK-England. 1962-1970. Lang.: Eng. 2149

Royal Shakespeare Company performances at the Barbican Theatre. UK-England: London. 1986. Lang.: Eng. 2152

Reconstruction of a number of Shakespeare plays staged and performed by Herbert Beerbohm Tree. UK-England: London. 1887-1917. Lang.: Eng. 2155

Actor Laurence Olivier's memoirs. UK-England: London. USA: New York, NY. 1907-1986. Lang.: Eng. 2170

Jonathan Pryce in the role of Macbeth. UK-England: Stratford. 1970-1986. Lang.: Eng. 2179

Detailed discussion of four successful Royal Shakespeare Company productions of Shakespeare's minor plays. UK-England: Stratford. 1946-1977. Lang.: Eng. 2182

Shakespearean productions by the National Theatre, Royal Shakespeare Company and Orange Tree Theatre. UK-England: Stratford, London. 1984-1985. Lang.: Eng. 2183

Analysis of predominant mode of staging final scene of *Othello* by William Shakespeare. UK-England: London. USA. 1760-1900. Lang.: Eng. 2184

Reviews of Shakespeare's *Twelfth Night*, staged by Wilford Leach. USA: New York, NY. 1986. Lang.: Eng. 2217

Reviews of Shakespeare's *Hamlet* staged by Liviu Ciulei. USA: New York, NY. 1986. Lang.: Eng. 2226

Margaret Webster's scenic approach to Shakespeare compared with those of Herbert Beerbohm Tree and Tyrone Guthrie. USA: New York, NY. 1910-1949. Lang.: Eng. 2293

Attempt to produce Quarto version of *King Lear* at University of Rochester. USA: Rochester, NY. 1985. Lang.: Eng. 2300

Robert Sturua of Georgian Academic Theatre directs Brecht and Shakespeare in Warsaw. USSR: Tbilisi. Poland: Warsaw. 1983. Lang.: Pol. 2336

Problems of producing Shakespeare on radio. UK-England. 1935-1980. Lang.: Eng. 3178

Self-referential elements in several film versions of Shakespeare's *King Lear*. UK. USA. 1916-1983. Lang.: Eng. 3227

The Franco Zeffirelli film of *Otello* by Giuseppe Verdi, an account of the production. Italy: Rome. 1985-1986. Lang.: Eng. 3758

Significance of the translation in recordings of Verdi's *Otello*. USA. 1902-1978. Lang.: Eng. 3812

Profile of and interview with Lee Hoiby, American composer of *The Tempest* with libretto by Mark Schulgasser. USA: Long Eddy, NJ. 1926-1986. Lang.: Eng. 3832

Plays/librettos/scripts

Envy in Shakespeare's *Othello* and Peter Shaffer's *Amadeus*. Canada: Montreal, PQ. Europe. 1604-1986. Lang.: Eng. 932

Comparison of natural and dramatic speech. England. USA. 1600-1986. Lang.: Eng. 939

Ballets based on works of William Shakespeare. USSR. Germany, West. 1980-1986. Lang.: Rus. 1322

Discusses Michel Garneau's *joual* translation of *Macbeth*. Canada: Montreal, PQ. 1978. Lang.: Eng. 2429

Environmental theatre version of *Hamlet*. Canada: Vancouver, BC. 1986. Lang.: Eng. 2435

Influence of middle class and of domestic comedy on the works of William Shakespeare. England. 1564-1616. Lang.: Eng. 2459

Shakespeare's influence on Beaumont and Fletcher's *Philaster*. England. 1609. Lang.: Eng. 2463

Ceremony distinguishes kings from peasants in Shakespeare's *Henry V*. England. 1598-1599. Lang.: Eng. 2464

Contrast between Shakespeare's England and the Vienna of *Measure for Measure*. England. 1604-1605. Lang.: Eng. 2465

Blessing and cursing in Shakespeare's *King Lear*. England. 1605-1606. Lang.: Eng. 2466

Semiotic analysis of Shakespeare's *King Lear*. England: London. 1605-1606. Lang.: Eng. 2467

Shakespeare, William — cont'd

Shakespeare's complex, unconventional heroines in *All's Well that Ends Well* and *Measure for Measure*. England. 1603. Lang.: Eng.
2469

Influence of Night Visit folk notif on Shakespeare's *Romeo and Juliet*. England: London. 1594-1597. Lang.: Eng.
2470

Heterosexual and homosexual desires in Shakespeare's *Troilus and Cressida*. England. 1602. Lang.: Eng.
2471

Analysis, *As You Like It* II:i by William Shakespeare. England. 1598. Lang.: Eng.
2474

Possible influence of Christopher Marlowe's plays upon those of William Shakespeare. England. 1580-1620. Lang.: Eng.
2478

Comparison of Shakespeare's *Antony and Cleopatra* and Ibsen's *Rosmersholm*. England. Norway. 1607-1885. Lang.: Eng.
2479

Similarities between *King Lear* by Shakespeare and *The Trimphs of Reunited Britannia* by Munday. England. 1605-1606. Lang.: Eng.
2480

Iconography of throne scene in Shakespeare's *Richard III*. England. 1591-1592. Lang.: Eng.
2481

Translation of two works by Northrop Frye on Shakespeare. England. 1564-1616. Lang.: Ita.
2484

Essays on Shakespeare's *All's Well that Ends Well*. England. 1603. Lang.: Eng, Fre.
2485

Shakespeare's *Henry VI* and Hall's *Chronicles*. England. 1542-1592. Lang.: Fre.
2488

Theme of redemption in Shakespeare's *The Winter's Tale*. England. 1611. Lang.: Eng.
2490

Role of Rosalind in Shakespeare's *As You Like It*. England. 1600-1986. Lang.: Eng.
2491

Analysis of *The Winter's Tale* by Shakespeare. England: London. 1604. Lang.: Eng.
2502

Interpretations of Shakespeare's *A Midsummer Night's Dream* based on Bottom's transformation. England. 1595-1986. Lang.: Eng.   2503

Adapting *Hamlet* for the nō theatre. England. Japan. 1600-1982. Lang.: Ita.
2506

Marxist analysis of colonialism in Shakespeare's *Othello*. England. South Africa, Republic of. 1597-1637. Lang.: Eng.
2507

Prophetic riddles in Shakespeare's *The Merchant of Venice*. England. 1598. Lang.: Eng.
2509

An appraisal of David Garrick's adaptation of Shakespeare's *King John*. England: London. 1736-1796. Lang.: Eng.
2510

Use of anachronism in William Shakespeare's history plays. England: London. 1590-1601. Lang.: Eng.
2511

Translation of *Shakespeare: His World and His Work* by M. M. Reese. England. 1564-1616. Lang.: Ita.
2514

Gift exchange and mercantilism in *The Merchant of Venice* by Shakespeare. England: London. 1594-1597. Lang.: Eng.
2520

Comparison of Shakespeare's *Othello* with New Comedy of Rome. England. 1604. Lang.: Eng.
2528

Essays on Shakespeare's *Romeo and Juliet*. England. 1595-1597. Lang.: Ita.
2529

Critics and directors on Shakespeare's *King Lear*. England. 1605. Lang.: Ita.
2530

Accuracy of portrayal of historical figures in Shakespeare and his adaptors. England. 1590-1940. Lang.: Eng.
2532

Senecan ideas in Shakespeare's *Timon of Athens*. England: London. 1601-1608. Lang.: Eng.
2533

Treatment of historical figures in plays by William Shakespeare, Christopher Marlowe and George Peele. England. 1560-1650. Lang.: Eng.
2534

Revision of dramaturgy and stagecraft in Restoration adaptations of Shakespeare. England: London. 1660-1690. Lang.: Eng.
2535

Modern criticism of Shakespeare's crowd scenes. England. 1590-1986. Lang.: Eng.
2536

Translations of plays by William Shakespeare into Amharic and Tegrenna. Ethiopia: Addis Ababa. 1941-1984. Lang.: Eng.
2537

Study of realism vs metadrama. Europe. 429 B.C.-1978 A.D. Lang.: Eng.
2540

Comparative analysis of the works of Maurice Maeterlinck and William Shakespeare. France. 1590-1911. Lang.: Eng.
2566

Treatment of Napoleon Bonaparte by French and English dramatists. France. England. 1797-1958. Lang.: Eng.
2568

Text of a lecture on Shakespeare's *King Lear* by Clifford Davidson. Hungary: Budapest. Lang.: Hun.
2643

Shakespeare's influence on playwright Wole Soyinka. Nigeria. UK-England: Leeds. 1957-1981. Lang.: Eng.
2725

Interpretation of Fortinbras in post-war productions of *Hamlet*. Poland. UK-England. 1945. Lang.: Eng.
2748

Translations of Shakespeare by Josep Maria de Sagarra. Spain-Catalonia: Barcelona. 1940-1964. Lang.: Cat.
2811

Short history of Catalan translations of plays. Spain-Catalonia. 1848-1984. Lang.: Fre.
2813

Beckettian elements in Shakespeare as seen by playwright Edward Bond. UK-England. 1971-1973. Lang.: Eng.
2833

Links between Shakespeare's *Macbeth* and Tom Stoppard's *Dogg's Hamlet, Cahoot's Macbeth*. UK-England. 1979-1986. Lang.: Eng.
2843

Brecht's ideas about the history play as justification for Edward Bond's *Bingo*. UK-England. 1974. Lang.: Eng.
2876

Correspondence between Bernhard Reich and Heinz-Uwe Haus. USSR. 1971-1972.
2966

Orson Welles' adaptation of Shakespeare's Falstaff scenes, *Chimes at Midnight*. UK-England. 1938-1965. Lang.: Eng.
3239

Sound effects and images of time in Orson Welles' film version of Shakespeare's *Othelllo*. USA. 1952. Lang.: Eng.
3241

Film versions of Shakespeare's *Macbeth* by Orson Welles, Akira Kurosawa and Roman Polanski. USA. Japan. 1948-1971. Lang.: Eng.
3243

Productions of Jane Howell and Elijah Moshinsky for the BBC Shakespeare series. UK-England: London. 1978-1985. Lang.: Eng.
3283

Review articles on the BBC Shakespeare series. UK-England: London. 1978-1985. Lang.: Eng.
3284

Development of Restoration musical theatre. England. 1642-1699. Lang.: Eng.
3496

Shakespeare's influence on Verdi's operas. Germany. Italy. Austria. 1750-1850. Lang.: Eng.
3878

Wagner's *Das Liebesverbot*, an operatic adaptation of *Measure for Measure*. Germany. 1834. Lang.: Eng.
3880

The Romeo and Juliet theme as interpreted in the musical and visual arts. Italy. 1476-1900. Lang.: Eng.
3886

Reference materials
Shakespeare on film. UK-England. USA. 1899-1984. Lang.: Eng.
3245

Relation to other fields
Concept of play in theatre and sport. Canada. 1972-1983. Lang.: Eng.
1071

Shakespearean allusions in political satire. Canada. 1798-1871. Lang.: Eng.
1074

Reports and discussions of restricted cultural communication. Lebanon. Spain-Catalonia. USA. 1985. Lang.: Fre, Spa, Cat.   1111

Shakespearean allusion in English caricature. UK-England. 1780-1820. Lang.: Eng.
3056

Theory/criticism
Ingmar Bergman production of *King Lear* and Asian influences. Spain-Catalonia: Barcelona. 1985. Lang.: Eng.
1219

Analysis of Goethe's criticism of Shakespeare. England. Germany. 1749-1832. Lang.: Rus.
3091

Pitfalls of a semiotic analysis of theatre. England. 1600-1921. Lang.: Eng.
3094

Coriolanus from Bertolt Brecht's viewpoint. Germany. 1898-1956. Lang.: Chi.
3105

Self-reflexivity in Shakespeare as seen by Lionel Abel, Sigurd Burckhardt and James L. Calderwood. USA. 1963-1983. Lang.: Eng.
3141

Shakespeare in media. UK-England. USA. Japan. 1899-1985. Lang.: Eng.
3172

Shamanism
Performance/production
Costumes, dance steps, and music in initiation rites of Yoruba priesthood. Western Africa. Lang.: Eng.
1373

Plays/librettos/scripts
Conceptions of the South Sea islands in works of Murnau, Artaud and Spies. Europe. USA. Indonesia. 1930. Lang.: Ita.
3231

Relation to other fields
Articles on anthropology of theatre. Lang.: Ita.
1056

Shamanism — cont'd

Influences of shamanism on Eastern and Western theatre. Greece. Asia. 500 B.C.-1986 A.D. Lang.: Ita. 1095

Origins of theatre in shamanistic ritual. Korea. 1900-1986. Lang.: Ita. 1110

Theatrical nature of shamanistic rituals. Zambia. 1985. Lang.: Eng. 1183

Shange, Ntozake
Reference materials
Current work of Audelco award-winning playwrights. USA: New York, NY. 1973-1984. Lang.: Eng. 3007

Shanghai Art Puppet Theatre (Shanghai)
Institutions
Report on state puppet theatre. China: Beijing, Shanghai. 1986. Lang.: Eng. 4015

Shanghai Drama Institute
Institutions
History of the Shanghai Drama Institute. China, People's Republic of: Shanghai. 1945-1982. Lang.: Chi. 1571

Shanley, John Patrick
Design/technology
Interview with set designer Adrianne Lobel. USA: New York, NY. 1986. Lang.: Eng. 1530
Performance/production
Interview with actor Stephen Ouimette. Canada. 1960-1986. Lang.: Eng. 1663

Shapiro, Mel
Performance/production
Productions of Dario Fo's *Morte accidentale di un anarchico* *(Accidental Death of an Anarchist)* in the light of Fo's political ideas. USA. Canada. Italy. 1970-1986. Lang.: Eng. 2262

Shapp, Richard
Performance/production
Opera greats reflect on performance highlights. USA: Philadelphia, PA, New York, NY. 1985. Lang.: Eng. 3841

Shared Experience
Performance/production
Director Mike Alfreds' interpretation of the plays of Čechov. UK-England: London. USSR. 1975-1986. Lang.: Eng. 2127

Shared Stage (Winnipeg, MB)
Institutions
History of the Shared Stage theatre company. Canada: Winnipeg, MB. 1980-1986. Lang.: Eng. 1555

Shaw Festival (Niagara-on-the-Lake, ON)
Administration
Resourcefulness of the Shaw Festival season. Canada: Niagara-on-the-Lake, ON. 1985. Lang.: Eng. 1430
Plays/librettos/scripts
Analysis of *As Is* by William Hoffman and *The Dolly* by Robert Locke. Canada: Toronto, ON. 1985. Lang.: Eng. 2419

Shaw, George Bernard
Performance/production
Letters to and from Harley Granville-Barker. UK-England. 1877-1946. Lang.: Eng. 807

Career of actress, manager and director Julia Arthur. Canada. UK-England. USA. 1869-1950. Lang.: Eng. 1675

Interview with Elisabeth Bergner and Jane Alexander on their portrayals of Joan of Arc. Germany, West: Berlin, West. UK-England: Malvern. USA: Washington, DC. Lang.: Eng. 1766

István Horvai directs *Megtört szivek háza (Heartbreak House)* by George Bernard Shaw at Pest National Theatre. Hungary: Budapest. 1985. Lang.: Hun. 1793

G.B. Shaw's *Megtörtszívek háza (Heartbreak House)* directed by István Horvai. Hungary: Budapest. 1985. Lang.: Hun. 1858

Performances of George Bernard Shaw's *Candida* and Čechov's *Diadia Vania (Uncle Vanya)*, under the title *Ványa bácsi*, at Pécs National Theatre. Hungary: Pécs. 1985. Lang.: Hun. 1893

Announcement of Margalith Prize winners. Israel: Jerusalem. 1986. Lang.: Heb. 1977

Collection of newspaper reviews by London theatre critics. UK. 1986. Lang.: Eng. 2099

Collection of newspaper reviews by London theatre critics. UK. 1986. Lang.: Eng. 2102

Collection of newspaper reviews by London theatre critics. UK-England: London. 1986. Lang.: Eng. 2119

Actresses Jane Lapotaire and Elizabeth Spriggs discuss their careers in the Royal Shakespeare Company. UK-England: London. 1970-1986. Lang.: Eng. 2147

Royal Shakespeare Company performances at the Barbican Theatre. UK-England: London. 1986. Lang.: Eng. 2152

Eileen Atkins, Judi Dench, Wendy Hiller and Barbara Jefford discuss playing Saint Joan in Shaw's play. UK-England: London. 1936-1983. Lang.: Eng. 2153

Reviews of *You Never Can Tell*, by George Bernard Shaw, staged by Stephen Porter. USA: New York, NY. 1986. Lang.: Eng. 2212

Plays/librettos/scripts
Treatment of Napoleon Bonaparte by French and English dramatists. France. England. 1797-1958. Lang.: Eng. 2568

Thematic analysis of *Candida* by George Bernard Shaw focusing on the spiritual development of Marchbanks. UK-England: London. 1894. Lang.: Eng. 2837

Reference of George Bernard Shaw to contemporary society. UK-England. 1856-1950. Lang.: Eng. 2862

Argument for coherence of *Arms and the Man* by George Bernard Shaw. UK-England: London. 1894. Lang.: Eng. 2863

Textual history of the final line of *Arms and the Man* by George Bernard Shaw. UK-England: London. 1894-1982. Lang.: Eng. 2873

Relation to other fields
Reports and discussions of restricted cultural communication. Lebanon. Spain-Catalonia. USA. 1985. Lang.: Fre, Spa, Cat. 1111

Theory/criticism
Shaw's use of devil's advocacy in his plays compared to deconstructionism. UK-England. 1900-1986. Lang.: Eng. 3135

Shaw, Robert
Performance/production
Collection of newspaper reviews by London theatre critics. UK-England: London. 1986. Lang.: Eng. 2121

Shawn, Wally
Plays/librettos/scripts
Discussion of issues raised in plays of 1985-86 season. USA: New York, NY. 1985-1986. Lang.: Eng. 2928

She Loves Me
Design/technology
Designers discuss regional productions of *She Loves Me*. USA. 1984-1986. Lang.: Eng. 3587

She Stoops to Conquer
Performance spaces
Technical review of *She Stoops to Conquer* by Oliver Goldsmith performed at the New Victoria Theatre. UK-England: Newcastle-under-Lyme. 1980-1986. Lang.: Eng. 1618

Shelagh, Delaney
Plays/librettos/scripts
Current state of women's playwriting. UK-England. 1985-1986. Lang.: Eng. 2830

Shell-Shocked
Plays/librettos/scripts
Analysis of plays by Canadian soldiers in World War I. Canada. UK. 1901-1918. Lang.: Eng. 936

Shelley, Mary Wollstonecraft
Performance/production
Controversy surrounding *Presumption, or The Fate of Frankenstein* by Richard Brinsley Peake. UK-England: London. 1818-1840. Lang.: Eng. 2142

Shelley, Sir Percy
Performance/production
Development and production of Sir Percy Shelley's amateur production of *The Doom of St. Querec*. UK-England: London. 1876. Lang.: Eng. 809

Shemilt-Duly, D.
Performance/production
Collection of newspaper reviews by London theatre critics. UK-England. 1986. Lang.: Eng. 2114

Shen, Ching
Plays/librettos/scripts
Life and works of playwright Shen Ching. China. 1368-1644. Lang.: Chi. 3526

Shen, Yao
Plays/librettos/scripts
Problems of adapting classic plays. China, People's Republic of. 1986. Lang.: Chi. 3543

Shepard, Sam
Performance/production
Director Robert Woodruff's shift from naturalism to greater theatricality. USA: San Francisco, CA, New York, NY, La Jolla, CA. 1976-1986. Lang.: Eng. 851

Shepard, Sam — cont'd

István Verebes directs *Valódi Vadnyugat (True West)* by Sam Shepard. Hungary: Budapest. 1986. Lang.: Hun.	1772

István Verebes directs *Valódi vadnyugat (True West)* by Sam Shepard at Radnóti Miklós Szinpad. Hungary: Budapest. 1986. Lang.: Hun.	1939

Biography of playwright and actor Sam Shepard. USA. 1943-1986. Lang.: Eng.	2295

Seduced by Sam Shepard, directed by George Nickas at Seven Stages. USA: Atlanta, GA. 1985. Lang.: Eng.	2302

Plays/librettos/scripts

Imagery and the role of women in Sam Shepard's *Buried Child*. USA. 1978. Lang.: Eng.	2899

Director John Lion on his work with playwright Sam Shepard. USA: San Francisco, CA, New York, NY. 1970-1984. Lang.: Eng.	2924

Interview with playwright Sam Shepard. USA. 1984. Lang.: Eng.	2925

Discussion of issues raised in plays of 1985-86 season. USA: New York, NY. 1985-1986. Lang.: Eng.	2928

Development of playwright Sam Shepard's style. USA. 1972-1985. Lang.: Eng.	2943

Sam Shepard's plays as a response to traditional American drama. USA. 1943-1986. Lang.: Eng.	2944

Argument of reversed chronology in Acts I and II of *La Turista* by Sam Shepard. USA. 1967. Lang.: Eng.	2951

Director George Ferencz and jazz musician Max Roach collaborate on music in trio of Sam Shepard plays. USA: New York, NY. 1984. Lang.: Eng.	2952

Relation to other fields

Comparison of works of playwright Sam Shepard and artist Robert Rauschenberg. USA. 1960-1980. Lang.: Eng.	3062

Playwright Sam Shepard's recent plays and super-realist painting. USA. 1978-1983. Lang.: Eng.	3069

Shepherd's Paradise, The

Plays/librettos/scripts

Female characterization in Nicholas Rowe's plays. England. 1629-1720. Lang.: Eng.	2475

Shepherds, The

SEE

Pastorets, Els.

Sheridan, Richard Brinsley

Performance/production

Lady Dufferin's amateur theatricals. Canada: Ottawa, ON. India. 1873-1888. Lang.: Eng.	671

Sherrin, Edward

Performance/production

Interview with Elisabeth Bergner and Jane Alexander on their portrayals of Joan of Arc. Germany, West: Berlin, West. UK-England: Malvern. USA: Washington, DC. Lang.: Eng.	1766

Sherrin, Robert

Institutions

History of the Neptune Theatre and its artistic directors. Canada: Halifax, NS. 1963-1983. Lang.: Eng.	483

Sherwood, Robert E.

Plays/librettos/scripts

Robert E. Sherwood's conception of history in *The Petrified Forest* and *Abe Lincoln in Illinois*. USA. 1930-1950. Lang.: Eng.	2949

Sherwood, Robert, E.

Performance/production

Survey of productions at the Kennedy Center's National Theatre. USA: Washington, DC. 1986. Lang.: Eng.	2247

Shimizu

Performance/production

Performing the *kyōgen* play *Shimizu* in English. USA. 1984.	1417

Shing, Fook

Performance/production

Chinese theatre companies on the Goldfields of Victoria. Australia. 1858-1870. Lang.: Eng.	1641

Shingeki

Performance/production

History of contemporary Japanese theatre. Japan: Tokyo. 1950-1986. Lang.: Jap.	757

Plays/librettos/scripts

Lives and works of major contemporary playwrights in Japan. Japan: Tokyo. 1900-1986. Lang.: Jap.	2719

Reference materials

Yearbook of major performances in all areas of Japanese theatre. Japan: Tokyo. 1986. Lang.: Jap.	1026

Dictionary of the life and work of Tsubouchi Shōyō. Japan: Tokyo. 1859-1986. Lang.: Jap.	1027

Shiomi, R.A.

Plays/librettos/scripts

Work of playwright R.A. Shiomi, including production history of *Yellow Fever*. Canada: Toronto, ON. USA: New York, NY. USA: San Francisco, CA. 1970-1986. Lang.: Eng.	2422

Ship's Company Theatre (Nova Scotia)

Performance spaces

Summer theatre on a restored cruise ship. Canada. 1982-1986. Lang.: Eng.	1614

Shiraishi, Kazoko

Performance/production

Suzuki's SCOT fuses diverse world cultures in ensemble theatre company. Japan: Toga. 1985. Lang.: Eng.	1404

Shirley Valentine or St. Joan of the Fitted Units

Performance/production

Collection of newspaper reviews by London theatre critics. UK. 1986. Lang.: Eng.	2103

Shirley, James

Basic theatrical documents

Prompt markings on a copy of James Shirley's *Loves Crueltie* performed by the King's Company. England: London. 1660-1669. Lang.: Eng.	1475

Plays/librettos/scripts

Image of poverty in Elizabethan and Stuart plays. England. 1558-1642. Lang.: Eng.	2482

Cast lists in James Shirley's *Six New Playes* suggest popularity of plays. England. 1653-1669. Lang.: Eng.	2504

Shopfront Theatre (Australia)

Performance/production

Dilemmas and prospects of youth theatre movement. Australia. 1982-1986. Lang.: Eng.	1639

Short Change

Performance/production

Collection of newspaper reviews by London theatre critics. UK-England: London. 1986. Lang.: Eng.	2122

Short Eyes

Plays/librettos/scripts

Race in prison dramas of Piñero, Camillo, Elder and Bullins. USA. 1970-1986. Lang.: Eng.	2912

Shouse, Jack

Design/technology

Designers discuss regional productions of *The Sound of Music*. USA. 1983-1986. Lang.: Eng.	3594

Show boats

Performance spaces

Summer theatre on a restored cruise ship. Canada. 1982-1986. Lang.: Eng.	1614

Showcase Code

Administration

Revisions in the Showcase Code by Actors' Equity Association. USA: New York, NY. 1982. Lang.: Eng.	165

Showtime Cable Network

Performance/production

Process and results of adapting plays from Off Broadway to TV. USA: New York, NY. 1980-1986. Lang.: Eng.	841

Shudraka

Performance/production

Collection of newspaper reviews by London theatre critics. UK: London. 1986. Lang.: Eng.	2100

Shusaku & Dormu Dance Theater

Performance/production

A photographic essay of 42 soloists and groups performing mime or gestural theatre. 1986.	3290

Sibitz, Bernd

Plays/librettos/scripts

Training for new playwrights in Austria. Austria: Vienna. 1985-1986. Lang.: Ger.	2392

Sid and Nancy

Design/technology

Cinematographer Roger Deakins discusses lighting for his work in the film *Sid and Nancy*. USA: New York, NY, Los Angeles, CA. UK-England: London. 1976-1986. Lang.: Eng.	3211

Siddons, Sarah

Performance/production

Illustrated analysis of 18th-century acting techniques. England. 1700-1985. Lang.: Eng.	694

Side-by-Side by Sondheim
Design/technology
Designers discuss regional productions of *Side-by-Side by Sondheim.*
USA. 1984. Lang.: Eng.   3593

Sidetrack Theatre Company (Sydney)
Administration
Malcolm Blaylock on theatre and government funding policy.
Australia. 1985. Lang.: Eng.   22

Performance/production
Community theatre as interpreted by the Sidetrack Theatre
Company. Australia: Sydney, N.S.W. 1980-1986. Lang.: Eng.   1638

Siedlecki, Franciszek
Relation to other fields
Views of designer and critic Franciszek Siedlecki. Poland. 1909-1934.
Lang.: Pol.   1116

Sielde, Caroline
Reference materials
Catalogue of an exhibition of costume designs for Broadway
musicals. USA: New York, NY. 1900-1925. Lang.: Eng, Ger.   3635

Sieveking, Alejandro
Plays/librettos/scripts
Chilean theatre in exile, Teatro del Angel. Chile. Costa Rica. 1955-
1984. Lang.: Eng.   2441

Siglo de Oro
SEE
Geographical-Chronological Index under Spain 1580-1680.

Sigrid, Jean
Basic theatrical documents
Playtext of Jean Sigrid's *L'ange couteau (Angel Knife)* in English
translation. Belgium. 1980. Lang.: Eng.   1463

Performance/production
Effect of dual-language society on Belgian theatre. Belgium: Brussels,
Liège. Lang.: Eng.   660

Plays/librettos/scripts
Biography and bibliography of playwright Jean Sigrid. Belgium.
1920-1986. Lang.: Eng.   2402

Sik, Ferenc
Performance/production
Ferenc Sik directs András Sütő's *Advent a Hargitán (Advent in the
Harghita Mountains)* at the National Theatre. Hungary: Budapest.
1984-1985. Lang.: Hun.   1779

Review of *Advent a Hargitán (Advent in the Harghita Mountains)*
by András Sütő, directed by Ferenc Sik. Hungary: Budapest. 1986.
Lang.: Hun.   1797

Ferenc Sik directs *A velencei Kalmár (The Merchant of Venice)* by
William Shakespeare. Hungary: Budapest. 1986. Lang.: Hun.   1853

Ferenc Sik directs Shakespeare's *A velencei kalmár (The Merchant of
Venice).* Hungary: Budapest. 1986. Lang.: Hun.   1907

Review of two performances of András Sütő's plays. Hungary:
Budapest. 1986. Lang.: Hun.   1913

Ferenc Sik directs two plays by Gyula Háy. Hungary: Veszprém,
Gyula. 1986. Lang.: Hun.   1943

Advent a Hargitán (Advent in the Harghita Mountains) by András
Sütő, directed at National Theatre by Ferenc Sik. Hungary:
Budapest. 1986. Lang.: Hun.   1956

Rehearsals of András Sütő's *Advent a Hargitán (Advent in the
Harghita Mountains)* at the National Theatre directed by Ferenc Sik.
Hungary: Budapest. 1985-1986. Lang.: Hun.   1963

András Sütő's *Advent a Hargitán (Advent in the Harghita
Mountains)* directed by Ferenc Sik. Hungary: Budapest. 1986. Lang.:
Hun.   1974

Silbersee, Der
Plays/librettos/scripts
Analysis of *Der Silbersee* by Kurt Weill and Georg Kaiser.
Germany: Leipzig. 1930-1933. Lang.: Eng.   3876

Silkeberg, Annika
Performance/production
Emblems of the 1980s in Swedish theatre. Sweden. 1980-1986.
Lang.: Swe.   796

Silver Tassie, The
Plays/librettos/scripts
Biography of playwright Teresa Deevy. Ireland. 1894-1963. Lang.:
Eng.   2665

Silver, Joan Micklin
Performance/production
Artists who began in dance, film or television move to Off
Broadway theatre. USA: New York, NY. 1982. Lang.: Eng.   2284

Silver, Rachel
Performance/production
Collection of newspaper reviews by London theatre critics. UK-
England. 1986. Lang.: Eng.   2114

Silverstein, Barbara
Institutions
The history and plans of the Pennsylvania Opera Theatre. USA:
Philadelphia, PA. 1976-1986. Lang.: Eng.   3680

Simándy, József
Performance/production
Autobiography of tenor József Simándy. Hungary. 1916-1984. Lang.:
Hun.   3753

Simkins, Al
Institutions
History of Black theater companies. USA: Philadelphia, PA. 1966-
1985. Lang.: Eng.   1608

Simon Boccanegra
Performance/production
Verdi's *Simon Boccanegra* and Puccini's *La Bohème* at the
Hungarian State Opera House and Erkel Theatre. Hungary:
Budapest. 1986. Lang.: Hun.   3747

The successful collaboration of Arrigo Boito and Giuseppe Verdi in
Simon Boccanegra. Italy. 1856-1881. Lang.: Eng.   3764

Photographs, cast list, synopsis, and discography of Metropolitan
Opera radio broadcast performances. USA: New York, NY. 1986.
Lang.: Eng.   3794

Plays/librettos/scripts
Why Verdi revised the 1857 version of *Simon Boccanegra.* Italy:
Milan. 1857-1881. Lang.: Eng.   3881

Creation of the 1857 version of *Simon Boccanegra* by Verdi, libretto
by Piave. Italy: Venice. 1856-1881. Lang.: Eng.   3882

The historical Simon Boccanegra. Italy: Genoa. 900-1857. Lang.:
Eng.   3888

Simon, Neil
Performance/production
Collection of newspaper reviews by London theatre critics. UK-
England. 1986. Lang.: Eng.   2120

Reviews of *Broadway Bound*, by Neil Simon, staged by Gene Saks.
USA: New York, NY. 1986. Lang.: Eng.   2206

Reviews of *Sweet Charity* by Neil Simon, staged and choreographed
by Bob Fosse. USA: New York, NY. 1986. Lang.: Eng.   3611

Plays/librettos/scripts
Symbolism and allusion in *Boiler Room Suite* by Rex Deverell.
Canada: Regina, SK. 1977. Lang.: Eng.   934

Interview with playwright Neil Simon. USA: New York, NY. 1927-
1986. Lang.: Eng.   2931

Simon, Zsuzsa
Training
Experiences of acting teacher Zsuzsa Simon. Hungary. 1945-1985.
Lang.: Hun.   3158

Simone Marchard
Performance/production
Director Peter Sellars talks about staging Brecht's plays. USA. 1983.
   2290

Simoneau, Leopold
Performance/production
Leopold Simoneau on Mozartian style. Lang.: Eng.   3686

Simons, Beverley
Plays/librettos/scripts
Influence of oriental theatre on playwright Beverley Simons. Canada:
Vancouver, BC. 1962-1975. Lang.: Eng.   928

Simonson, Lee
Design/technology
Adolphe Appia's influence on Lee Simonson. USA. 1900-1950.
Lang.: Eng.   416

Performance/production
Origins of radically simplified stage in modern productions. USA.
1912-1922. Lang.: Eng.   831

Analysis of reviews of 1929 *Dynamo* by Eugene O'Neill suggest
strong production of a weak play. USA: New York, NY. 1929.
Lang.: Eng.   2311

Simpson, Dave
Performance/production
Collection of newspaper reviews by London theatre critics. UK.
1986. Lang.: Eng.   2103

SUBJECT INDEX

Simpson, Michael
  Performance/production
  Collection of newspaper reviews by London theatre critics. UK-England: London. 1986. Lang.: Eng.   2118
Simukov, A.
  Theory/criticism
  Playwright A. Simukov discusses his craft. USSR. 1986. Lang.: Rus.
                                                                1249
Sinatra, Frank
  Performance/production
  Music critic Derek Jewell traces Frank Sinatra's career along with his own. USA. 1900-1986. Lang.: Eng.   3179
  Biography of singer Frank Sinatra. USA. 1915-1984. Lang.: Eng.
                                                                3180
Sinclair, Carol
  Performance/production
  Actress compares advantages of small-town and metropolitan careers. Canada. 1986. Lang.: Eng.   1677
Sing for St. Ned
  Plays/librettos/scripts
  Comparison of plays about Ned Kelly of Australia and Louis Riel of Canada. Canada. Australia. 1900-1976. Lang.: Eng. 2421
Singers
  SEE
  Singing.
Singing
  Institutions
  The survival and prosperity of the Santa Fe Opera Company. USA: Santa Fe, NM. 1957-1986. Lang.: Eng.   3678

  Performance/production
  Development of and influences on theatre and other regional entertainments. England. 1840-1870. Lang.: Eng.   688
  Interview with Peter Brook's designer, musician, and costumer for *Mahabharata*. France: Avignon. 1973-1985. Lang.: Eng.   1359
  Memoir of writer, critic, theatre director Béla Abody. Hungary. 1970-1980. Lang.: Hun.   1780
  Life and work of cabaret singer and stage director Leon Schiller. Poland. 1887-1954. Lang.: Eng, Fre.   2014
  Andrei Serban discusses the vibration of a sound and its effect on the listener. USA. 1976. Lang.: Eng.   2304
  Music critic Derek Jewell traces Frank Sinatra's career along with his own. USA. 1900-1986. Lang.: Eng.   3179
  Biography of singer Frank Sinatra. USA. 1915-1984. Lang.: Eng.
                                                                3180
  Biography of singer/actress Judy Garland. USA. 1922-1969. Lang.: Eng.   3229
  Types of costumes, dances, and songs of Dodo masquerades during Ramadan. Upper Volta: Ouagadougou. Lang.: Eng.   3428
  Imprisoned Nigerian pop musician Fela Anikulapo-Kuti. Nigeria: Lagos. 1960-1985. Lang.: Eng.   3468
  Four nightclub entertainers on their particular acts and the atmosphere of the late night clubs and theaters in Harlem. USA: New York, NY, Savannah, GA. 1930-1950. Lang.: Eng.   3470
  Dakota Stanton discusses her career as a singer and dancer in nightclubs and reviews. USA: Pittsburgh, PA, New York, NY. 1950-1980. Lang.: Eng.   3471
  Comprehensive history of singing and singers. 1901-1985. Lang.: Ger.   3482
  Elisabeth Kales and her performance in the main role of Leo Fall's operetta *Madame Pompadour*. Austria: Vienna. 1955-1986. Lang.: Ger.   3484
  Contemporary musical-dramatic performance. USSR. 1980-1986. Lang.: Rus.   3494
  Interview with composer Aleksej Ribnikov. USSR. 1986. Lang.: Rus.
                                                                3495
  Origins of Southern Sung drama (*Nanxi*). China: Wenzhou. 1127-1234. Lang.: Chi.   3512
  Ch'in opera and its influences. China: Beijing. 1795-1850. Lang.: Chi.   3518
  DeVina Barajas discusses performing the songs of Brecht. Switzerland. Germany, West. USA. 1978-1985.   3607
  Problems in the development of Soviet musical theatre. USSR. 1980-1986. Lang.: Rus.   3625
  Leopold Simoneau on Mozartian style. Lang.: Eng.   3686

Evidence that Enrico Caruso sang the baritone prologue to *I Pagliacci*. Argentina: Buenos Aires. 1906-1917. Lang.: Eng.   3687
Appreciation of the career of Joan Sutherland. Australia: Sydney, N.S.W. 1926-1986. Lang.: Eng.   3689
Performance rules of Mozart's time as guidance for singers. Austria: Vienna. 1700-1799. Lang.: Ger.   3691
Interviews with various artists of the Viennese State Opera. Austria: Vienna. 1909-1986. Lang.: Ger.   3692
Profile of and interview with soprano Leonie Rysanek. Austria: Vienna. 1926-1986. Lang.: Eng.   3693
Opera singer Giuseppe Taddei and his work at the Staatsoper. Austria: Vienna. Italy. Europe. 1916-1986. Lang.: Ger. 3694
Opera singer Oskar Czerwenka and his opinions. Austria: Vienna. 1924-1986. Lang.: Ger.   3695
Opera singer Leonie Rysanek and her career. Austria: Vienna. USA: New York, NY. 1926-1986. Lang.: Ger.   3697
Opera singer Ferruccio Furlanetto and his career. Austria: Salzburg. Italy. 1946-1949. Lang.: Ger.   3698
Life and career of actress-singer Lili Neményi. Austro-Hungarian Empire. Hungary. 1908-1986. Lang.: Hun.   3705
Opera singer Maureen Forrester tells of her switch from serious roles to character and comic roles. Canada. 1970-1984. Lang.: Eng.   3706
Review of Toronto performances of *Colas and Colinette*. Canada: Toronto, ON, Montreal, PQ. 1986. Lang.: Eng.   3707
Interview with mezzo-sporano Judith Forst. Canada. 1975-1986. Lang.: Eng.   3708
Interview with baritone John Fanning. Canada: Toronto, ON. 1980-1986. Lang.: Eng.   3709
Interview with soprano Joanne Kolomyjec. Canada: Toronto, ON. 1986. Lang.: Eng.   3710
Interview with baritone Gino Quilico. Canada: Toronto, ON. 1984-1986. Lang.: Eng.   3711
Discusses the opera *Winthrop*, by composer Istvan Anhalt. Canada: Toronto, ON. 1949-1985. Lang.: Eng.   3712
Profile of and interview with tenor Jon Vickers about his career and his leading role in *Samson* by George Frideric Handel. Canada: Prince Albert, AB. 1926-1986. Lang.: Eng.   3713
Artistic and technological differences in presenting opera for stage and television. Canada. 1960-1980. Lang.: Eng. 3714
Opera singer Peter Dvorsky: his life and work. Czechoslovakia: Bratislava. Austria: Vienna. 1951-1986. Lang.: Ger. 3716
Productions of Handel's *Muzio Scevola* and analysis of score and characters. England: London. 1718-1980. Lang.: Eng.   3720
Biographical dictionary of opera singers. Europe. 1600-1820. Lang.: Fre.   3722
Profile of and interview with Finnish bass Martti Talvela. Finland. 1935-1986. Lang.: Eng.   3723
Performance analysis of the title role of *Carmen*. France. 1875-1986. Lang.: Eng.   3725
Careers of young Parisian prima donnas. France: Paris. 1830-1850. Lang.: Eng.   3728
Reasons for the decline of French opera and singing. France. 1950-1986. Lang.: Eng.   3729
Diva as sociocultural phenomenon. France. Italy. USA. 1830-1970. Lang.: Fre.   3730
The first singers to perform *Tristan und Isolde*. Germany: Munich. 1857-1869. Lang.: Eng.   3733
Collection of interviews with Walter Felsenstein. Germany: Berlin. 1921-1971. Lang.: Ger.   3735
Harry Kupfer: his work and career as singer and director. Germany, East: Dresden, Berlin, East. 1970-1985. Lang.: Ger. 3738
Overview of Maria Callas' early career. Greece: Athens. 1937-1945. Lang.: Eng.   3741
Review of repertory season at the Hungarian State Opera House. Hungary: Budapest. 1985-1986. Lang.: Hun.   3744
Autobiography of tenor József Simándy. Hungary. 1916-1984. Lang.: Hun.   3753
Careers of three Hungarian opera stars. Hungary. 1925-1979. Lang.: Hun.   3755
Maurizio Tiberi and his Tima Club records of operatic rarities. Italy: Castelnuovo del Porto. 1950-1986. Lang.: Eng.   3756

506   International Bibliography of Theatre: 1986

Singing — cont'd

Physical, social and theatrical aspects of *castrati*. Italy: Rome, Venice. England: London. 1700-1799. Lang.: Ger.   3757

Opera-singer Mirella Freni: her roles and plans. Italy. Austria. 1935-1986. Lang.: Ger.   3759

Profile of and interview with Italian tenor Luciano Pavarotti. Italy: Modena. 1935-1986. Lang.: Eng.   3760

History of *castrati* in opera. Italy. 1599-1797. Lang.: Eng.   3761

Life and career of singer Giuseppina Cobelli. Italy. 1898-1948. Lang.: Eng.   3762

Profile of and interview with Italian baritone Leo Nucci. Italy: Castiglione del Pepoli. 1943-1986. Lang.: Eng.   3766

The growth and development of the Italian tenor singing style. Italy: Bergamo. 1788-1860. Lang.: Eng.   3767

Profile of and interview with New Zealand soprano Kiri Te Kanawa. New Zealand: Gisborne. USA: New York, NY. 1944-1986. Lang.: Eng.   3768

Life and career of singer Fëdor J. Šaljapin. Russia: Moscow. 1873-1938. Lang.: Rus.   3773

Biographical materials on Bolšoj singer Mark Rejzen. Russia: Moscow. 1895-1986. Lang.: Rus.   3774

Biography of singer N.A. Obychova. Russia. 1886-1961. Lang.: Rus.   3776

Profile of and interview with Spanish soprano Pilar Lorengar. Spain: Zaragoza. USA: San Francisco, CA. 1928-1986. Lang.: Eng.   3778

Interview with tenor and conductor Plácido Domingo. Spain: Madrid. 1941-1986. Lang.: Eng.   3779

Life and career of singer Peter Pears. UK-England: London. 1937-1986. Lang.: Eng.   3784

Appreciation and obituary of the late English tenor Sir Peter Pears. UK-England: Aldeburgh. 1910-1986. Lang.: Eng.   3785

Profile of and interview with Welsh soprano Gwyneth Jones. UK-Wales: Pontnewynydd. 1936-1986. Lang.: Eng.   3788

Stills from telecast performances of *Elektra*. List of principals, conductor and production staff included. USA: New York, NY. 1986. Lang.: Eng.   3790

Stills from telecast performance of *Goya*. List of principals, conductor and production staff included. USA: Washington, DC. 1986. Lang.: Eng.   3791

Reviews of 10 vintage recordings of complete operas on LP. USA. 1906-1925. Lang.: Eng.   3792

Profile of and interview with American soprano June Anderson. USA: New York, NY. 1955-1986. Lang.: Eng.   3793

Photographs, cast list, synopsis, and discography of Metropolitan Opera radio broadcast performances. USA: New York, NY. 1986. Lang.: Eng.   3794

Stills from telecast performances. List of principals, conductor and production staff included. USA: New York, NY. 1986. Lang.: Eng.   3795

Stills from telecast performance of *Candide* by New York City Opera. USA: New York, NY. 1986. Lang.: Eng.   3796

Photographs, cast list, synopsis, and discography of Metropolitan Opera radio broadcast performances. USA: New York, NY. 1986. Lang.: Eng.   3797

Review of Prokofiëv's *Love for Three Oranges*. USA: Cincinnati, OH. 1986. Lang.: Eng.   3798

Marilyn Zschau discusses her singing career and life. USA: Chicago, IL. 1976-1986. Lang.: Eng.   3804

Interview with mezzo Teresa Berganza. USA: Chicago, IL. 1984. Lang.: Eng.   3806

Interview with opera basso Terry Cook. USA: Chicago, IL. 1985. Lang.: Eng.   3807

History and achievements of the Brevard Music Center on the occasion of its fiftieth season. USA: Charlotte, NC. 1936-1986. Lang.: Eng.   3808

Famous sopranos discuss their interpretations of Tosca. USA. 1935-1986. Lang.: Eng.   3811

Significance of the translation in recordings of Verdi's *Otello*. USA. 1902-1978. Lang.: Eng.   3812

Review of Robert Downard's opera *Martin Audéich: A Christmas Miracle*. USA: Denver, CO. 1985. Lang.: Eng.   3813

Profile of and interview with American soprano Benita Valente. USA. 1940-1986. Lang.: Eng.   3816

Profile of and interview with American soprano Carol Vaness. USA: San Diego, CA. 1950-1986. Lang.: Eng.   3817

Profile of and interview with American tenor Jerry Hadley. USA: New York, NY. 1952-1986. Lang.: Eng.   3818

Details of Luigi Arditi's U.S. and Canada tour with the New York Opera Company. USA. Canada: Montreal, PQ, Toronto, ON. 1853-1854. Lang.: Eng.   3819

Interview with singer Nancy Evans and writer Eric Crozier discussing their association with Benjamin Britten. USA: Columbia, MO. UK-England: London. 1940-1985. Lang.: Eng.   3820

Review of the world premiere of the opera *Three Sisters*. USA: Columbus, OH. 1968-1986. Lang.: Eng.   3822

Obituary of soprano Dusolina Giannini. USA: Philadelphia, PA. 1902-1986. Lang.: Eng.   3823

Women's roles in the operas of Benjamin Britten. USA. 1940-1979. Lang.: Eng.   3824

Memoir of Dr. Eugen Grabscheid, throat specialist. USA: New York, NY. 1938-1986. Lang.: Eng.   3830

Appreciation and obituary of the late baritone of the Metropolitan Opera, George Cehanovsky. USA: New York, NY. 1892-1986. Lang.: Eng.   3833

Black opera stars and companies. USA: Enid, OK, New York, NY. 1961-1985. Lang.: Eng.   3839

Opera greats reflect on performance highlights. USA: Philadelphia, PA, New York, NY. 1985. Lang.: Eng.   3841

Problems in the performance and production of opera in Soviet theatres. USSR. 1980-1986. Lang.: Rus.   3844

Condition of operatic art in USSR: repertoire, acting, staging. USSR. 1980-1986. Lang.: Rus.   3845

Singer I. Archipova on tasks of Soviet opera. USSR. 1980-1986. Lang.: Rus.   3846

Biography of singer Ivan Jeršov. USSR. 1867-1943. Lang.: Rus.   3847

The staging of G. Kančeli's opera *Muzyka dlja živych (Music for the Living)* at the Z. Paliašvili theater. USSR: Tbilisi. 1980-1986. Lang.: Rus.   3848

Review of opera season and discussion of problems. USSR: Leningrad. 1985-1986. Lang.: Rus.   3850

Profile of actress Sári Fedák. Austro-Hungarian Empire. 1879-1955. Lang.: Hun.   3940

Plays/librettos/scripts

Description of *p'ansori*, a traditional Korean entertainment. Korea. Lang.: Eng.   3499

Examination of the text and music of Thomas Durfey's opera *Cinthia and Endimion*. England. 1690-1701. Lang.: Eng.   3861

Study of all aspects of Italian opera. Italy. 1810-1920. Lang.: Fre.   3889

Reference materials

Stills from telecast performances of *Hänsel und Gretel*. List of principals, conductor and production staff included. Austria: Vienna. 1986. Lang.: Eng.   3909

Relation to other fields

Study of agriculture-related songs and dances. Japan: Tokyo. 1986. Lang.: Jap.   3360

Psychological and sociological study of *The Widows* by Smetana and Züngel. Czechoslovakia-Bohemia. 1877-1878. Lang.: Eng.   3915

Research/historiography

Problems of research methodology applied to traditional singing styles. China. 1600-1980. Lang.: Chi.   3553

Theory/criticism

Analyzes the singing style of Szechuan opera. China. 1866-1952. Lang.: Chi.   3563

Training

Results of sonographic analysis of covered and uncovered singing. Austria. 1980-1984. Lang.: Ger.   3933

Psychological aspects of the voice teacher's work. Austria: Vienna. 1980-1984. Lang.: Ger.   3934

Psychological aspects of voice training. Austria. USA. 1750-1984. Lang.: Ger.   3935

Collected papers from a conference on voice training. Austria: Vienna. Italy: Rome. England: London. 1700-1984. Lang.: Ger. 3936

Physiological regulation for correct breathing and singing. Europe. North America. 1929-1984. Lang.: Ger.   3937

Medical examination of covered singing. Europe. 1980-1984. Lang.: Ger.   3938

Singing — cont'd

Seminar on training of opera and musical theatre performers. USSR. 1986. Lang.: Rus.   3939

Sinise, Gary
Performance/production
Collection of newspaper reviews by London theatre critics. UK. 1986. Lang.: Eng.   2103

Collection of newspaper reviews by London theatre critics. UK-England: London. 1986. Lang.: Eng.   2123

Sinkó, Ervin
Performance/production
Janez Pipan directs *Confiteor* by Slobodan Šnajder at National Theatre of Belgrade. Yugoslavia: Belgrade. 1986. Lang.: Hun.   2344

Sip a tökre (Play a Trump in Diamonds)
Performance/production
Sip a tökre (Play a Trump in Diamonds) by Péter Tömöry, directed by Imre Halasi. Hungary: Kisvárda. 1986. Lang.: Hun.   1859

Sir Salomon
Plays/librettos/scripts
Comparison of John Caryll's *Sir Salomon* with its source, *L'École des femmes (The School for Wives)* by Molière. England. France. 1662-1669. Lang.: Eng.   2527

Sircon, Malcolm
Performance/production
Interviews with playwrights Louise Page, Charles McKeown and Malcolm Sircon. UK-England: London. 1986. Lang.: Eng.   2133

Siren Theatre Company (London)
Performance/production
Collection of newspaper reviews by London theatre critics. UK-England: London. 1986. Lang.: Eng.   2109

Sirena varada, La (Beached Mermaid, The)
Plays/librettos/scripts
Discusses Christian outlook in plays by Alejandro Casona. Spain. 1940-1980. Lang.: Eng.   2795

Sirens, The
Reference materials
Current work of Audelco award-winning playwrights. USA: New York, NY. 1973-1984. Lang.: Eng.   3007

Sisters of Eve
Plays/librettos/scripts
Historical background of *Sisters of Eve* by Tricia Burden. Eire. 1984-1986. Lang.: Eng.   2455

Six Characters in Search of an Author
SEE
Sei personaggi in cerca d'autore.

Sixteenth Round, The
Plays/librettos/scripts
Biographical sketch of playwright/performer Samm-Art Williams. USA: Burgaw, NC, New York, NY. 1940-1986. Lang.: Eng.   2946

Sjöberg, Martin
Design/technology
Swedish set designers discuss their working methods. Sweden. 1980-1986. Lang.: Swe.   312

Skånska Teatern (Landskrona)
Administration
Role of Skånska Teatron in the community. Sweden: Landskrona, Malmö. 1963-1986. Lang.: Swe.   62

Skazka (Leningrad)
Performance/production
Round-table on puppet theatre. USSR: Moscow, Leningrad. 1986. Lang.: Rus.   3985

Skelton, Tom
Design/technology
A profile of lighting designer James Ingalls. USA. 1980-1986.   374

Lighting designer Tom Skelton discussing his work on the recent revival of *The Iceman Cometh*. USA: New York, NY. 1985-1986. Lang.: Eng.   1531

Skipitares, Theodora
Basic theatrical documents
Text of *The Age of Invention* by Theodora Skipitares. USA: New York, NY. 1985. Lang.: Eng.   3248

Performance/production
Interview with the mixed-media artist and puppeteer Theodora Skipitares. USA. 1974-1985. Lang.: Eng.   3251

Theodora Skipitares' puppet trilogy *Age of Invention*. USA: New York, NY. 1985.   4013

Sklar, George
Plays/librettos/scripts
Career of Marxist playwright George Sklar. USA: New York, NY. 1920-1967. Lang.: Eng.   985

Skoda, Albin
Performance/production
Playing Hamlet at the Burgtheater. Austria: Vienna. 1803-1985. Lang.: Ger.   1654

Skotorenko, V.S.
Administration
Artistic director of Union of State Circuses comments on new programs. USSR. 1986. Lang.: Rus.   3379

Skottes Musikteater (Gävle)
Institutions
How Skottes Musiktéater operates on a small government budget. Sweden: Gävle. 1976-1986. Lang.: Swe.   522

Skwark, Józef
Performance/production
Józef Skwark directs Gorkij's *Dačniki (Summer Folk)* under the title *Letnicy*. Poland: Warsaw. 1984. Lang.: Pol.   2045

Slade, Peter
Relation to other fields
Curricular authority for drama-in-education program. UK. Lang.: Eng.   3054

Slave Ship, The
Plays/librettos/scripts
Ritual function of *The Slave Ship* by LeRoi Jones (Amiri Baraka) and *Quinta Temporada (Fifth Season)* by Luis Valdez. USA. 1965-1967. Lang.: Eng.   2906

Sleep
Plays/librettos/scripts
Overview of playwright John Coulter's later career. Canada: Toronto, ON. UK-England: London. 1951-1957. Lang.: Eng.   2415

Slezak, Leo
Reference materials
Costumes of famous Viennese actors. Austria: Vienna. 1831-1960. Lang.: Ger.   1003

Slight Ache, A
Plays/librettos/scripts
Comparison of the radio and staged versions of Harold Pinter's *A Slight Ache*. UK-England. 1959-1961. Lang.: Eng.   2880

Slovak National Theatre (Bratislava)
SEE
Slovenske Narodni Divadlo.

Slovenske Narodni Divadlo (Bratislava)
Design/technology
Central workshops of the Slovak National Theatre. Czechoslovakia: Bratislava. 1960-1986. Lang.: Hun.   255

Słowacki, Juliusz
Administration
Russian censorship of classic repertory in Polish theatres. Poland: Warsaw. Russia. 1873-1907. Lang.: Rus, Pol.   1438

Performance/production
Krystyna Meissner directs Juliusz Słowacki's *Balladyna*, Teatr Horzycy. Poland: Toruń. 1984. Lang.: Pol.   2035

Plays/librettos/scripts
School use of Juliusz Słowacki's dramas in Polish high schools as a reflection of the political situation. Poland. 1945-1984. Lang.: Fre.   2743

Śluby Panienskie (Maiden Vows)
Performance/production
Andrzej Łapicki directs Aleksander Fredro's *Śluby Panienskie (Maiden Vows)*, Teatr Polski. Poland: Warsaw. 1984. Lang.: Pol.   2031

Small Craft Warnings
Basic theatrical documents
Catalan translation of *Small Craft Warnings* by Tennessee Williams. USA. 1972. Lang.: Cat.   1512

Plays/librettos/scripts
Analysis of *Small Craft Warnings*, and report of audience reactions. USA: New York, NY. Spain-Catalonia: Barcelona. 1972-1983. Lang.: Cat.   2929

Small Theatre (Leningrad)
SEE
Malyj Dramatičeskij Teat'r.

Small Theatre (Moscow)
SEE
Malyj Teat'r.

Sociology — cont'd

Argument against government involvement in the arts. USA. 1983. Lang.: Eng.   173

Problems of theatres in USSR-Russian SFSR. USSR. 1980-1986. Lang.: Rus.   196

Audience
Moral objections to children's attendance of theatres. USA: New York, NY. 1900-1910. Lang.: Eng.   202

Articles on social role of urban theatres. USSR. 1950-1985. Lang.: Rus.   205

Conference on low theatrical attendance. USSR: Kujbyšev. 1980-1986.   207

Results of a study of Minsk theatre audiences. USSR: Minsk. 1983-1984. Lang.: Rus.   208

On the role of the theatre in the life of contemporary youth. USSR. 1980-1986. Lang.: Rus.   209

Socio-aesthetic notes on contemporary theatre and audiences. USSR. 1970-1980. Lang.: Rus.   210

Overview of Moscow theatrical life. USSR: Moscow. 1980-1986. Lang.: Rus.   211

Sociological studies of Ukrainian theatrical life. USSR. 1920. Lang.: Ukr.   212

Effect of official educational and cultural policies on theatre. France. Germany. UK-England. 1789-1986. Lang.: Fre.   1446

Various aspects of audience/performer relationship. Germany, East: Leipzig, Schwerin, Helle. 1980-1983. Lang.: Ger.   1448

Postmodern concepts of individual, audience, public. USA. 1985-1986. Lang.: Eng.   1454

Reception of Lorraine Hansberry's *A Raisin in the Sun*. USA. 1959-1986. Lang.: Eng.   1456

Claques as viewed by French writers. France. 1800-1899. Lang.: Fre.   3647

Basic theatrical documents
Jean Vilar's diary compared to polemics against him. France: Paris. 1951-1981. Lang.: Fre.   221

Design/technology
Native American masks and headgear in various types of performances. USA. 1800-1900. Lang.: Eng.   402

Institutions
Playwright Jack Hibberd's analysis of nationalist and English-derived theatrical cultures. Australia: Melbourne, Sydney. 1850-1986. Lang.: Eng.   439

French-language theatre and the Acadian tradition. Canada. 1969-1986. Lang.: Eng.   1544

Introduction to the minority-language and 'Garrison theatre'. Canada. 1986. Lang.: Eng.   1565

Minority-language theatres in Canada. Canada: Montreal, PQ, Toronto, ON. 1986. Lang.: Eng.   1566

History of the Shanghai Drama Institute. China, People's Republic of: Shanghai. 1945-1982. Lang.: Chi.   1571

Performance spaces
Social role of theatre and theatrical space. USSR. Lang.: Rus.   647

Performance/production
Dangers of assimilation of French-Canadian theatre into Anglophone culture. Canada. 1985. Lang.: Fre.   668

Canadian theatre and its relations with U.S. theatre. Canada. USA. 1985. Lang.: Fre.   669

Poetry as performing art and political tool. Caribbean. 1937-1985. Lang.: Eng.   674

Gender roles in the work of female theatre professionals. USA. 1985. Lang.: Eng.   836

Soviet actor, poet and singer Vladimir Vysockij. USSR. 1938-1980. Lang.: Rus.   861

Essay on actor's place in society. USSR. 1980-1986. Lang.: Rus. 865

Social role of Georgian theatre today. USSR. 1980-1986. Lang.: Rus.   879

Description of *butō*, avant-garde dance movement of Japan. Japan. 1960-1986. Lang.: Eng.   1279

Dance in the Malaysian culture. Malaysia. 1950-1984. Lang.: Eng.   1333

Costumes, satiric dances and processions of the Ijebu Yoruba masquerades. Western Africa. Lang.: Eng.   1372

Costumes, dance steps, and music in initiation rites of Yoruba priesthood. Western Africa. Lang.: Eng.   1373

Origins of *malipenga*, a form of dance-drama combining Western and African elements. Zambia: Malawi. 1914-1985. Lang.: Eng. 1374

Meaning in dramatic texts as a function of performance. Lang.: Eng.   1630

Reflection of modern society in Antoine Vitez's production of Sophocles' *Electra* at Théâtre National Populaire. France: Paris. 1981-1986. Lang.: Swe.   1743

Director John Dillon on his Japanese production of *Death of a Salesman* by Arthur Miller. Japan. 1984. Lang.: Eng.   2005

Visits to Poland by Russian theatre troupes. Poland. Russia. 1882-1913. Lang.: Pol.   2043

Dramaturg Oskar Eustis on confronting social and aesthetic problems. USA: San Francisco, CA. 1975-1986. Lang.: Eng.   2250

Origins of Southern Sung drama (*Nanxi*). China: Wenzhou. 1127-1234. Lang.: Chi.   3512

Diva as sociocultural phenomenon. France. Italy. USA. 1830-1970. Lang.: Fre.   3730

Physical, social and theatrical aspects of *castrati*. Italy: Rome, Venice. England: London. 1700-1799. Lang.: Ger.   3757

History of *castrati* in opera. Italy. 1599-1797. Lang.: Eng.   3761

Shadow puppetry as a way of passing on Balinese culture. Bali. 1976-1985. Lang.: Eng.   4017

Plays/librettos/scripts
Analysis of the plays of Sharon Pollock. Canada. 1971-1983. Lang.: Eng.   935

Treatment of social problems in the plays of Lillian Hellman and Clifford Odets. USA. 1930-1939. Lang.: Eng.   984

Sociological problems in contemporary drama. USSR. 1980-1986. Lang.: Rus.   993

Poverty in plays by Michel Tremblay and David Fennario. Canada: Quebec, PQ. 1970-1980. Lang.: Eng.   2410

The plays of Antonine Maillet and the revival of Acadian theatre. Canada. 1971-1979. Lang.: Eng.   2423

La Storia and *La Storia II* performed in Italian and English by the Acting Company. Canada: Toronto, ON. 1984-1985. Lang.: Eng.   2424

Use of group aggression in Ben Jonson's comedies. England. 1575-1600. Lang.: Eng.   2508

Origin of Spanish setting in Middleton and Rowley's *The Changeling*. England. 1607-1622. Lang.: Eng.   2513

Gift exchange and mercantilism in *The Merchant of Venice* by Shakespeare. England: London. 1594-1597. Lang.: Eng.   2520

Aristocratic culture and 'country-house' poetic theme in Massinger's *A New Way to Pay Old Debts*. England. 1621. Lang.: Eng.   2531

Personal and social relationships in Goldoni's comedies. Italy. 1743-1760. Lang.: Ita.   2681

Individual and society in *Die Nag van Legio (The Night of Legio)* by P.G. du Plessis and *Der Besuch der alten Dame (The Visit)* by Friedrich Dürrenmatt. South Africa, Republic of. Switzerland. 1955-1970. Lang.: Afr.   2774

Influence of working class on form and content of theatre of resistance. South Africa, Republic of: Soweto. 1976-1986. Lang.: Eng.   2777

Reference of George Bernard Shaw to contemporary society. UK-England. 1856-1950. Lang.: Eng.   2862

Ritual function of *The Slave Ship* by LeRoi Jones (Amiri Baraka) and *Quinta Temporada (Fifth Season)* by Luis Valdez. USA. 1965-1967. Lang.: Eng.   2906

Interview with playwright Lorraine Hansberry. USA. 1959. Lang.: Eng.   2945

Philosophy of wealth in gilded age plays. USA: New York, NY. 1870-1889. Lang.: Eng.   2950

Conceptions of the South Sea islands in works of Murnau, Artaud and Spies. Europe. USA. Indonesia. 1930. Lang.: Ita.   3231

Schopenhauerian pessimism in Wagner's *Ring* and *Götterdämmerung*. Germany. 1852-1856. Lang.: Eng.   3873

Reference materials
Accounts of non-English-speaking artists. Australia. 1986. Lang.: Eng.   1001

Profile and problems of Korean theatre people. Korea. 1985-1986. Lang.: Kor.   1029

Description of popular entertainments, both sacred and secular. Spain-Catalonia. 1947-1986. Lang.: Cat.   3355

Sociology — cont'd

Encyclopedia of cabaret in German. Germany. Switzerland. Austria. 1900-1965. Lang.: Ger. 3369

Relation to other fields

Suggestions for reviving political theatre. Lang.: Fre. 1051

Political issues for Black performers. 1986. Lang.: Eng. 1052

Negative cultural effects of free trade between the U.S. and Canada. 1985-1986. Lang.: Eng. 1054

Articles on anthropology of theatre. Lang.: Ita. 1056

Translation of *Bodywatching* by Desmond Morris. Lang.: Ita. 1057

Translation of *From Ritual to Theatre* by Victor Turner. Lang.: Ita. 1060

Difficulties of distinction between 'high' and 'popular' culture. Australia. 1860-1930. Lang.: Eng. 1063

Concept of play in theatre and sport. Canada. 1972-1983. Lang.: Eng. 1071

Recommended ethical values for artists in a socialist country. China. 1949-1982. Lang.: Chi. 1076

Anecdotes about caricaturist Liao Bingxiong and comedian Chen Baichen. China, People's Republic of. 1942-1981. Lang.: Chi. 1078

Social critique and influence of Jacobean drama. England: London. 1603-1613. Lang.: Eng. 1081

Enthnography of a Hungarian village. Hungary: Zsámbok. 1930-1985. Lang.: Hun. 1099

Contribution to the discussion on theatre structure analyzing the function of theatre in society. Hungary. Lang.: Hun. 1100

Views of designer and critic Franciszek Siedlecki. Poland. 1909-1934. Lang.: Pol. 1116

Actor-director Juliusz Osterwa's ideas about theatre's role in society. Poland. 1918-1947. Lang.: Pol. 1118

Actor Stanisław Kwaskowski talks about the first years of independent Poland. Poland. 1918-1920. Lang.: Pol. 1121

Ancient Russian rituals linked with the 'ship of souls' theme in world culture. Russia. Lang.: Rus. 1124

Reflections and influence of arts and race relations. South Africa, Republic of. Lang.: Afr. 1125

Socio-historical basis of worker plays. South Africa, Republic of. 1985. 1126

Role of theatre after the Arusha Declaration. Tanzania. 1967-1984. Lang.: Eng. 1134

Proposals on theatre in education. UK-England: London, Greenwich. 1986. Lang.: Hun. 1137

The work of disabled theatre companies in England. UK-England. 1979-1986. Lang.: Eng. 1139

Anthropological approach to performance and language. USA. Japan. 1982. Lang.: Eng. 1140

Professional equality in theatrical careers for men and women. USA: New York, NY. 1850-1870. Lang.: Eng. 1143

Development of educational theatre program dealing with child sexual abuse. USA: St. Louis, MO. 1976-1984. Lang.: Eng. 1145

Style in children's theatre in light of theories of Philippe Ariès. USA. UK. France. 1600-1980. Lang.: Eng. 1162

Interview with director Oleg Jefremov of Moscow Art Theatre on social goals of theatre. USSR. 1986. Lang.: Rus. 1174

Statistical index of theatre attendance in the regional and provincial centers of the USSR-Russian SFSR. USSR. 1985. Lang.: Rus. 1175

Sociological view of audience-performer relationship. USSR. 1980. Lang.: Rus. 1176

The role of theatre and television in the moral education of society. USSR. 1980-1986. Lang.: Rus. 1177

Reaction of theatre to changed social conditions. USSR. 1980-1986. Lang.: Rus. 1180

Reflections on the role of theatre in society. USSR. 1980-1986. Lang.: Rus. 1181

Workshops in Canada on 'Theatre for the Oppressed'. Canada: Toronto, ON. 1986. Lang.: Eng. 3022

Theatre and society in post-revolutionary Cuba. Cuba. 1960-1986. Lang.: Rus. 3024

Sociological analysis of city comedy and revenge tragedy. England: London. 1576-1980. Lang.: Eng. 3025

Political and sociological aspects of the dramaturgy of Polish émigrés. Europe. 1820-1986. Lang.: Pol. 3028

Theatre as a force of social change in turn-of-the-century France. France. 1897-1901. Lang.: Eng. 3029

Analysis of contemporary drama from various viewpoints. Poland. 1945-1986. Lang.: Pol. 3049

Political situation and new plays on the Polish stage. Poland. 1958-1962. Lang.: Pol. 3051

Interview with actress Maria Aitken on a revival of *The Women* by Clare Boothe Luce. UK-England: London. 1936-1986. Lang.: Eng. 3061

Sociocultural elements of Black theatre. USA. 1960-1985. Lang.: Eng. 3063

Destructiveness in dramatic literature. USA. Lang.: Eng. 3066

Contrasts between culture and mass media. Italy. 1980-1986. Lang.: Ita. 3171

Social function of radio drama. Canada. 1950-1955. Lang.: Eng. 3187

Examples of Puritan attempts to ban legal entertainments. England: Cheshire. 1560-1641. Lang.: Eng. 3356

History of English penny theatres. England: London. 1820-1839. Lang.: Eng. 3357

Study of agriculture-related songs and dances. Japan: Tokyo. 1986. Lang.: Jap. 3360

Function of carnival in society. Europe. 1986. Lang.: Eng. 3376

Reflections of social and historical conditions in the carnival celebration of a small Emilian town. Italy: Guastalla. 1857-1895. Lang.: Ita. 3377

Circus as a cultural phenomenon. 1980-1986. Lang.: Rus. 3404

Analysis of Northern Sung theatrical artifacts. 1032-1126. Lang.: Chi. 3546

Role of Beijing opera today. China, People's Republic of: Beijing. 1985. Lang.: Chi. 3547

Mao's policy on theatre in revolution. China, People's Republic of: Beijing. 1920-1985. Lang.: Chi. 3549

Psychological and sociological study of *The Widows* by Smetana and Züngel. Czechoslovakia-Bohemia. 1877-1878. Lang.: Eng. 3915

Commentary on *Diabel włoski (Italian Devil)* by Stanisław Potocki. Poland. 1772-1821. Lang.: Pol. 3922

Critical analysis of composer William Grant Still. USA. 1895-1978. Lang.: Eng. 3924

Reflections on a 3-day workshop on using puppet theatre for social action and communication. UK-England: London. 1986. Lang.: Eng. 3993

Research/historiography

Ritual origins of the classical dance drama of Cambodia. Cambodia. 4 B.C.-1986 A.D. Lang.: Eng. 1336

Theory/criticism

Essays on the sociology of art and semiotics. Lang.: Hun. 1192

Survey on the major trends of theatre theory in the 1980s. 1977-1986. Lang.: Hun. 1195

History of theatre in its social context. Lang.: Hun. 1197

Purpose of literature and art, and the role of the artist. China, People's Republic of: Shanghai, Yan'an. 1942-1982. Lang.: Chi. 1203

Influences on the development of European and Japanese theatre. Japan. Europe. 500 B.C.-1986 A.D. Lang.: Ita. 1213

Technology and the spiritual/aesthetic role of the actor. USA. Lang.: Eng. 1230

National features of Russian literature and dramaturgy. USSR. 1986. Lang.: Rus. 1248

Pina Bausch seen as heir of epic theater of Bertolt Brecht. Germany, West. 1977-1985. Lang.: Eng. 1289

Attitudes toward sports in serious Australian drama. Australia. 1876-1965. Lang.: Eng. 3084

Social and political conditions of Greek society as sources for dramatic material. Greece: Athens. 450 B.C. Lang.: Eng. 3113

The popularity of Charles Dicken's *A Christmas Carol* in American theatres. USA. 1984. Lang.: Eng. 3143

Defense of Chinese traditional theatre. China. 200 B.C.-1982 A.D. Lang.: Chi. 3562

Sockolitch, Bob
Design/technology
A lighting designer discusses the unique problems of lighting symphony orchestras. USA: Washington, DC, Boston, MA, New York, NY. 1910-1986. Lang.: Eng.   3478

Söderberg, Roland
Design/technology
Swedish set designers discuss their working methods. Sweden. 1980-1986. Lang.: Swe.   312

Södertälje Teateramatörer (STA, Södertälje)
Institutions
The history of the Södertälje Teateramatörer. Sweden: Södertälje. 1953-1986. Lang.: Swe.   520

Sodomieter op (Netherlands)
Performance/production
Report from an international amateur theatre festival where music and dance were prominent. Denmark: Copenhagen. 1986. Lang.: Swe.   683

Soho Poly Theatre (London)
Performance/production
Collection of newspaper reviews by London theatre critics. UK-England: London. 1986. Lang.: Eng.   2110

Collection of newspaper reviews by London theatre critics. UK-England: London. 1986. Lang.: Eng.   2113

Collection of newspaper reviews by London theatre critics. UK-England: London. 1986. Lang.: Eng.   2124

Soho Repertory Company (New York, NY)
Institutions
Several nonprofit theatres secure new spaces. USA: New York, NY. 1984. Lang.: Eng.   544

Soif et la faim, La (Hunger and Thirst)
Plays/librettos/scripts
Intervening and pure theatre according to Eugène Ionesco. France. 1949-1970. Lang.: Chi.   2547

Soirée des murmures, La (Evening of Murmurs, The)
Performance/production
La Soirée des murmures (The Evening of Murmurs), a performance art piece by Le Théâtre Expérimental des Femmes. Canada: Montreal, PQ. 1986. Lang.: Eng.   3443

Sojuzgoscirk (Union of State Circuses)
Administration
Artistic director of Union of State Circuses comments on new programs. USSR. 1986. Lang.: Rus.   3379

Performance/production
Interview with V.A. Noskov of Union of State Circuses on international circus conference. France: Paris. 1986. Lang.: Rus.   3384

Sol
Performance/production
A photographic essay of 42 soloists and groups performing mime or gestural theatre. 1986.   3290

Soldier's Play, A
Institutions
History of two major Black touring companies. USA: New York, NY. 1969-1982. Lang.: Eng.   1598

Reference materials
Current work of Audelco award-winning playwrights. USA: New York, NY. 1973-1984. Lang.: Eng.   3007

Soler i Rovirosa, Francesc
Design/technology
History of Catalan scenography. Spain-Catalonia. 200 B.C.-1986 A.D. Lang.: Cat.   311

Introduction to facsimile edition of set designs by Fracesc Soler i Rovirosa. Spain-Catalonia: Barcelona, Valencia, Madrid. 1832-1900. Lang.: Cat.   3313

Facsimile edition of scene design drawings by Francesc Soler i Rovirosa for La almoneda del diablo (The Devil's Auction) by Rafael M. Liern. Spain-Catalonia: Barcelona. 1878. Lang.: Cat.   3314

Soler, Frederic
SEE
Pitarra, Serafía (Soler, Frederic).

Basic theatrical documents
Anthology and study of writings of Josep Maria de Sagarra. Spain-Catalonia. 1917-1964. Lang.: Cat.   1501

Plays/librettos/scripts
Evaluation of the literary and dramatic work of Josep Maria de Sagarra. Spain-Catalonia. 1917-1955. Lang.: Cat.   2810

Solheim, Wilhelm G.
Research/historiography
Ritual origins of the classical dance drama of Cambodia. Cambodia. 4 B.C.-1986 A.D. Lang.: Eng.   1336

Solovjëv, Jurij
Performance/production
Careers of four Russian 'apostles of dance'. USSR. Lang.: Rus.   1320

Solti, Georg
Reference materials
Stills from telecast performances of Hänsel und Gretel. List of principals, conductor and production staff included. Austria: Vienna. 1986. Lang.: Eng.   3909

Somelymes, Myles
Performance/production
Brief investigation of the lives of seven actors. England. 1526-1587. Lang.: Eng.   691

Somersaults
Performance/production
Production analysis of four plays by Peter Barnes. UK-England. 1981-1986. Lang.: Eng.   805

Sommarteatern (Södertälje)
Institutions
Sommarteatern, using both amateur and professional actors, will attempt a year-round season. Sweden: Södertälje. 1980-1986. Lang.: Swe.   1585

Sondheim, Stephen
Performance/production
Career of Broadway composer Stephen Sondheim. USA: New York, NY. 1930-1986. Lang.: Eng.   3624

Song of a Goat
Theory/criticism
Analysis of Wole Soyinka's major critical essays. Nigeria. 1960-1980. Lang.: Eng.   3124

Songs of the Morning
Plays/librettos/scripts
Study of heroism in verse dramas by Douglas Stewart, Tom Inglis Moore and Catherine Duncan. Australia. 1941-1943. Lang.: Eng.   2383

Sonnenthal, Adolf von
Performance/production
Playing Hamlet at the Burgtheater. Austria: Vienna. 1803-1985. Lang.: Ger.   1654

Sons of Cain
Plays/librettos/scripts
Interview with playwright David Williamson. Australia. 1986. Lang.: Eng.   2369

Interview with playwright David Williamson. Australia. 1986. Lang.: Eng.   2378

Analysis of plays by David Williamson. Australia. 1976-1985. Lang.: Eng.   2379

Sophisticated Ladies
Performance/production
Tap dancing career of Maurice Hines and the creation of his new company Balletap, USA. USA: New York, NY. 1949-1986. Lang.: Eng.   3623

Sophocles
Performance/production
Sophocles' Electra staged by Antoine Vitez as a conflict of deceit. France: Paris. 1986. Lang.: Swe.   1732

Reflection of modern society in Antoine Vitez's production of Sophocles' Electra at Théâtre National Populaire. France: Paris. 1981-1986. Lang.: Swe.   1743

Hungary: Szolnok. 1986. Lang.: Hun.   1968

Andrzej Wajda directs Sophocles' Antigone, Stary Teatr. Poland: Cracow. 1984. Lang.: Pol.   2058

Survey of productions at the Kennedy Center's National Theatre. USA: Washington, DC. 1986. Lang.: Eng.   2247

Robert Auletta's updated version of Sophocles' Ajax. USA: Washington, DC. 1986. Lang.: Eng.   2276

Plays/librettos/scripts
Semiotic analysis of a production of Antigone by Sophocles. Australia: Perth, W.A. 1986. Lang.: Eng.   923

Study of realism vs metadrama. Europe. 429 B.C.-1978 A.D. Lang.: Eng.   2540

Marguerite Yourcenar's treatment of Electra story compared to other versions. France. 1944-1954. Lang.: Fre.   2554

Sophocles — cont'd

Comparative analysis of *Elektra* by Hugo von Hofmannsthal and its sources. Germany. 1909. Lang.: Eng.　2603

Interpretation of final scenes of Sophocles' *Philoctetes*. Greece. 409 B.C. Lang.: Heb.　2630

Chorus in ancient Greek comedy and drama. Greece. 450-425 B.C. Lang.: Ita.　2633

Masked god as tragic subject in works of Aeschylus, Sophocles and Euripides. Greece. 499-401 B.C. Lang.: Fre.　2636

Playwright Robert Auletta on his adaptation of Sophocles' *Ajax*. USA: Washington, DC. 1986. Lang.: Eng.　2891

Theory/criticism

Social and political conditions of Greek society as sources for dramatic material. Greece: Athens. 450 B.C. Lang.: Eng.　3113

Šostakovič, Dimitrij

Plays/librettos/scripts

History and aesthetics of Soviet opera. USSR: Moscow. 1917-1941. Lang.: Ger.　3905

Soulier de Satin, Le (Satin Slipper, The)

Plays/librettos/scripts

Poetic and dramatic language in version of *Le Soulier de Satin (The Satin Slipper)* by Paul Claudel. France. 1928. Lang.: Fre.　2587

Sound

Design/technology

Details of new electrical system of rebuilt Szeged National Theatre. Hungary: Szeged. 1983-1986. Lang.: Hun.　277

The sound and video systems at the Szeged National Theatre. Hungary: Szeged. 1986. Lang.: Hun.　282

The history of a small sound and lighting equipment manufacturing enterprise. Hungary. 1983-1986. Lang.: Hun.　286

Comparison of British and North America theatre sound systems. North America. UK-England. 1980-1987. Lang.: Eng.　305

Overview of performance technology show at Riverside Studios. UK-England: London. 1986. Lang.: Eng.　323

ABTT technical guidelines for sound and communications systems in the theatre. UK-England. Lang.: Eng.　324

Sound design for Lily Tomlin's *The Search for Signs of Intelligent Life in the Universe*. USA: New York, NY. 1986. Lang.: Eng.　335

Construction of realistic-sounding concussion mortar. USA. 1986. Lang.: Eng.　346

Description of USITT trade show. USA. 1986. Lang.: Eng.　352

Sound designers at resident theatres on stage reinforcement. USA. 1986.　364

Sound reduction door added to shop at Seattle Repertory Theatre. USA: Seattle, WA. 1986. Lang.: Eng.　381

Sound desigers at regional theatres evaluate new equipment. USA. 1986.　409

Creating reverberation effects with a piano. USA. 1983. Lang.: Eng.　410

Interview with sound designer Abe Jacob. USA: New York, NY. 1986. Lang.: Eng.　414

Capabilities of available computer-controlled sound systems. USA. 1986.　421

Renovation of the Alhambra Theatre. UK-England: Bradford. 1980-1987. Lang.: Eng.　1521

Techniques and aesthetics of using biofeedback to create electronic music. USA. 1986. Lang.: Eng.　3176

An introduction to the Nagra IV Stereo Time Code Portable Recorder. Lang.: Eng.　3198

Problems faced by sound designer Chris Newman in filming *A Chorus Line*. USA: New York, NY. 1986.　3205

Les Immatériaux, multimedia exhibit by Jean-François Lyotard. France: Paris. 1986. Lang.: Eng.　3249

Use of music in film and theatre. Canada: Toronto, ON. 1985. Lang.: Eng.　3477

Technical details of producing *La Cage aux Folles* on a small budget. Sweden: Malmö. 1985. Lang.: Swe.　3581

Choosing music and sound effects for puppet theatre. USA. Lang.: Eng.　3953

Performance spaces

Technical design features of New Victoria Theatre. UK-England: Stoke-on-Trent. 1980-1986. Lang.: Eng.　624

Performance/production

Production description of the symbolist drama *La navaja (The Razor)* by Eduardo Quiles. Spain. 1980. Lang.: Spa.　2074

Sound of Music, The

Design/technology

Designers discuss regional productions of *The Sound of Music*. USA. 1983-1986. Lang.: Eng.　3594

Soundworks Festival (Sydney)

Performance/production

Overview of the Soundworks Festival. Australia. 1986. Lang.: Eng.　3439

South Coast Repertory (Los Angeles, CA)

Design/technology

A profile of Cliff Faulkner, resident designer at South Coast Repertory. USA: Los Angeles, CA. 1977-1986.　365

Institutions

A profile of South Coast Repertory. USA: Los Angeles, CA. 1964-1986.　569

Southern, Richard

Design/technology

Charles Kean's period production of Shakespeare's *Richard III*. UK-England: London. 1857. Lang.: Eng.　1525

Sovremennik (Moscow)

Performance/production

Career of actor-director Oleg Tabakov. USSR: Moscow. 1950-1986. Lang.: Rus.　904

Soyinka, Wole

Plays/librettos/scripts

Ritualistic elements in the structure of Wole Soyinka's *Death and the King's Horseman*. Africa. 1975. Lang.: Eng.　2359

Shakespeare's influence on playwright Wole Soyinka. Nigeria. UK-England: Leeds. 1957-1981. Lang.: Eng.　2725

Relation to other fields

Interview with playwright Wole Soyinka. Nigeria. USA: New Haven, CT. 1967-1984. Lang.: Eng.　3047

Sociocultural elements of Black theatre. USA. 1960-1985. Lang.: Eng.　3063

Theory/criticism

History of theatre in Africa. Africa. 1400-1985. Lang.: Ger.　1199

Analysis of Wole Soyinka's major critical essays. Nigeria. 1960-1980. Lang.: Eng.　3124

Spain/36

Performance/production

Review of *Spain/36* by San Francisco Mime Troupe. Spain. USA: San Francisco, CA. 1936-1986. Lang.: Eng.　790

Spanish Bawd, The

Performance/production

Collection of newspaper reviews by London theatre critics. UK: London. 1986. Lang.: Eng.　2100

Spanish Tragedy, The

Performance/production

Reconstruction of staging of Act I, *The Spanish Tragedy* by Thomas Kyd. England: London. 1592. Lang.: Eng.　1703

Plays/librettos/scripts

Bullfighting and revenge in *The Spanish Tragedy* by Thomas Kyd. England. 1500-1600. Lang.: Eng.　2458

Connection between character Senex in Thomas Kyd's *The Spanish Tragedy* and Senecan drama. England. 1587. Lang.: Eng.　2473

Spányik, Éva

Performance/production

Interview with actress Éva Spányik. Hungary. 1957-1985. Lang.: Hun.　1837

Spare Tyre (UK)

Performance/production

Interview with Lesbian feminist theatre company Hard Corps. UK-England. 1984-1986. Lang.: Eng.　2164

Sparks, Jake Posey

Performance/production

The effect of disease on circus animals. USA. France. 1890-1985. Lang.: Eng.　3389

Specht, Wayne

Performance/production

Increased use of physical aspects of theatre in Vancouver. Canada: Vancouver, BC. 1986. Lang.: Eng.　1664

Special Delivery Moving Theatre (Vancouver, BC)

Performance/production

Development of works by the Special Delivery Moving Theatre. Canada: Vancouver, BC. 1976-1986. Lang.: Eng.　3294

Special effects
Design/technology
Works by and about designers Jacopo Fabris and Citoyen Boullet. Denmark: Copenhagen. France: Paris. 1760-1801. Lang.: Eng.   256

Folio drawings by Jacopo Fabris illustrating how to paint perspective scenery and build theatrical machinery. Denmark: Copenhagen. Italy. 1760-1801. Lang.: Eng.   257

Early rope and pulley devices for ascending and descending. England. 1576-1595. Lang.: Eng.   258

Nineteenth-century special effects. Europe. North America. 1986. 1890-1920. Lang.: Swe.   262

Comparison of British and North America theatre sound systems. North America. UK-England. 1980-1987. Lang.: Eng.   305

Report on the leading brands of stage blood. USA. 1986. Lang.: Eng.   334

Prices, quantities and manufacturers' official line on stage blood. USA. 1986. Lang.: Eng.   337

Construction of realistic-sounding concussion mortar. USA. 1986. Lang.: Eng.   346

Remote-controlled portable water source. USA. 1982. Lang.: Eng.   354

Ammonium chloride used to produce stage smoke. USA. 1982. Lang.: Eng.   366

Making stage blood. USA. 1982. Lang.: Eng.   368

Application of stage blood. USA. 1986. Lang.: Eng.   373

Bran Ferren's special effects for *The Manhattan Project*. USA. 1986.   377

Safe method of controlling live fire onstage from remote position. USA. 1984. Lang.: Eng.   380

Operation of special effects without sophisticated electronics. USA. 1985. Lang.: Eng.   391

Touch-tone relay controller for special effects. USA. 1986. Lang.: Eng.   401

Creating snowballs for stage use. USA. 1976. Lang.: Eng.   405

Charles Kean's period production of Shakespeare's *Richard III*. UK-England: London. 1857. Lang.: Eng.   1525

Designer and special effects supervisor make sleigh fly in *Santa Claus—The Movie*. Greenland. 1986.   3199

Making of the movie *Return to Oz*, focusing on its special effects and creature design. USA.   3206

Special effects in the film *From Beyond*. USA. 1986. Lang.: Eng.   3208

Special effects in the film version of *Little Shop of Horrors*. USA. Lang.: Eng.   3212

Mechanical bears in film, *Clan of the Cave Bear*. USA. 1985-1986. Lang.: Eng.   3214

Editing and post production on the documentary film *Ornette: Made in America*. USA. Lang.: Eng.   3215

Les Immatériaux, multimedia exhibit by Jean-François Lyotard. France: Paris. 1986. Lang.: Eng.   3249

Details of the lighting arrangements for the four-day Statue of Liberty centennial celebration. USA: New York, NY. 1986. Lang.: Eng.   3318

Lighting designer John Ingram discusses his lighting for the Coca-Cola centennial. USA: Atlanta, GA. 1986. Lang.: Eng.   3319

Interview with manager Tony Smith and lighting designer Alan Owen of the rock band Genesis focusing on the lighting technology used on their latest tour. USA. 1968-1986. Lang.: Eng.   3320

Analysis of the technological aspects of *Les Misérables*. UK-England: London. 1980-1987. Lang.: Eng.   3582

Special institutions
SEE
Institutions, special.

Spectaculum 1986 (Vienna)
Institutions
Spectaculum 1986 and the concept for this festival. Austria: Vienna. 1986. Lang.: Ger.   3480

Spenser, Richard
Performance/production
Brief investigation of the lives of seven actors. England. 1526-1587. Lang.: Eng.   691

Spicer, Graham
Institutions
Role of the Canadian Actors' Equity Association. Canada: Toronto, ON. 1983-1986. Lang.: Eng.   1548

Spielberg, Stephen
Design/technology
Production design for Stephen Spielberg's series *Amazing Stories*. USA. 1986. Lang.: Eng.   3258

Spies, Walter
Plays/librettos/scripts
Conceptions of the South Sea islands in works of Murnau, Artaud and Spies. Europe. USA. Indonesia. 1930. Lang.: Ita.   3231

Spinning a Yarn
Performance/production
Collection of newspaper reviews by London theatre critics. UK-England. 1986. Lang.: Eng.   2114

Spirito della Morte, Lo (Spirit of Death, The)
Plays/librettos/scripts
Theme of death-wish in plays of Pier Maria Rosso di San Secondo. Italy. 1918-1919. Lang.: Ita.   2705

Spirits, The
SEE
Esprits, Les.

Spiró, György
Plays/librettos/scripts
Notes on György Spiró's play about actor, director, manager and playwright Wojciech Bogusławski. Hungary. 1983. Lang.: Hun.   2659

Spoleto/USA Festival (Charleston, SC)
Performance/production
Profile of and interview with Romanian-born conductor Christian Berea. Romania. USA: New York, NY. 1950-1986. Lang.: Eng. 3771

Collaboration of Italian composer Rafaello de Banfield and American playwright Tennessee Williams on the opera *Lord Byron's Love Letter*. USA: Charleston, SC. 1986. Lang.: Eng.   3810

Spoor, Will
Performance/production
A photographic essay of 42 soloists and groups performing mime or gestural theatre. 1986.   3290

Spriggs, Elizabeth
Performance/production
Actresses Jane Lapotaire and Elizabeth Spriggs discuss their careers in the Royal Shakespeare Company. UK-England: London. 1970-1986. Lang.: Eng.   2147

Springate, Michael
Institutions
Limited opportunities for English-language playwrights in Montreal. Canada: Montreal, PQ. 1976-1986. Lang.: Eng.   1561

Sprung, Guy
Design/technology
Use of music in film and theatre. Canada: Toronto, ON. 1985. Lang.: Eng.   3477

Performance/production
Description of an outdoor Shakespeare theatre project. Canada: Toronto, ON. 1983-1986. Lang.: Eng.   1678

Squarzina, Luigi
Plays/librettos/scripts
Letters of playwright Diego Fabbri. Italy. 1960-1978. Lang.: Ita.   2672

Theory/criticism
Decreasing importance of the playwright in Italian theatre. Italy. 1900-1984. Lang.: Fre.   3119

St. Francisco
SEE
Borgia, Francesco.

Staatsoper (Dresden)
SEE
Dresdner Hoftheater.

Staatsoper (Vienna)
Design/technology
Sceneshops of the Burgtheater, Staatsoper and Volksoper. Austria: Vienna. 1963-1980. Lang.: Hun.   237

Institutions
Tours of the Österreichische Bundestheater in Austria. Austria. 1976-1986. Lang.: Ger.   455

Wiener Sommer 1986 promoted by Teletheater-Gesellschaft. Austria: Vienna. 1986. Lang.: Ger.   3479

Staging — cont'd

Staging — cont'd

Staging — cont'd

Production of *L'Histoire terrible mais inachevé de Norodom Sihanouk, roi du Cambodge (The Terrible but Unfinished History of Norodom Sihanouk, King of Cambodia)* by Hélène Cixous. France: Paris. 1985. Lang.: Eng.   1737

History of staging of *Le Menteur (The Liar)* by Pierre Corneille. France: Paris. 1644-1985. Lang.: Fre.   1738

Analysis of two productions of plays by Marivaux. France: Nanterre. Germany, West: Berlin, West. 1985. Lang.: Swe.   1739

Comédie-Française seen through its records for one year. France: Paris. 1778. Lang.: Fre.   1740

Information on theatrical productions. France: Paris. 1944-1960. Lang.: Fre.   1741

Polemic surrounding Sacha Stavisky's production of Shakespeare's *Coriolanus* at the Comédie-Française. France: Paris. 1934. Lang.: Eng, Fre.   1742

Reflection of modern society in Antoine Vitez's production of Sophocles' *Electra* at Théâtre National Populaire. France: Paris. 1981-1986. Lang.: Swe.   1743

Actor, director and teacher Jean-Pierre Vincent. France. 1955-1986. Lang.: Fre.   1744

Analysis of theoretical writings of Jean Vilar. France. 1871-1912. Lang.: Ita.   1745

Staging of plays by Marivaux compared to textual analysis. France. 1723-1981. Lang.: Fre.   1746

Critical essays on major productions and aesthetics. France. 1970-1985. Lang.: Fre.   1747

Relationship between theatre and early photography. France. 1818-1899. Lang.: Fre.   1748

Eastern influences on a production of *Richard II*. France: Paris. 1981. Lang.: Ita.   1749

Reciprocal influences of French and Japanese theatre. France. Japan. 1900-1945. Lang.: Fre.   1750

Collaboration of Hélène Cixous and Ariane Mnouchkine. France. Cambodia. 1964-1986. Lang.: Eng.   1752

Peter Brook's *The Mahabharata* at the Théâtre aux Bouffes du Nord. France: Avignon, Paris. 1985-1986. Lang.: Eng.   1753

Stage adaptation of *La Mort de Judas (The Death of Judas)* by Paul Claudel. France: Brangues. 1985. Lang.: Fre.   1754

Difficulties in staging the plays of Paul Claudel. France. 1910-1931. Lang.: Fre.   1755

Reception of Pirandello's plays in Germany. Germany. Italy. 1924-1931. Lang.: Ita.   1756

Max Reinhardt's work with his contemporaries. Germany. Austria. 1890-1938. Lang.: Eng, Ger.   1757

Max Reinhardt's notes on his production of *Sei personaggi in cerca d'autore (Six Characters in Search of an Author)* by Luigi Pirandello. Germany. Italy. 1924-1934. Lang.: Ita.   1759

Analysis of Shakespeare's influence on Weimar, German neoclassicism. Germany: Weimar. 1771-1812. Lang.: Eng.   1760

Photographic record of forty years of the Berliner Ensemble. Germany, East: Berlin, East. 1949-1984. Lang.: Eng.   1761

Description of Georg Büchner's *Dantons Tod (Danton's Death)* staged by Alexander Lang at Deutsches Theater. Germany, East: Berlin, East. 1984. Lang.: Ger.   1763

Brecht and the Berliner Ensemble. Germany, East: Berlin, East. 1950-1956. Lang.: Ger.   1765

Interview with Elisabeth Bergner and Jane Alexander on their portrayals of Joan of Arc. Germany, West: Berlin, West. UK-England: Malvern. USA: Washington, DC. Lang.: Eng.   1766

Biography of Bertolt Brecht. Germany, West: Augsburg. Germany, East: Berlin, East. USA. 1898-1956. Lang.: Ger.   1767

Peter Stein directs Aeschylus' *Oresteia* in Warsaw. Germany, West: Berlin, West. Poland: Warsaw. 1983. Lang.: Pol.   1768

Program notes for the Athens Ensemble production of *Baal* by Bertolt Brecht. Greece: Athens. 1983. Lang.: Eng.   1769

István Paál directs Shakespeare's *Szeget szeggel (Measure for Measure)*. Hungary: Veszprém. 1985. Lang.: Hun.   1770

Performances of *Alice Csodaországban (Alice in Wonderland)*, *A Két Veronai nemes (The Two Gentlemen of Verona)* and *Tobbsincs királyfi (No More Crown Prince)*. Hungary: Pécs, Budapest. 1985. Lang.: Hun.   1771

István Verebes directs *Valódi Vadnyugat (True West)* by Sam Shepard. Hungary: Budapest. 1986. Lang.: Hun.   1772

Production analysis of a montage of sketches about Electra by Stúdió K. Hungary: Budapest. 1986. Lang.: Hun.   1773

Interview with director Mátyás Giricz. Hungary. 1986. Lang.: Hun. 1774

Interview with actor, director and manager Tamás Major. Hungary. 1910-1986. Lang.: Hun.   1776

Magda Szabó's *A macskák szerdája (Cat Wednesday)* at Csokonai Theatre directed by László Gali. Hungary: Debrecen. 1986. Lang.: Hun.   1777

Tamás Ascher directs *Ördögök (The Devils)*, an adaptation of *Besy (The Possessed)* by Dostojêvskij. Hungary: Budapest. 1986. Lang.: Hun.   1778

Ferenc Sik directs András Sütő's *Advent a Hargitán (Advent in the Harghita Mountains)* at the National Theatre. Hungary: Budapest. 1984-1985. Lang.: Hun.   1779

Memoir of writer, critic, theatre director Béla Abody. Hungary. 1970-1980. Lang.: Hun.   1780

A farkas (The Wolf) by Ferenc Molnár, directed by István Verebes at Vigszinház. Hungary: Budapest. 1985. Lang.: Hun.   1781

Öreg hölgy látogatása (The Visit) by Friedrich Dürrenmatt, directed by Péter Gothár at Vigszinház. Hungary: Budapest. 1986. Lang.: Hun.   1782

Ivan Vasiljêvič by Michajl Afanasjêvič Bulgakov directed by László Marton at Vigszinház under the title *Iván, a rettentő*. Hungary: Budapest. 1986. Lang.: Hun.   1783

Čechov's *Višněvyj sad (The Cherry Orchard)* directed at the National Theatre of Miskolc by Imre Csiszár as *Cseresznyéshert*. Hungary: Miskolc. 1986. Lang.: Hun.   1784

Szeget szeggel (Measure for Measure) by William Shakespeare directed by Tamás Szirtes at Madách Kamaraszinház. Hungary: Budapest. 1985. Lang.: Hun.   1785

Ki van a képen? (Who Is in the Picture?) by Károly Szakonyi directed by Tamás Szirtes at Madách Kamaraszinház. Hungary: Budapest. 1986. Lang.: Hun.   1786

Production by György Emőd of Friedrich Dürrenmatt's *A Öreg hölgy látogatása (The Visit)*. Hungary: Győr. 1985. Lang.: Hun. 1788

Tamás Szirtes directs *Szeget szeggel (Measure for Measure)* by Shakespeare. Hungary: Budapest. 1985. Lang.: Hun.   1789

IV. Henrik (Henry IV) by Shakespeare, directed by János Sándor. Hungary: Szeged. 1985. Lang.: Hun.   1791

Review of *A trójai nők (The Trojan Women)* adapted from Euripides and Sartre by Gyula Illyés, directed by László Vámos. Hungary: Budapest. 1986. Lang.: Hun.   1792

István Horvai directs *Megtört szivek háza (Heartbreak House)* by George Bernard Shaw at Pest National Theatre. Hungary: Budapest. 1985. Lang.: Hun.   1793

Ének Phaedráért (Song for Phaedra) by Per Olof Enquist directed by Imre Csiszár. Hungary: Miskolc. 1985. Lang.: Hun.   1794

Az esőcsináló (The Rainmaker) by N. Richard Nash, directed by Mátyás Giricz. Hungary: Békéscsaba. 1986. Lang.: Hun.   1795

Review of *Advent a Hargitán (Advent in the Harghita Mountains)* by András Sütő, directed by Ferenc Sik. Hungary: Budapest. 1986. Lang.: Hun.   1797

David Rabe's play *Sticks and Bones* presented at the Pesti Theatre in Hungary. Hungary: Budapest. 1971-1975. Lang.: Hun.   1799

Premiere of László Kolozsvári Papp's *Hazánk fiai (Sons of Our Country)*. Hungary: Budapest. 1985. Lang.: Hun.   1800

Notes on performances of *Hongkongi paróka (Wig Made in Hong Kong)*, *Egérút (Narrow Escape)* and *Róza néni (Aunt Rosa)*. Hungary: Budapest. 1985. Lang.: Hun.   1801

Career of actor/director György Várady. Hungary. Romania. 1945-1980. Lang.: Hun.   1802

Evaluation of the season's studio theatre productions. Hungary. 1985-1986. Lang.: Hun.   1803

Lanford Wilson's play, *Talley's Folly (Mint két tojás)* directed by András Bálint. Hungary: Dunaújváros. 1986. Lang.: Hun.   1804

István Verebes' production of *A farkas (The Wolf)* by Ferenc Molnár at the Vigszinház. Hungary: Budapest. 1985. Lang.: Hun.   1805

Review of *Alkony (Sunset)* by Isaak Babel, directed by Károly Kazimir at Thália Szinház. Hungary: Budapest. 1985. Lang.: Hun.   1806

Staging — cont'd

Stage adaptation of Erich Kästner's novel *Emil und die Detektive (Emil and the Detectives)* directed by István Keleti. Hungary: Budapest. 1986. Lang.: Hun.   1807

Review of Géza Páskándi's *Átkozottak (The Damned)* directed by László Romhányi. Hungary: Kőszeg. 1986. Lang.: Hun.   1808

Macska a forró bádogtetőn (Cat on a Hot Tin Roof) by Tennessee Williams, directed by Miklós Szurdi at Városzinház. Hungary: Budapest. 1985. Lang.: Hun.   1809

Der Hofmeister (The Tutor), Jakob Lenz's drama adapted by Bertolt Brecht, directed by Gábor Máté. Hungary: Kaposvár. 1985. Lang.: Hun.   1810

Review of Ivan Kušan's musical comedy *Čaruga (Death Cap)*, directed by Miklós Benedek, Katona József Theatre, as *Galócza*, includes discussion of acting and dramatic art. Hungary: Budapest. 1986. Lang.: Hun.   1811

Endre Vészi's *Don Quijote utolsó kalandja (Don Quixote's Last Adventure)* directed by Imre Kerényi, Gyula Várszinház. Hungary: Gyula. 1986. Lang.: Hun.   1812

István Szőke directs *Oszlopos Simeon (The Man on the Pillar)* by Imre Sarkadi at Miskolc National Theatre. Hungary: Miskolc. 1986. Lang.: Hun.   1813

Performances of Sławomir Mrożek's *Mészárszék (The Slaughterhouse)* and *Ház a határon (The Home on the Border)*. Hungary: Budapest. 1986. Lang.: Hun.   1817

Villa Negra by Anikó and Katalin Vajda directed by Miklós Szurdi. Hungary: Budapest. 1986. Lang.: Hun.   1818

Mihály Vörösmarty's *Csongor és Tünde (Csongor and Tünde)* directed by László Gergely. Hungary: Debrecen. 1986. Lang.: Hun.   1820

Anatoly Ivanov directs Gogol's *Ženitba (The Marriage)* at Jókai Szinház under the title *Háztűznéző*. Hungary: Békéscsaba. 1985. Lang.: Hun.   1821

Geza Páskándi's *Átkozottak (The Damned)* directed by László Romhányi at Kőszegi Várszinház. Hungary: Kőszeg. 1986. Lang.: Hun.   1822

Rostand's *Cyrano de Bergerac* directed by György Lengyel. Hungary: Budapest. 1985. Lang.: Hun.   1825

Review of *Bűnhődés (Punishment)*, a stage adaptation of *The Idiot* by Dostojévskij. Hungary: Budapest. Lang.: Hun.   1826

László Gali directs Shakespeare's *Hamlet*. Hungary: Debrecen. 1986. Lang.: Hun.   1827

A kis herceg (The Little Prince) by Antoine de Saint-Exupéry adapted and staged by Anna Belia and Péter Valló. Hungary: Budapest. 1985. Lang.: Hun.   1828

New director of Radnóti Miklós Theatre, András Bálint. Hungary: Budapest. 1985. Lang.: Hun.   1830

Gábor Berényi's production of *Macskajáték (Catsplay)* by István Örkény at the Magyar Játékszin. Hungary: Budapest. 1985. Lang.: Hun.   1832

Productions of *Deficit* by István Csurka. Hungary: Szolnok, Budapest. 1970-1985. Lang.: Hun.   1833

Premiere of Tibor Déry's *A Tanúk (The Witnesses)*, directed by Tibor Csizmadia. Hungary: Szolnok. 1945-1985. Lang.: Hun.   1834

Ki van a képen (Who Is in the Picture?) by Tamás Szirtes at Madách Studio Theatre. Hungary: Budapest. 1986. Lang.: Hun.   1835

Production of *A nevelő (The Tutor)* by Bertolt Brecht. Hungary: Kaposvár. 1985. Lang.: Hun.   1840

Ottó Adám directs *Egy lócsiszár virágvasárnapja (The Palm Sunday of a Horse Dealer)* by András Sütő after Kleist. Hungary: Budapest. 1986. Lang.: Hun.   1843

Gábor Görgey's *Huzatos ház (Drafty House)* directed by Gyula Bodrogi, Vidám Szinpad. Hungary: Budapest. 1986. Lang.: Hun.   1845

János Pelle's *Casanova* directed by Károly Kazimir at the Körszinház. Hungary: Budapest. 1986. Lang.: Hun.   1846

Segitség (Help) by György Schwajda, directed by István Pinczés, Csokonai Szinház. Hungary: Debrecen. 1986. Lang.: Hun.   1848

András Béhés directs *Légy jó mindhalálig (Be Good Till Death)* by Zsigmond Móricz at Nemzeti Szinház. Hungary: Budapest. 1986. Lang.: Hun.   1849

Alkony (Sunset) by Isaak Babel, directed by Károly Kazimir at Thália Szinház. Hungary: Budapest. 1985. Lang.: Hun.   1850

András Matkócsik directs *Mondd, Joe! (Eh, Joe!)* and *Az utlosó tekercs (Krapp's Last Tape)* by Samuel Beckett. Hungary: Budapest. 1985. Lang.: Hun.   1851

Ferenc Sik directs *A velencei Kalmár (The Merchant of Venice)* by William Shakespeare. Hungary: Budapest. 1986. Lang.: Hun.   1853

Ágyrajárók (Night Lodgers) by Péter Szántó, directed by György Emőd at Kisfaludy Studio Theatre. Hungary: Győr. 1985. Lang.: Hun.   1854

Review of *Trójai Nők (The Trojan Women)* by Jean-Paul Sartre, produced at Nemzeti Szinház. Hungary: Budapest. 1986. Lang.: Hun.   1855

Gábor Görgey's *Huzatos ház (Drafty House)* directed by Gyula Bodrogi at Vidám Színpad. Hungary: Budapest. 1986. Lang.: Hun.   1856

History of Hungarian productions and interpretations of *Death of a Salesman (Az ügynök halála)* by Arthur Miller and *A Streetcar Named Desire (A vágy villamos)* by Tennessee Williams. Hungary. 1959-1983. Lang.: Hun.   1857

G.B. Shaw's *Megtörtszívek háza (Heartbreak House)* directed by István Horvai. Hungary: Budapest. 1985. Lang.: Hun.   1858

Sip a tökre (Play a Trump in Diamonds) by Péter Tömöry, directed by Imre Halasi. Hungary: Kisvárda. 1986. Lang.: Hun.   1859

Reviews of Hungarian and other plays. Hungary. 1979-1983. Lang.: Hun.   1860

A collection of Tamás Koltai's critical reviews of productions and performances. Hungary. 1976-1983. Lang.: Hun.   1861

Review of Alex Koenigsmark's *Adié, milacku! (Good-bye, Darling!)* directed by Péter Gothár at Csiky Gergely Theatre under the title *Agyő, kedvesem*. Hungary: Kaposvár. 1985. Lang.: Hun.   1862

Reprinted preface to biography of Tamás Major. Hungary. 1930-1986. Lang.: Hun.   1863

Rzeźnia (The Slaughterhouse) by Sławomir Mrożek, directed by Sándor Beke at Józsefvárosi Szinház under the title *Mészárszék*. Hungary: Budapest. 1985. Lang.: Hun.   1865

Ahogy tetszik (As You Like It) by William Shakespeare directed by István Szőke. Hungary: Miskolc. 1986. Lang.: Hun.   1866

Review of László Teleki's *A Kegyenc (The Favorite)* as directed by József Ruszt, Hevesi Sándor Theatre. Hungary: Zalaegerszeg. 1986. Lang.: Hun.   1867

Interview with Tamás Major, director and actor. Hungary. 1945-1986. Lang.: Hun.   1868

Reviews of performances at Csiky Gergely Theatre. Hungary: Kaposvár. 1985-1986. Lang.: Hun.   1869

Adaptation for the stage by Anikó Vagda and Katalin Vajda of Imre Dobozy's screenplay *Villa Negra*, directed at Játékszin by Miklós Szurdi. Hungary: Budapest. 1986. Lang.: Hun.   1870

Production of Shakespeare's *Szeget szeggel (Measure for Measure)* directed by István Paál. Hungary: Veszprém. 1985. Lang.: Hun. 1872

István Szőke, directs *Ahogy tetszik (As You Like It)* by Shakespeare. Hungary: Miskolc. 1986. Lang.: Hun.   1873

János Ács directs *Kozma* by Mihály Kornis. Hungary: Kaposvár. 1986. Lang.: Hun.   1874

Géza Tordy directs *Császári futam (Imperial Round)* by Miklós Gyárfás at Gyulai Várszinház. Hungary: Gyula. 1986. Lang.: Hun. 1875

Review of József Katona's *Bánk Bán* directed by János Ács at Szigligeti Szinház. Hungary: Szolnok. 1986. Lang.: Hun.   1876

Csongor és Tünde (Csongor and Tünde) by Mihály Vörösmarty, directed by János Szikora at Gárdonyi Géza Szinház. Hungary: Eger. 1985. Lang.: Hun.   1877

Recollections of actor, director and theatre manager Tamás Major. Hungary. 1910-1986. Lang.: Hun.   1879

László Salamon Suba's production of *Urának hű szolgája (A Faithful Servant of His Lord)* by Franz Grillparzer. Hungary: Nyiregyháza. 1985. Lang.: Hun.   1881

Imre Csiszár directs *Az éjszaka a nappal anyja (Night is the Mother of the Day)* by Lars Norén. Hungary: Dunaújváros. 1986. Lang.: Hun.   1882

Gyula Gazdag directs *A vihar (The Tempest)* by William Shakespeare, Csiky Gergely Theatre. Hungary: Kaposvár. 1986. Lang.: Hun.   1883

Bánk Bán by József Katona at Szigligeti Theatre directed by János Ács. Hungary: Szolnok. 1986. Lang.: Hun.   1884

Staging — cont'd

Kozma by Mihály Kornis directed by János Ács, Csiky Gergely Szinház. Hungary: Kaposvár. 1986. Lang.: Hun.   1885

Reviews of Shakespeare productions written by Hungarian realist writer, Zsigmond Móricz. Hungary: Budapest. 1923. Lang.: Hun.   1887

Ivo Brešan's *Paraszt Hamlet (The Peasant Hamlet)* directed by Béla Merő. Hungary: Zalaegerszeg. 1986. Lang.: Hun.   1888

Péter Gothár's production of *A Öreg hölgy látogatósa (The Visit)* by Friedrich Dürrenmatt. Hungary: Budapest. 1986. Lang.: Hun.   1889

Notes on *Čaruga (Death Cap)*, by Ivan Kušan, directed by Miklós Benedek, Katona József Theatre, under the title *Galócza*. Hungary: Budapest. 1986. Lang.: Hun.   1890

Review of László Teleki's *A Kegyenc (The Favorite)* directed by József Ruszt. Hungary: Zalaegerszeg. 1986. Lang.: Hun.   1891

Knock by Jules Romains directed by Gábor Máté at Csiky Gergely Theatre. Hungary: Kaposvár. 1986. Lang.: Hun.   1892

Performances of George Bernard Shaw's *Candida* and Čechov's *Diadia Vania (Uncle Vanya)*, under the title *Ványa bácsi*, at Pécs National Theatre. Hungary: Pécs. 1985. Lang.: Hun.   1893

Péter Gothár directs *Agyő, kedvesem (Goodbye, Darling!)* by Alex Koenigsmark, at Csiky Gergely Theatre. Hungary: Kaposvár. 1985. Lang.: Hun.   1894

Review of collection of essays by drama critic Tamás Koltai. Hungary. 1978-1983. Lang.: Hun.   1895

Magda Szabó's *Szent Bertalan nappala (Saint Bartholomew's Day)* directed by György Lengyel at Madách Szinház. Hungary: Budapest. 1986. Lang.: Hun.   1896

Dezső Szomory's *Bella* at the Pécs National Theatre directed by István Jeney. Hungary: Pécs. 1986. Lang.: Hun.   1897

Productions of plays by Edward Bond, Gyula Hernádi and Lope de Vega at the Pécs National Theatre. Hungary: Pécs. 1986. Lang.: Hun.   1898

Review of Biblical passion play by National Theatre of Budapest. Hungary: Budapest. Poland: Warsaw. 1983. Lang.: Pol.   1899

Mátyás Giricz directs *A kertész kutyája (The Gardener's Dog)* by Lope de Vega. Hungary: Budapest. 1985. Lang.: Hun.   1900

Milán Füst's *Margit kisasszony (Miss Margit)* directed by István Dégi at Játékszin. Hungary: Budapest. 1986. Lang.: Hun.   1901

Selected reviews of *Segitsd a király! (Help the King!)* by József Ratkó. Hungary: Nyiregyháza. 1985. Lang.: Hun.   1902

Two productions of Čechov's *Három Nővér (Three Sisters)*. Hungary: Zalaegerszeg, Budapest. 1985. Lang.: Hun.   1903

Overview of children's theatre offerings. Hungary. 1985-1986. Lang.: Hun.   1904

János Ács directs *A kőszívű ember fiai (The Sons of the Stone-Hearted Man)* by Mór Jókai. Hungary: Zalaegerszeg. 1986. Lang.: Hun.   1905

Survey of various Hungarian amateur theatres and workshops. Hungary. 1960-1980. Lang.: Hun.   1906

Ferenc Sik directs Shakespeare's *A velencei kalmár (The Merchant of Venice)*. Hungary: Budapest. 1986. Lang.: Hun.   1907

Forgatókönyv (Film Script) by István Örkény directed by Gábor Balogh. Hungary: Békéscsaba. 1986. Lang.: Hun.   1908

Troádes (The Trojan Women) directed by László Gergely at Csokonai Theatre. Hungary: Debrecen. 1985. Lang.: Hun.   1909

Die dreigroschenoper (The Three Penny Opera) directed by István Pinczés at Csokonai Theatre. Hungary: Debrecen. 1986. Lang.: Hun.   1910

Tamás Ascher directs *A kopasz éneksnő (The Bald Soprano)* and *Különóra (The Lesson)* by Eugène Ionesco. Hungary: Kaposvár. 1986. Lang.: Hun.   1912

Review of two performances of András Sütő's plays. Hungary: Budapest. 1986. Lang.: Hun.   1913

Tamás Ascher directs Čechov's *Tri sestry (Three Sisters)* at Katona József Theatre under the title *Három nővér*. Hungary: Budapest. 1985. Lang.: Hun.   1914

Reviews of *Margit kisasszony (Miss Margit)*, *Az Ibolya (The Violet)*, *Az Árny (The Ghost)* and *Róza néni (Aunt Rosa)*. Hungary: Budapest. 1985-1986. Lang.: Hun.   1916

Production of *Ványa bácsi (Uncle Vanya)* by Čechov. Hungary: Pécs. 1985. Lang.: Hun.   1918

Miklós Mészöly's *Bunker* at Népszinház directed by Mátyás Giricz. Hungary: Budapest. 1985. Lang.: Hun.   1919

Čechov's *Višněvyj sad (The Cherry Orchard)* directed by Imre Csiszár under the title *Cseresznyéskert*. Hungary: Miskolc. 1986. Lang.: Hun.   1921

Stage adaptations of Dostojévskij novels *A Félkesgyelmü (The Idiot)* and *A Karamazov testvérek (The Brothers Karamazov)*. Hungary: Budapest, Debrecen. 1985. Lang.: Hun.   1922

Mihály Vörösmarty's *Csongor and Tünde* at Gárdonyi Géza Theatre directed by János Szikora. Hungary: Eger. 1985. Lang.: Hun.   1923

Criticizes stage adaptation of *Hangok komédiája (Comedy of Sounds)* by Miklós Gyárfás. Hungary: Budapest. 1985. Lang.: Hun.   1924

Production of Bengt Ahlfors' *Szinházkomédia (Theatre Comedy)* directed by András Márton. Hungary: Debrecen. 1985. Lang.: Hun.   1925

Study of *A Kétfejü fenerad (The Two-Headed Beast)*. Hungary. Lang.: Hun.   1926

Evaluation of József Ruszt's direction at Hevesi Sándor Theatre. Hungary: Zalaegerszeg. 1983-1986. Lang.: Hun.   1927

Interview with director János Szikora. Hungary. 1982-1986. Lang.: Hun.   1928

János Pelle's *Casanova* directed by Károly Kazimir at Körszinház. Hungary: Budapest. 1986. Lang.: Hun.   1929

Péter Gellért's production of *Urhatnám polgár (The Bourgeois Gentleman)* at Móricz Zsigmond Szinház. Hungary: Nyiregyháza. 1986. Lang.: Hun.   1931

Review of *Kettős ünnep (A Double Holiday)*, written and staged by István Verebes. Hungary: Budapest. 1986. Lang.: Hun.   1932

Performances of *Pán Peter (Peter Pan)* by J. M. Barrie, directed by Géza Pártos. Hungary: Kaposvár. 1985. Lang.: Hun.   1934

A kis herceg (The Little Prince) by Saint-Exupéry adapted and staged by Anna Belia and Péter Valló. Hungary: Budapest. 1985. Lang.: Hun.   1935

Dezső Szomory's *Bella* at Pécs National Theatre directed by István Jeney. Hungary: Pécs. 1986. Lang.: Hun.   1936

Ének Phaedráért (Song for Phaedra) by Per Olof Enquist, directed by Imre Csiszár at the National Theatre of Miskolc. Hungary: Miskolc. 1985. Lang.: Hun.   1937

István Paál directs *Szeget szeggel (Measure for Measure)* by Shakespeare at Petőfi Szinház. Hungary: Veszprém. 1985. Lang.: Hun.   1938

István Verebes directs *Valódi vadnyugat (True West)* by Sam Shepard at Radnóti Miklós Szinpad. Hungary: Budapest. 1986. Lang.: Hun.   1939

Kinn vagyunk a vízből (Saved) by Edward Bond directed by István Szőke. Hungary: Pécs. 1986. Lang.: Hun.   1940

Review of *Margit kisasszony (Miss Margit)* directed by István Dégi. Hungary: Budapest. 1986. Lang.: Hun.   1941

László Fábián's *Levéltetvek az akasztófán (Plant-Lice on the Gallows)* directed by István Szőke. Hungary: Miskolc. 1986. Lang.: Hun.   1942

Ferenc Sik directs two plays by Gyula Háy. Hungary: Veszprém, Gyula. 1986. Lang.: Hun.   1943

Theatrical career of Ede Paulay. Hungary: Budapest. 1878-1894. Lang.: Hun.   1944

Interview with actor, director and dramaturg Imre Katona of the Gropius Társulat. Hungary: Budapest. 1961-1985. Lang.: Hun.   1945

Hungarian performance of Edward Albee's play *Nem félünk a farkastól (Who's Afraid of Virginia Woolf?)*. Hungary. 1963-1984. Lang.: Hun.   1946

Aleksej Dudarëv's *Večer (An Evening)* directed by Mátyas Giricz at Józsefvárosi Theatre. Hungary: Budapest. 1986. Lang.: Hun.   1947

Stage adaptations of prose works by Gogol and Gončarov. Hungary: Veszprém, Békéscsaba. 1985. Lang.: Hun.   1948

Hagyaték (Legacy) by Gyula Hernádi, directed by Menyhért Szegvári. Hungary: Pécs. 1986. Lang.: Hun.   1949

Nő a körúton (Woman on the Boulevard) by István Gáll directed by Péter Léner at Móricz Zsigmond Theatre. Hungary: Nyiregyháza. 1986. Lang.: Hun.   1950

Endre Vészi's *Don Quijote utolsó kalandja (Don Quixote's Last Adventure)* directed by Imre Kerényi. Hungary: Gyula. 1986. Lang.: Hun.   1951

Imre Sarkadi's *Oszlopos Simeon (The Man on the Pillar)* directed by István Szőke at Nemzeti Szinház. Hungary: Miskolc. 1986. Lang.: Hun.   1952

Staging — cont'd

Cyrano de Bergerac by Edmond Rostand, directed by György Lengyel at Madách Szinház. Hungary: Budapest. 1985. Lang.: Hun.
1953

World premiere of *A tanúk (The Witnesses)* by the late Tibor Déry directed at Szigligeti Theatre by Tibor Csizmadia. Hungary: Szolnok. 1986. Lang.: Hun.
1954

Advent a Hargitán (Advent in the Harghita Mountains) by András Sütő, directed at National Theatre by Ferenc Sik. Hungary: Budapest. 1986. Lang.: Hun.
1956

Scapin furfangjai (Scapin's Tricks) by Molière, directed by László Vámos at Szentendrei Teátrum. Hungary: Szentendre. 1986. Lang.: Hun.
1957

Reviews of two plays by Arthur Schnitzler directed by Imre Halasi. Hungary: Budapest, Zalaegerszeg. 1986. Lang.: Hun.
1958

Performances of *Hair*, directed by János Sándor, and *Desire Under the Elms*, directed by Géza Bodolay at the National Theatre of Szeged. Hungary: Szeged. 1986. Lang.: Hun.
1959

Review of Gyula Gazdag's production of *A Vihar (The Tempest)* by Shakespeare, Csiky Gergely Theatre. Hungary: Kaposvár. 1986. Lang.: Hun.
1960

Isván Szőke directs *Letvéltetvek az akasztófán (Plant-Lice on the Gallows)* by László Fábián. Hungary: Miskolc. 1986. Lang.: Hun.
1961

Macskajáték (Catsplay) by István Örkény, directed by Gábor Berényi, at Magyar Játékszin. Hungary: Budapest. 1985. Lang.: Hun.
1962

Rehearsals of András Sütő's *Advent a Hargitán (Advent in the Harghita Mountains)* at the National Theatre directed by Ferenc Sik. Hungary: Budapest. 1985-1986. Lang.: Hun.
1963

Comparison of two Hungarian productions of *Háram nővér (Three Sisters)* by Anton Pavlovič Čechov. Hungary: Budapest, Zalaegerszeg. 1985. Lang.: Hun.
1964

Wariat i zakonnica (The Madman and the Nun) by Stanisław Ignacy Witkiewicz, directed by János Sándor at Szeged National Theatre under the title *Az őrült és az apáca*. Hungary: Szeged. 1986. Lang.: Hun.
1965

Gábor Máté directs Brecht's *Der Hofmeister (The Tutor)* at Csiky Gergely Theatre under the title *A nevelő*. Hungary: Kaposvár. 1985. Lang.: Hun.
1966

Synthesis of music, dance, song and speech in *Ayrus Leánya (Ayrus' Daughter)* by Ödön Palasovszky. Hungary: Budapest. 1931. Lang.: Hun.
1967

Hungary: Szolnok. 1986. Lang.: Hun.
1968

Performance of Shakespeare's *Richard II* at Várszinház, directed by Imre Kerényi. Hungary: Budapest. 1986. Lang.: Hun.
1970

A kegyenc (The Favorite) by Gyula Illyés, directed by János Sándor, National Theatre of Miskolc. Hungary: Miskolc. 1985. Lang.: Hun.
1971

Tizenkét dühós ember (Twelve Angry Men) by Reginald Rose directed by András Béhés. Hungary: Budapest. 1985. Lang.: Hun.
1972

István Gáll's *Nő a körúton (Woman on the Boulevard)* directed by Péter Léner at Móricz Zsigmond Szinház. Hungary: Nyiregyháza. 1986. Lang.: Hun.
1973

András Sütő's *Advent a Hargitán (Advent in the Harghita Mountains)* directed by Ferenc Sik. Hungary: Budapest. 1986. Lang.: Hun.
1974

Description of several *Bhavāī* performances. India. 1980-1986. Lang.: Eng.
1976

Announcement of Margalith Prize winners. Israel: Jerusalem. 1986. Lang.: Heb.
1977

Artistic cooperation between playwright Dan Horowitz and director Ya'akov Raz. Israel. 1978-1986. Lang.: Heb.
1978

Jurij Petrivič Liubimov directs Isaak Babel's *Hashhia (Sunset)*. Israel: Tel-Aviv. 1984-1986. Lang.: Heb.
1979

Notes on the process of staging *Eiolf Hakatan*, a Hebrew translation of Henrik Ibsen's *Lille Eyolf (Little Eyolf)*, directed by Yossi Israeli at the Kahn theatre. Israel: Jerusalem. 1986. Lang.: Heb.
1980

Daniel Lanzini's notes on writing and staging his play *Hazaiot Kamot Bamizrah (Fantasies Awakening in the East)* at the Acre Theatre Festival. Israel: Acre. 1986. Lang.: Heb.
1981

Obituary of director Raphael Zvi. Israel. 1898-1985. Lang.: Heb.
1984

Documentation on Arno Holz's *Ignorabimus* directed by Luca Ronconi. Italy: Prato. 1986. Lang.: Ita.
1985

Reconstruction of *Comedia Tinellaria* by Torres Naharro. Italy: Rome, Venice. 1508-1537. Lang.: Spa.
1986

Luigi Pirandello's concerns with staging in *Sei personaggi in cerca d'autore (Six Characters in Search of an Author)* and *Enrico Quarto (Henry IV)*. Italy. 1921-1986. Lang.: Fre.
1990

Working environment of director Memè Perlini. Italy. 1978. Lang.: Eng.
1991

Collaboration of director Virgilio Talli and playwright Pier Maria Rosso di San Secondo. Italy. 1917-1920. Lang.: Ita.
1992

Pirandello's dealings with actor, manager and director Virgilio Talli. Italy. 1917-1921. Lang.: Ita.
1993

Overview of productions in Italy. Italy: Milan. 1986. Lang.: Eng.
1994

Notes on the first production of Luigi Pirandello's *L'uomo, la bestia, e la virtù (Man, Animal and Virtue)*. Italy. 1919. Lang.: Ita.
1997

Creative development of director Jurij Liubimov in Italy. Italy. USSR. 1973-1986. Lang.: Ita.
2003

Luigi Pirandello's staging of his own works at the Teatro d'Arte. Italy: Rome. 1925-1928. Lang.: Ita.
2004

Director John Dillon on his Japanese production of *Death of a Salesman* by Arthur Miller. Japan. 1984. Lang.: Eng.
2005

Bungei-za performs *Tóték (The Tót Family)* by István Örkény. Japan: Toyama. 1985. Lang.: Hun.
2006

Reviews of the play productions at the National Theatre Festival. Korea. 1986. Lang.: Eng.
2009

Review of the play productions at the National Theatre Festival. Korea. 1985. Lang.: Eng.
2010

Performance conditions of specific theatrical genres. Lebanon. 1918-1985. Lang.: Fre.
2011

Performance of Comédie-Française actors in Amsterdam. Netherlands. 1811. Lang.: Fre.
2012

Andrzej Marczewski directs Andrzejewski's *Popiol i Diament (Ashes and Diamonds)*, Teatr Rozmaitości. Poland: Warsaw. 1984. Lang.: Pol.
2013

Life and work of cabaret singer and stage director Leon Schiller. Poland. 1887-1954. Lang.: Eng, Fre.
2014

Director Kazimierz Braun on his adaptation of *La Peste (The Plague)* by Albert Camus. Poland: Wrocław. 1976-1983. Lang.: Eng.
2015

Recollections of actor-directors Irena and Tadeusz Byrski. Poland: Vilna. 1930-1939. Lang.: Pol.
2017

Adam Hanuszkiewicz directs Corneille's *Le Cid* at Teatr Ateneum. Poland: Warsaw. 1984. Lang.: Pol.
2021

Overview of correspondence between Leon Schiller and Edward Gordon Craig. Poland: Warsaw. France: Paris. 1900-1954. Lang.: Eng, Fre.
2022

Othello, translated by Bohdan Drozdowski and directed by Wilfred Harrison at the Wilama Horzycy Theatre. Poland: Toruń. 1980. Lang.: Eng.
2023

Description of performances by touring companies from Vilna. Poland. 1789-1864. Lang.: Pol.
2026

Djrector Andrzei Wajda's work, accessibility to Polish audiences. Poland: Warsaw. 1926-1986. Lang.: Swe.
2027

Career and philosophy of director Tadeusz Kantor. Poland. 1915-1985. Lang.: Eng.
2028

Interview with director Tadeusz Kantor. Poland. 1967-1985. Lang.: Eng.
2029

Description of first translations and adaptations of Shakespeare's dramas on the Polish stage. Poland: Vilna. 1786-1864. Lang.: Pol.
2030

Andrzej Łapicki directs Aleksander Fredro's *Śluby Panienskie (Maiden Vows)*, Teatr Polski. Poland: Warsaw. 1984. Lang.: Pol.
2031

Adaptation of Dostojévskij's *Prestuplenijė i nakazanijė (Crime and Punishment)* directed by Andrzej Wajda at Teatr Stary under the title *Zdrodnia i Kara*. Poland: Cracow. 1984. Lang.: Pol.
2032

Tadeusz Łomnicki directs Pasolini's *Affabulazione* at Centrum Sztuki Studio. Poland: Warsaw. 1984. Lang.: Pol.
2033

Krystyna Meissner directs Juliusz Słowacki's *Balladyna*, Teatr Horzycy. Poland: Toruń. 1984. Lang.: Pol.
2035

Staging — cont'd

Repertory and artistic achievements of the Na Pohulance Theatre.
Poland: Vilna. 1938-1940. Lang.: Pol.   2036

Artistic profile and main achievements of Akademia Ruchu. Poland:
Warsaw. 1973-1986. Lang.: Pol.   2037

Andrzej Pawłowski directs Gombrowicz's *Pornografia (Pornography)*.
Poland: Warsaw. 1983. Lang.: Pol.   2038

Janusz Nyczak directs Michał Pałucki's *Dom Otwarty (Open House)*
at Teatr Nowy. Poland: Poznań. 1984. Lang.: Pol.   2039

Krzysztof Babicki directs Różewicz's *Pułapka (Trap)*. Poland:
Gdansk. 1984. Lang.: Pol.   2040

Laco Adamik directs Ferdinand Brückner's *Elisabeth von England*
under the title *Elzbieta, Królowa Anglii*. Poland: Cracow. 1984.
Lang.: Pol.   2041

Krzysztof Rościszewski directs Gombrowicz's *Iwona, Księzniczka
Burgundia (Ivona, Princess of Burgundia)*, Teatr Polski. Poland:
Bydgoszcz. 1984. Lang.: Pol.   2042

Analysis of the directorial style of Jerzy Grotowski. Poland:
Wrocław. 1959-1984. Lang.: Pol.   2044

Józef Skwark directs Gorkij's *Dačniki (Summer Folk)* under the title
Letnicy. Poland: Warsaw. 1984. Lang.: Pol.   2045

Mikołaj Grabowski directs *Irydion* by Zygmunt Krasiński. Poland:
Cracow. 1983. Lang.: Pol.   2046

The achievements and style of director Krzysztof Babicki. Poland.
1982-1986. Lang.: Pol.   2047

Jerzy Krasowski of Teatr Mały directs Ryszard Frelka's *Jalta
(Yalta)*. Poland: Warsaw. 1984. Lang.: Pol.   2048

Description of the festival of Russian and Soviet drama with reviews
of performances. Poland: Katowice. USSR. 1985. Lang.: Eng, Fre.
                                                         2049

A stage history of the work of Bertolt Brecht. Poland. 1923-1984.
                                                         2050

Shakespeare's *Hamlet* directed by Janusz Warmiński. Poland:
Warsaw. 1983. Lang.: Pol.   2051

Zygmunt Hübner directs Gombrowicz's *Iwona, Ksiezniczka Burgundia
(Ivona, Princess of Burgundia)*. Poland: Warsaw. 1983. Lang.: Pol.
                                                         2052

Jerzy Grzegorzewski directs Różewicz's *Pułapka (Trap)* at Centrum
Sztuki Studio. Poland: Warsaw. 1984. Lang.: Pol.   2053

Overview of the career of Jerzy Grotowski, his theatrical
experiments, training methodology and thoughts on the purpose of
theatre. Poland. 1958-1986. Lang.: Eng.   2054

Interview with director Tadeusz Kantor. Poland. 1942-1985. Lang.:
Hun.   2055

Tubieński's *Śmieré Komandura (The Death of the Commander)*
directed by Eugeniusz Korin, Teatr Polski. Poland: Wrocław. 1984.
Lang.: Pol.   2056

Kazimierz Dejmek directs Wyspiański's *Wesele (The Wedding)*, Teatr
Polski. Poland: Warsaw. 1984. Lang.: Pol.   2057

Andrzej Wajda directs Sophocles' *Antigone*, Stary Teatr. Poland:
Cracow. 1984. Lang.: Pol.   2058

Ignacy Gogolewski of Teatr Osterwy directs Wyspiański's *Wesele
(The Wedding)*. Poland: Lublin. 1984. Lang.: Pol.   2059

Tadeusz Kantor directs his *Gdzie sa Niegdysiejsze Śniegi (Where Are
the Snows of Yesteryear)*, Cricot 2. Poland: Cracow. 1984. Lang.:
Pol.   2061

Michał Ratyński directs Różewicz's *Kartoteka (Card Index)*, Teatr
Powszechny. Poland: Warsaw. 1984. Lang.: Pol.   2062

Notes on production of the Állami Magyar Szinház and its late
director György Harag. Romania: Cluj. 1984-1985. Lang.: Hun. 2063

Interview with director György Harag. Romania: Tîrgu-Mures. 1925-
1985. Lang.: Hun.   2064

Mejerchol'd's influence on Bertolt Brecht. Russia: Moscow. Germany,
East: Berlin, East. 1903-1957. Lang.: Eng.   2065

Career of director and playwright, Nikolaj Nikolajėvič Jėvreinov.
Russia. USSR. 1879-1953. Lang.: Hun.   2066

Collaboration of Nikolaj Gogol in first production of *Revizor (The
Inspector General)*. Russia. 1836. Lang.: Ita.   2069

Documentation on Stanislavskij's productions of Čechov plays.
Russia. 1901-1904. Lang.: Ita.   2070

Account of a production of *Ane Satyre of the Thrie Estaitis* by
David Lindsay. Scotland: Cupar. 1552-1554. Lang.: Eng.   2072

Production description of the symbolist drama *La navaja (The
Razor)* by Eduardo Quiles. Spain. 1980. Lang.: Spa.   2074

Use of stagehands in production of modern passion play. Spain.
1951-1986. Lang.: Eng.   2075

Playwright Antonio Martínez Ballesteros discusses the production
history of his play *Los Comediantes (The Players)*. Spain: Toledo.
USA: Cincinnati, OH. 1982-1985. Lang.: Spa.   2076

Directing career of Josefina Molina. Spain. 1952-1985. Lang.: Eng.
                                                         2078

Production history of *Hay que deshacer la casa (Undoing the
Housework)*, winner of Lope de Vega prize. Spain: Madrid. USA:
Miami, FL. 1983-1985. Lang.: Eng.   2079

Role of the director working with classics today. Spain-Catalonia.
1984. Lang.: Cat.   2080

Interview with director Jorge Lavelli of Estudio Faixat. Spain-
Catalonia: Barcelona. 1983. Lang.: Pol.   2081

Savannah Bay and *Reigen (Round)* produced by Centre Dramàtic.
Spain-Catalonia: Barcelona. 1986. Lang.: Cat.   2082

Articles on the 1986-87 theatre season. Spain-Catalonia: Barcelona.
France. 1986. Lang.: Cat.   2083

Articles about the productions of the Centre Dramàtic. Spain-
Catalonia: Barcelona. 1976-1986. Lang.: Cat.   2084

Rehearsals of *Kött och kärlek (Flesh and Love)* by Juoko Turkka.
Sweden: Gothenburg. 1986. Lang.: Swe.   2085

Reviews of regional productions. Sweden: Stockholm. 1985-1986.
Lang.: Swe.   2087

Regional theatre productions in Sweden. Sweden: Stockholm,
Gothenburg. 1985-1986. Lang.: Swe.   2088

Survey of summer theatre offerings. Sweden: Stockholm, Södertälje,
Karlskrona. 1986. Lang.: Swe.   2089

Reviews of three productions of *Fröken Julie (Miss Julie)* by August
Strindberg. Sweden: Stockholm. Denmark: Copenhagen. South Africa,
Republic of. 1985-1986. Lang.: Swe.   2090

Interview with actress Agneta Ekmanner. Sweden: Stockholm. 1950-
1986. Lang.: Swe.   2092

August Strindberg's theoretical writings. Sweden. 1887-1910. Lang.:
Ita.   2093

The cooperation between amateurs and professionals in Fria
Proteatern's staging of Brecht's *Turandot*. Sweden: Stockholm. 1986.
Lang.: Swe.   2095

Contribution of stage directions concerning stage design and directing
to producing plays by Friedrich Dürrenmatt. Switzerland. 1949-1986.
Lang.: Eng.   2097

Director, producer Wu Jing-Jyi discusses his life and career in
theatre. Taiwan. USA: Minneapolis, MN, New York, NY. 1939-
1980. Lang.: Eng.   2098

Collection of newspaper reviews by London theatre critics. UK.
1986. Lang.: Eng.   2099

Collection of newspaper reviews by London theatre critics. UK:
London. 1986. Lang.: Eng.   2100

Collection of newspaper reviews by London theatre critics. UK.
1986. Lang.: Eng.   2101

Collection of newspaper reviews by London theatre critics. UK.
1986. Lang.: Eng.   2102

Collection of newspaper reviews by London theatre critics. UK.
1986. Lang.: Eng.   2103

Political difficulties in staging two touring productions of
Shakespeare's *The Taming of the Shrew*. UK. 1985-1986. Lang.:
Eng.   2104

Solutions to staging the final scene of Shakespeare's *The Merry
Wives of Windsor*. UK. 1874-1985. Lang.: Eng.   2105

Theatre season in London. UK-England: London. 1986. Lang.: Eng.
                                                         2107

Review of alternative theatre productions. UK-England: London.
1986. Lang.: Eng.   2108

Collection of newspaper reviews by London theatre critics. UK-
England: London. 1986. Lang.: Eng.   2109

Collection of newspaper reviews by London theatre critics. UK-
England: London. 1986. Lang.: Eng.   2110

Collection of newspaper reviews by London theatre critics. UK-
England: London. 1986. Lang.: Eng.   2111

Collection of newspaper reviews by London theatre critics. UK-
England: London. 1986. Lang.: Eng.   2112

Collection of newspaper reviews by London theatre critics. UK-
England: London. 1986. Lang.: Eng.   2113

Staging — cont'd

Collection of newspaper reviews by London theatre critics. UK-England. 1986. Lang.: Eng.　2114

Collection of newspaper reviews by London theatre critics. UK-England. 1986. Lang.: Eng.　2115

Collection of newspaper reviews by London theatre critics. UK-England: London. 1986. Lang.: Eng.　2116

Collection of newspaper reviews by London theatre critics. UK-England: London. 1986. Lang.: Eng.　2117

Collection of newspaper reviews by London theatre critics. UK-England: London. 1986. Lang.: Eng.　2118

Collection of newspaper reviews by London theatre critics. UK-England: London. 1986. Lang.: Eng.　2119

Collection of newspaper reviews by London theatre critics. UK-England. 1986. Lang.: Eng.　2120

Collection of newspaper reviews by London theatre critics. UK-England: London. 1986. Lang.: Eng.　2121

Collection of newspaper reviews by London theatre critics. UK-England: London. 1986. Lang.: Eng.　2122

Collection of newspaper reviews by London theatre critics. UK-England: London. 1986. Lang.: Eng.　2123

Collection of newspaper reviews by London theatre critics. UK-England: London. 1986. Lang.: Eng.　2124

Collection of newspaper reviews by London theatre critics. UK-England: London. 1986. Lang.: Eng.　2125

Collection of newspaper reviews by London theatre critics. UK-England: London. 1986. Lang.: Eng.　2126

Director Mike Alfreds' interpretation of the plays of Čechov. UK-England: London. USSR. 1975-1986. Lang.: Eng.　2127

Doubling of roles in Shakespeare's *Hamlet*. UK-England: London. 1900-1985. Lang.: Eng.　2129

Survey of the season at the National Theatre. UK-England: London. 1986. Lang.: Eng.　2130

Michael Coveney surveys the London season. UK-England: London. 1986. Lang.: Eng.　2135

Impact and influence of the tour by black American actor Ira Aldridge. UK-England: Manchester. 1827. Lang.: Eng.　2136

Director Simon Curtis discusses his production of *Road*. UK-England: London. 1986. Lang.: Eng.　2137

Roger Rees, associate director at Bristol Old Vic discusses his career and the season. UK-England: Bristol. 1970-1986. Lang.: Eng.　2138

Director Simon Callow talks about his production of Jean Cocteau's *The Infernal Machine*. UK-England: London. 1986. Lang.: Eng.　2139

Reviews of three Shakespearean productions. UK-England: London, Stratford. USA: Ashland, OR. 1985. Lang.: Eng.　2140

Controversy surrounding *Presumption, or The Fate of Frankenstein* by Richard Brinsley Peake. UK-England: London. 1818-1840. Lang.: Eng.　2142

Overview of performances transferred from The Royal Court, Greenwich, and Lyric Hammersmith theatres. UK-England: London. 1986. Lang.: Eng.　2143

Director John Dexter and impresario Eddie Kulukundis discuss the formation of the New Theatre Company. UK-England: London. 1986. Lang.: Eng.　2144

Actress Julie McKenzie discusses her role in *Woman in Mind* by Alan Ayckbourn. UK-England: London. Lang.: Eng.　2145

Performance by Joculatores Lancastrienses of Thomas Garter's interlude, *Commody of the Moste Vertuous and Godlye Susanna*. UK-England: Lancaster. 1985. Lang.: Eng.　2148

Comparison of stage production and film version of Shakespeare's *King Lear*, both directed by Peter Brook. UK-England. 1962-1970. Lang.: Eng.　2149

Survey of theatrical performances in the low country. UK-England. 1986. Lang.: Eng.　2150

Royal Shakespeare Company performances at the Barbican Theatre. UK-England: London. 1986. Lang.: Eng.　2152

Reconstruction of a number of Shakespeare plays staged and performed by Herbert Beerbohm Tree. UK-England: London. 1887-1917. Lang.: Eng.　2155

Survey of theatre season in Merseyside. UK-England. 1986. Lang.: Eng.　2157

Playwright Alan Ayckbourn's directing stint at the National Theatre. UK-England: London. 1986. Lang.: Eng.　2158

Jonathan Miller's production of Eugene O'Neill's *Long Day's Journey Into Night*. UK-England: London. 1941-1986. Lang.: Eng.　2159

Director Jonathan Lynn discusses his works performed at the National Theatre. UK-England: London. UK-England: Cambridge. 1986. Lang.: Eng.　2160

Biographical notes on choreographer and director Gillian Lynne. UK-England: London. USA. 1940-1986. Lang.: Eng.　2161

Proposal to include theatre critics in pre-production evaluation of plays. UK-England. USA. Lang.: Eng.　2162

Comparative analysis of productions of *Summer* by Edward Bond. UK-England: London. 1982. Lang.: Eng.　2163

Thomas Garter's *Commody of the Moste Vertuous and Godlye Susana* performed before orignial screen in timberframed gothic hall. UK-England. 1986. Lang.: Eng.　2165

Interview with Pip Broughton of Paines Plough Theatre Company. UK-England. 1980-1986. Lang.: Eng.　2166

Director Lou Stein discusses his policy at the Watford Palace Theatre. UK-England: Watford. 1982-1986. Lang.: Eng.　2167

Survey of performances in England's Northeast. UK-England. 1986. Lang.: Eng.　2173

Overview of the season at the new Swan Theatre. UK-England: Stratford. 1986. Lang.: Eng.　2174

Nuria Espert talks about Federico García Lorca and her production of *The House of Bernarda Alba*. UK-England: London. Spain. Lang.: Eng.　2178

Detailed discussion of four successful Royal Shakespeare Company productions of Shakespeare's minor plays. UK-England: Stratford. 1946-1977. Lang.: Eng.　2182

Shakespearean productions by the National Theatre, Royal Shakespeare Company and Orange Tree Theatre. UK-England: Stratford, London. 1984-1985. Lang.: Eng.　2183

Analysis of predominant mode of staging final scene of *Othello* by William Shakespeare. UK-England: London. USA. 1760-1900. Lang.: Eng.　2184

Survey of the Chichester Festival. UK-England: Chichester. 1986. Lang.: Eng.　2185

Review of Tennessee Williams' *Sweet Bird of Youth* starring Lauren Bacall, directed by Harold Pinter. UK-England: London. 1985. Lang.: Eng.　2186

Chronological study of the work of director Peter Brook. UK-England. France. 1964-1980. Lang.: Eng.　2187

Interview with Borderline Theatre Company artistic director Morag Fullarton. UK-Scotland. 1979-1986. Lang.: Eng.　2190

Career of Anne Downie. UK-Scotland. 1970-1986. Lang.: Eng.　2191

Interview with director David Hayman of the Scottish Theatre Company. UK-Scotland. 1986. Lang.: Eng.　2192

Interview with Jules Cranfield on Focus Theatre Group. UK-Scotland. 1973-1986. Lang.: Eng.　2193

Survey of the year in Scottish theatre. UK-Scotland. 1986. Lang.: Eng.　2194

Interview with director Jurij Liubimov. USA: Washington, DC. USSR: Moscow. 1986. Lang.: Eng.　2196

Profile of theatre companies featured in Festival Latino de Nueva York. USA: New York, NY. 1984. Lang.: Eng.　2197

Review of *As Is*, a play about AIDS by William Hoffman. USA: New York, NY. 1985. Lang.: Eng.　2198

Reviews of *Coastal Disturbances*, by Tina Howe, staged by Carole Rothman. USA: New York, NY. 1986. Lang.: Eng.　2200

Reviews of *Grouch: A Life in Revue*, by Arthur Marx and Robert Fisher, staged by Arthur Marx. USA: New York, NY. 1986. Lang.: Eng.　2201

Reviews of *The Common Pursuit*, by Simon Gray, staged by Simon Gray and Michael McGuire. USA: New York, NY. 1986. Lang.: Eng.　2202

Reviews of *The Colored Museum*, by George C. Wolfe, staged by L. Kenneth Richardson. USA: New York, NY. 1986. Lang.: Eng.　2203

Reviews of *Lily Dale*, by Horton Foote, staged by William Alderson. USA: New York, NY. 1986. Lang.: Eng.　2204

Reviews of *Wild Honey*, by Michael Frayn after Čechov, conceived and staged by Christopher Morahan. USA: New York, NY. 1986. Lang.: Eng.　2205

Staging — cont'd

SUBJECT INDEX

Staging — cont'd

Achievements and problems of the contemporary circus. USSR. 1980-1986. Lang.: Rus.   3400

Interview with Carlo Boso on *commedia dell'arte* reconstruction. UK-England. Italy. 1947-1986. Lang.: Eng.   3415

Importance of records of a provincial masque. England: Shipton. 1600-1650. Lang.: Eng.   3419

Documenting evidence about a court entertainment of Henry VIII. England: Greenwich. 1504-1516. Lang.: Eng.   3420

Classification and description of Quebec pageants. Canada. 1900-1960. Lang.: Fre.   3423

Documents of religious processions and plays. France: Saint-Omer. 1200-1600. Lang.: Eng.   3424

Comparison of Holy Week Processions of Seville with English Mystery plays. Spain: Seville. 1986. Lang.: Eng.   3426

Instances of dramatic action and costume in Holy Week processions. Spain. 1986. Lang.: Eng.   3427

Overview of the Soundworks Festival. Australia. 1986. Lang.: Eng.   3439

Interview with performance artist Mike Mullins. Australia. 1986. Lang.: Eng.   3440

La Soirée des murmures (The Evening of Murmurs), a performance art piece by Le Théâtre Expérimental des Femmes. Canada: Montreal, PQ. 1986. Lang.: Eng.   3443

Interviews with performance artists. Canada: Toronto, ON. USA: New York, NY. 1980-1986. Lang.: Eng.   3444

Interview with performance artist Mona Hatoum. UK-England. 1975-1986. Lang.: Eng.   3452

Interview with performance artist Rose English. UK-England. 1970-1986. Lang.: Eng.   3453

Changes in East Village performance scene. USA: New York, NY. 1975-1985. Lang.: Eng.   3458

A profile of performance artist George Coates. USA: Berkeley, CA. 1986.   3460

Four nightclub entertainers on their particular acts and the atmosphere of the late night clubs and theaters in Harlem. USA: New York, NY, Savannah, GA. 1930-1950. Lang.: Eng.   3470

Description of *The Princess and the Stars* by R. Murray Schafer. Canada: Banff, AB. 1985. Lang.: Eng.   3485

Rehearsal of *Die Dreigroschenoper (The Three Penny Opera)* directed by Giorgio Strehler. France: Paris. 1986. Lang.: Eng. 3486

Melyrepülés (Flying at Low Altitude) by Tamás Cseh and Dénes Csengey. Hungary: Budapest. 1986. Lang.: Hun.   3487

Reviews of three musicals about the 1960s. Hungary. 1985-1986. Lang.: Hun.   3488

Review of rock opera *István a király (King Stephen)* at the National Theatre. Hungary: Budapest. 1985. Lang.: Hun.   3489

Abraham Goldfaden's *Sen O Goldfadenie (Dream About Goldfaden)* directed by Jacob Rotbaum, Teatr Zydowski. Poland: Warsaw. 1984. Lang.: Pol.   3490

Contemporary performance of the traditional *Festa d'Elx*. Spain: Elche. 1370-1985. Lang.: Eng.   3491

Performance by Sequentia of *Ordo Virtutum* by Hildegard of Bingen. USA: Stanford, CA. 1986. Lang.: Eng.   3493

Guide for producing traditional Beijing opera. China: Suzhou. 1574-1646. Lang.: Chi.   3508

Staging during the Ming dynasty. China: Suzhou. 1574-1646. Lang.: Chi.   3509

Influence of Beijing opera performer Mei Lanfang on European acting and staging traditions. China, People's Republic of. USSR. Germany. 1900-1935. Lang.: Eng.   3521

Detailed instructions on the mounting of a musical. 1986. Lang.: Eng.   3598

Elzéar Labelle's operetta *La Conversion d'un pêcheur de la Nouvelle-Écosse (The Conversion of a Nova Scotian Fisherman)* as an example of the move toward public performance. Canada: Quebec, PQ. 1837-1867. Lang.: Eng.   3599

Lakat alá lányokat (Lock Up Your Daughters), a stage adaptation of Henry Fielding's *Rape Upon Rape*, directed by Imre Halasi. Hungary: Diósgyőr. 1986. Lang.: Hun.   3600

Hungarian performance of *My Fair Lady*. Hungary. 1966-1970. Lang.: Hun.   3601

Ivan Vas-Zoltán directs *Vértestvérek (Blood Brothers)* by Willy Russell. Hungary: Pécs. 1986. Lang.: Hun.   3602

Éva Pataki's *Edith és Marlene (Edith and Marlene)* directed by Márta Mészáros, Pest National Theatre. Hungary: Budapest. 1986. Lang.: Hun.   3603

Jézus Krisztus Szupersztar (Jesus Christ Superstar) by Andrew Lloyd Webber and Tim Rice directed by János Szikora (Rock Szinház). Hungary: Szeged. 1986. Lang.: Hun.   3604

Summer productions of *Jézus Krisztus Szupersztár*. Hungary: Szeged, Budapest. 1986. Lang.: Hun.   3605

Three Swedish musical theatre productions. Sweden. 1985-1986. Lang.: Swe.   3606

Adapting and staging of *Les Misérables* by Victor Hugo. UK-England. 1980. Lang.: Eng.   3609

Reviews of musicals. UK-England: London. 1986. Lang.: Eng.   3610

Reviews of *Sweet Charity* by Neil Simon, staged and choreographed by Bob Fosse. USA: New York, NY. 1986. Lang.: Eng.   3611

Reviews of *Honky Tonk Nights*, book and lyrics by Ralph Allen and David Campbell, staged and choreographed by Ernest O. Flatt. USA: New York, NY. 1986. Lang.: Eng.   3612

Reviews of *Smile*, music by Marvin Hamlisch, book by Howard Ashman. USA: New York, NY. 1986. Lang.: Eng.   3613

Reviews of *Raggedy Ann*, book by William Gibon, music and lyrics by Joe Raposo, staged and choreographed by Patricia Birch. USA: New York, NY. 1986. Lang.: Eng.   3614

Reviews of *Into the Light*, book by Jeff Tamborniro, music by Lee Holdridge, lyrics by John Forster, staged by Michael Maurer. USA: New York, NY. 1986. Lang.: Eng.   3615

Reviews of *Oh Coward!*, lyrics and music by Noël Coward, devised and staged by Roderick Cook. USA: New York, NY. 1986. Lang.: Eng.   3616

Reviews of *Rags*, book by Joseph Stein, music by Charles Strouse, lyrics by Stephen Schwartz, staged by Gene Saks. USA: New York, NY. 1986. Lang.: Eng.   3617

Review of *Me and My Girl*, book and lyrics by L. Arthur Rose and Douglas Furber, staged by Mike Ockrent. USA: New York, NY. 1986. Lang.: Eng.   3618

Reviews of *Brigadoon*, by Alan Jay Lerner, Frederick Loewe, staged by Gerald Freedman. USA: New York, NY. 1986. Lang.: Eng.   3619

Choreography in musical theatre. USA: New York, NY. 1944-1981. Lang.: Eng.   3620

Career of Broadway composer Stephen Sondheim. USA: New York, NY. 1930-1986. Lang.: Eng.   3624

History and current state of Australian Opera at the Sydney Opera House. Australia: Sydney, N.S.W. 1973-1986. Lang.: Eng.   3688

Interviews with various artists of the Viennese State Opera. Austria: Vienna. 1909-1986. Lang.: Ger.   3692

Harry Kupfer and his ideas for staging operas. Austria. Germany, East. 1935-1985. Lang.: Ger.   3696

Interview with Jean-Pierre Ponnelle discussing his directing technique and set designs. Austria: Salzburg. 1984. Lang.: Eng.   3699

Performance history of *Die Fledermaus* by Richard Strauss. Austria: Vienna. 1874-1986. Lang.: Eng.   3704

Review of Toronto performances of *Colas and Colinette*. Canada: Toronto, ON, Montreal, PQ. 1986. Lang.: Eng.   3707

Discusses the opera *Winthrop*, by composer Istvan Anhalt. Canada: Toronto, ON. 1949-1985. Lang.: Eng.   3712

Artistic and technological differences in presenting opera for stage and television. Canada. 1960-1980. Lang.: Eng.   3714

Account of the neglected opera *Libuše* by Jan Smetana on the occasion of its New York premiere. Czechoslovakia: Prague. USA: New York, NY. 1883-1986. Lang.: Eng.   3715

Semiology of opera. Europe. 1600-1985. Lang.: Eng, Fre.   3721

Interview with composer and director of the Finnish National opera Ilkka Kuusisto. Finland: Helsinki, Suomussalmi. 1967-1986. Lang.: Eng, Fre.   3724

Profile of Bernard Lefort, former Intendant of the Palais Garnier of Paris. France: Paris. 1960-1985. Lang.: Eng.   3727

Peter Brook's direction and adaptation of the opera *Carmen* by Georges Bizet. France: Paris. 1981-1983. Lang.: Heb.   3731

Psychoanalytic study of staging as language. Germany. 1800-1909. Lang.: Fre.   3734

Collection of interviews with Walter Felsenstein. Germany: Berlin. 1921-1971. Lang.: Ger.   3735

Staging — cont'd

Nazi persecution of conductor Fritz Busch. Germany. USA. 1922-
1949. Lang.: Eng. 3736

Harry Kupfer: his work and career as singer and director. Germany,
East: Dresden, Berlin, East. 1970-1985. Lang.: Ger. 3738

Interview with director Harry Kupfer of Komische Oper. Germany,
East: Berlin, East. 1981-1986. Lang.: Hun. 3739

Interview with Wolfgang Wagner on his staging of 3 Wagnerian
operas at the Bayreuth Festspiele. Germany, West: Bayreuth. 1975-
1985. Lang.: Hun. 3740

Critical essays, studies and recording reviews of opera performances.
Hungary. 1982-1985. Lang.: Hun. 3742

Puccini's opera *Manon Lescaut* at the Hungarian State Opera House.
Hungary: Budapest. 1985. Lang.: Hun. 3743

Review of repertory season at the Hungarian State Opera House.
Hungary: Budapest. 1985-1986. Lang.: Hun. 3744

András Mikó directs Strauss' *Der Rosenkavalier* at the Hungarian
State Opera House. Hungary: Budapest. 1985. Lang.: Hun. 3745

András Fehér directs Verdi's *Un ballo in maschera* at the Hungarian
State Opera House. Hungary: Budapest. 1986. Lang.: Hun. 3746

Verdi's *Simon Boccanegra* and Puccini's *La Bohème* at the
Hungarian State Opera House and Erkel Theatre. Hungary:
Budapest. 1986. Lang.: Hun. 3747

Géza Oberfrank directs Bizet's *Carmen* at Szegedi Nemzeti Szinház.
Hungary: Szeged. 1985. Lang.: Hun. 3748

László Kertész directs Rossini's *L'occasione fa il ladro* at
Népszinház. Hungary: Budapest. 1986. Lang.: Hun. 3749

József Bor directs Verdi's opera *Il Trovatore* at Kisfaludy Theatre.
Hungary: Győr. 1985. Lang.: Hun. 3750

Zoltán Horváth directs Donizetti's *Don Pasquale* at the Pécsi
Nemzeti Szinház. Hungary: Pécs. 1985. Lang.: Hun. 3751

Hungarian translation of *L'Opera nel Settecento* by Giorgio Lise.
Hungary: Budapest. 1700-1800. Lang.: Hun. 3752

Gyula Kertész directs Puccini's *Tosca* at the Csokonai Theatre.
Hungary: Debrecen. 1985. Lang.: Hun. 3754

The Franco Zeffirelli film of *Otello* by Giuseppe Verdi, an account
of the production. Italy: Rome. 1985-1986. Lang.: Eng. 3758

Productions of operas at La Scala by Luca Ronconi. Italy: Milan.
1985. Lang.: Ita. 3763

Report on the North American opera season. North America. 1985-
1986. Lang.: Eng. 3769

Andrzej Straszyński directs Donizetti's *Lucia di Lammermoor*, Teatr
Wielki. Poland: Warsaw. 1984. Lang.: Pol. 3770

Mussorgskij's opera *Boris Godunov* at the Mariinskij Theatre. Russia:
St. Petersburg. 1874. Lang.: Eng. 3775

Premiere of *Der magische Kreis (The Magic Circle)*, an opera by
Gion Derungs and Lothar Deplazes. Switzerland: Chur. 1986. Lang.:
Ger. 3780

Claudio Monteverdi's *L'incoronazione di Poppea (The Coronation of
Poppea)* directed by Jonathan Hale at the Kent Opera. UK-England:
Kent. 1986. Lang.: Eng. 3781

Christopher Renshaw talks about his production of Benjamin
Britten's opera *A Midsummer Night's Dream* at Covent Garden. UK-
England: London. 1986. Lang.: Eng. 3782

The Metropolitan Opera Guild Teacher Workshop demonstrates its
techniques for London teachers. UK-England: London. 1986. Lang.:
Eng. 3786

Andrei Serban discusses his production of Beethoven's *Fidelio*. UK-
England: London. 1986. Lang.: Eng. 3787

Interview with Peter Stein about his production of Verdi's *Otello*.
UK-Wales: Cardiff. 1986. Lang.: Eng. 3789

Stills from telecast performances of *Elektra*. List of principals,
conductor and production staff included. USA: New York, NY.
1986. Lang.: Eng. 3790

Stills from telecast performance of *Goya*. List of principals, conductor
and production staff included. USA: Washington, DC. 1986. Lang.:
Eng. 3791

Photographs, cast list, synopsis, and discography of Metropolitan
Opera radio broadcast performances. USA: New York, NY. 1986.
Lang.: Eng. 3794

Stills from telecast performances. List of principals, conductor and
production staff included. USA: New York, NY. 1986. Lang.: Eng.
3795

Stills from telecast performance of *Candide* by New York City
Opera. USA: New York, NY. 1986. Lang.: Eng. 3796

Photographs, cast list, synopsis, and discography of Metropolitan
Opera radio broadcast performances. USA: New York, NY. 1986.
Lang.: Eng. 3797

Review of Prokofièv's *Love for Three Oranges*. USA: Cincinnati,
OH. 1986. Lang.: Eng. 3798

Reviews of *Death in the Family*, *Viaggio a Reims*, *Abduction from
the Seraglio* and *Tales of Hoffmann*. USA: St. Louis, MO. 1975-
1986. Lang.: Eng. 3799

History of *Opera News* in its fiftieth year. USA: New York, NY.
1936-1986. Lang.: Eng. 3802

Opera director Nathaniel Merrill on his productions. USA: New
York, NY. 1958-1986. Lang.: Eng. 3805

Collaboration of Italian composer Rafaello de Banfield and
American playwright Tennessee Williams on the opera *Lord Byron's
Love Letter*. USA: Charleston, SC. 1986. Lang.: Eng. 3810

Review of Robert Downard's opera *Martin Audéich: A Christmas
Miracle*. USA: Denver, CO. 1985. Lang.: Eng. 3813

The operations of the Hawaii Opera Theatre. USA: Honolulu, HI.
1950-1985. Lang.: Eng. 3814

Peter Sellars' production of Mozart's *Così fan tutte*. USA: Purchase,
NY. 1986. Lang.: Eng. 3815

Controversy over Jonathan Miller's production of *Rigoletto*. USA.
1984. Lang.: Eng. 3821

Review of the world premiere of the opera *Three Sisters*. USA:
Columbus, OH. 1968-1986. Lang.: Eng. 3822

Directors revitalizing opera. USA: New York, NY. 1970-1986. Lang.:
Eng. 3826

The videotaped opera showings at the Museum of Broadcasting.
USA: New York, NY. 1985-1986. Lang.: Eng. 3828

Samson, by George Frideric Handel is staged at the Metropolitan
Opera. USA: New York, NY. 1986. Lang.: Eng. 3831

Collaboration of Peter Hemmings and Götz Friedrich in Los
Angeles' opera season. USA: Los Angeles, CA. 1985. Lang.: Eng.
3836

New designs for the Seattle Opera production of *Der Ring des
Nibelungen* by Richard Wagner. USA: Seattle, WA. 1986. Lang.:
Eng. 3837

Review of premiere performance of Myron Fink's opera *Chinchilla*.
USA: Binghamton, NY. 1986. Lang.: Eng. 3840

Problems in the performance and production of opera in Soviet
theatres. USSR. 1980-1986. Lang.: Rus. 3844

Condition of operatic art in USSR: repertoire, acting, staging. USSR.
1980-1986. Lang.: Rus. 3845

The staging of G. Kančeli's opera *Muzyka dlja živych (Music for the
Living)* at the Z. Paliašvili theater. USSR: Tbilisi. 1980-1986. Lang.:
Rus. 3848

Review of opera season and discussion of problems. USSR:
Leningrad. 1985-1986. Lang.: Rus. 3850

Mágnás Miska (Miska the Magnate) by Albert Szirmai directed by
László Bagossy. Hungary: Pécs. 1986. Lang.: Hun. 3942

Jan Wolkowski directs an adaptation of a folk legend about Jedrzej
Wowrze. Poland: Szczecin. 1983. Lang.: Pol. 3968

Peter Schumann and his work with the Bread and Puppet Theatre.
USA: New York, NY. 1968-1986. Lang.: Eng. 3973

Festival of puppet theatre. USSR-Russian SFSR. 1986. Lang.: Rus.
3987

Development of *Anerca* by Figures of Speech Theater. USA:
Freeport, ME. 1985. Lang.: Eng. 3999

Puppet production of Mozart's opera *Die Zauberflöte*. USA. 1986.
Lang.: Eng. 4008

Plays/librettos/scripts

Revisionist view of twentieth-century Québec theatre based on
published works. Canada. 1900-1980. Lang.: Fre. 926

Development of the title character of *The Ecstasy of Rita Joe* by
George Ryga, seen in successive drafts. Canada: Vancouver, BC.
1966-1982. Lang.: Eng. 929

Envy in Shakespeare's *Othello* and Peter Shaffer's *Amadeus*. Canada:
Montreal, PQ. Europe. 1604-1986. Lang.: Eng. 932

Review essay on *Li jus de Robin et Marion (The Play of Robin and
Marion)* directed by Jean Asselin. Canada: Montreal, PQ. 1986.
Lang.: Fre. 937

Staging — cont'd

SUBJECT INDEX

Stanislavskij, Konstantin Sergejèvič — cont'd

Theatricality on and off-stage. Lang.: Eng. 649

Directorial process as seen through major productions of Stanislavskij, Brecht, Kazan and Brook. 1898-1964. Lang.: Eng. 650

Theory, practice and body-training for the beginning actor. Korea: Seoul. Lang.: Kor. 758

Physical nature of acting. USA. 1986. Lang.: Eng. 825

Interview with producer, director, actor Robert Lewis. USA: New York, NY. 1930-1986. Lang.: Eng. 844

Biography of K.S. Stanislavskij. USSR. 1863-1938. Lang.: Rus. 897

Notebooks of Konstantin Stanislavskij. USSR. 1888-1938. Lang.: Rus. 901

Historical development of acting and directing techniques. 1898-1986. Lang.: Eng. 1632

Last lecture of director Zhu Duanjun. 1890-1978. Lang.: Chi. 1635

Objectives and action in staging of director Wang Xiaoping. China: Shanghai. 1900-1982. Lang.: Chi. 1689

On the goal of acting. China, People's Republic of. 1978-1982. Lang.: Chi. 1693

Documentation on Stanislavskij's productions of Čechov plays. Russia. 1901-1904. Lang.: Ita. 2070

Discussion of basic theatrical issues during Stanislavskij symposium. Sweden: Stockholm. 1986. Lang.: Swe. 2086

Discussion of Stanislavskij's influence by a number of artists. Sweden. 1890-1986. Lang.: Swe. 2094

Modern and traditional performance styles compared. China. 1598-1984. Lang.: Chi. 3511

What spoken drama actors can learn from Sung drama. China. 1100-1980. Lang.: Chi. 3513

Influence of Beijing opera performer Mei Lanfang on European acting and staging traditions. China, People's Republic of. USSR. Germany. 1900-1935. Lang.: Eng. 3521

Plays/librettos/scripts

Great dramatic works considered in light of modern theatre and social reponsibility. France. Italy. Germany, West. 1700-1964. Lang.: Fre. 2560

Stanislavskij's method for the role of Othello. USSR. 1929-1930. Lang.: Swe. 2968

Relation to other fields

Curricular authority for drama-in-education program. UK. Lang.: Eng. 3054

Theory/criticism

Live theatre gives the spectator a choice of focus. 1600-1986. Lang.: Eng. 1190

Excerpts from writings of critics and theatre professionals on theory of theatre. Europe. 1880-1985. Lang.: Ita. 1204

Stanislavskij's aesthetic criteria. Russia. 1863-1938. Lang.: Rus. 1218

Stanislavskij in Russian and Soviet criticism. USSR: Russia. 1888-1986. Lang.: Rus. 1242

Selection from Peter Brook's *The Empty Space*. EUROPE. 1929-1982. Lang.: Chi. 3095

Aesthetic theory of interpretation. Europe. North America. 1900-1985. Lang.: Fre. 3097

Selections from Jerzy Grotowski's *Towards a Poor Theatre*. Poland. 1933-1982. Lang.: Chi. 3126

Training

Stanislavskij system in Romanian theatre. USSR. Romania. 1980-1986. Lang.: Rus. 1264

Discussion of archival material relating to translation and U.S. publication of books by Stanislavskij. USA. USSR. 1928-1986. Lang.: Eng. 3160

Effect of changing ideas about psychology and creativity on the Stanislavskij system. USSR: Moscow. 1900-1986. Lang.: Eng. 3162

Interview with director and teacher Zinovy Korogodskij. USSR: Moscow, Leningrad. 1970-1984. Lang.: Eng. 3163

Stanton, Dakota

Performance/production

Dakota Stanton discusses her career as a singer and dancer in nightclubs and reviews. USA: Pittsburgh, PA, New York, NY. 1950-1980. Lang.: Eng. 3471

Staple of Newes, The

Plays/librettos/scripts

Use of group aggression in Ben Jonson's comedies. England. 1575-1600. Lang.: Eng. 2508

Staret Directors Company (New York, NY)

Training

Lack of opportunities, programs and training for beginning directors. USA: New York, NY. 1985. Lang.: Eng. 1260

Staruska

SEE

Latino, Staruska.

Stary Teatr (Cracow)

Performance/production

Adaptation of Dostojèvskij's *Prestuplenijè i nakazanijè (Crime and Punishment)* directed by Andrzej Wajda at Teatr Stary under the title *Zdrodnia i Kara*. Poland: Cracow. 1984. Lang.: Pol. 2032

Andrzej Wajda directs Sophocles' *Antigone*, Stary Teatr. Poland: Cracow. 1984. Lang.: Pol. 2058

State Puppet Theatre (Budapest)

SEE

Állami Bábszínház.

State Puppet Theatre (Moscow)

SEE

Gosudarstvènnyj Centralnyj Teat'r Kukol.

State Theatre Institute (Moscow)

SEE

Gosudarstvènnyj Institut Teatralnovo Iskusstva.

Statistics

Administration

Statistics of income and expenses of New York Off and Off-off Broadway nonprofit theatres. USA: New York, NY. 1980-1983. Lang.: Eng. 167

Performance/production

Report on the North American opera season. North America. 1985-1986. Lang.: Eng. 3769

Relation to other fields

Statistical index of theatre attendance in the regional and provincial centers of the USSR-Russian SFSR. USSR. 1985. Lang.: Rus. 1175

Statistics, audience

Audience

Conference on low theatrical attendance. USSR: Kujbyšev. 1980-1986. 207

Reference materials

Overview of French-language productions. Canada: Montreal, PQ. 1958-1968. Lang.: Eng. 2984

Statue of Liberty (New York, NY)

Design/technology

Howard Brandston's approach to lighting the Statue of Liberty. USA: New York, NY. 1986. Lang.: Eng. 3317

Details of the lighting arrangements for the four-day Statue of Liberty centennial celebration. USA: New York, NY. 1986. Lang.: Eng. 3318

Stavis, Barrie

Plays/librettos/scripts

Survey of the achievements of American theatre of the 1960s. USA. 1960-1979. Lang.: Eng. 987

Stavisky, Sacha

Performance/production

Polemic surrounding Sacha Stavisky's production of Shakespeare's *Coriolanus* at the Comédie-Française. France: Paris. 1934. Lang.: Eng, Fre. 1742

Steckel, Leonard

Performance/production

Photographic record of forty years of the Berliner Ensemble. Germany, East: Berlin, East. 1949-1984. Lang.: Eng. 1761

Stedman, Edmund C.

Performance/production

Career of actor Lawrence Barrett. USA: New York, NY. 1871-1909. Lang.: Eng. 2261

Stefenson, Lena

Performance/production

Emblems of the 1980s in Swedish theatre. Sweden. 1980-1986. Lang.: Swe. 796

Stein, Gertrude

Basic theatrical documents

Correspondence between Gertrude Stein and Virgil Thomson regarding their collaboration on *The Mother of Us All*. France. USA. 1926-1946. Lang.: Eng. 222

Stein, Joseph

Performance/production

Reviews of *Rags*, book by Joseph Stein, music by Charles Strouse, lyrics by Stephen Schwartz, staged by Gene Saks. USA: New York, NY. 1986. Lang.: Eng. 3617

Stoppard, Tom — cont'd

Relation to other fields
Influence of Marcel Duchamp's work on Tom Stoppard's radio play, *Artist Descending a Staircase*. UK-England. 1913-1972. Lang.: Eng.
3059

Storia, La

Theory/criticism
Semiotic analysis of *La Storia*. Italy. 1985. Lang.: Eng.   3118

Storia, La (I & II)

Plays/librettos/scripts
La Storia and *La Storia II* performed in Italian and English by the Acting Company. Canada: Toronto, ON. 1984-1985. Lang.: Eng.
2424

Stormare, Peter

Performance/production
Survey of summer theatre offerings. Sweden: Stockholm, Södertälje, Karlskrona. 1986. Lang.: Swe.   2089

Storr, Sue

Performance/production
Interview with Pip Broughton of Paines Plough Theatre Company. UK-England. 1980-1986. Lang.: Eng.   2166

Story of Oxala, The

Theory/criticism
Analysis of Wole Soyinka's major critical essays. Nigeria. 1960-1980. Lang.: Eng.   3124

Story of the Eye and the Tooth, The

Performance/production
Collection of newspaper reviews by London theatre critics. UK-England: London. 1986. Lang.: Eng.   2109

Story-telling

Performance/production
Dramatic techniques in traditional Xhosa storytelling. South Africa, Republic of. 1800-1985. Lang.: Eng.   788

Narrator in *Katari* story-telling tradition. Japan. 1960-1983. Lang.: Eng.   1366

Relation to other fields
Theatrical conventions in religious story-telling. Asia. 700-1200. Lang.: Eng.   1061

Folklorist Tekla Dömötör includes traditional material in her popular work. Hungary. 1986. Lang.: Hun.   1098

Enthnography of a Hungarian village. Hungary: Zsámbok. 1930-1985. Lang.: Hun.   1099

Stowe Brothers Circus (USA)

Performance/production
Detailed history of the Stowe Brothers (family) Circus. USA. 1850-1920. Lang.: Eng.   3396

Strachan, Alan

Performance/production
Collection of newspaper reviews by London theatre critics. UK-England: London. 1986. Lang.: Eng.   2118

Strand Lighting

SEE
Rank Strand Ltd. Lighting.

Strand Lighting (Rancho Dominguez, CA)

Design/technology
Examination of the latest Strand TV lighting console in Studio A at BBC Scotland. UK-Scotland: Glasgow. 1980-1986. Lang.: Eng.   3256

Strand Theatre (Shreveport, LA)

Performance spaces
History of the Strand theatre. USA: Shreveport, LA. 1925-1986. Lang.: Eng.   3219

Strandmark, Katarina

Institutions
Recent outdoor productions of Gamla Stans Teater. Sweden: Stockholm. 1933-1986. Lang.: Swe.   524

Strange Interlude

Plays/librettos/scripts
Repetition and negativism in plays of Jean Anouilh and Eugene O'Neill. France. USA. 1922-1960. Lang.: Eng.   2578

Strasberg, Lee

Administration
Cheryl Crawford's producing career discussed in light of her latest Broadway show. USA: New York, NY, Atlanta, GA. 1936-1986. Lang.: Eng.   117

Performance/production
Interview with producer, director, actor Robert Lewis. USA: New York, NY. 1930-1986. Lang.: Eng.   844

Theory/criticism
Aesthetic theory of interpretation. Europe. North America. 1900-1985. Lang.: Fre.   3097

Straszyński, Andrzej

Performance/production
Andrzej Straszyński directs Donizetti's *Lucia di Lammermoor*, Teatr Wielki. Poland: Warsaw. 1984. Lang.: Pol.   3770

Stratford Festival (Stratford, ON)

Administration
John Hirsch's final season as artistic director of the Stratford Festival. Canada: Stratford, ON. 1985. Lang.: Eng.   1431

Basic theatrical documents
Videotape of Shakespeare's *As You Like It* with study guide and edition of the play. Canada: Stratford, ON. 1983. Lang.: Eng.   219

Design/technology
Profile of theatre designer Tanya Moiseiwitsch. 1934-1986. Lang.: Eng.   227

Institutions
Artistic director John Neville discusses future plans for the Stratford Festival. Canada: Stratford, ON. 1985. Lang.: Eng.   1551

History of music performances, mainly opera, at the Stratford Festival. Canada: Stratford, ON. 1951-1985. Lang.: Eng.   3671

Performance/production
Production analysis of *The Merchant of Venice* directed by Mark Lamos. Canada: Stratford, ON. 1984. Lang.: Eng.   667

John Neville's productions of *The Winter's Tale*, *Pericles*, and *Cymbeline*. Canada: Stratford, ON. 1974-1986. Lang.: Eng.   1657

Interview with actor Stephen Ouimette. Canada. 1960-1986. Lang.: Eng.   1663

Stratford Festival dramaturg discusses workshop trend. Canada: Stratford, ON. 1986. Lang.: Eng.   1665

Robin Phillips' staging of Shakespeare's *Richard III*. Canada: Stratford, ON. 1977. Lang.: Eng.   1668

John Hirsch's artistic career at the Stratford Festival Theatre. Canada: Stratford, ON. 1981-1985. Lang.: Eng.   1683

Strathcona Theatre Company (UK)

Relation to other fields
The work of disabled theatre companies in England. UK-England. 1979-1986. Lang.: Eng.   1139

Strauss, Johann

Performance spaces
Plans for using the Ronacher theatre after its renovation. Austria: Vienna. 1871-1986. Lang.: Ger.   584

Strauss, Richard

Performance/production
The love-music of *Der Rosenkavalier* by Richard Strauss. Austria: Vienna. 1911-1986. Lang.: Eng.   3703

Performance history of *Die Fledermaus* by Richard Strauss. Austria: Vienna. 1874-1986. Lang.: Eng.   3704

Harry Kupfer: his work and career as singer and director. Germany, East: Dresden, Berlin, East. 1970-1985. Lang.: Ger.   3738

András Mikó directs Strauss' *Der Rosenkavalier* at the Hungarian State Opera House. Hungary: Budapest. 1985. Lang.: Hun.   3745

Stills from telecast performances of *Elektra*. List of principals, conductor and production staff included. USA: New York, NY. 1986. Lang.: Eng.   3790

Reviews of 10 vintage recordings of complete operas on LP. USA. 1906-1925. Lang.: Eng.   3792

Photographs, cast list, synopsis, and discography of Metropolitan Opera radio broadcast performances. USA: New York, NY. 1986. Lang.: Eng.   3794

Stills from telecast performances. List of principals, conductor and production staff included. USA: New York, NY. 1986. Lang.: Eng.   3795

Profile of and interview with American conductor Jeffrey Tate, concerning his approach to *Die Fledermaus* by Richard Strauss. USA: New York, NY. 1940-1946. Lang.: Eng.   3827

Stravinsky, Igor

Reference materials
The purchase and eventual exhibition of a collection of Stravinsky's work. Switzerland: Basel. USA: New York, NY. 1930-1985. Lang.: Eng.   3500

Stravinsky, Theodore
Reference materials
The purchase and eventual exhibition of a collection of Stravinsky's work. Switzerland: Basel. USA: New York, NY. 1930-1985. Lang.: Eng.   3500

Streamers
Performance/production
Review of the Steppenwolf Theatre Company's production of *Streamers* by David Rabe. USA: Washington, DC. 1985. Lang.: Eng.   2297

Street Sounds
Plays/librettos/scripts
Race in prison dramas of Piñero, Camillo, Elder and Bullins. USA. 1970-1986. Lang.: Eng.   2912

Street theatre
Performance/production
Career of director/choreographer Mike Malone. USA: Washington, DC, Cleveland, OH. 1968-1985. Lang.: Eng.   2275

Resurgence of street theatre productions and companies. USA: New York, NY. 1960-1982. Lang.: Eng.   2285

Distinctive style of Canadian clowns. Canada: Toronto, ON, Vancouver, BC. 1967-1986. Lang.: Eng.   3328

Street theatre at Expo 86. Canada: Vancouver, BC. 1986. Lang.: Eng.   3330

Description of street theatre festival. Poland: Jelenia Góra. 1985. Lang.: Eng, Fre.   3344

Peter Schumann and his work with the Bread and Puppet Theatre. USA: New York, NY. 1968-1986. Lang.: Eng.   3973

Plays/librettos/scripts
Identifies dramatic elements unique to street theatre. USA. 1968-1986. Lang.: Eng.   3354

Theory/criticism
Theory and origin of traditional street plays. Korea: Seoul. 200 B.C.-1986 A.D. Lang.: Kor.   3122

Streetcar Named Desire, A
Performance/production
Directorial process as seen through major productions of Stanislavskij, Brecht, Kazan and Brook. 1898-1964. Lang.: Eng.   650

History of Hungarian productions and interpretations of *Death of a Salesman (Az ügynök halála)* by Arthur Miller and *A Streetcar Named Desire (A vágy villamos)* by Tennessee Williams. Hungary. 1959-1983. Lang.: Hun.   1857

Plays/librettos/scripts
Authority and victimization in *A Streetcar Named Desire* by Tennessee Williams. USA. 1960-1980. Lang.: Eng.   2947

Strehler, Giorgio
Performance/production
Productions of plays by Luigi Pirandello after World War II. Italy. 1947-1985. Lang.: Ita.   1987

Overview of productions in Italy. Italy: Milan. 1986. Lang.: Eng.   1994

Collection of newspaper reviews by London theatre critics. UK-England: London. 1986. Lang.: Eng.   2126

Rehearsal of *Die Dreigroschenoper (The Three Penny Opera)* directed by Giorgio Strehler. France: Paris. 1986. Lang.: Eng.   3486

Plays/librettos/scripts
Great dramatic works considered in light of modern theatre and social reponsibility. France. Italy. Germany, West. 1700-1964. Lang.: Fre.   2560

Stretch of the Imagination, A
Plays/librettos/scripts
Individualism and male-female relationships as themes in Australian drama. Australia. 1940-1980. Lang.: Eng.   2373

Stricker, Toni
Institutions
Concept and functions of Schlossspiele Kobersdorf. Austria: Burgenland. 1983-1986. Lang.: Ger.   458

Strike While the Iron is Hot
Performance/production
Brechtian technique in the contemporary feminist drama of Caryl Churchill, Claire Luckham and others. UK-England. 1956-1979. Lang.: Eng.   815

Striking Silence
Performance/production
Collection of newspaper reviews by London theatre critics. UK-England: London. 1986. Lang.: Eng.   2110

Strindberg, August
Audience
Analysis of *Dödsdansen (The Dance of Death)*. Sweden. 1900. Lang.: Eng.   1452

Performance/production
Survey of summer theatre offerings. Sweden: Stockholm, Södertälje, Karlskrona. 1986. Lang.: Swe.   2089

Reviews of three productions of *Fröken Julie (Miss Julie)* by August Strindberg. Sweden: Stockholm. Denmark: Copenhagen. South Africa, Republic of. 1985-1986. Lang.: Swe.   2090

The staging of an amateur performance of *Leka med elden (Playing With Fire)*. Sweden: Hedemora. 1985-1986. Lang.: Swe.   2091

Interview with actress Agneta Ekmanner. Sweden: Stockholm. 1950-1986. Lang.: Swe.   2092

August Strindberg's theoretical writings. Sweden. 1887-1910. Lang.: Ita.   2093

Plays/librettos/scripts
Study of realism vs metadrama. Europe. 429 B.C.-1978 A.D. Lang.: Eng.   2540

The presentation of atheism in August Strindberg's *The Father*. Sweden. 1887. Lang.: Eng.   2821

Biblical and Swedenborgian influences on the development of August Strindberg's chamber play *Påsk (Easter)*. Sweden. 1900. Lang.: Eng.   2827

Scandinavian drama on Canadian radio. Canada. Scandinavia. 1939-1982. Lang.: Eng.   3182

Theory/criticism
Semiotic analysis of audience involvement in *Fröken Julie (Miss Julie)* by August Strindberg. Sweden. 1889-1986. Lang.: Ita.   3133

Strittmatter, Erwin
Performance/production
Photographic record of forty years of the Berliner Ensemble. Germany, East: Berlin, East. 1949-1984. Lang.: Eng.   1761

Strouse, Charles
Performance/production
Reviews of *Rags*, book by Joseph Stein, music by Charles Strouse, lyrics by Stephen Schwartz, staged by Gene Saks. USA: New York, NY. 1986. Lang.: Eng.   3617

Structuralism
Plays/librettos/scripts
Study of realism vs metadrama. Europe. 429 B.C.-1978 A.D. Lang.: Eng.   2540

Structuralist analysis of Georg Büchner's *Leonce und Lena*. Germany. 1836. Lang.: Eng.   2604

Analysis of the plays of William Vaughn Moody. USA. 1869-1910. Lang.: Eng.   2917

Structure
SEE
Dramatic structure.

Strut: On Demand
Institutions
Overview of the productions and goals of Catalyst Theatre. Canada: Edmonton, AB. 1977-1983. Lang.: Eng.   464

Stuart theatre
Plays/librettos/scripts
Image of poverty in Elizabethan and Stuart plays. England. 1558-1642. Lang.: Eng.   2482

Stúdió K (Budapest)
Performance/production
Production analysis of a montage of sketches about Electra by Stúdió K. Hungary: Budapest. 1986. Lang.: Hun.   1773

Studioteatern (Malmö)
Performance/production
Interview with judge and amateur actor Bo Severin. Sweden: Malmö. 1985-1986. Lang.: Swe.   802

Sturm und Drang
SEE ALSO
Geographical-Chronological Index under Germany 1767-1787.

Plays/librettos/scripts
Analysis of *Die Zwillinge (The Twins)* by Friedrich Maximilian Klinger and the dilemma of the *Sturm und Drang* movement. Germany. 1775. Lang.: Ger.   2609

Theory/criticism
Concept of *Standpunkt* in J.M.R. Lenz's poetics and the search for identity in the 'Sturm und Drang' period. Germany. 1774. Lang.: Eng.   1209

Sturm und Drang — cont'd

Analysis of Friedrich Schiller's dramatic and theoretical works.
Germany. 1759-1805. Lang.: Cat.   3109

Sturua, Robert
Performance/production
Robert Sturua of Georgian Academic Theatre directs Brecht and
Shakespeare in Warsaw. USSR: Tbilisi. Poland: Warsaw. 1983.
Lang.: Pol.   2336

The staging of G. Kančeli's opera *Muzyka dlja živych (Music for the
Living)* at the Z. Paliašvili theater. USSR: Tbilisi. 1980-1986. Lang.:
Rus.   3848

Stwosz, Wit
Plays/librettos/scripts
Tadeusz Kantor comments on his play *Niech szezna artyszi (Let the
Artists Die)*. Poland. 1985. Lang.: Eng, Fre.   2751

Styles and Functions of Theatre for Youth in Asia (Manila)
Institutions
Reports on theatre conferences and festivals in Asia. Philippines:
Manila. Malaysia: Kuala Lumpur. Japan: Toga. India: Calcutta.
1981-1984. Lang.: Eng.   510

Su, Kuojung
Plays/librettos/scripts
Problems of adapting classic plays. China, People's Republic of.
1986. Lang.: Chi.   3543

Subject
SEE
Plot/subject/theme.

Subjects of Some Italian Comedies
SEE
Sujets de plusieurs comédies italiennes.

Subsidies
SEE
Funding, government.

Suchet, David
Performance/production
Actors Ben Kingsley and David Suchet discuss their roles in
Shakespeare's *Othello*. UK-England. 1986. Lang.: Eng.   2128

Sue, Chin
Performance/production
Chinese theatre companies on the Goldfields of Victoria. Australia.
1858-1870. Lang.: Eng.   1641

Sueño de la razón, El (Sleep of Reason, The)
Plays/librettos/scripts
Self-reflexivity in Antonio Buero Vallejo's play *El Sueño de la razón
(The Sleep of Reason)* and Victor Erice's film *El Espíritu de la
colmena (The Spirit of the Beehive)*. Spain. 1970-1973. Lang.: Eng.
                                                                     2781

Suicide in B-flat
Plays/librettos/scripts
Director George Ferencz and jazz musician Max Roach collaborate
on music in trio of Sam Shepard plays. USA: New York, NY. 1984.
Lang.: Eng.   2952

Sujets de plusieurs comédies italiennes (Subjects of Some Italian Comedies)
Reference materials
Current state of research on the manuscript *Sujets de plusieurs
comédies italiennes (Subjects of Some Italian Comedies)*. France.
Italy. 1670-1740. Lang.: Fre.   2988

Sullivan, Arthur
Basic theatrical documents
Text of plays by James Robinson Planché, with introduction on his
influence. UK-England. 1818-1872. Lang.: Eng.   226

Sullivan, Dan
Administration
Seattle Repertory's artistic director discusses producing musicals.
USA: Seattle, WA. Lang.: Eng.   3574

Sullivan, Gary
Design/technology
Designers discuss regional productions of *Oklahoma*. USA. 1984-
1986. Lang.: Eng.   3596

Sullivan, Thomas
Performance/production
Description of first stage adaptation of Robert Louis Stevenson's *Dr.
Jekyll and Mr. Hyde*. USA: New York, NY. USA: Boston, MA.
1886-1888. Lang.: Eng.   2298

Sumarokov, Aleksand'r
Performance/production
Dance-pantomime dramas based on the plots of plays by Aleksand'r
Sumarokov. Russia. 1717-1777. Lang.: Rus.   1367

Summer and Smoke
Performance/production
Profile of and interview with Lee Hoiby, American composer of *The
Tempest* with libretto by Mark Schulgasser. USA: Long Eddy, NJ.
1926-1986. Lang.: Eng.   3832

Summer Folk
SEE
Dačniki.

Summer of the Seventeenth Doll
Plays/librettos/scripts
Individualism and male-female relationships as themes in Australian
drama. Australia. 1940-1980. Lang.: Eng.   2373

Analysis of Ray Lawler's *Summer of the Seventeenth Doll* in the
context of his later plays. Australia. 1955-1977. Lang.: Eng.   2377

Impact of Ray Lawler's *Summer of the Seventeenth Doll* on
Australian theatre. Australia. 1959-1983. Lang.: Eng.   2381

Summer theatre
Institutions
The first decade of White Rock Summer Theatre in British
Columbia. Canada: White Rock, BC. 1976-1985. Lang.: Eng.   1560

Performance spaces
Summer theatre on a restored cruise ship. Canada. 1982-1986. Lang.:
Eng.   1614

Sumurun
Performance/production
Max Reinhardt's music-drama *Sumurun*. USA: New York, NY.
1912. Lang.: Ita.   1369

Sun, Chentai
Research/historiography
Analysis of three ancient types of dance-drama. China. 1032-1420.
Lang.: Chi.   3551

Sun, Kai
Plays/librettos/scripts
Profiles of Yuan dynasty playwrights. China. 1256-1341. Lang.: Chi.
                                                                     2445

Sung opera
Performance/production
What spoken drama actors can learn from Sung drama. China.
1100-1980. Lang.: Chi.   3513

Sunset
SEE
Zakat.

Suomen Harrastajateatterilitto (Amateur Theatre Union of Finland)
Performance/production
History of amateur theatre in Finland. Finland. 1920-1986. Lang.:
Swe.   706

Suomen Kansallisoopera (Helsinki)
Performance/production
Interview with composer and director of the Finnish National opera
Ilkka Kuusisto. Finland: Helsinki, Suomussalmi. 1967-1986. Lang.:
Eng, Fre.   3724

Suomen Kansallisteatteri (Helsinki)
Performance/production
Career of actor Jalmari Rinne. Finland: Helsinki, Tampere, Turku.
1893-1985. Lang.: Eng, Fre.   1719

Support areas
Design/technology
Theatre workshops of the Budapest Central Scene Shop Project.
Hungary: Budapest. 1953-1986. Lang.: Hun.   290

Description of plans for new central theatre scene shops and storage
areas. Hungary: Budapest. 1980. Lang.: Hun.   292

Report on new heating, plumbing and air-conditioning at
reconstructed Szeged National Theatre. Hungary: Szeged. 1978-1986.
Lang.: Hun.   293

Description of planned renovation for scene shop and production
building. Hungary: Budapest. 1984. Lang.: Hun.   295

Sale of textile shops permitted rebuilding and renovation of scene
shops. Hungary: Budapest. 1986. Lang.: Hun.   296

Performance spaces
Semper Depot and its history. Austria: Vienna. 1872-1986. Lang.:
Ger.   583

Overview of pub theatres. UK-England: London. 1980-1987. Lang.:
Eng.   626

Guide to locating and designing performance spaces for non-
traditional theatre. USA: New York, NY. 1979. Lang.: Eng.   636

Sweet Bird of Youth
Performance/production
Review of Tennessee Williams' *Sweet Bird of Youth* starring Lauren Bacall, directed by Harold Pinter. UK-England: London. 1985. Lang.: Eng. 2186

Plays/librettos/scripts
Genesis of *Sweet Bird of Youth* by Tennessee Williams. USA. 1958. Lang.: Eng. 2904

Sweet Charity
Performance/production
Reviews of *Sweet Charity* by Neil Simon, staged and choreographed by Bob Fosse. USA: New York, NY. 1986. Lang.: Eng. 3611

Sweet, Jeffrey
Performance/production
Current trend of productions moving from Chicago to New York. USA: New York, NY, Chicago, IL. 1984. Lang.: Eng. 853

Plays/librettos/scripts
Discussion among several playwrights on ethics and playwriting. 1986. 917

Swinarski, Konrad
Performance/production
Director Andrzei Wajda's work, accessibility to Polish audiences. Poland: Warsaw. 1926-1986. Lang.: Swe. 2027

Swine, The
Plays/librettos/scripts
Interview with playwright Stefan Schütz. Germany, West. 1970-1986. Lang.: Eng. 2628

Swiss Union of Theatre Makers
SEE
Vereinigten Theaterschaffenden der Schweiz.

Sydney Opera House
Performance spaces
Problematic dimensions of the Sydney Opera House's Drama Theatre. Australia: Sydney, N.S.W. 1980-1986. Lang.: Eng. 1612

Performance/production
History and current state of Australian Opera at the Sydney Opera House. Australia: Sydney, N.S.W. 1973-1986. Lang.: Eng. 3688

Sydney Theatre Company
Performance spaces
Sydney Theatre Company headquarters in converted wharf. Australia: Sydney, N.S.W. 1986. Lang.: Eng. 580

Symbolism
Performance/production
Career of director and playwright, Nikolaj Nikolajèvič Jèvreinov. Russia. USSR. 1879-1953. Lang.: Hun. 2066

Production description of the symbolist drama *La navaja (The Razor)* by Eduardo Quiles. Spain. 1980. Lang.: Spa. 2074

Influence of Richard Wagner on the work of the French Symbolists. France: Paris. Germany, West: Bayreuth. 1860-1986. Lang.: Eng. 3726

Plays/librettos/scripts
Analysis of religious symbolism in *Riel* by John Coulter. Canada. 1950. Lang.: Eng. 2407

Relation of 'New Drama'—from Büchner to Beckett—to Afrikaans drama. Europe. South Africa, Republic of. 1800-1985. Lang.: Afr. 2539

Symbolism in Derek Walcott's *Dream on Monkey Mountain*. Jamaica. 1967. Lang.: Eng. 2718

Theory/criticism
Evolution and symbolism of the Mask-Dance drama. Korea: Seoul. 700-1986. Lang.: Kor. 1379

Andrej Belyj's views on Symbolist and Realist theatre, dramaturgy. Russia. 1880-1934. Lang.: Rus. 3129

Symbolist poet Valerij Brjusov's ideas on theatre. Russia. 1873-1924. Lang.: Ita. 3131

Dramatic structure in Beijing opera. China, People's Republic of. 1955-1985. Lang.: Chi. 3566

Symphony Space (New York, NY)
Administration
Favorable ruling from Court of Appeals assisted arts organizations paying municipal property taxes. USA: New York, NY. 1979-1983. Lang.: Eng. 160

Symphony: A Drama of Motion and Light for a New Theatre
Relation to other fields
Analysis of *Symphony* by Herman Voaden and Lowrie Warrener. Canada. 1914-1933. Lang.: Eng. 1075

Synge, John Millington
Plays/librettos/scripts
Louis Esson's attempts to create an Australian national drama based on the Irish model. Australia. Eire. 1905-1943. Lang.: Eng. 2380

Syrokomla, Władysław
Relation to other fields
Poet, dramatist, critic and satirist Władysław Syrokomla. Poland: Vilna, Warsaw. 1844-1861. Lang.: Pol. 3052

Szabados, György
Performance/production
Analysis of choreography of *A szarvassá változott fiak (The Sons Who Turned Into Stags)*. Hungary: Győr. 1985-1986. Lang.: Hun. 1277

Szabó, Magda
Performance/production
Magda Szabó's *A macskák szerdája (Cat Wednesday)* at Csokonai Theatre directed by László Gali. Hungary: Debrecen. 1986. Lang.: Hun. 1777

Szent Bertalan nappala (Saint Bartholomew's Day) by Magda Szabó directed by György Lengyel. Hungary: Budapest. 1986. Lang.: Hun. 1790

Magda Szabó's *Szent Bertalan nappala (Saint Bartholomew's Day)* directed by György Lengyel at Madách Szinház. Hungary: Budapest. 1986. Lang.: Hun. 1896

Szakonyi, Károly
Performance/production
Ki van a képen? (Who Is in the Picture?) by Károly Szakonyi directed by Tamás Szirtes at Madách Kamaraszinház. Hungary: Budapest. 1986. Lang.: Hun. 1786

Notes on performances of *Hongkongi paróka (Wig Made in Hong Kong)*, *Egérút (Narrow Escape)* and *Róza néni (Aunt Rosa)*. Hungary: Budapest. 1985. Lang.: Hun. 1801

Ki van a képen (Who Is in the Picture?) by Tamás Szirtes at Madách Studio Theatre. Hungary: Budapest. 1986. Lang.: Hun. 1835

Plays/librettos/scripts
Comparison of plays and short stories by Károly Szakonyi. Hungary. 1963-1982. Lang.: Hun. 2646

Szaniawski, Jerzy
Plays/librettos/scripts
Analysis of plays of Kruczkowski, Szaniawski and Gałczyński. Poland. 1940-1949. Lang.: Pol. 2746

Overview of major productions of playwright Jerzy Szaniawski. Poland. 1886-1970. Lang.: Eng, Fre. 2753

Szántó, Péter
Performance/production
Ágyrajárók (Night Lodgers) by Péter Szántó, directed by György Emőd at Kisfaludy Studio Theatre. Hungary: Győr. 1985. Lang.: Hun. 1854

Szarvassá változott fiak, A (Sons Who Turned into Stags, The)
Performance/production
Analysis of choreography of *A szarvassá változott fiak (The Sons Who Turned Into Stags)*. Hungary: Győr. 1985-1986. Lang.: Hun. 1277

Szechuan opera
Performance/production
Ch'in opera and its influences. China: Beijing. 1795-1850. Lang.: Chi. 3518

Wei Ch'angsheng: actor of Szechuan opera, not Shensi opera. China. 1700-1800. Lang.: Chi. 3519

Theory/criticism
Analyzes the singing style of Szechuan opera. China. 1866-1952. Lang.: Chi. 3563

Characteristics of Chinese opera in Szechuan province. China, People's Republic of. 1963-1985. Lang.: Chi. 3570

Szegedi Nemzeti Szinház (Szeged)
Design/technology
Details of new electrical system of rebuilt Szeged National Theatre. Hungary: Szeged. 1983-1986. Lang.: Hun. 277

The sound and video systems at the Szeged National Theatre. Hungary: Szeged. 1986. Lang.: Hun. 282

Reconstruction of mechanical equipment at the Szeged National Theatre. Hungary: Szeged. 1981-1986. Lang.: Hun. 288

Report on new heating, plumbing and air-conditioning at reconstructed Szeged National Theatre. Hungary: Szeged. 1978-1986. Lang.: Hun. 293

Szegedi Nemzeti Szinház (Szeged) — cont'd

Performance spaces

Renovation of the Szeged National Theatre. Hungary: Szeged. 1978-1986. Lang.: Hun.   599

The burning of the Szeged National Theatre. Hungary: Szeged. 1885. Lang.: Hun.   600

Structural design problems and their solutions at the Szeged National Theatre in Hungary. Hungary: Szeged. 1977-1986. Lang.: Hun.   602

The history of the theatre building used by Szegedi Nemzeti Színhaz. Hungary: Szeged. 1800-1883. Lang.: Hun.   603

Reconstruction of the Szeged National Theatre. Hungary: Szeged. 1948-1980. Lang.: Hun.   604

Design and construction of rebuilt Szeged National Theatre. Hungary: Szeged. 1978-1986. Lang.: Hun.   605

Director of Szegedi Nemzeti Színhaz on reconstructed theatre. Hungary: Szeged. 1978-1986. Lang.: Hun.   607

Design of the Szeged National Theatre renovation. Hungary: Szeged. 1981-1986. Lang.: Hun.   608

Performance/production

IV. Henrik (Henry IV) by Shakespeare, directed by János Sándor. Hungary: Szeged. 1985. Lang.: Hun.   1791

Performances of *Hair*, directed by János Sándor, and *Desire Under the Elms*, directed by Géza Bodolay at the National Theatre of Szeged. Hungary: Szeged. 1986. Lang.: Hun.   1959

Wariat i zakonnica (The Madman and the Nun) by Stanisław Ignacy Witkiewicz, directed by János Sándor at Szeged National Theatre under the title *Az őrült és az apáca*. Hungary: Szeged. 1986. Lang.: Hun.   1965

Géza Oberfrank directs Bizet's *Carmen* at Szegedi Nemzeti Színház. Hungary: Szeged. 1985. Lang.: Hun.   3748

Szegedi Szabadtéri Játékok (Szeged)

Performance/production

Review of Gábor Görgey's *Mikszáth különös házassága (Mikszáth and His Peculiar Marriage)* directed by János Sándor. Hungary: Szeged. 1986. Lang.: Hun.   1819

Jézus Krisztus Szupersztar (Jesus Christ Superstar) by Andrew Lloyd Webber and Tim Rice directed by János Szikora (Rock Színház). Hungary: Szeged. 1986. Lang.: Hun.   3604

Summer productions of *Jézus Krisztus Szupersztár*. Hungary: Szeged, Budapest. 1986. Lang.: Hun.   3605

Szegvári, Menyhért

Performance/production

Productions of plays by Edward Bond, Gyula Hernádi and Lope de Vega at the Pécs National Theatre. Hungary: Pécs. 1986. Lang.: Hun.   1898

Hagyaték (Legacy) by Gyula Hernádi, directed by Menyhért Szegvári. Hungary: Pécs. 1986. Lang.: Hun.   1949

Székely, Mihály

Performance/production

Careers of three Hungarian opera stars. Hungary. 1925-1979. Lang.: Hun.   3755

Szent Bertalan nappala (Saint Bartholomew's Day)

Performance/production

Szent Bertalan nappala (Saint Bartholomew's Day) by Magda Szabó directed by György Lengyel. Hungary: Budapest. 1986. Lang.: Hun.   1790

Magda Szabó's *Szent Bertalan nappala (Saint Bartholomew's Day)* directed by György Lengyel at Madách Színház. Hungary: Budapest. 1986. Lang.: Hun.   1896

Szentendrei Teátrum (Szentendre)

Performance/production

Interview with actor Pál Mácsai on his role in *Scapin furfangjai (Scapin's Tricks)* by Molière. Hungary: Szentendre. 1986. Lang.: Hun.   1775

Scapin furfangjai (Scapin's Tricks) by Molière, directed by László Vámos at Szentendrei Teátrum. Hungary: Szentendre. 1986. Lang.: Hun.   1957

Szigligeti Színház (Szolnok)

Performance/production

Productions of *Deficit* by István Csurka. Hungary: Szolnok, Budapest. 1970-1985. Lang.: Hun.   1833

Premiere of Tibor Déry's *A Tanúk (The Witnesses)*, directed by Tibor Csizmadia. Hungary: Szolnok. 1945-1985. Lang.: Hun.   1834

Review of József Katona's *Bánk Bán* directed by János Ács at Szigligeti Színház. Hungary: Szolnok. 1986. Lang.: Hun.   1876

Bánk Bán by József Katona at Szigligeti Theatre directed by János Ács. Hungary: Szolnok. 1986. Lang.: Hun.   1884

World premiere of *A tanúk (The Witnesses)* by the late Tibor Déry directed at Szigligeti Theatre by Tibor Csizmadia. Hungary: Szolnok. 1986. Lang.: Hun.   1954

Janika (Our Son) by Géza Csáth, directed by Tamás Fodor and starring György Kézdy. Hungary: Szolnok. 1986. Lang.: Hun.   1955

Hungary: Szolnok. 1986. Lang.: Hun.   1968

Reviews of three musicals about the 1960s. Hungary. 1985-1986. Lang.: Hun.   3488

Sziki, Károly

Performance/production

Review of Shakespeare's *Hamlet* directed by László Gali at Csokonai Theatre, with attention to Károly Sziki's performance as Hamlet. Hungary: Debrecen. 1986. Lang.: Hun.   1844

Szikora, János

Performance/production

Csongor és Tünde (Csongor and Tünde) by Mihály Vörösmarty, directed by János Szikora at Gárdonyi Géza Színház. Hungary: Eger. 1985. Lang.: Hun.   1877

Mihály Vörösmarty's *Csongor and Tünde* at Gárdonyi Géza Theatre directed by János Szikora. Hungary: Eger. 1985. Lang.: Hun.   1923

Interview with director János Szikora. Hungary. 1982-1986. Lang.: Hun.   1928

Reviews of three musicals about the 1960s. Hungary. 1985-1986. Lang.: Hun.   3488

Jézus Krisztus Szupersztar (Jesus Christ Superstar) by Andrew Lloyd Webber and Tim Rice directed by János Szikora (Rock Színház). Hungary: Szeged. 1986. Lang.: Hun.   3604

Summer productions of *Jézus Krisztus Szupersztár*. Hungary: Szeged, Budapest. 1986. Lang.: Hun.   3605

Szinházak Központi Mütermei (Budapest)

Design/technology

Theatre workshops of the Budapest Central Scene Shop Project. Hungary: Budapest. 1953-1986. Lang.: Hun.   290

The renovation and modernization of the theatre production building. Hungary: Budapest. 1976. Lang.: Hun.   291

Sale of textile shops permitted rebuilding and renovation of scene shops. Hungary: Budapest. 1986. Lang.: Hun.   296

Szinházi műhelytitkok (Theatre Workshop Secrets)

Plays/librettos/scripts

Reviews of books on Hungarian theatre. Hungary. 1952-1984. Lang.: Hun.   958

Szinházkomédia (Theatre Comedy)

Performance/production

Production of Bengt Ahlfors' *Szinházkomédia (Theatre Comedy)* directed by András Márton. Hungary: Debrecen. 1985. Lang.: Hun.   1925

Szinmüvészeti Főiskola (Budapest)

Training

Experiences of acting teacher Zsuzsa Simon. Hungary. 1945-1985. Lang.: Hun.   3158

Szirmai, Albert

Performance/production

Mágnás Miska (Miska the Magnate) by Albert Szirmai directed by László Bagossy. Hungary: Pécs. 1986. Lang.: Hun.   3942

Szirtes, Tamás

Performance/production

Szeget szeggel (Measure for Measure) by William Shakespeare directed by Tamás Szirtes at Madách Kamaraszínház. Hungary: Budapest. 1985. Lang.: Hun.   1785

Ki van a képen? (Who Is in the Picture?) by Károly Szakonyi directed by Tamás Szirtes at Madách Kamaraszínház. Hungary: Budapest. 1986. Lang.: Hun.   1786

Tamás Szirtes directs *Szeget szeggel (Measure for Measure)* by Shakespeare. Hungary: Budapest. 1985. Lang.: Hun.   1789

Ki van a képen (Who Is in the Picture?) by Tamás Szirtes at Madách Studio Theatre. Hungary: Budapest. 1986. Lang.: Hun.   1835

Szkéné (Budapest)

Performance/production

Meeting of experimental theatre groups at Szkéné Theatre. Hungary: Budapest. 1985. Lang.: Hun.   736

Review of *Bűnhődés (Punishment)*, a stage adaptation of *The Idiot* by Dostojévskij. Hungary: Budapest. Lang.: Hun.   1826

Szobaszinház (Szolnok)
Performance/production
Janika (Our Son) by Géza Csáth, directed by Tamás Fodor and
starring György Kézdy. Hungary: Szolnok. 1986. Lang.: Hun. 1955

Szőke, István
Performance/production
István Szőke directs *Oszlopos Simeon (The Man on the Pillar)* by
Imre Sarkadi at Miskolc National Theatre. Hungary: Miskolc. 1986.
Lang.: Hun. 1813

Ahogy tetszik (As You Like It) by William Shakespeare directed by
István Szőke. Hungary: Miskolc. 1986. Lang.: Hun. 1866

István Szőke, directs *Ahogy tetszik (As You Like It)* by Shakespeare.
Hungary: Miskolc. 1986. Lang.: Hun. 1873

Productions of plays by Edward Bond, Gyula Hernádi and Lope de
Vega at the Pécs National Theatre. Hungary: Pécs. 1986. Lang.:
Hun. 1898

Kinn vagyunk a vízből (Saved) by Edward Bond directed by István
Szőke. Hungary: Pécs. 1986. Lang.: Hun. 1940

László Fábián's *Levéltetvek az akasztófán (Plant-Lice on the
Gallows)* directed by István Szőke. Hungary: Miskolc. 1986. Lang.:
Hun. 1942

Imre Sarkadi's *Oszlopos Simeon (The Man on the Pillar)* directed by
István Szőke at Nemzeti Szinház. Hungary: Miskolc. 1986. Lang.:
Hun. 1952

Isván Szőke directs *Letvéltetvek az akasztófán (Plant-Lice on the
Gallows)* by László Fábián. Hungary: Miskolc. 1986. Lang.: Hun.
1961

Szomory, Dezső
Performance/production
Dezső Szomory's *Bella* at the Pécs National Theatre directed by
István Jeney. Hungary: Pécs. 1986. Lang.: Hun. 1897

Dezső Szomory's *Bella* at Pécs National Theatre directed by István
Jeney. Hungary: Pécs. 1986. Lang.: Hun. 1936

Szörényi, Levente
Performance/production
Review of rock opera *István a király (King Stephen)* at the National
Theatre. Hungary: Budapest. 1985. Lang.: Hun. 3489

Szurdi, Miklós
Performance/production
Macska a forró bádogtetőn (Cat on a Hot Tin Roof) by Tennessee
Williams, directed by Miklós Szurdi at Városzinház. Hungary:
Budapest. 1985. Lang.: Hun. 1809

Villa Negra by Anikó and Katalin Vajda directed by Miklós Szurdi.
Hungary: Budapest. 1986. Lang.: Hun. 1818

Adaptation for the stage by Anikó Vagda and Katalin Vajda of
Imre Dobozy's screenplay *Villa Negra*, directed at Játékszin by
Miklós Szurdi. Hungary: Budapest. 1986. Lang.: Hun. 1870

Szydlowski, Roman
Performance/production
A stage history of the work of Bertolt Brecht. Poland. 1923-1984.
2050

Tabakov, Oleg
Performance/production
Stage adaptations of prose works by Gogol and Gončarov. Hungary:
Veszprém, Békéscsaba. 1985. Lang.: Hun. 1948

Four performances in Budapest by the students of Oleg Tabakov of
GITIS, the Institute of Dramatic Art, Moscow. USSR: Moscow.
Hungary: Budapest. 1986. Lang.: Hun. 2318

Tabard Theatre (London)
Performance/production
Collection of newspaper reviews by London theatre critics. UK-
England: London. 1986. Lang.: Eng. 2110

Tabori, George
Institutions
On concept of the new group, Der Kreis. Austria: Vienna. 1986-
1987. Lang.: Ger. 1536

Performance/production
Playwright and director George Tabori and his work. Austria:
Vienna. Germany, West. 1914-1985. Lang.: Ger. 658

Taddei, Giuseppe
Performance/production
Opera singer Giuseppe Taddei and his work at the Staatsoper.
Austria: Vienna. Italy. Europe. 1916-1986. Lang.: Ger. 3694

Taganka Theatre
SEE
Teat'r na Tagankė.

Tage der Kommune, Die (Days of the Commune, The)
Plays/librettos/scripts
Brecht's concept of *Naivität* in *Die Tage der Kommune (The Days
of the Commune)*. Germany, East. 1948-1956. 2621

Tagore, Rabindranath
Plays/librettos/scripts
Translations of three plays by Rabindranath Tagore, with critical
commentary. India. 1861-1941. Lang.: Eng. 2662

Tajo de Alacrán (Puerto Rico)
Plays/librettos/scripts
Development of recent Puerto Rican drama. Puerto Rico. 1960-1980.
Lang.: Spa. 2760

Takabayashi, Kōji
Performance/production
Nō actor discusses the centrality of *Okina* to his repertory. Japan.
Lang.: Eng. 1399

Tale of the Possessors Self-Dispossessed, A
Plays/librettos/scripts
Gender role-reversal in the Cycle plays of Eugene O'Neill. USA.
1927-1953. Lang.: Eng. 2896

Tales of Hoffman, The
SEE
Contes d'Hoffman, Les.

Taliesin Arts Centre (Swansea, Wales)
Performance/production
Collection of newspaper reviews by London theatre critics. UK:
London. 1986. Lang.: Eng. 2100

Tall Tales
Design/technology
Design concepts for television series *Tall Tales*. USA. 1986. Lang.:
Eng. 3261

Talley's Folly
Performance/production
Lanford Wilson's play, *Talley's Folly (Mint két tojás)* directed by
András Bálint. Hungary: Dunaújváros. 1986. Lang.: Hun. 1804

Talli, Virgilio
Performance/production
Collaboration of director Virgilio Talli and playwright Pier Maria
Rosso di San Secondo. Italy. 1917-1920. Lang.: Ita. 1992

Pirandello's dealings with actor, manager and director Virgilio Talli.
Italy. 1917-1921. Lang.: Ita. 1993

Talma, François-Joseph
Institutions
Views of Parisian theatre from the journals of August von Kotzebue.
France: Paris. Germany. 1790-1804. Lang.: Eng. 496

Performance/production
Performance of Comédie-Française actors in Amsterdam.
Netherlands. 1811. Lang.: Fre. 2012

Talmage, Fauntleroy
Performance/production
Productions of Handel's *Muzio Scevola* and analysis of score and
characters. England: London. 1718-1980. Lang.: Eng. 3720

Talvela, Martti
Performance/production
Profile of and interview with Finnish bass Martti Talvela. Finland.
1935-1986. Lang.: Eng. 3723

Tamagno, Francesco
Performance/production
Significance of the translation in recordings of Verdi's *Otello*. USA.
1902-1978. Lang.: Eng. 3812

Tamahnous Theatre (Vancouver, BC)
Plays/librettos/scripts
Environmental theatre version of *Hamlet*. Canada: Vancouver, BC.
1986. Lang.: Eng. 2435

Tamborniro, Jeff
Performance/production
Reviews of *Into the Light*, book by Jeff Tamborniro, music by Lee
Holdridge, lyrics by John Forster, staged by Michael Maurer. USA:
New York, NY. 1986. Lang.: Eng. 3615

Tamburlane the Great
Plays/librettos/scripts
Possible influence of Christopher Marlowe's plays upon those of
William Shakespeare. England. 1580-1620. Lang.: Eng. 2478

Contemporary responses to *Tamburlane the Great* by Christopher
Marlowe. England. 1984. Lang.: Eng. 2501

Taming of the Shrew, The
Performance/production
Director Charles Marowitz on the role of the director. USA. 1965-
1985. Lang.: Eng. 843
Political difficulties in staging two touring productions of
Shakespeare's *The Taming of the Shrew*. UK. 1985-1986. Lang.:
Eng. 2104
Tanaka, Chikao
Plays/librettos/scripts
Lives and works of major contemporary playwrights in Japan.
Japan: Tokyo. 1900-1986. Lang.: Jap. 2719
Tanaka, Min
Basic theatrical documents
Poem by Tanaka Min about his reasons for dancing. Japan. 1985.
Lang.: Eng. 1267
Homage to *butō* dancer Hijikata Tatsumi by Tanaka Min. Japan.
1976-1985. Lang.: Eng. 1268
Performance/production
Butō dancer Tanaka Min speaks of early influences of Ohno and
Hojikata. Japan. 1950-1985. Lang.: Eng. 1280
Brief autobiography of dancer Tanaka Min. Japan: Tokyo. 1945-
1985. Lang.: Eng. 1281
A photographic essay of 42 soloists and groups performing mime or
gestural theatre. 1986. 3290
Táncdalfestival '66 (Dance Music Festival '66)
Performance/production
Reviews of three musicals about the 1960s. Hungary. 1985-1986.
Lang.: Hun. 3488
TANDEM (Munich)
Research/historiography
Development of two databases, TANDEM and IBT to aid in
international theatre research. UK-England. 1985. Lang.: Eng. 1187
Tandy, Jessica
Performance/production
Interview with actors Jessica Tandy and Hume Cronyn. USA. 1932-
1984. Lang.: Eng. 2260
Tang, Chengpo
Performance/production
Use of early performance records to infer theatre activities of a later
period. China. 1868-1935. Lang.: Chi. 3505
Tang, Hsientsu
Performance/production
Modern and traditional performance styles compared. China. 1598-
1984. Lang.: Chi. 3511
Theory/criticism
Use of anxiety about fate in Beijing opera. China: Beijing. 5 B.C.-
1985 A.D. Lang.: Chi. 3558
Influence of Tuan Anchieh's aesthetics. China. 800-1644. Lang.: Chi.
3561
Tang, Xianzu
Plays/librettos/scripts
Playwright Wu Bing mocks *The Peony Pavilion* by Tang Xianzu.
China. 1600-1980. Lang.: Chi. 3531
Tannhäuser
Basic theatrical documents
The influence of *Euryanthe* by Carl Maria von Weber on Richard
Wagner. Germany: Dresden. 1824-1879. Lang.: Eng. 3649
Design/technology
Lighting techniques for Wagnerian operas. Germany, West: Bayreuth.
1981-1986. Lang.: Eng. 3651
Performance/production
Interview with Wolfgang Wagner on his staging of 3 Wagnerian
operas at the Bayreuth Festspiele. Germany, West: Bayreuth. 1975-
1985. Lang.: Hun. 3740
Reviews of 10 vintage recordings of complete operas on LP. USA.
1906-1925. Lang.: Eng. 3792
Tantinyà, Pere
Performance/production
Detailed description of the performance titled *Accions (Actions)* by
La Fura dels Baus. Spain-Catalonia. 1979-1984. Lang.: Cat. 3445
Tanúk, A (Witnesses, The)
Performance/production
Premiere of Tibor Déry's *A Tanúk (The Witnesses)*, directed by
Tibor Csizmadia. Hungary: Szolnok. 1945-1985. Lang.: Hun. 1834
World premiere of *A tanúk (The Witnesses)* by the late Tibor Déry
directed at Szigligeti Theatre by Tibor Csizmadia. Hungary: Szolnok.
1986. Lang.: Hun. 1954

Tanz '86 (Vienna)
Institutions
Tanz '86 festival. Austria: Vienna. 1986. Lang.: Ger. 1269
Tanztheater Wuppertal
SEE
Wuppertal Tanztheater.
TAP
SEE
CentreStage.
Tapatī
Plays/librettos/scripts
Translations of three plays by Rabindranath Tagore, with critical
commentary. India. 1861-1941. Lang.: Eng. 2662
Tarasoff, Misha N.
Performance spaces
Planning of 18 performance venues for Expo 86. Canada:
Vancouver, BC. 1986. Lang.: Eng. 589
Tardieu, Jean
Plays/librettos/scripts
Sexual metaphors in plays of Jean Tardieu. France. 1955. Lang.:
Fre. 2577
Tarn, Adam
Institutions
Thirty years of the Polish theatrical monthly *Dialog*. Poland:
Warsaw. 1956-1986. Lang.: Pol. 511
Tarragon Theatre (Toronto, ON)
Performance/production
Career of director Bill Glassco. Canada: Toronto, ON. 1965-1986.
Lang.: Eng. 1674
Tartuffe
Plays/librettos/scripts
Psychoanalytic and post-structuralist analysis of Molière's *Tartuffe*.
France. 1660-1669. Lang.: Eng. 948
Examination of the first Hebrew adaptation of Molière's *Tartuffe* by
David Vexler. France. 1874. Lang.: Heb. 2569
Overview of Hebrew adaptations and translations of *Tartuffe* by
Molière. Israel. France. 1794-1985. Lang.: Heb. 2667
Tasso
Plays/librettos/scripts
Brecht's interpretational legacy is best understood on West German
stages. Germany, West. 1956-1986. 2627
Tasso, Il
Plays/librettos/scripts
Playwright Carlo Goldoni's personality seen through autobiographical
comedies. Italy. 1751-1755. Lang.: Ita. 2687
Taste of Orton, A
Performance/production
Collection of newspaper reviews by London theatre critics. UK-
England: London. 1986. Lang.: Eng. 2119
**Tatarskij Gosudarstvĕnnyj Akademičeskij Teat'r im. Kamala
(Kazan')**
Performance/production
Description of the major activities of the Tatar State Academic
Theatre, known as the Kamal Theatre. USSR: Kazan. 1906-1985.
Lang.: Rus. 857
Tate, Allen
Plays/librettos/scripts
Revision of dramaturgy and stagecraft in Restoration adaptations of
Shakespeare. England: London. 1660-1690. Lang.: Eng. 2535
Tate, Jeffrey
Performance/production
Profile of and interview with American conductor Jeffrey Tate,
concerning his approach to *Die Fledermaus* by Richard Strauss.
USA: New York, NY. 1940-1946. Lang.: Eng. 3827
Taxes
Administration
Effect of 1986 tax law on charitable contributions. USA. 1986-1987.
Lang.: Eng. 85
Taylor, Elizabeth
Performance/production
Biography of Richard Burton. UK-Wales. 1925-1984. Lang.: Eng.
820
Taylor, William
Administration
Account of grievance petition by Opera House performers. England:
London. 1799. Lang.: Eng. 34

Taymor, Julie
Performance/production
Influence of Asian theatre traditions on American artists. USA: New York, NY. Indonesia. 1952-1985. Lang.: Eng.   1335

Puppeteer Julie Taymor adapts *Die vertauschten Köpfe (The Transposed Heads)* by Thomas Mann for performance at the Ark Theatre. USA: New York, NY. 1984. Lang.: Eng.   3977

The training and career of puppeteer Julie Taymor. USA. 1970-1984. Lang.: Eng.   3982

Te Kanawa, Kiri
Performance/production
Profile of and interview with New Zealand soprano Kiri Te Kanawa. New Zealand: Gisborne. USA: New York, NY. 1944-1986. Lang.: Eng.   3768

Famous sopranos discuss their interpretations of Tosca. USA. 1935-1986. Lang.: Eng.   3811

Teace, Jeff
Performance/production
Collection of newspaper reviews by London theatre critics. UK-England: London. 1986. Lang.: Eng.   2124

Teaching methods
Audience
Several New York theatres discuss their student outreach programs. USA: New York, NY. 1984. Lang.: Eng.   201

Institutions
Academics in theatre discuss the role of theatre in education. Canada. 1984. Lang.: Fre.   476

Reminiscences of study at Moscow Art Theatre. USSR. Lang.: Rus.   578

History of the teaching of acting at the Conservatoire national d'art dramatique. France: Paris. 1786-1986. Lang.: Fre.   1576

Performance/production
Analysis of career and methods of director Jerzy Grotowski. Poland. 1959-1984. Lang.: Hun.   771

Interview with producer, director, actor Robert Lewis. USA: New York, NY. 1930-1986. Lang.: Eng.   844

Actor training methods. USSR. Lang.: Rus.   866

Professionalism and training of actors. USSR. 1980-1986. Lang.: Rus.   867

Biographical study of actor/teacher/director Maxim Mazumdar. Canada: Wolfville, NS. 1985-1986. Lang.: Eng.   1662

Four performances in Budapest by the students of Oleg Tabakov of GITIS, the Institute of Dramatic Art, Moscow. USSR: Moscow. Hungary: Budapest. 1986. Lang.: Hun.   2318

The Metropolitan Opera Guild Teacher Workshop demonstrates its techniques for London teachers. UK-England: London. 1986. Lang.: Eng.   3786

Relation to other fields
Dissolution of Jerzy Grotowski's Laboratory Theatre. Poland: Wrocław. 1959-1985. Lang.: Eng.   1117

Black history and folklore taught in theatre workshops and productions. USA: New York, NY, Omaha, NE, Washington, DC. 1986. Lang.: Eng.   3068

Training
Review of training materials in Hungary and elsewhere since antiquity. Lang.: Hun.   1251

Numerous exercises with physiological explanations for phonation in harmony with breath rhythmics. Austria. 1985. Lang.: Ger.   1253

Potential use of Chinese actor-training methods in the West. China. Europe. Lang.: Ita.   1254

Actor training methods of Luce Berthomme. France: Paris. 1984. Lang.: Eng.   1256

Training of disabled students in theatre arts. USA. 1986. Lang.: Eng.   1258

Interview with actress and acting trainer Kristin Linklater. USA: New York, NY. UK-England: London. 1954-1985. Lang.: Eng.   1261
USSR. 1894-1977. Lang.: Rus.   1263

Stanislavskij system in Romanian theatre. USSR. Romania. 1980-1986. Lang.: Rus.   1264

Use of *nō* masks in actor training. USA. 1984.   1424

Guide for teachers on getting a full-length play together. 1980-1982. Lang.: Chi.   3154

Actor-training approach based on imitation of animals. China, People's Republic of: Shanghai. 1949-1982. Lang.: Chi.   3155

Xiong Foxi, playwright and teacher. China, People's Republic of: Ch'eng-tu. 1928-1940. Lang.: Chi.   3156

Physical aspects of actor training. Europe. North America. 1985. Lang.: Eng.   3157

Experiences of acting teacher Zsuzsa Simon. Hungary. 1945-1985. Lang.: Hun.   3158

Transcription of a course on how theatrical texts are written. Italy: Rome. 1981-1982. Lang.: Ita.   3159

History of the Performance Group. USA. 1960. Lang.: Eng.   3161

Effect of changing ideas about psychology and creativity on the Stanislavskij system. USSR: Moscow. 1900-1986. Lang.: Eng.   3162

Interview with director and teacher Zinovy Korogodskij. USSR: Moscow, Leningrad. 1970-1984. Lang.: Eng.   3163

Instructional television programming for the advancement of arts in education. USA: University Park, IL. 1986. Lang.: Eng.   3287

Results of sonographic analysis of covered and uncovered singing. Austria. 1980-1984. Lang.: Ger.   3933

Psychological aspects of voice training. Austria. USA. 1750-1984. Lang.: Ger.   3935

Collected papers from a conference on voice training. Austria: Vienna. Italy: Rome. England: London. 1700-1984. Lang.: Ger.   3936

Physiological regulation for correct breathing and singing. Europe. North America. 1929-1984. Lang.: Ger.   3937

Medical examination of covered singing. Europe. 1980-1984. Lang.: Ger.   3938

Tears of Joy Puppet Theatre (Vancouver, WA)
Institutions
Management techniques for growth at Tears of Joy Puppet Theatre. USA: Vancouver, WA. 1974-1985. Lang.: Eng.   549

Teat'r Baleta SSSR (Moscow)
Performance/production
Artistic directors of Soviet Ballet Theatre on plans for the future. USSR: Moscow. 1980-1985. Lang.: Rus.   1318

Teat'r Dramy i Komedii (Moscow)
SEE
Teat'r na Taganke.

Teat'r Dramy im. Karla Marksa (Saratov)
SEE
Oblastnoj Dramatičeskij Teat'r im. K. Marksa.

Teat'r im. Je. Vachtangova (Moscow)
Performance/production
Biographical materials on actress C.L. Mansurova. USSR. 1920-1986. Lang.: Rus.   884

Actor M. Ul'janov on tasks of Soviet theatre. USSR: Moscow. 1986. Lang.: Rus.   905

Actor M.A. Ul'janov in *I dol'še veka dlitsja den' (A Day Lasts Longer than a Century)* at Teat'r im. Je. Vachtangova. USSR: Moscow. 1980-1986. Lang.: Rus.   2327

Teat'r im. Kamala
SEE
Tatarskij Gosudarstvennyj Akademičeskij Teat'r im. Kamala.

Teat'r im. Leninskovo Komsomola (Moscow)
Performance/production
Director of Lenin Comsomol Theatre discusses theatre's history and repertory, Ribnikov's *Juno és Avosz (Juno and Avos)*. USSR: Moscow. 1927-1985. Lang.: Hun.   909

Komsomol Theatre director Mark Zacharov on his profession. USSR: Moscow. 1980-1986. Lang.: Rus.   910

Director Mark Zacharov of the Komsomol Theatre discusses his work. USSR: Moscow. 1980-1986. Lang.: Rus.   912

Plays by Ribnikov and Višnevskij performed by Moscow Theatre of Lenin Comsomal. USSR: Moscow. Hungary: Budapest. 1985. Lang.: Hun.   2329

Teat'r im. Mossovėta (Moscow)
Performance/production
Faina Ranevskaja's role in *Pravda—chorošo, a sčast'e lučše (Truth is Good, But Happiness is Better)* by A.N. Ostrovskij. USSR: Moscow. 1896-1984. Lang.: Rus.   2324

Vinotavye (The Guilty) at Teat'r im. Mossovėta. USSR: Moscow. 1986. Lang.: Rus.   2339

Teat'r im. V. Majakovskovo (Moscow)
Performance/production
Interview with actor A. Džigorchanjan. USSR: Moscow. 1980. Lang.: Rus.   902

Teatr Współczésny (Wrocław)
Plays/librettos/scripts
Interview with director of Teatr Współczésny about children's drama
competition. Poland: Wrocław. 1986. Lang.: Hun.   2736
Teatr Wybrzeže (Sopot)
Performance/production
Krzysztof Babicki directs Róžewicz's *Pulapka (Trap)*. Poland:
Gdansk. 1984. Lang.: Pol.   2040
Teatr Zydowski (Warsaw)
Performance/production
Abraham Goldfaden's *Sen O Goldfadenie (Dream About Goldfaden)*
directed by Jacob Rotbaum, Teatr Zydowski. Poland: Warsaw. 1984.
Lang.: Pol.   3490
Teatre Grec (Barcelona)
Performance/production
Savannah Bay and *Reigen (Round)* produced by Centre Dramàtic.
Spain-Catalonia: Barcelona. 1986. Lang.: Cat.   2082
Teatre Lliure (Barcelona)
Basic theatrical documents
Text of *Primera història d'Esther (First Story of Esther)* by Salvador
Espriu, with introduction on the author and the play. Spain-
Catalonia: Barcelona. 1913-1985. Lang.: Spa, Cat.   1496

Performance/production
Articles about the productions of the Centre Dramàtic. Spain-
Catalonia: Barcelona. 1976-1986. Lang.: Cat.   2084

Plays/librettos/scripts
Analysis of *Small Craft Warnings*, and report of audience reactions.
USA: New York, NY. Spain-Catalonia: Barcelona. 1972-1983. Lang.:
Cat.   2929
Teatre Principal (Barcelona)
Design/technology
Introduction to facsimile edition of set designs by Fracesc Soler i
Rovirosa. Spain-Catalonia: Barcelona, Valencia, Madrid. 1832-1900.
Lang.: Cat.   3313
Teatre Romea (Barcelona)
Performance/production
Articles on the 1986-87 theatre season. Spain-Catalonia: Barcelona.
France. 1986. Lang.: Cat.   2083

Articles about the productions of the Centre Dramàtic. Spain-
Catalonia: Barcelona. 1976-1986. Lang.: Cat.   2084
Teatre Victòria (Barcelona)
Design/technology
Introduction to facsimile of Oleguer Junyent's set design for *L'Auca
del senyor Esteve (Mr. Esteve's 'Auca')* by Santiago Rusiñol. Spain-
Catalonia: Barcelona. 1861-1984. Lang.: Cat.   1518
Teatret La Luna (Århus)
Performance/production
Amateur theatre festival initiated by Teatret La Luna (Århus). Italy:
Amandola. 1980-1986. Lang.: Swe.   747
Teatro alla Scala (Milan)
Institutions
History of the Teatro alla Scala. Italy: Milan. 1898-1986. Lang.:
Eng.   3677

Performance/production
Collaboration of choreographer Aurél Milloss and scene designer
Giorgio de Chirico. Hungary. Italy: Milan, Rome. 1942-1945. Lang.:
Hun.   1275

Productions of operas at La Scala by Luca Ronconi. Italy: Milan.
1985. Lang.: Ita.   3763
Teatro Arena (São Paulo)
Theory/criticism
Augusto Boal's concept of theatre of the oppressed. Brazil. France.
1956-1978. Lang.: Eng.   1201
Teatro Campesino (California)
Institutions
Origins and evolution of Teatro Campesino. USA. Mexico. 1965-
1986. Lang.: Eng.   547
Teatro Carlo Felice (Genoa)
Reference materials
Catalogue of an exhibit on the Carlo Felice Theatre, destroyed in
World War II, and its proposed reconstruction. Italy: Genoa. 1600-
1985. Lang.: Ita.   1024
Teatro Cuatro (New York, NY)
Performance/production
Profile of theatre companies featured in Festival Latino de Nueva
York. USA: New York, NY. 1984. Lang.: Eng.   2197

Teatro d'Arte (Rome)
Performance/production
Luigi Pirandello's concerns with staging in *Sei personaggi in cerca
d'autore (Six Characters in Search of an Author)* and *Enrico Quarto
(Henry IV)*. Italy. 1921-1986. Lang.: Fre.   1990

Luigi Pirandello's staging of his own works at the Teatro d'Arte.
Italy: Rome. 1925-1928. Lang.: Ita.   2004
Teatro de la Comedia (Madrid)
Performance/production
Production history of *Hay que deshacer la casa (Undoing the
Housework)*, winner of Lope de Vega prize. Spain: Madrid. USA:
Miami, FL. 1983-1985. Lang.: Eng.   2079
Teatro del Angel (Costa Rica)
Plays/librettos/scripts
Chilean theatre in exile, Teatro del Angel. Chile. Costa Rica. 1955-
1984. Lang.: Eng.   2441
Teatro del Ateneo Puertorriqueño
Plays/librettos/scripts
Development of recent Puerto Rican drama. Puerto Rico. 1960-1980.
Lang.: Spa.   2760
Teatro del Bosque (Buenos Aires)
Plays/librettos/scripts
Pacho O'Donnell's play *Vincent y los cuervos (Vincent and the
Crows)*. Argentina: Buenos Aires. 1984. Lang.: Eng.   2363
Teatro delle Novità (Bergamo)
Plays/librettos/scripts
Study of the librettos of operas premiered at the Teatro delle
Novità festival. Italy: Bergamo. 1950-1973. Lang.: Ita.   3883
Teatro Irrumpe (Cuba)
Plays/librettos/scripts
Interviews with actress Pilar Romero and director Roberto Blanco at
the Festival de Théâtre des Amériques. Canada: Montreal, PQ. 1985.
Lang.: Eng.   2426
Teatro La Fenice (Venice)
Institutions
Innovation at Teatro La Fenice under the directorship of Italo
Gomez. Italy: Venice. 1980-1986. Lang.: Eng.   3676
Teatro Popular de Sala y Alcoba (Barcelona)
Institutions
Three personal views of the evolution of the Catalan company La
Pipironda. Spain-Catalonia: Barcelona. 1958-1986. Lang.: Cat.   1583
Teatro Repertorio Español (New York, NY)
Performance/production
Producing *Café Con Leche (Coffee with Milk)* in Spanish. USA:
New York, NY. 1986.   2269
Teatro Stabile (Turin)
Performance/production
Program of *L'isola dei pappagalli (The Island of Parrots)* by Sergio
Tofano at the Teatro Stabile in Turin. Italy: Turin. 1986. Lang.: Ita.
                                                                   743
Teatro Studio di Caserta (Caserta)
Relation to other fields
Contrasts between culture and mass media. Italy. 1980-1986. Lang.:
Ita.   3171
Teatron HaIroni (Haifa)
Administration
Interview with directors of Teatron HaIroni. Israel: Haifa. 1982-1986.
Lang.: Heb.   52
Teatron Ironi šel Beer-Ševa (Beer Sheeba)
Plays/librettos/scripts
Introductory note on the first translation of *Lille Eyolf (Little Eyolf)*
into Hebrew. Norway. Israel. 1884-1985. Lang.: Heb.   962
Teatrul C.I. Nottara (Bucharest)
Performance/production
Reviews of performances at various theatres. Romania: Bucharest.
1980. Lang.: Rus.   779
Teatrul Lucia Sturdza Bulandra (Bucharest)
Performance/production
Reviews of performances at various theatres. Romania: Bucharest.
1980. Lang.: Rus.   779
Teatrul Mic (Bucharest)
Performance/production
Reviews of performances at various theatres. Romania: Bucharest.
1980. Lang.: Rus.   779
Tebaldi, Renata
Performance/production
Famous sopranos discuss their interpretations of Tosca. USA. 1935-
1986. Lang.: Eng.   3811

Terentius Afer, Publius
  Plays/librettos/scripts
    Critical problems in *Henno* by Johannes Reuchlin. Germany: Heidelberg. 1497-1522. Lang.: Eng.   2605
  Relation to other fields
    Influence of the plays of Terence on writings of Bishop Liutprando of Cremona. Italy: Cremona. 920-972. Lang.: Ita.   3041
Terenzio (Terence)
  Plays/librettos/scripts
    Playwright Carlo Goldoni's personality seen through autobiographical comedies. Italy. 1751-1755. Lang.: Ita.   2687
Terkel, Studs
  Plays/librettos/scripts
    Interview with playwright Lorraine Hansberry. USA. 1959. Lang.: Eng.   2945
Terlecki, Tymon
  Theory/criticism
    Analysis of critic Tymon Terlecki's theoretical concepts. Poland. 1905-1986. Lang.: Pol.   3128
Terra Baixa (Low Land)
  Theory/criticism
    Historical difficulties in creating a paradigm for Catalan theatre. Spain-Catalonia. 1400-1963. Lang.: Cat.   1220
Terrors of Pleasure
  Performance/production
    Reviews of *Terrors of Pleasure*, a monologue by Spalding Gray. USA: New York, NY. 1986. Lang.: Eng.   2208
Thacker, David
  Performance/production
    Collection of newspaper reviews by London theatre critics. UK-England. 1986. Lang.: Eng.   2115
Thahouser, Edwin
  Performance/production
    Self-referential elements in several film versions of Shakespeare's *King Lear*. UK. USA. 1916-1983. Lang.: Eng.   3227
Thaïs
  Plays/librettos/scripts
    'Meditation' theme as a dramatic element in Massenet's *Thaïs*. France. 1894. Lang.: Eng.   3867
Thália Stúdió (Budapest)
  Performance/production
    Criticizes stage adaptation of *Hangok komédiája (Comedy of Sounds)* by Miklós Gyárfás. Hungary: Budapest. 1985. Lang.: Hun.   1924
    Reviews of two plays by Arthur Schnitzler directed by Imre Halasi. Hungary: Budapest, Zalaegerszeg. 1986. Lang.: Hun.   1958
Thália Színház (Budapest)
  Design/technology
    Report on exhibition in Warsaw, especially on the S20 dimmer used by the lighting director of the Thália Theatre in Budapest. Poland: Warsaw. Hungary: Budapest. 1986. Lang.: Hun.   308
  Performance/production
    Review of *Alkony (Sunset)* by Isaak Babel, directed by Károly Kazimir at Thália Színház. Hungary: Budapest. 1985. Lang.: Hun.   1806
    Alkony (Sunset) by Isaak Babel, directed by Károly Kazimir at Thália Színház. Hungary: Budapest. 1985. Lang.: Hun.   1850
    Review of *Kettős ünnep (A Double Holiday)*, written and staged by István Verebes. Hungary: Budapest. 1986. Lang.: Hun.   1932
Thalia Theatre (New York, NY)
  Performance spaces
    The varied history of the Bowery Theatres. USA: New York, NY. 1826-1929. Lang.: Eng.   1624
Thang, Doan Anh
  Performance/production
    József Katona's *Bánk Bán* presented by the Hanoi Tuong Theatre directed by Doan Anh Thang. Vietnam: Hanoi. 1986. Lang.: Hun.   2340
Tharp, Twyla
  Design/technology
    Strategies of lighting dance performances on a limited budget. 1985-1986. Lang.: Eng.   1340
  Performance/production
    Analysis of Twyla Tharp's *Fait Accompli*. USA. 1984. Lang.: Eng.   1370
Thatcher, Margaret
  Plays/librettos/scripts
    Interview with playwright Howard Barker. UK-England. 1981-1985. Lang.: Eng.   2845

Thate, Hilmar
  Performance/production
    Actor Hilmar Thate on Brecht. Germany, West. Germany, East. 1949-1984.   732
Theater an der Wien (Vienna)
  Institutions
    Union of three theaters in Vienna to the Verbund Wiener Theatre. Austria: Vienna. 1986. Lang.: Ger.   449
Theater Brett (Vienna)
  Institutions
    Program of Theater Brett for the 1986/87 season. Austria: Vienna. 1986-1987. Lang.: Ger.   3288
Theater für Vorarlberg (Bregenz)
    History of the Theater für Vorarlberg. Austria: Bregenz. 1818-1986. Lang.: Ger.   3
Theater im Künstlerhaus (Vienna)
  Institutions
    New concept for using the Theater im Künstlerhaus for the Opernwerkstatt productions. Austria: Vienna. 1986-1987. Lang.: Ger.   3665
Theater in der Josefstadt (Vienna)
  Administration
    Manager Heinrich Kraus and his work. Austria: Vienna. 1930-1986. Lang.: Ger.   1426
    Manager, actor and director Boy Gobert: his plans for managing the Theater in der Josefstadt. Austria: Vienna. Germany, West. 1925-1986. Lang.: Ger.   1427
Theatre
  Design/technology
    Works by and about designers Jacopo Fabris and Citoyen Boullet. Denmark: Copenhagen. France: Paris. 1760-1801. Lang.: Eng.   256
Theatre After All (Prince Edward Island)
  Institutions
    Fragile alternatives to Charlottetown Festival. Canada: Charlottetown, PE. 1982-1986. Lang.: Eng.   1540
Theatre Alba (Scotland)
  Performance/production
    Survey of the year in Scottish theatre. UK-Scotland. 1986. Lang.: Eng.   2194
Theatre at St. Peter's Church (New York, NY)
  Performance spaces
    Descriptions of newly constructed Off Broadway theatres. USA: New York, NY. 1984. Lang.: Eng.   644
Théâtre aux Bouffes du Nord
  SEE
    Bouffes du Nord.
Theatre Bandwagon (Prince Edward Island)
  Institutions
    Fragile alternatives to Charlottetown Festival. Canada: Charlottetown, PE. 1982-1986. Lang.: Eng.   1540
Theatre Books
  Reference materials
    Three Manhattan theatre bookshops. USA: New York, NY. 1986. Lang.: Eng.   1047
Theatre Clwyd (Mold, Wales)
  Administration
    Artistic directors of Everyman Theatre and Theatre Clwyd discuss their theatres. UK-England: Cheltenham. UK-Wales: Mold. 1986. Lang.: Eng.   82
  Performance/production
    Collection of newspaper reviews by London theatre critics. UK. 1986. Lang.: Eng.   2099
    Collection of newspaper reviews by London theatre critics. UK. 1986. Lang.: Eng.   2102
Theatre Communications Group (TCG, New York, NY)
  Administration
    Statistics of income and expenses of New York Off and Off-off Broadway nonprofit theatres. USA: New York, NY. 1980-1983. Lang.: Eng.   167
  Reference materials
    Listing of repertory schedules, contact and contract information. USA. 1986. Lang.: Eng.   1045
    Productions, dates and directors at TCG constituent theatres. USA. 1984-1985. Lang.: Eng.   3004
  Theory/criticism
    National Conference of Theatre Communications Group (TCG). USA: Amherst, MA. Lang.: Eng.   1233

Theatre Contact (Fredericton, NB)
Institutions
Theatre Contact, alternative stage of Theatre New Brunswick. Canada. 1985-1986. Lang.: Eng. 1562

Théâtre d'en Face
Performance/production
A photographic essay of 42 soloists and groups performing mime or gestural theatre. 1986. 3290

Théâtre d'la Vieille 17 (Ottawa, ON)
Institutions
The development of French-language theatre in Ontario. Canada. 1968-1986. Lang.: Eng. 1567

Théâtre de Bretagne
Performance/production
A photographic essay of 42 soloists and groups performing mime or gestural theatre. 1986. 3290

Théâtre de l'Oeil (Montreal, PQ)
Institutions
Report on International Festival of Theatre for Young Audiences. Canada. Japan. 1985. Lang.: Fre. 482

Théâtre de la Bordée de Québec (Montreal, PQ)
Relation to other fields
Report of conference on theatre and economics. Canada: Quebec, PQ. 1985. Lang.: Fre. 1072

Théâtre de la Corvée (Ottawa, ON)
Institutions
The development of French-language theatre in Ontario. Canada. 1968-1986. Lang.: Eng. 1567

Théâtre de la Fenêtre Ouverte (Joliette, PQ)
Institutions
Techniques and philosophy of children's theatre compared to theatre for adults. Canada. 1980-1984. Lang.: Fre. 468

Théâtre de la Marmaille (Quebec, PQ)
Institutions
History of the Théâtre de la Marmaille. Canada: Quebec, PQ. 1973-1986. Lang.: Eng. 1552

Théâtre de la Marmaille (Toronto, ON)
Basic theatrical documents
Text of *Umiak* by Théâtre de la Marmaille. Canada: Toronto, ON. 1983. Lang.: Eng. 1467

Plays/librettos/scripts
Umiak by Théâtre de la Marmaille of Toronto, based on Inuit tradition. Canada. 1982-1983. Lang.: Eng. 2434

Théâtre de la Mie de Pain
Performance/production
A photographic essay of 42 soloists and groups performing mime or gestural theatre. 1986. 3290

Théâtre de la Rue-L (Montreal, PQ)
Institutions
Techniques and philosophy of children's theatre compared to theatre for adults. Canada. 1980-1984. Lang.: Fre. 468

Théâtre de la Ville (Paris)
Performance/production
Hungarian reviewer discusses Paris performances. France: Paris. 1986. Lang.: Hun. 1734

Théâtre des Jeunes Années (Lyons)
Institutions
Assessment of theatre for adolescents. France. 1968-1984. Lang.: Fre. 495

Théâtre du Gros Caillon (Caen)
Institutions
Assessment of theatre for adolescents. France. 1968-1984. Lang.: Fre. 495

Théâtre du Mouvement
Theory/criticism
The aesthetics of movement theatre. Europe. 1975-1986. 3301

Théâtre du Nouveau Monde (TNM, Montreal, PQ)
Plays/librettos/scripts
Envy in Shakespeare's *Othello* and Peter Shaffer's *Amadeus*. Canada: Montreal, PQ. Europe. 1604-1986. Lang.: Eng. 932

Relation to other fields
Report of conference on theatre and economics. Canada: Quebec, PQ. 1985. Lang.: Fre. 1072

Théâtre du Nouvel-Ontario (Sudbury, ON)
Institutions
The development of French-language theatre in Ontario. Canada. 1968-1986. Lang.: Eng. 1567

Plays/librettos/scripts
Life and work of Francophone playwright Paul-André Paiement. Canada. 1970-1978. Lang.: Fre. 2417

Théâtre du P'tit Bonheur (Toronto, ON)
Institutions
Minority-language theatres in Canada. Canada: Montreal, PQ, Toronto, ON. 1986. Lang.: Eng. 1566
The development of French-language theatre in Ontario. Canada. 1968-1986. Lang.: Eng. 1567

Performance spaces
Troubles faced by Adelaide Court theatre complex. Canada: Toronto, ON. 1979-1983. Lang.: En . 587

Théâtre du Rideau (Brussels)
Performance/production
Effect of dual-language society on Belgian theatre. Belgium: Brussels, Liège. Lang.: Eng. 660

Théâtre du Rond-Point (Paris)
Performance/production
Production journal of *La Musica deuxième* by Marguerite Duras. France: Paris. 1985. Lang.: Fre. 1733

Théâtre du Soleil (Paris)
Design/technology
Théâtre du Soleil set for *Norodom Sihanouk*. France: Paris. 1986. 267

Origins and development of *commedia dell'arte* detailing the costume and attributes of the stock characters. Italy. Europe. USA. 1500-1986. Lang.: Eng. 3407

Institutions
Overview of Ariane Mnouchkine's work with Théâtre du Soleil. France: Paris. 1959-1985. Lang.: Eng. 497
History of the Théâtre du Soleil. France: Paris. 1963-1985. Lang.: Eng. 1574
Work and distinctive qualities of the Théâtre du Soleil. France: Paris. 1964-1986. Lang.: Eng. 1575

Performance/production
Shakespearean form, Asian content in *Norodom Sihanouk* by Ariane Mnouchkine's Théâtre du Soleil. France: Paris. 1964-1986. Lang.: Eng. 709
Hungarian reviewer discusses Paris performances. France: Paris. 1986. Lang.: Hun. 1734
Production of *L'Histoire terrible mais inachevé de Norodom Sihanouk, roi du Cambodge (The Terrible but Unfinished History of Norodom Sihanouk, King of Cambodia)* by Hélène Cixous. France: Paris. 1985. Lang.: Eng. 1737
Eastern influences on a production of *Richard II*. France: Paris. 1981. Lang.: Ita. 1749
Collaboration of Hélène Cixous and Ariane Mnouchkine. France. Cambodia. 1964-1986. Lang.: Eng. 1752

Plays/librettos/scripts
Analysis of *L'Histoire terrible mais inachevé de Norodom Sihanouk, roi du Cambodge (The Terrible but Unfinished History of Norodom Sihanouk, King of Cambodia)* by Hélène Cixous. France: Paris. 1985. Lang.: Eng. 2570

Relation to other fields
Critique of the relation between politics and theatre in Klaus Mann's *Mephisto* performed by Théâtre du Soleil. France: Paris. 1979. Lang.: Eng. 1085

Théâtre du Trident (Montreal, PQ)
Relation to other fields
Report of conference on theatre and economics. Canada: Quebec, PQ. 1985. Lang.: Fre. 1072

Théâtre du Vaudeville (Paris)
Performance/production
Account of *Poisson Chez Colbert* as performed at Théâtre du Vaudeville with a discussion of the popularity of vaudeville in Paris. France: Paris. 1808. Lang.: Eng. 3941

Théâtre Expérimental des Femmes (Montreal, PQ)
Relation to other fields
Report of conference on theatre and economics. Canada: Quebec, PQ. 1985. Lang.: Fre. 1072

Théâtre Expérimental des Femmes, Le (Montreal, PQ)
Performance/production
La Soirée des murmures (The Evening of Murmurs), a performance art piece by Le Théâtre Expérimental des Femmes. Canada: Montreal, PQ. 1986. Lang.: Eng. 3443

Theatre for the New City (New York, NY)
Basic theatrical documents
Text of *The Age of Invention* by Theodora Skipitares. USA: New York, NY. 1985. Lang.: Eng. 3248

Institutions
Several nonprofit theatres secure new spaces. USA: New York, NY. 1984. Lang.: Eng. 544

Goals and accomplishments of Theatre for the New City. USA: New York, NY. 1970-1983. Lang.: Eng. 570

Performance spaces
Architectural design for new performance spaces for Theatre for the New City and the Vineyard Theatre. USA: New York, NY. 1986. Lang.: Eng. 639

Performance/production
Interview with development director Harvey Seifter on German theatre. USA: New York, NY. Germany, West. 1984. Lang.: Eng. 840

Resurgence of street theatre productions and companies. USA: New York, NY. 1960-1982. Lang.: Eng. 2285

Reference materials
Summer performance schedules for several New York companies. USA: New York, NY. 1984. Lang.: Eng. 3011

Théâtre Français (Montreal, PQ)
Institutions
Compares two Canadian stock companies. Canada: Montreal, PQ, Toronto, ON. 1890-1940. Lang.: Eng. 466

Théâtre français d'Edmonton (Edmonton, AB)
Institutions
A history of two French language theatres. Canada: Edmonton, AB. 1970-1986. Lang.: Eng. 1542

Théâtre Gremier (Paris)
Performance/production
Hungarian reviewer discusses Paris performances. France: Paris. 1986. Lang.: Hun. 1734

Theatre in education
Plays/librettos/scripts
Interview with playwright Carl Otto Ewers on writing for children. Sweden. 1986. Lang.: Swe. 2822

Relation to other fields
Drama handbook for secondary school teachers. Australia. 1974-1985. Lang.: Eng. 1062

Training course for teacher/actors. Switzerland: Zurich. 1980-1986. Lang.: Ger. 1132

Theatre in the Round (Budapest)
SEE
Körszinház.

Theatre Institute (London)
SEE
Royal Academy of Dramatic Arts.
London Academy of Music and Dramatic Art.

Theatre Institute (Moscow)
SEE
Gosudarstvěnnyj Institut Teatralnovo Iskusstva.

Theatre Institute (Paris)
SEE
Conservatoire National Supérieur d'Art Dramatique.
École d'Art Dramatique.

Theatre Institute (Rome)
SEE
Accademia Nazionale d'Arte Dramatica.

Théâtre Laboratoire Vicinal (Brussels)
Performance/production
Effect of dual-language society on Belgian theatre. Belgium: Brussels, Liège. Lang.: Eng. 660

Théâtre LaFontaine (Lille)
Institutions
Assessment of theatre for adolescents. France. 1968-1984. Lang.: Fre. 495

Théâtre Libre (Paris)
Performance/production
The Independent Theatre of Jacob Thomas Grein, established in imitation of André Antoine's Théâtre Libre. UK-England: London. 1891. Lang.: Rus. 818

Théâtre Marigny (Paris)
Performance/production
Recollection of Jean-Louis Barrault's career as actor and director. France. 1943-1956. Lang.: Fre. 711

Théâtre National de l'Odéon (Paris)
Performance/production
Interview with actor, director Jean-Pierre Miquel. France: Paris. 1950-1986. Lang.: Fre. 723

Théâtre National de l'Opéra (Paris)
Institutions
Illustrated discussion of the opening of the Théâtre National de l'Opéra. France: Paris. 1875. Lang.: Fre. 3674

Théâtre National Français de Montréal
Institutions
Founding of Théâtre National Français de Montréal. Canada: Montreal, PQ. 1889-1901. Lang.: Fre. 469

Théâtre National Populaire (Paris)
Administration
Jean Vilar's development of a working class audience for the Théâtre National Populaire. France: Paris. 1948-1968. Lang.: Fre. 38

Audience
Jean Vilar's view of the revolutionary power of the classics. France: Paris. 1951-1963. Lang.: Fre. 198

Basic theatrical documents
Jean Vilar's diary compared to polemics against him. France: Paris. 1951-1981. Lang.: Fre. 221

Performance/production
Recollections of Jean Vilar and his work. France: Paris. 1912-1971. Lang.: Fre. 712

Reflection of modern society in Antoine Vitez's production of Sophocles' *Electra* at Théâtre National Populaire. France: Paris. 1981-1986. Lang.: Swe. 1743

Theatre New Brunswick (TNB, Fredericton, NB)
Institutions
Theatre Contact, alternative stage of Theatre New Brunswick. Canada. 1985-1986. Lang.: Eng. 1562

Performance/production
Introduction to series of articles on small theatre companies. Canada. 1986. Lang.: Eng. 1669

Theatre of Action (Toronto, ON)
Relation to other fields
Circumstances surrounding a banned Workers' Experimental Theatre play. Canada: Toronto, ON. 1931-1933. Lang.: Eng. 3018

Theatre of Cruelty
Plays/librettos/scripts
Structuralist analysis of works of Albert Camus, Antonin Artaud and Gaston Bachelard. France. Lang.: Fre. 2575

Theatre of Nations Festival
Performance/production
Theatre of Nations Festival reviewed. USA: Baltimore, MD. 1986. Lang.: Hun. 833

Theatre of the Eighth Day
SEE
Teatr Osmego Dnia (Poland).

Theatre of the Oppressed (France)
Relation to other fields
Interview with Augusto Boal. Canada: Montreal, PQ. France. Brazil: São Paulo. 1952-1986. Lang.: Eng. 3019

Workshops in Canada on 'Theatre for the Oppressed'. Canada: Toronto, ON. 1986. Lang.: Eng. 3022

Theatre workshops led by Augusto Boal. Canada: Montreal, PQ. 1985. Lang.: Eng. 3023

Theatre of the Revolution
SEE
Teat'r im. V. Majakovskova.

Théâtre Ohel (Paris)
Performance/production
Paul Claudel's Biblical scripts for Ida Rubinstein. France. 1934-1936. Lang.: Fre. 1346

Theatre Passe Muraille
SEE
Passe Muraille, Theatre.

Théâtre Petit à Petit (Montreal, PQ)
Institutions
Théâtre Petit à Petit and their production of *Où est-ce qu'elle est ma gang (Where's My Gang?)* by Louis-Dominique Lavigne. Canada: Montreal, PQ. France. 1981-1984. Lang.: Fre. 474

Relation to other fields
Theatre professionals' round-table on issues in theatre for adolescents. Canada: Quebec, PQ. 1984. Lang.: Fre. 1068

Theatres — cont'd

Performance/production

Reference materials

Theatrum

Institutions

Thee Thy Thou Thine

Performance/production

Their Very Own and Golden City

Plays/librettos/scripts

Theme

SEE

Plot/subject/theme.

Theme parks

SEE

Amusement parks.

Theophany

Plays/librettos/scripts

Theory/criticism

SEE ALSO

Classed Entries.

Administration

Theory/criticism — cont'd

Audience
Articles on social role of urban theatres. USSR. 1950-1985. Lang.: Rus. 205

Aesthetic education through theatre. USSR. 1980-1986. Lang.: Rus. 214

Context and design of some lesbian performances. USA: New York, NY. 1985. Lang.: Eng. 1455

The growth of musical theatre and opera since World War II. North America. 1950-1986. Lang.: Eng. 3577

Basic theatrical documents
Jean Vilar's diary compared to polemics against him. France: Paris. 1951-1981. Lang.: Fre. 221

Letter from Luigi Pirandello to Silvio D'Amico. Italy: Agrigento. 1927. Lang.: Fre. 224

Texts of three political dramas, with discussion. Canada. 1833-1879. Lang.: Eng. 1472

The influence of *Euryanthe* by Carl Maria von Weber on Richard Wagner. Germany: Dresden. 1824-1879. Lang.: Eng. 3649

Design/technology
Elements of set design and their emotional impact. China, People's Republic of. 1960-1982. Lang.: Chi. 250

Scene designs and theoretical texts of futurist painters working in the theatre. Italy. 1910-1928. Lang.: Ita. 1517

Institutions
Techniques and philosophy of children's theatre compared to theatre for adults. Canada. 1980-1984. Lang.: Fre. 468

Overview of the 16th Quebec Children's Theatre Festival. Canada. 1985. Lang.: Fre. 479

Structure and political viewpoint of Great Canadian Theatre Company. Canada: Ottawa, ON. 1975-1986. Lang.: Eng. 486

Thirty years of the Polish theatrical monthly *Dialog*. Poland: Warsaw. 1956-1986. Lang.: Pol. 511

Foundation and brief history of Moscow Art Theatre. Russia: Moscow. 1898-1986. Lang.: Rus. 513

Production history and techniques of the Living Theatre. USA. 1964. Lang.: Eng. 546

Criticism of *Canadian Theatre Review*. Canada. 1985. Lang.: Fre. 1554

Theories on incorporating traditional theatrical forms into popular theatre. Canada: Toronto, ON. 1970-1986. Lang.: Eng. 3408

Performance spaces
Analysis of trends in theatre design. UK-England. 1986. Lang.: Eng. 628

Performance/production
Image of the indigène. Australia. New Zealand. Canada. 1830-1980. Lang.: Eng. 656

Reception of the Kembles' Canadian tour. Canada. 1832-1834. Lang.: Eng. 663

Canadian theatre and its relations with U.S. theatre. Canada. USA. 1985. Lang.: Fre. 669

Adaptation of Eastern theatre for the Western stage. China. Europe. Lang.: Ita. 676

Theories of medieval production and acting techniques. England. 1400-1500. Lang.: Eng. 698

Attempts to raise the professional status of acting. France: Paris. 1700-1799. Lang.: Eng. 715

Parisian criticism of Quebec theatre as French regional theatre. France: Paris. Canada. 1955-1985. Lang.: Fre. 719

Examination of German versions of Shakespeare's *Hamlet*. Germany: Hamburg. 1770-1811. Lang.: Eng. 728

Occidental nature of Israeli theatre. Israel. 1920-1986. Lang.: Ita. 742

Comparison of Eastern and Western theatre. Italy: Rome. 1986. Lang.: Ita. 748

Western actors and the energy of Oriental performance. Japan. Lang.: Ita. 756

19 critics, directors and dramaturgs tell which of the season's performances affected them most. Sweden. 1986. Lang.: Swe. 798

Volume 2 of complete works of Adolphe Appia. Switzerland. 1895-1905. Lang.: Fre, Ger. 804

Comprehensive survey of ten years of theatre in New York City. USA: New York, NY. 1970-1980. Lang.: Eng. 837

Comparison of Soviet theatre of the 1960s and 1980s. USSR: Moscow. 1960-1986. Lang.: Rus. 860

Analysis of choreography of *A szarvassá változott fiak (The Sons Who Turned Into Stags)*. Hungary: Győr. 1985-1986. Lang.: Hun. 1277

Analysis of Twyla Tharp's *Fait Accompli*. USA. 1984. Lang.: Eng. 1370

Zeami's theories of performance technique. Japan. 1363-1443. Lang.: Ita. 1401

Meaning in dramatic texts as a function of performance. Lang.: Eng. 1630

Objectives and action in staging of director Wang Xiaoping. China: Shanghai. 1900-1982. Lang.: Chi. 1689

Analysis of theoretical writings of Jean Vilar. France. 1871-1912. Lang.: Ita. 1745

Critical essays on major productions and aesthetics. France. 1970-1985. Lang.: Fre. 1747

Application of Brechtian concepts by Eckhardt Schall. Germany, East: Berlin, East. UK-England: London. 1952-1986. Lang.: Eng. 1762

David Rabe's play *Sticks and Bones* presented at the Pesti Theatre in Hungary. Hungary: Budapest. 1971-1975. Lang.: Hun. 1799

History of Hungarian productions and interpretations of *Death of a Salesman (Az ügynök halála)* by Arthur Miller and *A Streetcar Named Desire (A vágy villamos)* by Tennessee Williams. Hungary. 1959-1983. Lang.: Hun. 1857

Review of László Teleki's *A Kegyenc (The Favorite)* as directed by József Ruszt, Hevesi Sándor Theatre. Hungary: Zalaegerszeg. 1986. Lang.: Hun. 1867

Consideration of actor's place in a director's theatre. Hungary. 1985. Lang.: Hun. 1880

Review of collection of essays by drama critic Tamás Koltai. Hungary. 1978-1983. Lang.: Hun. 1895

Writings of Zaccaria Seriman on the theatre of his time. Italy: Venice. 1708-1784. Lang.: Ita. 1989

Conference and theatrical theory and practice sponsored by Pirandellian Studies Center. Italy: Agrigento. 1900-1940. Lang.: Spa. 2002

Essays by Suzuki Tadashi encompassing his approach to theatre, training, and performance. Japan. 1980-1983. Lang.: Eng. 2007

Collection of articles by critic and theatre historian Wiktor Brumer. Poland. 1765-1930. Lang.: Pol. 2016

Collection of articles by critic and theatre historian Stanisław Marczak-Oborski. Poland. 1918-1986. Lang.: Pol. 2034

Overview of the career of Jerzy Grotowski, his theatrical experiments, training methodology and thoughts on the purpose of theatre. Poland. 1958-1986. Lang.: Eng. 2054

Notes on production of the Állami Magyar Szinház and its late director György Harag. Romania: Cluj. 1984-1985. Lang.: Hun. 2063

August Strindberg's theoretical writings. Sweden. 1887-1910. Lang.: Ita. 2093

Discussion of Stanislavskij's influence by a number of artists. Sweden. 1890-1986. Lang.: Swe. 2094

Proposal to include theatre critics in pre-production evaluation of plays. UK-England. USA. Lang.: Eng. 2162

Interview with dramaturg Arthur Ballet. USA. 1950-1986. Lang.: Eng. 2248

Martin Esslin discusses dramaturg's need to balance roles of naive spectator and informed academic. USA: Waterford, CT, San Francisco, CA. 1936-1986. Lang.: Eng. 2249

Dramaturg Oskar Eustis on confronting social and aesthetic problems. USA: San Francisco, CA. 1975-1986. Lang.: Eng. 2250

Gitta Honegger on training dramaturgs and the European tradition of dramaturgy. USA: New Haven, CT. 1960-1986. Lang.: Eng. 2251

Dramaturg Richard Nelson on communicating with different kinds of directors. USA: New York, NY. 1979-1986. Lang.: Eng. 2252

Interview with dramaturg Russell Vandenbroucke. USA: Los Angeles, CA. 1974-1985. Lang.: Eng. 2253

Interview with dramaturg Anne Cattaneo. USA: New York, NY. 1971-1986. Lang.: Eng. 2254

Aesthetics, styles, rehearsal techniques of director Richard Foreman. USA. 1974-1986. Lang.: Eng. 2263

Chicago dramaturgs acknowledge a common ground in educating their audience. USA: Chicago, IL. 1984-1986. Lang.: Eng. 2274

SUBJECT INDEX

Theory/criticism — cont'd

Explorative structure and manner of performance in avant-garde theatre. USA. 1965. Lang.: Eng. 2277

Beckett's direction of *Krapp's Last Tape* at San Quentin Drama Workshop. USA. 1985. Lang.: Hun. 2279

Mark Bly on the dramaturg's responsibility to question. USA: Minneapolis, MN. 1981-1986. Lang.: Eng. 2294

Music critic Derek Jewell traces Frank Sinatra's career along with his own. USA. 1900-1986. Lang.: Eng. 3179

Diana McIntosh on her performance pieces involving contemporary music. Canada: Winnipeg, MB. 1979-1986. Lang.: Eng. 3250

Influence of Beijing opera performer Mei Lanfang on European acting and staging traditions. China, People's Republic of. USSR. Germany. 1900-1935. Lang.: Eng. 3521

Semiology of opera. Europe. 1600-1985. Lang.: Eng, Fre. 3721

Psychoanalytic study of staging as language. Germany. 1800-1909. Lang.: Fre. 3734

Critical essays, studies and recording reviews of opera performances. Hungary. 1982-1985. Lang.: Hun. 3742

Collected articles and reviews by composer Pëtr Iljič Čajkovskij. Russia. 1850-1900. Lang.: Rus. 3772

Review of the world premiere of the opera *Three Sisters*. USA: Columbus, OH. 1968-1986. Lang.: Eng. 3822

Plays/librettos/scripts

Semiotic analysis of a production of *Antigone* by Sophocles. Australia: Perth, W.A. 1986. Lang.: Eng. 923

Envy in Shakespeare's *Othello* and Peter Shaffer's *Amadeus*. Canada: Montreal, PQ. Europe. 1604-1986. Lang.: Eng. 932

Psychoanalytic and post-structuralist analysis of Molière's *Tartuffe*. France. 1660-1669. Lang.: Eng. 948

Bertolt Brecht and the Expressionists. Germany. 1919-1944. Lang.: Eng. 955

Reviews of books on Hungarian theatre. Hungary. 1952-1984. Lang.: Hun. 958

English theatrical representation of political struggle in Northern Ireland. UK-Ireland. 1980-1986. Lang.: Rus. 977

Analysis of Čechov's plays. Lang.: Hun. 2346

Proposed computerized playwrighting system. Lang.: Eng. 2350

Analysis of the characters of *Bánk Bán* by József Katona. Lang.: Hun. 2351

Theory of translation, using ideas of Eric Bentley and plays of Samuel Beckett. 1950-1986. Lang.: Eng. 2352

Theoretical discussion of audience participation techniques to break through theatrical illusion. 1985. Lang.: Afr. 2353

Use of violent language in the plays of Griselda Gambaro. Argentina. 1950-1980. Lang.: Eng. 2362

Chronotopic analysis of *El beso de la mujer araña (The Kiss of the Spider Woman)* by Manuel Puigi. Argentina. 1976-1986. Lang.: Spa. 2364

Analysis of *The Bushrangers* by Charles Harpur. Australia. 1835-1853. Lang.: Eng. 2370

Translations, adaptations and the Australian theatre. Australia: Armidale, N.S.W. 1985. Lang.: Eng. 2371

Analysis of *The Touch of Silk* and *Granite Peak* by Betty Roland. Australia. 1928-1981. Lang.: Eng. 2387

Language as an instrument of tyranny in Athayde's *Apareceua Margarida (Miss Margarida's Way)*. Brazil. 1808-1973. Lang.: Eng. 2405

Criticizes the plays in the collection *Five From the Fringe*. Canada: Edmonton, AB. 1986. Lang.: Eng. 2425

Post-structuralist insights on sexuality and transgression in transvestite roles in Jacobean plays. England: London. 1600-1625. Lang.: Eng. 2476

Possible influence of Christopher Marlowe's plays upon those of William Shakespeare. England. 1580-1620. Lang.: Eng. 2478

Reflections of Ben Jonson's personal life in his poems and plays. England: London. 1596-1604. Lang.: Eng. 2515

Essays on Shakespeare's *Romeo and Juliet*. England. 1595-1597. Lang.: Ita. 2529

Critics and directors on Shakespeare's *King Lear*. England. 1605. Lang.: Ita. 2530

Modern criticism of Shakespeare's crowd scenes. England. 1590-1986. Lang.: Eng. 2536

Various implications of 'waiting' in Samuel Beckett's *Waiting for Godot*. France. 1953. Lang.: Eng. 2555

Structuralist analysis of works of Albert Camus, Antonin Artaud and Gaston Bachelard. France. Lang.: Fre. 2575

Evolution of concept of the State in the tragedies of Pierre Corneille. France. 1636-1674. Lang.: Fre. 2582

Patriarchy in *Le Voyageur sans bagage (Traveler Without Luggage)* by Jean Anouilh. France. 1937. Lang.: Eng. 2586

The role of the double in Georg Kaiser's *Zweimal Amphitryon (Amphitryon x 2)* and other works. Germany. 1943. Lang.: Eng. 2589

Critical problems in *Henno* by Johannes Reuchlin. Germany: Heidelberg. 1497-1522. Lang.: Eng. 2605

Analysis of *Leben des Galilei (The Life of Galileo)* by Bertolt Brecht. Germany. 1938. Lang.: Rus. 2606

History in Goethe's *Götz von Berlichingen*. Germany. 1773. Lang.: Eng. 2610

Essays on Lessing and Lessing criticism. Germany. 1748-1984. Lang.: Ger. 2611

Applying Brecht's dramatic principles to the plays of Euripides. Germany, East. Greece. 450 B.C.-1956 A.D. 2614

Interpretation of final scenes of Sophocles' *Philoctetes*. Greece. 409 B.C. Lang.: Heb. 2630

Text of a lecture on Shakespeare's *King Lear* by Clifford Davidson. Hungary: Budapest. Lang.: Hun. 2643

Analysis of László Németh's study of *Bánk Bán* by József Katona and a portrait of the playwright. Hungary. 1985. Lang.: Hun. 2647

Young playwright's conference. Hungary: Zalaegerszeg. 1985. Lang.: Hun. 2650

Study of Tibor Gyurkovics' eight plays. Hungary. 1976-1985. Lang.: Hun. 2654

Works of playwright István Sárospataky. Hungary. 1974-1985. Lang.: Hun. 2660

Influence of German expressionism on the plays of Luigi Pirandello. Italy. Germany. 1917-1930. Lang.: Ita. 2682

Tension between text and realization in Pirandello's *Sei personaggi in cerca d'autore (Six Characters in Search of an Author)*. Italy. 1911-1929. Lang.: Eng. 2685

Critical notes on *La nuova colonia (The New Colony)* by Luigi Pirandello. Italy. 1928. Lang.: Ita. 2702

Nō and Beckett compared. Japan. France. 1954-1986. Lang.: Ita. 2721

Overview of symposium on playwright Stanisław Ignacy Witkiewicz. Poland. 1985. Lang.: Eng, Fre. 2747

Overview of major productions of playwright Jerzy Szaniawski. Poland. 1886-1970. Lang.: Eng, Fre. 2753

Analysis of the plays of Ivan Turgenjev. Russia. 1818-1883. Lang.: Rus. 2770

Interview with playwright Athol Fugard. South Africa, Republic of. USA: New Haven, CT. 1984. Lang.: Eng. 2775

Alfonso Sastre's theory of complex tragedy in *La Celestina (The Nun)*. Spain. 1978. Lang.: Spa. 2807

Narratological analysis of Harold Pinter's *Old Times*. UK-England. 1971. Lang.: Eng. 2842

Links between Shakespeare's *Macbeth* and Tom Stoppard's *Dogg's Hamlet, Cahoot's Macbeth*. UK-England. 1979-1986. Lang.: Eng. 2843

Articles on work of playwright Harold Pinter. UK-England. 1957-1984. Lang.: Eng. 2851

History of Harold Pinter's work and critical reception. UK-England. 1975-1983. Lang.: Eng. 2860

A comparison between Oscar Wilde's *The Importance of Being Earnest* and Tom Stoppard's *Travesties*. UK-England. 1895-1974. Lang.: Eng. 2872

Brecht's ideas about the history play as justification for Edward Bond's *Bingo*. UK-England. 1974. Lang.: Eng. 2876

T. S. Eliot's *Murder in the Cathedral* dramatizes Christian theory of history. UK-England. 1935. Lang.: Eng. 2878

Richard Foreman, founder of Ontological-Hysteric Theater Company. USA. 1960-1986. Lang.: Swe. 2890

Popularity and relevance of Eugene O'Neill. USA. Lang.: Eng. 2894

Theory/criticism — cont'd

Gender role-reversal in the Cycle plays of Eugene O'Neill. USA. 1927-1953. Lang.: Eng. 2896

Concept of tragic character in Eugene O'Neill's *Desire Under the Elms*. USA. 1924. Lang.: Eng. 2907

Influence of Gordon Craig on American theatre and his recognition of Eugene O'Neill's importance. USA. UK-England. 1912-1928. Lang.: Eng. 2908

Analysis of the plays of Edward Albee. USA. 1960-1970. Lang.: Rus. 2914

Similarities of *Hughie* by Eugene O'Neill and *The Zoo Story* by Edward Albee. USA: New York, NY. 1941-1958. Lang.: Eng. 2919

Analysis of the plays of Rosalyn Drexler. USA. 1964-1985. Lang.: Eng. 2920

Director John Lion on his work with playwright Sam Shepard. USA: San Francisco, CA, New York, NY. 1970-1984. Lang.: Eng. 2924

The Peasants by Władysław Reymont as possible source for O'Neill's version of the lustful stepmother play. USA. 1902-1924. Lang.: Eng. 2930

Interview with theatre professionals on successful writing and production. USA. 1986. Lang.: Eng. 2932

Theme and narrative structure in plays of Eugene O'Neill, David Belasco, and James A. Herne. USA. 1879-1918. Lang.: Eng. 2933

Development of playwright Sam Shepard's style. USA. 1972-1985. Lang.: Eng. 2943

Sam Shepard's plays as a response to traditional American drama. USA. 1943-1986. Lang.: Eng. 2944

Discussion of the hero in modern drama. USSR. 1980-1986. Lang.: Rus. 2969

Moral and ethical themes in contemporary drama. USSR. 1980-1986. Lang.: Rus. 2970

The positive hero in contemporary drama. USSR. 1980-1986. Lang.: Rus. 2971

Plays by women on the CBC radio network. Canada. 1985-1986. Lang.: Eng. 3185

Analysis of two versions of a screenplay by Luigi Pirandello. Italy. 1925-1928. Lang.: Ita. 3235

Critical debate over Timothy Findley's *The Paper People*. Canada. 1967. Lang.: Eng. 3280

Playwright Wu Bing mocks *The Peony Pavilion* by Tang Xianzu. China. 1600-1980. Lang.: Chi. 3531

Shakespeare's influence on Verdi's operas. Germany. Italy. Austria. 1750-1850. Lang.: Eng. 3878

Use of the tale of Patient Griselda in *Griselda* by Angelo Anelli and Niccolo Piccinni. Italy: Venice. Austria: Vienna. 1770-1800. Lang.: Eng. 3885

Study of all aspects of Italian opera. Italy. 1810-1920. Lang.: Fre. 3889

Gian Carlo Menotti's reactions to harsh criticism of his operas. USA: New York, NY. UK-Scotland: Edinburgh. Italy: Cadegliano. 1938-1988. Lang.: Eng. 3902

Reference materials

Comprehensive bibliography of scholarship, criticism and commentary on modern world drama. 1985. Lang.: Eng. 2976

Exhibition catalogue about context of the work and influence of Karl Kraus. Austria: Vienna. USA: New York, NY. France: Paris. 1874-1986. Lang.: Ger. 2980

Relation to other fields

Review of Iván Sándor's essays on Hungarian theatre. 1986. Lang.: Hun. 1049

Translation of *From Ritual to Theatre* by Victor Turner. Lang.: Ita. 1060

Analysis of Bertolt Brecht's love poetry. Germany, East. 1898-1956. 1092

Essays on literary and theatrical languages. Italy. 800-1985. Lang.: Ita. 1103

Reports and discussions of restricted cultural communication. Lebanon. Spain-Catalonia. USA. 1985. Lang.: Fre, Spa, Cat. 1111

Views of designer and critic Franciszek Siedlecki. Poland. 1909-1934. Lang.: Pol. 1116

Proposals on theatre in education. UK-England: London, Greenwich. 1986. Lang.: Hun. 1137

Comparison of Olympiad Arts Festival and the 1984 Olympic Games. USA: Los Angeles, CA. 1984. Lang.: Eng. 1148

Conceptions of humankind as seen in contemporary theatre. USSR. 1980. Lang.: Rus. 1171

Relates theatrical art and progressive scientific thought. USSR. 1980-1986. Lang.: Rus. 1172

Reflections on the role of theatre in society. USSR. 1980-1986. Lang.: Rus. 1181

Drama as a genre of literature. Lang.: Rus. 3012

Karl Kraus, a reflection of Viennese culture and literature history. Austria: Vienna. 1874-1936. Lang.: Ger. 3014

Collection of obituary notes for the critic and dramatist Karl Kraus. Austria: Vienna. 1933-1937. Lang.: Ger. 3015

Situation of playwrights in Austria. Austria: Vienna. 1971-1986. Lang.: Ger. 3016

Life and work of playwright and critic Karl Kraus. Austria: Vienna. 1874-1936. Lang.: Ger. 3017

Interview with Augusto Boal. Canada: Montreal, PQ. France. Brazil: São Paulo. 1952-1986. Lang.: Eng. 3019

Cardinal Richelieu's theatrical policies. France. 1634-1642. Lang.: Fre. 3030

Feminist criticism of plays written by women. Germany. Switzerland. Austria. 1900-1986. Lang.: Ger. 3033

Critical articles on playwright Luigi Pirandello. Italy. 1867-1936. Lang.: Ita. 3039

Comparison of playwright Luigi Pirandello and novelist Miguel de Cervantes. Italy. Spain. 1615-1936. Lang.: Ita. 3040

Study on the reception of critic and playwright Karl Kraus in Italy. Italy. Austria: Vienna. 1911-1985. Lang.: Ger. 3044

Analysis of contemporary drama from various viewpoints. Poland. 1945-1986. Lang.: Pol. 3049

The reception of critic and playwright Karl Kraus in the English speaking world. USA: New York, NY. Austria: Vienna. UK-Scotland: Glasgow. 1909-1985. Lang.: Ger. 3067

Nonfictional writings of Albin Zollinger, Max Frisch and Friedrich Dürrenmatt. Lang.: Ger. 3169

Historical function of cabaret entertainment. Germany. 1896-1945. Lang.: Ger. 3371

Research/historiography

Analysis and description in reviews of performances. USSR. 1970-1980. Lang.: Rus. 3072

Origins and evolution of today's Beijing opera. China, People's Republic of: Beijing. 1755-1984. Lang.: Chi. 3556

Theory/criticism

Low standard of much Australian theatre reviewing. Australia. 1985. Lang.: Eng. 3085

Reprints of Herbert Whittaker's theatre reviews. Canada. 1944-1975. Lang.: Eng. 3086

Selection from Peter Brook's *The Empty Space*. EUROPE. 1929-1982. Lang.: Chi. 3095

Selections from Jerzy Grotowski's *Towards a Poor Theatre*. Poland. 1933-1982. Lang.: Chi. 3126

Thespian Oracle or Monthly Mirror

Reference materials

Theatrical materials in five early American magazines. Colonial America. 1758-1800. Lang.: Eng. 1012

Thief of Souls

SEE

Ladro di anime, Il.

Thirkield, Rob

Institutions

History of Circle Repertory Company. USA: New York, NY. 1969-1984. Lang.: Eng. 1606

Thirty Pieces of Silver

Relation to other fields

The premiere of Howard Fast's play under the title *Harminc ezüstpénz* (*Thirty Pieces of Silver*) in Hungary. Hungary. 1951-1986. Lang.: Hun. 3036

This Is Not Broadway (Ez nem Broadway)

Performance/production

Interview with Mario Delgado Vásquez, director of Cuatrotablas. Peru: Lima. 1971-1985. Lang.: Hun. 769

Thomas England of Woodstock

Basic theatrical documents

Examination of promptbooks and notes for *Thomas England of Woodstock*. 1594-1633. Lang.: Eng. 1458

Torquemada
Plays/librettos/scripts
Interplay of signs of violence in Augusto Boal's *Torquemada*. Brazil. 1971. Lang.: Eng.   2404

Torres Naharro, Bartolomé de
Performance/production
Reconstruction of *Comedia Tinellaria* by Torres Naharro. Italy: Rome, Venice. 1508-1537. Lang.: Spa.   1986

Plays/librettos/scripts
Mutual influences between *commedia dell'arte* and Spanish literature. Spain. Italy. 1330-1623. Lang.: Spa.   2805

Tórtolas, crepúsculo y ...telón (Turtledoves, Twilight and ...Curtain)
Plays/librettos/scripts
Artaud's concept of theatre of cruelty in Francisco Nieva's *Tórtolas, crepúscula y ...telón (Turtledoves, Twilight and ...Curtain)*. Spain. 1953. Lang.: Spa.   2790

Toru, Tada
Institutions
The Kaze-no-Ko: professional travelling children's theatre of Japan. Japan. 1950-1984. Lang.: Eng.   507

Tosca
Performance/production
Gyula Kertész directs Puccini's *Tosca* at the Csokonai Theatre. Hungary: Debrecen. 1985. Lang.: Hun.   3754

Photographs, cast list, synopsis, and discography of Metropolitan Opera radio broadcast performances. USA: New York, NY. 1986. Lang.: Eng.   3794

Famous sopranos discuss their interpretations of Tosca. USA. 1935-1986. Lang.: Eng.   3811

Toscanini, Arturo
Institutions
History of the Teatro alla Scala. Italy: Milan. 1898-1986. Lang.: Eng.   3677

Tót Family, The
SEE
Tóték.

Totally Foxed
Performance/production
Collection of newspaper reviews by London theatre critics. UK. 1986. Lang.: Eng.   2099

Tote Stadt, Die (Dead Town, The)
Reference materials
Photos of the new opera productions at the Staatsoper. Austria: Vienna. 1985-1986. Lang.: Ger.   3910

Tóték (Tót Family, The)
Performance/production
Bungei-za performs *Tóték (The Tót Family)* by István Örkény. Japan: Toyama. 1985. Lang.: Hun.   2006

Totem (Cádiz)
Performance/production
Report from an international amateur theatre festival where music and dance were prominent. Denmark: Copenhagen. 1986. Lang.: Swe.   683

Totisesti totisesti (Verily Verily)
Basic theatrical documents
Text of Inkeri Kilpinen's *Totisesti totisesti (Verily Verily)* in English translation. Finland. 1982-1983. Lang.: Eng, Fin.   1476

Tou Erh Yüan (Injustice of Miss Tou, The)
Plays/librettos/scripts
Plots and themes in adaptations of *Tou Erh Yüan (The Injustice of Miss Tou)*. China. 1360-1960. Lang.: Chi.   3525

Touch of Silk, The
Plays/librettos/scripts
Analysis of *The Touch of Silk* and *Granite Peak* by Betty Roland. Australia. 1928-1981. Lang.: Eng.   2387

Touch of the Poet, A
Plays/librettos/scripts
Gender role-reversal in the Cycle plays of Eugene O'Neill. USA. 1927-1953. Lang.: Eng.   2896

Tour de Babel, La (Tower of Babel, The)
Plays/librettos/scripts
Politics and aesthetics in three plays of Fernando Arrabal. Spain. France. Lang.: Fre.   2801

Tourangeau, Rémi
Plays/librettos/scripts
Book review of *125 Ans de Theatre au Seminaire de Trois-Rivières*. Canada: Trois-Rivières, PQ. 1985. Lang.: Fre.   2427

Touring companies
Administration
Interview with director and tour manager of Royal Shakespeare Company about touring. UK. 1986. Lang.: Eng.   72

Use of sources in analyzing shift from resident to touring companies. USA. 1850-1900. Lang.: Eng.   86

Design/technology
Interview with Beverly Emmons, lighting designer for Mummenschanz's USA tour. USA: New York, NY. 1986. Lang.: Eng.   3305

Institutions
Tours of the Österreichische Bundestheater in Austria. Austria. 1976-1986. Lang.: Ger.   455

How Skottes Musiktéater operates on a small government budget. Sweden: Gävle. 1976-1986. Lang.: Swe.   522

Founding member discusses dinner-theatre Comedy Asylum. Canada: Fredericton, NB. 1982-1986. Lang.: Eng.   1559

Actor Michael Pennington and director Michael Bogdanov discuss the formation of the English Shakespeare Company. UK-England. 1986. Lang.: Eng.   1592

Analysis of documentation on Jefferson theatre company. USA. 1830-1845. Lang.: Eng.   1597

Collection of essays on the evolution of Chicano theatre. USA. 1850-1985. Lang.: Eng.   1599

Performance spaces
Touring production of *Cyrano de Bergerac* seen from crew's point of view. Sweden. 1986. Lang.: Swe.   617

Touring stage of ballet company Cullbergbaletten. Sweden. 1986. Lang.: Swe.   1300

Performance/production
Parisian criticism of Quebec theatre as French regional theatre. France: Paris. Canada. 1955-1985. Lang.: Fre.   719

Actor-director Edmund Wierciński on Reduta Theatre. Poland. 1924. Lang.: Pol.   775

Profile of actor-entrepeneur George Coppin. Canada: Victoria, BC. 1864. Lang.: Eng.   1666

Career of actress, manager and director Julia Arthur. Canada. UK-England. USA. 1869-1950. Lang.: Eng.   1675

Study of Hungarian actor Ede Paulay. Hungary: Győr. 1855. Lang.: Hun.   1823

Details of Wileński Touring Theatre. Poland: Vilna. 1935-1936. Lang.: Pol.   2020

Description of performances by touring companies from Vilna. Poland. 1789-1864. Lang.: Pol.   2026

Establishment of the English Shakespeare Company. UK-England. 1986. Lang.: Eng.   2131

Spalding Gray's memories of the development and tour of Richard Schechner's *Commune*. USA. France. Poland. 1970. Lang.: Eng. 2270

Touring exhibition 'Artists in the Theatre': influence of visual artists in the development of performance art. UK. 1900-1986. Lang.: Eng. 3447

Tournaments
Performance/production
Analysis and interpretation of the staging of *The Castle of Perseverance* based on original stage plan drawing. England. 1343-1554. Lang.: Eng.   1708

Evidence for performance of a mock tournament of the type described in a 15th-century poem. England: Exeter. 1432. Lang.: Eng.   3331

Tovstonogov, Georgij Aleksandrovič
Performance/production
Stage adaptations of Dostojévskij novels *A Fēlkesgyelmü (The Idiot)* and *A Karamazov testvérek (The Brothers Karamazov)*. Hungary: Budapest, Debrecen. 1985. Lang.: Hun.   1922

Toweal Theatre (Seoul)
Institutions
History of Korea's first theatre production company. Korea: Seoul. 1922-1924. Lang.: Kor.   509

Tower of Babel, The
SEE
Tour de Babel, La.

Town Theatre (Ottawa, ON)
Administration
History of the Town Theatre. Canada: Ottawa, ON. 1948-1970. Lang.: Eng.   29

Towneley Cycle
  Performance/production
  Performance of *Towneley Cycle* in Victoria College Quadrangle.
  Canada: Toronto, ON. 1985. Lang.: Eng.   1673
  Plays/librettos/scripts
  Dramatic dynamics of Chester cycle play, *The Fall of Lucifer.*
  England. 1400-1550. Lang.: Eng.   2499
Townsend, Sue
  Institutions
  Progress and aims of Women's Playhouse Trust. UK-England:
  London. 1984-1986. Lang.: Eng.   1590
  Performance/production
  Collection of newspaper reviews by London theatre critics. UK.
  1986. Lang.: Eng.   2099
Toy Theatre (Vienna)
  Reference materials
  Adaptation of Ferdinand Raimund's dramas for children's theatre.
  Austria: Vienna. 1790-1836. Lang.: Ger.   2979
Trafford Tanzi, Her Hopes, Her Fears, Her Early Years
  Performance/production
  Brechtian technique in the contemporary feminist drama of Caryl
  Churchill, Claire Luckham and others. UK-England. 1956-1979.
  Lang.: Eng.   815
Trafic, Carlos
  Performance/production
  A photographic essay of 42 soloists and groups performing mime or
  gestural theatre. 1986.   3290
Tragédie du roi Christophe, La (Tragedy of King Christopher, The)
  Plays/librettos/scripts
  Precursors of revolutionary black theatre. Haiti. Jamaica. 1820-1970.
  Lang.: Eng.   956
  Analysis of *La Tragédie du roi Christophe (The Tragedy of King
  Christopher)* by Aimé Césaire. Haiti. Africa. Martinique. 1939. Lang.:
  Fre.   2637
Tragedy
  Performance/production
  History of Edward Moore's *The Gamester* on London stages.
  England: London. 1771-1871. Lang.: Eng.   1700
  Othello, translated by Bohdan Drozdowski and directed by Wilfred
  Harrison at the Wilama Horzycy Theatre. Poland: Toruń. 1980.
  Lang.: Eng.   2023
  Greek tragedy on the New York stage. USA: New York, NY. 1854-
  1984. Lang.: Eng.   2301
  Ukrainian performances of classical Western tragedies. USSR. 1920-
  1930. Lang.: Rus.   2317
  Plays by Ribnikov and Višnevskij performed by Moscow Theatre of
  Lenin Comsomal. USSR: Moscow. Hungary: Budapest. 1985. Lang.:
  Hun.   2329
  Plays/librettos/scripts
  Similar dramatic techniques in Ben Jonson's masques and tragedies.
  England. 1597-1637. Lang.: Eng.   941
  Rise of English landowners reflected in *Arden of Faversham.*
  England. 1536-1592. Lang.: Eng.   943
  Blessing and cursing in Shakespeare's *King Lear.* England. 1605-
  1606. Lang.: Eng.   2466
  Semiotic analysis of Shakespeare's *King Lear.* England: London.
  1605-1606. Lang.: Eng.   2467
  Comparison of Shakespeare's *Antony and Cleopatra* and Ibsen's
  Rosmersholm. England. Norway. 1607-1885. Lang.: Eng.   2479
  Shakespeare's *Henry VI* and Hall's *Chronicles.* England. 1542-1592.
  Lang.: Fre.   2488
  Marxist analysis of colonialism in Shakespeare's *Othello.* England.
  South Africa, Republic of. 1597-1637. Lang.: Eng.   2507
  Analysis of the final scene of *The Broken Heart* by John Ford.
  England. 1629. Lang.: Eng.   2526
  Comparison of Shakespeare's *Othello* with New Comedy of Rome.
  England. 1604. Lang.: Eng.   2528
  Stoicism and modern elements in Senecan drama. Europe. 65-1986.
  Lang.: Eng.   2542
  Modern thought in works of Jean Racine. France. 1664-1691. Lang.:
  Fre.   2553
  Marguerite Yourcenar's treatment of Electra story compared to other
  versions. France. 1944-1954. Lang.: Fre.   2554
  Commonplace as rhetorical device in plays of Jean Racine. France.
  1650-1986. Lang.: Fre.   2559

Evolution of concept of the State in the tragedies of Pierre
Corneille. France. 1636-1674. Lang.: Fre.   2582
The tragic in plays of Heinrich von Kleist. Germany. 1777-1811.
Lang.: Rus.   2601
Chorus in ancient Greek comedy and drama. Greece. 450-425 B.C.
Lang.: Ita.   2633
Masked god as tragic subject in works of Aeschylus, Sophocles and
Euripides. Greece. 499-401 B.C. Lang.: Fre.   2636
The tragedy in the plays of Aleksand'r Nikolajèvič Ostrovskij.
Russia. 1823-1886. Lang.: Rus.   2771
Salvador Espriu's tragic vision in *Ronda de Mort a Sinera (Death
Round at Sinera).* Spain. 1965. Lang.: Eng.   2784
Alfonso Sastre's theory of complex tragedy in *La Celestina (The
Nun).* Spain. 1978. Lang.: Spa.   2807
Analysis of Josep Palau's plays and theoretical writings. Spain-
Catalonia. 1917-1982. Lang.: Cat.   2814
Concept of tragic character in Eugene O'Neill's *Desire Under the
Elms.* USA. 1924. Lang.: Eng.   2907
  Reference materials
  List and location of school playtexts and programs. France. 1601-
  1700. Lang.: Fre.   2987
  Relation to other fields
  Sociological analysis of city comedy and revenge tragedy. England:
  London. 1576-1980. Lang.: Eng.   3025
  Theory/criticism
  Influence of literary theory on Greek theatre studies. Greece. UK-
  England. Germany. Lang.: Afr.   1210
  Phenomenological study of *The White Devil* by John Webster.
  England: London. 1610-1612. Lang.: Eng.   3093
Tragedy of a Man
  SEE
  Ember tragédiája, Az.
Tragedy of Carmen
  Performance/production
  Overview of the career and work of director Peter Brook. USA:
  New York, NY. 1948-1984. Lang.: Eng.   829
Tragedy of Thierry and Theodoret, The
  Plays/librettos/scripts
  Female characterization in Nicholas Rowe's plays. England. 1629-
  1720. Lang.: Eng.   2475
Training
  SEE ALSO
  Classed Entries.
  Administration
  Current problems in theatrical organizations. 1980-1986. Lang.: Rus.
                                                              20
  Training of amateurs coordinated by Folkteatern in Gävleborgs Län.
  Sweden: Gävle. 1984-1986. Lang.: Swe.   60
  Ukrainian actors and teachers on rebuilding theatre business. USSR.
  1980-1986. Lang.: Ukr.   192
  Theatrical activity on various Vancouver stages. Canada: Vancouver,
  BC. 1986. Lang.: Heb.   1429
  Design/technology
  Commemoration of theatre expert Paul Jähnichen. Germany, East:
  Berlin, East. 1935-1986. Lang.: Hun.   271
  Interview with scene designer Sándor Bishof. Hungary: Zalaegerszeg.
  1983-1986. Lang.: Hun.   284
  Theory and practice in the training of theatre technicians at
  Dramatiska Institutet. Sweden: Stockholm. 1985-1986. Lang.: Swe.
                                                             316
  Institutions
  Overview of current theatre scene. Denmark: Copenhagen. 1976-
  1986. Lang.: Swe.   490
  Activities of the audience-society, Gesellschaft der Freunde der
  Ballettschule der Österreichischen Bundestheater. Austria: Vienna.
  1985-1986. Lang.: Ger.   1294
  Artistic director John Neville discusses future plans for the Stratford
  Festival. Canada: Stratford, ON. 1985. Lang.: Eng.   1551
  Performance/production
  Training of Chinese students for a production of *The Tempest* by
  William Shakespeare. China, People's Republic of: Beijing. 1981-
  1985. Lang.: Eng.   679
  Interview with Mario Delgado Vásquez, director of Cuatrotablas.
  Peru: Lima. 1971-1985. Lang.: Hun.   769
  Analysis of career and methods of director Jerzy Grotowski. Poland.
  1959-1984. Lang.: Hun.   771

Training — cont'd

Overview of the career and work of director Peter Brook. USA: New York, NY. 1948-1984. Lang.: Eng.   829

The *kyōgen* actor's goals, relationship to mask work and training. Japan. 1984.   1409

Experimental training method used by Kaméleon Szinház Csoport. Hungary: Kurd. 1982-1985. Lang.: Hun.   1798

Circus clown discusses his training and work with puppets.   3382

Career of lion tamer Captain Terrell Jacobs. USA. 1903-1943. Lang.: Eng.   3393

Plays/librettos/scripts

Cooperation between theatres in Austria and playwrights-in-training. Austria. 1980-1986. Lang.: Ger.   2393

Interview with leaders of playwrights' seminar. USSR: Picunde. 1986. Lang.: Rus.   2955

Interview with composer Wolfgang Rihm. Switzerland. 1974-1986. Lang.: Ger.   3893

Reference materials

Guide to theatrical services and productions. UK-England. 1985-1986. Lang.: Eng.   1035

Relation to other fields

Argument for the establishment of graduate programs in children's theatre. USA. 1985. Lang.: Eng.   1168

Theory/criticism

Spiritual dimension of *nō* actor training. Japan. 1363-1470. Lang.: Ita.   1421

Training aids

Relation to other fields

Typical characteristics of laughing and crying. Germany. USA. 1935-1983. Lang.: Ger.   1088

Training

Review of training materials in Hungary and elsewhere since antiquity. Lang.: Hun.   1251

Numerous exercises with physiological explanations for phonation in harmony with breath rhythmics. Austria. 1985. Lang.: Ger.   1253

Use of *nō* masks in actor training. USA. 1984.   1424

Results of sonographic analysis of covered and uncovered singing. Austria. 1980-1984. Lang.: Ger.   3933

Psychological aspects of the voice teacher's work. Austria: Vienna. 1980-1984. Lang.: Ger.   3934

Psychological aspects of voice training. Austria. USA. 1750-1984. Lang.: Ger.   3935

Collected papers from a conference on voice training. Austria: Vienna. Italy: Rome. England: London. 1700-1984. Lang.: Ger. 3936

Physiological regulation for correct breathing and singing. Europe. North America. 1929-1984. Lang.: Ger.   3937

Medical examination of covered singing. Europe. 1980-1984. Lang.: Ger.   3938

Training institutions

SEE

Institutions, training.

Training methods

Training

Psychological aspects of the voice teacher's work. Austria: Vienna. 1980-1984. Lang.: Ger.   3934

Training, actor

Administration

Training of amateurs coordinated by Folkteatern in Gävleborgs Län. Sweden: Gävle. 1984-1986. Lang.: Swe.   60

Notes on theatre business following meeting of All-Union Theatre Society. USSR. 1986. Lang.: Rus.   183

Institutions

Collection of texts referring to drama schools. Europe. 1888-1985. Lang.: Ita.   492

Training for amateur theatre leaders at Marieborg Folkhögskola. Sweden: Norrköping. 1960-1986. Lang.: Swe.   528

Training and use of child performers. USA. 1949-1985. Lang.: Eng.   565

Reminiscences of study at Moscow Art Theatre. USSR. Lang.: Rus.   578

Former students remember Xiong Foxi. China, People's Republic of: Chengdu. 1901-1981. Lang.: Chi.   1568

Recollections of a student actor under Xiong Foxi's direction. China, People's Republic of: Jinan, Chengdu. 1901-1982. Lang.: Chi. 1569

History of the teaching of acting at the Conservatoire national d'art dramatique. France: Paris. 1786-1986. Lang.: Fre.   1576

The Reduta theatre as the predecessor of Grotowski's Laboratory. Poland: Warsaw. 1919-1939. Lang.: Fre.   1581

Curriculum and expectation of students in Eubie Blake's Children's Theatre Company. USA: New York, NY. 1986. Lang.: Eng. 1602

History of Circle Repertory Company. USA: New York, NY. 1969-1984. Lang.: Eng.   1606

Director of school of mime and theatre on gesture and image in theatrical representation. France: Paris. 1962-1985. Lang.: Fre. 3289

Performance/production

Directing techniques of Wu Renzhi. China. 1930-1980. Lang.: Chi.   678

Report on the Third European Child Acting Workshop. Denmark: Vordingborg. 1986. Lang.: Hun.   684

Study of the history of acting theory. Europe. North America. 1700-1985. Lang.: Eng.   704

Essays by and about Charles Dullin. France. 1885-1949. Lang.: Ita.   714

Interview with actor, director Jean-Pierre Miquel. France: Paris. 1950-1986. Lang.: Fre.   723

Interview with actor, director and teacher Daniel Mesguich. France: Paris. 1985. Lang.: Fre.   725

Theory, practice and body-training for the beginning actor. Korea: Seoul. Lang.: Kor.   758

Impressions of Warsaw's theatres and the training of Polish actors. Poland: Warsaw. 1986. Lang.: Swe.   770

Career of director Jerzy Grotowski. Poland. 1933-1976. Lang.: Eng.   773

Literary legacy of Michajl A. Čechov. Russia. USA. 1891-1955. Lang.: Rus.   781

The artistic director of the Arena Stage discusses the place of the actor in contemporary theatre. USA: Washington, DC. 1951-1986. Lang.: Eng.   832

Guide to finding acting jobs in theatre, film and television. USA. 1986. Lang.: Eng.   835

Changes in ensemble theatre practice. USA. Lang.: Eng.   842

Interview with producer, director, actor Robert Lewis. USA: New York, NY. 1930-1986. Lang.: Eng.   844

Guidelines for working with deaf actors and sign interpreters. USA. 1984-1986. Lang.: Eng.   848

Actor training methods. USSR. Lang.: Rus.   866

Professionalism and training of actors. USSR. 1980-1986. Lang.: Rus.   867

On the physical training of actors. USSR. 1986. Lang.: Rus.   872

Biography of K.S. Stanislavskij. USSR. 1863-1938. Lang.: Rus. 897

Issues in speech pronunciation in performance. USSR. 1980-1986. Lang.: Rus.   898

Actors' round table on the problems facing young actors. USSR: Moscow. 1986. Lang.: Rus.   900

Career of actor-director Oleg Tabakov. USSR: Moscow. 1950-1986. Lang.: Rus.   904

Creative work of Il'chom studio theatre. USSR: Taškent. 1980-1986. Lang.: Rus.   907

Suzuki's SCOT fuses diverse world cultures in ensemble theatre company. Japan: Toga. 1985. Lang.: Eng.   1404

Interview with *nō* actor Kongō Iwao. Japan. Lang.: Eng.   1411

Last lecture of director Zhu Duanjun. 1890-1978. Lang.: Chi. 1635

On actor and playwright Gabriel Barylli. Austria: Vienna. 1957-1986. Lang.: Ger.   1646

Actress Elisabeth Orth, her life and work. Austria. 1936-1986. Lang.: Ger.   1650

Actress Lu Xiaoyan's experiences in preparing to play a role in *The Little Foxes*. China. USA. 1939-1982. Lang.: Chi.   1687

Exploring the world of emotion in acting. China. 1850-1981. Lang.: Chi.   1691

On the goal of acting. China, People's Republic of. 1978-1982. Lang.: Chi.   1693

Essays by Suzuki Tadashi encompassing his approach to theatre, training, and performance. Japan. 1980-1983. Lang.: Eng.   2007

Discussion of Stanislavskij's influence by a number of artists. Sweden. 1890-1986. Lang.: Swe.   2094

Training, actor — cont'd

Four performances in Budapest by the students of Oleg Tabakov of GITIS, the Institute of Dramatic Art, Moscow. USSR: Moscow. Hungary: Budapest. 1986. Lang.: Hun.   2318

Handbook for acting in television commercials. USA. 1977-1986. Lang.: Eng.   3271

Development of works by the Special Delivery Moving Theatre. Canada: Vancouver, BC. 1976-1986. Lang.: Eng.   3294

Licedej Studio, directed by Viačeslav Polunin. USSR: Leningrad. 1980-1986. Lang.: Rus.   3307

What spoken drama actors can learn from Sung drama. China. 1100-1980. Lang.: Chi.   3513

Reference materials
Bibliography of Xiong Foxi's writings. China, People's Republic of. 1917-1963. Lang.: Chi.   1011

Relation to other fields
Training course for teacher/actors. Switzerland: Zurich. 1980-1986. Lang.: Ger.   1132

Workshops in Canada on 'Theatre for the Oppressed'. Canada: Toronto, ON. 1986. Lang.: Eng.   3022

Theatre workshops led by Augusto Boal. Canada: Montreal, PQ. 1985. Lang.: Eng.   3023

Training
Concept of negation in actor training. Lang.: Fre.   1252

Potential use of Chinese actor-training methods in the West. China. Europe. Lang.: Ita.   1254

Overview of spoken drama training programs. China, People's Republic of. 1907-1982. Lang.: Chi.   1255

Actor training methods of Luce Berthomme. France: Paris. 1984. Lang.: Eng.   1256

Interview with actress and acting trainer Kristin Linklater. USA: New York, NY. UK-England: London. 1954-1985. Lang.: Eng. 1261

Collected articles on the theory and practice of actor training. USSR. 1980-1986. Lang.: Rus.   1262

Stanislavskij system in Romanian theatre. USSR. Romania. 1980-1986. Lang.: Rus.   1264

Guide for teachers on getting a full-length play together. 1980-1982. Lang.: Chi.   3154

Actor-training approach based on imitation of animals. China, People's Republic of: Shanghai. 1949-1982. Lang.: Chi.   3155

Xiong Foxi, playwright and teacher. China, People's Republic of: Ch'eng-tu. 1928-1940. Lang.: Chi.   3156

Physical aspects of actor training. Europe. North America. 1985. Lang.: Eng.   3157

Experiences of acting teacher Zsuzsa Simon. Hungary. 1945-1985. Lang.: Hun.   3158

Effect of changing ideas about psychology and creativity on the Stanislavskij system. USSR: Moscow. 1900-1986. Lang.: Eng. 3162

Interview with director and teacher Zinovy Korogodskij. USSR: Moscow, Leningrad. 1970-1984. Lang.: Eng.   3163

Education for the actor-singer. USSR. 1980. Lang.: Rus.   3502

Training, dance
Institutions
Current state of ballet theatre, including choreographic training. China: Beijing. 1980-1986. Lang.: Rus.   1297

Performance/production
Dance in the Malaysian culture. Malaysia. 1950-1984. Lang.: Eng.   1333

History of classical Cambodian dance. Cambodia. 1860-1985. Lang.: Eng.   1358

Dakota Stanton discusses her career as a singer and dancer in nightclubs and reviews. USA: Pittsburgh, PA, New York, NY. 1950-1980. Lang.: Eng.   3471

Training, director
Institutions
Training for amateur theatre leaders at Marieborg Folkhögskola. Sweden: Norrköping. 1960-1986. Lang.: Swe.   528

Performance/production
Training of English directors. UK-England. 1850-1900. Lang.: Rus.   813

Training
Argument for better director training. UK-England. 1986. Lang.: Eng.   1257

Training, singer
Performance/production
Comprehensive history of singing and singers. 1901-1985. Lang.: Ger.   3482

Interview with baritone John Fanning. Canada: Toronto, ON. 1980-1986. Lang.: Eng.   3709

Interview with soprano Joanne Kolomyjec. Canada: Toronto, ON. 1986. Lang.: Eng.   3710

Interview with baritone Gino Quilico. Canada: Toronto, ON. 1984-1986. Lang.: Eng.   3711

Reasons for the decline of French opera and singing. France. 1950-1986. Lang.: Eng.   3729

Collection of interviews with Walter Felsenstein. Germany: Berlin. 1921-1971. Lang.: Ger.   3735

Profile of and interview with American soprano June Anderson. USA: New York, NY. 1955-1986. Lang.: Eng.   3793

History and achievements of the Brevard Music Center on the occasion of its fiftieth season. USA: Charlotte, NC. 1936-1986. Lang.: Eng.   3808

Profile of and interview with American soprano Carol Vaness. USA: San Diego, CA. 1950-1986. Lang.: Eng.   3817

Profile of and interview with American tenor Jerry Hadley. USA: New York, NY. 1952-1986. Lang.: Eng.   3818

Biography of singer Ivan Jeršov. USSR. 1867-1943. Lang.: Rus. 3847

Training
Results of sonographic analysis of covered and uncovered singing. Austria. 1980-1984. Lang.: Ger.   3933

Psychological aspects of voice training. Austria. USA. 1750-1984. Lang.: Ger.   3935

Collected papers from a conference on voice training. Austria: Vienna. Italy: Rome. England: London. 1700-1984. Lang.: Ger. 3936

Physiological regulation for correct breathing and singing. Europe. North America. 1929-1984. Lang.: Ger.   3937

Medical examination of covered singing. Europe. 1980-1984. Lang.: Ger.   3938

Training, teacher
Relation to other fields
Training course for teacher/actors. Switzerland: Zurich. 1980-1986. Lang.: Ger.   1132

Creative drama content in college language arts textbooks. USA. 1986. Lang.: Eng.   1166

Training, technician
Administration
Summary of the Cork report with recommendations on how the results can be used. UK. 1986. Lang.: Eng.   70

Design/technology
Training course for theatre technicians at Dramatiska Institutet. Sweden: Stockholm. 1985. Lang.: Swe.   318

Institutions
History of the Swedish Society for Theatre Technicians. Sweden. 1976-1986. Lang.: Swe.   521

Traitors
Performance/production
Collection of newspaper reviews by London theatre critics. UK-England: London. 1986. Lang.: Eng.   2117

Tramway Road
Performance/production
Director discusses *Tramway Road* by Ronald Harwood. South Africa, Republic of. UK-England: London. 1986. Lang.: Eng. 2073

Transformtheater (Berlin, West)
Institutions
Production of Jürgen Lederach's *Japanische Spiele (Japanese Play)* by Transformtheater. Germany, West: Berlin, West. 1981-1986. Lang.: Swe.   499

Translations
Basic theatrical documents
Text of *Karimkutty* by K. N. Panikkar in English translation. India. 1983. Lang.: Eng.   1355

Text of *Kasan ogwangdae (The Five Buffoons of Kasan)* in English translation. Korea: Kasan. 1975. Lang.: Eng.   1356

Playtext of Jacques de Decker's *Jeu d'intérieur (Indoor Games)* in English translation. Belgium. 1979. Lang.: Eng.   1461

Playtext of René Kalisky's *Sur les ruines de Carthage (On the Ruins of Carthage)* in English translation. Belgium. 1980. Lang.: Eng. 1462

Translations — cont'd

Playtext of Jean Sigrid's *L'ange couteau (Angel Knife)* in English translation. Belgium. 1980. Lang.: Eng.   1463

Playtext of Paul Willems' play *Il pleut dans ma maison (It's Raining in My House)* in English translation. Belgium. 1963. Lang.: Eng.   1464

Text of Inkeri Kilpinen's *Totisesti totisesti (Verily Verily)* in English translation. Finland. 1982-1983. Lang.: Eng, Fin.   1476

Catalan translations of plays by Tankred Dorst, with critical introduction. Germany. 1961. Lang.: Cat.   1482

New German translation of Shakespeare's *As You Like It*. Germany, East. 1986. Lang.: Ger.   1483

English translation of *Az óriáscsecsemö (The Giant Baby)* by Tibor Déry. Hungary. 1894-1977. Lang.: Eng, Hun.   1484

Catalan translation of *Il giuoco delle parti (The Rules of the Game)* by Luigi Pirandello. Italy. 1918. Lang.: Cat.   1485

English translation of *Coppia aperta, quasì spalancata (An Open Couple—Very Open)* by Dario Fo and Franca Rame. Italy: Trieste. 1983. Lang.: Eng.   1486

Catalan translation of *Madame de Sade* by Mishima Yukio. Japan. 1960-1970. Lang.: Cat.   1487

English translation of *Pequeña historia de horror (Little Tale of Horror)*. Mexico. 1932. Lang.: Eng.   1488

Text of *Eiolf Hakatan*, Gad Kaynar's Hebrew translation of *Lille Eyolf (Little Eyolf)* by Henrik Ibsen. Norway. Israel. 1884-1985. Lang.: Heb.   1489

Text of Čechov's *Platonov* in a version by Michael Frayn. Russia. 1878. Lang.: Cat.   1492

English translation of *El desconfiado prodigioso (The Remarkable Misanthrope)* by Max Aub. Spain. 1903-1972. Lang.: Eng, Spa.   1493

Text of *Tu i l'hipòcrita (You and the Hypocrite)*, by Maria Aurélia Capmany, translated into Castilian Spanish by L. Teresa Valdivieso as *Tú y el hipócrita*. Spain-Catalonia: Barcelona. 1959. Lang.: Spa.
1495

Text of *Primera història d'Esther (First Story of Esther)* by Salvador Espriu, with introduction on the author and the play. Spain-Catalonia: Barcelona. 1913-1985. Lang.: Spa, Cat.   1496

English translation of *L'ús de la matèria (The Use of Matter)* by Manuel de Pedrolo. Spain-Catalonia. 1963. Lang.: Cat, Eng.   1500

Anthology and study of writings of Josep Maria de Sagarra. Spain-Catalonia. 1917-1964. Lang.: Cat.   1501

Josep Maria de Sagarra's translations of Shakespeare with scholarly introduction. Spain-Catalonia. UK-England. 1590-1986. Lang.: Cat.
1502

Catalan translation of *Look Back in Anger* by John Osborne. UK-England. 1956. Lang.: Cat.   1506

Catalan translation of *The Homecoming* by Harold Pinter. UK-England. 1965. Lang.: Cat.   1507

Catalan translation of *Chicken Soup with Barley* by Arnold Wesker. UK-England. 1958. Lang.: Cat.   1509

English translation of Mario Benedetti's *Pedro y el capitán (Pedro and the Captain)*. Uruguay. 1979. Lang.: Eng.   1510

Catalan translation of *A View From the Bridge* by Arthur Miller. USA. 1955. Lang.: Cat.   1511

Catalan translation of *Small Craft Warnings* by Tennessee Williams. USA. 1972. Lang.: Cat.   1512

Text of *bunraku* play in English translation. Japan. 1760-1770. Lang.: Eng.   3996

Performance/production

Translation of *Belly-dancing* by Wendy Buonaventura. Europe. Asia. Africa. Lang.: Ita.   1330

Theatre Plus production of Santander's *Two Brothers*. Canada: Toronto, ON. Mexico. 1986. Lang.: Eng.   1679

Notes on the process of staging *Eiolf Hakatan*, a Hebrew translation of Henrik Ibsen's *Lille Eyolf (Little Eyolf)*, directed by Yossi Israeli at the Kahn theatre. Israel: Jerusalem. 1986. Lang.: Heb.   1980

Notes on the rehearsals of Henrik Ibsen's *Lille Eyolf (Little Eyolf)* directed by Yossi Israeli, at the Kahn Theatre. Israel: Jerusalem. 1986. Lang.: Heb.   1982

Othello, translated by Bohdan Drozdowski and directed by Wilfred Harrison at the Wilama Horzycy Theatre. Poland: Toruń. 1980. Lang.: Eng.   2023

Description of first translations and adaptations of Shakespeare's dramas on the Polish stage. Poland: Vilna. 1786-1864. Lang.: Pol.
2030

Hungarian translation of *L'Opera nel Settecento* by Giorgio Lise. Hungary: Budapest. 1700-1800. Lang.: Hun.   3752

Plays/librettos/scripts

Analysis of various theatrical forms of francophone Africa. Africa. 1985. Lang.: Fre.   919

Historical information on Oscar Wilde's *Vera, or The Nihilists*. England. Russia. USA: New York, NY. 1883. Lang.: Rus.   944

Introductory note on the first translation of *Lille Eyolf (Little Eyolf)* into Hebrew. Norway. Israel. 1884-1985. Lang.: Heb.   962

Theory of translation, using ideas of Eric Bentley and plays of Samuel Beckett. 1950-1986. Lang.: Eng.   2352

Eric Bentley on playwriting, translating and adapting. 1986. Lang.: Eng.   2355

Translations, adaptations and the Australian theatre. Australia: Armidale, N.S.W. 1985. Lang.: Eng.   2371

Difficulties in French translation of Karl Kraus's *Die Letzten Tage der Menschheit (The Last Days of Mankind)*. Austria: Vienna. France: Paris. 1918-1986. Lang.: Ger.   2397

Discusses Michel Garneau's *joual* translation of *Macbeth*. Canada: Montreal, PQ. 1978. Lang.: Eng.   2429

Translation of two works by Northrop Frye on Shakespeare. England. 1564-1616. Lang.: Ita.   2484

Translation of *Shakespeare: His World and His Work* by M. M. Reese. England. 1564-1616. Lang.: Ita.   2514

Translations of plays by William Shakespeare into Amharic and Tegrenna. Ethiopia: Addis Ababa. 1941-1984. Lang.: Eng.   2537

Interview with Josy Eisenberg, translator of *Le Cantique des cantiques (The Song of Songs)* for the Comédie-Française. France: Paris. 1986. Lang.: Fre.   2544

Analysis of *L'Aigle à deux têtes (The Eagle With Two Heads)* by Jean Cocteau. France. 1889-1963. Lang.: Cat.   2565

Examination of the first Hebrew adaptation of Molière's *Tartuffe* by David Vexler. France. 1874. Lang.: Heb.   2569

Introduction to plays by Tankred Dorst. Germany. 1925-1982. Lang.: Cat.   2591

Criteria for evaluating translations, using the example of Brecht's *Galileo*. Germany, East. 1938-1953.   2616

Translations of three plays by Rabindranath Tagore, with critical commentary. India. 1861-1941. Lang.: Eng.   2662

Overview of Hebrew adaptations and translations of *Tartuffe* by Molière. Israel. France. 1794-1985. Lang.: Heb.   2667

Influence of Luigi Pirandello's work in Catalonia. Italy. Spain-Catalonia. 1867-1985. Lang.: Spa, Cat.   2706

Translator discusses her Spanish version of Maria Aurelia Capmany's Catalan play, *Tu i l'hipócrita (You and the Hypocrite)*. Spain. 1959-1976. Lang.: Spa.   2806

Translations of Shakespeare by Josep Maria de Sagarra. Spain-Catalonia: Barcelona. 1940-1964. Lang.: Cat.   2811

Short history of Catalan translations of plays. Spain-Catalonia. 1848-1984. Lang.: Fre.   2813

Plays translated into Catalan by Pompeu Fabra. Spain-Catalonia. 1890-1905. Lang.: Cat.   2818

Memoir concerning playwright Joan Oliver. Spain-Catalonia. 1920-1986. Lang.: Cat.   2820

Interview with Gillian Hanna about *Elisabetta: Quasì per caso una donna (Elizabeth: Almost by Chance a Woman)*. UK-England: London. Italy. 1986. Lang.: Eng.   2875

Eric Bentley as one of the major forces in the subversion of Brecht. USA.   2903

Analysis of *Small Craft Warnings*, and report of audience reactions. USA: New York, NY. Spain-Catalonia: Barcelona. 1972-1983. Lang.: Cat.   2929

Auden and Kallman's English translation of *Die Zauberflöte (The Magic Flute)*. USA. 1951-1956. Lang.: Eng.   3903

Reference materials

Exhibition catalogue about context of the work and influence of Karl Kraus. Austria: Vienna. USA: New York, NY. France: Paris. 1874-1986. Lang.: Ger.   2980

Bibliography of Hungarian writer and translator Jenő Mohácsi. Hungary. 1886-1944. Lang.: Hun.   2991

Triomphe de l'amour, Le (Triumph of Love, The)
Performance/production
Analysis of two productions of plays by Marivaux. France: Nanterre. Germany, West: Berlin, West. 1985. Lang.: Swe.   1739

Triptychon (Triptych)
Plays/librettos/scripts
Analysis of plays by Max Frisch, and influences of Thornton Wilder. Switzerland. 1939-1983. Lang.: Eng.   2829

Tristan und Isolde
Performance/production
The first singers to perform *Tristan und Isolde*. Germany: Munich. 1857-1869. Lang.: Eng.   3733

Triumph of Intrigue, The
Basic theatrical documents
Texts of three political dramas, with discussion. Canada. 1833-1879. Lang.: Eng.   1472

Triumphs of Reunited Brittania, The
Plays/librettos/scripts
Similarities between *King Lear* by Shakespeare and *The Trimphs of Reunited Britannia* by Munday. England. 1605-1606. Lang.: Eng.   2480

Troádes (Trojan Women, The)
Audience
HaBimah Theatre production of *Troádes (The Trojan Women)* by Euripides. Israel: Tel-Aviv. 1982-1983. Lang.: Eng.   199

Performance/production
Troádes (The Trojan Women) directed by László Gergely at Csokonai Theatre. Hungary: Debrecen. 1985. Lang.: Hun.   1909

Troia no onna (Trojan Women, The)
Performance/production
Suzuki's SCOT fuses diverse world cultures in ensemble theatre company. Japan: Toga. 1985. Lang.: Eng.   1404

Troilus and Cressida
Performance/production
Visual patterns of staging in Shakespeare's *Troilus and Cressida*. England: London. 1597-1600. Lang.: Eng.   1704

Reviews of three Shakespearean productions. UK-England: London, Stratford. USA: Ashland, OR. 1985. Lang.: Eng.   2140

Detailed discussion of four successful Royal Shakespeare Company productions of Shakespeare's minor plays. UK-England: Stratford. 1946-1977. Lang.: Eng.   2182

Shakespearean productions by the National Theatre, Royal Shakespeare Company and Orange Tree Theatre. UK-England: Stratford, London. 1984-1985. Lang.: Eng.   2183

Plays/librettos/scripts
Heterosexual and homosexual desires in Shakespeare's *Troilus and Cressida*. England. 1602. Lang.: Eng.   2471

Trojan Women
SEE
Troia no onna.
Troyennes, Les.
Troádes.

Trommeln in der Nacht (Drums in the Night)
Plays/librettos/scripts
Bertolt Brecht and the Expressionists. Germany. 1919-1944. Lang.: Eng.   955

Tron Theatre (Glasgow)
Performance/production
Survey of the year in Scottish theatre. UK-Scotland. 1986. Lang.: Eng.   2194

Troni (Venice)
Institutions
Relations between the 'Confidenti' company and their patron Don Giovanni dei Medici. Italy: Venice. 1613-1621. Lang.: Ita.   1580

Troubridge, Una
Performance/production
Interview with Lesbian feminist theatre company Hard Corps. UK-England. 1984-1986. Lang.: Eng.   2164

Troughton, Michael
Performance/production
Political difficulties in staging two touring productions of Shakespeare's *The Taming of the Shrew*. UK. 1985-1986. Lang.: Eng.   2104

Trovatore, Il
Performance/production
József Bor directs Verdi's opera *Il Trovatore* at Kisfaludy Theatre. Hungary: Győr. 1985. Lang.: Hun.   3750

Troyennes, Les
Performance/production
Review of *Trójai Nők (The Trojan Women)* by Jean-Paul Sartre, produced at Nemzeti Szinház. Hungary: Budapest. 1986. Lang.: Hun.   1855

Troyennes, Les (Trojan Women, The)
Performance/production
Review of *A trójai nők (The Trojan Women)* adapted from Euripides and Sartre by Gyula Illyés, directed by László Vámos. Hungary: Budapest. 1986. Lang.: Hun.   1792

TRTC
SEE
Ridiculous Theatre Company, The.

True Stories
Plays/librettos/scripts
How David Byrne constructed a script for *True Stories*. USA. 1986.   3242

True West
Performance/production
István Verebes directs *Valódi Vadnyugat (True West)* by Sam Shepard. Hungary: Budapest. 1986. Lang.: Hun.   1772

István Verebes directs *Valódi vadnyugat (True West)* by Sam Shepard at Radnóti Miklós Szinpad. Hungary: Budapest. 1986. Lang.: Hun.   1939

Plays/librettos/scripts
Interview with playwright Sam Shepard. USA. 1984. Lang.: Eng.   2925

Development of playwright Sam Shepard's style. USA. 1972-1985. Lang.: Eng.   2943

Relation to other fields
Playwright Sam Shepard's recent plays and super-realist painting. USA. 1978-1983. Lang.: Eng.   3069

Trujkis, L.
Design/technology
Opera set designs by L. Trujkis. USSR. Lithuania. 1986. Lang.: Rus.   3664

Tsaplia (Heron, The)
Plays/librettos/scripts
Analysis of *Grupa Laokoona (The Laocoön Group)* by Tadeusz Różewicz and *Tsaplia (The Heron)* by Vasilij Aksënov. Poland. USSR. 1961-1979. Lang.: Eng.   2738

Tsubouchi, Shikō
Reference materials
Dictionary of the life and work of Tsubouchi Shōyō. Japan: Tokyo. 1859-1986. Lang.: Jap.   1027

Tsubouchi, Shōyō
Reference materials
Dictionary of the life and work of Tsubouchi Shōyō. Japan: Tokyo. 1859-1986. Lang.: Jap.   1027

Tsumura, Reijirō
Performance/production
Nō actor's preparation and rehearsal for the play, *Dōjōji*. Japan. 1983. Lang.: Eng.   1413

Tu i l'hipócrita (You and the Hypocrite)
Basic theatrical documents
Text of *Tu i l'hipócrita (You and the Hypocrite)*, by Maria Aurélia Capmany, translated into Castilian Spanish by L. Teresa Valdivieso as *Tú y el hipócrita*. Spain-Catalonia: Barcelona. 1959. Lang.: Spa.   1495

Plays/librettos/scripts
Translator discusses her Spanish version of Maria Aurelia Capmany's Catalan play, *Tu i l'hipócrita (You and the Hypocrite)*. Spain. 1959-1976. Lang.: Spa.   2806

Tu, Long
Performance/production
Modern and traditional performance styles compared. China. 1598-1984. Lang.: Chi.   3511

Tu, Sanfu
Relation to other fields
Analysis of Northern Sung theatrical artifacts. 1032-1126. Lang.: Chi.   3546

Tuan, Anchieh
Theory/criticism
Influence of Tuan Anchieh's aesthetics. China. 800-1644. Lang.: Chi.   3561

Tubieński, Tomasz
Performance/production
Tubieński's *Śmieré Komandura (The Death of the Commander)* directed by Eugeniusz Korin, Teatr Polski. Poland: Wrocław. 1984. Lang.: Pol. 2056

Tubman, Harriet
Performance/production
Review of *Harriet, the Woman Called Moses*, an opera by Thea Musgrave, staged by Gordon Davidson. USA: Norfolk, VA. 1985. Lang.: Eng. 3835

Tulloch, Richard
Performance/production
Dilemmas and prospects of youth theatre movement. Australia. 1982-1986. Lang.: Eng. 1639

Tun, Hsiehyuan
Research/historiography
Origins and evolution of today's Beijing opera. China, People's Republic of: Beijing. 1755-1984. Lang.: Chi. 3556

Tungsram Rt. (Budapest)
Design/technology
Interviews at Tungsram Rt. electronics factory. Hungary: Budapest. 1980-1986. Lang.: Hun. 283

Tupa, A Vinganca (Tupa, Vengeance)
Performance/production
Survey of productions in 1985/86. Brazil: Rio de Janeiro. 1985-1986. Lang.: Eng. 1656

Turandot (Brecht)
Performance/production
The cooperation between amateurs and professionals in Fria Proteatern's staging of Brecht's *Turandot*. Sweden: Stockholm. 1986. Lang.: Swe. 2095

Turca, La (Turkish Woman, The)
Plays/librettos/scripts
Giovan Battista Andreini's problems in publishing *La Turca (The Turkish Woman)*. Italy. 1611. Lang.: Ita. 2692

Turgenjev, Ivan Sergejèvič
Plays/librettos/scripts
Dramaturgy of Turgenjev. Russia. 1842-1852. Lang.: Rus. 2768

Analysis of the plays of Ivan Turgenjev. Russia. 1818-1883. Lang.: Rus. 2770

Investigates whether Brahms wrote music for an opera. Austria: Vienna. 1863-1985. Lang.: Eng. 3856

Turista, La
Plays/librettos/scripts
Argument of reversed chronology in Acts I and II of *La Turista* by Sam Shepard. USA. 1967. Lang.: Eng. 2951

Turkka, Juoko
Institutions
Career of dramaturgist and teacher Outi Nyytäjä. Finland: Helsinki. 1967-1986. Lang.: Eng, Fre. 493

Performance/production
Interview with Juoko Turkka on acting and directing. Finland. 1986. Lang.: Swe. 1720

Rehearsals of *Kött och kärlek (Flesh and Love)* by Juoko Turkka. Sweden: Gothenburg. 1986. Lang.: Swe. 2085

Discussion of Stanislavskij's influence by a number of artists. Sweden. 1890-1986. Lang.: Swe. 2094

Turn of the Screw, The
Plays/librettos/scripts
A chronology and analysis of the compositions of Benjamin Britten. UK-England: London. 1946-1976. Lang.: Eng. 3896

Character analysis in Britten's opera *The Turn of the Screw*. UK-England. 1954. Lang.: Eng. 3898

Turner, Eva
Performance/production
Famous sopranos discuss their interpretations of Tosca. USA. 1935-1986. Lang.: Eng. 3811

Turner, Jessica
Institutions
Place of women in Britain's National Theatre. UK-England: London. 1986. Lang.: Eng. 1588

Turner, John
Performance/production
Collection of newspaper reviews by London theatre critics. UK-England: London. 1986. Lang.: Eng. 2126

Turner, Victor
Performance/production
Types of costumes, dances, and songs of Dodo masquerades during Ramadan. Upper Volta: Ouagadougou. Lang.: Eng. 3428

Plays/librettos/scripts
Bertolt Brecht and the Expressionists. Germany. 1919-1944. Lang.: Eng. 955

Ritual function of *The Slave Ship* by LeRoi Jones (Amiri Baraka) and *Quinta Temporada (Fifth Season)* by Luis Valdez. USA. 1965-1967. Lang.: Eng. 2906

Relation to other fields
Translation of *From Ritual to Theatre* by Victor Turner. Lang.: Ita. 1060

Turoev, G.
Performance/production
Round-table on puppet theatre. USSR: Moscow, Leningrad. 1986. Lang.: Rus. 3985

Turp, Gilbert
Performance/production
Three directors' versions of *Les cauchemars du grand monde (Nightmares of High Society)* by Gilbert Turp. Canada: Montreal, PQ. 1984. Lang.: Fre. 1672

TURteaterns (Kärrtorp)
Performance/production
Mats Ödeen's *Det ende raka (The Only Straight Thing)* performed by TURteaterns amatörteatergrupp. Sweden: Stockholm. 1979-1986. Lang.: Swe. 801

Tutin, Dorothy
Performance/production
Interview with actress Dorothy Tutin. UK-England: Chichester. 1986. Lang.: Eng. 2132

Tutta casa letto e chiesa (She's All Home, Bed and Church)
Performance/production
Life and work of actress-playwright Franca Rame. Italy. 1929-1983. Lang.: Eng. 1988

Twain, Mark
Plays/librettos/scripts
Philosophy of wealth in gilded age plays. USA: New York, NY. 1870-1889. Lang.: Eng. 2950

Twelfth Night
Performance spaces
Overview of the hall in which Shakespeare's *Twelfth Night* was performed. England: London. 1602. Lang.: Eng. 1616

Performance/production
Shakespearean form, Asian content in *Norodom Sihanouk* by Ariane Mnouchkine's Théâtre du Soleil. France: Paris. 1964-1986. Lang.: Eng. 709

Innovative Shakespeare stagings of Harley Granville-Barker. UK-England. 1912-1940. Lang.: Eng. 806

Significance of 'boy-actresses' in role of Viola in Shakespeare's *Twelfth Night*. England. 1601. Lang.: Eng. 1714

Reconstruction of a number of Shakespeare plays staged and performed by Herbert Beerbohm Tree. UK-England: London. 1887-1917. Lang.: Eng. 2155

Reviews of Shakespeare's *Twelfth Night*, staged by Wilford Leach. USA: New York, NY. 1986. Lang.: Eng. 2217

Plays/librettos/scripts
Shakespeare's influence on Beaumont and Fletcher's *Philaster*. England. 1609. Lang.: Eng. 2463

Twelve Angry Men
Performance/production
Tizenkét dühös ember (Twelve Angry Men) by Reginald Rose directed by András Béhés. Hungary: Budapest. 1985. Lang.: Hun. 1972

Twenty-one Hours at Munich
Plays/librettos/scripts
Analysis of television docudramas as a melodrama genre. USA. 1965-1986. Lang.: Eng. 3285

Twilight of the Gods, The
SEE
Gotterdammerung.

Two Brothers
Performance/production
Theatre Plus production of Santander's *Two Brothers*. Canada: Toronto, ON. Mexico. 1986. Lang.: Eng. 1679

Two Figures in Dense Violet Light
Performance/production
Survey of productions at the Kennedy Center's National Theatre.
USA: Washington, DC. 1986. Lang.: Eng. 2247

Two Gentlemen of Verona, The
Performance/production
John Hirsch's artistic career at the Stratford Festival Theatre.
Canada: Stratford, ON. 1981-1985. Lang.: Eng. 1683

Performances of *Alice Csodaországban (Alice in Wonderland), A Két Veronai nemes (The Two Gentlemen of Verona)* and *Tobbsincs királyfi (No More Crown Prince)*. Hungary: Pécs, Budapest. 1985. Lang.: Hun. 1771

Two Noble Kinsmen, The
Reference materials
List of 37 productions of 23 Renaissance plays, with commentary.
UK. USA. New Zealand. 1986. Lang.: Eng. 3000

Two-Headed Monster, The
SEE
Kétfejü fenevad, A.

Tynan, Kenneth
Performance/production
Overview of the career and work of director Peter Brook. USA:
New York, NY. 1948-1984. Lang.: Eng. 829

Photographic record of forty years of the Berliner Ensemble.
Germany, East: Berlin, East. 1949-1984. Lang.: Eng. 1761

Theory/criticism
Assessment of critic Kenneth Tynan's works. UK-England. 1950-
1960. Lang.: Eng. 3136

Tyne Weare Company (Newcastle, UK)
Performance/production
Survey of performances in England's Northeast. UK-England. 1986.
Lang.: Eng. 2173

Tyoväen Näyltämöiden Liitto (TNL, Workers' Theatre Union)
Performance/production
History of amateur theatre in Finland. Finland. 1920-1986. Lang.:
Swe. 706

Tzuyuan, Ma
Theory/criticism
Ma Tzuyuan's use of poetic elements in Chinese opera. China:
Beijing. 1279-1368. Lang.: Chi. 3559

U.S. Small Business Administration
Institutions
Report issued by Small Business Administration claims unfair
competition form nonprofit organizations. USA. 1984. Lang.: Eng.
556

Ubangi Club (New York, NY)
Performance/production
Four nightclub entertainers on their particular acts and the
atmosphere of the late night clubs and theaters in Harlem. USA:
New York, NY, Savannah, GA. 1930-1950. Lang.: Eng. 3470

Ubu roi
Performance/production
Amateur production of Alfred Jarry's *Kung Ubu (Ubu roi)* by
Kristianstad Musikteater. Sweden: Kristianstad. 1986. Lang.: Swe.
797

Production analysis of *Ubu roi* by Alfred Jarry staged for the first
time in Hungary by Gábor Zsámbéki at the József Katona Theatre.
Hungary: Budapest. 1984. Lang.: Hun. 1969

Udaka, Michishige
Design/technology
Nō actor talks about his work as a mask carver. Japan. Lang.: Eng.
1395

Ujima Youtheatre (Omaha, NE)
Relation to other fields
Black history and folklore taught in theatre workshops and
productions. USA: New York, NY, Omaha, NE, Washington, DC.
1986. Lang.: Eng. 3068

Ul'janov, M.A.
Performance/production
Actor M. Ul'janov on tasks of Soviet theatre. USSR: Moscow. 1986.
Lang.: Rus. 905

Actor M.A. Ul'janov in *I dol'še veka dlitsja den' (A Day Lasts
Longer than a Century)* at Teat'r im. Je. Vachtangova. USSR:
Moscow. 1980-1986. Lang.: Rus. 2327

Ulfsson, Birgitta
Institutions
History of Swedish language Lilla-teatern (Little Theatre). Finland:
Helsinki. 1940-1986. Lang.: Eng, Fre. 494

Ulises no vuelve (Ulysses Does Not Return)
Plays/librettos/scripts
Thematic and stylistic comparison of three plays influenced by the
Odyssey. Spain. 1952-1983. Lang.: Eng. 2792

Ullmann, Liv
Performance/production
Mariann Csernus' stage adaptations and performance in works of
Simone de Beauvoir and Liv Ullmann. Hungary: Budapest. 1985.
Lang.: Hun. 1816

Ultimatte
Design/technology
Discussion of ultimatte, a television matting technique. USA. 1986.
Lang.: Eng. 3260

Umberto D.
Plays/librettos/scripts
Comparison of screenplay and film of *Umberto D.,* directed by
Vittorio De Sica. Italy. 1952. Lang.: Fre. 3236

Umerla Klasa (Dead Class, The)
Performance/production
Career and philosophy of director Tadeusz Kantor. Poland. 1915-
1985. Lang.: Eng. 2028

Interview with director Tadeusz Kantor. Poland. 1967-1985. Lang.:
Eng. 2029

Umiak
Basic theatrical documents
Text of *Umiak* by Théâtre de la Marmaille. Canada: Toronto, ON.
1983. Lang.: Eng. 1467

Plays/librettos/scripts
Umiak by Théâtre de la Marmaille of Toronto, based on Inuit
tradition. Canada. 1982-1983. Lang.: Eng. 2434

Uncle Vanya
SEE
Diadia Vania.

Undivine Comedy, The
SEE
Ne-boska komedia.

Unger, Heinz Rudolf
Plays/librettos/scripts
Cooperation between playwright Heinz Rudolf Unger and the
Volkstheater. Austria: Vienna. 1938-1986. Lang.: Ger. 2394

UNIMA (Union Internationale de la Marionette)
Performance/production
Productions presented at the first regional puppet forum. France:
Gareoult. 1986. Lang.: Hun. 3965

Union County Arts Center (Rahway, NJ)
Performance spaces
History of the Rahway Theatre, now the Union County Arts Center.
USA: Rahway, NJ. 1926-1986. Lang.: Eng. 3218

Unions
Administration
Management and unions in collective bargaining. USA. 1986. Lang.:
Eng. 99

United States
Theory/criticism
Semiotic analysis of Laurie Anderson's *United States.* USA. 1984.
Lang.: Eng. 3462

United States Institute for Theatre Technology (USITT)
Design/technology
Stage machinery guidelines. Lang.: Eng. 228

Contemporary theatre architecture. USA. 1976-1987. Lang.: Eng. 342

Description of USITT trade show. USA. 1986. Lang.: Eng. 352

Unity Players (Glasgow)
Design/technology
Life of stage designer Tom MacDonald. UK-Scotland: Glasgow.
1914-1985. Lang.: Eng. 1526

Universal Jazz Coalition (New York, NY)
Performance/production
Dakota Stanton discusses her career as a singer and dancer in
nightclubs and reviews. USA: Pittsburgh, PA, New York, NY. 1950-
1980. Lang.: Eng. 3471

Universitas Együttes (Budapest)
Performance/production
Interview with actor, director and dramaturg Imre Katona of the
Gropius Társulat. Hungary: Budapest. 1961-1985. Lang.: Hun. 1945

University of California (Irvine, CA)
Performance/production
Account of University of California at Irvine production of a nativity play with composite text drawn from York, N-town and Wakefield cycles. USA: Irvine, CA. 1986. Lang.: Eng.   2307

University of Rochester (Rochester, NY)
Performance/production
Attempt to produce Quarto version of *King Lear* at University of Rochester. USA: Rochester, NY. 1985. Lang.: Eng.   2300

University of São Paulo
Plays/librettos/scripts
Ritual and archetypal communication in *La noche de los asesinos (The Night of the Assassins)* by José Triana. Cuba. Brazil. 1973-1974. Lang.: Eng.   2450

University of Toronto (Toronto, ON)
Performance/production
Interview with baritone John Fanning. Canada: Toronto, ON. 1980-1986. Lang.: Eng.   3709

Interview with soprano Joanne Kolomyjec. Canada: Toronto, ON. 1986. Lang.: Eng.   3710

Unnamable
Plays/librettos/scripts
Language and the permanent dialectic of truth and lie in the plays of Samuel Beckett. France. 1930-1980. Lang.: Fre.   2549

Unruh, Fritz von
Performance/production
Max Reinhardt's work with his contemporaries. Germany. Austria. 1890-1938. Lang.: Eng, Ger.   1757

Unwin, Paul
Performance/production
Collection of newspaper reviews by London theatre critics. UK-England. 1986. Lang.: Eng.   2120

Uomo, la bestia, e la virtù, L' (Man, Animal and Virtue)
Performance/production
Notes on the first production of Luigi Pirandello's *L'uomo, la bestia, e la virtù (Man, Animal and Virtue)*. Italy. 1919. Lang.: Ita.   1997

Upshaw, Dawn
Performance/production
Reviews of *Death in the Family, Viaggio a Reims, Abduction from the Seraglio* and *Tales of Hoffmann*. USA: St. Louis, MO. 1975-1986. Lang.: Eng.   3799

Upsy-Daisy, We Are Alive
SEE
Hoppla, wir leben!.

Uptown...It's Hot
Performance/production
Reviews of *Uptown...It's Hot*, staged, choreographed and conceived by Maurice Hines. USA: New York, NY. 1986. Lang.: Eng.   1284

Tap dancing career of Maurice Hines and the creation of his new company Balletap, USA. USA: New York, NY. 1949-1986. Lang.: Eng.   3623

Urban, Keith
Institutions
Careers of choreographers Maria Formolo and Keith Urban. Canada: Regina, SK, Edmonton, AB. 1980-1983. Lang.: Eng.   1343

Urfaust
Performance/production
Brecht and the Berliner Ensemble. Germany, East: Berlin, East. 1950-1956. Lang.: Ger.   1765

Ús de la matèria, L' (Use of Matter, The)
Basic theatrical documents
English translation of *L'ús de la matèria (The Use of Matter)* by Manuel de Pedrolo. Spain-Catalonia. 1963. Lang.: Cat, Eng.   1500

Usher, Simon
Performance/production
Collection of newspaper reviews by London theatre critics. UK-England. 1986. Lang.: Eng.   2115

Usigli, Rodolfo
Plays/librettos/scripts
Corona de luz (Crown of Light) by Rodolfo Usigli as a self-reflexive comment on the process of dramatizing an historical event. Mexico. 1960-1980. Lang.: Eng.   2722

Use of language in *El Gesticulador (The Gesticulator)* by Rodolfo Usigli. Mexico. 1970-1980. Lang.: Spa.   2723

Reflections and influence of playwrights Rodolfo Usigli of Mexico and Antonio Buero Vallejo of Spain on theatre in their native countries. Spain. Mexico. Lang.: Spa.   2803

Uspenskij, J.
Performance/production
Interview on puppet theatre playwriting with B. Goldovskij and J. Uspenskij. USSR: Moscow. 1986. Lang.: Rus.   3986

Vacationists, The
SEE
Dačniki.

Vachtangov, Jevgenij Bogrationovič
Performance/production
Biographical materials on actress C.L. Mansurova. USSR. 1920-1986. Lang.: Rus.   884

Vajda, Anikó
Performance/production
Villa Negra by Anikó and Katalin Vajda directed by Miklós Szurdi. Hungary: Budapest. 1986. Lang.: Hun.   1818

Adaptation for the stage by Anikó Vagda and Katalin Vajda of Imre Dobozy's screenplay *Villa Negra*, directed at Játékszin by Miklós Szurdi. Hungary: Budapest. 1986. Lang.: Hun.   1870

Vajda, Katalin
Performance/production
Villa Negra by Anikó and Katalin Vajda directed by Miklós Szurdi. Hungary: Budapest. 1986. Lang.: Hun.   1818

Adaptation for the stage by Anikó Vagda and Katalin Vajda of Imre Dobozy's screenplay *Villa Negra*, directed at Játékszin by Miklós Szurdi. Hungary: Budapest. 1986. Lang.: Hun.   1870

Vajda, László
Performance/production
Čechov's *Három nővér (Three Sisters)* directed by Tamás Ascher. Hungary: Budapest. 1985. Lang.: Hun.   1814

Vakhtangov Theatre
SEE
Teat'r im. Je. Vachtangova.

Valdez, Luis
Institutions
Origins and evolution of Teatro Campesino. USA. Mexico. 1965-1986. Lang.: Eng.   547

Collection of essays on the evolution of Chicano theatre. USA. 1850-1985. Lang.: Eng.   1599

Performance/production
Annual festival of Latin American plays at the Public Theatre. USA: New York, NY. 1985. Lang.: Eng.   2310

Plays/librettos/scripts
Ritual function of *The Slave Ship* by LeRoi Jones (Amiri Baraka) and *Quinta Temporada (Fifth Season)* by Luis Valdez. USA. 1965-1967. Lang.: Eng.   2906

Valdivieso, L. Teresa
Basic theatrical documents
Text of *Tu i l'hipócrita (You and the Hypocrite)*, by Maria Aurélia Capmany, translated into Castilian Spanish by L. Teresa Valdivieso as *Tú y el hipócrita*. Spain-Catalonia: Barcelona. 1959. Lang.: Spa.   1495

Plays/librettos/scripts
Translator discusses her Spanish version of Maria Aurelia Capmany's Catalan play, *Tu i l'hipócrita (You and the Hypocrite)*. Spain. 1959-1976. Lang.: Spa.   2806

Valente, Benita
Performance/production
Profile of and interview with American soprano Benita Valente. USA. 1940-1986. Lang.: Eng.   3816

Valéry, Paul
Performance/production
Collaboration of choreographer Aurél Milloss and scene designer Giorgio de Chirico. Hungary. Italy: Milan, Rome. 1942-1945. Lang.: Hun.   1275

Influence of Richard Wagner on the work of the French Symbolists. France: Paris. Germany, West: Bayreuth. 1860-1986. Lang.: Eng.   3726

Valesio, Francesco
Design/technology
Costume design in a 16th century production in Milan of Guarini's *Il Pastor Fido*. Italy: Mantua. 1500-1600. Lang.: Eng.   298

Valle-Inclán, Ramón María del
Plays/librettos/scripts
Salvador Espriu's tragic vision in *Ronda de Mort a Sinera (Death Round at Sinera)*. Spain. 1965. Lang.: Eng.   2784

Parody and satire in Ramón del Valle-Inclán's *La Cabeza del dragón (The Dragon's Head)*. Spain. 1909. Lang.: Eng.   2798

Vaudeville — cont'd

Design/technology
Costumes at New York International Clown Festival. USA: New York, NY. 1984. Lang.: Eng.   3316

Performance spaces
History of the Bushwick Theatre. USA: New York, NY. 1911-1986. Lang.: Eng.   3465

Performance/production
History of Yiddish theatre district. USA: New York, NY. 1900-1939. Lang.: Eng.   827

A scholarly study of the careers of Alfred Lunt and Lynn Fontanne. USA. 1922-1972. Lang.: Eng.   2257

Account of *Poisson Chez Colbert* as performed at Théâtre du Vaudeville with a discussion of the popularity of vaudeville in Paris. France: Paris. 1808. Lang.: Eng.   3941

Relation to other fields
Style in children's theatre in light of theories of Philippe Ariès. USA. UK. France. 1600-1980. Lang.: Eng.   1162

Vaudeville Theatre (Stratford)

Performance/production
Collection of newspaper reviews by London theatre critics. UK-England: London. 1986. Lang.: Eng.   2113

Vaughan Williams, Ralph

Performance/production
Interview with singer Nancy Evans and writer Eric Crozier discussing their association with Benjamin Britten. USA: Columbia, MO. UK-England: London. 1940-1985. Lang.: Eng.   3820

Vay, Sarolta

Relation to other fields
Selected cultural-historical sketches of Countess Sarolta Vay published in 1900 including several of theatrical interest. Austro-Hungarian Empire. 1740-1848. Lang.: Hun.   1065

Vázlatsor (Series of Sketches)

Performance/production
Production analysis of a montage of sketches about Electra by Stúdió K. Hungary: Budapest. 1986. Lang.: Hun.   1773

Večer (Evening, An)

Performance/production
Aleksej Dudarëv's *Večer (An Evening)* directed by Mátyás Giricz at Józsefvárosi Theatre. Hungary: Budapest. 1986. Lang.: Hun.   1947

Vega Carpio, Lope Félix de

Performance/production
Productions of plays by Edward Bond, Gyula Hernádi and Lope de Vega at the Pécs National Theatre. Hungary: Pécs. 1986. Lang.: Hun.   1898

Mátyás Giricz directs *A kertész kutyája (The Gardener's Dog)* by Lope de Vega. Hungary: Budapest. 1985. Lang.: Hun.   1900

Plays/librettos/scripts
Luis de Góngora's plays as a response to Lope de Vega. Spain. 1561-1627. Lang.: Eng.   968

Conservative and reactionary nature of the Spanish *Comedia*. Spain. 1600-1700. Lang.: Eng.   2782

Juan del Enzina's defence of pastoral vs. courtly genre. Spain. 1469-1529. Lang.: Spa.   2785

Examples of playwrights whose work was poorly received by theatrical audiences in Madrid. Spain: Madrid. 1609-1950. Lang.: Spa.   2786

Reconstructs from historical sources the rebellion depicted in *Fuente Ovejuna (The Sheep Well)* by Lope de Vega as ritual behavior. Spain. 1476. Lang.: Eng.   2794

Lope de Vega's characterization of the converted Jew. Spain. 1562-1635. Lang.: Spa.   2804

Mutual influences between *commedia dell'arte* and Spanish literature. Spain. Italy. 1330-1623. Lang.: Spa.   2805

Theory/criticism
Lope de Vega's theories of comedy. Spain. 1609-1624. Lang.: Spa.   3132

Vega, Lope de

SEE
Vega Carpio, Lope Félix de.

Veitch, Patrick

Performance/production
History and current state of Australian Opera at the Sydney Opera House. Australia: Sydney, N.S.W. 1973-1986. Lang.: Eng.   3688

Venables, Clare

Performance/production
Collection of newspaper reviews by London theatre critics. UK. 1986. Lang.: Eng.   2103

Venice Preserved

Performance/production
Reception of the Kembles' Canadian tour. Canada. 1832-1834. Lang.: Eng.   663

Ventriloquism

Reference materials
A profile of a museum of ventriloquism lore. USA: Fort Mitchell, KY. 1985.   3989

Vera, or The Nihilists

Plays/librettos/scripts
Historical information on Oscar Wilde's *Vera, or The Nihilists*. England. Russia. USA: New York, NY. 1883. Lang.: Rus.   944

Verbund Wiener Theatre (Vienna)

Institutions
Union of three theaters in Vienna to the Verbund Wiener Theatre. Austria: Vienna. 1986. Lang.: Ger.   449

Verdaguer, Jacint

Plays/librettos/scripts
A defense of Àngel Guimerà's language. Spain-Catalonia. 1860-1967. Lang.: Cat.   2817

Verdi, Giuseppe

Performance/production
András Fehér directs Verdi's *Un ballo in maschera* at the Hungarian State Opera House. Hungary: Budapest. 1986. Lang.: Hun.   3746

Verdi's *Simon Boccanegra* and Puccini's *La Bohème* at the Hungarian State Opera House and Erkel Theatre. Hungary: Budapest. 1986. Lang.: Hun.   3747

József Bor directs Verdi's opera *Il Trovatore* at Kisfaludy Theatre. Hungary: Győr. 1985. Lang.: Hun.   3750

The Franco Zeffirelli film of *Otello* by Giuseppe Verdi, an account of the production. Italy: Rome. 1985-1986. Lang.: Eng.   3758

Productions of operas at La Scala by Luca Ronconi. Italy: Milan. 1985. Lang.: Ita.   3763

The successful collaboration of Arrigo Boito and Giuseppe Verdi in *Simon Boccanegra*. Italy. 1856-1881. Lang.: Eng.   3764

Interview with Peter Stein about his production of Verdi's *Otello*. UK-Wales: Cardiff. 1986. Lang.: Eng.   3789

Reviews of 10 vintage recordings of complete operas on LP. USA. 1906-1925. Lang.: Eng.   3792

Photographs, cast list, synopsis, and discography of Metropolitan Opera radio broadcast performances. USA: New York, NY. 1986. Lang.: Eng.   3794

Opera director Nathaniel Merrill on his productions. USA: New York, NY. 1958-1986. Lang.: Eng.   3805

Significance of the translation in recordings of Verdi's *Otello*. USA. 1902-1978. Lang.: Eng.   3812

Controversy over Jonathan Miller's production of *Rigoletto*. USA. 1984. Lang.: Eng.   3821

Plays/librettos/scripts
Discussion of plays about Verdi and Puccini by Julian Mitchell and Robin Ray. UK-England: London. Italy. 1986. Lang.: Eng.   3628

Operatic facsimiles by Mozart, Bellini and Verdi. Europe. 1814-1985. Lang.: Eng.   3863

Origins of the characters Rigoletto and Marullo in Verdi's *Rigoletto*. France. 1496-1851. Lang.: Eng.   3869

Shakespeare's influence on Verdi's operas. Germany. Italy. Austria. 1750-1850. Lang.: Eng.   3878

Why Verdi revised the 1857 version of *Simon Boccanegra*. Italy: Milan. 1857-1881. Lang.: Eng.   3881

Creation of the 1857 version of *Simon Boccanegra* by Verdi, libretto by Piave. Italy: Venice. 1856-1881. Lang.: Eng.   3882

Changes from the Friedrich von Schiller source in *Don Carlo* by Giuseppe Verdi. Italy. 1867-1883. Lang.: Eng.   3887

The historical Simon Boccanegra. Italy: Genoa. 900-1857. Lang.: Eng.   3888

Relation to other fields
Comparison between insanity defense and opera productions with audience as jury. USA. 1980-1985. Lang.: Eng.   3925

Verdict, The

SEE
Veredicto, El.

Verebes, István

Performance/production
Director István Verebes discusses staging from the actor's viewpoint. Hungary. Lang.: Hun.   739

Verebes, István — cont'd

István Verebes directs *Valódi Vadnyugat (True West)* by Sam Shepard. Hungary: Budapest. 1986. Lang.: Hun.   1772

A farkas (The Wolf) by Ferenc Molnár, directed by István Verebes at Vigszinház. Hungary: Budapest. 1985. Lang.: Hun.   1781

István Verebes' production of *A farkas (The Wolf)* by Ferenc Molnár at the Vigszinház. Hungary: Budapest. 1985. Lang.: Hun.   1805

Review of *Kettős ünnep (A Double Holiday)*, written and staged by István Verebes. Hungary: Budapest. 1986. Lang.: Hun.   1932

István Verebes directs *Valódi vadnyugat (True West)* by Sam Shepard at Radnóti Miklós Szinpad. Hungary: Budapest. 1986. Lang.: Hun.   1939

Vereinigten Theaterschaffenden der Schweiz (VTS, Switzerland)
Institutions
Support for non-mainstream theatre. Switzerland. 1983-1986. Lang.: Fre, Ger.   531

Verfredungseffekt
Performance/production
Application of Brechtian concepts by Eckhardt Schall. Germany, East: Berlin, East. UK-England: London. 1952-1986. Lang.: Eng.   1762

Verga, Giovanni
Relation to other fields
Conference on novelist Giovanni Verga and the theatre. Italy. 1840-1922. Lang.: Ita.   3037

Verge, The
Plays/librettos/scripts
Imagery of gender compared in works by Susan Glaspell and Eugene O'Neill. USA: New York, NY, Provincetown, MA. 1916-1922. Lang.: Eng.   2893

Vergonzoso en palacio, El (Shy Man at Court, The)
Plays/librettos/scripts
Female sexuality in Tirso de Molina's *El vergonzoso en palacio (The Shy Man at Court)*. Spain. 1580-1648. Lang.: Eng.   969

Verhaeren, Emile
Performance/production
Playwright Emile Verhaeren's travels in Russia. Russia. Belgium. 1912-1914. Lang.: Rus.   783

Verkommenes Ufer Medeamaterial Landschaft mit Argonauten (Deserted Shore Matter for Medea Landscape with Argonauts)
Plays/librettos/scripts
History, poetry and violence in plays by Tankred Dorst, Heiner Müller and Jean Genet. Europe. Lang.: Fre.   2538

Verma, Jatinder
Performance/production
Collection of newspaper reviews by London theatre critics. UK: London. 1986. Lang.: Eng.   2100

Collection of newspaper reviews by London theatre critics. UK-England: London. 1986. Lang.: Eng.   2109

Verschwörung des Fiesko zu Gena (Fiesko)
Theory/criticism
Analysis of Friedrich Schiller's dramatic and theoretical works. Germany. 1759-1805. Lang.: Cat.   3109

Verse drama
Plays/librettos/scripts
Study of heroism in verse dramas by Douglas Stewart, Tom Inglis Moore and Catherine Duncan. Australia. 1941-1943. Lang.: Eng.   2383

Analysis of plays by Charles Jury and Ray Mathew. Australia. 1905-1967. Lang.: Eng.   2384

Vertauschten Köpfe, Die (Transposed Heads, The)
Performance/production
Puppeteer Julie Taymor adapts *Die vertauschten Köpfe (The Transposed Heads)* by Thomas Mann for performance at the Ark Theatre. USA: New York, NY. 1984. Lang.: Eng.   3977

The training and career of puppeteer Julie Taymor. USA. 1970-1984. Lang.: Eng.   3982

Vertical Mobility
Performance/production
Aesthetics, styles, rehearsal techniques of director Richard Foreman. USA. 1974-1986. Lang.: Eng.   2263

Vesely, Bob
Performance/production
Interview with puppeteers Roger Dennis and Bob Vesely. USA: Cleveland, OH. 1968-1986. Lang.: Eng.   3972

Vészi, Endre
Performance/production
Endre Vészi's *Don Quijote utolsó kalandja (Don Quixote's Last Adventure)* directed by Imre Kerényi, Gyula Várszinház. Hungary: Gyula. 1986. Lang.: Hun.   1812

Endre Vészi's *Don Quijote utolsó kalandja (Don Quixote's Last Adventure)* directed by Imre Kerényi. Hungary: Gyula. 1986. Lang.: Hun.   1951

Vexler, David
Plays/librettos/scripts
Examination of the first Hebrew adaptation of Molière's *Tartuffe* by David Vexler. France. 1874. Lang.: Heb.   2569

Vi-Ton-Ka Medicine Show, The
Performance/production
Recreation of a medicine show featuring 'Doc' Bloodgood, staged by American Place Theatre. USA. 1983. Lang.: Eng.   3375

Via Crucis
Performance/production
Productions based on sacred music of Franz Liszt. Hungary: Zalaegerszeg, Budapest. 1986. Lang.: Hun.   1308

Viaggio a Reims, Il
Performance/production
Productions of operas at La Scala by Luca Ronconi. Italy: Milan. 1985. Lang.: Ita.   3763

Reviews of *Death in the Family*, *Viaggio a Reims*, *Abduction from the Seraglio* and *Tales of Hoffmann*. USA: St. Louis, MO. 1975-1986. Lang.: Eng.   3799

Viale, Oscar
Performance/production
Overview of recent Argentine theatre. Argentina: Buenos Aires. 1978-1983. Lang.: Fre.   651

Plays/librettos/scripts
Development in the genre of the *sainete*, or comic afterpiece. Argentina. 1800-1980. Lang.: Spa.   2365

Vickers, Jon
Performance/production
Profile of and interview with tenor Jon Vickers about his career and his leading role in *Samson* by George Frideric Handel. Canada: Prince Albert, AB. 1926-1986. Lang.: Eng.   3713

Opera greats reflect on performance highlights. USA: Philadelphia, PA, New York, NY. 1985. Lang.: Eng.   3841

Victims of Duty
SEE
Victimes du devoir.

Victorian Playhouse (Victoria-by-the-Sea, PE)
Institutions
Development of community-based theatre on Prince Edward Island. Canada. 1981-1986. Lang.: Eng.   1556

Victorian theatre
SEE ALSO
Geographical-Chronological Index under England 1837-1901.

Administration
Legislation for the protection of Victorian child-actors. UK. 1837-1901. Lang.: Eng.   1439

Plays/librettos/scripts
Reference of George Bernard Shaw to contemporary society. UK-England. 1856-1950. Lang.: Eng.   2862

Victory at Entebbe
Plays/librettos/scripts
Analysis of television docudramas as a melodrama genre. USA. 1965-1986. Lang.: Eng.   3285

Vida es sueño, La (Life Is a Dream)
Design/technology
Unusual production of *Life Is a Dream* by Kungliga Dramatiska Teatern. Sweden: Stockholm. 1927. Lang.: Swe.   1520

Plays/librettos/scripts
Thematic analysis of *La vida es sueño (Life Is a Dream)* by Pedro Calderón de la Barca. Spain. 1635-1681. Lang.: Eng.   2788

Interview with Irena Kraus about her play *Lilla livet (The Little Life)*, based on *La vida es sueño (Life Is a Dream)* by Calderón. Sweden: Malmö. 1985-1986. Lang.: Swe.   2824

Vidal i Valenciano, Eduard
Plays/librettos/scripts
History of Catalan literature, including playwrights. Spain-Catalonia. France. 1800-1926. Lang.: Cat.   973

Vidám Színpad (Budapest)
Performance/production
Gábor Görgey's *Huzatos ház (Drafty House)* directed by Gyula Bodrogi, Vidám Színpad. Hungary: Budapest. 1986. Lang.: Hun. 1845

Gábor Görgey's *Huzatos ház (Drafty House)* directed by Gyula Bodrogi at Vidám Színpad. Hungary: Budapest. 1986. Lang.: Hun. 1856

Video forms
SEE ALSO
Classed Entries under MEDIA–Video forms: 3252-3287.

Administration
Overview of public broadcasting management. USA. 1986. Lang.: Eng. 3165
History of source licensing for television and film scores. USA. 1897-1987. Lang.: Eng. 3195

Basic theatrical documents
Videotape of Shakespeare's *As You Like It* with study guide and edition of the play. Canada: Stratford, ON. 1983. Lang.: Eng. 219

Design/technology
The differences in scene and costume design for television versus theatre. Hungary: Budapest. 1986. Lang.: Hun. 278
Career of costume and stage designer Eugenio Guglielminetti. Italy. 1946-1986. Lang.: Ita. 299
Technique for transferring film to black and white videotape. USA. 1986. 3209
Editing and post production on the documentary film *Ornette: Made in America*. USA. Lang.: Eng. 3215
Lighting techniques and equipment used at theme park. USA: Baltimore, MD. 1971-1986. Lang.: Eng. 3315
A lighting designer discusses the unique problems of lighting symphony orchestras. USA: Washington, DC, Boston, MA, New York, NY. 1910-1986. Lang.: Eng. 3478
Creating overhead shadow sequence for puppet production. USA. 4014

Institutions
Productions in 1986 of Ars Electronica. Austria: Linz. 1979-1986. Lang.: Ger. 3321

Performance/production
Acting for theatre, film and television. Germany, East. 1983. Lang.: Ger. 730
Process and results of adapting plays from Off Broadway to TV. USA: New York, NY. 1980-1986. Lang.: Eng. 841
Actor discusses work in recitation programs. USSR: Moscow. 1980-1986. Lang.: Rus. 888
Reviews of three productions of *Fröken Julie (Miss Julie)* by August Strindberg. Sweden: Stockholm. Denmark: Copenhagen. South Africa, Republic of. 1985-1986. Lang.: Swe. 2090
Interpretation of classics for theatre and television. USSR. 1980-1986. Lang.: Rus. 2337
Career of film and television actress Lucille Ball. USA. 1911-1986. Lang.: Eng. 3167
On the 'theatricalization' of film. USSR. 1980-1986. Lang.: Rus. 3230
Videotaped performances and interviews of San Francisco Mime Troupe. USA: San Francisco, CA. 1960-1986. Lang.: Eng. 3306
Comedienne Joan Rivers' account of her life and career. USA: New York, NY. 1928-1965. Lang.: Eng. 3352
Career of popular entertainer Bill Cosby. USA. 1937-1986. Lang.: Eng. 3353
Case-study of *Sweet and Sour* by the Australian Broadcasting Corporation. Australia: Sydney, N.S.W. 1980-1984. Lang.: Eng. 3483
Artistic and technological differences in presenting opera for stage and television. Canada. 1960-1980. Lang.: Eng. 3714

Plays/librettos/scripts
Popularity of dramatic monologue on stage and television. Australia. 1985. Lang.: Eng. 921
Interview with playwright Alex Buzo. Australia. 1986. Lang.: Eng. 2385
Interview with playwright Arthur Miller. USA. 1985. Lang.: Eng. 2921
History and practice of the documentary in radio, television, and film. UK-England. 1928-1986. Lang.: Eng. 3168

Reference materials
Yearbook of theatre, including radio and television drama. Sweden. 1985-1986. Lang.: Swe. 1031

Relation to other fields
The role of theatre and television in the moral education of society. USSR. 1980-1986. Lang.: Rus. 1177

Theory/criticism
Theoretical writings and reviews on the performing arts. Hungary. 1971-1983. Lang.: Hun. 1211
Theatre professionals challenge assertions that theatre is a weaker form of communication than film. USA: New York, NY. 1985. Lang.: Eng. 1225
Mutual influences of theatre, film, and television. USSR. 1980-1986. Lang.: Rus. 1250
Melodrama as an aesthetic theatre form. Australia. 1850-1986. Lang.: Eng. 3083
Shakespeare in media. UK-England. USA. Japan. 1899-1985. Lang.: Eng. 3172

Vie et le temps de Médéric Boileau, La (Life and Times of Médéric Boileau, The)
Plays/librettos/scripts
Life and work of Francophone playwright Paul-André Paiement. Canada. 1970-1978. Lang.: Fre. 2417

Vie et mort du Roi Boiteaux (Life and Death of King Boiteaux)
Plays/librettos/scripts
Analysis of *Vie et mort du Roi Boiteaux (Life and Death of King Boiteaux)* by Jean-Pierre Ronfard. Canada: Montreal, PQ. 1983. Lang.: Fre. 933

Viejo criado, El (Old Servant, The)
Performance/production
Overview of recent Argentine theatre. Argentina: Buenos Aires. 1978-1983. Lang.: Fre. 651

Vienna Boys Choir
Reference materials
Stills from telecast performances of *Hänsel und Gretel*. List of principals, conductor and production staff included. Austria: Vienna. 1986. Lang.: Eng. 3909

Vienna Philharmonic Orchestra
Reference materials
Stills from telecast performances of *Hänsel und Gretel*. List of principals, conductor and production staff included. Austria: Vienna. 1986. Lang.: Eng. 3909

Vienna: Lusthaus
Performance/production
Reviews of *Vienna: Lusthaus*, conceived and staged by Martha Clarke. USA: New York, NY. 1986. Lang.: Eng. 2209

View From the Bridge, A
Basic theatrical documents
Catalan translation of *A View From the Bridge* by Arthur Miller. USA. 1955. Lang.: Cat. 1511

Plays/librettos/scripts
Analysis of *A View From the Bridge* by Arthur Miller. USA: New York, NY. UK-England: London. 1915-1985. Lang.: Cat. 2901

Vigszinház (Budapest)
Institutions
History of Vigszinház (Comedy Theatre). Hungary: Budapest. 1896-1916. Lang.: Hun. 502

Performance/production
Tamás Ascher directs *Ördögök (The Devils)*, an adaptation of *Besy (The Possessed)* by Dostojévskij. Hungary: Budapest. 1986. Lang.: Hun. 1778
A farkas (The Wolf) by Ferenc Molnár, directed by István Verebes at Vigszinház. Hungary: Budapest. 1985. Lang.: Hun. 1781
Öreg hölgy látogatása (The Visit) by Friedrich Dürrenmatt, directed by Péter Gothár at Vigszinház. Hungary: Budapest. 1986. Lang.: Hun. 1782
Ivan Vasiljévič by Michajl Afanasjévič Bulgakov directed by László Marton at Vigszinház under the title *Iván, a rettentő*. Hungary: Budapest. 1986. Lang.: Hun. 1783
István Verebes' production of *A farkas (The Wolf)* by Ferenc Molnár at the Vigszinház. Hungary: Budapest. 1985. Lang.: Hun. 1805
Review of *Bűnhődés (Punishment)*, a stage adaptation of *The Idiot* by Dostojévskij. Hungary: Budapest. Lang.: Hun. 1826
Edith és Marlene (Edith and Marlene) by Éva Pataki at Comedy Theatre. Hungary: Budapest. 1986. Lang.: Hun. 1831

SUBJECT INDEX

Vigszinház (Budapest) — cont'd

András Matkócsik directs *Mondd, Joe! (Eh, Joe!)* and *Az utlosó tekercs (Krapp's Last Tape)* by Samuel Beckett. Hungary: Budapest. 1985. Lang.: Hun. 1851

Péter Gothár's production of *A Öreg hölgy látogatósa (The Visit)* by Friedrich Dürrenmatt. Hungary: Budapest. 1986. Lang.: Hun. 1889

Plays by Ribnikov and Višnevskij performed by Moscow Theatre of Lenin Comsomal. USSR: Moscow. Hungary: Budapest. 1985. Lang.: Hun. 2329

Plays/librettos/scripts

Review of study of experimental plays and playwrights. Hungary. 1967-1983. Lang.: Hun. 2641

Viimeiset kiusaukset (Last Temptation, The)

Plays/librettos/scripts

Analysis of thematic trends in recent Finnish Opera. Finland: Helsinki, Savonlinna. 1909-1986. Lang.: Eng, Fre. 3865

Interview with opera composer Aulis Sallinen on his current work. Finland: Helsinki. 1975-1986. Lang.: Eng, Fre. 3866

Vilalta, Maruxa

Basic theatrical documents

English translation of *Pequeña historia de horror (Little Tale of Horror)*. Mexico. 1932. Lang.: Eng. 1488

Vilar, Jean

Administration

Jean Vilar's development of a working class audience for the Théâtre National Populaire. France: Paris. 1948-1968. Lang.: Fre. 38

Audience

Jean Vilar's view of the revolutionary power of the classics. France: Paris. 1951-1963. Lang.: Fre. 198

Basic theatrical documents

Jean Vilar's diary compared to polemics against him. France: Paris. 1951-1981. Lang.: Fre. 221

Performance/production

Recollections of Jean Vilar and his work. France: Paris. 1912-1971. Lang.: Fre. 712

Interpretation of the theatrical work of Jean Vilar. France. 1912-1971. Lang.: Ita. 713

Theatrical illusion in *Sei personaggi in cerca d'autore (Six Characters in Search of an Author)* by Luigi Pirandello. France: Paris. 1951-1986. Lang.: Fre. 1730

An emotional account of Jean Vilar's early career by a young spectator. France. Lang.: Ita. 1731

Jean Vilar's staging of plays by Bertolt Brecht. France. 1951-1960. Lang.: Ita. 1736

Analysis of theoretical writings of Jean Vilar. France. 1871-1912. Lang.: Ita. 1745

Vildanden (Wild Duck, The)

Plays/librettos/scripts

Self-transcendence through grace embodied in Henrik Ibsen's female characters. Norway. 1849-1899. Lang.: Eng. 2726

Absence of the author in Henrik Ibsen's *Vildanden (The Wild Duck)*. Norway. 1882. Lang.: Eng. 2729

Theory/criticism

Influence of Henrik Ibsen on Korean theatre. Korea: Seoul. Norway. 1884-1986. Lang.: Kor. 3120

Villa Negra

Performance/production

Villa Negra by Anikó and Katalin Vajda directed by Miklós Szurdi. Hungary: Budapest. 1986. Lang.: Hun. 1818

Adaptation for the stage by Anikó Vagda and Katalin Vajda of Imre Dobozy's screenplay *Villa Negra*, directed at Játékszin by Miklós Szurdi. Hungary: Budapest. 1986. Lang.: Hun. 1870

Village Gate Theatre (New York, NY)

Performance/production

Reviews of National Lampoon's *Class of 86*, staged by Jerry Adler. USA: New York, NY. 1986. Lang.: Eng. 3348

Villiers de l'Isle-Adam, Auguste

Audience

Claques as viewed by French writers. France. 1800-1899. Lang.: Fre. 3647

Plays/librettos/scripts

Forerunner of contemporary theatre: *Axël* by Villiers de l'Isle-Adam. France. 1862-1894. Lang.: Fre. 2579

Vilomara i Virgili, Maurici

Design/technology

History of Catalan scenography. Spain-Catalonia. 200 B.C.-1986 A.D. Lang.: Cat. 311

Introduction to facsimile of Oleguer Junyent's set design for *L'Auca del senyor Esteve (Mr. Esteve's 'Auca')* by Santiago Rusiñol. Spain-Catalonia: Barcelona. 1861-1984. Lang.: Cat. 1518

Vincent y los cuervos (Vincent and the Crows)

Plays/librettos/scripts

Pacho O'Donnell's play *Vincent y los cuervos (Vincent and the Crows)*. Argentina: Buenos Aires. 1984. Lang.: Eng. 2363

Vincent, Jean-Pierre

Performance/production

Actor, director and teacher Jean-Pierre Vincent. France. 1955-1986. Lang.: Fre. 1744

Vincent, Mrs. J.R.

Relation to other fields

Professional equality in theatrical careers for men and women. USA: New York, NY. 1850-1870. Lang.: Eng. 1143

Vinegar Tom

Performance/production

Brechtian technique in the contemporary feminist drama of Caryl Churchill, Claire Luckham and others. UK-England. 1956-1979. Lang.: Eng. 815

Vineyard Theatre (New York, NY)

Performance spaces

Architectural design for new performance spaces for Theatre for the New City and the Vineyard Theatre. USA: New York, NY. 1986. Lang.: Eng. 639

Vinogradov, O.

Administration

Principal choreographer of Kirov Theatre on problems of Soviet ballet theatre. USSR. 1980-1986. Lang.: Rus. 1293

Vinotavye (Guilty, The)

Performance/production

Vinotavye (The Guilty) at Teat'r im. Mossovèta. USSR: Moscow. 1986. Lang.: Rus. 2339

Virgin Martyr, The

Plays/librettos/scripts

Religion and popular entertainment in *The Virgin Martyr* by Philip Massinger and Thomas Dekker. England: London. 1620-1625. Lang.: Eng. 2468

Virginia Opera Association (Norfolk, VA)

Performance/production

Review of *Harriet, the Woman Called Moses*, an opera by Thea Musgrave, staged by Gordon Davidson. USA: Norfolk, VA. 1985. Lang.: Eng. 3835

Virginia Theatre (New York, NY)

Performance/production

Reviews of *Wild Honey*, by Michael Frayn after Čechov, conceived and staged by Christopher Morahan. USA: New York, NY. 1986. Lang.: Eng. 2205

Reviews of *Execution of Justice*, written and staged by Emily Mann. USA: New York, NY. 1986. Lang.: Eng. 2230

Visakhadatta

Performance/production

Collection of newspaper reviews by London theatre critics. UK. 1986. Lang.: Eng. 2102

Collection of newspaper reviews by London theatre critics. UK-England. 1986. Lang.: Eng. 2114

Visconti, Luchino

Design/technology

Illustrated description of Umberto Tirelli costume collection. Europe. 1700-1984. Lang.: Ita. 263

Vishnevskaya, Galina

Performance/production

Famous sopranos discuss their interpretations of Tosca. USA. 1935-1986. Lang.: Eng. 3811

Visions

SEE

Látomások.

Visit, The

SEE

Besuch der alten Dame, Der.

Višnevskij, Vsevolod Vitaljèvič

Performance/production

Plays by Ribnikov and Višnevskij performed by Moscow Theatre of Lenin Comsomal. USSR: Moscow. Hungary: Budapest. 1985. Lang.: Hun. 2329

Plays/librettos/scripts

Analysis of the plays of Vsevolod Vitaljèvič Višnevskij. USSR. 1920-1959. Lang.: Rus. 2964

Višněvy sad (Cherry Orchard, The)
Performance/production
Čechov's *Višněvyj sad (The Cherry Orchard)* directed by Imre Csiszár under the title *Cseresznyéskert*. Hungary: Miskolc. 1986. Lang.: Hun. 1921

Višněvyj sad (Cherry Orchard, The)
Performance/production
Čechov's *Višněvyj sad (The Cherry Orchard)* directed at the National Theatre of Miskolc by Imre Csiszár as *Cseresznyéshert*. Hungary: Miskolc. 1986. Lang.: Hun. 1784

Interview with director György Harag. Romania: Tîrgu-Mures. 1925-1985. Lang.: Hun. 2064

Documentation on Stanislavskij's productions of Čechov plays. Russia. 1901-1904. Lang.: Ita. 2070

Collection of newspaper reviews by London theatre critics. UK. 1986. Lang.: Eng. 2101

Collection of newspaper reviews by London theatre critics. UK-England: London. 1986. Lang.: Eng. 2112

Survey of the season at the National Theatre. UK-England: London. 1986. Lang.: Eng. 2130

Actress Sheila Hancock discusses role of Madame Ranevskaya in Čechov's *Višněvyj sad (The Cherry Orchard)*. UK-England: London. 1986. Lang.: Eng. 2180

Plays/librettos/scripts
Analysis of Čechov's plays. Lang.: Hun. 2346

Study of the dramatic nature of Čechov's plays. Lang.: Hun. 2347

Visser, David
Institutions
History of two major Black touring companies. USA: New York, NY. 1969-1982. Lang.: Eng. 1598

Vitez, Antoine
Performance/production
The functions of rhythm in reading and performance. Europe. 1900-1984. Lang.: Fre. 1717

Sophocles' *Electra* staged by Antoine Vitez as a conflict of deceit. France: Paris. 1986. Lang.: Swe. 1732

Reflection of modern society in Antoine Vitez's production of Sophocles' *Electra* at Théâtre National Populaire. France: Paris. 1981-1986. Lang.: Swe. 1743

Viv'en, Leonid
Performance/production
The career of actor-director Leonid Viv'en, focusing on his work at Teat'r Dramy im. A.S. Puškina. USSR: Leningrad. 1887-1966. Lang.: Rus. 903

Vivian Beaumont Theatre (New York, NY)
Performance spaces
Technical facilities and labor practices at several U.S. theatres as seen by a Swedish visitor. USA: Chicago, IL, New York, NY. 1986. Lang.: Swe. 642

Performance/production
Overview of the career and work of director Peter Brook. USA: New York, NY. 1948-1984. Lang.: Eng. 829

Reviews of *The Front Page*, by Ben Hecht and Charles MacArthur, staged by Jerry Zaks. USA: New York, NY. 1986. Lang.: Eng. 2214

Reviews of *The House of Blue Leaves* by John Guare, staged by Jerry Zaks. USA: New York, NY. 1986. Lang.: Eng. 2220

Reviews of *Juggling and Cheap Theatrics* with the Flying Karamazov Brothers, staged by George Mosher. USA: New York, NY. 1986. Lang.: Eng. 3349

Voaden, Herman
Basic theatrical documents
Text of *Within* by Bertram Brooker. Canada: Toronto, ON. 1935. Lang.: Eng. 217

Text of *The Dragon* by Bertram Brooker. Canada: Toronto, ON. 1936. Lang.: Eng. 1466

Plays/librettos/scripts
Introduction to the plays of Bertram Brooker. Canada. 1928-1936. Lang.: Eng. 927

Career of expressionist playwright Bertram Brooker. Canada: Toronto, ON. 1888-1949. Lang.: Eng. 2418

The immigrant in plays by Herman Voaden and Robertson Davies. Canada. 1934-1950. Lang.: Eng. 2431

Reference materials
Collected reviews of 31 major Canadian plays. Canada. 1934-1983. Lang.: Eng. 1009

Relation to other fields
Analysis of *Symphony* by Herman Voaden and Lowrie Warrener. Canada. 1914-1933. Lang.: Eng. 1075

Philosophical context of the plays of Herman Voaden. Canada: Toronto, ON. 1929-1943. Lang.: Eng. 3170

Vocations
Plays/librettos/scripts
Interview with playwright Alma de Groen. Australia. Lang.: Eng. 2367

Vogels, Fritz
Theory/criticism
The aesthetics of movement theatre. Europe. 1975-1986. 3301

Voice
Training
Numerous exercises with physiological explanations for phonation in harmony with breath rhythmics. Austria. 1985. Lang.: Ger. 1253

Voina i mir (War and Peace)
Institutions
Erwin Piscator's work at the Dramatic Workshop of the New School for Social Research. USA: New York, NY. 1939-1951. Lang.: Ger. 1600

Plays/librettos/scripts
History and aesthetics of Soviet opera. USSR: Moscow. 1917-1941. Lang.: Ger. 3905

Volkov, Fëdor Grigorjevič
Performance/production
Career of actor Fëdor Grigorjevič Volkov. Russia. 1729-1763. Lang.: Rus. 786

Volksbühne (East Berlin)
Relation to other fields
Response of Freie Volksbühne to police pressure. Germany: Berlin. 1890-1912. Lang.: Fre. 3034

Volksoper (Vienna)
Design/technology
Sceneshops of the Burgtheater, Staatsoper and Volksoper. Austria: Vienna. 1963-1980. Lang.: Hun. 237

Institutions
Tours of the Österreichische Bundestheater in Austria. Austria. 1976-1986. Lang.: Ger. 455

Wiener Sommer 1986 promoted by Teletheater-Gesellschaft. Austria: Vienna. 1986. Lang.: Ger. 3479

Performance/production
Biography of Burgtheater actor Richard Eybner. Austria: Vienna. 1896-1986. Lang.: Ger. 1653

Elisabeth Kales and her performance in the main role of Leo Fall's operetta *Madame Pompadour*. Austria: Vienna. 1955-1986. Lang.: Ger. 3484

Volkstheater (Vienna)
Institutions
Paul Blaha's management of the Volkstheater. Austria: Vienna. 1986-1987. Lang.: Ger. 1538

Performance/production
On actor Heinz Petters and the production of *Der Raub der Sabinerinnen* at the Volkstheater. Austria: Vienna. 1938-1986. Lang.: Ger. 1644

Biography of actor and stage manager Franz Reichert. Austria: Vienna. Germany: Berlin. Czechoslovakia: Prague. 1925-1950. Lang.: Ger. 1652

Plays/librettos/scripts
Training for new playwrights in Austria. Austria: Vienna. 1985-1986. Lang.: Ger. 2392

Cooperation between playwright Heinz Rudolf Unger and the Volkstheater. Austria: Vienna. 1938-1986. Lang.: Ger. 2394

Relation to other fields
Life and work of playwright and critic Karl Kraus. Austria: Vienna. 1874-1936. Lang.: Ger. 3017

Volpone
Plays/librettos/scripts
Ben Jonson's use of romance in *Volpone*. England. 1575-1600. Lang.: Eng. 2461

Use of group aggression in Ben Jonson's comedies. England. 1575-1600. Lang.: Eng. 2508

Violation of genre divisions in the plays of Ben Jonson. England: London. 1606-1610. Lang.: Eng. 2525

Reference materials
List of 37 productions of 23 Renaissance plays, with commentary. UK. USA. New Zealand. 1986. Lang.: Eng. 3000

SUBJECT INDEX

Voltaire, Jean
Plays/librettos/scripts
Enlightenment narrative and French dramatists. France. 1700-1800.
Lang.: Eng. 2552

Vörös, Róbert
Performance/production
Hungary: Szolnok. 1986. Lang.: Hun. 1968

Vörösmarty, Mihály
Performance/production
Mihály Vörösmarty's *Csongor és Tünde (Csongor and Tünde)*
directed by László Gergely. Hungary: Debrecen. 1986. Lang.: Hun.
1820

Csongor és Tünde (Csongor and Tünde) by Mihály Vörösmarty,
directed by János Szikora at Gárdonyi Géza Szinház. Hungary: Eger.
1985. Lang.: Hun. 1877

Mihály Vörösmarty's *Csongor and Tünde* at Gárdonyi Géza Theatre
directed by János Szikora. Hungary: Eger. 1985. Lang.: Hun. 1923

Plays/librettos/scripts
Analysis of Mihály Vörösmarty's *A bújdosók (Refugees)*. Hungary.
1800-1855. Lang.: Hun. 2639

Voss
Traditional innovation in *Voss* by Richard Meale and David Malouf.
Australia. 1980-1986. Lang.: Eng. 3636

Voss, Gert
Performance/production
On actor Gert Voss and his work. Austria: Vienna. Germany, West.
1941-1986. Lang.: Ger. 1649

Vouyoucas, Andonis
Performance/production
Directors discuss staging of plays by Paul Claudel. France. Belgium.
1985. Lang.: Fre. 1723

Voyageur sans bagage, Le (Traveller Without Luggage)
Plays/librettos/scripts
Patriarchy in *Le Voyageur sans bagage (Traveler Without Luggage)*
by Jean Anouilh. France. 1937. Lang.: Eng. 2586

Vsesojuznyj teatral'nyj obščestvo (USSR)
Administration
Notes on theatre business following meeting of All-Union Theatre
Society. USSR. 1986. Lang.: Rus. 183

Vulgar Lives or Burlesque as a Way of Life
Plays/librettos/scripts
Analysis of the plays of Rosalyn Drexler. USA. 1964-1985. Lang.:
Eng. 2920

Vysockij, Vladimir
Performance/production
Soviet actor, poet and singer Vladimir Vysockij. USSR. 1938-1980.
Lang.: Rus. 861

Vysokoe naprjaženic (High Tension)
Plays/librettos/scripts
Analysis of A. Platonov's comedy *Vysokoe naprjaženic (High
Tension)*. Russia. 1899-1951. Lang.: Rus. 966

Wager, Douglas
Performance/production
Productions of Dario Fo's *Morte accidentale di un anarchico
(Accidental Death of an Anarchist)* in the light of Fo's political
ideas. USA. Canada. Italy. 1970-1986. Lang.: Eng. 2262

Wagner Community College (New York, NY)
Design/technology
Designers discuss regional productions of *Oklahoma*. USA. 1984-
1986. Lang.: Eng. 3596

Wagner, Betty Jane
Administration
Community funding of residency for children's theatre performer,
Aurand Harris. USA: Cleveland, OH. 1985-1986. Lang.: Eng. 145

Wagner, Jane
Audience
Context and design of some lesbian performances. USA: New York,
NY. 1985. Lang.: Eng. 1455

Wagner, Josef
Performance/production
Playing Hamlet at the Burgtheater. Austria: Vienna. 1803-1985.
Lang.: Ger. 1654

Wagner, Richard
Influence of Wagner on the music of contemporary Chinese opera.
China, People's Republic of. 1949-1980. Lang.: Chi. 3503

Basic theatrical documents
The influence of *Euryanthe* by Carl Maria von Weber on Richard
Wagner. Germany: Dresden. 1824-1879. Lang.: Eng. 3649

Design/technology
Lighting techniques for Wagnerian operas. Germany, West: Bayreuth.
1981-1986. Lang.: Eng. 3651

Adolphe Appia's theory of Wagner's *Ring* and present-day
evaluation. Switzerland: Geneva. 1862-1928. Lang.: Ger. 3653

Set designer John Conklin and the San Francisco Opera production
of Wagner's *Ring*. USA: San Francisco, CA. 1986. Lang.: Eng. 3662

Performance/production
Changes in English life reflected in 1883 theatre season. UK-
England: London. 1883. Lang.: Eng. 810

Influence of Richard Wagner on the work of the French Symbolists.
France: Paris. Germany, West: Bayreuth. 1860-1986. Lang.: Eng.
3726

Wilhelm Furtwängler's development as a Wagnerian conductor.
Germany: Bayreuth. Italy: Milan, Rome. 1901-1954. Lang.: Eng.
3732

The first singers to perform *Tristan und Isolde*. Germany: Munich.
1857-1869. Lang.: Eng. 3733

Psychoanalytic study of staging as language. Germany. 1800-1909.
Lang.: Fre. 3734

Collection of statements about the life and career of conductor
Wilhelm Furtwängler. Germany: Berlin. Austria: Salzburg. 1886-1986.
Lang.: Ger. 3737

Interview with Wolfgang Wagner on his staging of 3 Wagnerian
operas at the Bayreuth Festspiele. Germany, West: Bayreuth. 1975-
1985. Lang.: Hun. 3740

Reviews of 10 vintage recordings of complete operas on LP. USA.
1906-1925. Lang.: Eng. 3792

Photographs, cast list, synopsis, and discography of Metropolitan
Opera radio broadcast performances. USA: New York, NY. 1986.
Lang.: Eng. 3794

Stills from telecast performances. List of principals, conductor and
production staff included. USA: New York, NY. 1986. Lang.: Eng.
3795

Review of Wagner's *Die Walküre* staged by François Rochaix. USA:
Seattle, WA. 1985. Lang.: Eng. 3801

New designs for the Seattle Opera production of *Der Ring des
Nibelungen* by Richard Wagner. USA: Seattle, WA. 1986. Lang.:
Eng. 3837

Plays/librettos/scripts
Schopenhauerian pessimism in Wagner's *Ring* and *Götterdämmerung*.
Germany. 1852-1856. Lang.: Eng. 3873

Wagner's *Das Liebesverbot*, an operatic adaptation of *Measure for
Measure*. Germany. 1834. Lang.: Eng. 3880

Relation to other fields
Théophile Gautier's views about opera. France. 1811-1917. Lang.:
Eng. 3917

Theory/criticism
The concept of *Gesamtkunstwerk*. Germany. 1797-1953. Lang.: Eng.
3929

Influence of Greek theatre on Richard Wagner's music-drama.
Germany. 1813-1883. Lang.: Eng. 3930

Wagner, Wieland
Performance/production
Profile of and interview with soprano Leonie Rysanek. Austria:
Vienna. 1926-1986. Lang.: Eng. 3693

Wagner, Wolfgang
Performance/production
Interview with Wolfgang Wagner on his staging of 3 Wagnerian
operas at the Bayreuth Festspiele. Germany, West: Bayreuth. 1975-
1985. Lang.: Hun. 3740

Waiting for Godot
SEE
En attendant Godot.

Wajda, Andrzej
Performance/production
Tamás Ascher directs *Ördögök (The Devils)*, an adaptation of *Besy
(The Possessed)* by Dostojèvskij. Hungary: Budapest. 1986. Lang.:
Hun. 1778

Review of *Bűnhődés (Punishment)*, a stage adaptation of *The Idiot*
by Dostojèvskij. Hungary: Budapest. Lang.: Hun. 1826

Interview with director and cast of Wajda's *Crime and Punishment*.
Poland: Cracow. USA. 1986. Lang.: Eng. 2025

Director Andrzei Wajda's work, accessibility to Polish audiences.
Poland: Warsaw. 1926-1986. Lang.: Swe. 2027

Wajda, Andrzej — cont'd

Adaptation of Dostojèvskij's *Prestuplenijè i nakazanijè (Crime and Punishment)* directed by Andrzej Wajda at Teatr Stary under the title *Zdrodnia i Kara*. Poland: Cracow. 1984. Lang.: Pol.　2032

Andrzej Wajda directs Sophocles' *Antigone*, Stary Teatr. Poland: Cracow. 1984. Lang.: Pol.　2058

Wakefield cycle
Performance/production
Account of University of California at Irvine production of a nativity play with composite text drawn from York, N-town and Wakefield cycles. USA: Irvine, CA. 1986. Lang.: Eng.　2307

Wakefield Theatre Royal and Opera House (Wakefield, UK)
Performance spaces
Restoration of Wakefield Theatre Royal and Opera House. UK-England: Wakefield. 1954-1986. Lang.: Eng.　630

Walch, Garnet
Performance/production
Apprenticeship of playwright Garnet Walch. Australia: Sydney, N.S.W. 1860-1890. Lang.: Eng.　1640

Walcott, Derek
Plays/librettos/scripts
Symbolism in Derek Walcott's *Dream on Monkey Mountain*. Jamaica. 1967. Lang.: Eng.　2718

Wales, Terry
Performance/production
Collection of newspaper reviews by London theatre critics. UK-England. 1986. Lang.: Eng.　2111

Walford, Glen
Performance/production
Collection of newspaper reviews by London theatre critics. UK. 1986. Lang.: Eng.　2103

Walker, George F.
Plays/librettos/scripts
Development of playwright George F. Walker. Canada: Toronto, ON. 1970-1984. Lang.: Eng.　931

Walker, Joseph
Reference materials
Current work of Audelco award-winning playwrights. USA: New York, NY. 1973-1984. Lang.: Eng.　3007

Walker, Mark
Design/technology
Designers discuss regional productions of *Oklahoma*. USA. 1984-1986. Lang.: Eng.　3596

Walker, Robert
Performance/production
Collection of newspaper reviews by London theatre critics. UK-England: London. 1986. Lang.: Eng.　2110

Walküre, Die
Performance/production
Review of Wagner's *Die Walküre* staged by François Rochaix. USA: Seattle, WA. 1985. Lang.: Eng.　3801

Wallace Brothers Circus (York, SC)
Performance/production
History of Great Wallace Circus. USA. 1913. Lang.: Eng.　3387

Wallace, Benjamin E.
Performance/production
History of Great Wallace Circus. USA. 1913. Lang.: Eng.　3387

Wallace, Ian
Performance/production
Distinctive style of Canadian clowns. Canada: Toronto, ON, Vancouver, BC. 1967-1986. Lang.: Eng.　3328

Wallenstein
Theory/criticism
Analysis of Friedrich Schiller's dramatic and theoretical works. Germany. 1759-1805. Lang.: Cat.　3109

Walling, Savannah
Performance/production
Development of works by the Special Delivery Moving Theatre. Canada: Vancouver, BC. 1976-1986. Lang.: Eng.　3294

Walnut Street Theatre (Philadelphia, PA)
Administration
Walnut Street Theatre's executive producer discusses producing musicals. USA: Philadelphia, PA. Lang.: Eng.　3575

Design/technology
Designers discuss regional productions of *Gypsy*. USA. 1984-1986. Lang.: Eng.　3588

Designers discuss regional productions of *The Music Man*. USA. 1983-1986. Lang.: Eng.　3589

Designers discuss regional productions of *The Sound of Music*. USA. 1983-1986. Lang.: Eng.　3594

Walser, Karl
Design/technology
Contribution of designer Ernst Stern to modern scenography. Germany: Berlin. UK-England: London. 1905. Lang.: Eng.　1516

Walsh
Plays/librettos/scripts
Amerindian and aborigine characters in the works of white playwrights. Canada. Australia. 1606-1975. Lang.: Eng.　930

Analysis of the plays of Sharon Pollock. Canada. 1971-1983. Lang.: Eng.　935

Walsom, John
Performance spaces
Design and construction of Grand Cayman's National Theatre. Cayman Islands. UK-England. 1986. Lang.: Eng.　590

Walter, Harriet
Institutions
Progress and aims of Women's Playhouse Trust. UK-England: London. 1984-1986. Lang.: Eng.　1590

Walters, Eugene
Plays/librettos/scripts
David Belasco's influence on Eugene O'Neill. USA: New York, NY. 1908-1922. Lang.: Eng.　2927

Walters, Sam
Performance/production
Collection of newspaper reviews by London theatre critics. UK-England: London. 1986. Lang.: Eng.　2122

Shakespearean productions by the National Theatre, Royal Shakespeare Company and Orange Tree Theatre. UK-England: Stratford, London. 1984-1985. Lang.: Eng.　2183

Wandor, Michelene
Plays/librettos/scripts
Interview with playwright Kathleen Betsko. England: Coventry. USA. 1960-1986. Lang.: Eng.　2487

Wang, Chien
Plays/librettos/scripts
Differences between *Chan Ta* and *Chuan Ta* drama. China. 1200-1986. Lang.: Chi.　3527

Wang, Chungwei
Plays/librettos/scripts
Profiles of Yuan dynasty playwrights. China. 1256-1341. Lang.: Chi.　2445

Wang, Gide
Theory/criticism
Dramatic structure in Beijing opera. China, People's Republic of. 1955-1985. Lang.: Chi.　3566

Wang, Ji-De
Plays/librettos/scripts
Comparison of the works of Wang Ji-De and Xu Wei. China. 1620-1752. Lang.: Chi.　3534

Wang, Kuowei
Plays/librettos/scripts
Differences between *Chan Ta* and *Chuan Ta* drama. China. 1200-1986. Lang.: Chi.　3527

Relation to other fields
Analysis of Northern Sung theatrical artifacts. 1032-1126. Lang.: Chi.　3546

Research/historiography
Origins and evolution of today's Beijing opera. China, People's Republic of: Beijing. 1755-1984. Lang.: Chi.　3556

Theory/criticism
Influence of Tuan Anchieh's aesthetics. China. 800-1644. Lang.: Chi.　3561

Dramatic structure in Beijing opera. China, People's Republic of. 1955-1985. Lang.: Chi.　3566

Wang, Shihfu
Plays/librettos/scripts
Profiles of Yuan dynasty playwrights. China. 1256-1341. Lang.: Chi.　2445

Differences among 32 extant editions of *Xi Xiang Zhu*. China. 1669-1843. Lang.: Chi.　3528

Research/historiography
Controversy over identities of Tien Kuei-pu and Lu Kuei-pu. China. 1500-1644. Lang.: Chi.　3550

Origins and evolution of today's Beijing opera. China, People's Republic of: Beijing. 1755-1984. Lang.: Chi.　3556

Wang, Shihfu — cont'd

Theory/criticism
Influence of Tuan Anchieh's aesthetics. China. 800-1644. Lang.: Chi.
3561

Wang, Shou
Theory/criticism
Analyzes works of four dramatists from Fuchien province. China,
People's Republic of. 1981-1985. Lang.: Chi.
3569

Wang, Xiaoping
Performance/production
Objectives and action in staging of director Wang Xiaoping. China:
Shanghai. 1900-1982. Lang.: Chi.
1689

Waniek, Herbert
Performance/production
Biography of actor and stage manager Franz Reichert. Austria:
Vienna. Germany: Berlin. Czechoslovakia: Prague. 1925-1950. Lang.:
Ger.
1652

Reference materials
Interpretation of Ferdinand Raimund's dramas after his death.
Austria: Vienna. 1790-1986. Lang.: Ger.
2981

Wanselius, Bengt
Performance/production
Stage photographs with comment by photographers. Sweden. 1985-
1986. Lang.: Swe.
794

War Babies
Plays/librettos/scripts
Review of five published plays by Margaret Hollingsworth. Canada.
Lang.: Eng.
2440

War Memorial Opera House
SEE
San Francisco Opera.

War on the Waterfront
Basic theatrical documents
Text of *War on the Waterfront* by Betty Roland. Australia. 1939.
Lang.: Eng.
1459

War Plays, The
Plays/librettos/scripts
Evaluation of *The War Plays* by Edward Bond. UK-England:
London. 1986. Lang.: Eng.
2853

Ward, Douglas Turner
Administration
Alternative funding for small theatres previously dependent on
government subsidy. USA: St. Louis, MO, New York, NY, Los
Angeles, CA, Detroit, MI. 1985. Lang.: Eng.
103

Warfel, William
Design/technology
Interview with lighting designer William Warfel. USA: New Haven,
CT. 1985-1986. Lang.: Eng.
1527

Wariat i zakonnica (Madman and the Nun, The)
Performance/production
Wariat i zakonnica (The Madman and the Nun) by Stanisław Ignacy
Witkiewicz, directed by János Sándor at Szeged National Theatre
under the title *Az őrült és az apáca*. Hungary: Szeged. 1986. Lang.:
Hun.
1965

Warmiński, Janusz
Performance/production
Shakespeare's *Hamlet* directed by Janusz Warmiński. Poland:
Warsaw. 1983. Lang.: Pol.
2051

Warner, Deborah
Performance/production
Director Deborah Warner of KICK on her production of
Shakespeare's *Coriolanus* and limited public funding for the non-
touring company. UK-England: London. 1985-1986. Lang.: Eng. 812

Wārqnäh, Sara
Plays/librettos/scripts
Translations of plays by William Shakespeare into Amharic and
Tegrenna. Ethiopia: Addis Ababa. 1941-1984. Lang.: Eng.
2537

Warren, Jim
Performance/production
Distinctive style of Canadian clowns. Canada: Toronto, ON,
Vancouver, BC. 1967-1986. Lang.: Eng.
3328

Warrener, Lowrie
Relation to other fields
Analysis of *Symphony* by Herman Voaden and Lowrie Warrener.
Canada. 1914-1933. Lang.: Eng.
1075

Warwich Arts Centre
Performance/production
Collection of newspaper reviews by London theatre critics. UK:
London. 1986. Lang.: Eng.
2100

Wasserstein, Wendy
Plays/librettos/scripts
Discussion among several playwrights on ethics and playwriting.
1986.
917

Watanabe, Tamotsu
Performance/production
Collection of pictures of famous *onnagata*. Japan: Tokyo. Lang.: Jap.
1381

Water Hen, The
SEE
Kurka vodna.

Water, Sam
Performance/production
Collection of newspaper reviews by London theatre critics. UK-
England: London. 1986. Lang.: Eng.
2117

Watermans Theatre (Brentford)
Performance/production
Collection of newspaper reviews by London theatre critics. UK-
England: London. 1986. Lang.: Eng.
2109
Collection of newspaper reviews by London theatre critics. UK-
England. 1986. Lang.: Eng.
2115

Waters, Leo
Performance/production
Reviews of *Rum and Coke*, by Keith Reddin, staged by Leo Waters.
USA: New York, NY. 1986. Lang.: Eng.
2241

Way, Brian
Institutions
Educational theatre in Iraq. Iraq. 1885-1985. Lang.: Eng.
505

Wayang
Performance/production
Description of characters and techniques of *Wayang* puppetry.
Indonesia. 1983-1986. Lang.: Fre.
4018

Plays/librettos/scripts
Influences on Asian theatrical genres. Asia. 500-1985. Lang.: Eng.
920

Relation to other fields
Analyses of *Wayang cepak* play, *Gusti Sinuhan*, and its role in the
Hindu religion. Indonesia. 1045-1986. Lang.: Eng.
3992

We're Going Through
Plays/librettos/scripts
Study of heroism in verse dramas by Douglas Stewart, Tom Inglis
Moore and Catherine Duncan. Australia. 1941-1943. Lang.: Eng.
2383

We've Come Through
Performance/production
Productions of plays by Edward Bond, Gyula Hernádi and Lope de
Vega at the Pécs National Theatre. Hungary: Pécs. 1986. Lang.:
Hun.
1898

Weaver, William
Reference materials
Catalogue of an exhibition of costume designs for Broadway
musicals. USA: New York, NY. 1900-1925. Lang.: Eng, Ger. 3635

Weavers, The
SEE
Weber, Die.

Web, The
Plays/librettos/scripts
David Belasco's influence on Eugene O'Neill. USA: New York, NY.
1908-1922. Lang.: Eng.
2927

Webb, Chloe
Design/technology
Cinematographer Roger Deakins discusses lighting for his work in
the film *Sid and Nancy*. USA: New York, NY, Los Angeles, CA.
UK-England: London. 1976-1986. Lang.: Eng.
3211

Weber, Carl
Performance/production
Interview with individuals involved in production of *Alcestis* by
Euripides. USA: Cambridge, MA. 1986. Lang.: Eng.
2266

Weber, Carl Maria von
Composer Carl Maria von Weber and productions of his operas in
Vienna. Austria: Vienna. Germany. 1803-1826. Lang.: Ger.
3637

Basic theatrical documents
The influence of *Euryanthe* by Carl Maria von Weber on Richard
Wagner. Germany: Dresden. 1824-1879. Lang.: Eng.
3649

Weber, Die (Weavers, The)
Performance/production
American productions of Hauptmann's *Die Weber (The Weavers)*.
USA. Germany. 1892-1900. Lang.: Ger.
2272

Weber, Die (Weavers, The) — cont'd

Plays/librettos/scripts
Fox symbolism in plays of Bertolt Brecht, Max Frisch and Gerhart Hauptmann. Germany. Switzerland. 1700-1976. Lang.: Ger. 2598

Webster, John
Relation to other fields
Social critique and influence of Jacobean drama. England: London. 1603-1613. Lang.: Eng. 1081

Theory/criticism
Phenomenological study of *The White Devil* by John Webster. England: London. 1610-1612. Lang.: Eng. 3093

Webster, Margaret
Performance/production
History of the Margaret Webster-Paul Robeson production of *Othello*. USA: New York, NY. 1942-1944. Lang.: Eng. 852

Margaret Webster's scenic approach to Shakespeare compared with those of Herbert Beerbohm Tree and Tyrone Guthrie. USA: New York, NY. 1910-1949. Lang.: Eng. 2293

Wechsler, Gil
Design/technology
Interview with lighting designer Gil Wechsler of the Metropolitan Opera. USA: New York, NY. 1883-1986. Lang.: Eng. 3654

Weck, Peter
Institutions
Union of three theaters in Vienna to the Verbund Wiener Theatre. Austria: Vienna. 1986. Lang.: Ger. 449

Wedding in Texas
Performance/production
Playwright and performer Cathy Jones. Canada: St. John's, NF. 1986. Lang.: Eng. 1660

Wedekind, Frank
Performance/production
Max Reinhardt's work with his contemporaries. Germany. Austria. 1890-1938. Lang.: Eng, Ger. 1757

Plays/librettos/scripts
Title character in Alban Berg's *Lulu*. Austria: Vienna. 1891-1979. Lang.: Eng. 3857

Influences on Alban Berg's *Lulu*. Austria: Vienna. 1907-1979. Lang.: Eng. 3859

Wederzijds (Amsterdam)
Performance/production
Youth theatre productions by Optater and Wederzijds. Netherlands: Amsterdam. 1986. Lang.: Eng. 766

Wegeler, Richard
History of the Theater für Vorarlberg. Austria: Bregenz. 1818-1986. Lang.: Ger. 3

Wei, Ch'angsheng
Performance/production
Life and influence of Wei Ch'angsheng, actor and playwright. China. 1795-1850. Lang.: Chi. 3506

Wei Ch'angsheng: actor of Szechuan opera, not Shensi opera. China. 1700-1800. Lang.: Chi. 3519

Wei, Liangfu
Relation to other fields
Mao's policy on theatre in revolution. China, People's Republic of: Beijing. 1920-1985. Lang.: Chi. 3549

Weigel, Helene
Performance/production
An exploration of Brecht's *Gestus*. Germany. Lang.: Eng. 1758

Photographic record of forty years of the Berliner Ensemble. Germany, East: Berlin, East. 1949-1984. Lang.: Eng. 1761

Application of Brechtian concepts by Eckhardt Schall. Germany, East: Berlin, East. UK-England: London. 1952-1986. Lang.: Eng. 1762

Brecht and the Berliner Ensemble. Germany, East: Berlin, East. 1950-1956. Lang.: Ger. 1765

Biography of Bertolt Brecht. Germany, West: Augsburg. Germany, East: Berlin, East. USA. 1898-1956. Lang.: Ger. 1767

Weill, Kurt
Performance/production
Die dreigroschenoper (The Three Penny Opera) directed by István Pinczés at Csokonai Theatre. Hungary: Debrecen. 1986. Lang.: Hun. 1910

Collection of newspaper reviews by London theatre critics. UK-England: London. 1986. Lang.: Eng. 2124

Plays/librettos/scripts
The power of music to transform the play into living theatre, examples from the work of Paul Green, Clifford Odets, and Maxwell Anderson. USA: New York, NY. 1936. Lang.: Eng. 3632

Premiere of Kurt Weill's landmark opera *Der Zar lässt sich photographieren*. Germany: Berlin. 1926-1929. Lang.: Eng. 3872

Collaboration of Kurt Weill, Alban Berg and Arnold Schönberg on *Lulu*. Germany. 1920-1932. Lang.: Eng. 3875

Analysis of *Der Silbersee* by Kurt Weill and Georg Kaiser. Germany: Leipzig. 1930-1933. Lang.: Eng. 3876

Essays on Kurt Weill's art and life. Germany: Berlin, Leipzig. 1900-1950. Lang.: Eng. 3877

Mahler's influence on Kurt Weill's career. Germany: Berlin. 1756-1950. Lang.: Eng. 3879

Analysis of the operetta *Firebrand* by Kurt Weill and Ira Gershwin. USA: New York, NY. Italy: Florence. 1945. Lang.: Eng. 3944

Relation to other fields
Mutual influence of Kurt Weill and Arnold Schönberg. Germany. 1909-1940. Lang.: Eng. 3918

Kurt Weill's relationship with his publisher. Germany: Berlin. 1924-1931. Lang.: Eng. 3919

Kurt Weill and German expressionism. Germany: Berlin. 1923-1930. Lang.: Eng. 3920

Socialism and Kurt Weill's operatic reforms. Germany: Berlin. 1920-1959. Lang.: Eng. 3921

Research/historiography
Inadequacy of research on the life of Kurt Weill. Germany: Berlin. 1925-1926. Lang.: Eng. 3927

Weimar Classicism
Performance/production
Analysis of Shakespeare's influence on Weimar, German neoclassicism. Germany: Weimar. 1771-1812. Lang.: Eng. 1760

Weinheber, Josef
Performance/production
Biography of Burgtheater actor Richard Eybner. Austria: Vienna. 1896-1986. Lang.: Ger. 1653

Weiss, Ehrich (Houdini, Harry)
Institutions
History of the Dime Museums. USA: Milwaukee, WI. 1882-1916. Lang.: Eng. 3324

Weiss, Kathleen
Performance/production
Increased use of physical aspects of theatre in Vancouver. Canada: Vancouver, BC. 1986. Lang.: Eng. 1664

Weiss, Peter
Performance/production
Directorial process as seen through major productions of Stanislavskij, Brecht, Kazan and Brook. 1898-1964. Lang.: Eng. 650

Relation to other fields
A portrait of Brecht in Peter Weiss's *Die Ästhetik des Widerstands*. Sweden: Stockholm. 1939-1940. Lang.: Eng. 1130

Weiss, Peter Eliot
Basic theatrical documents
Text of *Sex Tips for Modern Girls* by Peter Eliot Weiss. Canada: Vancouver, BC. 1985. Lang.: Eng. 3578

Performance/production
Increased use of physical aspects of theatre in Vancouver. Canada: Vancouver, BC. 1986. Lang.: Eng. 1664

Interview with playwright Peter Eliot Weiss. Canada: Vancouver, BC. 1986. Lang.: Eng. 1680

Playwright/dramaturg Peter Eliot Weiss discusses *Sex Tips for Modern Girls*. Canada: Vancouver, BC. 1984-1985. Lang.: Eng. 1684

Development of works by the Special Delivery Moving Theatre. Canada: Vancouver, BC. 1976-1986. Lang.: Eng. 3294

Plays/librettos/scripts
Environmental theatre version of *Hamlet*. Canada: Vancouver, BC. 1986. Lang.: Eng. 2435

Weiss, William
Research/historiography
Challenge to assertion that hyper-realism dominated theatre of the 1970s. Canada. 1970-1980. Lang.: Eng. 1184

Wekwerth, Manfred
Performance/production
Application of Brechtian concepts by Eckhardt Schall. Germany, East: Berlin, East. UK-England: London. 1952-1986. Lang.: Eng. 1762

Welcome to Black River
Plays/librettos/scripts
Biographical sketch of playwright/performer Samm-Art Williams. USA: Burgaw, NC, New York, NY. 1940-1986. Lang.: Eng. 2946

Welfare State International (Ulverston, UK)
Institutions
Function of the Welfare State Theater. UK. 1977. Lang.: Eng. 532

Performance/production
English alternative theatre group Welfare State International works with Tanzanian performers. UK-England. Tanzania. 1970-1986. Lang.: Eng. 814

Welitsch, Ljuba
Performance/production
Famous sopranos discuss their interpretations of Tosca. USA. 1935-1986. Lang.: Eng. 3811

Weller, Michael
Plays/librettos/scripts
Review of adaptations for the stage of short stories by Čechov. USA: New York, NY. 1986. Lang.: Eng. 2922

Welles, Orson
Institutions
John Houseman discusses Federal Theatre Project. USA: New York, NY, Washington, DC. 1935-1940. Lang.: Eng. 559

Performance/production
Pieces related to performance at Comédie-Française of *Un Chapeau de Paille d'Italie (An Italian Straw Hat)* by Eugène Labiche. France: Paris. 1850-1986. Lang.: Fre. 1725

Plays/librettos/scripts
Orson Welles' adaptation of Shakespeare's Falstaff scenes, *Chimes at Midnight*. UK-England. 1938-1965. Lang.: Eng. 3239

Sound effects and images of time in Orson Welles' film version of Shakespeare's *Othello*. USA. 1952. Lang.: Eng. 3241

Film versions of Shakespeare's *Macbeth* by Orson Welles, Akira Kurosawa and Roman Polanski. USA. Japan. 1948-1971. Lang.: Eng. 3243

Reference materials
Shakespeare on film. UK-England. USA. 1899-1984. Lang.: Eng. 3245

Theory/criticism
Shakespeare in media. UK-England. USA. Japan. 1899-1985. Lang.: Eng. 3172

Wells, Linda
Performance/production
Influence of the Joy Puppeteers on the television program *Hickory Hideout*. USA: Cleveland, OH. 1982-1986. Lang.: Eng. 3275

Wells, Win
Performance/production
Reviews of *Gertrude Stein and a Companion*, by Win Wells, staged by Ira Cirker. USA: New York, NY. 1986. Lang.: Eng. 2238

Wenig, Josef
Performance/production
Technical innovation, scenography and cabaret in relation to political and social conditions. Czechoslovakia. 1781-1986. Lang.: Eng. 1697

Weöres, Sándor
Performance/production
Study of *A Kétfejű fenerad (The Two-Headed Beast)*. Hungary. Lang.: Hun. 1926

Wer durchs Laub geht (Through the Leaves)
Performance/production
Life and technique of Franz Xaver Kroetz. USA: New York, NY. Germany, West. 1984. Lang.: Eng. 2287

Werfel, Franz
Relation to other fields
Life and work of playwright and critic Karl Kraus. Austria: Vienna. 1874-1936. Lang.: Ger. 3017

Wertenbaker, Timberlake
Institutions
Place of women in Britain's National Theatre. UK-England: London. 1986. Lang.: Eng. 1588

Plays/librettos/scripts
Current state of women's playwriting. UK-England. 1985-1986. Lang.: Eng. 2830

Wesele (Wedding, The)
Performance/production
Kazimierz Dejmek directs Wyspiański's *Wesele (The Wedding)*, Teatr Polski. Poland: Warsaw. 1984. Lang.: Pol. 2057

Ignacy Gogolewski of Teatr Osterwy directs Wyspiański's *Wesele (The Wedding)*. Poland: Lublin. 1984. Lang.: Pol. 2059

Plays/librettos/scripts
Material derived from Stanisław Wyspiański's *Wesele (The Wedding)* by various Polish playwrights. Poland. 1901-1984. Lang.: Fre. 2741

Wesker, Arnold
Basic theatrical documents
Catalan translation of *Chicken Soup with Barley* by Arnold Wesker. UK-England. 1958. Lang.: Cat. 1509

Institutions
Work and distinctive qualities of the Théâtre du Soleil. France: Paris. 1964-1986. Lang.: Eng. 1575

Plays/librettos/scripts
Analysis of Arnold Wesker's *Chicken Soup with Barley*. UK-England: London. 1932-1986. Lang.: Cat. 2864

Playwright Arnold Wesker discusses the writing of dialogue. UK-England. 1950-1986. Lang.: Eng. 2881

Utopia in early plays by Arnold Wesker. UK-England. 1958-1970. Lang.: Eng. 2884

Relation to other fields
Non-dramatic writings of playwright Arnold Wesker. UK-England. 1932-1986. Lang.: Eng. 3058

Theory/criticism
Assessment of critic Kenneth Tynan's works. UK-England. 1950-1960. Lang.: Eng. 3136

Wesley, Richard
Reference materials
Current work of Audelco award-winning playwrights. USA: New York, NY. 1973-1984. Lang.: Eng. 3007

Wessely, Paula
Performance/production
Life and films of actor and director Willi Forst. Austria: Vienna. Germany: Berlin. 1903-1980. Lang.: Ger. 3223

West End
Performance/production
Interview with playwright Peter Eliot Weiss. Canada: Vancouver, BC. 1986. Lang.: Eng. 1680

Western Michigan University (Kalamazoo, MI)
Plays/librettos/scripts
Text of a lecture on Shakespeare's *King Lear* by Clifford Davidson. Hungary: Budapest. Lang.: Hun. 2643

Westlake, Hilary
Institutions
Interview with Hilary Westlake of Lumière & Son. UK-England: London. 1973-1986. Lang.: Swe. 536

Weston-super-Mare Theatre (UK)
Performance/production
Survey of theatrical performances in the low country. UK-England. 1986. Lang.: Eng. 2150

Wharf Theatre (Sydney)
Performance spaces
Sydney Theatre Company headquarters in converted wharf. Australia: Sydney, N.S.W. 1986. Lang.: Eng. 580

What the Butler Saw
Plays/librettos/scripts
Joe Orton's redefinition of farce as a genre. UK-England. 1960-1969. Lang.: Eng. 2840

What Where
Plays/librettos/scripts
Comparison of the stage and television versions of *What Where* by Samuel Beckett. France. 1983-1985. Lang.: Eng. 3282

When the Chickens Come Home to Roost
Reference materials
Current work of Audelco award-winning playwrights. USA: New York, NY. 1973-1984. Lang.: Eng. 3007

When We Are Married
Performance/production
Collection of newspaper reviews by London theatre critics. UK-England: London. 1986. Lang.: Eng. 2122

When We Dead Awaken
SEE
Når vi døde vågner.

Where the Cross Is Made
Plays/librettos/scripts
David Belasco's influence on Eugene O'Neill. USA: New York, NY. 1908-1922. Lang.: Eng. 2927

Where Yellow River Flows, Fertility Follows
Performance/production
Director, producer Wu Jing-Jyi discusses his life and career in theatre. Taiwan. USA: Minneapolis, MN, New York, NY. 1939-1980. Lang.: Eng. 2098

White Devil
Reference materials
List of 37 productions of 23 Renaissance plays, with commentary. UK. USA. New Zealand. 1986. Lang.: Eng.   3000

White Devil, The
Theory/criticism
Phenomenological study of *The White Devil* by John Webster. England: London. 1610-1612. Lang.: Eng.   3093

White Rock Summer Theatre (White Rock, BC)
Institutions
The first decade of White Rock Summer Theatre in British Columbia. Canada: White Rock, BC. 1976-1985. Lang.: Eng.   1560

White, Miles
Design/technology
Costume designs for musical comedy by Miles White. USA: New York, NY. 1944-1960. Lang.: Eng.   1529

White, Patrick
Traditional innovation in *Voss* by Richard Meale and David Malouf. Australia. 1980-1986. Lang.: Eng.   3636

Whitefriars Playhouse (London)
Administration
History and management of Whitefriars Playhouse. England: London. 1607-1614. Lang.: Eng.   1432

Whitehall Theatre (London)
Performance spaces
Restoration of the Whitehall Theatre. UK-England: London. 1930-1986. Lang.: Eng.   625

Performance/production
Collection of newspaper reviews by London theatre critics. UK-England: London. 1986. Lang.: Eng.   2122

Whitehead, Graham
Performance/production
Staging techniques employed at the Mermaid Theatre. Canada: Wolfville, NS. 1972-1985. Lang.: Eng.   665

Whitehead, Robert
Performance/production
Reviews of *Lillian* by William Luce, staged by Robert Whitehead. USA: New York, NY. 1986. Lang.: Eng.   2245

Greek tragedy on the New York stage. USA: New York, NY. 1854-1984. Lang.: Eng.   2301

Whitelaw, Billie
Performance/production
Career of actress Billie Whitelaw, interpreter of Samuel Beckett's plays. UK-England. 1956-1986. Lang.: Eng.   2172

Whitfield, Vantile E.
Administration
Alternative funding for small theatres previously dependent on government subsidy. USA: St. Louis, MO, New York, NY, Los Angeles, CA, Detroit, MI. 1985. Lang.: Eng.   103

Whiting, John
Plays/librettos/scripts
Musical use of language conveys meaning in John Whiting's *Saint's Day*. UK-England. 1951. Lang.: Eng.   2857

Whiting, Maggie
Design/technology
Overview of the costume department of the National Theatre. UK-England: London. 1950-1986. Lang.: Eng.   1523

Whitlam, Gough
Administration
Malcolm Blaylock on theatre and government funding policy. Australia. 1985. Lang.: Eng.   22

Whittaker, Herbert
Basic theatrical documents
Autobiographical essays by drama critic Herbert Whittaker. Canada: Montreal, PQ. 1910-1949. Lang.: Eng.   1473

Theory/criticism
Reprints of Herbert Whittaker's theatre reviews. Canada. 1944-1975. Lang.: Eng.   3086

Book review of *Whittaker's Theatre: A Critic Looks at Stages in Canada and Thereabouts: 1944-1975*, ed. Ronald Bryden and Boyd Neil. Canada: Toronto, ON. 1944-1985. Lang.: Eng.   3087

Who's Afraid of Virginia Woolf?
Performance/production
Biography of Richard Burton. UK-Wales. 1925-1984. Lang.: Eng.   820

Hungarian performance of Edward Albee's play *Nem félünk a farkastól (Who's Afraid of Virginia Woolf?)*. Hungary. 1963-1984. Lang.: Hun.   1946

Director of original production discusses Edward Albee's *Who's Afraid of Virginia Woolf?*. USA: New York, NY. 1962. Lang.: Eng.   2303

Who's Got His
Performance/production
Lloyd Richard's career as an actor, director, artistic director and academic dean. USA: Detroit, MI, New York, NY, New Haven, CT. 1920-1980. Lang.: Eng.   2308

Widoff, Anders
Design/technology
Swedish set designers discuss their working methods. Sweden. 1980-1986. Lang.: Swe.   312

Widows, The
Relation to other fields
Psychological and sociological study of *The Widows* by Smetana and Züngel. Czechoslovakia-Bohemia. 1877-1878. Lang.: Eng.   3915

Wieland, Christoph Martin
Performance/production
Examination of German versions of Shakespeare's *Hamlet*. Germany: Hamburg. 1770-1811. Lang.: Eng.   728

Wielopole-Wielopole
Performance/production
Career and philosophy of director Tadeusz Kantor. Poland. 1915-1985. Lang.: Eng.   2028

Interview with director Tadeusz Kantor. Poland. 1967-1985. Lang.: Eng.   2029

Plays/librettos/scripts
Influence of politics and personal history on Tadeusz Kantor and his Cricot 2 theatre company. Poland: Cracow. 1944-1986. Lang.: Eng.   2744

Wiener Festwochen (Vienna)
Institutions
Wiener Festwochen 1986: Mozart and Modern Art. Austria: Vienna. 1986. Lang.: Ger.   441

Report on the Microtheater Festival in the Wiener Festwochen. Austria: Vienna. 1986. Lang.: Ger.   447

Themes of productions at the Wiener Festwochen. Austria: Vienna. 1986. Lang.: Ger.   453

The Festival of Clowns in the Wiener Festwochen. Austria: Vienna. 1983-1986. Lang.: Ger.   3380

Wiener Kammeroper (Vienna)
Institutions
Wiener Sommer 1986 promoted by Teletheater-Gesellschaft. Austria: Vienna. 1986. Lang.: Ger.   3479

Performance/production
Playwright and director George Tabori and his work. Austria: Vienna. Germany, West. 1914-1985. Lang.: Ger.   658

Wiener Kinderoper (Vienna)
Institutions
On new activities of groups or persons producing theatre for children. Austria: Vienna. 1986. Lang.: Ger.   454

Wiener Sommer (Vienna)
Institutions
Wiener Sommer 1986 promoted by Teletheater-Gesellschaft. Austria: Vienna. 1986. Lang.: Ger.   3479

Wierciński, Edmund
Performance/production
Actor-director Edmund Wierciński on Reduta Theatre. Poland. 1924. Lang.: Pol.   775

Wigman, Mary
Performance/production
Biography of modern dancer Mary Wigman. Germany. Switzerland. 1886-1973. Lang.: Ger.   1348

Choreographer Mary Wigman's theory of dance. Germany. 1914-1961. Lang.: Fre.   1349

Wigs
Design/technology
Technical details of producing *La Cage aux Folles* on a small budget. Sweden: Malmö. 1985. Lang.: Swe.   3581

The wigmaker's role in regional opera houses. USA. Lang.: Eng.   3658

Wilama Horzycy Theatre (Toruń)
Performance/production
Othello, translated by Bohdan Drozdowski and directed by Wilfred Harrison at the Wilama Horzycy Theatre. Poland: Toruń. 1980. Lang.: Eng.   2023

Wild Duck, The
SEE
Vildanden.
Wild Goose, The
Plays/librettos/scripts
Biography of playwright Teresa Deevy. Ireland. 1894-1963. Lang.:
Eng.   2665
Wild Honey
SEE
Platonov.
Wilde, Oscar
Performance/production
Orientalism in four productions of Wilde's *Salome*. Italy. 1904-1963.
Lang.: Ita.   750
Collection of newspaper reviews by London theatre critics. UK-
England. 1986. Lang.: Eng.   2111

Plays/librettos/scripts
Historical information on Oscar Wilde's *Vera, or The Nihilists*.
England. Russia. USA: New York, NY. 1883. Lang.: Rus.   944
Comparative analysis of *Elektra* by Hugo von Hofmannsthal and its
sources. Germany. 1909. Lang.: Eng.   2603
A comparison between Oscar Wilde's *The Importance of Being
Earnest* and Tom Stoppard's *Travesties*. UK-England. 1895-1974.
Lang.: Eng.   2872
Wilder, Thornton
Plays/librettos/scripts
Tom Stoppard's *On the Razzle*, an adaptation of *Einen Jux will er
sich machen* by Johann Nestroy. England. Austria: Vienna. 1927-
1981. Lang.: Eng.   2462
Analysis of plays by Max Frisch, and influences of Thornton Wilder.
Switzerland. 1939-1983. Lang.: Eng.   2829

Theory/criticism
Aesthetic considerations in the plays and essays of Thornton Wilder.
USA. 1930-1949. Lang.: Rus.   3149
Wileński Teatr Objazdowy (Vilna)
Performance/production
Details of Wileński Touring Theatre. Poland: Vilna. 1935-1936.
Lang.: Pol.   2020
Wiles, David
Performance/production
Collection of newspaper reviews by London theatre critics. UK-
England: London. 1986. Lang.: Eng.   2122
Wilhelm, Kurt
Design/technology
Designers discuss regional productions of *Guys and Dolls*. USA.
1984-1986. Lang.: Eng.   3586
Will You Still Need Me
Plays/librettos/scripts
A description of Ena Lamont Stewart's trilogy *Will you Still Need
Me*. UK-Scotland. 1940-1985. Lang.: Eng.   2886
Willems, Paul
Basic theatrical documents
Playtext of Paul Willems' play *Il pleut dans ma maison (It's
Raining in My House)* in English translation. Belgium. 1963. Lang.:
Eng.   1464

Performance/production
Effect of dual-language society on Belgian theatre. Belgium: Brussels,
Liège. Lang.: Eng.   660

Plays/librettos/scripts
Biography and bibliography of playwright Paul Willems. Belgium.
1912-1986. Lang.: Eng.   2403
Willett, John
Theory/criticism
Critique of James Fenton's review of two books on Bertolt Brecht.
USA. 1974.   1236
Williams and Walker
Performance/production
Reviews of *Williams and Walker* by Vincent D. Smith, staged by
Shaunelle Percy. USA: New York, NY. 1986. Lang.: Eng.   2225
Williams, Alan
Plays/librettos/scripts
Interview with actor-playwright Alan Williams. Canada: Toronto,
ON, Winnipeg, MB. UK-England: Hull. 1976-1986. Lang.: Eng. 2438
Williams, Billy
Design/technology
Interview with cinematographer Billy Williams. USA. 1986.   3210

Williams, Bob
Design/technology
Mechanical bears in film, *Clan of the Cave Bear*. USA. 1985-1986.
Lang.: Eng.   3214
Williams, Percy
Performance spaces
History of the Bushwick Theatre. USA: New York, NY. 1911-1986.
Lang.: Eng.   3465
Williams, Raymond
Relation to other fields
Curricular authority for drama-in-education program. UK. Lang.:
Eng.   3054
Williams, Richard
Performance/production
Collection of newspaper reviews by London theatre critics. UK-
England. 1986. Lang.: Eng.   2111
Collection of newspaper reviews by London theatre critics. UK-
England: London. 1986. Lang.: Eng.   2118
Williams, Samm-Art
Plays/librettos/scripts
Review of adaptations for the stage of short stories by Čechov.
USA: New York, NY. 1986. Lang.: Eng.   2922
Biographical sketch of playwright/performer Samm-Art Williams.
USA: Burgaw, NC, New York, NY. 1940-1986. Lang.: Eng.   2946

Reference materials
Current work of Audelco award-winning playwrights. USA: New
York, NY. 1973-1984. Lang.: Eng.   3007
Williams, Tennessee
Basic theatrical documents
Catalan translation of *Small Craft Warnings* by Tennessee Williams.
USA. 1972. Lang.: Cat.   1512

Institutions
Interview with Adrian Hall, artistic director of both Trinity Square
Repertory Theatre and Dallas Theatre Center. USA: Providence, RI,
Dallas, TX. 1966-1986. Lang.: Eng.   548

Performance/production
Directorial process as seen through major productions of
Stanislavskij, Brecht, Kazan and Brook. 1898-1964. Lang.: Eng.   650
Collaboration of Tennessee Williams and Elia Kazan. Australia.
Lang.: Eng.   1637
Macska a forró bádogtetőn (Cat on a Hot Tin Roof) by Tennessee
Williams, directed by Miklós Szurdi at Városzinház. Hungary:
Budapest. 1985. Lang.: Hun.   1809
History of Hungarian productions and interpretations of *Death of a
Salesman (Az ügynök halála)* by Arthur Miller and *A Streetcar
Named Desire (A vágy villamos)* by Tennessee Williams. Hungary.
1959-1983. Lang.: Hun.   1857
Review of Tennessee Williams' *Sweet Bird of Youth* starring Lauren
Bacall, directed by Harold Pinter. UK-England: London. 1985.
Lang.: Eng.   2186
Collaboration of Italian composer Rafaello de Banfield and
American playwright Tennessee Williams on the opera *Lord Byron's
Love Letter*. USA: Charleston, SC. 1986. Lang.: Eng.   3810
Profile of and interview with Lee Hoiby, American composer of *The
Tempest* with libretto by Mark Schulgasser. USA: Long Eddy, NJ.
1926-1986. Lang.: Eng.   3832

Plays/librettos/scripts
Comparison of natural and dramatic speech. England. USA. 1600-
1986. Lang.: Eng.   939
Genesis of *Sweet Bird of Youth* by Tennessee Williams. USA. 1958.
Lang.: Eng.   2904
Comparison of plays by Tennessee Williams, Arthur Miller and
Eugene O'Neill. USA. 1949-1956. Lang.: Eng.   2926
Analysis of *Small Craft Warnings*, and report of audience reactions.
USA: New York, NY. Spain-Catalonia: Barcelona. 1972-1983. Lang.:
Cat.   2929
Authority and victimization in *A Streetcar Named Desire* by
Tennessee Williams. USA. 1960-1980. Lang.: Eng.   2947

Theory/criticism
Assessment of critic Kenneth Tynan's works. UK-England. 1950-
1960. Lang.: Eng.   3136
Williamson, C.J.
Plays/librettos/scripts
Developments in Australian playwriting since 1975. Australia. 1975-
1986. Lang.: Eng.   2374

SUBJECT INDEX

Witkiewicz, Stanisław Ignacy — cont'd

Description of international symposium discussing the work of Stanisław Ignacy Witkiewicz. Poland. 1985. Lang.: Eng, Fre.   2733

Material derived from Stanisław Wyspiański's *Wesele (The Wedding)* by various Polish playwrights. Poland. 1901-1984. Lang.: Fre.   2741

Overview of symposium on playwright Stanisław Ignacy Witkiewicz. Poland. 1985. Lang.: Eng, Fre.   2747

Production history of plays by Stanisław Ignacy Witkiewicz. Poland. 1921-1985. Lang.: Eng, Fre.   2754

Analysis of animal-like characters in Witkiewicz's dramas. Poland. 1920-1935. Lang.: Pol.   2757

Relation to other fields
Suicide of playwright Stanisław Witkiewicz. Poland. 1931-1939. Lang.: Pol.   3050

Wittig, Monique
Plays/librettos/scripts
Mythology in the works of Hélène Cixous, Andrée Chedid, Monique Wittig and Marguerite Yourcenar. France. Lang.: Eng.   2580

Wlasehin, Ken
Administration
Directors of the film festival Filmex discuss their plans for the future. USA: Los Angeles, CA. 1986. Lang.: Eng.   3190

Wochinz, Herbert
Institutions
Concept for programs at the Stadttheater. Austria: Klagenfurt. 1985-1987. Lang.: Ger.   443

Woe from Wit
SEE
Gore ot uma.

Wojewodski, Stan
Administration
A profile of Center Stage. USA: Baltimore, MD. 1963-1986. Lang.: Eng.   109

Center Stage's resident set designer Hugh Landwehr. USA: Baltimore, MD. 1977-1986. Lang.: Eng.   111

Wolf, Christa
Performance/production
Photographic record of forty years of the Berliner Ensemble. Germany, East: Berlin, East. 1949-1984. Lang.: Eng.   1761

Wolf, Friedrich
Plays/librettos/scripts
Reflections on Max Zweig's dramas. Austria: Vienna. Germany: Berlin. Israel: Tel Aviv. 1892-1986. Lang.: Ger.   2389

Wolfe, George C.
Performance/production
Reviews of *The Colored Museum*, by George C. Wolfe, staged by L. Kenneth Richardson. USA: New York, NY. 1986. Lang.: Eng.   2203

Wolff, Beverly
Performance/production
Opera greats reflect on performance highlights. USA: Philadelphia, PA, New York, NY. 1985. Lang.: Eng.   3841

Wolff, Egon
Plays/librettos/scripts
Marginal characters in plays of Jorge Díaz, Egon Wolff and Luis Alberto Heiremans. Chile. 1960-1971. Lang.: Eng.   2442

Wolkowski, Jan
Performance/production
Jan Wolkowski directs an adaptation of a folk legend about Jedrzej Wowrze. Poland: Szczecin. 1983. Lang.: Pol.   3968

Wolter, Charlotte
Reference materials
Costumes of famous Viennese actors. Austria: Vienna. 1831-1960. Lang.: Ger.   1003

Woman from the Sea, A
Basic theatrical documents
Playtext of *A Woman from the Sea* by Cindy Cowan. Canada. 1986. Lang.: Eng.   1468

Woman in Mind
Performance/production
Actress Julie McKenzie discusses her role in *Woman in Mind* by Alan Ayckbourn. UK-England: London. Lang.: Eng.   2145

Woman Killed with Kindness, A
Plays/librettos/scripts
Moral issues in *A Woman Killed with Kindness* by Thomas Heywood. England. 1560. Lang.: Eng.   2498

Woman of Paradise
SEE
Donna del Paradiso.

Woman of Paris, The
SEE
Parisienne, La.
Woman, The
Plays/librettos/scripts
Playwright Edward Bond's use of Greek models in *The Woman.* UK-England. 1978. Lang.: Eng.   2834

Women Beware Women
Performance/production
Collection of newspaper reviews by London theatre critics. UK-England. 1986. Lang.: Eng.   2114
Reference materials
List of 37 productions of 23 Renaissance plays, with commentary. UK. USA. New Zealand. 1986. Lang.: Eng.   3000

Women in theatre
Basic theatrical documents
Text of *Tu i l'hipócrita (You and the Hypocrite)*, by Maria Aurélia Capmany, translated into Castilian Spanish by L. Teresa Valdivieso as *Tú y el hipócrita*. Spain-Catalonia: Barcelona. 1959. Lang.: Spa.   1495

Design/technology
Interview with three female lighting designers. USA. 1946-1983. Lang.: Eng.   357

Panel held on women's roles in the field of design. USA: New York, NY. 1985. Lang.: Eng.   427
Institutions
Interview with Julia Miles, director of the Women's Project, American Place Theatre. USA: New York, NY. 1978-1985. Lang.: Eng.   558

Place of women in Britain's National Theatre. UK-England: London. 1986. Lang.: Eng.   1588

Progress and aims of Women's Playhouse Trust. UK-England: London. 1984-1986. Lang.: Eng.   1590
Performance/production
Discussion of women's comedy by one of its practitioners. Australia: Melbourne. 1986. Lang.: Eng.   657

Development of women's and Maori theatre. New Zealand. 1980-1986. Lang.: Eng.   767

Gender roles in the work of female theatre professionals. USA. 1985. Lang.: Eng.   836

Mariann Csernus' stage adaptations and performance in works of Simone de Beauvoir and Liv Ullmann. Hungary: Budapest. 1985. Lang.: Hun.   1816

Life and work of actress-playwright Franca Rame. Italy. 1929-1983. Lang.: Eng.   1988

Performances by women on women's issues. Australia: Sydney, N.S.W. 1986. Lang.: Eng.   3442

Overview of an international festival of performance art by women. UK-England. 1986. Lang.: Eng.   3449

Careers of fifty successful female comics. 1900-1986. Lang.: Eng.   3467

Plays/librettos/scripts
Discussion of plays and themes concerning the Women's Movement. USA. 1971-1986. Lang.: Eng.   982

Discusses feminist theatre with themes concerning the female body. Canada: Quebec, PQ. 1969-1985. Lang.: Eng.   2428

Interview with playwright Kathleen Betsko. England: Coventry. USA. 1960-1986. Lang.: Eng.   2487

Women's issues in Italian theatre. Italy. 1985. Lang.: Cat.   2710

Women's roles in New Zealand theatre. New Zealand. 1950-1984. Lang.: Eng.   2724

Translator discusses her Spanish version of Maria Aurelia Capmany's Catalan play, *Tu i l'hipócrita (You and the Hypocrite)*. Spain. 1959-1976. Lang.: Spa.   2806

Life and work of Caterina Albert, known as Víctor Català. Spain-Catalonia. 1869-1966. Lang.: Cat.   2816

Roles of women in middle-class Catalonian society as reflected in the plays of Carme Montoriol and Maria Aurélia Capmany. Spain-Catalonia. 1700-1960. Lang.: Spa.   2819

Current state of women's playwriting. UK-England. 1985-1986. Lang.: Eng.   2830

Introduction to and overview of articles contained in Volume 40 of *Theatre Annual.* USA. 1900-1985. Lang.: Eng.   2898

Discussion of issues raised in plays of 1985-86 season. USA: New York, NY. 1985-1986. Lang.: Eng.   2928

Women in theatre — cont'd

Theory/criticism
Lack of representation of women in theatre. USA: New York, NY. 1982-1986. Lang.: Eng. 1227

Women of Manhattan
Design/technology
Interview with set designer Adrianne Lobel. USA: New York, NY. 1986. Lang.: Eng. 1530

Women of the Town, The
Plays/librettos/scripts
Biographical sketch of playwright/performer Samm-Art Williams. USA: Burgaw, NC, New York, NY. 1940-1986. Lang.: Eng. 2946

Women, The
Relation to other fields
Interview with actress Maria Aitken on a revival of *The Women* by Clare Boothe Luce. UK-England: London. 1936-1986. Lang.: Eng. 3061

Women's Playhouse Trust (London)

Institutions
Progress and aims of Women's Playhouse Trust. UK-England: London. 1984-1986. Lang.: Eng. 1590

Performance/production
Collection of newspaper reviews by London theatre critics. UK. 1986. Lang.: Eng. 2101

Collection of newspaper reviews by London theatre critics. UK-England. 1986. Lang.: Eng. 2111

Plays/librettos/scripts
Current state of women's playwriting. UK-England. 1985-1986. Lang.: Eng. 2830

Interview with Gillian Hanna about *Elisabetta: Quasi per caso una donna (Elizabeth: Almost by Chance a Woman)*. UK-England: London. Italy. 1986. Lang.: Eng. 2875

Women's Theatre Group (UK)

Performance/production
Interview with Lesbian feminist theatre company Hard Corps. UK-England. 1984-1986. Lang.: Eng. 2164

Plays/librettos/scripts
Current state of women's playwriting. UK-England. 1985-1986. Lang.: Eng. 2830

Won Ton Soup
Performance/production
Director, producer Wu Jing-Jyi discusses his life and career in theatre. Taiwan. USA: Minneapolis, MN, New York, NY. 1939-1980. Lang.: Eng. 2098

Wonder, Erich

Design/technology
Profile of set and lighting designer Erich Wonder. Germany, West. 1944-1986. Lang.: Eng. 274

Wonderful Town
Performance/production
Reviews of musicals. UK-England: London. 1986. Lang.: Eng. 3610

Wood, Charles

Performance/production
Collection of newspaper reviews by London theatre critics. UK-England: London. 1986. Lang.: Eng. 2121

Wood, John

Institutions
History of the Neptune Theatre and its artistic directors. Canada: Halifax, NS. 1963-1983. Lang.: Eng. 483

Wood, Mrs. John (Mathilda Charlotte Vining)

Relation to other fields
Professional equality in theatrical careers for men and women. USA: New York, NY. 1850-1870. Lang.: Eng. 1143

Wood, Peter

Performance/production
Collection of newspaper reviews by London theatre critics. UK-England: London. 1986. Lang.: Eng. 2124

Woodes, Nathaniel

Plays/librettos/scripts
Tradition and individualism in Renaissance drama. England: London. 1575-1600. Lang.: Eng. 2496

Woodford, Thomas

Administration
History and management of Whitefriars Playhouse. England: London. 1607-1614. Lang.: Eng. 1432

Woodrow, Carol

Performance/production
Dilemmas and prospects of youth theatre movement. Australia. 1982-1986. Lang.: Eng. 1639

Woodruff, Robert

Performance/production
Director Robert Woodruff's shift from naturalism to greater theatricality. USA: San Francisco, CA, New York, NY, La Jolla, CA. 1976-1986. Lang.: Eng. 851

Woolf, Benjamin

Plays/librettos/scripts
Philosophy of wealth in gilded age plays. USA: New York, NY. 1870-1889. Lang.: Eng. 2950

Wooster Group (New York, NY)

Design/technology
Interview with set designer Jim Clayburgh. USA: New York, NY. 1972-1983. Lang.: Eng. 390

Institutions
Development of several companies funded by the NEA's Ongoing Ensembles Program. USA: New York, NY. 1986. Lang.: Eng. 553

Performance/production
History of the Wooster Group. USA: New York, NY. 1975-1985. Lang.: Eng. 849

Wooster Group retrospective of original works. USA: New York, NY. 1975-1986. Lang.: Eng. 850

Interview with Wooster Group's artistic director Elizabeth LeCompte. USA: New York, NY. 1984. Lang.: Eng. 2288

Performance art and its current characteristic tone. USA. Lang.: Eng. 3459

Plays/librettos/scripts
Discussion of issues raised in plays of 1985-86 season. USA: New York, NY. 1985-1986. Lang.: Eng. 2928

Contributing sources to Wooster Group's *Saint Anthony*. USA: New York, NY, Boston, MA, Washington, DC. 1983-1986. Lang.: Eng. 2940

Wopmann, Alfred

Institutions
Solving the financial problems of the Bregenzer Festspiele. Austria: Bregenz. 1986-1987. Lang.: Ger. 442

Workers' Art Club (Australia)

Institutions
Historical perspective of the New Theatre. Australia: Sydney, N.S.W. 1932-1986. Lang.: Eng. 438

Workers' Experimental Theatre (Toronto, ON)

Relation to other fields
Circumstances surrounding a banned Workers' Experimental Theatre play. Canada: Toronto, ON. 1931-1933. Lang.: Eng. 3018

Workers' theatre

Performance/production
History of amateur theatre in Finland. Finland. 1920-1986. Lang.: Swe. 706

People's theatre groups in the provinces of Shansi, Kansu and Liaoning. China, People's Republic of. 1938-1940. Lang.: Chi. 1692

Relation to other fields
History of workers' theatre. USSR. Germany. UK-England. 1917-1934. Lang.: Eng. 1179

Wotruba, Fritz

Reference materials
Costumes of famous Viennese actors. Austria: Vienna. 1831-1960. Lang.: Ger. 1003

WOW Cafe (New York, NY)

Audience
Context and design of some lesbian performances. USA: New York, NY. 1985. Lang.: Eng. 1455

Woyzeck
Plays/librettos/scripts
Study of realism vs metadrama. Europe. 429 B.C.-1978 A.D. Lang.: Eng. 2540

Origins and influences of *Woyzeck* on Berg's opera *Wozzeck*. Austria: Vienna. 1821-1925. Lang.: Eng. 3855

Wozzeck
Plays/librettos/scripts
The search for morality in *Wozzeck* by Alban Berg. 1821. Lang.: Eng. 3851

Origins and influences of *Woyzeck* on Berg's opera *Wozzeck*. Austria: Vienna. 1821-1925. Lang.: Eng. 3855

Relation to other fields
Influence of political and artistic movements on composer Alban Berg. Austria: Vienna. 1894-1935. Lang.: Eng. 3914

Comparison between insanity defense and opera productions with audience as jury. USA. 1980-1985. Lang.: Eng. 3925

SUBJECT INDEX

WPA Federal Theatre Project
Performance/production
Puppets in Performance, part of the 50th anniversary celebration of the WPA Federal Theatre Project. USA. 1986. 3974

WPA Theatre (New York, NY)
Administration
Transfer of plays from nonprofit to commercial theatre as experienced by WPA Theatre's artistic director Kyle Renick. USA: New York, NY. 1983. Lang.: Eng. 1443

Design/technology
The WPA Theatre's resident designer, Edward Gianfrancesco. USA: New York, NY. 1977-1986. 382

Institutions
Artistic director of WPA Theatre Kyle Renick discusses institutionalization of theatre companies. USA: New York, NY. 1977-1986. Lang.: Eng. 566

Performance/production
Director Kyle Renick's personal experiences with playwright Lillian Hellman. USA: New York, NY. 1984. Lang.: Eng. 2299

Wright, Alice
Performance/production
Acting style in plays by Henrik Ibsen. 1885-1905. Lang.: Eng. 1627

Wright, John
Performance/production
History of The Little Angel Marionette Theatre. UK-England: London. 1961-1986. Lang.: Eng. 4007

Wright, Jules
Performance/production
Collection of newspaper reviews by London theatre critics. UK. 1986. Lang.: Eng. 2101
Collection of newspaper reviews by London theatre critics. UK-England. 1986. Lang.: Eng. 2111

Writer's Opera, The
Plays/librettos/scripts
Analysis of the plays of Rosalyn Drexler. USA. 1964-1985. Lang.: Eng. 2920

Writers Theatre (New York, NY)
Institutions
Profile of Writers Theatre, an organization focusing on adaptations of poetry and literature for theatre. USA: New York, NY. 1975-1983. Lang.: Eng. 562

Wu, Bing
Plays/librettos/scripts
Playwright Wu Bing mocks The Peony Pavilion by Tang Xianzu. China. 1600-1980. Lang.: Chi. 3531

Wu, Jing-jyi
Performance/production
Director, producer Wu Jing-Jyi discusses his life and career in theatre. Taiwan. USA: Minneapolis, MN, New York, NY. 1939-1980. Lang.: Eng. 2098

Wunschkonzert (Request Concert)
Performance/production
Adaptation of Kroetz's Wunschkonzert (Request Concert). India: Calcutta, Madras, Bombay. Lang.: Eng. 1975

Wuppertal Tanztheater
Performance/production
Symposium on the violence in Pina Bausch's Tanztheater. Germany, West. 1973-1985. Lang.: Eng. 1272
Interview with choreographer Mechthild Grossman. Germany, West. 1984-1985. Lang.: Eng. 1273
Illustrated interview with choreographer Pina Bausch. Germany. 1970-1985. Lang.: Fre. 1347

Relation to other fields
The impact of the Third Reich on modern dance. Germany. 1902-1985. Lang.: Eng. 1353

Theory/criticism
Pina Bausch seen as heir of epic theater of Bertolt Brecht. Germany, West. 1977-1985. Lang.: Eng. 1289
American criticisms of German Tanztheater. Germany, West. USA. 1933-1985. Lang.: Eng. 1290
American dance critics' reviews of Pina Bausch's work. USA. Germany, West. 1984-1986. Lang.: Eng. 1291

Württemberg State Theatre (Stuttgart)
Performance spaces
The renovation of the Württemberg State Theatre by the citizens of Stuttgart. Germany, West: Stuttgart. 1909-1976. Lang.: Eng. 3683

Wus, Jerry
Design/technology
Designers discuss regional productions of Fiddler on the Roof. USA. 1984-1986. Lang.: Eng. 3595

Wyatt, Eliza
Performance/production
Call for playwrights to hold character conferences with actors in rehearsal. 1986. 1634

Wydro, Ken
Institutions
Vi Higginsen's Mama I Want to Sing and history of the Mumbo-Jumbo Theatre Company. USA: New York, NY. 1980-1986. Lang.: Eng. 1601

Wylie, Betty Jane
Performance/production
Playwright Betty Jane Wylie's advice on workshopping new plays. Canada. 1986. Lang.: Eng. 1685

Wyllie, George
Performance/production
Collection of newspaper reviews by London theatre critics. UK-England: London. 1986. Lang.: Eng. 2116

Wyndham's Theatre (London)
Performance/production
Collection of newspaper reviews by London theatre critics. UK-England: London. 1986. Lang.: Eng. 2124

Wyspiański, Stanisław
Performance/production
Kazimierz Dejmek directs Wyspiański's Wesele (The Wedding), Teatr Polski. Poland: Warsaw. 1984. Lang.: Pol. 2057
Ignacy Gogolewski of Teatr Osterwy directs Wyspiański's Wesele (The Wedding). Poland: Lublin. 1984. Lang.: Pol. 2059

Plays/librettos/scripts
Material derived from Stanisław Wyspiański's Wesele (The Wedding) by various Polish playwrights. Poland. 1901-1984. Lang.: Fre. 2741
Literary and theatrical history of Eastern Europe. Poland. Hungary. Czechoslovakia. 1800-1915. Lang.: Hun. 2755

Wyzewa, Téodore de
Performance/production
Influence of Richard Wagner on the work of the French Symbolists. France: Paris. Germany, West: Bayreuth. 1860-1986. Lang.: Eng. 3726

X
Performance/production
Profile of and interview with Anthony Davis, composer of the opera X, on the life and times of Malcolm X. USA: New York, NY. Lang.: Eng. 3834

Xenakis, Jannis
Performance/production
Discussion of Persepolis and Orghast at Persepolis-Shiraz festival. Iran: Shiraz. 1971. Lang.: Ita. 741

Xhosa dance
Research/historiography
System for describing ethnic dance based on Xhosa dances. South Africa, Republic of. 1980-1985. Lang.: Eng. 1337

Xi Xiang Zhu
Plays/librettos/scripts
Differences among 32 extant editions of Xi Xiang Zhu. China. 1669-1843. Lang.: Chi. 3528

Xiong, Foxi
Institutions
Former students remember Xiong Foxi. China, People's Republic of: Chengdu. 1901-1981. Lang.: Chi. 1568

Plays/librettos/scripts
Career of Xiong Foxi. China, People's Republic of: Beijing, Shanghai. USA: New York, NY. 1901-1965. Lang.: Chi. 2449

Reference materials
Bibliography of Xiong Foxi's writings. China, People's Republic of. 1917-1963. Lang.: Chi. 1011

Theory/criticism
Playwright Xiong Foxi's concept of theatre. China, People's Republic of. 1920-1965. Lang.: Chi. 3089

Training
Xiong Foxi, playwright and teacher. China, People's Republic of: Ch'eng-tu. 1928-1940. Lang.: Chi. 3156

GEOGRAPHICAL - CHRONOLOGICAL INDEX

Australia — cont'd

1835-1853. **Plays/librettos/scripts.**
Analysis of *The Bushrangers* by Charles Harpur. Lang.: Eng.
2370

1850-1986. **Institutions.**
Playwright Jack Hibberd's analysis of nationalist and
English-derived theatrical cultures. Melbourne. Sydney. Lang.:
Eng.
439

1850-1986. **Theory/criticism.**
Melodrama as an aesthetic theatre form. Lang.: Eng.   3083

1858-1870. **Performance/production.**
Chinese theatre companies on the Goldfields of Victoria.
Lang.: Eng.
1641

1860-1890. **Performance/production.**
Apprenticeship of playwright Garnet Walch. Sydney, N.S.W.
Lang.: Eng.
1640

1860-1930. **Relation to other fields.**
Difficulties of distinction between 'high' and 'popular'
culture. Lang.: Eng.
1063

1866. **Reference materials.**
Description of the theatrical library of writer James Smith.
Melbourne. Lang.: Eng.
1002

1870-1969. **Reference materials.**
Description of Australian archives relating to theatre and
film. Lang.: Eng.
1000

1876-1965. **Theory/criticism.**
Attitudes toward sports in serious Australian drama. Lang.:
Eng.
3084

1892-1954. **Performance/production.**
Career of vaudeville comedian Roy Rene, creator of 'Mo'.
Lang.: Eng.
3327

1900-1976. **Plays/librettos/scripts.**
Comparison of plays about Ned Kelly of Australia and
Louis Riel of Canada. Canada. Lang.: Eng.
2421

1905-1943. **Plays/librettos/scripts.**
Louis Esson's attempts to create an Australian national
drama based on the Irish model. Eire. Lang.: Eng.
2380

1905-1967. **Plays/librettos/scripts.**
Analysis of plays by Charles Jury and Ray Mathew. Lang.:
Eng.
2384

1909-1966. **Plays/librettos/scripts.**
Political plays of Katharine Susannah Prichard and Ric
Throssell. Lang.: Eng.
2388

1914-1939. **Administration.**
Causes of decline in number of commercially produced plays.
Sydney. Lang.: Eng.
24

1920-1955. **Reference materials.**
Description of a collection of unpublished Australian plays.
Lang.: Eng.
2977

1926-1986. **Performance/production.**
Appreciation of the career of Joan Sutherland. Sydney,
N.S.W. Lang.: Eng.
3689

1928-1981. **Plays/librettos/scripts.**
Analysis of *The Touch of Silk* and *Granite Peak* by Betty
Roland. Lang.: Eng.
2387

1928-1985. **Plays/librettos/scripts.**
Betty Roland's life and stage work. Sydney, N.S.W. Lang.:
Eng.
2382

1932-1955. **Institutions.**
Account of New Theatre movement by a participant. Sydney.
Melbourne. Lang.: Eng.
437

1932-1968. **Plays/librettos/scripts.**
Playwright Mona Brand's work with New Theatre movement.
Sydney, N.S.W. Lang.: Eng.
924

1932-1986. **Institutions.**
Historical perspective of the New Theatre. Sydney, N.S.W.
Lang.: Eng.
438

1938. **Basic theatrical documents.**
Act I, Scene 3 of *Are You Ready Comrade?* by Betty
Roland. Lang.: Eng.
1460

1939. **Basic theatrical documents.**
Text of *War on the Waterfront* by Betty Roland. Lang.:
Eng.
1459

1940-1980. **Plays/librettos/scripts.**
Individualism and male-female relationships as themes in
Australian drama. Lang.: Eng.
2373

1941-1943. **Plays/librettos/scripts.**
Study of heroism in verse dramas by Douglas Stewart, Tom
Inglis Moore and Catherine Duncan. Lang.: Eng.   2383

1942-1958. **Plays/librettos/scripts.**
Analysis of the plays of Oriel Gray. Lang.: Eng.   2376

1950-1986. **Plays/librettos/scripts.**
Interview with satirist Barry Humphries. UK-England. Lang.:
Eng.
922

1955-1977. **Plays/librettos/scripts.**
Analysis of Ray Lawler's *Summer of the Seventeenth Doll* in
the context of his later plays. Lang.: Eng.   2377

1959-1983. **Plays/librettos/scripts.**
Impact of Ray Lawler's *Summer of the Seventeenth Doll* on
Australian theatre. Lang.: Eng.
2381

1960-1970. **Plays/librettos/scripts.**
Ron Blair: considerations in writing for the theatre. Lang.:
Eng.
2372

1973-1986. **Performance/production.**
History and current state of Australian Opera at the Sydney
Opera House. Sydney, N.S.W. Lang.: Eng.
3688

1974-1985. **Relation to other fields.**
Drama handbook for secondary school teachers. Lang.: Eng.
1062

1974-1986. **Performance spaces.**
History of the Experimental Art Foundation as an alternative
space. Adelaide. Lang.: Eng.
3437

1975-1986. **Plays/librettos/scripts.**
Developments in Australian playwriting since 1975. Lang.:
Eng.
2374

1976-1985. **Plays/librettos/scripts.**
Analysis of plays by David Williamson. Lang.: Eng.   2379

1980-1984. **Performance/production.**
Case-study of *Sweet and Sour* by the Australian Broadcasting
Corporation. Sydney, N.S.W. Lang.: Eng.
3483

1980-1986. **Performance/production.**
Traditional innovation in *Voss* by Richard Meale and David
Malouf. Lang.: Eng.
3636

1980-1986. **Performance spaces.**
Problematic dimensions of the Sydney Opera House's Drama
Theatre. Sydney, N.S.W. Lang.: Eng.
1612

1980-1986. **Performance/production.**
Community theatre as interpreted by the Sidetrack Theatre
Company. Sydney, N.S.W. Lang.: Eng.
1638

1981-1986. **Performance/production.**
Influence of *kata* principle on Western acting technique.
Japan. Denmark. Lang.: Ita.
1365

1982-1986. **Performance/production.**
Dilemmas and prospects of youth theatre movement. Lang.:
Eng.
1639

1983-1986. **Plays/librettos/scripts.**
Analysis of *Balmain Boys Don't Cry*, a political satire.
Sydney, N.S.W. Lang.: Eng.
3368

1984. **Plays/librettos/scripts.**
Interview with playwright Ray Lawler. Melbourne. Lang.:
Eng.
2386

1985. **Administration.**
Malcolm Blaylock on theatre and government funding policy.
Lang.: Eng.
22

1985. **Plays/librettos/scripts.**
Popularity of dramatic monologue on stage and television.
Lang.: Eng.
921

Translations, adaptations and the Australian theatre.
Armidale, N.S.W. Lang.: Eng.
2371

Interview with scriptwriter Peter Yeldham. Sydney, N.S.W.
Lang.: Eng.
3278

1985. **Theory/criticism.**
Low standard of much Australian theatre reviewing. Lang.:
Eng.
3085

1986. **Administration.**
Economic conditions of the arts in Australia. Lang.: Eng.   23

1986. **Performance spaces.**
Sydney Theatre Company headquarters in converted wharf.
Sydney, N.S.W. Lang.: Eng.
580

Overview of performance spaces in several Australian cities.
Lang.: Eng.
3438

1986. **Performance/production.**
Interview with political satirist Max Gillies. Lang.: Eng.   654

Collaboration of playwright Jack Davis and director Andrew
Ross. Lang.: Eng.
655

Discussion of women's comedy by one of its practitioners.
Melbourne. Lang.: Eng.
657

Overview of the Soundworks Festival. Lang.: Eng.   3439

Interview with performance artist Mike Mullins. Lang.: Eng.
3440

Australia — cont'd

Interview with performance artist Jill Scott. Lang.: Eng. 3441

Performances by women on women's issues. Sydney, N.S.W. Lang.: Eng. 3442

1986. **Plays/librettos/scripts.**
Semiotic analysis of a production of *Antigone* by Sophocles. Perth, W.A. Lang.: Eng. 923

Interview with playwright Dorothy Hewett. Sydney, N.S.W. Lang.: Eng. 2368

Interview with playwright David Williamson. Lang.: Eng. 2369

Interview with playwright David Williamson. Lang.: Eng. 2378

Interview with playwright Alex Buzo. Lang.: Eng. 2385

1986. **Reference materials.**
Accounts of non-English-speaking artists. Lang.: Eng. 1001

Austria

Performance/production.
On manager and director Claus Helmut Drese. Vienna. Switzerland. Germany, West. Lang.: Ger. 659

Photos of famous conductors during their rehearsals. Vienna. Salzburg. Lang.: Ger. 3701

1700-1799. **Performance/production.**
Performance rules of Mozart's time as guidance for singers. Vienna. Lang.: Ger. 3691

1700-1984. **Training.**
Collected papers from a conference on voice training. Vienna. Rome. London. Lang.: Ger. 3936

1734-1789. **Plays/librettos/scripts.**
Appearance of Franz Anton Mesmer as a character in Mozart's *Così fan tutte*. Paris. Vienna. Lang.: Eng. 3871

1750-1850. **Plays/librettos/scripts.**
Shakespeare's influence on Verdi's operas. Germany. Italy. Lang.: Eng. 3878

1750-1984. **Training.**
Psychological aspects of voice training. USA. Lang.: Ger. 3935

1770-1800. **Plays/librettos/scripts.**
Use of the tale of Patient Griselda in *Griselda* by Angelo Anelli and Niccolo Piccinni. Venice. Vienna. Lang.: Eng. 3885

1776-1986. **Institutions.**
Ten years of the Burgtheater under the auspices of Achim Benning. Vienna. Lang.: Ger. 1533

1780. **Performance/production.**
The innovative quality of *Idomeneo*. Vienna. Lang.: Eng. 3702

1782-1791. **Plays/librettos/scripts.**
The theme of clemency in the final operas of Mozart. Vienna. Lang.: Cat. 3860

1790-1836. **Reference materials.**
Adaptation of Ferdinand Raimund's dramas for children's theatre. Vienna. Lang.: Ger. 2979

1790-1986. **Reference materials.**
Interpretation of Ferdinand Raimund's dramas after his death. Vienna. Lang.: Ger. 2981

1803-1826. **Reference materials.**
Composer Carl Maria von Weber and productions of his operas in Vienna. Vienna. Germany. Lang.: Ger. 3637

1803-1985. **Performance/production.**
Playing Hamlet at the Burgtheater. Vienna. Lang.: Ger. 1654

1818-1986. **Performance/production.**
History of the Theater für Vorarlberg. Bregenz. Lang.: Ger. 3

1821-1925. **Plays/librettos/scripts.**
Origins and influences of *Woyzeck* on Berg's opera *Wozzeck*. Vienna. Lang.: Ger. 3855

1831-1960. **Reference materials.**
Costumes of famous Viennese actors. Vienna. Lang.: Ger. 1003

1863-1985. **Plays/librettos/scripts.**
Investigates whether Brahms wrote music for an opera. Vienna. Lang.: Eng. 3856

1871-1986. **Performance spaces.**
Plans for using the Ronacher theatre after its renovation. Vienna. Lang.: Ger. 584

1872-1986. **Performance spaces.**
Semper Depot and its history. Vienna. Lang.: Ger. 583

1874-1936. **Relation to other fields.**
Karl Kraus, a reflection of Viennese culture and literature history. Vienna. Lang.: Ger. 3014

Life and work of playwright and critic Karl Kraus. Vienna. Lang.: Ger. 3017

1874-1986. **Performance/production.**
Performance history of *Die Fledermaus* by Richard Strauss. Vienna. Lang.: Eng. 3704

1874-1986. **Reference materials.**
Exhibition catalogue about context of the work and influence of Karl Kraus. Vienna. New York, NY. Paris. Lang.: Ger. 2980

1878-1982. **Reference materials.**
Bibliography on and about the playwright-author Ferenc Molnár. Vienna. Budapest. New York, NY. Lang.: Eng. 2982

1880-1935. **Reference materials.**
Exhibit on life and work of actor Alessandro Moissi. Trieste. Lang.: Ita. 2993

1886-1986. **Performance/production.**
Collection of statements about the life and career of conductor Wilhelm Furtwängler. Berlin. Salzburg. Lang.: Ger. 3737

1890-1938. **Performance/production.**
Max Reinhardt's work with his contemporaries. Germany. Lang.: Eng, Ger. 1757

1890-1945. **Performance/production.**
History of the Viennese cabaret. Vienna. Lang.: Ger. 3364

1891-1933. **Plays/librettos/scripts.**
Essays on all facets of Expressionism including theatre and dance. Germany. Lang.: Ger, Ita. 953

1891-1979. **Plays/librettos/scripts.**
Title character in Alban Berg's *Lulu*. Vienna. Lang.: Eng. 3857

1892-1986. **Plays/librettos/scripts.**
Reflections on Max Zweig's dramas. Vienna. Berlin. Tel Aviv. Lang.: Ger. 2389

1894-1935. **Relation to other fields.**
Influence of political and artistic movements on composer Alban Berg. Vienna. Lang.: Eng. 3914

1896-1986. **Performance/production.**
Biography of Burgtheater actor Richard Eybner. Vienna. Lang.: Ger. 1653

1900-1965. **Reference materials.**
Encyclopedia of cabaret in German. Germany. Switzerland. Lang.: Ger. 3369

1900-1986. **Relation to other fields.**
Feminist criticism of plays written by women. Germany. Switzerland. Lang.: Ger. 3033

1903-1980. **Performance/production.**
Life and films of actor and director Willi Forst. Vienna. Berlin. Lang.: Ger. 3223

1904-1930. **Design/technology.**
Travelling exhibitions of Edward Gordon Craig and his first book *The Art of the Theatre*. Germany. USA. Lang.: Eng. 1515

1907-1979. **Plays/librettos/scripts.**
Influences on Alban Berg's *Lulu*. Vienna. Lang.: Eng. 3859

1909-1985. **Relation to other fields.**
The reception of critic and playwright Karl Kraus in the English speaking world. New York, NY. Vienna. Glasgow. Lang.: Ger. 3067

1909-1986. **Performance/production.**
Interviews with various artists of the Viennese State Opera. Vienna. Lang.: Ger. 3692

1911-1985. **Relation to other fields.**
Study on the reception of critic and playwright Karl Kraus in Italy. Italy. Vienna. Lang.: Ger. 3044

1911-1986. **Performance/production.**
The love-music of *Der Rosenkavalier* by Richard Strauss. Vienna. Lang.: Eng. 3703

1913-1945. **Reference materials.**
Influence of stage director Max Reinhardt on film production. Berlin. Vienna. Lang.: Ger. 3244

1913-1986. **Plays/librettos/scripts.**
Details on performances of plays by Paul Claudel in German-speaking countries. Germany. Switzerland. Lang.: Ger. 2599

1914-1985. **Performance/production.**
Playwright and director George Tabori and his work. Vienna. Germany, West. Lang.: Ger. 658

1916-1986. **Performance/production.**
Opera singer Giuseppe Taddei and his work at the Staatsoper. Vienna. Italy. Europe. Lang.: Ger. 3694

Austria — cont'd

1918-1986. **Plays/librettos/scripts.**
Difficulties in French translation of Karl Kraus's *Die Letzten Tage der Menschheit (The Last Days of Mankind)*. Vienna. Paris. Lang.: Ger. 2397

1920-1939. **Plays/librettos/scripts.**
Life and work of playwright Franz Csokor. Lang.: Rus. 2396

1921. **Plays/librettos/scripts.**
Language in *Der Schwierige (The Difficult Man)* by Hugo von Hofmannsthal. Lang.: Ger. 2390

1922-1986. **Performance/production.**
Benno Besson and his staging of *Don Juan* at the Burgtheater. Vienna. Switzerland. Germany, East. Lang.: Ger. 1642

1924-1986. **Performance/production.**
Otto Grünmandl and his satiric revues. Lang.: Ger. 3363
Opera singer Oskar Czerwenka and his opinions. Vienna. Lang.: Ger. 3695

1925-1950. **Performance/production.**
Biography of actor and stage manager Franz Reichert. Vienna. Berlin. Prague. Lang.: Ger. 1652

1925-1986. **Administration.**
Manager, actor and director Boy Gobert: his plans for managing the Theater in der Josefstadt. Vienna. Germany, West. Lang.: Ger. 1427

1926-1986. **Performance/production.**
Profile of and interview with soprano Leonie Rysanek. Vienna. Lang.: Eng. 3693
Opera singer Leonie Rysanek and her career. Vienna. New York, NY. Lang.: Ger. 3697

1927-1981. **Plays/librettos/scripts.**
Tom Stoppard's *On the Razzle*, an adaptation of *Einen Jux will er sich machen* by Johann Nestroy. England. Vienna. Lang.: Eng. 2462

1928-1986. **Administration.**
Robert Jungbluth and his management of the Österreichische Bundestheater. Vienna. Lang.: Ger. 25

1928-1986. **Plays/librettos/scripts.**
Interview with playwright, director and actor Pavel Kohout. Prague. Vienna. Lang.: Swe. 2454

1930-1986. **Administration.**
Manager Heinrich Kraus and his work. Vienna. Lang.: Ger. 1426

1930-1986. **Institutions.**
Claus Helmut Drese and his plans for managing the Vienna Staatsoper. Vienna. Germany, West. Switzerland. Lang.: Ger. 3670

1933-1937. **Relation to other fields.**
Collection of obituary notes for the critic and dramatist Karl Kraus. Vienna. Lang.: Ger. 3015

1933-1986. **Performance/production.**
Composer Krzystof Penderecki and his new opera *Die schwarze Maske (The Black Mask)*, based upon a play by Gerhart Hauptmann. Salzburg. Poland. Lang.: Ger. 3700

1935-1985. **Performance/production.**
Harry Kupfer and his ideas for staging operas. Germany, East. Lang.: Ger. 3696

1935-1986. **Performance/production.**
Opera-singer Mirella Freni: her roles and plans. Italy. Lang.: Ger. 3759

1936-1986. **Performance/production.**
Actress Elisabeth Orth, her life and work. Lang.: Ger. 1650

1938-1986. **Performance/production.**
On actor Heinz Petters and the production of *Der Raub der Sabinerinnen* at the Volkstheater. Vienna. Lang.: Ger. 1644

1938-1986. **Plays/librettos/scripts.**
Cooperation between playwright Heinz Rudolf Unger and the Volkstheater. Vienna. Lang.: Ger. 2394

1939-1976. **Reference materials.**
Christl Zimmerl's career as prima ballerina at the Vienna State Opera. Vienna. Lang.: Ger. 1324

1941-1986. **Performance/production.**
On actor Gert Voss and his work. Vienna. Germany, West. Lang.: Ger. 1649

1944-1986. **Performance/production.**
Klaus Maria Brandauer as Hamlet. Vienna. Lang.: Ger. 1648

1945-1960. **Performance/production.**
Viennese cellar theatres as alternative theatre spaces. Vienna. Lang.: Ger. 1645

1945-1985. **Performance/production.**
Comparative history of German-language theatre. Germany. Switzerland. Lang.: Ger. 727

1945-1986. **Design/technology.**
On scene designer Hans Schavernoch and his work. Vienna. Lang.: Ger. 239

1946-1949. **Performance/production.**
Opera singer Ferruccio Furlanetto and his career. Salzburg. Italy. Lang.: Ger. 3698

1946-1986. **Performance/production.**
Actor Franz Morak and his work at the Burgtheater. Vienna. Lang.: Ger. 1647

1947-1986. **Institutions.**
On the audience-society, Salzburger Kulturvereinigung. Salzburg. Lang.: Ger. 446

1950-1986. **Performance/production.**
Conductor Claudio Abbado and his work at the Staatsoper. Vienna. Italy. Lang.: Ger. 3690

1951-1986. **Performance/production.**
Opera singer Peter Dvorsky: his life and work. Bratislava. Vienna. Lang.: Ger. 3716

1955-1986. **Performance/production.**
Elisabeth Kales and her performance in the main role of Leo Fall's operetta *Madame Pompadour*. Vienna. Lang.: Ger. 3484

1957-1986. **Institutions.**
The new secretary-general of the Salzburger Festspiele, Franz Willnauer. Salzburg. Germany, West. Lang.: Ger. 444

1957-1986. **Performance/production.**
On actor and playwright Gabriel Barylli. Vienna. Lang.: Ger. 1646

1963-1980. **Design/technology.**
Sceneshops of the Burgtheater, Staatsoper and Volksoper. Vienna. Lang.: Hun. 237

1964-1986. **Institutions.**
History of the Salzburger Osterfestspiele. Salzburg. Lang.: Ger. 3666

1968. **Relation to other fields.**
Gertrud Schattner, a founder of drama therapy, and her work at Bellevue Hospital. New York, NY. Lang.: Eng. 3064

1970-1986. **Plays/librettos/scripts.**
Distinguishes between the natural flow of words and present forms of linguistic alienation. USA. Lang.: Eng. 2913

1971-1986. **Relation to other fields.**
Situation of playwrights in Austria. Vienna. Lang.: Ger. 3016

1976-1986. **Institutions.**
Tours of the Österreichische Bundestheater in Austria. Lang.: Ger. 455
Achim Benning's management of the Burgtheater. Vienna. Lang.: Ger. 1537

1976-1986. **Performance/production.**
Playwright Václav Havel's experience with the Burgtheater. Vienna. Czechoslovakia. Lang.: Ger. 1643

1976-1986. **Plays/librettos/scripts.**
New playwrights in Austria and their difficulties of getting performed or published. Lang.: Ger. 2395

1978-1986. **Institutions.**
Photos of productions at the Schauspielhaus under the leadership of Hans Gratzer. Vienna. Lang.: Ger. 1534

1979-1986. **Institutions.**
Productions in 1986 of Ars Electronica. Linz. Lang.: Ger. 3321

1980-1984. **Training.**
Results of sonographic analysis of covered and uncovered singing. Lang.: Ger. 3933
Psychological aspects of the voice teacher's work. Vienna. Lang.: Ger. 3934

1980-1986. **Institutions.**
Niederösterreichischer Theatersommer: producing summer theatre at festivals in different places. Lang.: Ger. 448

1980-1986. **Plays/librettos/scripts.**
Cooperation between theatres in Austria and playwrights-in-training. Lang.: Ger. 2393

1983-1986. **Institutions.**
Concept and functions of Schlossspiele Kobersdorf. Burgenland. Lang.: Ger. 458
The Festival of Clowns in the Wiener Festwochen. Vienna. Lang.: Ger. 3380

1984. **Performance/production.**
Interview with Jean-Pierre Ponnelle discussing his directing technique and set designs. Salzburg. Lang.: Eng. 3699

Belgium — cont'd

1936-1981.   **Plays/librettos/scripts.**
Biography and bibliography of playwright René Kalisky.
Lang.: Eng.   2401

1943-1985.   **Performance/production.**
Actors discuss performing in plays by Paul Claudel. France.
Lang.: Fre.   1722

1945-1986.   **Plays/librettos/scripts.**
Biography and bibliography of playwright Jacques de Decker.
Lang.: Eng.   2400

1963.   **Basic theatrical documents.**
Playtext of Paul Willems' play *Il pleut dans ma maison (It's Raining in My House)* in English translation. Lang.: Eng.
    1464

1979.   **Basic theatrical documents.**
Playtext of Jacques de Decker's *Jeu d'intérieur (Indoor Games)* in English translation. Lang.: Eng.   1461

1980.   **Basic theatrical documents.**
Playtext of René Kalisky's *Sur les ruines de Carthage (On the Ruins of Carthage)* in English translation. Lang.: Eng.
    1462

Playtext of Jean Sigrid's *L'ange couteau (Angel Knife)* in English translation. Lang.: Eng.   1463

1980-1986.   **Relation to other fields.**
Use of marionettes in psychotherapy. France. Lang.: Fre.
    4011

1981-1982.   **Reference materials.**
Theatre productions in the French community of Belgium.
Lang.: Fre.   1004

1982-1983.   **Reference materials.**
Theatre productions in the French community of Belgium.
Lang.: Fre.   1005

1983-1984.   **Administration.**
Theatre as a generator of products, consumers, and financial flow. Lang.: Fre.   26

1983-1984.   **Reference materials.**
Theatre productions in the French community of Belgium.
Lang.: Fre.   1006

1984-1985.   **Reference materials.**
Theatre productions in the French community of Belgium.
Lang.: Fre.   1007

1985.   **Performance/production.**
Recent French-language theatre. Lang.: Fre.   661

Directors discuss staging of plays by Paul Claudel. France.
Lang.: Fre.   1723

1985.   **Relation to other fields.**
Political theatre in Wallonia. Lang.: Fre.   1066

1986.   **Design/technology.**
Description of portable cruciform theatre. Lang.: Eng.   240

Bohemia

ALSO SEE
Czechoslovakia.

Brazil

1808-1973.   **Plays/librettos/scripts.**
Language as an instrument of tyranny in Athayde's *Apareceua Margarida (Miss Margarida's Way)*. Lang.: Eng.
    2405

1952-1986.   **Relation to other fields.**
Interview with Augusto Boal. Montreal, PQ. France. São Paulo. Lang.: Eng.   3019

1956-1978.   **Theory/criticism.**
Augusto Boal's concept of theatre of the oppressed. France.
Lang.: Eng.   1201

1971.   **Plays/librettos/scripts.**
Interplay of signs of violence in Augusto Boal's *Torquemada*.
Lang.: Eng.   2404

1973-1974.   **Plays/librettos/scripts.**
Ritual and archetypal communication in *La noche de los asesinos (The Night of the Assassins)* by José Triana. Cuba.
Lang.: Eng.   2450

1985-1986.   **Performance/production.**
Survey of productions in 1985/86. Rio de Janeiro. Lang.: Eng.   1656

Bulgaria

1945-1986.   **Plays/librettos/scripts.**
Bulgarian drama after World War II. Lang.: Pol.   2406

1966-1985.   **Institutions.**
Festival for children and youth. Stara Zagora. Lang.: Ger.
    463

1980-1986.   **Performance/production.**
Notes on Bulgarian theatre. Lang.: Rus.   662

1983-1985.   **Performance spaces.**
Description of Lyudmila Zhivkova, the palace of culture.
Sofia. Lang.: Swe.   585

1986.   **Plays/librettos/scripts.**
Replies to questionnaire by five Soviet playwrights. USSR.
Lang.: Rus.   2958

Cambodia

4 B.C.-1986 A.D.   **Research/historiography.**
Ritual origins of the classical dance drama of Cambodia.
Lang.: Eng.   1336

1860-1985.   **Performance/production.**
History of classical Cambodian dance. Lang.: Eng.   1358

1964-1986.   **Performance/production.**
Collaboration of Hélène Cixous and Ariane Mnouchkine.
France. Lang.: Eng.   1752

Cameroon

1930-1986.   **Plays/librettos/scripts.**
Interview with playwright René Philombe on the educative function of theatre. Lang.: Eng.   925

1940-1985.   **Reference materials.**
Bibliography of plays by Cameroonians. Lang.: Fre.   2983

Canada

    Basic theatrical documents.
A collection of satirical monologues by playwright Corey Reay. Lang.: Eng.   1471

    Design/technology.
Working with robots to promote Expo '86.   3950

    Plays/librettos/scripts.
Review of five published plays by Margaret Hollingsworth.
Lang.: Eng.   2440

1604-1986.   **Plays/librettos/scripts.**
Envy in Shakespeare's *Othello* and Peter Shaffer's *Amadeus*.
Montreal, PQ. Europe. Lang.: Eng.   932

1606-1975.   **Plays/librettos/scripts.**
Amerindian and aborigine characters in the works of white playwrights. Australia. Lang.: Eng.   930

1759-1901.   **Plays/librettos/scripts.**
French-Canadian nationalism in *Le Drapeau de Carillon (The Flag of Carillon)*. Montreal, PQ. Lang.: Eng.   2433

1798-1871.   **Relation to other fields.**
Shakespearean allusions in political satire. Lang.: Eng.   1074

1800-1900.   **Relation to other fields.**
Theatricals used by temperance societies. Lang.: Eng.   1067

1800-1967.   **Reference materials.**
Bibliography of Canadian drama. Lang.: Eng.   2985

1809-1859.   **Basic theatrical documents.**
Text of radio play about a woman doctor who masqueraded as a man. Montreal, PQ. Edinburgh. Cape Town. Lang.: Eng.   3175

1830-1980.   **Performance/production.**
Image of the indigène. Australia. New Zealand. Lang.: Eng.   656

1832-1834.   **Performance/production.**
Reception of the Kembles' Canadian tour. Lang.: Eng.   663

1833.   **Plays/librettos/scripts.**
William Rufus Blake's *Fitzallan* as the first play written and produced in Canada. Halifax, NS. Lang.: Eng.   2430

1833-1879.   **Basic theatrical documents.**
Texts of three political dramas, with discussion. Lang.: Eng.
    1472

1837-1867.   **Performance/production.**
Elzéar Labelle's operetta *La Conversion d'un pêcheur de la Nouvelle-Écosse (The Conversion of a Nova Scotian Fisherman)* as an example of the move toward public performance. Quebec, PQ. Lang.: Eng.   3599

1838-1848.   **Basic theatrical documents.**
Text of *The Miser Outwitted*, attributed to Major John Richardson, with introduction. Dublin. Lang.: Eng.   1465

1845.   **Relation to other fields.**
Theatre riot provoked by Thomas Hill's *The Provincial Association*. St. John, NB. Lang.: Eng.   1073

1851-1887.   **Basic theatrical documents.**
Musical setting for operetta *La conversion d'un pêcheur de la Nouvelle-Écosse (The Conversion of a Nova Scotian Fisherman)*. Lang.: Eng.   3579

1853-1854.   **Performance/production.**
Details of Luigi Arditi's U.S. and Canada tour with the New York Opera Company. USA. Montreal, PQ. Toronto, ON.
Lang.: Eng.   3819

GEOGRAPHICAL - CHRONOLOGICAL INDEX

Canada — cont'd

1960-1980.   Performance/production.
Artistic and technological differences in presenting opera for stage and television. Lang.: Eng.   3714

1960-1986.   Performance/production.
Interview with actor Stephen Ouimette. Lang.: Eng.   1663

1960-1986.   Plays/librettos/scripts.
Actor and prose-poet Walter Borden's play *Tight Rope Time*. Halifax, NS. Lang.: Eng.   2409

1962-1975.   Plays/librettos/scripts.
Influence of oriental theatre on playwright Beverley Simons. Vancouver, BC. Lang.: Eng.   928

1962-1986.   Institutions.
Several short-lived alternative theatre companies to the Neptune Theatre. Halifax, NS. Lang.: Eng.   1557

1963-1983.   Institutions.
History of the Neptune Theatre and its artistic directors. Halifax, NS. Lang.: Eng.   483

1964-1984.   Institutions.
Interview with Françoise Graton and Gilles Pelletier of Nouvelle Compagnie Théâtrale. Montreal, PQ. Lang.: Fre.   477

Repertory of the Nouvelle Compagnie Théâtrale. Montreal, PQ. Lang.: Fre.   481

1965-1983.   Plays/librettos/scripts.
Ideology of commercial television. USA. Lang.: Eng.   3281

1965-1986.   Performance/production.
Career of director Bill Glassco. Toronto, ON. Lang.: Eng.   1674

1966-1982.   Plays/librettos/scripts.
Development of the title character of *The Ecstasy of Rita Joe* by George Ryga, seen in successive drafts. Vancouver, BC. Lang.: Eng.   929

1966-1984.   Institutions.
Overview of Festival de Créations Jeunesse. Montreal, PQ. Lang.: Fre.   467

1967.   Basic theatrical documents.
Text of *The Paper People* by Timothy Findley. Lang.: Eng.   3252

1967.   Plays/librettos/scripts.
Critical debate over Timothy Findley's *The Paper People*. Lang.: Eng.   3280

1967-1983.   Institutions.
Goals of Eric Bruhn, new artistic director of National Ballet of Canada. Toronto, ON. Lang.: Eng.   1296

1967-1986.   Performance/production.
Distinctive style of Canadian clowns. Toronto, ON. Vancouver, BC. Lang.: Eng.   3328

1968-1971.   Relation to other fields.
Controversy about *Captives of the Faceless Drummer* by George Ryga. Vancouver, BC. Lang.: Eng.   3021

1968-1975.   Plays/librettos/scripts.
Acadian characters of playwright Antonine Maillet contrasted with Longfellow's romantic myth. Lang.: Eng.   2439

1968-1982.   Institutions.
Problems of Toronto Dance Theatre. Toronto, ON. Lang.: Eng.   1344

1968-1986.   Institutions.
The development of French-language theatre in Ontario. Lang.: Eng.   1567

1968-1986.   Plays/librettos/scripts.
A review of radio plays written by Linda Zwicker. Lang.: Eng.   3184

1969-1985.   Institutions.
Productions and policies of National Art Centre. Ottawa, ON. Lang.: Eng.   480

1969-1985.   Plays/librettos/scripts.
Discusses feminist theatre with themes concerning the female body. Quebec, PQ. Lang.: Eng.   2428

1969-1986.   Institutions.
French-language theatre and the Acadian tradition. Lang.: Eng.   1544

1970.   Basic theatrical documents.
Text of *The Journey* by Timothy Findley. Lang.: Eng.   3173

1970-1978.   Plays/librettos/scripts.
Life and work of Francophone playwright Paul-André Paiement. Lang.: Fre.   2417

1970-1980.   Plays/librettos/scripts.
Poverty in plays by Michel Tremblay and David Fennario. Quebec, PQ. Lang.: Eng.   2410

1970-1980.   Research/historiography.
Challenge to assertion that hyper-realism dominated theatre of the 1970s. Lang.: Eng.   1184

1970-1983.   Design/technology.
Career of lighting designer Nicholas Cernovitch. Montreal, PQ. Lang.: Eng.   244

1970-1983.   Plays/librettos/scripts.
Cultural models and types in docudrama. Lang.: Eng.   3279

1970-1984.   Performance/production.
Opera singer Maureen Forrester tells of her switch from serious roles to character and comic roles. Lang.: Eng.   3706

1970-1984.   Plays/librettos/scripts.
Development of playwright George F. Walker. Toronto, ON. Lang.: Eng.   931

1970-1986.   Institutions.
A history of two French language theatres. Edmonton, AB. Lang.: Eng.   1542

Theories on incorporating traditional theatrical forms into popular theatre. Toronto, ON. Lang.: Eng.   3408

1970-1986.   Performance/production.
Productions of Dario Fo's *Morte accidentale di un anarchico (Accidental Death of an Anarchist)* in the light of Fo's political ideas. USA. Italy. Lang.: Eng.   2262

1970-1986.   Plays/librettos/scripts.
Work of playwright R.A. Shiomi, including production history of *Yellow Fever*. Toronto, ON. New York, NY. San Francisco, CA. Lang.: Eng.   2422

1970-1988.   Performance/production.
History of the Omnibus mime troupe. Montreal, PQ. Lang.: Eng.   3291

1971-1979.   Plays/librettos/scripts.
The plays of Antonine Maillet and the revival of Acadian theatre. Lang.: Eng.   2423

1971-1983.   Plays/librettos/scripts.
Analysis of the plays of Sharon Pollock. Lang.: Eng.   935

1972-1982.   Institutions.
Overview of Festival Lennoxville and the role of anglophone drama in Quebec. Lennoxville, PQ. Lang.: Eng.   485

1972-1983.   Design/technology.
Careers of stage designers, Murray Laufer, Michael Eagan and Susan Benson. Lang.: Eng.   241

1972-1983.   Reference materials.
Overview of Charlottetown Festival productions. Charlottetown, PE. Lang.: Eng.   1008

1972-1983.   Relation to other fields.
Concept of play in theatre and sport. Lang.: Eng.   1071

1972-1985.   Performance/production.
Staging techniques employed at the Mermaid Theatre. Wolfville, NS. Lang.: Eng.   665

1973-1986.   Institutions.
History of the Théâtre de la Marmaille. Quebec, PQ. Lang.: Eng.   1552

1974-1986.   Institutions.
Shift in emphasis at Banff Centre. Banff, AB. Lang.: Eng.   1543

1974-1986.   Performance/production.
John Neville's productions of *The Winter's Tale, Pericles,* and *Cymbeline*. Stratford, ON. Lang.: Eng.   1657

1975.   Plays/librettos/scripts.
Structure and characterization in the plays of W.O. Mitchell. Lang.: Eng.   2408

1975-1982.   Institutions.
Account of the firing of Alexander Grant, artistic director of National Ballet of Canada. Toronto, ON. Lang.: Eng.   1295

1975-1984.   Institutions.
Interview with Dennis Foon, director of Green Thumb Theatre for Young People. Vancouver, BC. Lang.: Fre.   473

1975-1986.   Institutions.
Structure and political viewpoint of Great Canadian Theatre Company. Ottawa, ON. Lang.: Eng.   486

History of the Green Thumb Theatre. Vancouver, BC. Lang.: Eng.   1541

1975-1986.   Performance/production.
Interview with mezzo-sporano Judith Forst. Lang.: Eng.   3708

1976-1981.   Plays/librettos/scripts.
Literary and popular theatrical forms in the plays of Rick Salutin. Montreal, PQ. Toronto, ON. Lang.: Eng.   2411

1976-1985.   Institutions.
The first decade of White Rock Summer Theatre in British Columbia. White Rock, BC. Lang.: Eng.   1560

Canada — cont'd

1976-1986.   Institutions.
Successful alternative theatre groups in Newfoundland. Lang.:
Eng.   1550
History of the Dramatists' Co-op of Nova Scotia. Lang.:
Eng.   1558
Limited opportunities for English-language playwrights in
Montreal. Montreal, PQ. Lang.: Eng.   1561
1976-1986.   Performance/production.
Development of works by the Special Delivery Moving
Theatre. Vancouver, BC. Lang.: Eng.   3294
1976-1986.   Plays/librettos/scripts.
Interview with actor-playwright Alan Williams. Toronto, ON.
Winnipeg, MB. Hull. Lang.: Eng.   2438
1977.   Performance/production.
Robin Phillips' staging of Shakespeare's *Richard III.*
Stratford, ON. Lang.: Eng.   1668
1977.   Plays/librettos/scripts.
Symbolism and allusion in *Boiler Room Suite* by Rex
Deverell. Regina, SK. Lang.: Eng.   934
1977-1983.   Institutions.
Overview of the productions and goals of Catalyst Theatre.
Edmonton, AB. Lang.: Eng.   464
1977-1985.   Audience.
History of the Mulgrave Road Co-op theatre. Guysborough,
NS. Lang.: Eng.   1444
1978.   Plays/librettos/scripts.
Discusses Michel Garneau's *joual* translation of *Macbeth.*
Montreal, PQ. Lang.: Eng.   2429
1978-1985.   Institutions.
Description of new arts district. Calgary, AB. Lang.: Eng.
                                                                                    484
1979-1983.   Administration.
John Neville's administration of the Neptune Theatre.
Halifax, NS. Lang.: Eng.   27
1979-1983.   Performance spaces.
Troubles faced by Adelaide Court theatre complex. Toronto,
ON. Lang.: En .   587
1979-1986.   Institutions.
Founder Sky Gilbert discusses aesthetic goals of Rhubarb
Festival. Toronto, ON. Lang.: Eng.   475
1979-1986.   Performance/production.
Diana McIntosh on her performance pieces involving
contemporary music. Winnipeg, MB. Lang.: Eng.   3250
1980.   Plays/librettos/scripts.
Examines *Ne blâmez jamais les Bédouins (Don't Blame It on
the Bedouins)* as a post-modernist play. Lang.: Fre.   2432
1980-1983.   Institutions.
Careers of choreographers Maria Formolo and Keith Urban.
Regina, SK. Edmonton, AB. Lang.: Eng.   1343
1980-1984.   Institutions.
Techniques and philosophy of children's theatre compared to
theatre for adults. Lang.: Fre.   468
1980-1986.   Institutions.
New leadership in Montreal's English-speaking theatres.
Montreal, PQ. Lang.: Eng.   1539
History of the Shared Stage theatre company. Winnipeg, MB.
Lang.: Eng.   1555
1980-1986.   Performance/production.
Playwright David Fennario's commitment to working-class
community theatre. Montreal, PQ. Lang.: Eng.   1661
Interviews with performance artists. Toronto, ON. New York,
NY. Lang.: Eng.   3444
Interview with baritone John Fanning. Toronto, ON. Lang.:
Eng.   3709
1981-1982.   Institutions.
Negative evaluation of recent Canadian Broadcasting
Corporation drama. Lang.: Eng.   3177
1981-1984.   Institutions.
Théâtre Petit à Petit and their production of *Où est-ce
qu'elle est ma gang (Where's My Gang?)* by Louis-Dominique
Lavigne. Montreal, PQ. France. Lang.: Fre.   474
1981-1985.   Performance/production.
John Hirsch's artistic career at the Stratford Festival Theatre.
Stratford, ON. Lang.: Eng.   1683
1981-1986.   Institutions.
Development of community-based theatre on Prince Edward
Island. Lang.: Eng.   1556
1982.   Reference materials.
Survey of Canadian theatre publications. Lang.: Eng.   1010

1982.   Relation to other fields.
Interactive theatre in *It's About Time* by Catalyst Theatre.
Edmonton, AB. Lang.: Eng.   1069
1982-1983.   Institutions.
Significance of Applebaum-Hébert report on Canadian
cultural policy. Lang.: Eng.   465
Career of Walter Learning, artistic director, Vancouver
Playhouse. Vancouver, BC. Lang.: Eng.   470
1982-1983.   Plays/librettos/scripts.
Umiak by Théâtre de la Marmaille of Toronto, based on
Inuit tradition. Lang.: Eng.   2434
1982-1986.   Institutions.
Fragile alternatives to Charlottetown Festival. Charlottetown,
PE. Lang.: Eng.   1540
Founding member discusses dinner-theatre Comedy Asylum.
Fredericton, NB. Lang.: Eng.   1559
1982-1986.   Performance spaces.
Summer theatre on a restored cruise ship. Lang.: Eng.   1614
1983.   Basic theatrical documents.
Videotape of Shakespeare's *As You Like It* with study guide
and edition of the play. Stratford, ON. Lang.: Eng.   219
Text of *Umiak* by Théâtre de la Marmaille. Toronto, ON.
Lang.: Eng.   1467
1983.   Institutions.
Argument that Canadian theatre awards are too numerous.
Toronto, ON. Lang.: Eng.   472
1983.   Plays/librettos/scripts.
Analysis of *Vie et mort du Roi Boiteaux (Life and Death of
King Boiteaux)* by Jean-Pierre Ronfard. Montreal, PQ. Lang.:
Fre.   933
Analysis of *RA* by R. Murray Schafer, performed by Comus
Music Theatre. Toronto, ON. Lang.: Eng.   2416
1983-1986.   Institutions.
Founding directors explain history and principles of
Enterprise Theatre. Lang.: Eng.   1546
Role of the Canadian Actors' Equity Association. Toronto,
ON. Lang.: Eng.   1548
1983-1986.   Performance/production.
Opposition to realism in plays from Francophone Manitoba.
Lang.: Fre.   670
Theatrical productions on local topics in small Inuit
communities. Lang.: Eng.   1658
Description of an outdoor Shakespeare theatre project.
Toronto, ON. Lang.: Eng.   1678
History of the International Mime Festival. Winnipeg, MB.
Lang.: Eng.   3293
1984.   Institutions.
Academics in theatre discuss the role of theatre in education.
Lang.: Fre.   476
1984.   Performance/production.
Production analysis of *The Merchant of Venice* directed by
Mark Lamos. Stratford, ON. Lang.: Eng.   667
Three directors' versions of *Les cauchemars du grand monde
(Nightmares of High Society)* by Gilbert Turp. Montreal, PQ.
Lang.: Fre.   1672
Behind-the-scenes look at *Fraggle Rock.* Toronto, ON. Lang.:
Eng.   3269
1984.   Plays/librettos/scripts.
Compares Michel Tremblay's *Albertine en cinq temps
(Albertine in Five Times)* to Marcel Proust's *À la recherche
du temps perdu (Remembrance of Things Past).*   2436
1984.   Relation to other fields.
Theatre professionals' round-table on issues in theatre for
adolescents. Quebec, PQ. Lang.: Fre.   1068
1984-1985.   Performance/production.
Playwright/dramaturg Peter Eliot Weiss discusses *Sex Tips
for Modern Girls.* Vancouver, BC. Lang.: Eng.   1684
1984-1985.   Plays/librettos/scripts.
Playwright Christopher Heide's research on high school
students. Lang.: Eng.   2420
La Storia and *La Storia II* performed in Italian and English
by the Acting Company. Toronto, ON. Lang.: Eng.   2424
1984-1986.   Performance/production.
Influences upon the post-modern mime troupe, Cirque du
Soleil. Montreal, PQ. Lang.: Eng.   3292
Interview with baritone Gino Quilico. Toronto, ON. Lang.:
Eng.   3711

Canada — cont'd

1986. **Plays/librettos/scripts.**
Review essay on *Li jus de Robin et Marion (The Play of Robin and Marion)* directed by Jean Asselin. Montreal, PQ. Lang.: Fre. 937

Criticizes the plays in the collection *Five From the Fringe.* Edmonton, AB. Lang.: Eng. 2425

Environmental theatre version of *Hamlet.* Vancouver, BC. Lang.: Eng. 2435

1986. **Relation to other fields.**
Workshops in Canada on 'Theatre for the Oppressed'. Toronto, ON. Lang.: Eng. 3022

Caribbean
1937-1985. **Performance/production.**
Poetry as performing art and political tool. Lang.: Eng. 674

Catalonia
SEE
Spain-Catalonia.

Cayman Islands
1986. **Performance spaces.**
Design and construction of Grand Cayman's National Theatre. UK-England. Lang.: Eng. 590

Chile
1940-1986. **Plays/librettos/scripts.**
Metaphoric style in the political drama of Jean-Paul Sartre, Athol Fugard and Juan Radrigán. France. South Africa, Republic of. Lang.: Eng. 951

1953-1986. **Performance/production.**
Interview with actor, director, playwright and filmmaker Ramón Griffero. Santiago. Lang.: Spa. 675

1955-1984. **Plays/librettos/scripts.**
Chilean theatre in exile, Teatro del Angel. Costa Rica. Lang.: Eng. 2441

1956-1985. **Plays/librettos/scripts.**
Interview with Chilean playwright Jaime Miranda. Venezuela. USA. Lang.: Eng. 2973

1960-1971. **Plays/librettos/scripts.**
Marginal characters in plays of Jorge Díaz, Egon Wolff and Luis Alberto Heiremans. Lang.: Eng. 2442

1984-1985. **Performance/production.**
Humorous and political trends in Chilean theatre season. Lang.: Spa. 1686

China
Performance/production.
Adaptation of Eastern theatre for the Western stage. Europe. Lang.: Ita. 676

Training.
Potential use of Chinese actor-training methods in the West. Europe. Lang.: Ita. 1254

600 B.C.-1985 A.D. **Training.**
History of classical Chinese theatre. Lang.: Eng. 4

300 B.C.-1980 A.D. **Design/technology.**
Pheasant feathers in warrior's helmets in Chinese theatre. Lang.: Chi. 3504

202 B.C.-220 A.D. **Design/technology.**
Profile of costuming during the Han dynasty. Nanyang. Lang.: Chi. 3310

200 B.C.-1982 A.D. **Theory/criticism.**
Use of red, white and black colors in Chinese traditional theatre. Lang.: Chi. 3560

Defense of Chinese traditional theatre. Lang.: Chi. 3562

5 B.C.-1985 A.D. **Theory/criticism.**
Use of anxiety about fate in Beijing opera. Beijing. Lang.: Chi. 3558

200-1986. **Theory/criticism.**
Development and characteristics of Oriental theatre. Seoul. Tokyo. Beijing. Lang.: Kor. 1215

618-1580. **Plays/librettos/scripts.**
Definition and characteristics of *Hsiao* role. Lang.: Chi. 3530

700-1980. **Design/technology.**
Use of audience imagination to complement a set design. Lang.: Chi. 246

710-905. **Performance spaces.**
Theatre activities during the Tang dynasty. Lang.: Chi. 591

800-1644. **Theory/criticism.**
Influence of Tuan Anchieh's aesthetics. Lang.: Chi. 3561

800-1986. **Performance/production.**
History of the Beijing Opera. Beijing. Lang.: Cat. 3507

960-1983. **Plays/librettos/scripts.**
Use of history in Chinese traditional drama. Lang.: Chi. 2444

1030-1984. **Plays/librettos/scripts.**
Use of poetic elements to create mood in Beijing opera. Beijing. Lang.: Chi. 3529

1032-1420. **Research/historiography.**
Analysis of three ancient types of dance-drama. Lang.: Chi. 3551

1100-1980. **Performance/production.**
What spoken drama actors can learn from Sung drama. Lang.: Chi. 3513

1101-1250. **Performance/production.**
Acting during the Southern Sung dynasty. Wenzhou. Lang.: Chi. 3510

1127-1234. **Performance/production.**
Origins of Southern Sung drama (*Nanxi*). Wenzhou. Lang.: Chi. 3512

1127-1278. **Performance/production.**
Origins of the stylized acting in Southern drama (Nanxi). Lang.: Chi. 3517

1127-1980. **Performance/production.**
Differences in portraying time and locale in Sung drama and in contemporary *spoken drama.* Lang.: Chi. 1688

1200-1986. **Plays/librettos/scripts.**
Differences between *Chan Ta* and *Chuan Ta* drama. Lang.: Chi. 3527

1256-1341. **Plays/librettos/scripts.**
Profiles of Yuan dynasty playwrights. Lang.: Chi. 2445

1271-1368. **Research/historiography.**
Great playwrights of the Yüan dynasty. Lang.: Chi. 3552

1279-1368. **Theory/criticism.**
Ma Tzuyuan's use of poetic elements in Chinese opera. Beijing. Lang.: Chi. 3559

1308-1982. **Design/technology.**
Visual imagery and metaphor in scenery and lighting. Lang.: Chi. 245

1349-1949. **Performance/production.**
Origins and staging of the traditional Tan Tan play. Lang.: Chi. 3520

1360-1960. **Plays/librettos/scripts.**
Plots and themes in adaptations of *Tou Erh Yüan (The Injustice of Miss Tou).* Lang.: Chi. 3525

1368-1644. **Plays/librettos/scripts.**
Life and works of playwright Shen Ching. Lang.: Chi. 3526

1400-1982. **Theory/criticism.**
Comparison of Brechtian theatre and Chinese traditional theatre. Germany. Lang.: Chi. 3111

1400-1986. **Theory/criticism.**
Styles of mask-dance drama in Asia. Seoul. Tokyo. Beijing. Lang.: Kor. 1378

1500-1600. **Performance/production.**
On Western impressions of Eastern performances. Japan. Lang.: Ita. 677

1500-1644. **Research/historiography.**
Controversy over identities of Tien Kuei-pu and Lu Kuei-pu. Lang.: Chi. 3550

1500-1980. **Plays/librettos/scripts.**
Analysis of one-act play structures. Lang.: Chi. 2447

1574-1646. **Performance/production.**
Guide for producing traditional Beijing opera. Suzhou. Lang.: Chi. 3508

Staging during the Ming dynasty. Suzhou. Lang.: Chi. 3509

1598-1984. **Performance/production.**
Modern and traditional performance styles compared. Lang.: Chi. 3511

1600-1980. **Plays/librettos/scripts.**
Playwright Wu Bing mocks *The Peony Pavilion* by Tang Xianzu. Lang.: Chi. 3531

1600-1980. **Research/historiography.**
Problems of research methodology applied to traditional singing styles. Lang.: Chi. 3553

1611-1930. **Plays/librettos/scripts.**
Analysis of the work of playwright Li Yu. Lang.: Chi. 3533

1620-1752. **Plays/librettos/scripts.**
Comparison of the works of Wang Ji-De and Xu Wei. Lang.: Chi. 3534

1669-1843. **Plays/librettos/scripts.**
Differences among 32 extant editions of *Xi Xiang Zhu.* Lang.: Chi. 3528

1674-1985. **Research/historiography.**
Transformation of traditional music notation into modern notation for four Chinese operas. Beijing. Lang.: Chi. 3554

China — cont'd

1700-1800. **Performance/production.**
Wei Ch'angsheng: actor of Szechuan opera, not Shensi
opera. Lang.: Chi. 3519
1700-1981. **Performance/production.**
Influence of Tibetan drama on Chinese theatre. Tibet. Lang.:
Chi. 3515
1795-1850. **Performance/production.**
Life and influence of Wei Ch'angsheng, actor and
playwright. Lang.: Chi. 3506
Ch'in opera and its influences. Beijing. Lang.: Chi. 3518
1817-1974. **Reference materials.**
Annotated list of English-language research on Chinese
opera. Lang.: Chi. 3544
1850-1981. **Performance/production.**
Exploring the world of emotion in acting. Lang.: Chi. 1691
1866-1952. **Theory/criticism.**
Analyzes the singing style of Szechuan opera. Lang.: Chi.
3563
1868-1935. **Performance/production.**
Use of early performance records to infer theatre activities of
a later period. Lang.: Chi. 3505
1898-1968. **Plays/librettos/scripts.**
Life and work of playwright Tian Han. Lang.: Eng. 2443
1900-1950. **Plays/librettos/scripts.**
Influence of Chinese theatre on Bertolt Brecht. Berlin. Lang.:
Ita. 2608
1900-1980. **Plays/librettos/scripts.**
Characteristics and influences of Fan Ts'ui-T'ing's plays.
Lang.: Chi. 3532
1900-1982. **Performance/production.**
Objectives and action in staging of director Wang Xiaoping.
Shanghai. Lang.: Chi. 1689
1912-1936. **Performance/production.**
Descendants of Confucius and Chinese opera after the Ching
dynasty. Beijing. Lang.: Chi. 3516
1920-1963. **Theory/criticism.**
Influence of Western theory on Chinese drama of Gu
Zhongyi. Lang.: Chi. 1202
1920-1983. **Performance/production.**
Career of Beijing opera actor, Hou Hsijui. Lang.: Chi. 3514
1923-1962. **Plays/librettos/scripts.**
Influence of Western and Chinese traditional theatre upon
works of Ding Xilin. Lang.: Chi. 2446
1930-1980. **Performance/production.**
Directing techniques of Wu Renzhi. Lang.: Chi. 678
1935-1956. **Plays/librettos/scripts.**
Chinese influences on Bertolt Brecht. Berlin, East. Lang.:
Eng. 2619
1939-1982. **Performance/production.**
Actress Lu Xiaoyan's experiences in preparing to play a role
in *The Little Foxes*. USA. Lang.: Chi. 1687
1949-1982. **Relation to other fields.**
Recommended ethical values for artists in a socialist country.
Lang.: Chi. 1076
1980-1986. **Institutions.**
Current state of ballet theatre, including choreographic
training. Beijing. Lang.: Rus. 1297
1982. **Performance/production.**
Directorial design for Dürrenmatt's *Die Physiker (The
Physicists)*. Shanghai. Lang.: Chi. 1690
1986. **Institutions.**
Report on state puppet theatre. Beijing. Shanghai. Lang.:
Eng. 4015

China, People's Republic of
1265-1981. **Design/technology.**
Symbolism in set design. Lang.: Chi. 247
1755-1984. **Research/historiography.**
Origins and evolution of today's Beijing opera. Beijing.
Lang.: Chi. 3556
1876-1983. **Plays/librettos/scripts.**
Introduction to Sichuan opera, including translation of a new
play. Lang.: Eng. 3542
1885-1948. **Research/historiography.**
Rise of the *Ping Hsi* form in Tienchin. Tienchin. Lang.: Chi.
3557
1885-1985. **Research/historiography.**
Development of Cantonese opera and its influence. Kuang
Tung. Lang.: Chi. 3555

1900-1935. **Performance/production.**
Influence of Beijing opera performer Mei Lanfang on
European acting and staging traditions. USSR. Germany.
Lang.: Eng. 3521
1900-1982. **Design/technology.**
Effect of changes in scenery and lighting onstage. Lang.: Chi.
249
1901-1965. **Plays/librettos/scripts.**
Career of Xiong Foxi. Beijing. Shanghai. New York, NY.
Lang.: Chi. 2449
1901-1981. **Institutions.**
Former students remember Xiong Foxi. Chengdu. Lang.: Chi.
1568
1901-1982. **Institutions.**
Recollections of a student actor under Xiong Foxi's direction.
Jinan. Chengdu. Lang.: Chi. 1569
1903-1985. **Plays/librettos/scripts.**
Origins, characteristics and structures of Beijing operas.
Beijing. Lang.: Chi. 3541
1907-1951. **Institutions.**
History of Zhang Boling's spoken drama company. Tianjin.
Lang.: Chi. 1570
1907-1980. **Design/technology.**
Theatre make-up compared to painting. Lang.: Chi. 251
1907-1982. **Training.**
Overview of spoken drama training programs. Lang.: Chi.
1255
1908-1986. **Administration.**
Berne Convention in People's Republic of China. Lang.: Eng.
30
1911-1945. **Plays/librettos/scripts.**
Career of He Mengfu, playwright and director. Lang.: Chi.
2448
1912-1931. **Institutions.**
Beginnings of performing arts labor organizations. Shanghai.
Lang.: Chi. 488
1913-1986. **Plays/librettos/scripts.**
Innovations of playwright Chen Jenchien. Lang.: Chi. 3539
1917-1963. **Reference materials.**
Bibliography of Xiong Foxi's writings. Lang.: Chi. 1011
1920-1965. **Theory/criticism.**
Playwright Xiong Foxi's concept of theatre. Lang.: Chi. 3089
1920-1985. **Relation to other fields.**
Mao's policy on theatre in revolution. Beijing. Lang.: Chi.
3549
1928-1940. **Training.**
Xiong Foxi, playwright and teacher. Ch'eng-tu. Lang.: Chi.
3156
1935-1985. **Theory/criticism.**
Symbolism and aesthetics in the performance styles of
Chinese opera. Beijing. Lang.: Chi. 3564
Strengths and weaknesses of Beijing opera. Beijing. Lang.:
Chi. 3565
Influence of Western dramatic theories on Beijing opera.
Beijing. Lang.: Chi. 3567
1938-1940. **Performance/production.**
People's theatre groups in the provinces of Shansi, Kansu
and Liaoning. Lang.: Chi. 1692
1942-1981. **Relation to other fields.**
Anecdotes about caricaturist Liao Bingxiong and comedian
Chen Baichen. Lang.: Chi. 1078
1942-1982. **Theory/criticism.**
Purpose of literature and art, and the role of the artist.
Shanghai. Yan'an. Lang.: Chi. 1203
1945-1982. **Institutions.**
History of the Shanghai Drama Institute. Shanghai. Lang.:
Chi. 1571
1949-1980. **Institutions.**
Influence of Wagner on the music of contemporary Chinese
opera. Lang.: Chi. 3503
1949-1980. **Plays/librettos/scripts.**
Play sequels and their characteristics. Lang.: Chi. 3540
1949-1982. **Relation to other fields.**
Importance of teaching proper values to theatre students.
Lang.: Chi. 1077
1949-1982. **Training.**
Actor-training approach based on imitation of animals.
Shanghai. Lang.: Chi. 3155
1951-1985. **Plays/librettos/scripts.**
Ma Ke's contribution and influence on Beijing opera. Beijing.
Lang.: Chi. 3536

China, People's Republic of — cont'd

1952-1985. Plays/librettos/scripts.
Analysis of playwright Xu Jin's work. Beijing. Lang.: Chi.
3535

1955-1985. Theory/criticism.
Dramatic structure in Beijing opera. Lang.: Chi. 3566

1959-1980. Performance/production.
Development of opera in Liaoning province. Lang.: Chi.
3523

1960-1981. Theory/criticism.
Experimental theatres to offset the impact of film and theatre. Lang.: Chi. 3090

1960-1982. Design/technology.
Realism and fantasy in set design. Lang.: Chi. 248
Elements of set design and their emotional impact. Lang.: Chi. 250

1962-1985. Plays/librettos/scripts.
Introduction to the folk play, *Mu Lian*. Beijing. Lang.: Chi.
3538

1963-1985. Theory/criticism.
Characteristics of Chinese opera in Szechuan province. Lang.: Chi. 3570

1964-1985. Performance/production.
Techniques of comedians in modern Beijing opera. Beijing. Lang.: Chi. 3524

1970-1983. Theory/criticism.
Comparison of Chinese play, *Kan Chien Nu*, with plays of Molière. Beijing. Lang.: Chi. 3568

1978-1982. Performance/production.
On the goal of acting. Lang.: Chi. 1693

1981-1985. Performance/production.
Training of Chinese students for a production of *The Tempest* by William Shakespeare. Beijing. Lang.: Eng. 679

1981-1985. Theory/criticism.
Analyzes works of four dramatists from Fuchien province. Lang.: Chi. 3569

1983. Plays/librettos/scripts.
Structure of Beijing opera. Beijing. Lang.: Chi. 3537

1984-1985. Performance/production.
On André Heller's project *Begnadete Körper (Blessed Bodies)*. Europe. Lang.: Ger. 3383

1985. Performance/production.
Review of the 1985 season of the Chinese National Opera. Beijing. Lang.: Chi. 3522

1985. Reference materials.
Review of 1985 dissertations. Beijing. Lang.: Chi. 3545

1985. Relation to other fields.
Role of Beijing opera today. Beijing. Lang.: Chi. 3547
Political goals for Beijing opera. Beijing. Lang.: Chi. 3548

1986. Plays/librettos/scripts.
Problems of adapting classic plays. Lang.: Chi. 3543

Colombia
1985. Performance/production.
Account of eighth International Theatre Festival. Manizales. Lang.: Spa. 1694

Colonial America
ALSO SEE
USA.
1758-1800. Reference materials.
Theatrical materials in five early American magazines. Lang.: Eng. 1012

Costa Rica
1955-1984. Plays/librettos/scripts.
Chilean theatre in exile, Teatro del Angel. Chile. Lang.: Eng.
2441

Cuba
1838-1972. Performance/production.
Short history of the activities of the family Robreño. Spain-Catalonia. Lang.: Cat. 680

1958-1964. Plays/librettos/scripts.
Cuban theatre in transition exemplified in the plays of Virgilio Piñera and Abelardo Estorino. Lang.: Eng. 2452

1959-1986. Plays/librettos/scripts.
The history of Cuban exile theatre. New York, NY. Lang.: Spa. 2451

1960-1986. Relation to other fields.
Theatre and society in post-revolutionary Cuba. Lang.: Rus.
3024

1973-1974. Plays/librettos/scripts.
Ritual and archetypal communication in *La noche de los asesinos (The Night of the Assassins)* by José Triana. Brazil. Lang.: Eng. 2450

1980-1986. Performance/production.
Survey of articles on Cuban theatre. Lang.: Rus. 681

Czechoslovakia
ALSO SEE
Slovakia.
ALSO SEE
Moravia.
ALSO SEE
Bohemia.
ALSO SEE
Austro-Hungarian Empire.
1781-1986. Performance/production.
Technical innovation, scenography and cabaret in relation to political and social conditions. Lang.: Eng. 1697

1787-1985. Institutions.
Development of Prague National Theatre. Prague. Lang.: Eng.
3672

1800-1910. Performance/production.
The native roots of Czechoslovakian literature and music. Lang.: Eng. 3717

1800-1915. Plays/librettos/scripts.
Literary and theatrical history of Eastern Europe. Poland. Hungary. Lang.: Hun. 2755

1880-1900. Plays/librettos/scripts.
Evaluation of the dramatic work of Gabriela Preissová, author of the source play for *Jenufa* by Leoš Janáček. Brno. Lang.: Eng. 2453

1883-1986. Performance/production.
Account of the neglected opera *Libuše* by Jan Smetana on the occasion of its New York premiere. Prague. New York, NY. Lang.: Eng. 3715

1887-1982. Design/technology.
Survey of Joseph Svoboda's lighting and design work. Lang.: Chi. 252

1894-1903. Performance/production.
Thematic, character and musical analysis of *Jenufa* by Leoš Janáček. Brno. Lang.: Eng. 3718

1921. Performance/production.
An evening of Italian futurist theatre. Prague. Lang.: Ita.
1696

1925-1950. Performance/production.
Biography of actor and stage manager Franz Reichert. Vienna. Berlin. Prague. Lang.: Ger. 1652

1928-1986. Plays/librettos/scripts.
Interview with playwright, director and actor Pavel Kohout. Prague. Vienna. Lang.: Swe. 2454

1951-1986. Performance/production.
Opera singer Peter Dvorsky: his life and work. Bratislava. Vienna. Lang.: Ger. 3716

1960-1979. Design/technology.
Constructivism in Czech stage design. Lang.: Rus. 253

1960-1986. Design/technology.
Central workshops of the Slovak National Theatre. Bratislava. Lang.: Hun. 255

1976-1986. Performance/production.
Playwright Václav Havel's experience with the Burgtheater. Vienna. Lang.: Ger. 1643

1985. Design/technology.
Master class by scene designer Josef Svoboda. Banff, AB. Lang.: Eng. 254

1986. Performance/production.
Notes on the amateur theatre festival of Pisek. Pisek. Lang.: Hun. 682
Overview of the season's productions, with emphasis on Czechoslovakian authors. Prague. Brno. Warsaw. Lang.: Hun.
1695
Overview of productions by the city's studio theatres. Prague. Lang.: Hun. 1698

Czechoslovakia-Bohemia
ALSO SEE
Bohemia.
1877-1878. Relation to other fields.
Psychological and sociological study of *The Widows* by Smetana and Züngel. Lang.: Eng. 3915

Czechoslovakia-Slovakia
ALSO SEE
Slovakia.

Denmark
1760-1801. Design/technology.
Works by and about designers Jacopo Fabris and Citoyen Boullet. Copenhagen. Paris. Lang.: Eng. 256

Denmark — cont'd

Folio drawings by Jacopo Fabris illustrating how to paint perspective scenery and build theatrical machinery. Copenhagen. Italy. Lang.: Eng.   257

1885-1985.   Relation to other fields.
Introduction to *The Revenge of Truth* by Isak Dinesen. Kenya. Lang.: Eng.   4010

1914.   Basic theatrical documents.
Annotated text of *The Revenge of Truth* by Isak Dinesen. Lang.: Eng.   4002

1976-1986.   Institutions.
Overview of current theatre scene. Copenhagen. Lang.: Swe.   490

1981-1986.   Performance/production.
Influence of *kata* principle on Western acting technique. Japan. Australia. Lang.: Ita.   1365

1985.   Performance/production.
Feminist criticism of theatre anthropology conference on women's roles. USA. Lang.: Eng.   845

1985-1986.   Performance/production.
Reviews of three productions of *Fröken Julie (Miss Julie)* by August Strindberg. Stockholm. Copenhagen. South Africa, Republic of. Lang.: Swe.   2090

1986.   Institutions.
A report from the European drama camp for children. Vordingborg. Lang.: Swe.   489

1986.   Performance/production.
Report from an international amateur theatre festival where music and dance were prominent. Copenhagen. Lang.: Swe.   683

Report on the Third European Child Acting Workshop. Vordingborg. Lang.: Hun.   684

Egypt

1798-1986.   Performance/production.
European and Arabic influences on Egyptian theatre. Lang.: Ita.   685

Eire

ALSO SEE
UK-Ireland.
ALSO SEE
Ireland.

1905-1943.   Plays/librettos/scripts.
Louis Esson's attempts to create an Australian national drama based on the Irish model. Australia. Lang.: Eng. 2380

1924.   Plays/librettos/scripts.
Pessimism of Sean O'Casey's *Juno and the Paycock*. Lang.: Eng.   2457

1926-1986.   Plays/librettos/scripts.
Limited perception in *The Plough and the Stars* by Sean O'Casey. Lang.: Eng.   2456

1984-1986.   Plays/librettos/scripts.
Historical background of *Sisters of Eve* by Tricia Burden. Lang.: Eng.   2455

1985.   Performance/production.
Survey of the 1985 Dublin theatre season. Dublin. Lang.: Eng.   686

England

ALSO SEE
UK-England.

**   Plays/librettos/scripts.**
Political ideas expressed in Elizabethan drama, particularly the work of Christopher Marlowe. London. Lang.: Eng. 2521

43 B.C.-1611 A.D.   Plays/librettos/scripts.
Comparison of Ben Jonson's *Catiline* with its Latin prose source by Sallust. Italy. Lang.: Eng.   2518

1200-1600.   Performance/production.
New evidence on the appearance of professional actors. London. Lang.: Eng.   699

1244-1985.   Performance/production.
History of Maypole dancing. Lang.: Eng.   1329

1300-1642.   Theory/criticism.
Attempts to define such terms as 'emblematic' and 'iconographic' with respect to Renaissance theatre. Lang.: Eng.   3092

1343-1554.   Performance/production.
Analysis and interpretation of the staging of *The Castle of Perseverance* based on original stage plan drawing. Lang.: Eng.   1708

The Castle of Perseverance examined for clues to audience placement and physical plan of original production. Lang.: Eng.   1709

1350-1550.   Plays/librettos/scripts.
Analysis of theophany in English *Corpus Christi* plays. Lang.: Eng.   2472

1377-1392.   Design/technology.
Construction of castle for goldsmith's guild pageant. London. Lang.: Eng.   3422

1400-1499.   Plays/librettos/scripts.
Function of humor and violence in the *Play of the Sacrament* (Croxton). Lang.: Eng.   2493

1400-1500.   Performance/production.
Theories of medieval production and acting techniques. Lang.: Eng.   698

1400-1550.   Plays/librettos/scripts.
Dramatic dynamics of Chester cycle play, *The Fall of Lucifer*. Lang.: Eng.   2499

1432.   Performance/production.
Evidence for performance of a mock tournament of the type described in a 15th-century poem. Exeter. Lang.: Eng. 3331

1445-1575.   Performance spaces.
Outdoor performance spaces surveyed through fragmentary records. Shrewsbury. Lang.: Eng.   593

1463-1544.   Relation to other fields.
Costuming evidence on carved baptismal fonts. Lang.: Eng.   3026

1475-1588.   Performance/production.
Analysis of Robin Hood entertainments in the parish of Yeovil. Lang.: Eng.   1712

1500-1600.   Plays/librettos/scripts.
Bullfighting and revenge in *The Spanish Tragedy* by Thomas Kyd. Lang.: Eng.   2458

1504-1516.   Performance/production.
Documenting evidence about a court entertainment of Henry VIII. Greenwich. Lang.: Eng.   3420

1504-1524.   Institutions.
Importance of Chapel Royal in early Tudor court entertainment. London. Lang.: Eng.   3418

1504-1538.   Administration.
Survey of records relating to performances of Robin Hood and King Games. Kingston. Lang.: Eng.   3309

1510-1559.   Administration.
Organization and operation of Office of Revels mainly under Thomas Cawarden. London. Lang.: Eng.   3417

1514-1980.   Research/historiography.
Review of recent editions of Revels plays, including George Peele's *The Old Wives Tale*. London. Lang.: Eng.   3071

1519-1639.   Plays/librettos/scripts.
Political use of biblical references in pageantry. Lang.: Eng.   3429

1526-1587.   Performance/production.
Brief investigation of the lives of seven actors. Lang.: Eng.   691

1536-1592.   Plays/librettos/scripts.
Rise of English landowners reflected in *Arden of Faversham*. Lang.: Eng.   943

1540-1560.   Performance/production.
Use of puppets in liturgical plays and ceremonies. London. Witney. Lang.: Eng.   3963

1542-1592.   Plays/librettos/scripts.
Shakespeare's *Henry VI* and Hall's *Chronicles*. Lang.: Fre.   2488

1558-1603.   Performance spaces.
Conjectural reconstruction of the Boar's Head Playhouse. London. Lang.: Eng.   592

1558-1642.   Plays/librettos/scripts.
Image of poverty in Elizabethan and Stuart plays. Lang.: Eng.   2482

1560.   Plays/librettos/scripts.
Moral issues in *A Woman Killed with Kindness* by Thomas Heywood. Lang.: Eng.   2498

1560-1600.   Plays/librettos/scripts.
Compares pageant-wagon play about Edward IV with version by Thomas Heywood. Coventry. London. Lang.: Eng.   3430

1560-1641.   Relation to other fields.
Examples of Puritan attempts to ban legal entertainments. Cheshire. Lang.: Eng.   3356

1560-1650.   Plays/librettos/scripts.
Treatment of historical figures in plays by William Shakespeare, Christopher Marlowe and George Peele. Lang.: Eng.   2534

England — cont'd

1563.   **Plays/librettos/scripts.**
Legalistic aspect of *Commody of the Moste Vertuous and Godlye Susana* by Thomas Garter. London. Lang.: Eng. 2494

1564-1616.   **Plays/librettos/scripts.**
Influence of middle class and of domestic comedy on the works of William Shakespeare. Lang.: Eng.   2459

Translation of two works by Northrop Frye on Shakespeare. Lang.: Ita.   2484

Translation of *Shakespeare: His World and His Work* by M. M. Reese. Lang.: Ita.   2514

1575-1600.   **Plays/librettos/scripts.**
Ben Jonson's use of romance in *Volpone*. Lang.: Eng.   2461

Tradition and individualism in Renaissance drama. London. Lang.: Eng.   2496

Use of group aggression in Ben Jonson's comedies. Lang.: Eng.   2508

1575-1920.   **Plays/librettos/scripts.**
Punctuation in *Gammer Gurton's Needle* indicates style of performance.   2489

1576-1595.   **Design/technology.**
Early rope and pulley devices for ascending and descending. Lang.: Eng.   258

1576-1980.   **Relation to other fields.**
Sociological analysis of city comedy and revenge tragedy. London. Lang.: Eng.   3025

1580-1620.   **Plays/librettos/scripts.**
Possible influence of Christopher Marlowe's plays upon those of William Shakespeare. Lang.: Eng.   2478

1584-1607.   **Plays/librettos/scripts.**
Machiavellian ideas in *The Devil's Charter* by Barnaby Barnes. Lang.: Eng.   2500

1587.   **Plays/librettos/scripts.**
Connection between character Senex in Thomas Kyd's *The Spanish Tragedy* and Senecan drama. Lang.: Eng.   2473

1589-1816.   **Performance/production.**
Use of the term 'fiddler' in early works. Lang.: Eng.   3332

1590-1600.   **Plays/librettos/scripts.**
Defense of *The Malcontent* by John Marston as a well-constructed satire. Lang.: Eng.   938

1590-1601.   **Plays/librettos/scripts.**
Use of anachronism in William Shakespeare's history plays. London. Lang.: Eng.   2511

1590-1940.   **Plays/librettos/scripts.**
Accuracy of portrayal of historical figures in Shakespeare and his adaptors. Lang.: Eng.   2532

1590-1986.   **Plays/librettos/scripts.**
Modern criticism of Shakespeare's crowd scenes. Lang.: Eng.   2536

1591-1592.   **Plays/librettos/scripts.**
Iconography of throne scene in Shakespeare's *Richard III*. Lang.: Eng.   2481

1592.   **Performance/production.**
Reconstruction of staging of Act I, *The Spanish Tragedy* by Thomas Kyd. London. Lang.: Eng.   1703

1593-1603.   **Administration.**
Effect of censorship on Shakespeare's *Richard III* and *Henry IV*. Lang.: Pol.   1435

1594-1597.   **Plays/librettos/scripts.**
Influence of Night Visit folk notif on Shakespeare's *Romeo and Juliet*. London. Lang.: Eng.   2470

Gift exchange and mercantilism in *The Merchant of Venice* by Shakespeare. London. Lang.: Eng.   2520

1595-1597.   **Plays/librettos/scripts.**
Essays on Shakespeare's *Romeo and Juliet*. Lang.: Ita.   2529

1595-1609.   **Plays/librettos/scripts.**
Religious ideas in the satirical plays of John Marston. Lang.: Eng.   940

1595-1986.   **Plays/librettos/scripts.**
Interpretations of Shakespeare's *A Midsummer Night's Dream* based on Bottom's transformation. Lang.: Eng.   2503

1596-1604.   **Plays/librettos/scripts.**
Reflections of Ben Jonson's personal life in his poems and plays. London. Lang.: Eng.   2515

1597-1600.   **Performance/production.**
Visual patterns of staging in Shakespeare's *Troilus and Cressida*. London. Lang.: Eng.   1704

1597-1637.   **Plays/librettos/scripts.**
Similar dramatic techniques in Ben Jonson's masques and tragedies. Lang.: Eng.   941

Marxist analysis of colonialism in Shakespeare's *Othello*. South Africa, Republic of. Lang.: Eng.   2507

1598.   **Plays/librettos/scripts.**
Analysis, *As You Like It* II:i by William Shakespeare. Lang.: Eng.   2474

Prophetic riddles in Shakespeare's *The Merchant of Venice*. Lang.: Eng.   2509

1598-1599.   **Plays/librettos/scripts.**
Ceremony distinguishes kings from peasants in Shakespeare's *Henry V*. Lang.: Eng.   2464

1600-1625.   **Plays/librettos/scripts.**
Post-structuralist insights on sexuality and transgression in transvestite roles in Jacobean plays. London. Lang.: Eng.   2476

1600-1650.   **Performance/production.**
Importance of records of a provincial masque. Shipton. Lang.: Eng.   3419

1600-1921.   **Theory/criticism.**
Pitfalls of a semiotic analysis of theatre. Lang.: Eng.   3094

1600-1980.   **Research/historiography.**
Review of introductions to the plays of Thomas Dekker by Cyrus Hoy. London. USA. Lang.: Eng.   1185

1600-1982.   **Plays/librettos/scripts.**
Adapting *Hamlet* for the nō theatre. Japan. Lang.: Ita.   2506

1600-1986.   **Performance spaces.**
Reconstructing a theatrical organization at Saint James Palace (London). London. Lang.: Eng.   1615

1600-1986.   **Plays/librettos/scripts.**
Comparison of natural and dramatic speech. USA. Lang.: Eng.   939

Role of Rosalind in Shakespeare's *As You Like It*. Lang.: Eng.   2491

1601.   **Performance/production.**
Significance of 'boy-actresses' in role of Viola in Shakespeare's *Twelfth Night*. Lang.: Eng.   1714

1601-1608.   **Plays/librettos/scripts.**
Senecan ideas in Shakespeare's *Timon of Athens*. London. Lang.: Eng.   2533

1602.   **Performance spaces.**
Overview of the hall in which Shakespeare's *Twelfth Night* was performed. London. Lang.: Eng.   1616

1602.   **Plays/librettos/scripts.**
Heterosexual and homosexual desires in Shakespeare's *Troilus and Cressida*. Lang.: Eng.   2471

1603.   **Plays/librettos/scripts.**
Critical confusion regarding *The Revenge of Bussy d'Ambois* by George Chapman. Lang.: Eng.   942

Shakespeare's complex, unconventional heroines in *All's Well that Ends Well* and *Measure for Measure*. Lang.: Eng.   2469

Essays on Shakespeare's *All's Well that Ends Well*. Lang.: Eng, Fre.   2485

1603-1613.   **Relation to other fields.**
Social critique and influence of Jacobean drama. London. Lang.: Eng.   1081

1603-1747.   **Administration.**
Development of the afterpiece. London. Lang.: Eng.   1434

1604.   **Plays/librettos/scripts.**
Analysis of *The Winter's Tale* by Shakespeare. London. Lang.: Eng.   2502

Comparison of Shakespeare's *Othello* with New Comedy of Rome. Lang.: Eng.   2528

1604-1605.   **Plays/librettos/scripts.**
Contrast between Shakespeare's England and the Vienna of *Measure for Measure*. Lang.: Eng.   2465

1605.   **Plays/librettos/scripts.**
Critics and directors on Shakespeare's *King Lear*. Lang.: Ita.   2530

1605-1606.   **Plays/librettos/scripts.**
Blessing and cursing in Shakespeare's *King Lear*. Lang.: Eng.   2466

Semiotic analysis of Shakespeare's *King Lear*. London. Lang.: Eng.   2467

Similarities between *King Lear* by Shakespeare and *The Trimphs of Reunited Britannia* by Munday. Lang.: Eng.   2480

1605-1631.   **Plays/librettos/scripts.**
George Chapman's *Caesar and Pompey* as a disguised version of the story of Prince Henry. Lang.: Eng.   2523

England — cont'd

1606-1610. **Plays/librettos/scripts.**
Violation of genre divisions in the plays of Ben Jonson. London. Lang.: Eng. 2525

1607-1614. **Administration.**
History and management of Whitefriars Playhouse. London. Lang.: Eng. 1432

1607-1622. **Plays/librettos/scripts.**
Origin of Spanish setting in Middleton and Rowley's *The Changeling.* Lang.: Eng. 2513

1607-1885. **Plays/librettos/scripts.**
Comparison of Shakespeare's *Antony and Cleopatra* and Ibsen's *Rosmersholm.* Norway. Lang.: Eng. 2479

1608. **Administration.**
Involvement of Robert Keysar with Harry Evans and Blackfriars' Children's Company. London. Lang.: Eng. 1433

1608-1611. **Plays/librettos/scripts.**
Passion in early plays of Beaumont and Fletcher. Lang.: Eng. 945

1609. **Plays/librettos/scripts.**
Shakespeare's influence on Beaumont and Fletcher's *Philaster.* Lang.: Eng. 2463
Use of language in Beaumont and Fletcher's *Philaster.* Lang.: Eng. 2512

1609-1668. **Plays/librettos/scripts.**
Sounds in Ben Jonson's *Epicoene.* London. Lang.: Eng. 2483

1609-1909. **Plays/librettos/scripts.**
Gender roles in *Epicoene* by Ben Jonson. London. Lang.: Eng. 2505

1610. **Plays/librettos/scripts.**
Theme of Puritanism in *The Alchemist* by Ben Jonson. Lang.: Eng. 2519

1610-1612. **Theory/criticism.**
Phenomenological study of *The White Devil* by John Webster. London. Lang.: Eng. 3093

1611. **Plays/librettos/scripts.**
Language in *The Second Maiden's Tragedy.* London. Lang.: Eng. 2460
Theme of redemption in Shakespeare's *The Winter's Tale.* Lang.: Eng. 2490
Herpetological imagery in Jonson's *Catiline.* Lang.: Eng. 2517

1613-1847. **Performance/production.**
History of productions of *Cardenio* by William Shakespeare and John Fletcher. London. Lang.: Eng. 1705

1619-1661. **Performance/production.**
Original staging of Thomas Middleton's *Hengist, King of Kent.* London. Lang.: Eng. 1713

1620-1625. **Plays/librettos/scripts.**
Religion and popular entertainment in *The Virgin Martyr* by Philip Massinger and Thomas Dekker. London. Lang.: Eng. 2468

1621. **Plays/librettos/scripts.**
Aristocratic culture and 'country-house' poetic theme in Massinger's *A New Way to Pay Old Debts.* Lang.: Eng. 2531

1629. **Plays/librettos/scripts.**
Analysis of the final scene of *The Broken Heart* by John Ford. Lang.: Eng. 2526

1629-1720. **Plays/librettos/scripts.**
Female characterization in Nicholas Rowe's plays. Lang.: Eng. 2475

1633. **Plays/librettos/scripts.**
Allegorical romantic conventions in John Ford's *The Broken Heart.* Lang.: Eng. 2497

1634. **Performance/production.**
Historical context of *The Late Lancaster Witches* by Thomas Heywood and Richard Brome. Lang.: Eng. 689

1636. **Administration.**
An expense account in Christ Church details production expenses. Oxford. Lang.: Eng. 31

1636. **Performance/production.**
Analysis of the document detailing expenses for performances given at Christ Church (Oxford) for Charles I, suggesting involvement by Inigo Jones as stage director. Oxford. Lang.: Eng. 1701

1642-1671. **Performance/production.**
New determination of birthdate of actress Nell Gwyn. London. Lang.: Eng. 690

1642-1699. **Plays/librettos/scripts.**
Development of Restoration musical theatre. Lang.: Eng. 3496

1651-1800. **Plays/librettos/scripts.**
Contrasting treatment of history in *Carolus Stuardus* by Andreas Gryphius and *Maria Stuart* by Friedrich von Schiller. Germany. Lang.: Eng. 2590

1653-1669. **Plays/librettos/scripts.**
Cast lists in James Shirley's *Six New Playes* suggest popularity of plays. Lang.: Eng. 2504

1659-1695. **Plays/librettos/scripts.**
English traditions in works of Henry Purcell. Lang.: Rus. 3497

1660-1669. **Basic theatrical documents.**
Prompt markings on a copy of James Shirley's *Loves Crueltie* performed by the King's Company. London. Lang.: Eng. 1475

1660-1690. **Plays/librettos/scripts.**
Revision of dramaturgy and stagecraft in Restoration adaptations of Shakespeare. London. Lang.: Eng. 2535

1660-1708. **Performance/production.**
Restoration era cast lists of the King's Company. London. Lang.: Eng. 1711

1660-1737. **Performance/production.**
History of English theatre. Lang.: Rus. 5

1660-1986. **Performance/production.**
Performance-oriented study of Restoration comedy. Lang.: Eng. 696

1661-1684. **Basic theatrical documents.**
Transcription of manuscript assigning shares in the King's Company. Lang.: Eng. 220

1662-1669. **Plays/librettos/scripts.**
Comparison of John Caryll's *Sir Salomon* with its source, *L'École des femmes (The School for Wives)* by Molière. France. Lang.: Eng. 2527

1664. **Plays/librettos/scripts.**
Analysis of George Etherege's play, *The Comical Revenge.* Lang.: Eng. 2486

1664-1715. **Performance/production.**
Career of actress Elizabeth Bowtell, who first acted under her maiden name of Davenport. Lang.: Eng. 1706

1680-1779. **Performance/production.**
Changing attitudes toward madness reflected in David Garrick's adaptation of Shakespeare's *King Lear.* Lang.: Eng. 1715

1685-1985. **Research/historiography.**
The life of Handel and his influence in making Italian opera popular in England. Italy. London. Germany. Lang.: Eng. 3928

1690-1701. **Plays/librettos/scripts.**
Examination of the text and music of Thomas Durfey's opera *Cinthia and Endimion.* Lang.: Eng. 3861

1696. **Plays/librettos/scripts.**
Language and society in Colley Cibber's *Love's Last Shift* and Sir John Vanbrugh's *The Relapse.* Lang.: Eng. 2495

1700-1799. **Basic theatrical documents.**
Promptbooks for three Dryden plays. Lang.: Eng. 1474

1700-1799. **Performance/production.**
Physical, social and theatrical aspects of *castrati.* Rome. Venice. London. Lang.: Ger. 3757

1700-1900. **Relation to other fields.**
Impact of painting and sculpture on theatre. Lang.: Eng. 1079

1700-1984. **Training.**
Collected papers from a conference on voice training. Vienna. Rome. London. Lang.: Ger. 3936

1700-1985. **Performance/production.**
Illustrated analysis of 18th-century acting techniques. Lang.: Eng. 694

1705. **Administration.**
Analysis of petition drawn up by actors of the Drury Lane Theatre. Lang.: Eng. 32

1713-1714. **Performance/production.**
Study of first production of *Jane Shore* by Nicholas Rowe at Drury Lane Theatre. London. Lang.: Eng. 693

1717-1779. **Performance/production.**
Biography of actor David Garrick. London. Lang.: Eng. 692

1718. **Design/technology.**
Comparison of lighting in English theatres and Comédie-Française. London. Hampton Court. Lang.: Eng. 259

1718-1980. **Performance/production.**
Productions of Handel's *Muzio Scevola* and analysis of score and characters. London. Lang.: Eng. 3720

England — cont'd

1720-1737. **Institutions.**
List of actors and companies using Little Haymarket Theatre. London. Lang.: Eng. 491

1727-1760. **Administration.**
Royal theatrical patronage during the reign of George II. London. Lang.: Eng. 33

1729-1739. **Administration.**
Reconsideration of George Frideric Handel's declining success. London. Lang.: Eng. 3640

1730. **Plays/librettos/scripts.**
Analysis of Henry Fielding's play *The Author's Farce.* Lang.: Eng. 2516

1730-1759. **Plays/librettos/scripts.**
Liberated female characters in the plays of George Lillo. Lang.: Eng. 2477

1734-1745. **Administration.**
The Drury Lane Theatre under the management of Charles Fleetwood. London. Lang.: Eng. 35

1734-1779. **Performance/production.**
Influence of mechanical physiology on David Garrick. Lang.: Eng. 695

1736-1796. **Plays/librettos/scripts.**
An appraisal of David Garrick's adaptation of Shakespeare's *King John.* London. Lang.: Eng. 2510

1737-1764. **Relation to other fields.**
William Popple's career in literature and politics. Lang.: Eng. 1080

1740-1900. **Research/historiography.**
Comparison of oratorio and opera styles as developed by Handel. London. Lang.: Eng. 3926

1741-1986. **Performance/production.**
The mixture of opera and oratory in *Samson* by George Frideric Handel. London. Lang.: Eng. 3719

1743. **Plays/librettos/scripts.**
Comparison of the *Samson Agonistes* of John Milton and the *Samson* of George Frideric Handel. London. Lang.: Eng. 3862

1749-1832. **Theory/criticism.**
Analysis of Goethe's criticism of Shakespeare. Germany. Lang.: Rus. 3091

1760-1840. **Relation to other fields.**
Influence of Mozart's operas on the 'Cockney' school of writers. London. Lang.: Eng. 3916

1768-1774. **Plays/librettos/scripts.**
Character source for Dr. Last in Samuel Foote's play *The Devil Upon Two Sticks.* Lang.: Eng. 2522

1771-1871. **Performance/production.**
History of Edward Moore's *The Gamester* on London stages. London. Lang.: Eng. 1700

1787-1791. **Plays/librettos/scripts.**
Dramatic spectacles relating to Botany Bay. London. Australia. Lang.: Eng. 2492

1793-1867. **Design/technology.**
Recently discovered sketches by set designer Clarkson Stanfield. London. Lang.: Eng. 1513

1797-1958. **Plays/librettos/scripts.**
Treatment of Napoleon Bonaparte by French and English dramatists. France. Lang.: Eng. 2568

1799. **Administration.**
Account of grievance petition by Opera House performers. London. Lang.: Eng. 34

1800-1986. **Performance/production.**
History of the British and American stage. USA. Lang.: Eng. 826

1808-1858. **Performance/production.**
Unsuccessful career of actor Charles Freer. London. New York, NY. Lang.: Eng. 1707

1813-1890. **Performance/production.**
The portrayal of Cleopatra by various actresses. Lang.: Eng. 1699

1820-1839. **Relation to other fields.**
History of English penny theatres. London. Lang.: Eng. 3357

1822-1906. **Performance/production.**
English-language performances of Italian actress Adelaide Ristori. Italy. USA. Lang.: Ita. 2000

1840-1848. **Performance/production.**
Tom Robertson as a theatrical innovator and as a character in Arthur Wing Pinero's *Trelawny of the Wells.* London. Lang.: Eng. 1702

1840-1870. **Performance/production.**
Development of regional theatre and other entertainments. Lang.: Eng. 687

Development of and influences on theatre and other regional entertainments. Lang.: Eng. 688

1858-1877. **Institutions.**
Royal Dramatic College's charity for retired theatre professionals. London. Lang.: Eng. 3322

1860-1869. **Performance/production.**
Marionette theatre history in Northern England. Sunderland. Lang.: Eng. 4006

1883. **Plays/librettos/scripts.**
Historical information on Oscar Wilde's *Vera, or The Nihilists.* Russia. New York, NY. Lang.: Rus. 944

1927-1981. **Plays/librettos/scripts.**
Tom Stoppard's *On the Razzle*, an adaptation of *Einen Jux will er sich machen* by Johann Nestroy. Vienna. Lang.: Eng. 2462

1960-1986. **Plays/librettos/scripts.**
Interview with playwright Kathleen Betsko. Coventry. USA. Lang.: Eng. 2487

1961-1986. **Performance/production.**
Review of director Jonathan Miller's career in theatre. London. Lang.: Eng. 697

1970-1980. **Plays/librettos/scripts.**
Analysis of *Magnificence* by Howard Brenton. Lang.: Eng. 2524

1984. **Plays/librettos/scripts.**
Contemporary responses to *Tamburlane the Great* by Christopher Marlowe. Lang.: Eng. 2501

1986. **Performance/production.**
Interview with actor-turned-director Michael Leech. London. Lang.: Eng. 1710

Estonia

1882-1913. **Performance/production.**
Documents on amateur theatre. Tartu. Lang.: Rus. 700

Ethiopia

1941-1984. **Plays/librettos/scripts.**
Translations of plays by William Shakespeare into Amharic and Tegrenna. Addis Ababa. Lang.: Eng. 2537

Europe

Design/technology.
Survey of the use of masks in theatre. Asia. Africa. Lang.: Ita. 236

Performance/production.
Adaptation of Eastern theatre for the Western stage. China. Lang.: Ita. 676

Role of the mask in popular theatre. Japan. Africa. Lang.: Ita. 755

Translation of *Belly-dancing* by Wendy Buonaventura. Asia. Africa. Lang.: Ita. 1330

Plays/librettos/scripts.
History, poetry and violence in plays by Tankred Dorst, Heiner Müller and Jean Genet. Lang.: Fre. 2538

Theory/criticism.
Characteristics of Eastern and Western theatre. Asia. Lang.: Kor. 1200

Training.
Potential use of Chinese actor-training methods in the West. China. Lang.: Ita. 1254

600 B.C.-1986 A.D. **Reference materials.**
Western theatre from ancient times to the present. Lang.: Ger. 1013

600 B.C.-1986 A.D. **Relation to other fields.**
Overview of political impact of puppet theatre. Lang.: Eng. 3990

500 B.C.-1986 A.D. **Theory/criticism.**
Influences on the development of European and Japanese theatre. Japan. Lang.: Ita. 1213

429 B.C.-1978 A.D. **Plays/librettos/scripts.**
Study of realism vs metadrama. Lang.: Eng. 2540

375 B.C.-1983 A.D. **Plays/librettos/scripts.**
Treatment of history in drama. North America. Indonesia. Lang.: Eng. 2541

65-1986. **Plays/librettos/scripts.**
Stoicism and modern elements in Senecan drama. Lang.: Eng. 2542

1480-1630. **Audience.**
Audience of the humanistic, religious and school-theatre of the European Renaissance. Lang.: Ger. 1445

Europe — cont'd

1500-1986.   **Design/technology.**
Origins and development of *commedia dell'arte* detailing the costume and attributes of the stock characters. Italy. USA. Lang.: Eng.   3407

1500-1986.   **Performance/production.**
Interview with clown, writer and teacher Philippe Gaulier. Lang.: Fre.   3333

1560-1979.   **Performance/production.**
Study of white actors who performed in blackface, with emphasis on *Othello*. USA. Lang.: Eng.   702

1600-1820.   **Performance/production.**
Biographical dictionary of opera singers. Lang.: Fre.   3722

1600-1985.   **Performance/production.**
Semiology of opera. Lang.: Eng, Fre.   3721

1600-1985.   **Relation to other fields.**
Nativity puppet plays in Eastern Europe. Lang.: Hun.   3991

1604-1986.   **Plays/librettos/scripts.**
Envy in Shakespeare's *Othello* and Peter Shaffer's *Amadeus*. Montreal, PQ. Lang.: Eng.   932

1700-1950.   **Performance/production.**
Innovative stagings of Shakespeare's *Hamlet*. Lang.: Rus.   1716

1700-1984.   **Design/technology.**
Illustrated description of Umberto Tirelli costume collection. Lang.: Ita.   263

1700-1985.   **Performance/production.**
Study of the history of acting theory. North America. Lang.: Eng.   704

1709-1886.   **Administration.**
History of Berne Convention and copyright laws. Lang.: Eng.   37

1800-1985.   **Plays/librettos/scripts.**
Relation of 'New Drama'—from Büchner to Beckett—to Afrikaans drama. South Africa, Republic of. Lang.: Afr. 2539

1814-1985.   **Plays/librettos/scripts.**
Operatic facsimiles by Mozart, Bellini and Verdi. Lang.: Eng.   3863

1820-1986.   **Relation to other fields.**
Political and sociological aspects of the dramaturgy of Polish émigrés. Lang.: Pol.   3028

1860-1909.   **Plays/librettos/scripts.**
Biography of composer Isaac Albèniz. Lang.: Cat.   3864

1880-1985.   **Theory/criticism.**
Excerpts from writings of critics and theatre professionals on theory of theatre. Lang.: Ita.   1204

1884-1986.   **Performance/production.**
Influence of Indian theatre on Western drama. India. Lang.: Ita.   703

1888-1985.   **Institutions.**
Collection of texts referring to drama schools. Lang.: Ita. 492

1890-1910.   **Performance/production.**
Influence of Oriental theatre on European directors. Asia. Lang.: Rus.   705

1890-1980.   **Design/technology.**
Painters as designers for the theatrical productions. Lang.: Fre.   260

1893-1939.   **Relation to other fields.**
Political influence of Ernst Toller's plays. Lang.: Pol.   3027

1898-1986.   **Reference materials.**
Modern plays using mythic themes, grouped according to subject. USA. Lang.: Eng.   2986

1900-1930.   **Relation to other fields.**
Artistic, literary and theatrical avant-garde movements. Lang.: Ita.   1083

1900-1984.   **Performance/production.**
The functions of rhythm in reading and performance. Lang.: Fre.   1717

1900-1985.   **Relation to other fields.**
Study of attempts to create a 'visual' music using light instead of sound. USA. Lang.: Ita.   1082

1900-1985.   **Theory/criticism.**
Aesthetic theory of interpretation. North America. Lang.: Fre.   3097

1900-1986.   **Performance/production.**
Improvisation in East and West. Asia. Lang.: Ita.   653

1907-1986.   **Performance/production.**
Biography of mime Angna Enters. USA. Lang.: Eng.   3295

1908-1986.   **Administration.**
Berne Convention and compulsory licensing. Lang.: Eng.   36

1916-1986.   **Performance/production.**
Opera singer Giuseppe Taddei and his work at the Staatsoper. Vienna. Italy. Lang.: Ger.   3694

1917-1986.   **Performance/production.**
Memoirs of Vera Zorina, star of stage and screen. Lang.: Eng.   1303

1920-1985.   **Performance spaces.**
An architect discusses theory of theatre construction. North America. Lang.: Hun.   594

1925-1985.   **Performance/production.**
Writings by and about Julian Beck, founder of Living Theatre. USA. Lang.: Ita.   2309

1929-1984.   **Training.**
Physiological regulation for correct breathing and singing. North America. Lang.: Ger.   3937

1929-1982.   **Theory/criticism.**
Selection from Peter Brook's *The Empty Space*. Lang.: Chi.   3095

1929-1986.   **Performance/production.**
Career of choreographer Kenneth MacMillan. USA. Lang.: Eng.   1302

1930.   **Plays/librettos/scripts.**
Conceptions of the South Sea islands in works of Murnau, Artaud and Spies. USA. Indonesia. Lang.: Ita.   3231

1950-1972.   **Performance/production.**
History of the American Conservatory Theatre. USA. Lang.: Eng.   856

1960-1980.   **Performance/production.**
Analyses of the major trends in theatre, film and other art forms. USA. Lang.: Rus.   701

1960-1985.   **Performance/production.**
Extracts from unpublished writings by Julian Beck. USA. Lang.: Ita.   824

1975-1986.   **Theory/criticism.**
The aesthetics of movement theatre.   3301

1979.   **Theory/criticism.**
Semiotic analysis of theatrical elements. Lang.: Eng.   3461

1980-1984.   **Training.**
Medical examination of covered singing. Lang.: Ger.   3938

1984.   **Plays/librettos/scripts.**
Interview with founders of Internationale Nieuwe Scene. 2543

1984-1985.   **Performance/production.**
On André Heller's project *Begnadete Körper (Blessed Bodies)*. China, People's Republic of. Lang.: Ger.   3383

1985.   **Performance/production.**
Interview with Eugenio Barba, director of Odin Teatret. Lang.: Hun.   1718

Interview with Carlo Boso, expert on *commedia dell'arte*. Lang.: Fre.   3409

1985.   **Plays/librettos/scripts.**
Conference on eighteenth-century theatre and culture. Lang.: Ita.   946

1985.   **Training.**
Physical aspects of actor training. North America. Lang.: Eng.   3157

1986.   **Design/technology.**
Directions for making various masks, with historical information. Lang.: Cat.   261

1986.   **Reference materials.**
Index of operas, artists, contributors, etc. UK-England. USA. Lang.: Eng.   3911

1986.   **Relation to other fields.**
Function of carnival in society. Lang.: Eng.   3376

1986.   **Theory/criticism.**
Primacy of idea over performance. Lang.: Ita.   3096

Eastern and western myths explaining the origin of theatre. Asia. Lang.: Ita.   3098

1986.   **Design/technology.**
Nineteenth-century special effects. North America. Lang.: Swe.   262

Federal Republic of Germany
SEE
Germany, West.

Finland

1893-1985.   **Performance/production.**
Career of actor Jalmari Rinne. Helsinki. Tampere. Turku. Lang.: Eng, Fre.   1719

1909-1986.   **Plays/librettos/scripts.**
Analysis of thematic trends in recent Finnish Opera. Helsinki. Savonlinna. Lang.: Eng, Fre.   3865

Finland — cont'd

1920-1986. **Performance/production.**
History of amateur theatre in Finland. Lang.: Swe.   706
1935-1986. **Performance/production.**
Profile of and interview with Finnish bass Martti Talvela.
Lang.: Eng.   3723
1940-1986. **Institutions.**
History of Swedish language Lilla-teatern (Little Theatre).
Helsinki. Lang.: Eng, Fre.   494
1957-1985. **Institutions.**
Obituary of theatre manager, director, critic and scholar
Timo Tiusanen. Helsinki. Lang.: Eng, Fre.   1572
1963-1986. **Design/technology.**
Career of designer Ralf Forsström discussing his influences
and stylistic preferences. Helsinki. Lang.: Eng, Fre.   3650
1967-1986. **Institutions.**
Career of dramaturgist and teacher Outi Nyytäjä. Helsinki.
Lang.: Eng, Fre.   493
1967-1986. **Performance/production.**
Interview with composer and director of the Finnish National
opera Ilkka Kuusisto. Helsinki. Suomussalmi. Lang.: Eng, Fre.
3724
1975-1986. **Plays/librettos/scripts.**
Interview with opera composer Aulis Sallinen on his current
work. Helsinki. Lang.: Eng, Fre.   3866
1982-1983. **Basic theatrical documents.**
Text of Inkeri Kilpinen's *Totisesti totisesti (Verily Verily)* in
English translation. Lang.: Eng, Fin.   1476
1986. **Performance/production.**
Review of *Finlandia*, produced by Ryhmäteatteri. Helsinki.
Lang.: Swe.   707
Interview with Juoko Turkka on acting and directing. Lang.:
Swe.   1720
1986. **Theory/criticism.**
Lecture on the nature of theatre. Tammerfors. Lang.: Swe.
1205

France
Performance/production.
An emotional account of Jean Vilar's early career by a
young spectator. Lang.: Ita.   1731
Report on international puppet festival. Lang.: Rus.   3964
Plays/librettos/scripts.
Structuralist analysis of works of Albert Camus, Antonin
Artaud and Gaston Bachelard. Lang.: Fre.   2575
Mythology in the works of Hélène Cixous, Andrée Chedid,
Monique Wittig and Marguerite Yourcenar. Lang.: Eng.   2580
Deconstructionist analysis of *Riccardo III* by Carmelo Bene.
Italy. Lang.: Eng.   2690
Politics and aesthetics in three plays of Fernando Arrabal.
Spain. Lang.: Fre.   2801
Attitudes toward sexuality in plays from French sources. UK-
England. Lang.: Eng.   2852
Aesthetic considerations in *Lélio* by Hector Berlioz. Lang.:
Fre.   3868
Theory/criticism.
An imagined dialogue on the work of Roland Barthes.
Lang.: Eng.   1207
500 B.C.-1726 A.D. **Performance spaces.**
Development of theatres, stages and the Italianate
proscenium arch theatre. Italy. Lang.: Eng, Fre.   596
500-900. **Plays/librettos/scripts.**
Argument that the Gallican liturgy was a form of drama.
Lang.: Eng.   949
674-1963. **Relation to other fields.**
Popular theatrical forms in the Basque country. Spain. Lang.:
Spa.   3361
900-999. **Relation to other fields.**
Review article on Johann Drumbl's *Quem Quaeritis: Teatro
Sacro dell'Alto Mediaevo*. Italy. Lang.: Eng.   3031
900-1499. **Performance/production.**
Actors and roles in medieval French theatre. Lang.: Rus.   721
1200-1600. **Performance/production.**
Documents of religious processions and plays. Saint-Omer.
Lang.: Eng.   3424
1450-1500. **Plays/librettos/scripts.**
Study of playtexts and illustrations in Lille plays manuscript.
Lille. Lang.: Eng.   3431
1485-1970. **Plays/librettos/scripts.**
Textual study of *La Farce de Maître Pierre Pathelin (The
Farce of Master Pierre Pathelin)*. Lang.: Fre.   2561

1496-1851. **Plays/librettos/scripts.**
Origins of the characters Rigoletto and Marullo in Verdi's
Rigoletto. Lang.: Eng.   3869
1500-1985. **Plays/librettos/scripts.**
Essays on dramatic form, genre and language. Lang.: Fre.
2545
1550-1600. **Performance/production.**
Comic actor Tristano Martinelli, probable creator of the
character Harlequin. Italy. Lang.: Ita.   3412
1568-1600. **Performance spaces.**
Ceremonies celebrating the marriage of Maria dei Medici to
Henri IV. Florence. Lyon. Lang.: Ita.   3325
1570-1953. **Plays/librettos/scripts.**
Adaptation by Albert Camus of *Les Esprits (The Spirits)* by
Pierre de Larivey. Lang.: Fre.   2571
1575-1670. **Performance/production.**
Interpretive technique of *commedia dell'arte* actors. Lang.: Ita.
3410
1590-1911. **Plays/librettos/scripts.**
Comparative analysis of the works of Maurice Maeterlinck
and William Shakespeare. Lang.: Eng.   2566
1600-1634. **Basic theatrical documents.**
Identity of actor Bruscambille, or Des Louriers. Lang.: Fre.
1480
1600-1700. **Plays/librettos/scripts.**
Use of the present tense in some tragedies of Corneille and
Racine. Lang.: Fre.   2564
1600-1700. **Theory/criticism.**
Corneille, Racine and Molière as neoclassisists. Lang.: Kor.
3102
1600-1980. **Relation to other fields.**
Style in children's theatre in light of theories of Philippe
Ariès. USA. UK. Lang.: Eng.   1162
1601-1700. **Reference materials.**
List and location of school playtexts and programs. Lang.:
Fre.   2987
1606-1636. **Plays/librettos/scripts.**
Style in the plays of Pierre Corneille. Lang.: Rus.   947
1620-1930. **Design/technology.**
Relationship between high fashion and costume design. Paris.
Lang.: Fre.   266
1622-1673. **Plays/librettos/scripts.**
Biography of Molière as seen through his plays. Lang.: Fre.
2573
1630-1980. **Plays/librettos/scripts.**
Don Juan legend in literature and film. Lang.: Eng.   2581
1634-1642. **Relation to other fields.**
Cardinal Richelieu's theatrical policies. Lang.: Fre.   3030
1636-1674. **Plays/librettos/scripts.**
Evolution of concept of the State in the tragedies of Pierre
Corneille. Lang.: Fre.   2582
1636-1986. **Theory/criticism.**
Influence of pastoral myth on works of Pierre Corneille.
Lang.: Fre.   3100
1644-1985. **Performance/production.**
Pieces related to performance at the Comédie-Française of
Le Menteur (The Liar) by Pierre Corneille. Paris. Lang.: Fre.
1735
History of staging of *Le Menteur (The Liar)* by Pierre
Corneille. Paris. Lang.: Fre.   1738
1650-1986. **Plays/librettos/scripts.**
Commonplace as rhetorical device in plays of Jean Racine.
Lang.: Fre.   2559
1657-1682. **Plays/librettos/scripts.**
Study of six French versions of the Don Juan legend. Lang.:
Ita.   2548
1660-1669. **Plays/librettos/scripts.**
Psychoanalytic and post-structuralist analysis of Molière's
Tartuffe. Lang.: Eng.   948
1660-1986. **Basic theatrical documents.**
Text of comedies and pamphlets about Molière. Lang.: Fre.
1481
1660-1986. **Plays/librettos/scripts.**
Molière's character Dom Juan reinterpreted. Lang.: Fre.   2551
1662-1669. **Plays/librettos/scripts.**
Comparison of John Caryll's *Sir Salomon* with its source,
L'École des femmes (The School for Wives) by Molière.
England. Lang.: Eng.   2527
1663. **Basic theatrical documents.**
Details of polemical impromptus about Molière's *L'école des
Femmes (The School for Wives)*. Lang.: Fre.   1479

France — cont'd

1663. **Performance/production.**
Analysis of actor/character relationship in *L'impromptu de Versailles (The Impromptu of Versailles)* by Molière. Lang.: Eng. 726

1664-1691. **Plays/librettos/scripts.**
Modern thought in works of Jean Racine. Lang.: Fre. 2553

1666. **Plays/librettos/scripts.**
Dialectical method in the plays of Molière. Lang.: Eng. 2567

1670-1691. **Plays/librettos/scripts.**
Study of *Bérénice, Athalie* and *Bajazet* by Jean Racine. Lang.: Fre. 2583

1670-1740. **Reference materials.**
Current state of research on the manuscript *Sujets de plusieurs comédies italiennes (Subjects of Some Italian Comedies)*. Italy. Lang.: Fre. 2988

1673-1722. **Relation to other fields.**
The work of painter and scene designer Claude Gillot. Lang.: Ita. 1084

1676-1753. **Performance/production.**
Career of Luigi Riccoboni, actor, author and theatre historian. Italy. Lang.: Ita. 745

1680-1986. **Administration.**
History of Comédie-Française administration. Paris. Lang.: Fre. 41

1683-1764. **Performance/production.**
On productions of lyric comedies and opera ballets by Jean-Philippe Rameau. Lang.: Rus. 1304

1700-1799. **Performance/production.**
Attempts to raise the professional status of acting. Paris. Lang.: Eng. 715

1700-1799. **Relation to other fields.**
Eighteenth-century prints depict dancers Marie Sallé and Marie Anne de Cupis de Camargo. Lang.: Rus. 1327

1700-1800. **Plays/librettos/scripts.**
Enlightenment narrative and French dramatists. Lang.: Eng. 2552

Theatrical renderings of the experiences of French travelers in Italy and vice-versa. Italy. Lang.: Ita. 2686

1700-1964. **Plays/librettos/scripts.**
Great dramatic works considered in light of modern theatre and social reponsibility. Italy. Germany, West. Lang.: Fre. 2560

1712-1778. **Plays/librettos/scripts.**
Love in the plays and operas of Jean-Jacques Rousseau. Switzerland. Lang.: Fre. 2563

1713-1834. **Theory/criticism.**
Selection and analysis of Diderot's theoretical writings about theatre. Lang.: Cat. 3101

1723-1981. **Performance/production.**
Staging of plays by Marivaux compared to textual analysis. Lang.: Fre. 1746

1734-1789. **Plays/librettos/scripts.**
Appearance of Franz Anton Mesmer as a character in Mozart's *Così fan tutte*. Paris. Vienna. Lang.: Eng. 3871

1739-1985. **Performance spaces.**
History of the theatres of Nîmes. Nîmes. Lang.: Fre. 595

1750-1820. **Relation to other fields.**
Translation of *Les métamorphoses de la fête en Provence de 1750 à 1820* (Paris 1976) by Michel Vovelle. Lang.: Ita. 3358

1753-1832. **Plays/librettos/scripts.**
Introduction to *Jesús batejat per Sant Joan Baptista (Jesus Christ Baptized by St. John the Baptist)*. Lang.: Cat. 2585

1760-1801. **Design/technology.**
Works by and about designers Jacopo Fabris and Citoyen Boullet. Copenhagen. Paris. Lang.: Eng. 256

Translation of eighteenth-century treatise on stage machinery and construction. Paris. Lang.: Eng. 264

1778. **Performance/production.**
Comédie-Française seen through its records for one year. Paris. Lang.: Fre. 1740

1786-1986. **Institutions.**
History of the teaching of acting at the Conservatoire national d'art dramatique. Paris. Lang.: Fre. 1576

1789-1986. **Audience.**
Effect of official educational and cultural policies on theatre. Germany. UK-England. Lang.: Fre. 1446

1790-1804. **Institutions.**
Views of Parisian theatre from the journals of August von Kotzebue. Paris. Germany. Lang.: Eng. 496

1790-1848. **Institutions.**
Development of ballet at Opéra de Paris. Paris. Lang.: Eng. 1298

1791-1891. **Administration.**
Censorship in post-Revolutionary France. Paris. Lang.: Eng. 39

1794-1985. **Plays/librettos/scripts.**
Overview of Hebrew adaptations and translations of *Tartuffe* by Molière. Israel. Lang.: Heb. 2667

1797-1958. **Plays/librettos/scripts.**
Treatment of Napoleon Bonaparte by French and English dramatists. England. Lang.: Eng. 2568

1800. **Audience.**
Claques as a theatrical institution. Lang.: Fre. 1447

1800-1899. **Audience.**
Claques as viewed by French writers. Lang.: Fre. 3647

1800-1926. **Plays/librettos/scripts.**
History of Catalan literature, including playwrights. Spain-Catalonia. Lang.: Cat. 973

1808. **Performance/production.**
Account of *Poisson Chez Colbert* as performed at Théâtre du Vaudeville with a discussion of the popularity of vaudeville in Paris. Paris. Lang.: Eng. 3941

1811-1872. **Relation to other fields.**
Théophile Gautier's ideas on theatre and performance. Lang.: Rus. 1086

1811-1917. **Relation to other fields.**
Théophile Gautier's views about opera. Lang.: Eng. 3917

1818-1899. **Performance/production.**
Relationship between theatre and early photography. Lang.: Fre. 1748

1830-1844. **Plays/librettos/scripts.**
Political aspects of George Sand's *Père va-tout-seul (Old Man Go-It-Alone)*. Lang.: Eng. 2574

1830-1850. **Performance/production.**
Careers of young Parisian prima donnas. Paris. Lang.: Eng. 3728

1830-1970. **Performance/production.**
Diva as sociocultural phenomenon. Italy. USA. Lang.: Fre. 3730

1834. **Plays/librettos/scripts.**
Theme of fragmentation in *Lorenzaccio* by Alfred de Musset. Lang.: Eng. 2558

1845-1983. **Plays/librettos/scripts.**
Adaptations of *Carmen* by Prosper Mérimée. Spain. Lang.: Fre. 3870

1846-1949. **Theory/criticism.**
Eastern influences on the work of Antonin Artaud. Lang.: Rus. 1208

1850-1986. **Performance/production.**
Pieces related to performance at Comédie-Française of *Un Chapeau de Paille d'Italie (An Italian Straw Hat)* by Eugène Labiche. Paris. Lang.: Fre. 1725

1860-1986. **Performance/production.**
Influence of Richard Wagner on the work of the French Symbolists. Paris. Bayreuth. Lang.: Eng. 3726

1862-1894. **Plays/librettos/scripts.**
Forerunner of contemporary theatre: *Axël* by Villiers de l'Isle-Adam. Lang.: Fre. 2579

1868-1955. **Plays/librettos/scripts.**
Influence of *Nō* on Paul Claudel. Lang.: Ita. 2556

1871-1912. **Performance/production.**
Analysis of theoretical writings of Jean Vilar. Lang.: Ita. 1745

1872-1929. **Performance/production.**
European career of Serge de Diaghilew. Russia. Lang.: Ita. 1312

1872-1986. **Performance/production.**
Development of stage photography. Lang.: Fre. 720

1874. **Plays/librettos/scripts.**
Examination of the first Hebrew adaptation of Molière's *Tartuffe* by David Vexler. Lang.: Heb. 2569

1874-1986. **Reference materials.**
Exhibition catalogue about context of the work and influence of Karl Kraus. Vienna. New York, NY. Paris. Lang.: Ger. 2980

1875. **Institutions.**
Illustrated discussion of the opening of the Théâtre National de l'Opéra. Paris. Lang.: Fre. 3674

France — cont'd

1875-1986.   **Performance/production.**
Performance analysis of the title role of *Carmen*. Lang.: Eng.
         3725

1885-1949.   **Performance/production.**
Essays by and about Charles Dullin. Lang.: Ita.   714

1885-1960.   **Performance/production.**
On the career of dancer and actress Ida Rubinstein, member
of Diaghilew's 'Russian Seasons'. Russia. Lang.: Rus.   1311

1889-1963.   **Plays/librettos/scripts.**
Analysis of *L'Aigle à deux têtes (The Eagle With Two
Heads)* by Jean Cocteau. Lang.: Cat.   2565

1890-1985.   **Performance/production.**
The effect of disease on circus animals. USA. Lang.: Eng.
         3389

1894.   **Plays/librettos/scripts.**
'Meditation' theme as a dramatic element in Massenet's
Thaïs. Lang.: Eng.   3867

1896-1949.   **Theory/criticism.**
Selections from Antonin Artaud's *The Theatre and Its
Double*. Lang.: Chi.   3099

1897-1901.   **Relation to other fields.**
Theatre as a force of social change in turn-of-the-century
France. Lang.: Eng.   3029

1900-1945.   **Performance/production.**
Reciprocal influences of French and Japanese theatre. Japan.
Lang.: Fre.   1750

1900-1954.   **Performance/production.**
Overview of correspondence between Leon Schiller and
Edward Gordon Craig. Warsaw. Paris. Lang.: Eng, Fre. 2022

1903.   **Design/technology.**
Adolphe Appia's use of some innovative lighting techniques
of Mariano Fortuny. Lang.: Ita.   1514

1910-1931.   **Performance/production.**
Difficulties in staging the plays of Paul Claudel. Lang.: Fre.
         1755

1910-1985.   **Plays/librettos/scripts.**
Biographical information on Jean Genet. Lang.: Fre.   2588

1912-1971.   **Performance/production.**
Recollections of Jean Vilar and his work. Paris. Lang.: Fre.
         712

Interpretation of the theatrical work of Jean Vilar. Lang.: Ita.
         713

1913-1978.   **Plays/librettos/scripts.**
Comparison of Harold Pinter and Marcel Proust, focusing on
Pinter's filmscript *The Proust Screenplay*. UK-England. Lang.:
Eng.   3232

1918-1986.   **Plays/librettos/scripts.**
Difficulties in French translation of Karl Kraus's *Die Letzten
Tage der Menschheit (The Last Days of Mankind)*. Vienna.
Paris. Lang.: Ger.   2397

1920-1925.   **Performance/production.**
Study of four works by Ballets Suédois. Paris. Lang.: Eng.
         1271

1920-1960.   **Performance/production.**
Survey of the career of director Michel Saint-Denis. UK-
England. Lang.: Hun.   718

1922-1960.   **Plays/librettos/scripts.**
Repetition and negativism in plays of Jean Anouilh and
Eugene O'Neill. USA. Lang.: Eng.   2578

1923-1986.   **Theory/criticism.**
Interview with semiologist Patrice Pavis about the theatre
institute at the Sorbonne, his semiotic approach to theatre
and modern French theatre. Paris. Lang.: Heb.   1206

1925-1986.   **Performance/production.**
Arguments for typecasting. Lang.: Fre.   710

1926-1946.   **Basic theatrical documents.**
Correspondence between Gertrude Stein and Virgil Thomson
regarding their collaboration on *The Mother of Us All*. USA.
Lang.: Eng.   222

1928.   **Plays/librettos/scripts.**
Poetic and dramatic language in version of *Le Soulier de
Satin (The Satin Slipper)* by Paul Claudel. Lang.: Fre. 2587

1930-1980.   **Plays/librettos/scripts.**
Language and the permanent dialectic of truth and lie in the
plays of Samuel Beckett. Lang.: Fre.   2549

1930-1983.   **Performance/production.**
Reminiscences of actor-director Roger Blin. Lang.: Fre. 1726

1931-1958.   **Plays/librettos/scripts.**
Waiting for Godot as an assessment of the quality of life of
the couple. UK-Ireland. Lang.: Eng.   2557

1931-1986.   **Performance/production.**
Recollections of actress Edwige Feuillère. Lang.: Fre.   716

1934.   **Performance/production.**
Polemic surrounding Sacha Stavisky's production of
Shakespeare's *Coriolanus* at the Comédie-Française. Paris.
Lang.: Eng, Fre.   1742

1934-1936.   **Performance/production.**
Paul Claudel's Biblical scripts for Ida Rubinstein. Lang.: Fre.
         1346

1935-1944.   **Plays/librettos/scripts.**
Superficial and reductive use of classical myth in modern
French theatre. Lang.: Eng.   2550

1936.   **Basic theatrical documents.**
Journal of playwright and general administrator of Comédie-
Française. Paris. Lang.: Fre.   1477

1937.   **Plays/librettos/scripts.**
Patriarchy in *Le Voyageur sans bagage (Traveler Without
Luggage)* by Jean Anouilh. Lang.: Eng.   2586

1938-1973.   **Performance/production.**
Notes, interviews and evolution of actor/director Jean-Marie
Serreau. Lang.: Fre.   1724

1940-1952.   **Administration.**
Development of regional theatre companies. Lang.: Eng.   44

1940-1986.   **Performance/production.**
Arguments against typecasting. Lang.: Fre.   722

1940-1986.   **Plays/librettos/scripts.**
Metaphoric style in the political drama of Jean-Paul Sartre,
Athol Fugard and Juan Radrigán. South Africa, Republic of.
Chile. Lang.: Eng.   951

1943-1956.   **Performance/production.**
Recollection of Jean-Louis Barrault's career as actor and
director. Lang.: Fre.   711

1943-1985.   **Performance/production.**
Actors discuss performing in plays by Paul Claudel. Belgium.
Lang.: Fre.   1722

1944-1954.   **Plays/librettos/scripts.**
Marguerite Yourcenar's treatment of Electra story compared
to other versions. Lang.: Fre.   2554

1944-1960.   **Performance/production.**
Information on theatrical productions. Paris. Lang.: Fre. 1741

1945-1956.   **Theory/criticism.**
Introduction of the work and influence of Bertolt Brecht.
Lang.: Fre.   3103

1945-1970.   **Plays/librettos/scripts.**
Influence of artist Jack Yeats on playwright Samuel Beckett.
Ireland. Lang.: Eng.   2663

1945-1985.   **Administration.**
Theatrical legislation. Lang.: Fre.   42

1946.   **Basic theatrical documents.**
Catalan translation of *L'aigle à deux têtes (The Eagle With
Two Heads)* by Jean Cocteau. Lang.: Cat.   1478

1946-1967.   **Plays/librettos/scripts.**
Personal memoir of playwright Antonin Artaud. Lang.: Fre.
         2584

1946-1986.   **Institutions.**
Retrospective of activities of Compagnie Renaud-Barrault.
Paris. Lang.: Fre.   1573

1947-1985.   **Plays/librettos/scripts.**
Beckett as writer and director. UK. Lang.: Fre.   2546

1948-1968.   **Administration.**
Jean Vilar's development of a working class audience for the
Théâtre National Populaire. Paris. Lang.: Fre.   38

1949-1970.   **Plays/librettos/scripts.**
Intervening and pure theatre according to Eugène Ionesco.
Lang.: Chi.   2547

1950.   **Performance/production.**
Albert Camus' appreciation of actress Madeleine Renaud.
Lang.: Fre.   1728

1950-1980.   **Plays/librettos/scripts.**
Essentialism and avant-garde in the plays of Eugène Ionesco.
Lang.: Fre.   2576

1950-1986.   **Performance/production.**
Interview with actor, director Jean-Pierre Miquel. Paris.
Lang.: Fre.   723

Advantages to actor and audience of multiple roles. Lang.:
Fre.   724

Reasons for the decline of French opera and singing. Lang.:
Eng.   3729

1951-1960.   **Performance/production.**
Jean Vilar's staging of plays by Bertolt Brecht. Lang.: Ita.
         1736

France — cont'd

1951-1963.   **Audience.**
Jean Vilar's view of the revolutionary power of the classics.
Paris. Lang.: Fre.   198

1951-1981.   **Basic theatrical documents.**
Jean Vilar's diary compared to polemics against him. Paris.
Lang.: Fre.   221

1951-1986.   **Performance/production.**
Theatrical illusion in *Sei personaggi in cerca d'autore (Six Characters in Search of an Author)* by Luigi Pirandello.
Paris. Lang.: Fre.   1730

1952-1986.   **Relation to other fields.**
Interview with Augusto Boal. Montreal, PQ. São Paulo.
Lang.: Eng.   3019

1953.   **Plays/librettos/scripts.**
Various implications of 'waiting' in Samuel Beckett's *Waiting for Godot.* Lang.: Eng.   2555
Rhetorical analysis of Samuel Beckett's *Waiting for Godot.*
Lang.: Eng.   2562

1953-1986.   **Plays/librettos/scripts.**
Multiple role of 'I' in plays of Sanuel Beckett. Lang.: Eng.
     2572

1954-1986.   **Plays/librettos/scripts.**
Nō and Beckett compared. Japan. Lang.: Ita.   2721

1955.   **Plays/librettos/scripts.**
Sexual metaphors in plays of Jean Tardieu. Lang.: Fre.   2577

1955-1985.   **Performance/production.**
Parisian criticism of Quebec theatre as French regional
theatre. Paris. Canada. Lang.: Fre.   719

1955-1986.   **Performance/production.**
Actor, director and teacher Jean-Pierre Vincent. Lang.: Fre.
     1744

1956-1978.   **Theory/criticism.**
Augusto Boal's concept of theatre of the oppressed. Brazil.
Lang.: Eng.   1201

1957-1986.   **Administration.**
Laws governing contracts and copyright. Lang.: Fre.   40

1958-1986.   **Plays/librettos/scripts.**
Notes on film treatments of plays by Samuel Beckett.
Ireland. Lang.: Ita.   3234

1959-1984.   **Design/technology.**
Costumes by Yves Saint-Laurent. Lang.: Fre.   1341

1959-1985.   **Institutions.**
Overview of Ariane Mnouchkine's work with Théâtre du
Soleil. Paris. Lang.: Eng.   497

1960.   **Institutions.**
Discussions of opera at the festival of Aix-en-Provence. Aix-
en-Provence. Lang.: Fre.   3673

1960-1985.   **Performance/production.**
Profile of Bernard Lefort, former Intendant of the Palais
Garnier of Paris. Paris. Lang.: Eng.   3727

1961-1986.   **Design/technology.**
Recollections of workers who maintain costumes at the
Comédie-Française. Lang.: Fre.   265

1962-1985.   **Institutions.**
Director of school of mime and theatre on gesture and
image in theatrical representation. Paris. Lang.: Fre.   3289

1963-1985.   **Institutions.**
History of the Théâtre du Soleil. Paris. Lang.: Eng.   1574

1964-1980.   **Performance/production.**
Chronological study of the work of director Peter Brook.
UK-England. Lang.: Eng.   2187

1964-1986.   **Institutions.**
Work and distinctive qualities of the Théâtre du Soleil. Paris.
Lang.: Eng.   1575

1964-1986.   **Performance/production.**
Shakespearean form, Asian content in *Norodom Sihanouk* by
Ariane Mnouchkine's Théâtre du Soleil. Paris. Lang.: Eng.
     709
Collaboration of Hélène Cixous and Ariane Mnouchkine.
Cambodia. Lang.: Eng.   1752

1965-1986.   **Performance/production.**
Peter Brook discusses development of *The Mahabharata.*
Avignon. India. Lang.: Eng.   1361

1968-1984.   **Institutions.**
Assessment of theatre for adolescents. Lang.: Fre.   495

1970.   **Performance/production.**
Spalding Gray's memories of the development and tour of
Richard Schechner's *Commune.* USA. Poland. Lang.: Eng.
     2270

1970-1985.   **Performance/production.**
Critical essays on major productions and aesthetics. Lang.:
Fre.   1747

1971-1986.   **Administration.**
Protection of rights existing before Berne Convention. Lang.:
Eng.   43

1973-1985.   **Performance/production.**
Interview with Peter Brook's designer, musician, and
costumer for *Mahabharata.* Avignon. Lang.: Eng.   1359

1976-1985.   **Administration.**
Performers' rights in the United States, England and France.
USA. UK-England. Lang.: Eng.   3164

1979.   **Relation to other fields.**
Critique of the relation between politics and theatre in Klaus
Mann's *Mephisto* performed by Théâtre du Soleil. Paris.
Lang.: Eng.   1085

1980-1986.   **Performance/production.**
Problems of contemporary French theatre. Lang.: Rus.   717

1980-1986.   **Relation to other fields.**
Use of marionettes in psychotherapy. Belgium. Lang.: Fre.
     4011

1981.   **Performance/production.**
Eastern influences on a production of *Richard II.* Paris.
Lang.: Ita.   1749

1981-1983.   **Performance/production.**
Peter Brook's direction and adaptation of the opera *Carmen*
by Georges Bizet. Paris. Lang.: Heb.   3731

1981-1984.   **Institutions.**
Théâtre Petit à Petit and their production of *Où est-ce qu'elle est ma gang (Where's My Gang?)* by Louis-Dominique
Lavigne. Montreal, PQ. Lang.: Fre.   474

1981-1985.   **Performance/production.**
Photos and interviews of dance company l'Esquisse. Paris.
Lang.: Fre.   1345

1981-1986.   **Performance spaces.**
Description of the new home of the Paris Opéra, L'Opéra
Bastille. Paris. Lang.: Eng.   3682

1981-1986.   **Performance/production.**
Reflection of modern society in Antoine Vitez's production of
Sophocles' *Electra* at Théâtre National Populaire. Paris.
Lang.: Swe.   1743

1982-1986.   **Plays/librettos/scripts.**
Theatre festival and playwriting competition. Metz. Lang.:
Hun.   950

1983-1985.   **Plays/librettos/scripts.**
Comparison of the stage and television versions of *What Where* by Samuel Beckett. Lang.: Eng.   3282

1984.   **Training.**
Actor training methods of Luce Berthomme. Paris. Lang.:
Eng.   1256

1985.   **Performance/production.**
On international festival of children's theatre and youth
theatre. Lyons. Lang.: Ukr.   708
Interview with actor, director and teacher Daniel Mesguich.
Paris. Lang.: Fre.   725
Interviews with actors in Peter Brook's *Mahabharata.*
Avignon. Lang.: Eng.   1360
Directors discuss staging of plays by Paul Claudel. Belgium.
Lang.: Fre.   1723
Production journal of *La Musica deuxième* by Marguerite
Duras. Paris. Lang.: Fre.   1733
Production of *L'Histoire terrible mais inachevé de Norodom Sihanouk, roi du Cambodge (The Terrible but Unfinished History of Norodom Sihanouk, King of Cambodia)* by Hélène
Cixous. Paris. Lang.: Eng.   1737
Analysis of two productions of plays by Marivaux. Nanterre.
Berlin, West. Lang.: Swe.   1739
Stage adaptation of *La Mort de Judas (The Death of Judas)*
by Paul Claudel. Brangues. Lang.: Fre.   1754

1985.   **Plays/librettos/scripts.**
Analysis of *L'Histoire terrible mais inachevé de Norodom Sihanouk, roi du Cambodge (The Terrible but Unfinished History of Norodom Sihanouk, King of Cambodia)* by Hélène
Cixous. Paris. Lang.: Eng.   2570

1985.   **Relation to other fields.**
On Peter Brook's *Mahabharata,* produced by the
International Center of Theatre Research. Paris. Lang.: Rus.
     3032

France — cont'd

1985-1986. **Performance/production.**
Peter Brook's *The Mahabharata* at the Théâtre aux Bouffes
du Nord. Avignon. Paris. Lang.: Eng. 1753
1986. **Design/technology.**
Théâtre du Soleil set for *Norodom Sihanouk*. Paris. 267
Les Immatériaux, multimedia exhibit by Jean-François
Lyotard. Paris. Lang.: Eng. 3249
1986. **Institutions.**
The French-American Film Workshop, designed to showcase
the work of independents and encourage cultural exchange.
Avignon. Lang.: Eng. 3216
1986. **Performance/production.**
Evolution of *Le Cantique des cantiques (The Song of Songs)*
directed by Jacques Destoop at Comédie-Française. Paris.
Lang.: Fre. 1721
Production photos of *Un Chapeau de Paille d'Italie (An
Italian Straw Hat)* by Eugène Labiche. Paris. Lang.: Fre.
1727
Production photographs of Pierre Corneille's *Le Menteur
(The Liar)* at the Comédie-Française. Paris. Lang.: Fre. 1729
Sophocles' *Electra* staged by Antoine Vitez as a conflict of
deceit. Paris. Lang.: Swe. 1732
Hungarian reviewer discusses Paris performances. Paris.
Lang.: Hun. 1734
Interview with Comédie-Française actress Dominique
Constanza. Paris. Lang.: Fre. 1751
Articles on the 1986-87 theatre season. Barcelona. Lang.: Cat.
2083
Descriptions of productions of *Li Jus de Robin et Marion
(The Play of Robin and Marion)*, *The Comedy of Virtuous
and Godly Susanna* and *The Second Shepherds Play*.
Washington, DC. Lancaster. Perpignan. Lang.: Eng. 2289
Interview with V.A. Noskov of Union of State Circuses on
international circus conference. Paris. Lang.: Rus. 3384
Rehearsal of *Die Dreigroschenoper (The Three Penny Opera)*
directed by Giorgio Strehler. Paris. Lang.: Eng. 3486
Productions presented at the first regional puppet forum.
Gareoult. Lang.: Hun. 3965
1986. **Plays/librettos/scripts.**
Interview with Josy Eisenberg, translator of *Le Cantique des
cantiques (The Song of Songs)* for the Comédie-Française.
Paris. Lang.: Fre. 2544
1986. **Theory/criticism.**
Classical, modern and postmodern theatre and their
delineation through opposites. Lang.: Eng. 3104

German Democratic Republic
SEE
Germany, East.
Germany
Performance/production.
An exploration of Brecht's *Gestus*. Lang.: Eng. 1758
Theory/criticism.
Influence of literary theory on Greek theatre studies. Greece.
UK-England. Lang.: Afr. 1210
1151. **Plays/librettos/scripts.**
Analysis of Hildegard of Bingen's *Ordo Virtutum* as a
morality play. Bingen. Lang.: Eng. 3498
1400-1982. **Theory/criticism.**
Comparison of Brechtian theatre and Chinese traditional
theatre. China. Lang.: Chi. 3111
1497-1522. **Plays/librettos/scripts.**
Critical problems in *Henno* by Johannes Reuchlin.
Heidelberg. Lang.: Eng. 2605
1651-1800. **Plays/librettos/scripts.**
Contrasting treatment of history in *Carolus Stuardus* by
Andreas Gryphius and *Maria Stuart* by Friedrich von
Schiller. England. Lang.: Eng. 2590
1685-1985. **Research/historiography.**
The life of Handel and his influence in making Italian opera
popular in England. Italy. London. Lang.: Eng. 3928
1700-1976. **Plays/librettos/scripts.**
Fox symbolism in plays of Bertolt Brecht, Max Frisch and
Gerhart Hauptmann. Switzerland. Lang.: Ger. 2598
1748-1984. **Plays/librettos/scripts.**
Essays on Lessing and Lessing criticism. Lang.: Ger. 2611
1749-1832. **Theory/criticism.**
Analysis of Goethe's criticism of Shakespeare. England.
Lang.: Rus. 3091

1750-1850. **Plays/librettos/scripts.**
Shakespeare's influence on Verdi's operas. Italy. Austria.
Lang.: Eng. 3878
1751-1792. **Plays/librettos/scripts.**
Biography of playwright Jakob Lenz. Moscow. Lang.: Ger.
2594
1756-1950. **Plays/librettos/scripts.**
Mahler's influence on Kurt Weill's career. Berlin. Lang.: Eng.
3879
1759-1805. **Theory/criticism.**
Analysis of Friedrich Schiller's dramatic and theoretical
works. Lang.: Cat. 3109
Selection of Schiller's writings about drama. Lang.: Cat. 3110
1761-1819. **Plays/librettos/scripts.**
Biography of playwright August von Kotzebue. Weimar. St.
Petersburg. Lang.: Ger. 2596
1770-1811. **Performance/production.**
Examination of German versions of Shakespeare's *Hamlet*.
Hamburg. Lang.: Eng. 728
1770-1982. **Theory/criticism.**
Hegel's theory of theatre and its application by 20th-century
dramatists. Lang.: Chi. 3106
1771-1812. **Performance/production.**
Analysis of Shakespeare's influence on Weimar, German
neoclassicism. Weimar. Lang.: Eng. 1760
1773. **Plays/librettos/scripts.**
History in Goethe's *Götz von Berlichingen*. Lang.: Eng. 2610
1774. **Theory/criticism.**
Concept of *Standpunkt* in J.M.R. Lenz's poetics and the
search for identity in the 'Sturm und Drang' period. Lang.:
Eng. 1209
1775. **Plays/librettos/scripts.**
Analysis of *Die Zwillinge (The Twins)* by Friedrich
Maximilian Klinger and the dilemma of the *Sturm und
Drang* movement. Lang.: Ger. 2609
1777-1811. **Plays/librettos/scripts.**
The idea of grace in the life and work of Heinrich von
Kleist. Lang.: Eng. 2593
The tragic in plays of Heinrich von Kleist. Lang.: Rus. 2601
1789-1986. **Audience.**
Effect of official educational and cultural policies on theatre.
France. UK-England. Lang.: Fre. 1446
1790-1804. **Institutions.**
Views of Parisian theatre from the journals of August von
Kotzebue. Paris. Lang.: Eng. 496
1795-1850. **Plays/librettos/scripts.**
Comedies of Tieck and Brentano representing German
Romanticism. Lang.: Rus. 2602
1796-1840. **Plays/librettos/scripts.**
Playwright Karl Immermann's creative method. Lang.: Rus.
2592
1797-1953. **Theory/criticism.**
The concept of *Gesamtkunstwerk*. Lang.: Eng. 3929
1800-1909. **Performance/production.**
Psychoanalytic study of staging as language. Lang.: Fre. 3734
1801-1836. **Plays/librettos/scripts.**
Biography of playwright Christian Dietrich Grabbe. Lang.:
Ger. 2595
1801-1946. **Relation to other fields.**
Nazi ideology and the revival of plays by Christian Dietrich
Grabbe. Lang.: Eng. 1087
1803-1826. **Relation to other fields.**
Composer Carl Maria von Weber and productions of his
operas in Vienna. Vienna. Lang.: Ger. 3637
1810-1811. **Relation to other fields.**
Translation of works on puppetry by Heinrich von Kleist.
Lang.: Ita. 4012
1813-1883. **Theory/criticism.**
Influence of Greek theatre on Richard Wagner's music-
drama. Lang.: Eng. 3930
1824-1879. **Basic theatrical documents.**
The influence of *Euryanthe* by Carl Maria von Weber on
Richard Wagner. Dresden. Lang.: Eng. 3649
1834. **Plays/librettos/scripts.**
Wagner's *Das Liebesverbot*, an operatic adaptation of
Measure for Measure. Lang.: Eng. 3880
1836. **Plays/librettos/scripts.**
Structuralist analysis of Georg Büchner's *Leonce und Lena*.
Lang.: Eng. 2604

Germany — cont'd

1852-1856. **Plays/librettos/scripts.**
Schopenhauerian pessimism in Wagner's *Ring* and
Götterdämmerung. Lang.: Eng. 3873

1857-1869. **Performance/production.**
The first singers to perform *Tristan und Isolde*. Munich.
Lang.: Eng. 3733

1863-1929. **Plays/librettos/scripts.**
Reflections on the works of Arno Holz. Lang.: Ita. 2607

1872. **Theory/criticism.**
Hungarian translation of Nietzsche's *Birth of Tragedy*. Lang.:
Hun. 3108

1878-1921. **Relation to other fields.**
Children's paper theatres as educational tools. Lang.: Ger.
1090

1884-1955. **Institutions.**
Autobiographical documents by personnel of the Deutsches
Theater. Berlin. Lang.: Ger. 1577

1886-1973. **Performance/production.**
Biography of modern dancer Mary Wigman. Switzerland.
Lang.: Ger. 1348

1886-1986. **Performance/production.**
Collection of statements about the life and career of
conductor Wilhelm Furtwängler. Berlin. Salzburg. Lang.: Ger.
3737

1890-1912. **Relation to other fields.**
Response of Freie Volksbühne to police pressure. Berlin.
Lang.: Fre. 3034

1890-1928. **Plays/librettos/scripts.**
Influence of Japanese drama on the works of Klabund.
Lang.: Ita. 954

1890-1938. **Performance/production.**
Max Reinhardt's work with his contemporaries. Austria.
Lang.: Eng, Ger. 1757

1891-1933. **Plays/librettos/scripts.**
Essays on all facets of Expressionism including theatre and
dance. Austria. Lang.: Ger, Ita. 953

1892-1900. **Performance/production.**
American productions of Hauptmann's *Die Weber (The
Weavers)*. USA. Lang.: Ger. 2272

1892-1986. **Plays/librettos/scripts.**
Reflections on Max Zweig's dramas. Vienna. Berlin. Tel
Aviv. Lang.: Ger. 2389

1896-1945. **Relation to other fields.**
Historical function of cabaret entertainment. Lang.: Ger. 3371

1898-1956. **Theory/criticism.**
Coriolanus from Bertolt Brecht's viewpoint. Lang.: Chi. 3105

1900-1935. **Performance/production.**
Influence of Beijing opera performer Mei Lanfang on
European acting and staging traditions. China, People's
Republic of. USSR. Lang.: Eng. 3521

1900-1950. **Plays/librettos/scripts.**
Japanese influences on works of Brecht and Klabund. Japan.
Lang.: Ita. 952

Influence of Chinese theatre on Bertolt Brecht. Berlin. China.
Lang.: Ita. 2608

Essays on Kurt Weill's art and life. Berlin. Leipzig. Lang.:
Eng. 3877

1900-1965. **Reference materials.**
Encyclopedia of cabaret in German. Switzerland. Austria.
Lang.: Ger. 3369

1900-1986. **Plays/librettos/scripts.**
Compares contemporary Canadian theatre with German and
Russian theatre of the early 20th century. Canada. Moscow.
Lang.: Eng. 2412

1900-1986. **Relation to other fields.**
Feminist criticism of plays written by women. Switzerland.
Austria. Lang.: Ger. 3033

1901-1938. **Reference materials.**
Checklist of plays by Ödön von Horváth and their
productions. Lang.: Eng. 2989

1901-1954. **Performance/production.**
Wilhelm Furtwängler's development as a Wagnerian
conductor. Bayreuth. Milan. Rome. Lang.: Eng. 3732

1902-1985. **Relation to other fields.**
The impact of the Third Reich on modern dance. Lang.:
Eng. 1353

1903-1980. **Performance/production.**
Life and films of actor and director Willi Forst. Vienna.
Berlin. Lang.: Ger. 3223

1904-1930. **Design/technology.**
Travelling exhibitions of Edward Gordon Craig and his first
book *The Art of the Theatre*. Austria. USA. Lang.: Eng.
1515

1905. **Design/technology.**
Contribution of designer Ernst Stern to modern scenography.
Berlin. London. Lang.: Eng. 1516

1909. **Plays/librettos/scripts.**
Comparative analysis of *Elektra* by Hugo von Hofmannsthal
and its sources. Lang.: Eng. 2603

1909-1940. **Relation to other fields.**
Mutual influence of Kurt Weill and Arnold Schönberg.
Lang.: Eng. 3918

1911-1970. **Plays/librettos/scripts.**
Treatment of homosexuality in *Death in Venice*. UK-England.
Lang.: Eng. 3874

1913-1918. **Relation to other fields.**
The young Brecht's use of the Bible to criticize the Church
and society. 1089

1913-1945. **Reference materials.**
Influence of stage director Max Reinhardt on film
production. Berlin. Vienna. Lang.: Ger. 3244

1913-1986. **Plays/librettos/scripts.**
Details on performances of plays by Paul Claudel in
German-speaking countries. Switzerland. Austria. Lang.: Ger.
2599

1914-1934. **Theory/criticism.**
Solipsism, expressionism and aesthetics in the anti-rational
dramas of Gottfried Benn. Berlin. Lang.: Eng. 3107

1914-1961. **Performance/production.**
Choreographer Mary Wigman's theory of dance. Lang.: Fre.
1349

1917-1930. **Plays/librettos/scripts.**
Influence of German expressionism on the plays of Luigi
Pirandello. Italy. Lang.: Ita. 2682

1917-1934. **Relation to other fields.**
History of workers' theatre. USSR. UK-England. Lang.: Eng.
1179

1919-1944. **Plays/librettos/scripts.**
Bertolt Brecht and the Expressionists. Lang.: Eng. 955

1920-1932. **Plays/librettos/scripts.**
Collaboration of Kurt Weill, Alban Berg and Arnold
Schönberg on *Lulu*. Lang.: Eng. 3875

1920-1959. **Relation to other fields.**
Socialism and Kurt Weill's operatic reforms. Berlin. Lang.:
Eng. 3921

1920-1977. **Plays/librettos/scripts.**
Biographical notes on playwright Carl Zuckmayer.
Switzerland. Lang.: Ger. 2597

1921-1971. **Performance/production.**
Collection of interviews with Walter Felsenstein. Berlin.
Lang.: Ger. 3735

1922-1949. **Performance/production.**
Nazi persecution of conductor Fritz Busch. USA. Lang.: Eng.
3736

1923-1930. **Relation to other fields.**
Kurt Weill and German expressionism. Berlin. Lang.: Eng.
3920

1924-1931. **Performance/production.**
Reception of Pirandello's plays in Germany. Italy. Lang.: Ita.
1756

1924-1931. **Relation to other fields.**
Kurt Weill's relationship with his publisher. Berlin. Lang.:
Eng. 3919

1924-1934. **Performance/production.**
Max Reinhardt's notes on his production of *Sei personaggi
in cerca d'autore (Six Characters in Search of an Author)* by
Luigi Pirandello. Italy. Lang.: Ita. 1759

1925-1926. **Research/historiography.**
Inadequacy of research on the life of Kurt Weill. Berlin.
Lang.: Eng. 3927

1925-1950. **Performance/production.**
Biography of actor and stage manager Franz Reichert.
Vienna. Berlin. Prague. Lang.: Ger. 1652

1925-1982. **Plays/librettos/scripts.**
Introduction to plays by Tankred Dorst. Lang.: Cat. 2591

1926-1929. **Plays/librettos/scripts.**
Premiere of Kurt Weill's landmark opera *Der Zar lässt sich
photographieren*. Berlin. Lang.: Eng. 3872

Germany — cont'd

1930-1933.   Plays/librettos/scripts.
Analysis of *Der Silbersee* by Kurt Weill and Georg Kaiser.
Leipzig. Lang.: Eng.   3876
1933-1944.   Relation to other fields.
Study of Fascist theatrical policies. Berlin. Lang.: Ger.   1091
1933-1944.   Relation to other fields.
History of anti-Nazi satire. Zurich. Lang.: Ger.   3370
1935-1983.   Relation to other fields.
Typical characteristics of laughing and crying. USA. Lang.:
Ger.   1088
1937-1947.   Relation to other fields.
Refugee artists from Nazi Germany in Britain. UK-England.
Lang.: Eng.   1135
1938.   Plays/librettos/scripts.
Analysis of *Leben des Galilei (The Life of Galileo)* by
Bertolt Brecht. Lang.: Rus.   2606
1938-1955.   Plays/librettos/scripts.
Distortion of historical fact in Brecht's *Leben des Galilei
(The Life of Galileo)*. Lang.: Eng.   2600
1940.   Plays/librettos/scripts.
Nazi ideology and Hans Schweikart's film adaptation of
Lessing's *Minna von Barnhelm*. Lang.: Ger.   3233
1943.   Plays/librettos/scripts.
The role of the double in Georg Kaiser's *Zweimal
Amphitryon (Amphitryon x 2)* and other works. Lang.: Eng.
                                                        2589
1945-1985.   Performance/production.
Comparative history of German-language theatre. Switzerland.
Austria. Lang.: Ger.   727
1961.   Basic theatrical documents.
Catalan translations of plays by Tankred Dorst, with critical
introduction. Lang.: Cat.   1482
1970-1985.   Performance/production.
Illustrated interview with choreographer Pina Bausch. Lang.:
Fre.   1347

Germany, East
                    Plays/librettos/scripts.
Dialogue analysis of *Die Gewehre der Frau Carrar (Señora
Carrar's Rifles)* by Bertolt Brecht. Lang.: Ger.   2612
Brecht's patriarchal view of women as seen in the character
of Jenny in *Die Dreigroschenoper (The Three Penny Opera)*.
                                                        2615
450 B.C.-1956 A.D. Plays/librettos/scripts.
Applying Brecht's dramatic principles to the plays of
Euripides. Greece.   2614
1898-1956.   Performance/production.
Biography of Bertolt Brecht. Augsburg. Berlin, East. USA.
Lang.: Ger.   1767
1898-1956.   Plays/librettos/scripts.
Brecht's life and work. Augsburg. Berlin, East. Los Angeles,
CA. Lang.: Ger.   2626
1898-1956.   Relation to other fields.
Analysis of Bertolt Brecht's love poetry.   1092
A review of the 5-volume edition of Bertolt Brecht's poetry.
                                                        1093
Critique of two articles which examine Brecht's love poetry
from a feminist perspective.   1094
1903-1957.   Performance/production.
Mejerchol'd's influence on Bertolt Brecht. Moscow. Berlin,
East. Lang.: Eng.   2065
1922-1986.   Performance/production.
Benno Besson and his staging of *Don Juan* at the
Burgtheater. Vienna. Switzerland. Lang.: Ger.   1642
1930-1985.   Plays/librettos/scripts.
Comparison of Heiner Müller's *Der Auftrag (The Mission)*
and Bertolt Brecht's *Die Massnahme (The Measures Taken)*.
Lang.: Eng.   2622
1930-1986.   Institutions.
Work of the Berliner Ensemble group. Berlin, East. Lang.:
Eng.   1578
1935-1956.   Plays/librettos/scripts.
Chinese influences on Bertolt Brecht. Berlin, East. China.
Lang.: Eng.   2619
1935-1985.   Performance/production.
Harry Kupfer and his ideas for staging operas. Austria.
Lang.: Ger.   3696
1935-1986.   Design/technology.
Commemoration of theatre expert Paul Jähnichen. Berlin,
East. Lang.: Hun.   271

1938-1953.   Plays/librettos/scripts.
Criteria for evaluating translations, using the example of
Brecht's *Galileo*.   2616
1945-1984.   Plays/librettos/scripts.
Premiere of Ernst Toller's play *Hoppla, wir leben! (Upsy
Daisy, We Are Alive)*. Lang.: Eng.   2617
1948-1956.   Plays/librettos/scripts.
Brecht's concept of *Naivität* in *Die Tage der Kommune (The
Days of the Commune)*.   2621
1949-1984.   Performance/production.
Actor Hilmar Thate on Brecht. Germany, West.   732
Photographic record of forty years of the Berliner Ensemble.
Berlin, East. Lang.: Eng.   1761
1950-1956.   Performance/production.
Brecht and the Berliner Ensemble. Berlin, East. Lang.: Ger.
                                                        1765
1952-1986.   Performance/production.
Application of Brechtian concepts by Eckhardt Schall. Berlin,
East. London. Lang.: Eng.   1762
1964.   Performance/production.
Production of Shakespeare's *Coriolanus* by the Berliner
Ensemble. Berlin, East. Lang.: Eng.   729
1970-1985.   Performance/production.
Harry Kupfer: his work and career as singer and director.
Dresden. Berlin, East. Lang.: Ger.   3738
1970-1986.   Institutions.
History of drama ensemble Mecklenburgisches Staatstheater
Schwerin. Schwerin. Lang.: Ger.   498
1977-1981.   Design/technology.
Sceneshop of Semperoper. Dresden. Lang.: Hun.   270
1980-1983.   Audience.
Various aspects of audience/performer relationship. Leipzig.
Schwerin. Helle. Lang.: Ger.   1448
1980-1984.   Performance/production.
Essays on acting by Wolfgang Heinz. Berlin, East. Lang.:
Ger.   1764
1981-1986.   Performance/production.
Interview with director Harry Kupfer of Komische Oper.
Berlin, East. Lang.: Hun.   3739
1983.   Performance/production.
Acting for theatre, film and television. Lang.: Ger. 730
1984.   Performance/production.
The development and production of Robert Wilson's *CIVIL
warS*. USA. Lang.: Eng.   838
Description of Georg Büchner's *Dantons Tod (Danton's
Death)* staged by Alexander Lang at Deutsches Theater.
Berlin, East. Lang.: Ger.   1763
1984.   Plays/librettos/scripts.
Demystification of the feminine myth in Brecht's plays. 2618
Work of Bertolt Brecht should be re-examined according to
the current historical perspective.   2620
1985.   Design/technology.
Shows of models by Eduard Fischer of Berliner Ensemble.
Berlin, East. Budapest. Lang.: Hun.   269
1985.   Plays/librettos/scripts.
Revising Brecht's plays to insure socially relevant
productions.   2613
1986.   Basic theatrical documents.
New German translation of Shakespeare's *As You Like It*.
Lang.: Ger.   1483
1986.   Design/technology.
Report on development of theatrical equipment in Socialist
countries. Berlin, East. Lang.: Hun.   268
Activities of committee on development of theatre technology.
Berlin, East. Lang.: Hun.   272

Germany, West
                    Performance/production.
On manager and director Claus Helmut Drese. Vienna.
Switzerland. Lang.: Ger.   659
Interview with Elisabeth Bergner and Jane Alexander on
their portrayals of Joan of Arc. Berlin, West. Malvern.
Washington, DC. Lang.: Eng.   1766
1689-1986.   Institutions.
History of the former Royal Opera House of Hanover and
its plans for the future. Hanover. Lang.: Eng.   3675
1700-1964.   Plays/librettos/scripts.
Great dramatic works considered in light of modern theatre
and social reponsibility. France. Italy. Lang.: Fre. 2560

Germany, West — cont'd

1860-1986.   Performance/production.
Influence of Richard Wagner on the work of the French
Symbolists. Paris. Bayreuth. Lang.: Eng.   3726

1898-1956.   Performance/production.
Biography of Bertolt Brecht. Augsburg. Berlin, East. USA.
Lang.: Ger.   1767

1898-1956.   Plays/librettos/scripts.
Brecht's life and work. Augsburg. Berlin, East. Los Angeles,
CA. Lang.: Ger.   2626

1909-1976.   Performance spaces.
The renovation of the Württemberg State Theatre by the
citizens of Stuttgart. Stuttgart. Lang.: Eng.   3683

1914-1985.   Performance/production.
Playwright and director George Tabori and his work. Vienna.
Lang.: Ger.   658

1921-1986.   Performance/production.
Homage to dancer and choreographer Roger George.
Switzerland. Lang.: Ger.   1351

1925-1986.   Administration.
Manager, actor and director Boy Gobert: his plans for
managing the Theater in der Josefstadt. Vienna. Lang.: Ger.
1427

1930-1986.   Institutions.
Claus Helmut Drese and his plans for managing the Vienna
Staatsoper. Vienna. Switzerland. Lang.: Ger.   3670

1933-1985.   Theory/criticism.
American criticisms of German *Tanztheater*. USA. Lang.:
Eng.   1290

1941-1986.   Performance/production.
On actor Gert Voss and his work. Vienna. Lang.: Ger.   1649

1942-1986.   Plays/librettos/scripts.
A *laudatio* in honor of playwright Friedrich Dürrenmatt,
recipient of the 1986 Büchner Prize. Darmstadt. Neuchâtel.
Lang.: Ger.   2624

1944-1986.   Design/technology.
Profile of set and lighting designer Erich Wonder. Lang.:
Eng.   274

1944-1986.   Plays/librettos/scripts.
Work of playwright Stefan Schütz. Lang.: Eng.   2625

1949-1984.   Performance/production.
Actor Hilmar Thate on Brecht. Germany, East.   732

1956-1986.   Plays/librettos/scripts.
Brecht's interpretational legacy is best understood on West
German stages.   2627

1957-1986.   Institutions.
The new secretary-general of the Salzburger Festspiele, Franz
Willnauer. Salzburg. Lang.: Ger.   444

1970-1986.   Plays/librettos/scripts.
Interview with playwright Stefan Schütz. Lang.: Eng.   2628

1973-1985.   Performance/production.
Symposium on the violence in Pina Bausch's *Tanztheater*.
Lang.: Eng.   1272

1975-1985.   Performance/production.
Interview with Wolfgang Wagner on his staging of 3
Wagnerian operas at the Bayreuth Festspiele. Bayreuth.
Lang.: Hun.   3740

1977-1985.   Theory/criticism.
Pina Bausch seen as heir of epic theater of Bertolt Brecht.
Lang.: Eng.   1289

1978-1985.   Performance/production.
DeVina Barajas discusses performing the songs of Brecht.
Switzerland. USA.   3607

1979.   Theory/criticism.
Limited usefulness of dramaturgy in staging. Lang.: Eng.
3112

1980-1986.   Plays/librettos/scripts.
Ballets based on works of William Shakespeare. USSR.
Lang.: Rus.   1322

1981-1986.   Design/technology.
Lighting techniques for Wagnerian operas. Bayreuth. Lang.:
Eng.   3651

1981-1986.   Institutions.
Production of Jürgen Lederach's *Japanische Spiele (Japanese
Play)* by Transformtheater. Berlin, West. Lang.: Swe.   499

1983.   Design/technology.
Details of the new production building at the Bayerische
Staatsoper. Munich. Lang.: Hun.   275

1983.   Performance/production.
Peter Stein directs Aeschylus' *Oresteia* in Warsaw. Berlin,
West. Warsaw. Lang.: Pol.   1768

1984.   Performance/production.
Interview with Peter Stein, director of Schaubühne am
Helleschen Ufer. Berlin, West. Warsaw. Lang.: Pol.   731
Interview with development director Harvey Seifter on
German theatre. New York, NY. Lang.: Eng.   840
Life and technique of Franz Xaver Kroetz. New York, NY.
Lang.: Eng.   2287

1984-1985.   Performance/production.
Interview with choreographer Mechthild Grossman. Lang.:
Eng.   1273

1984-1986.   Plays/librettos/scripts.
Characterization in *Furcht und Hoffnung der BRD (Help
Wanted)* by Franz Xaver Kroetz. Lang.: Eng.   2623

1984-1986.   Theory/criticism.
American dance critics' reviews of Pina Bausch's work. USA.
Lang.: Eng.   1291

1985.   Performance/production.
Analysis of two productions of plays by Marivaux. Nanterre.
Berlin, West. Lang.: Swe.   1739

1986.   Design/technology.
Reports on Showtech conference. Berlin, West. Lang.: Hun.
273
Text of a lecture on international technical cooperation in
theatre. Hungary. Berlin, West. Lang.: Hun.   289

1986.   Performance/production.
Director Dieter Dorn and his idea for staging *Der
zerbrochene Krug (The Broken Jug)*. Salzburg. Munich. Lang.:
Ger.   1651

Greece

**   Theory/criticism.**
Influence of literary theory on Greek theatre studies. UK-
England. Germany. Lang.: Afr.   1210

600-400 B.C.   Performance spaces.
Ambiguous translations of ancient Greek theatrical
documentation. Rome. Lang.: Eng.   597

500 B.C.-1986 A.D.   Relation to other fields.
Influences of shamanism on Eastern and Western theatre.
Asia. Lang.: Ita.   1095

499-401 B.C.   Plays/librettos/scripts.
Masked god as tragic subject in works of Aeschylus,
Sophocles and Euripides. Lang.: Fre.   2636

475-375 B.C.   Relation to other fields.
Factors that discouraged historical drama in the classical
period. Athens. Lang.: Eng.   3035

472-458 B.C.   Plays/librettos/scripts.
Cosmic themes in the works of Aeschylus. Lang.: Fre.   2629

458 B.C.   Plays/librettos/scripts.
Topicality of Aeschylus' *Oresteia*. Lang.: Fre.   2632

450 B.C.   Theory/criticism.
Social and political conditions of Greek society as sources for
dramatic material. Athens. Lang.: Eng.   3113

450-425 B.C.   Plays/librettos/scripts.
Chorus in ancient Greek comedy and drama. Lang.: Ita.
2633

450 B.C.-1956 A.D.   Plays/librettos/scripts.
Applying Brecht's dramatic principles to the plays of
Euripides. Germany, East.   2614

446-385 B.C.   Plays/librettos/scripts.
Aristophanes and his conception of comedy. Lang.: Fre. 2635

438-408 B.C.   Plays/librettos/scripts.
Moral and political crises reflected in the plays of Euripides.
Athens. Lang.: Fre.   2634

409 B.C.   Plays/librettos/scripts.
Interpretation of final scenes of Sophocles' *Philoctetes*. Lang.:
Heb.   2630

1937-1945.   Performance/production.
Overview of Maria Callas' early career. Athens. Lang.: Eng.
3741

1983.   Performance/production.
Program notes for the Athens Ensemble production of *Baal*
by Bertolt Brecht. Athens.   1769

1985.   Plays/librettos/scripts.
Program notes from Heinz-Uwe Haus's production of *Arturo
Ui*.   2631

1985-1986.   Plays/librettos/scripts.
Interview with Peter Handke about his play *Prometheus
gefesselt*. Salzburg. Lang.: Ger.   2398

Greenland

1986.   **Design/technology.**
Designer and special effects supervisor make sleigh fly in *Santa Claus—The Movie*.   3199

Haiti

1820-1970.   **Plays/librettos/scripts.**
Precursors of revolutionary black theatre. Jamaica. Lang.: Eng.   956

1939.   **Plays/librettos/scripts.**
Analysis of *La Tragédie du roi Christophe (The Tragedy of King Christopher)* by Aimé Césaire. Africa. Martinique. Lang.: Fre.   2637

1970-1979.   **Plays/librettos/scripts.**
The influence of Brecht on Haiti's exiled playwright Frank Fouché and the group Kovidor.   2638

Holland

SEE

Netherlands.

Hungary

ALSO SEE

Austro-Hungarian Empire.
Summary of articles on Hungarian theatre structure. Lang.: Hun.   6

                      Performance/production.
Director István Verebes discusses staging from the actor's viewpoint. Lang.: Hun.   739

Review of *Bűnhődés (Punishment)*, a stage adaptation of *The Idiot* by Dostojèvskij. Budapest. Lang.: Hun.   1826

Study of *A Kétfejü fenerad (The Two-Headed Beast)*. Lang.: Hun.   1926

                      Plays/librettos/scripts.
Problems of modern dramatury exemplified in current Hungarian theatre. Lang.: Hun.   2640

Text of a lecture on Shakespeare's *King Lear* by Clifford Davidson. Budapest. Lang.: Hun.   2643

Analysis of István Örkény's play, *Pisti a vérzivatarban (Steve in the Bloodbath)*. Lang.: Hun.   2652

Plot, structure and national character of *Bánk Bán* by József Katona. Lang.: Hun.   2655

                      Relation to other fields.
Contribution to the discussion on theatre structure analyzing the function of theatre in society. Lang.: Hun.   1100

                      Theory/criticism.
Role of theatrical habit in Hungarian theatre history. Lang.: Hun.   1212

1610-1850.   **Performance/production.**
Review of the Theatre History Collection exhibition in the Széchényi National Library. Lang.: Hun.   734

1700-1730.   **Basic theatrical documents.**
Edited text of a traditional Nativity play. Kézdivásárhely. Lang.: Hun.   223

1700-1800.   **Performance/production.**
Hungarian translation of *L'Opera nel Settecento* by Giorgio Lise. Budapest. Lang.: Hun.   3752

1731-1982.   **Performance/production.**
Historical data on actor Ede Paulay and his family. Lang.: Hun.   1852

1773-1985.   **Institutions.**
History of puppetry and the Hungarian State Puppet Theatre. Lang.: Hun.   3956

1773-1985.   **Performance/production.**
Adaptation of folk dance to the stage. Lang.: Hun.   1331

1800-1855.   **Plays/librettos/scripts.**
Analysis of Mihály Vörösmarty's *A bújdosók (Refugees)*. Lang.: Hun.   2639

1800-1883.   **Performance spaces.**
The history of the theatre building used by Szegedi Nemzeti Színhaz. Szeged. Lang.: Hun.   603

1800-1915.   **Plays/librettos/scripts.**
Literary and theatrical history of Eastern Europe. Poland. Czechoslovakia. Lang.: Hun.   2755

1810-1893.   **Reference materials.**
Guide to Ferenc Erkel opera museum. Gyula. Lang.: Hun.   3912

1833-1840.   **Reference materials.**
Source materials on the history of Hungarian dance. Pest. Lang.: Hun.   1286

1833-1938.   **Performance/production.**
Theatrical recollections focusing on the career of actress Kornélia Prielle. Máramarossziget. Lang.: Hun.   1878

1847-1880.   **Performance/production.**
Stage history of *Giselle* by Adolphe Adam at Pest National Theatre. Pest. Lang.: Hun.   1306

1850-1986.   **Reference materials.**
Illustrated guide to Actor's Museum. Budapest. Lang.: Hun.   2990

1852-1864.   **Performance/production.**
Career of theatrical professional Ede Paulay. Budapest. Lang.: Hun.   1824

1855.   **Performance/production.**
Study of Hungarian actor Ede Paulay. Győr. Lang.: Hun.   1823

1878-1894.   **Performance/production.**
Theatrical career of Ede Paulay. Budapest. Lang.: Hun.   1944

1878-1982.   **Reference materials.**
Bibliography on and about the playwright-author Ferenc Molnár. Vienna. Budapest. New York, NY. Lang.: Eng. 2982

1883-1983.   **Plays/librettos/scripts.**
Philosophy and morality of Imre Madách's classical dramatic poem *Az ember tragédiája (The Tragedy of a Man)*. Lang.: Hun.   2644

1885.   **Performance spaces.**
The burning of the Szeged National Theatre. Szeged. Lang.: Hun.   600

1886-1944.   **Reference materials.**
Bibliography of Hungarian writer and translator Jenő Mohácsi. Lang.: Hun.   2991

1894-1977.   **Basic theatrical documents.**
English translation of *Az óriáscsecsemö (The Giant Baby)* by Tibor Déry. Lang.: Eng, Hun.   1484

1896-1916.   **Institutions.**
History of Vigszinház (Comedy Theatre). Budapest. Lang.: Hun.   502

1906-1985.   **Performance/production.**
Notes on the choreography of Aurél Milloss. Italy. Lang.: Ita.   1310

1907-1986.   **Performance/production.**
Career of actress Margit Dajka. Lang.: Hun.   1787

1908-1986.   **Performance/production.**
Life and career of actress-singer Lili Neményi. Austro-Hungarian Empire. Lang.: Hun.   3705

1910-1986.   **Performance/production.**
Interview with actor, director and manager Tamás Major. Lang.: Hun.   1776

Recollections of actor, director and theatre manager Tamás Major. Lang.: Hun.   1879

1916-1984.   **Performance/production.**
Autobiography of tenor József Simándy. Lang.: Hun.   3753

1917-1986.   **Administration.**
Berne Convention and copyright in socialist countries. Lang.: Eng.   46

1921-1974.   **Performance/production.**
Life and career of choreographer Miklós Rábai. Lang.: Hun.   1332

1923.   **Performance/production.**
Reviews of Shakespeare productions written by Hungarian realist writer, Zsigmond Móricz. Budapest. Lang.: Hun. 1887

1925-1979.   **Performance/production.**
Careers of three Hungarian opera stars. Lang.: Hun.   3755

1927-1984.   **Plays/librettos/scripts.**
Review of a monograph on András Sütő. Romania. Lang.: Hun.   2657

1927-1986.   **Performance/production.**
Career of actress Éva Ruttkai. Lang.: Hun.   1871

1928-1950.   **Performance/production.**
Memoir of actress and poetry recitalist Mariann Csernus. Lang.: Hun.   1815

1929-1986.   **Performance/production.**
Tribute to late actress Margit Dajka. Lang.: Hun.   1915

Recollections of actress Margit Dajka. Lang.: Hun.   1930

1930-1985.   **Relation to other fields.**
Enthnography of a Hungarian village. Zsámbok. Lang.: Hun.   1099

1930-1986.   **Performance/production.**
Reprinted preface to biography of Tamás Major. Lang.: Hun.   1863

1931.   **Performance/production.**
Synthesis of music, dance, song and speech in *Ayrus Leánya (Ayrus' Daughter)* by Ödön Palasovszky. Budapest. Lang.: Hun.   1967

Hungary — cont'd

1932-1938. **Performance/production.**
History of Hungarian theatre in the 1930s. Lang.: Hun. 738

1934-1976. **Performance/production.**
Biography of actress Éva Ruttkai. Lang.: Hun. 3224

1935-1938. **Performance/production.**
Choreography by Aurél Milloss for dramatic productions directed by Antal Németh at the National Theatre in Budapest. Budapest. Lang.: Hun. 1847

1938-1939. **Performance/production.**
Hungarian folksongs and dance adapted to the stage in *Magyar Csupajáték (Hungarian All-Play)*. Budapest. Lang.: Hun. 1274

1942-1945. **Performance/production.**
Collaboration of choreographer Aurél Milloss and scene designer Giorgio de Chirico. Milan. Rome. Lang.: Hun. 1275

1944-1985. **Performance/production.**
Selected short comic prose sketches of Róbert Rátony, actor, showman and writer. Lang.: Hun. 1920

1944-1986. **Performance/production.**
Recollections of actor Péter Huszti. Lang.: Hun. 1842

1945-1980. **Performance/production.**
Career of actor/director György Várady. Romania. Lang.: Hun. 1802

1945-1985. **Performance/production.**
Premiere of Tibor Déry's *A Tanúk (The Witnesses)*, directed by Tibor Csizmadia. Szolnok. Lang.: Hun. 1834

1945-1985. **Training.**
Experiences of acting teacher Zsuzsa Simon. Lang.: Hun. 3158

1945-1986. **Performance/production.**
Autobiographical recollections of Cecilia Esztergályos, ballet-dancer turned actress. Lang.: Hun. 1829

Interview with Tamás Major, director and actor. Lang.: Hun. 1868

1947-1979. **Plays/librettos/scripts.**
The grotesque in the plays of István Örkény. Lang.: Ger. 2651

1948-1980. **Performance spaces.**
Reconstruction of the Szeged National Theatre. Szeged. Lang.: Hun. 604

1950-1984. **Plays/librettos/scripts.**
Study of author and playwright András Sütő. Romania. Lang.: Hun. 2762

1951-1986. **Relation to other fields.**
The premiere of Howard Fast's play under the title *Harminc ezüstpénz (Thirty Pieces of Silver)* in Hungary. Lang.: Hun. 3036

1952-1977. **Plays/librettos/scripts.**
Reconstruction of the three versions and productions of the operetta *Állami Áruház (State Stores)*. Lang.: Hun. 3943

1952-1984. **Plays/librettos/scripts.**
Reviews of books on Hungarian theatre. Lang.: Hun. 958

1953-1986. **Design/technology.**
Theatre workshops of the Budapest Central Scene Shop Project. Budapest. Lang.: Hun. 290

1954-1985. **Performance/production.**
Interview with actor István Avar. Lang.: Hun. 1836

Actress/poetry recitalist Erzsi Palotai recalls her life and career. Lang.: Hun. 1911

1955-1980. **Plays/librettos/scripts.**
Loss of identity in plays by István Örkény's and Sławomir Mrożek. Poland. Lang.: Hun. 2752

1956-1985. **Performance/production.**
Production history of Bela Bartók's ballet *A csodálatos mandarin (The Miraculous Mandarin)* on Hungarian stages. Lang.: Hun. 1305

1956-1986. **Performance/production.**
The life and career of actress Mari Tórőcsik. Lang.: Hun. 1933

1957-1970. **Design/technology.**
Development of modern Hungarian set and costume design. Lang.: Hun. 279

1957-1985. **Performance/production.**
Interview with actress Éva Spányik. Lang.: Hun. 1837

1958-1986. **Institutions.**
Recollections of director Károly Kazimir, of Körszinház. Budapest. Lang.: Hun. 501

1959-1983. **Performance/production.**
History of Hungarian productions and interpretations of *Death of a Salesman (Az ügynók halála)* by Arthur Miller

and *A Streetcar Named Desire (A vágy villamos)* by Tennessee Williams. Lang.: Hun. 1857

1960-1980. **Performance/production.**
Survey of various Hungarian amateur theatres and workshops. Lang.: Hun. 1906

1960-1980. **Plays/librettos/scripts.**
Dramatizations of the life of politician Endre Bajcsy-Zsilinszky. Lang.: Hun. 2661

1960-1985. **Plays/librettos/scripts.**
Survey of the development of Hungarian drama. Lang.: Hun. 2645

1961-1985. **Performance/production.**
Interview with actor, director and dramaturg Imre Katona of the Gropius Társulat. Budapest. Lang.: Hun. 1945

1961-1986. **Institutions.**
History of Bóbita Puppet Theatre. Pécs. Lang.: Hun. 3957

1963-1982. **Plays/librettos/scripts.**
Comparison of plays and short stories by Károly Szakonyi. Lang.: Hun. 2646

1963-1984. **Performance/production.**
Hungarian performance of Edward Albee's play *Nem félünk a farkastól (Who's Afraid of Virginia Woolf?)*. Lang.: Hun. 1946

1965-1980. **Design/technology.**
Historical overview of scene and costume design. Lang.: Hun. 280

1965-1985. **Plays/librettos/scripts.**
Interview with playwright András Sütő. Romania. Lang.: Hun. 957

1965-1986. **Performance/production.**
Interview with actor András Bálint. Lang.: Hun. 1839

1966-1970. **Performance/production.**
Hungarian performance of *My Fair Lady*. Lang.: Hun. 3601

1967-1983. **Plays/librettos/scripts.**
Review of study of experimental plays and playwrights. Lang.: Hun. 2641

Review of a book on modern dramaturgy by playwright Zsuzsa Radnóti. Lang.: Hun. 2642

1967-1986. **Performance/production.**
Review and notes on Festival Days for students. Csurgó. Lang.: Hun. 737

1969-1984. **Plays/librettos/scripts.**
Excerpts from playwright Miklós Hubay's diary. Lang.: Hun. 2649

1970-1980. **Basic theatrical documents.**
Text of a Nativity puppet play. Balatonberényi. Lang.: Hun. 3945

1970-1980. **Performance/production.**
Memoir of writer, critic, theatre director Béla Abody. Lang.: Hun. 1780

Interview with actor Erzsi Pásztor. Lang.: Hun. 1838

1970-1985. **Performance/production.**
Productions of *Deficit* by István Csurka. Szolnok. Budapest. Lang.: Hun. 1833

1971-1975. **Performance/production.**
David Rabe's play *Sticks and Bones* presented at the Pesti Theatre in Hungary. Budapest. Lang.: Hun. 1799

1971-1983. **Theory/criticism.**
Theoretical writings and reviews on the performing arts. Lang.: Hun. 1211

1974-1985. **Plays/librettos/scripts.**
Works of playwright István Sárospataky. Lang.: Hun. 2660

1974-1986. **Institutions.**
Interviews with former managing directors of Csokonai Theatre. Debrecen. Lang.: Hun. 503

1976. **Design/technology.**
The renovation and modernization of the theatre production building. Budapest. Lang.: Hun. 291

1976-1983. **Performance/production.**
A collection of Tamás Koltai's critical reviews of productions and performances. Lang.: Hun. 1861

1976-1984. **Plays/librettos/scripts.**
Monodramas of playwright István Kocsis. Romania. Lang.: Hun. 2761

1976-1985. **Plays/librettos/scripts.**
Study of Tibor Gyurkovics' eight plays. Lang.: Hun. 2654

1977-1986. **Design/technology.**
Interviews with technicians Gyula Ember and Gyula Asztalos about theatre technology. Lang.: Hun. 285

Hungary — cont'd

A kis herceg (The Little Prince) by Antoine de Saint-Exupéry adapted and staged by Anna Belia and Péter Valló. Budapest. Lang.: Hun. 1828

New director of Radnóti Miklós Theatre, András Bálint. Budapest. Lang.: Hun. 1830

Gábor Berényi's production of *Macskajáték (Catsplay)* by István Örkény at the Magyar Játékszin. Budapest. Lang.: Hun. 1832

Production of *A nevelő (The Tutor)* by Bertolt Brecht. Kaposvár. Lang.: Hun. 1840

Account of nation-wide theatre conference. Budapest. Lang.: Hun. 1841

Alkony (Sunset) by Isaak Babel, directed by Károly Kazimir at Thália Szinház. Budapest. Lang.: Hun. 1850

András Matkócsik directs *Mondd, Joe! (Eh, Joe!)* and *Az utlosó tekercs (Krapp's Last Tape)* by Samuel Beckett. Budapest. Lang.: Hun. 1851

Ágyrajárók (Night Lodgers) by Péter Szántó, directed by György Emöd at Kisfaludy Studio Theatre. Győr. Lang.: Hun. 1854

G.B. Shaw's *Megtörtszívek háza (Heartbreak House)* directed by István Horvai. Budapest. Lang.: Hun. 1858

Review of Alex Koenigsmark's *Adié, milacku! (Good-bye, Darling!)* directed by Péter Gothár at Csiky Gergely Theatre under the title *Agyó, kedvesem.* Kaposvár. Lang.: Hun. 1862

Rzeźnia (The Slaughterhouse) by Sławomir Mrożek, directed by Sándor Beke at Józsefvárosi Szinház under the title *Mészárszék.* Budapest. Lang.: Hun. 1865

Production of Shakespeare's *Szeget szeggel (Measure for Measure)* directed by István Paál. Veszprém. Lang.: Hun. 1872

Csongor és Tünde (Csongor and Tünde) by Mihály Vörösmarty, directed by János Szikora at Gárdonyi Géza Szinház. Eger. Lang.: Hun. 1877

Consideration of actor's place in a director's theatre. Lang.: Hun. 1880

László Salamon Suba's production of *Urának hű szolgája (A Faithful Servant of His Lord)* by Franz Grillparzer. Nyiregyháza. Lang.: Hun. 1881

Performances of George Bernard Shaw's *Candida* and Čechov's *Diadia Vania (Uncle Vanya)*, under the title *Ványa bácsi*, at Pécs National Theatre. Pécs. Lang.: Hun. 1893

Péter Gothár directs *Agyó, kedvesem (Goodbye, Darling!)* by Alex Koenigsmark, at Csiky Gergely Theatre. Kaposvár. Lang.: Hun. 1894

Mátyás Giricz directs *A kertész kutyája (The Gardener's Dog)* by Lope de Vega. Budapest. Lang.: Hun. 1900

Selected reviews of *Segitsd a király! (Help the King!)* by József Ratkó. Nyiregyháza. Lang.: Hun. 1902

Two productions of Čechov's *Három Nővér (Three Sisters)*. Zalaegerszeg. Budapest. Lang.: Hun. 1903

Troádes (The Trojan Women) directed by László Gergely at Csokonai Theatre. Debrecen. Lang.: Hun. 1909

Tamás Ascher directs Čechov's *Tri sestry (Three Sisters)* at Katona József Theatre under the title *Három nővér.* Budapest. Lang.: Hun. 1914

Production of *Ványa bácsi (Uncle Vanya)* by Čechov. Pécs. Lang.: Hun. 1918

Miklós Mészöly's *Bunker* at Népszinház directed by Mátyás Giricz. Budapest. Lang.: Hun. 1919

Stage adaptations of Dostojévskij novels *A Félkesgyelmű (The Idiot)* and *A Karamazov testvérek (The Brothers Karamazov).* Budapest. Debrecen. Lang.: Hun. 1922

Mihály Vörösmarty's *Csongor and Tünde* at Gárdonyi Géza Theatre directed by János Szikora. Eger. Lang.: Hun. 1923

Criticizes stage adaptation of *Hangok komédiája (Comedy of Sounds)* by Miklós Gyárfás. Budapest. Lang.: Hun. 1924

Production of Bengt Ahlfors' *Szinházkomédia (Theatre Comedy)* directed by András Márton. Debrecen. Lang.: Hun. 1925

Performances of *Pán Peter (Peter Pan)* by J. M. Barrie, directed by Géza Pártos. Kaposvár. Lang.: Hun. 1934

A kis herceg (The Little Prince) by Saint-Exupéry adapted and staged by Anna Belia and Péter Valló. Budapest. Lang.: Hun. 1935

Ének Phaedráért (Song for Phaedra) by Per Olof Enquist, directed by Imre Csiszár at the National Theatre of Miskolc. Miskolc. Lang.: Hun. 1937

István Paál directs *Szeget szeggel (Measure for Measure)* by Shakespeare at Petőfi Szinház. Veszprém. Lang.: Hun. 1938

Stage adaptations of prose works by Gogol and Gončarov. Veszprém. Békéscsaba. Lang.: Hun. 1948

Cyrano de Bergerac by Edmond Rostand, directed by György Lengyel at Madách Szinház. Budapest. Lang.: Hun. 1953

Macskajáték (Catsplay) by István Örkény, directed by Gábor Berényi, at Magyar Játékszin. Budapest. Lang.: Hun. 1962

Comparison of two Hungarian productions of *Háram nővér (Three Sisters)* by Anton Pavlovič Čechov. Budapest. Lang.: Hun. 1964

Gábor Máté directs Brecht's *Der Hofmeister (The Tutor)* at Csiky Gergely Theatre under the title *A nevelő.* Kaposvár. Lang.: Hun. 1966

A kegyenc (The Favorite) by Gyula Illyés, directed by János Sándor, National Theatre of Miskolc. Miskolc. Lang.: Hun. 1971

Tizenkét dühós ember (Twelve Angry Men) by Reginald Rose directed by András Béhés. Budapest. Lang.: Hun. 1972

Plays by Ribnikov and Višnevskij performed by Moscow Theatre of Lenin Comsomal. Moscow. Budapest. Lang.: Hun. 2329

Review of *Mágiarakás (Magic Heap)* by humorist György Sándor. Budapest. Lang.: Hun. 3334

Review of rock opera *István a király (King Stephen)* at the National Theatre. Budapest. Lang.: Hun. 3489

Puccini's opera *Manon Lescaut* at the Hungarian State Opera House. Budapest. Lang.: Hun. 3743

András Mikó directs Strauss' *Der Rosenkavalier* at the Hungarian State Opera House. Budapest. Lang.: Hun. 3745

Géza Oberfrank directs Bizet's *Carmen* at Szegedi Nemzeti Szinház. Szeged. Lang.: Hun. 3748

József Bor directs Verdi's opera *Il Trovatore* at Kisfaludy Theatre. Győr. Lang.: Hun. 3750

Zoltán Horváth directs Donizetti's *Don Pasquale* at the Pécsi Nemzeti Szinház. Pécs. Lang.: Hun. 3751

Gyula Kertész directs Puccini's *Tosca* at the Csokonai Theatre. Debrecen. Lang.: Hun. 3754

1985.   **Plays/librettos/scripts.**
Analysis of László Németh's study of *Bánk Bán* by József Katona and a portrait of the playwright. Lang.: Hun. 2647

Young playwright's conference. Zalaegerszeg. Lang.: Hun. 2650

Notes on the Open Forum in Zalaegerszeg. Zalaegerszeg. Lang.: Hun. 2653

Conference on the problems of adapting, interpreting and staging the classics. Italy. Lang.: Hun. 2656

1985.   **Reference materials.**
Catalogue from an exhibit of theatrical and ballet art by Zsuzsi Roboz. Budapest. Lang.: Hun. 1325

1985-1986.   **Administration.**
Contribution to the discussion on the Hungarian theatre structure. Lang.: Hun. 45

Problems in the structural organization of Hungarian theatre. Lang.: Hun. 48

Contribution to the discussion on theatre structure in Hungary. Lang.: Hun. 49

Contribution to the discussion on the Hungarian theatre structure. Lang.: Hun. 50

Economic problems of Hungarian theatre. Lang.: Hun. 51

1985-1986.   **Performance spaces.**
Design of concert hall in part of a major railway station. Budapest. Lang.: Hun. 598

1985-1986.   **Performance/production.**
Hungarian critics' awards for best actors, play, costume, scenery, etc. of the season. Lang.: Hun. 733

Commemoration of actor László Márkus. Lang.: Hun. 1864

Ahogy tetszik (As You Like It) by William Shakespeare directed by István Szőke. Miskolc. Lang.: Hun. 1866

Review of László Teleki's *A Kegyenc (The Favorite)* as directed by József Ruszt, Hevesi Sándor Theatre. Zalaegerszeg. Lang.: Hun. 1867

Adaptation for the stage by Anikó Vagda and Katalin Vajda of Imre Dobozy's screenplay *Villa Negra*, directed at Játékszin by Miklós Szurdi. Budapest. Lang.: Hun. 1870

István Szőke, directs *Ahogy tetszik (As You Like It)* by Shakespeare. Miskolc. Lang.: Hun. 1873

János Ács directs *Kozma* by Mihály Kornis. Kaposvár. Lang.: Hun. 1874

Géza Tordy directs *Császári futam (Imperial Round)* by Miklós Gyárfás at Gyulai Várszinház. Gyula. Lang.: Hun. 1875

Review of József Katona's *Bánk Bán* directed by János Ács at Szigligeti Szinház. Szolnok. Lang.: Hun. 1876

Imre Csiszár directs *Az éjszaka a nappal anyja (Night is the Mother of the Day)* by Lars Norén. Dunaújváros. Lang.: Hun. 1882

Gyula Gazdag directs *A vihar (The Tempest)* by William Shakespeare, Csiky Gergely Theatre. Kaposvár. Lang.: Hun. 1883

Bánk Bán by József Katona at Szigligeti Theatre directed by János Ács. Szolnok. Lang.: Hun. 1884

Kozma by Mihály Kornis directed by János Ács, Csiky Gergely Szinház. Kaposvár. Lang.: Hun. 1885

Recollections of actress Margit Dajka. Lang.: Hun. 1886

Ivo Brešan's *Paraszt Hamlet (The Peasant Hamlet)* directed by Béla Merő. Zalaegerszeg. Lang.: Hun. 1888

Péter Gothár's production of *A Öreg hölgy látogatósa (The Visit)* by Friedrich Dürrenmatt. Budapest. Lang.: Hun. 1889

Notes on *Čaruga (Death Cap)*, by Ivan Kušan, directed by Miklós Benedek, Katona József Theatre, under the title *Galócza*. Budapest. Lang.: Hun. 1890

Review of László Teleki's *A Kegyenc (The Favorite)* directed by József Ruszt. Zalaegerszeg. Lang.: Hun. 1891

Knock by Jules Romains directed by Gábor Máté at Csiky Gergely Theatre. Kaposvár. Lang.: Hun. 1892

Magda Szabó's *Szent Bertalan nappala (Saint Bartholomew's Day)* directed by György Lengyel at Madách Szinház. Budapest. Lang.: Hun. 1896

Dezső Szomory's *Bella* at the Pécs National Theatre directed by István Jeney. Pécs. Lang.: Hun. 1897

Productions of plays by Edward Bond, Gyula Hernádi and Lope de Vega at the Pécs National Theatre. Pécs. Lang.: Hun. 1898

Milán Füst's *Margit kisasszony (Miss Margit)* directed by István Dégi at Játékszin. Budapest. Lang.: Hun. 1901

János Ács directs *A kőszívű ember fiai (The Sons of the Stone-Hearted Man)* by Mór Jókai. Zalaegerszeg. Lang.: Hun. 1905

Ferenc Sik directs Shakespeare's *A velencei kalmár (The Merchant of Venice)*. Budapest. Lang.: Hun. 1907

Forgatókönyv (Film Script) by István Örkény directed by Gábor Balogh. Békéscsaba. Lang.: Hun. 1908

Die dreigroschenoper (The Three Penny Opera) directed by István Pinczés at Csokonai Theatre. Debrecen. Lang.: Hun. 1910

Tamás Ascher directs *A kopasz éneksnő (The Bald Soprano)* and *Különóra (The Lesson)* by Eugène Ionesco. Kaposvár. Lang.: Hun. 1912

Review of two performances of András Sütő's plays. Budapest. Lang.: Hun. 1913

Interview with actor Imre Kulcsár. Miskolc. Lang.: Hun. 1917

Čechov's *Višněvyj sad (The Cherry Orchard)* directed by Imre Csiszár under the title *Cseresznyéskert*. Miskolc. Lang.: Hun. 1921

János Pelle's *Casanova* directed by Károly Kazimir at Körszinház. Budapest. Lang.: Hun. 1929

Péter Gellért's production of *Urhatnám polgár (The Bourgeois Gentleman)* at Móricz Zsigmond Szinház. Nyiregyháza. Lang.: Hun. 1931

Review of *Kettős ünnep (A Double Holiday)*, written and staged by István Verebes. Budapest. Lang.: Hun. 1932

Dezső Szomory's *Bella* at Pécs National Theatre directed by István Jeney. Pécs. Lang.: Hun. 1936

István Verebes directs *Valódi vadnyugat (True West)* by Sam Shepard at Radnóti Miklós Szinpad. Budapest. Lang.: Hun. 1939

Kinn vagyunk a vízből (Saved) by Edward Bond directed by István Szőke. Pécs. Lang.: Hun. 1940

Review of *Margit kisasszony (Miss Margit)* directed by István Dégi. Budapest. Lang.: Hun. 1941

László Fábián's *Levéltetvek az akasztófán (Plant-Lice on the Gallows)* directed by István Szőke. Miskolc. Lang.: Hun. 1942

Ferenc Sik directs two plays by Gyula Háy. Veszprém. Gyula. Lang.: Hun. 1943

Aleksej Dudarёv's *Večer (An Evening)* directed by Mátyas Giricz at Józsefvárosi Theatre. Budapest. Lang.: Hun. 1947

Hagyaték (Legacy) by Gyula Hernádi, directed by Menyhért Szegvári. Pécs. Lang.: Hun. 1949

Nő a körúton (Woman on the Boulevard) by István Gáll directed by Péter Léner at Móricz Zsigmond Theatre. Nyiregyháza. Lang.: Hun. 1950

Endre Vészi's *Don Quijote utolsó kalandja (Don Quixote's Last Adventure)* directed by Imre Kerényi. Gyula. Lang.: Hun. 1951

Imre Sarkadi's *Oszlopos Simeon (The Man on the Pillar)* directed by István Szőke at Nemzeti Szinház. Miskolc. Lang.: Hun. 1952

World premiere of *A tanúk (The Witnesses)* by the late Tibor Déry directed at Szigligeti Theatre by Tibor Csizmadia. Szolnok. Lang.: Hun. 1954

Janika (Our Son) by Géza Csáth, directed by Tamás Fodor and starring György Kézdy. Szolnok. Lang.: Hun. 1955

Advent a Hargitán (Advent in the Harghita Mountains) by András Sütő, directed at National Theatre by Ferenc Sik. Budapest. Lang.: Hun. 1956

Scapin furfangjai (Scapin's Tricks) by Molière, directed by László Vámos at Szentendrei Teátrum. Szentendre. Lang.: Hun. 1957

Reviews of two plays by Arthur Schnitzler directed by Imre Halasi. Budapest. Zalaegerszeg. Lang.: Hun. 1958

Performances of *Hair*, directed by János Sándor, and *Desire Under the Elms*, directed by Géza Bodolay at the National Theatre of Szeged. Szeged. Lang.: Hun. 1959

Review of Gyula Gazdag's production of *A Vihar (The Tempest)* by Shakespeare, Csiky Gergely Theatre. Kaposvár. Lang.: Hun. 1960

Isván Szőke directs *Letvéltetvek az akasztófán (Plant-Lice on the Gallows)* by László Fábián. Miskolc. Lang.: Hun. 1961

Wariat i zakonnica (The Madman and the Nun) by Stanisław Ignacy Witkiewicz, directed by János Sándor at Szeged National Theatre under the title *Az őrült és az apáca*. Szeged. Lang.: Hun. 1965 ENDSzolnok. Lang.: Hun. 1968

Performance of Shakespeare's *Richard II* at Várszinház, directed by Imre Kerényi. Budapest. Lang.: Hun. 1970

István Gáll's *Nő a körúton (Woman on the Boulevard)* directed by Péter Léner at Móricz Zsigmond Szinház. Nyiregyháza. Lang.: Hun. 1973

András Sütő's *Advent a Hargitán (Advent in the Harghita Mountains)* directed by Ferenc Sik. Budapest. Lang.: Hun. 1974

Four performances in Budapest by the students of Oleg Tabakov of GITIS, the Institute of Dramatic Art, Moscow. Moscow. Budapest. Lang.: Hun. 2318

Melyrepülés (Flying at Low Altitude) by Tamás Cseh and Dénes Csengey. Budapest. Lang.: Hun. 3487

Lakat alá lányokat (Lock Up Your Daughters), a stage adaptation of Henry Fielding's *Rape Upon Rape*, directed by Imre Halasi. Diósgyőr. Lang.: Hun. 3600

Ivan Vas-Zoltán directs *Vértestvérek (Blood Brothers)* by Willy Russell. Pécs. Lang.: Hun. 3602

Hungary — cont'd

Éva Pataki's *Edith és Marlene (Edith and Marlene)* directed by Márta Mészáros, Pest National Theatre. Budapest. Lang.: Hun. 3603

Jézus Krisztus Szupersztar (Jesus Christ Superstar) by Andrew Lloyd Webber and Tim Rice directed by János Szikora (Rock Szinház). Szeged. Lang.: Hun. 3604

Summer productions of *Jézus Krisztus Szupersztár.* Szeged. Budapest. Lang.: Hun. 3605

András Fehér directs Verdi's *Un ballo in maschera* at the Hungarian State Opera House. Budapest. Lang.: Hun. 3746

Verdi's *Simon Boccanegra* and Puccini's *La Bohème* at the Hungarian State Opera House and Erkel Theatre. Budapest. Lang.: Hun. 3747

László Kertész directs Rossini's *L'occasione fa il ladro* at Népszinház. Budapest. Lang.: Hun. 3749

Mágnás Miska (Miska the Magnate) by Albert Szirmai directed by László Bagossy. Pécs. Lang.: Hun. 3942

1986.   Relation to other fields.
Edward Albee on government censorship and freedom of artistic expression. Budapest. 1096

Interview with designer of theatrical posters Győző Varga. Lang.: Hun. 1097

Folklorist Tekla Dömötör includes traditional material in her popular work. Lang.: Hun. 1098

1986.   Theory/criticism.
Review of *Mi lesz velünk Anton Pavlovics? (What Will Become of Us, Anton Pavlovič?)* by Miklós Almási. Lang.: Hun. 3114

Tamás Bécsy's theory of the theatre. Lang.: Hun. 3115

Reviews of books on Hungarian theatre. Lang.: Hun. 3116

Iceland
1986.   Performance/production.
Nordic Festival of Amateur Theatre now includes Iceland and Greenland. Reykjavik. Lang.: Swe. 740

India
**   Performance/production.**
Adaptation of Kroetz's *Wunschkonzert (Request Concert).* Calcutta. Madras. Bombay. Lang.: Eng. 1975

200 B.C.   Performance spaces.
Ancient Indian theatre and its conventions. Lang.: Ita. 609

1861-1941.   Plays/librettos/scripts.
Translations of three plays by Rabindranath Tagore, with critical commentary. Lang.: Eng. 2662

1873-1888.   Performance/production.
Lady Dufferin's amateur theatricals. Ottawa, ON. Lang.: Eng. 671

1884-1986.   Performance/production.
Influence of Indian theatre on Western drama. Europe. Lang.: Ita. 703

1895-1985.   Institutions.
History of Museum Theatre. Madras. Lang.: Eng. 504

1940-1985.   Performance/production.
Life and work of an Indian street performer. Rajasthan. Lang.: Eng. 3335

1965-1986.   Performance/production.
Peter Brook discusses development of *The Mahabharata.* Avignon. Lang.: Eng. 1361

1974-1980.   Performance/production.
Hindu world view reflected in Sanskrit theatre. Lang.: Eng. 1362

1980-1985.   Research/historiography.
Indian theatre professionals criticize Peter Brook's *Mahabharata.* Kerala. Calcutta. Lang.: Eng. 1376

1980-1986.   Performance/production.
Description of several *Bhavāī* performances. Lang.: Eng. 1976

1981-1984.   Institutions.
Reports on theatre conferences and festivals in Asia. Manila. Kuala Lumpur. Toga. Calcutta. Lang.: Eng. 510

1983.   Basic theatrical documents.
Text of *Karimkutty* by K. N. Panikkar in English translation. Lang.: Eng. 1355

Indonesia
**   Relation to other fields.**
Uses of religious ritual in traditional theatre. Lang.: Rus. 1102

Religious, communal and artistic functions of Hindu *odalan* festival. Lang.: Eng. 3359

375 B.C.-1983 A.D.   Plays/librettos/scripts.
Treatment of history in drama. Europe. North America. Lang.: Eng. 2541

1045-1986.   Relation to other fields.
Analyses of *Wayang cepak* play, *Gusti Sinuhan*, and its role in the Hindu religion. Lang.: Eng. 3992

1930.   Plays/librettos/scripts.
Conceptions of the South Sea islands in works of Murnau, Artaud and Spies. Europe. USA. Lang.: Ita. 3231

1952-1985.   Performance/production.
Influence of Asian theatre traditions on American artists. New York, NY. Lang.: Eng. 1335

1977-1982.   Performance/production.
Trance dance compared to role of dance in conventional theatre. Lang.: Eng. 1363

1983-1986.   Performance/production.
Description of characters and techniques of *Wayang* puppetry. Lang.: Fre. 4018

Iran
1971.   Performance/production.
Discussion of *Persepolis* and *Orghast* at Persepolis-Shiraz festival. Shiraz. Lang.: Ita. 741

Iraq
1885-1985.   Institutions.
Educational theatre in Iraq. Lang.: Eng. 505

Ireland
ALSO SEE
Eire.
ALSO SEE
UK-Ireland.

1602.   Plays/librettos/scripts.
Possible source of cock fight in Henry Medwall's *Fulgens and Lucres.* Lang.: Eng. 2664

1894-1963.   Plays/librettos/scripts.
Biography of playwright Teresa Deevy. Lang.: Eng. 2665

1945-1970.   Plays/librettos/scripts.
Influence of artist Jack Yeats on playwright Samuel Beckett. France. Lang.: Eng. 2663

1950-1972.   Plays/librettos/scripts.
The place of *The Island of the Mighty* in the John Arden canon. UK. Lang.: Eng. 2666

1958-1986.   Plays/librettos/scripts.
Notes on film treatments of plays by Samuel Beckett. France. Lang.: Ita. 3234

Israel
1794-1985.   Plays/librettos/scripts.
Overview of Hebrew adaptations and translations of *Tartuffe* by Molière. France. Lang.: Heb. 2667

1884-1985.   Basic theatrical documents.
Text of *Eiolf Hakatan*, Gad Kaynar's Hebrew translation of *Lille Eyolf (Little Eyolf)* by Henrik Ibsen. Norway. Lang.: Heb. 1489

1884-1985.   Plays/librettos/scripts.
Introductory note on the first translation of *Lille Eyolf (Little Eyolf)* into Hebrew. Norway. Lang.: Heb. 962

1892-1986.   Plays/librettos/scripts.
Reflections on Max Zweig's dramas. Vienna. Berlin. Tel Aviv. Lang.: Ger. 2389

1898-1985.   Performance/production.
Obituary of director Raphael Zvi. Lang.: Heb. 1984

1920-1986.   Performance/production.
Occidental nature of Israeli theatre. Lang.: Ita. 742

1925-1971.   Reference materials.
Betzalel London's archive deposited at Hebrew University. Jerusalem. Lang.: Heb. 1014

1935-1986.   Performance/production.
Interview with actress Rachel Marcus. Tel-Aviv. Lang.: Heb. 1983

1955-1971.   Design/technology.
Photographs of settings designed by set designer Arnon Adar. Tel-Aviv. Lang.: Eng. 297

1978-1986.   Performance/production.
Artistic cooperation between playwright Dan Horowitz and director Ya'akov Raz. Lang.: Heb. 1978

1982-1983.   Audience.
HaBimah Theatre production of *Troádes (The Trojan Women)* by Euripides. Tel-Aviv. Lang.: Eng. 199

1982-1986.   Administration.
Interview with directors of Teatron HaIroni. Haifa. Lang.: Heb. 52

Israel — cont'd

1983-1985.   **Reference materials.**
Bibliography of book reviews. Tel-Aviv. Lang.: Heb.   1018
1984-1986.   **Performance/production.**
Jurij Petrivič Liubimov directs Isaak Babel's *Hashhia
(Sunset)*. Tel-Aviv. Lang.: Heb.   1979
Puppeteer Eric Bass of Hakaron Puppet Theatre. Jerusalem.
Lang.: Heb.   3966
1985-1986.   **Reference materials.**
A list of opening nights of the theatrical season in Israel.
Lang.: Heb.   1016
Overview of seven newly published Israeli plays. Lang.: Heb.
          2992
1986.   **Audience.**
The semiotics of dramatic dialogue. Lang.: Eng.   1449
Organization of audience response. Lang.: Eng.   1450
1986.   **Performance/production.**
Announcement of Margalith Prize winners. Jerusalem. Lang.:
Heb.   1977
Notes on the process of staging *Eiolf Hakatan*, a Hebrew
translation of Henrik Ibsen's *Lille Eyolf (Little Eyolf)*,
directed by Yossi Israeli at the Kahn theatre. Jerusalem.
Lang.: Heb.   1980
Daniel Lanzini's notes on writing and staging his play
Hazaiot Kamot Bamizrah (Fantasies Awakening in the East)
at the Acre Theatre Festival. Acre. Lang.: Heb.   1981
Notes on the rehearsals of Henrik Ibsen's *Lille Eyolf (Little
Eyolf)* directed by Yossi Israeli, at the Kahn Theatre.
Jerusalem. Lang.: Heb.   1982
1986.   **Reference materials.**
List of the season's opening nights. Lang.: Heb.   1015
A list of opening nights of the theatrical season in Israel.
Lang.: Heb.   1017
Speech given by Benjamin Zemach on the deposition of
Nachum Zemach's archive at Hebrew University. Jerusalem.
Lang.: Heb.   1019

Italy

          Plays/librettos/scripts.
Deconstructionist analysis of *Riccardo III* by Carmelo Bene.
France. Lang.: Eng.   2690
600-400 B.C.   **Performance spaces.**
Ambiguous translations of ancient Greek theatrical
documentation. Greece. Rome. Lang.: Eng.   597
500 B.C.-1726 A.D.   **Performance spaces.**
Development of theatres, stages and the Italianate
proscenium arch theatre. France. Lang.: Eng, Fre.   596
55 B.C.-1983 A.D.   **Performance spaces.**
Descriptions and photos of theatres. Rome. Lang.: Ita.   610
43 B.C.-1611 A.D.   **Plays/librettos/scripts.**
Comparison of Ben Jonson's *Catiline* with its Latin prose
source by Sallust. England. Lang.: Eng.   2518
800-1985.   **Relation to other fields.**
Essays on literary and theatrical languages. Lang.: Ita.   1103
900-999.   **Relation to other fields.**
Review article on Johann Drumbl's *Quem Quaeritis: Teatro
Sacro dell'Alto Mediaevo*. France. Lang.: Eng.   3031
900-1857.   **Plays/librettos/scripts.**
The historical Simon Boccanegra. Genoa. Lang.: Eng.   3888
920-972.   **Relation to other fields.**
Influence of the plays of Terence on writings of Bishop
Liutprando of Cremona. Cremona. Lang.: Ita.   3041
1000-1680.   **Relation to other fields.**
Proceedings of a symposium on theatre during the Middle
Ages and the Renaissance. Spain. Lang.: Cat, Spa, Ita.   12
1200-1400.   **Relation to other fields.**
Literary origins of the 'lauda drammatica'. Lang.: Ita.   1109
1200-1906.   **Relation to other fields.**
Playwright Luigi Pirandello on the dynamics of humor.
Lang.: Ita.   1108
1330-1623.   **Plays/librettos/scripts.**
Mutual influences between *commedia dell'arte* and Spanish
literature. Spain. Lang.: Spa.   2805
1350-1550.   **Relation to other fields.**
Reciprocal influence of Italian comedy and Boccaccio's *The
Decameron*. Lang.: Ita.   3045
1388-1538.   **Performance spaces.**
Spatial orientation in medieval Catalan religious productions.
Spain-Catalonia. Florence. Lang.: Cat.   616

1400-1503.   **Performance/production.**
Reconstruction of religious dramatic spectacles. Ravello.
Lang.: Ita.   3339
1400-1600.   **Design/technology.**
Description of scenery, machinery and performance of
Renaissance Italian feast. Lang.: Ita.   3311
1400-1620.   **Performance/production.**
Precursors of *commedia dell'arte*. Venice. Lang.: Eng.   3414
1476-1900.   **Plays/librettos/scripts.**
The Romeo and Juliet theme as interpreted in the musical
and visual arts. Lang.: Eng.   3886
1494-1600.   **Performance/production.**
Reconstruction of triumphal entry pageants. Lang.: Eng.   3425
1500-1540.   **Performance/production.**
Career of comic author and clown Zuanpolo Leopardi.
Venice. Lang.: Ita.   3336
1500-1600.   **Design/technology.**
Costume design in a 16th century production in Milan of
Guarini's *Il Pastor Fido*. Mantua. Lang.: Eng.   298
1500-1986.   **Design/technology.**
Origins and development of *commedia dell'arte* detailing the
costume and attributes of the stock characters. Europe. USA.
Lang.: Eng.   3407
1508-1537.   **Performance/production.**
Reconstruction of *Comedia Tinellaria* by Torres Naharro.
Rome. Venice. Lang.: Spa.   1986
1550-1600.   **Performance/production.**
Comic actor Tristano Martinelli, probable creator of the
character Harlequin. France. Lang.: Ita.   3412
1550-1650.   **Performance/production.**
Oriental influences on *commedia dell'arte*. Lang.: Ita.   3413
1565-1634.   **Performance/production.**
Life and works of actor and playwright Silvio Fiorillo. Lang.:
Ita.   3411
1568-1600.   **Performance spaces.**
Ceremonies celebrating the marriage of Maria dei Medici to
Henri IV. Florence. Lyon. Lang.: Ita.   3325
1576-1646.   **Plays/librettos/scripts.**
Analysis of *commedia dell'arte* text of Carlo Cantú's
Cicalamento. Lang.: Ita.   3416
1585-1589.   **Plays/librettos/scripts.**
Discussion of *L'esaltazione della croce (The Exaltation of the
Cross)* by Giovanni Maria Cecchi. Lang.: Ita.   2683
1599-1797.   **Performance/production.**
History of *castrati* in opera. Lang.: Eng.   3761
1600-1985.   **Reference materials.**
Catalogue of an exhibit on the Carlo Felice Theatre,
destroyed in World War II, and its proposed reconstruction.
Genoa. Lang.: Ita.   1024
1611.   **Plays/librettos/scripts.**
Giovan Battista Andreini's problems in publishing *La Turca
(The Turkish Woman)*. Lang.: Ita.   2692
1613-1621.   **Institutions.**
Relations between the 'Confidenti' company and their patron
Don Giovanni dei Medici. Venice. Lang.: Ita.   1580
1615-1936.   **Relation to other fields.**
Comparison of playwright Luigi Pirandello and novelist
Miguel de Cervantes. Spain. Lang.: Ita.   3040
1637-1700.   **Plays/librettos/scripts.**
Influence of Asian theatre on work of Filippo Acciajoli.
Lang.: Ita.   2713
1651-1986.   **Plays/librettos/scripts.**
Cultural and popular elements in a traditional nativity
puppet performance. Sicily. Naples. Lang.: Eng.   4009
1670-1740.   **Reference materials.**
Current state of research on the manuscript *Sujets de
plusieurs comédies italiennes (Subjects of Some Italian
Comedies)*. France. Lang.: Fre.   2988
1676-1753.   **Performance/production.**
Career of Luigi Riccoboni, actor, author and theatre
historian. France. Lang.: Ita.   745
1685-1985.   **Research/historiography.**
The life of Handel and his influence in making Italian opera
popular in England. London. Germany. Lang.: Eng.   3928
1700-1799.   **Research/historiography.**
Conference on aspects of theatre and opera in Emilia.
Emilia. Lang.: Ita.   7
1700-1799.   **Administration.**
Privatization and management of theatrical activity. Venice.
Lang.: Ita.   54

Italy — cont'd

1935-1986. **Performance/production.**
Opera-singer Mirella Freni: her roles and plans. Austria. Lang.: Ger. 3759

Profile of and interview with Italian tenor Luciano Pavarotti. Modena. Lang.: Eng. 3760

1937. **Performance/production.**
Premiere of Luigi Pirandello's *I giganti della montagna (The Giants of the Mountain)*. Florence. Lang.: Ita. 1998

1938-1988. **Plays/libretto/scripts.**
Gian Carlo Menotti's reactions to harsh criticism of his operas. New York, NY. Edinburgh. Cadegliano. Lang.: Eng. 3902

1942-1945. **Performance/production.**
Collaboration of choreographer Aurél Milloss and scene designer Giorgio de Chirico. Hungary. Milan. Rome. Lang.: Hun. 1275

1943-1986. **Performance/production.**
Profile of and interview with Italian baritone Leo Nucci. Castiglione del Pepoli. Lang.: Eng. 3766

1945. **Plays/libretto/scripts.**
Analysis of the operetta *Firebrand* by Kurt Weill and Ira Gershwin. New York, NY. Florence. Lang.: Eng. 3944

1946. **Plays/libretto/scripts.**
Realism and fantasy in *Questi fantasmi! (These Phantoms!)* by Eduardo De Filippo. Lang.: Ita. 2676

1946-1949. **Performance/production.**
Opera singer Ferruccio Furlanetto and his career. Salzburg. Lang.: Ger. 3698

1946-1986. **Design/technology.**
Career of costume and stage designer Eugenio Guglielminetti. Lang.: Ita. 299

1947-1950. **Plays/libretto/scripts.**
Correspondence of Alberto Savinio, author of *Alcesti di Samuele (Alcesti of Samuel)*. Lang.: Ita. 2716

1947-1985. **Performance/production.**
Productions of plays by Luigi Pirandello after World War II. Lang.: Ita. 1987

1947-1986. **Performance/production.**
Interview with Carlo Boso on *commedia dell'arte* reconstruction. UK-England. Lang.: Eng. 3415

1948. **Plays/libretto/scripts.**
Critical discussion of *La grande magia (The Great Magic)* by Eduardo De Filippo. Lang.: Ita. 2678

1950-1973. **Plays/libretto/scripts.**
Study of the librettos of operas premiered at the Teatro delle Novità festival. Bergamo. Lang.: Ita. 3883

1950-1986. **Performance/production.**
Conductor Claudio Abbado and his work at the Staatsoper. Vienna. Lang.: Ger. 3690

Maurizio Tiberi and his Tima Club records of operatic rarities. Castelnuovo del Porto. Lang.: Eng. 3756

1952. **Plays/libretto/scripts.**
Comparison of screenplay and film of *Umberto D.*, directed by Vittorio De Sica. Lang.: Fre. 3236

1956. **Plays/libretto/scripts.**
Italo Calvino's first libretto is based on one of his Marcovaldo stories. Lang.: Ita. 3884

1960-1978. **Plays/libretto/scripts.**
Letters of playwright Diego Fabbri. Lang.: Ita. 2672

1960-1986. **Performance/production.**
Dario Fo's fusion of slapstick and politics. Lang.: Eng. 749

1970-1985. **Performance/production.**
Examination of Italian avant-garde theatre. Lang.: Ita. 751

1970-1985. **Relation to other fields.**
Modern business methods in show business. Lang.: Ita. 1105

1970-1986. **Performance/production.**
Productions of Dario Fo's *Morte accidentale di un anarchico (Accidental Death of an Anarchist)* in the light of Fo's political ideas. USA. Canada. Lang.: Eng. 2262

1973. **Plays/libretto/scripts.**
Notes on Pier Paolo Pasolini's *Calderón*. Lang.: Ita. 2689

1973-1986. **Performance/production.**
Creative development of director Jurij Liubimov in Italy. USSR. Lang.: Ita. 2003

1976-1986. **Institutions.**
History of Compagnia Teatroinaria. Lang.: Ita. 506

1978. **Performance/production.**
Working environment of director Memè Perlini. Lang.: Eng. 1991

1980-1986. **Institutions.**
Innovation at Teatro La Fenice under the directorship of Italo Gomez. Venice. Lang.: Eng. 3676

1980-1986. **Performance/production.**
Amateur theatre festival initiated by Teatret La Luna (Århus). Amandola. Lang.: Swe. 747

1980-1986. **Relation to other fields.**
Contrasts between culture and mass media. Lang.: Ita. 3171

1981-1982. **Training.**
Transcription of a course on how theatrical texts are written. Rome. Lang.: Ita. 3159

1982-1986. **Institutions.**
Experimental productions of classical works by Collettivo di Parma. Parma. Lang.: Eng. 1579

1983. **Basic theatrical documents.**
English translation of *Coppia aperta, quasì spalancata (An Open Couple—Very Open)* by Dario Fo and Franca Rame. Trieste. Lang.: Eng. 1486

1984. **Performance/production.**
Discussion of international congress 'Theatre East and West'. Rome. Asia. Lang.: Eng. 744

Papers presented at a conference on puppets. Lang.: Ita. 3967

1984. **Reference materials.**
Yearbook of statistics on film, television, theatre and sports. Lang.: Ita. 1023

1984-1985. **Reference materials.**
Yearbook of information on the Italian theatre season. Lang.: Ita. 1022

1985. **Performance/production.**
Productions of operas at La Scala by Luca Ronconi. Milan. Lang.: Ita. 3763

1985. **Plays/libretto/scripts.**
Conference on the problems of adapting, interpreting and staging the classics. Hungary. Lang.: Hun. 2656

Women's issues in Italian theatre. Lang.: Cat. 2710

1985. **Reference materials.**
Books on theatre, film, music and dance published in Italy in 1985. Lang.: Ita. 1021

1985. **Theory/criticism.**
Semiotic analysis of *La Storia*. Lang.: Eng. 3118

1985-1986. **Performance/production.**
The Franco Zeffirelli film of *Otello* by Giuseppe Verdi, an account of the production. Rome. Lang.: Eng. 3758

1986. **Design/technology.**
Handbook of mask and puppet construction. Lang.: Ita. 3951

1986. **Performance/production.**
Program of *L'isola dei pappagalli (The Island of Parrots)* by Sergio Tofano at the Teatro Stabile in Turin. Turin. Lang.: Ita. 743

Comparison of Eastern and Western theatre. Rome. Lang.: Ita. 748

Documentation on Arno Holz's *Ignorabimus* directed by Luca Ronconi. Prato. Lang.: Ita. 1985

Overview of productions in Italy. Milan. Lang.: Eng. 1994

1986. **Plays/libretto/scripts.**
The link between comic and survival instincts. Lang.: Eng. 2688

Interview with Gillian Hanna about *Elisabetta: Quasì per caso una donna (Elizabeth: Almost by Chance a Woman)*. London. Lang.: Eng. 2875

Discussion of plays about Verdi and Puccini by Julian Mitchell and Robin Ray. London. Lang.: Eng. 3628

The town of Rimini and its attachment to *Francesca da Rimini*. Rimini. Lang.: Ita. 3890

1986. **Reference materials.**
Program of European Actors' Meeting, including criticism, texts and performances. Parma. Lang.: Ita. 1020

Yearbook of Italian theatrical productions. Lang.: Ita. 1025

Ivory Coast

Performance/production.
Maskers and masquerades of We tribal rituals. Lang.: Eng. 3341

Jamaica

1820-1970. **Plays/libretto/scripts.**
Precursors of revolutionary black theatre. Haiti. Lang.: Eng. 956

Jamaica — cont'd

1967.   **Plays/librettos/scripts.**
Symbolism in Derek Walcott's *Dream on Monkey Mountain.*
Lang.: Eng.   2718

Japan

Basic theatrical documents.
Notes on the sources of inspiration for Ohno Kazuo dances.
Lang.: Eng.   1265
                      Design/technology.
Nō actors make interpretive costume choices.   1386
The aesthetic qualities of the Yuki *no ko-omote* mask. Lang.:
Eng.   1388
The development of *nō* and *kyōgen* masks and the concerns
of the mask carver.   1390
Characteristics of different *nō* masks. Lang.: Eng.   1392
The meaning and significance of the *nō* mask. Lang.: Eng.
                                                                    1393
Carving techniques used in making the *ko-omote* mask.
Lang.: Eng.   1394
Nō actor talks about his work as a mask carver. Lang.: Eng.
                                                                    1395
Collection of pictures of *bunraku* puppet heads. Tokyo.
Lang.: Jap.   3997
                      Performance/production.
Role of the mask in popular theatre. Africa. Europe. Lang.:
Ita.   755
Western actors and the energy of Oriental performance.
Lang.: Ita.   756
Collection of pictures of famous *onnagata.* Tokyo. Lang.: Jap.
                                                                    1381
Nō actor discusses the centrality of *Okina* to his repertory.
Lang.: Eng.   1399
Nō actor Kanze Hisao and the actor's relationship with the
mask. Lang.: Eng.   1402
Kyōgen actor on the difference between *nō* and *kyōgen.* 1406
Career of *nō* artist Kitashichidayū Nagayoshi. Lang.: Jap.
                                                                    1407
The relationship between the *nō* actor and the mask. Lang.:
Eng.   1408
Interview with *nō* actor Kongō Iwao. Lang.: Eng.   1411
Introduction to *nō* and *kyōgen.*   1412
Special performances of *kyōgen* presented at the Mibu
Temple. Kyoto. Lang.: Jap.   1414
Dramaturgy and performance of *nō* drama. Lang.: Jap. 1415
500 B.C.-1986 A.D.   Theory/criticism.
Influences on the development of European and Japanese
theatre. Europe. Lang.: Ita.   1213
200-1986.   Theory/criticism.
Development and characteristics of Oriental theatre. Seoul.
Tokyo. Beijing. Lang.: Kor.   1215
800-899.   Performance/production.
Ancient sources relating to *nō* drama. Lang.: Jap.   1403
1060-1982.   Basic theatrical documents.
Kyōgen: history, training, and promotion. Lang.: Eng. 1384
1200-1500.   Reference materials.
Listing of theatrical productions. Tokyo. Lang.: Jap. 1028
1300-1400.   Performance/production.
Performances of *nō* plays dealing with Chinese subject
matter. Lang.: Jap.   1405
1300-1986.   Design/technology.
Collection of pictures of *nō* costumes. Lang.: Jap.   1389
1300-1986.   Theory/criticism.
Various aspects of *kyōgen.* Lang.: Jap.   1422
1350-1986.   Performance/production.
Collection of pictures about *nō* theatre. Lang.: Jap. 1400
1357-1441.   Performance/production.
Novel about founders of *nō* theatre. Lang.: Eng.   1397
1363-1443.   Basic theatrical documents.
Edition of Zeami's essays on *nō* theatre, organized by
subject. Lang.: Eng.   1385
1363-1443.   Performance/production.
Zeami's theories of performance technique. Lang.: Ita. 1401
1363-1470.   Theory/criticism.
Spiritual dimension of *nō* actor training. Lang.: Ita. 1421
1363-1986.   Design/technology.
Description of how *Nō* masks are made. Lang.: Eng.   1387

1363-1986.   Performance/production.
An outline formula of performance as derived from Asian
theatre. Lang.: Ita.   1364
1364-1443.   Performance/production.
Aesthetic evaluation of Zeami's techniques and work. Lang.:
Jap.   1410
1364-1443.   Theory/criticism.
Life and work of Zeami Motokiyo. Lang.: Jap.   1420
1400-1600.   Theory/criticism.
Influence of Korean mask-dance theatre in Japan. Seoul.
Lang.: Kor.   1377
1400-1986.   Theory/criticism.
Styles of mask-dance drama in Asia. Seoul. Tokyo. Beijing.
Lang.: Kor.   1378
1430.   Theory/criticism.
Translation and discussion of Zeami's *Sarugaku dangi.* Lang.:
Eng.   1423
1500-1600.   Performance/production.
On Western impressions of Eastern performances. China.
Lang.: Ita.   677
1596-1941.   Performance/production.
Development of performing arts related to formation of
Japanese national culture. Lang.: Rus.   8
1600-1800.   Plays/librettos/scripts.
A study of the *ai-kyōgen* texts in the Okura school. Lang.:
Jap.   1418
1600-1980.   Basic theatrical documents.
Collection of *kabuki* texts. Tokyo. Lang.: Jap.   1380
1600-1982.   Plays/librettos/scripts.
Adapting *Hamlet* for the *nō* theatre. England. Lang.: Ita.
                                                                    2506
1653-1724.   Basic theatrical documents.
Works of playwright Chikamatsu Monzaemon. Tokyo. Lang.:
Jap.   3995
1653-1725.   Plays/librettos/scripts.
Musical structure of dramas of Chikamatsu. Lang.: Eng. 4000
1760-1770.   Basic theatrical documents.
Text of *bunraku* play in English translation. Lang.: Eng.
                                                                    3996
1859-1986.   Reference materials.
Dictionary of the life and work of Tsubouchi Shōyō. Tokyo.
Lang.: Jap.   1027
1885-1972.   Relation to other fields.
Work of Ezra Pound and his relationship to *nō.* Lang.: Jap.
                                                                    1419
1899-1985.   Theory/criticism.
Shakespeare in media. UK-England. USA. Lang.: Eng. 3172
1900-1945.   Performance/production.
Reciprocal influences of French and Japanese theatre. France.
Lang.: Fre.   1750
1900-1950.   Plays/librettos/scripts.
Japanese influences on works of Brecht and Klabund.
Germany. Lang.: Ita.   952
1900-1986.   Performance/production.
Plays from Japan performed in Romania. Romania. Lang.:
Ita.   778
1900-1986.   Plays/librettos/scripts.
Lives and works of major contemporary playwrights in
Japan. Tokyo. Lang.: Jap.   2719
1906-1985.   Performance/production.
Interview with choreographer Ohno Kazuo. Lang.: Eng. 1278
1945-1964.   Performance/production.
History of schism in *Bunraku* puppetry. Lang.: Eng. 3998
1945-1985.   Performance/production.
Brief autobiography of dancer Tanaka Min. Tokyo. Lang.:
Eng.   1281
1948-1971.   Plays/librettos/scripts.
Film versions of Shakespeare's *Macbeth* by Orson Welles,
Akira Kurosawa and Roman Polanski. USA. Lang.: Eng.
                                                                    3243
1950-1984.   Institutions.
The Kaze-no-Ko: professional travelling children's theatre of
Japan. Lang.: Eng.   507
1950-1985.   Performance/production.
Butō dancer Tanaka Min speaks of early influences of Ohno
and Hojikata. Lang.: Eng.   1280
1950-1986.   Performance/production.
History of contemporary Japanese theatre. Tokyo. Lang.: Jap.
                                                                    757
1954-1986.   Plays/librettos/scripts.
Nō and Beckett compared. France. Lang.: Ita.   2721

Japan — cont'd

1959-1984.   Reference materials.
Chronology of major *butō* works and choreographers. Lang.:
Eng.   1287
1960-1970.   Basic theatrical documents.
Catalan translation of *Madame de Sade* by Mishima Yukio.
Lang.: Cat.   1487
1960-1970.   Plays/librettos/scripts.
Themes and characterization in *Madame de Sade* by
Mishima Yukio. Lang.: Cat.   2720
1960-1983.   Performance/production.
Narrator in *Katari* story-telling tradition. Lang.: Eng.   1366
1960-1986.   Performance/production.
Description of *butō*, avant-garde dance movement of Japan.
Lang.: Eng.   1279
1976-1985.   Basic theatrical documents.
Homage to *butō* dancer Hijikata Tatsumi by Tanaka Min.
Lang.: Eng.   1268
1979-1986.   Performance/production.
Discusses *Marie Antoinette Tonight!* by puppeteer Bruce D.
Schwartz. Los Angeles, CA. Tokyo. Lang.: Eng.   3981
1980-1983.   Performance/production.
Essays by Suzuki Tadashi encompassing his approach to
theatre, training, and performance. Lang.: Eng.   2007
1981-1984.   Institutions.
Reports on theatre conferences and festivals in Asia. Manila.
Kuala Lumpur. Toga. Calcutta. Lang.: Eng.   510
1981-1986.   Performance/production.
Influence of *kata* principle on Western acting technique.
Denmark. Australia. Lang.: Ita.   1365
1982.   Relation to other fields.
Anthropological approach to performance and language.
USA. Lang.: Eng.   1140
1983.   Performance/production.
Nō actor's preparation and rehearsal for the play, *Dōjōji*.
Lang.: Eng.   1413
1983-1984.   Performance/production.
Old and new forms in Japanese theatre. Lang.: Eng.   1382
1984.   Design/technology.
Carving, back finishing and coloring of *nō* masks.   1391
1984.   Performance/production.
The *kyōgen* actor's goals, relationship to mask work and
training.   1409
Director John Dillon on his Japanese production of *Death of
a Salesman* by Arthur Miller. Lang.: Eng.   2005
Tour of puppet show *The Return of the Bounce* by Jean
Mattson and Joan King. Seattle, WA. Lang.: Eng.   3979
A production of *At the Hawk's Well* using *nō* techniques.
Kyoto. Tokyo.   1396
1984-1985.   Basic theatrical documents.
Playtext of *Drifting Fires* by Janine Beichman, with author's
afterword on use of *Nō* elements. Ibaraki. Lang.: Eng.   1383
1985.   Basic theatrical documents.
Poem by Tanaka Min about his reasons for dancing. Lang.:
Eng.   1267
1985.   Design/technology.
Technical aspects relating to Toyota's showing of its new
automobile designs. Tokyo. Lang.: Eng.   3312
1985.   Institutions.
Report on International Festival of Theatre for Young
Audiences. Canada. Lang.: Fre.   482
1985.   Performance/production.
Suzuki's SCOT fuses diverse world cultures in ensemble
theatre company. Toga. Lang.: Eng.   1404
Bungei-za performs *Tóték (The Tót Family)* by István
Örkény. Toyama. Lang.: Hun.   2006
1985-1986.   Design/technology.
Lighting designer Kazuo Inoue discusses his lighting for a
rock concert. Yokohama. Lang.: Eng.   3434
1986.   Basic theatrical documents.
Notes for a *butō* dance. Lang.: Eng.   1266
1986.   Design/technology.
Film director Akira Kurosawa discusses designing *Ran*.
Lang.: Eng.   3200
1986.   Performance/production.
Essays on Japanese theatre. Lang.: Fre.   1398
Anthology of Japanese popular entertainments. Tokyo. Lang.:
Jap.   3342
The popular entertainment of *Inadani* in Nagano province.
Iida. Lang.: Jap.   3343

1986.   Reference materials.
Yearbook of major performances in all areas of Japanese
theatre. Tokyo. Lang.: Jap.   1026
1986.   Relation to other fields.
Study of agriculture-related songs and dances. Tokyo. Lang.:
Jap.   3360

Kenya

1885-1985.   Relation to other fields.
Introduction to *The Revenge of Truth* by Isak Dinesen.
Denmark. Lang.: Eng.   4010

Korea

**   Performance/production.**
Theory, practice and body-training for the beginning actor.
Seoul. Lang.: Kor.   758
**   Plays/librettos/scripts.**
Description of *p'ansori*, a traditional Korean entertainment.
Lang.: Eng.   3499
200 B.C.-1986 A.D.   Theory/criticism.
Theory and history of Korean theatre. Seoul. Lang.: Kor.
                                                              1214
Theory and origin of traditional street plays. Seoul. Lang.:
Kor.   3122
57 B.C.-1945 A.D.   Theory/criticism.
History of Korean theatre up to 1945. Lang.: Kor.   9
200-1986.   Theory/criticism.
Development and characteristics of Oriental theatre. Seoul.
Tokyo. Beijing. Lang.: Kor.   1215
700-1986.   Theory/criticism.
Evolution and symbolism of the Mask-Dance drama. Seoul.
Lang.: Kor.   1379
1400-1600.   Theory/criticism.
Influence of Korean mask-dance theatre in Japan. Seoul.
Japan. Lang.: Kor.   1377
1400-1986.   Theory/criticism.
Styles of mask-dance drama in Asia. Seoul. Tokyo. Beijing.
Lang.: Kor.   1378
1700-1900.   Plays/librettos/scripts.
Role analysis of the mask-dance play, *Yängjubyulsändae* and
the theories of Choe Sang-Su. Yängju. Lang.: Kor.   1375
1800-1950.   Theory/criticism.
Theories about the stage for the traditional *chäng-gük* play.
Seoul. Lang.: Kor.   3931
1884-1986.   Theory/criticism.
Influence of Henrik Ibsen on Korean theatre. Seoul. Norway.
Lang.: Kor.   3120
1900-1986.   Relation to other fields.
Origins of theatre in shamanistic ritual. Lang.: Ita.   1110
1920-1929.   Theory/criticism.
Theatre criticism of Kim Woo-Jin. Seoul. Lang.: Kor.   1216
1922-1924.   Institutions.
History of Korea's first theatre production company. Seoul.
Lang.: Kor.   509
1945-1986.   Design/technology.
Korean stage settings. Seoul. Lang.: Kor.   302
1950-1986.   Performance/production.
History of Korea's small theatre movement. Lang.: Kor.   759
1970-1979.   Theory/criticism.
Problems in Korean drama. Seoul. Lang.: Kor.   3121
1975.   Basic theatrical documents.
Text of *Kasan ogwangdae (The Five Buffoons of Kasan)* in
English translation. Kasan. Lang.: Eng.   1356
1975-1985.   Audience.
Survey of audience preferences for commercial theatre. Seoul.
Lang.: Kor.   200
1983-1984.   Performance/production.
Reviews of plays performed in the 1983-84 Seoul theatre
season. Seoul. Lang.: Eng.   2008
1985.   Administration.
Repertories of Korean Traditional Art Masters Festival.
Seoul. Lang.: Kor.   57
1985.   Performance/production.
Review of the play productions at the National Theatre
Festival. Lang.: Eng.   2010
1985-1986.   Institutions.
Future of the Korean National Theatre Association. Lang.:
Kor.   508
1985-1986.   Reference materials.
Profile and problems of Korean theatre people. Lang.: Kor.
                                                              1029
1986.   Administration.
Managing the Korean Theatre Festival. Lang.: Kor.   55

Korea — cont'd

Copyright protection in Korea. USA. Lang.: Kor.   56

Account of the International Folklore Festival. Seoul. Lang.: Kor.   58

1986.   **Design/technology.**
Set design and the current state of Korean theatre. Lang.: Kor.   303

1986.   **Performance/production.**
Directing and the current state of Korean theatre. Lang.: Kor.   760

Acting and the current state of Korean theatre. Lang.: Kor.   761

Theatre activities outside of Seoul. Lang.: Kor.   762

Reviews of the play productions at the National Theatre Festival. Lang.: Eng.   2009

1986.   **Plays/librettos/scripts.**
Playwriting and the current state of Korean theatre. Lang.: Kor.   961

Latin America
      Performance/production.
The New Theatre movement combines methodologies of collective creation with the Brechtian epic.   763

1185.   **Relation to other fields.**
Reports and discussions on theatre and colonialism. Spain. Lang.: Eng, Fre, Spa, Cat.   1128

Lebanon
1918-1985.   **Performance/production.**
Performance conditions of specific theatrical genres. Lang.: Fre.   2011

1980-1986.   **Performance/production.**
Contemporary Lebanese directing. Lang.: Rus.   764

1985.   **Relation to other fields.**
Reports and discussions of restricted cultural communication. Spain-Catalonia. USA. Lang.: Fre, Spa, Cat.   1111

Lithuania
ALSO SEE
USSR-Lithuanian SSR.

1986.   **Design/technology.**
Opera set designs by L. Trujkis. USSR. Lang.: Rus.   3664

Malaysia
1930-1985.   **Relation to other fields.**
Traditional Malay and European elements in children's theatre. Lang.: Eng.   1112

1950-1984.   **Performance/production.**
Dance in the Malaysian culture. Lang.: Eng.   1333

1981-1984.   **Institutions.**
Reports on theatre conferences and festivals in Asia. Manila. Kuala Lumpur. Toga. Calcutta. Lang.: Eng.   510

Martinique
1939.   **Plays/librettos/scripts.**
Analysis of *La Tragédie du roi Christophe (The Tragedy of King Christopher)* by Aimé Césaire. Haiti. Africa. Lang.: Fre.   2637

Mexico
      Plays/librettos/scripts.
Reflections and influence of playwrights Rodolfo Usigli of Mexico and Antonio Buero Vallejo of Spain on theatre in their native countries. Spain. Lang.: Spa.   2803

1519-1559.   **Relation to other fields.**
Assimilation of dramatic elements of Aztec worship in Christianization process. Spain. Lang.: Eng.   3046

1600-1680.   **Plays/librettos/scripts.**
Calderón's *El gran duque de Gandía (The Grand Duke of Gandía)* and its Mexican source. Spain. Lang.: Eng.   2789

1932.   **Basic theatrical documents.**
English translation of *Pequeña historia de horror (Little Tale of Horror)*. Lang.: Eng.   1488

1947-1985.   **Relation to other fields.**
Interview with Socorro Merlin, director of the Institute of Fine Arts. Mexico City. Lang.: Eng.   1113

1960-1980.   **Plays/librettos/scripts.**
Corona de luz (Crown of Light) by Rodolfo Usigli as a self-reflexive comment on the process of dramatizing an historical event. Lang.: Eng.   2722

1965-1986.   **Institutions.**
Origins and evolution of Teatro Campesino. USA. Lang.: Eng.   547

1970-1980.   **Plays/librettos/scripts.**
Use of language in *El Gesticulador (The Gesticulator)* by Rodolfo Usigli. Lang.: Spa.   2723

1982-1986.   **Theory/criticism.**
A semiotic reading of Carlos Fuentes' play *Orquídeas a la luz de la luna (Orchids in the Moonlight)*. Lang.: Eng.   3123

1986.   **Performance/production.**
Theatre Plus production of Santander's *Two Brothers*. Toronto, ON. Lang.: Eng.   1679

Monaco
1893-1951.   **Administration.**
Raoul Gunsbourg, director of Monte Carlo Opera for 59 years. Monte Carlo. Lang.: Eng.   3641

Moravia
ALSO SEE
Austro-Hungarian Empire.
ALSO SEE
Czechoslovakia.

Netherlands
1811.   **Performance/production.**
Performance of Comédie-Française actors in Amsterdam. Lang.: Fre.   2012

1980-1987.   **Institutions.**
History of Pantijn Muziekpoppentheater. Amsterdam. Lang.: Eng.   3958

1986.   **Design/technology.**
Account of meeting of OISTAT Executive Committee. Amsterdam. Lang.: Hun.   304

1986.   **Performance/production.**
Overview of performances, 'Holland '86'. Amsterdam. Lang.: Hun.   765

Youth theatre productions by Optater and Wederzijds. Amsterdam. Lang.: Eng.   766

New Zealand
1830-1980.   **Performance/production.**
Image of the indigène. Australia. Canada. Lang.: Eng.   656

1944-1986.   **Performance/production.**
Profile of and interview with New Zealand soprano Kiri Te Kanawa. Gisborne. New York, NY. Lang.: Eng.   3768

1950-1984.   **Plays/librettos/scripts.**
Women's roles in New Zealand theatre. Lang.: Eng.   2724

1980-1986.   **Performance/production.**
Development of women's and Maori theatre. Lang.: Eng.   767

1986.   **Reference materials.**
List of 37 productions of 23 Renaissance plays, with commentary. UK. USA. Lang.: Eng.   3000

Nicaragua
1983.   **Relation to other fields.**
The role of culture in Nicaragua since the revolution. Lang.: Eng.   1115

1985.   **Relation to other fields.**
Director Alan Bolt of the Nicaraguan National Theater Workshop discusses the process of theatre.   1114

Nigeria
1826-1986.   **Research/historiography.**
Examination of Joel Adedeji's thesis on *alárìnjó*, a Yoruba theatrical art form. Lang.: Eng.   1186

1957-1981.   **Plays/librettos/scripts.**
Shakespeare's influence on playwright Wole Soyinka. Leeds. Lang.: Eng.   2725

1960-1980.   **Theory/criticism.**
Analysis of Wole Soyinka's major critical essays. Lang.: Eng.   3124

1960-1985.   **Performance/production.**
Imprisoned Nigerian pop musician Fela Anikulapo-Kuti. Lagos. Lang.: Eng.   3468

1967-1984.   **Relation to other fields.**
Interview with playwright Wole Soyinka. New Haven, CT. Lang.: Eng.   3047

North America
375 B.C.-1983 A.D.   **Plays/librettos/scripts.**
Treatment of history in drama. Europe. Indonesia. Lang.: Eng.   2541

1700-1985.   **Performance/production.**
Study of the history of acting theory. Europe. Lang.: Eng.   704

1900-1985.   **Theory/criticism.**
Aesthetic theory of interpretation. Europe. Lang.: Fre.   3097

1920-1985.   **Performance spaces.**
An architect discusses theory of theatre construction. Europe. Lang.: Hun.   594

North America — cont'd

1929-1984. **Training.**
Physiological regulation for correct breathing and singing.
Europe. Lang.: Ger. 3937

1938-1986. **Performance/production.**
Antonin Artaud's conception of gesture and movement.
Lang.: Eng. 768

1950-1986. **Audience.**
The growth of musical theatre and opera since World War
II. Lang.: Eng. 3577

1980-1987. **Design/technology.**
Comparison of British and North America theatre sound
systems. UK-England. Lang.: Eng. 305

1983-1985. **Performance/production.**
Interview with choreographer Trisha Brown. Lang.: Eng.
1350

1985. **Training.**
Physical aspects of actor training. Europe. Lang.: Eng. 3157

1985-1986. **Performance/production.**
Report on the North American opera season. Lang.: Eng.
3769

1986. **Reference materials.**
Calendar of opera performances scheduled for the 1986-87
season throughout North America. Lang.: Eng. 3913

1986. **Design/technology.**
Nineteenth-century special effects. Europe. Lang.: Swe. 262

Norway

1607-1885. **Plays/librettos/scripts.**
Comparison of Shakespeare's *Antony and Cleopatra* and
Ibsen's *Rosmersholm*. England. Lang.: Eng. 2479

1849-1899. **Plays/librettos/scripts.**
Self-transcendence through grace embodied in Henrik Ibsen's
female characters. Lang.: Eng. 2726

1879. **Plays/librettos/scripts.**
Narcissism in *Et Dukkehjem (A Doll's House)* by Henrik
Ibsen. Lang.: Eng. 2727

1882. **Plays/librettos/scripts.**
Analysis of *En Folkefiende (An Enemy of the People)* by
Henrik Ibsen. Lang.: Eng. 2728

Absence of the author in Henrik Ibsen's *Vildanden (The
Wild Duck)*. Lang.: Eng. 2729

1884-1985. **Basic theatrical documents.**
Text of *Eiolf Hakatan*, Gad Kaynar's Hebrew translation of
Lille Eyolf (Little Eyolf) by Henrik Ibsen. Israel. Lang.: Heb.
1489

1884-1985. **Plays/librettos/scripts.**
Introductory note on the first translation of *Lille Eyolf (Little
Eyolf)* into Hebrew. Israel. Lang.: Heb. 962

1884-1986. **Theory/criticism.**
Influence of Henrik Ibsen on Korean theatre. Seoul. Lang.:
Kor. 3120

1986. **Design/technology.**
Translation of a report on NOTT conference. Geilo. Lang.:
Hun. 306

Ottoman Empire
SEE
Turkey.

Peru

Plays/librettos/scripts.
Levels of time in *La señorita de Tacna (The Lady from
Tacna)* by Mario Vargas Llosa. Lang.: Spa. 2731

1599-1620. **Basic theatrical documents.**
Contract of first known theatre company in America. Lima.
Lang.: Spa. 225

1970-1984. **Plays/librettos/scripts.**
Influence and development of the plays of Julio Ortega.
Lang.: Eng. 2730

1971-1985. **Performance/production.**
Interview with Mario Delgado Vásquez, director of
Cuatrotablas. Lima. Lang.: Hun. 769

Philippines

1981-1984. **Institutions.**
Reports on theatre conferences and festivals in Asia. Manila.
Kuala Lumpur. Toga. Calcutta. Lang.: Eng. 510

1983-1985. **Plays/librettos/scripts.**
Prison camp passion play with Christ as a labor organizer.
Davao City. Lang.: Eng. 2732

Poland

Theory/criticism.
Andrzej Hausbrandt (critic) and Gustaw Holoubek (actor)
discuss their views on general problems of theatre. Lang.:
Pol. 1217

1600-1984. **Plays/librettos/scripts.**
Collection of essays on dramatic text and performance.
Lang.: Fre. 2742

1765-1930. **Performance/production.**
Collection of articles by critic and theatre historian Wiktor
Brumer. Lang.: Pol. 2016

1772-1821. **Relation to other fields.**
Commentary on *Diabel włoski (Italian Devil)* by Stanisław
Potocki. Lang.: Pol. 3922

1779-1833. **Design/technology.**
Description of the decor equipment used in the Narodowy
Theatre. Warsaw. Lang.: Pol. 309

1782-1793. **Institutions.**
Foundation of Polish theatre in Poznań in 1783, its
repertoire and political contexts. Poznań. Lang.: Pol. 512

1786-1864. **Performance/production.**
Description of first translations and adaptations of
Shakespeare's dramas on the Polish stage. Vilna. Lang.: Pol.
2030

1789-1864. **Performance/production.**
Description of performances by touring companies from
Vilna. Lang.: Pol. 2026

1798-1855. **Theory/criticism.**
Adam Mickiewicz's theory of theatrical poetry. Lang.: Eng.
3125

1799-1883. **Performance/production.**
Business dealings of actor Adam Dmuszewski. Lang.: Pol.
2018

1800-1863. **Basic theatrical documents.**
Photographs of playbills from Soviet archives. Vilna. Lang.:
Pol. 1491

1800-1915. **Plays/librettos/scripts.**
Literary and theatrical history of Eastern Europe. Hungary.
Czechoslovakia. Lang.: Hun. 2755

1800-1978. **Reference materials.**
Theatre documents and listing of playtexts in the Polish
theatre in Lvov. Lvov. Katowice. Lang.: Pol. 2996

1835-1976. **Plays/librettos/scripts.**
Polish drama performed in Sweden. Sweden. Lang.: Pol. 975

1835-1984. **Plays/librettos/scripts.**
Different interpretations of Zygmunt Krasiński's *Ne-boska
komedia (Undivine Comedy)*. Lang.: Fre. 2756

1844-1861. **Relation to other fields.**
Poet, dramatist, critic and satirist Władysław Syrokomla.
Vilna. Warsaw. Lang.: Pol. 3052

1873-1907. **Administration.**
Russian censorship of classic repertory in Polish theatres.
Warsaw. Russia. Lang.: Rus, Pol. 1438

1878-1914. **Performance/production.**
Review of book on Polish proletarian theatre society. Lang.:
Pol. 774

1880-1985. **Performance spaces.**
Description of theatre buildings designed by architect
Czesław Przybylski. Warsaw. Vilna. Kalisz. Lang.: Pol. 611

1882-1913. **Performance/production.**
Visits to Poland by Russian theatre troupes. Russia. Lang.:
Pol. 2043

1886-1970. **Plays/librettos/scripts.**
Overview of major productions of playwright Jerzy
Szaniawski. Lang.: Eng, Fre. 2753

1887-1954. **Performance/production.**
Life and work of cabaret singer and stage director Leon
Schiller. Lang.: Eng, Fre. 2014

1900-1954. **Performance/production.**
Overview of correspondence between Leon Schiller and
Edward Gordon Craig. Warsaw. Paris. Lang.: Eng, Fre. 2022

1901-1984. **Plays/librettos/scripts.**
Material derived from Stanisław Wyspiański's *Wesele (The
Wedding)* by various Polish playwrights. Lang.: Fre. 2741

1905. **Relation to other fields.**
Reopening of Polish theatre after over forty years of
repression. Vilna. Lang.: Pol. 1120

1905-1986. **Theory/criticism.**
Analysis of critic Tymon Terlecki's theoretical concepts.
Lang.: Pol. 3128

1908-1986. **Theory/criticism.**
Description of various theatrical activities. Vilna. Lang.: Pol.
10

1909-1934. **Relation to other fields.**
Views of designer and critic Franciszek Siedlecki. Lang.: Pol.
1116

GEOGRAPHICAL - CHRONOLOGICAL INDEX

Poland — cont'd

1915-1985. **Performance/production.**
Career and philosophy of director Tadeusz Kantor. Lang.:
Eng. 2028

1918-1920. **Relation to other fields.**
Actor Stanisław Kwaskowski talks about the first years of
independent Poland. Lang.: Pol. 1121

1918-1947. **Relation to other fields.**
Actor-director Juliusz Osterwa's ideas about theatre's role in
society. Lang.: Pol. 1118

1918-1986. **Performance/production.**
Collection of articles by critic and theatre historian Stanisław
Marczak-Oborski. Lang.: Pol. 2034

1919-1939. **Institutions.**
The Reduta theatre as the predecessor of Grotowski's
Laboratory. Warsaw. Lang.: Fre. 1581

1920-1935. **Plays/librettos/scripts.**
Analysis of animal-like characters in Witkiewicz's dramas.
Lang.: Pol. 2757

1920-1986. **Performance/production.**
Recollections of actor, director and professor Aleksander
Zelwerowicz. Lang.: Pol. 772

1920-1986. **Plays/librettos/scripts.**
Philosophy and obscenity in the plays of Tadeusz Różewicz.
Lang.: Pol. 2750

1921-1933. **Design/technology.**
Irena Pikiel, Polish puppet theatre stage-designer, describes
her years in satirical performances. Vilna. Lang.: Pol. 3952

1921-1985. **Plays/librettos/scripts.**
Production history of plays by Stanisław Ignacy Witkiewicz.
Lang.: Eng, Fre. 2754

1923-1984. **Performance/production.**
A stage history of the work of Bertolt Brecht. 2050

1924. **Performance/production.**
Actor-director Edmund Wierciński on Reduta Theatre. Lang.:
Pol. 775

1926-1986. **Performance/production.**
Djrector Andrzei Wajda's work, accessibility to Polish
audiences. Warsaw. Lang.: Swe. 2027

1929-1986. **Plays/librettos/scripts.**
Philosophical aspects and structure of plays by Bogusław
Schaeffer. Lang.: Pol. 2749

1930-1939. **Performance/production.**
Recollections of actor-directors Irena and Tadeusz Byrski.
Vilna. Lang.: Pol. 2017

1931-1939. **Relation to other fields.**
Suicide of playwright Stanisław Witkiewicz. Lang.: Pol. 3050

1933-1976. **Performance/production.**
Career of director Jerzy Grotowski. Lang.: Eng. 773

1933-1982. **Theory/criticism.**
Selections from Jerzy Grotowski's *Towards a Poor Theatre*.
Lang.: Chi. 3126

1933-1986. **Performance/production.**
Composer Krzysztof Penderecki and his new opera *Die
schwarze Maske (The Black Mask)*, based upon a play by
Gerhart Hauptmann. Salzburg. Lang.: Ger. 3700

1935-1936. **Performance/production.**
Details of Wileński Touring Theatre. Vilna. Lang.: Pol. 2020

1938-1940. **Performance/production.**
Repertory and artistic achievements of the Na Pohulance
Theatre. Vilna. Lang.: Pol. 2036

1940-1944. **Institutions.**
Cultural activities in the Lodz ghetto. Łódź. Lang.: Heb.
3323

1940-1947. **Relation to other fields.**
Actor-director Juliusz Osterwa's views of historical processes.
Lang.: Pol. 1122

1940-1949. **Plays/librettos/scripts.**
Analysis of plays of Kruczkowski, Szaniawski and Gałczyński.
Lang.: Pol. 2746

1942-1985. **Performance/production.**
Interview with director Tadeusz Kantor. Lang.: Hun. 2055

1944-1986. **Plays/librettos/scripts.**
Influence of politics and personal history on Tadeusz Kantor
and his Cricot 2 theatre company. Cracow. Lang.: Eng. 2744

1945. **Plays/librettos/scripts.**
Interpretation of Fortinbras in post-war productions of
Hamlet. UK-England. Lang.: Eng. 2748

1945-1955. **Plays/librettos/scripts.**
World War II and post-war life as major subjects of Polish
dramaturgy. Lang.: Pol. 2745

1945-1984. **Plays/librettos/scripts.**
School use of Juliusz Słowacki's dramas in Polish high
schools as a reflection of the political situation. Lang.: Fre.
2743

1945-1986. **Relation to other fields.**
Analysis of contemporary drama from various viewpoints.
Lang.: Pol. 3049

1946-1986. **Reference materials.**
Writings by and about director Tadeusz Kantor. Lang.: Eng.
2995

1955-1980. **Plays/librettos/scripts.**
Loss of identity in plays by István Örkény's and Sławomir
Mrożek. Hungary. Lang.: Hun. 2752

1956-1985. **Basic theatrical documents.**
Writings by Tadeusz Kantor on the nature of theatre. Lang.:
Eng. 1490

1956-1986. **Institutions.**
Thirty years of the Polish theatrical monthly *Dialog*. Warsaw.
Lang.: Pol. 511

1958. **Plays/librettos/scripts.**
Mrożek's *Policja (The Police)* as read by the censor. Lang.:
Fre. 2735

1958-1962. **Relation to other fields.**
Political situation and new plays on the Polish stage. Lang.:
Pol. 3051

1958-1986. **Performance/production.**
Overview of the career of Jerzy Grotowski, his theatrical
experiments, training methodology and thoughts on the
purpose of theatre. Lang.: Eng. 2054

1959-1984. **Performance/production.**
Analysis of career and methods of director Jerzy Grotowski.
Lang.: Hun. 771

Analysis of the directorial style of Jerzy Grotowski. Wrocław.
Lang.: Pol. 2044

1959-1985. **Relation to other fields.**
Dissolution of Jerzy Grotowski's Laboratory Theatre.
Wrocław. Lang.: Eng. 1117

1960-1986. **Relation to other fields.**
Alternative theatre and the political situation. Lang.: Pol.
1119

1961-1979. **Plays/librettos/scripts.**
Analysis of *Grupa Laokoona (The Laocoön Group)* by
Tadeusz Różewicz and *Tsaplia (The Heron)* by Vasilij
Aksënov. USSR. Lang.: Eng. 2738

1963-1985. **Performance/production.**
Interviews with Polish theatre professionals. Poznań. Lang.:
Eng. 2024

1964. **Plays/librettos/scripts.**
Jerzy Grotowski and his adaptation of *Doctor Faustus*. Lang.:
Eng. 2740

1967-1985. **Performance/production.**
Interview with director Tadeusz Kantor. Lang.: Eng. 2029

1968-1985. **Relation to other fields.**
Interview with director Lech Raczak of Theatre of the
Eighth Day. Poznań. Lang.: Eng. 3048

1970. **Performance/production.**
Spalding Gray's memories of the development and tour of
Richard Schechner's *Commune*. USA. France. Lang.: Eng.
2270

1973-1983. **Plays/librettos/scripts.**
Analysis of the theatrical ideas of Tadeusz Kantor. Cracow.
Lang.: Pol. 2759

1973-1986. **Performance/production.**
Artistic profile and main achievements of Akademia Ruchu.
Warsaw. Lang.: Pol. 2037

1976-1983. **Performance/production.**
Director Kazimierz Braun on his adaptation of *La Peste
(The Plague)* by Albert Camus. Wrocław. Lang.: Eng. 2015

1980. **Performance/production.**
Othello, translated by Bohdan Drozdowski and directed by
Wilfred Harrison at the Wilama Horzycy Theatre. Toruń.
Lang.: Eng. 2023

1982-1986. **Performance/production.**
The achievements and style of director Krzysztof Babicki.
Lang.: Pol. 2047

1983. **Performance/production.**
Peter Stein directs Aeschylus' *Oresteia* in Warsaw. Berlin,
West. Warsaw. Lang.: Pol. 1768

Review of Biblical passion play by National Theatre of
Budapest. Budapest. Warsaw. Lang.: Pol. 1899

Poland — cont'd

Andrzej Pawłowski directs Gombrowicz's *Pornografia (Pornography)*. Warsaw. Lang.: Pol.   2038

Mikołaj Grabowski directs *Irydion* by Zygmunt Krasiński. Cracow. Lang.: Pol.   2046

Shakespeare's *Hamlet* directed by Janusz Warmiński. Warsaw. Lang.: Pol.   2051

Zygmunt Hübner directs Gombrowicz's *Iwona, Ksiezniczka Burgundia (Ivona, Princess of Burgundia)*. Warsaw. Lang.: Pol.   2052

Robert Sturua of Georgian Academic Theatre directs Brecht and Shakespeare in Warsaw. Tbilisi. Warsaw. Lang.: Pol.   2336

Jan Wolkowski directs an adaptation of a folk legend about Jedrzej Wowrze. Szczecin. Lang.: Pol.   3968

1984.   Performance/production.

Interview with Peter Stein, director of Schaubühne am Helleschen Ufer. Berlin, West. Warsaw. Lang.: Pol.   731

Andrzej Marczewski directs Andrzejewski's *Popioł i Diament (Ashes and Diamonds)*, Teatr Rozmaitości. Warsaw. Lang.: Pol.   2013

Adam Hanuszkiewicz directs Corneille's *Le Cid* at Teatr Ateneum. Warsaw. Lang.: Pol.   2021

Andrzej Łapicki directs Aleksander Fredro's *Śluby Panienskie (Maiden Vows)*, Teatr Polski. Warsaw. Lang.: Pol.   2031

Adaptation of Dostojévskij's *Prestuplenijė i nakazanijė (Crime and Punishment)* directed by Andrzej Wajda at Teatr Stary under the title *Zdrodnia i Kara*. Cracow. Lang.: Pol.   2032

Tadeusz Łomnicki directs Pasolini's *Affabulazione* at Centrum Sztuki Studio. Warsaw. Lang.: Pol.   2033

Krystyna Meissner directs Juliusz Słowacki's *Balladyna*, Teatr Horzycy. Toruń. Lang.: Pol.   2035

Janusz Nyczak directs Michał Pałucki's *Dom Otwarty (Open House)* at Teatr Nowy. Poznań. Lang.: Pol.   2039

Krzysztof Babicki directs Różewicz's *Pułapka (Trap)*. Gdansk. Lang.: Pol.   2040

Laco Adamik directs Ferdinand Brückner's *Elisabeth von England* under the title *Elzbieta, Królowa Anglii*. Cracow. Lang.: Pol.   2041

Krzysztof Rościszewski directs Gombrowicz's *Iwona, Księzniczka Burgundia (Ivona, Princess of Burgundia)*, Teatr Polski. Bydgoszcz. Lang.: Pol.   2042

Józef Skwark directs Gorkij's *Dačniki (Summer Folk)* under the title *Letnicy*. Warsaw. Lang.: Pol.   2045

Jerzy Krasowski of Teatr Mały directs Ryszard Frelka's *Jalta (Yalta)*. Warsaw. Lang.: Pol.   2048

Jerzy Grzegorzewski directs Różewicz's *Pułapka (Trap)* at Centrum Sztuki Studio. Warsaw. Lang.: Pol.   2053

Tubieński's *Śmieré Komandura (The Death of the Commander)* directed by Eugeniusz Korin, Teatr Polski. Wrocław. Lang.: Pol.   2056

Kazimierz Dejmek directs Wyspiański's *Wesele (The Wedding)*, Teatr Polski. Warsaw. Lang.: Pol.   2057

Andrzej Wajda directs Sophocles' *Antigone*, Stary Teatr. Cracow. Lang.: Pol.   2058

Ignacy Gogolewski of Teatr Osterwy directs Wyspiański's *Wesele (The Wedding)*. Lublin. Lang.: Pol.   2059

Tadeusz Kantor directs his *Gdzie sa Niegdysiejsze Śniegi (Where Are the Snows of Yesteryear)*, Cricot 2. Cracow. Lang.: Pol.   2061

Michał Ratyński directs Różewicz's *Kartoteka (Card Index)*, Teatr Powszechny. Warsaw. Lang.: Pol.   2062

Abraham Goldfaden's *Sen O Goldfadenie (Dream About Goldfaden)* directed by Jacob Rotbaum, Teatr Zydowski. Warsaw. Lang.: Pol.   3490

Andrzej Straszyński directs Donizetti's *Lucia di Lammermoor*, Teatr Wielki. Warsaw. Lang.: Pol.   3770

1984.   Relation to other fields.

Polish theatre posters. Lang.: Pol.   1123

1985.   Performance/production.

Description of the festival of Russian and Soviet drama with reviews of performances. Katowice. USSR. Lang.: Eng, Fre.   2049

Description of street theatre festival. Jelenia Góra. Lang.: Eng, Fre.   3344

1985.   Plays/librettos/scripts.

Description of international symposium discussing the work of Stanisław Ignacy Witkiewicz. Lang.: Eng, Fre.   2733

Overview of symposium on playwright Stanisław Ignacy Witkiewicz. Lang.: Eng, Fre.   2747

Tadeusz Kantor comments on his play *Niech szezna artyszi (Let the Artists Die)*. Lang.: Eng, Fre.   2751

1985.   Theory/criticism.

Conferences on theory of performance. USA. Lang.: Eng, Fre.   3127

1986.   Audience.

Reactions of Polish teenagers to the plays (1920s) of poet and playwright Tadeusz Różewicz. Lang.: Pol.   1451

1986.   Design/technology.

Overview of conference on visual art in theatre. Lang.: Eng, Fre.   307

Report on exhibition in Warsaw, especially on the S20 dimmer used by the lighting director of the Thália Theatre in Budapest. Warsaw. Budapest. Lang.: Hun.   308

Account of meeting of OISTAT technicians' committee. Warsaw. Lang.: Hun.   310

1986.   Performance/production.

Impressions of Warsaw's theatres and the training of Polish actors. Warsaw. Lang.: Swe.   770

Overview of the season's productions, with emphasis on Czechoslovakian authors. Prague. Brno. Warsaw. Lang.: Hun.   1695

Performances of the 15th festival of contemporary Polish drama. Wrocław. Lang.: Hun.   2019

Interview with director and cast of Wajda's *Crime and Punishment*. Cracow. USA. Lang.: Eng.   2025

On the Tenth Festival of Russian and Soviet Theatre in Poland. Katowice. USSR. Lang.: Rus.   2060

1986.   Plays/librettos/scripts.

Analysis of Tomasz Łubieński's plays. Lang.: Pol.   2734

Interview with director of Teatr Współczésny about children's drama competition. Wrocław. Lang.: Hun.   2736

Death in the plays of Tadeusz Różewicz. Lang.: Pol.   2737

Analysis of contemporary Polish plays dealing with solitude. Lang.: Pol.   2739

Analysis of the play *Operetka (Operetta)* by Witold Gombrowicz. Lang.: Pol.   2758

Portugal

1985.   Performance/production.

Survey of Portuguese theatrical life, including discussion of both large and small theatres. Lang.: Hun.   776

Prussia

SEE

Germany.

Puerto Rico

1960-1980.   Plays/librettos/scripts.

Development of recent Puerto Rican drama. Lang.: Spa.   2760

Roman Republic

100 B.C.   Performance/production.

Translation of *The Roman Stage* by William Beare. Rome. Lang.: Ita.   777

Romania

1900-1986.   Performance/production.

Plays from Japan performed in Romania. Japan. Lang.: Ita.   778

1925-1985.   Performance/production.

Interview with director György Harag. Tîrgu-Mures. Lang.: Hun.   2064

1927-1984.   Plays/librettos/scripts.

Review of a monograph on András Sütő. Hungary. Lang.: Hun.   2657

1945-1980.   Performance/production.

Career of actor/director György Várady. Hungary. Lang.: Hun.   1802

1950-1984.   Plays/librettos/scripts.

Study of author and playwright András Sütő. Hungary. Lang.: Hun.   2762

Review of a study of playwright and novelist András Sütő. Lang.: Hun.   2763

1950-1986.   Performance/production.

Profile of and interview with Romanian-born conductor Christian Berea. New York, NY. Lang.: Eng.   3771

Romania — cont'd

1965-1985. **Plays/librettos/scripts.**
Interview with playwright András Sütő. Hungary. Lang.: Hun.
957

1976-1984. **Plays/librettos/scripts.**
Monodramas of playwright István Kocsis. Hungary. Lang.:
Hun. 2761

1978. **Plays/librettos/scripts.**
Dramatic elements in wedding celebrations. Armăseni. Lang.:
Hun. 963

1980. **Performance/production.**
Reviews of performances at various theatres. Bucharest.
Lang.: Rus. 779

1980-1986. **Training.**
Stanislavskij system in Romanian theatre. USSR. Lang.: Rus.
1264

1984-1985. **Performance/production.**
Notes on production of the Állami Magyar Szinház and its
late director György Harag. Cluj. Lang.: Hun. 2063

Russia

ALSO SEE
USSR-Russian SFSR.
Relation to other fields.
Ancient Russian rituals linked with the 'ship of souls' theme
in world culture. Lang.: Rus. 1124
Theory/criticism.
Relation of short story and drama in the plays of Anton
Pavlovič Čechov and Eugene O'Neill. USA. Lang.: Eng.
3130

1700-1985. **Plays/librettos/scripts.**
History of Russian opera, with detailed articles on individual
works and composers. Lang.: Ger. 3892

1712-1914. **Plays/librettos/scripts.**
Report on exhibit at State Historical Museum, Leningrad,
dedicated to pre- and post-Lenten public festivals. St.
Petersburg. Lang.: Rus. 3373

1717-1777. **Performance/production.**
Dance-pantomime dramas based on the plots of plays by
Aleksand'r Sumarokov. Lang.: Rus. 1367

1729-1763. **Performance/production.**
Career of actor Fëdor Grigorjèvič Volkov. Lang.: Rus. 786

1751-1792. **Plays/librettos/scripts.**
Biography of playwright Jakob Lenz. Germany. Moscow.
Lang.: Ger. 2594

1761-1819. **Plays/librettos/scripts.**
Biography of playwright August von Kotzebue. Weimar. St.
Petersburg. Lang.: Ger. 2596

1766-1826. **Plays/librettos/scripts.**
Western European influences on playwright Nikolaj M.
Karamzin. Lang.: Rus. 965

1768-1803. **Performance/production.**
Serf actress P.I. Žemčugova. Lang.: Rus. 2071

1800-1850. **Relation to other fields.**
Sources of Ukrainian dramaturgy. Lang.: Rus. 3053

1800-1917. **Performance/production.**
Careers of Sadovskije acting family. Moscow. Lang.: Rus.
784

Development of the *raëk* or gallery as a folk entertainment.
Lang.: Rus. 3345

1808-1816. **Performance/production.**
History of theatre in Char'kov and Poltava. Char'kov.
Poltava. Lang.: Ukr. 11

1818-1883. **Plays/librettos/scripts.**
Analysis of the plays of Ivan Turgenjev. Lang.: Rus. 2770

1821-1881. **Plays/librettos/scripts.**
Life and work of playwright Aleksej Feofilaktovič Pisemskij.
Lang.: Rus. 2767

1823-1886. **Plays/librettos/scripts.**
The tragedy in the plays of Aleksand'r Nikolajèvič
Ostrovskij. Lang.: Rus. 2771

System of genres in the work of A.N. Ostrovskij. Lang.: Rus.
2772

1833-1890. **Plays/librettos/scripts.**
Puškin's *Queen of Spades* adapted for opera by Čajkovskij.
Lang.: Eng. 3891

1836. **Performance/production.**
Collaboration of Nikolaj Gogol in first production of *Revizor*
(The Inspector General). Lang.: Ita. 2069

1842-1852. **Plays/librettos/scripts.**
Dramaturgy of Turgenjev. Lang.: Rus. 2768

1845-1900. **Performance/production.**
History of productions of A.S. Griboedov's *Gore ot uma (Wit
Works Woe)*. Lang.: Rus. 780

1850-1890. **Performance/production.**
The alcoholism of Modest Pavlovič Mussorgskij prevented the
completion of *Chovanščina*. St. Petersburg. Lang.: Eng. 3777

1850-1900. **Performance/production.**
Collected articles and reviews by composer Pëtr Iljič
Čajkovskij. Lang.: Rus. 3772

1860-1904. **Plays/librettos/scripts.**
Recollections of Anton Pavlovič Čechov by some of his
contemporaries. Lang.: Rus. 2765

1860-1986. **Performance/production.**
Plays of Čechov interpreted in theatre and ballet. Lang.:
Rus. 2068

1863-1938. **Theory/criticism.**
Stanislavskij's aesthetic criteria. Lang.: Rus. 1218

1868-1936. **Plays/librettos/scripts.**
Analysis of the major plays of Maksim Gorkij. Lang.: Chi.
2769

1869. **Performance/production.**
Performance history of *Gorjačego serdca (The Burning Heart)*
by Aleksand'r Nikolajèvič Ostrovskij. Lang.: Rus. 2067

1872-1929. **Performance/production.**
European career of Serge de Diaghilew. France. Lang.: Ita.
1312

1873-1907. **Administration.**
Russian censorship of classic repertory in Polish theatres.
Warsaw. Lang.: Rus, Pol. 1438

1873-1924. **Theory/criticism.**
Symbolist poet Valerij Brjusov's ideas on theatre. Lang.: Ita.
3131

1873-1938. **Performance/production.**
Life and career of singer Fëdor J. Šaljapin. Moscow. Lang.:
Rus. 3773

1874. **Performance/production.**
Mussorgskij's opera *Boris Godunov* at the Mariinskij Theatre.
St. Petersburg. Lang.: Eng. 3775

1878. **Basic theatrical documents.**
Text of Čechov's *Platonov* in a version by Michael Frayn.
Lang.: Cat. 1492

1878-1960. **Plays/librettos/scripts.**
History of the writing and diffusion of Čechov's *Platonov
(Wild Honey)*. USSR. Lang.: Cat. 2764

1879-1953. **Performance/production.**
Career of director and playwright, Nikolaj Nikolajèvič
Jèvreinov. USSR. Lang.: Hun. 2066

1880-1921. **Plays/librettos/scripts.**
Poetic and dramatic elements in the plays of Aleksand'r
Blok. Lang.: Rus. 2766

1880-1934. **Theory/criticism.**
Andrej Belyj's views on Symbolist and Realist theatre,
dramaturgy. Lang.: Rus. 3129

1882-1913. **Performance/production.**
Visits to Poland by Russian theatre troupes. Poland. Lang.:
Pol. 2043

1883. **Plays/librettos/scripts.**
Historical information on Oscar Wilde's *Vera, or The
Nihilists*. England. New York, NY. Lang.: Rus. 944

1885-1922. **Plays/librettos/scripts.**
Poetic language in plays of Velimir Chlebnikov. Lang.: Rus.
964

1885-1960. **Performance/production.**
On the career of dancer and actress Ida Rubinstein, member
of Diaghilew's 'Russian Seasons'. France. Lang.: Rus. 1311

1886-1961. **Performance/production.**
Biography of singer N.A. Obychova. Lang.: Rus. 3776

1891-1940. **Performance/production.**
Michajl Bulgakov's ties with Moscow Art Theatre. Moscow.
Lang.: Rus. 785

1891-1955. **Performance/production.**
Literary legacy of Michajl A. Čechov. USA. Lang.: Rus. 781

1895-1986. **Performance/production.**
Biographical materials on Bolšoj singer Mark Rejzen.
Moscow. Lang.: Rus. 3774

1898-1948. **Performance/production.**
Eastern and Western elements in Sergej Eisenstein's work.
Lang.: Ita. 3225

1898-1986. **Institutions.**
Foundation and brief history of Moscow Art Theatre.
Moscow. Lang.: Rus. 513

Spain — cont'd

1562-1635.   Plays/librettos/scripts.
Lope de Vega's characterization of the converted Jew. Lang.:
Spa.   2804

1580-1648.   Plays/librettos/scripts.
Female sexuality in Tirso de Molina's *El vergonzoso en
palacio (The Shy Man at Court)*. Lang.: Eng.   969
Emblematic pictorialism in *La mujer que manda en casa
(The Woman Who Rules the Roost)* by Tirso de Molina.
Lang.: Eng.   970

1600-1680.   Plays/librettos/scripts.
Prophecy in Calderón's *Eco y Narciso (Echo and Narcissus)*.
Lang.: Eng.   2787
Calderón's *El gran duque de Gandía (The Grand Duke of
Gandía)* and its Mexican source. Mexico. Lang.: Eng.   2789

1600-1699.   Plays/librettos/scripts.
The institution of slavery as presented in *Entremés de los
negros (Play of the Blacks)*. Lang.: Eng.   2796

1600-1700.   Plays/librettos/scripts.
Conservative and reactionary nature of the Spanish *Comedia*.
Lang.: Eng.   2782

1609-1624.   Theory/criticism.
Lope de Vega's theories of comedy. Lang.: Spa.   3132

1609-1950.   Plays/librettos/scripts.
Examples of playwrights whose work was poorly received by
theatrical audiences in Madrid. Madrid. Lang.: Spa.   2786

1615-1936.   Relation to other fields.
Comparison of playwright Luigi Pirandello and novelist
Miguel de Cervantes. Italy. Lang.: Ita.   3040

1635-1681.   Plays/librettos/scripts.
Thematic analysis of *La vida es sueño (Life Is a Dream)* by
Pedro Calderón de la Barca. Lang.: Eng.   2788

1817-1982.   Institutions.
History of theatre in Valencia area focusing on Civil War
period. Valencia. Lang.: Cat.   514

1845-1983.   Plays/librettos/scripts.
Adaptations of *Carmen* by Prosper Mérimée. France. Lang.:
Fre.   3870

1898-1936.   Plays/librettos/scripts.
Biographical study of playwright Federico García Lorca.
Granada. Madrid. New York, NY. Lang.: Eng.   971

1903-1972.   Basic theatrical documents.
English translation of *El desconfiado prodigioso (The
Remarkable Misanthrope)* by Max Aub. Lang.: Eng, Spa.
                                                                                    1493

1909.   Plays/librettos/scripts.
Parody and satire in Ramón del Valle-Inclán's *La Cabeza
del dragón (The Dragon's Head)*. Lang.: Eng.   2798

1928-1986.   Performance/production.
Profile of and interview with Spanish soprano Pilar
Lorengar. Zaragoza. San Francisco, CA. Lang.: Eng.   3778

1936-1986.   Performance/production.
Review of *Spain/36* by San Francisco Mime Troupe. San
Francisco, CA. Lang.: Eng.   790

1940-1980.   Plays/librettos/scripts.
Discusses Christian outlook in plays by Alejandro Casona.
Lang.: Eng.   2795

1940-1985.   Plays/librettos/scripts.
Description of plays by Eduardo Quiles including *La navaja
(The Razor)* a tragicomedy for two actors and puppets.
Lang.: Spa.   2780

1941-1986.   Performance/production.
Interview with tenor and conductor Plácido Domingo.
Madrid. Lang.: Eng.   3779

1951-1986.   Performance/production.
Use of stagehands in production of modern passion play.
Lang.: Eng.   2075

1952-1983.   Plays/librettos/scripts.
Thematic and stylistic comparison of three plays influenced
by the *Odyssey*. Lang.: Eng.   2792

1952-1985.   Performance/production.
Directing career of Josefina Molina. Lang.: Eng.   2078

1953.   Plays/librettos/scripts.
Artaud's concept of theatre of cruelty in Francisco Nieva's
*Tórtolas, crepúscula y ...telón (Turtledoves, Twilight and
...Curtain)*. Lang.: Spa.   2790

1959-1976.   Plays/librettos/scripts.
Translator discusses her Spanish version of Maria Aurelia
Capmany's Catalan play, *Tu i l'hipócrita (You and the
Hypocrite)*. Lang.: Spa.   2806

1959-1984.   Institutions.
Discussion of public theatre in Europe, especially Spain.
Valencia. Lang.: Fre, Eng, Spa, Ita, Cat.   516

1959-1985.   Institutions.
Trend toward independent Spanish theatres. Lang.: Spa.   515

1963-1985.   Plays/librettos/scripts.
Current thematic trends in the plays of Antonio Gala. Lang.:
Spa.   2783

1965.   Plays/librettos/scripts.
Salvador Espriu's tragic vision in *Ronda de Mort a Sinera
(Death Round at Sinera)*. Lang.: Eng.   2784

1970-1973.   Plays/librettos/scripts.
Self-reflexivity in Antonio Buero Vallejo's play *El Sueño de
la razón (The Sleep of Reason)* and Victor Erice's film *El
Espíritu de la colmena (The Spirit of the Beehive)*. Lang.:
Eng.   2781

1971-1984.   Plays/librettos/scripts.
Thematic analysis of *La Jaula (The Cage)* by José Fernando
Dicenta. Lang.: Eng.   2800

1972-1985.   Plays/librettos/scripts.
Reasons for the lack of new Spanish drama and the few
recent significant realistic and experimental plays. Lang.: Spa.
                                                                                    2793

1974-1979.   Plays/librettos/scripts.
Radical subjectivism in three plays by Antonio Buero
Vallejo: *La Fundación (The Foundation), La Detonación (The
Detonation)* and *Jueces en la noche (Judges at Night)*. Lang.:
Eng.   2797

1975-1985.   Institutions.
Factors leading to the decline of Spanish theatre. Lang.: Spa.
                                                                                    1582

1978.   Plays/librettos/scripts.
Alfonso Sastre's theory of complex tragedy in *La Celestina
(The Nun)*. Lang.: Spa.   2807

1980.   Performance/production.
Production description of the symbolist drama *La navaja
(The Razor)* by Eduardo Quiles. Lang.: Spa.   2074

1980-1985.   Plays/librettos/scripts.
Description of a staged reading of *The Cock's Short Flight*
by Jaime Salom. New York, NY. Lang.: Eng.   2808

1982.   Basic theatrical documents.
Playtext of *Los Comediantes (The Players)* by Antonio
Martínez Ballesteros. Lang.: Spa.   1494

1982-1985.   Performance/production.
Playwright Antonio Martínez Ballesteros discusses the
production history of his play *Los Comediantes (The Players)*.
Toledo. Cincinnati, OH. Lang.: Spa.   2076

1983-1985.   Performance/production.
Production history of *Hay que deshacer la casa (Undoing the
Housework)*, winner of Lope de Vega prize. Madrid. Miami,
FL. Lang.: Eng.   2079

1983-1986.   Plays/librettos/scripts.
Playwright Alfonso Sastre discusses three of his recent plays.
Lang.: Spa.   2802

1984.   Plays/librettos/scripts.
Poor reception of *Diálogo secreto (Secret Dialogue)* by
Antonio Buero Vallejo in Spain. Madrid. Lang.: Eng.   2791
Refutes critical position that Antonio Buero Vallejo's *Diálogo
secreto (Secret Dialogue)* is unbelievable. Madrid. Lang.: Eng.
                                                                                    2799

1984.   Reference materials.
Bibliography of twentieth century Spanish drama. Lang.: Spa.
                                                                                    2997

1985.   Performance/production.
Reports and discussions on nonverbal communication in
theatre. Lang.: Eng, Fre, Spa.   789

1985.   Plays/librettos/scripts.
Analysis of Pedro Corradi's *Retrato de señora con espejo—
Vida y pasión de Margarita Xirgu (Portrait of a Lady with
Mirror—The Life and Passion of Margarita Xirgu)*. Uruguay.
Madrid. Lang.: Spa.   2887

1986.   Performance/production.
Review of international theatre festivals. Montreal, PQ.
Toronto, ON. Lang.: Eng.   2077
Comparison of Holy Week Processions of Seville with
English Mystery plays. Seville. Lang.: Eng.   3426
Instances of dramatic action and costume in Holy Week
processions. Lang.: Eng.   3427

Spain-Catalonia

200 B.C.-1986 A.D.   Design/technology.
History of Catalan scenography. Lang.: Cat.   311

1000-1709.   Performance/production.
Medieval style Assumption plays. Lang.: Cat.   792

1264-1986.   Relation to other fields.
Christian and pre-Christian elements of Corpus Christi
celebration. Berga. Lang.: Cat.   3432

1330-1970.   Relation to other fields.
Renaissance theatre at Valencia court, Catalan festivals.
Valencia. Lang.: Spa.   3362

1350-1388.   Performance/production.
Comparison of Catalan Assumption plays. Tarragona. Lang.:
Cat.   3346

1388-1538.   Performance spaces.
Spatial orientation in medieval Catalan religious productions.
Florence. Lang.: Cat.   616

1400-1599.   Plays/librettos/scripts.
Analysis of Catalan Nativity plays. Lang.: Cat.   972

1400-1880.   Basic theatrical documents.
Edition and introduction to Catalan religious tragedy of Saint
Sebastian. Riudoms. Lang.: Cat.   1498

1400-1963.   Theory/criticism.
Historical difficulties in creating a paradigm for Catalan
theatre. Lang.: Cat.   1220

1510-1514.   Plays/librettos/scripts.
Linguistic study of *Auto de Pasión (Passion Play)* by Lucas
Fernández. Lang.: Cat.   2812

1590-1986.   Basic theatrical documents.
Josep Maria de Sagarra's translations of Shakespeare with
scholarly introduction. UK-England. Lang.: Cat.   1502

1625-1680.   Basic theatrical documents.
Edition of *La famosa comèdia de la gala està en son punt
(The Famous Comedy of the Gala Done to a Turn)*, with
analysis. Lang.: Cat.   1497

1700-1960.   Plays/librettos/scripts.
Roles of women in middle-class Catalonian society as
reflected in the plays of Carme Montoriol and Maria Aurélia
Capmany. Lang.: Spa.   2819

1800-1926.   Plays/librettos/scripts.
History of Catalan literature, including playwrights. France.
Lang.: Cat.   973

1800-1974.   Plays/librettos/scripts.
History of Catalan literature, including playwrights and
theatre. Lang.: Cat.   974

1832-1900.   Design/technology.
Introduction to facsimile edition of set designs by Fracesc
Soler i Rovirosa. Barcelona. Valencia. Madrid. Lang.: Cat.
3313

1838-1972.   Performance/production.
Short history of the activities of the family Robreño. Cuba.
Lang.: Cat.   680

1845-1986.   Performance spaces.
Children's history of the Gran Teatre del Liceo opera house.
Barcelona. Lang.: Cat.   3684

1848-1984.   Plays/librettos/scripts.
Short history of Catalan translations of plays. Lang.: Fre.
2813

1848-1986.   Reference materials.
Guide to Catalan theatres. Lang.: Cat.   1030

1860-1967.   Plays/librettos/scripts.
A defense of Àngel Guimerà's language. Lang.: Cat.   2817

1861-1984.   Design/technology.
Introduction to facsimile of Oleguer Junyent's set design for
L'Auca del senyor Esteve (Mr. Esteve's 'Auca') by Santiago
Rusiñol. Barcelona. Lang.: Cat.   1518

1867-1985.   Plays/librettos/scripts.
Influence of Luigi Pirandello's work in Catalonia. Italy.
Lang.: Spa, Cat.   2706

1869-1966.   Plays/librettos/scripts.
Life and work of Caterina Albert, known as Víctor Català.
Lang.: Cat.   2816

1878.   Design/technology.
Facsimile edition of scene design drawings by Francesc Soler
i Rovirosa for *La almoneda del diablo (The Devil's Auction)*
by Rafael M. Liern. Barcelona. Lang.: Cat.   3314

1890-1905.   Plays/librettos/scripts.
Plays translated into Catalan by Pompeu Fabra. Lang.: Cat.
2818

1897-1907.   Plays/librettos/scripts.
Analysis of *La Santa Espina (The Holy Thorn)* by Àngel
Guimerà. Lang.: Cat.   2815

1913-1985.   Basic theatrical documents.
Text of *Primera història d'Esther (First Story of Esther)* by
Salvador Espriu, with introduction on the author and the
play. Barcelona. Lang.: Spa, Cat.   1496

1917.   Design/technology.
Facsimile edition of scene design drawings by Oleguer
Junyent for *L'auca del senyor Esteve (Mr. Esteve's 'Auca')* by
Santiago Rusiñol. Barcelona. Lang.: Cat.   1519

1917-1955.   Plays/librettos/scripts.
Evaluation of the literary and dramatic work of Josep Maria
de Sagarra. Lang.: Cat.   2810

1917-1964.   Basic theatrical documents.
Anthology and study of writings of Josep Maria de Sagarra.
Lang.: Cat.   1501

1917-1982.   Basic theatrical documents.
Texts of *Avui, Romeo i Julieta (Today, Romeo and Juliet)*
and *El porter i el penalty (The Goalkeeper and the Penalty)*
by Josep Palau i Fabre. Lang.: Cat.   1499

1917-1982.   Plays/librettos/scripts.
Analysis of Josep Palau's plays and theoretical writings.
Lang.: Cat.   2814

1920-1986.   Plays/librettos/scripts.
Memoir concerning playwright Joan Oliver. Lang.: Cat.   2820

1940-1964.   Plays/librettos/scripts.
Translations of Shakespeare by Josep Maria de Sagarra.
Barcelona. Lang.: Cat.   2811

1947-1986.   Reference materials.
Description of popular entertainments, both sacred and
secular. Lang.: Cat.   3355

1958-1986.   Institutions.
Three personal views of the evolution of the Catalan
company La Pipironda. Barcelona. Lang.: Cat.   1583

1959.   Basic theatrical documents.
Text of *Tu i l'hipócrita (You and the Hypocrite)*, by Maria
Aurélia Capmany, translated into Castilian Spanish by L.
Teresa Valdivieso as *Tú y el hipócrita*. Barcelona. Lang.:
Spa.   1495

1963.   Basic theatrical documents.
English translation of *L'ús de la matèria (The Use of
Matter)* by Manuel de Pedrolo. Lang.: Cat, Eng.   1500

1970-1985.   Basic theatrical documents.
Text of *David, rei (David, King)* by Jordi Teixidor. Lang.:
Cat.   1503

1970-1985.   Plays/librettos/scripts.
Analysis of the six published dramatic works by Jordi
Teixidor. Lang.: Cat.   2809

1972-1982.   Institutions.
Activities of Rialles, including children's theatre and
puppetry. Terrassa. Lang.: Cat.   517

1972-1983.   Plays/librettos/scripts.
Analysis of *Small Craft Warnings*, and report of audience
reactions. New York, NY. Barcelona. Lang.: Cat.   2929

1976-1986.   Performance/production.
Articles about the productions of the Centre Dramàtic.
Barcelona. Lang.: Cat.   2084

1979-1984.   Performance/production.
Detailed description of the performance titled *Accions
(Actions)* by La Fura dels Baus. Lang.: Cat.   3445

1983.   Performance/production.
Interview with director Jorge Lavelli of Estudio Faixat.
Barcelona. Lang.: Pol.   2081

1984.   Performance/production.
Role of the director working with classics today. Lang.: Cat.
2080

1985.   Performance/production.
Report on International Theatre Congress. Barcelona. Lang.:
Rus.   793

1985.   Relation to other fields.
Reports and discussions of restricted cultural communication.
Lebanon. USA. Lang.: Fre, Spa, Cat.   1111

1985.   Theory/criticism.
Ingmar Bergman production of *King Lear* and Asian
influences. Barcelona. Lang.: Eng.   1219

1985-1986.   Performance/production.
Collected reviews of theatre season. Barcelona. Lang.: Cat.
791

Spain-Catalonia — cont'd

1986.   **Performance/production.**
Savannah Bay and *Reigen (Round)* produced by Centre
Dramàtic. Barcelona. Lang.: Cat.   2082
Articles on the 1986-87 theatre season. Barcelona. France.
Lang.: Cat.   2083

Sweden

1835-1976.   **Plays/librettos/scripts.**
Polish drama performed in Sweden. Poland. Lang.: Pol. 975
1887.   **Plays/librettos/scripts.**
The presentation of atheism in August Strindberg's *The
Father*. Lang.: Eng.   2821
1887-1910.   **Performance/production.**
August Strindberg's theoretical writings. Lang.: Ita. 2093
1889-1986.   **Theory/criticism.**
Semiotic analysis of audience involvement in *Fröken Julie
(Miss Julie)* by August Strindberg. Lang.: Ita.   3133
1890-1986.   **Performance/production.**
Discussion of Stanislavskij's influence by a number of artists.
Lang.: Swe.   2094
1900.   **Audience.**
Analysis of *Dödsdansen (The Dance of Death)*. Lang.: Eng.
                    1452
1900.   **Plays/librettos/scripts.**
Biblical and Swedenborgian influences on the development of
August Strindberg's chamber play *Påsk (Easter)*. Lang.: Eng.
                    2827
1905-1985.   **Performance/production.**
Life and career of film star Greta Garbo. Hollywood, CA.
Lang.: Hun.   3226
1918-1986.   **Institutions.**
Interview with Einar Bergvin, founder of amateur theatre
groups and publication. Fagersta. Lang.: Swe.   519
1927.   **Design/technology.**
Unusual production of *Life Is a Dream* by Kungliga
Dramatiska Teatern. Stockholm. Lang.: Swe.   1520
1928-1985.   **Performance spaces.**
Details of renovation of Husumgården auditorium. Husum.
Lang.: Swe.   621
1933-1986.   **Institutions.**
Recent outdoor productions of Gamla Stans Teater.
Stockholm. Lang.: Swe.   524
1939-1940.   **Relation to other fields.**
A portrait of Brecht in Peter Weiss's *Die Ästhetik des
Widerstands*. Stockholm.   1130
1940-1986.   **Design/technology.**
Comparison of manual and computerized dimmer systems.
Lang.: Swe.   313
1950-1986.   **Design/technology.**
Contrasts the boldness of scene designs for the Royal Opera
from the 1950s and 1960s to the present. Stockholm. Lang.:
Swe.   3652
1950-1986.   **Performance/production.**
Interview with actress Agneta Ekmanner. Stockholm. Lang.:
Swe.   2092
1952-1986.   **Design/technology.**
Innovator and scene designer Carl-Eric Sandgren. Gävle.
Lang.: Swe.   314
1953-1986.   **Institutions.**
The history of the Södertälje Teateramatörer. Södertälje.
Lang.: Swe.   520
1957-1961.   **Institutions.**
Intertextual analysis of Eugene O'Neill's play *Long Day's
Journey Into Night* and Ingmar Bergman's film, *Through a
Glass Darkly*. USA. Lang.: Eng.   1425
1960-1986.   **Institutions.**
Liturgical drama and dance performed by amateur theatre
group. Lund. Lang.: Swe.   526
Training for amateur theatre leaders at Marieborg
Folkhögskola. Norrköping. Lang.: Swe.   528
1963-1986.   **Administration.**
Role of Skånska Teatron in the community. Landskrona.
Malmö. Lang.: Swe.   62
1966-1986.   **Administration.**
Interview with Bernt Thorell, president of Svensk
Teaterteknisk Förening. Lang.: Swe.   63
1970-1986.   **Institutions.**
Seminar on local plays and worker's theatre. Norrköping.
Lang.: Swe.   527
1972-1986.   **Plays/librettos/scripts.**
Interview with actor, director, playwright Staffan Göthe.
Luleå. Lang.: Swe.   2826

1975-1985.   **Relation to other fields.**
Participation of disabled children in Vår Teater. Stockholm.
Lang.: Eng.   1129
1976-1986.   **Institutions.**
Recent collaborations between technical directors and
technicians. Lang.: Swe.   518
History of the Swedish Society for Theatre Technicians.
Lang.: Swe.   521
How Skottes Musiktéater operates on a small government
budget. Gävle. Lang.: Swe.   522
Role of the Swedish Society for Theatre Technicians in
recent theatre architecture. Lang.: Swe.   523
1977-1986.   **Institutions.**
Activities of the Folkkulturcentrum Festival. Stockholm.
Lang.: Swe.   529
1977-1986.   **Reference materials.**
A list of all articles that have appeared in *STTF-
medlemsblad* 1977-1985 and *ProScen* 1986. Lang.: Swe. 1032
1979-1986.   **Performance/production.**
Mats Ödeen's *Det ende raka (The Only Straight Thing)*
performed by TURteaterns amatörteatergrupp. Stockholm.
Lang.: Swe.   801
1980-1986.   **Design/technology.**
Swedish set designers discuss their working methods. Lang.:
Swe.   312
Absence of stylization in scene design. Lang.: Swe.   315
High-tech trends in scene design. Stockholm. Lang.: Swe. 317
1980-1986.   **Institutions.**
Sommarteatern, using both amateur and professional actors,
will attempt a year-round season. Södertälje. Lang.: Swe.
                    1585
1980-1986.   **Performance/production.**
Emblems of the 1980s in Swedish theatre. Lang.: Swe. 796
1981-1986.   **Plays/librettos/scripts.**
Innerst inne (At Heart) dramatizes political and economic
dilemma. Karlskoga. Lang.: Swe.   2825
1982-1986.   **Institutions.**
Amateur production of García Lorca's *La Casa de Bernarda
Alba (The House of Bernarda Alba)*. Handen. Lang.: Swe.
                    1584
1982-1986.   **Performance/production.**
De dövas historia (The Story of the Deaf) staged by
Ändockgruppen using both hearing and deaf amateurs.
Vänersborg. Lang.: Swe.   799
1983-1986.   **Performance spaces.**
Description of Orionteatern, a former factory. Stockholm.
Lang.: Swe.   618
1984-1986.   **Administration.**
Training of amateurs coordinated by Folkteatern in
Gävleborgs Län. Gävle. Lang.: Swe.   60
1984-1986.   **Performance/production.**
Outsidern (The Outsider), a production by Mimensemblan,
based on Hermann Hesse's *Steppenwolf*. Stockholm. Lang.:
Swe.   3296
1984-1986.   **Plays/librettos/scripts.**
Interview with Ingegerd Monthan, author of *Drottningmötet
(The Meeting of the Queens)*. Lang.: Swe.   2823
1985.   **Design/technology.**
Training course for theatre technicians at Dramatiska
Institutet. Stockholm. Lang.: Swe.   318
Technical details of producing *La Cage aux Folles* on a
small budget. Malmö. Lang.: Swe.   3581
1985.   **Performance spaces.**
Technical problems of using tents for performances.
Stockholm. Lang.: Swe.   3326
1985-1986.   **Administration.**
Poorly designed and produced programs of theatrical
performances. Lang.: Swe.   61
1985-1986.   **Design/technology.**
Theory and practice in the training of theatre technicians at
Dramatiska Institutet. Stockholm. Lang.: Swe.   316
1985-1986.   **Performance/production.**
Stage photographs with comment by photographers. Lang.:
Swe.   794
Interview with judge and amateur actor Bo Severin. Malmö.
Lang.: Swe.   802
Reviews of regional productions. Stockholm. Lang.: Swe.
                    2087

Switzerland — cont'd

1982-1986. **Relation to other fields.**
Critique of government support and funding for the arts.
Lang.: Ger. 1133
1983-1986. **Administration.**
Evaluation of a program of financial support for Swiss
playwrights. Lang.: Fre, Ger. 65
1983-1986. **Institutions.**
Support for non-mainstream theatre. Lang.: Fre, Ger. 531
1984. **Performance/production.**
A profile of the three performers known collectively as
Mummenschanz. Zurich. USA. Lang.: Eng. 3297
1985. **Theory/criticism.**
Interview on the nature of humor with comedian Emil
Steinberger. Lang.: Ger. 3372
1986. **Administration.**
Draft copyright laws of World Intellectual Property
Organization. Lang.: Eng. 64
Discussion of dance theatre subsidy. Boswil. Lang.: Fre, Ger. 1339
1986. **Institutions.**
The effect of subsidization on private and public professional
ballet schools in Switzerland. Lang.: Fre. 1299
1986. **Performance/production.**
Premiere of *Der magische Kreis (The Magic Circle)*, an
opera by Gion Derungs and Lothar Deplazes. Chur. Lang.:
Ger. 3780
1986. **Plays/librettos/scripts.**
Interview with playwright Friedrich Dürrenmatt. Lang.: Ger. 2828
1986. **Reference materials.**
Catalogue of exhibition on dancer Serge Lifar. Lausanne.
Lang.: Fre. 1326
1986-1987. **Administration.**
Contractual problems in theatrical professions. Lang.: Ger. 66
1986-1987. **Reference materials.**
Annual guide to Swiss theatrical productions. Lang.: Ger,
Fre, Ita. 1033

Taiwan
1939-1980. **Performance/production.**
Director, producer Wu Jing-Jyi discusses his life and career
in theatre. Minneapolis, MN. New York, NY. Lang.: Eng. 2098

Tanzania
1967-1984. **Relation to other fields.**
Role of theatre after the Arusha Declaration. Lang.: Eng. 1134
1970-1986. **Performance/production.**
English alternative theatre group Welfare State International
works with Tanzanian performers. UK-England. Lang.: Eng. 814

Tibet
1700-1981. **Performance/production.**
Influence of Tibetan drama on Chinese theatre. China.
Lang.: Chi. 3515
1986. **Relation to other fields.**
Cinematographer David Breashears climbs Mt. Everest. 3246

Tunisia
1986. **Design/technology.**
Pierre Guffroy's design of a functional ship for Polanski's
Pirates. Lang.: Eng. 3201

Turkey
ALSO SEE
Ottoman Empire.
1000-1986. **Theory/criticism.**
Eastern and Western influences on Turkish theatre. Lang.:
Ita. 1222
1524-1986. **Theory/criticism.**
Western influences on theatrical development in Turkey.
Lang.: Ita. 1221

Ukraine
ALSO SEE
USSR-Ukrainian SSR.

Upper Volta
Performance/production.
Types of costumes, dances, and songs of Dodo masquerades
during Ramadan. Ouagadougou. Lang.: Eng. 3428

Uruguay
1979. **Basic theatrical documents.**
English translation of Mario Benedetti's *Pedro y el capitán
(Pedro and the Captain)*. Lang.: Eng. 1510

1985. **Plays/librettos/scripts.**
Analysis of Pedro Corradi's *Retrato de señora con espejo—
Vida y pasión de Margarita Xirgu (Portrait of a Lady with
Mirror—The Life and Passion of Margarita Xirgu)*. Madrid.
Lang.: Spa. 2887

UK
Relation to other fields.
Curricular authority for drama-in-education program. Lang.:
Eng. 3054
Discussion of theatre-in-education. Lang.: Eng. 3055
1600-1986. **Relation to other fields.**
Style in children's theatre in light of theories of Philippe
Ariès. USA. France. Lang.: Eng. 1162
1717-1986. **Reference materials.**
Theatrical careers of famous actors. USA. Lang.: Eng. 3010
1769-1985. **Performance/production.**
Development of clowning to include parody. Lang.: Fre. 3347
1837-1901. **Administration.**
Legislation for the protection of Victorian child-actors. Lang.:
Eng. 1439
1850-1986. **Administration.**
Copyright before and after Berne Convention. Lang.: Eng. 68
1874-1985. **Performance/production.**
Solutions to staging the final scene of Shakespeare's *The
Merry Wives of Windsor*. Lang.: Eng. 2105
1886-1986. **Administration.**
Berne Convention and copyright in market economy. USA.
Lang.: Eng. 69
Berne Convention and public interest. Lang.: Eng. 75
1900-1986. **Performance/production.**
Touring exhibition 'Artists in the Theatre': influence of visual
artists in the development of performance art. Lang.: Eng. 3447
1901-1918. **Plays/librettos/scripts.**
Analysis of plays by Canadian soldiers in World War I.
Canada. Lang.: Eng. 936
1914-1985. **Performance/production.**
Autobiography of actor Alec Guinness. USA. Lang.: Eng. 2106
1916-1983. **Performance/production.**
Self-referential elements in several film versions of
Shakespeare's *King Lear*. USA. Lang.: Eng. 3227
1945-1986. **Administration.**
Subsidized theatre in England. Lang.: Eng. 74
1946-1986. **Design/technology.**
Amateur lighting technician describes his work in schools,
colleges and churches over the last forty years. Lang.: Eng. 320
1947-1985. **Plays/librettos/scripts.**
Beckett as writer and director. France. Lang.: Fre. 2546
1949-1985. **Audience.**
Critical reception of British productions of Canadian plays.
Canada. Lang.: Eng. 1453
1950-1972. **Plays/librettos/scripts.**
The place of *The Island of the Mighty* in the John Arden
canon. Ireland. Lang.: Eng. 2666
1956-1986. **Administration.**
Problems of copyright protection for computer programs.
USA. Lang.: Eng. 73
1957-1986. **Theory/criticism.**
Overview of Pinter criticism with emphasis on the works'
inherent uncertainty. Lang.: Eng. 3134
1965-1986. **Performance/production.**
Interview with a performance artist undergoing training as a
deep-sea diver. Lang.: Eng. 3446
1971-1986. **Administration.**
Effect of copyright on new broadcast technologies. Lang.:
Eng. 71
1977. **Institutions.**
Function of the Welfare State Theater. Lang.: Eng. 532
1978-1986. **Administration.**
Financial problems in British art centers. Lang.: Eng. 78
1980-1986. **Administration.**
Description of computerized ticketing and administration
system. Lang.: Eng. 77
1981-1985. **Reference materials.**
Bibliography of English drama. Lang.: Rus. 2999
1985-1986. **Performance/production.**
Political difficulties in staging two touring productions of
Shakespeare's *The Taming of the Shrew*. Lang.: Eng. 2104

UK — cont'd

1985-1986. **Reference materials.**
Lists 292 research collections and information sources, most of which are open to the public. Lang.: Eng. 1034

1986. **Administration.**
Identification of important British officials responsible for most government policies. Lang.: Eng. 67

Summary of the Cork report with recommendations on how the results can be used. Lang.: Eng. 70

Interview with director and tour manager of Royal Shakespeare Company about touring. Lang.: Eng. 72

Formation and development of the Association of British Theatre Technicians (ABTT). Lang.: Eng. 76

1986. **Performance/production.**
Collection of newspaper reviews by London theatre critics. Lang.: Eng. 2099

Collection of newspaper reviews by London theatre critics. London. Lang.: Eng. 2100

Collection of newspaper reviews by London theatre critics. Lang.: Eng. 2101

Collection of newspaper reviews by London theatre critics. Lang.: Eng. 2102

Collection of newspaper reviews by London theatre critics. Lang.: Eng. 2103

1986. **Reference materials.**
List of 37 productions of 23 Renaissance plays, with commentary. USA. New Zealand. Lang.: Eng. 3000

UK-England

ALSO SEE
England.

Design/technology.
Lighting tips for amateur theatre groups working in church and community halls and schools. Lang.: Eng. 322

ABTT technical guidelines for sound and communications systems in the theatre. Lang.: Eng. 324

Performance spaces.
Outlines the technical and architectural features of the Swan Theatre at Stratford-upon-Avon. Stratford. Lang.: Eng. 1617

Performance/production.
Interview with Elisabeth Bergner and Jane Alexander on their portrayals of Joan of Arc. Berlin, West. Malvern. Washington, DC. Lang.: Eng. 1766

Actress Julie McKenzie discusses her role in *Woman in Mind* by Alan Ayckbourn. London. Lang.: Eng. 2145

Proposal to include theatre critics in pre-production evaluation of plays. USA. Lang.: Eng. 2162

Nuria Espert talks about Federico García Lorca and her production of *The House of Bernarda Alba*. London. Spain. Lang.: Eng. 2178

Plays/librettos/scripts.
Attitudes toward sexuality in plays from French sources. France. Lang.: Eng. 2852

Relation to other fields.
Current style of theatre-in-education. Lang.: Eng. 3057

Theory/criticism.
Influence of literary theory on Greek theatre studies. Greece. Germany. Lang.: Afr. 1210

1580-1600. **Basic theatrical documents.**
Text of *Edmund Ironside*, attributed to Shakespeare. London. Lang.: Eng. 1508

1590-1986. **Basic theatrical documents.**
Josep Maria de Sagarra's translations of Shakespeare with scholarly introduction. Spain-Catalonia. Lang.: Cat. 1502

1633-1986. **Performance/production.**
Actors' memorials at St. Paul's Church in Covent Garden. London. Lang.: Eng. 817

1760-1900. **Performance/production.**
Analysis of predominant mode of staging final scene of *Othello* by William Shakespeare. London. USA. Lang.: Eng. 2184

1780-1820. **Relation to other fields.**
Shakespearean allusion in English caricature. Lang.: Eng. 3056

1789-1986. **Audience.**
Effect of official educational and cultural policies on theatre. France. Germany. Lang.: Fre. 1446

1790-1986. **Design/technology.**
Broad survey of costuming in England. London. Lang.: Eng. 1524

1818-1840. **Performance/production.**
Controversy surrounding *Presumption, or The Fate of Frankenstein* by Richard Brinsley Peake. London. Lang.: Eng. 2142

1818-1872. **Basic theatrical documents.**
Text of plays by James Robinson Planché, with introduction on his influence. Lang.: Eng. 226

1823-1826. **Plays/librettos/scripts.**
Treatment of the Frankenstein myth in three gothic melodramas. France. Lang.: Eng. 2847

1827. **Performance/production.**
Impact and influence of the tour by black American actor Ira Aldridge. Manchester. Lang.: Eng. 2136

1850-1900. **Performance/production.**
Training of English directors. Lang.: Rus. 813

1856-1950. **Plays/librettos/scripts.**
Reference of George Bernard Shaw to contemporary society. Lang.: Eng. 2862

1857. **Design/technology.**
Charles Kean's period production of Shakespeare's *Richard III*. London. Lang.: Eng. 1525

1869-1950. **Performance/production.**
Career of actress, manager and director Julia Arthur. Canada. USA. Lang.: Eng. 1675

1875-1900. **Plays/librettos/scripts.**
Development and subsequent decline of the three-act farce. Lang.: Eng. 976

1875-1986. **Performance spaces.**
Alexander Palace Theatre as pantomime stage. London. Lang.: Eng. 627

1876. **Performance/production.**
Development and production of Sir Percy Shelley's amateur production of *The Doom of St. Querec*. London. Lang.: Eng. 809

1877-1946. **Performance/production.**
Letters to and from Harley Granville-Barker. Lang.: Eng. 807

1883. **Performance/production.**
Changes in English life reflected in 1883 theatre season. London. Lang.: Eng. 810

1887-1917. **Performance/production.**
Reconstruction of a number of Shakespeare plays staged and performed by Herbert Beerbohm Tree. London. Lang.: Eng. 2155

1891. **Performance/production.**
The Independent Theatre of Jacob Thomas Grein, established in imitation of André Antoine's Théâtre Libre. London. Lang.: Rus. 818

1894. **Plays/librettos/scripts.**
Thematic analysis of *Candida* by George Bernard Shaw focusing on the spiritual development of Marchbanks. London. Lang.: Eng. 2837

Argument for coherence of *Arms and the Man* by George Bernard Shaw. London. Lang.: Eng. 2863

1894-1982. **Plays/librettos/scripts.**
Textual history of the final line of *Arms and the Man* by George Bernard Shaw. London. Lang.: Eng. 2873

1895-1974. **Plays/librettos/scripts.**
A comparison between Oscar Wilde's *The Importance of Being Earnest* and Tom Stoppard's *Travesties*. Lang.: Eng. 2872

1899-1984. **Reference materials.**
Shakespeare on film. USA. Lang.: Eng. 3245

1899-1986. **Theory/criticism.**
Shakespeare in media. USA. Japan. Lang.: Eng. 3172

1900. **Performance/production.**
Recollection of performances by music-hall comedian Billy Danvers. Lang.: Eng. 3469

1900-1930. **Reference materials.**
Update of Allardyce Nicoll's handlist of plays. London. Lang.: Eng. 3003

1900-1985. **Performance/production.**
Doubling of roles in Shakespeare's *Hamlet*. London. Lang.: Eng. 2129

Informal history of musical theatre. New York, NY. London. Lang.: Eng. 3621

1900-1986. **Theory/criticism.**
Shaw's use of devil's advocacy in his plays compared to deconstructionism. Lang.: Eng. 3135

1905. **Design/technology.**
Contribution of designer Ernst Stern to modern scenography. Berlin. London. Lang.: Eng. 1516

UK-England — cont'd

1907-1920.   Design/technology.
Influence of Hampstead Garden Suburb pageant on the
Russian Proletkult movement. Russia. London. Lang.: Eng.
3421

1907-1986.   Performance/production.
Actor Laurence Olivier's memoirs. London. New York, NY.
Lang.: Eng.   2170

1910-1986.   Performance/production.
Appreciation and obituary of the late English tenor Sir Peter
Pears. Aldeburgh. Lang.: Eng.   3785

1911-1970.   Plays/librettos/scripts.
Treatment of homosexuality in *Death in Venice*. Germany.
Lang.: Eng.   3874

1911-1986.   Administration.
Conflicts between reproduction permission and authors'
rights. Lang.: Eng.   79

1912-1928.   Plays/librettos/scripts.
Influence of Gordon Craig on American theatre and his
recognition of Eugene O'Neill's importance. USA. Lang.:
Eng.   2908

1912-1940.   Performance/production.
Innovative Shakespeare stagings of Harley Granville-Barker.
Lang.: Eng.   806

1913-1967.   Performance/production.
Hungarian translation of *Vivien Leigh: A Biography*. Lang.:
Hun.   2141

1913-1972.   Relation to other fields.
Influence of Marcel Duchamp's work on Tom Stoppard's
radio play, *Artist Descending a Staircase*. Lang.: Eng.   3059

1913-1976.   Plays/librettos/scripts.
The life, career and compositions of Benjamin Britten.
London. Lang.: Eng.   3899

1913-1978.   Plays/librettos/scripts.
Comparison of Harold Pinter and Marcel Proust, focusing on
Pinter's filmscript *The Proust Screenplay*. France. Lang.: Eng.
3232

1914-1986.   Performance spaces.
Modernization of the Alhambra Theatre. Bradford. Lang.:
Eng.   623

1915-1985.   Plays/librettos/scripts.
Analysis of *A View From the Bridge* by Arthur Miller. New
York, NY. London. Lang.: Cat.   2901

1917-1934.   Relation to other fields.
History of workers' theatre. USSR. Germany. Lang.: Eng.
1179

1917-1986.   Plays/librettos/scripts.
Interview with playwright Stephen MacDonald. London.
Lang.: Eng.   2879

1918-1986.   Plays/librettos/scripts.
Career of lyricist Alan Jay Lerner. New York, NY. Lang.:
Eng.   3629

1920-1960.   Performance/production.
Survey of the career of director Michel Saint-Denis. France.
Lang.: Hun.   718

1923-1986.   Performance/production.
Director Zeffirelli recounts his work with notable actors and
singers. Italy. Lang.: Eng.   754

1928-1986.   Plays/librettos/scripts.
History and practice of the documentary in radio, television,
and film. Lang.: Eng.   3168

1929-1978.   Plays/librettos/scripts.
Analysis of John Osborne's *Look Back in Anger*. London.
Lang.: Cat.   2866

1930-1933.   Performance/production.
History of the Edward Dunstan Shakespearean Company, a
touring company. Lang.: Eng.   2156

1930-1960.   Design/technology.
Lighting control in early live TV productions. Lang.: Eng.
3253

1930-1985.   Plays/librettos/scripts.
Analysis of the plot, characters and structure of *The
Homecoming* by Harold Pinter. London. Lang.: Cat.   2865

1930-1986.   Performance spaces.
Restoration of the Whitehall Theatre. London. Lang.: Eng.
625

1932-1986.   Institutions.
Exhibit on stages and staging by Royal Shakespeare
Company. Stratford. Lang.: Eng.   1591

1932-1986.   Plays/librettos/scripts.
Relation of Harold Pinter's plays to modern developments in
science and philosophy. Lang.: Eng.   2849

Analysis of Arnold Wesker's *Chicken Soup with Barley*.
London. Lang.: Cat.   2864

1932-1986.   Relation to other fields.
Non-dramatic writings of playwright Arnold Wesker. Lang.:
Eng.   3058

1933-1984.   Performance/production.
Career and religious convictions of actor Alec Guinness.
Lang.: Eng.   808

1935.   Plays/librettos/scripts.
T. S. Eliot's *Murder in the Cathedral* dramatizes Christian
theory of history. Lang.: Eng.   2878

1935-1980.   Performance/production.
Problems of producing Shakespeare on radio. Lang.: Eng.
3178

1935-1986.   Design/technology.
Details the installation and use of a 1935 Strand lighting
console. London. Lang.: Eng.   321

1936-1983.   Performance/production.
Eileen Atkins, Judi Dench, Wendy Hiller and Barbara
Jefford discuss playing Saint Joan in Shaw's play. London.
Lang.: Eng.   2153

1936-1986.   Institutions.
History of variety act playhouse, the Players Theatre.
London. Lang.: Eng.   3463

1936-1986.   Performance/production.
Interview with John Mills on his acting career. London.
Lang.: Eng.   811

1936-1986.   Relation to other fields.
Interview with actress Maria Aitken on a revival of *The
Women* by Clare Boothe Luce. London. Lang.: Eng.   3061

1937-1947.   Relation to other fields.
Refugee artists from Nazi Germany in Britain. Germany.
Lang.: Eng.   1135

1937-1986.   Performance/production.
Life and career of singer Peter Pears. London. Lang.: Eng.
3784

1938-1965.   Plays/librettos/scripts.
Orson Welles' adaptation of Shakespeare's Falstaff scenes,
Chimes at Midnight. Lang.: Eng.   3239

1940-1985.   Performance/production.
Interview with singer Nancy Evans and writer Eric Crozier
discussing their association with Benjamin Britten. Columbia,
MO. London. Lang.: Eng.   3820

1940-1986.   Performance/production.
Biographical notes on choreographer and director Gillian
Lynne. London. USA. Lang.: Eng.   2161

1941-1986.   Performance/production.
Jonathan Miller's production of Eugene O'Neill's *Long Day's
Journey Into Night*. London. Lang.: Eng.   2159

1945.   Plays/librettos/scripts.
Interpretation of Fortinbras in post-war productions of
Hamlet. Poland. Lang.: Eng.   2748

1945-1983.   Plays/librettos/scripts.
World War II as a theme in post-war British drama. Lang.:
Eng.   2868

1945-1986.   Design/technology.
Interview with designer Ralph Koltai. Lang.: Eng.   331

1945-1986.   Performance/production.
An assessment of actor Paul Scofield. Lang.: Eng.   2154

1945-1986.   Reference materials.
Guide to postwar British theatre. Lang.: Eng.   3001

1946-1976.   Plays/librettos/scripts.
A chronology and analysis of the compositions of Benjamin
Britten. London. Lang.: Eng.   3896

1946-1977.   Performance/production.
Detailed discussion of four successful Royal Shakespeare
Company productions of Shakespeare's minor plays.
Stratford. Lang.: Eng.   2182

1947.   Plays/librettos/scripts.
Analysis of Benjamin Britten's opera *Albert Herring*. London.
Lang.: Eng.   3897

1947-1986.   Performance/production.
Interview with Carlo Boso on *commedia dell'arte*
reconstruction. Italy. Lang.: Eng.   3415

1948-1986.   Performance/production.
Actress Rosemary Harris discusses her work in *The Petition*.
London. New York, NY. Lang.: Eng.   2177

1949-1964.   Plays/librettos/scripts.
Collaboration of authors and composers of *Billy Budd*.
London. Lang.: Eng.   3895

UK-England — cont'd

1972. **Plays/librettos/scripts.**
Analysis of Harold Pinter's technique in adapting *A la Recherche du Temps Perdu (Remembrance of Things Past)* by Marcel Proust as a screenplay. Lang.: Eng.   3240

1973-1986. **Institutions.**
Interview with Hilary Westlake of Lumière & Son. London. Lang.: Swe.   536

1973-1986. **Plays/librettos/scripts.**
Political views of Howard Brenton as evidenced in his adaptations. Lang.: Eng.   2883

1974. **Plays/librettos/scripts.**
Brecht's ideas about the history play as justification for Edward Bond's *Bingo*. Lang.: Eng.   2876

1975-1983. **Plays/librettos/scripts.**
History of Harold Pinter's work and critical reception. Lang.: Eng.   2860

1975-1986. **Performance/production.**
Director Mike Alfreds' interpretation of the plays of Čechov. London. USSR. Lang.: Eng.   2127

Interview with performance artist Mona Hatoum. Lang.: Eng.   3452

1976-1985. **Administration.**
Performers' rights in the United States, England and France. USA. France. Lang.: Eng.   3164

1976-1986. **Design/technology.**
Cinematographer Roger Deakins discusses lighting for his work in the film *Sid and Nancy*. New York, NY. Los Angeles, CA. London. Lang.: Eng.   3211

1976-1986. **Institutions.**
Community documentary plays of Living Archive Project. Milton Keynes. Lang.: Eng.   1589

Experiences of a couple who converted a coal barge into a touring puppet theatre. London. Lang.: Eng.   4005

1976-1986. **Plays/librettos/scripts.**
Interview with actor-playwright Alan Williams. Toronto, ON. Winnipeg, MB. Hull. Lang.: Eng.   2438

1977-1986. **Performance spaces.**
History of the new Swan Theatre. Stratford. Lang.: Ger.   632

1978. **Plays/librettos/scripts.**
Playwright Edward Bond's use of Greek models in *The Woman*. Lang.: Eng.   2834

Theme of renewal in Harold Pinter's *Betrayal*.   2835

1978-1985. **Performance spaces.**
Description of the new Swan Theatre. Stratford. Lang.: Eng.   1619

1978-1985. **Plays/librettos/scripts.**
Productions of Jane Howell and Elijah Moshinsky for the BBC Shakespeare series. London. Lang.: Eng.   3283

Review articles on the BBC Shakespeare series. London. Lang.: Eng.   3284

1978-1986. **Performance/production.**
Horse and Bamboo Theatre, specializing in community puppet theatre. Rossendale. Lang.: Eng.   3970

1979-1986. **Performance/production.**
Discussion of increasingly popular comedy cabaret. Lang.: Eng.   3366

1979-1986. **Plays/librettos/scripts.**
Links between Shakespeare's *Macbeth* and Tom Stoppard's *Dogg's Hamlet, Cahoot's Macbeth*. Lang.: Eng.   2843

Interview with playwright Louise Page. Lang.: Eng.   2882

1979-1986. **Relation to other fields.**
The work of disabled theatre companies in England. Lang.: Eng.   1139

1980. **Performance/production.**
Adapting and staging of *Les Misérables* by Victor Hugo. Lang.: Eng.   3609

1980. **Plays/librettos/scripts.**
Interview with playwright Dusty Hughes about his play, *The Futurists*. Lang.: Eng.   2867

Caryl Churchill combines Brecht's alienation effect with traditional comic structure in *Cloud 9*.   2871

1980-1986. **Design/technology.**
Lighting concerts, plays and pantomimes in a church hall with minimum lighting facilities. Stratford. Lang.: Eng.   326

Lighting outline for a unique production of *Godspell*. Lang.: Eng.   327

Amateur technician describes how three one-act plays can be lit with four lanterns. Lang.: Eng.   1522

Overview of a suspension lighting system for the drama area of a small video studio. Lang.: Eng.   3254

Amateur lighting designer describes her first job. Brighton. Lang.: Eng.   3302

Outlines the lighting of an amateur pantomime. Lang.: Eng.   3303

Amateur technician outlines his experience of lighting a pantomime in a hall with a ceiling 8 feet high. Brighton. Lang.: Eng.   3304

Interview with designer John Napier. London. Lang.: Eng.   3585

1980-1986. **Institutions.**
Administrators seen as destroying the fringe theatre. London. Lang.: Swe.   535

1980-1986. **Performance spaces.**
Technical design features of New Victoria Theatre. Stoke-on-Trent. Lang.: Eng.   624

Technical review of *She Stoops to Conquer* by Oliver Goldsmith performed at the New Victoria Theatre. Newcastle-under-Lyme. Lang.: Eng.   1618

1980-1986. **Performance/production.**
Interview with Pip Broughton of Paines Plough Theatre Company. Lang.: Eng.   2166

Profile of the work of Lumière & Son Circus (London). Lang.: Eng.   3454

1980-1987. **Design/technology.**
Comparison of British and North America theatre sound systems. North America. Lang.: Eng.   305

Renovation of the Alhambra Theatre. Bradford. Lang.: Eng.   1521

Analysis of the technological aspects of *Les Misérables*. London. Lang.: Eng.   3582

1980-1987. **Performance spaces.**
Overview of pub theatres. London. Lang.: Eng.   626

1981-1985. **Plays/librettos/scripts.**
Interview with playwright Howard Barker. Lang.: Eng.   2845

1981-1986. **Administration.**
Dissolution of the Greater London Council and its effect on theatre funding. London. Lang.: Eng.   81

1981-1986. **Institutions.**
Comparison of the creative process in theatre and in research. London. Lang.: Eng.   1586

1981-1986. **Performance/production.**
Production analysis of four plays by Peter Barnes. Lang.: Eng.   805

1981-1986. **Research/historiography.**
Characteristics of radio drama. Lang.: Eng.   3188

1982. **Performance/production.**
Comparative analysis of productions of *Summer* by Edward Bond. London. Lang.: Eng.   2163

1982-1986. **Performance/production.**
Director Lou Stein discusses his policy at the Watford Palace Theatre. Watford. Lang.: Eng.   2167

1983. **Plays/librettos/scripts.**
Playwright Simon Gray's journal about the production of his play *The Common Pursuit*. Lang.: Eng.   2858

1983-1985. **Design/technology.**
Translation of article on theatre technicians in England from ABTT News. Lang.: Hun.   330

1983-1986. **Performance/production.**
Interview with actor/playwright Harvey Fierstein. London. New York. Lang.: Eng.   2175

1984-1985. **Performance/production.**
Shakespearean productions by the National Theatre, Royal Shakespeare Company and Orange Tree Theatre. Stratford. London. Lang.: Eng.   2183

1984-1986. **Institutions.**
Progress and aims of Women's Playhouse Trust. London. Lang.: Eng.   1590

1984-1986. **Performance/production.**
Interview with Lesbian feminist theatre company Hard Corps. Lang.: Eng.   2164

1985. **Performance/production.**
Interview with actress Glenda Jackson. Lang.: Eng.   2134

Reviews of three Shakespearean productions. London. Stratford. Ashland, OR. Lang.: Eng.   2140

UK-England — cont'd

Performance by Joculatores Lancastrienses of Thomas Garter's interlude, *Commody of the Moste Vertuous and Godlye Susanna*. Lancaster. Lang.: Eng.   2148

Review of Tennessee Williams' *Sweet Bird of Youth* starring Lauren Bacall, directed by Harold Pinter. London. Lang.: Eng.   2186

1985.   **Reference materials.**
Chronological list of 407 London productions mounted in 1985 with an index to actors, writers and production personnel. London. Lang.: Eng.   3002

1985.   **Relation to other fields.**
Influence of Sir Keith Joseph upon the education system. Lang.: Eng.   1138

References to operas in the novels of Agatha Christie. Lang.: Eng.   3923

1985.   **Research/historiography.**
Development of two databases, TANDEM and IBT to aid in international theatre research. Lang.: Eng.   1187

Computer databases for theatre studies. London. Lang.: Eng.   1188

1985-1986.   **Performance/production.**
Director Deborah Warner of KICK on her production of Shakespeare's *Coriolanus* and limited public funding for the non-touring company. London. Lang.: Eng.   812

1985-1986.   **Plays/librettos/scripts.**
Current state of women's playwriting. Lang.: Eng.   2830

Diary of a playwright at Royal Shakespeare Company. Lang.: Eng.   2854

1985-1986.   **Reference materials.**
Guide to theatrical services and productions. Lang.: Eng.   1035

1986.   **Administration.**
Discussion of Berne Convention (1886) establishing copyright agreement. London. Lang.: Eng.   80

Artistic directors of Everyman Theatre and Theatre Clwyd discuss their theatres. Cheltenham. Mold. Lang.: Eng.   82

1986.   **Audience.**
Audience reaction to performance art productions. Newcastle. Lang.: Eng.   3433

1986.   **Design/technology.**
Overview of performance technology show at Riverside Studios. London. Lang.: Eng.   323

Report on the first European subsidiary of Rosco Laboratories. London. Lang.: Hun.   328

Information on Rank Strand Ltd. Lighting and its subsidiaries. Lang.: Hun.   329

The making of the film *My Beautiful Laundrette*. London.   3202

Design challenges of the film *Absolute Beginners*. London. Lang.: Eng.   3203

Lighting requirements for television production of *Lost Empires*. Lang.: Eng.   3255

Set designer John Napier's work on *Les Misérables*. London.   3583

William Dudley's life-like replica of the Bounty for David Essex's *Mutiny!*. London. Lang.: Eng.   3584

1986.   **Institutions.**
Survey of nine repertory theatres. Lang.: Eng.   533

Overview of the *Not the RSC Festival* at the Almeida Theatre. London. Lang.: Eng.   534

David Porter, the new artistic director of Leicester Haymarket Theatre, discusses his policy. Leicester. Lang.: Eng.   1587

Place of women in Britain's National Theatre. London. Lang.: Eng.   1588

Actor Michael Pennington and director Michael Bogdanov discuss the formation of the English Shakespeare Company. Lang.: Eng.   1592

1986.   **Performance spaces.**
Design and construction of Grand Cayman's National Theatre. Cayman Islands. Lang.: Eng.   590

Analysis of trends in theatre design. Lang.: Eng.   628

Description of the new Swan Theatre and Shakespeare-related buildings. Stratford. Lang.: Eng.   631

Impact of Swan Theatre on actors, audiences. Stratford. Lang.: Eng.   1620

1986.   **Performance/production.**
Director discusses *Tramway Road* by Ronald Harwood. South Africa, Republic of. London. Lang.: Eng.   2073

Theatre season in London. London. Lang.: Eng.   2107

Review of alternative theatre productions. London. Lang.: Eng.   2108

Collection of newspaper reviews by London theatre critics. London. Lang.: Eng.   2109

Collection of newspaper reviews by London theatre critics. London. Lang.: Eng.   2110

Collection of newspaper reviews by London theatre critics. Lang.: Eng.   2111

Collection of newspaper reviews by London theatre critics. London. Lang.: Eng.   2112

Collection of newspaper reviews by London theatre critics. London. Lang.: Eng.   2113

Collection of newspaper reviews by London theatre critics. Lang.: Eng.   2114

Collection of newspaper reviews by London theatre critics. Lang.: Eng.   2115

Collection of newspaper reviews by London theatre critics. London. Lang.: Eng.   2116

Collection of newspaper reviews by London theatre critics. London. Lang.: Eng.   2117

Collection of newspaper reviews by London theatre critics. London. Lang.: Eng.   2118

Collection of newspaper reviews by London theatre critics. London. Lang.: Eng.   2119

Collection of newspaper reviews by London theatre critics. Lang.: Eng.   2120

Collection of newspaper reviews by London theatre critics. London. Lang.: Eng.   2121

Collection of newspaper reviews by London theatre critics. London. Lang.: Eng.   2122

Collection of newspaper reviews by London theatre critics. London. Lang.: Eng.   2123

Collection of newspaper reviews by London theatre critics. London. Lang.: Eng.   2124

Collection of newspaper reviews by London theatre critics. London. Lang.: Eng.   2125

Collection of newspaper reviews by London theatre critics. London. Lang.: Eng.   2126

Actors Ben Kingsley and David Suchet discuss their roles in Shakespeare's *Othello*. Lang.: Eng.   2128

Survey of the season at the National Theatre. London. Lang.: Eng.   2130

Establishment of the English Shakespeare Company. Lang.: Eng.   2131

Interview with actress Dorothy Tutin. Chichester. Lang.: Eng.   2132

Interviews with playwrights Louise Page, Charles McKeown and Malcolm Sircon. London. Lang.: Eng.   2133

Michael Coveney surveys the London season. London. Lang.: Eng.   2135

Director Simon Curtis discusses his production of *Road*. London. Lang.: Eng.   2137

Director Simon Callow talks about his production of Jean Cocteau's *The Infernal Machine*. London. Lang.: Eng.   2139

Overview of performances transferred from The Royal Court, Greenwich, and Lyric Hammersmith theatres. London. Lang.: Eng.   2143

Director John Dexter and impresario Eddie Kulukundis discuss the formation of the New Theatre Company. London. Lang.: Eng.   2144

Actress Frances de la Tour discusses her work in *Lillian* by William Luce. London. USA. Lang.: Eng.   2146

Survey of theatrical performances in the low country. Lang.: Eng.   2150

Royal Shakespeare Company performances at the Barbican Theatre. London. Lang.: Eng.   2152

Survey of theatre season in Merseyside. Lang.: Eng.   2157

USA — cont'd

1900-1985. **Performance/production.**
Informal history of musical theatre. New York, NY. London.
Lang.: Eng. 3621

1900-1985. **Plays/librettos/scripts.**
Successful Broadway playwrights, lyricists, and composers
discuss their hits. New York, NY. Lang.: Eng. 3631

1900-1986. **Reference materials.**
Biographical encyclopedia of stand-up comics and comedy
teams. Lang.: Eng. 3472

1901-1965. **Plays/librettos/scripts.**
Career of Xiong Foxi. Beijing. Shanghai. New York, NY.
Lang.: Chi. 2449

1902-1924. **Plays/librettos/scripts.**
The Peasants by Władysław Reymont as possible source for
O'Neill's version of the lustful stepmother play. Lang.: Eng.
2930

1902-1986. **Performance/production.**
Obituary of soprano Dusolina Giannini. Philadelphia, PA.
Lang.: Eng. 3823

1903-1985. **Reference materials.**
Alphabetically arranged profiles and history of professional
and amateur theatres for children. Lang.: Eng. 1046

1903-1985. **Relation to other fields.**
Development of forms and goals in the children's theatre
movement. Lang.: Eng. 1158

1904-1983. **Administration.**
'Sense of place' in developing arts policy. Lang.: Eng. 147

1904-1986. **Performance/production.**
Biography of actor James Cagney. Lang.: Eng. 3228

1907-1986. **Performance/production.**
Actor Laurence Olivier's memoirs. London. New York, NY.
Lang.: Eng. 2170

1908-1922. **Plays/librettos/scripts.**
David Belasco's influence on Eugene O'Neill. New York,
NY. Lang.: Eng. 2927

1909-1985. **Relation to other fields.**
The reception of critic and playwright Karl Kraus in the
English speaking world. New York, NY. Vienna. Glasgow.
Lang.: Ger. 3067

1911-1986. **Administration.**
Edward Downes on his life in the opera. New York, NY.
Lang.: Eng. 3643

1911-1986. **Performance/production.**
Career of film and television actress Lucille Ball. Lang.: Eng.
3167

1912. **Performance/production.**
Max Reinhardt's music-drama *Sumurun*. New York, NY.
Lang.: Ita. 1369

1912-1928. **Plays/librettos/scripts.**
Influence of Gordon Craig on American theatre and his
recognition of Eugene O'Neill's importance. UK-England.
Lang.: Eng. 2908

1915-1984. **Performance/production.**
Biography of singer Frank Sinatra. Lang.: Eng. 3180

1915-1985. **Plays/librettos/scripts.**
Analysis of *A View From the Bridge* by Arthur Miller. New
York, NY. London. Lang.: Cat. 2901

1917-1967. **Plays/librettos/scripts.**
Correlation between short stories and plays by Carson
McCullers. Lang.: Rus. 2889

1920-1943. **Basic theatrical documents.**
Text of Lorenz Hart lyrics. Lang.: Eng. 3580

1922-1969. **Performance/production.**
Biography of singer/actress Judy Garland. Lang.: Eng. 3229

1922-1972. **Performance/production.**
A scholarly study of the careers of Alfred Lunt and Lynn
Fontanne. Lang.: Eng. 2257

1924. **Plays/librettos/scripts.**
Concept of tragic character in Eugene O'Neill's *Desire Under
the Elms*. Lang.: Eng. 2907

1926-1946. **Basic theatrical documents.**
Correspondence between Gertrude Stein and Virgil Thomson
regarding their collaboration on *The Mother of Us All*.
France. Lang.: Eng. 222

1927-1953. **Plays/librettos/scripts.**
Gender role-reversal in the Cycle plays of Eugene O'Neill.
Lang.: Eng. 2896

1928-1965. **Performance/production.**
Comedienne Joan Rivers' account of her life and career.
New York, NY. Lang.: Eng. 3352

1929. **Performance/production.**
Analysis of reviews of 1929 *Dynamo* by Eugene O'Neill
suggest strong production of a weak play. New York, NY.
Lang.: Eng. 2311

1929-1986. **Performance/production.**
Career of choreographer Kenneth MacMillan. Europe. Lang.:
Eng. 1302

1930. **Plays/librettos/scripts.**
Conceptions of the South Sea islands in works of Murnau,
Artaud and Spies. Europe. Indonesia. Lang.: Ita. 3231

1930-1939. **Performance/production.**
Biography of actor Richard B. Harrison, who played God in
The Green Pastures. Lang.: Eng. 828

1930-1939. **Plays/librettos/scripts.**
Treatment of social problems in the plays of Lillian Hellman
and Clifford Odets. Lang.: Eng. 984

1930-1949. **Theory/criticism.**
Aesthetic considerations in the plays and essays of Thornton
Wilder. Lang.: Rus. 3149

1930-1986. **Performance/production.**
Interview with producer, director, actor Robert Lewis. New
York, NY. Lang.: Eng. 844

Career of Broadway composer Stephen Sondheim. New
York, NY. Lang.: Eng. 3624

1932-1985. **Performance/production.**
Profile of puppeteer Blanche Hardig. 3976

1933-1953. **Institutions.**
Eva LeGallienne on Civic Repertory and American Repertory
Theatres. New York, NY. Lang.: Eng. 560

1935-1939. **Plays/librettos/scripts.**
Attitudes toward technology reflected in some Living
Newspaper productions of the Federal Theatre Project.
Lang.: Eng. 2905

1935-1940. **Institutions.**
John Houseman discusses Federal Theatre Project. New
York, NY. Washington, DC. Lang.: Eng. 559

1936-1986. **Administration.**
Cheryl Crawford's producing career discussed in light of her
latest Broadway show. New York, NY. Atlanta, GA. Lang.:
Eng. 117

1936-1986. **Performance/production.**
Review of *Spain/36* by San Francisco Mime Troupe. Spain.
San Francisco, CA. Lang.: Eng. 790

1938. **Performance/production.**
Michael Chekhov's theories of acting and directing. Moscow.
Ridgefield, CT. Lang.: Eng. 887

1938-1988. **Plays/librettos/scripts.**
Gian Carlo Menotti's reactions to harsh criticism of his
operas. New York, NY. Edinburgh. Cadegliano. Lang.: Eng.
3902

1939-1982. **Performance/production.**
Actress Lu Xiaoyan's experiences in preparing to play a role
in *The Little Foxes*. China. Lang.: Chi. 1687

1940-1979. **Performance/production.**
Women's roles in the operas of Benjamin Britten. Lang.:
Eng. 3824

1940-1983. **Administration.**
Strategies for funding under Reagan's Economic Recovery
Act. Lang.: Eng. 98

1940-1984. **Relation to other fields.**
Methods and goals of Children's Theatre Association of
America. Lang.: Eng. 1163

1941-1958. **Plays/librettos/scripts.**
Similarities of *Hughie* by Eugene O'Neill and *The Zoo Story*
by Edward Albee. New York, NY. Lang.: Eng. 2919

1942-1944. **Performance/production.**
History of the Margaret Webster-Paul Robeson production of
Othello. New York, NY. Lang.: Eng. 852

1943-1986. **Performance/production.**
Biography of playwright and actor Sam Shepard. Lang.: Eng.
2295

1944-1985. **Relation to other fields.**
Argument for 'dramatic literacy' as part of 'cultural literacy'.
Lang.: Eng. 1142

1946-1983. **Design/technology.**
Interview with three female lighting designers. Lang.: Eng.
357

1949-1985. **Institutions.**
Training and use of child performers. Lang.: Eng. 565

USA — cont'd

Proposal for using creative drama with museum visits and a study of the visual arts. Austin, TX. Lang.: Eng.   1159

Argument for the establishment of graduate programs in children's theatre. Lang.: Eng.   1168

1985-1986.   Audience.
Postmodern concepts of individual, audience, public. Lang.: Eng.   1454

1985-1986.   Design/technology.
Creating the proportions and constructing a pattern plan for marionettes.   4003

1985-1986.   Plays/librettos/scripts.
Discussion of issues raised in plays of 1985-86 season. New York, NY. Lang.: Eng.   2928

1986.   Administration.
Copyright protection in Korea. Korea. Lang.: Kor.   56

Zelda Fichandler discusses artistic risk and funding. Washington, DC. Lang.: Eng.   101

Ken Copel's transition to independent filmmaker. Lang.: Eng.   3191

The popularity of musical revues in regional theatre. Lang.: Eng.   3576

Account of an international symposium on the future of opera. New York, NY. Lang.: Eng.   3646

1986.   Design/technology.
Theatre Craft's annual directory of theatre equipment and manufacturers. Lang.: Eng.   336

Prices, quantities and manufacturers' official line on stage blood. Lang.: Eng.   337

Interview with lighting designers Arden Fingerhut, Tharon Musser and Jennifer Tipton. Lang.: Eng.   340

Construction of realistic-sounding concussion mortar. Lang.: Eng.   346

Modification in the nylon roller construction explained in TB 1137 by Ray Forton. Lang.: Eng.   348

Construction of terrain platforms. Lang.: Eng.   358

Charles Ludlam's role as set designer, artistic director and lead actor of The Ridiculous Theatre Company. New York, NY.   360

Construction of a pantograph. Lang.: Eng.   361

Construction of non-skid ground cloth. Lang.: Eng.   371

How to frost plexiglass. Lang.: Eng.   375

A profile of non-union scene shops. New York, NY.   396

Touch-tone relay controller for special effects. Lang.: Eng.   401

An equipment buyer's guide to followspots.   411

Interview with sound designer Abe Jacob. New York, NY. Lang.: Eng.   414

Capabilities of available computer-controlled sound systems.   421

Construction of stage turntables. Lang.: Eng.   423

Production design for Stephen Spielberg's series *Amazing Stories*. Lang.: Eng.   3258

1986.   Institutions.
The few New York theatres that promote international plays and companies. New York, NY. Lang.: Eng.   561

1986.   Performance spaces.
Results of an Off Broadway survey on the crisis of limited space and real estate costs. New York, NY. Lang.: Eng. 638

1986.   Performance/production.
Psychological elements of stage fright. Lang.: Eng.   822

Physical nature of acting. Lang.: Eng.   825

Guide to auditioning for dramatic and musical productions. Lang.: Eng.   830

Interview with director and cast of Wajda's *Crime and Punishment*. Cracow. Lang.: Eng.   2025

Interview with individuals involved in production of *Alcestis* by Euripides. Cambridge, MA. Lang.: Eng.   2266

Interview with Peter Gallagher on his portrayal of Edmund in *Long Day's Journey Into Night*. New York, NY. New London, CT. Lang.: Eng.   2268

Robert Auletta's updated version of Sophocles' *Ajax*. Washington, DC. Lang.: Eng.   2276

Account of competition in producing Spanish Golden Age plays. El Paso, TX. Lang.: Eng.   2280

Robert Wilson's production of *Alcestis* at the American Repertory Theatre. Cambridge, MA.   2306

Profile of actor Bill Cosby. Lang.: Eng.   3274

Review of Prokofiêv's *Love for Three Oranges*. Cincinnati, OH. Lang.: Eng.   3798

Peter Sellars' production of Mozart's *Così fan tutte*. Purchase, NY. Lang.: Eng.   3815

Review of premiere performance of Myron Fink's opera *Chinchilla*. Binghamton, NY. Lang.: Eng.   3840

Puppets in Performance, part of the 50th anniversary celebration of the WPA Federal Theatre Project.   3974

1986.   Plays/librettos/scripts.
Playwright Robert Auletta on his adaptation of Sophocles'*Ajax*. Washington, DC. Lang.: Eng.   2891

Review of adaptations for the stage of short stories by Čechov. New York, NY. Lang.: Eng.   2922

Interview with theatre professionals on successful writing and production. Lang.: Eng.   2932

A group of playwrights discuss the one-act play as a form.   2937

How David Byrne constructed a script for *True Stories*. 3242

1986.   Reference materials.
Directory of member organizations of ART/NY. New York, NY. Lang.: Eng.   1037

A directory of services available to Dramatists Guild members.   1038

1986.   Relation to other fields.
Effect of playmaking on sixth and seventh grade pupils. New York, NY. Lang.: Eng.   1157

1986.   Theory/criticism.
Essays on artistic media by playwright David Mamet. New York, NY. Los Angeles, CA. Lang.: Eng.   3144

USA, cont: Part 2

Administration.
Alternate programs produced by opera houses. Lang.: Eng.   3642

Design/technology.
Review of the leading manufacturers of remote controlled luminaires.   412

Interview with scene designer Ming Cho Lee. New Haven, CT. Lang.: Eng.   1528

Special effects in the film version of *Little Shop of Horrors*. Lang.: Eng.   3212

Portland Opera's resident designer discusses set recycling. Lang.: Eng.   3663

Choosing music and sound effects for puppet theatre. Lang.: Eng.   3953

Creating overhead shadow sequence for puppet production.   4014

Performance/production.
Changes in ensemble theatre practice. Lang.: Eng.   842

Interview with Elisabeth Bergner and Jane Alexander on their portrayals of Joan of Arc. Berlin, West. Malvern. Washington, DC. Lang.: Eng.   1766

Proposal to include theatre critics in pre-production evaluation of plays. UK-England. Lang.: Eng.   2162

Performance art and its current characteristic tone. Lang.: Eng.   3459

Profile of and interview with Anthony Davis, composer of the opera *X*, on the life and times of Malcolm X. New York, NY. Lang.: Eng.   3834

Plays/librettos/scripts.
Richard Foreman's ideas about playwriting. Lang.: Swe.   980

Popularity and relevance of Eugene O'Neill. Lang.: Eng.   2894

Reference materials.
Comprehensive list of rehearsal and performance spaces. New York, NY. Lang.: Eng.   1042

Relation to other fields.
Destructiveness in dramatic literature. Lang.: Eng.   3066

Theory/criticism.
Technology and the spiritual/aesthetic role of the actor. Lang.: Eng.   1230

National Conference of Theatre Communications Group (TCG). Amherst, MA. Lang.: Eng.   1233

1958. **Plays/librettos/scripts.**
Genesis of *Sweet Bird of Youth* by Tennessee Williams.
Lang.: Eng. 2904

1959. **Plays/librettos/scripts.**
Interview with playwright Lorraine Hansberry. Lang.: Eng.
2945

1959-1986. **Plays/librettos/scripts.**
The history of Cuban exile theatre. Cuba. New York, NY.
Lang.: Spa. 2451

1960. **Training.**
History of the Performance Group. Lang.: Eng. 3161

1960-1980. **Relation to other fields.**
Comparison of works of playwright Sam Shepard and artist
Robert Rauschenberg. Lang.: Eng. 3062

1960-1982. **Performance/production.**
Resurgence of street theatre productions and companies. New
York, NY. Lang.: Eng. 2285

1960-1984. **Administration.**
Growing activity and changing role of Black regional theatre
companies. Lang.: Eng. 1440

1960-1985. **Performance/production.**
Extracts from unpublished writings by Julian Beck. Europe.
Lang.: Ita. 824

1960-1985. **Relation to other fields.**
Sociocultural elements of Black theatre. Lang.: Eng. 3063

1960-1986. **Performance/production.**
Gitta Honegger on training dramaturgs and the European
tradition of dramaturgy. New Haven, CT. Lang.: Eng. 2251

1960-1986. **Plays/librettos/scripts.**
Interview with playwright Kathleen Betsko. Coventry. Lang.:
Eng. 2487

Richard Foreman, founder of Ontological-Hysteric Theater
Company. Lang.: Swe. 2890

1960-1986. **Theory/criticism.**
Analysis of the essentials of art, especially in theatre. Lang.:
Eng. 3142

1961-1978. **Institutions.**
Discussion of techniques and theories of Bread and Puppet
Theatre. New York, NY. Lang.: Ita. 3960

1961-1985. **Performance/production.**
Black opera stars and companies. Enid, OK. New York, NY.
Lang.: Eng. 3839

1962-1986. **Theory/criticism.**
Influence of drama critic Eric Bentley. Lang.: Eng. 1229

1963-1983. **Theory/criticism.**
Self-reflexivity in Shakespeare as seen by Lionel Abel, Sigurd
Burckhardt and James L. Calderwood. Lang.: Eng. 3141

1963-1985. **Plays/librettos/scripts.**
Themes and structures of the plays of Lanford Wilson.
Lang.: Eng. 2936

1963-1986. **Administration.**
A profile of Center Stage. Baltimore, MD. Lang.: Eng. 109

1963-1986. **Theory/criticism.**
Intents and purposes of *The Drama Review*. Lang.: Eng.
3150

1964. **Institutions.**
Production history and techniques of the Living Theatre.
Lang.: Eng. 546

1964-1980. **Theory/criticism.**
Edward Albee's development of realistic setting for absurdist
drama. Lang.: Eng. 3148

1964-1984. **Performance/production.**
Interview with choreographer Meredith Monk. New York,
NY. Lang.: Eng. 1368

1964-1984. **Theory/criticism.**
Arthur Miller's *After the Fall* seen an monomyth. Lang.:
Eng. 3138

1964-1986. **Theory/criticism.**
Forums: Dispute regarding content and aims of *The Drama
Review*. Lang.: Eng. 3139

1965. **Performance/production.**
Modern dancer Ann Halprin and her work with artists in
other media. Lang.: Eng. 1352

Explorative structure and manner of performance in avant-
garde theatre. Lang.: Eng. 2277

1965. **Plays/librettos/scripts.**
God as image and symbol in Edward Albee's *Tiny Alice*.
Lang.: Eng. 2911

1965. **Theory/criticism.**
John Cage discusses his struggle to define art. Lang.: Eng.
1231

1965-1984. **Design/technology.**
Career of scenic designer Eugene Lee. Providence, RI. Lang.:
Eng. 339

1965-1985. **Plays/librettos/scripts.**
Correspondence and personal contact with Sir Michael
Tippett. Dallas, TX. Lang.: Eng. 3900

1965-1985. **Reference materials.**
Chronological listing of 20 theatre seasons. New York, NY.
Lang.: Eng. 3009

1965-1986. **Institutions.**
Origins and evolution of Teatro Campesino. Mexico. Lang.:
Eng. 547

1965-1986. **Plays/librettos/scripts.**
Analysis of television docudramas as a melodrama genre.
Lang.: Eng. 3285

1966. **Institutions.**
Reprint of an article by Douglas Turner Ward that resulted
in the founding of the Negro Ensemble Company. New
York, NY. Lang.: Eng. 572

1966. **Theory/criticism.**
Details ten-year anniversary celebration of *The Drama
Review* and reasons for its longevity. Lang.: Eng. 3140

1966-1985. **Institutions.**
History of Black theater companies. Philadelphia, PA. Lang.:
Eng. 1608

1967. **Plays/librettos/scripts.**
Argument of reversed chronology in Acts I and II of *La
Turista* by Sam Shepard. Lang.: Eng. 2951

1967-1984. **Relation to other fields.**
Interview with playwright Wole Soyinka. Nigeria. New
Haven, CT. Lang.: Eng. 3047

1968. **Relation to other fields.**
Gertrud Schattner, a founder of drama therapy, and her
work at Bellevue Hospital. New York, NY. Austria. Lang.:
Eng. 3064

1968-1973. **Plays/librettos/scripts.**
Summary and discussion of the plays of Ed Bullins. Lang.:
Eng. 2900

1968-1985. **Performance/production.**
Career of director/choreographer Mike Malone. Washington,
DC. Cleveland, OH. Lang.: Eng. 2275

1968-1986. **Design/technology.**
Interview with manager Tony Smith and lighting designer
Alan Owen of the rock band Genesis focusing on the
lighting technology used on their latest tour. Lang.: Eng.
3320

1968-1986. **Performance/production.**
Interview with puppeteers Roger Dennis and Bob Vesely.
Cleveland, OH. Lang.: Eng. 3972

Peter Schumann and his work with the Bread and Puppet
Theatre. New York, NY. Lang.: Eng. 3973

1968-1986. **Plays/librettos/scripts.**
Identifies dramatic elements unique to street theatre. Lang.:
Eng. 3354

1968-1986. **Theory/criticism.**
Six rules which render socially desirable elements of
performance superfluous. Lang.: Eng. 3151

1969. **Plays/librettos/scripts.**
Mosaic structure of Arthur Kopit's *Indians*. 2935

1969-1982. **Institutions.**
History of two major Black touring companies. New York,
NY. Lang.: Eng. 1598

1969-1984. **Institutions.**
History of Circle Repertory Company. New York, NY.
Lang.: Eng. 1606

1969-1984. **Audience.**
Susceptibility of American audiences to media manipulation
by the bureaucratic establishment. Lang.: Eng. 3166

1969-1986. **Theory/criticism.**
Richard Schechner bids farewell to *The Drama Review* and
suggests areas of future theatrical investigation. Lang.: Eng.
1234

1970-1983. **Institutions.**
Goals and accomplishments of Theatre for the New City.
New York, NY. Lang.: Eng. 570

1970-1983. **Performance/production.**
Avant-garde theatre companies from Britain perform in New
York festival. New York, NY. Lang.: Eng. 2286

1970-1984. **Performance/production.**
The training and career of puppeteer Julie Taymor. Lang.:
Eng. 3982

1970-1984. **Plays/librettos/scripts.**
Director John Lion on his work with playwright Sam
Shepard. San Francisco, CA. New York, NY. Lang.: Eng.
2924

1970-1985. **Design/technology.**
Tomie DePaola's work in puppetry. New London, NH.
Lang.: Eng. 3955

1970-1986. **Institutions.**
History of Black Spectrum. New York, NY. Lang.: Eng.
1603

Brief histories of the H.A.D.L.E.Y. Players and the Cynthia
Belgrave Theatre Workshop. New York, NY. Lang.: Eng.
1604

1970-1986. **Performance/production.**
Productions of Dario Fo's *Morte accidentale di un anarchico*
(Accidental Death of an Anarchist) in the light of Fo's
political ideas. Canada. Italy. Lang.: Eng. 2262

Gary Jones, and the Black Street, USA Puppet Theatre.
Chicago, IL. Los Angeles, CA. Lang.: Eng. 3978

1970-1986. **Plays/librettos/scripts.**
Work of playwright R.A. Shiomi, including production history
of *Yellow Fever*. Toronto, ON. New York, NY. San
Francisco, CA. Lang.: Eng. 2422

Race in prison dramas of Piñero, Camillo, Elder and Bullins.
Lang.: Eng. 2912

Distinguishes between the natural flow of words and present
forms of linguistic alienation. Austria. Lang.: Eng. 2913

1971. **Plays/librettos/scripts.**
Playwright David Rabe's treatment of cliche in *Sticks and
Bones*. Lang.: Eng. 2902

1971-1986. **Design/technology.**
Lighting techniques and equipment used at theme park.
Baltimore, MD. Lang.: Eng. 3315

1971-1986. **Institutions.**
Brief history of the McCree Theatre. Flint, MI. Lang.: Eng.
1609

1971-1986. **Performance/production.**
Interview with dramaturg Anne Cattaneo. New York, NY.
Lang.: Eng. 2254

1971-1986. **Plays/librettos/scripts.**
Discussion of plays and themes concerning the Women's
Movement. Lang.: Eng. 982

1971-1986. **Theory/criticism.**
Michael Kirby defends the liberal outlook of *The Drama
Review*. Lang.: Eng. 1232

1972-1983. **Design/technology.**
Interview with set designer Jim Clayburgh. New York, NY.
Lang.: Eng. 390

1972-1985. **Plays/librettos/scripts.**
Development of playwright Sam Shepard's style. Lang.: Eng.
2943

1972-1986. **Administration.**
Lynne Meadow, artistic director of the Manhattan Theatre
Club, describes her fourteen years on the job. New York,
NY. Lang.: Eng. 1442

1972-1986. **Design/technology.**
Career of lighting designer Beverly Emmons. 333

1972-1986. **Performance spaces.**
History of the Alabama Shakespeare Festival and new
theatre. Montgomery, AL. Lang.: Eng. 1621

1973-1984. **Reference materials.**
Current work of Audelco award-winning playwrights. New
York, NY. Lang.: Eng. 3007

1973-1986. **Institutions.**
Career of Marjorie Moon, artistic director of Billie Holliday
Theatre. New York, NY. Cleveland, OH. Lang.: Eng. 1610

1973-1986. **Performance/production.**
Profile of and interview with opera parodist Charles Ludlam
of The Ridiculous Theatre Company. New York, NY. Lang.:
Eng. 3825

1973-1986. **Reference materials.**
David Mamet bibliography. Lang.: Eng. 3008

1974. **Theory/criticism.**
Critique of James Fenton's review of two books on Bertolt
Brecht. 1236

1974-1985. **Institutions.**
Management techniques for growth at Tears of Joy Puppet
Theatre. Vancouver, WA. Lang.: Eng. 549

1974-1985. **Performance/production.**
Interview with dramaturg Russell Vandenbroucke. Los
Angeles, CA. Lang.: Eng. 2253

1974-1986. **Performance/production.**
Aesthetics, styles, rehearsal techniques of director Richard
Foreman. Lang.: Eng. 2263

1975-1983. **Institutions.**
Profile of Writers Theatre, an organization focusing on
adaptations of poetry and literature for theatre. New York,
NY. Lang.: Eng. 562

1975-1984. **Institutions.**
Profile of Merry Enterprises Theatre. New York, NY. Lang.:
Eng. 543

1975-1985. **Performance/production.**
Changes in East Village performance scene. New York, NY.
Lang.: Eng. 3458

1975-1986. **Design/technology.**
Interview with director and former designer Wilford Leach.
New York, NY. 344

1975-1986. **Performance/production.**
Merce Cunningham, Alwin Nikolais, Meredith Monk and
Yvonne Rainer on post-modern dance. Lang.: Eng. 1285

Dramaturg Oskar Eustis on confronting social and aesthetic
problems. San Francisco, CA. Lang.: Eng. 2250

1976. **Performance/production.**
Andrei Serban discusses the vibration of a sound and its
effect on the listener. Lang.: Eng. 2304

1976-1984. **Performance/production.**
Revival of Philip Glass and Robert Wilson's *Einstein on the
Beach* and opportunities to improve the piece. New York,
NY. Lang.: Eng. 2305

1976-1985. **Administration.**
Copyright licensing agreement between museums and artists.
Lang.: Eng. 144

Injunctions in copyright infringement cases. Lang.: Eng. 146

Performers' rights in the United States, England and France.
UK-England. France. Lang.: Eng. 3164

1976-1986. **Design/technology.**
Cinematographer Roger Deakins discusses lighting for his
work in the film *Sid and Nancy*. New York, NY. Los
Angeles, CA. London. Lang.: Eng. 3211

1976-1986. **Institutions.**
New administrative personnel at the Opera Theatre of St.
Louis. St. Louis, MO. Lang.: Eng. 3679

The history and plans of the Pennsylvania Opera Theatre.
Philadelphia, PA. Lang.: Eng. 3680

1976-1986. **Theory/criticism.**
Critical profile of *Performing Arts Journal* and of recent
theatrical trends. Lang.: Pol. 1228

1976-1987. **Design/technology.**
Contemporary theatre architecture. Lang.: Eng. 342

1977-1986. **Design/technology.**
The WPA Theatre's resident designer, Edward Gianfrancesco.
New York, NY. 382

1977-1986. **Institutions.**
Artistic director of WPA Theatre Kyle Renick discusses
institutionalization of theatre companies. New York, NY.
Lang.: Eng. 566

1977-1986. **Performance/production.**
Handbook for acting in television commercials. Lang.: Eng.
3271

1978. **Plays/librettos/scripts.**
Imagery and the role of women in Sam Shepard's *Buried
Child*. Lang.: Eng. 2899

1978-1983. **Institutions.**
Profile of Economy Tires Theatre, producing arm of Dance
Theatre Workshop. New York, NY. Lang.: Eng. 563

1978-1983. **Relation to other fields.**
Playwright Sam Shepard's recent plays and super-realist
painting. Lang.: Eng. 3069

1978-1985. **Performance/production.**
DeVina Barajas discusses performing the songs of Brecht.
Switzerland. Germany, West. 3607

1979-1983. **Administration.**
Favorable ruling from Court of Appeals assisted arts
organizations paying municipal property taxes. New York,
NY. Lang.: Eng. 160

1979-1984. **Performance/production.**
Martha Clarke's production of *The Garden of Earthly
Delights*. New York, NY. Lang.: Eng. 1371

GEOGRAPHICAL - CHRONOLOGICAL INDEX

1935-1985.   Performance/production.
Jubilee of Avarskij Musykal'no-Dramatičeskij Teat'r im. G.
Cadasy. Lang.: Rus.   873
1938.   Performance/production.
Michael Chekhov's theories of acting and directing. Moscow.
Ridgefield, CT. Lang.: Eng.   887
1938-1980.   Performance/production.
Soviet actor, poet and singer Vladimir Vysockij. Lang.: Rus.
                                                       861
1940-1980.   Performance/production.
Autobiography of B.G. Golubovskij, director of the Gogol
Theatre. Moscow. Lang.: Rus.   2322
1947-1971.   Performance/production.
Recollections of children's theatre in two Soviet cities.
Leningrad. Novosidirsk. Lang.: Rus.   2333
1950-1979.   Performance/production.
Development of Armenian directing. Lang.: Rus.   896
1950-1979.   Plays/librettos/scripts.
Trends in Russian Soviet dramaturgy. Lang.: Rus.   2961
1950-1985.   Audience.
Articles on social role of urban theatres. Lang.: Rus. 205
1950-1985.   Performance/production.
Creative development of ballerina Irina Kolpakova.
Leningrad. Lang.: Rus.   1317
1950-1986.   Performance/production.
Career of actor-director Oleg Tabakov. Moscow. Lang.: Rus.
                                                       904
1960-1980.   Performance/production.
Development of a system of stage appearance for actors.
Lang.: Rus.   880
1960-1986.   Design/technology.
Work of F.F. Nirod, principal designer of the Teat'r Opery i
Baleta im. T.G. Sevčenko. Kiev. Lang.: Rus.   432
1960-1986.   Performance/production.
Comparison of Soviet theatre of the 1960s and 1980s.
Moscow. Lang.: Rus.   860
USA-USSR cultural ties, including theatre. USA. Lang.: Rus.
                                                       863
1961-1979.   Plays/librettos/scripts.
Analysis of *Grupa Laokoona (The Laocoön Group)* by
Tadeusz Różewicz and *Tsaplia (The Heron)* by Vasilij
Aksënov. Poland. Lang.: Eng.   2738
1970-1979.   Performance/production.
Influence of playwright A.V. Vampilov. Lang.: Rus.   2319
1970-1980.   Audience.
Socio-aesthetic notes on contemporary theatre and audiences.
Lang.: Rus.   210
1970-1980.   Plays/librettos/scripts.
Conflict and characterization in recent Soviet dramaturgy.
Lang.: Rus.   2967
1970-1980.   Research/historiography.
Analysis and description in reviews of performances. Lang.:
Rus.   3072
1970-1984.   Training.
Interview with director and teacher Zinovy Korogodskij.
Moscow. Leningrad. Lang.: Eng.   3163
1970-1985.   Performance/production.
Staging of Uzbek comedy. Lang.: Rus.   2326
1970-1986.   Performance/production.
On developments in the theatres of the Ukraine. Lang.: Rus.
                                                       862
1971-1972.   Plays/librettos/scripts.
Correspondence between Bernhard Reich and Heinz-Uwe
Haus.   2966
1973-1986.   Performance/production.
Creative development of director Jurij Liubimov in Italy.
Italy. Lang.: Ita.   2003
1975-1986.   Performance/production.
Director Mike Alfreds' interpretation of the plays of Čechov.
London. Lang.: Eng.   2127
1980.   Administration.
Interview with V.R. Beljakovič, manager of Teat'r-studija na
Jugo-Zapade. Moscow. Lang.: Rus.   185
1980.   Performance/production.
Interview with actor A. Džigorchanjan. Moscow. Lang.: Rus.
                                                       902
1980.   Relation to other fields.
Conceptions of humankind as seen in contemporary theatre.
Lang.: Rus.   1171
Sociological view of audience-performer relationship. Lang.:
Rus.   1176

New tendencies in Soviet theatre. Lang.: Rus.   1178
1980.   Theory/criticism.
Reflections on theatre criticism. Lang.: Rus.   1247
1980.   Training.
Education for the actor-singer. Lang.: Rus.   3502
1980-1985.   Performance/production.
Artistic directors of Soviet Ballet Theatre on plans for the
future. Moscow. Lang.: Rus.   1318
1980-1986.   Performance/production.
Research on the theatre and dramaturgy of Soviet
Azerbajdžan. Lang.: Rus.   15
1980-1986.   Administration.
Independent financing of experimental theatre. Lang.: Rus.
                                                       182
Need for change in the organization of theatrical
management. Lang.: Rus.   186
Personnel problems in theatres. Lang.: Rus.   188
Effect of group planning on the creativity of regional
theatres. Lang.: Rus.   189
Amateur theatre groups' transition to professional status.
Moscow. Lang.: Rus.   191
Ukrainian actors and teachers on rebuilding theatre business.
Lang.: Ukr.   192
Problems of present-day reality in Ukrainian theatres. Lang.:
Ukr.   193
Articles on the organizational problems of theatre. Lang.:
Rus.   194
Experiments with broadening creative independence and
reestablishing economic basis of theatre operations. Lang.:
Rus.   195
Problems of theatres in USSR-Russian SFSR. Lang.: Rus.
                                                       196
Principal choreographer of Kirov Theatre on problems of
Soviet ballet theatre. Lang.: Rus.   1293
1980-1986.   Audience.
Absence of an audience for non-mainstream theatre. Lang.:
Rus.   206
Conference on low theatrical attendance. Kujbyšev.   207
On the role of the theatre in the life of contemporary youth.
Lang.: Rus.   209
Overview of Moscow theatrical life. Moscow. Lang.: Rus. 211
Aesthetic education through theatre. Lang.: Rus.   214
1980-1986.   Design/technology.
Designing for the small stage. Lang.: Rus.   428
Guide to materials necessary for theatrical performances.
Lang.: Rus.   430
Recent Soviet set design and designers. Lang.: Rus.   433
Problems and goals of designers for theatre and film. Lang.:
Rus.   434
Role of stage design in production as an artistic whole.
Lang.: Rus.   436
The art of set design for television. Lang.: Rus.   3266
1980-1986.   Institutions.
The State Institute of Theatrical Art. Moscow. Lang.: Rus.
                                                       576
Actor and artistic director of the Puškin Theatre on the
theatre collective. Leningrad. Lang.: Rus.   577
1980-1986.   Performance spaces.
Problems of designing and building theatrical buildings.
Lang.: Rus.   646
1980-1986.   Performance/production.
Problems of contemporary theatre. Lang.: Rus.   858
Working life of theatrical collective Teat'r-studija na Jugo-
Zapade. Moscow. Lang.: Rus.   864
Essay on actor's place in society. Lang.: Rus.   865
Professionalism and training of actors. Lang.: Rus.   867
Problems of experimental theatre. Lang.: Rus.   869
Director Anatolij Efros on theatrical conventions, audience
and perception. Lang.: Rus.   871
Plastic aspects of the actor's appearance on stage. Lang.:
Rus.   875
Performances of adolescents. Moscow. Lang.: Rus.   877
Social role of Georgian theatre today. Lang.: Rus.   879

USSR — cont'd

1986. **Administration.**
Notes on theatre business following meeting of All-Union
Theatre Society. Lang.: Rus.   183
On the need for radical change in theatrical management
and financing. Lang.: Rus.   184
Problems of funding cultural institutions, including theatres.
Lang.: Rus.   187
Proposals for the reorganization of theatrical business. Lang.:
Rus.   190
General director of Bolšoj Ballet on problems of the future.
Moscow. Lang.: Rus.   1292
Artistic director of Union of State Circuses comments on new
programs. Lang.: Rus.   3379
1986. **Audience.**
Audience-performer relationship in experimental theatre.
Moscow. Lang.: Rus.   204
Study of the reality and misconception about opera
audiences. Lang.: Rus.   3648
1986. **Design/technology.**
Scene designer E. Kočergin discusses his work. Lang.: Rus.
                                                               431
Opera set designs by L. Trujkis. Lithuania. Lang.: Rus. 3664
1986. **Institutions.**
Description of a theatre museum. Penze. Lang.: Rus.   575
1986. **Performance/production.**
Interview about the acting profession with T. Zabozlaeva and
G. Karelina. Lang.: Rus.   859
Elements of theatrical expression. Lang.: Rus.   868
Discussion of director's role in a theatrical company. Lang.:
Rus.   870
On the physical training of actors. Lang.: Rus.   872
Actor professionalism and the spoken word. Lang.: Ukr.   874
Paralinguistic and communicative aspects of stage speech.
Lang.: Rus.   893
Actors' round table on the problems facing young actors.
Moscow. Lang.: Rus.   900
Actor M. Ul'janov on tasks of Soviet theatre. Moscow.
Lang.: Rus.   905
On the Tenth Festival of Russian and Soviet Theatre in
Poland. Katowice. Lang.: Rus.   2060
Interview with director Jurij Liubimov. Washington, DC.
Moscow. Lang.: Eng.   2196
Four performances in Budapest by the students of Oleg
Tabakov of GITIS, the Institute of Dramatic Art, Moscow.
Moscow. Budapest. Lang.: Hun.   2318
Interview with actor-director S. Jurskij. Lang.: Rus.   2325
Vinotavye (The Guilty) at Teat'r im. Mossověta. Moscow.
Lang.: Rus.   2339
Problems of the contemporary circus. Lang.: Rus.   3398
Excerpt from book by manager of Durov Theatre of Wild
Animals. Moscow. Lang.: Rus.   3399
Notes on comic stunts. Lang.: Rus.   3403
Interview with composer Aleksej Ribnikov. Lang.: Rus. 3495
Round-table on puppet theatre. Moscow. Leningrad. Lang.:
Rus.   3985
Interview on puppet theatre playwriting with B. Goldovskij
and J. Uspenskij. Moscow. Lang.: Rus.   3986
1986. **Plays/librettos/scripts.**
Critical analysis of *Tri devuški v golubom (Three Girls in
Blue)* by Ljudmila Petruševskaja. Lang.: Rus.   989
On the necessity of preserving the actor's text in a play.
Lang.: Rus.   992
Analyses of the plays of Ljudmila Petruševskaja. Lang.: Rus.
                                                               994
Interview with leaders of playwrights' seminar. Picunde.
Lang.: Rus.   2955
Problems of contemporary dramaturgy. Lang.: Rus.   2956
Excerpts from speeches by playwrights, 8th Congress of
Soviet Writers. Moscow. Lang.: Rus.   2957
Replies to questionnaire by five Soviet playwrights. Bulgaria.
Lang.: Rus.   2958

Analysis of the plays of Aleksej Gel'man. Lang.: Rus.   2959
Report of drama commission, 8th Congress of Soviet Writers.
Moscow. Lang.: Rus.   2960
1986. **Relation to other fields.**
Interview with director Oleg Jěfremov of Moscow Art
Theatre on social goals of theatre. Lang.: Rus.   1174
1986. **Theory/criticism.**
'New Wave' drama and contemporary Soviet dramaturgy.
Lang.: Rus.   1237
Correlation of word and image in dramaturgy. Lang.: Rus.
                                                             1239
Synthesis of the arts in the theatrical process. Moscow.
Lang.: Rus.   1240
Problems, tendencies and basic features of Soviet dramaturgy.
Lang.: Rus.   1246
National features of Russian literature and dramaturgy.
Lang.: Rus.   1248
Playwright A. Simukov discusses his craft. Lang.: Rus. 1249
1986. **Training.**
Seminar on training of opera and musical theatre performers.
Lang.: Rus.   3939

USSR-Russian SFSR
1986. **Performance/production.**
Festival of puppet theatre. Lang.: Rus.   3987

Venezuela
1956-1985. **Plays/librettos/scripts.**
Interview with Chilean playwright Jaime Miranda. Chile.
USA. Lang.: Eng.   2973
1958-1980. **Plays/librettos/scripts.**
Traces development of political trends in Venezuelan drama.
Lang.: Spa.   2972
1969-1986. **Performance/production.**
Interview with director Carlos Gimenez. Argentina. Caracas.
Lang.: Eng.   1636

Vietnam
1940-1986. **Plays/librettos/scripts.**
Vietnamese drama focusing on its origins from traditional
forms. Lang.: Swe.   2974
1986. **Performance/production.**
Review and discussion of Vietnamese performance in
Hungary. Thai Binh. Hungary. Lang.: Hun.   915
József Katona's *Bánk Bán* presented by the Hanoi Tuong
Theatre directed by Doan Anh Thang. Hanoi. Lang.: Hun.
                                                             2340

Wales
SEE
UK-Wales.
Western Africa
Performance/production.
Costumes, satiric dances and processions of the Ijebu Yoruba
masquerades. Lang.: Eng.   1372
Costumes, dance steps, and music in initiation rites of
Yoruba priesthood. Lang.: Eng.   1373

Yugoslavia
1980. **Performance/production.**
Survey of plays from 21st festival of Yugoslavian theatre.
Lang.: Rus.   2342
1984-1985. **Performance/production.**
Preview of Dubrovnik Summer Theatre Festival, 1985.
Dubrovnik. Lang.: Hun.   2345
1985. **Performance/production.**
Notes on theatrical events of nineteenth annual international
theatre festival. Belgrade. Lang.: Hun.   2341
Theatrical events of nineteenth annual international theatre
festival. Lang.: Hun.   2343
1986. **Performance/production.**
Review of children's theatre festival. Šibenik. Lang.: Hun.
                                                             916
Janez Pipan directs *Confiteor* by Slobodan Šnajder at
National Theatre of Belgrade. Belgrade. Lang.: Hun.   2344

Zambia
1914-1985. **Performance/production.**
Origins of *malipenga*, a form of dance-drama combining
Western and African elements. Malawi. Lang.: Eng.   1374
1985. **Relation to other fields.**
Theatrical nature of shamanistic rituals. Lang.: Eng.   1183

DOCUMENT AUTHORS INDEX

Copfermann, Émile. 1128, 1201
Corbella, Jordi. 517
Cormack, Randy. 305
Corner, John, ed. 3168
Corrigan, Robert. 3139, 3140
Corsinovi, Graziella. 2682
Corson, Richard. 229
Costigan, Daniel M. 3218
Cotarella, Lia. 3951
Cots, Joan. 517
Coudrin, Gildas-Louis. 4018
Couprie, Alain. 3100
Courtney, Richard. 3070
Cousin, Geraldine. 2104
Couton, Georges. 3030
Coveney, Michael. 1579, 2135
Cowan, Cindy. 1468, 1545
Cowhig, Ruth M. 2136
Crabb, Michael. 1295, 1296
Cramer, James Douglas. 2472
Crass, Randall F. 3468
Cravath, Paul. 1336, 1358
Cro, Stelio. 3040
Crohn Schmitt, Natalie. 3162
Crowthers, Malcolm. 3786
Crozier, Eric. 3784, 3895
Cruciani, Fabrizio, ed. 1204
Crum, Jane Ann. 357
Crystal, Billy. 3350
Csáki, Judit. 1803, 1804, 1805, 1806, 1807,
    1808, 1809, 1810, 1811, 1812, 1813,
    3487, 3602
Császár, Miklós. 282
Csengery, Judit. 3226
Cserje, Zsuzsa. 1814
Csernus, Mariann. 1815
Csik, István. 1097, 2019, 2736
Csillag, Ilona. 1050
Csizner, Ildikó. 1816, 1817, 1818, 1819, 1820,
    2318
Cummings, Scott. 979
Cummings, Scott T. 2623, 3390
Cuneo, Anne. 3374
Cunningham, David. 358
Curell, Mireia, transl. 2710
Currell, David. 3961
Curry, Richard Jerome. 1258
Curtis, A. Ross. 3941
Curtis, Simon. 2137
Cusatelli, Giorgio, ed. 4012
Cushman, Robert. 3610
Cusson, Chantal. 482, 1068
Cypkin, Diane. 827
Cyr, René Richard. 474
Czeglédi, Imre. 3912
Czinege-Károly, Anna. 963
Czinner, Karolina. 47
Daalder, Joost. 2473
Dace, Tish. 359, 360, 2260
Dachs, Robert. 3223
Dahlberg, Christer. 60, 683
Dahle, Terje Nils, ed. 579, 996
Dahlinger, Fred, Jr. 3391
Dai, Ling, transl. 3542
Dai, Ping. 3564
Daley, A. Stuart. 2474
Daly, Ann. 1272
Damkjaer, Nils. 747
Damm, Sigrid. 2594
Dammers, Richard H. 2475
Dan'ko, L. 3638
Daniel, Walter C. 828
Danilevskij, R. Ju., ed. 965
Danilova, L., comp. 782
Darcy, William. 3873
Dasgupta, Gautam. 1194
Daverio, John J. 3929
Davidson, Clifford. 2643, 3092, 3963

Davidson, Erika. 3890
Davidson, Jim, ed. 439
Davies, Anthony. 3172
Davies, Ronald Austin. 1087
Davis, Ivor. 68
Davis, J. Madison. 3008
Davis, Jim. 3322
Davis, Peter A. 2261
Davis, Peter G. 3785, 3802
Davis, R.G. 2262, 2613, 2903
Davis, Tracy C. 1627
Davis, Tracy G. 1439
Davlekamova, S. 1315
Davoli, Susi, ed. 7
Davril, Anselme. 3031
Davy, Kate. 1455, 2263
Davydov, V.G. 868
Day, Barbara. 1697
De Angelis, Maria Pia, transl. 2484
De Beaumarchais, Jean-Pierre. 1725
De Dancan, Llyn. 1333
De Filippo, Eduardo. 3159
de Freitas, Denis. 69
de Marinis, Marco. 789
De Nonno, Mario, transl. 777
De Poorter, Erika. 1423
De Santi, Pier Marco. 299
Deák, Attila. 1821, 1822, 3224
Deák, Tamás. 2644
Dean, Joan F. 2840
Dean, Laura. 171
Debusscher, Gilbert. 2904
Decker, Jacques de. 1461
Declercq, Gilles. 2559
Deforge, Bernard. 2629
del Ministro, Maurizio. 3225
Delamothe, Tony. 81, 83, 2138, 2139, 2841
Delcampe, Armand. 221
Deldime, Roger. 1051
Delgado, Eduard, intro. 261
Demidov, A. 869
Demin, G.G. 2319
Demin, V. 576
Demo, Mary Penasack. 1144
Demur, Guy. 711
Dennstaedt, Jeffrey V. 361
Dereuck, J.A. 2842
Déry, Tibor. 1484
Desai, Rupin W. 3093
Desgraves, Louis. 2987
Deshoulière, Christophe. 3647
Dessen, Alan C. 2140
Desson, Jim. 1661
Detels, Claire. 3881, 3882
Deverell, Rex. 218
Deverell, Rita Shelton. 1052
Devet, Donald. 4016
Devine, Michael. 2412, 3018
Dezseran, Catherine. 1145
Di Palma, Guido. 3337
Di Puccio, Denise M. 2722
Di-Nur, Shlomo. 1018
Diamond, Elin. 2843
Díaz, Néstor Gustavo. 1694
Dibble, Peter David. 3619
Dibia, I Wayan. 3359
Diderot, Denis. 3101
Didym, Eric. 1729
Dieterle, Regina, ed. 1339
Dietrich, Margret, comp. 997
Dietrich, Richard F. 3135
Díez Borque, José María. 2785, 2812
Dillon, John. 2005
DiMaggio, Paul. 98
Dinesen, Isak. 4002
Ding, Daoxi. 3560
Ding, Luonan. 3089
Dmitriev, Ju. 3398

Dmitrievskij, V. 207
Dmitrijevskaja, E.R. 3773
Dmitrijevskij, V. 3773
Dobson, Warwick. 3057
Docker, John. 3083
Dodin, L. 870
Dohmen, William F. 2844
Doi, Yuriko. 1416
Dolan, Jill. 362, 363, 1227
Dolan, Jill, ed. 532, 547, 982, 1140, 1231,
    1232, 1234, 1285, 1352, 1991, 2263,
    2277, 2304, 2740, 2913, 3139, 3140,
    3142, 3145, 3150, 3151, 3152, 3166,
    3354, 3461, 3973
Dollimore, Jonathan. 2476
Dōmoto, Masaki. 1420
Dömötör, Tekla. 1098
Donesky, Finlay. 2845
Donin-Janz, Beatrice. 3883, 3884
Donner, Franz. 3933
Dorr, Donald. 3924
Dorst, Tankred. 1482
Dort, Bernard. 712, 713, 1628, 1990, 2560
Doucette, L.E. 2413, 3599
Douglas, James B. 2320
Dowling, John. 2786
Downton, Dawn Rae. 1662
Doyle, John. 82
Doyle, Sandra. 3293
Dreier, Martin. 3653
Drese, Claus Helmut. 727
Dressler, Roland. 1448
Drewel, Henry John. 1372
Drewel, Margaret Thompson. 1373
Drewnowski, Tadeusz. 511
Driggers, Sam. 3803
Drohocka, Halina. 2020
Drozdov, G. 184
Drucker, Trudy. 2264, 2477
Drueding, Alice. 3913
Duane, Carol Leventen. 2478
Dudzik, Wojciech. 1116
Duffie, Bruce. 3643, 3804, 3805, 3806, 3807
Duffy, Bernard K. 2905
Duffy, Susan. 2905
Dufournet, Jean. 2561
Dugulin, Adriano, ed. 2993
Duhaime, Julien. 1563
Dukore, Bernard F. 805, 2846
Dullin, Charles. 714
Dumur, Guy. 1730, 1731
Dunn, E. Catherine. 949
Dunn, Tom. 1146
Dupuccio, Denise. 2787
Durang, Christopher. 917
Durbach, Errol. 2479
Durham, Weldon B. 551
Duro, Dan. 364
Duró, Győző. 915
Durova, N. 3399
Dürrenmatt, Friedrich. 1504
Dusek, Peter. 3692
Dusting, Gillian. 470
Dutton, Richard. 2480
Dymkowski, Christine. 806
Dziewulska, Małgorzata. 1228
Dzjubinskaja, O. 662
Džofri, P. 1319
Easterbrook, Anthony. 1617
Eaton, Katherine Bliss. 2065
Ebert, Fa Chu. 3966
Edelman, Susanne Popper. 3869
Eder, Richard. 829
Edmondson, Belinda, ed. 856
Edwards, Anne. 2141
Edwards, Christopher. 1187
Edwards, Philip. 323
Edwards, Susanna. 1720, 2085

Giannini, Vera. 3736
Giantvalley, Scott. 2855
Gibbs, James. 2725
Gibson, June V., transl. 3521
Giday, Kálmán. 600
Gilbert, Huguette. 1479
Gilbert, Michael. 3501
Gilbert, Michael, transl. 1092
Gilbert, Sky. 475, 1549
Gillen, Francis. 2856
Gillespie, Fern. 103
Gilman, Richard. 1148, 1229
Gilmour, Dean. 3408
Gilsing, Monika. 1533
Gilula, Dvora. 1018, 2630
Gin, Sue-Jeung. 552
Ginsburg, Loren. 1259
Gioia, Joseph. 3192
Giovanelli, Paola. 1436
Gisselbrecht, André. 1736
Gissenwehrer, Michael. 1254
Gitovič, N.I., comp. 2765
Gladil'ščikov, Ju. 2321
Gladyševa, A. 874
Glagoleva, V.S., comp. 430
Glasheen, Anne-Marie. 2400, 2401, 2402, 2403
Glasheen, Anne-Marie, transl. 1462, 1463, 1464
Gleber, Anke. 3233
Glerum, Jay O., ed. 228
Gleuck, Germaine. 615, 1282
Gobin, Alain. 40
Godden, Jerry. 484
Godfrey, Marian A. 104, 105, 553, 554
Godin, Jean Cléo, intro. 1469
Godin, Jean-Cléo. 926
Godlewska, Joanna. 2021, 2022, 2739
Goetz, Ruth. 2348
Gold, Sylviane. 2200, 2202, 2204, 2208, 2209, 2215, 2222, 2224, 2232, 2240, 2242, 3298
Goldbard, Arlene. 106
Goldberg, Marianne. 1350
Goldberg, Moses. 1149
Golden, Joseph. 107
Goldie, Terry. 656, 1550
Goldstein, Imre, transl. 1484
Golodner, Jack. 108
Golubovskij, B. 194
Golubovskij, B.G. 875, 2322
Gomery, Douglas. 3220
Gómez Grande, Fernando, ed. 516
Gomez Lara, Manuel. 3427
González Vilar, José Manuel. 789
Gonzalez, Gloria. 2269
González, Josep Maria. 261
Goodall, Jane. 2857
Goodden, Angelica. 715
Goodwin, Dorothy A. 1150
Goodwin, Michael. 1574
Gorbačëv, I. 577
Gordon, Steve. 3286
Gorier, Jacquie. 230
Görömbei, András. 2762
Gourdon, Anne-Marie, ed. 1446
Gourgey, Annette F. 1151
Gourtney, Cathy. 2487
Gow, Gordon. 2144, 2145, 2146, 2147
Gowin, Steve. 3209, 3260
Goy-Blanquet, Dominique. 2488
Goyet, Thérèse. 2564
Gozenpud, A.A. 3847, 3907
Grace-Warrick, Christa. 1664, 3330
Grace, Sherrill E. 927, 2418
Gràcia, Josep, ed. 1030
Graells, Guillem-Jordi. 1518, 2565, 3313

Graells, Guillem-Jordi, intro. 1478, 1519, 3314
Graff, Yveta Synek. 2453, 3715, 3811
Graham-White, Anthony. 2489
Graham, Bill. 324, 1521
Graham, Billy. 1598
Graham, Jaylene. 369
Graham, Robert. 1416
Graham, Tony. 3055
Grammer, Charles. 370
Grancy, Christine de. 1533
Grantley, Darryll. 2490
Granville-Barker, Harley. 807
Graver, David. 1737, 3107
Gray, Herman. 3272
Gray, Simon. 2858
Gray, Spalding. 2270
Gray, Stephen. 2773
Gredeby, Nils. 798
Green, Adolph. 3626
Green, London. 3812, 3857
Green, William. 1369
Greene, Susan. 3851
Greenhaigh, Jill. 3449
Greenwald, Michael L. 325
Gregor, Joseph, gen. ed. 997
Greiner, Bernhard. 2390
Grezsa, Ferenc. 2647
Grieshofer, Franz. 2979
Grilli, Giuseppe. 1111, 1220
Grin, Claude. 530
Grinšpun, I.A. 876
Griševa, L.D. 8
Griswold, Wendy. 3025
Groenewald, H.C., ed. 1125
Groppali, Enrico. 2910
Groševa, E.A., comp. 3774
Grossman, Harry. 240
Grote, David. 2349, 3598
Grotowski, Jerzy. 748, 2740, 3126
Gruber, William E. 1630
Grulin, Adrien. 476
Grunes, Dennis. 2911
Gruslin, Adrien. 477, 668
Gu, Zhongyi. 1202
Guare, John. 3626
Guccini, Gerardo. 2686
Guccini, Gerardo, ed. 746
Guccini, Gerardo, transl. 714
Gudkova, V. 2323
Guernsey, Otis L. 3009, 3631
Guglielmino, Salvatore, intro. 1108
Guibert, Noëlle. 41, 266, 1725, 1738
Guifreu, Patrick. 2720
Guifreu, Patrick, ed. 2720
Guillamón, Julià. 2814
Guillamón, Julià, intro. 1499
Guinness, Alec. 2106
Gul'čenko, V. 877, 2342
Gul'janc, E.I. 3774
Gulčenko, V. 878
Gulli, Caterina, transl. 1082
Guntheret, André. 265
Guo, Bing-zhen. 3555
Guo, Liang. 3510
Gurbanidze, N. 879
Gurney, A.R., Jr. 1225
Gusejnov, G. 647
Gussow, Mel. 2201, 2208, 2217, 2222, 2225, 2226, 2227, 2228, 2230, 2238, 2271, 3349, 3612, 3616
Gustafson, Ann, transl. 747
Guszpit, Ireneusz. 1118
Guszpit, Ireneusz, ed. 1122
Guthrie, Tyrone. 555
György, Péter. 1840
Habermann, Günther. 1088, 3757, 3936
Hacker, Philip E. 371

Hägglund, Kent. 62, 798, 2089, 3606
Haigh, Anthony Russell. 3058
Hailey, Christopher. 3919
Halász, Péter. 3748, 3749
Halcomb, Richard. 1529
Hale, Alice M. 109, 110, 111, 112, 154, 372, 373, 374, 637, 1259, 3572, 3573, 3586, 3587, 3588, 3656
Halizev, V.E. 3012
Hall, John C., Jr. 95
Hall, Robin. 507
Halverson, Rachel, transl. 1092
Hamer, Mary. 2491
Hampton, Christopher. 2859
Han, Rixin, ed. 1011
Han, Seong-ju. 762
Hanley, P.L. 332
Hanna, Cliff. 2492
Hannah, Donald, transl. 4002
Hannan, Ted. 2197
Hannowa, Anna. 1451
Hanrahan, Thomas. 2789
Hapgood, Robert. 3239
Happé, Peter. 2148
Har'el, Vered. 52, 1206
Hardison, Curtis. 375
Harlén, Carl. 798
Harmer, Wendy. 657
Harms, Klaus B. 2828
Harris, Dale. 3577
Harris, Laurilyn J. 2149
Harris, Max. 3327
Harris, Richard. 3254, 3256
Harris, Stephen. 1622
Harris, William. 113, 114, 3193, 3202, 3251
Harris, Wilson. 3376
Harrison, David. 2150
Harrison, James. 1054, 1551, 2419, 3020, 3118
Harrison, John. 3813
Harrison, Wayne. 1612
Harrison, Wilfred. 2023
Harrow, Gustave. 115
Hart, Charles. 2190
Hart, Dorothy, ed. 3580
Hart, Lorenz. 3580
Hart, Steven. 2912
Hart, William D. 92
Harter, Patricia. 510
Hartwig, Edward, photo. 2759
Harvey, Donald A. 376
Hatch, Christopher. 3916
Hatch, Jim. 2098
Hauger, George. 3142
Hauptfleisch, Temple, ed. 1125
Haus, Heinz-Uwe. 1769, 2631, 2966
Hausbrandt, Andrzej. 1217
Havel, Václav. 1643
Havlicèk, Franklin J. 116
Hawałej, Adam, photo. 2056
Hawkins, Bobbie. 2151
Haye, Bethany. 377, 378, 3201, 3210, 3583
Hayes, Elliott. 1665
Hays, Michael. 2566
Hayward, Bill. 3760, 3816
He, Wei. 3536
Headley, Robert K. 1623, 3196
Heaney, Michael. 3332
Hébert, Anne. 3174
Hébert, Lorraine. 669
Heckenberg, Pamela. 24
Heed, Sven Åke. 1739
Hees, Edwin. 941
Heffernan, James. 3795
Hegedüs, Sándor, ed. 1841
Heide, Christopher. 2420
Heinz, Wolfgang. 730, 1764
Heinze, Mona, transl. 3112

FINDING LIST OF PERIODICAL TITLES WITH ACRONYMS

Canadian Literature/Littérature Canadienne ... CanL
Canadian Theatre Review (Toronto) ... CTR
Canadian Theatre Checklist ... CTCheck
Canadian Theatre Review Yearbook (Downsview) ... CTRY
Caratula ... Caratula
Castelets ... Castelets
Celcit ... Celcit
Central Opera Service Bulletin ... COS
Ceskoslovenski Loutkar ... CeskL
Chhaya Nat. ... Chhaya
Children's Theatre Review ... ChTR
Chinese Literature ... ChinL
Chronico ... Chronico
Cineschedario: Letture Drammatiche ... CineLD
Circus-Parade ... CircusP
Circuszeitung, Die ... Cz
Cirque dans l'Univers, Le ... CU
Città Aperta ... CittaA
City Arts Monthly ... CAM
City Limits ... CityL
Claudel Studies ... ClaudelS
CLSU Journal of the Arts ... CLSUJ
Coleçao Teatro ... ColecaoT
College English ... CE
College Language Association Journal ... CLAJ
Columbia-VLA Journal of Law & the Arts ... ColJL&A
Comédie de l'Ouest ... CO
Comédie-Française ... CF
Comedy ... Comedy
Communications from the International Brecht Society ... ComIBS
Comparative Drama ... CompD
Confessio ... Confes
Confluent ... Cfl
Conjunto: Revista de Teatro Latinamericano ... Cjo
Connoisseur ... Con
Contact Quarterly ... ContactQ
Contemporary French Civilization ... CFT
Contenido ... Contenido
CORD Dance Research Annual ... CORD
Corps écrit ... CorpsE
Costume Society of America ... CSAN
Costume: The Journal of the Costume Society ... Costume
Courrier Dramatique de l'Ouest ... CDO
Courrier du Centre international d'études poétiques ... CCIEP
Creative Drama ... CreD
Crépuscule, Le ... Crepuscl
Crisis ... Crisis
Critical Arts ... CrAr
Critical Digest ... CritD
Critical Quarterly ... CritQ
Critique ... CritNY
Cuadernos El Publico ... Cuaderno
Cue New York ... CueNY
Cue, The ... CueM
Cue: Technical Theatre Review ... Cue
Cultural Post ... CuPo
Culture et Communication ... CetC
Culture ... Culture
C'wan t'ong Xiju Yishu/Art of Traditional Opera ... CTXY
Dalnij Vostok: (Far East) ... DalVostok
Dance and Dancers ... D&D
Dance Australia ... DA
Dance Chronicle ... DnC
Dance in Canada/Danse au Canada ... DC
Dance Magazine ... Dm
Dance Research ... DRs
Dance Research Journal ... DRJ
Dance Theatre Journal ... DTJ
Dancing Times ... DTi
Dekorativnojė Iskusstvo SSR ... DekorIsk
Detskaja Literatura ... DetLit
Deutsche Bühne, Die ... DB
Deutsche Zeitschrift für Philosophie ... DZP
Deutsches Bühnenjahrbuch ... DBj
Deutsches Institut für Puppenspiel Forschung und Lehre ... DIPFL
Devlet Tijatrolari (State Theatres) ... Devlet
Dewan Budaya ... Dewan
Dialog: Miesiecznik Poswiecony Dramaturgii Wspolczesnej ... DialogW
Dialog ... DialogA
Dialogue: Canadian Philosophical Review ... Dialogue
Dialogue (Tunisia) ... DialogTu
Dioniso ... Dioniso
Directors Notes ... DirNotes
Diskurs ... Diskurs
Diskurs ... DRostock
Divadelni Noviny ... DiN
Divadlo ve Svete ... DvS
Divadlo: (Theatre) ... DTh
Dix-Huitième Siècle ... DHS
Dix-Septième Siècle ... DSS
Dockteatereko ... Dockt
Documentation Théâtrale ... DocTh
Documents del Centre Dramatic ... DCD
DOE ... DOE
Dokumenti Slovenskega Gledaliskega Muzeja ... DSGM
Don Saturio: Boletin Informativo de Teatro Gallego ... DSat
Dong-Guk Dramatic Art ... DongukDA
Drama and the School ... DSchool
Drama and Theater ... D&T
Drama and Theatre Newsletter ... DTN
Drama Review, The ... TDR
Drama Review ... DrRev
Drama: Nordisk dramapedagogisk Tidskrift ... DNDT
Drama: The Quarterly Theatre Review ... Drama
Drama ... DramaY
Dramatherapy: SEE: Journal of Dramatherapy (JDt) ... Dtherapy
Dramatics ... DMC
Dramatists Guild Quarterly ... DGQ
Dramatists Sourcebook ... DSo
Dramaturgi: Tedri Og Praksis ... DTOP
Dramma ... DrammaR
Dramma: Il Mensile dello Spettacolo ... DrammaT
Dress ... Dress
Družba ... Druzba
Družba Narodov ... DruzNar
Ebony ... Ebony
Echanges ... Echanges
Economic Efficiency and the Performing Arts ... EE&PA
Economic History Review ... EHR
EDAM Newsletter ... EDAM
Editorial Nuevo Grupo ... ENG
Educational Theatre News ... ETN
Eire-Ireland ... Eire
Elet és Irodalom: irodalmi es politkai hetilap ... Ell
Eletunk ... Elet
Elizabethan Theatre ... ETh
Empirical Research in Theatre ... ERT
Enact: monthly theatre magazine ... Enact
Encore (Australia) ... EncoreA
Encore (Georgia) ... Encore
Engekikai: Theatre World ... Egk
English Academy Review, The ... EAR
English Literary Renaissance Journal ... ELR
English Studies in Africa ... ESA
Entertainment and Arts Manager ... E&AM
Entré ... Entre
Envers du Décor, L' ... ED
Epic Theatre ... EpicT
Equity Journal ... EquityJ
Equity News ... EN
Escena: Informativo Teatral ... EIT
Escena ... Escena
Espill, L' ... Espill
Esprit Créateur, L' ... ECR
Esprit ... Esprit
Essays in Theatre ... ET
Essence ... Essence
Estafeta Literaria: La Revista ... EstLit
Estreno: Journal on the Contemporary Spanish Theater ... Estreno
Estudis Escenics ... EECIT
Etoile de la Foire ... Etoile
Eugene O'Neill Newsletter, The ... EON
Europe: Revue Littéraire Mensuelle ... Europe
Evento Teatrale ... Evento
Exchange ... Exchange
Ežėgodnik MChAT ... MChAT
Farsa, La ... Farsa
Federal One ... FO
Feminist Review ... FemR
Fight Master, The ... FMa
Figurentheater ... Ftr
Film a Divadlo ... FDi
Film, Szinház, Muzsika ... FSM
Filologičeskije Nauki ... FN
Filológiai Közlöny ... FiloK
FIRT/SIBMAS Bulletin d'information ... FIRTSIB
Footnotes ... Fnotes
Forrás ... Forras
France Théâtre ... FranceT
Freedomways: A Quarterly Review of the Freedom Movement ... Fds
Fremantle Gazette ... FG
French Forum ... FrF
French Review, The ... FR
French Studies ... FS
Fundarte ... Fundarte
Gambit ... Gambit
Gap, The ... Gap
Garcin: Libro de Cultura ... Garcin
Gazette des Beaux Arts ... GdBA
Gazette du Français ... GdF
Gazette Officielle du Spectacle ... GOS
Gazit ... Gazit
George Spelvin's Theatre Book ... GSTB
Georgia Review ... GaR
German Life and Letters ... GL&L
German Quarterly ... GQ
German Studies Review ... GerSR
Gestus: A Quarterly Journal of Brechtian Studies ... Gestus
Gilbert and Sullivan Journal ... GSJ
Giornale dello Spettacolo ... GdS
Gosteri: Performance ... Gosteri
Grande République ... GrandR
Grupo Teatral Antifaz: Revista ... GTAR
Guida dello Spettacolo ... Guida
Guidateatro: Estera ... GtE
Guidateatro: Italiana ... GtI
Hamlet Studies ... HSt
Harlekijn ... Harlekijn
Hecate: Women's Interdisciplinary Journal ... Hecate
Helikon: Vilagirodalmi ... Helik
Hermes: Zeitschrift ... Hermes
Higeki Kigeki: Tragedy and Comedy ... HgK
High Performance ... HP
Hispanic Arts ... HispArts
Historical Journal of Film, TV, Radio ... HJFTR
Historical Studies ... HisSt
History Workshop ... HW
Horisont ... Horis
Hungarian Theatre/Hungarian Drama ... HTHD
Ibsen News & Comments ... INC
Ibsenårboken/Ibsen Yearbook ... IA
Impressum ... Impressum
In Sachen Spiel und Theatre ... ISST
In the Arts: Search, Research, and Discovery ... InArts
Independent Shavian ... IndSh
Indonesia ... Indonesia

Opernwelt....Opw
Opuscula....Opuscula
Organon....Organon
Österreichische Dramatiker der Gegenwart....ODG
Overture....OvA
Pamiętnik Teatralny....PaT
Pamir....Pamir
Pantallas y Escenarios....Pantallas
Pantuflas del Obispo....PdO
Paraules al Ven....PaV
Parnass....Parnass
Parnasso....Parnasso
Passing Show....PasShow
Past and Present....Pa&Pr
Performance Magazine, The....PM
Performance: A Handbook of the Performing Arts in New Zealand....PerfNZ
Performance....Pe
Performing Arts Annual....PAA
Performing Arts in Canada....PAC
Performing Arts Journal....PerAJ
Performing Arts Magazine....PArtsSF
Performing Arts Resources....PAR
Performing Arts: The Music and Theatre Monthly....PArts
Performing Arts Year Book of Australia....PAYBA
Perlicko-Perlacko....Perlicko
Pesti Műsor....PeM
Peuples noirs, peuples africains....Pnpa
Philippine Quarterly of Culture and Society....PQCS
Philological Quarterly....PQ
Philosophy and Literature....P&L
Pipirijaina....Pja
Plateaux....Plateaux
Platform....Pf
Play....Play
Playbill....Pb
Players Magazine....PlayM
Plays and Players....PlPl
Plays in Process....PiP
Plays International....PI
Plays....Plays
PLUG....PLUG
PMLA....PMLA
Podium: Zeitschrift für Bühnenbildner und Theatertechnik....PodiumB
Podium....Podium
Poppenspelbereichten....Poppen
Pozorište (Novi Sad)....PozL
Pozorište (Tuzla)....Pozorište
Préface....Preface
Présence Africaine....PA
Présence Francophone....PFr
Pratiques Théâtrales....PrTh
Premiery Ceskoslovenskych Divadel....PCD
Premijera: List Narodnog Pozorista Sombor....Premijera
Primer Acto....PrAc
Profile....Prof
Programa....Programa
Prolog: Revija za dramsku umjetnost....Prolog
Prolog....PrologTX
Prologue....Prologue
Prompts....Prompts
ProScen....ProScen
Proszenium....Pz
Publico, El....ElPu
Publiekstheaterkrant....Ptk
Puppenspiel-Information....PInfo
Puppenspiel und Puppenspieler....Pusp
Puppet Master....PupM
Puppetry Journal....PuJ
Quaderni del Teatro Stabile di Torino....QTST
Quaderni di Teatro....QT
Quarta Parete....Quarta
Quellen zur Theatergeschichte....QuellenT
Raduga....Raduga
Rajatabla....Raja
Rampelyset....Rampel
Randa....Randa
Rangarupa....Rangarupa
Rangayan....Rangayan
Rangbharati....Rbharati
Rangyog....Rangyog
Raritan....Raritan
Rassegna dello Spettacolo....RdS
Rassegna di Diritto Cinematografico, Teatrale e della Televisione....RdD
Rassegna Melodrammatica....RMelo
Recorder, The....Recorder
Records of Early English Drama Newsletter....REEDN
Red Letters....RLtrs
Renaissance Drama....RenD
Renmin Xiju: People's Theatre....Renmin
Repliikki....Repliikki
Research in African Literature....RAL
Research Opportunities in Renaissance Drama....RORD
Restoration and Eighteenth Century Theatre Research....Restor
Revista d'Art....RdArt
Revista de Estudios de Teatro: Boletin....REsT
Revue d'esthétique....RE
Revue d'Histoire du Théâtre....RHT
Revue de l'Art....RdA
Revue de Littérature Comparée....RLC
Revue Roumaine d'Histoire de l'Art....RHSTMC
Revue....Revue
Ridotto: Rassegna Mensile di Teatro....RRMT
Rivista di Studi Pirandelliani....RSP
Rivista Italiana di Drammaturgia....RIDr
Roda Lyktan....Roda
Rouge et Noir....RN
Russkaja Literatura....RLit
SAADYT Journal....SAADYT
Sage: A Scholarly Journal on Black Women....Sage
Sahne (The Stage)....Sahne
SAITT Focus....SAITT
Sanajans Cagdas....SCagdas
Sanat Olayi (Art Event)....SanatO
Sangeet Natak: Journal of the Performing Arts....SNJPA
Scen och Salong....ScenoS
Scena (East Berlin)....ScenaB
Scena (Milan)....ScenaM
Scena (Warsaw)....ScenaW
Scena IDI, La....ScIDI
Scena: Časopis za pozorišnu umetnost....Scena
Scena: Theatre Arts Review....ScenaE
Scenaria....Scenaria
Scenarium....Scenarium
Scene Changes....ScCh
Scene, Die....Scene
Sceničeskaja Technika i Technologija....STT
Scenograficky Obzor....SObzor
Scenografie....Scenograf
Schauspielfuehrer....Schaus
Schriften der Gesellschaft für Theatergeschichte....SGT
Schweizer Theaterjahrbuch....SchwT
Schweizerische Gesellschaft für Theaterkultur Jahrbücher....SGTJ
Schweizerische Gesellschaft für Theaterkultur Schriften....SGTS
Scottish Opera News....SON
Scottish Theater News....STN
Screen....Screen
SCYPT Journal....SCYPT
Sean O'Casey Review, The....SORev
Secondary School Theater Journal....SSTJ
Segismundo....Segmundo
Sehir Tijatrolari (City Theatre)....Sehir
Sembianza....Sembianza
Serra d'Or....SdO
Shahaab....Shahaab
Shakespeare Jahrbuch....SJW
Shakespeare Newsletter....ShN
Shakespeare on Film Newsletter....SFN
Shakespeare Quarterly....SQ
Shakespeare Studies (Nashville)....ShakSN
Shakespeare Studies (New York)....ShakS
Shakespeare Survey....ShS
Shavian....Shavian
Shaw: The Annual of Bernard Shaw Studies....ShawR
Shilpakala....Spa
Shingeki....Sg
Show....Show
Sight and Sound....SiSo
Sightline: The Journal of Theatre Technology and Design....Sin
Sightlines....Sis
Silex....Silex
Sinn und Form: Beiträge zur Literatur....SuF
Sipario....Sipario
Sirp ja Vasar....SjV
Skript....Skript
Slavic & East European Arts....SEEA
Slovenské Divadlo....SDi
Smena....Smena
Sobcota Chelovneta....SobCh
Sobesednik....Sobesednik
Social History....SocH
Somogy....Somo
SourceMonthly: The Resource for Mimes, Clowns, Jugglers, and Puppeteers....SMR
South African Journal of African Languages....SAJAL
South African Theatre Journal....SATJ
Southerly....SOUTHERLY
Southern Quarterly, The....SoQ
Southern Sawdust....SoSaw
Southern Theatre....SoTh
Southwest Review....SWR
Sovèckaja Estrada i Cirk....SovEC
Sovèckaja Ethnografia....SovEt
Sovèckaja Kultura....SovKult
Sovèckaja Muzyka: (Soviet Music)....SovMuzyka
Sovèckij Balet....SovBal
Sovèckij Teat'r/Soviet Theatre....SovT
Sovèckojè Slavjanovèdènjè: (Soviet Slavonic Studies)....SovSlav
Sovetskie Arkhivy....SovAr
Sovetskoe Gosudarstvo i Pravo....SGIP
Soviet and East-European Drama, Theatre and Film....SEEDTF
Sovremènnaja Dramaturgija....SovD
Speak....Speak
Speaking of Mime....SoM
Spectacles Magazine....SM
Spettacolo in Italia, Lo....SpIt
Spettacolo, Lo....Spettacolo
Spettacolo Viaggiante....SpViag
Spielplan, Der....Spl
Spirale: Art, letters, spectacles, sciences humaines....Spirale
Staffrider....Staff
Stage....StageZ
Standpunte....Standpunte
Sterijino Pozorje: Informativno Glasilo....Sterijino
Stikord....Stikord
STILB....STILB
Stratford-upon-Avon Studies....SuAS
Strindbergiana....Strind
Studenčeskij Meridian....StudM
Studia i Materialy do Dziejow Teatru Polskiego....StudiaP
Studies in American Drama, 1945-Present....SAD
Studies in Philology....StPh
Studies in Popular Culture....SPC
Studii si Cercetari de Istoria Artel....StudiiR
STYolainen....STYol
Suffløren....Suffloren

Suid-Afrikaan, Die ....SuidAfr
Swedish Theater/Théâtre Suédois................SwTS
Szene Schweiz/Scène-Suisse/Scena
   Svizzera ....SSSS
Szene: Fachzeitschrift der DDR..............SzeneAT
Szene..Szene
Szinház (Theatre) ....Sz
Szinháztechnikai Fórum........................SFo
Szinháztudomanyi Szemle......................SzSz
Tablas: Cuban Theatre...........................Tablas
Tabs..Tabs
Talent Management................................Talent
TamKang Review ....TkR
Tampereen Tyovaen Teatteri ....Tampereen
Tanecni Listy..Tanecni
Tantsovo Izkustvo..................................TantI
Tanz und Gymnastik ....TanzG
TCG National Working Conference
   Proceedings.....................................TCGNWCP
Teat'r žurnal dramaturgii i teatra.............TeatrM
Teatarski Glasnik...................................TGlasnik
Teater Film & TV..................................TF&TV
Teater i Danmark: Theatre in Denmark..TeaterD
Teater Jaarboek voor Vlaanderen.................TJV
Teater, Musika, Kyno.............................TMK
Teaterårsboken.......................................TArsb
Teaterforum (Sweden)............................Teaterf
Teaterforum (South Africa).....................TF
Teatern..Teatern
Teatervetenskap.....................................Tv
Teatervidenskabelige Studier...................TSt
Teatoro..Teatoro
Teatr Lalek ....TeatL
Teatr ....TeatrW
Teatralnaja Žizn....................................TeatZ
Teatraluri Moambe................................TeatM
Teatras..Teatras
Teatro Archivio......................................TArch
Teatro Clásico: Boletin...........................TCB
Teatro Contemporaneo ....TeatrC
Teatro del Siglo de Oro: Ediciones Críticas..TSO
Teatro del Siglo de Oro: Estudios de
   Literatura...TSOL
Teatro e Cinema....................................TeC
Teatro e Storia......................................TeatroS
Teatro en España...................................TeatrE
Teatron..TeatY
Teatron..Teatron
TeatroSM...TeatroSM
Teatrul..Teatrul
Teatteri..Teat
Teatur..TeaturS
Technical Briefs.....................................TechB
Tenaz Talks Teatro ....TTT
Tennessee Williams Review.....................TWNew
Textual..Textual
Textuel..Textuel
Théâtre de l'Est Parisien ....TEP
Théâtre en Europe.................................ThE
Théâtre Enfance et Jeunesse....................TEJ
Théâtre et Animation.............................TAnim
Théâtre et université ....TU
Théâtre International...............................TI
Théâtre National de Strasbourg: Actualité.....TNS
Théâtre Ouvert/Ecritures ....TOE

Théâtre Professionnel..............................TProf
Théâtre..Th
Théâtre Public..ThPu
Theater Across America ....TAAm
Theater Computer Users Group Notes........TCUG
Theater der Zeit ....TZ
Theater Heute..THeute
Theater in Graz.....................................TGraz
Theater Magazine...................................ThM
Theater Rundschau..................................TR
Theaterarbeit in der DDR ....TDDR
Theaterbuch...Tbuch
Theaterpaedagogische Bibliothek................TpaedB
Theaterwissenschaftlicher Informationsdienst...TWI
Theaterwork...Tk
Theaterzeitschrift ....Tzs
Theatre Annual......................................TA
Theatre Australia ....TAus
Theatre Chicago.....................................TChicago
Theatre Communications...........................TCom
Theatre Crafts.......................................ThCr
Theatre Design and Technology ....TD&T
Theatre History in Canada/Histoire du
   Théâtre..THC
Theatre History Studies...........................THSt
Theatre in Poland/Théâtre en Pologne.............TP
Theatre in the GDR................................TGDR
Theatre Insight......................................TInsight
Theatre Ireland......................................ThIr
Theatre Journal......................................TJ
Theatre Movement Journal........................TMJ
Theatre News...ThNe
Theatre Notebook ....TN
Theatre Notes..TNotes
Theatre Papers ....ThPa
Theatre Quarterly...................................TQ
Theatre Research International....................ThR
Theatre SA: Quarterly for South African
   Theater..TSA
Theatre Southwest..................................ThSw
Theatre Studies.......................................TheatreS
Theatre Survey.......................................ThS
Theatre Times.......................................TT
Theatre Today.......................................ThToday
Theatre Year...ThYear
Theatre: Ex...TheatreEx
Theatre: News from the Finnish Theatre.......NFT
Theatrecraft...TCraft
Theatrephile..ThPh
Theatrika..Tka
Theatro..Theatro
Theatron..Theatron
Theatrum: A Theatre Journal..................Theatrum
Themes in Drama...................................TID
Theoria..Theoria
Thespis..Thespis
Tijatro Arastirmalari Dergisi (Theatre Research
   Magazine)...TAD
Tijatro..Tijatro
Tijdschrift voor Theaterwetenschap.............TvT
Tiszatáj..Tisz
Toneel Teatraal......................................Toneel
Tournées de Spectacles............................Tournees
Tréteaux..Treteaux
Traces..Traces

Tramoya: Cuaderno de teatro ....Tramoya
Travail Théâtral......................................TTh
Trujaman..Trujaman
Tvorchestvo...TVOR
Tydskrif vir Letterkunde.........................TvL
Tydskrif vir Volkskunde en Volkstaal..........TvVV
Ufahamu..Ufa
Uj Irás..UjIras
Ukrainskij Teat'r...................................UTeatr
UNIMA France ....UNIMA
Unisa English Studies..............................UES
Universidad de Murcia Catedra de Teatro
   Cuadernos ....UMurcia
Universitas Tarraconensis.........................UTarra
University of Dar es Salaam.................UDSalaam
Unterhaltungskunst ....UZ
Upstart Crow, The.................................UCrow
Usbu Al-Masrah.....................................Usbu
USITT Newsletter...................................USITT
Uusi-Laulu..Uusi
V sovĕckom teatrĕ..................................VSov
Valóság..Valo
Valiverho..Valivero
Vantage Point: Issues in American Arts.....VantageP
Vestnik MGU: Series 9-Filologia.............VMGUf
Victorian Studies....................................VS
Vigilia..Vig
Világszínház..Vilag
Voprosy filosofii....................................VFil
Voprosy Literatury..................................VLit
Voprosy Teatra......................................Voprosy
Vyakat..Vyakat
Waiguo Xiju..Waiguo
Washington International Arts.....................WIAL
Weimarer Beiträge..................................WB
West Coast Plays....................................WCP
Western Journal of Black Studies ....WJBS
White Tops...WTops
Wiener Forschungen zur Theater und
   Medienwissenschaft ....WFTM
Wiener Gesellschaft für Theaterforschung
   Jahrbuch...WGTJ
WIJ, Poppenspelers................................WijP
Women & Performance ....WPerf
Women's Review ....WomenR
World Literature Today............................WLT
World of Opera......................................WOpera
World Premieres Listing...........................WPList
Xiju Luncong: Selected Essays of Theatre.XLunc
Xiju Xuexi: Theatre...............................XXuexi
Xiju Yishu: Theatre Arts.........................XYishu
Xiqu Yanjiu..XYanj
Yorick: Revista e Teatro ....Yorick
Young Cinema & Theatre/Jeune Cinéma et
   Théâtre..YCT
Youth Theatre Journal.............................YTJ
Zahranicni Divadlo: (Theatre Abroad)............ZDi
Zeitschrift für Anglistik und Amerikanistik....ZAA
Zeitschrift für Kulturaustausch..................ZfK
Zeitschrift für Germanistik ....ZG
Zeitschrift für Slawistik ....ZS
Znamya..Znamya
Zpravy..Zpravy
Zreliščnyjë Iskusstva (Performing Arts).....ZreIssk
Zvezda..Zvezda

LIST OF PERIODICALS

The following list is an attempt to provide an updated and comprehensive listing of periodical literature, current and recent past, devoted to theatre and related subjects.

This Bibliography provides full coverage of materials published in periodicals marked "Full" and selected coverage of those marked "Scan".

We have not dropped periodicals that are no longer published for the sake of researchers for whom that information can be valuable. We also note and list title changes.

A&A   *Art & Artists*. Freq: 12; Cov: Scan; Lang: Eng; Subj: Related.
ISSN: 0004-3001
■Artist Publishing Co.; 102 High St.; TN30 6HT Tenderden, Kent; UK.

A&B   *Architect & Builder*. Freq: 12; Began: 1951; Cov: Scan; Lang: Eng; Subj: Related.   ISSN: 0003-8407
■Laurie Wale (Pty) Ltd.; Box 4591; Cape Town; SOUTH AFRICA.

A&AR   *Art and Artists*. Formerly: *Art Workers News; Art Workers Newsletter*. Freq: 10; Began: 1971; Lang: Eng; Subj: Related.
ISSN: 0740-5723
■Foundation for the Community of Artists; 280 Broadway, Ste 412; New York, NY 10007; USA.

A&L   *Art and the Law*: Columbia Journal of Art and the Law. Freq: 4; Began: 1974; Ceased: 1985; Cov: Full; Lang: Eng; Subj: Related.   ISSN: 0743-5266
■Volunteer Lawyers for the Arts; 435 West 116th St.; New York, NY 10027; USA.

AAinNYLH   *Afro-Americans in New York Life and History*. Freq: 2; Began: 1977; Cov: Scan; Lang: Eng; Subj: Related. ISSN: 0364-2437
■Afro-American Historical Assoc. of the, Niagara Frontier; Box 1663, Hertel Station; Buffalo, NY 14216; USA.

AATTN   *AATT News*. Freq: 11; Began: 1976; Lang: Eng; Subj: Theatre.
■Australian Assoc. for Theatre Tech.; 40 Wave Avenue Mountain; 3149 Waverly; AUSTRALIA.

Abel   *Abel*: Panem et Circenses/Bread and Circuses. Freq: 12; Began: 1969; Lang: Eng; Subj: Theatre.   ISSN: 0001-3153
■Abel News Agencies; 300 West 17th Street; New York, NY 10011; USA.

AbhC   *Abhinaya*. Freq: 12; Lang: Ben; Subj: Theatre.
■121 Harish Mukherjee Road; Calcutta; INDIA.

AbhD   *Abhinaya*. Freq: 25; Lang: Hin; Subj: Theatre.
■Yuvamanch; 4526 Amirchand Marg; Delhi; INDIA.

AbqN   *Arabesque*: A magazine of international dance. Freq: 6; Began: 1975; Cov: Scan; Lang: Eng; Subj: Related. ISSN: 0148-5865

■Ibrahim Farrah Inc.; One Sherman Square, Suite 22F; New York, NY 10023; USA.

ACH   *Australian Cultural History*. Freq: 1; Began: 1982; Cov: Scan; Lang: Eng; Subj: Related.   ISSN: 0728-8433
■University of New South Wales; School of History; P.O. Box 1; Kensington 2033; AUSTRALIA.

ACCTV   *Almanacco della Canzone e del Cinema e della TV*. Lang: Ita; Subj: Theatre.
■Viale del Vignola 105; Rome; ITALY.

ACom   *Art Com*: Contemporary Art Communication. Formerly: *Mamelle Magazine: Art Contemporary*. Freq: 4; Began: 1975; Cov: Scan; Lang: Eng; Subj: Related.
ISSN: 0732-2852
■Contemporary Arts Press; Box 3123; San Francisco, CA 94119; USA.

Act   *Act*: Theatre in New Zealand. Formerly: *Theatre*. Freq: 6; Began: 1976; Lang: Eng; Subj: Theatre. ISSN: 0010-0106
■Playmarket Inc.; Box 9767; Wellington; NEW ZEALAND.

ACTA   *Acta Classica (Proceedings of the Classical Association of South Africa)*. Freq: 1; Began: 1958; Cov: Scan; Lang: Eng.; Subj: Related.   ISSN: 0065-1141
■Classical Association of South Africa; P.O. Box 392; Pretoria 0001; SOUTH AFRICA.

Acteurs   *Acteurs/Auteurs*.   Formerly: *Acteurs*. Freq: 10; Began: 1982; Cov: Scan; Lang: Fre; Subj: Theatre.
■28, rue Sevin-Vincent; 92210 Saint-Cloud; FRANCE.

ActS   *Actualité de la Scénographie*. Freq: 6; Began: 1977; Lang: Fre; Subj: Theatre.
■Assoc. Belgique des Scenographes et Techniciens de Théâtre; Avenue Herbert Hoover 5; 1320 Genval; BELGIUM.

ActT   *Action Théâtre*. Lang: Fre; Subj: Theatre.
■Action Culturelle de Sud-Est; 4 rue du Théâtre Français; 13001 Marseille; FRANCE.

Actualites   *Actualités*. Lang: Fre; Subj: Theatre.
■Actualités Spectacles; 1 rue Marietta Martin; 75016 Paris; FRANCE.

AD   *After Dark*. Freq: 12; Began: 1968; Lang: Eng; Subj: Theatre.
ISSN: 0002-0702
■After Dark Magazine, Inc.; 175 Fifth Avenue; New York, NY 10010; USA.

ADoc   *Arts Documentation Monthly*. Freq: 12; Began: 1979; Lang: Eng; Subj: Theatre.   ISSN: 0140-6965
■The Arts Council of Great Britain Library, Information and Research Section; 105 Piccadilly; W1V 0AU London; UK.

AdP   *Atti dello Psicodramma*. Freq: 1; Began: 1976; Lang: Ita; Subj: Related.
■Rome; ITALY.

ADS   *Australasian Drama Studies*. Freq: 2; Began: 1982; Lang: Eng; Subj: Theatre.
ISSN: 0810-4123
■Australasia Drama Studies, English Dept., University of Queensland; Q 4067 St. Lucia; AUSTRALIA.

AdSpect   *Annuaire du Spectacle*. Freq: 1; Began: 1956; Lang: Fre; Subj: Theatre.
ISSN: 0066-3026
■Editions Raoult; 17 Fauberg Montmartre; 75009 Paris; FRANCE.

AdT   *Art du Théâtre, L'*. Freq: 3; Began: 1985; Cov: Full; Lang: Fre; Subj: Theatre.
■Théâtre National de Chaillot; 1 Place du Tracadero; 75116 Paris; FRANCE.

AdTI   *Annuario del Teatro Italiano*. Freq: 1; Began: 1934; Lang: Ita; Subj: Theatre.
■S.I.A.E. - I.D.I.; Viale della Letteratura 30; 00100 Rome; ITALY.

AETR   *AET Revista*. Lang: Spa; Subj: Theatre.
■Associacion de Estudiantes de Teatro; Viamonte 1443; Buenos Aires; ARGENTINA.

AfAmArt   *African American Art*. Formerly: *Black American Quarterly*. Freq: 4; Cov: Scan; Lang: Eng; Subj: Related. ISSN: 0145-8116
■Los Angeles, CA; USA.

Afr   *Afrasia*. Lang: Eng; Subj: Theatre.
■42 Commercial Buildings; Shahrah-e-Quaid-e-Azam; Lahore; PAKISTAN.

AfrA   *African Arts*. Freq: 4; Began: 1967; Cov: Scan; Lang: Eng; Subj: Related.
ISSN: 0001-9933

■African Studies Center, Univ. of California, Los Angeles; 405 Hilgard Avenue; Los Angeles, CA 90024; USA.

AfricaP   *Africa Perspective*. Freq: 2; Began: 1976; Cov: Scan; Lang: Eng; Subj: Related.   ISSN: 0145-5311
■Students' African Studies Society, Univ. of Witwatersrand; 1 Jan Smuts Ave; 2001 Johannesburg; SOUTH AFRICA.

AfTR   *African Theatre Review*. Freq: IRR; Began: 1985; Lang: Eng; Subj: Theatre.
■Dept. of African Literature, Fac. of Letters & Social Science; University Yaoumde, PO Box 755; Yaounde; CAMEROON.

AG   *An Gael*: Irish Traditional Culture Alive in America Today. Freq: 4; Began: 1975; Lang: Eng; Subj: Related.
■An Claidheamh Soluis, The Irish Arts Center; 553 W. 51st Street; New York, NY 10019; USA.

AHA   *Aha! Hispanic Arts News*. Freq: 10; Began: 1976; Lang: Eng/Spa; Subj: Related.
■Association of Hispanic Arts; 200 E. 87 St.; New York, NY 10038; USA.

AHAT   *Al-Hayat At-T'aqafiyya*. Lang: Ara; Subj: Theatre.
■Ministère des Affaires Culturelles; La Kasbah; Tunis; TUNISIA.

AInf   *Artist and Influence*. Freq: 1; Began: 1981; Cov: Scan; Lang: Eng; Subj: Related.
■Hatch-Billops Collection, Inc.; 691 Broadway; New York, NY; USA.

AIT   *Annuaire International du Théâtre*: SEE: Miedzynarodowny Rocznik Teatralny (Acro: MRT). Freq: 1; Began: 1977; Lang: Fre/Eng; Subj: Theatre.
■Warsaw; POLAND.

AIWAT   *Al-Idaa Wa At-Talfaza*. Lang: Ara; Subj: Theatre.
■R.T.T.; 71 Avenue de la Liberté; Tunis; TUNISIA.

AJCS   *Australian Journal of Cultural Studies*. Freq: 2; Began: 1983; Ceased: 1987; Cov: Scan; Lang: Eng; Subj: Related.   ISSN: 0810-9648
■School of English; Western Australian Institute of Technology; Bentley, Western Australia 6102; AUSTRALIA.

AKT   *AKT*: Aktuelles Theater. Freq: 12; Began: 1969; Lang: Ger; Subj: Theatre.
■Frankfurter Bund für Volksbildung GmbH; Eschersheimer Landstrasse 2; 6000 Frankfurt/M 1; WEST GERMANY.

AL   *American Literature*. Freq: 4; Began: 1929; Cov: Scan; Lang: Eng; Subj: Related.   ISSN: 0002-9831
■Duke Univ. Press, Box 6697; College Station; Durham, NC 27708; USA.

Alfold   *Alföld*. Freq: 12; Began: 1954; Cov: Scan; Lang: Hun; Subj: Related.   ISSN: 0401-3174
■Hajdu Megyei Lapkiado Vallalat; Vörös Hadsereg útja 26/A I. em.; 4024 Debrecen; HUNGARY.

Alif   *Alif*. Lang: Fre; Subj: Theatre.
■24 rue Gamel Abdel-Nasser; Tunis; TUNISIA.

Alive   *Alive*: The New Performance Magazine. Freq: 24; Began: 1982; Lang: Eng; Subj: Theatre.
■New York, NY; USA.

Almanach   *Almanach Sceny Polskiej*. Freq: 1; Began: 1961; Lang: Pol; Subj: Theatre.
■Wydawbictwa Artystyczne i Filmowe; Pulawska 61; 02 595 Warsaw; POLAND.

ALS   *Australian Literary Studies*. Freq: 2; Began: 1963; Cov: Scan; Lang: Eng; Subj: Related.   ISSN: 0004-9697
■Univ. of Queensland, Dept. of English; Box 88; St. Lucia; Queensland 4067; AUSTRALIA.

AltT   *Alternatives Théâtrales*. Freq: 4; Began: 1979; Cov: Scan; Lang: Fre; Subj: Theatre.
■18 Place de Chatelain; 1050 Brussels; BELGIUM.

AmatS   *Amateur Stage*. Freq: 11; Began: 1946; Lang: Eng; Subj: Theatre.   ISSN: 0002-6867
■Team Publishing; Bretton St.; WF12 9BL Dewsbury, W Yorks; UK.

AMN   *Arts Management Newsletter*. Freq: 5; Began: 1962; Lang: Eng; Subj: Related.   ISSN: 0004-4067
■Radius Group, Inc.; 408 W. 57th Street; New York, NY 10019; USA.

AmS   *Amaterska Scena*: Ochotnicke divadlo. Freq: 12; Began: 1965; Lang: Cze; Subj: Theatre.   ISSN: 0002-6786
■Panorama; Vinchradsk 46; 12041 Prague 2; CZECHOSLOVAKIA.

AmTh   *American Theatre*. Formerly: Theatre Communications. Freq: 11; Began: 1984; Cov: Full; Lang: Eng; Subj: Theatre.   ISSN: 0275-5971
■Theatre Communications Group; 355 Lexington Avenue; New York, NY 10017; USA.

Amyri   *Amyri*. Freq: 4; Lang: Fin; Subj: Theatre.
■Suomen Nayttelijaliitto r.y.; Arkadiankatu 12 A 18; 00100 Helsinki 10/52; FINLAND.

Anim   *Animations*: Review of Puppets and Related Theatre. Freq: 6; Began: 1977; Cov: Scan; Lang: Eng; Subj: Theatre.   ISSN: 0140-7740
■Puppet Centre Trust, Battersea Arts Centre; Lavender Hill; SW11 5TJ London; UK.

Annuel   *Annuel de Théâtre*. Freq: 1; Lang: Fre; Subj: Theatre.
■Association Loi de 1901; 30, rue de la Belgique; 92190 Meudon; FRANCE.

AnSt   *Another Standard*. Freq: 6; Ceased: 1986; Cov: Scan; Lang: Eng; Subj: Related.
■PO Box 900; B70 6JP West Bromwich; UK.

AnT   *Annuaire Théâtral, L'*. Freq: 1; Lang: Fre; Subj: Theatre.
■Montreal, PQ; CANADA.

Apollo   *Apollo*: The international magazine of art and antiques. Freq: 12; Began: 1925; Cov: Scan; Lang: Eng; Subj: Related.   ISSN: 0003-6536
■Apollo Magazine Ltd.; 22 Davies Street; W1 London; UK.

Apuntes   *Apuntes*. Freq: 2; Began: 1960; Lang: Spa; Subj: Theatre.
■Universidad Católica de Chile, Escuela Artes de la Comunicacion; Diagonal Oriente 3300, Casilla 114D; Santiago; CHILE.

AQ   *American Quarterly*. Freq: 24; Began: 1949; Cov: Scan; Lang: Eng; Subj: Related.   ISSN: 0003-0678
■Univ. of Philadelphia; 307 College Hall; Philadelphia, PA 19104 6303; USA.

Araldo   *Araldo dello Spettacolo, L'*. Lang: Ita; Subj: Theatre.
■Via Aureliana 63; Rome; ITALY.

Archivio   *Archivio del Teatro Italiano*. Freq: IRR; Began: 1968; Lang: Ita; Subj: Theatre.   ISSN: 0066-6661
■Edizioni Il Polifilo; Via Borgonuovo2; 20121 Milan; ITALY.

Arco   *Arcoscenico*. Freq: 12; Began: 1945; Lang: Ita; Subj: Theatre.
■Via Ormisda 10; Rome; ITALY.

AReview   *Arts Review*. Freq: 4; Began: 1983; Lang: Eng; Subj: Related.
■National Endowment for the Arts; 1100 Pennsylvania Avenue NW; Washington, DC 20506; USA.

Ariel   *Ariel*. Freq: 3; Began: 1986; Cov: Full; Lang: Ita; Subj: Theatre.
■Rome; ITALY.

Ark   *Arkkitehti*: The Finnish Architectural Review. Freq: 8; Began: 1903; Cov: Scan; Lang: Fin; Subj: Related.
■Association of Finnish Architects; Etelaesplanacli 22A; 00130 Helsinki 13; FINLAND.

ArNy   *Arte Nyt*. Lang: Dut; Subj: Related.
■Teaterudvalget for Storkobenhavn; Hj. Brantings Plads 8; 2100 Copenhagen; DENMARK.

Arrel   *Arrel*. Freq: 4; Cov: Scan; Lang: Spa; Subj: Theatre.
■Disputacio de Barcelona; Placa de Sant Juame 1; 08002 Barcelona; SPAIN.

ArsU   *Ars-Uomo*. Freq: 12; Began: 1975; Lang: Ita; Subj: Theatre.
■Bulzoni Editore; Via F. Cocco Ortu 120; 00139 Rome; ITALY.

ArtP   *Art-Press (International)*. Freq: 12; Cov: Scan; Lang: Fre; Subj: Related.
■Paris; FRANCE.

ArtsAtl   *Arts Atlantic*: Atlantic Canada's Journal of the Arts. Freq: 4; Began: 1977; Cov: Scan; Lang: Eng; Subj: Related.   ISSN: 0704-7916
■Confederation Centre, Art Gallery and Museum; P.O.Box 848; Charlottetown, PE C1A 7L9; CANADA.

ArtsRS   *Arts Reporting Service, The*. Freq: 24; Began: 1970; Lang: Eng; Subj: Theatre.
■Charles Christopher Mark; PO Box 39008; Washington, DC 20016; USA.

ASabah   *As-Sabah*. Lang: Ara; Subj: Theatre.
■4 rue Ali Bach Hamba; Tunis; TUNISIA.

ASamvad   *Abhnaya Samvad*. Freq: 12; Lang: Hin; Subj: Theatre.
■20 Muktaram Babu Street; Calcutta; INDIA.

ASBelg   *Arts du Spectacle en Belgique*. Formerly: *Centre d'Etudes Theatrales, Louvain: Annuaire*. Freq: IRR; Began: 1968; Lang: Fre; Subj: Theatre.   ISSN: 0069-1860
■Université Catholique de Louvain, Centre d'Etudes Théâtrales; 1, place de l'Université; 1348 Louvain-la-Neuve; BELGIUM.

AScene   *Autre Scène, L'*. Lang: Fre; Subj: Theatre.
■Editions Albatros; 14 rue de l'Amérique; 75015 Paris; FRANCE.

ASCFB   *Annuaire du Spectacle de la Communauté Française de Belgique*. Freq: 1; Began: 1981; Lang: Fre; Subj: Theatre.
■Archives et Musée de la Littérature, ASBL; 4 Bd de l'Empereur; 1000 Brussels; BELGIUM.

ASInt   *American Studies International*. Freq: 4; Cov: Scan; Lang: Eng; Subj: Related.   ISSN: 0003-1321
■American Studies Program, George Washington University; Washington, DC 20052; USA.

ASO   *Avant Scène Opéra, L'*. Freq: 6; Began: 1976; Lang: Fre; Subj: Theatre.
■27 rue St. André des Arts; 75006 Paris; FRANCE.

ASSAPHc   *ASSAPH*: Section C. Freq: 1; Began: 1984; Cov: Full; Lang: Eng; Subj: Theatre.   ISSN: 0334-5963
■Dept. of Theatre Arts, Tel Aviv University; 69978 Ramat Aviv; ISRAEL.

AST   *Avant Scène Théâtre, L'*. Freq: 20; Began: 1949; Lang: Fre; Subj: Theatre.   ISSN: 0045-1169
■Editions de l'Avant Scène; 1, rue Lord Byron; 75008 Paris; FRANCE.

AStage   *American Stage*. Freq: 10; Began: 1979; Lang: Eng; Subj: Theatre.
■American Stage Publishing Company; 217 East 28th Street; New York, NY 10016; USA.

ASTRN   *ASTR Newsletter*. Freq: 2; Began: 1972; Cov: Scan; Lang: Eng; Subj: Theatre.   ISSN: 0044-7927
■American Society for Theatre Research, C.W. Post College; Department of English; Brookvale, NY 11548; USA.

ATAC   *Aujourd'hui Tendances Art Culture*. Formerly: *Partenaires*. Lang: Fre; Subj: Related.
■FRANCE.

ATArg   *Annuario del Teatro Argentino*. Freq: 1; Lang: Spa; Subj: Theatre.
■F.N.A.; Calle Alsina 673; Buenos Aires; ARGENTINA.

ATB   *Annuario do Teatro Brasileiro*. Freq: 1; Began: 1976; Lang: Por; Subj: Theatre.
■Ministerio da Educacao e Cultura; Service Nacional de Teatro; Rio de Janeiro; BRAZIL.

AThR   *Australian Theatre Review*. Lang: Eng; Subj: Theatre.   ISSN: 0310-6381
■Australian Centre of the ITI, c/o School of Drama; University of NSW; NSW 2066 Kensington; AUSTRALIA.

ATJ   *Asian Theatre Journal*. Formerly: *Asian Theatre Reports*. Freq: 2; Began: 1984; Cov: Full; Lang: Eng; Subj: Theatre.   ISSN: 0742-5457
■Univ. of Hawaii Press; 2840 Kolowalu Street; Honolulu, HI 96822; USA.

ATR   *Australian Theatre Record*. Freq: 12; Began: 1987; Lang: Eng; Subj: Theatre.   ISSN: 0819-1182
■Australian Studies Theatre Centre of ITI, University of New South Wales; POBox 1; NSW 2033 Kensington; AUSTRALIA.

ATT   *Amers Theatrical Times*. Freq: 12; Began: 1976; Lang: Eng; Subj: Related.
■William Amer (Pty) Ltd.; 15 Montgomery Avenue; NSW 2142 South Granville; AUSTRALIA.

Audiences   *Audiences Magazine*. Freq: 12; Lang: Fre; Subj: Theatre.
■55 avenue Jean Jaures; 75019 Paris; FRANCE.

AULLA   *Journal of the Australian Universities Language & Literature Association*. Freq: 2; Began: 1953; Cov: Scan; Lang: Eng; Subj: Related.   ISSN: 0001-2793
■Australasian Universities Language & Literature Association; Monash University; Clayton, Victoria 3168; AUSTRALIA.

Autores   *Autores*. Freq: 4; Lang: Por; Subj: Theatre.
■Sociedade Portuguesa de Autores; Av. Duque de Loule, 31; 1098 Lisbon Codex; PORTUGAL.

Avrora   *Avrora*. Freq: 12; Began: 1969; Cov: Scan; Lang: Rus; Subj: Related.
■Leningrad; USSR.

Baal   *Baal Rangmanch*. Freq: 12; Lang: Hin; Subj: Theatre.
■325 Shradanand Nagar (Bashirat Gunj); Lucknow; INDIA.

Bahub   *Bahubacana*. Began: 1978; Lang: Ben; Subj: Theatre.
■Bahubacana Natyagoshthi; 11/2 Jaynag Road, Bakshi Bazaar; Dacca; BANGLADESH.

BaI   *Ballett International*: Aktuelle Monatszeitung für Ballett und Tanztheater. Formerly: *Ballett Info*. Freq: 12; Began: 1978; Lang: Ger/Eng; Subj: Related.   ISSN: 0722-6268
■Ballett International Verlags GmbH, P.O. Box 270 443; Richard-Wagner Strasse 33; D5000 Cologne 1; WEST GERMANY.

BALF   *Black American Literature Forum*. Formerly: *Negro American Literature*. Freq: 4; Began: 1967; Cov: Scan; Lang: Eng; Subj: Related.   ISSN: 0148-6179
■English Dept., Indiana State Univ.; Terre Haute, IN 47809; USA.

Bamah   *Bamah*: Educational Theatre Review. Freq: 4; Began: 1959; Cov: Full; Lang: Heb; Subj: Theatre.   ISSN: 0045-138X
■Bamah Association; PO Box 4069; 91040 Jerusalem; ISRAEL.

BAMu   *Buenos Aires Musical*. Lang: Spa; Subj: Theatre.
■Calle Alsina 912; Buenos Aires; ARGENTINA.

Band   *Bandwagon*. Freq: 6; Began: 1939; Cov: Scan; Lang: Eng; Subj: Theatre.   ISSN: 0005-4968
■Circus Historical Society; 2515 Dorset Road; Columbus, OH 43221; USA.

BaNe   *Ballet News*. Freq: 12; Began: 1979; Lang: Eng; Subj: Related.   ISSN: 0191-2690

■Metropolitan Opera Guild, Inc.; 1865 Broadway; New York, NY 10023; USA.

BASSITEJ   *Bulletin ASSITEJ*. Formerly: *Bulletin d'Information ASSITEJ*. Freq: 3; Began: 1966; Lang: Fre/Eng/Rus; Subj: Theatre.
■ASSITEJ; Celetna 17; 110 01 Prague 1; CZECHOSLOVAKIA.

BCl   *Beckett Circle / Cercle de Beckett*. Freq: 2; Began: 1978; Lang: Eng/Fre; Subj: Theatre.
■Samuel Beckett Society; University of California at Los Angeles; Los Angeles, CA 90024; USA.

BCom   *Bulletin of the Commediantes*. Freq: 2; Began: 1949; Lang: Eng; Subj: Theatre.
■James A. Parr, Dept. of Spa. & Portuguese; University of California; Los Angeles, CA 90007; USA.

BelgITI   *Bulletin*: Van het Belgisch Centrum ITI. Lang: Fre; Subj: Theatre.
■Belgisch Centrum van het ITI, c/o Mark Hermans; Rudolfstraat 33; B 2000 Antwerp; BELGIUM.

Bergens   *Bergens Theatermuseum Skrifter*. Began: 1970; Lang: Nor; Subj: Theatre.
■Bergens Theatermuseum, Kolstadgt 1; Box 2959 Toeyen; 6 Oslo; NORWAY.

Bericht   *Bericht*. Lang: Ger; Subj: Theatre.   ISSN: 0067-6047
■UMLOsterreichischer Bundestheaterverband; Goethegasse 1; A 1010 Vienna; AUSTRIA.

BFant   *Botteghe della Fantasia, Le*. Lang: Ita; Subj: Theatre.
■Via S. Manlio 13; Milan; ITALY.

BGs   *Bühnengenossenschaft*. Freq: 10; Began: 1949; Lang: Ger; Subj: Theatre.   ISSN: 0007-3083
■Bühnenschriften-Vertriebs-Gesellschaft; Feldsbrunnenstrasse 74; 2000 Hamburg 13; WEST GERMANY.

BGTA   *Bibliographic Guide to Theatre Arts*. Freq: 1; Lang: Eng; Subj: Theatre.   ISSN: 0360-2788
■G. K. Hall & Co.; 70 Lincoln Street; Boston, MA 02111; USA.

BIINET   *Boletin Informativo del Instituto Nacional de Estudios de Teatro*. Freq: 10; Began: 1978; Lang: Spa; Subj: Theatre.
■1055 Avenida Cordoba; 1199 Buenos Aires; ARGENTINA.

Biladi   *Biladi*. Lang: Ara; Subj: Theatre.
■Parti Socialiste Desourien, Maison du Parti, BP 1033; Blvd. du 9 Avril, La Kasbah; Tunis; TUNISIA.

BiT   *Biblioteca Teatrale*. Freq: 4; Began: 1986; Cov: Full; Lang: Ita; Subj: Theatre.   ISSN: 0045-1959
■Bulzoni Editore; Via dei Liburni 14; 00185I Rome; ITALY.

BITIJ   *Boletin Iberoamericano de Teatro para la Infancia y la Juventud*. Lang: Spa; Subj: Theatre.
■Associacion Espanola de Teatro para la Infancia y la Juventud; Claudio Coello 141; 6 Madrid; SPAIN.

BK   *Bauten der Kultur*. Freq: 4; Began: 1976; Lang: Ger; Subj: Related.   ISSN: 0323-5696

■Institut für Kulturbauten; Clara-Zetkin-Strasse 105; 1080 Berlin; WEST GERMANY.

BlackM   *Black Masks*. Freq: 12; Began: 1984; Cov: Scan; Lang: Eng; Subj: Related.
■New York, NY; USA.

BlC   *Black Collegian, The*: The National Magazine of Black College Students. Formerly: *Expressions*. Freq: IRR; Began: 1970; Cov: Scan; Lang: Eng; Subj: Related.
         ISSN: 0192-3757
■Black Collegiate Services, Inc.; 1240 Broad Street; New Orleans, LA 70125; USA.

BM   *Burlington Magazine*. Freq: 12; Began: 1903; Cov: Scan; Lang: Eng; Subj: Related.   ISSN: 0007-6287
■Burlington Magazine Publications, Elm House; 10-16 Elm Street; WC1X 0BP London; UK.

BMT   *Biuletyn Mlodego Teatru*. Began: 1978; Lang: Pol; Subj: Theatre.
■Gwido Zlatkes; Bednarska 24 m; 00 321 Warsaw; POLAND.

BNJMtd   *Biblioteca Nacional José Marti*: Informacion y Documentacion de la Cultura. Serie Teatro y Danza. Freq: 12; Lang: Spa; Subj: Theatre.
■Biblioteca Nacional José Marti, Dept. Info. y Doc. de Cultura; Plaza de la Revolución; Havana; CUBA.

BNS   *Builder N.S.* Formerly: *Builder N.S.W.*. Freq: 12; Began: 1907; Cov: Scan; Lang: Eng; Subj: Related.
■Master Builders Asso. of New South Wales; Private Bag 9; Broadway; N.S.W. 2007; AUSTRALIA.Tel: 660-7188

BooksC   *Books in Canada*. Freq: 9; Began: 1971; Cov: Scan; Lang: Eng/Fre; Subj: Related.   ISSN: 0045-2564
■Canadian Review of Books; 366 Adelaide Street East, Suite 432; Toronto, ON M5A 3X9; CANADA.

Bouff   *Bouffonneries*. Lang: Fre; Subj: Theatre.
■Domaine de Lestanière; 11000 Cazilhac; FRANCE.

BPAN   *British Performing Arts Newsletter*. Ceased: 1980; Lang: Eng; Subj: Related.
■London; UK.

BPM   *Black Perspective in Music*. Freq: 2; Began: 1973; Cov: Scan; Lang: Eng; Subj: Related.   ISSN: 0090-7790
■Foundation for Research in the Afro-American Creative Arts; P.O. Drawer One; Cambria Heights, NY 11411; USA.

BPTV   *Bühne und Parkett*: Theater Journal Volksbühnen-Spiegel. Formerly: *Volksbuhnen-Spiegel*. Freq: 3; Began: 1955; Lang: Ger; Subj: Theatre.   ISSN: 0172-1321
■Verband der deutschen Volksbühne e.v.; Bismarckstrasse 17; 1000 Berlin 12; WEST GERMANY.

BR   *Ballet Review*. Freq: 4; Began: 1965; Lang: Eng; Subj: Related.
        ISSN: 0522-0653
■Dance Research Foundation, Inc.; 46 Morton Street; New York, NY 10014; USA.

BrechtJ   *Brecht Jahrbuch*. Freq: 1; Began: 1971; Lang: Ger/Eng/Fre; Subj: Theatre.
■Program in Comparative Literature, Foreign Language Bldg, Room 3202; Univ. of Maryland; College Park, MD 20742; USA.

Brs   *Broadside*. Freq: 4; Began: 1940; Lang: Eng; Subj: Theatre. ISSN: 0068-2748
■Theatre Library Assoc.; 111 Amsterdam Avenue; New York, NY 10023; USA.

BSOAS   *Bulletin of the School of Oriental & African Studies*. Lang: Eng; Subj: Related.
■London; UK.

BSPC   *Bulletin de la Société Paul Claudel*. Freq: 4; Cov: Scan; Lang: Fre; Subj: Related.
■13, rue du Pont Louis-Philippe; 75004 Paris; FRANCE.

BSSJ   *Bernard Shaw Newsletter*. Formerly: *Newsletter & Journal of the Shaw Society of London*. Freq: 1; Began: 1976; Lang: Eng; Subj: Related.
■Bernard Shaw Centre, High Orchard; 125 Markyate Road; EM8 2LB Dagenahm, Essex; UK.

BTA   *Børneteateravisen*. Freq: 4; Began: 1972; Lang: Dan; Subj: Theatre.
■Samarbejdsudvalget; Frederiksborggade 20; 1360 Copenhagen; DENMARK.

BTlog   *British Theatrelog*. Freq: 4; Began: 1978; Ceased: 1980; Lang: Eng; Subj: Theatre.   ISSN: 0141-9056
■Associate British Centre of the ITI; 44 Earlham St.; WC2H 9LA London; UK.

BtR   *Bühnentechnische Rundschau*: Zeitschrift für Theatertechnik, Bühnenbau und Bühnengestaltung. Freq: 6; Began: 1907; Lang: Ger; Subj: Theatre.
■Orell Fuessli & Friedrich Verlag; Dietzingerstrasse 3; CH8036 Zurich; SWITZERLAND.

Buhne   *Bühne, Die*. Freq: 12; Began: 1958; Cov: Full; Lang: Ger; Subj: Theatre.   ISSN: 0007-3075
■Zeitschriftenverlag Austria Int'l.; Wallnerstrasse 8; A1014 Vienna; AUSTRIA.

CahiersC   *Cahiers Césairiens*. Freq: 2; Began: 1974; Lang: Eng/Fre; Subj: Theatre.
■Pennsylvania State University, Dept. of French; University Park, PA 16802; USA.

CahiersCC   *Cahiers CERT/CIRCE*. Lang: Fre; Subj: Theatre.
■Centre Etudes Recherches Théâtrale, Université de Bordeaux III; Esplanade des Antilles; 33405 Talence; FRANCE.

Callaloo   *Callaloo*: A Black South Journal of Arts and Letters. Freq: 3; Began: 1976; Cov: Scan; Lang: Eng; Subj: Related.
        ISSN: 0161-2492
■University of Kentucky, Dept. of English; Lexington, KY 40506; USA.

CallB   *Call Boy, The*: Journal of the British Music Hall Society. Freq: 4; Began: 1963; Lang: Eng; Subj: Theatre.
■British Music Hall Society; 32 Hazelbourne Road; SW12 London; UK.

Callboard   *Callboard*. Freq: 4; Began: 1951; Lang: Eng; Subj: Theatre. ISSN: 0045-4044
■Nova Scotia Drama League; 5516 Spring Garden Road, Suite 305; Halifax, NS B3J 1G6; CANADA.

Calliope   *Calliope*. Freq: 12; Began: 1964; Lang: Eng; Subj: Theatre.
■Clowns of America Inc.; 717 Beverley Road; Baltimore, MD 21222; USA.

CAM   *City Arts Monthly*. Freq: 12; Lang: Eng; Subj: Related.
■640 Natoma St.; San Francisco, CA 94103; USA.

CanL   *Canadian Literature/Littérature Canadienne*: A Quarterly of Criticism and Review. Freq: 4; Began: 1959; Cov: Scan; Lang: Eng/Fre; Subj: Related.
        ISSN: 0008-4360
■University of British Columbia; 223-2029 West Mall; Vancouver, BC V6T 1W5; CANADA.

Caratula   *Caratula*. Freq: 12; Lang: Spa; Subj: Theatre.
■Sanchez Pacheco 83; 2 Madrid; SPAIN.

Castelets   *Castelets*. Lang: Fre; Subj: Theatre.
■Centre Belge de l'UNIMA, Section francophone; 66 rue de Lot; 1650 Beersel; BELGIUM.

CaTheatre   *Cahiers Théâtre*. Freq: 1; Began: 1968; Lang: Fre; Subj: Theatre.
        ISSN: 0068-5232
■Université Catholique de Louvain, Centre d'Etudes Théâtrales; 1 Place de l'Université; 1348 Louvain-la-Neuve; BELGIUM.

CB   *Call Board*. Formerly: *Monthly Theatre Magazine of TCCBA*. Freq: IRR; Began: 1931; Lang: Eng; Subj: Theatre.
        ISSN: 0008-1701
■Theatre Communications Center of the Bay Area; 2940 16th St., Suite 102; San Francisco, CA 94103; USA.

CBGB   *Cahiers de la Bibliothèque Gaston Baty*. Lang: Fre; Subj: Related.
■Paris; FRANCE.

CCIEP   *Courrier du Centre international d'études poétiques*. Freq: 6; Cov: Scan; Lang: Fre; Subj: Theatre.
■Centre d'études poétiques; Bibliothèque royale; Boulevard de l'empereur, 4; 1000 Bruxelles; BELGIUM.

CDO   *Courrier Dramatique de l'Ouest*. Freq: 4; Began: 1973; Lang: Fre; Subj: Theatre.
■Théâtre du Bout du Monde, Ctre Dramatique Natl de l'Ouest; 9B Avenue Janvier; 35100 Rennes; FRANCE.

CDr   *Canadian Drama/Art Dramatique Canadien*. Freq: 2; Began: 1975; Cov: Full; Lang: Eng/Fre; Subj: Theatre.
        ISSN: 0317-9044
■Dept. of English, University of Waterloo; Waterloo, ON N2L 3G1; CANADA.

CdRideau   *Cahiers du Rideau*. Freq: 3; Began: 1976; Lang: Fre; Subj: Theatre.
■Rideau de Bruxelles; 23 rue Ravenstein; B 1000 Bruxelles; BELGIUM.

CE   *College English*. Freq: 8; Began: 1937; Cov: Scan; Lang: Eng; Subj: Related.
        ISSN: 0010-0994
■National Council of Teachers of English; 1111 Kenyon Road; Urbana, IL 61801; USA.

Celcit   *Celcit*. Lang: Spa; Subj: Theatre.
■Apartado 662; 105 Caracas; VENEZUELA.

CeskL   *Ceskoslovenski Loutkar*. Began: 1913; Lang: Cze; Subj: Theatre.
■Panorama; Mrstikova 23; 10 000 Prague 10; CZECHOSLOVAKIA.

CetC   *Culture et Communication*. Freq: 10; Lang: Fre; Subj: Theatre.
■Min. de la Culture et de la Documentation; 3 rue de Valois; 75001 Paris; FRANCE.

CF   *Comédie-Française*. Freq: 10; Began: 1971; Cov: Full; Lang: Fre; Subj: Theatre.
■1 Place Colette; 75001 Paris; FRANCE.

Cfl   *Confluent*. Freq: 9; Began: 1974; Lang: Fre; Subj: Related. ISSN: 0150-2441
■Maison de la Culture de Rennes; 1, rue St. Helier; 35008 Rennes; FRANCE.

CFT   *Contemporary French Civilization*. Freq: 3; Began: 1976; Cov: Scan; Lang: Fre/ Eng; Subj: Related. ISSN: 0147-9156
■Dept. of Modern Languages, Montana State University; Bozeman, MT 59717; USA.

Chhaya   *Chhaya Nat*. Freq: 4; Lang: Hin; Subj: Theatre.
■U.P. Sangeet Natak Akademi; Lucknow; INDIA.

ChinL   *Chinese Literature*. Freq: 4; Began: 1951; Cov: Scan; Lang: Eng; Subj: Related. ISSN: 0009-4617
■Bai Wan Zhuang; Peking 37; CHINA.

Chronico   *Chronico*. Lang: Gre; Subj: Theatre.
■'Horo'; Xenofontos 7; Athens; GREECE.

ChTR   *Children's Theatre Review*. Freq: 4; Began: 1952; Cov: Full; Ceased: 1985; Lang: Eng; Subj: Theatre. ISSN: 0009-4196
■c/o Milton W. Hamlin, Shoreline High School; 18560 1st Avenue N.E.; Seattle, WA 98155; USA.

CineLD   *Cineschedario*: Letture Drammatiche. Freq: 12; Began: 1964; Lang: Ita; Subj: Related. ISSN: 0024-1458
■Centro Salesiano dello Spettacolo; Via M. Ausiliatrice 32; Turin 10121; ITALY.

CIQ   *Callahan's Irish Quarterly*. Freq: 4; Ceased: 1983; Cov: Scan; Lang: Eng; Subj: Related.
■P.O. Box 5935; Berkeley, CA 94705; USA.

CircusP   *Circus-Parade*. Freq: 12; Began: 1976; Lang: Ger; Subj: Theatre.
■Circus-Club International; Klosterhof 10; 2308 Preetz; WEST GERMANY.

CittaA   *Città Aperta*. Freq: 1; Began: 1981; Lang: Ita; Subj: Theatre.
■Associazione Piccolo Teatro; Via Cesalpino 20; 52100 Arezzo; ITALY.

CityL   *City Limits*. Freq: 10; Began: 1976; Cov: Scan; Lang: Eng; Subj: Related. ISSN: 0199-0330
■City Limits, Community Information Services; 424 W. 33rd Street; New York, NY 10001; USA.

CJC   *Cahiers Jean Cocteau*. Freq: 1; Began: 1969; Lang: Fre; Subj: Theatre. ISSN: 0068-5178
■6 rue Bonaparte; 75006 Paris; FRANCE.

CJG   *Cahiers Jean Giraudoux*. Freq: 1; Began: 1972; Lang: Fre; Subj: Theatre.
■Editions Bernard Grasset; 61, rue des Saints-Pères; 75006 Paris; FRANCE.

Cjo   *Conjunto*: Revista de Teatro Latinamericano. Freq: 4; Began: 1964; Cov: Full; Lang: Spa; Subj: Theatre. ISSN: 0010-5937
■Departamento de Teatro Latino Americano, Casa de las Americas; Tercera y G, El Vedado; Havana; CUBA.

CLAJ   *College Language Association Journal*. Freq: 4; Began: 1957; Lang: Eng; Subj: Related. ISSN: 0007-8549
■College Language Assoc., c/o Cason Hill; Morehouse College; Atlanta, GA 30314; USA.

ClaudelS   *Claudel Studies*. Freq: 2; Began: 1972; Cov: Scan; Lang: Eng; Subj: Related. ISSN: 0090-1237
■University of Dallas, Dept. of French; PO Box 464; Irving, TX 75061; USA.

CLSUJ   *CLSU Journal of the Arts*. Freq: 1; Began: 1981; Lang: Eng/Phi; Subj: Theatre.
■Central Luzon State University, Publications House; Munoz; Nueva Ecija; PHILIPPINES.

CMJV   *Cahiers de la Maison Jean Vilar*. Lang: Fre; Subj: Theatre.
■Avignon; FRANCE.

CNCT   *Cahiers de la NCT*. Freq: 3; Began: 1965; Cov: Scan; Lang: Fre; Subj: Theatre.
■Nouvelle Compagnie Théâtrale; 4353 rue Ste. Catherine est.; Montreal, PQ H1V 1F2; CANADA.

CO   *Comédie de l'Ouest*. Lang: Fre; Subj: Theatre.
■Rennes; FRANCE.

ColecaoT   *Coleçao Teatro*. Freq: IRR; Began: 1974; Lang: Por; Subj: Theatre.
■Universidade Federal do Rio Grande do Sul; Porto Alegre; BRAZIL.

ColJL&A   *Columbia-VLA Journal of Law & the Arts*. Formerly: *Art & the Law*. Freq: 4; Began: 1985; Cov: Full; Lang: Eng; Subj: Related. ISSN: 0743-5226
■Columbia University School of Law &, Volunteer Lawyers for the Arts; 435 West 116 Street; New York, NY 10027; USA.

Comedy   *Comedy*. Freq: 4; Began: 1980; Lang: Eng; Subj: Theatre.
■Trite Explanations Ltd.; Box 505, Canal Street Station; New York, NY 10013; USA.

ComIBS   *Communications from the International Brecht Society*: The Global Brecht. Freq: 2; Began: 1970; Cov: Scan; Lang: Eng/Ger; Subj: Theatre. ISSN: 0740-8943
■Editor of the Communications from the IBS, Dep. Foreign Langs & Literatures; Valparaiso University; Valparaiso, IN 46383; USA.

CompD   *Comparative Drama*. Freq: 4; Began: 1967; Cov: Full; Lang: Eng; Subj: Theatre. ISSN: 0010-4078
■Department of English, Western Michigan University; Kalamazoo, MI 49008; USA.

Con   *Connoisseur*. Freq: 12; Began: 1901; Cov: Scan; Lang: Eng; Subj: Related. ISSN: 0010-6275
■Hearst Magazines, Connoisseur; 250 W. 55th St.; New York, NY 10019; USA.

Confes   *Confessio*. Freq: 4; Began: 1976; Cov: Scan; Lang: Hun; Subj: Related.
■Bulletin of the Hungarian Reformed Church; XIV. Abonyi u. 21.; 1146 Budapest; HUNGARY.

ContactQ   *Contact Quarterly*. Freq: 3; Began: 1975; Lang: Eng; Subj: Theatre. ISSN: 0198-9634
■Contact Collaborations Inc.; Box 603; Northampton, MA 01061; USA.

Contenido   *Contenido*. Lang: Spa; Subj: Theatre.
■Centro Venezolano del ITI; Apartado 51-456; 105 Caracas; VENEZUELA.

CORD   *CORD Dance Research Annual*. Lang: Eng; Subj: Related.
■CORD Editorial Board, NYU Dance and Dance Educ. Dept.; 35 W. 4th St., Room 675; New York, NY 10003; USA.

CorpsE   *Corps écrit*. Freq: 4; Cov: Scan; Lang: Fre; Subj: Theatre.
■Presses Universitaires de France; 12, rue Jean de Beauvais; 75005 Paris; FRANCE.

COS   *Central Opera Service Bulletin*. Freq: 4; Began: 1954; Lang: Eng; Subj: Theatre. ISSN: 0008-9508
■Metropolitan Opera Nat'l Council, Central Opera Service; Lincoln Center; New York, NY 10023; USA.

Costume   *Costume*: The Journal of the Costume Society. Freq: 1; Began: 1967; Cov: Scan; Lang: Eng; Subj: Related. ISSN: 0590-8876
■c/o Miss Anne Brogden; 63 Salisbury Road; LI9 0PH Liverpool; UK.

CrAr   *Critical Arts*. Freq: 3; Began: 1980; Cov: Scan; Lang: Eng; Subj: Related.
■Critial Arts Study Group, c/o Dept. of Journalism & Media; Rhodes University; 6140 Grahamstown; SOUTH AFRICA.

CRB   *Cahiers Renaud Barrault*. Freq: 4; Began: 1953; Cov: Scan; Lang: Fre; Subj: Theatre. ISSN: 0008-0470
■Editions Gallimard; 5 rue Sebastien-Bottin; 75007 Paris; FRANCE.

CreD   *Creative Drama*. Freq: 1; Began: 1949; Lang: Eng; Subj: Theatre. ISSN: 0011-0892
■Educational Drama Association, c/o Stacey Publications; 1 Hawthorndene Road; BR2 7DZ Kent; UK.

Crepuscl   *Crépuscule, Le*. Ceased: 1979; Lang: Fre; Subj: Theatre.
■Théâtre du Crepuscule; rue Scailquin 30; Brussels 3; BELGIUM.

Crisis   *Crisis*. Freq: 6; Began: 1910; Cov: Scan; Lang: Eng; Subj: Related. ISSN: 0011-1422
■Crisis Publishing Co.; 186 Remsen St.; Brooklyn, NY 11201; USA.

CritD   *Critical Digest*. Freq: 24; Began: 1948; Lang: Eng; Subj: Theatre.
■225 West 34th Street, Room 918; New York, NY 10001; USA.

CritNY   *Critique*. Freq: 4; Began: 1976; Lang: Eng; Subj: Theatre.
■417 Convent Avenue; New York, NY 10031; USA.

CritQ   *Critical Quarterly*. Freq: 4; Began: 1959; Lang: Eng; Subj: Related. ISSN: 0011-1562
■Manchester University Press; Oxford Road; M13 9PL Manchester; UK.

CRT *Cabra, La*: Revista de Teatro. Lang: Spa; Subj: Theatre. ■Mexico City; MEXICO.

CS *Canada on Stage*. Freq: 1; Began: 1975; Lang: Eng; Subj: Theatre. ISSN: 0380-9455 ■Drama Department, University of Guelph; Guelph, ON N1G 2W1; CANADA.

CSAN *Costume Society of America Newsletter*. Lang: Eng; Subj: Related. ■Englishtown, NJ; USA.

CShav *Californian Shavian*. Freq: 6; Began: 1958; Lang: Eng; Subj: Theatre. ISSN: 0008-154X ■Shaw Society of California; 1933 S. Broadway; Los Angeles, CA 90007; USA.

CTA *California Theatre Annual*. Freq: 1; Lang: Eng; Subj: Theatre. ISSN: 0733-5806 ■Performing Arts Network; 9025 Wilshire Blvd.; Beverly Hills, CA 90211; USA.

CTCheck *Canadian Theatre Checklist*. Formerly: *Checklist of Canadian Theatres*. Freq: 1; Began: 1979; Ceased: 1983; Lang: Eng; Subj: Theatre. ISSN: 0226-5125 ■University of Toronto Press; 63A St. George Street; Toronto, ON M5S 1A6; CANADA.

CTL *Cahiers Théâtre Louvain*. Freq: 4; Began: 1968; Cov: Full; Lang: Fre; Subj: Theatre. ■Office International de Libraries; 30 avenue de Marnix; 1050 Brussels; BELGIUM.

CTPA *Cahiers du Théâtre Populaire d'Amiens*. Began: 1984; Lang: Fre; Subj: Theatre. ■Amiens; FRANCE.

CTR *Canadian Theatre Review*. Freq: 4; Began: 1974; Cov: Full; Lang: Eng; Subj: Theatre. ISSN: 0315-0836 ■CTR, c/o Department of English, Glendon College; 2275 Bayview Avenue; Toronto, ON M4N 3M6; CANADA.

CTRY *Canadian Theatre Review Yearbook*. Freq: 1; Began: 1974; Lang: Eng; Subj: Theatre. ISSN: 0380-9455 ■Canadian Theatre Review Publications, 222 Admin. Studies; York University; Downsview, ON M3J 1P3; CANADA.

CTXY *C'wan t'ong Xiju Yishu/Art of Traditional Opera*. Freq: 4; Began: 1979; Lang: Chi; Subj: Theatre. ■Institute of Traditional Chinese Opera; Peking; CHINA.

CU *Cirque dans l'Univers, Le*. Freq: 4; Began: 1950; Cov: Scan; Lang: Fre; Subj: Theatre. ISSN: 0009-7373 ■Club du Cirque; 11, rue Ch-Silvestri; 94300 Vincennes; FRANCE.

Cuaderno *Cuadernos El Publico*. Began: 1985; Lang: Spa/Cat; Subj: Theatre. ISSN: 8602-3573 ■Centro de Documentacion Teatral, Organismo Autonomo Teatros Ncnl; c/ Capitan Haya 44; 28020 Madrid; SPAIN.

Cue *Cue*: Technical Theatre Review. Freq: 6; Began: 1979; Cov: Full; Lang: Eng; Subj: Theatre. ISSN: 0144-6088 ■Twynam Publishing Ltd.; SN7 8HR Kitemore; UK.

CueM *Cue, The*. Freq: 2; Began: 1928; Cov: Scan; Lang: Eng; Subj: Theatre. ISSN: 0011-2666 ■Theta Alpha Phi Fraternity, Dept. of Speech/Theatre; Montclair State College; Upper Montclair, NJ 07043; USA.

CueNY *Cue New York*. Freq: 26; Began: 1932; Lang: Eng; Subj: Theatre. ISSN: 0011-2658 ■North American Publishing Company; 545 Madison Avenue; New York, NY 10022; USA.

Culture *Culture*. Freq: 12; Lang: Fre; Subj: Theatre. ■Maison de la Culture de La Rochelle; 11 rue Chef-de-Ville; 17000 La Rochelle; FRANCE.

CuPo *Cultural Post*. Lang: Eng; Subj: Related. ■National Endowment for the Arts; 1100 Pennsylvania Avenue N.W.; Washington, DC 20506; USA.

Cz *Circuszeitung, Die*. Freq: 12; Began: 1955; Lang: Ger; Subj: Theatre. ■Gesellschaft für Circusfreunde; Klosterhof 10; 2308 Preetz; WEST GERMANY.

D&D *Dance and Dancers*. Freq: 12; Began: 1950; Lang: Eng; Subj: Related. ISSN: 0011-5983 ■Brevet Publishing Ltd.; 43B Gloucester Rd.; CR0 2DH Croydon, Surrey; UK.

D&T *Drama and Theater*. Freq: 3; Began: 1968; Lang: Eng; Subj: Theatre. ■Dept. of English, State University; Fredonia, NY 14063; USA.

DA *Dance Australia*. Freq: 4; Began: 1980; Cov: Scan; Lang: Eng; Subj: Related. ISSN: 0159-6330 ■Dance Australia Publications; 2 Yaralla Court; 3173 Keysborough; AUSTRALIA.

DalVostok *Dalnij Vostok*: (Far East). Freq: 12; Began: 1933; Cov: Scan; Lang: Rus; Subj: Related. ISSN: 0130-3023 ■Khabarovsk; USSR.

DB *Deutsche Bühne, Die*. Freq: 12; Began: 1909; Cov: Scan; Lang: Ger; Subj: Theatre. ISSN: 0011-975X ■Verlag Rommerskirchen und Co. KG, Rolandshof; 5480 Remagen-Rolandsec; WEST GERMANY.

DBj *Deutsches Bühnenjahrbuch*. Freq: 1; Lang: Ger; Subj: Theatre. ■Buhnenschriften-Vertrieb-Gesellschaft; Feldbrunnenstrasse 74; 2000 Hamburg 13; WEST GERMANY.

DC *Dance in Canada/Danse au Canada*. Freq: 4; Began: 1973; Lang: Eng/Fre; Subj: Theatre. ISSN: 0317-9737 ■Dance in Canada Association; 4700 Keele St.; Downsview, ON M3J 1P3; CANADA.

DCD *Documents del Centre Dramatic*. Freq: 4; Cov: Scan; Lang: Spa; Subj: Theatre. ■c/o Hospital, 51, 1er; Barcelona 08001; SPAIN.

DekorIsk *Dekorativnoje Iskusstvo SSR*. Freq: 12; Began: 1957; Cov: Scan; Lang: Rus; Subj: Related. ISSN: 0418-5153 ■Soveckij Chudožnik; Moscow; USSR.

DetLit *Detskaja Literatura*. Freq: 12; Began: 1932; Cov: Scan; Lang: Rus; Subj: Related. ISSN: 0130-3104

■Moscow; USSR.

Devlet *Devlet Tijatrolari (State Theatres)*. Freq: 4; Lang: Tur; Subj: Theatre. ■Genel Mudurugu; Ankara; TURKEY.

Dewan *Dewan Budaya*. Freq: 12; Began: 1979; Lang: Mal; Subj: Theatre. ISSN: 0126-8473 ■Peti Surat 803; Kuala Lumpur; MALAYSIA.

DGQ *Dramatists Guild Quarterly*. Freq: 4; Began: 1964; Cov: Scan; Lang: Eng; Subj: Theatre. ISSN: 0012-6004 ■The Dramatists Guild, Inc.; 234 W. 44th St.; New York, NY 10036; USA.

DHS *Dix-Huitième Siècle*. Freq: 1; Began: 1969; Cov: Scan; Lang: Fre; Subj: Related. ISSN: 0070-6760 ■Soc. Française d'Etude du 18e Siecle; 23 Quai de Grenelle; 75015 Paris; FRANCE.

DialogA *Dialog*. Freq: 10; Began: 1973; Lang: Ger; Subj: Theatre. ISSN: 0378-6935 ■Verlag Sauerländer; Laurenzenvorstadt 89; CH 5001 Aarau; SWITZERLAND.

DialogTu *Dialogue*. Lang: Fre; Subj: Theatre. ■Parti Socialiste Desourien, Maison du Parti, BP 1033; Blvd. du 9 Avril, La Kasbah; Tunis; TUNISIA.

Dialogue *Dialogue*: Canadian Philosophical Review/Revue Canadienne de Philosophie. Freq: 4; Began: 1962; Lang: Eng; Subj: Related. ISSN: 0012-2173 ■Montreal, PQ; CANADA.

DialogW *Dialog*: Miesiecznik Poswiecony Dramaturgii Wspolczesnej. Freq: 12; Began: 1956; Cov: Full; Lang: Pol; Subj: Theatre. ISSN: 0012-2041 ■Wydawnictwa Artystyczno-Graficzne, RSW Prasa-Ksiazka-Ruch; Ul. Smolna 10; Warsaw; POLAND.

DiN *Divadelni Noviny*. Freq: 26; Began: 1970; Lang: Cze; Subj: Theatre. ISSN: 0012-4141 ■Svaz Ceskoslovenskych Divadelnich a Rozhlasovych Umelcu; Valdstejnske nam. 3; Prague 1; CZECHOSLOVAKIA.

Dioniso *Dioniso*. Freq: 1; Began: 1929; Lang: Ita/Eng/Fre/Spa; Subj: Theatre. ■Instituto Nazionale del Dramma Antico; Corso Matteoti 29; Siracusa; ITALY.

DIPFL *Deutsches Institut für Puppenspiel Forschung und Lehre*. Freq: IRR; Began: 1964; Lang: Ger; Subj: Theatre. ISSN: 0070-4490 ■Deutsches Institut für Puppenspiel; Bergstrasse 115; 4630 Bochum; WEST GERMANY.

DirNotes *Directors Notes*. Lang: Eng; Subj: Theatre. ■American Directors Institute; 248 W. 74th St., Suite 10; New York, NY 10023; USA.

Diskurs *Diskurs*. Freq: 4; Lang: Ger; Subj: Theatre. ■Schauble Verlag; Waldgurtel 5; 506 Bensberg; WEST GERMANY.

Dm *Dance Magazine*. Freq: 12; Began: 1926; Lang: Eng; Subj: Related. ISSN: 0011-6009 ■Dance Magazine, Inc.; 33 W. 60th St.; New York, NY 10023; USA.

DMC   *Dramatics*. Freq: 9; Began: 1929; Lang: Eng; Subj: Theatre. ISSN: 0012-5989 ■International Thespian Society; 3368 Central Parkway; Cincinnati, OH 45225; USA.

DnC   *Dance Chronicle: Studies in Dance & the Related Arts*. Freq: 2; Began: 1978; Cov: Scan; Lang: Eng; Subj: Theatre. ISSN: 0147-2526 ■Marcel Dekker Journals; 270 Madison Avenue; New York, NY 10016; USA.

DNDT   *Drama*: Nordisk dramapedagogisk Tidskrift. Freq: 4; Began: 1963; Lang: Nor/Swe/Dan; Subj: Theatre. ■Landslaget Drama i skolen, Jerikoveien 97A; Furuset; 10 Oslo; NORWAY.

Dockt   *Dockteatereko*. Freq: 4; Began: 1971; Lang: Swe; Subj: Theatre. ISSN: 0349-9944 ■Dockteaterforeningen; Sandavagen 10; 14032 Grodinge; SWEDEN.

DocTh   *Documentation Théâtrale*. Began: 1974; Lang: Fre; Subj: Theatre. ■Centre d'Etudes Théâtrales, Université Paris X; 200 Avenue de la République; 92000 Nanterre; FRANCE.

DOE   *DOE*. Formerly: *Speel*. Freq: 24; Began: 1951; Lang: Dut; Subj: Theatre. ISSN: 0038-7258 ■Stichting 'Ons Leekenspel'; Gudelalaan 2; Bussum; NETHERLANDS.

DongukDA   *Dong-Guk Dramatic Art*. Freq: 1; Began: 1970; Cov: Full; Lang: Kor; Subj: Theatre. ■Department of Drama & Cinema, Dong-guk University; Seoul; KOREA.

Drama   *Drama: The Quarterly Theatre Review*: Third Series. Formerly: *Drama*. Freq: 4; Began: 1919; Cov: Scan; Lang: Eng; Subj: Theatre. ISSN: 0012-5946 ■British Theatre Association, Cranbourn Mansions; Cranbourn Street; London WC2H 7AG; UK.

DramaY   *Drama*. Lang: Slo; Subj: Theatre. ■Erjavceva; Ljubljana; YUGOSLAVIA.

DrammaR   *Dramma*. Freq: 12; Began: 1925; Cov: Scan; Lang: Ita; Subj: Theatre. ISSN: 0012-6004 ■Romana Teatri s.r.l.; Via Torino 29; 00184 Rome; ITALY.

DrammaT   *Dramma*: Il Mensile dello Spettacolo. Freq: 12; Lang: Ita; Subj: Theatre. ■I.L.T.E.; Corso Bramante 20; Turin; ITALY.

Dress   *Dress*. Freq: 1; Lang: Eng; Subj: Related. ■Costume Society of America; 15 Little John Road, PO Box 761; Englishtown, NJ 07726; USA.

DRJ   *Dance Research Journal*. Freq: 2; Began: 1967; Lang: Eng; Subj: Related. ISSN: 0149-7677 ■Congress on Research in Dance, NYU Dept. Dance Education 675D; 35 W. 4th St.; New York, NY 10003; USA.

DRostock   *Diskurs*. Freq: 3; Began: 1973; Lang: Ger; Subj: Theatre. ■Volkstheater Rostock; Patriotischer Weg 33; 25 Rostock; EAST GERMANY.

DrRev   *Drama Review*. Freq: 2; Began: 1970; Lang: Kor; Subj: Theatre. ■Yonguk-pyongron-sa; 131-51 Nokbun-dong, Eunpyong-ku; 122 Seoul; SOUTH KOREA.

DRs   *Dance Research*. Freq: 2; Lang: Eng; Subj: Related. ■17 Dules's Road; WC 1H 9AB London; UK.

Druzba   *Družba*. Freq: 6; Began: 1977; Cov: Scan; Lang: Rus/Bul; Subj: Related. ISSN: 0320-1021 ■Moscow;.

DruzNar   *Družba Narodov*. Freq: 12; Began: 1939; Cov: Scan; Lang: Rus; Subj: Related. ISSN: 0012-6756 ■Moscow; USSR.

DSat   *Don Saturio: Boletin Informativo de Teatro Gallego*. Lang: Spa; Subj: Theatre. ■Coruna 70-30; Esda; SPAIN.

DSchool   *Drama and the School*. Freq: 2; Began: 1948; Lang: Eng; Subj: Theatre. ■Whitehall Productions; 63 Elizabeth Bay Road; NSW 2011 Elizabeth Bay; AUSTRALIA.

DSGM   *Dokumenti Slovenskega Gledaliskega Muzeja*. Freq: 2; Began: 1964; Lang: Slo; Subj: Theatre. ■Slovenski Gledaliski in Filski muzej; Cankarjeva 11; Ljubljana; YUGOSLAVIA.

DSo   *Dramatists Sourcebook*. Formerly: *Information for Playwrights*. Freq: 1; Began: 1981; Cov: Scan; Lang: Eng; Subj: Theatre. ISSN: 0733-1606 ■Theatre Comm. Group, Inc; 355 Lexington Ave.; New York, NY 10017; USA.

DSS   *Dix-Septième Siècle*. Freq: 4; Began: 1949; Cov: Scan; Lang: Fre; Subj: Related. ISSN: 0012-4273 ■Commission des Publications, c/o Collège de France; 11 Place M. Berthelot; 75005 Paris; FRANCE.

DTh   *Divadlo*: (Theatre). Freq: 2; Lang: Slo; Subj: Theatre. ■Prague; CZECHOSLOVAKIA.

Dtherapy   *Dramatherapy*: SEE: Journal of Dramatherapy (JDt). Cov: Scan; Lang: Eng; Subj: Theatre. ■Herfordshire; St. Albans; UK.

DTi   *Dancing Times*. Freq: 12; Began: 1910; Lang: Eng; Subj: Theatre. ISSN: 0011-605X ■Dancing Times Ltd., Clerkenwell House; 45-47 Clerkenwell Green; EC1R 0BE London; UK.

DTJ   *Dance Theatre Journal*. Freq: 4; Began: 1983; Cov: Scan; Lang: Eng; Subj: Theatre. ■Laban Centre for Movement & Dance, Goldsmiths' College; SE15 6NW London; UK.

DTN   *Drama and Theatre Newsletter*. Freq: 4; Began: 1975; Ceased: 1982; Lang: Eng; Subj: Theatre. ■British Theatre Institute; 30 Clareville Street; SW7 5AW London; UK.

DTOP   *Dramaturgi: Tedri Og Praksis*. Lang: Dan; Subj: Theatre. ■Akademisk Forlag; St. Kannikestraede 8; 1169 Copenhagen; DENMARK.

DvS   *Divadlo ve Svete*. Lang: Cze; Subj: Theatre. ■Celetna 17; 100 01 Prague 1; CZECHOSLOVAKIA.

DZP   *Deutsche Zeitschrift für Philosophie*. Freq: 12; Began: 1953; Cov: Scan; Lang: Ger; Subj: Related. ISSN: 0012-1045 ■VEB Deutscher Verlag der Wissenschaften; Johannes-Dieckmann-Str. 10, Postfach 1216; 1080 Berlin; EAST GERMANY.

E&AM   *Entertainment and Arts Manager*. Formerly: *Entertainment and Arts Management*. Freq: 4; Began: 1973; Cov: Scan; Lang: Eng; Subj: Theatre. ISSN: 0143-8980 ■Assoc. of Entertainment & Arts Mangement, T.G. Scott and Son Ltd.; 30-32 Southampton St., Covent Garden; WC2E 7HR London; UK.

EAR   *English Academy Review, The*. Began: 1983; Cov: Scan; Lang: Eng; Subj: Related. ■English Academy of Southern Africa, Bollater House; 35 Melle St., Braamfontein; 2001 Johannesburg; SOUTH AFRICA.

Ebony   *Ebony*. Freq: 12; Began: 1945; Cov: Scan; Lang: Eng; Subj: Related. ISSN: 0012-9011 ■820 S. Michigan; Chicago, IL 60605; USA.

Echanges   *Echanges*. Freq: 12; Lang: Fre; Subj: Theatre. ■Théâtre Romain-Rolland; rue Eugène Varlin; 94 Villejuif; FRANCE.

ECr   *Esprit Créateur, L'*. Freq: 4; Began: 1961; Lang: Fre; Subj: Theatre. ISSN: 0014-0767 ■John D. Erickson; Box 222; Lawrence, KS 66044; USA.

ECrit   *Essays in Criticism*. Freq: 4; Began: 1951; Lang: Eng; Subj: Related. ISSN: 0014-0856 ■6A Rawlinson Rd.; Oxford OX2 6UE; UK.

ED   *Envers du Décor, L'*. Freq: 6; Began: 1973; Lang: Fre; Subj: Theatre. ISSN: 0319-8650 ■Théâtre du Nouveau Monde; 84 Ouest, Rue Ste-Catharine; Montreal, PQ H2X 1Z6; CANADA.

EDAM   *EDAM Newsletter*. Freq: 2; Began: 1978; Cov: Scan; Lang: Eng; Subj: Theatre. ISSN: 0196-5816 ■Medieval Institute Publications; Western Michigan University; Kalamazoo, MI 49008; USA.

EE&PA   *Economic Efficiency and the Performing Arts*. Lang: Eng; Subj: Theatre. ■Association for Cultural Economics, University of Akron; Akron, OH 44235; USA.

EECIT   *Estudis Escenics*. Freq: 2; Began: 1979; Cov: Full; Lang: Cat; Subj: Theatre. ISSN: 0212-3819 ■Inst. del Theatre de Barcelona, c/o Nou de la Rambla; 08001 Barcelona 3; SPAIN.

Egk   *Engekikai*: Theatre World. Freq: 12; Began: 1940; Lang: Jap; Subj: Theatre. ■Engeki Shuppan-sha, Chiyoda-ku; 2-11 Kanda-Jinpo-cho; Tokyo 101; JAPAN.

EHR   *Economic History Review*. Freq: 4; Began: 1927; Cov: Scan; Lang: Eng; Subj: Related. ISSN: 0013-0117

■Economic History Society, University of Birmingham; Faculty of Commerce & Social Science; Birmingham; UK.

Eire   *Eire-Ireland*. Freq: 4; Began: 1966; Cov: Scan; Lang: Eng; Subj: Related.
ISSN: 0013-2683
■Irish American Cultural Institute; 683 Osceola Ave.; St. Paul, MN 55105; USA.

EIT   *Escena*: Informativo Teatral. Freq: 4; Began: 1979; Lang: Spa; Subj: Theatre.
■Universidad de Costa Rica, Teatro Universitario, Apt. 92; San Pedro de Montes de Oca; San José; COSTA RICA.

Elet   *Eletünk*. Freq: 04; Began: 1963; Cov: Scan; Lang: Hun; Subj: Related.
ISSN: 0133-4751
■Vas Megyei Lapkiado Vallalat; P.O.B. 168; 9701 Szombathely; HUNGARY.

EIl   *Elet és Irodalom*: irodalmi es politkai hetilap. Freq: 52; Began: 1957; Lang: Hun; Subj: Related.   ISSN: 0424-8848
■Ft. Lapkiado Vallalat; Széchenyi rkp. 1; 1054 Budapest V; HUNGARY.

EIM   *Marges, El*. Freq: 3; Cov: Scan; Lang: Cat; Subj: Related.
■Curial Edicions Catalanes del Bruc; 144 Baixos; 08037 Barcelona; SPAIN.

ElPu   *Publico, El*: Periodico mensual de teatro. Freq: 12; Began: 1983; Cov: Scan; Lang: Spa; Subj: Theatre. ISSN: 0213-4926
■Centro de Documentación Teatral; c/ Capitán Haya, 44; 28020 Madrid; SPAIN.

ELR   *English Literary Renaissance Journal*. Cov: Scan; Lang: Eng; Subj: Related.
■University of Massachusetts; Boston, MA 02125; USA.

EN   *Equity News*. Freq: 12; Began: 1915; Cov: Scan; Lang: Eng; Subj: Theatre.
ISSN: 0013-9890
■Actors Equity Association; 165 W. 46 St.; New York, NY 10036; USA.

Enact   *Enact*: monthly theatre magazine. Freq: 12; Began: 1967; Cov: Scan; Lang: Eng; Subj: Theatre.   ISSN: 0013-6980
■Paul's Press, E44-11; Okhla Industrial Area, Phase II; 110020 New Delhi; INDIA.

Encore   *Encore*. Lang: Eng; Subj: Theatre.
■Fort Valley State College; Fort Valley, GA 31030; USA.

EncoreA   *Encore*. Freq: 12; Began: 1976; Lang: Eng; Subj: Theatre.
■PO Box 247; NSW 2154 Castle Hill; AUSTRALIA.

ENG   *Editorial Nuevo Grupo*. Lang: Spa; Subj: Theatre.
■Avenida La Colina, Prolongación Los Manolos; La Florida; 105 Caracas; VENEZUELA.

Entre   *Entré*. Freq: 6; Began: 1974; Cov: Full; Lang: Swe; Subj: Theatre.
ISSN: 0345-2581
■Svenska Riksteatern, Swedish National Theatre Centre; Raasundav 150; Solna S-171 30; SWEDEN.

EON   *Eugene O'Neill Newsletter, The*. Freq: 3; Began: 1977; Cov: Full; Lang: Eng; Subj: Theatre.   ISSN: 0733-0456
■Suffolk University, Department of English; Boston, MA 02114; USA.

EpicT   *Epic Theatre*. Freq: 4; Lang: Ben; Subj: Theatre.
■140/24 Netaji Subhashchandra Bose Road; Calcutta; INDIA.

EquityJ   *Equity Journal*. Freq: 4; Began: 1971; Lang: Eng; Subj: Theatre.
ISSN: 0141-3147
■British Actor's Equity Association; 8 Harley St.; London W1N 2AB; UK.

ERT   *Empirical Research in Theatre*. Freq: 1; Began: 1971; Ceased: 1984; Cov: Full; Lang: Eng; Subj: Theatre.
ISSN: 0361-2767
■Center for Communications Research; Bowling Green State University; Bowling Green, OH 43403; USA.

ESA   *English Studies in Africa: A Journal of the Humanities*. Freq: 2; Began: 1958; Cov: Scan; Lang: Eng; Subj: Related.
ISSN: 0013-8398
■Witwatersrand Univ. Press; Jan Smuts Ave.; Johannesburg 2001; SOUTH AFRICA.

Escena   *Escena*. Lang: Spa; Subj: Theatre.
■Departamento de Publicaciones, Consejo Nacional de la Cultura; Calle Paris, Edificio Macanao 3er. Piso; 106 Caracas; VENEZUELA.

Espill   *Espill, L'*. Freq: 4; Cov: Scan; Lang: Cat; Subj: Related.
■Editorial 3 i 4, c/o Moratin 15; Porta 3; 46002 Valencia; SPAIN.

Esprit   *Esprit*. Freq: 12; Began: 1932; Lang: Fre; Subj: Related.   ISSN: 0014-0759
■19, rue Jacob; 75006 Paris; FRANCE.

Essence   *Essence*. Freq: 12; Began: 1970; Cov: Scan; Lang: Eng; Subj: Related.
ISSN: 0014-0880
■Essence Comm., Inc.; 1500 Broadway; New York, NY 10036; USA.

EstLit   *Estafeta Literaria*: La Revista Quincenal de Libros, Artes y Espetáculos. Freq: 24; Began: 1958; Lang: Spa; Subj: Theatre.   ISSN: 0014-1186
■Avda. de José Antonio, 62; 13 Madrid; SPAIN.

Estreno   *Estreno*: Journal on the Contemporary Spanish Theater. Freq: 2; Began: 1975; Cov: Full; Lang: Eng/Spa; Subj: Theatre.
ISSN: 0097-8663
■University of Cincinnati, Dept. of Romance Languages & Lit; Cincinnati, OH 45221; USA.

ET   *Essays in Theatre*. Freq: 2; Began: 1982; Cov: Full; Lang: Eng; Subj: Theatre.
ISSN: 0821-4425
■University of Guelph, Department of Drama; Guelph, ON N1G 2W1; CANADA.

ETh   *Elizabethan Theatre*. Began: 1968; Lang: Eng; Subj: Theatre.
ISSN: 0071-0032
■Archon Books; 995 Sherman Avenue; Hamden, CT 06514; USA.

ETN   *Educational Theatre News*. Freq: 6; Began: 1953; Lang: Eng; Subj: Theatre.
ISSN: 0013-1997
■Southern California Education Theatre Association; 9811 Pounds Avenue; Whittier, CA 90603; USA.

Etoile   *Etoile de la Foire*. Freq: 12; Began: 1945; Lang: Fle/Fre; Subj: Theatre.
ISSN: 0014-1895

■15 rue Vanderlinden; Brussels 3; BELGIUM.

Europe   *Europe*: Revue Littéraire Mensuelle. Freq: 8; Began: 1923; Cov: Scan; Lang: Fre; Subj: Related.   ISSN: 0014-2751
■146, rue du Fg. Poisonnière; 75010 Paris; FRANCE.

Evento   *Evento Teatrale*. Freq: 3; Began: 1975; Lang: Ita; Subj: Theatre.
■A.BE.TE.spa; Via Presentina 683; 00155 Rome; ITALY.

Exchange   *Exchange*. Freq: 3; Began: 1977; Lang: Eng; Subj: Theatre.
■University of Missouri: Columbia, Dept. of Speech/Drama; 129 Fine Arts Centre; Columbia, MS 65211; USA.

Farsa   *Farsa, La*. Freq: 20; Lang: Spa; Subj: Theatre.
■Pza. de los Mostenses 11; 9 Madrid; SPAIN.

FDi   *Film a Divadlo*. Freq: 26; Lang: Cze; Subj: Related.
■Theatre Intitute in Bratislava; Obzor, Ceskoslovenskej Armady 35; Bratislava 815 85; CZECHOSLOVAKIA.

Fds   *Freedomways*: A Quarterly Review of the Freedom Movement. Freq: 4; Began: 1961; Cov: Scan; Lang: Eng; Subj: Related.   ISSN: 0016-061X
■Freedomways Assoc., Inc.; 799 Broadway; New York, NY 10003 6849; USA.

FemR   *Feminist Review*. Freq: 3; Began: 1979; Cov: Scan; Lang: Eng; Subj: Related.
ISSN: 0141-7789
■11 Carleton Gardens, Brecknock Rd.; London N19 5AQ; UK.

FG   *Fremantle Gazette*. Freq: 24; Began: 1977; Cov: Scan; Lang: Eng; Subj: Related.
■Community Newspapers; 7 High Street; Fremantle WA 6160; AUSTRALIA.

Fikr   *Al Fikr*. Lang: Ara; Subj: Theatre.
■Rue Dar Eg-gild; Tunis; TUNISIA.

FiloK   *Filológiai Közlöny*: Philological Review. Freq: 4; Began: 1955; Cov: Scan; Lang: Hun; Subj: Related. ISSN: 0015-1785
■Akademiai Kiado, Hungarian Academy of Sciences; Pesti Barnabás u. 1. IV. em 5-6; 1052 Budapest V; HUNGARY.

FIRTSIB   *FIRT/SIBMAS Bulletin d'information*. Freq: 4; Began: 1977; Lang: Fre/Eng; Subj: Theatre.
■c/o Netherlands Theatre Institute; Herengracht 166-168; 1016 BP Amsterdam; NETHERLANDS.

FMa   *Fight Master, The*. Freq: 4; Lang: Eng; Subj: Theatre.
■Society of American Fight Directors; 1551 York Ave., Suite 5N; New York, NY 10028; USA.

FN   *Filologičeskije Nauki*. Freq: 6; Began: 1958; Cov: Scan; Lang: Rus; Subj: Related.   ISSN: 0470-4649
■Izdatelstvo VysšajaŠkola; Prospekt Marksa 18; 103009 Moscow K-9; USSR.

Fnotes   *Footnotes*. Freq: 1; Began: 1975; Lang: Eng; Subj: Theatre.
■F. Randolph Associates; 1300 Arch Street; Philadelphia, PA 19107; USA.

FO   *Federal One*. Freq: IRR; Began: 1975; Cov: Scan; Lang: Eng; Subj: Related.
■George Mason University; 4400 University Dr.; Fairfax, VA 22030; USA.

Forras   *Forrás*. Freq: 10; Began: 1969; Cov: Scan; Lang: Hun; Subj: Related.
■Bacs Kiskun Megyei, Lapkiado Vallalat; Szabadság tér l/a; 6001 Kecskemét; HUNGARY.

FR   *French Review, The*. Freq: 6; Began: 1927; Lang: Fre/Eng; Subj: Related. ISSN: 0016-111X
■American Association of Teachers of French; 57 E. Armory Ave.; Champaign, IL 61820; USA.

FranceT   *France Théâtre*. Freq: 24; Began: 1957; Lang: Fre; Subj: Theatre. ISSN: 0015-9433
■Syndicat National des Agences; 16 Avenue l'Opéra; 75001 Paris; FRANCE.

FrF   *French Forum*. Freq: 3; Began: 1976; Lang: Fre/Eng; Subj: Related. ISSN: 0098-9355
■French Forum Publishers, Inc.; Box 5108; Lexington, KY 40505; USA.

FS   *French Studies*: A quarterly review. Freq: 4; Began: 1947; Cov: Scan; Lang: Eng; Subj: Related. ISSN: 0016-1128
■Society for French Studies; c/o M.J. Tilby; Selwyn College; CB3 9DQ Cambridge; UK.

FSM   *Film, Szinház, Muzsika*. Freq: 52; Began: 1957; Cov: Scan; Lang: Hun; Subj: Theatre. ISSN: 0015-1416
■Lapkiado Vallalat; Lenin korut 9-11; 1073 Budapest VII; HUNGARY.

Ftr   *Figurentheater*. Freq: IRR; Began: 1930; Lang: Ger; Subj: Theatre. ISSN: 0070-4490
■Deutsches Institut für Puppenspiel; Bergstrasse 115; 4630 Bochum; WEST GERMANY.

Fundarte   *Fundarte*. Lang: Spa; Subj: Theatre.
■Edificio Tajamar, P.H., Parque Central; Avenida Lecuna; 105 Caracas; VENEZUELA.

Funoun   *Al Funoun*: The Arts. Freq: 12; Lang: Ara; Subj: Theatre.
■Ministry of Information, Dept. of Culture and Arts; PO Box 6140; Amman; JORDAN.

Gambit   *Gambit*. Freq: IRR; Began: 1963; Cov: Scan; Lang: Eng; Subj: Theatre. ISSN: 0016-4283
■John Calder, Ltd.; 18 Brewer Street; W1R 4AS London; UK.

Gap   *Gap, The*. Cov: Scan; Lang: Eng; Subj: Related.
■Washington, DC; USA.

GaR   *Georgia Review*. Freq: 4; Began: 1947; Lang: Eng; Subj: Related. ISSN: 0016-8386
■University of Georgia; Athens, GA 30602; USA.

Garcin   *Garcin: Libro de Cultura*. Freq: 12; Began: 1981; Lang: Spa; Subj: Related.
■Acali Editoria; Ituzaingo 1495; Montevideo; URUGUAY.

Gazit   *Gazit*. Lang: Heb; Subj: Theatre.
■8 Brook Street; Tel Aviv; ISRAEL.

GdBA   *Gazette des Beaux Arts*. Freq: 10; Began: 1859; Cov: Scan; Lang: Fre; Subj: Related.
■Imprimerie Louis Jean, B.P. 87; Gap Cedex 05002; SWITZERLAND.

GdF   *Gazette du Français*. Lang: Fre; Subj: Related.
■Paris; FRANCE.

GdS   *Giornale dello Spettacolo*. Freq: 52; Lang: Ita; Subj: Theatre. ISSN: 0017-0232
■Associazione Generale Italiana dello Spettacolo; Via di Villa Patrizi 10; 00161 Rome; ITALY.

GerSR   *German Studies Review*. Freq: 3; Began: 1978; Cov: Scan; Lang: Ger; Subj: Related. ISSN: 0149-7952
■German Studies Association, c/o Prof. Gerald R. Kleinfeld; Arizona State University; Tempe, AZ 85287; USA.

Gestus   *Gestus*: A Quarterly Journal of Brechtian Studies. Freq: 4; Began: 1985; Cov: Full; Lang: Eng/Ger/Fre/Ita/Spa; Subj: Theatre. ISSN: 0749-7644
■Brecht Society of America; 59 S. New St.; Dover, DE 19901; USA.

GL&L   *German Life and Letters*. Freq: 4; Began: 1936; Cov: Scan; Lang: Eng; Subj: Related. ISSN: 0016-8777
■Basil Blackwell Publisher, Ltd.; 108 Cowley Road; 0X4 1JF Oxford; UK.

GOS   *Gazette Officielle du Spectacle*. Freq: 36; Began: 1969; Lang: Fre; Subj: Theatre.
■Office des Nouvelles Internationales; 12 rue de Miromesnil; 75008 Paris; FRANCE.

Gosteri   *Gosteri*: Performance. Freq: 12; Lang: Tur; Subj: Theatre.
■Uluslararasi Sanat Gosterileri A.S.; Narlpbahce Sok. 15; Cagaloglu-Istanbul; TURKEY.

GQ   *German Quarterly*. Freq: 4; Began: 1928; Cov: Scan; Lang: Ger; Subj: Related. ISSN: 0016-8831
■American Assoc. of Teachers of German; 523 Building, Suite 201, Rt. 38; Cherry Hill, NJ 08034; USA.

GrandR   *Grande République*. Formerly: *Pratiques Théâtrales*. Freq: 3; Began: 1978; Ceased: 1981; Lang: Fre; Subj: Theatre. ISSN: 0714-8178
■University of Québec; 200 Rue Sherbrooke Ouest; Montreal, PQ H2X 3P2; CANADA.

GSJ   *Gilbert and Sullivan Journal*. Freq: 3; Began: 1925; Ceased: 1986; Lang: Eng; Subj: Theatre. ISSN: 0016-9951
■Gilbert and Sullivan Society; 23 Burnside, Sawbridgeworth; CM21 OEP Hertfordshire; UK.

GSTB   *George Spelvin's Theatre Book*. Freq: 3; Began: 1978; Cov: Scan; Lang: Eng; Subj: Theatre. ISSN: 0730-6431
■Proscenium Press; Box 361; Newark, NJ 19711; USA.

GTAR   *Grupo Teatral Antifaz: Revista*. Freq: 12; Lang: Spa; Subj: Theatre.
■San Addres 146; 16 Barcelona; SPAIN.

GtE   *Guidateatro: Estera*. Freq: 1; Began: 1967; Lang: Ita; Subj: Theatre.
■Edizione Teatron; Via Fabiola 1; 00152 Rome; ITALY.

GtI   *Guidateatro: Italiana*. Freq: 1; Began: 1967; Lang: Ita; Subj: Theatre.
■Edizione Teatron; Via Fabiola 1; 00152 Rome; ITALY.

Guida   *Guida dello Spettacolo*. Lang: Ita; Subj: Theatre.
■Via Palombini 6; Rome; ITALY.

Harlekijn   *Harlekijn*. Freq: 4; Began: 1970; Lang: Dut; Subj: Theatre.
■Kerkdijk 11; 3615 BA Westbroek; NETHERLANDS.

Hecate   *Hecate: Women's Interdisciplinary Journal*. Freq: 2; Began: 1975; Cov: Scan; Lang: Eng; Subj: Related. ISSN: 0311-4198
■Hecate Press; English Dept., University of Queensland; St. Lucia, Qld. 4067; AUSTRALIA.

Helik   *Helikon*: Vilagirodalmi Figyelo. Freq: 4; Began: 1955; Lang: Hun; Subj: Related. ISSN: 0017-999X
■Akademiai Kiado,; Ménesi u. 11-13; 1118 Budapest; HUNGARY.

Hermes   *Hermes: Zeitschrift für Klassische Philologie*. Freq: 4; Began: 1866; Cov: Scan; Lang: Ger; Subj: Related. ISSN: 0018-0777
■Franz Steiner Verlag Wiesbaden GmbH; Birkenwaldstr. 44; Postfach 347; D-7000; Stuttgart 1; WEST GERMANY.

HgK   *Higeki Kigeki*: Tragedy and Comedy. Freq: 12; Began: 1948; Lang: Jap; Subj: Theatre.
■Hayakawa-Shobo, Chiyoda-ku; 2-2 Kanda-Tacho; 101 Tokyo; JAPAN.

HispArts   *Hispanic Arts*. Freq: 5; Began: 1976; Lang: Spa/Eng; Subj: Theatre.
■Association of Hispanic Arts Inc.; 200 East 87th Street; New York, NY 10028; USA.

HisSt   *Historical Studies*. Formerly: *Historical Studies: Australia and New Zealand*. Freq: 2; Began: 1940; Lang: Eng; Subj: Related. ISSN: 0018-2559
■University of Melbourne, Dept. of History; Parkville 3052; AUSTRALIA.

HJFTR   *Historical Journal of Film, TV, Radio*. Freq: 2; Began: 1980; Lang: Eng; Subj: Related. ISSN: 0143-9685
■Carfax Pulbishing Co.; Box 25; OX14 3UE Abingdon; UK.

Horis   *Horisont*. Freq: 6; Began: 1954; Cov: Scan; Lang: Swe; Subj: Related. ISSN: 0439-5530
■Svenska Oesterbottens Litteratur.; Fasanvagen 4; S 775 00 Krylbo; SWEDEN.

HP   *High Performance*. Freq: 4; Began: 1978; Lang: Eng; Subj: Related. ISSN: 0160-9769
■Astro Artz; 240 S. Broadway, 5th Floor; Los Angeles, CA 90012; USA.

HSt   *Hamlet Studies*. Freq: 2; Began: 1978; Lang: Eng; Subj: Related. ISSN: 0256-2480
■Rangoon Villa; 1/10 West Patel Nagar; 110 008 New Delhi; INDIA.

HTHD   *Hungarian Theatre/Hungarian Drama*. Freq: 1; Began: 1981; Lang: Eng; Subj: Theatre. ISSN: 0230-1237
■Hungarian Theatre Institute; Kriszina krt. 57; 1016 Budapest; HUNGARY.

HW *History Workshop*. Freq: 2; Began: 1976; Cov: Scan; Lang: Eng; Subj: Related. ISSN: 0309-2984
■Routledge & Kegan Paul Ltd., Broadway House; Newton Rd.; RG9 1EN Henley-on-Thames; UK.

IA *Ibsenårboken / Ibsen Yearbook*: Contemporary Approaches to Ibsen. Freq: 1; Began: 1952; Cov: Full; Lang: Nor/Eng; Subj: Theatre. ISSN: 0073-4365
■Universitetssorleget; Box 2959; 0608 Oslo 6; NORWAY.

IAS *Interscena / Acta Scaenographica*. Freq: 2; Lang: Eng/Fre/Ger; Subj: Theatre.
■Divadelni Ustav; Celetna 17; Prague 1; CZECHOSLOVAKIA.

IdS *Information du Spectacle, L'*. Freq: 11; Lang: Fre; Subj: Theatre.
■7 rue du Helder; 75009 Paris; FRANCE.

IDSelect *Irish Drama Selections*. Freq: IRR; Began: 1982; Lang: Eng; Subj: Theatre. ISSN: 0260-7964
■Colin Smythe Ltd., Box 6; Gerrards Cross; SL9 8XA Buckinghamshire; UK.

IHoL *Irodalomtörténet*. Freq: 4; Began: 1912; Cov: Scan; Lang: Hun; Subj: Related. ISSN: 0021-1478
■Akademiai Kiado, Pub. Hse. of Hung. Acad. Science; Pesti Barnabás u.1; 1052 Budapest V; HUNGARY.

IHS *Irish Historical Studies*. Freq: 2; Began: 1938; Lang: Eng; Subj: Related. ISSN: 0021-1214
■Irish Historical Society, Dept. of Modern Irish History; Arts-Commerce Bldg, University College; Dublin 4; IRELAND.

IITBI *Instituto Internacional del Teatro, Centro Espanol*: Boletin Informativo. Freq: 4; Lang: Spa; Subj: Theatre.
■Paseo de Recoletos 18-60; 1 Madrid; SPAIN.

IK *Irodalomtudományi Közlemények*. Freq: 24; Began: 1891; Cov: Scan; Lang: Hun; Subj: Related. ISSN: 0021-1486
■Akademiai Kiado, Hungarian Academy of Sciences; Ménesi u. 11-13; 1118 Budapest XI; HUNGARY.

Impressum *Impressum*. Freq: 4; Lang: Ger; Subj: Related.
■Henschelverlag Kunst und Gesellschaft; Oranienburger Strasse 67/68; 1040 Berlin; EAST GERMANY.

InArts *In the Arts*: Search, Research, and Discovery. Began: 1978; Lang: Eng; Subj: Related.
■Ohio State University, College of the Arts; Columbus, OH 43210; USA.

INC *Ibsen News & Comments*. Freq: 1; Began: 1980; Cov: Scan; Lang: Eng; Subj: Theatre.
■Ibsen Society in America, Mellon Programs, Dekalb Hall 3; Pratt Institute; Brooklyn, NY 11205; USA.

Indonesia *Indonesia*. Freq: 2; Began: 1966; Cov: Scan; Lang: Eng; Subj: Related. ISSN: 0019-7289
■Cornell University, Southeast Asia Program; 120 Uris Hall; Ithaca, NY 14853; USA.

IndSh *Independent Shavian*. Freq: 3; Began: 1962; Lang: Eng; Subj: Theatre. ISSN: 0019-3763

■The Bernard Shaw Society; Box 1373, Grand Central Station; New York, NY 10163; USA.

Info *Information*. Lang: Eng; Subj: Theatre. ISSN: 0133-2902
■Hungarian Centre of the ITI; Hevesi Sandor ter. 2; 1077 Budapest VII; HUNGARY.

InoLit *Inostrannaja Literatura*: (Foreign Literature). Freq: 12; Began: 1955; Cov: Scan; Lang: Rus; Subj: Related. ISSN: 0130-6545
■Moscow; USSR.

ISK *Iskusstvo Kino*. Freq: 12; Cov: Scan; Lang: Rus; Subj: Related. ISSN: 0021-1788

Iskusstvo *Iskusstvo*. Freq: 12; Began: 1918; Cov: Scan; Lang: Rus; Subj: Related. ISSN: 0131-2278
■Tsvetnoi Bulvar 25; K 51 Moscow; USSR.

ISPTC *Istituto di Studi Pirandelliani e sul Teatro Contemporaneo*. Freq: 1; Began: 1967; Lang: Ita; Subj: Theatre. ISSN: 0075-1480
■Casa Editrice Felice le Monnier; Via Scipione Ammirato 100; 50136 Florence; ITALY.

ISST *In Sachen Spiel und Theater*. Freq: 6; Began: 1949; Lang: Ger; Subj: Theatre.
■Höfling Verlag, Dr. V. Mayer; Postfach 1421; 6940 Weinheim; WEST GERMANY.

ITY *International Theatre Yearbook*: SEE: Miedzynarodowny Rocznik Teatralny (Acro: MRT). Lang: Pol; Subj: Theatre.
■Warsaw; POLAND.

IUR *Irish University Review*. Freq: 2; Began: 1970; Cov: Scan; Lang: Eng; Subj: Related. ISSN: 0021-1427
■Wolfhound Press, University College; Room J210, Belfield; Dublin 4; IRELAND.

IW *Ireland of the Welcomes*. Freq: 24; Began: 1952; Cov: Scan; Lang: Eng; Subj: Related. ISSN: 0021-0943
■Bord Failte - Irish Tourist Board; Baggot St. Bridge; Dublin 2; IRELAND.

JAC *Journal of American Culture*. Freq: 4; Began: 1978; Cov: Scan; Lang: Eng; Subj: Related. ISSN: 0191-1813
■American Culture Association, Bowling Green State University; Popular Culture Center; Bowling Green, OH 43403; USA.

JADT *Journal of American Drama and Theatre, The*. Freq: 3; Began: 1989; Lang: Eng; Subj: Theatre.
■CASTA, Grad. School and Univ. Centre, City University of New York; 33 West 42nd Street; New York, NY 10036; USA.

JAfS *Journal of African Studies*. Freq: 4; Began: 1974; Cov: Scan; Lang: Eng; Subj: Related. ISSN: 0095-4993
■Heldref Publications; 4000 Albemarle St, N.W.; Wasington, DC 20016; USA.

JAML *Journal of Arts Management and Law*. Freq: 4; Began: 1969; Cov: Full; Lang: Eng; Subj: Related. ISSN: 0733-5113
■Heldref Publications; 400 Albemarle St., N.W.; Washington, DC 20016; USA.

JAP&M *Journal of Arts Policy and Mangement*. Freq: 3; Began: 1984; Cov: Full; Lang: Eng; Subj: Theatre. ISSN: 0265-0924
■John Offord Publications; 12 The Avenue; BN21 3YA Eastbourne; UK.

JASt *Journal of Asian Studies*. Freq: 4; Began: 1941; Cov: Scan; Lang: Eng; Subj: Related. ISSN: 0021-9118
■Association for Asian Studies, Inc., University of Michigan; One Lane Hall; Ann Arbor, MI 48109; USA.

Javisko *Javisko*. Freq: 12; Lang: Cze; Subj: Related.
■Cultural Institute in Bratislava; Obzor, Ceskoslovenskij Armady 35; 815 85 Bratislava; CZECHOSLOVAKIA.

JBeckS *Journal of Beckett Studies*. Freq: 2; Began: 1976; Cov: Full; Lang: Eng; Subj: Theatre. ISSN: 0309-5207
■Dept. of English, University of California; Riverside, CA 92521; USA.

JCNREC *Journal of Canadian Studies / Revue d'études canadiennes*. Freq: 4; Began: 1966; Cov: Scan; Lang: Eng/Fre; Subj: Related. ISSN: 0021-9495
■Trent Uiversity; Peterborough, ON K9J 7B8; CANADA.

JCSt *Journal of Caribbean Studies*. Freq: 2; Began: 1970; Cov: Scan; Lang: Eng/Fre/Spa; Subj: Related. ISSN: 0190-2008
■Association of Caribbean Studies; Box 248231; Coral Gables, FL 33124; USA.

JCT *Jeu*: Cahiers de Théâtre. Freq: 4; Began: 1976; Cov: Full; Lang: Fre; Subj: Theatre.
■Cahiers de Theatre Jeu Inc.; P.O. Box 1600, Station E; Montreal, PQ H2T 3B1; CANADA.

JdCh *Journal de Chaillot*. Freq: 8; Began: 1974; Cov: Scan; Lang: Fre; Subj: Related.
■Chaillot Théâtre National; Place du Tracadero; 75116 Paris; FRANCE.

JDS *Jacobean Drama Studies*. Freq: IRR; Began: 1972; Lang: Eng; Subj: Theatre.
■Universität Salzburg, Institut für Englische Sprach; Akademiestr. 24; A 5020 Salzburg; AUSTRIA.

JDSh *Jahrbuch der Deutsche Shakespeare-Gesellschaft*. Cov: Scan; Lang: Ger; Subj: Theatre.
■Deutsche Shakespeare-Gesellschaft West; Rathaus; D 4630 Bochum; WEST GERMANY.

JDt *Journal of Dramatherapy*. Formerly: *Dramatherapy*. Freq: 2; Began: 1977; Cov: Scan; Lang: Eng; Subj: Related. ISSN: 0263-0672
■David Powley, British Association for Dramatherapy; PO Box 98; YD6 6EX Kirkbymoorside; UK.

JDTC *Journal of Dramatic Theory and Criticism*. Freq: 2; Began: 1986; Cov: Full; Lang: Eng; Subj: Theatre.
■University of Kansas, Dept. of Theatre and Media Arts; Murphy Hall; Lawrence, KS 66045; USA.

JEBT *JEB Théâtre*. Lang: Fre; Ceased: 1982; Subj: Theatre.
■Documentation Générale de la jeunes, des Loisirs; Galerie Ravenstein 78; 1000 Brussels; BELGIUM.

Jelenkor *Jelenkor*. Freq: 12; Began: 1958; Cov: Scan; Lang: Hun; Subj: Related. ISSN: 0447-6425

■Ft. Baranya Megyei, Lapkiado Vallalat; Széchenyi tér 17.I.; 7621 Pécs; HUNGARY.

JENS *Journal of the Eighteen Nineties Society.* Freq: 1; Began: 1970; Lang: Eng; Subj: Related. ISSN: 0144-008X
■28 Carlingford Rd., Hampstead; NW3 1RQ London; UK.

JGG *Jahrbuch der Grillparzer-Gesellschaft.* Lang: Ger; Cov: Scan; Subj: Related.
■Grillparzer-Gesellschaft; Gumpendorfer Strasse 15/1; A 1060 Vienna; AUSTRIA.

JGT *Journal du Grenier de Toulouse.* Freq: 12; Lang: Fre; Subj: Theatre.
■Grenier de Toulouse; 3, rue de la Digue; 31300 Toulouse; FRANCE.

JITT *JITT.* Lang: Jap; Subj: Theatre.
■Japanese Institute for Theatre Technology; 4-437 Ikebukuro, Toshima-ku; Tokyo; JAPAN.

JJS *Journal of Japanese Studies.* Freq: 2; Began: 1974; Lang: Eng; Subj: Related. ISSN: 0095-6848
■Society for Japanese Studies, University of Washington; Thomson Hall DR-05; Seattle, WA 98195; USA.

JLS/TLW *Journal of Literary Studies/ Tydskrif vir Literatuurwetenskap.* Freq: 4; Began: 1985; Cov: Scan; Lang: Eng/Afr; Subj: Related.
■South African Society for, General Literary Studies; Pretoria; SOUTH AFRICA.

JMH *Journal of Magic History.* Lang: Eng; Subj: Related.
■Toledo, OH; USA.

JNZL *Journal of New Zealand Literature.* Lang: Eng; Subj: Related.
■Wellington; NEW ZEALAND.

JPC *Journal of Popular Culture.* Freq: 4; Began: 1967; Cov: Scan; Lang: Eng; Subj: Related. ISSN: 0022-3840
■Popular Culture Association, Bowling Green State University; 100 University Hall; Bowling Green, OH 43402; USA.

JRASM *Journal of the Royal Asiatic Society of Malaysia.* Lang: Eng; Subj: Related.
■Kuala Lumpur; MALAYSIA.

JSH *Journal of Social History.* Freq: 4; Began: 1967; Cov: Scan; Lang: Eng; Subj: Related. ISSN: 0022-4529
■Carnegie-Mellon University Press; Schenley Park; Pittsburgh, PA 15213; USA.

JSSB *Journal of the Siam Society.* Cov: Scan; Lang: Tha; Subj: Related.
■131 Soi Asoki; Sukhumvit Rd.; Bangkok; THAILAND.

JT *Jeune Théâtre.* Began: 1970; Ceased: 1982; Lang: Fre; Subj: Theatre. ISSN: 0315-0402
■Assoc. Québecoise du, Jeune Théâtre; 952 rue Cherrier; Montreal, PQ H2L 1H7; CANADA.

JTPR *Journal du Théâtre Populaire Romand.* Freq: 8; Began: 1962; Lang: Fre; Subj: Theatre.
■Case Postale 80; 2301 La Chaux-de-Fonds; SWITZERLAND.

JTV *Journal du Théâtre de la Ville.* Freq: 4; Began: 1968; Lang: Fre; Subj: Theatre.

■Theatre de la Ville; 16 quai de Gesvres; Paris; FRANCE.

Juben *Juben*: (Playtexts). Freq: 12; Began: 1956; Lang: Chi; Subj: Theatre.
■52 Dongai Batiao; Beijing; CHINA.

JugoIgre *Jugoslovenske*: Pozorišne Igre. Began: 1962; Lang: Ser; Subj: Theatre.
■Sterijino Pozorje; Zmaj Jovina 22; Novi Sad; YUGOSLAVIA.

Junkanoo *Junkanoo.* Freq: 12; Lang: Eng; Subj: Theatre.
■Junkanoo Publications; Box N 4923; Nassau; BAHAMAS.

JWCI *Journal of the Warburg & Courtauld Institutes.* Freq: 1; Began: 1937; Cov: Scan; Lang: Eng; Subj: Related.
■Woburn Square; WC1H OAB London; UK.

JWGT *Jahrbuch der Wiener Gesellschaft für Theaterforschung.* Freq: 1; Lang: Ger; Subj: Related.
■Vienna; AUSTRIA.

Kabuki *Kabuki.* Lang: Jap; Subj: Theatre.
■4-12-15 Ginza; 104 Chuo-ku, Tokyo; JAPAN.

Kalak *Kalakalpam.* Freq: 2; Began: 1966; Lang: Eng; Subj: Theatre.
■Karyalaya Matya Kala Institute; 30-A Paddapukur Road; 20 Calcutta; INDIA.

Kanava *Kanava.* Formerly: *Aika.* Freq: 9; Began: 1932; Cov: Scan; Lang: Fin; Subj: Related. ISSN: 0355-0303
■Yhtyneet Kuvalehdet Oy; Hietalahdenranta 13; 00180 Helsinki 18; FINLAND.

KAPM *Kassette*: Almanach für Bühne, Podium und Manege. Freq: 1; Lang: Ger; Subj: Theatre.
■Berlin; EAST GERMANY.

Kathakali *Kathakali.* Freq: 4; Began: 1969; Lang: Eng/Hin; Subj: Theatre. ISSN: 0022-9326
■International Centre for Kathakali; 1-84 Rajandra Nagar; New Delhi; INDIA.

Kazal *Kazaliste.* Freq: 26; Began: 1965; Lang: Yug; Subj: Theatre.
■Prolaz Radoslava Bacica 1; Osijek; YUGOSLAVIA.

KB *Kunst Bulletin.* Freq: 12; Cov: Scan; Subj: Related.
■Fr. Hallwag AG; Nording 4; 4001 Bern; SWITZERLAND.

Keshet *Keshet.* Lang: Heb; Subj: Theatre.
■9 Bialik Street; Tel Aviv; ISRAEL.

KesK *Kultura és Közösség.* Freq: 6; Began: 1974; Cov: Scan; Lang: Hun; Subj: Related.
■Corvin tér 8; 1011 Budapest I; HUNGARY.

KingP *King Pole Circus Magazine.* Freq: 4; Began: 1934; Cov: Scan; Lang: Eng; Subj: Theatre.
■Circus Fans' Assoc. of UK; 53 Park Court; Harlow, Essex; UK.

KJAZU *Kronika*: Zavoda za kniževnost i teatrologiju. Began: 1976; Lang: Slo; Subj: Theatre.
■Jugosl. Akad. Znanosti i Umjetnosti; Opatička 18; Zagreb; YUGOSLAVIA.

Klub *Klub i Chudožestvennaja Samodejetelnost.* Freq: 26; Lang: Rus; Subj: Theatre.
■Profizdat; Ulitza Korova 13; Moscow; USSR.

KMFB *KMFB.* Freq: 11; Began: 1945; Lang: Ger; Subj: Theatre.
■UMLOsterreichischer Gewerkschaftsbund, Gewrkshft. Kunst, Medien, Berufe; Maria-Theresienstrasse 11; A 1090 Vienna; AUSTRIA.

KoJ *Korea Journal.* Freq: 12; Began: 1961; Cov: Scan; Lang: Kor; Subj: Related. ISSN: 0023-3900
■Korean Natl. Comm. for UNESCO; Box Central 64; Seoul; SOUTH KOREA.

Kommunist *Kommunist.* Began: 1924; Cov: Scan; Lang: Rus; Subj: Related. ISSN: 0131-1212
■Moscow; USSR.

KoreanD *Korean Drama.* Lang: Kor; Subj: Theatre.
■National Drama Association of Korea, Insadong, Jongno-gu; Fed. of Arts & Cult. Org. Building; 110 Seoul; SOUTH KOREA.

Kortars *Kortárs.* Freq: 12; Began: 1957; Cov: Scan; Lang: Hun; Subj: Related. ISSN: 0023-415X
■Lapkiado Vallalat; Széchényi rkp. 1; 1054 Budapest V; HUNGARY.

KPR *Kulturno-Prosvetitelnaja Rabota.* Freq: 12; Lang: Rus; Subj: Related.
■Sověckaja Rossija; Bersenevskaja Naberežnaja 22; Moscow; USSR.

Krit *Kritika.* Freq: 12; Began: 1963; Cov: Scan; Lang: Hun; Subj: Related. ISSN: 0023-4818
■Lapkiado Vallalat; Blahah Lujza tér 3; 1085 Budapest VIII; HUNGARY.

KSF *Korean Studies Forum.* Freq: 2; Began: 1976; Lang: Kor; Subj: Related. ISSN: 0147-6335
■Korean-American Educ. Commission, Garden Towers; No. 1803, 98-78 Wooni-Dong, Chongro-Ku; Seoul 110; SOUTH KOREA.

KSGT *Kleine Schriften der Gesellschaft für Theatergeschichte.* Lang: Ger; Subj: Theatre.
■Gesellschaft für Theatergeschichte; 1 Berlin; WEST GERMANY.

KTJ *Korean Theatre Journal.* Freq: 12; Lang: Kor; Cov: Scan; Subj: Theatre.
■Korean National Theatre Association;

Kulis *Kulis.* Freq: 12; Began: 1946; Lang: Arm; Subj: Theatre.
■H. Ayvaz; PK 83; 10 A Cagaloglu Yokusu; TURKEY.

Kvihkot *Kultuurivihkot.* Freq: 8; Began: 1973; Lang: Fin/Swe; Subj: Theatre.
■Kultuurityontekijain Liitto; Korkeavuorenkatu 4 C 15; 00130 Helsinki; FINLAND.

KWN *Kurt Weill Newsletter.* Freq: 2; Began: 1983; Cov: Scan; Lang: Eng; Subj: Related.
■Kurt Weill Foundation for Music, Lincoln Towers; 142 West End Avenue, Suite 1-R; New York, NY 10023; USA.

KZ *Kultura i Žizn.* (Culture and Life). Freq: 12; Began: 1957; Cov: Scan; Lang: Rus/Eng/Ger/Fre/Spa; Subj: Related. ISSN: 0023-5199

■Sovĕckaja Rossija; Projĕzd Sapunova 13-15; Moscow K-12; USSR.

L&DA   *Lighting Design & Application.* Freq: 12; Began: 1906; Cov: Scan; Lang: Eng; Subj: Theatre.   ISSN: 0360-6325 ■Illuminating Engineering Society; 345 E. 47th St.; New York, NY 10017; USA.

L&H   *Literature & History.* Freq: 2; Began: 1975; Cov: Scan; Lang: Eng; Subj: Related.   ISSN: 0306-1973 ■Thames Polytechnic, Dept. of Humanities; Wellington Street; SE18 3PF London; UK.

Laien   *Laientheater.* Freq: 12; Began: 1972; Lang: Ger; Subj: Theatre. ■Schweizerischen Volkstheater; 30 Bern; SWITZERLAND.

LAQ   *Livres et Auteurs Québecois.* Freq: 1; Began: 1969; Lang: Fre; Subj: Related.   ISSN: 0316-2621 ■Presses de l'Université Laval, Cité Universitaire; Québec, PQ G1K 7R4; CANADA.

LATR   *Latin American Theatre Review.* Freq: 2; Began: 1967; Cov: Full; Lang: Eng/Spa/Por; Subj: Theatre.   ISSN: 0023-8813 ■University of Kansas, Center of Latin American Studies; 107 Lippincott Hall; Lawrence, KS 66044; USA.

LDim   *Lighting Dimensions*: For the Entertainment Lighting Industry. Freq: 6; Began: 1977; Cov: Full; Lang: Eng; Subj: Theatre. ■Lighting Dimensions Publishing; 1590 S. Coast Highway, Suite 8; Laguna, CA 92651; USA.

LetQu   *Lettres Québecoises.* Freq: 4; Began: 1976; Lang: Fre; Subj: Related.   ISSN: 0382-084X ■Editions Jumonville; Box 1840, Succarsale B; Montreal, PQ H3B 3L4; CANADA.

Letture   *Letture*: Libro e spettacolo, mensile di studi e rassegne. Freq: 10; Began: 1946; Lang: Ita; Subj: Related. ISSN: 0024-144X ■Edizioni Letture; Piazza San Fedele 4; 20121 Milan; ITALY.

LFQ   *Literature/Film Quarterly.* Freq: 4; Began: 1973; Lang: Eng; Subj: Related.   ISSN: 0090-4260 ■Salisbury State College; Salisbury, MD 21801; USA.

Light   *Light.* Freq: 24; Began: 1921; Lang: Eng; Subj: Theatre. ■Ahmadiyya Building; Brandreth Road; Lahore; PAKISTAN.

LiNQ   *Literature in North Queensland.* Freq: 3; Began: 1971; Cov: Scan; Lang: Eng; Subj: Related. ■Dept. of English; James Cook University of North Queensland; Townsville, 4811; AUSTRALIA.

LinzerT   *Linzer Theaterzeitung.* Freq: 10; Began: 1955; Lang: Ger; Subj: Theatre.   ISSN: 0024-4139 ■Landestheater Linz; Promenade 39; A 4010 Linz; AUSTRIA.

Lipika   *Lipika.* Freq: 4; Began: 1972; Lang: Eng; Subj: Theatre. ■F-20 Nizzamudin West; 10013 New Delhi; INDIA.

Literatura   *Literatura.* Freq: 4; Began: 1974; Lang: Hun; Subj: Related. ISSN: 0133-2368 ■Akademiai Kiado, Hungarian Academy of Sciences; Ménesi u. 11-13; 1118 Budapest XI; HUNGARY.

LitGruzia   *Literaturnaja Gruzia.* Freq: 12; Began: 1957; Cov: Scan; Lang: Rus; Subj: Related.   ISSN: 0130-3600 ■Tbilisi, Georg. SSR; USSR.

Live   *Live.* Freq: 4; Lang: Eng; Subj: Related. ■New York, NY; USA.

LLJ   *La Trobe Library Journal.* Freq: 2; Began: 1968; Cov: Scan; Lang: Eng; Subj: Related.   ISSN: 0041-3151 ■Friends of the State Library of Victoria; State Library of Victoria; Swanston Street; Melbourne, 3000; AUSTRALIA.

LO   *Literaturnojë Obozrenijë.* Freq: 12; Began: 1973; Cov: Scan; Lang: Rus; Subj: Related.   ISSN: 0321-2904 ■Sojuz Pisatelej SSSR; 9/10 ul. Dobroliubova; 127254 Moscow I-254; USSR.

Loisir   *Loisir.* Freq: 4; Began: 1962; Lang: Fre; Subj: Theatre. ■Comédie de Caen; 120 rue St. Pierre; 1400 Caen; FRANCE.

LokK   *Lok Kala.* Freq: 2; Lang: Hin; Subj: Theatre. ■Bharatiya Lok Kala Mandal; Udaipur; INDIA.

Lowdown   *Lowdown.* Freq: 6; Began: 1979; Lang: Eng; Subj: Theatre. ■Australian Youth Performing Arts Assoc., c/o Theatre Workshop; University of Sydney; NSW 2006 Sydney; AUSTRALIA.

LPer   *Literature in Performance.* Freq: 2; Began: 1980; Lang: Eng; Subj: Theatre.   ISSN: 0734-0796 ■Inter. Div.,Speech Comm. Assoc., Dept. of Speech Communication; U. of NC, 115 Bingham Hall; Chapel Hall, NC 27514; USA.

LTR   *London Theatre Record.* Freq: 26; Began: 1981; Cov: Full; Lang: Eng; Subj: Theatre.   ISSN: 0261-5282 ■4 Cross Deep Gardens; TW1 4QU Twickenham, Midlsex; UK.

Ludus   *Ludus*: List Udruženja Dramskih Umetnika Srbije. Freq: 6; Began: 1983; Lang: Ser; Subj: Theatre. ■Udruženja Dramskih Umetnika Srbije; Terazije 26; Belgrade; YUGOSLAVIA.

Lutka   *Lutka*: Revija za lutkovno kulturo. Freq: 3; Began: 1966; Lang: Slo; Subj: Theatre.   ISSN: 0350-9303 ■Zveza kulturnih organizacij Slovenije; Kidričeva 5; Ljubljana; YUGOSLAVIA.

M&T   *Musik & Teater.* Freq: 6; Began: 1979; Lang: Dan; Subj: Theatre. ■Bagsvard Horedgade 9914E; 2800 Bagsvard; DENMARK.

Maksla   *Maksla.* Lang: Lat; Subj: Related. ■Riga, Latvian SSR; USSR.

MAL   *Modern Austrian Literature.* Freq: 4; Began: 1961; Lang: Eng/Ger; Subj: Related.   ISSN: 0026-7503 ■Intl A. Schnitzler Research Assoc., c/o Donald G. Daviau, Ed.; Dept. of Lit. & Langs; Univ. of CA; Riverside, CA 92521; USA.

Mamulengo   *Mamulengo.* Lang: Por; Subj: Theatre. ■Assoc. Brasileira de Teatro de Bonecos; Rua Barata Ribeiro; 60 C 01 Guanabara; BRAZIL.

Manip   *Manipulation.* Lang: Eng; Subj: Theatre. ■Mrs. Maeve Vella; 28 Macarthur Place; 3053 Carlton, Victoria; AUSTRALIA.

MarqJTHS   *Marquee*: The Journal of the Theatre Historical Society. Freq: 4; Began: 1969; Cov: Scan; Lang: Eng; Subj: Theatre.   ISSN: 0025-3928 ■P. O. Box 15428; Columbus, OH 43215; USA.

Marquee   *Marquee.* Freq: 8; Began: 1976; Lang: Eng; Subj: Related. ISSN: 0700-5008 ■Marquee Communications Inc.; 277 Richmond St. W.; Toronto, ON M5V 1X1; CANADA.

Mask   *Mask.* Freq: 6; Began: 1967; Lang: Eng; Subj: Theatre. ISSN: 0726-9072 ■Simon Pryor, Executive Officer, VADIE; 117 Bouverie Street; 3053 Carlton; AUSTRALIA.

Maske   *Maske.* Began: 1985; Lang: Slo; Subj: Theatre.   ISSN: 0352-7913 ■Zveza kulturnih organizacij Slovenije; Ljubljana; YUGOSLAVIA.

Masque   *Masque.* Freq: 24; Began: 1967; Lang: Eng; Subj: Theatre. ISSN: 0025-469X ■Masque Publications; 22 Steam Mill St.; 2000 Sydney NSW; AUSTRALIA.

Mast   *Masterstvo.* Freq: 6; Lang: Ukr; Subj: Theatre. ■Pouchkineskaia Street 5; Kiev; USSR.

Matya   *Matya Prasanga.* Freq: 12; Lang: Ben; Subj: Theatre. ■54/1 B Patuatola Lane; Emherst Street; Calcutta; INDIA.

MAvilia   *Monte Avilia.* Freq: 12; Began: 1980; Lang: Spa; Subj: Theatre. ■Apartado 70-712; 107 Caracas; VENEZUELA.

MBB   *Mala Biblioteka Baletowa.* Began: 1957; Lang: Pol; Subj: Theatre. ■Polskie Wydawnictwo Muzyczne; Al. Krasiskiego 11; Cracow; POLAND.

MC&S   *Media, Culture and Society.* Freq: 4; Began: 1979; Cov: Scan; Lang: Eng; Subj: Related.   ISSN: 0163-4437 ■Academic Press Ltd.; 24-28 Oval Road; NW1 7DX London; UK.

MChAT   *Ezĕgodnik MChAT.* Freq: 1; Lang: Rus; Subj: Theatre. ■Association of Soviet Writers; Hertsen 49; Moscow; USSR.

MD   *Modern Drama.* Freq: 4; Began: 1958; Cov: Full; Lang: Eng; Subj: Theatre.   ISSN: 0026-7694 ■A.M. Hakkert Limited; 554 Spadina Crescent; Toronto, ON M5S 2J9; CANADA.

MdVO   *Mitteilungen der Vereinigung Österreichischer Bibliotheken.* Lang: Ger; Subj: Related. ■Vienna; AUSTRIA.

Meanjin   *Meanjin.* Formerly: *Meanjin Quarterly* Freq: 3; Began: 1940; Cov: Scan; Lang: Eng; Subj: Related. ISSN: 0025-6293 ■Meanjin Co. Ltd.; Parkville; Victoria 3052; AUSTRALIA.

MeisterP *Meister des Puppenspiels*. Freq: IRR; Began: 1959; Lang: Ger; Subj: Theatre. ISSN: 0076-6216
■Deutsches Institut für Puppenspiel; Bergstr. 115; 4630 Bochum; WEST GERMANY.

Merker *Merker, Der*. Lang: Ger; Subj: Theatre.
■Kurt Grisold; Karlplusgasse 1-39/Stg. 10; A 1100 Vienna; AUSTRIA.

MET *Medieval English Theatre*. Freq: 2; Began: 1979; Cov: Full; Lang: Eng; Subj: Theatre. ISSN: 0143-3784
■c/o M. Twycross, Dept. of English, Language and Medieval Literature; University of Lancaster; LA1 4YT Lancaster; UK.

MGL *Mestno Gledalisce Ljubljansko*. Began: 1959; Lang: Yug; Subj: Theatre.
■Ljubljana; 14 Copova; YUGOSLAVIA.

MHall *Music Hall*. Freq: 6; Began: 1978; Cov: Scan; Lang: Eng; Subj: Theatre.
■Tony Barker; 50 Reperton Road; SW6 London; UK.

MID *Modern International Drama*: Magazine for Contemporary International Drama in Translation. Freq: 2; Began: 1967; Cov: Full; Lang: Eng; Subj: Theatre. ISSN: 0026-4385
■State University of NY; Max Reinhardt Archive; Binghamton, NY 13901; USA.

Mim *Mim: Revija za glumu i glumište*: Glasilo Udruženja dramskih umjetnika Hrvatske. Freq: 12; Began: 1984; Lang: Cro; Subj: Theatre.
■Udruž. Dramskih Umjetnika Hravatske; Ilica 42; Zagreb; YUGOSLAVIA.

MimeJ *Mime Journal*. Freq: 1; Began: 1974; Cov: Full; Lang: Eng; Subj: Theatre. ISSN: 0145-787X
■Pamona College Theater Department, Claremont Colleges; Claremont, CA 91711; USA.

MimeN *Mime News*. Freq: 5; Cov: Scan; Lang: Eng; Subj: Theatre.
■National Mime Association; PO Box 5574; Atlanta, GA 30307; USA.

Mimos *Mimos*. Freq: 4; Began: 1949; Cov: Scan; Lang: Ger; Subj: Theatre. ISSN: 0026-4385
■Swiss Assoc. for Theatre Research, c/o Lydia Benz-Burger; Herenholzweg 33; 8906 Bonstetten; SWITZERLAND.

MK *Molodoi Kommunist*. Freq: 12; Began: 1918; Cov: Scan; Lang: Rus; Subj: Related. ISSN: 0026-9077
■Izdatel'stvo Molodaya Gvardiya, Ul.; Sushevskaya, 21; Moscow A-55; Russian S.F.S.R.; U.S.S.R.

MLet *Music & Letters*. Freq: 4; Began: 1920; Cov: Scan; Lang: Eng; Subj: Related. ISSN: 0027-4224
■Oxford University Press; Walton Street; OX2 6DP Oxford; UK.

MLR *Modern Language Review*. Freq: 4; Began: 1905; Cov: Scan; Lang: Eng; Subj: Related. ISSN: 0026-7937
■Modern Humanities Research Assoc.; King's College; WC2 R 2LS London; UK.

MMDN *Medieval Music-Drama News*. Freq: 2; Lang: Eng; Subj: Related.
■Staunton, VA; USA.

MMDTA *Monographs on Music, Dance and Theater in Asia*. Freq: 1; Began: 1971; Lang: Eng; Subj: Theatre.
■The Asia Society, Performing Arts Program; 133 East 58th Street; New York, NY 10022; USA.

MN *Monumenta Nipponica*: Studies in Japanese Culture. Freq: 4; Began: 1938; Cov: Scan; Lang: Eng; Subj: Related. ISSN: 0027-0741
■Sophia University, 7-1 Kioi-cho; Chiyoda-ku; 102 Tokyo; JAPAN.

Mobile *Mobile*. Freq: 12; Lang: Fre; Subj: Theatre.
■Maison de la Culture d'Amiens; Place Léon Gontier; 80000 Amiens; FRANCE.

MoD *Monthly Diary*. Lang: Eng; Subj: Theatre.
■Sydney; AUSTRALIA.

MolGvar *Molodaja Gvardija*. Freq: 12; Began: 1922; Cov: Scan; Lang: Rus; Subj: Related. ISSN: 0131-1225
■Moscow; USSR.

Monsalvat *Monsalvat*. Freq: 11; Began: 1973; Lang: Spa; Subj: Theatre.
■Ediciones de Nuevo Arte; Plaza Gala Placidia 1; 6 Barcelona; SPAIN.

Mosk *Moskva*. Freq: 12; Began: 1957; Cov: Scan; Lang: Rus; Subj: Related. ISSN: 0027-1411
■24 Rub. Soyuz Pisatelei Rossiiskoi S.F.S.R.; Moscow Russia S.F.S.R.; U.S.S.R.

Mozgo *Mozgó Világ*. Freq: 12; Began: 1971; Cov: Scan; Lang: Hun; Subj: Related.
■Münnich F. u. 26; 1051 Budapest V; HUNGARY.

MP *Modern Philology*: Research in Medieval and Modern Literature. Freq: 4; Began: 1903; Cov: Scan; Lang: Eng; Subj: Related. ISSN: 0026-8232
■University of Chicago Press; 5801 S. Ellis Avenue; Chicago, IL 60637; USA.

MPI *Manadens Premiarer och Information*. Lang: Swe; Subj: Related.
■Stockholm; SWEDEN.

MPSKD *Mitteilungen der Puppentheatersammlung der Staatlicher Kunstsammlungen Dresden*. Freq: 4; Began: 1958; Lang: Ger; Subj: Theatre.
■Rolf Maser; Barkengasse 6; 8122 Radebeul; EAST GERMANY.

MRenD *Medieval and Renaissance Drama*. Lang: Eng; Began: 1984; Cov: Full; Subj: Theatre.
■AMS Press; 56 E. 13th Street; New York, NY 10003; USA.

MRT *Miedzynarodowny Rocznik Teatralny*: Annuaire Intl. du Théâtre/Intl. Theatre Yearbook. Freq: 1; Began: 1977; Lang: Pol/Fre/Eng; Subj: Theatre.
■International Association of Theatre Critics; ul. Moliera 1; 00 076 Warsaw; POLAND.

MSD *Milliyet Sanat Dergisi*. Freq: 26; Lang: Tur; Subj: Theatre.
■Aydin Dogan; Nurosmaniye Cad. 65/67; Cagaloglu-Istanbul; TURKEY.

MT *Material zum Theater*. Freq: 12; Began: 1970; Lang: Ger; Subj: Theatre.
■Verband der Theaterschaffended der DDR; Hermann-Matern-Strasse 18; 1040 Berlin; EAST GERMANY.

MuD *MusikDramatik*. Freq: 4; Cov: Full; Lang: Swe; Subj: Theatre.
■Stockholm; SWEDEN.

Muhely *Mühely*. Freq: 12; Began: 1978; Lang: Hun; Cov: Scan; Subj: Related.
■Tanácsköztársaság útja 51.II10; 9022 Györ; HUNGARY.

MuK *Maske und Kothurn*: Internationale Beiträge zur Theaterwissenschaft. Freq: 4; Began: 1955; Cov: Full; Lang: Ger/Eng/Fre; Subj: Theatre. ISSN: 0025-4606
■Hermann Boehlaus Nachf., c/o Dr. Karl Lueger Ring 12; A 1010 Vienna; AUSTRIA.

MuQ *Musical Quarterly*. Freq: 4; Began: 1915; Cov: Scan; Lang: Eng; Subj: Related. ISSN: 0027-4631
■G. Schirmer, Inc.; 866 Third Avenue; New York, NY 10022; USA.

MusGes *Musik und Gesellschaft*. Freq: 12; Began: 1951; Cov: Scan; Lang: Ger; Subj: Related. ISSN: 0027-4755
■Henschelverlag Kunst und Gesellschaft; Oranienburger Str. 67/68; 1040 Berlin; EAST GERMANY.

MuT *Musik und Theater*: Die aktuelle schweizerische Kulturzeitschrift. Freq: 12; Began: 1980; Cov: Scan; Lang: Ger; Subj: Theatre.
■Postfach 926; 9001 St. Gallen; SWITZERLAND.

MuZizn *Muzykalnaja Žizn*: (Musical Life). Freq: 24; Began: 1957; Cov: Scan; Lang: Rus; Subj: Related. ISSN: 0131-2303
■Moscow; USSR.

Muzsika *Muzsika*. Freq: 12; Began: 1958; Cov: Scan; Lang: Hun; Subj: Related. ISSN: 0027-5336
■Lapkiado Vallalat; Lenin korut 9-11; 1073 Budapest VII; HUNGARY.

Muzyka *Muzyka*. Freq: 12; Began: 1973; Cov: Full; Lang: Rus; Subj: Related. ISSN: 0208-3086
■Gos. Biblioteka SSSR im. Lenina, NIO Informkultura; Prospekt Kalinina; 101000 Moscow; USSR.

MV *Minority Voices*: An Interdisciplinary Journal of Literature & Arts. Freq: 2; Began: 1977; Lang: Eng; Subj: Theatre.
■Paul Robeson Cultural Center, 101 Walnut Bldg.; Pennsylvania State Univ.; University Park, PA 16802; USA.

Mykenae *Mykenae*. Freq: 36; Began: 1950; Lang: Ger; Subj: Theatre.
■Mykenae Verlag; Ahastrasse 9; 6100 Darmstadt; WEST GERMANY.

Napj *Napjaink*. Freq: 12; Began: 1962; Cov: Scan; Lang: Hun; Subj: Related. ISSN: 0027-7819
■Borsod Megyei Lapkiado Vallalat; Korvin Ottó u. 1; 3530 Miskolc; HUNGARY.

NasSovr *Naš Sovremennik*. Freq: 12; Began: 1933; Cov: Scan; Lang: Rus; Subj: Related. ISSN: 0027-8238
■Moscow; USSR.

Natrang *Natrang*. Freq: 4; Lang: Hin; Subj: Theatre.
■I-47 Jangoura Extension; New Delhi; INDIA.

Natya *Natya*. Freq: 4; Began: 1969; Lang: Eng; Subj: Theatre. ISSN: 0028-1115
■Bharatiya Natya Sangh; 34 New Central Market; New Delhi; INDIA.

Nayt *Naytelmauutiset*. Lang: Fin; Subj: Theatre.
■Tyovaen Nayttamoiden; Vuoritaku 6 A 7; Liitti; FINLAND.

NBT *Neue Blätter des Theaters in Der Josefstadt*. Freq: 6; Began: 1953; Lang: Ger/Eng/Fre; Subj: Theatre. ISSN: 0028-3096
■Theater in der Josefstadt, Direktion; Josefstaedterstrasse 26; A 1082 Vienna; AUSTRIA.

NCBSBV *Netherlands Centraal Bureau Voor de Statistiek*: Bezoek aan Vermakelukheidsinstellingen. Freq: 1; Began: 1940; Lang: Dut/Eng; Subj: Related. ISSN: 0077-6688
■Centraal Bureau voor de Statistiek; Prinses Beatrixlaan 428; Voorburg; NETHERLANDS.

NCBSMT *Netherlands Centraal Bureau voor de Statistiek*: Muziek en Theater. Formerly: *Statistiek van het Gesubsidieerde Toneel*. Lang: Dut; Subj: Theatre.
■Centraal Bureau voor de Statistiek; Prinses Beatrixlaan 428; Voorburg; NETHERLANDS.

NCM *Nineteenth Century Music*. Cov: Scan; Lang: Eng; Subj: Related.
■University of California; Berkeley, CA; USA.

NConL *Notes on Contemporary Literature*. Freq: 4; Began: 1971; Lang: Eng; Subj: Related. ISSN: 0029-4047
■English Department, West Georgia College; Carollton, GA 30118; USA.

NCPA *National Center for the Performing Arts*: Quarterly Journal. Freq: 4; Began: 1972; Lang: Eng; Subj: Related.
■Natl Cter for the Performing Arts; Nariman Point; 400021 Bombay; INDIA.

NCT *Nineteenth Century Theatre*. Formerly: *Nineteenth Century Theatre Research*. Freq: 2; Began: 1987; Lang: Eng; Subj: Theatre. ISSN: 0893-3766
■Amherst, MA; USA.

NCTR *Nineteenth Century Theatre Research*. Freq: 2; Began: 1973; Ceased: 1986; Cov: Full; Lang: Eng; Subj: Theatre. ISSN: 0316-5329
■Department of English, University of Arizona; Tuscon, AZ 85721; USA.

Neva *Neva*. Freq: 12; Began: 1955; Cov: Scan; Lang: Rus; Subj: Related. ISSN: 0130-741X
■Leningrad; USSR.

NewPerf *New Performance*. Freq: 4; Lang: Eng; Subj: Theatre.
■1159 DeHaro Street; San Francisco, CA 94107; USA.

NFT *Theatre*: News from the Finnish Theatre. Formerly: *News from the Finnish Theatre*. Freq: IRR; Began: 1958; Cov: Scan; Lang: Eng/Fre; Subj: Theatre. ISSN: 0358-3627
■Finnish Center of the ITI; Vuorikatu 6 A3; 00100 Helsinki 10; FINLAND.

NihonU *Nihon-Unima*. Lang: Jap; Subj: Theatre.
■Taoko Kawajiri, Puppet Theatre PUK; 2-12 Yoyogi, Shibuya; 151 Tokyo; JAPAN.

NIMBZ *Notate*: Informations-und-Mitteilungsblatt des Brecht-Zentrums der DDR. Lang: Ger; Subj: Theatre.
■Brecht Zentrum der DDR; Chausseestrasse 125; 1040 Berlin; EAST GERMANY.

NiR *Nauka i Religija*: (Science and Religion). Freq: 12; Began: 1959; Cov: Scan; Lang: Rus; Subj: Related. ISSN: 0130-7045
■Moscow; USSR.

Nk *Näköpiiri*. Ceased: 1983; Lang: Fin; Subj: Theatre.
■Osuuskunta Näköpiiri; Annakatu 13 B; 00120 Helsinki 12; FINLAND.

NKala *Natya Kala*. Freq: 12; Lang: Tel; Subj: Theatre.
■Kala Bhavan; Saifabad; Hyderabad; INDIA.

NNews *Natya News*. Freq: 4; Lang: Eng; Subj: Theatre.
■F. 34 New Central Market; New Delhi; INDIA.

NO *New Observations*. Freq: 10; Lang: Eng; Subj: Related.
■144 Greene Street; New York, NY 10012; USA.

Noh *Noh*. Freq: 12; Lang: Jap; Subj: Theatre.
■Ginza-Nohgakudo Building; 6-5-15 Ginza, Chuo-Ku; 104 Tokyo; JAPAN.

NoK *Nōgaku-kenkyū*. Freq: Irreg. exchange basis; Began: 1916; Cov: Scan; Lang: Jap; Subj: Related. ISSN: 0029-0874
■Okayama Univ.; Ohara Institute fuer Landwirtschaftliche Biologie-Ohara Institute for Agricultural Biology; 2-20-1 Chuo; Kurashiki 710; JAPAN.

NovyjMir *Novyj Mir*. Freq: 12; Began: 1925; Cov: Scan; Lang: Rus; Subj: Related. ISSN: 0130-7673
■Moscow; USSR.

Ns *Nestroyana*: Blätter der Internationalen Nestroy-Gesellschaft. Freq: 4; Began: 1979; Cov: Scan; Lang: Ger; Subj: Theatre.
■Internationale Nestroy-Gesellschaft, Volkstheater; Neustiftgasse 1; A 1070 Vienna; AUSTRIA.

NT *Nya Teatertidningen*. Freq: 4; Began: 1977; Cov: Full; Lang: Swe; Subj: Theatre. ISSN: 0348-0119
■Teatercentrum, Bjorkhagens Skola; Karlskrondvagen 10; 121 52 Johanneshov; SWEDEN.

NTE *Narodna Tvorcist' ta Ethnohrafija*. Freq: 6; Began: 1925; Lang: Ukr; Subj: Related. ISSN: 0130-6936
■Naukova Dumka; Repina 3; Kiev, Ukrainian SSR; USSR.

NTimes *Nohgaku Times*. Freq: 12; Began: 1953; Lang: Jap; Subj: Theatre.
■Nohgaku Shorin Ltd.; 3-6 Kanda-Jinpo-cho, Chiyoda-ku; 101 Tokyo; JAPAN.

NTQ *New Theatre Quarterly*. Freq: 4; Began: 1985; Cov: Full; Lang: Eng; Subj: Theatre. ISSN: 0266-464X
■Cambridge University Press; 32 E. 57th Street; New York, NY 10022; USA.

NTS *Nordic Theatre Studies*: Yearbook for Theatre Research in Scandinavia. Freq: 1; Began: 1988; Lang: Eng; Subj: Theatre.
■Munksgaard; Postbox 2148; 1016 Copenhagen K; DENMARK.

NTTJ *Nederlands Theatre-en-Televisie Jaarboek*. Freq: 1; Lang: Dut; Subj: Theatre.
■Amsterdam; NETHERLANDS.

Numero *Numero*. Freq: 12; Lang: Spa; Subj: Related.
■Apt. Post. 75570; El Marques; Caracas; VENEZUELA.

NVarta *Natya Varta*. Freq: 12; Lang: Hin; Subj: Theatre.
■Anakima; 4 Bishop Lefroy Road; Calcutta; INDIA.

Nvilag *Nagyvilág*. Freq: 12; Began: 1956; Cov: Scan; Lang: Hun; Subj: Related. ISSN: 1613-1547
■Széchenyi rkp. 1; 1054 Budapest V; HUNGARY.

NWR *NeWest Review*: A Journal of Culture and Current Events in the West. Freq: 12; Began: 1975; Lang: Eng; Subj: Theatre. ISSN: 0380-2817
■NeWest Publishers Ltd.; Box 394, Sub Post Office 6; Saskatoon, SK S7N 0W0; CANADA.

NYO *New York Onstage*. Freq: 12; Lang: Eng; Subj: Theatre.
■New York, NY; USA.

NYTCR *New York Theatre Critics Review*. Freq: 30; Began: 1940; Cov: Full; Lang: Eng; Subj: Theatre.
■Critics Theatre Review; 4 Park Avenue, Suite 21; New York, NY 10016; USA.

NYTR *New York Theatre Reviews*. Began: 1977; Ceased: 1980; Lang: Eng; Subj: Theatre.
■Ira J. Bilowit; 55 West 42nd Street; New York, NY 10036; USA.

Obliques *Obliques*. Lang: Fre; Subj: Related.
■Roger Borderie; BP1, Les Pilles; 26110 Lyons; FRANCE.

OC *Opera Canada*. Freq: 4; Began: 1960; Cov: Scan; Lang: Eng; Subj: Theatre. ISSN: 0030-3577
■Foundation for Coast to Coast, Opera Publication; 366 Adelaide Street E., Suite 433; Toronto, ON M5A 3X9; CANADA.

OCA *O'Casey Annual*. Freq: 1; Began: 1982; Cov: Scan; Lang: Eng; Subj: Theatre.
■MacMillan Publishers Ltd.; 4 Little Essex Street; WC2R 3LF London; UK.

ODG *Österreichische Dramatiker der Gegenwart*. Lang: Ger; Subj: Theatre.
■Inst. für Österreichische Dramaturgie; Singerstrasse 26; A 1010 Vienna; AUSTRIA.

OI *Opéra International*. Freq: 12; Began: 1963; Lang: Fre; Subj: Theatre.
■10 Galerie Vero-Dodat; 75001 Paris; FRANCE.

OJ *Opera Journal*. Freq: 4; Began: 1968; Cov: Scan; Lang: Eng; Subj: Theatre. ISSN: 0030-3585
■National Opera Association, Inc., University of Mississippi; Division of Continuing Ed. and Extension; University, MS 38677; USA.

OK   *Oper und Konzert*. Freq: 12; Began: 1963; Lang: Ger; Subj: Theatre.
ISSN: 0030-3518
■A. Hanuschik; Ungererstrasse 19/VI (Fuchsbau); 8000 Munich 40; WEST GERMANY.

Oktiabr   *Oktiabr*. Freq: 12; Began: 1924; Cov: Scan; Lang: Rus; Subj: Related.
ISSN: 0132-0637
■Moscow; USSR.

Opal   *Opal*. Freq: 6; Began: 1962; Lang: Eng; Subj: Theatre. ISSN: 0030-3062
■Ontario Puppetry Association; 171 Avondale Avenue; Willowdale, ON M2N 2V4; CANADA.

Oper   *Oper*. Freq: 1; Lang: Ger; Subj: Theatre.
■Zurich; SWITZERLAND.

Opera   *Opera*. Freq: 12; Began: 1950; Cov: Scan; Lang: Eng; Subj: Theatre.
ISSN: 0030-3542
■Seymour Press Ltd.; 336 Woodland Rise; N10 3UH London; UK.

OperaA   *Opera Australia*. Freq: 12; Began: 1978; Lang: Eng; Subj: Theatre.
ISSN: 0155-4980
■PO Box R361; NSW 2000 Royal Exchange; AUSTRALIA.

OperaCT   *Opera*. Freq: 4; Began: 1974; Lang: Eng/Afr; Subj: Theatre.
■Cape Performing Arts Board; POB 4107; 8000 Cape Town; SOUTH AFRICA.

OperaR   *Opera*. Freq: 4; Began: 1965; Lang: Ita/Eng/Fre/Ger/Spa; Subj: Theatre.
ISSN: 0030-3542
■Editoriale Fenarete; Via Beruto 7; Milan; ITALY.

OperH   *Oper Heute*. Lang: Ger; Subj: Theatre.
■East Berlin; EAST GERMANY.

OpN   *Opera News*. Freq: 12; Began: 1936; Cov: Full; Lang: Eng; Subj: Theatre.
ISSN: 0030-3607
■Metropolitan Opera Guild, Inc.; 1865 Broadway; New York, NY 10023; USA.

Opuscula   *Opuscula*. Freq: 3; Began: 1976; Lang: Dan; Subj: Theatre.
■Det Teatervidenskabelige Institot; Fredericingade 18; 1310 Copenhagen; DENMARK.

Opw   *Opernwelt*: Die deutsche Opernzeitschrift. Freq: 12; Began: 1963; Cov: Scan; Lang: Ger; Subj: Theatre.
ISSN: 0030-3690
■Orell Fuessli & Friedrich Verlag; Dietzingerstrasse 3; CH 8036 Zurich; SWITZERLAND.

OQ   *Opera Quarterly*. Freq: 4; Began: 1983; Cov: Full; Lang: Eng; Subj: Theatre.
ISSN: 0736-0053
■University of North Carolina Press; Box 2288; Chapel Hill, NC 27514; USA.

Organon   *Organon*. Freq: 1; Began: 1975; Lang: Fre; Subj: Theatre.
■Ctre de Recherches Théâtrales, Univ. Lyon II; Ensemble Univ., Ave. de l'Universite; 69500 Bron; FRANCE.

OSS   *On-Stage Studies*. Formerly: *Colorado Shakespeare Festival Annual*. Freq: 1; Began: 1977; Cov: Full; Lang: Eng; Subj: Theatre.

■Colorado Shakespeare Festival, Campus Box 261; University of Colorado; Boulder, CO 80309 0261; USA.

OvA   *Overture*. Freq: 12; Began: 1919; Cov: Scan; Lang: Eng; Subj: Theatre.
ISSN: 0030-7556
■American Federation of Musicians, Local 47, AFL-CIO; 817 N. Vine Street; Los Angeles, CA 90038; USA.

P&L   *Philosophy and Literature*. Freq: 2; Began: 1976; Lang: Eng; Subj: Theatre.
ISSN: 0190-0013
■University of Michigan; Dearborn, MI 48128; USA.

PA   *Présence Africaine*. Freq: 4; Began: 1947; Lang: Fre/Eng; Subj: Related.
ISSN: 0032-7638
■Nouvelle Société Presence Africaine; 25 bis rue des Ecoles; Paris 75005; FRANCE.

Pa&Pr   *Past and Present*: A Journal of Historical Studies. Freq: 4; Began: 1952; Cov: Scan; Lang: Eng; Subj: Related.
ISSN: 0031-2746
■Past and Present Society; Corpus Christi College; Oxford; UK.

PAA   *Performing Arts Annual*. Freq: 1; Began: 1986; Cov: Full; Lang: Eng; Subj: Theatre.
ISSN: 0887-8234
■Library of Congress, Performing Arts Library Resources; Dist. by G.O.P.; Washington, DC 20540; USA.

PAC   *Performing Arts in Canada*. Freq: 4; Began: 1961; Cov: Full; Lang: Eng; Subj: Theatre.
ISSN: 0031-5230
■Canadian Stage & Arts Publ.; 52 Avenue Road, 2nd floor; Toronto, ON M5R 2G2; CANADA.

Pamir   *Pamir*. Freq: 12; Began: 1949; Cov: Scan; Lang: Rus; Subj: Related.
ISSN: 0131-2650
■Dushanbe; USSR.

Pantallas   *Pantallas y Escenarios*. Freq: 5; Lang: Spa; Subj: Theatre.
■Maria Lostal 24; 8 Zaragoza; SPAIN.

PAR   *Performing Arts Resources*. Freq: 1; Began: 1974; Cov: Scan; Lang: Eng; Subj: Theatre.
■Theatre Library Association, NYU School of the Arts; 51 W. 4th St., Room 300; New York, NY 10023; USA.

Parnass   *Parnass*: Die Österreichische Kunst- und Kulturzeitschrift. Freq: 6; Began: 1981; Cov: Scan; Lang: Ger; Subj: Theatre.
■C & E Grosser, Druckerei Verlag; Wiener Strasse 290; A 4020 Linz; AUSTRIA.

Parnasso   *Parnasso*. Freq: 8; Began: 1951; Lang: Fin; Subj: Theatre.
■Yhtyneet Kuvalehdet; Hietalahdenranta 13; 00180 Helsinki 18; FINLAND.

PArts   *Performing Arts*: The Music and Theatre Monthly. Freq: 12; Began: 1967; Ceased: 1983; Lang: Eng; Subj: Theatre.
ISSN: 0031-5222
■K & K Publishing Inc.; 2999 Overland Avenue, No. 201; Los Angeles, CA 90046 4243; USA.

PArtsSF   *Performing Arts Magazine*: San Francisco Music & Theatre Monthly. Freq: 12; Began: 1967; Lang: Eng; Subj: Theatre.
ISSN: 0480-0257

■Theatre Publications, Inc.; 1232 Market; San Francisco, CA 94102; USA.

PasShow   *Passing Show*. Freq: IRR; Began: 1981; Lang: Eng; Subj: Theatre.
ISSN: 0706-1897
■Performing Arts Museum, Victorian Arts Centre; 1 City Rd; 3205 S. Melbourne, Victoria; AUSTRALIA.

PaT   *Pamiętnik Teatralny*: Poswiecony historii i krytyce teatru. Freq: 4; Began: 1952; Cov: Full; Lang: Pol; Subj: Theatre.
ISSN: 0031-0522
■Ossolineum, Polish Academy of Sciences; Rynek 9; Wroclaw; POLAND.

PaV   *Paraules al Vent*. Freq: 12; Cov: Scan; Lang: Spa; Subj: Related.
■Associació de Joves 'Paraules al Vent'; Casal de Sant Jordi; Sant Jordi Desvalls; SPAIN.

PAYBA   *Performing Arts Year Book of Australia*. Freq: 1; Began: 1977; Lang: Eng; Subj: Theatre.
■Showcast Publications Ltd; Box 141; 2088 Spit Junction N.S.W; AUSTRALIA.

Pb   *Playbill*: A National Magazine of the Theatre. Freq: 12; Began: 1982; Lang: Eng; Subj: Theatre. ISSN: 0032-146X
■Playbill Incorporated; 71 Vanderbilt Avenue; New York, NY 10169; USA.

PCD   *Premiery Ceskoslovenskych Divadel*. Freq: 12; Lang: Cze; Subj: Theatre.
■Valdstejnske 3; Prague 1; CZECHOSLOVAKIA.

PdO   *Pantuflas del Obispo*. Began: 1966; Lang: Spa; Subj: Theatre.
■Semanario Sabado; Vargas 219; Quito; ECUADOR.

Pe   *Performance*. Freq: 6; Began: 1981; Lang: Eng; Subj: Related.
■Brevet Publishing Ltd.; 445 Brighton Road; CR2 6EU South Croydon; UK.

PeM   *Pesti Müsor*. Freq: 52; Began: 1957; Lang: Hun; Subj: Theatre.
■Garay u.5; 1076 Budapest VII; HUNGARY.

PerAJ   *Performing Arts Journal*. Freq: 3; Began: 1976; Cov: Full; Lang: Eng; Subj: Theatre. ISSN: 0735-8393
■Performing Arts Journal, Inc.; 325 Spring Street, Room 318; New York, NY 10013; USA.

PerfNZ   *Performance: A Handbook of the Performing Arts in New Zealand*. Freq: 5; Began: 1980; Cov: Full; Lang: Eng; Subj: Theatre.
ISSN: 0112-0654
■Association of Community Theatres; P.O. 68-257; Newton, Aukland; NEW ZEALAND.

Perlicko   *Perlicko-Perlacko*. Began: 1950; Lang: Ger; Subj: Theatre.
■Dr. Hans R. Purschke; Postfach 550135; 6000 Frankfurt; WEST GERMANY.

Pf   *Platform*. Freq: 2; Began: 1979; Ceased: 1983; Cov: Scan; Lang: Eng; Subj: Theatre.
■Dept of Literature, University of Essex; Wivenhoe Park; Colchester; UK.

PFr   *Présence Francophone*. Freq: 2; Began: 1970; Ceased: 1970; Cov: Scan; Lang: Fre; Subj: Related. ISSN: 0048-5195
■Université de Sherbrooke; Sherbrooke, PQ J1K 2R1; CANADA.

PI   *Plays International.* Formerly: *Plays/Plays International.* Freq: 12; Began: 1985; Cov: Scan; Lang: Eng; Subj: Theatre. ■Chancery Publications Ltd.; 55 Hatton Garden; ECIN 8HP London; UK.

PInfo   *Puppenspiel-Information.* Began: 1967; Lang: Ger; Subj: Theatre. ■Hans Scheu; Stahlsberg 46; 5600 Wuppertal 2; WEST GERMANY.

PiP   *Plays in Process.* Lang: Eng; Subj: Theatre. ■New York, NY; USA.

Pja   *Pipirijaina.* Freq: 6; Began: 1979; Lang: Spa; Subj: Theatre. ■c/o San Enrique 16; 20 Madrid; SPAIN.

Plateaux   *Plateaux.* Formerly: *Bulletin de l'Union des Artistes.* Freq: 6; Began: 1925; Lang: Fre; Subj: Theatre. ■Syndicat Français des Artistes et Interpretes; 21 bis, rue Victor-Masse; 75009 Paris; FRANCE.

Play   *Play.* Freq: 12; Began: 1974; Lang: Eng; Subj: Theatre. ISSN: 0311-4031 ■Main Street; PO Box 67; 5245 Hahndorf; SOUTH AFRICA.

PlayM   *Players Magazine.* Freq: 22; Began: 1924; Lang: Eng; Subj: Theatre.   ISSN: 0032-1486 ■National Collegiate Players, Northern Illinois University; University Theatre; Dekalb, IL 60115; USA.

Plays   *Plays:* (In 1985 became part of *Plays and Players*). Formerly: *Plays/Plays International.* Freq: 12; Began: 1983; Ceased: 1985; Cov: Scan; Lang: Eng; Subj: Theatre. ■Ocean Publications; 34 Buckingham Palace Road; SW1 London; UK.

PlPl   *Plays and Players.* Freq: 12; Began: 1953; Cov: Scan; Lang: Eng; Subj: Theatre.   ISSN: 0032-1540 ■Brevet Publishing Ltd.; 43B Gloucester Rd.; CR0 2DH Croyden, Surrey; UK.

PLUG   *PLUG:* Maandelijks informatieblad van het Cultureel Jongeren Paspoort. Freq: 12; Began: 1967; Lang: Dut; Subj: Theatre.   ISSN: 0032-1621 ■Cultureel Jongeren Paspoort; Kleine Gartmanplts. 10; 1017 RR Amsterdam; NETHERLANDS.

PM   *Performance Magazine, The.* Freq: 6; Began: 1979; Cov: Full; Lang: Eng; Subj: Theatre.   ISSN: 0144-5901 ■Performance Magazine Ltd.; 14 Peto Place; NW1 London; UK.

PMLA   *PMLA:* Publications of the Modern Language Assoc. of America. Freq: 6; Began: 1929; Cov: Scan; Lang: Eng; Subj: Related.   ISSN: 0030-8129 ■Modern Language Assoc. of America; 62 5th Avenue; New York, NY 10011; USA.

Pnpa   *Peuples noirs, peuples africains.* Freq: 4; Began: 1977; Cov: Scan; Lang: Fre; Subj: Related. ■82, avenue de la Porte-des-Champs; 76000 Rouen; FRANCE.

Podium   *Podium.* Lang: Dut; Subj: Theatre. ■Rijswijk; NETHERLANDS.

PodiumB   *Podium:* Zeitschrift für Bühnenbildner und Theatertechnik. Freq: 4; Lang: Ger; Subj: Theatre. ■Abteilung Berufsbildung; Munzstrasse 21; 1020 Berlin; EAST GERMANY.

Poppen   *Poppenspelbereichten.* Freq: 4; Lang: Dut; Subj: Theatre. ■Mechelen; BELGIUM.

PozL   *Pozorište:* List Srpskog narodnog pozorišta. Freq: 10; Began: 1871; Lang: Ser; Subj: Theatre. ■Srpsko narodno pozorište; Novi Sad; YUGOSLAVIA.

Pozoriste   *Pozorište:* Časopis za pozorišnu umjetnost. Freq: 8; Began: 1959; Lang: Cro; Subj: Theatre.   ISSN: 0032-616X ■Narodno Pozorište; Matija Gupca 6; 75000 Tuzla; YUGOSLAVIA.

PQ   *Philological Quarterly:* Investigation of Classical & Modern Langs. and Lit.. Freq: 4; Began: 1922; Cov: Scan; Lang: Eng; Subj: Related.   ISSN: 0031-7977 ■Editor, Philological Quarterly; University of Iowa; Iowa City, IA 52242; USA.

PQCS   *Philippine Quarterly of Culture and Society.* Freq: 4; Began: 1973; Lang: Eng; Subj: Related.   ISSN: 0115-0243 ■San Carlos Publications; 6401 Cebu City; PHILIPPINES.

PrAc   *Primer Acto.* Freq: 5; Began: 1957; Lang: Spa; Subj: Theatre. ■Pza. de los Mostenses 11; 8 Madrid; SPAIN.

Preface   *Préface.* Freq: 12; Lang: Fre; Subj: Theatre. ■Centre National Nice-Côte d'Azur; Esplanade des Victoires; 06300 Nice; FRANCE.

Premijera   *Premijera:* List Narodnog Pozorišta Sombor. Lang: Ser; Subj: Theatre. ■Koste Trifkovica 2; Sombor; YUGOSLAVIA.

Prof   *Profile:* The Newsletter of the New Zealand Assoc. of Theatre Technicians. Freq: 4; Lang: Eng; Subj: Related. ■Ponsonby, Auckland; NEW ZEALAND.

Programa   *Programa.* Began: 1978; Lang: Por; Subj: Theatre. ■Grupo de Teatro de Campolide; 43, 20 D. Cde. Antas; Lisbon; PORTUGAL.

Prolog   *Prolog:* Revija za dramsku umjetnost. In 1986 became Novi Prolog. Freq: 2; Began: 1968; Lang: Cro; Subj: Theatre. ■Centar za kulturnu djelatnost; Mihanoviceva 28/1; 41000 Zagreb; YUGOSLAVIA.

PrologTX   *Prolog.* Freq: 4; Began: 1973; Lang: Eng; Subj: Theatre. ISSN: 0271-7743 ■Theatre Sources Inc., c/o Michael Firth; 104 North St. Mary; Dallas, TX 75214; USA.

Prologue   *Prologue.* Freq: 4; Began: 1944; Lang: Eng; Subj: Theatre. ISSN: 0033-1007 ■Arena Theater; Tufts University; Medford, MA 02155; USA.

Prompts   *Prompts.* Freq: IRR; Began: 1981; Lang: Eng; Subj: Theatre. ■Irish Theatre Archive, Archives Division; City Hall; 2 Dublin; IRELAND.

ProScen   *ProScen.* Freq: 4; Began: 1986; Cov: Full; Lang: Swe; Subj: Theatre. ■Svensk Teaterteknisk Sörening, Section of OISTT; P.O. Box 45003; 10430 Stockholm 45; SWEDEN.

PrTh   *Pratiques Théâtrales:* In 1978 became Grande République. Freq: 3; Ceased: 1978; Lang: Fre; Subj: Theatre. ■200 Ouest rue Sherbrooke; Montreal, PQ H2Y 3P2; CANADA.

Ptk   *Publiekstheaterkrant.* Freq: 5; Began: 1978; Lang: Dut; Subj: Theatre. ■Publiekstheater; Marnixstraat 427; 1017 PK Amsterdam; NETHERLANDS.

PuJ   *Puppetry Journal.* Freq: 4; Began: 1949; Cov: Full; Lang: Eng; Subj: Theatre.   ISSN: 0033-4405 ■Puppeteers of America; 6216 N. Morgan St.; Alexandria, VA 22312; USA.

PupM   *Puppet Master.* Began: 1946; Lang: Eng; Subj: Theatre. ■British Puppet and Model Theatre Guild, c/o Gordon Shapley (Hon. Sec.); 18 Maple Road, Yeading, Nr Hayes; Middlesex; UK.

Pusp   *Puppenspiel und Puppenspieler.* Freq: 2; Began: 1960; Lang: Ger/Fre; Subj: Theatre.   ISSN: 0033-4405 ■Schweiz. Vereinigung Puppenspiel, c/o Gustav Gysin, Ed.; Roggenstr. 1; Riehen CH-4125; SWITZERLAND.

Pz   *Proszenium.* Lang: Ger; Subj: Theatre. ■Zurich; SWITZERLAND.

QT   *Quaderni di Teatro:* Rivista Trimestrale del Teatro Regionale Toscano. Freq: 4; Began: 1978; Cov: Full; Lang: Ita; Subj: Theatre. ■Vallecchi Editore; Volta dei Mercanti 1; Florence; ITALY.

QTST   *Quaderni del Teatro Stabile di Torino.* Freq: IRR; Lang: Ita; Subj: Theatre. ■Teatro Stabile di Torino; Turin; ITALY.

Quarta   *Quarta Parete.* Freq: 4; Lang: Ita; Subj: Theatre. ■Via Sant'Ottavio 15; Turin; ITALY.

QuellenT   *Quellen zur Theatergeschichte.* Freq: IRR; Began: 1981; Lang: Ger; Subj: Theatre. ■Verband der Wissenschaftlichen, Gesellschaften Oesterreichs; Lindengasse 37; A1070 Vienna; AUSTRIA.

Raduga   *Raduga.* Freq: 12; Began: 1986; Cov: Scan; Lang: Rus; Subj: Related.   ISSN: 0234-8179 ■Talin, Eston. SSR; USSR.

Raja   *Rajatabla.* Lang: Spa; Subj: Theatre. ■Apartado 662; 105 Caracas; VENEZUELA.

RAL   *Research in African Literature.* Freq: 4; Began: 1970; Cov: Scan; Lang: Eng; Subj: Related.   ISSN: 0034-5210 ■University of Texas Press; Box 7819; Austin, TX 78712; USA.

Rampel   *Rampelyset.* Freq: 6; Began: 1948; Lang: Dan; Subj: Theatre. ■Danske Amatør Teater Samvirke; Box 70; DK 6300 Grasten; DENMARK.

Randa   *Randa.* Freq: 2; Cov: Scan; Lang: Spa; Subj: Related. ■Curial Edicions Catalanes, c/o Bruc; 144 Baixos; 08037 Barcelona; SPAIN.

Rangarupa *Rangarupa*. Began: 1976; Lang: Ben; Subj: Theatre.
■Rangarup Natya Academy; 27/76 Central Rd.; Dhanmondi, Dacca; BANGLADESH.

Rangayan *Rangayan*. Freq: 12; Lang: Hin; Subj: Theatre.
■Bharatiya Lok Kala Mandal; Udaipur; INDIA.

Rangyog *Rangyog*. Freq: 4; Lang: Hin; Subj: Theatre.
■Rajasthan Sangeet Natak Adademi; Paota; Jodhpur; INDIA.

Raritan *Raritan*. Freq: 4; Began: 1981; Lang: Eng; Subj: Related. ISSN: 0275-1607
■Rutgers University; 165 College Ave.; New Brunswick, NJ 08903; USA.

Rbharati *Rangbharati*. Freq: 12; Lang: Hin; Subj: Theatre.
■Bharatendu Rangmanch; Chowk; Lucknow; INDIA.

RdA *Revue de l'Art*. Freq: 4; Began: 1968; Cov: Scan; Lang: Fre; Subj: Related. ISSN: 0035-1326
■Editions du CNRS; 15 quai Anatole France; 75700 Paris; FRANCE.

RdArt *Revista d'Art*. Freq: 1; Cov: Scan; Lang: Spa; Subj: Related.
■c/o Baldiri Reixac, Departament d'Historia de l'Art; Facultat de Geografia i Historia; 08028 Barcelona; SPAIN.

RdD *Rassegna di Diritto Cinematografico, Teatrale e della Televisione*. Lang: Ita; Subj: Theatre.
■Via Ennio Quirino Visconti 99; Rome; ITALY.

RdS *Rassegna dello Spettacolo*. Began: 1953; Lang: Ita; Subj: Theatre.
ISSN: 0033-9474
■Assoc. Gen. Italiana dello Spettacolo; Via di Villa Patrizi 10; 00161 Rome; ITALY.

RE *Revue d'esthétique*. Freq 4; Cov: Scan; Lang: Fre; Subj: Theatre.
■Privat et Cie; 14, rue des Arts; 31068 Toulouse CEDEX; FRANCE.

Recorder *Recorder, The: A Journal of the American Irish Historical Society*. Freq: 2; Began: 1985; Cov: Scan; Lang: Eng; Subj: Related.
■American Irish Historical Society; 991 Fifth Avenue; New York, NY 10028; USA.

REEDN *Records of Early English Drama Newsletter*. Freq: 2; Began: 1976; Cov: Full; Lang: Eng; Subj: Theatre. ISSN: 0070-9283
■University of Toronto, Erindale College, English Section; Mississauga, ON L5L 1C6; CANADA.

RenD *Renaissance Drama*. Freq: 1; Began: 1964; Cov: Full; Lang: Eng; Subj: Theatre. ISSN: 0486-3739
■English Dept.; Northwestern University; Evanston, IL 60201; USA.

Renmin *Renmin Xiju*: People's Theatre. Freq: 12; Began: 1950; Lang: Chi; Subj: Theatre.
■52 Dongai Batiao; Peking; CHINA.

Repliikki *Repliikki*. Freq: 4; Began: 1970; Lang: Fin; Subj: Theatre.
■Suomen Harrastajateatteriliitto; r.y. Museokatu 7B12; 00100 Helsinki 10; FINLAND.

REsT *Revista de Estudios de Teatro*: Boletin. Freq: 3; Began: 1964; Lang: Spa; Subj: Theatre. ISSN: 0034-8171
■Instituto Nacional de Estudios de Teatro; Cordoba 1199; Buenos Aires; ARGENTINA.

Restor *Restoration and Eighteenth Century Theatre Research*. Freq: 2; Began: 1962; Cov: Full; Lang: Eng; Subj: Theatre.
ISSN: 0034-5822
■Loyola University of Chicago, Dept. of English; 6525 North Sheridan Road; Chicago, IL 60626; USA.

Revue *Revue*. Freq: 6; Lang: Fre; Subj: Theatre.
■Theatre de la Commune, BP 157; 2 rue Edouard Poisson; 93304 Aubervilliers; FRANCE.

RHSTMC *Revue Roumaine d'Histoire de l'Art*: Série Théâtre, Musique, Cinéma. Freq: 4; Began: 1980; Lang: Fre; Subj: Related.
■Ed. Academiei Rep. Soc. Romania; Calea Victoriei 125; 79717 Bucharest; ROMANIA.

RHT *Revue d'Histoire du Théâtre*. Freq: 4; Began: 1948; Cov: Full; Lang: Fre; Subj: Theatre. ISSN: 0035-2373
■Société d'Histoire du Théâtre; 98 Boulevard Kellermann; 75013 Paris; FRANCE.

RIDr *Rivista Italiana di Drammaturgia*. Freq: 4; Began: 1976; Lang: Ita; Subj: Theatre.
■Istituto del Dramma Italiano; Via Monte della Farina 42; Rome; ITALY.

RLC *Revue de Littérature Comparée*. Freq: 4; Began: 1921; Cov: Scan; Lang: Fre/Eng/Ger; Subj: Related. ISSN: 0035-1466
■F. Didier Erudition; 6 rue de la Sorbonne; 75005 Paris; FRANCE.

RLit *Russkaja Literatura: Istoriko-Literaturnyj Žurnal*: (Russian Literature: Historical Literary Journal). Freq: 4; Began: 1958; Cov: Scan; Lang: Rus; Subj: Related.
ISSN: 0557-5362
■Inst. Russkoj Lit. Akademii Nauk SSSR, Puškinskij Dom; Nab. Makarova 4; 199164 Leningrad; USSR.

RLtrs *Red Letters*. Freq: 3; Began: 1976; Cov: Scan; Lang: Eng; Subj: Related.
ISSN: 0308-6852
■A Journal of Cultural Politics; 16 St. John Street; EC1M 4AY London; UK.

RMelo *Rassegna Melodrammatica*. Lang: Ita; Subj: Theatre.
■Corso di Porta Romana 80; Milan; ITALY.

RN *Rouge et Noir*. Freq: 9; Began: 1968; Lang: Fre; Subj: Related.
■Maison de la Culture de Grenoble; BP 70-40; 38020 Grenoble; FRANCE.

Roda *Roda Lyktan*. Freq: 1; Began: 1976; Lang: Swe; Subj: Theatre.
ISSN: 0040-0750
■Skanska Teatern; Osterg 31; 26134 Landskrona; SWEDEN.

RORD *Research Opportunities in Renaissance Drama*. Freq: 1/2 yrs; Began: 1956; Cov: Full; Lang: Eng; Subj: Theatre.
■Department of English; University of Kansas; Lawrence, KS 66045; USA.

RRMT *Ridotto*: Rassegna Mensile di Teatro. Freq: 12; Began: 1951; Cov: Scan; Lang: Ita; Subj: Theatre. ISSN: 0035-5186

■Società Italiana Autori Drammatici; Via Po 10; 00198 Rome; ITALY.

RSP *Rivista di Studi Pirandelliani*. Freq: 3; Began: 1978; Cov: Scan; Lang: Ita; Subj: Theatre.
■Centro Nazionale di Studi Pirandelliani; Agrigento; ITALY.

SAADYT *SAADYT Journal*. Formerly: *SAADYT Newsletter*. Began: 1979; Cov: Scan; Lang: Eng/Afr; Subj: Theatre.
■South African Assoc. for Drama and, Youth Theatre; Private Bag X41; Pretoria; SOUTH AFRICA.

SAD *Studies in American Drama, 1945-Present*. Freq: 1; Began: 1986; Cov: Full; Lang: Eng; Subj: Theatre. ISSN: 0886-7097
■University of Southern Mississippi, Department of English; Hattiesburg, MS 39406 4319; USA.

Sage *Sage*: A Scholarly Journal on Black Women. Freq: 2; Began: 1984; Cov: Scan; Lang: Eng; Subj: Related.
ISSN: 0741-8369
■Sage Women's Educational Press, Inc.; Box 42741; Atlanta, GA 30311 0741; USA.

Sahne *Sahne (The Stage)*. Freq: 12; Began: 1981; Lang: Tur; Subj: Theatre.
■Nes'e Altiner; Cagaloglu Yokusu 2; Istanbul; TURKEY.

SAITT *SAITT Focus*. Freq: IRR; Began: 1969; Lang: Eng/Afr; Subj: Theatre.
■S. African Inst. for Theatre Technology; Pretoria; SOUTH AFRICA.

SAJAL *South African Journal of African Languages*. Freq: 4; Began: 1981; Lang: Eng & Afrikaans; Subj: Related. ISSN: 0257-2117
■African Languages Asso. of Southern Africa; Bureau for Scientific Publications; Box 1758; Pretoria 0001; SOUTH AFRICA.

SanatO *Sanat Olayi (Art Event)*. Freq: 12; Lang: Tur; Subj: Theatre.
■Karacan Yayinlari; Basin Sarayi; Cagaloglu-Istanbul; TURKEY.

SATJ *South African Theatre Journal*. Freq: 2; Began: 1987; Lang: Eng; Subj: Theatre.
■Drama Department; University of Witwatersrand; WITS 2050; SOUTH AFRICA.

SCagdas *Sanajans Cagdas*. Freq: 12; Lang: Tur; Subj: Theatre.
■Istiklal Caddesi Botter Han; 475/479 Kat. 3; Istanbul; TURKEY.

ScCh *Scene Changes*. Freq: 9; Began: 1973; Ceased: 1981; Cov: Scan; Lang: Eng; Subj: Theatre. ISSN: 0381-8098
■Theatre Ontario; 8 York Street, 7th floor; Toronto, ON M5R 1J2; CANADA.

Scena *Scena*: Časopis za pozorišnu umetnost. Freq: 6; Began: 1965; Lang: Ser; Subj: Theatre. ISSN: 0036-5734
■Sterijino Pozorje; Zmaj Jovina 22; 21000 Novi Sad; YUGOSLAVIA.

ScenaB *Scena*. Freq: 4; Began: 1962; Lang: Ger; Subj: Theatre. ISSN: 0036-5726
■Institut für Technologie Kultureller Einrichtung; Clara Zetkin-Str. 1205; 108 Berlin; EAST GERMANY.

ScenaE *Scena*: Theatre Arts Review. Freq: 1; Began: 1978; Lang: Eng; Subj: Theatre.
■Sterijino Pozorje; Novi Sad; YUGOSLAVIA.

ScenaM *Scena*. Freq: 12; Began: 1976; Lang: Ita; Subj: Theatre.
■Morrison Hotel; Via Modena 16; 20129 Milan; ITALY.

Scenaria *Scenaria*. Freq: 24; Began: 1977; Cov: Scan; Lang: Eng; Subj: Theatre.
■Triad Publishers Ltd.; Box 72161, Parkview 2122; Johannesburg; SOUTH AFRICA.

Scenarium *Scenarium*. Freq: 1; Began: 1977; Lang: Dut; Subj: Theatre.
■De Walburg Pres; P.O. Box 222; 7200 AE Zutphen; NETHERLANDS.

ScenaW *Scena*. Formerly: *Poradnik Teatrow, Lirnik Wioskowy*. Freq: 48; Began: 1908; Lang: Pol; Subj: Theatre.
■Wydawnictwo Prasa ZSL; ul. Reja 9; 02 053 Warsaw; POLAND.

Scene *Scene, De*. Freq: 10; Began: 1959; Lang: Dut; Subj: Theatre.
■Theatercentrum; Jan van Rijswijcklaan 28; B 2000 Antwerpen; BELGIUM.

Scenograf *Scenografie*. Freq: 4; Began: 1963; Lang: Cze; Subj: Theatre.
ISSN: 0036-5815
■Divadelni Ustav; Valdstejnske 3; Prague 1; CZECHOSLOVAKIA.

ScenoS *Scen och Salong*. Freq: 12; Began: 1915; Lang: Swe; Subj: Theatre.
ISSN: 0036-5718
■Folkparkernas Centralorganisation; Svedenborgsgatan 1; S 116 48 Stockholm; SWEDEN.

Schaus *Schauspielfuehrer*. Der Inhalt der wichtigsten Theaterstuecke aus aller Welt. Freq: IRR; Began: 1953; Lang: Ger; Subj: Theatre.
ISSN: 0342-4553
■Anton Hiersemann Verlag, Rosenbergstr 113; Postfach 723; 7000 Stuttgart 1; WEST GERMANY.

SchwT *Schweizer Theaterjahrbuch*. Freq: 1; Lang: Ger; Subj: Related.
■Bonstetten; SWITZERLAND.

ScIDI *Scena IDI, La*. Freq: 4; Began: 1971; Lang: Ita; Subj: Theatre.
■Bulzoni Editore; Via Liburni 14; 00185 Rome; ITALY.

Screen *Screen*. Freq: 24; Began: 1959; Cov: Scan; Lang: Eng; Subj: Related.
ISSN: 0036-9543
■Society for Educ. in Film & TV; 29 Old Compton St.; W1V 5PL London; UK.

SCYPT *SCYPT Journal*. Freq: 2; Began: 1977; Cov: Scan; Lang: Eng; Subj: Theatre.
■Standing Conf. on Young People's Theatre, c/o Cockpit Theatre; Gateforth Street; NW8 London; UK.

SDi *Slovenské Divadlo*. Freq: 4; Began: 1952; Cov: Full; Lang: Slo; Subj: Theatre.
ISSN: 0037-699X
■Slovanian Acad. of Sciences; Klemensova 19; 814 30 Bratislava; CZECHOSLOVAKIA.

SdO *Serra d'Or*. Freq: 12; Began: 1959; Cov: Scan; Lang: Spa; Subj: Related.
ISSN: 0037-2501

■Publicacions de l'Abadia de Montser, Ausias March 92-98; Apdo. 244; 13 Barcelona; SPAIN.

SEEA *Slavic & East European Arts*. Freq: 2; Began: 1982; Cov: Full; Lang: Eng; Subj: Related.
■State Univ. of NY, Stonybrook, Dept. of Germanic & Slavic Lang.; Slavic & East European Arts; Stonybrook, NY 11794; USA.

SEEDTF *Soviet and East-European Drama, Theatre and Film*. Formerly: *Newsnotes on Soviet & East European Drama &Theatre*. Freq: 3; Began: 1981; Cov: Scan; Lang: Eng; Subj: Theatre.
■Inst. for Contemporary East European and Soviet Drama and Theatre; Graduate Ctre, CUNY, 33 West 42nd St., Room 1206A; New York, NY 10036; USA.

Segmundo *Segismundo*. Freq: 6; Began: 1965; Lang: Spa; Subj: Theatre.
■Consejo Superior de Investigaciones Cientificas; Vitruvio 8, Apartado 14.458; Madrid 6; SPAIN.

Sehir *Sehir Tijatrolari (City Theatre)*. Freq: 12; Began: 1930; Lang: Tur; Subj: Theatre.
■Sunusi Tekiner; Basin ve Halka Iliskiler Danismanligi; Harbiye-Istanbul; TURKEY.

Sembianza *Sembianza*. Freq: 6; Began: 1981; Lang: Ita; Subj: Theatre.
■Via Manzoni 14; 20121 Milan; ITALY.

SFN *Shakespeare on Film Newsletter*. Freq: 2; Began: 1977; Cov: Scan; Lang: Eng; Subj: Related.
■Dept. of English; Nassau Community College; Garden City, NY 11530; USA.

SFo *Szinháztechnikai Fórum*. Freq: 4; Began: 1977; Cov: Full; Lang: Hun; Subj: Theatre.
ISSN: 0139-1542
■OPAKFI; Anker köz. 1; 1061 Budapest VII; HUNGARY.

Sg *Shingeki*. Freq: 12; Began: 1954; Lang: Jap; Subj: Theatre.
■Hakusui-sha, Chiyoda-ku; 3-24 Kanda-Ogawamachi; 101 Tokyo; JAPAN.

SGIP *Sovetskoe Gosudarstvo i Pravo*. Freq: 12; Began: 1927; Cov: Scan; Lang: Rus; Subj: Related.
ISSN: 0038-5204
■Akad. Nauk S.S.S.R.; Inst. Gosudarstva i Prava; Izdatel'stvo Nauka; Podsosenskii Per., 21; Moscow K-62; Russian S.F.S.R.; U.S.S.R.

SGT *Schriften der Gesellschaft für Theatergeschichte*. Lang: Ger; Subj: Theatre.
■Berlin; WEST GERMANY.

SGTJ *Schweizerische Gesellschaft für Theaterkultur Jahrbücher*. Freq: IRR; Began: 1928; Ceased: 1982; Lang: Ger; Subj: Theatre.
■Swiss Association for Theatre Research, c/o Lydis Benz-Burger; Herenholzweg 33; 8906 Bonstetten; SWITZERLAND.

SGTS *Schweizerische Gesellschaft für Theaterkultur Schriften*. Freq: IRR; Began: 1928; Ceased: 1982; Lang: Ger; Subj: Theatre.
■Swiss Association for Theatre Research, c/o Lydia Benz-Burger; Herenholzweg 33; 8906 Bonstetten; SWITZERLAND.

Shahaab *Shahaab*. Lang: Ara; Subj: Theatre.
■Hayassat Building; Cooper Road; Rawlpindi; PAKISTAN.

ShakS *Shakespeare Studies*. Freq: 1; Lang: Eng; Subj: Theatre.
■New York, NY; USA.

ShakSN *Shakespeare Studies*. Lang: Eng; Subj: Theatre.
■Nashville, TN; USA.

Shavian *Shavian*. Freq: 1; Began: 1946; Lang: Eng; Subj: Theatre. ISSN: 0037-3346
■High Orchard Press, High Orchard; 125 Markyate Rd.; RM8 2LB Dgenham, Essex; UK.

ShawR *Shaw*: The Annual of Bernard Shaw Studies. Formerly: *Shaw Review (ISSN: 0037-3354)*. Freq: 1; Began: 1981; Cov: Scan; Lang: Eng; Subj: Theatre. ISSN: 0741-5842
■Pennsylvania State Univ. Press; S234 Burrowes Bldg South; University Park, PA 16802; USA.

ShN *Shakespeare Newsletter*. Freq: 4; Began: 1951; Lang: Eng; Subj: Theatre.
ISSN: 0037-3214
■Louis Marder, Ed. & Pub.; 1217 Ashland Ave.; Evanston, IL 60202; USA.

Show *Show*. Lang: Eng; Subj: Theatre.
■9/2 Nazimabad; Karachi; PAKISTAN.

ShS *Shakespeare Survey*. Freq: 1; Began: 1948; Cov: Full; Lang: Eng; Subj: Theatre. ISSN: 0080-9152
■Cambridge University Press, The Edinburgh Building; Shaftesbury Road; CB2 2RU Cambridge; UK.

Silex *Silex*. Lang: Fre; Subj: Theatre.
■BP 554 RP; 38013 Grenoble; FRANCE.

Sin *Sightline*: The Journal of Theatre Technology and Design. Freq: 2; Began: 1974; Cov: Full; Lang: Eng; Subj: Theatre.
ISSN: 0265-9808
■Assoc. of British Theatre Technicians; 4 Gt. Pulteney Street; W1R 3DF London; UK.

Sipario *Sipario*. Freq: 12; Began: 1946; Lang: Ita; Subj: Theatre.
■Sipario Editrice S.R.L.; Via Flaminia 167; 00196 Rome; ITALY.

Sis *Sightlines*. Freq: 4; Began: 1967; Cov: Scan; Lang: Eng; Subj: Related.
ISSN: 0037-4830
■Educ. Film Library Assoc.,Inc.; 45 John Street, Suite 301; New York, NY 10038; USA.

SiSo *Sight and Sound*. Freq: 4; Began: 1932; Cov: Scan; Lang: Eng; Subj: Related.
ISSN: 0037-4806
■British Film Institute; 127 Charing Cross Rd.; WC2H 0EA London; UK.

SjV *Sirp ja Vasar*. Freq: 52; Began: 1940; Lang: Est; Subj: Theatre.
■Postkast 388, Pikk t. 40; 200 001 Talin, Estonian SSR; USSR.

SJW *Shakespeare Jahrbuch*. Freq: 1; Began: 1865; Cov: Scan; Lang: Ger; Subj: Theatre. ISSN: 0080-9128
■Deutsche Shakespeare Gesellschaft, Hermann Bohlaus Nachfolger; Meyerstrasse 50a; 53 Weimar; EAST GERMANY.

Skript *Skript*. Freq: 10; Lang: Dut; Subj: Theatre.
■N.C.A.; Postbus 64; 3600 AB Maarssen; NETHERLANDS.

SM *Spectacles Magazine*. Freq: 12; Lang: Fre; Subj: Theatre.
■42 Blvd. du Temple; 75011 Paris; FRANCE.

Smena *Smena*. Freq: 12; Began: 1924; Cov: Scan; Lang: Rus; Subj: Related.
ISSN: 0131-6656
■Moscow; USSR.

SMR *SourceMonthly*: The Resource for Mimes, Clowns, Jugglers, and Puppeteers. Freq: 12; Cov: Scan; Lang: Eng; Subj: Theatre.
■Mimesource Inc.; 125 Sherman Str.; Brooklyn, NY 11218; USA.

SNJPA *Sangeet Natak*: Journal of the Performing Arts. Freq: 4; Began: 1965; Cov: Scan; Lang: Eng; Subj: Theatre.
ISSN: 0036-4339
■Sangeet Natak Akademi, Rabindra Bhavan; Ferozeshah Rd.; 110001 New Delhi; INDIA.

SobCh *Sobcota Chelovneta*. Lang: Geo; Subj: Theatre.
■Tbilisi, Georg. SSR; USSR.

Sobesednik *Sobesednik*. Freq: 12; Began: 1949; Cov: Scan; Lang: Rus; Subj: Related.
ISSN: 0202-3180
■Moscow; USSE.

SObzor *Scenograficky Obzor*. Freq: 6; Lang: Cze; Subj: Theatre.
■Vinohradska 2; Prague 1; CZECHO-SLOVAKIA.

SocH *Social History*. Freq: 3; Began: 1976; Cov: Scan; Lang: Eng; Subj: Related.
ISSN: 0307-1022
■Methuen and Co. Ltd.; 11 New Fetter Lane; EC4P 4EE London; UK.

SoM *Speaking of Mime*. Freq: IRR; Began: 1976; Lang: Eng; Subj: Theatre.
■Canadian Mime Council; Niagara, ON L0S 1J0; CANADA.

Somo *Somogy*. Freq: 6; Began: 1970; Cov: Scan; Lang: Hun; Subj: Related.
■Május 1. u. 10; 7400 Kaposvár; HUNGARY.

SON *Scottish Opera News*. Freq: 12; Lang: Eng; Subj: Theatre. ISSN: 0309-7323
■Scottish Opera Club; Elmbank Crescent; G2 4PT Glasgow; UK.

SoQ *Southern Quarterly, The*: A Journal of the Arts in the South. Freq: 4; Began: 1962; Lang: Eng; Subj: Related.
ISSN: 0038-4496
■PO Box 5078 Southern Station; Hattiesburg, MS 39401; USA.

SORev *Sean O'Casey Review, The*. Freq: 2; Began: 1974; Lang: Eng; Subj: Theatre.
ISSN: 0365-2245
■O'Casey Studies; PO Box 333; Holbrook, NY 11741; USA.

SoSaw *Southern Sawdust*. Freq: 4; Began: 1954; Lang: Eng; Subj: Theatre.
ISSN: 0038-4542
■L. Wilson Poarch Jr.; 2965 Freeman Avenue; Sarasota, FL 33580; USA.

SoTh *Southern Theatre*. Began: 1960; Cov: Scan; Lang: Eng; Subj: Theatre.
■Greensboro, NC; USA.

SOUTHERLY *Southerly: A Review of Australian Literature*. Freq: 4; Began: 1939; Cov: Scan; Lang: Eng; Subj: Related. ISSN: 0038-3732
■Dept. of English; Univ. of Sydney; Sydney N.S.W. 2006; AUSTRALIA.

SovAr *Sovetskie Arkhivy*. Freq: 6; Began: 1966; Cov: Scan; Lang: Rus; Subj: Related.
ISSN: 0038-5166
■Glavnoe Arkhivnoe Upravlenie; Pirogovskaya 17; Moscow G-435; Russian S.F.S.R.; U.S.S.R.

SovBal *Sovèckij Balet*. Cov: Scan; Lang: Rus; Subj: Theatre.
■Moscow; USSR.

SovD *Sovremènnaja Dramaturgija*. Freq: 4; Began: 1982; Cov: Scan; Lang: Rus; Subj: Theatre. ISSN: 6207-7698
■Moscow; USSR.

SovEC *Sovèckaja Estrada i Cirk*. Freq: 12; Cov: Scan; Lang: Rus; Subj: Theatre.
■Moscow; USSR.

SovEt *Sovèckaja Ethnografia*. Freq: 6; Began: 1926; Cov: Scan; Lang: Rus; Subj: Related. ISSN: 0038-5050
■Ulica D. Uljanova 19; B 36 Moscow; USSR.

SovKult *Sovèckaja Kultura*. Cov: Scan; Lang: Rus; Subj: Related.
■Novoslobodskaja ul. 73; K 55 Moscow; USSR.

SovMuzyka *Sovèckaja Muzyka*: (Soviet Music). Freq: 12; Began: 1933; Cov: Scan; Lang: Rus; Subj: Related. ISSN: 0131-6818
■Moscow; USSR.

SovSlav *Sovèckojè Slavjanovèdènjè*: (Soviet Slavonic Studies). Freq: 6; Began: 1965; Cov: Scan; Lang: Rus; Subj: Related.
ISSN: 0584-5394
■Izdatel'stvo Nauka; Podsosenskii Per. 21; K 62 Moscow; USSR.

SovT *Sovèckij Teat'r/Soviet Theatre*. Freq: 4; Began: 1976; Cov: Scan; Lang: Rus/Ger/Eng/Fre/Spa; Subj: Theatre.
■Copyright Agency of the USSR; 6a Bolshaya Bronnaya St.; K 104 Moscow 103670; USSR.

Spa *Shilpakala*. Lang: Ben; Subj: Related.
■Dacca; BANGLADESH.

SPC *Studies in Popular Culture*. Freq: 2; Began: 1977; Lang: Eng; Subj: Related.
■Popular Culture Association in the South, Florida State Univ., English Dp.; Tallahassee, FL 32306; USA.

Speak *Speak*. Began: 1977; Lang: Eng; Subj: Theatre.
■PO Box 126, Newlands; 7725 Cape Town; SOUTH AFRICA.

Spettacolo *Spettacolo, Lo*. Freq: 4; Began: 1951; Lang: Ita; Subj: Theatre.
ISSN: 0038-738X
■S.I.A.E.; Viale della Letteratura 30; 00100 Rome; ITALY.

Spirale *Spirale: Art, letters, spectacles, sciences humaines*. Freq: 12; Began: 1979; Lang: Fre; Subj: Theatre. ISSN: 0225-9004
■C.P. 98, Succ. E; Montreal, PQ; CANADA.

SpIt *Spettacolo in Italia, Lo*. Freq: 1; Began: 1936; Lang: Ita; Subj: Theatre.
■S.I.A.E.; Viale della Letteratura 30; 00100 Rome; ITALY.

Spl *Spielplan, Der*. Freq: 12; Began: 1954; Lang: Ger; Subj: Theatre.
ISSN: 0038-7517
■P.-A. Schmueking; Kastanienallee 2a; 3300 Braunschweig; WEST GERMANY.

SpViag *Spettacolo Viaggiante*. Began: 1948; Lang: Ita; Subj: Theatre.
■Assoc. Naz. Eserc. Spet. Viaggianti; Via di Villa Patrizi 10; 00161 Rome; ITALY.

SQ *Shakespeare Quarterly*. Freq: 4; Began: 1950; Cov: Scan; Lang: Eng; Subj: Related. ISSN: 0037-3222
■Folger Shakespeare Library; 201 E. Capitol St. S.E.; Washington, DC 20003; USA.

SSSS *Szene Schweiz/Scène Suisse/Scena Svizzera*. Freq: 1; Began: 1973; Cov: Scan; Lang: Ger/Fre/Ita; Subj: Theatre.
■Theaterkultur Verlag; Herenholzweg 33; CH 8906 Bonstetten; SWITZERLAND.

SSTJ *Secondary School Theater Journal*. Freq: 3; Began: 1962; Lang: Eng; Subj: Theatre.
■American Theatre Association, Secondary School Theatre Assoc.; 1010 Wisconsin Ave., N.W., Suite 630; Washington, DC 20007; USA.

Staff *Staffrider*. Freq: 4; Began: 1978; Lang: Eng; Subj: Related.
■Ravan Press Ltd.; Box 31134; 2017 Braamfontein; SOUTH AFRICA.

StageZ *Stage*. Freq: IRR; Began: 1956; Lang: Eng; Subj: Theatre.
■Lusaka Theatre Club Ltd; Box 30615; Lusaka; ZAMBIA.

Standpunte *Standpunte*. Freq: 6; Began: 1945; Cov: Scan; Lang: Afr; Subj: Related.
ISSN: 0038-9730
■Tafelberg Publishers; c/o J.C. Kannemeyer, Ed.; P.O. Box 91073; Auckland Park 2006; SOUTH AFRICA.

Sterijino *Sterijino Pozorje*: Informativno Glasilo. Freq: IRR; Began: 1982; Lang: Ser; Subj: Theatre.
■Sterijino Pozorje; Zmaj Jovina 22; Novi Sad; YUGOSLAVIA.

Stikord *Stikord*. Freq: 4; Began: 1981; Lang: Dan; Subj: Theatre. ISSN: 0107-6582
■Foreningen Hidovre Teater; Hidovre Strandvej 70A; 2650 Hidovre; DENMARK.

STILB *STILB*. Freq: 5; Began: 1981; Lang: Ita; Subj: Theatre.
■Via della Fosse di Castello 6; 00193 Rome; ITALY.

STN *Scottish Theater News*. Freq: 12; Began: 1981; Ceased: 1986; Cov: Scan; Lang: Eng; Subj: Theatre.
ISSN: 0261-4057
■Scottish Society of Playwrights; 346 Sauchiehall St.; G2 3JD Glasgow; UK.

StPh *Studies in Philology*. Freq: 3; Began: 1906; Cov: Scan; Lang: Eng; Subj: Related. ISSN: 0039-3738
■University of North Carolina Press; Box 2288; Chapel Hill, NC 27514; USA.

Strind *Strindbergiana*: Meddelanden från Strindbergssällskapet. Formerly: *Meddelanden från Strindbergssällskapet*. Freq: 1; Began: 1985; Cov: Full; Lang: Swe; Subj: Theatre.

■Strindbergssällskapet, c/o C. R. Smedmark; Drottninggatan 85; 111 60 Stockholm; SWEDEN.

STT *Sceničeskaja Technika i Technologija*. Freq: 6; Began: 1963; Cov: Full; Lang: Rus; Subj: Theatre. ISSN: 0131-9248 ■Serebriančeskij Per. 2/5; 109028 Moscow; USSR.

StudiaP *Studia i Materialy do Dziejow Teatru Polskiego*. Formerly: *Studia i Materialy z Dziejow Teatru Polskiego*. Freq: IRR; Began: 1957; Lang: Pol; Subj: Theatre. ISSN: 0208-404X ■Polish Academy of Sciences; Rynek 9; Wroclaw; POLAND.

StudiiR *Studii si Cercetari de Istoria Artel*: Seria Teatru-Muzica-Cinematografie. Freq: 1; Began: 1954; Lang: Rom; Subj: Theatre. ISSN: 0039-3991 ■Academia Rep. Soc. Romania; Calea Victoriei 125; 79717 Bucharest; ROMANIA.

StudM *Studenčeskij Meridian*. Freq: 12; Began: 1924; Cov: Scan; Lang: Rus; Subj: Related. ISSN: 0321-3803 ■Moscow; USSR.

STYol *STYolainen*. Freq: 6; Began: 1975; Lang: Fin; Subj: Theatre. ■Suomen Teatterityontekijain, Yhteisjarjesto; Maneesikatu 4c; 00170 Helsinki 17; FINLAND.

SuAS *Stratford-upon-Avon Studies*. Freq: IRR; Began: 1961; Lang: Eng; Subj: Theatre. ■Edward Arnold Ltd; 41 Bedford Square; WC1B 3DQ London; UK.

SuF *Sinn und Form: Beiträge zur Literatur*. Freq: 6; Began: 1949; Cov: Scan; Lang: Ger; Subj: Related. ISSN: 0037-5756 ■Verlag Rütten & Loening; Französische Str. 32; 1080 Berlin; EAST GERMANY.

Suffloren *Suffloren*. Lang: Dan; Subj: Theatre. ■Medlemsblad for Dansk Dukketeaterforening; Vestergrade 3; 1456 Copenhagen; DENMARK.

SuidAfr *Suid-Afrikaan, Die*. Began: 1985; Cov: Scan; Lang: Afr; Subj: Related. ■Die Suid-Afrikaan; P.O. Box 7010; 7610 Dalsig Stellembosch; SOUTH AFRICA.

SWR *Southwest Review*. Freq: 4; Began: 1924; Lang: Eng; Subj: Related. ISSN: 0038-4712 ■Southern Methodist University; Dallas, TX 75275; USA.

SwTS *Swedish Theater/Théâtre Suédois*. Lang: Eng/Fre; Subj: Theatre. ■Stockholm; SWEDEN.

Sz *Szinház*: (Theatre). Freq: 12; Began: 1968; Cov: Full; Lang: Hun; Subj: Theatre. ISSN: 0039-8136 ■Lapkiado Vallalat; Báthori u.10; 1054 Budapest V; HUNGARY.

Szene *Szene*. Lang: Ger; Subj: Theatre. ■UMLOsterreichischer Bundestheaterverband; Goethegasse 1; A 1010 Vienna; AUSTRIA.

SzeneAT *Szene: Fachzeitschrift der DDR Amateur-theater, -kabarett, -puppenspiel und -pantomime*. Freq: 4; Began: 1966; Cov: Scan; Lang: Ger; Subj: Theatre. ISSN: 0039-811X

■Zentralhaus für Kulturarbeit, Dittrichring 4; Postfach 1051; 7010 Leipzig; EAST GERMANY.

SzSz *Szinháztudomanyi Szemle*. Freq: 3; Began: 1977; Cov: Full; Lang: Hun; Subj: Theatre. ■Hungarian Theatre Institute; Krisztina Krt. 57; 1016 Budapest I; HUNGARY.

TA *Theatre Annual*. Freq: 1; Began: 1942; Cov: Full; Lang: Eng; Subj: Theatre. ISSN: 0082-3821 ■Dept. of Music, Theatre, and Dance, University of Akron; Akron, OH 44235; USA.

TAAm *Theater Across America*. Freq: 5; Began: 1975; Lang: Eng; Subj: Theatre. ■Theatre Sources Inc.; 104 North St. Mary; Dallas, TX 75214; USA.

Tablas *Tablas*: Cuban Theatre. Freq: 4; Began: 1982; Lang: Spa; Subj: Theatre. ■Unidad Presupuestada de Teatro y Danza, Ed. Cubanas Publc. y Promocion; Obispo No 461, Apartado 605; Habana; CUBA.

Tabs *Tabs*. Freq: 2; Began: 1937; Ceased: 1986; Cov: Scan; Lang: Eng; Subj: Theatre. ISSN: 0306-9389 ■Rank Strand Ltd., P.O. Box 51, Great West Road; Brentford; TW8 9HR Middlesex; UK.

TAD *Tijatro Arastirmalari Dergisi (Theatre Research Magazine)*. Freq: 1; Began: 1970; Lang: Tur/Eng/Fre; Subj: Theatre. ■Tijatro Arastirmalari Enstitusu, Ankara Universitesi D.T.C.; Fakultesi; Shhiye; Ankara; TURKEY.

Talent *Talent Management*. Freq: 12; Began: 1981; Lang: Eng; Subj: Related. ■T M Publishing; 1501 Broadway; New York, NY 10036; USA.

Tampereen *Tampereen Tyovaen Teatteri*. Lang: Fin; Subj: Theatre. ■Hallituskatu 19; 33003 Tampere 300; FINLAND.

Tanecni *Tanecni Listy*. Freq: 10; Began: 1963; Lang: Cze; Subj: Theatre. ISSN: 0039-937X ■Panorama; Halkova 1; 120 72 Prague 2; CZECHOSLOVAKIA.

TAnim *Théâtre et Animation*. Freq: 4; Began: 1976; Lang: Fre; Subj: Theatre. ■Fédération National du Théâtre et d'Animation; 12 rue de la Chaussée d'Antin; 75441 Paris Cedex 19; FRANCE.

TantI *Tantsovo Izkustvo*. Freq: 12; Began: 1954; Lang: Bul; Subj: Theatre. ■Izdatelstvo Nauka i Izkustvo; 6 Rouski Blvd; Sofia; BULGARIA.

TanzG *Tanz und Gymnastik*. Freq: 4; Began: 1944; Cov: Scan; Lang: Ger; Subj: Theatre. ■Schweizerischer Berufsverband für Tanz und Gymnastik; Riedbergstrasse 1; 4059 Basel; SWITZERLAND.

TArch *Teatro Archivio*. Formerly: *Bolletino del Museo Biblioteca dell'attore*. Freq: IRR; Began: 1979; Cov: Full; Lang: Ita; Subj: Theatre. ■Civico Museo Biblioteca dell'attore, Teatro Stabile di Genova; Viale IV Novembre 3; Genoa; ITALY.

TArsb *Teaterårsboken*. Freq: 1; Began: 1982; Cov: Scan; Lang: Swe; Subj: Theatre. ■Svenska Riksteatern; Råsundavägen 150; S 171 30 Solna; SWEDEN.

TAus *Theatre Australia*. Freq: 12; Began: 1976; Lang: Eng; Subj: Theatre. ■Theatre Publications Ltd.; 80 Elizabeth Street; NSW 2304 Mayfield; AUSTRALIA.

Tbuch *Theaterbuch*. Freq: 1; Lang: Ger; Subj: Theatre. ■Munich; WEST GERMANY.

TCB *Teatro Clásico: Boletin*. Freq: 1; Lang: Spa; Subj: Theatre. ■Teatro Clásico de Mexico; Apartado 61-077; MEXICO.

TCGNWCP *TCG National Working Conference Proceedings*. Freq: IRR; Began: 1976; Lang: Eng; Subj: Theatre. ■Theatre Communications Group; 355 Lexington Ave; New York, NY 10017; USA.

TChicago *Theatre Chicago*. Freq: 12; Began: 1986; Lang: Eng; Subj: Theatre. ■22 W Monroe, Suite 801; 60603 Chicago;.

TCom *Theatre Communications*. Freq: 12; Began: 1979; Lang: Eng; Subj: Theatre. ISSN: 0275-5971 ■Theatre Communications Group Inc; 355 Lexington Avenue; New York, NY 10017; USA.

TCraft *Theatrecraft*. Freq: 12; Began: 1964; Lang: Eng; Subj: Theatre. ■G. Hilton, Victoria Drama League, First Floor; 256 Flindera Street; Melbourne, Victoria; AUSTRALIA.

TCUG *Theater Computer Users Group Notes*. Began: 1978; Lang: Eng; Subj: Theatre. ■Theatre Sources Inc.; 104 N Sait Mary; Dallas, TX 76214; USA.

TD&T *Theatre Design and Technology*. Freq: 4; Began: 1965; Cov: Full; Lang: Eng; Subj: Theatre. ISSN: 0040-5477 ■US Inst. for Theatre Technology; 330 W. 42nd St. Suite 1702; New York, NY 10036; USA.

TDDR *Theaterarbeit in der DDR*. Freq: 3; Began: 1979; Lang: Ger; Subj: Theatre. ■Verband der Theaterschaffended der DDR; Hermann-Matern-Strasse 18; 1040 Berlin; EAST GERMANY.

TDR *Drama Review, The*. Freq: 4; Began: 1955; Cov: Full; Lang: Eng; Subj: Theatre. ISSN: 0012-5962 ■MIT Press; 28 Carleton St.; Cambridge, MA 02142; USA.

Teat *Teatteri*. Freq: 12; Began: 1945; Cov: Full; Lang: Fin; Subj: Theatre. ■Kustannus Oy Teatteri; Vuorikatu 6 A 8; 00100 Helsinki 10; FINLAND.

TeaterD *Teater i Danmark*: Theatre in Denmark. Freq: 1; Began: 1980; Lang: Dan; Subj: Theatre. ISSN: 0106-7672 ■Bibliotekscentralen; Telegrafvej 5; DK 2750 Ballerup; DENMARK.

Teaterf *Teaterforum*. Freq: 6; Began: 1968; Cov: Full; Lang: Swe; Subj: Theatre. ■Swedish Society for Amateur Theatres; Von Rosens Väg 1A; 77300 Fagersta; SWEDEN.

Teatern *Teatern*. Freq: 4; Began: 1934; Lang: Swe; Subj: Theatre. ISSN: 0040-0750 ■Riksteatern; Rasundavagen 150; S 171 30 Solna; SWEDEN.

TeatL *Teatr Lalek*. Lang: Pol; Subj: Theatre. ■Warsaw; POLAND.

TeatM *Teatraluri Moambe*. Lang: Geo; Subj: Theatre. ■Tbilisi, Georgian S; USSR.

Teatoro *Teatoro*. Freq: 12; Began: 1944; Lang: Jap; Subj: Theatre. ■c/o Hagiwara Building, 2-3-1 Sarugaku-cho; Chiyoda-ku; 101 Tokyo; JAPAN.

Teatras *Teatras*. Lang: Lit; Subj: Theatre. ■Vilnius, Lithuanian, SSR; USSR.

TeatrC *Teatro Contemporaneo*. Freq: 3; Began: 1982; Cov: Full; Lang: Ita; Subj: Theatre. ■Via Trionfale 8406; 00135 Rome; ITALY.

TeatrE *Teatro en España*. Lang: Spa; Subj: Theatre. ■Madrid; SPAIN.

TeatrM *Teat'r*. žurnal dramaturgii i teatra. Freq: 12; Began: 1937; Cov: Full; Lang: Rus; Subj: Theatre. ISSN: 0040-0777 ■Izdatel'stvo Iskusstvo; Tsvetnoi bulvar 25; Moscow K-51; USSR.

Teatron *Teatron*. Began: 1962; Lang: Heb; Subj: Theatre. ■Municipal Theatre; 20 Pevsner Street; Haifa; ISRAEL.

TeatroS *Teatro e Storia*. Began: 1984; Cov: Scan; Lang: Ita; Subj: Theatre. ■Rome; ITALY.

TeatroSM *TeatroSM*. Began: 1980; Lang: Spa; Subj: Theatre. ■Teatro Municipal General San Martin; Ave. Corrientes 1530, 50 piso; 1042 Buenos Aires; ARGENTINA.

Teatrul *Teatrul*. Freq: 12; Began: 1956; Lang: Rom; Subj: Theatre. ISSN: 0040-0815 ■Consiliul Culturii si Educatiei Socialiste; Calea Victoriei 174; Bucharest; ROMANIA.

TeatrW *Teatr*. Freq: 26; Began: 1946; Cov: Scan; Lang: Pol; Subj: Theatre. ISSN: 0040-0769 ■Wydawnictwa Artystyczno-Graficzne, RSW Prasa-Ksiazka-Ruch; Ul. Smolna 10; Warsaw; POLAND.

TeaturS *Teatur*. Freq: 12; Began: 1946; Cov: Full; Lang: Bul; Subj: Theatre. ISSN: 0204-6253 ■Komitet za Izkustvo i Kultura; 39 Dondukov Blvd.; Sofia; BULGARIA.

TeatY *Teatron*: Časopis za pozirišnu istoriju i teatrologiju. Began: 1974; Lang: Ser; Subj: Theatre. ■Muzej Pozorišne umetnosti SR Srbije; Gospodar Jevremova 19; 11000 Belgrade; YUGOSLAVIA.

TeatZ *Teatralnaja Žizn*. Freq: 24; Began: 1958; Cov: Scan; Lang: Rus; Subj: Theatre. ISSN: 0040-0785 ■Vserossij. Teatr. Obščestvo; Moscow; USSR.

TeC *Teatro e Cinema*. Freq: 4; Began: 1968; Lang: Ita; Subj: Theatre. ISSN: 0040-0807 ■Silva Editore; Viale Salita Salvatore 1; 28 16128 Genoa; ITALY.

TechB *Technical Briefs*. Freq: 3; Began: 1973; Cov: Full; Lang: Eng; Subj: Theatre. ■TD&P Dept., Yale School of Drama; 222 York St.; New Haven, CT 06520; USA.

TEJ *Théâtre Enfance et Jeunesse*. Freq: 2; Began: 1963; Lang: Fre/Eng; Subj: Theatre. ■Assoc. du Théâtre pour l'Enfance, et la Jeunesse; 98 Blvd. Kellermann; 75013 Paris; FRANCE.

TEP *Théâtre de l'Est Parisien*: TEP Actualité. Lang: Fre; Subj: Theatre. ■Paris; FRANCE.

Textual *Textual*. Lang: Spa; Subj: Theatre. ■I.N.C.; Ancash; 390 Idma; PERU.

Textuel *Textuel*. Freq: 2; Cov: Scan; Lang: Fre; Subj: Theatre. ■Université de Paris VII; 2, place Jussieu; 75221 Paris CEDEX 05; FRANCE.

TF *Teaterforum*. Freq: 2; Began: 1980; Cov: Scan; Lang: Eng/Afr; Subj: Theatre. ■University of Potchefstroom, Departement Spraakler en Drama; Potchefstroom; SOUTH AFRICA.

TF&TV *Teater Film & TV*. Freq: 8; Began: 1974; Lang: Dan; Subj: Theatre. ■Faellesforbundet for Teater Film & TV; Ny Oestergade 12; DK 1101 Copenhagen; DENMARK.

TGDR *Theatre in the GDR*. Lang: Ger; Subj: Theatre. ■Berlin; EAST GERMANY.

TGlasnik *Teatarski Glasnik*: Spisanie na teatrite vo SR Makedonija. Freq: 2; Began: 1977; Lang: Slo; Subj: Theatre. ■Dramski Teatar Skopje;Šekspirova 15; 91000 Skopje; YUGOSLAVIA.

TGraz *Theater in Graz*. Freq: 4; Began: 1952; Lang: Ger; Subj: Theatre. ■Vereinigte Bühnen Graz; Burggasse 16; A 8010 Graz; AUSTRIA.

Th *Théâtre*. Formerly: *Théâtre du Trident*. Lang: Fre; Subj: Theatre. ■Théâtre du Trident, Edifice Palais Montcalm; 975 Place d'Youville; Quebec, PQ; CANADA.

THC *Theatre History in Canada/ Histoire du Théâtre*. Freq: 2; Began: 1980; Cov: Full; Lang: Eng/Fre; Subj: Theatre. ISSN: 0226-5761 ■Graduate Centre for the Study of Drama, University of Toronto; 214 College Street; Toronto, ON M5T 2Z9; CANADA.

ThCr *Theatre Crafts*. Freq: 9; Began: 1967; Cov: Full; Lang: Eng; Subj: Theatre. ISSN: 0040-5469 ■Theatre Crafts Associates; 135 Fifth Avenue; New York, NY 10010; USA.

ThE *Théâtre en Europe*. Freq: 4; Began: 1984; Cov: Scan; Lang: Fre; Subj: Theatre. ■Place Paul Claudel; 70056 Paris; FRANCE.

TheatreEx *Theatre: Ex*. Freq: 3; Began: 1985; Lang: Eng; Subj: Theatre. ■104 E. 4th Street; New York, NY 10003; USA.

TheatreS *Theatre Studies*. Freq: 1; Began: 1954; Cov: Full; Lang: Eng; Subj: Theatre. ISSN: 0362-0964 ■Ohio State Univ., Lawrence and Lee, Theatre Research Institute; 1430 Lincoln Tower, 1800 Cannon Drive; Columbus, OH 43210 1234; USA.

Theatro *Theatro*. Lang: Gre; Subj: Theatre. ■Kosta Nitsos; Christou Lada 5-7; Athens; GREECE.

Theatron *Theatron*: Rivista quindicinale di cultura, documentazione ed informazione teatrale. Freq: 26; Began: 1961; Lang: Ita/Eng/ Ger; Subj: Theatre. ISSN: 0040-5604 ■Centro Teatrale Intl. di Documentazione e Collaborazione tra Teatri di Ricerca e Univ.; Via Fabiola 1; 00152 Rome; ITALY.

Theatrum *Theatrum: A Theatre Journal*. Freq: 3; Began: 1985; Cov: Full; Lang: Eng; Subj: Theatre. ■Theatrum; P.O. Box 688, Station C; Toronto, ON M6J 3S1; CANADA.

Theoria *Theoria*: A Journal of Studies in the Arts, Humanities and Social Studies. Freq: 2; Began: 1947; Cov: Scan; Lang: Eng; Subj: Related. ISSN: 0040-5817 ■University of Natal Press; Box 375; Pietermaritzburg; SOUTH AFRICA.

Thespis *Thespis*. Lang: Gre; Subj: Theatre. ■Greek Centre of the ITI; Anthinou Gazi 9; Athens; GREECE.

THeute *Theater Heute*. Freq: 12; Began: 1960; Cov: Scan; Lang: Ger; Subj: Theatre. ISSN: 0040-5507 ■Orell Fuessli & Friedrich Verlag; Dietzingerstr. 3; CH 8036 Zurich; SWITZERLAND.

ThIr *Theatre Ireland*. Freq: 3; Began: 1982; Cov: Scan; Lang: Eng; Subj: Theatre. ISSN: 0263-6344 ■Theatre Ireland, Ltd; 172 Upper Newtownards Road; BT4 3ES Belfast; IRELAND.

ThM *Theater Magazine*. Freq: 3; Began: 1968; Cov: Full; Lang: Eng; Subj: Theatre. ISSN: 0160-0775 ■Yale University, School of Theater; Box 2046 Yale Station; New Haven, CT 06520; USA.

ThNe *Theatre News*. Freq: 6; Began: 1968; Ceased: 1985; Cov: Scan; Lang: Eng; Subj: Theatre. ISSN: 0563-4040 ■American Theatre Association; 1010 Wisconsin Ave., NW, Suite 620; Washington, DC 20007; USA.

ThPa *Theatre Papers*. Freq: 1; Began: 1977; Cov: Full; Lang: Eng; Subj: Theatre. ISSN: 0309-8036 ■Documentation Unit, Dartington College of Arts; Totnes; TQ9 6EJ Devon; UK.

ThPh *Theatrephile*. Freq: 4; Began: 1983; Ceased: 1985; Cov: Full; Lang: Eng; Subj: Theatre. ISSN: 0265-2609 ■D. Cheshire & S. McCarthy Eds. & Publ.; 5 Dryden Street, Covent Garden; WC2E 9NW London; UK.

ThPu   *Théâtre Public*. Freq: 6; Began: 1974; Cov: Scan; Lang: Fre; Subj: Theatre.   ISSN: 0335-2927 ▪Théâtre de Gennevilliers; 41, avenue des Gresillons; 92230 Gennevilliers; FRANCE.

ThR   *Theatre Research International*. Freq: 3; Began: 1958; Cov: Full; Lang: Eng; Subj: Theatre.   ISSN: 0307-8833 ▪Oxford University Press; Walton Street; OX2 6DP Oxford; UK.

ThS   *Theatre Survey*. Freq: 2; Began: 1960; Cov: Full; Lang: Eng; Subj: Theatre.   ISSN: 0040-5574 ▪ASTR; Ph.D. Program in Theatre; Graduate Center of CUNY; 33 W 42st.; NY. NY. 10036; USA.

THSt   *Theatre History Studies*. Freq: 1; Began: 1981; Cov: Full; Lang: Eng; Subj: Theatre.   ISSN: 0733-2033 ▪Dept. of Theatre Arts; Univ. of North Dakota; Grand Forks, ND 58202; USA.

ThSw   *Theatre Southwest*. Freq: 3; Began: 1974; Cov: Full; Lang: Eng; Subj: Theatre. ▪Oklahoma State University; 102 Seretean Center; Stillwater, OK 74078; USA.

ThToday   *Theatre Today*. Lang: Eng; Subj: Theatre. ▪Advanced Institute for Development, American Repertory Theatre; 245 West 52nd Street; New York, NY 10019; USA.

ThYear   *Theatre Year*. Freq: 1; Began: 1980; Ceased: 1983; Cov: Scan; Lang: Eng; Subj: Theatre.   ISSN: 0261-2348 ▪In (Parenthesis) Ltd.; 21 Wellington Street; WC2E 7DN London; UK.

TI   *Théâtre International*. Freq: 4; Began: 1981; Ceased: 1984; Lang: Eng/Fre; Subj: Theatre. ▪British Centre of the ITI; 31 Shelton Street; WC2H 9HT London; UK.

TID   *Themes in Drama*. Freq: 1; Began: 1979; Cov: Full; Lang: Eng; Subj: Theatre.   ISSN: 0263-676X ▪Westfield College, University of London; NW3 7ST London; UK.

Tijatro   *Tijatro*. Freq: 12; Began: 1970; Lang: Tur; Subj: Theatre. ▪PK 58; Besiktas-Istanbul; TURKEY.

TInsight   *Theatre Insight*: A Journal of Contemporary Performance Thought. Freq: 3; Began: 1988; Lang: Eng; Subj: Theatre. ▪Program in Theatre History and Criticism, Univ. of Texas; Winshop Building; Austin, TX 78712; USA.

Tisz   *Tiszatáj*. Freq: 12; Began: 1947; Cov: Scan; Lang: Hun; Subj: Theatre. ▪Csongrad Megyei Lapkidiado Vallalat; Tanácsköztársasag útja l0; 6720 Szeged; HUNGARY.

TJ   *Theatre Journal*. Formerly: *Educational Theatre Journal*. Freq: 4; Began: 1949; Cov: Full; Lang: Eng; Subj: Theatre.   ISSN: 0192-2282 ▪Univ./College Theatre Assoc., The Johns Hopkins Univ. Press; 701 West 40th St. Suite 275; Baltimore, MD 21211; USA.

TJV   *Teater Jaarboek voor Vlaanderen*. Lang: Dut; Subj: Theatre. ▪Antwerp; BELGIUM.

Tk   *Theaterwork*. Freq: 6; Began: 1980; Ceased: 1983; Cov: Full; Lang: Eng; Subj: Theatre.   ISSN: 0735-1895 ▪Theaterwork; 120 South Broad St.; Mankato, MN 56001; USA.

Tka   *Theatrika*. Freq: 52; Lang: Eng; Subj: Theatre. ▪Athens; GREECE.

TkR   *TamKang Review*: Comparative Studies Between Chinese & Foreign Literature. Freq: 4; Began: 1970; Lang: Eng; Subj: Related. ▪Tamkang University, Grad. Inst. of West. Langs & Lit.; Tamsui; Taipei Hsien 251; TAIWAN.

TMJ   *Theatre Movement Journal*. Lang: Eng; Subj: Theatre. ▪Ohio State University, Dept. of Theatre; 1849 Cannon Drive; Columbus, OH 43210; USA.

TMK   *Teater, Musika, Kyno*. Lang: Est; Subj: Theatre. ▪Talin, Estonian SSR; USSR.

TN   *Theatre Notebook*: Journal of the History and Technique of the British Theatre. Freq: 3; Began: 1946; Cov: Full; Lang: Eng; Subj: Theatre.   ISSN: 0040-5523 ▪The Society for Theatre Research; 77 Kinnerton Street; SW1X 8ED London; UK.

TNotes   *Theatre Notes*. Freq: 10; Began: 1970; Lang: Eng; Subj: Theatre. ▪US Centre of the ITI; 1860 Broadway, Suite 1510; New York, NY 10023; USA.

TNS   *Théâtre National de Strasbourg*: Actualité. Lang: Fre; Subj: Theatre. ▪Théâtre National; Strasbourg; FRANCE.

TOE   *Théâtre Ouvert/Ecritures*. Freq: 4; Began: 1978; Lang: Fre; Subj: Theatre.   ISSN: 0181-5393 ▪21 rue Cassette; 75006 Paris; FRANCE.

Toneel   *Toneel Teatraal*. Formerly: *Mickery Mouth and Toneel Teatraal*. Freq: 10; Began: 1879; Lang: Dut; Subj: Theatre.   ISSN: 0040-9170 ▪Nederlands Theaterinstituut; Herengracht 166-168; 1016 BP Amsterdam; NETHERLANDS.

Tournees   *Tournées de Spectacles*. Freq: 12; Began: 1975; Cov: Scan; Lang: Fre; Subj: Theatre.   ISSN: 0317-5979 ▪Conseil des Arts du Canada; Office des Tournées; Ottawa, ON; CANADA.

TP   *Theatre in Poland/Théâtre en Pologne*. Freq: 12; Began: 1958; Cov: Full; Lang: Eng/Fre; Subj: Theatre.   ISSN: 0040-5493 ▪ITI, Polish Center; Ul. Moliera 1; 00 072 Warsaw; POLAND.

TpaedB   *Theaterpaedagogische Bibliothek*. Freq: IRR; Began: 1983; Lang: Ger; Subj: Theatre. ▪Heinrichshofens Verlag; Liebigstr 16; 2940 Wilhelmshaven; WEST GERMANY.

TProf   *Théâtre Professionnel*. Lang: Fre; Subj: Theatre. ▪14 rue de la Promenade; Asnieres; FRANCE.

TQ   *Theatre Quarterly*: Since 1985 published as New Theatre Quarterly (NTQ). Freq: 4; Began: 1971; Ceased: 1981; Lang: Eng; Subj: Theatre.   ISSN: 0049-3600

▪TQ Publications, Ltd.; 44 Earlham Street; WC2 9LA London; UK.

TR   *Theater Rundschau*. Freq: 12; Began: 1955; Lang: Ger; Subj: Theatre.   ISSN: 0040-5442 ▪Bund der Theatergemeinden e.V. Bonn, Theater Rundschau Verlagsgesell.; Bonner Talweg 10; 5300 Bonn; WEST GERMANY.

Traces   *Traces*. Freq: 6; Lang: Fre; Subj: Theatre. ▪Comédie de Rennes; Théâtre de la Parcheminerie; 35100 Rennes; FRANCE.

Tramoya   *Tramoya*: Cuaderno de teatro. Freq: 4; Lang: Spa; Subj: Theatre. ▪Universidad Veracruzana; Clavijero 10; Xalapa; MEXICO.

Treteaux   *Tréteaux*. Freq: 2; Lang: Eng; Subj: Theatre.   ISSN: 0161-4479 ▪University of Maine at Orono Press; University of Maine; Farmington, ME 04938; USA.

Trujaman   *Trujaman*. Lang: Spa; Subj: Theatre. ▪Casilla de Correos 3234; Buenos Aires; ARGENTINA.

TSA   *Theatre SA*: Quarterly for South African Theater. Freq: 4; Began: 1968; Lang: Eng; Subj: Theatre. ▪PO Box 2153; Cape Town; SOUTH AFRICA.

TSO   *Teatro del Siglo de Oro: Ediciones Críticas*. Freq: 2; Began: 1982; Lang: Eng/Spa/Fre; Subj: Theatre.   ISSN: 7188-4400 ▪Edition Reichenberger; Pfannkuchstr. 4; D 3500 Kassel; WEST GERMANY.

TSOL   *Teatro del Siglo de Oro: Estudios de Literatura*. Freq: IRR; Began: 1984; Lang: Spa/Eng; Subj: Theatre.   ISSN: 7200-9300 ▪Edition Reichenberger; Pfannkuchstr. 4; D 3500 Kassel; WEST GERMANY.

TSt   *Teatervidenskabelige Studier*. Freq: 1; Began: 1974; Lang: Dan; Subj: Theatre. ▪Akademisk Forlag; St. Kannikestraede 8; 1169 Copenhagen; DENMARK.

TT   *Theatre Times*. Formerly: *OOBA Newsletter (OOBA Guidebook to Theatre)*. Freq: 6; Began: 1982; Cov: Scan; Lang: Eng; Subj: Theatre.   ISSN: 0732-300X ▪Alliance of Resident Theatres; 325 Spring Street, Room 315; New York, NY 10013; USA.

TTh   *Travail Théâtral*. Freq: 4; Began: 1970; Lang: Fre; Subj: Theatre.   ISSN: 0049-4534 ▪Editions l'Age d'Homme-la Cite; Case Postale 263; 1000 Lausanne 9; SWITZERLAND.

TTT   *Tenaz Talks Teatro*. Freq: 4; Began: 1977; Lang: Eng/Spa; Subj: Theatre. ▪University of California-La Jolla, Chicano Studies Program, D-009; La Jolla, CA 92093; USA.

TU   *Théâtre et université*. Lang: Fre; Subj: Theatre. ▪Centre Universitaire International, Form. & Recherche Dramatique; Nancy; FRANCE.

Tv   *Teatervetenskap*. Freq: 2; Began: 1968; Lang: Swe/Eng; Subj: Theatre. ▪Inst. for Teater & Filmvetenskap; Box 27026; S 102 Stockholm 27; SWEDEN.

TvL   *Tydskrif vir Letterkunde*. Freq: 4; Began: 1951; Cov: Scan; Lang: Eng & Afrikaans; Subj: Related. ISSN: 0041-476X
■Elize Botha; Posbus 1758; Pretoria; SOUTH AFRICA.

TVOR   *Tvorchestvo*. Freq: 12; Began: 1957; Cov: Scan; Lang: Rus; Subj: Related. ISSN: 0041-4565
■Izdatel'stvo Sovetskii Khudozhnik; Ul. Chernyakhovskogo; 4A; Moscow; U.S.S.R.

TvT   *Tijdschrift voor Theaterweten- schap*. Freq: 4; Lang: Dut; Subj: Theatre.
■Instituut voor Wetenschap, Nw.; Doelenstraat 16; 1012 CP Amsterdam; NETHERLANDS.

TvVV   *Tydskrif vir Volkskunde en Volkstaal*. Freq: 3; Began: 1944; Cov: Scan; Lang: Eng. & Afrikaans; Subj: Related. ISSN: 0049-4933
■Genootskap vir Afrikaanse Volkskunde; Box 4585; Johannesburg 2000; SOUTH AFRICA.

TWI   *Theaterwissenschaftlicher Infor- mationsdienst*. Lang: Ger; Subj: Theatre.
■Theaterhochschule 'Hans Otto'; Sec. für Theaterwissenschaftliche Dok.; Leipzig; EAST GERMANY.

TWNew   *Tennessee Williams Review*. For- merly: *Tennessee Williams Newsletter*. Freq: 2; Began: 1980; Ceased: 1982; Lang: Eng; Subj: Theatre. ISSN: 0276-993X
■University of Michigan, Department of Hu- manities; Ann Arbor, MI; USA.

TZ   *Theater der Zeit*. Freq: 12; Began: 1946; Cov: Full; Lang: Ger; Subj: Theatre. ISSN: 0040-5418
■Henschelverlag Kunst und Gesellschaft; Orienburger Strasse 67/68; 1040 Berlin; EAST GERMANY.

Tzs   *Theaterzeitschrift*: Beiträge zu Theater, Medien, Kulturpolitik. Cov: Scan; Lang: Ger; Subj: Theatre.
■Verein zur Erforschung theatraler Verkehrsformen; Grossbeerenstrasse 13A; D 1000 Berlin 61; WEST GERMANY.

UCrow   *Upstart Crow, The*. Freq: 1; Began: 1978; Lang: Eng; Subj: Theatre.
■P.O. Box 740; Martin, TN 38237; USA.

UDSalaam   *University of Dar es Salaam: The- atre Arts Department*: Annual Report. Freq: 1; Lang: Eng; Subj: Theatre.
■University of Dar es Salaam, Theatre Arts Department; Box 35091; Dar es Salaam; TANZANIA.

UES   *Unisa English Studies: Journal of the Department of English*. Freq: 2; Began: 1963; Cov: Scan; Lang: Eng & Afr; Subj: Related. ISSN: 0041-5359
■S.G. Kossick, Ed.; Dept. of English; Univ. of South Africa; P.O. Box 392; 0001 Pretoria; SOUTH AFRICA.

Ufa   *Ufahamu*: Journal of the African Activist Association. Freq: 3; Began: 1970; Cov: Scan; Lang: Eng; Subj: Related. ISSN: 0041-5715
■University of California, African Studies Cen- ter; 405 Hilgard Ave.; Los Angeles, CA 90024; USA.

UjIras   *Uj Irás*. Freq: 12; Began: 1961; Cov: Scan; Lang: Hun; Subj: Related. ISSN: 0041-5952

■Lapkiado Vallalat; Lenin krt. 9-11; 1073 Budapest VII; HUNGARY.

UMurcia   *Universidad de Murcia Catedra de Teatro Cuadernos*. Freq: IRR; Began: 1978; Lang: Spa; Subj: Theatre.
■Universidad de Murcia, Catedra de Teatro; Santo Cristo 1; Murcia; SPAIN.

UNIMA   *UNIMA France*. Freq: 4; Began: 1962; Lang: Fre; Subj: Theatre.
■Union Internationale de la Marionette, Sec- tion Française; 7 Rue du Helder; 75009 Paris; FRANCE.

Usbu   *Usbu Al-Masrah*. Lang: Ara; Subj: Theatre.
■Ministère des Affaires Culturelles; La Kas- bah; Tunis; TUNISIA.

USITT   *USITT Newsletter*. Freq: 4; Began: 1965; Cov: Scan; Lang: Eng; Subj: Theatre. ISSN: 0565-6311
■US Inst. for Theatre Technology; 330 W. 42nd St., Suite 1702; New York, NY 10036; USA.

UTarra   *Universitas Tarraconensis*. Freq: 1; Cov: Scan; Lang: Spa; Subj: Related.
■División de Filologia; Placa Imperial Tarraco, 1; 43005 Tarragona; SPAIN.

UTeatr   *Ukrainskij Teat'r*. Lang: Ukr; Subj: Related.
■Kiev, Ukrainian SSR; USSR.

Uusi   *Uusi-Laulu*. Lang: Fin; Subj: Theatre.
■Uusi-Laulu-yhdistys; Eerikinkatu 14 A 9; 00100 Helsinki 10; FINLAND.

UZ   *Unterhaltungskunst*: Zeitschrift für Bühne, Podium und Manege. Freq: 12; Began: 1969; Lang: Ger; Subj: Related. ISSN: 0042-0565
■Henschelverlag Kunst und, Gesellschaft; Oranienburger Strasse 67/68; 104 Berlin; EAST GERMANY.

Valivero   *Valiverho*. Freq: 3; Lang: Fin; Subj: Theatre.
■Helsinki; FINLAND.

Valo   *Valóság*. Freq: 12; Began: 1964; Cov: Scan; Lang: Hun; Subj: Related.
■Kirlapkiado; Lenin krt. 5; 1073 Budapest VII; HUNGARY.

VantageP   *Vantage Point*: Issues in American Arts. Formerly: *American Arts*. Freq: 6; Began: 1984; Cov: Scan; Lang: Eng; Subj: Related. ISSN: 0194-1305
■American Council for the Arts; 570 Seventh Ave; New York, NY 10018; USA.

VFil   *Voprosy filosofii*. Freq: 12; Began: 1947; Lang: Eng/Rus; Subj: Related. ISSN: 0042-8744
■Akademiya Nauk S.S.S.R., Institut Filosofii; Izdatel'stvo Pravda, Ul. Pravdy, 24; Moscow 125047; USSR.

Vig   *Vigília*. Freq: 12; Began: 1935; Cov: Scan; Lang: Hun; Subj: Related.
■Actio Catholica; Kossuth L. u. 1; 1053 Buda- pest V; HUNGARY.

Vilag   *Világszinház*: A magyar szinházi intézet havi folyóirata. Formerly: *Dramatur- gical News 1965-1982*. Freq: 12; Began: 1982; Cov: Full; Lang: Hun; Subj: Theatre. ISSN: 0231-4541

■Hungarian Theatre Institute; Krisztina krt. 57; 1016 Budapest I; HUNGARY.

VLit   *Voprosy Literaty*. Freq: 12; Began: 1957; Cov: Scan; Lang: Rus; Subj: Related. ISSN: 0042-8795
■Sojuz Pisatelej SSSR, Inst. Mirovoj Litera- tury; Bolšoj Gnezdnikovskij per 10; 103009 Moscow; USSR.

VMGUf   *Vestnik MGU*: Series 9-Filologia. Freq: 6; Began: 1946; Cov: Scan; Lang: Rus; Subj: Related. ISSN: 0579-9449
■Moscow State University; Ul. Gercena 5/7; 103009 Moscow; USSR.

Voprosy   *Voprosy Teatra*. Freq: 1; Lang: Rus; Subj: Theatre.
■VTO (All-Russia Theatre Society); Kiselny Tupik 1; 103045 Moscow I-45; USSR.

VS   *Victorian Studies*: A Journal of the Humanities, Arts and Sciences. Freq: 4; Began: 1957; Cov: Scan; Lang: Eng; Subj: Related. ISSN: 0042-5222
■Program for Victorian Studies, Indiana Uni- versity; Ballantine Hall; Bloomington, IN 47405; USA.

VSov   *V sovéckom teatré*. Cov: Scan; Lang: Rus; Subj: Theatre.
■Moscow; USSR.

Vyakat   *Vyakat*. Freq: 4; Lang: Eng; Subj: Theatre.
■A-28 Nizamuddin West; New Delhi; INDIA.

Waiguo   *Waiguo Xiju*. Freq: 4; Began: 1962; Lang: Chi; Subj: Theatre.
■52 Dongai Ba tiao; Beijing; CHINA.

WB   *Weimarer Beiträge*: Zeitschrift für Literaturwissenschaft, Aesthetik und Kultur. Freq: 12; Began: 1955; Cov: Scan; Lang: Ger; Subj: Related. ISSN: 0043-2199
■Aufbau-Verlag Berlin und Weimar; Fran- zösische Strasse 32; 1080 Berlin; EAST GERMANY.

WCP   *West Coast Plays*. Freq: 2; Began: 1977; Lang: Eng; Subj: Theatre. ISSN: 0147-4502
■California Theatre Council, Eastern Columbia Building; 849 S. Broadway, Suite 621; Los Angeles, CA 90014; USA.

WFTM   *Wiener Forschungen zur Theater und Medienwissenschaft*. Freq: IRR; Began: 1972; Lang: Ger; Subj: Theatre.
■Universitäts-Verlagsbuchhandlung Gmb; Ser- vitengasse 5; A1092 Vienna; AUSTRIA.

WGTJ   *Wiener Gesellschaft für Theater- forschung Jahrbuch*. Freq: IRR; Began: 1944; Ceased: 1984; Lang: Ger; Subj: Theatre.
■Verband der Wissenshaftlichen, Gesell- schaften Oesterreichs; Lindengasse 37; A1070 Vienna; AUSTRIA.

WIAL   *Washington International Arts Letter*. Freq: 10; Began: 1962; Lang: Eng; Subj: Related. ISSN: 0043-0609
■Box 9005; Washington, DC 20003; USA.

WijP   *WIJ, Poppenspelers*. Lang: Dut; Subj: Theatre.
■M. Ruth van der Steenhoven; Westeinde 252; 3351 AS Papendrecht; NETHERLANDS.

WJBS   *Western Journal of Black Studies*. Freq: 4; Began: 1977; Cov: Scan; Lang: Eng; Subj: Related. ISSN: 0197-4327

■Washington State Univ. Press; Pullman, WA 99164 5910; USA.

WLT *World Literature Today*: a literary quarterly of the University of Oklahoma. Formerly: *Books Abroad*. Freq: 4; Began: 1927; Lang: Eng; Subj: Related.
■University of Oklahoma Press; 110 Monnet Hall; Norman, OK 73019; USA.

WomenR *Women's Review*. Freq: 12; Began: 1985; Ceased: 1986; Cov: Scan; Lang: Eng; Subj: Related.
ISSN: 0267-5080
■1-4 Christina St.; EC2A 4PA London; UK.

WOpera *World of Opera*. Freq: 6; Lang: Eng; Subj: Theatre. ISSN: 0160-8673
■Marcel Dekker Inc.; 270 Madison Avenue; New York, NY 10016; USA.

WPerf *Women & Performance*: A Journal of Feminist Theory. Freq: 2; Began: 1983; Cov: Scan; Lang: Eng; Subj: Theatre.
ISSN: 0740-770X
■NYU Tisch School of the Arts, Dept. of Performance Studies; 51 W 4th St., 300 South Bldg.; New York, NY 10012; USA.

WPList *World Premieres Listing*. Began: 1981; Lang: Eng; Subj: Theatre.
■Hungarian Centre of the ITI; Hevesi Sandor Ter. 2; 1077 Budapest VII; HUNGARY.

WTops *White Tops*. Freq: 6; Began: 1927; Lang: Eng; Subj: Theatre.
ISSN: 0043-499X
■Circus Fans Assoc. of America; 4 Center Drive; Camp Hill, PA 17011; USA.

XLunc *Xiju Luncong*: Selected Essays of Theatre. Freq: 4; Began: 1957; Cov: Full; Lang: Chi; Subj: Theatre.
■52 Dongai Ba tiao; Beijing; CHINA.

XXuexi *Xiju Xuexi*: Theatre. Freq: 4; Began: 1957; Lang: Chi; Subj: Theatre.
■Central Institute for Modern Theatre; Jiaonan Qitiao; Beijing; CHINA.

XYanj *Xiqu Yanjiu*. Freq: 4; Began: 1980; Cov: Full; Lang: Chi; Subj: Theatre.
■Cultural and Artistic Publishing; 17 Qianhai Xijie; Beijing; CHINA.

XYishu *Xiju Yishu*: Theatre Arts. Freq: 4; Began: 1978; Cov: Full; Lang: Chi; Subj: Theatre.
■630 Huashan Road; 4 274 Shanghai; CHINA.

YCT *Young Cinema & Theatre/Jeune Cinéma et Théâtre*: Cultural Magazine of the IUS. Freq: 4; Began: 1964; Lang: Eng/Fre/Spa; Subj: Theatre.
■International Union of Students; 17th November Street; 110 01 Prague 1; CZECHO-SLOVAKIA.

Yorick *Yorick*: Revista de Teatro. Lang: Spa; Subj: Theatre.
■Via Layetana 30; 3 Barcelona; SPAIN.

YTJ *Youth Theatre Journal*. Freq: 4; Began: 1986; Lang: Eng; Formerly: *Children's Theatre Review;* Subj: Theatre.
ISSN: 0009-4196
■American Association Theatre Youth; Virginia Tech/Theatre Arts Department; Blacksburg, VA 24061; USA.

ZAA *Zeitschrift für Anglistik und Amerikanistik*. Freq: 4; Began: 1953; Cov: Scan; Lang: Ger/Eng; Subj: Related.
ISSN: 0044-2305
■Verlag Enzyklopädie; Gerichtsweg 26; 7010 Leipzig; EAST GERMANY.

ZDi *Zahranicni Divadlo*: (Theatre Abroad). Lang: Cze; Subj: Theatre.
■Prague; CZECHOSLOVAKIA.

ZfK *Zeitschrift für Kulturaustausch*. Freq: 4; Lang: Ger; Subj: Theatre.
ISSN: 0044-2976
■Horst Erdmann Verlag für, Internationalen-Kulturaustausch; Hartmeyerstrasse 117; 7400 Tübingen 1; WEST GERMANY.

ZG *Zeitschrift für Germanistik*. Freq: 6; Began: 1980; Cov: Scan; Lang: Ger; Subj: Related. ISSN: 0323-7982
■Verlag Enzyklopädie; Gerichtsweg 26; 7010 Leipzig; EAST GERMANY.

Znamya *Znamya*. Freq: 12; Began: 1931; Lang: Rus; Subj: Related. ISSN: 0044-4898
■Soyuz Pisatelei S.S.S.R.; Moscow; USSR.

Zpravy *Zpravy*. Freq: 3; Lang: Cze/Eng; Subj: Theatre.
■Dilia Theatrical and Literary Agency; Vysehradska 28; 128 24 Prague 2; CZECHOSLOVAKIA.

ZreIssk *Zreliščnyjë Iskusstva* (Performing Arts). Freq: 12; Began: 1983; Cov: Full; Lang: Rus; Subj: Theatre. ISSN: 0207-9739
■Gos. Biblioteka SSSR im. Lenina, NIO Informkultura; Prospekt Kalinina 3; 101000 Moscow; USSR.

ZS *Zeitschrift für Slawistik*. Freq: 6; Began: 1956; Cov: Scan; Lang: Ger/Rus; Subj: Related. ISSN: 0044-3506
■Akademie der Wissenschaften der DDR, Inst. für Literaturgeschichte; Akademie-Verlag, Leipziger Str. 3-4; 1086 Berlin; EAST GERMANY.

Zvezda *Zvezda*. Freq: 12; Began: 1924; Cov: Scan; Lang: Rus; Subj: Related.
ISSN: 0039-7105
■Izdatel. Chudožestvennaja Literatura; Mochovaja 20; 192028 Leningrad; USSR.

Photocomposition and printing services for this volume
of the *International Bibliography of Theatre* were
provided by Volt Information Sciences Inc.,

Cover Design by Irving M. Brown

International Bibliography of Theatre: 1986